CRESCENT CITY

HOUSE of EARTH and BLOOD

Books by Sarah J. Maas

The Throne of Glass series

The Assassin's Blade
Throne of Glass
Crown of Midnight
Heir of Fire
Queen of Shadows
Empire of Storms
Tower of Dawn
Kingdom of Ash

•

The Throne of Glass Coloring Book

The Court of Thorns and Roses series

A Court of Thorns and Roses
A Court of Mist and Fury
A Court of Wings and Ruin
A Court of Frost and Starlight
A Court of Silver Flames

•

A Court of Thorns and Roses Coloring Book

The Crescent City series

House of Earth and Blood
House of Sky and Breath
House of Flame and Shadow

CRESCENT CITY

HOUSE of EARTH and BLOOD

SARAH J. MAAS

BLOOMSBURY PUBLISHING
NEW YORK • LONDON • OXFORD • NEW DELHI • SYDNEY

BLOOMSBURY PUBLISHING
Bloomsbury Publishing Inc.
1385 Broadway, New York, NY 10018, USA
29 Earlsfort Terrace, Dublin 2, Ireland

BLOOMSBURY, BLOOMSBURY PUBLISHING, and the Diana logo are trademarks of Bloomsbury Publishing Plc

First published in the United States 2020

Map by Virginia Allyn
Endpapers and interior art by Carlos Quevedo

ISBN: HB: 978-1-63557-404-3; eBook 978-1-63557-405-0
exclusive 978-1-63557-617-7; special 978-1-63557-618-4

Library of Congress Cataloging-in-Publication Data is available

14 16 18 20 19 17 15

Typeset by Westchester Publishing Services
Printed in Great Britain by CPI (UK) ltd, Croydon CR0 4YY

For Taran—
The brightest star in my sky

LUNATHION

CRESCENT CITY

THE ANGELS' GATE

CENTRAL BUSINESS DISTRICT

THE MEAT MARKET

THE MERCHANTS' GATE

WESTERN ROAD

ISTROS RIVER

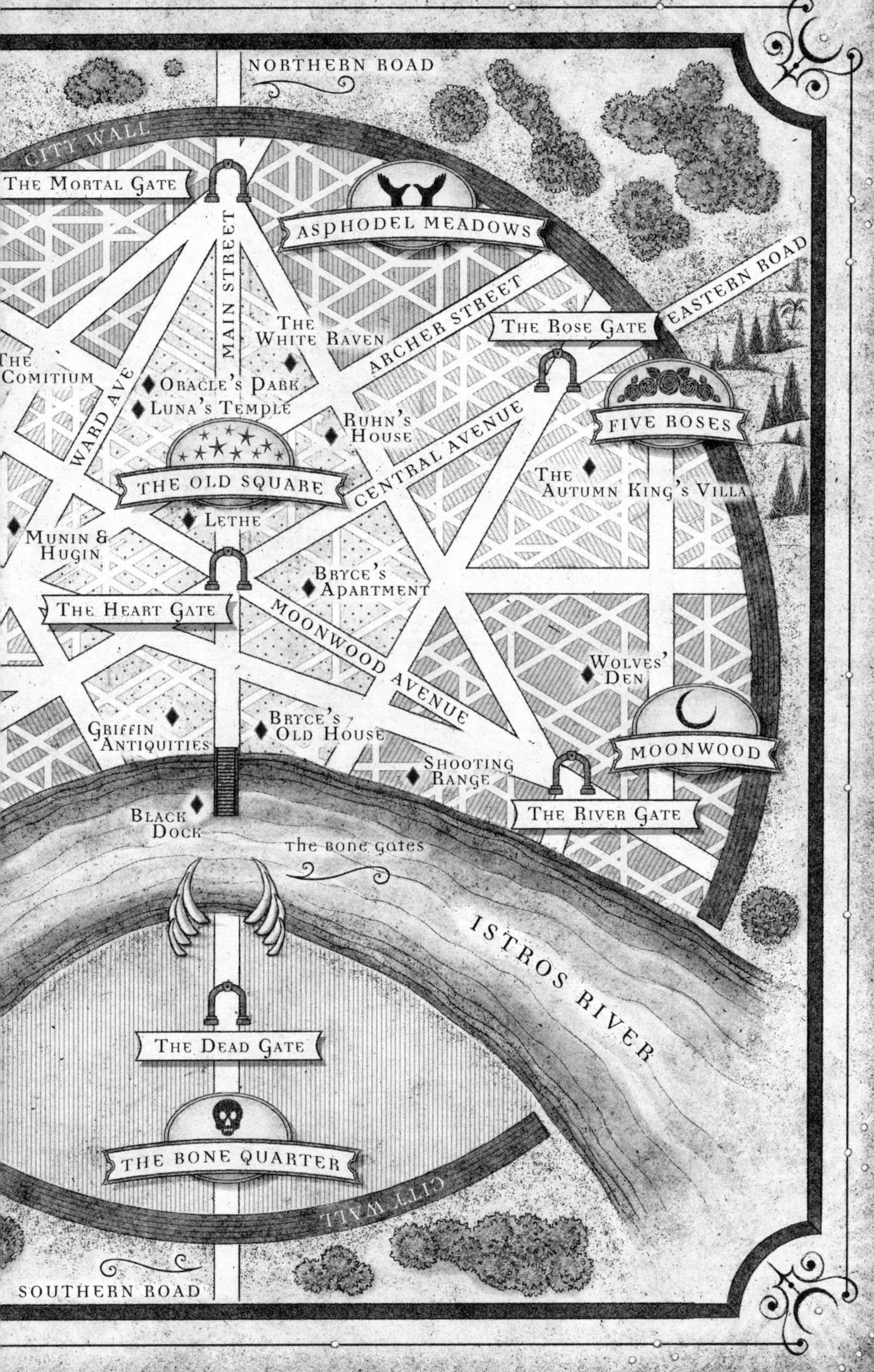

NORTHERN ROAD
CITY WALL
THE MORTAL GATE
ASPHODEL MEADOWS
MAIN STREET
EASTERN ROAD
ARCHER STREET
THE ROSE GATE
THE WHITE RAVEN
THE COMITIUM
WARD AVE
ORACLE'S PARK
LUNA'S TEMPLE
RUHN'S HOUSE
FIVE ROSES
CENTRAL AVENUE
THE OLD SQUARE
THE AUTUMN KING'S VILLA
LETHE
MUNIN & HUGIN
BRYCE'S APARTMENT
THE HEART GATE
MOONWOOD AVENUE
WOLVES' DEN
GRIFFIN ANTIQUITIES
BRYCE'S OLD HOUSE
MOONWOOD
SHOOTING RANGE
BLACK DOCK
THE RIVER GATE
the bone gates
ISTROS RIVER
THE DEAD GATE
THE BONE QUARTER
CITY WALL
SOUTHERN ROAD

THE FOUR HOUSES OF MIDGARD

As decreed in 33 V.E. by the Imperial Senate in the Eternal City

HOUSE OF EARTH AND BLOOD

Shifters, humans, witches, ordinary animals, and many others to whom Cthona calls, as well as some chosen by Luna

HOUSE OF SKY AND BREATH

Malakim (angels), Fae, elementals, sprites,* and those who are blessed by Solas, along with some favored by Luna

HOUSE OF MANY WATERS

River-spirits, mer, water beasts, nymphs, kelpies, nøkks, and others watched over by Ogenas

HOUSE OF FLAME AND SHADOW

Daemonaki, Reapers, wraiths, vampyrs, draki, dragons, necromancers, and many wicked and unnamed things that even Urd herself cannot see

**Sprites were kicked out of their House as a result of their participation in the Fall, and are now considered Lowers, though many of them refuse to accept this.*

PART I

THE HOLLOW

1

There was a wolf at the gallery door.

Which meant it must be Thursday, which meant Bryce had to be *really* gods-damned tired if she relied on Danika's comings and goings to figure out what day it was.

The heavy metal door to Griffin Antiquities thudded with the impact of the wolf's fist—a fist that Bryce knew ended in metallic-purple painted nails in dire need of a manicure. A heartbeat later, a female voice barked, half-muffled through the steel, "Open the Hel up, B. It's hot as shit out here!"

Seated at the desk in the modest gallery showroom, Bryce smirked and pulled up the front door's video feed. Tucking a strand of her wine-red hair behind a pointed ear, she asked into the intercom, "Why are you covered in dirt? You look like you've been rootling through the garbage."

"What the fuck does *rootling* mean?" Danika hopped from foot to foot, sweat gleaming on her brow. She wiped at it with a filthy hand, smearing the black liquid splattered there.

"You'd know if you ever picked up a book, Danika." Glad for the break in what had been a morning of tedious research, Bryce smiled as she rose from the desk. With no exterior windows, the gallery's extensive surveillance equipment served as her only warning of who stood beyond its thick walls. Even with her sharp half-Fae hearing, she couldn't make out much beyond the iron door save for the occasional banging fist. The building's unadorned sandstone walls belied the latest tech and grade A spellwork that kept it operational and preserved many of the books in the archives below.

As if merely thinking about the level beneath Bryce's high heels had summoned her, a little voice asked from behind the six-inch-thick archives door to her left, "Is that Danika?"

"Yes, Lehabah." Bryce wrapped her hand around the front door's handle. The enchantments on it hummed against her palm, slithering like smoke over her freckled golden skin. She gritted her teeth and withstood it, still unused to the sensation even after a year of working at the gallery.

From the other side of the deceptively simple metal door to the archives, Lehabah warned, "Jesiba doesn't like her in here."

"*You* don't like her in here," Bryce amended, her amber eyes narrowing toward the archives door and the tiny fire sprite she knew was hovering just on the other side, eavesdropping as she always did whenever someone stood out front. "Go back to work."

Lehabah didn't answer, presumably drifting back downstairs to guard the books below. Rolling her eyes, Bryce yanked open the front door, getting a face full of heat so dry it threatened to suck the life from her. And summer had only just begun.

Danika didn't just look like she'd been rootling through the garbage. She smelled like it, too.

Wisps of her silvery blond hair—normally a straight, silken sheet—curled from her tight, long braid, the streaks of amethyst, sapphire, and rose splattered with some dark, oily substance that reeked of metal and ammonia.

"Took you long enough," Danika groused, and swaggered into the gallery, the sword strapped at her back bobbing with each step. Her braid had become tangled in its worn leather hilt, and as she stopped before the desk, Bryce took the liberty of prying the plait free.

She'd barely untangled it before Danika's slim fingers were unbuckling the straps that kept the sword sheathed across her worn leather motorcycle jacket. "I need to dump this here for a few hours," she said, pulling the sword off her back and aiming for the supply closet hidden behind a wooden panel across the showroom.

Bryce leaned against the lip of the desk and crossed her arms, fingers brushing against the stretchy black fabric of her skintight dress. "Your gym bag's already stinking up the place. Jesiba's due back later this afternoon—she'll throw your shit in the dumpster again if it's still here."

It was the mildest Hel Jesiba Roga could unleash if provoked.

A four-hundred-year-old enchantress who'd been born a witch and defected, Jesiba had joined the House of Flame and Shadow and now answered only to the Under-King himself. Flame and Shadow suited her well—she possessed an arsenal of spells to rival any sorcerer or necromancer in the darkest of the Houses. She'd been known to change people into animals when irritated enough. Bryce had never dared ask if the small animals in the dozen tanks and terrariums had always been animals.

And Bryce tried never to irritate her. Not that there were any safe sides when the Vanir were involved. Even the least powerful of the Vanir—a group that covered every being on Midgard aside from humans and ordinary animals—could be deadly.

"I'll get it later," Danika promised, pushing on the hidden panel to spring it open. Bryce had warned her three times now that the showroom supply closet wasn't her personal locker. Yet Danika always countered that the gallery, located in the heart of the Old Square, was more centrally located than the wolves' Den over in Moonwood. And that was that.

The supply closet opened, and Danika waved a hand in front of her face. "*My* gym bag's stinking up the place?" With a black boot, she toed the sagging duffel that held Bryce's dance gear, currently wedged between the mop and bucket. "When the fuck did you last wash those clothes?"

Bryce wrinkled her nose at the reek of old shoes and sweaty clothing that wafted out. Right—she'd forgotten to bring home the leotard and tights to wash after a lunchtime class two days ago. Mostly thanks to Danika sending her a video of a heap of mirthroot on their kitchen counter, music already blasting from the beat-up boom box by the windows, along with a command to hurry home quick. Bryce had obeyed. They'd smoked enough that there was a good chance Bryce had still been high yesterday morning when she'd stumbled into work.

There was really no other explanation for why it had taken ten minutes to type out a two-sentence email that day. Letter by letter.

"Never mind that," Bryce said. "I have a bone to pick with you."

Danika rearranged the crap in the closet to make space for her own. "I told you I was sorry I ate your leftover noodles. I'll buy you more tonight."

"It's not that, dumbass, though again: fuck you. That was my lunch for today." Danika chuckled. "This tattoo hurts like Hel," Bryce complained. "I can't even lean against my chair."

Danika countered in a singsong voice, "The artist warned you it'd be sore for a few days."

"I was so drunk I spelled my name wrong on the waiver. I'd hardly say I was in a good place to understand what 'sore for a few days' meant." Danika, who'd gotten a matching tattoo of the text now scrolling down Bryce's back, had already healed. One of the benefits to being a full-blooded Vanir: swift recovery time compared to humans—or a half-human like Bryce.

Danika shoved her sword into the mess of the closet. "I promise I'll help you ice your sore back tonight. Just let me take a shower and I'll be out of here in ten."

It wasn't unusual for her friend to pop into the gallery, especially on Thursdays, when her morning patrol ended just a few blocks away, but she'd never used the full bathroom in the archives downstairs. Bryce motioned to the dirt and grease. "What *is* that on you?"

Danika scowled, the angular planes of her face scrunching. "I had to break up a fight between a satyr and a nightstalker." She bared her white teeth at the black substance crusting her hands. "Guess which one spewed its *juices* onto me."

Bryce snorted and gestured to the archives door. "Shower's yours. There are some clean clothes in the bottom drawer of the desk down there."

Danika's filthy fingers began pulling the handle of the archives door. Her jaw tightened, the older tattoo on her neck—the horned, grinning wolf that served as the sigil for the Pack of Devils—rippling with tension.

Not from the effort, Bryce realized as she noted Danika's stiff back. Bryce glanced to the supply closet, which Danika had not bothered to shut. The sword, famed both in this city and far beyond it, leaned against the push broom and mop, its ancient leather scabbard nearly obscured by the full container of gasoline used to fuel the electric generator out back.

Bryce had always wondered why Jesiba bothered with an old-fashioned generator—until the citywide firstlight outage last week. When the power had failed, only the generator had kept the mechanical locks in place during the looting that followed, when creeps had rushed in from the Meat Market, bombarding the gallery's front door with counterspells to break through the enchantments.

But—Danika ditching the sword in the office. Danika needing to take a shower. Her stiff back.

Bryce asked, "You've got a meeting with the City Heads?"

In the five years since they'd met as freshmen at Crescent City University, Bryce could count on one hand the number of times Danika had been called in for a meeting with the seven people important enough to merit a shower and change of clothes. Even while delivering reports to Danika's grandfather, the Prime of the Valbaran wolves, and to Sabine, her mother, Danika usually wore that leather jacket, jeans, and whatever vintage band T-shirt wasn't dirty.

Of course, it pissed off Sabine to no end, but *everything* about Danika—and Bryce—pissed off the Alpha of the Scythe Moon Pack, chief among the shifter units in the city's Auxiliary.

It didn't matter that Sabine was the Prime Apparent of the Valbaran wolves and had been her aging father's heir for centuries, or that Danika was officially second in line to the title. Not when whispers had swirled for years that Danika should be tapped to be the Prime Apparent, bypassing her mother. Not when the old wolf had given his granddaughter their family's heirloom sword after centuries of promising it to Sabine only upon his death. The blade had called to Danika on her eighteenth birthday like a howl on a moonlit night, the Prime had said to explain his unexpected decision.

Sabine had never forgotten that humiliation. Especially when Danika carried the blade nearly everywhere—especially in front of her mother.

Danika paused in the gaping archway, atop the green carpeted steps that led down to the archives beneath the gallery—where the true treasure in this place lay, guarded by Lehabah day and night. It was the real reason why Danika, who'd been a history major at CCU, liked to drop by so often, just to browse the ancient art and books, despite Bryce's teasing about her reading habits.

Danika turned, her caramel eyes shuttered. "Philip Briggs is being released today."

Bryce started. "*What?*"

"They're letting him go on some gods-damned technicality. Someone fucked up the paperwork. We're getting the full update in the meeting." She clenched her slim jaw, the glow from the first-lights in the glass sconces along the stairwell bouncing off her dirty hair. "It's so fucked up."

Bryce's stomach churned. The human rebellion remained confined to the northern reaches of Pangera, the sprawling territory across the Haldren Sea, but Philip Briggs had done his best to bring it over to Valbara. "You and the pack busted him right in his little rebel bomb lab, though."

Danika tapped her booted foot on the green carpet. "Bureaucratic fucking nonsense."

"He was going to blow up a *club*. You literally found his blueprints for blowing up the White Raven." As one of the most popular nightclubs in the city, the loss of life would have been catastrophic. Briggs's previous bombings had been smaller, but no less deadly, all designed to trigger a war between the humans and Vanir to match the one raging in Pangera's colder climes. Briggs made no secret of his goal: a global conflict that would cost the lives of millions on either side. Lives that were expendable if it meant a possibility for humans to overthrow those who oppressed them—the magically gifted and long-lived Vanir and, above them, the Asteri, who ruled the planet Midgard from the Eternal City in Pangera.

But Danika and the Pack of Devils had stopped the plot. She'd busted Briggs and his top supporters, all part of the Keres rebels, and spared innocents from their brand of fanaticism.

As one of the most elite shifter units in Crescent City's Auxiliary, the Pack of Devils patrolled the Old Square, making sure drunken, handsy tourists didn't become drunken, dead tourists when they approached the wrong person. Making sure the bars and cafés and music halls and shops stayed safe from whatever lowlife had crawled into town that day. And making sure people like Briggs were in prison.

The 33rd Imperial Legion claimed to do the same, but the angels who made up the fabled ranks of the Governor's personal army just glowered and promised Hel if challenged.

"Believe me," Danika said, stomping down the stairs, "I'm going to make it perfectly fucking clear in this meeting that Briggs's release is unacceptable."

She would. Even if Danika had to snarl in Micah Domitus's face, she'd get her point across. There weren't many who'd dare piss off the Archangel of Crescent City, but Danika wouldn't hesitate. And given that all seven Heads of the City would be at this meeting, the odds of that happening were high. Things tended to escalate swiftly when they were in one room. There was little love lost between the six lower Heads in Crescent City, the metropolis formally known as Lunathion. Each Head controlled a specific part of the city: the Prime of the wolves in Moonwood, the Fae Autumn King in Five Roses, the Under-King in the Bone Quarter, the Viper Queen in the Meat Market, the Oracle in the Old Square, and the River Queen—who very rarely made an appearance—representing the House of Many Waters and her Blue Court far beneath the Istros River's turquoise surface. She seldom deigned to leave it.

The humans in Asphodel Meadows had no Head. No seat at the table. Philip Briggs had found more than a few sympathizers because of it.

But Micah, Head of the Central Business District, ruled over them all. Beyond his city titles, he was Archangel of Valbara. Ruler of this entire fucking territory, and answerable only to the six Asteri in the Eternal City, the capital and beating heart of Pangera. Of the entire planet of Midgard. If anyone could keep Briggs in prison, it would be him.

Danika reached the bottom of the stairs, so far below that she was cut off from sight by the slope of the ceiling. Bryce lingered in the archway, listening as Danika said, "Hey, Syrinx." A little yip of delight from the thirty-pound chimera rose up the stairs.

Jesiba had purchased the Lower creature two months ago, to Bryce's delight. *He is not a pet*, Jesiba had warned her. *He's an expensive, rare creature bought for the sole purpose of assisting Lehabah in guarding these books. Do not interfere with his duties.*

Bryce had so far failed to inform Jesiba that Syrinx was more interested in eating, sleeping, and getting belly rubs than monitoring the precious books. No matter that her boss might see that at any point, should she bother to check the dozens of camera feeds in the library.

Danika drawled, the smirk audible in her voice, "What's got your panties in a twist, Lehabah?"

The fire sprite grumbled, "I don't wear panties. Or clothes. They don't pair well when you're made of flame, Danika."

Danika snickered. Before Bryce could decide whether to go downstairs to referee the match between the fire sprite and the wolf, the phone on the desk began ringing. She had a good idea who it would be.

Heels sinking into the plush carpeting, Bryce reached the phone before it went to audiomail, sparing herself a five-minute lecture. "Hi, Jesiba."

A beautiful, lilting female voice answered, "Please tell Danika Fendyr that if she continues to use the supply closet as her own personal locker, I *will* turn her into a lizard."

2

By the time Danika emerged on the gallery's showroom floor, Bryce had endured a mildly threatening reprimand from Jesiba about her ineptitude, one email from a fussy client demanding Bryce expedite the paperwork on the ancient urn she'd bought so she could show it off to her equally fussy friends at her cocktail party on Monday, and two messages from members of Danika's pack inquiring about whether their Alpha was about to kill someone over Briggs's release.

Nathalie, Danika's Third, had gotten straight to the point: *Has she lost her shit about Briggs yet?*

Connor Holstrom, Danika's Second, took a little more care with what he sent out into the ether. There was always a chance of a leak. *Have you spoken to Danika?* was all he'd asked.

Bryce was writing back to Connor—*Yes. I've got it covered*—when a gray wolf the size of a small horse pushed the iron archives door shut with a paw, claws clicking on the metal.

"You hated my clothes that much?" Bryce asked, rising from her seat. Only Danika's caramel eyes remained the same in this form—and only those eyes softened the pure menace and grace the wolf radiated with each step toward the desk.

"I've got them on, don't worry." Long, sharp fangs flashed with each word. Danika cocked her fuzzy ears, taking in the computer that had been shut down, the purse Bryce had set on the desk. "You're coming out with me?"

"I've got to do some sleuthing for Jesiba." Bryce grabbed the ring of keys that opened doors into various parts of her life. "She's been hounding me about finding Luna's Horn again. As if I haven't been trying to find it nonstop for the last week."

Danika glanced to one of the visible cameras in the showroom, mounted behind a decapitated statue of a dancing faun dating back ten thousand years. Her bushy tail swished once. "Why does she even want it?"

Bryce shrugged. "I haven't had the balls to ask."

Danika stalked to the front door, careful not to let her claws snag a single thread in the carpet. "I doubt she's going to return it to the temple out of the goodness of her heart."

"I have a feeling Jesiba would leverage its return to her advantage," Bryce said. They strode onto the quiet street a block off the Istros, the midday sun baking the cobblestones, Danika a solid wall of fur and muscle between Bryce and the curb.

The theft of the sacred horn during the power outage had been the biggest news story out of the disaster: looters had used the cover of darkness to break into Luna's Temple and swipe the ancient Fae relic from its resting place atop the lap of the massive, enthroned deity.

The Archangel Micah himself had offered a hefty reward for any information regarding its return and promised that the sacrilegious bastard who'd stolen it would be brought to justice.

Also known as public crucifixion.

Bryce always made a point of not going near the square in the CBD, where they were usually held. On certain days, depending on the wind and heat, the smell of blood and rotting flesh could carry for blocks.

Bryce fell into step beside Danika as the massive wolf scanned the street, nostrils sniffing for any hint of a threat. Bryce, as half-Fae, could scent people in greater detail than the average human. She'd entertained her parents endlessly as a kid by describing the scents of everyone in their little mountain town, Nidaros—humans possessed no such way to interpret the world. But her abilities had nothing on her friend's.

As Danika scented the street, her tail wagged once—and not from happiness.

"Chill," Bryce said. "You'll make your case to the Heads, then they'll figure it out."

Danika's ears flattened. "It's all fucked, B. All of it."

Bryce frowned. "You really mean to tell me that any of the Heads want a rebel like Briggs at large? They'll find some technicality and throw his ass right back in jail." She added, because Danika still wouldn't look at her, "There's no way the 33rd's not monitoring his every breath. Briggs so much as blinks wrong and he'll see what kind of pain angels can rain down on us all. Hel, the Governor might even send the Umbra Mortis after him." Micah's personal assassin, with the rare gift of lightning in his veins, could eliminate almost any threat.

Danika snarled, teeth gleaming. "I can handle Briggs myself."

"I know you can. Everyone knows you can, Danika."

Danika surveyed the street ahead, glancing past a poster of the six enthroned Asteri tacked up on a wall—with an empty throne to honor their fallen sister—but loosed a breath.

She would always have burdens and expectations to shoulder that Bryce would never have to endure, and Bryce was thankful as Hel for that privilege. When Bryce fucked up, Jesiba usually griped for a few minutes and that was that. When Danika fucked up, it was blasted on news reports and across the interweb.

Sabine made sure of it.

Bryce and Sabine had hated each other from the moment the Alpha had sneered at her only child's improper, half-breed roommate that first day at CCU. And Bryce had loved Danika from the moment her new roommate had offered her a hand in greeting anyway, and then said Sabine was just pissy because she'd been hoping for a muscle-bound vampyr to drool over.

Danika rarely let the opinions of others—especially Sabine—eat away at her swagger and joy, yet on rough days like this . . . Bryce lifted a hand and ran it down Danika's muscled ribs, a comforting, sweeping stroke.

"Do you think Briggs will come after you or the pack?" Bryce asked, her stomach twisting. Danika hadn't busted Briggs alone—he had a score to settle with all of them.

Danika's snout wrinkled. "I don't know."

The words echoed between them. In hand-to-hand combat, Briggs would never survive against Danika. But one of those bombs would change everything. If Danika had made the Drop into immortality, she'd probably survive. But since she hadn't—since she was the only one of the Pack of Devils who hadn't yet done it . . . Bryce's mouth turned dry.

"Be careful," Bryce said quietly.

"I will," Danika said, her warm eyes still full of shadows. But then she tossed her head, as if shaking it free of water—the movement purely canine. Bryce often marveled at this, that Danika could clear away her fears, or at least bury them, enough to move onward. Indeed, Danika changed the subject. "Your brother will be at the meeting today."

Half brother. Bryce didn't bother to correct her. *Half brother and full-Fae prick.* "And?"

"Just thought I'd warn you that I'll be seeing him." The wolf's face softened slightly. "He's going to ask me how you're doing."

"Tell Ruhn I'm busy doing important shit and to go to Hel."

Danika huffed a laugh. "Where, exactly, are you doing this sleuthing for the Horn?"

"The temple," Bryce said with a sigh. "Honestly, I've been looking into this thing for days on end, and can't figure out anything. No suspects, no murmurings at the Meat Market about it being for sale, no motive for who'd even bother with it. It's famous enough that whoever's got it has it wrapped up *tight.*" She frowned at the clear sky. "I almost wonder if the power outage was tied to it—if someone shut down the city's grid to steal it in the chaos. There are about twenty people in this city capable of being that crafty, and half of them possess the resources to pull it off."

Danika's tail twitched. "If they're able to do something like that, I'd suggest staying away. Lead Jesiba around a bit, make her think you're looking for it, and then let it drop. Either the Horn will show up by then, or she'll move on to her next stupid quest."

Bryce admitted, "I just . . . It'd be good to find the Horn. For my own career." Whatever the Hel that would be. A year of working at the gallery hadn't sparked anything beyond disgust at the obscene amounts of money that rich people squandered on old-ass shit.

Danika's eyes flickered. "Yeah, I know."

Bryce zipped a tiny golden pendant—a knot of three entwined circles—along the delicate chain around her neck.

Danika went on patrol armed with claws, a sword, and guns, but Bryce's daily armor consisted solely of this: an Archesian amulet barely the size of her thumbnail, gifted by Jesiba on the first day of work.

A hazmat suit in a necklace, Danika had marveled when Bryce had shown off the amulet's considerable protections against the influence of various magical objects. Archesian amulets didn't come cheap, but Bryce didn't bother to delude herself into thinking her boss's gift was given out of anything but self-interest. It would have been an insurance nightmare if Bryce didn't have one.

Danika nodded to the necklace. "Don't take that off. Especially if you're looking into shit like the Horn." Even though the Horn's mighty powers had long been dead—if it had been stolen by someone powerful, she'd need every magical defense against them.

"Yeah, yeah," Bryce said, though Danika was right. She'd never taken the necklace off since getting it. If Jesiba ever kicked her to the curb, she knew she'd have to find some way to make sure the necklace came with her. Danika had said as much several times, unable to stop that Alpha wolf's instinct to protect at all costs. It was part of why Bryce loved her—and why her chest tightened in that moment with that same love and gratitude.

Bryce's phone buzzed in her purse, and she fished it out. Danika peered over, noted who was calling, and wagged her tail, ears perking up.

"Do not say a word about Briggs," Bryce warned, and accepted the call. "Hi, Mom."

"Hey, sweetie." Ember Quinlan's clear voice filled her ear, drawing a smile from Bryce even with three hundred miles between them. "I wanted to double-check that next weekend is still okay to visit."

"Hi, Mommy!" Danika barked toward the phone.

Ember laughed. Ember had always been *Mom* to Danika, even from their first meeting. And Ember, who had never borne any children beyond Bryce, had been more than glad to find herself with a second—equally willful and troublesome—daughter. "Danika's with you?"

Bryce rolled her eyes and held out the phone to her friend. Between one step and the next, Danika shifted in a flash of light, the massive wolf shrinking into the lithe humanoid form.

Snatching the phone from Bryce, Danika pinned it between her ear and shoulder as she adjusted the white silk blouse Bryce had loaned her, tucking it into her stained jeans. She'd managed to wipe a good amount of the nightstalker gunk off both the pants and leather jacket, but the T-shirt had apparently been a lost cause. Danika said into the phone, "Bryce and I are taking a walk."

With Bryce's arched ears, she could hear her mother perfectly as she said, "Where?"

Ember Quinlan made overprotectiveness a competitive sport.

Moving here, to Lunathion, had been a test of wills. Ember had only relented when she'd learned who Bryce's freshman-year roommate was—and then gave Danika a lecture on how to make sure Bryce stayed safe. Randall, Bryce's stepfather, had mercifully cut his wife off after thirty minutes.

Bryce knows how to defend herself, Randall had reminded Ember. *We saw to that. And Bryce will keep up her training while she's here, won't she?*

Bryce certainly had. She'd hit up the gun range just a few days ago, going through the motions Randall—her true father, as far as she was concerned—had taught her since childhood: assembling a gun, taking aim at a target, controlling her breathing.

Most days, she found guns to be brutal killing machines, and felt grateful that they were highly regulated by the Republic. But given that she had little more to defend herself beyond speed and a few well-placed maneuvers, she'd learned that for a human, a gun could mean the difference between life and slaughter.

Danika fibbed, "We're just heading to one of the hawker stalls in the Old Square—we wanted some lamb kofta."

Before Ember could continue the interrogation, Danika added, "Hey, B must have forgotten to tell you that we're actually heading down to Kalaxos next weekend—Ithan's got a sunball game there, and we're all going to cheer him on."

A half-truth. The game was happening, but there had been no discussion of going to watch Connor's younger brother, CCU's star player. This afternoon, the Pack of Devils was actually heading over to the CCU arena to cheer for Ithan, but Bryce and Danika hadn't bothered to attend an away game since sophomore year, when Danika had been sleeping with one of the defensemen.

"That's too bad," Ember said. Bryce could practically hear the frown in her mother's tone. "We were really looking forward to it."

Burning Solas, this woman was a master of the guilt trip. Bryce cringed and snatched back the phone. "So were we, but let's reschedule for next month."

"But that's so long from now—"

"Shit, a client's coming down the street," Bryce lied. "I gotta go."

"Bryce Adelaide Quinlan—"

"Bye, Mom."

"Bye, Mom!" Danika echoed, just as Bryce hung up.

Bryce sighed toward the sky, ignoring the angels soaring and flapping past, their shadows dancing over the sun-washed streets. "Message incoming in three, two . . ."

Her phone buzzed.

Ember had written, *If I didn't know better, I'd think you were avoiding us, Bryce. Your father will be very hurt.*

Danika let out a whistle. "Oh, she's good."

Bryce groaned. "I'm not letting them come to the city if Briggs is running free."

Danika's smile faded. "I know. We'll keep pushing them off until it's sorted out." Thank Cthona for Danika—she always had a plan for everything.

Bryce slid her phone into her purse, leaving her mother's message unanswered.

When they reached the Gate at the heart of the Old Square, its quartz archway as clear as a frozen pond, the sun was just hitting its upper edge, refracting and casting small rainbows against one of the buildings flanking it. On Summer Solstice, when the sun lined up perfectly with the Gate, it filled the entire square with rainbows, so many that it was like walking inside a diamond.

Tourists milled about, a line of them snaking across the square itself, all waiting for the chance at a photo with the twenty-foot-high landmark.

One of seven in this city, all carved from enormous blocks of quartz hewn from the Laconian Mountains to the north, the Old Square Gate was often called the Heart Gate, thanks to its location in the dead center of Lunathion, with the other six Gates located equidistant from it, each one opening onto a road out of the walled city.

"They should make a special access lane for residents to cross the square," Bryce muttered as they edged around tourists and hawkers.

"And give tourists fines for slow walking," Danika muttered back, but flashed a lupine grin at a young human couple that recognized her, gawked, and began snapping photos.

"I wonder what they'd think if they knew that nightstalker's special sauce is all over you," Bryce murmured.

Danika elbowed her. "Asshole." She threw a friendly wave to the tourists and continued on.

On the other side of the Heart Gate, amid a small army of vendors selling food and touristy crap, a second line of people waited to access the golden block sticking out of its southern side. "We'll have to cut through them to get across," Bryce said, scowling at the tourists idling in the wilting heat.

But Danika halted, her angular face turned to the Gate and the plaque. "Let's make a wish."

"I'm not waiting in that line." Usually, they just shouted their wishes drunkenly into the ether late at night when they were staggering home from the White Raven and the square was empty. Bryce checked the time on her phone. "Don't you have to get over to the Comitium?" The Governor's five-towered stronghold was at least a fifteen-minute walk away.

"I've got time," Danika said, and grabbed Bryce's hand, tugging her through the crowds and toward the real tourist draw of the Gate.

Jutting out of the quartz about four feet off the ground lay the dial pad: a solid-gold block embedded with seven different gems, each for a different quarter of the city, the insignia of each district etched beneath it.

Emerald and a rose for Five Roses. Opal and a pair of wings for the CBD. Ruby and a heart for the Old Square. Sapphire and an oak tree for Moonwood. Amethyst and a human hand for Asphodel Meadows. Tiger's-eye and a serpent for the Meat Market. And onyx—so black it gobbled the light—and a set of skull and crossbones for the Bone Quarter.

Beneath the arc of stones and etched emblems, a small, round disk rose up slightly, its metal worn down by countless hands and paws and fins and any other manner of limb.

A sign beside it read: *Touch at your own risk. Do not use between sundown and sunrise. Violators will be fined.*

The people in line, waiting for access to the disk, seemed to have no problem with the risks.

A pair of giggling teenage male shifters—some kind of feline from their scents—goaded each other forward, elbowing and taunting, daring the other to touch the disk.

"Pathetic," Danika said, striding past the line, the ropes, and a bored-looking city guard—a young Fae female—to the very front. She fished a badge from inside her leather coat and flashed it at the guard, who stiffened as she realized who'd cut the line. She didn't even look at the golden emblem of the crescent moon bow with an arrow nocked through it before stepping back.

"Official Aux business," Danika declared with an unnervingly straight face. "It'll just be a minute."

Bryce stifled her laughter, well aware of the glares fixed on their backs from the line.

Danika drawled to the teenage boys, "If you're not going to do it, then clear off."

They whirled toward her, and went white as death.

Danika smiled, showing nearly all her teeth. It wasn't a pleasant sight.

"Holy shit," whispered one of them.

Bryce hid her smile as well. It never got old—the awe. Mostly because she knew Danika had earned it. Every damned day, Danika earned the awe that bloomed across the faces of strangers when they spotted her corn-silk hair and that neck tattoo. And the fear that made the lowlifes in this city think twice before fucking with her and the Pack of Devils.

Except for Philip Briggs. Bryce sent a prayer to Ogenas's blue depths that the sea goddess would whisper her wisdom to Briggs to keep his distance from Danika if he ever really did walk free.

The boys stepped aside, and it only took a few milliseconds for them to notice Bryce, too. The awe on their faces turned to blatant interest.

Bryce snorted. *Keep dreaming.*

One of them stammered, turning his attention from Bryce to Danika, "My—my history teacher said the Gates were originally communication devices."

"I bet you get all the ladies with those stellar factoids," Danika said without looking back at them, unimpressed and uninterested.

Message received, they slunk back to the line. Bryce smirked and stepped up to her friend's side, peering down at the dial pad.

The teenager was right, though. The seven Gates of this city, each set along a ley line running through Lunathion, had been designed as a quick way for the guards in the districts to speak to each other centuries ago. When someone merely placed a hand against the golden disk in the center of the pad and spoke, the wielder's voice would travel to the other Gates, a gem lighting up with the district from which the voice originated.

Of course, it required a drop of magic to do so—literally sucked it like a vampyr from the veins of the person who touched the pad, a tickling *zap* of power, gone forever.

Bryce raised her eyes to the bronze plaque above her head. The quartz Gates were memorials, though she didn't know for which conflict or war. But each bore the same plaque: *The power shall always belong to those who give their lives to the city.*

Considering it was a statement that could be construed as being in opposition to the Asteri's rule, Bryce was always surprised that they allowed the Gates to continue to stand. But after becoming obsolete with the advent of phones, the Gates had found a second life when kids and tourists began using them, having their friends go to the other Gates in the city so they could whisper dirty words or marvel at the sheer novelty of such an antiquated method of communication. Not surprisingly, come weekends, drunk assholes—a category to which Bryce and Danika firmly belonged—became such a pain in the ass with their shouting through the Gates that the city had instituted hours of operation.

And then dumb superstition grew, claiming the Gate could make wishes come true, and that to give over a droplet of your power was to make an offering to the five gods.

It was bullshit, Bryce knew—but if it made Danika not dread Briggs's release so much, well, it was worth it.

"What are you going to wish for?" Bryce asked when Danika stared down at the disk, the gems dark above it.

The emerald for FiRo lit up, a young female voice coming through to shriek, "*Titties!*"

People laughed around them, the sound like water trickling over stone, and Bryce chuckled.

But Danika's face had gone solemn. "I've got too many things to wish for," she said. Before Bryce could ask, Danika shrugged. "But I think I'll wish for Ithan to win his sunball game tonight."

With that, she set her palm onto the disk. Bryce watched as her friend let out a shiver and quietly laughed, stepping back. Her caramel eyes shone. "Your turn."

"You know I have barely any magic worth taking, but okay," Bryce said, not to be outdone, even by an Alpha wolf. From the moment Bryce walked into her dorm room freshman year, they'd done everything together. Just the two of them, as it always would be.

They even planned to make the Drop together—to freeze into immortality at the same breath, with members of the Pack of Devils Anchoring them.

Technically, it wasn't true immortality—the Vanir did age and die, either of natural causes or other methods, but the aging process was so slowed after the Drop that, depending on one's species, it could take centuries to show a wrinkle. The Fae could last a thousand years, the shifters and witches usually five centuries, the angels somewhere between. Full humans did not make the Drop, as they bore no magic. And compared to humans, with their ordinary life spans and slow healing, the Vanir *were* essentially immortal—some species bore children who didn't even enter maturity until they were in their eighties. And most were very, very hard to kill.

But Bryce had rarely thought about where she'd fall on that spectrum—whether her half-Fae heritage would grant her a hundred years or a thousand. It didn't matter, so long as Danika was there for all of it. Starting with the Drop. They'd take the deadly plunge into their matured power together, encounter whatever lay at the bottom of their souls, and then race back up to life before the lack of oxygen rendered them brain-dead. Or just plain dead.

Yet while Bryce would inherit barely enough power to do cool party tricks, Danika was expected to claim a sea of power that would put her ranking far past Sabine's—likely equal to that of Fae royalty, maybe even beyond the Autumn King himself.

It was unheard of, for a shifter to have that sort of power, yet all the standard childhood tests had confirmed it: once Danika Dropped, she'd become a considerable power among the wolves, the likes of which had not been seen since the elder days across the sea.

Danika wouldn't just become the Prime of the Crescent City

wolves. No, she had the potential to be the Alpha of *all* wolves. On the fucking planet.

Danika never seemed to give two shits about it. Didn't plan for her future based on it.

Twenty-seven was the ideal age to make the Drop, they'd decided together, after years of mercilessly judging the various immortals who marked their lives by centuries and millennia. Right before any permanent lines or wrinkles or gray hairs. They merely said to anyone who inquired, *What's the point of being immortal badasses if we have sagging tits?*

Vain assholes, Fury had hissed when they'd explained it the first time.

Fury, who had made the Drop at age twenty-one, hadn't chosen the age for herself. It'd just happened, or had been forced upon her—they didn't know for sure. Fury's attendance at CCU had only been a front for a mission; most of her time was spent doing *truly* fucked-up things for disgusting amounts of money over in Pangera. She made it a point never to give details.

Assassin, Danika claimed. Even sweet Juniper, the faun who occupied the fourth side of their little friendship-square, admitted the odds were that Fury was a merc. Whether Fury was occasionally employed by the Asteri and their puppet Imperial Senate was up for debate, too. But none of them really cared—not when Fury always had their back when they needed it. And even when they didn't.

Bryce's hand hovered over the golden disk. Danika's gaze was a cool weight on her.

"Come on, B, don't be a wimp."

Bryce sighed, and set her hand on the pad. "I wish Danika would get a manicure. Her nails look like shit."

Lightning zapped through her, a slight vacuuming around her belly button, and then Danika was laughing, shoving her. "You fucking *dick*."

Bryce slung an arm around Danika's shoulders. "You deserved it."

Danika thanked the security guard, who beamed at the attention, and ignored the tourists still snapping photos. They didn't speak until they reached the northern edge of the square—where Danika would head toward the angel-filled skies and towers of the CBD, to the sprawling Comitium complex in its heart, and Bryce toward Luna's Temple, three blocks up.

Danika jerked her chin toward the streets behind Bryce. "I'll see you at home, all right?"

"Be careful." Bryce blew out a breath, trying to shake her unease.

"I know how to look out for myself, B," Danika said, but love shone in her eyes—gratitude that crushed Bryce's chest—merely for the fact that someone cared whether she lived or died.

Sabine was a piece of shit. Had never whispered or hinted who Danika's father might be—so Danika had grown up with absolutely no one except her grandfather, who was too old and withdrawn to spare Danika from her mother's cruelty.

Bryce inclined her head toward the CBD. "Good luck. Don't piss off too many people."

"You know I will," Danika said with a grin that didn't meet her eyes.

3

The Pack of Devils was already at her apartment by the time Bryce got home from work.

It had been impossible to miss the roaring laughter that met her before she'd even cleared the second-floor stairwell landing—as well as the canine yips of amusement. Both had continued as she ascended the remaining level of the walk-up apartment building, during which time Bryce grumbled to herself about her plans for a quiet evening on the couch being ruined.

Chanting a string of curses that would make her mother proud, Bryce unlocked the blue-painted iron door to the apartment, bracing for the onslaught of lupine bossiness, arrogance, and general nosiness in all matters of her life. And that was just Danika.

Danika's pack made each of those things an art form. Mostly because they claimed Bryce as one of their own, even if she didn't bear the tattoo of their sigil down the side of her neck.

Sometimes she felt bad for Danika's future mate, whoever that would be. The poor bastard wouldn't know what hit him when he bound himself to her. Unless he was wolf-kind himself—though Danika had about as much interest in sleeping with a wolf as Bryce did.

That is to say, not a gods-damned shred.

Giving the door a good shove with her shoulder—its warped edges got stuck more often than not, mostly thanks to the romping of the hellions currently spread across the several sagging couches and armchairs—Bryce sighed as she found six pairs of eyes fixed on her. And six grins.

"How was the game?" she asked no one in particular, chucking her keys into the lopsided ceramic bowl Danika had half-assed during a fluff pottery course in college. She'd heard nothing from Danika regarding the Briggs meeting beyond a general *I'll tell you at home*.

It couldn't have been that bad, if Danika made it to the sunball game. She'd even sent Bryce a photo of the whole pack in front of the field, with Ithan a small, helmeted figure in the background.

A message from the star player himself had popped up later: *Next time, you better be with them, Quinlan.*

She'd written back, *Did baby pup miss me?*

You know it, Ithan had answered.

"We won," Connor drawled from where he lounged on *her* favorite spot on the couch, his gray CCU sunball T-shirt rumpled enough to reveal the cut of muscle and golden skin.

"Ithan scored the winning goal," Bronson said, still wearing a blue-and-silver jersey with *Holstrom* on the back.

Connor's little brother, Ithan, held an unofficial membership in the Pack of Devils. Ithan also happened to be Bryce's second-favorite person after Danika. Their message chain was an endless stream of snark and teasing, swapped photos, and good-natured grousing about Connor's bossiness.

"Again?" Bryce asked, kicking off her four-inch, pearl-white heels. "Can't Ithan share some of the glory with the other boys?" Normally, Ithan would have been sitting right on that couch beside his brother, forcing Bryce to wedge herself between them while they watched whatever TV show was on, but on game nights, he usually opted to party with his teammates.

A half smile tugged at a corner of Connor's mouth as Bryce held his stare for longer than most people considered wise. His five packmates, two still in wolf form with bushy tails swishing, wisely kept their mouths and maws shut.

It was common knowledge that Connor would have been Alpha of the Pack of Devils if Danika weren't around. But Connor didn't resent it. His ambitions didn't run that way. Unlike Sabine's.

Bryce nudged her backup dance bag over on the coatrack to make room for her purse, and asked the wolves, "What are you watching tonight?" Whatever it was, she'd already decided to curl up with a romance novel in her room. With the door shut.

Nathalie, flipping through celebrity gossip magazines on the couch, didn't lift her head as she answered, "Some new legal procedural about a pack of lions taking on an evil Fae corporation."

"Sounds like a real award winner," Bryce said. Bronson grunted his disapproval. The massive male's tastes skewed more toward art house flicks and documentaries. Unsurprisingly, he was never allowed to select the entertainment for Pack Night.

Connor ran a calloused finger down the rolled arm of the couch. "You're home late."

"I have a job," Bryce said. "You might want to get one. Stop being a leech on my couch."

This wasn't exactly fair. As Danika's Second, Connor acted as her enforcer. To keep this city safe, he'd killed, tortured, maimed, and then gone back out and done it again before the moon had even set.

He never complained about it. None of them did.

What's the point in bitching, Danika had said when Bryce asked how she endured the brutality, *when there's no choice in joining the Auxiliary?* The predator-born shifters were destined for certain Aux packs before they were even born.

Bryce tried not to glance at the horned wolf tattooed on the side of Connor's neck—proof of that predestined lifetime of service. Of his eternal loyalty to Danika, the Pack of Devils, and the Aux.

Connor just looked Bryce over with that half smile. It set her teeth to grinding. "Danika's in the kitchen. Eating half the pizza before we can get a bite."

"*I am not!*" was the muffled reply.

Connor's smile grew.

Bryce's breathing turned a shade uneven at that smile, the wicked light in his eyes.

The rest of the pack remained dutifully focused on the television screen, pretending to watch the nightly news.

Swallowing, Bryce asked him, "Anything I should know?" Translation: *Was the Briggs meeting a disaster?*

Connor knew what she meant. He always did. He jerked his head to the kitchen. "You'll see."

Translation: *Not great.*

Bryce winced, and managed to tear her gaze away from him so she could pad into the galley kitchen. She felt Connor's stare on her every step of the way.

And maybe she swished her hips. Only a tiny bit.

Danika was indeed shoveling a slice down her throat, her eyes wide in warning for Bryce to keep her mouth shut. Bryce noted the unspoken plea, and merely nodded.

A half-empty bottle of beer dripped condensation onto the white plastic counter Danika leaned against, her borrowed silk shirt damp with sweat around the collar. Her braid drooped over her slim shoulder, the few colorful streaks unusually muted. Even her pale skin, usually flushed with color and health, seemed ashen.

Granted, the crappy kitchen lighting—two meager recessed orbs of firstlight—wasn't exactly favorable to anyone, but . . . Beer. Food. The pack keeping their distance. And that hollow weariness in her friend's eyes—yeah, some shit had gone down in that meeting.

Bryce tugged open the fridge, grabbing a beer for herself. The pack all had different preferences, and were prone to coming over whenever they felt like it, so the fridge was crammed with bottles and cans and what she could have sworn was a jug of . . . mead? Must be Bronson's.

Bryce grabbed one of Nathalie's favorites—a cloudy, milky-tasting beer, heavy on the hops—and twisted off the top. "Briggs?"

"Officially released. Micah, the Autumn King, and the Oracle pored over every law and bylaw and still couldn't find a way around that loophole. Ruhn even had Declan run some of his fancy tech searches and found nothing. Sabine ordered the Scythe Moon Pack to watch Briggs tonight, along with some of the 33rd." The packs had mandatory nights off once a week, and this was the Pack of Devils'—no negotiating. Otherwise, Bryce knew Danika would be out there, watching Briggs's every move.

"So you're all in agreement," Bryce said. "At least that's good."

"Yeah, until Briggs blows something or someone up." Danika shook her head with disgust. "It's fucking bullshit."

Bryce studied her friend carefully. The tension around her mouth, her sweaty neck. "What's wrong?"

"Nothing's wrong."

The words were spoken too quickly to be believable. "Something's been eating at you. Shit like this thing with Briggs is big, but you always bounce back." Bryce narrowed her eyes. "What aren't you telling me?"

Danika's eyes gleamed. "Nothing." She swigged from her beer.

There was only one other answer. "I take it Sabine was in rare form this afternoon."

Danika just tore into her pizza.

Bryce swallowed two mouthfuls of beer, watching Danika blankly consider the teal cabinets above the counter, the paint chipping at the edges.

Her friend chewed slowly, then said around a mouthful of bread and cheese, "Sabine cornered me after the meeting. Right in the hall outside Micah's office. So everyone could hear her tell me that two CCU research students got killed near Luna's Temple last week during the blackout. My shift. My section. My fault."

Bryce winced. "It took a *week* to hear about this?"

"Apparently."

"Who killed them?"

Crescent City University students were *always* out in the Old Square, always causing trouble. Even as alums Bryce and Danika often bemoaned the fact that there wasn't a sky-high electric fence penning CCU students into their corner of the city. Just to keep them from puking and pissing all over the Old Square every Friday night to Sunday morning.

Danika drank again. "No clue who did it." A shiver, her caramel eyes darkening. "Even with their scents marking them as human, it took twenty minutes to identify who they were. They were ripped to shreds and partially eaten."

Bryce tried not to imagine it. "Motive?"

Danika's throat bobbed. "No idea, either. But Sabine told me in front of everyone exactly what she thought of such a public butchering happening on my watch."

Bryce asked, "What'd the Prime say about it?"

"Nothing," Danika said. "The old man fell asleep during the meeting, and Sabine didn't bother to wake him before cornering me." It would be soon now, everyone said—only a matter of a year or two until the current Prime of the wolves, nearly four hundred years old, had his Sailing across the Istros to the Bone Quarter for his final sleep. There was no way the black boat would tip for him during the final rite—no way his soul would be deemed unworthy and given to the river. He'd be welcomed into the Under-King's realm, granted access to its mist-veiled shores . . . and then Sabine's reign would begin.

Gods spare them all.

"It's not your fault, you know," Bryce said, flipping open the cardboard lids of the two closest pizza boxes. Sausage, pepperoni, and meatball in one. The other held cured meats and stinky cheeses—Bronson's choice, no doubt.

"I know," Danika muttered, draining the last of her beer, clunking the bottle in the sink, and rooting around in the fridge for another. Every muscle in her lean body seemed taut—on a hair trigger. She slammed the fridge shut and leaned against it. Danika didn't meet Bryce's eyes as she breathed, "I was three blocks away that night. *Three*. And I didn't hear or see or smell them being shredded."

Bryce became aware of the silence from the other room. Keen hearing in both human and wolf form meant endless, *entitled* eavesdropping.

They could finish this conversation later.

Bryce flipped open the rest of the pizza boxes, surveying the culinary landscape. "Shouldn't you put them out of their misery and let them get a bite before you demolish the rest?"

She'd had the pleasure of witnessing Danika eat three large pies in one sitting. In this sort of mood, Danika might very well break her record and hit four.

"Please let us eat," begged Bronson's deep, rumbling voice from the other room.

Danika swigged from her beer. "Come get it, mongrels."

The wolves rushed in.

In the frenzy, Bryce was nearly flattened against the back wall of the kitchen, the monthly calendar pinned to it crumpling behind her.

Damn it—she loved that calendar: *Hottest Bachelors of Crescent City: Clothing-Optional Edition.* This month had the most gorgeous daemonaki she'd ever seen, his propped leg on a stool the only thing keeping *everything* from being shown. She smoothed out the new wrinkles in all the tan skin and muscles, the curling horns, and then turned to scowl at the wolves.

A step away, Danika stood among her pack like a stone in a river. She smirked at Bryce. "Any update on your hunt for the Horn?"

"No."

"Jesiba must be thrilled."

Bryce grimaced. "Overjoyed." She'd seen Jesiba for all of two minutes this afternoon before the sorceress threatened to turn Bryce into a donkey, and then vanished in a chauffeured sedan to the gods knew where. Maybe off on some errand for the Under-King and the dark House he ruled.

Danika grinned. "Don't you have that date with what's-his-face tonight?"

The question clanged through Bryce. "Shit. *Shit.* Yes." She winced at the kitchen clock. "In an hour."

Connor, taking an entire pizza box for himself, stiffened. He'd made his thoughts on Bryce's rich-ass boyfriend clear since the first date two months ago. Just as Bryce had made it perfectly clear she did not give a fuck about Connor's opinion regarding her love life.

Bryce took in his muscled back as Connor stalked out, rolling his broad shoulders. Danika frowned. She never missed a fucking thing.

"I need to get dressed," Bryce said, scowling. "And his name is Reid, and you know it."

A wolfish smile. "Reid's a stupid fucking name," Danika said.

"One, *I* think it's a hot name. And two, *Reid* is hot." Gods help her, Reid Redner was hot as Hel. Though the sex was . . . fine. Standard. She'd gotten off, but she'd really had to work for it. And not in the way she sometimes *liked* to work for it. More in the sense of *Slow down, Put that here, Can we switch positions?* But she'd slept with him only twice. And she told herself that it could take time to find the right rhythm with a partner. Even if . . .

Danika just said it. "If he grabs his phone to check his messages before his dick's barely out of you again, please have the self-respect to kick his balls across the room and come home to me."

"Fucking Hel, Danika!" Bryce hissed. "Say it a little gods-damn louder."

The wolves had gone silent. Even their munching had stopped. Then resumed just a decibel too loudly.

"At least he's got a good job," Bryce said to Danika, who crossed her slender arms—arms that hid tremendous, ferocious strength—and gave her a look. A look that said, *Yeah, one that Reid's daddy gave him*. Bryce added, "And at least he's not some psychotic alphahole who will demand a three-day sex marathon and then call me his mate, lock me in his house, and never let me out again." Which was why Reid—human, okay-at-sex Reid—was perfect.

"You could use a three-day sex marathon," Danika quipped.

"You're to blame for this, you know."

Danika waved a hand. "Yeah, yeah. My first and last mistake: setting you two up."

Danika knew Reid casually through the part-time security work she did for his father's business—a massive human-owned magitech company in the Central Business District. Danika claimed that the work was too boring to bother explaining, but paid well enough that she couldn't say no. And more than that—it was a job she *chose.* Not the life she'd been shoved into. So between her patrols and obligations with the Aux, Danika was often at the towering skyscraper in the CBD—pretending she had a shot at a normal life. It was unheard of for any Aux member to have a secondary job—for an Alpha, especially—but Danika made it work.

It didn't hurt that everyone wanted a piece of Redner Industries these days. Even Micah Domitus was a major investor in its cutting-edge experiments. It was nothing out of the ordinary, when the Governor invested in everything from tech to vineyards to schools, but since Micah was on Sabine's eternal shit list, pissing off her mother by working for a human company he supported was likely even better for Danika than the sense of free will and generous pay.

Danika and Reid had been in the same presentation one afternoon months ago—exactly when Bryce had been single and complaining constantly about it. Danika had given Bryce's number to Reid in a last-ditch effort to preserve her sanity.

Bryce smoothed a hand over her dress. "I need to change. Save me a slice."

"Aren't you going out for dinner?"

Bryce cringed. "Yeah. To one of those frilly spots—where they give you salmon mousse on a cracker and call it a meal."

Danika shuddered. "Definitely fill up before, then."

"A slice," Bryce said, pointing at Danika. "Remember my slice." She eyed the one remaining box and padded out of the kitchen.

The Pack of Devils were now all in human form—save for Zelda—pizza boxes balanced on knees or spread on the worn blue rug. Bronson was indeed swigging from the ceramic jug of mead, his brown eyes fixed on the nightly news broadcast. The news about Briggs's release—along with grainy footage of the human male being escorted out of the jail complex in a white jumpsuit—began blasting. Whoever held the remote quickly changed the channel to a documentary on the Black River delta.

Nathalie gave Bryce a shit-eating grin as she strode for her bedroom door at the opposite end of the living room. Oh, Bryce wouldn't live down that little tidbit about Reid's performance in the bedroom anytime soon. Especially when Nathalie was sure to make it a reflection on Bryce's skills.

"Don't even start," Bryce warned her. Nathalie clamped her lips together, like she could hardly keep the howl of wicked amusement contained. Her sleek black hair seemed to quiver with the effort of holding in her laughter, her onyx eyes near-glowing.

Bryce pointedly ignored Connor's heavy golden stare as he tracked her across the space.

Wolves. Gods-damned wolves shoving their noses into her business.

There would never be any mistaking them for humans, though their forms were nearly identical. Too tall, too muscled, too still. Even the way they tore into their pizzas, each movement deliberate and graceful, was a silent reminder of what they could do to anyone who crossed them.

Bryce walked over Zach's sprawled, long legs, and carefully avoided stepping on Zelda's snow-white tail, where she lay on the floor beside her brother. The twin white wolves, both slender and dark-haired in human form, were utterly terrifying when they shifted. *The Ghosts*—the whispered nickname followed them everywhere.

So, yeah. Bryce tried really hard not to step on Zelda's fluffy tail.

Thorne, at least, threw Bryce a sympathetic smile from where he sat in the half-rotted leather armchair near the television, his CCU sunball hat turned backward. He was the only other person in the apartment who understood how meddlesome the pack could be. And who cared as much about Danika's moods. About Sabine's ruthlessness.

It was a long shot for an Omega like Thorne to ever be noticed by an Alpha like Danika. Not that Thorne had ever so much as hinted at it to any of them. But Bryce saw it—the gravitational pull that seemed to happen whenever Danika and Thorne were in a room together, like they were two stars orbiting each other.

Mercifully, Bryce reached her bedroom without any comments

regarding her sort-of boyfriend's prowess, and shut the door behind her firmly enough to tell them all to fuck off.

She made it three steps toward her sagging green dresser before laughter barked through the apartment. It was silenced a moment later by a vicious, not-quite-human snarl. Deep and rumbling and utterly lethal.

Not Danika's snarl, which was like death incarnate, soft and husky and cold. This was Connor's. Full of heat and temper and feeling.

Bryce showered off the dust and grime that seemed to coat her whenever she made the fifteen-block walk between the apartment and the slim sandstone building that Griffin Antiquities occupied.

A few carefully placed pins erased the end-of-day limpness that usually plagued her heavy sheet of wine-red hair, and she hastily applied a fresh coat of mascara to bring some life back into her amber eyes. From shower to sliding on her black stiletto heels, it was a grand total of twenty minutes.

Proof, she realized, of how little she really cared about this date. She spent a gods-damned *hour* on her hair and makeup every morning. Not counting the thirty-minute shower to get herself gleaming, shaved, and moisturized. But twenty minutes? For dinner at the Pearl and Rose?

Yeah, Danika had a point. And Bryce knew the bitch was watching the clock, and would probably ask if the short prep time was reflective of how long, exactly, Reid could keep it going.

Bryce glared in the direction of the wolves beyond the door of her cozy bedroom before surveying the quiet haven around her. Every wall was bedecked in posters of legendary performances at the Crescent City Ballet. Once, she'd imagined herself up there among the lithe Vanir, exploding across the stage in turn after turn, or making audiences weep with an agonizing death scene. Once, she'd imagined there might be a spot for a half-human female on that stage.

Even being told, over and over, that she had the *wrong body type* hadn't stopped her from loving to dance. Hadn't stopped that heady rush seeing a dance performed live, or her taking amateur classes after work, or her following CCB's dancers the way Connor, Ithan, and Thorne followed sports teams. Nothing could ever stop her from craving that soaring sensation she found when she was dancing, whether in class or at a club or even on the gods-damned street.

Juniper, at least, hadn't been deterred. Had decided that she was in it for the long haul, that a faun *would* defy the odds and grace a stage built for Fae and nymphs and sylphs—and leave them all in her dust. She'd done it, too.

Bryce loosed a long sigh. Time to go. It was a twenty-minute walk to the Pearl and Rose, and in these heels, it'd take her twenty-five. No point in getting a taxi during the chaos and congestion of Thursday night in the Old Square when the car would just *sit* there.

She stabbed pearl studs into her ears, hoping half-heartedly that they'd add some class to what might be considered a somewhat scandalous dress. But she was twenty-three, and she might as well enjoy her generously curved figure. She gave her gold-dusted legs a little smile as she twisted in front of the full-length mirror propped against the wall to admire the slope of her ass in the skintight gray dress, the hint of text from that still-sore new tattoo peeking over the plunging back, before she stepped into the living room again.

Danika let out a wicked laugh that rumbled over the nature show the wolves were watching. "I bet fifty silver marks the bouncers don't let you through the doors looking like that."

Bryce flipped off her friend as the pack chuckled. "I'm sorry if I make you feel self-conscious about your bony ass, Danika."

Thorne barked a laugh. "At least Danika makes up for it with her winning personality."

Bryce smirked at the handsome Omega. "That must explain why I have a date and she hasn't been on one in . . . what's it now? Three years?"

Thorne winked, his blue eyes sliding toward Danika's scowling face. "Must be why."

Danika slouched in her chair and propped her bare feet on the coffee table. Each toenail was painted a different color. "It's only been two years," she muttered. "Assholes."

Bryce patted Danika's silken head as she passed. Danika nipped at her fingers, teeth flashing.

Bryce chuckled, entering the narrow kitchen. She pawed through the upper cabinets, glass rattling as she searched for the—

Ah. The gin.

She knocked back a shot. Then another.

"Rough night ahead?" Connor asked from where he leaned against the kitchen doorway, arms crossed over his muscular chest.

A drop of gin had landed on her chin. Bryce narrowly avoided wiping the sin-red lipstick off her mouth with the back of her wrist and instead opted for patting it away with a leftover napkin from the pizza place. Like a proper person.

That color should be called Blow Job Red, Danika had said the first time Bryce had worn it. *Because that's all any male will think about when you wear it.* Indeed, Connor's eyes had dipped right to her lips. So Bryce said as nonchalantly as she could, "You know I like to enjoy my Thursday nights. Why not kick it off early?"

She balanced on her toes as she put the gin back in the upper cupboard, the hem of her dress rising precariously high. Connor studied the ceiling as if it were immensely interesting, his gaze only snapping to hers as she settled on her feet again. In the other room, someone turned the volume on the television up to an apartment-rattling level.

Thank you, Danika.

Even wolf hearing couldn't sort through that cacophony to eavesdrop.

Connor's sensuous mouth twitched upward, but he remained in the doorway.

Bryce swallowed, wondering how gross it would be to chase away the burn of the gin with the beer she'd left warming on the counter.

Connor said, "Look. We've known each other a while . . ."

"Is this a rehearsed speech?"

He straightened, color staining his cheeks. The Second in the Pack of Devils, the most feared and lethal of all the Auxiliary units, was *blushing*. "No."

"That sounded like a rehearsed introduction to me."

"Can you let me ask you out, or do I need to get into a fight with you about my phrasing first?"

She snorted, but her guts twisted. "I don't date wolves."

Connor threw her a cocky grin. "Make an exception."

"No." But she smiled slightly.

Connor merely said with the unwavering arrogance that only an immortal predator could achieve, "You want me. I want you. It's been that way for a while, and playing with these human males hasn't done a damn thing to make you forget that, has it?"

No, it hadn't. But she said, her voice mercifully calm despite her thundering heart, "Connor, I'm not going out with you. Danika is bossy enough. I don't need another wolf, especially a *male* wolf, trying to run my life. I don't need any more Vanir shoving into my business."

His golden eyes dimmed. "I'm not your father."

He didn't mean Randall.

She shoved off the counter, marching toward him. And the apartment door beyond. She was going to be late. "That has nothing to do with this—with you. My answer is no."

Connor didn't move, and she halted mere inches away. Even in heels, even though she fell on the taller side of average height, he towered over her. Dominated the entire space just by breathing.

Like any alphahole would. Like what her Fae father had done to nineteen-year-old Ember Quinlan, when he'd pursued her, seduced her, tried to keep her, and gone so far into possessive territory that the moment Ember had realized she was carrying his child—carrying *Bryce*—she ran before he could scent it and lock her up in his villa in FiRo until she grew too old to interest him.

Which was something Bryce didn't let herself consider. Not after the blood tests had been done and she'd walked out of the medwitch's office knowing that she'd taken after her Fae father in more ways than the red hair and pointed ears.

She would have to bury her mother one day, bury Randall, too. Which was utterly expected, if you were a human. But the fact that she'd go on living for a few more centuries, with only photos and videos to remind her of their voices and faces, made her stomach twist.

She should have had a third shot of gin.

Connor remained unmoving in the doorway. "One date won't send me into a territorial hissy fit. It doesn't even have to be a date. Just . . . pizza," he finished, glancing at the stacked boxes.

"You and I go out plenty." They did—on nights when Danika was called in to meet with Sabine or the other Aux commanders, he often brought over food, or he met up with her at one of the many restaurants lining the apartment's lively block. "If it's not a date, then how is it different?"

"It'd be a trial run. For a date," Connor said through his teeth.

She lifted a brow. "A date to decide if I want to date you?"

"You're impossible." He pushed off the doorjamb. "See you later."

Smiling to herself, she trailed him out of the kitchen, cringing at the monstrously loud television the wolves were all watching very, *very* intently.

Even Danika knew there were limits to how far she could push Connor without serious consequences.

For a heartbeat, Bryce debated grabbing the Second by the shoulder and explaining that he'd be better off finding a nice, sweet wolf who wanted to have a litter of pups, and that he didn't really want someone who was ten kinds of fucked-up, still liked to party until she was no better than a puking-in-an-alley CCU student, and wasn't entirely sure if she *could* love someone, not when Danika was all she really needed anyway.

But she didn't grab Connor, and by the time Bryce scooped her keys from the bowl beside the door, he'd slumped onto the couch—again, in *her* spot—and was staring pointedly at the screen. "Bye," she said to no one in particular.

Danika met her gaze from across the room, her eyes still wary but faintly amused. She winked. "Light it up, bitch."

"Light it up, asshole," Bryce replied, the farewell sliding off her tongue with the ease of years of usage.

But it was Danika's added "Love you" as Bryce slipped out into the grimy hallway that made her hesitate with her hand on the knob.

It'd taken Danika a few years to say those words, and she still used them sparingly. Danika had initially hated it when Bryce said them to her—even when Bryce explained that she'd spent most of her life saying it, just in case it *was* the last time. In case she wouldn't get to say goodbye to the people who mattered most. And it had taken one of their more fucked-up adventures—a trashed motorcycle, and literally having guns pointed at their heads—to get Danika to utter the words, but at least she now said them. Sometimes.

Forget Briggs's release. Sabine must have really done a number on Danika.

Bryce's heels clacked on the worn tile floor as she headed for the stairs at the end of the hall. Maybe she should cancel on Reid. She could grab some buckets of ice cream from the corner market and cuddle in bed with Danika while they watched their favorite absurd comedies.

Maybe she'd call up Fury and see if she could pay a little visit to Sabine.

But—she'd never ask that of Fury. Fury kept her professional shit out of their lives, and they knew better than to ask too many questions. Only Juniper could get away with it.

Honestly, it made no sense that any of them were friends: the future Alpha of all wolves, an assassin for high-paying clients waging war across the sea, a stunningly talented dancer and the only faun *ever* to grace the stage of the Crescent City Ballet, and . . . her.

Bryce Quinlan. Assistant to a sorceress. Would-be, *wrong-body-type* dancer. Chronic dater of preening, breakable human men who had no idea what to do with her. Let alone what to do with Danika, if they ever got far enough into the dating crucible.

Bryce clomped down the stairs, scowling at one of the orbs of firstlight that cast the crumbling gray-blue paint in flickering relief. The landlord went as cheap as possible on the firstlight, likely siphoning it off the grid rather than paying the city for it like everyone else.

Everything in this apartment building was a piece of shit, to be honest.

Danika could afford better. Bryce certainly couldn't. And Danika knew her well enough not to even suggest that she alone pay for one of the high-rise, glossy apartments by the river's edge or in the CBD. So after graduation, they'd only looked at places Bryce could swing with her paycheck—this particular shithole being the least miserable of them.

Sometimes, Bryce wished she'd accepted her monstrous father's money—wished she hadn't decided to develop some semblance of morals at the exact moment the creep had offered her mountains of gold marks in exchange for her eternal silence about him. At least then she'd currently be lounging by some sky-high pool deck, ogling oiled-up angels as they swaggered past, and not avoiding the letch of a janitor who leered at her chest anytime she had to complain about the trash chute being blocked yet again.

The glass door at the bottom of the stairwell led onto the night-darkened street, already packed with tourists, revelers, and bleary-eyed residents trying to squeeze their way home through the rowdy crowds after a long, hot summer day. A draki male clad in a suit and tie rushed past, messenger bag bobbing at his hip as he wove his way around a family of some sort of equine shifters—perhaps horses, judging by their scents full of open skies and green fields—all so busy snapping photos of everything that they remained oblivious to anyone trying to get somewhere.

At the corner, a pair of bored malakim clad in the black armor of the 33rd kept their wings tucked in tight to their powerful bodies, no doubt to avoid any harried commuter or drunk idiot touching them. Touch an angel's wings without permission and you'd be lucky to lose just a hand.

Firmly shutting the glass door behind her, Bryce soaked in the tangle of sensations that was this ancient, vibrant city: the dry summer heat that threatened to bake her very bones; the honk of car horns slicing through the steady hiss and dribble of music leaking from the revel halls; the wind off the Istros River, three blocks away, rustling the swaying palms and cypresses; the hint of brine from the nearby turquoise sea; the seductive, night-soft smell of the crawling jasmine wrapped around the iron park fence nearby; the tang of puke and piss and stale beer; the beckoning, smoky spices crusting the slow-roasting lamb at the vendor's cart on the corner . . . It all hit her in one awakening kiss.

Trying not to snap her ankles on the cobblestones, Bryce breathed in the nightly offering of Crescent City, drank it deep, and vanished down the teeming street.

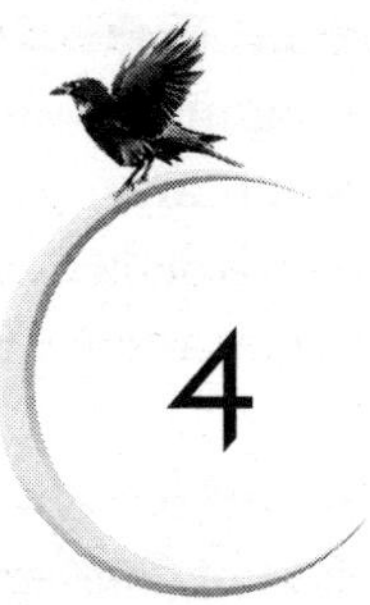

4

The Pearl and Rose was everything Bryce hated about this city.

But at least Danika now owed her fifty silver marks.

The bouncers had let her stride past them, up the three steps, and through the open bronze-plated doors of the restaurant.

But even fifty silver marks wouldn't put so much as a dent in paying for this meal. No, this would be firmly in the *gold* zone.

Reid could certainly afford it. Given the size of his bank account, he likely wouldn't even glance at the check before handing over his black card.

Seated at a table in the heart of the gilded dining room, under the crystal chandeliers dangling from the intricately painted ceiling, Bryce went through two glasses of water and half a bottle of wine while she waited.

Twenty minutes in, her phone buzzed in her black silk clutch. If Reid was canceling on her, she'd kill him. There was no fucking way she could afford to pay for the wine—not without having to give up dance classes for the next month. Two months, actually.

But the messages weren't from Reid, and Bryce read them three times before chucking her phone back in her purse and pouring another glass of very, very expensive wine.

Reid was rich *and* he was late. He owed her.

Especially since the upper echelons of Crescent City were entertaining themselves by sneering at her dress, the skin on display, the Fae ears but clearly human body.

Half-breed—she could nearly hear the hateful term as they thought it. They considered her a lowly worker at best. Prey and dumpster fodder at worst.

Bryce took out her phone and read the messages a fourth time.

Connor had written, *You know I'm shit with talking. But what I wanted to say—before you tried to get into a fight with me instead, by the way—was that I think it's worth it. You and me. Giving us a shot.*

He'd added: *I'm crazy about you. I don't want anyone else. I haven't for a long while. One date. If it doesn't work, then we'll deal with it. But just give me a chance. Please.*

Bryce was still staring at the messages, her head spinning from all that gods-damned wine, when Reid finally appeared. Forty-five minutes late.

"Sorry, babe," he said, leaning in to kiss her cheek before sliding onto his chair. His charcoal-gray suit remained immaculate, his golden skin glowing above the collar of his white shirt. Not one dark brown hair on his head was out of place.

Reid had the easy manners of someone brought up with money, education, and no doors locked to his desires. The Redners were one of the few human families who had risen into Vanir high society—and dressed for the part. Reid was meticulous about his appearance, down to the very last detail. Every tie he wore, she'd learned, was selected to bring out the green in his hazel eyes. His suits were always impeccably cut to his toned body. She might have called him vain, had she not put such consideration into her own outfits. Had she not known that Reid worked with a personal trainer for the exact reason that she kept dancing—beyond her love for it—making sure her body was primed for when its strength might be needed to escape any would-be predator hunting the streets.

Since the day the Vanir had crawled through the Northern Rift and overtaken Midgard eons ago, an event historians called the Crossing, running was the best option if a Vanir decided to make a meal of you. That is, if you didn't have a gun or bombs or any of the horrid things people like Philip Briggs had developed to kill even a long-lived, quick-healing creature.

She often wondered about it: what it had been like before this planet had found itself occupied by creatures from so many different worlds, all of them far more advanced and *civilized* than this one, when it was just humans and ordinary animals. Even their calendar system hearkened to the Crossing, and the time before and after it: H.E. and V.E.—*Human Era* and *Vanir Era*.

Reid lifted his dark brows at the mostly empty bottle of wine. "Nice choice."

Forty-five minutes. Without a call or a message to tell her he'd be late.

Bryce gritted her teeth. "Something came up at work?"

Reid shrugged, scanning the restaurant for high-ranking officials to hobnob with. As the son of a man who had his name displayed in twenty-foot letters on three buildings in the CBD, people usually lined up to chat with him. "Some of the malakim are restless about developments in the Pangeran conflict. They needed reassurance their investments were still sound. The call ran long."

The Pangeran conflict—the fighting Briggs so badly wanted to bring to this territory. The wine that had gone to her head eddied into an oily pool in her gut. "The angels think the war might spread here?"

Spying no one of interest in the restaurant, Reid flipped open his leather-bound menu. "No. The Asteri wouldn't let that happen."

"The Asteri let it happen over there."

His lips twitched downward. "It's a complicated issue, Bryce."

Conversation over. She let him go back to studying the menu.

Reports of the territory across the Haldren Sea were grim: the human resistance was prepared to wipe themselves out rather than submit to the Asteri and their "elected" Senate's rule. For forty years now, the war had raged in the vast Pangeran territory, wrecking cities, creeping toward the stormy sea. Should the conflict cross it, Crescent City, sitting on Valbara's southeastern coast—midway up a peninsula called the Hand for the shape of the arid, mountainous land that jutted out—would be one of the first places in its path.

Fury refused to talk about what she saw over there. What she did over there. What side she fought for. Most Vanir did not find a challenge to more than fifteen thousand years of their reign amusing.

Most humans did not find fifteen thousand years of near-slavery, of being prey and food and whores, to be all that amusing, either. Never mind that in recent centuries, the Imperial Senate had granted humans more rights—with the Asteri's approval, of course. The fact remained that anyone who stepped out of line was thrown right back to where they'd started: literal slaves to the Republic.

The slaves, at least, existed mostly in Pangera. A few lived in Crescent City, namely among the warrior-angels in the 33rd, the Governor's personal legion, marked by the *SPQM* slave tattoo on their wrists. But they blended in, for the most part.

Crescent City, for all that its wealthiest were grade A assholes, was still a melting pot. One of the rare places where being a human didn't necessarily mean a lifetime of menial labor. Though it didn't entitle you to much else.

A dark-haired, blue-eyed Fae female caught Bryce's cursory glance around the room, her boy toy across the table marking her as some sort of noble.

Bryce had never decided whom she hated more: the winged malakim or the Fae. The Fae, probably, whose considerable magic and grace made them think they were allowed to do what they pleased, with anyone they pleased. A trait shared by many members of the House of Sky and Breath: the swaggering angels, the lofty sylphs, and the simmering elementals.

House of Shitheads and Bastards, Danika always called them. Though her own allegiance to the House of Earth and Blood might have shaded her opinion a bit—especially when the shifters and Fae were forever at odds.

Born of two Houses, Bryce had been forced to yield her allegiance to the House of Earth and Blood as part of accepting the civitas rank her father had gotten her. It had been the price paid for accepting the coveted citizen status: he'd petition for full citizenship, but she would have to claim Sky and Breath as her House.

She'd resented it, resented the bastard for making her choose, but even her mother had seen that the benefits outweighed the costs.

Not that there were many advantages or protections for humans within the House of Earth and Blood, either. Certainly not for the young man seated with the Fae female.

Beautiful, blond, no more than twenty, he was likely a tenth of his Fae companion's age. The tanned skin of his wrists held no hint of the four-lettered slave tattoo. So he had to be with her through his own free will, then—or desire for whatever she offered: sex, money, influence. It was a fool's bargain, though. She'd use him until she was bored, or he grew too old, and then dump his ass at the curb, still craving those Fae riches.

Bryce inclined her head to the noblewoman, who bared her too-white teeth at the insolence. The Fae female was beautiful—but most of the Fae were.

She found Reid watching, a frown on his handsome face. He shook his head—at *her*—and resumed reading the menu.

Bryce sipped her wine. Signaled the waiter to bring over another bottle.

I'm crazy about you.

Connor wouldn't tolerate the sneering, the whispering. Neither would Danika. Bryce had witnessed *both* of them rip into the stupid assholes who'd hissed slurs at her, or who mistook her for one of the many half-Vanir females who scraped a living in the Meat Market by selling their bodies.

Most of those women didn't get the chance to complete the Drop—either because they didn't make it to the threshold of maturity or because they got the short end of the stick with a mortal life span. There were predators, both born and trained, who used the Meat Market as a personal hunting ground.

Bryce's phone buzzed, right as the waiter finally made his way over, fresh bottle of wine in hand. Reid frowned again, his disapproval heavy enough that she refrained from reading the message until she'd ordered her beef-with-cheese-foam sandwich.

Danika had written, *Dump the limp-dicked bastard and put Connor out of his misery. A date with him won't kill you. He's been waiting years, Bryce. Years. Give me something to smile about tonight.*

Bryce cringed as she shoved her phone back into her bag. She looked up to find Reid on his own phone, thumbs flying, his chiseled features illuminated by the dim screen. Their invention five decades ago had occurred right in Redner Industries' famed tech lab, and vaulted the company into unprecedented fortune. A new era of linking the world, everyone claimed. Bryce thought they just gave people an excuse not to make eye contact. Or be bad dates.

"Reid," she said. He just held up a finger.

Bryce tapped a red nail on the base of her wineglass. She kept her nails long—and took a daily elixir to keep them strong. Not as effective as talons or claws, but they could do some damage. At least enough to potentially get away from an assailant.

"Reid," she said again. He kept typing, and looked up only when the first course appeared.

It was indeed a salmon mousse. Over a crisp of bread, and encaged in some latticework of curling green plants. Small ferns, perhaps. She swallowed her laugh.

"Go ahead and dig in," Reid said distantly, typing again. "Don't wait for me."

"One bite and I'll be done," she muttered, lifting her fork but wondering how the Hel to eat the thing. No one around them used their fingers, but . . . The Fae female sneered again.

Bryce set down the fork. Folded her napkin into a neat square before she rose. "I'm going."

"All right," Reid said, eyes fixed on his screen. He clearly thought she was going to the bathroom. She could feel the eyes of a well-dressed angel at the next table travel up her expanse of bare leg, then heard the chair groan as he leaned back to admire the view of her ass.

Exactly why she kept her nails strong.

But she said to Reid, "No—I'm leaving. Thank you for dinner."

That made him look up. "What? Bryce, sit down. Eat."

As if his being late, being on the phone, weren't part of this. As if she were just something he needed to feed before he fucked. She said clearly, "This isn't working out."

His mouth tightened. "Excuse me?"

She doubted he'd ever been dumped. She said with a sweet smile, "Bye, Reid. Good luck with work."

"Bryce."

But she had enough gods-damned self-respect not to let him explain, not to accept sex that was merely okay basically in exchange for meals at restaurants she could never afford, and a man who had indeed rolled off her and gotten right back on that phone. So she swiped the bottle of wine and stepped away from the table, but not toward the exit.

She went up to the sneering Fae female and her human plaything and said in a cool voice that would have made even Danika back away, "Like what you see?"

The female gave her a sweeping glance, from Bryce's heels to her red hair to the bottle of wine dangling from her fingers. The Fae female shrugged, setting the black stones in her long dress sparkling. "I'll pay a gold mark to watch you two." She inclined her head to the human at her table.

He offered Bryce a smile, his vacant face suggesting he was soaring high on some drug.

Bryce smirked at the female. "I didn't know Fae females had gotten so cheap. Word on the street used to be that you'd pay us gold by the armful to pretend you're not lifeless as Reapers between the sheets."

The female's tan face went white. Glossy, flesh-shredding nails snagged on the tablecloth. The man across from her didn't so much as flinch.

Bryce put a hand on the man's shoulder—in comfort or to piss off the female, she wasn't sure. She squeezed lightly, again inclining her head toward the female, and strode out.

She swigged from the bottle of wine and flipped off the preening hostess on her way through the bronze doors. Then snatched a handful of matchbooks from the bowl atop the stand, too.

Reid's breathless apologies to the noble drifted behind her as Bryce stepped onto the hot, dry street.

Well, shit. It was nine o'clock, she was decently dressed, and if she went back to that apartment, she'd pace around until Danika bit her head off. And the wolves would shove their noses into her business, which she didn't want to discuss with them *at all*.

Which left one option. Her favorite option, fortunately.

Fury picked up on the first ring. "What."

"Are you on this side of the Haldren or the wrong one?"

"I'm in Five Roses." The flat, cool voice was laced with a hint of amusement—practically outright laughter, coming from Fury. "But I'm not watching television with the pups."

"Who the Hel would want to do that?"

A pause on the line. Bryce leaned against the pale stone exterior of the Pearl and Rose. "I thought you had a date with what's-his-face."

"You and Danika are the worst, you know that?"

She practically heard Fury's wicked smile through the line. "I'll meet you at the Raven in thirty minutes. I need to finish up a job."

"Go easy on the poor bastard."

"That's not what I was paid to do."

The line went dead. Bryce swore and prayed Fury wouldn't reek of blood when she got to their preferred club. She dialed another number.

Juniper was breathless when she picked up on the fifth ring, right before it went to audiomail. She must have been in the studio, practicing after-hours. As she always did. As Bryce loved to do whenever she had a spare moment herself. To dance and dance and dance, the world fading into nothing but music and breath and sweat. "Oh, you dumped him, didn't you?"

"Did motherfucking Danika send a message to *everyone*?"

"No," the sweet, lovely faun replied, "but you've been on your date for only an hour. Since the recap calls usually happen the morning after . . ."

"We're going to the Raven," Bryce snapped. "Be there in thirty." She hung up before Juniper's quicksilver laugh set her cursing.

Oh, she'd find a way to punish Danika for telling them. Even though she knew it'd been meant as a warning, to prepare them for any picking up the pieces, if necessary. Just as Bryce had checked in with Connor regarding Danika's state earlier that evening.

The White Raven was only a five-minute walk away, right in the heart of the Old Square. Which left Bryce with enough time to either really, truly get into trouble, or face what she'd been avoiding for an hour now.

She opted for trouble.

Lots of trouble, enough to empty out the seven hard-earned gold marks in her purse as she handed them over to a grinning draki female, who slipped everything Bryce asked for into her waiting palm. The female had tried to sell her on some new party drug—*Synth will make you feel like a god*, she said—but the thirty gold marks for a single dose had been well above Bryce's pay grade.

She was still left with five minutes. Standing across from the White Raven, the club still teeming with revelers despite Briggs's failed plan to blast it apart, Bryce pulled out her phone and opened the thread with Connor. She'd bet all the money she'd just blown on mirthroot that he was checking his phone every two seconds.

Cars crawled past, the bass of their sound systems thumping over the cobblestones and cypresses, windows down to reveal passengers eager to start their Thursday: drinking; smoking; singing along to the music; messaging friends, dealers, whoever might get them into one of the dozen clubs that lined Archer Street. Queues already snaked from the doors, including the Raven's. Vanir peered up in anticipation at the white marble facade, well-dressed pilgrims waiting at the gates of a temple.

The Raven was just that: a temple. Or it had been. A building now encased the ruins, but the dance floor remained the original, ancient stones of some long-forgotten god's temple, and the carved stone pillars throughout still stood from that time. To dance inside was to worship that nameless god, hinted at in the age-worn carvings of satyrs and fauns drinking and dancing and fucking amid grapevines. A temple to pleasure—that's what it had once been. And what it had become again.

A cluster of young mountain-lion shifters prowled past, a few twisting back to growl in invitation. Bryce ignored them and sidled over to an alcove at the left of the Raven's service doors. She leaned against the slick stone, tucked the wine into the crook of her arm, braced a foot on the wall behind her as she bobbed her head to the music pouring out of a nearby car, and finally typed: *Pizza. Saturday night at six. If you're late, it's over.*

Instantly, Connor began typing in reply. Then the bubble paused. Then started again.

Then finally, the message came.

I'll never keep you waiting.

She rolled her eyes and wrote, *Don't make promises you can't keep.*

More typing, deleting, typing. Then, *You mean it—about the pizza?*

Do I look like I'm joking, Connor?

You looked delicious when you left the apartment.

Heat curled in her, and she bit her lip. Charming, arrogant bastard. *Tell Danika I'm going to the Raven with Juniper and Fury. I'll see you in two days.*

Done. What about what's-his-face?

REID is officially dumped.

Good. I was getting worried I'd have to kill him.

Her gut churned.

He quickly added, *Kidding, Bryce. I won't go alphahole on you, I promise.*

Before she could answer, her phone buzzed again.

Danika, this time. *HOW DARE YOU GO TO THE RAVEN WITHOUT ME. TRAITOR.*

Bryce snorted. *Enjoy Pack Night, loser.*

DO NOT HAVE FUN WITHOUT ME. I FORBID YOU.

She knew that as much as it killed Danika to stay in, she wouldn't leave the pack. Not on the one night they all had together, the night they used to keep the bonds between them strong. Not after this shitstorm of a day. And especially not while Briggs was on the loose, with a reason to get back at the whole Pack of Devils.

That loyalty was why they loved Danika, why they fought so fiercely for her, went to the mat for her again and again when Sabine publicly wondered if her daughter was worthy of the responsibilities and status as second in line. The power hierarchy among the wolves of Crescent City was dictated by dominance alone—but the three-generation lineage that made up the Prime of the wolves, Prime Apparent, and whatever Danika was (the Apparent Prime Apparent?) was a rarity. Powerful, ancient bloodlines was the usual explanation.

Danika had spent countless hours looking into the history of the dominant shifter packs in other cities—why lions had come to rule in Hilene, why tigers oversaw Korinth, why falcons reigned in Oia. Whether the dominance that determined the Prime Alpha status passed through families or skipped around. Non-predatory shifters could head up a city's Aux, but it was rare. Honestly, most of it bored Bryce to tears. And if Danika had ever learned why the Fendyr family claimed such a large share of the dominance pie, she'd never told Bryce.

Bryce wrote back to Connor, *Good luck handling Danika.*

He simply replied, *She's telling me the same about you.*

Bryce was about to put her phone away when the screen flashed again. Connor had added, *You won't regret this. I've had a long while to figure out all the ways I'm going to spoil you. All the fun we're going to have.*

Stalker. But she smiled.

Go enjoy yourself. I'll see you in a few days. Message me when you're home safe.

She reread the conversation twice because she really was an absolute fucking loser, and was debating asking Connor to skip waiting and just meet her *now*, when something cool and metal pressed against her throat.

"And you're dead," crooned a female voice.

Bryce yelped, trying to calm the heart that had gone from stupid-giddy to stupid-scared in the span of one beat.

"Don't fucking *do* that," she hissed at Fury as the female lowered the knife from Bryce's throat and sheathed it across her back.

"Don't be a walking target," Fury said coolly, her long onyx hair tied high in a ponytail that brought out the sharp lines of her light brown face. She scanned the line into the Raven, her deep-set chestnut eyes marking everything and promising death to anyone who crossed her. But beneath that . . . mercifully, the black leather leggings, skintight velvet top, and ass-kicking boots did *not* smell of blood. Fury gave Bryce a once-over. "You barely put on any makeup. That little human should have taken one look at you and known you were about to dump his ass."

"He was too busy on his phone to notice."

Fury glanced pointedly at Bryce's own phone, still clenched in a death grip in her hand. "Danika's going to nail your balls to the wall when I tell her I caught you distracted like that."

"It's her own damn fault," Bryce snapped.

A sharp smile was her only response. Bryce knew Fury was Vanir, but she had no idea what kind. No idea what House Fury belonged to, either. Asking wasn't polite, and Fury, aside from her preternatural speed, grace, and reflexes, had never revealed another form, nor any inkling of magic beyond the most basic.

But she was a civitas. A full citizen, which meant she had to be something they deemed worthy. Given her skill set, the House of Flame and Shadow was the likeliest place for her—even if Fury was certainly not a daemonaki, vampyr, or even a wraith. Definitely not a witch-turned-sorceress like Jesiba, either. Or a necromancer, since her gifts seemed to be taking life, not illegally bringing it back.

"Where's the leggy one?" Fury asked, taking the wine bottle from Bryce and swigging as she scanned the teeming clubs and bars along Archer Street.

"Hel if I know," Bryce said. She winked at Fury and held up the plastic bag of mirthroot, jostling the twelve rolled black cigarettes. "I got us some goodies."

Fury's grin was a flash of red lips and straight white teeth. She reached into the back pocket of her leggings and held up a small bag of white powder that glittered with a fiery iridescence in the glow of the streetlamp. "So did I."

Bryce squinted at the powder. "Is that what the dealer just tried to sell me?"

Fury went still. "What'd she say it was?"

"Some new party drug—gives you a godlike high, I don't know. Super expensive."

Fury frowned. "Synth? Stay away from it. That's some bad shit."

"All right." She trusted Fury enough to heed the warning. Bryce peered at the powder Fury still held in her hand. "I can't take anything that makes me hallucinate for days, please. I have work tomorrow." When she had to at least pretend she had some idea how to find that gods-damned Horn.

Fury tucked the bag into her black bra. She swigged from the wine again before passing it back to Bryce. "Jesiba won't be able to scent it on you, don't worry."

Bryce linked elbows with the slender assassin. "Then let's go make our ancestors roll over in their graves."

5

Going on a date with Connor in a few days didn't mean she had to behave.

So within the inner sanctum of the White Raven, Bryce savored every delight it offered.

Fury knew the owner, Riso, either through work or whatever the Hel she did in her personal life, and as such, they never had to wait in line. The flamboyant butterfly shifter always left a booth open for them.

None of the smiling, colorfully dressed waiters who brought over their drinks so much as blinked at the lines of glittering white powder Fury arranged with a sweep of her hand or the plumes of smoke that rippled from Bryce's parted lips as she tipped her head back to the domed, mirrored ceiling and laughed.

Juniper had a studio class at dawn, so she abstained from the powder and smoke and booze. But it didn't stop her from sneaking away for a good twenty minutes with a broad-chested Fae male who took in the dark brown skin, the exquisite face and curling black hair, the long legs that ended in delicate hooves, and practically begged on his knees for the faun to touch him.

Bryce reduced herself into the pulsing beat of the music, to the euphoria glittering through her blood faster than an angel diving out of the sky, to the sweat sliding down her body as she writhed on the ancient dance floor. She would barely be able to walk tomorrow, would have half a brain, but holy shit—*more, more, more.*

Laughing, she swooped over the low-lying table in their private booth between two half-crumbling pillars; laughing, she arched away, a red nail releasing its hold on one nostril as she sagged against the dark leather bench; laughing, she knocked back water and elderberry wine and stumbled again into the dancing throng.

Life was good. Life was fucking *good*, and she couldn't godsdamn wait to make the Drop with Danika and do this until the earth crumbled into dust.

She found Juniper dancing amid a pack of sylph females celebrating a friend's successful Drop. Their silvery heads were adorned with circlets of neon glow sticks chock-full of their friend's designated allotment of her own firstlight, which she'd generated when she successfully completed the Drop. Juniper had managed to swipe a glow-stick halo for herself, and her hair shone with blue light as she extended her hands to Bryce, their fingers linking as they danced.

Bryce's blood pulsed in time to the music, as if she had been crafted just for this: the moment when she *became* the notes and rhythm and the bass, when she became song given form. Juniper's glittering eyes told Bryce that she understood, had always understood the particular freedom and joy and unleashing that came from dancing. Like their bodies were so full of sound they could barely contain it, could barely stand it, and only *dance* could express it, ease it, honor it.

Males and females gathered to watch, their lust coating Bryce's skin like sweat. Juniper's every movement matched hers without so much as a lick of hesitation, as if they were question and answer, sun and moon.

Quiet, pretty Juniper Andromeda—the exhibitionist. Even dancing in the sacred, ancient heart of the Raven, she was sweet and mild, but she shone.

Or maybe that was all the lightseeker Bryce had ingested up her nose.

Her hair clung to her sweaty neck, her feet were utterly numb thanks to the steep angle of her heels, her throat was ravaged from screaming along to the songs that blasted through the club.

She managed to shoot a few messages to Danika—and one video, because she could barely read any of what was coming in anyway.

She'd be so royally fucked if she showed up at work tomorrow unable to *read*.

Time slowed and bled. Here, dancing among the pillars and upon the timeworn stones of the temple that had been reborn, no time existed at all.

Maybe she'd live here.

Quit her job at the gallery and live in the club. They could hire her to dance in one of the steel cages dangling from the glass ceiling high above the temple ruins that made up the dance floor. They certainly wouldn't spew bullshit about a *wrong body type*. No, they'd pay her to do what she loved, what made her come alive like nothing else.

It seemed like a reasonable enough plan, Bryce thought as she stumbled down her own street later with no recollection of leaving the Raven, saying goodbye to her friends, or of how the Hel she'd even gotten here. Taxi? She'd blown all her marks on the drugs. Unless someone had paid . . .

Whatever. She'd think about it tomorrow. If she could even sleep. She wanted to stay awake, to dance for-gods-damn-*ever*. Only . . . oh, her feet fucking *hurt*. And they were near-black and *sticky*—

Bryce paused outside her building door and groaned as she unstrapped her heels and gathered them in a hand. A code. Her building had a code to get in.

Bryce contemplated the keypad as if it'd open a pair of eyes and tell her. Some buildings did that.

Shit. Shiiit. She pulled out her phone, the glaring screen light burning her eyes. Squinting, she could make out a few dozen message alerts. They blurred, her eyes trying and failing to focus enough to read one single coherent letter. Even if she somehow managed to call Danika, her friend would rip her head off.

The screech of the building buzzer would piss off Danika even more. Bryce cringed, hopping from foot to foot.

What was the code? The code, the code, the cooooode . . .

Oh, there it was. Tucked into a back pocket of her mind.

She cheerfully punched in the numbers, then heard the buzz as the lock opened with a faint, tinny sound.

She scowled at the reek of the stairwell. That gods-damned janitor. She'd kick his ass. Impale him with these useless, cheap stilettos that had wrecked her feet—

Bryce set a bare foot on the stairs and winced. This was going to hurt. Walking-on-glass hurt.

She let her heels clunk to the tile floor, whispering a fervent promise to find them tomorrow, and gripped the black-painted metal banister with both hands. Maybe she could straddle the banister and scoot herself up the stairs.

Gods, it stunk. What did the people in this building *eat*? Or, for that matter, *who* did they eat? Hopefully not wasted, stupid-high, half-Fae females who couldn't manage to walk up the stairs.

If Fury had laced the lightseeker with something else, she'd fucking *kill* her.

Snorting at the idea of even attempting to kill the infamous Fury Axtar, Bryce hauled herself up the stairs, step by step.

She debated sleeping on the second-level landing, but the stench was overwhelming.

Maybe she'd get lucky and Connor would still be at the apartment. And then she'd *really* get lucky.

Gods, she wanted good sex. No-holds-barred, scream-your-lungs-out sex. Break-the-bed sex. She knew Connor would be like that. More than that. It'd go far beyond the physical with him. It might honestly melt whatever was left of her mind after tonight.

It was why she'd been a coward, why she'd avoided thinking about it from the moment he'd leaned in her doorway five years ago, having come to say hi to Danika and meet her new roommate, and they'd just . . . stared at each other.

Having Connor living four doors down freshman year had been

the worst sort of temptation. But Danika had given the order to stay away until Bryce approached *him*, and even though they hadn't yet formed the Pack of Devils, Connor obeyed. It seemed Danika had lifted the order tonight.

Lovely, wicked Danika. Bryce smiled as she half crawled onto the third-floor landing, found her balance, and dug her keys out of her purse—which she'd managed to hold on to by some miracle. She took a few swaying steps down the hall they shared with one other apartment.

Oh, Danika was going to be so pissed. *So* pissed that Bryce had not only had fun without her, but that she'd gotten so wasted she couldn't remember how to read. Or the code to the building.

The flickering firstlight stung her eyes enough that she again squinted them to near-darkness and staggered down the hall. She should shower, if she could remember how to operate the handles. Wash off her filthy, numb feet.

Especially after she stepped in a cold puddle beneath some dripping ceiling pipe. She shuddered, bracing a hand on the wall, but kept staggering ahead.

Fuck. Too many drugs. Even her Fae blood couldn't clear them out fast enough.

But there was her door. Keys. Right—she had them in her hand already.

There were six. Which one was hers? One opened the gallery; one opened the various tanks and cages in the archives; one opened Syrinx's crate; one was to the chain on her scooter; one was *to* her scooter . . . and one was to the door. This door.

The brass keys tinkled and swayed, shining in the firstlights, then blending with the painted metal of the hall. They slipped out of her slackening fingers, clanking on the tile.

"*Fuuuuuuck.*" The word was a long exhale.

Bracing a hand on the doorframe to keep from falling clean on her ass, Bryce stooped to pick up the keys.

Something cool and wet met her fingertips.

Bryce closed her eyes, willing the world to stop spinning. When she opened them, she focused on the tile before the door.

Red. And the smell—it wasn't the reek of before.

It was blood.

And the apartment door was already open.

The lock had been mangled, the handle wrenched off completely.

Iron—the door was *iron*, and enchanted with the best spells money could buy to keep out any unwanted guests, attackers, or magic. Those spells were the one thing Bryce had ever allowed Danika to purchase on her behalf. She hadn't wanted to know how much they'd cost, not when it was likely double her parents' annual salary.

But the door now looked like a crumpled piece of paper.

Blinking furiously, Bryce straightened. Fuck the drugs in her system—fuck Fury. She'd promised no hallucinations.

Bryce was *never* drinking or polluting her body with those drugs *ever again*. She'd tell Danika first thing tomorrow. No more. No. More.

She rubbed her eyes, mascara smearing on her fingertips. On her blood-soaked fingertips—

The blood remained. The mangled door, too.

"Danika?" she croaked. If the attacker was still inside . . . "Danika?"

That bloody hand—her own hand—pushed the half-crumpled door open farther.

Blackness greeted her.

The coppery tang of blood, and that festering odor, slammed into her.

Her entire body seized, every muscle going on alert, every instinct screaming to *run, run, run*—

But her Fae eyes adjusted to the dark, revealing the apartment.

What was left of it.

What was left of them.

Help—she needed to get *help*, but—

She staggered into the trashed apartment.

"Danika?" The word was a raw, broken sound.

The wolves had fought. There wasn't a piece of furniture that was intact, that wasn't shredded and splintered.

There wasn't a body intact, either. Piles and clumps were all that remained.

"DanikaDanikaDanika—"

She needed to call someone, needed to scream for help, needed to get Fury, or her brother, her father, needed Sabine—

Bryce's bedroom door was destroyed, the threshold painted in blood. The ballet posters hung in ribbons. And on the bed . . .

She knew in her bones it was not a hallucination, what lay on that bed, knew in her bones that what bled out inside her chest was her heart.

Danika lay there. In pieces.

And at the foot of the bed, littering the torn carpet in even smaller pieces, as if he'd gone down defending Danika . . . she knew that was Connor.

Knew the heap just to the right of the bed, closest to Danika . . . That was Thorne.

Bryce stared. And stared.

Perhaps time stopped. Perhaps she was dead. She couldn't feel her body.

A clanging, echoing *thunk* sounded from outside. Not from the apartment, but the hall.

She moved. The apartment warped, shrinking and expanding as if it were breathing, the floors rising with each inhale, but she managed to move.

The small kitchen table lay in fragments. Her blood-slick, shaking fingers wrapped around one of its wooden legs, silently lifting it over her shoulder. She peered into the hall.

It took a few blinks to clear her contracting vision. The godsdamned drugs—

The trash chute hatch lay open. Blood that smelled of wolf coated the rusty metal door, and prints that did not belong to a human stained the tile floor, aiming toward the stairs.

It was real. She blinked, over and over, swaying against the door—

Real. Which meant—

From far away, she saw herself launch into the hallway.

Saw herself slam into the opposite wall and rebound off it, then scramble into a sprint toward the stairwell.

Whatever had killed them must have heard her coming and hidden inside the trash chute, waiting for the chance to leap out at her or slink away unnoticed—

Bryce hit the stairs, a glowing white haze creeping over her vision. It blazed through every inhibition, disregarded every warning bell.

The glass door at the bottom of the stairs was already shattered. People screamed outside.

Bryce leapt from the top of the landing.

Her knees popped and buckled as she cleared the stairs, her bare feet shredding on the glass littering the lobby floor. Then they ripped open more as she hurtled through the door and into the street, scanning—

People were gasping to the right. Others were screaming. Cars had halted, drivers and passengers all staring toward a narrow alley between the building and its neighbor.

Their faces blurred and stretched, twisting their horror into something grotesque, something strange and primordial and—

This was no hallucination.

Bryce sprinted across the street, following the screams, the *reek*—

Her breath tore apart her lungs as she hurtled along the alley, dodging piles of trash. Whatever she was chasing had gotten only a brief head start.

Where was it, where was it?

Every logical thought was a ribbon floating above her head. She read them, as if following a stock ticker mounted on a building's side in the CBD.

One glimpse, even if she couldn't kill it. One glimpse, just to ID it, for Danika—

Bryce cleared the alley, careening onto bustling Central Avenue, the street full of fleeing people and honking cars. She leapt over their hoods, scaling them one after another, every movement as smooth as one of her dance steps. *Leap, twirl, arch*—her body did not fail her. Not as she followed the creature's rotting stench to another alley. Another and another.

They were almost at the Istros. A snarl and roar rent the air ahead. It had come from another connected alley, more of a dead-end alcove between two brick buildings.

She hefted the table leg, wishing she'd grabbed Danika's sword instead, wondering if Danika had even had time to unsheathe it—

No. The sword was in the gallery, where Danika had ignored Jesiba's warning and left it in the supply closet. Bryce launched herself around the alley's corner.

Blood everywhere. *Everywhere.*

And the thing halfway down the alley . . . not Vanir. Not one she'd encountered before.

A demon? Some feral thing with smooth, near-translucent gray skin. It crawled on four long, spindly limbs, but looked vaguely humanoid. And it was feasting on someone else.

On—on a malakh.

Blood covered the angel's face, soaking his hair and veiling the swollen, battered features beneath. His white wings were splayed and snapped, his powerful body arced in agony as the beast ripped at his chest with a maw of clear, crystalline fangs that easily dug through skin and bone—

She did not think, did not feel.

She moved, fast like Randall had taught her, brutal like he'd made her learn to be.

She slammed the table leg into the creature's head so hard that bone and wood cracked.

It was thrown off the angel and whirled, its back legs twisting beneath it while its front legs—*arms*—gouged lines in the cobblestones.

The creature had no eyes. Only smooth planes of bone above deep slits—its nose.

And the blood that leaked from its temple . . . it was clear, not red.

Bryce panted, the malakh male groaning some wordless plea as the creature sniffed at her.

She blinked and blinked, willing the lightseeker and mirthroot out of her system, willing the image ahead to stop blurring—

The creature lunged. Not for her—but the angel. Right back to the chest and heart it was trying to get to. The more considerable prey.

Bryce launched forward, table leg swinging again. The reverberations against bone bit into her palm. The creature roared, blindly surging at her.

She dodged, but its sharp, clear fangs ripped her thigh clean open as she twisted away.

She screamed, losing her balance, and swung upward as it leapt again, this time for her throat.

Wood smashed those clear teeth. The demon shrieked, so loudly that her Fae ears nearly ruptured, and she dared all of one blink—

Claws scraped, hissing sounded, and then it was gone.

It was just clearing the lip of the brick building the malakh lay slumped against. She could track it from the streets, could keep it in sight long enough for the Aux or 33rd to come—

Bryce had dared one step when the angel groaned again. His hand was against his chest, pushing weakly. Not hard enough to stop the death-bite from gushing blood. Even with his fast healing, even if he'd made the Drop, the injuries were substantial enough to be fatal.

Someone screamed in a nearby street as the creature jumped between buildings.

Go, go, *go*.

The angel's face was so battered it was barely more than a slab of swollen flesh.

The table leg clattered into a puddle of the angel's blood as she dove for him, biting down her scream at the burning gash in her thigh. Someone had poured *acid* onto her skin, her bones.

Unbearable, impenetrable darkness swept through her, blanketing everything within.

But she shoved her hand against the angel's wound, not allowing herself to feel the wet, torn flesh, the jagged bone of his cleaved sternum. The creature had been eating its way into his heart—

"Phone," she panted. "Do you have a phone?"

The angel's white wing was so shredded it was mostly red splinters. But it shifted slightly to reveal the pocket of his black jeans. The square lump in them.

How she managed to pull out the phone with one hand was beyond her. Time was still snagging, speeding and stopping. Pain lanced through her leg with every breath.

But she gripped the sleek black device in her wrecked hands, her red nails almost snapping with the force as she punched in the emergency number.

A male voice answered on the first ring. "Crescent City Rescue—"

"Help." Her voice broke. *"Help."*

A pause. "Miss, I need you to specify where you are, what the situation is."

"Old Square. River—off the river, near Cygnet Street . . ." But that was where she lived. She was blocks away from that. Didn't know the cross streets. "Please—please help."

The angel's blood soaked her lap. Her knees were bleeding, scraped raw.

And Danika was

And Danika was

And Danika was

"Miss, I need you to tell me where you are—we can have wolves on the scene in a minute."

She sobbed then, and the angel's limp fingers brushed against her torn knee. As if in comfort.

"Phone," she managed, interrupting the responder. "His phone—track it, track us. Find us."

"Miss, are you—"

"Track this phone number."

"Miss, I need a moment to—"

She pulled up the main screen of the phone, clicking through pages in a haze until she found the number herself. *"112 03 0577."*

"Miss, the records are—"

"112 03 0577!" she screamed into the phone. Over and over. *"112 03 0577!"*

It was all she could remember. That stupid number.

"Miss—holy gods." The line crackled. "They're coming," the responder breathed.

He tried to inquire about the injuries on the male, but she dropped the angel's phone as the drugs pulled her back, yanked her down, and she swayed. The alley warped and rippled.

The angel's gaze met hers, so full of agony she thought it was what her soul must look like.

His blood poured out between her fingers. It did not stop.

6

The half-Fae female looked like Hel.

No, not Hel, Isaiah Tiberian realized as he studied her through the one-way mirror in the legion's holding center. She looked like death.

Looked like the soldiers he'd seen crawl off the blood-drenched battlefields of Pangera.

She sat at the metal table in the center of the interrogation room, staring at nothing. Just as she had done for hours now.

A far cry from the screaming, thrashing female Isaiah and his unit had found in the Old Square alley, her gray dress ripped, her left thigh gushing enough blood that he wondered if she'd faint. She'd been half-wild, either from the sheer terror of what had occurred, the grief sinking in, or the drugs that had been coursing through her system.

Likely a combination of all three. And considering that she was not only a source of information regarding the attack, but also currently a danger to herself, Isaiah had made the call to bring her into the sterile, subterranean processing center a few blocks from the Comitium. A witness, he'd made damn sure the records stated. Not a suspect.

He blew out a long breath, resisting the urge to rest his forehead against the observation window. Only the incessant hum of the firstlights overhead filled the space.

The first bit of quiet he'd had in hours. He had little doubt it would end soon.

As if the thought had tempted Urd herself, a rough male voice spoke from the door behind him. "She's still not talking?"

It took all two centuries of Isaiah's training on and off the battlefield to avoid flinching at that voice. To turn slowly toward the angel he knew would be leaning against the doorway, wearing his usual black battle-suit—an angel who reason and history reminded him was an ally, though every instinct roared the opposite.

Predator. Killer. Monster.

Hunt Athalar's angular dark eyes, however, remained fixed on the window. On Bryce Quinlan. Not one gray feather on his wings rustled. Ever since their first days in the 17th Legion in southern Pangera, Isaiah had tried to ignore the fact that Hunt seemed to exist within a permanent ripple of stillness. It was the bated silence before a thunderclap, like the entire land held its breath when he was near.

Given what he'd seen Hunt do to his enemies and chosen targets, it came as no surprise.

Hunt's stare slid toward him.

Right. He'd been asked a question. Isaiah shifted his white wings. "She hasn't said a word since she was brought in."

Hunt again regarded the female through the window. "Has the order come down yet to move her to another room?"

Isaiah knew exactly what sort of room Hunt referred to. Rooms designed to get people to talk. Even witnesses.

Isaiah straightened his black silk tie and offered up a half-hearted plea to the five gods that his charcoal business suit wouldn't be stained with blood by sunrise. "Not yet."

Hunt nodded once, his golden-brown face betraying nothing.

Isaiah scanned the angel, since Hunt sure as Hel wasn't going to volunteer anything without being prompted. No sign of the skull-faced helmet that had earned Hunt a nickname whispered down every corridor and street in Crescent City: the Umbra Mortis.

The Shadow of Death.

Unable to decide whether to be relieved or worried at the absence of Hunt's infamous helmet, Isaiah wordlessly handed Micah's personal assassin a thin file.

He made sure his dark brown fingers didn't touch Hunt's gloved ones. Not when blood still coated the leather, its scent creeping through the room. He recognized the angelic scent in that blood, so the other scent had to be Bryce Quinlan's.

Isaiah jerked his chin to the white-tiled interrogation room. "Bryce Quinlan, twenty-three years old, half-Fae, half-human. Blood test from ten years ago confirmed she'll have an immortal life span. Power rating near-negligible. Hasn't made the Drop yet. Listed as a full civitas. Found in the alley with one of our own, trying to keep his heart from falling out with her bare hands."

The words sounded so damn clinical. But he knew Hunt was well versed in the details. They both were. They'd been in that alley, after all. And they knew that even here, in the secure observation room, they'd be fools to risk saying anything delicate aloud.

It had taken both of them to get Bryce to her feet, only for her to collapse against Isaiah—not from grief but from pain.

Hunt had realized it first: her thigh had been shredded open.

She'd still been nearly feral, had thrashed as they guided her back to the ground, Isaiah calling for a medwitch as the blood gushed out of her thigh. An artery had been hit. It was a godsdamn miracle she wasn't dead before they arrived.

Hunt had cursed up a storm as he knelt before her, and she'd bucked, nearly kicking him in the balls. But then he'd pulled off his helmet. Looked her right in the eye.

And told her to calm the fuck down.

She'd fallen completely silent. Just stared at Hunt, blank and hollow. She didn't so much as flinch with each punch of the staple gun Hunt had pulled from the small medkit built into his battlesuit. She just stared and stared and stared at the Umbra Mortis.

Yet Hunt hadn't lingered after he'd stapled her leg shut—he'd launched into the night to do what he did best: find their enemies and obliterate them.

As if noticing the blood on his gloves, Hunt swore and peeled them off, dumping them into the metal trash can by the door.

Then the male leafed through Quinlan's thin file, his shoulder-length black hair slipping over his unreadable face.

"Seems like she's your standard spoiled party girl," he said, turning the pages. A corner of Hunt's mouth curved upward, anything but amused. "And what a surprise: she's Danika Fendyr's roommate. The Party Princess herself."

No one but the 33rd used that term—because no one else in Lunathion, not even the Fae royals, would have dared. But Isaiah motioned to keep reading. Hunt had left the alley before he'd learned the entire scope of this disaster.

Hunt kept reading. His brows rose. "Holy fucking Urd."

Isaiah waited for it.

Hunt's dark eyes widened. "Danika Fendyr is dead?" He read further. "Along with the entire Pack of Devils." He shook his head and repeated, "Holy fucking Urd."

Isaiah took back the file. "It is totally and completely fucked, my friend."

Hunt's jaw clenched. "I didn't find any trace of the demon that did this."

"I know." At Hunt's questioning glance, Isaiah clarified, "If you had, you'd be holding a severed head in your hands right now and not a file."

Isaiah had been there—on many occasions—when Hunt had done just that, returning triumphant from a demon-hunting mission he'd been ordered to go on by whatever Archangel currently held their reins.

Hunt's mouth twitched slightly, as if remembering the last time he'd presented a kill in such a manner, but he crossed his powerful arms. Isaiah ignored the inherent dominance in the position. There was a pecking order among them, the five-warrior team who made up the triarii—the most elite of all the Imperial Legion units. Micah's little cabal.

Though Micah had appointed Isaiah the Commander of the 33rd, he'd never formally declared him its leader. But Isaiah had always assumed he stood right at the top, the unspoken finest soldier of the triarii, despite his fancy suit and tie.

Where Hunt fell, however . . . no one had really decided in the two years since he'd arrived from Pangera. Isaiah wasn't entirely sure he really wanted to know, either.

Tracking down and eliminating any demons who crept through cracks in the Northern Rift or entered this world through an illegal summoning was his official role, and one well suited to Hunt's particular skill set. The gods knew how many of them he'd tracked down over the centuries, starting from that very first Pangeran unit they'd been in together—the 17th—dedicated to sending the creatures into the afterlife.

But the work Hunt did in the shadows for the Archangels—for Micah, currently—that was what had earned him his nickname. Hunt answered directly to Micah, and the rest of them stayed out of his way.

"Naomi just arrested Philip Briggs for the murders," Isaiah said, naming the captain of the 33rd's infantry. "Briggs got out of jail today—and Danika and the Pack of Devils were the ones who busted him in the first place." That the honor hadn't gone to the 33rd had irked Isaiah to no end. At least Naomi had been the one to apprehend him tonight. "How the fuck a human like Briggs could summon a demon that powerful, I don't know."

"I suppose we'll find out soon enough," Hunt said darkly.

Yeah, they fucking would. "Briggs has to be ten kinds of stupid to have been released only to go for a kill that big." The leader of the Keres rebels—an offshoot of the larger rebellion movement, the Ophion—hadn't seemed dumb, though. Just a fanatic hell-bent on starting a conflict to mirror the war raging across the sea.

"Or maybe Briggs acted on the sole chance of freedom he had before we found an excuse to bring him back into custody," Hunt countered. "He knew his time was limited and wanted to make sure he got one up on the Vanir first."

Isaiah shook his head. "What a mess." Understatement of the century.

Hunt blew out a breath. "Has the press gotten wind of anything?"

"Not yet," Isaiah said. "And I got the order a few minutes ago that we're to keep it quiet—even if it'll be all over the news tomorrow morning."

Hunt's eyes gleamed. "I've got no one to tell."

Indeed, Hunt and the concept of *friends* didn't mesh well. Even among the triarii, even after being here for two years, Hunt still kept to himself. Still worked relentlessly toward one thing: freedom. Or rather, the slim chance of it.

Isaiah sighed. "How soon until Sabine gets here?"

Hunt checked his phone. "Sabine's on her way downstairs right—" The door blew open. Hunt's eyes flickered. "Now."

Sabine looked barely older than Bryce Quinlan, with her fine-boned face and long, silvery blond hair, but there was only an immortal's rage in her blue eyes. "Where is that half-breed whore—" She simmered as she spotted Bryce through the window. "I'll fucking *kill* her—"

Isaiah extended a white wing to block the Prime Apparent's path back out the door and into the interrogation room, a few steps to its left.

Hunt fell into a casual stance on her other side. Lightning danced along his knuckles.

A mild showing of the power Isaiah had witnessed being unleashed upon their enemies: lightning, capable of bringing down a building.

Whether ordinary angel or Archangel, the power was always some variation of the same: rain, storms, the occasional tornado—Isaiah himself could summon wind capable of keeping a charging enemy at bay, but none in living memory possessed Hunt's ability to harness lightning to his will. Or the depth of power to make it truly destructive. It had been Hunt's salvation and destruction.

Isaiah let one of his cold breezes sift through Sabine's corn-silk hair, over to Hunt.

They'd always worked well together—Micah had known it when he put Hunt with Isaiah two years ago, despite the entwined thorns tattooed across both their brows. Most of Hunt's mark was hidden by his dark hair, but there was no concealing the thin black band on his forehead.

Isaiah could barely remember what his friend had looked like before those Pangeran witches had branded him, working their infernal spells into the ink itself so they might never let his crimes be forgotten, so the witch-magic bound the majority of his power.

The halo, they called it—a mockery of the divine auras early humans had once portrayed angels as possessing.

There was no hiding it on Isaiah's brow, either, the tattoo on it the same as on Hunt's, and on the brows of the nearly two thousand rebel angels who had been such idealistic, brave fools two centuries ago.

The Asteri had created the angels to be their perfect soldiers and loyal servants. The angels, gifted with such power, had relished their role in the world. Until Shahar, the Archangel they'd once called the Daystar. Until Hunt and the others who'd flown in Shahar's elite 18th Legion.

Their rebellion had failed—only for the humans to begin their own forty years ago. A different cause, a different group and species of fighters, but the sentiment was essentially the same: the Republic was the enemy, the rigid hierarchies utter bullshit.

When the human rebels had started their war, one of the idiots should have asked the Fallen angels how their rebellion had failed, long before those humans were even born. Isaiah certainly could have given them some pointers on what not to do. And enlightened them about the consequences.

For there was also no hiding the second tattoo, stamped on their right wrists: *SPQM*.

It adorned every flag and letterhead of the Republic—the four letters encircled with seven stars—and adorned the wrist of every being owned by it. Even if Isaiah chopped off his arm, the limb that regrew would bear the mark. Such was the power of the witch-ink.

A fate worse than death: to become an eternal servant to those they'd sought to overthrow.

Deciding to spare Sabine from Hunt's way of dealing with things, Isaiah asked mildly, "I understand you are grieving, but do you have reason, Sabine, to want Bryce dead?"

Sabine snarled, pointing at Bryce, "She took the sword. That wannabe wolf took Danika's sword. I know she did, it's not at the apartment—and it's *mine*."

Isaiah had seen those details: that the heirloom of the Fendyr family was missing. But there was no sign of Bryce Quinlan possessing it. "What does the sword have to do with your daughter's death?"

Rage and grief warred in that feral face. Sabine shook her head, ignoring his question, and said, "Danika couldn't stay out of trouble. She could never keep her mouth *shut* and know when to be quiet around her enemies. And look what became of her. That stupid little bitch in there is still breathing, and Danika is *not*." Her voice nearly cracked. "Danika should have known better."

Hunt asked a shade more gently, "Known better about what?"

"All of it," Sabine snapped, and again shook her head, clearing her grief away. "Starting with that slut of a roommate." She whirled on Isaiah, the portrait of wrath. "Tell me *everything*."

Hunt said coolly, "He doesn't have to tell you shit, Fendyr."

As Commander of the 33rd Imperial Legion, Isaiah held an equal rank to Sabine: they both sat on the same governing councils, both answered to males of power within their own ranks and their own Houses.

Sabine's canines lengthened as she surveyed Hunt. "Did I fucking speak to you, Athalar?"

Hunt's eyes glittered. But Isaiah pulled out his phone, typing as he cut in calmly, "We're still getting the reports in. Viktoria is coming to talk to Miss Quinlan right now."

"I'll talk to her," Sabine seethed. Her fingers curled, as if ready to rip out Hunt's throat. Hunt gave her a sharp smile that told her to just try, the lightning around his knuckles twining up his wrist.

And fortunately for Isaiah, the interrogation room's door opened and a dark-haired woman in an immaculately tailored navy suit walked in.

They were a front, those suits that he and Viktoria wore. A sort of armor, yes, but also a last attempt to pretend that they were even remotely normal.

It was no wonder Hunt never bothered with them.

As Viktoria made her graceful approach, Bryce gave no acknowledgment of the stunning female who usually made people of *all* Houses do a double take.

But Bryce had been that way for hours now. Blood still stained the white bandage around her bare thigh. Viktoria sniffed delicately, her pale green eyes narrowing beneath the halo's dark tattoo on her brow. The wraith had been one of the few non-malakim who had rebelled with them two centuries ago. She'd been given to Micah soon afterward, and her punishment had gone beyond the brow tattoo and slave markings. Not nearly as brutal as what Isaiah and Hunt had endured in the Asteri's dungeons, and then in various Archangels' dungeons for years afterward, but its own form of torment that lasted even when their own had stopped.

Viktoria said, "Miss Quinlan."

She didn't respond.

The wraith dragged over a steel chair from the wall and set it on the other side of the table. Pulling a file from her jacket, Viktoria crossed her long legs as she perched on the seat.

"Can you tell me who is responsible for the bloodshed tonight?"

Not even a hitch of breath. Sabine growled softly.

The wraith folded her alabaster hands in her lap, the unnatural elegance the only sign of the ancient power that rippled beneath the calm surface.

Vik had no body of her own. Though she'd fought in the 18th, Isaiah had learned her history only when he'd arrived here ten years ago. How Viktoria had acquired this particular body, who it had once belonged to, he didn't ask. She hadn't told him. Wraiths wore bodies the way some people owned cars. Vainer wraiths switched them often, usually at the first sign of aging, but Viktoria had held on to this one for longer than usual, liking its build and movement, she'd said.

Now she held on to it because she had no choice. It had been Micah's punishment for her rebellion: to trap her within this body. Forever. No more changing, no more trading up for something newer and sleeker. For two hundred years, Vik had been contained, forced to weather the slow erosion of the body, now plainly visible: the thin lines starting to carve themselves around her eyes, the crease now etched in her forehead above the tattoo's twining band of thorns.

"Quinlan's gone into shock," Hunt observed, monitoring Bryce's every breath. "She's not going to talk."

Isaiah was inclined to agree, until Viktoria opened the file, scanned a piece of paper, and said, "I, for one, believe that you are not in full control of your body or actions right now."

And then she read a shopping list of a cocktail of drugs and alcohol that would stop a human's heart dead. Stop a lesser Vanir's heart, too, for that matter.

Hunt swore again. "Is there anything she didn't snort or smoke tonight?"

Sabine bristled. "Half-breed trash—"

Isaiah threw Hunt a look. All that was needed to convey the request.

Never an order—he'd never dared to order Hunt around. Not when the male possessed a hair-trigger temper that had left entire imperial fighting units in smoldering cinders. Even with the spells of the halo binding that lightning to a tenth of its full strength, Hunt's skills as a warrior made up for it.

But Hunt's chin dipped, his only sign that he'd agreed to Isaiah's request. "You'll need to complete some paperwork upstairs, Sabine." Hunt blew out a breath, as if reminding himself that Sabine was a mother who had lost her only child tonight, and added, "If you want time to yourself, you can take it, but you need to sign—"

"Fuck signing things and fuck time to myself. Crucify the bitch if you have to, but get her to give a statement." Sabine spat on the tiles at Hunt's booted feet.

Ether coated Isaiah's tongue as Hunt gave her the cool stare that served as his only warning to opponents on a battlefield. None had ever survived what happened next.

Sabine seemed to remember that, and wisely stormed into the hall. She flexed her hand as she did, four razor-sharp claws appearing, and slashed them through the metal door.

Hunt smiled at her disappearing figure. A target marked. Not today, not even tomorrow, but at one point in the future . . .

And people claimed the shifters got along better with the angels than the Fae.

Viktoria was saying gently to Bryce, "We have video footage from the White Raven, confirming your whereabouts. We have footage of you walking home."

Cameras covered all of Lunathion, with unparalleled visual and audio coverage, but Bryce's apartment building was old, and the mandatory monitors in the hallways hadn't been repaired in decades. The landlord would be getting a visit tonight for the code violations that had fucked this entire investigation. One tiny sliver of audio was all the building cameras had managed to catch—just the audio. It held nothing beyond what they already knew. The phones of the Pack of Devils had all been destroyed in the attack. Not one message had gone out.

"What we don't have footage of, Bryce," Viktoria went on, "is what happened in that apartment. Can you tell me?"

Slowly, as if she drifted back into her battered body, Bryce turned her amber eyes to Viktoria.

"Where's her family?" Hunt asked roughly.

"Human mother lives with the stepfather in one of the mountain towns up north—both peregrini," Isaiah said. "The sire wasn't registered or refused to acknowledge paternity. Fae, obviously. And likely one with some standing, since he bothered to get her civitas status."

Most of the offspring born to human mothers took their peregrini rank. And though Bryce had something of the Fae's elegant beauty, her face marked her as human—the gold-dusted skin, the smattering of freckles over her nose and high cheekbones, the full mouth. Even if the silken flow of red hair and arched ears were pure Fae.

"Have the human parents been notified?"

Isaiah dragged a hand over his tight brown curls. He'd been awoken by his phone's shrill ringing at two in the morning, hurtled from the barracks a minute after that, and was now starting to feel the effects of a sleepless night. Dawn was likely not far off. "Her mother was hysterical. She asked over and over if we knew why they'd attacked the apartment, or if it was Philip Briggs. She saw on the news that he'd been released on a technicality and was certain he did this. I have a patrol from the 31st flying out right now; the parents will be airborne within the hour."

Viktoria's voice slid through the intercom as she continued her interview. "Can you describe the creature that attacked your friends?"

But Quinlan was gone again, her eyes vacant.

They had fuzzy footage thanks to the street cameras, but the demon had moved faster than the wind and had known to keep out of lens range. They hadn't been able to ID it yet—even Hunt's extensive knowledge hadn't helped. All they had of it was a vague, grayish blur no slowdown could clarify. And Bryce Quinlan, charging barefoot through the city streets.

"That girl isn't ready to give a statement," Hunt said. "This is a waste of our time."

But Isaiah asked him, "Why does Sabine hate Bryce so much—why imply she's to blame for all this?" When Hunt didn't answer, Isaiah jerked his chin toward two files on the edge of the desk. "Look at Quinlan's. Only one standing crime before this—for public indecency during a Summer Solstice parade. She got a little frisky against a wall and was caught in the act. Holding cell overnight, paid the fine the next day, did community service for a month to get it wiped off any permanent record." Isaiah could have sworn a ghost of a smile appeared on Hunt's mouth.

But Isaiah tapped a calloused finger on the impressively thick stack beside it. "This is part *one* of Danika Fendyr's file. Of seven. Starts with petty theft when she was ten, continues until she reached her majority five years ago. Then it goes eerily quiet. If you ask me, Bryce was the one who was led down a road of ruination—and then maybe led Danika out of hers."

"Not far enough to keep from snorting enough lightseeker to kill a horse," Hunt said. "I'm assuming she didn't party alone. Were there any other friends with her tonight?"

"Two others. Juniper Andromeda, a faun who's a soloist at the City Ballet, and . . ." Isaiah flipped open the case file and muttered a prayer. "Fury Axtar."

Hunt swore softly at the mercenary's name.

Fury Axtar was licensed to kill in half a dozen countries. Including this one.

Hunt asked, "Fury was with Quinlan tonight?"

They'd crossed paths with the merc enough to know to stay the Hel away. Micah had even ordered Hunt to kill her. Twice.

But she had too many high-powered allies. Some, it was whispered, on the Imperial Senate. So both times, Micah had decided that the fallout over the Umbra Mortis turning Fury Axtar into veritable toast would be more trouble than it was worth.

"Yes," Isaiah said. "Fury was with her at the club."

Hunt frowned. But Viktoria leaned in to speak to Bryce once more.

"We're trying to find who did this. Can you give us the information we need?"

Only a shell sat before the wraith.

Viktoria said, in that luxurious purr that usually had people eating out of her palm, "I want to help you. I want to find who did this. And punish them."

Viktoria reached into her pocket, pulled out her phone, and set it faceup on the table. Instantly, its digital feed appeared on the small screen in the room with Isaiah and Hunt. They glanced between the wraith and the screen as a series of messages opened.

"We downloaded the data from your phone. Can you walk me through these?"

Glassy eyes tracked a small screen that rose from a hidden compartment in the linoleum floor. It displayed the same messages Isaiah and Hunt now read.

The first one, sent from Bryce, read, *TV nights are for waggle-tailed pups. Come play with the big bitches.*

And then a short, dark video, shaking as someone roared with laughter while Bryce flipped off the camera, leaned over a line of white powder—lightseeker—and sniffed it right up her freckled nose. She was laughing, so bright and alive that the woman in the room before them looked like a gutted corpse, and she shrieked into the camera, "LIGHT IT UP, DANIKAAAAA!"

Danika's written reply was precisely what Isaiah expected from the Prime Apparent of the wolves, whom he'd seen only from a distance at formal events and who had seemed poised to start trouble wherever she went: *I FUCKING HATE YOU. STOP DOING LIGHTSEEKER WITHOUT ME. ASSHOLE.*

Party Princess, indeed.

Bryce had written back twenty minutes later, *I just hooked up with someone in the bathroom. Don't tell Connor.*

Hunt shook his head.

But Bryce sat there as Viktoria read the messages aloud, the wraith stone-faced.

Danika wrote back, *Was it good?!!?*

Only good enough to take the edge off.

"This isn't relevant," Hunt murmured. "Pull in Viktoria."

"We have our orders."

"Fuck the orders. That woman is about to break, and not in a good way."

Then Bryce stopped responding to Danika.

But Danika kept messaging. One after another. Over the next two hours.

The show's over. Where are you assholes?

Why aren't you picking up your phone? I'm calling Fury.

Where the FUCK is Fury?

Juniper never brings her phone, so I'm not even gonna bother with her. Where are you?!!!

Should I come to the club? The pack's leaving in ten. Stop fucking strangers in the bathroom, because Connor's coming with me.

BRYYYYCE. When you look at your phone, I hope the 1,000 alerts piss you off.

Thorne is telling me to stop messaging you. I told him to mind his own fucking business.

Connor says to grow the Hel up and stop doing shady-ass drugs, because only losers do that shit. He wasn't happy when I said I'm not sure I can let you date a holier-than-thou priss.

Okay, we're leaving in five. See you soon, cocksucker. Light it up.

Bryce stared at the screen unblinkingly, her torn face sickly pale in the light of the monitor.

"The building's cameras are mostly broken, but the one in the hall was still able to record some audio, though its video footage was down," Viktoria said calmly. "Shall I play it?"

No response. So Viktoria played it.

Muffled snarling and screaming filled the speakers—quiet enough that it was clear the hall camera had picked up only the loudest noises coming from the apartment. And then someone was roaring—a feral wolf's roar. "*Please, please—*"

The words were cut off. But the hall camera's audio wasn't.

Danika Fendyr screamed. Something tumbled and crashed in the background—as if she'd been thrown into furniture. And the hall camera kept recording.

The screaming went on, and on, and on. Interrupted only by the camera's fritzed system. The muffled grunts and growls were wet and vicious, and Danika was begging, sobbing as she pleaded for mercy, wept and screamed for it to stop—

"Turn it off," Hunt ordered, stalking from the room. "Turn it off *now*." He was out so fast Isaiah couldn't stop him, instantly crossing the space to the door beside theirs and flinging it open before Isaiah had cleared the room.

But there was Danika, audio crackling in and out, the sound of her voice still pleading for mercy coming from the speakers in the ceiling. Danika, being devoured and shredded.

The silence from the murderer was as chilling as Danika's sobbing screams.

Viktoria twisted toward the door as Hunt barreled in, his face dark with fury, wings spreading. The Shadow of Death unleashed.

Isaiah tasted ether. Lightning writhed at Hunt's fingertips.

Danika's unending, half-muffled screams filled the room.

Isaiah stepped into the chamber in time to see Bryce explode.

He summoned a wall of wind around himself and Vik, Hunt no doubt doing the same, as Bryce shot out of her chair and flipped the table. It soared over Viktoria's head and slammed into the observation window.

A feral growl filled the room as she grabbed the chair she'd been sitting on, hurling it against the wall, so hard its metal frame dented and crumpled.

She vomited all over the floor. If his power hadn't been around Viktoria, it would have showered her absurdly expensive bespoke heels.

The audio finally cut off when the hall camera went on the fritz again—and stayed that way.

Bryce panted, staring at her mess. Then fell to her knees in it.

She puked again. And again. And then curled over her knees, her silky hair falling into the vomit as she rocked herself in the stunned silence.

She was half-Fae, assessed at a power level barely on the grid. What she'd just done to the table and chair . . . Pure, physical rage. Even the most aloof of the Fae couldn't halt an eruption of primal wrath when it overtook them.

Unfazed, Hunt approached her, his gray wings high to avoid dragging through the vomit.

"Hey." Hunt knelt at Bryce's side. He reached for her shoulder, but lowered his hand. How many people ever saw the hands of the Umbra Mortis reach for them with no hint of violence?

Hunt nodded toward the destroyed table and chair. "Impressive."

Bryce bowed farther over herself, her tan fingers near-white as they dug into her back hard enough to bruise. Her voice was a broken rasp. "I want to go home."

Hunt's dark eyes flickered. But he said nothing more.

Viktoria, frowning at the mess, slipped away to find someone to clean it.

Isaiah said, "You can't go home, I'm afraid. It's an active crime scene." And it was so wrecked that even if they scrubbed it with bleach, no Vanir would be able to walk in and not scent the slaughter. "It's not safe for you to return until we've found who did this. And why they did it."

Then Bryce breathed, "Does S-Sabine—"

"Yes," Isaiah said gently. "Everyone who was in Danika's life has been notified."

The entire world would know in a few hours.

Still kneeling beside her, Hunt said roughly, "We can move you to a room with a cot and a bathroom. Get you some clothes."

Her dress was so torn that most of her skin was on display, a rip along the waist revealing the hint of a dark tattoo down her back. He'd seen whores in the Meat Market wearing more modest clothes.

The phone in Isaiah's pocket buzzed. Naomi. The voice of the captain of the 33rd's infantry was strained when Isaiah answered. "Let the girl go. Right now. Get her out of this building, and for all our sakes, do *not* put anyone on her tail. Especially Hunt."

"Why? The Governor gave us the opposite order."

"I got a phone call," Naomi said. "From Ruhn fucking Danaan. He's livid that we didn't notify Sky and Breath about bringing in the girl. Says it falls under the Fae's jurisdiction and whatever the fuck else. So screw what the Governor wants—he'll thank us later for avoiding this enormous fucking headache. Let the girl go *now*. She can come back in with a Fae escort, if that's what those assholes want."

Hunt, having heard the entire conversation, studied Bryce Quinlan with a predator's unflinching assessment. As one of the triarii, Naomi Boreas answered only to Micah and owed them no explanation, but to disregard his direct order in favor of the Fae . . . Naomi added, "Do it, Isaiah." Then she hung up.

Despite Bryce's pointed Fae ears, her glazed eyes registered no sign that she'd heard.

Isaiah pocketed his phone. "You're free to go."

She uncurled on surprisingly steady legs, despite the bandage on one of them. Yet blood and dirt caked her bare feet. Enough of the former that Hunt said, "We've got a medwitch on-site."

But Bryce ignored him and limped out, through the open door and into the hall.

His eyes fixed on the doorway as the scuffle-hop of her steps faded.

For a long minute, neither of them spoke. Then Hunt blew out a breath and rose. "What room is Naomi putting Briggs in?"

Isaiah didn't get the chance to answer before footsteps sounded down the hall, approaching fast. Definitely not Bryce's.

Even in one of the most secure places in this city, Isaiah and Hunt positioned their hands within easy reach of their weapons, the former crossing his arms so that he might draw the gun hidden beneath his suit jacket, the latter letting his hand dangle at his thigh, inches from the black-hilted knife sheathed there. Lightning again writhed at Hunt's fingers.

A dark-haired Fae male burst through the interrogation room door. Even with a silver hoop through his lower lip, even with one side of his long raven-black hair buzzed, even with the sleeves of tattoos beneath the leather jacket, there was no disguising the heritage the strikingly handsome face broadcasted.

Ruhn Danaan, Crown Prince of the Valbaran Fae. Son of the Autumn King and the current possessor of the Starsword, fabled dark blade of the ancient Starborn Fae. Proof of the prince's Chosen One status among the Fae—whatever the Hel that meant.

That sword was currently strapped across Ruhn's back, its black hilt devouring the glaring firstlights. Isaiah had once heard someone say the sword was made from iridium mined from a meteorite, forged in another world—before the Fae had come through the Northern Rift.

Danaan's blue eyes simmered like the heart of a flame—though Ruhn himself bore no such magic. Fire magic was common among the Valbaran Fae, wielded by the Autumn King himself. But rumor claimed Ruhn's magic was more like those of his kin who ruled the sacred Fae isle of Avallen across the sea: power to summon shadows or mist that could not only veil the physical world, but the mind as well. Perhaps even telepathy.

Ruhn glanced at the vomit, scenting the female who'd just left. "Where the fuck is she?"

Hunt went still at the cold command in the prince's voice.

"Bryce Quinlan has been released," Isaiah said. "We sent her upstairs a few minutes ago."

Ruhn had to have taken a side entrance if he'd missed her, and they hadn't been warned by the front desk of his arrival. Perhaps he'd used that magic of his to worm through the shadows.

The prince turned toward the doorway, but Hunt said, "What's it to you?"

Ruhn bristled. "She's my cousin, asshole. We take care of our own."

A distant cousin, since the Autumn King had no siblings, but apparently the prince knew Bryce well enough to intervene.

Hunt threw Ruhn a grin. "Where were you tonight?"

"Fuck you, Athalar." Ruhn bared his teeth. "I suppose you heard that Danika and I got into it over Briggs at the Head meeting. What a lead. Good job." Each word came out more clipped than the last. "If I wanted to kill Danika, I wouldn't summon a fucking demon to do it. Where the fuck is Briggs? I want to talk to him."

"He's incoming." Hunt was still smiling. That lightning still danced at his knuckles. "And you don't get the first shot at him." Then he added, "Daddy's clout and cash only get you so far, Prince."

It made no difference that Ruhn headed up the Fae division of the Aux, and was as well trained as any of their elite fighters. Or that the sword on his back wasn't merely decorative.

It didn't matter to Hunt. Not where royals and rigid hierarchies were concerned.

Ruhn said, "Keep talking, Athalar. Let's see where it gets you."

Hunt smirked. "I'm shaking."

Isaiah cleared his throat. Burning Solas, the last thing he needed tonight was a brawl between one of his triarii and a prince of the Fae. He said to Ruhn, "Can you tell us if Miss Quinlan's behavior before the murder tonight was unusual or—"

"The Raven's owner told me she was drunk and had snorted a pile of lightseeker," Ruhn snapped. "But you'll find Bryce with that kind of shit in her system at least one night a week."

"Why does she do it at all?" Isaiah asked.

Ruhn crossed his arms. "She does what she wants. She always has." There was enough bitterness there to suggest history—bad history.

Hunt drawled, "Just how close are you two?"

"If you're asking whether I'm fucking her," Ruhn seethed, "the answer, asshole, is no. She's family."

"Distant family," Hunt pointed out. "I heard the Fae like to keep their bloodline undiluted."

Ruhn held his stare. And as Hunt smiled again, ether filled the room, the promise of a storm skittering over Isaiah's skin.

Wondering if he'd be dumb enough to get between them when Ruhn attempted to bash in Hunt's teeth and Hunt turned the prince into a pile of smoldering bones, Isaiah said quickly, "We're just trying to do our job, Prince."

"If you assholes had kept an eye on Briggs like you were supposed to, maybe this wouldn't have happened at all."

Hunt's gray wings flared slightly—a malakh's usual stance when preparing for a physical fight. And those dark eyes . . . They were the eyes of the feared warrior, the Fallen angel. The one who had smashed apart the battlefields he'd been ordered to fight on. The one who killed on an Archangel's whim, and did it so well they called him the Shadow of Death.

"Careful," Hunt said.

"Stay the fuck away from Bryce," Ruhn snarled before striding back through the door, presumably after his cousin. At least Bryce would have an escort.

Hunt flipped off the empty doorway. After a moment, he murmured, "The tracking device in the water Quinlan drank when she got here. What's the time frame on it?"

"Three days," Isaiah replied.

Hunt studied the knife sheathed at his thigh. "Danika Fendyr was one of the strongest Vanir in the city, even without making the Drop. She begged like a human by the end."

Sabine would never recover from the shame.

"I don't know of a demon that kills like that," Hunt mused. "Or disappears that easily. I couldn't find a trace. It's like it vanished back to Hel."

Isaiah said, "If Briggs is behind it, we'll learn what the demon is soon enough."

If Briggs talked at all. He certainly hadn't when he'd been busted in his bomb lab, despite the best efforts of the 33rd's interrogators and the Aux.

Isaiah added, "I'll have every available patrol quietly looking out for other young packs in the Auxiliary. If it winds up not being related to Briggs, then it could be the start of a pattern."

Hunt asked darkly, "If we find the demon?"

Isaiah shrugged. "Then make sure it's not a problem anymore, Hunt."

Hunt's eyes sharpened into lethal focus. "And Bryce Quinlan—after the three days are up?"

Isaiah frowned at the table, the crumpled chair. "If she's smart, she'll lie low and not attract the attention of any other powerful immortals for the rest of her life."

7

The black steps ringing the foggy shore of the Bone Quarter bit into Bryce's knees as she knelt before the towering ivory gates.

The Istros spread like a gray mirror behind her, silent in the predawn light.

As quiet and still as she had gone, hollowed out and drifting.

Mist curled around her, veiling all but the obsidian steps she knelt on and the carved bone gates looming overhead. The rotting black boat at her back was her only companion, its moldy, ancient rope draped over the steps in lieu of a mooring. She'd paid the fee—the boat would linger here until she was done. Until she had said what she needed to say.

The living realm remained a world away, the spires and skyscrapers of the city hidden by that swirling mist, its car horns and array of voices rendered mute. She'd left behind any mortal possessions. They would have no value here, among the Reapers and the dead.

She'd been glad to leave them—especially her phone, so full of anger and hatred.

Ithan's latest audiomail had come only an hour ago, stirring her from the unsleeping stupor in which she'd spent the past six nights, staring at the dark ceiling of the hotel room she was sharing with her mother. Ignoring every call and message.

Ithan's words had lingered, though, when she'd slipped into the hotel bathroom to listen.

Don't come to the Sailing tomorrow. You're not welcome there.

She'd listened to it over and over, the first words to echo in her silent head.

Her mother hadn't woken from the bed beside hers when Bryce had exited the hotel room on Fae-soft feet, taking the service elevator and leaving through the unwatched alley door. She hadn't left that room for six days, just sat staring vacantly at the floral hotel wallpaper. And now, with the seventh dawning . . . Only for this would she leave. Would she remember how to move her body, how to speak.

Danika's Sailing would commence at dawn, and the Sailings for the rest of the pack would follow. Bryce would not be there to witness them. Even without the wolves banning her from it, she couldn't have endured it. To see the black boat pushed from the dock, all that was left of Danika with it, her soul to be judged either worthy or unworthy of entering the sacred isle across the river.

There was only silence here. Silence and mist.

Was this death? Silence and fog?

Bryce ran her tongue over her dry, chapped lips. She did not remember the last time she'd drunk anything. Had a meal. Only her mother coaxing her to take a sip of water.

A light had gone out inside her. A light had been extinguished.

She might as well have been staring inside herself: Darkness. Silence. Mist.

Bryce lifted her head, peering up toward the carved bone gates, hewn from the ribs of a long-dead leviathan who'd prowled the deep seas of the north. The mist swirled tighter, the temperature dropping. Announcing the arrival of something ancient and terrible.

Bryce remained kneeling. Bowed her head.

She was not welcome at the Sailing. So she had come here to say goodbye. To give Danika this one last thing.

The creature that dwelt in the mist emerged, and even the river at her back trembled.

Bryce opened her eyes. And slowly lifted her gaze.

PART II
THE TRENCH

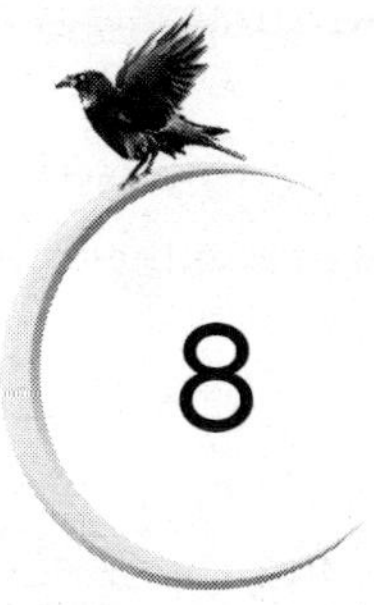

8

TWENTY-TWO MONTHS LATER

Bryce Quinlan stumbled from the White Raven's bathroom, a lion shifter nuzzling her neck, his broad hands grabbing at her waist.

It was easily the best sex she'd had in three months. Maybe longer than that. Maybe she'd keep him for a while.

Maybe she should learn his name first. Not that it mattered. Her meeting was at the VIP bar across the club in . . . well, shit. Right now.

The beat of the music pounded against her bones, echoing off the carved pillars, an incessant summons that Bryce ignored, denied. Just as she had every day for the past two years.

"Let's dance." The golden-haired lion's words rumbled against her ear as he gripped her hand to drag her toward the teeming throng on the ancient stones of the dance floor.

She planted her feet as firmly as her four-inch stilettos would allow. "No, thanks. I've got a business meeting." Not a lie, though she would have turned him down regardless.

The corner of the lion's lip twitched as he surveyed her short-as-sin black dress, the bare legs she'd had wrapped around his waist moments ago. Urd spare her, his cheekbones were unreal. So were those golden eyes, now narrowing in amusement. "You go to business meetings looking like that?"

She did when her boss's clients insisted on meeting in a neutral space like the Raven, fearful of whatever monitoring or spells Jesiba had at the gallery.

Bryce never would have come here—had so rarely come back here at all—on her own. She'd been sipping sparkling water at the *normal* bar within the club, not the VIP one she was supposed to be sitting at on the mezzanine, when the lion approached her with that easy smile and those broad shoulders. She'd been in such need of a distraction from the tension building in her with each moment in here that she'd barely finished her glass before she'd dragged him into the bathroom. He'd been all too happy to oblige her.

Bryce said to the lion, "Thanks for the ride." *Whatever your name is.*

It took him a blink to realize she was serious about the business meeting. Red crept over his tanned cheeks. Then he blurted, "I can't pay you."

It was her turn to blink. Then she tipped her head back and laughed.

Just perfect: he thought she was one of the whores in Riso's employ. *Sacred* prostitution, Riso had once explained—since the club lay on the ruins of a temple to pleasure, it was his duty to continue its traditions.

"Consider it on the house," she crooned, patting him on the cheek before she turned toward the glowing golden bar on the glass mezzanine hovering over the cavernous space.

She didn't let herself look toward the booth tucked between two age-worn pillars. Didn't let herself see who might now be occupying it. Not Juniper, who was too busy these days for more than the occasional brunch, and certainly not Fury, who didn't bother to take her calls, or answer messages, or even visit this city.

Bryce rolled her shoulders, shoving the thoughts away.

The jaguar shifters standing guard atop the illuminated golden staircase that linked the VIP mezzanine with the converted temple pulled aside their black velvet rope to let her pass.

Twenty glass stools flanked the solid gold bar, and only a third of them were occupied. Vanir of every House sat in them. No humans, though.

Except for her, if she even counted.

Her client was already seated at the far end of the bar, his dark suit tight over his bulky frame, long black hair slicked back to reveal a sharp-boned face and inky eyes.

Bryce rattled off his details to herself as she sauntered up to him, praying he wasn't the sort to mark that she was technically two minutes late.

Maximus Tertian: two-hundred-year-old vampyr; unwed and unmated; son of Lord Cedrian, richest of the Pangeran vamps and the most monstrous, if rumor was to be believed. Known for filling bathtubs with the blood of human maidens in his frosty mountain keep, bathing in their youth—

Not helpful. Bryce plastered on a smile and claimed the stool beside his, ordering a sparkling water from the bartender. "Mr. Tertian," she said by way of greeting, extending her hand.

The vampyr's smile was so smooth she knew ten thousand pairs of underwear had likely dropped at the sight of it over the centuries. "Miss Quinlan," he purred, taking her hand and brushing a kiss to the back of it. His lips lingered just long enough that she suppressed the urge to yank her fingers back. "A pleasure to meet you in the flesh." His eyes dipped toward her neck, then the cleavage exposed by her dress. "Your employer might have a gallery full of art, but you are the true masterpiece."

Oh please.

Bryce ducked her head, making herself smile. "You say that to all the girls."

"Only the mouthwatering ones."

An offer for how this night could end, if she wanted: being sucked and fucked. She didn't bother to inform him she'd already had that particular need scratched, minus the sucking. She liked her blood where it was, thank you very much.

She reached into her purse, pulling out a narrow leather folio—an exact replica of what the Raven used to hand out steep bills to its most exclusive patrons. "Your drink's on me." She slid the folio toward him with a smile.

Maximus peered at the ownership papers for the five-thousand-year-old onyx bust of a long-dead vampyr lord. The deal had been a triumph for Bryce after weeks of sending out feelers to potential buyers, taunting them with the chance to buy a rare artifact before any of their rivals. She'd had her eye on Maximus, and during their endless phone calls and messages, she'd played him well, drawing upon his hatred for other vampyr lords, his fragile ego, his unbearable arrogance.

It was an effort now to suppress her smile as Maximus—*never Max*—nodded while he read. Giving him the illusion of privacy, Bryce pivoted on the stool to peer at the teeming club below.

A cluster of young females adorned in firstlight glow-stick halos danced together near a pillar, laughing and singing and passing a bottle of sparkling wine among them.

Bryce's chest tightened. She'd once planned to have her Drop party at the Raven. Had planned to be as obnoxious as those females down there, partying with her friends from the moment she emerged from the Ascent until she either passed out or was kicked to the curb.

The party, honestly, was what she'd wanted to focus on. What most people tried to focus on. Rather than the sheer terror of the Drop ritual itself.

But it was a necessary rite. Because the firstlight grid's power was generated by the pure, undiluted light each Vanir emitted while making the Drop. And it was only during the Drop that the flash of firstlight appeared—raw, unfiltered magic. It could heal and destroy and do everything in between.

Captured and bottled, the first glow was always used for healing, then the rest of it was handed over to the energy plants to fuel their lights and cars and machines and tech; some of it was used for spells, and some was reserved for whatever shady shit the Republic wanted.

The "donation" of the firstlight by each citizen was a key element of the Drop ritual, part of why it was always done in a government center: a sterile room, where the light from the person making the Drop was gobbled up during the transition into immortality and true power. All tracked by the Eleusian system, able to monitor every moment of it through vibrations in the world's magic. Indeed, family members sometimes watched the feeds in an adjacent room.

The Drop was the easy part: falling into one's power. But once the bottom was reached, one's mortal body expired. And then the clock began counting down.

Mere minutes were allowed for the race back up to life—before the brain shut down permanently from lack of oxygen. Six minutes to start barreling down a psychic runway along the bottom of one's power, a single desperate shot at launching skyward toward life. The alternative to successfully making that leap: tumbling into an endless black pit and awaiting death. The alternative to getting enough momentum on that runway: tumbling into an endless black pit and awaiting death.

Which was why someone else had to act as an Anchor: a beacon, a lifeline, a bungee cord that would snap their companion back up to life once they leapt off the runway. To make the Drop alone was to die—to reach the bottom of one's power, to have one's heart stop beating upon hitting that nadir. No one knew if the soul continued living down there, lost forever, or if it died along with the body left in life.

It was why Anchors were usually family—parents or siblings—or trusted friends. Someone who wouldn't leave you stranded. Or a government employee who had a legal obligation not to do so. Some claimed those six minutes were called the Search—that during that time, you faced the very depths of your soul. But beyond that, there was no hope of survival.

It was only upon making the Ascent and reaching that threshold back to life, brimming with new power, that immortality was attained, the aging process slowed to a glacial drip and the body rendered near-indestructible as it was bathed in all that ensuing firstlight, so bright it could blind the naked eye. And at the end of it, when the Drop Center's sleek energy panels had siphoned off that firstlight, all any of them were left with to mark the occasion was a mere pinprick of that light in a bottle. A pretty souvenir.

These days, with Drop parties like the one below all the rage, the newly immortal often used their allotment of their own firstlight to make party favors to hand out to their friends. Bryce had planned for glow sticks and key chains that said *Kiss My Sparkly Ass!* Danika had just wanted shot glasses.

Bryce tucked away that old ache in her chest as Maximus shut the folio with a snap, his reading done. A matching folio appeared in his hand, then he nudged it across the shining gold surface of the bar.

Bryce glanced at the check within—for a mind-boggling sum that he handed over as if passing her an empty gum wrapper—and smiled again. Even as some small part of her cringed at the tiny fact that she wouldn't receive any part of her commission on the piece. On any art in Jesiba's gallery. That money went elsewhere.

"A pleasure doing business with you, Mr. Tertian."

There. Done. Time to go home and climb into bed and snuggle with Syrinx. The best form of celebrating she could think of these days.

But a pale, strong hand landed on the folio. "Going so soon?" Maximus's smile grew again. "It'd be a shame for a pretty thing like you to leave when I was about to order a bottle of Serat." The sparkling wine from the south of Valbara started at roughly a hundred gold marks a bottle. And apparently made pricks like him believe they were entitled to female company.

Bryce gave him a wink, trying to pull the folio with the check toward her awaiting purse. "I think you'd be the one feeling sorry if a pretty thing like me left, Mr. Tertian."

His hand remained on the folio. "For what I paid your boss, I'd think some perks came with this deal."

Well, it had to be a record: being mistaken for a whore twice within ten minutes. She had no disdain for the world's oldest profession, only respect and sometimes pity, but being mistaken for one of them had led to more unfortunate incidents than she liked. Yet Bryce managed to say calmly, "I'm afraid I have another meeting."

Maximus's hand slipped to her wrist, gripping hard enough to demonstrate that he could snap every bone inside it with barely a thought.

She refused to allow her scent to shift as her stomach hollowed out. She had dealt with his kind and worse. "Take your hand off me, please."

She added the last word because she owed it to Jesiba to at least sound polite—just once.

But Maximus surveyed her body with all the male, immortal entitlement in the world. "Some like their prey to play hard to get." He smiled up at her again. "I happen to be one of them. I'll make it good for you, you know."

She met his stare, hating that some small part of her wanted to recoil. That it recognized him as a predator and her as his prey and she'd be lucky to even get the chance to run before she was eaten whole. "No, thank you."

The VIP mezzanine went quiet, the ripple of silence a sure sign that some bigger, badder predator had prowled in. Good.

Maybe it'd distract the vampyr long enough for her to snatch her wrist back. And that check. Jesiba would flay her alive if she left without it.

Indeed, Maximus's gaze drifted over her shoulder to whoever had entered. His hand tightened on Bryce's. Just hard enough that Bryce looked.

A dark-haired Fae male stalked up to the other end of the bar. Looking right at her.

She tried not to groan. And not the way she'd groaned with that lion shifter.

The Fae male kept looking at her as Maximus's upper lip pulled back from his teeth, revealing the elongated canines he so badly wanted to sink into her. Maximus snarled in warning. "You are mine." The words were so guttural she could barely understand him.

Bryce sighed through her nose as the Fae male took a seat at the bar, murmuring his drink order to the silver-haired sylph behind it. "That's my cousin," Bryce said. "Relax."

The vampyr blinked. "What?"

His surprise cost him: his grip loosened, and Bryce stashed the folio with the check in her purse as she stepped back. At least her Fae heritage was good for moving quickly when necessary. Walking away, Bryce purred over a shoulder, "Just so you know—I don't do possessive and aggressive."

Maximus snarled again, but he'd seen who her "cousin" was. He didn't dare follow.

Even when the world thought they were only distantly related, one didn't fuck with the relatives of Ruhn Danaan.

If they had known Ruhn was her brother—well, technically her half brother—no male would ever go near her. But thankfully, the world thought he was her cousin, and she was glad to keep it that way. Not just because of who their sire was and the secrecy that she'd long ago sworn to maintain. Not just because Ruhn was the legitimate child, the fucking Chosen One, and she was . . . not.

Ruhn was already sipping from his whiskey, his striking blue eyes fixed on Maximus. Promising death.

She was half-tempted to let Ruhn send Maximus scurrying back to his daddy's castle of horrors, but she'd worked so hard on the deal, had tricked the asshole into paying nearly a third more than the bust was worth. All it would take was one phone call from Maximus to his banker and that check in her purse would be dead on arrival.

So Bryce went up to Ruhn, drawing his attention from the vampyr at last.

Her brother's black T-shirt and dark jeans were tight enough to show off the muscles Fae went to pieces over, and that plenty of people on the VIP level were now ogling. The tattooed sleeves on his golden-skinned arms, however, were colorful and beautiful enough to piss off their father. Along with the line of rings in one arched ear, and the straight black hair that flowed to his waist save for one shaved side. All painting a glaring billboard that said *Fuck You, Dad!*

But Ruhn was still a Fae male. Still fifty years older than her. Still a domineering dick whenever she ran into him or his friends. Which was whenever she couldn't avoid it.

"Well, well, well," Bryce said, nodding her thanks to the

bartender as another sparkling water appeared before her. She took a swig, swishing the bubbles to rinse away the lingering taste of lion and alphahole. "Look who decided to stop frequenting poseur rock clubs and start hanging with the cool kids. Seems like the Chosen One's finally getting hip."

"I always forget how annoying you are," Ruhn said by way of greeting. "And not that it's any of your business, but I'm not here to party."

Bryce surveyed her brother. No sign of the Starsword tonight—and, glancing at him, beyond the telltale physical heritage of the Starborn line, little declared that he'd been anointed by Luna or genetics to usher their people to greater heights. But it had been years since they'd really spoken. Maybe Ruhn had crawled back into the fold. It'd be a shame, considering the shit that had gone down to pull him out of it in the first place.

Bryce asked, "Is there a reason why you're here, other than to ruin my night?"

Ruhn snorted. "Still happy playing slutty secretary, I see."

Spoiled prick. For a few glittering years, they'd been best friends, a dynamic duo against Motherfucker Number One—aka the Fae male who'd sired them—but that was ancient history. Ruhn had seen to that.

She frowned at the packed club below, scanning the crowd for any sign of the two friends who trailed Ruhn everywhere, both pains in her ass. "How'd you get in here, anyway?" Even a Fae Prince had to wait in line at the Raven. Bryce had once delighted in watching preening Fae assholes be turned away at the doors.

"Riso's my buddy," Ruhn said. "He and I play poker on Tuesday nights."

Of course Ruhn had somehow managed to befriend the club's owner. A rare breed of butterfly shifter, what Riso lacked in size he made up for with sheer personality, always laughing, always flitting about the club and dancing above the crowd. Feeding off its merriment as if it were nectar. He was picky about his close circle, though—he liked to cultivate *interesting* groups of people to entertain him. Bryce and Danika had never made the cut, but odds were that Fury was in that poker group. Too bad Fury didn't answer her calls for Bryce to even ask about it.

Ruhn bared his teeth at Maximus as the glowering vamp headed toward the golden steps. "Riso called me a few minutes ago and said you were here. With that fucking creep."

"Excuse me?" Her voice sharpened. It had nothing to do with the fact that she highly doubted the diplomatic club owner had used those terms. Riso was more the type to say, *She's with someone who might cause the dancing to cease.* Which would have been Riso's idea of Hel.

Ruhn said, "Riso can't risk tossing Tertian to the curb—he implied the prick was being handsy and you needed backup." A purely predatory gleam entered her brother's eyes. "Don't you know what Tertian's father *does*?"

She grinned, and knew it didn't reach her eyes. None of her smiles did these days. "I do," she said sweetly.

Ruhn shook his head in disgust. Bryce leaned forward to grab her drink, each movement controlled—if only to keep from taking the water and throwing it in his face.

"Shouldn't you be home?" Ruhn asked. "It's a weekday. You've got *work* in six hours."

"Thanks, Mom," she said. But getting home and taking off her bra did sound fantastic. She'd been up before dawn again, sweat-soaked and breathless, and the day hadn't improved from there. Maybe she'd be exhausted enough tonight to actually sleep.

But when Ruhn made no move to leave, Bryce sighed. "Let's hear it, then."

There had to be another reason why Ruhn had bothered to come—there always was, considering who had sired them.

Ruhn sipped from his drink. "The Autumn King wants you to lie low. The Summit meeting is in just over a month, and he wants any loose cannons tied down."

"What does the Summit meeting have to do with me?" They occurred every ten years, a gathering of Valbara's ruling powers to debate whatever issues or policies the Asteri ordered them to deal with. Each territory in the Republic held its own Summit meeting on a rotating schedule, so that one occurred in the world each year—and Bryce had paid attention to exactly zero of them.

"The Autumn King wants everyone associated with the Fae on their best behavior—rumor says the Asteri are sending over some of their favored commanders, and he wants us all looking like good, obedient subjects. Honestly, I don't fucking care, Bryce. I was just ordered to tell you to not . . . get into trouble until the meeting's over."

"You mean, don't do anything embarrassing."

"Basically," he said, drinking again. "And look: beyond that, shit always gets intense around the Summit meetings, so be careful, okay? People come out of the woodwork to make their agendas known. Be on your guard."

"I didn't know Daddy bothered to care about my safety." He never had before.

"He doesn't," Ruhn said, lips thinning, the silver hoop through the bottom one shifting with the movement. "But I'll make him care about it."

She considered the rage in his blue eyes—it wasn't directed at her. Ruhn hadn't yet fallen in line, then. Hadn't bought into his Chosen One greatness. She took another sip of water. "Since when does he listen to you?"

"Bryce. Just stay out of trouble—on all fronts. For whatever reason, this Summit is important to him. He's been on edge about it—beyond the whole everyone-needing-to-behave-themselves bullcrap." He sighed. "I haven't seen him this riled since two years ago . . ."

The words trailed off as he caught himself. But she got his meaning. Since two years ago. Since Danika. And Connor.

The glass in her hands cracked.

"Easy," Ruhn murmured. "Easy."

She couldn't stop clutching the glass, couldn't get her body to back down from the primal fury that surged up, up—

The heavy crystal glass exploded in her hands, water spraying across the golden bar. The bartender whirled, but kept away. No one along the bar dared look for more than a breath—not at the Crown Prince of the Valbaran Fae.

Ruhn gripped Bryce's face with a hand. *"Take a fucking breath."*

That horrible, useless Fae side of her obeyed the dominance in his command, her body falling back on instincts that had been bred into her, despite her best attempts to ignore them.

Bryce sucked in a breath, then another. Gasping, shuddering sounds.

But with each breath, the blinding wrath receded. Eddied away.

Ruhn held her gaze until she stopped snarling, until she could see clearly. Then he slowly released her face—and took a deep breath of his own. "Fuck, Bryce."

She stood on wobbling legs and adjusted the strap of her purse over her shoulder, making sure Maximus's outrageous check was still inside. "Message received. I'll lie low and act my classiest until the Summit."

Ruhn scowled and slid off the stool with familiar Fae grace. "Let me walk you home."

"I don't need you to." Besides, no one went to her apartment. Which wasn't technically even *her* apartment, but that was beside the point. Only her mom and Randall, and occasionally Juniper if she ever left the dance studio, but no one else was allowed inside. It was her sanctuary, and she didn't want Fae scents anywhere near it.

But Ruhn ignored her refusal and scanned the bar. "Where's your coat?"

She clenched her jaw. "I didn't bring one."

"It's barely spring."

She stomped past him, wishing she'd worn boots instead of stilettos. "Then it's a good thing I have my alcohol sweater on, isn't it?" A lie. She hadn't touched a drink in nearly two years.

Ruhn didn't know that, though. Nor did anyone else.

He trailed her. "You're hilarious. Glad all those tuition dollars went to something."

She strode down the stairs. "At least I went to college and didn't sit at home on a pile of Daddy's cash, playing video games with my dickbag friends."

Ruhn growled, but Bryce was already halfway down the

staircase to the dance floor. Moments later, she was elbowing her way through the crowds between the pillars, then breezing down the few steps into the glass-enclosed courtyard—still flanked on two sides by the temple's original stone walls—and toward the enormous iron doors. She didn't wait to see if Ruhn still trailed before she slipped out, waving at the half-wolf, half-daemonaki bouncers, who returned the gesture.

They were good guys—years ago, on rougher nights, they had always made sure Bryce got into a taxi. And that the driver knew exactly what would happen if she didn't get home in one piece.

She made it a block before she sensed Ruhn catching up, a storm of temper behind her. Not close enough for someone to know they were together, but near enough for her senses to be full of his scent, his annoyance.

At least it kept any would-be predators from approaching her.

When Bryce reached the glass-and-marble lobby of her building, Marrin, the ursine shifter behind the front desk, buzzed her through the double doors with a friendly wave. Pausing with a hand on the glass doors, she glanced over a shoulder to where Ruhn leaned against a black-painted lamppost. He lifted a hand in farewell—a mockery of one.

She flipped him off and walked into her building. A quick hello to Marrin, an elevator ride up to the penthouse, five levels above, and the small cream-colored hallway appeared. She sighed, heels sinking into the plush cobalt runner that flowed between her apartment and the one across the hall, and opened her purse. She found her keys by the glow of the firstlight orb in the bowl atop the blackwood table against the wall, its radiance gilding the white orchid drooping over it.

Bryce unlocked her door, first by key, then by the finger pad beside the knob. The heavy locks and spells hissed as they faded away, and she stepped into her dark apartment. The scent of lilac oil from her diffuser caressed her as Syrinx yowled his greeting and demanded to be immediately released from his crate. But Bryce leaned back against the door.

She hated knowing that Ruhn still lurked on the street below, the Crown Fucking Prince of Possessive and Aggressive Alphaholes, staring at the massive floor-to-ceiling wall of windows across the great room before her, waiting for the lights to come on.

His banging on the door in three minutes would be inevitable if she refused to turn on the lights. Marrin wouldn't be stupid enough to stop him. Not Ruhn Danaan. There had never been a door shut for him, not once in his entire life.

But she wasn't in the mood for that battle. Not tonight.

Bryce flicked on the panel of lights beside the door, illuminating the pale wood floors, the white plush furniture, the matching white walls. All of it as pristine as the day she'd moved in, almost two years ago—all of it far above her pay grade.

All of it paid for by Danika. By that stupid fucking will.

Syrinx grumbled, his cage rattling. Another possessive and aggressive alphahole. But a small, fuzzy one, at least.

With a sigh, Bryce kicked off her heels, unhooked her bra at last, and went to let the little beast out of his cage.

9

"Please."

The male's whimper was barely discernible with the blood filling his mouth, his nostrils. But he still tried again. "Please."

Hunt Athalar's sword dripped blood onto the soaked carpet of the dingy apartment in the Meadows. Splatters of it coated the visor of his helmet, speckling his line of vision as he surveyed the lone male standing.

Kneeling, technically.

The male's friends littered the living room floor, one of them still spurting blood from what was now his stump of a neck. His severed head lay on the sagging sofa, gaping face rolled into the age-flattened cushions.

"I'll tell you everything," the male pleaded, sobbing as he pressed his hand against the gash on his shoulder. "They didn't tell you all of it, but I can."

The male's terror filled the room, overpowering the scent of blood, its reek as bad as stale piss in an alley.

Hunt's gloved hand tightened on his blade. The male noted it and began shaking, a stain paler than blood leaking across his pants. "I'll tell you more," the man tried again.

Hunt braced his feet, rooting his strength into the floor, and slashed his blade.

The male's innards spilled onto the carpet with a wet slap. Still the male kept screaming.

So Hunt kept working.

Hunt made it to the Comitium barracks without anyone seeing him.

At this hour, the city at least appeared asleep. The five buildings that made up the Comitium's complex did, too. But the cameras throughout the 33rd Legion's barracks—the second of the Comitium's spire-capped towers—saw everything. Heard everything.

The white-tiled halls were dim, no hint of the hustle that would fill them come dawn.

The helmet's visor cast everything into stark relief, its audio receptors picking up sounds from behind the shut bedroom doors lining either side of hallway: low-level sentries playing some video game, doing their best to keep their voices down as they cursed at each other; a female sentry talking on the phone; two angels fucking each other's brains out; and several snorers.

Hunt passed his own door, instead aiming for the shared bathroom in the center of the long hallway, accessible only through the common room. Any hope for an unnoticed return vanished at the sight of the golden light leaking from beneath the shut door and the sound of voices beyond it.

Too tired, too filthy, Hunt didn't bother to say hello as he entered the common room, prowling past the scattering of couches and chairs toward the bathroom.

Naomi was sprawled on the worn green couch before the TV, her black wings spread. Viktoria lounged in the armchair next to her, watching the day's sports highlights, and on the other end of the couch sat Justinian, still in his black legionary armor.

Their conversation stalled as Hunt entered.

"Hey," Naomi said, her inky braid draping over her shoulder. She wore her usual black—the triarii's usual black—though there was no trace of her wicked weapons or their holsters.

Viktoria seemed content to let Hunt pass without greeting. It was why he liked the wraith more than nearly anyone else in

Micah Domitus's inner circle of warriors, had liked her since those early days in the 18th, when she'd been one of the few non-angel Vanir to join their cause. Vik never pushed when Hunt didn't want to be bothered. But Justinian—

The angel sniffed, scenting the blood on Hunt's clothes, his weapons. How many different people it belonged to. Justinian blew out a whistle. "You are one sick fuck, you know that?"

Hunt continued toward the bathroom door. His lightning didn't so much as hiss inside him.

Justinian went on, "A gun would have been a Hel of a lot cleaner."

"Micah didn't want a gun for this," Hunt said, his voice hollow even to his ears. It had been that way for centuries now; but tonight, these kills he'd made, what they'd done to earn the wrath of the Archangel . . . "They didn't deserve a gun," he amended. Or the swift bolt of his lightning.

"I don't want to know," Naomi grumbled, punching up the volume of the TV. She pointed with the remote at Justinian, the youngest in the triarii. "And neither do you, so shut it."

No, they really didn't want to know.

Naomi—the only one of the triarii who was not Fallen—said to Hunt, "Isaiah told me that Micah wants you two playing investigators tomorrow for some shit in the Old Square. Isaiah will call you after breakfast with the details."

The words barely registered. Isaiah. Tomorrow. Old Square.

Justinian snorted. "Good luck, man." He swigged from his beer. "I hate the Old Square—it's all university brats and tourist creeps." Naomi and Viktoria grunted their agreement.

Hunt didn't ask why they were up, or where Isaiah was, given that he couldn't deliver the message. The angel was likely with whatever handsome male he was currently dating.

As Commander of the 33rd, acquired by Micah to shore up Crescent City's defenses, Isaiah had enjoyed every second here since he'd arrived more than a decade ago. In four years, Hunt hadn't seen the city's appeal beyond it being a cleaner, more organized version of any Pangeran metropolis, with streets in clean lines rather than meandering curves that often doubled back on themselves, as if in no hurry to get anywhere.

But at least it wasn't Ravilis. And at least it was Micah ruling over it, not Sandriel.

Sandriel—the Archangel and Governor of the northwestern quadrant of Pangera, and Hunt's former owner before Micah had traded with her, desiring to have Hunt clear Crescent City of any enemies. Sandriel—his dead lover's twin sister.

The formal papers declared that Hunt's duties would be to track down and dispatch any loose demons. But considering that those sorts of disasters happened only once or twice a year, it was glaringly obvious why he'd really been brought over. He'd done most of the assassinating for Sandriel, the Archangel who bore the same face as his beloved, for the fifty-three years she'd possessed him.

A rare occurrence, for both siblings to bear an Archangel's title and power. A good omen, people had believed. Until Shahar—until Hunt, leading her forces—had rebelled against everything the angels stood for. And betrayed her sister in the process.

Sandriel had been the third of his owners after the defeat at Mount Hermon, and had been arrogant enough to believe that despite the two Archangels before her who had failed to do so, she might be the one to break him. First in her horror show of a dungeon. Then in her blood-soaked arena in the heart of Ravilis, pitting him against warriors who never stood a chance. Then by commanding him to do what he did best: slipping into a room and ending lives. One after another after another, year after year, decade after decade.

Sandriel certainly had motivation to break him. During that too-short battle at Hermon, it was her forces that Hunt had decimated, his lightning that turned soldier after soldier into charred husks before they could draw their swords. Sandriel had been Shahar's prime target, and Hunt had been ordered to take her out. By whatever means necessary.

And Shahar had good reason to go after her sister. Their parents had both been Archangels, whose titles had passed to their daughters after an assassin had somehow managed to rip them to shreds.

He'd never forget Shahar's theory: that Sandriel had killed their parents and framed the assassin. That she'd done it for herself and her sister, so they might rule without *interference*. There had never been proof to pin it on Sandriel, but Shahar believed it to her dying day.

Shahar, the Daystar, had rebelled against her fellow Archangels and the Asteri because of it. She'd wanted a world free of rigid hierarchies, yes—would have brought their rebellion right to the crystal palace of the Asteri if it had been successful. But she'd also wanted to make her sister pay. So Hunt had been unleashed.

Fools. They had all been fools.

It made no difference if he'd admitted his folly. Sandriel believed he'd lured her twin into the rebellion, that *he* had turned Shahar against her. That somehow, when sister had drawn blade against sister, so nearly identical in face and build and fighting technique that it was like watching someone battle their reflection, it was *his fucking fault* that it had ended with one of them dead.

At least Micah had offered him the chance to redeem himself. To prove his utter loyalty and submission to the Archangels, to the empire, and then one day get the halo removed. Decades from now, possibly centuries, but considering that the oldest angels lived to be nearly eight hundred . . . maybe he'd earn back his freedom in time to be old. He could potentially die free.

Micah had offered Hunt the bargain from his first day in Crescent City four years ago: a kill for every life he'd taken that bloody day on Mount Hermon. Every angel he'd slaughtered during that doomed battle, he was to pay back. In the form of more death. *A death for a death,* Micah had said. *When you've fulfilled the debt, Athalar, we'll discuss removing that tattoo on your brow.*

Hunt had never known the tally—how many he'd killed that day. But Micah, who'd been on that battlefield, who'd watched while Shahar fell at her twin sister's hand, had the list. They'd had to pay out commissions for all the legionaries. Hunt had been about to ask how they'd been able to determine which killing blows had been made by his blade and not someone else's, when he'd seen the number.

Two thousand two hundred and seventeen.

It was impossible for him to have personally killed that many in one battle. Yes, his lightning had been unleashed; yes, he'd blasted apart entire units, but that many?

He'd gaped. *You were Shahar's general,* Micah said. *You commanded the 18th. So you will atone, Athalar, not only for the lives you took, but those your traitorous legion took as well.* At Hunt's silence, Micah had added, *This is not some impossible task. Some of my missions will count for more than one life. Behave, obey, and you will be able to reach this number.*

For four years now, he had behaved. He had obeyed. And tonight had put him at a grand total of eighty-fucking-two.

It was the best he could hope for. All he worked for. No other Archangel had ever offered him the chance. It was why he'd done everything Micah had ordered him to do tonight. Why every thought felt distant, his body pulled from him, his head full of a dull roaring.

Micah was an Archangel. A Governor appointed by the Asteri. He was a king among angels, and law unto himself, especially in Valbara—so far from the seven hills of the Eternal City. If he deemed someone a threat or in need of justice, then there would be no investigation, no trial.

Just his command. Usually to Hunt.

It would arrive in the form of a file in his barracks mailbox, the imperial crest on its front. No mention of his name. Just *SPQM*, and the seven stars surrounding the letters.

The file contained all he needed: names, dates, crimes, and a timeline for Hunt to do what he did best. Plus any requests from Micah regarding the method employed.

Tonight it had been simple enough—no guns. Hunt understood the unwritten words: make them suffer. So he had.

"There's a beer with your name on it when you come out," Viktoria said, her eyes meeting Hunt's even with the helmet on. Nothing but a casual, cool invitation.

Hunt continued into the bathroom, the firstlights fluttering to life as he shouldered his way through the door and approached one of the shower stalls. He cranked the water to full heat before stalking back to the row of pedestal sinks.

In the mirror above one, the being who stared back was as bad as a Reaper. Worse.

Blood splattered the helmet, right over the painted silver skull's face. It gleamed faintly on the intricate leather scales of his battle-suit, on his black gloves, on the twin swords peeking above his shoulders. Flecks of it even stained his gray wings.

Hunt peeled off the helmet and braced his hands on the sink.

In the harsh bathroom firstlights, his light brown skin was pallid under the black band of thorns across his brow. The tattoo, he'd learned to live with. But he shrank from the look in his dark eyes. Glazed. Empty. Like staring into Hel.

Orion, his mother had named him. Hunter. He doubted she would have done so, would have so lovingly called him Hunt instead, if she'd known what he'd become.

Hunt glanced to where his gloves had left red stains on the porcelain sink.

Tugging off the gloves with brutal efficiency, Hunt prowled to the shower stall, where the water had reached near-scalding temperatures. He removed his weapons, then his battle-suit, leaving more streaks of blood on the tiles.

Hunt stepped under the spray, and submitted himself to its relentless burning.

10

It was barely ten in the morning, and Tuesday was already fucked.

Keeping a smile pasted on her face, Bryce lingered by her ironwood desk in the showroom of the gallery while a Fae couple browsed.

The elegant plucking of violins trickled through the hidden speakers in the two-level, wood-paneled space, the opening movement of a symphony that she'd switched on as soon as the intercom had buzzed. Given the couple's attire—a pleated tan skirt and white silk blouse for the female, a gray suit for the male—she'd doubted they'd appreciate the thumping bass of her morning workout mix.

But they'd been browsing the art for ten minutes now, which was enough time for her to politely inquire, "Are you here for anything in particular, or just to browse?"

The blond Fae male, older-looking for one of his kind, waved a dismissive hand, leading his companion toward the nearest display: a partial marble relief from the ruins of Morrah, salvaged from a wrecked temple. The piece was about the size of a coffee table, with a rearing hippocamp filling most of it. The half-horse, half-fish creatures had once dwelled in the cerulean waters of the Rhagan Sea in Pangera, until ancient wars had destroyed them.

"Browsing," the male replied coldly, his hand coming to rest on his companion's slender back as they studied the waves carved in strikingly precise detail.

Bryce summoned another smile. "Take your time. I'm at your disposal."

The female nodded her thanks, but the male sneered his dismissal. His companion frowned deeply at him.

The silence in the small gallery turned palpable.

Bryce had gleaned from the moment they'd walked through the door that the male was here to impress the female, either by buying something outrageously expensive or pretending he could. Perhaps this was an arranged pairing, testing out the waters before committing to anything further.

Had Bryce been full-blooded Fae, had her father claimed her as his offspring, she might have been subjected to such things. Ruhn, especially with his Starborn status, would one day have to submit to an arranged marriage, when a young female deemed suitable to continue the precious royal bloodline came along.

Ruhn might sire a few children before then, but they wouldn't be acknowledged as royalty unless their father chose that path. Unless they were *worthy* of it.

The Fae couple passed the mosaic from the courtyard of the once-great palace in Altium, then studied the intricate jade puzzle box that had belonged to a princess in a forgotten northern land.

Jesiba did most of the art acquisitions, which was why she was away so often, but Bryce herself had tracked down and purchased a good number of the pieces. And then resold them at a steep profit.

The couple had reached a set of fertility statues from Setmek when the front door buzzed.

Bryce glanced toward the clock on her desk. The afternoon client appointment wasn't for another three hours. To have multiple browsers in the gallery was an oddity given the notoriously steep price tags of the art in here, but—maybe she'd get lucky and sell something today.

"Excuse me," Bryce murmured, ducking around the massive desk and pulling up the outside camera feed on the computer. She'd barely clicked the icon when the buzzer rang again.

Bryce beheld who was standing on the sidewalk and froze.

Tuesday was indeed fucked.

No windows lined the sandstone facade of the slender two-story building a block off the Istros River. Only a bronze plaque to the right of the heavy iron door revealed to Hunt Athalar that it was a business of any sort.

Griffin Antiquities had been etched there in archaic, bold lettering, the words adorned with a set of glaring owl eyes beneath them, as if daring any shoppers to enter. An intercom with a matching bronze button lay beneath.

Isaiah, in his usual suit and tie, had been staring at the buzzer for long enough that Hunt finally drawled, "There aren't any enchantments on it, you know." Despite the identity of its owner.

Isaiah shot him a look, straightening his tie. "I should have had a second cup of coffee," he muttered before stabbing a finger onto the metal button. A faint buzzing sounded through the door.

No one answered.

Hunt scanned the building exterior for a hidden camera. Not a gleam or hint. The nearest one, in fact, was mounted on the chrome door of the bomb shelter halfway down the block.

Hunt scanned the sandstone facade again. There was no way Jesiba Roga wouldn't have cameras covering every inch, both outside and within.

Hunt unleashed a crackle of his power, small tongues of lightning tasting for energy fields.

Nearly invisible in the sunny morning, the lightning bounced off a skintight enchantment coating the stone, the mortar, the door. A cold, clever spell that seemed to laugh softly at any attempt to enter.

Hunt murmured, "Roga isn't screwing around, is she?"

Isaiah pushed the buzzer again, harder than necessary. They had their orders—ones that were pressing enough that even Isaiah, regardless of the lack of coffee, was on a short fuse.

Though it could also have been due to the fact that Isaiah had been out until four in the morning. Hunt hadn't asked about it, though. Had only heard Naomi and Justinian gossiping in the common room, wondering if this new boyfriend meant Isaiah was finally moving on.

Hunt hadn't bothered to tell them there was no fucking way. Not when Isaiah obeyed Micah only because of the generous weekly salary that Micah gave them all, when the law declared that slaves weren't owed a paycheck. The money Isaiah amassed would buy someone else's freedom. Just as the shit Hunt did for Micah went toward earning his own.

Isaiah rang the buzzer a third time. "Maybe she's not in."

"She's here," Hunt said. The scent of her still lingered on the sidewalk, lilac and nutmeg and something he couldn't quite place—like the gleam of the first stars at nightfall.

And indeed, a moment later, a silky female voice that definitely did not belong to the gallery's owner crackled through the intercom. "I didn't order a pizza."

Despite himself, despite the mental clock ticking away, Hunt choked on a laugh.

Isaiah rustled his white wings, plastering on a charming smile, and said into the intercom, "We're from the 33rd Legion. We're here to see Bryce Quinlan."

The voice sharpened. "I'm with clients. Come back later."

Hunt was pretty sure that "come back later" meant "go fuck yourselves."

Isaiah's charming smile strained. "This is a matter of some urgency, Miss Quinlan."

A low hum. "I'm sorry, but you'll have to make an appointment. How about . . . three weeks? I've got the twenty-eighth of April free. I'll pencil you in for noon."

Well, she had balls, Hunt would give her that much.

Isaiah widened his stance. Typical legion fighting position, beaten into them from their earliest days as grunts. "We need to talk right now, I'm afraid."

No answer came. Like she'd just walked away from the intercom.

Hunt's snarl sent the poor faun walking behind them bolting down the street, his delicate hooves clopping on the cobblestones. "She's a spoiled party girl. What did you expect?"

"She's not stupid, Hunt," Isaiah countered.

"Everything I've seen and heard suggests otherwise." What he'd seen when he skimmed her file two years ago, combined with what he'd read this morning and the pictures he'd gone through, all painted a portrait that told him precisely how this meeting would go. Too bad for her it was about to get a Hel of a lot more serious.

Hunt jerked his chin toward the door. "Let's see if a client's even in there." He stalked back across the street, where he leaned against a parked blue car. Some drunken reveler had used its hood as a canvas to spray-paint an unnecessarily detailed, massive cock—with wings. A mockery of the 33rd's logo of a winged sword, he realized. Or merely the logo stripped down to its true meaning.

Isaiah noted it as well and chuckled, following Hunt's lead and leaning against the car.

A minute passed. Hunt didn't move an inch. Didn't take his gaze away from the iron door. He had better things to do with this day than play games with a brat, but orders were orders. After five minutes, a sleek black sedan rolled up and the iron door opened.

The Fae driver of the car, which was worth more than most human families saw in a lifetime, got out. He was around the other side of the vehicle in a heartbeat, opening the back passenger door. Two Fae paraded out of the gallery, a male and a female. The pretty female's every breath radiated the easy confidence gained from a lifetime of wealth and privilege.

Around her slim neck lay a strand of diamonds, each as large as Hunt's fingernail. Worth as much as the car—more. The male climbed into the sedan, face tight as he slammed the door before his driver could do it for him. The well-heeled female just rushed down the street, phone already to her ear, grousing to whoever was on the line about *No more blind dates, for Urd's sake.*

Hunt's attention returned to the gallery door, where a curvy, red-haired woman stood.

Only when the car rounded the corner did Bryce slide her eyes toward them.

She angled her head, her silken sheet of hair sliding over the shoulder of her white skintight dress, and smiled brightly. Waved. The delicate gold amulet around her tan neck glinted.

Hunt pushed off the parked car and stalked toward her, his gray wings flaring wide.

A flick of Bryce's amber eyes took in Hunt from his tattoo to his ass-kicking boot tips. Her smile grew. "See you in three weeks," she said cheerfully, and slammed the door shut.

Hunt cleared the street in a matter of steps. A car screeched to a stop, but the driver wasn't stupid enough to blast the horn. Not when lightning wreathed Hunt's fist as he pounded it into the intercom button. "Don't waste my fucking time, Quinlan."

Isaiah let the near-frantic driver pass before coming up behind Hunt, his brown eyes narrowing. But Bryce replied sweetly, "My boss doesn't like legionaries in her place. Sorry."

Hunt slammed his fist into the iron door. That same blow had smashed cars, shattered walls, and splintered bones. And that was without the aid of the storm in his veins. The iron didn't so much as shudder; his lightning skittered off it.

To Hel with threats, then. He'd go for the jugular, as deep and sure as any of his physical kills. So Hunt said into the intercom, "We're here about a murder."

Isaiah winced, scanning the street and skies for anyone who might have heard.

Hunt crossed his arms as the silence spread.

Then the iron door hissed and clicked, and inched open.

Bull's-fucking-eye.

It took Hunt a heartbeat to adjust from the sunlight to the dimmer interior, and he used that first step into the gallery to note every angle and exit and detail.

Plush pine-green carpets went wall to wood-paneled wall in the two-story showroom. Alcoves with soft-lit art displays dotted the edges of the room: chunks of ancient frescoes, paintings, and statues of Vanir so strange and rare even Hunt didn't know their names.

Bryce Quinlan leaned against the large ironwood desk in the center of the space, her snow-white dress clinging to every generous curve and dip.

Hunt smiled slowly, showing all his teeth.

He waited for it: the realization of who he was. Waited for her to shrink back, to fumble for the panic button or gun or whatever the fuck she thought might save her from the likes of him.

But maybe she was stupid, after all, because her answering smile was saccharine in the extreme. Her red-tinted nails idly tapped on the pristine wood surface. "You have fifteen minutes."

Hunt didn't tell her that this meeting would likely take a good deal longer than that.

Isaiah turned to shut the door, but Hunt knew it was already locked. Just as he knew, thanks to legion intel gathered over the years, that the small wood door behind the desk led upstairs to Jesiba Roga's office—where a floor-to-ceiling internal window overlooked the showroom they stood in—and the simple iron door to their right led down into another full level, stocked with things that legionaries weren't supposed to find. The enchantments on those two doors were probably even more intense than those outside.

Isaiah loosed one of his long-suffering sighs. "A murder occurred on the outskirts of the Meat Market last night. We believe you knew the victim."

Hunt marked every reaction that flitted across her face as she maintained her perch on the edge of the desk: the slight widening of her eyes, the pause in those tapping nails, the sole blink that suggested she had a short list of possible victims and none of the options were good.

"Who?" was all she said, her voice steady. Wisps of smoke from the conical diffuser beside the computer drifted past her, carrying the bright, clean scent of peppermint. Of course she was one of those aromatherapy zealots, conned into handing over her marks for the promise of feeling happier, or being better in bed, or growing another half a brain to match the half she already had.

"Maximus Tertian," Isaiah told her. "We have reports that you had a meeting with him in the VIP mezzanine of the White Raven two hours before his death."

Hunt could have sworn Bryce's shoulders sagged slightly. She said, "Maximus Tertian is dead." They nodded. She angled her head. "Who did it?"

"That's what we're trying to figure out," Isaiah said neutrally.

Hunt had heard of Tertian—a creep of a vamp who couldn't take no for an answer, and whose rich, sadistic father had taught him well. And shielded him from any fallout from his hideous behavior. If Hunt was being honest, Midgard was better off without him. Except for the headache they'd now have to endure when Tertian's father got word that his favored son had been killed . . . Today's meeting would be just the start.

Isaiah went on, "You might have been one of the last people to see him alive. Can you walk us through your encounter with him? No detail is too small."

Bryce glanced between them. "Is this your way of feeling out whether I killed him?"

Hunt smiled slightly. "You don't seem too cut up that Tertian's dead."

Those amber eyes slid to him, annoyance lighting them.

He'd admit it: males would do a lot of fucked-up things for someone who looked like that.

He'd done precisely those sort of things for Shahar once. Now he bore the halo tattooed across his brow and the slave tattoo on his wrist because of it. His chest tightened.

Bryce said, "I'm sure someone's already said that Maximus and I parted on unfriendly terms. We met to finish up a deal for the gallery, and when it was done, he thought he was entitled to some . . . personal time with me."

Hunt understood her perfectly. It lined up with everything he'd heard regarding Tertian and his father. It also offered a good amount of motive.

Bryce went on, "I don't know where he went after the Raven. If he was killed on the outskirts of the Meat Market, I'd assume he was heading there to purchase what he wanted to take from me." Cold, sharp words.

Isaiah's expression grew stony. "Was his behavior last night different from how he acted during previous meetings?"

"We only interacted over emails and the phone, but I'd say no. Last night was our first face-to-face, and he acted exactly as his past behavior would indicate."

Hunt asked, "Why not meet here? Why the Raven?"

"He got off on the thrill of acting like our deal was secretive. He claimed he didn't trust that my boss wasn't recording the meeting, but he really just wanted people to notice him—to see him doing deals. I had to slide him the paperwork in a bill folio, and he swapped it with one of his own, that sort of thing." She met Hunt's stare. "How did he die?"

The question was blunt, and she didn't smile or blink. A girl used to being answered, obeyed, heeded. Her parents weren't wealthy—or so her file said—yet her apartment fifteen blocks away suggested outrageous wealth. Either from this job or some shady shit that had escaped even the legion's watchful eyes.

Isaiah sighed. "Those details are classified."

She shook her head. "I can't help you. Tertian and I did the deal, he got handsy, and he left."

Every bit of the camera footage and eyewitness reports from the Raven confirmed that. But that wasn't why they were here. What they'd been sent over to do.

Isaiah said, "And when did Prince Ruhn Danaan show up?"

"If you know everything, why bother asking me?" She didn't wait for them to answer before she said, "You know, you two never told me your names."

Hunt couldn't read her expression, her relaxed body language. They hadn't initiated contact since that night in the legion's holding center—and neither of them had introduced themselves then. Had she even registered their faces in that drug-induced haze?

Isaiah adjusted his pristine white wings. "I'm Isaiah Tiberian, Commander of the 33rd Imperial Legion. This is Hunt Athalar, my—"

Isaiah tripped up, as if realizing that it had been a damn long time since they'd had to introduce themselves with any sort of rank attached. So Hunt did Isaiah a favor and finished with, "His Second."

If Isaiah was surprised to hear it, that calm, pretty-boy face didn't let on. Isaiah was, technically, his superior in the triarii and in the 33rd as a whole, even if the shit Hunt did for Micah made him directly answerable to the Governor.

Isaiah had never pulled rank, though. As if he remembered those days before the Fall, and who'd been in charge then.

As if it fucking mattered now.

No, all that mattered about that shit was that Isaiah had killed at least three dozen Imperial Legionaries that day on Mount Hermon. And Hunt now bore the burden of paying back each one of those lives to the Republic. To fulfill Micah's bargain.

Bryce's eyes flicked to their brows—the tattoos there. Hunt braced for the sneering remark, for any of the bullshit comments people still liked to make about the Fallen Legion and their failed rebellion. But she only said, "So, what—you two investigate crimes on the side? I thought that was Auxiliary territory. Don't you have better things to do in the 33rd than play buddy cop?"

Isaiah, apparently not amused that there was one person in this city who didn't fall at his feet, said a tad stiffly, "Do you have people who can verify your whereabouts after you left the White Raven?"

Bryce held Isaiah's gaze. Then flicked her eyes to Hunt. And he still couldn't read her mask of boredom as she pushed off the desk and took a few deliberate steps toward them before crossing her arms.

"Just my doorman . . . and Ruhn Danaan, but you already knew that."

How anyone could walk in heels that high was beyond him. How anyone could breathe in a dress that tight was also a mystery. It was long enough that it covered the area on her thigh where the scar from that night two years ago would be—that is, if she hadn't paid some medwitch to erase it. For someone who clearly took pains to dress nicely, he had little doubt she'd gotten it removed immediately.

Party girls didn't like scars messing with how they looked in a swimsuit.

Isaiah's white wings shifted. "Would you call Ruhn Danaan a friend?"

Bryce shrugged. "He's a distant cousin."

But apparently invested enough to have charged into the interrogation room two years ago. And shown up at the VIP bar last night. If he was that protective of Quinlan, that might be one Hel of a motive, too. Even if Ruhn and his father would make the interrogation a nightmare.

Bryce smiled sharply, as if she remembered that fact, too. "Have fun talking to him."

Hunt clenched his jaw, but she strode for the front door, hips swishing like she knew precisely how spectacular her ass was.

"Just a moment, Miss Quinlan," Isaiah said. The commander's voice was calm, but take-no-shit.

Hunt hid his smile. Seeing Isaiah angry was always a good show. So long as you weren't on the receiving end.

Quinlan hadn't realized that yet as she glanced over a shoulder. "Yes?"

Hunt eyed her as Isaiah at last voiced their true reason for this little visit. "We weren't just sent here to ask you about your whereabouts."

She gestured to the gallery. "You want to buy something pretty for the Governor?"

Hunt's mouth twitched upward. "Funny you should mention him. He's on his way here right now."

A slow blink. Again, no sign or scent of fear. "Why?"

"Micah just told us to get information from you about last night, and then make sure you were available and have you get your boss on the line." Given how infrequently Hunt was asked to help out on investigations, he'd been shocked as Hel to get the order. But considering that he and Isaiah had been there that night in the alley, he supposed that made them the top choices to head this sort of thing up.

"Micah is coming here." Her throat bobbed once.

"He'll be here in ten minutes," Isaiah said. He nodded toward her phone. "I suggest you call your boss, Miss Quinlan."

Her breathing turned slightly shallow. "Why?"

Hunt dropped the bomb at last. "Because Maximus Tertian's injuries were identical to the ones inflicted upon Danika Fendyr and the Pack of Devils." Pulped and dismembered.

Her eyes shuttered. "But—Philip Briggs killed them. He summoned that demon to kill them. And he's in prison." Her voice sharpened. "He's been in prison for *two years*."

In a place worse than prison, but that was beside the point.

"We know," Hunt said, keeping his face devoid of any reaction.

"He can't have killed Tertian. How could he possibly summon the demon from jail?" Bryce said. "He . . ." She swallowed, catching herself. Realizing, perhaps, why Micah was coming. Several people she'd known had been killed, all within hours of interacting with her. "You think Briggs didn't do it. Didn't kill Danika and her pack."

"We don't know that for sure," Isaiah cut in. "But the specific details of how they all died never leaked, so we have good reason to believe this wasn't a copycat murder."

Bryce asked flatly, "Have you met with Sabine?"

Hunt said, "Have *you*?"

"We do our best to stay out of each other's way."

It was perhaps the only smart thing Bryce Quinlan had ever decided to do. Hunt remembered Sabine's venom as she'd glared through the window at Bryce in the observation room two years ago, and he had no doubt Sabine was just waiting for enough time to pass for Quinlan's unfortunate and untimely death to be considered nothing more than a fluke.

Bryce walked back to her desk, giving them a wide berth. To her credit, her gait remained unhurried and solid. She picked up the phone without so much as looking at them.

"We'll wait outside," Isaiah offered. Hunt opened his mouth to object, but Isaiah shot him a warning look.

Fine. He and Quinlan could spar later.

Phone held in a white-knuckled grip, Bryce listened to the other end ring. Twice. Then—

"Morning, Bryce."

Bryce's heartbeat pounded in her arms, her legs, her stomach. "Two legionaries are here." She swallowed. "The Commander of the 33rd and . . ." She blew out a breath. "The Umbra Mortis."

She'd recognized Isaiah Tiberian—he graced the nightly news and gossip columns often enough that there would never be any mistaking the 33rd's beautiful Commander.

And she'd recognized Hunt Athalar, too, though he was never on television. Everyone knew who Hunt Athalar was. She'd heard of him even while growing up in Nidaros, when Randall would talk about his battles in Pangera and whispered when he mentioned Hunt. The Umbra Mortis. The Shadow of Death.

Then, the angel hadn't worked for Micah Domitus and his legion, but for the Archangel Sandriel—he'd flown in her 45th Legion. Demon-hunting, rumor claimed his job was. And worse.

Jesiba hissed, "Why?"

Bryce clutched the phone. "Maximus Tertian was murdered last night."

"Burning *Solas*—"

"The same way as Danika and the pack."

Bryce shut out every hazy image, breathing in the bright, calming scent of the peppermint vapors rippling from the diffuser on her desk. She'd bought the stupid plastic cone two months after Danika had been killed, figuring it couldn't hurt to try some aromatherapy during the long, quiet hours of the day, when her thoughts swarmed and descended, eating her up from the inside out. By the end of the week, she'd bought three more and placed them throughout her house.

Bryce breathed, "It seems like Philip Briggs might not have killed Danika."

For two years, part of her had clung to it—that in the days following the murder, they'd found enough evidence to convict Briggs, who'd wanted Danika dead for busting his rebel bomb ring. Briggs had denied it, but it had added up: He'd been caught purchasing black summoning salts in the weeks before his initial arrest, apparently to fuel some sort of new, horrible weapon.

That Danika had then been murdered by a Pit-level demon—which would have required the deadly black salt to summon it into this world—couldn't have been a coincidence. It seemed quite clear that Briggs had been released, gotten his hands on the black salt, summoned the demon, and set it loose upon Danika and the Pack of Devils. It had attacked the 33rd soldier who'd been patrolling the alleyway, and when its work was done, it had been sent back to Hel by Briggs. Though he'd never confessed to it, or what the breed even was, the fact remained that the demon hadn't been seen again in two years. Since Briggs had been locked up. Case closed.

For two years, Bryce had clung to those facts. That even though her world had fallen apart, the person responsible was behind bars. Forever. Deserving of every horror his jailors inflicted on him.

Jesiba let out a long, long breath. "Did the angels accuse you of anything?"

"No." Not quite. "The Governor is coming here."

Another pause. "To interrogate you?"

"I hope not." She liked her body parts where they were. "He wants to talk to you, too."

"Does Tertian's father know he's dead?"

"I don't know."

"I need to make some phone calls," Jesiba said, more to herself. "Before the Governor comes." Bryce understood her meaning well enough: So Maximus's father didn't show up at the gallery, demanding answers. Blaming Bryce for his death. It'd be a mess.

Bryce wiped her sweaty palms on her thighs. "The Governor will be here soon."

Faint tapping sounded on the iron archives door before Lehabah whispered, "BB? Are you all right?"

Bryce put a hand over the mouthpiece of her phone. "Go back to your post, Lele."

"Were those two angels?"

Bryce ground her teeth. "Yes. Go downstairs. Keep Syrinx quiet."

Lehabah let out a sigh, audible through six inches of iron. But the fire sprite didn't speak further, suggesting she'd either returned to the archives beneath the gallery or was still eavesdropping. Bryce didn't care, as long as she and the chimera stayed quiet.

Jesiba was asking, "When does Micah get there?"

"Eight minutes."

Jesiba considered. "All right." Bryce tried not to gape at the fact that she didn't push for more time—especially with a client's death in the balance.

But even Jesiba knew not to screw around with an Archangel. Or maybe she'd finally found a scrap of empathy where Danika's murder was concerned. She sure as Hel hadn't demonstrated it when she'd ordered Bryce to get back to work or be turned into a pig two weeks after Danika's death.

Jesiba said, "I don't need to tell you to make sure everything is on lockdown."

"I'll double-check." But she'd made sure before the angels had even set foot in the gallery.

"Then you know what to do, Quinlan," Jesiba said, the sound of rustling sheets or clothes filling the background. Two male voices grumbled in protest. Then the line went dead.

Blowing out a breath, Bryce launched into motion.

11

The Archangel rang the buzzer precisely seven minutes later.

Calming her panting, Bryce scanned the gallery for the tenth time, confirming that all was in place, the art dust-free, any contraband stored below—

Her legs felt spindly, the old ache in her thigh clawing at the bone, but her hands remained steady as she reached the front door and hauled it open.

The Archangel was gorgeous. Horrifically, indecently gorgeous.

Hunt Athalar and Isaiah Tiberian stood behind him—almost as good-looking; the latter giving her another bland smile he obviously believed was charming. The former . . . Hunt's dark eyes missed nothing.

Bryce lowered her head to the Governor, stepping back, her stupid heels wobbling on the carpet. "Welcome, Your Grace. Please come in."

Micah Domitus's brown eyes devoured her. His power pressed against her skin, ripped the air from the room, her lungs. Filled the space with midnight storms, sex and death entwined.

"I assume your employer will be joining us through the vidscreen," the Archangel said, stepping in from the glaringly bright street.

Fucking Hel, his *voice*—silk and steel and ancient stone. He could probably make someone come by merely whispering filthy things in their ear.

Even without that voice, it would have been impossible to forget what Micah was, what the Governor radiated with every breath, every blink. There were currently ten Archangels who ruled the various territories of the Republic, all bearing the title of Governor—all answering only to the Asteri. An ordinary angel's magic might level a building if they were considered powerful. An Archangel's power could level an entire metropolis. There was no predicting where the extra strength that separated Archangel from angel came from—sometimes, it was passed on, usually upon the careful breeding orders of the Asteri. Other times, it popped up in unremarkable bloodlines.

She didn't know much about Micah's history—had never paid attention during history class, too busy drooling over the unfairly perfect face currently before her to listen to her teacher's droning.

"Miss Roga is waiting for our call," she managed to say, and tried not to breathe too loudly as the Governor of Valbara swept past. One of his pristine white feathers brushed her bare collarbone. She might have shuddered—were it not for the two angels behind him.

Isaiah just gave her a nod as he trailed Micah toward the chairs before the desk.

Hunt Athalar, however, lingered. Holding her gaze—before he glanced at her collarbone. As if the feather had left a mark. The tattoo of thorns across his forehead seemed to turn darker.

And just like that, that scent of sex rippling off the Archangel turned to rot.

The Asteri and the Archangels could have easily found another way to hobble the power of the Fallen, yet they'd enslaved them with the witch spells woven into magical tattoos stamped onto their foreheads like fucked-up crowns. And the tattoos on their wrists: *SPQM*.

Senatus Populusque Midgard.

The Midgard Senate and People. Total fucking bullshit. As if the Senate was anything but a puppet ruling body. As if the Asteri weren't their emperors and empresses, ruling over everything and everyone for eternity, their rotted souls regenerating from one form to the next.

Bryce shoved the thought from her mind as she shut the iron door behind Hunt, just barely missing his gray feathers. His black eyes flashed with warning.

She gave him a smile to convey everything she didn't dare say aloud regarding her feelings about this ambush. *I've faced worse than you, Umbra Mortis. Glower and snarl all you like.*

Hunt blinked, the only sign of his surprise, but Bryce was already turning toward her desk, trying not to limp as pain speared through her leg. She'd dragged up a third chair from the library, which had aggravated her leg further.

She didn't dare rub at the thick, curving scar across her upper thigh, hidden under her white dress. "Can I get you anything, Your Grace? Coffee? Tea? Something stronger?" She'd already laid out bottled sparkling water on the small tables between the chairs.

The Archangel had claimed the middle seat, and as she smiled politely at him, the weight of his gaze pressed on her like a silken blanket. "I'm fine." Bryce looked to Hunt and Isaiah, who slid into their chairs. "They're fine, too," Micah said.

Very well, then. She strode around the desk, sliding her hand beneath its ledge to push a brass button and sending up a prayer to merciful Cthona that her voice remained calm, even as her mind kept circling back to the same thought, over and over: *Briggs didn't kill Danika, Briggs didn't kill Danika, Briggs didn't kill Danika—*

The wood panel in the wall behind her split open, revealing a large screen. As it flickered to life, she picked up the desk phone and dialed.

Briggs had been a monster who had planned to hurt people, and he deserved to be in jail, but—he'd been wrongly accused of the murder.

Danika's killer was still out there.

Jesiba answered on the first ring. "Is the screen ready?"

"Whenever you are." Bryce typed the codes into her computer, trying to ignore the Governor staring at her like she was a steak and he was . . . something that ate steak. Raw. And moaning. "I'm dialing you in," she declared.

Jesiba Roga appeared on the screen an instant later—and they both hung up their phones.

Behind the sorceress, the hotel suite was decorated in Pangeran splendor: paneled white walls with gilded molding, plush cream carpets and pale pink silk drapes, a four-poster oak bed big enough for her and the two males Bryce had heard when she called before.

Jesiba played as hard as she worked while over on the massive territory, seeking out more art for the gallery, either through visiting various archaeological digs or courting high-powered clients who already possessed them.

Despite having less than ten minutes, and despite using most of that time to make some very important calls, Jesiba's flowing navy dress was immaculate, revealing tantalizing glimpses of a lush female body adorned with freshwater pearls at her ears and throat. Her cropped ash-blond hair glowed in the golden firstlight lamps—cut shorter on the sides, longer on the top. Effortlessly chic and casual. Her face . . .

Her face was both young and wise, bedroom-soft yet foreboding. Her pale gray eyes gleamed with glittering magic, alluring and deadly.

Bryce had never dared ask why Jesiba had defected from the witches centuries ago. Why she'd aligned herself with the House of Flame and Shadow and its leader, the Under-King—and what she did for him. She called herself a sorceress now. Never a witch.

"Morning, Micah," Jesiba said mildly. A pleasant, disarming voice compared to that of other members of Flame and Shadow—the hoarse rasp of Reapers, or the silken tones of vampyrs.

"Jesiba," Micah purred.

Jesiba gave him a slight smile, as if she'd heard that purr a thousand different times, from a thousand different males. "Pleased as I am to see your handsome face, I'd like to know why you called this meeting. Unless the Danika thing was an excuse to talk to sweet Bryce."

The Danika thing. Bryce kept her face neutral, even as she felt

Hunt watching her carefully. As if he could hear her heart thundering, scent the sweat now coating her palms.

But Bryce gave him a bored look in return.

Micah leaned back in his chair, crossing his long legs, and said without so much as glancing at Bryce, "Tempting as your assistant is, we have important matters to discuss."

She ignored the outright entitlement, the timbre of that sensual voice. *Tempting*—as if she were a piece of dessert on a platter. She was used to it, but . . . these gods-damned Vanir males.

Jesiba waved with ethereal grace to continue, silver nails sparkling in the hotel's lamplight.

Micah said smoothly, "I believe my triarii informed Miss Quinlan of the murder last night. One that was an exact match for the deaths of Danika Fendyr and the Pack of Devils two years ago."

Bryce kept herself still, unfeeling. She took a subtle inhale of the soothing peppermint wisps from the infuser a few inches away.

Micah went on, "What they did not mention was the other connection."

The two angels flanking the Governor stiffened almost imperceptibly. This was clearly the first they were hearing of this as well.

"Oh?" Jesiba said. "And do I have to pay for this information?"

Vast, cold power crackled in the gallery, but the Archangel's face remained unreadable. "I am sharing this information so we might combine resources."

Jesiba arched a blond brow with preternatural smoothness. "To do what?"

Micah said, "For Bryce Quinlan to find the true murderer behind this, of course."

12

Bryce had gone still as death—so unmoving that Hunt wondered if she knew it was a solid tell. Not about her own nerves, but about her heritage. Only the Fae could go that still.

Her boss, the young-faced sorceress, sighed. "Is your 33rd so incompetent these days that you truly need my assistant's help?" Her lovely voice hardly softened her question. "Though I suppose I already have my answer, if you falsely convicted Philip Briggs."

Hunt didn't dare grin at her outright challenge. Few people could get away with speaking to Micah Domitus, let alone any Archangel, like that.

He considered the four-hundred-year-old sorceress on the screen. He'd heard the rumors: that Jesiba answered to the Under-King, that she could transform people into common animals if they provoked her, that she'd once been a witch who'd left her clan for reasons still unknown. Most likely bad ones, if she'd wound up a member of the House of Flame and Shadow.

Bryce breathed, "I don't know anything about this. Or who wanted to kill Tertian."

Jesiba sharpened her gaze. "Regardless, you are *my* assistant. You don't work for the 33rd."

Micah's mouth tightened. Hunt braced himself. "I invited you to this meeting, Jesiba, as a courtesy." His brown eyes narrowed with distaste. "It does indeed appear that Philip Briggs was wrongly convicted. But the fact remains that Danika Fendyr and the Pack of Devils apprehended him in his laboratory, with undeniable evidence regarding his intention to bomb innocents at the White Raven nightclub. And though he was initially released due to a loophole, in the past two years, enough evidence has been found for his earlier crimes that he has been convicted of them, too. As such, he will remain behind bars and serve out the sentence for those earlier crimes as leader of the now-inactive Keres sect, and his participation in the larger human rebellion."

Quinlan seemed to sag with relief.

But then Micah went on, "However, this means a dangerous murderer remains loose in this city, able to summon a lethal demon—for sport or revenge, we do not know. I will admit that my 33rd and the Auxiliary have exhausted their resources. But the Summit is in just over a month. There are individuals attending who will see these murders as proof that I am not in control of my city, let alone this territory, and seek to use it against me."

Of course it wasn't about catching a deadly killer. No, this was pure PR.

Even with the Summit so far off, Hunt and the other triarii had been prepping for weeks now, getting the units in the 33rd ready for the pomp and bullshit that surrounded the gathering of Valbaran powers every ten years. Leaders from across the territory would attend, airing their grievances, with maybe a few guest appearances from the ruling assholes across the Haldren.

Hunt hadn't yet attended one in Valbara, but he'd been through plenty of other Summits in Pangera, with rulers who all pretended they had some semblance of free will. The Summit meetings usually amounted to a week of powerful Vanir arguing until the overseeing Archangel laid down the law. He had little doubt Micah would be any different. Isaiah had experienced one already, and had warned him that the Archangel liked to flex his military might at the Summits—liked to have the 33rd in marching and flying formation, decked out in imperial regalia.

Hunt's golden breastplate was already being cleaned. The thought of donning the formal armor, the seven stars of the Asteri's crest displayed across his heart, made him want to puke.

Jesiba examined her silver nails. "Anything exciting happening at the Summit this time?"

Micah seemed to weigh Jesiba's casual expression as he said, "The new witch-queen will be formally recognized."

Jesiba didn't let one speck of emotion show. "I heard of Hecuba's passing," the sorceress said. No tinge of grief or satisfaction. Just fact.

But Quinlan tensed, as if she'd shout at them to get back to the murder. Micah added, "And the Asteri are sending Sandriel to deliver a report from the Senate regarding the rebel conflict."

Every thought eddied out of Hunt's head. Even the usually unflappable Isaiah went rigid.

Sandriel was coming *here.*

Micah was saying, "Sandriel will arrive at the Comitium next week, and at the Asteri's request, she will be my guest until the Summit."

A month. That fucking monster would be in this city for a month.

Jesiba angled her head with unnerving grace. She might not have been a Reaper, but she sure as shit moved like one. "What does my assistant have to offer in finding the murderer?"

Hunt shoved it down—the roaring, the trembling, the stillness. Shoved it down and down and down until it was just another wave in the black, roiling pit inside himself. Forced himself to concentrate on the conversation. And not on the psychopath on her way to this city.

Micah's stare settled on Bryce, who had turned so pale her freckles were like splattered blood across the bridge of her nose. "Miss Quinlan is, thus far, the only person alive to have witnessed the demon the murderer summoned."

Bryce had the nerve to ask, "What about the angel in the alley?"

Micah's face remained unchanged. "He had no memories of the attack. It was an ambush." Before Bryce could push, he went on, "Considering the delicate nature of this investigation, I am now willing to look outside the box, as they say, for assistance in solving these murders before they become a true problem."

Meaning, the Archangel needed to look good in front of the powers that be. In front of Sandriel, who would report it all to the Asteri and their puppet Senate.

A murderer on the loose, capable of summoning a demon that could kill Vanir as easily as humans? Oh, it'd be precisely the sort of shit Sandriel would delight in telling the Asteri. Especially if it cost Micah his position. And if she gained it for herself. What was the northwestern quadrant of Pangera compared to *all* of Valbara? And Micah losing everything meant his slaves—Hunt, Isaiah, Justinian, and so many others—went to whoever inherited his Governor's title.

Sandriel would never honor Micah's bargain with Hunt.

Micah turned to Hunt, a cruel tilt to his lips. "You can guess, Athalar, who Sandriel will be bringing with her." Hunt went rigid. "Pollux would be all too happy to report his findings as well."

Hunt fought to master his breathing, to keep his face neutral.

Pollux Antonius, Sandriel's triarii commander—the Malleus, they called him. The Hammer. As cruel and merciless as Sandriel. And an absolute motherfucking asshole.

Jesiba cleared her throat. "And you still don't know what kind of demon it was?" She leaned back in her chair, a frown on her full mouth.

"No," Micah said through his teeth.

It was true. Even Hunt hadn't been able to identify it, and he'd had the distinct pleasure of killing more demons than he could count. They came in endless breeds and levels of intelligence, ranging from the beasts that resembled feline-canine hybrids to the humanoid, shape-shifting princes who ruled over Hel's seven territories, each one darker than the last: the Hollow, the Trench, the Canyon, the Ravine, the Chasm, the Abyss, and the worst of them all—the Pit.

Even without a specific identification, though, given its speed and what it had done, the demon fit with something belonging to the Pit, perhaps a pet of the Star-Eater himself. Only in the depths of the Pit could something like that evolve—a creature who had never seen light, never needed it.

It didn't matter, Hunt supposed. Whether the demon was accustomed to light or not, his particular skills could still turn it into chunks of sizzling meat. A quick flash of light and a demon would either turn tail or writhe in pain.

Quinlan's voice cut through the storm in Hunt's head. "You said that there was another connection between the murders then and the one now. Beyond the . . . style."

Micah looked at her. To her credit, Quinlan didn't lower her eyes. "Maximus Tertian and Danika Fendyr were friends."

Bryce's brows twitched toward each other. "Danika didn't know Tertian."

Micah sighed toward the wood-paneled ceiling high above. "I suspect there might have been a good deal about which she didn't inform you."

"I would have known if she was friends with Maximus Tertian," Quinlan ground out.

Micah's power murmured through the room. "Careful, Miss Quinlan."

No one took that kind of tone with an Archangel, at least not anyone with nearly zero power in their veins. It was enough to get Hunt to set aside Sandriel's visit and focus on the conversation.

Micah went on, "There is also the fact that *you* knew both Danika and Maximus Tertian. That you were at the White Raven nightclub on each of the nights the murders happened. The similarity is enough to be . . . of interest."

Jesiba straightened. "Are you saying that Bryce is a suspect?"

"Not yet," Micah said coldly. "But anything is possible."

Quinlan's fingers curled into fists, her knuckles going white as she no doubt tried to restrain herself from spitting at the Archangel. She opted to change the subject instead. "What about investigating the others in the Pack of Devils? None of them might have been a target?"

"It has already been looked into and dismissed. Danika remains our focus."

Bryce asked tightly, "You honestly think I can find anything, when the Aux and 33rd couldn't? Why not get the Asteri to send over someone like the Hind?"

The question rippled through the room. Surely Quinlan wasn't dumb enough to wish for that. Jesiba threw a warning look at her assistant.

Micah, unfazed by the mention of Lidia Cervos, the Republic's most notorious spy-hunter—and breaker—replied, "As I said, I do not wish for knowledge of these . . . events to pass beyond the walls of my city."

Hunt heard what Micah left unspoken: despite being part of Sandriel's triarii, the deer shifter known as the Hind reported directly to the Asteri and was known to be Pollux's lover.

The Hammer and the Hind—the smasher of battlefields and the destroyer of the Republic's enemies. Hunt had seen the Hind a few times in Sandriel's stronghold and always walked away unnerved by her unreadable golden eyes. Lidia was as beautiful as she was ruthless in her pursuit of rebel spies. A perfect match for Pollux. The only one who might have suited Pollux more than the Hind was the Harpy, but Hunt tried not to think about the second in command of Sandriel's triarii when he could avoid it.

Hunt smothered his rising dread. Micah was saying, "Crime statistics suggest that it's likely Danika knew her killer." Another pointed silence that left Quinlan bristling. "And despite the things she might not have told you, you remain the person who knew Danika Fendyr better than anyone. I believe you can provide unparalleled insight."

Jesiba leaned toward the screen in her plush hotel room, all grace and restrained power. "All right, Governor. Let's say you commandeer Bryce to look into this. I'd like compensation."

Micah smiled, a sharp, thrilling thing that Hunt had witnessed only before the Archangel blasted someone into wind-torn smithereens. "Regardless of your allegiance to the Under-King, and the protection you believe it affords you, you remain a citizen of the Republic."

And you will answer to me, he didn't need to add.

Jesiba said simply, "I'd think you'd be well versed in the bylaws, Governor. Section Fifty-Seven: If a government official requires the services of an outside contractor, they are to pay—"

"Fine. You will send your invoice to me." Micah's wings rustled, the only sign of his impatience. But his voice was kind, at least, as he turned to Quinlan. "I am out of options, and shall soon be out of time. If there is someone who might retrace Danika's steps in her final days and discover who murdered her, it would be you. You are the only tie between the victims." She just gaped. "I believe your position here at the gallery also grants you access to individuals who might not be willing to talk to the 33rd or Auxiliary. Isaiah Tiberian will report to me on any progress you make, and keep a keen eye on this investigation." His brown eyes appraised Hunt, as if he could read every line of tension on his body, the panic seeping through his veins at the news of Sandriel's arrival. "Hunt Athalar is experienced in hunting demons. He shall be on protection duty, guarding you during your search for the person behind this."

Bryce's eyes narrowed, but Hunt didn't dare say a word. To blink his displeasure—and relief.

At least he would have an excuse not to be at the Comitium while Sandriel and Pollux were around. But to be a glorified babysitter, to not be able to work toward earning back his *debts* . . .

"Very well," Jesiba said. Her gaze slid to her assistant. "Bryce?"

Bryce said quietly, her amber eyes full of cold fire, "I'll find them." She met the Archangel's gaze. "And then I want you to wipe them off the fucking planet."

Yeah, Quinlan had balls. She was stupid and brash, but at least she had nerve. The combination, however, would likely see her dead before she completed the Drop.

Micah smiled, as if realizing that, too. "What is done with the murderer will be up to our justice system." Mild, bureaucratic nonsense, even as the Archangel's power thundered through the room, as if promising Quinlan he'd do exactly as she wished.

Bryce muttered, "Fine."

Jesiba Roga frowned at her assistant, noting that her face still burned with that cold fire. "Do try not to die, Bryce. I'd hate to endure the inconvenience of training someone new." The feed cut off.

Bryce stood in those absurd shoes. Walking around the desk, she swept the silky curtain of red hair over a shoulder, the slightly curled ends almost brushing the generous curve of her ass.

Micah stood, eyes sliding down Bryce as if he, too, noted that particular detail, but said to none of them in particular, "We're done here."

Bryce's dress was so tight that Hunt could see the muscles in her thighs strain as she hauled open the iron door for the Archangel. A faint wince passed over her face—then vanished.

Hunt reached her as the Archangel and his Commander paused outside. She only gave Hunt a winning, bland smile and began closing the door on him before he could step onto the dusty street. He wedged a foot between the door and jamb, and the enchantments zinged and snapped against his skin as they tried to align around him. Her amber eyes flared. "*What.*"

Hunt gave her a sharp grin. "Make a list of suspects today. Anyone who might have wanted Danika and her pack dead." If Danika knew her murderer, odds were that Bryce probably did, too. "And make a list of Danika's locations and activities during the last few days of her life."

Bryce only smiled again, as if she hadn't heard a damn word he said. But then she hit some button beside the door that had the enchantments *burning* like acid—

Hunt jumped back, his lightning flaring, defending against an enemy that was not there.

The door shut. She purred through the intercom, "I'll call you. Don't bother me until then."

Urd fucking spare him.

13

Atop the roof of the gallery a moment later, Isaiah silent at his side, Hunt watched the late morning sunlight gild Micah's pristine white wings and set the strands of gold in his hair to near-glowing as the Archangel inspected the walled city sprawled around them.

Hunt instead surveyed the flat roof, broken up only by equipment and the doorway to the gallery below.

Micah's wings shifted, his only warning that he was about to speak. "Time is not our ally."

Hunt just said, "Do you really think Quinlan can find whoever is behind this?" He let the question convey the extent of his own faith in her.

Micah angled his head. An ancient, lethal predator sizing up prey. "I think this is a matter that requires us to use every weapon in our arsenal, no matter how unorthodox." He sighed as he looked out at the city again.

Lunathion had been built as a model of the ancient coastal cities around the Rhagan Sea, a near-exact replica that included its sandstone walls, the arid climate, the olive groves and little farms that lined distant hills beyond the city borders to the north, even the great temple to a patron goddess in the very center. But unlike those cities, this one had been allowed to adapt: streets lay in an orderly grid, not a tangle; and modern buildings jutted up like lances in the heart of the CBD, far surpassing the strict height codes of Pangera.

Micah had been responsible for it—for seeing this city as a tribute to the old model, but also a place for the future to thrive. He'd even embraced using the name Crescent City over Lunathion.

A male of progress. Of tolerance, they said.

Hunt often wondered what it would feel like to rip out his throat.

He'd contemplated it so many times he'd lost count. Had contemplated blasting a bolt of his lightning into that beautiful face, that perfect mask for the brutal, demanding bastard inside.

Maybe it was unfair. Micah had been born into his power, had never known a life as anything but one of the major forces on this planet. A near-god who was unused to having his authority questioned and would put down any threats to it.

A rebellion led by a fellow Archangel and three thousand warriors had been just that. Even though nearly all of his triarii was now made up of the Fallen. Offering them a second chance, apparently. Hunt couldn't fathom why he'd bother being that merciful.

Micah said, "Sabine is certainly already putting her people on this case and will be visiting my office to tell me precisely what she thinks of the fuckup with Briggs." An icy glance between them. "I want *us* to find the murderer, not the wolves."

Hunt said coolly, "Dead or alive?"

"Alive, preferably. But dead is better than letting the person run free."

Hunt dared ask, "And will this investigation count toward my quota? It could take months."

Isaiah tensed. But Micah's mouth curled upward. For a long moment, he said nothing. Hunt didn't so much as blink.

Then Micah said, "How about this incentive, Athalar: you solve this case quickly—you solve it before the Summit, and I'll lower your debts to ten."

The very wind seemed to halt.

"Ten," Hunt managed to say, "more assignments?"

It was outrageous. Micah had no reason to offer him anything. Not when his word was all that was needed for Hunt to obey.

"Ten more assignments," Micah said, as if he hadn't dropped a fucking bomb into the middle of Hunt's life.

It could be a fool's bargain. Micah might draw out those ten assignments over decades, but . . . Burning fucking Solas.

The Archangel added, "You tell no one about this, Athalar." That he didn't bother to also warn Isaiah suggested enough about how much he trusted his commander.

Hunt said, as calmly as he could, "All right."

Micah's stare turned merciless, though. He scanned Hunt from head to toe. Then the gallery beneath their booted feet. The assistant within it. Micah growled, "Keep your dick in your pants and your hands to yourself. Or you'll find yourself without either for a long while."

Hunt would regrow both, of course. Any immortal who made the Drop could regrow just about anything if they weren't beheaded or severely mutilated, with arteries bleeding out, but . . . the recovery would be painful. Slow. And being dickless, even for a few months, wasn't high up on Hunt's to-do list.

Fucking around with a half-human assistant was the least of his priorities, anyway, with freedom potentially ten kills away.

Isaiah nodded for both of them. "We'll keep it professional."

Micah twisted toward the CBD, assessing the river breeze, his pristine wings twitching. He said to Isaiah, "Be in my office in an hour."

Isaiah bowed at the waist to the Archangel, a Pangeran gesture that made Hunt's hackles rise. He'd been forced to do that, at the risk of having his feathers pulled out, burned off, sliced apart. Those initial decades after the Fall had not been kind.

The wings he knew were mounted to the wall in the Asteri throne room were proof.

But Isaiah had always known how to play the game, how to stomach their protocols and hierarchies. How to dress like them, dine and fuck like them. He'd Fallen and risen back to the rank of commander because of it. It wouldn't surprise anyone if Micah recommended that Isaiah's halo be removed at the next Governors' Council with the Asteri after the Winter Solstice.

No assassinating, butchering, or torturing required.

Micah didn't so much as glance at them before he shot into the skies. Within seconds he'd become a white speck in the sea of blue.

Isaiah blew out a breath, frowning toward the spires atop the five towers of the Comitium, a glass-and-steel crown rising from the heart of the CBD.

"You think there's a catch?" Hunt asked his friend.

"He doesn't scheme like that." Like Sandriel and most of the other Archangels. "He means what he says. He's got to be desperate, if he wants to give you that kind of motivation."

"He owns me. His word is my command."

"With Sandriel coming, maybe he realized it'd be advantageous if you were inclined to be . . . loyal."

"Again: slave."

"Then I don't fucking know, Hunt. Maybe he was just feeling generous." Isaiah shook his head again. "Don't question the hand Urd dealt you."

Hunt blew out a breath. "I know." Odds were, the truth was a combination of those things.

Isaiah arched a brow. "You think you can find whoever is behind this?"

"I don't have a choice." Not with this new bargain on the table. He tasted the dry wind, half listening to its rasping song through the sacred cypresses lining the street below—the thousands of them in this city planted in honor of its patron goddess.

"You'll find them," Isaiah said. "I know you will."

"If I can stop thinking about Sandriel's visit." Hunt blew out a breath, dragging his hands through his hair. "I can't believe she's coming *here*. With that piece of shit Pollux."

Isaiah said carefully, "Tell me you realize that Micah threw you *another* big fucking bone just now in stationing you to protect Quinlan instead of keeping you around the Comitium with Sandriel there."

Hunt knew that, knew Micah was well aware of how Hunt felt about Sandriel and Pollux, but rolled his eyes. "Whatever. Trumpet all you want about how fantastic Micah is, but remember that the bastard is welcoming her with open arms."

"The Asteri ordered her to come for the Summit," Isaiah countered. "It's standard for them to send one of the Archangels as their emissary to these meetings. Governor Ephraim came to the last one here. Micah welcomed him, too."

Hunt said, "The fact remains that she'll be here for a whole month. In that fucking complex." He pointed to the five buildings of the Comitium. "Lunathion isn't her scene. There's nothing to amuse her here."

With most of the Fallen either scattered to the four winds or dead, Sandriel enjoyed nothing better than strolling through her castle dungeons, crammed full of human rebels, and selecting one, two, or three at a time. The arena at the heart of her city was just for the pleasure of destroying these prisoners in various ways. Battles to the death, public torture, unleashing Lowers and basic animals against them . . . There was no end to her creativity. Hunt had seen and endured it all.

With the conflict currently surging, those dungeons were sure to be packed. Sandriel and Pollux must have been enjoying the Hel out of the pain that flowed from that arena.

The thought made Hunt stiffen. "Pollux will be a fucking menace in this city." The Hammer was well known for his favorite activities: slaughter and torture.

"Pollux will be dealt with. Micah knows what he's like—what he does. The Asteri might have ordered him to welcome Sandriel, but he isn't going to let her give Pollux free rein." Isaiah paused, eyes going distant as he seemed to weigh something internally. "But I can make you unavailable while Sandriel visits—permanently."

Hunt lifted an eyebrow. "If you're referring to Micah's promise to make me dickless, I'll pass."

Isaiah laughed quietly. "Micah gave you an order to investigate with Quinlan. Orders that will make you very, very busy. Especially if he wants Bryce protected."

Hunt threw him a half grin. "So busy that I won't have time to be around the Comitium."

"So busy that you'll be staying on the roof across from Quinlan's building to monitor her."

"I've slept in worse conditions." So had Isaiah. "And it'd be an easy cover for keeping an eye on Quinlan for more than protection."

Isaiah frowned. "You honestly mark her as a suspect?"

"I'm not ruling it out," Hunt said, shrugging. "Micah didn't clear her, either. So until she proves otherwise, she's not off *my* list." He wondered who the Hel might make it onto Quinlan's list of suspects. When Isaiah only nodded, Hunt asked, "You're not going to tell Micah I'm watching her around the clock?"

"If he notices that you're not sleeping at the barracks, I'll tell him. But until then, what he doesn't know won't hurt him."

"Thanks." It wasn't a word in Hunt's normal vocabulary, not to anyone with wings, but he meant it. Isaiah had always been the best of them—the best of the Fallen, and all the legionaries Hunt had ever served with. Isaiah should have been in the Asterian Guard, with those skills and those pristine white wings, but like Hunt, Isaiah had come from the gutter. Only the highborn would do for the Asteri's elite private legion. Even if it meant passing over good soldiers like Isaiah.

Hunt, with his gray wings and common blood, despite his lightning, had never even been in the running. Being asked to join Shahar's elite 18th had been privilege enough. He'd loved her almost instantly for seeing his worth—and Isaiah's. All of the 18th had been like that: soldiers she'd selected not for their status, but their skills. Their true value.

Isaiah gestured toward the CBD and the Comitium within it. "Grab your gear from the barracks. I need to make a stop before I meet with Micah." At Hunt's blink, Isaiah winced. "I owe Prince Ruhn a visit to confirm Quinlan's alibi."

It was the last fucking thing Hunt wanted to do, and the last fucking thing he knew Isaiah wanted to do, but protocols were protocols. "You want me to go with you?" Hunt offered. It was the least he could offer.

The corner of Isaiah's mouth lifted. "Considering that you broke Danaan's nose the last time you were in a room together, I'm going to say no."

Wise move. Hunt drawled, "He deserved it."

Micah, mercifully, had found the entire event—the Incident, as Naomi called it—amusing. It wasn't every day that the Fae had their asses handed to them, so even the Governor had discreetly gloated over the altercation at the Spring Equinox celebrations the previous year. He'd given Hunt a whole week off for it. *A suspension*, Micah had claimed—but that suspension had come with an especially padded paycheck. And three less deaths to atone for.

Isaiah said, "I'll call you later to check in."

"Good luck."

Isaiah threw him a weary, worn smile—the only hint of the grind of all these years with those two tattoos—and went to track down Ruhn Danaan, the Crown Prince of the Fae.

Bryce paced the showroom once, hissed at the pain in her leg, and kicked off her heels hard enough that one slammed into the wall, setting an ancient vase shuddering.

A cool voice asked behind her, "When you nail Hunt Athalar's balls to the wall, will you do me a favor and take a picture?"

She glared at the vidscreen that had come on again—and the sorceress still sitting there. "You really want to get mixed up in this, boss?"

Jesiba leaned back in her gilded chair, a queen at ease. "Good old-fashioned revenge doesn't hold any appeal?"

"I have no idea who wanted Danika and the pack dead. None." It had made sense when it seemed like Briggs had summoned the demon to do it: he'd been released that day, Danika was on edge and upset about it, and then she had died. But if it wasn't Briggs, and with Maximus Tertian killed . . . She didn't know where to start.

But she'd do it. Find whoever had done this. A small part of it was just to make Micah Domitus eat his words hinting that she might be *of interest* in this case, but . . . She ground her teeth. She'd find whoever had done this and make them regret ever being born.

Bryce walked over to the desk, stifling the limp. She perched on the edge. "The Governor must be desperate." And insane, if he was asking for her help.

"I don't care about the Governor's agenda," Jesiba said. "Play vengeful detective all you want, Bryce, but do remember that you have a job. Client meetings will not take a back seat."

"I know." Bryce chewed on the inside of her cheek. "If whoever is behind this is strong enough to summon a demon like that to do their dirty work, I'll likely wind up dead, too." Very likely, given that she hadn't decided if or when to make the Drop yet.

Those gray glittering eyes roved over her face. "Then keep Athalar close."

Bryce bristled. As if she were some little female in need of a big, strong warrior to guard her.

Even if it *was* partially true. Mostly true.

Totally and definitely true, if that demon was being summoned again.

But—make a list of suspects, indeed. And the other task he'd given her, to make a list of Danika's last locations . . . Her body tightened at the thought.

She might accept Athalar's protection, but she didn't need to make it easy for the swaggering asshole.

Jesiba's phone rang. Thc female glanced at the screen. "It's Tertian's father." She threw Bryce a warning glare. "If I start losing money because you're off playing detective with the Umbra Mortis, I'll turn you into a turtle." She lifted the phone to her ear and the feed ended.

Bryce blew out a long breath before she hit the button to close the screen into the wall.

The silence of the gallery twined around her, gnawing at her bones.

Lehabah for once, seemed to not be eavesdropping. No tapping on the iron door filled the thrumming silence. Not a whisper of the tiny, incurably nosy fire sprite.

Bryce braced her arm on the cool surface of the desk, cupping her forehead in her hand.

Danika had never mentioned knowing Tertian. They'd never even spoken of him—not once. And that was all she had to go on?

Without Briggs as the summoner-killer, the murder didn't make sense. Why had the demon chosen their apartment, when it was three stories up and located in a supposedly monitored building? It had to be intentional. Danika and the others, Tertian included, must have been targeted, with Bryce's connection to the latter a sick coincidence.

Bryce toyed with the amulet on the end of her golden chain, zipping it back and forth.

Later. She'd think it over tonight, because—she glanced at the clock. Shit.

She had another client coming in forty-five minutes, which meant she should get through the tsunami of paperwork for the Svadgard wood carving purchased yesterday.

Or maybe she should work on that job application she'd kept in a secret, deceptively named file on her computer: *Paper Vendor Spreadsheets*.

Jesiba, who left her in charge of everything from restocking toilet paper to ordering printer paper, would never open the file. She'd never see that among the actual documents Bryce had thrown in there, there was one folder—*March Office Supply Invoices*—that didn't contain a spreadsheet. It held a cover letter, a résumé, and half-completed applications for positions at about ten different places.

Some were long shots. *Crescent City Art Museum Associate Curator.* As if she'd ever get that job, when she had neither an art nor a history degree. And when most museums believed places like Griffin Antiquities should be illegal.

Other positions—*Personal Assistant to Miss Fancypants Lawyer*—would be more of the same. Different setting and boss, but same old bullshit.

But they were a way out. Yeah, she'd have to find some kind of arrangement with Jesiba regarding her debts, and avoid finding out if just mentioning she wanted to leave would get her turned into some slithering animal, but dicking around with the applications, endlessly tweaking her résumé—it made her feel better, at least. Some days.

But if Danika's murderer had resurfaced, if being in this dead-end job could help . . . Those résumés were a waste of time.

Her phone's dark screen barely reflected the lights high, high above.

Sighing again, Bryce punched in her security code, and opened the message thread.

You won't regret this. I've had a long while to figure out all the ways I'm going to spoil you. All the fun we're going to have.

She could have recited Connor's messages from memory, but it hurt more to see them. Hurt enough to feel through every part of her body, the dark remnants of her soul. So she always looked.

Go enjoy yourself. I'll see you in a few days.

The white screen burned her eyes. *Message me when you're home safe.*

She shut that window. And didn't dare open up her audiomail. She usually had to be in one of her monthly emotional death-spirals to do that. To hear Danika's laughing voice again.

Bryce loosed a long breath, then another, then another.

She'd find the person behind this. For Danika, for the Pack of Devils, she'd do it. Do anything.

She opened up her phone again and began typing out a group message to Juniper and Fury. Not that Fury ever replied—no, the thread was a two-way conversation between Bryce and June. She'd written out half of her message: *Philip Briggs didn't kill Danika. The murders are starting again and I'm—* when she deleted it. Micah had given an order to keep this quiet, and if her phone was hacked . . . She wouldn't jeopardize being taken off the case.

Fury had to know about it already. That her so-called *friend* hadn't contacted her . . . Bryce shoved the thought away. She'd tell Juniper face-to-face. If Micah was right and there was somehow a connection between Bryce and how the victims were chosen, she couldn't risk leaving Juniper unaware. Wouldn't lose anyone else.

Bryce glanced at the sealed iron door. Rubbed the deep ache in her leg once before standing.

Silence walked beside her during the entire trip downstairs.

14

Ruhn Danaan stood before the towering oak doors to his father's study and took a bracing, cooling breath.

It had nothing to do with the thirty-block run he'd made from his unofficial office above a dive bar in the Old Square over to his father's sprawling marble villa in the heart of FiRo. Ruhn let out a breath and knocked.

He knew better than to barge in.

"Enter." The cold male voice leached through the doors, through Ruhn. But he shoved aside any indication of his thundering heart and slid into the room, shutting the door behind him.

The Autumn King's personal study was larger than most single-family houses. Bookshelves rose two stories on every wall, crammed with tomes and artifacts both old and new, magic and ordinary. A golden balcony bisected the rectangular space, accessible by either of the spiral staircases at the front and back, and heavy black velvet curtains currently blocked the morning light from the tall windows overlooking the interior courtyard of the villa.

The orrery in the far back of the space drew Ruhn's eye: a working model of their seven planets, moons, and sun. Made from solid gold. Ruhn had been mesmerized by it as a boy, back when he'd been stupid enough to believe his father actually gave a shit about him, spending hours in here watching the male make whatever observations and calculations he jotted down in his black leather notebooks. He'd asked only once about what his father was looking for, exactly.

Patterns was all his father said.

The Autumn King sat at one of the four massive worktables, each littered with books and an array of glass and metal devices. Experiments for whatever the fuck his father did with those *patterns.* Ruhn passed one of the tables, where iridescent liquid bubbled within a glass orb set over a burner—the flame likely of his father's making—puffs of violet smoke curling from it.

"Should I be wearing a hazmat suit?" Ruhn asked, aiming for the worktable where his father peered through a foot-long prism ensconced in some delicate silver contraption.

"State your business, Prince," his father said shortly, an amber eye fixed to the viewing apparatus atop the prism.

Ruhn refrained from commenting about how the taxpaying people of this city would feel if they knew how one of their seven Heads spent his days. The six lower Heads were all appointed by Micah, not elected by any democratic process. There were councils within councils, designed to give people the illusion of control, but the main order of things was simple: The Governor ruled, and the City Heads led their own districts under him. Beyond that, the 33rd Legion answered only to the Governor, while the Aux obeyed the City Heads, divided into units based upon districts and species. It grew murkier from there. The wolves claimed the shifter packs were the commanders of the Aux—but the Fae insisted that this distinction belonged to them, instead. It made dividing—*claiming*—responsibilities difficult.

Ruhn had been heading up the Fae division of the Aux for fifteen years now. His father had given the command, and he had obeyed. He had little choice. Good thing he'd trained his entire life to be a lethal, efficient killer.

Not that it brought him any particular joy.

"Some major shit is going down," Ruhn said, halting on the other side of the table. "I just got a visit from Isaiah Tiberian. Maximus Tertian was murdered last night—in exactly the same way that Danika and her pack were killed."

His father adjusted some dial on the prism device. "I received the report earlier this morning. It appears Philip Briggs wasn't the murderer."

Ruhn stiffened. "You were going to tell me when?"

His father glanced up from the prism device. "Am I beholden to you, Prince?"

The bastard certainly wasn't, his title aside. Though they were close in depth of power, the fact remained that Ruhn, despite his Starborn status and possession of the Starsword, would always have just a little less than his father. He'd never decided, after he'd gone through his Ordeal and made the Drop fifty years ago, whether it was a relief or a curse to have come up short on the power ranking. On the one hand, had he surpassed his father, the playing field would have tipped in his favor. On the other, it would have established him firmly as a rival.

Having seen what his father did to rivals, it was better to not be on that list.

"This information is vital. I already put out a call to Flynn and Declan to amp up patrols in FiRo. We'll have every street watched."

"Then it does not appear that I needed to tell you, does it?"

His father was nearing five hundred years old, had worn the golden crown of the Autumn King for most of that time, and had been an asshole for all of it. And he still showed no signs of aging—not as the Fae did, with their gradual fading into death, like a shirt washed too many times.

So it'd be another few centuries of this. Playing prince. Having to knock on a door and wait for permission to enter. Having to kneel and obey.

Ruhn was one of about a dozen Fae Princes across the whole planet Midgard—and had met most of the others over the decades. But he stood apart as the only Starborn among them. Among all the Fae.

Like Ruhn, the other princes served under preening, vain kings stationed in the various territories as Heads of city districts or swaths of wilderness. Some of them had been waiting for their thrones for centuries, counting down each decade as if it were mere months.

It disgusted him. Always had. Along with the fact that everything he had was bankrolled by the bastard before him: the office above the dive bar, the villa in FiRo adorned with priceless antiques that his father had gifted him upon winning the Starsword during his Ordeal. Ruhn never stayed at the villa, instead choosing to live in a house he shared with his two best friends near the Old Square.

Also purchased with his father's money.

Officially, the money came from the "salary" Ruhn received for heading up the Fae Auxiliary patrols. But his father's signature authorized that weekly check.

The Autumn King lifted the prism device. "Did the Commander of the 33rd say anything of note?"

The meeting had been one step short of a disaster.

First, Tiberian had grilled him about Bryce's whereabouts last night, until Ruhn was about one breath away from beating the shit out of the angel, Commander of the 33rd or no. Then Tiberian had the balls to ask about *Ruhn's* whereabouts.

Ruhn had refrained from informing the commander that pummeling Maximus Tertian for grabbing Bryce's hand had been tempting.

She'd have bitten his head off for it. And she'd been able to handle herself, sparing Ruhn the political nightmare of setting off a blood feud between their two Houses. Not just between Sky and Breath and Flame and Shadow, but between the Danaans and the Tertians. And thus every Fae and vampyr living in Valbara and Pangera. The Fae didn't fuck around with their blood feuds. Neither did the vamps.

"No," Ruhn said. "Though Maximus Tertian died a few hours after having a business meeting with Bryce."

His father set down the prism, his lip curling. "I told you to warn that girl to stay *quiet*."

That girl. Bryce was always *that girl*, or *the girl*, to their father.

Ruhn hadn't heard the male speak her name in twelve years. Not since her first and last visit to this villa.

Everything had changed after that visit. Bryce had come here for the first time, a coltish thirteen-year-old ready to finally meet her father and his people. To meet Ruhn, who had been intrigued at the prospect of finding he had a half sister after more than sixty years of being an only child.

The Autumn King had insisted that the visit be discreet—not saying the obvious: *until the Oracle whispers of your future*. What had gone down had been an unmitigated disaster not only for Bryce, but for Ruhn as well. His chest still ached when he remembered her leaving the villa in tears of rage, refusing to look back over her shoulder even once. His father's treatment of Bryce had opened Ruhn's eyes to the Autumn King's true nature . . . and the cold Fae male before him had never forgotten this fact.

Ruhn had visited Bryce frequently at her parents' place over the next three years. She'd been a bright spot—the brightest spot, if he felt like being honest. Until that stupid, shameful fight between them that had left things in such shambles that Bryce still hated his guts. He didn't blame her—not with the words he'd said, that he'd immediately regretted as soon as they'd burst from him.

Now Ruhn said, "*Bryce's* meeting with Maximus preceded my warning to behave. I arrived right as she was wrapping up." When he'd gotten that call from Riso Sergatto, the butterfly shifter's laughing voice unusually grave, he'd sprinted over to the White Raven, not giving himself time to second-guess the wisdom of it. "I'm her alibi, according to Tiberian—I told him that I walked her home, and stayed there until well after Tertian's time of death."

His father's face revealed nothing. "And yet it still does not seem very flattering that the girl was at the club on both nights, and interacted with the victims hours before."

Ruhn said tightly, "Bryce had nothing to do with the murders. Despite the alibi shit, the Governor must believe it, too, because Tiberian swore Bryce is being guarded by the 33rd."

It might have been admirable that they bothered to do so, had all the angels not been arrogant assholes. Luckily, the most arrogant of those assholes hadn't been the one to pay Ruhn this particular visit.

"That girl has always possessed a spectacular talent for being where she shouldn't."

Ruhn controlled the anger thrumming through him, his shadow magic seeking to veil him, shield him from sight. Another reason his father resented him: beyond his Starborn gifts, the bulk of his magic skewed toward his mother's kin—the Fae who ruled Avallen, the mist-shrouded isle in the north. The sacred heart of Faedom. His father would have burned Avallen into ashes if he could. That Ruhn did not possess his father's flames, the flames of most of the Valbaran Fae, that he instead possessed Avallen abilities—more than Ruhn ever let on—to summon and walk through shadows, had been an unforgivable insult.

Silence rippled between father and son, interrupted only by the ticking metal of the orrery at the other end of the room as the planets inched around their orbit.

His father picked up the prism, holding it up to the firstlights twinkling in one of the three crystal chandeliers.

Ruhn said tightly, "Tiberian said the Governor wants these murders kept quiet, but I'd like your permission to warn my mother." Every word grated. *I'd like your permission.*

His father waved a hand. "Permission granted. She'll heed the warning."

Just as Ruhn's mother had obeyed everyone her entire life.

She'd listen and lie low, and no doubt gladly accept the extra guards sent to her villa, down the block from his own, until this shit was sorted out. Maybe he'd even stay with her tonight.

She wasn't queen—wasn't even a consort or mate. No, his sweet, kind mother had been selected for one purpose: breeding. The Autumn King had decided, after a few centuries of ruling, that he wanted an heir. As the daughter of a prominent noble house that had defected from Avallen's court, she'd done her duty gladly, grateful for the eternal privilege it offered. In all of Ruhn's seventy-five years of life, he'd never heard her speak one ill word about his father. About the life she'd been conscripted to.

Even when Ember and his father had their secret, disastrous relationship, his mother had not been jealous. There had been so many other females before her, and after her. Yet none had been formally chosen, not as she was, to continue the royal bloodline. And when Bryce had come along, the few times his mother had met her, she'd been kind. Doting, even.

Ruhn couldn't tell if he admired his mother for never questioning the gilded cage she lived in. If something was wrong with *him* for resenting it.

He might never understand his mother, yet it didn't stop his fierce pride that he took after her bloodline, that his shadow-walking set him apart from the asshole in front of him, a constant, welcome reminder that he didn't *have* to turn into a domineering prick. Even if most of his mother's kin in Avallen were little better. His cousins especially.

"Perhaps you should call her," Ruhn said, "give the warning yourself. She'd appreciate your concern."

"I'm otherwise engaged," his father said calmly. It had always astonished Ruhn: how cold his father was, when those flames burned in his veins. "You may inform her yourself. And you will refrain from telling me how to manage my relationship with your mother."

"You don't have a relationship. You bred her like a mare and sent her out to pasture."

Cinders sparked through the room. "You benefited quite well from that *breeding*, Starborn."

Ruhn didn't dare voice the words that tried to spring from his mouth. *Even as my stupid fucking* title *brought you further influence in the empire and among your fellow kings, it still chafed, didn't it? That your son, not you, retrieved the Starsword from the Cave of Princes in Avallen's dark heart. That your son, not you, stood among the long-dead Starborn Princes asleep in their sarcophagi and was deemed worthy to pull the sword from its sheath. How many times did you try to draw the sword when you were young? How much research did you do in this very study to find ways to wield it without being chosen?*

His father curled a finger toward him. "I have need of your *gift*."

"Why?" His Starborn abilities were little more than a sparkle of starlight in his palm. His shadow talents were the more interesting gift. Even the temperature monitors on the high-tech cameras in this city couldn't detect him when he shadow-walked.

His father held up the prism. "Direct a beam of your starlight through this." Not waiting for an answer, his father again put an eye to the metal viewing contraption atop the prism.

It ordinarily took Ruhn a good amount of concentration to summon his starlight, and it usually left him with a headache for hours afterward, but . . . He was intrigued enough to try.

Setting his index finger onto the crystal of the prism, Ruhn closed his eyes and focused upon his breathing. Let the clicking metal of the orrery guide him down, down, down into the black pit within himself, past the churning well of his shadows, to the little hollow beneath them. There, curled upon itself like some hibernating creature, lay the single seed of iridescent light.

He gently cupped it with a mental palm, stirring it awake as he carefully brought it upward, as if he were carrying water in his hands. Up through himself, the power shimmering with anticipation, warm and lovely and just about the only part of himself he liked.

Ruhn opened his eyes to find the starlight dancing at his fingertip, refracting through the prism.

His father adjusted a few dials on the device, jotting down notes with his other hand.

The starlight seed became slippery, disintegrating into the air around them.

"Just another moment," the king ordered.

Ruhn gritted his teeth, as if it'd somehow keep the starlight from dissolving.

Another click of the device, and another jotted note in an ancient, rigid hand. The Old Language of the Fae—his father recorded everything in the half-forgotten language their people had used when they had first come to Midgard through the Northern Rift.

The starlight shivered, flared, and faded into nothing. The

Autumn King grunted in annoyance, but Ruhn barely heard it over his pounding head.

He'd mastered himself enough to pay attention as his father finished his notes. "What are you even doing with that thing?"

"Studying how light moves through the world. How it can be shaped."

"Don't we have scientists over at CCU doing this shit?"

"Their interests are not the same as mine." His father surveyed him. And then said, without a hint of warning, "It is time to consider females for an appropriate marriage."

Ruhn blinked. "For you?"

"Don't play stupid." His father shut his notebook and leaned back in his chair. "You owe it to our bloodline to produce an heir—and to expand our alliances. The Oracle decreed you would be a fair and just king. This is the first step in that direction."

All Fae, male and female, made a visit to the city's Oracle at age thirteen as one of the two Great Rites to enter adulthood: first the Oracle, and then the Ordeal—a few years or decades later.

Ruhn's stomach churned at the memory of that first Rite, far worse than his harrowing Ordeal in so many ways. "I'm not getting married."

"Marriage is a political contract. Sire an heir, then go back to fucking whomever you please."

Ruhn snarled. "I am *not* getting married. Certainly not in an arranged marriage."

"You will do as you are told."

"You're not fucking married."

"I did not need the alliance."

"But now we do?"

"There is a war raging overseas, in case you weren't aware. It worsens by the day, and it may very well spread here. I do not plan to enter it without insurance."

Pulse hammering, Ruhn stared at his father. He was completely serious.

Ruhn managed to say, "You plan to make me marry so we have solid allies in the war? Aren't we the Asteri's allies?"

"We are. But war is a liminal time. Power rankings can easily be reshuffled. We must demonstrate how vital and influential we are."

Ruhn considered the words. "You're talking about a marriage to someone not of the Fae." His father had to be worried, to even consider something so rare.

"Queen Hecuba died last month. Her daughter, Hypaxia, has been crowned the new witch-queen of Valbara."

Ruhn had seen the news reports. Hypaxia Enador was young, no more than twenty-six. No photos of her existed, as her mother had kept her cloistered in her mountain fortress.

His father went on, "Her reign will be officially recognized by the Asteri at the Summit next month. I will tie her to the Fae soon after that."

"You're forgetting that Hypaxia will have a say in this. She might very well laugh you off."

"My spies tell me she will heed her mother's old friendship with us—and will be skittish enough as a new ruler to accept the friendly hand we offer."

Ruhn had the distinct feeling of being led into a web, the Autumn King drawing him ever closer to its heart. "I'm not marrying her."

"You are the Crown Prince of the Valbaran Fae. You do not have a choice." His father's cold face became so like Bryce's that Ruhn turned away, unable to stomach it. It was a miracle no one had figured out their secret yet. "Luna's Horn remains at large."

Ruhn twisted back to his father. "So? What does one have to do with the other?"

"I want you to find it."

Ruhn glanced to the notebooks, the prism. "It went missing two years ago."

"And I now have an interest in locating it. The Horn belonged to the Fae first. Public interest in retrieving it has waned; now is the right time to attain it."

His father tapped a finger on the table. Something had riled him. Ruhn considered what he'd seen on his father's schedule this morning when he'd done his cursory scan of it as commander of the Fae Auxiliary. Meetings with preening Fae nobility, a workout with his private guard, and— "The meeting with Micah went well this morning, I take it."

His father's silence confirmed his suspicions. The Autumn King pinned him with his amber eyes, weighing Ruhn's stance, his expression, all of it. Ruhn knew he'd always come up short, but his father said, "Micah wished to discuss shoring up our city's defenses should the conflict overseas spread here. He made it clear the Fae are . . . not as they once were."

Ruhn stiffened. "The Fae Aux units are in just as good shape as the wolves are."

"It is not about our strength of arms, but rather our strength as a people." His father's voice dripped with disgust. "The Fae have long been fading—our magic wanes with each generation, like watered-down wine." He frowned at Ruhn. "The first Starborn Prince could blind an enemy with a flash of his starlight. You can barely summon a sparkle for an instant."

Ruhn clenched his jaw. "The Governor pushed your buttons. So what?"

"He insulted our strength." His father's hair simmered with fire, as if the strands had gone molten. "He said we gave up the Horn in the first place, then let it be lost two years ago."

"It was stolen from Luna's Temple. We didn't fucking *lose* it." Ruhn barely knew anything about the object, hadn't even cared when it went missing two years ago.

"We let a sacred artifact of our people be used as a cheap tourist attraction," his father snapped. "And I want *you* to find it again." So his father could rub it in Micah's face.

Petty, brittle male. That's all his father was.

"The Horn has no power," Ruhn reminded him.

"It is a symbol—and symbols will always wield power of their own." His father's hair burned brighter.

Ruhn suppressed his urge to cringe, his body tensing with the memory of how the king's burning hand had felt wrapped around his arm, sizzling through his flesh. No shadows had ever been able to hide him from it. "Find the Horn, Ruhn. If war comes to these shores, our people will need it in more ways than one."

His father's amber eyes blazed. There was more the male wasn't telling him.

Ruhn could think of only one other thing to cause this much aggravation: Micah again suggesting that Ruhn replace his father as City Head of FiRo. Whispers had swirled for years, and Ruhn had no doubt the Archangel was smart enough to know how much it'd anger the Autumn King. With the Summit nearing, Micah knew pissing off the Fae King with a reference to his fading power was a good way to ensure the Fae Aux was up to snuff before it, regardless of any war.

Ruhn tucked that information aside. "Why don't *you* look for the Horn?"

His father loosed a breath through his long, thin nose, and the fire in him banked to embers. The king nodded toward Ruhn's hand, where the starlight had been. "I have been looking. For two years." Ruhn blinked, but his father went on, "The Horn was originally the possession of Pelias, the first Starborn Prince. You may find that like calls to like—merely researching it could reveal things to you that were hidden from others."

Ruhn hardly bothered to read anything these days beyond the news and the Aux reports. The prospect of poring over ancient tomes just in case something jumped out at him while a murderer ran loose . . . "We'll get into a lot of trouble with the Governor if we take the Horn for ourselves."

"Then keep it quiet, Prince." His father opened his notebook again. Conversation over.

Yeah, this was nothing more than political ego-stroking. Micah had taunted his father, insulted his strength—and now his father would show him precisely where the Fae stood.

Ruhn ground his teeth. He needed a drink. A strong fucking drink.

His head roiled as he headed for the door, the pain from summoning the starlight eddying with every word thrown at him.

I told you to warn that girl to stay quiet.

Find the Horn.

Like calls to like.

An appropriate marriage.

Produce an heir.

You owe it to our bloodline.

Ruhn slammed the door behind him. Only when he'd gotten halfway down the hall did he laugh, a harsh, rasping sound. At least the asshole still didn't know that he'd lied about what the Oracle had told him all those decades ago.

With every step out of his father's villa, Ruhn could once more hear the Oracle's unearthly whispering, reading the smoke while he'd trembled in her dim marble chamber:

The royal bloodline shall end with you, Prince.

15

Syrinx pawed at the window, his scrunched-up face smooshed against the glass. He'd been hissing incessantly for the past ten minutes, and Bryce, more than ready to settle into the plush cushions of the L-shaped couch and watch her favorite Tuesday night reality show, finally twisted to see what all the fuss was about.

Slightly bigger than a terrier, the chimera huffed and pawed at the floor-to-ceiling glass, the setting sun gilding his wiry golden coat. The long tail, tufted with dark fur at the end like a lion's, waved back and forth. His folded little ears were flat to his round, fuzzy head, his wrinkles of fat and the longer hair at his neck—not quite a mane—were vibrating with his growling, and his too-big paws, which ended in birdlike talons, were now—

"*Stop that!* You're scratching the glass!"

Syrinx looked over a rounded, muscled shoulder, his squished face more dog than anything, and narrowed his dark eyes. Bryce glared right back.

The rest of her day had been long and weird and exhausting, especially after she'd gotten a message from Juniper, saying Fury had alerted her about Briggs's innocence and the new murder, and warning Bryce to be careful. She doubted either friend knew of her involvement in finding the murderer, or of the angel who'd been assigned to work with her, but it had stung—just a bit. That Fury hadn't bothered to contact her personally. That even June had done it over messaging and not face-to-face.

Bryce had a feeling tomorrow would be just as draining—if not worse. So throwing in a battle of wills with a thirty-pound chimera wasn't her definition of a much-needed unwinding.

"You just got a walk," she reminded Syrinx. "*And* an extra helping of dinner."

Syrinx gave a *hmmph* and scratched the window again.

"*Bad!*" she hissed. Half-heartedly, sure, but she *tried* to sound authoritative.

Where the little beast was concerned, dominance was a quality they both pretended she had.

Groaning, Bryce hauled herself from the nest of cushions and padded across wood and carpet to the window. On the street below, cars inched past, a few late commuters trudged home, and some dinner patrons strolled arm-in-arm to one of the fine restaurants along the river at the end of the block. Above them, the setting sun smeared the sky red and gold and pink, the palm trees and cypresses swayed in the balmy spring breeze, and . . . And that was a winged male sitting on the opposite roof. Staring right at her.

She knew those gray wings, and the dark, shoulder-length hair, and the cut of those broad shoulders.

Protection duty, Micah had said.

Bullshit. She had a strong feeling the Governor still didn't trust her, alibi or no.

Bryce gave Hunt Athalar a dazzling smile and slashed the heavy curtains shut.

Syrinx yowled as he was caught in them, reversing his stout little body out of the folds. His tail lashed from side to side, and she braced her hands on her hips. "You were *enjoying* the sight?"

Syrinx showed all his pointy teeth as he let out another yowl, trotted to the couch, and threw himself onto the warmed cushions where she'd been sitting. The portrait of despair.

A moment later, her phone buzzed on the coffee table. Right as her show began.

She didn't know the number, but she wasn't at all surprised when she picked up, plopping down onto the cushions, and Hunt growled, "Open the curtains. I want to watch the show."

She propped both bare feet on the table. "I didn't know angels deigned to watch trash TV."

"I'd rather watch the sunball game that's on right now, but I'll take what I can get."

The idea of the Umbra Mortis watching a dating competition was laughable enough that Bryce hit pause on the live show. At least she could now speed through commercials. "What are you doing on that roof, Athalar?"

"What I was ordered to do."

Gods spare her. "Protecting me doesn't entitle you to invade my privacy." She could admit to the wisdom in letting him guard her, but she didn't have to yield all sense of boundaries.

"Other people would disagree." She opened her mouth, but he cut her off. "I've got my orders. I can't disobey them."

Her stomach tightened. No, Hunt Athalar certainly could not disobey his orders.

No slave could, whether Vanir or human. So she instead asked, "And how, exactly, did you get this number?"

"It's in your file."

She tapped her foot on the table. "Did you pay Prince Ruhn a visit?" She would have handed over a gold mark to watch her brother go head-to-head with Micah's personal assassin.

Hunt grunted, "Isaiah did." She smiled. "It was standard protocol."

"So even after your boss tasked me with finding this murderer, you felt the need to look into whether my alibi checked out?"

"I didn't write the fucking rules, Quinlan."

"Hmm."

"Open the curtains."

"No, thank you."

"Or you could invite me in and make my job easier."

"Definitely no."

"Why?"

"Because you can do your job just as well from that roof."

Hunt's chuckle skittered along her bones. "We've been ordered to get to the bottom of these murders. So I hate to tell you this, sweetheart, but we're about to get real up close and personal."

The way he said *sweetheart*—full of demeaning, condescending swagger—made her grind her teeth.

Bryce rose, padding to the floor-to-ceiling window under Syrinx's careful watch, and tugged the curtains back enough to see the angel standing on the opposite roof, phone to his ear, gray wings slightly flared, as if balancing against the wind. "I'm sure you get off on the whole protector-of-damsels thing, but *I* was asked to head this case. You're the backup."

Even from across the street, she could see him roll his eyes. "Can we skip this pecking-order bullshit?"

Syrinx nudged at her calves, then shoved his face past her legs to peer at the angel.

"What *is* that pet of yours?"

"He's a chimera."

"Looks expensive."

"He was."

"Your apartment looks pretty damn expensive, too. That sorceress must pay you well."

"She does." Truth and lie.

His wings flared. "You have my number now. Call it if something goes wrong, or feels wrong, or if you need anything."

"Like a pizza?"

She clearly saw the middle finger Hunt lifted above his head. Shadow of Death, indeed.

Bryce purred, "You *would* make a good delivery boy with those wings." Angels in Lunathion never stooped to such work, though. Ever.

"Keep the damn curtains open, Quinlan." He hung up.

She just gave him a mocking wave. And shut the curtains entirely.

Her phone buzzed with a message just as she plopped down again.

Do you have enchantments guarding your apartment?

She rolled her eyes, typing back, *Do I look stupid?*

Hunt fired back, *Some shit is going down in this city and you've been gifted with grade A protection against it—yet you're busting my balls about boundaries. I think that's answer enough regarding your intelligence.*

Her thumbs flew over the screen as she scowled and wrote, *Kindly fly the fuck off.*

She hit send before she could debate the wisdom of saying that to the Umbra Mortis.

He didn't reply. With a smug smile, she picked up her remote.

A *thud* against the window had her leaping out of her skin, sending Syrinx scrambling in a mad dash toward the curtains, yowling his fuzzy head off.

She stormed around the couch, whipping the curtains back, wondering what the fuck he'd thrown at her window—

The Fallen angel hovered right there. Glaring at her.

She refused to back away, even as her heart thundered. Refused to do anything but shove open the window, the wind off his mighty wings stirring her hair. "*What?*"

His dark eyes didn't so much as blink. Striking—that was the only word Bryce could think of to describe his handsome face, full of powerful lines and sharp cheekbones. "You can make this investigation easy, or you can make it hard."

"I don't—"

"Spare me." Hunt's dark hair shifted in the wind. The rustle and beat of his wings overpowered the traffic below—and the humans and Vanir now gawking up at him. "You don't appreciate being watched, or coddled, or whatever." He crossed his muscled arms. "Neither of us gets a say in this arrangement. So rather than waste your breath arguing about boundaries, why don't you make that list of suspects and Danika's movements?"

"Why don't you stop telling me what I should be doing with my time?"

She could have sworn she tasted ether as he growled, "I'm going to be straight with you."

"Goody."

His nostrils flared. "I will do whatever the Hel it takes to solve this case. Even if it means tying you to a fucking chair until you write those lists."

She smirked. "Bondage. Nice."

Hunt's eyes darkened. "Do. Not. Fuck. With. Me."

"Yeah, yeah, you're the Umbra Mortis."

His teeth flashed. "I don't care what you call me, Quinlan, so long as you do what you're told."

Fucking alphahole.

"Immortality is a long time to have a giant stick up your ass." Bryce put her hands on her hips. Never mind that she was completely undermined by Syrinx dancing at her feet, prancing in place.

Dragging his stare away from her, the angel surveyed her pet with raised brows. Syrinx's tail waved and bobbed. Hunt snorted, as if despite himself. "You're a smart beastie, aren't you?" He threw a scornful glance to Bryce. "Smarter than your owner, it seems."

Make that the King of Alphaholes.

But Syrinx preened. And Bryce had the stupid, overwhelming urge to hide Syrinx from Hunt, from anyone, from anything. He was *hers*, and no one else's, and she didn't particularly like the thought of anyone coming into their little bubble—

Hunt's stare lifted to her own again. "Do you own any weapons?" The purely male gleam in his eye told her that he assumed she didn't.

"Bother me again," she said sweetly, just before she shut the window in his face, "and you'll find out."

Hunt wondered how much trouble he'd get in if he chucked Bryce Quinlan into the Istros.

After the morning he'd had, any punishment from Micah or being turned into a pig by Jesiba Roga was starting to seem well worth it.

Leaning against a lamppost, his face coated with the misting rain that drifted through the city, Hunt clenched his jaw hard enough to hurt. At this hour, commuters packed the narrow streets of the Old Square—some heading to jobs in the countless shops and galleries, others aiming for the spires of the CBD, half a mile westward. All of them, however, noted his wings, his face, and gave him a wide berth.

Hunt ignored them and glanced at the clock on his phone. Eight fifteen.

He'd waited long enough to make the call. He dialed the number and held the phone to his ear, listening to it ring once, twice—

"Please tell me Bryce is alive," said Isaiah, his voice breathless in a way that told Hunt he was either at the barracks gym or enjoying his boyfriend's company.

"For the moment."

A machine beeped, like Isaiah was dialing down the speed of a treadmill. "Do I want to know why I'm getting a call this soon?" A pause. "Why are you on Samson Street?"

Though Isaiah probably tracked his location through the beacon on Hunt's phone, Hunt still scowled toward the nearest visible camera. There were likely ones hidden in the cypresses and palm trees flanking the sidewalks, too, or disguised as sprinkler heads popping from the soggy grass of the flower beds, or built into the iron lampposts like the one he leaned against.

Someone was always watching. In this entire fucking city, territory, and world, someone was always watching, the cameras so bespelled and warded that they were bombproof. Even if this city turned to rubble under the lethal magic of the Asterian Guard's brimstone missiles, the cameras would keep recording.

"Are you aware," Hunt said, his voice a low rasp as a bevy of quails snaked across the street—some tiny shifter family, no doubt—"that chimeras are able to pick locks, open doors, and jump between two places as if they were walking from one room to another?"

"No . . . ?" Isaiah said, panting.

Apparently, Quinlan wasn't, either, if she bothered to have a crate for her beast. Though maybe the damn thing was more to give the chimera a designated comfort space, like people did with their dogs. Since there was no way he would stay contained without a whole host of enchantments.

The Lowers, the class of Vanir to which the chimera belonged, had all sorts of interesting, small powers like that. It was part of why they demanded such high prices on the market. And why, even millennia later, the Senate and Asteri had shot down any attempts to change the laws that branded them as property to be traded. The Lowers were too dangerous, they'd claimed—unable to understand the laws, with powers that could be disruptive if left unchecked by the various spells and magic-infused tattoos that held them.

And too lucrative, especially for the ruling powers whose families profited from their trade.

So they remained Lowers.

Hunt tucked his wings in one at a time. Water beaded off the gray feathers like clear jewels. "This is already a nightmare."

Isaiah coughed. "You watched Quinlan for one night."

"Ten hours, to be exact. Right until her pet chimera just *appeared* next to me at dawn, bit me in the ass for looking like I was dozing off, and then vanished again—right back into the apartment. Just as Quinlan came out of her bedroom and opened the curtains to see me grabbing my own ass like a fucking idiot. Do you *know* how sharp a chimera's teeth are?"

"No." Hunt could have sworn he heard a smile in Isaiah's voice.

"When I flew over to explain, she blasted her music and ignored me like a fucking brat." With enough enchantments around her apartment to keep out a host of angels, Hunt hadn't even tried to get in through a window, since he'd tested them all overnight. So he'd been forced to glower through the glass—returning to the roof only after she'd emerged from her bedroom in nothing but a black sports bra and thong. Her smirk at his backtracking wings had been nothing short of feline. "I didn't see her again until she went for a run. She flipped me off as she left."

"So you went to Samson Street to brood? What's the emergency?"

"The emergency, asshole, is that I might kill her before we find the real murderer." He had too much riding on this case.

"You're just pissed she's not cowering or fawning."

"Like I fucking want anyone to *fawn*—"

"Where's Quinlan now?"

"Getting her nails done."

Isaiah's pause sounded a Hel of a lot like he was about to burst out laughing. "Hence your presence on Samson Street before nine."

"Gazing through the window of a *nail salon* like a gods-damned stalker."

The fact that Quinlan wasn't gunning for the murderer grated as much as her behavior. And Hunt couldn't help being suspicious. He didn't know how or why she might have killed Danika, her pack, and Tertian, but she'd been connected to all of them. Had gone to the same place on the nights they'd been murdered. She knew something—or had done something.

"I'm hanging up now." The bastard was smiling. Hunt knew it. "You've faced down enemy armies, survived Sandriel's arena, gone toe-to-toe with Archangels." Isaiah chuckled. "Surely a party girl isn't as difficult as all that." The line cut off.

Hunt ground his teeth. Through the glass window of the salon, he could perfectly make out Bryce seated at one of the marble workstations, hands outstretched to a pretty reddish-gold-scaled draki female who was putting yet *another* coat of polish on her nails. How many did she *need*?

At this hour, only a few other patrons were seated inside, nails or talons or claws in the process of being filed and painted and whatever the Hel they did to them in there. But all of them kept glancing through the window. To him.

He'd already earned a glare from the teal-haired falcon shifter at the welcome counter, but she hadn't dared come out to ask him to stop making her clients nervous and leave.

Bryce sat there, wholly ignoring him. Chatting and laughing with the female doing her nails.

It had taken Hunt a matter of moments to launch into the skies when Bryce had left her apartment. He'd trailed overhead, well aware of the morning commuters who would film him if he landed beside her in the middle of the street and wrapped his hands around her throat.

Her run took her fifteen blocks away, apparently. She had barely broken a sweat by the time she jogged up to the nail salon, her skin-tight athletic clothes damp with the misting rain, and threw him a look that warned him to stay outside.

That had been an hour ago. A full hour of drills and files and scissors being applied to her nails in a way that would make the Hind herself cringe. Pure torture.

Five minutes. Quinlan had five more fucking minutes, then he'd drag her out. Micah must have lost his mind—that was the only explanation for asking her to help, especially if she prioritized her *nails* over solving her friends' murder.

He didn't know why it came as a surprise. After all he'd seen, everyone he'd met and endured, this sort of shit should have ceased to bother him long ago.

Someone with Quinlan's looks would become accustomed to the doors that face and body of hers opened without so much as a squeak of protest. Being half-human had some disadvantages, yes—a lot of them, if he was being honest about the state of the world. But she'd done well. Really fucking well, if that apartment was any indication.

The draki female set aside the bottle and flicked her claw-tipped fingers over Bryce's nails. Magic sparked, Bryce's ponytail shifting as if a dry wind had blown by.

Like that of the Valbaran Fae, draki magic skewed toward flame and wind. In the northern climes of Pangera, though, he'd met draki and Fae whose power could summon water, rain, mist—element-based magic. But even among the reclusive draki and the Fae, no one bore lightning. He knew, because he'd looked—desperate in his youth for anyone who might teach him how to control it. He'd had to teach himself in the end.

Bryce examined her nails, and smiled. And then hugged the female. Fucking *hugged* her. Like she was some sort of gods-damned war hero for the job she'd done.

Hunt was surprised his teeth weren't ground to stumps by the time she headed for the door, waving goodbye to the smiling falcon shifter at the front desk, who handed her a clear umbrella, presumably to borrow against the rain.

The glass door opened, and Bryce's eyes at last met Hunt's.

"Are you fucking *kidding* me?" The words exploded out of him.

She popped open the umbrella, nearly taking out his eye. "Did you have something better to do with your time?"

"You made me wait in the rain."

"You're a big, tough male. I think you can handle a little water."

Hunt fell into step beside her. "I told you to make those two lists. Not go to a motherfucking beauty salon."

She paused at an intersection, waiting for the bumper-to-bumper cars to crawl past, and straightened to her full height. Not anywhere close to his, but she somehow managed to look down her nose at him while still looking *up* at him. "If you're so good at investigating, why don't you look into it and spare me the effort?"

"You were given an order by the Governor." The words sounded ridiculous even to him. She crossed the street, and he followed. "And I'd think you'd be personally motivated to figure out who's behind this."

"Don't assume anything about my motivations." She dodged around a puddle of either rain or piss. In the Old Square, it was impossible to tell.

He refrained from pushing her into that puddle. "Do you have a problem with me?"

"I don't really care about you enough to have a problem with you."

"Likewise."

Her eyes really did glow then, as if a distant fire simmered within. She surveyed him, sizing up every inch and somehow—some-fucking-how—making him feel about three inches tall.

He said nothing until they turned down her street at last. He growled, "You need to make the list of suspects and the list of Danika's last week of activities."

She examined her nails, now painted in some sort of color

gradient that went from pink to periwinkle tips. Like the sky at twilight. "No one likes a nag, Athalar."

They reached the arched glass entry of her apartment building—structured like a fish's fin, he'd realized last night—and the doors slid open. Ponytail swishing, she said cheerfully, "Bye."

Hunt drawled, "People might see you dicking around like this, Quinlan, and think you were trying to hinder an official investigation." If he couldn't bully her into working on this case, maybe he could scare her into it.

Especially with the truth: She wasn't off the hook. Not even close.

Her eyes flared again, and damn if it wasn't satisfying. So Hunt just added, mouth curving into a half smile, "Better hurry. You wouldn't want to be late for work."

Going to the nail salon had been worth it on so many levels, but perhaps the biggest benefit had been pissing off Athalar.

"I don't see why you can't let the angel in," moped Lehabah, perched atop an old pillar candle. "He's so handsome."

In the bowels of the gallery library, client paperwork spread on the table before her, Bryce cast a sidelong glare at the female-shaped flame. "Do *not* drip wax on these documents, Lele."

The fire sprite grumbled, and plopped her ass on the candle's wick anyway. Wax dribbled down the sides, her tangle of yellow hair floating above her head—as if she were indeed a flame given a plump female shape. "He's just sitting on the roof in the dreary weather. Let him rest on the couch down here. Syrinx says the angel can brush his coat if he needs something to do."

Bryce sighed at the painted ceiling—the night sky rendered in loving care. The giant gold chandelier that hung down the center of the space was fashioned after an exploding sun, with all the other dangling lights in perfect alignment of the seven planets. "The angel," she said, frowning toward Syrinx's slumbering form on the green velvet couch, "is not allowed in here."

Lehabah let out a sad little noise. "One day, the boss will trade my services to some lecherous old creep, and you'll regret ever denying me anything."

"One day, that lecherous old creep will actually make you do your job and guard his books, and you'll regret spending all these hours of relative freedom moping."

Wax sizzled on the table. Bryce whipped her head up.

Lehabah was sprawled belly-down on the candle, an idle hand hanging off the side. Dangerously near the documents Bryce had spent the past three hours poring over.

"Do *not*."

Lehabah rotated her arm so that the tattoo inked amid the simmering flesh was visible. It had been stamped on her arm within moments of her birth, Lehabah had said. *SPQM*. It was inked on the flesh of every sprite—fire or water or earth, it didn't matter. Punishment for joining the angels' rebellion two hundred years ago, when the sprites had dared protest their status as peregrini. As Lowers. The Asteri had gone even further than their enslavement and torture of the angels. They'd decreed after the rebellion that every sprite—not only the ones who'd joined Shahar and her legion—would be enslaved, and cast from the House of Sky and Breath. All of their descendants would be wanderers and slaves, too. Forever.

It was one of the more spectacularly fucked episodes of the Republic's history.

Lehabah sighed. "Buy my freedom from Jesiba. Then I can go live at your apartment and keep your baths and all your food warm."

She could do far more than that, Bryce knew. Technically, Lehabah's magic outranked Bryce's own. But most non-humans could claim the same. And even while it was greater than Bryce's, Lehabah's power was still an ember compared to the Fae's flames. Her father's flames.

Bryce set down the client's purchase papers. "It's not that easy, Lele."

"Syrinx told me you're lonely. I could cheer you up."

In answer, the chimera rolled onto his back, tongue dangling from his mouth, and snored.

"One, my building doesn't allow fire sprites. *Or* water sprites. It's an insurance nightmare. Two, it's not as simple as asking Jesiba. She might very well get rid of you *because* I ask."

Lehabah cupped her round chin in her hand and dripped another freckle of wax dangerously close to the paperwork. "She gave you Syrie."

Cthona give her patience. "She *let* me *buy* Syr*inx* because my life was fucked up, and I lost it when she got bored with him and tried to sell him off."

The fire sprite said quietly, "Because Danika died."

Bryce closed her eyes for a second, then said, "Yeah."

"You shouldn't curse so much, BB."

"Then you really won't like the angel."

"He led my people into battle—*and* he's a member of my House. I deserve to meet him."

"Last I checked, that battle went rather poorly, and the fire sprites were kicked out of Sky and Breath thanks to it."

Lehabah sat up, legs crossed. "Membership in the Houses is not something a government can decree. Our expulsion was in name only."

It was true. But Bryce still said, "What the Asteri and their Senate say goes."

Lehabah had been guardian of the gallery's library for decades. Logic insisted that ordering a fire sprite to watch over a library was a poor idea, but when a third of the books in the place would like nothing more than to escape, kill someone, or eat them—in varying orders—having a living flame keeping them in line was worth any risk. Even the endless chatter, it seemed.

Something thumped on the mezzanine. As if a book had dived off the shelf of its own accord.

Lehabah hissed toward it, turning a deep blue. Paper and leather whispered as the errant book found its place once again.

Bryce smiled, and then the office phone rang. One glance at the screen had her reaching for the phone and hissing at the sprite, "Back on your perch *now*."

Lehabah had just reached the glass dome where she maintained her fiery vigil over the library's wandering books when Bryce answered. "Afternoon, boss."

"Any progress?"

"Still investigating. How's Pangera?"

Jesiba didn't bother answering, instead saying, "I've got a client coming in at two o'clock. Be ready. And stop letting Lehabah prattle. She has a job to do." The line went dead.

Bryce rose from the desk where she'd been working all morning. The oak panels of the library beneath the gallery looked old, but they were wired with the latest tech and best enchantments money could buy. Not to mention, there was a killer sound system that she often put to good use when Jesiba was on the other side of the Haldren.

Not that she danced down here—not anymore. Nowadays, the music was mostly to keep the thrumming of the firstlights from driving her insane. Or for drowning out Lehabah's monologues.

Bookshelves lined every wall, interrupted only by a dozen or so small tanks and terrariums, occupied by all manner of small common animals: lizards and snakes and turtles and various rodents. Bryce often wondered if they were all people who'd pissed off Jesiba. None showed any sign of awareness, which was even more horrifying if it was true. They'd not only been turned into animals, but had also forgotten they were something else entirely.

Naturally, Lehabah had named all of them, each one more ridiculous than the last. *Nutmeg* and *Ginger* were the names of the geckos in the tank closest to Bryce. Sisters, Lehabah claimed. *Miss Poppy* was the name of the black-and-white snake on the mezzanine.

Lehabah never named anything in the biggest tank, though. The massive one that occupied an entire wall of the library, and whose glass expanse revealed a watery gloom. Mercifully, the tank was currently empty.

Last year, Bryce lobbied on Lehabah's behalf for a few iris eels to brighten the murky blue with their shimmering rainbow light. Jesiba had said no, and instead bought a pet kelpie that had humped the glass with all the finesse of a wasted college guy.

Bryce had made sure that motherfucker was given to a client as a gift *really* quickly.

Bryce braced herself for the work before her. Not the paperwork or the client—but what she had to do tonight. Gods fucking help her when Athalar got wind of it.

But the thought of his face when he realized what she had planned . . . Yeah, it'd be satisfying.

If she survived.

16

The mirthroot Ruhn had smoked ten minutes ago with Flynn might have been more potent than his friend had let on.

Lying on his bed, specially shaped Fae headphones over his arched ears, Ruhn closed his eyes and let the thumping bass and sizzling, soaring synthesizer of the music send him drifting.

His booted foot tapped in time to the steady beat, the drumming fingers he'd interlaced over his stomach echoing each flutter of notes high, high above. Every breath pulled him further back from consciousness, as if his very mind had been yanked a good few feet away from where it normally rested like a captain at the helm of a ship.

Heavy relaxation melted him, bone and blood morphing to liquid gold. Each note sent it rippling through him. Every stressor and sharp word and aggravation leaked from him, slithered off the bed like a snake.

He flipped off those feelings as they slid away. He was well aware that he'd taken the hits of Flynn's mirthroot thanks to the hours he'd spent brooding over his father's bullshit orders.

His father could go to Hel.

The mirthroot wrapped soft, sweet arms around his mind and dragged him into its shimmering pool.

Ruhn let himself drown in it, too mellow to do anything but let the music wash over him, his body sinking into the mattress, until he was falling through shadows and starlight. The strings of the song hovered overhead, golden threads that glittered with sound. Was he still moving his body? His eyelids were too heavy to lift to check.

A scent like lilac and nutmeg filled the room. Female, Fae . . .

If one of the females partying downstairs had shown herself into his room, thinking she'd get a nice, sweaty ride with a Prince of the Fae, she'd be sorely disappointed. He was in no shape for fucking right now. At least not any fucking that would be worthwhile.

His eyelids were so incredibly heavy. He should open them. Where the Hel were the controls to his body? Even his shadows had drifted away, too far to summon.

The scent grew stronger. He knew that scent. Knew it as well as—

Ruhn jerked upward, eyes flying open to find his sister standing at the foot of his bed.

Bryce's mouth was moving, whiskey-colored eyes full of dry amusement, but he couldn't hear a word she said, not a word—

Oh. Right. The headphones. Blasting music.

Blinking furiously, gritting his teeth against the drug trying to haul him back down, down, down, Ruhn removed the headphones and hit pause on his phone. "What?"

Bryce leaned against his chipped wood dresser. At least she was in normal clothes for once. Even if the jeans were painted on and the cream-colored sweater left little to the imagination. "I said, you'll blow out your eardrums listening to music that loud."

Ruhn's head spun as he narrowed his eyes at her, blinking at the halo of starlight that danced around her head, at her feet. He blinked again, pushing past the auras clouding his vision, and it was gone. Another blink, and it was there.

Bryce snorted. "You're not hallucinating. I'm standing here."

His mouth was a thousand miles away, but he managed to ask, "Who let you in?" Declan and Flynn were downstairs, along with half a dozen of their top Fae warriors. A few of them people he didn't want within a block of his sister.

Bryce ignored his question, frowning toward the corner of his room. Toward the pile of unwashed laundry and the Starsword he'd chucked atop it. The sword glimmered with starlight, too. He could have sworn the damn thing was singing. Ruhn shook his head, as if it'd clear out his ears, as Bryce said, "I need to talk to you."

The last time Bryce had been in this room, she'd been sixteen and he'd spent hours beforehand cleaning it—and the whole house. Every bong and bottle of liquor, every pair of female underwear that had never been returned to its owner, every trace and scent of sex and drugs and all the stupid shit they did here had been hidden.

And she'd stood right there, during that last visit. Stood there as they screamed at each other.

Then and now blurred, Bryce's form shrinking and expanding, her adult face blending into teenage softness, the light in her amber eyes warming and cooling, his vision surrounding the scene glinting with starlight, starlight, starlight.

"Fucking Hel," Bryce muttered, and aimed for the door. "You're pathetic."

He managed to say, "Where are you going?"

"To get you water." She flung the door open. "I can't talk to you like this."

It occurred to him then that this had to be important if she was not only here, but eager to get him to focus. And that there might still be a chance he was hallucinating, but he wasn't going to let her venture into the warren of sin unaccompanied.

On legs that felt ten miles long, feet that weighed a thousand pounds, he staggered after her. The dim hallway hid most of the various stains on the white paint—all thanks to the various parties he and his friends had thrown in fifty years of being roommates. Well, they'd had this house for twenty years—and had only moved because their first one had literally started to fall apart. This house might not last another two years, if he was being honest.

Bryce was halfway down the curving grand staircase, the firstlights of the crystal chandelier bouncing off her red hair in that shimmering halo. How had he not noticed the chandelier was hanging askew? Must be from when Declan had leapt off the stair railing onto it, swinging around and swigging from his bottle of whiskey. He'd fallen off a moment later, too drunk to hold on.

If the Autumn King knew the shit they did in this house, there was no way he or any other City Head would allow them to lead the Fae Aux division. No way Micah would ever tap him to take his father's place on that council.

But getting wasted was for off-nights only. Never when on duty or on call.

Bryce hit the worn oak floor of the first level, edging around the beer pong table occupying most of the foyer. A few cups littered its stained plywood surface, painted by Flynn with what they'd all deemed was high-class art: an enormous Fae male head devouring an angel whole, only frayed wings visible through the snapped-shut teeth. It seemed to ripple with movement as Ruhn cleared the stairs. He could have sworn the painting winked at him.

Yeah, water. He needed water.

Bryce showed herself through the living room, where the music blasted so loud it made Ruhn's teeth rattle in his skull.

He entered in time to see Bryce striding past the pool table in the rear of the long, cavernous space. A few Aux warriors stood around it, females with them, deep in a game.

Tristan Flynn, son of Lord Hawthorne, presided over it from a nearby armchair, a pretty dryad on his lap. The glazed light in his brown eyes mirrored Ruhn's own. Flynn gave Bryce a crooked grin as she approached. All it usually took was one look and females crawled into Tristan Flynn's lap just like the tree nymph, or—if the look was more of a glower—any enemies outright bolted.

Charming as all Hel and lethal as fuck. It should have been the Flynn family motto.

Bryce didn't stop as she passed him, unfazed by his classic Fae beauty and considerable muscles, but demanded over her shoulder, "What the fuck did you give him?"

Flynn leaned forward, prying his short chestnut hair free from the dryad's long fingers. "How do you know it was me?"

Bryce walked toward the kitchen at the back of the room, accessible through an archway. "Because you look high off your ass, too."

Declan called from the sectional couch at the other end of the living room, a laptop on his knee and a *very* interested draki male half-sprawled over him, running clawed fingers through Dec's dark red hair, "Hey, Bryce. To what do we owe the pleasure?"

Bryce jerked her thumb back at Ruhn. "Checking on the Chosen One. How's your fancy tech crap going, Dec?"

Declan Emmet didn't usually appreciate anyone belittling the lucrative career he'd built on a foundation of hacking into Republic websites and then charging them ungodly amounts of money to reveal their critical weaknesses, but he grinned. "Still raking in the marks."

"Nice," Bryce said, continuing into the kitchen and out of sight.

Some of the Aux warriors were staring toward the kitchen now, blatant interest in their eyes. Flynn growled softly, "She's off-limits, assholes."

That was all it took. Not even a snapping vine of Flynn's earth magic, rare among the fire-prone Valbaran Fae. The others immediately returned their attention to the pool game. Ruhn threw his friend a grateful look and followed Bryce—

But she was already back in the doorway, water bottle in hand. "Your fridge is worse than mine," she said, shoving the bottle toward him and entering the living room again. Ruhn sipped as the stereo system in the back thumped the opening notes of a song, guitars wailing, and she angled her head, listening, weighing.

Fae impulse—to be drawn to music, and to love it. Perhaps the one side of her heritage she didn't mind. He remembered her showing him her dance routines as a young teenager. She'd always looked so unbelievably happy. He'd never had the chance to ask why she stopped.

Ruhn sighed, forcing himself to *focus*, and said to Bryce, "Why are you here?"

She stopped near the sectional. "I told you: I need to talk to you."

Ruhn kept his face blank. He couldn't remember the last time she'd bothered finding him.

"Why would your cousin need an excuse to chat with us?" Flynn asked, murmuring something in the dryad's delicate ear that had her heading for the cluster of her three friends at the pool table, her narrow hips swishing in a reminder of what he'd miss if he waited too long. Flynn drawled, "She knows we're the most charming males in town."

Neither of his friends ever guessed the truth—or at least voiced any suspicions. Bryce tossed her hair over a shoulder as Flynn rose from his armchair. "I have better things to do—"

"Than hang out with Fae losers," Flynn finished for her, heading to the built-in bar against the far wall. "Yeah, yeah. You've said so a hundred times now. But look at that: here you are, hanging with us in our humble abode."

Despite his carefree demeanor, Flynn would one day inherit his father's title: Lord Hawthorne. Which meant that for the past several decades, Flynn had done everything he could to forget that little fact—and the centuries of responsibilities it would entail. He poured himself a drink, then a second one that he handed to Bryce. "Drink up, honeycakes."

Ruhn rolled his eyes. But—it was nearly midnight, and she was at their house, on one of the rougher streets in the Old Square, with a murderer on the loose. Ruhn hissed, "You were given an order to *lie low*—"

She waved a hand, not touching the whiskey in her other. "My imperial escort is outside. Scaring everyone away, don't worry."

Both his friends went still. The draki male took that as an invitation to drift away, aiming for the billiards game behind them as Declan twisted to look at her. Ruhn just said, "Who."

A little smile. Bryce asked, swirling the whiskey in its glass, "Is this house really befitting of the Chosen One?"

Flynn's mouth twitched. Ruhn shot him a warning glare, just daring him to bring up the Starborn shit right now. Outside of his father's villa and court, all that had gotten Ruhn was a lifetime of teasing from his friends.

Ruhn ground out, "Let's hear it, Bryce." Odds were, she'd come here just to piss him off.

She didn't respond immediately, though. No, Bryce traced a circle on a cushion, utterly unfazed by the three Fae warriors watching her every breath. Tristan and Declan had been Ruhn's best friends for as long as he could remember, and always had his back, no questions asked. That they were highly trained and efficient warriors was beside the point, though they'd saved each other's asses more times than Ruhn could count. Going through their Ordeals together had only cemented that bond.

The Ordeal itself varied depending on the person: for some, it might be as simple as overcoming an illness or a bit of personal strife. For others, it might be slaying a wyrm or a demon. The greater the Fae, the greater the Ordeal.

Ruhn had been learning to wield his shadows from his hateful cousins in Avallen, his two friends with him, when they'd all gone through their Ordeal, nearly dying in the process. It had culminated in Ruhn entering the mist-shrouded Cave of Princes, and emerging with the Starsword—and saving them all.

And when he'd made the Drop weeks later, it had been Flynn, fresh from his own Drop, who'd Anchored him.

Declan asked, his deep voice rumbling over the music and chatter, "What's going on?"

For a second, Bryce's swagger faltered. She glanced at them: their casual clothes, the places where she knew their guns were hidden even in their own home, their black boots and the knives tucked inside them. Bryce's eyes met Ruhn's.

"I know what that look means," Flynn groaned. "It means you don't want us to hear."

Bryce didn't take her eyes away from Ruhn as she said, "Yep."

Declan slammed his laptop shut. "You're really gonna go all mysterious and shit?"

She looked between Declan and Flynn, who had been inseparable since birth. "You two dickbags have the biggest mouths in town."

Flynn winked. "I thought you liked my mouth."

"Keep dreaming, lordling." Bryce smirked.

Declan chuckled, earning a sharp elbow from Flynn and the glass of whiskey from Bryce.

Ruhn swigged from his water, willing his head to clear further.

"Enough of this crap," he bit out. All that mirthroot threatened to turn on him as he pulled Bryce toward his bedroom again.

When they arrived, he took up a spot by the bed. "Well?"

Bryce leaned against the door, the wood peppered with holes from all the knives he'd chucked at it for idle target practice. "I need you to tell me if you've heard anything about what the Viper Queen's been up to."

This could not be good. "Why?"

"Because I need to talk to her."

"Are you fucking *nuts*?"

Again, that annoying-ass smile. "Maximus Tertian was killed on her turf. Did the Aux get any intel about her movements that night?"

"Your boss put you up to this?" It reeked of Roga.

"Maybe. Do you know anything?" She angled her head again, that silky sheet of hair—the same as their father's—shifting with the movement.

"Yes. Tertian's murder was . . . the same as Danika's and the pack's."

Any trace of a smile faded from her face. "Philip Briggs didn't do it. I want to know what the Viper Queen was up to that night. If the Aux has any knowledge of her movements."

Ruhn shook his head. "Why are you involved in this?"

"Because I was asked to look into it."

"Don't fuck with this case. Tell your boss to lay off. This is a matter for the Governor."

"And the Governor commandeered me to look for the murderer. He thinks I'm the link between them."

Great. Absolutely fantastic. Isaiah Tiberian had failed to mention that little fact. "You spoke to the Governor."

"Just answer my question. Does the Aux know anything about the Viper Queen's whereabouts on the night of Tertian's death?"

Ruhn blew out a breath. "No. I've heard that she pulled her people from the streets. Something spooked her. But that's all I know. And even if I knew the Viper Queen's alibis, I wouldn't tell you. Stay the fuck out of this. I'll call the Governor to tell him you're done being his personal investigator."

That icy look—their father's look—passed over her face. The sort of look that told him there was a wild, wicked storm raging beneath that cold exterior. And the power and thrill for both father and daughter lay not in sheer force, but in the control over the self, over those impulses.

The outside world saw his sister as reckless, unchecked—but he knew she'd been the master of her fate since before he'd met her. Bryce was just one of those people who, once she'd set her sights on what she wanted, didn't let anything get in her way. If she wanted to sleep around, she did it. If she wanted to party for three days straight, she did it. If she wanted to catch Danika's murderer . . .

"I am going to find the person behind this," she said with quiet fury. "If you try to interfere with it, I will make your life a living Hel."

"The demon that murderer is using is *lethal*." He'd seen the crime scene photos. The thought that Bryce had been saved by mere minutes, by sheer drunken stupidity, still twisted him up. Ruhn continued before she could answer. "The Autumn King *told* you to lie low until the Summit—this is the fucking opposite, Bryce."

"Well, it's now part of my job. Jesiba signed off on it. I can't very well refuse, can I?"

No. *No one* could say no to that sorceress.

He slid his hands into the back pockets of his jeans. "She ever tell you anything about Luna's Horn?"

Bryce's brows lifted at the shift in subject, but considering Jesiba Roga's field of work, she'd be the one to ask.

"She had me look for it two years ago," Bryce said warily. "But it was a dead end. Why?"

"Never mind." He eyed the small gold amulet around his sister's neck. At least Jesiba gave her that much protection. Expensive protection, too—and powerful. Archesian amulets didn't come cheap, not when there were only a few in the world. He nodded to it. "Don't take that off."

Bryce rolled her eyes. "Does everyone in this city think I'm dumb?"

"I mean it. Beyond the shit you do for work, if you're looking for someone strong enough to summon a demon like that, don't take that necklace off." At least he could remind her to be smart.

She just opened the door. "If you hear anything about the Viper Queen, call me."

Ruhn stiffened, his heart thundering. "Do *not* provoke her."

"Bye, Ruhn."

He was desperate enough that he said, "I'll go with you to—"

"Bye." Then she was down the stairs, waving in that annoying-as-fuck way at Declan and Flynn, before swaggering out the front door.

His friends threw inquisitive looks to where Ruhn stood on the second-floor landing. Declan's whiskey was still raised to his lips.

Ruhn counted to ten, if only to keep from snapping the nearest object in half, and then vaulted over the railing, landing so hard that the scuffed oak planks shuddered.

He felt, more than saw, his friends fall into place behind him, hands within easy reach of their hidden weapons, drinks discarded as they read the fury on his face. Ruhn stormed through the front door and out into the brisk night.

Just in time to see Bryce strut across the street. To Hunt fucking Athalar.

"What the actual Hel," Declan breathed, halting beside Ruhn on the porch.

The Umbra Mortis looked pissed, his arms crossed and wings flaring slightly, but Bryce just breezed past him without so much as a glance. Causing Athalar to *slowly* turn, arms slackening at his sides, as if such a thing had never happened in his long, miserable life.

And wasn't that enough to put Ruhn in a killing sort of mood.

Ruhn cleared the porch and front lawn and stepped into the street, holding out a hand to the car that skidded to a screeching halt. His hand hit the hood, fingers curving. Metal dented beneath it.

The driver, wisely, didn't scream.

Ruhn strode between two parked sedans, Declan and Flynn close behind, just as Hunt turned to see what the fuss was about.

Understanding flashed in Hunt's eyes, quickly replaced by a half smile. "Prince."

"What the fuck are you doing here?"

Hunt jerked his chin toward Bryce, already disappearing down the street. "Protection duty."

"Like Hel you're watching her." Isaiah Tiberian had failed to mention *this*, too.

A shrug. "Not my call." The halo across his brow seemed to darken as he sized up Declan and Flynn. Athalar's mouth twitched upward, onyx eyes glinting with an unspoken challenge.

Flynn's gathering power had the earth beneath the pavement rumbling. Hunt's shit-eating grin only spread.

Ruhn said, "Tell the Governor to put someone else on the case."

Hunt's grin sharpened. "Not an option. Not when it plays to my expertise."

Ruhn bristled at the arrogance. Sure, Athalar was one of the best demon-hunters out there, but fuck, he'd even take Tiberian on this case over the Umbra Mortis.

A year ago, the Commander of the 33rd hadn't been dumb enough to get between them when Ruhn had launched himself at Athalar, having had enough of his snide remarks at the fancy-ass Spring Equinox party Micah threw every March. He'd broken a few of Athalar's ribs, but the asshole had gotten in a punch that had left Ruhn's nose shattered and gushing blood all over the marble floors of the Comitium's penthouse ballroom. Neither of them had been pissed enough to unleash their power in the middle of a crowded room, but fists had done just fine.

Ruhn calculated how much trouble he'd be in if he punched the Governor's personal assassin again. Maybe it'd be enough to get Hypaxia Enador to refuse to consider marrying him.

Ruhn demanded, "Did you figure out what kind of demon did it?"

"Something that eats little princes for breakfast," Hunt crooned.

Ruhn bared his teeth. "Blow me, Athalar."

Lightning danced over the angel's fingers. "Must be easy to run your mouth when you're bankrolled by your father." Hunt pointed to the white house. "He buy that for you, too?"

Ruhn's shadows rose to meet the lightning wreathing Athalar's fists, setting the parked cars behind him shuddering. He'd learned from his cousins in Avallen how to make the shadows solidify—how to wield them as whips and shields and pure torment. Physical and mental.

But mixing magic and drugs was never a good idea. Fists it would have to be, then. And all it would take was one swing, right into Athalar's face—

Declan growled, "This isn't the time or place."

No, it wasn't. Even Athalar seemed to remember the gawking people, the upraised phones recording everything. And the red-haired female nearing the end of the block. Hunt smirked. "Bye, assholes." He followed Bryce, lightning skittering over the pavement in his wake.

Ruhn growled at the angel's back, "Do not fucking let her go to the Viper Queen."

Athalar glanced over a shoulder, his gray wings tucking in. His blink told Ruhn that he hadn't been aware of Bryce's agenda. A shiver of satisfaction ran through Ruhn. But Athalar continued down the street, people pressing themselves against buildings to give him a wide berth. The warrior's focus remained on Bryce's exposed neck.

Flynn shook his head like a wet dog. "I literally can't tell if I'm hallucinating right now."

"I wish I were," Ruhn muttered. He'd need to smoke another mountain of mirthroot to mellow the Hel out again. But if Hunt Athalar was watching Bryce . . . He'd heard enough rumors to know what Hunt could do to an opponent. That he, in addition to being a prime bastard, was relentless, single-minded, and utterly brutal when it came to eliminating threats.

Hunt had to obey the order to protect her. No matter what.

Ruhn studied them as they walked away. Bryce would speed up; Hunt would match her pace. She'd drop back; he'd do the same. She'd edge him to the right, right, right—off the curb and into oncoming traffic; he'd narrowly avoid a swerving car and step back onto the sidewalk.

Ruhn was half-tempted to trail them, just to watch the battle of wills.

"I need a drink," Declan muttered. Flynn agreed and the two of them headed back toward the house, leaving Ruhn alone on the street.

Could it really be a coincidence that the murders were starting again at the same time his father had given the order to find an object that had gone missing a week before Danika's death?

It felt . . . odd. Like Urd was whispering, nudging them all.

Ruhn planned to find out why. Starting with finding that Horn.

17

Bryce had just succeeded in nudging Hunt into oncoming traffic when he asked, "Do I get an explanation for why I've had to trail you like a dog all night?"

Bryce shoved her hand into the pocket of her jeans and pulled out a piece of paper. Then silently handed it to Hunt.

His brow furrowed. "What's this?"

"My list of suspects," she said, letting him glance at the names before she snatched it away.

"When did you make this?"

She said sweetly, "Last night. On the couch."

A muscle ticked in his jaw. "And you were going to tell me when?"

"After you'd spent a whole day assuming I was a dumb, vapid female more interested in getting my nails done than solving this case."

"You *did* get your nails done."

She waved her pretty ombre fingernails in his face. He looked half-inclined to bite them. "Do you know what *else* I did last night?" His silence was delightful. "I looked up Maximus Tertian some more. Because despite what the Governor says, there was no fucking way Danika knew him. And you know what? I was right. And you know how I know I'm right?"

"Cthona fucking save me," Hunt muttered.

"Because I looked up his profile on Spark."

"The dating site?"

"The dating site. Turns out even creepy vamps are looking for love, deep down. And it showed that he was in a relationship. Which apparently did nothing to stop him from hitting on me, but that's beside the point. So I did some *more* digging. And found his girlfriend."

"Fuck."

"Aren't there people at the 33rd who should be doing this shit?" When he refused to answer, she grinned. "Guess where Tertian's girlfriend works."

Hunt's eyes simmered. He said through his teeth, "At the nail salon on Samson."

"And guess who did my nails and got to chatting about the terrible loss of her rich-ass boyfriend?"

He ran his hands through his hair, looking so disbelieving that she chuckled. He snarled, "Stop with the fucking questions and just tell me, Quinlan."

She examined her gorgeous new nails. "Tertian's girlfriend didn't know anything about who might have wanted to murder him. She said the 33rd did vaguely question her, but that was it. So I told her that I'd lost someone, too." It was an effort to keep her voice steady as the memory of that bloody apartment flashed. "She asked me who, I told her, and she looked so shocked that I asked if Tertian was friends with Danika. She told me no. She said she would have known if Maximus was, because Danika was famous enough that he'd have been bragging about it. The closest to Danika she or Tertian got was through two degrees of separation—through the Viper Queen. Whose nails she does on Sundays."

"Danika knew the Viper Queen?"

Bryce held up the list. "Danika's job in the Aux made her a friend and enemy to a lot of people. The Viper Queen was one of them."

Hunt paled. "You honestly think the Viper Queen killed Danika?"

"Tertian was found dead just over her borders. Ruhn said she pulled her people in last night. And no one knows what kind of powers she has. She could have summoned that demon."

"That is a big fucking accusation to make."

"Which is why we need to feel her out. This is the only clue we have to go on."

Hunt shook his head. "All right. I can buy the possibility. But we need to go through the right channels to contact her. It could be days or weeks before she deigns to meet with us. Longer, if she gets a whiff that we're onto her."

With someone like the Viper Queen, even the law was flexible.

Bryce scoffed. "Don't be such a stickler for the rules."

"The rules are there to keep us alive. We follow them, or we don't go after her at all."

She waved a hand. "Fine."

A muscle ticked in his jaw again. "And what about Ruhn? You just dragged your cousin into our business."

"My cousin," she said tightly, "will be unable to resist the urge to inform his father that a member of the Fae race has been commandeered for an imperial investigation. How he reacts, who he contacts, might be worth noting."

"What—you think the Autumn King could have done this?"

"No. But Ruhn was given an order to warn me to keep out of trouble the night of Maximus's murder—maybe the old bastard knew something, too. I'd suggest telling your people to watch him. See what he does and where he goes."

"Gods," Hunt breathed, striding past gawking pedestrians. "You want me to just put a tail on the Autumn King like it's not a violation of about ten different laws?"

"Micah said to do whatever was necessary."

"The Autumn King has free rein to kill anyone found stalking him like that."

"Then you better tell your spies to keep themselves hidden."

Hunt snapped his wings. "Don't play games again. If you know something, tell me."

"I was going to tell you everything when I finished up at the nail salon this morning." She put her hands on her hips. "But then you bit my head off."

"Whatever, Quinlan. Don't do it again. You *tell me* before you make a move."

"I'm getting real bored with you giving me orders and forbidding me to do things."

"Whatever," he said again. She rolled her eyes, but they'd reached her building. Neither bothered to say goodbye before Hunt leapt into the skies, aiming for the adjacent roof, a phone already at his ear.

Bryce rode the elevator up to her floor, mulling everything over in the silence. She'd meant what she said to Hunt—she didn't think her father was behind Danika's and the pack's deaths. She had little doubt he'd killed others, though. And would do anything to keep his crown.

The Autumn King was a courtesy title in addition to her father's role as a City Head—as for all the seven Fae Kings. No kingdom was truly their own. Even Avallen, the green isle ruled by the Stag King, still bowed to the Republic.

The Fae had coexisted with the Republic since its founding, answerable to its laws, but ultimately left to govern themselves and retain their ancient titles of kings and princes and the like. Still respected by all—and feared. Not as much as the angels, with their destructive, hideous storm-and-sky powers, but they could inflict pain if they wished. Choke the air from your lungs or freeze you or burn you from the inside out. Solas knew Ruhn and his two friends could raise Hel when provoked.

But she wasn't looking to raise Hel tonight. She was looking to quietly slip into its Midgard equivalent.

Which was precisely why she waited thirty minutes before tucking a knife into her black leather ankle boots, and placed something that packed a bigger punch into the back of her dark jeans, hidden beneath her leather jacket. She kept the lights and television on, the curtains partially closed—just enough to block Hunt's view of her front door as she left.

Sneaking out the rear stairwell of her building to the small alley where her scooter was chained, Bryce took a swift, bracing breath before fitting on her helmet.

Traffic wasn't moving as she unchained the ivory Firebright 3500 scooter from the alley lamppost and waddled it onto the cobblestones. She waited for other scooters, pedicabs, and motorcycles to zip past, then launched into the flow, the world stark through the visor of her helmet.

Her mother still complained about the scooter, begging her to use a car until after the Drop, but Randall had always insisted Bryce was fine. Of course, she never told them of the various *incidents* on this scooter, but . . . her mother had a mortal life span. Bryce didn't need to shave off any more years than necessary.

Bryce cruised down one of the city's main arteries, losing herself in the rhythm of weaving between cars and swerving around pedestrians. The world was a blur of golden light and deep shadows, neon glaring above, all of it accented by pops and flittering shimmers of street magic. Even the little bridges she crossed, spanning the countless tributaries to the Istros, were strung with sparkling lights that danced on the dim, drifting water below.

High above Main Street, a silvery sheen filled the night sky, limning the drifting clouds where the malakim partied and dined. Only a flare of red interrupted the pale glow, courtesy of Redner Industries' massive sign atop their skyscraper in the heart of the district.

Few people walked the streets of the CBD at this hour, and Bryce made sure to get through its canyons of high-rises as swiftly as possible. She knew she'd entered the Meat Market not by any street or marker, but by the shift in the darkness.

No lights stained the skies above the low brick buildings crammed together. And here the shadows became permanent, tucked into alleys and under cars, the streetlamps mostly shattered and never repaired.

Bryce pulled down a cramped street where a few dented delivery trucks were in the process of unloading boxes of spiky green fruit and crates of crustacean-looking creatures that seemed far too aware of their captivity and oncoming demise via boiling pots of water in one of the food stalls.

Bryce tried not to meet their googly black eyes pleading with her through the wooden bars as she parked a few feet away from a nondescript warehouse, removed her helmet, and waited.

Vendors and shoppers alike eyed her to glean if she was selling or for sale. In the warrens below, carved deep into Midgard's womb, lay three different levels just for flesh. Mostly human; mostly living, though she'd heard of some places that specialized in certain tastes. Every fetish could be bought; no taboo was too foul. Half-breeds were prized: they could heal faster and better than full-humans. A smarter long-term investment. And occasional Vanir were enslaved and bound with so many enchantments that they had no hope of escape. Only the wealthiest could afford to purchase a few hours with them.

Bryce checked the time on her scooter's dash clock. Crossing her arms, she leaned against the black leather seat.

The Umbra Mortis slammed to the ground, cracking the cobblestones in a rippling circle.

Hunt's eyes practically glowed as he said, in full view of those cowering along the street, "*I am going to kill you.*"

18

Hunt stormed toward Bryce, stepping over the cobblestones fragmented from his landing. He'd detected her lilac-and-nutmeg scent on the wind the moment she'd stepped outside the back door of her building, and when he'd discovered where, precisely, she was driving on that scooter . . .

Bryce had the nerve to push back the sleeve of her leather jacket, frown at her bare wrist as if she were reading a gods-damned watch, and say, "You're two minutes late."

He was going to throttle her. Someone should have done it a long fucking time ago.

Bryce smiled in a way that said she'd like to see him try, and sauntered toward him, scooter and helmet left behind.

Unbelievable. Un-fucking-believable.

Hunt growled, "There's no way that scooter is there when we get back."

Bryce batted her eyelashes, fluffing out her helmet hair. "Good thing you've made such a big entrance. No one would dare touch it now. Not with the Umbra Mortis as my wrathful companion."

Indeed, people shrank from his gaze, some stepping behind the stacked crates as Bryce aimed for one of the open doors into the labyrinth of subterraneanly interconnected warehouses that made up the blocks of the district.

Even Micah didn't station legionaries here. The Meat Market had its own laws and methods of enforcing them.

Hunt ground out, "I told you that there are protocols to follow if we want to stand a chance of contacting the Viper Queen—"

"I'm not here to contact the Viper Queen."

"What?" The Viper Queen had ruled the Meat Market for longer than anyone could remember. Hunt made a point—all the angels, whether civilians or legionaries, made a point—of staying the fuck away from the serpentine shifter, whose snake form, rumor claimed, was a true horror to behold. Before Bryce could answer, Hunt said, "I'm growing tired of this bullshit, Quinlan."

She bared her teeth. "I'm sorry," she seethed, "if your fragile ego can't handle that *I know what I'm fucking doing*."

Hunt opened and closed his mouth. Fine, he'd misjudged her earlier today, but she hadn't exactly given him any hint of being remotely interested in this investigation. Or that she wasn't trying to hinder it.

Bryce continued through the open doors to the warehouse without saying another word.

Being in the 33rd—or any legion—was as good as putting a target on your back, and Hunt checked that his weapons were in place in the cleverly constructed sheaths along his suit as he followed her.

The reek of bodies and smoke coated his face like oil. Hunt tucked in his wings tightly.

Whatever fear he'd instilled in people on the streets was of no consequence inside the market, packed with ramshackle stalls and vendors and food stands, smoke drifting throughout, the tang of blood and spark of magic acrid in his nostrils. And above it all, against the far wall of the enormous space, was a towering mosaic, the tiles taken from an ancient temple in Pangera, restored and re-created here in loving detail, despite its gruesome depiction: cloaked and hooded death, the skeleton's face grinning out from the cowl, a scythe in one hand and an hourglass in the other. Above its head, words had been crafted in the Republic's most ancient language:

Memento Mori.

Remember that you will die. It was meant to be an invitation for merriment, to seize each moment as if it were one's last, as if tomorrow were not guaranteed, even for slow-aging Vanir. *Remember that you will die, and enjoy each pleasure the world has to offer. Remember that you will die, and none of this illegal shit will matter anyway. Remember that you will die, so who cares how many people suffer from your actions?*

Bryce swept past it, her swaying hair shining like the heart of a ruby. The lights illuminated the worn black leather of her jacket, bringing into stark relief the painted words along the back in feminine, colorful script. It was instinct to translate—also from the ancient language, as if Urd herself had chosen this moment to lay the two ancient phrases before him.

Through love, all is possible.

Such a pretty phrase was a fucking joke in a place like this. Glimmering eyes that tracked Quinlan from the stalls and shadows quickly looked away when they noticed him at her side.

It was an effort not to haul her out of this shithole. Even though he wanted this case solved, having only ten beautiful kills standing between him and freedom, coming here was a colossal risk. What was the use of his freedom if he was left in a dumpster behind one of these warehouses?

Maybe that was what she wanted. To lure him here—use the Meat Market itself to kill him. It seemed unlikely, but he kept one eye on her.

Bryce knew her way around. Knew a few of the vendors, from the nods they exchanged. Hunt marked each one: a metalworker specializing in intricate little mechanisms; a fruit vendor with exotic produce for sale; an owl-faced female who had a spread of scrolls and books bound in materials that were everything but cow leather.

"The metalworker helps me identify if an artifact is a fake," Bryce said under her breath as they wound through the steam and smoke of a food pit. How she'd noticed his observing, he had no idea. "And the fruit lady gets shipments of durian in the early spring and fall—Syrinx's favorite food. Stinks up the whole house, but he goes nuts for it." She edged around a garbage pail near-overflowing with discarded plates and bones and soiled napkins before ascending a rickety set of stairs to the mezzanine flanking either side of the warehouse floor, doors stationed every few feet.

"The books?" Hunt couldn't help asking. She seemed to be counting doors, rather than looking at the numbers. There *were* no numbers, he realized.

"The books," Bryce said, "are a story for another time." She paused outside a pea-green door, chipped and deeply gouged in spots. Hunt sniffed, trying to detect what lay beyond. Nothing, as far as he could detect. He subtly braced himself, keeping his hands within range of his weapons.

Bryce opened the door, not bothering to knock, revealing flickering candles and—brine. Salt. Smoke and something that dried out his eyes.

Bryce stalked down the cramped hallway to the open, rotting sitting room beyond. Scowling, he shut the door and followed, wings tucked in to keep from brushing the oily, crumbling walls. If Quinlan died, Micah's offer would be off the table.

White and ivory candles guttered as Bryce walked onto the worn green carpet, and Hunt held in his cringe. A sagging, ripped couch was shoved against a wall, a filthy leather armchair with half its stuffing bursting from it sat against the other, and around the room, on tables and stacks of books and half-broken chairs, were jars and bowls and cups full of salt.

White salt, black salt, gray salt—in grains of every size: from near-powder to flakes to great, rough hunks of it. Salts for protection against darker powers. Against demons. Many Vanir built their houses with slabs of salt at the cornerstones. Rumor claimed that the entire base of the Asteri's crystal palace was a slab of salt. That it had been built atop a natural deposit.

Fucking Hel. He'd never seen such an assortment. As Bryce peered down the darkened hall to the left, where the shadows yielded three doors, Hunt hissed, "Please tell me—"

"Just keep your snarling and eye rolling to yourself," she snapped at him, and called into the gloom, "I'm here to buy, not collect."

One of the doors cracked open, and a pale-skinned, dark-haired satyr hobbled toward them, his furred legs hidden by trousers. His pageboy hat must have hid little, curling horns. The clopping of the hooves gave him away.

The male barely came up to Bryce's chest, his shrunken, twisted body half the size of the bulls that Hunt had witnessed tearing people into shreds on battlefields. And that he had faced himself in Sandriel's arena. The male's slitted pupils, knobbed at either side like a goat's, expanded.

Fear—and not at Hunt's presence, he realized with a jolt.

Bryce dipped her fingers into a lead bowl of pink salt, plucking up a few pieces and letting them drop into the dish with faint, hollow cracks. "I need the obsidian."

The satyr shifted, hooves clopping faintly, rubbing his hairy, pale neck. "Don't deal in that."

She smiled slightly. "Oh?" She went over to another bowl, stirring the powder-fine black salt in there. "Grade A, whole-rock obsidian salt. Seven pounds, seven ounces. Now."

The male's throat bobbed. "It's illegal."

"Are you quoting the motto of the Meat Market, or trying to tell me that you somehow *don't* have precisely what I need?"

Hunt scanned the room. White salt for purification; pink for protection; gray for spellwork; red for . . . he forgot what the Hel red was for. But obsidian . . . Shit.

Hunt fell back on centuries of training to keep the shock off his face. Black salts were used for summoning demons directly—bypassing the Northern Rift entirely—or for various dark spellwork. A salt that went beyond black, a salt like the *obsidian* . . . It could summon something big.

Hel was severed from them by time and space, but still accessible through the twin sealed portals at the north and south poles—the Northern Rift and the Southern Rift, respectively. Or by idiots who tried to summon demons through salts of varying powers.

A lot of fucked-up shit, Hunt had always thought. The benefit of using salts, at least, was that only one demon could be summoned at a time. Though if things went badly, the summoner could wind up dead. And a demon could wind up stuck in Midgard, hungry.

It was why the creeps existed in their world at all: most had been hunted after those long-ago wars between realms, but every so often, demons got loose. Reproduced, usually by force.

The result of those horrible unions: the daemonaki. Most walking the streets were diluted, weaker incarnations and hybrids of the purebred demons in Hel. Many were pariahs, through no fault of their own beyond genetics, and they usually worked hard to integrate into the Republic. But the lowest-level purebred demon fresh out of Hel could bring an entire city to a standstill as it went on a rampage. And for centuries now, Hunt had been tasked with tracking them down.

This satyr had to be a big-time dealer then, if he peddled obsidian salt.

Bryce took a step toward the satyr. The male retreated. Her amber eyes gleamed with feral amusement, no doubt from her Fae side. A far cry from the party girl getting her nails done.

Hunt tensed. She couldn't be that foolish, could she? To show him that she knew how to and could easily acquire the same type of salt that had probably been used to summon the demon that killed Tertian and Danika? Another tally scratched itself into the Suspect column in his mind.

Bryce shrugged with one shoulder. "I could call your queen. See what she makes of it."

"You—you don't have the rank to summon *her*."

"No," Bryce said, "I don't. But I bet if I go down to the main floor and start screaming for the Viper Queen, she'll drag herself out of that fighting pit to see what the fuss is about."

Burning Solas, she was serious, wasn't she?

Sweat beaded the satyr's brow. "Obsidian's too dangerous. I can't in good conscience sell it."

Bryce crooned, "Did you say that when you sold it to Philip Briggs for his bombs?"

Hunt stilled, and the male went a sickly white. He glanced to Hunt, noting the tattoo across his brow, the armor he wore. "I don't know what you're talking about. I—I was cleared by the investigators. I never sold Briggs anything."

"I'm sure he paid you in cash to hide the money trail," Bryce said. She yawned. "Look, I'm tired and hungry, and I don't feel like playing this game. Name your price so I can be on my way."

Those goatlike eyes snapped to hers. "Fifty thousand gold marks."

Bryce smiled as Hunt held in his curse. "Do you know my boss paid fifty thousand to watch a pack of Helhounds rip apart a satyr? Said it was the best minute of her miserable life."

"Forty-five."

"Don't waste my time with nonsense offers."

"I won't go below thirty. Not for that much obsidian."

"Ten." Ten thousand gold marks was still outrageous. But summoning salts were extraordinarily valuable. How many demons had he hunted because of them? How many dismembered bodies had he seen from summonings gone wrong? Or right, if it was a targeted attack?

Bryce held up her phone. "In five minutes, I'm expected to call Jesiba, and say that the obsidian salt is in my possession. In six minutes, if I do *not* make that phone call, someone will knock on that door. And it will not be someone for me."

Hunt honestly couldn't tell if Quinlan was bluffing. She likely wouldn't have told him—could have gotten that order from her boss while he was sitting on the roof. If Jesiba Roga was dealing with whatever shit the obsidian implied, either for her own uses or on behalf of the Under-King . . . Maybe Bryce hadn't committed the murder, but rather abetted it.

"Four minutes," Bryce said.

Sweat slid down the satyr's temple and into his thick beard. Silence.

Despite his suspicions, Hunt had the creeping feeling that this assignment was either going to be a fuck-ton of fun or a nightmare. If it got him to his end goal, he didn't care one way or another.

Bryce perched on the rotting arm of the chair and began typing into her phone, no more than a bored young woman avoiding social interaction.

The satyr whirled toward Hunt. "You're the Umbra Mortis." He swallowed audibly. "You're one of the triarii. You protect us—you serve the Governor."

Before Hunt could reply, Bryce lifted her phone to show him a photo of two fat, roly-poly puppies. "Look what my cousin just adopted," she told him. "That one is Osirys, and the one on the right is Set." She lowered the phone before he could come up with a response, thumbs flying.

But she glanced at Hunt from under her thick lashes. *Play along, please,* she seemed to say.

So Hunt said, "Cute dogs."

The satyr let out a small whine of distress. Bryce lifted her head, curtain of red hair limned with silver in her screen's light. "I thought you'd be running to get the salt by now. Maybe you should, considering you've got"—a glance at the phone, fingers flying—"oh. Ninety seconds."

She opened what looked like a message thread and began typing.

The satyr whispered, "T-twenty thousand."

She held up a finger. "I'm writing back to my cousin. Give me two seconds." The satyr was trembling enough that Hunt almost felt bad. Almost, until—

"Ten, ten, damn you! Ten!"

Bryce smiled. "No need to shout," she purred, pressing a button that had her phone ringing.

"Yes?" The sorceress picked up after the first ring.

"Call off your dogs."

A breathy, feminine laugh. "Done."

Bryce lowered the phone. "Well?"

The satyr rushed to the back, hooves thumping on the worn floors, and procured a wrapped bundle a moment later. It reeked of mold and dirt. Bryce lifted a brow. "Put it in a bag."

"I don't have a—" Bryce gave him a look. The satyr found one. A stained, reusable grocery bag, but better than holding the slab in public.

Bryce weighed the salt in her hands. "It's two ounces over."

"It's seven and seven! Just what you asked for! It's all cut to sevens."

Seven—the holy number. Or unholy, depending on who was worshipping. Seven Asteri, seven hills in their Eternal City, seven neighborhoods and seven Gates in Crescent City; seven planets, and seven circles in Hel, with seven princes who ruled them, each darker than the last.

Bryce inclined her head. "If I measure it and it's not—"

"It is!" the satyr cried. "Dark Hel, it is!"

Bryce tapped some buttons on her phone. "Ten grand, transferred right to you."

Hunt kept at her back as she strode out, the satyr half-seething, half-trembling behind them.

She opened the door, grinning to herself, and Hunt was about to start demanding answers when she halted. When he also beheld who stood outside.

The tall, moon-skinned woman was dressed in a gold jumpsuit, emerald hoop earrings hanging lower than her chin-length black bob. Her full lips were painted in purple so dark it was nearly black, and her remarkable green eyes . . . Hunt knew her by the eyes alone.

Humanoid in every aspect, but for them. Green entirely, marbled with veins of jade and gold. Interrupted only by a slitted pupil now razor-thin in the warehouse lights. A snake's eyes.

Or a Viper Queen's.

19

Bryce shouldered the canvas bag, surveying the Viper Queen. "Nice outfit."

The serpentine shifter smiled, revealing bright white teeth—and canines that were slightly too elongated. And slightly too thin. "Nice bodyguard."

Bryce shrugged as those snake's eyes dragged over every inch of Hunt. "Nothing going on upstairs, but everything happening where it counts."

Hunt stiffened. But the female's purple lips curved upward. "I've never heard Hunt Athalar described that way, but I'm sure the general appreciates it."

At the near-forgotten title, Hunt's jaw tightened. Yes, the Viper Queen had likely been alive during the Fall. Would have known Hunt not as one of the 33rd's triarii or the Shadow of Death, but as General Hunt Athalar, High Commander of all the Archangel Shahar's legions.

And Bryce had strung him along for two days. She glanced over a shoulder, finding Hunt assessing the Viper Queen and the four Fae males flanking her. Defectors from her father's court—trained assassins in not just weapons, but the queen's specialty: venoms and poisons.

None of them deigned to acknowledge her.

The Viper Queen tilted her head to the side, the razor-sharp bob shifting like black silk. On the ground below, patrons milled about, unaware that their ruler had graced them with her presence. "Looks like you were doing some shopping."

Bryce gave a half shrug. "Bargain hunting is a hobby. Your realm is the best place for it."

"I thought your boss paid you too well for you to stoop to cutting costs. And using salts."

Bryce forced herself to smile, to keep her heartbeat steady, knowing full well the female could pick up on it. Could taste fear. Could likely taste what variety of salt, exactly, sat in the bag dangling from her shoulder. "Just because I make money doesn't mean I have to get ripped off."

The Viper Queen glanced between her and Hunt. "I heard you two have been spotted around town together."

Hunt growled, "It's classified."

The Viper Queen arched a well-groomed black eyebrow, the small beauty mark just beneath the outer corner of her eye shifting with the movement. Her gold-painted nails glinted as she reached a hand into the pocket of her jumpsuit, fishing out a lighter encrusted with rubies forming the shape of a striking asp. A cigarette appeared between her purple lips a moment later, and they watched in silence, her guards monitoring every breath they made, as she lit up and inhaled deeply. Smoke rippled from those dark lips as she said, "Shit's getting interesting these days."

Bryce pivoted toward the exit. "Yep. Let's go, Hunt."

One of the guards stepped in front of her, six and a half feet of Fae grace and muscle.

Bryce stopped short, Hunt nearly slamming into her—his growl likely his first and last warning to the male. But the guard merely gazed at his queen, vacant and beholden. Likely addicted to the venom she secreted and doled out to her inner circle.

Bryce looked over her shoulder at the Viper Queen, still leaning against the rail, still smoking that cigarette. "It's a good time for business," the queen observed, "when key players converge for the Summit. So many ruling-class elites, all with their own . . . interests."

Hunt was close enough to Bryce's back that she could feel the tremor that ran through his powerful body, could have sworn lightning tingled over her spine. But he said nothing.

The Viper Queen merely extended a hand to the walkway behind her, gold nails flashing in the light. "My office, if you will."

"No," Hunt said. "We're going."

Bryce stepped closer to the Viper Queen. "Lead the way, Majesty."

She did. Hunt was bristling at her side, but Bryce kept her eyes on the swaying, glossy bob of the female ahead of them. Her guards kept a few feet behind—far enough away that Hunt deemed it safe to mutter, "This is a terrible idea."

"You were bitching this morning that I wasn't doing anything of value," Bryce muttered back as they trailed the Viper Queen through an archway and down a back set of stairs. From below, roaring and cheers rose to meet them. "And now that I am doing something, you're bitching about it, too?" She snorted. "Get your shit together, Athalar."

His jaw tightened again. But he glanced at her bag, the block of salt weighing it down. "You bought the salt because you knew it'd attract her attention."

"You told me that it'd take weeks to get a meeting with her. I decided to bypass all the bullshit." She tapped the bag, the salt thumping hollowly beneath her hand.

"Cthona's tits," he muttered, shaking his head. They exited the stairwell a level down, the walls solid concrete. Behind them, the roar of the fighting pit echoed down the corridor. But the Viper Queen glided ahead, passing rusty metal doors. Until she opened an unmarked one and swept in without so much as looking back. Bryce couldn't help her smug smile.

"Don't look so fucking satisfied," Hunt hissed. "We might not even walk out of this place alive." True. "I'll ask the questions."

"No."

They glowered at each other, and Bryce could have sworn

lightning forked across his eyes. But they'd reached the door, which opened into—

She'd been expecting the plush opulence of Griffin Antiquities hidden behind that door: gilded mirrors and velvet divans and silk drapes and a carved oak desk as old as this city.

Not this . . . mess. It was barely better than the stockroom of a dive bar. A dented metal desk occupied most of the cramped space, a scratched purple chair behind it—tufts of stuffing poking out of the upper corner, and the pale green paint peeled off the wall in half a dozen spots. Not to mention the water stain gracing the ceiling, made worse by the thrumming fluorescent firstlights. Against one wall stood an open shelving unit filled with everything from files to crates of liquor to discarded guns; on the opposite, stacked cardboard boxes rose above her head.

One glance at Hunt and Bryce knew he was thinking the same: the Viper Queen, mistress of the underworld, feared poisons expert and ruler of the Meat Market, claimed this hovel as an office?

The female slid into the chair, interlacing her fingers atop the mess of papers strewn across the desk. A computer that was about twenty years out of date sat like a fat rock before her, a little statue of Luna poised atop it, the goddess's bow aimed at the shifter's face.

One of her guards shut the door, prompting Hunt's hand to slide toward his hip, but Bryce had already taken a seat in one of the cheap aluminum chairs.

"Not as fancy as your boss's place," the Viper Queen said, reading the disbelief on Bryce's face, "but it does the trick."

Bryce didn't bother agreeing that the space was far from anything befitting a serpentine shifter whose snake form was a moon-white cobra with scales that gleamed like opals—and whose power was rumored to be . . . different. Something *extra* that mixed with her venom, something strange and old.

Hunt took a seat beside her, twisting the chair frontward to accommodate his wings. Roaring from the fighting pit rumbled through the concrete floor beneath their feet.

The Viper Queen lit another cigarette. "You're here to ask about Danika Fendyr."

Bryce kept her face neutral. To his credit, Athalar did, too.

Hunt said carefully, "We're trying to get a clearer picture of everything."

Her remarkable eyes narrowed with pleasure. "If that's what you want to claim, then sure." Smoke rippled from her lips. "I'll spare you the bullshit, though. Danika was a threat to me, and in more ways than perhaps you know. But she was smart. Our relationship was a working one." Another inhale. "I'm sure Athalar can back me up on this," she drawled, earning a warning glare from him, "but to get shit done, sometimes the Aux and 33rd have to work with those of us who dwell in the shadows."

Hunt said, "And Maximus Tertian? He was killed on the outskirts of your territory."

"Maximus Tertian was a spoiled little bitch, but I would never be stupid enough to pick a fight with his father like that. I'd only stand to gain a headache."

"Who killed him?" Bryce asked. "I heard you pulled in your people. You know something."

"Just a precaution." She flicked her tongue over her bottom teeth. "Us serps can taste when shit is about to go down. Like a charge in the air. I can taste it now—all over this city."

Hunt's lightning grumbled in the room. "You didn't think to warn anyone?"

"I warned my people. As long as trouble doesn't pass through my district, I don't care what goes on in the rest of Lunathion."

Hunt said, "Real noble of you."

Bryce asked again, "Who do you think killed Tertian?"

She shrugged. "Honestly? It's the Meat Market. Shit happens. He was probably coming here for drugs, and this is the price he paid."

"What kind of drugs?" Bryce asked, but Hunt said, "Toxicology report says there were no drugs in his system."

"Then I can't help you," the shifter said. "Your guess is as good as mine." Bryce didn't bother to ask about camera footage, not when the 33rd would have already combed through it.

The Viper Queen pulled something from a drawer and chucked

it on the desk. A flash drive. "My alibis from the night Tertian was killed and from the days before and during Danika and her pack's murders."

Bryce didn't touch the tiny metal drive, no bigger than a lipstick tube.

The Viper Queen's lips curved again. "I was at the spa the night of Tertian's murder. And as for Danika and the Pack of Devils, one of my associates threw a Drop party for his daughter that night. Turned into three days of . . . well, you'll see."

"This drive contains footage of you at a three-day orgy?" Hunt demanded.

"Let me know if it gets you hot and bothered, Athalar." The Viper Queen took another hit of the cigarette. Her green eyes drifted toward his lap. "I hear you're one Hel of a ride when you pause the brooding long enough."

Oh please. Hunt's teeth flashed as he bared them in a silent snarl, so Bryce said, "Orgy and Hunt's bedroom prowess aside, you've got a salt vendor in this market." She tapped the bag balanced on her knees.

The Viper Queen tore her eyes from a still-snarling Hunt and said sharply to Bryce, "I don't use what I sell. Though I don't think you live by that rule over at your fancy gallery." She winked. "You ever get sick of crawling for that sorceress, come find me. I have a stable of clients who'd crawl for you. And pay to do it."

Hunt's hand was warm on her shoulder. "She's not for sale."

Bryce leaned out of his grip, throwing him a warning glare.

The Viper Queen said, "Everyone, General, is for sale. You just have to figure out the asking price." Smoke flared from her nostrils, a dragon huffing flames. "Give me a day or two, Athalar, and I'll figure out yours."

Hunt's smile was a thing of deadly beauty. "Maybe I've figured out yours already."

The Viper Queen smiled. "I certainly hope so." She stubbed out the cigarette and met Bryce's stare. "Here's a pro tip for your little investigation." Bryce stiffened at the cool mockery. "Look toward where it hurts the most. That's always where the answers are."

"Thanks for the advice," Bryce gritted out.

The shifter merely snapped her gold-tipped fingers. The office door opened, those venom-addicted Fae males peering in. "They're done," the Viper Queen said, turning on her antique of a computer. "Make sure they get outside." *And don't go poking about.*

Bryce shouldered the block of salt as Hunt snatched up the flash drive, pocketing it.

The guard was smart enough to step away as Hunt nudged Bryce through the door. Bryce made it three steps before the Viper Queen said, "Don't underestimate the obsidian salt, Quinlan. It can bring over the very worst of Hel."

A chill snaked down her spine. But Bryce merely lifted a hand in an over-the-shoulder wave as she entered the hall. "Well, at least I'll be entertained, won't I?"

They left the Meat Market in one piece, thank the five fucking gods—especially Urd herself. Hunt wasn't entirely sure how they'd managed to walk away from the Viper Queen without their guts pumped full of poisoned bullets, but . . . He frowned at the red-haired woman now inspecting her white scooter for damage. Even the helmet had been left untouched.

Hunt said, "I believe her." No way in Hel was he watching the video on that flash drive. He'd be sending it right over to Viktoria. "I don't think she had anything to do with this."

Quinlan and Roga, however . . . He hadn't yet crossed them off his mental list.

Bryce tucked the helmet into the crook of her arm. "I agree."

"So that brings us back to square one." He suppressed the urge to pace, picturing his kill count still in the thousands.

"No," Bryce countered. "It doesn't." She fastened the bag of salt into the small compartment on the back of her scooter. "She said to look where it hurts most for answers."

"She was just spewing some bullshit to mess with us."

"Probably," Bryce said, fitting the helmet over her head before flicking up the visor to reveal those amber eyes. "But maybe she was unintentionally right. Tomorrow . . ." Her eyes shuttered. "I've got to do some thinking tomorrow. At the gallery, or else Jesiba will throw a fit."

He was intrigued enough that he said, "You think you have a lead?"

"Not yet. A general direction, though. It's better than nothing."

He jerked his chin toward the compartment of her scooter. "What's the obsidian salt for?" She had to have another purpose for it. Even if he prayed she wasn't dumb enough to use it.

Bryce just said blandly, "Seasoning my burgers."

Fine. He'd walked into that. "How'd you afford the salt, anyway?" He doubted she had ten grand just sitting around in her bank account.

Bryce zipped up her leather jacket. "I put it on Jesiba's account. She spends more money on beauty products in a month, so I doubt she'll notice."

Hunt had no idea how to even respond to any of that, so he gritted his teeth and surveyed her atop her ride. "You know, even a scooter is a dumb fucking thing to drive before making the Drop."

"Thanks, Mom."

"You should take the bus."

She just let out a barking laugh, and zoomed off into the night.

20

Look toward where it hurts the most.

Bryce had refrained from telling Athalar how accurate the Viper Queen's tip had been. She'd already given him her list of suspects—but he hadn't asked about the other demand he'd made.

So that's what she'd decided to do: compile a list of every one of Danika's movements from the week before her death. But the moment she'd finished opening up the gallery for the day, the moment she'd come down to the library to make the list . . . Nausea had hit her.

She turned on her laptop instead, and began combing through her emails with Maximus Tertian, dating back six weeks. Perhaps she'd find some sort of connection there—or at least a hint of his plans for that night.

Yet with each professional, bland email she reread, the memories from Danika's last days clawed at the welded-shut door of her mind. Like looming specters, they hissed and whispered, and she tried to ignore them, tried to focus on Tertian's emails, but—

Lehabah looked over from where she'd sprawled on the tiny fainting couch Bryce had given her years ago—courtesy of a dollhouse from her childhood—watching her favorite Vanir drama on her tablet. Her glass dome sat behind her atop a stack of books, the plumes of a purple orchid arching over it. "You could let the angel down here and work together on whatever is causing you such difficulty."

Bryce rolled her eyes. "Your fascination with Athalar is taking on stalkerish levels."

Lehabah sighed. "Do you know what Hunt Athalar *looks* like?"

"Considering that he's living on the roof across from my apartment, I'd say yes."

Lehabah hit pause on her show, leaning her head against the backrest of her little fainting couch. "He's *dreamy*."

"Yeah, just ask him." Bryce clicked out of the email she'd been reading—one of about a hundred between her and Tertian, and the first where he'd been mildly flirty with her.

"Hunt's handsome enough to be on this show." Lehabah pointed with a dainty toe toward the tablet propped before her.

"Unfortunately, I don't think the size differences between you and Athalar would work in the bedroom. You're barely big enough to wrap your arms around his dick."

Smoke swirled around Lehabah at her puff of embarrassment, and the sprite waved her little hands to clear it away. "BB!"

Bryce chuckled, then she gestured to the tablet. "I'm not the one who's bingeing a show that's basically porn with a plot. What's it called again? *Fangs and Bangs*?"

Lehabah turned purple. "It's not called that and you know it! And it's *artistic*. They make *love*. They don't . . ." She choked.

"Fuck?" Bryce suggested dryly.

"Exactly," Lehabah said with a prim nod.

Bryce laughed, letting it chase away the swarming ghosts of the past, and the sprite, despite her prudishness, joined her. Bryce said, "I doubt Hunt Athalar is the *making love* type."

Lehabah hid her face behind her hands, humming with mortification.

Just to torture her a bit more, Bryce added, "He's the type to bend you over a desk and—"

The phone rang.

She glanced at the ceiling, wondering if Athalar had somehow heard, but—no. It was worse.

"Hi, Jesiba," she said, motioning Lehabah back to her guardian's perch in case the sorceress was monitoring through the library's cameras.

"Bryce. Glad to see Lehabah is hard at work."

Lehabah quickly shut down the tablet and did her best to look alert. Bryce said, "It was her midmorning break. She's entitled to one."

Lehabah threw her a grateful glance that cut right to the bone.

Jesiba just began rattling off commands.

Thirty minutes later, at the desk in the gallery showroom, Bryce stared toward the shut front door. The ticking of the clock filled the space, a steady reminder of each second lost. Each second that Danika and the pack's killer roamed the streets while she sat in here, checking bullshit paperwork.

Unacceptable. Yet the thought of prying open the door to those memories . . .

She knew she'd regret it. Knew it was probably ten kinds of stupid. But she dialed the number before she could second-guess it.

"What's wrong." Hunt's voice was already sharp, full of storms.

"Why do you assume something's wrong?"

"Because you've never called me before, Quinlan."

This was stupid—really fucking stupid. She cleared her throat to make up some excuse about ordering food for lunch, but he said, "You found something?"

For Danika, for the Pack of Devils, she could do this. Would do this. Pride had no place here. "I need you to . . . help me with something."

"With what?" But before his words finished sounding, a fist banged on the door. She knew it was him without pulling up the camera feed.

She opened the door, getting a face full of wings and rain-kissed cedar. Hunt asked wryly, "Are you going to give me shit about coming in or can we spare ourselves that song and dance?"

"Just get inside." Bryce left Hunt in the doorway and walked to her desk, where she hauled open the bottom drawer to yank out a reusable bottle. She drank straight from it.

Hunt shut the door after himself. "A little early to be drinking, isn't it?"

She didn't bother to correct him, just took another sip and slid into her chair.

He eyed her. "You gonna tell me what this is about?"

A polite but insistent *thump-thump-thump* came from the iron door down to the library. Hunt's wings snapped shut as he turned his head toward the heavy metal slab.

Another *tap-tap-tap* filled the showroom atrium. "BB," Lehabah said mournfully through the door. "BB, are you all right?"

Bryce rolled her eyes. Cthona spare her.

Hunt asked too casually, "Who is that?"

A third little *knock-knock-knock*. "BB? BB, please say you're all right."

"I'm fine," Bryce called. "Go back downstairs and do your job."

"I want to see you with my own eyes," Lehabah said, sounding for all the world like a concerned aunt. "I can't focus on my work until then."

Hunt's brows twitched toward each other—even as his lips tugged outward.

Bryce said to him, "One, hyperbole is an art form for her."

"Oh, BB, you can be so terribly cruel—"

"*Two,* very few people are allowed downstairs, so if you report to Micah about it, we're done."

"I promise," Hunt said warily. "Though Micah can make me talk if he insists."

"Then don't give him a reason to be curious about it." She set the bottle on her desk, and found her legs were surprisingly sturdy. Hunt still towered over her. The horrible twining thorns tattooed across his brow seemed to suck the light from the room.

But Hunt rubbed his jaw. "A lot of the stuff down there is contraband, isn't it."

"Surely you've realized *most* of the shit in here is contraband. Some of these books and scrolls are the last known copies in existence." She pursed her lips, then added quietly, "A lot of people suffered and died to preserve what's in the library downstairs."

More than that, she wouldn't say. She hadn't been able to read most of the books, since they were in long-dead languages or in codes so clever only highly trained linguists or historians might decipher them, but she'd finally learned last year what most of them were. Knew the Asteri and the Senate would order them destroyed. Had destroyed all other copies. There were normal books in there, too, which Jesiba acquired mostly for her own uses—possibly even for the Under-King. But the ones that Lehabah guarded . . . those were the ones people would kill for. Had killed for.

Hunt nodded. "I won't breathe a word."

She assessed him for a moment, then turned to the iron door. "Consider this your birthday present, Lele," she muttered through the metal.

The iron door opened on a sigh, revealing the pine-green carpeted staircase that led straight down into the library. Hunt almost crashed into her as Lehabah floated up between them, her fire shining bright, and purred, "Hello."

The angel examined the fire sprite hovering a foot away from his face. She was no longer than Bryce's hand, her flaming hair twirling above her head.

"Well, aren't you beautiful," Hunt said, his voice low and soft in a way that made every instinct in Bryce sit up straight.

Lehabah flared as she wrapped her plump arms around herself and ducked her head.

Bryce shook off the effects of Hunt's voice. "Stop pretending to be shy."

Lehabah cut her a simmering glare, but Hunt lifted a finger for her to perch on. "Shall we?"

Lehabah shone ruby red, but floated over to his scarred finger and sat, smiling at him beneath her lashes. "He is very nice, BB," Lehabah observed as Bryce walked down the stairs, the sun-chandelier blinking to life again. "I don't see why you complain so much about him."

Bryce scowled over her shoulder. But Lehabah was making

mooncalf eyes at the angel, who gave Bryce a wry smile as he trailed her into the library's heart.

Bryce looked ahead quickly.

Maybe Lehabah had a point about Athalar's looks.

Bryce was aware of every step downward, every rustle of Hunt's wings mere steps behind her. Every bit of air that he filled with his breath, his power, his will.

Other than Jesiba, Syrinx, and Lehabah, only Danika had been down here with her before.

Syrinx stirred enough from his nap to see that they had a guest—and his little lion's tail whacked against the velvet sofa. "Syrie says you can brush him now," Lehabah told Hunt.

"Hunt is busy," Bryce said, heading for the table where she'd left the book open.

"Syrie talks, does he?"

"According to her, he does," Bryce muttered, scanning the table for—right, she'd put the list on Lehabah's table. She aimed for it, heels sinking deep into the carpet.

"There must be thousands of books in here," Hunt said, surveying the towering shelves.

"Oh yes," Lehabah said. "But half of this is also Jesiba's private collection. Some of the books date all the way back to—"

"*Ahem*," Bryce said.

Lehabah stuck out her tongue and said in a conspiratorial whisper to Hunt, "BB is cranky because she hasn't been able to make her list."

"I'm cranky because I'm hungry and you've been a pain in my ass all morning."

Lehabah floated off Hunt's finger to rush to her table, where she plopped on her doll's couch and said to the angel, who looked torn between wincing and laughing, "BB pretends to be mean, but she's a softie. She bought Syrie because Jesiba was going to gift him to a warlord client in the Farkaan mountains—"

"*Lehabah*—"

"It's true."

Hunt examined the various tanks throughout the room and the assortment of reptiles within them, then the empty waters of the massive aquarium. "I thought he was some designer pet."

"Oh, he is," Lehabah said. "Syrinx was stolen from his mother as a cub, then traded for ten years around the world, then Jesiba bought him to be her pet, then *Bryce* bought him—his freedom, I mean. She even had proof of his freedom certified. No one can ever buy him again." She pointed to the chimera. "You can't see it with him lying down like that, but he's got the freed brand on his front right paw. The official *C* and everything."

Hunt twisted from the gloomy water to look Bryce over.

She crossed her arms. "What? You did the assuming."

His eyes flickered. Whatever the fuck that meant.

She tried not to look at his own wrist, though—the *SPQM* stamped there. She wondered if he was resisting the same urge; if he was contemplating whether he'd ever get that *C* one day.

But then Lehabah said to Hunt, "How much do *you* cost to buy, Athie?"

Bryce cut in, "Lele, that's rude. And don't call him Athie."

She sent up a puff of smoke. "He and I are of the same House, and are both slaves. My great-grandmother fought in his 18th Legion during their rebellion. I am allowed to ask."

Hunt's face wholly shuttered at the mention of the rebellion, but he approached the couch, let Syrinx sniff his fingers, then scratched the beast behind his velvety ears. Syrinx let out a low growl of pleasure, his lion's tail going limp.

Bryce tried to block out the squeezing sensation in her chest at the sight of it.

Hunt's wings rustled. "I was sold to Micah for eighty-five million gold marks."

Bryce's heel snagged on the carpet as she reached Lehabah's little station and grabbed the tablet. Lehabah again floated over to the angel. "I cost ninety thousand gold marks," Lehabah confided. "Syrie was two hundred thirty-three thousand gold marks."

Hunt's eyes snapped to Bryce. "You paid that?"

Bryce sat at the worktable and pointed to the empty chair beside hers. Hunt followed obediently, for once. "I got a fifteen percent employee discount. And we came to an arrangement."

Let that be that.

Until Lehabah declared, "Jesiba takes some out of each paycheck." Bryce growled, reining in the instinct to smother the sprite with a pillow. "BB will be paying it off until she's three hundred. Unless she doesn't make the Drop. Then she'll die first."

Hunt dropped into his seat, his wing brushing her arm. Softer than velvet, smoother than silk. He snapped it in tight at the touch, as if he couldn't bear the contact. "Why?"

Bryce said, "Because that warlord wanted to hurt and break him until he was a fighting beast, and Syrinx is my friend, and I was sick of losing friends."

"I thought you were loaded."

"Nope." She finished the word on a popping noise.

Hunt's brow furrowed. "But your apartment—"

"The apartment is Danika's." Bryce couldn't meet his gaze. "She bought it as an investment. Had its ownership written in our names. I didn't even know it existed until after she died. And I would have just sold it, but it had top-notch security, and grade A enchantments—"

"I get it," he said again, and she shrank from the kindness in his eyes. The pity.

Danika had died, and she was alone, and—Bryce couldn't breathe.

She'd refused to go to therapy. Her mother had set up appointment after appointment for the first year, and Bryce had bailed on all of them. She'd bought herself an aromatherapy diffuser, had read up on breathing techniques, and that had been that.

She knew she should have gone. Therapy helped so many people—saved so many lives. Juniper had been seeing a therapist since she was a teenager and would tell anyone who would listen about how vital and brilliant it was.

But Bryce hadn't shown up—not because she didn't believe it

would work. No, she knew it would work, and help, and probably make her feel better. Or at least give her the tools to try to do so.

That was precisely why she hadn't gone.

From the way Hunt was staring at her, she wondered if he knew it—realized why she blew out a long breath.

Look toward where it hurts the most.

Fucker. The Viper Queen could go to Hel with her pro tips.

She turned on Lehabah's electronic tablet. The screen revealed a vampyr and wolf tangled in each other, groaning, naked—

Bryce laughed. "You stopped watching in the middle of *this* to come bother me, Lele?"

The air in the room lightened, as if Bryce's sorrow had cracked at the sight of the wolf pounding into the moaning vampyr female.

Lehabah burned ruby. "I wanted to meet Athie," she muttered, slinking back to her couch.

Hunt, as if despite himself, chuckled. "You watch *Fangs and Bangs*?"

Lehabah shot upright. "That is *not* what it's called! Did you tell him to say that, Bryce?"

Bryce bit her lip to keep from laughing and grabbed her laptop instead, bringing up her emails with Tertian on the screen. "No, I didn't."

Hunt raised a brow, with that wary amusement.

"I'm taking a nap with Syrie," Lehabah declared to no one in particular. Almost as soon as she said it, something heavy thumped on the mezzanine.

Hunt's hand went to his side, presumably for the gun there, but Lehabah hissed toward the railing, "*Do not interrupt my nap.*"

A heavy slithering filled the library, followed by a thump and rustle. It didn't come from Miss Poppy's tank.

Lehabah said to Hunt, "Don't let the books sweet-talk you into taking them home."

He threw her a half smile. "You're doing a fine job ensuring that doesn't happen."

Lehabah beamed, curling along Syrinx's side. He purred with

delight at her warmth. "They'll do anything to get out of here: sneak into your bag, the pocket of your coat, even flop up the stairs. They're desperate to get into the world again." She flowed toward the distant shelves behind them, where a book had landed on the steps. "*Bad!*" she seethed.

Hunt's hand slid within easy reach of the knife at his thigh as the book, as if carried by invisible hands, drifted up the steps, floated to the shelf, and found its place again, humming once with golden light—as if in annoyance.

Lehabah cast a warning simmer toward it, then wrapped Syrinx's tail around herself like a fur shawl.

Bryce shook her head, but a sidelong glance told her that Hunt was now staring at her. Not in the way that males tended to stare at her. He said, "What's up with all the little critters?"

"They're Jesiba's former lovers and rivals," Lehabah whispered from her fur-blanket.

Hunt's wings rustled. "I'd heard the rumors."

"I've never seen her transform anyone into an animal," Bryce said, "but I try to stay on her good side. I'd really prefer not to be turned into a pig if Jesiba gets pissed at me for fucking up a deal."

Hunt's lips twitched upward, as if caught between amusement and horror.

Lehabah opened her mouth, presumably to tell Hunt all the names she'd given the creatures in the library, but Bryce cut her off, saying to Hunt, "I called you because I started to make that list of all of Danika's movements during her final days." She patted the page she'd started writing on.

"Yeah?" His dark eyes remained on her face.

Bryce cleared her throat and admitted, "It's, um, hard. To make myself remember. I thought . . . maybe you could ask me some questions. Help get the . . . memories flowing."

"Ah. Okay." Silence rippled again as she waited for him to remind her that time wasn't on their side, that he had a fucking job to do and she shouldn't be such a wimp, blah blah.

But Hunt surveyed the books; the tanks; the door to the bathroom at the back of the space; the lights high above, disguised like the stars painted across the ceiling. And then, rather than ask her about Danika, he said, "Did you study antiquities at school?"

"I took a few classes, yeah. I liked learning about old crap. I was a classical literature major." She added, "I learned the Old Language of the Fae when I was a kid." She'd taught herself out of a sudden interest in learning more about her heritage. When she'd gone to her father's house a year later—for the first time in her life—she'd hoped to use it to impress him. After everything went to shit, she'd refused to learn another language. Childish, but she didn't care.

Though knowing the most ancient of the Fae languages had been helpful for this job, at least. For the few Fae antiquities that weren't hoarded in their glittering troves.

Hunt again surveyed the space. "How'd you get this job?"

"After I graduated, I couldn't get a job anywhere. The museums didn't want me because I didn't have enough experience, and the other art galleries in town were run by creeps who thought I was . . . appetizing." His eyes darkened, and she made herself ignore the rage she beheld there on her behalf. "But my friend Fury . . ." Hunt stiffened slightly at the name—he clearly knew her reputation. "Well, she and Jesiba worked together in Pangera at some point. And when Jesiba mentioned that she needed a new assistant, Fury basically shoved my résumé down her throat." Bryce snorted at the memory. "Jesiba offered me the job because she didn't want an uptight priss. The work is too dirty, customers too shady. She needed someone with social skills as well as a little background in ancient art. And that was that."

Hunt considered, then asked, "What's your deal with Fury Axtar?"

"She's in Pangera. Doing what Fury does best." It wasn't really an answer.

"Axtar ever tell you what she gets up to over there?"

"No. And I like it to stay that way. My dad told me enough stories about what it's like. I don't enjoy imagining what Fury sees and deals with." Blood and mud and death, science versus magic, machines versus Vanir, bombs of chemicals and firstlight, bullets and fangs.

Randall's own service had been mandatory, a condition of life for any non-Lower in the peregrini class: all humans had to serve in the military for three years. Randall had never said it, but she'd always known the years on the front had left deep scars beyond those visible on him. Being forced to kill your own kind was no small task. But the Asteri's threat remained: Should any refuse, their lives would be forfeit. And then the lives of their families. Any survivors would be slaves, their wrists forever inked with the same letters that marred Hunt's skin.

"There's no chance Danika's murderer might have been connected to—"

"No." Bryce growled. She and Fury might be totally fucked up right now, but she knew that. "Fury's enemies weren't Danika's enemies. Once Briggs was behind bars, she bailed." Bryce hadn't seen her since.

Searching for anything to change the topic, Bryce asked, "How old are you?"

"Two hundred thirty-three."

She did the math, frowning. "You were that young when you rebelled? And already commanded a legion?" The angels' failed rebellion had been two hundred years ago; he'd have been incredibly young—by Vanir standards—to have led it.

"My gifts made me invaluable to people." He held up a hand, lightning writhing around his fingers. "Too good at killing." She grunted her agreement. Hunt eyed her. "You ever killed before?"

"Yes."

Surprise lit his eyes. But she didn't want to go into it—what had happened with Danika senior year that had left them both in the hospital, her arm shattered, and a stolen motorcycle little more than scrap.

Lehabah cut in from across the library, "BB, stop being cryptic! I've wanted to know for years, Athie, but she never tells me anything good—"

"Leave it, Lehabah." The memories of that trip pelted her. Danika's smiling face in the hospital bed beside hers. How Thorne carried Danika up the stairs of their dorm when they got home, despite her protests. How the pack had fussed over them for a week, Nathalie and Zelda kicking the males out one night so they could have a girls-only moviefest. But none of it had compared to what had changed between her and Danika on that trip. The final barrier that had fallen, the truth laid bare.

I love you, Bryce. I'm so sorry.

Close your eyes, Danika.

A hole tore open in her chest, gaping and howling.

Lehabah was still grousing. But Hunt was watching Bryce's face. He asked, "What's one happy memory you have with Danika from the last week of her life?"

Her blood pounded through her entire body. "I—I have a lot of them from that week."

"Pick one, and we'll start with that."

"Is this how you get witnesses to talk?"

He leaned back in his seat, wings adjusting around its low back. "It's how you and I are going to make this list."

She weighed his stare, his solid, thrumming presence. She swallowed. "The tattoo on my back—she and I got it done that week. We got stupid drunk one night, and I was so out of it I didn't even know what the fuck she put on my back until I'd gotten over my hangover."

His lips twitched. "I hope it was something good, at least."

Her chest ached, but she smiled. "It was."

Hunt sat forward and tapped the paper. "Write it down."

She did. He asked, "What'd Danika do during that day before you got the tattoo?"

The question was calm, but he weighed her every movement. As if he were reading something, assessing something that she couldn't see.

Eager to avoid that too-aware look, Bryce picked up the pen, and began writing, one memory after another. Kept writing her recollections of Danika's whereabouts that week: that silly wish on the Old Square Gate, the pizza she and Danika had devoured while standing at the counter of the shop, swigging from bottles of beer and talking shit; the hair salon where Bryce flipped through gossip magazines while Danika had gotten her purple, blue, and pink streaks touched up; the grocery store two blocks down where she and Thorne had found Danika stuffing her face with a bag of chips she hadn't yet paid for and teased her for hours afterward; the CCU sunball arena where she and Danika had ogled the hot players on Ithan's team during practice and called dibs on them . . . She kept writing and writing, until the walls pressed in again.

Her knee bounced relentlessly beneath the table. "I think we can stop there for today."

Hunt opened his mouth, glancing to the list—but her phone buzzed.

Thanking Urd for the well-timed intervention, Bryce glanced at the message on the screen and scowled. The expression was apparently intriguing enough that Hunt peered over her shoulder.

Ruhn had written, *Meet me at Luna's Temple in thirty minutes.*

Hunt asked, "Think it's got to do with last night?"

Bryce didn't answer as she typed back, *Why?*

Ruhn replied. *Because it's one of the few places in this city without cameras.*

"Interesting," she murmured. "You think I should give him a heads-up that you're coming?"

Hunt's grin was pure wickedness. "Hel no."

Bryce couldn't keep herself from grinning back.

21

Ruhn Danaan leaned against one of the marble pillars of the inner sanctum of Luna's Temple and waited for his sister to arrive. Tourists drifted past, snapping photos, none marking his presence, thanks to the shadow veil he'd pulled around himself.

The chamber was long, its ceiling lofty. It had to be, to accommodate the statue enthroned at the back.

Thirty feet high, Luna sat in a carved golden throne, the goddess lovingly rendered in shimmering moonstone. A silver tiara of a full moon held by two crescent ones graced her upswept curling hair. At her sandaled feet lay twin wolves, their baleful eyes daring any pilgrim to come closer. Across the back of her throne, a bow of solid gold had been slung, its quiver full of silver arrows. The pleats of her thigh-length robe draped across her lap, veiling the slim fingers resting there.

Both wolves and Fae claimed Luna as their patron goddess—had gone to war over whom she favored in millennia long past. And while the wolves' connection to her had been carved into the statue with stunning detail, the nod to the Fae had been missing for two years. Maybe the Autumn King had a point about restoring the Fae to glory. Not in the haughty, sneering way his father intended, but . . . the lack of Fae heritage on the statue raked down Ruhn's nerves.

Footsteps scuffed in the courtyard beyond the sanctum doors, followed by excited whispers and the click of cameras.

"The courtyard itself is modeled after the one in the Eternal City," a female voice was saying as a new flock of tourists entered the temple, trailing their guide like ducklings.

And at the rear of the group—a wine-red head of hair.

And a too-recognizable pair of gray wings.

Ruhn gritted his teeth, keeping hidden in the shadows. At least she'd shown up.

The tour group stopped in the center of the inner sanctum, the guide speaking loudly as everyone spread out, cameras flashing like Athalar's lightning in the gloom. "And here it is, folks: the statue of Luna herself. Lunathion's patron goddess was crafted from a single block of marble hewn from the famed Caliprian Quarries by the Melanthos River up north. This temple was the first thing built upon the city's founding five hundred years ago; the location of this city was selected precisely because of the way the Istros River bends through the land. Can anyone tell me what shape the river makes?"

"A crescent!" someone called out, the words echoing off the marble pillars, wending through the curling smoke from the bowl of incense laid between the wolves at the goddess's feet.

Ruhn saw Bryce and Hunt scan the sanctum for him, and he let the shadows peel back long enough for them to spy his location. Bryce's face revealed nothing. Athalar just grinned.

Fan-fucking-tastic.

With all the tourists focused on their guide, no one noticed the unusual pair crossing the space. Ruhn kept the shadows at bay until Bryce and Hunt reached him—and then willed them to encompass them as well.

Hunt just said, "Fancy trick."

Bryce said nothing. Ruhn tried not to remember how delighted she'd once been whenever he'd demonstrated how his shadows and starlight worked—both halves of his power working as one.

Ruhn said to her, "I asked you to come. Not him."

Bryce linked her arm through Athalar's, the portrait they painted laughable: Bryce in her fancy work dress and heels, the angel in his black battle-suit. "We're joined at the hip now, unfortunately for you. Best, best friends."

"The best," Hunt echoed, his grin unfading.

Luna shoot him dead. This would not end well.

Bryce nodded to the tour group still trailing their leader through the temple. "This place might not have any cameras, but they do."

"They're focused on their guide," Ruhn said. "And the noise they're making will mask any conversation we have." The shadows could only hide him from sight, not sound.

Through thin ripples in the shadows, they could make out a young couple edging around the statue, so busy snapping photos they didn't note the denser bit of darkness in the far corner. But Ruhn fell silent, and Bryce and Athalar followed suit.

As they waited for the couple to pass, the tour guide went on, "We'll dive more into the architectural wonders of the inner sanctum in a minute, but let's direct our attention to the statue. The quiver, of course, is real gold, the arrows pure silver with tips of diamond."

Someone let out an appreciative whistle. "Indeed," the tour guide agreed. "They were donated by the Archangel Micah, who is a patron and investor in various charities, foundations, and innovative companies." The tour guide went on, "Unfortunately, two years ago, the third of Luna's treasures was stolen from this temple. Can anyone tell me what it was?"

"The Horn," someone said. "It was all over the news."

"It was a terrible theft. An artifact that cannot be replaced easily."

The couple moved on, and Ruhn uncrossed his arms.

Hunt said, "All right, Danaan. Get to the point. Why'd you ask Bryce to come?"

Ruhn gestured to where the tourists were snapping photos of the goddess's hand. Specifically, the fingers that now curled around air, where a cracked ivory hunting horn had once lain.

"Because I was tasked by the Autumn King to find Luna's Horn."

Athalar angled his head, but Bryce snorted. "Is that why you asked about it last night?"

They were interrupted again by the tour guide saying, as she moved toward the rear of the room, "If you'll follow me, we've been granted special permission to see the chamber where the stag sacrifices are prepared to be burned in Luna's honor." Through the murky shadows, Bryce could make out a small door opening in the wall.

When they'd filtered out, Hunt asked, eyes narrowing, "What is the Horn, exactly?"

"A bunch of fairy-tale bullcrap," Bryce muttered. "You really dragged me here for this? To what—help you impress your daddy?"

Growling, Ruhn pulled out his phone, making sure the shadows held around them, and brought up the photos he'd snapped in the Fae Archives last night.

But he didn't share them, not before he said to Athalar, "Luna's Horn was a weapon wielded by Pelias, the first Starborn Prince, during the First Wars. The Fae forged it in their home world, named it for the goddess in their new one, and used it to battle the demon hordes once they made the Crossing. Pelias wielded the Horn until he died." Ruhn put a hand on his chest. "My ancestor—whose power flows in my veins. I don't know how it worked, how Pelias used it with his magic, but the Horn became enough of a nuisance for the demon princes that they did everything they could to retrieve it from him."

Ruhn held out his phone, the picture of the illuminated manuscript glaringly bright in the thick shadows. The illustration of the carved horn lifted to the lips of a helmeted Fae male was as pristine as it had been when inked millennia ago. Above the figure gleamed an eight-pointed star, the emblem of the Starborn.

Bryce went wholly still. The stillness of the Fae, like a stag halting in a wood.

Ruhn went on, "The Star-Eater himself bred a new horror just to hunt the Horn, using some blood he managed to spill from Prince Pelias on a battlefield and his own terrible essence. A beast twisted out of the collision of light and darkness." Ruhn swiped on his phone, and the next illustration appeared. The reason he'd had her come here—had taken this gamble.

Bryce recoiled at the grotesque, pale body, the clear teeth bared in a roar.

"You recognize it," Ruhn said softly.

Bryce shook herself, as if to bring herself back to reality, and rubbed her thigh absently. "That's the demon I found attacking the angel in the alley on that night."

Hunt gave her a sharp look. "The one that attacked you, too?"

Bryce gave a small, affirmative nod. "What is it?"

"It dwells in the darkest depths of the Pit," Ruhn answered. "So lightless that the Star-Eater named it the kristallos, for its clear blood and teeth."

Athalar said, "I've never heard of it."

Bryce contemplated the drawing. "It . . . There was never a mention of a fucking *demon* in the research I did on the Horn." She met his gaze. "No one put this together two years ago?"

"I think it's *taken* two years to put it together," Ruhn said carefully. "This volume was deep in the Fae Archives, with the stuff that's not allowed to be scanned. None of your research would have ever pulled it up. The entire damn thing was in the Old Language of the Fae." And had taken him most of the night to translate. Throwing in the lingering fog of the mirthroot hadn't helped.

Bryce's brow furrowed. "But the Horn was broken—it basically became a dud, right?"

"Right," Ruhn said. "During the final battle of the First Wars, Prince Pelias and the Prince of the Pit faced each other. The two of them fought for like three fucking days, until the Star-Eater struck the fatal blow. But not before Pelias was able to summon all the Horn's strength, and banished the Prince of the Pit, his brethren, and their armies back to Hel. He sealed the Northern Rift forever—so only small cracks in it or summonings with salt can bring them over now."

Athalar frowned. "So you mean to tell me this deadly artifact, which the Prince of the Pit *literally* bred a new demon species to hunt, was just sitting here? In this temple? And *no one* from this world or Hel tried to take it until that blackout? Why?"

Bryce met Hunt's disbelieving stare. "The Horn cracked in two when Pelias sealed the Northern Rift. Its power was broken. The Fae and Asteri tried for years to renew it through magic and spells and all that crap, but no luck. It was given a place of honor in the Asteri Archives, but when they established Lunathion a few millennia later, they had it dedicated to the temple here."

Ruhn shook his head. "That the Fae allowed for the artifact to be given over suggests they'd dismissed its worth—that even my father might have forgotten its importance." Until it was stolen—and he'd gotten it into his head that it would be a rallying symbol of power during a possible war.

Bryce added, "I thought it was just a replica until Jesiba made me start looking for it." She turned to Ruhn. "So you think someone has been summoning this demon to hunt for the Horn? But why, when it no longer has any power? And how does it explain any of the deaths? You think the victims somehow . . . had contact with the Horn, and it brought the kristallos right to them?" She went on before either of them could answer, "And why the two-year gap?"

Hunt mused, "Maybe the murderer waited until things calmed down enough to resume searching."

"Your guess is as good as mine," Ruhn admitted. "It doesn't seem like coincidence that the Horn went missing right before this demon showed up, though, and for the murders to be starting again—"

"Could mean someone is hunting for the Horn once more," Bryce finished, frowning.

Hunt said, "The kristallos's presence in Lunathion suggests the Horn is still inside the city walls."

Bryce pinned Ruhn with a look. "Why does the Autumn King suddenly want it?"

Ruhn chose his words carefully. "Call it pride. He wants it returned to the Fae. And wants me to find it quietly."

Athalar asked him, "But why ask *you* to look for the Horn?"

The shadows veiling them rippled. "Because Prince Pelias's Starborn power was woven into the Horn itself. And it's in my blood.

My father thinks I might have some sort of preternatural gift to find it." He admitted, "When I was browsing the archives last night, this book . . . jumped out at me."

"Literally?" Bryce asked, brows high.

Ruhn said, "It just felt like it . . . shimmered. I don't fucking know. All I know is I was down there for hours, and then I sensed the book, and when I saw that illustration of the Horn . . . There it was. The crap I translated confirmed it."

"So the kristallos can track the Horn," Bryce said, eyes glittering. "But so can *you*."

Athalar's mouth curled in a crooked grin, catching Bryce's drift. "We find the demon, we find who's behind this. And if we have the Horn . . ."

Ruhn grimaced. "The kristallos will come to us."

Bryce glanced to the empty-handed statue behind them. "Better get cracking, Ruhn."

Hunt leaned against the entry pillars atop the steps leading into Luna's Temple, his phone at his ear. He'd left Quinlan inside with her cousin, needing to make this phone call before they could sort out logistics. He would have made the call right there, but the moment he'd pulled up his contacts list, he'd earned a snipe from Bryce about mobile phones in sacred spaces.

Cthona spare him. Declining to tell her to fuck off, he'd decided to spare them a public scene and stalked out through the cypress-lined courtyard and to the front steps.

Five temple acolytes emerged from the sprawling villa behind the temple itself, bearing brooms and hoses to clean the temple steps and the flagstones beyond it for their midday washing.

Unnecessary, he wanted to tell the young females. With the misting rain yet again gracing the city, the hoses were superfluous.

Teeth gritted, he listened to the phone ring and ring. "Pick the fuck up," he muttered.

A dark-skinned temple acolyte—black-haired, white-robed, and no more than twelve—gaped at him as she walked past, clutching a broom to her chest. He nearly winced, realizing the portrait of wrath he now presented, and checked his expression.

The Fae girl still kept back, the golden crescent moon dangling from a delicate chain across her brow glinting in the gray light. A waxing moon—until she became a full-fledged priestess upon reaching maturity, when she would trade the crescent for the full circle of Luna. And whenever her immortal body began to age and fade, her cycle vanishing with it, she would again trade the charm, this time for a waning crescent.

The priestesses all had their own reasons for offering themselves to Luna. For forsaking their lives beyond the temple grounds and embracing the goddess's eternal maidenhood. Just as Luna had no mate or lover, so they would live.

Hunt had always thought celibacy seemed like a bore. Until Shahar had ruined him for anyone else.

Hunt offered the shrinking acolyte his best attempt at a smile. To his surprise, the Fae girl offered a small one back. The girl had courage.

Justinian Gelos answered on the sixth ring. "How's babysitting?"

Hunt straightened. "Don't sound so amused."

Justinian huffed a laugh. "You sure Micah's not punishing you?"

Hunt had considered the question a great deal in the past two days. Across the empty street, the palm trees dotting the rain-soft grasses of the Oracle's Park shone in the gray light, the domed onyx building of the Oracle's Temple veiled in the mists that had rolled in over the river.

Even at midday, the Oracle's Park was near-empty, save for the hunched, slumbering forms of the desperate Vanir and humans who wandered the paths and gardens, waiting for their turn to enter the incense-filled hallways.

And if the answers they sought weren't what they'd hoped . . . Well, the white-stoned temple on whose steps Hunt now stood could offer some solace.

Hunt glanced over his shoulder to the dim temple interior just visible through the towering bronze doors. In the firstlight from a row of shimmering braziers, he could just barely make out the gleam of red hair in the quiet gloom of the inner sanctum, shining like molten metal as Bryce talked animatedly with Ruhn.

"No," Hunt said at last. "I don't think this assignment was punishment. He was out of options and knew I'd cause more trouble if he stationed me on guard duty around Sandriel." And Pollux.

He didn't mention the bargain he'd struck with Micah. Not when Justinian bore the halo as well and Micah had never shown much interest in him beyond his popularity with the grunt troops of the 33rd. If there was any sort of deal to earn his freedom, Justinian had never said a word.

Justinian blew out a breath. "Yeah—shit's getting intense around here right now. People are on edge and she hasn't even arrived yet. You're better off where you are."

A glassy-eyed Fae male stumbled past the steps of the temple, got a good look at who was barring entry into the temple itself—and aimed for the street, staggering toward the Oracle's Park and the domed building in its heart. Another lost soul looking for answers in smoke and whispers.

"I'm not so sure of that," Hunt said. "I need you to look up something for me—an old-school demon. The kristallos. Just search through the databases and see if anything pops up." He'd have asked Vik, but she was already busy going through the alibi footage from the Viper Queen.

"I'll get on it," Justinian said. "I'll message over any results." He added, "Good luck."

"I'll need it," Hunt admitted. In a hundred fucking ways.

Justinian added slyly, "Though it doesn't hurt that your *partner* is easy on the eyes."

"I gotta go."

"No one gets a medal for suffering the most, you know," Justinian pushed, his voice slipping into uncharacteristic seriousness. "It's been two centuries since Shahar died, Hunt."

"Whatever." He didn't want to have this conversation. Not with Justinian or anyone.

"It's admirable that you're still holding out for her, but let's be realistic about—"

Hunt hung up. Debated throwing his phone against a pillar.

He had to call Isaiah and Micah about the Horn. Fuck. When it had gone missing two years ago, top inspectors from the 33rd and the Aux had combed this temple. They'd found nothing. And since no cameras were allowed within the temple walls, there had been no hint of who might have taken it. It had been nothing more than a stupid prank, everyone had claimed.

Everyone except for the Autumn King, it seemed.

Hunt hadn't paid much attention to the theft of the Horn, and sure as fuck hadn't listened during history lessons as a boy about the First Wars. And after Danika's and the Pack of Devils' murders, they'd had bigger things to worry about.

He couldn't tell what was worse: the Horn possibly being a vital piece of this case, or the fact that he'd now have to work alongside Ruhn Danaan to find it.

22

Bryce waited until Hunt's muscled back and beautiful wings had disappeared through the inner sanctum's gates before she whirled on Ruhn. "Did the Autumn King do it?"

Ruhn's blue eyes glimmered in his shadow-nest or whatever the fuck he called it. "No. He's a monster in so many ways, but he wouldn't kill Danika."

She'd come to that conclusion the other night, but she asked, "How can you be so sure? You have no idea what the Hel his long-term agenda is."

Ruhn crossed his arms. "Why ask me to hunt for the Horn if he's summoning the kristallos?"

"Two trackers are better than one?" Her heart thundered.

"He's not behind this. He's just trying to take advantage of the situation—to restore the Fae to their former glory. You know how he likes to delude himself with that kind of crap."

Bryce trailed her fingers through the wall of shadows, the darkness running over her skin like mist. "Does he know you came to meet with me?"

"No."

She held her brother's stare. "Why . . ." She struggled for words. "Why bother?"

"Because I want to help you. Because this shit puts the entire city at risk."

"How very Chosen One of you."

Silence stretched between them, so taut it trembled. She blurted, "Just because we're working together doesn't mean anything changes between us. You'll find the Horn, and I'll find who's behind this. End of story."

"Fine," Ruhn said, his eyes cold. "I wouldn't expect you to consider listening to me anyway."

"Why would I listen to you?" she seethed. "I'm just a *half-breed slut*, right?"

Ruhn stiffened, a flush flaring. "You know it was a dumb fight and I didn't *mean* that—"

"Yes, you fucking did," she spat, and turned on her heel. "You might dress like you're a punk rebelling against Daddy's rules, but deep down, you're no better than the rest of the Fae shitheads who kiss your Chosen One ass."

Ruhn snarled, but Bryce didn't wait before shoving through the shadows, blinking at the flood of light that greeted her, and aiming for where Hunt had paused at the doors.

"Let's go," she said. She didn't care what he'd overheard.

Hunt lingered in place, his black eyes flickering as he gazed toward the shadowed back of the room, where her so-called cousin was again veiled in darkness. But the angel thankfully said nothing as he fell into step beside her, and she said nothing more to him.

Bryce practically ran back to the gallery. In part to start researching the Horn again, but also thanks to the flurry of messages from Jesiba, demanding to know where she was, whether she still wanted her job, and whether she'd prefer to be turned into a rat or a pigeon. And then an order to get back *now* to greet a client.

Five minutes after Bryce got there, Jesiba's client—a raging asshole of a leopard shifter who believed he was entitled to put his paws all over her ass—prowled in and purchased a small statue of Solas and Cthona, portrayed as a sun with male features burying his face in a pair of mountain-shaped breasts. The holy image was known simply as the Embrace. Her mother even wore its simplified symbol—a circle nestled atop two triangles—as a silver pendant. But Bryce had always found the Embrace cheesy and cliché in every incarnation. Thirty minutes and two blatant rejections to his slimy come-ons later, Bryce was mercifully alone again.

But in the hours she looked, the gallery's databases for Luna's Horn revealed nothing beyond what she already knew, and what her brother had claimed that morning. Even Lehabah, gossip queen extraordinaire, didn't know anything about the Horn.

With Ruhn heading back to the Fae Archives to see if any more information appealed to his Starborn sensibilities, she supposed she'd have to wait for an update.

Hunt had gone to take watch on the roof, apparently needing to make calls to his boss—or whatever Micah pretended he was—and Isaiah regarding the Horn. He hadn't tried to come back down to the library, as if sensing she needed space.

Look toward where it hurts the most. That's always where the answers are.

Bryce found herself staring down at the half-finished list she'd started that morning.

She might not be able to find much on the Horn itself, but maybe she could figure out how the Hel Danika factored into all of it.

Hands shaking, she made herself finish the list of Danika's locations—as far as she knew.

By the time the sun was near setting, and Syrinx was ready to be walked home, Bryce would have traded what was left of her soul to a Reaper just for the quiet comfort of her bed. It had been a long fucking day, full of information she needed to process, and a list that she'd left in her desk drawer.

It must have been a long day for Athalar, too, because he trailed her and Syrinx from the skies without saying a word to her.

She was in bed by eight, and didn't even remember falling asleep.

23

The next morning, Bryce was sitting at the reception desk in the gallery's showroom, staring at her list of Danika's last locations, when her phone rang.

"The deal with the leopard went through," she said to Jesiba by way of greeting. The paperwork had been finalized an hour ago.

"I need you to go up into my office and send me a file from my computer."

Bryce rolled her eyes, refraining from snipping, *You're welcome*, and asked, "You don't have access to it?"

"I made sure this one wasn't on the network."

Nostrils flaring, Bryce rose, her leg throbbing slightly, and walked to the small door in the wall adjacent to the desk. A hand on the metal panel beside it had the enchantments unlocking, the door swinging open to reveal the tight, carpeted staircase upward.

"When I want things done, Bryce, you're to do them. No questions."

"Yes, Jesiba," Bryce muttered, climbing the stairs. Dodging the reaching hands of the leopard shifter yesterday had twinged something in her bad leg.

"Would you like to be a worm, Bryce?" Jesiba purred, voice sliding into something eerily close to a Reaper's rasp. At least Jesiba wasn't one of them—even if Bryce knew the sorceress often dealt with them in the House of Flame and Shadow. Thank the gods none had ever shown up at the gallery, though. "Would you like to be a dung beetle or a centipede?"

"I'd prefer to be a dragonfly." Bryce entered the small, plush office upstairs. One wall was a pane of glass that overlooked the gallery floor a level below, the material utterly soundproof.

"Be careful what you ask of me," Jesiba went on. "You'd find that smart mouth of yours shut up fairly quickly if I transform you. You wouldn't have any voice at all."

Bryce calculated the time difference between Lunathion and the western shores of Pangera and realized Jesiba had probably just come back from dinner. "That Pangeran red wine is heady stuff, isn't it?" She was almost to the wooden desk when the firstlights flicked on. A rack of them illuminated the dismantled gun hanging on the wall behind the desk, the Godslayer Rifle gleaming as fresh as it had the day it'd been forged. She could have sworn a faint whine radiated from the gold and steel—like the legendary, lethal gun was still ringing after a shot.

It unnerved her that it was in here, despite the fact that Jesiba had split it into four pieces, mounted like a work of art behind her desk. Four pieces that could still be easily assembled, but it put her clients at ease, even while it reminded them that she was in charge.

Bryce knew the sorceress never told them about the six-inch engraved golden bullet in the safe beside the painting on the right wall. Jesiba had shown it to her just once, letting her read the words etched onto the bullet: *Memento Mori*.

The same words that appeared in the mosaic in the Meat Market.

It'd seemed melodramatic, but some part of her had marveled at it—at the bullet and at the rifle, so rare only a few existed in Midgard.

Bryce powered up Jesiba's computer, letting the female rattle off instructions before sending the file. Bryce was halfway down the stairs again when she asked her boss, "Have you heard anything new about Luna's Horn?"

A long, contemplative pause. "Does it have to do with this investigation of yours?"

"Maybe."

Jesiba's low, cold voice was an embodiment of the House she served. "I haven't heard anything." Then she hung up. Bryce gritted her teeth as she headed back to her desk on the showroom floor.

Lehabah interrupted her by whispering through the iron door, "Can I see Athie now?"

"No, Lele."

He'd kept his distance this morning, too. Good.

Look toward where it hurts the most.

She had her list of Danika's locations. Unfortunately, she knew what she had to do next. What she'd woken up this morning dreading. Her phone rang in her clenched hand, and Bryce steeled herself for Jesiba calling to bitch that she'd fucked up the file, but it was Hunt.

"Yeah?" she asked by way of greeting.

"There's been another murder." His voice was tight—cold.

She nearly dropped the phone. "Who—"

"I'm still getting the details. But it was about ten blocks from here—near the Gate in the Old Square."

Her heart beat so fast she could scarcely draw breath to say, "Any witnesses?"

"No. But let's go over there."

Her hands shook. "I'm busy," she lied.

Hunt paused. "I'm not fucking around, Quinlan."

No. No, she couldn't do it, endure it, see it again—

Bryce forced herself to breathe, practically inhaling the peppermint vapors from the diffuser. "There's a client coming—"

He banged on the gallery door, sealing her fate. "We're leaving."

Bryce's entire body was taut to the point of near-trembling as she and Hunt approached the magi-screens blocking the alley a few blocks away from the Old Square Gate.

She tried to breathe through it, tried all the techniques she'd read and heard about regarding reining in her dread, that sickening plunging feeling in her stomach. None of them worked.

Angels and Fae and shifters milled about the alley, some on radios or phones.

"A jogger found the remains," Hunt said as people parted to let him pass. "They think it happened sometime last night." He added carefully, "The 33rd's still working on getting an ID, but from the clothes, it looks like an acolyte from Luna's Temple. Isaiah is already asking the temple priestesses who might be missing."

All sounds turned into a blaring drone. She didn't entirely remember the walk over.

Hunt edged around the magi-screen blocking the crime scene from view, took one look at what lay there, and swore. He whirled toward her, as if realizing what he was dragging her back into, but too late.

Blood had splashed across the bricks of the building, pooled on the cracked stones of the alley floor, splattered on the sides of the dumpster. And beside that dumpster, as if someone had chucked them out of a bucket, sat clumps of red pulp. A torn robe lay beside the carnage.

The droning turned into a roar. Her body pulled farther away.

Danika howling with laughter, Connor winking at her, Bronson and Zach and Zelda and Nathalie and Thorne all in hysterics—

Then nothing but red pulp. All of them, all they had been, all she had been with them, became nothing more than piles of red pulp.

Gone, gone, gone—

A hand gripped her shoulder. But not Athalar's. No, Hunt remained where he was, face now hard as stone.

She flinched as Ruhn said at her ear, "You don't need to see this."

This was another murder. Another body. Another year.

A medwitch even knelt before the body, a wand buzzing with firstlight in her hands, trying to piece the corpse—the *girl*—back together.

Ruhn tugged her away, toward the screen and open air beyond—

The movement shook her loose. Snapped the droning in her ears.

She yanked her body free from his grip, not caring if anyone else saw, not caring that he, as head of the Fae Aux units, had the right to be here. "Don't fucking touch me."

Ruhn's mouth tightened. But he looked over her shoulder to Hunt. "You're an asshole."

Hunt's eyes glittered. "I warned her on the walk over what she'd see." He added a touch ruefully, "I didn't realize what a mess it'd be." He had warned her, hadn't he? She'd drifted so far away that she'd barely listened to Hunt on the walk. As dazed as if she'd snorted a heap of lightseeker. Hunt added, "She's a grown woman. She doesn't need you deciding what she can handle." He nodded toward the alley exit. "Shouldn't you be researching? We'll call you if you're needed, princeling."

"Fuck you," Ruhn shot back, shadows twining through his hair. Others were noticing now. "You don't think it's more than a coincidence that an acolyte was killed right after we went to the temple?"

Their words didn't register. None of it registered.

Bryce turned from the alley, the swarming investigators. Ruhn said, "Bryce—"

"Leave me alone," she said quietly, and kept walking. She shouldn't have let Athalar bully her into coming, shouldn't have seen this, shouldn't have had to remember.

Once, she might have gone right to the dance studio. Would have danced and moved until the world made sense again. It had always been her haven, her way of puzzling out the world. She'd gone to the studio whenever she'd had a shit day.

It had been two years since she'd set foot in one. She'd thrown out all her dance clothes and shoes. Her bags. The one at the apartment had all been splattered with blood anyway—Danika's, Connor's, and Thorne's on the clothes in the bedroom, and Zelda's and Bronson's on her secondary bag, which had been left hanging beside the door. Blood patterns just like—

A rain-kissed scent brushed her nose as Hunt fell into step beside her. And there he was. Another memory from that night.

"Hey," Hunt said.

Hey, he'd said to her, so long ago. She'd been a wreck, a ghost, and then he'd been there, kneeling beside her, those dark eyes unreadable as he'd said, *Hey.*

She hadn't told him—that she remembered that night in the interrogation room. She sure as Hel didn't feel like telling him now.

If she had to talk to someone, she'd explode. If she had to do *anything* right now, she'd sink into one of those primal Fae wraths and—

The haze started to creep over her vision, her muscles seizing painfully, her fingertips curled as if imagining shredding into someone—

"Walk it off," Hunt murmured.

"Leave me alone, Athalar." She wouldn't look at him. Couldn't stand him or her brother or *anyone.* If the acolyte's murder *had* been because of their presence at the temple, either as a warning or because the girl might have seen something related to the Horn, if they'd accidentally brought her death about . . . Her legs kept moving, swifter and swifter. Hunt didn't falter for a beat.

She wouldn't cry. Wouldn't dissolve into a hyperventilating mess on the street corner. Wouldn't scream or puke or—

After another block, Hunt said roughly, "I was there that night."

She kept walking, her heels eating up the pavement.

Hunt asked, "How did you survive the kristallos?"

He'd no doubt been looking at the body just now and wondering this. How did she, a pathetic half-breed, survive when full-blooded Vanir hadn't?

"I didn't survive," she mumbled, crossing a street and edging around a car idling in the intersection. "It got away."

"But the kristallos pinned Micah, ripped open his chest—"

She nearly tripped over the curb, and whipped around to gape at him. "That was Micah?"

24

She had saved Micah Domitus that night.

Not some random legionary, but the gods-damned Archangel himself. No wonder the emergency responder had launched into action when he traced the phone number.

The knowledge rippled through her, warping and clearing some of the fog around her memories. "I saved the Governor in the alley."

Hunt just gave her a slow, wincing nod.

Her voice sharpened. "Why was it a secret?"

Hunt waited until a flock of tourists had passed before saying, "For his sake. If word got out that the Governor had his ass handed to him, it wouldn't have looked good."

"Especially when he was saved by a half-breed?"

"No one in our group *ever* used that term—you know that, right? But yes. We did consider how it'd look if a twenty-three-year-old human-Fae female who hadn't made the Drop had saved the Archangel when he couldn't save himself."

Her blood roared in her ears. "Why not tell *me*, though? I looked in all the hospitals, just to see if he'd made it." More than that, actually. She'd demanded answers about how the warrior was recovering, but she'd been put on hold or ignored or asked to leave.

"I know," Hunt said, scanning her face. "It was deemed wiser to keep it a secret. Especially when your phone got hacked right after—"

"So I was just going to live in ignorance forever—"

"Did you want a medal or something? A parade?"

She halted so quickly that Hunt had to splay his wings to pause, too. "*Go fuck yourself.* What I wanted . . ." She tried to stop the sharp, jagged breaths that blinded her, built and built under her skin— "What I wanted," she hissed, resuming her walk as he just stared at her, "was to know that *something* I did made a difference that night. I assumed you'd dumped him in the Istros—some legionary grunt not worth the honor of a Sailing."

Hunt shook his head. "Look, I know it was shitty. And I'm sorry, okay? I'm sorry for all of it, Quinlan. I'm sorry we didn't tell you, and I'm sorry you're on my suspect list, and I'm sorry—"

"I'm on your *what*?" she spat. Red washed over her vision as she bared her teeth. "After all of *this*," she seethed, "you think I am a *fucking suspect*?" She screamed the last words, only pure will keeping her from leaping on him and shredding his face off.

Hunt held up his hands. "That—fuck, Bryce. That didn't come out right. Look—I had to consider every angle, every possibility, but I know now . . . Solas, when I saw your face in that alley, I realized it couldn't ever have been you, and—"

"Get *the fuck* out of my sight."

He watched her, assessing, then spread his wings. She refused to back up a step, teeth still bared. The wind off his wings stirred her hair, throwing his cedar-and-rain scent into her face as he leapt into the skies.

Look toward where it hurts the most.

Fuck the Viper Queen. Fuck *everything*.

Bryce launched into a run—a steady, swift run, despite the flimsy flats she'd switched into at the gallery. A run not toward anything or from anything, but just . . . movement. The pounding of her feet on pavement, the heaving of her breath.

Bryce ran and ran, until sounds returned and the haze receded and she could escape the screaming labyrinth of her mind. It wasn't dancing, but it would do.

* * *

Bryce ran until her body screamed to stop. Ran until her phone buzzed and she wondered if Urd herself had extended a golden hand. The phone call was swift, breathless.

Minutes later, Bryce slowed to a walk as she approached the White Raven. And then stopped entirely before the alcove tucked into the wall just beside its service doors. Sweat ran down her neck, into her dress, soaking the green fabric as she again pulled out her phone.

But she didn't call Hunt. He hadn't interrupted her, but she knew he was overhead.

A few drops of rain splattered the pavement. She hoped it poured on Athalar all night.

Her fingers hesitated on the screen, and she sighed, knowing she shouldn't.

But she did. Standing there in that same alcove where she'd exchanged some of her final messages with Danika, she pulled up the thread. It burned her eyes.

She scrolled upward, past all those final, happy words and teasing. To the photo Danika had sent that afternoon of herself and the pack at the sunball game, decked out in CCU gear. In the background, Bryce could make out the players on the field—Ithan's powerful form among them.

But her gaze drifted to Danika's face. That broad smile she'd known as well as her own.

I love you, Bryce. The worn memory of that mid-May day during their senior year tugged at her, sucked her in.

The hot road bit into Bryce's knees through her torn jeans, her scraped hands trembling as she kept them interlocked behind her head, where she'd been ordered to hold them. The pain in her arm sliced like a knife. Broken. The males had made her put her hands up anyway.

The stolen motorcycle was no more than scrap metal on the dusty highway, the unmarked semitruck pulled over twenty feet away left idle. The rifle had been thrown into the olive grove beyond the mountain road, wrenched from Bryce's hands in the accident that had led them here. The accident Danika had shielded her from, wrapping her body around Bryce's. Danika had taken the shredding of the asphalt for them both.

Ten feet away, hands also behind her head, Danika bled from so many places her clothes were soaked with it. How had it come to this? How had things gone so terribly wrong?

"Where are those fucking *bullets?" the male from the truck shrieked to his cronies, his empty gun—that blessedly, unexpectedly empty gun—clenched in his hand.*

Danika's caramel eyes were wide, searching, as they remained on Bryce's face. Sorrow and pain and fear and regret—all of it was written there.

"I love you, Bryce." Tears rolled down Danika's face. "And I'm sorry."

She had never said those words before. Ever. Bryce had teased her for the past three years about it, but Danika had refused to say them.

Motion caught Bryce's attention to their left. Bullets had been found in the truck's cab. But her gaze remained on Danika. On that beautiful, fierce face.

She let go, like a key turning in a lock. The first rays of the sun over the horizon.

And Bryce whispered, as those bullets came closer to that awaiting gun and the monstrous male who wielded it, "Close your eyes, Danika."

Bryce blinked, the shimmering memory replaced by the photo still glaring from her screen. Of Danika and the Pack of Devils years later—so happy and young and alive.

Mere hours from their true end.

The skies opened, and wings rustled above, reminding her of Athalar's hovering presence. But she didn't bother to look as she strode into the club.

25

Hunt knew he'd fucked up. And he was in deep shit with Micah—*if* Micah found out that he'd revealed the truth about that night.

He doubted Quinlan had made that call—either to the sorceress or to Micah's office—and he'd make sure she didn't. Maybe he'd bribe her with a new pair of shoes or some purse or whatever the fuck might be enticing enough to keep her mouth shut. One fuckup, one misstep, and he had few illusions about how Micah would react.

He let Quinlan run through the city, trailing her from the Old Square into the dark wasteland of Asphodel Meadows, then into the CBD, and back to the Old Square again.

Hunt flew above her, listening to the symphony of honking cars, thumping bass, and the brisk April wind whispering through the palms and cypresses. Witches on brooms soared down the streets, some close enough to touch the roofs of the cars they passed. So different from the angels, Hunt included, who always kept above the buildings when flying. As if the witches wanted to be a part of the bustle the angels defined themselves by avoiding.

While he'd trailed Quinlan, Justinian had called with the information on the kristallos, which amounted to a whole lot of nothing. A few myths that matched with what they already knew. Vik had called five minutes after that: the Viper Queen's alibis checked out.

Then Isaiah had called, confirming that the victim in the alley was indeed a missing acolyte. He knew Danaan's suspicions were right: it couldn't be coincidence that they'd been at the temple yesterday, talking about the Horn and the demon that had slaughtered Danika and the Pack of Devils, and now one of its acolytes had died at the kristallos's claws.

A Fae girl. Barely more than a child. Acid burned through his stomach at the thought.

He shouldn't have brought Quinlan to the murder scene. Shouldn't have pushed her into going, so blinded by his damn need to get this investigation solved quickly that he hadn't thought twice about her hesitation.

He hadn't realized until he'd seen her look at the pulped body, until her face had gone white as death, that her quiet wasn't calm at all. It was shock. Trauma. Horror. And he'd shoved her into it.

He'd fucked up, and Ruhn had been right to call him on that, but—shit.

He'd taken one look at Quinlan's ashen face and known she hadn't been behind these murders, or even remotely involved. And he was a giant fucking asshole for even entertaining the idea. For even *telling* her she'd been on his list.

He rubbed his face. He wished Shahar were here, soaring beside him. She'd always let him talk out various strategies or issues during the five years he'd been with her 18th, always listened, and asked questions. Challenged him in a way no one else had.

By the time an hour had passed and the rain had begun, Hunt had planned a whole speech. He doubted Quinlan wanted to hear it, or would admit what she'd felt today, but he owed her an apology. He'd lost so many essential parts of himself over these centuries of enslavement and war, but he liked to think he hadn't lost his basic decency. At least not yet.

After completing those two thousand–plus kills he still had to make if he failed to solve this case, however, he couldn't imagine he'd have even that left. Whether the person he'd be at that point would deserve freedom, he didn't know. Didn't want to think about it.

But then Bryce got a phone call—got one, didn't make one,

thank fuck—and didn't break her stride to answer it. Too high up to hear, he could only watch as she'd shifted directions again and aimed—he realized ten minutes later—for Archer Street.

Just as the rain increased, she'd paused outside the White Raven and spent a few minutes on her phone. But despite his eagle-sharp eyesight, he couldn't make out what she was doing on it. So he'd watched from the adjacent roof, and must have checked his own phone a dozen times in those five minutes like a pathetic fucking loser, hoping she'd message him.

And right when the rain turned to a downpour, she put her phone away, walked past the bouncers with a little wave, and vanished into the White Raven without so much as a look upward.

Hunt landed, sending Vanir and humans skittering down the sidewalk. And the half-wolf, half-daemonaki bouncer had the nerve to actually hold out a hand. "Line's to the right," the male to his left rumbled.

"I'm with Bryce," he said.

The other bouncer said, "Tough shit. Line's on the right."

The line, despite the early hour, was already down the block. "I'm here on legion business," Hunt said, fishing for his badge, wherever the fuck he'd put it—

The door cracked open, and a stunning Fae waitress peeked out. "Riso says he's in, Crucius."

The bouncer who'd first spoken just held Hunt's stare.

Hunt smirked. "Some other time." Then he followed the female inside.

The scent of sex and booze and sweat that hit him had every instinct rising with dizzying speed as they crossed the glass-framed courtyard and ascended the steps. The half-crumbled pillars were uplit by purple lights.

He'd never set foot in the club—always made Isaiah or one of the others do it. Mostly because he knew it was no better than the palaces and country villas of the Pangeran Archangels, where feasts turned to orgies that lasted for days. All while people starved mere steps from those villas—humans and Vanir alike rooting through garbage piles for anything to fill their children's bellies. He knew his temper and triggers well enough to stay the fuck away.

Some people whispered as he walked by. He just kept his eyes on Bryce, who was already in a booth between two carved pillars, sipping at a glass of something clear—either vodka or gin. With all the scents in here, he couldn't make it out.

Her eyes lifted to him from the rim of her glass as she sipped. "How'd *you* get in?"

"It's a public place, isn't it?"

She said nothing. Hunt sighed, and was about to sit down to make that apology when he scented jasmine and vanilla, and—

"Excuse me, sir—oh. Um. Erm." He found himself looking at a lovely faun, dressed in a white tank top and skirt short enough to show off her long, striped legs and delicate hooves. Her gently arcing horns were nearly hidden in curly hair that was pulled back into a coiled bun, her brown skin dusted with gold that flickered in the club lights. Gods, she was beautiful.

Juniper Andromeda: Bryce's friend in the ballet. He'd read her file, too. The dancer glanced between Hunt and Quinlan. "I—I hope I'm not interrupting anything—"

"He was just leaving," Bryce said, draining her glass.

He finally slid into the booth. "I was just arriving." He extended a hand to the faun. "It's nice to meet you. I'm Hunt."

"I know who you are," the faun said, her voice husky.

Juniper's grip was light but solid. Bryce refilled her glass from a decanter of clear liquid and drank deep. Juniper asked her, "Did you order food? Rehearsal just let out and I'm *starving*." Though the faun was thin, she was leanly muscled, strong as Hel beneath that graceful exterior.

Bryce held up her drink. "I'm having a liquid dinner."

Juniper frowned. But she asked Hunt, "You want food?"

"Hel yes."

"You can order whatever you want—they'll get it for you." She raised a hand, signaling a waitress. "I'll have a veggie burger, no cheese, with a side of fries, vegetable oil only to cook them, and two pieces of pizza—plant-based cheese on it, please." She bit her lip, then explained to Hunt, "I don't eat animal products."

As a faun, meat and dairy were abhorrent. Milk was only for nursing babies.

"Got it," he said. "You mind if I do?" He'd fought alongside fauns over the centuries. Some hadn't been able to stand the sight of meat. Some hadn't cared. It was always worth asking.

Juniper blinked, but shook her head.

He offered the waitress a smile as he said, "I'll have . . . a bone-in rib eye and roasted green beans." What the Hel. He glanced at Bryce, who was guzzling her booze like it was a protein shake.

She hadn't eaten dinner yet, and even though he'd been distracted this morning when she'd emerged from her bedroom in nothing but a lacy hot-pink bra and matching underwear, he'd noted through the living room window that she'd also forgone breakfast, and since she hadn't brought lunch with her or ordered in, he was willing to bet she hadn't eaten that, either.

So Hunt said, "She'll have lamb kofta with rice, roasted chickpeas, and pickles on the side. Thanks." He'd watched her go for lunch a few times now, and had scented precisely what was inside her takeaway bags. Bryce opened her mouth, but the waitress was already gone. Juniper surveyed them nervously. Like she knew precisely what Bryce was about to—

"Are you going to cut my food, too?"

"What?"

"Just because you're some big, tough asshole doesn't mean you get the right to decide when I should eat—or when *I'm* not taking care of my body. I'm the one who lives in it, *I* know when I fucking want to eat. So keep your possessive and aggressive bullshit to yourself."

Juniper's swallow was audible over the music. "Long day at work, Bryce?"

Bryce reached for her drink again. But Hunt moved faster, his hand wrapping around her wrist and pinning it to the table before she could guzzle down more booze.

"Get your fucking hand off me," she snarled.

Hunt threw her a half smile. "Don't be such a cliché." Her eyes simmered. "You have a rough day and you come to drown yourself in vodka?" He snorted, letting go of her wrist and grabbing her glass. He lifted it to his lips, holding her stare over the rim as he said, "At least tell me you have good taste in—" He sniffed the liquor. Tasted it. "This is water."

Her fingers curled into fists on the table. "I don't drink."

Juniper said, "I invited Bryce tonight. It's been a while since we've seen each other, and I have to meet some of the company members here later, so—"

"Why don't you drink?" Hunt asked Bryce.

"You're the Umbra Mortis. I'm sure you can figure it out." Bryce scooted out of the booth, forcing Juniper to get up. "Though considering you thought I killed my best friend, maybe you can't." Hunt bristled, but Bryce just declared, "I'm going to the bathroom." Then she walked right into the throng on the ancient dance floor, the crowd swallowing her as she wove her way toward a distant door between two pillars at the back of the space.

Juniper's face was tight. "I'll go with her."

Then she was gone, moving swift and light, two males gaping as she passed. Juniper ignored them. She caught up to Bryce midway across the dance floor, halting her with a hand on her arm. Juniper smiled—bright as the lights around them—and began speaking, gesturing to the booth, the club. Bryce's face remained cold as stone. Colder.

Males approached, saw that expression, and didn't venture closer.

"Well, if she's pissed at you, it'll make me look better," drawled a male voice beside him.

Hunt didn't bother to look pleasant. "Tell me you've found something."

The Crown Prince of the Valbaran Fae leaned against the edge of the booth, his strikingly blue eyes lingering on his cousin. He'd no doubt used those shadows of his to creep up without Hunt's notice. "Negative. I got a call from the Raven's owner that she was here. She was in bad enough shape when she left the crime scene that I wanted to make sure she was all right."

Hunt couldn't argue with that. So he said nothing.

Ruhn nodded toward where the females stood motionless in the middle of a sea of dancers. "She used to dance, you know. If she'd been able, she would have gone into the ballet like Juniper."

He hadn't known—not really. Those facts had been blips on her file. "Why'd she drop it?"

"You'll have to ask her. But she stopped dancing completely after Danika died."

"And drinking, it seems." Hunt glanced toward her discarded glass of water.

Ruhn followed his line of sight. If he was surprised, the prince didn't let on.

Hunt took a sip of Bryce's water and shook his head. Not a party girl at all—just content to let the world believe the worst of her.

Including him. Hunt rolled his shoulders, wings moving with him, as he watched her on the dance floor. Yeah, he'd fucked up. Royally.

Bryce looked toward the booth and when she saw her cousin there . . . There were trenches of Hel warmer than the look she gave Ruhn.

Juniper tracked her gaze.

Bryce took all of one step toward the booth before the club exploded.

26

One minute, Athalar and Ruhn were talking. One minute, Bryce was about to go rip into both of them for their alphahole protectiveness, smothering her even from afar. One minute, she was just trying not to drown in the weight that had yanked her under that too-familiar black surface. No amount of running could free her from it, buy her a sip of air.

The next, her ears hollowed out, the ground ripped from beneath her, the ceiling rained down, people screamed, blood sprayed, fear scented the air, and she was twisting, lunging for Juniper—

Shrill, incessant ringing filled her head.

The world had been tipped on its side.

Or maybe that was because she lay sprawled on the wrecked floor, debris and shrapnel and *body parts* around her.

But Bryce kept down, stayed arched over Juniper, who might have been screaming—

That shrill ringing wouldn't stop. It drowned out every other sound. Coppery slickness in her mouth—blood. Plaster coated her skin.

"Get up." Hunt's voice cut through the ringing, the screaming,

the shrieking, and his strong hands wrapped around her shoulders. She thrashed against him, reaching for Juniper—

But Ruhn was already there, blood running from his temple as he helped her friend stand—

Bryce looked over every inch of Juniper: plaster and dust and someone else's green blood, but not a scratch, not a scratch, not a scratch—

Bryce swayed back into Hunt, who gripped her shoulders. "We need to get out—*now*," the angel was saying to Ruhn, ordering her brother like a foot soldier. "There could be more."

Juniper pushed out of Ruhn's grip and screamed at Bryce, "*Are you out of your mind?*"

Her ears—her ears wouldn't stop ringing, and maybe her brain was leaking because she couldn't talk, couldn't seem to remember how to use her limbs—

Juniper swung. Bryce didn't feel the impact on her cheek. Juniper sobbed as if her body would break apart. "*I made the Drop, Bryce! Two years ago! You haven't! Have you completely lost it?*"

A warm, strong arm slid across her abdomen, holding her upright. Hunt said, his mouth near her ear, "Juniper, she's shell-shocked. Give it a rest."

Juniper snapped at him, "*Stay out of this!*" But people were wailing, screaming, and debris was still raining down. Pillars lay like fallen trees around them. June seemed to notice, to realize—

Her body, gods, her body wouldn't work—

Hunt didn't object when Ruhn gave them an address nearby and told them to go wait for him there. It was closer than her apartment, but frankly, Hunt wasn't entirely sure Bryce would let him in—and if she went into shock and he couldn't get past those enchantments . . . Well, Micah would spike his head to the front gates of the Comitium if she died on his watch.

He might very well do that just for not sensing that the attack was about to happen.

Quinlan didn't seem to notice he was carrying her. She was heavier than she looked—her tan skin covered more muscle than he'd thought.

Hunt found the familiar white-columned house a few blocks away; the key Ruhn had given him opened a green-painted door. The cavernous foyer was laced with two male scents other than the prince's. A flick of the light switch revealed a grand staircase that looked like it'd been through a war zone, scuffed oak floors, and a crystal chandelier hanging precariously.

Beneath it: a beer pong table painted with remarkable skill—portraying a gigantic Fae male swallowing an angel whole.

Ignoring that particular *fuck you* to his kind, Hunt aimed for the living room to the left of the entry. A stained sectional lay against the far wall of the long room, and Hunt set Bryce down there as he hurried for the equally worn wet bar midway down the far wall. Water—she needed some water.

There hadn't been an attack in the city for years now—since Briggs. He'd felt the bomb's power as it rippled through the club, shredding the former temple and its inhabitants apart. He'd leave it to the investigators to see what exactly it was, but—

Even his lightning hadn't been fast enough to stop it, not that it would have been any protection against a bomb, not in an ambush like that. He'd destroyed enough on battlefields to know how to intercept them with his power, how to match death with death, but this hadn't been some long-range missile fired from a tank.

It had been planted somewhere in the club, and detonated at a predetermined moment. There were a handful of people who might be capable of such a thing, and at the top of Hunt's list . . . there was Philip Briggs again. Or his followers, at least—Briggs himself was still imprisoned at the Adrestia Prison. He'd think on it later, when his head wasn't still spinning, and his lightning wasn't still a crackle in his blood, hungry for an enemy to obliterate.

Hunt turned his attention to the woman who sat on the couch, staring at nothing.

Bryce's green dress was wrecked, her skin was covered in plaster and someone else's blood, her face pale—save for the red mark on her cheek.

Hunt grabbed an ice pack from the freezer under the bar counter and a dish towel to wrap it in. He set the glass of water on the stained wood coffee table, then handed her the ice. "She slugged you pretty damn good."

Those amber eyes lifted slowly to him. Dried blood crusted inside her ears.

A moment's searching in the sorry-looking kitchen and bathroom cabinet revealed more towels and a first aid kit.

He knelt on the worn gray carpet before her, tucking his wings in tight to keep them from tangling with the beer cans that littered the coffee table.

She kept staring at nothing as he cleaned out her bloody ears.

He didn't have med-magic like a witch, but he knew enough battlefield healing to assess her arched ears. The Fae hearing would have made that explosion horrific—the human bloodline then slowing down the healing process. Mercifully, he found no signs of continued bleeding or damage.

He started on the left ear. And when he'd finished, he noticed her knees were scraped raw, with shards of stone embedded in them.

"Juniper stands a shot of being promoted to principal," Bryce rasped at last. "The first faun ever. The summer season starts soon—she's an understudy for the main roles in two of the ballets. A soloist in all five of them. This season is crucial. If she got injured, it could interfere."

"She made the Drop. She would have bounced back quickly." He pulled a pair of tweezers from the kit.

"Still."

She hissed as he carefully pried out some shards of metal and stone from her knee. She'd hit the ground hard. Even with the club exploding, he'd seen her move.

She'd thrown herself right over Juniper, shielding her from the blast.

"This will sting," he told her, frowning at the bottle of healing solution. Fancy, high-priced stuff. Surprising that it was even here, given that the prince and his roommates had all made the Drop. "But it'll keep it from scarring."

She shrugged, studying the massive, dark television screen over his shoulder.

Hunt doused her leg with the solution, and she jerked. He gripped her calf hard enough to keep her down, even as she cursed. "I warned you."

She pushed a breath out between clenched teeth. The hem of her already short dress had ridden up with her movements, and Hunt told himself he looked only to assess if there were other injuries, but—

The thick, angry scar cut across an otherwise sleek, unnervingly perfect thigh.

Hunt stilled. She'd never gotten it healed.

And every limp he'd sometimes caught her making from the corner of his eye . . . Not from her dumb fucking shoes. But from this. From *him*. From his clumsy battlefield instincts to staple her up like a soldier.

"When males are kneeling between my legs, Athalar," she said, "they're not usually grimacing."

"What?" But her words registered, just at the moment he realized his hand still gripped her calf, the silky skin beneath brushing against the calluses on his palms. Just as he realized that he was indeed kneeling between her thighs, and had leaned closer to her lap to see that scar.

Hunt reeled back, unable to help the heat rising to his face. He removed his hand from her leg. "Sorry," he ground out.

Any amusement faded from her eyes as she said, "Who do you think did it—the club?"

The heat of her soft skin still stained his palm. "No idea."

"Could it have anything to do with us looking into this case?" Guilt already dampened her eyes, and he knew the body of the acolyte flashed through her mind.

He shook his head. "Probably not. If someone wanted to stop us, a bullet in the head's a lot more precise than blowing up a club.

It could easily have been some rival of the club's owner. Or the remaining Keres members looking to start more shit in this city."

Bryce asked, "You think we'll have war here?"

"Some humans want us to. Some Vanir want us to. To get rid of the humans, they say."

"They've destroyed parts of Pangera with the war there," she mumbled. "I've seen the footage." She looked at him, letting her unspoken question hang. *How bad was it?*

Hunt just said, "Magic and machines. Never a good mix."

The words rippled between them. "I want to go home," she breathed. He peeled off his jacket and settled it around her shoulders. It nearly devoured her. "I want to shower all this off." She gestured at the blood on her bare skin.

"Okay." But the front door in the foyer opened. One set of booted feet.

Hunt had his gun out, hidden against his thigh as he turned, when Ruhn walked in, shadows in his wake. "You're not going to like this," the prince said.

She wanted to go home. Wanted to call Juniper. Wanted to call her mom and Randall just to hear their voices. Wanted to call Fury and learn what she knew, even if Fury wouldn't pick up or answer her messages. Wanted to call Jesiba and *make her* find out what had happened. But she mostly just wanted to *go home and shower.*

Ruhn, stone-faced and blood-splattered, halted in the archway.

Hunt slid the handgun back into its holster at his thigh before sitting on the couch beside her.

Ruhn went to the wet bar and filled a glass of water from the sink. Every movement was stiff, shadows whispering around him. But the prince exhaled and the shadows, the tension, vanished.

Hunt spared her from demanding that Ruhn elaborate. "I'm assuming this has to do with whoever bombed the club?"

Ruhn nodded and tossed back a gulp of water. "All signs point to the human rebels." Bryce's blood chilled. She and Hunt swapped glances. Their discussion moments ago hadn't been far from the mark. "The bomb was smuggled into the club through some new exploding liquid hidden in a delivery of wine. They left the calling card on the crate—their own logo."

Hunt cut in. "Any potential connection to Philip Briggs?"

Ruhn said, "Briggs is still behind bars." A polite way of describing the punishment the rebel leader now endured at Vanir hands in Adrestia Prison.

"The rest of his Keres group isn't," Bryce croaked. "Danika was the one who made the raid on Briggs in the first place. Even if he didn't kill her, he's still doing time for his rebel crimes. He could have instructed his followers to carry out this bombing."

Ruhn frowned. "I thought they'd disbanded—joined other factions or returned to Pangera. But here's the part you're not going to like. Next to the logo on the crate was a branded image. My team and your team thought it was a warped *C* for Crescent City, but I looked at the footage of the storage area before the bomb went off. It's hard to make out, but it could also be depicting a curved horn."

"What does the Horn have to do with the human rebellion?" Bryce asked. Then her mouth dried out. "Wait. Do you think that Horn image was a message to *us*? To warn us away from looking for the Horn? As if that acolyte wasn't enough?"

Hunt mused, "It can't just be coincidence that the club was bombed when we were there. Or that one of the images on the crate seems like it could be the Horn, when we're knee-deep in a search for it. Before Danika busted him, Briggs planned to blow up the Raven. The Keres sect has been inactive since he went to prison, but . . ."

"They could be coming back," Bryce insisted. "Looking to pick up where Briggs left off, or somehow getting directions from him even now."

Hunt looked somber. "Or it was one of Briggs's followers all along—the planned bombing, Danika's murder, *this* bombing . . . Briggs might not be guilty, but maybe he knows who is. He could be protecting someone." He pulled out his phone. "We need to talk to him."

Ruhn said, "Are you fucking nuts?"

Hunt ignored him and dialed a number, rising to his feet. "He's in Adrestia Prison, so the request might take a few days," he said to Bryce.

"Fine." She blocked out the thought of what, exactly, this meeting would be like. Danika had been unnerved by Briggs's fanaticism toward the human cause, and had rarely wanted to talk about him. Busting him and his Keres group—an offshoot of the main Ophion rebellion—had been a triumph, a legitimization of the Pack of Devils. It still hadn't been enough to win Sabine's approval.

Hunt tucked the phone to his ear. "Hey, Isaiah. Yeah, I'm all right." He stepped into the foyer, and Bryce watched him go.

Ruhn said quietly, "The Autumn King knows I've involved you in looking for the Horn."

She lifted heavy eyes to her brother. "How pissed is he?"

Ruhn's grim smile wasn't comforting. "He warned me of the *poison* you'd spew in my ear."

"I should take that as a compliment, I suppose."

Ruhn didn't smile this time. "He wants to know what you'll do with the Horn if it's found."

"Use it as my new drinking mug on game day."

Hunt gave a snort of laughter as he entered the room, call over. Ruhn just said, "He was serious."

"I'll give it back to the temple," Bryce said. "Not to him."

Ruhn looked at both of them as Hunt again sat on the couch. "My father said that since I have now involved you in something so dangerous, Bryce, you need a guard to . . . remain with you at all times. Live with you. I volunteered."

Every part of her battered body ached. "Over my dead fucking corpse."

Hunt crossed his arms. "Why does your king care if Quinlan lives or dies?"

Ruhn's eyes grew cold. "I asked him the same. He said that she falls under his jurisdiction, as half-Fae, and he doesn't want to have to clean up any messy situations. *The girl is a liability*, he said." Bryce could hear the cruel tones in every word Ruhn mimicked. Could see her father's face as he spoke them. She often imagined how it'd feel to beat in that perfect face with her fists. To give him a scar like the one her mother bore along her cheekbone—small and slender, no longer than a fingernail, but a reminder of the blow he'd given her when his hideous rage drove him too far.

The blow that had sent Ember Quinlan running—pregnant with Bryce.

Creep. Old, hateful creep.

"So he's just concerned about the PR nightmare of Quinlan's death before the Summit," Hunt said roughly, disgust tightening his face.

"Don't look so shocked," Ruhn said, then added to Bryce, "I'm only the messenger. Consider whether it's wise to pick this as your big battle with him."

No chance in Hel was she letting *Ruhn* into her apartment to order her around. Especially with those friends of his. It was bad enough she had to work with him on this case.

Gods, her head was pounding. "Fine," she said, simmering. "He said I needed a guard—not you specifically, right?" At Ruhn's tense silence, Bryce went on, "That's what I thought. Athalar stays with me instead. Order fulfilled. Happy?"

"He won't like that."

Bryce smiled smugly, even as her blood simmered. "He didn't say who the guard had to be. The bastard should have been more precise with his wording."

Even Ruhn couldn't argue against that.

If Athalar was shocked at Bryce's choice of roommates, he didn't let on.

Ruhn watched the angel glance between them—carefully.

Fuck. Had Athalar finally started putting it together—that they were more entwined than cousins should be, that Ruhn's father *shouldn't* be taking such an interest in her?

Bryce seethed at Ruhn, "Did you put your father up to this?"

"No," Ruhn said. His father had cornered him about the temple visit right as he left the ruined club. Honestly, given how pissed the male had been, it was a miracle Ruhn wasn't dead in a gutter. "He's got a network of spies that even I don't know about."

Bryce scowled, but it morphed into a wince as she got off the couch, Athalar keeping a hand within easy reach of her elbow, should she need it.

Ruhn's phone buzzed, and he pulled it from his pocket long enough to read the message on the screen. And the others that began flying in.

Declan had written in the group chain with Flynn, *What the fuck happened?*

Flynn replied, *I'm at the club. Sabine sent Amelie Ravenscroft to head the Aux packs hauling away debris and helping the wounded. Amelie said she saw you leave, Ruhn. You all right?*

Ruhn answered, just so they wouldn't call. *I'm fine. I'll meet you at the club soon.* He squeezed the phone in his fist as Bryce made her way toward the front door and the Helscape beyond. Blue and red sirens blared, casting their light on the oak floors of the foyer.

But his sister paused before reaching for the handle, twisting to ask him, "Why were you at the Raven earlier?"

And here it was. If he mentioned the call Riso had made to him, that Ruhn had been keeping tabs on her, he'd get his head bitten off. So Ruhn half lied, "I want to check out your boss's library."

Hunt paused, a step behind Bryce. It was impressive, really, to watch both of them plaster confused expressions on their faces.

"What library?" she asked, the portrait of innocence.

Ruhn could have sworn Athalar was trying not to smile. But he said tightly, "The one everyone says is beneath the gallery."

"First I've heard of it," Hunt said with a shrug.

"Fuck off, Athalar." Ruhn's jaw ached from clenching it so hard.

Bryce said, "Look, I get that you want in on our little cool kids' club, but there's a strict membership-vetting process."

Yeah, Athalar was trying really hard not to smile.

Ruhn growled, "I want to look at the books there. See if anything about the Horn jumps out." She paused at the tone in his voice, the bit of dominance Ruhn threw into it. He wasn't above pulling rank. Not where this was concerned.

Though Athalar was glaring daggers at him, Ruhn said to his sister, "I've been through the Fae Archives twice, and . . ." He shook his head. "I just kept thinking about the gallery. So maybe there's something there."

"I searched it," she said. "There's nothing about the Horn beyond vague mentions."

Ruhn gave her a half smile. "So you admit there's a library."

Bryce frowned at him. He knew that contemplative look. "What."

Bryce flipped her hair over a dirty, torn shoulder. "I'll make a bargain with you: you can come hunt for the Horn at the gallery, and I'll help in whatever way I can. If—" Athalar whipped his head to her, the outrage on his face almost delightful. Bryce went on, nodding to the phone in Ruhn's hand, "*If* you put Declan at my disposal."

"I'll have to tell him about this case, then. And what he knows, Flynn will learn two seconds later."

"Fine. Go ahead and fill them in. But tell Dec I need intel about Danika's last movements."

"I don't know where he can get that," Ruhn admitted.

"The Den would have it," Hunt said, eyeing Bryce with something like admiration. "Tell Emmet to hack the Den archives."

So Ruhn nodded. "Fine. I'll ask him later."

Bryce gave him that smile that didn't meet her eyes. "Then come by the gallery tomorrow."

Ruhn had to give himself a moment to master his shock at how easy it had been to get access. Then he said, "Be careful out there."

If she and Athalar were right and it *was* some Keres rebels acting on Briggs's request or in his honor . . . the political mess would be a nightmare. And if he hadn't been wrong about that *C* actually being an image of the Horn, if this bombing and the acolyte's murder were targeted warnings to them regarding their search for it . . . then the threat to all of them had just become a Hel of a lot deadlier.

Bryce said sweetly before continuing on, "Tell your daddy we say hello—and that he can go fuck himself."

Ruhn gritted his teeth again, earning another grin from Athalar. Winged asshole.

The two of them strode through the door, and Ruhn's phone rang a heartbeat after that.

"Yeah," he said.

Ruhn could have sworn he could hear his father tense before the male drawled, "Is that how you speak to your king?"

Ruhn didn't bother replying. His father said, "Since you couldn't stop yourself from revealing my business, I wish to make one thing clear regarding the Horn." Ruhn braced himself. "I don't want the angels getting it."

"Fine." If Ruhn had anything to say about it, *no one* would get the Horn. It would go straight back to the temple, with a permanent Fae guard.

"Keep an eye on that girl."

"Both eyes."

"I mean it, boy."

"So do I." He let his father hear the growl of sincerity in his voice.

His father went on, "You, as Crown Prince, revealed the secrets of your king to the girl and Athalar. I have every right to punish you for this, you know."

Go ahead, he wanted to say. *Go ahead and do it. Do me a favor and take my title while you're at it. The royal bloodline ends with me anyway.*

Ruhn had puked after hearing it the first time when he was thirteen, sent to the Oracle for a glimpse of his future, like all Fae. The ritual had once been to foretell marriages and alliances. Today, it was more to get a feel for a child's career and whether they'd amount to anything. For Ruhn—and for Bryce, years later—it had been a disaster.

Ruhn had begged the Oracle to tell him whether she meant he'd die before he could sire a child, or if she meant he was infertile. She only repeated her words. *The royal bloodline shall end with you, Prince.*

He'd been too much of a coward to tell his king what he'd learned. So he'd fed his father a lie, unable to bear the male's disappointment and rage. *The Oracle said I would be a fair and just king.*

His father had been disappointed, but only that the fake prophecy hadn't been mightier.

So, yeah. If his father wanted to strip him of his title, he'd be doing him a favor. Or even unwittingly fulfilling that prophecy at last.

Ruhn had truly worried about its meaning once—the day he'd learned he had a little sister. He'd thought it might foretell an untimely death for her. But his fears had been assuaged by the fact that she was not and would never be formally recognized as part of the royal bloodline. To his relief, she'd never questioned why, in those early years when they were still close, Ruhn hadn't lobbied their father to publicly accept her.

The Autumn King continued, "Unfortunately, the punishment you deserve would render you unable to look for the Horn."

Ruhn's shadows drifted around him. "I'll take a rain check, then."

His father snarled, but Ruhn hung up.

27

The streets were packed with Vanir streaming from the still-chaotic White Raven, all looking for answers about what the Hel had happened. Various legionaries, Fae, and Aux pack members had erected a barricade around the site, a thrumming, opaque magic wall, but the crowds still converged.

Hunt glanced to where Bryce walked beside him, silent, glassy-eyed. Barefoot, he realized.

How long had she been barefoot? She must have lost her shoes in the explosion.

He debated offering to carry her again, or suggesting that he fly them to her apartment, but she held her arms so tightly around herself that he had a feeling one word would send her into a rage-spiral with no bottom.

The look she gave Ruhn before walking out . . . It made Hunt glad she wasn't an acid-spitting viper. The male's face would have *melted*.

Gods help them when the prince arrived at the gallery tomorrow.

Bryce's doorman leapt out of his seat as they walked into the pristine lobby, asking if she was all right, if she'd been in the club. She mumbled that she was fine, and the ursine shifter surveyed Hunt with a predator's focus. Noticing that look, she waved a hand at him, punching the elevator button, and introduced them. *Hunt, this is Marrin; Marrin, this is Hunt; he's staying with me for the foreseeable future, unfortunately.* Then she was padding into the elevator, where she had to lean against the chrome rail along the back, as if she were about to collapse—

Hunt squeezed in as the doors were closing. The box was too small, too tight with his wings, and he kept them close as they shot up to the penthouse—

Bryce's head sagged, her shoulders curving inward—

Hunt blurted, "Why won't you make the Drop?"

The elevator doors opened and she slumped against them before she entered the elegant cream-and-cobalt hallway. But she halted at her apartment door. Then turned to him.

"My keys were in my purse."

Her purse was now in the ruin of the club.

"Does the doorman have a spare?"

She grunted her confirmation, eyeing the elevator as if it were a mountain to climb.

Marrin busted Hunt's balls for a good minute, checking that Bryce was alive in the hallway, asking into the hall vidcom if she approved—to which he got a thumbs-up.

When Hunt returned, he found her sitting against her door, legs up and spread enough to show a pair of hot-pink underwear. Thankfully, the hall cameras couldn't see at that angle, but he had no doubt the shifter monitored them as Hunt helped her to her feet and handed her the spare keys.

She slowly slid in the key, then put her palm to the bespelled finger pad beside the door.

"I was waiting," she murmured as the locks clicked open and the dim apartment lights flickered on. "We were supposed to make the Drop together. We picked two years from now."

He knew who she meant. The reason why she no longer drank, or danced, or really seemed to live her life. The reason why she must keep that scar on her pretty, sleek thigh. Ogenas and all her sacred Mysteries knew that Hunt had punished himself for a damn long while after the colossal failure that had been the Battle of Mount Hermon. Even while he'd been tortured in the Asteri's dungeons, he'd punished himself, flaying his own soul in a way no imperial interrogator ever could.

So maybe it was a stupid question, but he asked as they entered the apartment, "Why bother waiting now?"

Hunt stepped inside and got a good look at the place Quinlan called home. The open-concept apartment had looked nice from outside the windows, but inside . . .

Either she or Danika had decorated it without sparing any expense: a white deep-cushioned couch lay in the right third of the great room, set before a reclaimed wood coffee table and the massive television atop a carved oak console. A fogged-glass dining table with white leather chairs took up the left third of the space, and the center third of it went to the kitchen—white cabinets, chrome appliances, and white marble counters. All of it impeccably clean, soft, and welcoming.

Hunt took it in, standing like a piece of baggage by the kitchen island while Bryce padded down a pale oak hallway to release Syrinx from where he yowled from his crate.

She was halfway down the hallway when she said without looking back, "Without Danika . . . We were supposed to make the Drop together," she said again. "Connor and Thorne were going to Anchor us."

The choice of Anchor during the Drop was pivotal—and a deeply personal choice. But Hunt shoved aside the thoughts of the sour-faced government employee he'd been appointed, since he sure as fuck hadn't had any family or friends left to Anchor him. Not when his mother had died only days before.

Syrinx flung himself through the apartment, claws clicking on the light wood floors, yipping as he leapt upon Hunt, licking his hands. Each one of Bryce's returning steps dragged on her way to the kitchen counter.

The silence pressed on him enough that he asked, "Were you and Danika lovers?"

He'd been told two years ago that they weren't, but friends didn't mourn each other the way Bryce seemed to have so thoroughly shut down every part of herself. The way he had for Shahar.

The patter of kibble hitting tin filled the apartment before Bryce plunked down the bowl, and Syrinx, abandoning Hunt, half threw himself inside it as he gobbled it down.

Hunt turned in place as Bryce padded around the other end of the kitchen island, flinging open the enormous metal fridge to examine its meager contents. "No," she said, her voice flat and cold. "Danika and I weren't like that." Her grip on the fridge's handle tightened, her knuckles going white. "Connor and I—Connor Holstrom, I mean. He and I . . ." She trailed off. "It was complicated. When Danika died, when they all died . . . a light went out in me."

He remembered the details about her and the elder of the Holstrom brothers. Ithan hadn't been there that night, either—and was now Second in Amelie Ravenscroft's pack. A sorry replacement for what the Pack of Devils had once been. This city had also lost something that night.

Hunt opened his mouth to tell Quinlan he understood. Not just the complicated relationship thing, but the loss. To wake up one morning surrounded by friends and his lover—and then to end the day with all of them dead. He understood how it gnawed on bones and blood and the very soul of a person. How nothing could ever make it right.

How cutting out the alcohol and the drugs, how refusing to do the thing she loved most—the dancing—still couldn't make it right. But the words stalled in his throat. He hadn't felt like talking about it two hundred years ago, and sure as Hel didn't feel like talking about it now.

A landline phone somewhere in the house began ringing, and a pleasant female voice trilled, *Call from . . . Home.*

Bryce closed her eyes, as if rallying herself, then padded down the darkened hallway that led to her bedroom. A moment later, she said with a cheerfulness that should have earned her an award for Best Fucking Actor in Midgard, "Hey, Mom." A mattress groaned. "No, I wasn't there. My phone fell in the toilet at work—yep, totally dead. I'll get a new one tomorrow. Yeah, I'm fine. June wasn't there, either. We're all good." A pause. "I know—it was just a long day at work." Another pause. "Look, I've got company." A rough laugh.

"Not that kind. Don't get your hopes up. I'm serious. Yes, I let him into my house willingly. Please don't call the front desk. His name? I'm not telling you." Just the slightest hesitation. "*Mom.* I will call you tomorrow. I'm not telling him hello. Bye—*bye*, Mom. Love you."

Syrinx had finished his food and was staring expectantly at Hunt—silently pleading for more, that lion's tail waggling. "*No,*" he hissed at the beast just as Bryce walked back into the main room.

"Oh," she said, as if she'd forgotten he was there. "I'm going to take a shower. Guest room is yours. Use whatever you need."

"I'll swing by the Comitium tomorrow to get more clothes." Bryce just nodded like her head weighed a thousand pounds. "Why'd you lie?" He'd let her decide which one she wanted to explain.

She paused, Syrinx trotting ahead down the hall to her bedroom. "My mom would only worry and come visit. I don't want her around if things are getting bad. And I didn't tell her who you were because that would lead to questions, too. It's easier this way."

Easier to not let herself enjoy life, easier to keep everyone at arm's length.

The mark on her cheek from Juniper's slap had barely faded. Easier to throw herself on top of a friend as a bomb exploded, rather than risk losing them.

She said quietly, "I need to find who did this, Hunt."

He met her raw, aching stare. "I know."

"No," she said hoarsely. "You don't. I don't care what Micah's motives are—if I don't find this fucking person, it is going to *eat me alive*." Not the murderer or the demon, but the pain and grief that he was only starting to realize dwelled inside her. "I need to find who did this."

"We will," he promised.

"How can you know that?" She shook her head.

"Because we don't have another choice. *I* don't have another choice." At her confused look, Hunt blew out a breath and said, "Micah offered me a deal."

Her eyes turned wary. "What sort of deal?"

Hunt clenched his jaw. She'd offered up a piece of herself, so he could do the same. Especially if they were now gods-damned roommates. "When I first came here, Micah offered me a bargain: if I could make up for every life the 18th took that day on Mount Hermon, I'd get my freedom back. All two thousand two hundred and seventeen lives." He steeled himself, willing her to hear what he couldn't quite say.

She chewed on her lip. "I'm assuming that *make up* means . . ."

"Yes," he ground out. "It means doing what I'm good at. A death for a death."

"Micah has more than two thousand people for you to assassinate?"

Hunt let out a harsh laugh. "Micah is a Governor of an entire territory, and he will live for at least another two hundred years. He'll probably have double that number of people on his shit list before he's done." Horror crept into her eyes, and he scrambled for a way to get rid of it, unsure why. "It comes with the job. His job, and mine." He ran a hand through his hair. "Look, it's awful, but he offered me a way out, at least. And when the killings started again, he offered me a different bargain: find the murderer before the Summit meeting, and he'd reduce the debts I owe to ten."

He waited for her judgment, her disgust with him and Micah. But she angled her head. "That's why you've been a bullish pain in the ass."

"Yes," he said tightly. "Micah ordered me not to say anything, though. So if you breathe one word about it—"

"His offer will be rescinded."

Hunt nodded, scanning her battered face. She said nothing more. After a heartbeat, he demanded, "Well?"

"Well, what?" She again began walking toward her bedroom.

"Well, aren't you going to say that I'm a self-serving piece of shit?"

She paused again, a faint ray of light entering her eyes. "Why bother, Athalar, when you just said it for me?"

He couldn't help it then. Even though she was bloodied and covered in debris, he looked her over. Every inch and curve. Tried not to think about the hot-pink underwear beneath that tight green dress. But he said, "I'm sorry I thought you were a suspect. And more than that, I'm sorry I judged you. I thought you were just a party girl, and I acted like an asshole."

"There's nothing wrong with being a party girl. I don't get why the world thinks there is." But she considered his words. "It's easier for me—when people assume the worst about what I am. It lets me see who they really are."

"So you're saying you think I'm really an asshole?" A corner of his mouth curled up.

But her eyes were dead serious. "I've met and dealt with a lot of assholes, Hunt. You're not one of them."

"You weren't singing that tune earlier."

She just aimed for her room once more. So Hunt asked, "Want me to get food?"

Again, she paused. She looked like she was about to say no, but then rasped, "Cheeseburger—with cheese fries. And a chocolate milkshake."

Hunt smiled. "You got it."

The elegant guest room on the other side of the kitchen was spacious, decorated in shades of gray and cream accented with pale rose and cornflower blue. The bed was big enough for Hunt's wings, thankfully—definitely bought with Vanir in mind—and a few photos in expensive-looking frames were propped next to a lopsided, chipped ceramic blue bowl, all adorning a chest of drawers to the right of the door.

He'd gotten them both burgers and fries, and Bryce had torn into hers with a ferocity that Hunt had seen only among lions gathered around a fresh kill. He'd tossed the whining Syrinx a few fries under the white glass table, since she sure as shit wasn't sharing anything.

Exhaustion had set in so thoroughly that neither of them spoke, and once she'd finished slurping down the milkshake, she'd merely gathered up the trash, dumped it into the bin, and headed to her room. Leaving Hunt to enter his.

A mortal scent lingered that he assumed was courtesy of her parents, and as Hunt opened the drawers, he found some of them full of clothes—light sweaters, socks, pants, athletic-looking gear . . . He was snooping. Granted, it was part of the job description, but it was still snooping.

He shut the drawers and studied the framed photos.

Ember Quinlan had been a knockout. No wonder that Fae asshole had pursued her to the point where she'd bailed. Long black hair framed a face that could have been on a billboard: freckled skin, full lips, and high cheekbones that made the dark, depthless eyes above them striking.

It was Bryce's face—the coloring was just different. An equally attractive brown-skinned, dark-haired human male stood beside her, arm slung around her slim shoulders, grinning like a fiend at whoever was behind the camera. Hunt could just barely make out the writing on the silver dog tags dipping over the man's gray button-up.

Well, holy shit.

Randall Silago was Bryce's adoptive father? The legendary war hero and sharpshooter? He had no idea how he'd missed that fact in her file, though he supposed he had been skimming when he'd read it years ago.

No wonder his daughter was so fearless. And there, to the right of Ember, stood Bryce.

She was barely past three, that red hair pulled high into two floppy pigtails. Ember was looking at her daughter—the expression a bit exasperated—as if Bryce was *supposed* to be in the nice clothes that the two adults were wearing. But there she was, giving her mother an equally sassy look, hands on her chubby hips, legs set apart in an unmistakable fighting stance. Covered head to toe in mud.

Hunt snickered and turned to the other photo on the dresser.

It was a beautiful shot of two women—girls, really—sitting on some red rocks atop a desert mountain, their backs to the camera, shoulder-to-shoulder as they faced the scrub and sand far below. One was Bryce—he could tell from her sheet of red hair. The other was in a familiar leather jacket, the back painted with those words in the Republic's most ancient language. *Through love, all is possible.*

It had to be Bryce and Danika. And—that was Danika's jacket that Bryce now wore.

She had no other photos of Danika in the apartment.

Through love, all is possible. It was an ancient saying, dating back to some god he couldn't remember. Cthona, probably—what with all the mother-goddess stuff she presided over. Hunt had long since stopped visiting temples, or paying much attention to the overzealous priestesses who popped up on the morning talk shows every now and then. None of the five gods had ever helped him—or anyone he cared about. Urd, especially, had fucked him over often enough.

Danika's blond ponytail draped down Bryce's back as she leaned her head against her friend's shoulder. Bryce wore a loose white T-shirt, showing a bandaged arm braced on her knee. Bruises peppered her body. And gods—that was a sword lying to Danika's left. Sheathed and clean, but—he knew that sword.

Sabine had gone ballistic searching for it when it was discovered to be missing from the apartment where her daughter had been murdered. Apparently it was some wolf heirloom. But there it lay, beside Bryce and Danika in the desert.

Sitting there on those rocks, perched over the world, they seemed like two soldiers who had just walked through the darkest halls of Hel and were taking a well-earned break.

Hunt turned from the picture and rubbed at the tattoo on his brow. A flick of his power had the heavy gray curtains sliding shut over the floor-to-ceiling windows on a chill wind. He peeled off his clothes one by one, and found the bathroom was just as spacious as the bedroom.

Hunt showered quickly and fell into bed with his skin still drying. The last thing he saw before sleep overtook him was the photo of Bryce and Danika, frozen forever in a moment of peace.

28

Hunt woke the moment he scented a male in his room, his fingers wrapping around the knife under his pillow. He opened an eye, grip tightening on the hilt, remembering every window and doorway, every possible would-be weapon that he could wield to his advantage—

He found Syrinx sitting on the pillow beside his, the chimera's smooshed-up face peering into his own.

Hunt groaned, a breath exploding out of him. Syrinx just swatted at his face.

Hunt rolled out of reach. "Good morning to you, too," he mumbled, scanning the room. He'd *definitely* shut the door last night. It now gaped wide open. He glanced at the clock.

Seven. He hadn't noticed Bryce get up for work—hadn't heard her buzzing about the apartment or the music he knew she liked to play.

Granted, he hadn't heard his own door open, either. He'd slept like the dead. Syrinx rested his head on Hunt's shoulder, and huffed a mournful sigh.

Solas spare him. "Why do I get the feeling that if I give you breakfast, it'll actually be your second or third meal of the day?"

An innocent blink of those round eyes.

Unable to help himself, Hunt scratched the little beast behind his silly ears.

The sunny apartment beyond his room was silent, the light warming the pale wood floors. He eased from the bed, hauling on his pants. His shirt was a wreck from last night's events, so he left it on the floor, and— Shit. His phone. He grabbed it from the bedside table and flicked through the messages. Nothing new, no *missions* from Micah, thank the gods.

He left the phone on the dresser beside the door and padded into the great room.

No sign or sound. If Quinlan had just *left*—

He stormed across the space, to the hall on the other side. Her bedroom door was cracked, as if Syrinx had seen himself out, and—

Sound asleep. The heap of blankets had been twisted and tossed around, and Quinlan lay belly-down on the bed, wrapped around a pillow. The position was almost identical to the one she'd been in last night in the club, flung over Juniper.

Hunt was pretty sure most people would consider the low-backed gray nightgown, edged with pale pink lace, to be a shirt. Syrinx trotted past, leaping on the bed and nosing her bare shoulder.

The tattoo down her back—scrolling, beautiful lines in some alphabet he didn't recognize—rose and fell with each deep breath. Bruises he hadn't noted last night peppered her golden skin, already greenish thanks to the Fae blood in her.

And he was staring at her. Like a fucking creep.

Hunt twisted for the hall, his wings suddenly too big, his skin too tight, when the front door swung open. A smooth movement had his knife angled behind him—

Juniper breezed in, a brown bag of what smelled like chocolate pastries in one hand, a spare set of keys in another. She stopped dead as she spied him in the bedroom hallway.

Her mouth popped open in a silent *Oh*.

She looked him over—not in the way some females did until they noted the tattoos, but in the way that told him she realized a half-naked *male* stood in Bryce's apartment at seven in the morning.

He opened his mouth to say it wasn't how it looked, but Juniper just strutted past, her delicate hooves clipping on the wood floors. She shoved into the bedroom, jostling the bag, and Syrinx went wild, curly tail wagging as Juniper trilled, "I brought chocolate croissants, so get that bare ass out of bed and into some pants."

Bryce lifted her head to see Juniper, then Hunt in the hall. She didn't bother to tug the hem of her nightgown over her teal lace underwear as she squinted. "What?"

Juniper strode to the bed and looked like she was about to plop onto it, but glanced at him.

Hunt stiffened. "It's not what it seems."

Juniper gave him a sweet smile. "Then some privacy would be nice."

He backed down the hall, into the kitchen. Coffee. That sounded like a good plan.

He opened a cabinet, fishing out some mugs. Their voices flitted out to him anyway.

"I tried calling you, but your phone wasn't on—I figured you probably lost it," Juniper said.

Blankets rustled. "Are you all right?"

"Totally fine. News reports are still speculating, but they think human rebels from Pangera did it, wanting to start trouble here. There's video footage from the loading dock that shows their insignia on a case of wine. They think that's how the bomb got in."

So the theory had held overnight. Whether it was truly connected to the Horn remained to be seen. Hunt made a note to check with Isaiah about the request to meet with Briggs as soon as Juniper left.

"Is the Raven totally wrecked?"

A sigh. "Yeah—really bad. No idea when it'll be open again. I finally got a hold of Fury last night, and she said Riso's mad enough that he put a bounty on the head of whoever was responsible."

No surprise there. Hunt had heard that despite his laughing nature, when the butterfly shifter got pissed, he went all in. Juniper went on, "Fury's probably coming home because of it. You know she can't resist a challenge."

Burning Solas. Throwing Fury Axtar into this mess was a bad

fucking idea. Hunt spooned coffee beans into the gleaming chrome machine built into the kitchen wall.

Quinlan asked tightly, "So she'll come back home for a bounty, but not to see us?"

A silence. Then, "You weren't the only one who lost Danika that night, B. We all dealt with it in different ways. Fury's answer to her pain was to bail."

"Your therapist tell you that?"

"I'm not fighting with you about this again."

More silence. Juniper cleared her throat. "B, I'm sorry for what I did. You've got a bruise—"

"It's fine."

"No, it's not—"

"It is. I get it, I—"

Hunt turned on the machine's coffee grinder to give them some privacy. He might have ground the beans into a fine powder instead of rough shards, but when he finished, Juniper was saying, "So, the gorgeous angel who's making you coffee right now—"

Hunt grinned at the coffee machine. It had been a long, long while since anyone had bothered describing him as anything but *Umbra Mortis, the Knife of the Archangels*.

"No, no, and no," Bryce cut her off. "Jesiba is having me do a classified job, and Hunt was assigned to protect me."

"Is being shirtless in your house part of that assignment?"

"You know how these Vanir males are. They live to show off their muscles."

Hunt rolled his eyes as Juniper laughed. "I'm shocked you're even letting him stay here, B."

"I didn't really have a choice."

"Hmmm."

A thump of bare feet on the ground. "You know he's listening, right? His feathers are probably so puffed up he won't be able to fit through the door."

Hunt leaned against the counter, the coffee machine doing the growling for him as Bryce stalked into the hallway. "Puffed up?"

She certainly hadn't bothered to fulfill her friend's pants request.

Each step had the pale pink lace of the nightgown's hem brushing against her upper thighs, tugging up slightly to reveal that thick, brutal scar on the left leg. His stomach twisted at the sight of what he'd done to her.

"Eyes up here, Athalar," she drawled. Hunt scowled.

But Juniper was following closely on Bryce's heels, her hooves clopping lightly on the wood floors as she held up the pastry bag. "I just wanted to drop these off. I've got rehearsal in . . ." She fished her phone from the pocket of her tight black leggings. "Oh shit. *Now*. Bye, B." She rushed to the door, chucking the pastry bag on the table with impressive aim.

"Good luck—call me later," Bryce said, already going to inspect her friend's peace offering.

Juniper lingered in the doorway long enough to say to him, "Do your job, *Umbra*."

Then she was gone.

Bryce slid into one of the white leather chairs at the glass table and sighed as she pulled out a chocolate croissant. She bit in and moaned. "Do legionaries eat croissants?"

He remained leaning against the counter. "Is that an actual question?"

Crunch-munch-swallow. "Why are you up so early?"

"It's nearly seven thirty. Hardly early by anyone's count. But your chimera nearly sat on my face, so how could I *not* be up? And how many people, exactly, have keys to this place?"

She finished off her croissant. "My parents, Juniper, and the doorman. Speaking of which . . . I need to give those keys back—and get another copy made."

"And get me a set."

The second croissant was halfway to her mouth when she set it down. "Not going to happen."

He held her stare. "Yes, it is. And you'll change the enchantments so I can get access—"

She bit into the croissant. "Isn't it *exhausting* to be an alphahole all the time? Do you guys have a handbook for it? Maybe secret support groups?"

"An alpha-*what*?"

"Alphahole. Possessive and aggressive." She waved a hand at his bare torso. "You know—you males who rip your shirt off at the slightest provocation, who know how to kill people in twenty different ways, who have females falling over themselves to be with you; and when you finally bang one, you go full-on mating-frenzy with her, refusing to let another male look at or talk to her, deciding what and when she needs to eat, what she should wear, when she sees her friends—"

"What the *fuck* are you talking about?"

"Your favorite hobbies are brooding, fighting, and roaring; you've perfected about thirty different types of snarls and growls; you've got a cabal of hot friends, and the moment one of you mates, the others fall like dominoes, too, and gods help you when you all start having babies—"

He snatched the croissant out of her hand. That shut her up.

Bryce gaped at him, then at the pastry, and Hunt wondered if she'd bite him as he lifted it to his mouth. Damn, but it was good.

"One," he told her, yanking over a chair and turning it backward for him to straddle. "The *last* thing I want to do is fuck you, so we can take the whole Sex, Mating, and Baby option off the table. *Two*, I don't have friends, so there sure as fuck will be no couples-retreat lifestyle anytime soon. *Three*, if we're complaining about people who are clothing-optional . . ." He finished the croissant and gave her a pointed look. "I'm not the one who parades around this apartment in a bra and underwear every morning while getting dressed."

He'd worked hard to forget that particular detail. How after her morning run, she did her hair and makeup in a routine that took her more than an hour from start to finish. Wearing only what seemed to be an extensive, and rather spectacular, assortment of lingerie.

Hunt supposed if he looked the way she did, he'd wear that shit, too.

Bryce only glared at him—his mouth, his hand—and grumbled, "That was my croissant."

The coffee machine beeped, but he kept his ass planted in the chair. "You're going to get me a new set of keys. And add me to the enchantments. Because it's part of my *job*, and being assertive isn't the first sign of being an *alphahole*—it's a sign of me wanting to make sure you don't wind up *dead*."

"Stop cursing so much. You're upsetting Syrinx."

He leaned close enough to note gold flecks in her amber eyes. "You have the dirtiest mouth I've ever heard, sweetheart. And from the way *you* act, I think *you* might be the alphahole here."

She hissed.

"See?" he drawled. "What was it you said? An assortment of snarls and growls?" He waved a hand. "Well, there you go."

She tapped her dusk-sky nails on the glass table. "Don't ever eat my croissant again. And stop calling me sweetheart."

Hunt threw her a smirk and rose. "I need to head to the Comitium for my clothes. Where are you going to be?"

Bryce scowled and said nothing.

"The answer," Hunt went on, "is with me. Anywhere you or I go, we go together from now on. Got it?"

She flipped him off. But she didn't argue further.

29

Micah Domitus might have been an asshole, but at least he gave his triarii the weekend off—or its equivalent if a particular duty required them to work through it.

Jesiba Roga, no surprise, didn't seem to believe in weekends. And since Quinlan was expected at work, Hunt had decided they'd hit the barracks at the Comitium during lunch, while most people were distracted.

The thick veils of morning mist hadn't burned off by the time Hunt trailed Bryce on her way to work. No new updates had been delivered to him on the bombing, and there was no mention of further attacks that matched the kristallos's usual methods.

But Hunt still kept his focus sharp, assessing every person who passed the redhead below. Most people spotted Syrinx, prancing at the end of his leash, and gave her a healthy berth. Chimeras were volatile pets—prone to small magics and biting. No matter that Syrinx seemed more interested in whatever food he could swindle out of people.

Bryce wore a little black dress today, her makeup more subdued, heavier on the eyes, lighter on the lipstick . . . Armor, he realized as she and Syrinx wound through other commuters and tourists, dodging cars already honking with impatience at the usual Old

Square traffic. The clothes, the hair, the makeup—they were like the leather and steel and guns he donned every morning.

Except he didn't wear lingerie beneath it.

For whatever reason, he found himself dropping onto the cobblestones behind her. She didn't so much as flinch, her sky-high black heels unfaltering. Impressive as Hel, for her to walk on the ancient streets without snapping an ankle. Syrinx huffed his greeting and kept trotting, proud as an imperial parade horse. "Your boss ever give you a day off?"

She sipped from the coffee she balanced in her free hand. She drank a surely illegal amount of the stuff throughout the day. Starting with no less than three cups before they'd left the apartment. "I get Sundays off," she said. Palm fronds hissed in the chill breeze above them. The tan skin of her legs pebbled with the cold. "Many of our clients are busy enough that they can't come in during the workweek. Saturday is their day of leisure."

"Do you get holidays off at least?"

"The store is closed on the major ones." She idly jangled the triknot amulet around her neck.

An Archesian charm like that had to cost . . . Burning Solas, it had to cost a fuck-ton. Hunt thought about the heavy iron door to the archives. Perhaps it hadn't been put there to keep thieves out . . . but to keep things *in*.

He had a feeling she wouldn't tell him any details about why the art required her to wear such an amulet, so he instead asked, "What's the deal with you and your cousin?" Who would be arriving at the gallery at some point this morning.

Bryce gently pulled on Syrinx's leash when he lunged for a squirrel scampering up a palm tree. "Ruhn and I were close for a few years when I was a teenager, and then we had a big fight. I stopped speaking to him after that. And things have been . . . well, you see how things are now."

"What'd you fight about?"

The morning mist swirled past as she fell quiet, as if debating what to reveal. She said, "It started off as a fight about his father.

What a piece of shit the Autumn King is, and how Ruhn was wrapped around his finger. It devolved into a screaming match about each other's flaws. I walked out when Ruhn said that I was flirting with his friends like a shameless hussy and to stay away from them."

Ruhn had said far worse than that, Hunt recalled. At Luna's Temple, he'd heard Bryce refer to him calling her a *half-breed slut*. "I've always known Danaan was an asshole, but even for him, that's low."

"It was," she admitted softly, "But . . . honestly, I think he was being protective of me. That's what the argument was about, really. He was acting like every other domineering Fae asshole out there. And just like my father."

Hunt asked, "You ever have contact with him?" There were a few dozen Fae nobles that might be monstrous enough to have prompted Ember Quinlan to bail all those years ago.

"Only when I can't avoid it. I think I hate him more than anyone else in Midgard. Except for Sabine." She sighed skyward, watching angels and witches zoom past above the buildings around them. "Who's number one on your shit list?"

Hunt waited until they'd passed a reptilian-looking Vanir typing on their phone before he replied, mindful of every camera mounted on the buildings or hidden in trees or garbage cans. "Sandriel."

"Ah." Only Sandriel's first name was necessary for anyone on Midgard. "From what I've seen on TV, she seems . . ." Bryce grimaced.

"Whatever you've seen is the pleasant version. The reality is ten times worse. She's a sadistic monster." To say the least. He added, "I was forced to . . . work for her for more than half a century. Until Micah." He couldn't say the word—*owned*. He'd never let Sandriel have that kind of power over him. "She and the commander of her triarii, Pollux, take cruelty and punishment to new levels." He clenched his jaw, shaking off the blood-soaked memories. "They're not stories to tell on a busy street." Or at all.

But she eyed him. "You ever want to talk about it, Athalar, I'm here."

She said it casually, but he could read the sincerity in her face. He nodded. "Likewise."

They passed the Old Square Gate, tourists already queued to take photos or touch the disk on the dial pad, gleefully handing over a drop of their power as they did so. None seemed aware of the body that had been found a few blocks away. In the drifting mist, the quartz Gate was almost ethereal, like it had been carved from ancient ice. Not one rainbow graced the buildings around it—not in the fog.

Syrinx sniffed at a trash can overflowing with food waste from the stands around the square. "You ever touch the disk and make a wish?" Bryce asked.

He shook his head. "I thought it was something only kids and tourists did."

"It is. But it's fun." She tossed her hair over a shoulder, smiling to herself. "I made a wish here when I was thirteen—when I visited the city for the first time. Ruhn took me."

Hunt lifted a brow. "What'd you wish for?"

"For my boobs to get bigger."

A laugh burst out of him, chasing away any lingering shadows that talk of Sandriel dragged up. But Hunt avoided looking at Bryce's chest as he said, "Seems your wish paid off, Quinlan." Understatement. Big, fucking, lace-covered understatement.

She chuckled. "Crescent City: Where dreams come true."

Hunt elbowed her ribs, unable to stop himself from making physical contact.

She batted him away. "What would you wish for, if you knew it'd come true?"

For his mother to be alive and safe and happy. For Sandriel and Micah and all the Archangels and Asteri to be dead. For his bargain with Micah to be over and the halo and slave tattoos removed. For the rigid hierarchies of the malakim to come crashing down.

But he couldn't say any of that. Wasn't ready to say those things aloud to her.

So Hunt said, "Since I'm perfectly happy with the size of *my* assets, I'd wish for you to stop being such a pain in my ass."

"Jerk." But Bryce grinned, and damn if the morning sun didn't finally make an appearance at the sight of it.

The library beneath Griffin Antiquities would have made even the Autumn King jealous.

Ruhn Danaan sat at the giant worktable in its heart, still needing a moment to take in the space—and the fire sprite who'd batted her eyelashes and asked if all his piercings had hurt.

Bryce and Athalar sat on the other side of the table, the former typing at a laptop, the latter leafing through a pile of old tomes. Lehabah lay on what seemed to be a doll's fainting couch, a digital tablet propped up before her, watching one of the more popular Vanir dramas.

"So," Bryce said without glancing up from the computer, "are you going to look around or sit there and gawk?"

Athalar snickered, but said nothing, his finger tracing over a line of text.

Ruhn glared at him. "What are you doing?"

"Researching the kristallos," Hunt said, his dark eyes lifting from the book. "I've killed about a dozen Type-Six demons over the centuries, and I want to see if there are any similarities."

"Is the kristallos a Type-Six?" Ruhn asked.

"I'm assuming it is," Hunt replied, studying the book again. "Type-Seven is only for the princes themselves, and given what this thing can do, I'd bet it'd be deemed a Six." He drummed his fingers on the ancient page. "I haven't seen any similarities, though."

Bryce hummed. "Maybe you're looking in the wrong spot. Maybe . . ." She angled her laptop toward Athalar, fingers flying. "We're looking for info on something that hasn't entered this world in fifteen thousand years. The fact that no one could ID it suggests it might not have made it into many of the history books, and only a handful of those books survived this long. But . . ." More typing, and Ruhn craned his neck to see the database she pulled up. "Where are we right now?" she asked Athalar.

"A library."

"An *antiquities* gallery, dumbass." A page loaded, full of images of ancient vases and amphorae, mosaics, and statues. She'd typed *demon + Fae* into the search bar. Bryce slid the laptop to Hunt. "Maybe we can find the kristallos in ancient art."

Hunt grumbled, but Ruhn noted the impressed gleam in his eyes before he began scanning through the pages of results.

"I've never met a prince before," Lehabah sighed from the couch.

"They're overrated," Ruhn said over a shoulder.

Athalar grunted his agreement.

"What is it like," the sprite asked, propping her fiery head on a burning fist, "to be the Chosen One?"

"Boring," Ruhn admitted. "Beyond the sword and some party tricks, there's not much to it."

"Can I see the Starsword?"

"I left it at home. I didn't feel like having to deal with tourists stopping me on every block, wanting to take pictures."

"Poor little prince," Bryce cooed.

Hunt grunted his agreement again, and Ruhn bit out, "You got something to say, Athalar?"

The angel's eyes lifted from the laptop. "She said it all."

Ruhn snarled, but Bryce asked, surveying them, "What's the deal with you two?"

"Oh, do tell," Lehabah pleaded, pausing her show to perk up on the couch.

Hunt went back to perusing the results. "We beat the shit out of each other at a party. Danaan's still sore about it."

Bryce's grin was the definition of shit-eating. "Why'd you fight?"

Ruhn snapped, "Because he's an arrogant asshole."

"Likewise," Hunt said, mouth curling in a half smile.

Bryce threw Lehabah a knowing look. "Boys and their pissing contests."

Lehabah made a prim little sound. "Not nearly as advanced as us ladies."

Ruhn rolled his eyes, surprised to find Athalar doing the same.

Bryce gestured to the endless shelves that filled the library. "Well, cousin," she said, "have at it. Let your Starborn powers guide you to enlightenment."

"Funny," he said, but began walking toward the shelves, scanning the titles. He paused at the various tanks and terrariums built into the bookcases, the small animals within wholly uninterested in his presence. He didn't dare ask if the rumors about them were true, especially not when Lehabah called over from her couch, "The tortoise is named Marlene."

Ruhn gave his sister an alarmed look, but Bryce was doing something on her phone.

Music began playing a moment later, trickling in from speakers hidden in the wood panels. Ruhn listened to the first strains of the song—just a guitar and two soaring, haunting female voices. "You're still into this band?" As a kid, she'd been obsessed with the sister folk duo.

"Josie and Laurel keep making good music, so I keep listening." She swiped at her phone.

Ruhn continued his idle browsing. "You always had really good taste." He tossed it out there—a rope into the stormy sea that was their relationship.

She didn't look up, but she said a shade quietly, "Thanks."

Athalar, wisely, didn't say a word.

Ruhn scanned the shelves, waiting to feel a tug toward anything beyond the sister who'd spoken more to him in the past few days than she had in nine years. The titles were in the common language, the Old Language of the Fae, the mer, and a few other alphabets he didn't recognize. "This collection is amazing."

Ruhn reached for a blue tome whose spine glittered with gold foil. *Words of the Gods*.

"Don't touch it," Lehabah warned. "It might bite."

Ruhn snatched back his hand as the book stirred, rumbling on the shelf. His shadows murmured inside him, readying to strike. He willed them to settle. "Why does the book *move*?"

"Because they're special—" Lehabah began.

"Enough, Lele," Bryce warned. "Ruhn, don't touch anything without permission."

"From you or the book?"

"Both," she said. As if in answer, a book high up on the shelf rustled. Ruhn craned his head to look, and saw a green tome . . . shining. Beckoning. His shadows murmured, as if in urging. All right, then.

It was a matter of moments to drag over the brass ladder and scale it. Bryce said, seemingly to the library itself, "Don't bother him," before Ruhn pulled the book from its resting place. He rolled his eyes at the title. *Great Romances of the Fae.*

Starborn power indeed. Tucking the book into the crook of his arm, he descended the ladder and returned to the table.

Bryce choked on a laugh at the title. "You sure that Starborn power isn't for finding smut?" She called to Lehabah, "This one's right up your alley."

Lehabah burned to a raspberry pink. "BB, you're horrible."

Athalar winked at him. "Enjoy."

"I will," Ruhn shot back, flipping open the book. His phone buzzed before he could begin. He fished it from his back pocket and glanced at the screen. "Dec's got the intel you wanted."

Bryce and Athalar went still. Ruhn opened the email, then his fingers hovered over the forwarding screen. "I, uh . . . is your email still the same?" he asked her. "And I don't have yours, Athalar."

Hunt rattled his off, but Bryce frowned at Ruhn for a long moment, as if weighing whether she wanted to open yet another door into her life. She then sighed and answered, "Yes, it's the same."

"Sent," Ruhn said, and opened up the attachment Declan had emailed over.

It was full of coordinates and their correlating locations. Danika's daily routine as Alpha of the Pack of Devils had her moving throughout the Old Square and beyond. Not to mention her healthy social life after sundown. The list covered everything from the apartment, the Den, the City Head office at the Comitium, a tattoo parlor, a burger joint, too many pizza places to count, bars, a concert venue, the CCU sunball arena, hair salons, the gym . . . Fuck, had she ever gotten any sleep? The list dated back two weeks prior to her death. From the silence around the table, he knew Bryce and Hunt were also skimming over the locations. Then—

Surprise lit Hunt's dark eyes as he looked to her. Bryce murmured, "Danika wasn't merely on duty near Luna's Temple around that time—this says Danika was stationed *at* the temple for the two days before the Horn was stolen. And during the night of the blackout."

Hunt asked, "You think she saw whoever took it and they killed her to cover it up?"

Could it be that easy? Ruhn prayed it was.

Bryce shook her head. "If Danika saw the Horn being stolen, she would have reported it." She sighed again. "Danika wasn't usually stationed at the temple, but Sabine often switched her schedule around for spite. Maybe Danika had some of the Horn's scent on her from being on duty and the demon tracked her down."

"Go through it again," Ruhn urged. "Maybe there's something you're missing."

Bryce's mouth twisted to the side, the portrait of skepticism, but Hunt said, "Better than nothing." Bryce held the angel's stare for longer than most people deemed wise.

Nothing good could come of it—Bryce and Athalar working together. Living together.

But Ruhn kept his mouth shut, and began reading.

"Any good sex scenes yet?" Bryce asked Ruhn idly, going over Danika's location data for the third time. The first few of those locations, she'd realized, had been to Philip Briggs's bomb lab just outside the city walls. Including the night of the bust itself.

She still remembered Danika and Connor limping into the apartment that night, after making the bust on Briggs and his Keres group two years ago. Danika had been fine, but Connor had sported a split lip and black eye that screamed some shit had gone down. They never told her what, and she hadn't asked. She'd just made Connor sit at that piece-of-shit kitchen table and let her clean him up.

He'd kept his eyes fixed on her face, her mouth, the entire time she'd gently dabbed his lip. She'd known then and there that it was coming—that Connor was done waiting. That five years of friendship, of dancing around each other, was now going to change, and he'd make his move soon. It didn't matter that she'd been dating Reid. Connor had let her take care of him, his eyes near-glowing, and she'd known it was time.

When Ruhn didn't immediately respond to her taunting, Bryce looked up from the laptop. Her brother had kept reading—and didn't seem to hear her. "Ruhn."

Hunt halted his own searching through the gallery database. "Danaan."

Ruhn snapped his head up, blinking. Bryce asked, "You found something?"

"Yes and no," Ruhn said, sitting back in his chair. "This is just a three-page account of Prince Pelias and his bride, Lady Helena. But I didn't realize that Pelias was actually the high general for a Fae Queen named Theia when they entered this world during the Crossing—and Helena was her daughter. From what it sounds like, Queen Theia was *also* Starborn, and her daughter possessed the same power. Theia had a younger daughter with the same gift, but only Lady Helena gets mentioned." Ruhn cleared his throat and read, "*Night-haired Helena, from whose golden skin poured starlight and shadows.* It seems like Pelias was one of several Fae back then with the Starborn power."

Bryce blinked. "So? What does it have to do with the Horn?"

"It mentions here that the sacred objects were made only for Fae like them. That the Horn worked only when that starlight flowed through it, when it was filled with power. This claims that the Starborn magic, in addition to a bunch of other crap, can be channeled through the sacred objects—bringing them to life. I sure as fuck have never been able to do anything like that, even with the Starsword. But it says that's why the Prince of the Pit had to steal Pelias's blood to make the kristallos to hunt the Horn—it contained that essence. I think the Horn could have been wielded by any of them, though."

Hunt said, "But if the Prince of the Pit had gotten his hands on the Horn, he wouldn't be able to use it unless he had a Starborn Fae to operate it." He nodded to Ruhn. "Even if whoever wants the Horn now finds it, they'd have to use you."

Ruhn considered. "But let's not forget that whoever is summoning the demon to track the Horn—and kill these people—doesn't *have* the Horn. Someone else stole it. So we're essentially looking for two different people: the killer and whoever has the Horn."

"Well, the Horn is broken anyway," Bryce said.

Ruhn tapped the book. "Permanently broken, apparently. It says here that once it was cracked, the Fae claimed it could only be repaired by *light that is not light; magic that is not magic*. Basically a convoluted way of saying there's no chance in Hel of it ever working again."

Hunt said, "So we need to find out why someone would want it, then." He frowned at Ruhn. "Your father wants it for what—some Fae PR campaign about the good old days of Faedom?"

Ruhn snorted, and Bryce smiled slightly. With lines like that, Athalar was in danger of becoming one of her favorite people. Ruhn said, "Basically, yeah. The Fae have been *declining*, according to him, for the past several thousand years. He claims our ancestors could burn entire forests to ash with half a thought—while he can probably torch a grove, and not much more." Ruhn's jaw tightened. "It drives him nuts that my Chosen One powers are barely more than a kernel."

Bryce knew her own lack of power had been part of her father's disgust with her.

Proof of the Fae's failing influence.

She felt Hunt's eyes on her, as if he could sense the bitterness that rippled through her. She half lied to him, "My own father never had a lick of interest in me for the same reason."

"Especially after your visit to the Oracle," Ruhn said.

Hunt's brows rose, but Bryce shook her head at him, scowling. "It's a long story."

Hunt again looked at her in that considering, all-seeing way. So

Bryce peered over at Ruhn's tome, skimmed a few lines, and then looked back up at Ruhn. "This whole section is about your fancy Avallen cousins. Shadow-walking, mind-reading . . . I'm surprised they don't claim they're Starborn."

"They wish they were," Ruhn muttered. "They're a bunch of pricks."

She had a vague memory of Ruhn telling her the details about why, exactly, he felt that way, but asked, "No mind-reading for you?"

"It's mind-speaking," he grumbled, "and it has nothing to do with the Starborn stuff. Or this case."

Hunt, apparently, seemed to agree, because he cut in, "What if we asked the Oracle about the Horn? Maybe she could see why someone would want a broken relic."

Bryce and Ruhn straightened. But she said, "We'd be better off going to the mystics."

Hunt cringed. "The mystics are some dark, fucked-up shit. We'll try the Oracle first."

"Well, I'm not going," Bryce said quickly.

Hunt's eyes darkened. "Because of what happened at your visit?"

"Right," she said tightly.

Ruhn cut in and said to Hunt, "You go, then."

Hunt snickered. "You have a bad experience, too, Danaan?"

Bryce found herself carefully watching her brother. Ruhn had never mentioned the Oracle to her. But he just shrugged and said, "Yeah."

Hunt threw up his hands. "Fine, assholes. I'll go. I've never been. It always seemed too gimmicky."

It wasn't. Bryce blocked out the image of the golden sphinx who'd sat before the hole in the floor of her dim, black chamber—how that human woman's face had monitored her every breath.

"You'll need an appointment," she managed to say.

Silence fell. A buzzing interrupted it, and Hunt sighed as he pulled out his phone. "I gotta take this," he said, and didn't wait for them to reply before striding up the stairs out of the library. A moment later, the front door to the gallery shut.

With Lehabah still watching her show behind them, Ruhn quietly said to Bryce, "Your power levels never mattered to me, Bryce. You know that, right?"

She went back to looking through Danika's data. "Yeah. I know." She lifted an eyebrow. "What's your deal with the Oracle?"

His face shuttered. "Nothing. She told me everything the Autumn King wanted to hear."

"What—you're upset that it wasn't something as disastrous as mine?"

Ruhn rose from his seat, piercings glittering in the firstlights. "Look, I've got an Aux meeting this afternoon that I need to prep for, but I'll see you later."

"Sure."

Ruhn paused, as if debating saying something else, but continued toward the stairs and out.

"Your cousin is dreamy," Lehabah sighed from her couch.

"I thought Athalar was your one true love," Bryce said.

"Can't they both be?"

"Considering how terrible they are at sharing, I don't think it'll end well for any of you."

Her email pinged on the laptop. Since her phone was in shards in the rubble of the Raven, Hunt had emailed, *Saw your cousin leave. We're heading to the Comitium in five minutes.*

She wrote back, *Don't give me orders, Athalar.*

Four minutes, sweetheart.

I told you: don't call me sweetheart.

Three minutes.

Growling, she stood from the table, rubbing her leg. Her heels were already killing her, and knowing Athalar, he'd make her walk the entire Comitium complex. Her dress would look ridiculous with a different set of shoes, but fortunately, she kept a change of clothes in the bottom drawer of the library desk, mostly in case of a rainy day that threatened to ruin whatever she was wearing.

Lehabah said, "It's nice—to have company down here."

Something in Bryce's chest wrenched, but she said, "I'll be back later."

30

Hunt kept a casual distance from Bryce as she walked beside him through the Comitium lobby to the bank of elevators that would take them up to the 33rd's barracks. The other elevator bays dispersed through the centralized, glass-enclosed atrium led to the four other towers of the complex: one for the City Heads' meeting rooms and the running of Lunathion, one for Micah as both residence and official office, one for general administrative bullshit, and one for public meetings and events. Thousands upon thousands of people lived and worked within its walls, but even with the bustling lobby, Quinlan somehow managed to stand out.

She'd changed into red suede flats and a button-up white blouse tucked into tight jeans, and tied her silken mass of hair into a high ponytail that swayed sassily with every step she took, matching Hunt stride for stride.

He placed his palm against the round disk next to the elevator doors, clearing him for access to his floor thirty levels up. Usually, he flew to the barracks' landing balcony—half for ease, half to avoid the busybodies who were now gawking at them across the lobby floor, no doubt wondering if Hunt was bringing Quinlan here to fuck her or interrogate her.

The legionary who lounged on a low-lying couch wasn't particularly skilled in stealing covert glances at her ass. Bryce looked over a shoulder, as if some extra sense told her someone was watching, and gave the soldier a smile.

The legionary stiffened. Bryce bit her lower lip, her lashes lowering slightly.

Hunt punched the elevator button, hard, even as the male gave Bryce a half smile Hunt was pretty sure the bastard threw at any female who came his way. As low-level grunts in a very large machine, legionaries—even those in the famed 33rd—couldn't be picky.

The elevator doors opened, and legionaries and business types filed out, those without wings careful not to step on anyone's feathers. And all of them careful not to look Hunt in the eye.

It wasn't that he was unfriendly. If someone offered him a smile, he usually made an attempt at returning it. But they'd all heard the stories. All knew whom he worked for—every one of his *masters*—and what he did for them.

They'd be more comfortable getting into an elevator with a starved tiger.

So Hunt kept back, minimizing any chance of contact. Bryce whirled to face the elevator, that ponytail nearly whipping him in the face.

"Watch that thing," Hunt snapped as the elevator finally emptied and they walked in. "You'll take my eye out."

She leaned nonchalantly against the far glass wall. Mercifully, no one got inside with them. Hunt wasn't stupid enough to think that it was by pure chance.

They'd made only one stop on their way here, to buy her a replacement phone for the one she'd lost at the club. She'd even coughed up a few extra marks for a standard protection spell package on the phone.

The glass-and-chrome store had been mostly empty, but he hadn't failed to notice how many would-be shoppers spied him through the windows and kept far away. Bryce hadn't seemed to notice, and while they'd waited for the employee to bring out a new phone for her, she'd asked him for his own, so she could trawl the news feeds for any updates on the club attack. Somehow, she'd wound up going through his photos. Or lack of them.

"There are thirty-six photos on this phone," she said flatly.

Hunt had frowned. "So?"

She scrolled through the paltry collection. "Going back *four years*." To when he'd arrived in Lunathion and gotten his first phone and taste of life without a monster ruling over him. Bryce had gagged as she opened a photo of a severed leg on a bloody carpet. "What the *fuck*?"

"I sometimes get called to crime scenes and have to snap a few for evidence."

"Are any of these people from your bargain with—"

"No," he said. "I don't take pictures of them."

"There are thirty-six photos on your four-year-old phone, and all of them are of dismembered bodies," she said. Someone gasped across the store.

Hunt gritted his teeth. "Say it a little louder, Quinlan."

She frowned. "You never take any others?"

"Of what?"

"Oh, I don't know—of *life*? A pretty flower or good meal or something?"

"What's the point?"

She'd blinked, then shook her head. "Weirdo."

And before he could stop her, she'd angled his phone in front of her, beamed from ear to ear, and snapped a photo of herself before she handed it back to him. "There. One non-corpse photo."

Hunt had rolled his eyes, but pocketed the phone.

The elevator hummed around them, shooting upward. Bryce watched the numbers rise. "Do you know who that legionary was?" she asked casually.

"Which one? There was the one drooling on the Traskian carpet, the one with his tongue rolled out on the floor, or the one who was staring at your ass like it was going to talk to him?"

She laughed. "They must keep you all starved for sex in these barracks if the presence of one female sends them into such a tizzy. So—do you know his name? The one who wanted to have a chat with my ass."

"No. There are three thousand of us in the 33rd alone." He

glanced at her sidelong, watching her monitor the rising floor numbers. "Maybe some guy that checks out your ass before he says hello isn't someone worth knowing."

Her brows lifted as the elevator stopped and the doors opened. "That is *precisely* the kind of person I'm looking for." She stepped into the simple hallway, and he followed her—realizing as she paused that *he* knew where they were going, and she only faked it.

He turned left. Their footsteps echoed off the tan granite tile of the long corridor. The stone was cracked and chipped in spots—from dropped weapons, magical pissing contests, actual brawls—but still polished enough that he could see both their reflections.

Quinlan took in the hall, the names on each door. "Males only, or are you mixed?"

"Mixed," he told her. "Though there are more males than females in the 33rd."

"Do you have a girlfriend? Boyfriend? Someone whose ass *you* gawk at?"

He shook his head, trying to fight the ice in his veins as he stopped before his door, opened it, and let her inside. Trying to block out the image of Shahar plunging to the earth, Sandriel's sword through her sternum, both angels' white wings streaming blood. Both sisters screaming, faces nearly mirror images of each other. "I was born a bastard." He shut the door behind them, watching her survey the small room. The bed was big enough to fit his wings, but there wasn't space for much else beyond an armoire and dresser, a desk stacked with books and papers, and discarded weapons.

"So?"

"So my mother had no money, and no distinguished bloodline that might have made up for it. I don't exactly have females lining up for me, despite this face of mine." His laugh was bitter as he opened the cheap pine armoire and pulled out a large duffel. "I had someone once, someone who didn't care about status, but it didn't end well." Each word singed his tongue.

Bryce wrapped her arms around herself, nails digging into the filmy silk of her shirt. She seemed to realize whom he'd alluded to.

She glanced around, as if casting for things to say, and somehow settled on, "When did you make the Drop?"

"I was twenty-eight."

"Why then?"

"My mother had just died." Sorrow filled her eyes, and he couldn't stand the look, couldn't stand to open up the wound, so he added, "I was reeling afterward. So I got a public Anchor and made the Drop. But it didn't make a difference. If I'd inherited the power of an Archangel or a dormouse, once the tattoos got inked on me five years later, it cut me off at the knees."

He could hear her hand stroke his blanket. "You ever regret the angels' rebellion?"

Hunt glanced over a shoulder to find her leaning against the bed. "No one's ever asked me that." No one dared. But she held his stare. Hunt admitted, "I don't know what I think."

He let his stare convey the rest. *And I wouldn't say a fucking word about it in this place.*

She nodded. Then looked at the walls—no artwork, no posters. "Not one to decorate?"

He stuffed clothes into the duffel, remembering she had a washing machine in the apartment. "Micah can trade me whenever he wants. It's asking for bad luck to put down roots like that."

She rubbed her arms, even though the room was warm, almost stuffy. "If he'd died that night, what would have happened to you? To every Fallen and slave he owns?"

"Our deed of ownership passes on to whoever replaces him." He hated every word out of his mouth. "If he doesn't have anyone listed, the assets get divided among the other Archangels."

"Who wouldn't honor his bargain with you."

"Definitely not." Hunt started on the weapons stashed in his desk drawers.

He could feel her watching his every movement, as if counting each blade and gun he pulled out. She asked, "If you achieved your freedom, what would you do?"

Hunt checked the ammo for the guns he had on his desk, and

she wandered over to watch. He tossed a few into his bag. She picked up a long knife as if it were a dirty sock. "I heard your lightning is unique among the angels—even the Archangels can't produce it."

He tucked in his wings. "Yeah?"

A shrug. "So why is Isaiah the Commander of the 33rd?"

He took the knife from her and set it in his bag. "Because I piss off too many people and don't give a shit that I do." It had been that way even before Mount Hermon. Yet Shahar had seen it as a strength. Made him her general. He'd tried and failed to live up to that honor.

Bryce gave him a conspirator's smile. "We have something in common after all, Athalar."

Fine. The angel wasn't so bad. He had patched her up after the bombing with no male swaggering. And he had one Hel of a reason to want this case solved. And he pissed Ruhn off to no end.

As he'd finished packing, he'd gotten a call from Isaiah, who said that their request to see Briggs had been approved—but that it would take a few days to get Briggs cleaned up and brought over from Adrestia Prison. Bryce had chosen to ignore what, exactly, that implied about Briggs's current state.

The only bright spot was that Isaiah informed Hunt that the Oracle had made room for him on her schedule first thing tomorrow.

Bryce eyed Hunt as they boarded the elevator once again, her stomach flipping as they plunged toward the central lobby of the Comitium. Whatever clearance Hunt had, it somehow included overriding the elevator commands to stop at other floors. Sweet.

She'd never really known any of the malakim beyond seeing the legionaries on patrol, or their rich elite strutting like peacocks around town. Most preferred the rooftop lounges in the CBD. And since half-breed sluts weren't allowed into those, she'd never had a chance to take one home.

Well, now she *was* taking one home, though not in the way she'd once imagined while ogling their muscles. She and Danika had once spent two solid summer weeks of lunch breaks sitting on a rooftop adjacent to a legion training space. With the heat, the male angels had stripped down to their pants while they sparred. And then got sweaty. Very, very sweaty.

She and Danika would have kept going every lunch hour if they hadn't been caught by the building's janitor, who called them perverts and permanently locked access to the roof.

The elevator slowed to a stop, setting her stomach flipping again. The doors opened, and they were greeted by a wall of impatient-looking legionaries—who all made sure to rearrange their expressions to carefully noncommittal when they beheld Hunt.

The Shadow of Death. She'd spied the infamous helmet in his room, sitting beside his desk. He'd left it behind, thank the gods.

The Comitium lobby beyond the elevators was packed. Full of wings and halos and those enticing muscled bodies, all facing the front doors, craning their necks to see over each other but none launching into the atrium airspace—

Hunt went rigid at the edge of the crowd that had nearly blocked off the barracks elevator bank. Bryce made it all of one step toward him before the elevator to their right opened and Isaiah rushed out, halting as he spied Hunt. "I just heard—"

The ripple of power at the other end of the lobby made her legs buckle.

As if that power had knocked the crowd to the ground, everyone knelt and bowed their heads.

Leaving the three of them with a perfect view of the Archangel who stood at the giant glass doors of the atrium, Micah at her side.

31

Sandriel turned toward Hunt, Bryce, and Isaiah at the same moment Micah did. Recognition flared in the dark-haired female's eyes as that gaze landed on Hunt, skipped Bryce entirely, and took in Isaiah.

Bryce recognized her, of course. She was on television often enough that no one on the planet wouldn't recognize her.

A step ahead, Hunt was a trembling live wire. She'd never seen him like this.

"Get down," Isaiah murmured, and knelt.

Hunt didn't move. Wouldn't, Bryce realized. People looked over their shoulders as they remained on their knees.

Isaiah muttered, "Pollux isn't with her. Just fucking kneel."

Pollux—the Hammer. Some of the tension went out of Hunt, but he remained standing.

He looked lost, stranded, somewhere between rage and terror. Not even a flicker of lightning at his fingertips. Bryce stepped closer to his side, flicking her ponytail over a shoulder. She took her brand-new phone out of her pocket, making sure the sound was cranked up.

So everyone could hear the loud *click click click* as she snapped photos of the two Archangels, then turned, angling herself and the phone, to get a shot with herself *and* the Governors in the background—

People murmured in shock. Bryce tilted her head to the side, smiling wide, and snapped another.

Then she turned to Hunt, who was still trembling, and said as flippantly as she could muster, "Thanks for bringing me to see them. Shall we?"

She didn't give Hunt the chance to do anything as she looped her arm through his, turned them both around before taking a photo with him and the stone-faced Archangels and the gawking crowd in the background, and then tugged him back toward the elevator bank.

That's why some legionaries had been rushing to get on. To flee.

Maybe there was another exit beyond the wall of glass doors. The crowd rose to their feet.

She pushed the button, praying it gave her access to any of the tower's floors. Hunt was still shaking. Bryce gripped his arm tight, tapping her foot on the tiles as—

"Explain yourself." Micah stood behind them, blocking the crowd from the elevator bank.

Hunt closed his eyes.

Bryce swallowed and turned, nearly whipping Hunt in the face with her hair again. "Well, I heard that you had a special guest, so I asked Hunt to bring me so I could get a photo—"

"Do not lie."

Hunt opened his eyes, then slowly turned to the Governor. "I had to pick up supplies and clothes. Isaiah gave me the go-ahead to bring her here."

As if speaking his name had summoned him, the Commander of the 33rd pushed through the line of guards. Isaiah said, "It's true, Your Grace. Hunt was grabbing necessities, and didn't want to risk leaving Miss Quinlan alone while he did it."

The Archangel looked at Isaiah, then Hunt. Then her.

Micah's gaze roved over her body. Her face. She knew that gaze, that slow study.

Too fucking bad that Micah was about as warm as a fish at the bottom of a mountain lake.

Too fucking bad he'd used Hunt like a weapon, dangling his freedom like a dog treat.

Too fucking bad he often worked with her father on city matters, and on House business—too bad he *reminded* her of her father.

Boo. Fucking. Hoo.

She said to Micah, "It was nice to see you again, Your Grace." Then the elevator doors opened, as if some god had willed them to make a good exit.

She nudged Hunt inside, and was following him in when a cold, strong hand gripped her elbow. She batted her eyelashes up at Micah as he stopped her between the elevator doors. Hunt didn't seem to be breathing.

As if he were waiting for the Governor to rescind his deal.

But Micah purred, "I would like to take you to dinner, Bryce Quinlan."

She pulled out of his grip, joining Hunt in the elevator. And as the doors closed, she looked the Archangel of Valbara full in the face. "Not interested," she said.

Hunt had known Sandriel was coming, but running into her today . . . She must have wanted to surprise them all, if Isaiah hadn't known. Wanted to catch the Governor and the legion off guard and see what this place was like *before* the pomp and circumstance made their defenses seem stronger, their wealth deeper. *Before* Micah could call in one of his other legions to make them look that much more impressive.

What piss-poor fucking luck that they'd run into her.

But at least Pollux hadn't been there. Not yet.

The elevator shot up again, and Bryce stayed silent. Holding herself.

Not interested.

He doubted Micah Domitus had ever heard those words before.

He doubted Sandriel ever had someone snap photos of her like that.

All he'd been able to think about while he beheld Sandriel was the weight of his knife at his side. All he could smell was the reek of her arena, blood and shit and piss and sand—

Then Bryce had made her move. Played that irreverent, vapid party girl she wanted them to believe she was, that he'd believed she was, snapping those photos, giving him an out—

Hunt placed his hand against the disk beside the button panel and punched in a different floor, overriding wherever the elevator had been taking them. "We can leave from the landing." His voice was like gravel. He always forgot—just how similar Sandriel and Shahar looked. Not identical twins, but their coloring and build had been nearly the same. "I'll have to carry you, though."

She twirled the silken length of her ponytail around a wrist, unaware that she bared the golden column of her throat to him with the movement.

Not interested.

She'd sounded certain. Not gleeful, not gloating, but . . . firm.

Hunt didn't dare consider how this rejection might affect his bargain with Micah—to wonder if Micah would somehow blame Hunt for it.

Bryce asked, "No back door?"

"There is, but we'd have to go down again."

He could feel her questions bubbling up, and before she could ask any of them he said, "Sandriel's Second, Pollux, is even worse than she is. When he arrives, avoid him at all costs."

He couldn't bring himself to dredge up the list of horrors Pollux had inflicted on innocents.

Bryce clicked her tongue. "Like my path will ever cross theirs if I can help it."

After that show in the lobby, it might. But Hunt didn't tell her that Sandriel wasn't above petty revenge for slights and minor offenses. Didn't tell her that Sandriel would likely never forget Bryce's face. Might already be asking Micah who she was.

The doors opened onto a quiet upper level. The halls were dim, hushed, and he led her into a labyrinth of gym equipment. A broad path cut through the gear directly to the wall of windows—and the launch balcony beyond. There was no railing, just an open jut of stone. She balked.

"I've never dropped anyone," he promised.

She gingerly followed him outside. The dry wind whipped at them. Far below, the city street was packed with onlookers and news vans. Above them, angels were flying, some fleeing outright, some circling the five spires of the Comitium to get a glimpse of Sandriel from afar.

Hunt bent, sliding a hand under Bryce's knees, bracing another on her back, and picked her up. Her scent filled his senses, washing away the last of the memory of that reeking dungeon.

"Thank you," he said, meeting her stare. "For bailing me out back there."

She shrugged as best she could in his grip, but winced as he stepped closer to the edge.

"That was fast thinking," he went on. "Ridiculous on so many levels, but I owe you."

She slid her arms around his neck, her grip near-strangling. "You helped me out last night. We're even."

Hunt didn't give her a chance to change her mind as he beat his wings in a powerful push and leapt off the edge. She clung to him, tight enough to hurt, and he held her firmly, the duffel strapped across his chest awkwardly banging against his thigh.

"Are you even watching?" he asked over the wind as he sent them sailing hard and fast, flying up, up, up the side of the adjacent skyscraper in the Central Business District.

"Absolutely not," she said in his ear.

He chuckled as they leveled out, cruising above the reaching pinnacles of the CBD, the Istros a winding sparkle to their right, the mist-shrouded isle of the Bone Quarter looming behind it. To the left, he could just make out the walls of the city, and then the wide-open land beyond the Angels' Gate. No houses or buildings or roads out there. Nothing but the aerialport. But at the Gate to their right—the Merchants' Gate in the Meat Market—the broad, pale line of the Western Road shot into the rolling, cypress-dotted hills.

A pleasant, beautiful city—in the midst of pleasant, beautiful countryside.

In Pangera, the cities were little more than pens for the Vanir to trap and feed on the humans—and their children. No wonder the humans had risen up. No wonder they were shredding that territory with their chemical bombs and machines.

A shiver of rage ran down his spine at the thought of those children, and he made himself look toward the city again. The Central Business District was separated from the Old Square by the clear dividing line of Ward Avenue. The sunlight glowed off the white stones of Luna's Temple—and, as if in a mirror reflection directly across from it, seemed to be absorbed by the black-domed Oracle's Temple. His destination tomorrow morning.

But Hunt looked beyond the Old Square, to where the green of Five Roses sparkled in the muggy haze. Towering cypresses and palms rose up, along with glittering bursts of magic. In Moonwood, more oak trees—less magic frills. Hunt didn't bother looking anywhere else. Asphodel Meadows wasn't much to behold. Yet the Meadows was a luxury development compared to the human districts in Pangera.

"Why'd you want to live in the Old Square?" he asked after several minutes of flying in silence, with only the song of the wind to listen to.

She still wasn't looking, and he began a gentle descent toward her little section of the Old Square, just a block off the river and a few blocks from the Heart Gate. Even from that distance, he could see it, the clear quartz glinting like an icy spear toward the gray sky.

"It's the heart of the city," she said, "why not be there?"

"FiRo is cleaner."

"And full of Fae peacocks who sneer at *half-breeds*." She spat out the term.

"Moonwood?"

"Sabine's territory?" A harsh laugh, and she pulled back to look at him. Her smattering of freckles crinkled as she scrunched her face. "Honestly, the Old Square is about the only safe place for someone like me. Plus, it's close to work *and* I've got my pick of restaurants, music halls, and museums. I never need to leave."

"But you do—you go all over the city on your morning runs. Why a different route so often?"

"Keeps it fresh and fun."

Her building became clearer, the roof empty. A firepit, some lounge chairs, and a grill occupied most of it. Hunt banked, circling back, and smoothly landed, carefully setting her down. She clung to him long enough to get her legs steady, then stepped back.

He adjusted the duffel, heading for the roof door. He held it open for her, firstlight warming the stairwell beyond. "Did you mean what you said—to Micah?"

She plunked down the stairs, the ponytail bobbing. "Of course I did. Why the Hel would I want to go out with him?"

"He's the Governor of Valbara."

"So? Just because I saved his life, that doesn't mean I'm destined to be his girlfriend. It'd be like banging a statue anyway."

Hunt smirked. "In all fairness, the females who have been with him say otherwise."

She unlocked her door, mouth twisting. "Like I said, not interested."

"You sure it's not because you're just avoiding—"

"See, that right there is the problem. You and the whole rest of the world seem to think I exist *just* to find someone like him. That *of course* I can't be genuinely *not* interested, because why *wouldn't* I want a big, strong male to protect me? Surely if I'm pretty and single, the second *any* powerful Vanir shows interest, I'm *bound* to drop my panties. In fact, I didn't even have a *life* until he showed up—never had good sex, never felt *alive*—"

Darkest Hel, this woman. "You've got a real chip on your shoulder there, you know."

Bryce snickered. "You make it really fucking easy, *you know*."

Hunt crossed his arms. She crossed hers.

That stupid fucking ponytail seemed to cross its proverbial arms, too.

"So," Hunt said through his teeth as he dumped his duffel on the ground, clothes and weapons thumping hard. "You gonna come with me to the Oracle tomorrow or what?"

"Oh no, Athalar." Her purred words ran over his skin, and her smile was pure wickedness. Hunt braced himself for whatever was about to come out of her mouth. Even as he found himself looking forward to it. "You get to deal with her alone."

32

After dropping off his gear at the apartment, Hunt trailed Bryce back to work, where she said she intended to look through Danika's location data from Declan and cross-reference it with her own list—and the murder scenes so far.

But the thought of sitting underground for another few hours grated enough that he found himself sitting on the roof instead. He needed the fresh, open air. Even if angels were still flying past—leaving the city. He made a point not to look toward the Comitium, looming at his back.

Just before sundown, Syrinx in tow, Bryce emerged from the gallery with a grim expression that matched Hunt's own.

"Nothing?" he asked, landing on the sidewalk beside her.

"Nothing," she confirmed.

"We'll look tomorrow with fresh eyes." Maybe there was something they were missing. Today had been long and awful and weird, and he was more than ready to collapse on her couch.

He asked as casually as he could, "There's a big sunball game on tonight. You mind if I watch it?"

She glanced at him sidelong, her brows rising.

"What?" he asked, unable to keep the corner of his mouth from twitching upward.

"It's just . . . you're such . . . a *guy*." She waved a hand at him. "With the sports and stuff."

"Females like sports as much as males."

She rolled her eyes. "This sunball-watching person doesn't fit with my mental image of the Shadow of Death."

"Sorry to disappoint." Hunt's turn to lift a brow. "What *do* you think I do with my spare time?"

"I don't know. I assumed you cursed at the stars and brooded and plotted revenge on all your enemies."

She didn't know the half of it. But Hunt let out a low chuckle. "Again, sorry to disappoint."

Her eyes crinkled with amusement, the last of the day's sun lighting them into liquid gold. He forced himself to monitor the streets around them.

They were a block from Bryce's apartment when Hunt's phone rang. She tensed, peering at his screen the same moment he did.

The phone rang a second time. They both stared at the name that popped up, pedestrians streaming past.

"You gonna answer it?" Bryce asked quietly.

It rang a third time.

Hunt knew. Before he hit the button, he knew.

Which was why he stepped away from Quinlan, putting the phone to his ear just as he said blandly, "Hi, boss."

"I have work for you tonight," Micah said.

Hunt's gut twisted. "Sure."

"I hope I'm not interrupting your fun with Miss Quinlan."

"We're good," Hunt said tightly.

Micah's pause was loaded. "What occurred in the lobby this morning is never to happen again. Understood?"

"Yes." He bit out the word. But he said it—and meant it—because the alternative to Micah was now staying at the Governor's residence in the Comitium. Because Sandriel would have drawn out his punishment for refusing to bow, for embarrassing her, for days, weeks. Months.

But Micah would give him this warning, and make him do this job tonight to remind him where the fuck he stood in the pecking order, and then that would be that.

"Good," Micah said. "The file's waiting at your room in the barracks." He paused, as if sensing the question now burning through Hunt. "The offer still stands, Athalar. Don't make me reconsider." The call ended.

Hunt clenched his jaw hard enough to hurt.

Quinlan's forehead wrinkled with concern. "Everything okay?"

Hunt slid the phone into his pocket. "It's fine." He resumed walking. "Just legion business." Not a lie. Not entirely.

The glass doors to her building opened. Hunt nodded toward the lobby. "You head up. I've got something to do. I'll call if we get the date and time for Briggs."

Her amber eyes narrowed. Yeah, she saw right through it. Or rather, heard everything he wasn't saying. Knew what Micah had ordered him to do.

But she said, "All right." She turned toward the lobby, but added over her shoulder, "Good luck."

He didn't bother answering before he shot into the skies, phone already to his ear as he called Justinian to ask him to play sentry for a few hours. Justinian whined about missing the sunball game, but Hunt pulled rank, earning a grumbled promise that the angel would be at the adjacent rooftop in ten minutes.

Justinian arrived in eight. Leaving his brother-in-arms to it, Hunt sucked in a breath of dusty, dry air, the Istros a teal ribbon to his left, and went to do what he did best.

"Please."

It was always the same word. The only word people tended to say when the Umbra Mortis stood before them.

Through the blood splattered on his helmet, Hunt regarded the male cougar shifter cowering before him. His clawed hands shook as he left them upraised. "Please," the man sobbed.

Every utterance dragged Hunt further away. Until the arm he

outstretched was distant, until the gun he aimed at the male's head was just a bit of metal.

A death for a death.

"Please."

The male had done horrible things. Unspeakable things. He deserved this. Deserved worse.

"Pleasepleaseplease."

Hunt was nothing but a shadow, a wisp of life, an instrument of death.

He was nothing and no one at all.

"Ple—"

Hunt's finger curled on the trigger.

Hunt returned early. Well, early for him.

Thankfully, no one was in the barracks bathroom while he showered off the blood. Then sat under the scalding spray for so long that he lost track of time.

He would have stayed longer had he not known that Justinian was waiting.

So he patched himself up, pieced himself together. Half crawled out of the boiling-hot shower and into the person he was when he wasn't forced to put a bullet between someone's eyes.

He made a few stops before getting back to Bryce's apartment. But he made it back, relieving Justinian from his duties, and walked through Bryce's door at eleven.

She was in her bedroom, the door shut, but Syrinx let out a little yowl of welcome from within. Her scolding hush was proof that she'd heard Hunt return. Hunt prayed she wouldn't come into the hall. Words were still beyond him.

Her doorknob turned. But Hunt was already at his room, and didn't dare look across the expanse of the great room as she said tightly, "You're back."

"Yeah," he choked out.

Even across the room, he could feel her questions. But she said softly, "I recorded the game for you. If you still want to watch it."

Something tightened unbearably in his chest. But Hunt didn't look back.

He slipped into his room with a mumbled "Night," and shut the door behind him.

33

The Oracle's black chamber reeked of sulfur and roasted meat—the former from the natural gases rising from the hole in the center of the space, the latter from the pile of bull bones currently smoldering atop the altar against the far wall, an offering to Ogenas, Keeper of Mysteries.

After last night, what he'd done, a sacred temple was the last place he wanted to be. The last place he deserved to be.

The twenty-foot doors shut behind Hunt as he strode across the silent chamber, aiming for the hole in the center and wall of smoke behind it. His eyes burned with the various acrid scents, and he summoned a wind to keep them out of his face.

Behind the smoke, a figure moved. "I wondered when the Shadow of Death would darken my chamber," a lovely voice said. Young, full of light and amusement—and yet tinged with ancient cruelty.

Hunt halted at the edge of the hole, avoiding the urge to peer into the endless blackness. "I won't take much of your time," he said, his voice swallowed by the room, the pit, the smoke.

"I shall give you what time Ogenas offers." The smoke parted, and he sucked in a breath at the being that emerged.

Sphinxes were rare—only a few dozen walked the earth, and all of them had been called to the service of the gods. No one knew how old they were, and this one before him . . . She was so beautiful he forgot what to do with his body. The golden lioness's form moved with fluid grace, pacing the other side of the hole, weaving in and out of the mist. Golden wings lay folded against the slender body, shimmering as if they were crafted from molten metal. And above that winged lion's body . . . the golden-haired woman's face was as flawless as Shahar's had been.

No one knew her name. She was simply her title: Oracle. He wondered if she was so old that she'd forgotten her true name.

The sphinx blinked large brown eyes at him, lashes brushing against her light brown cheeks. "Ask me your question, and I shall tell you what the smoke whispers to me." The words rumbled over his bones, luring him in. Not in the way he sometimes let himself be lured in by beautiful females, but in the manner that a spider might lure a fly to its web.

Maybe Quinlan and her cousin had a point about not wanting to come here. Hel, Quinlan had refused to even set foot in the park surrounding the black-stoned temple, opting to wait on a bench at its edge with Ruhn.

"What I say here is confidential, right?" he asked.

"Once the gods speak, I become the conduit through which their words pass." She arranged herself on the floor before the hole, folding her front paws, claws glinting in the dim light of the braziers smoldering to either side of them. "But yes—this shall be confidential."

It sounded like a whole bunch of bullshit, but he blew out a breath, meeting those large brown eyes, and said, "Why does someone want Luna's Horn?"

He didn't ask who had taken it—he knew from the reports that she had already been asked that question two years ago and had refused to answer.

She blinked, wings rustling as if in surprise, but settled herself. Breathed in the fumes rising from the hole. Minutes passed, and Hunt's head began to throb with the various scents—especially the reeking sulfur.

Smoke swirled, masking the sphinx from sight even though she sat only ten feet away.

Hunt forced himself to keep still.

A rasping voice slithered out of the smoke. "To open the doorway between worlds." A chill seized Hunt. "They wish to use the Horn to reopen the Northern Rift. The Horn's purpose wasn't merely to close doors—it opens them, too. It depends on what the bearer wishes."

"But the Horn is broken."

"It can be healed."

Hunt's heart stalled. "How?"

A long, long pause. Then, "It is veiled. I cannot see. None can see."

"The Fae legends say it can't be repaired."

"Those are legends. This is truth. The Horn can be repaired."

"Who wants to do this?" He had to ask, even if it was foolish.

"This, too, is veiled."

"Helpful."

"Be grateful, Lord of Lightning, that you learned anything at all." That voice—that title . . . His mouth went dry. "Do you wish to know what I see in your future, Orion Athalar?"

He recoiled at the sound of his birth name like he'd been punched in the gut. "No one has spoken that name in two hundred years," he whispered.

"The name your mother gave you."

"Yes," he ground out, his gut twisting at the memory of his mother's face, the love that had always shone in her eyes for him. Utterly undeserved, that love—especially when he had not been there to protect her.

The Oracle whispered, "Shall I tell you what I see, Orion?"

"I'm not sure I want to know."

The smoke peeled back enough for him to see her sensuous lips part in a cruel smile that did not wholly belong in this world. "People come from across Midgard to plead for my visions, yet you do not wish to know?"

The hair on the back of his neck stood. "I thank you, but no." Thanks seemed wise—like something that might appease a god.

Her teeth shone, her canines long enough to shred flesh. "Did Bryce Quinlan tell you what occurred when she stood in this chamber twelve years ago?"

His blood turned to ice. "That's Quinlan's business."

That smile didn't falter. "You do not wish to know what I saw for her, either?"

"No." He spoke from his heart. "It's her business," he repeated. His lightning rose within him, rallying against a foe he could not slay.

The Oracle blinked, a slow bob of those thick lashes. "You remind me of that which was lost long ago," she said quietly. "I had not realized it might ever appear again."

Before Hunt dared ask what that meant, her lion's tail—a larger version of Syrinx's—swayed over the floor. The doors behind him opened on a phantom wind, his dismissal clear. But the Oracle said before stalking into the vapors, "Do yourself a favor, Orion Athalar: keep well away from Bryce Quinlan."

34

Bryce and Ruhn had waited at the edge of the Oracle's Park for Hunt, each minute dripping by. And when he'd emerged again, eyes searching every inch of her face . . . Bryce knew it was bad. Whatever he'd learned.

Hunt waited until they'd walked down a quiet residential block bordering the park before he told them what the Oracle had said about the Horn.

His words were still hanging in the bright morning air around them as Bryce blew out a breath. Hunt did the same beside her and then said, "If someone has learned how to repair the Horn after so long, then they can do the opposite of what Prince Pelias did. They can *open* the Northern Rift. It seems like one Hel of a motive to kill anyone who might rat them out."

Ruhn ran a hand over the buzzed side of his hair. "Like the acolyte at the temple—either as a warning to us to stay the fuck away from the Horn or to keep her from saying anything, if she'd found out somehow."

Hunt nodded. "Isaiah questioned the others at the temple—they said the girl was the only acolyte on duty the night the Horn was stolen, and was interviewed then, but claimed she didn't know anything about it."

Guilt twisted and writhed within Bryce.

Ruhn said, "Maybe she was scared to say anything. And when we showed up . . ."

Hunt finished, "Whoever is looking for the Horn doesn't want us anywhere near it. They could have learned she'd been on duty that night and gone to extract information from her. They'd have wanted to make sure she didn't reveal what she knew to anyone else—to make sure she stayed silent. Permanently."

Bryce added the girl's death to the list of others she'd repay before this was finished.

Then she asked, "If that mark on the crate really was the Horn, maybe the Ophion—or even just the Keres sect—is seeking the Horn to aid in their rebellion. To open a portal to Hel, and bring the demon princes back here in some sort of alliance to overthrow the Asteri." She shuddered. "Millions would die." At their chilled silence, she went on, "Maybe Danika caught on to their plans about the Horn—and was killed for it. And the acolyte, too."

Hunt rubbed the back of his neck, his face ashen. "They'd need help from a Vanir to summon a demon like that, but it's a possibility. There are some Vanir pledged to their cause. Or maybe one of the witches summoned it. The new witch queen could be testing her power, or something."

"Unlikely that a witch was involved," Ruhn said a shade tightly, piercings along his ear glinting in the sun. "The witches obey the Asteri—they've had millennia of unbroken loyalty."

Bryce said, "But the Horn can only be used by a Starborn Fae—by you, Ruhn."

Hunt's wings rustled. "So maybe they're looking for some way around the Starborn shit."

"Honestly," Ruhn said, "I'm not sure I *could* use the Horn. Prince Pelias possessed what was basically an ocean of starlight at his disposal." Her brother's brow furrowed, and a pinprick of light appeared at his fingertip. "This is about as good as it gets for me."

"Well, you're not going to use the Horn, even if we find it, so it won't matter," Bryce said.

Ruhn crossed his arms. "If someone can repair the Horn . . . I don't even know how that would be possible. I read some mentions of the Horn having a sort of sentience to it—almost like it was alive. Maybe a healing power of some sort would be applicable? A med-witch might have some insight."

Bryce countered, "They heal people, not objects. And the book you found in the gallery's library said the Horn could only be repaired by light that is not light, magic that is not magic."

"Legends," said Hunt. "Not truth."

"It's worth looking into," Ruhn said, and halted, glancing between Bryce and Hunt, who was watching her warily from the corner of his eye. Whatever the fuck that meant. Ruhn said, "I'll look up a few medwitches and pay some discreet visits."

"Fine," she said. When he stiffened, she amended, "That sounds good."

Even if nothing else about this case did.

Bryce tuned out the sound of Lehabah watching one of her dramas and tried to concentrate on the map of Danika's locations. Tried but failed, since she could feel Hunt's eyes lingering on her from across the library table. For the hundredth time in that hour alone. She met his stare, and he looked away quickly. "What?"

He shook his head and went back to his research.

"You've been staring at me all afternoon with that weird fucking look on your face."

He drummed his fingers on the table, then blurted, "You want to tell me why the Oracle warned me to stay the Hel away from you?"

Bryce let out a short laugh. "Is that why you seemed all freaked when you left the temple?"

"She said she'd reveal her vision for you—like she has a damned bone to pick with you."

A shiver crawled down Bryce's spine at that. "I don't blame her if she's still pissed."

Hunt paled, but Bryce said, "In Fae culture, there's a custom: when girls get their cycle for the first time, or when they turn thirteen, they go to an Oracle. The visit provides a glimpse toward what sort of power they might ascend to when mature, so their parents can plan unions years before the actual Drop. Boys go, too—at age thirteen. These days, if the parents are progressive, it's just an old tradition to figure out a career for their children. Soldiers or healers or whatever Fae do if they can't afford to lounge around eating grapes all day."

"The Fae and malakim might hate each other, but they have a lot of bullshit in common."

Bryce hummed her agreement. "My cycle started when I was a few weeks shy of thirteen. And my mom had this . . . I don't know. Crisis? This sudden fear that she'd shut me off from a part of my heritage. She got in touch with my biological father. Two weeks later, the documents showed up, declaring me a full civitas. It came with a catch, though: I had to claim Sky and Breath as my House. I refused, but my mom actually insisted I do it. She saw it as some kind of . . . protection. I don't know. Apparently, she was convinced enough of his intention to protect me that she asked if he wanted to meet me. For the first time. And I eventually cooled down enough from the whole House allegiance thing to realize I wanted to meet him, too."

Hunt read her beat of silence. "It didn't go well."

"No. That visit was the first time I met Ruhn, too. I came here—stayed in FiRo for the summer. I met the Autumn King." The lie was easy. "Met my father, too," she added. "In the initial few days, the visit wasn't as bad as my mother had feared. I liked what I saw. Even if some of the other Fae children whispered that I was a half-breed, I knew what I was. I've never not been proud of it—being human, I mean. And I knew my father had invited me, so he at least wanted me there. I didn't mind what others thought. Until the Oracle."

He winced. "I have a bad feeling about this."

"It was catastrophic." She swallowed against the memory. "When the Oracle looked into her smoke, she screamed. Clawed at her eyes." There was no point hiding it. The event had been known in some circles. "I heard later that she went blind for a week."

"Holy shit."

Bryce laughed to herself. "Apparently, my future is *that* bad."

Hunt didn't smile. "What happened?"

"I returned to the petitioners' antechamber. All you could hear was the Oracle screaming and cursing me—the acolytes rushed in."

"I meant with your father."

"He called me a worthless disgrace, stormed out of the temple's VIP exit so no one could know who he was to me, and by the time I caught up, he'd taken the car and left. When I got back to his house, I found my bags on the curb."

"Asshole. Danaan had nothing to say about him kicking his cousin to the curb?"

"The king forbade Ruhn to interfere." She examined her nails. "Believe me, Ruhn tried to fight. But the king bound him. So I got a cab to the train station. Ruhn managed to shove money for the fares into my hand."

"Your mom must have gone ballistic."

"She did." Bryce paused a moment and then said, "Seems like the Oracle's still pissed."

He threw her a half smile. "I'd consider it a badge of honor."

Bryce, despite herself, smiled back. "You're probably the only one who thinks that." His eyes lingered on her face again, and she knew it had nothing to do with what the Oracle had said.

Bryce cleared her throat. "Find anything?"

Catching her request to drop the subject, Hunt pivoted the laptop toward her. "I've been looking at this ancient shit for days—and this is all I've found."

The terra-cotta vase dated back nearly fifteen thousand years. After Prince Pelias by about a century, but the kristallos hadn't yet faded from common memory. She read the brief catalog copy and said, "It's at a gallery in Mirsia." Which put it a sea and two thousand miles beyond that from Lunathion. She pulled the computer to her and clicked on the thumbnail. "But these photos should be enough."

"I might have been born before computers, Quinlan, but I do know how to use them."

"I'm just trying to spare you from further ruining your badass image as the Umbra Mortis. We can't have word getting out that you're a computer nerd."

"Thanks for your concern." His eyes met hers, the corner of his mouth kicking up.

Her toes might have curled in her heels. Slightly.

Bryce straightened. "All right. Tell me what I'm looking at."

"A good sign." Hunt pointed at the image, rendered in black paint against the burnt orange of the terra-cotta, of the kristallos demon roaring as a sword was driven through its head by a helmeted male warrior.

She leaned toward the screen. "How so?"

"That the kristallos can be killed the old-fashioned way. As far as I can tell, there's no magic or special artifact being used to kill it here. Just plain brute force."

Her gut tightened. "This vase could be an artistic interpretation. That thing killed Danika and the Pack of Devils, and knocked Micah on his ass, too. And you mean to tell me some ancient warrior killed it with just a sword through the head?"

Though Lehabah's show kept playing, Bryce knew the sprite was listening to every word.

Hunt said, "Maybe the kristallos had the element of surprise on its side that night."

She tried and failed to block out the red pulped piles, the spray of blood on the walls, the way her entire body had seemed to plummet downward even while standing still as she stared at what was left of her friends. "Or maybe this is just a bullshit rendering by an artist who heard an embellished song around a fire and did their own take on it." She began tapping her foot under the table, as if it'd somehow calm her staccato heartbeat.

He held her stare, his black eyes stark and honest. "All right." She waited for him to push, to pry, but Hunt slid the computer back to his side of the table. He squinted. "That's odd. It says the vase is originally from Parthos." He angled his head. "I thought Parthos was a myth. A human fairy tale."

"Because humans were no better than rock-banging animals until the Asteri arrived?"

"Tell me you don't believe that conspiracy crap about an ancient library in the heart of a pre-existing human civilization?" When she didn't answer, Hunt challenged, "If something like that *did* exist, where's the evidence?"

Bryce zipped her amulet along its chain and nodded toward the image on the screen.

"This vase was made by a nymph," he said. "Not some mythical, enlightened human."

"Maybe Parthos hadn't been wiped off the map entirely at that point."

Hunt looked at her from under lowered brows. "Really, Quinlan?" When she again didn't answer, he jerked his chin at her digital tablet. "Where are you with the data about Danika's locations?"

Hunt's phone buzzed before she could reply, but Bryce said, reeling herself back together as that image of the slain kristallos bled with what had been done to Danika, what had been left of her, "I'm still ruling out the things that were likely unconnected, but . . . Really, the only outlier here is the fact that Danika was on sentry duty at Luna's Temple. She was sometimes stationed in the general area, but never specifically at the temple itself. And somehow, days before she died, she got put on watch there? And data shows her being *right there* when the Horn was stolen. The acolyte was *also* there that night. It's all got to tie together somehow."

Hunt set down his phone. "Maybe Philip Briggs will enlighten us tonight."

Her head snapped up. "Tonight?"

Lehabah completely stopped watching her show at that.

"Just got the message from Viktoria. They transferred him from Adrestia. We're meeting him in an hour in a holding cell under the Comitium." He surveyed the data spread before them. "He's going to be difficult."

"I know."

He leaned back in the chair. "He's not going to have nice things to say about Danika. You sure you can handle hearing his kind of venom?"

"I'm fine."

"Really? Because that vase just set you off, and I doubt coming face-to-face with this guy is going to be any easier."

The walls began swelling around her. "Get out." Her words cut between them. "Just because we're working together doesn't mean you're entitled to push into my personal matters."

Hunt merely looked her over. Saw all of that. But he said roughly, "I want to head to the Comitium in twenty. I'll wait for you outside."

Bryce trailed Hunt out, making sure he didn't touch any of the books and that they didn't grab for him, then shut the door before he'd fully walked onto the street beyond.

She sank against the iron until she sat on the carpet, and braced her forearms on her knees.

They were gone—all of them. Thanks to that demon depicted on an ancient vase. They were gone, and there would be no more wolves in her life. No more hanging out in the apartment. No more drunken, stupid dancing on street corners, or blasting music at three in the morning until their neighbors threatened to call the 33rd.

No friends who would say *I love you* and mean it. Syrinx and Lele came creeping in, the chimera curling up beneath her bent legs, the sprite lying belly-down on Bryce's forearm.

"Don't blame Athie. I think he wants to be our friend."

"I don't give a shit what Hunt Athalar wants."

"June is busy with ballet, and Fury is as good as gone. Maybe it's time for more friends, BB. You seem sad again. Like you were two winters ago. Fine one minute, then not fine the next. You don't dance, you don't hang out with anyone, you don't—"

"Leave it, Lehabah."

"Hunt is nice. And Prince Ruhn is nice. But Danika was never nice to me. Always biting and snarling. Or she ignored me."

"*Watch it.*"

The sprite crawled off her arm and floated in front of her, arms wrapping across her round belly. "You can be cold as a Reaper,

Bryce." Then she was gone, whizzing off to stop a thick leather-bound tome from crawling its way up the stairs.

Bryce blew out a long breath, trying to piece the hole in her chest together.

Twenty minutes, Hunt had said. She had twenty minutes before going to question Briggs. Twenty minutes to get her shit together. Or at least pretend she had.

35

The fluorescent wands of firstlight hummed through the white-paneled, pristine corridor far beneath the Comitium. Hunt was a storm of black and gray against the shining white tiles, his steps unfaltering as he aimed for one of the sealed metal doors at the end of the long hall.

A step behind him, Bryce simply watched Hunt move—the way he cut through the world, the way the guards in the entry room hadn't so much as checked his ID before waving them through.

She hadn't realized that this place existed beneath the five shining towers of the Comitium. That they had cells. Interrogation rooms.

The one she'd been in the night Danika had died had been five blocks from here. A facility governed by protocols. But this place . . . She tried not to think about what this place was for. What laws stopped applying once one crossed over the threshold.

The lack of any scent except bleach suggested it was scrubbed down often. The drains she noted every few feet suggested—

She didn't want to know what the drains suggested.

They reached a room without windows, and Hunt laid a palm against the circular metal lock to its left. A hum and hiss, and he shouldered open the door, peering inside before nodding to her.

The firstlights above droned like hornets. What would her own firstlight go toward, small mote that it would be? With Hunt, the explosion of energy-filled light that had probably erupted from him when he'd made the Drop had likely gone toward fueling an entire city.

She sometimes wondered about it: whose firstlight was powering her phone, or the stereo, or her coffee machine.

And now was not the time to think about random shit, she chided herself as she followed Hunt into the cell and beheld the pale-skinned man sitting there.

Two seats had been set before the metal table in the center of the room—where Briggs's shackles were currently chained. His white jumpsuit was pristine, but—

Bryce beheld the state of his gaunt, hollow face and willed herself not to flinch. His dark hair was buzzed close to his scalp, and though not a bruise or scratch marred his skin, his deep blue eyes . . . empty and hopeless.

Briggs said nothing as she and Hunt claimed the seats across the table. Cameras blinked red lights in every corner, and she had no doubt someone was listening in a control room a few doors down.

"We won't take much of your time," Hunt said, as if noting those haunted eyes as well.

"Time is all I have now, angel. And being here is better than being . . . there."

There, where they kept him in Adrestia Prison. Where they did the things to him that resulted in those broken, awful eyes.

Bryce could feel Hunt silently urging her to ask the first of their questions, and she took a breath, bracing herself to fill this humming, too-small room with her voice.

But Briggs asked, "What month is it? What's today's date?"

Horror coiled in her gut. This man had wanted to kill people, she reminded herself. Even if it seemed he hadn't killed Danika, he had planned to kill plenty of others, to ignite a larger-scale war between the human and Vanir. To overthrow the Asteri. It was why he remained behind bars.

"It's the twelfth of April," Hunt said, his voice low, "in the year 15035."

"It's only been two years?"

Bryce swallowed against the dryness in her mouth. "We came to ask you about some things related to two years ago. As well as some recent events."

Briggs looked at her then. Really looked. "Why?"

Hunt leaned back, a silent indication that this was now her show to run. "The White Raven nightclub was bombed a few days ago. Considering that it was one of your prime targets a few years ago, evidence points toward Keres being active again."

"And you think I'm behind it?" A bitter smile curved the angular, harsh face. Hunt tensed. "I don't know what *year* it is, girl. And you think I'm somehow able to make outside contact?"

"What about your followers?" Hunt said carefully. "Would they have done it in your name?"

"Why bother?" Briggs reclined in his chair. "I failed them. I failed our people." He nodded toward Bryce. "And failed people like you—the undesirables."

"You never represented me," Bryce said quietly. "I abhor what you tried to do."

Briggs laughed, a broken rasp. "When the Vanir tell you you're not good enough for any job because of your human blood, when males like this asshole next to you just see you as a piece of ass to be fucked and then discarded, when you see your mother—it is a human mother for you, isn't it? It always is—being treated like trash . . . You'll find those self-righteous feelings fading real fast."

She refused to reply. To think about the times she'd seen her mother ignored or sneered at—

Hunt said, "So you're saying you're not behind this bombing."

"Again," Briggs said, tugging on his shackles, "the only people I see on a daily basis are the ones who take me apart like a cadaver, and then stitch me up again before nightfall, their medwitches smoothing everything away."

Her stomach churned. Even Hunt's throat bobbed as he swallowed.

"Your followers wouldn't have considered bombing the nightclub in revenge?"

Briggs demanded, "Against who?"

"Us. For investigating Danika Fendyr's murder and looking for Luna's Horn."

Briggs's blue eyes shuttered. "So the assholes in the 33rd finally realized I didn't kill her."

"You haven't been officially cleared of anything," Hunt said roughly.

Briggs shook his head, staring at the wall to his left. "I don't know anything about Luna's Horn, and I'm sure as shit no Keres soldier did either, but I liked Danika Fendyr. Even when she busted me, I liked her."

Hunt stared at the gaunt, haunted man—a shell of the powerfully built adult he'd been two years ago. What they were doing to him in that prison . . . Fucking Hel.

Hunt could take a few guesses about the manner of torture. The memories of it being inflicted upon him still dragged him from sleep.

Bryce was blinking at Briggs. "What do you mean, you *liked* her?"

Briggs smiled, savoring Quinlan's surprise. "She circled me and my agents for weeks. She even met with me twice. Told me to stop my plans—or else she'd have to bring me in. Well, that was the first time. The second time she warned me that she had enough evidence against me that she *had* to bring me in, but I could get off easy if I admitted to my plotting and ended it then and there. I didn't listen then, either. That third time . . . She brought her pack, and that was that."

Hunt reined in his emotions, setting his features into neutrality.

"Danika went easy on you?" Bryce's face had drained of color. It took a surprising amount of effort not to touch her hand.

"She tried to." Briggs ran gnarled fingers down his pristine jumpsuit. "For a Vanir, she was fair. I don't think she necessarily disagreed with us. With my methods, yes, but I thought she might have been a sympathizer." He surveyed Bryce again with a starkness that had Hunt's hackles rising.

Hunt suppressed a growl at the term. "Your followers knew this?"

"Yes. I think she even let some of them get away that night."

Hunt blew out a breath. "That is a big fucking claim to make against an Aux leader."

"She's dead, isn't she? Who cares?"

Bryce flinched. Enough so that Hunt didn't hold back his growl this time.

"Danika wasn't a rebel sympathizer," Bryce hissed.

Briggs looked down his nose at her. "Not yet, maybe," he agreed, "but Danika could have been starting down that path. Maybe *she* saw how her pretty, half-breed friend was treated by others and didn't like it too much, either." He smiled knowingly when Bryce blinked at his correct guess regarding her relationship to Danika. The emotions he'd probably read in her face.

Briggs went on, "My followers knew Danika was a potential asset. We'd discussed it, right up until the raid. And that night, Danika and her pack were fair with us. We fought, and even managed to get in a few good blows on that Second of hers." He whistled. "Connor Holstrom." Bryce went utterly rigid. "Guy was a bruiser." From the cruel curve of his lips, he'd clearly noticed how stiff she'd gone at the mention of Connor's name. "Was Holstrom your boyfriend? Pity."

"That's none of your business." The words were flat as Briggs's eyes.

They tightened something in Hunt's chest, her words. The vacancy in her voice.

Hunt asked him, "You never mentioned any of this when you were initially arrested?"

Briggs spat, "Why the *fuck* would I ever rat out a potentially sympathetic, incredibly powerful Vanir like Danika Fendyr? I might have been headed for *this*"—he gestured to the cell around them—"but the cause would live on. It *had* to live on, and I knew that someone like Danika could be a mighty ally to have on our side."

Hunt cut in, "But why not mention any of this during your murder trial?"

"My trial? You mean that two-day sham they televised? With that *lawyer* the Governor assigned me?" Briggs laughed and laughed. Hunt had to remind himself that this was an imprisoned man, enduring unspeakable torture. And not someone he could punch in the face. Not even for the way his laugh made Quinlan shift in her seat. "I knew they'd pin it on me no matter what. Knew that even if I told the truth, I'd wind up here. So on the chance that Danika might have friends still living who shared her sentiments, I kept her secrets to myself."

"You're ratting her out now," Bryce said.

But Briggs didn't reply to that, and instead studied the dented metal table. "I said it two years ago, and I'll say it again now: Keres didn't kill Danika or the Pack of Devils. The White Raven bombing, though—they might have managed that. Good for them if they did."

Hunt ground his teeth. Had he been this out of touch with reality when he'd followed Shahar? Had it been this level of fanaticism that prompted him to lead the angels of the 18th to Mount Hermon? In those last days, would he have even *listened* to anyone if they'd advised against it?

A hazy memory surfaced, of Isaiah doing just that, screaming in Hunt's war tent. Fuck.

Briggs asked, "Did a lot of Vanir die in the bombing?"

Disgust curdled Bryce's face. "No," she said, standing from her chair. "Not a single one." She spoke with the imperiousness of a queen. Hunt could only rise with her.

Briggs tsked. "Too bad."

Hunt's fingers balled into fists. He'd been so wildly in love with Shahar, with the cause—had he been no better than this man?

Bryce said tightly, "Thank you for answering our questions." Without waiting for Briggs to reply, she hurried for the door. Hunt kept a step behind her, even with Briggs anchored to the table.

That she'd ended the meeting so quickly showed Hunt that Bryce shared his opinion: Briggs truly hadn't killed Danika.

He'd nearly reached the open doorway when Briggs said to him, "You're one of the Fallen, huh?" Hunt paused. Briggs smiled.

"Tons of respect for you, man." He surveyed Hunt from head to toe. "What part of the 18th did you serve in?"

Hunt said nothing. But Briggs's blue eyes shone. "We'll bring the bastards down someday, brother."

Hunt glanced toward Bryce, already halfway down the hallway, her steps swift. Like she couldn't stand to breathe the same air as the man chained to the table, like she had to get out of this awful place. Hunt himself had been here, interrogated people, more often than he cared to remember.

And the kill he'd made last night . . . It had lingered. Ticked off another life-debt, but it had lingered.

Briggs was still staring at him, waiting for Hunt to speak. The agreement that Hunt would have voiced weeks ago now dissolved on his tongue.

No, he'd been no better than this man.

He didn't know where that put him.

"So Briggs and his followers are off the list," Bryce said, folding her feet beneath her on her living room couch. Syrinx was already snoring beside her. "Unless you think he was lying?"

Hunt, seated at the other end of the sectional, frowned at the sunball game just starting on TV. "He was telling the truth. I've dealt with enough . . . prisoners to sense when someone's lying."

The words were clipped. He'd been on edge since they'd left the Comitium through the same unmarked street door they'd used to enter. No chance of running into Sandriel that way.

Hunt pointed to the papers Bryce had brought from the gallery, noting some of Danika's movements and the list of names she'd compiled. "Remind me who's the next suspect on your list?"

Bryce didn't answer as she observed his profile, the light of the screen bouncing off his cheekbones, deepening the shadow beneath his strong jaw.

He truly was pretty. And really seemed to be in a piss-poor mood. "What's wrong?"

"Nothing."

"Says the guy who's grinding his teeth so hard I can hear them."

Hunt cut her a glare and spread a muscled arm along the back of the couch. He'd changed when they'd returned thirty minutes ago, having grabbed a quick bite at a noodles-and-dumplings food cart just down the block, and now wore a soft gray T-shirt, black sweats, and a white sunball cap turned backward.

It was the hat that had proven the most confusing—so ordinary and . . . *guy-ish*, for lack of a better word, that she'd been stealing glances at him for the past fifteen minutes. Stray locks of his dark hair curled around the edges, the adjustable band nearly covered the tattoo over his brow, and she had no idea why, but it was all just . . . Disgustingly distracting.

"What?" he asked, noting her gaze.

Bryce reached forward, her long braid slipping over a shoulder, and grabbed his phone from the coffee table. She snapped a photo of him and sent a copy to herself, mostly because she doubted anyone would believe her that Hunt fucking Athalar was sitting on her couch in casual clothes, sunball hat on backward, watching TV and drinking a beer.

The Shadow of Death, everyone.

"That's annoying," he said through his teeth.

"So is your face," she said sweetly, tossing the phone to him. Hunt picked it up, snapped a photo of *her*, and then set it down, eyes on the game again.

She let him watch for another minute before she said, "You've been broody since Briggs."

His mouth twisted toward the side. "Sorry."

"Why are you apologizing?"

His fingers traced a circle along the couch cushion. "It brought up some bad shit. About—about the way I helped lead Shahar's rebellion."

She considered, retracing every horrid word and exchange in that cell beneath the Comitium.

Oh. *Oh.* She said carefully, "You're nothing like Briggs, Hunt."

His dark eyes slid toward her. "You don't know me well enough to say that."

"Did you willingly and gleefully risk innocent lives to further your rebellion?"

His mouth thinned. "No."

"Well, there you have it."

Again, his jaw worked. Then he said, "But I was blind. About a lot of things."

"Like what?"

"Just a lot," he hedged. "Looking at Briggs, what they're doing to him . . . I don't know why it bothered me this time. I've been down there often enough with other prisoners that—I mean . . ." His knee bounced. He said without looking at her, "You know what kinda shit I have to do."

She said gently, "Yeah."

"But for whatever reason, seeing Briggs like that today, it just made me remember my own . . ." He trailed off again and swigged from his beer.

Icy, oily dread filled her stomach, twisting with the fried noodles she'd inhaled thirty minutes ago. "How long did they do that to you—after Mount Hermon?"

"Seven years."

She closed her eyes as the weight of those words rippled through her.

Hunt said, "I lost track of time, too. The Asteri dungeons are so far beneath the earth, so lightless, that days are years and years are days and . . . When they let me out, I went right to the Archangel Ramuel. My first . . . *handler.* He continued the pattern for two years, got bored with it, and realized that I'd be more useful dispatching demons and doing his bidding than rotting away in his torture chambers."

"Burning Solas, Hunt," she whispered.

He still didn't look at her. "By the time Ramuel decided to let me serve as his assassin, it had been nine years since I'd seen sunlight. Since I'd heard the wind or smelled the rain. Since I'd seen grass, or a river, or a mountain. Since I'd flown."

Her hands shook enough that she crossed her arms, tucking her fingers tight to her body. "I—I am so sorry."

His eyes turned distant, glazed. "Hatred was the only thing that fueled me through it. Briggs's kind of hatred. Not hope, not love. Only unrelenting, raging hatred. For the Archangels. For the Asteri. For all of it." He finally looked at her, his eyes as hollow as Briggs's had been. "So, yeah. I might not have ever been willing to kill innocents to help Shahar's rebellion, but that's the only difference between me and Briggs. Still is."

She didn't let herself reconsider before she took his hand.

She hadn't realized how much bigger Hunt's hand was until hers coiled around it. Hadn't realized how many calluses lay on his palms and fingers until they rasped against her skin.

Hunt glanced down at their hands, her dusk-painted nails contrasting with the deep gold of his skin. She found herself holding her breath, waiting for him to snatch his hand back, and asked, "Do you still feel like hatred is all that gets you through the day?"

"No," he said, eyes lifting from their hands to scan her face. "Sometimes, for some things, yes, but . . . No, Quinlan."

She nodded, but he was still watching her, so she reached for the spreadsheets.

"You have nothing else to say?" Hunt's mouth twisted to the side. "You, the person who has an opinion on everything and everyone, have nothing else to say about what I just told you?"

She pushed her braid over her shoulder. "You're not like Briggs," she said simply.

He frowned. And began to withdraw his hand from hers.

Bryce clamped her fingers around his. "You might see yourself that way, but I see you, too, Athalar. I see your kindness and your . . . whatever." She squeezed his hand for emphasis. "I see all the shit you conveniently forget. Briggs is a bad person. He might have once gotten into the human rebellion for the right reasons, but he is a *bad person*. You aren't. You will never be. End of story."

"This bargain I've got with Micah suggests otherwise—"

"You're not like him."

The weight of his stare pressed on her skin, warmed her face.

She withdrew her hand as casually as she could, trying not to note how his own fingers seemed hesitant to let go. But she leaned forward, stretching out her arm, and flicked his hat. "What's up with this, by the way?"

He batted her away. "It's a hat."

"It doesn't fit with your whole predator-in-the-night image."

For a heartbeat, he was utterly silent. Then he laughed, tipping back his head. The strong tan column of his throat worked with the movement, and Bryce crossed her arms again.

"Ah, Quinlan," he said, shaking his head. He swept the hat off his head and plunked it down atop her own. "You're merciless."

She grinned, twisting the cap backward the way he'd worn it, and primly shuffled the papers. "Let's look this over again. Since Briggs was a bust, and the Viper Queen's out . . . maybe there's something with Danika at Luna's Temple the night the Horn was stolen that we're missing."

He drifted closer, his thigh grazing her bent knee, and peered at the papers in her lap. She watched his eyes slide over them as he studied the list of locations. And tried not to think about the warmth of that thigh against her leg. The solid muscle of it.

Then he lifted his head.

He was close enough that she realized his eyes weren't black after all, but rather a shade of darkest brown. "We're idiots."

"At least you said *we*."

He snickered, but didn't pull back. Didn't move that powerful leg of his. "The temple has exterior cameras. They would have been recording the night the Horn was stolen."

"You make it sound as if the 33rd didn't check that two years ago. They said the blackout rendered any footage essentially useless."

"Maybe we didn't run the right tests on the footage. Look at the right fields. Ask the right people to examine it. If Danika was there that night, why didn't anyone know that? Why didn't *she* come forward about being at the temple when the Horn was stolen? Why didn't the acolyte say anything about her presence?"

Bryce chewed on her lip. Hunt's eyes dipped to it. She could have sworn they darkened. That his thigh pressed harder into hers. As if in challenge—a dare to see if she'd back down.

She didn't, but her voice turned hoarse as she said, "You think

Danika might have known who took the Horn—and she tried to hide it?" She shook her head. "Danika wouldn't have done that. She barely seemed to care that the Horn had been stolen at all."

"I don't know," he said. "But let's start by looking at the footage, even if it's a whole lot of nothing. And send it to someone who can give us a more comprehensive analysis." He swiped his hat off her head, and put it back on his own—still backward, still with those little curling pieces of hair peeking around the edges. As if for good measure, he tugged the end of her braid, then folded his hands behind his head as he went back to watching the game.

The absence of his leg against hers was like a cold slap. "Who do you have in mind?"

His mouth just curved upward.

36

The three-level shooting range in Moonwood catered to a lethal, creative clientele. Occupying a converted warehouse that stretched four city blocks along the Istros, it boasted the only sniper-length gallery in the city.

Hunt stopped by every few weeks to keep his skills sharp, usually in the dead of night when no one could gawk at the Umbra Mortis donning a pair of earmuffs and military-grade glasses as he walked through the concrete hallways to one of the private galleries.

It had been late when he'd gotten the idea for this meeting, and then Jesiba had slammed Quinlan with work the next day, so they'd decided to wait until nightfall to see where their quarry wound up. Hunt had bet Bryce a gold mark it'd be a tattoo parlor, and she'd raised him to two gold marks that it'd be a fake-grungy rock bar. But when she'd gotten the reply to her message, it had led them here.

The sniper gallery lay on the northern end of the building, accessible through a heavy metal door that sealed off any sound. They grabbed electronic earmuffs that would stifle the boom of the guns—but still allow them to hear each other's voices—on the way in. Before he entered the gallery, Hunt glanced over a shoulder at Bryce, checking that her earmuffs were in place.

She noted his assessing look and chuckled. "Mother hen."

"I wouldn't want your pretty little ears to get blown out, Quinlan." He didn't give her the chance to reply as he opened the door, thumping music blasting to greet them, and beheld the three males lined up along a waist-high glass barrier.

Lord Tristan Flynn had a sniper rifle aimed toward a person-shaped paper target at the far, far end of the space, so distant a mortal could barely make it out. He'd opted out of using the scope, instead relying on his keen Fae eyesight as Danaan and Declan Emmet stood near him, their own rifles hanging off their shoulders.

Ruhn nodded their way, and motioned to wait a moment.

"He's gonna miss," Emmet observed over the bumping bass of the music, barely sparing Hunt and Bryce a glance. "Off by a half inch."

"Screw you, Dec," Flynn muttered, and fired. The gunshot erupted through the space, the sound absorbed by the padding along the ceiling and walls, and at the far end of the gallery, the piece of paper swayed, the torso rippling.

Flynn lowered the rifle. "Straight shot to the balls, dickbags." He held out his palm toward Ruhn. "Pay up."

Ruhn rolled his eyes and slammed a gold coin into it as he turned to Hunt and Bryce.

Hunt glanced at the prince's two friends, who were now sizing him up as they pulled off their earmuffs and eye gear. He and Bryce followed suit.

He didn't expect the tinge of envy curdling in his gut at the sight of the friends together. A glance at Quinlan's stiff shoulders had him wondering if she felt the same—if she was remembering nights with Danika and the Pack of Devils when they'd had nothing better to do than give each other grief over nonsense.

Bryce shook it off faster than Hunt did as she drawled, "Sorry to interrupt you boys playing commando, but we have some adult things to discuss."

Ruhn set his rifle on the metal table to his left and leaned against the glass barrier. "You could have called."

Bryce strode to the table to examine the gun her cousin had set down. Her nails glimmered against the matte black. Stealth weapons, designed to blend into shadows and not give away their bearer with a gleam. "I didn't want this intel out there in the networks."

Flynn flashed a grin. "Cloak-and-dagger shit. Nice." He sidled up to her at the table, close enough that Hunt found himself tensing. "Color me intrigued."

Quinlan's gift of looking down her nose at males who towered above her usually grated on Hunt to no end. But seeing it used on someone else was a true delight.

Yet that imperious look only seemed to make Flynn's grin grow wider, especially as Bryce said, "I'm not here to talk to you."

"You wound me, Bryce," Flynn drawled.

Declan Emmet snickered. "You up to do some more hacking shit?" Quinlan asked him.

"Call it shit again, Bryce, and see if I help you," Declan said coolly.

"Sorry, sorry. Your technology . . . stuff." She waved a hand. "We need analysis of some footage from Luna's Temple the night the Horn was stolen."

Ruhn went still, his blue eyes flaring as he said to Hunt, "You've got a lead on the Horn?"

Hunt said, "Just laying out the puzzle pieces."

Declan rubbed his neck. "All right. What are you looking for exactly?"

"Everything," Hunt said. "Anything that might come up on the audio or thermal, or if there's a way to make the video any clearer despite the blackout."

Declan set down his rifle beside Ruhn's. "I might have some software that can help, but no promises. If the investigators didn't find anything two years ago, the odds are slim I'll find any anomalies now."

"We know," Bryce said. "How long would it take you to look?"

He seemed to do some mental calculations. "Give me a few days. I'll see what I can find."

"Thank you."

Flynn let out an exaggerated gasp. "I think that's the first time you've ever said those words to us, B."

"Don't get used to it." She surveyed them again with that cool, mocking indifference that made Hunt's pulse begin to pound as drivingly as the beat of the music playing through the chamber's speakers. "Why are you three even here?"

"We do actually work for the Aux, Bryce. That requires the occasional bit of training."

"So where's the rest of your unit?" She made a show of looking around. Hunt didn't bother to hide his mirth. "Or was this a roomies-only kind of thing?"

Declan chuckled. "This was an invite-only session."

Bryce rolled her eyes and said to Ruhn, "I'm sure the Autumn King told you he wants reports on our movements." She crossed her arms. "Keep this"—she gestured to all of them—"quiet for a few days."

"You're asking me to lie to my king," Ruhn said, frowning.

"I'm asking you not to tell him about this for the moment," Bryce said.

Flynn lifted a brow. "Are you saying the Autumn King is one of your suspects?"

"I'm saying I want shit kept quiet." She grinned at Ruhn, showing all her white teeth, the expression more savage than amused. "I'm saying if you three morons leak any of this to your Aux buddies or drunken hookups, I am going to be *very* unhappy."

Honestly, Hunt would have liked nothing more than to grab some popcorn and a beer, kick back in a chair, and watch her verbally fillet these assholes.

"Sounds like a whole lot of big talk," Ruhn said, then indicated the target at the back of the room. "Why don't you put on a little demonstration for Athalar, Bryce?"

She smirked. "I don't need to prove I can handle a big gun to run with the boys' club." Hunt's skin tightened at the feral delight in her eyes as she said *big gun*. Other parts of him tightened, too.

Tristan Flynn said, "Twenty gold marks says we outshoot you."

"Only rich-ass pieces of shit have twenty gold marks to blow on bullshit contests," Bryce said, amber eyes dancing with amusement as she winked at Hunt. His blood thrummed, his body tensing as surely as if she'd gripped his cock. But her gaze already drifted to the distant target.

She snapped the earmuffs over her arched ears.

Flynn rubbed his hands together. "Here we fuckin' go."

Bryce popped on the glasses, adjusted her ponytail, and hefted Ruhn's rifle into her hands. She weighed it in her arms, and Hunt couldn't drag his eyes away from the way her fingers brushed over the chassis, stroking all the way down to the butt plate.

He swallowed hard, but she merely fitted the gun to her shoulder, each movement as comfortable as he'd expect from someone raised by a legendary sharpshooter. She clicked off the safety and didn't bother to use the scope as she said to none of them in particular, "Allow me to demonstrate why you all can kiss my fucking ass."

Three shots cracked over the music, one after another, her body absorbing the kickback of the gun like a champ. Hunt's mouth dried out entirely.

They all peered up at the screen with the feed of the target.

"You only landed one," Flynn snorted, eyeing the hole through the heart of the target.

"No, she didn't," Emmet murmured, just as Hunt saw it, too: the circle wasn't perfect. No, two of its edges bulged outward—barely noticeable.

Three shots, so precise that they'd passed through the same small space.

A chill skittered down Hunt's body that had nothing to do with fear as Bryce merely reset the safety, placed the rifle on the table, and removed the earmuffs and glasses.

She turned, and her eyes met Hunt's again—a new sort of vulnerability shining beneath the self-satisfied narrowing. A challenge thrown down. Waiting to see how he'd react.

How many males had run from this part of her, their alphahole egos threatened by it? Hunt hated them all merely for putting the question in her eyes.

He didn't hear whatever shit Flynn was saying as he put on the earmuffs and eye gear and took up the rifle Bryce had set down, the metal still warm from her body. He didn't hear Ruhn asking him something as he lined up his shot.

No, Hunt only met Bryce's stare as he clicked off the safety.

That click reverberated between them, loud as a thunderclap. Her throat bobbed.

Hunt pulled his gaze from hers and fired one round. With his eagle-sharp vision, he didn't need the scope to see the bullet pass through the hole she'd made.

When he lowered the gun, he found Bryce's cheeks flushed, her eyes like warm whiskey. A quiet sort of light shone in them.

He still didn't hear any of what the males were saying, only had the vague notion of even Ruhn cursing with appreciation. Hunt just held Bryce's stare.

I see you, Quinlan, he silently conveyed to her. *And I like all of it.*

Right back at you, her half smile seemed to say.

Hunt's phone rang, dragging his eyes from the smile that made the floor a little uneven. He fished it from his pocket with fingers that were surprisingly shaky. *Isaiah Tiberian* flashed on the screen. He answered instantly. "What's up?"

Hunt knew Bryce and the Fae males could hear every word as Isaiah said, "Get your asses over to Asphodel Meadows. There's been another murder."

37

Where?" Hunt demanded into the phone, one eye on Quinlan, her arms crossed tight as she listened. All that light had vanished from her eyes.

Isaiah told him the address. A good two miles away. "We've got a team already setting up camp," the commander said.

"We'll be there in a few," Hunt answered, and hung up.

The three Fae males, having heard as well, began packing their gear with swift efficiency. Well trained. Total pains in his ass, but they were well trained.

But Bryce fidgeted, hands twitching at her sides. He'd seen that stark look before. And the fake-ass calm that crept over her as Ruhn and his friends glanced at her.

Then, Hunt had bought into it, essentially bullied her into going to that other murder scene.

Hunt said without looking at the males, "I take it you heard the address." He didn't wait for any of them to confirm before he ordered, "We'll meet you there." Quinlan's eyes flickered, but Hunt didn't take his focus off her as he walked closer. He sensed Danaan, Flynn, and Emmet leaving the gallery, but didn't look to confirm as he halted before her.

The cold emptiness of the sniper range yawned around them.

Again, Quinlan's hands curled, fingers wiggling at her sides.

Like she could shake the dread and pain away. Hunt said calmly, "You want me to handle it?"

Color crept over her freckled cheeks. She pointed to the door with a shaking finger. "Someone *died* while we were dicking around tonight."

Hunt wrapped his hand around her finger. Lowered it to the space between them. "This guilt isn't on you. It's on whoever is doing this."

People like him, butchering in the night.

She tried to yank her finger back, and he let go, remembering her wariness of male Vanir. Of alphaholes.

Bryce's throat bobbed, and she peered around his wing. "I want to go to the scene of the crime." He waited for the rest of it. She blew out an uneven breath. "I need to go," she said, more to herself. Her foot tapped on the concrete floor, in time to the beat of the still-thumping music. She winced. "But I don't want Ruhn or his friends seeing me like this."

"Like what?" It was normal, expected, to be screwed up by what she'd endured.

"Like a fucking mess." Her eyes glowed.

"Why?"

"Because it's none of their business, but they'll make it their business if they see. They're Fae males—sticking their noses into places they don't belong is an art form for them."

Hunt huffed a laugh. "True."

She exhaled again. "Okay," she murmured. "Okay." Her hands still shook, as if her bloody memories swarmed her.

It was instinct to take her hands in his own.

They trembled like glasses rattling on a shelf. Felt as delicate, even with the slick, clammy sweat coating them.

"Take a breath," Hunt said, squeezing her fingers gently.

Bryce closed her eyes, head bowing as she obeyed.

"Another," he commanded.

She did.

"Another."

So Quinlan breathed, Hunt not letting go of her hands until the sweat dried. Until she lifted her head. "Okay," she said again, and this time, the word was solid.

"You good?"

"As good as I'll ever be," she said, but her gaze had cleared.

Unable to help himself, he brushed back a loose tendril of her hair. It slid like cool silk against his fingers as he hooked it behind her arched ear. "You and me both, Quinlan."

Bryce let Hunt fly her to the crime scene. The alley in the Asphodel Meadows was about as seedy as they came: overflowing dumpster, suspect puddles of liquid gleaming, rail-thin animals rooting through the trash, broken glass sparkling in the firstlight from the rusting lamppost.

Glowing blue magi-screens already blocked off the alley entrance. A few technicians and legionaries were on the scene, Isaiah Tiberian, Ruhn, and his friends among them.

The alley lay just off Main Street, in the shadow of the North Gate—the Mortal Gate, most people called it. Apartment buildings loomed, most of them public, all in dire need of repairs. The noises from the cramped avenue beyond the alley echoed off the crumbling brick walls, the cloying reek of trash stuffing itself up her nose. Bryce tried not to inhale too much.

Hunt surveyed the alley and murmured, a strong hand on the small of her back, "You don't need to look, Bryce."

What he'd done for her just now in that shooting range . . . She'd never let anyone, even her parents, see her like that before. Those moments when she couldn't breathe. She usually went into a bathroom or bailed for a few hours or went for a run.

The instinct to flee had been nearly as overwhelming as the panic and dread searing her chest, but . . . she'd seen Hunt come in from his mission the other night. Knew he of all people might get it.

He had. And hadn't balked for one second.

Just as he hadn't balked from seeing her shoot that target, and instead answered it with a shot of his own. Like they were two of a kind, like she could throw anything at him and he'd catch it. Would meet every challenge with that wicked, feral grin.

She could have sworn the warmth from his hands still lingered on her own.

Whatever conversation they'd been having with Isaiah over, Flynn and Declan strode for the magi-screen. Ruhn stood ten feet beyond them, talking to a beautiful, dark-haired medwitch. No doubt asking about what she'd assessed.

Peering around the glowing blue edge to the body hidden beyond, Flynn and Declan swore.

Her stomach bottomed out. Maybe coming here had been a bad idea. She leaned slightly into Hunt's touch.

His fingers dug into her back in silent reassurance before he murmured, "I can look for us."

Us, like they were a unit against this fucking mess of a world.

"I'm fine," she said, her voice mercifully calm. But she didn't move toward the screen.

Flynn pulled away from the blocked-off body and asked Isaiah, "How fresh is this kill?"

"We're putting the TOD at thirty minutes ago," Isaiah answered gravely. "From the remains of the clothes, it looks like it was one of the guards at Luna's Temple. He was on his way home."

Silence rippled around them. Bryce's stomach dropped.

Hunt swore. "I'm gonna take a guess and say he was on duty the night the Horn was stolen?"

Isaiah nodded. "It was the first thing I checked."

Bryce swallowed and said, "We have to be getting close to something, then. Or the murderer is already one step ahead of us, interrogating and then killing anyone who might have known where the Horn disappeared to."

"None of the cameras caught anything?" Flynn asked, his handsome face unusually serious.

"Nothing," Isaiah said. "It's like it knew where they were. Or whoever summoned it did. It stayed out of sight."

Hunt ran his hand up the length of her spine, a solid, calming sweep, and then stepped toward the Commander of the 33rd, his voice low as he said, "To know every camera in this city, especially the hidden ones, would require some clearance." His words hung there, none of them daring to say more, not in public. Hunt asked, "Did anyone report a sighting of a demon?"

A DNA technician emerged from the screen, blood staining the knees of her white jumpsuit. Like she'd knelt in it while she gathered the sample kit dangling from her gloved fingers.

Bryce glanced away again, back toward Main Street.

Isaiah shook his head. "No reports from civilians or patrols yet."

Bryce barely heard him as the facts poured into her mind. Main Street.

She pulled out her phone, drawing up the map of the city. Her location pinged, a red dot on the network of streets.

The males were still talking about the scant evidence when she placed a few pins in the map, then squinted at the ground beneath them. Ruhn had drifted over, falling into conversation with his friends as she tuned them out.

But Hunt noted her focus and turned toward her, his dark brows high. "What?"

She leaned into the shadow of his wing, and could have sworn he folded it more closely around her. "Here's a map of where all the murders happened."

She allowed Ruhn and his friends to prowl near. Even deigned to show them her screen, her hands shaking slightly.

"This one," she said, pointing to the blinking dot, "is us." She pointed to another, close by. "This is where Maximus Tertian died." She pointed to another, this one near Central Avenue. "This is the acolyte's murder." Her throat constricted, but she pushed past it as she pointed to the other dot, a few blocks due north. "Here's where . . ." The words burned. Fuck. Fuck, she had to say it, voice it—

"Danika and the Pack of Devils were killed," Hunt supplied.

Bryce threw him a grateful glance. "Yes. Do you see what I see?"

"No?" Flynn said.

"Didn't you go to some fancy Fae prep school?" she asked. At

Flynn's scowl, she sighed, zooming out on the screen. "Look: all of them took place within steps of one of the major avenues. On top of the ley lines—natural channels for the firstlight to travel through the city."

"Highways of power," Hunt said, his eyes shining. "They flow right through the Gates." Yeah, Athalar got it. He aimed for where Isaiah stood twenty feet away, talking to a tall, blond nymph in a forensics jacket.

Bryce said to the Fae males, to her wide-eyed brother, "Maybe whoever is summoning this demon is drawing upon the power of these ley lines under the city to have the strength to summon it. If all the murders take place near them, maybe that's how the demon appeared."

One of the Aux team called Ruhn's name, and her brother merely gave her an impressed nod before going over to them. She ignored what that admiration did to her, turning her gaze to Hunt instead as he kept walking down the alley, the powerful muscles of his legs shifting. She heard him call to Isaiah as he walked toward the commander, "Have Viktoria run a search on the cameras along Main, Central, and Ward. See if they catch any blip of power—any small surge or drop in temperature that might happen if a demon were summoned." The kristallos might stay out of sight, but surely the cameras would pick up a slight disturbance in the power flow or temperature. "And have her look at the firstlight grid around those times, too. See if anything registered."

Declan watched the angel stride off, then said to Bryce, "You know what he does, right?"

"Look really good in black?" she said sweetly.

Declan growled. "That demon-hunting is a front. He does the Governor's dirty work." His chiseled jaw clenched for a second. "Hunt Athalar is bad news."

She batted her eyelashes. "Good thing I like bad boys."

Flynn let out a low whistle.

But Declan shook his head. "The angels don't give a shit about anyone, B. His goals are not *your* goals. Athalar's goals might not even be the same as Micah's. Be careful."

She nodded to where her brother was again speaking with the stunning medwitch. "I already got the pep talk from Ruhn, don't worry."

Down the alley, Hunt was saying to Isaiah, "Call me if Viktoria gets any video of it." Then he added, as if not quite used to it, "Thanks."

In the distance, clouds gathered. Rain had been predicted for the middle of the night, but it seemed it was arriving sooner.

Hunt stalked back toward them. "They're on it."

"We'll see if the 33rd follows through this time," Declan muttered. "I'm not holding my breath."

Hunt straightened. Bryce waited for his defense, but the angel shrugged. "Me neither."

Flynn jerked his head toward the angels working the scene. "No loyalty?"

Hunt read a message that flashed on his phone's screen, then pocketed it. "I don't have any choice but to be loyal."

And to tick off those deaths one by one. Bryce's stomach twisted.

Declan's amber eyes dropped to the tattoo on Hunt's wrist. "It's fucked up."

Flynn grumbled his agreement. At least her brother's friends were on the same page as her regarding the politics of the Asteri.

Hunt looked the males over again. Assessing. "Yeah," he said quietly. "It is."

"Understatement of the century." Bryce surveyed the murder scene, her body tightening again, not wanting to look. Hunt met her eyes, as if sensing that tightening, the shift in her scent. He gave her a subtle nod.

Bryce lifted her chin and declared, "We're going now."

Declan waved. "I'll call you soon, B."

Flynn blew her a kiss.

She rolled her eyes. "Bye." She caught Ruhn's stare and motioned her farewell. Her brother threw her a wave, and continued talking to the witch.

They made it all of one block before Hunt said, a little too casually, "You and Tristan Flynn ever hook up?"

Bryce blinked. "Why would you ask that?"

He tucked in his wings. "Because he flirts with you nonstop."

She snorted. "You wanna tell me about everyone you've ever hooked up with, Athalar?"

His silence told her enough. She smirked.

But then the angel said, as if he needed something to distract him from the pulped remains they'd left behind, "None of my *hookups* are worth mentioning." He paused again, taking a breath before continuing. "But that's because Shahar ruined me for anyone else."

Ruined me. The words clanged through Bryce.

Hunt went on, eyes swimming with memory, "I grew up in Shahar's territory in the southeast of Pangera, and as I worked my way up the ranks of her legions, I fell in love with her. With her vision for the world. With her ideas about how the angel hierarchies might change." He swallowed. "Shahar was the only one who ever suggested to me that I'd been denied anything by being born a bastard. She promoted me through her ranks, until I served as her right hand. Until I was her lover." He blew out a long breath. "She led the rebellion against the Asteri, and I led her forces—the 18th Legion. You know how it ended."

Everyone in Midgard did. The Daystar would have led the angels—maybe everyone—to a freer world, but she'd been extinguished. Another dreamer crushed under the boot heel of the Asteri.

Hunt said, "So you and Flynn . . . ?"

"You tell me this tragic love story and expect me to answer it with my bullshit?" His silence was answer enough. She sighed. But—fine. She, too, needed to talk about *something* to shake off that murder scene. And to dispel the shadows that had filled his eyes when he'd spoken of Shahar.

For that alone she said, "No. Flynn and I never hooked up." She smiled slightly. "When I visited Ruhn as a teenager, I was barely able to *function* in Flynn's and Declan's presence." Hunt's mouth curled upward. "They indulged my outrageous flirting, and for a while, I had a fanatic's conviction that Flynn would be my husband one day."

Hunt snickered, and Bryce elbowed him. "It's true. I wrote *Lady Bryce Flynn* on all my school notebooks for two years straight."

He gaped. "You did not."

"I so did. I can prove it: I still have all my notebooks at my parents' house because my mom refuses to throw anything away." Her amusement faltered. She didn't tell him about that time senior year of college when she and Danika ran into Flynn and Declan at a bar. How Danika had gone home with Flynn, because Bryce hadn't wanted to mess up anything between him and Ruhn.

"Want to hear my worst hookup?" she asked, throwing him a forced grin.

He chuckled. "I'm half-afraid to hear it, but sure."

"I dated a vampyr for like three weeks. My first and only hookup with anyone in Flame and Shadow."

The vamps had worked hard to get people to forget the tiny fact that they'd all come from Hel, lesser demons themselves. That their ancestors had defected from their seven princes during the First Wars, and fed the Asteri Imperial Legions vital intel that aided in their victory. Traitors and turncoats—who still held a demon's craving for blood.

Hunt lifted a brow. "And?"

Bryce winced. "And I couldn't stop wondering what part of me he wanted more: blood or . . . you know. And then he suggested eating *while* eating, if you know what I mean?"

It took Hunt a second to sort it out. Then his dark eyes widened. "Oh fuck. *Really?*" She didn't fail to note his glance to her legs—between them. The way his eyes seemed to darken further, something within them sharpening. "Wouldn't that hurt?"

"I didn't want to find out."

Hunt shook his head, and she wondered if he was unsure whether to cringe or laugh. But the light had come back to his eyes. "No more vamps after that?"

"Definitely not. He claimed the finest pleasure was always edged in pain, but I showed him the door."

Hunt grunted his approval. Bryce knew she probably shouldn't, but asked carefully, "You still have a thing for Shahar?"

A muscle feathered in his jaw. He scanned the skies. "Until the day I die."

No longing or sorrow graced the words, but she still wasn't entirely sure what to do with the dropping sensation in her stomach.

Hunt's eyes slid to hers at last. Bleak and lightless. "I don't see how I can move on from loving her when she gave up *everything* for me. For the cause." He shook his head. "Every time I hook up, I remember it."

"Ah." No arguing with that. Anything she said against it would sound selfish and whiny. And maybe she was dumb, for letting herself read into his leg touching hers or the way he'd looked at her at the shooting range or coaxed her through her panic or any of it.

He was staring at her. As if seeing all of that. His throat bobbed. "Quinlan, that isn't to say that I'm not—"

His words were cut off by a cluster of people approaching from the other end of the street.

She glimpsed silvery blond hair and couldn't breathe. Hunt swore. "Let's get airborne—"

But Sabine had spotted them. Her narrow, pale face twisted in a snarl.

Bryce hated the shaking that overtook her hands. The trembling in her knees.

Hunt warned Sabine, "Keep moving, Fendyr."

Sabine ignored him. Her stare was like being pelted with shards of ice. "I heard you've been showing your face again," she seethed at Bryce. "Where the *fuck* is my sword, Quinlan?"

Bryce couldn't think of anything to say, any retort or explanation. She just let Hunt lead her past Sabine, the angel a veritable wall of muscle between them.

Hunt's hand rested on Bryce's back as he nudged her along. "Let's go."

"Stupid slut," Sabine hissed, spitting at Bryce's feet as she passed.

Hunt stiffened, a growl slipping out, but Bryce gripped his arm in a silent plea to let it go.

His teeth gleamed as he bared them over a shoulder at Sabine, but Bryce whispered, "Please."

He scanned her face, mouth opening to object. She made them keep walking, even as Sabine's sneer branded itself into her back.

"Please," Bryce whispered again.

His chest heaved, as if it took every bit of effort to reel in his rage, but he faced forward. Sabine's low, smug laugh rippled toward them.

Hunt's body locked up, and Bryce squeezed his arm tighter, misery coiling around her gut.

Maybe he scented it, maybe he read it on her face, but Hunt's steps evened out. His hand again warmed her lower back, a steady presence as they walked, finally crossing the street.

They were halfway across Main when Hunt scooped her into his arms, not saying a word as he launched into the brisk skies.

She leaned her head against his chest. Let the wind drown out the roaring in her mind.

They landed on the roof of her building five minutes later, and she would have gone right down to the apartment had he not gripped her arm to stop her.

Hunt again scanned her face. Her eyes.

Us, he'd said earlier. A unit. A team. A two-person pack.

Hunt's wings shifted slightly in the wind off the Istros. "We're going to find whoever is behind all this, Bryce. I promise."

And for some reason, she believed him.

She was brushing her teeth when her phone rang.

Declan Emmet.

She spat out her toothpaste before answering. "Hi."

"You still have my number saved? I'm touched, B."

"Yeah, yeah, yeah. What's up?"

"I found something interesting in the footage. The taxpaying residents of this city should revolt at how their money's being blown on second-rate analysts instead of people like me."

Bryce padded into the hall, then into the great room—then to

Hunt's door. She knocked on it once, and said to Declan, "Are you going to tell me or just gloat about it?"

Hunt opened the door.

Burning. Fucking. Solas.

He wasn't wearing a shirt, and from the look of it, had been in the middle of brushing his teeth, too. But she didn't give a shit about his dental hygiene when he looked like *that.*

Muscles upon muscles upon muscles, all covered by golden-brown skin that glowed in the firstlights. It was outrageous. She'd seen him shirtless before, but she hadn't noticed—not like this.

She'd seen more than her fair share of cut, beautiful male bodies, but Hunt Athalar's blew them all away.

He was pining for a lost love, she reminded herself. Had made that *very* clear earlier tonight. Through an effort of will, she lifted her eyes and found a shit-eating smirk on his face.

But his smug-ass smile faded when she put Declan on speaker. Dec said, "I don't know if I should tell you to sit down or not."

Hunt stepped into the great room, frowning. "Just tell me," Bryce said.

"Okay, so I'll admit someone could easily have made a mistake. Thanks to the blackout, the footage is just darkness with some sounds. Ordinary city sounds of people reacting to the blackout. So I pulled apart each audio thread from the street outside the temple. Amped up the ones in the background that the government computers might not have had the tech to hear. You know what I heard? People giggling, goading each other to *touch it.*"

"Please tell me this isn't going to end grossly," Bryce said. Hunt snorted.

"It was people at the Rose Gate. I could hear people at the Rose Gate in FiRo daring each other to touch the disk on the dial pad in the blackout, to see if it still worked. It did, by the way. But I could also hear them *ooh*ing about the night-blooming flowers on the Gate itself."

Hunt leaned in, his scent wrapping around her, dizzying her, as he said into the phone, "The Rose Gate is halfway across the city from Luna's Temple."

Declan chuckled. "Hey, Athalar. Enjoying playing houseguest with Bryce?"

"Just tell us," Bryce said, grinding her teeth. Taking a big, careful step away from Hunt.

"Someone swapped the footage of the temple during the time of the Horn's theft. It was clever fucking work—they patched it right in so that there isn't so much as a flicker in the time stamp. They picked audio footage that was a near-match for what it would have sounded like at the temple, with the angle of the buildings and everything. Really smart shit. But not smart enough. The 33rd should have come to me. I'd have found an error like that."

Bryce's heart pounded. "Can you find who did this?"

"I already did." Any smugness faded from Declan's voice. "I looked at who was responsible for heading up the investigation of the video footage that night. They'd be the only one with the clearance to make a swap like that."

Bryce tapped her foot on the ground, and Athalar brushed his wing against her shoulder in quiet reassurance. "Who *is* it, Dec?"

Declan sighed. "Look, I'm not saying it's this person one hundred percent . . . but the official who headed up that part of the investigation was Sabine Fendyr."

PART III
THE CANYON

38

It makes sense," Hunt said carefully, watching Bryce where she sat on the rolled arm of her sofa, chewing on her lower lip. She'd barely thanked Declan before hanging up.

Hunt said, "The demon has been staying out of view of the cameras in the city. Sabine would know where those cameras are, especially if she had the authority to oversee the video footage of criminal cases."

Sabine's behavior earlier tonight . . . He'd wanted to kill her.

He'd seen Bryce laugh in the face of the Viper Queen, go toe-to-toe with Philip Briggs, and taunt three of the most lethal Fae warriors in this city—and yet she'd trembled before Sabine.

He hadn't been able to stand it, her fear and misery and guilt.

When Bryce didn't reply, he said again, "It makes sense that Sabine could be behind this." He sat beside her on the sectional. He'd put on a shirt a moment ago, even though he'd enjoyed the look of pure admiration on Bryce's face as she got an eyeful of him.

"Sabine wouldn't have killed her own daughter."

"You really believe that?"

Bryce wrapped her arms around her knees. "No." In a pair of sleeping shorts and an oversize, worn T-shirt, she looked young. Small. Tired.

Hunt said, "Everyone knows that the Prime was considering skipping over Sabine to tap Danika to be his heir. That seems like a good fucking motive to me." He considered again, an old memory snagging his attention. He pulled out his phone and said, "Hold on."

Isaiah answered on the third ring. "Yeah?"

"How easily can you access your notes from the observation room the night Danika died?" He didn't let Isaiah reply before he said, "Specifically, did you write down what Sabine said to us?"

Isaiah's pause was fraught. "Tell me you don't think Sabine killed her."

"Can you get me the notes?" Hunt pushed. Isaiah swore, but a moment later he said, "All right, I've got it." Hunt moved closer to Quinlan so she could hear the commander's voice as he said, "You want me to recite this whole thing?"

"Just what she said about Danika. Did you catch it?"

He knew Isaiah had. The male took extensive notes on everything.

"Sabine said, *Danika couldn't stay out of trouble.*" Bryce stiffened, and Hunt laid his free hand on her knee, squeezing once. "*She could never keep her mouth* shut *and know when to be quiet around her enemies. And look what became of her. That stupid little bitch in there is still breathing, and Danika is* not. *Danika should have known better.* Hunt, you then asked her what Danika should have known better about, and Sabine said, *All of it. Starting with that slut of a roommate.*"

Bryce flinched, and Hunt rubbed his thumb over her knee. "Thanks, Isaiah."

Isaiah cleared his throat. "Be careful." The call ended.

Bryce's wide eyes glimmered. "What Sabine said could be construed a lot of ways," she admitted. "But—"

"It sounds like Sabine wanted Danika to keep quiet about something. Maybe Danika threatened to talk about the Horn's theft, and Sabine killed her for it. "

Bryce's throat bobbed as she nodded. "Why wait two years, though?"

"I suppose that's what we'll find out from her."

"What would Sabine want with a broken artifact? And even if she knew how to repair it, what would she do with it?"

"I don't know. And I don't know if someone else has it and she wants it, but—"

"If Danika saw Sabine steal it, it'd make sense that Danika never said anything. Same with the guard and the acolyte. They were probably too scared to come forward."

"It would explain why Sabine swapped the footage. And why it freaked her out when we showed up at the temple, causing her to kill anyone who might have seen anything that night. The bomb at the club was probably a way to either intimidate us or kill us while making it look like humans were behind it."

"But . . . I don't think she has it," Bryce mused, toying with her toes. They were painted a deep ruby. Ridiculous, he told himself. Not the alternative. The one that had him imagining tasting each and every one of those toes before slowly working his way up those sleek, bare legs of hers. Bare legs that were mere inches from him, golden skin gleaming in the firstlights. He forced himself to withdraw his hand from her knee, even as his fingers begged to move, to stroke along her thigh. Higher.

Bryce went on, oblivious to his filthy train of thoughts, "I don't see why Sabine would have the Horn and still summon the kristallos."

Hunt cleared his throat. It'd been a long fucking day. A weird one, if this was where his thoughts had drifted. Honestly, they'd been drifting in this direction since the gun range. Since he'd seen her hold that gun like a gods-damned pro.

He forced himself to focus. Consider the conversation at hand and not contemplate whether Quinlan's legs would feel as soft beneath his mouth as they looked. "Don't forget that Sabine hates Micah's guts. Beyond silencing the victims, the killings now could also be to undermine him. You saw how tied up he is about getting this solved before the Summit. Murders like these, caused by an unknown demon, when Sandriel is here? It'll make a mockery of him. Maximus Tertian was high profile enough to create a political headache for Micah—Tertian's death might have just been to fuck with Micah's standing. For fuck's sake, she and Sandriel might even be in on it together, hoping to weaken him in the Asteri's eyes, so they appoint Sandriel to Valbara instead. She could easily make Sabine the Prime of all Valbaran shifters—not just wolves."

Bryce's face blanched. No such title existed, but it was within a Governor's right to create it. "Sabine isn't that type. She's power hungry, but not on that scale. She thinks petty—*is* petty. You heard her bitching about Danika's missing sword." Bryce idly braided her long hair. "We shouldn't waste our breath guessing her motives. It could be anything."

"You're right. We've got a damn good reason for thinking she killed Danika, but nothing solid enough to explain these new murders." He watched her long, delicate fingers twine through her hair. Made himself look at the darkened television screen instead. "Catching her with the demon would prove her involvement."

"You think Viktoria can find that footage we requested?"

"I hope so," he said. Hunt mulled it over. Sabine—fuck, if it was her . . .

Bryce rose from the couch. "I'm going for a run."

"It's one in the morning."

"I need to run for a bit, or I won't be able to fall asleep."

Hunt shot to his feet. "We just came from the scene of a murder, and Sabine was out for your blood, Bryce—"

She aimed for her bedroom and didn't look back.

She emerged two minutes later in her exercise clothes and found him standing by the door in workout gear of his own. She frowned. "I want to run alone."

Hunt opened the door and stepped into the hall. "Too fucking bad."

There was her breathing, and the pounding of her feet on the slick streets, and the blaring music in her ears. She'd turned it up so loud it was mostly just noise. Deafening noise with a beat. She never played it this loud during her morning runs, but with Hunt keeping a steady pace beside her, she could blast her music and not worry about some predator taking advantage of it.

So she ran. Down the broad avenues, the alleys, and side streets. Hunt moved with her, every motion graceful and rippling with power. She could have sworn lightning trailed in their wake.

Sabine. Had she killed Danika?

Bryce couldn't wrap her mind around it. Each breath was like shards of glass.

They needed to catch her in the act. Find evidence against her.

Her leg began to ache, an acidic burn along her upper thigh-bone. She ignored it.

Bryce cut toward Asphodel Meadows, the route so familiar that she was surprised her footprints hadn't been worn into the cobble-stones. She rounded a corner sharply, biting down on the groan of pain as her leg objected. Hunt's gaze snapped to her, but she didn't look at him.

Sabine. Sabine. Sabine.

Her leg burned, but she kept going. Through the Meadows. Through FiRo.

Kept running. Kept breathing. She didn't dare stop.

Bryce knew Hunt was making a concerted effort to keep his mouth shut when they finally returned to her apartment an hour later. She had to grip the doorway to keep upright.

His eyes narrowed, but he said nothing. He didn't mention that her limp had been so bad she'd barely been able to run the last ten blocks. Bryce knew the limp and pain would be worse by morning. Each step drew a cry to her throat that she swallowed down and down and down.

"All right?" he asked tightly, lifting his shirt to wipe the sweat from his face. She had a too-brief glimpse of those ridiculous stom-ach muscles, gleaming with sweat. He'd stayed by her side the entire time—hadn't complained or spoken. Had just kept pace.

Bryce made a point not to lean on the wall as she walked toward her bedroom.

"I'm fine," she said breathlessly. "Just needed to run it out."

He reached for her leg, a muscle ticking in his jaw. "That happen often?"

"No," she lied.

Hunt just gave her a look.

She couldn't stop her next limping step. "Sometimes," she amended, wincing. "I'll ice it. It'll be fine by morning." If she'd been full-blooded Fae, it would have healed in an hour or two. Then again, if she were full-blooded Fae, the injury wouldn't have lingered like this.

His voice was hoarse as he asked, "You ever get it checked out?"

"Yep," she lied again, and rubbed at her sweaty neck. Before he could call her on it, she said, "Thanks for coming."

"Yeah." Not quite an answer, but Hunt mercifully said nothing else as she limped down the hallway and shut the door to her room.

39

Despite its entrance facing the bustle of the Old Square, Ruhn found the medwitch clinic blissfully quiet. The white-painted walls of the waiting room glowed with the sunshine leaking through the windows that looked onto the semipermanent traffic, and the trickle of a small quartz fountain atop the white marble counter blended pleasantly with the symphony playing through the ceiling's speakers.

He'd been waiting for five minutes now, while the witch he'd come to see finished up with a patient, and had been perfectly content to bask in the tendrils of lavender-scented steam from the diffuser on the small table beside his chair. Even his shadows slumbered inside him.

Magazines and pamphlets had been spread across the white oak coffee table before him, the latter advertising everything from fertility treatments to scar therapy to arthritis relief.

A door down the narrow hallway beyond the counter opened, and a dark head of softly curling hair emerged, a musical voice saying, "Please do call if you have any further symptoms." The door clicked shut, presumably to give the patient privacy.

Ruhn stood, feeling out of place in his head-to-toe black clothes in the midst of the soft whites and creams of the clinic, and kept himself perfectly still as the medwitch approached the counter.

At the crime scene last night, he'd gone over to inquire as to whether she'd noted anything interesting about the corpse. He'd been impressed enough by her clear-eyed intelligence that he'd asked to stop by this morning.

The medwitch smiled slightly as she reached the other side of the counter, her dark eyes lighting with welcome.

Then there was that. Her arresting face. Not the cultivated beauty of a movie star or model—no, this was beauty in its rawest form, from her large brown eyes to her full mouth to her high cheekbones, all in near-perfect symmetry. All radiating a cool serenity and awareness. He'd been unable to stop looking at her, even with a splattered corpse behind them.

"Good morning, Prince." And there was that, too. Her fair, beautiful voice. Fae were sensitive about sounds, thanks to their heightened hearing. They could hear notes within notes, chords within chords. Ruhn had once nearly run from a date with a young nymph when her high-pitched giggling had sounded more like a porpoise's squeal. And in bed . . . fuck, how many partners had he never called again not because the sex had been bad, but because the sounds they'd made had been unbearable? Too many to count.

Ruhn offered the medwitch a smile. "Hi." He nodded toward the hall. "I know you're busy, but I was hoping you could spare a few minutes to chat about this case I'm working on."

Clad in loose navy pants and a white cotton shirt with quarter-length sleeves that brought out her glowing brown skin, the medwitch stood with an impressive level of stillness.

They were a strange, unique group, the witches. Though they looked like humans, their considerable magic and long lives marked them as Vanir, their power mostly passed through the female line. All of them deemed civitas. The power was inherited, from some ancient source that the witches claimed was a three-faced goddess, but witches did pop up in non-magical families every now and then. Their gifts were varied, from seers to warriors to potion-makers, but healers were the most visible in Crescent City. Their schooling was thorough and long enough that the young witch before him was unusual. She had to be skilled to be already working in a clinic when she couldn't have been a day over thirty.

"I have another patient coming soon," she said, glancing over his shoulder to the busy street beyond. "But I have lunch after that. Do you mind waiting half an hour?" She gestured to the hall behind her, where sunlight leaked in through a glass door at its other end. "We have a courtyard garden. The day is fine enough that you could wait out there."

Ruhn agreed, glancing to the nameplate on the counter. "Thank you, Miss Solomon."

She blinked, those thick, velvety lashes bobbing in surprise. "Oh—I am not . . . This is my sister's clinic. She went on holiday, and asked me to cover for her while she's gone." She gestured again to the hallway, graceful as a queen.

Ruhn followed her down the hall, trying not to breathe in her eucalyptus-and-lavender scent too deeply.

Don't be a fucking creep.

The sunlight tangled in her thick night-dark hair as she reached the courtyard door and shouldered it open, revealing a slate-covered patio surrounded by terraced herb gardens. The day was indeed lovely, the river breeze making the plants rustle and sway, spreading their soothing fragrances.

She pointed to a wrought-iron table and chairs set by a bed of mint. "I'll be out shortly."

"Okay," he said, and she didn't wait for him to take a seat before disappearing inside.

The thirty minutes passed quickly, mostly thanks to a flurry of calls he got from Dec and Flynn, along with a few of his Aux captains. By the time the glass door opened again, he had just set down his phone, intending on enjoying a few minutes of sweet-smelling silence.

He shot to his feet at the sight of the heavy tray the witch bore, laden with a steaming teapot, cups, and a plate of cheese, honey, and bread. "I thought that if I'm stopping for lunch, we might as well eat together," she said as Ruhn took the tray.

"You didn't need to bring me anything," he said, careful not to upset the teapot as he set the tray on the table.

"It was no trouble. I don't like to eat alone anyway." She took the seat across from him, and began distributing the silverware.

"Where's your accent from?" She didn't speak with the fast-paced diction of someone in this city, but rather like someone who selected each word carefully.

She spread some cheese onto a slice of bread. "My tutors were from an old part of Pelium—by the Rhagan Sea. It rubbed off on me, I suppose."

Ruhn poured himself some of the tea, then filled her cup. "All of that area is old."

Her brown eyes gleamed. "Indeed."

He waited until she'd taken a sip of tea before saying, "I've spoken about this to a few other medwitches around town, but no one's been able to give me an answer. I'm fully aware that I might be grasping at straws here. But before I say anything, I'd like to ask for your . . . discretion."

She pulled a few grapes and dates onto her plate. "You may ask what you wish. I will not speak a word of it."

He inhaled the scent of his tea—peppermint and licorice and something else, a whisper of vanilla and something . . . woodsy. He leaned back in his chair. "All right. I know your time is limited, so I'll be direct: can you think of any way a magical object that was broken might be repaired when no one—not witches, not the Fae, not the Asteri themselves—has been able to fix it? A way it might be . . . healed?"

She drizzled honey atop her cheese. "Was the object made from magic, or was it an ordinary item that was imbued with power afterward?"

"Legend says it was made with magic—and could only be used with the Starborn gifts."

"Ah." Her clear eyes scanned him, noting his coloring. "So it is a Fae artifact."

"Yes. From the First Wars."

"You speak of Luna's Horn?" None of the other witches had gotten to it so quickly.

"Maybe," he hedged, letting her see the truth in his eyes.

"Magic and the power of the seven holy stars could not repair it," she said. "And far wiser witches than I have looked at it and found it an impossible task."

Disappointment dropped in his stomach. "I just figured that the medwitches might have some idea how to heal it, considering your field of expertise."

"I see why you might think that. This clinic is full of marvels that I did not know existed—that my tutors did not know existed. Lasers and cameras and machines that can peer inside your body in the same way my magic can." Her eyes brightened with each word, and for the life of him, Ruhn couldn't look away. "And maybe . . ." She angled her head, staring into a swaying bed of lavender.

Ruhn kept his mouth shut, letting her think. His phone buzzed with an incoming message, and he quickly silenced it.

The witch went still. Her slender fingers contracted on the table. Just one movement, one ripple of reaction, to suggest something had clicked in that pretty head of hers. But she said nothing.

When she met his stare again, her eyes were dark. Full of warning. "It is possible that with all the medical advancements today, someone might have found a way to repair a broken object of power. To treat the artifact not as something inert, but as a living thing."

"So, what—they'd use some sort of laser to repair it?"

"A laser, a drug, a skin graft, a transplant . . . current research has opened many doors."

Shit. "Would it ring any bells if I said the ancient Fae claimed the Horn could only be repaired by light that was not light, magic that was not magic? Does it sound like any modern tech?"

"In that, I will admit I am not as well-versed as my sisters. My knowledge of healing is rooted in our oldest ways."

"It's all right," he said, and rose from his chair. "Thanks for your time."

She met his eyes with a surprising frankness. Utterly unafraid of or impressed by him. "I am certain you will do so already, but I'd advise you to proceed with caution, Prince."

"I know. Thanks." He rubbed the back of his neck, bracing himself. "Do you think your queen might have an answer?"

The medwitch's head angled again, all that glorious hair spilling over her shoulder. "My . . . Oh." He could have sworn sorrow clouded her eyes. "You mean the new queen."

"Hypaxia." Her name shimmered on his tongue. "I'm sorry about the loss of your old queen."

"So am I," the witch said. For a moment, her shoulders seemed to curve inward, her head bowing under a phantom weight. Hecuba had been beloved by her people—her loss would linger. The witch blew out a breath through her nose and straightened again, as if shaking off the mantle of sorrow. "Hypaxia has been in mourning for her mother. She will not receive visitors until she makes her appearance at the Summit." She smiled slightly. "Perhaps you can ask her yourself then."

Ruhn winced. On the one hand, at least he didn't have to go see the woman his father wanted him to marry. "Unfortunately, this case is pressing enough that it can't wait until the Summit."

"I will pray to Cthona that you find your answers elsewhere, then."

"Hopefully she'll listen." He took a few steps toward the door.

"I hope to see you again, Prince," the medwitch said, returning to her lunch.

The words weren't a come-on, some not-so-subtle invitation. But even later, as he sat in the Fae Archives researching medical breakthroughs, he still pondered the tone and promise of her farewell.

And realized he'd never gotten her name.

40

It took Viktoria two days to find anything unusual on the city cameras and the power grid. But when she did, she didn't call Hunt. No, she sent a messenger.

"Vik told me to get your ass to her office—the one at the lab," Isaiah said by way of greeting as he landed on the roof of the gallery.

Leaning against the doorway that led downstairs, Hunt sized up his commander. Isaiah's usual glow had dimmed, and shadows lay beneath his eyes. "It's that bad with Sandriel there?"

Isaiah folded in his wings. Tightly. "Micah's keeping her in check, but I was up all night dealing with petrified people."

"Soldiers?"

"Soldiers, staff, employees, nearby residents . . . She's rattled them." Isaiah shook his head. "She's keeping the timing of Pollux's arrival quiet, too, to put us all on edge. She knows what kind of fear he drags up."

"Maybe we'll get lucky and that piece of shit will stay in Pangera."

"We're never that lucky, are we?"

"No. We're not." Hunt let out a bitter laugh. "The Summit's still a month away." A month of enduring Sandriel's presence. "I . . . If you need anything from me, let me know."

Isaiah blinked, surveying Hunt from head to boot tip. It shouldn't have shamed him, that surprise on the commander's face at his offer. Isaiah's gaze shifted to the tiled roof beneath their matching boots, as if contemplating what or who might be responsible for his turn toward the altruistic. But Isaiah just asked, "Do you think Roga really turns her exes and enemies into animals?"

Having observed the creatures in the small tanks throughout the library, Hunt could only say, "I hope not." Especially for the sake of the assistant who had been pretending she wasn't falling asleep at her desk when he'd called to check in twenty minutes ago.

Since Declan had dropped the bomb about Sabine, she'd been broody. Hunt had advised her to be cautious about going after the future Prime, and she'd seemed inclined to wait for Viktoria to find any hint of the demon's patterns—any proof that Sabine was indeed using the power of the ley lines to summon it, since her own power levels weren't strong enough. Most shifters' powers weren't, though Danika had been an exception. Another reason for her mother's jealousy—and motive.

They'd heard nothing from Ruhn, only a message yesterday about doing more research on the Horn. But if Vik had found something . . . Hunt asked, "Vik can't come here with the news?"

"She wanted to show you in person. And I doubt Jesiba will be pleased if Vik comes here."

"Considerate of you."

Isaiah shrugged. "Jesiba is assisting us—we need her resources. It'd be stupid to push her limits. I have no interest in seeing any of you turned into pigs if we step on her toes too much."

And there it was. The meaningful, too-long glance.

Hunt held up his hands with a grin. "No need to worry on my front."

"Micah will come down on you like a hammer if you jeopardize this."

"Bryce already told Micah she wasn't interested."

"He won't forget that anytime soon." Fuck, Hunt certainly knew that. The kill Micah had ordered last week as punishment for Hunt and Bryce embarrassing him in the Comitium lobby . . . It had lingered. "But I don't mean that. I meant if we don't find out who's behind this, if it turns out you're wrong about Sabine—not only will your reduced sentence be off the table, but Micah will find *you* responsible."

"Of course he will." Hunt's phone buzzed, and he pulled it from his pocket.

He choked. Not just at the message from Bryce: *The gallery roof isn't a pigeon roost, you know,* but what she'd changed her contact name to, presumably when he'd gone to the bathroom or showered or just left his phone on the coffee table: *Bryce Rocks My Socks.*

And there, beneath the ridiculous name, she'd added a photo to her contact: the one she'd snapped of herself in the phone store, grinning from ear to ear.

Hunt suppressed a growl of irritation and typed back, *Shouldn't you be working?*

Bryce Rocks My Socks wrote back a second later, *How can I work when you two are thumping around up there?*

He wrote back, *How'd you get my password?* She hadn't needed it to activate the camera feature, but to have gotten into his contacts, she would have needed the seven-digit combination.

I paid attention. She added a second later, *And might have observed you typing it in a few times while you were watching some dumb sunball game.*

Hunt rolled his eyes and pocketed his phone without replying. Well, at least she was coming out of that quiet cloud she'd been in for days.

He found Isaiah watching him carefully. "There are worse fates than death, you know."

Hunt looked toward the Comitium, the female Archangel lurking in it. "I know."

Bryce frowned out the gallery door. "The forecast didn't call for rain." She scowled at the sky. "*Someone* must be throwing a tantrum."

"It's illegal to interfere with the weather," Hunt recited from beside her, thumbing a message into his phone. He hadn't changed the new contact name she'd given herself, Bryce had noticed. Or erased that absurd photo she'd added to her contact listing.

She silently mimicked his words, then said, "I don't have an umbrella."

"It's not a far flight to the lab."

"It'd be easier to call a car."

"At this hour? In the rain?" He sent off his message and pocketed his phone. "It'll take you an hour just to cross Central Avenue."

The rain swept through the city in sheets. "I could get electrocuted up there."

Hunt's eyes glittered as he offered her a hand. "Good thing I can keep you safe."

With all that lightning in his veins, she supposed it was true.

Bryce sighed and frowned at her dress, the black suede heels that would surely be ruined. "I'm not in flying-appropriate attire—"

The word ended on a yelp as Hunt hauled her into the sky.

She clung to him, hissing like a cat. "We have to go back before closing for Syrinx."

Hunt soared over the congested, rain-battered streets as Vanir and humans ducked into doorways and under awnings to escape the weather. The only ones on the streets were those with umbrellas or magical shields up. Bryce buried her face against his chest, as if it'd shield her from the rain—and the terrible drop. What it amounted to was a face full of his scent and the warmth of his body against her cheek.

"Slow down," she ordered, fingers digging into his shoulders and neck.

"Don't be a baby," he crooned in her ear, the richness of his voice skittering over every bone of her body. "Look around, Quinlan. Enjoy the view." He added, "I like the city in the rain."

When she kept her head ducked against his chest, he gave her a squeeze. "Come on," he teased over the honking horns and splash of tires through puddles. He added, voice nearly a purr, "I'll buy you a milkshake if you do."

Her toes curled in her shoes at the low, coaxing voice.

"Only for ice cream," she muttered, earning a chuckle from him, and cracked open an eye. She forced the other one open, too. Clutching his shoulders nearly hard enough to pierce through to his skin, working against every instinct that screamed for her body to lock up, she squinted through the water lashing her face at the passing city.

In the rain, the marble buildings gleamed like they were made from moonstone, the gray cobblestone streets appeared polished a silvery blue splashed with the gold of the firstlight lamps. To her right, the Gates in the Old Square, Moonwood, and FiRo rose through the sprawl, like the humped spine of some twining beast breaking the surface of a lake, their crystal gleaming like melting ice. From this high, the avenues that linked them all—the ley lines beneath them—shot like spears through the city.

The wind rattled the palms, tossing the fronds to and fro, their hissing almost drowning out the cranky honking of drivers now in a traffic standstill. The whole city, in fact, seemed to have stopped for a moment—except for them, swiftly passing above it all.

"Not so bad, huh?"

She pinched Athalar's neck, and his answering laugh brushed over her ear. She might have pressed her body a little harder against the solid wall of his. He might have tightened his grip, too. Just a bit.

In silence, they watched the buildings shift from ancient stone and brick to sleek metal and glass. The cars turned fancier, too—worn taxis exchanged for black sedans with tinted windows, uniformed drivers idling in the front seats while they waited in lines outside the towering high-rises. Fewer people occupied the much-cleaner streets—certainly there was no music or restaurants overflowing with food and drink and laughter. This was a sanitized, orderly pocket of the city, where the point was not to look around, but to look *up*. High in the rain-veiled gloom that wreathed the upper portions of the buildings, lights and shimmering whorls of color stained the mists. A splotch of red gleamed to her left, and she didn't need to look to know it came from Redner Industries' headquarters. She hadn't seen or heard from Reid in the two years since Danika's murder—he'd never even sent his condolences afterward. Even though Danika herself had worked part-time at the company. Prick.

Hunt steered for a solid concrete building that Bryce had tried to block from her memory, landing smoothly on a second-story balcony. Hunt was opening the glass doors, flashing some sort of entry ID into a scanner, when he said to her, "Viktoria's a wraith."

She almost said *I know*, but only nodded, following him inside. She and Hunt had barely spoken about that night. About what she remembered.

The air-conditioning was on full blast, and she instantly wrapped her arms around herself, teeth chattering at the shock of going from the storm into crisp cold.

"Walk fast" was the only help Hunt offered, wiping the rain off his face.

A cramped elevator ride and two hallways later, Bryce found herself shivering in the doorway of a spacious office overlooking a small park.

Watching as Hunt and Viktoria clasped hands over the wraith's curved glass desk.

Hunt gestured to her, "Bryce Quinlan, this is Viktoria Vargos."

Viktoria, to her credit, pretended to be meeting her for the first time.

So much of that night was a blur. But Bryce remembered the sanitized room. Remembered Viktoria playing that recording.

At least Bryce could now appreciate the beauty before her: the dark hair and pale skin and stunning green eyes were all Pangeran heritage, speaking of vineyards and carved marble palaces. But the grace with which Viktoria moved . . . Viktoria must have been old as Hel to have that sort of fluid beauty. To be able to steer her body so smoothly.

A halo had been tattooed on her brow as well. Bryce hid her surprise—her memory had failed to provide that detail. She knew the sprites had fought in the angels' rebellion, but hadn't realized any other non-malakim had marched under Shahar's Daystar banner.

Warmth glowed in Viktoria's eyes as she purred, "Pleasure."

Somehow, Athalar only looked better soaked with rain, his shirt clinging to every hard, sculpted muscle. Bryce was all too aware, as she extended a hand, of how her hair now lay flat on her head thanks to the rain, of the makeup that had probably smeared down her face.

Viktoria took Bryce's hand, her grip firm but friendly, and smiled. Winked.

Hunt grumbled, "She does that flirty smile with everyone, so don't bother being flattered."

Bryce settled into one of the twin black leather seats on the other side of the desk, batting her eyelashes at Hunt. "Does she do it for you, too?"

Viktoria barked a laugh, the sound rich and lovely. "You earned that one, Athalar."

Hunt scowled, dropping into another chair—one with the back cut low, Bryce realized, to accommodate anyone with wings.

"Isaiah said you found something," Hunt said, crossing an ankle over a knee.

"Yes, though not quite what you requested." Viktoria came around the desk and handed a file to Bryce. Hunt leaned in to peer over her shoulder. His wing brushed against the back of Bryce's head, but he didn't remove it.

Bryce squinted at the grainy photo, the sole clawed foot in the lower right corner. "Is that—"

"Spotted in Moonwood just last night. I was tracking temperature fluctuations around the main avenues like you said, and noticed a dip—just for two seconds."

"A summoning," Hunt said.

"Yes," Viktoria said. "The camera only got this tiny image of the foot—it mostly stayed out of sight. But it was just off a main avenue, like you suspected. We have a few more grainy captures from other locations last night, but those show it even less—a talon, rather than this entire foot."

The photo was blurry, but there it was—those shredding claws she'd never forget.

It was an effort not to touch her leg. To remember the clear teeth that had ripped into it.

Both of them looked to her. Waiting. Bryce managed to say, "That's a kristallos demon."

Hunt's wing spread a little farther around her, but he said nothing.

"I couldn't find temperature fluctuations from the night of every murder," Vik said, face turning grim. "But I did find one from when Maximus Tertian died. Ten minutes and two blocks away from him. No video footage, but it was the same seventy-seven-degree dip, made in the span of two seconds."

"Did it attack anyone last night?" Bryce's voice had turned a bit distant—even to her ears.

"No," Viktoria said. "Not as far as we know."

Hunt kept studying the image. "Did the kristallos go anywhere specific?"

Viktoria handed over another document. It was a map of Moonwood, full of sprawling parks and riverfront walkways, palatial villas and complexes for Vanir and a few wealthy humans, peppered with the best schools and many of the fanciest restaurants in town. In its heart: the Den. About six red dots surrounded it. The creature had crawled around its towering walls. Right in the heart of Sabine's territory.

"Burning Solas," Bryce breathed, a chill slithering along her spine.

"It would have found a way inside the Den's walls if what it hunts was there," Hunt mused quietly. "Maybe it was just following an old scent."

Bryce traced a finger between the various dots. "No bigger pattern, though?"

"I ran it through the system and nothing came up beyond what you two figured out about the proximity to the ley lines beneath those roads and the temperature dips." Viktoria sighed. "It seems like it was looking for something. Or someone."

Blood and bone and gore, sprayed and shredded and in chunks—

Glass ripping into her feet; fangs ripping into her skin—

A warm, strong hand gently gripped her thigh. Squeezed once.

But when Bryce looked over at Hunt, his attention was upon Viktoria—even as his hand remained upon her bare leg, his wing still slightly curved around her. "How'd you lose track of it?"

"It was simply there one moment, and gone the next."

Hunt's thumb stroked her leg, just above her knee. An idle, reassuring touch.

One that was far too distracting as Viktoria leaned forward to tap another spot on the map, her green eyes lifting from it only to note Hunt's hand as well. Wariness flooded her stare, but she said, "This was its last known location, at least as far as what our cameras could find." The Rose Gate in FiRo. Nowhere near Sabine's territory. "As I said, one moment it was there, then it was gone. I've had two different units and one Auxiliary pack hunting for it all day, but no luck."

Hunt's hand slid from her leg, leaving a cold spot in its wake. A glance at his face and she saw the cause: Viktoria now held his gaze, her own full of warning.

Bryce tapped her dusky nails on the chrome arm of the chair.

Well, at least she knew what they were doing after dinner tonight.

41

The rain didn't halt.

Hunt couldn't decide if it was a blessing, since it kept the streets mostly empty of all save Vanir affiliated with water, or if it was shit-poor luck, since it certainly wiped away any chance of a scent from the demon prowling the streets.

"Come . . . *on*," Bryce grunted.

Leaning against the wall beside the front door of the gallery, sunset mere minutes away, Hunt debated pulling out his phone to film the scene before him: Syrinx with his claws embedded in the carpet, yowling his head off, and Bryce trying to haul him by the back legs toward the door.

"It's. Just. *Water!*" she gritted out, tugging again.

"*Eeettzzz!*" Syrinx wailed back.

Bryce had declared that they were dropping off Syrinx at her apartment before going out to FiRo to investigate.

She grunted again, legs straining as she heaved the chimera. "We. Are. Going. *Home!*"

The green carpet began to lift, nails popping free as Syrinx clung for dear life.

Cthona spare him. Snickering, Hunt did Jesiba Roga a favor before Syrinx started on the wood panels, and wrapped a cool breeze around the chimera. Brow scrunching with concentration, he hoisted Syrinx from the carpet, floating him on a storm-wind straight to Hunt's open arms.

Syrinx blinked at him, then bristled, his tiny white teeth bared.

Hunt said calmly, "None of that, beastie."

Syrinx harrumphed, then went boneless.

Hunt found Bryce blinking, too. He threw her a grin. "Any more screeching from you?"

She grumbled, her words muffled by the rain-blasted night. Syrinx tensed in Hunt's arms as they emerged into the wet evening, Bryce shutting and locking the door behind them. She limped slightly. As if her tug-of-war with the chimera had strained her thigh again.

Hunt kept his mouth shut as he handed Syrinx over to her, the chimera practically clawing holes in Bryce's dress. He knew her leg bothered her. Knew he'd been the cause, with his battlefield stapling. But if she was going to be stupid and not get it looked at, then fine. Fine.

He didn't say any of that as Bryce wrapped her arms around Syrinx, hair already plastered to her head, and stepped closer to him. Hunt was keenly aware of every part of his body that met every part of hers as he scooped her into his arms, flapped his wings, and shot them into the storming skies, Syrinx huffing and hissing.

Syrinx forgave them both by the time they stood, dripping water, in the kitchen, and Bryce earned redemption points for the additional food she dumped into his bowl.

An outfit change for Bryce into athletic gear, and thirty minutes later, they stood in front of the Rose Gate. Its roses, wisteria, and countless other flowers gleamed with rain in the firstlight from lampposts flanking the traffic circle beyond it. A few cars wound past to disperse either into the city streets or along Central Avenue, which crossed through the Gate and became the long, dark expanse of the Eastern Road.

Hunt and Bryce squinted through the rain to peer at the square, the Gate, the traffic circle.

No hint of the demon that had been creeping through Vik's feeds.

From the corner of his eye, he watched Bryce rub her upper

thigh, reining in her wince. He ground his teeth, but bit back his reprimand.

He didn't feel like getting another lecture on domineering alphahole behavior.

"Right," Bryce said, the ends of her ponytail curling in the damp. "Since you're the sicko with dozens of crime scene photos on your phone, I'll let you do the investigating."

"Funny." Hunt pulled out his phone, snapped a photo of her standing in the rain and looking pissy, and then pulled up a photo he'd taken of the printouts Vik had made.

Bryce pressed closer to study the photo on his phone, the heat of her body a beckoning song. He kept perfectly still, refusing to heed it, as she lifted her head. "That camera there," she said, pointing to one of the ten mounted on the Gate itself. "That's the one that got the little blur."

Hunt nodded, surveying the Rose Gate and its surroundings. No sign of Sabine. Not that he expected the future Prime to be standing out in the open, summoning demons like some city-square charlatan. Especially not in such a public place, usually packed with tourists.

In the centuries since the Fae had decided to cover their Gate with flowers and climbing plants, the Rose Gate had become one of the biggest tourist draws, with thousands of people flocking there each day to give a drop of power to make a wish on its dial pad, nearly hidden beneath ivy, and to snap photos of the stunning little creatures who now made their nests and homes within the tangle of green. But at this hour, in this weather, even the Rose Gate was quiet. Dark.

Bryce rubbed her gods-damned thigh again. He swallowed down his annoyance and asked, "You think the demon headed out of the city?"

"I'm praying it didn't." The broad Eastern Road speared into dark, rolling hills and cypresses. A few golden firstlights gleamed among them, the only indication of the farms and villas interspersed throughout the vineyards, grazing lands, and olive groves. All good places to hide.

Bryce kept close as they crossed the street, into the heart of the small park in the center of the traffic circle. She scanned the rain-slick trees around them. "Anything?"

Hunt began to shake his head, but paused. He saw something on the other side of the marble circle on which the Gate stood. He took out his phone, the screen light bouncing off the strong planes of his face. "Maybe we were wrong. About the ley lines."

"What do you mean?"

He showed her the map of the city he'd pulled up, running a finger over Ward Avenue. Then Central. Main. "The kristallos appeared near all these streets. We thought it was because they were close to the ley lines. But we forgot what lies right beneath the streets, allowing the demon to appear and vanish without anyone noticing. The perfect place for Sabine to summon something and order it to move around the city." He pointed to the other side of the Gate. To a sewer grate.

Bryce groaned. "You've got to be kidding."

"Gods, it reeks," Bryce hissed over the rushing water below, pressing her face into her elbow as she knelt beside Hunt and peered into the open sewer. "What the fuck."

Soaked from the rain and kneeling in Ogenas knew what on the sidewalk, Hunt hid his smile as the beam of his flashlight skimmed over the slick bricks of the tunnel below in a careful sweep, then over the cloudy, dark river, surging thanks to the waterfalls of rain that poured in through the grates. "It's a sewer," he said. "What did you expect?"

She flipped him off. "You're the warrior-investigator-whatever. Can't you go down there and find some clues?"

"You really think Sabine left an easy trail like that?"

"Maybe there are claw marks or whatever." She surveyed the ancient stone. Hunt didn't know why she bothered. There were claw marks and scratches *everywhere*. Likely from whatever lowlifes had dwelled and hunted down here for centuries.

"This isn't some crime-scene investigative drama, Quinlan. It's not that easy."

"No one likes a condescending asshole, *Athalar*."

His mouth curved upward. Bryce studied the gloom below, mouth tightening as if she'd will the kristallos or Sabine to appear. He'd already sent a message to Isaiah and Vik to get extra cameras on the Gate and the sewer grate, along with any others in the vicinity. If one so much as shifted an inch, they'd know. He didn't dare ask them to follow Sabine. Not yet.

"We should go down there," Bryce declared. "Maybe we can pick up her scent."

He said carefully, "You haven't made the Drop."

"Spare me the protective bullshit."

Dark Hel, this woman. "I'm not going down there unless we have a fuck-ton more weapons." He only had two guns and a knife. "Demon aside, if Sabine's down there . . ." He might outrank Sabine in terms of power, but with the witches' spells hobbling most of his might through the halo's ink, he had his proverbial hands tied.

So it'd come down to brute strength, and while he had the advantage there, too, Sabine was lethal. Motivated. And mean as an adder.

Bryce scowled. "I can handle myself." After the shooting range, he certainly knew that.

"It's not about you, sweetheart. It's about *me* not wanting to wind up dead."

"Can't you use your lightning-thing to protect us?"

He suppressed another smile at *lightning-thing*, but he said, "There's water down there. Adding lightning to the mix doesn't seem wise."

She cut him a glare. Hunt gave one right back.

Hunt had the feeling he'd passed some test when she smiled slightly.

Avoiding that little smile, Hunt scanned the river of filth running below. "All sewers lead to the Istros. Maybe the Many Waters folk have seen something."

Bryce's brows rose. "Why would they?"

"A river's a good place to dump a corpse."

"The demon left remains, though. It—or Sabine—doesn't seem

to be interested in hiding them. Not if she wants to do this as part of some scheme to jeopardize Micah's image."

"That's only a theory right now," Hunt countered. "I have a Many Waters contact who might have intel."

"Let's head to the docks, then. We'll be less likely to be noticed at night anyway."

"But twice as likely to encounter a predator searching for a meal. We'll wait until daylight." The gods knew they'd already risked enough in coming down here. Hunt placed the metal lid back on the sewer with a *thud*. He got one look at her annoyed, dirty face and chuckled. Before he could reconsider, he said, "I have fun with you, Quinlan. Despite how terrible this case is, despite all of it, I haven't had fun like this in a while." In *ever*.

He could have sworn she blushed. "Hang with me, Athalar," she said, trying to wipe the grime off her legs and hands from kneeling at the grate entrance, "and you might get rid of that stick up your ass after all."

He didn't answer. There was just a *click*.

She whirled toward him to find his phone out. Snapping a photo of her.

Hunt's grin was a slash of white in the rainy gloom. "I'd rather have a stick up my ass than look like a drowned rat."

Bryce used the spigot on the roof to wash off her shoes, her hands. She had no desire to track the filth of the street into her house. She went so far as to make Hunt take off his boots in the hallway, and didn't look to see if he was planning on taking a shower before she ran for her own room and had the water going in seconds.

She left her clothes in a pile in the corner, turned the heat as high as she could tolerate, and began a process of scrubbing and foaming and scrubbing some more. Remembering how she'd knelt on the filthy city street and breathed in a face full of sewer air, she scrubbed herself again.

Hunt knocked twenty minutes later. "Don't forget to clean between your toes."

Even with the shut door, she covered herself. "Fuck off."

His chuckle rumbled to her over the sound of the water. He said, "The soap in the guest room is out. Do you have another bar?"

"There's some in the hall linen closet. Just take whatever."

He grunted his thanks, and was gone a heartbeat later. Bryce washed and lathered herself again. Gross. This city was so gross. The rain only made it worse.

Then Hunt knocked again. "Quinlan."

His grave tone had her shutting off the water. "What's wrong?"

She whipped a towel around herself, sliding across the marble tiles as she reached the door. Hunt was shirtless, leaning against the doorjamb to her bedroom. She might have ogled the muscles the guy was sporting if his face hadn't been serious as Hel. "You want to tell me something?"

She gulped, scanning him from head to toe. "About what?"

"About what the fuck this is?" He extended his hand. Opened up his big fist.

A purple glittery unicorn lay in it.

She snatched the toy from his hand. His dark eyes lit with amusement as Bryce demanded, "Why are you snooping through my things?"

"Why do you have a box of unicorns in your linen closet?"

"This one is a unicorn-*pegasus*." She stroked the lilac mane. "Jelly Jubilee."

He just stared at her. Bryce shoved past him into the hall, where the linen closet door was still ajar, her box of toys now on one of the lower shelves. Hunt followed a step behind. Still shirtless.

"The soap is *right there*," she said, pointing to the stack directly at his eye level. "And yet you took down a box from the highest shelf?"

She could have sworn color stained his cheeks. "I saw purple glitter."

She blinked at him. "You thought it was a sex toy, didn't you?"

He said nothing.

"You think I keep my vibrator in my *linen closet*?"

He crossed his arms. "What I want to know is why you have a box of these things."

"Because I love them." She gently set Jelly Jubilee in the box, but pulled out an orange-and-yellow toy. "This is my pegasus, Peaches and Dreams."

"You're twenty-five years old."

"And? They're sparkly and squishy." She gave P&D a little squeeze, then put her back in the box and pulled out the third one, a slender-legged unicorn with a mint-green coat and rose-colored mane. "And this is Princess Creampuff." She almost laughed at the juxtaposition as she held up the sparkly toy in front of the Umbra Mortis.

"That name doesn't even match her coloring. What's up with the food names?"

She ran a finger over the purple glitter sprayed across the doll's flank. "It's because they're so cute you could eat them. Which I did when I was six."

His mouth twitched. "You didn't."

"Her name was Pineapple Shimmer and her legs were all squishy and glittery and I couldn't resist anymore and just . . . took a bite. Turns out the inside of them really is jelly. But not the edible kind. My mom had to call poison control."

He surveyed the box. "And you still have these because . . . ?"

"Because they make me happy." At his still-bemused look she added, "All right. If you want to get deep about it, Athalar, playing with them was the first time the other kids didn't treat me like a total freak. The Starlight Fancy horses were the number one toy on every girl's Winter Solstice wish list when I was five. And they were *not* all made equal. Poor Princess Creampuff here was common as a hoptoad. But Jelly Jubilee . . ." She smiled at the purple unicorn-pegasus, the memory it summoned. "My mom left Nidaros for the first time in years to buy her from one of the big towns two hours away. She was the ultimate Starlight Fancy conquest. Not just a unicorn, not just a pegasus—but *both*. I flashed this baby at school and was instantly accepted."

His eyes shone as she gently set the box on the high shelf. "I'll never laugh at them again."

"Good." She turned back to him, remembering that she still

wore only her towel, and he was still shirtless. She grabbed a box of soap and shoved it toward him. "Here. Next time you want to check out my vibrators, just ask, Athalar." She inclined her head toward her bedroom door and winked. "They're in the left nightstand."

Again, his cheeks reddened. "I wasn't—you're a pain in the ass, you know that?"

She shut the linen closet door with her hip and sauntered back to her bedroom. "I'd rather be a pain in the ass," she said slyly over her bare shoulder, "than a snooping pervert."

His snarl followed her all the way back into the bathroom.

42

In the midmorning light, the Istros River gleamed a deep blue, its waters clear enough to see the detritus sprinkled among the pale rocks and waving grasses. Centuries of Crescent City artifacts rusted away down there, picked over again and again by the various creatures who eked out a living by scavenging the crap hurled into the river.

Rumor had it that city officials had once tried to institute heavy fines for anyone caught dumping things in the river, but the scavengers had caught wind of it and put up such a fuss that the River Queen had no choice but to shut the bill down when it was officially proposed.

Overhead, angels, witches, and winged shifters soared by, keeping clear of the misty gloom of the Bone Quarter. Last night's rain had cleared to a pleasant spring day—no hint of the flickering lights that often drifted beneath the river's surface, visible only once night fell.

Bryce frowned down at a crustacean—some type of mammoth blue crab—picking its way along the floor beside the quay's stone block, sorting through a pile of beer bottles. The remnants of last night's drunken revels. "Have you ever been down to the mer-city?"

"No." Hunt rustled his wings, one brushing against her

shoulder. "Happy to stay above the surface." The river breeze drifted past, chill despite the warm day. "You?"

She rubbed her hands down her arms along the smooth leather of Danika's old jacket, trying to coax some warmth into them. "Never got an invite."

Most never would. The river folk were notoriously secretive, their city beneath the surface—the Blue Court—a place few who dwelled on land would ever see. One glass sub went in and out per day, and those on it traveled by invitation only. And even if they possessed the lung capacity or artificial means, no one was stupid enough to swim down. Not with what prowled these waters.

An auburn head of hair broke the surface a couple hundred yards out, and a partially scaled, muscled arm waved before vanishing, fingers tipped in sharp gray nails glinting in the sun.

Hunt glanced to Bryce. "Do you know any mer?"

Bryce lifted a corner of her mouth. "One lived down the hall my freshman year at CCU. She partied harder than all of us combined."

The mer could shift into fully human bodies for short periods of time, but if they went too long, the shift would be permanent, their scales drying up and flaking away into dust, their gills shrinking to nothing. The mer down the hall had been granted an oversize tub in her dorm room so she didn't need to interrupt her studies to return to the Istros once a day.

By the end of the first month of school, the mer had turned it into a party suite. Parties that Bryce and Danika gleefully attended, Connor and Thorne in tow. At the end of that year, their entire floor had been so wrecked that every one of them was slapped with a hefty fine for damages.

Bryce made sure she intercepted the letter before her parents got it out of the mailbox and quietly paid the fine with the marks she earned that summer scooping ice cream at the town parlor.

Sabine had gotten the letter, paid the fine, and made Danika spend the whole summer picking up trash in the Meadows.

Act like trash, Sabine had told her daughter, *and you can spend your days with it.*

Naturally, the following fall, Bryce and Danika had dressed as trash cans for the Autumnal Equinox.

The water of the Istros was clear enough for Bryce and Hunt to see the powerful male body swim closer, the reddish-brown scales of his long tail catching the light like burnished copper. Black stripes slashed through them, the pattern continuing up his torso and along his arms. Like some sort of aquatic tiger. The bare skin of his upper arms and chest was heavily tanned, suggesting hours spent near the surface or basking on the rocks of some hidden cove along the coast.

The male's head broke the water, and his taloned hands brushed back his jaw-length auburn hair as he flashed Hunt a grin. "Long time no see."

Hunt smiled at the mer male treading water. "Glad you weren't too busy with your fancy new title to say hello."

The mer waved a hand in dismissal, and Hunt beckoned Bryce forward. "Bryce, this is Tharion Ketos." She stepped closer to the concrete edge of the quay. "An old friend."

Tharion grinned at Hunt again. "Not as old as you."

Bryce gave the male a half smile. "Nice to meet you."

Tharion's light brown eyes glittered. "The pleasure, Bryce, is all mine."

Gods spare him. Hunt cleared his throat. "We're here on official business."

Tharion swam the remaining few feet to the quay's edge, knocking the crustacean into the drifting blue with a careless brush of his tail. Planting his talon-tipped hands on the concrete, he easily heaved his massive body from the water, the gills beneath his ears sealing in as he switched control of his breathing to his nose and mouth. He patted the now-wet concrete next to him and winked at Bryce. "Take a seat, Legs, and tell me all about it."

Bryce huffed a laugh. "You're trouble."

"It's my middle name, actually."

Hunt rolled his eyes. But Bryce sat beside the male, apparently not caring that the water would surely soak into the green dress she wore beneath the leather jacket. She pulled off her beige heels and dipped her feet in the water, splashing softly. Normally, he'd have dragged her away from the river's edge, and told her she'd be lucky to lose just the leg if she put a foot in the water. But with Tharion beside them, none of the river's denizens would dare approach.

Tharion asked Bryce, "Are you in the 33rd or the Auxiliary?"

"Neither. I'm working with Hunt as a consultant on a case."

Tharion hummed. "What does your boyfriend think of you working with the famed Umbra Mortis?"

Hunt sat down on the male's other side. "Real subtle, Tharion."

Yet Bryce's mouth bloomed into a full smile.

It was a near-twin to the one she'd given him this morning, when he'd popped his head into her room to see if she was ready to leave. Of course, his eyes had gone directly to the left nightstand. And then that smile had turned feral, like she knew exactly what he was wondering about.

He certainly had not been looking for any of her sex toys when he'd opened up the linen closet last night. But he'd spied a flash of purple sparkles, and—fine, maybe the thought had crossed his mind—he'd just pulled down the box before he could really think.

And now that he knew where they were, he couldn't help but look at that nightstand and imagine her there, in that bed. Leaning against the pillows and—

It might have made sleeping a shade uncomfortable last night.

Tharion leaned back on his hands, displaying his muscled abdomen as he asked innocently, "What did I say?"

Bryce laughed, making no attempt to hide her blatant ogling of the mer's cut body. "I don't have a boyfriend. You want the job?"

Tharion smirked. "You like to swim?"

And that was about as much as Hunt could take with only one cup of coffee in his system. "I know you're busy, Tharion," he said through his teeth with just enough edge that the mer peeled his attention away from Bryce, "so we'll keep this quick."

"Oh, take your time," Tharion said, eyes dancing with pure male challenge. "The River Queen gave me the morning off, so I'm all yours."

"You work for the River Queen?" Bryce asked.

"I'm a lowly peon in her court, but yes."

Hunt leaned forward to catch Bryce's stare. "Tharion's just been promoted to her Captain of Intelligence. Don't let the charm and irreverence fool you."

"Charm and irreverence happen to be my two favorite traits," Bryce said with a wink for Tharion this time.

The mer's smile deepened. "Careful, Bryce. I might decide I like you and bring you Beneath."

Hunt gave Tharion a warning look. Some of the darker mer had done just that, long ago. Carried human brides down to their undersea courts and kept them there, trapped within the massive air bubbles that contained parts of their palaces and cities, unable to reach the surface.

Bryce waved off the awful history. "We have a few questions for you, if that's all right."

Tharion gestured lazily with a claw-tipped, webbed hand. The markings on the mer were varied and vibrant: different coloring, stripes or specks or solids, their tails long-finned or short or wispy. Their magic mostly involved the element in which they lived, though some could summon tempests. The River Queen, part mer, part river-spirit, could summon far worse, they said. Possibly wash away all of Lunathion, if provoked.

She was a daughter of Ogenas, according to legend, born from the mighty river-that-encircles-the-world, and sister to the Ocean Queen, the reclusive ruler of the five great seas of Midgard. There was a fifty-fifty chance the goddess thing was true of the River Queen, Hunt supposed. But regardless, the residents of this city did their best not to piss her off. Even Micah maintained a healthy, respectful relationship with her.

Hunt asked, "You see anything unusual lately?"

Tharion's tail idly stirred the sparkling water. "What kind of case is this? Murder?"

"Yes," Hunt said. Bryce's face tightened.

Tharion's claws clicked on the concrete. "Serial killer?"

"Just answer the question, asshole."

Tharion peered at Bryce. "If he talks to you like that, I hope you kick him in the balls."

"She'd enjoy it," Hunt muttered.

"Hunt has learned his lesson about pissing me off," Bryce said sweetly.

Tharion's smile was sly. "*That* is a story I'd like to hear."

"Of course you would," Hunt grumbled.

"Does this have to do with the Viper Queen pulling in her people the other week?"

"Yes," Hunt said carefully.

Tharion's eyes darkened, a reminder that the male could be lethal when the mood struck him, and that there was a good reason the creatures of the river didn't fuck with the mer. "Some bad shit's going down, isn't it."

"We're trying to stop it," Hunt said.

The mer nodded gravely. "Let me ask around."

"Covertly, Tharion. The less people who know something's happening the better."

Tharion slipped back into the water, again disturbing the poor crab who'd clawed his way back to the quay. The mer's powerful tail thrashed, keeping him effortlessly in place as he surveyed Hunt and Bryce. "Do I tell my queen to pull in our people, too?"

"Doesn't fit the pattern so far," Hunt said, "but it wouldn't hurt to give a warning."

"What should I be warning her about?"

"An old-school demon called the kristallos," Bryce said softly. "A monster straight from the Pit, bred by the Star-Eater himself."

For a moment, Tharion said nothing, his tan face going pale. Then, "Fuck." He ran a hand through his wet hair. "I'll ask around," he promised again. Far down the river, motion drew Hunt's eye. A black boat drifted toward the mist of the Bone Quarter.

On the Black Dock, jutting from the city's bright shoreline

like a dark sword, a group of mourners huddled beneath the inky arches, praying for the boat to safely bear the veiled pine coffin across the water.

Around the wooden vessel, broad, scaled backs broke the river's surface, writhing and circling. Waiting for final judgment—and lunch.

Tharion followed his line of sight. "Five marks says it tips."

"That's disgusting," Bryce hissed.

Tharion swished his tail, playfully splashing Bryce's legs with water. "I won't bet on your Sailing, Legs. I promise." He flicked some water toward Hunt. "And we already know *your* boat is going to tip right the fuck over before it's even left the shore."

"Funny."

Behind them, an otter in a reflective yellow vest loped past, a sealed wax message tube held in its fanged mouth. It barely glanced their way before leaping into the river and vanishing. Bryce bit her lip, a high-pitched squeal cracking from her.

The fearless, fuzzy messengers were hard to resist, even for Hunt. While true animals and not shifters, they possessed an uncanny level of intelligence, thanks to the old magic in their veins. They'd found their place in the city by relaying tech-free communication between those who lived in the three realms that made up Crescent City: the mer in the river, the Reapers in the Bone Quarter, and the residents of Lunathion proper.

Tharion laughed at the naked delight on Bryce's face. "Do you think the Reapers fall to pieces over them, too?"

"I bet even the Under-King himself squeals when he sees them," Bryce said. "They were part of why I wanted to move here in the first place."

Hunt lifted a brow. "Really?"

"I saw them when I was a kid and thought they were the most magical thing I'd ever seen." She beamed. "I still do."

"Considering your line of work, that's saying something."

Tharion angled his head at them. "What manner of work is that?"

"Antiquities," Bryce said. "If you ever find anything interesting in the depths, let me know."

"I'll send an otter right to you."

Hunt got to his feet, offering a hand to help Bryce rise. "Keep us posted."

Tharion gave him an irreverent salute. "I'll see you when I see you," he said, gills flaring, and dove beneath the surface. They watched him swim out toward the deep heart of the river, following the same path as the otter, then plunge down, down—to those distant, twinkling lights.

"He's a charmer," Bryce murmured as Hunt hauled her to her feet, his other hand coming to her elbow.

Hunt's hand lingered, the heat of it searing her even through the leather of the jacket. "Just wait until you see him in his human form. He causes riots."

She laughed. "How'd you even meet him?"

"We had a string of mer murders last year." Her eyes darkened in recognition. It'd been all over the news. "Tharion's little sister was one of the victims. It was high-profile enough that Micah assigned me to help out. Tharion and I worked on the case together for the few weeks it lasted."

Micah had traded him three whole *debts* for it.

She winced. "It was you two who caught the killer? They never said on the news—just that he'd been apprehended. Nothing more—not even who it was."

Hunt let go of her elbow. "We did. A rogue panther shifter. I handed him over to Tharion."

"I'm assuming the panther didn't make it down to the Blue Court."

Hunt surveyed the shimmering expanse of water. "No, he didn't."

"Is Bryce being nice to you, Athie?"

Seated at the front desk of the gallery showroom, Bryce

muttered, "Oh please," and kept clicking through the paperwork Jesiba had sent over.

Hunt, sprawled in the chair across the desk from her, the portrait of angelic arrogance, merely asked the fire sprite lurking in the open iron door, "What would you do if I said she wasn't, Lehabah?"

Lehabah floated in the archway, not daring to come into the showroom. Not when Jesiba would likely see. "I'd burn all her lunches for a month."

Hunt chuckled, the sound sliding along her bones. Bryce, despite herself, smiled.

Something heavy thumped, audible even a level above the library, and Lehabah zoomed down the stairs, hissing, "*Bad!*"

Bryce looked at Hunt as he sifted through the photos of the demon from a few nights ago. His hair hung over his brow, the sable strands gleaming like black silk. Her fingers curled on the keyboard.

Hunt lifted his head. "We need more intel on Sabine. The fact that she swapped the footage of the Horn's theft from the temple is suspicious, and what she said in the observation room that night is pretty suspicious, too, but they don't necessarily mean she's a murderer. I can't approach Micah without concrete proof."

She rubbed the back of her neck. "Ruhn hasn't gotten any leads on finding the Horn, either, so that we can lure the kristallos."

Silence fell. Hunt crossed an ankle over a knee, then stretched out a hand to where she'd discarded Danika's jacket on the chair beside him, too lazy to bother hanging it. "I saw Danika wearing this in the photo in your guest room. Why'd you keep it?"

Bryce let out a long breath, thankful for his shift in subject. "Danika used to store her stuff in the supply closet here, rather than bothering to go back to the apartment or over to the Den. She'd stashed the jacket here the day . . ." She blew out a breath and glanced toward the bathroom in the back of the space, where Danika had changed only hours before her death. "I didn't want Sabine to have it. She would have read the back of it and thrown it in the trash."

Hunt picked up the jacket and read, "Through love, all is possible."

Bryce nodded. "The tattoo on my back says the same thing. Well, in some fancy alphabet that she dug up online, but . . . Danika had a thing about that phrase. It was all the Oracle told her, apparently. Which makes no sense, because Danika was one of the least lovey-dovey people I've ever met, but . . ." Bryce toyed with the amulet around her neck, zipping it along the chain. "Something about it resonated with her. So after she died, I kept the jacket. And started wearing it."

Hunt carefully set the jacket back on the chair. "I get it—about the personal effects." He seemed like he wasn't going to say more, but then he continued, "That sunball hat you made fun of?"

"I didn't make fun of it. You just don't seem like the kind of male who *wears* such a thing."

He chuckled again—in that same way that slid over her skin. "That hat was the first thing I bought when I came here. With the first paycheck I ever received from Micah." The corner of his mouth turned upward. "I saw it in an athletic shop, and it just seemed so ordinary. You have no idea how different Lunathion is from the Eternal City. From anything in Pangera. And that hat just . . ."

"Represented that?"

"Yeah. It seemed like a new beginning. A step toward a more normal existence. Well, as normal an existence as someone like me can have."

She made an effort not to look at his wrist. "So you have your hat—and I have Jelly Jubilee."

His smile lit up the dimness of the gallery. "I'm surprised you don't have a tattoo of Jelly Jubilee somewhere." His eyes skimmed over her, lingering on the short, tight green dress.

Her toes curled. "Who says I don't have a tattoo of her somewhere you can't see, Athalar?"

She watched him sort through everything he had *already* seen. Since he'd moved in, she'd stopped parading about the apartment in her underwear while getting dressed, but she knew he'd spotted her through the window in the days before. Knew he realized there was a limited, very intimate, number of places where another tattoo might be hidden.

She could have sworn his voice dropped an octave or two as he asked, "Do you?"

With any other male, she would have said, *Why don't you come find out?*

With any other male, she would have already been on the other side of the desk. Crawling into his lap. Unbuckling his belt. And then sinking down onto his cock, riding him until they were both moaning and breathless and—

She made herself go back to her paperwork. "There are a few males who can answer that question, if you're so curious." How her voice was so steady, she had no idea.

Hunt's silence was palpable. She didn't dare look over her computer screen.

But his eyes remained focused on her, burning her like a brand.

Her heart thundered throughout her body. Dangerous, stupid, reckless—

Hunt let out a long, tight breath. The chair he sat in groaned as he shifted in it, his wings rustling. She still didn't dare look. She honestly didn't know what she'd do if she looked.

But then Hunt said, his voice gravelly, "We need to focus on Sabine."

Hearing her name was like being doused with ice water.

Right. Yes. Of course. Because hooking up with the Umbra Mortis wasn't a possibility. The reasons for that started with him pining for a lost love and ended with the fact that he was owned by the gods-damned Governor. With a million other obstacles in between.

She still couldn't look at him as Hunt asked, "Any thoughts on how we can get more intel on her? Even just a glimpse into her current state of mind?"

Needing something to do with her hands, her too-warm body, Bryce printed out, then signed and dated, the paperwork Jesiba had sent. "We can't bring in Sabine for formal questioning without making her aware that we're onto her," Bryce said, at last looking at Hunt.

His face was flushed, and his eyes . . . Fucking Solas, his black eyes glittered, wholly fixed on her face. Like he was thinking of touching her.

Tasting her.

"Okay," he said roughly, running a hand through his hair. His eyes settled, the dark fire in them banking. Thank the gods.

An idea dawned upon her, and Bryce said in a strangled voice, her stomach twisting with dread, "So I think we have to bring the questions to Sabine."

43

The wolves' Den in Moonwood occupied ten entire city blocks, a sprawling villa built around a wild tangle of forest and grass that legend claimed had grown there since before anyone had touched these lands. Through the iron gates built into the towering limestone arches, Bryce could see through to the private park, where morning sunlight coaxed drowsy flowers into opening up for the day. Wolf pups bounded, pouncing on each other, chasing their tails, watched over by gray-muzzled elders whose brutal days in the Aux were long behind them.

Her gut twisted, enough to make her grateful she'd forgone breakfast. She'd barely slept last night, as she considered and reconsidered this plan. Hunt had offered to do it himself, but she'd refused. She had to come here—had to step up. For Danika.

In his usual battle-suit, Hunt stood a step away, silent as he'd been on the walk over here. As if he knew she could barely keep her legs from shaking. She wished she'd worn sneakers. The steep angle of her heels had irritated the wound in her thigh. Bryce clenched her jaw against the pain as they stood before the Den.

Hunt kept his dark eyes fixed upon the four sentries stationed at the gates.

Three females, one male. All in humanoid form, all in black, all armed with guns and sheathed swords down their backs. A tattoo of an onyx rose with three claw marks slashed through its petals adorned the sides of their necks, marking them as members of the Black Rose Wolf Pack.

Her stomach roiled at the hilts peeking over their armored shoulders. But she pushed away the memory of a braid of silvery-blond hair streaked with purple and pink, constantly snagging in the hilt of an ancient, priceless blade.

Though young, the Pack of Devils had been revered, the most talented wolves in generations. Led by the most powerful Alpha to grace Midgard's soil.

The Black Rose Pack was a far cry from that. A far fucking cry.

Their eyes lit with predatory delight as they spotted Bryce.

Her mouth went dry. And turned positively arid as a fifth wolf appeared from the glass security vestibule to the left of the gate.

The Alpha's dark hair had been pulled into a tight braid, accentuating the sharp angles of her face as she sneered toward Bryce and Hunt. Athalar's hand casually drifted to the knife at his thigh.

Bryce said as casually as she could, "Hi, Amelie."

Amelie Ravenscroft bared her teeth. "What the fuck do you want?"

Hunt bared his teeth right back. "We're here to see the Prime." He flashed his legion badge, the gold twinkling in the sun. "On behalf of the Governor."

Amelie flicked her gold eyes to Hunt, over his tattooed halo. Over his hand on the knife and the *SPQM* she surely knew was tattooed on the other side of his wrist. Her lip curled. "Well, at least you picked interesting company, Quinlan. Danika would have approved. Hel, you might have even done him together." Amelie leaned a shoulder against the vestibule's side. "You used to do that, right? I heard about you guys and those two daemonaki. Classic."

Bryce smiled blandly. "It was three daemonaki, actually."

"Stupid slut," Amelie snarled.

"Watch it," Hunt growled back.

Amelie's pack members lingered behind her, eyeing Hunt and keeping back. The benefit of hanging with the Umbra Mortis, apparently.

Amelie laughed, a sound filled with loathing. Not merely hatred for her, Bryce realized. But for the angels. The Houses of Earth and Blood and Sky and Breath were rivals on a good day, enemies on a bad one. "Or what? You'll use your lightning on me?" she said to Hunt. "If you do, you'll be in such deep shit that your *master* will bury you alive in it." A little smile at the tattoo across his brow.

Hunt went still. And as interesting as it would have been to finally see how Hunt Athalar killed, they had a reason for being here. So Bryce said to the pack leader, "You're a delight, Amelie Ravenscroft. Radio your boss that we're here to see the Prime." She flicked her brows in emphasis of the dismissal she knew would make the Alpha see red.

"Shut that mouth of yours," Amelie said, "before I rip out your tongue."

A brown-haired male wolf standing behind Amelie taunted, "Why don't you go fuck someone in a bathroom again, Quinlan?"

She blocked out every word. But Hunt huffed a laugh that promised broken bones. "I told you to watch it."

"Go ahead, angel," Amelie sneered. "Let's see what you can do."

Bryce could barely move around the panic and dread pushing in, could barely breathe, but Hunt said quietly, "There are six pups playing in sight of this gate. You really want to expose them to the kind of fight we'd have, Amelie?"

Bryce blinked. Hunt didn't so much as glance her way as he continued addressing a seething Amelie. "I'm not going to beat the shit out of you in front of children. So either you let us in, or we'll come back with a warrant." His gaze didn't falter. "I don't think Sabine Fendyr would be particularly happy with Option B."

Amelie held his stare, even as the others tensed. That haughty arrogance had made Sabine tap her as Alpha of the Black Rose Pack, even over Ithan Holstrom, now Amelie's Second. But Sabine had wanted someone just like herself, regardless of Ithan's higher power ranking. And perhaps someone a little less Alpha, too—so she'd have them firmly under her claws.

Bryce waited for Amelie to call Hunt's bluff about the warrant. Waited for a snide remark or the appearance of fangs.

Yet Amelie plucked the radio from her belt and said into it, "Guests are here for the Prime. Come get them."

She had once breezed through the doors beyond Amelie's dark head, had spent hours playing with the pups in the grass and trees beyond it whenever Danika had been given babysitting duty.

She shut out the memory of what it had been like—to watch Danika playing with the fuzzy pups or shrieking children, who had all worshipped the ground she walked upon. Their future leader, their protector, who would take the wolves to new heights.

Bryce's chest constricted to the point of pain. Hunt glanced her way then, his brows rising.

She couldn't do this. Be here. Enter this place.

Amelie smiled, as if realizing that. Scenting her dread and pain.

And the sight of the fucking bitch standing there, where Danika had once been . . . Red washed over Bryce's vision as she drawled, "It's good to see that crime has gone down so much, if all you have to do with your day, Amelie, is play guard at the front door."

Amelie smiled slowly. Footsteps sounded on the other side of the gate, just before they swung open, but Bryce didn't dare look. Not as Amelie said, "You know, sometimes I think I should thank you—they say if Danika hadn't been so distracted by messaging you about your drunk bullshit, she might have anticipated the attack. And then I wouldn't be where I am, would I."

Bryce's nails cut into her palms. But her voice, thank the gods, was steady as she said, "Danika was a thousand times the wolf you are. No matter *where you are*, you'll never be where *she* was."

Amelie went white with rage, her nose crinkling, lips pulling back to expose her now-lengthening teeth—

"Amelie," a male voice growled from the shadows of the gate archway.

Oh gods. Bryce curled her fingers into fists to keep from shaking as she looked toward the young male wolf.

But Ithan Holstrom's eyes darted between her and Amelie as he approached his Alpha. "It's not worth it." The unspoken words simmered in his eyes. *Bryce isn't worth it.*

Amelie snorted, turning back to the vestibule, a shorter, brown-haired female following her. The pack's Omega, if memory served. Amelie sneered over a shoulder to Bryce, "Go back to the dumpster you crawled out of."

Then she shut the door. Leaving Bryce standing before Connor's younger brother.

There was nothing kind on Ithan's tan face. His golden-brown hair was longer than the last time she'd seen him, but he'd been a sophomore playing sunball for CCU then.

This towering, muscled male before them had made the Drop. Had stepped into his brother's shoes and joined the pack that had replaced Connor's.

A brush of Hunt's velvet-soft wings against her arm had her walking. Every step toward the wolf ratcheted up her heartbeat.

"Ithan," Bryce managed to say.

Connor's younger brother said nothing as he turned toward the pillars flanking the walkway.

She was going to puke. All over everything: the limestone tiles, the pale pillars, the glass doors that opened into the park in the center of the villa.

She shouldn't have let Athalar come. Should have made him stay on the roof somewhere so he couldn't witness the spectacular meltdown that she was three seconds away from having.

Ithan Holstrom's steps were unhurried, his gray T-shirt pulling across the considerable expanse of his muscled back. He'd been a cocky twenty-year-old when Connor died, a history major like Danika and the star of CCU's sunball team, rumored to be going pro as soon as his brother gave the nod. He could have gone pro right after high school, but Connor, who had raised Ithan since their parents had died five years earlier, had insisted that a degree came first, sports second. Ithan, who had idolized Connor, had always folded on it, despite Bronson's pleas with Connor to let the kid go pro.

Connor's Shadow, they'd teased Ithan.

He'd filled out since then. At last started truly resembling his older brother—even the shade of his golden-brown hair was like a spike through her chest.

I'm crazy about you. I don't want anyone else. I haven't for a long while.

She couldn't breathe. Couldn't stop seeing, hearing those words, feeling the giant fucking rip in the space-time continuum where Connor should have been, in a world where nothing bad could ever, ever happen—

Ithan stopped before another set of glass doors. He opened one, the muscles in his long arm rippling as he held it for them.

Hunt went first, no doubt scanning the space in the span of a blink.

Bryce managed to look up at Ithan as she passed.

His white teeth shone as he bared them at her.

Gone was the cocky boy she'd teased; gone was the boy who'd tried out flirting on her so he could use the techniques on Nathalie, who had laughed when Ithan asked her out but told him to wait a few more years; gone was the boy who had relentlessly questioned Bryce about when she'd finally start dating his brother and wouldn't take *never* for an answer.

A honed predator now stood in his place. Who had surely not forgotten the leaked messages she'd sent and received that horrible night. That she'd been fucking some random in the club bathroom while Connor—Connor, who had just spilled his heart to her—was slaughtered.

Bryce lowered her eyes, hating it, hating every second of this fucked-up visit.

Ithan smiled, as if savoring her shame.

He'd dropped out of CCU after Connor had died. Quit playing sunball. She only knew because she'd caught a game on TV one night two months later and the commentators had still been discussing it. No one, not his coaches, not his friends, not his packmates, could convince him to return. He'd walked away from the sport and never looked back, apparently.

She hadn't seen him since the days right before the murders.

Her last photo of him was the one Danika had taken at his game, playing in the background. The one she'd tortured herself with last night for hours while bracing herself for what the dawn would bring.

Before that, though, there had been hundreds of photos of the two of them together. They still sat on her phone like a basket full of snakes, waiting to bite if she so much as opened the lid.

Ithan's cruel smile didn't waver as he shut the door behind them. "The Prime's taking a nap. Sabine will meet with you."

Bryce glanced at Hunt, who gave her a shallow nod. Precisely as they'd planned.

Bryce was aware of Ithan's every breath at her back as they aimed for the stairs that Bryce knew would take them up a level to Sabine's office. Hunt seemed aware of Ithan, too, and let enough lightning wreathe his hands, his wrists, that the young wolf took a step away.

At least alphaholes were good for something.

Ithan didn't leave. No, it seemed he was to be their guard and silent tormentor for the duration of this miserable trip.

Bryce knew every step toward Sabine's office on the second level, but Ithan led the way: up the sprawling limestone stairs marred with so many scratches and gouges no one bothered to fix them anymore; down the high-ceilinged, bright hall whose windows overlooked the busy street outside; and finally to the worn wood door. Danika had grown up here—and moved out as soon as she'd gone to CCU. After graduation, she'd stayed only during formal wolf events and holidays.

Ithan's pace was leisurely. As if he could scent Bryce's misery, and wanted to make her endure it for every possible second.

She supposed she deserved it. *Knew* she deserved it.

She tried to block out the memory that flashed.

The twenty-one ignored calls from Ithan, all in the first few days following the murder. The half-dozen audiomails. The first had been sobbing, panicked, left in the hours afterward. *Is it true, Bryce? Are they dead?*

And then the messages had shifted to worry. *Where are you? Are you okay? I called the major hospitals and you're not listed, but no one is talking. Please call me.*

And then, by the end, that last audiomail from Ithan, nothing but razor-sharp coldness. *The Legion inspectors showed me all the messages. Connor practically told you that he loved you, and you finally agreed to go out with him, and then you fucked some stranger in the Raven bathroom? While he was* dying*? Are you kidding me with this shit? Don't come to the Sailing tomorrow. You're not welcome there.*

She'd never written back, never sought him out. Hadn't been able to endure the thought of facing him. Seeing the grief and pain in his face. Loyalty was the most prized of all wolf traits. In their eyes, she and Connor had been inevitable. Nearly mated. Just a question of time. Her hookups before that hadn't mattered, and neither had his, because nothing had been declared yet.

Until he'd asked her out at last. And she had said yes. Had started down that road.

To the wolves, she was Connor's, and he was hers.

Message me when you're home safe.

Her chest tightened and tightened, the walls pushing in, squeezing—

She forced herself to take a long breath. To inhale to the point where her ribs strained from holding it in. Then to exhale, pushing-pushing-pushing, until she was heaving out the pure gut-shredding panic that burned through her whole body like acid.

Bryce wasn't a wolf. She didn't play by their rules of courtship. And she'd been stupid and scared of what agreeing to that date had meant, and Danika certainly didn't care one way or another if Bryce had some meaningless hookup, but—Bryce hadn't ever worked up the nerve to explain to Ithan after she'd seen and heard his messages.

She'd kept them all. Listening to them was a solid central arc of her emotional death-spiral routine. The culmination of it, of course, being Danika's last, foolishly happy messages.

Ithan knocked on Sabine's door, letting it swing wide to reveal a sunny white office whose windows looked into the verdant greenery of the Den's park. Sabine sat at her desk, her corn-silk hair near-glowing in the light. "You have some nerve coming here."

Words dried up in Bryce's throat as she took in the pale face, the slender hands interlaced on the oak desk, the narrow shoulders that belied her tremendous strength. Danika had been pure wildfire; her mother was solid ice. And if Sabine had killed her, if Sabine had done this . . .

Roaring began in Bryce's head.

Hunt must have sensed it, scented it, because he stepped up to Bryce's side, Ithan lingering in the hall, and said, "We wanted to meet with the Prime."

Irritation flickered in Sabine's eyes. "About?"

"About your daughter's murder."

"Stay the fuck out of our business," Sabine barked, setting the glass on her table rattling. Bile burned Bryce's throat, and she focused on not screaming or launching herself at the woman.

Hunt's wing brushed Bryce's back, a casual gesture to anyone watching, but that warmth and softness steadied her. Danika. For Danika, she'd do this.

Sabine's eyes blazed. "Where the Hel is my sword?"

Bryce refused to answer, to even snap that the sword was and would always be Danika's, and said, "We have intel that suggests Danika was stationed at Luna's Temple the night the Horn was stolen. We need the Prime to confirm." Bryce kept her eyes on the carpet, the portrait of terrified, shameful submission, and let Sabine dig her own grave.

Sabine demanded, "What the fuck does this have to do with her death?"

Hunt said calmly, "We're putting together a picture of Danika's movements before the kristallos demon killed her. Who she might have met, what she might have seen or done."

Another bit of bait: to see her reaction to the demon's breed, when it hadn't yet been made public. Sabine didn't so much as blink. Like she was already familiar with it—perhaps because she'd been summoning it all along. Though she might just not have cared, Bryce supposed. Sabine hissed, "Danika wasn't at the temple that night. She had nothing to do with the Horn being stolen."

Bryce avoided the urge to close her eyes at the lie that confirmed everything.

Claws slid from Sabine's knuckles, embedding in her desk. "Who told you Danika was at the temple?"

"No one," Bryce lied. "I thought I might have remembered her mentioning—"

"You *thought*?" Sabine sneered, voice rising to imitate Bryce's. "It's hard to remember, isn't it, when you were high, drunk, and fucking strangers."

"You're right," Bryce breathed, even as Hunt growled. "This was a mistake." She didn't give Hunt time to object before she turned on a heel and left, gasping for breath.

How she kept her back straight, her stomach inside her body, she had no idea.

She barely heard Hunt as he fell into step behind her. Couldn't stand to look at Ithan as she entered the hallway and found him waiting against the far wall.

Back down the stairs. She didn't dare look at the wolves she passed.

She knew Ithan trailed, but she didn't care, didn't care—

"Quinlan." Hunt's voice cut through the marble stairwell. She made it down another flight when he said again, "*Quinlan*."

It was sharp enough that she paused. Looked up over a shoulder. Hunt's eyes scanned her face—worry, not triumph at Sabine's blatant lie, shining there.

But Ithan stood between them on the steps, eyes hard as stones. "Tell me what this is about."

Hunt drawled, "It's classified, asshole."

Ithan's snarl rumbled through the stairwell.

"It's starting again," Bryce said quietly, aware of all the cameras, of Micah's order to keep this quiet. Her voice was rasping. "We're trying to figure out why and who's behind it. Three murders so far. The same way. Be careful—warn your pack to be careful."

Ithan's face remained unreadable. That had been one of his assets as a sunball player—his ability to keep from broadcasting moves to his opponents. He'd been brilliant, and cocky as fuck, yes, but that arrogance had been well earned through hours of practice and brutal discipline.

Ithan's face remained cold. "I'll let you know if I hear anything."

"Do you need our numbers?" Hunt asked coolly.

Ithan's lip curled. "I have hers." She struggled to meet his stare, especially as he asked, "Are you going to bother to reply this time?"

She turned on her heel and rushed down the stairs into the reception hall.

The Prime of the wolves stood in it now. Talking to the receptionist, hunched over his redwood cane, Danika's grandfather lifted his withered face as she came to an abrupt halt in front of him.

His warm brown eyes—those were Danika's eyes, staring out at her.

The ancient male offered her a sad, kind smile. It was worse than any of the sneers or snarls.

Bryce managed to bow her head before she bolted through the glass doors.

She made it to the gates without running into anyone else. Had almost made it onto the street when Ithan caught up to her, Hunt a step behind. Ithan said, "You never deserved him."

He might as well have drawn the knife she knew was hidden in his boot and plunged it into her chest. "I know," she rasped.

The pups were still playing, bounding through the high grasses. He nodded to the second level, to where Sabine's office overlooked the greenery. "You made some dumb fucking choices, Bryce, but I never pegged you for stupid. She wants you dead." Another confirmation, perhaps.

The words snapped something in her. "Likewise." She pointed to the gates, unable to stop the rage boiling in her as she realized that all signs pointed toward Sabine. "Connor would be ashamed of you for letting Amelie run rampant. For letting a piece of shit like that be your Alpha."

Claws glinted at Ithan's knuckles. "Don't you *ever* say his name again."

"Walk away," Hunt said softly to him. Lightning licked along his wings.

Ithan looked inclined to rip out his throat, but Hunt was already at Bryce's side, following her onto the sun-drenched street. She didn't dare look at Amelie or her pack at the gates, sneering and snickering at them.

"You're trash, Quinlan!" Amelie shouted as they passed by, and her friends roared with laughter.

Bryce couldn't bear to see if Ithan laughed with them.

44

Sabine lied about Danika not being at the temple. But we need a solid plan for catching her if she's summoning this demon," Hunt said to Bryce twenty minutes later over lunch. The angel devoured no less than three bowls of cereal, one after another. She hadn't spoken on the way back to the apartment. Had needed the entire walk here to reel herself back together.

Bryce pushed at the puffed rice floating around in her own bowl. She had zero interest in eating. "I'm sick of waiting. Just arrest her."

"She's the unofficial Head of Moonwood and basically the Prime of the wolves," Hunt cautioned. "If not in title, then in every other way. We have to be careful how we approach this. The fallout could be catastrophic."

"Sure." Bryce poked at her cereal again. She knew she should be screaming, knew she should be marching back to the Den to kill that fucking bitch. Bryce ground her teeth. They'd had no word from Tharion or Ruhn, either.

Hunt tapped a finger on the glass table, weighing her expression. Then he mercifully switched subjects. "I get Ithan's history, but what's Amelie's problem with you?"

Maybe Bryce was just tired, but she wound up saying, "Did you ever see them—the messages from that night? Every newspaper had them on the front page after they leaked."

Hunt stilled. "Yeah," he said gently. "I did."

She shrugged, swirling the cereal in her bowl. Around and around.

"Amelie had . . . a thing. For Connor. Since they were kids. I think she still does."

"Ah."

"And—you know about me and Connor."

"Yeah. I'm sorry."

She hated those two words. Had heard them so many times she just fucking *hated* them. She said, "When she saw the messages from that night, I think Amelie finally realized why he had never returned her feelings."

He frowned. "It's been two years."

"So?" It sure as shit hadn't done anything to help her feel better about it.

Hunt shook his head. "People still bring them up? Those messages?"

"Of course." She snorted, shaking her head. "Just look me up online, Athalar. I had to shut down every account I had." The thought made her stomach churn, nauseating panic tightening every muscle and vein in her body. She'd gotten better about managing it—that feeling—but not by much. "People hate me. Literally *hate* me. Some of the wolf packs even wrote a song and put it online—they called it 'I Just Hooked Up with Someone in the Bathroom, Don't Tell Connor.' They sing it whenever they see me."

His face had gone cold as ice. "Which packs?"

She shook her head. She certainly wouldn't name them, not with that murderous expression on his face. "It doesn't matter. People are assholes."

It was as simple as that, she'd learned. Most people were assholes, and this city was rife with them.

She sometimes wondered what they'd say if they knew about that time two winters ago when someone had sent a thousand printed-out lyric sheets of the song to her new apartment, along with mock album artwork taken from the photos she'd snapped that night. If they knew she had gone up to the roof to burn them all—but instead wound up staring over the ledge. She wondered what would have happened if Juniper, on a whim, hadn't called just to check in that night. Right as Bryce had braced her hands on the rail.

Only that friendly voice on the other end of the line kept Bryce from walking right off the roof.

Juniper had kept Bryce on the phone—babbling about nothing. Right until her cab had pulled up in front of the apartment. Juniper refused to hang up until she was on the roof with Bryce, laughing it off. She'd only known where to find her because Bryce had mumbled something about sitting there. And perhaps she'd rushed over because of how hollow Bryce's voice had been when she'd said it.

Juniper had stayed to burn the copies of the song, then gone downstairs to the apartment, where they'd watched TV in bed until they fell asleep. Bryce had risen at one point to turn off the TV and use the bathroom; when she'd come back, Juniper had been awake, waiting.

Her friend didn't leave her side for three days.

They'd never spoken of it. But Bryce wondered if Juniper had later told Fury how close it had been, how hard she'd worked to keep that phone call going while she raced over without alerting Bryce, sensing that something was wrong-wrong-wrong.

Bryce didn't like to think about that winter. That night. But she would never stop being grateful for Juniper for that sense—that love that had kept her from making such a terrible, stupid mistake.

"Yeah," Hunt said, "people are assholes."

She supposed he'd had it worse than her. A lot worse.

Two centuries of slavery that was barely disguised as some sort of twisted path to redemption. Micah's bargain with him, reduced or no, was a disgrace.

She made herself take a bite of her now-soggy cereal. Made herself ask something, anything, to clear her head a bit. "Did you make up your nickname? The Shadow of Death?"

Hunt set down his spoon. "Do I look like the sort of person who needs to make up nicknames for myself?"

"No," Bryce admitted.

"They only call me that because I'm ordered to do that sort of shit. And I do it well." He shrugged. "They'd be better off calling me Slave of Death."

She bit her lip and took another bite of cereal.

Hunt cleared his throat. "I know that visit today was hard. And I know I didn't act like it at first, Quinlan, but I'm glad you got put on this case. You've been . . . really great."

She tucked away what his praise did to her heart, how it lifted the fog that had settled on her. "My dad was a Dracon captain in the 25th Legion. They stationed him at the front for the entire three years of his military service. He taught me a few things."

"I know. Not about you being taught, I mean. But about your dad. Randall Silago, right? He's the one who taught you to shoot."

She nodded, an odd sort of pride wending its way through her.

Hunt said, "I never fought beside him, but I heard of him the last time I was sent to the front—around twenty-six years ago. Heard about his sharpshooting, I mean. What does he think about . . ." A wave of his hand to her, the city around them.

"He wants me to move back home. I had to go to the mat with him—literally—to win the fight about going to CCU."

"You physically fought him?"

"Yeah. He said if I could pin him, then I knew enough about defense to hold my own in the city. Turns out, I'd been paying more attention than I'd let him believe."

Hunt's low laugh skittered over her skin. "And he taught you how to shoot a sniper rifle?"

"Rifles, handguns, knives, swords." But guns were Randall's specialty. He'd taught her ruthlessly, over and over and over again.

"You ever use any outside of practice?"

I love you, Bryce.

Close your eyes, Danika.

"When I had to," she rasped. Not that it had made a difference when it mattered.

Her phone buzzed. She glanced at the message from Jesiba and groaned.

A client is coming in thirty minutes. Be there or you've got a one-way ticket to life as a vole.

Bryce set down her spoon, aware of Hunt watching her, and began to type. *I'll be at—*

Jesiba added another message before Bryce could reply. *And where is that paperwork from yesterday?*

Bryce deleted what she'd written, and began writing, *I'll get it—*

Another message from Jesiba: *I want it done by noon.*

"Someone's pissed off," Hunt observed, and Bryce grimaced, grabbing up her bowl and hurrying to the sink.

The messages kept coming in on the walk over, along with half a dozen threats to turn her into various pathetic creatures, suggesting someone had indeed royally pissed off Jesiba. When they reached the gallery door, Bryce unlocked the physical and magical locks and sighed. "Maybe you should stay on the roof this afternoon. She's probably going to be monitoring me on the cameras. I don't know if she's seen you inside before, but . . ."

He clapped a hand on her shoulder. "Got it, Quinlan." His black jacket buzzed, and he pulled out his phone. "It's Isaiah," he murmured, and nodded to the now-open door of the gallery, through which they could see Syrinx scratching at the library door, yowling his greeting to Lehabah. "I'll check in later," he said.

He waited to fly to the roof, she knew, until she'd locked the gallery door behind herself. A message from him appeared fifteen minutes later. *Isaiah needs me for an opinion on a different case. Heading over now. Justinian's watching you. I'll be back in a few hours.*

She wrote back, *Is Justinian hot?*

He answered, *Who's the pervert now?*

A smile pulled at her mouth.

Her thumbs were hovering over the keyboard to reply when her phone rang. Sighing, she raised it to her ear to answer.

"Why aren't you ready for the client?" Jesiba demanded.

This morning had been a wreck. Standing guard on the roof of the gallery hours later, Hunt couldn't stop thinking it. Yes, they'd caught Sabine in her lie, and all signs pointed toward her as the murderer, but . . . Fuck. He hadn't realized how rough it'd be on Quinlan, even knowing Sabine hated her. Hadn't realized the other wolves had it out for Bryce, too. He should never have brought her. Should have gone himself.

The hours ticked by, one by one, as he mulled it all over.

Hunt made sure no one was flying over the roof before he pulled up the video footage, accessed from the 33rd's archives. Someone had compiled the short reel, no doubt an attempt to get a better image of the demon than a toe or a claw.

The kristallos was a gray blur as it exploded from the front door of the apartment building. They hadn't been able to get footage of it actually entering the building, which suggested it had either been summoned on-site or had snuck through the roof, and no nearby cameras had picked it up, either. But here it was, shattering the front door, so fast it was just gray smoke.

And then—there *she* was. Bryce. Hurtling through the door, barefoot and running on shards of glass, table leg in her hand, pure rage twisting her face.

He'd seen the footage two years ago, but it made slightly more sense now, knowing that Randall Silago had trained her. Watching her leap over cars, careening down streets, as fast as a Fae male. Her face was smeared with blood, her lips curled in a snarl he couldn't hear.

But even in the grainy video footage, her eyes were hazy. Still fighting those drugs.

She definitely didn't remember that he'd been in that interrogation room with her, if she'd asked about the messages during lunch. And, fuck—he'd known everything from her phone had leaked, but he'd never thought about what it must have been like.

She was right: people were assholes.

Bryce cleared Main Street, sliding over the hood of a car, and then the footage ended.

Hunt blew out a breath. If it really was Sabine behind this . . . Micah had given him permission to take out the culprit. But Bryce might very well do it herself.

Hunt frowned toward the wall of fog just visible across the river, the mists impenetrable even in the afternoon sunlight. The Bone Quarter.

No one knew what went on in the Sleeping City. If the dead roamed through the mausoleums, if the Reapers patrolled and ruled like kings, if it was merely mist and carved stone and silence. No one flew over it—no one dared.

But Hunt sometimes felt like the Bone Quarter watched them, and some people claimed that their beloved dead could communicate through the Oracle or cheap market psychics.

Two years ago, Bryce hadn't been at Danika's Sailing. He'd looked. The most important people in Crescent City had gone, but she hadn't been there. Either to avoid Sabine killing her on sight, or for reasons of her own. After what he'd seen today, his money was on the former.

So she hadn't witnessed Sabine pushing the ancient black boat into the Istros, the gray silk-shrouded box—all that remained of Danika's body—in its center. Hadn't counted the seconds as it drifted into the muddy waters, holding her breath with all those on shore to see if the boat would be picked up by that swift current that would bring it to the shores of the Bone Quarter, or if it would overturn, Danika's unworthy remains given to the river and the beasts who swam within it.

But Danika's boat headed straight for the mist-shrouded island across the river, the Under-King deeming her worthy, and more than one person had heaved a sigh. The audio from the apartment building's shitty hall camera of Danika begging for mercy had leaked a day before.

Hunt had suspected that half the people who'd come to her Sailing hoped Danika's begging meant she'd be given to the river, that they could deem the haughty and wild former Alpha a coward.

Sabine, clearly aware of those anticipating such an outcome, had only waited until the river gates opened to reveal the swirling mists of the Bone Quarter, the boat tugged inside by invisible hands, and then left. She didn't wait to see the Sailings for the rest of the Pack of Devils.

But Hunt and everyone else had. It had been the last time he'd seen Ithan Holstrom. Weeping as he pushed his brother's remains into the blue waters, so distraught his sunball teammates had been forced to hold him up. The cold-eyed male who'd served as escort today was a wholly different person from that boy.

Talented, Hunt had heard Naomi say of Ithan in her endless running commentary about the Aux packs and how they stacked up to the 33rd. Beyond his skill on the sunball field, Ithan Holstrom was a gifted warrior, who had made the Drop and come within spitting distance of Connor's power. Naomi always said that despite being cocky, Ithan was a solid male: fair-minded, smart, and loyal.

And a fucking prick, it seemed.

Hunt shook his head, again staring toward the Bone Quarter.

Did Danika Fendyr roam that misty island? Or part of her, at least? Did she remember the friend who, even so long after her death, took no shit from anyone who insulted her memory? Did she know that Bryce would do anything, possibly descend to the level of rage forever preserved in the video, to destroy her killer? Even if that killer was Danika's own mother?

Loyal unto death and beyond.

Hunt's phone rang, Isaiah's name popping up again, but Hunt didn't immediately answer. Not as he glanced at the gallery roof beneath his boots and wondered what it was like—to have a friend like that.

45

So do you think you'll get promoted to principal after the season?" Her shoulder wedging her phone against her ear, Bryce toed off her shoes at her apartment door and strode for the wall of windows. Syrinx, freed of his leash, ran for his food bowl to await his dinner.

"Doubtful," Juniper said, her voice soft and quiet. "Eugenie is really killing it this year. I think she'll be tapped for principal next. I've been a little off in some of my solos, I can feel it."

Bryce peered out the window, spotted Hunt precisely where he said he'd wait until she signaled that she was safe and sound in her apartment, and waved. "You know you've been awesome. Don't pretend that you're not killing it, too."

Hunt lifted a hand and launched skyward, winking at her as he flew past the window, then headed to the Munin and Hugin.

He hadn't been able to convince her to join his triarii companions at the bar, and had made her swear on all five gods that she wouldn't leave her apartment or open the door for anyone while he was gone.

Well, for *almost* anyone.

From their brief conversation, she'd gleaned that Hunt was invited often to the bar, but had never gone. Why he was going tonight for the first time . . . Maybe she was driving him nuts. She hadn't sensed that, but maybe he just needed a night off.

"I've been doing all right, I guess," Juniper admitted.

Bryce clicked her tongue. "You're so full of shit with that 'all right' crap."

"I was thinking, B," Juniper said carefully. "My instructor mentioned that she's starting a dance class that's open to the general public. You could go."

"Your instructor is the most in-demand teacher in this city. No way I'd get in," Bryce deflected, watching the cars and pedestrians stream past below her window.

"I know," Juniper said. "That's why I asked her to save you a spot."

Bryce stilled. "I've got a lot going on right now."

"It's a two-hour class, twice a week. After work hours."

"Thanks, but I'm good."

"You were, Bryce. You were *good*."

Bryce clenched her teeth. "Not fucking good enough."

"It didn't matter to you before Danika died. Just go to the class. It's not an audition—it's literally just a class for people who love to dance. Which you do."

"Which I *did*."

Juniper's breath rattled the phone. "Danika would be heartbroken to hear you don't dance anymore. Even for fun."

Bryce made a show of humming with consideration. "I'll think about it."

"Good," Juniper said. "I'm sending you the details."

Bryce changed the subject. "You wanna come over and watch some trashy TV? *Beach House Hookup* is on tonight at nine."

Juniper asked slyly, "Is the angel there?"

"He's out for beers with his little cabal of killers."

"They're called the triarii, Bryce."

"Yeah, just ask them." Bryce turned from the window and aimed for the kitchen. Syrinx still waited at his food bowl, lion's tail wagging. "Would it make a difference if Hunt was here?"

"I'd be over a Hel of a lot faster."

Bryce laughed. "Shameless." She scooped Syrinx's food into his bowl. His claws clicked as he pranced in place, counting each kibble piece. "Unfortunately for you, I think he's hung up on someone."

"Unfortunately for *you.*"

"Please." She opened the fridge and pulled out an assortment of food. A grazer's dinner it was. "I met a mer the other day who was so hot you could have fried an egg on his ten billion abs."

"None of what you said makes any sort of sense, but I think I get the point."

Bryce laughed again. "Should I get a veggie burger warmed up for you, or what?"

"I wish I could, but—"

"But you have to practice."

Juniper sighed. "I'm not going to be made principal by lounging on a couch all night."

"You'll get injured if you push yourself too hard. You're already doing eight shows a week."

The soft voice sharpened. "I'm fine. Maybe Sunday, okay?" The only day the dance company didn't perform.

"Sure," Bryce said. Her chest tightened, enough that she said, "Call me when you're free."

"Will do."

Their goodbyes were quick, and Bryce had barely hung up when she dialed another number.

Fury's phone went right to audiomail. Not bothering to leave a message, Bryce set down her phone and pried open the container of hummus, then leftover noodles, then some possibly rotten pork stew. Magic kept most of the food in her fridge fresh, but there were rational limits.

Grunting, she dumped the stew into the trash. Syrinx frowned up at her.

"Even you wouldn't eat that, my friend," she said.

Syrinx waggled his tail again and bounded for the couch.

The silence of her apartment grew heavy.

One friend—that was what her social circle had become. Fury had made it clear she had no interest in bothering with her anymore.

So now, with her solitary friend too busy with her career to hang out on a reliable schedule, especially in the upcoming summer months when the company performed throughout the week . . . Bryce supposed she was down to zero.

Bryce half-heartedly ate the hummus, dipping slightly slimy carrots into the spread. The crunch of them filled the silence of the apartment.

That too-familiar surge of self-pity came creeping in, and Bryce chucked the carrots and hummus in the garbage before padding for the couch.

She flipped through the channels until she found the local news. Syrinx peered up at her expectantly. "Just you and me tonight, bud," she said, plopping down next to him.

On the news, Rigelus, Bright Hand of the Asteri, appeared, giving some speech on new trade laws at a gilded podium. Behind him, the five other Asteri sat enthroned in their crystal chamber, cold-faced and radiating wealth and power. As always, the seventh throne sat empty in honor of their long-dead sister. Bryce changed the channel again, this time to another news station, blasting footage of lines of human-built mech-suits going toe-to-toe with elite Imperial Legions on a muddy battlefield. Another channel showed starving humans lined up for bread in the Eternal City, their children wailing with hunger.

Bryce switched to a show about buying vacation houses unseen and watched without really processing it.

When was the last time she'd read a book? Not for work or research, but for pleasure? She'd read loads before everything with Danika, but that part of her brain had just turned off afterward.

She'd wanted to drown out any sort of calm and quiet. The blaring television had become her companion to drive the silence away. The dumber the show, the better.

She nestled into the cushions, Syrinx curling up tightly against her leg as she scratched at his velvet-soft ears. He wriggled in a request for more.

The silence pushed in, tighter and thicker. Her mouth dried out, her limbs going light and hollow. The events at the Den threatened to begin looping, Ithan's cold face at the forefront.

She peered at the clock. Barely five thirty.

Bryce blew out a long breath. Lehabah was wrong—this wasn't like that winter. Nothing could ever be as bad as that first winter without Danika. She wouldn't let it.

She stood, Syrinx huffing with annoyance at being disturbed.

"I'll be back soon," she promised, pointing toward the hall and his crate.

Throwing her a baleful look, the chimera saw himself into his cage, yanking the metal door shut with a hooked claw.

Bryce locked it, reassuring him again that she wouldn't be out for long, and slipped back into her heels. She'd promised Hunt she would stay put—had sworn it on the gods.

Too bad the angel didn't know that she no longer prayed to any of them.

Hunt had drunk all of half a beer when his phone rang.

He knew exactly what had happened before he picked up. "She left, didn't she?"

Naomi let out a quiet laugh. "Yeah. All glammed up, too."

"That's how she usually is," he grumbled, rubbing his temple.

Down the carved oak bar, Vik arched a graceful eyebrow, her halo shifting with the movement. Hunt shook his head and reached for his wallet. He shouldn't have come out tonight. The offer had been thrown to him so many times these past four years, and he'd never gone, not when it had felt so much like being in the 18th again. But this time, when Isaiah had called with his standard caveat (*I know you'll say no, but . . .*) he'd said yes.

He didn't know why, but he'd gone.

Hunt asked, "Where'd she head?"

"I'm tracking her now," Naomi said, the wind rustling on her end of the line. She hadn't asked questions when Hunt had called her an hour ago to ask that she guard Bryce—and give up her spot in tonight's hangout. "Looks like she's headed toward FiRo."

Maybe she was seeking out her cousin for an update. "Stay close, and keep your guard up," he said. He knew he didn't need to say it. Naomi was one of the most talented warriors he'd ever encountered, and took no shit from anyone. One look at her tightly braided black hair, the colorful tattoo that covered her hands, and the array of weapons on her muscled body and most people didn't dare to tangle with her. Maybe even Bryce would have obeyed an order to stay put, if Naomi had been the one to give it. "Send me your coordinates."

"Will do." The line went dead.

Hunt sighed. Viktoria said, "You should have known better, friend."

Hunt ran his hands through his hair. "Yeah."

Beside him, Isaiah swigged from his beer. "You could let Naomi handle her."

"I have a feeling that would result in them unleashing Hel together, and I'd still need to go end their fun."

Vik and Isaiah chuckled, and Hunt dropped a silver mark on the bar. Viktoria held up a hand in protest, but Hunt ignored it. They might all be slaves, but he could pay for his own damn drink. "I'll see you two later."

Isaiah raised his beer in salute, and Viktoria gave him a knowing smile before Hunt elbowed his way through the packed bar. Justinian, playing pool in the back, lifted a hand in farewell. Hunt had never asked why all of them preferred the tight quarters of the street-level bar to one of the rooftop lounges most angels frequented. He supposed he wouldn't get the chance to learn why tonight.

Hunt wasn't surprised that Bryce had bailed. Frankly, the only thing that surprised him was that she'd waited this long.

He shouldered through the leaded glass door and out onto the muggy street beyond. Patrons drank at reclaimed oak barrels, and a raucous group of some sort of shifter pack—perhaps wolves or one of the big cats—puffed away on cigarettes.

Hunt scowled at the reek that chased him into the sky, then frowned again at the clouds rolling in from the west, the heavy scent of rain already on the wind. Fantastic.

Naomi sent over her coordinates in Five Roses, and a five-minute flight had Hunt arriving at one of the night gardens, just beginning to awaken with the fading light. Naomi's black wings were a stain against the creeping darkness as she hovered in place above a fountain filled with moon lilies, the bioluminescent flowers already open and glowing pale blue.

"That way," Naomi said, the harsh planes of her face gilded by the soft light from the plants.

Hunt nodded to the angel. "Thanks."

"Good luck." The words were enough to set him on edge, and Hunt didn't bother saying goodbye before soaring down the path. Star oaks lined it, their leaves glittering in a living canopy overhead. The gentle illumination danced on Bryce's hair as she ambled down the stone path, night-blooming flowers opening around her. Jasmine lay heavy in the twilight air, sweet and beckoning.

"You couldn't give me an hour of peace?"

Bryce didn't flinch as he dropped into step beside her. "I wanted some fresh air." She admired an unfurling fern, its fronds lit from within to illuminate every vein.

"Were you going somewhere in particular?"

"Just—out."

"Ah."

"I'm waiting for you to start yelling." She continued past beds of night crocuses, their purple petals shimmering amid the vibrant moss. The garden seemed to awaken for her, welcome her.

"I'll yell when I find out what was so important that you broke your promise."

"Nothing."

"Nothing?"

"Nothing is important."

She said the words with enough quiet that he watched her carefully. "You all right?"

"Yeah." Definitely *no*, then.

She admitted, "The quiet bothers me sometimes."

"I invited you to the bar."

"I didn't want to go to a bar with a bunch of triarii."

"Why not?"

She cut him a sidelong glance. "I'm a civilian. They wouldn't be able to relax."

Hunt opened his mouth to deny it, but she gave him a look. "Fine," he admitted. "Maybe."

They walked in silence for a few steps. "You could go back to your drinking, you know. That ominous-looking angel you sent to babysit me can handle it."

"Naomi left."

"She looks intense."

"She is."

Bryce threw him a hint of a smile. "You two . . . ?"

"No." Though Naomi had hinted about it on occasion. "It'd complicate things."

"Mmm."

"Were you on your way to meet your friends?"

She shook her head. "Just the one friend these days, Athalar. And she's too busy."

"So you were going out alone. To do what?"

"Walk through this garden."

"Alone."

"I knew you'd send a babysitter."

Hunt moved before he could think, gripping her elbow.

She peered up into his face. "Is this the part where you start yelling?"

Lightning cracked through the sky, and echoed in his veins as he leaned closer and purred, "Would you like me to yell, Bryce Quinlan?"

Her throat bobbed, her eyes glowing with golden fire. "Maybe?"

Hunt let out a low laugh. Didn't try to stop the heat that flooded him. "That can be arranged."

All of his focus narrowed on the dip of her eyes to his mouth. The blush that bloomed over her freckled cheeks, inviting him to taste every rosy inch.

No one and nothing existed but this—but her.

He never heard the night-dark bushes behind him rustling. Never heard the branches cracking.

Not until the kristallos crashed into him and sank its teeth into his shoulder.

46

The kristallos slammed into Hunt with the force of an SUV.

Bryce knew he only had enough time to either draw a weapon or shove her out of the way. Hunt chose her.

She hit the asphalt several feet from him, bones barking, and froze. Angel and demon went down, the kristallos pinning Hunt with a roar that sent the night garden shuddering.

It was worse. So much worse than that night.

Blood sprayed, and a knife glinted as Hunt pulled it from its sheath and plunged it into the grayish, near-translucent hide.

Veins of lightning wreathed Hunt's hands—and faded into blackness.

People screamed and bolted down the path, cries to *run!* ringing through the glowing flora. Bryce barely heard them as she climbed to her knees.

Hunt rolled, flipping the creature off him and onto the pathway, wrenching his knife free in the process. Clear blood dripped down the blade as Hunt angled it in front of himself, his shredded arm outflung to protect Bryce. Lightning flared and sputtered at his fingertips.

"Call for backup," he panted without taking his focus off the demon, who paced a step, a clawed hand—crystalline talons glinting—going to the wound in its side.

She'd never seen anything like it. Anything so unearthly, so primal and raging. Her memory of that night was fogged with rage and grief and drugs, so this, the real, undiluted thing—

Bryce reached for her phone, but the creature lunged for Hunt.

The angel's blade drove home. It made no difference.

They again toppled to the path, and Hunt bellowed as the demon's jaws wrapped around his forearm and *crunched*.

His lightning died out entirely.

Move. *Move*, she had to *move*—

Hunt's free fist slammed into the creature's face hard enough to crack bone, but the crystal teeth remained clamped.

This thing pinned him down so easily. Had it done just this to Danika? Shredding and shredding?

Hunt grunted, brow bunched in pain and concentration. His lightning had vanished. Not one flicker of it rose again.

Every part of her shook.

Hunt punched the demon's face again, "*Bryce*—"

She scrambled into movement. Not for her phone, but for the gun holstered at Hunt's hip.

The blind demon sensed her, its nostrils flaring as her fingers wrapped around the handgun. She freed the safety, hauling it up as she uncoiled to her feet.

The creature released Hunt's arm and leapt for her. Bryce fired, but too slow. The demon lunged to the side, dodging her bullet. Bryce fell back as it roared and leapt for her again—

Its head snapped to the side, clear blood spraying like rain as a knife embedded itself to the hilt just above its mouth.

Hunt was upon it again, drawing another long knife from a hidden panel down the back of his battle-suit and plunging the blade right into the skull and toward the spine.

The creature struggled, snapping for Bryce, its clear teeth stained red with Hunt's blood. She'd wound up on the pavement somehow, and crawled backward as it tried to lunge for her. Failed to, as Hunt wrapped his hands around the blade and *twisted*.

The crack of its severing neck was muffled by the moss-shrouded trees.

Bryce still aimed the handgun. "Get out of the way."

Hunt released his grip, letting the creature slump to the mossy path. Its black tongue lolled from its clear-fanged mouth.

"Just in case," Bryce said, and fired. She didn't miss this time.

Sirens wailed, and wings filled the air. Ringing droned in her head.

Hunt withdrew his blade from the creature's skull and brought it down with a mighty, one-armed sweep. The severed head tumbled away. Hunt moved again, and the head split in half. Then quarters.

Another plunge and the hateful heart was skewered, too. Clear blood leaked everywhere, like a spilled vial of serum.

Bryce stared and stared at its ruined head, the horrible, monstrous body.

Powerful forms landed among them, that black-winged malakh instantly at Hunt's side. "Holy shit, Hunt, what—"

Bryce barely heard the words. Someone helped her to her feet. Blue light flared, and a magi-screen encompassed the site, blocking it from the view of any who hadn't yet fled. She should have been screaming, should have been leaping for the demon, ripping apart its corpse with her bare hands. But only a thrumming silence filled her head.

She looked around the park, stupidly and slowly, as if she might see Sabine there.

Hunt groaned, and she whirled as he tumbled face-first to the ground. The dark-winged angel caught him, her powerful body easily bearing his weight. "Get a medwitch here *now*!"

His shoulder was gushing blood. So was his forearm. Blood, and some sort of silvery slime.

She knew the burn of that slime, like living fire.

A head of sleek black curls streamed past, and Bryce blinked as a curvy young woman in a medwitch's blue jumpsuit unhooked the bag across her chest and slid to her knees beside Hunt.

He was bent over, a hand at his forearm, panting heavily. His gray wings sagged, splattered with both clear and red blood.

The medwitch asked him something, the broom-and-bell insignia on her right arm catching the blue light of the screens. Her brown hands didn't falter as she used a pair of tweezers to extract what looked to be a small worm from a glass jar full of damp moss and set it on Hunt's forearm.

He winced, teeth flashing.

"Sucking out the venom," a female voice explained beside Bryce. The dark-winged angel. Naomi. She pointed a tattooed finger toward Hunt. "They're mithridate leeches."

The leech's black body swiftly swelled. The witch set another on Hunt's shoulder wound. Then another on his forearm.

Bryce said nothing.

Hunt's face was pale, his eyes shut as he seemed to focus on his breathing. "I think the venom nullified my power. As soon as it bit me . . ." He hissed at whatever agony worked through his body. "I couldn't summon my lightning."

Recognition jolted through her. It explained so much. Why the kristallos had been able to pin Micah, for one thing. If it had ambushed the Archangel and gotten a good bite, he would have been left with only physical strength. Micah had probably never even realized what happened. Had likely written it off as shock or the swiftness of the attack. Perhaps the bite had nullified the preternatural strength of Danika and the Pack of Devils, too.

"Hey." Naomi put a hand on Bryce's shoulder. "You hurt?"

The medwitch peeled a poison-eating leech from Hunt's shoulder, threw it back in the glass jar, then replaced it with another. Pale light wreathed her hands as she assessed Hunt's other injuries, then began the process of healing them. She didn't bother with the vials of firstlight glowing in her bag—a cure-all for many medics. As if she preferred using the magic in her own veins.

"I'm fine."

Hunt's body might have been able to heal itself, but it would have taken longer. With the venom in those wounds, Bryce knew too well that it might not really heal at all.

Naomi ran a hand over her inky hair. "You should let that medwitch examine you."

"No."

Her onyx eyes sharpened. "If Hunt can let the medwitch work on him, then you—"

Vast, cold power erupted through the site, the garden, the whole quarter of the city. Naomi whirled as Micah landed. Silence fell, Vanir of all types backing away as the Archangel prowled toward the fallen demon and Hunt.

Naomi was the only one with enough balls to approach him. "I was on watch right before Hunt arrived and there was no sign—"

Micah stalked past her, his eyes pinned on the demon. The medwitch, to her credit, didn't halt her ministrations, but Hunt managed to lift his head to meet Micah's interrogation.

"What happened."

"Ambush," Hunt said, his voice gravelly.

Micah's white wings seemed to glow with power. And for all the ringing silence in Bryce's head, all the distance she now felt between her body and what remained of her soul, she stepped up. Like Hel would this jeopardize Micah's bargain with Hunt. Bryce said, "It came out of the shadows."

The Archangel raked his eyes over her. "Which one of you did it attack?"

Bryce pointed to Hunt. "Him."

"And which one of you killed it?"

Bryce began to repeat "Him," but Hunt cut in, "It was a joint effort." Bryce shot him a look to keep quiet, but Micah had already pivoted to the demon's corpse. He toed it with his boot, frowning.

"We can't let the press get wind of this," Micah ordered. "Or the others coming in for the Summit." The unspoken part of that statement lingered. *Sandriel doesn't hear a word.*

"We'll keep it out of the papers," Naomi promised.

But Micah shook his head, and extended a hand.

Before Bryce could so much as blink, white flame erupted around the demon and its head. Within a second, it was nothing more than ash.

Hunt started. "We needed to examine it for evidence—"

"No press," Micah said, then turned toward a cluster of angel commanders.

The medwitch began removing her leeches and bandaging Hunt. Each of the silk strips was imbued with her power, willing the skin and muscle to knit back together and staving off infection. They'd dissolve once the wounds had healed, as if they'd never existed.

The pile of ashes still lay there, mockingly soft considering the true terror the kristallos had wrought. Had this demon been the one to kill Danika, or merely one of thousands waiting on the other side of the Northern Rift?

Was the Horn here, in this park? Had she somehow, unwittingly, come near it? Or maybe whoever was looking for it—Sabine?—simply sent the kristallos as another message. They were nowhere near Moonwood, but Sabine's patrols took her all over the city.

The sting of the gun still bit into Bryce's palms, its kickback zinging along her bones.

The medwitch removed her bloody gloves. A crackle of lightning at Hunt's knuckles showed his returning power. "Thanks," he said to the witch, who waved him off. Within a few seconds, she'd packed the poison-swollen leeches in their jars and swept behind the magi-screens.

Hunt's stare met Bryce's. The ashes and busy officials and warriors around them faded away into white noise.

Naomi approached, braid swaying behind her. "Why'd it target you?"

"Everyone wants to take a bite out of me," Hunt deflected.

Naomi gave them both a look that told Bryce she didn't buy it for one second, but moved off to talk to a Fae female in the Aux.

Hunt tried to ease to his feet, and Bryce stepped in to offer a hand up. He shook his head, grimacing as he braced a hand on his knee and rose. "I guess we hit a nerve with Sabine," he said. "She must have figured out we're onto her. This was either a warning like the club bombing or a failed attempt to take care of a problem like she did with the acolyte and guard."

She didn't answer. A wind drifted by, stirring the ashes.

"Bryce." Hunt stepped closer, his dark eyes clear despite his injury.

"It doesn't make any sense," she whispered at last. "You—we killed it so quickly."

Hunt didn't reply, giving her the space to think through it, to say it.

She said, "Danika was strong. Connor was strong. Either one of them could have taken on that demon and walked away. But the entire Pack of Devils was there that night. Even if its venom nullified some of their powers, the entire pack could have . . ." Her throat tightened.

"Even Mic—" Hunt caught himself, glancing toward the Archangel still talking to commanders off to the side. "He didn't walk away from it."

"But I did. Twice now."

"Maybe it's got some Fae weakness."

She shook her head. "I don't think so. It just . . . it's not adding up."

"We'll lay it all out tomorrow." Hunt nodded toward Micah. "I think tonight just proved it's time to tell him our suspicions about Sabine."

She was going to be sick. But she nodded back.

They waited until most of Micah's commanders had peeled off on their various assignments before approaching, Hunt wincing with each step.

Hunt grunted, "We need to talk to you."

Micah only crossed his arms. And then Hunt, briskly and efficiently, told him. About the Horn, about Sabine, about their suspicions. About the Horn possibly being repaired—though they still didn't know why she'd want or need to open a portal to another world.

Micah's eyes went from annoyed to enraged to outright glacial.

When Hunt was done, the Governor looked between them. "You need more evidence."

"We'll get it," Hunt promised.

Micah surveyed them, his face dark as the Pit. "Come to me when you have concrete proof. Or if you find that Horn. If someone's gone to so much trouble over it, there's a damn good chance they've found a way to repair it. I won't have this city endangered by a power-hungry bitch." Bryce could have sworn the thorns tattooed across Hunt's brow darkened as his eyes met the Archangel's. "Don't fuck this up for me, Athalar." Without a further word, he flapped his wings and shot into the night sky.

Hunt blew out a breath, staring at the pile of ashes. "Prick."

Bryce rubbed her hands over her arms. Hunt's eyes darted toward her, noting the movement. The cold creeping over her that had nothing to do with the spring night. Or the storm that was moments from unleashing itself.

"Come on," he said gently, rotating his injured arm to test its strength. "I think I can manage flying us back to your place."

She surveyed the busy crew, the tracker shifters already moving off into the trees to hunt for prints before the rain wiped them away. "Don't we need to answer questions?"

He extended a hand. "They know where to find us."

Ruhn got to the night garden moments after his sister and Athalar left, according to Naomi Boreas, captain of the 33rd's infantry. The take-no-shit angel had merely said both of them were fine, and pivoted to receive an update from a unit captain under her command.

All that was left of the kristallos was a burnt stain and a few sprayed drops of clear blood, like beaded rainwater on the stones and moss.

Ruhn approached a carved boulder just off the path. Squatting, he freed the knife in his boot and angled the blade toward a splash of the unusual blood clinging to some ancient moss.

"I wouldn't do that."

He knew that fair voice—its steady, calm cadence. He peered over his shoulder to find the medwitch from the clinic standing behind him, her curly dark hair loose around her striking face. But her eyes were upon the blood. "Its venom lies in its saliva," she said, "but we don't know what other horrors might be in the blood itself."

"It hasn't affected the moss," he said.

"Yes, but this was a demon bred for specific purposes. Its blood might be harmless to non-sentient life, but be dangerous to everything else."

Ruhn started. "You recognized the demon?"

The witch blinked, as if she'd been caught. "I had very old tutors, as I told you. They required me to study ancient texts."

Ruhn rose to his feet. "We could have used you years ago."

"I had not completed my training then." A nonanswer. Ruhn's brow furrowed. The witch took a step back. "I was thinking, Prince," she said, continuing her retreat. "About what you asked me. I looked into it, and there is some potential . . . research. I have to leave the city for a few days to attend to a personal matter, but when I return and fully review it, I will send it to you."

"Ruhn!" Flynn's shout cut through the chaos of the investigatory team around them.

Ruhn glanced over a shoulder to tell his friend to wait for two gods-damned seconds, but motion from the witch caught his eye.

He hadn't seen the broom she'd stashed beside the tree, but he certainly saw it now as she shot into the night sky, her hair a dark curtain behind her.

"Who was that?" Flynn asked, nodding toward the vanishing witch.

"I don't know," Ruhn said quietly, staring after her into the night.

47

The storm hit when they were two blocks from Bryce's building, soaking them within seconds. Pain lanced through Hunt's forearm and shoulder as he landed on the roof, but he swallowed it down. Bryce was still shaking, her face distant enough that he didn't immediately let go when he set her upon the rain-soaked tiles.

She peered up at him when his arms remained around her waist.

Hunt couldn't help the thumb he swept over her ribs. Couldn't stop himself from doing it a second time.

She swallowed, and he tracked every movement of her throat. The raindrop that ran over her neck, her pulse pounding delicately beneath it.

Before he could react, she leaned forward, wrapping her arms around him. Held him tightly. "Tonight sucked," she said against his soaked chest.

Hunt slid his arms around her, willing his warmth into her trembling body. "It did."

"I'm glad you're not dead."

Hunt chuckled, letting himself bury his face against her neck. "So am I."

Bryce's fingers curled against his spine, exploring and gentle.

Every single one of his senses narrowed to that touch. Came roaring awake. "We should get out of the rain," she murmured.

"We should," he replied. And made no move.

"Hunt."

He couldn't tell if his name was a warning or a request or something more. Didn't care as he grazed his nose against the rain-slick column of her neck. Fuck, she smelled good.

He did it again, unable to help himself or get enough of that scent. She tipped her chin up slightly. Just enough to expose more of her neck to him.

Hel, yes. Hunt almost groaned the words as he let himself nuzzle into that soft, delicious neck, as greedy as a fucking vampyr to be there, smell her, taste her.

It overrode every instinct, every pained memory, every vow he'd sworn.

Bryce's fingers tightened on his back—then began stroking. He nearly purred.

He didn't let himself think, not as he brushed his lips over the spot he'd nuzzled. She arched slightly against him. Into the hardness that ached behind the reinforced leather of his battle-suit.

Swallowing another groan against her neck, Hunt tightened his arms around her warm, soft body, and ran his hands downward, toward that perfect, sweet ass that had tortured him since day fucking one, and—

The metal door to the roof opened. Hunt already had his gun drawn and aimed toward it as Sabine stepped out and snarled, "*Back the fuck up.*"

48

Hunt weighed his options carefully.

He had a gun pointed at Sabine's head. She had a gun pointed at Bryce's heart.

Which of them was faster? The question buzzed in his skull.

Bryce obeyed Sabine's command, her hands raised. Hunt could only follow, stepping behind Bryce so she was up against his chest, so he could snake his free hand around her waist, pinning her against him. Could he get into the air fast enough to avoid a bullet?

Bryce wouldn't survive a close-range shot to the heart. She'd be dead in seconds.

Bryce managed to ask over the drumming rain, "Where's your little demon friend?"

Sabine kicked the door to the roof shut. The cameras had all been disabled, he realized. They had to be, or the legion would already be here, having been tipped off by Marrin. The feeds had to be looping on harmless footage—just as she'd done at Luna's Temple. Which meant no one, absolutely no one, knew what was happening.

Hunt slowly began to bring his good arm up Bryce's shaking, soaked body.

Sabine spat. "Don't fucking think about it, Athalar."

He stopped his arm before it could cover Bryce's breasts—the heart beating beneath them. His battle-suit had enough armor to deflect a bullet. To let him absorb the impact. Better for him to lose an arm that he could regrow than for her to—

He couldn't think the last word.

Sabine hissed, "I told you to stay away from this. And yet you just couldn't listen—you had to show up at the Den, asking questions you have *no right* to ask."

Bryce snarled, "We were asking those questions because you killed Danika, you fucking psycho."

Sabine went wholly still. Nearly as still as the Fae could go. "You think I did *what*?"

Hunt knew Sabine wore every emotion on her face and had never once bothered to hide it. Her shock was genuine. Rain dripped off the narrow angles of her face as she seethed, "You think I killed my own daughter?"

Bryce was shaking so hard that Hunt had to tighten his grip, and she snapped, "You killed her because she was going to take your place as future Prime, you stole the Horn to undermine her, and you've been using that demon to kill anyone who might have seen you and to humiliate Micah before the Summit—"

Sabine laughed, low and hollow. "What utter bullshit."

Hunt growled, "You wiped the footage of the Horn's theft from the temple. We have it confirmed. You lied to us about Danika being there that night. And ranted about your daughter not keeping her mouth shut the night she died. All we need to prove you killed Danika is to tie you to the kristallos demon."

Sabine lowered her gun, putting the safety back on. She trembled with barely restrained rage. "I didn't steal anything, you stupid fucks. And I didn't kill my daughter."

Hunt didn't dare lower his gun. Didn't dare let go of Bryce.

Not as Sabine said, cold and joyless, "I was protecting her. *Danika* stole the Horn."

49

Danika didn't steal anything," Bryce whispered, cold lurching through her. Only Hunt's arm around her middle kept her upright, his body a warm wall at her back.

Sabine's light brown eyes—the same shade Danika's had been but void of their warmth—were merciless. "Why do you think I swapped the footage? She thought the blackout would hide her, but was too dumb to consider that there might be audio still rolling that picked up each one of her disappearing footsteps as she left her post to steal the Horn, then reappeared a minute later, going back on patrol, as if she hadn't spat in our goddess's face. Whether she caused the blackout to steal it or if she took advantage of an opportunity, I don't know."

"Why would she take it?" Bryce could barely get the words out.

"Because Danika was a brat who wanted to see what she could get away with. As soon as I got the alert that the Horn had been stolen, I looked into the videos and swapped the footage on every database." Sabine's smile was a cruel slash. "I cleaned up her mess—just like I did for her entire life. And you two, in asking your *questions*, have threatened the shred of a legacy that she stands to leave."

Hunt's wings flared slightly. "You sent that demon after us tonight—"

Sabine's pale brows snapped together. "What demon? I've been waiting for you here all night. I thought about your stupid fucking visit to *my* Den, and decided you needed a real reminder to stay the Hel out of this case." She bared her teeth. "Amelie Ravenscroft is standing across the street, waiting to make the call if you step out of line, Athalar. She says you two were putting on quite the show a moment ago." A vicious, knowing smile.

Bryce flushed, and let Hunt look to confirm. From the way he tensed, she knew it was true.

Sabine said, "And as for what I said the night she died: Danika *couldn't* keep her mouth shut—about anything. I knew she'd stolen the Horn, and knew someone probably killed her for it because she couldn't keep it quiet." Another cold laugh. "Everything I did was to protect my daughter. My reckless, arrogant daughter. Everything *you* did encouraged the worst in her."

Hunt's growl rent the night. "Careful, Sabine."

But the Alpha just snorted. "You'll regret crossing me." She strolled for the edge of the roof, her power thrumming in a faint glow around her as she assessed the same leap that Bryce had so stupidly considered a year and a half ago. Only, Sabine would be able to gracefully land on the pavement. Sabine looked back over a thin shoulder, her lengthening teeth gleaming as she said, "I didn't kill my daughter. But if you jeopardize her legacy, I will kill *you*."

And then she jumped, shifting with a soft flash of light as she went. Hunt sprinted for the edge, but Bryce knew what he'd see: a wolf landing lightly on the pavement and streaking away into the darkness.

50

Hunt didn't realize just how badly Sabine's bombshell had hit Bryce until the next morning. She didn't run. Nearly didn't get up in time for work.

She drank a cup of coffee but refused the eggs he made. Barely said three words to him.

He knew she wasn't mad at him. Knew that she was just . . . processing.

Whether that processing also had to do with what they'd done on the roof, he didn't dare ask. It wasn't the time. Even though he'd had to take a cold, cold shower afterward. And take matters into his own hands. It was to Bryce's face, the memory of her scent and that breathy moan she'd made as she arched against him, that he'd come, hard enough he'd seen stars.

But it was the least of his concerns, this thing between them. Whatever it was.

Mercifully, nothing had leaked to the press about the attack in the park.

Bryce barely spoke after work. He'd made her dinner and she'd poked at it, then gone to sleep before nine. There sure as fuck were no more hugs that led to nuzzling.

The next day was the same. And the next.

He was willing to give her space. The gods knew he'd sometimes needed it. Every time he killed for Micah he needed it.

He knew better than to suggest Sabine could be lying, since there was no easier person to accuse than a dead one. Sabine was a monster, but Hunt had never known her to be a liar.

The investigation was full of dead ends, and Danika had died—for what? For an ancient artifact that didn't work. That hadn't worked in fifteen thousand years and never would again.

Had Danika herself wanted to repair and use the Horn? Though why, he had no idea.

He knew those thoughts weighed on Bryce. For five fucking days, she barely ate. Just went to work, slept, and went to work again.

Every morning he made her breakfast. Every morning she ignored the plate he laid out.

Micah called only once, to ask if they'd gotten proof on Sabine. Hunt had merely said, "It was a dead end," and the Governor had hung up, his rage at the unsolved case palpable.

That had been two days ago. Hunt was still waiting for the other shoe to drop.

"I thought hunting for ancient, deadly weapons would be exciting," Lehabah groused from where she sat on her little divan, half watching truly inane daytime television.

"Me too," Bryce muttered.

Hunt looked up from the evidence report he'd been skimming and was about to answer when the front doorbell rang. Ruhn's face appeared on the camera feed, and Bryce let out a long, long sigh before silently buzzing him in.

Hunt rotated his stiff shoulder. His arm still throbbed a bit, an echo of the lethal venom that had ripped his magic right from his body.

The prince's black boots appeared on the green carpeted steps seconds later, apparently taking a hint about their location thanks to the open library door. Lehabah was instantly zooming across the space, sparks in her wake, as she beamed and said, "*Your Highness!*"

Ruhn offered her a half smile, his eyes going right to Quinlan.

They missed none of the quiet, brooding exhaustion. Or the tone in Bryce's voice as she said, "To what do we owe this pleasure?"

Ruhn slid into a seat across from them at the book-strewn table. The Starsword sheathed down his back didn't reflect the lights in the library. "I wanted to check in. Anything new?"

Neither of them had told him about Sabine. And apparently Declan hadn't, either.

"No," Bryce said. "Anything about the Horn?"

Ruhn ignored her question. "What's wrong?"

"Nothing." Her spine stiffened.

Ruhn looked ready to get into it with his cousin, so Hunt did both of them—and himself, if he was being honest—a favor and said, "We've been waiting on a Many Waters contact to get back to us about a possible pattern with the demon attacks. Have you come across any information about the kristallos negating magic?" Days later, he couldn't stop thinking about it—how it'd felt for his power to just sputter and die in his veins.

"No. I still haven't found anything about the creation of the kristallos except that it was made from the blood of the first Starborn Prince and the essence of the Star-Eater himself. Nothing about it negating magic." Ruhn nodded at him. "You've never come across a demon that can do that?"

"Not one. Witch spells and gorsian stones negate magic, but this was different." He'd dealt with both. Before they'd bound him using the witch-ink on his brow, they'd shackled him with manacles hewn from the gorsian stones of the Dolos Mountains, a rare metal whose properties numbed one's access to magic. They were used on high-profile enemies of the empire—the Hind herself was particularly fond of using them as she and her interrogators broke the Vanir among the rebel spies and leaders. But for years now, rumors had swirled in the 33rd's barracks that rebels were experimenting with ways to render the metal into a spray that could be unleashed upon Vanir warriors on the battlefields.

Ruhn motioned to the ancient book he'd left on the table days ago, still open to a passage about the Starborn Fae. "If the Star-Eater himself put his essence in the kristallos, that's probably what gave the demon the ability to eat magic. Just as Prince Pelias's blood gave it the ability to look for the Horn."

Bryce frowned. "So that Chosen One sense of yours hasn't detected a trace of the Horn?"

Ruhn tugged at the silver ring through his bottom lip. "No. But I got a message this morning from a medwitch I met the other day—the one who stitched up Hunt in the night garden. It's a shot in the dark, but she mentioned that there's a relatively new drug on the market that's just starting to come into use. It's a synthetic healing magic." Hunt and Bryce straightened. "It can have some wicked side effects if not carefully controlled. She didn't have access to its exact formula or the trials, but she said research showed it capable of healing at rates nearly double that of firstlight."

Bryce said, "You think something like that could repair the Horn?"

"It's a possibility. It'd fit with that stupid riddle about light that's not light, magic that's not magic repairing the Horn. That's kind of what a synthetic compound like that is."

Her eyes flickered. "And it's . . . readily available?"

"It entered the market at some point in the past few years, apparently. No one has tested it on inanimate objects, but who knows? If real magic couldn't heal it, maybe a synthetic compound could."

"I've never heard of synthetic magic," Hunt said.

"Neither have I," Ruhn admitted.

"So we have a potential way to repair the Horn," Bryce mused, "but not the Horn itself." She sighed. "And we still don't know if Danika stole the Horn on a lark or for some actual purpose."

Ruhn started. "Danika did *what*?"

Bryce winced, then filled the prince in on all they'd learned. When she finished, Ruhn leaned back in his chair, shock written on every line of his face.

Hunt said into the silence, "Regardless of whether Danika stole the Horn for fun or to do something with it, the fact remains that she stole it."

Ruhn asked carefully, "Do you think she wanted it for herself? To repair it and use it?"

"No," Bryce said quietly. "No, Danika might have kept things from me, but I knew her heart. She never would have sought a weapon as dangerous as the Horn—something that could jeopardize the world like that." She ran her hands over her face. "Her killer is still out there. Danika must have taken the Horn to keep them from getting it. They killed her for it, but they must not have found it, if they're still using the kristallos to search for it." She waved a hand at Ruhn's sword. "That thing can't help you find it? I still think luring the killer with the Horn is probably the most surefire way to find them."

Ruhn shook his head. "The sword doesn't work like that. Aside from being picky about who draws it, the sword has no power without the knife."

"The knife?" Hunt asked.

Ruhn drew the sword, the metal whining, and laid it on the table between them. Bryce leaned back, away from it, as a bead of starlight sang down the fuller and sparkled at the tip.

"Fancy," Hunt said, earning a glare from Ruhn, who had raised a brow at Bryce, no doubt expecting some kind of reverence from her at a sword that was older than this city, older than the Vanir's first step in Midgard.

"The sword was part of a pair," Ruhn said to him. "A long-bladed knife was forged from the iridium mined from the same meteorite, which fell on our old world." The world the Fae had left to travel through the Northern Rift and into Midgard. "But we lost the knife eons ago. Even the Fae Archives have no record of how it might have been lost, but it seems to have been sometime during the First Wars."

"It's another of the Fae's countless inane prophecies," Bryce muttered. "*When knife and sword are reunited, so shall our people be.*"

"It's literally carved above the Fae Archives entrance—whatever the fuck it means," Ruhn said. Bryce gave a small smile at that.

Hunt grinned. Her little smile was like seeing the sun after days of rain.

Bryce pretended not to notice his grin, but Ruhn gave him a sharp look.

Like he knew every filthy thing Hunt had thought about Bryce, everything he'd done to pleasure himself while imagining it was her mouth around him, her hands, her soft body.

Shit—he was in such deep, unrelenting shit.

Ruhn only snorted, as if he knew that, too, and sheathed the sword again.

"I'd like to see the Fae Archives," Lehabah sighed. "Think of all that ancient history, all those glorious objects."

"Kept locked away, only for their pure-blooded heirs to see," Bryce finished with a pointed glance at Ruhn.

Ruhn held up his hands. "I've tried to get them to change the rules," he said. "No luck."

"They let in visitors on the major holidays," Lehabah said.

"Only from an approved list," Bryce said. "And fire sprites are *not* on it."

Lehabah rolled over onto her side, propping her head up with a fiery hand. "They would let me in. I am a descendant of Queen Ranthia Drahl."

"Yeah, and I'm the seventh Asteri," Bryce said dryly.

Hunt was careful not to react at the tone. The first bit of spark he'd seen in days.

"I am," Lehabah insisted, turning to Ruhn. "She was my six-times-great-grandmother, dethroned in the Elemental Wars. Our family was cast from favor—"

"The story changes every time," Bryce told Hunt, whose lips twitched.

"It does not," Lehabah whined. Ruhn was smiling now, too. "We stood a chance at earning back our title, but my great-great-grandmother was booted from the Eternal City for—"

"Booted."

"Yes, *booted*. For a completely false accusation of trying to steal the royal consort from the impostor queen. She'd be thrashing in her ashes if she knew what had become of her last scion. Little more than a bird in a cage."

Bryce sipped from her water. "This is the point, boys, where she solicits you for cash to purchase her freedom."

Lehabah turned crimson. "That is *not* true." She pointed her finger at Bryce. "My *great*-grandmother fought with Hunt against the angels—and *that* was the end of my entire people's freedom."

The words cracked through Hunt. All of them looked at him now. "I'm sorry." He had no other words in his head.

"Oh, Athie," Lehabah said, zooming over to him and turning rose pink. "I didn't mean to . . ." She cupped her cheeks in her hands. "I do not blame *you*."

"I led everyone into battle. I don't see how there's anyone else to blame for what happened to your people because of it." His words sounded as hollow as they felt.

"But Shahar led *you*," Danaan said, his blue eyes missing nothing.

Hunt bristled at the sound of her name on the prince's lips. But he found himself looking to Quinlan, to torture himself with the damning agreement he'd find on her face.

Only sorrow lay there. And something like understanding. Like she saw him, as he'd seen her in that shooting gallery, marked every broken shard and didn't mind the jagged bits. Under the table, the toe of her high heel brushed against his boot. A little confirmation that yes—she saw his guilt, the pain, and she wouldn't shy from it. His chest tightened.

Lehabah cleared her throat and asked Ruhn, "Have you ever visited the Fae Archives on Avallen? I heard they're grander than what was brought over here." She twirled her curl of flame around a finger.

"No," Ruhn said. "But the Fae on that misty island are even less welcoming than the ones here."

"They do like to hoard all their wealth, don't they," Lehabah said, eyeing Bryce. "Just like you, BB. Only spending on yourself, and never anything nice for me."

Bryce removed her foot. "Do I not buy you strawberry shisha every other week?"

Lehabah crossed her arms. "That's barely a gift."

"Says the sprite who hotboxes herself in that little glass dome and burns it all night and tells me not to bother her until she's done." She leaned back in her chair, smug as a cat, and Hunt nearly grinned again at the spark in her eyes.

Bryce grabbed his phone from the table and snapped a photo of him before he could object. Then one of Lehabah. And another of Syrinx.

If Ruhn noticed she didn't bother with a photo of him, he said nothing. Though Hunt could have sworn the shadows in the room deepened.

"All I want, BB," Lehabah said, "is a little appreciation."

"Gods spare me," Bryce muttered. Even Ruhn smiled at that.

The prince's phone rang, and he picked up before Hunt could see who it was. "Flynn."

Hunt heard Flynn's voice faintly. "You're needed at the barracks. Some bullshit fight broke out about somebody's girlfriend sleeping with someone else and I honestly don't give two fucks about it, but they bloodied each other up pretty damn good."

Ruhn sighed. "I'll be there in fifteen," he said, and hung up.

Hunt asked, "You really have to moderate petty fights like that?"

Ruhn ran a hand down the hilt of the Starsword. "Why not?"

"You're a prince."

"I don't understand why you make that sound like an insult," Ruhn growled.

Hunt said, "Why not do . . . bigger shit?"

Bryce answered for him. "Because his daddy is scared of him."

Ruhn shot her a warning look. "He outranks me power-wise *and* title-wise."

"And yet he made sure to get you under his thumb as early as possible—as if you were some sort of animal to be tamed." She said the words mildly, but Ruhn tensed.

"It was going well," Ruhn said tightly, "until you came along."

Hunt braced himself for the brewing storm.

Bryce said, "He was alive the last time a Starborn Prince appeared, you know. You ever ask what happened to him? Why he died before he made the Drop?"

Ruhn paled. "Don't be stupid. That was an accident during his Ordeal."

Hunt kept his face neutral, but Bryce just leaned back in her chair. "If you say so."

"You still believe this shit you tried to sell me as a kid?"

She crossed her arms. "I wanted your eyes open to what he really is before it was too late for you, too."

Ruhn blinked, but straightened, shaking his head as he rose from the table. "Trust me, Bryce, I've known for a while what he is. I had to fucking live with him." Ruhn nodded toward the messy table. "If I hear anything new about the Horn or this synthetic healing magic, I'll let you know." He met Hunt's stare and added, "Be careful."

Hunt gave him a half smile that told the prince he knew exactly what that *be careful* was about. And didn't give a shit.

Two minutes after Ruhn left, the front door buzzed again.

"What does he fucking want now?" Bryce muttered, grabbing the tablet Lehabah had been using to watch her trash TV and pulling up the video feed for the front cameras.

A squeal escaped her. An otter in a reflective yellow vest stood on its hind legs, a little paw on the lower buzzer she'd had Jesiba install for shorter patrons. Out of the hope that one day, somehow, she'd find a fuzzy, whiskery messenger standing on the doorstep.

Bryce bolted from her chair a second later, her heels eating up the carpet as she ran upstairs.

The message the otter bore from Tharion was short and sweet.

I think you'll find this of interest. Kisses, Tharion

"Kisses?" Hunt asked.

"They're for you, obviously," Bryce said, still smiling about the otter. She'd handed him a silver mark, for which she'd earned a twitch of the whiskers and a little fanged grin.

Easily the highlight of her day. Week. Year.

Honestly, her entire life.

At the desk in the showroom, Bryce removed Tharion's letter from the top of the pile, while Hunt began to leaf through some of the pages beneath.

The blood rushed from her face at a photograph in Hunt's hand. "Is that a body?"

Hunt grunted. "It's what's left of one after Tharion pried it from a sobek's lair."

Bryce couldn't stop the shudder down her spine. Clocking in at more than twenty-five feet and nearly three thousand pounds of scale-covered muscle, sobeks were among the worst of the apex predators who prowled the river. Mean, strong, and with teeth that could snap you in two, a full-grown male sobek could make most Vanir back away. "He's insane."

Hunt chuckled. "Oh, he most certainly is."

Bryce frowned at the gruesome photo, then read through Tharion's notes. "He says the bite marks on the torso aren't consistent with sobek teeth. This person was already dead when they were dumped into the Istros. The sobek must have seen an easy meal and hauled it down to its lair to eat later." She swallowed the dryness in her mouth and again looked at the body. A dryad female. Her chest cavity had been ripped open, heart and internal organs removed, and bite marks peppered—

"These wounds look like the ones you got from the kristallos. And the mer's lab figured this body was probably five days old, judging by the level of decay."

"The night we were attacked."

Bryce studied the analysis. "There was clear venom in the wounds. Tharion says he could feel it inside the corpse even before the mer did tests on it." Most of those in the House of Many Waters could sense what flowed in someone's body—illnesses and weaknesses and, apparently, venom. "But when they tested it . . ." She blew out a breath. "It negated magic." It had to be the kristallos. Bryce cringed, reading on, "He looked into records of all unidentified bodies the mer found in the past couple years. They found two with identical wounds and this clear venom right around the time of . . ." She swallowed. "Around when Danika and the pack died.

A dryad and a fox shifter male. Both reported missing. This month, they've found *five* with these marks and the venom. All reported missing, but a few weeks after the fact."

"So they're people who might not have had many close friends or family," Hunt said.

"Maybe." Bryce again studied the photograph. Made herself look at the wounds. Silence fell, interrupted only by the distant sounds of Lehabah's show downstairs.

She said quietly, "That's not the creature that killed Danika."

Hunt ran a hand through his hair. "There might have been multiple kristallos—"

"No," she insisted, setting down the papers. "The kristallos isn't what killed Danika."

Hunt's brow furrowed. "You were on the scene, though. You saw it."

"I saw it in the hall, not in the apartment. Danika, the pack, and the other three recent victims were in *piles*." She could barely stand to say it, to think about it again.

These past five days had been . . . not easy. Putting one foot in front of the other had been the only thing to get her through it after the disaster with Sabine. After the bomb she'd dropped about Danika. And if they'd been looking for the wrong fucking thing all this time . . .

Bryce held up the photo. "These wounds aren't the same. The kristallos wanted to get at your heart, your organs. Not turn you into a—a heap. Danika, the Pack of Devils, Tertian, the acolyte and temple guard—*none* of them had wounds like this. And *none* had this venom in their system." Hunt just blinked at her. Bryce's voice cracked. "What if something else came through? What if the kristallos was summoned to look for the Horn, but something worse was also there that night? If you had the power to summon the kristallos, why not summon multiple types of demons?"

Hunt considered. "I can't think of a demon that demolishes its victims like that, though. Unless it's another ancient horror straight from the Pit." He rubbed his neck. "If the kristallos killed this dryad—killed these people whose bodies washed into the river through the sewers—then *why* summon two kinds of demons? The kristallos is already lethal as Hel." Literally.

Bryce threw up her hands. "I have no idea. But if everything we know about Danika's death is wrong, then we need to figure out *how* she died. We need someone who can weigh in."

He rubbed his jaw. "Any ideas?"

She nodded slowly, dread curling in her gut. "Promise me you won't go ballistic."

51

Summoning a demon is a bad fucking idea," Hunt breathed as night fell beyond the apartment's shut curtains. "Especially considering that's what started this mess in the first place."

They stood in her great room, lights dimmed and candles flickering around them, Syrinx bundled in blankets and locked in his crate in Bryce's bedroom, surrounded by a protective circle of white salt.

What lay around and before them on the pale floors, reeking of mold and rotten earth, was the opposite of that.

Bryce had ground the block of obsidian salt down at some point—presumably using her fucking food processor. For something she'd dropped ten grand on, Bryce didn't treat it with any particular reverence. She'd chucked it into a kitchen cabinet as if it were a bag of chips.

He hadn't realized she'd only been biding her time until she needed it.

Now, she'd crafted two circles with the obsidian salt. The one near the windows was perhaps five feet in diameter. The other was big enough to hold herself and Hunt.

Bryce said, "I'm not going to waste my time snooping around town for answers about what kind of demon killed Danika. Going right to the source will save me a headache."

"Going right to the source will get you splattered on a wall. And if not, arrested for summoning a demon into a residential zone." Shit. *He* should arrest her, shouldn't he?

"No one likes a narc, Athalar."

"I *am* a narc."

A dark red eyebrow arched. "Could've fooled me, Shadow of Death." She joined him in the salt circle. Her long ponytail pooled in the collar of her leather jacket, the candlelight gilding the red strands.

His fingers twitched, as if they'd reach for that silken length of hair. Run it between them. Wrap it around his fist and draw her head back, exposing that neck of hers again to his mouth. His tongue. Teeth.

Hunt growled, "You do know that it is my *job* to stop these demons from entering this world."

"We're not setting the demon loose," she hissed back. "This is as safe as a phone call."

"Are you going to summon it with its unholy number, then?" Many demons had numbers associated with them, like some sort of ancient email address.

"No, I don't need it. I know how to find this demon." He started to answer, but she cut him off. "The obsidian salt will hold it."

Hunt eyed the circles she'd made, then sighed. Fine. Even though arguing with her was nearly as enticing as foreplay, he didn't feel like wasting time, either.

But then the temperature in the room began to drop. Rapidly.

And as Hunt's breath began to cloud the air, as a humanoid male appeared, thrumming with dark power that made his stomach roil . . .

Bryce grinned up at Hunt as his heart stopped dead. "Surprise."

She'd lost her fucking mind. He would kill her for this—if they weren't both killed in the next few seconds.

"Who is that?" Ice formed in the room. No clothing could protect against the cold this demon brought with him. It pierced through every layer, snatching the breath from Hunt's chest with clawed fingers. A shuddering inhale was the only sign of Bryce's discomfort as she remained facing the circle on the other side of the room. The male now contained inside its dark border.

"Aidas," she said softly.

Hunt had always imagined the Prince of the Chasm as similar to the lower-level demons he'd hunted over the centuries: scales or fangs or claws, brute muscle and snarling with blind animal rage.

Not this slender, pale-skinned . . . pretty boy.

Aidas's blond hair fell to his shoulders in soft waves, loose, yet well cut around his fine-boned face. Undoubtedly to show off the eyes like blue opals, framed by thick, golden lashes. Those lashes bobbed once in a cursory blink. Then his full, sensuous mouth parted in a smile to reveal a row of too-white teeth. "Bryce Quinlan."

Hunt's hand drifted to his gun. The Prince of the Chasm knew her name—her face. And the way he'd spoken her name was as much greeting as it was question, his voice velvet-soft.

Aidas occupied the fifth level of Hel—the Chasm. He yielded only to two others: the Prince of the Abyss, and the Prince of the Pit, the seventh and mightiest of the demon princes. The Star-Eater himself, whose name was never uttered on this side of the Northern Rift.

No one would dare say his name, not after the Prince of the Pit became the first and only being to ever kill an Asteri. His butchering of the seventh holy star—Sirius, the Wolf Star—during the First Wars remained a favorite ballad around war-camp fires. And what he'd done to Sirius after slaying her had earned him that awful title: Star-Eater.

"You appeared as a cat the last time" was all Bryce said.

All. She. Said.

Hunt dared take his eyes off the Prince of the Chasm to find Bryce bowing her head.

Aidas slid his slender hands into the pockets of his closely tailored jacket and pants—the material blacker than the Chasm in which he resided. "You were very young then."

Hunt had to plant his feet to keep from swaying. She'd met the prince before—how?

His shock must have been written on his face because she shot him a look that he could only interpret as *Calm the fuck down*, but said, "I was thirteen—not *that* young."

Hunt reined in his grunt that would have suggested otherwise.

Aidas tilted his head to one side. "You were very sad then as well."

It took Hunt a moment to process it—the words. The bit of history, and the bit of now.

Bryce rubbed her hands together. "Let's talk about *you*, Your Highness."

"I am always happy to do so."

The cold burned Hunt's lungs. They could last only minutes at this temperature before their healing abilities started churning. And despite Bryce's Fae blood, there was a good chance that she might not recover at all. Without having made the Drop, the frostbite would be permanent for Bryce. As would any digits or limbs lost.

She said to the demon prince, "You and your colleagues seem to be getting restless in the dark."

"Is that so?" Aidas frowned at his polished leather shoes as if he could see all the way down to the Pit. "Perhaps you summoned the wrong prince, for this is the first I've heard of it."

"Who is summoning the kristallos demon to hunt through this city?" Flat, cutting words. "And what killed Danika Fendyr?"

"Ah yes, we heard of that—how Danika screamed as she was shredded apart."

Bryce's beat of silence told Hunt enough about the internal wound that Aidas had pressed. From the smile gracing Aidas's face, the Prince of the Chasm knew it as well.

She went on, "Do you know what demon did it?"

"Despite what your mythologies claim, I am not privy to the movements of every being in Hel."

She said tightly, "Do you know, though? Or know who summoned it?"

His golden lashes shimmered as he blinked. "You believe I dispatched it?"

"You would not be standing there if I did."

Aidas laughed softly. "No tears from you this time."

Bryce smiled slightly. "You told me not to let them see me cry. I took the advice to heart."

What the Hel had gone on during that meeting twelve years ago?

"Information is not free."

"What is your price?" A bluish tint crept over her lips. They'd have to cut the connection soon.

Hunt kept perfectly still as Aidas studied her. Then his eyes registered Hunt.

He blinked—once. As if he had not really marked his presence until this moment. As if he hadn't cared to notice, with Bryce before him. Hunt tucked away that fact, just as Aidas murmured, "Who are you."

A command.

"He's eye candy," Bryce said, looping her arm through Hunt's and pressing close. For warmth or steadiness, he didn't know. She was shaking. "And he is not for sale." She pointed to the halo across Hunt's brow.

"My pets like to rip out feathers—it would be a good trade."

Hunt leveled a stare at the prince. Bryce threw Hunt a sidelong glare, the effect of which was negated by her chattering teeth.

Aidas smiled, looking him over again. "A Fallen warrior with the power of . . ." Aidas's groomed brows lifted in surprise. His blue opal eyes narrowed to slits—then simmered like the hottest flame. "What are *you* doing with a black crown around your brow?"

Hunt didn't dare let his surprise at the question show. He'd never heard it called that before—a black crown. Halo, witch-ink, mark-of-shame, but never that.

Aidas looked between them now. Carefully. He didn't bother to let Hunt answer his question before that awful smile returned. "The seven princes dwell in darkness and do not stir. We have no interest in your realm."

"I'd believe it if you and your brethren hadn't been rattling the

Northern Rift for the past two decades," Hunt said. "And if I hadn't been cleaning up after it."

Aidas sucked in a breath, as if tasting the air on which Hunt's words had been delivered to him. "You do realize that it might not be my people? The Northern Rift opens to other places—other realms, yes, but other planets as well. What is Hel but a distant planet bound to yours by a ripple in space and time?"

"Hel is a planet?" Hunt's brows lowered. Most of the demons he'd killed and dealt with hadn't been able to or inclined to speak.

Aidas shrugged with one shoulder. "It is as real a place as Midgard, though most of us would have you believe it wasn't." The prince pointed to him. "Your kind, Fallen, were made in Midgard by the Asteri. But the Fae, the shifters, and many others came from their own worlds. The universe is massive. Some believe it has no end. Or that our universe might be one in a multitude, as bountiful as the stars in the sky or the sand on a beach."

Bryce threw Hunt a look that told him she, too, was wondering what the Hel the demon prince was smoking in the Chasm. "You're trying to distract us," Bryce said, arms crossing. Hoarfrost crept across the floors. "You're not rattling the Northern Rift?"

"The lesser princes do that—levels one through four," Aidas said, head angling again. "Those of us in the true dark have no need or interest in sunshine. But even they did not send the kristallos. Our plans do not involve such things."

Hunt growled, "Your kind wanted to live here, once upon a time. Why would that change?"

Aidas chuckled. "It is dreadfully amusing to hear the stories the Asteri have spun for you." He smiled at Bryce. "What blinds an Oracle?"

All color leached from Bryce's face at the mention of her visit to the Oracle. How Aidas knew about it, Hunt could only guess, but she countered, "What sort of cat visits an Oracle?"

"Winning first words." Aidas slid his hands into his pockets again. "I did not know what you might prefer now that you are grown." A smirk at Hunt. "But I may appear more like that, if it pleases you, Bryce Quinlan."

"Better yet: don't appear again at all," Hunt said to the demon prince.

Bryce squeezed his arm. He stepped on her foot hard enough to get her to cut it out.

But Aidas chuckled. "Your temperature drops. I shall depart."

"Please," Bryce said. "Just tell me if you know what killed Danika. Please."

A soft laugh. "Run the tests again. Find what is in-between."

He began to fade, as if a phone call were indeed breaking up.

"Aidas," she blurted, stepping right to the edge of their circle. Hunt fought the urge to tuck her to his side. Especially as darkness frayed the edges of Aidas's body. "Thank you. For that day."

The Prince of the Chasm paused, as if clinging to this world. "Make the Drop, Bryce Quinlan." He flickered. "And find me when you are done."

Aidas had nearly vanished into nothing when he added, the words a ghost slithering through the room, "The Oracle did not see. But I did."

Silence pulsed in his wake as the room thawed, frost vanishing.

Hunt whirled on Bryce. "First of all," he seethed, "*fuck you* for that surprise."

She rubbed her hands together, working warmth back into them. "You never would have let me summon Aidas if I'd told you first."

"Because we should be fucking *dead* right now!" He gaped at her. "Are you insane?"

"I knew he wouldn't hurt me. Or anyone with me."

"You want to tell me how you *met* Aidas when you were thirteen?"

"I . . . I told you how badly things ended between me and my biological father after my Oracle visit." His anger banked at the lingering pain in her face. "So afterward, when I was crying my little heart out on one of the park benches outside the temple, this white cat appeared next to me. It had the most unnatural blue eyes. I knew, even before it spoke, that it wasn't a cat—and wasn't a shifter."

"Who summoned him that time?"

"I don't know. Jesiba told me that the princes can sneak through cracks in either Rift, taking the form of common animals. But then they're confined to those forms—with none of their own power, save the ability to speak. And they can only stay for a few hours at a time."

A shudder worked its way down his gray wings. "What did Aidas say?"

"He asked me: *What blinds an Oracle?* And I replied: *What sort of cat visits an Oracle?* He'd heard the screaming on his way in. I suppose it intrigued him. He told me to stop crying. Said it would only satisfy those who had wronged me. That I shouldn't give them the gift of my sorrow."

"Why was the Prince of the Chasm at the Oracle?"

"He never told me. But he sat with me until I worked up the nerve to walk back to my father's house. By the time I remembered to thank him, he was gone."

"Strange." And—fine, he could understand why she hadn't balked from summoning him, if he'd been kind to her in the past.

"Perhaps some of the feline body wore off on him and he was merely curious about me."

"Apparently, he's missed you." A leading question.

"Apparently," she hedged. "Though he barely gave us anything to go on."

Her gaze turned distant as she looked at the empty circle before them, then took her phone out of her pocket. Hunt caught a glimpse of who she dialed—*Declan Emmet.*

"Hi, B." In the background, music thumped and male laughter roared.

Bryce didn't bother with niceties. "We've been tipped off that we should run various tests again—I'm assuming that means the ones on the victims and crime scenes a few years ago. Can you think of anything that should be reexamined?"

In the background, Ruhn asked, *Is that Bryce?* But Declan said, "I'd definitely run a scent diagnostic. You'll need clothes."

Bryce said, "They must have done a scent diagnostic two years ago."

Declan said, "Was it the common one, or the Mimir?"

Hunt's stomach tightened. Especially as Bryce said, "What's the difference?"

"The Mimir is better. It's relatively new."

Bryce looked at Hunt, and he shook his head slowly. She said quietly into the phone, "No one did a Mimir test."

Declan hesitated. "Well . . . it's Fae tech mostly. We loan it out to the legion for their major cases." A pause. "Someone should have said something."

Hunt braced himself. Bryce asked, "You had access to this sort of thing two years ago?"

Declan paused again. "Ah—shit." Then Ruhn came on the line. "Bryce, a direct order was given not to pursue it through those channels. It was deemed a matter that the Fae should stay out of."

Devastation, rage, grief—all exploded across her face. Her fingers curled at her sides.

Hunt said, knowing Ruhn could hear it, "The Autumn King is a real prick, you know that?"

Bryce snarled, "I'm going to tell him just that." She hung up.

Hunt demanded, "What?" But she was already running out of the apartment.

52

Bryce's blood roared as she sprinted through the Old Square, down rain-soaked streets, all the way to Five Roses. The villas glowed in the rain, palatial homes with immaculate lawns and gardens, all fenced with wrought iron. Stone-faced Fae or shifter sentries from the Auxiliary were posted at every corner.

As if the residents here lived in abject terror that the peregrini and few slaves of Crescent City were poised to loot at any moment.

She hurtled past the marble behemoth that was the Fae Archives, the building covered in drooping veils of flowers that ran down its many columns. Roses, jasmine, wisteria—all in perpetual bloom, no matter the season.

She sprinted all the way to the sprawling white villa covered in pink roses, and to the wrought-iron gate around it guarded by four Fae warriors.

They stepped into her path as she skidded to a halt, the flagstone street slick with rain.

"Let me in," she said through her teeth, panting.

They didn't so much as blink. "Do you have an appointment with His Majesty?" one asked.

"Let me in," she said again.

He'd known. Her father had known there were tests to assess

what had killed Danika and had done *nothing.* Had deliberately stayed out of it.

She had to see him. Had to hear it from him. She didn't care what time it was.

The polished black door was shut, but the lights were on. He was home. He had to be.

"Not without an appointment," said the same guard.

Bryce took a step toward them and rebounded—hard. A wall of heat surrounded the compound, no doubt generated by the Fae males before her. One of the guards snickered. Her face grew hot, her eyes stinging.

"Go tell your *king* that Bryce Quinlan needs a word. *Now.*"

"Come back when you have an appointment, half-breed," one of the sentries said.

Bryce smacked her hand against their shield. It didn't so much as ripple. "*Tell him*—"

The guards stiffened as power, dark and mighty, pulsed from behind her. Lightning skittered over the cobblestones. The guards' hands drifted to their swords.

Hunt said, voice like thunder, "The lady wants an audience with His Majesty."

"His Majesty is unavailable." The guard who spoke had clearly noted the halo at Hunt's brow. The sneer that spread across his face was one of the most hideous things Bryce had ever seen. "Especially for Fallen scum and half-human skanks."

Hunt took a step toward them. "Say that again."

The guard's sneer remained. "Once wasn't enough?"

Hunt's hand fisted at his side. He'd do it, she realized. He'd pummel these assholes into dust for her, fight his way inside the gates so she could have a chat with the king.

Down the block, Ruhn appeared, wreathed in shadow, his black hair plastered to his head. Flynn and Declan followed close behind him. "Stand down," Ruhn ordered the guards. "Stand the fuck down."

They did no such thing. "Even you, Prince, are not authorized to order that."

Ruhn's shadows swirled at his shoulders like a phantom pair of wings, but he said to Bryce, "There are other battles worth fighting with him. This isn't one of them."

Bryce stalked a few feet from the gate, even though the guards could likely hear every word. "He deliberately chose not to help with what happened to Danika."

Hunt said, "Some might consider that to be interference with an imperial investigation."

"Fuck off, Athalar," Ruhn growled. He reached for Bryce's arm, but she stepped back. He clenched his jaw. "You are considered a member of this court, you know. You were involved in a colossal mess. He decided the best thing for your safety was to let the case drop, not dig further."

"As if he's ever given two shits about my safety."

"He gave enough of a shit about you to want me to be your live-in guard. But you wanted Athalar to play sexy roomie."

"He wants to find the Horn for *himself*," she snapped. "It has *nothing* to do with me." She pointed to the house beyond the iron fence. "You go in there and tell that piece of shit that I won't forget this. *Ever.* I doubt he'll care, but you tell him."

Ruhn's shadows stilled, draping from his shoulders. "I'm sorry, Bryce. About Danika—"

"Do *not*," she seethed, "ever say her name to me. Never say her name to me again."

She could have sworn hurt that even his shadows couldn't hide flashed across her brother's face, but she turned, finding Hunt watching with crossed arms. "I'll see you at the apartment," she said to him, and didn't bother to say more before launching back into a run.

It had been fucked up to not warn Hunt whom she was summoning. She'd admit it.

But not as fucked up as the Fae tests her father had *declined* to provide access to.

Bryce didn't go home. Halfway there, she decided she'd head

somewhere else. The White Raven was shut down, but her old favorite whiskey bar would do just fine.

Lethe was open and serving. Which was good, because her leg throbbed mercilessly and her feet were blistered from running in her stupid flats. She took them off the moment she hopped onto the leather stool at the bar, and sighed as her bare feet touched the cool brass footrest running the length of the dark wood counter.

Lethe hadn't changed in the two years since she'd last set foot on the floor that lent itself to an optical illusion, painted with black, gray, and white cubes. The cherrywood pillars still rose like trees to form the carved, arched ceiling high above, looming over a bar made from fogged glass and black metal, all clean lines and square edges.

She'd messaged Juniper five minutes ago, inviting her for a drink. She still hadn't heard back. So she'd watched the news on the screen above the bar, flashing to the muddy battlefields in Pangera, the husks of mech-suits littering them like broken toys, bodies both human and Vanir sprawled for miles, the crows already feasting.

Even the human busboy had stopped to look, his face tight as he beheld the carnage. A barked order from the bartender had kept him moving, but Bryce had seen the gleam in the young man's brown eyes. The fury and determination.

"What the Hel," she muttered, and knocked back a mouthful of the whiskey in front of her.

It tasted as acrid and vile as she remembered—burned all the way down. Precisely what she wanted. Bryce took another swig.

A bottle of some sort of purple tonic plunked onto the counter beside her tumbler. "For your leg," Hunt said, sliding onto the stool beside hers. "Drink up."

She eyed the glass vial. "You went to a medwitch?"

"There's a clinic around the corner. I figured you weren't leaving here anytime soon."

Bryce sipped her whiskey. "You guessed right."

He nudged the tonic closer. "Have it before you finish the rest."

"No comment about breaking my No Drinking rule?"

He leaned on the bar, tucking in his wings. "It's your rule—you can end it whenever you like."

Whatever. She reached for the tonic, uncorking and knocking it back. She grimaced. "Tastes like grape soda."

"I told her to make it sweet."

She batted her eyelashes. "Because I'm so sweet, Athalar?"

"Because I knew you wouldn't drink it if it tasted like rubbing alcohol."

She lifted her whiskey. "I beg to differ."

Hunt signaled the bartender, ordered a water, and said to Bryce, "So, tonight went well."

She chuckled, sipping the whiskey again. Gods, it tasted awful. Why had she ever guzzled this stuff down? "Superb."

Hunt drank from his water. Watched her for a long moment before he said, "Look, I'll sit here while you get stupid drunk if that's what you want, but I'll just say this first: there are better ways to deal with everything."

"Thanks, Mom."

"I mean it."

The bartender set another whiskey before her, but Bryce didn't drink.

Hunt said carefully, "You're not the only person to have lost someone you love."

She propped her head on a hand. "Tell me all about her, Hunt. Let's hear the full, unabridged sob story at last."

He held her gaze. "Don't be an asshole. I'm trying to talk to you."

"And I'm trying to drink," she said, lifting her glass to do so.

Her phone buzzed, and both of them glanced at it. Juniper had finally written back.

Can't, sorry. Practice. Then another buzz from Juniper. *Wait—why are you drinking at Lethe? Are you drinking again? What happened?*

Hunt said quietly, "Maybe your friend is trying to tell you something, too."

Bryce's fingers curled into fists, but she set her phone facedown on the glowing, fogged glass. "Weren't you going to tell me your heartbreaking story about your amazing girlfriend? What would *she* think about the way you manhandled me and practically devoured my neck the other night?"

She regretted the words the moment they were out. For so many reasons, she regretted them, the least of which being that she hadn't been able to stop thinking about that moment of insanity on the roof, when his mouth had been on her neck and she'd started to completely unravel.

How good it had felt—*he* had felt.

Hunt stared her down for a long moment. Heat rose to her face.

But all he said was "I'll see you at home." The word echoed between them as he set another purple tonic on the counter. "Drink that one in thirty minutes."

Then he was gone, prowling through the empty bar and onto the street beyond.

Hunt had just settled onto the couch to watch the sunball game when Bryce walked into the apartment, two bags of groceries in her hands. About fucking time.

Syrinx flung himself off the couch and bounded to her, rising onto his back legs to demand kisses. She obliged him, ruffling his golden fur before looking up at where Hunt sat on the couch. He just sipped from his beer and gave her a terse nod.

She nodded back, not quite meeting his eyes, and strode for the kitchen. The limp was better, but not wholly gone.

He'd sent Naomi to monitor the street outside that fancy whiskey bar while he hit the gym to work off his temper.

Manhandled. The word had lingered. Along with the truth: he hadn't thought about Shahar for a second while they'd been on the roof. Or in the days following. And when he'd had his hand wrapped around his cock in the shower that night, and every night since, it hadn't been the Archangel he'd thought of. Not even close.

Quinlan had to know that. She had to know what wound she'd hit.

So the options had been to yell at her, or to exercise. He'd picked the latter.

That had been two hours ago. He'd cleaned up all the obsidian salt, walked and fed Syrinx, and then sat on the couch to wait.

Bryce set her bags onto the counter, Syrinx lingering at her feet to inspect every purchase. In between plays, Hunt stole glances at what she unpacked. Vegetables, fruits, meat, oat milk, cow's milk, rice, a loaf of brown bread—

"Are we having company?" he asked.

She yanked out a skillet and plunked it on the burner. "I figured I'd make a late dinner."

Her back was stiff, her shoulders straight. He might have thought she was pissed, but the fact that she was making dinner for them suggested otherwise. "Is it wise to cook when you've been pounding whiskey?"

She shot him a glare over a shoulder. "I'm trying to do something nice, and you're not making it easy."

Hunt held up his hands. "All right. Sorry."

She went back to the stove, adjusted the heat, and opened a package of some sort of ground meat. "I wasn't pounding whiskey," she said. "I left Lethe soon after you did."

"Where'd you go?"

"Out to a storage unit near Moonwood." She began gathering spices. "I stashed a lot of Danika's stuff there. Sabine was going to chuck it, but I took it before she did." She dumped some ground meat in the skillet and gestured to a third bag she'd left by the door. "I just wanted to make sure there was no hint of the Horn there, anything I might not have noticed at the time. And to grab some of Danika's clothes—ones that were in my bedroom that night that Evidence didn't take. I know they already have clothes from before, but I thought . . . Maybe there's something on these, too."

Hunt opened his mouth to say something—what, exactly, he didn't know—but Bryce went on. "After that, I went to the market. Since condiments aren't food, apparently."

Hunt brought his beer with him as he padded to the kitchen. "Want help?"

"No. This is an apology meal. Go watch your game."

"You don't need to apologize."

"I acted like an asshole. Let me cook something for you to make up for it."

"Based on how much chili powder you just dumped into that pan, I'm not sure I want to accept this particular apology."

"Fuck, I forgot to add the cumin!" She whirled toward the skillet, turning down the heat and adding the spice, stirring it into what smelled like ground turkey. She sighed. "I'm a mess."

He waited, letting her gather her words.

She began cutting an onion, her motions easy and smooth.

"Honestly, I was a bit of a mess before what happened to Danika, and . . ." She sliced the onion into neat rings. "It didn't get any better."

"Why were you a mess before she died?"

Bryce slid the onion into the skillet. "I'm a half-human with a near-useless college degree. All my friends were going somewhere, doing something with themselves." Her mouth quirked to the side. "I'm a glorified secretary. With no long-term plan for anything." She stirred the onion around. "The partying and stuff—it was the only time when the four of us were on equal footing. When it didn't matter that Fury's some kind of merc or Juniper's so amazingly talented or Danika would one day be this all-powerful wolf."

"They ever hold that against you?"

"No." Her amber eyes scanned his face. "No, they would never have done that. But I couldn't ever forget it."

"Your cousin said you used to dance. That you stopped after Danika died. You never wanted to follow that road?"

She pointed to the sweep of her hips. "I was told my half-human body was *too clunky*. I was also told that my boobs were too big, and my ass could be used as an aerialport landing pad."

"Your ass is perfect." The words slipped out. He refrained from commenting on just how much he liked the other parts of her, too. How much he wanted to worship them. Starting with that ass of hers.

Color bloomed on her cheeks. "Well, thank you." She stirred the contents of the skillet.

"But you don't dance for fun anymore?"

"No." Her eyes went cold at that. "I don't."

"And you never thought of doing anything else?"

"Of course I have. I've got ten job applications hidden on my work computer, but I can't focus enough to finish them. It's been so long since I saw the job postings that they're probably filled by now anyway. It doesn't even matter that I'd also have to find some way to convince Jesiba that I'll keep paying off my debt to her." She kept stirring. "A human life span seems like a long time to fill, but an immortal one?" She hooked her hair behind an ear. "I have no idea what to do."

"I'm two hundred thirty-three years old, and I'm still figuring it out."

"Yeah, but you—you *did* something. You fought for something. You *are* someone."

He tapped the slave tattoo on his wrist. "And look where I wound up."

She turned from the stove. "Hunt, I really am sorry for what I said about Shahar."

"Don't worry about it."

Bryce jerked her chin toward Hunt's open bedroom door, the photo of her and Danika just barely visible on the dresser. "My mom took that the day we got out of the hospital in Rosque."

He knew she was building to something, and was willing to play along. "Why were you in the hospital?"

"Danika's senior thesis was on the history of the illegal animal trade. She uncovered a real smuggling ring, but no one in the Aux or the 33rd would help her, so she and I went to deal with it ourselves." Bryce snorted. "The operation was run by five asp shifters, who caught us trying to free their stock. We called them asp-holes, and things went downhill from there."

Of course they did. "How downhill?"

"A motorcycle chase and crash, my right arm broken in three places, Danika's pelvis fractured. Danika got shot twice in the leg."

"Gods."

"You should have seen the asp-holes."

"You killed them?"

Her eyes darkened, nothing but pure Fae predator shining

there. "Some. The ones who shot Danika . . . I took care of them. The police got the rest." Burning Solas. He had a feeling there was far more to the story. "I know people think Danika was a reckless partier with mommy issues, I know Sabine thinks that, but . . . Danika went to free those animals because she literally couldn't sleep at night knowing they were in cages, terrified and alone."

The Party Princess, Hunt and the triarii had mocked her behind her back.

Bryce went on, "Danika was always doing that kind of thing—helping people Sabine thought were beneath them. Some part of her might have done it to piss off her mom, yeah, but most of it was because she wanted to help. That's why she went easy on Philip Briggs and his group, why she gave him so many chances." She let out a long breath. "She was difficult, but she was good."

"And what about you?" he asked carefully.

She ran a hand through her hair. "Most days, I feel cold as it was in here with Aidas. Most days, all I want is to go back. To how it was before. I can't bear to keep going forward."

Hunt gazed at her for a long moment. "There were some of the Fallen who accepted the halo and slave tattoo, you know. After a few decades, they accepted it. Stopped fighting it."

"Why have you never stopped?"

"Because we were right then, and we're still right now. Shahar was only the spear point. I followed her blindly into a battle we could never have won, but I believed in what she stood for."

"If you could do it over, march under Shahar's banner again—would you?"

Hunt considered that. He didn't normally let himself dwell too long on what had happened, what had occurred since then. "If I hadn't rebelled with her, I'd probably have been noticed by another Archangel for my lightning. I'd likely now be serving as a commander in one of Pangera's cities, hoping to one day earn enough to buy my way out of service. But they'd never let someone with my gifts go. And I had little choice but to join a legion. It was the path I was pushed onto, and the lightning, the killing—I never asked to be good at it. I'd give it up in a heartbeat if I could."

Her eyes flickered with understanding. "I know." He lifted a brow. She clarified, "The being good at something you don't want to be good at. That talent you'd let go of in a heartbeat." He angled his head. "I mean, look at me: I'm *amazing* at attracting assholes."

Hunt huffed a laugh. She said, "You didn't answer my question. Would you still rebel if you knew what would happen?"

Hunt sighed. "That's what I was starting to say: even if I hadn't rebelled, I'd wind up in a sugarcoated version of my life now. Because I'm still a legionary being used for my so-called gifts—just now *officially* a slave, rather than being forced into service by a lack of other options. The only other difference is that I'm serving in Valbara, in a fool's bargain with an Archangel, hoping to one day be forgiven for my supposed sins."

"You don't think they were sins."

"No. I think the angel hierarchies are bullshit. We were right to rebel."

"Even though it cost you everything?"

"Yeah. So I guess that's my answer. I'd still do it, even knowing what would happen. And if I ever get free . . ." Bryce halted her stirring. Met his stare unblinkingly as Hunt said, "I remember every one of them who was there on the battlefield, who brought down Shahar. And all the angels, the Asteri, the Senate, the Governors—all of them, who were there at our sentencing." He leaned against the counter behind them and swigged from his beer, letting her fill in the rest.

"And after you've killed them all? What then?"

He blinked at the lack of fear, of judgment. "Assuming I live through it, you mean."

"Assuming you live through taking on the Archangels and Asteri, what then?"

"I don't know." He gave her a half smile. "Maybe you and I can figure it out, Quinlan. We'll have centuries to do it."

"If I make the Drop."

He started. "You would choose not to?" It was rare—so, so rare for a Vanir to refuse to make the Drop and live only a mortal life span.

She added more vegetables and seasoning to the pan before throwing a packet of instant rice into the microwave. "I don't know. I'd need an Anchor."

"What about Ruhn?" Her cousin, even if neither of them would admit it, would take on every beast in the Pit itself to protect her.

She threw him a look dripping with disdain. "No fucking way."

"Juniper, then?" Someone she truly trusted, loved.

"She'd do it, but it doesn't feel right. And using one of the public Anchors isn't for me."

"I used one. It was fine." He spied the questions brimming in her eyes and cut her off before she could voice them. "Maybe you'll change your mind."

"Maybe." She chewed on her lip. "I'm sorry you lost your friends."

"I'm sorry you lost yours."

Bryce nodded her thanks, going back to stirring. "I know people don't get it. It's just . . . a light went out inside me when it happened. Danika wasn't my sister, or my lover. But she was the one person I could be myself around and never feel judged. The one person that I knew would always pick up the phone, or call me back. She was the one person who made me feel brave because no matter what happened, no matter how bad or embarrassing or shitty it was, I knew that I had her in my corner. That if it all went to Hel, I could talk to her and it would be fine."

Her eyes gleamed, and it was all he could do to not cross the few feet between them and grab her hand as she continued. "But it . . . It's not fine. I will *never* talk to her again. I think people expect me to be over it by now. But I can't. Anytime I get anywhere close to the truth of my new reality, I want to space out again. To not have to *be* me. I can't fucking dance anymore because it reminds me of her—of all the dancing we did together in clubs or on the streets or in our apartment or dorm. I *won't* let myself dance anymore because it brought me joy, and . . . And I didn't, I don't, want to feel those things." She swallowed. "I know it sounds pathetic."

"It's not," he said quietly.

"I'm sorry I dumped my baggage in your lap."

A corner of his mouth turned up. "You can dump your baggage in my lap anytime, Quinlan."

She snorted, shaking her head. "You made it sound gross."

"You said it first." Her mouth twitched. Damn, if the smile didn't make his chest tighten.

But Hunt just said, "I know you'll keep going forward, Quinlan—even if it sucks."

"What makes you so sure of it?"

His feet were silent as he crossed the kitchen. She tipped back her head to hold his stare. "Because you pretend to be irreverent and lazy, but deep down, you don't give up. Because you know that if you do, then they win. All the asp-holes, as you called them, win. So living, and living well—it's the greatest *fuck you* that you can ever give them."

"That's why you're still fighting."

He ran a hand over the tattoo on his brow. "Yes."

She let out a *hmm*, stirring the mixture in the pan again. "Well then, Athalar. I guess it'll be you and me in the trenches for a while longer."

He smiled at her, more openly than he'd dared do with anyone in a long while. "You know," he said, "I think I like the sound of that."

Her eyes warmed further, a blush stealing across her freckled cheeks. "You said *home* earlier. At the bar."

He had. He'd tried not to think about it.

She went on, "I know you're supposed to live in the barracks or whatever Micah insists on, but if we somehow solve this case . . . that room is yours, if you want it."

The offer rippled through him. And he couldn't think of a single word beyond "Thanks." It was all that was necessary, he realized.

The rice finished cooking, and she divvied it into two bowls before dumping the meat mixture on top of it. She extended one to him. "Nothing gourmet, but . . . here. I'm sorry for earlier."

Hunt studied the steaming heap of meat and rice. He'd seen dogs served fancier meals. But he smiled slightly, his chest inexplicably tightening again. "Apology accepted, Quinlan."

* * *

A cat was sitting on her dresser.

Exhaustion weighed her eyelids, so heavily she could barely raise them.

Eyes like the sky before dawn pinned her to the spot.

What blinds an Oracle, Bryce Quinlan?

Her mouth formed a word, but sleep tugged her back into its embrace.

The cat's blue eyes simmered. *What blinds an Oracle?*

She fought to keep her eyes open at the question, the urgency.

You know, she tried to say.

The Autumn King's only daughter—thrown out like rubbish.

The cat had either guessed it at the temple all those years ago, or followed her home to confirm whose villa she had tried to enter.

He'll kill me if he knows.

The cat licked a paw. *Then make the Drop.*

She tried to speak again. Sleep held her firm, but she finally managed, *And what then?*

The cat's whiskers twitched. *I told you. Come find me.*

Her eyelids drooped—a final descent toward sleep. *Why?*

The cat angled its head. *So we can finish this.*

53

It was still raining the next morning, which Bryce decided was an omen.

Today would suck. Last night had sucked.

Syrinx refused to emerge from under the sheets, even though Bryce tried to coax him with the promise of breakfast *before* his walk, and by the time Bryce finally hauled him to the street below, Hunt monitoring from the windows, the rain had gone from a pleasant patter to an outright deluge.

A fat hoptoad squatted in the corner of the building doorway, under the slight overhang, waiting for any small, unfortunate Vanir to fly past. He eyed Bryce and Syrinx as they splashed by, earning a whiskery huff from the latter, and sidled closer to the side of the building.

"Creep," she murmured above the drumming rain on the hood of her coat, feeling the hoptoad watch them down the block. For a creature no bigger than her fist, they found ways to be menaces. Namely to all manner of sprites. Even confined to the library, Lehabah loathed and dreaded them.

Despite her navy raincoat, her black leggings and white T-shirt were soon soaked. As if the rain somehow went *up* from the ground. It pooled in her green rain boots, too, squelching with every step she made through the lashing rain, the palms swaying and hissing overhead.

The rainiest spring on record, the news had proclaimed last night. She didn't doubt it.

The hoptoad was still there when they returned, Syrinx having completed his morning routine in record time, and Bryce might or might not have gone out of her way to stomp in a nearby puddle.

The hoptoad had stuck out his tongue at her, but flopped away.

Hunt was standing at the stove, cooking something that smelled like bacon. He glanced over his shoulder while she removed her raincoat, dripping all over the floor. "You hungry?"

"I'm good."

His eyes narrowed. "You should eat something before we go."

She waved him off, scooping food into Syrinx's bowl.

When she stood, she found Hunt extending a plate toward her. Bacon and eggs and thick brown toast. "I watched you pick at your food for five days this past week," he said roughly. "We're not starting down that road again."

She rolled her eyes. "I don't need a male telling me when to eat."

"How about a friend telling you that you had an understandably rough night, and you get mean as shit when you're hungry?"

Bryce scowled. Hunt just kept holding out the plate.

"It's all right to be nervous, you know," he said. He nodded toward the paper bag she'd left by the door—Danika's clothes, folded and ready for analysis. She'd overheard Hunt calling Viktoria thirty minutes ago, asking her to get the Mimir tech from the Fae. She'd said Declan already sent it.

Bryce said, "I'm not nervous. They're just clothes." He only stared at her. Bryce growled. "I'm not. Let them lose the clothes in Evidence or whatever."

"Then eat."

"I don't like eggs."

His mouth twitched upward. "I've seen you eat about three dozen of them."

Their gazes met and held. "Who taught you to cook, anyway?"

He sure as Hel was a better cook than she was. The pitiful dinner she'd made him last night was proof.

"I taught myself. It's a useful skill for a soldier. Makes you a popular person in any legion camp. Besides, I've got two centuries under my belt. It'd be pathetic not to know how to cook at this point." He held the plate closer. "Eat up, Quinlan. I won't let anyone lose those clothes."

She debated throwing the plate in his face, but finally took it and plunked into the seat at the head of the dining table. Syrinx trotted over to her, already gazing expectantly at the bacon.

A cup of coffee appeared on the table a heartbeat later, the cream still swirling inside.

Hunt smirked at her. "Wouldn't want you to head out to the world without the proper provisions."

Bryce flipped him off, took his phone from where he'd left it on the table, and snapped a few pictures: the breakfast, the coffee, his stupid smirking face, Syrinx sitting beside her, and her own scowl. But she drank the coffee anyway.

By the time she put her mug into the sink, Hunt finishing up his meal at the table behind her, she found her steps feeling lighter than they had in a while.

"Don't lose those," Hunt warned Viktoria as she sifted through the bag on her desk.

The wraith looked up from the faded gray band T-shirt with a wailing, robed figure on the front. *The Banshees.* "We've got clothes in Evidence for Danika Fendyr and the other victims."

"Fine, but use these, too," Hunt said. Just in case someone had tampered with the evidence here—and to let Quinlan feel as if she'd helped with this. Bryce was at the gallery dealing with some snooty customer, with Naomi watching. "You got the Mimir tech from Declan?"

"As I said on the phone: yes." Vik peered into the bag again. "I'll give you a call if anything comes up."

Hunt stretched a piece of paper across the desk. "See if traces of any of these come up, too."

Viktoria took one look at the words on it and went pale, her halo stark over her brow. "You think it's one of these demons?"

"I hope not."

He'd made a list of potential demons that might be working in conjunction with the kristallos, all ancient and terrible, his dread deepening with each new name he added. Many of them were nightmares that prowled bedtime stories. All of them were catastrophic if they entered Midgard. He'd faced two of them before—and barely made it through the encounters.

Hunt nodded toward the bag again. "I mean it: don't lose those clothes," he said again.

"Going soft, Athalar?"

Hunt rolled his eyes and aimed for the doorway. "I just like my balls where they are."

Viktoria notified Hunt that evening that she was still running the diagnostic. The Fae's Mimir tech was thorough enough that it'd take a good while to run.

He prayed the results wouldn't be as devastating as he expected.

He'd messaged Bryce about it while she finished up work, chuckling when he saw that she'd again changed her contact information in his phone: *Bryce Is a Queen.*

They stayed up until midnight binge-watching a reality show about a bunch of hot young Vanir working at a beach club in the Coronal Islands. He'd refused at first—but by the end of the first hour, he'd been the one pressing play on the next episode. Then the next.

It hadn't hurt that they'd gone from sitting on opposite ends of the sectional to being side by side, his thigh pressed against hers. He might have toyed with her braid. She might have let him.

The next morning, Hunt was just following Bryce toward the apartment elevator when his phone rang. He took one look at the number and grimaced before picking up. "Hi, Micah."

"My office. Fifteen minutes."

Bryce pressed the elevator button, but Hunt pointed to the roof door. He'd fly her to the gallery, then head to the CBD. "All right," he said carefully. "Do you want Miss Quinlan to join us?"

"Just you." The line went dead.

54

Hunt took a back entrance into the tower, careful to avoid any area that Sandriel might be frequenting. Isaiah hadn't picked up, and he knew better than to keep calling until he did.

Micah was staring out the window when he arrived, his power already a brewing storm in the room. "Why," the Archangel asked, "are you running Fae tests on old evidence down at the lab?"

"We have good reason to think the demon we identified isn't the one behind Danika Fendyr's death. If we can find what actually did kill her, it might lead us to whoever summoned it."

"The Summit is in two weeks."

"I know. We're working as hard as we can."

"Are you? Drinking at a whiskey bar with Bryce Quinlan counts as working?"

Asshole. "We're on it. Don't worry."

"Sabine Fendyr called my office, you know. To rip my head off about being a *suspect*." There was nothing humane behind those eyes. Only cold predator.

"It was a mistake, and we'll own up to that, but we had sufficient cause to believe—"

"Get. The. Job. Done."

Hunt gritted out, "We will."

Micah surveyed him coolly. Then he said, "Sandriel has

been asking about you—about Miss Quinlan, too. She's made me a few generous offers to trade again." Hunt's stomach became leaden. "I've turned her down so far. I told her that you're too valuable to me."

Micah threw a file on the table, then turned back to the window. "Don't make me reconsider, Hunt."

Hunt read through the file—the silent order it conveyed. His punishment. For Sabine, for taking too long, for just existing. A death for a death.

He stopped at the barracks to pick up his helmet.

Micah had written a note in the margin of the list of targets, their crimes. *No guns.*

So Hunt grabbed a few more of his black-hilted daggers, and his long-handled knife, too.

Every movement was careful. Deliberate. Every shift of his body as he donned his black battle-suit quieted his mind, pulling him farther and farther from himself.

His phone buzzed on his desk, and he glanced at it only long enough to see that *Bryce Is a Queen* had written to him: *Everything okay?*

Hunt slid on his black gloves.

His phone buzzed again.

I'm going to order in dumpling soup for lunch. Want some?

Hunt turned the phone over, blocking the screen from view. As if it'd somehow stop her from learning what he was doing. He gathered his weapons with centuries of efficiency. And then donned the helmet.

The world descended into cool calculations, its colors dimmed.

Only then did he pick up his phone and write back to Bryce, *I'm good. I'll see you later.*

She'd written back by the time he reached the barracks landing pad. He'd watched the typing bubble pop up, vanish, then pop up again. Like she'd written out ten different replies before settling on *Okay.*

Hunt shut off his phone as he shouldered his way through the doors and into the open air.

He was a stain against the brightness. A shadow standing against the sun.

A flap of his wings had him skyborne. And he did not look back.

Something was wrong.

Bryce had known it the moment she realized she hadn't heard from him after an hour in the Comitium.

The feeling had only worsened at his vague response to her message. No mention of why he'd been called in, what he was up to.

As if someone else had written it for him.

She'd typed out a dozen different replies to that not-Hunt message.

Please tell me everything is okay.

Type 1 if you need help.

Did I do something to upset you?

What's wrong?

Do you need me to come to the Comitium?

Turning down an offer of dumpling soup—did someone steal this phone?

On and on, writing and deleting, until she'd written, *I'm worried. Please call me.* But she had no right to be worried, to demand those things of him.

So she'd settled with a pathetic *Okay.*

And had not heard back from him. She'd checked her phone obsessively the whole workday.

Nothing.

Worry was a writhing knot in her stomach. She didn't even order the soup. A glance at the roof cameras showed Naomi sitting there all day, her face tight.

Bryce had gone up there around three. "Do you have any idea where he might have gone?" she asked, her arms wrapped tightly around herself.

Naomi looked her over. "Hunt is fine," she said. "He . . ." She stopped herself, reading something on Bryce's face. Surprise flickered in her eyes. "He's fine," the angel said gently.

By the time Bryce got home, with Naomi stationed on the adjacent rooftop, she had stopped believing her.

So she'd decided to Hel with it. To Hel with caution or looking cool or any of it.

Standing in her kitchen as the clock crept toward eight, she wrote to Hunt, *Please call me. I'm worried about you.*

There. Let it shoot into the ether or wherever the messages floated.

She walked Syrinx one final time for the night, her phone clutched in her hand. As if the harder she gripped it, the more likely he'd be to respond.

It was eleven by the time she broke, and dialed a familiar number. Ruhn picked up on the first ring. "What's wrong?"

How he knew, she didn't care. "I . . ." She swallowed.

"Bryce." Ruhn's voice sharpened. Music was playing in the background, but it began to shift, as if he were moving to a quieter part of wherever he was.

"Have you seen Hunt anywhere today?" Her voice sounded thin and high.

In the background, Flynn asked, "Is everything okay?"

Ruhn just asked her, "What happened?"

"Like, have you seen Hunt at the gun range, or anywhere—"

The music faded. A door slammed. "Where are you?"

"Home." It hit her then, the rush of how stupid this was, calling him, asking if Ruhn, of all people, knew what the Governor's personal assassin was doing.

"Give me five minutes—"

"No, I don't need you here. I'm fine. I just . . ." Her throat burned. "I can't find him." What if Hunt was lying in a pile of bones and flesh and blood?

When her silence dragged on, Ruhn said with quiet intensity, "I'll put Dec and Flynn on it right—"

The enchantments hummed, and the front door unlocked.

Bryce went still as the door slowly opened. As Hunt, clad in battle-black and wearing that famed helmet, walked in.

Every step seemed like it took all of his concentration. And his scent—

Blood.

Not his own.

"Bryce?"

"He's back," she breathed into the phone. "I'll call you tomorrow," she said to her brother, and hung up.

Hunt paused in the center of the room.

Blood stained his wings. Shone on his leather suit. Splattered the visor of his helmet.

"What—what happened?" she managed to get out.

He began walking again. Walked straight past her, the scent of all that blood—several different types of blood—staining the air. He didn't say a word.

"Hunt." Any relief that had surged through her now transformed into something sharper.

He headed for his room and did not stop. She didn't dare to move. He was a wraith, a demon, a—a shadow of death.

This male, helmeted and in his battle clothes . . . she didn't know him.

Hunt reached his room, not even looking at her as he shut the door behind him.

He couldn't stand it.

He couldn't stand the look of pure, knee-wobbling relief on her face when he'd walked into the apartment. He'd come right back here after he'd finished because he thought she'd be asleep and he could wash off the blood without having to go back to the Comitium barracks first, but she'd been just standing in the living room. Waiting for him.

And as he'd stepped into the apartment and she'd seen and smelled the blood . . .

He couldn't stand the horror and pain on her face, either.

You see what this life has done to me? he wanted to ask. But he had been beyond words. There had been only screaming until now. From the three males he'd spent hours ending, all of it done to Micah's specifications.

Hunt strode for the bathroom and turned the shower up to scalding. He removed the helmet, the bright lights stinging his eyes without the visor's cooling tones. Then he removed his gloves.

She had looked so horrified. It was no surprise. She couldn't have really understood what he was, who he was, until now. Why people shied away from him. Didn't meet his eyes.

Hunt peeled his suit off, his bruised skin already healing. The drug lords he'd ended tonight had gotten in a few blows before he'd subdued them. Before he'd pinned them to the ground, impaled on his blades.

And left them there, shrieking in pain, for hours.

Naked, he stepped into the shower, the white tiles already sweating with steam.

The scalding water blasted his skin like acid.

He swallowed his scream, his sob, his whimper, and didn't balk from the boiling torrent.

Didn't do anything as he let it burn everything away.

Micah had sent him on a mission. Had ordered Hunt to kill someone. Several people, from the different scents on him. Did each one of those lives count toward his hideous *debt*?

It was his job, his path to freedom, what he did for the Governor, and yet . . . And yet Bryce had never really considered it. What it did to him. What the consequences were.

It wasn't a path to freedom. It was a path to Hel.

Bryce lingered in the living room, waiting for him to finish showering. The water kept running. Twenty minutes. Thirty. Forty.

When the clock crept up on an hour, she found herself knocking on his door. "Hunt?"

No answer. The water continued.

She cracked the door, peering into the dim bedroom. The

bathroom door stood open, steam wafting out. So much steam that the bedroom had turned muggy.

"Hunt?" She pushed forward, craning her neck to see into the bright bathroom. No sign of him in the shower—

A hint of a soaked gray wing rose from behind the shower glass.

She moved, not thinking. Not caring.

She was in the bathroom in a heartbeat, his name on her lips, bracing for the worst, wishing she'd grabbed her phone from the kitchen counter—

But there he was. Sitting naked on the floor of the shower, his head bowed between his knees. Water pounded into his back, his wings, dripping off his hair. His gold-dusted brown skin gleamed an angry red.

Bryce took one step into the shower and hissed. The water was scalding. Burning hot.

"Hunt," she said. He didn't so much as blink.

She glanced between him and the showerhead. His body was healing the burns—healing and then scalding, healing and scalding. It had to be torturous.

She bit down on her yelp as she reached into the shower, the near-boiling water soaking her shirt, her pants, and lowered the temperature.

He didn't move. Didn't even look at her. He'd done this many times, she realized. Every time Micah had sent him out, and for all the Archangels he'd served before that.

Syrinx came to investigate, sniffed at the bloody clothes, then sprawled himself on the bath mat, head on his front paws.

Hunt made no indication that he knew she stood there.

But his breathing deepened. Became easier.

And she couldn't explain why she did it, but she grabbed a bottle of shampoo and the block of lavender soap from the nook in the tiles. Then knelt before him.

"I'm going to clean you off," she said quietly. "If that's all right."

A slight but terribly clear nod was his only response. Like words were still too hard.

So Bryce poured the shampoo into her hands, and then laced

her fingers into his hair. The thick strands were heavy, and she gently scrubbed, tipping his head back to rinse it. His eyes lifted at last. Met hers, as his head leaned back into the stream of water.

"You look how I feel," she whispered, her throat tight. "Every day."

He blinked, his only sign that he'd heard.

She removed her hands from his hair, and picked up the bar of soap. He was naked, she realized, having somehow forgotten. Utterly naked. She didn't let herself contemplate it as she began lathering his neck, his powerful shoulders, his muscled arms. "I'll leave your bottom half for you to enjoy," she said, her face heating.

He was just watching her with that raw openness. More intimate than any touch of his lips on her neck. Like he indeed saw everything she was and had been and might yet become.

She scrubbed down his upper body as best she could. "I can't clean your wings with you sitting against the wall."

Hunt rose to his feet in a mighty, graceful push.

She kept her eyes averted from what, exactly, this brought into her direct line of vision. The very considerable something that he didn't seem to notice or care about.

So she wouldn't care about it, either. She stood, water splattering her, and gently turned him. She didn't let herself admire the view from behind, either. The muscles and perfection of him.

Your ass is perfect, he'd said to her.

Likewise, she could now attest.

She soaped his wings, now dark gray in the water.

He towered over her, enough that she had to rise to her toes to reach the apex of his wings. In silence, she washed him, and Hunt braced his hands against the tiles, his head hanging. He needed rest, and the comfort of oblivion. So Bryce rinsed off the soap, making sure each and every feather was clean, and then reached around the angel to turn off the shower.

Only the dribbling of water eddying into the drain filled the steamy bathroom.

Bryce grabbed a towel, keeping her eyes up as Hunt turned to face her. She slung it around his hips, yanked a second towel off the bar just outside the shower stall, and ran it over his tan skin. Gently patted his wings dry. Then rubbed his hair.

"Come on," she murmured. "Bed."

His face became more alert, but he didn't object when she tugged him from the shower, dripping water from her sodden clothes and hair. Didn't object when she led him into the bedroom, to the chest of drawers where he'd put his things.

She pulled out a pair of black undershorts and stooped down, eyes firmly on the ground as she stretched out the waistband. "Step in."

Hunt obeyed, first one foot and then the other. She rose, sliding the shorts up his powerful thighs and releasing the elastic waist with a soft snap. Bryce snatched a white T-shirt from another drawer, frowned at the complicated slats on the back to fit his wings, and set it down again. "Underwear it is," she declared, pulling back the blanket on the bed he so dutifully made each morning. She patted the mattress. "Get some sleep, Hunt."

Again, he obeyed, sliding between the sheets with a soft groan.

She shut off the bathroom light, darkening the bedroom, and returned to where he now lay, still staring at her. Daring to stroke his damp hair away from his brow, Bryce's fingers grazed over the hateful tattoo. His eyes closed.

"I was so worried about you," she whispered, stroking his hair again. "I . . ." She couldn't finish the sentence. So she made to step back, to head to her room and change into dry clothes and maybe get some sleep herself.

But a warm, strong hand gripped her wrist. Halted her.

She looked back, and found Hunt staring at her again. "What?"

A slight tug on her wrist told her everything.

Stay.

Her chest squeezed to the point of pain. "Okay." She took a breath. "Okay, sure."

And for some reason, the thought of going all the way to her bedroom, of leaving him for even a moment, seemed too risky. Like he might vanish again if she left to change.

So she grabbed the white T-shirt she'd intended to give him, and twisted away, peeling off her own shirt and bra and chucking them into the bathroom. They landed with a slap on the tiles, drowning out the rustle of his soft shirt as she slid it over herself. It hung down to her knees, providing enough coverage that she shucked off her wet sweats and underwear and threw them into the bathroom, too.

Syrinx had leapt into the bed, curling at the foot. And Hunt had moved over, giving her ample room. "Okay," she said again, more to herself.

The sheets were warm, and smelled of him—rain-kissed cedar. She tried not to breathe it in too obviously as she took up a sitting position against the headboard. And she tried not to look too shocked when he laid his head on her thigh, his arm coming across her to rest on the pillow.

A child laying his head on his mother's lap. A friend looking for any sort of reassuring contact to remind him that he was a living being. A good person, no matter what they made him do.

Bryce tentatively brushed the hair from his brow again.

Hunt's eyes closed, but he leaned slightly into the touch. A silent request.

So Bryce continued stroking his hair, over and over, until his breathing deepened and steadied, until his powerful body grew limp beside hers.

It smelled like paradise. Like home and eternity and like exactly where he was meant to be.

Hunt opened his eyes to feminine softness and warmth and gentle breathing.

In the dim light, he found himself half-sprawled across Bryce's lap, the woman herself passed out against the headboard, head lolling to the side. Her hand still lingered in his hair, the other in the sheets by his arm.

The clock read three thirty. It wasn't the time that surprised him, but the fact that he was clearheaded enough to notice.

She'd taken care of him. Washed and clothed and soothed him. He couldn't remember the last time anyone had done that.

Hunt carefully peeled his face from her lap, realizing that her legs were bare. That she wasn't wearing anything beneath his T-shirt. And his face had been mere inches away.

His muscles protested only slightly as he rose upward. Bryce didn't so much as stir.

She'd put him in his underwear, for fuck's sake.

His cheeks warmed, but he eased from the bed, Syrinx opening an eye to see what the commotion was about. He waved the beastie off and padded to Bryce's side of the mattress.

She stirred only slightly as he scooped her into his arms and carried her to her own room. He laid her on her bed, and she grumbled, protesting at the cool sheets, but he swiftly tossed the down comforter over her and left before she could awaken.

He was halfway across the living area when her phone, discarded on the kitchen counter, glared with light. Hunt looked at it, unable to help himself.

A chain of messages from Ruhn filled the screen, all from the past few hours.

Is Athalar all right? Later, *Are you all right?*

Then, an hour ago, *I called the front desk of your building, and the doorman reassured me that you're both up there, so I'm assuming you two are fine. But call me in the morning.*

And then from thirty seconds ago, as if it were an afterthought, *I'm glad you called me tonight. I know things are fucked up between us, and I know a lot of that is my fault, but if you ever need me, I'm here. Anytime at all, Bryce.*

Hunt glanced toward her bedroom hallway. She'd called Ruhn—that's who she'd been on the phone with when he got back. He rubbed at his chest.

He fell back asleep in his own bed, where the scent of her still lingered, like a phantom, warming touch.

55

The golden rays of dawn coaxed Bryce awake. The blankets were warm, and the bed soft, and Syrinx was still snoring—

Her room. Her bed.

She sat up, jostling Syrinx awake. He yowled in annoyance and slithered deeper under the covers, kicking her in the ribs with his hind legs for good measure.

Bryce left him to it, sliding from bed and leaving her room within seconds. Hunt must have moved her at some point. He'd been in no shape to do anything like that, and if he'd somehow been forced to go back out again—

She sighed as she glimpsed a gray wing draped over the guest room bed. The golden-brown skin of a muscled back. Rising and falling. Still asleep.

Thank the gods. Rubbing her hands over her face, sleep a lost cause, she padded for the kitchen and began to make coffee. She needed a strong cup of it, then a quick run. She let muscle memory take over, and as the coffee maker buzzed and rattled away, she scooped up her phone from the counter.

Ruhn's messages occupied most of her alerts. She read through them twice.

He would have dropped everything to come over. Put his friends on the task of finding Hunt. Would have done it without question. She knew that—had made herself forget it.

She knew why, too. Had been well aware that her reaction to their argument years ago had been justified, but overblown. He'd tried to apologize, and she had only used it against him. And he must have felt guilty enough that he'd never questioned why she'd cut him out of her life. That he'd never realized that it hadn't just been some slight hurt that had forced her to shut him off from her life, but fear. Absolute terror.

He'd wounded her, and it had scared the Hel out of her that he held such power. That she had wanted so many things from him, imagined so many things with her brother—adventures and holidays and ordinary moments—and he had the ability to rip it all away.

Bryce's thumbs hovered over the keyboard on her phone, as if searching for the right words. *Thank you* would be good. Or even *I'll call you later* would suffice, since maybe she should actually say those words aloud.

But her thumbs remained aloft, the words slipping and tumbling past.

So she let them fall by, and turned to the other message she'd received—from Juniper.

Madame Kyrah told me that you never showed up to her class. What the Hel, Bryce? I had to beg her to hold that spot for you. She was really mad.

Bryce ground her teeth. She wrote back, *Sorry. Tell her I'm in the middle of working on something for the Governor and got called away.*

Bryce set down the phone and turned to the coffee machine. Her phone buzzed a second later. Juniper had to be on her way to morning practice, then.

This woman does not peddle in excuses. I worked hard to get her to like me, Bryce.

June was definitely pissed if she was calling her *Bryce* instead of *B*.

Bryce wrote back, *I'm sorry, okay? I told you I was a maybe. You shouldn't have let her think I'd be there.*

Juniper sniped back, *Whatever. I gotta go.*

Bryce blew out a breath, forcing herself to unclench her fingers from around her phone. She cradled her mug of hot coffee.

"Hey."

She whirled to find Hunt leaning a hip against the marble island. For someone heavily muscled and winged, the angel was stealthy, she had to admit. He'd put on a shirt and pants, but his hair was still sleep-mussed.

She rasped, her knees wobbling only slightly, "How are you feeling?"

"Fine." The word held no bite, only a quiet resignation and a request not to push. So Bryce fished out another mug, set it in the coffee machine, and hit a few buttons that had it brewing.

His gaze brushed over every part of her like a physical touch. She peered down at herself and realized why. "Sorry I took one of your shirts," she said, bunching the white fabric in a hand. Gods, she wasn't wearing any underwear. Did he know?

His eyes dipped toward her bare legs and went a shade darker. He definitely knew.

Hunt pushed off the island, stalking toward her, and Bryce braced herself. For what, she didn't know, but—

He just strode past. Right to the fridge, where he pulled out eggs and the slab of bacon. "At the risk of sounding like an alphahole cliché," he said without looking at her as he set the skillet on the stove, "I like seeing you in my shirt."

"Total alphahole cliché," she said, even as her toes curled on the pale wood floor.

Hunt cracked the eggs into a bowl. "We always seem to end up in the kitchen."

"I don't mind," Bryce said, sipping her coffee, "as long as you're cooking."

Hunt snorted, then stilled. "Thanks," he said quietly. "For what you did."

"Don't mention it," she said, taking another sip of coffee. Remembering the one she'd brewed for him, she reached for the now-full mug.

Hunt turned from the stove as she extended the coffee to him. Glanced between the outstretched mug and her face.

And as his large hand wrapped around the mug, he leaned in,

closing the space between them. His mouth brushed over her cheek. Brief and light and sweet.

"Thank you," he said again, pulling back and returning to the stove. As if he didn't notice that she couldn't move a single muscle, couldn't find a single word to utter.

The urge to grab him, to pull his face down to hers and taste every part of him practically blinded her. Her fingers twitched at her sides, nearly able to feel those hard muscles beneath them.

He had a long-lost love he was still holding a torch for. And she'd just gone too long without sex. Cthona's tits, it'd been weeks since that hookup with the lion shifter in the Raven's bathroom. And with Hunt here, she hadn't dared open up her left nightstand to take care of herself.

Keep telling yourself all that, a small voice said.

The muscles in Hunt's back stiffened. His hands paused whatever they were doing.

Shit, he could smell this kind of thing, couldn't he? Most Vanir males could. The shifts in a person's scent: fear and arousal being the two big ones.

He was the Umbra Mortis. Off-limits in ten million ways. And the Umbra Mortis didn't date—no, it'd be all or nothing with him.

Hunt asked, voice like gravel, "What are you thinking about?" He didn't turn from the stove.

You. Like a fucking idiot, I'm thinking about you.

"There's a sample sale at one of the designer stores this afternoon," she lied.

Hunt glanced over his shoulder. Fuck, his eyes were dark. "Is that so?"

Was that a purr in his voice?

She couldn't help the step she took back, bumping into the kitchen island. "Yes," she said, unable to look away.

Hunt's eyes darkened further. He said nothing.

She couldn't breathe properly with that stare fixed on her. That stare that told her he scented everything going on in her body.

Her nipples pebbled under that stare.

Hunt went preternaturally still. His eyes dipped downward. Saw her breasts. The thighs she now clamped together—as if it'd stop the throbbing beginning to torture her between them.

His face went positively feral. A mountain cat ready to pounce. "I didn't know clothing sales got you so hot and bothered, Quinlan."

She nearly whimpered. Forced herself to keep still. "It's the little things in life, Athalar."

"Is that what you think about when you open up that left nightstand? Clothing sales?" He faced her fully now. She didn't dare let her gaze drop.

"Yes," she breathed. "All those clothes, all over my body." She had no idea what the fuck was coming out of her mouth.

How was it possible all the air in the apartment, the city, had been sucked out?

"Maybe you should buy some new underwear," he murmured, nodding to her bare legs. "Seems like you're out."

She couldn't stop it—the image that blazed over her senses: Hunt putting those big hands on her waist and hoisting her onto the counter currently pressing into her spine, shoving her T-shirt over her midriff—his T-shirt, actually—and spreading her legs wide. Fucking her with his tongue, then his cock, until she was sobbing in pleasure, screaming with it, she didn't care just so long as he was touching her, inside her—

"Quinlan." He seemed to be shaking now. As if only a tether of pure will kept him in place. As if he'd seen the same burning image and was just waiting for her nod.

It'd complicate everything. The investigation, whatever he felt for Shahar, her own life—

To fucking Hel with all that. They'd figure it out later. They'd—

Burning smoke filled the air between them. Gross, nose-stinging smoke.

"Fuck," Hunt hissed, whirling to the stove and the eggs he'd left on the burner.

As if a witch spell had snapped, Bryce blinked, the dizzying heat vanishing. Oh gods. His emotions had to be all over the place after last night, and hers were a mess on a good day, and—

"I have to get dressed for work," she managed to say, and hurried toward her bedroom before he could turn from the burning breakfast.

She'd lost her mind, she told herself in the shower, in the bathroom, on the too-quiet walk to work with Syrinx, Hunt trailing overhead. Keeping his distance. As if he realized the same thing.

Let someone in, give them the power to hurt you, and they'd do exactly that, in the end.

She couldn't do it. Endure it.

Bryce had resigned herself to that fact by the time she reached the gallery. A glance upward showed Hunt making his descent as Syrinx yipped happily, and the thought of a day in an enclosed space with him, with only Lehabah as a buffer . . .

Thank fucking Urd, her phone rang as she opened the gallery door. But it wasn't Ruhn calling to check in, and it wasn't Juniper with an earful about missing the dance class. "Jesiba."

The sorceress didn't bother with pleasantries. "Get the back door open. Now."

"Oh, it's horrible, BB," Lehabah whispered in the dimness of the library. "Just horrible."

Staring up at the massive, dimly lit tank, Bryce felt her arm hair stand on end as she watched their new addition explore its environment. Hunt crossed his arms and peered into the gloom. Any thoughts of getting naked with him had vanished an hour ago.

A dark, scaled hand slapped against the thick glass, ivory claws scraping. Bryce swallowed. "I want to know where anyone even found a nøkk in these waters." From what she'd heard, they existed only in the icy seas of the north, and mostly in Pangera.

"I preferred the kelpie," Lehabah whispered, shrinking behind her little divan, her flame a quivering yellow.

As if it had heard them, the nøkk paused before the glass and smiled.

At more than eight feet long, the nøkk might have very well been the Helish twin to a mer male. But instead of humanoid features, the nøkk presented a jutting lower jaw with a too-wide, lipless mouth, full of needle-thin teeth. Its overlarge eyes were milky, like some of the fishes of the deep. Its tail was mostly translucent—bony and sharp—and above it, a warped, muscled torso rose.

No hair covered its chest or head, and its four-fingered hands ended in daggerlike claws.

With the tank spanning the entire length of one side of the library, there would be no escaping its presence, unless the nøkk went down to the cluster of dark rocks at the bottom. The creature dragged those claws over the glass again. The inked *SPQM* gleamed stark white on his greenish-gray wrist.

Bryce lifted her phone to her ear. Jesiba picked up on the first ring. "Yes?"

"We have a problem."

"With the Korsaki contract?" Jesiba's voice was low, as if she didn't want to be overheard.

"No." Bryce scowled at the nøkk. "The creep in the aquarium needs to go."

"I'm in a meeting."

"Lehabah is scared as Hel."

Air was lethal to nøkks—if one was exposed for more than a few seconds, its vital organs would begin shutting down, its skin peeling away as if burned. But Bryce had still gone up the small stairwell to the right of the tank to ensure that the feeding hatch built into the grate atop the water was thoroughly locked. The hatch itself was a square platform that could be raised and lowered into the water, operated by a panel of controls in the rear of the space atop the tank, and Bryce had triple-checked that the machine was completely turned off.

When she'd returned to the library, she'd found Lehabah curled into a ball behind a book, the sprite's flame a sputtering yellow.

Lehabah whispered from her couch, "He's a hateful, horrible creature."

Bryce shushed her. "Can't you gift him to some macho loser in Pangera?"

"I'm hanging up now."

"But he's—"

The line went dead. Bryce slumped into her seat at the table. "Now she'll just keep him forever," she told the sprite.

"What are you going to feed it?" Hunt asked as the nøkk again tested the glass wall, feeling with those terrible hands.

"It loves humans," Lehabah whispered. "They drag swimmers under the surface of ponds and lakes and drown them, then slowly feast on their corpses over days and days—"

"Beef," Bryce said, her stomach turning as she glanced at the small door to access the stairwell to the top of the tank. "He'll get a few steaks a day."

Lehabah cowered. "Can't we put up a curtain?"

"Jesiba will just rip it down."

Hunt offered, "I could pile some books on this table—block your view of him instead."

"He'll still know where I am, though." Lehabah pouted at Bryce. "I can't sleep with it in here."

Bryce sighed. "What if you just pretend he's an enchanted prince or something?"

The sprite pointed toward the tank. To the nøkk hovering in the water, tail thrashing. Smiling at them. "A prince from Hel."

"Who would want a nøkk for a pet?" Hunt asked, sprawling himself across from Bryce at the desk.

"A sorceress who chose to join Flame and Shadow and turns her enemies into animals." Bryce motioned to the smaller tanks and terrariums built into the shelves around them, then rubbed at the persistent ache in her thigh beneath her pink dress. When she'd finally worked up the nerve to emerge from her bedroom this morning after the kitchen fiasco, Hunt had looked at her for a long, long moment. But he'd said nothing.

"You should see a medwitch about that leg," he said now. Hunt didn't look up from where he was leafing through some report Justinian had sent over that morning for a second opinion. She'd asked what it was, but he'd told her it was classified, and that was that.

"My leg is fine." She didn't bother to turn from where she once again began typing in the details for the Korsaki contract Jesiba was so eager to have finalized. Mindless busywork, but work that had to be done at some point.

Especially since they were again at a dead end. No word had arrived from Viktoria about the Mimir test results. Why Danika had stolen the Horn, who wanted it so badly that they'd kill her for it . . . Bryce still had no idea. But if Ruhn was right about a method to heal the Horn . . . It all had to tie together somehow.

And she knew that while they'd killed the one kristallos demon, there were other kristallos waiting in Hel that could still be summoned to hunt the Horn. And if its kind had failed so far, when the breed had literally been created by the Princes of Hel to track the Horn . . . How could she even hope to find it?

Then there was the matter of those gruesome, pulping killings . . . which hadn't been done by a kristallos. Hunt had already put in a request to have the footage checked again, but nothing had come through.

Hunt's phone buzzed, and he fished it from his pocket, glimpsed at the screen, then put it away. From across the desk, she could just barely make out the text box of a message on the screen.

"Not going to write back?"

His mouth twisted to the side. "Just one of my colleagues, busting my balls." His eyes flickered when he looked at her, though. And when she smiled at him, shrugging, his throat bobbed—just slightly.

Hunt said a bit roughly, "I gotta head out for a while. Naomi will come to stand guard. I'll pick you up when you're ready to leave."

Before she could ask about it, he was gone.

* * *

"I know it's been a while," Bryce said, her phone wedged between her shoulder and ear.

Hunt had been waiting outside the gallery while she locked up, smiling at Syrinx scratching at the door. The chimera yowled in protest when he realized Bryce wasn't bringing him along yet, and Hunt stooped to scratch his fuzzy golden head before Bryce shut the door, locking him in.

"I'll have to look at my calendar," Bryce was saying, nodding her hello to Hunt.

She looked beautiful today, in a rose-pink dress, pearls at her ears, and hair swept back on either side with matching pearl combs.

Fuck, *beautiful* wasn't even the right word for it.

She'd emerged from her bedroom and he'd been struck stupid.

She hadn't seemed to notice that *he'd* noticed, though he supposed she knew that she looked gorgeous every day. Yet there was a light to her today, a color that hadn't been there before, a glow in her amber eyes and flush to her skin.

But that pink dress . . . It had distracted him all day.

So had their encounter in the kitchen this morning. He'd done his best to ignore it—to forget about how close he'd come to begging her to touch him, to let him touch her. It hadn't stopped him from being in a state of semi-arousal all day.

He had to get his shit together. Considering that their investigation had slowed this past week, he couldn't afford distractions. Couldn't afford to ogle her every time she wasn't looking. This afternoon, she'd been rising up onto her toes, arm straining to grab some book on a high shelf in the library, and it was like that color pink was the fucking Horn, and he was a kristallos demon.

He'd been out of his chair in an instant, at her side a heartbeat after that, and had pulled the book off the shelf for her.

She'd stood there, though, when he'd held the book out. Hadn't backed up a step as she looked between the outstretched book and his face. His blood had begun pounding in his ears, his skin becoming too tight. Just like it had this morning when he'd seen her breasts peak, and had scented how filthy her own thoughts had turned.

But she'd just taken the book and walked away. Unfazed and unaware of his sheer stupidity.

It hadn't improved as the hours had passed. And when she'd smiled at him earlier . . . He'd been half-relieved to be called away from the gallery a minute later. It was while he was heading back, breathing in the brisk air off the Istros, that Viktoria sent him a message: *I found something. Meet me at Munin and Hugin in 15.*

He debated telling the wraith to wait. To delay the inevitable bad news coming their way, to go just a few more days with that beautiful smile on Bryce's face and that desire starting to smolder in her eyes, but . . . Micah's warnings rang in his ears. The Summit was still two weeks away, but Hunt knew Sandriel's presence had stretched Micah's patience thinner than usual. That if he delayed much longer, he'd find his bargain null and void.

So whatever intel Vik had, however bad . . . he'd find a way to deal with it. He called *Bryce Kicks Ass* and told her to get *her* ass outside to meet him.

"I don't know, Mom," Bryce was saying into her phone, falling into step with Hunt as they started down the street. The setting sun bathed the city in gold and orange, gilding even the puddles of filth. "Of course I miss you, but maybe next month?"

They passed an alley a few blocks away, neon signs pointing to the small tea bars and ancient food stalls cramming its length. Several tattoo shops lay interspersed, some of the artists or patrons smoking outside before the evening rush of drunken idiots.

"What—*this* weekend? Well, I have a guest—" She clicked her tongue. "No, it's a long story. He's like . . . a roommate? His name? Uh, Athie. *No*, Mom." She sighed. "This weekend *really* doesn't work. No, I'm not blowing you guys off again." She gritted her teeth. "What about a video chat, then? Mmhmm, yeah, of course I'll make the time." Bryce winced again. "Okay, Mom. Bye."

Bryce turned to him, grimacing.

"Your mom seems . . . insistent," Hunt said carefully.

"I'm video chatting with my parents at seven." She sighed at the sky. "They want to meet you."

Viktoria was at the bar when they arrived, a glass of whiskey in front of her. She offered them both a grave smile, then slid a file over as they seated themselves to her left.

"What did you find?" Bryce asked, opening the cream-colored folder.

"Read it," Viktoria said, then glanced toward the cameras in the bar. Recording everything.

Bryce nodded, taking the warning, and Hunt leaned closer as her head dipped to read, unable to stop himself from stretching out his wing, ever so slightly, around her back.

He forgot about it, though, when he beheld the test results. "This can't be right," he said quietly.

"That's what I said," Viktoria said, her narrow face impassive.

There, on the Fae's Mimir screening, lay the results: small bits of something synthetic. Not organic, not technological, not magic—but a combination of all three.

Find what is in-between, Aidas had said.

"Danika freelanced for Redner Industries," Bryce said. "They do all sorts of experiments. Would that explain this?"

"It might," Viktoria said. "But I'm running the Mimir on every other sample we have—from the others. Initial tests also came up positive on Maximus Tertian's clothes." The tattoo on Viktoria's brow bunched as she frowned. "It's not pure magic, or tech, or organic. It's a hybrid, with its other traces causing it to be canceled out in the other categories. A cloaking device, almost."

Bryce frowned. "What is it, exactly?"

Hunt knew Viktoria well enough to read the caution in the wraith's eyes. She said to Bryce, "It's some sort of . . . drug. From what I can find, it looks like it's mostly used for medical purposes in very small doses, but might have leaked onto the streets—which led to doses that are far from safe."

"Danika wouldn't have taken a drug like that."

"Of course not," Viktoria said quickly. "But she was exposed to it—all her clothes were. Whether that was upon her death or before it, however, is unclear. We're about to run the test on the samples we took from the Pack of Devils and the two most recent victims."

"Tertian was in the Meat Market," Hunt murmured. "He might have taken it."

But Bryce demanded, "What's it called? This thing?"

Viktoria pointed to the results. "Exactly what it sounds like. Synth."

Bryce whipped her head around to look at Hunt. "Ruhn said that medwitch mentioned a synthetic healing compound that could possibly repair . . ." She didn't finish the statement.

Hunt's eyes were dark as the Pit, a haunted look in them. "It might be the same one."

Viktoria held up her hands. "Again, I'm still testing the other victims, but . . . I just thought you should know."

Bryce hopped off the stool. "Thanks."

Hunt let her reach the front door before he murmured to the wraith, "Keep it quiet, Vik."

"Already wiped the files from the legion database," Vik said.

They barely spoke while they returned to the gallery, grabbed Syrinx, and headed home. Only when they stood in her kitchen, Hunt leaning against the counter, did he say, "Investigations can take time. We're getting closer. That's a good thing."

She dumped food in Syrinx's bowl, face unreadable. "What do you think about this synth?"

Hunt considered his words carefully. "As you said, it could have just been exposure Danika had at Redner. Tertian could have just taken it as a recreational drug right before he died. And we're still waiting to find out if it shows up on the clothes of the remaining victims."

"I want to know about it," she said, pulling out her phone and dialing.

"It might not be worth our—"

Ruhn picked up. "Yeah?"

"That synthetic healing drug you heard about from the medwitch. What do you know about it?"

"She sent over some research a couple days ago. A lot of it's been redacted by Redner Industries, but I'm going through it. Why?"

Bryce glanced toward Hunt's open bedroom door—to the photo of her and Danika on the dresser, Hunt realized. "There were traces of something called synth on Danika's clothes—it's a relatively new synthetic medicine. And it sounds like it's leaked onto the streets and is being used in higher concentrations as an illegal substance. I'm wondering if it's the same thing."

"Yeah, this research is on synth." Pages rustled in the background. "It can do some pretty amazing things. There's a list of ingredients here—again, a lot of it was redacted, but . . ."

Ruhn's silence was like a bomb dropping.

"But what?" Hunt said into the phone, leaning close enough to hear Bryce's thundering heart.

"Obsidian salt is listed as one of the ingredients."

"Obsidian . . ." Bryce blinked at Hunt. "Could the synth be used to summon a demon? If someone didn't have the power on their own, could the obsidian salt in the drug let them call on something like the kristallos?"

"I'm not sure," Ruhn said. "I'll read through this and let you know what I find."

"Okay." Bryce blew out a breath, and Hunt pulled a step away as she began pacing again. "Thanks, Ruhn."

Ruhn's pause was different this time. "No problem, Bryce." He hung up.

Hunt met her stare. She said, "We need to figure out who's selling this stuff. Tertian must have known before he died. We're going to the Meat Market." Because if there was one place in this city where a drug like that might be available, it'd be in that cesspit.

Hunt swallowed. "We need to be *careful*—"

"I want answers." She aimed for the front closet.

Hunt stepped into her path. "We'll go tomorrow." She drew up short, mouth opening. But Hunt shook his head. "Take tonight off."

"It can't—"

"Yes, it can wait, Bryce. Talk to your parents tonight. I'll put on some real clothes," he added, gesturing to his battle-suit. "And then tomorrow, we'll go to the Meat Market to ask around. It can wait." Hunt, despite himself, grabbed her hand. Ran his thumb over the back of it. "Enjoy talking to your parents, Bryce. They're *alive.* Don't miss out on a moment of it. Not for this." She still looked like she'd object, insist they go hunt down the synth, so he said, "I wish I had that luxury."

She looked down at his hand, gripping hers, for a second—for a lifetime. She asked, "What happened to your parents?"

He said, throat tight, "My mother never told me who my father is. And she . . . She was a low-ranking angel. She cleaned the villas of some of the more powerful angels, because they didn't trust humans or other Vanir to do it." His chest ached at the memory of his mother's beautiful, gentle face. Her soft smile and dark, angular eyes. The lullabies he could still hear, more than two hundred years later.

"She worked day and night to keep me fed and never once complained, because she knew that if she did, she'd be out of a job and she had me to think about. When I was a foot soldier, and sending home every copper I made, she refused to spend it. Apparently, someone heard I was doing that, thought she had tons of money hidden in her apartment, and broke in one night. Killed her and took the money. All five hundred silver marks she'd amassed over her life, and the fifty gold marks I'd managed to send her after five years in service."

"I am so sorry, Hunt."

"None of the angels—the powerful, adored angels—that my mother worked for bothered to care that she'd been killed. No one investigated who did it, and no one granted me leave to mourn. She was nothing to them. But she was . . . she was everything to me." His throat ached. "I made the Drop and joined Shahar's cause soon after that. I battled on Mount Hermon that day for her—my mother. In her memory." Shahar had taken those memories and made them into weapons.

Bryce's fingers pressed his. "It sounds like she was a remarkable person."

"She was." He pulled his hand away at last.

But she still smiled at him, his chest tightening to the point of pain as she said, "All right. I'll video chat my parents. Playing legionary with you can wait."

Bryce spent most of the evening cleaning. Hunt helped her, offering to fly over to the nearest apothecary and get an insta-clean spell, but Bryce waved him off. Her mom was such a neat freak, she claimed, that she could tell the difference between magically cleaned bathrooms and hand-scrubbed ones. Even on video chat.

It's that bleach smell that tells me it's been done properly, Bryce, her daughter had imitated to Hunt in a flat, no-nonsense voice that made him just a little nervous.

Bryce had used his phone throughout, snapping photos of him cleaning, of Syrinx taking the toilet paper rolls from their container and shredding them on the carpet they'd just vacuumed, of herself with Hunt stooped over his toilet behind her, brushing down the inside.

By the time he'd snatched the phone out of her gloved hands, she'd again changed her contact name, this time to *Bryce Is Cooler Than Me.*

But despite the smile it brought to his face, Hunt kept hearing Micah's voice, threats both spoken and implied. *Find who is behind this. Get. The. Job. Done. Don't make me reconsider our bargain. Before I take you off this case. Before I sell you back to Sandriel. Before I make you and Bryce Quinlan regret it.*

Once he solved this case, it would be over, wouldn't it? He'd still have ten kills left for Micah, which could easily take years to fulfill. He'd have to go back to the Comitium. To the 33rd.

He found himself looking at her while they cleaned. Taking out his phone and snapping some photos of her as well.

He knew too much. Had learned too much. About all of it. About what he might have had, without the halo and slave tattoos.

"I can open a bottle of wine, if you need some liquid courage," Bryce was saying as they sat before her computer at the kitchen island, the video chat service dialing her parents. She'd bought a bag of pastries from the corner market on their way home—a stress-coping device, he assumed.

Hunt just scanned her face. This—calling her parents, sitting thigh-to-thigh with her . . . Fucking Hel.

He was on a one-way collision course. He couldn't bring himself to stop it.

Before Hunt could open his mouth to suggest that this might be a mistake, a female voice said, "And why exactly would he need liquid courage, Bryce Adelaide Quinlan?"

56

A stunning woman in her mid-forties appeared on the screen, her sheet of black hair still untouched by gray, her freckled face just beginning to show the signs of a mortal life span.

From what Hunt could see, Ember Quinlan was seated on a worn green couch situated against oak-paneled walls, her long, jeans-clad legs folded beneath her.

Bryce rolled her eyes. "I'd say most people need liquid courage when dealing with you, Mom." But she smiled. One of those broad smiles that did funny things to Hunt's sense of balance.

Ember's dark eyes shifted toward Hunt. "I think Bryce is confusing me with herself."

Bryce waved off the comment. "Where's Dad?"

"He had a long day at work—he's making some coffee so he doesn't fall asleep."

Even through the video feed, Ember possessed a grounded sort of presence that commanded attention. She said, "You must be Athie."

Before he could answer, a male eased onto the couch beside Ember.

Bryce beamed in a way Hunt hadn't seen before. "Hey, Dad."

Randall Silago held two coffees, one of which he handed to Ember as he grinned back at his daughter. Unlike his wife, the years or the war had left their mark on him: his black braided hair was streaked with silver, his brown skin marred with a few brutal scars. But his dark eyes were friendly as he sipped from his mug—a chipped white one that said *Insert Cliché Dad Joke Here*. "I'm still scared of that fancy coffee machine you bought us for Winter Solstice," he said by way of greeting.

"I've shown you how to use it literally three times."

Her mother chuckled, toying with a silver pendant around her neck. "He's old-school."

Hunt had looked up how much the built-in machine in this apartment cost—if Bryce had bought them anything remotely similar, she must have dumped a considerable portion of her paycheck on it. Money she did not have. Not with her debt to Jesiba.

He doubted her parents knew that, doubted they'd have accepted that machine if they'd known the money could have gone toward paying back her debts to the sorceress.

Randall's eyes shifted to Hunt, the warmth cooling to something harder. The eyes of the fabled sharpshooter—the man who'd taught his daughter how to defend herself. "You must be Bryce's sort-of roommate." Hunt saw the man notice his tattoos—on his brow, on his wrist. Recognition flared across Randall's face.

Yet he didn't sneer. Didn't cringe.

Bryce elbowed Hunt in the ribs, reminding him to actually *speak*. "I'm Hunt Athalar," he said, glancing at Bryce. "Or Athie, as she and Lehabah call me."

Randall slowly set down his coffee. Yeah, that had been recognition in the man's face a moment ago. But Randall narrowed his eyes at his daughter. "You were going to mention this when, exactly?"

Bryce rootled through the pastry bag on the counter and pulled out a chocolate croissant. She bit in and said around it, "He's not as cool as you think, Dad."

Hunt snorted. "Thanks."

Ember said nothing. Didn't even move. But she watched every bite Bryce took.

Randall met Hunt's stare through the feed. "You were stationed at Meridan when I was over there. I was running recon the day you took on that battalion."

"Rough battle" was all Hunt said.

Shadows darkened Randall's eyes. "Yeah, it was."

Hunt shut out the memory of that one-sided massacre, of how many humans and their few Vanir allies hadn't walked away from his sword or lightning. He'd been serving Sandriel then, and her orders had been brutal: no prisoners. She'd sent him and Pollux out that day, ahead of her legion, to intercept the small rebel force camped in a mountain pass.

Hunt had worked around her order as best he could. He'd made the deaths quick.

Pollux had taken his time. And enjoyed every second of it.

And when Hunt could no longer listen to people screaming for Pollux's mercy, he'd ended their lives, too. Pollux had raged, the brawl between them leaving both angels spitting blood onto the rocky earth. Sandriel had been delighted by it, even if she'd thrown Hunt into her dungeons for a few days as punishment for ending Pollux's fun too soon.

Beneath the counter, Bryce brushed her crumb-covered hand over Hunt's. There had been no one, after that battle, to wash away the blood and put him in bed. Would it have been better or worse to have known Bryce then? To have fought, knowing he could return to her?

Bryce squeezed his fingers, leaving a trail of buttery flakes, and opened the bag for a second croissant.

Ember watched her daughter dig through the pastries and again toyed with the silver pendant—a circle set atop two triangles. The Embrace, Hunt realized. The union of Solas and Cthona. Ember frowned. "Why," she asked Bryce, "is Hunt Athalar your roommate?"

"He was booted from the 33rd for his questionable fashion sense," she said, munching on the croissant. "I told him his boring black clothes don't bother me, and let him stay here."

Ember rolled her eyes. The exact same expression he'd seen on Bryce's face moments before. "Do you ever manage to get a straight answer out of her, Hunt? Because I've known her for twenty-five years and she's never given me one."

Bryce glared at her mother, then turned to Hunt. "Do not feel obligated to answer that."

Ember let out an outraged click of her tongue. "I wish I could say that the big city corrupted my lovely daughter, but she was this rude even before she left for university."

Hunt couldn't help his low chuckle. Randall leaned back on the couch. "It's true," Randall said. "You should have seen their fights. I don't think there was a single person in Nidaros who didn't hear them hollering at each other. It echoed off the gods-damned mountains."

Both Quinlan women scowled at him. That expression was the same, too.

Ember seemed to peer over their shoulders. "When was the last time you cleaned, Bryce Adelaide Quinlan?"

Bryce stiffened. *"Twenty minutes ago."*

"I can see dust on that coffee table."

"You. Can. Not."

Ember's eyes danced with devilish delight. "Does Athie know about JJ?"

Hunt couldn't stop himself from going rigid. JJ—an ex? She hadn't ever mentioned—Oh. Right. Hunt smirked. "Jelly Jubilee and I are good friends."

Bryce grumbled something he chose not to hear.

Ember leaned closer to the screen. "All right, Hunt. If she showed you JJ, then she's got to like you." Bryce, mercifully, refrained from mentioning to her parents how he'd discovered her doll collection in the first place. Ember continued, "So tell me about yourself."

Randall said flatly to his wife. "He's Hunt Athalar."

"I know," Ember said. "But all I've heard are horrible war stories. I want to know about the real male. And get a straight answer about why you're living in my daughter's guest room."

Bryce had warned him while they cleaned: *Do* not *say a word about the murders.*

But he had a feeling that Ember Quinlan could sniff out lies like a bloodhound, so Hunt smudged the truth. "Jesiba is working with my boss to find a stolen relic. With the Summit happening in two weeks, the barracks are overloaded with guests, so Bryce generously offered me a room to make working together easier."

"Sure," Ember said. "My daughter, who never once shared her precious Starlight Fancy toys with a single kid in Nidaros, but only let them *look* at the stupid things, offered up the entire guest room of her own goodwill."

Randall nudged his wife with a knee, a silent warning, perhaps, of a man used to keeping the peace between two highly opinionated women.

Bryce said, "This is why I told him to have a drink before we dialed you."

Ember sipped from her coffee. Randall picked up a newspaper from the table and began to flip through it. Ember asked, "So you won't let us come visit this weekend because of this case?"

Bryce winced. "Yes. It's not the sort of thing you guys could tag along on."

A hint of the warrior shone through as Randall's eyes sharpened. "It's dangerous?"

"No," Bryce lied. "But we need to be a little stealthy."

"And bringing along two humans," Ember said testily, "is the opposite of that?"

Bryce sighed at the ceiling. "Bringing along my *parents*," she countered, "would undermine my image as a cool antiquities dealer."

"*Assistant* antiquities dealer," her mother corrected.

"Ember," Randall warned.

Bryce's mouth tightened. Apparently, this was a conversation they'd had before. He wondered if Ember saw the flicker of hurt in her daughter's eyes.

It was enough that Hunt found himself saying, "Bryce knows more people in this city than I do—she's a pro at navigating all this. She's a real asset to the 33rd."

Ember considered him, her gaze frank. "Micah is your boss, isn't he?"

A polite way of putting what Micah was to him.

"Yeah," Hunt said. Randall was watching him now. "The best I've had."

Ember's stare fell on the tattoo across his brow. "That's not saying much."

"Mom, can we not?" Bryce sighed. "How's the pottery business?"

Ember opened her mouth, but Randall nudged her knee again, a silent plea to let it drop. "Business," Ember said tightly, "is going great."

Bryce knew her mother was a brewing tempest.

Hunt was kind to them, friendly even, well aware that her mom was now on a mission to figure out why he was here, and what existed between them. But he asked Randall about his job as co-head of an organization to help humans traumatized by their military service and asked her mom about her roadside stand selling pottery of fat babies lolling in various beds of vegetables.

Her mom and Hunt were currently debating which sunball players were best this season, and Randall was still flipping through the newspaper and chiming in every now and then.

It had gutted her to hear what had happened to Hunt's own mother. She kept the call going longer than usual because of it. Because he was right. Rubbing her aching leg beneath the table—she'd strained it again at some point during their cleaning—Bryce dug into her third croissant and said to Randall, "This still isn't as good as yours."

"Move back home," her dad said, "and you could have them every day."

"Yeah, yeah," she said, eating another mouthful. She massaged her thigh. "I thought you were supposed to be the cool parent. You've become even worse than Mom with the nagging."

"I was always worse than your mother," he said mildly. "I was just better at hiding it."

Bryce said to Hunt, "This is why my parents have to ambush me if they want to visit. I'd never let them through the door."

Hunt just glanced at her lap—her thigh—before he asked Ember, "Have you tried to get her to a medwitch for that leg?"

Bryce froze at exactly the same heartbeat as her mother.

"What's wrong with her leg?" Ember's eyes dropped to the lower half of her screen as if she could somehow see Bryce's leg beneath the camera's range, Randall following suit.

"Nothing," Bryce said, glaring at Hunt. "A busybody angel, that's what."

"It's the wound she got two years ago," Hunt answered. "It still hurts her." He rustled his wings, as if unable to help the impatient gesture. "And she still insists on running."

Ember's eyes filled with alarm. "Why would you do that, Bryce?"

Bryce set down her croissant. "It's none of anyone's business."

"Bryce," Randall said. "If it bothers you, you should see a medwitch."

"It doesn't bother me," Bryce said through her teeth.

"Then why have you been rubbing your leg under the counter?" Hunt drawled.

"Because I was trying to convince it not to kick you in the face, asshole," Bryce hissed.

"*Bryce,*" her mother gasped. Randall's eyes widened.

But Hunt laughed. He rose, picking up the empty pastry bag and squishing it into a ball before tossing it into the trash can with the skill of one of his beloved sunball players. "I think the wound still has venom lingering from the demon who attacked her. If she doesn't get it checked out before the Drop, she'll be in pain for centuries."

Bryce shot to her feet, hiding her wince at the ripple of pain in her thigh. They'd never discussed it—that the kristallos's venom might indeed still be in her leg. "I don't need you deciding what is best for me, you—"

"Alphahole?" Hunt supplied, going to the sink and turning on the water. "We're partners. Partners look out for each other. If you won't listen to me about your gods-damned leg, then maybe you'll listen to your parents."

"How bad is it?" Randall asked quietly.

Bryce whirled back to the computer. "It's *fine.*"

Randall pointed to the floor behind her. "Balance on that leg and tell me that again."

Bryce refused to move. Filling a glass of water, Hunt smiled, pure male satisfaction.

Ember reached for her phone, which she'd discarded on the cushions beside her. "I'll find the nearest medwitch and see if she can squeeze you in tomorrow—"

"I am not going to a medwitch," Bryce snarled, and grabbed the rim of the laptop. "It was great chatting with you. I'm tired. Good night."

Randall began to object, eyes shooting daggers at Ember, but Bryce slammed the laptop shut.

At the sink, Hunt was the portrait of smug, angelic arrogance. She aimed for her bedroom.

Ember, at least, waited two minutes before video-calling Bryce on her phone.

"Is your father behind this *case*?" Ember asked, venom coating each word. Even through the camera, her rage was palpable.

"Randall is not behind this," Bryce said dryly, flopping onto her bed.

"Your *other* father," Ember snapped. "This sort of arrangement reeks of him."

Bryce kept her face neutral. "No. Jesiba and Micah are working together. Hunt and I are mere pawns."

"Micah Domitus is a monster," Ember breathed.

"All the Archangels are. He's an arrogant ass, but not that bad."

Ember's eyes simmered. "Are you being careful?"

"I'm still taking birth control, yes."

"Bryce Adelaide Quinlan, you know what I mean."

"Hunt has my back." Even if he'd thrown her under the bus by mentioning her leg to them.

Her mom was having none of it. "I have no doubt that sorceress would push you into harm's way if it made her more money. Micah's no better. Hunt might have your back, but don't forget that these Vanir only look out for themselves. He's Micah's personal assassin, for fuck's sake. And one of the Fallen. The Asteri *hate* him. He's a slave because of it."

"He's a slave because we live in a fucked-up world." Hazy wrath fogged her vision, but she blinked it away.

Her dad called out from the kitchen, asking where the microwave popcorn was. Ember hollered back that it was in the same exact place it always was, her eyes never leaving the phone's camera. "I know you'll bite my head off for it, but let me just say this."

"Gods, Mom—"

"Hunt might be a good roommate, and he might be nice to look at, but remember that he's a Vanir male. A very, *very* powerful Vanir male, even with those tattoos keeping him in line. He and every male like him is lethal."

"Yeah, and you never let me forget it." It was an effort not to look at the tiny scar on her mom's cheekbone.

Old shadows banked the light in her mom's eyes, and Bryce winced. "Seeing you with an older Vanir male—"

"I'm not *with* him, Mom—"

"It brings me back to that place, Bryce." She ran a hand through her dark hair. "I'm sorry."

Her mom might as well have punched her in the heart.

Bryce wished she could reach through the camera and wrap her arms around her, breathing in her honeysuckle-and-nutmeg scent.

Then Ember said, "I'll make some calls and get that medwitch appointment for your leg."

Bryce scowled. "No, thanks."

"You're going to that appointment, Bryce."

Bryce turned the phone and stretched out her leg over the covers so her mother could see. She rotated her foot. "See? No problems."

Her mother's face hardened to steel that matched the wedding band on her finger. "Just because Danika died doesn't mean you need to suffer, too."

Bryce stared at her mother, who was always so good at cutting to the heart of everything, at rendering her into rubble with a few words. "It doesn't have anything to do with that."

"*Bullshit*, Bryce." Her mom's eyes glazed with tears. "You think

Danika would want you limping in pain for the rest of your existence? You think she would've wanted you to stop dancing?"

"I don't want to talk about Danika." Her voice trembled.

Ember shook her head in disgust. "I'll message the medwitch's address and number when I get the appointment for you. Good night."

She hung up without another word.

57

Thirty minutes later, Bryce had changed into her sleep shorts and was brooding on her bed when a knock thumped on the door. "You're a fucking traitor, Athalar," she called.

Hunt opened the door and leaned against its frame. "No wonder you moved here, if you and your mom fight so much."

The instinct to strangle him was overwhelming, but she said, "I've never seen my mom back down from a fight. It rubbed off, I guess." She scowled at him. "What do you want?"

Hunt pushed off the door and approached. The room became too small with each step closer. Too airless. He stopped at the foot of her mattress. "I'll go to the medwitch appointment with you."

"I'm not going."

"Why?"

She sucked in a breath. And then it all burst out. "Because once that wound is gone, once it stops hurting, then *Danika* is gone. The Pack of Devils is gone." She shoved back the blankets, revealing her bare legs, and hitched up her silk sleep shorts so the full, twisting scar was visible. "It will all be some memory, some dream that happened for a flash and then was gone. But this scar and the pain . . ." Her eyes stung. "I can't let it be erased. I can't let *them* be erased."

Hunt slowly sat beside her on the bed, as if giving her time to object. His hair skimmed his brow, the tattoo, as he studied the scar. And ran a calloused finger over it.

The touch left her skin prickling in its wake.

"You're not going to erase Danika and the pack if you help yourself."

Bryce shook her head, looking toward the window, but his fingers closed around her chin. He gently turned her face back to his. His dark, depthless eyes were soft. Understanding.

How many people ever saw those eyes this way? Ever saw *him* this way?

"Your mother loves you. She cannot—literally, on a biological level, Bryce—bear the thought of you in pain." He let go of her chin, but his eyes remained on hers. "Neither can I."

"You barely know me."

"You're my friend." The words hung between them. His head dipped again, as if he could hide the expression on his face as he amended, "If you would like me to be."

For a moment, she stared at him. The offer thrown out there. The quiet vulnerability. It erased any annoyance still in her veins.

"Didn't you know, Athalar?" The tentative hope in his face nearly destroyed her. "We've been friends from the moment you thought Jelly Jubilee was a dildo."

He tipped back his head and laughed, and Bryce scooted back on the bed. Propped up the pillows and turned on the TV. She patted the space beside her.

Grinning, eyes full of light in a way she'd never seen before, he sat beside her. Then he pulled out his phone and snapped a picture of her.

Bryce blew out a breath, her smile fading as she surveyed him. "My mom went through a lot. I know she's not easy to deal with, but thanks for being so cool with her."

"I like your mom," Hunt said, and she believed him. "How'd she and your dad meet?"

Bryce knew he meant Randall. "My mom ran from my biological father before he found out she was pregnant. She wound up at a temple to Cthona in Korinth, and knew the priestesses there would take her in—shield her—since she was a holy pregnant vessel or whatever." Bryce snorted. "She gave birth to me there, and I spent the first three years of my life cloistered behind the temple walls. My mom did their laundry to earn our keep. Long story short, my biological father heard a rumor that she had a child and sent goons to hunt her down." She ground her teeth. "He told them that if there was a child that was undoubtedly his, they were to bring me to him. At any cost."

Hunt's mouth thinned. "Shit."

"They had eyes at every depot, but the priestesses got us out of the city—with the hope of getting us all the way to the House of Earth and Blood headquarters in Hilene, where my mom could beg for asylum. Even my father wouldn't dare infringe on their territory. But it's a three-day drive, and none of the Korinth priestesses had the ability to defend us against Fae warriors. So we drove the five hours to Solas's Temple in Oia, partially to rest, but also to pick up our holy guard."

"Randall." Hunt smiled. But he arched a brow. "Wait—Randall was a sun-priest?"

"Not quite. He'd gotten back from the front a year before, but the stuff he did and saw while he was serving . . . It messed with him. Really badly. He didn't want to go home, couldn't face his family. So he'd offered himself as an acolyte to Solas, hoping that it'd somehow atone for his past. He was two weeks away from swearing his vows when the High Priest asked him to escort us to Hilene. Many of the priests are trained warriors, but Randall was the only human, and the High Priest guessed my mother wouldn't trust a Vanir male. Right before we reached Hilene, my father's people caught up with us. They expected to find a helpless, hysterical female." Bryce smiled again. "What they found was a legendary sharpshooter and a mother who would move the earth itself to keep her daughter."

Hunt straightened. "What happened?"

"What you might expect. My parents dealt with the mess afterward." She glanced at him. "Please don't tell that to anyone. It . . . There were never any questions about the Fae that didn't return to Crescent City. I don't want any to come up now."

"I won't say a word."

Bryce smiled grimly. "After that, the House of Earth and Blood literally deemed my mother a vessel for Cthona and Randall a vessel for Solas, and blah blah religious crap, but it basically amounted to an official order of protection that my father didn't dare fuck with. And Randall finally went home, bringing us with him, and obviously didn't swear his vows to Solas." Her smile warmed. "He proposed by the end of the year. They've been disgustingly in love ever since."

Hunt smiled back. "It's nice to hear that sometimes things work out for good people."

"Yeah. Sometimes." A taut silence stretched between them. In her bed—they were in her bed, and just this morning, she'd fantasized about him going down on her atop the kitchen counter—

Bryce swallowed hard. "*Fangs and Bangs* is on in five minutes. You want to watch?"

Hunt smiled slowly, as if he knew precisely why she'd swallowed, but lay back on the pillows, his wings sprawled beneath him. A predator content to wait for his prey to come to him.

Fucking Hel. But Hunt winked at her, tucking an arm behind his head. The motion made the muscles down his biceps ripple. His eyes glittered, as if he was well aware of that, too. "Hel yes."

Hunt hadn't realized how badly he needed to ask it. How badly he'd needed her answer.

Friends. It didn't remotely cover whatever was between them, but it was true.

He leaned against the towering headboard, the two of them watching the raunchy show. But by the time they reached the halfway point of the episode, she'd begun to make comments about the inane plot. And he'd begun to join her.

Another show came on, a reality competition with different Vanir performing feats of strength and agility, and it felt only natural to watch that, too. All of it felt only natural. He let himself settle into the feeling.

And wasn't that the most dangerous thing he'd ever done.

58

Her mother messaged while she was dressing for work the next morning, with the time and location of a medwitch appointment. *Eleven today. It's five blocks from the gallery. Please go.*

Bryce didn't write back. She certainly wouldn't be going to the appointment.

Not when she had another one scheduled with the Meat Market.

Hunt had wanted to wait until night, but Bryce knew that the vendors would be much more likely to chat during the quieter daytime hours, when they wouldn't be trying to entice the usual evening buyers.

"You're quiet again today," Bryce murmured as they wove through the cramped pathways of the warehouse. This was the third they'd visited so far—the other two had quickly proven fruitless.

No, the vendors didn't know anything about drugs. No, that was a stereotype of the Meat Market that they did not appreciate. No, they did not know anyone who might help them. No, they were not interested in marks for information, because they really did not know anything useful at all.

Hunt had stayed a few stalls away during every discussion, because no one would talk with a legionary and Fallen slave.

Hunt held his wings tucked in tight. "Don't think I've forgotten that we're missing that medwitch appointment right now."

She never should have mentioned it.

"I don't remember giving you permission to shove your nose into my business."

"We're back to that?" He huffed a laugh. "I'd think cuddling in front of the TV allowed me to at least be able to *voice* my opinions without getting my head bitten off."

She rolled her eyes. "We didn't cuddle."

"What is it you want, exactly?" Hunt asked, surveying a stall full of ancient knives. "A boyfriend or mate or husband who will just sit there, with no opinions, and agree to everything you say, and never dare to ask you for anything?"

"Of course not."

"Just because I'm male and have an opinion doesn't make me into some psychotic, domineering prick."

She shoved her hands into the pockets of Danika's leather jacket. "Look, my mom went through a lot thanks to some psychotic, domineering pricks."

"I know." His eyes softened. "But even so, look at her and your dad. He voices his opinions. And he seems pretty damn psychotic when it comes to protecting both of you."

"You have no idea," Bryce grumbled. "I didn't go on a single date until I got to CCU."

Hunt's brows rose. "Really? I would have thought . . ." He shook his head.

"Thought what?"

He shrugged. "That the human boys would have been crawling around after you."

It was an effort not to glance at him, with the way he said *human boys*, as if they were some other breed than him—a full-grown malakh male.

She supposed they were, technically, but that hint of masculine arrogance . . . "Well, if they wanted to, they didn't dare show it. Randall was practically a god to them, and though he never said anything, they all got it into their heads that I was firmly off-limits."

"That wouldn't have been a good enough reason for me to stay away."

Her cheeks heated at the way his voice lowered. "Well, idolizing Randall aside, I was also different." She gestured to her pointed ears. Her tall body. "Too Fae for humans. Woe is me, right?"

"It builds character," he said, examining a stall full of opals of every color: white, black, red, blue, green. Iridescent veins ran through them, like preserved arteries from the earth itself.

"What are these for?" he asked the black-feathered, humanoid female at the stall. A magpie.

"They're luck charms," the magpie said, waving a feathery hand over the trays of gems. "White is for joy; green for wealth; red for love and fertility; blue for wisdom . . . Take your pick."

Hunt asked, "What's the black for?"

The magpie's onyx-colored mouth curved upward. "For the opposite of luck." She tapped one of the black opals, kept contained within a glass dome. "Slip it under the pillow of your enemy and see what happens to them."

Bryce cleared her throat. "Interesting as that may be—"

Hunt held out a silver mark. "For the white."

Bryce's brows rose, but the magpie swept up the mark, and plunked the white opal into Hunt's awaiting palm. They left, ignoring her gratitude for their business.

"I didn't peg you for superstitious," Bryce said.

But Hunt paused at the end of the row of stalls and took her hand. He pressed the opal into it, the stone warm from his touch. The size of a crow's egg, it shimmered in the firstlights high above.

"You could use some joy," Hunt said quietly.

Something bright sparked in her chest. "So could you," she said, attempting to press the opal back into his palm.

But Hunt stepped away. "It's a gift."

Bryce's face warmed again, and she looked anywhere but at him as she smiled. Even though she could feel his gaze lingering on her face while she slid the opal into the pocket of her jacket.

* * *

The opal had been stupid. Impulsive.

Likely bullshit, but Bryce had pocketed it, at least. She hadn't commented on how rusty his skills were, since it had been two hundred years since he'd last thought to buy something for a female.

Shahar would have smiled at the opal—and forgotten about it soon after. She'd had troves of jewels in her alabaster palace: diamonds the size of sunballs; solid blocks of emerald stacked like bricks; veritable bathtubs filled with rubies. A small white opal, even for joy, would have been like a grain of sand on a miles-long beach. She'd have appreciated the gift but, ultimately, let it disappear into a drawer somewhere. And he, so dedicated to their cause, would probably have forgotten about it, too.

Hunt clenched his jaw as Bryce strode for a hide stall. The teenager—a feline shifter from her scent—was in her lanky humanoid form and watched them approach from where she perched on a stool. Her brown braid draped over a shoulder, nearly grazing the phone idly held in her hands.

"Hey," Bryce said, pointing toward a pile of shaggy rugs. "How much for one of them?"

"Twenty silvers," the shifter said, sounding as bored as she looked.

Bryce smirked, running a hand over the white pelt. Hunt's skin tightened over his bones. He'd felt that touch the other night, stroking him to sleep. And could feel it now as she petted the sheepskin. "Twenty silvers for a snowsheep hide? Isn't that a little low?"

"My mom makes me work weekends. It'd piss her off to sell it for what it's actually worth."

"Loyal of you," Bryce said, chuckling. She leaned in, her voice dropping. "This is going to sound *so* random, but I have a question for you."

Hunt kept back, watching her work. The irreverent, down-to-earth party girl, merely looking to score some new drugs.

The shifter barely looked up. "Yeah?"

Bryce said, "You know where I can get anything . . . fun around here?"

The girl rolled her chestnut-colored eyes. "All right. Let's hear it."

"Hear what?" Bryce asked innocently.

The shifter lifted her phone, typing away with rainbow-painted nails. "That fake-ass act you gave everyone else here, and in the two other warehouses." She held up her phone. "We're all on a group chat." She gestured to everyone in the market around them. "I got, like, ten warnings you two would be coming through here, asking cheesy questions about drugs or whatever."

It was, perhaps, the first time Hunt had seen Bryce at a loss for words. So he stepped up to her side. "All right," he said to the teenager. "But *do* you know anything?"

The girl looked him over. "You think the Vipe would allow shit like that synth in here?"

"She allows every other depravity and crime," Hunt said through his teeth.

"Yeah, but she's not dumb," the shifter said, tossing her braid over a shoulder.

"So you've heard of it," Bryce said.

"The Vipe told me to tell you that it's nasty, and she doesn't deal in it, and never will."

"But someone does?" Bryce said tightly.

This was bad. This would not end well at all—

"The Vipe also told me to say you should check the river." She went back to her phone, presumably to tell *the Vipe* that she'd conveyed the message. "That's the place for that kinda shit."

"What do you mean?" Bryce asked.

A shrug. "Ask the mer."

"We should lay out the facts," Hunt said as Bryce stormed for the Meat Market's docks. "Before we run to the mer, accusing them of being drug dealers."

"Too late," Bryce said.

He hadn't been able to stop her from sending a message via otter to Tharion twenty minutes ago, and sure as Hel hadn't been able to stop her from heading for the river's edge to wait.

Hunt gripped her arm, the dock mere steps away. "Bryce, the mer do *not* take kindly to being falsely accused—"

"Who said it's false?"

"Tharion isn't a drug dealer, and he sure as shit isn't selling something as bad as synth seems to be."

"He might know someone who is." She shrugged out of his grasp. "We've been dicking around for long enough. I want answers. Now." She narrowed her eyes. "Don't you want to get this over with? So you can have your *sentence* reduced?"

He did, but he said, "The synth probably has *nothing* to do with this. We shouldn't—"

But she'd already reached the wood slats of the dock, not daring to look into the eddying water beneath. The Meat Market's docks were notorious dumping grounds. And feeding troughs for aquatic scavengers.

Water splashed, and then a powerful male body was sitting on the end of the dock. "This part of the river is gross," Tharion said by way of greeting.

Bryce didn't smile. Didn't say anything other than, "Who's selling synth in the river?"

The grin vanished from Tharion's face. Hunt began to object, but the mer said, "Not in, Legs." He shook his head. "*On* the river."

"So it's true, then. It's—it's what? A healing drug that leaked from a lab? Who's behind it?"

Hunt stepped up to her side. "Tharion—"

"Danika Fendyr," Tharion said, his eyes soft. Like he knew who Danika had been to her. "The intel came in a day before her death. She was spotted doing a deal on a boat just past here."

59

What do you mean, *Danika* was selling it?"

Tharion shook his head. "I don't know if she was selling it or buying it or what, but right before synth started appearing on the streets, she was spotted on an Auxiliary boat in the dead of night. There was a crate of synth on board."

Hunt murmured, "It always comes back to Danika."

Above the roaring in her head, Bryce said, "Maybe she was confiscating it."

"Maybe," Tharion admitted, then ran a hand through his auburn hair. "But that synth—it's some bad shit, Bryce. If Danika was involved in it—"

"She wasn't. She never would have done something like that." Her heart was racing so fast she thought she'd puke. She turned to Hunt. "But it explains why there were traces of it on her clothes, if she had to confiscate it for the Aux."

Hunt's face was grim. "Maybe."

She crossed her arms. "What is it, exactly?"

"It's synthetic magic," Tharion said, eyes darting between them. "It started off as an aid for healing, but someone apparently realized that in super-concentrated doses, it can give humans strength greater than most Vanir. For short bursts, but it's potent. They've tried to make it for centuries, but it seemed impossible. Most people thought it was akin to alchemy—just as unlikely as turning something into gold. But apparently modern science made it work this time." He angled his head. "Does this have to do with the demon you were hunting?"

"It's a possibility," Hunt said.

"I'll let you know if I get any other reports," Tharion said, and didn't wait for a farewell before diving back into the water.

Bryce stared out at the river in the midday sun, gripping the white opal in her pocket.

"I know it wasn't what you wanted to hear," Hunt said cautiously beside her.

"Was she killed by whoever is creating the synth? If she was on that boat to seize their shipment?" She tucked a strand of hair behind her ear. "Could the person selling the synth and the person searching for the Horn be the same, if the synth can possibly repair the Horn?"

He rubbed his chin. "I guess. But this could also be a dead end."

She sighed. "I don't get why she never mentioned it."

"Maybe it wasn't worth mentioning," he suggested.

"Maybe," she murmured. "Maybe."

Bryce waited until Hunt hit the gym in her apartment building before she dialed Fury.

She didn't know why she bothered. Fury hadn't taken a call from her in months.

The call nearly went to audiomail before she answered. "Hey."

Bryce slumped against her bed and blurted, "I'm shocked you picked up."

"You caught me between jobs."

Or maybe Juniper had bitten Fury's head off about bailing.

Bryce said, "I thought you were coming back to hunt down whoever was behind the Raven's bombing."

"I thought so, too, but it turned out I didn't need to cross the Haldren to do it."

Bryce leaned against her headboard, stretching out her legs. "So it really was the human rebellion behind it?" Maybe that *C* on the crates Ruhn thought was the Horn was just that: a letter.

"Yeah. Specifics and names are classified, though."

Fury had said that to her so many times in the past that she'd lost count. "At least tell me if you found them?"

There was a good chance that Fury was sharpening her arsenal of weapons on the desk of whatever fancy hotel she was holed up in right now. "I said I was between jobs, didn't I?"

"Congratulations?"

A soft laugh that still freaked Bryce the fuck out. "Sure." Fury paused. "What's up, B."

As if that somehow erased two years of near-silence. "Did Danika ever mention synth to you?"

Bryce could have sworn something heavy and metallic clunked in the background. Fury said softly, "Who told you about synth?"

Bryce straightened. "I think it's getting spread around here. I met a mer today who said Danika was seen on an Aux boat with a crate of it, right before she died." She blew out a breath.

"It's dangerous, Bryce. Really dangerous. Don't fuck around with it."

"I'm not." Gods. "I haven't touched any drugs in two years." Then she added, unable to stop herself, "If you'd bothered to take my calls or visit, you would have known that."

"I've been busy."

Liar. Fucking liar and coward. Bryce ground out, "Look, I wanted to know if Danika had ever mentioned synth to you before she died, because she didn't mention it to me."

Another one of those pauses.

"She did, didn't she." Even now, Bryce wasn't sure why jealousy seared her chest.

"She might have said that there was some nasty shit being sold," Fury said.

"You never thought to mention it to anyone?"

"I did. To you. At the White Raven the night Danika died. Someone tried to sell it to you then, for fuck's sake. I told you to stay the Hel away from it."

"And you still didn't find the chance to mention then or after Danika died that she warned you about it in the first place?"

"A demon ripped her to shreds, Bryce. Drug busts didn't seem connected to it."

"And what if it was?"

"How?"

"I don't know, I just . . ." Bryce tapped her foot on the bed. "Why wouldn't she have told me?"

"Because . . ." Fury stopped herself.

"Because *what*?" Bryce snapped.

"All right," Fury said, her voice sharpening. "Danika didn't want to tell you because she didn't want you getting near it. Even *thinking* about trying synth."

Bryce shot to her feet. "Why the *fuck* would I ever—"

"Because we have literally seen you take everything."

"You've been right there, taking everything with me, you—"

"Synth is *synthetic magic*, Bryce. To replace *real* magic. Of which you have *none*. It gives humans Vanir powers and strength for like an hour. And then it can seriously fuck you up. Make you addicted and worse. For the Vanir, it's even riskier—a crazy high and superstrength, but it can easily turn bad. Danika didn't want you even knowing something like that existed."

"As if I'm so desperate to be like you big, tough Vanir that I'd take something—"

"Her goal was to protect you. *Always*. Even from yourself."

The words struck like a slap to the face. Bryce's throat closed up.

Fury blew out a breath. "Look, I know that came out harsh. But take my word for it: don't mess with synth. If they've actually managed to mass-produce the stuff outside of an official lab and make it in even stronger concentrations, then it's bad news. Stay away from it, and anyone who deals in it."

Bryce's hands shook, but she managed to say "All right" without sounding like she was one breath away from crying.

"Look, I gotta go," Fury said. "I've got something to do tonight. But I'll be back in Lunathion in a few days. I'm wanted at the

Summit in two weeks—it's at some compound a few hours outside the city."

Bryce didn't ask why Fury Axtar would attend a Summit of various Valbaran leaders. She didn't really care that Fury would be coming back at all.

"Maybe we can grab a meal," Fury said.

"Sure."

"Bryce." Her name was both a reprimand and an apology. Fury sighed. "I'll see you."

Her throat burned, but she hung up. Took a few long breaths. Fury could go to Hel.

Bryce waited to call her brother until she'd plunked her ass down on the couch, opened her laptop, and pulled up the search engine. He answered on the second ring. "Yeah?"

"I want you to spare me the lectures and the warnings and all that shit, okay?"

Ruhn paused. "Okay."

She put the call on speaker and leaned her forearms on her knees, the cursor hanging over the search bar.

Ruhn asked, "What's going on with you and Athalar?"

"Nothing," Bryce said, rubbing her eyes. "He's not my type."

"I was asking about why he's not on the call, not whether you're dating, but that's good to know."

She gritted her teeth and typed *synthetic magic* in the search bar. As the results filtered in, she said, "*Athalar* is off making those muscles of his even nicer." Ruhn huffed a laugh.

She skimmed the results: small, short articles about the uses of a synthetic healing magic to aid in human healing. "That medwitch who sent you the information about synthetic magic—did she offer any thoughts on why or how it got onto the streets?"

"No. I think she's more concerned about its origins—and an antidote. She told me she actually tested some of the kristallos venom she got out of Athalar from the other night against the synth, trying to formulate one. She thinks her healing magic can act like some kind of stabilizer for the venom to make the antidote, but she needs more of the venom to keep testing it out. I don't know. It sounded like some complex shit." He added wryly, "If you run into a kristallos, ask it for some venom, would you?"

"Got a crush, Ruhn?"

He snorted. "She's done us a huge favor. I'd like to repay her in whatever way we can."

"All right." She clicked through more results, including a patent filing from Redner Industries for the drug, dating back ten years. Way before Danika's time working there.

"The research papers say only tiny amounts are released, even for the medwitches and their healing. It's incredibly expensive and difficult to make."

"What if . . . what if the formula and a shipment leaked two years ago from Redner, and Danika was sent out to track it down. And maybe she realized whoever wanted to steal the synth planned to use it to repair the Horn, and she stole the Horn before they could. And then they killed her for it."

"But why keep it a secret?" Ruhn asked. "Why not bust the person behind it?"

"I don't know. It's just a theory." Better than nothing.

Ruhn went quiet again. She had the feeling a Serious Talk was coming and braced herself. "I think it's admirable, Bryce. That you still care enough about Danika and the Pack of Devils to keep looking into this."

"I was ordered to by my boss and the Governor, remember?"

"You would have looked once you heard it wasn't Briggs anyway." He sighed. "You know, Danika nearly beat the shit out of me once."

"No she didn't."

"Oh, she did. We ran into each other in Redner Tower's lobby when I went to meet up with Declan after some fancy meeting he was having with their top people. Wait—you dated that prick son of Redner's, didn't you?"

"I did," she said tightly.

"Gross. Just gross, Bryce."

"Tell me about Danika wiping the floor with your pathetic ass."

She could nearly hear his smile through the phone. "I don't know how we got into it about you, but we did."

"What'd you say?"

"Why are you assuming I did the instigating? Did you ever meet Danika? She had a mouth on her like I've never seen." He clicked his tongue, the admiration in the noise making Bryce's chest clench. "Anyway, I told her to tell you that I was sorry. She told me to go fuck myself, and fuck my apology."

Bryce blinked. "She never told me she ran into you."

"*Ran into* is an understatement." He whistled. "She hadn't even made the Drop, and she nearly kicked my balls across the lobby. Declan had to . . . involve himself to stop it."

It sounded like Danika all right. Even if everything else she'd learned lately didn't.

60

It's a stretch," Hunt said an hour later from his spot beside her on the sectional. She'd filled him in on her latest theory, his brows rising with each word out of her mouth.

Bryce clicked through the pages on Redner Industries' website. "Danika worked part-time at Redner. She rarely talked about the shit she did for them. Some kind of security division." She pulled up the login page. "Maybe her old work account still has info on her assignments."

Her fingers shook only slightly as she typed in Danika's username, having seen it so many times on her phone in the past: *dfendyr.*

DFendyr—Defender. She'd never realized it until now. Fury's harsh words rang through her head. Bryce ignored them.

She typed in one of Danika's usual half-assed passwords: 1234567. Nothing.

"Again," Hunt said warily, "it's a stretch." He leaned back against the cushions. "We're better off doubling down with Danaan on looking for the Horn, not chasing down this drug."

Bryce countered, "Danika was involved in this synth stuff and never said a word. You don't think that's weird? You don't think there might be something more here?"

"She also didn't tell you the truth about Philip Briggs," Hunt said carefully. "Or that she stole the Horn. Keeping things from you could have been standard for her."

Bryce just typed in another password. Then another. And another.

"We need the full picture, Hunt," she said, trying again. *She* needed the full picture. "It all ties together somehow."

But every password failed. Every one of Danika's usual combinations.

Bryce shut her eyes, foot bouncing on the carpet as she recited, "The Horn could possibly be healed by the synth in a large enough dose. Synthetic magic has obsidian salt as one of its ingredients. The kristallos can be summoned by obsidian salt . . ." Hunt remained silent as she thought it through. "The kristallos was bred to track the Horn. The kristallos's venom can eat away at magic. The medwitch wants some venom to test if it's possible to create an antidote to synth with her magic or something."

"What?"

Her eyes opened. "Ruhn told me." She filled him in on Ruhn's half-joking request for more venom to give the medwitch.

Hunt's eyes darkened. "Interesting. If the synth is on the verge of becoming a deadly street drug . . . we should help her get the venom."

"What about the Horn?"

His jaw tightened. "We'll keep looking. But if this drug explodes—not just in this city but across the territory, the world . . . that antidote is vital." He scanned her face. "How can we get our hands on some venom for her?"

Bryce breathed, "If we summon a kristallos—"

"We don't take that risk," Hunt snarled. "We'll figure out how to get the venom another way."

"I can handle myself—"

"*I* can't fucking handle myself, Quinlan. Not if you might be in danger."

His words rippled between them. Emotion glinted in his eyes, if she dared to read what was there.

But Hunt's phone buzzed, and he lifted his hips off the couch to pull it from the back pocket of his pants. He glanced at the screen, and his wings shifted, tucking in slightly.

"Micah?" she dared ask.

"Just some legion shit," he murmured, and stood. "I gotta head out for a few. Naomi will take watch." He gestured to the computer. "Keep trying if you want, but let's *think*, Bryce, before we do anything drastic to get our hands on that venom."

"Yeah, yeah."

It was apparently acceptance enough for Hunt to leave, but not before ruffling her hair and leaning down to whisper, his lips brushing the curve of her ear, "JJ would be proud of you." Her toes curled in her slippers, and stayed that way long after he'd left.

After trying another few password options, Bryce sighed and shut the computer. They were narrowing in on it—the truth. She could feel it.

But would she be ready for it?

Her cycle arrived the next morning like a gods-damned train barreling into her body, which Bryce decided was fitting, given what day it was.

She stepped into the great room to find Hunt making breakfast, his hair still mussed with sleep. He stiffened at her approach, though. Then he turned, his eyes darting over her. His preternatural sense of smell missed nothing. "You're bleeding."

"Every three months, like clockwork." Pure-blooded Fae rarely had a cycle at all; humans had it monthly—she'd somehow settled somewhere in between.

She slid onto a stool at the kitchen counter. A glance at her phone showed no messages from Juniper or Fury. Not even a message from her mom biting her head off about bailing on the medwitch appointment.

"You need anything?" Hunt extended a plate of eggs and bacon toward her. Then a cup of coffee.

"I took something for the cramps." She sipped her coffee. "But thanks."

He grunted, going back to plating his own breakfast. He stood on the other side of the counter and wolfed down a few bites before he said, "Beyond the synth stuff and the antidote, I think the Horn ties everything together. We should concentrate on looking for it. There hasn't been a murder since the temple guard, but I doubt the person has dropped the search for it since they've already gone to such trouble. If we get our hands on the Horn, I still feel like the killer will save us the trouble of looking for them and come right to us."

"Or maybe they found wherever Danika hid it already." She took another bite. "Maybe they're just waiting until the Summit or something."

"Maybe. If that's the case, then we need to figure out who has it. Immediately."

"But even Ruhn can't find it. Danika didn't leave any hint of where she hid it. None of her last known locations were likely hiding spots."

"So maybe today we go back to square one. Look at everything we've learned and—"

"I can't today." She finished off her breakfast and brought the plate over to the sink. "I've got some meetings."

"Reschedule them."

"Jesiba needs them held today."

He looked at her for a long moment, as if he could see through everything she'd said, but finally nodded.

She ignored the disappointment and concern in his face, his tone, as he said, "All right."

Lehabah sighed. "You're being mean today, BB. And don't blame it on your cycle."

Seated at the table in the heart of the gallery's library, Bryce massaged her brows with her thumb and forefinger. "Sorry."

Her phone lay dark and quiet on the table beside her.

"You didn't invite Athie down here for lunch."

"I didn't need the distraction." The lie was smooth. Hunt hadn't called her on the other lie, either—that Jesiba was watching the gallery cameras today, so he should stay on the roof.

But despite needing him, needing everyone, at arm's length today, and despite claiming she couldn't look for the Horn, she'd been combing over various texts regarding it for hours now. There was nothing in them but the same information, over and over.

A faint scratching sound stretched across the entire length of the library. Bryce pulled over Lehabah's tablet and cranked up the volume on the speakers, blasting music through the space.

A loud, angry *thump* sounded. From the corner of her eye, she watched the nøkk swim off, its translucent tail slashing through the dim water.

Pop music: Who would have thought it was such a strong deterrent for the creature?

"He wants to kill me," Lehabah whispered. "I can tell."

"I doubt you'd make a very satisfying snack," Bryce said. "Not even a mouthful."

"He knows that if I'm submerged in water, I'm dead in a heartbeat."

It was another form of torture for the sprite, Bryce had realized early on. A way for Jesiba to keep Lehabah in line down here, caged within a cage, as surely as all the other animals throughout the space. No better way to intimidate a fire sprite than to have a hundred-thousand-gallon tank looming.

"He wants to kill you, too," Lehabah whispered. "You ignore him, and he hates that. I can see the rage and hunger in his eyes when he looks at you, BB. Be careful when you feed him."

"I am." The feeding hatch was too small for it to fit through anyway. And since the nøkk wouldn't dare bring its head above the water for fear of the air, only its arms were a threat if the hatch was opened and the feeding platform was lowered into the water. But it kept to the bottom of the tank, hiding among the rocks whenever she dumped in the steaks, letting them drift lazily down.

It wanted to hunt. Wanted something big, juicy, and frightened.

Bryce glanced toward the dim tank, illuminated by three

built-in spotlights. "Jesiba will get bored with him soon and gift him to a client," she lied to Lehabah.

"Why does she collect us at all?" the sprite whispered. "Am I not a person, too?" She pointed to the tattoo on her wrist. "Why do they insist on this?"

"Because we live in a republic that has decided that threats to its order have to be punished—and punished so thoroughly that it makes others hesitate to rebel, too." Her words were flat. Cold.

"Have you ever thought of what it might be like—without the Asteri?"

Bryce shot her a look. "Be quiet, Lehabah."

"But BB—"

"Be *quiet*, Lehabah." There were cameras everywhere in this library, all with audio. They were exclusive to Jesiba, yes, but to speak of it here . . .

Lehabah drifted to her little couch. "Athie would talk to me about it."

"Athie is a slave with little left to lose."

"Don't say such things, BB," Lehabah hissed. "There is *always* something left to lose."

Bryce was in a foul spirit. Maybe there was something going on with Ruhn or Juniper. Hunt had seen her checking her phone frequently this morning, as if waiting for a call or message. None had come. At least, as far as he could tell on the walk to the gallery. And, judging by the distant, sharp look still on her face as she left just before sunset, none had come in during the day, either.

But she didn't head home. She went to a bakery.

Hunt kept to the rooftops nearby, watching while she walked into the aqua-painted interior and walked out three minutes later with a white box in her hands.

Then she turned her steps toward the river, dodging workers and tourists and shoppers all enjoying the end of the day. If she was aware that he followed, she didn't seem to care. Didn't even look up once as she aimed for a wooden bench along the river walkway.

The setting sun gilded the mists veiling the Bone Quarter. A few feet down the paved walkway, the dark arches of the Black Dock loomed. No mourning families stood beneath them today, waiting for the onyx boat to take their coffin.

Bryce sat on the bench overlooking the river and the Sleeping City, the white bakery box beside her, and checked her phone again.

Sick of waiting until she deigned to talk to him about whatever was eating her up, Hunt landed quietly before sliding onto the bench's wooden planks, the box between them. "What's up?"

Bryce stared out at the river. She looked drained. Like that first night he'd seen her, in the legion's holding center.

She still wasn't looking at him when she said, "Danika would have been twenty-five today."

Hunt went still. "It's . . . Today's Danika's birthday."

She glanced to her phone, discarded at her side. "No one remembered. Not Juniper or Fury—not even my mom. Last year, they remembered, but . . . I guess it was a onetime thing."

"You could have asked them."

"I know they're busy. And . . ." She ran a hand through her hair. "Honestly, I thought they'd remember. I *wanted* them to remember. Even just a message saying something bullshitty, like *I miss her* or whatever."

"What's in the box?"

"Chocolate croissants," she said hoarsely. "Danika always wanted them on her birthday. They were her favorite."

Hunt looked from the box to her, then to the looming Bone Quarter across the river. How many croissants had he seen her eating these weeks? Perhaps in part because they connected her to Danika the same way that scar on her thigh did. When he looked back at her, her mouth was a tight, trembling line.

"It sucks," she said, her voice thick. "It sucks that everyone just . . . moves on, and forgets. They expect me to forget. But I can't." She rubbed at her chest. "I *can't* forget. And maybe it's fucking weird that I bought my dead friend a bunch of birthday croissants. But the world moved on. Like she never existed."

He watched her for a long moment. Then he said, "Shahar was that for me. I'd never met anyone like her. I think I loved her from the moment I laid eyes on her in her palace, even though she was so high above me that she might as well have been the moon. But she saw me too. And somehow, she picked me. Out of all of them, she picked me." He shook his head, the words creaking from him as they crept from that box he'd locked them in all this while. "I would have done anything for her. I *did* anything for her. Anything she asked. And when it all went to Hel, when they told me it was over, I refused to believe it. How could she be gone? It was like saying the sun was gone. It just . . . there was nothing left if she wasn't there." He ran a hand through his hair. "This won't be a consolation, but it took me about fifty years before I really believed it. That it was over. Yet even now . . ."

"You still love her that much?"

He held her gaze, unflinching. "After my mother died, I basically fell into my grief. But Shahar—she brought me out of that. Made me feel alive for the first time. Aware of myself, of my potential. I'll always love her, if only for that."

She looked to the river. "I never realized it," she murmured. "That you and I are mirrors."

He hadn't, either. But a voice floated back to him. *You look how I feel every day*, she'd whispered when she'd cleaned him up after Micah's latest assignment. "Is it a bad thing?"

A half smile tugged at a corner of her mouth. "No. No, it isn't."

"No issue with the Umbra Mortis being your emotional twin?"

But her face grew serious again. "That's what they call you, but that's not who you are."

"And who am I?"

"A pain in my ass." Her smile was brighter than the setting sun on the river. He laughed, but she added, "You're my friend. Who watches trashy TV with me and puts up with my shit. You're the person I don't need to explain myself to—not when it matters. You see everything I am, and you don't run away from it."

He smiled at her, let it convey everything that glowed inside him at her words. "I like that."

Color stained her cheeks, but she blew out a breath as she turned toward the box. "Well, Danika," she said. "Happy birthday."

She peeled off the tape and flipped back the top.

Her smile vanished. She shut the lid before Hunt could see what was inside.

"What is it?"

She shook her head, making to grab the box—but Hunt grabbed it first, pulling it onto his lap and opening the lid.

Inside lay half a dozen croissants, carefully arranged in a pile. And on the top one, artfully written in a chocolate drizzle, was one word: *Trash*.

It wasn't the hateful word that tore through him. No, it was the way Bryce's hands shook, the way her face turned red, and her mouth became a thin line.

"Just throw it out," she whispered.

No hint of the loyal defiance and anger. Just exhausted, humiliated pain.

His head went quiet. Terribly, terribly quiet.

"Just throw it out, Hunt," she whispered again. Tears shone in her eyes.

So Hunt took the box. And he stood.

He had a good idea of who had done it. Who'd had the message altered. Who had shouted that same word—*trash*—at Bryce the other week, when they'd left the Den.

"Don't," Bryce pleaded. But Hunt was already airborne.

Amelie Ravenscroft was laughing with her friends, swigging from a beer, when Hunt exploded into the Moonwood bar. People screamed and fell back, magic flaring.

But Hunt only saw her. Saw her claws form as she smirked at him. He set the pastry box on the wooden bar with careful precision.

A phone call to the Aux had given him the info he needed about the shifter's whereabouts. And Amelie seemed to have been waiting for him, or at least Bryce, when she leaned back against the bar and sneered, "Well, isn't this—"

Hunt pinned her against the wall by the throat.

The growls and attempted attacks of her pack against the wall of rippling lightning he threw up were background noise. Fear gleamed in Amelie's wide, shocked eyes as Hunt snarled in her face.

But he said softly, "You don't speak to her, you don't go near her, you don't even fucking *think* about her again." He sent enough of his lightning through his touch that he knew pain lashed through her body. Amelie choked. "Do you understand me?"

People were on their phones, dialing for the 33rd Legion or the Auxiliary.

Amelie scratched at his wrists, her boots kicking at his shins. He only tightened his grip. Lightning wrapped around her throat. "Do you understand?" His voice was frozen. Utterly calm. The voice of the Umbra Mortis.

A male approached his periphery. Ithan Holstrom.

But Ithan's eyes were on Amelie as he breathed, "What did you do, Amelie?"

Hunt only said, snarling again in Amelie's face, "Don't play dumb, Holstrom."

Ithan noticed the pastry box on the bar then. Amelie thrashed, but Hunt held her still as her Second opened the lid and looked inside. Ithan asked softly, "What is this?"

"Ask your Alpha," Hunt ground out.

Ithan went utterly still. But whatever he was thinking wasn't Hunt's concern, not as he met Amelic's burning stare again. Hunt said, "You leave her the fuck alone. *Forever.* Got it?"

Amelie looked like she'd spit on him, but he sent another casual zap of power into her, flaying her from the inside out. She winced, hissing and gagging. But nodded.

Hunt immediately released her, but his power kept her pinned against the wall. He surveyed her, then her pack. Then Ithan, whose face had gone from horror to something near grief as he must have realized what day it was and pieced enough of it together—thought about who had always wanted chocolate croissants on this day, at least.

Hunt said, "You're all pathetic."

And then he walked out. Took a damn while flying home.

Bryce was waiting for him on the roof. A phone in her hand. "No," she was saying to someone on the line. "No, he's back."

"Good," he heard Isaiah say, and it sounded like the male was about to add something else when she hung up.

Bryce wrapped her arms around herself. "You're a fucking idiot."

Hunt didn't deny it.

"Is Amelie dead?" There was fear—actual fear—in her face.

"No." The word rumbled from him, lightning hissing in its wake.

"You . . ." She rubbed at her face. "I didn't—"

"Don't tell me I'm an alphahole, or possessive and aggressive or whatever terms you use."

She lowered her hands, her face stark with dread. "You'll get in so much trouble for this, Hunt. There's no way you won't—"

It was fear *for* him. Terror for *him*.

Hunt crossed the distance between them. Took her hands. "You're my mirror. You said so yourself."

He was shaking. For some reason, he was shaking as he waited for her to respond.

Bryce looked at her hands, gripped in his, as she answered, "Yes."

The next morning, Bryce messaged her brother. *What's your medwitch's number?*

Ruhn sent it immediately, no questions asked.

Bryce called her office a minute later, hands shaking. The fair-voiced medwitch could squeeze her in—immediately. So Bryce didn't give herself the time to reconsider as she slid on her running shorts and a T-shirt, then messaged Jesiba:

Medical appointment this morning. Be at the gallery by lunch.

She found Hunt making breakfast. His brows rose when she just stared at him.

"I know where we can get kristallos venom for the medwitch's antidote tests," she said.

61

The medwitch's immaculately clean white clinic was small, not like the larger practices Bryce had visited in the past. And rather than the standard blue neon sign that jutted over nearly every other block in this city, the broom-and-bell insignia had been rendered in loving care on a gilded wooden sign hanging outside. About the only old-school-looking thing about the place.

The door down the hallway behind the counter opened, and the medwitch appeared, her curly dark hair pulled back into a bun that showed off her elegant brown face. "You must be Bryce," the woman said, her full smile instantly setting Bryce at ease. She glanced to Hunt, giving him a shallow nod of recognition. But she made no mention of their encounter in the night garden before she said to Bryce, "Your partner can come back with you if you would like. The treatment room can accommodate his wings."

Hunt looked at Bryce, and she saw the question in his expression: *Do you want me with you?*

Bryce smiled at the witch. "My partner would love to come."

The white treatment room, despite the clinic's small size, contained all the latest technology. A bank of computers sat against one wall, the long mechanical arm of a surgical light was set against the other.

The third wall held a shelf of various tonics and potions and powders in sleek glass vials, and a chrome cabinet on the fourth wall likely possessed the actual surgical instruments.

A far cry from the wood-paneled shops Hunt had visited in Pangera, where witches still made their own potions in iron cauldrons that had been passed down through the generations.

The witch idly patted the white leather examination table in the center of the room. Hidden panels gleamed in its plastic sides, extensions for Vanir of all shapes and sizes.

Hunt claimed the lone wooden chair by the cabinet as Bryce hopped onto the table, her face slightly pale.

"You said on the phone that you received this wound from a kristallos demon, and it was never healed—the venom is still in you."

"Yes," Bryce said quietly. Hunt hated every bit of pain that laced that word.

"And you give me permission to use the venom I extract in my experiments as I search for a synth antidote?"

Bryce glanced at him, and he nodded his encouragement. "An antidote to synth seems pretty damn important to have," she said, "so yes, you have my permission."

"Good. Thank you." The medwitch rifled through a chart, presumably the one Bryce had filled out on the woman's website, along with the medical records that were tied to her file as a civitas. "I see that the trauma to your leg occurred nearly two years ago?"

Bryce fiddled with the hem of her shirt. "Yes. It, um—it closed up, but still hurts. When I run or walk too much, it burns, right along my bone." Hunt refrained from grunting his annoyance.

The witch's brow creased, and she looked up from the file to glance at Bryce's leg. "How long has the pain been present?"

"Since the start," Bryce said, not looking at him.

The medwitch glanced at Hunt. "Were you there for this attack as well?"

Bryce opened her mouth to answer, but Hunt said, "Yes." Bryce whipped her head around to look at him. He kept his eyes on the witch. "I arrived three minutes after it occurred. Her leg was ripped open across the thigh, courtesy of the kristallos's teeth." The words tumbled out, the confession spilling from his lips. "I used one of the legion's medical staplers to seal the wound as best I could." Hunt went on, unsure why his heart was thundering, "The medical note about the injury is from me. She didn't receive any treatment after that. It's why the scar . . ." He swallowed against the guilt working its way up his throat. "It's why it looks the way it does." He met Bryce's eyes, letting her see the apology there. "It's my fault."

Bryce stared at him. Not a trace of damnation on her face—just raw understanding.

The witch glanced between them, as if debating whether to give them a moment. But she asked Bryce, "So you did not see a medwitch after that night?"

Bryce still held Hunt's gaze as she said to the woman, "No."

"Why?"

Her eyes still didn't leave his as she rasped, "Because I wanted to hurt. I wanted it to remind me every day." Those were tears in her eyes. Tears forming, and he didn't know why.

The witch kindly ignored her tears. "Very well. The *why*s and *how*s aren't as important as what remains in the wound." She frowned. "I can treat you today, and if you stick around afterward, you're welcome to watch me test your sample. The venom, in order to be an effective antidote, needs to be stabilized so it can interact with the synth and reverse its effects. My healing magic can do that, but I need to be present in order to hold that stability. I'm trying to find a way for the magic to permanently hold the stabilization so it can be sent out into the world and widely used."

"Sounds like some tricky stuff," Bryce said, looking away from Hunt at last. He felt the absence of her stare as if a warm flame had been extinguished.

The witch lifted her hands, white light shining at her fingertips then fading away, as if giving a quick check of her magic's readiness. "I was raised by tutors versed in our oldest forms of magic. They taught me an array of specialized knowledge."

Bryce let out a breath through her nose. "All right. Let's get on with it, then."

But the witch's face grew grave. "Bryce, I have to open the wound. I can numb you so you don't feel that part, but the venom, if it's as deep as I suspect . . . I cannot use mithridate leeches to extract it." She gestured to Hunt. "With his wound the other night, the poison had not yet taken root. With an injury like yours, deep and old . . . The venom is a kind of organism. It feeds off you. It won't want to go easily, especially after so long meshing itself to your body. I shall have to use my own magic to pull it from your body. And the venom might very well try to convince you to get me to stop. Through pain."

"It's going to hurt her?" Hunt asked.

The witch winced. "Badly enough that the local anesthesia cannot help. If you like, I can get a surgical center booked and put you under, but it could take a day or two—"

"We do it today. Right now," Bryce said, her eyes meeting Hunt's again. He could only offer her a solid nod in return.

"All right," the witch said, striding gracefully to the sink to wash her hands. "Let's get started."

The damage was as bad as she'd feared. Worse.

The witch was able to scan Bryce's leg, first with a machine, then with her power, the two combining to form an image on the screen against the far wall.

"You see the dark band along your femur?" The witch pointed to a jagged line like forked lightning through Bryce's thigh. "That's the venom. Every time you run or walk too long, it creeps into the surrounding area and hurts you." She pointed to a white area above it. "That's all scar tissue. I need to cut through it first, but that should be fast. The extraction is what might take a while."

Bryce tried to hide her trembling as she nodded. She'd already signed half a dozen waivers.

Hunt sat in the chair, watching.

"Right," the witch said, washing her hands again. "Change into a gown, and we can begin." She reached for the metal cabinet near Hunt, and Bryce removed her shorts. Her shirt.

Hunt looked away, and the witch helped Bryce step into a light cotton shift, tying it at the back for her.

"Your tattoo is lovely," the medwitch said. "I don't recognize the alphabet, though—what does it say?"

Bryce could still feel every needle prick that had made the scrolling lines of text on her back. "*Through love, all is possible.* Basically: my best friend and I will never be parted."

A hum of approval as the medwitch looked between Bryce and Hunt. "You two have such a powerful bond." Bryce didn't bother to correct her assumption that the tattoo was about Hunt. The tattoo that Danika had drunkenly insisted they get one night, claiming that putting the vow of eternal friendship in another language would make it less cheesy.

Hunt turned back to them, and the witch asked him, "Does the halo hurt you?"

"Only when it went on."

"What witch inked it?"

"Some imperial hag," Hunt said through his teeth. "One of the Old Ones."

The witch's face tightened. "It is a darker aspect of our work—that we bind individuals through the halo. It should be halted entirely."

He threw her a half smile that didn't reach his eyes. "Want to take it off for me?"

The witch went wholly still, and Bryce's breath caught in her throat. "What would you do if I did?" the witch asked softly, her dark eyes glimmering with interest—and ancient power. "Would you punish those who have held you captive?"

Bryce opened her mouth to warn them that this was a dangerous conversation, but Hunt thankfully said, "I'm not here to talk about my tattoo."

It lay in his eyes, though—his answer. The confirmation. Yes, he'd kill the people who'd done this. The witch inclined her head slightly, as if she saw that answer.

She turned back to Bryce and patted the examination table. "Very well. Lie on your back, Miss Quinlan."

Bryce began shaking as she obeyed. As the witch strapped down her upper body, then her legs, and adjusted the arm of the surgical light. A cart rattled as the witch hauled over a tray of various gleaming silver instruments, cotton pads, and an empty glass vial.

"I'm going to numb you first," the witch said, and then a needle was in her gloved hands.

Bryce shook harder.

"Deep breaths," the witch said, tapping the air bubbles from the needle.

A chair scraped, and then a warm, calloused hand wrapped around Bryce's.

Hunt's eyes locked on hers. "Deep breath, Bryce."

She sucked one in. The needle sank into her thigh, its prick drawing tears. She squeezed Hunt's hand hard enough to feel bones grinding. He didn't so much as flinch.

The pain swiftly faded, numbness tingling over her leg. Deep inside it.

"Do you feel this?" the witch asked.

"Feel what?"

"Good," the witch declared. "I'm starting now. I can put up a little curtain if you—"

"No," Bryce gritted out. "Just do it."

No delays. No waiting.

She saw the witch lift the scalpel, and then a slight, firm pressure pushed against her leg. Bryce shook again, blasting a breath through her clenched teeth.

"Steady now," the witch said. "I'm cutting through the scar tissue."

Hunt's dark eyes held hers, and she forced herself to think of him instead of her leg. He had been there that night. In the alley.

The memory surfaced, the fog of pain and terror and grief clearing slightly. Strong, warm hands gripping her. Just as he held her hand now. A voice speaking to her. Then utter stillness, as if his voice had been a bell. And then those strong, warm hands on her thigh, holding her as she sobbed and screamed.

I've got you, he'd said over and over. *I've got you.*

"I believe I can remove most of this scar tissue," the witch observed. "But . . ." She swore softly. "Luna above, look at this."

Bryce refused to look, but Hunt's eyes slid to the screen behind her, where her bloody wound was on display. A muscle ticked in his jaw. It said enough about what was inside the wound.

"I don't understand how you're walking," the witch murmured. "You said you weren't taking painkillers to manage it?"

"Only during flare-ups," Bryce whispered.

"Bryce . . ." The witch hesitated. "I'm going to need you to hold very still. And to breathe as deeply as you can."

"Okay." Her voice sounded small.

Hunt's hand clasped hers. Bryce took a steadying breath—

Someone poured acid into her leg, and her skin was sizzling, bones melting away—

In and out, out and in, her breath sliced through her teeth. Oh gods, oh gods—

Hunt interlaced their fingers, squeezing.

It burned and burned and burned and burned—

"When I got to the alley that night," he said above the rush of her frantic breathing, "you were bleeding everywhere. Yet you tried to protect him first. You wouldn't let us get near until we showed you our badges and proved we were from the legion."

She whimpered, her breathing unable to outrun the razor-sharp digging, digging, digging—

Hunt's fingers stroked over her brow. "I thought to myself, *There's someone I want guarding my back. There's a friend I'd like to have.* I think I gave you such a hard time when we met up again because . . . because some part of me knew that, and was afraid of what it'd mean."

She couldn't stop the tears sliding down her face.

His eyes didn't waver from hers. "I was there in the interrogation room, too." His fingers drifted through her hair, gentle and calming. "I was there for all of it."

The pain struck deep, and she couldn't help the scream that worked its way out of her.

Hunt leaned forward, putting his cool brow against hers. "I've known who you were this whole time. I never forgot you."

"I'm beginning extraction and stabilization of the venom," the witch said. "It will worsen, but it's almost over."

Bryce couldn't breathe. Couldn't think beyond Hunt and his words and the pain in her leg, the scar across her very soul.

Hunt whispered, "You've got this. You've got this, Bryce."

She didn't. And the Hel that erupted in her leg had her arching against the restraints, her vocal cords straining as her screaming filled the room.

Hunt's grip never wavered.

"It's almost out," the witch hissed, grunting with effort. "Hang on, Bryce."

She did. To Hunt, to his hand, to that softness in his eyes, she held on. With all she had.

"I've got you," he murmured. "Sweetheart, I've got you."

He'd never said it like that before—that word. It had always been mocking, teasing. She'd always found it just this side of annoying.

Not this time. Not when he held her hand and her gaze and everything she was. Riding out the pain with her.

"Breathe," he ordered her. "You can do it. We can get through this."

Get through it—together. Get through this mess of a life together. Through this mess of a world. Bryce sobbed, not entirely from pain this time.

And Hunt, as if he sensed it, too, leaned forward again. Brushed his mouth against hers.

Just a hint of a kiss—a feather-soft glancing of his lips over hers.

A star bloomed inside her at that kiss. A long-slumbering light began to fill her chest, her veins.

"Burning Solas," the witch whispered, and the pain ceased.

Like a switch had been flipped, the pain was gone. It was startling enough that Bryce turned away from Hunt and peered at her body, the blood on it, the gaping wound. She might have fainted at the sight of a good six inches of her leg lying open were it not for the thing that the witch held between a set of pincers, as if it were indeed a worm.

"If my magic wasn't stabilizing the venom like this, it'd be liquid," the witch said, carefully moving the venom—a clear, wriggling worm with black flecks—toward a glass jar. It writhed, like a living thing.

The witch deposited it in the jar and shut the lid, magic humming. The poison instantly dissolved into a puddle within, but still vibrated. As if looking for a way out.

Hunt's eyes were still on Bryce's face. As they'd been the entire time. Had never left.

"Let me clean you out and stitch you up, and then we'll test the antidote," the witch said.

Bryce barely heard the woman as she nodded. Barely heard anything beyond Hunt's lingering words. *I've got you.*

Her fingers curled around his. She let her eyes tell him everything her ravaged throat couldn't. *I've got you, too.*

Thirty minutes later, Bryce was sitting up, Hunt's arm and wing around her, both of them watching as the witch's glowing, pale magic wrapped around the puddle of venom in the vial and warped it into a thin thread.

"You'll forgive me if my method of antidote testing fails to qualify as a proper medical experiment," she declared as she walked over to where an ordinary white pill sat in a clear plastic box. Lifting the lid, she dropped the thread of venom in. It fluttered like a ribbon, hovering above the pill before the witch shut the lid again. "What is being used on the street is a much more potent version of this," she said, "but I want to see if this amount of my healing magic, holding the venom in place and merging with it, will do the trick against the synth."

The witch carefully let the thread of the magic-infused venom alight on the tablet. It vanished within a blink, sucked into the pill.

But the witch's face remained bunched in concentration. As if focused on whatever was happening within the pill.

Bryce asked, "So your magic is currently stabilizing the venom in that tablet? Making it stop the synth?"

"Essentially," the witch said distantly, still focused on the pill. "It takes most of my concentration to keep it stable long enough to halt the synth. Which is why I'd like to find a way to remove myself from the equation—so it can be used by anyone, even without me."

Bryce fell silent after that, letting the witch work in peace.

Nothing happened. The pill merely sat there.

One minute passed. Two. And just as it was nearing three minutes—

The pill turned gray. And then dissolved into nothing but minuscule particles that then faded away, too. Until there was nothing left.

Hunt said into the silence, "It worked?"

The witch blinked at the now-empty box. "It would appear so." She turned to Bryce, sweat gleaming on her brow. "I'd like to continue testing this, and try to find some way for the antidote to work without my magic stabilizing the venom. I can send over a vial for you when I'm finished, though, if you'd like. Some people want to keep such reminders of their struggles."

Bryce nodded blankly. And realized she had absolutely no idea what to do next.

62

Jesiba hadn't seemed to care when Bryce explained that she needed the rest of the day off. She'd just demanded that Bryce be in first thing tomorrow or be turned into a donkey.

Hunt flew her home from the medwitch's office, going so far as to carry her down the stairs from the roof of the apartment building and through her door. He deposited her on the couch, where he insisted she stay for the remainder of the day, curled up beside him, snuggled into his warmth.

She might have stayed there all afternoon and evening if Hunt's phone hadn't rung.

He'd been in the midst of making her lunch when he picked up. "Hi, Micah."

Even from across the room, Bryce could hear the Archangel's cold, beautiful voice. "My office. Immediately. Bring Bryce Quinlan with you."

While he dressed in his battle-suit and gathered his helmet and weapons, Hunt debated telling Bryce to get on a train and get the fuck out of the city. He knew this meeting with Micah wasn't going to be pleasant.

Bryce was limping, her wound still tender enough that he'd

grabbed her a pair of loose workout pants and helped her put them on in the middle of the living room. She'd registered for a follow-up appointment in a month, and it only now occurred to Hunt that he might not be there to see it.

Either because this case had wrapped up, or because of whatever the fuck was about to go down in the Comitium.

Bryce tried to take all of one step before Hunt picked her up, carrying her out of the apartment and into the skies. She barely spoke, and neither did he. After this morning, what use were words? That too-brief kiss he'd given her had said enough. So had the light he could have sworn glowed in her eyes as he'd pulled away.

A line had been crossed, one from which there was no walking away.

Hunt landed on a balcony of the Governor's spire—the central of the Comitium's five. The usually bustling hall of his public office was hushed. Bad sign. He carried Bryce toward the chamber. If people had run, or Micah ordered them out . . .

If he saw Sandriel right now, if she realized Bryce was injured . . .

Hunt's temper became a living, deadly thing. His lightning pushed against his skin, coiling through him, a cobra readying to strike.

He gently set Bryce down before the shut fogged-glass office doors. Made sure she was steady on her feet before he let go, stepping back to study every inch of her face.

Worry shone in her eyes, enough of it that he leaned in, brushing a kiss over her temple. "Chin up, Quinlan," he murmured against her soft skin. "Let's see you do that fancy trick where you somehow look down your nose at people a foot taller than you."

She chuckled, smacking him lightly on the arm. Hunt pulled away with a half smile of his own before opening the doors and guiding Bryce through with a hand on her back. He knew it would likely be his last smile for a long while. But he'd be damned if he let Quinlan know it. Even as they beheld who stood in Micah's office.

To the left of the Governor's desk stood Sabine, arms crossed and spine rigid, the portrait of cold fury. A tight-faced Amelie lingered at her side.

He knew precisely what this meeting was about.

Micah stood at the window, his face glacial with distaste. Isaiah and Viktoria flanked his desk. The former's eyes flashed with warning.

Bryce glanced between them all and hesitated.

Hunt said quietly to Micah, to Sabine, "Quinlan doesn't need to be here for this."

Sabine's silvery blond hair shimmered in the firstlight lamps as she said, "Oh, she does. I want her here for every second."

"I won't bother asking if it's true," Micah said to Hunt as he and Bryce stopped in the center of the room. The doors shut behind them. Locking.

Hunt braced himself.

Micah said, "There were six cameras in the bar. They all captured what you did and said to Amelie Ravenscroft. She reported your behavior to Sabine, and Sabine brought it directly to me."

Amelie flushed. "I just mentioned it to her," she amended. "I didn't howl like a pup about it."

"It is unacceptable," Sabine hissed to Micah. "You think you can set your assassin on a member of one of *my* packs? My heir?"

"I will tell you again, Sabine," Micah said, bored, "I did not set Hunt Athalar upon her. He acted of his own free will." A glance at Bryce. "He acted on behalf of his companion."

Hunt said quickly, "Bryce had nothing to do with this. Amelie pulled a bullshit prank and I decided to pay her a visit." He bared his teeth at the young Alpha, who swallowed hard.

Sabine snapped, "You assaulted my captain."

"I told Amelie to stay the fuck away," Hunt bit out. "To leave her alone." He angled his head, unable to stop the words. "Or are you unaware that Amelie has been gunning for Bryce since your daughter died? Taunting her about it? Calling her trash?"

Sabine's face didn't so much as flinch. "What does it matter, if it's true?"

Hunt's head filled with roaring. But Bryce just stood there. And lowered her eyes.

Sabine said to Micah, "This cannot go unpunished. You fumbled the investigation of my daughter's murder. You allowed these two to poke their noses into it, to accuse *me* of killing her. And now this. I'm one breath away from telling this city how your *slaves* cannot even stay in line. I'm sure your current guest will be highly interested in that little fact."

Micah's power rumbled at the mention of Sandriel. "Athalar will be punished."

"Now. Here." Sabine's face was positively lupine. "Where I can see it."

"Sabine," Amelie murmured. Sabine growled at her young captain.

Sabine had been hoping for this moment—had used Amelie as an excuse. No doubt dragged the wolf here. Sabine had sworn they'd pay for accusing her of murdering Danika. And Sabine was, Hunt supposed, a female of her word.

"Your position among the wolves," Micah said with terrifying calm, "does not entitle you to tell a Governor of the Republic what to do."

Sabine didn't back down. Not an inch.

Micah just loosed a long breath. He met Hunt's eyes, disappointed. "You acted foolishly. I'd have thought you, at least, would know better."

Bryce was shaking. But Hunt didn't dare touch her.

"History indicates that a slave assaulting a free citizen should automatically forfeit their life."

Hunt suppressed a bitter laugh at her words. Wasn't that what he'd been doing for the Archangels for centuries now?

"Please," Bryce whispered.

And perhaps it was sympathy that softened the Archangel's face as Micah said, "Those are old traditions. For Pangera, not Valbara." Sabine opened her mouth, objecting, but Micah lifted a hand. "Hunt Athalar will be punished. And he shall die—in the way that angels die."

Bryce lurched a limping step toward Micah. Hunt grabbed her by the shoulder, halting her.

Micah said, "The Living Death."

Hunt's blood chilled. But he bowed his head. He had been ready to face the consequences since he'd shot into the skies yesterday, pastry box in his hands.

Bryce looked at Isaiah, whose face was grim, for an explanation. The commander said to her, to the confused Amelie, "The Living Death is when an angel's wings are cut off."

Bryce shook her head. "No, please—"

But Hunt met Micah's rock-solid stare, read the fairness in it. He lowered himself to his knees and removed his jacket, then his shirt.

"I don't need to press charges," Amelie insisted. "Sabine, *I don't want this.* Let it go."

Micah stalked toward Hunt, a shining double-edged sword appearing in his hand.

Bryce flung herself in the Archangel's path. "Please—*please*—" The scent of her tears filled the office.

Viktoria instantly appeared at her side. Holding her back. The wraith's whisper was so quiet Hunt barely heard it. "They will grow back. In several weeks, his wings will grow back."

But it would hurt like Hel. Hurt so badly that Hunt now took steadying, bracing breaths. Plunged down into himself, into that place where he rode out everything that had ever been done to him, every task he'd been assigned, every life he'd been ordered to take.

"Sabine, *no*," Amelie insisted. "It's gone far enough."

Sabine said nothing. Just stood there.

Hunt spread his wings and lifted them, holding them high over his back so the slice might be clean.

Bryce began shouting something, but Hunt only looked at Micah. "Do it."

Micah didn't so much as nod before his sword moved.

Pain, such as Hunt had not experienced in two hundred years, raced through him, short-circuiting every—

* * *

Hunt jolted into consciousness to Bryce screaming.

It was enough of a summons that he forced his head to clear, even around the agony down his back, his soul.

He must have blacked out only for a moment, because his wings were still spurting blood from where they lay like two fallen branches on the floor of Micah's office.

Amelie looked like she was going to be sick; Sabine was smirking, and Bryce was now at his side, his blood soaking her pants, her hands, as she sobbed, "*Oh gods, oh gods—*"

"We're settled," Sabine said to Micah, who punched a button on his phone to call for a medwitch.

He'd paid for his actions, and it was over, and he could go home with Bryce—

"You are a disgrace, Sabine." Bryce's words speared through the room as she bared her teeth at the Prime Apparent. "You are a disgrace to every wolf who has ever walked this planet."

Sabine said, "I don't care what a half-breed thinks of me."

"You didn't deserve Danika," Bryce growled, shaking. "You didn't deserve her for one second."

Sabine halted. "I didn't deserve a selfish, spineless brat for a daughter, but that's not how it turned out, is it?"

Dimly, from far away, Bryce's snarl cut through Hunt's pain. He couldn't reach her in time, though, as she surged to her feet, wincing in agony at her still-healing leg.

Micah stepped in front of her. Bryce panted, sobbing through her teeth. But Micah stood there, immovable as a mountain. "Take Athalar out of here," the Archangel said calmly, the dismissal clear. "To your home, the barracks, I don't care."

But Sabine, it seemed, had decided to stay. To give Bryce a piece of her vicious mind.

Sabine said to her, low and venomous, "I sought out the Under-King last winter, did you know that? To get answers from my daughter, with whatever speck of her energy lives on in the Sleeping City."

Bryce stilled. The pure stillness of the Fae. Dread filled her eyes.

"Do you know what he told me?" Sabine's face was inhuman.

"He said that Danika would not come. She would not obey my summons. My pathetic daughter would not even deign to meet me in her afterlife. For the *shame* of what she did. How she died, helpless and screaming, begging like one of *you*." Sabine seemed to hum with rage. "And do you know what the Under-King told me when I demanded again that he summon her?"

No one else dared speak.

"He told me that *you*, you piece of trash, had made a bargain with him. For *her*. That *you* had gone to him after her death and traded your spot in the Bone Quarter in exchange for Danika's passage. That you worried she would be denied access because of her cowardly death and *begged* him to take her in your stead."

Even Hunt's pain paused at that.

"That wasn't why I went!" Bryce snapped. "Danika wasn't a coward for one *fucking* moment of her life!" Her voice broke as she shouted the last words.

"You had *no right*," Sabine exploded. "She *was* a coward, and died like one, and deserved to be dumped into the river!" The Alpha was screaming. "And now she is left with eons of *shame* because of you! Because she should not *be there*, you *stupid* whore. And now she must *suffer* for it!"

"That's enough," Micah said, his words conveying his order. *Get out.*

Sabine just let out a dead, cold laugh and turned on her heel.

Bryce was still sobbing when Sabine strutted out, a stunned Amelie on her heels. The latter murmured as she shut the door, "I'm sorry."

Bryce spat at her.

It was the last thing Hunt saw before darkness swept in again.

She would never forgive them. Any of them.

Hunt remained unconscious while the medwitches worked on him in Micah's office, stitching him up so that the stumps where his wings had been stopped spurting blood onto the floor, then dressing the wounds in bandages that would promote quick growth.

No firstlight—apparently, its aid in healing wasn't allowed for the Living Death. It would delegitimize the punishment.

Bryce knelt with Hunt the entire time, his head in her lap. She didn't hear Micah telling her how the alternative was Hunt being dead—officially and irrevocably dead.

She stroked Hunt's hair as they lay in her bed an hour later, his breathing still deep and even. *Give him the healing potion every six hours,* the medwitch ordered her. *It will stave off the pain, too.*

Isaiah and Naomi had carried them home, and she'd barely let them lay Hunt facedown on her mattress before she'd ordered them to get out.

She hadn't expected Sabine to understand why she'd given up her place in the Bone Quarter for Danika. Sabine never listened when Danika spoke about how she'd one day be buried there, in full honor, with all the other great heroes of her House. Living on, as that small speck of energy, for eternity. Still a part of the city she loved so much.

Bryce had seen people's boats tip. Would never forget Danika's half-muffled pleading on the audio of the apartment building's hall camera.

Bryce hadn't been willing to make the gamble that the boat might not reach the far shore. Not for Danika.

She'd tossed a Death Mark into the Istros, payment to the Under-King—a coin of pure iron from an ancient, long-gone kingdom across the sea. Passage for a mortal on a boat.

And then she'd knelt on the crumbling stone steps, the river mere feet behind her, the arches of the bone gates above her, and waited.

The Under-King, veiled in black and silent as death, had appeared moments later.

It has been an age since a mortal dared set foot on my isle.

The voice had been old and young, male and female, kind and full of hatred. She'd never heard anything so hideous—and beckoning.

I wish to trade my place.

I know why you are here, Bryce Quinlan. Whose passage you seek to barter. An amused pause. *Do you not wish to one day dwell here among the honored dead? Your balance remains skewed toward acceptance—continue on your path, and you shall be welcomed when your time comes.*

I wish to trade my place. For Danika Fendyr.

Do this and know that no other Quiet Realms of Midgard shall be open to you. Not the Bone Quarter, not the Catacombs of the Eternal City, not the Summer Isles of the north. None, Bryce Quinlan. To barter your resting place here is to barter your place everywhere.

I wish to trade my place.

You are young, and you are weighed with grief. Consider that your life may seem long, but it is a mere flutter of eternity.

I wish to trade my place.

Are you so certain Danika Fendyr will be denied welcome? Have you so little faith in her actions and deeds that you must make this bargain?

I wish to trade my place. She'd sobbed the words.

There is no undoing this.

I wish to trade my place.

Then say it, Bryce Quinlan, and let the trade be done. Say it a seventh and final time, and let the gods and the dead and all those between hear your vow. Say it, and it shall be done.

She hadn't hesitated, knowing this was the ancient rite. She'd looked it up in the gallery archives. Had stolen the Death Mark from there, too. It had been given to Jesiba by the Under-King himself, the sorceress had told her, when she'd sworn fealty to the House of Flame and Shadow.

I wish to trade my place.

And so it had been done.

Bryce had not felt any different afterward, when she'd been sent back over the river. Or in the days after that. Even her mother had not been able to tell—hadn't noticed that Bryce had snuck from her hotel room in the dead of night.

In the two years since, Bryce had sometimes wondered if she'd dreamed it, but then she'd look through the drawer in the gallery where all the old coins were kept and see the empty, dark spot where the Death Mark had been. Jesiba had never noticed it was gone.

Bryce liked to think of her chance at eternal rest as missing with it. To imagine the coins nestled in their velvet compartments in the drawer as all the souls of those she loved, dwelling together forever. And there was hers—missing and drifting, wiped away the moment she died.

But what Sabine had claimed about Danika suffering in the Bone Quarter . . . Bryce refused to believe it. Because the alternative—No. Danika had deserved to go to the Bone Quarter, had nothing to be ashamed about, whether Sabine or the other assholes disagreed or not. Whether the Under-King or whoever the Hel deemed their souls *worthy* disagreed or not.

Bryce ran her hand through Hunt's silken hair, the sounds of his breathing filling the room.

It sucked. This stupid fucking world they lived in.

It sucked, and it was full of awful people. And the good ones always paid for it.

She pulled her phone from the nightstand and began typing out a message.

She fired it off a moment later, not giving herself time to reconsider what she'd written to Ithan. Her first message to him in two years. His frantic messages from that horrible night, then his cold order to stay away, were still the last things in a thread that went back five years before that.

You tell your Alpha that Connor never bothered to notice her because he always knew what a piece of shit she was. And tell Sabine that if I see her again, I will kill her.

Bryce lay down next to Hunt, not daring to touch his ravaged back.

Her phone buzzed. Ithan had written, *I had no part in what went down today.*

Bryce wrote back, *You disgust me. All of you.*

Ithan didn't reply, and she put her phone on silent before she let out a long breath and leaned her brow against Hunt's shoulder.

She'd find a way to make this right. Somehow. Someday.

* * *

Hunt's eyes cracked open, pain a steady throb through him. Its sharpness was dulled—likely by some sort of potion or concoction of drugs.

The steady counterweight that should have been on his back was gone. The emptiness hit him like a semitruck. But soft, feminine breathing filled the darkness. A scent like paradise filled his nose, settled him. Soothed the pain.

His eyes adjusted to the dark enough to know that he was in Bryce's bedroom. That she was lying beside him. Medical supplies and vials lay next to the bed. All for him, many looking used. The clock read four in the morning. How many hours had she sat up, tending to him?

Her hands were tucked in at her chest, as if she had fallen asleep beseeching the gods.

He mouthed her name, his tongue as dry as sandpaper.

Pain rippled through his body, but he managed to stretch out an arm. Managed to slide it over her waist and tuck her into him. She made a soft sound and nuzzled her head into his neck.

Something deep in him shifted and settled. What she'd said and done today, what she'd revealed to the world in her pleading for him . . . It was dangerous. For both of them. So, so dangerous.

If he were wise, he'd find somehow to pull away. Before this thing between them met its inevitable, horrible end. As all things in the Republic met a horrible end.

And yet Hunt couldn't bring himself to remove his arm. To avoid the instinct to breathe in her scent and listen to her soft breathing.

He didn't regret it, what he'd done. Not one bit of it.

But there might come a day when that wouldn't be true. A day that might dawn very soon.

So Hunt savored the feel of Bryce. Her scent and breathing.

Savored every second of it.

63

Is Athie okay, BB?"

Bryce rubbed her eyes as she studied the computer screen in the gallery library. "He's sleeping it off."

Lehabah had cried this morning when Bryce had trudged in to tell her what had occurred. She'd barely noticed that her leg had no pain—not a whisper. She'd wanted to stay home, to care for Hunt, but when she'd called Jesiba, the answer had been clear: *No.*

She'd spent the first half of the morning filling out job applications.

And had sent each and every one of them in.

She didn't know where the Hel she would end up, but getting out of this place was the first step. Of many.

She'd taken a few more today.

Ruhn had picked up on the first ring, and come right over to the apartment.

Hunt had still been asleep when she'd left him in her brother's care. She didn't want anyone from that fucking legion in her house. Didn't want to see Isaiah or Viktoria or any of the triarii anytime soon.

Ruhn had taken one glance at Hunt's mutilated back and gagged. But he'd promised to stay on the pills-and-wound-care schedule she laid out for him.

"Micah went easy on him," Ruhn said when she stopped by at lunch, toying with one of his earrings. "Really fucking easy. Sabine had the right to call for his death." As a slave, Hunt had no rights whatsoever. None.

"I will never forget it as long as I live," Bryce answered, her voice dull. The flash of Micah's sword. Hunt's scream, as if his soul was being shredded. Sabine's smile.

"I should have been the one to shut Amelie up." Shadows flickered in the room.

"Well, you weren't." She measured the potion for Ruhn to give Hunt at the top of the hour.

Ruhn stretched an arm over the back of the sofa. "I'd like to be, Bryce."

She met her brother's gaze. "Why?"

"Because you're my sister."

She didn't have a response—not yet.

She could have sworn hurt flashed in his eyes at her silence. She was out of her apartment in another minute, and barely reached the gallery before Jesiba had called, raging about how Bryce wasn't ready for the two o'clock meeting with the owl shifter who was ready to buy a marble statuette worth three million gold marks.

Bryce executed the meeting, and the sale, and didn't hear half of what was said.

Sign, stamp, goodbye.

She returned to the library by three. Lehabah warmed her shoulder as she opened her laptop. "Why are you on Redner Industries' site?"

Bryce just stared at the two small fields:

Username. Password.

She typed in *dfendyr.* The cursor hovered over the password.

Someone might be tipped off that she was trying to get in. And if she did get access, someone might very well receive an alert. But . . . It was a risk worth taking. She was out of options.

Lehabah read the username. "Does this somehow tie in to the Horn?"

"Danika knew something—something big," Bryce mused.

Password. What would Danika's password be?

Redner Industries would have told her to write something random and full of symbols.

Danika would have hated being told what to do, and would have done the opposite.

Bryce typed in *SabineSucks.*

No luck. Though she'd done it the other day, she again typed in Danika's birthday. Her own birthday. The holy numbers. Nothing.

Her phone buzzed, and a message from Ruhn lit up her screen.

He woke up, took his potions like a good boy, and demanded to know where you were.

Ruhn added, *He's not a bad male.*

She wrote back, *No, he's not.*

Ruhn replied, *He's sleeping again, but seemed in good enough spirits, all things considered.*

A pause, and then her brother wrote, *He told me to tell you thanks. For everything.*

Bryce read the messages three times before she looked at the interface again. And typed in the only other password she could think of. The words written on the back of a leather jacket she'd worn constantly for the last two years. The words inked on her own back in an ancient alphabet. Danika's favorite phrase, whispered to her by the Oracle on her sixteenth birthday.

The Old Language of the Fae didn't work. Neither did the formal tongue of the Asteri.

So she wrote it in the common language.

Through love, all is possible.

The login screen vanished. And a list of files appeared.

Most were reports on Redner's latest projects: improving tracking quality on phones; comparing the speed at which shifters could change forms; analyzing the healing rates of witch magic versus Redner medicines. Boring everyday science.

She'd almost given up when she noticed a subfolder: *Party Invites.*

Danika had never been organized enough to keep such things, let alone put them in a folder. She either deleted them right away or let them rot in her inbox, unanswered.

It was enough of an anomaly that Bryce clicked on it and found a list of folders within. Including one titled *Bryce*.

A file with her name on it. Hidden in another file. Exactly as Bryce had hidden her own job applications on this computer.

"What is that?" Lehabah whispered at her shoulder.

Bryce opened the file. "I don't know. I never sent invites to her work address."

The folder contained a single photo.

"Why does she have a picture of her old jacket?" Lehabah asked. "Was she going to sell it?"

Bryce stared and stared at the image. Then she moved, logging out of the account before running up the stairs to the showroom, where she grabbed the leather jacket from her chair.

"It was a clue," she said breathlessly to Lehabah as she flew back down the stairs, fingers running and pawing over every seam of the jacket. "The photo is a fucking clue—"

Something hard snagged her fingers. A lump. Right along the vertical line of the *L* in *love*.

"Through love, all is possible," Bryce whispered, and grabbed a pair of scissors from the cup on the table. Danika had even tattooed the hint on Bryce's fucking *back*, for fuck's sake. Lehabah peered over her shoulder as Bryce cut into the leather.

A small, thin metal rectangle fell onto the table. A flash drive.

"Why would she hide that in her coat?" Lehabah asked, but Bryce was already moving again, hands shaking as she fitted the drive into the slot on her laptop.

Three unmarked videos lay within.

She opened the first video. She and Lehabah watched in silence.

Lehabah's whisper filled the library, even over the scratching of the nøkk.

"Gods spare us."

64

Hunt had managed to get out of bed and prove himself alive enough that Ruhn Danaan had finally left. He had no doubt the Fae Prince had called his cousin to inform her, but it didn't matter: Bryce was home in fifteen minutes.

Her face was white as death, so ashen that her freckles stood out like splattered blood. No sign of anything else amiss, not one thread on her black dress out of place.

"What." He was instantly at the door, wincing as he surged from where he'd been on the couch watching the evening news coverage of Rigelus, Bright Hand of the Asteri, giving a pretty speech about the rebel conflict in Pangera. It'd be another day or two before he could walk without pain. Another several weeks until his wings grew back. A few days after that until he could test out flying. Tomorrow, probably, the insufferable itching would begin.

He remembered every miserable second from the first time he'd had his wings cut off. All the surviving Fallen had endured it. Along with the insult of having their wings displayed in the crystal palace of the Asteri as trophies and warnings.

But she first asked, "How are you feeling?"

"Fine." Lie. Syrinx pranced at his feet, showering his hand with kisses. "What's wrong?"

Bryce wordlessly closed the door. Shut the curtains. Yanked out her phone from her jacket pocket, pulled up an email—from herself to herself—and clicked on an attached file. "Danika had a flash drive hidden in the lining of her jacket," Bryce said, voice shaking, and led him back to the couch, helping him to sit as the video loaded. Syrinx leapt onto the cushions, curling up beside him. Bryce sat on his other side, so close their thighs pressed together. She didn't seem to notice. After a heartbeat, Hunt didn't, either.

It was grainy, soundless footage of a padded cell.

At the bottom of the video, a ticker read: *Artificial Amplification for Power Dysfunction, Test Subject 7.*

A too-thin human female sat in the room in a med-gown. "What the fuck is this?" Hunt asked. But he already knew.

Synth. These were the synth research trials.

Bryce grunted—*keep watching.*

A young draki male in a lab coat entered the room, bearing a tray of supplies. The video sped up, as if someone had increased the speed of the footage for the sake of urgency. The draki male took her vitals and then injected something into her arm.

Then he left. Locked the door.

"Are they . . ." Hunt swallowed. "Did he just inject her with synth?"

Bryce made a small, confirming noise in her throat.

The camera kept rolling. A minute passed. Five. Ten.

Two Vanir walked into the room. Two large serpentine shifters who sized up the human female locked in alone with them. Hunt's stomach turned. Turned further at the slave tattoos on their arms, and knew that they were prisoners. Knew, from the way they smiled at the human female shrinking against the wall, why they had been locked up.

They lunged for her.

But the human female lunged, too.

It happened so fast that Hunt could barely track it. The person who had edited the footage went back and slowed it, too.

So he watched, blow by blow, as the human female launched herself at the two Vanir males.

And ripped them to pieces.

It was impossible. Utterly impossible. Unless—

Tharion had said synth could temporarily grant humans powers greater than most Vanir. Powers enough to kill.

"Do you know how badly the human rebels would want this?" Hunt said. Bryce just jerked her chin toward the screen. Where the footage kept going.

They sent in two other males. Bigger than the last. And they, too, wound up in pieces.

Piles.

Oh gods.

Another two. Then three. Then five.

Until the entire room was red. Until the Vanir were clawing at the doors, begging to be let out. Begging as their companions, then they themselves, were slaughtered.

The human female was screaming, her head tilted to the ceiling. Screaming in rage or pain or what, he couldn't tell without the sound.

Hunt knew what was coming next. Knew, and couldn't stop himself from watching.

She turned on herself. Ripped herself apart. Until she, too, was a pile on the floor.

The footage cut out.

Bryce said softly, "Danika must have figured out what they were working on in the labs. I think someone involved in these tests . . . Could they have sold the formula to some drug boss? Whoever killed Danika and the pack and the others must have been high on this synth. Or injected someone with it and sicced them on the victims."

Hunt shook his head. "Maybe, but how does it tie in to the demons and the Horn?"

"Maybe they summoned the kristallos for the antidote in its venom—and nothing more. They wanted to try to make an antidote of their own, in case the synth ever turned on them. Maybe it doesn't connect to the Horn at all," Bryce said. "Maybe this is what we were meant to find. There are two other videos like this, of two different human subjects. Danika left them for *me*. She must have known someone was coming for her. Must have known when she was on that Aux boat, confiscating that crate of synth, that they'd come after her soon. There was no second type of demon hunting alongside the kristallos. Just a person—from *this* world. Someone who was high on the synth and used its power to break through our apartment's enchantments. And then had the strength to kill Danika and the whole pack."

Hunt considered his next words carefully, fighting against his racing mind. "It could work, Bryce. But the Horn is still out there, with a drug that might be able to repair it, coincidence or no. And we're no closer to finding it." No, this just led them a Hel of a lot closer to trouble. He added, "Micah already demonstrated what it means to set one foot out of line. We need to go slow on the synth hunt. Make sure we're certain this time. And careful."

"*None* of you were able to find out anything like this. Why should I go slow with the only clue I have about who killed Danika and the Pack of Devils? This ties in, Hunt. I know it does."

And because she was opening her mouth to object again, he said what he knew would stop her. "Bryce, if we pursue this and we're wrong, if Micah learns about another fuckup, forget the bargain being over. I might not walk away from his next punishment."

She flinched.

His entire body protested as he reached a hand to touch her knee. "This synth shit is horrific, Bryce. I . . . I've never seen anything like it." It changed everything. *Everything.* He didn't even know where to begin sorting out all he'd seen. He should make some phone calls—*needed* to make some phone calls about this. "But to find the murderer and maybe the Horn, and to make sure there's an afterward for you and me"—because there would be a *you and me* for them; he'd do whatever it took to ensure it—"we need to be *smart.*" He nodded to the footage. "Forward that to me. I'll make sure it gets to Vik on our encrypted server. See what she can dig up about these trials."

Bryce scanned his face. The openness in her expression nearly sent him to his knees before her. Hunt waited for her to argue, to defy him. To tell him he was an idiot.

But she only said, "Okay." She let out a long breath, slumping back against the cushions.

She was so fucking beautiful he could barely stand it. Could barely stand to hear her ask quietly, "What sort of an afterward for you and me do you have in mind, Athalar?"

He didn't balk from her searching gaze. "The good kind," he said with equal quiet.

She didn't ask, though. About how it would be possible. How any of it would be possible for him, for them. What he'd do to make it so.

Her lips curved upward. "Sounds like a plan to me."

For a moment, an eternity, they stared at each other.

And despite what they'd just watched, what lurked in the world beyond the apartment, Hunt said, "Yeah?"

"Yeah." She toyed with the ends of her hair. "Hunt. You kissed me—at the medwitch's office."

He knew he shouldn't, knew it was ten kinds of stupid, but he said, "What about it?"

"Did you mean it?"

"Yes." He'd never said anything more true. "Did you want me to mean it?"

His heart began to race, fast enough that he nearly forgot the pain along his back as she said, "You know the answer to that, Athalar."

"Do you want me to do it again?" Fuck, his voice had dropped an octave.

Her eyes were clear, bright. Fearless and hopeful and everything that had always made it impossible for him to think about anything else if she was around. "*I* want to do it." She added, "If that's all right with you."

Hel, yes. He made himself throw her a half smile. "Do your worst, Quinlan."

She let out a breathy little laugh and turned her face up toward his. Hunt didn't so much as inhale too deeply for fear of startling her. Syrinx, apparently taking the hint, saw himself into his crate.

Bryce's hands shook as they lifted to his hair, brushed back a strand, then ran over the band of the halo.

Hunt gripped her trembling fingers. "What's this about?" he murmured, unable to help himself from pressing his mouth to the dusky nails. How many times had he thought about these hands on him? Caressing his face, stroking down his chest, wrapped around his cock?

Her swallow was audible. He pressed another kiss to her fingers.

"This wasn't supposed to happen—between us," she whispered.

"I know," he said, kissing her shaking fingers again. He gently unfurled them, exposing the heart of her palm. He pressed his mouth there, too. "But thank fucking Urd it did."

Her hands stopped shaking. Hunt lifted his eyes from her hand to find her own lined with silver—and full of fire. He interlaced their fingers. "For fuck's sake, just kiss me, Quinlan."

She did. Dark Hel, she did. His words had barely finished sounding when she slid her hand over his jaw, around his neck, and hauled his lips to hers.

The moment Hunt's lips met her own, Bryce erupted.

She didn't know if it was weeks without sex or Hunt himself, but she unleashed herself. That was the only way to describe it as she drove her hands into his hair and slanted her mouth against his.

No tentative, sweet kisses. Not for them. Never for them.

Her mouth opened at that first contact, and his tongue swept in, tasting her in savage, unrelenting strokes. Hunt groaned at that first taste—and the sound was kindling.

Rising onto her knees, fingers digging into his soft hair, she couldn't get enough, taste enough of him—rain and cedar and salt and pure lightning. His hands skimmed over her hips, slow and steady despite the mouth that ravaged hers with fierce, deep kisses.

His tongue danced with her own. She whimpered, and he let out a dark laugh as his hand wandered under the back of her dress, down the length of her spine, his calluses scraping. She arched into the touch, and he tore his mouth away.

Before she could grab his face back to hers, his lips found her neck. He pressed openmouthed kisses to it, nipped at the sensitive skin beneath her ears. "Tell me what you want, Quinlan."

"All of it." There was no doubt in her. None.

Hunt dragged his teeth along the side of her neck, and she panted, her entire consciousness narrowing to the sensation. "All of it?"

She slid her hand down his front. To his pants—the hard, considerable length straining against them. Urd spare her. She palmed his cock, eliciting a hiss from him. "All of it, Athalar."

"Thank fuck," he breathed against her neck, and she laughed.

Her laugh died as he put his mouth on hers again, as if he needed to taste the sound, too.

Tongues and teeth and breath, his hands artfully unhooking her bra under her dress. She wound up straddling his lap, wound up grinding herself over that beautiful, perfect hardness in his lap. Wound up with her dress peeled down to her waist, her bra gone, and then Hunt's mouth and teeth were around her breast, suckling and biting and kissing, and nothing, nothing, nothing had ever felt this good, this right.

Bryce didn't care that she was moaning loud enough for every demon in the Pit to hear. Not as Hunt switched to her other breast, sucking her nipple deep into his mouth. She drove her hips down on his, release already a rising wave in her. "Fuck, Bryce," he murmured against her breast.

She only dove her hand beneath the waist of his pants. His hand wrapped around her wrist, though. Halted her millimeters from what she'd wanted in her hands, her mouth, her body for weeks.

"Not yet," he growled, dragging his tongue along the underside of her breast. Content to feast on her. "Not until I've had my turn."

The words short-circuited every logical thought. And any objections died as he slipped a hand up her dress, running it over her thigh. Higher. His mouth found her neck again as a finger explored the lacy front of her underwear.

He hissed again as he found it utterly soaked, the lace doing nothing to hide the proof of just how badly she wanted this, wanted him. He ran his finger down the length of her—and back up again.

Then that finger landed on that spot at the apex of her thighs. His thumb gently pressed on it over the fabric, drawing a moan deep from her throat.

She felt him smile against her neck. His thumb slowly circled, every sweep a torturous blessing.

"Hunt." She didn't know if his name was a plea or a question.

He just tugged aside her underwear and put his fingers directly on her.

She moaned again, and Hunt stroked her, two fingers dragging up and down with teeth-grinding lightness. He licked up the side of her throat, fingers playing mercilessly with her. He whispered against her skin, "Do you taste as good as you feel, Bryce?"

"Please find out immediately," she managed to gasp.

His laugh rumbled through her, but his fingers didn't halt their leisurely exploration. "Not yet, Quinlan."

One of his fingers found her entrance and lingered, circling. "Do it," she said. If she didn't feel him inside her—his fingers or his cock, anything—she might start begging.

"So bossy," Hunt purred against her neck, then claimed her mouth again. And as his lips settled over hers, nipping and taunting, he slid that finger deep into her.

Both of them groaned. "Fuck, Bryce," he said again. "Fuck."

Her eyes nearly rolled back into her head at the feeling of that finger. She rocked her hips, desperate to drive him deeper, and he obliged her, pulling out his finger nearly all the way, adding a second, and plunging both back into her.

She bucked, her nails digging into his chest. His thunderous heartbeat raged against her palms. She buried her face in his neck, biting and licking, starving for any taste of him while he pumped his hand into her again.

Hunt breathed into her ear, "I am going to fuck you until you can't remember your gods-damned name."

Gods, yes. "Likewise," she croaked.

Release shimmered in her, a wild and reckless song, and she rode his hand toward it. His other hand cupped her backside. "Don't think I've forgotten this particular asset," he murmured, squeezing for emphasis. "I have plans for this beautiful ass, Bryce. Filthy, filthy plans."

She moaned again, and his fingers stroked into her, over and over.

"Come for me, sweetheart," he purred against her breast, his tongue flicking over her nipple just as one of his fingers curled inside her, hitting that gods-damned spot.

Bryce did. Hunt's name on her lips, she tipped her head back and let go, riding his hand with abandon, driving them both into the couch cushions.

He groaned, and she swallowed the sound with an openmouthed kiss as every nerve in her body exploded into glorious starlight.

Then there was only breathing, and him—his body, his scent, that strength.

The starlight receded, and she opened her eyes to find him with his head tipped back, teeth bared.

Not in pleasure. In pain.

She'd driven him into the cushions. Shoved his wounded back right up against the couch.

Horror lurched through her like ice water, dousing any heat in her veins. "Oh gods. I am so sorry—"

He cracked his eyes open. That groan he'd made as she came had been *pain*, and she'd been so fucking wild for him that she hadn't noticed—

"Are you hurt?" she demanded, hoisting herself up from his lap, reaching to remove his fingers, still deep inside her.

He halted her with his other hand on her wrist. "I'll survive." His eyes darkened as he looked at her bare breasts, still inches from his mouth. The dress shoved halfway down her body. "I have other things to distract me," he murmured, leaning down for her peaked nipple.

Or trying to. A grimace passed over his face.

"Dark Hel, Hunt," she barked, yanking out of his grip, off his fingers, nearly falling from his lap. He didn't even fight her as she grabbed his shoulder and peered at his back.

Fresh blood leaked through his bandages.

"Are you out of your mind?" she shouted, searching for anything in the immediate vicinity to press against the blood. "Why didn't you tell me?"

"As you like to say," he panted, shaking slightly, "it's my body. I decide its limits."

She reined in the urge to strangle him, grabbing for her phone. "I'm calling a medwitch."

He gripped her wrist again. "We're not done here."

"Oh yes we fucking are," she seethed. "I'm not having sex with you when you're spouting blood like a fountain." An exaggeration, but still.

His eyes were dark—burning. So Bryce poked his back, a good six inches beneath his wound. His answering wince of pain settled the argument.

Setting her underwear to rights and sliding her dress back over her chest and arms, she dialed the public medwitch number.

The medwitch arrived and was gone within an hour. Hunt's wound was fine, she'd declared, to Bryce's knee-wobbling relief.

Then Hunt had the nerve to ask if he was cleared for sex.

The witch, to her credit, didn't laugh. Just said, *When you're able to fly again, then I'd say it's safe for you to be sexually active as well.* She nodded toward the couch cushions—the bloodstain that would require a magi-spell to erase. *I'd suggest whatever . . . interaction caused tonight's injury also be postponed until your wings are healed.*

Hunt had looked ready to argue, but Bryce had hurried the witch out of the apartment. And then helped him to his bed. For all his questions, he swayed with each step. Nearly collapsed onto his bed. He answered a few messages on his phone, and was asleep before she'd shut off the lights.

Cleared for sex, indeed.

Bryce slept heavily in her own bed, despite what she'd learned and seen about the synth.

But she woke at three. And knew what she had to do.

She fired off an email with her request, and regardless of the late hour, received one back within twenty minutes: she'd need to wait until her request was approved by the 33rd. Bryce frowned. She didn't have time for that.

She crept from her room. Hunt's door was shut, his room dark beyond it. He didn't so much as come to investigate as she slipped out of the apartment.

And headed for her old one.

She hadn't been on this block in two years.

But as she rounded the corner and saw the flashing lights and terrified crowds, she knew.

Knew what building burned midway down the block.

Someone must have noticed that she'd logged on to Danika's account at Redner Industries today. Or perhaps someone had been monitoring her email account—and seen the message she'd sent to the building's landlord. Whoever had done this must have acted quickly, realizing that she'd wanted to come hunt for any other clues Danika might have left around the apartment.

There had to be more. Danika was smart enough to not have put everything she'd discovered in one place.

Terrified, weeping people—her old neighbors—had clustered on the street, hugging each other and gazing up at the blaze in disbelief. Fire licked at every windowsill.

She'd done this—brought this upon the people watching their homes burn. Her chest tightened, the pain barely eased by overhearing a passing water nymph announce to her firefighting squad that every resident was accounted for.

She had caused this.

But—it meant she was getting close. *Look toward where it hurts the most,* the Viper Queen had advised her all those weeks ago. She'd thought the shifter meant what hurt her. But maybe it had been about the murderer all along.

And by circling in on the synth . . . Apparently, she'd hit a nerve.

Bryce was halfway home when her phone buzzed. She pulled it from her hastily repaired jacket, the white opal in the pocket clinking against the screen, already bracing herself for Hunt's questions.

But it was from Tharion.

There's a deal going down on the river right now. A boat is out there, signaling. Just past the Black Dock. Be there in five and I can get you out to see it.

She clenched the white opal in her fist and wrote back, *A synth deal?*

Tharion answered, *No, a cotton candy deal.*

She rolled her eyes. *I'll be there in three.*

And then she broke into a run. She didn't call Hunt. Or Ruhn.

She knew what they'd say. *Do not fucking go there without me, Bryce. Wait.*

But she didn't have time to waste.

65

Bryce gripped Tharion's waist so hard it was a wonder he didn't have difficulty breathing. Beneath them, the wave skimmer bobbed on the river's current. Only the occasional passing glow under the dark surface indicated that there was anything or anyone around them.

She'd hesitated when the mer arrived at the pier, the matte black wave skimmer idling. *It's either this or swimming, Legs*, he'd informed her.

She'd opted for the wave skimmer, but had spent the last five minutes regretting it.

"Up there," the mer male murmured, cutting the already quiet engine. It must have been a stealth vehicle from the River Queen's stash. Or Tharion's own, as her Captain of Intelligence.

Bryce beheld the small barge idling on the river. Mist drifted around them, turning the few firstlights on the barge into bobbing orbs.

"I count six people," Tharion observed.

She peered into the gloom ahead. "I can't make out what they are. Humanoid shapes."

Tharion's body hummed, and the wave skimmer drifted forward, carried on a current of his own making.

"Neat trick," she murmured.

"It always gets the ladies," he muttered back.

Bryce might have chuckled had they not neared the barge. "Keep downwind so they can't scent us."

"I know how to remain unseen, Legs." But he obeyed her.

The people on the boat were hooded against the misting rain, but as they drifted closer—

"It's the Viper Queen," Bryce said, her voice hushed. No one else in this city would have the swagger to wear that ridiculous purple raincoat. "Lying *asshole*. She said she didn't deal in synth."

"No surprise," Tharion growled. "She's always up to shady shit."

"Yeah, but is she buying or selling this time?"

"Only one way to find out."

They drifted closer. The barge, they realized, was painted with a pair of snake eyes. And the crates piled on the rear of the barge . . . "Selling," Tharion observed. He jerked his chin to a tall figure facing the Viper Queen, apparently in a heated discussion with someone beside them. "Those are the buyers." A nod to the person half-hidden in the shadows, arguing with the tall figure. "Disagreeing about what it's worth, probably."

The Viper Queen was selling synth. Had it really been her this entire time? Behind Danika and the pack's deaths, too, despite that alibi? Or had she merely gotten her hands on the substance once it leaked from the lab?

The arguing buyer shook their head with clear disgust. But their associate seemed to ignore whatever was said and chucked the Viper Queen what looked like a dark sack. She peered inside, and pulled something out. Gold flashed in the mist.

"That is a fuck-ton of money," Tharion murmured. "Enough for that entire shipment, I bet."

"Can you get closer so we can hear?"

Tharion nodded, and they drifted again. The barge loomed, the attention of all aboard fixed on the deal going down rather than the shadows beyond it.

The Viper Queen was saying to them, "I think you'll find this to be sufficient for your goals."

Bryce knew she should call Hunt and Ruhn and get every

legionary and Aux member over here to shut this down before more synth flooded the streets or wound up in worse hands. In the hands of fanatics like Philip Briggs and his ilk.

She pulled her phone from her jacket pocket, flicking a button to keep the screen from lighting up. A push of another button had the camera function appearing. She snapped a few photos of the boat, the Viper Queen, and the tall, dark figure she faced. Human, shifter, or Fae, she couldn't tell with the jacket and hood.

Bryce pulled up Hunt's number.

The Viper Queen said to the buyers, "I think this is the start of a beautiful friendship, don't you?"

The tallest buyer didn't reply. Just stiffly turned back to their companions, displeasure written in every movement as the first-lights illuminated the face beneath the hood.

"Holy fuck," Tharion whispered.

Every thought eddied out of Bryce's head.

There was nothing left in her but roaring silence as Hunt's face became clear.

66

Bryce didn't know how she wound up on the barge. What she said to Tharion to make him pull up. How she climbed off the wave skimmer and onto the boat itself.

But it happened fast. Fast enough that Hunt had made it only three steps before Bryce was there, soaked and wondering if she'd puke.

Guns clicked, pointing at her. She didn't see them.

She only saw Hunt whirl toward her, his eyes wide.

Of course she hadn't recognized him from a distance. He had no wings. But the powerful build, the height, the angle of his head . . . That was all him.

And his colleague behind him, the one who'd handed over the money—Viktoria. Justinian emerged from the shadows beyond them, his wings painted black to conceal them in the moonlight.

Bryce was distantly aware of Tharion behind her, telling the Viper Queen that she was under arrest on behalf of the River Queen. Distantly aware of the Viper Queen chuckling.

But all she heard was Hunt breathe, "Bryce."

"What the fuck is this?" she whispered. Rain slashed her face. She couldn't hear, couldn't get any air down, couldn't think as she said again, her voice breaking, "What the *fuck* is this, Hunt?"

"It is exactly what it looks like," a cold, deep voice said behind her.

In a storm of white wings, Micah emerged from the mists and landed, flanked by Isaiah, Naomi, and six other angels, all armed to the teeth and in legion black. But they made no move to incapacitate the Viper Queen or her cronies.

No, they all faced Hunt and his companions. Aimed their guns toward them.

Hunt looked at the Governor—then at the Viper Queen. He snarled softly, "You fucking bitch."

The Viper Queen chuckled. She said to Micah, "You owe me a favor now, Governor."

Micah jerked his chin in confirmation.

Viktoria hissed at her, halo crinkling on her brow, "You set us up."

The Viper Queen crossed her arms. "I knew it would be worth my while to see who came sniffing around for this shit when word leaked that I got my hands on a shipment," she said, motioning toward the synth. Her smile was pure poison as she looked at Hunt. "I was hoping it'd be you, Umbra Mortis."

Bryce's heart thundered. "What are you talking about?"

Hunt pivoted to her, his face bleak in the floodlights. "It wasn't supposed to go down like this, Bryce. Maybe at first, but I saw that video tonight and I tried to stop it, stop them, but they wouldn't fucking *listen*—"

"These three thought synth would be an easy way to regain what was taken from them," the Viper Queen said. A vicious pause. "The power to overthrow their masters."

The world shifted beneath her. Bryce said, "I don't believe you."

But the flicker of pain in Hunt's eyes told her that her blind, stupid faith in his innocence had gutted him.

"It's true," Micah said, his voice like ice. "These three learned of the synth days ago, and have since been seeking a way to purchase it—and to distribute it among their fellow would-be rebels. To attain its powers long enough to break their halos, and finish what Shahar started on Mount Hermon." He nodded toward the Viper Queen. "She was gracious enough to inform me of this plan, after Justinian tried to recruit a female under her . . . influence."

Bryce shook her head. She was trembling so hard that Tharion gripped her around the waist.

"I told you I'd figure out your asking price, Athalar," the Viper Queen said.

Bryce began crying. She hated every tear, every shuddering, stupid gasp. Hated the pain in Hunt's eyes as he stared at her, only her, and said, "I'm sorry."

But Bryce just asked, "*Days* ago?"

Silence.

She said again, "You knew about the synth *days* ago?"

Her heart—it was her stupid fucking heart that was cracking and cracking and cracking . . .

Hunt said, "Micah assigned me some targets. Three drug lords. They told me that two years ago, a small amount of synth leaked from the Redner lab and onto the streets. But it ran out fast—too fast. They said that finally, after two years of trying to replicate it, someone had figured out the formula at last, and it was now being made—and would be capable of amping up our power. I didn't think it had anything to do with the case—not until recently. I didn't know the truth of what the Hel it could even *do* until I saw that footage of the trials."

"How." Her word cut through the rain. "How did it leak?"

Hunt shook his head. "It doesn't matter."

Micah said coldly, "Danika Fendyr."

Bryce backed up a step, into Tharion's grip. "That's not possible."

Hunt said with a gentleness that decimated her, "Danika sold it, Bryce. It's why she was spotted on that boat with the crate of it. I figured it out nearly a week ago. She stole the formula for it, sold the stock, and—" He stopped himself.

"And *what*?" Bryce whispered. "And *what*, Hunt?"

"And Danika used it herself. Was addicted to it."

She was going to be sick. "Danika would *never* have done that. She never would have done *any* of this."

Hunt shook his head. "She did, Bryce."

"No."

When Micah didn't interrupt them, Hunt said, "Look at the

evidence." His voice was sharp as knives. "Look at the last messages between you. The drugs we found in your system that night—that was standard shit for you two. So what was one more kind of drug? One that in small doses could give an even more intense high? One that could take the edge off for Danika after a long day, after Sabine had ripped her apart yet again? One that gave her a taste of what it'd be like to be Prime of the wolves, *gave* her that power, since she was waiting to make the Drop with you?"

"*No.*"

Hunt's voice cracked. "She took it, Bryce. All signs point to her killing those two CCU students the night the Horn was stolen. They saw her stealing the Horn and she chased them down and killed them."

Bryce remembered Danika's pallor when she'd told her about the students' deaths, her haunted eyes.

"It's not true."

Hunt shook his head. As if he could undo it, unlearn it. "Those drug lords I killed said Danika was seen around the Meat Market. Talking about synth. It was how Danika knew Maximus Tertian—he was an addict like her. His girlfriend had no idea."

"No."

But Hunt looked to Micah. "I assume we're going now." He held out his wrists. For cuffs. Indeed, those were gorsian stones—thick, magic-killing manacles—gleaming in Isaiah's hands.

The Archangel said, "Aren't you going to tell her the rest?"

Hunt stilled. "It's not necessary. Let's go."

"Tell me what," Bryce whispered. Tharion's hands tightened on her arms in warning.

"That he already knows the truth about Danika's murder," the Archangel said coldly. Bored. As if he'd done this a thousand times, in a thousand variations. As if he'd already guessed.

Bryce looked at Hunt and saw it in his eyes. She began shaking her head, weeping. "No."

Hunt said, "Danika took the synth the night she died. Took too much of it. It drove her out of her mind. She slaughtered her own pack. And then herself."

Only Tharion's grip was keeping her upright. "No, no, no—"

Hunt said, "It's why there was never any audio of the killer, Bryce."

"She was begging for her life—"

"She was begging herself to stop," Hunt said. "The only snarls on the recording were hers."

Danika. Danika had killed the pack. Killed Thorne. Killed Connor.

And then ripped herself to shreds.

"But the Horn—"

"She must have stolen it just to piss off Sabine. And then probably sold it on the black market. It had nothing to do with any of this. It was always about the synth for her."

Micah cut in, "I have it on good authority that Danika stole footage of the synth trials from Redner's lab."

"But the kristallos—"

"A side effect of the synth, when used in high doses," Micah said. "The surge of powerful magic it grants the user also brings the ability to open portals, thanks to the obsidian salt in its formula. Danika did just that, accidentally summoning the kristallos. The black salt in the synth can have a mind of its own. A sentience. Its measurement in the synth's formula matches the unholy number of the kristallos. With high doses of synth, the power of the salt gains control and can summon the kristallos. That's why we've been seeing them recently—the drug is on the streets now, in doses often higher than recommended. Like you suspected, the kristallos feeds on vital organs, using the sewers to deposit bodies into the waterway. The two recent murder victims—the acolyte and the temple guard—were the unfortunate victims of someone high on the synth."

Silence fell again. And Bryce turned once more to Hunt. "You knew."

He held her stare. "I'm sorry."

Her voice rose to a scream. *"You knew!"*

Hunt lunged—one step toward her.

A gun gleamed in the dark, pressed against his head, and halted him in his tracks.

Bryce knew that handgun. The engraved silver wings on the black barrel.

"You move, angel, and you fucking die."

Hunt held up his hands. But his eyes did not leave Bryce as Fury Axtar emerged from the shadows beyond the crates of synth.

Bryce didn't question how Fury had arrived without even Micah noticing or how she knew to come. Fury Axtar was liquid night—she'd made herself infamous for knowing the world's secrets.

Fury edged around Hunt, backing up to Bryce's side. She pocketed the gun in the holster at her thigh, her usual skintight black suit gleaming with rain and her chin-length black hair dripping with it, but said to the Viper Queen, "Get the fuck out of my sight."

A sly smile. "It's my boat."

"Then go somewhere I can't see your face."

Bryce didn't have it in her to be shocked that the Viper Queen obeyed Fury's order.

Didn't have it in her to do anything but stare at Hunt. "You knew," she said again.

Hunt's eyes scanned hers. "I never wanted you to be hurt. I never wanted you to know—"

"You knew, you knew, you knew!" He'd figured out the truth, and for nearly a week, he'd said nothing to her. Had let her go on and on about how much she loved her friend, how great Danika had been, and had led her in fucking *circles*. "All your talk about the synth being a waste of my time to look into . . ." She could barely get the words out. "Because you realized the truth already. Because you *lied*." She threw out an arm to the crates of drugs. "Because you learned the truth and then realized you wanted the synth for yourself? And when you wanted to help the medwitch find an antidote . . . It was for *yourself*. And all of this for what—to rebel again?"

Hunt slid to his knees, as if he'd beg her forgiveness. "At first, yes, but it was all just based on a rumor of what it could do. Then tonight I saw that footage you found, and I wanted to pull out from the deal. I knew it wasn't right—any of it. Even with the antidote, it was too dangerous. I realized *all* this was the wrong path. But you and me, Bryce . . . *You* are where I want to end up. A life—with *you*. *You* are my fucking path." He pointed to Justinian and Viktoria, stone-faced and handcuffed. "I messaged them that it was over, but they got spooked, contacted the Viper Queen, and insisted it was going down *tonight*. I swear, I came here only to stop it, to put a fucking *end* to it before it became a disaster. I *never*—"

She grabbed the white opal from her pocket and hurled it at him.

Hurled it so hard it slammed into Hunt's head. Blood flowed from his temple. As if the halo itself were bleeding.

"I never want to see you again," she whispered as Hunt gazed at the blood-splattered opal on the deck.

"That won't be a problem," Micah said, and Isaiah stepped forward, gorsian stone manacles gleaming like amethyst fire. The same as those around Viktoria's and Justinian's wrists.

Bryce couldn't stop shaking as she leaned back into Tharion, Fury a silent force beside her.

"Bryce, I'm sorry," Hunt said as a grim-looking Isaiah clapped the shackles on him. "I couldn't bear the thought of you—"

"That's enough," Fury said. "You've said and done enough." She looked to Micah. "She's done with you. All of you." She tugged Bryce toward her wave skimmer idling beside Tharion's, the mer male guarding their backs. "You bother her again and I'll pay *you* a visit, Governor."

Bryce didn't notice as she was eased onto the wave skimmer. As Fury got on in front of her and gunned the engine. As Tharion slipped onto his and trailed, to guard the way back to shore.

"Bryce," Hunt tried again as she wrapped her arms around Fury's tiny waist. "Your heart was already so broken, and the last thing I ever wanted to do was—"

She didn't look back at him as the wind whipped her hair and the wave skimmer launched into the rain and darkness.

"*BRYCE!*" Hunt roared.

She didn't look back.

67

Ruhn was in the apartment lobby when Fury dropped her off. Tharion left them at the docks, saying he was going to help haul in the seized synth shipment, and Fury departed fast enough that Bryce knew she was heading out to make sure the Viper Queen didn't abscond with any of it, either.

Ruhn said nothing as they rode the elevator.

But she knew Fury had told him. Summoned him here.

Her friend had been messaging someone on the walk back from the docks. And she'd spied Flynn and Declan standing guard on the rooftops of her block, armed with their long-range rifles.

Her brother didn't speak until they were in the apartment, the place dark and hollow and foreign. Every piece of clothing and gear belonging to Hunt was like an asp, ready to strike. That bloodstain on the couch was the worst of all.

Bryce made it halfway across the great room before she puked all over the carpet.

Ruhn was instantly there, his arms and shadows around her.

She could feel her sobs, hear them, but they were distant. The entire world was distant as Ruhn picked her up and carried her to the couch, keeping away from that spot where she'd yielded herself entirely to Hunt. But he made no comment about the bloodstain or any lingering scent.

It wasn't true. It couldn't be true.

No better than a bunch of drug addicts. That's what Hunt had implied. She and Danika had been no better than two addicts, inhaling and snorting everything they could get their hands on.

It wasn't like that. Hadn't ever been like that. It had been stupid, but it had been for fun, for distraction and release, never for something dark—

She was shaking so hard she thought her bones might snap.

Ruhn's grip on her tightened, like he could keep her together.

Hunt must have known she was getting close to learning the truth when she'd shown him the trial videos. So he'd spun her lies about a happy ending for the two of them, a *future* for them, had distracted her with his mouth and hands. And then, as one of the triarii, he'd gotten the alert from her old landlord about her request to visit the apartment—and snuck out, letting her think he was asleep. A bolt of his lightning had probably sparked the flame.

She remembered the water nymph saying that there hadn't been any casualties—had some shred of decency in Hunt made him trigger the fire alarms in an attempt to warn people? She had to believe it.

But once Hunt had burned the building down so there was no hint of evidence left, he'd met with the Viper Queen to barter for what he needed to fuel his rebellion. She didn't believe his bullshit about pulling out of the deal. Not for a heartbeat. He knew the world of hurt about to come down on him. He'd have said anything.

Danika had killed the Pack of Devils. Killed Thorne and Connor. And then herself.

And now Danika lived on, in shame, among the mausoleums of the Sleeping City. Suffering. Because of Bryce.

It wasn't true. It couldn't be true.

By the time Fury came back, Bryce had been staring at the same spot on the wall for hours. Ruhn left her on the couch to talk to the assassin in the kitchen.

Bryce heard their whispering anyway.

Athalar's in one of the holding cells under the Comitium, Fury said.

Micah didn't execute him?

No. Justinian and Viktoria . . . He crucified the angel, and did some fucked-up shit to the wraith.

They're dead?

Worse. Justinian's still bleeding out in the Comitium lobby. They gave him some shit to slow his healing. He'll be dead soon enough if he's lucky.

What about the wraith?

Micah ripped her from her body and shoved her essence into a glass box. Put it at the base of Justinian's crucifix. Rumor says he's going to dump the box—Viktoria—into the Melinoë Trench and let her fall right to the bottom of the sea to go insane from the isolation and darkness.

Fucking Hel. You can't do anything?

They're traitors to the Republic. They were caught conspiring against it. So, no.

But Athalar's not crucified beside Justinian?

I think Micah came up with a different punishment for him. Something worse.

What could be worse than what the other two are enduring?

A long, horrible pause. *A lot of things, Ruhn Danaan.*

Bryce let the words wash over her. She sat on the couch and stared at the dark screen of the television. And stared into the black pit inside herself.

PART IV

THE RAVINE

68

For some reason, Hunt had expected a stone dungeon.

He didn't know why, since he'd been in these holding cells beneath the Comitium countless times to deposit the few enemies Micah wanted left alive, but he'd somehow pictured his capture to be the mirror of what had gone down in Pangera: the dark, filthy dungeons of the Asteri, the ones that were so similar in Sandriel's palace.

Not this white cell, the chrome bars humming with magic to nullify his own. A screen on the wall of the hallway showed a feed of the Comitium atrium: the one body spiked to the iron crucifix in its center, and the glass box, covered in dripping blood, sitting at its feet.

Justinian still groaned every now and then, his toes or fingers twitching as he slowly asphyxiated, his body trying and failing to heal his taxed lungs. His wings had already been cut off. Left on the marble floor beneath him.

Viktoria, her essence invisible within that glass box, was forced to watch. To endure Justinian's blood dripping on the lid of her container.

Hunt had sat on the small cot and watched every second of what had been done to them. How Viktoria had screamed while Micah ripped her from that body she'd been trapped in for so long. How

Justinian had fought, even as they held down his brutalized body on the crucifix, even as the iron spikes went into him. Even as they raised the crucifix, and he'd begun screaming at the pain.

A door clanged open down the hallway. Hunt didn't rise from the cot to see who approached. The wound on his temple had healed, but he hadn't bothered to wash away the blood streaking down his cheek and jaw.

The footsteps down the hall were steady, unhurried. Isaiah.

Hunt remained seated as his old companion paused before the bars.

"Why." There was nothing charming, nothing warm on the handsome face. Just anger, exhaustion, and fear.

Hunt said, aware of every camera and not caring, "Because it has to stop at some point."

"It stops when you're *dead*. When *everyone we love* is dead." Isaiah pointed to the screen behind him, to Justinian's ravaged body and Viktoria's blood-soaked box. "Does this make you feel like you're on the right path, Hunt? Was this worth it?"

When he'd gotten Justinian's message that the deal was going down, as he climbed into bed, he'd realized it *wasn't* worth it. Not even with the medwitch's antidote. Not after these weeks with Bryce. Not after what they'd done on that couch. But Hunt said, because it was still true, "Nothing's changed since Mount Hermon, Isaiah. Nothing has gotten better."

"How long have you three been planning this shit?"

"Since I killed those three drug lords. Since they told me about the synth and what it could do. Since they told me what kind of power it gave Danika Fendyr when she took it in the right doses. We decided it was time. No more fucking bargains with Micah. No more deaths for deaths. Just the ones *we* choose."

The three of them had known there was one place, one person, who might get the synth. He'd paid the Viper Queen a private visit a few days ago. Had found her in her den of poisons and told her what he wanted. Vik had the gold, thanks to the paychecks she'd saved up for centuries.

It hadn't occurred to him that the snake would be in the Archangel's pocket. Or looking for a way into it.

Isaiah shook his head. "And you thought that *you*, you and Vik and Justinian and whatever idiots would follow you, could take the synth and do what? Kill Micah? Sandriel? All of them?"

"That was the idea." They'd planned to do it at the Summit. And afterward, they'd make their way to Pangera. To the Eternal City. And finish what was started so long ago.

"What if it turned on you—what if you took too much and ripped yourself to shreds instead?"

"I was working on getting my hands on an antidote." Hunt shrugged. "But I've already confessed to everything, so spare me the interrogation."

Isaiah banged a hand on the cell bars. Wind howled in the corridor around him. "You couldn't have let it go, couldn't serve and prove yourself and—"

"I tried to stop it, for fuck's sake. I was on that barge because I realized . . ." He shook his head. "It makes no difference at this point. But I did try. I saw that footage of what it really did to someone who took it, and even with an antidote, it was too fucking dangerous. But Justinian and Vik refused to quit. By the time Vik gave the Viper Queen the gold, I just wanted us to go our separate ways."

Isaiah shook his head in disgust.

Hunt spat, "You might be able to accept the bit in your mouth, but I *never* will."

"I don't," Isaiah hissed. "But I have a reason to work for my freedom, Hunt." A flash of his eyes. "I thought you did, too."

Hunt's stomach twisted. "Bryce had nothing to do with this."

"Of course she didn't. You shattered her fucking heart in front of everyone. It was obvious she had no idea."

Hunt flinched, his chest aching. "Micah won't go after her to—"

"No. You're lucky as fuck, but no. He won't crucify her to punish you. Though don't be naïve enough to believe the thought didn't cross his mind."

Hunt couldn't stop his shudder of relief.

Isaiah said, "Micah knows that you tried to stop the deal. Saw the messages between you and Justinian about it. That's why they're in the lobby right now and you're here."

"What's he going to do with me?"

"He hasn't declared it yet." His face softened slightly. "I came down to say goodbye. Just in case we can't later on."

Hunt nodded. He'd accepted his fate. He'd tried, and failed, and would pay the price. Again.

It was a better end than the slow death of his soul as he took one life after another for Micah. "Tell her I'm sorry," Hunt said. "Please."

At the end of the day, despite Vik and Justinian, despite the brutal end that would come his way, it was the sight of Bryce's face that haunted him. The sight of the tears he'd caused.

He'd promised her a future and then brought that pain and despair and sorrow to her face. He'd never hated himself more.

Isaiah's fingers lifted toward the bars, as if he'd reach for Hunt's hand, but then lowered back to his side. "I will."

"It's been three days," Lehabah said. "And the Governor hasn't announced what he's doing with Athie."

Bryce looked up from the book she was reading in the library. "Turn off that television."

Lehabah did no such thing, her glowing face fixed on the tablet's screen. The news footage of the Comitium lobby and the now-rotting corpse of the triarii soldier crucified there. The blood-crusted glass box beneath it. Despite the endless bullshitting by the news anchors and analysts, no information had leaked regarding why two of Micah's top soldiers had been so brutally executed. *A failed coup* was all that had been suggested. No mention of Hunt. Whether he lived.

"He's alive," Lehabah whispered. "I know he is. I can feel it."

Bryce ran a finger over a line of text. It was the tenth time she'd attempted to read it in the twenty minutes since the messenger had left, dropping off a vial of the antidote from the medwitch who'd taken the kristallos venom from her leg. Apparently, she'd found the way to make the antidote work without her being present. But Bryce didn't marvel. Not when the vial was just a silent reminder of what she and Hunt had shared that day.

She'd debated throwing it out, but had opted to lock the antidote in the safe in Jesiba's office, right next to that six-inch golden bullet for the Godslayer Rifle. Life and death, salvation and destruction, now entombed there together.

"Violet Kappel said on the morning news that there might be more would-be rebels—"

"Turn off that screen, Lehabah, before I throw it in the fucking tank."

Her sharp words cut through the library. The rustling creatures in their cages stilled. Even Syrinx stirred from his nap.

Lehabah dimmed to a faint pink. "Are you sure there's nothing we can—"

Bryce slammed the book shut and hauled it with her, aiming for the stairs.

She didn't hear Lehabah's next words over the front door's buzzer. Work had proved busier than usual, a grand total of six shoppers wasting her time asking about shit they had no interest in buying. If she had to deal with one more idiot today—

She glanced at the monitors. And froze.

The Autumn King surveyed the gallery, the showroom stocked with priceless artifacts, the door that led up to Jesiba's office and the window in it that overlooked the floor. He stared at the window for long enough that Bryce wondered if he could somehow see through the one-way glass, all the way to the Godslayer Rifle mounted on the wall behind Jesiba's desk. Sense its deadly presence, and that of the golden bullet in the wall safe beside it. But his eyes drifted on, to the iron door sealed to her right, and finally, finally to Bryce herself.

He'd never come to see her. In all these years, he'd never come. Why bother?

"There are cameras everywhere," she said, staying seated behind her desk, hating every whiff of his ashes-and-nutmeg scent that dragged her back twelve years, to the weeping thirteen-year-old she'd been the last time she'd spoken to him. "In case you're thinking of stealing something."

He ignored the taunt and slid his hands into the pockets of his black jeans, still conducting his silent survey of the gallery. He was gorgeous, her father. Tall, muscled, with an impossibly beautiful face beneath that long red hair, the exact same shade and silken texture as her own. He looked just a few years older than her, too—dressed like a young man, with those black jeans and a matching long-sleeved T-shirt. But his amber eyes were ancient and cruel as he said at last, "My son told me what occurred on the river on Wednesday night."

How he managed to make that slight emphasis on *my son* into an insult was beyond her.

"Ruhn is a good dog."

"*Prince* Ruhn deemed it necessary that I know, since you might be . . . in peril."

"And yet you waited three days? Were you hoping I'd be crucified, too?"

Her father's eyes flashed. "I have come to tell you that your security has been assured, and that the Governor knows you were innocent in the matter and will not dare to harm you. Even to punish Hunt Athalar."

She snorted. Her father stilled. "You are incredibly foolish if you think that would not be enough to break Athalar at last."

Ruhn must have told him about that, too. The disaster that had been this thing between her and Hunt. Whatever it had been. Whatever using her like that could be called.

"I don't want to talk about this." Not with him, not with anyone. Fury had disappeared again, and while Juniper had messaged, Bryce kept the conversation brief. Then the calls from her mother and Randall had started. And the big lies had begun.

She didn't know why she'd lied about Hunt's involvement. Maybe because explaining her own idiocy in letting Hunt in—being so fucking *blind* to the fact that he'd led her around when everyone had warned her, that he'd even *told her* he would love Shahar until the day he died—was too much. It gutted her to know he'd chosen the Archangel and their rebellion over her, over *them* . . . She couldn't talk to her mom about it. Not without completely losing what was left of her ability to function.

So Bryce had gone back to work, because what else was there to do? She'd heard nothing from the places where she'd applied for new jobs.

"I'm *not* talking about this," she repeated.

"You will talk about this. With your king." A crackling ember of his power set the firstlights guttering.

"You are not my king."

"Legally, I am," her father said. "You are listed as a half-Fae citizen. That places you under my jurisdiction both in this city and as a member of the House of Sky and Breath."

She clicked her nails together. "So what is it you want to talk about, *Your Majesty*?"

"Have you stopped looking for the Horn?"

She blinked. "Does it matter now?"

"It is a deadly artifact. Just because you learned the truth regarding Danika and Athalar doesn't mean whoever wishes to use it is done."

"Didn't Ruhn tell you? Danika stole the Horn on a lark. Ditched it somewhere in one of her flying-high-as-a-fucking-kite moments. It was a dead end." At her father's frown, she explained, "The kristallos were all accidentally summoned by Danika and the others who took synth, thanks to the black salt in it. We were wrong in even looking for the Horn. There was no one pursuing it."

She couldn't decide whom she hated more: Hunt, Danika, or herself for not seeing their lies. Not *wanting* to see any of it. It haunted every step, every breath, that loathing. Burned deep inside.

"Even if no enemy seeks it, it is worth ensuring that the Horn does not fall into the wrong hands."

"Only Fae hands, right?" She smiled coldly. "I thought your Chosen One son was put on its tail."

"He is otherwise occupied." Ruhn must have told him to go fuck himself.

"Well, if you can think where Danika unloaded it in her synth-high stupor, I'm all ears."

"It is no trivial matter. Even if the Horn is long defunct, it still holds a special place in Fae history. It will mean a great deal to my people if it is recovered. I'd think with your *professional expertise*, such a search would be of interest to you. And your employer."

She looked back at her computer screen. "Whatever."

He paused, and then his power buzzed, warping every audio feed before he said, "I loved your mother very much, you know."

"Yeah, so much you left a scar on her face."

She could have sworn he flinched. "Do not think I have not spent every moment since then regretting my actions. Living in shame."

"Could have fooled me."

His power rumbled through the room. "You are so much like her. More than you know. She never forgave anyone for anything."

"I take that as a compliment." That fire burned and raged inside her head, her bones.

Her father said quietly, "I would have made her my queen. I had the paperwork ready."

She blinked. "How surprisingly un-elitist of you." Her mother had never suggested, never hinted at it. "She would have hated being queen. She would have said no."

"She loved me enough to have said yes." Absolute certainty laced his words.

"You think that somehow erases what you did?"

"No. Nothing shall ever erase what I did."

"Let's skip the woe-is-me bullshit. You came here after all these years to tell me this crap?"

Her father looked at her for a long moment. Then strode for the door, opening it in silence. But he said before he stepped into the street, his red hair gleaming in the afternoon sunlight, "I came here after all these years to tell you that you may be like your mother, but you are also more like me than you realize." His amber eyes—her own—flickered. "And that is not a good thing."

The door shut, the gallery darkening. Bryce stared at the computer screen before her, then typed in a few words.

There was still nothing on Hunt. No mention of him in the news. Not a whisper about whether the Umbra Mortis was imprisoned or tortured or alive or dead.

As if he had never existed. As if she had dreamed him up.

69

Hunt ate only because his body demanded it, slept because there was nothing else to do, and watched the TV screen in the hall beyond his cell bars because he'd brought this upon himself and Vik and Justinian and there was no undoing it.

Micah had left the latter's body up. Justinian would hang there for seven full days and then be pulled off the crucifix—and dumped into the Istros. No Sailings for traitors. Just the bellies of the river beasts.

Viktoria's box had already been dumped into the Melinoë Trench.

The thought of her trapped on the seafloor, the deepest place in Midgard, nothing but dark and silence and that tight, tight space . . .

Dreams of her suffering had launched Hunt over to the toilet, puking up his guts.

And then the itching began. Deep in his back, radiating through the framework now beginning to regrow, it itched and itched and itched. His fledgling wings remained sore enough that scratching them resulted in near-blinding pain, and as the hours ticked by, each new bit of growth had him clenching his jaw against it.

A waste, he silently told his body. A big fucking waste to

regrow his wings, when he was likely hours or days away from an execution.

He'd had no visitors since Isaiah six days ago. He'd tracked the time by watching the sunlight shift in the atrium on the TV feed.

Not a whisper from Bryce. Not that he dared hope she'd somehow find a way to see him, if only to let him beg on his knees for her forgiveness. To tell her what he needed to say.

Maybe Micah would let him rot down here. Let him go mad like Vik, buried beneath the earth, unable to fly, unable to feel fresh air on his face.

The doors down the hall hissed, and Hunt blinked, rising from his silence. Even his miserably itching wings halted their torture.

But the female scent that hit him a heartbeat later was not Bryce's.

It was a scent he knew just as well—would never forget as long as he lived. A scent that stalked his nightmares, whetted his rage into a thing that made it impossible to think.

The Archangel of northwestern Pangera smiled as she appeared before his cell. He'd never get used to it: how much she looked like Shahar. "This seems familiar," Sandriel said. Her voice was soft, beautiful. Like music. Her face was, too.

And yet her eyes, the color of fresh-tilled soil, gave her away. They were sharp, honed by millennia of cruelty and near-unchecked power. Eyes that delighted in pain and bloodshed and despair. That had always been the difference between her and Shahar—their eyes. Warmth in one; death in the other.

"I heard you want to kill me, Hunt," the Archangel said, crossing her thin arms. She clicked her tongue. "Are we really back to that old game?"

He said nothing. Just sat on his cot and held her gaze.

"You know, when you had your belongings confiscated, they found some interesting things, which Micah was kind enough to share." She pulled an object from her pocket. His phone. "This in particular."

She waved a hand and his phone screen appeared on the TV behind her, its wireless connection showing every movement of her fingers through the various programs. "Your email, of course, was dull as dirt. Do you never delete anything?" She didn't wait for his response before she went on. "But your messages . . ." Her lips curled, and she clicked on the most recent chain.

Bryce had changed her contact name one last time, it seemed. *Bryce Thinks Hunt Is the Best* had written:

I know you're not going to see this. I don't even know why I'm writing to you.

She'd messaged a minute after that, *I just . . .* Then another pause. *Never mind. Whoever is screening this, never mind. Ignore this.*

Then nothing. His head became so, so quiet.

"And you know what I found absolutely fascinating?" Sandriel was saying, clicking away from the messages and going into his photos. "These." She chuckled. "*Look* at all of this. Who knew you could act so . . . *commonly*?"

She hit the slideshow function. Hunt just sat there as photos began appearing on the screen.

He'd never looked through them. The photos that he and Bryce had taken these weeks.

There he was, drinking a beer on her couch, petting Syrinx while watching a sunball game.

There he was, making her breakfast because he'd come to enjoy knowing that he could take care of her like that. She'd snapped another photo of him working in the kitchen: of his ass. With her own hand in the foreground, giving a thumbs-up of approval.

He might have laughed, might have smiled, had the next photo not popped up. A photo he'd taken this time, of her mid-sentence.

Then one of him and her on the street, Hunt looking notably annoyed at having his photo taken, while she grinned obnoxiously.

The photo he'd snapped of her dirty and drenched by the sewer grate, spitting mad.

A photo of Syrinx sleeping on his back, limbs splayed. A photo of Lehabah in the library, posing like a pinup girl on her little couch. Then a photo he'd gotten of the river at sunset as he flew overhead. A photo of Bryce's tattooed back in the bathroom mirror, while she gave a saucy wink over her shoulder. A photo he'd taken of an otter in its yellow vest, then one he'd managed to grab a second later of Bryce's delighted face.

He didn't hear what Sandriel was saying.

The photos had begun as an ongoing joke, but they'd become real. Enjoyable. There were more of the two of them. And more photos that Hunt had taken, too. Of the food they'd eaten, interesting graffiti along the alleys, of clouds and things he normally never bothered to notice but had suddenly wanted to capture. And then ones where he looked into the camera and smiled.

Ones where Bryce's face seemed to glow brighter, her smile softer.

The dates drew closer to the present. There they were, on her couch, her head on his shoulder, smiling broadly while he rolled his eyes. But his arm was around her. His fingers casually tangled in her hair. Then a photo he'd taken of her in his sunball hat. Then a ridiculous medley she'd taken of Jelly Jubilee and Peaches and Dreams and Princess Creampuff tucked into his bed. Posed on his dresser. In his bathroom.

And then some by the river again. He had a vague memory of her asking a passing tourist to snap a few. One by one, the various shots unfolded.

First, a photo with Bryce still talking and him grimacing.

Then one with her smiling and Hunt looking at her.

The third was of her still smiling—and Hunt still looking at her. Like she was the only person on the planet. In the galaxy.

His heart thundered. In the next few, her face had turned toward him. Their eyes had met. Her smile had faltered.

As if realizing how he was looking at her.

In the next, she was smiling at the ground, his eyes still on her. A secret, soft smile. Like she knew, and didn't mind one bit.

And then in the last, she had leaned her head against his chest, and wrapped her arms around his middle. He'd put his arm and wing around her. And they had both smiled.

True, broad smiles. Belonging to the people they might have been without the tattoo on his brow and the grief in her heart and this whole stupid fucking world around them.

A life. These were the photos of someone with a *life*, and a good one at that. A reminder of what it had felt like to have a home, and someone who cared whether he lived or died. Someone who made him smile just by entering a room.

He'd never had that before. With anyone.

The screen went dark, and then the photos began again.

And he could see it, this time. How her eyes—they had been so cold at the start. How even with her ridiculous pictures and poses, that smile hadn't reached her eyes. But with each photo, more light had crept into them. Brightened them. Brightened his eyes, too. Until those last photos. When Bryce was near-glowing with joy.

She was the most beautiful thing he had ever seen.

Sandriel was smirking like a cat. "Is this really what you wanted in the end, Hunt?" She gestured to the photos. To Bryce's smiling face. "To be freed one day, to marry the girl, to live out some ordinary, basic life?" She chuckled. "Whatever would Shahar say?"

Her name didn't clang. And the guilt he thought would sear him didn't so much as sizzle.

Sandriel's full lips curved upward, a mockery of her twin's smile. "Such simple, sweet wishes, Hunt. But that's not how these things work out. Not for people like you."

His stomach twisted. The photos were torture, he realized. To remind him of the life he might have had. What he'd tasted on the couch with Bryce the other night. What he'd pissed away.

"You know," Sandriel said, "if you had played the obedient dog, Micah would have eventually petitioned for your freedom." The words pelted him. "But you couldn't be patient. Couldn't be smart. Couldn't choose this"—she gestured to their photos—"over your own petty revenge." Another snake's smile. "So here we are. Here *you* are." She studied a photo Hunt had taken of Bryce with Syrinx, the chimera's pointed little teeth bared in something terrifyingly close to a grin. "The girl will probably cry her little heart out for a while. But then she'll forget you, and she'll find someone else. Maybe there will be some Fae male who can stomach an inferior pairing."

Hunt's senses pricked, his temper stirring.

Sandriel shrugged. "Or she'll wind up in a dumpster with the other half-breeds."

His fingers curled into fists. There was no threat in Sandriel's words. Just the terrible practicality of how their world treated people like Bryce.

"The point is," Sandriel continued, "she will go on. And you and I will go on, Hunt."

At last, at last, he dragged his eyes from Bryce and the photos of the life, the home, they'd made. The life he still so desperately, stupidly wanted. His wings resumed their itching. "What."

Sandriel's smile sharpened. "Didn't they tell you?"

Dread curled as he looked at his phone in her hands. As he realized why he'd been left alive, and why Sandriel had been allowed to take his belongings.

They were *her* belongings now.

Bryce entered the near-empty bar just after eleven. The lack of a brooding male presence guarding her back was like a phantom limb, but she ignored it, made herself forget about it as she spotted Ruhn sitting at the counter, sipping his whiskey.

Only Flynn had joined him, the male too busy seducing the female currently playing billiards with him to give Bryce more than a wary, pitying nod. She ignored it and slid onto the stool beside Ruhn, her dress squeaking against the leather. "Hi."

Ruhn glanced sidelong at her. "Hey."

The bartender strode over, brows raised in silent question. Bryce shook her head. She didn't plan to be here long enough for a drink, water or otherwise. She wanted this over with as quickly as possible so she could go back home, take off her bra, and put on her sweats.

Bryce said, "I wanted to come by to say thanks." Ruhn only stared at her. She watched the sunball game on the TV above the bar. "For the other day. Night. For looking out for me."

Ruhn squinted at the tiled ceiling.

"What?" she asked.

"I'm just checking to see if the sky's falling, since you're thanking me for something."

She shoved his shoulder. "Asshole."

"You could have called or messaged." He sipped from his whiskey.

"I thought it'd be more adultlike to do it face-to-face."

Her brother surveyed her carefully. "How are you holding up?"

"I've been better." She admitted, "I feel like a fucking idiot."

"You're not."

"Oh yeah? Half a dozen people warned me, you included, to be on my guard around Hunt, and I laughed in all your faces." She blew out a breath. "I should have seen it."

"In your defense, I didn't think Athalar was still that ruthless." His blue eyes blazed. "I thought his priorities had shifted lately."

She rolled her eyes. "Yeah, you and dear old Dad."

"He visited you?"

"Yep. Told me I'm just as big a piece of shit as he himself is. Like father, like daughter. Like calls to like or whatever."

"You're nothing like him."

"Don't bullshit a bullshitter, Ruhn." She tapped the bar. "Anyway, that's all I came to say." She noted the Starsword hanging at his side, its black hilt not reflecting the firstlights in the room. "You on patrol tonight?"

"Not until midnight." With his Fae metabolism, the whiskey would be out of his system long before then.

"Well . . . good luck." She hopped off the stool, but Ruhn halted her with a hand on her elbow.

"I'm having some people over at my place in a couple weeks to watch the big sunball game. Why don't you come over?"

"Pass."

"Just come for the first period. If it isn't your thing, no problem. Leave when you want."

She scanned his face, weighing the offer there. The hand extended.

"Why?" she asked quietly. "Why keep bothering?"

"Why keep pushing me away, Bryce?" His voice strained. "It wasn't just about that fight."

She swallowed, her throat thick. "You were my best friend," she said. "Before Danika, you were my best friend. And I . . . It doesn't matter now." She'd realized back then that the truth didn't matter—she wouldn't *let* it matter. She shrugged, as if it'd help lighten the crushing weight in her chest. "Maybe we could start over. On a trial basis *only*."

Ruhn started to smile. "So you'll come watch the game?"

"Juniper was supposed to come over that day, but I'll see if she's up for it." Ruhn's blue eyes twinkled like stars, but Bryce cut in, "No promises, though."

He was still grinning when she rose from her barstool. "I'll save a seat for you."

70

Fury was sitting on the couch when Bryce returned from the bar. In the exact spot where she'd gotten used to seeing Hunt.

Bryce chucked her keys onto the table beside the front door, loosed Syrinx upon her friend, and said, "Hey."

"Hey, yourself." Fury gave Syrinx a look that stopped him in his tracks. That made him sit his fluffy butt down on the carpet, lion's tail swaying, and wait until she deigned to greet *him*. Fury did so after a heartbeat, ruffling his velvety, folded ears.

"What's up?" Bryce toed off her heels, rotated her aching feet a few times, and reached back to tug at the zipper to her dress. Gods, it was incredible to have no pain in her leg—not even a flicker. She padded for her bedroom before Fury could answer, knowing she'd hear anyway.

"I got some news," Fury said casually.

Bryce peeled off her dress, sighing as she took off her bra, and changed into a pair of sweats and an old T-shirt before pulling her hair into a ponytail. "Let me guess," she said from the bedroom, shoving her feet into slippers, "you finally realized that black all the time is boring and want me to help you find some real-person clothes?"

A quiet laugh. "Smart-ass." Bryce emerged from the bedroom, and Fury eyed her with that swift assassin's stare. So unlike Hunt's.

Even when she and Fury had been out partying, Fury never really lost that cold gleam. That calculation and distance. But Hunt's stare—

She shut out the thought. The comparison. That roaring fire in her veins flared.

"Look," Fury said, standing from the couch. "I'm heading out a few days early to the Summit. So I just thought you should know something before I go."

"You love me and you'll write often?"

"Gods, you're the worst," Fury said, running a hand through her sleek bob. Bryce missed the long ponytail her friend had worn in college. The new look made Fury seem even more lethal, somehow. "Ever since I met you in that dumb-ass class, you've been the worst."

"Yeah, but you find it delightful." Bryce aimed for the fridge.

A huff. "Look, I'm going to tell you this, but I want you to first promise me that you won't do anything stupid."

Bryce froze with her fingers grasping the handle of the fridge. "As you've told me so often, *stupid* is my middle name."

"I mean it this time. I don't even think anything can be done, but I need you to promise."

"I promise."

Fury studied her face, then leaned against the kitchen counter. "Micah gave Hunt away."

That fire in her veins withered to ash. "To whom?"

"Who do you think? Fucking Sandriel, that's who."

She couldn't feel her arms, her legs. "When."

"You said you wouldn't do anything stupid."

"Is asking for details stupid?"

Fury shook her head. "This afternoon. That bastard knew giving Hunt back to Sandriel was a bigger punishment than publicly crucifying him or shoving his soul into a box and dumping it into the sea."

It was. For so many reasons.

Fury went on, "She and the other angels are heading to the Summit tomorrow afternoon. And I have it on good authority that once the meeting's done next week, she'll go back to Pangera to keep dealing with the Ophion rebels. With Hunt in tow."

And he'd never be free again. What Sandriel would do to him . . . He deserved it. He fucking deserved *everything*.

Bryce said, "If you're so concerned I'll do something stupid, why tell me at all?"

Fury's dark eyes scanned her again. "Because . . . I just thought you should know."

Bryce turned to the fridge. Yanked it open. "Hunt dug his own grave."

"So you two weren't . . ."

"No."

"His scent is on you, though."

"We lived in this apartment together for a month. I'd think it'd be on me."

She'd handed over a hideous number of silver marks to have his blood removed from the couch. Along with all traces of what they'd done there.

A small, strong hand slammed the fridge door shut. Fury glared up at her. "Don't bullshit me, Quinlan."

"I'm not." Bryce let her friend see her true face. The one her father had talked about. The one that did not laugh and did not care for anybody or anything. "Hunt is a liar. He *lied* to me."

"Danika did some fucked-up stuff, Bryce. You know that. You always knew it and laughed it off, looked the other way. I'm not so sure Hunt was lying about that."

Bryce bared her teeth. "I'm over it."

"Over what?"

"All of it." She yanked open the fridge again, nudging Fury out of the way. To her surprise, Fury let her. "Why don't you go back to Pangera and ignore me for another two years?"

"I didn't ignore you."

"You fucking *did*," Bryce spat. "You talk to June all the time, and yet you dodge my calls and barely reply to my messages?"

"June is different."

"Yeah, I know. The special one."

Fury blinked at her. "You nearly *died* that night, Bryce. And Danika *did* die." The assassin's throat bobbed. "I gave you drugs—"

"I bought that mirthroot."

"And I bought the lightseeker. I don't fucking care, Bryce. I got too close to all of you, and *bad things* happen when I do that with people."

"And yet you can still talk to Juniper?" Bryce's throat closed up. "I wasn't worth the risk to you?"

Fury hissed, "Juniper and I have something that is *none* of your fucking business." Bryce refrained from gaping. Juniper had never hinted, never suggested—"I could no sooner stop talking to her than I could rip out my own fucking heart, okay?"

"I get it, I get it," Bryce said. She blew out a long breath. "Love trumps all."

Too fucking bad Hunt hadn't realized that. Or he had, but he'd just chosen the Archangel who still held his heart and their *cause*. Too fucking bad Bryce had still been stupid enough to believe nonsense about love—and let it blind her.

Fury's voice broke. "You and Danika were my friends. You were these two stupid fucking *puppies* that came bounding into my perfectly fine life, and then one of you was slaughtered." Fury bared her teeth. "And. I. Couldn't. Fucking. Deal."

"I needed you. I needed you *here*. Danika died, but it was like I lost you, too." Bryce didn't fight the burning in her eyes. "You walked away like it was nothing."

"It wasn't." Fury blew out a breath. "Fuck, did Juniper not tell you *anything*?" At Bryce's silence, she swore again. "Look, she and I have been working through a lot of my shit, okay? I know it was fucked up that I bailed like that." She dragged her fingers through her hair. "It's all just . . . it's more fucked than you know, Bryce."

"Whatever."

Fury angled her head. "Do I need to call Juniper?"

"No."

"Is this a repeat of two winters ago?"

"No." Juniper must have told her about that night on the roof. They told each other everything, apparently.

Bryce grabbed a jar of almond butter, screwed off the lid, and dug in with a spoon. "Well, have fun at the Summit. See you in another two years."

Fury didn't smile. "Don't make me regret telling you all this."

She met her friend's dark stare. "I'm over it," she said again.

Fury sighed. "All right." Her phone buzzed and she peered at the screen before saying, "I'll be back in a week. Let's hang then, okay? Maybe without screaming at each other."

"Sure."

Fury stalked for the door, but paused on the threshold. "It'll get better, Bryce. I know the past two years have been shit, but it will get better. I've been there, and I promise you it does."

"Okay." Bryce added, because real concern shone on Fury's normally cold face, "Thanks."

Fury had the phone to her ear before she'd shut the door. "Yeah, I'm on my way," she said. "Well, why don't you shut the fuck up and let me drive so I can get there on time, dickbag?"

Through the peephole, Bryce watched her get onto the elevator. Then crossed the room and watched from the window as Fury climbed into a fancy black sports car, gunned the engine, and roared off into the streets.

Bryce peered at Syrinx. The chimera wagged his little lion's tail.

Hunt had been given away. To the monster he hated and feared above all others.

"I *am* over it," she said to Syrinx.

She looked toward the couch, and could nearly see Hunt sitting there, that sunball cap on backward, watching a game on TV. Could nearly see his smile as he looked over his shoulder at her.

That roaring fire in her veins halted—and redirected. She wouldn't lose another friend.

Especially not Hunt. Never Hunt.

No matter what he had done, what and who he'd chosen, even if this was the last she would ever see of him . . . she wouldn't let this happen. He could go to Hel afterward, but she would do this. For him.

Syrinx whined, pacing in a circle, claws clicking on the wood floor.

"I promised Fury not to do anything *stupid*," Bryce said, her eyes on Syrinx's branded-out tattoo. "I didn't say I wouldn't do something smart."

71

Hunt had a night to puke out his guts.

One night in that cell, likely the last bit of security he'd have for the rest of his existence.

He knew what would happen after the Summit. When Sandriel took him back to her castle in the misty, mountainous wilds of northwestern Pangera. To the gray-stoned city in its heart.

He'd lived it for more than fifty years, after all.

She'd left the photo feed up on the hallway TV screen, so he could see Bryce over and over and over. See the way Bryce had looked at him by the end, like he wasn't a complete waste of life.

It wasn't just to torture him with what he'd lost.

It was a reminder. Of who would be targeted if he disobeyed. If he resisted. If he fought back.

By dawn, he'd stopped puking. Had washed his face in the small sink. A change of clothes had arrived for him. His usual black armor. No helmet.

His back itched incessantly as he dressed, the cloth scraping against the wings that were taking form. Soon they'd be fully regenerated. A week of careful physical therapy after that and he'd be in the skies.

If Sandriel ever let him out of her dungeons.

She'd lost him once, to pay off her debts. He had few illusions that she'd allow it to happen again. Not until she found a way to break him for how he'd targeted her forces on Mount Hermon. How he and Shahar had come so close to destroying her completely.

It wasn't until nearly sunset that they came for him. As if Sandriel wanted him stewing all day.

Hunt let them shackle him again with the gorsian stones. He knew what the stones would do if he so much as moved wrong. Disintegration of blood and bone, his brain turned into soup before it leaked out his nose.

The armed guard, ten deep, led him from the cell and into the elevator. Where Pollux Antonius, the golden-haired commander of Sandriel's triarii, waited, a smile on his tan face.

Hunt knew that dead, cruel smile well. Had tried his best to forget it.

"Miss me, Athalar?" Pollux asked, his clear voice belying the monster lurking within. The Hammer could smash through battlefields and delighted in every second of carnage. Of fear and pain. Most Vanir never walked away. No humans ever had.

But Hunt didn't let his rage, his hatred for that smirking, handsome visage so much as flicker across his face. A glimmer of annoyance flashed in Pollux's cobalt eyes, his white wings shifting.

Sandriel waited in the Comitium lobby, the last of the sunlight shining in her curling hair.

The lobby. Not the landing pad levels above. So he might see—

Might see—

Justinian still hung from the crucifix. Rotting away.

"We thought you might want to say goodbye," Pollux purred in his ear as they crossed the lobby. "The wraith, of course, is at the bottom of the sea, but I'm sure she knows you'll miss her."

Hunt let the male's words flow through him, out of him. They would only be the start. Both from the Malleus and from Sandriel herself.

The Archangel smiled at Hunt as they approached, the cruelty on her face making Pollux's smirk look downright pleasant. But she said nothing as she turned on her heel toward the lobby doors.

An armed transport van idled outside, back doors flung wide. Waiting for him, since he sure as fuck couldn't fly. From the mocking gleam in Pollux's eyes, Hunt had a feeling he knew who would be accompanying him.

Angels from the Comitium's five buildings filled the lobby.

He noted Micah's absence—coward. The bastard probably didn't want to sully himself by witnessing the horror he'd inflicted. But Isaiah stood near the heart of the gathered crowd, his expression grim. Naomi gave Hunt a grave nod.

It was all she dared, the only farewell they could make.

The angels silently watched Sandriel. Pollux. Him. They hadn't come to taunt, to witness his despair and humiliation. They, too, had come to say goodbye.

Every step toward the glass doors was a lifetime, was impossible. Every step was abhorrent.

He had done this, brought this upon himself and his companions, and he would pay for it over and over and—

"*Wait!*" The female voice rang out from across the lobby.

Hunt froze. Everyone froze.

"*Wait!*"

No. No, she couldn't be here. He couldn't bear for her to see him like this, knees wobbling and a breath away from puking again. Because Pollux strode beside him, and Sandriel prowled in front of him, and they would destroy her—

But there was Bryce. Running toward them. Toward him.

Fear and pain tightened her face, but her wide eyes were trained on him as she shouted again, to Sandriel, to the entire lobby full of angels, "*Wait!*"

She was breathless as the crowd parted. Sandriel halted, Pollux and the guards instantly on alert, forcing Hunt to pause with them, too.

Bryce skidded to a stop before the Archangel. "Please," she

panted, bracing her hands on her knees, her ponytail drooping over a shoulder as she tried to catch her breath. No sign of that limp. "Please, wait."

Sandriel surveyed her like she would a gnat buzzing about her head. "Yes, Bryce Quinlan?"

Bryce straightened, still panting. Looked at Hunt for a long moment, for eternity, before she said to the Archangel of northwestern Pangera, "Please don't take him."

Hunt could barely stand to hear the plea in her voice. Pollux let out a soft, hateful laugh.

Sandriel was not amused. "He has been gifted to me. The papers were signed yesterday."

Bryce pulled something from her pocket, causing the guards around them to reach for their weapons. Pollux's sword was instantly in his hand, angled toward her with lethal efficiency.

But it wasn't a gun or a knife. It was a piece of paper.

"Then let me buy him from you."

Utter silence.

Sandriel laughed then, the sound rich and lilting. "Do you know how much—"

"I'll pay you ninety-seven million gold marks."

The floor rocked beneath Hunt. People gasped. Pollux blinked, eyeing Bryce again.

Bryce extended a piece of paper toward Sandriel, though the malakh didn't take it. Even from a few feet behind the Archangel, Hunt's sharp eyesight could make out the writing.

Proof of funds. A check from the bank, made out to Sandriel. For nearly a hundred million marks.

A check from Jesiba Roga.

Horror sluiced through him, rendering him speechless. How many years had Bryce added to her debt?

He didn't deserve it. Didn't deserve her. Not for a heartbeat. Not in a thousand years—

Bryce waved the check toward Sandriel. "Twelve million more than his asking price when you sold him, right? You'll—"

"I know how to do the mathematics."

Bryce remained with her arm outstretched. Hope in her beautiful face. Then she reached up, Pollux and the guards tensing again. But it was to just unclasp the golden amulet from around her neck. "Here. To sweeten the deal. An Archesian amulet. It's fifteen thousand years old, and fetches around three million gold marks on the market."

That tiny necklace was worth three *million* gold marks?

Bryce extended both the necklace and the paper, the gold glinting. "Please."

He couldn't let her do it. Not even for what remained of his soul. Hunt opened his mouth, but the Archangel took the dangling necklace from Bryce's fingers. Sandriel glanced between them. Read everything on Hunt's face. A snake's smile curled her mouth. "Your loyalty to my sister was the one good thing about you, Athalar." She clenched her fist around the amulet. "But it seems those photographs did not lie."

The Archesian amulet melted into streams of gold on the floor.

Something ruptured in Hunt's chest at the devastation that crumpled Bryce's face.

He said quietly to her, his first words all day, "Get out of here, Bryce."

But Bryce pocketed the check. And slid to her knees.

"Then take me."

Terror rocked him, so violently he had no words when Bryce looked up at Sandriel, tears filling her eyes as she said, "Take me in his place."

A slow grin spread across Pollux's face.

No. She'd already traded her eternal resting place in the Bone Quarter for Danika. He couldn't let her trade her mortal life for him. Not for him—

"Don't you dare!" The male bellow cracked across the space. Then Ruhn was there, wreathed in shadows, Declan and Flynn flanking him. They weren't foolish enough to reach for their guns as they sized up Sandriel's guards. Realized that Pollux Antonius, the

Malleus, stood there, sword angled to punch through Bryce's chest if Sandriel so much as gave the nod.

The Crown Prince of the Fae pointed at Bryce. "Get off the floor."

Bryce didn't move. She just repeated to Sandriel, "Take me in his place."

Hunt snapped at Bryce, "*Be quiet*," just as Ruhn snarled at the Archangel, "Don't listen to a word she says—"

Sandriel took a step toward Bryce. Another. Until she stood before her, peering down into Bryce's flushed face.

Hunt pleaded, "Sandriel—"

"You offer your life," Sandriel said to Bryce. "Under no coercion, no force."

Ruhn lunged forward, shadows unfurling around him, but Sandriel raised a hand and a wall of wind held him in check. It choked off the prince's shadows, shredding them into nothing.

It held Hunt in check, too, as Bryce met Sandriel's stare and said, "Yes. In exchange for Hunt's freedom, I offer myself in his place." Her voice shook, cracking. She knew how he'd suffered at the Archangel's hands. Knew what awaited her would be even worse.

"Everyone here would call me a fool to take this bargain," Sandriel mused. "A half-breed with no true power or hope to come into it—in exchange for the freedom of one of the most powerful malakim to ever darken the skies. The only warrior on Midgard who can wield lightning."

"Sandriel, *please*," Hunt begged. The air ripping from his throat choked off his words.

Pollux smiled again. Hunt bared his teeth at him as Sandriel stroked a hand over Bryce's cheek, wiping away her tears. "But I know your secret, Bryce Quinlan," Sandriel whispered. "I know what a prize you are."

Ruhn cut in, "That is *enough*—"

Sandriel stroked Bryce's face again. "The only daughter of the Autumn King."

Hunt's knees wobbled.

"Holy fuck," Tristan Flynn breathed. Declan had gone pale as death.

Sandriel purred at Bryce, "Yes, what a prize you would be to possess."

Her cousin's face was stark with terror.

Not cousin. *Brother.* Ruhn was her brother. And Bryce was . . .

"What does your father think of his bastard daughter borrowing such a vast amount from Jesiba Roga?" Sandriel went on, chuckling as Bryce began crying in earnest now. "What shame it would bring upon his royal household, knowing you sold your life away to a half-rate sorceress."

Bryce's pleading eyes met his. The amber eyes of the Autumn King.

Sandriel said, "You thought you were safe from *me*? That after you pulled your little stunt when I arrived, I wouldn't look into your history? My spies are second to none. They found what could not be found. Including your life span test from twelve years ago, and whom it exposed as your father. Even though he paid steeply to bury it."

Ruhn stepped forward, either pushing past Sandriel's wind or being allowed to do so. He grabbed Bryce under the arm and hauled her to her feet. "She is a female member of the Fae royal household and a full civitas of the Republic. I lay claim to her as my sister and kin."

Ancient words. From laws that had never been changed, though public sentiment had.

Bryce whirled on him. *"You have no right—"*

"Based upon the laws of the Fae, as approved by the Asteri," Ruhn charged on, "she is *my* property. My father's. And I do not permit her to trade herself in exchange for Athalar."

Hunt's legs almost gave out with relief. Even as Bryce shoved at Ruhn, clawed at him, and growled, "I'm no property of yours—"

"You are a Fae female of my bloodline," Ruhn said coldly. "You are my property and our father's until you marry."

She looked to Declan, to Flynn, whose solemn faces must have told her she'd find no allies among them. She hissed at Ruhn, "I will *never* forgive you. I will *never*—"

"We're done here," Ruhn said to Sandriel.

He tugged Bryce away, his friends falling into formation around them, and Hunt tried to memorize her face, even with despair and rage twisting it.

Ruhn tugged her again, but she thrashed against him.

"Hunt," she pleaded, stretching a hand for him, "I'll find a way."

Pollux laughed. Sandriel just began to turn from them, bored.

But Bryce continued to reach for him, even as Ruhn tried to drag her toward the doors.

Hunt stared at her outstretched fingers. The desperate hope in her eyes.

No one had ever fought for him. No one had ever cared enough to do so.

"*Hunt,*" Bryce begged, shaking. Her fingers strained. *"I'll find a way to save you."*

"*Stop it,*" Ruhn ordered, and grabbed for her waist.

Sandriel walked toward the lobby doors and the awaiting motorcade. She said to Ruhn, "You should have slit your sister's throat when you had the chance, Prince. I speak from personal experience."

Bryce's wrenching sobs ripped at Hunt as Pollux shoved him into movement.

She'd never stop fighting for him, would never give up hope. So Hunt went in for the kill as he passed her, even as each word broke him apart, "I owe you nothing, and you owe me nothing. Don't ever come looking for me again."

Bryce mouthed his name. As if he were the sole person in the room. The city. The planet.

And it was only when Hunt was loaded onto the armored truck, when his chains were anchored to the metal sides and Pollux was smirking across from him, when the driver had embarked on the five-hour drive to the town in the heart of the Psamathe Desert where the Summit would be held in five days, that he let himself take a breath.

* * *

Ruhn watched as Pollux loaded Athalar into that prison van. Watched as it rumbled to life and sped off, watched as the crowd in the lobby dispersed, marking the end of this fucking disaster.

Until Bryce wrenched out of his grip. Until Ruhn let her. Pure, undiluted hatred twisted her features as she said again, "I will *never* forgive you for this."

Ruhn said coldly, "Do you have any idea what Sandriel does to her slaves? Do you know that was Pollux Antonius, the fucking *Hammer*, with her?"

"Yes. Hunt told me everything."

"Then you're a fucking idiot." She advanced on him, but Ruhn seethed, "I will not apologize for protecting you—not from her, and not from yourself. I get it, I do. Hunt was your—whatever he was to you. But the last thing he would ever want is—"

"Go fuck yourself." Her breathing turned jagged. *"Go fuck yourself, Ruhn."*

Ruhn jerked his chin toward the lobby doors in dismissal. "Cry about it to someone else. You'll have a hard time finding anyone who'll agree with you."

Her fingers curled at her sides. As if she'd punch him, claw him, shred him.

But she just spat at Ruhn's feet and stalked away. Bryce reached her scooter and didn't look back as she zoomed off.

Flynn said, voice low, "What the fuck, Ruhn."

Ruhn sucked in a breath. He didn't even want to think about what kind of bargain she'd struck with the sorceress to get that kind of money.

Declan was shaking his head. And Flynn . . . disappointment and hurt flickered on his face. "Why didn't you tell us? Your *sister*, Ruhn?" Flynn pointed to the glass doors. "She's our fucking *princess*."

"She is not," Ruhn growled. "The Autumn King has not recognized her, nor will he ever."

"Why?" Dec demanded.

"Because she's his bastard child. Because he doesn't like her.

I don't fucking know," Ruhn spat. He couldn't—wouldn't—ever tell them his own motivations for it. That deep-rooted fear of what the Oracle's prophecy might mean for Bryce should she ever be granted a royal title. For if the royal bloodline was to end with Ruhn, and Bryce was officially a princess of their family . . . She would have to be out of the picture for it to come to pass. Permanently. He'd do whatever was necessary to keep her safe from that particular doom. Even if the world hated him for it.

Indeed, at his friends' disapproving frowns, he snapped, "All I know is that I was given an order never to reveal it, even to you."

Flynn crossed his arms. "You think we would have told anyone?"

"No. But I couldn't take the risk of him finding out. And *she* didn't want anyone to know." And now wasn't the time or place to speak about this. Ruhn said, "I need to talk to her."

What came *after* he spoke with Bryce, he didn't know if he could handle.

Bryce rode to the river. To the arches of the Black Dock.

Darkness had fallen by the time she chained her scooter to a lamppost, the night balmy enough that she was grateful for Danika's leather jacket keeping her warm as she stood on the dark dock and stared across the Istros.

Slowly, she sank to her knees, bowing her head. "It's so fucked," she whispered, hoping the words would carry across the water, to the tombs and mausoleums hidden behind the wall of mist. "It is all so, so fucked, Danika."

She'd failed. Utterly and completely failed. And Hunt was . . . he was . . .

Bryce buried her face in her hands. For a while, the only sounds were the wind hissing through the palms and the lapping of the river against the dock.

"I wish you were here," Bryce finally allowed herself to say. "Every day, I wish that, but today especially."

The wind quieted, the palms going still. Even the river seemed to halt.

A chill crept toward her, through her. Every sense, Fae and human, went on alert. She scanned the mists, waiting, praying for a black boat. She was so busy looking that she didn't see the attack coming.

Didn't twist to see a kristallos demon leaping from the shadows, jaws open, before it tackled her into the eddying waters.

72

Claws and teeth were everywhere. Ripping at her, snatching her, dragging her down.

The river was pitch-black, and there was no one, no one at all, who'd seen or would know—

Something burned along her arm, and she screamed, water rushing down her throat.

Then the claws splayed. Loosened.

Bryce kicked, shoving blindly away, the surface somewhere—in any direction—oh gods, she was going to pick wrong—

Something grabbed her by the shoulder, dragging her away, and she would have screamed if there had been any air left in her lungs—

Air broke around her face, open and fresh, and then there was a male voice at her ear saying, "I've got you, I've got you."

She might have sobbed, if she hadn't spewed water, hadn't launched into a coughing fit. Hunt had said those words to her, and now Hunt was gone, and the male voice at her ear—Declan Emmet.

Ruhn shouted from a few feet away, "It's down."

She thrashed, but Declan held her firm, murmuring, "It's all right."

It wasn't fucking all right. Hunt should have been there. He should have been with her, he should have been freed, and she should have found a way to help him—

It took half a moment for Declan to heave her out of the water. Ruhn, his face grim, hauled her the rest of the way, cursing up a storm while she shuddered on the dock.

"What the fucking fuck," Tristan Flynn was panting, rifle aimed at the black water, ready to unload a hail of bullets at the slightest ripple.

"Are you all right?" Declan asked, water streaming down his face, red hair plastered to his head.

Bryce drew back into herself enough to survey her body. A gash sliced down her arm, but it had been made with claws, not those venomous teeth. Other slices peppered her, but . . .

Declan didn't wait before kneeling before her, hands wreathed in light as he held them over the gash in her arm. It was rare—the Fae healing gift. Not as powerful as the talent of a medwitch, but a valuable strength to possess. She'd never known Dec had the ability.

Ruhn asked, "Why the *fuck* were you standing on the Black Dock after sundown?"

"I was kneeling," she muttered.

"Same fucking question."

She met her brother's gaze as her wounds healed shut. "I needed a breather."

Flynn muttered something.

"What?" She narrowed her eyes at him.

Flynn crossed his arms. "I said I've known that you're a princess for all of an hour and you're already a pain in my ass."

"I'm not a princess," she said at the same moment Ruhn snapped, "She's not a princess."

Declan snorted. "Whatever, assholes." He pulled back from Bryce, healing complete. "We should have realized. You're the only one who even comes close to getting under Ruhn's skin as easily as his father does."

Flynn cut in, "Where did that thing come from?"

"Apparently," she said, "people who take large quantities of synth can inadvertently summon a kristallos demon. It was probably a freak accident."

"Or a targeted attack," Flynn challenged.

"The case is over," Bryce said flatly. "It's done."

The Fae lord's eyes flashed with a rare show of anger. "Maybe it isn't."

Ruhn wiped the water off his face. "On the chance Flynn's right, you're staying with me."

"Over my dead fucking body." Bryce stood, water pouring off her. "Look, thanks for rescuing me. And thanks for royally fucking me and Hunt over back there. But you know what?" She bared her teeth and pulled out her phone, wiping water from it, praying the protective spell she'd paid good money for had held. It had. She scrolled through screens until she got to Ruhn's contact info. She showed it to him. "You?" She swiped her finger, and it was deleted. "Are *dead* to me."

She could have sworn her brother, her fuck-you-world brother, flinched.

She looked at Dec and Flynn. "Thanks for saving my ass."

They didn't come after her. Bryce could barely stop shaking long enough to steer her scooter home, but she somehow made it. Made it upstairs, walked Syrinx.

The apartment was too quiet without Hunt in it. No one had come to take his things. If they had, they'd have found that sunball hat missing. Hidden in the box alongside Jelly Jubilee.

Exhausted, Bryce peeled off her clothes and stared at herself in the bathroom mirror. She lifted a palm to her chest, where the weight of the Archesian amulet had been for the past three years.

Red, angry lines marred her skin where the kristallos had swiped, but with Declan's magic still working on her, they'd be faded to nothing by morning.

She twisted, bracing herself to see the damage to the tattoo on her back. This last shred of Danika. If that fucking demon had wrecked it . . .

She nearly wept to see it intact. To look at the lines in that ancient, unreadable alphabet and know that even with everything gone to Hel, this still remained: The words Danika had insisted they ink there, with Bryce too plastered to object. Danika had picked the alphabet out of some booklet at the shop, though it sure as fuck didn't look like any Bryce recognized. Maybe the artist had just made it up, and told them it said what Danika had wanted:

Through love, all is possible.

The same words on the jacket in a pile at her feet. The same words that had been a clue—to her Redner account, to finding that flash drive.

Nonsense. It was all fucking nonsense. The tattoo, the jacket, losing that amulet, losing Danika, losing Connor and the Pack of Devils, losing Hunt—

Bryce tried and failed to wrest herself from the cycle of thoughts, the maelstrom that brought them around and around and around, until they all eddied together.

73

The last Summit Hunt had attended had been in an ancient, sprawling palace in Pangera, bedecked in the riches of the empire: silk tapestries and sconces of pure gold, goblets twinkling with precious stones, and succulent meats crusted in the rarest spices.

This one was held in a conference center.

The glass and metal space was sprawling, its layout reminding Hunt of a bunch of shoeboxes stacked beside and atop each other. Its central hall rose three stories high, the stairs and escalators at the back of the space adorned with the crimson banners of the Republic, the long pathway leading to them carpeted in white.

Each territory in Midgard held their own Summit every ten years, attended by various leaders within their borders, along with a representative of the Asteri and a few visiting dignitaries relevant to whatever issues would be discussed. This one was no different, save for its smaller scope: Though Valbara was far smaller than Pangera, Micah held four different Summit meetings, each for a separate quadrant of his realm. This one, for the southeastern holdings—with Lunathion's leaders at its heart—was the first.

The site, located in the heart of the Psamathe Desert, a good five-hour drive from Crescent City—an hour for an angel at top flying speeds or a mere half hour by helicopter—had its own holding cells for dangerous Vanir.

He'd spent the last five days there, marking them by the shift in his food: breakfast, lunch, dinner. At least Sandriel and Pollux had not come to taunt him. At least he had that small reprieve. He'd barely listened to the Hammer's attempts to bait him during the drive. He'd barely felt or heard anything at all.

Yet this morning, a set of black clothes had arrived with his breakfast tray. No weapons, but the uniform was clear enough. So was the message: he was about to be displayed, a mockery of an imperial Triumphus parade, for Sandriel to gloat about regaining ownership of him.

But he'd obediently dressed, and let Sandriel's guards fit the gorsian manacles on him, rendering his power null and void.

He followed the guards silently, up through the elevator, and into the grand lobby itself, bedecked in imperial regalia.

Vanir of every House filled the space, most dressed in business clothes or what had once been known as courtly attire. Angels, shifters, Fae, witches . . . Delegations flanked either side of the red runner leading toward the stairs. Fury Axtar stood among the crowd, clad in her usual assassin leathers, watching everyone. She didn't look his way.

Hunt was led toward a delegation of angels near the staircase—members of Sandriel's 45th Legion. Her triarii. Pollux stood in front of them, his commander status marked by his gold armor, his cobalt cape, his smirking face.

That smirk only grew as Hunt took up his position nearby, wedged between her guards.

Her other triarii were nearly as bad as the Hammer. Hunt would never forget any of them: the thin, pale-skinned, dark-haired female known as the Harpy; the stone-faced, black-winged male called the Helhound; and the haughty, cold-eyed angel named the Hawk. But they ignored him. Which, he'd learned, was better than their attention.

No sign of the Hind, the final member of the triarii—though maybe her work as a spy-breaker in Pangera was too valuable to the Asteri for Sandriel to be allowed to drag her here.

Across the runner stood Isaiah and the 33rd. What remained

of its triarii. Naomi was stunning in her uniform, her chin high and right hand on the hilt of her formal legion sword, its winged cross guard glinting in the morning light.

Isaiah's eyes drifted over to his. Hunt, in his black armor, was practically naked compared to the full uniform of the Commander of the 33rd: the bronze breastplate, the epaulets, the greaves and vambraces . . . Hunt still remembered how heavy it was. How stupid he'd always felt decked out in the full regalia of the Imperial Army. Like some prize warhorse.

The Autumn King's Auxiliary forces stood to the left of the angels, their armor lighter but no less ornate. Across from them were the shifters, in their finest clothes. Amelie Ravenscroft didn't so much as dare look in his direction. Smaller groups of Vanir filled the rest of the space: mer and daemonaki. No sign of any humans. Certainly no one with mixed heritage, either.

Hunt tried not to think of Bryce. Of what had gone down in the lobby.

Princess of the Fae. Bastard princess was more like it, but she was still the only daughter of the Autumn King.

She might have been furious at him for lying, but she'd lied plenty to him as well.

Drummers—fucking Hel, the gods-damned drummers—sounded the beat. The trumpeters began a moment later. The rolling, hateful anthem of the Republic filled the cavernous glass space. Everyone straightened as a motorcade pulled up beyond the doors.

Hunt sucked in a breath as Jesiba Roga emerged first, clad in a thigh-length black dress cut to her curvy body, ancient gold glittering at her ears and throat, a diaphanous midnight cape flowing behind her on a phantom wind. Even in towering high heels, she moved with the eerie smoothness of the House of Flame and Shadow.

Maybe she'd been the one who told Bryce how to sell her soul to the ruler of the Sleeping City.

The blond sorceress kept her gray eyes on the three flags hanging above the stairs as she moved toward them: on the left, the flag of Valbara; on the right, the insignia of Lunathion with its crescent moon bow and arrow. And in the center, the *SPQM* and its twin branches of stars—the flag of the Republic.

The witches came next, their steps ringing out. A young, brown-skinned female in flowing azure robes strode down the carpet, her braided black hair gleaming like spun night.

Queen Hypaxia. She'd worn her mother's gold-and-red crown of cloudberries for barely three months, and though her face was unlined and beautiful, there was a weariness to her dark eyes that spoke volumes about her lingering grief.

Rumor had it that Queen Hecuba had raised her deep in the boreal forest of the Heliruna Mountains, far from the corruption of the Republic. Hunt might have expected that such a person would shy from the gathered crowd and imperial splendor, or at least gape a little, but her chin remained high, her steps unfaltering. As if she had done this a dozen times.

She was to be formally recognized as Queen of the Valbaran Witches when the Summit officially began. Her final bit of pageantry before truly inheriting her throne. But—

Hunt got a look at her face as she neared.

He knew her: the medwitch from the clinic. She acknowledged Hunt with a swift sidelong glance as she passed.

Had Ruhn known? Who he'd met with, who had fed him research about the synth?

The mer leaders arrived, Tharion in a charcoal suit beside a female in a flowing, gauzy teal gown. Not the River Queen—she rarely left the Istros. But the beautiful, dark-skinned female might as well have been her daughter. Probably was her daughter, in the way that all mer claimed the River Queen as their mother.

Tharion's red-brown hair was slicked back, with a few escaped strands hanging over his brow. He'd swapped his fins for legs, but they didn't falter as his eyes slid toward Hunt. Sympathy shone there.

Hunt ignored it. He hadn't forgotten just who had brought Bryce to the barge that night.

Tharion, to his credit, didn't balk from Hunt's stare. He just gave him a sad smile and looked ahead, following the witches to the mezzanine level and open conference room doors beyond.

Then came the wolves. Sabine walked beside the hunched figure of the Prime, helping the old male along. His brown eyes were milky with age, his once-strong body bent over his cane. Sabine, clad in a dove-gray suit, sneered at Hunt, steering the ancient Prime toward the escalator rather than the steps.

But the Prime halted upon seeing where she planned to bring him. Drew her to the stairs. And began the ascent, step by painful step.

Proud bastard.

The Fae left their black cars, stalking onto the carpet. The Autumn King emerged, an onyx crown upon his red hair, the ancient stone like a piece of night even in the light of morning.

Hunt didn't know how he hadn't seen it before. Bryce looked more like her father than Ruhn did. Granted, plenty of the Fae had that coloring, but the coldness on the Autumn King's face . . . He'd seen Bryce make that expression countless times.

The Autumn King, not some prick lordling, had been the one to go with her to the Oracle that day. The one to kick a thirteen-year-old to the curb.

Hunt's fingers curled at his sides. He couldn't blame Ember Quinlan for running the moment she'd seen the monster beneath the surface. Felt its cold violence.

And realized she was carrying its child. A potential heir to the throne—one that might complicate things for his pure-blooded, Chosen One son. No wonder the Autumn King had hunted them down so ruthlessly.

Ruhn, a step behind his father, was a shock to the senses. In his princely raiment, the Starsword at his side, he could have very well been one of the first Starborn with that coloring of his. Might have been one of the first through the Northern Rift, so long ago.

They passed Hunt, and the king didn't so much as glance his way. But Ruhn did.

Ruhn looked to the shackles on Hunt's wrists, the 45th's triarii around him. And subtly shook his head. To any observer, it was in disgust, in reprimand. But Hunt saw the message.

I'm sorry.

Hunt kept his face unmoved, neutral. Ruhn moved on, the circlet of gilded birch leaves atop his head glinting.

And then the atrium seemed to inhale. To pause.

The angels did not arrive in cars. No, they dropped from the skies.

Forty-nine angels in the Asterian Guard, in full white-and-gold regalia, marched into the lobby, spears in their gloved hands and white wings shining. Each had been bred, hand-selected, for this life of service. Only the whitest, purest of wings would do. Not one speck of color on them.

Hunt had always thought they were swaggering assholes.

They took up spots along the carpet, standing at attention, wings high and spears pointing at the glass ceiling, their snowy capes draping to the floor. The white plumes of horsehair on their golden helmets gleamed as if freshly brushed, and the visors remained down.

They'd been sent from Pangera as a reminder to all of them, the Governors included, that the ones who held their leashes still monitored everything.

Micah and Sandriel arrived next, side by side. Each in their Governor's armor.

The Vanir sank to a knee before them. Yet the Asterian Guard—who would bow only for their six masters—remained standing, their spears like twin walls of thorns that the Governors paraded between.

No one dared speak. No one dared breathe as the two Archangels passed by.

They were all fucking worms at their feet.

Sandriel's smile seared Hunt as she breezed past. Almost as badly as Micah's utter disappointment and weariness.

Micah had picked his method of torture well, Hunt would give him that. There was no way Sandriel would let him die quickly. The torment when he returned to Pangera would last decades. No chance of a new death-bargain or a buyout.

And if he so much as stepped out of line, she'd know where to strike first. Who to strike.

The Governors swept up the stairs, their wings nearly touching. Why the two of them hadn't become a mated pair was beyond Hunt. Micah was decent enough that he likely found Sandriel as abhorrent as everyone else did. But it was still a wonder the Asteri hadn't ordered the bloodlines merged. It wouldn't have been unusual. Sandriel and Shahar had been the result of such a union.

Though perhaps the fact that Sandriel had likely killed her own parents to seize power for her and her sister had made the Asteri put a halt to the practice.

Only when the Governors reached the conference room did those assembled in the lobby move, first the angels peeling off for the stairs, the rest of the assembly falling into line behind them.

Hunt was kept wedged between two of the 45th's triarii—the Helhound and the Hawk, who both sneered at him—and took in as many details as he could when they entered the meeting room.

It was cavernous, with rings of tables flowing down to a central floor and round table where the leaders would sit.

The Pit of Hel. That's what it was. It was a wonder none of its princes stood there.

The Prime of Wolves, the Autumn King, the two Governors, the River Queen's fair daughter, Queen Hypaxia, and Jesiba all took seats at that central table. Their seconds—Sabine, Ruhn, Tharion, an older-looking witch—all claimed spots in the ring of tables around them. No one else from the House of Flame and Shadow had come with Jesiba, not even a vampyr. The ranks fell into place beyond that, each ring of tables growing larger and larger, seven in total. The Asterian Guard lined the uppermost level, standing against the wall, two at each of the room's three exits.

The seven levels of Hel indeed.

Vidscreens were interspersed throughout the room, two hanging from the ceiling itself, and computers lined the tables, presumably for references. Fury Axtar, to his surprise, took up a spot in the third circle, leaning back in her chair. No one else accompanied her.

Hunt was led to a spot against the wall, nestled between two Asterian Guards who ignored him completely. Thank fuck the angle blocked his view of Pollux and the rest of Sandriel's triarii.

Hunt braced himself as the vidscreens flicked on. The room went quiet at what appeared.

He knew those crystal halls, torches of firstlight dancing on the carved quartz pillars rising toward the arched ceiling stories above. Knew the seven crystal thrones arranged in a curve on the golden dais, the one empty throne at its far end. Knew the twinkling city beyond them, the hills rolling away into the dimming light, the Tiber a dark band wending between them.

Everyone rose from their seats as the Asteri came into view. And everyone knelt.

Even from nearly six thousand miles away, Hunt could have sworn their power rippled into the conference room. Could have sworn it sucked out the warmth, the air, the life.

The first time he'd been before them, he'd thought he'd never experienced anything worse. Shahar's blood had still coated his armor, his throat had still been ravaged from screaming during the battle, and yet he had never encountered anything so horrific. So unearthly. As if his entire existence were but a mayfly, his power but a wisp of breeze in the face of their hurricane. As if he'd been hurled into deep space.

They each held the power of a sacred star, each could level this planet to dust, yet there was no light in their cold eyes.

Through lowered lashes, Hunt marked who else dared to lift their eyes from the gray carpet as the six Asteri surveyed them: Tharion and Ruhn. Declan Emmet. And Queen Hypaxia.

No others. Not even Fury or Jesiba.

Ruhn met Hunt's stare. And a quiet male voice said in his head, *Bold move.*

Hunt held in his shock. He'd known there were occasional telepaths out there among the Fae, especially the ones who dwelled in

Avallen. But he'd never had a conversation with one. Certainly not inside his head. *Neat trick.*

A gift from my mother's kin—one I've kept quiet.

And you trust me with this secret?

Ruhn was silent for a moment. *I can't be seen talking to you. If you need anything, let me know. I'll do what I can for you.*

Another shock, as physical as his lightning zapping through him. *Why would you help me?*

Because you would have done everything in your power to keep Bryce from trading herself to Sandriel. I could see it on your face. Ruhn hesitated, then added, a shade uncertainly, *And because I don't think you're quite as much of an asshole now.*

The corner of Hunt's mouth lifted. *Likewise.*

Is that a compliment? Another pause. *How are you holding up, Athalar?*

Fine. How is she?

Back at work, according to the eyes I have on her.

Good. He didn't think he could endure any more talk of Bryce without completely falling apart, so he said, *Did you know that med-witch was Queen Hypaxia?*

No. I fucking didn't.

Ruhn might have gone on, but the Asteri began to speak. As one, like they always did. Telepaths in their own regard. "You have converged to discuss matters pertaining to your region. We grant you our leave." They looked to Hypaxia.

Impressively, the witch didn't flinch, didn't so much as tremble as the six Asteri looked upon her, the world watching with them, and said, "We formally recognize you as the heir of the late Queen Hecuba Enador, and with her passing, now anoint you Queen of the Valbaran Witches."

Hypaxia bowed her head, her face grave. Jesiba's face revealed nothing. Not even a hint of sorrow or anger for the heritage she'd walked away from. So Hunt dared a look at Ruhn, who was frowning.

The Asteri again surveyed the room, none more haughtily than

Rigelus, the Bright Hand. That slim teenage boy's body was a mockery of the monstrous power within. As one the Asteri continued, "You may begin. May the blessings of the gods and all the stars in the heavens shine upon you."

Heads bowed further, in thanks for merely being allowed to exist in their presence.

"It is our hope that you discuss a way to end this inane war. Governor Sandriel will prove a valuable witness to its destruction." A slow, horrible scan through the room followed. And Hunt knew their eyes were upon him as they said, "And there are others here who may also provide their testimony."

There was only one testimony to provide: that the humans were wasteful and foolish, and the war was their fault, their fault, their fault, and must be ended. Must be avoided here at all costs. There was to be no sympathy for the human rebellion, no hearing of the humans' plight. There was only the Vanir side, the good side, and no other.

Hunt held Rigelus's dead stare on the central screen. A zap of icy wind through his body courtesy of Sandriel warned him to avert his eyes. He did not. He could have sworn the Head of the Asteri smiled. Hunt's blood turned to ice, not just from Sandriel's wind, and he lowered his eyes.

This empire had been built to last for eternity. In more than fifteen thousand years, it had not broken. This war would not be the thing that ended it.

The Asteri said together, "Farewell." Another small smile from all of them—the worst being Rigelus's, still directed at Hunt. The screens went dark.

Everyone in the room, the two Governors included, blew out a breath. Someone puked, by the sound and reek from the far corner. Sure enough, a leopard shifter bolted through the doors, a hand over his mouth.

Micah leaned back in his chair, his eyes on the wood table before him. For a moment, no one spoke. As if they all needed to reel themselves back in. Even Sandriel.

Then Micah straightened, his wings rustling, and declared in a deep, clear voice, "I hereby commence this Valbaran Summit. All hail the Asteri and the stars they possess."

The room echoed the words, albeit half-heartedly. As if everyone remembered that even in this land across the sea from Pangera, so far from the muddy battlefields and the shining crystal palace in a city of seven hills, even here, there was no escaping.

74

Bryce tried not to dwell on the fact that Hunt and the world knew what and who she really was. At least the press hadn't caught wind of it, for whatever small mercy that was.

As if being a bastard princess meant anything. As if it said anything about her as a person. The shock on Hunt's face was precisely why she hadn't told him.

She'd torn up Jesiba's check, and with it the centuries of debts.

None of it mattered now anyway. Hunt was gone.

She knew he was alive. She'd seen the news footage of the Summit's opening procession. Hunt had looked just as he had before everything went to shit. Another small mercy.

She'd barely noticed the others arriving: Jesiba, Tharion, her sire, her brother . . . No, she'd just kept her eyes on that spot in the crowd, those gray wings that had now regrown.

Pathetic. She was utterly pathetic.

She would have done it. Would have gladly traded places with Hunt, even knowing what Sandriel would do to her. What Pollux would do to her.

Maybe it made her an idiot, as Ruhn said. Naïve.

Maybe she was lucky to have walked out of the Comitium lobby still breathing.

Maybe being attacked by that kristallos was payment for her fuckups.

She'd spent the past few days looking through the laws to see if there was anything to be done for Hunt. There wasn't. She'd done the only two things that might have granted him his freedom: offered to buy him, and offered herself in his stead.

She didn't believe Hunt's bullshit last words to her. She would have said the same had she been in his place. Would have been as nasty as she could, if it would have gotten him to safety.

Bryce sat at the front desk in the showroom, staring at the blank computer screen. The city had been quiet these past two days. As if everyone's attention was on the Summit, even though only a few of Crescent City's leaders and citizens had gone.

She'd watched the news recaps only to catch another glimpse of Hunt—without any luck.

She slept in his room every night. Had put on one of his T-shirts and crawled between the sheets that smelled of him and pretended he was lying in the dark beside her.

An envelope with the Comitium listed as its return address had arrived at the gallery three days ago. Her heart had thundered as she'd ripped it open, wondering if he'd been able to get a message out—

The white opal had fallen to the desk. Isaiah had written a reserved note, as if aware that every piece of mail was read:

Naomi found this on the barge. Thought you might want it back.

Then he'd added, as if on second thought, *He's sorry.*

She'd slid the stone into her desk drawer.

Sighing, Bryce opened it now, peering at the milky gem. She ran her finger over its cool surface.

"Athie looks miserable," Lehabah observed, floating by Bryce's head. She pointed to the tablet, where Bryce had paused her third replay of the opening procession on Hunt's face. "So do you, BB."

"Thank you."

At her feet, Syrinx stretched out, yawning. His curved claws glinted.

"So what do we do now?"

Bryce's brow furrowed. "What do you mean?"

Lehabah wrapped her arms around herself, floating in midair. "We just go back to normal?"

"Yes."

Her flickering eyes met Bryce's. "What is *normal*, anyway?"

"Seems boring to me."

Lehabah smiled slightly, turning a soft rose color.

Bryce offered one in return. "You're a good friend, Lele. A really good friend." She sighed again, setting the sprite's flame guttering. "I'm sorry if I haven't been such a good one to you at times."

Lehabah waved a hand, going scarlet. "We'll get through this, BB." She perched on Bryce's shoulder, her warmth seeping into skin Bryce hadn't realized was so cold. "You, me, and Syrie. Together, we'll get through this."

Bryce held up a finger, letting Lehabah take it in both of her tiny, shimmering hands. "Deal."

75

Ruhn had anticipated that the Summit would be intense, vicious, flat-out dangerous—each moment spent wondering whether someone's throat would be ripped out. Just as it was at every one he'd attended.

This time, his only enemy seemed to be boredom.

It had taken Sandriel all of two hours to tell them that the Asteri had ordered more troops to the front from every House. There was no point in arguing. It wasn't going to change. The order had come from the Asteri.

Talk turned to the new trade proposals. And then circled and circled and circled, even Micah getting caught in the semantics of who did what and got what and on and on until Ruhn was wondering if the Asteri had come up with this meeting as some form of torture.

He wondered how many of the Asterian Guard were sleeping behind their masks. He'd caught a few of the lesser members of the various delegations nodding off. But Athalar was alert—every minute, the assassin seemed to be listening. Watching.

Maybe that was what the Governors wanted: all of them so bored and desperate to end this meeting that they eventually agreed to terms that weren't to their advantage.

There were a few holdouts, still. Ruhn's father being one, along with the mer and the witches.

One witch in particular.

Queen Hypaxia spoke little, but he noticed that she, too, listened to every word being bandied about, her rich brown eyes full of wary intelligence despite her youth.

It had been a shock to see her the first day—that familiar face in this setting, with her crown and royal robes. To know he'd been talking to his would-be betrothed for weeks now with no fucking idea.

He'd managed to slip between two of her coven members as they filed into the dining hall the first day, and, like an asshole, demanded, "Why didn't you say anything? About who you really are?"

Hypaxia held her lunch tray with a grace better suited to holding a scepter. "You didn't ask."

"What the Hel were you doing in that shop?"

Her dark eyes shuttered. "My sources told me that evil was stirring in the city. I came to see for myself—discreetly." It was why she'd been at the scene of the temple guard's murder, he realized. And there the night Athalar and Bryce had been attacked in the park. "I also came to see what it was like to be . . . ordinary. Before this." She waved with a hand toward her crown.

"Do you know what my father expects of you? And me?"

"I have my suspicions," she said coolly. "But I am not considering such . . . changes in my life right now." She gave him a nod before walking away. "Not with anyone."

And that was it. His ass had been handed to him.

Today, at least, he'd tried to pay attention. To not look at the witch who had absolutely zero interest in marrying him, thank fuck. With her healing gifts, could she sense whatever was wrong inside him that would mean he was the last of the bloodline? He didn't want to find out. Ruhn shoved away the memory of the Oracle's prophecy. He wasn't the only one ignoring Hypaxia, at least. Jesiba Roga hadn't spoken one word to her.

Granted, the sorceress hadn't said much, other than to assert that the House of Flame and Shadow thrived on death and chaos, and had no quarrel with a long, devastating war. Reapers were always happy to ferry the souls of the dead, she said. Even the Archangels had looked disconcerted at that.

As the clock struck nine and all took their seats in the room, Sandriel announced, "Micah has been called away, and will be joining us later."

Only one person—well, six of them—could summon Micah away from this meeting. Sandriel seemed content to rule over the day's proceedings, and declared, "We will begin with the mer explaining their shortsighted resistance to the building of a canal for the transportation of our tanks and the continuation of the supply lines."

The River Queen's daughter bit her bottom lip, hesitating. But it was Captain Tharion Ketos who drawled to Sandriel, "I'd say that when your war machines rip up our oyster beds and kelp forests, it's not shortsighted to say that it will destroy our fishing industry."

Sandriel's eyes flashed. But she said sweetly, "You will be compensated."

Tharion didn't back down. "It is not just about the money. It is about the care of this planet."

"War requires sacrifice."

Tharion crossed his arms, muscles rippling beneath his black long-sleeved T-shirt. After the initial parade and that first day of endless meetings, most of them had donned far less formal wear for the rest of the talks. "I know the costs of war, Governor."

Bold male, to say that, to look Sandriel dead in the eye.

Queen Hypaxia said, her voice soft but unflinching, "Tharion's concern has merit. And precedent." Ruhn straightened as all eyes slid toward the witch-queen. She, too, did not back down from the storms in Sandriel's eyes. "Along the eastern borders of the Rhagan Sea, the coral and kelp beds that were destroyed in the Sorvakkian Wars two thousand years ago have still not returned. The mer who farmed them were compensated, as you claim. But only for a few seasons." Utter silence in the meeting room. "Will you pay, Governor, for a thousand seasons? Two thousand seasons? What of the creatures who make their homes in places you propose to destroy? How shall you pay them?"

"They are Lowers. Lower than the Lowers," Sandriel said coldly, unmoved.

"They are children of Midgard. Children of Cthona," the witch-queen said.

Sandriel smiled, all teeth. "Spare me your bleeding-heart nonsense."

Hypaxia didn't smile back. She just held Sandriel's stare. No challenge in it, but frank assessment.

To Ruhn's eternal shock, it was Sandriel who looked away first, rolling her eyes and shuffling her papers. Even his father blinked at it. And assessed the young queen with a narrowed gaze. No doubt wondering how a twenty-six-year-old witch had the nerve. Or what Hypaxia might have on Sandriel to make an Archangel yield to her.

Wondering if the witch-queen would indeed be a good bride for Ruhn—or a thorn in his side.

Across the table, Jesiba Roga smiled slightly at Hypaxia. Her first acknowledgment of the young witch.

"The canal," Sandriel said tightly, setting down her papers, "we shall discuss later. The supply lines . . ." The Archangel launched into another speech about her plans to streamline the war.

Hypaxia went back to the papers before her. But her eyes lifted to the second ring of tables.

To Tharion.

The mer male gave her a slight, secret smile—gratitude and acknowledgment.

The witch-queen nodded back, barely a dip of her chin.

The mer male just casually lifted his paper, flashing what looked like about twenty rows of markings—counting something.

Hypaxia's eyes widened, bright with reproach and disbelief, and Tharion lowered the paper before anyone else noticed. Added another slash to it.

A flush crept over the witch-queen's cheeks.

His father, however, began speaking, so Ruhn ignored their antics and squared his shoulders, trying his best to look like he was paying attention. Like he cared.

None of it would matter, in the end. Sandriel and Micah would get what they wanted.

And everything would remain the same.

Hunt was so bored he honestly thought his brain was going to bleed out his ears.

But he tried to savor these last days of calm and relative comfort, even with Pollux monitoring everything from across the room. Waiting until he could stop appearing civilized. Hunt knew Pollux was counting down the hours until he'd be unleashed upon him.

So every time the asshole smiled at him, Hunt grinned right back.

Hunt's wings, at least, had healed. He'd been testing them as much as he could, stretching and flexing. If Sandriel allowed him to get airborne, he knew they'd carry him. Probably.

Standing against the wall, dissecting each word spoken, was its own form of torture, but Hunt listened. Paid attention, even when it seemed like so many others were fighting sleep.

He hoped the delegations who held out—the Fae, the mer, the witches—would last until the end of the Summit before remembering that control was an illusion and the Asteri could simply issue an edict regarding the new trade laws. Just as they had with the war update.

A few more days, that was all Hunt wanted. That's what he told himself.

76

Bryce had camped out in the gallery library for the past three days, staying well after closing and returning at dawn. There was no point in spending much time at the apartment, since her fridge was empty and Syrinx was always with her. She figured she might as well be at the office until she stopped feeling like her home was just an empty shell.

Jesiba, busy with the Summit, didn't check the gallery video feeds. Didn't see the takeout containers littering every surface of the library, the mini fridge mostly full of cheese, or the fact that Bryce had started wearing her athletic clothes into the office. Or that she'd begun showering in the bathroom in the back of the library. Or that she'd canceled all their client meetings. And taken a new Archesian amulet right from the wall safe in Jesiba's office—the very last one in the territory. One of five left in the entire world.

It was only a matter of time, however, until Jesiba got bored and pulled up the dozens of feeds to see everything. Or looked at their calendar and saw all the rescheduled appointments.

Bryce had heard back about two potential new jobs, and had interviews lined up. She'd need to invent some excuse to feed Jesiba, of course. A medwitch appointment or teeth cleaning or something else normal but necessary. And if she got one of those jobs, she'd have to come up with a plan for repaying her debt for Syrinx—something that would please Jesiba's ego enough to keep her from transforming Bryce into some awful creature just for asking to leave.

Bryce sighed, running a hand over an ancient tome full of legal jargon that required a degree to decipher. She'd never seen so many *ergo*s and *therefore*s and *hence the following*s and *shall be included but not limited to*s. But she kept looking.

So did Lehabah. "What about this, BB?" The sprite flared, pointing to a page before her. "It says here, *A criminal's sentence may be commuted to service if*—"

"We saw that one two days ago," Bryce said. "It leads us right back to slavery."

A faint scratching filled the room. Bryce glanced at the nøkk from under her lashes, careful not to let him see her attention.

The creature was grinning at her anyway. Like it knew something she didn't.

She found out why a moment later.

"There's another case beneath it," Lehabah said. "The human woman was freed after—"

Syrinx growled. Not at the tank. At the green-carpeted stairs.

Casual footsteps thudded. Bryce was instantly standing, reaching for her phone.

A pair of boots, then dark jeans, and then—

Snow-white wings. An unfairly beautiful face.

Micah.

Every thought short-circuited as he stepped into the library, surveying its shelves and the stairs leading to the brass mezzanines and alcoves, the tank and the nøkk who was still grinning, the exploding-sun light high above.

He couldn't be down here. Couldn't see these books—

"Your Grace," Bryce blurted.

"The front door was open," he said. The sheer power behind his stare was like being hit in the face with a brick.

Of course the locks and enchantments hadn't kept him out. Nothing could ever keep him out.

She calmed her racing heart enough to say, "I'd be happy to meet with you upstairs, Your Grace, if you want me to phone Jesiba."

Jesiba, who is at the Summit where you *are currently supposed to be.*

"Down here is fine." He slowly stalked over to one of the towering shelves.

Syrinx was shaking on the couch; Lehabah hid behind a small stack of books. Even the animals in their various cages and small tanks cowered. Only the nøkk kept smiling.

"Why don't you have a seat, Your Grace?" Bryce said, scooping takeout containers into her arms, not caring if she got chili oil on her white T-shirt, only that Micah got the fuck away from the shelves and those precious books.

He ignored her, examining the titles at eye level.

Urd save her. Bryce dumped the takeout containers into the overflowing trash can. "We have some fascinating art upstairs. Perhaps you can tell me what you're looking for." She glanced at Lehabah, who had turned a startling shade of cyan, and shook her head in a silent warning to be careful.

Micah folded his wings, and turned to her. "What I'm looking for?"

"Yes," she breathed. "I—"

He pinned her with those icy eyes. "I'm looking for you."

Today's meeting was by far the worst. The slowest.

Sandriel delighted in leading them in circles, lies and half-truths spewing from her lips, as if savoring the kill soon to come: the moment they yielded everything to her and the Asteri's wishes.

Hunt leaned against the wall, standing between the Asterian Guards in their full regalia, and watched the clock inch toward four. Ruhn looked like he'd fallen asleep half an hour ago. Most of the lower-level parties had been dismissed, leaving the room barely occupied. Even Naomi had been sent back to Lunathion to make sure the 33rd remained in shape. Only skeleton staff and their leaders remained. As if everyone now knew this was over. That this *republic* was a sham. Either one ruled or one bowed.

"Opening a new port along the eastern coastline of Valbara," Sandriel said for the hundredth time, "would allow us to build a secure facility for our aquatic legion—"

A phone buzzed.

Jesiba Roga, to his surprise, pulled it from an inner pocket of the gray blazer she wore over a matching dress. She shifted in her seat, angling the phone away from the curious male to her left.

A few of the other leaders had noticed Roga's change in attention. Sandriel kept talking, unaware, but Ruhn had stirred at the sound and was looking at the woman. So was Fury, seated two rows behind her.

Jesiba's thumbs flew over her phone, her red-painted mouth tightening as she lifted a hand. Even Sandriel shut up.

Roga said, "I'm sorry to interrupt, Governor, but there's something that you—that all of us—need to see."

He had no rational reason for the dread that began to curl in his stomach. Whatever was on her phone could have been about anything. Yet his mouth dried up.

"What?" Sabine demanded from across the room.

Jesiba ignored her, and glanced to Declan Emmet. "Can you link what's on my phone to these screens?" She indicated the array of them throughout the room.

Declan, who had been half-asleep in the circle behind Ruhn, instantly straightened. "Yeah, no problem." He was smart enough to look to Sandriel first—and the Archangel rolled her eyes but nodded. Declan's laptop was open a heartbeat later. He frowned at what popped up on the laptop, but then he hit a button.

And revealed dozens of different video feeds—all from Griffin Antiquities. In the lower right corner, in a familiar library . . . Hunt forgot to breathe entirely.

Especially as Jesiba's phone buzzed again, and a message—a continuation of a previous conversation, it seemed—popped up on the screens. His heart stalled at the name: *Bryce Quinlan.*

His heart wholly stopped at the message. *Are the feeds on yet?*

"What the fuck?" Ruhn hissed.

Bryce was standing in front of the camera, pouring what seemed to be a glass of wine. And behind her, seated at the main table of the library, was Micah.

Sandriel murmured, "He said he had a meeting . . ."

The camera was hidden inside one of the books, just above Bryce's head.

Declan hit a few keys on his computer, pulling up that particular feed. Another keystroke and its audio filled the conference room.

Bryce was saying over her shoulder, throwing Micah a casual smile, "Would you like some food with your wine? Cheese?"

Micah lounged at the table, surveying a spread of books. "That would be appreciated."

Bryce hummed, covertly typing on her phone as she fiddled on the refreshment cart.

The next message to Jesiba blared across the conference room screens.

One word that had Hunt's blood going cold.

Help.

It was not a cheeky, charming plea. Not as Bryce lifted her gaze to the camera.

Fear shone there. Stark, bright fear. Every instinct in Hunt went on roaring alert.

"Governor," the Autumn King said to Sandriel, "I would like an explanation."

But before Sandriel could reply, Ruhn quietly ordered, with eyes glued to the feeds, "Flynn, send an Aux unit to Griffin Antiquities. Right now."

Flynn instantly had his phone out, fingers flying.

"Micah has not done anything wrong," Sandriel snapped at the Fae Prince. "Except demonstrate his poor choice in females."

Hunt's snarl ripped from him.

It would have earned him a whip of cold wind from Sandriel, he knew, had the sound not been hidden by matching snarls from Declan and Ruhn.

Tristan Flynn was snapping at someone, "Get over to Griffin Antiquities right now. Yes, in the Old Square. No—just go. That is a *fucking* order."

Ruhn barked another command at the Fae lord, but Micah began speaking again.

"You've certainly been busy." Micah motioned to the table. "Looking for a loophole?"

Bryce swallowed as she began assembling a plate for Micah. "Hunt is my friend."

Those were—those were law books on the table. Hunt's stomach dropped to his feet.

"Ah yes," Micah said, leaning back in his chair. "I admire that about you."

"What the fuck is going on?" Fury bit out.

"Loyal unto death—and beyond," Micah continued. "Even with all the proof in the world, you still didn't believe Danika was little better than a drug-addicted whore."

Sabine and several wolves growled. Hunt heard Amelie Ravenscroft say to Sabine, "We should send a wolf pack."

"All the top packs are here," Sabine murmured, eyes fixed on the feed. "Every top security force is here. I only left a few behind."

But like a struck match, Bryce's entire countenance shifted. Fear pivoted into bright, sharp anger. Hunt ordinarily thrilled to see that blazing look. Not now.

Use your fucking head, he silently begged her. *Be smart.*

Bryce let Micah's insult settle, surveying the platter of cheese and grapes she was assembling. "Who knows what the truth is?" she asked blandly.

"The philosophers in this library certainly had opinions on the matter."

"On Danika?"

"Don't play stupid." Micah's smile widened. He gestured to the books around them. "Do you know that harboring these volumes earns you a one-way ticket to execution?"

"Seems like a lot of fuss over some books."

"Humans died for these books," Micah purred, motioning to the shelves towering around them. "Banned titles, if I'm not mistaken, many of them supposed to only exist in the Asteri Archives. Evolution, mathematics, theories to disprove the superiority of the

Vanir and Asteri. Some from philosophers people claimed existed *before* the Asteri arrived." A soft, awful laugh. "Liars and heretics, who admitted they were wrong when the Asteri tortured them for the truth. They were burned alive with the heretical works used as kindling. And yet here, they survive. All the knowledge of the ancient world. Of a world before Asteri. And theories of a world in which the Vanir are not your masters."

"Interesting," Bryce said. She still did not turn to face him.

Ruhn said to Jesiba, "What, exactly, is in that library?"

Jesiba said nothing. Absolutely nothing. Her gray eyes promised cold death, though.

Micah went on, unwittingly answering the prince's question. "Do you even know what you are surrounded by, Bryce Quinlan? This is the Great Library of Parthos."

The words clanged through the room. Jesiba refused to so much as open her mouth.

Bryce, to her credit, said, "Sounds like a lot of conspiracy theory crap. Parthos is a bedtime story for humans."

Micah chuckled. "Says the female with the Archesian amulet around her neck. The amulet of the priestesses who once served and guarded Parthos. I think you know what's here—that you spend your days in the midst of all that remains of the library after most of it burned at Vanir hands fifteen thousand years ago."

Hunt's stomach turned. He could have sworn a chill breeze drifted from Jesiba.

Micah went on idly, "Did you know that during the First Wars, when the Asteri gave the order, it was at Parthos that a doomed human army made its final stand against the Vanir? To save proof of what they were before the Rifts opened—to save the *books*. A hundred thousand humans marched that day knowing they would die, and lose the war." Micah's smile grew. "All to buy the priestesses time to grab the most vital volumes. They loaded them onto ships and vanished. I am curious to learn how they landed with Jesiba Roga."

The sorceress watching her truth unfold on the screens still did not speak. To acknowledge what had been suggested. Did it have something to do with why she'd left the witches? Or why she'd joined the Under-King?

Micah leaned back in his seat, wings rustling. "I've long suspected that the remains of Parthos were housed here—a record of two thousand years of human knowledge before the Asteri arrived. I took one look at some of the titles on the shelves and knew it to be true."

No one so much as blinked as the truth settled. But Jesiba pointed to the screens and said to Tristan Flynn, to Sabine, her voice shaking, "Tell the Aux to move their fucking asses. Save those books. I *beg* you."

Hunt ground his teeth. Of course the books were more important to her than Bryce.

"The Aux shall do no such thing," Sandriel said coldly. She smiled at Jesiba as the female went rigid. "And whatever Micah has in mind for your little assistant is going to look mild compared to what the Asteri do to *you* for harboring that lying rubbish—"

But Bryce picked up the cheese tray and glass of wine. "Look, I only work here, Governor."

She faced Micah at last. She was wearing athletic clothes: leggings and a long-sleeved white T-shirt. Her neon-pink sneakers shone like firstlight in the dim library.

"Run," Flynn urged to the screen, as if Bryce could hear him. "Fucking *run*, Bryce."

Sandriel glared at the Fae warrior. "You dare accuse a Governor of foul play?" But doubt shone in her eyes.

The Fae lord ignored her, his eyes again on the screens.

Hunt couldn't move. Not as Bryce set down the cheese platter, the wine, and said to Micah, "You came here looking for me, and here I am." A half smile. "That Summit must have been a real bore." She crossed her arms behind her back, the portrait of casualness. She winked. "Are you going to ask me out again?"

Micah didn't see the angle of the second feed that Declan pulled up—how her fingers began flicking behind her back. Pointing to the stairs. A silent, frantic order to Lehabah and Syrinx to flee. Neither moved.

"As you once said to me," Micah replied smoothly, "I'm not interested."

"Too bad." Silence throbbed in the conference room.

Bryce gestured again behind her back, her fingers shaking now. *Please*, those hands seemed to say. *Please run. While he's distracted by me.*

"Have a seat," Micah said, gesturing to the chair across the table. "We might as well be civilized about it."

Bryce obeyed, batting her eyelashes. "About what?"

"About you giving me Luna's Horn."

77

Bryce knew there was little chance of this ending well.

But if Jesiba had seen her messages, maybe it wouldn't be in vain. Maybe everyone would know what had happened to her. Maybe they could save the books, if the protective spells on them held out against an Archangel's wrath. Even if the gallery's enchantments had not.

Bryce said smoothly to Micah, "I have no idea where the Horn is."

His smile didn't waver. "Try again."

"I have no idea where the Horn is, *Governor*?"

He braced his powerful forearms on the table. "Do you want to know what I think?"

"No, but you're going to tell me anyway?" Her heart raced and raced.

Micah chuckled. "I think you figured it out. Likely at the same moment I did a few days ago."

"I'm flattered you think I'm that smart."

"Not you." Another cold laugh. "Danika Fendyr was the smart one. She stole the Horn from the temple, and you knew her well enough to finally realize what she did with it."

"Why would Danika have ever wanted the Horn?" Bryce asked innocently. "It's broken."

"It was cleaved. And I'm guessing you already learned what could repair it at last." Her heart thundered as Micah growled, "*Synth.*"

She got to her feet, her knees shaking only slightly. "Governor or not, this is private property. If you want to burn me at the stake with all these books, you'll need a warrant."

Bryce reached the steps. Syrinx and Lehabah hadn't moved, though.

"Hand over the Horn."

"I told you, I don't know where it is."

She put one foot on the steps, and then Micah was there, his hand at the collar of her shirt. He hissed, "*Do not lie.*"

Hunt staggered all of one step down the stairs before Sandriel stopped him, her wind shoving him back against the wall. It snaked down his throat, clamping on to his vocal cords. Rendering him silent to watch what unfolded on the screens.

Micah growled in Bryce's ear, more animal than angel, "Do you want to know how I figured it out?"

She trembled as the Governor ran a possessive hand down the curve of her spine.

Hunt saw red at that touch, the entitlement in it, the sheer dread that widened her eyes.

Bryce wasn't stupid enough to try to run as Micah ran his fingers back up her spine, intent in every stroke.

Hunt's jaw clenched so hard it hurt, his breath coming out in great, bellowing pants. He'd kill him. He'd find a way to get free of Sandriel, and fucking *kill* Micah for that touch—

Micah trailed his fingers over the delicate chain of her necklace. A new one, Hunt realized.

Micah purred, unaware of the camera mere feet away, "I saw the footage of you in the Comitium lobby. You gave your Archesian amulet to Sandriel. And she destroyed it." His broad hand clamped around her neck, and Bryce squeezed her eyes shut. "That's how I realized. How you realized the truth, too."

"I don't know what you're talking about," Bryce whispered.

Micah's hand tightened, and it might as well have been his hand on Hunt's throat for all the difficulty he had breathing. "For three years, you wore that amulet. Every single day, every single hour. Danika knew that. Knew you were without ambition, too, and would never have the drive to leave this job. And thus never take off the amulet."

"You're insane," Bryce managed to say.

"Am I? Then explain to me why, within an hour after you took off the amulet, that kristallos demon attacked you."

Hunt stilled. A demon had *attacked* her that day? He found Ruhn's stare, and the prince nodded, his face deathly pale. *We got to her in time* was all Danaan said to him, mind-to-mind.

"Bad luck?" Bryce tried.

Micah didn't so much as smile, his hand still clamped on her neck. "You don't just have the Horn. You *are* the Horn." His hand again ran down her back. "You became its bearer the night Danika had it ground into a fine powder, mixed it with witch-ink, and then got you so drunk you didn't ask questions when she had it tattooed onto your back."

"*What?*" Fury Axtar barked.

Holy fucking gods. Hunt bared his teeth, still forbidden from speaking.

But Bryce said, "Cool as that sounds, Governor, this tattoo says—"

"The language is beyond that of this world. It is the language of *universes*. And it spells out a direct command to activate the Horn through a blast of raw power upon the tattoo itself. Just as it once did for the Starborn Prince. You may not possess his gifts like your brother, but I believe your bloodline and the synth shall compensate for it when I use my power upon you. To fill the tattoo—to fill *you*—with power is, in essence, to blow the Horn."

Bryce's nostrils flared. "Blow *me*, asshole." She snapped her head back, fast enough that even Micah couldn't stop the collision of her skull with his nose. He stumbled, buying her time to twist and flee—

His hand didn't let go, though.

And with a shove, her shirt ripping down the back, Micah hurled her to the floor.

Hunt's shout was lodged in his throat, but Ruhn's echoed through the conference room as Bryce skidded across the carpet.

Lehabah screamed as Syrinx roared, and Bryce managed to snap, "*Hide.*"

But the Archangel halted, surveying the woman sprawled on the floor before him.

The tattoo down her back. Luna's Horn contained within its dark ink.

Bryce scrambled to her feet, as if there were anywhere to go, anywhere to hide from the Governor and his terrible power. She made it across the room, to the steps up to the mezzanine—

Micah moved fast as the wind. He wrapped a hand around her ankle and tossed her across the room.

Bryce's scream as she collided with the wood table and it shattered beneath her was the worst sound Hunt had ever heard.

Ruhn breathed, "He's going to fucking kill her."

Bryce crawled backward through the debris of the table, blood running from her mouth as she whispered to Micah, "You killed Danika and the pack."

Micah smiled. "I enjoyed every second of it."

The conference room shook. Or maybe that was just Hunt himself.

And then the Archangel was upon her, and Hunt couldn't bear it, the sight of him grabbing Bryce by the neck and throwing her across the room again, into those shelves.

"Where is the *fucking* Aux?" Ruhn screamed at Flynn. At Sabine.

But her eyes were wide. Stunned.

So slowly, Bryce crawled backward, up the mezzanine stairs again, clawing at the books to heave herself along. A gash leaked blood onto her leggings, bone gleaming beneath a protruding shard of wood. She panted, half sobbing, "Why?"

Lehabah had crept to the metal bathroom door in the back of the library and managed to open it, as if silently signaling Bryce to get there—so they could lock themselves inside until help arrived.

"Did you learn, in all your research, that I am an investor in Redner Industries? That I have access to all its experiments?"

"Oh fuck," Isaiah said from across the pit.

"And did you ever learn," Micah went on, "what Danika *did* for Redner Industries?"

Bryce still crawled backward up the stairs. There was nowhere to go, though. "She did part-time security work."

"Is that how she sanitized it for you?" He smirked. "Danika tracked down the people that Redner wanted her to find. People who didn't want to be found. Including a group of Ophion rebels who had been experimenting with a formula for synthetic magic—to assist in the humans' treachery. They'd dug into long-forgotten history and learned that the kristallos demons' venom nullified magic—*our* magic. So these clever rebels decided to look into why, isolating the proteins that were targeted by that venom. The source of magic. Redner's human spies tipped him off, and out Danika went to bring in the research—and the people behind it."

Bryce gasped for breath, still slowly crawling upward. No one spoke in the conference room as she said, "The Asteri don't approve of synthetic magic. How did Redner even get away with doing the research on it?"

Hunt shook. She was buying herself time.

Micah seemed all too happy to indulge her. "Because Redner knew the Asteri would shut down any synthetic magic research, that *I* would shut their experiments down, they spun synth experiments as a drug for healing. Redner invited me to invest. The earliest trials were a success: with it, humans could heal faster than with any medwitch or Fae power. But later trials did not go according to plan. Vanir, we learned, went out of their minds when given it. And humans who took too much synth . . . well. Danika used her security clearance to steal footage of the trials—and I suspect she left it for you, didn't she?"

Burning Solas. Up and up, Bryce crawled along the stairs, fingers scrabbling over those ancient, precious books. "How did she learn what you were really up to?"

"She always stuck her nose where it didn't belong. Always wanting to protect the meek."

"From monsters like *you*," Bryce spat, still inching upward. Still buying herself time.

Micah's smile was hideous. "She made no secret that she kept an eye on the synth trials, because she was keen to find a way to help her weak, vulnerable, half-human friend. You, who would inherit no power—she wondered if it might give you a fighting chance against the predators who rule this world. And when she saw the horrors the synth could bring about, she became *concerned* for the test subjects. Concerned for what it'd do to humans if it leaked into the world. But Redner's employees said Danika had her own research there, too. No one knew what, but she spent time in their labs outside of her own duties."

All of it had to be on the flash drive Bryce had found. Hunt prayed she'd put it somewhere safe. Wondered what other bombshells might be on it.

Bryce said, "She was never selling the synth on that boat, was she?"

"No. By that point, I'd realized I needed someone with unrestricted access to the temple to take the Horn—I would be too easily noticed. So when she stole the synth trial footage, I had my chance to use her."

Bryce made it up another step. "You dumped the synth into the streets."

Micah kept trailing her. "Yes. I knew Danika's constant need to be the hero would send her running after it, to save the lowlifes of Lunathion from destroying themselves with it. She got most of it, but not all. When I told her I'd seen her on the river, when I claimed no one would believe the Party Princess was trying to get drugs off the streets, her hands were tied. I told her I'd forget about it, if she did one little favor for me, at just the right moment."

"You caused the blackout that night she stole the Horn."

"I did. But I underestimated Danika. She'd been wary of my interest in the synth long before I leaked it onto the streets, and when I blackmailed her into stealing the Horn, she must have realized the connection between the two. That the Horn could be repaired by synth."

"So you killed her for it?" Another step, another question to buy herself time.

"I killed her because she hid the Horn before I could repair it with the synth. And thus help my people."

"I'd think your power alone would be enough for that," Bryce said, as if trying flattery to save herself.

The Archangel looked truly sad for a moment. "Even my power is not enough to help them. To keep war from Valbara's shores. For that, I need help from beyond our own world. The Horn will open a portal—and allow me to summon an army to decimate the human rebels and end their wanton destruction."

"What world?" Bryce asked, blanching. "Hel?"

"Hel would resist kneeling to me. But ancient lore whispers of other worlds that exist that would bow to a power like mine—and bow to the Horn." He smiled, cold as a deep-sea fish. "The one who possesses the Horn at full power can do anything. Perhaps establish oneself as an Asteri."

"Their power is born, not made," Bryce snapped, even as her face turned ashen.

"With the Horn, you would not need to inherit a star's might to rule. And the Asteri would recognize that. Welcome me as one of them." Another soft laugh.

"You killed those two CCU students."

"No. They were slaughtered by a satyr high on synth—while Danika was busy stealing the Horn that night. I'm sure the guilt of it ate her up."

Bryce was shaking. Hunt was, too. "So you went to the apartment and killed her and the Pack of Devils?"

"I waited until Philip Briggs was released."

She murmured, "He had the black salt in his lab that would incriminate him."

"Yes. Once he was again on the streets, I went to Danika's apartment—your apartment—disabled the Pack of Devils with my power, and injected her with the synth. And watched as she ripped them apart before turning on herself."

Bryce was crying in earnest now. "She didn't tell you, though. Where the Horn was."

Micah shrugged. "She held out."

"And what—you summoned the kristallos afterward to cover your tracks? Let it attack you in the alley to keep your triarii from suspecting you? Or just to give yourself a reason to monitor this case so closely without raising any eyebrows? And then you waited two fucking years?"

He frowned. "I have spent these past two years looking for the Horn, calling kristallos demons to track it down for me, but I couldn't find a trace of it. Until I realized *I* didn't have to do the legwork. Because you, Bryce Quinlan, were the key to finding the Horn. I knew Danika had hidden it somewhere, and *you,* if I gave you a chance for vengeance, would lead me to it. All my power couldn't find it, but you—you loved her. And the power of your love would bring the Horn to me. Would fuel your need for justice and lead you right to it." He snorted. "But there was a chance you might not get that far—not alone. So I planted a seed in the mind of the Autumn King."

Everyone in the room looked to the stone-faced Fae male.

Ruhn growled at his father, "He played you like a fucking fiddle."

The Autumn King's amber eyes flashed with white-hot rage. But Micah went on before he could speak. "I knew a bit of taunting about the Fae's waning power, about the loss of the Horn, would rankle his pride *just* enough for him to order his Starborn son to look for it."

Bryce let out a long breath. "So if I couldn't find it, then Ruhn might."

Ruhn blinked. "I—every time I went to look for the Horn . . ." He paled. "I always had the urge to go to Bryce." He twisted in his seat to meet Hunt's stare and said to him mind-to-mind, *I thought it was the gallery, some knowledge in there, but . . . fuck, it was her.*

Your Starborn connection to her and the Horn must have overcome even the masking power of the Archesian amulet, Hunt answered. *That's quite a bond, Prince.*

Bryce demanded, "And summoning the kristallos these months? The murders?"

Micah drawled, "I summoned the kristallos to nudge you both along, making sure it kept just enough out of camera range, knowing its connection to the Horn would lead you toward it. Injecting Tertian, the acolyte, and the temple guard with the synth—letting them rip themselves apart—was also to prompt you. Tertian, to give us an excuse to come to you for this investigation, and the others to keep pointing you toward the Horn. I targeted two people from the temple that were on duty the night Danika stole it."

"And the bombing at the White Raven, with an image of the Horn on the crate? Another *nudge*?"

"Yes, and to raise suspicions that humans were behind everything. I planted bombs throughout the city, in places I thought you might go. When Athalar's phone location pinged at the club, I knew the gods were helping me along. So I remotely detonated it."

"I could have died."

"Maybe. But I was willing to bet Athalar would shield you. And why not cause a little chaos, to stir more resentment between the humans and Vanir? It would only make it easier to convince others of the wisdom of my plan to end this conflict. Especially at a cost most would deem too high."

Hunt's head swam. No one in the room spoke.

Bryce slowed her retreat as she winced in pain, "And the apartment building? I thought it was Hunt, but it wasn't, was it? It was you."

"Yes. Your landlord's request went to all of my triarii. And to me. I knew Danika had left nothing there. But by that time, Bryce Quinlan, I was enjoying watching you squirm. I knew Athalar's plan to acquire the synth would soon be exposed—and I took a guess that you'd be willing to believe the worst of him. That he'd used the lightning in his veins to endanger innocent people. He's a killer. I thought you might need a reminder. That it played into Athalar's guilt was an unexpected boon."

Hunt ignored the eyes that glanced his way. The fucking asshole had never planned to honor his bargain. If he'd solved the case, Micah would have killed him. Killed them both. He'd been played like a fucking fool.

Bryce asked, voice raw, "When did you start to think it was me?"

"That night it attacked Athalar in the garden. I realized only later that he'd probably come into contact with one of Danika's personal items, which must have come into contact with the Horn."

Hunt had touched Danika's leather jacket that day. Gotten its scent on him.

"Once I got Athalar off the streets, I summoned the kristallos again—and it went right to you. The only thing that had changed was that you finally, finally took that amulet off. And then . . ." He chuckled. "I looked at Hunt Athalar's photos of your time together. Including that one of your back. The tattoo you had inked there, days before Danika's death, according to the list of Danika's last locations Ruhn Danaan sent to you and Athalar—whose account is easily accessible to me."

Bryce's fingers curled into the carpet, as if she'd sprout claws. "How do you know the Horn will even work now that it's in my back?"

"The Horn's physical shape doesn't matter. Whether it is fashioned as a horn or a necklace or a powder mixed with witch-ink, its power remains."

Hunt silently swore. He and Bryce had never visited the tattoo parlor. Bryce had said she knew why Danika was there.

Micah went on, "Danika knew the Archesian amulet would hide you from any detection, magical or demonic. With that amulet, you were *invisible* to the kristallos, bred to hunt the Horn. I suspect she knew that Jesiba Roga has similar enchantments upon this gallery, and perhaps Danika placed some upon your apartments—your old one and the one she left to you—to make sure you would be even more veiled from it."

Hunt scanned the gallery camera feeds from the street. Where the fuck was the Aux?

Bryce spat, "And you thought no one would figure this out? What about Briggs's testimony?"

"Briggs is a raving fanatic who'd been caught by Danika before a planned bombing. No one would listen to his pleas of innocence." Especially when his lawyer had been provided by Micah.

Bryce glanced up at the camera. As if checking that it was on.

Sabine whispered, "She's been leading him along to get a full confession."

Despite the terror tightening his body, pride flared through Hunt.

Micah smiled again. "So here we are."

"You're a piece of shit," Bryce said.

But then Micah reached into his jacket pocket. Pulled out a needle. Full of clear liquid. "Calling me names isn't going to stop me from using the Horn."

Hunt's breath sawed through his chest.

Micah advanced on her. "The Horn's remnants are now embedded in your flesh. When I inject you with synth, the healing properties in it will target and fix whatever it finds to be broken. And the Horn will again be whole. Ready for me to learn if it works at last."

"You'd risk opening a portal to another fucking world in the middle of Crescent City," she spat, inching farther away, "just to *learn if it works*?"

"If I am correct, the benefits shall far outweigh any casualties," Micah answered mildly as a bead of liquid gleamed on the syringe's tip. "Too bad you will not survive the synth's side effects in order to see for yourself."

Bryce lunged for a book on a low-lying shelf along the stairs, but Micah halted her with a leash of wind.

Her face crumpled as the Archangel knelt over her. "*No*."

This couldn't happen; Hunt couldn't *let* this happen.

But Bryce could do nothing, Hunt could do nothing, as Micah stabbed the needle into her thigh. Drained it to the hilt. She screamed, thrashing, but Micah stepped back.

His power must have lessened its hold on her, because she sagged to the carpeted steps.

The bastard glanced at the clock. Assessing how much time remained until she tore herself apart. And slowly, the wounds on her battered body began to seal. Her split lip healed fully—though the bone-deep gash in her thigh knit far more slowly.

Smiling, Micah reached for the tattoo on her exposed back. "Shall we?"

But Bryce moved again—and this time Micah's power didn't catch her before she grabbed a book from the shelf and clutched it tight.

Golden light erupted from the book, a bubble against which Micah's hand bounced harmlessly off. He pushed. The bubble would not yield.

Thank the gods. If it could buy her just a few more minutes until help came . . . But what could an Aux pack do against an Archangel? Hunt strained against his invisible bonds. Scoured his memory for anything that could be done, anyone left in the fucking city who might help—

"Very well," Micah said, that smile remaining as he again tested the golden barrier. "There are other ways to get you to yield."

Bryce was shaking in her golden bubble. Hunt's heart stopped as Micah strode down the mezzanine steps. Heading straight for where Syrinx cowered behind the couch. "No," Bryce breathed. "*No—*"

The chimera thrashed, biting at the Archangel, who grabbed him by the scruff of his neck.

Bryce dropped the book. The golden bubble vanished. But when she tried to rise on her still-healing leg, it collapsed. Even the synth couldn't heal fast enough for it to bear weight.

Micah just carried Syrinx along. Over to the tank.

"*PLEASE,*" Bryce screamed. Again, she tried to move. Again, again, again.

But Micah didn't even falter as he opened the door to the small stairs that led to the top of the nøkk's tank. Bryce's screaming was unending.

Declan switched the feed over to a camera atop the tank—just as Micah flipped open the feeding hatch. And threw Syrinx into the water.

78

He couldn't swim.

Syrinx couldn't swim. He didn't stand a chance of getting out, getting free of the nøkk—

From her angle below, Bryce could only glimpse the bottoms of Syrinx's frantic, desperate legs as he struggled to stay at the surface. She dropped the book, the golden bubble rupturing, and tried to rise to her feet.

Micah emerged from the door to the tank stairwell. His power hit her a moment later.

It flipped her, pinning her facedown on the carpeted stairs. Exposing her back to him.

She writhed, the ebbing pain in her leg secondary to the tingling numbness creeping through her blood. Syrinx was drowning, he was—

Micah loomed over her. She stretched her arm out—toward the shelf. Her tingling fingers brushed over the titles. *On the Divine Number*; *The Walking Dead*; *The Book of Breathings*; *The Queen with Many Faces* . . .

Syrinx was thrashing and thrashing, still fighting so hard—

And then Micah sent a blast of white-hot flame straight into her back. Into the Horn.

She screamed, even as the fire didn't burn, but rather absorbed into the ink, raw power filling her, flame turning to ice and cracking through her blood like shifting glaciers.

The air in the room seemed to suck in on itself, tighter and tighter and tighter—

It blasted outward in a violent ripple. Bryce screamed, hoarfrost in her veins sizzling into burning agony. Upstairs, glass shattered. Then nothing.

Nothing. She shuddered on the ground, tingling ice and searing flame spasming through her.

Micah looked around. Waited.

Bryce could barely breathe, trembling as she waited for a portal to open, for some hole to another world to appear. But nothing occurred.

Disappointment flickered in Micah's eyes before he said, "Interesting."

The word told her enough: he'd try again. And again. It wouldn't matter if she was alive or a pile of self-destructed pulp. Her body would still bear the Horn's ink—the Horn itself. He'd lug around her corpse if he had to until he found a way to open a portal to another world.

She'd figured it out in the hours after the kristallos's attack at the docks, when she'd seen herself in the mirror. And began to suspect that the tattoo on her back was not in any alphabet she knew because it was *not* an alphabet. Not one from Midgard. She'd looked again at all the locations Danika had visited that last week, and saw that only the tattoo shop had gone unchecked. Then she'd realized the amulet was gone, and she had been attacked. Just as Hunt had been attacked by the kristallos in the park—after he'd touched Danika's jacket in the gallery. Touched Danika's scent, full of the Horn.

Bryce strained, hauling herself against the invisible grip of Micah's power. Her fingers brushed a dark purple book spine.

Syrinx, Syrinx, Syrinx—

"Maybe carving the Horn from you will be more effective," Micah murmured. A knife hummed free from its sheath at his thigh. "This will hurt, I'm afraid."

Bryce's finger hooked on the lip of the book's spine. *Please.*

It did not move. Micah knelt over her.

Please, she begged the book. *Please.*

It slid toward her fingers.

Bryce whipped the book from its shelf and splayed open its pages.

Greenish light blasted from it. Right into Micah's chest.

It sent him rocketing back across the library, a clear shot to the open entry to the bathroom.

To where Lehabah waited in the shadows of the bathroom door, a small book in her own hands, whose pages she opened to unleash another blast of power against the door, propelling it shut.

The book's power hissed over the bathroom door, sealing it tight. Locking the Archangel within.

Ruhn had not woken up this morning expecting to watch his sister die.

And his father . . . Ruhn's father said nothing at the horror that unfolded.

For three heartbeats, Bryce lay on the steps as the last of her leg stitched itself together, while she stared at the shut bathroom door. It might have been funny, the idea of locking a near-god inside a bathroom, had it not been so fucking terrifying.

A strangled voice growled behind Ruhn, "Help her."

Hunt. The muscles of his neck were bulging, fighting Sandriel's grip on him. Indeed, Hunt's eyes were on Sandriel as he snarled, "*Help her.*"

The metal bathroom door, even with the book's power sealing it, wouldn't hold Micah for long. Minutes, if that. And the synth in Bryce's system . . . How long did she have until she turned herself into bloody ribbons?

Lehabah rushed over to Bryce just as Hunt again growled at Sandriel, "*Go stop him.*"

No matter that even at ungodly speeds, it would take Sandriel an hour to fly there. Thirty minutes by helicopter.

A choking sound filled the air as Sandriel clamped down on her power, silencing Hunt's voice. "This is Micah's territory. I do not have the authority to intervene in his business."

Athalar still managed to get out, dark eyes blazing, "*Fuck. You.*"

All of Sandriel's triarii fixed their lethal attention on Hunt. He didn't seem to give a shit, though. Not as Bryce gasped to Lehabah, "*Get the tank's feeding dock running.*"

The gaping wound in her thigh finally sealed shut thanks to the synth shooting through her blood. And then Bryce was up and running.

The bathroom door shuddered. She didn't so much as look back as she sprinted, still limping, for the stairs to the tank. She grabbed a knife off the ground. Micah's knife.

Ruhn had to remind himself to take a breath as Bryce hit the stairs, ripping a piece from her torn shirt, wrapping it around her thigh to bind the knife to her. A makeshift sheath.

Declan switched the feed to the small chamber atop the tank, the water sloshing through the grated floor. A three-foot square in the center opened into the gloom, the small platform on a chain anchored to the top of the tank. Lehabah floated at the controls. "It's not attacking him," the sprite wept. "Syrie's just limp there, he's dead—"

Bryce knelt, and began taking swift, deep breaths. Fast, fast, fast—

"What's she doing?" Queen Hypaxia asked.

"She's hyperventilating," Tharion murmured back. "To get more air into her lungs."

"Bryce," Lehabah pleaded. "It's a—"

But then Bryce sucked in one last, mighty breath, and plunged beneath the surface.

Into the nøkk's lair. The feeding platform dropped with her, chain unraveling into the gloom, and as it raced past Bryce, she gripped the iron links, swimming down, down, down—

Bryce had no magic. No strength nor immortality to shield her. Not against the nøkk in the tank with her; not against the Archangel likely only a minute away from breaking through that bathroom door. Not against the synth that would destroy her if the rest didn't.

His sister, his brash, wild sister—knew all that and still went to save her friend.

"It's her Ordeal," Flynn murmured. "This is her fucking Ordeal."

79

The frigid water threatened to snatch the precious little breath from her lungs.

Bryce refused to think of the cold, of the lingering pain in her healed leg, of the two monsters in this library with her. One, at least, had been contained behind the bathroom door.

The other . . .

Bryce kept her focus upon Syrinx, refusing to let her terror take over, to let it rob her of breath as she reached the chimera's limp body.

She would not accept this. Not for a moment.

Her lungs began burning, a growing tightness that she fought against as she bore Syrinx back toward the feeding platform, her lifeline out of the water, away from the nøkk. Her fingers latched into the chain links as the dock rose back toward the surface.

Lungs constricting, Bryce held Syrinx on the platform, letting it propel them up, up—

From the shadows of the rocks at the bottom, the nøkk burst forth. It was already smiling.

The nøkk knew she'd come for Syrinx. It had been watching her in the library for weeks now.

But the feeding platform broke the surface, Bryce with it, and she gasped down sweet, life-saving air as she heaved Syrinx over the edge and gasped to Lehabah, "Chest compressions—"

Clawed hands wrapped around her ankles, slicing her skin as they yanked her back. Her brow smashed into the metal rim of the platform before the cold water swallowed her once more.

Hunt couldn't breathe as the nøkk slammed Bryce into the glass of the tank so hard it cracked.

The impact shook her from her stunned stupor, just as the nøkk snapped for her face.

She dodged left, but it still had its talons on her shoulders, cutting into her skin. She reached for the knife she'd tied to her thigh—

The nøkk grabbed the knife from her hands, tossing it into the watery gloom.

This was it. This was how she'd die. Not at Micah's hand, not from the synth in her body, but by being ripped to shreds by the nøkk.

Hunt could do nothing, nothing, nothing as it again snapped for her face—

Bryce moved again. Lunging not for a hidden weapon, but another sort of attack.

She punched her right hand low into the nøkk's abdomen—and dug inside the nearly invisible front fold. It happened so fast Hunt wasn't sure what she'd done. Until she twisted her wrist, and the nøkk arched in pain.

Bubbles leaked from Bryce's mouth as she wrenched its balls harder—

Every male in the pit flinched.

The nøkk let go, falling to the bottom. It was the opening Bryce needed. She drifted back against the cracked glass, braced her legs, and pushed.

It launched her into the open water. Blood from her head wound streamed in her wake, even as the synth healed the gash and prevented the blow from rendering her unconscious.

The platform dropped into the water again. Lehabah had sent

it down. A final lifeline. Bryce dolphin-kicked for it, her arms pointed in front of her. Blood swirled with each undulating kick.

At the rocky bottom of the tank, the nøkk had recovered—and now bared its teeth up at the fleeing woman. Molten rage gleamed in its milky eyes.

"*Swim, Bryce,*" Tharion growled. "Don't look back."

The platform hit its lowest level. Bryce swam, her teeth gritted. The instinct to take a breath had to be horrendous.

Come on, Hunt prayed. *Come on.*

Bryce's fingers wrapped around the bottom of the platform. Then the rim. The nøkk charged up from the depths, fury and death blazing in its monstrous face.

"Don't stop, Bryce," Fury Axtar warned the screen.

Bryce didn't. Hand by hand by hand, she climbed the ascending chain, fighting for each foot gained toward the surface.

Ten feet from the top. The nøkk reached the platform base.

Five. The nøkk shot up the chain, closing in on her heels.

Bryce broke the surface with a sharp gasp, her arms grappling, hauling, hauling—

She got her chest out. Her stomach. Her legs.

The nøkk's hands broke from the water, reaching.

But Bryce had cleared its range. And now panted, dripping water into the churning surface beneath the grated floor. Head healed without a trace.

The nøkk, unable to stand the touch of the air, dropped beneath the surface just as the feeding platform halted, sealing access to the water beneath.

"Fucking Hel," Fury whispered, running her shaking hands over her face. "Fucking Hel."

Bryce rushed to the unresponsive Syrinx and demanded from Lehabah, "Anything?"

"No, it's—"

Bryce began chest compressions, two fingers on the center of the chimera's sodden chest. She closed his jaws and blew into his nostrils. Did it again. Again. Again.

She didn't speak. Didn't beg any of the gods as she tried to resuscitate him.

On a feed across the room, the bathroom door fizzled beneath Micah's assaults. She had to get out. Had to run now, or she'd be ruptured into shards of bone—

Bryce stayed. Kept fighting for the chimera's life.

"Can you speak through the audio?" Ruhn asked Declan and Jesiba. "Can you patch us through?" He pointed to the screen. "Tell her to *get the fuck out now.*"

Jesiba said quietly, her face ashen, "It's only one-way."

Bryce kept up the chest compressions, her soaking hair dripping, her skin bluish in the light from the tank, as if she were a corpse herself. And scrawled on her back, cut off only by her black sports bra—the Horn.

Even if she got free of the gallery, if she somehow survived the synth, Micah would . . .

Syrinx thrashed, vomiting water. Bryce let out a sob, but turned the chimera over, letting him cough it out. He convulsed, vomiting again, gasping for every breath.

Lehabah had dragged a shirt up the steps from one of the desk drawers. She handed it to her, and Bryce swapped it with her ruined shirt before gathering the still-weak Syrinx in her arms and trying to stand.

She moaned in pain, nearly dropping Syrinx as her leg gushed blood into the water below.

Hunt had been so focused on the head wound he hadn't seen the nøkk slash her calf—where the flesh visible through her leggings remained half-shredded. Still slowly healing. The nøkk must have dug its claws in to the bone if the injury was so severe the synth was still stitching it together.

Bryce said, "We have to run. Now. Before he gets out." She didn't wait for Lehabah to reply as she managed to get upright, carrying Syrinx.

She limped—badly. And she moved so, so slowly toward the stairs.

The bathroom door heated again, the metal red-hot as Micah attempted to melt his way through.

Bryce panted through her teeth, a controlled *hiss-hiss-hiss* with each step. Trying to master the pain the synth hadn't yet taken away. Trying to drag a thirty-pound chimera down a set of steps on a shredded leg.

The bathroom door pulsed with light, sparks flying from its cracks. Bryce reached the library, took a limping step toward the main stairs up to the showroom, and whimpered.

"Leave it," the Autumn King growled. "Leave the chimera."

Hunt knew, even before Bryce took another step, that she would not. That she'd rather have her back peeled off by an Archangel than leave Syrinx behind.

And he could see that Lehabah knew it, too.

Bryce was a third of the way up the stairs, sparks flying from the seams of the bathroom door across the library behind them, when she realized Lehabah was not with her.

Bryce halted, gasping around the pain in her calf that even the synth could not dull, and looked back at the base of the library stairs. "Forget the books, Lehabah," she pleaded.

If they survived, she'd kill Jesiba for even making the sprite hesitate. *Kill her.*

Yet Lehabah did not move. "Lehabah," Bryce said, the name an order.

Lehabah said softly, sadly, "You won't make it in time, BB."

Bryce took one step up, pain flaring up her calf. Each movement kept ripping it open, an uphill battle against the synth attempting to heal her. Before it'd rip apart her sanity. She swallowed her scream and said, "We have to try."

"Not we," Lehabah whispered. "You."

Bryce felt her face drain of any remaining color. "You can't." Her voice cracked.

"I can," Lehabah said. "The enchantments won't hold him much longer. Let me buy you time."

Bryce kept moving, gritting her teeth. "We can figure this out. We can get out together—"

"No."

Bryce looked back to find Lehabah smiling softly. Still at the base of the stairs. "Let me do this for you, BB. For you, and for Syrinx."

Bryce couldn't stop the sob that wrenched its way out of her. "You're free, Lehabah."

The words rippled through the library as Bryce wept. "I traded with Jesiba for your freedom last week. I have the papers in my desk. I wanted to throw a party for it—to surprise you." The bathroom door began warping, bending. Bryce sobbed, "I bought you, and now I set you free, Lehabah."

Lehabah's smile didn't falter. "I know," she said. "I peeked in your drawer."

And despite the monster trying to break loose behind them, Bryce choked on a laugh before she begged, "You are a free person—you do not have to do this. You are *free*, Lehabah."

Yet Lehabah remained at the foot of the stairs. "Then let the world know that my first act of freedom was to help my friends."

Syrinx shifted in Bryce's arms, a low, pained sound breaking from him. Bryce thought it might be the sound her own soul was making as she whispered, unable to bear this choice, this moment, "I love you, Lehabah."

The only words that ever mattered.

"And I will love you always, BB." The fire sprite breathed, "Go."

So Bryce did. Gritting her teeth, a scream breaking from her, Bryce heaved herself and Syrinx up the stairs. Toward the iron door at the top. And whatever time it'd buy them, if the synth didn't destroy her first.

The bathroom door groaned.

Bryce glanced back—just once. To the friend who had stayed by her when no one else had. Who had refused to be anything but cheerful, even in the face of the darkness that had swallowed Bryce whole.

Lehabah burned a deep, unfaltering ruby and began to move.

First, a sweep of her arm upward. Then an arc down. A twirl, hair spiraling above her head. A dance, to summon her power. Whatever kernel of it a fire sprite might have.

A glow spread along Lehabah's body.

So Bryce climbed. And with each painful step upward, she could hear Lehabah whisper, almost chanting, "I am a descendant of Ranthia Drahl, Queen of Embers. She is with me now and I am not afraid."

Bryce reached the top of the stairs.

Lehabah whispered, "My friends are behind me, and I will protect them."

Screaming, Bryce shoved the library door. Until it clanged shut, the enchantments sealing, cutting off Lehabah's voice with it, and Bryce leaned against it, sliding to the floor as she sobbed through her teeth.

Bryce had made it up to the showroom and locked the iron door behind her. Thank the gods for that—thank the fucking gods.

Yet Hunt couldn't take his eyes off the library feed, where Lehabah still moved, still summoned her power, repeating the words over and over:

"*I am a descendant of Ranthia Drahl, Queen of Embers. She is with me now and I am not afraid.*"

Lehabah glowed, bright as the heart of a star.

"*My friends are behind me, and I will protect them.*"

The top of the bathroom door began to curl open.

And Lehabah unleashed her power. Three blows. Perfectly aimed.

Not to the bathroom door and Archangel behind it. No, Lehabah couldn't slow Micah.

But a hundred thousand gallons of water would.

Lehabah's shimmering blasts of power slammed into the glass tank. Right on top of the crack that Bryce had made when the nøkk threw her into it.

The creature, sensing the commotion, rose from the rocks. And recoiled in horror as Lehabah struck again. Again. The glass cracked further.

And then Lehabah hurled herself against it. Pushed her tiny body against the crack.

She kept whispering the words over and over again. They morphed together into one sentence, a prayer, a challenge.

"My friends are with me and I am not afraid."

Hunt wrested control of his body enough that he was able to put a hand over his heart. The only salute he could make as Lehabah's words whispered through the speakers.

"My friends are with me and I am not afraid."

One by one, the angels in the 33rd rose to their feet. Then Ruhn and his friends. And they, too, put their hands on their hearts as the smallest of their House pushed and pushed against the glass wall, burning gold as the nøkk tried to flee to any place it might survive what was about to come.

Over and over, Lehabah whispered, *"My friends are with me and I am not afraid."*

The glass spiderwebbed.

Everyone in the conference room rose to their feet. Only Sandriel, her attention fixed on the screen, did not notice. They all stood, and bore witness to the sprite who brought her death down upon herself, upon the nøkk—to save her friends. It was all they could offer her, this final respect and honor.

Lehabah still pushed. Still shook with terror. Yet she did not stop. Not for one heartbeat.

"My friends are with me and I am not afraid."

The bathroom door tore open, metal curling aside to reveal Micah, glowing as if newly forged, as if he'd rend this world apart. He surveyed the library, eyes landing on Lehabah and the cracked tank wall.

The sprite whirled, back pressed against the glass. She hissed at Micah, "This is for Syrinx."

She slammed her little burning palm into the glass.

And a hundred thousand gallons of water exploded into the library.

80

Flashing red lights erupted, casting the world into flickering color. A roar rose from below, the gallery shuddering.

Bryce knew.

She knew the tank had exploded, and that Lehabah had been wiped away with it. Knew the nøkk, exposed to the air, had been killed, too. Knew that Micah would only be slowed for so long.

Syrinx was still whimpering in her arms. Glass littered the gallery floor, the window to Jesiba's office shattered a level above.

Lehabah was dead.

Bryce's fingers curled into claws at her side. The red light of the warning alarms washed over her vision. She welcomed the synth into her heart. Every destructive, raging, frozen ounce of it.

Bryce crawled for the front door, broken glass tinkling. Power, hollow and cold, thrummed at her fingertips.

She grabbed the handle and hoisted herself upright. Yanked the door open to the golden light of late afternoon.

But she did not go through it.

That was not what Lehabah had bought her time to do.

Hunt knew Lehabah was killed instantly, as surely as a torch plunged into a bucket of water.

The tidal wave threw the nøkk onto the mezzanine, where it thrashed, choking on the air as it ate away its skin. It even blasted Micah back into the bathroom.

Hunt just stared and stared. The sprite was gone.

"Shit," Ruhn was whispering.

"Where's Bryce?" Fury asked.

The main floor of the gallery was empty. The front door lay open, but—

"Holy fuck," Flynn whispered.

Bryce was sprinting up the stairs. To Jesiba's office. Only synth fueled that sprint. Only that kind of drug could override pain. And reason.

Bryce set Syrinx on the ground as she entered the office—and then leapt over the desk. To the disassembled gun mounted on the wall above it.

The Godslayer Rifle.

"She's going to kill him," Ruhn whispered. "She's going to kill him for what he did to Danika and the pack." Before she succumbed to the synth, Bryce would offer her friends nothing less than this. Her final moments of clarity. Of her life.

Sabine was silent as death. But she trembled wildly.

Hunt's knees buckled. He couldn't watch this. Wouldn't watch it.

Micah's power rumbled in the library. Parted the water as he plowed across the space.

Bryce grabbed the four parts of the Godslayer Rifle mounted on the wall and chucked them onto the desk. Unlocked the safe door and reached inside. She pulled out a glass vial and knocked back some sort of potion—another drug? Who knew what the sorceress kept in there?—and then pulled out a slender golden bullet.

It was six inches long, its surface engraved with a grinning, winged skull on one side. On the other, two simple words:

Memento Mori.

Remember that you will die. They now seemed more of a promise than the mild reminder from the Meat Market.

Bryce clenched the bullet between her teeth as she hauled the first piece of the rifle toward her. Fitted the second.

Micah surged up the stairs, death incarnate.

Bryce whirled toward the open interior window. She threw out a hand, and the third piece of the rifle—the barrel—flew from the desk into her splayed fingers, borne on magic she did not naturally possess, thanks to the synth coursing through her veins. A few movements had her locking it into place.

She ran for the shattered window, assembling the rifle as she went, summoning the final piece from the desk on an invisible wind, that golden bullet still clenched in her teeth.

Hunt had never seen anyone assemble a gun without looking at it, running toward a target. As if she had done it a thousand times.

She had, Hunt remembered.

Bryce might have been fathered by the Autumn King, but she was Randall Silago's daughter. And the legendary sharpshooter had taught her well.

Bryce clicked the last piece into place and dropped into a slide, finally loading the bullet. She careened into a stop before the gaping window, rising onto her knees as she braced the Godslayer against her shoulder.

And in the two seconds it took Bryce to line up her shot, in the two seconds it took for her to loose a steadying breath, Hunt knew those seconds were Lehabah's. Knew that's what the sprite's life had bought her friend. What Lehabah had offered to Bryce, and Bryce had accepted, understanding.

Not a chance to run. No, there would never be any escaping Micah.

Lehabah had offered Bryce the two extra seconds needed to kill an Archangel.

Micah exploded out of the iron door. Metal embedded in the wood paneling of the gallery. The Governor whirled toward the open front door. To the trap Bryce had laid in opening it.

So he wouldn't look up. So he didn't have time to even glance in Bryce's direction before her finger curled on the trigger.

And she shot that bullet right through Micah's fucking head.

81

Time warped and stretched.

Hunt had the distinct feeling of falling backward, even though he was already against a wall and hadn't so much as moved a muscle.

Yet the coffee in the mug on the nearest table tilted, the liquid endlessly rocking, rocking, rocking to one side—

The death of an Archangel, of a world power, could shudder through time and space. A second could last an hour. A day. A year.

So Hunt saw everything. Saw the endlessly slow movements of everyone in the room, the gaping shock that rippled, Sandriel's outrage, Pollux's white-faced disbelief, Ruhn's terror—

The Godslayer bullet was still burrowing through Micah's skull. Still twisting through bone and brain matter, dragging time in its wake.

Then Bryce stood at the office's blown-out window. A sword in both hands.

Danika's sword—she must have left it in the gallery on her last day alive. And Bryce must have stashed it in Jesiba's office, where it had stayed hidden for two years. Hunt saw every minute expression on Sabine's face, the widening of her pupils, the flow of her corn-silk hair as she reeled at the sight of the missing heirloom—

Bryce leapt from the window and into the showroom below. Hunt saw each movement of her body, arcing as she raised the sword above her head, then brought it back down as she fell.

He could have sworn the ancient steel cut the very air itself. And then it cut through Micah.

Sliced his head in two as Bryce drove it through, the sword cleaving a path into his body. Peeling him apart. Only Danika's sword would do for this task.

Hunt savored these final moments of her life, before the synth took over. Was this the first sign of it—this madness, this pure, frenzied rage?

Bryce. His Bryce. His friend and . . . everything they had that was more than that. She was his and he was hers, and he should have told her that, should have told her in the Comitium lobby that she was the only person who mattered, who would ever matter to him, and he'd find her again, even if it took him a thousand years, he'd find her and do everything Sandriel had mocked him about.

Bryce still leapt, still kept cutting through Micah's body. His blood rained upward.

In normal time, it would have splattered. But in this warped existence, the Archangel's blood rose like ruby bubbles, showering Bryce's face, filling her screaming mouth.

In this warped existence, he could see the synth heal every sliced, bruised place on Bryce as she cut her way down through Micah. Cut him in half.

She landed on the green carpet. Hunt expected to hear bone cracking. But her calf was wholly healed. The last gift of the synth before it destroyed her. Yet in her eyes . . . he saw no haze of insanity, of self-destructive frenzy. Only cold, glittering vengeance.

The two halves of Micah's body fell away from each other and Bryce moved again. Another swipe. Across his torso. And then another to his head.

The red alarm lights were still blaring, but there was no mistaking the blood on Bryce. The white shirt that was now crimson. Her eyes remained clear, though. Still the synth did not take control.

Hypaxia murmured, "The antidote is working. It's working on her."

Hunt swayed then. He said to the witch, "I thought you were only sending over the venom."

Hypaxia didn't take her eyes off the screen. "I figured out how to stabilize the venom without needing to be present, and—I sent the antidote to her instead. Just . . . just in case."

And they'd watched Bryce down it like a bottle of whiskey.

It had taken almost three minutes for the antidote to wholly destroy the synth in Hypaxia's clinic. Neither Hunt nor the witch-queen took their eyes off Bryce long enough to count the minutes until the synth had vanished from her body entirely.

Bryce walked calmly to the hidden supply closet. Pulled out a red plastic container. And dumped the entire gallon of gasoline on the Governor's dismembered corpse.

"Holy fuck," Ruhn whispered, over and over. "Holy fuck."

The rest of the room didn't so much as breathe too loudly. Even Sandriel had no words as Bryce grabbed a pack of matches from a drawer in her desk.

She struck one, and tossed it onto the Governor's body.

Flames erupted. The fireproofing enchantments on the art around her shimmered.

There would be no chance of salvation. Of healing. Not for Micah. Not after what he had done to Danika Fendyr. To the Pack of Devils. And Lehabah.

Bryce stared at the fire, her face still splattered with the Archangel's blood. And finally, she lifted her eyes. Right to the camera. To the world watching.

Vengeance incarnate. Wrath's bruised heart. She would bow for no one. Hunt's lightning sang at the sight of that brutal, beautiful face.

Time sped up, the flames devouring Micah's body, crisping his wings to cinders. They spat him out as ashes.

Sirens wailed outside the gallery as the Auxiliary pulled up at last.

Bryce slammed the front door shut as the first of the Fae units and wolf packs appeared.

No one, not even Sandriel, spoke a word as Bryce took out the vacuum from the supply closet. And erased the last trace of Micah from the world.

82

A gas explosion, she told the Aux through the intercom, who apparently hadn't been informed of the details by their superiors. She was fine. Just a private mess to deal with.

No mention of the Archangel. Of the ashes she'd vacuumed, then dumped in the bin out back.

She'd gone up to Jesiba's office afterward, to hold Syrinx, stroking his fur, kissing his still-damp head, whispering repeatedly, "It's okay. You're okay."

He'd eventually fallen asleep in her lap, and when she'd assured herself that his breathing was unlabored, she'd finally pulled her phone from the pocket in the back of her leggings.

She had seven missed calls, all from Jesiba. And a string of messages. She barely comprehended the earlier ones, but the one that had arrived a minute ago said, *Tell me that you are all right.*

Her fingers were distant, her blood pounded in her ears. But she wrote back, *Fine. Did you see what happened?*

Jesiba's reply came a moment later.

Yes. The entire thing. Then the sorceress added, *Everyone at the Summit did.*

Bryce just wrote back, *Good.*

She put her phone on silent, tucking it back in her pocket, and ventured down to the watery ruin of the archives.

There was no trace of Lehabah in the mostly submerged library. Not even a smudge of ash.

The nøkk's corpse lay sprawled on the mezzanine, its dried-out skin flaking away, one clawed hand still gripping the iron bars of the balcony rail.

Jesiba had enough spells on the library that the books and the small tanks and terrariums had been shielded from the wave, though their occupants were near-frantic, but the building itself . . .

The silence roared around her.

Lehabah was gone. There was no voice at her shoulder, grousing about the mess.

And Danika . . . She tucked away the truth Micah had revealed. The Horn on her back, healed and functional again. She felt no different—wouldn't have known it was awake were it not for the horrific blast the Archangel had unleashed. At least a portal hadn't opened. At least she had that.

She knew the world was coming. It would arrive on her doorstep soon.

And she might very well burn for what she'd just done.

So Bryce trudged back upstairs. Her leg was healed. Every ache was gone; the synth was cleansed from her system—

Bryce puked into the trash can beside her desk. The venom in the antidote had burned as fiercely as it had gone down, but she didn't stop. Not until there was nothing left but spittle.

She should call someone. Anyone.

Still, the doorbell did not ring. No one came to punish her for what she'd done. Syrinx was still sleeping, curled into a tight ball. Bryce crossed the gallery and opened the door for the world.

It was then that she heard the screaming. She grabbed Syrinx and ran toward it.

And when she arrived, she realized why no one had come for her, or for the Horn inked in her flesh.

They had far bigger problems to deal with.

* * *

Chaos reigned at the Summit. The Asterian Guard had flown off, presumably to get instructions from their masters, and Sandriel just gaped at the feed that had shown Bryce Quinlan casually vacuuming up the ashes of a Governor as if she'd spilled chips on the carpet.

She was distracted enough that Hunt was able to finally move. He slid into the empty seat beside Ruhn and Flynn. His voice was low. "This just went from bad to worse."

Indeed, the Autumn King had Declan Emmet and two other techs on six different computers, monitoring everything from the gallery to the news to the movements of the Aux through the city. Tristan Flynn was again on his phone, arguing with someone in the Fae command post.

Ruhn rubbed his face. "They'll kill her for this."

For murdering a Governor. For proving a sprite and a half-human woman could take on a Governor and win. It was absurd. As likely as a minnow slaying a shark.

Sabine still stared at the screens, unseeing as the ancient Prime, currently dozing in his chair beside her. A tired, weary wolf ready for his last slumber. Amelie Ravenscroft, still pale and shaky, handed Sabine a glass of water. The future Prime ignored it.

Across the room, Sandriel rose, a phone to her ear. She looked at none of them as she ascended the steps out of the pit and left, her triarii falling into rank around her, Pollux already mastering himself enough to recover his swagger.

Hunt's stomach churned as he wondered if Sandriel was moments away from being crowned Archangel of Valbara. Pollux was grinning widely enough to confirm the possibility. Fuck.

Ruhn glanced at Hunt. "We need to figure out a plan, Athalar."

For Bryce. To somehow shield her from the fallout of this. If such a thing were even possible. If the Asteri weren't already moving against her, already telling Sandriel what to do. To eliminate the threat Bryce had just made herself into, even without the Horn inked in her back.

At least Micah's *experiment* had failed. At least they had that.

Ruhn said again, more to himself, "They'll kill her for this."

Queen Hypaxia took a seat at Hunt's other side, giving him a warning look as she held up a key. She fitted it into Hunt's manacles and the gorsian stones thumped to the table. "I believe they have bigger issues at hand," she said, gesturing to the city cameras Declan had pulled up.

Quiet rippled through the conference room.

"Tell me that's not what I think it is," Ruhn said.

Micah's experiment with the Horn hadn't failed at all.

83

Bryce took one look at the Heart Gate in the Old Square and sprinted home, Syrinx in her arms.

Micah had indeed wielded the Horn successfully. And it had opened a portal right through the mouth of the Heart Gate, drawing upon the magic in its quartz walls. Bryce had taken one look at what sailed out of the void suspended in the Heart Gate and knew Micah had not opened a portal to unknown worlds, as he'd intended. This one went straight to Hel.

People screamed as winged, scaled demons soared out of the Gate—demons from the Pit itself.

At her building, she yelled at Marrin to get into the basement, along with any tenants he could bring with him. And to call his family, his friends, and warn them to get somewhere secure—the bomb shelters, if they could—and hunker down with whatever weapons were available.

She left Syrinx in the apartment, laid down a massive bowl of water, and took the lid off the food bin entirely. He could feed himself. She piled blankets on the couch, tucking him into them, and kissed him once on his furry head before she grabbed what she needed and ran out the door again.

She raced to the roof, shrugging on Danika's leather jacket, then tying the Fendyr family's sword across her back. She tucked one of

Hunt's handguns into the waist of her jeans, shouldered his rifle, and slid as many packs of ammo as she could into her pockets. She surveyed the city and her blood turned to ice. It was worse—so much worse—than she'd imagined.

Micah hadn't just opened a portal to Hel in the Heart Gate. He'd opened one in *every* Gate. Every one of the seven quartz arches was a doorway to Hel.

Screams from below rose as the demons raced from the voids and into the defenseless city.

A siren wailed. A warning cry—and an order.

Bomb shelters opened, their automatic foot-thick doors sliding aside to let in those already gathered. Bryce lifted her phone to her ear.

Juniper, for once, picked up on the first ring. "Oh gods, Bryce—"

"Get somewhere safe!"

"I am, I am," Juniper sobbed. "We were having a dress rehearsal with some big donors, and we're all in the shelter down the block, and—" Another sob. "Bryce, they're saying they're going to shut the door early."

Horror lurched through her. "People need to get in. They need every moment you can spare."

Juniper wept. "I told them that, but they're frantic and won't listen. They won't let humans in."

"Fucking bastards," Bryce breathed, studying the shelter still open down her block—the people streaming inside. The shelters could be shut manually at any time, but all would close within an hour. Sealed until the threat was dealt with.

Juniper's voice crackled. "I'll *make* them hold the doors. But Bryce, it's—" Reception cut out as she presumably moved farther into the shelter, and Bryce glanced northward, toward the theaters. Mere blocks from the Heart Gate. "Mess of—" Another crackle. "Safe?"

"I'm safe," Bryce lied. "Stay in the shelter. Hold the doors for as long as you can."

But Juniper, sweet and determined and brave, wouldn't be able to calm a panicked crowd. Especially one draped in finery—and convinced of their right to live at the expense of all others.

Juniper's voice crackled again, so Bryce just said, "I love you, June." And hung up.

She fired off a message to Jesiba about the literal Hel being unleashed, and when she received no instantaneous reply, added another saying that she was heading out into it. Because someone had to.

Demons soared into the skies from the Moonwood Gate. Bryce could only pray the Den had gone into lockdown already. But the Den had guards by the dozen and powerful enchantments. Parts of this city had no protection at all.

It was enough to send her sprinting for the stairs off the roof. Down through the building.

And into the chaotic streets below.

"Demons are coming out of every Gate," Declan reported over the clamor of various leaders and their teams shouting into their phones. The Gates now held black voids within their archways. As if an invisible set of doors had been opened within them.

He could only see six of them on his screens, since the Bone Quarter had no cameras, but Declan supposed he could safely assume the Dead Gate across the Istros held the same darkness. Jesiba Roga made no attempt to contact the Under-King, but kept her eyes fixed on the feeds. Her face was ashen.

It didn't matter, Hunt thought, looking over Declan's shoulder. The denizens of the Bone Quarter were already dead.

Calls were going out—many weren't being answered. Sabine barked orders at Amelie, both of them pressing phones to their ears as they tried to reach the Alphas of the city packs.

On every screen in the conference center, cameras from around Crescent City revealed a land of nightmares. Hunt didn't know where to look. Each new image was more awful than the last. Demons he recognized with chilling clarity—the worst of the worst—poured into the city through the Gates. Demons that had been an effort for *him* to kill. The people of Lunathion didn't stand a chance.

Not the urbane, clever demons like Aidas. No, these were the grunts. The beasts of the Pit. Its wild dogs, hungry for easy prey.

In FiRo, the iridescent bubbles of the villas' defense enchantments already gleamed. Locking out anyone poor or unlucky enough to be on the streets. It was there, in front of the ironclad walls of the city's richest citizens, that the Aux had been ordered to go. To protect the already safe.

Hunt snarled at Sabine, "Tell your packs there are defenseless homes where they're needed—"

"These are the protocols," Sabine snarled back. Amelie Ravenscroft, at least, had the decency to flush with shame and lower her head. But she didn't dare speak out of turn.

Hunt growled, "Fuck the protocols." He pointed to the screens. "Those assholes have enchantments *and* panic rooms in their villas. The people on the streets have *nothing*."

Sabine ignored him. But Ruhn ordered his father, "Pull our forces from FiRo. Send them where they're needed."

The Autumn King's jaw worked. But he said, "The protocols are in place for a reason. We will not abandon them to chaos."

Hunt demanded, "Are you both fucking kidding me?"

The afternoon sun inched toward the horizon. He didn't want to think about how much worse it would get once night fell.

"I don't care if they don't want to," Tharion was yelling into his phone. "Tell them to *go to shore*." A pause. "*Then tell them to take anyone they can carry under the surface!*"

Isaiah was on the phone across the room. "No, that time warp was just some spell that went wrong, Naomi. Yeah, it caused the Gates to open. No, get the 33rd to the Old Square. *Get them to the Old Square Gate right now. I don't care if they all get ripped to shreds—*" Isaiah pulled his phone away from his ear, blinking at the screen.

Isaiah's eyes met Hunt's. "The CBD is under siege. The 33rd are being slaughtered." He didn't muse whether Naomi had just been one of them, or had merely lost her phone in the fight.

Ruhn and Flynn dialed number after number. No one answered. As if the Fae leaders left in the city were all dead, too.

Sabine got through. "Ithan—report."

Declan wordlessly patched Sabine's number through to the room's speakers. Ithan Holstrom's panting filled the space, his location pinging from outside the bespelled and impenetrable Den. Unearthly, feral growls that did not belong to wolves cut between his words. "They're fucking *everywhere.* We can barely keep them away—"

"Hold positions," Sabine commanded. *"Hold your positions and await further orders."*

Humans and Vanir alike were running, children in their arms, to any open shelter they could find. Many were already shut, sealed by the frantic people inside.

Hunt asked Isaiah, "How long until the 32nd can make it down from Hilene?"

"An hour," the angel replied, eyes on the screen. On the slaughter, on the panicking city. "They'll be too late." And if Naomi was down, either injured or dead . . . *Fuck.*

Flynn thundered at someone on the phone, "Get the Rose Gate surrounded *now.* You're just *handing* the city to them."

Hunt surveyed the bloodshed and sorted through the city's few options. They'd need armies to surround all seven Gates that opened to Hel—and find some way to close those portals.

Hypaxia had risen from her seat. She studied the screens with grim determination and said calmly into her phone, "Suit up and move out. We're heading in."

Everyone turned toward her. The young queen didn't seem to notice. She just ordered whoever was on the line, "To the city. Now."

Sabine hissed, "You'll all be slaughtered." And too late, Hunt didn't say.

Hypaxia ended the call and pointed to a screen on the left wall, its footage of the Old Square. "I would rather die like her than watch innocents die while I'm sitting in here."

Hunt turned to where she'd pointed, the hair on his neck rising. As if knowing what he'd see.

There, racing through the streets in Danika's leather jacket, sword in one hand and gun in the other, was Bryce.

Running not from the danger, but into it.

She roared something, over and over. Declan locked into the feeds, changing from camera to camera to follow her down the street. "I think I can pull up her audio and isolate her voice against the ambient noise," he said to no one in particular. And then—

"*Get into the shelters!*" she was screaming. Her words echoed off every part of the room.

Duck, slash, shoot. She moved like she'd trained with the Aux her entire life.

"*Get inside now!*" she bellowed, whirling to aim at a winged demon blotting out the mockingly golden afternoon sun. Her gun fired, and the creature screeched, careening into an alley. Declan's fingers flew on the keyboard as he kept her on-screen.

"Where the fuck is she going?" Fury said.

Bryce kept running. Kept firing. She did not miss.

Hunt looked at her surroundings, and realized where she was headed.

To the most defenseless place in Crescent City, full of humans with no magic. No preternatural gifts or strength.

"She's going to the Meadows," Hunt said.

It was worse than anything Bryce had imagined.

Her arm was numb from the bite of the gun every time she fired, reeking blood covered her, and there was no end to the snapping teeth; the leathery wings; the raging, lightless eyes. The afternoon bled toward a vibrant sunset, the sky soon matching the gore in the streets.

Bryce sprinted, her breath sharp as a knife in her chest.

Her handgun ran out. She didn't waste time feeling for ammo she didn't have left. No, she just hurled the gun at a winged black demon that swooped for her, knocking it off-kilter, and unslung the rifle from her shoulder. Hunt's rifle. His cedar-and-rain scent wrapped around her as she pumped the barrel, and by the time the demon had whirled back her way, jaws snapping, she'd fired.

Its head was blasted off in a spray of red.

Still she ran on, working her way into the city. Past the few still-open shelters, whose occupants were doing their best to defend the entrances. To buy others time to make it inside.

Another demon launched from a rooftop, curved claws reaching for her—

Bryce swiped Danika's sword upward, splitting the demon's mottled gray skin from gut to neck. It crashed into the pavement behind her, leathery wings snapping beneath it, but she was already moving again.

Keep going. She had to keep going.

All her training with Randall, every hour between the boulders and pines of the mountains around her home, every hour in the town rec hall, all of it had been for this.

84

Hunt couldn't take his eyes from the feed of Bryce battling her way through the city. Hypaxia's phone rang somewhere off to his left, and the witch-queen answered before the first ring had ended. Listened. "What do you mean, the brooms are destroyed?"

Declan patched her call through to the speakers, so they could all hear the shaking voice of the witch on the other end of the line. "They're all in splinters, Your Majesty. The conference center armory, too. The guns, the swords—the helicopters, too. The cars. All of it, wrecked."

Dread curdled in Hunt's gut as the Autumn King murmured, "Micah." The Archangel must have done it before he left, quietly and unseen. Anticipating keeping them at bay while he experimented with the Horn's power. With Bryce.

"I have a helicopter," Fury said. "I kept it off-site."

Ruhn got to his feet. "Then we move out now." It would still take thirty minutes to get there.

"The city is a slaughterhouse," Sabine was saying into the phone. "Hold your posts in Moonwood and FiRo!"

Every pack in the Aux was linked to the call, able to hear each other. With a few keystrokes, Declan had linked Sabine's phone to the system in the conference room so the Aux might hear them all as well. But some packs had stopped responding altogether.

Hunt snapped at Sabine, "*Get a fucking wolf pack to the Old Square now!*" Even with Fury's helicopter, he'd be too late. But if help could at least reach Bryce before she headed solo into the charnel house that would be the Meadows—

Sabine snapped back at him, "*There are no wolves left for the Old Square!*"

But the Prime of the wolves had stirred at last, and pointed an ancient, gnarled finger to the screen. To the feeds. And he said, "One wolf remains in the Old Square."

Everyone looked then. To where he'd pointed. Whom he'd pointed to.

Bryce raced through the carnage, sword glinting with each swipe and duck and slash.

Sabine choked. "That's Danika's sword you're sensing, Father—"

The Prime's age-worn eyes blinked unseeingly at the screen. His hand curled on his chest. "A wolf." He tapped his heart. Still Bryce fought onward toward the Meadows, still she ran interference for anyone fleeing for the shelters, buying them a path to safety. "A true wolf."

Hunt's throat tightened to the point of pain. He extended his hand to Isaiah. "Give me your phone."

Isaiah didn't question him, and didn't say a word as he handed it over. Hunt dialed a number he'd memorized, since he hadn't dared to store it in his contacts. The call rang and rang before it finally went through. "I'm guessing this is important?"

Hunt didn't bother to identify himself as he growled, "You owe me a gods-damned favor."

The Viper Queen only said, amusement coating her rich voice, "Oh?"

Two minutes later, Hunt had risen from his seat, intent on following Ruhn to Fury's helicopter, when Jesiba's phone rang. The sorceress announced, voice strained, "It's Bryce."

Hunt whipped his head to the camera feed, and sure enough, Bryce had tucked her phone into her bra strap over her shoulder, presumably leaving it on speaker. She wove around abandoned cars as she crossed the border into Asphodel Meadows. The sun began to set, as if Solas himself was abandoning them.

"Bring it up on the speakers and merge the call with the Aux lines," Jesiba ordered Declan, and answered the phone. "Bryce?"

Bryce's panting was labored. Her rifle cracked like breaking thunder. "Tell whoever's at the Summit that I need backup in the Meadows—I'm heading for the shelter near the Mortal Gate."

Ruhn vaulted down the stairs and ran right to the speaker in the center of the table. He said to it, "Bryce, it's a massacre. Get inside that shelter before they all shut—"

Her rifle boomed, and another demon went down. But more swept through the Gates and into the city, staining the streets with blood as surely as the vibrant sunset now stained the sky.

Bryce ducked behind a dumpster for cover as she fired again and again. Reloaded.

"There's no backup for Asphodel Meadows," Sabine said. "Every pack is stationed—"

"*There are children here!*" Bryce screamed. "There are *babies*!"

The room fell silent. A deeper sort of horror spread through Hunt like ink in water.

And then a male voice panted over the speakers, "I'm coming, Bryce."

Bryce's bloodied face crumpled as she whispered, "Ithan?"

Sabine snarled, "Holstrom, stay at your *fucking* post—"

But Ithan said again, more urgently this time, "Bryce, I'm coming. *Hang on*." A pause. Then he added, "We're all coming."

Hunt's knees wobbled as Sabine bellowed at Ithan, "*You are disobeying a direct order from your—*"

Ithan cut off her call. And every wolf under his command ended their connection, too.

The wolves could be at the Meadows in three minutes.

Three minutes through Hel, through the slaughter and death.

Three minutes in a flat-out run, a sprint to save the most defenseless among them.

The human children.

The jackals joined them. The coyotes. The wild dogs and common dogs. The hyenas and dingoes. The foxes. It was who they were. Who they had always been. Defenders of those who could not protect themselves. Defenders of the small, the young.

Shifter or true animal, that truth lay etched in the soul of every canine.

Ithan Holstrom sprinted toward Asphodel Meadows with the weight of that history behind him, burning in his heart. He prayed he was not too late.

85

Bryce knew it was stupid luck that kept her alive. And pure adrenaline that made her focus her aim so clearly. Calmly.

But with each block she cleared as the sunset deepened, her legs moved more slowly. Her reactions lagged. Her arms ached, becoming leaden. Every pull of the trigger took a bit more effort.

Just a little longer—that was all she needed. Just a little longer, until she could make sure that everyone in Asphodel Meadows got into a shelter before they all closed. It wouldn't be long now.

The shelter halfway down the block remained open, figures holding the line in front of it while human families rushed in. The Mortal Gate lay a few blocks northward—still open to Hel.

So Bryce planted herself at the intersection, sheathing Danika's sword as she again raised Hunt's rifle to her shoulder. She had six rounds left.

Ithan would be here soon. Any moment now.

A demon surged from around a corner, taloned fingers gouging lines into the cobblestones. The rifle bit into her shoulder as she fired. The demon was still falling, sliding across the ground, when she angled the rifle and fired again. Another demon went down.

Four bullets left.

Behind her, humans screamed orders. *Hurry! Into the shelter! Drop the bag and run!*

Bryce fired at a demon soaring across the intersection, right for the shelter. The demon went down twenty feet from the entrance. The humans finished it off.

Inside the shelter's open mouth, children shrieked, babies wailed.

Bryce fired again. Again. Again.

Another demon barreled around the corner, sprinting for her. The trigger clicked.

Out. Done. Empty.

The demon leapt, jaws opening wide to reveal twin rows of dagger-sharp teeth. Aiming for her throat. Bryce barely had time to lift the rifle and wedge it between those gaping jaws. Metal and wood groaned, and the world tilted with the impact.

She and the demon slammed into the cobblestones, her bones barking in pain. The demon clamped down on the rifle. It snapped in two.

Bryce managed to hurl herself backward from under the demon as it spat out the pieces of the rifle. Maw leaking saliva on the blood-ied streets, it advanced on her. Seemed to savor each step.

With her sheathed sword pinned beneath her, Bryce reached for the knife at her thigh. As if it would do anything, as if it would stop this—

The demon sank onto its haunches, readying for the kill.

The ground shook behind her as Bryce angled her wrist, blade tilting upward—

A sword plunged through the demon's gray head.

A massive sword, at least four feet long, borne by a towering, armored male figure. Blue lights glowed along the blade. More glared along sleek black body armor and a matching helmet. And across the male's chest, an emblem of a striking cobra glowed.

One of the Viper Queen's Fae bodyguards.

Six others raced past him, the cobblestones shaking beneath their feet, guns and swords drawn. No venom-addled stupor to be seen. Just lethal precision.

And with the Viper Queen's Fae guards, wolves and foxes and canines of every breed flowed by, launching into the fray.

Bryce scrambled to her feet, nodding to the warrior who'd saved her. The Fae male only whirled, his metal-encased hands grabbing a demon by the shoulders and wrenching it apart with a mighty yell. He tore the demon in two.

But more of Hel's worst thundered and soared for them. So Bryce freed Danika's sword again from across her back.

She willed strength to her arm, bracing her feet as another demon galloped down the street for her. Canine shifters engaged demons all around, forming a barrier of fur and teeth and claws between the oncoming horde and the shelter behind them.

Bryce feinted left, swiping her sword up as the demon fell for her fake-out. But the blade didn't break through bone and to the soft, vulnerable organs beneath. The creature roared, pivoting, and lunged again. She gritted her teeth, and lifted her sword in challenge, the demon too frenzied to notice that she'd let herself become the distraction.

While the massive gray wolf attacked from behind.

Ithan ripped into the demon in an explosion of teeth and claws, so fast and brutal it momentarily stunned her. She'd forgotten how enormous he was in this form—all the shifters were at least three times the size of normal animals, but Ithan had always been larger. Exactly like his brother.

Ithan spat out the demon's throat and shifted, wolf becoming a tall male in a flash of light. Blood coated his navy T-shirt and jeans as much as it did her own clothes, but before they could speak, his brown eyes flared with alarm. Bryce twisted, met by the rancid breath of a demon as it dive-bombed her.

She ducked and thrust the sword upward, the demon's shriek nearly bursting her ears as she let the beast drag its belly down the blade. Gutting it.

Gore splattered her sneakers, her torn leggings, but she made sure the demon's head was rolling before whirling to Ithan. Just as he drew a sword from a sheath on his back and split another demon apart.

Their stares held, and all the words she'd needed to say hung there. She saw them in his eyes, too, as he realized whose jacket and sword she bore.

But she offered a grim smile. Later. If they somehow survived this, if they could last another few minutes and get into the shelter . . . They'd speak then.

Ithan nodded, understanding.

Bryce knew it wasn't adrenaline alone that powered her as she launched back into the carnage.

"Shelters close in four minutes," Declan announced to the conference room.

"Why hasn't your helicopter arrived?" Ruhn asked Fury. He stood, Flynn rising with him.

Axtar checked her phone. "It's on its way over from—"

The doors at the top of the pit burst open, and Sandriel entered on a storm wind. And there was no sign of her triarii or Pollux as she strode down the stairs. No one spoke.

Hunt prepared himself as she glanced his way, seated between a now-standing Ruhn and Hypaxia. The gorsian manacles lay on the table before him.

But she merely returned to her seat at the lowermost table. She had bigger concerns at hand, he supposed. Her attention darting between the screens and feeds and updates, Sandriel said, "There is nothing we can do for the city with the Gates open to Hel. We are under orders to remain here."

Ruhn started. "We are *needed*—"

"We are to *remain here*." The words rumbled like thunder through the room. "The Asteri are sending help."

Hunt sagged in his seat, and Ruhn sank down beside him. "Thank fuck," the prince muttered, rubbing shaking hands over his face.

They must have dispatched the Asterian Guard, then. And further reinforcements. Perhaps Sandriel's triarii had gone to Lunathion. They might all be psychotic assholes, but at least they could hold their own in a fight. Fuck, the Hammer alone would be a blessing to the city right now.

"Three minutes until shelter lockdown," Declan said.

In the general chaos of the audio feed Declan had pulled up, a shifter's howl went out, warning everyone to get to safety. To abandon the boundary they'd established against the horde and run like Hel for the still-open metal door.

Humans were still fleeing, though. Adults carrying children and pets sprinted for the opening, hardly bigger than a single-car garage door. The Viper Queen's warriors and a few of the wolves remained at the intersection.

"Two minutes," Declan said.

Bryce and Ithan fought side by side. Where one stumbled, the other did not fail. Where one baited a demon, the other executed it.

A siren blared in the city. A warning. Still Bryce and Ithan held the corner.

"Thirty seconds," Declan said.

"Go," Hunt urged. "Go, Bryce."

She gutted a demon, whirling toward the shelter at last, Ithan moving with her. Good, she'd get inside, and could wait it out until the Asterian Guard arrived to wipe these fuckers away. Maybe they'd know how to seal the voids in the Gates.

The shelter door began closing.

"They're too far," Fury said quietly.

"They'll make it," Hunt ground out, even as he eyed the distance between the slowly closing door and the two figures racing for it, Bryce's red hair a banner behind her.

Ithan stumbled, and Bryce grabbed his hand before he could go down. A nasty gash gleamed in Ithan's side, blood soaking his T-shirt. How the male was even running—

The door was halfway closed. Losing inches every second.

A clawed, humanoid hand from inside wrapped around its edge. Multiple pairs.

And then a young, brown-haired wolf was there, her teeth gritted, her face lupine, roaring as she heaved against the inevitable. As every one of the wolves behind her grabbed the sliding door and tried to slow it.

"Fifteen seconds," Declan whispered.

Bryce ran and ran and ran.

One by one, the wolves of Ithan's pack lost their grip on the door.

Until only that one young female was holding it back, a foot braced against the concrete wall, bellowing in defiance—

Ithan and Bryce charged for the shelter, the wolf's focus solely on the shelter door.

Only three feet of space remained. Not enough room for both of them. Bryce's stare shot to Ithan's face. Sorrow filled her eyes. And determination.

"No," Hunt breathed. Knowing exactly what she'd do.

Bryce dropped behind just a step. Just enough to draw upon her Fae strength to shove Ithan forward. To save Connor Holstrom's brother.

Ithan twisted toward Bryce, eyes flaring with rage and despair and grief, hand outstretched, but too late.

The metal door shut with a boom that seemed to echo across the city.

That *was* echoed across the city, as every shelter door shut at last.

Her momentum was too great to slow. Bryce slammed into the metal door, grunting in pain.

She turned in place, face leached of color. Searching for options and coming up empty.

Hunt read it on her face, then. For the first time, Bryce had no idea what to do.

Every part of Bryce shook as she took cover in the slight alcove before the shelter, the sunset a vibrant wash of orange and ruby—like the final battle cry of the world before the oncoming night.

The demons had moved on, but more would be coming. Soon. As long as the Gates held those portals to Hel, they would never stop coming.

Someone—Ithan, probably—began pounding on the shelter door behind her. As if he'd claw his way through, open up a passage for her to get inside. She ignored the sound.

The Viper Queen's warriors were flashes of metal and light far down the street, still fighting. Some had fallen, heaps of steaming armor and blood.

If she could make it to her apartment, it had enchantments enough to protect her and any others she could get inside. But it was twenty blocks away. It might as well have been twenty miles.

An idea flared, and she weighed it, considering. She could try. She had to try.

Bryce took a bracing breath. In her hand, Danika's sword shook like a reed in the wind.

She could make it. Somehow, she'd find a way.

She leapt into the blood-slick streets, sword held ready to attack. She didn't look back at the shelter behind her as she began to run, blind memory of the city grid sinking in to guide her on the fastest route. A snarl rumbled from around a corner, and Bryce barely brought up her sword in time to intercept the demon. She partially severed its neck, and was running again before it fully hit the ground. She had to keep moving. Had to get to the Old Square—

Dead shifters and the Viper Queen's soldiers lay in the streets. Even more dead humans around them. Most in pieces.

Another demon barreled from the red sky—

She screamed as it knocked her back, slamming her into a car so hard the windows shattered. She had all of a second to wrench open the passenger-side door and climb in before it landed again. Attacked the car.

Bryce scrambled over the armrests and stick shift, fumbling for the driver's-side door. She yanked on the handle and half fell into the street, the demon so distracted with shredding the tires on the opposite side that it didn't see her lurch into a sprint.

The Old Square. If she could make it to the Old Square—

Two demons raced for her. The only thing she could do was run as the light began to fade.

Alone. She was alone out here.

86

The city was starting to go quiet. Every time Declan checked the audio in another district, more screams had diminished, cut off one by one.

Not from any calm or salvation, Hunt knew.

The voids in the Gates remained open. The sunset gave way to bruised purple skies. When true night fell, he could imagine what sort of horrors Hel would send through. The kind that did not like the light, that had been bred and learned to hunt in the dark.

Bryce was still out there. One mistake, one misstep, and she would be dead.

There would be no healing, no regeneration. Not without the Drop.

She made it over the border of the Old Square. But she didn't run for safety. No, she seemed to be running for the Heart Gate, where the flow of demons had halted. As if Hel were indeed waiting for true night to begin before its second round.

His heart thundered as she paused down the block from the Gate. As she ducked into the alcove of a nearby shelter. Illuminated by the firstlight lamp mounted outside it, she slid to the ground, her sword loosely gripped in one hand.

Hunt knew that position, that angle of the head.

A soldier who had fought a good, hard battle. A soldier who was exhausted, but would take this moment, this last moment, to rally before their final stand.

Hunt bared his teeth at the screen, "*Get up, Bryce.*"

Ruhn was shaking his head, terror stark on his face. The Autumn King said nothing. Did nothing as he watched his daughter on the feed Declan placed on the main screen.

Bryce reached into her shirt to pull out her phone. Her hands were shaking so hard she could barely hold it. But she hit a button on the screen and lifted it to her ear. Hunt knew what that was, too. Her final chance to say goodbye to her parents, her loved ones.

A faint ringing sounded in the conference room. From the table at its center. Hunt looked to Jesiba, but her phone remained dark. Ruhn's stayed dark as well. Everyone went silent as Sandriel pulled a phone from her pocket. Hunt's phone.

Sandriel glanced toward him, shock slackening her face. Every thought eddied from Hunt's head.

"Give him the phone," Ruhn said softly.

Sandriel just stared at the screen. Debating.

"*Give him the fucking phone,*" Ruhn ordered her.

Sandriel, to Hunt's shock, did. With trembling hands, he picked up.

"Bryce?"

On the video feed, he could see her wide eyes. "Hunt?" Her voice was so raw. "I—I thought it would go to audiomail—"

"Help is coming soon, Bryce."

The stark terror on her face as she surveyed the last of the sunlight destroyed him. "No—no, it'll be too late."

"It won't. I need you to get up, Bryce. Get to a safer location. Do *not* go any closer to that Gate."

She bit her lip, trembling. "It's still wide open—"

"*Go to your apartment and stay there until help comes.*" The panicked terror on her face hardened into something calm at his order. Focused. Good.

"Hunt, I need you to call my mom."

"Don't start making those kinds of goodbyes—"

"I need you to call my mom," she said quietly. "I need you to tell her that I love her, and that everything I am is because of her. Her strength and her courage and her love. And I'm sorry for all the bullshit I put her through."

"Stop—"

"Tell my dad . . . ," she whispered. The Autumn King stiffened. Looked back toward Hunt. "Tell Randall," she clarified, "that I'm so proud I got to call him my father. That he was the only one that ever mattered."

Hunt could have sworn something like shame flitted across the Autumn King's face. But Hunt implored, "Bryce, you need to move to safer ground *now*."

She did no such thing. "Tell Fury I'm sorry I lied. That I would have told her the truth eventually." Across the room, the assassin had tears running down her face. "Tell Juniper . . ." Bryce's voice broke. "Tell her thank you—for that night on the roof." She swallowed a sob. "Tell her that I know now why she stopped me from jumping. It was so I could get here—to help today."

Hunt's heart cracked entirely. He hadn't known, hadn't guessed that things had ever been that bad for her—

From the pure devastation on Ruhn's face, her brother hadn't known, either.

"Tell Ruhn I forgive him," Bryce said, shaking again. Tears streamed down the prince's face.

"I forgave him a long time ago," Bryce said. "I just didn't know how to tell him. Tell him I'm sorry I hid the truth, and that I only did it because I love him and didn't want to take anything away from him. He'll always be the better one of us."

The agony on Ruhn's face turned to confusion.

But Hunt couldn't bear it. He couldn't take another word of this. "Bryce, please—"

"Hunt." The entire world went quiet. "I was waiting for you."

"Bryce, sweetheart, just get back to your apartment and give me an hour and—"

"No," she whispered, closing her eyes. She put her hand on her chest. Over her heart. "I was waiting for you—in here."

Hunt couldn't stop his own tears then. "I was waiting for you, too."

She smiled, even as she sobbed again.

"Please," Hunt begged. "Please, Bryce. You have to go *now*. Before more come through."

She opened her eyes and got to her feet as true night fell. Faced the Gate halfway down the block. "I forgive you—for the shit with the synth. For all of it. None of it matters. Not anymore." She ended the call and leaned Danika's sword against the wall of the shelter alcove. Placed her phone carefully on the ground next to it.

Hunt shot from his seat. "*BRYCE—*"

She ran for the Gate.

87

No," Ruhn was saying, over and over. "No, *no*—"

But Hunt heard nothing. Felt nothing. It had all crumbled inside him the moment she'd hung up.

Bryce leapt the fence around the Gate and halted before its towering archway. Before the terrible black void within it.

A faint white radiance began to glow around her.

"What is that?" Fury whispered.

It flickered, growing brighter in the night.

Enough to illuminate her slender hands cupping a sparkling, pulsing light before her chest.

The light was coming *from* her chest—had been pulled from inside it. Like it had dwelled inside her all along. Bryce's eyes were closed, her face serene.

Her hair drifted above her head. Bits of debris floated up around her, too. As if gravity had ceased to exist.

The light she held was so stark it cast the rest of the world into grays and blacks. Slowly, her eyes opened, amber blazing like the first pure rays of dawn. A soft, secret smile graced her mouth.

Her eyes lifted to the Gate looming above her. The light between her hands grew stronger.

Ruhn fell to his knees.

"I am Bryce Quinlan," she said to the Gate, to the void, to all of

Hel behind it. Her voice was serene—wise and laughing. "Heir to the Starborn Fae."

The ground slid out from under Hunt as the light between her hands, the star she'd drawn from her shattered heart, flared as bright as the sun.

Danika knelt on the asphalt, hands interlocked behind her blood-soaked hair. The two gunshot wounds to her leg had stopped leaking blood, but Bryce knew the bullets remained lodged in her upper thigh. The pain from kneeling had to be unbearable.

"You stupid cunt," the asp shifter spat at her, opening the chamber of his handgun with brutal precision. Bullets were on the way—as soon as his associate found them, that gun would be loaded.

The agony in Bryce's injured arm was secondary. All of it was secondary to that gun.

The motorcycle smoldered thirty feet away, the rifle thrown even farther into the arid scrub. Down the road, the semitruck idled, its cargo hold filled with all those petrified animals on their way to gods knew where.

They had failed. Their wild rescue attempt had failed.

Danika's caramel eyes met the asp shifter's. The leader of this horrific smuggling ring. The male responsible for this moment, when the shootout that had taken place at a hundred miles an hour had turned on them. Danika had been steering the motorcycle, an arm looped through Bryce's leg to hold her steady as she'd aimed her rifle. Taken out the asps' two sedans full of equally hateful males intent on hurting and selling those animals. They'd been nearing the racing semi when the male before them had managed a shot to the motorcycle's tires.

The motorcycle had flipped, and Danika had reacted with a wolf's speed. She had wrapped her body around Bryce. And taken the brunt of the impact.

Her shredded skin, the fractured pelvis—all thanks to that.

"Bryce," Danika whispered, tears running down her face now as the reality of this colossal fuckup set in. "Bryce, I love you. And I'm sorry."

Bryce shook her head. "I don't regret it." The truth.

And then the asp shifter's associate arrived, bullets in hand. Their clink as they loaded into the gun echoed through Bryce's bones.

Danika sobbed. "I love you, Bryce."

The words rippled between them. Cleaved Bryce's heart wide open.

"I love you," Danika said again.

Danika had never said those words to her. Not once in four years of college. Not once to anyone, Bryce knew. Not even Sabine.

Especially not Sabine.

Bryce watched the tears roll down Danika's proud, fierce face. A lock clicked open in Bryce's heart. Her soul.

"Close your eyes, Danika," she said softly. Danika just stared at her.

Only for this. Only for Danika would she do this, risk this.

The gravel around Bryce began to shiver. Began to float upward. Danika's eyes widened. Bryce's hair drifted as if underwater. In deep space.

The asp shifter finished loading the bullets and pointed the gun at Danika's face. His colleague smirked from a step behind him.

Bryce held Danika's stare. Did not look away as she said again, "Danika, close your eyes." Trembling, Danika obeyed. Squeezed them shut.

The asp shifter clicked off the gun's safety, not even glancing at Bryce and the debris that floated toward the sky. "Yeah, you'd better close your eyes, you—"

Bryce exploded. White, blinding light ruptured from her, unleashed from that secret place in her heart.

Right into the eyes of the asp shifter. He screamed, clawing at his face. Blazing bright as the sun, Bryce moved.

Pain forgotten, she had his arm in her hands in a heartbeat. Twisted it so he dropped the gun into her waiting palm. Another movement and he was sprawled on the asphalt.

Where she fired that bullet meant for Danika into his heart.

His accomplice was screaming, on his knees and clawing at his eyes. Bryce fired again.

He stopped screaming.

But Bryce did not stop burning. Not as she raced for the semi's cab—for the final asp now trying to start its engine. Danika trembled on the ground, hands over her head, eyes squeezed shut against the brightness.

The asp shifter gave up on the engine and fled the cab, sprinting down the road. Bryce took aim, just as Randall had taught her, and waited for the shot to come to her.

Another crack of the gun. The male dropped.

Bryce blazed for a long moment, the world bleached into blinding white.

Slowly, carefully, she spooled the light back into herself. Smothered it, the secret she and her parents had kept for so long. From her sire, from the Asteri, from Midgard.

From Ruhn.

The pure light of a star—from another world. From long, long ago. The gift of the ancient Fae, reborn again. Light, but nothing more than that. Not an Asteri, who possessed brute power of the stars. Just light.

It meant nothing to her. But the Starborn gifts, the title—they had always meant something to Ruhn. And that first time she'd met him, she'd intended to share her secret with him. He'd been kind, joyful at finding a new sister. She'd instantly known she could trust him with this secret, hidden thing.

But then she'd seen their father's cruelty. Seen how that Starborn gift gave her brother just the slightest edge against that fucking monster. Seen the pride her brother denied but undoubtedly felt at being Starborn, blessed and chosen by Urd.

She couldn't bring herself to tell Ruhn the truth. Even after things fell apart, she hid it. Would never tell anyone—anyone at all. Except Danika.

Blue skies and olive trees filtered back in, color returning to the world as Bryce hid the last of her starlight inside her chest. Danika still trembled on the asphalt.

"Danika," Bryce said.

Danika lowered her hands from her face. Opened her eyes. Bryce waited for the terror her mother had warned about, should someone learn what she bore. The strange, terrible light that had come from another world.

But there was only wonder on Danika's face.

Wonder—and love.

Bryce stood before the Gate, holding the star she'd kept hidden within her heart, and let the light build. Let it flow out of her chest, untethered and pure.

Even with the void mere feet away, Hel just a step beyond it, a strange sense of calm wended through her. She'd kept this light a secret for so long, had lived in such utter terror of anyone finding out, that despite everything, relief filled her.

There had been so many times these weeks when she was sure Ruhn would realize it at last. Her blatant disinterest in learning about anything related to the first Starborn, Prince Pelias and Queen Theia, had bordered on suspicious, she'd feared. And when he'd laid the Starsword on the table in the gallery library and it had hummed, shimmering, she'd had to physically pull back to avoid the instinct to touch it, to answer its silent, lovely song.

Her sword—it was her sword, and Ruhn's. And with that light in her veins, with the star that slumbered inside her heart, the Starsword had recognized her not as a royal, worthy Fae, but as *kin*. Kin to those who had forged it so long ago.

Like called to like. Even the kristallos's venom in her leg had not been able to stifle the essence of what she was. It had blocked her access to the light, but not what lay stamped in her blood. The moment the venom had come out of her leg, as Hunt's lips had met hers that first time, she'd felt it awaken again. Freed.

And now here she was, the starlight building within her hands.

It was a useless gift, she'd decided as a child. It couldn't do much at all beyond blinding people, as she'd done to her father's men when they came after her and her mother and Randall, as had happened to the Oracle when the seer peered into her future and beheld only her blazing light, as she'd done to those asp-hole smugglers.

Only her father's unfaltering Fae arrogance and snobbery had kept him from realizing it after her Oracle visit. The male was incapable of imagining anyone but pure Fae being blessed by fate.

Blessed—as if this gift made her something special. It didn't. It was an old power and nothing more. She had no interest in the throne or crown or palace that could come with it. None.

But Ruhn . . . He might have claimed otherwise, but the first time he'd told her about his Ordeal, when he'd won the sword from its ancient resting place in Avallen, she'd seen how his face had glowed with pride that he'd been able to draw the sword from its sheath.

So she'd let him have it, the title and the sword. Had tried to open Ruhn's eyes to their father's true nature as often as she could, even if it made her father resent her further.

She would have kept this burning, shining secret inside her until her dying day. But she'd realized what she had to do for her city. This world.

The dregs of the light flowed out of her chest, all of it now cupped between her palms.

She'd never done it before—wholly removed the star itself. She'd only glowed and blinded, never summoned its burning core from inside her. Her knees wobbled, and she gritted her teeth against the strain of holding the light in place.

At least she'd spoken to Hunt one last time. She hadn't expected him to be able to pick up. Had thought the phone would go right to audiomail where she could say everything she wanted. The words she still hadn't said aloud to him.

She didn't let herself think of it as she took the final step to the Gate's quartz archway.

She was Starborn, and the Horn lay within her, repaired and now filled with her light.

This had to work.

The quartz of the Gate was a conduit. A prism. Able to take light and power and refract them. She closed her eyes, remembering the rainbows this Gate had been adorned with on the last day of Danika's life, when they'd come here together. Made their wishes.

This had to work. A final wish.

"*Close*," Bryce whispered, shaking.

And she thrust her starlight into the Gate's clear stone.

88

Hunt had no words in his head, his heart, as Bryce shoved her burning starlight into the Gate.

White light blasted from the Gate's clear stone.

It filled the square, shooting outward for blocks. Demons caught in its path screamed as they were blinded, then fled. Like they remembered whom it had once belonged to. How the Starborn Prince had battled their hordes with it.

The Starborn line had bred true—twice.

Ruhn's face drained of color as he remained kneeling and beheld his sister, the blazing Gate. What she'd declared to the world. What she'd revealed herself to be.

His rival. A threat to all he stood to inherit.

Hunt knew what the Fae did to settle disputes to the throne.

Bryce possessed the light of a star, such as hadn't been witnessed since the First Wars. Jesiba looked like she'd seen a ghost. Fury gaped at the screen. When the flare dimmed, Hunt's breath caught in his throat.

The void within the Heart Gate was gone. She'd channeled her light through the Horn somehow—and sealed the portal.

In the stunned silence of the conference room, they watched Bryce pant, leaning against one side of the Gate before sliding to the slate tiles. The crystal archway still shone. A temporary haven that would make any demons think twice before approaching, fearful of a Starborn descendant.

But the rest of the Gates in the city remained open.

A phone rang—an outgoing call, linked to the room's speakers. Hunt scanned the room for the culprit and found the Autumn King with his phone in his hands. But the male was apparently too lost in the rage crinkling his face to care that the call was audible to everyone. Declan Emmet showed no sign of even trying to make the call private as Ember Quinlan picked up the phone and said, "Who is—"

"You've known she was Starborn Fae all these years and *lied* to me about it," the king bit out.

Ember didn't miss a beat. "I've been waiting for this call for more than twenty years."

"You *bitch*—"

A low, agonized laugh. "Who do you think ended your goons all those years ago? Not me and Randall. They had her in their grasp—by the neck. And they had *us* at gunpoint." Another laugh. "She realized what they were going to do to me. To Randall. And she fucking *blinded* them."

What blinds an Oracle?

Light. Light the way the Starborn had possessed it.

Bryce still sat against the archway, breathing hard. Like summoning that star, wielding the Horn, had taken everything out of her.

Ruhn murmured, more to himself than anyone, "Those books claimed there were multiple Starborn in the First Wars. I told her, and she . . ." He blinked slowly. "She already knew."

"She lied because she loves you," Hunt ground out. "So you could keep your title."

Because compared to the Starborn powers he'd seen from Ruhn . . . Bryce's were the real deal. Ruhn's ashen face contorted with pain.

"Who knew?" the Autumn King demanded of Ember. "Those fucking priestesses?"

"No. Only me and Randall," Ember said. "And Danika. She and

Bryce got into some serious trouble in college and it came out then. She blinded the males that time, too."

Hunt remembered the photo on the guest room dresser—taken in the aftermath of that. Their closeness and exhaustion the result not just of a battle fought and won but of a deadly secret revealed at last.

"Her tests showed no power," the Autumn King spat.

"Yes," Ember said quietly. "They were correct."

"Explain."

"It is a gift of starlight. Light, and nothing more. It never meant anything to us, but to your people . . ." Ember paused. "When Bryce was thirteen, she agreed to visit you. To meet you—to see if you could be trusted to know what she possessed and not be threatened by it."

To see if he could handle that such a gift had gone to a half-human bastard and not Ruhn.

Hunt saw no fear on the prince's face, though. No envy or doubt. Only sorrow.

"But then she met your son. And she told me that when she saw his pride in his Chosen One status, she realized she couldn't take it away from him. Not when she also saw that was the only value *you* placed in him. Even if it meant she would be denied everything she was due, even if revealing herself would have meant she could lord it over you, she wouldn't do that to Ruhn. Because she loved him that much more than she hated you."

Ruhn's face crumpled.

Ember spat at the Autumn King, *"And then you left her on the curb like garbage."* She let out another broken laugh. "I hope she finally returns the favor, you fucking asshole." She hung up.

The Autumn King hurled a pitcher of water before him across the room, so hard it shattered against the wall.

Hunt's blood thrummed through him as a conversation from weeks ago flitted back to him: how he'd spoken of having gifts he didn't really want. Bryce had agreed, to his surprise, and then seemed to catch herself before joking about attracting assholes. Deflecting, hiding the truth.

A soft female hand landed atop Hunt's. Queen Hypaxia. Her dark brown eyes glowed when he looked over in surprise. Her power was a song of warmth through him. It was a hammer to every wall and obstacle placed on him. And he felt that power focus on the halo's spell upon his brow.

She'd asked him weeks ago what he'd do if she removed it. Whom he'd kill.

His first target was in this room with them. His eyes darted toward Sandriel, and Hypaxia's chin dipped, as if in confirmation.

Still Bryce sat against the Gate. As if trying to rally herself. As if wondering how she could possibly do this six more times.

Demons in adjacent streets beheld the starlight still glowing from the Old Square Gate and stayed back. Yes, they remembered the Starborn. Or knew the myths.

Aidas had known. Had watched her all these years, waiting for her to reveal herself.

Hypaxia's power flowed silently and unnoticed into Hunt.

Sandriel slid her phone into her pocket. As if she'd been using it under the table.

Ruhn saw it, too. The Crown Prince of the Fae asked with savage quiet, "What did you do?"

Sandriel smiled. "I took care of a problem."

Hunt's power growled within him. She'd have told the Asteri all she'd seen. Not only what glowed in Bryce's veins—but about the Horn, too.

They were likely already moving on the information. Quickly. Before anyone else could ponder Bryce's gifts. What it might mean to the people of the world if they knew a half-human female, heir to the Starborn line, now bore the Horn in her very body. Able to be used only by her—

The truth clicked into place.

It was why Danika had inked it on Bryce. *Only* the Starborn line could use the Horn.

Micah had believed the synth and Bryce's bloodline would be enough to let him use the Horn, overriding the need for the true Starborn power. The Horn had indeed been healed—but it only worked because Bryce was heir to the Starborn line. Object and wielder had become one.

If Bryce willed it, the Horn could open a portal to any world, any realm. Just as Micah had wanted to do. But that kind of power—belonging to a half-human, no less—could endanger the sovereignty of the Asteri. And the Asteri would take out any threat to their authority.

A roar began building in Hunt's bones.

Ruhn snarled, "They *can't* kill her. She's the only one who can shut those fucking Gates."

Sandriel leaned back in her chair. "She hasn't made the Drop yet, Prince. So they most certainly can." She added, "And it looks like she's wholly drained anyway. I doubt she'll be able to close a second Gate, let alone six more."

Hunt's fingers curled.

Hypaxia met his stare again and smiled slightly. An invitation and challenge. Her magic shimmered through him, over his forehead.

Sandriel had informed the Asteri—so they'd kill Bryce.

His Bryce. Hunt's attention narrowed on the back of Sandriel's neck.

And he rose to his feet as Hypaxia's magic dissolved the halo from his brow.

89

The conference room shook.

Ruhn had kept Sandriel distracted, kept her talking while Queen Hypaxia had freed Hunt from the halo's grip. He'd sensed the ripple of her power down the table, then seen Athalar's halo begin to glow, and had understood what the witch, her hand on Hunt's, was doing.

There was nothing but cold death in Hunt's eyes as the halo tattoo flaked away from his brow. The true face of the Umbra Mortis.

Sandriel whirled, realizing too late who now stood at her back. No mark across his brow. Something like pure terror crossed the Archangel's face as Hunt bared his teeth.

Lightning gathered around his hands. The walls cracked. Debris rained from the ceiling.

Sandriel was too slow.

Ruhn knew Sandriel had signed her own death warrant when she didn't bring her triarii back with her. And stamped the official seal on it the moment she'd revealed that she'd put Bryce in the Asteri's line of fire.

Even her Archangel's might couldn't protect her from Athalar. From what he felt for Bryce.

Athalar's lightning skittered over the floors. Sandriel barely had time to lift her arms and summon a gale-force wind before Hunt was upon her.

Lightning erupted, the entire room cracking with it.

Ruhn threw himself under a table, grabbing Hypaxia with him. Slabs of stone slammed onto the surface above them. Flynn swore up a storm beside him, and Declan crouched low, curled around a laptop. A cloud of debris filled the space, choking them. Ether coated Ruhn's tongue.

Lightning flared, licking and crackling through the room.

Then time shifted and slowed, sliding by, by, by—

"*Fuck,*" Flynn was saying between pants, each word an eternity and a flash, the world tipping over again, slowing and dragging. "*Fuck.*"

Then the lightning stopped. The cloud of debris pulsed and hummed.

Time began its normal pace, and Ruhn crawled out from under the table. He knew what he'd find within the whirling, electrified cloud everyone gaped at. Fury Axtar had a gun pointed at where the Archangel and Hunt had stood, debris whitening her dark hair.

Hypaxia helped Ruhn to his feet. Her eyes were wide as they scanned the cloud. The witch-queen had undoubtedly known that Sandriel would kill her for freeing Hunt. She'd taken a gamble that the Umbra Mortis would be the one to walk away.

The cloud of debris cleared, lightning fading into the dust-choked air. Her gamble had paid off. Blood splattered Hunt's face as his feathers fluttered on a phantom wind.

And from his hand, gripped by the hair, dangled Sandriel's severed head.

Her mouth was still open in a scream, smoke rippling from her lips, the skin of her neck so damaged Ruhn knew Hunt had torn it off with his bare hands.

Hunt slowly lifted the head before him, as if he were one of the ancient heroes of the Rhagan Sea surveying a slain creature. A monster.

He let the Archangel's head drop. It thumped and lolled to

the side, smoke still trickling from the mouth, the nostrils. He'd flayed her with his lightning from the inside out.

The angels in the room all knelt on one knee. Bowed. Even a wide-eyed Isaiah Tiberian. No one on the planet had that sort of power. No one had seen it fully unleashed in centuries.

Two Governors dead in one day. Slain by his sister and his sister's . . . whatever Hunt was. From the awe and fear on his father's face, Ruhn knew the Autumn King was wondering about it. Wondering if Hunt would kill him next, for how he'd treated Bryce.

Bryce, his Starborn sister.

Ruhn didn't know what to think about it. That she'd thought he valued the Chosen One bullshit more than her. And when that fight had happened, had she let things rupture between them to keep him from ever learning what she was? She'd walked away from the privilege and honor and glory—for him.

And all those warnings she'd given him about the Autumn King, about their father killing the last Starborn . . . She'd lived with that fear, too.

Hunt threw the Autumn King a feral grin.

Ruhn felt a sick amount of satisfaction as his father went pale.

But then Hunt looked to Fury, who was pulling debris from her dark hair, and growled, "Fuck the Asteri. Get your gods-damned helicopter over here."

Every decision, every order flowed from a long-quiet place within Hunt.

He sizzled with power, the lightning in his veins roaring to crack free into the world, to burn and sunder. He suppressed it, promised it he'd allow it to flow unchecked as soon as they reached the city—but they had to reach the city first.

Fury shook slightly—as if even she had forgotten what he could do. What he'd done to Sandriel with primal satisfaction, sinking into a place of such rage that there had only been his lightning and his enemy and the threat she posed to Bryce. But Fury said, "The helicopter is landing on the roof now."

Hunt nodded and ordered the remaining angels without looking at them, "We move out."

Not one of them objected to his command. He hadn't given a shit that they'd bowed—whatever the fuck that meant. He'd only cared that they flew to Lunathion as fast as they could.

Fury was already at the exit, phone at her ear. Hunt strode after her, through the room full of rustling wings and stomping feet, but looked back over his shoulder. "Danaan, Ketos—you in?" He needed them.

Ruhn shot to his feet without question; Tharion waited until he got the nod from the River Queen's daughter before rising. Amelie Ravenscroft stepped forward, ignoring Sabine's glare, and said, "I'm going with you, too." Hunt nodded again.

Flynn was already moving, not needing to voice that he'd join his prince—to save his princess. Declan pointed to the screens. "I'll be your eyes in the field."

"Good," Hunt said, aiming for the door.

The Autumn King and the Prime of the wolves, the only City Heads present, remained in the pit, along with Sabine. Jesiba and Hypaxia would have to keep them honest. Neither of the females so much as acknowledged the other, but no animosity sparked between them, either. Hunt didn't care.

He silently scaled the stairs toward the roof, his companions behind him. They were thirty minutes by helicopter from the city. So much could go wrong before they reached it. And when they got there . . . it would be pure slaughter.

The helicopter's blades whipped Fury's black hair as she crossed the landing pad. Flynn trailed close behind, sizing up their ride, and let out an impressed whistle.

It wasn't a luxury transport. It was a military-grade helicopter. Complete with two gunners on either door and a cache of assorted guns and weapons in duffels strapped to the floor.

Fury Axtar had not come to this meeting expecting it to be

friendly. She grabbed the headset from the departing pilot before slinging her slender body into the cockpit.

"I'm with you," Hunt said, gesturing to the helicopter as the angels took off around them. "My wings can't handle the flight yet."

Ruhn leapt into the helicopter behind Flynn and Amelie, Tharion claiming the left gunner. Hunt remained on the roof, shouting orders to the departing angels. *Establish a perimeter around the city. Scout team: investigate the portal. Send survivors to triage at least five miles beyond city walls.* He didn't let himself think about how easy it was to slip back into a commander's role.

Then Hunt was in the helicopter, taking up the right gunner. Fury flicked switch after switch on the control panel. Hunt asked her, his voice hoarse, "Did you know about what happened on the roof with Bryce and Juniper?"

It had fucking gutted him to hear Bryce allude to it—that she'd considered jumping. To hear that he'd come so close to losing her before he even knew her. Ruhn turned toward them, his agonized face confirming that he felt the same.

Fury didn't stop her prep. "Bryce was a ghost for a long while, Hunt. She pretended she wasn't, but she was." The helicopter finally pulled into the air. "You brought her back to life."

90

Bryce's entire body trembled as she leaned against the glowing quartz of the Gate, exhaustion rooting her to the spot.

It had worked. Somehow, it had worked.

She didn't let herself marvel over it—or dread its implications, when her father and the Asteri found out. Not when she had no idea how long her starlight would remain glowing in the Gate. But maybe it would hold long enough for help to come. Maybe this had made a difference.

Maybe she had made a difference.

Each breath burned in her chest. Not much longer now. For help to come, for her end, she didn't know.

But it would be soon. Whichever way it ended, Bryce knew it would be soon.

"Declan says Bryce is still at the Old Square Gate," Fury reported over a shoulder.

Hunt just kept his eyes on the star-filled horizon. The city was a dark shadow, interrupted only by a faint glowing in its heart. The Old Square Gate. Bryce.

"And Hypaxia says Bryce can barely move," Fury added, a note of surprise in her flat voice. "It looks like she's drained. She's not going to be able to get to the next Gate without help."

"But the light from the Gate is keeping her safe?" Ruhn called over the wind.

"Until the demons stop fearing the Starborn light." Fury switched the call to the helicopter's speakers. "Emmet, radar's picking up three war machines from the west. Any read on them?"

Thank fuck. Someone else was coming to help after all. If they could bring Bryce to each Gate and she could just muster enough starlight to flow through the Horn, they'd stop the carnage.

Declan took a moment to reply, his voice crackling through the speakers above Hunt. "They're registering as imperial tanks." His pause had Hunt's grip tightening on the gunner.

Hypaxia clarified, "It's the Asterian Guard. With brimstone missile launchers." Her voice sharpened as she said to the Autumn King and Prime of the wolves, "*Get your forces out of the city.*"

The blood in Hunt's veins went cold.

The Asteri had sent someone to deal with the demons. And with Bryce.

They were going to blast the city into dust.

The brimstone missiles weren't ordinary bombs of chemicals and metal. They were pure magic, made by the Asterian Guard: a combination of their angelic powers of wind and rain and fire into one hyperconcentrated entity, bound with firstlight and fired through machinery. Where they struck, destruction bloomed.

To make them even deadlier, they were laced with spells to slow healing. Even for Vanir. The only comfort for any on their receiving end was that the missiles took a while to make, offering reprieve between rounds. A small, fool's comfort.

Fury flicked buttons on the switchboard. "Copy Asterian Units One, Two, and Three, this is Fury Axtar speaking. Pull back." No answer. "I repeat, *pull back*. Abort mission."

Nothing. Declan said, "They're the Asterian Guard. They won't answer to you."

The Autumn King's voice crackled through the speakers. "No one at Imperial Command is answering our calls."

Fury angled the helicopter, sweeping southward. Hunt saw them then. The black tanks breaking over the horizon, each as large as a small house. The imperial insignia painted on their flanks. All three gunning for Crescent City.

They halted just outside its border. The metal launchers atop them angled into position.

The brimstone missiles shot from the launchers and arced over the walls, blazing with golden light. As the first of them hit, he prayed that Bryce had left the Gate to find shelter.

Bryce choked on dust and debris, chest heaving. She tried to move—and failed. Her spine—

No, that was her leg, pinned in a tangle of concrete and iron. She'd heard the boom a minute ago, recognized the golden, arcing plume as brimstone thanks to news coverage of the Pangeran wars, and had sprinted halfway across the square, aiming for the open door of the brick music hall there, hoping it had a basement, when it hit.

Her ears were roaring, buzzing. Shrieking.

The Gate still stood, still shielded her with its light. Her light, technically.

The nearest brimstone missile had hit a neighborhood away, it seemed. It had been enough to trash the square, to reduce some buildings to rubble, but not enough to decimate it.

Move. She had to move. The other Gates still lay open. She had to find some way to get there; shut them, too.

She tugged at her leg. To her surprise, the minor wounds were already healing—far faster than she'd ever experienced. Maybe the Horn in her back helped speed it along.

She reached forward to haul the concrete slab off her. It didn't budge.

She panted through her teeth, trying again. They'd unleashed brimstone upon the city. The Asterian Guard had blindly fired it over the walls to either destroy the Gates or kill the demons. But they'd fired on their own people, not caring who they hit—

Bryce took deep, steadying breaths. It did nothing to settle her.

She tried again, fingernails cracking on the concrete. But short of cutting off her foot, she wasn't getting free.

The Asterian Guard was reloading their missile launchers atop the tanks. Hyperconcentrated magic flared around them, as if the brimstone was straining to be free of its firstlight constraints. Eager to unleash angelic ruin upon the helpless city.

"They're going to fire again," Ruhn whispered.

"The brimstone landed mostly in Moonwood," Declan told them. "Bryce is alive but in trouble. She's trapped under a piece of concrete. Struggling like Hel to free herself, though."

Fury screamed into the microphone, "*ABORT MISSION*."

No one answered. The launchers cocked skyward again, pivoting to new targets.

As if they knew Bryce still lived. They'd keep bombarding the city until she was dead, killing anything in their path. Perhaps hoping that if they took out the Gates, too, the voids would vanish.

An icy, brutal calm settled over Hunt.

He said to Fury, "Go high. High as the helicopter can handle."

She saw what he intended. He couldn't fly, not on weak wings. But he didn't need to.

"Grab something," Fury said, and angled the helicopter sharply. It went up, up, up, all of them gritting their teeth against the weight trying to shove them earthward.

Hunt braced himself, settling into that place that had seen him through battles and years in dungeons and Sandriel's arena.

"Get ready, Athalar," Fury called. The war machines halted, launchers primed.

The helicopter flew over Lunathion's walls. Hunt unstrapped himself from the gunner. The Bone Quarter was a misty swirl below as they crossed the Istros.

Gratitude shone in Danaan's eyes. Understanding what only Hunt could do.

The Old Square and glowing Gate at its heart became visible. The only signal he needed. There was no hesitation in Hunt. No fear.

Hunt leapt out of the helicopter, his wings tucked in tight. A one-way ticket. His last flight.

Far below, his sharp eyes could just make out Bryce as she curled herself into a ball, as if it'd save her from the death soon to blast her apart.

The brimstone missiles launched one after another after another, the closest arcing toward the Old Square, shimmering with lethal golden power. Even as Hunt plunged to the earth, he knew its angle was off—it'd strike probably ten blocks away. But it was still too close. Still left her in the blast zone, where all that compressed angelic power would splatter her apart.

The brimstone hit, the entire city bouncing beneath its unholy impact. Block after block ruptured in a tidal wave of death.

Wings splaying, lightning erupting, Hunt threw himself over Bryce as the world shattered.

91

She should be dead.

But those were her fingers, curling on the rubble. That was her breath, sawing in and out.

The brimstone had decimated the square, the city was now in smoldering ruins, yet the Gate still stood. Her light had gone out, though, the quartz again an icy white. Fires sputtered around her, lighting the damage in flickering relief.

Clumps of ashes rained down, mixing with the embers.

Bryce's ears buzzed faintly, yet not as badly as they had after the first blast.

It wasn't possible. She'd spied the shimmering golden brimstone missile arcing past, knew it'd strike a few blocks away, and that death would soon find her. The Gate must have shielded her, somehow.

Bryce eased into a kneeling position with a groan. The bombardment, at least, had ceased. Only a few buildings stood. The skeletons of cars still burned around her. The acrid smoke rose in a column that blotted out the first of the evening stars.

And—and in the shadows, those were stirring demons. Bile burned her throat. She had to get up. Had to move while they were down.

Her legs wouldn't cooperate. She wiggled her toes inside her sneakers, just to make sure they could work, but . . . she couldn't rise off the ground. Her body refused to obey.

A clump of ash landed on the torn knee of her leggings.

Her hands began to shake. It wasn't a piece of ash.

It was a gray feather.

Bryce twisted to look behind herself. Her head emptied out. A scream broke from her, rising from so deep that she wondered if it was the sound of the world shredding apart.

Hunt lay sprawled on the ground, his back a bloodied, burned mess, and his legs . . .

There was nothing left of them but ribbons. Nothing left of his right arm but splattered blood on pavement. And through his back, where his wings had been—

That was a bloody, gaping hole.

She moved on instinct, scrambling over concrete and metal and blood.

He'd shielded her against the brimstone. Had somehow escaped Sandriel and come here. To save her.

"*Pleasepleasepleaseplease*"

She turned him over, searching for any hint of life, of breathing—

His mouth moved. Just slightly.

Bryce sobbed, pulling his head into her lap. "Help!" she called. No answer beyond an unearthly baying in the fire-licked darkness. "Help!" she yelled again, but her voice was so hoarse it barely carried across the square. Randall had told her about the terrible power of the Asterian Guard's brimstone missiles. How the spells woven into the condensed angelic magic slowed healing in Vanir long enough for them to bleed out. To die.

Blood coated so much of Hunt's face that she could barely see the skin beneath. Only the faint flutter of his throat told her he still lived.

And the wounds that should have been healing . . . they leaked and gushed blood. Arteries had been severed. Vital arteries—

"*HELP!*" she screamed.

But no one answered.

The brimstone's blasts had downed the helicopter.

Only Fury's skill kept them alive, though they'd still crashed, flipping twice, before landing somewhere in Moonwood.

Tharion bled from his head, Fury had a gash in her leg, Flynn and Amelie both bore broken bones, and Ruhn . . . He didn't bother to think about his own wounds. Not as the smoke-filled, burning night became laced with approaching snarls. But the brimstone had halted—at least they had that. He prayed the Asterian Guard would need a good while before they could muster the power to form more of them.

Ruhn forced himself into movement by sheer will.

Two of the duffels of weapons had come free of their bindings and been lost in the crash. Flynn and Fury began divvying out the remaining guns and knives, working quickly while Ruhn assessed the state of the one intact machine gun he'd ripped from the chopper's floor.

Hypaxia's voice cracked over the miraculously undamaged radio, "We have eyes on the Old Square Gate," she said. Ruhn paused, waiting for the news. Not daring to hope.

The last Ruhn had seen of Athalar was the angel plunging toward Bryce while the Asterian Guard fired those glowing golden missiles over the walls like some sick fireworks show. Then the citywide explosions had sundered the world.

"Athalar is down," Declan announced gravely. "Bryce lives." Ruhn offered up a silent prayer of thanks to Cthona for her mercy. Another pause. "Correction, Athalar made it, but barely. His injuries are . . . Shit." His swallow was audible. "I don't think there's any chance of survival."

Tharion cocked a rifle to his shoulder, peering through the scope into the darkness. "We've got about a dozen demons sizing us up from that brick building over there."

"Six more over here," Fury said, also using the scope on her rifle. Amelie Ravenscroft limped badly as she shifted into wolf form with a flash of light and bared her teeth at the darkness.

If they didn't shut the portals in the other Gates, only two options existed: retreat or death.

"They're getting curious," Flynn murmured without taking his eye from the scope of his gun. "Do we have a plan?"

"The river's at our backs," Tharion said. "If we're lucky, my people might come to our aid." The Blue Court lay far enough below the surface to have avoided the brimstone's wrath. They could rally.

But Bryce and Hunt remained in the Old Square. Ruhn said, "We're thirty blocks from the Heart Gate. We go down the riverwalk, then cut inland at Main." He added, "That's where I'm headed, at least." They all nodded, grim-faced.

Tell Ruhn I forgive him—for all of it.

The words echoed through Ruhn's blood. They had to keep going, even if the demons picked them off one by one. He just hoped they'd reach his sister in time to find something to save.

Bryce knelt over Hunt, his life spilling out all around her. And in the smoldering, acrid quiet, she began whispering.

"I believe it happened for a reason. I believe it all happened for a reason." She stroked his bloody hair, her voice shaking. "I believe it wasn't for nothing."

She looked toward the Gate. Gently set Hunt down amid the rubble. She whispered again, rising to her feet, "I believe it happened for a reason. I believe it all happened for a reason. I believe it wasn't for nothing."

She walked from Hunt's body as he bled behind her. Wended her way through the debris and rubble. The fence around the Gate had been warped, peeled away. But the quartz archway still stood, its bronze plaque and the dial pad's gems intact as she halted before them.

Bryce whispered again, "I believe it wasn't for nothing."

She laid her palm on the dial pad's bronze disk.

The metal was warm against Bryce's fingers, as it had been

when she'd touched it that final day with Danika. Its power zinged through her, sucking the fee for the usage: a drop of her magic.

The Gates had been used as communication devices in the past—but the only reason words could pass between them was the power that connected them. They all sat atop linked ley lines. A veritable matrix of energy.

The Gate wasn't just a prism. It was a conduit. And she had the Horn in her very skin. Had proved it could close a portal to Hel.

Bryce whispered into the little intercom in the center of the pad's arc of gems, "Hello?"

No one answered. She said, "If you can hear me, come to the Gate. Any Gate."

Still nothing. She said, "My name is Bryce Quinlan. I'm in the Old Square. And . . . and I think I've figured out how we can stop this. How we can fix this."

Silence. None of the other gems lit up to indicate the presence or voice of another person in another district, touching the disk on their end.

"I know it's bad right now," she tried again. "I know it's so, so bad, and dark, and . . . I know it feels impossible. But if you can make it to another Gate, just . . . please. Please come."

She took a shuddering breath.

"You don't need to do anything," she said. "All you need to do is just put your hand on the disk. That's all I need—just another person on the line." Her hand shook, and she pressed it harder to the metal. "The Gate is a conduit of power—a lightning rod that feeds into every other Gate throughout the city. And I need someone on the other end, linked to me through that vein." She swallowed. "I need someone to Anchor me. So I can make the Drop."

The words whispered out into the world.

Bryce's rasping voice overrode the sounds of the demons rallying again around her. "The firstlight I'll generate by making the Drop will spread from this Gate to the others. It'll light up *everything*, send those demons racing away. It'll heal everything it touches. Every*one* it touches. And I—" She took a deep breath. "I am

Starborn Fae, and I bear Luna's Horn in my body. With the power of the firstlight I generate, I can shut the portals to Hel. I did it here—I can do it everywhere else. But I need a link—and the power from my Drop to do it."

Still no one answered. No life stirred, beyond the beasts in the deepest shadows.

"Please," Bryce begged, her voice breaking.

Silently, she prayed for any one of those six other gems to light up, to show that just one person, in any district, would answer her plea.

But there was only the crackling nothingness.

She was alone. And Hunt was dying.

Bryce waited five seconds. Ten seconds. No one answered. No one came.

Swallowing another sob, she took a shuddering breath and let go of the disk.

Hunt's breaths had grown few and far between. She crawled back to him, hands shaking. But her voice was calm as she again slid his head into her lap. Stroked his blood-soaked face. "It's going to be all right," she said. "Help is coming, Hunt. The medwitches are on their way." She shut her eyes against her tears. "We're going to be all right," she lied. "We're going to go home, where Syrinx is waiting for us. We're going to go home. You and me. Together. We'll have that afterward, like you promised. But only if you hold on, Hunt."

His breathing rattled in his chest. A death rattle. She bent over him, inhaling his scent, the strength in him. And then she said it—the three words that meant more than anything. She whispered them into his ear, sending them with all she had left in her.

The final truth, the one she needed him to hear.

Hunt's breathing spread and thinned. Not much longer.

Bryce couldn't stop her tears as they dropped onto Hunt's cheeks, cleaning away the blood in clear tracks.

Light it up, Danika whispered to her. Into her heart.

"I tried," she whispered back. "Danika, I tried."

Light it up.

Bryce wept. "It didn't work."

Light it up. Urgency sharpened the words. As if . . . As if . . .

Bryce lifted her head. Looked toward the Gate. To the plaque and its gems.

She waited. Counted her breaths. *One. Two. Three.*

The gems remained dark. *Four. Five. Six.*

Nothing at all. Bryce swallowed hard and turned back to Hunt. One last time. He'd go, and then she'd follow, once more brimstone fell or the demons worked up the courage to attack her.

She took another breath. *Seven.*

"Light it up." The words filled the Old Square. Filled every square in the city.

Bryce whipped her head around to look at the Gate as Danika's voice sounded again. "Light it up, Bryce."

The onyx stone of the Bone Quarter glowed like a dark star.

92

Bryce's face crumpled as she lurched to her feet, sprinting to the Gate.

She didn't care how it was possible as Danika said again, "*Light it up.*"

Then Bryce was laughing and sobbing as she screamed, "*LIGHT IT UP, DANIKA! LIGHT IT UP, LIGHT IT UP, LIGHT IT UP*!"

Bryce slammed her palm onto the bronze disk of the Gate.

And soul to soul with the friend whom she had not forgotten, the friend who had not forgotten her, even in death, Bryce made the Drop.

Stunned silence filled the conference room as Bryce plunged into her power.

Declan Emmet didn't look up from the feeds he monitored, his heart thundering.

"It's not possible," the Autumn King said. Declan was inclined to agree.

Sabine Fendyr murmured, "Danika had a small kernel of energy left, the Under-King said. A bit of self that remained."

"Can a dead soul even serve as an Anchor?" Queen Hypaxia asked.

"No," Jesiba replied, with all the finality of the Under-King's emissary. "No, it can't."

Silence rippled through the room as they realized what they were witnessing. An untethered, solo Drop. Utter free fall. Bryce might as well have leapt from a cliff and hoped to land safely.

Declan drew his eyes from the video feed and scanned the graph on one of his three computers—the one charting Bryce's Drop, courtesy of the Eleusian system. "She's approaching her power level." Barely a blip past zero on the scale.

Hypaxia peered over his shoulder to study the graph. "She's not slowing, though."

Declan squinted at the screen. "She's gaining speed." He shook his head. "But—but she's classified as a low-level." Near-negligible, if he felt like being a dick about it.

Hypaxia said quietly, "But the Gate is not."

Sabine demanded, "What do you mean?"

Hypaxia whispered, "I don't think it's a memorial plaque. On the Gate." The witch pointed to the sign mounted on the glowing quartz, the bronze stark against the incandescent stone. "*The power shall always belong to those who give their lives to the city.*"

Bryce dropped further into power. Past the normal, respectable levels.

Queen Hypaxia said, "The plaque is a blessing."

Declan's breathing was uneven as he murmured, "The power of the Gates—the power given over by every soul who has ever touched it . . . every soul who has handed over a drop of their magic."

He tried and failed to calculate just how many people, over how many centuries, had touched the Gates in the city. Had handed over a drop of their power, like a coin tossed in a fountain. Made a wish on that drop of yielded power.

People of every House. Every race. Millions and millions of drops of power fueled this solo Drop.

Bryce passed level after level after level. The Autumn King's face went pale.

Hypaxia said, "Look at the Gates."

The quartz Gates across the city began to glow. Red, then orange, then gold, then white.

Firstlight erupted from them. Lines of it speared out in every direction.

The lights flowed down the ley lines between the Gates, connecting them along the main avenues. It formed a perfect, six-pointed star.

The lines of light began to spread. Curving around the city walls. Cutting off the demons now aiming for the lands beyond.

Light met light met light met light.

Until the city was ringed with it. Until every street was glowing.

And Bryce was still making the Drop.

It was joy and life and death and pain and song and silence.

Bryce tumbled into power, and power tumbled into her, and she didn't care, didn't care, didn't care, because it was Danika falling with her, Danika laughing with her as their souls twined.

She was here, she was here, she was here—

Bryce plunged into the golden light and song at the heart of the universe.

Danika let out a howl of joy, and Bryce echoed it.

Danika was here. It was enough.

"She's passing Ruhn's level," Declan breathed, not believing it. That his friend's party-girl sister had surpassed the prince himself. Surpassed Ruhn fucking Danaan.

Declan's king was still as death as Bryce smashed past Ruhn's ranking. This could change their very order. A powerful half-human princess with a star's light in her veins . . . Fucking Hel.

Bryce began slowing at last. Nearing the Autumn King's level. Declan swallowed.

The city was awash with her light. Demons fled from it, racing back through the voids, opting to brave the glowing Gates rather than be trapped in Midgard.

Light shot up from the Gates, seven bolts becoming one in the heart of the city—above the Old Square Gate. A highway of power. Of Bryce's will.

The voids between Midgard and Hel began to shrink. As if the light itself was abhorrent. As if that pure, unrestrained firstlight could heal the world.

And it did. Buildings shattered by brimstone slid back into place. Rubble gathered into walls and streets and fountains. Wounded people became whole again.

Bryce slowed further.

Declan ground his teeth. The voids within the Gates became smaller and smaller.

Demons rushed back to Hel through the shrinking doorways. More and more of the city healed as the Horn closed the portals. As *Bryce* sealed the portals, the Horn's power flowing through her, amplified by the firstlight she was generating.

"Holy gods," someone was whispering.

The voids between worlds became slivers. Then nothing at all.

The Gates stood empty. The portals gone.

Bryce stopped at last. Declan studied the precise number of her power, just a decimal point above that of the Autumn King.

Declan let out a soft laugh, wishing Ruhn were here to see the male's shocked expression.

The Autumn King's face tightened and he growled at Declan, "I would not be so smug, boy."

Declan tensed. "Why?"

The Autumn King hissed, "Because that girl may have used the Gates' power to Drop to unforeseen levels, but she will not be able to make the Ascent."

Declan's fingers stilled on the keys of his laptop.

The Autumn King laughed mirthlessly. Not from malice, Declan realized—but something like pain. He'd never known the prick could feel such a thing.

Bryce slumped to the stones beside the Gate. Declan didn't need medical monitors to know her heart had flatlined.

Her mortal body had died.

A clock on the computer showing the Eleusian system began counting down from a six-minute marker. The indicator of how long she had to make the Search and the Ascent, to let her mortal, aging body die, to face what lay within her soul, and race back up to life, into her full power. And emerge an immortal.

If she made the Ascent, the Eleusian system would register it, track it.

The Autumn King said hoarsely, "She made the Drop alone. Danika Fendyr is dead—she is not a true Anchor. Bryce has no way back to life."

93

This was the cradle of all life, this place.

There was a physical ground beneath her, and she had the sense of an entire world above her, full of distant, twinkling lights. But this was the bottom of the sea. The dark trench that cut through the skin of the earth.

It didn't matter. Nothing mattered at all. Not with Danika standing before her. Holding her.

Bryce peeled away far enough to look at her beautiful, angular face. The corn-silk hair. It was the same, right down to the amethyst, sapphire, and rose streaks. She'd somehow forgotten the exact features of Danika's face, but . . . there they were.

Bryce said, "You came."

Danika's smile was soft. "You asked for help."

"Are you . . . are you alive? Over there, I mean."

"No." Danika shook her head. "No, Bryce. This, what you see . . ." She gestured to herself. The familiar jeans and old band T-shirt. "This is just the spark that's left. What was resting over there."

"But it's you. This is *you*."

"Yes." Danika peered at the churning darkness above them, the entire ocean above. "And you don't have much time to make the Ascent, Bryce."

Bryce snorted. "I'm not making the Ascent."

Danika blinked. "What do you mean?"

Bryce stepped back. "I'm not making it." Because this was where her homeless soul would stay, if she failed. Her body would die in the world above, and her soul that she'd traded away to the Under-King would be left to wander this place. With Danika.

Danika crossed her arms. "Why?"

Bryce blinked furiously. "Because it got too hard. Without you. It *is* too hard without you."

"That's bullshit," Danika snarled. "So you'll just give up on everything? Bryce, I am *dead*. I am *gone*. And you'll trade your entire life for this tiny piece of me that's left?" Disappointment shuttered her caramel eyes. "The friend I knew wouldn't have done that."

Bryce's voice broke as she said, "We were supposed to do this together. We were supposed to live out our lives together."

Danika's face softened. "I know, B." She took her hand. "But that's not how it turned out."

Bryce bowed her head, thinking she'd crack apart. "I miss you. Every moment of every day."

"I know," Danika said again, and put a hand over her heart. "And I've felt it. I've seen it."

"Why did you lie—about the Horn?"

"I didn't lie," Danika said simply. "I just didn't tell you."

"You lied about the tattoo," Bryce countered.

"To keep you safe," Danika said. "To keep the Horn safe, yeah, but mostly to keep you safe in case the worst happened to me."

"Well, the worst did happen to you," Bryce said, instantly regretting it when Danika flinched.

But then Danika said, "You traded your place in the Bone Quarter for me."

Bryce began crying. "It was the least I could do."

Tears formed in Danika's eyes. "You didn't think I'd make it?" She threw her a sharp, pained grin. "Asshole."

But Bryce shook with the force of her weeping. "I couldn't . . . I couldn't take that risk."

Danika brushed back a piece of Bryce's hair.

Bryce sniffled and said, "I killed Micah for what he did. To you. To Lehabah." Her heart strained. "Is—is she over in the Bone Quarter?"

"I don't know. And yeah—I saw what happened in the gallery." Danika didn't explain more about the particulars. "We all saw."

That word snagged. *We.*

Bryce's lips trembled. "Is Connor with you?"

"He is. And the rest of the pack. They bought me time with the Reapers. To get to the Gate. They're holding them off, but not for long, Bryce. I can't stay here with you." She shook her head. "Connor would have wanted more for you than this." She stroked the back of Bryce's hand with her thumb. "He wouldn't have wanted you to stop fighting."

Bryce wiped at her face again. "I didn't. Not until now. But now I'm . . . It's all just *fucked*. And I'm so *tired* of it feeling that way. I'm done."

Danika asked softly, "What about the angel?"

Bryce's head snapped up. "What about him?"

Danika gave her a knowing smile. "If you want to ignore the fact that you've got your family who loves you no matter what, fine—but the angel remains."

Bryce withdrew her hand from Danika's. "You're really trying to convince me to make the Ascent for a guy?"

"Is Hunt Athalar really just some guy to you?" Danika's smile turned gentle. "And why is it somehow a mark against your strength to admit that there is someone, who happens to be male, worth returning to? Someone who I know made you feel like things are *far* from fucked."

Bryce crossed her arms. "So what."

"He's healed, Bryce," Danika said. "You healed him with the firstlight."

Bryce's breath shuddered out of her. She'd done all of this for that wild hope.

She swallowed, looking at the ground that was not earth, but the very base of Self, of the world. She whispered, "I'm scared."

Danika grabbed her hand again. "That's the point of it, Bryce.

Of *life*. To live, to love, knowing that it might all vanish tomorrow. It makes everything that much more precious." She took Bryce's face in her hands and pressed their brows together.

Bryce closed her eyes and inhaled Danika's scent, somehow still present even in this form. "I don't think I can make it. Back up."

Danika pulled away, peering at the impossible distance overhead. Then at the road that stretched before them. The runway. Its end was a free fall into eternal darkness. Into nothingness. But she said, "Just try, Bryce. One try. I'll be with you every step of the way. Even if you can't see me. I will *always* be with you."

Bryce didn't look at that too-short runway. The endless ocean above them, separating her from life. She just memorized the lines of Danika's face, as she had not had the chance to do before. "I love you, Danika," she whispered.

Danika's throat bobbed. She cocked her head, the movement purely lupine. As if listening to something. "Bryce, you have to hurry." She grabbed her hand, squeezing. "You have to decide now."

The timer on Bryce's life showed two minutes left.

Her dead body lay sprawled on the stones beside the faintly glowing Gate.

Declan ran a hand over his chest. He didn't dare contact Ruhn. Not yet. Couldn't bear to.

"There's no way to help her?" Hypaxia whispered to the silent room. "No way at all?"

No. Declan had used the past four minutes to run a search of every public and private database in Midgard for a miracle. He'd found nothing.

"Beyond being without an Anchor," the Autumn King said, "she used an artificial power source to bring her to that level. Her body is not biologically equipped to make the Ascent. Even with a true Anchor, she wouldn't be able to gain enough momentum for that first jump upward."

Jesiba gravely nodded her confirmation, but the sorceress said nothing.

Declan's memories of his Drop and Ascent were murky, frightening. He'd gone farther than anticipated, but had at least stayed within his own range. Even with Flynn Anchoring him, he'd been petrified he wouldn't make it back.

Despite registering on the system as a blip of energy beside Bryce, Danika Fendyr was not a tether to life, not a true Anchor. She had no life of her own. Danika was merely the thing that had given Bryce enough courage to attempt the Drop alone.

The Autumn King went on, "I've looked. I've spent centuries looking. Thousands of people throughout the ages have attempted to go past their own intended levels through artificial means. None of them ever made it back to life."

One minute remained, the seconds flying off the countdown clock.

Bryce had still not Ascended. Was still making the Search, facing whatever lay within her. The timer would have halted if she had begun her attempt at the Ascent, marking her entrance into the Between—the liminal place between death and life. But the timer kept going. Winding down.

It didn't matter, though. Bryce would die whether she attempted it or not.

Thirty seconds left. The remaining dignitaries in the room bowed their heads.

Ten seconds. The Autumn King rubbed at his face, then watched the clock count down. The remainder of Bryce's life.

Five. Four. Three. Two.

One. The milliseconds raced toward zero. True death.

The clock stopped at 0.003.

A red line shot across the bottom of the Eleusian system's graph, along the runway toward oblivion.

Declan whispered, "She's running."

"Faster, Bryce!" Danika raced at her heels.

Step after step after step, Bryce barreled down that mental runway. Toward the ever-nearing end of it.

"*Faster!*" Danika roared.

One shot. She had one shot at this.

Bryce ran. Ran and ran and ran, arms pumping, gritting her teeth.

The odds were impossible, the likelihood slim.

But she tried. With Danika beside her, this last time, she could try.

She had made the Drop solo, but she was not alone.

She had never been alone. She never would be.

Not with Danika in her heart, and not with Hunt beside her.

The end of the runway neared. She had to get airborne. Had to start the Ascent, or she'd fall into nothingness. Forever.

"*Don't stop!*" Danika screamed.

So Bryce didn't.

She charged onward. Toward that very final, deadly end point.

She used every foot of the runway. Every last inch.

And then blasted upward.

Declan couldn't believe what he was seeing as the Autumn King fell to his knees. As Bryce rose, lifted on a surge of power.

She cleared the deepest levels.

"It's not . . . ," the Autumn King breathed. "It's not *possible*. She is *alone*."

Tears streamed down Sabine's harsh face as she whispered, "No, she isn't."

The force that was Danika Fendyr, the force that had given Bryce that boost upward, faded away into nothing.

Declan knew it would never return, in this world or on a mist-veiled isle.

It might still have been too long for Bryce's brain to be without oxygen, even if she could make it the entire way back to life. But his princess fought for every bit of progress upward, her power shifting, traces of everyone who'd given it to her coming through: mer, shifter, draki, human, angel, sprite, Fae . . .

"How," the Autumn King asked no one in particular. "*How?*"

It was the ancient Prime of the wolves who answered, his

withered voice rising above the pinging of the graph. "With the strength of the most powerful force in the world. The most powerful force in any realm." He pointed to the screen. "What brings loyalty beyond death, undimming despite the years. What remains unwavering in the face of hopelessness."

The Autumn King twisted toward the ancient Prime, shaking his head. Still not understanding.

Bryce was at the level of ordinary witches now. But still too far from life.

Motion caught Declan's eye, and he whirled toward the feed of the Old Square.

Wreathed in lightning, healed and whole, Hunt Athalar was kneeling over Bryce's dead body. Pumping her torso with his hands—chest compressions.

Hunt hissed to Bryce through his gritted teeth, thunder cracking above him, "I heard what you said." *Pump, pump, pump* went his powerful arms. "What you waited to admit until I was almost *dead,* you fucking coward." His lightning surged into her, sending her body arcing off the ground as he tried to jump-start her heart. He snarled in her ear, "*Now come say it to my face.*"

Sabine whispered a sentence to the room, to the Autumn King, and Declan's heart rose, hearing it.

It was the answer to the ancient Prime's words. To the Autumn King's question of how, against every statistic blaring on Declan's computer, they were even witnessing Hunt Athalar fight like Hel to keep Bryce Quinlan's heart beating.

Through love, all is possible.

94

She was sea and sky and stone and blood and wings and earth and stars and darkness and light and bone and flame.

Danika was gone. She had given over what remained of her soul, her power, to get Bryce off the runway, and for that initial rocketing Ascent.

Danika had whispered, *"I love you,"* before fading into nothing, her hand sliding from Bryce's.

And it had not destroyed Bryce, to make that final goodbye.

The roar she had emitted was not one of pain. But of challenge.

Bryce barreled higher. She could feel the surface nearby. The thin veil between this place and life. Her power shifted, dancing between forms and gifts. She thrust upward with a push of a mighty tail. Twisted and rose with a sweep of vast wings. She was all things—and yet herself.

And then she heard it. His voice. His answering challenge to her call.

He was there. Waiting for her.

Fighting to keep her heart going. She was close enough to the veil to see it now.

Even before she had come to lie dead before him, he'd fought to keep her heart going.

Bryce smiled, in this place between, and at last careened toward Hunt.

"*Come on*," Hunt grunted, continuing the chest compressions, counting Bryce's breaths until he could shock her again with his lighting.

He didn't know how long she had been down, but she'd been dead when he'd awoken, healed and whole, to a repaired city. As if no magic bombs, no demons, had ever harmed it.

He saw the glowing Gate, the blazing light—the *firstlight*—and knew only someone making the Drop could generate that kind of power. And when he'd seen her lifeless body before the Gate, he'd known she'd somehow found a way to make the Drop, to unleash that healing firstlight, to use the Horn to seal the portals to Hel at the other Gates.

So he'd acted on instinct. Did the only thing he could think of.

He'd saved her and she'd saved him, and he—

His power felt it coming a moment later. Recognized her, like seeing itself in a mirror.

How she was bringing up this much power, how she was making the Ascent alone . . . he didn't care about that. He had Fallen, he had survived, he had gone through every trial and torture and horror—all for this moment. So he could be here.

It had all been for her. For Bryce.

Closer and closer, her power neared. Hunt braced himself, and sent another shock of lightning into her heart. She arced off the ground once more, body lifeless.

"Come on," he repeated, pumping her chest again with his hands. "I'm waiting for you."

He'd been waiting for her from the moment he'd been born.

And as if she'd heard him, Bryce exploded into life.

She was warm, and she was safe, and she was home.

There was light—around her, from her, in her heart.

Bryce realized she was breathing. And her heart was beating.

Both were secondary. Would always be secondary around Hunt.

She dimly registered that they were kneeling in the Old Square. His gray wings glowed like embers as they curved around them both, holding her tightly to him. And inside the wall of velvet-soft wings, like a sun contained inside a flower bud, Bryce shone.

She slowly lifted her head, pulling away only far enough to look at his face.

Hunt already stared down at her, his wings unfurling like petals at dawn. No tattoo marked his brow. The halo was gone.

She ran her shaking fingers over the smooth skin. Hunt silently brushed away her tears.

She smiled at him. Smiled at him with the lightness in her heart, her soul. Hunt slid his hand along her jaw, cupping her face. The tenderness in his eyes wiped away any lingering doubts.

She laid her palm over his thundering heart. "Did you just call me a fucking coward?"

Hunt tipped his head to the stars and laughed. "So what if I did?"

She angled her face closer to his. "Too bad all that healing firstlight didn't turn you into a decent person."

"Where would the fun be in that, Quinlan?"

Her toes curled at the way he said her name. "I suppose I'll just have to—"

A door opened down the street. Then another and another. And stumbling, weeping with relief or silent in shock, the people of Crescent City emerged. Gaped at what they beheld. At Bryce and Hunt.

She let go of him and rose. Her power was a strange, vast well beneath her. Belonging not only to her—but to all of them.

She peered up at Hunt, who was now gazing at her as if he couldn't quite believe his eyes. She took his hand. Interlaced their fingers.

And together, they stepped forward to greet the world.

95

Syrinx was sitting in her apartment's open front doorway, whining with worry, as Bryce and Hunt stepped off the elevator.

Bryce scanned the empty hall, the chimera. "I left that door shut . . ." she began, earning a knowing chuckle from Hunt, but Syrinx was already sprinting for her.

"I'll explain his *gifts* later," Hunt murmured as Bryce herded a hysterical Syrinx into the apartment and knelt before the beast, flinging her arms around him.

She and Hunt had stayed in the Old Square for all of two minutes before the wailing began—from the people who stumbled from the shelters to discover that it had been too late for their loved ones.

The Horn inked into her back had done its job well. Not one void remained in the Gates. And her firstlight—through those Gates—had been able to heal everything: people, buildings, the world itself.

Yet it could not do the impossible. It could not bring back the dead.

And there were many, many bodies in the streets. Most only in pieces.

Bryce tightened her arms around Sryinx. "It's okay," she whispered, letting him lick her face.

But it wasn't okay. Not even close. What had happened, what she'd done and revealed, the Horn in her body, all those people dead, Lehabah dead, and seeing Danika, Danika, Danika—

Her breathless words turned into pants, and then shuddering sobs. Hunt, standing behind her as if he'd been waiting for this, just scooped her and Syrinx into his arms.

Hunt brought her to her bedroom, sitting down on the edge of the mattress, keeping his arms around her and Syrinx, who pried his way free from Bryce's arms to lick Hunt's face, too.

His hand slipped into her hair, fingers twining through it, and Bryce leaned into him, soaking up that strength, that familiar scent, marveling that they had even gotten here, had somehow made it—

She glanced at his wrist. No sign of the halo on his brow, yet the slave tattoo remained.

Hunt noticed the shift in her attention. He said quietly, "I killed Sandriel."

His eyes were so calm—clear. Fixed wholly on hers.

"I killed Micah," she whispered.

"I know." The corner of his mouth curled upward. "Remind me to never get on your bad side."

"It's not funny."

"Oh, I know it's not." His fingers drifted through her hair, casually and gently. "I could barely stand to watch."

She could barely stand to remember it. "How did you manage to kill her? To get rid of the tattoo?"

"It's a long story," he said. "I'd rather you fill in the details of yours."

"You first."

"Not a chance. I want to hear how you hid the fact that you've got a star inside you."

He looked down at her chest then, as if he'd glimpse it shimmering beneath her skin. But when his eyebrows flicked upward, Bryce followed his line of sight.

"Well," she said with a sigh, "that's new." Indeed, just visible down the V-neck of her T-shirt, a white splotch—an eight-pointed star—now scarred the place between her breasts.

Hunt chuckled. "I like it."

Some small part of her did, too. But she said, "You know it's just the Starborn light—not true power."

"Yeah, except now you've got that, too." He pinched her side. "A good amount from what I can sense. And the fucking Horn—" He ran his hand down her spine for emphasis.

She rolled her eyes. "Whatever."

But his face grew grave. "You're going to have to learn to control it."

"We save the city, and you're already telling me I need to get back to work?"

He chuckled. "Old habits, Bryce."

Their eyes met again, and she glanced at his mouth, so close to hers, so perfectly formed. At his eyes, now staring so intently into her own.

It had all happened for a reason. She believed that. For this—for him.

And though the path she'd been thrust onto was royally fucked, and had led her through the lightless halls of grief and despair . . . Here, here before her, was light. True light. What she'd raced toward during the Ascent.

And she wanted to be kissed by that light. Now.

Wanted to kiss him back, and tell Syrinx to go wait in his crate for a while.

Hunt's dark eyes turned near-feral. As if he could read those thoughts on her face, in her scent. "We have some unfinished business, Quinlan," he said, voice roughening. He threw Syrinx a Look, and the chimera leapt from the bed and trotted out into the hall, lion's tail waggling as if to say, *It's about time.*

When Bryce looked back at Hunt, she found his focus on her lips. And became hyperaware of the fact that she was sitting across his lap. On her bed. From the hardness starting to poke into her backside, she knew he'd realized it, too.

Still they said nothing as they stared at each other.

So Bryce wriggled slightly against his erection, drawing a hiss from him. She huffed a laugh. "I throw one smoldering look at you and you're already—what was it you said to me a few weeks ago? Hot and bothered?"

One of his hands traced down her spine again, intent in every inch of it. "I've been hot and bothered for you for a long time now." His hand halted on her waist, his thumb beginning a gentle, torturous stroking along her rib cage. With each sweep, the building ache between her legs ratcheted.

Hunt smiled slowly, as if well aware of that. Then he leaned in, pressing a kiss to the underside of her jaw. He said against her flushed skin, "You ready to do this?"

"Gods, yes," she breathed. And when he kissed just beneath her ear, making her back arch slightly, she said, "I recall you promising to fuck me until I couldn't remember my own name."

He shifted his hips, grinding his cock into her, searing her even with the clothing still between them. "If that's what you want, sweetheart, that's what I'll give you."

Oh gods. She couldn't get a solid breath down. Couldn't think around his roving mouth on her neck and his hands and that massive, beautiful cock digging into her. She had to get him inside her. Right now. She needed to feel him, needed to have his heat and strength around her. In her.

Bryce shifted to straddle his lap, lining herself up with all of him. She met all of him, satisfied to find his breathing as ragged as her own. His hands bracketed her waist, thumbs stroking, stroking, stroking, as if he were an engine waiting to roar into movement upon her command.

Bryce leaned in, brushing her mouth over his. Once. Twice.

Hunt began shaking with the force of his restraint as he let her explore his mouth.

But she pulled back, meeting his hazy, burning gaze. The words she wanted to say clogged in her throat, so she hoped he understood them as she pressed a kiss to his now-clear brow. Sketched a line of soft, glancing kisses over every inch where the tattoo had been.

Hunt slid a shaking hand from her waist and laid it over her thundering heart.

She swallowed thickly, surprised to find her eyes stinging. Surprised to see silver lining his eyes as well. They had made it; they were here. Together.

Hunt leaned in, slanting his mouth over hers. She met him halfway, arms snaking around his neck, fingers burying themselves in his thick, silken hair.

A shrill ringing filled the apartment.

She could ignore it, ignore the world—

Call from . . . Home.

Bryce pulled back, panting hard.

"You gonna get that?" Hunt's voice was guttural.

Yes. No. Maybe.

Call from . . . Home.

"She'll just keep calling until I pick up," Bryce murmured.

Her limbs were stiff as she peeled herself from Hunt's lap, his fingers trailing over her back as she stood. She tried not to think about the promise in that touch, as if he was as reluctant to let go of her as she was of him.

She ran to the great room and picked up the phone before it went to audiomail.

"Bryce?" Her mom was crying. It was enough to douse a bucket of ice water over any lingering arousal. "Bryce?"

She blew out a breath, returned to the bedroom, and threw Hunt an apologetic look that he waved off before he slumped back on the bed, wings rustling. "Hi, Mom."

Her mom's sobbing threatened to make her start again, so she kept moving, aiming for her bathroom. She was filthy—her pink sneakers were near-black, her pants torn and bloody, her shirt almost in ruins. Apparently, the firstlight had only gone so far in fixing everything.

"Are you all right? Are you safe?"

"I'm fine," Bryce said, turning on the shower. Leaving it on cold. She peeled off her clothes. "I'm doing fine."

"What's that water?"

"My shower."

"You save a city and make the Drop and can't even give me your full attention?"

Bryce chuckled and put the phone on speaker before setting it on the sink. "How much do you know?" She hissed at the icy blast as she stepped into the spray. But it shocked away any lingering heat between her legs and the heady desire clouding her mind.

"Your biological father had Declan Emmet call to fill me in on everything. I guess the bastard finally realized he owed me that much, at least."

Bryce turned up the heat at last as she shampooed her hair. "How pissed is he?"

"Furious, I'm sure." She added, "The news also just broke a story about—about who your father is." Bryce could practically hear her mother grinding her teeth. "They know the exact amount of power you got. As much as he has, Bryce. *More* than him. That's a big deal."

Bryce tried not to reel at it—where her power had landed her. She tucked away that factoid for later. She rinsed the shampoo from her hair, reaching for the conditioner. "I know."

"What are you going to do with it?"

"Open a chain of beach-themed restaurants."

"It was too much to hope that achieving that much power would give you a sense of dignity."

Bryce stuck out her tongue even though her mom couldn't see it, and plopped conditioner into her palm. "Look, can we shelve the whole *mighty power, mighty burdens* discussion until tomorrow?"

"Yes, except *tomorrow* in your vocabulary means *never.*" Her mother sighed. "You closed those portals, Bryce. And I can't even talk about what Danika did for you without . . ." Her voice broke. "We can talk about that *tomorrow,* too."

Bryce rinsed out the conditioner. And realized that her mother didn't know—about Micah. What she'd done to him. Or what Micah had done to Danika.

Ember kept talking, and Bryce kept listening, while dread grew like ivy inside her, creeping through her veins, wrapping around her bones and squeezing tight.

Hunt took a swift, icy shower of his own and changed into different clothes, smiling slightly to himself as Bryce's shower shut off and she kept talking to her mother.

"Yeah, Hunt's here." Her words floated down the hall, through the great room, and into his own room. "No, I didn't, Mom. And no, he didn't, either." A drawer slammed. "*That* is none of your business, and please never ask me anything like that again."

Hunt had a good idea of what Ember had asked her daughter. And wouldn't you know, he'd been about to do just that with Bryce when she'd called.

He hadn't cared that an entire city was looking on: he'd wanted to kiss her when the light of her power had faded, when Hunt had lowered his wings to find her in his arms, looking up at him like he was worth something. Like he was all she needed. End of story.

No one had ever looked at him like that.

And when they'd come back here, and he'd had her on his lap on her bed and seen the way her cheeks became pink as she looked at his mouth, he'd been ready to cross that final bridge with her. To spend all day and night doing so.

Considering how her firstlight had healed him, he'd most definitely say he was cleared for sex. Aching for it—for her.

Bryce groaned. "You're a pervert, Mom. You know that?" She growled. "Well, if you're so fucking invested in it, why did you *call me*? Didn't you think I might be *busy*?"

Hunt smiled, going half-hard again at the sass in her tone. He could listen to her snark all fucking day. He wondered how much of it would make an appearance when he got her naked again. Got her moaning.

The first time, she'd come on his hand. This time . . . This time, he had *plans* for all the other ways he'd get her to make that beautiful, breathless sound as she'd orgasmed.

Leaving Bryce to deal with her mother, willing his cock to calm the fuck down, Hunt grabbed a burner phone from his underwear drawer and dialed Isaiah, one of the few numbers he'd memorized.

"Thank the fucking gods," Isaiah said when he heard Hunt's voice.

Hunt smiled at the male's uncharacteristic relief. "What's happening on your end?"

"My end?" Isaiah barked a laugh. "What the fuck is happening on *your* end?"

Too much to say. "Are you at the Comitium?"

"Yeah, and it's a gods-damned madhouse. I just realized *I'm* in charge now."

With Micah a bunch of ashes in a vacuum and Sandriel not much better, Isaiah, as Micah's Commander of the 33rd, was indeed in charge.

"Congrats on the promotion, man."

"Promotion my ass. I'm not an Archangel. And these assholes know it." Isaiah snapped at someone in the background, "*Then call fucking maintenance to clean it up.*" He sighed.

Hunt asked, "What happened to the Asterian fuckheads who sent their brimstone over the walls?" He had half a mind to fly out there and start unleashing his lightning on those tanks.

"Gone. Already moved off." Isaiah's dark tone told Hunt he'd be down for some good old-fashioned retribution, too.

Hunt asked, bracing himself, "Naomi?"

"Alive." Hunt uttered a silent prayer of thanks to Cthona for that mercy. Then Isaiah said, "Look, I know you're exhausted, but can you get over here? I could use your help to sort this shit out. All these pissing contests will end pretty damn fast if they see us both in charge."

Hunt tried not to bristle. Bryce and him getting naked, it seemed, would have to wait.

Because the slave tattoo on his wrist meant he still had to obey the Republic, still belonged to someone other than himself. The list of possibilities wasn't good. He'd be lucky if he got to stay in

Lunathion as the possession of whoever took Micah's spot, and maybe see Bryce in stolen moments. If he was even allowed outside the Comitium.

Fuck, if they even allowed him to *live* after what he'd done to Sandriel.

Hunt's hands began to shake. Any trace of arousal vanished.

But he shrugged a shirt over his head. He'd find some way to survive—some way back to this life with Quinlan he'd barely begun to savor. Unable to help himself, he glanced at his wrist.

He blinked once. Twice.

Bryce was just saying goodbye to her deviant mother when the phone beeped with another call. It was from an unknown number, which meant it was probably Jesiba, so Bryce promised Ember they'd talk tomorrow and switched over. "Hey."

A young, male voice asked, "Is that how you greet all your callers, Bryce Quinlan?"

She knew that voice. Knew the lanky teenage body it belonged to, a shell to house an ancient behemoth. To house an Asteri. She'd seen and heard it on TV so many times she'd lost count.

"Hello, Your Brilliance," she whispered.

96

Rigelus, the Bright Hand of the Asteri, had called her house. Bryce's hands shook so badly she could barely keep the phone to her ear.

"We beheld your actions today and wished to extend our gratitude," the lilting voice said.

She swallowed, wondering if the mightiest of the Asteri somehow knew she was standing in a towel, hair dripping onto the carpet. "You're . . . welcome?"

Rigelus laughed softly. "You have had quite a day, Miss Quinlan."

"Yes, Your Brilliance."

"It was a day full of many surprises, for all of us."

We know what you are, what you did.

Bryce forced her legs to move, to head to the great room. To where Hunt was standing in the doorway of his bedroom, his face pale. His arms slack at his sides.

"To show you how deep our gratitude goes, we would like to grant you a favor."

She wondered if the brimstone had been a *favor*, too. But she said, "That's not necessary—"

"It is already done. We trust you will find it satisfactory."

She knew Hunt could hear the voice on the line as he walked over.

But he just held out his wrist. His tattooed wrist, with a *C* stamped over the slave's mark.

Freed.

"I . . ." Bryce gripped Hunt's wrist, then scanned his face. But it was not joy she saw there—not as he heard the voice on the line and understood who had gifted him his freedom.

"We also trust that this favor will serve as a reminder for you and Hunt Athalar. It is our deepest wish that you remain in the city, and live out your days in peace and contentment. That you use your ancestors' gift to bring yourself joy. And refrain from using the other gift inked upon you."

Use your starlight as a party trick and never, ever use the Horn.

It made her the biggest idiot in Midgard, but she said, "What about Micah and Sandriel?"

"Governor Micah went rogue and threatened to destroy innocent citizens of this empire with his high-handed approach to the rebel conflict. Governor Sandriel got what she deserved in being so lax with her control over her slaves."

Fear gleamed in Hunt's eyes. In her own, too, Bryce was sure. Nothing was ever this easy—this simple. There had to be a catch.

"These are, of course, sensitive issues, Miss Quinlan. Ones that, were they publicly announced, would result in a great deal of trouble for all involved."

For you. We will destroy you.

"All the witnesses to both events have been notified of the potential fallout."

"Okay," Bryce whispered.

"And as for the unfortunate destruction of Lunathion, we do accept full responsibility. We were informed by Sandriel that the city had been evacuated, and sent the Asterian Guard to wipe away the demon infestation. The brimstone missiles were a last resort, intended to save us all. It was incredibly fortunate that you found a solution."

Liar. Ancient, awful liar. He'd picked the perfect scapegoat: a dead one. The rage that flickered over Hunt's face told her he shared her opinion.

"I was truly lucky," Bryce managed to say.

"Yes, perhaps because of the power in your veins. Such a gift can have tremendous consequences, if not handled wisely." A pause, as if he were smiling. "I trust you shall learn to wield both your unexpected strength and the light within you with . . . discretion."

Stay in your lane.

"I will," Bryce murmured.

"Good," Rigelus said. "And do you believe it necessary that I contact your mother, Ember Quinlan, to ask for her discretion, too?" The threat gleamed, sharp as a knife. One step out of line, and they knew where to strike first. Hunt's hands curled into fists.

"No," Bryce said. "She doesn't know about the Governors."

"And she never will. No one else will ever know, Bryce Quinlan."

Bryce swallowed again. "Yes."

A soft laugh. "Then you and Hunt Athalar have our blessing."

The line went dead. Bryce stared at the phone like it was going to sprout wings and fly around the room.

Hunt slumped on the couch, rubbing his face. "Live quietly and normally, keep your mouths shut, never use the Horn, and we won't fucking kill you and everyone you love."

Bryce sat on the rolled arm of the couch. "Slay a few enemies, gain twice as many in return." Hunt grunted. She angled her head. "Why are your boots on?"

"Isaiah needs me at the Comitium. He's up to his neck in angels wanting to challenge his authority and needs backup." He arched a brow. "Want to come play Scary Asshole with me?"

Despite everything, despite the Asteri watching and all that had occurred, Bryce smiled. "I have just the outfit."

Bryce and Hunt made it two steps onto the roof before she caught the familiar scent. Peered over the edge and saw who ran down the street below. A glance at Hunt, and he swept her into his arms, flying her down to the sidewalk. She might have snuck a deep inhale of him, her nose grazing the strong column of his neck.

Hunt's caress down her spine a moment before he set her down told her he'd caught that little sniff. But then Bryce was standing before Ruhn. Before Fury and Tristan Flynn.

Fury barely gave her a moment before she leapt upon Bryce, hugging her so tightly her bones groaned. "You are one lucky idiot," Fury said, laughing softly. "And one smart bitch."

Bryce smiled, her laugh caught in her throat as Fury pulled away. But a thought struck her, and Bryce reached for her phone—no, it was left somewhere in this city. "Juniper—"

"She's safe. I'm going to check on her now." Fury squeezed her hand and then nodded to Hunt. "Well done, angel." And then her friend was sprinting off, blending into the night itself.

Bryce turned back to Ruhn and Flynn. The latter just gaped at her. But Bryce looked to her brother, wholly still and silent. His clothes torn enough to tell her that before the firstlight had healed everything, he'd been in bad shape. Had probably fought his way through this city.

Then Ruhn began babbling. "Tharion went off to help get the evacuees out of the Blue Court, and Amelie ran to the Den to make sure the pups were okay, but we were nearly . . . we were half a mile away when I heard the Moonwood Gate. Heard you talking through it, I mean. There were so many demons I couldn't get there, but then I heard Danika, and all that light erupted and . . ." He halted, swallowing hard. His blue eyes gleamed in the streetlights, dawn still far off. A breeze off the Istros ruffled his black hair. And it was the tears that filled his eyes, the wonder in them, that had Bryce launching forward. Had her throwing her arms around her brother and holding him tightly.

Ruhn didn't hesitate before his arms came around her. He shook so badly that she knew he was crying.

A scuff of steps told her Flynn was giving them privacy; a cedar-scented breeze flitting past suggested that Hunt had gone airborne to wait for her.

"I thought you were dead," Ruhn said, his voice shaking as much as his body. "Like ten fucking times, I thought you were dead."

She chuckled. "I'm glad to disappoint you."

"Shut up, Bryce." He scanned her face, his cheeks wet. "Are you . . . are you all right?"

"I don't know," she admitted. Concern flared in his face, but she didn't dare give any specifics, not after Rigelus's phone call. Not with all the cameras around. Ruhn gave her a knowing grimace. Yes, they'd talk about that strange, ancient starlight within her veins later. What it meant for both of them. "Thank you for coming for me."

"You're my sister." Ruhn didn't bother to keep his voice down. No, there was pride in his voice. And damn if that didn't hit her in the heart. "Of course I'd come to save your ass."

She punched his arm, but Ruhn's smile turned tentative. "Did you mean what you said to Athalar? About me?" *Tell Ruhn I forgive him.*

"Yes," she said without a moment of hesitation. "I meant all of it."

"Bryce." His face grew grave. "You really thought that I would care more about the Starborn shit than about *you*? You honestly think I care which one of us it is?"

"It's both of us," she said. "Those books you read said such things once happened."

"I don't give a shit," he said, smiling slightly. "I don't care if I'm called Prince or Starborn or the Chosen One or any of that." He grabbed her hand. "The only thing I want to be called right now is your brother." He added softly, "If you'll have me."

She winked, even as her heart tightened unbearably. "I'll think about it."

Ruhn grinned before his face turned grave once more. "You know the Autumn King will want to meet with you. Be ready."

"Doesn't getting a bunch of fancy-ass power mean I don't have to obey anyone? And just because I forgive you doesn't mean I forgive him." She would never do that.

"I know." Ruhn's eyes gleamed. "But you need to be on your guard."

She arched a brow, tucking away the warning, and said, "Hunt told me about the mind-reading." He'd mentioned it briefly—along with a recap of the Summit and everything that had gone down—on the walk up to the roof.

Ruhn glared at the adjacent rooftop where Hunt stood. "Athalar has a big fucking mouth."

One she'd like to put to good use on various parts of her body, she didn't say. She didn't need Ruhn puking on her clean clothes.

Ruhn went on, "And it's not mind-reading. Just . . . mind-talking. Telepathy."

"Does dear old Dad know?"

"No." And then her brother said into her head, *And I'd like to keep it that way.*

She started. *Creepy. Kindly stay the fuck out of my head, brother.*

Gladly. His phone rang, and he glanced at the screen before wincing. "I gotta take this."

Right, because they all had work to do to get this city to rights—starting with tending to the dead. The sheer number of Sailings would be . . . she didn't want to think about it.

Ruhn let the phone ring again. "Can I come over tomorrow?"

"Yes," she said, smirking. "I'll get your name added to the guest list."

"Yeah, yeah, you're a fucking hotshot." He rolled his eyes and answered the call. "Hey, Dec." He strode down the street to where Flynn waited, throwing Bryce a parting grin.

Bryce looked to the rooftop across the street. Where the angel still waited for her, a shadow against the night.

But no longer the Shadow of Death.

97

Hunt stayed at the Comitium barracks that night. Bryce had lost track of the hours they'd worked, first through the night, then into the cloudless day, and finally at sunset she'd been dragging so much that he'd ordered Naomi to fly her home. And presumably ordered her to stand watch, since a dark-winged figure still stood on the adjacent rooftop in the gray light before dawn, and a peek into Hunt's room revealed that his bed remained made.

But Bryce didn't dwell on all the work they'd done yesterday, or all that lay ahead. Reorganizing the city's leadership, Sailings for the dead, and waiting for the big announcement: which Archangel would be tapped by the Asteri to rule over Valbara.

Odds of them being decent were slim to none, but Bryce didn't dwell on that, either, as she slipped into the still-dim streets, Syrinx tugging on his leash as she tucked her new phone into her pocket. She'd defied the odds yesterday, so maybe the gods would throw them another bone and convince the Asteri to send someone who wasn't a psychopath.

At the very least, there would be no more death bargains for Hunt. Nothing more to *atone* for. No, he would be a free and true member of the triarii, if he wished. He had yet to decide.

Bryce waved to Naomi, and the angel waved back. She'd been too tired yesterday to object to having a guard, since Hunt didn't trust the Asteri, her father, or any other power brokers to stay the Hel away. After letting Syrinx do his business, she shook her head when the chimera made to turn back toward the apartment. "No breakfast yet, buddy," she said, aiming for the river.

Syrinx yowled with displeasure, but trotted along, sniffing at everything in his path until the broad band of the Istros appeared, its riverside walkway empty at this early hour. Tharion had called her yesterday, promising the River Queen's full support for any resources she needed.

Bryce hadn't the nerve to ask whether that support was due to her being the bastard daughter of the Autumn King, a Starborn Fae, or the bearer of Luna's Horn. Perhaps all of them.

Bryce settled onto one of the wooden benches along the quay, the Bone Quarter a swirling, misty wall across the water. The mer had come—had helped so many escape. Even the otters had grabbed the smallest of the city's residents and carried them down to the Blue Court. The House of Many Waters had risen to the occasion. The shifters had risen to it.

But the Fae . . . FiRo had sustained the least damage. The Fae had suffered the fewest casualties. It was no surprise, when their shields had been the first to go up. And had not opened to allow anyone inside.

Bryce blocked out the thought as Syrinx leapt onto the bench beside her, nails clicking on the wood, and plopped his furry butt next to hers. Bryce slid her phone from her pocket and wrote to Juniper, *Tell Madame Kyrah I'll be at her next dance class.*

June wrote back almost immediately. *The city was attacked and this is what you're thinking about?* A few seconds later she added, *But I will.*

Bryce smiled. For long minutes, she and Syrinx sat in silence, watching the light bleed to gray, then to the palest blue. And then a golden thread of light appeared along the Istros's calm surface.

Bryce unlocked her phone. And read Danika's final, happy messages one last time.

The light built on the river, gilding its surface.

Bryce's eyes stung as she smiled softly, then read through Connor's last words to her.

Message me when you're home safe.

Bryce began typing. The answer it had taken her two years, nearly to the day, to write.

I'm home.

She sent the message into the ether, willed it to find its way across the gilded river and to the misty isle beyond.

And then she deleted the thread. Deleted Danika's messages, too. Each swipe of her finger had her heart lightening, lifting with the rising sun.

When they were gone, when she had set them free, she stood, Syrinx leaping to the pavement beside her. She made to turn home, but a glimmer of light across the river caught her eye.

For a heartbeat, just one, the dawn parted the mists of the Bone Quarter. Revealing a grassy shore. Rolling, serene hills beyond. Not a land of stone and gloom, but of light and green. And standing on that lovely shore, smiling at her . . .

A gift from the Under-King for saving the city.

Tears began rolling down her face as she beheld the near-invisible figures. All six of them—the seventh gone forever, having yielded her eternity. But the tallest of them, standing in the middle with his hand lifted in greeting . . .

Bryce brought her hand to her mouth, blowing a gentle kiss.

As swiftly as they parted, the mists closed. But Bryce kept smiling, all the way back to the apartment. Her phone buzzed, and Hunt's message popped up. *I'm home. Where are you?*

She could barely type as Syrinx tugged her along. *Walking Syrinx. I'll be there in a minute.*

Good. I'm making breakfast.

Bryce's grin nearly split her face in two as she hurried her steps, Syrinx launching into a flat-out sprint. As if he, too, knew what awaited them. *Who* awaited them.

There was an angel in her apartment. Which meant it must be any gods-damned day of the week. Which meant she had joy in her heart, and her eyes set on the wide-open road ahead.

EPILOGUE

The white cat with eyes like blue opals sat on a bench in the Oracle's Park and licked his front paw.

"You know you're not a true cat, don't you?" Jesiba Roga clicked her tongue. "You don't need to lick yourself."

Aidas, Prince of the Chasm, lifted his head. "Who says I don't enjoy licking myself?"

Amusement tugged on Jesiba's thin mouth, but she shifted her stare to the quiet park, the towering cypresses still gleaming with dew. "Why didn't you tell me about Bryce?"

He flexed his claws. "I didn't trust anyone. Even you."

"I thought Theia's light was forever extinguished."

"So did I. I thought they'd made sure she and her power died on that last battlefield under Prince Pelias's blade." His eyes glowed with ancient rage. "But Bryce Quinlan bears her light."

"You can tell the difference between Bryce's starlight and her brother's?"

"I shall never forget the exact shine and hue of Theia's light. It is still a song in my blood."

Jesiba studied him for a long moment, then frowned. "And Hunt Athalar?"

Aidas fell silent as a petitioner stumbled past, hoping to beat the crowds that had filled the Oracle's Park and Luna's Temple since portals to his world had opened within the quartz Gates and the beasts of the Pit had taken full advantage of it. Any who had managed to return were currently being punished by one of Aidas's brothers. He would soon return to join them in it.

Aidas said at last, "I think Athalar's father would have been proud."

"Sentimental of you."

Aidas shrugged as best his feline body would allow. "Feel free to disagree, of course," he said, leaping off the bench. "You knew the male best." His whiskers twitched as he angled his head. "What of the library?"

"It has already been moved."

He knew better than to ask where she had hidden it. So he merely said, "Good."

Jesiba didn't speak again until the fifth Prince of Hel had stalked a few feet away. "Don't fuck us over this time, Aidas."

"I do not plan to," he said, fading into the space between realms, Hel a dark song beckoning him home. "Not when things are about to get so interesting."

ACKNOWLEDGMENTS

This book has been such a tremendous labor of love from the very start, and because of that, I have far too many people to thank than can possibly fit within these few pages, but I shall do my best! My endless gratitude and love to:

Noa Wheeler, editor extraordinaire. Noa, how can I even begin to thank you? You transformed this book into something I'm proud of, challenged me to be a better writer, and worked your ass off at every single stage. You are brilliant and just a joy to work with, and I'm so honored to call you my editor.

Tamar Rydzinski: Thank you for having my back through each step of this (long, long) journey. You are a badass *queen*.

To the entire team at Bloombury: Laura Keefe, Nicole Jarvis, Valentina Rice, Emily Fisher, Lucy Mackay-Sim, Rebecca McNally, Kathleen Farrar, Amanda Shipp, Emma Hopkin, Nicola Hill, Ros Ellis, Nigel Newton, Cindy Loh, Alona Fryman, Donna Gauthier, Erica Barmash, Faye Bi, Beth Eller, Jenny Collins, Phoebe Dyer, Lily Yengle, Frank Bumbalo, Donna Mark, John Candell, Yelena Safronova, Melissa Kavonic, Oona Patrick, Nick Sweeney, Diane Aronson, Kerry Johnson, Christine Ma, Bridget McCusker, Nicholas Church, Claire Henry, Elise Burns, Andrea Kearney, Maia Fjord, Laura Main Ellen, Sian Robertson, Emily Moran, Ian Lamb,

Emma Bradshaw, Fabia Ma, Grace Whooley, Alice Grigg, Joanna Everard, Jacqueline Sells, Tram-Anh Doan, Beatrice Cross, Jade Westwood, Cesca Hopwood, Jet Purdie, Saskia Dunn, Sonia Palmisano, Catriona Feeney, Hermione Davis, Hannah Temby, Grainne Reidy, Kate Sederstrom, Jennifer Gonzalez, Veronica Gonzalez, Elizabeth Tzetzo. It is a privilege to be published by you. Thank you for all of your support, and thank you especially to Kamilla Benko and Grace McNamee for their hard work on this book!

To my foreign publishers: Record, Egmont Bulgaria, Albatros, DTV, Konyvmolykepzo, Mondadori, De Boekerij, Foksal, Azbooka Atticus, Slovart, Alfaguara, and Dogan Egmont. Thank you so much for bringing my books to your countries and to your amazing readers!

A giant hug and round of applause for Elizabeth Evans, the audiobook narrator who so faithfully and lovingly brings my characters to life. It's a delight and privilege to work with you!

Thank you to the incredibly talented Carlos Quevedo for the cover artwork that so perfectly captured the spirit of this book, and to Virginia Allyn, for her fantastic map of the city!

I literally would not have gotten through writing this book without my friends and family.

So thank you from the bottom of my heart to J. R. Ward, for sharing your wisdom when I needed it most, for your unbelievable kindness, and for being an inspiration to me (and not minding that we both have a Ruhn!).

To Lynette Noni: You are the actual best. The BEST. Your clever feedback, your generosity, your general awesomeness—girl, I love you something fierce.

Jenn Kelly, I don't know what I would do without you. You have become a part of my family, and I am grateful for you every day! To Steph Brown, my dear friend, fellow hockey fan, and the person who never fails to make me laugh—I adore you.

Thank you to Julie Eshbaugh, Elle Kennedy, Alice Fanchiang, Louisse Ang, Laura Ashforth, and Jennifer Armentrout, for being true rays of light in my life. As always: thank you, Cassie Homer, for everything! A massive hug and thank-you to Jillian Stein, for all your help. A heartfelt thank-you to the immensely talented and cool Qusai Akoud, for your kickass vision and unparalleled website-building skills. And a *huge* thank-you to Danielle Jensen for reading and providing such vital feedback!

Endless gratitude to my family (both by birth and through marriage!) for their support and unwavering love. (And to Linda, who prefers chocolate croissants on her birthday.)

To my brilliant, lovely, and marvelous readers: How can I begin to thank you? You guys are the reason I do this, the reason I get out of bed each morning excited to write. I will never stop being grateful for each and every one of you.

To Annie, who sat by my side/at my feet/in my lap while I worked on this book for years, and served as the inspiration for Syrinx in so many ways. I love you forever and ever, babypup.

To Josh: I don't think I can convey everything I feel for you even if I had another 800 pages to write it out. You are my best friend, my soul mate, and the reason I can write about true love. You held me together this past year, walking alongside me through some of the hardest moments I've ever encountered, and I have no words for what that means to me. The luckiest day of my life was the one when I met you, and I am so blessed to have you as my husband—and as such a wonderful father to our son.

And lastly, to Taran: You truly are the brightest star in my sky. When things were hard, when things were dark, it was you I'd think about—your smile, your laugh, your beautiful face—and it carried me through. You probably won't read this for a long, long while, but know that you give me purpose, and motivation, and joy—so much joy that my heart is full to bursting every single day. I love you, I love you, I love you, and I will always be so proud to be your mom.

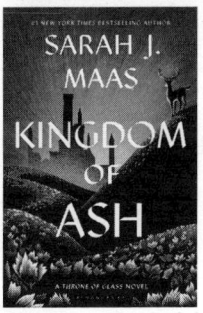

CRESCENT CITY

HOUSE
of
SKY
and
BREATH

Books by Sarah J. Maas

The Throne of Glass series

The Assassin's Blade
Throne of Glass
Crown of Midnight
Heir of Fire
Queen of Shadows
Empire of Storms
Tower of Dawn
Kingdom of Ash
•
The Throne of Glass Coloring Book

The Court of Thorns and Roses series

A Court of Thorns and Roses
A Court of Mist and Fury
A Court of Wings and Ruin
A Court of Frost and Starlight
A Court of Silver Flames
•
A Court of Thorns and Roses Coloring Book

The Crescent City series

House of Earth and Blood
House of Sky and Breath
House of Flame and Shadow

CRESCENT CITY

HOUSE of SKY and BREATH

SARAH J. MAAS

BLOOMSBURY PUBLISHING
NEW YORK • LONDON • OXFORD • NEW DELHI • SYDNEY

BLOOMSBURY PUBLISHING
Bloomsbury Publishing Inc.
1385 Broadway, New York, NY 10018, USA
29 Earlsfort Terrace, Dublin 2, Ireland

BLOOMSBURY, BLOOMSBURY PUBLISHING, and the Diana logo are trademarks of Bloomsbury Publishing Plc

First published in the United States 2022

Map by Virginia Allyn
Endpapers and interior art by Carlos Quevedo

ISBN: HB: 978-1-63557-407-4; eBook 978-1-63557-408-1
Special editions: 978-1-63557-942-0; 978-1-63557-941-3; 978-1-63557-943-7; 978-1-63557-944-4; 978-1-63557-945-1; 978-1-63557-946-8; 978-1-63557-947-5; 978-1-63557-948-2

Library of Congress Cataloging-in-Publication Data is available

6 8 10 9 7

Typeset by Westchester Publishing Services
Printed and bound in Great Britain by CPI (UK) Ltd, Croydon CR0 4YY

To find out more about our authors and books visit www.bloomsbury.com and sign up for our newsletters, including news about Sarah J. Maas.

Bloomsbury books may be purchased for business or promotional use. For information on bulk purchases please contact Macmillan Corporate and Premium Sales Department at specialmarkets@macmillan.com.

For Robin Rue,
fearless agent and true friend

LUNATHION

CRESCENT CITY

THE ANGELS' GATE

CENTRAL BUSINESS DISTRICT

THE MEAT MARKET

THE MERCHANTS' GATE

WESTERN ROAD

ISTROS RIVER

Northern Road
City Wall
The Mortal Gate
Asphodel Meadows
Main Street
Urd's Temple
The White Raven
Archer Street
Eastern Road
The Rose Gate
The Comitium
Ward Ave
Oracle's Park
Luna's Temple
Ruhn's House
Five Roses
The Astronomer
The Old Square
Central Avenue
The Autumn King's Villa
Mugin & Hugin
Lethe
The Archives
Crescent City Ballet
Bryce's Apartment
Laurel Avenue
The Heart Gate
Moonwood Avenue
Crone Street
Wolves' Den
Bryce's Old House
Griffin Antiquities
Aux Training Center
Moonwood
Shooting Range
Black Dock
The River Gate
The bone gates
Istros River
Blue Court
The Dead Gate
The Bone Quarter
City Wall
Southern Road

THE FOUR HOUSES OF MIDGARD

As decreed in 33 V.E. by the Imperial Senate in the Eternal City

HOUSE OF EARTH AND BLOOD

Shifters, humans, witches, ordinary animals, and many others to whom Cthona calls, as well as some chosen by Luna

HOUSE OF SKY AND BREATH

Malakim (angels), Fae, elementals, sprites,* and those who are blessed by Solas, along with some favored by Luna

HOUSE OF MANY WATERS

River-spirits, mer, water beasts, nymphs, kelpies, nøkks, and others watched over by Ogenas

HOUSE OF FLAME AND SHADOW

Daemonaki, Reapers, wraiths, vampyrs, draki, dragons, necromancers, and many wicked and unnamed things that even Urd herself cannot see

**Sprites were kicked out of their House as a result of their participation in the Fall, and are now considered Lowers, though many of them refuse to accept this.*

PROLOGUE

Sofie had survived in the Kavalla death camp for two weeks.

Two weeks, and still the guards—dreadwolves, all of them—had not sniffed her out. Everything had gone according to plan. The reek of the days crammed into the cattle car had covered the telltale scent in her blood. It had also veiled her when they'd marched her and the others between the brick buildings of the camp, this new Hel that was only a small model of what the Asteri planned to do if the war continued.

Two weeks here, and that reek had become etched into her very skin, blinding even the wolves' keen noses. She'd stood mere feet from a guard in the breakfast line this morning and he hadn't so much as sniffed in her direction.

A small victory. One she'd gladly take these days.

Half of the Ophion rebel bases had fallen. More would soon. But only two places existed for her now: here, and the port of Servast, her destination tonight. Alone, even on foot, she could have easily made it. A rare benefit of being able to switch between human and Vanir identities—and of being a rare human who'd made the Drop.

It technically made her Vanir. Granted her a long life span and all the benefits that came from it that her human family did not and would never have. She might not have bothered to make the Drop had her parents not encouraged it—with the healing abilities she would gain, it provided extra armor in a world designed to kill her kind. So she'd done it under the radar, in a back-alley, highly illegal Drop center, where a leering satyr had been her Anchor, and handing over her firstlight had been the cost of the ritual. She'd spent the years since then learning to wear her humanity like a cloak, inside and out. She might have all the traits of the Vanir, but she'd never *be* Vanir. Not in her heart, her soul.

Yet tonight . . . tonight, Sofie did not mind letting a little of the monster loose.

It would not be an easy journey, thanks to the dozen small forms crouched behind her in the mud before the barbed-wire fence.

Five boys and six girls gathered by her thirteen-year-old brother, who now stood watch over them like a shepherd with his flock. Emile had gotten all of them out of the bunks, aided by a gentle human sun-priest, who was currently serving as lookout at the shed ten yards away.

The children were gray-skinned, gaunt. Eyes too big, too hopeless.

Sofie didn't need to know their stories. They were likely the same as hers: rebel human parents who'd either been caught or sold out. Hers had been the latter.

Pure dumb luck had kept Sofie out of the dreadwolves' clutches, too—at least until now. Three years ago, she'd been studying late at the university library with her friends. Arriving home after midnight, she'd spied the broken windows and shattered front door, the spray paint on the siding of their ordinary suburban house—*REBEL SHITS*—and begun running. She could only credit Urd for the fact that the dreadwolf guard posted at the front door hadn't seen her.

Later, she'd managed to confirm that her parents were dead. Tortured until the brutal end by the Hind or her elite squadron of dreadwolf interrogators. The report Sofie spent months working her way up through Ophion to attain had also revealed that her grandparents had been herded off upon reaching the Bracchus camp in the north, and shot in a lineup of other elders, their bodies left to crumple into a mass grave.

And her brother . . . Sofie hadn't been able to find anything on

Emile until now. For years, she'd been working with the Ophion rebels in exchange for any snippet of information about him, about her family. She didn't let herself think about what she'd done in return for that information. The spying, the people she'd killed to collect whatever intel Ophion wanted—these things weighed on her soul like a leaden cloak.

But she'd finally done enough for Ophion that they'd informed her Emile had been sent here, and survived against all odds. At last, she had a location for him. Convincing Command to let her come here . . . that had been another labyrinth to navigate.

In the end, it had required Pippa's support. Command listened to Pippa, their faithful and fervent soldier, leader of the elite Lightfall unit. Especially now that Ophion's numbers had taken such steep hits. Sort-of-human Sofie, on the other hand . . . She knew she was an asset, but with the Vanir blood in her veins, they'd never fully trust her. So she occasionally needed Pippa. Just as much as Pippa's Lightfall missions had needed Sofie's powers.

Pippa's help hadn't been due to friendship. Sofie was fairly certain that friends didn't exist within the Ophion rebel network. But Pippa was an opportunist—and she knew what she stood to gain should this op go smoothly, the doors that would further open to her within Command if Sofie returned triumphant.

A week after Command had approved the plan, over three years after her family had been snatched from their home, Sofie walked into Kavalla.

She'd waited until a local dreadwolf patrol was marching by and stumbled into their path, a mere mile from here. They immediately found the fake rebel documents she'd planted in her coat. They had no idea that Sofie also carried with her, hidden in her head, information that could very well be the final piece of this war against the Asteri.

The blow that could end it.

Ophion had found out too late that before she'd gone into Kavalla, she'd finally accomplished the mission she'd spent years preparing for. She'd made sure before she was picked up that Pippa and Ophion knew she'd acquired that intel. Now they wouldn't back out of their promises to retrieve her and Emile. She knew there would be Hel to pay for it—that she'd gone in secret to gather the information, and was now using it as collateral.

But that would come later.

The dreadwolf patrol interrogated her for two days. Two days, and then they'd thrown her into the cattle car with the others, convinced she was a foolish human girl who'd been given the documents by a lover who'd used her.

She'd never thought her minor in theater would come in handy. That she'd hear her favorite professor's voice critiquing her performance while someone was ripping out her fingernails. That she'd feign a confession with all the sincerity she'd once brought to the stage.

She wondered if Command knew she'd used those acting abilities on them, too.

That wasn't her concern, either. At least, not until tomorrow. Tonight, all that mattered was the desperate plan that would now come to fruition. If she had not been betrayed, if Command had not realized the truth, then a boat waited twenty miles away to ferry them out of Pangera. She looked down at the children around her and prayed the boat had room for more than the three passengers she'd claimed would be arriving.

She'd spent her first week and a half in Kavalla waiting for a glimpse of her brother—a hint of where he might be in the sprawling camp. And then, a few days ago, she'd spotted him in the food line. She'd faked a stumble to cover her shock and joy and sorrow.

He'd gotten so tall. As tall as their father. He was all gangly limbs and bones, a far cry from the healthy thirteen-year-old he should have been, but his face . . . it was the face she'd grown up with. But beginning to show the first hints of manhood on the horizon.

Tonight, she'd seized her chance to sneak into his bunk. And despite the three years and the countless miseries they'd endured, he knew her in an instant, too. Sofie would have spirited him away that moment had he not begged her to bring the others.

Now twelve children crouched behind her.

The alarms would be blaring soon. They had different sirens

for everything here, she'd learned. To signal their wake-ups, their meals, random inspections.

A mournful bird's call fluttered through the low-hanging mist. *All clear.*

With a silent prayer of thanks to the sun-priest and the god he served, Sofie lifted her mangled hand to the electrified fence. She did not glance at her missing fingernails, or the welts, or even feel how numb and stiff her hands were, not as the fence's power crackled through her.

Through her, into her, *becoming* her. Becoming hers to use as she wished.

A thought, and the fence's power turned outward again, her fingertips sparking where they curled against the metal. The metal turned orange, then red beneath her hand.

She sliced her palm down, skin so blisteringly hot it cleaved metal and wire. Emile whispered to the others to keep them from crying out, but she heard one of the boys murmur, "*Witch.*"

A typical human's fear of those with Vanir gifts—of the females who held such tremendous power. She did not turn to tell him that it was not a witch's power that flowed through her. It was something far more rare.

The cold earth met her hand as she rent the last of the fence and peeled the two flaps apart, barely wide enough for her to fit through. The children edged forward, but she signaled for them to halt, scanning the open dirt beyond. The road separating the camp from the ferns and towering pines lay empty.

But the threat would come from behind. She pivoted toward the watchtowers at the corners of the camp, which housed guards with sniper rifles forever trained on the road.

Sofie took a breath, and the power she'd sucked from the fence again shuddered through her. Across the camp, the spotlights ruptured in a shower of sparks that had the guards whirling toward it, shouting.

Sofie peeled the fence apart wider, arms straining, metal biting into her palms, grunting at the children to *run, run, run*—

Little shadows, their light gray uniforms tattered and stained and too bright in the near-full moon, hurried through the fence and across the muddy road to the dense ferns and steep gully beyond. Emile went last, his taller, bony body still a shock to her system, as brutal as any power she could wield.

Sofie did not let herself think of it. She raced after him, weak from the lack of food, the grueling labor, the soul-draining misery of this place. Mud and rocks cut into her bare feet, but the pain was distant as she took in the dozen pale faces peering from the ferns. "*Hurry, hurry, hurry,*" she whispered.

The van would wait only so long.

One of the girls swayed as she got to her feet, aiming for the slope beyond, but Sofie gripped her beneath a bony shoulder, keeping her upright as they staggered along, ferns brushing their legs, roots tangling their feet. Faster. They had to be *faster*—

A siren wailed.

This one, Sofie had not heard before. But she knew its blaring screech for what it was: *Escape*.

Flashlight beams shot through the trees as Sofie and the children crested the lip of a hill, half falling into the fern-laden gully. The dreadwolves were in their humanoid forms, then. Good—their eyes weren't as sharp in the dark this way. Bad, because it meant they carried guns.

Sofie's breathing hitched, but she focused, and sent her power slicing behind her. The flashlights went dark. Even firstlight could not stand against her power. Shouting rose—male, vicious.

Sofie hurried to the front of the group and Emile fell to the back to make sure none were forgotten. Pride swelled in her chest, even as it mingled with terror.

She knew they'd never make it back to the camp alive if they were caught.

Thighs burning, Sofie sprinted up the steep side of the gully. She didn't want to think what the children were enduring, not when their knobbly-kneed legs looked barely able to hold them up. They reached the top of the hill just as the dreadwolves howled, an inhuman sound breaking from humanoid throats. A summons to the hunt.

She pushed the children faster. Mist and ferns and trees and stones—

When one of the boys collapsed, Sofie carried him, focusing on the too-delicate hands gripping the front of her shift.

Hurry, hurry, hurry—

And then there was the road, and the van. Agent Silverbow had waited.

She didn't know his real name. Had refused to let him tell her, though she had a good idea of what—who—he was. But he'd always be Silver to her. And he had waited.

He'd said he wouldn't. Had said Ophion would kill him for abandoning his current mission. *Pippa* would kill him. Or order one of her Lightfall soldiers to do it.

But he'd come with Sofie, had hidden out these two weeks, until Sofie had sent forth the ripple of firstlight last night—the one signal she'd dared make with the Vanir prowling the death camp—to tell him to be here in twenty-four hours.

She'd told him not to use his powers. Even if it would've made this far safer and easier, it would have drained him too much for the escape. And she needed him at full strength now.

In the moonlight, Silver's face was pale above the imperial uniform he'd stolen, his hair slicked back like any preening officer. He grimaced at Emile, then at the eleven other kids—clearly calculating how many could fit into the nondescript white van.

"All," Sofie said as she hurtled for the vehicle, her voice raw. "All, Silver."

He understood. He'd always understood her.

He leapt out of the car with preternatural grace and opened the rear doors. A minute later, squeezed against Silver in the front of the van, his warmth heating her through her threadbare clothes, Sofie could hardly draw breath fast enough as he floored the gas pedal. His thumb brushed over her shoulder, again and again, as if reassuring himself that she was there, that she'd made it.

None of the children spoke. None of them cried.

As the van barreled into the night, Sofie found herself wondering if they still could.

It took them thirty minutes to reach the port city of Servast.

Sofie leaned on Silver, who saw to it, even while racing down the bumpy, winding country road, that the children found the food in the bags he'd stashed in the back. Only enough for three, but the children knew how to stretch a scant spread. He made sure Sofie ate, too. Two weeks in that camp had nearly wrecked her. She didn't understand how these children had survived months. Years. Her brother had survived *three years*.

Silver said quietly as they rounded a sharp curve, "The Hind is close by. I received a report this morning that she was in Alcene." A small city not two hours away—one of the vital depots along the Spine, the north-south network of train tracks that provided ammo and supplies to the imperial troops. "Our spies indicated she was headed this way."

Sofie's stomach tightened, but she focused on donning the clothes and shoes Silver had brought for her to change into. "Then let's hope we make it to the coast before she does."

His throat bobbed. She dared ask, "Pippa?"

A muscle ticked in his jaw. He and Pippa had been jockeying for a promotion into Command's inner ranks for years now. *A crazed fanatic*, Silver had called Pippa on more than one occasion, usually after her Lightfall squadron had led a brutal attack that left no survivors. But Sofie understood Pippa's devotion—she herself had grown up passing as fully human, after all. Had learned exactly how they were treated—how Pippa had likely been treated by the Vanir her entire life. Some things, some experiences, Silver could never understand.

Silver said, "No word yet. She'd better be where she promised to be." Disapproval and distrust laced every word.

Sofie said nothing else as they drove. She wouldn't tell him the details of the intelligence she'd gathered, for all that he had done and meant to her, despite the silent hours spent together, bodies and souls merging. She wouldn't tell anyone—not until Command came through on their promises.

The Asteri had probably realized what she'd discovered. They'd no doubt sent the Hind after her to stop her from telling anyone else.

But the more immediate threat came from the dreadwolves closing in with every mile they hurried toward Servast, hounds on a scent. Silver's frequent glances in the rearview mirror told her that he knew it, too.

The two of them could take on perhaps a handful of wolf shifters—they'd done so before. But there would be more than a handful for an escape from Kavalla. Far more than they could face and live.

She'd prepared for that eventuality. Had already handed over her comm-crystal to Command before entering Kavalla. That precious, sole line of communication to their most valued spy. She knew they'd keep the small chunk of quartz safe. Just as Silver would keep Emile safe. He'd given her his word.

When they emerged from the van, mist wreathed the narrow docks of Servast, writhing over the chill, night-dark waters of the Haldren Sea. It wended around the ancient stone houses of the port town, the firstlight in the few lampposts above the cobblestone streets flickering. No lights shone behind the shuttered windows; not one car or pedestrian moved in the deep shadows and fog.

It was as if the streets of Servast had been emptied in advance of their arrival. As if its citizens—mostly poor fisher-folk, both human and Vanir allied with the House of Many Waters—had hunkered down, some instinct bleating that the fog was not to be braved. Not this night.

Not with dreadwolves on the prowl.

Silver led the way, hair peeking from beneath the cap he'd donned, his attention darting this way and that, his gun within easy reach at his side. She'd seen him kill efficiently with his power, but sometimes a gun was easier.

Emile kept close to Sofie as they crept down the age-worn

streets, through the empty markets. She could feel eyes on her from behind the closed shutters. But no one opened a door to offer help.

Sofie didn't care. As long as that boat waited where she'd been told it would be, the world could go to Hel.

Mercifully, the *Bodegraven* was idling at the end of a long wooden dock three blocks ahead, silver letters bright against her black hull. A few firstlights glowed in the small steamer's port-holes, but the decks remained quiet. Emile gasped, as if it were a vision from Luna.

Sofie prayed the other Ophion boats would be waiting beyond the harbor to provide backup, exactly as Command had promised in return for the valuable asset she'd gone into the camp to retrieve. They hadn't cared that the valuable asset was her brother. Only what she told them he could do.

She scanned the streets, the docks, the skies.

The power in her veins thrummed in time to her heart. A counter-beat. A bone-drum, a death knell. A warning.

They had to go *now*.

She started, but Silver's broad hand clamped on her shoulder.

"They're here," he said in his northern accent. With his sharp senses, he could detect the wolves better than she could.

Sofie surveyed the sloping rooftops, the cobblestones, the fog. "How close?"

Dread filled Silver's handsome face. "Everywhere. They're fucking everywhere."

Only three blocks separated them from salvation. Shouts echoed off the stones a block away. "*There! There!*"

One heartbeat to decide. One heartbeat—Emile halted, fear bright in his dark eyes.

No more fear. No more pain.

Sofie hissed at Silver, "*Run.*" Silver reached for his gun, but she shoved his hand down, getting in his face. "Get the kids to the boat and go. I'll hold the wolves off and meet you there."

Some of the children were already bolting for the dock. Emile waited. "Run!" she told Silver again. He touched her cheek—the softest of caresses—and sprinted after the children, roaring for the captain to rev the engines. None of them would survive if they didn't depart now.

She whirled to Emile. "Get on that boat."

His eyes—their mother's eyes—widened. "But how will you—"

"I promise I will find you again, Emile. Remember all I told you. *Go.*"

When she embraced his lanky, bony body, she let herself inhale one breath of his scent, the one that lay beneath the acrid layers of dirt and waste from the camp. Then Emile staggered away, half tripping over himself as he marked the lingering power building at her fingertips.

But her brother said softly, "*Make them pay.*"

She closed her eyes, readying herself. Gathering her power. Lights went out on the block around her. When she opened her eyes to the newfound darkness, Emile had reached the dock. Silver waited at the ramp, beckoning beneath the one streetlight that remained lit. Her stare met Silver's.

She nodded once—hoping it conveyed all that was within her heart—and aimed for the dreadwolves' howls.

Sofie sprinted right into the golden beams of the headlights of four cars emblazoned with the Asteri's symbol: *SPQM* and its wreath of seven stars. All crammed full of dreadwolves in imperial uniforms, guns out.

Sofie instantly spied the golden-haired female lounging in the front of the military convertible. A silver torque glimmered against her neck.

The Hind.

The deer shifter had two snipers poised beside her in the open-air car, rifles trained on Sofie. Even in the darkness, Lidia Cervos's hair shimmered, her beautiful face passive and cold. Amber eyes fixed on Sofie, lit with smug amusement. Triumph.

Sofie whipped around a corner before their shots cracked like thunder. The snarl of the Hind's dreadwolves rumbled in the mist behind her as she charged into Servast proper, away from the harbor. From that ship and the children. From Emile.

Silver couldn't use his power to get her. He had no idea where she was.

Sofie's breath sawed out of her chest as she sprinted down the empty, murky streets. A blast from the boat's horn blared through the misty night, as if pleading with her to hurry.

In answer, half a dozen unearthly howls rose up behind her. All closing in.

Some had taken their wolf form, then.

Claws thundered against the pavement nearby, and Sofie gritted her teeth, cutting down another alley, heading for the one place all the maps she'd studied suggested she might stand a chance. The ship's horn blasted again, a final warning that it would leave.

If she could only make it a bit deeper into the city—a bit deeper—

Fangs gnashed behind her.

Keep moving. Not only away from the Vanir on her tail, but from the snipers on the ground, waiting for the open shot. From the Hind, who must know what information Sofie bore. Sofie supposed she should be flattered the Hind herself had come to oversee this.

The small market square appeared ahead, and Sofie barreled for the fountain in its center, punching a line of her power straight for it, shearing through rock and metal until water sprayed, a geyser coating the market square. Wolves splashed into the water as they surged from the surrounding streets, shifting as they cornered her.

In the center of the flooded square, Sofie paused.

The wolves in human forms wore imperial uniforms. Tiny silver darts glimmered along their collars. A dart for every rebel spy broken. Her stomach flipped. Only one type of dreadwolf had those silver darts. The Hind's private guard. The most elite of the shifters.

A throaty whistle sounded through the port. A warning and a farewell.

So Sofie leapt onto the lip of the fountain and smiled at the wolves closing in. They wouldn't kill her. Not when the Hind was waiting to interrogate her. Too bad they didn't know what Sofie truly was. Not a human, nor a witch.

She let the power she'd gathered by the docks unspool.

Crackling energy curled at her fingertips and amid the strands of her short brown hair. One of the dreadwolves understood then—matched what he was seeing with the myths Vanir whispered to their children.

"*She's a fucking thunderbird!*" the wolf roared—just as Sofie unleashed the power she'd gathered on the water flooding the square. On the dreadwolves standing ankle-deep in it.

They didn't stand a chance.

Sofie pivoted toward the docks as the electricity finished slithering over the stones, hardly sparing a glance for the smoking, half-submerged carcasses. The silver darts along their collars glowed molten-hot.

Another whistle. She could still make it.

Sofie splashed through the flooded square, breath ragged in her throat.

The dreadwolf had been only half-right. She was part thunderbird—her great-grandmother had mated with a human long ago, before being executed. The gift, more legend than truth these days, had resurfaced in Sofie.

It was why the rebels had wanted her so badly, why they'd sent her out on such dangerous missions. Why Pippa had come to value her. Sofie smelled like and could pass for a human, but in her veins lurked an ability that could kill in an instant. The Asteri had long ago hunted most thunderbirds to extinction. She'd never learned how her great-grandmother had survived, but the descendants had kept the bloodline secret. *She* had kept it secret.

Until that day three years ago when her family had been killed and taken. When she'd found the nearest Ophion base and showed them exactly what she could do. When she told them what she wanted them to do for her in exchange.

She hated them. Almost as much as she hated the Asteri and the world they'd built. For three years, Ophion had dangled Emile's whereabouts above her, promising to find him, to help her free him, if she could do *one more mission*. Pippa and Silver might believe in the cause, though they differed in their methods of how to fight for it, but Emile had always been Sofie's cause. A free world would be wonderful. But what did it matter if she had no family to share it with?

So many times, for those rebels, she had drawn up power from the grid, from lights and machines, and killed and killed, until her soul lay in tatters. She'd often debated going rogue and finding her brother herself, but she was no spy. She had no network. So she'd stayed, and covertly built up her own bait to dangle before Ophion. Made sure they knew the importance of what she'd gleaned before she entered Kavalla.

Faster, faster she pushed herself toward the dock. If she didn't make it, maybe there would be a smaller boat that she could take to the steamer. Maybe she'd just swim until she was close enough for Silver to spot her, and easily reach her with his power.

Half-crumbling houses and uneven streets passed; fog drifted in veils.

The stretch of wooden dock between Sofie and the steamer pulling away lay clear. She raced for it.

She could make out Silver on the *Bodegraven*'s deck, monitoring her approach. But why didn't he use his power to reach her? Another few feet closer, and she spied the hand pressed to his bleeding shoulder.

Cthona have mercy on him. Silver didn't appear badly hurt, but she had a feeling she knew what kind of bullet he'd been hit with. A bullet with a core of gorsian stone—one that would stifle magic.

His power was useless. But if a sniper had hit Silver on the ship . . . Sofie drew up short.

The convertible sat in the shadows of the building across from the docks. The Hind still lounged like a queen, a sniper beside her with his rifle trained on Sofie. Where the second had gone, she didn't know. Only this one mattered. This one, and his rifle.

It was likely chock-full of gorsian bullets. They'd bring her down in seconds.

The Hind's golden eyes glowed like coals in the dimness. Sofie gauged the distance to the end of the dock, the rope Silver had thrown down, trailing with every inch the *Bodegraven* chugged toward the open water.

The Hind inclined her head in challenge. A deceptively calm voice slid from between her red lips. "Are you faster than a bullet, thunderbird?"

Sofie didn't wait to banter. As swift as a wind through the fjords of her native land, she hurtled down the dock. She knew the sniper's rifle tracked her.

The end of the dock, the dark harbor beyond, loomed.

The rifle cracked.

Silver's roar cleaved the night before Sofie hit the wood planks, splinters cutting into her face, the impact ricocheting through one eye. Pain burst through her right thigh, leaving a wake of shredded flesh and shattered bone, so violent it robbed even the scream from her lungs.

Silver's bellow stopped abruptly—and then he yelled to the captain, "*Go, go, go, go!*"

Facedown on the dock, Sofie knew it was bad. She lifted her head, swallowing her shriek of pain, blood leaking from her nose. The droning hum of an Omega-boat's energy rocked through her even before she spied the approaching lights beneath the harbor's surface.

Four imperial submersible warships converged like sharks on the *Bodegraven*.

Pippa Spetsos stood aboard the rebel ship *Orrae*, the Haldren Sea a dark expanse around her. In the distance, the firstlights of the towns along Pangera's northern coast twinkled like gold stars.

But her attention remained fixed on the gleam of Servast. On the little light sailing toward them.

The *Bodegraven* was on time.

Pippa pressed a hand against the cold, hard armor covering her breast, right above the sinking sun insignia of the Lightfall unit. She would not loose that final breath of relief—not until she saw Sofie. Until she'd secured the assets Sofie carried with her: the boy and the intel.

Then she'd demonstrate to Sofie precisely how Command felt about being manipulated.

Agent Silverbow, the arrogant bastard, had followed the woman he loved. She knew the asset Sofie brought with her meant little to him. The fool. But the possibility of the intel that Sofie claimed to have spent years covertly gathering for Ophion . . . even Silverbow would want that.

Captain Richmond stepped up beside her. "Report," she ordered.

He'd learned the hard way not to disobey her. Learned exactly who in Command supported her, and would rain down Hel on her behalf. Monitoring the approaching vessel, Richmond said, "We've made radio contact. Your operative is not on that ship."

Pippa went still. "The brother?"

"The boy is there. And eleven other children from Kavalla. Sofie Renast stayed behind to buy them time. I'm sorry."

Sorry. Pippa had lost track of how many times she'd heard that fucking word.

But right now . . . Emile had made it to the ship. Was gaining him worth losing Sofie?

It was the gamble they'd taken in even allowing Sofie to go into Kavalla: possibly losing one valuable asset in the quest to seize another. But that was before Sofie had left—and then informed them, right before entering the camp, that she'd attained vital intel on their enemies. To lose Sofie now, with that crucial intel on the line . . .

She hissed at the captain, "I want—"

A human sailor barreled out the glass-enclosed bridge door, skin eerily pale in the moonlight. He faced the captain, then Pippa, uncertain whom to report to. "The *Bodegraven*'s got four Omegas on her tail, closing in fast. Agent Silverbow is down—gorsian bullet to the shoulder."

Pippa's blood chilled. Silverbow wouldn't be any help with a gorsian bullet in him. "They're going to sink that ship, rather than let those children go."

She had not yet become so numb to the horrors of this world that it didn't roil her stomach. Captain Richmond swore softly.

Pippa ordered, "Prepare the gunners." Even if the odds were slim that *they* would survive an assault by the Omegas, they could provide a distraction. The captain grunted his agreement. But the sailor who'd come rushing out of the bridge gasped and pointed.

On the horizon, each and every light in Servast was winking out. The wave of darkness swept inland.

"What in Hel—"

"Not Hel," Pippa murmured as the blackout spread.

Sofie. Or . . . Her eyes narrowed on the *Bodegraven*.

Pippa ran for the bridge's better view. She arrived, panting, Richmond beside her, in time to see the *Bodegraven* racing for them—the submerged lights of the four Omega-boats flickering behind, closing in.

But as they did, a mighty white light soared beneath the surface. It wrapped its long arms around the nearest Omega.

The white light leapt away a moment later, flying for the next boat. No submersible lights glowed in its wake. On the radar before her, the Omega-boat vanished.

"Holy gods," Richmond said.

Something like that, Pippa wanted to say. It was Sofie's strange gift: not only electricity, but firstlight power, too. Energy of any type was hers to command, to suck into herself. Her kind had been hunted to extinction by the Asteri centuries ago because of that mighty, unconquerable gift—or so it had seemed.

But now there were two of them.

Sofie said her brother's powers dwarfed her own. Powers Pippa now witnessed as the light leapt from the second boat—another blackout—and raced for the third.

She could make out no sign of Emile on the *Bodegraven*'s deck, but he had to be there.

"What can bring down an Omega with no torpedoes?" murmured one of the sailors. Closer now, the light swept beneath the surface for the third boat, and even with the distance, Pippa could see the core of long, bright white tendrils streaming from it—like wings.

"An angel?" someone whispered. Pippa scoffed privately. There were no angels among the few Vanir in Ophion. If Pippa had her way, there'd be no Vanir among them at all . . . save for ones like this. Vanir powers, but a human soul and body.

Emile was a great prize for the rebellion—Command would be pleased indeed.

The third Omega submersible went black, vanishing into the inky deep. Pippa's blood sang at the terrible glory of it. Only one Omega left.

"Come on," Pippa breathed. "Come on . . ." Too much rested on that boat. The balance of this war might hang on it.

"Two brimstone torpedoes fired from the remaining Omega," a sailor shouted.

But the white light slammed into the Omega, miles' worth of first-light sending the final ship spiraling into a watery abyss.

And then a leap outward, a whip of light illuminating the waves above it to turquoise. A stretching hand.

A sailor reported hoarsely, awe and anticipation in every word, "Brimstone torpedoes are gone from the radar. Vanished."

Only the lights of the *Bodegraven* remained, like dim stars in a sea of darkness.

"Commander Spetsos?" Richmond asked.

But Pippa ignored Richmond, and stalked into the warmth of the bridge's interior, yanking a pair of long-range binoculars from a hook just inside the door. Within seconds, she was out on the wind-whipped deck again, binoculars focused on the *Bodegraven*.

Emile stood there, aged but definitely the same child from Sofie's photos, no more than a lean figure alone at the prow. Staring toward the watery graveyard as they passed over it. Then to the land beyond. He slowly sank to his knees.

Smiling to herself, Pippa shifted the view on the binoculars and gazed toward the thorough blackness of Pangera.

Lying on her side, the lap of waves against the quay and the drip of her blood on the surface beneath the wooden slats the only sounds she could hear, Sofie waited to die.

Her arm dangled off the end of the dock as the *Bodegraven* sailed toward those savior lights on the sea. Toward Pippa. Pippa had brought battleships to guide the *Bodegraven* to safety. Likely to ensure Sofie was on it, along with Emile, but . . . Pippa had still come. Ophion had come.

Tears slid along her cheeks, onto the wood slats. Everything hurt.

She'd known this would happen, if she pushed too far, demanded too much power, as she had tonight. The firstlight always hurt so much worse than electricity. Charred her insides even as it left her craving more of its potent power. It was why she avoided it as much as possible. Why the idea of Emile had been so enticing to Command, to Pippa and her Lightfall squadron.

There was nothing left inside her now. Not one spark of power. And no one was coming to save her.

Footsteps thudded on the dock, rattling her body. Sofie bit her lip against the flashing pain.

Polished black boots stopped inches from her nose. Sofie shifted her good eye upward. The Hind's pale face peered down.

"Naughty girl," the Hind said in that fair voice. "Electrocuting my dreadwolves." She ran an amber eye over Sofie. "What a remarkable power you have. And what a remarkable power your brother has, downing my Omega-boats. It seems all the legends about your kind are true."

Sofie said nothing.

The spy-breaker smiled slightly. "Tell me who you passed the intel to, and I will walk off this dock and let you live. I'll let you see your darling little brother."

Sofie said through stiff lips, "No one."

The Hind merely said, "Let's go for a ride, Sofie Renast."

The dreadwolves bundled Sofie into a nondescript boat. No one spoke as it sailed out to sea. As an hour passed, and the sky lightened. Only when they were so far from the shore that it was no longer a darker shadow against the night sky did the Hind lift a hand. The engines cut off, and the boat bobbed in the waves.

Again, those polished, knee-high boots approached Sofie. She'd been bound, gorsian shackles around her wrists to stifle her power. Her leg had gone numb with agony.

With a nod to a wolf, the Hind ordered that Sofie should be hauled to her feet. Sofie bit down her cry of pain. Behind her, another wolf opened the transom gate, exposing the small platform off the boat's back. Sofie's throat closed up.

"Since your brother has bestowed such a death upon a multitude of imperial soldiers, this will be an apt punishment for you," the Hind said, stepping onto the platform, not seeming to care about the water splashing over her boots. She pulled a small white stone from her pocket, lifting it for Sofie to see, and then chucked it into the water. Observed it with her Vanir-sharp eyes as it dropped down, down, down into the inky blackness.

"At that depth, you'll likely drown before you hit the seafloor," the Hind observed, her golden hair shifting across her imperious face. She slid her hands into her pockets as the wolves knelt at Sofie's feet and bound them together with chains weighted with lead blocks.

"I'll ask you again," the Hind said, angling her head, silver torque glinting at her neck. "With whom did you share the intelligence you collected before you went into Kavalla?"

Sofie felt the ache of her missing fingernails. Saw the faces in that camp. The people she'd left behind. Her cause had been Emile—yet Ophion was right in so many ways. And some small part of her had been glad to kill for Ophion, to fight for those people. Would keep fighting for them, for Emile, now. She gritted out, "I told you: no one."

"Very well, then." The Hind pointed to the water. "You know how this ends."

Sofie kept her face blank to conceal her shock at her good luck, one last gift from Solas. Apparently, even the Hind was not as clever as she believed herself to be. She offered a swift, horrible death—but it was nothing compared to the endless torture Sofie had expected.

"Put her on the platform."

A dreadwolf—a hulking, dark-haired male—objected, sneering, "We'll get it out of her." Mordoc, the Hind's second in command. Almost as feared as his commander. Especially with his particular gifts.

The Hind didn't so much as look at him. "I'm not wasting my time on this. She says she didn't tell anyone, and I'm inclined to believe her." A slow smile. "So the intel will die with her."

It was all the Hind needed to say. The wolves hauled Sofie onto the platform. She swallowed a cry at the wave of agony that rippled through her thigh. Icy water sprayed, soaking through her clothes, burning and numbing.

Sofie couldn't stop her shaking. Tried to remember the kiss of the air, the scent of the sea, the gray of the sky before dawn. She would not see the sunrise, only minutes away. She'd never see another one again.

She had taken the beauty and simplicity of living for granted. How she wished she'd savored it more. Every single moment.

The deer shifter prowled closer. "Any last words?"

Emile had gotten away. It was all that mattered. He'd be kept safe now.

Sofie smiled crookedly at the Hind. "*Go to Hel.*"

Mordoc's clawed hands shoved her off the platform.

The frigid water hit Sofie like a bomb blast, and then the lead at her feet grabbed all that she was and might have been, and pulled her under.

The Hind stood, a phantom in the chilled mist of the Haldren Sea, and watched until Sofie Renast had been wrapped in Ogenas's embrace.

PART I
THE CHASM

1

For a Tuesday night at the Crescent City Ballet, the theater was unusually packed. The sight of the swarming masses in the lobby, drinking and chatting and mingling, filled Bryce Quinlan with a quiet sort of joy and pride.

There was only one reason why the theater was so packed tonight. With her Fae hearing, she could have sworn she heard the hundreds of voices all around her whispering, *Juniper Andromeda*. The star of tonight's performance.

Yet even with the crowd, an air of quiet reverence and serenity filled the space. As if it were a temple.

Bryce had the creeping sensation that the various ancient statues of the gods flanking the long lobby watched her. Or maybe that was the well-dressed older shifter couple standing by a reclining statue of Cthona, the earth goddess, naked and awaiting the embrace of her lover, Solas. The shifters—some sort of big cats, from their scents, and rich ones, judging by their watches and jewelry—blatantly ogled her.

Bryce offered them a bland, close-lipped smile.

Some variation of this had happened nearly every single day since the attack this past spring. The first few times had been overwhelming, unnerving—people coming up to her and sobbing with gratitude. Now they just stared.

Bryce didn't blame the people who wanted to speak to her, who *needed* to speak to her. The city had been healed—by her—but its people . . .

Scores had been dead by the time her firstlight erupted through Lunathion. Hunt had been lucky, had been taking his last breaths, when the firstlight saved him. Five thousand other people had not been so lucky.

Their families had not been so lucky.

So many dark boats had drifted across the Istros to the mists of the Bone Quarter that they had looked like a bevy of black swans. Hunt had carried her into the skies to see it. The quays along the river had teemed with people, their mourning cries rising to the low clouds where she and Hunt had glided.

Hunt had only held her tighter and flown them home.

"Take a picture," Ember Quinlan called now to the shifters from where she stood next to a marble torso of Ogenas rising from the waves, the ocean goddess's full breasts peaked and arms upraised. "Only ten gold marks. Fifteen, if you want to be in it."

"For fuck's sake, Mom," Bryce muttered. Ember stood with her hands on her hips, gorgeous in a silky gray gown and pashmina. "Please don't."

Ember opened her mouth, as if she'd say something else to the chastised shifters now hurrying toward the east staircase, but her husband interrupted her. "I second Bryce's request," Randall said, dashing in his navy suit.

Ember turned outraged dark eyes on Bryce's stepfather—her only father, as far as Bryce was concerned—but Randall pointed casually to a broad frieze behind them. "That one reminds me of Athalar."

Bryce arched a brow, grateful for the change of subject, and twisted toward where he'd pointed. On it, a powerful Fae male stood poised above an anvil, hammer raised skyward in one fist, lightning cracking from the skies, filling the hammer, and flowing down toward the object of the hammer's intended blow: a sword.

Its label read simply: *Unknown sculptor. Palmira, circa 125 V.E.*

Bryce lifted her mobile and snapped a photo, pulling up her messaging thread with *Hunt Athalar Is Better at Sunball Than I Am.*

She couldn't deny that. They'd gone to the local sunball field one sunny afternoon last week to play, and Hunt had promptly wiped the floor with her. He'd changed his name in her phone on the way home.

With a few sweeps of her thumbs, the picture zoomed off into the ether, along with her note: *Long-lost relative of yours?*

She slid her phone into her clutch to find her mother watching. "What?" Bryce muttered.

But Ember only motioned toward the frieze. "Who does it depict?"

Bryce checked the sliver of writing in the lower right corner. "It just says *The Making of the Sword.*"

Her mother peered at the half-faded etching. "In what language?"

Bryce tried to keep her posture relaxed. "The Old Language of the Fae."

"Ah." Ember pursed her lips, and Randall wisely drifted off through the crowd to study a towering statue of Luna aiming her bow toward the heavens, two hunting dogs at her feet and a stag nuzzling her hip. "You stayed fluent in it?"

"Yep," Bryce said. Then added, "It's come in handy."

"I'd imagine so." Ember tucked back a strand of her black hair.

Bryce moved to the next frieze dangling from the distant ceiling on near-invisible wires. "This one's of the First Wars." She scanned the relief carved into the ten-foot expanse of marble. "It's about . . ." She schooled her expression into neutrality.

"What?" Ember stepped closer to the depiction of an army of winged demons swooping down from the skies upon a terrestrial army gathered on the plain below.

"This one's about Hel's armies arriving to conquer Midgard during the First Wars," Bryce finished, trying to keep her voice bland. To block out the flash of talons and fangs and leathery wings—the boom of her rifle resounding through her bones, the rivers of blood in the streets, the screaming and screaming and—

"You'd think this one would be a popular piece these days," Randall observed, returning to their sides to study the frieze.

Bryce didn't reply. She didn't particularly enjoy discussing the events of the past spring with her parents. Especially not in the middle of a packed theater lobby.

Randall jerked his chin to the inscription. "What's this one say?"

Keenly aware of her mother marking her every blink, Bryce kept her stance unaffected as she skimmed the text in the Old Language of the Fae.

It wasn't that she was trying to hide what she'd endured. She *had* talked to her mom and dad about it a few times. But it always resulted in Ember crying, or ranting about the Vanir who'd locked out so many innocents, and the weight of all her mother's emotions on top of all of *hers* . . .

It was easier, Bryce had realized, to not bring it up. To let herself talk it out with Hunt, or sweat it out in Madame Kyrah's dance classes twice a week. Baby steps toward being ready for actual talk therapy, as Juniper kept suggesting, but both had helped immensely.

Bryce silently translated the text. "This is a piece from a larger collection—likely one that would have wrapped around the entire exterior of a building, each slab telling a different part of the story. This one says: *Thus the seven Princes of Hel looked in envy upon Midgard and unleashed their unholy hordes upon our united armies*."

"Apparently nothing's changed in fifteen thousand years," Ember said, shadows darkening her eyes.

Bryce kept her mouth shut. She'd never told her mom about Prince Aidas—how he'd helped her twice now, and had seemed unaware of his brothers' dark plans. If her mom knew she'd consorted with the fifth Prince of Hel, they'd have to redefine the concept of *going berserk*.

But then Ember said, "Couldn't you get a job *here*?" She gestured with a tan hand to the CCB's grand entrance, its ever-changing art exhibits in the lobby and on a few of the other levels. "You're qualified. This would have been perfect."

"There were no openings." True. And she didn't want to use her princess status to get one. She wanted to work at a place like the CCB's art department on her own merit.

Her job at the Fae Archives . . . Well, she definitely got that because they saw her as a Fae Princess. But it wasn't the same, somehow. Because she hadn't wanted to work there as badly.

"Did you even *try*?"

"Mom," Bryce said, voice sharpening.

"Bryce."

"Ladies," Randall said, a teasing remark designed to fracture the growing tension.

Bryce smiled gratefully at him but found her mother frowning. She sighed up at the starburst chandeliers above the glittering throng. "All right, Mom. Out with it."

"Out with what?" Ember asked innocently.

"Your opinion about my job." Bryce gritted her teeth. "For years, you ragged on me for being an assistant, but now that I'm doing something better, it's not good enough?"

This was so not the place, not with tons of people milling about within earshot, but she'd had it.

Ember didn't seem to care as she said, "It's not that it's not good enough. It's about where that job is."

"The Fae Archives operate independently of *him*."

"Oh? Because I remember him bragging that it was pretty much his personal library."

Bryce said tightly, "Mom. The gallery is gone. I need a job. Forgive me if the usual corporate nine-to-five isn't available to me right now. Or if CCB's art department isn't hiring."

"I just don't get why you couldn't work something out with Jesiba. She's still got that warehouse—surely she needs help with whatever she does there."

Bryce refrained from rolling her eyes. Within a day of the attack on the city this spring, Jesiba had cleared out the gallery—and the precious volumes that made up all that remained of the ancient Great Library of Parthos. Most of Jesiba's other pieces were now in a warehouse, many in crates, but Bryce had no idea where the sorceress had spirited off the Parthos books—one of the few remnants of the human world before the Asteri's arrival. Bryce hadn't dared question Jesiba about their current whereabouts. It was a miracle that the Asteri hadn't been tipped off about the contraband books' existence. "There are only so many times I can ask for a job without looking like I'm begging."

"And we can't have a princess do that."

She'd lost count of how often she'd told her mom she wasn't a princess. Didn't want to be, and the Autumn King sure as shit didn't want her to be, either. She hadn't spoken to the asshole since that last time he'd come to see her at the gallery, right before her confrontation with Micah. When she'd revealed what power coursed through her veins.

It was an effort not to glance down at her chest, to where the front of her gauzy, pale blue dress plunged to just below her breasts, displaying the star-shaped mark between them. Thankfully, the back was high enough to hide the Horn tattooed there. Like an old scar, the white mark stood out starkly against her freckled, golden-tan skin. It hadn't faded in the three months since the city had been attacked.

She'd already lost count of how many times she'd caught her mom staring at her star since arriving last night.

A cluster of gorgeous females—woodland nymphs, from their cedar-and-moss scents—meandered past, champagne in hand, and Bryce lowered her voice. "What do you want me to say? That I'll move back home to Nidaros and pretend to be normal?"

"What's so bad about normal?" Her mother's beautiful face blazed with an inner fire that never banked—never, ever died out. "I think Hunt would like living there."

"Hunt still works for the 33rd, Mom," Bryce said. "He's second in command, for fuck's sake. And while he might appease you by saying he'd *love* to live in Nidaros, don't think for one minute he means it."

"Way to throw him under the bus," Randall said while keeping his attention on a nearby information placard.

Before Bryce could answer, Ember said, "Don't think I haven't noticed things between you two are weird."

Trust her mom to bring up two topics she didn't want to talk about in the space of five minutes. "In what way?"

"You're together but not *together*," Ember said bluntly. "What's that about?"

"It's none of your business." It really wasn't. But as if he'd heard her, the phone in her clutch buzzed. She yanked it out and peered at the screen.

Hunt had written, *I can only hope to have abs like those one day.*

Bryce couldn't help her half smile as she peered back at the muscular Fae male on the frieze before answering. *I think you might have a few on him, actually . . .*

"Don't ignore me, Bryce Adelaide Quinlan."

Her phone buzzed again, but she didn't read Hunt's reply as she said to her mother, "Can you please drop it? And don't bring it up when Hunt gets here."

Ember's mouth popped open, but Randall said, "Agreed. No job or romance interrogations when Hunt arrives."

Her mother frowned doubtfully, but Bryce said, "Mom, just . . . stop, okay? I don't mind my job, and the thing between me and Hunt is what he and I agreed on. I'm doing fine. Let's leave it at that."

It was a lie. Sort of.

She actually *liked* her job—a lot. The private wing of the Fae Archives housed a trove of ancient artifacts that had been sorely neglected for centuries—now in need of researching and cataloging so they could be sent on a traveling exhibit next spring.

She set her own hours, answering only to the head of research, an owl shifter—one of the rare non-Fae staff—who only worked from dusk to dawn, so they barely overlapped. The worst part of her day was entering the sprawling complex through the main buildings, where the sentries all gawked at her. Some even bowed. And then she had to walk through the atrium, where the librarians and patrons tended to stare, too.

Everyone these days stared—she really fucking hated it. But Bryce didn't want to tell her mom any of that.

Ember said, "Fine. You know I just worry."

Something in Bryce's chest softened. "I know, Mom. And I know . . ." She struggled for the words. "It really helps to know that I can move back home if I want to. But not right now."

"Fair enough," Randall chimed in, giving Ember a pointed glance before looping his arm around her waist and steering her toward another frieze across the theater lobby.

Bryce used their distraction to take out her phone, and found that Hunt had written two messages:

Want to count my abs when we get home from the ballet?

Her stomach tightened, and she'd never been more grateful that her parents possessed a human sense of smell as her toes curled in her heels.

Hunt had added, *I'll be there in five, by the way. Isaiah held me up with a new case.*

She sent a thumbs-up, then replied: *Pleaaaaaase get here ASAP. I just got a major grilling about my job. And you.*

Hunt wrote back immediately, and Bryce read as she slowly trailed her parents to where they observed the frieze: *What about me?*

"Bryce," her mom called, pointing to the frieze before her. "Check out this one. It's JJ."

Bryce looked up from her phone and grinned. "Badass warrior Jelly Jubilee." There, hanging on the wall, was a rendering of a pegasus—though not a unicorn-pegasus, like Bryce's childhood toy—charging into battle. An armored figure, helmet obscuring any telltale features, rode atop the beast, sword upraised. Bryce snapped a photo and sent it to Hunt.

First Wars JJ, reporting for duty!

She was about to reply to Hunt's *What about me?* question when her mom said, "Tell Hunt to stop flirting and hurry up already."

Bryce scowled at her mom and put her phone away.

So many things had changed since revealing her heritage as the Autumn King's daughter and a Starborn heir: people gawking, the hat and sunglasses she now wore on the street to attain some level of anonymity, the job at the Fae Archives. But at least her mother remained the same.

Bryce couldn't decide whether that was a comfort or not.

Entering the private box in the angels' section of the theater—the stage-left boxes a level above the floor—Bryce grinned toward the heavy golden curtain blocking the stage from sight. Only ten minutes remained until the show began. Until the world could see how insanely talented Juniper was.

Ember gracefully sank into one of the red velvet chairs at the front of the box, Randall claiming the seat beside her. Bryce's mother didn't smile. Considering that the royal Fae boxes occupied the wing across from them, Bryce didn't blame her. And considering that many of the bejeweled and shining nobility were staring at Bryce, it was a miracle Ember hadn't flipped them off yet.

Randall whistled at the prime seats as he peered over the golden rail. "Nice view."

The air behind Bryce went electric, buzzing and alive. The hair on her arms prickled. A male voice sounded from the vestibule, "A benefit to having wings: no one wants to sit behind you."

Bryce had developed a keen awareness of Hunt's presence, like scenting lightning on the wind. He had only to enter a room and she'd know if he was there by that surge of power in her body. Like her magic, her very blood answered to his.

Now she found Hunt standing in the doorway, already tugging at the black tie around his neck.

Just . . . gods-damn.

He'd worn a black suit and white shirt, both cut to his powerful, muscled body, and the effect was devastating. Add in the gray wings framing it all and she was a goner.

Hunt smirked knowingly, but nodded to Randall. "You clean up good, man. Sorry I'm late." Bryce could barely hear her dad's reply as she surveyed the veritable malakim feast before her.

Hunt had cut his hair shorter last month. Not too short, since she'd staged an intervention with the stylist before the draki male could chop off all those beautiful locks, but gone was the shoulder-length hair. The shorter style suited him, but it was still a shock weeks later to find his hair neatly trimmed to his nape, with only a few pieces in the front still unruly enough to peek through the hole in his sunball hat. Tonight, however, he'd brushed it into submission, revealing the clear expanse of his forehead.

That was still a shock, too: no tattoo. No sign of the years of torment the angel had endured beyond the *C* stamped over the slave's tattoo on his right wrist, marking him a free male. Not a full citizen, but closer to it than the peregrini.

The mark was hidden by the cuff of his suit jacket and the shirt beneath, and Bryce lifted her gaze to Hunt's face. Her mouth went dry at the bald hunger filling his dark, angular eyes. "You look okay, too," he said, winking.

Randall coughed, but leafed through the playbill. Ember did the same beside him.

Bryce ran a hand down the front of her blue dress. "This old thing?"

Hunt chuckled, and tugged on his tie again.

Bryce sighed. "Please tell me you're not one of those big, tough males who makes a big fuss about how he hates getting dressed up."

It was Ember's turn to cough, but Hunt's eyes danced as he said to Bryce, "Good thing I don't have to do it that often, huh?"

A knock on the box door shut off her reply, and a satyr server appeared, carrying a tray of complimentary champagne. "From Miss Andromeda," the cloven-hoofed male announced.

Bryce grinned. "Wow." She made a mental note to double the size of the bouquet she'd planned to send to June tomorrow. She took the glass the satyr extended to her, but before she could raise it to her lips, Hunt halted her with a gentle hand on her wrist. She'd officially ended her No Drinking rule after this spring, but she suspected the touch had nothing to do with reminding her to go slow.

Arching a brow, she waited until the server had left before asking, "You want to make a toast?"

Hunt reached into an inner pocket of his suit and pulled out a small container of mints. Or what seemed like mints. She barely had time to react before he plopped a white pill into her glass.

"What the *Hel*—"

"Just testing." Hunt studied her glass. "If it's drugged or poisoned, it'll turn green."

Ember chimed in with her approval. "The satyr said the drinks are from Juniper, but how do you know, Bryce? Anything could be in it." Her mom nodded at Hunt. "Good thinking."

Bryce wanted to object, but . . . Hunt had a point. "And what am I supposed to do with it now? It's ruined."

"The pill is tasteless," Hunt said, clinking his flute against hers when the liquid remained pale gold. "Bottoms up."

"Classy," she said, but drank. It still tasted like champagne—no hint of the dissolved pill lingered.

The golden sconces and dangling starburst chandeliers dimmed twice in a five-minute warning, and Bryce and Hunt took their seats behind her parents. From this angle, she could barely make out Fury in the front row.

Hunt seemed to track the direction of her attention. "She didn't want to sit with us?"

"Nope." Bryce took in her friend's shining dark hair, her black suit. "She wants to see every drop of Juniper's sweat."

"I'd think she saw that every night," Hunt said wryly, and Bryce waggled her eyebrows.

But Ember twisted in her seat, a genuine smile lighting her face. "How are Fury and Juniper doing? Did they move in together yet?"

"Two weeks ago." Bryce craned her neck to study Fury, who seemed to be reading the playbill. "And they're really good. I think Fury's here to stay this time."

Her mom asked carefully, "And you and Fury? I know things were weird for a while."

Hunt did her a favor and made himself busy on his phone. Bryce idly flipped the pages of her playbill. "Working things out with Fury took some time. But we're good."

Randall asked, "Is Axtar still doing what she does best?"

"Yep." Bryce was content to leave her friend's mercenary business at that. "She's happy, though. And more important, June and Fury are happy together."

"Good," Ember said, smiling softly. "They make such a beautiful couple." And because her mom was . . . well, her mom, Ember sized up Bryce and Hunt and said with no shame whatsoever, "You two would as well, if you got your shit together."

Bryce slouched down in her seat, lifting her playbill to block her red-hot face. Why weren't the lights dimming yet? But Hunt took it in stride and said, "All good things come to those who wait, Ember."

Bryce scowled at the arrogance and amusement in his tone, throwing her playbill into her lap as she declared, "Tonight's a big deal for June. Try not to ruin it with nonsensical banter."

Ember patted Bryce's knee before twisting back to face the stage.

Hunt drained his champagne, and Bryce's mouth dried out again at the sight of the broad, strong column of his throat working as he swallowed, then said, "Here I was, thinking you loved the banter."

Bryce had the option of either drooling or turning away, so rather than ruin her dress, she observed the crowd filtering into their seats. More than one person peered toward her box.

Especially from the Fae boxes across the way. No sign of her father or Ruhn, but she recognized a few cold faces. Tristan Flynn's parents—Lord and Lady Hawthorne—were among them, their professional snob of a daughter Sathia sitting between them. None of the glittering nobility seemed pleased at Bryce's presence. Good.

"Tonight's a big deal for June, remember," Hunt murmured, lips quirking upward.

She glowered. "What?"

Hunt inclined his head toward the Fae nobility sneering across the space. "I can see you thinking about some way to piss them off."

"I was not."

He leaned in to whisper, his breath brushing her neck, "You were, and I know it because I was thinking the same thing." A few cameras flashed from above and below, and she knew people weren't snapping photos of the stage curtain.

Bryce peeled back to survey Hunt, the face she knew as well as her own. For a moment, for a too-brief eternity, they stared at each other. Bryce swallowed, but couldn't bring herself to move. To break the contact.

Hunt's throat bobbed. But he said nothing more, either.

Three fucking *months* of this torture. Stupid agreement. Friends, but more. More, but without any of the physical benefits.

Hunt said at last, voice thick, "It's really nice of you to be here for Juniper."

She tossed her hair over a shoulder. "You're making it sound like it's some big sacrifice."

He jerked his chin toward the still-sneering Fae nobility. "You can't wear a hat and sunglasses here, so . . . yeah."

She admitted, "I wish she'd gotten us seats in the nosebleed section."

Instead, Juniper—to accommodate Hunt's wings—had gotten them this box. Right where everyone could see the Starborn Princess and the Fallen Angel.

The orchestra began tuning up, and the sounds of slowly awakening violins and flutes drew Bryce's attention to the pit. Her muscles tensed of their own volition, as if priming to move. To dance.

Hunt leaned in again, voice a low purr, "You look beautiful, you know."

"Oh, I know," she said, even as she bit her lower lip to keep from grinning. The lights began dimming, so Bryce decided to Hel with it. "When do I get to count those abs, Athalar?"

The angel cleared his throat—once, twice—and shifted in his seat, feathers rustling. Bryce smiled smugly.

He murmured, "Four more months, Quinlan."

"And three days," she shot back.

His eyes shone in the growing darkness.

"What are you two talking about back there?" Ember asked, and Bryce replied without tearing her gaze from Hunt's, "Nothing."

But it wasn't nothing. It was the stupid bargain she'd made with Hunt: that rather than diving right into bed, they'd wait until Winter Solstice to act on their desires. Spend the summer and autumn getting to know each other without the burdens of a psychotic Archangel and demons on the prowl.

So they had. Torturing each other with flirting was allowed, but sometimes, tonight especially . . . she really wished she'd never suggested it. Wished she could drag him into the coat closet of the vestibule behind them and show him precisely how much she liked that suit.

Four months, three days, and . . . She peeked at the delicate watch on her wrist. Four hours. And at the stroke of midnight on Winter Solstice, *she* would be stroking—

"Burning fucking Solas, Quinlan," Hunt grunted, again shifting in his seat.

"Sorry," she muttered, thankful for the second time in an hour that her parents didn't have the sense of smell that Hunt possessed.

But Hunt laughed, sliding an arm along the back of her chair, fingers tangling in her unbound hair. He seemed contented. Assured of his place there.

She glanced at her parents, sitting with similar closeness, and couldn't help but smile. Her mom had taken a while to act on her desires with Randall, too. Well, there'd been some initial . . . stuff. That was as much as Bryce let herself think about them. But she knew it had been nearly a year before they'd made things official. And they'd turned out pretty damn well.

So these months with Hunt, she cherished them. As much as she cherished her dance classes with Madame Kyrah. No one except Hunt really understood what she'd gone through—only Hunt had been at the Gate.

She scanned his striking features, her lips curving again. How many nights had they stayed up, talking about everything and nothing? Ordering in dinner, watching movies or reality shows or sunball, playing video games, or sitting on the roof of the apartment building, observing malakim and witches and draki dart across the sky like shooting stars.

He'd shared so many things about his past, sad and horrible and joyous. She wanted to know all of it. And the more she learned, the more she found herself sharing, and the more she . . .

Light flared from the star on her chest.

Bryce clapped a hand over it. "I shouldn't have worn this stupid dress."

Her fingers could barely cover the star that was blaring white light through the dim theater, illuminating every face now turned her way as the orchestra quieted in anticipation of the conductor's approach.

She didn't dare look toward the Fae across the space. To see the disgust and disdain.

Ember and Randall twisted in their seats, her dad's face scrunched with concern, Ember's eyes wide with fear. Her mom knew those Fae were sneering, too. She'd hidden Bryce from them her whole life because of how they'd react to the power that now radiated from her.

Some jackass shouted from the audience below, "*Hey! Turn off the light!*" Bryce's face burned as a few people chuckled, then quickly went silent.

She could only assume Fury had been nearby.

Bryce cupped both hands over the star, which had taken to glowing at the *worst* fucking times—this was merely the most mortifying. "I don't know how to turn it off," she muttered, making to rise from her seat and flee into the vestibule behind the curtain.

But Hunt slid a warm, dry hand over her scar, fingers grazing her breasts. His palm was broad enough that it covered the mark, capturing the light within. It glowed through his fingers, casting his light brown skin into rosy gold, but he managed to contain the light.

"Admit it: you just wanted me to feel you up," Hunt whispered, and Bryce couldn't help her stupid, giddy laugh. She buried her face in Hunt's shoulder, the smooth material of his suit cool against her cheeks and brow. "Need a minute?" he asked, though she knew he was glaring daggers at all the assholes still gawking. The Fae nobility hissing about the *disgrace*.

"Should we go?" Ember asked, voice sharp with worry.

"No," Bryce said thickly, putting a hand over Hunt's. "I'm good."

"You can't sit there like that," Ember countered.

"I'm good, Mom."

Hunt didn't move his hand. "We're used to the staring. Right, Quinlan?" He flashed Ember a grin. "They won't fuck with us." An edge laced his smile, a reminder to anyone watching that he wasn't only Hunt Athalar, he was also the Umbra Mortis. The Shadow of Death.

He'd earned that name.

Ember nodded again approvingly as Randall offered Hunt a grateful dip of the chin. Mercifully, the conductor emerged then, and a smattering of applause filled the theater.

Bryce inhaled deeply, then slowly exhaled. She had zero control over when the star flared, or when it stopped. She sipped from her champagne, then said casually to Hunt, "The headline on the gossip sites tomorrow is going to be: *Horndog Umbra Mortis Gropes Starborn Princess at Ballet.*"

"Good," Hunt murmured. "It'll improve my standing in the 33rd."

She smiled, despite herself. It was one of his many gifts—making her laugh, even when the world seemed inclined to humiliate and shun her.

His fingers went dark at her chest, and Bryce heaved a sigh. "Thanks," she said as the conductor raised his baton.

Hunt slowly, so slowly, removed his hand from her chest. "Don't mention it, Quinlan."

She glanced sidelong at him again, wondering at the shift in his tone. But the orchestra began its lilting opening, and the curtain drew back, and Bryce leaned forward breathlessly to await her friend's grand entrance.

2

Bryce tried not to shiver with delight when Hunt knocked her with a wing while they walked up the sagging stairs to Ruhn's house.

A small get-together, Ruhn had said when he'd called to invite them to swing by after the ballet. Since the thought of her mother grilling her again about her job, sex life, and princess status was sure to drive her to drink anyway, Bryce and Hunt had dumped her parents back at their hotel, changed at the apartment—Hunt had insisted on that part with a grumbled *I need to get the fuck out of this suit*—and flown over here.

The entire Old Square had apparently turned up as well: Fae and shifters and people of all Houses drank and danced and talked. On the pathetic excuse for a front lawn, a cluster of green-haired river nymphs and fauns both male and female played cornhole. A cluster of Fae males behind them—Aux members, from their muscles and stick-up-the-ass posture—were engaged in what looked like an absolutely *riveting* game of bocce.

The arid day had yielded to a whisper-sweet night, warm enough that every bar and café and club in the Old Square—especially around Archer Street—teemed with revelers. Even with the booming music erupting from Ruhn's house, she could make out the thump of the bass from the other houses along the street, the bar at the corner, the cars driving by.

Everyone was celebrating being alive.

As they should be.

"Fury and June are already here," Bryce called to Hunt over the noise as they strode up the rickety, beer-splattered steps into Ruhn's house. "June said they're in the living room."

Hunt nodded, though his focus remained fixed on the partying crowd. Even here, people noted from all directions as the Starborn Princess and the Umbra Mortis arrived. The crowd parted for them, some even backing away. Bryce stiffened, but Hunt didn't halt his easy pace. He was accustomed to this shit—had been for a while now. And though he was no longer officially the Shadow of Death, people hadn't forgotten what he had once done. Who he'd once served.

Hunt aimed for the living room to the left of the foyer, the ridiculous muscles along his shoulders shifting with the movement. They were put on near-obscene display by the black tank top he wore. Bryce might have survived the sight of it, had it not been for the white sunball hat, twisted backward the way Hunt usually wore it.

She preferred that hat to the fancy suit, actually.

To her shock, Hunt didn't protest when a reveling air sprite floated past, crowning him and then Bryce with glow-stick necklaces made from firstlight. Bryce removed the plastic tube of light and looped it into a bracelet snaking up her arm. Hunt left his hanging over his chest, the light casting the deep muscles of his pectorals and shoulders in stark relief. Gods spare her.

Hunt had only taken one step into the living room when Tristan Flynn's voice boomed from the foyer behind them: "The *fuck*, Ruhn!"

Bryce snorted, and through the crowd she spied the Fae lord at one end of the beer pong table on which he'd painted an image of an enormous Fae head devouring an angel whole.

Ruhn stood at the other end of the table, both middle fingers raised to his opponents, his lip ring glinting in the dim lights of the foyer. "Pay up, assholes," her brother said, the rolled cigarette between his lips bobbing with his words.

Bryce reached a hand for Hunt, fingers grazing his downy soft wings. He went rigid, twisting to look at her. Angels' wings were highly sensitive. She might as well have grabbed him by the balls.

Face flushing, she jabbed a thumb toward her brother. "Tell June and Fury I'll be there in a sec," she called over the noise. "I want to say hi to Ruhn." She didn't wait for Hunt to reply before wending her way over.

Flynn let out a cheer as she appeared, obviously well on his way to being smashed. Typical Tuesday night for him. She considered sending a photo of his wasted ass to his parents and sister. They might not sneer so much at her, then.

Declan Emmet appeared slightly more sober as he said from Flynn's side, "Hey, B."

Bryce waved, not wanting to shout over the crowd gathered in what had once been a dining room. It had recently been transformed into a billiards and darts room. Absolutely fitting for the Crown Prince of the Valbaran Fae, Bryce thought with a half smile as she sidled up to the male beside her brother. "Hi, Marc."

The towering leopard shifter, all sleek muscle beneath his dark brown skin, peered down at her. His striking topaz eyes sparkled. Declan had been seeing Marc Rosarin for a month now, having met the tech entrepreneur during some fancy party at one of the big engineering companies in the Central Business District. "Hey, Princess."

Flynn demanded, "Since when do you let Marc get away with calling you Princess?"

"Since I like him better than you," Bryce shot back, earning a clap on the shoulder from Marc and a grin from Ruhn. She said to her brother, "*A small get-together*, huh?"

Ruhn shrugged, the tattoos along his arms shifting. "I blame Flynn."

Flynn lifted his last beer up in acknowledgment and chugged.

"Where's Athalar?" Declan asked.

"With June and Fury in the living room," Bryce said.

Ruhn waved his greeting to a passing partier before he asked, "How was the ballet?"

"Awesome. June killed her solos. Brought the house to its feet."

She'd had chills along her entire body while her friend had danced—and tears in her eyes when Juniper had received a standing ovation after finishing. Bryce had never heard the CCB so full of cheering, and from Juniper's flushed, joyous face as she'd bowed, Bryce knew her friend realized it, too. A promotion to principal was sure to come any day now.

"Hottest ticket in town," Marc said, whistling. "Half my office would have sold their souls to be there tonight."

"You should have told me," Bryce said. "We had a few extra seats in our box. We could have fit them."

Marc smiled appreciatively. "Next time."

Flynn began reracking the beer pong cups, and called to her, "How are Mommy and Daddy?"

"Good. They fed me a bottle of milk and read me a bedtime story before I left."

This earned a chuckle from Ruhn, who had once again become close with Ember. Her brother asked, "How many interrogations since they got here last night?"

"Six." Bryce pointed to the foyer and living room beyond. "Which is why I'm going to go have a drink with my friends."

"Open bar," Declan said, gesturing magnanimously behind him.

Bryce waved again, and she was off. Without Hunt's imposing form, far fewer people turned her way. But when they did . . . pockets of silence appeared. She tried to ignore them, and nearly sighed with relief when she spied a familiar pair of horns atop a head of gracefully curling hair tucked into Juniper's usual bun. She was seated on the stained living room sectional, thigh to thigh with Fury, their hands interlaced.

Hunt stood before them, wings held at a casual angle as he talked with her friends. He looked up as Bryce entered the living room, and she could have sworn his black eyes lit.

She reined in her joy at the sight as she plopped onto the cushions beside Juniper, cuddling close. She nuzzled June's shoulder. "Hi, my talented and brilliant and beautiful friend."

Juniper laughed, squeezing Bryce. "Right back at you."

Bryce said, "I was talking to Fury."

Juniper smacked Bryce's knee, and Fury laughed, observing, "Already acting like a prima donna."

Bryce sighed dramatically. "I can't wait to see June throw temper tantrums about the state of her dressing room."

"Oh, you're both horrible," Juniper said, but laughed along with them. "One, I won't even *have* a dressing room to myself for years. *Two*—"

"Here we go," Fury said, and when June made a noise of objection, she only chuckled and brushed her mouth over the faun's temple.

The casual, loving bit of intimacy had Bryce daring a glance toward Hunt, who was smiling faintly. Bryce avoided the urge to fidget, to think about how that could so easily be them, cuddling on the couch and kissing. Hunt just said, voice gravelly, "What can I get you, Quinlan?" He inclined his head toward the bar in the rear of the room, barely visible with the crowds mobbing the two bartenders.

"Whiskey, ginger beer, and lime."

"You got it." With a mockery of a salute, Hunt stalked off through the crowd.

"How's the whole no-sex thing going for you, Bryce?" Fury asked wryly, leaning forward to peer at her face.

Bryce slumped against the cushions. "Asshole."

June's laugh fizzled through her, and her friend patted her thigh. "Remind me why you two aren't hooking up?"

Bryce peered over the back of the couch to make sure Hunt still stood at the bar before she said, "Because I am a fucking idiot, and you two jerks know that."

Juniper and Fury snickered, the latter taking a sip of her vodka soda. "Tell him you've changed your mind," the merc said, resting the glass on her black leather-clad knee. How Fury could wear leather in this heat was beyond Bryce. Shorts, T-shirt, and sandals were all she could endure with the sizzling temperatures, even at night.

"And break our bargain before Winter Solstice?" Bryce hissed. "He'd never let me live it down."

"Athalar already knows you want to break it," Fury drawled.

"Oh, he totally knows," Juniper agreed.

Bryce crossed her arms. "Can we not talk about this?"

"Where would the fun be in that?" Fury asked.

Bryce kicked Fury's leather boot, wincing as her gold-sandaled foot collided with unforgiving metal. "Steel toes? Really?"

"This is a veritable frat party," Fury said, smirking. "There might be some asses to kick if someone makes a move on my girlfriend."

Juniper glowed at the term. *Girlfriend.*

Bryce didn't know what the Hel she was to Hunt. *Girlfriend* seemed ridiculous when talking about Hunt fucking Athalar. As if Hunt would ever do anything as normal and casual as dating.

Juniper poked Bryce in the arm. "I mean it. Remind me why you guys still need to wait for solstice to do the deed."

Bryce slouched, sinking down a few inches, her feet sending the empty beer cans under the coffee table clattering. "I just . . ."

That familiar buzz of power and maleness that was Hunt filled the air behind her, and Bryce shut her mouth a moment before a plastic cup of amber liquid garnished with a wedge of lime appeared before her. "Princess," Hunt crooned, and Bryce's toes curled—yet again. They seemed to have a habit of doing that around him.

"Do we get to use that term now?" June perked up with delight. "I've been *dying*—"

"Absolutely not." Bryce swigged from her drink. She gagged. "How much whiskey did you have the bartender *put* in here, Athalar?" She coughed, as if it'd do anything to ease the burn.

Hunt shrugged. "I thought you liked whiskey."

Fury snorted, but Bryce got to her feet. Lifted the cup toward Hunt in a silent toast, then lifted it to June. "To the next principal dancer of the CCB."

Then she knocked back the whole thing and let it burn right down to her soul.

Hunt let himself—just for one fucking second—look at Bryce. Admire the steady, unfaltering tap of her sandaled foot on the worn wood floor to the beat of the music; the long, muscled legs that gleamed in the neon firstlights, her white shorts offsetting her summer tan. No scars remained from the shit that had occurred this spring, aside from that mark on her chest, though the thick scar from years ago still curved along her thigh.

His fierce, strong, beautiful Bryce. He'd done his best not to gape at the shape of her ass in those shorts as they'd walked over here, the sway of her long hair against her lower back, the ample hips that swished with each step.

He was a stupid fucking animal. But he'd always been a stupid fucking animal around her.

He'd barely been able to focus on the ballet earlier—on June's dancing—because Bryce had looked so . . . delicious in that blue dress. Only her parents sitting a few feet in front of him had kept him from thinking too much about sliding his hand up her thigh and underneath that gauzy material.

But that wasn't part of the plan. Earlier this spring, he'd been fine with it. Aching for her, but fine with the concept of getting to know each other better before sex entered the equation. Yet that ache had only gotten worse these past months. Living together in their apartment was a slow kind of torture for both of them.

Bryce's whiskey-colored eyes shifted toward him. She opened her mouth, then shut it at whatever she beheld in his expression.

The memory of those days following Micah's and Sandriel's demises cooled his rising lust.

Let's take things slow, she'd requested. *I feel like we tumbled into all of this, and now that things are getting back to normal, I want to do this right with you. Get to know you in real time, not while we're running around the city trying to solve murders.*

He'd agreed, because what else could he do? Never mind that he'd come home from the Comitium that night planning to seduce Quinlan within an inch of her life. He hadn't even gotten to the kissing part when she'd announced she wanted to hit the brakes.

He knew more lay behind it. Knew it likely had something to do with the guilt she harbored for the thousands of people who hadn't been saved that day. Allowing herself to be with him, to be happy . . . She needed time to sort it out. And Hunt would give it to her. Anything Bryce wanted, anything she needed, he'd gladly give it to her. He had the freedom to do so now, thanks to the branded-out tattoo on his wrist.

But on nights like these, with her in those shorts . . . it was really gods-damned hard.

Bryce hopped up from the couch and padded over to him, leaving Juniper and Fury to chat, Fury busy reloading the arts page of the *Crescent City Times* for the review of Juniper's performance. "What's up?" Hunt said to Bryce as she took up a place beside him.

"Do you actually like coming to these parties?" Bryce asked, gesturing to the throng, firstlight glow stick around her wrist gleaming bright. "This doesn't disgust you?"

He tucked in his wings. "Why would it disgust me?"

"Because you've seen all the shit that's happening in the world, and been treated like dirt, and these people . . ." She tossed her sheet of hair over a shoulder. "A lot of them have no idea about it. Or just don't care."

Hunt studied her tight face. "Why do we come to these parties if it bothers you?"

"Well, tonight we're here to avoid my mom." Hunt chuckled, but she went on, "And because I want to celebrate June being a genius." She smiled at her friend on the couch. "And we're here because Ruhn asked me to come. But . . . I don't know. I want to feel normal, but then I feel guilty about that, and then I get mad at all these people who don't care enough to feel guilty, and I think the poison-testing pill you no doubt put in my whiskey had some sort of sad-sack potion in it because I don't know why I'm thinking about this right now."

Hunt huffed a laugh. "Sad-sack potion?"

"You know what I mean!" She glared. "This really doesn't bug you?"

"No." He assessed the party raging around them. "I prefer to see people enjoying their lives. And you can't assume that because they're here, it means they don't care. For all you know, a lot of them lost family and friends this spring. Sometimes people need stuff like this to feel alive again. To find a kind of release."

Wrong word. He sure as fuck hadn't found release recently, other than by his own hand. He tried not to think about whether Bryce had opened the drawer in her left nightstand, where she kept her toys, as often as he'd jacked off in the shower.

Four months left until Winter Solstice. Only four.

Bryce nodded, her mind clearly still on the conversation at hand. "I guess I just . . . Sometimes I catch myself enjoying a moment, and worry I'm enjoying it *too* much, you know? Like something could come along and ruin all of this if I let myself have too much fun or get too accustomed to feeling happy."

"I know the feeling." He couldn't stop himself from letting his fingers curl in the ends of her hair. "It's going to take time to adjust."

He was still adjusting, too. He couldn't get used to walking around without a pit in his stomach as he wondered what horrors the day would bring. Being in charge of himself, his future . . . The Asteri could take it all away again, if they wished. Had only let him live because he and Bryce were too public to kill—the Asteri wanted them to lie low forever. And if they didn't . . . Well, Rigelus had been very clear on his call to Bryce months ago: the Bright Hand of the Asteri would kill everyone Bryce and Hunt cared about if they stepped out of line. So lying low it would be.

Hunt was happy to do precisely that. To go to the ballet and these parties and pretend that he'd never known anything different. That Bryce didn't have the Horn tattooed into her back.

But each morning, when he donned his usual black armor for the 33rd, he remembered. Isaiah had asked him for backup right after Micah's death, and Hunt had gladly given it. He'd stayed on as Isaiah's unofficial commander—unofficial only because Hunt didn't want the paperwork that came with the real title.

The city had been quiet, though. Focused on healing. Hunt wasn't going to complain.

His phone buzzed in the back pocket of his black jeans, and he fished it out to find an email from Isaiah waiting for him. Hunt read it and went still. His heart dropped to his feet and back up again.

"What's wrong?" Bryce peered over his shoulder.

Hunt passed her the phone with a surprisingly steady hand. "New Archangels have been chosen for Micah's and Sandriel's territories."

Her eyes widened. "Who? How bad are they?"

He motioned for her to read Isaiah's email, and Bryce, that firstlight glow stick still coiled around her wrist, obeyed.

Roll out the welcome mat, Isaiah had written as his only comment on the forwarded email from the Asteri's imperial secretary announcing the new positions.

"They're not bad," Hunt said, staring blankly at the revelers now gathering around a Fae male doing a keg stand in the corner. "That's the problem."

Bryce's brows bunched as she scanned the email. "Ephraim—he currently shares Rodinia with Jakob. Yeah, he seems decent enough. But he's going to northern Pangera. Who . . . Oh. Who the Hel is Celestina?"

Hunt frowned. "She's stayed out of the spotlight. She oversees Nena—population, like, fifty. She has one legion under her command. *One.* She doesn't even have a triarii. The legion is literally controlled by the Asteri—all watchdogs for the Northern Rift. She's a figurehead."

"Big promotion, then."

Hunt grunted. "Everything I've heard about her sounds unusually nice."

"No chance it's true?"

"Where Archangels are concerned? No." He crossed his arms.

Fury said from the couch, "For what it's worth, Athalar, I haven't heard anything bad, either."

Juniper asked, "So this is promising, right?"

Hunt shook his head. This wasn't a conversation to have in public, but he said, "I can't figure out why the Asteri would appoint her *here,* when she's only handled a small territory until now. She must be their puppet."

Bryce tilted her head to the side, looking at him in that stark, all-seeing way that made his balls tighten. Gods, she was beautiful. "Maybe it's just a good thing, Hunt. So many shitty things have happened to us that we might not trust when something actually *is* good. But maybe we got lucky with Celestina's appointment."

"I'm inclined to think Urd's dealing us a decent hand," Juniper agreed.

Fury Axtar said nothing, her eyes shining as she thought. The merc would likely be the only one to fully grasp the workings of the Asteri. Not that she'd ever reveal the details of her dealings with them.

"Celestina wants to meet what remains of Micah's triarii when she arrives. Apparently, there's going to be some sort of restructuring," Hunt said as Bryce handed back his phone. "Whatever that means. The press release won't go live until tomorrow morning. So keep it quiet." The three females nodded, though he had a feeling Fury wouldn't keep her word. Whoever she answered to, whatever valuable clients she served, would likely hear before dawn.

Bryce hooked her red hair behind her pointed ears. "When's Celestina coming?"

"Tomorrow evening." His throat constricted.

Juniper and Fury fell into quiet conversation, as if to grant them privacy. Bryce, catching their drift, lowered her voice. "You're a free male, Hunt. She can't order you to do anything you don't want to do." Her warm fingers wrapped around his wrist, thumb brushing over the branded-out *SPQM*. "You *chose* to reenlist in the 33rd. You have the rights of a free citizen. If you don't like her, if you don't want to serve her, then you don't need to give her a reason in order to leave. You don't need her permission."

Hunt grunted his agreement, though he still had a fucking knot in his chest. "Celestina could make life very difficult for us."

Bryce held up a hand. Starlight radiated, turning her skin iridescent. A drunk asshole nearby let out an *ooooooh*. Bryce ignored him and said, "I'd like to see her try. I'm the Super Powerful and Special Magic Starborn Princess, remember?" He knew she was joking, but her mouth thinned. "I'll protect you."

"How could I forget, oh Magically Powerful and Super Special . . . whatever you said."

Bryce grinned, lowering her hand. She'd been meeting with Ruhn once a week to explore her magic—to learn more about what lay within her veins, fueled by the power of so many. Her magic only manifested as starlight—a purely Fae gift. No shadows, like Ruhn possessed, or fire, like her father. But the sheer force of her power came from all those who'd given a droplet of their magic to the Gates over the years. All combined to make some kind of fuel to increase the potency of her starlight. Or something like that. Bryce had tried to explain it—why the magic manifested as a Fae talent—but Hunt didn't care where it came from, so long as it kept her safe.

The magic was protection in a world designed to kill her. From a father who might very well want to eliminate the threat of a daughter who surpassed him in power, if only by a fraction.

Hunt still had trouble fathoming that the female standing beside him had become more powerful than the Autumn King. Hunt's power technically still outranked hers, and her father's, but with the Horn etched in her back, who really knew the depths of Bryce's power? Considering Rigelus's order to lie low, it wasn't like Bryce could explore how the Horn affected her magic, but given what it had done this spring . . . He doubted Bryce would ever be tempted to experiment with it anyway.

He caught Axtar watching Bryce, but the merc said nothing.

So Hunt continued, only loud enough to indicate that he wanted Fury and Juniper to also hear, "I don't know what this Celestina thing is about, but the Asteri do nothing out of the kindness of their hearts."

"They'd need hearts to do that," Juniper whispered with uncharacteristic venom.

Fury's voice lowered. "The war is getting worse in Pangera. Valbara is a key territory full of vital resources. Appointing someone who all reports claim is *nice* seems idiotic."

Juniper raised her brows. Not at the claim about the Asteri, Hunt guessed, but that Fury had willingly mentioned the war overseas. The merc rarely, if ever, talked about it. What she'd done over there. What she'd seen. Hunt, having fought in many of those battles, had a good idea of both.

"Maybe they really do want a puppet," Juniper said. "Someone who's a figurehead, so they can order all of Valbara's troops overseas with no resistance."

Fury tucked a strand of her hair behind an ear. From all appearances, Axtar seemed human. But she was definitely Vanir—of what breed, what House, Hunt had no idea. Flame and Shadow seemed likeliest, but more than that, he couldn't guess. The merc said, "Even Micah might have resisted that order."

Bryce's face paled at the bastard's name. Hunt repressed the urge to fold a wing around her. He hadn't told her of his own nightmares—of being forced to watch, over and over, as Micah brutalized her. And the nightmares of how she'd raced through the streets, demons from Hel's darkest pits swarming her. Of brimstone missiles shooting for her in the Old Square.

"We can guess all night," Bryce said, mastering herself. "But until you have that meeting tomorrow, Hunt, we won't know. Just go in there with an open mind."

"You mean, don't start a fight." His mouth twitched to the side. Fury snickered.

Bryce put a hand on her hip. "I mean, don't go in there playing Scary Asshole. Maybe try for an Approachable Asshole vibe."

Juniper laughed at that, and Hunt chuckled as well. Unable to stop himself from knocking Bryce with a wing for the second time that night, he promised, "Approachable Asshole it is, Quinlan."

3

Ruhn Danaan knew three things with absolute certainty:

1. He had smoked so much mirthroot that he couldn't feel his face. Which was a damn shame because there was a female currently sitting on it.
2. He had downed an obscene amount of whiskey, because he had no idea what the female's name was, or how they'd gotten to his bedroom, or how he'd wound up with his tongue between her legs.
3. He really fucking loved his life. At least . . . right now.

Ruhn dug his fingers into the soft, spotted flanks of the delectable creature moaning above him, dragging his lip ring across that spot he knew would—

Yeah. There it was. That groan of pure pleasure that shot right to his cock, currently aching behind the fly of his black jeans. He hadn't even undressed before going to town on the sweet faun who'd shyly approached him at the beer pong table. He'd gotten one look at her large green eyes, the long legs that ended in those pretty little hooves, and the creamy skin of her neck, above those high, perky breasts, and known precisely where he wanted this night to end.

Good thing she'd had the same idea. Had told him precisely what she wanted in that whisper-soft voice.

Ruhn flicked his tongue across the taut bud of her clit, savoring the meadow-soft taste of her in his mouth. She arched, thighs straining—and came with a series of breathy moans that nearly had him spilling in his pants.

Ruhn gripped her bare ass, letting her ride his face through each wave of pleasure, moaning himself as he slipped his tongue inside her to let her delicate inner muscles clench around him.

Fuck, this was hot. *She* was hot. Even through the haze of drugs and booze, he was ready to go. All he needed was the okay from those full lips and he'd be buried in her within seconds.

For a heartbeat, like an arrow of light fired through the blissed-out darkness of his mind, he remembered that he was, technically, betrothed. And not to some simpering Fae girl whose parents might be pissed at his behavior, but to the Queen of the Valbaran Witches. Granted, they'd sworn no vows of faithfulness—for fuck's sake, they'd barely spoken to each other during the Summit and in the months afterward—but . . . did it cross some line, to fuck around like this?

He knew the answer. The weight of it had lain heavy on him for months. And perhaps that was why he was here right now: it did cross a line, but a line he had no say in. And yes, he respected and admired Hypaxia Enador—she was alarmingly beautiful, brave, and intelligent—but until the High Priestess bound their hands at Luna's Temple, until that titanium ring went on his finger . . . he'd savor these last months of freedom.

He hoped it would be months, anyway. Hypaxia had not given his father any indication of a timeline.

The faun stilled, chest heaving, and Ruhn let his thoughts of his betrothed fade away as he swallowed the taste of the faun deep into his throat.

"Merciful Cthona," the faun breathed, rising on her knees to pull herself off his face. Ruhn released the firm cheeks of her ass, meeting her bright gaze as she peered at him, a flush across her high cheekbones.

Ruhn winked up at her, running a tongue over the corner of his mouth to get one final taste of her. Gods, she was delectable. Her throat bobbed, her pulse fluttering like a beckoning drum.

Ruhn ran his hands up her bare thighs, fingers grazing over her narrow hips and waist. "Do you want to—"

The door to his bedroom burst open, and Ruhn, pinned beneath the female, could do nothing but twist his head toward the male standing there.

Apparently, the sight of the Crown Prince of the Valbaran Fae with a female straddling his face was common enough that Tristan Flynn didn't so much as blink. Didn't even smirk, though the faun leapt off Ruhn with a squeak, hiding herself behind the bed.

"Get downstairs," Flynn said, his usually golden-brown skin pale. Gone was any hint of drunken revelry. Even his brown eyes were sharp.

"Why?" Ruhn asked, wishing he had time to talk to the female quickly gathering her clothes on the other side of the bed before he headed for the door.

But Flynn pointed to the far corner—the pile of dirty laundry, and the Starsword propped against the stained wall beside it. "Bring that."

Ruhn's raging hard-on had vanished, thankfully, by the time he made it to the top of the stairs above the foyer. Music still shook the floors of the house, people still drank and hooked up and smoked and did whatever bullshit they usually enjoyed during these parties.

No sign of danger, no sign of anything except—

There. A prickle at the back of his neck. Like a chill wind had skittered over the top of his spine.

"Dec's new security system picked up some kind of anomaly," Flynn said, scanning the party below. He'd gone into pure Aux mode. "It's making all the sensors go off. Some kind of aura—Dec said it felt like a storm was circling the house."

"Great," Ruhn said, the hilt of the Starsword cool against his back. "And it's not some drunk asshole dicking around with magic?"

Flynn assessed the crowds. "Dec didn't think so. He said from the way it circled the house, it seemed like it was surveilling the area."

Their friend and roommate had spent months designing a system to be placed around their house and the surrounding streets—one that could pick up things like the kristallos demon, formerly too fast for their technology to detect.

"Then let's see how it likes being watched, too," Ruhn said, wishing he was slightly less high and drunk as his shadows wobbled around him. Flynn sniggered.

The mirthroot took hold for a moment, and even Ruhn laughed as he moved for the staircase. But his amusement faded as he checked the rooms on either side of the foyer. Where the fuck was Bryce? He'd last seen her with Fury, Juniper, and Athalar in the living room, but from this angle atop the stairs, he couldn't see her—

Ruhn had made it three steps down the front staircase, dodging discarded beer cans and plastic cups and someone's zebra-print bra, when the open front doors darkened.

Or rather, the space within them darkened. Exactly as it had when those demons had stormed through the Gates.

Ruhn gaped for a moment at the portal to Hel that had just replaced his front doors.

Then he reached for the sword half-buckled at his back, working past his brain fog to gather shadows in his other hand. Laughter and singing and talking stopped, and the firstlights guttered. The music shut off as if someone had yanked the power cord from the wall.

Then Bryce and Athalar were at the archway into the living room, his sister now wearing Athalar's hat, and the angel armed with a gun discreetly tucked against his thigh. Athalar was the only person Ruhn would allow to bring a gun into one of his parties. And Axtar—who was now nowhere to be seen.

Ruhn drew his sword as he leapt down the rest of the stairs, managing to land gracefully on the other side of his sister. Flynn and Dec fell into place beside him. His shadows swirled up his left arm like twining snakes.

A faint light glowed from Bryce— No, that was the glow stick on her arm.

A figure stalked from the darkness in the doorway. Straight out of Hel. And in that moment, Ruhn knew three more things.

1. He wasn't looking at a portal to Hel after all. Shadows swirled there instead. Familiar, whispering shadows.
2. It wasn't just the glow stick coiled around Bryce's arm that was shining. The star-shaped scar beneath her T-shirt blazed with iridescent light.
3. As a familiar golden-haired Fae male strode from those shadows and into the foyer, Ruhn knew his night was about to take a turn for the worse.

4

"Oh, *come on*," Bryce hissed at the glowing scar between her breasts. Or what she could glimpse of it with the neckline of her T-shirt and her bra in the way. It lit up the fabric of both, and if she hadn't been facing the towering Fae male who'd appeared out of a cloud of shadows, she *might* have used the moment to ponder why and how it glowed.

Partygoers had stopped dead in their revelry. Waiting for whatever shit was about to go down.

And what asshole had turned off the music? Dramahounds.

"What the fuck are you doing here?" Ruhn prowled closer to the stranger.

The male's tan face might have been ruggedly good-looking were it not for the complete lack of feeling there. His light brown eyes were dead. Humorless. His thin white sweater over black jeans and combat boots told Bryce he'd come from somewhere colder.

The crowd seemed to sense danger, too, and backed away until only Hunt, Bryce, Ruhn, and his friends remained facing the stranger. She had no idea where Fury and Juniper were. The former was likely strategically positioned in the room to make sure she could intercept any danger before it reached her girlfriend. Good.

The stranger stalked forward, and Bryce braced herself, even as Hunt casually angled himself between her and the male. Bryce held in her grin at the gesture. And found that grin vanishing instantly when the blond spoke, his accent rolling and rich.

"I was invited."

The stranger turned to her and smirked, lifeless as a dead fish. "I don't believe we've met." A nod toward her—her chest. "Though I know who you are, of course." His eyes flicked over her. "You look better than expected. Not that I was expecting much."

"What the *fuck* are you doing here, Cormac?" Ruhn ground out, stepping closer. But he sheathed the Starsword down his back once more.

The blond—Cormac—faced her brother. He sniffed once, then chuckled. "You smell like cunt."

Bryce nearly gagged at the thought. Cormac went on as Ruhn bristled, "And I told you: I was invited."

"Not to this fucking house," Flynn said, moving to Ruhn's side, Declan flanking his other. A lethal unit.

Cormac assessed his surroundings. "You call this a house? I hadn't realized your standards had dropped so low, Lord Hawthorne."

Declan snarled. "Fuck off, Cormac." Marc came up behind him, teeth bared with silent menace.

Any other opponent, Bryce knew the group would likely obliterate, but this male was Avallen Fae: powerful, trained in combat from a young age, and merciless.

The male said, as if seeing her try to puzzle him out, "I'm your cousin, Bryce."

Hunt—the fucking bastard—snorted.

"I don't have any Fae cousins." Bryce snapped. If only the stupid scar would halt its glowing. If only people would go back to partying.

"That light says otherwise," Cormac said with blatant confidence. "I might be Ruhn's cousin directly through his mother's kin, but your father, King Einar, is Fae, and his line once crossed with ours long ago." He held up his hand, and flame wreathed his fingers before winking out.

Bryce blinked. Her mother had never once spoken the Autumn King's name, and Bryce had only learned it through the news when she was old enough to use a computer.

"Why are you here?" Ruhn bit out.

From the corner of her vision lightning sizzled at Hunt's fingertips. One strike, and Hunt could fry this fucker.

Yet Cormac smiled. His dead eyes gleamed with nothing but contempt as he bowed mockingly to Bryce. "I'm here to meet my bride."

The words shot through Hunt's mind fast enough that they doused his lightning, but Bryce tipped her head back and laughed.

No one else joined her.

And when Bryce had finished, she smirked at Cormac. "You're hilarious."

"It is no joke," Cormac said, face darkening. "It's been decreed."

"By who?" Hunt snapped.

The Avallen male sized up Hunt with palpable disdain. Not someone used to being questioned, then. Spoiled little prick. "By her sire, the Autumn King, and mine, the High King of the Avallen Fae." Making this shithead a Crown Prince.

Bryce said coolly, "Last I checked, I wasn't on the market."

Hunt crossed his arms, becoming a wall of muscle beside her. Let Cormac see precisely who he'd be tangling with if he took another step closer to Bryce. Hunt willed tendrils of his lightning to crackle along his shoulders, his wings.

"You're an unwed Fae female," Cormac said, unmoved. "That means you belong to your male kin until they decide to pass you to another. The decision has been made."

From the living room archway, a delicate, dark figure emerged. Axtar. She palmed a gun, but kept it at her thigh. No sign of Juniper—presumably, the faun was staying wherever Fury had instructed her to hide.

Cormac glanced toward the merc, and even his sneer faltered.

Every power broker on Midgard knew of Fury Axtar. What she was capable of, if provoked.

Ruhn pointed to the door and snarled at Cormac, "Get the fuck out of my house. I don't care if you use your shadows or your own feet, but get out."

Yet Cormac glowered at the Starsword peeking over Ruhn's broad shoulder. "Rumor has it that the sword sings for my bride, too."

A muscle feathered in Ruhn's jaw. Hunt didn't know what to make of that.

But Bryce stepped forward, star still blazing. "I'm not your bride, asshole. And I'm not going to be, so scuttle back to whatever hole you crawled out of and tell your kings to find someone else. And tell them—"

"You've got a mouth on you," Cormac murmured.

Hunt didn't particularly like the male's appreciative tone. But he kept his power reined in. Even a zap of lightning against Cormac could be seen as a declaration of war.

Fae were highly sensitive babies. Their tantrums could last centuries.

Bryce smiled sweetly at Cormac. "I get that you want to play Broody Prince, but don't ever fucking interrupt me again."

Cormac started. Hunt hid his smirk, even as his blood heated at Bryce's irreverence.

Bryce went on, "My brother told you to leave his house." Her skin began to glow. "You don't want *me* to have to ask you."

The hair on Hunt's neck rose. She'd blinded people with that power—and that had been before the Drop. With all that magic backing her starlight . . . He hadn't yet seen how it would manifest. Half hoped he'd find out now, with this asshole as a test subject.

Hunt eyed Flynn, Declan, and Marc—all of whom were tense and primed to leap into the fray. And Ruhn . . .

Hunt didn't know why Ruhn's apparent satisfaction surprised him. He'd expected wounded male pride, perhaps, at Bryce showing him up in his own home. Yet pride did shine from Ruhn's face—for Bryce. Like the prince had been waiting for his sister to step into her power for a while now and he was honored to have her at his side.

Hunt's attention shot back to Cormac as the Avallen Prince held up his hands and slowly smiled at Bryce. The expression was as dead as his eyes. "I've seen all I needed to."

"What the fuck are you talking about?" Ruhn demanded. Shadows rippled from his shoulders, a dark contrast to the light emanating from Bryce.

But shadows also swirled behind Cormac—darker, wilder than Ruhn's, like a stampede of stallions waiting to gallop over all of them. "I wanted to confirm that she has the gift. Thank you for demonstrating." He set one foot into those untamed shadows. Bowed his head to Bryce. "I'll see you at the altar."

Bryce's star winked out the moment he vanished, leaving only drifting embers behind.

Bryce was dimly aware of the party ending: people filtering out through the front door, the countless eyes on her as she stood in the foyer, typing into her phone.

"There's a train at seven tomorrow morning," Bryce announced to Hunt, who lingered at her side. As if afraid the Avallen male would reappear to snatch her away.

Not just any Avallen male: Prince Cormac. Her . . . fiancé.

"There's no way your mom will go," Hunt said. "If by some miracle she isn't suspicious that you're bumping them onto a train five hours earlier, then Randall will be."

Juniper scrolled on her phone at Bryce's other side. "Social channels are empty right now, but . . ."

"All it takes is one person," Fury finished from where she monitored the front of the house with the same vigilance as Hunt. "I think I made my point clear about the consequences of that, though."

Gods bless her, Fury really had. *If any of you post, talk, or so much as* think *about what went down here tonight,* she'd declared with quiet authority to the awed partygoers, *I'll hunt you down and make you regret it.*

No one had said anything, but Bryce had noticed more than a few people deleting pictures from their phones as they hurried out.

Hunt said, "Getting your parents out of the city without them being suspicious *or* finding out will be tricky, to say the least." He angled his head. "You sure it's not easier to tell them?"

"And risk my mom going ballistic? Doing something reckless?" And that was to say nothing about what Randall might do if he thought the Autumn King was threatening Bryce's happiness and control over her own life. Whatever her mom left of the Autumn King, Randall would be sure to put a bullet in it. "I'm not risking them like that."

"They're adults," Fury said. "You can trust them to make rational choices."

"Have you met my mom?" Bryce burst out. "Does *rational* ever spring to mind when you think about her? She makes sculptures of babies in beds of lettuce, for fuck's sake."

"I just think," June jumped in, "that they're going to find out anyway, so maybe it's better if it comes from you. Before they hear it from someone else."

Bryce shook her head. "Nope. I want to be far, far away when they find out. And get a few hundred miles between them and the Autumn King, too."

Hunt grunted his agreement, and she threw him a grateful nod.

The sound of Declan shutting the front door pulled her attention from the angel as the Fae male leaned back against it. "Well, my buzz is officially ruined."

Flynn slumped onto the lowest steps of the staircase, a bottle of whiskey in his hand. "Then we better start getting it back." He swigged deeply before passing it up to Ruhn, who leaned against the banister with crossed arms, his blue eyes blazing into a near-violet. He'd been quiet these last few minutes.

Bryce had no idea where to start with him. About Cormac, about the power she'd shown in Ruhn's own house, about the star glowing for the Avallen Prince . . . any of it. So she said, "I take it that's the cousin from your Ordeal."

Ruhn, Dec, and Flynn nodded gravely. Her brother drank from the bottle of whiskey.

"How close did Cormac get to killing you during your Ordeal?"

Hunt asked. Ruhn must have told him about it at some point this summer.

"Close," Flynn said, earning a glare from Ruhn.

But Ruhn admitted, "It was bad." Bryce could have sworn he didn't look at her as he added, "Cormac spent his whole life thinking he'd get the Starsword one day. That he'd go into the Cave of Princes and be proven worthy. He studied all the lore, learned all the lineage, pored over every account detailing the variations in the power. It, ah . . . didn't go down well when I got it instead."

"And now his fiancée has a claim to it, also," Flynn said, and it was Bryce's turn to glare at the lord. She could have lived without anyone bringing that up again.

Ruhn seemed to force himself to look at Bryce as he said, "It's true." So he'd seen her glare, then. "The sword's as much yours as it is mine."

Bryce waved a hand. "I'll take it on weekends and holidays, don't worry."

Hunt tossed in, "And it'll get *two* Winter Solstices, so . . . double the presents."

Ruhn and the others gawked at them like they had ten heads, but Bryce grinned at Hunt. He returned it with one of his own.

He got her—her humor, her fears, her hedging. Whatever it was, Athalar *got* her.

"Is it true?" Juniper looped her elbow through Bryce's and pressed close. "About the legality of an engagement against Bryce's will?"

That wiped the smile from Hunt's face. And Bryce's. Her mind raced, each thought as swift and dizzying as a shooting star.

"Tell me there's a way out of this, Ruhn." She walked to her brother and snatched the whiskey bottle from him. A faint light flared at his back—the Starsword. It hummed, a whining sound like a finger tracing the rim of a glass.

Ruhn's stare met hers, questioning and wary, but Bryce stepped back. The sword stopped singing.

It's not going to bite, you know.

Bryce nearly flinched as her brother's voice filled her mind. He used the mind-speaking rarely enough that she often entirely forgot he had the gift.

It's your sword. Not mine. You're as much a Starborn Prince as I am a princess.

He shot back, eyes glinting with stars, *I'm not the kind of male whose sense of pride is so brittle that I need to cling to a shiny weapon. If you want to use it, it's yours.*

She shook her head. *You retrieved the blade—and apparently had to deal with Cormac while doing it. That fact alone entitles you to keep it.*

Ruhn's laughter filled her mind, full of amusement and relief. But his face remained serious as he said to the group, now staring at them, "I didn't pay attention in class when we covered Fae law. Sorry."

"Well, I did," Marc said. "And I've already put some of my firm's associates on researching it. Any legal case or precedent that's been uploaded into a database, short of whatever's hidden in the Asteri Archives, we'll be able to comb through."

Declan added, "I'll go hunting, too." But even Dec, with his hacking skills, couldn't pierce the security around the private, ancient files of the Asteri.

"Thank you," Bryce said, but she didn't allow that shred of hope to balloon in her chest. "Update me when you have anything."

Ruhn started talking, but Bryce tuned him out, handing off the bottle of whiskey to Juniper before slipping out onto the sagging front porch, dodging discarded cups and cans. Hunt was a storm wind at her back as she strode onto the small slice of grassy front lawn and breathed in the bustle of the Old Square before her.

"Why are you being so calm about this?" Hunt asked, his arms crossed. The dry, warm night breeze ruffled his hair, his gray wings.

"Because this is some move in a game the Autumn King is playing," Bryce said. "He's anticipating that I'm going to run to his house and fight him. I'm trying to figure out why that would help him. What his endgame is."

And what her own might be.

"Connecting the two most powerful Fae royal bloodlines is a

pretty clear endgame," Hunt growled. "And you're Starborn on top of it—you told me you've got the gifts of one of the first of the Starborn. *And* you've got the Horn. That makes you a massive bargaining chip for more power."

"That's too simple for the Autumn King. His games play out over years—centuries. This engagement is the first step. Or maybe we're already several steps along." She just needed to find some way to get a few steps ahead of *that* without revealing her hand. The engagement would have to stand. For now.

"It's bullshit."

Bryce steeled her spine. "I was really enjoying this summer, you know. Today seems Hel-bent on ruining it for both of us."

Hunt ducked his head. "You'd almost think this was planned by the gods. They probably have a special task force: How to Fuck Over Bryce and Hunt in One Day."

Bryce chuckled. "Celestina might wind up being a blessing. But . . ." She asked Hunt, "You think the Autumn King might have timed this to coincide with you getting the news about Celestina?"

"To what end?"

"To rattle us. To make us act, I don't know." She dared say, "Maybe he thought you'd go after him, and it'd make you look bad in front of the new Archangel."

Hunt stilled, and Bryce became keenly aware of the distance between their bodies. "Again," he said, voice husky, "to what end?"

"If you did something illegal," Bryce mused, heart beginning to thunder as he stepped closer, "like . . ."

"Kill a Crown Prince of the Fae?"

Bryce chewed on her lip. "Celestina needs to set an example of how she plans to rule. And punishing a powerful angel, a *notorious* angel acting out of line . . . that'd be the perfect way to demonstrate her power. And thus get you out of the picture for the Autumn King. He knows we're a team."

"A team," Hunt said slowly. As if, out of everything she'd laid out, *that* was what he chose to dwell on.

"You know what I mean," Bryce said.

"I'm not sure I do." Had his voice dropped lower?

"We're roomies," she said, her own voice getting breathy.

"Roomies."

"Occasional Beer Pong Champions?"

Hunt snatched the hat off her head and plunked it back on his own, backward as usual. "Yes, the Autumn King truly fears our unholy beer pong alliance."

Bryce smiled, letting it chase away the darkness lurking in her soul. But Hunt added, "We can't forget that Avallen has their own angle. Why'd they agree to the union?"

"You know what?" Bryce said. "Who cares about any of them? My father, the Avallen Fae—screw them." Only with Hunt could she be dismissive about this. He'd have her back, no matter what. "At least until we get my parents onto that train."

"You still haven't given me a convincing plan for how *that* will happen. For all we know, they're learning about this on the news."

"Oh, my phone would already be exploding if my mother had heard." She ran a hand through her hair. "Maybe I should ask Fury to sneak into their hotel and disable their phones."

"Is it bad if I think she should go one step further and tie them up, throw them in the trunk of a car, and drive them home so they get there before the news breaks? Because that's what Fury will likely do if you send her to that hotel."

Bryce laughed, and the sound sang through her like silver bells. "Okay, no Fury." She looped her arm through Hunt's, savoring the muscled mass of him as she steered them toward the low gate and sidewalk beyond. "Let's watch old episodes of *Beach House Hookup* and come up with ways to trick my parents."

One of his wings brushed along her back in the softest of caresses. Every inch it touched lit up like firstlight. "Sounds like a normal Tuesday night."

They meandered home, and despite Bryce's flippant words, she found herself slipping into a state of roiling darkness and thoughts like shooting stars. She'd been a fool to think she could lie low forever. She'd been willing to follow the Asteri's order to lead a boring, normal life, but the rest of the world had different plans for her. And Hunt.

She was bringing her phone to her ear to call her parents with the news that *Oh, so sad, but Jesiba needs me to head over to her warehouse tomorrow and I think this might lead to a second chance at a job with her, so do you mind getting on the earlier train?* when she and Hunt walked off the elevator and found the door to their apartment ajar.

If her mom and Randall had come over unexpectedly . . .

Syrinx was barking inside, and Bryce lunged for the door, the memory of another night washing red over her senses. Now, as then, the scent of blood was a coppery tang in the air, in the hallway, on the threshold of her door—

Not again. Not her parents—

Hunt shoved her back as he angled himself at the doorway, gun out and lightning wreathing his other hand, violence written in every taut line of his body, his raised wings.

Surprise flared in his dark eyes, and then he lowered the gun. Bryce beheld what was in the center of the great room and swayed into Hunt with relief and shock.

Yes, the gods had clearly formed a How to Fuck Over Hunt and Bryce task force.

Inside lay Ithan Holstrom, bleeding all over her pale wood floors.

5

Tharion Ketos had royally fucked up.

Literally. The River Queen had been *pissed.*

Which was why he was now struggling to keep his feet on a small fishing vessel in a sea so stormy it made even his iron stomach churn. Up and down, down and up, the boat bobbed in the rain and swells, wind threatening to flay his skin to the bone, despite his thick black sweater and the tactical vest atop it.

He should be lounging on a rock in the Istros right now, preferably in plain sight of whatever females walked along the quay. He certainly enjoyed finding not-so-covert photos of him on social media, with captions like: *So hot it's a miracle he doesn't turn the Istros to steam!*

That had been a particular favorite. Too bad it had also landed him here. Punished by the River Queen because her daughter had cried over it.

He was accustomed to cold, had explored as deep as his mer's gifts would allow without his skull cracking like an egg, but this northern stretch of the Haldren Sea was different. It sucked the life from one's bones, its grayness creeping into the soul.

Though swimming would be a Hel of a lot less nauseating.

Tharion ducked his head against the lashing rain, his dark red hair plastered to his scalp, dripping icy water down his neck. Gods, he wanted to go home. Back to the dry, blistering heat of a Lunathion summer.

"Submersible's within range," the captain called. The female dolphin shifter was tucked in the safety of the command vestibule. Lucky asshole. "We're starting to get a live feed."

Barely able to maintain his grip on the rain-slick rail of the boat, Tharion aimed for the vestibule. It could only fit two people, so he had to wait until the first mate—a shark shifter—squeezed out before entering. The warmth was like a kiss from Solas himself, and Tharion sighed as he slid the door shut and observed the small screen beside the wheel.

The images from the trench were murky: flurries of floating bits in a whole lot of darkness. If they'd been on a battleship—Hel, even a yacht—they'd have had giant screens with crystal clarity. But this fishing boat, capable of slipping past the Pangeran navy's radar, had been the best bet.

The captain stood before the screen, pointing with a brown finger to a rising number in its upper right corner. "We're nearing the requested depth."

Tharion sank into the swivel chair anchored into the floor. Technically, it was the captain's chair, but he didn't care. He was paying for this expedition. Granted, it was with his Blue Court–issued credit card, but he could damn well sit where he wanted to.

The captain raised a dark brow. "You know what you're looking for?" She'd come highly recommended by a few spies in his employ—a discreet and bold female who wouldn't flee at the first hint of imperial battleships.

Tharion surveyed the screen. "A body."

The captain whistled. "You know the odds of that are—"

"She was tied to lead blocks and dropped into the water around here." By the Hind.

"If she's not in the House of Many Waters, she's long dead."

No shit. "I just need to find her." What remained of her, after two weeks at the bottom of the sea. Frankly, her bones and body had likely exploded from the pressure.

His queen had learned of the poor girl's fate through whatever the rivers and seas whispered to her. He'd known it was how the River Queen kept tabs on her sisters, who ruled the other bodies of water around Midgard, but he hadn't realized how precise the information could be—she'd been able to tell him to hunt for lead blocks, and where to look. And what manner of Vanir, exactly, Sofie was: a thunderbird. Ogenas have mercy on them all.

It was on the slim chance that Sofie's Vanir body had survived the plunge—and hadn't been picked apart yet by scavengers—that he'd come. His queen seemed to be under the impression that Sofie was an asset, even dead.

His queen had refused to tell him more than that. She'd only said that he was to retrieve the body and bring it back to the Blue Court. Presumably to search it for intel or weapons. He prayed he wouldn't be the one to do it.

"We're at depth," the captain announced, and the camera feed halted. More white bits swirled past as the camera pivoted to reveal the silty, alien seafloor. "Any idea where to start, Captain?"

Captain. Tharion still found the title ridiculous, and more than a little painful. The case that had earned him the recent promotion had been his sister's murder. He'd have traded in the title in a heartbeat if it meant he could have Lesia back. Hear his younger sister's boisterous laugh one more time. Catching and killing her murderer hadn't eased that feeling.

"Based on the current, she should have landed around here," Tharion said, letting his water magic drift to the bottom, cringing at the ocean's viciousness. Not at all like the clear calm of the Istros. Granted, plenty of monsters dwelled within the Blue River, but the turquoise water sang to him, laughed with him, cried with him. This sea only bellowed and raged.

Tharion monitored the camera feed. "Rotate the camera to the west—and move the submersible ahead about ten yards."

Through the glare of the firstlight beams atop the remote submersible, more fleshy white bits floated by. This was what the wraith Viktoria had been damned by Micah to endure. The former Archangel had shoved her essence into a magically sealed box while the wraith remained fully conscious despite having no corporeal form, and dropped her to the floor of the Melinoë Trench.

That the trench's bottom was another fifteen miles deeper than the seafloor before them sent a shiver along Tharion's tiger-striped forearms. The wraith's shoebox-sized Helhole had been bespelled against the pressure. And Viktoria, not needing food or water, would live forever. Trapped. Alone. No light, nothing but silence, not even the comfort of her own voice.

A fate worse than death. With Micah now sitting in a trash bag in some city dump, would anyone dare retrieve the wraith? Athalar had shown no signs of rebellion, and Bryce Quinlan, the last Tharion had heard, was content to return to a normal life.

Hel, after this spring, hadn't everyone wanted to return to normal?

The River Queen didn't seem to want to. She'd sent him hunting for a rebel spy's remains. To retrieve her Very Fucking Important corpse.

Even if the mere fact that the River Queen was searching for the body of a rebel spy could damn her. Damn all of them.

And he'd be first in the line of fire. But he never dared to challenge her about the contradictions of it: she punished him for making her daughter cry, yet what would happen should he be killed or harmed during one of her punishments? Wouldn't her daughter cry then?

Her daughter, as capricious as her mother—and as jealous. If she was a bit of a possessive monster, it was because her mother had taught her well.

He'd been a fool not to see it before he'd taken her maidenhead and sworn himself to her a decade ago. Before he'd ever made himself her betrothed. Beloved of the River Queen's daughter. A prince-in-training.

A fucking nightmare.

Judging by the fact that he had kept his job these ten years, and even been promoted, her mother apparently still had no idea what to do with him. Unless her daughter had intervened on his behalf, to keep him safe. The thought of that alone—that he had to stay on her good side—had made him keep his hands to himself and his cock in his pants. Fins. Whatever.

And he'd accepted the punishments, however unfair and undeserved and dangerous, that were thrown his way.

"I'm not seeing anything." The captain adjusted the control toggle on the dash.

"Keep moving. Do a complete scan within a one-mile perimeter." He wouldn't return to his queen empty-handed if he could help it.

"We'll be here for hours," the captain countered, frowning.

Tharion just settled into the chair, glancing to the first mate sheltering against the side of the vestibule.

They knew what they were getting into by coming here. Knew what kind of storms stalked these seas at this point in the year. If the shifter got tired of the wind and rain, he could jump beneath the waves.

Even if a shark in these waters was the least of the terrors.

Three and a half hours later, Tharion lifted a hand. "Go back to the right. No—yeah. There. Can you get closer?"

The remote submersible had floated past boiling-hot sea vents, past muck and rock and all manner of strange creatures. But there, tucked among a cluster of red-and-white tuber worms . . . a square rock.

Only Vanir or human hands could have made it.

"I'll be damned," the captain murmured, leaning toward the screen, the light illuminating her angular face. "Those are lead blocks."

He suppressed a shiver. The River Queen had been right. Down to the last detail. "Circle them."

But . . . Chains draped from the block onto the seafloor. They were empty.

The captain observed, "Whoever those chains held is long gone. They either got eaten or they exploded from the pressure."

Tharion marked the chains, nodding. But his gaze snagged on something.

He glanced at the captain to see if she'd noticed the anomaly, but her face revealed no sign of surprise. So Tharion kept silent, letting her bring the small submersible back up to the surface, where the first mate hauled it onto the deck.

Two hours later, back on land—soggy and muddy from the rain—Tharion calmed his chattering teeth long enough to call his queen.

The River Queen answered after the first ring. "Talk."

Used to the curt, yet ethereal voice, Tharion said, "I found the lead blocks. The chains were still attached."

"So?"

"There was no body." A sigh of disappointment. He shivered yet again—not entirely from the cold. "But the shackles had been unlocked."

The sigh paused. He'd learn to read her pauses, as varied as the life in her river. "You're sure of this?"

He refrained from asking why the currents hadn't told her about this particularly vital detail. Maybe they were as capricious as she. Tharion said mildly, "No signs of damage. At least as far as I could tell on the crappy screen."

"You think Sofie Renast freed herself?"

"I don't know." Tharion climbed into the black SUV that he'd drive to the private heliport in the north of Pangera, and turned the heat to full blast. It'd probably take the entire hour's drive inland to warm his frozen body. "But I sure as Hel don't think she ever made it to the seafloor."

Tharion drove down the rough road, mud spraying, windshield wipers swishing faintly.

His queen said, "Then either someone got there before us . . . or Sofie is alive. Interesting, that the water did not whisper of that. As if it were silenced." Tharion had a feeling he knew where this was going. "Find her," she ordered. "I'd bet my court that she's looking for her brother. She went to great lengths to free him from Kavalla. The sea whispered that he is as gifted as she. Find him, and we find her. And vice versa. But even if we only find the boy . . . he will be valuable indeed."

Tharion didn't dare ask why she wanted either of them. He could invent reasons for wanting the rebel, but the boy . . . Emile Renast had his sister's gift, and that was it. A powerful one, but he was a kid. Hadn't even made the Drop. And as far as Tharion knew, his queen wasn't in the habit of using child soldiers. But Tharion couldn't say anything other than: "I'll begin the search immediately."

6

Bryce tore through the cabinet beneath her sink. Bottles of hair products, old makeup palettes, dead blow-dryers flew out and scattered behind her. Where the *fuck* had she put it—

There. Bryce yanked out the white first aid kit, Syrinx doing a little dance next to her. As if the golden-furred chimera had found it himself. Cheeky pup.

Leaping to her feet as she opened the lid, she rifled through the antiseptic ointment, bandages, and vial of pain-relieving potion. She frowned down at Syrinx. "This stuff never goes bad, right?"

Syrinx scrunched his snout, huffing as if to say, *Beats me!*

Bryce scratched under his chin and returned to the great room to find Hunt crouching beside Ithan, whom they'd laid out on the coffee table. Ithan's face . . . Burning Solas.

Well, he was awake. And talking. She hoped he hadn't heard her and Hunt bickering over where to put his barely conscious form a moment ago. Hunt had wanted to set Ithan on the couch, and Bryce hadn't been able to stop herself from shrieking about ruining the white cushions. So the coffee table it was.

Hunt and Ithan were murmuring too low for Bryce to understand, and they halted as she approached. Though she could detect no outward sign of it, Hunt's lightning seemed to crackle in the air around him. Or maybe that was Hunt's presence, once again doing funny things to her senses. Bryce lifted the first aid kit. "Found it."

Ithan grunted. "It's . . . it's not as bad as it looks."

"Your mouth literally started bleeding again saying that," Bryce said, dropping the kit on the table next to Ithan before fishing inside for sterile wipes. She hadn't seen him since the attack last spring. Hadn't spoken to him.

Bryce waved a hand over the bruised and swollen face that held no resemblance to the handsome, charming features she'd once known so well. "I don't even know where to start with this . . . mess." She didn't just mean his face.

"You and me both," Ithan mumbled, and hissed as Bryce dabbed at a slice across his brow. He pulled his head from her reach. "It'll heal. That one's already smaller."

"I'd guess claws made that," Hunt said, arms crossed. Syrinx hopped onto the sectional, turned in a circle three times, then curled up in a ball.

Ithan said nothing. Bryce reached for the wound again, but he pulled his head farther back, wincing in pain.

"Why the fuck are you here, Ithan?" Hunt's voice was like gravel.

Ithan's brown eyes, one half-swollen, met Bryce's. Ire glowed in them. "I didn't tell them to bring me here. Perry . . . my pack's Omega . . . She arranged it."

A fuzzy memory of a brown-haired female emerged. Perry . . . Ravenscroft. Amelie's younger sister. "*She* did this to you?"

Ithan huffed a raw laugh, then winced. His ribs must be—

Bryce lifted Ithan's bloody gray T-shirt, revealing disgustingly carved abs and—"Holy shit, Ithan."

He yanked the shirt back over the extensive bruising. "It's fine."

"Those look like broken ribs," Hunt said wryly.

"Definitely broken ribs, Athalar," Bryce replied, sitting back on her heels. "And a broken arm, from the way he's cradling it."

"Skull fracture's healed," Hunt observed with equal distance, as if they were on one of his favorite Vanir crime procedurals. Ithan's eyes flashed again.

"I'm sensing hostility and a good dose of male pride," Bryce said.

"Throw in some stubbornness and I'd say we've got ourselves a classic case of stupidity," Hunt answered.

"What *the fuck* is wrong with you two?" Ithan demanded.

Bryce smiled at Hunt, all thoughts of the betrothal and her father and the Asteri vanishing at the amusement glittering in the angel's eyes. But she stopped smiling as she faced Ithan again.

"I promise to clean you up as quickly as possible, and you'll be on your way," she said.

"Take your time. It's not like I have anywhere to go."

Hunt stilled. "Amelie kicked you out?"

"Sabine kicked me out," Ithan growled. "She, Amelie, and the others did . . . this."

"Why?" Bryce managed to say.

Ithan met her stare. "Why do you think?" Bryce shook her head, disgust creeping through her. Ithan said, "You know how Sabine operates. Some reporter cornered me at a bar a few weeks ago about the attack last spring, and I talked about . . . what happened. How I helped you. The article came out this morning. Sabine apparently wasn't a fan."

"Oh?" Hunt lifted a brow.

Ithan's bruised throat bobbed. "I might have also defended you," he said to Bryce. "Against a nasty quote from Sabine."

Bryce resisted the urge to pull out her phone to search for the article. Nothing in there would make her feel better about this. So she said, "Sabine's a City Head. This is really what she wants to waste her time on?"

"Wolves don't talk shit about other wolves."

"But you did," Hunt countered.

"So did Sabine." He said sadly, wearily to Bryce, "The Prime called you a wolf. That's good enough for me. I, ah . . . It didn't sit well, what Sabine said. But I guess the article didn't sit well with her, either. So I'm out."

Bryce exhaled a long, long breath.

"Why bring you here?" Hunt asked.

Ithan grimaced with pain. "Perry remembered that we were friends, once upon a time." He tried and failed to rise. "But give me a few minutes, then I'll be gone."

"You're staying here," Bryce said. Honestly, after the night she'd had, it was the last thing she wanted. Especially when she still had to call her mom and convince her to get out of town. Gods, if Ember found out Ithan was here, she'd never leave. She'd loved him like a son. Bryce shook off the thought. "You're lucky Sabine didn't kill you."

"Trust me, she wanted to," Ithan said bitterly. "But I wasn't worth the legal headache that would cause."

Bryce swallowed. Connor's little brother had once been her best friend, after Danika. Fury and June had come after that. Gods, how many messages had she and Ithan swapped over the years? How many juvenile jokes had they shared? How many times had she bounced in the stands at one of his sunball games, screaming her lungs out for him?

The male before her was a stranger.

"I should go," Ithan said thickly. Like he remembered their history, too. Read it on her face.

"Sit the fuck down," Hunt said. "You can't even walk."

"Fine," Ithan conceded. "One night."

He had to be desperate, then.

Fighting the tightness in her chest, Bryce pulled out her phone. "Good." She noted the time. Almost midnight. Her parents were likely about to go to bed. "I have to make a call."

Hunt fixed a cup of decaf just to give himself something to do as Ithan lay bleeding on the coffee table behind him. Bryce's voice as she spoke to her parents filtered down the hall in bits and pieces.

We'll plan a long weekend next time. Maybe Hunt and I can come up to you guys. I think he'd love to finally see Nidaros.

Hunt's lips quirked upward. Bringing him home to her parents, huh? No matter that she was lying through her teeth.

The coffee machine finished a heartbeat before Bryce said, "All right. I'll meet you at your hotel at six. Yep. Bright and early. Okay. Love you. Bye."

Hunt blew on the steaming-hot coffee as Bryce padded back down the hall. "Everything good?" he asked her.

"Aside from the fact that I have to be up in a few hours, sure." Bryce slid her phone onto the kitchen counter. "Tickets are switched." She peered at Ithan, whose eyes were closed. But Hunt had no doubt the wolf was listening.

"Right," Bryce said. "Beds."

"I'm good on the couch," Ithan croaked.

Hunt was inclined to agree, but Bryce said, "Oh no. You're in my room. I won't have you bleeding all over my white couch."

Hunt said roughly, "I'll sleep on the couch. Holstrom, you can have my room."

"Nope," Bryce countered. "It's fine. My bed is big."

Hunt shot back, "Then *you* sleep on the couch and give Holstrom the bed."

"With my back problems?" Before Hunt could ask what the Hel she was talking about, she said, "I'm tired, and I don't want to argue. Conversation over."

Ithan cracked open an eye. Hunt reined in his growl of frustration.

Fifteen minutes later, Hunt lay in his own bed, teeth gritted as he stared at the ceiling, with only a snoring Syrinx for company.

It was fine. Totally fucking fine that Ithan Holstrom was sharing Bryce's bed.

Totally. Fucking. Fine.

His bed, his blood roared. Even if he hadn't been near it in months. His bed, *his* Bryce, who'd emerged from the bathroom in her sleep shorts and a faded, threadbare T-shirt that did nothing to hide the shadow of her nipples behind the purple fabric. Thankfully, Holstrom's eyes were too swollen for Hunt to notice if the male looked. Not that it really mattered. He trusted Bryce. Knew precisely what—and who—she wanted.

But . . . it didn't matter that Holstrom had come to Bryce's defense during the attack, or in some stupid article. He'd been a nasty fuck to her in the two years before that. And had let Amelie run rampant, tormenting Bryce over the death of his brother.

And fine—trust aside, maybe he was slightly on edge. Holstrom was good-looking, when he wasn't beaten to Hel and back. He'd been a star sunball player at CCU. Hunt remembered watching a few of the games in the 33rd's lounge in the Comitium, marveling at Holstrom's speed and agility. The male hadn't played the sport for two years now, but he was still built.

Stupid, jealous idiot. For fuck's sake, having Holstrom here bothered him more than that asshole Cormac claiming he'd marry Quinlan.

He hated himself just a little bit as he pulled his phone from the nightstand and typed in *Ithan Holstrom Sabine Fendyr Bryce Quinlan*.

The article popped up immediately.

Hunt skimmed it. Read what Sabine had said and focused on his breathing. On not leaping into the skies and shredding the Prime Apparent into pieces.

"Bryce Quinlan is nothing but a spoiled party girl who was conveniently in the right place during the attack. My wolves saved innocents. She's a pathetic fame-chaser."

Hunt ground his teeth so hard his jaw hurt. Toward the bottom, he found Holstrom's sound bite.

"The wolves only went to Asphodel Meadows because of Bryce. She got the call for help out, and held the line until we could provide backup. She saved this city. She's a hero, as far as I'm concerned. Don't let anyone convince you otherwise. Especially people who weren't even in this city during the attack."

Well, Hunt didn't blame Sabine for being pissed. The truth hurt.

Hunt sighed and was about to set his phone back onto the nightstand when it buzzed with a message from Isaiah. *Thoughts???*

He knew Isaiah was asking about Celestina's appointment. *Too early to tell,* he wrote back. *Too early for hope, too.*

Isaiah answered immediately. *She'll be here tomorrow evening at five. Try to play nice, Hunt. She's not Micah.*

Hunt sent back a thumbs-up. But sleep was a long time coming.

Bryce gazed at her bedroom ceiling, listening to the wet, labored breathing of the male beside her.

Her mom and dad had bought her lies—hook, line, and sinker. Of course, it meant she'd be getting up in four hours, but it was a price worth paying. No news about her engagement had been leaked yet. She could only pray it wouldn't until their train was out of the city.

Ithan shifted slightly, the sound of the blankets loud in the silence. It was strange to have him here, his scent filling her nose. So similar to Connor's scent—

"I could have slept on the couch," Ithan said into the darkness.

"I don't trust Athalar not to smother you with a pillow."

Ithan huffed a laugh. "He holds a grudge, huh?"

"You have no idea."

Silence fell again, thick and heavy. She'd wanted Ithan right where she could see him. It was as simple as that. Wards on this place or not, she wasn't about to leave him unguarded when Sabine and Amelie might change their minds about the paperwork being too much trouble. She'd lost one Holstrom already.

"Danika had me keyed to the locks," Ithan said. "Right before . . . everything. She showed me this place—wanted me in on the surprise. That's how I got in."

Bryce's throat clogged. "Oh."

"Is it true that Danika helped you make the Drop?"

Since her voice had been broadcast through the Gates into every part of the city, it was common knowledge that Danika Fendyr had something to do with Bryce's Drop, but rumors about exactly what ranged widely.

"Yeah," Bryce said. "She, ah . . . She was my Anchor."

"I didn't know that was possible."

"Me neither."

His breathing thinned. Bryce said, "I . . . Ithan, when I saw Danika during the Search, she told me that the others—Connor and Nathalie and the whole Pack of Devils—held off the Reapers to buy her time to be there with me. They saved me, too. Connor saved me."

Ithan said nothing for a long moment. When was the last time they'd spoken like this? Calm, quiet. Without hate spewing like acid, burning everything it touched? Then Ithan said, "He loved you more than anyone."

Her heart strained. "He loved *you* more than anyone."

"He thought you were his mate."

Bryce shut her eyes against the punch that slammed into her gut. "In the wolf sense of the word?"

"What other sense is there? Yeah, the wolf sense."

There were several definitions of the term *mate*—though Bryce supposed that to Ithan, to a shifter, only one mattered: one's true lover, predestined by Urd.

The Fae had a similar concept—a mate was a bond deeper than marriage, and beyond an individual's control. The angels, she knew, used the term far more lightly: for the malakim, it was akin to a marriage, and matings could be arranged. Like breeding animals in a zoo.

But for Connor, if he'd thought Bryce was his mate . . . Her stomach twisted again.

"Did you love him?" Ithan whispered.

"You know I did," Bryce said, voice thick.

"We waste so much time. Maybe it's our curse as immortals. To see time as a luxury, a never-ending ocean." He loosed a long breath. "I wasted a lot of it."

Bryce couldn't tell what he was referring to. "Real poetic of you." Ithan let out a soft laugh. In the air-conditioned dark, Bryce asked, "Why did you quit sunball?"

She felt Ithan tense, the mattress shifting. "Because it's a stupid game," he said, voice empty, and turned onto his side with a groan.

Bryce had no idea how to respond. So she closed her eyes, rubbing idly at the scar on her chest, and prayed for Luna to send her into a dreamless, heavy sleep.

7

This is bullshit." Ruhn paced the ornate rugs of his father's study as the grandfather clock in the corner chimed two in the morning. "You *know* it's total fucking bullshit."

Lounging in a crimson leather armchair by the darkened fireplace, the Autumn King said nothing. The experiments and nonsense he worked on day and night boiled and bubbled away, the sound a steady hum in the background.

"What's the matter, cousin? Feeling possessive of your sister?" Cormac smirked from where he leaned against the black marble mantel, white sweater stretched tight over his muscled chest. Not one golden hair on his head out of place.

Fucker.

Ruhn ignored Cormac's taunt and said to his father, "We live in a modern city. In modern times. There are lawyers by the dozen who have endless resources to challenge this—and courts that might be amenable to setting a new precedent that protects the rights of Fae females."

"Bryce will arrive willingly at the marriage altar," his father said. "As will you."

Cormac's mouth curled upward. "I hear you're engaged to Hypaxia Enador. Congratulations." Ruhn scowled at him. Cormac went on, sizing up Ruhn, "Of course, the marriage is unorthodox, considering your bride's family and bloodline."

Ruhn stiffened. "You've got some shit to spew about Hypaxia, then let's hear it."

But Cormac said to the Autumn King, "He doesn't know?"

His father, damn him, seemed bored as he said, "It didn't seem necessary. My order is law."

Ruhn glanced between them. "What is this?"

His father, features tightening with distaste—as if disappointed that Ruhn hadn't learned it himself—said, "The late Queen Hecuba had two daughters, from different sires. Hypaxia's sire, Hecuba's coven learned afterward, was a powerful necromancer from the House of Flame and Shadow. Hypaxia seems to have inherited his gifts alongside her mother's."

Ruhn blinked. Slowly. Hypaxia could raise and speak to the dead. All right. He could live with that. "Cool."

Flames danced along his father's hair, dancing over his shoulders. "Her older sister, however, was sired by a shape-shifting male. A stag."

"So?"

Cormac snorted. "Hypaxia's half sister is better known as the Hind." Ruhn gaped at him. How had he not known this? "She didn't inherit any witch gifts," Cormac continued, "and was handed over to her father's kin. The crown naturally went to Hypaxia. But it seems that since your bride has been crowned queen, the question of her necromancy has become . . . an issue for the witches."

"It's of no bearing on this conversation," his father said. "Ruhn shall marry her, necromancy or not, odious sister or not."

"My father found Hypaxia's background to be problematic," Cormac said.

"Then it is a good thing your father is not marrying her," the Autumn King countered.

Cormac shut his mouth, and Ruhn held in his grin of delight.

But his father went on, "Ruhn shall marry Hypaxia, and Bryce Quinlan shall marry you, Prince Cormac. There will be no more debate."

"You do remember that Bryce and Athalar are together?" Ruhn said. "Try to get between them, and you'll get a refresher course on why he was called the Umbra Mortis."

"Last my spies reported, she still does not bear his scent. So I can only assume they have not consummated their relationship."

Just talking about this with his father was gross.

Cormac cut in, "One day, she'll be Queen of Avallen. She'd be a fool to throw it away on a bastard angel."

Ruhn spat, "You need Bryce more than she needs either of you. She's Starborn."

The Autumn King's teeth flashed. "If Bryce wished to remain free of our household, then she should not have been so brazen about showing off her power."

"Is that what this is about?" Fire seared through Ruhn's veins. "That she *showed you up*? That she has more power than you? What—you needed to put her back in her place?"

"You're delusional," Cormac's grin promised violence. "I am stooping to marry your sister. Many of my people will consider the union a disgrace."

"Careful," the Autumn King warned, true anger sparking in his whiskey-colored eyes. "Regardless of her human lineage, Bryce is an heir to the Starborn line. More so than my son." He threw a frown dripping with disdain at Ruhn. "We have not seen starlight with such force for thousands of years. I do not take handing her over to Avallen lightly."

"What the fuck are you getting from it?" Nausea clawed its way up Ruhn's throat.

His father answered, "Your sister has one value to me: her breeding potential. Both of our royal houses will benefit from the union."

Cormac added, "And the continued commitment to the alliance between our peoples."

"Against what?" Had everyone lost their minds?

"A weakening of magic in the royal bloodline," Cormac said. "As recent generations have demonstrated." He waved with a flame-crusted hand toward Ruhn and his shadows.

"Fuck you," Ruhn hissed. "Is this about the war in Pangera? The rebellion?" He'd heard rumors recently that Ophion had taken out four Omega submersibles in the north. *Four.* Some insane shit had to be going on over there. His father had even hinted at it in the late spring, when he'd announced Ruhn's betrothal. That war was coming, and they needed to shore up allies.

"It is about ensuring that the Fae retain our power and birthright," his father said. His icy voice had always belied the merciless flame in his blood. "Your sister can imbue that into her offspring with Cormac."

Cormac grunted his agreement, flames winking out.

Ruhn tried again. "For fuck's sake, leave Bryce out of this. Don't we have other royals we can pair off to punch out some babies?"

"I didn't remember you whining so much, Ruhn," Cormac said.

"Before or after you tried to kill me? Or when you buried a sword in Dec's gut?"

Cormac's eyes gleamed like hot coals. "Just wanted to feel you boys out." He pushed off the mantel and strode for the shut doors. "You know," Cormac drawled over his shoulder, "the Starborn used to intermarry. Brother wed sister, aunt married nephew, and so on. All to keep the bloodline pure. Since you seem so heavily invested in who shares Bryce's bed, perhaps the old traditions could be revived for you two."

"Get the Hel out," Ruhn snarled. His shadows writhed at his fingertips, whips ready to snap for the Avallen Prince's neck.

"You might rebel all you like, Ruhn Danaan, but you are a Crown Prince, as I am. Our fates are the same. But I know which one of us will rise to meet it."

Then he was gone.

Our fates are the same. Cormac meant that they would both be kings, but Ruhn knew his fate was more complicated than that.

The royal bloodline shall end with you, Prince. The Oracle's voice floated through his mind, twisting up his insides. He might very well not live long enough to see himself crowned. His blood chilled. Was it because Cormac would lead some sort of coup?

He shook it off, turning to his father. "Why are you doing this?"

"That you have to ask shows me you're no true son of mine."

The words seared through him. Nothing could ever hurt worse than what had already been done to him by this male, the scars he bore on his arms from it, mostly covered by the sleeves of his tattoos. But the words . . . yeah, they stung.

Ruhn refused to let the old bastard see it, though. Would never let him see it. "And I suppose you think Cormac will become that true son by marrying Bryce."

His father's lips curled upward, eyes as lifeless as the Pit. "Cormac has always been the son I should have had. Rather than the one I was burdened with."

8

Today's the big day, huh?"

Hunt turned from where he'd been staring at the coffee machine, willing the grinding of the beans to drown out the thoughts roaring in his head. Bryce leaned against the white marble counter behind him, clad in leggings and an old T-shirt.

Hunt tucked in his gray wings and saluted. "Approachable Asshole, reporting for duty." Her lips curved upward, but he asked, "How'd it go with your parents?" She'd left well before he was up.

"Perfectly." She feigned brushing dirt off her shoulders. "Not a whisper about the engagement. I think Randall suspected *something*, but he was game to play along."

"Five gold marks says your mom calls before noon to start yelling."

Her grin was brighter than the morning sun streaming outside the windows. "You're on." She angled her head, surveying his daily uniform: his usual black battle-suit for the 33rd. "You should see the decorations that went up overnight—apparently, the city's rolling out the welcome mat, and sparing no expense. Banners, flowers, sparkly-clean streets, even in the Old Square. Not one drop of drunken-idiot vomit to be seen or smelled."

"The appointment of a new Governor is a pretty big deal," he said, wondering where she was going with this.

"Yep." Then Bryce asked casually, "Want me to come with you today?"

There it was. Something in his chest kindled at the offer. "No hand-holding needed, Quinlan. But thanks."

Bryce's eyes glowed—pure Fae predator lurking there. "Remember what we did to the last two Archangels, Hunt," she said quietly. That was new—the raw power that thundered beneath her words. "If Celestina does something fucked up, we'll react accordingly."

"Bloodthirsty, Quinlan?"

She didn't smile. "You might be heading in there without me today, but I'm a phone call away."

His chest ached. She'd do it—back him up against a fucking Archangel, Solas burn him. "Noted," he said thickly. He nodded toward the hallway. "How's our guest?"

"He looks a lot better this morning, though the broken ribs have some mending left to do. He was still sleeping when I left."

"What's the plan?" Hunt kept his voice neutral. He'd slept terribly last night, every sound sending him lurching from sleep. Bryce, of course, appeared as beautiful as ever.

"Ithan can stay as long as he wants," Bryce said simply. "I'm not turning him over to Sabine."

"Glad to hear it," Ithan said from behind her, and even Hunt started.

The male had crept up with preternatural silence. He *did* look better. Blood still crusted Holstrom's short golden-brown hair, but the swelling around his eyes had vanished, leaving only a few purple streaks. Most of the cuts were healed, except the thick slash across his brow. That'd take another day or two. Ithan pointed past Hunt. "Is that coffee?"

Hunt busied himself with pouring three cups, passing one to Quinlan first. "A drop of coffee in a cup of milk, just as you like it."

"Asshole." She swiped the mug. "I don't know how you drink it straight."

"Because I'm a grown-up." Hunt passed the second mug to Ithan, whose large hands engulfed the white ceramic cup that said *I*

Survived Class of 15032 Senior Week and All I Got Was This Stupid Mug!

Ithan peered at it, his mouth twitching. "I remember this mug."

Hunt fell silent as Bryce let out a breathy laugh. "I'm surprised you do, given how drunk you were. Even though you were a sweet baby frosh."

Ithan chuckled, a hint of the handsome, cocky male Hunt had heard about. "You and Danika had me doing keg stands at ten in the morning. How was I supposed to stay sober?" The wolf sipped from his coffee. "My last memory from that day is of you and Danika passed out drunk on a couch you'd moved right into the middle of the quad."

"And why was that your last memory?" Bryce asked sweetly.

"Because I passed out next to you," Ithan said, grinning now.

Bryce smiled, and damn if it didn't do something to Hunt's heart. A smile of pain and joy and loss and longing—and hope. But she cleared her throat, peering at the clock. "I need to get into the shower. I'll be late for work." With a swish of her hips, she padded down the hallway.

Syrinx scratched at Hunt's calf, and Hunt hissed, "Absolutely not. You had one breakfast already." Probably two, if Bryce had fed him before going to meet her parents. Syrinx flopped down beside his steel bowl and let out a whine. Hunt tried to ignore him.

He found Ithan watching him carefully. "What?" Hunt said, not bothering to sound pleasant.

Ithan only sipped from his mug again. "Nothing."

Hunt gulped a mouthful of coffee. Glanced down the hall to make sure Bryce was indeed in her room. His voice dropped to a low growl. "Allow me to repeat what I said to you last night. You bring trouble in here, to Bryce, and I will fucking gut you."

Ithan's mouth twitched upward. "I'm shaking, Athalar."

Hunt didn't smile back. "Are you suddenly cool with her because she's a princess? Because of the Horn and the Starborn shit?"

Ithan's nose crinkled with the beginnings of a snarl. "I don't care about any of that."

"Then why the fuck did you bother to defend her in that article? You had to know there'd be consequences with Sabine. You practically called Sabine out."

"Danika showed up for her. My brother and the rest of the Pack of Devils showed up for her this spring. If they're not holding a grudge, then how can I?"

"So you needed permission from your dead brother to be nice to her?"

Ithan's snarl rattled the cabinets. "Bryce was my best friend, you know. She had Danika, yeah, but I only had *her.* You've known Bryce for what—a few months? We were friends for five *years*. So don't fucking talk about me, my brother, or her as if you know anything about us. You don't know shit, *Umbra Mortis*."

"I know you were a dick to her for two years. I watched you stand by while Amelie Ravenscroft tormented her. Grow the fuck up."

Ithan bared his teeth. Hunt bared his own right back.

Syrinx hopped to his feet and whined, demanding more food.

Hunt couldn't help his exasperated laugh. "Fine, fine," he said to the chimera, reaching for his container of kibble.

Ithan's eyes burned him like a brand. Hunt had seen that same take-no-shit face during televised sunball games. "Connor was in love with her for those five years, you know." The wolf headed over to the couch and plopped onto the cushions. "Five years, and by the end of it, he'd only managed to get her to *agree* to go on a date with him."

Hunt kept his face unreadable as Syrinx devoured his second—potentially third—breakfast. "So?"

Ithan turned on the morning news before propping his feet on the coffee table and interlacing his hands behind his head. "You're at month five, bro. Good luck to you."

The Fae Archives hummed with activity—loud enough that Bryce had grown accustomed to keeping in her earbuds all day, even with the door to her tiny office on Sublevel Alpha shut.

It wasn't that it was *loud,* exactly—the archives had the usual hush of any library. But so many people visited or studied or worked in the cavernous atrium and surrounding stacks that there was a constant, underlying roar. The scuff of footsteps, the waterfall fountain pouring from the atrium's ceiling, the clack of keyboards blending with the crinkle of turning pages, the whispers of patrons and tourists mingling with the occasional giggle or snap of a camera.

It grated on her.

Gone were the solitary days in the gallery. The days of blasting her music through the sound system.

Lehabah was gone, too.

No incessant chatter about the latest episode of *Fangs and Bangs*. No whining about wanting to go outside. No dramatic monologues about Bryce's cruelty.

Bryce stared at the dark computer screen on her glass desk. She reached out a foot to stroke Syrinx's coat, but her toes only met air. Right—she'd left the chimera home to watch over Ithan.

She wondered if Syrinx even remembered Lehabah.

Bryce had visited the Black Dock during the days after the attack, searching for a tiny onyx boat among the mass of Sailings. None had appeared.

Lehabah had no remains anyway. The fire sprite had been snuffed out like a candle the moment a hundred thousand gallons of water had come crashing down upon her.

Bryce had gone over it, again and again. Usually during her dance classes with Madame Kyrah, amid her panting and sweating. She always arrived at the same conclusion: there was nothing she might have done to stop Lehabah's death.

Bryce understood it, could rationally talk about it, and yet . . . The thoughts still circled, as if dancing right along with her: *You might have found a way. Revealed yourself as Starborn earlier. Told Lehabah to run while you faced Micah.*

She'd talked about it with Hunt, too. And he'd pointed out that all of those options would have resulted in Bryce's own death, but . . . Bryce couldn't get past the question: Why was Lele's life any less valuable than Bryce's? Her Starborn Princess status meant nothing. If it came down to it, Lele had been the better person, who had suffered for decades in bondage. The fire sprite should be free. Alive, and free, and enjoying herself.

Bryce picked up the desktop phone, dialing. Jesiba answered on the third ring. "Another question, Quinlan? That's the third one this week."

Bryce drummed her fingers on her glass desk. "I've got a nine-thousand-year-old Rhodinian bust of Thurr here." Basically a broody male who was supposed to pass for the nearly forgotten minor storm deity. All that remained of him in their culture was the behemoth of a planet named after him. And Thursdays, apparently. Bryce had already sent a photo of it to Hunt, with the comment, *Bryce Quinlan Presents: The Original Alphahole Smolder.* "A museum is interested, but they're worried the former owner fudged some documents about its history. They want to make sure it's legit before showing it to the public. Any idea who to call in Rhodinia to verify?"

"If I'm doing your job for you, then why am I not being paid for it?"

Bryce ground her teeth. "Because we're friends?"

"Are we?"

"You tell me."

Jesiba huffed a soft laugh. The enchantress who'd defected from her witch-clan and sworn allegiance to the House of Flame and Shadow still lurked around Lunathion, but Bryce hadn't seen her in months. Not since the day Jesiba had found Bryce poking around the watery ruins of the gallery library and told her not to come back.

Not in a mean way. Just in a *This gallery is now permanently closed, and those books you're looking for are hidden away where no one will ever find them* sort of manner.

Jesiba said, "I suppose I should consider it an honor, to be called a friend by the Starborn Princess daughter of the Autumn King." A slight pause, and Bryce knew what was coming next. "And the future Queen of Avallen."

Bryce swiftly opened a news website as she hissed, "Who told you?"

"Some of the people I've turned into animals have remained in my employ, you know. They tell me what they overhear on the streets. Especially the sewer rats who hope to regain their true forms one day."

Bryce truly wasn't sure if Jesiba was serious. She sighed again. "I don't suppose you have any insights as to *why* the Autumn King suddenly decided to ruin my life."

Jesiba tsked. "Males will always try to control the females who scare them. Marriage and breeding are their go-to methods."

"Satisfying as it is to think of my father being afraid of me, that can't be it."

"Why not? It's been months. You've done nothing with your new power, your titles. Or the Horn in your back. He grew tired of waiting. I wouldn't be surprised if he did this just to learn how you'd react."

"Maybe." Bryce doodled on a piece of scrap paper beside her computer. A little heart that said *BQ + HA*.

"What *are* you going to do about it?" Jesiba asked, as if she couldn't help it.

"Pretend it's not happening until I can't any longer?"

Jesiba chuckled again. "I worried, you know, when I learned you were Starborn. I've watched many succumb to the allure of being the Chosen One. Perhaps you and your brother have more in common than I realized."

"I think that's a compliment?"

"It is. Ruhn Danaan is one of the few who's ever been strong enough to shun what he is." Bryce grunted. "You don't plan on doing anything with it, then," Jesiba asked, more quietly than Bryce had ever heard. "Your talent. Or the Horn."

"*Definitely* not the Horn. And it seems most of the Starborn power's value lies in what I can breed into the Fae bloodline." Bryce straightened, twirling her pencil between her fingers. "And what good does blinding people do? I mean, it *does* have its uses, but surely there are deadlier weapons to wield?" Like Hunt's lightning.

"You killed an Archangel without access to that power. I imagine that you can now do a great many things, Quinlan."

Bryce stiffened at the words, spoken so casually over an open line. She had no idea what Jesiba had done with the Godslayer Rifle. Honestly, she never wanted to see it again.

Bryce lowered her voice, even though she knew no one was near her little subterranean office. "I was given an order by the Asteri to lie low. Forever."

"How terribly boring of you to obey them."

Bryce opened her mouth, but the intercom on her desk buzzed. "Miss Quinlan, you're needed in the northern wing. Doctor Patrus wants your opinion on that sculpture from Delsus?"

Bryce pushed the button. "Be there in five." She said to Jesiba, "I'm going to send you some photos of this piece. I'd appreciate it if you'd deign to give me your opinion. And let me know if you have any contacts in Rhodinia who can help verify its authenticity."

"I'm busy."

"So am I."

"Perhaps I'll turn you into a toad."

"At least toads don't wear stupid heels to work," Bryce said, sliding her feet back into the white stilettos she'd chucked beneath her desk.

Jesiba let out another soft, wicked laugh. "A word of advice, Quinlan: think through the advantages of a marriage to Cormac Donnall before you decide to be a cliché and refuse."

Bryce stood, cradling the phone between her ear and shoulder. "Who says I'm not?"

There was a lengthy pause before the sorceress said, "Good girl," and hung up.

9

Anything?"

"Nothing at all—though you were right about the all-out decorations. I nearly flew into about six different banners and wreaths on my way over this morning. But no reports or sightings of the Governor. Pretty normal day so far, to be honest." Hunt's low voice ran invisible hands along Bryce's arms as she picked at the remnants of her lunch: a gyro grabbed from the archives' staff cafeteria. He added, "Though not if you count me receiving a photo of some marble abs while I was showing crime scene pictures to Naomi."

"Thought you'd enjoy that."

His laugh rumbled over the line. It shot through her like starlight. If he was able to laugh today, good. She'd do whatever she could to keep a smile on Hunt's face. He cleared his throat. "Thurr was pretty jacked, huh?"

"I'm petitioning for the exhibit to sell replicas in the gift shop. I think the old ladies will go wild over it." That earned her another beautiful laugh. She bit her lip against her broad smile. "So Celestina's now due to arrive at six, then?" Apparently, she'd been delayed by an hour.

"Yep." Any hint of amusement faded.

Bryce stirred her computer to life. So far, the news sites reported nothing beyond the headline that Lunathion—that all of Valbara—would have a new leader.

Bryce was willing to admit she'd spent a good hour skimming through various images of the beautiful Archangel, pondering what sort of boss she'd be for Hunt. She found no hint about any romantic entanglements, though Micah hadn't often broadcast who he'd been fucking. It wasn't that Bryce was *worried*, though she'd certainly felt a scrap of *something* when she'd seen precisely how stunning Celestina was, but . . . she needed a mental picture of who Hunt would be seeing day in and day out.

Bryce chucked her lunch into the trash beside her desk. "I could come over after work. Be with you for the grand arrival."

"It's all right. I'll fill you in afterward. It might take a while, though, so feel free to eat without me."

"But it's pizza night."

Hunt laughed. "Glad you've got your priorities straight." His wings rustled in the background. "Any word about Prince Dickhead?"

"Nothing on the news, nothing from my mom."

"Small blessing."

"You owe me five gold marks."

"Add it to my tab, Quinlan."

"Don't forget that my mom will probably be pissed at *you* for not telling her."

"I already have my bug-out bag packed and ready to flee to another territory."

She chuckled. "I think you'd have to go to Nena to escape her." Hunt laughed with her. "Don't you think she—"

A glow flared at her chest. From the scar.

"Bryce?" Hunt's voice sharpened.

"I, uh . . ." Bryce frowned down at the glowing star between her breasts, visible in her low-cut dress. Not again. Its glowing had been rare until now, but after last night—

She looked up.

"My boss is here. I'll call you back," she lied, and hung up before Hunt could reply.

Bryce lifted her chin and said to Cormac Donnall, lurking in the doorway, "If you're looking for *How Not to Be an Asshole,* it's shelved between *Bye, Loser* and *Get the Fuck Out.*"

The Crown Prince of Avallen had changed into a climate-appropriate gray T-shirt that did little to hide the considerable muscles of his arms. A tattoo of strange symbols encircled his left biceps, the black ink gleaming in the bright lights.

He examined her closet-sized office with typical Fae arrogance—and disapproval. "Your star glows in my presence because our union is predestined. In case you were wondering."

Bryce barked out a laugh. "Says who?"

"The Oracle."

"Which one?" There were twelve sphinxes around the world, each one bitchier than the last. The meanest of them, apparently, dwelled in the Ocean Queen's court Beneath.

"Does it matter?" Cormac turned, noting the shell-white dress Bryce wore, the gold bracelets, and, yes, her ample cleavage. Or was he gazing at the star? She supposed it made no difference.

"I just want to know whose ass to kick."

Cormac's mouth quirked upward. "I don't know why I expected a half-breed to be as docile as a pure-blooded female."

"You're not doing yourself any favors."

"I did not say I preferred a tamer female."

"Gross. What did the Oracle say to you, exactly?"

"What did she say to *you* before she began clawing at her blinded eyes?"

She didn't want to know how he'd found out. Maybe her father had told him—warned him about his bride. "Old news. I asked first."

Cormac glowered. "The Oracle of Avallen said I was destined to unite with a princess who possessed a star in her heart. That our mingling would bring great prosperity to our people."

Bryce drummed her fingers on her glass desk. "A lot of room for interpretation there." Trust an Oracle to call sex *mingling.*

"I disagree."

Bryce sighed. "Tell me why you're here, then leave, please. I have work to do."

Cormac studied the small torso of Thurr on her desk. "I wanted to see where my betrothed works. To gain some insight into your . . . life."

"You say that as if it's a foreign thing for females to have jobs."

"In Avallen, it is." He leaned against the doorjamb. "My people have let the old traditions remain untouched. You will need to adjust."

"Thanks, but no. I like my TV and phone. And I like being considered a person, not livestock for breeding."

"Like I said last night, you don't have a choice." His voice was flat, his eyes hollow.

Bryce crossed her arms, realized it put her cleavage and the star on better display, and lowered them to her sides once more. "Can I . . . pay you to drop this whole engagement thing?"

Cormac laughed. "I have more gold than I know what to do with. Money holds little power over me." He crossed his arms as well. "You have a chance to help your people and this world. Once you bear me a few heirs, you can take whatever lovers you wish. I will do the same. This marriage doesn't need to burden either of us."

"Except for the part where I have to sleep with you. And live in your backwater land."

His lips curled upward. "I think you'll find the first part to be rather enjoyable."

"Spoken with true male arrogance."

He shrugged, clearly confident that she *would* enjoy him. "I haven't had any complaints yet. And if our union helps our people, and strengthens the royal bloodlines, then I'll do it."

"The Fae are no people of mine." They never had been, and certainly not now, after they'd locked out innocent citizens in this city and refused to come to anyone's aid during the attack last spring. She pointed to the open door. "Bye."

He simmered with disgust. "Your father let you run wild for too long."

"My father's name is Randall Silago. The Autumn King is just a male who gave me genetic material. He will never have a place in my life. Neither will you."

Cormac took a step back from the doorway, shadows swirling. His golden hair glowed like molten metal. "You're immortal now, as well as Starborn. Time to act like it."

Bryce slammed the door in his face.

Hunt considered the beautiful Archangel seated at Micah's old desk. Glowing skin as dark as onyx brought out the light brown of her eyes, and her delicate mouth seemed permanently set in a patient smile. It was that smile—that gentle, kind smile—that threw him. "Take a seat, please," Celestina said to him, Naomi, and Isaiah.

Hunt nearly choked at the word. *Please*. Micah would never have said anything of the sort. Isaiah appeared equally baffled as they settled into the three chairs before the simple oak desk. Naomi kept her face wholly blank, her black wings rustling.

Behind the Governor's gleaming white wings, the wall of windows revealed an unusual number of angels soaring by. All hoping to catch a glimpse of the female who had entered the Comitium in a grand procession thirty minutes ago.

The lobby ceremony had been the start of Hunt's utter confusion. Rather than strutting magnanimously past the gathered crowd, the voluptuous, lush-bodied Archangel had taken her time, pausing to greet the malakim who stepped forward, asking for their names, saying things like *I'm so very happy to meet you* and *I look forward to working with you*. Cthona spare him, but Hunt honestly thought she might be serious.

He didn't let his guard down, though. Not when she'd reached him, Naomi, and Isaiah, standing before the elevator doors to escort her to her new residence and office; not when she'd taken his hand with genuine warmth; and certainly not now that they sat here for this private meeting.

Celestina surveyed them with unnerving clarity. "You three are all that remains of Micah's triarii."

None of them replied. Hunt didn't dare mention Vik—or beg the Archangel to pull her out of Melinoë's inky depths. To spare her from a living Hel. It had been months. Odds were that Vik had gone insane. Was likely begging for death with each moment in that box.

The Governor angled her head, her tightly curling black hair shifting with the movement. She wore pale pink-and-lilac robes, gauzy and ethereal, and the silver jewelry along her wrists and neck glowed as if lit by the moon. Where Micah had radiated dominance and might, she shimmered with feminine strength and beauty. She barely came up to Hunt's chest, yet . . . she had a presence that had Hunt eyeing her carefully.

"Not ones for talking, are you?" Her voice held a musical quality, as if it had been crafted from silver bells. "I suppose my predecessor had rules quite different from mine." She drummed her fingers on the desk, nails tinted a soft pink. "Allow me to make this clear: I do not wish for subservience. I want my triarii to be my partners. I want you to work alongside me to protect this city and territory, and help it meet its great potential."

A pretty little speech. Hunt said nothing. Did she know what he'd done to Sandriel? What Bryce had done to Micah? What Micah had done in his quest to supposedly protect this territory?

Celestina wrapped a curl around a finger, her immaculate wings shifting. "I see that I shall have to do a great deal of work to earn your trust."

Hunt kept his face bland, even as he wished that she'd be equally as forthright as Micah. He'd always hated his owners who'd disguised their dead souls in pretty speeches. This could easily be part of a game: to get them to trust her, come limping into her soft arms, and then spring the trap. Make them suffer.

Naomi's sharp chin lifted. "We don't wish to offend you, Your Grace—"

"Call me Celestina," the Archangel interrupted. "I abhor formalities." Micah had said the same thing once. Hunt had been a fool to buy it then.

Isaiah's wings shifted—like his friend was thinking the same.

His friend, who still bore the halo tattoo across his brow. Isaiah was the better male, the better leader—and still a slave. Rumors had swirled in the months before Micah's demise that the Archangel would free him soon. That possibility was now as dead as Micah himself.

Naomi nodded, and Hunt's heart tightened at the tentative hope in his friend's jet-black eyes. "We don't wish to offend you . . . Celestina. We and the 33rd are here to serve you."

Hunt suppressed his bristle. *Serve.*

"The only way you could offend me, Naomi Boreas, would be to withhold your feelings and thoughts. If something troubles you, I want to know about it. Even if the matter is due to my own behavior." She smiled again. "We're partners. I've found that such a partnership worked wonders on my legions in Nena. As opposed to the . . . systems my fellow Archangels prefer."

Torture and punishment and death. Hunt blocked out the sear of white-hot iron rods pounding his back, roasting his skin, splitting it down to the bone as Sandriel watched from her divan, popping grapes into her mouth—

Isaiah said, "We're honored to work with you, then."

Hunt pushed aside the bloody, screaming horrors of the past as another lovely smile bloomed on the Governor. "I've heard so many wonderful things about you, Isaiah Tiberian. I'd like you to stay on as leader of the 33rd, if that is what you wish."

Isaiah bowed his head in thanks, a tentative, answering smile gracing his face. Hunt tried not to gape. Was he the only asshole who didn't believe any of this?

Celestina turned her gaze upon him. "You have not yet spoken, Hunt Athalar. Or do you wish to go by Orion?"

"Hunt is fine." Only his mother had been allowed to call him Orion. He'd keep it that way.

She surveyed him again, elegant as a swan. "I understand that you and Micah did not necessarily see eye to eye." Hunt reined in his urge to growl in agreement. Celestina seemed to read his inclination. "On another day, I'd like to learn about your relationship with Micah and what went wrong. So we might avoid such a situation ourselves."

"What went wrong is that he tried to kill my—Bryce Quinlan." Hunt couldn't stop the words, or his stumble.

Naomi's brows nearly touched her hairline at his outburst, but Celestina sighed. "I heard about that. I'm sorry for any pain you and Miss Quinlan suffered as a result of Micah's actions."

The words hit him like stones. *I'm sorry.* He'd never, not in all the centuries he'd lived, heard an Archangel utter those words.

Celestina went on, "From what I've gathered, you have chosen to live with Miss Quinlan, rather than in the barracks tower."

Hunt kept his body loose. Refused to yield to the tension rising in him. "Yeah."

"I am perfectly fine with that arrangement," Celestina said, and Hunt nearly toppled out of his chair. Isaiah looked inclined to do the same. Especially as the Archangel said to Isaiah and Naomi, "If you should wish to dwell in your own residences, you are free to do so. The barracks are good for building bonds, but I believe the ones between you are quite unshakable. You are free to enjoy your own lives." She glanced at Isaiah, to the halo still tattooed on his brow. "I am not one to keep slaves," she said, disapproval tightening her face. "And though the Asteri might brand you as such, Isaiah, you are a free male in my eyes. I will endeavor to continue Micah's work in convincing them to free you."

Isaiah's throat worked, and Hunt studied the window—the shining city beyond—to give him privacy. Across the room, Naomi followed his lead.

Celestina couldn't be serious. This had to be an act.

"I'd like to hit the ground running," the Governor went on.

"Each morning, let's gather here so you can update me on any news, as well as your plans for the day. Should I have tasks for you or the 33rd, I shall convey them then." She folded her hands in her lap. "I am aware that you are skilled at hunting demons, and have been employed to do so in the past. If any break into this city, gods forbid, I'd like you to head up the containment and extermination unit against them."

Hunt jerked his chin in confirmation. Easy enough. Though this spring, dealing with the kristallos had been anything but easy.

Celestina finished, "And should an issue arise before our meeting tomorrow morning, my phone is always on."

Naomi nodded again. "What time tomorrow?"

"Let's say nine," Celestina said. "No need to drag ourselves out of bed simply to look busy." Hunt blinked at her. "And I'd like the others to get some rest after their journey."

"Others?" Isaiah asked.

The Archangel frowned slightly. "The rest of the triarii. They were delayed by a few hours due to some bad weather up north."

All three of them stilled. "What do you mean?" Hunt asked quietly.

"It was in the formal letter you received," she said to Isaiah, who shook his head.

Celestina's frown deepened. "The Asteri's Communications Minister is not usually one to make mistakes. I apologize on their behalf. The Asteri found themselves with a predicament after losing two Archangels, you see. You are all that remains of Micah's triarii, but Sandriel had a full stable in that regard. I had no triarii of my own in Nena, as the legion there technically answers to the Asteri, but Ephraim wanted to bring his own triarii with him. So rather than have his group get too large, it was split—since ours is so depleted."

Roaring erupted in Hunt's head. Sandriel's triarii. The actual scum of the universe.

They were coming here. To be part of *this* group. In *this* city.

A knock sounded on the door, and Hunt twisted as Celestina said, "Come in."

Lightning crackled at Hunt's fingertips. The door opened, and in swaggered Pollux Antonius and Baxian Argos.

The Hammer and the Helhound.

10

Absolute quiet settled over the Governor's office as Hunt and his friends took in the two newcomers.

One was dark-haired and brown-skinned, tall and finely muscled—the Helhound. His jet-black wings shimmered faintly, like a crow's feathers. But it was the wicked scar snaking down his neck, forking across the column of his throat, that snared the eye.

Hunt knew that scar—he'd given it to the Helhound thirty years ago. Some powers, it seemed, even immortality couldn't guard against.

Baxian's obsidian eyes simmered as they met Hunt's stare.

But Pollux's cobalt eyes lit with feral delight as he sized up Naomi, then Isaiah, and finally Hunt. Hunt allowed his lightning to flare as he stared down the golden-haired, golden-skinned leader of Sandriel's triarii. The most brutal, sadistic asshole to have ever walked Midgard's soil. Motherfucker Number One.

Pollux smirked, slow and satisfied. Celestina was saying something, but Hunt couldn't hear it.

Couldn't hear anything except Pollux drawling, "Hello, friends," before Hunt leapt from his chair and tackled him to the floor.

* * *

Ithan Holstrom dabbed a damp washcloth at the last of the cuts healing on his face, wincing. Bryce's bathroom was exactly as he'd expected it to be: full of at least three kinds of shampoos and conditioners, an array of hair treatments, brushes, curling rods of two different sizes, a blow-dryer left plugged into the wall, half-burned candles, and makeup scattered up and down the marble counter like some glittery bomb had gone off.

It was almost exactly the same as her bathroom at the old apartment. Just being here made his chest tighten. Just smelling this place, smelling *her* made his chest tighten.

He'd had little to distract himself today, sitting alone with her chimera—Syrinx, Athalar had called him—on the couch, nearly dying of boredom watching daytime TV. He didn't feel like trawling the news for hours, awaiting a glimpse of the new Archangel. None of the sports channels had interesting coverage on, and he had no desire to listen to those assholes talk anyway.

Ithan angled his face before the mirror to better see the cut lacing across his brow. This particular beauty had been from Sabine, a swipe of a claw-armed fist.

He had a feeling the blow had been intended for his eyes. Sure, they'd have healed after a few days or weeks, sooner if he'd gone to a medwitch, but being blinded wasn't at the top of his to-do list.

Not that he really had anything *else* on his to-do list today.

His phone buzzed on the counter, and Ithan peered down to see three different news alerts and photo essays about the arrival of Celestina. Had shit not gone down with Sabine, he'd probably be gearing up to meet the beautiful malakh as part of the wolves' formal welcome. And fealty-swearing bullshit.

But now he was a free agent. A wolf without a pack.

It wasn't common, but it did happen. Lone wolves existed, though most roamed the wilds and were left to their own devices. He'd just never thought he'd be one.

Ithan set down his phone, hanging up the washcloth on the already-crowded towel bar.

He willed the shift, inhaling sharply and bidding his bones to melt, his skin to ripple.

It occurred to him a moment after he took his wolf form that the bathroom wasn't quite large enough.

Indeed, a swish of his tail knocked over various bottles, sending them scattering across the marble floor. His claws clicked on the tiles, but he lifted his muzzle toward the mirror and met his reflection once more.

The horse-sized wolf that stared back was hollow-eyed, though his fur covered most of his bruising and the cuts, save for the slash along his brow.

He inhaled—and the breath stuck in his ribs. In some empty, strange pocket.

Wolf with no pack. Amelie and Sabine had not merely bloodied him, they'd exorcised him from their lives, from the Den. He backed into the towel rack, tossing his head this way and that.

Worse than an Omega. Friendless, kinless, unwanted—

Ithan shuddered back into his humanoid form. Panting, he braced his hands on the bathroom counter and waited until the nausea subsided. His phone buzzed again. Every muscle in his body tensed.

Perry Ravenscroft.

He might have ignored it had he not read the first part of the message as it appeared.

Please tell me you're alive.

Ithan sighed. Amelie's younger sister—the Omega of the Black Rose Pack—was technically the reason he'd made it here. Had said nothing about her sister and Sabine ripping him to shreds, but she'd carried him into the apartment. She was the only one of his former pack to bother to check in.

She added, *Just write back y/n.*

Ithan stared at the message for a long moment.

Wolves were social creatures. A wolf without a pack . . . it was a soul-wound. One that would cripple most wolves. But he'd been struck a soul-wound two years ago and had survived.

Even though he knew he couldn't endure taking his wolf form again anytime soon.

Ithan took in the bathroom, the various crap Bryce had left

lying around. She'd been a wolf without a pack for those two years, too. Yeah, she had Fury and Juniper, but it wasn't the same as Danika and Connor and the Pack of Devils. Nothing would ever be the same as that.

Ithan typed back *Yes*, then slid his phone into his pocket. Bryce would be home soon. And she'd mentioned something about pizza.

Ithan padded out into the airy apartment, Syrinx lifting his head from the couch to inspect him. The chimera lay back down with a puff of approval, lion's tail waggling.

The silence of the apartment pressed on Ithan. He'd never lived on his own. He'd always had the constant chaos and closeness of the Den, the insanity of his college dorm, or the hotels he'd stayed at with the CCU sunball team. This place might as well have been another planet.

He rubbed at his chest, as if it'd erase the tightness.

He'd known precisely why he'd disobeyed Sabine's order this spring when Bryce had screamed for help. The sound of her pleading had been unbearable. And when she'd mentioned children at risk, something had exploded in his brain. He had no regrets about what he'd done.

But could he endure its consequences? Not the beating—he could weather that shit any day. But being here, alone, adrift . . . He hadn't felt like this since Connor and the others had died. Since he'd walked away from his sunball team and stopped answering their calls.

He had no idea what the Hel he'd do now. Perhaps the answer wasn't some big, life-altering thing. Maybe it could be as simple as putting one foot in front of the other.

That's how you wound up following someone like Amelie, a voice that sounded an awful lot like Connor's growled. *Make better choices this time, pup. Assess. Decide what* you *want.*

But for now . . . one foot in front of the other. He could do that. If just for today.

Ithan walked to the door and pulled the leash off the hook on the wall beside it. "Want a walk?" he asked Syrinx. The beast rolled onto his side, as if saying, *Belly rub, please.*

Ithan slung the leash back onto its hook. "You got it, bud."

"Approachable Asshole, huh?"

Bryce leaned against the bars of the immaculate cell beneath the Comitium, frowning at where Hunt sat on a steel-framed cot, head hanging. He straightened at her words, gray wings tucking in. His face— Bryce stiffened. "What the *fuck,* Hunt?"

Black eye, swollen lip, cuts along his temple, his hairline . . . "I'm fine," he grumbled, even though he looked as bad as Ithan. "Who called you?"

"Your new boss—she filled me in. She sounds nice, by the way." Bryce pressed her face through the bars. "Definitely nice, since she hasn't kicked your ass to the curb yet."

"She did put me in this cell."

"Isaiah put you in the cell."

"Whatever."

"Don't *whatever* me." Gods, she sounded like her mother.

His voice sharpened. "I'll see you at home. You shouldn't be here."

"And you shouldn't have gotten into a stupid fight, but here you are."

Lightning forked down his wings. "Go home."

Was he—was he really pissed she was here? She snorted. "Were you intentionally trying to sabotage yourself today?"

Hunt shot to his feet, then winced at whatever pain it summoned in his battered body. "Why the fuck would I do that?"

A deep male voice answered, "Because you're a stupid bastard."

Bryce grimaced. She'd forgotten about Pollux.

Hunt snarled, "I don't want to hear your fucking voice."

"Get used to it," said another male voice from the elevator bay at the end of the white hall.

Bryce found a tall, lean angel approaching with a natural

elegance. Not beautiful, not in the way that Hunt and Pollux and Isaiah were, but . . . striking. Intense and focused.

Baxian Argos, the Helhound. An angel with the rare ability to shift into the form that had given him his nickname.

Hunt had told her about him, too. Baxian hadn't ever tortured Hunt or others, as far as she knew—but he'd done plenty of awful things in Sandriel's name. He'd been her chief spy-master and tracker.

Baxian bared his teeth in a fierce smile. Hunt bristled.

Like Hel would these males make her back down.

Pollux crooned from his cell, his pretty-boy face as battered as Hunt's, "Why don't you come a little closer, Bryce Quinlan?"

Hunt growled. "Don't talk to her."

Bryce snapped, "Spare me the protective alphahole act." Before Hunt could reply, she'd stalked over to Pollux's cell.

Pollux made a show of looking her over from head to stilettos. "I thought your kind usually worked the night shift."

Bryce snickered. "Any other outdated jabs to throw my way?" At Pollux's silence, Bryce said, "Sex work is a respectable profession in Crescent City. It's not my fault Pangera hasn't caught up with modern times."

Pollux brimmed with malice. "Micah should have killed you and been done with it."

She let her eyes glow—let him see that she knew all he'd done to Hunt, how much she detested him. "That's the best you can come up with? I thought the Hammer was supposed to be some kind of sadistic badass."

"And I thought half-breed whores were supposed to keep their mouths closed. Fortunately, I know the perfect thing to shove in that trap of yours to shut you up."

Bryce winked saucily. "Careful. I use teeth." Hunt coughed, and Bryce leaned forward—close enough that if Pollux extended an arm, his hand could wrap around her throat. Pollux's eyes flared, noting that fact. Bryce said sweetly, "I don't know who you pissed off to be sent to this city, but I'm going to make your life a living Hel if you touch him again."

Pollux lunged, fingers aiming for her neck.

She let her power surge, bright enough that Pollux reared back, an arm flung over his eyes. Bryce's lips quirked to the side. "I thought so."

She backed away a few steps, pivoting toward Hunt once more. He cocked an eyebrow, eyes shining beneath the bruises. "Fancy, Quinlan."

"I aim to impress."

A low laugh whispered behind her, and Bryce found the Helhound now leaning against the wall opposite the cells, beside a large TV.

"I take it I'll be seeing more of you than I'd like," Bryce said.

Baxian sketched a bow. He wore lightweight black armor made of overlapping plates. It reminded her of a reptilian version of Hunt's suit. "Maybe you'll give me a tour."

"Keep dreaming," Hunt muttered.

The Helhound's dark eyes gleamed. He turned on his heel and said before entering the elevator, "Glad someone finally put a bullet through Micah's head."

Bryce stared after him in stunned silence. Had he come down here for any reason other than to say that? Hunt whooshed out a breath. Pollux remained pointedly silent in his cell.

Bryce gripped the bars of Hunt's cell. "No more fights."

"If I say yes, can we go home now?" He gave her a mournful pout almost identical to Syrinx's begging.

Bryce suppressed her smile. "Not my call."

A fair female voice floated from an intercom in the ceiling. "I've seen enough. He's free to go, Miss Quinlan." The bars hissed, the door unlocking with a clank.

Bryce said to the ceiling, "Thank you."

Pollux growled from his cell, "And what of me? I didn't start this fight." The shithead had balls. Bryce would give him that.

Celestina answered coolly, "You also didn't do anything to defuse it."

"Forgive me for fighting back while being pummeled by a brute."

From the corner of her eye, Bryce could have sworn Hunt was grinning wickedly.

The Governor said, voice taking on a no-bullshit sharpness, "We shall discuss this later." Pollux was wise enough not to snap a reply. The Archangel went on, "Keep Athalar in line, Miss Quinlan."

Bryce waved at the camera mounted beside the TV. When Celestina didn't answer, Bryce stepped back to allow Hunt out of the cell. He limped toward her, badly enough that she looped her arm around his waist as they aimed for the elevator.

Pollux sneered from his cell, "You two mongrels deserve each other."

Bryce blew him a kiss.

11

Tharion needed a new job.

Honestly, even years into the position, he had no idea how he'd wound up in charge of the River Queen's intelligence. His schoolmates probably laughed every time his name came up: a thoroughly average, if not lazy, student, he'd gotten his passing grades mostly through charming his teachers. He had little interest in history or politics or foreign languages, and his favorite subject in school had been lunch.

Maybe that had primed him. People were far more inclined to talk over food. Though anytime he'd tortured an enemy, he'd puked his guts up afterward. Fortunately, he'd learned that a cold beer, some mirthroot, and a few rounds of poker usually got him what he needed.

And this: research.

Normally, he'd tap one of his analysts to pore over his current project, but the River Queen wanted this kept secret. As he sat before the computer in his office, all it took was a few keystrokes to access what he wanted: Sofie Renast's email account.

Declan Emmet had set up the system for him: capable of hacking into any non-imperial email within moments. Emmet had charged him an arm and a fin for it, but it had proved more than useful. The first time Tharion had used it had been to help track down his sister's murderer.

The sick fuck had emailed himself photos of his victims. Even what Tharion had done to him afterward hadn't erased the image seared into his brain of his sister's brutalized body.

Tharion swallowed, looking toward the wall of glass that opened into clear cobalt waters. An otter shot past, yellow vest blazingly bright in the river water, a sealed tube clenched between his little fangs.

A creature of both worlds. Some of the messenger otters dwelled here, in the Blue Court deep beneath the Istros, a small metropolis both exposed and sealed off from the water around them. Other otters lived Above, in the bustle and chaos of Crescent City proper.

Tharion couldn't ever move Above, he reminded himself. His duties required him here, at the River Queen's beck and call. Tharion peered at his bare feet, digging them into the cream shag carpet beneath his desk. He'd been in human form for nearly a day now. He'd have to enter the water soon or risk losing his fins.

His parents found it odd that he'd chosen to live in one of the dry glass-and-metal buildings anchored into a sprawling platform at the bottom of the river, and not near them in the network of underwater caves that doubled as apartments for the mer. But Tharion liked TV. Liked eating food that wasn't soggy at best, cold and wet at worst. He liked sleeping in a warm bed, sprawled over the covers and pillows, and not tucked into a seaweed hammock swinging in the currents. And since living on land wasn't an option, this underwater building had become his best bet.

The computer pinged, and Tharion pivoted back to the screen. His office was in one of the glass-domed bubbles that made up the Blue Court Investigative Unit's headquarters—the River Queen had only allowed their construction because computers had to stay dry.

Tharion himself had been forced to explain that simple fact.

His queen was almighty, beautiful, and wise—and, like so many of the older Vanir, had no idea how modern technology worked. Her daughter, at least, had adapted better. Tharion had been instructed to show her how to use a computer. Which was how he'd wound up here.

Well, not here in this office. But in this place. In his current life.

Tharion skimmed through Sofie Renast's email archive. Evidence of a normal existence: emails with friends about sports or TV or an upcoming party; emails from parents asking that she pick up groceries on her way home from school; emails from her little brother. Emile.

Those were the ones that he combed through the most carefully. Maybe he'd get lucky and there'd be some hint in here about where Sofie was headed.

On and on, Tharion read, keeping an eye on the clock. He had to get in the water soon, but . . . He kept reading. Hunting for any clue or hint of where Sofie and her brother might have gone. He came up empty.

Tharion finished Sofie's inbox, checked the junk folder, and then finally the trash. It was mostly empty. He clicked open her sent folder, and groaned at the tally. But he began reading again. Click after click after click.

His phone chimed with an alert: thirty minutes until he needed to get into the water. He could reach the air lock in five minutes, if he walked fast. He could get through another few emails before then. *Click, click, click.* Tharion's phone chimed again. Ten minutes.

But he'd halted on an email dated three years ago. It was so simple, so nonsensical that it stood out.

Subject: Re: Dusk's Truth

The subject line was weird. But the body of her email was even weirder.

Working on gaining access. Will take time.

That was it.

Tharion scanned downward, toward the original message that Sofie had replied to. It had been sent two weeks before her reply.

From: BansheeFan56

Subject: Dusk's Truth

Have you gotten inside yet? I want to know the full story.

Tharion scratched his head, opened another window, and searched for *Dusk's Truth.*

Nothing. No record of a movie or book or TV show. He did a search on the email system for the sender's name: *BansheeFan56.*

Another half-deleted chain. This one originating from BansheeFan56.

Subject: Project Thurr

Could be useful to you. Read it.

Sofie had replied: *Just did. I think it's a long shot. And the Six will kill me for it.*

He had a good feeling he knew who "the Six" referred to: the Asteri. But when Tharion searched online for *Project Thurr,* he found nothing. Only news reports on archaeological digs or art gallery exhibits featuring the ancient demigod. Interesting.

There was one other email—in the drafts folder.

BansheeFan56 had written: *When you find him, lie low in the place I told you about—where the weary souls find relief from their suffering in Lunathion. It's secure.*

A rendezvous spot? Tharion scanned what Sofie had started to reply, but never sent.

Thank you. I'll try to pass along the info to my

She'd never finished it. There were any number of ways that sentence could have ended. But Sofie must have needed a place where no one would think to look for her and her brother. If Sofie Renast had indeed survived the Hind, she might well have come here, to this very city, with the promise of a safe place to hide.

But this stuff about Project Thurr and Dusk's Truth . . . He tucked those tidbits away for later.

Tharion opened a search field within Declan's program and typed in the sender's address. He started as the result came in.

Danika Fendyr.

Tharion burst from his office, sprinting through the glass corridors that revealed all manner of river life: mer and otters and fish, diving birds and water sprites and the occasional winding sea serpent. He only had three minutes before he had to be in the water.

Thankfully, the hatch into the pressurization chamber was open when he arrived, and Tharion leapt in, slamming the round door behind him before punching the button beside it.

He'd barely sealed the door when water flooded his feet, rushing into the chamber with a sigh. Tharion sighed with it, slumping into the rising water and shucking off his pants, his body tingling as fins replaced skin and bone, his legs fusing, rippling with tiger-striped scales.

He pulled off his shirt, shuddering into the scales that rippled along his arms and halfway up his torso. Talons curled off his fingers as Tharion thrust them into his hair, slicking back the red strands.

Fucking inconvenient.

Tharion glanced at the digital clock above the air lock door. He was free to return to human form now, but he liked to wait a good five minutes. Just to make sure the transformation had been marked by the strange magic that guided the mer. It didn't matter that he could summon water from thin air—the shift only counted if he submerged completely in the currents of wild magic.

Danika Fendyr had known Sofie Renast. Had swapped emails during a six-month window leading up to Danika's death, all relating to something about Dusk's Truth and this Project Thurr, except that one detailing a secure spot.

But had Danika Fendyr known Emile as well? Had Emile been the person Sofie had meant to pass along the safe location info to? It was a stretch, but from what the River Queen had told him, everything Sofie had done before her death had been for her brother. Why wouldn't he be the person she was eager to hide, should she ever get him free from Kavalla? The trouble now was finding them somewhere in this city. *Where the weary souls find relief from their suffering*, apparently. Whatever that meant.

Tharion waited until five minutes had passed, then reached up with a muscled arm to hit the release button beside the air lock door. Water drained out, clearing the chamber, and Tharion remained seated, staring at his fins, waving idly in the air.

He willed the change, and light shimmered along his legs, pain lancing down them as his fin split in two, revealing his naked body.

His pants were soaked, but Tharion didn't particularly care as he shoved his legs back into them. At least he hadn't been wearing shoes. He'd lost countless pairs thanks to close calls like this over the years.

With a groan, he eased to his feet and opened the door once more. He donned one of the navy windbreakers hanging from the wall for warmth, BCIU written in yellow print on the back. Blue Court Investigative Unit. It was technically part of Lunathion's Auxiliary, but the River Queen liked to think of her realm as a separate entity.

He checked his phone as he stalked down the hall toward his office, skimming the field reports that had come in. He went still at one of them. Maybe Ogenas was looking out for him.

A kingfisher shifter had called in a report three hours ago—out in the Nelthian Marshes. A small, abandoned boat. Nothing unusual, but its registration had snagged his eye. It had made berth in Pangera. The rest of the report had Tharion hurrying to his office.

An adolescent-sized life vest with *Bodegraven* written on its back had been found in the boat. No one remained on board, but a scent lingered. Human, male, young.

What were the odds that a life jacket from the same ship Sofie Renast's brother had been on had appeared on a wholly different boat, near the very city the emails between her and Danika had indicated was safe to hide in?

Emile Renast had to have been on that boat. The question was: Did he have reason to suspect that his sister had survived the Hind? Were they currently en route to be reunited? Tharion had a few guesses for where Danika's cryptic instructions might imply—none of them good. He might have no idea what his queen wanted with either Sofie or Emile, enough that she'd wanted the former alive or dead, but he had little choice in following this lead.

He supposed he'd forfeited the right to choices long ago.

Tharion took a wave skimmer up the Istros, aiming for the marshland an hour north of the city. The river cut along the coast here, wending between the swaying, hissing reeds. Along one seemingly random curve, the small skiff had been driven up onto the grasses, and now tilted precariously to one side.

Birds swooped and soared overhead, and eyes monitored him unblinkingly from the grasses as he slowed the wave skimmer to examine the boat.

He shuddered. The river beasts nested in these marshes. Even Tharion had been careful about what watery paths he took through the grasses. The sobeks might know better than to fuck with the mer, but a female beast would go down snapping for her young.

A thirteen-year-old boy, however gifted, would be a rich dessert.

Tharion used his water magic to guide him right up to the boat, then hopped aboard. Empty cans of food and bottles of water clanked against each other with the impact of his landing. A sweep of the sleeping area below revealed a human, male scent, along with blankets and more food.

Small, muddy footprints marked the deck near the steering wheel. A child had indeed been on this boat. Had that child sailed from Pangera all the way here alone? Pity and dread stirred in Tharion's gut at all the abandoned trash.

He turned on the engine and discovered plenty of fuel—indicating that the boat hadn't run out of firstlight and been ditched here. So this must have been an intentional landing. Which suggested that Sofie must have passed that information about the meeting spot along to Emile after all. But if he'd discarded the boat here, in the heart of sobek territory . . . Tharion rubbed his jaw.

He made a slow circle of the reeds around the boat. Listening, scenting. And—fuck. Human blood. He braced himself for the worst as he approached a red-splattered section of reeds.

His relief was short-lived. The smell was adult, but . . . that was an arm. Ripped away from the body, which must have been dragged off. Trauma to the biceps in line with a sobek bite.

Fighting his roiling stomach, Tharion crept closer. Scented it again.

It was fresher than the boy's scent on the boat by a day or so. And maybe it was a coincidence that there was a human arm here, but Tharion knew the dark gray of the torn sleeve that remained on the arm. The patch of the golden sun bracketed by a gun and a blade still half-visible near the bite.

The Ophion insignia. And the additional red sinking sun above it . . . Their elite Lightfall squadron, led by Pippa Spetsos.

Carefully, as silently as he could, Tharion moved through the reeds, praying he didn't stumble into any sobek nests. The human scents were more numerous here. Several males and a female, all adult. All coming from inland—not the water. Ogenas, had Pippa Spetsos herself led the unit here to get the boy? They must have tried to creep up on the boat from the reeds. And apparently one of them had paid the ultimate price.

Ophion had sent their best unit here, despite their numerous recent losses. They needed Lightfall in Pangera—and yet they were expending resources on this hunt. So they likely weren't seeking the boy out of the goodness of their hearts. Had Emile abandoned the boat here not because Sofie had told him to, but because he'd sensed someone on his tail? Had he fled to this city not only to find his sister at the arranged spot, but also to get free of the rebels?

Tharion retraced his steps back to the boat, scanning it again. He slung himself belowdecks, pulling aside blankets and garbage, skimming, scanning—

There. A marked-up map of the Valbaran coast. With these marshes circled. These marshes . . . and one other marking. Tharion winced. If Emile Renast had fled on foot from here to Crescent City . . .

He pulled out his phone and dialed one of his officers. Ordered them to get to the marshes. To start at the boat and work their way by land toward the city. And bring guns—not just for the beasts in the reeds, but for the rebels who might be following the kid.

And if they found Emile . . . He ordered the officer to track him for a while. See who he met up with. Who the boy might lead them to.

If the boy had even walked out of these marshes alive.

12

Hunt stretched out his legs, adjusting his wings so he didn't crush them between his back and the wooden bench. Bryce sat beside him, pistachio ice cream melting down the sides of her cone, and Hunt tried not to stare as she licked away each dribbling green droplet.

Was this punishment for his fight with Pollux? To sit here and watch this?

Hunt focused instead on the scooter she'd apparently ridden at breakneck speed to the Comitium. She'd walked with him when they left, though, pushing it beside her all the way to the park. He cleared his throat and asked, "Something up with your bike?"

Bryce frowned. "It was making a weird noise earlier. Didn't seem wise to get back on it." She arched a brow. "Want to be a gentleman and carry it home for me?"

"I'd rather carry *you*, but sure." The scooter would be heavy, but nothing he couldn't deal with. He remembered his own ice cream—coffee—in time to lick away the melted bits. He tried not to note the way her eyes tracked each movement of his tongue. "What kind of noise was it making?"

"A kind of rasping sputter whenever I idled." She twisted to where her beloved bike leaned against a banner-adorned lamp-post. "It's gonna have to go into the shop, poor thing."

Hunt chuckled. "I can bring it up to the roof and check it out."

"So romantic. When do the wedding invites go out for you two?"

He laughed again. "I'm shocked Randall didn't make you learn how to fix your own bike."

"Oh, he tried. But I was a legal adult by that point and didn't have to listen." She glanced at him sidelong. "Seriously, though—you know how to fix a bike?"

Hunt's amusement slipped a notch. "Yeah. I, ah . . . know how to fix a lot of machines."

"Does your lightning give you an affinity for knowing how they work, or something?"

"Yeah." Hunt trained his gaze upon the Istros. The relentless sun was finally setting, casting the river in reds and golds and oranges. Far below the surface, little lights glowed, all that showed of the mighty, sprawling court beneath the water. He said quietly, "Sandriel took advantage of that—she often had me take apart Ophion's mech-suits after battles, so I could learn how they worked and then sabotage them before discreetly sending the machines back to the front for the rebels to use unwittingly." He couldn't look at her, especially when she remained silent as he added, almost confessing, "I learned a lot about how machines work. How to make them *not* work. Especially at key moments. A lot of people likely died because of that. Because of me."

He'd tried convincing himself that what he did was justified, that the suits themselves were monstrous: fifteen feet high and crafted of titanium, they were essentially exoskeletal armor that the human standing within could pilot as easily as moving their own body. Armed with seven-foot-long swords—some of them charged with firstlight—and massive guns, they could go head-to-maw with a wolf shifter and walk away intact. They were the human army's most valuable asset—and only way of withstanding a Vanir attack.

Sandriel ordering him to take apart and mess with the suits had nothing to do with that, though. It had been about pure cruelty and sick amusement—stealing the suits, sabotaging them, and returning them with the humans none the wiser. It was about watching with glee as the pilots squared off against Vanir forces, only to find that their mech-suits failed them.

Bryce laid a hand on his knee. "I'm sorry she made you do that, Hunt."

"So am I," Hunt said, exhaling deeply, as if it could somehow cleanse his soul.

Bryce seemed to sense his need to shift the subject, because she suddenly asked, "What the Hel are we going to do about Pollux and Baxian?" She threw him a wry look, drawing him out of the past. "Aside from pummeling them into tenderized meat."

Hunt snorted, silently thanking Urd for bringing Bryce into his life. "We can only hope Celestina keeps them in line."

"You don't sound so certain."

"I spoke to her for five minutes before Pollux came in. It wasn't enough to make a judgment."

"Isaiah and Naomi seem to like her."

"You talked to them?"

"On the way in. They're . . . concerned about you."

Hunt growled. "They should be concerned about those two psychopaths living here."

"Hunt."

The sun lit her eyes to a gold so brilliant it knocked the breath from him. She said, "I know your history with Pollux. I understand why you reacted this way. But it can't happen again."

"I know." He licked his ice cream again. "The Asteri sent him here for a reason. Probably to rile me like this."

"They told us to lie low. Why goad you out of doing so?"

"Maybe they changed their minds and want a public reason to arrest us."

"We killed two Archangels. They don't need any further charges to sign our death sentences."

"Maybe they do. Maybe they worry we *could* get away with it if it went to trial. And a public trial would mean admitting our roles in Micah's and Sandriel's deaths."

"I think the world could easily believe you killed an Archangel. But a widdle nobody half-human like me? *That's* the thing they don't want leaking out."

"I guess. But . . . I just have a hard time believing any of this.

That Pollux and Baxian being here isn't a sign of shit about to go down. That Celestina might actually be a decent person. I've got more than two hundred years of history telling me to be wary. I can't deprogram myself." Hunt shut his eyes.

A moment later, soft fingers tangled in his hair, idly brushing the strands. He nearly purred, but kept perfectly still as Bryce said, "We'll keep our guards up. But I think . . . I think we might need to start believing in our good luck."

"Ithan Holstrom's arrival is the exact opposite of that."

Bryce nudged him with a shoulder. "He's not so bad."

He cracked open an eye. "You've come around quickly on him."

"I don't have time to hold grudges."

"You're immortal now. I'd say you do."

She opened her mouth, but a bland male voice echoed through the park: *The Gates will be closing in ten minutes. Anyone not in line will not be granted access.*

She scowled. "I could have lived without them using the Gates to broadcast announcements all day."

"You're the one to blame for it, you know," he said, mouth kicking up at one corner.

Bryce sighed, but didn't argue.

It was true. Since she'd used the crystal Gates to contact Danika, it had awoken public interest in them, and revived awareness that they could be used to speak throughout the city. They were now mostly used to make announcements, ranging from the opening and closing times at the tourist sites to the occasional recording of an imperial announcement from Rigelus himself. Hunt hated those the most. *This is Rigelus, Bright Hand of the Asteri. We honor the fallen dead in beautiful Lunathion, and thank those who fought for their service.*

And we watch all of them like hawks, Hunt always thought when he heard the droning voice that disguised the ancient being within the teenage Fae body.

The Gate announcer fell quiet again, the gentle lapping of the Istros and whispering palm trees overhead filling the air once more.

Bryce's gaze drifted across the river, to the mists swirling on its opposite shore. She smiled sadly. "Do you think Lehabah is over there?"

"I hope so." He'd never stop being grateful for what the fire sprite had done.

"I miss her," she said quietly.

Hunt slid an arm around her, tucking her into his side. Savoring her warmth and offering his own. "Me too."

Bryce leaned her head against his shoulder. "I know Pollux is a monster; and you have every reason in the world to want to kill him. But please don't do anything to make the Governor punish you. I couldn't . . ." Her voice caught, and Hunt's chest strained with it. "Watching Micah cut off your wings . . . I can't see that again, Hunt. Or any other horror she might invent for you."

He ran a hand over her silken hair. "I shouldn't have lost control like that. I'm sorry."

"You don't need to apologize. Not for this. Just . . . be cautious."

"I will."

She ate more of her ice cream, but didn't move. So Hunt did the same, careful not to drip into her hair.

When they'd eaten it all, when the sun was near-vanished and the first stars had appeared, Bryce straightened. "We should go home. Ithan and Syrinx need dinner."

"I'd suggest not telling Holstrom that you group him with your pet."

Bryce chuckled, pulling away, and it was all Hunt could do to not reach for her.

He'd decided to Hel with it all when Bryce stiffened, her attention fixed on something beyond his wings. Hunt whirled, hand going to the knife at his thigh.

He swore. This was not an opponent he could fight against. No one could.

"Let's go," Hunt murmured, folding a wing around her as the black boat neared the quay. A Reaper stood atop it. Clothed and veiled in billowing black that hid all indication of whether the Reaper was male or female, old or young. Such things did not matter to Reapers.

Hunt's blood chilled to ice as the oarless, rudderless boat drifted right to the quay, utterly at odds with the elegant banners and flowers adorning every part of this city. The boat halted as if invisible hands tied it to the concrete walkway.

The Reaper stepped out, moving so fluidly it was as if it walked on air. Bryce trembled beside him. The city around them had gone quiet. Even the insects had ceased their humming. No wind stirred the palms lining the quay. The banners hanging from the lampposts had ceased their flapping. The ornate flower wreaths seemed to wither and brown.

But a phantom breeze fluttered the Reaper's robes and trailing veil as it aimed for the small park beyond the quay and the streets past that. It did not look their way, did not halt.

Reapers did not need to halt for anything, not even death. The Vanir might call themselves immortal, but they could die from trauma or sickness. Even the Asteri were killable. The Reapers, however . . .

You could not kill what was already dead. The Reaper drifted by, silence rippling in its wake, and vanished into the city.

Bryce braced her hands on her knees. "Ugh, ugh, *ughhh*."

"My sentiments exactly," Hunt murmured. Reapers dwelled on every eternal isle in the world: the Bone Quarter here, the Catacombs in the Eternal City, the Summerlands in Avallen . . . Each of the sacred, sleeping domains guarded by a fierce monarch. Hunt had never met the Under-King of Lunathion—and hoped he never would.

He had as little as possible to do with the Under-King's Reapers, too. Half-lifes, people called them. Humans and Vanir who had once been alive, who had faced death and offered their souls to the Under-King as his private guards and servants instead. The cost: to live forever, unaging and unkillable, but never again to be able to sleep, eat, fuck. Vanir did not mess with them.

"Let's go," Bryce said, shaking off her shiver. "I need more ice cream."

Hunt chuckled. "Fair enough." He was about to turn them from the river when the roar of a wave skimmer's engine sounded. He turned toward it on training and instinct, and halted when he marked the red-haired male atop it. The muscled arm that waved toward them. Not a friendly wave, but a frantic one.

"Tharion?" Bryce asked, seeing the direction of Hunt's focus as the mer male gunned for them, leaving roiling waves in his wake.

It was the work of a moment to reach them, and Tharion cut the engine and drifted for the quay, keeping well away from the black boat tied nearby.

"Where the fuck have *you* been this summer?" Hunt asked, crossing his arms.

But Tharion said breathlessly to Bryce, "We need to talk."

"How did you even find us?" Bryce asked as they rode the elevator in her apartment building minutes later.

"Spy-master, remember?" Tharion grinned. "I've got eyes everywhere." He followed Bryce and Hunt into the apartment.

Bryce's attention immediately shot to Ithan—who was exactly where she'd left him that morning: on the couch, Syrinx sprawled across his lap. His face had healed even more, the raw scar nearly vanished.

Ithan straightened as Tharion entered. "Relax," she said, and didn't spare the wolf another glance as Hunt and Tharion aimed for the couch.

Bryce let out a warning hiss at the mer's still-wet clothes.

Hunt rolled his eyes and sat at the dining table instead. "This is why people shouldn't get white couches," the angel grumbled, and Bryce scowled.

"Then *you* can clean off the river water and dirt," she shot back.

"That's what insta-clean spells are for," Hunt replied smoothly. Bryce scowled.

"Domestic bliss, I see," Tharion said.

Bryce snickered, but Ithan asked from the couch, "Who are you?"

Tharion flashed him a smile. "None of your business."

But Ithan sniffed. "Mer. Oh—yeah, I know you. Captain Whatever."

"Ketos," Tharion muttered.

Hunt tipped his head to Ithan. "You've landed a grave blow to Captain Whatever's ego, Holstrom."

"The gravest blow comes from my dearest friends failing to extol my many qualities when I'm challenged," Tharion said, pouting.

"Dearest friends?" Hunt asked, raising a brow.

"Prettiest friends," Tharion said, blowing a kiss to Bryce.

Bryce laughed and twisted away, putting her phone on silent before sending off a message to Ruhn. *Get over here ASAP.*

He replied instantly. *What's wrong?*

NOW.

Whatever it was that Tharion wanted with such urgency, Ruhn should know about it, too. She wanted him to know about it. Which was . . . weird. Yet nice.

Bryce slid her phone into her back pocket as Tharion gestured toward the neon-pink lace bra dangling off the folding door to the laundry machines. "Hot," the mer said.

"Don't get her started," Hunt muttered.

Bryce glared at him, but said to Tharion, "It's been a while." The mer was as attractive as she remembered. Perhaps more so, now that he was slightly disheveled and muddy.

"We talking about your sex life, or the time since I've seen you?" Tharion asked, glancing between her and Hunt. Hunt glowered, but Bryce smiled fiendishly. Tharion went on, heedless of Hunt's ire, "It's been a busy summer." He jumped onto a stool at the kitchen counter and patted the one beside him. "Sit, Legs. Let's have a chat."

Bryce plopped next to him, hooking her feet on the bar below.

Tharion asked, suddenly serious, "Did Danika ever talk about someone named Sofie?" Ithan grunted in surprise.

Bryce's mouth scrunched to the side. "Sofie who?"

Before she could ask more, Hunt demanded, "What the fuck is this about?"

Tharion said smoothly, "Just updating some old files."

Bryce drummed her fingers on the marble counter. "On Danika?"

Tharion shrugged. "Glamorous as my life might seem, Legs, there's a lot of grunt work behind the scenes." He winked. "Though not the sort of grunting I'd like to do with you, of course."

"Don't try to distract me with flirting," Bryce said. "Why are you asking about Danika? And who the Hel is Sofie?"

Tharion sighed at the ceiling. "There's a cold case I'm working on, and Danika—"

"Don't lie to her, Tharion," Hunt growled. Lightning danced along his wings.

A thrill shot through Bryce at it—not only the power, but knowing he had her back. She said to Tharion, "I'm not telling you shit until you give me more information." She jabbed a thumb toward Ithan. "And neither is he, so don't even ask."

Ithan only smiled slowly at the mer, as if daring him to.

Tharion sized them all up. To his credit, he didn't back down. A muscle ticked in his cheek, though. As if he waged some inner debate. Then the mer captain said, "I, ah . . . I was assigned to look into a human woman, Sofie Renast. She was a rebel who was captured by the Hind two weeks ago. But Sofie was no ordinary human, and neither was her younger brother—Emile. Both he and Sofie pass as human, yet they possess full thunderbird powers."

Bryce blew out a breath. Well, she hadn't been expecting *that.*

Hunt said, "I thought thunderbirds had been hunted to extinction by the Asteri." *Too dangerous and volatile to be allowed to live* was the history they'd been spoon-fed at school. *A grave threat to the empire.* "They're little more than myths now."

All true. Bryce remembered a Starlight Fancy horse called Thunderbird: a blue-and-white unicorn-pegasus who could wield all types of energy. She'd never gotten her hands on one, though she'd yearned to.

But Tharion went on, "Well, somehow, somewhere, one survived. And bred. Emile was captured three years ago and sent to the Kavalla death camp. His captors were unaware of what they'd grabbed, and he wisely kept his gifts hidden. Sofie went into Kavalla and freed him. But from what I was told, Sofie was caught by the Hind before she reached safety. Emile got away—only to run from Ophion as well. It seems like he came this way, but various parties are still *very* interested in the powers he possesses. And Sofie, too, if she survived."

"No one survives the Hind," Hunt said darkly.

"Yeah, I know. But the chains attached to the lead blocks at the bottom of the ocean were empty. Unlocked. Seems like Sofie made it. Or someone snatched her corpse."

Bryce frowned. "And the River Queen wants both the kid and Sofie? Why? And what does this have to do with Danika?"

"I don't know what my queen's ultimate goal is. All I know is that she's very keen on finding Sofie, alive or dead, and equally keen on attaining Emile. But despite what that suggests, she's not affiliated with Ophion in any way." Tharion rubbed at his jaw. "In the process of trying to figure out this clusterfuck, I found some emails between Sofie and Danika talking about a safe place in this city for Sofie to lie low should she ever need it."

"That's not possible," Ithan said.

Hunt rose from the table and stalked to Bryce's side. His power shimmered up her body, electrifying her very blood at his nearness. "Is the River Queen insane? Are *you* insane? Searching for rebels and not turning them in is a one-way ticket to crucifixion."

Tharion held his stare. "I don't really have a choice here. Orders are orders." He nodded to them. "Clearly you guys know nothing about this. Do me a favor and don't mention it to anyone, okay?" The mer stood and turned toward the door.

Bryce hopped off her stool and stepped into his path. "Oh, I don't think so." She let a fraction of her starlight shine around her. "You don't get to tell me that Danika was in contact with a known rebel and then waltz out of here."

Tharion chuckled, cold frosting his eyes. "Yeah, I do, Legs." He took a blatantly challenging step toward her.

Bryce held her ground. Was surprised and delighted that Hunt let her fight this battle without interfering. "Do you even care that this oh-so-powerful thunderbird is a kid? Who survived a fucking *death camp*? And is now scared and alone?"

Tharion blinked, and she could have strangled him.

"I know this is a dick thing to say," Ithan added, "but if the kid's got that power, why didn't he use it to get out of Kavalla himself?"

"Maybe he doesn't know how to use it yet," Tharion mused. "Maybe he was too weak or tired. I don't know. But I'll see you guys later." He made to step past Bryce.

She blocked him again. "Emile aside, Danika wasn't a rebel, and she didn't know anyone named Sofie Renast."

Ithan said, "I agree."

Tharion said firmly, "The email was linked to her. And the email address was *BansheeFan56*—Danika was clearly a Banshees fan. Skim through any of her old social media profiles and there are ten thousand references to her love of that band."

Solas, how many Banshees shirts and posters had Danika amassed over the years? Bryce had lost count.

Bryce tapped her foot, her blood at a steady simmer. Hadn't Philip Briggs said something similar when she and Hunt had interrogated the former leader of the Keres rebel sect in his prison cell? That Danika was a rebel sympathizer? "What did the emails say?"

Tharion kept his mouth shut.

Bryce bristled. "*What did the emails say?*"

Tharion snapped, a rare show of temper apparently getting the better of him, "Does Dusk's Truth mean anything to you? What about Project Thurr?" At her blank look, and Ithan's, the mer said, "I thought so."

Bryce clenched her jaw hard enough to hurt. After this spring, she'd realized she hadn't known as much about Danika as she'd believed, but to add even more to that list . . . She tried not to let it sting.

Tharion took another challenging step toward the door. But Bryce said, "You can't drop all that information and expect me not to do anything. Not to go looking for this kid."

Tharion arched a brow. "So softhearted. But stay out of it, Legs."

"No way," Bryce countered.

Hunt cut in, "Bryce. We were given an order by the Asteri—by Rigelus himself—to lie low."

"Then obey them," Tharion said.

Bryce glared at the mer, then at Hunt. But Hunt said, storms in his eyes, "The Asteri will slaughter us, along with your entire family, if word reaches them that you're involved with rebel activity in any way. Even if it's just helping to find a lost kid."

Bryce opened her mouth, but Hunt pushed, "We won't get a trial, Bryce. Only an execution."

Tharion crossed his arms. "Exactly. So, again: stay out of it, and I'll be on my way."

Before Bryce could snap her reply, the front door banged open, and Ruhn filled the doorway. "What the— Oh. Hey, Tharion."

"You invited him?" Tharion accused Bryce.

Bryce stayed silent, holding her ground.

"What's going on?" Ruhn asked, glancing to Hunt and Ithan. Ruhn startled at the sight of the wolf. "And what's *he* doing here?"

"Ithan's a free agent right now, so he's staying with us," Bryce said, and at Ruhn's puzzled look, added, "I'll fill you in later."

Ruhn asked, "Why's your heart racing?"

Bryce peered at her chest, half expecting her scar to be glowing. Mercifully, it lay dormant. "Well, apparently Tharion thinks Danika was involved with the rebels."

Ruhn gaped.

"Thanks, Bryce," Tharion muttered.

Bryce threw him a saccharine smile and explained Tharion's investigation to Ruhn.

"Well?" Ruhn asked when she'd finished, his face drained of color. "*Was* Danika a rebel?"

"No!" Bryce splayed her arms. "Solas, she was more interested in what junk food we had in our apartment."

"That's not all she was interested in," Ruhn corrected. "She stole the Horn and hid it from you. Hid it *on* you. And all that shit with Briggs and the synth . . ."

"Okay, fine. But the rebel stuff . . . She never even *talked* about the war."

"She would have known it'd endanger you," Tharion suggested.

Hunt said to Tharion, "And you're cool with being press-ganged into working on this shit?" His face remained paler than usual. Tharion just crossed his long, muscular arms. Hunt went on, voice lowering, "It won't end well, Tharion. Trust me on that. You're tangling in some dangerous shit."

Bryce avoided looking at the branded-out tattoo on Hunt's wrist.

Tharion's throat bobbed. "I'm sorry to have even come here. I know how you feel about this stuff, Athalar."

"You really think there's a chance Sofie is alive?" Ruhn asked.

"Yes," Tharion said.

"If she survived the Hind," Hunt said, "and the Hind hears about it, she'll come running."

"The Hind might already be headed this way," Tharion said thickly. "Regardless of Sofie, Emile and his powers remain a prize. Or something to be wiped out once and for all." He dragged his long fingers through his dark red hair. "I know I'm dropping a bomb on you guys." He winced at his unfortunate word choice, no doubt remembering what had happened last spring. "But I want to find this kid before anyone else."

"And do what with him?" Bryce asked. "Hand him over to your queen?"

"He'd be safe Beneath, Legs. It'd take a damn long while even for the Asteri to find him—and kill him."

"So he'd be used by your queen like some kind of weaponized battery instead? Like Hel am I going to let you do that."

"Again, I don't know what she wants with Emile. But she wouldn't harm him. And you'd be wise to keep out of her path."

Ithan cut in before Bryce could start spitting venom, "You really think the kid is coming here? That the Hind will follow?"

Hunt rubbed his jaw. "The 33rd hasn't heard anything about the Hind coming over. Or Ophion being in the area."

"Neither has the Aux," Ruhn confirmed.

"Well, unless one of the marsh sobeks swam all the way across the Haldren to take a bite out of an Ophion soldier, I can't think of any other reason why I found dismembered body parts of one here," Tharion said.

"I don't even know where to begin with that," Hunt said.

"Just trust me," Tharion said, "Ophion is on its way, if not already here. So I need to know as much as possible, and as quickly as possible. Find Emile, and we potentially find Sofie."

"And gain a nice child soldier, right?" Bryce said tightly.

Tharion turned pleading eyes on her. "Either the River Queen puts me in charge of hunting for them, or she assigns someone else, possibly someone less . . . independently minded. I'd rather it be me who finds Emile."

Ithan burst out, "Can we discuss that you guys are talking about *rebels* in this city? About *Danika* potentially being a rebel?" He snarled. "That's a serious fucking claim."

"Sofie and Danika exchanged a number of intentionally vague emails," Tharion said. "Ones that included an allusion to a safe hiding place here in Lunathion. A place *where the weary souls find relief from their suffering.* I'm guessing the Bone Quarter, though I'm not sure even Danika would be so reckless as to send them there. But anyway, it's not a claim. It's a fact."

Ithan shook his head, but it was Hunt who said, "This is a lethal game, Tharion. One I'd rather not play again." Bryce could have sworn his hands shook slightly. This had to be dragging up the worst of his memories and fears—he'd *been* a rebel, once. It had won him two hundred years of servitude.

And today had been long and weird and she hadn't even told Hunt about Cormac's visit at lunch.

But to let this boy be hunted by so many people . . . She couldn't sit by. Not for an instant. So Bryce said, "I can ask Fury tomorrow if she knows anything about Danika and Sofie. Maybe she can give some insight into where Danika might have suggested hiding."

"Ask her right now," Tharion said with unusual seriousness.

"It's Wednesday night. She and Juniper always have date night."

It was half a lie, and Hunt must have known it was for his sake, because his wing gently brushed over her shoulder.

But Tharion ordered, "Then interrupt it."

"Don't you know *anything* about Fury Axtar?" Bryce waved a hand. "I'll call her tomorrow morning. She's always in a better mood after she and June get it on."

Tharion glanced between her and Hunt, then to Ruhn and Ithan, both silently watching. The mer reached into his jacket and pulled out a folded stack of papers with a resigned sigh. "Here's a sampling of the emails," he said, handing them to Bryce, and aimed for the door again. He paused near Syrinx, then knelt down and petted his head, his thick neck. He straightened Syrinx's collar and earned a lick of thanks. Tharion's mouth curled up at the corners as he stood. "Cool pet." He opened the front door. "Don't put anything in writing. I'll be back around lunch tomorrow."

As soon as the mer shut the door, Hunt said to Bryce, "Getting involved with this is a bad idea."

Ruhn said, "I agree."

Bryce only clutched the papers tighter and turned to Ithan. "This is the part where you say you agree, too."

Ithan frowned deeply. "I can ignore the shit about Danika and Ophion, but there's a kid out there on the run. Who probably has nothing to do with Ophion and needs help."

"*Thank you,*" Bryce said, whirling on Hunt. "See?"

"It's Tharion's business. Leave it alone, Bryce," Hunt warned. "I don't even know why you had to ask about any of this."

"I don't know why you *wouldn't* ask," Bryce challenged.

Hunt pushed, "Is this really about finding the kid, or is it about learning something new about Danika?"

"Can't it be both?"

Hunt slowly shook his head.

Ruhn said, "Let's think this through, Bryce, before deciding to act. And maybe burn those emails."

"I've already decided," she announced. "I'm going to find Emile."

"And do what with him?" Hunt asked. "If the Asteri want him, you'd be harboring a rebel."

Bryce couldn't stop the light from shimmering around her. "He's thirteen years old. He's not a rebel. The rebels just *want* him to be."

Hunt said quietly, "I saw kids his age walk onto battlefields, Bryce."

Ruhn nodded solemnly. "Ophion doesn't turn away fighters based on their age."

Ithan said, "That's despicable."

"I'm not saying it isn't," Hunt countered. "But the Asteri won't care if he's thirteen or thirty, if he's a true rebel or not. You stand in their way, and they'll punish you."

Bryce opened her mouth, but—a muscle flickered in his cheek, making the bruise there all the more noticeable. Guilt punched through her, warring with her ire. "I'll think about it," she conceded, and stalked for her bedroom.

She needed a breather before she said or did more than she meant to. A moment to process the information she'd gotten out of Tharion. She hadn't put any stock in Briggs's claim about Danika and the rebels when he'd taunted her with it—he'd been trying to get at her in any way possible. But it seemed she'd been wrong.

She scoured her memory for any detail as she washed away her makeup, then brushed her hair. Male voices rumbled from the other side of the door, but Bryce ignored them, changing into her pajamas. Her stomach gurgled.

Was Emile hungry? He was a kid—alone in the world, having suffered in one of those gods-forsaken camps, no family left. He had to be terrified. Traumatized.

She hoped Sofie was alive. Not for any intel or amazing powers, but so Emile had someone left. Family who loved him for *him* and not for being some all-powerful chosen one whose people had long ago been hunted to extinction.

Bryce frowned in the mirror. Then at the stack of papers Tharion had handed her. The emails between Sofie and Danika—and a few between Sofie and Emile.

The former were exactly as Tharion had claimed. Vague mentions of things.

But Sofie and Emile's emails . . .

I had to leave your sunball game before the end, Sofie had written in one exchange more than three years ago, *but Mom told me you guys won! Congrats—you were amazing out there!*

Emile had replied, *I was ok. Missed 2 shots.*

Sofie had written back, at three in the morning—as if she'd been up late studying or partying—*I once had a game when I missed* ten *shots! So you're doing way better than me. :)*

The next morning, Emile had said, *Thanks, sis. Miss u.*

Bryce swallowed hard. Such an ordinary exchange—proof of a normal, decent life.

What had happened to them? How had he wound up in Kavalla? Part of her didn't want to know, and yet . . . She read the emails again. The loving, casual exchange between siblings.

Did any of the many people searching for Emile want to actually help him? Not use him, but just . . . protect him? Maybe he and Sofie would find each other at that rendezvous spot Danika had mentioned. Maybe they'd get lucky, and no one would ever find them.

Danika had always helped those who needed it. Bryce included.

And during the spring attack, when Bryce had run to Asphodel Meadows . . . it was the same feeling creeping over her now. The boy needed help. She wouldn't walk away from it. *Couldn't* walk away from it.

But how did Danika factor in to all of this? She needed to know.

Her stomach protested again. Right—dinner. With a silent prayer to Cthona to keep Emile safe, Bryce emerged from the bedroom and said, "I'm ordering pizza."

Ruhn said, "I'm in," as if he'd been invited, but Bryce glanced at the shut door to Hunt's bedroom.

If *she* needed a moment, he'd sure as Hel need a lot longer.

Hunt turned on the shower with a shaking hand. The blast and splatter of the water provided much-needed white noise, a quieting barrier against the world beyond his bathroom. He'd muttered something about needing a shower and walked in here, not caring what Danaan and Holstrom thought.

Hunt peeled out of his battle-suit, dimly aware of the bruises along his ribs and his face, the brawl with Pollux almost forgotten.

He couldn't stop shaking, couldn't stop the surge of acid through his veins that made every breath torturous.

Fucking Tharion. That stupid, arrogant asshole. Dragging them—dragging *Bryce*—into this. The River Queen might have no association with Ophion, but Emile was a rebel's brother. Danika had possibly been a rebel herself. It brought them far too close to Ophion's orbit.

Of course Bryce wouldn't have been able to drop it once she'd heard. He knew it was irrational to be pissed at her about it, because part of why he adored her was that she was the kind of person who *would* want to help, but . . . fucking Hel.

Hunt sucked in a breath, stepping into the now-warm stream, and clenched his jaw against the rising thunder in his blood and the memories that came with it.

Those strategy meetings in Shahar's war tent; the bloody, screaming chaos of battle; his roar as Shahar died, a piece of his heart dying with her; the bolt of unrelenting pain as his wings were sawed off tendon by tendon—

Hunt sucked in another breath, wings twitching, as if in an echo of that pain.

He couldn't let it happen again. If all of it had been for Bryce, to get here—then it had happened so that he'd know when to walk away, and keep her safe.

But he hadn't been able to find those words. Hunt focused on his breathing, on the sensation of his feet against the slick tiles, the dribble of water down his wings.

And couldn't help but think that warm water felt an awful lot like blood.

Thirty minutes later, they sat around the dining table, four boxes of pizza stacked before them.

"Carnivore's Delight," Bryce said with forced cheer to Hunt, sliding the meat-on-meat-on-meat pizza toward him. He offered a smile, but it didn't quite reach his eyes. She didn't ask about that haunted gleam, though. Not with Ruhn and Ithan here. Not when Hunt had already made it pretty clear what was going through his head.

They'd undoubtedly have it out the moment they were alone.

"Carnivore's Delight with extra sausage," she said to Ithan, winking as she handed over the box. She could have sworn Ithan blushed. "And pepperoni with grilled onions," she said to Ruhn.

"What'd you get?" her brother asked. An attempt at normalcy after Tharion's visit.

Hunt and Ithan said at the same time, "Sausage and onion with extra cheese."

Bryce laughed. "I don't know whether to be impressed or disturbed."

But Ithan and Hunt didn't smile. She caught Ruhn's glance from across the table, and her brother said into her mind, *Ignoring all the shit with Tharion and Emile, it's super fucking weird that Holstrom's here.*

She started on her pizza and sighed at the combination of meat and cheese and slightly sweet sauce. *I think it's super weird for him, too.*

Ruhn bit into his slice. *Honestly, don't flip the Hel out, but you're technically a Starborn Princess. And you're now harboring an exiled wolf. I hate this political crap, but . . . I wouldn't put it past Sabine to see this as an affront. The wolves are technically our allies.*

Bryce sipped from her beer. *It's not like he has any family left.* Her heart ached. *Believe me, he is fucking* miserable *that he has nowhere else to go.*

I can take him in. Her brother spoke with utter sincerity.

Isn't that the same political bullshit?

I can say that I'm hiring him to work for the Fae side of the Aux. Claim it's for a top secret investigation, which I suppose this stuff with Danika and Sofie and Emile is. Sabine can't get around that.

All right. But . . . give him a few days. I don't want him to think I'm kicking him out.

Why not? He was a dick to you.

There were five years before that when we were close.

So? He was a dick to you when you needed him most.

And I shut him out when he needed me *most.*

Bryce blinked, finding Hunt and Ithan watching her and Ruhn. The angel drawled, no hint of his previous haunted discomfort, "Some might consider it rude to have a silent conversation in front of other people."

Ithan raised his hand in agreement. How he'd figured out what was going on, she could only attribute to his keen wolf's abilities. Or his athlete's skill at reading opponents.

Bryce stuck out her tongue. "Sorry you're not magical, special Fae like us."

"Here we go," Hunt said, diving into his slice. "I was waiting for this day to come."

"What day?" Ithan swigged from his beer.

Hunt smirked. "When Bryce realizes how truly obnoxious being a princess allows her to be."

Bryce flipped him off. "If I have to suffer through the title, then you have to suffer through the effects."

Hunt opened his mouth, but Ithan said, "I heard you had your Ordeal that day this spring. Congrats?"

Bryce went still. "Yeah. Uh, thanks." She didn't want to think about it—the nøkk, Syrinx nearly drowning, the tank . . . Syrinx rubbed against her ankles, as if sensing her distress. And Hunt, also reading it, said to Ruhn, "You had your Ordeal in Avallen, right? And our new friend Cormac was there?"

Before Ruhn could answer, Flynn and Dec strode into the apartment with a key Bryce definitely hadn't authorized. She whipped her head to Ruhn. "You gave them fingerprint access and copies of my keys?"

Flynn slid into the chair beside hers and pulled her pizza toward himself. "We took Ruhn's fingerprints when he was passed out during the Summer Solstice, as a way into the system. Then Dec added ours alongside them."

Declan dropped into the chair beside Ruhn, taking one of her brother's slices and a beer from the bucket in the center of the table. "We made copies of the physical keys before he noticed they were gone."

"You're really making me look good, you two," Ruhn grumbled.

Bryce shoved out a hand. "I'm changing my fingerprint system to something more secure. Give me that key."

Flynn only slid it into his pocket. "Come get it, babycakes."

Hunt shot the Fae lord a glare, and Declan snickered. "Careful, Flynn," Dec warned.

Ithan snorted, and the two males eyed him up. Of course they'd already noticed him—they were trained warriors—but they hadn't yet deigned to acknowledge him.

Flynn flashed a charming smile full of teeth. "Hi, pup."

Ithan's fingers tightened into fists at the term. "Hey."

Declan gave a mirror grin to Flynn's. "Bryce needed a new pet?"

"Okay, okay," Bryce cut in. "Let's just say that we made a thousand dog jokes about Ithan, and he made a thousand Fae asshole jokes about you two idiots, and we now all thoroughly hate each other, but we can be adults and eat our food."

"I second that." Hunt dug into his third slice, using his other hand to clink beers with Bryce.

Flynn grinned again. "I thought I heard you ask Ruhn about his Ordeal. It was our Ordeal, too, you know."

"I know," Bryce said, flicking her hair over her shoulder. "But he won the prize sword, didn't he?"

"Ouch." Flynn clutched his chest.

"Cold, B," Declan said.

Ruhn chuckled and leaned back in his seat, finishing off his beer before he said, "I was twenty-seven. My—our father sent me to Avallen to . . . check out the ladies."

"There was a Fae female from a powerful family who the Autumn King wanted Ruhn to marry," Flynn explained. "Unfortunately, Cormac wanted to marry her, too. Neither married her in the end, of course."

Bryce groaned. "Please tell me all this tension between you two isn't over a girl."

"Only partially," Declan said. "It's also because Cormac and his twin cousins tried to kill us. Cormac literally put a sword through my gut." He patted his rock-hard abs.

"Aren't you Fae all . . . allies?" Ithan asked, brows raised.

Flynn nearly spat out his drink. "Valbaran Fae and Avallen Fae *hate* each other. The Avallen Fae are a bunch of backward assholes. Prince Cormac might be Ruhn's cousin, but he can drop dead for all we care."

"Strong family bonds, huh?" Hunt said.

Flynn shrugged. "They deserved what happened during the Ordeal."

"Which was what, exactly?" Bryce asked.

"Humiliation," Declan said with relish. "A few weeks into our visit, King Morven—Cormac's dad—ordered Ruhn to go see if he could retrieve the Starsword from the caves."

"Tell the whole story, Dec. *Why* did he order me to do that?" Ruhn growled.

Dec sheepishly grinned. "Because I bragged that you could."

Ruhn cracked open another beer. "And?"

"And I made fun of Cormac for not having gone to retrieve it yet."

"And?"

"And I said that one Valbaran Fae warrior was better than ten from Avallen."

Bryce laughed. "So Uncle Morven sent you off to teach you a lesson?"

"Yep," Flynn said. "All three of us. We didn't realize until we were in the mist—the caves are literally full of it—that he also sent Cormac and the asshole twins to hunt us in there."

"Starting blood feuds," Bryce said to Declan, raising her hand for a high five. "Nice work."

Declan clapped her hand, but Ithan asked, "So your Ordeals happened then?"

"Yeah," Ruhn said, face darkening. "We all got lost in the caves. There was some . . . scary shit in there. Ghouls and wraiths—they were old and wicked. The six of us went from trying to kill each other to trying to stay alive. Long story short, Flynn and Dec and I wound up in these catacombs deep beneath the cave—"

"Surrounded by bloodsucking spirits who were going to eat our bodies, then our souls," Flynn added. "Or was it our souls, then our bodies?"

Ruhn shook his head. "I got disarmed. So I looked in the sarcophagus in the center of the chamber where we were trapped, and . . . there it was. The Starsword. It was either die at the hands of those creatures or die trying to pull that sword from its sheath." He shrugged. "Thankfully, it worked."

Declan said, "Bastards ran screaming from the cave when Ruhn drew the sword. Right to where Cormac and the twins were hunting us." He grinned again. "The three of them had no choice but to flee back to their castle. King Morven was *not* happy. Especially when Ruhn returned with the Starsword and told him to go fuck himself."

Bryce lifted her brows at her brother. He smiled, lip ring glinting. "Not such a loser after all, huh?"

Bryce waved him off. "Whatever."

Flynn suddenly asked Ithan, gaze on his tattooed neck, "You gonna keep that ink?"

Ithan drained his beer. "What's it to you?"

Another charming grin. "Just want to know when I can tell you that Sabine and Amelie are two of the worst fucking people in this city."

Ithan grunted, but a ghost of a smile appeared on his lips.

Bryce glanced to Ruhn, who said into her mind, *Might not be such a bad idea for him to come stay with us.*

You really want to be roomies with a wolf?

Better than an angel.

Depends on what you're doing with that angel.

Gross, Bryce.

Bryce tuned back into the conversation as Declan asked with a wicked smile that told her he was about to start shit, "So, who's sleeping where in this apartment tonight?"

Bryce couldn't help glancing again at Hunt, who kept his face wholly neutral as he said, "I'm bunking with Bryce."

Bryce's mouth popped open, but Ithan said, "Good. She snores."

"Assholes," Bryce seethed. "You can both go sleep on the roof."

"Not enough distance from your snoring," Ithan said, smirking.

Bryce scowled, leaning down to pet Syrinx's velvety ears.

Hunt only winked. "I'll get earplugs."

13

Bryce barely slept. She was trying too hard to pretend that Hunt fucking Athalar was not sleeping beside her. The illusion was shattered every time she rolled over, got a face full of gray wings, and remembered that Hunt fucking Athalar was sleeping beside her.

They hadn't spoken about Tharion's visit. Or about her decision to find Emile. So any fight on that front was likely still on the horizon.

Naturally, Bryce woke up puffy-eyed, sweat-slicked, and with a pounding headache. Hunt was already up and making coffee, to guess by the sounds in the other room.

Bryce slithered out of bed, earning a disgruntled yip from Syrinx at being disturbed. Her ringing phone aggravated her headache, and it didn't get any better when she glanced at the caller ID.

She mustered her most chipper voice. "Hi, Mom."

"Hello, Bryce." Ember's voice was calm. Too calm.

Ithan smirked from the couch as she passed by, blindly walking toward the beckoning aroma of coffee. Gods, she needed some. Bryce asked her mom, "What's up? You guys get home okay?"

The wall of windows revealed a sunny day, witches and angels zooming by. And, Bryce realized in the morning light, the fact that she was still wearing her worn T-shirt that said *Nidaros Community Center Camp Summer 15023* and . . . little else. Oops. No wonder

Ithan was smirking. Her lilac lace demi-thong left little to the imagination. Bryce stifled the urge to tug her shirt's hem over her half-bare ass.

Hunt's eyes darkened, but he merely leaned against the counter and silently offered her a cup of coffee.

"Oh yes," Ember said. "We got home, had plenty of time to do some grocery shopping and run a few errands." Bryce put the phone on speaker and slid it onto the counter, backing away a few feet. Like it was a grenade of compressed firstlight about to explode.

"Great," Bryce said, and she could have sworn Hunt was trying not to laugh.

"We also had plenty of time," her mom went on, "to answer all the phone calls that we began to get, asking when the wedding is."

Hunt took a long sip of his coffee. Ithan just watched with a befuddled expression. Right. She hadn't told him.

Bryce gritted her teeth in an attempt at a smile. "You and Randall are renewing your vows?"

Her mom fell silent. A wave building, cresting, about to break. "Is this engagement some scheme to prompt Hunt to finally confess his love for you?"

Hunt choked on his coffee.

Oh gods. Bryce was half-tempted to pour the boiling coffee over her head and melt into nothing. "For fuck's sake," she hissed, snatching up her phone and taking it off speaker. Even if Hunt and Ithan, with their heightened hearing, could no doubt make out everything Ember said. "Look, it's not a *real* engagement—"

"It certainly sounds like it is, Bryce Adelaide Quinlan." Her mom's voice rose with each word. "And it sounds like you're engaged to the Crown Prince of Avallen! Do you *know* who his father is?"

"Mom, I'm not going to marry him."

"Then why do so many of my former school friends know about it? Why are there photos of you two having a private meeting at your office yesterday?"

Hunt's wings flared with alarm, and Bryce shook her head. *Later*, she tried to signal.

"Cormac ambushed me—"

"He did *what*?"

"In a nonphysical way. Nothing I couldn't handle. *And*," she said as her mom began objecting, "I have zero intention of marrying Prince Creepster, but you gotta trust me to deal with it." She gave Hunt a look as if to say, *You too.*

Hunt nodded, getting it. Drank some more coffee. Like he needed it.

Her mother, however, hissed, "Randall is in a *panic*."

"Randall, or you? Because last I checked, Dad knows I can take care of myself." Bryce couldn't help the sharpness in her tone.

"You're playing games with Fae royals who will outsmart you at every turn, who have likely anticipated your reticence—"

Bryce's phone buzzed. She skimmed the incoming message. Thank Urd.

"I appreciate your confidence, Mom. I have to go. I've got an important meeting."

"Don't you try to—"

"*Mom*." She couldn't stop herself, couldn't halt the roiling, rising power that made her body begin to shimmer, as if she were a pot boiling over with liquid starlight. "You don't get a say in what I do or don't do, and if you're smart, you'll stay the Hel out of this."

Stunned silence from her mother. From Hunt and Ithan, too.

The words kept flowing, though. "You have *no* fucking idea what I've been through, and faced, and what I'm now dealing with." Her mom and Randall would never know about what she'd done to Micah. She couldn't risk it. "But let me tell you that handling this bogus engagement is *nothing* compared to that. So *drop* it."

Another pause. Then her mother said, "I knew you bundled us off at the break of dawn for a reason. I want to *help* you, Bryce—"

"Thanks for the guilt trip," Bryce said. She could practically see her mother stiffening.

"Fine. We're still at your disposal should you need us, Your Highness."

Bryce started to answer, but her mother had hung up. She

slowly, slowly closed her eyes. Hunt said into the sudden, heavy quiet, "Cormac came by the archives?"

Bryce opened her eyes. "Only to swing his dick around." Hunt tensed, and Bryce added, "Not literally."

His expression turned wary. "Why didn't you tell me?"

"Because I got a phone call from Celestina that you were in a holding cell." She bared her teeth. "Spare me the territorial male act, okay?"

"Hide shit from your parents all you want, but don't keep stuff from me. We're a team."

"I just *forgot*. No big deal."

Hunt hesitated. "All right." He lifted his hands. "Okay. Sorry."

Silence fell, and she became keenly aware of Ithan's attention. "Hunt can fill you in on my joyous news," she said, glancing at the clock. "I do have a meeting, and I need to get dressed." Hunt arched a brow, but Bryce offered no explanation as she aimed for her bedroom.

She returned to the great room an hour later, showered and in work clothes. Hunt was already in his 33rd gear.

Bryce said to Ithan, who was doing push-ups in front of the TV with extraordinary ease, "I'll pop back in at lunch when Tharion swings by. Help yourself to whatever's in the fridge and call if you need anything."

"Thanks, Mom," Ithan said between reps, and Bryce stuck out her tongue.

Bryce unlocked the door, then buckled Syrinx's leash before slipping into the hall. She'd been lonely in the archives yesterday without his company. And maybe a little jealous about the fact that Syrinx had spent the day with Ithan.

And it would have been nice to watch him take a bite out of Prince Cormac's ass.

The elevator had just arrived when Hunt appeared behind her, and every muscle in her body turned electric. Had the elevator always been this small? Had his wings gotten larger overnight?

"Why are things so weird between us?" Hunt asked.

Going right for the throat, then. "Are things weird?"

"Don't play stupid. Come on—last night was weird. Right now is fucking weird."

Bryce leaned against the wall. "Sorry. Sorry." It was all she could think to say.

Hunt asked carefully, "When were you going to tell me about Cormac dropping by the archives? What the fuck did he say?"

"That you and I are losers and he thinks I'm an immature brat."

"Did he touch you?" Lightning skittered along Hunt's wings. The elevator lights guttered.

The elevator reached the ground floor before she could answer, and they fell silent as they passed Marrin, the doorman. The ursine shifter waved goodbye.

Only when they'd stepped onto the sizzling sidewalk did Bryce say, "No. Cormac's just a creep. Seems like this city is full of them these days." She gestured to the sky above, the angels soaring toward the sprawling complex of the Comitium in the CBD. The decorations in Celestina's honor seemed to have multiplied overnight. "No fights today, okay?"

"I'll try."

They reached the corner where Bryce would go right, Hunt to the left. "I mean it, Hunt. No more fights. We need to keep a low profile." Especially now. They were too close to Ophion for comfort.

"Fine. Only if you call me the moment Prince Asshole contacts you again."

"I will. Let me know if Tharion gets in touch. Or if you pick up anything about . . ." She glanced at the cameras mounted on the ornately decorated streetlamps and buildings. She couldn't say Emile's name here.

Hunt stiffened, wings tucking in. "We need to talk about that. I, ah . . ." Shadows darkened his eyes, and her heart strained, knowing what memories caused them. But here it was. The discussion she'd been waiting for. "I know you want to help, and I commend you for it, Bryce. But I think we really need to weigh everything before we jump in."

She couldn't resist the impulse to squeeze his hand. "Okay." His calluses brushed against her skin. "Good point."

"Tharion threw me off last night," he went on. "It dragged up a lot of old shit for me—and worries for you. But if you want to move forward with this . . . let's talk it through first."

"Okay," she said again. "But I'm still going to meet with Fury right now." She had too many questions *not* to meet with her.

"Sure," he said, though worry shone in his gaze. "Keep me updated." He slid his hand from hers. "And don't think we're done talking about this weirdness between us."

By the time Bryce had opened her mouth to answer, Hunt had already launched skyward.

Bryce slid onto a stool at the eight-seat counter that made up Tempest in a Teapot, her favorite tea bar in the city.

Nestled on Ink Street in the heart of the Old Square, most of the narrow, graffiti-painted alley was quiet, most of the shops shut. Only the tea bar and the tiny bakery operating out of a window between two tattoo parlors were open. Come lunch, the many eateries would roll up their doors and set out the little tables and benches that crowded either side of the street. Once the lunch crowd returned to their offices, the street would quiet again—until the after-work rush of people eager for a beer, a specialty cocktail, or more food. And sundown brought in a whole new crowd: drunk assholes.

"Morning, B," Juniper said, her curly hair pulled back into an elegant bun, brown skin glowing in the morning light. She stood alongside Fury, who'd perched herself on a barstool and was scrolling through her phone. "Just wanted to say hi before practice."

Bryce kissed her friend on her silken cheek. "Hi. You're gorgeous. I hate you."

Juniper laughed. "You should see me when I'm dripping with sweat in an hour."

"You'll still be gorgeous," Bryce said, and Fury nodded without taking her focus from her phone. "Did you guys order?"

"Yeah." Fury put away her phone. "So go ahead."

Juniper said, "Mine's to go, though." She tapped her navy dance bag, which was partially unzipped, the soft pink of her leotard peeking out. For a moment, Bryce allowed herself to look at her friend—really look at the beauty that was Juniper. Graceful and tall and thin, certainly not the *wrong body type*.

What would it have been like to be heading into morning practice? To have a dance bag full of gear and not a purse full of random crap on her shoulder? Heels braced on the rail beneath the bar, Bryce couldn't stop her feet from twitching, arching—as if testing the strength and pliancy of pointe shoes.

Bryce had known the high of performance well. Had craved it those years in Nidaros, dancing with her small team at the rec hall. She'd been the best dancer in town—in their entire mountainous region. Then she'd come to Lunathion and learned what a fragile bubble she'd been living inside. And, yeah, ultimately she didn't think she could have lasted as long as Juniper, but . . . seeing the faun standing there, some small part of her wondered. Yearned.

Bryce swallowed, then sighed, clearing away the cobwebs of her old dreams. Dancing in Madame Kyrah's class twice a week was pleasure enough. And though Kyrah had once graced the stage of CCB herself until she'd decided to open a studio, the dancer-turned-instructor understood.

So Bryce asked, "What are you guys rehearsing today?"

"*Marceline*," Juniper said, her eyes flickering. "But I don't have the lead."

Bryce's brows rose. "I thought you were rehearsing for it these last weeks."

Fury said tightly, "Apparently, Marceline's costume doesn't fit Juniper."

Bryce's mouth popped open.

"Roles are often determined that way," Juniper said quickly. "But I'm fine with soloist."

Bryce and Fury swapped a look. No, she wasn't. But after the disaster this spring, the CCB had put a hold on any "new" changes. Including June's promotion from soloist to principal.

Juniper had often wondered aloud over drinks or pastries whether that hold was because she'd been the only one in the bomb shelter to demand that they keep the doors open for humans to get in. Had gone hoof-to-toe with some of their wealthiest patrons, thinking nothing of the consequences for her career.

Of what it might mean for the first faun to ever grace the stage of that theater to curse out those patrons, to condemn them to their faces for their cowardice and selfishness.

Well, *this* was what it meant for her.

June slumped into the stool beside Bryce, stretching out her long legs. Another year of waiting in the wings for her chance to shine.

"So who got your shot at Marceline?" The group of principals and veteran soloists rotated through the main roles each night.

"Korinne," Juniper said, a shade too neutrally.

Bryce scoffed. "You're twenty times the dancer she is."

June laughed softly. "No way."

"Way," Fury added.

"Come on," Bryce said, elbowing Juniper. "No need to be humble."

June shrugged, then smiled at the barista as she handed over a green tea in a to-go cup. "Okay. Maybe *twice* the dancer she is."

Fury said, "There's my girl." She nodded her thanks to the barista as her own drink was deposited in a ceramic mug.

Juniper pulled off the lid of her to-go cup and blew on the steaming-hot brew inside.

Bryce asked, "Did you give any thought to that offer from the Heprin Company?"

"Yeah," June murmured. Fury suddenly became very interested in her drink.

"And?" Bryce pushed. "They're practically crawling to have you as principal." And so were about three other smaller dance companies in the city.

"They're great," June said quietly. "But they're still a step down."

Bryce nodded. She got it. She really did. For a dancer in Valbara, CCB was the pinnacle. The distant star to aspire to. And June had been *so close.* Close enough to touch that glimmer of principal dancer. Now she was in free fall.

"I want to hold out for another year," June said, putting the lid on her tea and standing. "Just to see if things change." Pain gleamed in her friend's large, beautiful eyes.

"They will," Bryce assured her, because hope was the only thing she could offer at the moment.

"Thanks," Juniper said. "I'm off. I'll see you at home later," she said to Fury, leaning in to kiss her swiftly. When she made to step away, however, Fury put a hand on her cheek, keeping her there. Deepened the kiss for a few heartbeats.

Then Fury pulled back, holding her girlfriend's stare, and said, "See you at home." Sensual promise laced every word.

Juniper was more than a bit breathless, her cheeks flushing, as she turned to Bryce and kissed her cheek. "Bye, B," she said, then was gone into the sun and dust.

Bryce glanced sidelong at Fury. "You've got it bad, huh?"

Fury snorted. "You have no idea."

"How was date night?" Bryce asked, waggling her eyebrows.

Fury Axtar sipped delicately from her tea. "Exquisite."

Pleasure and happiness quietly radiated from her friend, and Bryce smiled. "What are you drinking?"

"Chai with almond milk. It's good. Spicy."

"You've never been here?"

"Do I look like the kind of person who goes to tea bars?"

"Yes . . . ?"

Fury laughed, her dark hair swaying. She wore her usual head-to-toe black, despite the heat. "Fair enough. So, what's this urgent thing you need to talk to me about?"

Bryce waited until she'd ordered her matcha latte with oat milk before murmuring, "It's about Danika." She and Hunt might need to talk things over regarding Emile, but speaking about this with Fury wasn't a step toward anything, necessarily. She could learn the truth without being dragged into Ophion's orbit, right?

At this hour, only the barista and one other patron occupied the bar. The street was empty save for a few cats picking through piles of trash. Safe enough to talk without being overheard.

Fury kept her posture casual, uninterested. "Does it have to do with Ithan staying with you?"

"How did you even hear about that?" Fury smiled smugly, but Bryce shook her head. "Never mind. But no, that's separate."

"He's always had a thing for you, you know."

"Um, Ithan had a thing for Nathalie."

"Sure."

"Whatever." How to phrase any of this? "You knew about Danika and the synth stuff. I was wondering if there was anything else you might have been . . . keeping secret for her."

Fury sipped her chai. "Care to explain more?" Bryce made a face. "That wasn't really a request," Fury said, her voice lethally soft.

Bryce swallowed. And so quietly only Fury could hear, she told her about Sofie Renast and Tharion and the River Queen and the hunt to find Emile and all the power he possessed. About the abandoned boat in the marshes and Ophion hunting for the boy as well. About the potential meet-up location that Danika had hinted at three years ago and the vague mentions of Project Thurr and Dusk's Truth in those emails between Danika and Sofie.

When she'd finished, Fury drained her drink and said, "I'm going to need something a lot stronger than chai."

"I've been reeling since Tharion told me," Bryce admitted, voice still low. "But Danika and Sofie definitely knew each other. Well enough for Sofie to trust Danika to find her a potential place to hide, should she ever need one."

Fury drummed her fingers on the counter. "I believe you. But Danika never hinted at involvement with the rebels, and I never picked it up on my usual channels."

Bryce nearly sagged with relief. Maybe it hadn't gone too far, then. Maybe their acquaintance hadn't been related to Ophion at all. "Do you think the meeting location is the Bone Quarter?" She prayed it wasn't.

"Danika wouldn't have sent a kid there, even with thunderbird power in his veins. And she wouldn't be so stupid as to make it *that* obvious."

Bryce frowned. "Yeah. True."

"As for Dusk's Truth and Project Thurr . . ." Fury shrugged. "No idea. But Danika was always interested in weird, random shit. She could spend hours getting sucked into an interweb research hole."

Bryce smiled slightly. Also true. "But do you think Danika might have been keeping anything else a secret?"

Fury seemed to consider. Then said, "The only other secret I knew about Danika was that she was a bloodhound."

Bryce straightened. "A what?"

Fury signaled the barista for another chai. "A bloodhound—she could scent bloodlines, the secrets in them."

"I knew Danika had an intense sense of smell," Bryce acknowledged. "But I didn't realize it was *that* . . ." She trailed off, memory surfacing. "When she came home with me over winter break freshman year, she could pick out the family ties of everyone in Nidaros. I thought it was a wolf thing. It's special?"

"I only know about it because she confronted me when we first met. She scented me, and wanted to understand." Fury's eyes darkened. "We sorted our shit out, but Danika knew something dangerous about me, and I knew something dangerous about her."

It was as much as Fury had ever said about being . . . whatever she was.

"Why is it dangerous to be a bloodhound?"

"Because people will pay highly to use the gift and to kill anyone with it. Imagine being able to tell someone's true lineage—especially if that person is a politician or some royal whose parentage is in question. Apparently, the gift came from her sire's line."

Maybe that was another reason why Danika hadn't wanted to mention it. She'd never discussed the male who'd been ballsy enough to fuck Sabine.

Bryce asked, "You never thought to tell me this during the investigation?"

"It didn't seem relevant. It was only one of Danika's many powers."

Bryce lifted a hand to rub at her eyes, then halted, remembering her makeup. "What are the odds that Sofie knew that?"

"No idea," Fury said. "Slim, probably." Then she asked carefully, "You sure you want to start digging into this? Go after that kid?"

"It's not only for Emile's sake," Bryce confessed. "I want to know what Danika was up to. I feel like she was always two steps—more like *ten* steps—ahead. I want to know the full scope of it."

"She's dead, Bryce. Knowing or not knowing won't change that."

Bryce cringed at her friend's harsh words. "I know. But if Danika was tied up with Ophion, with Sofie . . . I want to find Sofie, if she's alive. Learn whatever it is that Sofie knew about Danika, and how they were even in contact. Whether Danika truly was aligned with Ophion."

"You're tangling in some dangerous shit."

"Hunt said the same thing. And . . . you're both right. Maybe that makes me stupid, for not walking away. But setting aside the fact that Emile is a kid being chased by some intense people, if I can locate him for Tharion—he'll lead me to Sofie, or the information about her. And her answers about Danika."

Fury saluted her thanks to the barista and sipped her second chai. "And what will you do once you learn the truth?"

Bryce chewed on her lip. "Pray to Cthona that I can accept it, I guess."

14

Hunt crossed his arms, trying to focus on the unit sparring in one of the Comitium's rooftop training areas and not the scorching heat threatening to singe his wings. Beside him, Isaiah also sweated away, dark eyes fixed on a pair of fighting soldiers. The female was faster and cleverer than the male she faced, but the male had a hundred pounds on her. Each of his blows must have felt like being hit by a semitruck.

"My money's on the male," Isaiah murmured.

"So's mine. She's too green to hold out much longer." Hunt wiped the sweat from his brow, grateful he'd cut his hair shorter before the heat had set in. Solas was slow-roasting them over a pit of coals. Thank fuck he'd changed in the barracks to shorts and a T-shirt.

"Won't really matter in the long run," Isaiah said as the male landed a blow to her jaw with the pommel of his sword. Blood sprayed from her mouth. "Not if we head into war."

The great equalizer.

Hunt said nothing. He'd barely slept last night. Hadn't been able to calm the thoughts that circled over and over. He'd wanted to talk to Bryce, but that acid in his veins had surged every time he'd gotten close, and dissolved all his words. Even this morning, all he'd been able to say was that they needed to talk.

But Bryce being Bryce, she'd seen all of that. Knew what haunted him. And held his hand as she said yes.

He checked his phone. Only an hour until Tharion would show up at the apartment to discuss things. Great.

"You think we'll wind up back there?" Isaiah went on, face distant. "On those battlefields?"

Hunt knew which ones he meant, though they'd fought on many. Sandriel had sent both him and Isaiah to slaughter human rebels decades ago, when Ophion had initially formed.

"I hope not," Hunt said, blocking out the images of those muddy massacres: the mech-suits smoldering with their pilots bleeding out inside them; heaps of broken wings piled high to the skies; some shifters going feral and feasting on the carrion alongside the crows.

He looked over at Isaiah. What would his friend say if he knew about Tharion? Isaiah's words from their last argument in Shahar's war tent still rang in his ears. *This is folly, Athalar! We fly into slaughter. We have no allies, no route of retreat—you two are going to* kill *us all!*

Hunt had ordered his friend out. Had curled up alongside Shahar, who'd listened to their argument from her bed behind the curtain of the tent. She'd promised him that Isaiah was wrong, that he was merely afraid, and Hunt had believed her. Because he was also afraid, he realized later. He'd believed her, and they'd fucked like animals, and a few hours after dawn, she was dead.

Hunt shook the memories of the past away and focused on the fight in front of him. The female ducked and slammed her fist into the male's gut. He went down like a sack of flour, and Hunt chuckled, memories and dread shaking loose. "A pleasant surprise," he said, turning his attention to the other soldiers paired off throughout the space. Sweat gleamed on bare skin, wings white and black and brown and gray rustled, and blood shone on more than a few faces.

Naomi was in the skies training a unit in dive-bombing maneuvers. It was an effort not to glance to the far ring, where Pollux and Baxian oversaw a unit practicing their shooting. The latter was currently in his large canine form, his coat a slick black.

It felt wrong to have those two pieces of shit here, instead of Vik and Justinian.

So wrong that he did look at them after all. Sized up the Helhound's animal form. He'd seen Baxian rip limbs from opponents with those jaws, and move as fast on land as he did in his malakh form. As if sensing his attention, Baxian turned his head. His dark eyes gleamed.

Hunt bristled at the blatant challenge in Baxian's gaze. It didn't lessen when Baxian shifted in a flash of light, a few angels nearby startling at the return of his humanoid form.

Isaiah murmured, "Relax," as Baxian said something to Pollux before stalking for them.

Baxian stood nearly as tall as Hunt, and despite the sweltering heat, he still wore head-to-toe black that matched his wings and his Helhound pelt. "I thought you were doing something far more interesting here in Valbara, Athalar. I'm surprised you haven't dropped dead from boredom."

Isaiah took that as a cue to check on the male who'd fallen, winking at Hunt as he left.

Traitor.

"Some of us crave a normal life, you know," Hunt said to Baxian.

Baxian snickered. "All those battles, all that glory you won for yourself, all that lightning in your veins . . . and you simply want a nine-to-five job?" He tapped the scar on his neck. "The male who gave me this would be horrified."

"The male who gave you that," Hunt said through his teeth, "always wanted peace."

"Didn't seem like it when your lightning flayed me."

"You handed over that rebel family to Sandriel without a second thought. I'd say you had it coming."

Baxian laughed, low and lifeless. The hot, dry breeze rustled his black wings. "You were always a literal sort of bastard. Couldn't read between the lines."

"What the fuck does that mean?" Hunt's power flared at his fingertips.

Baxian shrugged. "I might not have been a slave as you are—were." A nod toward his clear brow. "But I had as little choice in serving Sandriel as you did. Only I didn't make my displeasure known."

"Bullshit. You served her gladly. You don't get to rewrite your history now that you're here."

Baxian's wings rustled. "You never asked me why I was in her triarii, you know. Not once, in all those decades. You're like that with everyone, Athalar. Surface-level."

"Fuck off. Go back to your work."

"This is my work. The Governor just messaged me and told me to team up with you."

Hunt's stomach turned. Did Celestina somehow know about Tharion asking for help finding that thunderbird kid? What better way to monitor him than to shackle him to the Helhound? "Hel no," he said.

Baxian's mouth curled upward as he nodded toward Pollux. "I've been stuck with that prick for a hundred years. It's someone else's turn to deal with him." He pointed to Naomi.

Was it selfish to be glad he didn't have to deal with the Hammer? "Why not tell us during the meeting earlier?"

"I think she's been watching us this morning." Baxian inclined his head to the cameras. "Likely didn't want to alter our behavior before deciding who to pair up."

"To what end?"

As if in answer, Hunt's phone buzzed. He pulled it from his shorts to find a message from Celestina.

As Isaiah will be escorting me around the city to meet its various leaders, I am relying on you and Naomi to help our two new arrivals adjust. I'd like you to partner with Baxian. Show him the ropes. Not just the ins and outs of the 33rd, but also how this city operates. Ease him into life in Valbara.

Hunt considered, even as he inwardly groaned. He was acutely aware of those cameras—the Archangel might be observing his every expression. "She put Naomi in charge of helping Pollux adjust?"

Across the ring, Isaiah was now checking his phone, frowning deeply. He glanced to Hunt, face lit with alarm. Not at the honor of escorting the Governor, Hunt knew.

Hunt turned back to Baxian, who'd no doubt gleaned that Hunt had all the orders he needed. "There's no way Pollux will allow anyone to *show him the ropes*."

Baxian shrugged. "Let Pollux dig his own grave here. He's too pissed about being separated from the Hind to understand his new reality."

"I didn't realize the Hammer was capable of caring for anyone like that."

"He isn't. He just likes to have control over his . . . belongings."

"The Hind belongs to no one." Hunt hadn't known Lidia Cervos well—their time had only briefly overlapped when he'd served Sandriel, and the Hind had spent most of it off on missions for the Asteri. Rented out like some sort of field-worker to do their spy-hunting and rebel-breaking. Whenever Lidia had been at Sandriel's castle, she'd either been in secret meetings with the Archangel, or fucking Pollux in whatever room they felt like using. Thank the gods the Hind hadn't come here. Or the Harpy.

But if Emile Renast was heading for this city . . . Hunt asked, "The Hind's really not coming to Lunathion?"

"No. Pollux got a call from her this morning. He's been moody ever since."

"Mordoc finally making his move?" The head of the Hind's dreadwolves was as formidable as his mistress.

Baxian snorted. "He's not Lidia's type. And doesn't have the balls to go head-to-head with Pollux."

"Did Mordoc go with her to Ephraim?" He had to step carefully.

"Yeah," Baxian said, attention on Pollux. "They're all in Forvos right now. Ephraim's been keeping them close for the last few weeks—it's pissed off the Hind. The Harpy's even madder."

So the Hind wasn't in pursuit of Emile. At least, not at present. Which left the Ophion agents as the main danger to the boy, he supposed. He made a mental note to tell Tharion when he saw him later and said, "I thought you and the Harpy were a pair—you don't seem too hung up on not seeing her."

Baxian let out another one of those low laughs that skittered over Hunt's bones. "She and Pollux would be a better pair than him and Lidia." *Lidia.* Hunt had never heard Baxian use the Hind's given name, but he'd used it twice now. "She'll make Ephraim miserable," Baxian went on, smiling to himself. "Too bad I can't see it."

Hunt almost pitied Ephraim for inheriting the Harpy. "And the Hawk?"

"Doing what he does best: trying to outdo Pollux in cruelty and brutality." The hawk shifter had long been Pollux's main rival for power. Hunt had steered clear of him for decades. So had Baxian, he realized. He'd never seen them interact.

"You're a free male," Hunt said carefully. "Sandriel's gone. Why keep serving at all?"

Baxian ran a hand over his closely buzzed hair. "I could ask the same question of you."

"I need the money."

"Is that so?" Baxian clicked his tongue. "Bryce Quinlan's an expensive girlfriend, I take it. Princesses like pretty things."

Hunt knew better than to deny that Bryce was his girlfriend. Not if it'd open a door for Baxian to taunt him. "Exactly."

Baxian continued, "I like her. She's got balls."

Isaiah shouted Hunt's name from across the space, and Hunt nearly sagged with relief to have an excuse to get out of this conversation. "Here's the first rule of getting adjusted: don't fucking talk to me unless I talk to you." As Isaiah's Second, he outranked Baxian.

Baxian's eyes flared, as if realizing it. "I'm taking this assignment seriously, you know."

Hunt gave him a savage grin. "Oh, I know." If he had to help Baxian adjust, he'd happily drag him into the current century. Hopefully kicking and screaming. "So am I."

Baxian had the good sense to look a little nervous.

Tharion wanted to own Bryce Quinlan's apartment. Badly.

But he sure as shit didn't make enough to afford it, and the sun would shine in Hel before the River Queen allowed him to live

Above. The thought had him scowling as he knocked on the apartment door.

The lock clicked, and Ithan Holstrom peered out from the doorway, brows high. "Bryce isn't back yet."

"She already told me." Tharion held up his phone, displaying the brief exchange with the Fae Princess from a few minutes ago.

I'm at your apartment and ready to go through your underwear drawer.

She'd written back immediately, *You're early. I'll be there in ten. Don't leave drool stains on the lace ones. Or worse.*

No promises, he'd answered, and she'd replied, *Just spare the pink bra, please.*

To Tharion's surprise, Ithan checked that the number under her contact info was indeed Bryce's. Smart kid. Ithan's jaw worked before he said, "I thought she was involved with Athalar."

"Oh, she is," Tharion said, pocketing his phone. "But Legs and I have an understanding when it comes to her underwear." He stepped forward, a blatant demand to be let in.

Ithan stiffened, teeth flashing. Pure wolf. But the male opened the door wider, stepping aside. Tharion kept a healthy distance away as he entered. How many sunball games had Tharion watched where this male had scored the winning shot? How many times had he yelled at his TV, ordering Ithan to *throw that fucking ball*? It was weird to see him face-to-face. To go toe-to-toe with him.

Tharion plopped onto the ridiculously comfortable white couch, sinking deep into the cushions. "It occurred to me after I left last night that you didn't say much about Danika."

Ithan leaned against the counter. "What do you mean?"

Tharion smirked. "You might be a jock, but you're not dumb. I mean about what I told Bryce last night."

"Why would Danika tell me anything about knowing a rebel?"

"You were pretty damn close with her."

"She was my Alpha."

"You weren't part of the Pack of Devils."

"No, but I would have been."

Tharion toed off his shoes and propped his bare feet on the

coffee table. Sports news blared on the TV. "Weren't you all set to go pro?"

Ithan's face tightened. "That's none of your business."

"Right. I'm just Captain Whatever." Tharion gave him a salute. "But if you knew about any involvement Danika had, if there was a place Danika might have told Sofie was safe for hiding here in the city that sounds like it might be *where the weary souls find relief*, or even if your brother—"

"Don't talk about my brother." Ithan's snarl rattled the glasses in the kitchen cabinets.

Tharion held up his hands. "Noted. So you don't know anything."

"We didn't talk about the rebellion, or the war, or anything of the sort." A muscle ticked in Ithan's jaw. "I don't appreciate being dragged into this. Or having Bryce dragged into it, either. You're endangering her simply by mentioning it. Hunting for a missing kid is one thing, but the shit with Ophion is deadly."

Tharion gave the male a winning smile. "I have my orders, and I'm bound to obey them."

"You're an idiot if you don't see the risk in spreading this intel about your queen searching for Emile."

"Maybe, but what she'll do to me if I disobey will be a Hel of a lot worse than what Sabine and Amelie did to you." Another grin. "And I won't have pretty Bryce to kiss my wounds after."

Ithan snarled again. Did the wolf have any idea what he revealed with that snarl alone? He'd been such a smart sunball player, never broadcasting his moves. Seemed like he'd lost the skill.

But Tharion went on, "Danika did a lot of shady shit before she died. Bryce knows that. You're not protecting her by refusing to talk." Tharion eased to his feet, then stalked for the fridge, keenly aware of the wolf's every breath.

He'd opened the door to rummage for snacks when Ithan said, "She was a history major."

Tharion arched a brow. "Yeah?"

Ithan shrugged. "She once told me she was doing research on something that would likely land her in a heap of trouble. But when

I asked her later what she'd gotten on the paper, she said she'd changed subjects. I always thought it was weird."

Tharion shut the fridge door and lounged against it. "Why?"

"Because Danika was relentless. If she was interested in something, she didn't stop. I didn't really believe that she'd have changed the subject of her paper without good reason."

"You think a college student found something top secret that led her to Ophion?"

"Danika wasn't ever only a college student."

"The same way you weren't ever just a college sunball player, huh?"

Ithan ignored the barb. "You asked me about Danika. Aside from everything that went down with the synth, that's the only thing I can think of. Sorry if it's not what you hoped for."

Tharion just looked at the male leaning against the counter. Alone.

Maybe he was a sappy bastard, but Tharion pointed toward the TV. "I missed the sunball game against Korinth last night and want to see the highlights. Mind if I watch with you while we wait for the others?"

Ithan frowned, but Tharion put a hand on his heart. "No secret spying stuff, I swear." He sighed. "I could use a few minutes of peace."

Ithan weighed the words, Tharion's expression, with a keen-eyed sharpness that the wolf had used on his opponents. Perhaps the sunball player wasn't dead after all.

But Ithan only said, "There's leftover pizza if you're hungry."

15

Ruhn met his sister outside the Fae Archives right as the lunchtime crowds spilled into the warren of streets in Five Roses.

Amid the throng, few of the milling Fae noticed them, too focused on getting food or scrolling through their phones. Still, Bryce slid on a sunball cap and a pair of sunglasses as she stepped onto the blisteringly hot street that even the trees and greenery of FiRo couldn't entirely cool.

"I'm not wearing that getup," Ruhn said. Certainly not in Fae territory. "People are going to figure out who you are pretty damn fast."

"I can't take any more of the gawking."

"Comes with the territory."

Bryce grumbled something Ruhn chose not to hear. "So Tharion's back at the house?" he asked as they headed toward her apartment.

"Yep. Already grilling Ithan." Which was why she'd asked him to come as backup. A fact that gave him no small amount of satisfaction.

They crossed a busy intersection teeming with Fae and shifters, the occasional draki making their way past. Ruhn said, "I take it you didn't invite me to walk you home for some muscle in the mean streets of Crescent City." He wryly nodded to the angels and witches soaring overhead, the little otter in his yellow vest scooting by, the family of some sort of equine shifters trotting between the cars.

She glared at him over her sunglasses. "I wanted to discuss something with you—and I don't trust the phone. Or messages."

Ruhn blew out a breath. "I know the shit with Cormac is absurd—"

"It's not about Cormac. It's about Danika."

"Danika?"

"I saw Fury this morning. She told me Danika was a bloodhound. Do you know what that is?"

"Yes," Ruhn said, surprise shooting through him. "You're simply . . . telling me this?"

His sister waved a dismissive hand. "Danika kept a lot of things from me. And I don't see the point in keeping secrets anymore."

"It's okay to be pissed at her, you know."

"Spare me the self-help lecture, okay?"

"Fair enough." He rubbed his jaw. "I guess this explains how Danika knew we were siblings before anyone else." He'd never forget running into Bryce and Danika at that frat party—his first time seeing his sister in years. And how Danika had stared at him. Then looked at Bryce, brows high. He'd known in that moment that Danika had guessed what no one else had, even as Bryce introduced him as her cousin. He'd chalked it up to her uncanny observation skills.

"I thought she was just *good* at scenting," Bryce said, fanning her face against the heat. "Not a genius or whatever. Do you think this could have anything to do with her connection to Sofie?"

"It seems like a stretch. Danika was a powerful, influential Vanir regardless of that gift. She could have been sought out by Sofie or Ophion for a host of other reasons."

"I know." They fell silent until Bryce halted outside the glass doors of her apartment building. "Maybe Sofie thought Danika could help free her brother from Kavalla or something. It sounded like she was working on that for years before she was able to get to him. Maybe she imagined Danika had the influence."

Ruhn nodded. He couldn't begin to imagine what it had been like—for Emile to endure, and for Sofie to spend every moment of every day praying and working for his survival. That she hadn't given up, that she'd accomplished it . . . Ruhn had no words. "*Did* Danika have that kind of sway, though?" he asked.

Bryce shook her head. "I mean, she might have been able to, but she never tried to do anything like that, as far as I know. And I don't see why Sofie would contact Danika, of all people, when Danika was here and Sofie was over in Pangera. It doesn't add up." Bryce flipped her ponytail over a shoulder and grunted her frustration. "I want to know what Sofie knew about Danika."

"I get that," Ruhn said carefully. "And I get why you want to find Emile, too. But I'll say this one more time, Bryce: if I were you, I'd stay out of whatever game Tharion and the River Queen are playing in looking for the kid. Especially if Ophion is on the hunt for Emile as well."

Bryce opened the door to her building, air-conditioning smothering them like a frosty blanket, and waved to Marrin. The ursine shifter waved back from the front desk, and Ruhn offered a half smile to the male before he stepped into the elevator after his sister.

Ruhn waited until the doors had shut before he said softly, "I know Athalar already said this to you last night, but the Asteri could kill you for even getting involved. Even if it's something as seemingly harmless as finding this kid."

Bryce idly wrapped the length of her ponytail around a wrist. "They could have killed me this spring, but they didn't. I'm guessing they won't now."

Ruhn toyed with his lip ring, tugging on the silver hoop as the elevator doors opened and they stepped out onto her floor. "If they want you alive, I'd start wondering why that is. You have the Horn in your back. That's no small thing." He couldn't help himself from glancing at his sister's back as he said it, eyeing the upper tendrils of the tattoo visible above her dress. "You're a power player now, Bryce, whether you like it or not. And trust me, I get it—it *sucks* to want to be normal but to have all this other shit that keeps you from being that way." His voice turned hoarse and she looked over a shoulder at him, face neutral. "But you're Starborn and you have the Horn. And you have a lot of power thanks to the Drop. The Bryce before this spring might have searched for Emile with few repercussions, but the Bryce who exists now? Any move you make will be politicized, analyzed—viewed as an act of aggression or rebellion or outright war. No matter what you say."

Bryce sighed loudly—but her eyes had softened. Either at what he'd said, or what he'd admitted to her about his own life. "I know," she said before unlocking the front door to her apartment.

They found Tharion on the couch with Ithan, the TV blasting the latest sports stats. Tharion munched on a piece of pizza, long legs sprawled out in front of him, bare feet on the coffee table.

Ruhn might have stepped inside to grab a piece of that pizza had Bryce not gone still.

A Fae sort of stillness, sizing up a threat. His every instinct went on high alert, bellowing at him to defend, to attack, to slaughter any threat to his family. Ruhn suppressed it, held back the shadows begging to be unleashed, to hide Bryce from sight.

Ithan called over to them, "Pizza's on the counter if you want some."

Bryce remained silent as fear washed over her scent. Ruhn's fingers grazed the cool metal of the gun strapped to his thigh.

"Your cat's a sweetheart, by the way," Ithan went on, not taking his focus from the TV as he stroked the white cat curled on his lap. Bryce slowly shut the door behind her. "He scared the shit out of me when he leapt onto the counter a few minutes ago, the bastard." The wolf ran his fingers through the luxurious coat, earning a deep purr in response.

The cat had stunning blue eyes. They seemed keenly aware as they fixed on Bryce.

Ruhn's shadows gathered at his shoulders, snakes ready to strike. He subtly drew his gun.

Behind her, a familiar ripple of ether-laced power kissed over her skin. A small reassurance as Bryce croaked, "That's not a cat."

Hunt arrived at the apartment just in time to hear Bryce's words through the shut front door. He was inside in a moment, his lightning gathered at his fingers.

"Oh, calm yourself," the Prince of the Chasm said, leaping onto the coffee table.

Swearing, Ithan lunged from the couch and jumped over it with preternatural grace. Tharion went for a knife at his thigh, a wicked blade with a curved tip. Designed to do its worst damage on the way out.

But Aidas said to Hunt, little fangs glinting, "I thought we were friends, Orion."

"It's Hunt," he gritted out, lightning skittering over his teeth, zapping his tongue.

One move and he'd fry the prince. Or try to. He didn't dare take his focus off Aidas to check on Bryce's positioning. Ruhn would make sure she stayed back.

"Regardless," Aidas said, padding across the coffee table and jumping onto the carpet. A glowing light filled the corner of Hunt's vision, and he found Ruhn standing on Bryce's other side, Starsword in hand.

But Bryce, damn her, walked forward. Hunt tried to block her, but she easily sidestepped him, her chin high as she said, "Good to see you again, Aidas."

Ruhn, Tharion, and Ithan all seemed to inhale at once.

Hunt hardly breathed as the cat trotted up to her and wended between her legs, brushing against her shins. "Hello, Princess."

Hunt's blood chilled. The demon prince purred the word with such intent. Such delight. Like he had some sort of claim on her. Hunt's lightning flared.

Aidas trotted for the counter and jumped onto it in one

graceful spring, then surveyed all of them. His blue gaze returned to Bryce at last. "Why don't you know how to use your powers yet?"

Bryce rolled her shoulders, cracking her neck, and held out a hand. A kernel of starlight flared in her palm. "I can use them."

A soft, hissing laugh. "Party tricks. I meant your real powers. Your heritage."

Hunt's fingers tightened on his gun. Bryce challenged, "What powers?"

Aidas's eyes glowed like blue stars. "I remember the last Starborn Queen, Theia, and her powers." He seemed to shudder. "Your light is her light. I'd recognize that luster anywhere. I'm assuming you have her other gifts as well."

"You *knew* the last Starborn Queen?" Ruhn asked. Starlight glinted among Ruhn's shadows, shimmering down the length of his sword.

Aidas's eyes now flared with a strange sort of rage as he looked upon the Fae Prince. "I did. And I knew the sniveling prince whose light *you* bear." A ripple of stunned silence went through the room.

Ruhn, to his credit, didn't back down an inch. But from the corner of Hunt's vision, he noted Ithan and Tharion creeping into mirroring positions behind the Prince of the Chasm.

Bryce said, more to herself than to the demon prince, "I hadn't realized they'd have individualized starlight. I always thought mine was only . . . brighter than yours." She frowned at Ruhn. "I guess it makes sense that there could be nuances to the light amongst the Fae that got interbred. Theia's elder daughter, Helena, had the gift—and married Prince Pelias. Your ancestor."

"He's your ancestor, too," Ruhn muttered.

"Pelias was no true prince," Aidas spat, fangs bared. "He was Theia's high general and appointed himself prince after he forcibly wed Helena."

"I'm sorry," Ithan said, scrubbing at his face, "but what the fuck is this about?" He glanced at the pizza on the table, as if wondering whether it had been spiked with something.

Welcome to our lives, Hunt wanted to say.

But Bryce's face had gone pale. "Queen Theia allowed this?"

"Theia was dead by that point," Aidas said flatly. "Pelias slew her." He nodded to the Starsword in Ruhn's hand. "And stole her blade when he'd finished." He snarled. "That sword belongs to Theia's *female* heir. Not the male offspring who corrupted her line."

Bryce swallowed audibly, and Ruhn gaped at his blade. "I've never heard any of this," the Fae Prince protested.

Aidas laughed coldly. "Your celebrated Prince Pelias, the so-called first Starborn Prince, was an impostor. Theia's other daughter got away—vanished into the night. I never learned of her fate. Pelias used the Starsword and the Horn to set himself up as a prince, and passed them on to his offspring, the children Helena bore him through rape."

That very Horn that was now tattooed into Bryce's back. A chill went down Hunt's spine, and his wings twitched.

"Pelias's craven blood runs through both of your veins," Aidas said to Ruhn.

"So does Helena's," Ruhn shot back, then recited, "*Night-haired Helena, from whose golden skin poured starlight and shadows.*"

Bryce clicked her tongue, impressed. "You memorized that passage?"

Ruhn scowled, as if annoyed she'd focus on that when a demon prince was before them.

But Bryce asked Aidas, "Why are you telling us this now?"

Aidas shimmered with anger. "Because I was powerless to help then. I arrived too late, and was vastly outnumbered. After it was over—that's when I asked my eldest brother for a favor. To face Pelias on the battlefield and wipe him from this world." Aidas paced a few steps, tail swishing. "I tell you this now, Bryce Quinlan, so the past does not repeat itself. Are you doing anything to help in this endless war?"

"You mean the rebel cause?" Tharion asked, face taut with disbelief and dread.

Aidas didn't take his eyes off Bryce as he said, "It is the same war we fought fifteen thousand years ago, only renewed. The same war you fought, Hunt Athalar, in a different form. But the time is ripe again to make a push."

Ithan said slowly, "Hel is our enemy."

"Is it?" Aidas laughed, ears twitching. "Who wrote the history?"

"The Asteri," Tharion said darkly.

Aidas turned approving eyes on him. "You've heard the truth in some form, I take it."

"I know that the official history of this world is not necessarily to be believed."

Aidas leapt off the counter, trotting to the coffee table again. "The Asteri fed their lies to your ancestors. Made the scholars and philosophers write down their version of events under penalty of death. Erased Theia from the record. That library your former employer possesses," he said, turning to Bryce, "is what remains of the truth. Of the world before the Asteri, and the few brave souls who tried to voice that truth afterward. You knew that, Bryce Quinlan, and protected the books for years—yet you have done nothing with that knowledge."

"What the fuck?" Ithan asked Bryce.

Aidas only asked, "What was this world *before* the Asteri?"

Tharion said, "Ancient humans and their gods dwelled here. I've heard the ruins of their civilization are deep beneath the sea."

Aidas inclined his head. "And where did the Asteri come from? Where did the Fae, or the shifters, or the angels come from?"

Bryce cut in, "Enough with the questions. Why not just tell us? What does this have to do with my . . . gifts?" She seemed to choke on the word.

"The war approaches its crescendo. And your power isn't ready."

Bryce flicked the length of her ponytail over a shoulder. "How fucking cliché. Whatever my other powers are, I want nothing to do with them. Not if they somehow link me to you—the Asteri will consider that a serious threat. Rightly so."

"People died so you could have this power. People have been dying in this battle for fifteen thousand years so we could reach this point. Don't play the reluctant hero now. *That* is the cliché."

Bryce seemed at a loss for words, so Hunt stepped in. "What

about your eldest brother, with his armies? They seem perfectly content to slaughter innocent Midgardians."

"Those armies have always been to help you. Not to conquer."

"The attack on this city last spring suggests otherwise," Hunt argued.

"A mistake," Aidas said. "The beasts that swept in were . . . pets. Animals. Micah opened the doors to their pens. They ran amok as they saw fit. Fortunately, you took control of the situation before our intervention was required," he said, smiling at Bryce.

"A lot of people died," Ithan growled. "Children died."

"And more will soon die in this war," Aidas countered coolly. "Hel's armies shall strike at your command, Bryce Quinlan."

The words dropped like a bomb.

"Bullshit," Ruhn said, face crinkling as he snarled. "You're waiting for the right moment when we're all at war with each other, so you'll be able to find a way into this world at last."

"Not at all," Aidas said. "I already know the way into this world." He pointed with a paw to Bryce and inclined his head. "Through my lovely Bryce and the Horn on her back." Hunt suppressed a growl at the word *my* as all of them looked to her. Her eyes remained fixed on Aidas, her lips a thin line. The Prince of the Chasm said, "It's your choice in the end. It has always been your choice."

Bryce shook her head. "Allow me to get this straight: You're here to convince me to rebel against the Asteri in front of all these people? And what—sign up with Ophion? No, thank you."

Aidas only chuckled. "You should have looked more carefully at the cats picking through the trash in the alley of Ink Street this morning. Should have picked a more discreet location to discuss the rebellion with Fury Axtar." Bryce hissed, but said nothing as Aidas went on, "But yes—by all means, turn rebel. Help Ophion, if you need some authority to answer to. I can tell you before you undoubtedly ask, I have no information about the connection between Danika Fendyr and Sofie Renast."

Bryce growled, "I don't even *know* any Ophion rebels."

Aidas stretched out his front paws, back arching. "That's not true." Hunt stilled as the demon yawned. "There's one right behind you."

Bryce whirled, Hunt with her, lightning poised to strike.

Cormac Donnall stood in the doorway, shadows fading from his shoulders.

"Hello, Agent Silverbow," Aidas crooned, then vanished.

16

I'm sorry," Ruhn blurted, gaping at the Avallen Prince in the doorway, "you're *what*?" Bryce's gaze darted between her brother and their cousin. Ithan was sniffing delicately toward Cormac, clearly putting together who stood before them.

"Agent Silverbow?" Tharion demanded.

Ruhn went on, "Does your father know about this? Does *my* father?" Bryce swapped a glance with her brother. They could use this. Maybe she'd get out of the engagement—

Cormac's face darkened with menace. "No. Nor will they ever." Threat rumbled in every word.

Bryce might have joined in on the interrogation, had the star on her chest not flared through the fabric of her dress. She clapped a hand over it.

Trust Aidas to reveal Cormac's secret and then bail. Bryce had a strong feeling that the Prince of the Chasm had also let Cormac through the wards using his unholy power.

Fucking demon.

Cormac bristled as he glared around the room. "What the fuck do you know about Sofie Renast?"

Bryce pushed her hand harder against her chest, grinding against her sternum as she countered, "What the fuck do *you* know about Sofie Renast, *Agent Silverbow*?"

Cormac whirled on her, stalking closer. "Answer me."

Hunt casually stepped into his path. Lightning danced over his wings. Alphahole to the core, yet it warmed something in her.

Tharion slumped onto the couch, an arm slung lazily along the back cushions, and peered at his nails. He drawled to Cormac, "And you are?"

Shadows ran down Cormac's arms, trailing like smoke from his shoulders. Like Ruhn's shadows—only darker, more feral somehow. Some small part of her was impressed. The Avallen Prince growled, "Cormac Donnall. I'll ask one more time, mer. What do you know about Sofie?"

Tharion crossed an ankle over a knee. "How do you know I'm mer?" Solas, was Tharion riling him for the Hel of it?

"Because you reek of fish," Cormac spat, and Tharion, gods bless him, lifted an arm to sniff his armpit. Ithan chuckled. Most Vanir could detect when a mer was in their humanoid form by that scent of water and salt—not an unpleasant one, but definitely distinct.

Hunt and Ruhn weren't smiling. She had to admit her brother cut a rather imposing figure. Not that she'd ever tell him that.

Tharion smirked at Cormac. "I'm guessing Sofie is your . . . girlfriend?"

Bryce blinked. Cormac let out a snarl that echoed into her bones.

"Impressive," Hunt murmured to Bryce, but she didn't feel like smiling.

Cormac had turned on her once again. "You know Sofie."

"I don't—didn't," Bryce said, stepping to Hunt's side. "I never heard of her until yesterday, when *he* came to ask some questions." She shot a look at Tharion, who held up his long-fingered hands. "But I now have a Hel of a lot of my own questions to ask, so can we all just . . . sit down and talk? Instead of this weird standoff?" She shut the apartment door, and then claimed a seat at one of the stools by the kitchen counter, kicking off her heels beneath it. Ruhn slid onto the one at her left; Hunt perched on the one to the right. Leaving Cormac standing in the middle of the great room, eyeing all of them.

"Why do your shadows appear different from Ruhn's?" Bryce asked Cormac.

"*That*'s the first thing you want to know?" Hunt muttered. She ignored him.

"How do you know Sofie?" was Cormac's only reply.

Bryce rolled her eyes. "I already told you—I don't know her. Tharion, can you put him out of his misery?"

Tharion crossed his arms and settled into the couch cushions. "I was asked to confirm her death." Bryce noted that Tharion's answer could be interpreted as ensuring a dangerous rebel was dead. Smart male.

"And did you?" Cormac's voice had gone low. His body shook, as if he was restraining himself from leaping upon Tharion. Embers sparked in his hair.

But Hunt leaned back against the counter, elbows on the stone. Lightning snaked along his wings; his face was deathly calm. The embodiment of the Umbra Mortis. A thrill shot through Bryce's veins as Hunt spoke. "You have to realize that you're not getting any other answers or leaving here alive without convincing us of some key things."

Gods-damn. He meant it. Bryce's heart thundered.

"So take a breath," Hunt said to the prince. "Calm yourself." The angel smiled, showing all his teeth. "And listen to the lady's advice and sit the fuck down."

Bryce pressed her lips together to keep from smiling. But Cormac—he did indeed take a breath. Another. Bryce glanced at Ithan, but his attention remained on Cormac as the prince breathed, studying his every movement like he was an opponent on the sunball field.

Ruhn, however, met her stare, surprise lighting his features. He said into her head, *I did not see this coming.*

Bryce might have replied, but the shadows on Cormac's arms faded. His broad shoulders relaxed. Then he stalked to the dining table and sat. His eyes were clear—calmer.

The star on her chest winked out as well. As if reassured that all was well.

"Good," Hunt said in that take-no-shit tone that did funny things to her insides. "First things first: How'd you get in? This place is warded to Hel and back."

"That cat—or not-cat. That somehow knew who—what I am." A glimmer of displeasure in his face hinted that the prince was only leaving that question aside for the moment. "It left a gaping hole in the wards."

Hunt nodded, like this wasn't a big fucking deal. "And why did you come here, at this exact moment?" He'd gone into full-on interrogation mode. How many times had he done this in the 33rd?

Cormac pointed to Tharion. "Because I believe we're hunting for the same person: Emile Renast. I want to know what you know."

Bryce couldn't stop her low sound of surprise. But Tharion's face remained stony. The expression of the River Queen's Captain of Intelligence. He asked, "Did Pippa Spetsos send you?"

Cormac barked a laugh. "No. Pippa is the reason Emile fled the *Bodegraven*."

"So who sent you to find Emile?" Hunt asked.

"No one," Cormac said, taking another long breath. "I was sent to this city for another reason, for many reasons, but this matter of finding Emile . . ." His jaw worked. "Sofie and I were close. I helped her free Emile from Kavalla. And before she . . ." He swallowed. "I made her a promise—not only as one agent to another, but as a . . . friend. To look after Emile. I failed her. In every way, I failed her."

Either he's an amazing actor, Ruhn said into her head, *or he was in love with Sofie.*

Agreed, Bryce said.

"Why did Emile run from Pippa?" Tharion asked.

Cormac ran his hands through his blond hair. "He was afraid of her. He's wise to be. Pippa is a fanatic on a fast track to promotion into Ophion Command. With so many of our bases recently destroyed, Ophion is nervous enough to start considering her ideas—and I worry they'll soon start following her as well. There are no lines she and her unit of Lightfall soldiers won't cross. Did your news over here get wind of that story about the leopard massacre a year ago?"

Bryce couldn't stop her shudder. Ithan said quietly, "Yeah."

Cormac said, "That was Pippa's idea, carried out by Lightfall. To use those Vanir kids and babies to lure their parents out of their hidden dens—and then kill them all. Simply for sport. For the Hel of it. Because they were Vanir and *deserved* to die. Even the children. She said it was part of cleansing this world. Working their way up to the top: the Asteri. Hence the Lightfall name."

Hunt looked to Tharion—who nodded gravely. Apparently, the Captain of Intelligence had heard that, too.

Cormac went on, "Pippa sees Emile as a weapon. The night of the escape, he took down those imperial Omegas, and she was practically beside herself with excitement. She spooked him with her eagerness to get him onto a battlefield, and he fled on an escape boat before I could convince him that I was there to help. The boy sailed to the nearest port, then stole another boat."

"Resourceful kid," Ithan muttered.

"I tracked him as far as these shores." Cormac jerked his chin at Tharion. "I saw you in the marshes at the abandoned boat. I figured you were on his trail as well. And I watched you find the remains of the Lightfall soldier's body—so you must have at least guessed that Pippa wants Emile for her Lightfall unit. If she catches him, she'll drag him back to Ophion's main base and turn him into a weapon. Into exactly what the Asteri feared when they hunted down the thunderbirds centuries ago."

His gaze shifted to Hunt. "You asked why I came here, at this exact moment? Because when the mer kept returning here, I figured you lot might be involved somehow—some of the very people I was sent here to meet. I hoped Emile might even be here." Again, his jaw tightened. "If you know where Emile is, tell me. He's not safe."

"I don't understand," Ruhn said. "You and Pippa are both in Ophion, yet you're trying to find Emile to . . . keep him out of Ophion's hands?"

"Yes."

"Won't Ophion be pissed?"

"Command will never know of my involvement," Cormac said. "I have other tasks here to complete."

Bryce didn't like the sound of that for one moment. She slid off the stool, taking a step toward the dining table. Her mouth began moving before she could think through her words. "You expect us to trust you about all of this when you were so fucking obsessed with a stupid piece of metal that you wanted to kill my brother?" She flung a hand in the general direction of Ruhn and the Starsword in his grip.

Ruhn grunted with surprise as Cormac retorted, "That was fifty years ago. People change. Priorities change."

But Bryce took one step closer to the dining table, not caring if Cormac deemed it a challenge. "Fae don't change. Not you old-school losers."

Cormac glanced between her and Ruhn with palpable disdain. "You Valbaran Fae are such babies. Did you not learn something of yourself, your destiny, *Prince* Ruhn, because of me nipping at your heels?"

"You put a sword through Dec's gut," Ruhn said mildly. "I'd hardly call that *nipping*."

Tharion cut in, "Assuming we buy your story, why would a Fae Prince join Ophion?"

Cormac said, "I joined because I felt it was right. The details are unnecessary."

"Not if you might be working for the Asteri," Bryce said.

"You think I'd turn you over to the Asteri?" Cormac laughed, dead and cold. "I wouldn't wish that fate on anyone. The dungeons beneath their crystal palace are darker and deadlier than the Pit."

Hunt said icily, "I know. I was there."

Bryce hated the shadows in his eyes. Ones she'd do anything to help heal. Do anything to avoid renewing. Team Survive at All Costs—that was her team. She didn't care if that made her a coward.

Cormac went on, ignoring Hunt, "Sofie was an Ophion agent because the Asteri butchered her family. Her human family, and her thunderbird ancestors. All she wanted was to find her brother. Everything she did was for him."

Tharion opened his mouth, but Bryce lifted a hand, cutting him off as she said to Cormac, "Tharion came by yesterday to ask about a connection between someone I . . . knew and Sofie. He was being super shady"—a glare from Tharion at this—"so I managed to get some answers out of him, mainly that he's looking for Emile for the River Queen."

Cormac narrowed his stare on Tharion. "What does your queen want with the boy?"

Tharion shrugged.

Ruhn murmured, "Nothing good, I bet."

Tharion rumbled a warning growl at Ruhn, but Bryce continued, "I don't care about the politics. Emile's a kid, and lost—I want to find him." And get answers about Danika knowing Sofie, but . . . that could wait for a moment. She wanted to feel Cormac out first.

Indeed, the Avallen Prince's eyes softened a bit—with gratitude.

Could be faking that, Ruhn observed to her.

Could be, but my gut says he isn't, Bryce replied before she angled her head and asked Cormac, "The Hind's a pretty big deal. She went to all that trouble to kill Sofie just for freeing her brother? Or was it because Sofie's a thunderbird?"

Cormac's hands curled into fists at his side. "The Hind went to all that trouble because Sofie, as collateral to make sure the Ophion boat showed up for Emile, had gathered vital intel on the Asteri, and made sure Command knew it."

"What?" Hunt blurted, wings twitching.

"What kind of intel?" Tharion asked, face darkening.

Cormac shook his head. "Sofie was the only person who knew it. She just mentioned to me that it was something big—war-changing. That Ophion would kill to have it. And our enemies would kill to contain it."

Across the room, Ithan was wide-eyed. Had any of his training prepared him for this? Had any of hers?

Tharion said, "The Asteri probably sent the Hind to kill her before she could tell anyone else."

Cormac grimaced. "Yes. But I suspect the Hind knew Sofie could hold out against torture, and decided it was best the information die with her." He shuddered and said, "They ripped out her nails when she went into Kavalla, you know. She told me that they tore out the nails on one hand, and when they asked her for any information, she held out her other hand to them." He laughed to himself. "One of the guards fainted."

"Brave female," Ithan said softly, earning a thankful nod from Cormac that had Bryce wishing she'd said as much herself. Bryce studied her own manicured nails. Wondered if she'd be able to hold out if it ever came to that.

Cormac again turned to Tharion, his face bleak. "Tell me the Hind at least put a bullet in her head before she sent Sofie down to the deep."

"I don't know," Tharion said. "Her body wasn't there."

"What?" Shadows rippled from Cormac again.

Tharion went on, "The lead blocks, the chains were there. But Sofie's body was gone. And the shackles had all been unlocked."

Cormac shot to his feet. "Sofie is alive?"

Such raw hope filled his voice. Was it from genuine love? Or hope that the intel she carried lived on?

"I don't know," Tharion answered. Then he admitted, "But that's why I came to Bryce. She had a friend who knew Sofie years ago. I'm investigating any connections between them—I'm wondering if it might give us hints about Emile's whereabouts." Tharion shrugged. "I have good reason to believe that a safe meeting place was set up long ago for a scenario like this, and that Emile might be headed there—and Sofie, too, if she's alive."

Would Sofie have passed that vital intel to her brother? Bryce found Hunt giving her a *Don't even think about it* look.

Cormac said, pacing, "Sofie made the Drop—at an illegal center where it wouldn't be recorded. I thought that there was a chance she might have survived, but when she didn't contact me . . ." His eyes narrowed at the mer. "What else do you know?"

"I've told you everything," Tharion lied, crossing his legs.

Cormac gave a slashing, mocking grin. "And what of Danika Fendyr?"

Bryce stilled. "What about her?" Hunt gave her another look warning her to keep quiet.

Cormac said, "She and Sofie knew each other. She was the one who set up this safe place, wasn't she?"

"You don't know any of that for sure," Hunt said.

"I do," Cormac said, his gaze still on Bryce, on the star in her chest that had begun to glow dimly again. "It's why I agreed to marry Bryce."

Ruhn needed a moment to process everything. He watched his cousin warily.

But Bryce chuckled. "I thought you agreed to marry me because of my winning personality."

Cormac didn't smile. "I agreed to marry you because I needed access to you. And to you, cousin," he said to Ruhn.

Athalar demanded, "You couldn't just pay a friendly visit?"

"The Avallen Fae and the Valbaran Fae are not *friendly*. We are allies, but also rivals. I needed a reason to come here. I needed to come here to find Emile—it was a blessing from Urd that Ophion wanted me here for another mission, too."

Bryce glowered. "Forcing me into marriage seems extreme."

"It's the only currency I have. My breeding potential."

Ruhn snorted. He and his cousin had more in common than he'd realized. "Why do you need access to me?"

"Because you can mind-speak, can you not? It's how you and your friends survived in the Cave of Princes during your Ordeal. You fought as if you were of one mind. You never told my father, but he suspected. *I* suspected. It's a rare Starborn gift. A skill Ophion needs badly."

Ruhn said, "What about your cousins—the twins? They can mind-speak."

"They're not trustworthy. You know that."

Athalar cut in, "Don't let him rope you into whatever this is, Danaan. Searching for Emile independently is one thing. If you let him deliver his pitch, you're one step away from working with Ophion. The Asteri won't care whether you agree or reject his ass." He leveled a look at Cormac. "And let me remind you that Ophion is going up against legions that outrank them in power and size. If one of the Asteri walks onto a battlefield, you're all done."

The power of one Asteri, the holy star glowing within them, could level an entire army.

Hunt went on, "And if the Asteri catch wind that *Agent Silverbow* is trying to recruit Ruhn, we'll all be taken in for questioning. If we're lucky. If not, we'll be executed."

"You didn't seem to have such concerns when you rebelled, Fallen Angel," Cormac said.

"I learned the hard way," Hunt said through his teeth. Bryce stepped closer to him, fingers brushing his. "I'd prefer to protect my friends from learning that lesson."

It shouldn't have meant something to Ruhn, for Athalar to consider him a friend. But it did.

Hunt continued, "You're not only insane to tell us this—you're reckless. We could sell you out in a heartbeat."

Tharion added, "Or you're an Asteri mole seeking to entrap us."

Cormac drawled, "Trust me, I don't bandy about this information to just anyone." He sized up Athalar. "You might have made foolish mistakes in the past, Umbra Mortis, but I shall not."

"Fuck you." That one came from Bryce, her voice low and deadly.

Ruhn said to Cormac, hoping to take the temperature down a few degrees, "I'm not going to get involved with you or Ophion. I won't risk it. So don't even ask me to do whatever it is you want me to use my . . . mind-stuff for." He hated that his cousin knew. That Tharion was now watching him with a mixture of surprise, awe, and wariness.

Cormac laughed bitterly. "You can't risk your friends and family? What about the countless friends and family in Pangera who are tortured, enslaved, and murdered? I saw you entering this apartment earlier, and assumed you were assisting Captain Ketos in looking for Emile. I thought convincing you to help me might be that much easier. But it seems all of you wish to put your own lives before those of others."

"Fuck off," Hunt growled. "Did you see what happened here this spring?"

"Yes. It convinced me of your . . . compassion." He said to Bryce, "I saw that you raced to Asphodel Meadows. To the humans." He glanced at Ithan. "You too. I thought it meant you'd be sympathetic to their greater plight." He again addressed Bryce. "That's why I wanted to get near you. You and Danika saved this city. I realized you two were close. I wanted to see if you might have any insights—I've long suspected that Danika might have arranged a rendezvous spot for Sofie." He faced Tharion. "Where do you believe the meet-up point would be?"

"Nowhere good," Tharion muttered. Then he added, "You'll get the details when we're good and ready to tell you, princey."

Cormac bristled, flames sparking in his hair again, but Bryce cut in, "How did Danika and Sofie meet?" Apparently, Ruhn realized, this trumped everything else for his sister.

Cormac shook his head. "I'm not sure. But from what Sofie told me, Danika suspected something about the Asteri, and needed someone to go in to confirm those suspicions. Sofie was that person."

Bryce's eyes were bright—churning. It didn't bode well.

Bryce's brows knit, though. "Danika died two years ago. Sofie had this intel for that long?"

"No. From what I've gathered, three years ago, Danika needed Sofie to go in to get it, but it took Sofie that long to gain access. Danika died before Sofie could ever pass the information to her. When she finally got it, she decided to use it to manipulate Ophion into upholding their bargain to go help rescue Emile."

"So Danika worked for *Ophion*?" Ithan asked. The wolf's face was a portrait of shock.

"No," Cormac said. "She was connected to them, but didn't report to them. As far as I understood from Sofie, Danika had her own agenda."

Bryce watched Cormac, her head angled to the side. Ruhn knew that look.

Bryce was planning something. Had definitely already planned something.

Bryce stepped closer to Cormac. The padding of her bare feet was the only sound. Ruhn braced himself for whatever was about to come out of her mouth. "For what it's worth, I don't think Aidas is in the habit of allowing Asteri loyalists into my apartment."

"Aidas." Cormac started, face paling. "That cat was the Prince of the Chasm?"

"Yep," Bryce said. "And I think Aidas brought you here as a gift to me." Athalar blinked at her, but Bryce went on, "Talk all you like about tracking Tharion here, and wanting to recruit Ruhn, but don't for one minute think that Aidas wasn't involved in your being here at the exact moment he told me to learn about my powers." She crossed her arms. "What do you know about the Starborn gifts?"

Cormac said nothing. And Ruhn found himself saying, half in dread that Bryce was right, "I told you the other night that our cousin here was obsessed enough with the idea of getting the Starsword that he learned everything he could about Starborn powers. He's a veritable library of information."

Cormac cut him a glare. But he admitted, "I did spend . . . much of my youth reading about the various gifts."

Her lips curled upward. "Rebel prince and bookworm." Athalar looked at her like she'd lost her mind. "I'll make a deal with you."

Hunt growled his objection, but Ruhn's mind churned. This was the Bryce he knew—always angling for the advantage.

"No interest in helping out of the goodness of your heart, Princess?" Cormac taunted.

"I want out of this marriage," Bryce said smoothly, running a finger over the counter's edge. Ruhn pretended not to see Athalar's shudder. "But I know that if I end our engagement too soon, my . . . sire will send along someone who isn't as motivated to work with me." Truth. "So we'll team up with Tharion here to find Emile. And I'll even help you find out whatever intel it was that Danika wanted Sofie to learn. But I want this engagement ended when I say it's time. And I want you to teach me about my magic. If not, good luck to you. I'll be sure to point Pippa and her Lightfall unit right in your direction."

Hunt smirked. Ruhn avoided doing the same. Tharion just tucked his arms behind his head. Only Ithan seemed surprised. Like he'd never seen this side of Bryce.

"Fine," Cormac said. "But the engagement will only be broken once my work here for Ophion is done. I need the reason to be in Valbara."

Ruhn expected Bryce to object, but she seemed to think it over. "We do need the cover to be seen together," she mused. "Otherwise, anyone who knows what a piece of shit you are would wonder why the Hel I would stoop to hang with you. It'd be suspicious."

Hunt coughed into his shoulder.

Ruhn blurted, "Am I the only one here who thinks this is insane?"

Ithan said, "I think we're all dead meat for even talking about this."

But Hunt rubbed his jaw, solemn and weary. "We need to talk this over before deciding." Bryce's hand brushed over his once more.

Ruhn grunted his agreement and said to his cousin, "You've dropped a shit-ton of information on us. We need to process." He gestured toward the door in dismissal. "We'll contact you."

Cormac didn't move an inch. "I require your blood oath not to say a word of this."

Ruhn barked a laugh. "I'm not making a blood oath. You can trust us. Can we trust you?"

"If I can trust cowards who like painting their nails while the rest of the world suffers, then you can trust me."

Bryce said wryly, "Going in hard with the charm, Cormac."

"Swear a blood oath. And I'll leave."

"No," Bryce said with surprising calm. "I have a manicure in ten minutes."

Cormac glowered. "I'll require your answer tomorrow. In the meantime, I am entrusting my life to you." His eyes slid to Ruhn's. "Should you wish to hear my *pitch*, I'll be at the bar on Archer and Ward today. Your services would be . . . greatly valued."

Ruhn said nothing. The fucker could rot.

Cormac's eyes narrowed with cold amusement. "Your father remains unaware of your mind-speaking gifts, doesn't he?"

"Are you threatening me?" Ruhn snarled.

Cormac shrugged, walking toward the door. "Come meet me at the bar and find out."

"Asshole," Ithan murmured.

Cormac paused with his hand on the knob. He sucked in a breath, the powerful muscles of his back rippling. When he looked over his shoulder, the amusement and threats were gone. "Beyond Sofie, beyond Emile . . . This world could be so much more. This world could be *free*. I don't understand why you wouldn't want that."

"Hard to enjoy being free," Hunt countered darkly, "if you're dead."

Cormac opened the door, stepping into the swirling shadows. "I can think of no better reason to yield my life."

17

Does anyone else feel like they're about to wake up from a bad dream?" Ithan's question echoed into the fraught silence of the apartment.

Bryce checked the clock on her phone. Had it really been less than an hour since she'd walked down the teeming lunchtime streets with Ruhn? She rubbed idly at her star, still glowing faintly, and said to no one in particular, "I need to get back to the archives."

Ruhn exclaimed, "After all that, you're going back to *work*?"

But she strode across the room, throwing Hunt a glance that had him following. He always got her like that—they didn't need Ruhn's fancy mind-speaking to communicate.

She halted by the front door. None of Cormac's power lingered—not even a wisp of shadow. Not one ember. For a heartbeat, she wished she had the serenity of Lehabah to return to, the serenity of the gallery and its quiet library.

But those things were irrevocably gone.

Bryce said as calmly as she could to the males watching her, schooling her face into neutrality, "We just had a bomb dropped into our lives. A bomb that is now ticking away. I need to think. And I have a job that I'm contractually obligated to show up to."

Where she could close her office door and figure out if she wanted to run like Hel from that bomb or face its wrath.

Hunt put a hand on her shoulder, but said nothing. He'd leapt in front of a bomb for her months ago. Had shielded her body with his own against the brimstone missile. There was nothing he could do to shield her from this, though.

Bryce couldn't bear to see the worry and dread she knew would be etched on his face. He knew what they were walking into. The enemy and odds they faced.

She pivoted to Tharion instead. "What do you want to do, Tharion? Not because the River Queen is pulling your puppet strings—what do *you* want?"

"This apartment, for starters," Tharion said, leaning his head back against the cushions, muscled chest expanding as he heaved a breath. "I want to find answers. Regardless of my orders, I want the truth of what I am facing—the enemy at my front as well as my back. But I'm inclined to believe Cormac—he didn't display any signs of lying."

"Trust me," Ruhn growled, "he's more skilled than you know."

"I don't think he was lying, either," Hunt admitted.

Bryce rubbed at her neck—then straightened. "Any chance that Dusk's Truth is somehow related to the Lightfall squadron?"

Tharion arched a brow. "Why?"

Hunt picked up her thread immediately. "Lightfall. Also known as dusk."

"And Project Thurr . . . thunder god . . . Could it be related to the thunderbirds?" Bryce went on.

"You think it involved some kind of intel about Pippa's Lightfall squadron?" Ruhn asked.

"It seemed to be some sort of groundbreaking info," Tharion said. "And Thurr . . . It could have had something to do with the thunderbird stuff. Sofie sounded afraid of the Asteri's wrath in her reply to Danika . . . Maybe it was because she was afraid of them knowing she had the gift."

"These are all hypotheticals," Hunt said. "And big stretches. But they might lead somewhere. Sofie and Danika were certainly well aware of the threats posed by both Lightfall and the Asteri."

Ithan said, "Can we go back to how the Prince of the Chasm was *sitting on my lap*?"

"You've got a lot to catch up on," Hunt said, chuckling darkly. "Be glad you weren't here for the first summoning."

Bryce elbowed him. "I really do have to return to work."

Ruhn asked, "You don't think we should go to the Bone Quarter to look for Emile and Sofie?"

Bryce winced. "I'm not going to the Bone Quarter to look for *anyone* unless we're absolutely certain that they're there."

"Agreed," Tharion said. "It's too dangerous to go on a whim. We'll keep investigating. Maybe Danika meant something else by *weary souls*."

Bryce nodded. "None of us talks to anyone else. I think we all know we're going to be roasted on a spit if this leaks."

"One word from Cormac and we're dead," Ruhn said gravely.

"One word from us," Hunt countered, "and *he's* dead." He jerked his chin at Bryce. She finally met his stare, finding only razor-sharp calculation there. "Grab a gun."

Bryce scowled. "Absolutely not." She gestured to her tight dress. "Where would I hide it?"

"Then take the sword." He pointed to her bedroom hallway. "Use it as some sort of accessory. If anyone can pull it off, you can."

Bryce couldn't help her glance at Ithan. It gave away everything.

"You never gave Danika's sword back after the attack this spring?" the wolf asked a shade quietly.

"Sabine can fight me for it," Bryce said, and ignored Hunt's order to take the blade from its resting place in her closet. Bryce twisted the knob. "Let's take the day. Agree not to fuck each other over on this, pray Cormac isn't a lying sack of shit, and then reconvene tomorrow night."

"Done," Tharion said.

Bryce stepped into the hall, Hunt on her heels, and heard Ithan sigh behind her. "This was not how I expected my day to go," the wolf muttered to Tharion before ratcheting up the volume on the TV.

Same, Bryce thought, and shut the door.

Hunt's head spun as he and Bryce rode the elevator down to the apartment lobby. He'd been free for a few glorious months, only to wind up right back on the cusp of another rebellion.

The same war, Aidas had claimed. Just by a different name, with a different army. Hunt's hands slicked with sweat. He'd seen how this war turned out. Felt its cost for centuries.

He said to Bryce, unable to stop the trembling that now overtook him, the sense that the elevator walls were pushing in, "I don't know what to do."

She leaned against the rail. "Me neither."

They waited until they were out on the street, keeping their voices down, before Hunt continued, words falling out of his mouth, "This isn't something we can jump into for the Hel of it." He couldn't get a breath down. "I've seen wrecked mech-suits with their human pilots hanging out of the cockpit, organs dangling. I've seen wolves as strong as Ithan ripped in two. I've seen angels decimate battlefields without setting foot on the ground." He shuddered, picturing Bryce among all that. "I . . . Fuck."

She looped her arm through his, and he leaned into her warmth, finding himself frozen despite the hot day. "This sounds more like . . . spying than battle-fighting or whatever."

"I'd rather die on the battlefield than in one of the Hind's interrogation rooms." *I'd rather* you *die on a battlefield than in her hands.* Hunt swallowed. "Sofie was lucky that the Hind dumped her and was done with it." He halted at an alley, tugging Bryce into its shadows with him.

He let himself look at her face: pale enough that her freckles stood out, eyes wide. Scared. The scent hit him a moment later.

"We were never going to be allowed to live like normal people," Bryce breathed, and Hunt ran a hand through her hair, savoring the silken strands. "Trouble was always going to come find us."

He knew she was right. They weren't the sort of people who could live ordinary lives. Hunt fought past the shaking in his bones, the roaring in his mind.

She lifted a hand, and her warm palm cupped his cheek. He leaned into her touch, reining in a purr as her thumb brushed over his cheekbone. "You really don't think Cormac is luring us into a trap with this claim that Sofie knew some vital intel—the bait being that Danika was involved in some way?"

"It's possible," Hunt admitted. "But there was clearly a connection between Danika and Sofie—the emails prove it. And Cormac seemed pretty damned shocked to learn that Sofie was potentially alive. I think he believed the intel on the Asteri had died with Sofie. I wouldn't blame him for wondering if it could be in play once more."

"You think there's any chance Sofie told Emile before they were separated?"

Hunt shrugged. "They were in Kavalla together—she might have found an opportunity to tell him. And if he doesn't have the intel, and Sofie is alive, he might know where Sofie is headed right now. That makes Emile a pretty valuable asset. For everyone."

Bryce began counting on her fingers. "So we've got Ophion, Tharion, and Cormac all wanting to find him."

"If you want to find him, too, Bryce, then we need to navigate carefully. Consider if we really want to get involved at all."

Her mouth twisted to the side. "If there's a chance that we could discover what Sofie knew, what Danika guessed—separate from Cormac, from this shit with that Pippa woman and whatever the River Queen wants—I think that intel is worth the risk."

"But why? So we can keep the Asteri from fucking with us about Micah and Sandriel?"

"Yeah. When I met up with Fury this morning, she mentioned that Danika knew something dangerous about her, so Fury learned something big about Danika in return." Hunt didn't get the chance to ask what exactly that was before Bryce said, "Why not apply the same thinking to this? The Asteri know something dangerous about me. About you." That they'd killed two Archangels. "I want to even the playing field a bit." Hunt could have sworn her expression was one he'd glimpsed on the Autumn King's face as she went on, "So we'll learn something vital about *them.* We'll take steps to ensure that if they fuck with us, the information will leak to the broader world."

"This is a deadly game. I'm not convinced the Asteri will want to play."

"I know. But beyond that, Danika thought this intel might be important enough to send Sofie after it—to risk her life for it. If Sofie is dead, then someone else needs to secure that information."

"It's not your responsibility, Bryce."

"It is."

He wasn't going to touch that one. Not yet. "And what about the kid?"

"We find him, too. I don't give a shit if he's powerful—he's a kid and he's caught up in this giant mess." Her eyes softened, and his heart with them. Would Shahar have cared about the boy? Only in the way Ophion and the River Queen seemed to: as a weapon. Bryce asked, head tilting to the side, "And what about Cormac's talk of freeing the world from the Asteri? That doesn't hold any weight with you?"

"Of course it does." He slid a hand over her waist, tugging her closer. "A world without them, without the Archangels and the hierarchies . . . I'd like to see that world one day. But . . ." His throat dried up. "But I don't want to live in that world if the risk of creating it means . . ." *Get it out.* "If it means that *we* might not make it to that world."

Her eyes softened once more, and her thumb stroked over his cheek again. "Same, Athalar."

He huffed a laugh, bowing his head, but she lifted his chin with her other hand. His fingers tightened on her waist.

Bryce's whiskey-colored eyes glowed in the muted light of the alley. "Well, since we're dabbling in some seriously dangerous shit, now's probably as good a time as any to admit I don't want to wait until Winter Solstice."

"For what?" Fuck, his voice had dropped an octave.

"This," she murmured, and rose onto her toes to kiss him.

Hunt met her halfway, unable to contain his groan as he hauled her against him, lips finding hers at the same moment their bodies touched. He could have sworn the fucking world spun out from under him at the taste of her—

His head filled with fire and lightning and storms, and all he could think of was her mouth, her warm, luscious body, the aching of his cock pressing against his pants—pressing against *her* as her arms twined around his neck.

He was going to kick that wolf out of the apartment immediately.

Hunt twisted, pinning her against the wall, and her mouth opened wider on a gasp. He swept his tongue in, tasting the honeyed spice that was pure Bryce. She wrapped a leg around his waist, and Hunt took the invitation, hefting her thigh higher, pressing himself against her until they were both writhing.

Anyone might walk by the alley and see them. Lunchtime workers were streaming past. All it would take was one peek down the alley into the dusty shadows, *one* photograph, and this whole thing—

Hunt halted.

One photo, and her engagement to Cormac would be off. Along with the bargain Bryce had crafted with him.

Bryce asked, panting hard, "What's wrong?"

"We, ah . . ." Words had become foreign. All thought had gone between his legs. Between *her* legs.

He swallowed hard, then gently backed away, trying to master his jagged breathing. "You're engaged. Technically. You have to keep up that ruse with Cormac, at least in public."

She straightened her dress, and—shit. Was that a lilac lace bra peeking out from the neckline? Why the fuck hadn't he explored that just now? Bryce peered down the alley, lips swollen from his kisses, and some feral part of him howled in satisfaction to see that *he* had done that, *he* had brought that flush to her cheeks and wine-rich scent of arousal to her. She was *his*.

And he was hers. Utterly fucking hers.

"Are you suggesting we find a seedy motel instead?" Her lips curved, and Hunt's cock throbbed at the sight, as if begging for her mouth to slide over him.

He let out a strangled noise. "I'm suggesting . . ." Hel, what *was* he suggesting? "I don't know." He blew out a breath. "You're sure you want to do this now?" He gestured between them. "I know emotions are high after what we've learned. I . . ." He couldn't look at her. "Whatever you want, Quinlan. That's what I mean to say."

She was silent for a moment. Then her hand slid over his chest, landing upon his heart. "What do you want? Why is it only what I want?"

"Because you were the one who mentioned waiting until solstice."

"And?"

"And I want to make sure that you're fully on board with ending our . . . agreement."

"All right. But I also want to know what *you* want, Hunt."

He met her golden stare. "You know what I want." He couldn't stop his voice from lowering again. "I've never stopped wanting it—wanting you. I thought it was obvious."

Her heart was thundering. He could hear it. He glanced down at her ample chest and beheld a faint glimmering. "Your star . . ."

"Let's not even get started on this thing," she said, waving a hand at it. "Let's keep talking about how much you want me." She winked.

Hunt slung an arm around her shoulders, steering her back toward the bustling avenue. He whispered in her ear, "Why don't I just show you later?"

She laughed, the star's glow fading in the sunlight as they emerged onto the baking streets, and she slipped on her sunglasses and hat. "That's what I want, Hunt. That is *definitely* what I want."

18

Ithan rubbed at his face. This day had gotten . . . complicated.

"You look like you need a drink," Tharion said as he strode to the apartment door. Ruhn had left a moment ago. Ithan supposed he'd sit on his ass for a good few hours and contemplate the epic mess he'd somehow landed in the middle of. That Bryce seemed intent on involving herself in.

"How long have you guys been doing all this shit?"

"You know what happened during the Summit, right?"

"Demons wrecked the city, killed a lot of people. Two Archangels died. Everyone knows that."

Tharion's brows rose. "You ever learn how Micah and Sandriel died?"

Ithan blinked, bracing himself.

Tharion's expression was dead serious. "I am telling you this after I received a personal phone call from Rigelus three months ago, telling me to keep my mouth shut or I'd be killed, my parents with me. But as everything I'm doing these days seems to point toward that road anyway—you might as well know the truth, too. Since you'll likely wind up dead with us."

"Fantastic." Ithan wished Perry had dumped him anywhere but this apartment.

Tharion said, "Hunt ripped Sandriel's head from her shoulders after the Archangel threatened Bryce."

Ithan started. He'd known Athalar was intense as shit, but killing an Archangel—

"And Bryce slaughtered Micah after he bragged about killing Danika and the Pack of Devils."

Ithan's body went numb. "I . . ." He couldn't get a breath down. "Micah . . . what?"

By the time Tharion finished explaining, Ithan was shaking. "Why didn't she tell me?" That packless wolf inside him was howling with rage and pain.

Fuck, Sabine had no idea Micah had killed her daughter. Or . . . wait. Sabine *did* know. Sabine and Amelie had both been at the Summit, along with the Prime. They'd witnessed through the feeds what Tharion had just described.

And . . . and hadn't told him. The rest of the Den, fine, but Connor was his brother. The urge to shift, to bellow and roar, filled his blood, trembling along his bones. He suppressed it.

Tharion went on, unaware of the animal within trying to claw free. "The Asteri have made it clear to Bryce and Athalar: one word to anyone, and they're dead. The only reason they're not dead yet is because they've played nicely this summer."

Claws appeared at Ithan's fingertips. Tharion didn't fail to note them.

Through a mouth full of lengthening fangs, Ithan growled, "Micah killed my brother. And Bryce killed Micah because of it." He couldn't wrap his mind around it—that Bryce, *before* the Drop, had destroyed an Archangel.

It made no sense.

He'd had the audacity, the ignorance, to question her love for Danika and Connor. His claws and fangs retracted. That wolf inside ceased baying.

Ithan rubbed at his face again, shame an oily river through him that drowned that wolf inside his skin. "I need some time to process this." The wolf he used to be would have run to the sunball field to practice until he became nothing but breath and sweat and the thoughts sorted themselves out. But he hadn't set foot on one of those fields in two years. He wasn't going to start now.

Tharion headed for the door again. "I'm sure you do, but a word of advice: don't take too long. Urd works in strange ways, and I don't think it was a coincidence that you were brought here right as this shit started."

"So I'm supposed to go along with it on some hunch that fate is nudging me?"

"Maybe," the mer answered. He shrugged his powerful shoulders, honed from a lifetime of swimming. "But whenever you're tired of sitting on the couch feeling sorry for yourself, come find me. I could use a wolf's sense of smell."

"For what?"

Tharion's face turned grave. "I need to find Emile before Pippa Spetsos. Or Cormac."

The mer left him with that. For a long moment, Ithan sat in silence.

Had Connor known anything about Danika's involvement with Sofie Renast? Had Sabine? He doubted it, but . . . At least Bryce had been as much in the dark about this as he was.

Bryce, who had used Danika's sword during the attack on this city, and kept it ever since. Ithan glanced to the door.

He moved before he could second-guess the wisdom and morality of it, going right to the coat closet. Umbrellas, boxes of crap . . . nothing. The linen closet and the laundry closet didn't reveal anything, either.

Which left . . . He winced as he entered her bedroom.

He didn't know how he hadn't seen it the other night. Well, he'd been beaten to Hel and back, so that was excuse enough, but . . . the sword leaned against the chair beside her tall dresser, as if she'd left it there for decoration.

Ithan's mouth dried out, but he stalked for the ancient blade. Gifted to Danika by the Prime—an act that had infuriated Sabine, who'd long expected to inherit the family weapon.

He could still hear Sabine raging in the weeks after Danika's death, trying to find where Danika had left the sword. She'd practically torn that old apartment to pieces to find it. Ithan had thought it lost until he saw Bryce brandishing it this spring.

Breath tight in his chest, Ithan picked up the blade. It was light but perfectly balanced. He drew it from the sheath, the metal shining in the dim light.

Damn, it was gorgeous. Simple, yet impeccably made.

He blew out a long breath, chasing away the clinging cobwebs of memories—Danika carrying this sword everywhere, wielding it in practice, the blade somehow validation that even if Sabine sucked, with Danika, they had a bright future, with Danika, the wolves would become *more*—

He couldn't help it. He took up a defensive stance and swung the blade.

Yeah, it was perfect. A remarkable feat of craftsmanship.

Ithan pivoted, feinting and then striking at an invisible opponent. Sabine would lose her shit if she knew he was messing around with the blade. Whatever.

Ithan struck again at the shadows, shuddering at the beautiful song of the sword slicing through the air. And . . . what the Hel: he'd had a weird fucking morning. He needed to burn off some tension.

Lunging and parrying, leaping and rolling, Ithan sparred against an invisible enemy.

Maybe he'd gone crazy. Maybe this was what happened to wolves without a pack.

The sword was an extension of his arm, he thought. He slid over the glass dining table, taking on two, three, ten opponents—

Holstrom blocks; Holstrom presses—

Moving through the apartment, Ithan leapt up onto the coffee table in front of the sectional, wood shuddering beneath him, the narration loud and precise in his head. *Holstrom delivers the killing blow!*

He swiped the sword down in a triumphant arc.

The front door opened.

Bryce stared at him. Standing on the coffee table with Danika's sword.

"I forgot my work ID . . . ?" Bryce started, brows so high they seemed capable of touching her hairline. Ithan prayed Solas would melt him into the floor and boil his blood into steam.

It seemed the sun god was listening. The coffee table groaned. Then cracked.

And collapsed entirely beneath him.

Ithan might have continued to lie there, hoping some Reaper would come suck the soul from his body, had Bryce not rushed over. Not to him—not to help him up. But to investigate something just beyond his line of sight.

"What the Hel is this?" she asked, kneeling.

Ithan managed to move his ass off the debris, lifting his head to see her crouching over a stack of papers. "Was there a drawer in the table?"

"No. There must have been a secret compartment." Bryce flicked splinters of wood from the half-scattered pile. "This table was here when I moved in—all the furniture was Danika's." She lifted her gaze to him. "Why would she hide her old college papers in here?"

Ruhn held the Starsword to the grindstone. Black, iridescent sparks flew from the blade's edge. Behind him in the otherwise empty Aux armory, Flynn and Declan cleaned their array of guns at a worktable.

He'd planned to meet them here this afternoon. Had intended to hone the sword, clean and inspect his guns, and then cap the day off with a City Head meeting to discuss the new Archangel.

A normal day, in other words. Except for the colossal, life-threatening shit that had just gone down. Incredibly, the Prince of the Chasm was the least of his problems.

"Out with it," Flynn said without halting work on his handgun.

"What?" Ruhn asked, pulling the blade away.

Declan answered, "Whatever has kept you standing there in silence for ten minutes, not even complaining about Flynn's shitty playlist."

"Asshole," Flynn said to Dec, nodding toward where his phone blasted heavy metal. "This stuff is poetry."

"They've done studies where plants wither up and die when exposed to this music," Declan countered. "Which is precisely how I feel right now."

Flynn chuckled. "I'm guessing you're brooding about one of three things: horrible daddy, baby sister, or pretty fiancée."

"None of them, dickhead," Ruhn said, slumping into the chair across the table from them. He glanced to the doors, listening. When he was assured no one occupied the hall beyond, he said, "My lunch hour began with finding the Prince of the Chasm in feline form at Bryce's apartment, where he revealed that Cormac is an Ophion rebel, and it ended with learning that Cormac is on the hunt for a missing kid and the kid's spy sister. Who happens to be Cormac's girlfriend. And he's basically threatened to tell my father about my mind-speaking gifts if I don't meet him at some bar to hear his pitch for how I can be of use to Ophion."

His friends gaped. Declan said carefully, "Is everyone . . . alive?"

"Yes," Ruhn said, sighing. "I was sworn to secrecy, but . . ."

"So long as you didn't swear a blood oath, who cares?" Flynn said, gun forgotten on the table beside him.

"Trust me, Cormac tried. I refused."

"Good," Dec said. "Tell us everything."

They were the only two people in the world Ruhn would trust with this knowledge. Bryce—and Hunt—would kick his ass for saying anything, but too fucking bad. They had each other to vent to. So Ruhn opened his mouth and explained.

"And . . . that's where I'm at," Ruhn finished, toying with the ring through his lip.

Flynn rubbed his hands together. "This should be exciting." He was totally serious. Ruhn gawked at him.

But Declan was eyeing him thoughtfully. "I once hacked into an imperial military database and saw the uncensored footage from the battlefields and camps." Even Flynn's smile vanished. Declan went on, red hair gleaming in the firstlights, "It made me sick. I dreamed about it for weeks afterward."

"Why didn't you say anything?" Ruhn asked.

"Because there was nothing to be done about it. It seemed that way, at least." Declan nodded, as if to himself. "Whatever you need, I'm in."

"That easy, huh?" Ruhn said, brows lifting.

"That easy," Dec answered.

Ruhn had to take a moment. He had no idea what god he'd pleased enough to warrant being blessed with such friends. They were more than friends. They were his brothers. Ruhn finally said hoarsely, "We get caught, and we're dead. Our families with us." He added to Dec, "And Marc."

"Trust me, Marc would be the first one to say Hel yes to this. He hates the Asteri." Dec's smile turned subdued. "But . . . yeah, I think it's safer if he doesn't know." He frowned at Flynn. "Can you keep quiet?"

Flynn made an outraged sound.

"You talk when you're wasted," Ruhn chimed in. But he knew Flynn was a steel vault when he wanted to be.

Declan's voice deepened into a ridiculous mockery of Flynn as he said, "Oh, sexy nymph-writer, look at your boobs, they're so round, they remind me of these bombs the Aux is hiding in their armory in case of—"

"That was *not* what fucking happened!" Flynn hissed. "She was a reporter, first of all—"

"And it was twenty years ago," Ruhn cut him off before this could descend into further insanity. "I think you learned your lesson."

Flynn glowered. "So what now? You're going to go meet Cormac and hear him out?"

Ruhn blew out a breath and began cleaning the sword in earnest. Bryce was going to go ballistic. "I don't see how I have any other choice."

19

What the fuck *is* this?" Bryce whispered as she knelt in the ruins of her coffee table and leafed through the stack of papers that had apparently been hidden inside.

"It's not only college papers," Ithan said, fanning out the pages beside her. "These are documents and images of newspaper clippings." He peered at them. "They all seem like they're regarding firstlight's uses—mostly how it was made into weapons."

Bryce's hands shook. She sifted through a few academic articles—all full of redactions—theorizing on the origin of worlds and what the Asteri even *were*.

"She never mentioned any of this," Bryce said.

"Think this is what Sofie Renast discovered?" he asked. "Like, maybe Danika sniffed something out about the Asteri with her . . ." He trailed off, then added, "Gifts?"

Bryce lifted her gaze to his carefully neutral face as he tried to recover from a stumble. "You knew about her bloodhound gift?"

Ithan shifted on his knees. "It wasn't ever talked about, but . . . yeah. Connor and I knew."

Bryce flipped another page, tucking that factoid away. "Well, why would it even matter if Danika had sniffed out something regarding the Asteri? They're holy stars." Beings that possessed the force of an entire star within them, unaging and undying.

But as Bryce skimmed article after article, Ithan doing the same beside her, she began to see that they challenged that fact. She made herself keep breathing steadily. Danika had been a history major at CCU. None of this stuff was out of the ordinary—except that it had been hidden. Here.

All we have as proof of their so-called sacred power is their word, Bryce read. *Who has ever seen such a star manifest itself? If they are stars from the heavens, then they are fallen stars.*

A chill ran down Bryce's spine, one hand drifting to her chest. She had a star within her. Well, starlight that manifested as a star-shaped thing, but . . . What was the Asteri's power, then? The sun was a star—did they possess the power of an actual sun?

If so, this rebellion was fucked. Maybe Danika had wondered about it, and wanted Sofie to verify it somehow. Maybe that was what the intel was about, what Danika had suspected and dreaded and needed to officially confirm: there was no way to win. Ever.

Bryce wished Hunt were here, but she didn't dare call him with this info. Though after what had happened between them in the alley during lunch, maybe it was good they weren't in close quarters. She didn't trust herself to keep her hands off him.

Because *gods-damn.* That kiss. She hadn't hesitated. Had seen Hunt, that usually unflappable exterior melting away, and . . . she'd needed to kiss him.

The problem was that now she needed more. It was unfortunate that Ithan was staying with her, and the kind of sex she planned to have with Hunt would rattle the walls.

But . . . Urd must have sent her back to the apartment just now. For this. She exhaled. Ran a hand over the pages. The final papers in the pile made Bryce's breath catch.

"What is it?" Ithan asked.

Bryce shook her head, angling slightly away from him to read the text again.

Dusk's Truth.

The same project that had been mentioned in the emails between Sofie and Danika. That Danika had said would be of interest to Sofie.

Danika had been digging into it since *college*? Bryce inhaled and turned to the next page.

It was completely blank. Like Danika had never gotten to writing down any notes about it.

"Dusk's Truth was one of the things that Danika mentioned to Sofie," Bryce said quietly. "Dusk's Truth and Project Thurr."

"What is it?"

She shook her head again. "I don't know. But there has to be a connection between all of it." She tossed the Dusk's Truth document back onto the pile.

Ithan asked, "So what now?"

She sighed. "I gotta get back to work."

He arched a brow in question.

"Job, remember?" She got to her feet. "Maybe, um . . . find someplace to hide this stuff? And don't play Warrior Hero anymore. I liked that coffee table."

Ithan flushed. "I wasn't playing Warrior Hero," he muttered.

Bryce snickered and grabbed her ID from where she'd left it hanging beside the door, but then she sobered. "You looked good wielding it, Ithan."

"I was just screwing around." His tone was tense enough that she didn't say anything more before leaving.

Ruhn found Cormac at the pool hall in FiRo, losing to a satyr, an old rock song crackling from the jukebox on the other side of the concrete-lined space.

Cormac said, focusing on his shot, "I'd never tell your father, by the way."

"And yet here I am," Ruhn said. The satyr noted the expression on Ruhn's face and made himself scarce. "Seems like your threat worked."

"Desperate times," Cormac muttered.

Ruhn grabbed the cue the satyr had discarded, eyeing the pool table. He spotted the satyr's next shot immediately and smirked. "He was probably going to kick your ass."

Cormac again assessed his shot. “I was letting him win. It was the princely thing to do.”

Balls cracked, and Ruhn chuckled as they scattered. None found a pocket.

“Sure,” Ruhn said, aligning the cue ball. Two balls found their homes with a satisfying *plink*.

Cormac swore softly. “I have a feeling this is more your element than mine.”

“Guilty.”

“You seem like a male who spends his time in places like this.”

“As opposed to . . . ?”

“Doing things.”

“I head up the Aux. It’s not like I squat in dives all day.” Ruhn looked pointedly around the bar.

“That party suggested otherwise.”

“We like to enjoy ourselves here in sunny Lunathion.”

Cormac snorted. “Apparently.” He watched Ruhn pocket another ball, then blow his second shot by an inch. “You have more piercings since the last time I saw you. And more ink. Things must be dull around here if that’s what you spend your time on.”

“All right,” Ruhn said, leaning against his cue. “You’re a brooding hero and I’m a lazy asshole. Is that really how you want to start your pitch?”

Cormac made his move, one of the balls finally sinking into a pocket. But his second shot missed, leaving the angle Ruhn needed completely open. “Hear me out, cousin. That’s all I ask.”

“Fine.” Ruhn took his shot. “Let’s hear it.” His voice was barely more than a whisper.

Cormac leaned against his cue and studied the empty bar before saying, “Sofie was in contact with our most vital spy in the rebellion—Agent Daybright.”

Unease wended through Ruhn. He really, really didn’t want to know this.

Cormac went on, “Daybright has direct access to the Asteri—Ophion has long wondered whether Daybright is one of the Asteri themselves. Daybright and Sofie used codes on crystal-fueled radios to pass along messages. But with Sofie's . . . disappearance, it's become too dangerous to keep using the old methods of communicating. The fact that the Hind was able to be on the scene so quickly that night indicates that someone might have intercepted those messages and broken our codes. We need someone who can mind-speak to be in direct contact with Agent Daybright."

"And why the fuck would I ever agree to work with you?" Beyond the threat of Cormac telling his father about his talents.

The mind-speaking was a rare gift of the Avallen Fae, inherited from his mother's bloodline, and had always come naturally to him. He'd been four the first time he'd done it—he'd asked his mother for a sandwich. She'd screamed when she'd heard him in her mind, and in that moment, he'd known that the gift was something to hide, to keep secret. When she'd rubbed her head, clearly wondering if she'd imagined things, he'd kept quiet. And made sure she had no reason to bring him to his father, who he knew, even then, would have questioned and examined him and never let him go. Ruhn hadn't made that mistake again.

He wouldn't let his father control this piece of him, too. And even if Cormac had sworn he wouldn't reveal it . . . he'd be stupid to believe his cousin.

"Because it's the right thing to do," Cormac said. "I've seen those death camps. Seen what's left of the people who survive. The children who survive. It can't be allowed to go on."

Ruhn said, "The prison camps are nothing new. Why act now?"

"Because Daybright came along and started feeding us vital information that has led to successful strikes on supply lines, missions, encampments. Now that we have someone in the upper echelons of the Asteri's rule, it changes everything. The information Daybright would pass to you can save thousands of lives."

"And take them," Ruhn said darkly. "Did you tell Command about me?"

"No," Cormac said earnestly. "I only mentioned that I had a contact in Lunathion who might be useful in reestablishing our connection with Daybright, and was sent here."

Ruhn couldn't fault him for trying. While he couldn't read

thoughts or invade people's unguarded minds as some of his cousins could, he'd learned that he could talk to people on a sort of psychic bridge, as if his mind had formed it brick by brick between souls. It was perfect for a spy network.

But Ruhn asked, "And it was coincidence that it happened to line up with Emile coming here, too?"

A slight smile. "Two birds, one stone. I needed a reason to be here, to cover for my hunt for him. Seeking out your gifts offered that to Ophion. As does my engagement to your sister."

Ruhn frowned. "So you're asking me to what—help out this one time? Or for the rest of my fucking life?"

"I'm asking you, Ruhn, to pick up where Sofie left off. How long you decide to work with us is up to you. But right now, Ophion is desperate for Daybright's information. People's lives depend on it. Daybright has alerted us three times now before an imperial attack on one of our bases. Those warnings saved thousands of lives. We need you for the next few months—or at least until we've attained the intel that Sofie knew."

"I don't see how I have any choice but to say yes."

"I told you—I won't tell your father. I just needed to get you here. To get you to listen. I wouldn't ask this of you unless it was necessary."

"How'd you even get caught up in all this rebel business?" Cormac's life had been pretty cushy, as far as Ruhn could tell. But he supposed that to an outsider, his own life looked the same.

Cormac weighed the cue in his hands. "It's a long story. I linked up with them about four years ago."

"And what's your title with Ophion, exactly?"

"Field agent. Technically, I'm a field commander of the northwestern Pangeran spy network." He exhaled slowly. "Sofie was one of my agents."

"But now you're trying to keep Emile away from Ophion? Having doubts about the cause?"

"Never about the cause," Cormac said quietly. "Only about the people in it. After the heavy hits to the bases this year, Ophion has about ten thousand members left, controlled by a team of twenty in

Command. Most of them are humans, but some are Vanir. Any Vanir affiliated with Ophion, Command or not, are sworn to secrecy, perhaps to stricter standards than the humans."

Ruhn angled his head and asked baldly, "How do you know you can trust me?"

"Because your sister put a bullet through the head of an Archangel and you've all kept quiet about it."

Ruhn nodded toward a pocket, but missed his final shot. Yet he said calmly, "I don't know what you're talking about."

Cormac laughed softly. "Really? My father's spies learned of it before the Asteri shut the information down."

"Then why treat her like some party girl?"

"Because she went back to partying after what happened last spring."

"So did I." But they were getting off topic. "What do you know about Agent Daybright?"

"As much as you do." Cormac's ball went wide by an embarrassing margin.

"How do I make contact? And what's the process after I receive information?"

"You pass it to me. I know where to send it in Command."

"And again, I'm supposed to simply . . . trust you."

"I've trusted you with information that could land me in the Asteri's cells."

Not just any prison. For this kind of thing, for someone of Cormac's rank—Ruhn's rank—it'd be the notorious dungeons beneath the Asteri's crystal palace. A place so awful, so brutal, that rumor claimed there were no cameras. No record, no proof of atrocities. Except for rare witnesses and survivors like Athalar.

Ruhn again lined up his final shot and called the pocket, but paused before making it. "So how do I do it? Cast my mind into oblivion and hope someone answers?"

Cormac chuckled, swearing again as Ruhn sank his last ball. Ruhn wordlessly grabbed the wooden triangle and began to rerack the balls.

Ruhn broke the balls with a thunderous crack, starting the next round. The three and seven balls landed in opposite pockets—solids, then.

Cormac pulled a small quartz crystal from his pocket and tossed it to Ruhn. "It's all hypothetical right now, given that we've never worked with someone like you. But first try to contact Daybright by holding this. Daybright has the sister to this comm-crystal. It possesses the same communicative properties as the Gates in this city."

The comm-crystal was warm against Ruhn's skin as he pocketed it. "How does it work?"

"That's how our radios reached Daybright. Seven crystals all hewn from one rock—six in radios in our possession, the seventh in Daybright's radio. They're beacons—on the same precise frequency. Always desiring to connect into one whole again. This crystal is the last one that remains of our six. The other five were destroyed for safety. I'm hoping that if someone with your powers holds it in your hand, it might link you with Daybright when you cast your mind out. The same way the Gates here can send audio between them."

Cormac's gaze had gone hazy—pained. And Ruhn found himself asking, "Is this crystal from Sofie's radio?"

"Yes." Cormac's voice thickened. "She gave it to Command before she went into Kavalla. They gave it to me when I mentioned I might know someone who could use it."

Ruhn weighed the grief, the pain in his cousin's face before he softened his tone. "Sofie sounds like a remarkable person."

"She was. Is." Cormac's throat bobbed. "I need to find her. And Emile."

"You love her?"

Cormac's eyes burned with flame. "I don't try to delude myself into thinking that my father would ever approve of a union with a part-human—especially one with no fortune or name. But yes. I was hoping to find a way to spend my life with her."

"You really think she's here, trying to meet up with Emile?"

"The mer didn't rule it out. Why should I?" Again those walls rose in Cormac's eyes. "If your sister knows anything about whether Danika found a hiding place for them, I need to know."

Ruhn noted the faint hint of desperation—of dread and panic—and decided to put his cousin out of his misery. "We suspect Danika might have told Sofie to lie low in the Bone Quarter," he said.

Alarm flared across Cormac's face, but he nodded his gratitude to Ruhn. "Then we will need to find a way to secure safe passage there—and find some way to search unseen and undisturbed."

Well, Ruhn needed a drink. Thank Urd they were already in a bar. "All right." He surveyed his cousin, the perfect blond hair and handsome face. "For what it's worth, if we can find Sofie, I think you should marry her, if she feels the same way about you. Don't let your father tie you into some betrothal you don't want."

Cormac didn't smile. He observed Ruhn with the same clear-eyed scrutiny and said, "The witch-queen Hypaxia is beautiful and wise. You could do far worse, you know."

"I know." That was as much as Ruhn would say about it.

She *was* beautiful. Stunningly, distractingly beautiful. But she had zero interest in him. She'd made that clear in the months after the Summit. He didn't entirely blame her. Even if he'd had a glimpse of what life might have been like with her. Like peering through a keyhole.

Cormac cleared his throat. "When you connect with Daybright, say this to confirm your identity."

As his cousin rattled off the code phrases, Ruhn made shot after shot, until only two balls remained and he blew an easy one and scratched the cue ball to give his cousin a chance. He didn't know why he bothered.

Cormac handed the cue ball back to him. "I don't want a pity win."

Ruhn rolled his eyes but took the ball back, making another shot. "Is there any intel I should be asking Daybright about?"

"For months now, we've been trying to coordinate a hit on the Spine. Daybright is our main source of information regarding when and where to strike."

The Spine—the north-south railway that cut Pangera in half. The main artery for supplies in this war.

"Why risk the hit?" Ruhn asked. "To disrupt the supply lines?"

"That, and Daybright's been getting whispers for months now about the Asteri working on some sort of new mech-suit prototype."

"Different from the mech-suits the humans use?"

"Yes. This is a mech-suit designed for Vanir to pilot. For the imperial armies."

"Fuck." He could only imagine how dangerous they'd be.

"Exactly," Cormac said. He checked his watch. "I need to head toward the Black Dock—I want to know if there's any hint that Emile or Sofie have been there. But contact Daybright as soon as you can. We need to intercept the Vanir suit prototype to study its technology before it can be used to slaughter us."

Ruhn nodded, resigned. "All right. I'll help you."

"Your friends will not be pleased. Athalar in particular."

"Leave Athalar to me." He didn't answer to the angel. Though his sister . . .

Cormac observed him once more. "When you want out, I'll get you out. I promise."

Ruhn sank his last ball into his chosen pocket and leaned the stick against the concrete wall. "I'll hold you to that."

20

The water dripping from Tharion's wave skimmer onto the plastic floor of the dry dock in the Blue Court was the only sound as he repaired the vehicle. His sweat dripped along with it, despite the chamber's cool temperature. He'd stripped off his shirt within minutes of arriving here, even its soft cotton too confining against his skin as he worked. Reeds had gotten stuck in the engine during his trip out to the marshes the other day, and though the engineering team could have easily fixed the issue, he'd wanted to do it himself.

Wanted to give his mind some time to sort everything out.

When he'd awoken that morning, talking to the Prince of the Chasm—pretending to be a cat, for Urd's sake—hadn't been remotely near the list of possibilities for his day. Nor had finding out that an Avallen prince was an Ophion rebel searching for Sofie Renast's younger brother. Or that Danika Fendyr had sent Sofie to gather some vital intel on the Asteri. No, he'd awoken with only one goal: learn what Ithan Holstrom knew.

A whole lot of nothing, apparently.

Some Captain of Intelligence. *Captain Whatever,* Holstrom had called him. Tharion was half-inclined to get it etched into a plaque for his desk.

But at least Holstrom had agreed to help out should Tharion

need his nose to find the kid. If Pippa Spetsos was hunting for Emile as Cormac had claimed, politics and Sofie and his queen aside . . . they needed to find the kid first. If only to spare him from being forced to use those thunderbird powers in horrible ways. Holstrom would be a valuable asset in that endeavor.

And besides—the wolf seemed like he needed something to do.

The door to the dry dock room whooshed open, ushering in a scent of bubbling streams and water lilies. Tharion kept his attention on the engine, the wrench clenched in his hand.

"I heard you were here," said a lilting female voice, and Tharion plastered a smile on his face as he looked over a shoulder at the River Queen's daughter.

She wore her usual diaphanous pale blue gown, offsetting the warm brown of her skin. River pearls and shards of abalone gleamed in her thick black curls, cascading well past her slim shoulders to the small of her back. She glided toward him on bare feet, the chill water coating the floor seemingly not bothering her at all. She always moved like that: as if she were floating underwater. She had no mer form—was only a fraction mer, actually. She was some kind of elemental humanoid, as at home in the open air as she was beneath the surface. Part woman, part river.

Tharion held up his wrench, a strip of river weed tangled around the tip. "Repairs."

"Why do you still insist on doing them yourself?"

"Gives me a tangible task." He leaned against the wave skimmer on the lift behind him, the water beading its sides cool against his hot skin.

"Is your work for my mother so unfulfilling that you need such things?"

Tharion offered a charming smile. "I like to pretend I know what I'm doing around machines," he deflected.

She gave him a light laugh in return, coming closer. Tharion kept himself perfectly still, refusing to shy from the hand she laid on his bare chest. "I haven't seen much of you lately."

"Your mother's been keeping me busy." *Take it up with her.*

A small, shy smile. "I'd hoped we could . . ." She blushed, and Tharion caught the meaning.

They hadn't done *that* in years. Why now? Water-spirits were capricious—he'd figured she'd gotten him, had him, lost interest, and moved on. Even if the vows between them still bound them together irreparably.

Tharion covered her small hand with his own, brushing his thumb over the velvety skin. "It's late, and I have an early start."

"And yet you're here, toiling on this . . . machine." She took after her mother when it came to technology. Had barely mastered the concept of a computer, despite lessons with Tharion. He wondered if she even knew the name for the machine behind him.

"I need it for tomorrow's work." A lie.

"More than you need me?"

Yes. Definitely yes.

But Tharion gave another one of those grins. "Another time, I promise."

"I heard you went into the city today."

"I'm always in the city."

She eyed him, and he noted the jealous, wary gleam.

"Who did you see?"

"Some friends."

"Which ones?"

How many interrogations had begun like this and ended in her crying to her mother? The last one had been only a few days ago. Afterward, he'd wound up on that boat in the Haldren Sea, hunting for Sofie Renast's remains.

He said carefully, "Bryce Quinlan, Ruhn Danaan, Ithan Holstrom, and Hunt Athalar." No need to mention Aidas or Prince Cormac. They weren't his friends.

"Bryce Quinlan—the girl from this spring? With the star?"

He wasn't surprised she only asked about the female. "Yeah." Another wary look that Tharion pretended not to notice as he said casually, "She and Athalar are dating now, you know. A nice ending after everything that went down."

The River Queen's daughter relaxed visibly, shoulders slumping. "How sweet."

"I'd like to introduce you sometime." A blatant lie.

"I shall ask Mother."

He said, "I'm going to see them again tomorrow. You could join me." It was reckless, but . . . he'd spent ten years now avoiding her, dodging the truth. Maybe they could change it up a bit.

"Oh, Mother will need more time than that to prepare."

He bowed his head, the picture of understanding. "Just let me know when. It'll be a double date."

"What's that?"

Television didn't exist down here. Or at least in the River Queen's royal chambers. So popular culture, anything modern . . . they weren't even on her radar.

Not that theirs could be considered a true betrothal. It was more like indentured servitude.

"Two couples going out to a meal together. You know, a date . . . times two."

"Ah." A pretty smile. "I'd like that."

So would Athalar. Tharion would never hear the end of it. He glanced at the clock. "I do have an early start, and this engine is a mess . . ."

It was as close to a dismissal as he'd ever dare make. He did have a few rights: she could seek him out for sex—as she'd done—but he could say no without repercussions; and his duties as Captain of Intelligence were more important than seeing to her needs. He prayed she'd consider fixing a wave skimmer one of those duties.

Ogenas be thanked, she did. "I'll leave you to it, then."

And then she was gone, the scent of water lilies with her. As the doors slid open to let her through, Tharion glimpsed her four mer guards waiting on the other side—the River Queen's daughter never went anywhere alone. The broad-chested males would have fought to the death for the chance to share her bed. He knew they detested him for having and rejecting that access.

He'd happily yield his position. If only the River Queen would let him.

Alone again, Tharion sighed, leaning his forehead against the wave skimmer.

He didn't know how much more of this he could take. It could be weeks or years until she and her mother would start pushing for the wedding. And then for children. And he'd be locked in a cage, here below the surface, until even his Vanir life expired. Old and dreamless and forgotten.

A fate worse than death.

But if this thing with Sofie and Emile Renast was indeed playing out in a big way . . . he'd use it as his temporary escape. He didn't give a shit about the rebellion, not really. But his queen had given him a task, so he'd milk this investigation for all it was worth. Perhaps see what the intel Sofie had gathered could gain *him*.

Until his own stupid choices finally called in a debt.

"And here's the common room," Hunt said through his teeth to Baxian as he shouldered open the door to the barracks hangout area. "As you already know."

"Always nice to hear from a local," Baxian said, black wings folded in tightly as he noted the dim space: the little kitchenette to the left of the door, the sagging chairs and couches before the large TV, the door to the bathrooms straight ahead. "This is only for triarii?"

"All yours tonight," Hunt said, checking his phone. After ten. He'd been on his way out at seven when Celestina had called, asking him to give Baxian a tour of the Comitium. Considering the sheer size of the place . . . it had taken this long. Especially because Baxian had oh-so-many *questions*.

The bastard knew he was keeping Hunt here. Away from Bryce and that sweet, sumptuous mouth. Which was precisely why Hunt had opted to grin and bear it: he wouldn't give the shithead the satisfaction of knowing how much he was pissing him off. Or turning his balls blue.

But enough was enough. Hunt asked, "You need me to tuck you into bed, too?"

Baxian snorted, going up to the fridge and yanking it open. The light bounced off his wings, silvering their arches. "You guys have crap beer."

"Government salary," Hunt said, leaning against the doorway. "Menus for takeout are in the top drawer to your right; or you can call down to the canteen and see if they're still serving. Good? Great. Bye."

"What's that?" Baxian asked, and there was enough curiosity in his tone that Hunt didn't bite his head off. He followed the direction of the Helhound's gaze.

"Um. That's a TV. We watch stuff on it."

Baxian threw him a withering glare. "I know what a TV is, Athalar. I meant those wires and boxes beneath."

Hunt arched a brow. "That's an OptiCube." Baxian stared at him blankly. Hunt tried again. "Gaming system?" The Helhound shook his head.

For a moment, Hunt was standing in Baxian's place, assessing the same room, the same strange, new tech, Isaiah and Justinian explaining what a fucking mobile phone was. Hunt said roughly, "You play games on it. Racing games, first-person games . . . giant time suck, but fun."

Baxian looked like the word—*fun*—was foreign to him, too. Solas.

Sandriel hated technology. Had refused to allow even televisions in her palace. Baxian might as well have been transported here from three centuries ago. Hunt himself had encountered tech in other parts of the world, but when most of his duties had kept him focused on Sandriel or her missions, he hadn't really had time to learn about everyday shit.

From the hallway behind him, low voices murmured. Naomi—and Pollux. Isaiah's soothing tones wove between them. Thank the gods.

Hunt found Baxian observing him warily. He threw a flat stare back, one he'd perfected as the Umbra Mortis. Baxian just aimed for the hallway. Hunt gave him a wide berth.

The Hammer filled the doorway of Vik's room, talking to Isaiah and Naomi in the hall. It was Pollux's room now. Hunt's magic rumbled, lightning on the horizon. Pollux sneered at Hunt as he stalked past. Bags and boxes were piled high behind him, a miniature city dedicated to the Hammer's vanity.

Hunt, keenly aware of all the cameras, of Bryce's plea to behave, continued on, nodding at Naomi and Isaiah as he passed.

"Well, here you go," Hunt said to Baxian, pausing before Justinian's old room. Baxian opened the door. The room was as bare and empty as Hunt's had been.

A duffel lay beside the narrow bed. All of Baxian's belongings fit in one fucking bag.

It didn't make a difference. The Helhound was an asshole who had done shit that even Hunt couldn't stomach. For him to be in Justinian's room, filling his place—

The crucifix in the lobby flashed in Hunt's mind, Justinian's agonized face as he hung on it. Hunt tried to banish the thought, but failed. He'd fucked up. Twice now, he'd fucked up. First with the Fallen rebellion, then this spring with the Viper Queen, and now . . . Was he really going to allow himself and Bryce to be dragged into something similar? How many people would be destroyed by the end?

Baxian said, stepping into his room, "Thanks for the tour, Athalar."

Hunt again glimpsed that sad, empty little room behind the Helhound. Perhaps something like pity stirred him, because he said, "I'll give you a lesson on video games tomorrow. I gotta get home."

He could have sworn a shadow dimmed in Baxian's eyes that appeared a Hel of a lot like longing. "Thanks."

Hunt grunted. "We'll link up after the morning check-in. You can shadow me for the day."

"Real generous of you," Baxian said, and shut the door without further reply.

Fortunately, Pollux shut his own door right then—slammed it in Naomi's face. Leaving Hunt with his two friends.

They headed for the common room without needing to say a word, waiting until they'd closed the door and ensured no one was in the bathroom before sinking onto the couch. Hunt really wanted to go home, but . . . "So this fucking sucks," he said quietly.

"Pollux should be drawn and quartered," Naomi spat.

"I'm amazed you're both still alive," Isaiah said to her, propping his feet on the coffee table and loosening the gray tie around his neck. Judging by the suit, he must have recently gotten in from escorting Celestina somewhere. "But as your commander, I'm grateful you didn't brawl." He gave Hunt a pointed look.

Hunt snorted. But Naomi said, "The two of them defile those rooms by staying in there."

"They're only rooms," Isaiah said, though pain tightened his face. "All that Vik and Justinian were . . . it's not in there."

"Yeah, it's in a box at the bottom of a trench," Naomi said, crossing her arms. "And Justinian's ashes are on the wind."

"So are Micah's," Hunt said softly, and they looked at him.

Hunt just shrugged.

"Were you really going to rebel this spring?" Naomi asked. They hadn't once spoken about it these past months. The shit that had gone down.

"Not by the end," Hunt said. "I meant everything I said on the boat. I changed my mind; I realized that wasn't the path for me." He met Isaiah's disapproving frown. "I still mean it."

He did. If Sofie and Emile and Ophion and Cormac and all that shit went away right now, he wouldn't fucking think twice about it. Would be *glad* for it.

But that wasn't how things were playing out. It wasn't how Bryce wanted it to play out. He could barely stand the sight of Isaiah's tattooed brow.

"I know," Isaiah said at last. "You've got a lot more on the line now," he added, and Hunt wondered if he'd intended the slight tone of warning in the words.

Wondered if Isaiah remembered how he and the other angels in the Summit conference room had bowed to him after he'd ripped off Sandriel's head. What would his friends do if he told them about his recent contact with an Ophion rebel? His head spun.

Hunt changed the subject, nodding to the hall behind the shut door. "You two going to stay here or find places of your own?"

"Oh, I'm out," Isaiah said, practically beaming. "Signed a lease this morning on a place a few blocks from here. CBD, but closer to the Old Square."

"Nice," Hunt said, and lifted a brow at Naomi, who shook her head.

"Free rent," she said, "despite the new hallmates." Pollux and Baxian would be staying here until Celestina deemed them well adjusted enough to live in the city proper. Hunt shuddered to think of them loose.

"Do you trust that they're going to behave?" he asked Isaiah. "Because I fucking don't."

"We don't have any choice but to trust that they will," Isaiah said, sighing. "And hope that the Governor will see them for what they are."

"Will it make any difference if she knows?" Naomi asked, tucking her hands behind her head.

"I guess we'll see," Hunt said, and glanced at his phone again. "All right. I'm out." He paused at the doorway, however. Looked at his two friends, wholly unaware of the shit that was coming their way. It'd be huge for either of them—potentially freeing for Isaiah—to bust Ophion. To capture Sofie Renast and her brother and haul in Cormac.

If he spoke up now, spilled his guts, could he spare Bryce from the worst of it? Could he avoid crucifixion—avoid having an empty room being all that was left of him one day, too? If he played it right, could he save them both—and maybe Ruhn and Ithan—and live to tell the tale? Tharion was likely dead fucking meat for not telling the authorities about his mission, queen or no, as was the Crown Prince of Avallen. But . . .

Isaiah asked, "Something on your mind?"

Hunt cleared his throat.

The words sizzled on his tongue. A parachute, and now would be the exact moment to pull it open. *We have a major problem with rebels converging on this city and I need your help to make sure they play right into our hands.*

Hunt cleared his throat again. Shook his head.

And left.

21

Dusk's Truth, huh?" Hunt's deep voice rumbled across the bed to Bryce as they lay in the darkness, Syrinx already snoring between them.

"Danika definitely thought she was onto something," Bryce replied. Hunt had missed dinner, leaving her to an unbearably awkward meal with Ithan. He'd been quiet and contemplative, wearing the game face she'd seen before big matches. She'd said as much to him, but he hadn't wanted to talk.

So Bryce had combed through Danika's papers and clippings again. Had found nothing new. She'd only filled Hunt in when he'd finally gotten home from the Comitium and they'd readied for bed. Any thoughts of continuing what had gone down in that alley had vanished by the time she'd finished.

Hunt hummed, shifting onto his side. "So you're really going to help Cormac, then."

"It's not about wanting to help him—it's more about wanting to help Emile. But I meant what I said to you in the alley: this is also about getting what I can out of the situation for our own advantage." An end to the betrothal, and some training. "And," she admitted, "learning about Danika."

"Does it matter? About Danika, I mean?"

"It shouldn't. But it does. For some reason, it does." She said carefully, "I know we discussed this earlier, but . . . I can't do this without you, Hunt."

He said softly, "I know. I'm just . . . Fuck, Quinlan. The thought of anything happening to you scares the shit out of me. I understand, though. That's what prompted me this spring . . . what I was doing with Vik and Justinian. It was for Shahar."

Her heart strained. "I know." And he'd been willing to give that up for her—for *them*. "So you're in?"

"Yeah. Whatever help I can give, I'll offer it. But we need an exit strategy."

"We do," she agreed. "Let's talk about it tomorrow, though. I'm exhausted."

"All right." His wing brushed her bare shoulder and she turned her head to find him with his head propped on a fist.

"Don't *do* that."

"What?" His eyes sparkled in the dimness.

She turned onto her own side and waved a hand toward him. "Look so . . . like that."

His lips curled upward. "Sexy? Attractive? Seductive?"

"All of the above."

He flopped onto his back. "I feel weird doing anything with Holstrom a wall away."

She pointed to the aforementioned wall. "He's on the other side of the apartment."

"He's a wolf."

Bryce inhaled the musky, midnight scent of him. Arousal. "So let's be quiet, then."

Hunt's swallow was audible. "I . . . All right, I'll be straight with you, Quinlan."

She arched a brow.

He blew out a breath toward the ceiling. "It's been . . . a while. For me, I mean."

"Me too." The longest she'd ever gone without sex since her first time at seventeen. Well, ignoring what she and Hunt had done on the couch months ago—though that wasn't the kind of sex she wanted right now.

He said, "I guarantee that however long it's been for you, it's been longer for me."

"How long?"

Some part of her howled at the idea of anyone—any-fucking-one—putting their hands and mouth and other parts on him. Of *Hunt* touching anyone else. Wanting anyone else. Of him existing in a world where he hadn't known her, and some other female had been more important—

Some other female *had* been more important. Shahar. He'd loved her. Been willing to die for her.

He nearly died for you, too, a small voice whispered. But . . . this was different somehow.

Hunt grimaced. "Six months?"

Bryce laughed. "That's it?"

He growled. "It's a long time."

"I thought you were going to say *years*."

He gave her an affronted look. "I wasn't celibate, you know."

"So who was the lucky lady, then?" Or male, she supposed. She'd assumed he preferred females, but it was entirely possible he also—

"A nymph at a bar. She was from out of town and didn't recognize me."

Bryce's fingers curled, as if invisible claws appeared at their tips. "Nymph, huh."

Was that his type? Exactly like those dancers at the ballet? Delicate and svelte? Had Shahar been like that? Bryce had never searched for portraits of the dead Archangel—hadn't ever wanted to torture herself like that. But Sandriel had been beautiful as Hel, slim and tall, and Hunt had once mentioned that they were twins.

Bryce added, if only because she wanted him to feel a shred of the misery that now coursed through her, "Lion shifter. In a bathroom at the White Raven."

"The night of the bombing?" The words were sharp. As if her fucking someone while they'd known each other was unacceptable.

"Less than a week before," she said nonchalantly, quietly pleased at his sharpness.

"I thought you didn't like alphaholes."

"I like them for some things."

"Oh yeah?" He trailed a finger down her bare arm. "What, exactly?" His voice dropped to a purr. "You don't seem to enjoy males bossing you around."

She couldn't help her blush. "Every once in a while." It was all she could think to say as his fingers reached her wrist and he lifted her hand, bringing it to his mouth and pressing a kiss to her palm. "This one was especially good at being in charge."

"All right, Quinlan," he said against her skin. "I'm thoroughly jealous."

She chuckled. "So am I."

He kissed the inside of her wrist, lips grazing over sensitive flesh. "Before we went off on this stupid tangent, I was trying to warn you that it's been a while, so I might . . ."

"Be fast?"

He nipped at her wrist. "Be loud, asshole."

She laughed, running her fingers over his smooth, unmarked brow. "I could gag you."

Hunt barked out a laugh. "Please tell me you're not into that."

She let out a *hmmm*.

"For real?" He sat up slowly.

She lay back against the pillows, arms behind her head. "I'll try anything once."

A muscle throbbed in his neck. "All right. But let's start with the basics. If that gets boring, I promise to find ways to keep you interested."

"That doesn't get rid of the problem of Ithan's keen hearing."

He shifted against the bed, and Bryce found the blatant evidence of his interest pushing against his tight boxer briefs. Solas, he was huge.

She laughed softly, sitting up as well. "It really has been a while."

He trembled, though—with restraint. "Tell me yes, Bryce."

She went molten at the raw need in his words. "I want to touch you first."

"That's not a yes."

"I want *your* yes."

"Yes. Fuck yes. Now your turn."

She only smirked, pressing a surprisingly steady hand to his bare, muscled chest. He allowed her to push him back against the pillows. "I'll say yes when I've had my fill."

Hunt let out a low, rough noise.

"Not too late for a gag," Bryce murmured, pressing a kiss to his chest.

Hunt was going to burst out of his skin. He couldn't stand it: the sight of Bryce now straddling his thighs, wearing nothing but an old, soft T-shirt, the silken glide of her hair over his bare chest as she pressed a kiss between his pecs. Pressed another near his nipple.

There was another person in this apartment. One with exceptional hearing, and he—

Bryce's lips closed around his left nipple, wet heat sending Hunt's hips straining toward hers. She flicked her tongue across the taut bud, and Hunt hissed. "For fuck's sake."

She laughed around his nipple, then moved to the other. "Your chest is as big as mine," she muttered.

"That's the least sexy thing anyone has ever said to me," he managed to say.

She dug her long nails into his chest, the pain a light, singeing kiss. His cock throbbed in response. Gods spare him, he wouldn't last a minute.

Bryce kissed his right ribs. Ran her tongue along the muscles there. "How do you get these stupid muscles, anyway?"

"Exercise." Why was she talking? Why was *he* talking?

His hands shook, and he fisted them in the sheets. Syrinx had leapt off the bed, trotting to the bathroom and kicking the door shut with a hind leg. Smart chimera.

Her tongue teased over his left ribs, trailing downward as her fingers traced lines along his chest, his stomach. She kissed his belly button, and her head hovered mere inches from the edge of his boxer briefs, so close he was about to erupt at the sight of it—

"Aren't we supposed to do some kissing first?" His voice was guttural.

"Absolutely not," Bryce said, wholly focused on her task. Hunt couldn't get a breath down as her fingers curled on the waistband of his underwear and peeled it away. He could only let her do it, lifting his hips to accommodate her, baring all of him—

"Well, well, well," she crooned, sitting up. Hunt almost started whining at the distance she put between that mouth of hers and his cock. "This is a . . . big surprise."

"Stop playing, Quinlan." She had five seconds until he leapt on her and did everything he'd dreamed of for months now. Everything he'd planned to do during the longest night of the year.

She laid a finger on his lips. "Hush." She brushed her mouth over his. Slid her tongue along the seam of his lips. Hunt parted for her, and as her tongue slipped into his mouth, he caught it between his lips and sucked hard. Let her know precisely how he liked it.

Her whimper was a triumph. But Hunt kept still as she withdrew, straightening again, and lifted the shirt over her head.

Fuck, those breasts. Full and heavy and tipped in rosy nipples that had him seeing double—

He hadn't gotten enough of them that day they'd hooked up. Not even close. He needed to feast on these, needed their weight in his palms, those pretty nipples on his tongue—

She fisted her breasts, squeezing as she looked down at him. Hunt bucked his hips, driving his cock up before her in a silent request. Bryce only writhed, the plane of her stomach undulating as she squeezed her breasts again.

Hunt surged to grab her, to put his mouth where her hands were, but she held up a finger. "Not yet." Her eyes simmered like coals in the dimness. Her star began to glow faintly, as if it were under a black light. She traced her finger over the soft iridescence. "Please."

He panted through his teeth, chest heaving, but lay back on the pillows once more. "Well, when you put it so politely . . ."

She let out a sensuous laugh and leaned over him. Ran her nails along the shaft of his cock, then back down to its base. He shivered, pleasure singing along his spine as she said, "There's no way I can fit all of you in me."

He ground out, "Never know until we try."

Bryce smiled, and her head dipped as her fingers wrapped around his cock, barely able to grasp him fully. She squeezed his base right as her tongue lapped at his tip.

Hunt bucked, panting hard. Bryce laughed against his cock. "Quiet, remember?"

He was going to cut off Holstrom's ears. That would keep the wolf from hearing—

Bryce licked him again, tongue swirling, then slid his broad head into her mouth. Warm, wet heat enveloped him as she sucked tight and—

Hunt arched again, clapping a hand over his mouth as his eyes rolled back in his head. Yes. *Fuck* yes. Bryce withdrew, then slid her mouth further onto him. A few more strokes and he'd—

Hunt shifted, making to grab her, but she pinned his hips to the bed with a hand. Took him until he bumped against the back of her throat. He nearly flew out of his skin.

She sucked him hard, the pressure so perfect it was practically pain, withdrawing nearly to his tip before taking him all again. What didn't make it into her mouth was squeezed by her hand in flawless tandem.

Hunt took in the sight of his cock disappearing into her mouth, her hair whispering over his thighs, her breasts swaying—

"Quinlan," he groaned, a plea and a warning.

Bryce only slid him down her throat again, her free hand digging into the muscles of his thigh in silent permission. In her mouth—that was where she wanted him.

The thought alone unleashed him. Hunt couldn't stop himself as he raked his hands into her hair, fingers digging into her scalp, and rode her mouth. She met him thrust for thrust, moaning deep in her throat so that it echoed through him—

And then her hand slipped down to his balls, squeezing hard as her teeth grazed along his shaft—

Hunt shattered, biting down on his lip so hard the coppery tang of blood coated his tongue, bucking up into her, spilling down her throat.

Bryce swallowed as he came, the walls of her mouth fluttering against him, and he was going to fucking *die* from this, from her, from the pleasure she was wringing from him—

Hunt groaned, the last of himself shooting into her mouth. Then he was shaking and panting as she removed her mouth in one wet slide, then held his gaze.

She swallowed once more. Licked her lips.

Hunt tried and failed to get up. As if his body were stunned stupid.

Bryce smirked, a queen triumphant. Every fantasy he'd had of her these months—none of them came close to this. To what her mouth had been like, to what she looked like naked . . .

Hunt had managed to prop himself up on his elbows when Ithan yelled from the other side of the apartment, "*Please: have sex a little louder! I didn't hear everything that time!*"

Bryce burst out laughing, but Hunt could only stare at the little droplet that ran down her chin, gleaming in the dim light of her star. She noted the direction of his attention and wiped off her chin, rubbing her fingers together, then licking them clean.

Hunt growled, low and deep. "I'm going to fuck you senseless." Her nipples were hard as pebbles, and she squirmed against him. Nothing but those little lace panties separated her sweetness from his bare thighs.

But then Holstrom shouted, "*That sounds medically dangerous!*"

And Bryce laughed again, rolling off Hunt and reaching for his T-shirt. "Let's go to a sleazy motel tomorrow," she said, and promptly went to sleep.

Hunt, mind blasted apart, could only lie there naked, wondering if he'd imagined it all.

* * *

Hunt sat in a simple folding chair at the bottom of an abyss, nothing but blackness around him, the only light coming from the faint glow cast by his body. There was no beginning or end to the perpetual night.

He'd fallen asleep beside Quinlan, wondering if he should just slide his hand over her hip to reacquaint himself with that lovely spot between her legs. But Bryce wasn't there.

He didn't want Bryce in a place like this, so dark and empty and yet . . . awake. Wings rustled nearby—not the soft feathers of his wings, but something leathery. Dry.

Hunt stiffened, trying to shoot to his feet, but he couldn't. His ass stayed planted in the chair, though no ties bound him. His booted feet were glued to the black floor.

"Who's there?" The darkness absorbed his voice, muffling it. The leathery wings whispered again, and Hunt twisted his head toward the sound. Moving his head was about the only thing he could manage.

"A greater warrior would have freed himself from those bonds by now." The soft, deep voice slithered over his skin.

"Who the fuck are you?"

"Why do you not use the gifts in your blood to free yourself, Orion?"

Hunt gritted his teeth. "It's Hunt."

"I see. Because Orion was a hunter."

The voice came from everywhere. "What's *your* name?"

"Midgardians do not feel comfortable uttering my name on your side of the Rift."

Hunt stilled. There was only one being whose name was not uttered in Midgard.

The Prince of the Pit. Apollion.

His blood chilled. This was a fucked-up, weird-ass dream, no doubt caused by Quinlan literally blowing his mind into smithereens—

"It is no dream."

The seventh and most lethal of the demon princes of Hel was *in his mind—*

"I am not in your mind, though your thoughts ripple toward me like your world's radio waves. You and I are in a place between our worlds. A pocket-realm, as it were."

"What do you want?" Hunt's voice held steady, but—fuck. He needed to get out of here, to find some way back to Bryce. If the Prince of the Pit could get into Hunt's mind, then—

"If I went into her mind, my brother would be very angry with me. Again." Hunt could have sworn he heard a smile in the prince's voice. "You certainly worry a great deal about a female who is far safer than you at the moment."

"Why am I here?" Hunt forced out, willing his mind to clear of anything but the thought. It was difficult, though. This being before him, around him . . . This demon prince had killed the seventh Asteri. Had *devoured* the seventh Asteri.

The Star-Eater.

"I do like that name," Apollion said, chuckling softly. "But as for your question, you are here because I wished to meet you. To assess your progress."

"We got the pep talk from Aidas this afternoon, don't worry."

"My brother does not inform me of his movements. I do not know or care what he has or has not done."

Hunt lifted his chin with a bravado he didn't feel. "So let's hear it. Your proposal for how we should ally with you to overthrow the Asteri and set you up as our new masters."

"Is that what you think will happen?"

"Aidas already gave us a history lesson. Spare me."

The darkness rumbled with distant thunder. "You are foolish and arrogant."

"Takes one to know one, I suppose."

The darkness paused. "You are impertinent as well. Do you not know where I come from? My father was the Void, the Being That Existed Before. Chaos was his bride and my dam. It is to them that we shall all one day return, and their mighty powers that run in my blood."

"Fancy."

But Apollion said, "You're wasting the gifts that were given to you."

Hunt drawled, “Oh, I think I’ve put them to good use.”

“You don’t know a fraction of what you might do. You and the Starborn girl.”

“Again, Quinlan got the whole ‘master your powers’ talk from Aidas today, and that was boring enough, so let’s not repeat it.”

“Both of you would benefit from training. Your powers are more similar than you realize. Conduits, both of you. You have no idea how valuable you and the others like you are.”

Hunt arched a brow. “Oh yeah?”

The darkness rippled with displeasure. “If you are so dismissive of my assistance, perhaps I should send some . . . appetizers to test you and yours.”

Hunt flared his wings slightly. “Why summon me? Just to give me this shove?”

Apollion’s unholy essence whispered around him again. “The Northern Rift is groaning once more. I can smell war on the wind. I do not plan to lose this time.”

“Well, I don’t plan to have a demon prince for my ruler, so find a new five-year goal.”

A soft laugh. “You do amuse, Orion.”

Hunt snarled, and his lightning sizzled in answer. “I take it we’re done here—”

The seething darkness and those leathery wings vanished.

Hunt jolted awake. He was already reaching for the knife on the nightstand when he halted.

Quinlan slept beside him, Syrinx on her other side, both of them snoring softly. In the darkness, her red hair looked like fresh blood across her pillow.

The Prince of the Pit had spoken to him. Knew who he was, who Bryce was—

The Prince of the Pit was a liar and a monster, and it was entirely likely that he was trying to lure Hunt and Bryce into some fool’s quest with their powers. And yet . . . Fuck.

Hunt ran a shaking hand over his sweaty face, then settled back onto the pillows, brushing a knuckle down Bryce's soft cheek. She murmured, shifting closer, and Hunt obliged, sliding his arm over her waist and folding a wing around her. As if he could shield her from all that hunted them.

On both sides of the Northern Rift.

22

Ruhn finished off his beer, setting it on the coffee table before the massive TV in the living room. Declan, seated to his left, did the same. "All right," Dec said, "espionage time."

Flynn, smoking some mirthroot that Ruhn desperately needed a hit of, chuckled. "Our sweet son Ruhn is all grown up and spying for rebels."

"Shut up," Ruhn growled. "I knew I should have done this in private."

"Where would the fun be in that?" Dec asked. "Plus, shouldn't someone be here in case it's, I don't know, a trap or something?"

"Then why the fuck is he smoking?" Ruhn nodded to where Flynn blew smoke rings.

"Because I'm a self-destructive yet insanely charming idiot?" Flynn grinned.

"Emphasis on *insane*," Dec muttered.

But Ruhn wanted them with him tonight, when most of the city was asleep, as he attempted contact with Agent Daybright. He had the comm-crystal, though he wasn't exactly sure what to do with it—how to even begin connecting his abilities with its communication affinity. All hypotheticals, no guarantee of success. He couldn't decide whether or not it'd be a relief to fail. To be able to walk away from this.

"So, are we supposed to meditate with you or something?" Flynn set down the mirthroot.

"How the Hel would that help?" Ruhn asked.

"Solidarity?" Flynn suggested.

Ruhn snorted. "I'm good. Just . . . put a wooden spoon between my teeth if I go into some kind of fit."

Declan raised one. "Already thought of that."

Ruhn put his hand on his heart. "Thanks. I'm touched."

Flynn clapped Ruhn on the back. "We've got you. Do your thing."

There wasn't anything else to say, anything else Ruhn needed to hear, so he closed his eyes, leaning back against the cushions of the couch. He clenched the crystal in his fist, the stone eerily warm.

A mental bridge—that was how he always pictured the link he made between his mind and someone else's. So that was the image he summoned, funneling it through the crystal in his hand, as surely as Bryce had funneled her own powers through the crystal of the Gate this spring. Cormac had said the crystal had similar properties, so . . . why not?

Ruhn extended the bridge from himself, through the crystal, and then out into the vast unknown, sprawling into a darkness with no end. He clenched the crystal tighter, willing it to lead him where he needed to go, as if it were a prism filtering his powers out into the world.

Hello? His voice echoed down the bridge. Into nothing.

He visualized the crystal's milky core. Imagined a thread running from it, down along this mental bridge, out toward another end.

Hello? This is Agent . . .

Well, fuck. He should have come up with a code name. He sure as Hel couldn't risk his own name or identity, but he wanted something cool, damn it.

This is your new contact.

No answer from Daybright came. Ruhn kept extending the bridge, letting it span into nothingness. Pictured the crystal and its thread, letting himself follow its trail into the night.

I'm here to—

Yes?

Ruhn went still at the faint female voice. Light glowed down the bridge, and then there she was.

A female of pure flame. Or that was how she chose to appear. Not how Lehabah had been made of flame, with her body visible, but rather a female cloaked in it, only a flash of a bare wrist or an ankle or a shoulder through the veil. She was humanoid, but that was all he could glean. She looked like one of the radical sun-priests who'd gone rogue and immolated themselves to be close to their god.

Who are you? he asked.

Who are you? she challenged. Not one hint of her face.

I asked first.

Her flame flared, as if in annoyance. But she said, *The little black dog sleeps soundly on a wool blanket.*

Ruhn blew out a breath. There it was—the code phrase Cormac had given him to confirm her identity. He said, *And the gray tabby cleans her paws by the light of the moon.*

Utter nonsense.

But she said, *I'm Agent Daybright, in case that wasn't clear enough. Now . . . you are?*

Ruhn peered down at himself, swearing. He hadn't thought to hide his body—

But he found only a form of night and stars, galaxies and planets. As if his silhouette had been filled by them. He lifted a hand, finding not skin but the starry blanket of the sky covering his fingers. Had his mind instinctively shielded him? Or was this what he was, deep below the skin? Was this fire-being standing thirty feet down the mental bridge what *she* was, deep below her own skin? Or fur, he supposed.

She could be a faun or a satyr. Or a witch or a shifter. Or an Asteri, as Cormac had suggested. Maybe the fire was that of the holy star in her.

She merely stood there, burning. *Well?*

Her voice was beautiful. Like a golden song. It stirred his Fae soul, made it perk up. *I, ah . . . I hadn't gotten that far yet.*

She angled her head with what seemed like predatory intent. *They sent a novice?*

A chill skittered down his spine. She certainly spoke like one of the Asteri, regal and aloof. She looked over her shoulder. As if back toward the body connected to her mind.

Ruhn said, *Look, Agent Silverbow gave me this crystal, but had no idea if it could even work on a mind-to-mind level. So I wanted to attempt to make contact and let you know I'm here and this is the new mode of communication. So if it's an emergency, I don't need to waste time figuring out how to get in touch.*

That's fine.

He surveyed her again. *So, we trust each other that easily, then?* He couldn't stop his taunting question. *You're not at all worried the crystal fell into the wrong hands and the code phrases were compromised?*

Agents of the Asteri don't bumble about so much.

Damn. *I'll try harder to impress you the next time.*

Another soft laugh. *You already have, Agent Night.*

Did you just give me a code name? Night and Daybright. Night and Day—he liked that.

I figured I'd spare you the trouble of trying to invent something interesting. She turned back to her end of the bridge, flame flowing in her wake.

No messages for me to pass along? He didn't dare say Cormac's name. *Anything about the Spine?*

She kept walking. *No. But tell your commander that safe passage is granted under the cover of the waning moon.*

Ruhn bristled. Like Hel was Cormac his commander. *I don't know what that means.*

You're not supposed to. But Agent Silverbow will. And tell him I much *prefer this method of communicating.*

Then Daybright and her flame winked out, and Ruhn was alone.

"Why not tell me Agent Daybright was a female?" Ruhn asked Cormac the next morning, standing in his living room and gulping down his second cup of coffee, Flynn lounging beside him. He'd messaged his cousin to come here under the guise of wanting to discuss the terms of Bryce's engagement. Thankfully, his cousin hadn't needed much more than that before arriving.

Cormac shrugged, his gray T-shirt lightly coated in sweat, presumably from the scorching walk over here. "I thought you might share your father's outdated views that females should not be in the line of danger and balk at putting her at risk."

"Does anything I've ever done indicate I'd feel that way?"

"You're protective of your sister to a fault." Cormac frowned. "Did you *see* Daybright?"

"She appeared humanoid, cloaked in flame. I couldn't see anything, really."

"Good. I'm assuming you veiled yourself, too."

Only by pure dumb luck. "Yeah."

Cormac paced in front of the TV. "But she said nothing of Sofie?"

Ruhn hadn't even thought to ask. Guilt twisted in his gut. "No."

Cormac dragged his hands through his short blond hair. "And no updates on the Asteri's mech-suit prototype being sent along the Spine?"

"No. She only told me to tell you that safe passage is granted under the light of the waning moon."

Cormac sighed. Whatever that meant. But Declan asked as he emerged from the kitchen, cup of coffee in hand, "So what now? Ruhn waits for her to call with intel about this raid on the Spine?"

Cormac sneered at Declan. Avallen snob to the core. He said to Ruhn, "Remind me, cousin, why you felt the need to involve these two fools in our business?"

"Remind me," Ruhn countered, "why I'm working with someone who insults my brothers?"

Dec and Flynn smirked at Cormac, who seethed, but finally sighed. The Avallen Prince said, "To answer your question, Declan Emmet, yes: Ruhn will wait until Daybright contacts him with details on the Spine raid. Or until I have something for him to pass along, in which case he'll contact her again."

Flynn leaned back on the couch, propping his arms behind his head. "Sounds boring."

"Lives are at stake," Cormac gritted out. "This hit on the Spine, attaining that new mech-suit prototype before the Asteri can use it against us on the battlefields, will give us a fighting chance."

"Not to mention all the weapons you'll loot from the supply trains," Declan said darkly.

Cormac ignored his tone. "We don't do anything unless it's been approved by Command. So wait until you hear from me before you contact her again."

Fine. He could do that. Go about his life, pretending he wasn't a sort-of rebel. Only until he wanted out, Cormac had promised. And after that . . . he'd go back to what he'd been doing. To leading the Aux and hating his father yet dreading the day the male died. Until the next person who needed him for something came along.

Flynn grinned. "Bureaucracy at its finest."

Cormac scowled at the Fae lord, but stalked for the front door. "I need to head out."

"Hunting for Emile?" Ruhn asked. It was the middle of the morning—the kid would likely be lying low.

Cormac nodded. "Being a visiting prince allows me the cover of . . . sightseeing, as you call it here. And as a tourist, I've taken a keen interest in your Black Dock and its customs."

"Morbid," Declan said.

Ruhn blurted, "You can't think Emile's going to jump into one of the black boats in broad daylight."

"I'll look for him both by the light of the sun and the moon, until I find him. But I'd rather ask casual questions of the Reapers during the day."

"Are you insane?" Flynn said, laughing in disbelief.

Ruhn was inclined to agree. "Don't fuck with the Reapers, Cormac," he warned. "Even for Emile's sake."

Cormac patted a knife at his side. As if that would do anything to kill a creature that was already dead. "I know how to handle myself."

"I told you this would happen," Hunt snarled to Isaiah as their steps thundered along the hallway of Celestina's private residence atop the third tower of the Comitium. Celestina had called this meeting in her own home, rather than in the public office Micah had always used.

"We don't have the full scope yet," Isaiah shot back, adjusting his tie and the lapels of his gray suit.

Celestina had tried to ease the harsh modernism that Micah had favored: plush rugs now softened the white marble floors, angular statues had been replaced by lush-bodied effigies of Cthona, and vases of fluffy, vibrant flowers graced nearly every table and console they passed.

It was a nice contrast, Hunt might have thought. Had they not been called here for a reason.

He kept reminding himself of that reason, that this was a triarii meeting and not some one-on-one session. That he wasn't in Sandriel's castle of horrors, where a trip to her private chambers ended in blood and screaming.

He inhaled once, thinking of Bryce, of her scent, the warmth of her body against his. It settled the edge in him, even as something far more lethal opened an eye. What they were doing with Cormac, all this rebel shit they'd agreed to go through with last night . . .

Hunt glanced sidelong at Isaiah as the male knocked on the open double doors of Celestina's study. He could tell him. He needed someone like Isaiah, even-keeled and unflappable. Especially if Hel had a vested interest in the conflict. And Hunt himself.

He'd decided to ignore Apollion's commands. He had no interest in playing right into Hel's hands.

Celestina murmured her welcome, and Hunt braced himself as he followed Isaiah in.

Sunlight filled the glass-and-marble space, and all the hard-edged furniture had been replaced by lovely artisanal wood pieces, but Hunt only noted the two males sitting before the desk. Naomi leaned against the wall by the built-in bookcase to the right, face dark and lethal focus fixed upon the males.

Well, the one male. The reason they were here.

Pollux didn't turn as they entered, and Hunt aimed for the chair beside Baxian. Isaiah could sit next to Pollux. Isaiah threw him a *Thanks, asshole* look, but Hunt scanned Celestina's expression for clues.

Displeasure tightened the corners of her mouth, but her eyes were calm. Face full of contemplation. She wore pale purple robes, her curls spilling down her bare arms like a waterfall of night. She might have been a goddess, so still and lovely was she—might have been Cthona herself, voluptuous and full-bodied, were it not for the radiant wings that filled with the light of the sun shining through the windows behind her.

"I apologize for keeping my message brief," Celestina said to Hunt, Isaiah, and Naomi. "But I did not want the full account on the record."

Pollux and Baxian stared ahead at nothing. Or Hunt assumed that was the case, given that one of Baxian's eyes was swollen shut, and Pollux's face was one big magnificent bruise. That it remained this way after twelve hours suggested the initial damage had been impressive. He wished he could have seen it.

"We understand," Isaiah said in that take-no-shit commander's tone. "We share your disappointment."

Celestina sighed. "Perhaps I was naïve in believing that I could introduce two Pangerans to this city without a more thorough education in its ways. To hand over the responsibility"—she glanced at Naomi, then at Hunt—"was my mistake."

Hunt could have warned her about that. He kept his mouth shut.

"I would like to hear from you two, in your own words, about what happened," the Archangel ordered Pollux and Baxian. The tone was pleasant, yet her eyes glinted with hidden steel. "Pollux? Why don't you start?"

It was a thing of beauty, the way Pollux bristled in his seat, flowing golden hair still streaked with blood. The Hammer hated this. Absolutely fucking hated this, Hunt realized with no small amount of delight. Celestina's kindness, her fairness, her softness . . . Pollux was chafing even worse than Hunt. He'd served enthusiastically under Sandriel—had relished her cruelty and games. Perhaps sending him to Celestina had been a punishment that even the Asteri had not anticipated.

But Pollux growled, "I was having some fun at a tavern."

"Bar," Hunt drawled. "We call them bars here."

Pollux glared, but said, "The female was all over me. She *said* she wanted it."

"Wanted what?" Celestina's voice had taken on a decidedly icy tone.

"To fuck me." Pollux leaned back in his chair.

"She said no such thing," Baxian growled, wings shifting.

"And were you there every moment of the night?" Pollux demanded. "Though perhaps you were. You always pant after my scraps."

Hunt met Isaiah's wary stare. Some major tension had arisen between these two in the years since Hunt and Isaiah had left Sandriel's territory.

Baxian bared his teeth in a feral grin. "Here I was, thinking your *scraps* were panting after me. They always seem so . . . unsatisfied when they leave your room."

Pollux's power—standard malakim magic, but strong—rattled the pretty trinkets along the built-in bookcase.

Celestina cut in, "That is enough." Warm, summer-kissed power filled the room, smothering their own gifts. A feminine, unbreaking sort of magic—the kind that took no shit and would lay down the law if threatened. That was utterly unafraid of Pollux and the sort of male he was. She said to the Hammer, "Explain what happened."

"We went into the alley behind the *tavern*"—he threw that last word at Hunt—"and she was all over me, as I said. Then the bastard"—he threw that one at Baxian—"attacked me."

"And at what point did you not hear her say no?" Baxian challenged. "The first or the tenth time?"

Pollux snorted. "Some females say no when they want it. It's a game for them."

"You're fucking delusional," Naomi spat from across the room.

"Was I talking to you, hag?" Pollux snapped.

"*Enough.*" Celestina's power again filled the room, stifling any magic they might have summoned. She asked Baxian, "Why did you go into the alley after him?"

"Because I've spent decades with this asshole," Baxian seethed. "I knew what was about to happen. I wasn't going to let him go through with it."

"You did plenty of times under Sandriel," Isaiah said, voice low. "You and your whole triarii stood back."

"You don't know shit about what I did or didn't do," Baxian snapped at Isaiah, then said to Celestina, "Pollux deserved the beating I gave him."

The Hammer bared his teeth. Hunt could only watch in something like shock.

"That may be true," Celestina said, "but the fact remains that you two are in my triarii and your fight was filmed. And it's now online and being aired by every news station." Her gaze sharpened on Pollux. "I offered the female the chance to press charges—but she declined. I can only assume she is aware of what a circus it would be, and is frightened of the consequences for herself and her loved ones. I plan to fix that in this city. This territory. Even if it means making an example of one of my triarii."

Hunt's blood roiled, howling. Maybe this would be it. Maybe Pollux would finally get what was coming to him.

But Celestina's throat worked. "I received a call this morning, however, and have seen the wisdom in . . . granting you a second chance."

"*What?*" Hunt blurted.

Pollux bowed his head in a mockery of gratitude. "The Asteri are benevolent masters."

A muscle ticked in Celestina's smooth cheek. "They are indeed."

Naomi asked, "What about that one?" She gestured toward Baxian, who glared at her.

Celestina said, "I would like to grant you a second chance as well, Helhound."

"I *defended* that female," Baxian snapped.

"You did, and I commend you for that. But you did so in a public way that drew attention." Not only the city's attention. The Asteri's.

Again, Celestina's throat bobbed.

Isaiah asked a shade gently, "What can we do to help clean up this mess?"

She kept her stare on her wooden desk, thick lashes nearly grazing her high cheekbones. "It is already done. To give the media something else to focus on, the Asteri have blessed me with an opportunity. A gift."

Even Pollux dropped his simpering bullshit to angle his head. Hunt braced himself. This couldn't be good.

Celestina smiled, and Hunt saw it for the forced expression it was. "I am to mate Ephraim. With two Archangels now dead, there is a need to . . . replenish the ranks. On the Autumnal Equinox, we shall have our mating ceremony here in Lunathion."

A month away. The holiday known as Death's Day was a lively one, despite its name: it was a day of balance between the light and dark, when the veil between the living and dead was thinnest. Cthona began her preparations for her upcoming slumber then, but in Lunathion, raging costume parties were held along the Istros River at the various Sailing points. The biggest party of all surrounded the Black Dock, where lanterns were sent across the water to the Bone Quarter, along with offerings of food and drink. It had been a total shitshow every time Hunt had flown above the festivities. He could only imagine what Bryce would wear. Something as irreverent as possible, he imagined.

Celestina went on, "He shall stay here for a few weeks, then return to his territory. After that, he and I shall alternate visiting each other's territories." Until a baby was born, no doubt.

Naomi asked, "This is a good thing, right?"

Celestina again gave them that forced smile. "Ephraim has been my friend for many years and is a fair and wise male. I can think of no better partner."

Hunt sensed the lie. But such was the lot of Archangels: should the Asteri decide they were to breed, they obeyed.

"Congratulations?" Isaiah said, and Celestina laughed.

"Yes, I suppose those are in order," she said. But her amusement faded upon facing Pollux—the cause of this. He'd embarrassed this city, embarrassed her, and the Asteri had taken notice. And now she would pay. Not for what Pollux had tried to do to that female, but for getting caught by the public. The Asteri would take this opportunity to remind her exactly how much control they had over her. Her life. Her body.

Hunt didn't know why they bothered to care, why they'd gone so far out of their way to prove a point, but . . . nothing surprised him where they were concerned. Hunt's blood began to heat, his temper with it. Fucking monsters.

"With my mating announcement, we will have a media frenzy. The ceremony and party will be a high-profile event. Royals and dignitaries will attend, along with Ephraim's retinue."

Pollux straightened at that, delight in his bruised eyes. Celestina leveled that cold stare at him again. "I hope that with the Hind coming to visit, you will refrain from behaving as you did last night."

Baxian snorted. "Never stopped him before."

Pollux bared his teeth again, but Celestina went on, "Hunt, I'd like a word with you. The rest of you are dismissed." Hunt froze, but said nothing as the others filed out. Isaiah and Naomi gave him warning looks before shutting the doors behind them.

Alone with his Archangel, Hunt forced himself to breathe. To keep steady.

She was going to rip into him for not controlling Baxian last night. For not being there to stop him from brawling, even if he'd been given no order to watch over him at all hours of the day. The punishment was coming, he could sense it—

"The Autumn King informed me of Miss Quinlan's engagement to Crown Prince Cormac of Avallen," Celestina said.

Hunt blinked.

She continued, "I was hoping you could provide insight into the situation, considering that they will be expected to attend my mating celebration together."

He hadn't thought of that. That this would even be something to discuss. And after what they'd done last night . . . Could he stomach it, seeing her in the arms of another male, even if it was just pretend?

"It's an arranged marriage," Hunt said. "Their fathers insist."

"I'd assumed so." Celestina's mouth tightened. "I'm curious how *you* are feeling. You and Miss Quinlan are close."

"Yeah. We are." Hunt rubbed his neck. "We're dealing with it day by day," he admitted.

Celestina studied him, and Hunt made himself hold her gaze. Found nothing but . . . consideration and worry there. "You are exactly as I thought you'd be."

Hunt arched a brow.

Celestina's eyes fell to her hands, fingers twisting. "Shahar was my friend, you know. My dearest friend. We kept it quiet. The Asteri wouldn't have approved. Shahar was already defying them in small ways when she and I became close, and she thought they would see our friendship as an alliance and try to . . . stop it."

Hunt's heart stumbled. "She never said anything."

"Our correspondence over the years was covert. And when you rebelled . . . I had nothing to offer her. My legion in Nena is—was—an extension of the Asteri's forces."

"You could have offered your own power." Fuck, one more Archangel fighting with them that day—

"I have lived with the consequences of my choice since then," Celestina said.

"Why are you telling me this?"

"Because I heard the whispers that you did what I had longed to do since I learned about Shahar's death at Sandriel's hands. What I longed to do every time I had to sit in the Asteri's council room and listen to Sandriel spit on her sister's memory."

Holy shit.

"And I would like to apologize for my failure to extract you from the masters who held you in the years after Shahar fell."

"That's not your fault."

"I tried—but it wasn't enough."

Hunt's brows bunched. "What?"

She set her hands on the desk. Interlaced her fingers. "I amassed funds to . . . purchase you, but the Asteri denied me. I tried three times. I had to stop a century ago—it would have raised suspicions had I continued."

She had sympathized with the Fallen. With his cause. "All for Shahar?"

"I couldn't let someone she cared for rot away like that. I wish . . ." She blew out a breath. "I wish they'd let me buy you. So many things might be different now."

It could all be a lie. A lovely, clever lie to get him to trust her. If she'd sympathized with the Fallen, did she share the same sentiments about the Ophion rebels? If he told her all that was brewing in this city, would she damn them or help them?

"The doubt in your eyes shames me." For all the world, she sounded like she meant it.

"I just find it hard to believe that during all the shit I went through, someone was out there, trying to help me."

"I understand. But perhaps I might atone for my failures now. I'd like us to be . . . friends."

Hunt opened his mouth, then shut it. "Thank you." He meant it, he realized.

Celestina smiled, like she understood it, too. "I'm at your disposal should you need anything. Anything at all."

He weighed the kind expression on her face. Did she know about Ophion and Cormac and Sofie? She'd somehow learned about him killing Sandriel, so she clearly was able to attain secret information.

Hunt breathed deeply, calming himself as he said again, "Thank you." He rose from his chair. "Since we're being honest here . . . Sandriel's old triarii is poison. I don't know why Baxian is suddenly playing good guy, but I'm sorry I wasn't there to rein him in last night."

"I don't hold you accountable for that."

Something tight eased in Hunt's chest. He went on, "Okay, but the rest . . . They're dangerous people. Worse than the Princes of Hel."

She chuckled. "You compare them like you know from experience."

He did. But he hedged, "I hunted demons for years. I know a monster when I see one. So when the Harpy and the Hawk and the Hind come for the mating party . . . I'm begging you to be careful. To protect the people of this city. We might give Baxian shit about standing by while Pollux terrorized people, but . . . I had to stand by, too. I've seen what Pollux does, what he delights in. The Harpy is his female counterpart. The Hawk is secretive and dangerous. And the Hind . . ."

"I know very well what manner of threat Lidia Cervos poses."

Even Archangels feared the Hind. What she might learn. And Celestina, secret friend to Shahar, who still cared about her friend centuries later, who carried the guilt of not helping . . . "Whatever you need," Hunt said quietly, "anything you need to get through this mating ceremony, to deal with Sandriel's cabal, you let me know."

Perhaps the Asteri had redistributed Sandriel's triarii here not only to balance out the numbers, but to plant allies and spies. To report on Hunt—and Celestina.

She nodded solemnly. "Thank you, Hunt."

He strode for the door, tucking in his wings. He halted at the doorway. "You don't need to feel guilty, you know. About the shit that happened to me."

She angled her head. "Why?"

He gave her a half smile. "If I'd gone to you in Nena, I never would have come here. To Lunathion." His smile broadened as he walked out. "I never would have met Bryce."

And every horror, every nightmare . . . all of it had been worth it for her.

Hunt found Baxian waiting at the end of the hallway, the male's arms crossed, bruised face solemn. "How'd your special time go?" Baxian asked by way of greeting.

"What the fuck do you want?" Hunt strode toward the veranda

at the far end of the hall. He'd pay Bryce a lunchtime visit. Maybe they'd get naked. That sounded really fucking good.

"The old gang's getting back together in a few weeks. I assume you were warning Celestina about it."

"You're a bunch of sadistic psychos." Hunt stepped onto the empty veranda. The wind whipped at his hair, carrying the fresh scent of the Istros from across the city. Storm clouds gathered on the horizon, and lightning danced in his veins. "I'd hardly call you the *old gang*."

Baxian's mouth twitched upward, bruises stretching.

Hunt said, "I'm not buying whatever bullshit you're selling by beating the Hel out of Pollux."

"New city, new rules," Baxian said, black feathers rustling. "New boss, who doesn't seem to like Pollux all that much."

"So?" Hunt spread his wings.

"So I don't have to pretend anymore," Baxian said. He lifted his face to the darkening sky. "Storm's coming. Be careful up there."

"Thanks for your concern." Hunt flapped once, feet lifting.

"I'm not trying to fuck you over."

"You're trying to be a pain in my ass, then?"

Baxian snorted. "Yeah, I guess."

Hunt settled back to the ground. "What was that shit with you and Pollux—about his seconds?"

Baxian slid his hands into his pockets. "He's a jealous fucker. You know that."

Hunt could think of only one person Pollux had ever shown any preference for beyond Sandriel. "You have a thing for the Hind?"

Baxian barked a laugh. "Fuck no. Pollux is the only person insane enough to go near her. I wouldn't touch Lidia with a ten-foot pole."

Hunt studied the male who had been his enemy for so long he'd lost track of the years. Something had changed. Something big, and primal, and . . . "What the fuck went on with Sandriel after I left?"

Baxian smirked. "Who says it had anything to do with Sandriel?"

"Why can't anyone give me a direct answer these days?"

Baxian cocked a brow. Thunder growled its warning in the distance. "You tell me your secrets, Athalar, and I'll tell you mine."

Hunt flipped him off. He didn't bother saying goodbye before launching into the darkening sky.

But he couldn't shake the sense that Baxian continued to watch him. As if he'd left something vital hanging in the balance. It seemed only a matter of time before it returned to bite him in the ass.

23

Ithan kept a step back from the small crowd of mer emergency workers gathered around Captain Ketos—and the body. He'd scented death before they'd even approached the pristine stretch of the Istros an hour north of Lunathion, a pretty green spot amid the oaks of the small forest. They'd taken wave skimmers up the Blue, as this section of the river was nearly inaccessible by foot. He supposed he might have made the run easily in his wolf form, but after getting one sniff of the corpse from a mile downriver, he was glad not to be in that body.

"Selkie female," Tharion was saying to the small group assembled, wiping the sweat from his brow. Even in the shadow of the mighty oaks, the sun baked the forest into kindling.

Ithan swigged from his canteen. He should have worn shorts and sandals instead of the black jeans and boots of the Aux. He had no business wearing these clothes anyway.

Tharion went on, surveying the little heap by the river's edge. It had been found this morning by a passing otter. "Killed execution-style."

Death was nothing new. Ithan just wished he hadn't become so well acquainted with it that at age twenty-two, it was already something he barely batted an eye at. But that was the life of a wolf. Of a Holstrom.

Tharion pointed. "Gorsian bullet to the right thigh to keep her from shifting into her seal form, then a slow bleed-out from a slice to her left femoral artery. Repeated lacerations indicate the murderer reopened the thigh incision continuously to keep her bleeding until she died."

Cthona spare him. "Or until whoever it was got their answers," Ithan said.

The group—three of Tharion's people—turned his way. He'd been brought for one reason—to use his nose. Apparently, that hadn't included speaking.

"Or that," Tharion said, crossing his arms with a pointedness that said:

Keep it quiet; I have the same instinct you do about this.

At least, that was what Ithan thought it conveyed. He'd gotten pretty good at assessing others' expressions and tells thanks to his years on the sunball field.

Tharion said to the group, "Right. Continue documenting the scene, then let's see if we can find a name for her." People peeled away to follow his orders, and Tharion stepped aside to sniff the air.

A male voice spoke from Ithan's left. "Hey, you used to play sunball, right?" Ithan found a ruddy-faced mer in a blue BCIU windbreaker standing a few feet away, a walkie-talkie in hand.

Ithan grunted. "Yeah."

"For CCU—you were that Holstrom kid."

Were. Everything in his life was *were* these days. *You were Connor's brother. You were part of a pack. You were in the Aux. You were a sunball player. You were Bryce's friend. You were normal. You were happy.*

"One and only."

"Why'd you quit? You could be, like, MVP in the pros right now."

Ithan didn't smile, tried his best to appear disinterested. "Had other plans."

"Than playing sunball professionally?" The male gaped. As if a selkie's ravaged body didn't lie mere feet away.

Everyone was watching now. Ithan had grown up with eyes on him like that—had triumphed and failed spectacularly in front of thousands of people, day after day, for years. It didn't make it easier.

"Holstrom." Tharion's voice cut through the air, mercifully drawing him from the conversation. Ithan gave the male a nod and aimed for where the captain stood beside the river. Tharion murmured, "Smell anything?"

Ithan inhaled. Blood and rot and water and iron and—

Another sniff, taking him deeper, pulling back layers. Salt and water and seal. That was the selkie. Then— "There's a human scent here. On her." He pointed to the selkie left amid the leaves and bone-dry brush. "Two of them."

Tharion said nothing, idly twirling a ribbon of water between his fingers. The mer were similar to the water sprites in that regard—able to summon water from thin air.

Ithan began to pace through the clearing, careful of the tracks—noting and scenting the slight disturbances in the dirt and leaves and sticks.

He sniffed again, brain downloading and sorting all those scents.

"Wouldn't your wolf form be easier?" Tharion asked, leaning against a tree.

"No," Ithan lied, and kept moving. He couldn't bear to take that form, to feel that empty-souled wolf.

He sniffed a few more times, then stalked up to Tharion and said quietly, "There's a human female scent all over this scene. But the second scent—it's a human male. A little strange, but human." Exactly as Ithan would have described a part-thunderbird human. "It's only on the selkie. A little whiff."

"So what does that tell you?" Tharion asked with equal quiet, monitoring the others documenting the crime scene.

"My guess?"

"Yeah, tell me your gut impressions."

Ithan noted the mer around him. Their hearing might not be as keen as his, but . . . "I think we should be somewhere more secure."

Tharion made a *hmm* of contemplation. Then he called to the group of investigators, "Any further insights, kids?"

No one answered.

Tharion sighed. "All right. Let's get her bagged up and brought back to the lab. I want tests done as soon as possible, along with an ID."

The others broke apart, heading to the aquatic vehicles lined up along the Blue River's edge, tethered in place with their water magic. Leaving Ithan and Tharion with the body.

The mer male arched a brow. "I need to head to the Blue Court, but I'd like to hear your findings while they're fresh. Do you have time?"

"I got nothing but time," Ithan answered.

He wondered when having all that time would stop feeling like such a chore.

"So, let's hear it," Tharion said as he slumped into his office chair and turned on his computer.

Ithan Holstrom stood at the wall of glass, gazing out at the deep blue of the Istros, observing the fish and otters dart past. The wolf had said little while Tharion had brought him Beneath, though from his wide eyes, it was clear he'd never been here before.

Ithan said without turning, "Let's assume the players involved are the ones we think they are. I think the selkie found the kid, helped him on his way toward Lunathion. Not soon afterward, given how his scent is still on her clothes, the selkie was found and tortured by a human woman for intel on Emile's location. From what we know about her, my guess is Pippa Spetsos."

Tharion's mouth twisted to the side. "My techs said the kill was about a day old. That line up with your info?"

"Yeah, though probably less than a day. But the kid's scent on her clothes was older than that. Only by six hours or so."

"Why?" Tharion propped his chin on his hands.

"Because she couldn't have gone in the water—or changed her clothes, if the scent was still on her. As far as I know, selkies rarely go a day before shifting and swimming. The water would have washed the kid's scent from her."

Tharion considered, turning over the information in his mind. "We didn't pick up any tracks from the kid in the clearing, though."

"No," Ithan agreed, turning back to him. "Emile was never in that clearing. The selkie must have come there afterward."

Tharion peered at the map of Crescent City and its surrounding lands behind his desk. "That spot is between the boat I investigated and the city. If he linked up with the selkie somewhere around there, he is indeed moving toward Lunathion. And if that kill is less than a day old, he might have just gotten here."

"And Pippa Spetsos, if that's whose scent was on the female, could be here as well."

"Or one of her soldiers, I guess," Tharion admitted. "Either way, Lightfall is near. We need to be careful."

"Pippa is a human woman."

"She's a dangerous rebel, capable of killing Vanir thanks to those gorsian bullets. And a psychopath who delights in killing even the most innocent. We're not going near her without prep and thought." Hopefully they would find Emile first and not need to deal with Pippa at all.

Ithan snorted. "We can take her. My brother took down Philip Briggs."

"Something tells me Pippa might be worse than Briggs."

"Come on," Ithan said, scoffing.

Tharion didn't bother to keep the gravity from his face. "I like being alive. I'm not going to risk death because you've got an outsize view of your wolf skills."

"Fuck you."

Tharion shrugged. "My river, my rules, pup."

Thunder from far above echoed in the quiet halls, rattling even the thick glass.

"I can go after her on my own."

Tharion smirked. "Not while you're stuck down here."

Ithan sized him up. "Really? You'd trap me?"

"For your own safety, yeah. You know what Bryce would do to me if you wound up dead? I'd never get to fondle her underwear again."

Ithan gaped at him. Then burst out laughing. It was a rich sound, a little hoarse—like he hadn't done it in a while. "I'm surprised Athalar lets you live."

"You know what Bryce would do to Hunt if *I* wound up dead?" Tharion grinned. "My sweet Legs has my back."

"Why do you call her that?" Ithan asked cautiously.

Tharion shrugged again. "You really want me to answer that?"

"No."

Tharion smirked. "Anyway, the real question is whether Emile is headed toward the place Danika hinted at in her email."

Holstrom had already filled him in on the papers and news clippings he and Bryce had uncovered yesterday, but none had any link to a potential rendezvous location.

The door to Tharion's office opened, and one of his officers, Kendra, strode in. The blond sentinel stopped short upon seeing Ithan, hair swaying around her. She looked to Tharion, who nodded. She was free to speak around the wolf.

"Boss wants you in her quarters. She's, ah . . . in a mood."

Fuck. "I thought I heard thunder." Tharion jerked his chin at the door as Kendra left. "There's a lounge down this hall on the left. Feel free to watch TV, help yourself to snacks, whatever. I'll be back . . . soon. Then we can start sniffing around for the kid." And hopefully avoid Pippa Spetsos.

He used the walk to his queen's quarters to steady his nerves against whatever storm was brewing. It had to be bad, if it was raining Above during the dry summer months.

Bryce fanned her face in the summer heat, thanking Ogenas, Bringer of Storms, for the rain that was moments away from falling. Or whatever Vanir might be throwing a temper tantrum. Judging by how swiftly the storm had swept in to ruin the otherwise flawless blue sky, odds were on the latter.

"It's not *that* hot," Ruhn observed as they walked down the sidewalk toward the Aux training facility on the edge of the Old Square and Moonwood. The empty, cavernous chamber was usually used for large meetings, but he'd reserved it once a week at this hour for their standing training.

They'd have a newcomer today. At least, if Prince Cormac deigned to show up to begin her training, as he'd promised.

"I don't know how you're wearing a leather jacket," Bryce said, her sweaty thighs sticking together with each step.

"Gotta hide the weapons," Ruhn said, patting the holsters beneath the leather jacket. "Can't have the tourists getting skittish."

"You literally carry a sword."

"That has a different impact on people than a gun."

True. Randall had taught her that a long time ago. Swords could mean hope, resistance, strength. Guns meant death. They were to be respected, but only as weapons of killing, even in defense.

Bryce's phone rang, and she checked the caller ID before shutting off the ringer and sliding it into her pocket.

"Who's that?" Ruhn asked, glancing at her sidelong as thunder grumbled. People began clearing the streets, darting into shops and buildings to avoid the downpour. With the arid climate, summer storms were usually violent and swift, prone to flooding the streets.

"My mom," Bryce said. "I'll call her later." She fished out a postcard from her purse and waved it at Ruhn. "She's probably calling about this."

"A postcard?" On the front, it said *Greetings from Nidaros!* in a cheery font.

Bryce slid it back into her purse. "Yeah. It's a thing from when I was a kid. We'd get into a huge fight, and my mom would send me postcards as a weird kind of apology. Like, we might not be talking in person, but we'd start communicating again through postcards."

"But you were living in the same house?"

Bryce laughed again. "Yeah. She'd put them under my door and I'd put them under hers. We'd write about everything *but* the fight. We kept doing it when I went to CCU, and afterward." Bryce riffled through her bag and pulled out a blank postcard of an otter waving that said, *Keep It Fuzzy, Lunathion!* "I'm going to send her one later. Seems easier than a phone call."

He asked, "Are you going to tell her about . . . everything?"

"Are you crazy?"

"What about the engagement being a ruse? Surely that'd get her off your back."

"Why do you think I'm avoiding her calls?" Bryce asked. "She'll say I'm playing with fire. Literally, considering Cormac's power. There's no winning with her."

Ruhn chuckled. "You know, I would have really liked to have her as my stepmom."

Bryce snickered. "Weird. You're, like, twenty years older than her."

"Doesn't mean I don't need a mom to kick my ass every now and then." He said it with a grin, but . . . Ruhn's relationship with his own mother was strained. She wasn't cruel, merely out to lunch. Ruhn took care of her these days. He knew his father certainly wouldn't.

Bryce spoke before she had the chance to consider it. "I'm thinking of going home to Nidaros for the Winter Solstice. Hunt's coming. You want to join?" Now that she and Hunt had adjusted their timeline, Bryce supposed she could be a decent human being and go home for the holiday.

That is, if her mom forgave her for the engagement. And not telling her about it.

Rain splattered the pavement, but Ruhn stopped. His eyes filled with such hope and happiness that Bryce's chest hurt. But he said, "Bringing Hunt home, huh?"

She couldn't help her blush. "Yep."

"Big step, bringing home the boyfriend."

She waved him off, but cringed at the rain that now became a deluge. They still had five blocks to the training center. "Let's wait it out," she said, ducking under an empty restaurant's awning. The Istros lay a block away, close enough that Bryce could see the veils of rain lashing its surface. Even the mer weren't out in this.

Rain streamed off the awning, thick as a waterfall, joining the veritable river already flowing down to the gaping sewer entrance at the corner of the block. Ruhn said over the din, "You really want me to come home with you?"

"I wouldn't have asked if I didn't." Assuming they were still alive by December. If this rebellion shit hadn't killed them all.

Ruhn's tattooed throat bobbed. "Thanks. I normally spend it with Dec and his family, but . . . I don't think they'll mind if I skip this year."

She nodded, awkward silence setting in. They usually had the training to occupy them during any tense silences, but now, trapped by the rain . . . she kept quiet, waiting to see what Ruhn might say.

"Why won't you touch the Starsword?"

She twisted, gesturing to the black hilt of the blade peeking over his shoulder. "It's yours."

"It's yours, too."

"I've got Danika's sword. And you found it first. Doesn't seem fair of me to claim it."

"You're more Starborn than I am. You should have it."

"That's bullshit." She backed up a step. "I don't want it." She could have sworn the rain, the wind, paused. Seemed to listen. Even the temperature seemed to drop.

"Aidas said you've got the light of the true Starborn Queen. I'm just the heir to some rapist asshole."

"Does it matter? I like that you're the Chosen One."

"Why?"

"Because . . ." She hooked her hair behind her ears, then fiddled with the hem of her T-shirt. "I already have this star on my chest." She touched the scar gently. The hair on her arms rose as if in answer. "I don't need a fancy sword to add to it."

"But I do?"

"Honestly? I think you don't know how special you are, Ruhn."

His blue eyes flickered. "Thanks."

"I mean it." She grabbed his hand, and light flared from her chest. "The sword came to you first for a reason. When was the last time two Starborn royals lived peacefully side by side? There's that dumb prophecy that the Fae have: *When knife and sword are reunited, so shall our people be*. You have the Starsword. What if . . . I don't know. What if there's a knife out there for me? But beyond that, what's Urd playing at? Or is it Luna? What's the end goal?"

"You think the gods have something to do with all this?"

Again, the hair on her arms rose; the star on her chest dimmed and went dark. She turned to the rain-lashed street. "After this spring, I can't help but wonder if there *is* something out there. Guiding all this. If there's some game afoot that's . . . I don't know. Bigger than anything we can grasp."

"What do you mean?"

"Hel is another world. Another *planet.* Aidas said so—months ago, I mean. The demons worship different gods than we do, but what happens when the worlds overlap? When demons come here, do their gods come with them? And all of us, the Vanir . . . we all came from elsewhere. We were immigrants into Midgard. But what became of our home worlds? Our home gods? Do they still pay attention to us? Remember us?"

Ruhn rubbed his jaw. "This is some seriously sacrilegious shit for a lunchtime conversation. The postcards with your mom, I can handle. This? I need some coffee."

She shook her head and closed her eyes, unable to suppress the chill down her spine. "I just have this feeling." Ruhn said nothing, and she opened her eyes again.

Ruhn was gone.

A rotted, veilless Reaper, black cloak and robes clinging to its bony body, rain sluicing down its sagging, grayish face, was dragging her unconscious brother across the drenched street. Its acid-green eyes glowed as if lit by Helfire.

The rain must have covered the creature's approach. The hair on her arms had been raised but she'd chalked it up to their dangerous conversation. No one was on the street—was it because everyone had somehow sensed the Reaper?

With a roar, Bryce darted into the driving rain, but she was too late. The Reaper shoved Ruhn into the gaping sewer drain with too-long fingers that ended in cracked, jagged nails, and slithered in after him.

24

Ruhn drifted.

One breath, he'd been talking to Bryce about gods and fate and all that shit. The next, something cold and rotting had breathed in his ear and he'd found himself here in this black void, no up or down.

What the fuck had happened? Something had jumped him and *fuck*, Bryce—

Night.

The female voice flitted in from everywhere and nowhere.

Night, open your eyes.

He twisted toward the voice. *Daybright?*

Open your eyes. Wake up.

What happened? How did you find my mind? I don't have the crystal.

I have no idea what happened to you. Or how I found your mind. I simply felt . . . I don't know what I felt, but the bridge was suddenly there. I think you're in grave danger, wherever you are.

Her voice echoed from above, from below, from within his bones.

I don't know how to wake up.

Open your eyes.

No shit.

She barked, *Wake up! Now!*

Something familiar echoed in her voice—he couldn't place it.

And then she was there, burning flame, as if the link between their minds had solidified. Bright as a bonfire, her hair floated around her head. Like they were both underwater.

Get up! she roared, flames crackling.

Why do I know your voice?

I can assure you, you don't. And you are about to be dead *if you don't wake up.*

Your scent—

You can't smell me.

I can. I know it.

I have never met you, and you have never met me—

How can you know that, if you don't know who I am?

OPEN YOUR EYES!

There was blackness, and the bellow of pouring water. That was Bryce's first, pathetic assessment of the sewer as she plunged into the subterranean river rushing beneath the city.

She didn't let herself think of what swam or floated in the water as she splashed for the stone path running along its side, hauling herself up as she scanned for the Reaper. For Ruhn.

Nothing but dimness, the faint trickle of light from the sewer grates overhead. She peered inward, to the star in her chest. Inhaled sharply. And when she exhaled, light bloomed.

It cast the sewer in stark relief, silvering the stones, the brown water, the arched ceiling—

Well, she'd found her brother.

And five Reapers.

The Reapers floated over the sewer's river, black robes drifting. Ruhn, unconscious, dangled between two of them. The Starsword was still strapped to him. Either they were too stupid to disarm him, or they didn't want to touch it.

"What the fuck do you want?" Bryce stepped closer. Water poured from the grates above, the river rising swiftly.

"We bear a message," the Reapers intoned together. Like they were of one mind.

"Easier ways to send it than this," she spat, advancing another step.

"No further," they warned, and Ruhn dropped an inch for emphasis. Like they'd dump his unconscious ass into the water and let him drown.

One of the Reapers drifted closer to Ruhn as they caught him. The hilt of the Starsword brushed against its robes. It hissed, recoiling.

Okay, they definitely didn't want to touch the sword.

Yet that became the least of her worries as five more Reapers drifted out of the darkness behind her. She reached for the phone in her back pocket, but the Reapers holding Ruhn dropped him another inch. "None of that," they said, the sound echoing from all around.

Wake up, she willed Ruhn. *Wake the fuck up and rip these shitheads apart.*

"What do you want?" she asked again.

"The Prince of the Pit sent us."

Her blood chilled. "You don't serve him. I doubt your king would be happy about it."

"We bear his message nonetheless."

"Put Prince Ruhn down and we can talk."

"And have you use the star on us? We think not."

She pivoted, trying to keep them all in her sights. Ruhn might survive being dumped in the river, but there were limits. How long could a Vanir who'd made the Drop go without oxygen? Or would it be a torturous process of drowning, healing, and drowning again, until even their immortal strength was spent and they finally died?

She didn't want to find out.

"What's your message?" she demanded.

"Apollion, Prince of the Pit, is ready to strike."

Her blood iced over to hear the name spoken aloud. "He's going to launch a war?" Aidas had said something like that yesterday, but he'd indicated that the armies would be for *her*. She'd thought he meant to help in whatever insanity Hel had planned.

"The Prince of the Pit wants a worthy opponent this time. One who will not break so easily, as Prince Pelias did so long ago. He insists on facing *you*, Starborn, at your full power."

Bryce barked a laugh. "Tell him I was literally on my way to training before you half-lives interrupted me." But her bones quaked to say it, to think about who they represented. "Tell him you just knocked out my tutor."

"Train harder. Train better. He is waiting."

"Thanks for the pep talk."

"Your disrespect is not appreciated."

"Yeah, well, your kidnapping my brother is definitely not appreciated."

They seethed with ire and Bryce cringed. "The Prince of the Pit already hunts through the Bone Quarter's mists to find the other one who might be his worthy opponent . . . or his greatest weapon."

Bryce opened her mouth, but shut it before she could blurt *Emile?* But *fuck*—Apollion was hunting for the kid, too? Was the Bone Quarter what Danika had meant after all? Her mind raced, plan after plan spreading out, then she said, "I'm surprised the Under-King lets Apollion wander around his territory unchecked."

"Even the caretakers of the dead bow to the Prince of the Pit."

Bryce's heart sank. Emile *was* in the Bone Quarter. Or at least Apollion thought so. What the fuck had Danika been thinking, telling Sofie it was safe there?

Before Bryce could ask more, the Reapers said as one, "You sold your soul away, Bryce Quinlan. When it is your time, we shall come to rip it to shreds."

"It's a date." She had to find some way to grab Ruhn, to be faster, smarter than them—

"Perhaps we shall have a taste of you now." They surged forward.

Bryce flared her light, falling against the curved wall of the tunnel. Water lapped over the edge of the walkway, spilling toward her neon-pink sneakers.

The Reapers exploded back, but despite their threats, kept Ruhn between them. So Bryce rallied that power inside her, let it crest in a blink, and then—

Another blast. Not from her, but somewhere else. A blast of pure night.

One moment a Reaper stood close to her. Then it was gone. Vanished into nothing. The others screeched, but—

Bryce shouted as Cormac appeared out of nothing, hovering over the river, arms around another Reaper—and vanished once more.

Again, he appeared. Again, he took another Reaper with him and vanished.

What was already dead could not be killed. But they could be . . . removed. Or whatever the fuck he was doing.

Cormac appeared again, blond hair shining, and yelled, "*USE THE FUCKING LIGHT!*"

She caught the direction of his stare: Ruhn. The Reapers who still held him aloft.

Bryce punched out her power, flaring bright as a supernova. The Reapers screamed and made good on their threat, hurling Ruhn toward the raging water—

Cormac caught Ruhn before he hit the frothing surface. Vanished again.

The Reapers whirled, screeching and hissing. Bryce flared her light anew, and they scattered into the darkest shadows.

Then Cormac returned, and tossed something to her—the Starsword. He must have taken it from Ruhn. Bryce didn't stop to think as she unsheathed it. Starlight erupted from the black blade. Like its metal had been kindled with iridescent fire.

A Reaper lunged, and Bryce swept the sword up, a blind, unwieldy block that she knew would have horrified Randall.

But blade met cloth and rotting flesh and ancient bone. And for the first time, perhaps the only time in that world, a Reaper bled.

It screamed, the sound as piercing as a hawk's cry. The others keened in horror and rage.

The Starsword sang with light, her power flowing into it. Activating it. And nothing had ever felt so right, so easy, as plunging the blade into the bony chest of the wounded Reaper. It arced, bellowing, black blood spurting from its withered lips.

The others screamed then. So loud she thought the sewer might come down, so loud she nearly dropped the blade to cover her ears.

The Reapers surged, but Cormac appeared before her in a plume of shadows. He grabbed her around the middle, nearly tackling her, and they were gone.

Wind roared and the world spun out from beneath her, but—

They landed inside the Aux training center. Ruhn was coughing on the floor beside her, the polished pine scrubbed clean except where the three of them dripped sewer water.

"You can fucking *teleport*?" Bryce gasped out, twisting to where Cormac stood.

But Cormac's gaze was on the Starsword, his face ashen. Bryce peered at the blade she clenched in a white-knuckled grip. As if her hand refused to let go.

With shaking fingers, she put it back into its sheath. Dimmed its light. But the Starsword still sang, and Bryce had no idea what to make of it.

Of the blade that had slain that which was unkillable.

PART II

THE ABYSS

25

Tharion warily watched the two sobeks lounging at his queen's feet, their scaly, powerful bodies draped over the dais steps. With their shut eyes, only the bubbles drifting from their long snouts revealed they lived—and were capable of snapping his arm off in one swift bite.

The River Queen's throne had been carved into a towering mountain of river corals rising from the rocky floor. Lunathion lay close enough to the coast that the water in this part of the Istros had plenty of salt to support the vibrant corals, as well as the bouquets of anemones, waving lace sea fans, and the occasional rainbow ribbons of iris eels all adorning the mount around and above her. He had a feeling her magic had also created a good chunk of it.

Tail pumping against the strong current that flowed past, Tharion bowed his head. "Your Majesty." At this point, the effort against the current was second nature, but he knew she'd selected this location for her throne so that any person appearing before her would be a bit off-kilter—and perhaps less guarded as a result. "You summoned me?"

"It has come to my attention," his queen said, her dark hair drifting above her, "that you asked my daughter on a date."

Tharion focused on keeping his tail moving, holding him in place. "Yes. I thought she'd enjoy it."

"You asked her on a date *Above*. Above!"

Tharion lifted his chin, hands clasped behind his back. A subservient, vulnerable position that he knew his queen preferred, exposing the entirety of his chest to her. His heart lay in range of the jagged sea-glass knife resting on the arm of her throne, or the beasts drowsing at her feet. She had the power to destroy him in an instant, but he knew she liked the feel of the kill.

He'd never understood it, until he'd found his sister's murderer and opted to tear the panther shifter apart with his bare hands.

"I only meant to please her," Tharion said.

But the River Queen's fingers dug into the carved arms of her throne. "You know how overwhelmed she becomes. She is too fragile for such things."

Tharion sucked in a deep breath through his gills. Exhaled it before saying, "She handled herself well at the Summit." A half-lie. She'd done absolutely nothing of value at the Summit, but at least she hadn't been cowering the whole time.

Anemones shrank into themselves, a swift warning of his queen's ire before she said, "That was in an organized, guarded place. Lunathion is a wild forest of distraction and pleasure. It will devour her whole." The iris eels sensed her tone and darted into the cracks and crevices around the throne.

"I apologize for any distress the suggestion caused you or her." He didn't dare so much as curl his fingers into a fist.

The queen studied him with the concentration of one of the sobeks at her feet, when the beasts were poised to strike. "What of your progress with the Renast boy?"

"I have good reason to believe he's just arrived in this city. I have my people looking for him." They hadn't found any new bodies today—for better or worse. He could only pray it didn't mean Pippa Spetsos had gotten her hands on the boy.

"I want that boy at the Blue Court the moment he's found."

Pippa or the River Queen. Above or Beneath. Emile Renast's options were limited.

Once the kid was down here, he wouldn't get back Above unless the River Queen wished it. Or the Asteri dispatched one of their elite aquatic units to drag him out. But that would mean they'd learned of the River Queen's betrayal.

But Tharion only nodded. As he had always done. As he would always do. "We'll apprehend Emile soon."

"Before Ophion."

"Yes." He didn't dare ask why she was bothering with any of it. From the moment she'd heard the rumors about the boy who could bring down those Omegas with his power-draining magic, she'd wanted Emile. She didn't share her reasons. She never did.

"And before any other of the River Courts."

Tharion lifted his head at that. "You think they know about Emile, too?"

"The currents whispered to me about it. I don't see why my sisters wouldn't hear similar murmurings from the water."

The queens of Valbara's four great rivers, the Istros, the Melanthos, the Niveus, and the Rubellus—the Blue, the Black, the White, and the Red, respectively—had long been rivals: all mighty and gifted with magic. All vain and ancient and bored.

While Tharion might not be privy to his queen's most intimate plans, he could only assume she wanted the boy for the same reason Pippa Spetsos did: to use him as a weapon. One that could be used to get the queens of the Black, White, and Red Courts to yield. With the boy in her thrall, she could potentially use him to siphon their powers, to turn all that elemental energy against them and expand her influence.

But if they knew of Emile as well, then did they already scheme, thinking to take the Blue Court? And if the Queen of the Red Court wished to overthrow his queen, to use Emile's gifts to drain her of power . . . would he fight it?

Years ago, he would have said Hel yes.

But now . . .

Tharion lifted his face toward the surface. That distant, beckoning ribbon of light.

He found her studying him again. As if she could hear every

thought in his mind. The sobek at her left cracked open an eye, revealing a slitted pupil amid green-marbled citrine.

His queen asked, "Are things so wonderful Above that you resent your time Beneath?"

Tharion kept his face neutral, kept swishing his fins with an idle grace. "Can't both realms be wonderful?"

The second sobek opened an eye as well. Would they be opening their jaws next?

They ate anything and everything. Fresh meat, trash, and, perhaps most important, the bodies of the shameful dead. Having one's black boat overturned on its way to the Bone Quarter was the deepest sort of humiliation and judgment: a soul deemed unworthy of entering the holy resting place, its corpse given over to the river beasts to devour.

But Tharion kept his hands clasped behind him, kept his chest exposed, ready to be shredded apart. Let her see his utter subservience to her power.

His queen only said, "Keep searching for the boy. Report as soon as you hear anything new."

He bowed his head. "Of course." He swished his fin, readying to swim off the moment she gave the dismissal.

But the River Queen said, "And Tharion?"

He couldn't stop his swallow at the smooth, casual tone. "Yes, my queen?"

Her full lips curved into a smile. So much like the beasts at her feet. "Before you invite my daughter on a date Above again, I think you should witness firsthand the disrespect those Above show the citizens of the Beneath."

The River Queen picked her punishments well. Tharion would give her that.

Swimming along the Old Square's section of the quay an hour later, he kept his head down as he speared trash.

He was her Captain of Intelligence. How many of his people had already noticed him here or heard about this? He stabbed a discarded, half-decayed pizza box. It fell into three pieces before he could tuck it into the giant bag drifting behind him on the current.

The River Queen wanted Emile badly, Pippa Spetsos was leaving a trail of bodies in her hunt for the kid, and yet *this* was his queen's priority for him?

Water splashed twenty feet above, and Tharion lifted his head to find an empty beer bottle filling—and then drifting down. Through the surface, he could just make out a blond female laughing at him.

She'd tried to fucking *hit* him with that bottle. Tharion rallied his magic, smiling to himself as a plume of water showered the female, earning a host of shrieks and growls from those around her.

Ten more bottles came flying down at him.

Tharion sighed, bubbles flowing from his lips. Captain Whatever, indeed.

The River Queen fancied herself a benevolent ruler who wanted the best for her people, yet she treated her subjects as harshly as any Asteri. Tharion wended between the mussel-crusted pillars of a dock, various crabs and bottom-scavengers watching him from the shadows.

Something had to change. In this world, in the hierarchies. Not only in the way Ophion wanted, but . . . this imbalance of power across all Houses.

Tharion pried a bike tire—for fuck's sake—from between two rocks, muscles groaning. A giant blue crab scuttled over, waving its claws in reprimand. *Mine!* it seemed to shout. Tharion backed off, gesturing to the trash. *Have at it*, he conveyed with a wave of his hand, and with a powerful thrust of his tail, swam farther along the quay.

The glowing firstlights cast ripples on the surface. It was like swimming through gold.

Something had to change. For him, at least.

Ruhn laid the Starsword on his father's desk as the Autumn King stalked through the study doors.

The top buttons of his father's black shirt were undone, his ordinarily smooth red hair a bit out of place. Like someone had been running their hands through it. Ruhn shuddered.

His father eyed the sword. "What is so important that you interrupted my afternoon meeting?"

"Is that what you're calling it these days?"

His father threw him an admonishing glance as he slid into his desk chair, surveying the bare Starsword. "You smell like trash."

"Thanks. It's a new cologne I'm trying out." Considering the insanity of the last hour, it was a miracle he could even joke right then.

Agent Daybright had been in his mind, screaming at him to wake up. That was all he'd known before he'd started puking water and the gods knew what else—*he* certainly didn't want to know—on the Aux training center floor.

Cormac had left by the time Ruhn mastered himself, apparently wanting to quickly search the area for any hint of Emile or Sofie. Bryce had still been in shock when Ruhn managed to ask what the fuck had happened.

But she'd told him enough—then kicked the Starsword toward him in the empty training hall and left. Which was when he'd rushed over here.

Flame sparked at his father's fingers—the first warning of his impatience. So Ruhn asked, "What's the lore behind this sword?"

His father arched a brow. "You've been its bearer for decades. Now you want to know its history?"

Ruhn shrugged. His head still pounded from the blow the Reapers had given him; his stomach churned like he'd been drinking all night. "Does it have any special powers? Weird gifts?"

The Autumn King swept a cold look over Ruhn, from his waterlogged boots to his half-shaved head, the longer hair scraggly thanks to the sewer trip. "Something has happened."

"Some Reapers tried to jump me, and the sword . . . reacted."

A light way of putting it. Had Bryce stayed away from the sword all these years because she somehow sensed that in her hand, it would unleash horrors?

He didn't want to know what his father would do with the truth.

A sword that could kill the unkillable. How many rulers in Midgard would scheme and murder to attain it? Starting with his father and ending with the Asteri.

Maybe they'd get lucky and the information would be contained to the Reapers. But the Under-King . . .

His father stilled. "How did the sword react?"

"Shouldn't a father ask if his son is all right? And why the Reapers attacked?"

"You appear unharmed. And I assume you did something to offend them."

"Thanks for your vote of confidence."

"Did you?"

"No."

"How did the sword react in the presence of the Reapers?"

"It glowed. They ran from it." It was only a half-lie. "Any idea why?"

"They are already dead. Blades hold no threat to them."

"Yeah, well . . . they freaked."

His father reached for the black blade but halted, remembering himself. It wasn't his blade to touch.

Ruhn reined in his smirk of satisfaction. But his father watched the various globes and solar system models across his office for a long moment.

Ruhn spied their own solar system in the center of it all. Seven planets around a massive star. Seven Asteri—technically six now—to rule Midgard. Seven Princes of Hel to challenge them.

Seven Gates in this city through which Hel had tried to invade this spring.

Seven and seven and seven and seven—always that holy number. Always—

"It's an ancient sword," the Autumn King said at last, drawing Ruhn from his wandering thoughts, "from another world. Made from the metal of a fallen star—a meteorite. This sword exists beyond our planet's laws. Perhaps the Reapers sensed that and shied away."

The Reapers had learned precisely how outside the planet's laws the sword was. It could fucking *kill* them.

Ruhn opened his mouth, but his father sniffed him again. Frowned. "And when were you going to tell me your sister was involved in this incident? She's even more reckless than you."

Ruhn stifled the spike of anger in his gut. "Only fit for breeding, right?"

"She should consider herself lucky I believe her valuable enough for that."

"You should consider yourself lucky that she didn't come in here to kick your ass for the betrothal to Cormac."

His father stalked to the elegant wood liquor cabinet behind his desk and pulled out a crystal decanter of what looked and smelled like whiskey. "Oh, I've been waiting for days now." He poured himself a glass, not bothering to offer Ruhn any, and knocked it back. "I suppose you convinced her not to."

"She decided all on her own that you weren't worth the effort."

His father's eyes simmered as he set the glass and decanter on the edge of his desk. "If that sword is acting up," the Autumn King said, ignoring his barb, "I'd suggest keeping it far from your sister."

Too late. "I offered it to her already. She didn't want it. I don't think she's interested in your politics."

But she had run into a sewer teeming with Reapers after him. Ruhn's heart squeezed tight.

His father poured himself another glass of whiskey. The only sign that something about this conversation rattled him. But the Autumn King's voice was bland as he said, "In ancient times, Starborn rivals would slit each other's throats. Even those of the children. She is now more powerful than you and I are, as you like to remind me."

Ruhn resisted the urge to ask whether that had played any part in his father's slaying of the last Starborn heir. "Are you telling me to kill Bryce?"

His father sipped from the whiskey this time before replying, "If you had any backbone, you would have done it the moment you learned she was Starborn. Now what are you?" Another sip before he said mildly, "A second-rate prince who only possesses the sword because she allows you to have it."

"Pitting us against each other won't work." But those words—*second-rate prince*—those gouged something deep in him. "Bryce and I are good."

The Autumn King drained the glass. "Power attracts power. It is her fate to be tied to a powerful male to match her own strength. I would rather not learn what comes of her union with the Umbra Mortis."

"So you betrothed her to Cormac to avoid that?"

"To consolidate that power for the Fae."

Ruhn slowly picked up the Starsword. Refused to meet his father's stare while he sheathed it down his back. "So this is what being king is all about? That old shit about keeping friends close and enemies closer?"

"It remains to be seen whether your sister is an enemy to the Fae."

"I think the burden of that's on you. Overstepping your authority doesn't help."

His father returned the crystal decanter to the cabinet. "I am a King of the Fae. My word is law. I cannot overstep my authority—it has no limits."

"Maybe it should." The words were out before Ruhn could think.

His father went still in a way that always promised pain. "And who will impose them?"

"The Governor."

"That doe-eyed angel?" A mirthless laugh. "The Asteri knew what they were doing in appointing a lamb to rule a city of predators."

"Maybe, but I bet the Asteri would agree that there are limits to your power."

"Why don't you ask them, then, Prince?" He smiled slowly, cruelly. "Maybe they'll make you king instead."

Ruhn knew his answer would mean his life or death. So he shrugged again, nonchalant as always, and aimed for the door. "Maybe they'll find a way to make you live forever. I sure as fuck have no interest in the job."

He didn't dare to look back before he left.

26

Bryce leaned against the alley side of a brick building bordering the Black Dock, arms crossed and face stony. Hunt, gods bless him, stood at her side, mirroring her position. He'd come right over the moment she'd called him, sensing that her eerily calm voice meant something big had gone down.

She'd only managed to say something vague about Reapers before they'd found Cormac here, prowling for any hint of Emile.

Cormac lounged against the wall across the alley, focus on the quay beyond. Not even the vendors selling touristy crap came here. "Well?" the Avallen Prince asked, not taking his attention from the Black Dock.

"You can teleport," Bryce said, voice low. *That* made Hunt's eyes widen. He kept himself contained, though, solid and still as a statue, wings tucked in—but brimming with power. One blink, and Hunt would unleash lightning on the prince.

"What of it?" Cormac asked with no small hint of haughtiness.

"What did you do to the Reapers you teleported out?"

"Put them about half a mile up in the sky." The Avallen Prince smiled darkly. "They weren't happy."

Hunt's brows rose. But Bryce asked, "You can go that far? It's that precise?"

"I need to know the spot. If it's a trickier location—indoors, or a specific room—I need exact coordinates," Cormac said. "My accuracy is within two feet."

Well, that explained how he'd shown up at Ruhn's house party. Dec's tech had picked up Cormac teleporting around the house's perimeter to calculate where he wanted to appear to make his grand entrance. Once he'd had them, he'd simply walked right out of a shadow in the doorway.

Hunt pointed to a dumpster halfway down the alley. "Teleport there."

Cormac bowed mockingly. "Left side or right side?"

Hunt leveled a cool stare at him. "Left," he challenged. Bryce suppressed a smile.

But Cormac bowed at the waist again—and vanished.

Within a blink, he reappeared where Hunt had indicated.

"Well, fuck," Hunt muttered, rubbing the back of his neck. Then, Cormac reappeared before them, right where he'd been standing.

Bryce pushed off the wall. "How the Hel do you do that?"

Cormac slicked back his blond hair. "You have to picture where you want to go. Then simply allow yourself to take that step. As if you're folding two points on a piece of paper so that the two points can meet."

"Like a wormhole," Hunt mused, wings rustling.

Cormac waved a dismissive hand. "Wormhole, teleportation, yes. Whatever you want to call it."

Bryce blew out an impressed breath. But it didn't explain—"How'd you know where to find me and Ruhn?"

"I was on my way to meet you, remember?" Cormac rolled his eyes, as if she should have figured it out by now. Asshole. "I saw you run into the sewer, and I did some mental calculations for the jump. Thankfully, they were right."

Hunt let out an approving grunt, but said nothing.

So Bryce said, "You're going to teach me how to do that. Teleport."

Hunt whipped his head to her. But Cormac simply nodded. "If it's within your wheelhouse, I will."

Hunt blurted, "I'm sorry, but Fae can just *do* this shit?"

"*I* can do this shit," Cormac countered. "If Bryce has as much Starborn ability as she seems to, she might also be able to do this shit."

"Why?"

"Because I'm the Super Powerful and Special Magic Starborn Princess," Bryce answered, waggling her eyebrows.

Cormac said, "You should treat your title and gifts with the reverence they are due."

"You sound like a Reaper," she said, and leaned against Hunt. He tucked her into his side. Her clothes were still soaked. And smelled atrocious.

But Hunt didn't so much as sniff as he asked Cormac, "Where did you inherit the ability from?"

Cormac squared his shoulders, every inch the proud prince as he said, "It was once a gift of the Starborn. It was the reason I became so . . . focused on attaining the Starsword. I thought my ability to teleport meant that the bloodline had resurfaced in me, as I've never met anyone else who can do it." His eyes guttered as he added, "As you know, I was wrong. Some Starborn blood, apparently, but not enough to be worthy of the blade."

Bryce wasn't going to touch that one. So she retied her wet hair into a tight bun atop her head. "What are the odds that I have the gift, too?"

Cormac gave her a slashing smile. "Only one way to find out."

Bryce's eyes glowed with the challenge. "It would be handy."

Hunt murmured, his voice awed, "It would make you unstoppable."

Bryce winked at Hunt. "Hel yeah, it would. Especially if those Reapers weren't full of shit about the Prince of the Pit sending them to challenge me to some epic battlefield duel. Worthy opponent, my ass."

"You don't believe the Prince of the Pit sent them?" Cormac asked.

"I don't know what I believe," Bryce admitted. "But we need to confirm where those Reapers came from—who sent them—before we make any moves."

"Fair enough," Hunt said.

Bryce went on, "Beyond that, this is twice now that we've gotten warnings about Hel's armies being ready. Apollion's a little heavy-handed for my tastes, but I guess he *really* wants to get the point across. And wants me leveled up by the time all Hel breaks loose. Literally, I guess."

Bryce knew there was no fucking way she'd ever stand against the Star-Eater and live, not if she didn't expand her understanding of her power. Apollion had killed a fucking Asteri, for gods' sakes. He'd obliterate her.

She said to Cormac, "Tomorrow night. You. Me. Training center. We'll try out this teleporting thing."

"Fine," the prince said.

Bryce picked lingering dirt from beneath her nails and sighed. "I could have lived without Hel getting mixed up in this. Without Apollion apparently wanting in on Sofie's and Emile's powers."

"Their powers," Cormac said, face thunderous, "are a gift and a curse. I'm not surprised at all that so many people want them."

Hunt frowned. "And you really think you're going to find Emile just hanging around here?"

The prince glowered at the angel. "I don't see you combing the docks for him."

"No need," Hunt drawled. "We're going to search for him without lifting a finger."

Cormac sneered, "Using your lightning to survey the city?"

Hunt didn't fall for the taunt. "No. Using Declan Emmet."

Leaving the males to their posturing, Bryce pulled out her phone and dialed. Jesiba answered on the second ring. "What?"

Bryce smiled. Hunt half turned toward her at the sound of the sorceress's voice. "Got any Death Marks lying around?"

Hunt hissed, "You can't be serious."

Bryce ignored him as Jesiba answered, "I might. Plan on taking a trip, Quinlan?"

"I hear the Bone Quarter's gorgeous this time of year."

Jesiba chuckled, a rolling, sultry sound. "You do amuse me every now and then." Pause. "You have to pay for this one, you know."

"Send the bill to my brother." Ruhn would have a conniption, but he could deal.

Another soft chuckle. "I only have two. And it'll take until tomorrow morning for them to reach you."

"Fine. Thanks."

The sorceress said a shade gently, "You won't find any traces of Danika left in the Bone Quarter, you know."

Bryce tensed. "What does that have to do with anything?"

"I thought you were finally going to start asking questions about her."

Bryce clenched the phone hard enough for the plastic to groan. "What sort of questions?" What the fuck did Jesiba know?

A low laugh. "Why don't you start by wondering why she was always poking around the gallery?"

"To see me," Bryce said through her teeth.

"Sure," Jesiba said, and hung up.

Bryce swallowed hard and pocketed her phone.

Hunt was slowly shaking his head. "We're not going to the Bone Quarter."

"I agree," Cormac grumbled.

"You're not going at all," she said sweetly to Cormac. "We'll only have two fares, and Athalar is my plus-one." The prince bristled, but Bryce turned to Hunt. "When the coins arrive tomorrow, I want to be ready—have as much information as possible about where those Reapers came from."

Hunt folded his wings behind him, feathers rustling. "Why?"

"So the Under-King and I can have an informed heart-to-heart."

"What was that shit Jesiba said about Danika?" Hunt asked warily.

Bryce's mouth hardened into a thin line. Jesiba did and said nothing without reason. And while she knew she'd never get answers out of her old boss, at least this nudge was something to go on. "Turns out we're going to have to ask Declan for an additional favor."

* * *

That night, still reeling from the events of the day, Ruhn flipped through the channels on the TV until he found the sunball game, then set down the remote and swigged from his beer.

On the other end of the sectional couch in Bryce's apartment, Ithan Holstrom sat hunched over a laptop, Declan beside him with a laptop of his own. Bryce and Hunt stood behind the two, staring over their shoulders, the latter's face stormy.

Ruhn had told none of them, especially Bryce, about the conversation with his father.

Ithan typed away, then said, "I'm super rusty at this."

Dec said without breaking his attention from the computer, "If you took Kirfner's Intro to Systems and Matrices, you'll be fine."

Ruhn often forgot that Dec was friendly with people other than him and Flynn. While none of them had attended college, Dec had struck up a years-long friendship with the ornery CCU computer science professor, often consulting the satyr on some of his hacking ventures.

"He gave me a B minus in that class," Ithan muttered.

"From what he tells me, that's practically an A plus," Declan said.

"Okay, okay," Bryce said, "any idea how long this is going to take?"

Declan threw her an exasperated look. "You're asking us to do two things at once, and neither is easy, so . . . a while?"

She scowled. "How many cameras are even at the Black Dock?"

"A lot," Declan said, going back to his computer. He glanced to Holstrom's laptop. "Click that." He pointed to a mark on the screen that Ruhn couldn't see. "Now type this code in to identify the footage featuring Reapers."

How Dec managed to direct Ithan to comb through the footage around the Black Dock from earlier today while *also* creating a program to search through years of video footage of Danika at the gallery was beyond Ruhn.

"It's insane that you made this," Ithan said with no small bit of admiration.

"All in a day's work," Dec replied, typing away. Pulling any footage from the gallery featuring Danika could take days, he'd said.

But at least the footage from the Black Dock would only take minutes.

Ruhn carefully asked Bryce, "You sure you trust Jesiba enough to follow this lead? Or at all?"

"Jesiba literally has a collection of books that could get her killed," Bryce said tartly. "I trust that she knows how to stay out of . . . dangerous entanglements. And wouldn't shove me into one, either."

"Why not tell you to look at the footage during the investigation this spring?" Hunt asked.

"I don't know. But Jesiba must have had a good reason."

"She scares me," Ithan said, gaze fixed on the computer.

"She'll be happy to hear that," Bryce said, but her face was tight.

What's up? Ruhn asked her mind-to-mind.

Bryce frowned. *You want the honest answer?*

Yeah.

She tucked a strand of hair behind an ear. *I don't know how much more of this "Surprise! Danika had a big secret!" stuff I can take. It feels like . . . I don't even know. It feels like I never really knew her.*

She loved you, Bryce. That's not in doubt.

Yeah, I know. But did Danika know about the Parthos books—or the other contraband tomes—in the gallery? Jesiba made it sound like she did. Like she took a special interest in them.

You guys never talked about it?

Never. But Jesiba was always monitoring those cameras, so . . . maybe she saw something. Danika was down there without me plenty of times. Though Lehabah was usually there, too.

Ruhn noted the pain that filled his sister's face at the fire sprite's name.

We'll figure it out, Ruhn offered, and Bryce gave him a thankful smile in return.

"Don't forget to keep an eye out for Emile around the docks," Bryce said to Ithan. Cormac had turned down the invitation to join them here—he'd said he wanted to continue hunting for Emile on the ground.

"I already added it to the program," Declan said. "It'll flag any Reaper or any person whose facial features and build match the kid's." Dec had managed to pull a still from the security footage in the town of Servast the night Emile and Sofie had separated.

Ruhn again considered his sister, who was peering over Declan's shoulder with an intensity he recognized. She wouldn't let go of any of this.

Would she be able to teleport? She'd told him that Cormac had agreed to try to teach her. And wouldn't that be something for the Autumn King to chew on—Bryce plus teleporting plus Starborn power plus Starsword with crazy killing abilities plus Bryce magically outranking their father equaled . . .

Ruhn kept his face neutral, tucking away thoughts of what a leveled-up Bryce might mean for the Fae.

Ithan finished typing in the code, and said without looking up, "Hilene is going to win this one."

Ruhn checked the sunball game just beginning its first period. "I thought Ionia was favored."

Ithan stretched out his long legs, propping his bare feet on a cushioned stool Bryce had dragged over from the windows to be a temporary replacement for the coffee table. "Jason Regez has been off the last two games. I played with him at CCU—I can tell when he starts to get in a funk. He'll fuck it up for Ionia."

Ruhn eyed Ithan. A few years off the sunball field hadn't gotten rid of the muscles on the male. He'd somehow gotten even bigger since then.

"I hate Ionia anyway," Dec said. "They're all swaggering assholes."

"Pretty much." Ithan typed in the next line of code that Declan fed him.

Bryce yawned audibly. "Can't we watch *Veiled Love*?"

"No," everyone answered.

Bryce elbowed Hunt. "I thought we were a team."

Hunt snorted. "Sunball always trumps reality shows."

"Traitor."

Ithan snickered. "I remember a time when you knew all the players on the CCU team and their stats, Bryce."

"If you think that was because I was remotely interested in the actual sunball playing, you're delusional."

Hunt laughed, some of the tightness on the angel's face lightening, and Ruhn smiled, despite the old ache in his heart. He'd missed out on those years with Bryce. They hadn't been speaking then. Those had been formative, pivotal years. He should have been there.

Ithan flipped Bryce off, but said to Declan, "Okay, I'm in."

Bryce scanned the screen. "Do you see any Reapers crossing in boats?"

"This is showing nothing landing at the Black Dock at all today. Or last night."

Athalar asked, "When's the last time any Reaper docked?"

Ithan kept typing, and they all waited, the only additional sound the swift clack of Declan's fingers on the keys of his computer. The wolf said, "Yesterday morning." He grimaced. "These two look familiar?"

Bryce and Ruhn scanned the image Ithan had pulled up. Ruhn had no idea why the fuck he bothered, since he'd been unconscious, but a shiver went down his spine at the sagging, graying faces, the crepe-like skin so at odds with the jagged, sharp teeth that gleamed as the Reapers stepped from the boat. Both had pulled back their veils during the trip across the Istros, but tugged them over their faces as they stepped onto the Black Dock and drifted into the city.

Bryce said hoarsely, "No. Gods, they're awful. But no—those weren't the ones who attacked."

"They might have been hiding out for a few days," Athalar said. "The Prince of the Pit only threatened us the other night, but he might have had them in place already."

Ruhn had no idea how the angel spoke so calmly. If the Star-Eater had come to *him* and wanted to have a one-on-one chat, he'd still be shitting his pants.

"I'm not seeing any kids lurking around the Black Dock, either,"

Ithan muttered, scanning the results. He twisted to Bryce. "No sign of Emile at all."

Ruhn asked, "Possible the kid took another way over? Maybe Danika found some sort of back door into the Bone Quarter."

"Not possible," Athalar said. "Only one way in, one way out."

Ruhn bristled. "That's what we've been taught, but has anyone ever tried to get in some other way?"

Athalar snorted. "Why would they want to?"

Ruhn glared at the angel but said, "Fair enough."

Ithan stopped on an image. "What about this one? He didn't take a boat over, just appeared from within the city—"

"That's the one," Bryce hissed, her face paling.

They all studied the still—the Reaper was half-turned to the camera as it entered the frame from a street near the Black Dock. He was taller than the others, but had the same grayish, soft face and those terrifying teeth.

Athalar whistled. "You sure know how to pick them, Quinlan."

She scowled at the angel, but asked Dec, "Where's it coming from? Can you add its face to the program and run a search on the city's footage?"

Declan's brows rose. "You know how long *that* will take? Every camera in Lunathion? It's why we're not even doing it for Emile. It'd take . . . I can't even calculate how long we'd need."

"Okay, okay," Bryce said. "But can we . . . track this one for a while?" She directed the last bit at Ithan, but the wolf shook his head.

"There must be a logical reason for this—like a gap in the camera coverage or something—but that Reaper just seems to . . . appear."

"Micah had the kristallos stay in known camera gaps," Hunt said darkly. "These Reapers could know about them, too."

Ithan pointed to the screen. "Right here is where they first appear. Before that, nothing."

Ruhn pulled up a map of the city in his Aux app. "There should be a sewer entrance right behind them. Possible they came out of there?"

Ithan moved the footage around. "The cameras don't cover that sewer entrance."

Bryce said, "So they probably knew it'd be a good entry point. And it'd make sense, given that they dragged us into the sewers." Where there were no cameras at all.

"Let me look around a little more," Ithan offered, and clicked away.

Athalar asked none of them in particular, "You think they were waiting for you, or for Emile?"

"Or both?" Ruhn asked. "Clearly, they wanted to stay hidden."

"But did the Prince of the Pit send them, or did the Under-King?" Athalar pushed.

"Good thing we've got a date with the being who can answer that," Bryce said.

Ruhn winced. He'd paid for the Death Marks that Jesiba had promised, but he wasn't happy about it. The thought of Bryce confronting the Under-King scared the Hel out of him.

"We need a plan for how we question him," Athalar warned her. "I doubt he'll appreciate being questioned at all."

"Hence the research," Bryce shot back, gesturing to the computer. "You think I'm stupid enough to go in and fling accusations around? If we can confirm whether or not those Reapers came directly from the Bone Quarter, we'll have steadier footing when we question him. And if we can get any hint of Emile actually going over to the Bone Quarter, then we'll have a good reason to ask him about that, too."

Ithan added, "Considering what Tharion thinks Pippa Spetsos has done while hunting for Emile, I'm half hoping the kid's already in the Bone Quarter." He dragged a hand through his short brown hair. "What she did to that selkie we found this morning was no joke."

The wolf had filled them all in on the work he'd done with Tharion earlier—the tortured body they suspected had been left behind by the rebel fanatic.

Bryce pivoted and began pacing. Syrinx trotted at her heels, whining for a second dinner. Ruhn refrained from remarking on how similar the motion was to one he'd seen their father do so many times in his study. Unable to stand it, he turned back to the sunball game.

Then Ithan said to Ruhn, picking up the thread of conversation from earlier, "See? Regez should have nailed that shot, but he balked. He's second-guessing himself. He's too deep in his head."

Ruhn glanced sidelong at the male. "You've never thought about playing again?"

A muscle ticked in Ithan's jaw. "No."

"You miss it?"

"No."

It was an obvious lie. Ruhn didn't fail to note that Bryce's eyes had softened.

But Ithan didn't so much as look in her direction. So Ruhn nodded to the wolf. "If you ever want to play a pickup game, me, Dec, and Flynn usually play with some of the Aux in Oleander Park over in Moonwood on Sundays."

"Where's my invite?" Bryce asked, scowling.

But Ithan said roughly, "Thanks. I'll think about it."

Hunt asked, "I'm assuming I don't get an invite, either, Danaan?"

Ruhn snorted at the angel. "You want an excuse for me to beat the shit out of you, Athalar, then I'm down."

Athalar smirked, but his gaze drifted to Bryce, who was now staring over Declan's shoulder at the lightning-fast footage zooming by on his laptop. Footage of Danika from years ago.

She straightened suddenly. Cleared her throat. "I'm going down to the gym. Call me if you find anything." She aimed for her bedroom, presumably to change. Ruhn watched Hunt glance between her disappearing form and the sunball game. Weighing which one to follow.

It took Athalar all of thirty seconds to decide. He ducked into his room, saying he was going to change for the gym.

When Ruhn was alone with Dec and Ithan, his beer half-finished, Ithan said, "Connor would have picked the game."

Ruhn raised an eyebrow. "I didn't realize it was a competition between them." Between a dead male and a living one.

Ithan just typed away, eyes darting over the screen.

And for some reason, Ruhn dared ask, "What would you have picked?"

Ithan didn't hesitate. "Bryce."

27

Bryce didn't go to the gym. Not yet, anyway. She waited in front of the elevator, and when Hunt appeared, she tapped her wrist and said, "You're late. Let's go."

He halted. "We're not working out?"

She rolled her eyes, stepping into the elevator and hitting the Lobby button. "Honestly, Athalar. We've got a kid to find."

"You really think Emile is *here*? What about the Bone Quarter?" Hunt asked as Bryce strode through the warren of stalls that made up one of the Meat Market's many warehouses. There was no missing her, not with her neon-pink sneakers and athletic gear, that high ponytail that swished back and forth, brushing tantalizingly close to the glorious curve of her ass. "The Reapers practically told you that he and Sofie are lying low over there. You're having Emmet and Holstrom comb through footage *because* you think Emile's over there."

She paused at an open seating area, surveying the crammed array of tables and the diners hunched over them. "Forgive me if I don't take those half-lifes at their word. Or want to wait around while Declan and Ithan stare at their screens. Jesiba said the coins will arrive tomorrow, so why not look at alternatives in the meantime?

What Danika said . . . *Where the weary souls find relief* . . . Couldn't that be here, too?"

"Why would Danika tell them to lie low in the Meat Market?"

"Why tell them to lie low in the *Bone Quarter*?" She sniffed and sighed with longing toward a bowl of noodle soup.

Hunt said, "Even if Danika or Sofie told Emile it was safe to hide out, if I were a kid, I wouldn't have come here."

"You were a kid, like, a thousand years ago. Forgive me if my childhood is a little more relevant."

"Two hundred years ago," he muttered.

"Still old as fuck."

He pinched her ass and she squeaked, batting him away, drawing more than a few eyes. Not exactly inconspicuous. How long until the Viper Queen heard they were here? Hunt tried not to bristle at the thought. He had zero interest in dealing with the shapeshifter tonight.

Hunt marked the faces that turned their way, the ones who moved off into the stalls and shadows. "And if this is where Sofie told him to hide, Sofie was a fool for listening to Danika. Though I really doubt Danika would have suggested it as a rendezvous point."

Bryce glared at him over a shoulder. "This kid stole *two* boats and made it all the way here. I think he can handle the Meat Market."

"Okay, buying that, you think he's simply going to be sitting at a table, twiddling his thumbs? You're no better than Cormac, stomping around the docks for any sign of this kid." Hunt shook his head. "If you do find Emile, don't forget you'll have Tharion and Cormac fighting you for him."

She patted his cheek. "Then it's a good thing I have the Umbra Mortis at my side, huh?"

"Bryce," he growled. "Be reasonable. I mean, look at where we are right now. This market's huge. Are we going to search through every warehouse ourselves?"

"Nope." Bryce put her hands on her hips. "That's why I brought backup."

Hunt's brows rose. She lifted her hand, waving at someone across the space. He followed her line of attention. Let out a low growl. "You didn't."

"You're not the only badass I know, Athalar," she trilled, approaching Fury and Juniper, the former in her usual all black, the latter in tight jeans and a flowing white blouse. "Hi, friends," Bryce said, smiling. She kissed June's cheek as if they were meeting for brunch, then gave Fury a once-over. "I said casual clothes."

"These are her casual clothes," Juniper said, laughter in her eyes.

Fury crossed her arms, ignoring them as she said to Hunt, "Gym clothes? Really?"

"I thought I *was* going to the gym," he grumbled.

Bryce waved him off. "All right. We divide and conquer. Try not to attract too much attention." The last bit she directed at Hunt and Fury, and the merc glowered with impressive menace. "Don't ask questions. Just watch—listen. June, you take the east stalls, Fury the west ones, Hunt the south, and me . . ." Her gaze drifted to the northern wall, where *Memento Mori* had been painted. The stalls beneath it—beneath the walkway above—lay within range of the door to the Viper Queen's quarters.

Fury eyed her, but Bryce winked. "I'm a big girl, Fury. I'll be fine."

Hunt grunted, but suppressed any hint of objection.

"That's not what I'm worried about," Fury said. Then asked quietly, "Who is this kid again?"

"His name is Emile," Bryce whispered. "He's from Pangera. Thirteen years old."

"And possibly very, very dangerous," Hunt warned, glancing at Juniper. "If you spot him, come find us."

"I can take care of myself, angel," Juniper said with impressive cool.

"She's a big girl, too." Bryce high-fived her friend. "Right. Meet back here in thirty?"

They parted, and Hunt watched Bryce weave through the tables of the dining area—watched the many patrons note her, but keep well away—before slipping between the stalls. Gazes slid back to him, questioning. Hunt bared his teeth in a silent snarl.

Moving off toward the area she'd ordered him to sweep, Hunt opened his senses, calmed his breathing.

Thirty minutes later, he'd returned to the dining area, Juniper appearing a moment later. "Anything?" he asked the faun, who shook her head.

"Not a whisper." The dancer frowned. "I really hope that kid isn't here." She scowled at the warehouse. "I hate this place."

"That makes two of us," Hunt said.

Juniper rubbed at her chest. "You should talk to Celestina about it—the things that happen here. Not only that fighting pit and the warriors the Viper Queen practically enslaves . . ." The faun shook her head. "The other things, too."

"Even Micah let the Viper Queen do what she wanted," Hunt said. "I don't think the new Governor is going to challenge her anytime soon."

"Someone should," she said quietly, eyes drifting to the *Memento Mori* on the wall. "Someday, someone should."

Her words were haunted and strained enough that Hunt opened his mouth to ask more, but Fury sauntered up, smooth as a shadow, and said, "No sign of the kid."

Hunt searched the space for Bryce, and found her at a stall far too close to the Fae-guarded door to the Viper Queen's private living area. The towering Fae sentries a mere fifty feet from her didn't so much as blink at her presence, though. She had a bag swinging from her wrist, and she was chatting away.

Bryce finished and walked toward them. Again, too many eyes watched her.

"She's got some pep in her step," Juniper observed, chuckling. "She must have gotten a good bargain."

The tang of blood and bone and meat stuffed itself up Hunt's nose as Bryce approached. "I got some lamb bones from the butcher for Syrinx. He goes crazy for the marrow." She added to Juniper, "Sorry."

Right. The faun was a vegetarian. But Juniper shrugged. "Anything for the little guy."

Bryce smiled, then surveyed them all. "Nothing?"

"Nothing," Hunt said.

"Me neither," Bryce said, sighing.

"What now?" Fury asked, monitoring the crowd.

"Even if Declan and Ithan can't find any footage of Emile around the Black Dock," Bryce said, "the fact that there's no hint of him here at the Meat Market leads us right back to the Bone Quarter again. So it gives us a bit more reason to even ask the Under-King about whether Emile is there."

Hunt's blood sparked. When she talked like that, so sure and unflinching . . . His balls tightened. He couldn't wait to show her just how insanely that turned him on.

But Juniper whispered, "A little boy in the Bone Quarter . . ."

"We'll find him," Bryce assured her friend, and threw an arm around Juniper's shoulders, turning them toward the exit. Hunt swapped a look with Fury, and they followed. Hunt let Bryce and Juniper drift ahead a few feet, and then, when he was sure they wouldn't be overheard, asked Axtar, "Why does your girlfriend hate this place so much?"

Fury kept her attention on the shadows between the stalls, the vendors and shoppers. "Her brother was a fighter here."

Hunt started. "Does Bryce know?"

Fury nodded shallowly. "He was talented—Julius. The Viper Queen recruited him from his training gym, promised him riches, females, everything he wanted if he signed himself into her employ. What he got was an addiction to her venom, putting him in her thrall, and a contract with no way out." A muscle ticked in Fury's jaw. "June's parents tried everything to get him freed. *Everything.* Lawyers, money, pleas to Micah for intervention—none of it worked. Julius died in a fight ten years ago. June and her parents only learned about it because the Viper Queen's goons dumped his body on their doorstep with a note that said *Memento Mori* on it."

The elegant dancer strode arm-in-arm with Bryce. "I had no idea."

"June doesn't talk about it. Even with us. But she hates this place more than you can imagine."

"So why'd she come?" Why had Bryce even invited her?

"For Bryce," Fury said simply. "Bryce told her she didn't have to join, but she wanted to come with us. If there's a kid running around lost in this place, June would do anything to help find him. Even come here herself."

"Ah," Hunt said, nodding.

Fury's eyes glittered with dark promise. "I'll burn this place to the ground for her one day."

Hunt didn't doubt it.

An hour later, Bryce's arms and stomach trembled as she held her plank on the floor of her apartment building's gym, sweat dripping off her brow and onto the soft black mat beneath. Bryce focused on the droplet as it splattered, on the music thumping in her earbuds, on breathing through her nose—*anything* other than the clock.

Time itself had slowed. Ten seconds lasted a minute. She pushed her heels back, steadying her body. Two minutes down. Three more to go.

Before the Drop, she'd usually managed a decent minute in this position. After it, in her immortal body, five minutes should be nothing.

Master her powers, indeed. She needed to master her body first. Though she supposed magic was ideal for lazy people: she didn't need to be able to hold a plank for ten minutes if she could just unleash her power. Hel, she could blind someone while sitting down if she felt like it.

She chuckled at the idea, horrible as it was: her lounging in an oversize armchair, taking down enemies as easily as if she were changing the channel with a remote. And she *did* have enemies now, didn't she? She'd killed a fucking Reaper today.

As soon as those Death Marks arrived from Jesiba tomorrow morning, she'd demand answers from the Under-King.

It was why she'd come down here—not only to validate her excuse for leaving the apartment. Well, that and seeing Danika on Declan's laptop as it scanned through footage. Her head had begun spinning and acid had been burning through her veins, and sweating it all out seemed like a good idea. It always worked in Madame Kyrah's classes.

She owed June a massive box of pastries for coming tonight.

Bryce checked the clock on her phone. Two minutes fifteen seconds. Fuck this. She plopped onto her front, elbows splaying, and laid her face directly on the mat.

A moment later, a foot prodded her ribs. Since there was only one other person in the gym, she didn't bother to be alarmed as she craned her neck to peer up at Hunt. His lips were moving, sweat beading his brow and dampening his tight gray T-shirt—gods-damn it. How could he look so good?

She tugged an earbud out. "What?" she asked.

"I asked if you were alive."

"Barely."

His mouth twitched, and he lifted the hem of his T-shirt up to clean his dripping face. She was rewarded with a glimpse of sweat-slicked abs. Then he said, "You dropped like a corpse."

She cradled her arms, rubbing the sore muscles. "I prefer running. This is torture."

"Your dance classes are equally grueling."

"This isn't as fun."

He offered her a hand, and Bryce took it, her sweaty skin sliding against his as he hauled her to her feet.

She wiped at her face with the back of her arm, but found it to be equally sweaty. Hunt returned to the array of metal machines that seemed more like torture devices, adjusting the seat on one to accommodate his gray wings. She stood in the center of the room like a total creep for a moment, watching his back muscles ripple as he went through a series of pull-down exercises.

Burning fucking Solas.

She'd blown this male. Had slid down that beautiful, strong body and taken his ridiculously large cock in her mouth and had nearly come herself as he'd spilled on her tongue.

And she knew it was ten kinds of fucked up, considering how much shit they were juggling and all that lay ahead, but . . . *look* at him.

She wiped at the sweat rolling down her chest, leaving a spectacularly unsexy stain beneath her sports bra.

Hunt finished his set but kept gripping the bar above his head, arms extended high above him, stretching out his back and wings. Even in a T-shirt and gym shorts, he was formidable. And . . . she was still staring. Bryce twisted back to her mat, grimacing as she put in her earbud and it blasted music. But her body refused to move.

Water. She needed some water. Anything to delay going back to that plank.

She trudged for the wet bar built into the far wall of the gym. The beverage fridge beneath the white marble counter was stocked with glass water bottles and chilled towels, and Bryce helped herself to both. A bowl of green apples sat on the counter, along with a basket full of granola bars, and she took the former, teeth sinking into the crisp flesh.

Fuck doing planks.

Savoring the apple's tart kiss, she glanced over toward Hunt, but—Where was he? Even that telltale ripple of his power had faded away.

She scanned the expansive gym, the rows of machines, the treadmills and ellipticals before the wall of windows overlooking the bustle of the Old Square. How had he—

Hands wrapped around her waist, and Bryce shrieked, nearly leaping out of her skin. Light erupted from her chest, but with the music thumping in her ears, she couldn't hear anything—

"Fucking *Hel*, Quinlan!" Hunt said, prying her earbuds away. "Listen to your music a little louder, will you?"

She scowled, pivoting to find him right behind her. "It wouldn't matter if you didn't *sneak up on me*."

He flashed her a sweaty, wicked grin. "Just making sure my Shadow of Death skills don't get rusty before tomorrow's tea party with the Under-King. I thought I'd see if I could dim myself a bit."

Hence her inability to sense him creeping up. He rubbed at his eyes. "I didn't realize you'd be so . . . jumpy. Or *bright*."

"I thought you'd praise me for my quick reflexes."

"Good jump. You almost blinded me. Congrats."

She playfully slapped his chest, finding rock-hard muscles beneath the sweat-dampened shirt. "Solas, Hunt." She rapped her knuckles on his pecs. "You could bounce a gold mark off these things."

His wings rustled. "I'm taking that as a compliment."

She propped her elbows on the counter and bit into her apple again. Hunt extended a hand, and she wordlessly handed him one earbud. He fitted it to his ear, head angling as he listened to the song.

"No wonder you can't do a plank for more than two minutes, if you're listening to this sad-sack music."

"And your music is so much better?"

"I'm listening to a book."

She blinked. They'd often swapped music suggestions while working out, but this was new. "Which book?"

"Voran Tritus's memoir about growing up in the Eternal City and how he became, well . . . him." Tritus was one of the youngest late-night talk show hosts ever. And absurdly hot. Bryce knew the last fact had little to do with why Hunt tuned in religiously, but it certainly made her own viewing much more enjoyable.

"I'd say listening to a book while working out is even less motivational than this *sad-sack* music," she said.

"It's all muscle memory at this point. I only need to pass the time until I'm done."

"Asshole." She ate more of her apple, then changed the song. Something she'd first heard in the hallowed space of the White Raven dance club, a remix of a slower song that somehow managed to combine the song's original sensual appeal with a driving beat that demanded dancing.

The corner of Hunt's mouth kicked up. "You trying to seduce me with this music?"

She met his gaze as she chewed on another mouthful of apple. The gym was empty. But the cameras . . . "You're the one who snuck up to fondle me."

He laughed, the column of his throat working. A droplet of sweat ran down its powerful length, gleaming among all that golden-brown skin, and her breathing hitched. His nostrils flared, no doubt scenting everything that went hot and wet within the span of a breath.

He tucked in his wings, leaving the earbud in place as he took a step closer. Bryce leaned slightly against the counter, the marble digging into her overheated spine. But he only took the apple from her fingers. Held her gaze while he bit in, then slowly set the core on the counter.

Her toes curled in her sneakers. "This is even less private than my bedroom."

Hunt's hands slid onto her waist, and he hoisted her onto the counter in one easy movement. His lips found her neck, and she arched as his tongue slid up one side, as if licking away a bead of sweat. "Best be quiet, then, Quinlan," he said against her skin.

Lightning skittered around the room. She didn't need to look to know he'd severed the camera wires, and likely had a wall of power blocking the door. Didn't need to do anything other than enjoy the sensation of his tongue on her throat, teasing and tasting.

She couldn't stop the hands that slid into his hair, driving through the sweaty strands, all the way down his head until they landed on the nape of his neck. She drew him closer as she did so, and Hunt lifted his head from her neck to claim her mouth.

Her legs opened wider, and he settled between them, pressing hard as his tongue met hers.

Bryce groaned, tasting apple and that storm-kissed cedar scent that was pure Hunt, grinding herself against his demanding hardness. With his gym shorts and her skintight leggings, there was no hiding his erection, or the dampness that soaked through her pants.

His tongue tangled with hers, hands dropping from her waist

to cup her ass. She gasped as his fingers dug in, pulling her harder against him, and she hooked her legs around his middle. She couldn't taste him deep enough, fast enough.

His shirt came off, and then she was running her fingers over those absurd abs and side abs and pecs, down the shifting muscles of his back, frantic and desperate to touch all of him.

Her tank top peeled away, and then his teeth nipped at the swells of her breasts above the seafoam green of her sports bra, the fabric almost neon against her tan skin.

He bracketed her waist, calluses scraping her skin as he tilted her back, and Bryce let him lay her on the counter. She propped herself up on her elbows as he pulled away, graceful as an ebbing tide, hands running from her breasts to her sweaty stomach.

Hunt's fingers curled over the waistband of her black leggings, but paused. His gaze lifted to hers in silent request.

At the black fire she beheld there, the sheer beauty and size and perfection of him . . .

"Hel yes," she said, and Hunt grinned wickedly, rolling down her leggings. Exposing her midriff. Then her abdomen. Then the lacy top of her amethyst thong. Her pants and underwear were soaked with sweat—she didn't want to imagine what they smelled like—and she opened her mouth to tell him so, but he'd already knelt.

He pulled off her sneakers, then her socks, then the leggings. Then gently, so gently, he took her right ankle and kissed its inside. Licked at the bone. Then at her calf. The inside of her knee.

Oh gods. This was going to happen. Right here, in the middle of the building gym where anyone could fly past the wall of windows twenty feet away. He was going down on her right here, and she needed it more than she'd ever needed anything—

His tongue traced circles along the inside of her right thigh. Higher and higher, until she was shaking. But his hands slid up, looping through the waistband of her thong. He pressed a kiss to the front of her underwear, and she could have sworn he shuddered as he inhaled.

Bryce went liquid, unable to stop her writhe of demand, and Hunt huffed a warm laugh against her most sensitive place, kissing her again through the fabric of her underwear.

But then he kissed her left thigh, beginning a downward trajectory, pulling her underwear away as he went. And when the thong was completely gone, when she was bared to the world, Hunt's wings splayed above him, blocking her from the world's view.

Only his to see, his to devour.

Her breathing turned jagged as his mouth reached her left ankle, kissing again, and then he was sliding back up. He halted with his head between her thighs, though. Took her feet and propped them onto the counter.

Spread her legs wide.

Bryce moaned softly as Hunt surveyed her, the light glowing through his wings making him look like an avenging angel lit with inner fire.

"Look at you," he murmured, voice guttural with need.

She'd never felt so naked, yet so seen and cherished. Not as Hunt slid a finger through her wetness. "Fuck yeah," he growled, more to himself than to her, and she really, truly couldn't breathe as he knelt again, head poised where she needed him most.

Hunt softly, reverently, laid a hand on her, opening her for his own personal tasting. His tongue swept along her in an introductory *Hi, nice to fuck you* flit. She bit her lip, panting through her nose.

Yet Hunt bowed his head, brow resting just above her mound as his hands slid to her thighs once more. He inhaled and exhaled, shuddering, and she had no idea if he was savoring her scent or really needed a moment to calm the Hel down.

One or two more licks and she knew she'd lose her mind entirely.

Then Hunt pressed a kiss to the top of her sex. And another, as if he couldn't help it. His hands caressed her thighs. He kissed her a third time, raised wings twitching, and then his mouth drifted south, one hand with it.

Again, he parted her, and pressed his tongue flat against her as he dragged it up.

Stars sparked behind Bryce's eyes, her breasts aching so much she arched into the air, as if seeking invisible hands to touch them.

"That's it," Hunt said against her, and flicked his tongue over her clit with lethal precision.

She couldn't endure this. Couldn't handle one more second of this torture—

His tongue pushed into her, curling deep, and she bucked.

"You taste like gods-damn paradise," he growled, pulling back enough for her to note her wetness on his mouth, his chin. "I knew you'd taste like this."

Bryce clapped a hand over her mouth to keep from shouting as Hunt drove his tongue back into her, then dragged it all the way up to her clit. His teeth clamped down gently, and her eyes rolled back into her head. Burning Solas and merciful Cthona . . .

"Hunt," she managed to say, voice strangled.

He paused, ready to halt should she give the word. But that was the last thing she wanted.

Bryce met Hunt's blazing gaze, her chest heaving, head a dizzy, starry mess. She said the only thing in her head, her mind, her soul. "I love you."

She regretted the words the moment they left her mouth. She'd never said them to any male, hadn't even *thought* the words about Hunt, though she'd known for a while. Why they came out then, she had no idea, but—his eyes darkened again. His fingers tightened on her legs.

Oh gods. She'd fucked everything up. She was a stupid, horny idiot, and what the *fuck* had she been thinking, telling him that when they weren't even *dating*, for fuck's sake—

Hunt unleashed himself. Dipped his head back down between her thighs and feasted on her. Bryce could have sworn thunderstorms rumbled in the room. It was answer and acceptance of what she'd said. Like he was beyond words now.

Tongue and teeth and purring—all combined into a maelstrom of pleasure that had Bryce grinding against him. Hunt gripped her thighs hard enough to bruise and she loved it, needed it; she drove her hips into his face, pushing his tongue into her, and then something *zapped* right at her clit, as if Hunt had summoned a little spark of lightning, and her brain and body lit up like white fire, and oh gods, oh gods, oh gods—

Bryce was screaming the words, Hunt's wings still cocooning them as she came hard enough that she arced clean off the counter, fingers scrabbling in his hair, pulling hard. She was flaring with light inside and out, like a living beacon.

She could have sworn they fell through time and space, could have sworn they tumbled toward something, but she wanted to stay here, with him, in this body and this place—

Hunt licked her through every ripple, and when the climax eased, when the light she'd erupted with had faded, and that falling sensation had steadied, he lifted his head.

He met her stare from between her thighs, panting against her bare skin, lightning in his eyes. "I love you, too, Quinlan."

No one had said those words to Hunt in two centuries.

Shahar had never said them. Not once, though he'd stupidly offered the words to her. The last person had been his mother, a few weeks before her death. But hearing them from Quinlan . . .

Hunt lay beside her in bed thirty minutes later, the minty scent of their toothpaste and lavender of their shampoo mingling in the air. That had been weird enough: showering one after the other, then brushing their teeth side by side, those words echoing. Walking through the apartment, past Ruhn, Declan, and Ithan watching sunball analysts argue over tonight's game, wondering how so much and yet so little had changed in the span of a few minutes.

Going into the Bone Quarter tomorrow seemed like a far-off storm. A distant rumble of thunder. Any thought of their search at the Meat Market tonight dissolved like melting snow.

In the dimness, the TV still droning from the living room, Hunt stared at Bryce. She silently watched him back.

"One of us has got to say something," Hunt said, voice gravelly.

"What else is there to say?" she asked, propping her head on a fist, hair spilling over a shoulder in a red curtain.

"You said you love me."

"And?" She cocked an eyebrow.

Hunt's mouth twitched upward. "It was said under duress."

She bit her lip. He wanted to plant his teeth there. "Are you asking whether I meant it, or do you think you're that good with your mouth that I went out of my mind?"

He flicked her nose. "Smart-ass."

She flopped back onto the mattress. "They're both true."

Hunt's blood heated. "Yeah?"

"Oh, come on." She tucked her arms behind her head. "You have to know you're good at it. That *lightning* thing . . ."

Hunt held up a finger, a spark of lightning dancing at the tip. "Thought you'd enjoy that."

"If I'd known ahead of time, I might have been concerned about you deep-frying my favorite parts."

He laughed warmly. "I wouldn't dare. They're my favorite parts, too."

She lifted herself onto her elbows, unable to keep from fidgeting. "Does it weird you out? What I said?"

"Why should it? I reciprocated, didn't I?"

"Maybe you felt bad for me and wanted to make it less weird."

"I'm not the kind of person who lightly tosses those words around."

"Me neither." She reached over and Hunt leaned toward her hand, letting her brush her fingers through his hair. "I've never said it to anyone. I mean, like . . . romantically."

"Really?" His chest became unbearably full.

She blinked, her eyes like golden embers in the darkness. "Why the surprise?"

"I thought you and Connor . . ." He wasn't sure why he needed to know.

That fire banked slightly. "No. We might have one day, but it didn't get that far. I loved him as a friend, but . . . I still needed time." She smiled crookedly. "Who knows? Maybe I was just waiting for you."

He grabbed her hand, pressing a kiss to her knuckles. "I've been in love with you for a while. You know that, right?" His heart thundered, but he said, "I was . . . very attached to you during our investigation, but when Sandriel had me in that cell under the Comitium, she put on this fucked-up slideshow of all the photos on my phone. Of you and me. And I watched it and knew. I saw the photos of us toward the end, how I was looking at you and you were looking at me, and it was a done deal."

"Sealed with you jumping in front of a bomb for me."

"It's disturbing when you make jokes about that, Quinlan."

She chuckled, kissing his jaw. Hunt's body tensed, readying for another touch. Begging for another touch. She said, "I made the Drop for you. *And* offered to sell myself into slavery in your stead. I think I'm allowed to joke about this shit." He nipped at her nose. But she pulled back, gaze meeting his. Hunt let her see everything that lay there. "I knew the moment you went snooping for my dildos."

Hunt burst out laughing. "I can't tell if that's the truth."

"You handled Jelly Jubilee with such care. How could I not love you for it?"

He laughed again, ducking to brush a kiss to her warm throat. "I'll take that." He traced his fingers down her hip, the threadbare softness of her old T-shirt snagging against his callused skin. He kissed her collarbone, inhaling the scent of her, his cock stirring. "So what now?"

"Sex?"

He grinned. "No. I mean, fuck yes, but I don't want an audience." He gestured over his shoulder and wing to the wall behind him. "Shall we get a hotel room somewhere in the city?"

"Somewhere on another continent."

"Ah, Quinlan." He kissed her jaw, her cheek, her temple. He whispered into her ear, "I really want to fuck you right now."

She shuddered, arching against him. "Same."

His hand slid from her waist to cup her ass. "This is torture." He slipped his hand under her oversize shirt, finding her bare skin warm and soft. He traced his fingers along the seam of her lacy thong, down toward her thighs. Heat beckoned him, and she sucked in a breath as he halted millimeters short of where he wanted to be.

But she placed a hand on his chest. "What do I call you now?"

The words took a moment to register. "What?"

"I mean, what *are* we? Like, dating? Are you my boyfriend?"

He snorted. "You really want to say you're dating the Umbra Mortis?"

"I'm not keeping this private." She said it without an ounce of doubt. She brushed her fingers over his brow. Like she knew what it meant to him.

Hunt managed to ask, "What about Cormac and your ruse?"

"Well, after all that, I guess." If they survived. She whooshed out a breath. "*Boyfriend* sounds weird for you. It's so . . . young. But what else is there?"

If he had a star on his chest, Hunt knew it'd be glowing as he asked, "Partner?"

"Not sexy enough."

"Lover?"

"Does that come with a ruff and lute?"

He swept a wing over her bare thigh. "Anyone ever tell you that you're a pain in the ass?"

"Just ye olde lover."

Hunt hooked his finger under the strap of her thong and snapped it. She yowled, swatting away his hand.

But Hunt grabbed her fingers, laying them on his heart again. "What about *mate*?" Bryce stilled, and Hunt held his breath, wondering if he'd said the wrong thing. When she didn't reply, he went on, "Fae have mates, right? That's the term they use."

"Mates are . . . an intense thing for the Fae." She swallowed audibly. "It's a lifetime commitment. Something sworn between bodies and hearts and souls. It's a binding between beings. You say I'm your mate in front of any Fae, and it'll mean something big to them."

"And we don't mean something big like that?" he asked carefully, hardly daring to breathe. She held his heart in her hands. Had held it since day one.

"You mean *everything* to me," she breathed, and he exhaled

deeply. "But if we tell Ruhn that we're mates, we're as good as married. To the Fae, we're bound on a biological, molecular level. There's no undoing it."

"*Is* it a biological thing?"

"It can be. Some Fae claim they know their mates from the moment they meet them. That there's some kind of invisible link between them. A scent or soul-bond."

"Is it ever between species?"

"I don't know," she admitted, and ran her fingers over his chest in dizzying, taunting circles. "But if you're not my mate, Athalar, no one is."

"A winning declaration of love."

She scanned his face, earnest and open in a way she so rarely was with others. "I want you to understand what you're telling people, telling the Fae, if you say I'm your mate."

"Angels have mates. Not as . . . soul-magicky as the Fae, but we call life partners mates in lieu of husbands or wives." Shahar had never called him such a thing. They'd rarely even used the term *lover.*

"The Fae won't differentiate. They'll use their intense-ass definition."

He studied her contemplative face. "I feel like it fits. Like we're already bound on that biological level."

"Me too. And who knows? Maybe we're already mates."

It would explain a lot. How intense things had been between them from the start. And once they crossed that last physical barrier, he had a feeling the bond would be even further solidified.

So . . . maybe they *were* already mates, by that Fae definition. Maybe Urd had long ago bound their souls, and they'd needed all this time to realize it. But did it even matter? If it was fate or choice to be together?

Hunt asked, "Does it scare you? Calling me your mate?"

Her gaze dipped to the space between them, and she said quietly, "You're the one who's been defined by other people's terms for centuries." *Fallen. Slave. Umbra Mortis.* "I just want to make sure it's a title you're cool with having. Forever."

He kissed her temple, breathing in her scent. "Of everything I've ever been called, Quinlan, your mate will be the one I truly cherish."

Her lips curved. "Did you hear the *forever* part?"

"I thought that's what this thing between us is."

"We've known each other for, like, five months."

"So?"

"My mom will throw a fit. She'll say we should date for at least two years before calling ourselves mates."

"Who cares what other people think? None of their rules have ever applied to us anyway. And if we're some sort of predestined mates, then it doesn't make a difference at all."

She smiled again, and it lit up his entire chest. No, that was the star between her breasts. He laid a hand over the glowing scar, light shining through his fingers. "Why does it do that?"

"Maybe it likes you."

"It glowed for Cormac and Ruhn."

"I didn't say it was smart."

Hunt laughed and leaned to kiss the scar. "All right, my lovely mate. No sex tonight."

His mate. *His.*

And he was hers. It wouldn't have surprised him if her name were stamped on his heart. He wondered if his own were stamped on the glowing star in her chest.

"Tomorrow night. We'll get a hotel room."

He brushed another kiss against her scar. "Deal."

28

I'm glad to see you alive.

Ruhn stood on a familiar mental bridge, the lines of his body once more filled in with night and stars and planets. At the other end of the bridge waited that burning female figure. Long hair of pure flame floated around her as if underwater, and what he could make out of her mouth was curved upward in a half smile.

"So am I," he said. He must have passed out on the couch in Bryce's apartment. He'd still been there at two in the morning, watching old game highlights with Ithan. Dec had long since gone to spend the night at Marc's place. Neither had turned up any solid footage of Emile at the docks—or concrete proof of the Reapers being sent from the Under-King or Apollion. The search for Danika at the gallery would take days, Dec had said before leaving, and he did have other work to do. Ithan had instantly volunteered to keep combing through it.

The wolf pup wasn't bad. Ruhn could see them being friends, if their people weren't constantly at each other's throats. Literally.

Ruhn said to Agent Daybright, "Thanks for trying to wake me up."

"What happened?"

"Reapers."

Her flame guttered to a violet blue. "They attacked you?"

"Long story." He angled his head. "So I don't need the crystal to reach you? I can just be unconscious? Sleeping?"

"Perhaps the crystal was only needed to initiate contact between our minds—a beacon for your talents," she said. "Now that your mind—and mine—knows where to go, you don't require the crystal anymore, and can contact me even in . . . inopportune moments."

A pinprick of guilt poked at him. She was embedded in the higher ranks of the empire—had he endangered her when he'd been unconscious earlier, his mind blindly reaching for hers?

But Daybright said, "I have information for you to pass on."

"Yeah?"

She straightened. "Is that how Ophion agents speak these days? *Yeah?*"

She had to be old, then. One of the Vanir who'd lived for so long that modern lingo was like a foreign language. Or, gods, if she was an Asteri . . .

Ruhn wished he had a wall or a doorway or a counter to lean against as he crossed his arms. "So you're old-school Pangeran."

"Your position here isn't to learn about me. It's to pass along information. Who I am, who you are, is of no consequence." She gestured to her flames. "This should tell you enough."

"About what?"

Her flames pushed closer to her body, turning a vibrant orange—like the hottest embers. The kind that would burn to the bone. "About what shall happen if you ask too many prying questions."

He smiled slightly. "So what's the intel?"

"The hit on the Spine is a go."

Ruhn's smile faded. "When's the shipment?"

"Three days from now. It leaves from the Eternal City at six in the morning their time. No planned stops, no refueling. They'll travel swiftly northward, all the way to Forvos."

"The mech-suit prototype will be on the train?"

"Yes. And along with it, Imperial Transport is moving fifty crates of brimstone missiles to the northern front, along with a hundred and twelve crates of guns and about five hundred crates of ammunition."

Burning Solas. "You're going to stage a heist?"

"*I'm* not doing anything," Agent Daybright said. "Ophion will be responsible. I'd recommend destroying it all, though. Especially that new mech-suit. Don't waste time trying to unload anything from the trains or you'll be caught."

Ruhn refrained from mentioning that Cormac had suggested something different. He'd said Ophion wanted to attain the suit—to study it. And use those weapons in their war. "Where's the best place to intercept?"

He was really doing this, apparently. Pass this intel along, and he was officially aligning himself with the rebels.

"That's for Ophion Command to decide."

He asked carefully, "Will Pippa Spetsos be assigned to the hit?" Or was she in Lunathion looking for Emile, as Tharion suspected?

"Does it matter?"

Ruhn shrugged as nonchalantly as he could. "Just want to know whether we need to notify her."

"I'm not privy to who Command sends on their missions."

"Do you know where Pippa Spetsos is right now, though?"

Her flame guttered for a moment. "Why do you have such interest in her?"

He held up his hands. "No interest at all." He could sense her suspicion, though, so he asked, "Will there be armed guards with the shipment?"

"Yes. About a hundred wolves in and atop the cars, along with a dozen aerial angel scouts above. All armed with rifles, handguns, and knives."

Forested areas would be best for a strike, then, to avoid being seen by the malakim.

"Anything else?"

She angled her head. "None of this bothers you?"

"I've been in the Aux for a while. I'm used to coordinating shit." Nothing like this, though. Nothing that put him firmly in the Asteri's line of fire.

"That's a stupid thing to reveal. Ophion must have been desperate, if they sent someone as untrained as you to deal with me."

"Trust is a two-way street." He gestured to the space between them.

Another one of those soft laughs raked over his skin. "Do you have anything for me? What's this business with Pippa Spetsos?"

"Nothing at all. But—thanks for trying to save my ass earlier."

"I'd be a fool to let a valuable contact go to waste."

He bristled. "I'm touched."

She snorted. "You sound like a male used to being obeyed. Interesting."

"What the Hel is interesting about it?"

"The rebels must have something on you, to make you risk your position by doing this."

"I thought you didn't give a shit about my personal life."

"I don't. But knowledge is power. I'm curious about who you might be, if the Reapers tried to grab you. And why you allow the rebels to push you around."

"Maybe I wanted to join."

She laughed, the sound sharp as a blade. "I've found that the ruling class rarely do such things out of the kindness of their hearts."

"Cynical."

"Perhaps, but it's true."

"I could name a highly placed Vanir who's helping the rebels without being forced into it."

"Then they should put a bullet in your head."

Ruhn stiffened. "Excuse me?"

She waved a hand. "If you know their identity, if you're able to so blithely boast about it, if you are asking too many questions about Agent Spetsos, you're not an asset at all. You're a loose cannon. If the dreadwolves catch you, how long will it take for you to sing that person's name?"

"Fuck off."

"Have you ever been tortured? It's easy for people to claim they wouldn't break, but when your body is being pulled apart piece by piece, bone by bone, you'd be surprised what people offer to get the pain to stop, even for a second."

Ruhn's temper flared. "You don't know shit about me or what

I've been through." He was grateful the night and stars of his skin covered the marks his father's ministrations had left—the ones his ink couldn't hide.

Day's flame blazed brighter. "You should mind what you tell people, even among Ophion allies. They have ways of making people disappear."

"Like Sofie Renast?"

Her fire simmered. "Don't repeat her true name to anyone. Refer to her as Agent Cypress."

Ruhn gritted his teeth. "Do you know anything about Sofie?"

"I assumed she was dead, since you're now my contact."

"And if she isn't?"

"I don't understand."

"If she isn't dead, where would she go? Where would she hide?"

Daybright whirled back toward her end of the bridge. "This meeting is over." And before Ruhn could say another word, she vanished, leaving only drifting embers behind.

"Why the Hel would the Asteri create their own mech-suit for this war?" Hunt asked, rubbing his jaw as he leaned against the kitchen counter the next morning.

He tried not to look at the black box on the other end of the counter. But its presence seemed to . . . hum. Seemed to hollow out the air around it.

Considering the two Death Marks inside, it was no wonder.

Cormac sipped from his tea, face clouded. He'd arrived barely past dawn, apparently after Ruhn had called him to demand that he rush over, thus dragging Hunt from slumber—and Bryce's arms—with his knocking. "The suits are the one advantage we have. Well, that the humans have."

"I know that," Hunt countered tightly. "I've fought them. I know them inside and out."

And he'd taken them apart. And sabotaged them so their pilots didn't stand a chance.

He'd been content to let that knowledge serve him lately for stuff like fixing Bryce's bike—which he'd gone so far as to wash for her before handing it back over—but if the Asteri were making a mech-suit of their own for a Vanir soldier to use . . .

"I always forget," Ruhn murmured from where he sat on the couch beside Bryce, "that you fought in two wars." The one he'd waged and lost with the Fallen, and then the years spent fighting at Sandriel's command against the Ophion rebels.

"I don't," Hunt said, earning an apologetic wince from Ruhn. "We need to be careful. You're sure this information was real?"

"Yeah," Ruhn said.

Holstrom settled himself against the wall beside the counter, silently watching the exchange. His face revealed nothing. A laptop sat open on the couch, though, still combing through the years of gallery footage for any hint of Danika.

But this conversation with Cormac, this hit on the Spine . . . "You likely have double agents in Ophion," Hunt said to the Avallen Prince.

"Not Daybright," Cormac said with absolute certainty.

"Anyone can be bought," Hunt said.

Bryce said nothing, busy pretending that she was more interested in her pink toenails than this conversation. Hunt knew she was picking over every word.

He'd emerged from the bedroom intending to tell every single person who crossed his path that she was his mate, but Ruhn had been waiting with this news instead, apparently having slept on the couch.

"Regardless," Cormac said tightly, "I need to pass this information along."

"I'll go with you," Ruhn said. Bryce's mouth popped open in alarm.

"You could be walking right into a trap," Hunt warned.

"We don't have any choice," Cormac countered. "We can't risk losing this opportunity."

"And what do you risk losing if it's fake?" Lightning crackled at Hunt's fingers. Bryce's eyes flicked up to him at last, wary and full of caution.

She said before Cormac could answer, "This isn't our business, Hunt."

"Like Hel it isn't. We're tied into it, whether we want to be or not."

Golden fire filled her gaze. "Yes, but we have nothing to do with this hit; this intel. It's Ophion's problem to deal with." She straightened, giving Ruhn a scathing look that seemed to say, *You should stay out of it, too,* but faced Cormac. "So go report to Command and keep us out of it."

Cormac stared her down, his jaw working.

She gave him a slash of a smile that set Hunt's blood thrumming. "Not used to females giving you orders?"

"There are plenty of females in Command." Cormac's nostrils flared. "And I would advise you to behave as a Fae female ought to when we are seen together in public. It shall be hard enough to convince others of our betrothal thanks to that smell on you."

"What smell?" Bryce said, and Hunt braced his feet. She could take care of herself in a fight, but he'd still enjoy pummeling the bastard.

Cormac motioned between her and Hunt. "You think I can't scent what went down between you two?"

Bryce leaned back against the cushions. "You mean, that *he* went down on me?"

Hunt choked, and Ruhn let out a garbled string of curses. Ithan walked to the coffee machine and muttered something about it being too early.

Cormac, however, didn't so much as blush. He said gravely, "Your mingling scents will jeopardize this ruse."

"I'll take that into consideration," Bryce said, and then winked at Hunt.

Gods, she'd tasted like a dream. And the sweet, breathy sounds she made when she came . . . Hunt rolled out the tautness in his shoulders. They had a long day ahead of them. A dangerous day.

They were going to the Bone Quarter today, for fuck's sake. The street camera footage had pinpointed that the Reaper who'd attacked Bryce and Ruhn had been within a block of the Black Dock, but even with Declan's skills, they hadn't found any concrete proof of the Reaper sailing over. It was enough of a link that they'd question the Under-King about it, though. And if they got through that, then Hunt planned to have a long, long night. He'd already made a reservation at a fancy-ass hotel restaurant. And reserved a large suite. With rose petals and champagne.

Cormac drummed his fingers on the table and said to Bryce, "If you find Emile in the Bone Quarter, let me know immediately." Bryce, to Hunt's surprise, didn't object. Cormac pivoted to Ruhn, jerking his chin to the door. "We need to get going. If that supply train is leaving in three days, we can't waste a moment." He looked sharply at Hunt. "Even if it's bad intel."

"I'm ready." Ruhn got to his feet. He frowned at his sister. "Good hunting. Stay out of trouble today, please."

"Right back at you." Bryce grinned, though Hunt noted that her attention was on the Starsword—as if she were speaking to it, pleading with it to protect her brother. Then her gaze slid to Cormac, who already stood at the door. "Be careful," she said pointedly to Ruhn.

The warning was clear enough: *Don't trust Cormac entirely.*

Ruhn nodded slowly. The male might have claimed he'd changed since trying to kill the prince decades ago, but Hunt didn't trust him, either.

Ruhn turned toward Ithan as the wolf aimed for the discarded laptop on the couch. "Look, I hate to drag anyone else into our shit, but . . . you want to come?"

Holstrom jerked his chin toward the laptop. "What about the footage?"

"It can wait a few hours—you can look through any flagged sections when we get back. We could use your skills today."

"What skills?" Bryce demanded. Pure, protective alarm. "Being good at sunball doesn't count."

"Thanks, Bryce," Ithan grumbled, and before Ruhn could supply a reason for inviting the wolf, he said, "Sabine will have a fit if I'm caught helping you."

That was the least of what would happen if he was caught

aiding rebels. Hunt tried not to shift his wings, tried to halt the echo of agony through them.

"You don't answer to Sabine anymore," Ruhn countered.

Ithan considered. "I guess I'm already in this mess." Hunt could have sworn guilt and worry filled Bryce's face. She chewed her bottom lip, but didn't challenge Ithan further.

"Okay," Ithan continued, plugging in the laptop. "Let me get dressed."

Bryce turned warily toward the black box on the counter. The looming, thrumming Death Marks within. But she said, "Right, Athalar. Time to be on our way. Suit up."

Hunt followed Bryce back into her bedroom—their bedroom now, he supposed—to see her pick up a holster and prop her leg on the bed. Her short pink skirt slid back, revealing that lean, long expanse of golden leg. His mind went blank as she strapped the holster around her upper thigh.

Her fingers snagged on the buckle, and Hunt was instantly there to help, savoring the silken warmth of her bare skin. "You're really wearing this to the Bone Quarter?" He drifted a hand to toy with the soft pleats of the skirt. No matter that her gun would be useless against any Reapers that came their way.

"It's a thousand degrees today and humid. I'm not wearing pants."

"What if we get into trouble?" He might have taken far longer on the buckle than necessary. He knew she was letting him.

She smiled wickedly. "Then I suppose the Under-King will get a nice view of my ass."

He gave her a flat look.

Bryce rolled her eyes, but said, "Give me five minutes to change."

29

I think he knows we're coming," Bryce whispered to Hunt as they stood on the edge of the Black Dock and peered through the mist swarming the Istros. Thankfully, there had been no Sailings today. But a path through the mists spread ahead—an opening through which they'd sail to get to the Bone Quarter.

She knew, because she'd sailed through it herself once.

"Good," Hunt said, and Bryce caught his glance at the Starsword she'd sheathed down her back. Ruhn had left it for her with the note: *Bring it. Don't be stupid.*

For once in her life, she'd listened.

And Ruhn had listened when she'd encouraged him, in their swift mind-to-mind conversation, not to trust Cormac. His invitation to Ithan had been the result.

She could only pray they'd stay safe. And that Cormac was true to his word.

Bryce shifted, tucking the thoughts away, the half-rotted black wood beneath her shoes creaking. She'd wound up changing into black leggings and a gray T-shirt before leaving. Yet even with the mist, the heat somehow continued, turning her clothes into a sticky second skin. She should have stayed in the skirt. If only because it had allowed her to conceal the gun—which she'd left behind after Hunt had mortifyingly reminded her of its uselessness against anything they'd encounter in the Bone Quarter.

"Well, here goes," Bryce said, fishing out the onyx coin from the pocket in the back of her waistband. The stifling, earthen smell of mold stuffed itself up her nostrils, as if the coin itself were rotting.

Hunt pulled his coin from a compartment in his battle-suit and sniffed, frowning. "It smells worse the closer we get to the Bone Quarter."

"Then good riddance." Bryce flipped the Death Mark with her thumb into the fog-veiled water below. Hunt's followed. Both only made one ripple before they went rushing toward the Bone Quarter, hidden from view.

"I'm sure a few people have told you this," a male voice said behind them, "but that is a very bad idea."

Bryce whirled, but Hunt bristled. "What the fuck do you want, Baxian?"

The Helhound emerged like a wraith from the mist, wearing his own battle-suit. Shadows had settled beneath his dark eyes, like he hadn't slept in a while. "Why are you here?"

"I'd like to know the same," Hunt bit out.

Baxian shrugged. "Enjoying the sights," he said, and Bryce knew it for the lie it was. Had he followed them? "I thought we were supposed to be paired up, Athalar. You never showed. Does Celestina know about this?"

"It's my day off," Hunt said. Which was true. "So no. It's none of her business. Or yours. Go report to Isaiah. He'll give you something to do."

Baxian's attention shifted to Bryce, and she held his stare. His gaze dipped to the scar on her chest, only the upper spikes of the star visible above the neckline of her T-shirt. "Who are you going to see over there?" His voice had gone low, dangerous.

"The Under-King," Bryce said cheerfully. She could feel Hunt's wariness growing with each breath.

Baxian blinked slowly, as if reading the threat emanating from Athalar. "I can't tell if that's a joke, but if it isn't, you're the dumbest people I've ever met."

Something stirred behind them, and then a long, black boat appeared from the slender path in the mists, drifting toward the dock. Bryce reached out a hand for the prow. Her fingers curled over the screaming skeleton carved into its arch. "Guess you'll have to wait to find out," she said, and leapt in.

She didn't look back as Hunt climbed in after her, the boat rocking with his weight. It pulled away from the Black Dock along that narrow path, leaving Baxian behind to watch until the mists swallowed him.

"You think he'll say anything?" Bryce whispered into the gloom as the path ahead vanished, too.

Hunt's voice was strained, gravelly as it floated toward her. "I don't see why he would. You were attacked by Reapers yesterday. We're going to talk to the Under-King about it today. There's nothing wrong or suspicious about that."

"Right." This shit with Ophion had her overthinking every movement.

Neither of them spoke after that. Neither of them dared.

The boat sailed on, across the too-silent river, all the way to the dark and distant shore.

Hunt had never seen such a place. Knew in his bones he never wanted to see it again.

The boat advanced with no sail, no rudder, no rower or ferryman. As if it were pulled by invisible beasts toward the isle across the Istros. The temperature dropped with each foot, until Hunt could hear Bryce's teeth clacking through the mist, so thick her face was nearly obscured.

The memory of Baxian nagged at him. Snooping asshole.

But he had a feeling that the Helhound wouldn't go blabbing. Not yet. Baxian was more likely to gather intel, to shadow their every move and then strike when he had enough to damn them.

Hunt would turn him into smoldering cinders before he could do that, though. What a fucking mess.

The boat jolted, colliding with something with a *thunk*.

Hunt stiffened, lightning at his fingertips. But Bryce rose, graceful as a leopard, the Starsword's dark hilt muted and matte in the dimness.

The boat had stopped at the base of worn, crumbling steps. The mists above them parted to reveal an archway of carved, ancient bone, brown with age in spots. *Memento Mori*, it said across the top.

Hunt interpreted its meaning differently here than in the Meat Market: *Remember that you will die, and end here. Remember who your true masters are.*

The hair on Hunt's arms rose beneath his battle-suit. Bryce leapt from the boat with Fae elegance, twisting to offer a hand back to him. He took it, only because he wanted to touch her, feel her warmth in this lifeless place.

But her hands were icy, her skin drab and waxy. Even her shimmering hair had dulled. His own skin appeared paler, sickly. As if the Bone Quarter already sucked the life from them.

He interlaced their fingers as they strode up the seven steps to the archway and tucked all the worries and fears regarding Baxian, regarding this rebellion, deep within him. They'd only be a distraction.

His boots scuffed on the steps. Here, Bryce had once knelt. Right here, she'd traded her resting place for Danika's. He squeezed her hand tighter. Bryce squeezed back, leaning into him as they stepped under the archway.

Dry ground lay beyond. Mist, and grayness, and silence. Marble and granite obelisks rose like thick spears, many inscribed—but not with names. Just with strange symbols. Grave markers, or something else? Hunt scanned the gloom, ears straining for any hint of Reapers, of the ruler they sought.

And for any hint of Emile, or Sofie. But not one footprint marked the ground. Not one scent lingered in the mist.

The thought of the kid hiding out here . . . of any living being dwelling here . . . Fuck.

Bryce whispered, voice thick, "It's supposed to be green. I saw a land of green and sunlight." Hunt lifted a brow, but her eyes—now a flat yellow—searched the mists. "The Under-King showed me the Pack of Devils after the attack on the city." Her words shook. "Showed me that they rested here among shining meadows. Not . . . this."

"Maybe the living aren't allowed to see the truth unless the Under-King allows it." She nodded, but he read the doubt tightening her ashen face. He said, "No sign of Emile, unfortunately."

Bryce shook her head. "Nothing. Though I don't know why I thought it'd be easy. It's not like he'd be camped out here in a tent or something."

Hunt, despite himself, offered her a half smile. "So we head to the boss, then." He kept scanning the mists and earth for any hint of Emile or his sister as they continued on.

Bryce halted suddenly between two black obelisks, each engraved with a different array of those odd symbols. The obelisks—and dozens more beyond them—flanked what seemed to be a central walkway stretching into the mist.

She drew the Starsword, and Hunt didn't have time to stop her before she whacked it against the side of the closest obelisk. It clanked, its ringing echoing into the gloom. She did it again. Then a third time.

"Ringing the dinner bell?" Hunt asked.

"Worth a shot," Bryce muttered back. And smarter than running around shouting Emile's and Sofie's names. Though if they were as survival-savvy as they seemed, Hunt doubted either would come running to investigate.

As the noise faded, what remained of the light dimmed. What remained of the warmth turned to ice.

Someone—something—had answered.

The other being they sought here.

Their breath hung in the air, and Hunt angled himself in front of Bryce, monitoring the road ahead.

When the Under-King spoke, however, in a voice simultaneously ancient and youthful but cold and dry, the sound came from behind them. "This land is closed to you, Bryce Quinlan."

A tremor went through Bryce, and Hunt rallied his power, lightning crackling in his ears. But his mate said, "I don't get a VIP pass?"

The voice from the mist echoed around them. "Why have you come? And brought Orion Athalar with you?"

"Call him Hunt," Bryce drawled. "He gets huffy if you go all formal on him."

Hunt gave her an incredulous look. But the Under-King materialized from the mist, inch by inch.

He stood at least ten feet tall, robes of richest black velvet draping to the gravel. Darkness swirled on the ground before him, and his head . . . Something primal in him screamed to run, to bow, to fall on his knees and beg.

A desiccated corpse, half-rotted and crowned with gold and jewels, observed them. Hideous beyond belief, yet regal. Like a long-dead king of old left to rot in some barrow, who had emerged to make himself master of this land.

Bryce lifted her chin and said, bold as Luna herself, "We need to talk."

"Talk?" The lipless mouth pulled back, revealing teeth brown with age.

Hunt reminded himself firmly that the Under-King was feared, yes—but not evil.

Bryce replied, "About your goons grabbing my sweet brother and dragging him into the sewer. They claimed they were sent by Apollion." Hunt tensed as she spoke the Prince of the Pit's name. Bryce continued, utterly nonchalant, "But I don't see how they could have been sent by anyone but *you*."

The Under-King hissed. "Do not speak that name on this side of the Rift."

Hunt followed Bryce's irreverence. "Is this the part where you insist you knew nothing?"

"You have the nerve to cross the river, to take a black boat to my shores, and accuse me of this treachery?" The darkness behind the Under-King shivered. In fear or delight, Hunt couldn't tell.

"Some of your Reapers survived me," Bryce said. "Surely they've filled you in by now."

Silence fell, like the world in the aftermath of a boom of thunder.

The Under-King's milky, lidless eyes slid to the Starsword in Bryce's hand. "Some did *not* survive you?"

Bryce's swallow was audible. Hunt swore silently.

Bryce said, "Why did you feel the need to attack? To pretend the Reapers were messengers of—the Prince of the Pit." She clicked her tongue. "I thought we were friends."

"Death has no friends," the Under-King said, eerily calm. "I did not send any Reapers to attack you. But I do not tolerate those who falsely accuse me in my realm."

"And we're supposed to take you at your word that you're innocent?" Bryce pushed.

"Do you call me a liar, Bryce Quinlan?"

Bryce said, cool and calm as a queen, "You mean to tell me that there are Reapers who can simply defect and serve Hel?"

"From whence do you think the Reapers first came? Who first ruled them, ruled the vampyrs? The Reapers chose Midgard. But I am not surprised some have changed their minds."

Bryce demanded, "And you don't care if Hel steps into your territory?"

"Who said they were my Reapers to begin with? There are none unaccounted for here. There are many other necropolises they might hail from." And other half-life rulers they answered to.

"Reapers don't travel far beyond their realms," Hunt managed to say.

"A comforting lie for mortals." The Under-King smiled faintly.

"All right," Hunt said, fingers tightening around Bryce's. The Under-King seemed to be telling them the truth. Which meant . . . Well, fuck. Maybe Apollion *was* the one who'd sent the Reapers. And if that part was true, then what he'd said about Emile . . .

Bryce seemed to be following the same train of thought, because she said, "I'm looking for two people who might be hiding out here. Any insight?"

"I know all the dead who reside here."

"They're alive," Bryce said. "Humans—or part-humans."

The Under-King surveyed them once more. Right down to their souls. "No one enters this land without my knowledge."

"People can slip in," Hunt countered.

"No," the creature said, smiling again. "They cannot. Whoever you seek, they are not here."

Hunt pushed, "Why should we believe you?"

"I swear upon Cthona's dark crown that no living beings other than yourselves are currently on this island."

Well, vows didn't get much more serious than that. Even the Under-King wouldn't fuck with invoking the earth goddess's name in a vow.

But that left them back at square one. If Emile and Sofie weren't here, and couldn't even enter . . . Danika had to have known that. She'd have been smart enough to look into the rules before sending them here for hiding.

This was a dead end. But it still left Apollion looking for the kid—and them needing to find him before anyone else.

So Hunt said, "You've been enlightening. Thanks for your time."

But Bryce didn't move. Her face had gone stony. "Where's the green and sunlight you showed me? Was that another comforting lie?"

"You saw what you wished to see."

Bryce's lips went white with rage. "Where's the Pack of Devils?"

"You are not entitled to speak to them."

"Is Lehabah here?"

"I do not know of one with such a name."

"A fire sprite. Died three months ago. Is she here?"

"Fire sprites do not come to the Bone Quarter. The Lowers are of no use."

Hunt arched a brow. "No use for what?"

The Under-King smiled again—perhaps a shade ruefully. "Comforting lies, remember?"

Bryce pressed, "Did Danika Fendyr say anything to you before she . . . vanished this spring?"

"You mean before she traded her soul to save yours, as you did with your own."

Nausea surged through Hunt. He hadn't let himself think much on it—that Bryce would not be allowed here. That he wouldn't rest with her one day.

One day that might come very soon, if they were caught associating with rebels.

"Yes," Bryce said tightly. "Before Danika helped to save this city. Where's the Pack of Devils?" she asked again, voice hitching.

Something large growled and shifted in the shadows behind the Under-King, but remained hidden by the mists. Hunt's lightning zapped at his fingers in warning.

"Life is a beautiful ring of growth and decay," the Under-King said, the words echoing through the Sleeping City around them. "No part left to waste. What we receive upon birth, we give back in death. What is granted to you mortals in the Eternal Lands is merely another step in the cycle. A waypoint along your journey toward the Void."

Hunt growled. "Let me guess: You hail from Hel, too?"

"I hail from a place between stars, a place that has no name and never shall. But I know of the Void that the Princes of Hel worship. It birthed me, too."

The star in the center of Bryce's chest flared.

The Under-King smiled, and his horrific face turned ravenous. "I beheld your light across the river, that day. Had I only known when you first came to me—things might have been quite different."

Hunt's lightning surged, but he reined it in. "What do you want with her?"

"What I want from all souls who pass here. What I give back to the Dead Gate, to all of Midgard: energy, life, power. You did not give your power to the Eleusian system; you made the Drop outside of it. Thus, you still possess some firstlight. Raw, nutritious firstlight."

"Nutritious?" Bryce said.

The Under-King waved a bony hand. "Can you blame me for sampling the goods as they pass through the Dead Gate?"

Hunt's mouth dried up. "You . . . you feed on the souls of the dead?"

"Only those who are worthy. Who have enough energy. There is no judgment but that: whether a soul possesses enough residual power to make a hearty meal, both for myself and for the Dead Gate. As their souls pass through the Dead Gate, I take a . . . bite or two."

Hunt cringed inwardly. Maybe he had been too hasty in deeming the being before him not evil.

The Under-King went on, "The rituals were all invented by you. Your ancestors. To endure the horror of the offering."

"But Danika was here. She *answered* me." Bryce's voice broke.

"She was here. She and all of the newly dead from the past several centuries. Just long enough that their living descendants and loved ones either forget or don't come asking. They dwell here until then in relative comfort—unless they make themselves a nuisance and I decide to send them into the Gate sooner. But when the dead are forgotten, their names no longer whispered on the wind . . . then they are herded through the Gate to become firstlight. Or secondlight, as it is called when the power comes from the dead. Ashes to ashes and all that."

"The Sleeping City is a lie?" Hunt asked. His mother's face flashed before him.

"A comforting one, as I have said." The Under-King's voice again became sorrowful. "One for your benefit."

"And the Asteri know about this?" Hunt demanded.

"I would never presume to claim what the holy ones know or don't know."

"Why are you telling us any of this?" Bryce blanched with horror.

"Because he's not letting us leave here alive," Hunt breathed. And their souls wouldn't live on, either.

The light vanished entirely, and the voice of the Under-King echoed around them. "That is the first intelligent thing you've said."

A rumbling growl shook the ground. Reverberated up Hunt's legs. He clutched Bryce to him, snapping out his wings for a blind flight upward.

The Under-King crooned, "I should like to taste your light, Bryce Quinlan."

30

Ruhn had grown up in Crescent City. He knew it had places to avoid, yet it had always felt like home. Like his.

Until today.

"Ephraim must have arrived," Ithan murmured as they waited in the dimness of a dusty alley for Cormac to finish making the information drop. "And brought the Hind with him."

"And she brought her entire pack of dreadwolves? To what end?" Ruhn toyed with the ring through his bottom lip. They'd seen two of the elite imperial interrogators on the way to the meet-up near the Old Square.

Ruhn had veiled himself and Holstrom in shadows while Cormac spoke at the other end of the alley with the cloaked, hooded figure disguised as a begging vagrant. Ruhn could make out the outline of a gun strapped to the figure's thigh beneath the threadbare cloak.

Ithan eyed him. "You think the Hind's onto us?"

Us. Fuck, just that word freaked him out when it came to consorting with rebels. Ruhn monitored the bright street beyond the alley, willing his shadows to keep them hidden from what prowled the sidewalks.

Tourists and city dwellers alike kept a healthy distance from the dreadwolves. The wolf shifters were exactly as Ruhn had expected:

cold-eyed and harsh-faced above their pristine gray uniforms. A black-and-white patch of a wolf's skull and crossbones adorned that uniform's left arm. The seven golden stars of the Asteri shone on a red patch above their hearts. And on their starched, high collars—silver darts.

The number varied on each member. One dart for every rebel spy hunted down and broken. The two that Ruhn had passed had borne eight and fifteen darts, respectively.

"It's like the city's gone quiet," Ithan observed, head cocked. "Isn't this the *least* safe place for this meet-up?"

"Don't be paranoid," Ruhn said, though he'd thought the same.

Down the alley, Cormac finished and strode back to them. Within a blink, the hunched figure was gone, swallowed into the crowds teeming on the main avenue, all too focused on the dreadwolves slinking among them to remark on a hobbling vagrant.

Cormac had veiled his face in shadows, and they pulled away now as he met Ruhn's stare. "The agent told me they think the Asteri suspect that Emile came here after he fled Ophion. It's possible the Hind brought the dreadwolves to hunt for him."

"The sight of those wolves in this city is a disgrace," Ithan snarled. "No one's going to stomach this shit."

"You'd be surprised what people will stomach when they find their families threatened," Cormac said. "I've seen cities and towns fall silent in the wake of a dreadwolf pack's arrival. Places as vibrant as this, now warrens of fear and mistrust. They, too, thought no one would tolerate it. That someone would do something. Only when it was too late did they realize that *they* should have done something."

A chill ran up Ruhn's arms. "I have to make some calls. The Aux and the 33rd run this city. Not the Hind." Shit, he'd have to see his father. He might be a bastard, but the Autumn King wouldn't appreciate having the Hind infringe on his turf.

Ithan's jaw twitched. "I wonder what Sabine and the Prime will do about them."

"No loyalty among wolves?" Cormac asked.

"*We* are wolves," Ithan challenged. "The dreadwolves . . . they're demons in wolves' fur. Wolves in name only."

"And if the dreadwolves request to stay at the Den?" Cormac asked. "Will the Prime or Sabine find their morals holding firm?"

Ithan didn't answer.

Cormac went on, "This is what the Asteri do. This is Midgard's true reality. We believe we are free, we are powerful, we are near-immortals. But when it comes down to it, we're all the Asteri's slaves. And the illusion can be shattered this quickly."

"Then why the fuck are you trying to bring this shit here?" Ithan demanded.

"Because it has to end at some point," Ruhn murmured. He shuddered inwardly.

Cormac opened his mouth, surprise lighting his face—but whirled as a male—towering and muscle-bound and clad in the impeccable uniform of the dreadwolves—appeared at the other end of the alley. So many silver darts covered his collar that from a distance, it looked like a mouth full of razor-sharp teeth around his neck.

"Mordoc," Ithan breathed. Genuine fear laced his scent. Cormac motioned for the wolf to be silent.

Mordoc . . . Ruhn scanned his memory. The second in command to the Hind. Her chief butcher and enforcer. The dreadwolf monitored the alley with golden, glowing eyes. Dark claws glinted at his fingertips. As if he lived in some state between human and wolf.

Cormac's nose crinkled. The prince trembled, anger and violence leaking from him. Ruhn gripped his cousin's shoulder, fingers digging into the hard muscle.

Slowly, Mordoc prowled down the alley. Noting the brick walls, the dusty ground—

Fuck. They'd left tracks all over this alley. None of them dared to breathe too loudly as they pressed into the wall.

Mordoc angled his head, scalp gleaming through his buzzed hair, then crouched, muscles flexing beneath his gray uniform, and ran a thick finger through a footprint. He lifted the dirt to his nose and sniffed. His teeth—slightly too long—gleamed in the dimness of the alley.

Mind-to-mind, Ruhn asked Cormac, *Does Mordoc know your scent?*

I don't think so. Does he know yours?

No. I've never met him.

Ruhn said to Ithan, who jolted slightly at the sound of Ruhn's voice in his mind, *Do you know Mordoc? Have you met him before?*

Ithan's gaze remained on the powerful male now rising to sniff the air. *Yes. A long time ago. He came to visit the Den.*

Why?

Ithan at last responded, eyes wide and pained. *Because he's Danika's father.*

Bryce had enough presence of mind to draw the Starsword. To rally her power even though the thing before them . . . Oh gods.

"Allow me to introduce my shepherd," the Under-King said from the mist ahead, standing beside a ten-foot-tall black dog. Each of its fangs was as long as one of her fingers. All hooked—like a shark's. Designed to latch into flesh and hold tight while it ripped and shredded. Its eyes were milky white—sightless. Identical to the Under-King's.

Her light would have no effect on something that was already blind.

The dog's fur—sleek and iridescent enough that it almost resembled scales—flowed over bulky, bunched muscle. Claws like razor blades sliced into the dry ground.

Hunt's lightning crackled, skittering at Bryce's feet. "That's a demon," he ground out. He'd fought enough of them to know.

"An experiment of the Prince of the Ravine's, from the First Wars," the Under-King rasped. "Forgotten and abandoned here in Midgard during the aftermath. Now my faithful companion and helper. You'd be surprised how many souls do not wish to make their final offering to the Gate. The Shepherd . . . Well, it herds them for me. As it shall herd you."

"Fry this fucker," Bryce muttered to Hunt as the dog snarled.

"I'm assessing."

"Assess faster. *Roast it like a—*"

"Do *not* make a joke about—"

"Hot dog."

Bryce had no sooner finished saying the words than the hound lunged. Hunt struck, swift and sure, a lightning bolt spearing toward its neck.

It screamed, dodging to the left, an obelisk crumbling beneath it. Bryce pivoted to where the Under-King had been, but only mist remained.

Coward.

Hunt struck again, forked lightning splitting the sky before it slammed into the creature's back, but it rolled once more, shaking off the lightning.

"The *fuck*," Hunt panted, drawing his sword and gun as he moved in front of Bryce. The Shepherd halted, eyeing them. Then the hound peeled apart.

First its head split, two other heads joining the first. And then the three-headed dog continued to separate until three hounds snarled at them. Three beasts that shared one mind, one goal: *Kill*.

"Run," Hunt ordered, not taking his focus from the three dogs. "Get back to the river and fucking *swim*."

"Not without you."

"I'll be right behind."

"Just fly us—"

The dog to the left snarled, bristling. Bryce faced it, and in that blink, the one on the right leapt. Hunt's lightning snapped free, and Bryce didn't hesitate before she turned and ran.

Mist swallowed her, swallowed Hunt until he was nothing but light rippling behind her. She sped past obelisks and stone mausoleums. Resting places for the dead, or mere cages to keep them until they could become food, valuable for their firstlight? *Secondlight*.

Thunderous steps crunched behind her. She dared a glance over her shoulder.

One of the hounds rampaged at her heels, closing the distance. Hunt's lightning flashed behind it, along with his bellow of rage. That was her *mate* she was leaving behind—

Bryce cut inland. The beast, apparently convinced she was making a run for the river, pivoted too slowly. It crashed into a mausoleum, sending both structure and hound sprawling. Bryce kept running. Sprinted as fast as she could back toward Hunt.

But the mist was a labyrinth, and Hunt's lightning seemed to launch from everywhere. Obelisks loomed like giants.

Bryce slammed into something hard and smooth, her teeth punching through her lower lip and the Starsword clattering out of her hand. The coppery tang of blood filled her mouth as she hit the ground. Flipping over, she peered up to find herself sprawled before a crystal archway.

The Dead Gate.

A snarl rumbled the earth. Bryce twisted, crawling backward to the Gate. The Shepherd emerged from the mist.

And in the grayish dirt between them lay the Starsword, glowing faintly.

Ruhn's blood iced over at Ithan's declaration. Did Bryce know Mordoc was Danika's father? She'd have mentioned it if she did, right?

It wasn't spoken of, Ithan explained. *Sabine and the others tried to forget. Danika refused to acknowledge Mordoc. Never said his name, or that she even had a father. But a few of us were at the Den the only time he came to see his daughter. She was seventeen and refused to even see him. Afterward, she wouldn't talk about it except to say that she was nothing like him. She never mentioned Mordoc again.*

The male approached, and Ruhn scanned for any hint of Danika Fendyr in him. He found none. *They don't resemble each other at all.*

Ithan said warily, sadly, *The similarities run beneath the surface.* Ruhn waited for the blow. Knew it was coming even before Ithan explained, *He's a bloodhound.*

Ruhn said to Cormac, *Teleport us the fuck out of here.* He should have done it the moment they saw Mordoc coming.

I can only take one at a time.

Mordoc drew closer. *Take Ithan and* go.

I won't be able to pinpoint you in the shadows when I return, Cormac answered. *Be ready to run to the avenue on my signal.* Then he grabbed Ithan and vanished.

Ruhn kept perfectly still as the wolf prowled near. Sniffing, head swaying from side to side.

"I can smell you, Faeling," Mordoc growled, voice like stones cracking against each other. "I can smell the coffee on your breath."

Ruhn kept his shadows tight around him, blending into the dimness along the alley's far wall. He made each step silent, though the dusty ground threatened to betray him.

"What were you doing here, I wonder," Mordoc said, halting to turn in place. Tracking Ruhn. "I saw your agent go in—the vagabond. He slipped my net, but why did you stay?"

Where the Hel was Cormac? Considering that Bryce and Hunt were currently in the Bone Quarter, Ruhn had expected *them* to be the ones in major peril today.

He kept moving, slowly and silently. The bright, open street lay beyond. The crowd might hide him, but not his scent. And his shadows would be of no use out in the sunny open.

"Hunting you all down like vermin shall be diverting," Mordoc said, pivoting in place as if he could see Ruhn through the shadows. "This city has been coddled for far too long."

Ruhn's temper unsheathed its talons, but he willed it down.

"Ah, that annoys you. I can smell it." A savage smile. "I shall remember that smell."

At the other end of the alley, Ruhn's magic picked up the flicker of Cormac arriving—only long enough to scuff his shoes in the dirt—and then vanish.

Mordoc whirled toward it, and Ruhn ran, dropping the shadows around himself.

Cormac appeared in a writhing nest of darkness, grabbed his arm, and teleported them out. Ruhn could only pray to Luna that by the time Mordoc had faced the street again, nothing remained of his scent for the bloodhound to detect.

31

Ruhn nursed his glass of whiskey, trying to calm his frayed nerves. Ithan, seated across from him at a quiet bar in FiRo, was watching the sports highlights on the TV above the liquor display. Cormac had dropped them both here before teleporting away, presumably to warn his rebel counterparts about what had happened with Mordoc.

Danika's father. Bryce would have a fit.

Had her sire's involvement with the dreadwolves been part of what spurred Danika to work with the rebels? She was rebellious and defiant enough to do such a thing.

And Mordoc knew Ruhn's scent now. Knew Ithan's scent had been there. Which was why Cormac had brought them here—so there would be video proof of them far from the Old Square at the time Mordoc would claim Ithan had been in the alley.

Ithan said nothing as the minutes wore on, his whiskey vanishing with them. No matter that it was barely eleven in the morning and only one other person sat at the bar—a hunched female who looked like she'd seen better years. Decades.

Neither of them dared utter a word about what had happened. So Ruhn said to Ithan, "I asked you to join me here so we could chat about something."

Ithan blinked. "Yeah?"

Ruhn said to him, mind-to-mind, *Play along. I have no idea if the cameras have audio, but in case they do, I want our meeting here to seem planned.*

Ithan's face remained casual, intrigued. *Got it.*

Ruhn made sure his voice was loud enough to be picked up as he said, "How do you feel about moving in with me and the guys?"

Ithan angled his head. "What? Like—live with you?" His surprise seemed genuine.

Ruhn shrugged. "Why not?"

"You're Fae."

"Yeah, but we hate the angels more than we hate wolves, so . . . you're only our second-worst enemy."

Ithan chuckled, some color returning to his face. "A winning argument."

"I mean it," Ruhn said. "You honestly want to stay at Bryce's apartment and endure her and Hunt hooking up nonstop?"

Ithan snorted. "Hel no. But . . . why?" *Beyond an excuse for the cameras,* Ithan said silently.

Ruhn leaned back in his chair. "You seem like a decent male. You're helping Dec with the footage stuff. And you need a place to stay. Why not?"

Ithan seemed to weigh his response. "I'll think about it."

"Take all the time you need. The offer stands."

Ithan straightened, his attention darting behind Ruhn. He went wholly still. Ruhn didn't dare look. Not as light footsteps sounded, followed by a second thudding pair. Before he could ask Ithan mind-to-mind what he saw, Ruhn found himself faced with the most beautiful female he'd ever seen.

"Mind if I join?" Her voice was lovely, fair and cool—yet no light shone in her amber eyes.

A step behind her, a dark-haired, pale-faced female malakh grinned with wicked amusement. She was narrow-featured, black-winged, with a wildness like the western wind. "Hello, princeling. Pup."

Ruhn's blood chilled as the Harpy slid into the seat to his left.

An assortment of knives glinted on the belt at her slim waist. But Ruhn peered up again at the beautiful female, whose face he knew well thanks to the news and TV, though he'd never seen it in person. Her golden hair glinted in the dim lights as she sat on his right and signaled the bartender with an elegant hand.

"I thought we'd play a round of cards," the Hind said.

Two against one. Those odds were usually laughable for Hunt.

But not when his opponents were demons from Hel. One of the princes' cast-off experiments, now acting as the Under-King's enforcers, feeding long-dead souls into the Gate for secondlight energy. Like all they were, would ever be, was food to fuel the empire.

The demon to his left lunged, teeth snapping.

Hunt blasted his lightning, forks of it wrapping around the beast's thick neck. It bucked, bellowing, and the one to his right charged. Hunt lashed at it, another collar of lightning going around its neck, a leash of white light clenched in his fist.

Had Bryce made it to the river? The third demon had raced after her before he could stop it, but she was fast, and she was smart—

The demons before him halted. They shuddered and melted back into each other, becoming one beast again.

His lightning remained around its neck. But he could do nothing as it flexed—and shattered the lightning sizzling into its flesh. Something of that size and speed would use the two seconds of slowness it took him to get airborne and swallow him whole.

This wasn't how he'd expected the morning to go.

He rallied his power, focusing. He'd killed Sandriel with this lightning. A demon should be nothing. But before he could act, a scream rent the mists to the southeast. The beast twisted toward the sound, sniffing.

And before Hunt could stop it, faster than his lightning's whip, it raced off into the mist. After Bryce.

* * *

Bryce crouched beside the Dead Gate, sizing up the threats surrounding her. Not just the hound, but the two dozen Reapers who'd floated from the mists, encircling her.

The half-lifes' rotting flesh reeked; their acid-green eyes glowed through the mists. Their rasping whispers slithered like snakes over her skin. The Shepherd advanced, cutting her off further.

The crystal of the Dead Gate began to glow white. Not from her touch, but as if—

The Reapers were chanting. Awakening the Dead Gate, somehow.

During the attack on the city, it had channeled her magic against the demons, but today . . . today it would siphon off her power. Her soul. The Gates sucked magic from whoever touched them, and stored it. She'd inherited her power from that very force.

But this one fed that power right back into the power grid. Like some fucked-up rechargeable battery. Somehow, she'd become food. Was that what she'd traded away? A few centuries here, thinking she'd found eternal rest—and then meeting this end? Instead, she'd face a trip straight into the meat grinder of souls immediately when she died.

Which seemed likely to be soon.

There was a good chance that she could draw from the Gate as well, she supposed. But what if the Dead Gate was somehow different? What if she went to summon power, only to lose all of hers? She couldn't risk it.

Bryce got to her feet, hands shaking. The Starsword lay between her and the Shepherd.

Hunt's lightning had stopped. Where was he? Would a mate know, would a mate feel—

Another dog stepped from the mist. Then peeled apart into two—the ones Hunt had been fighting. No blood stained their muzzles, but Hunt wasn't with them. Not a sliver of his lightning graced the mists.

The three dogs advanced, sniffing for her location. The Reapers kept chanting as the Dead Gate glowed brighter. That teleporting of Cormac's would have been helpful—she could have grabbed Hunt five minutes ago and vanished.

She glanced at the sword. It was now or never. Live or die. Like, *really* die.

Bryce sucked in a breath, and didn't give herself a chance to second-guess her stupidity. She bolted for the hounds. They charged, leaping for her with three sets of snapping jaws—

Bryce dropped, the rocky ground shredding her face as she slid beneath them, until the Starsword was cradled to her body. Something burning shot down her back.

The world boomed with the impact of the three hounds landing and pivoting. Bryce tried to get up, to hold the sword out, but blood warmed her back. A claw must have raked up her spine while one of the hounds had leapt over her, and the splintering, blistering pain—

Hunt was out there somewhere. Possibly dying.

Bryce dug the tip of the Starsword into the earth, using it to shove herself up to her knees. Her back screamed in agony. She might have screamed with it. The three hounds, the Reapers beyond them, seemed to smile.

"Yeah," Bryce panted, heaving to her feet. "Fuck you, too."

Her legs wobbled, yet she managed to lift the black sword in front of her. The three beasts roared, threatening to split her ears. Bryce opened her mouth to roar back.

But someone else did it for her.

For Hunt, there was only Bryce, bleeding and hurt.

Bryce, who'd made that brash run for the sword, probably thinking it was her only shot. Bryce, who'd gotten to her feet anyway, and planned to go down swinging.

Bryce, his mate.

The three hounds merged back into one. Readying for the killing blow.

Hunt landed in the dirt beside her and let out a bellow that shook the Gate itself.

* * *

Wreathed in lightning from wing tip to toe, Hunt landed beside Bryce so hard the earth shuddered. The power rolling off him sent Bryce's hair floating upward. Primal rage poured from Hunt as he faced down the Shepherd. The Reapers.

She'd never seen anything of the sort—Hunt was the heart of a storm personified. The lightning around him turned blue, like the hottest part of a flame.

An image blasted through her mind. She *had* seen this before, carved in stone in the lobby of the CCB. A Fae male posed like an avenging god, hammer raised to the sky, a channel for his power—

Hunt unleashed his lightning at the Shepherd, the Reapers observing with wide eyes.

Bryce was too fast, even for him, as she leapt in front of the blow, Starsword extended. A wild theory, only half-formed, but—

Hunt's lightning hit the Starsword, and the world erupted.

32

Hunt screamed as Bryce leapt in front of his power. As his lightning hit the black blade, exploding from the metal, flowing up into her arm, her body, her heart. Light flashed, blinding—

No, that was Bryce.

Power crackled from every inch of her, and from the Starsword she clenched in one hand as she barreled toward the Shepherd. It split into three hounds again, and as the first beast landed, Bryce struck. The glowing Starsword pierced the thick hide. Lightning exploded across the beast's body. The other two screamed, and Reapers began scattering into the mist beyond the obelisks.

Bryce whirled as Hunt reached her and said, eyes white with light, "Watch out!"

Too late. The beast who'd fallen snapped its tail at Hunt, catching him in the gut and hurling him into the Dead Gate. He hit the stone and crumpled, his power fizzing out.

Bryce shouted his name as she held her ground against the remaining two beasts. The one she'd injured died, twitching on the ground. Hunt gasped for breath, trying to rise.

She lifted the sword, crackling with remnants of power. Not much. Like the first blow had exhausted most of it. Hunt braced a hand on the Dead Gate's brass plaque as he tried to raise himself once more.

Power sucked from his fingers, pulled into the stone. He snatched his hand back. One of the beasts lunged for Bryce, but bounced away at a swipe of her sword. She needed more power—

Hunt peered at the Dead Gate's archway above him. Firstlight flowed both ways. Into the Dead Gate and out of it.

And here, where the last power of the dead was fed into it . . . here was a well, like the one Bryce had used during the attack last spring.

Sofie and Emile Renast could channel energy, too—and lightning. Hunt was no thunderbird, but could he do the same?

Lightning flowed in his veins. His body was equipped to handle raw, sizzling energy. Was this what Apollion had hinted at—why the prince wanted not only him and Bryce, but Emile and Sofie? Had the Prince of the Pit engineered this situation, manipulating them into coming to the Bone Quarter so that Hunt would be forced to realize what he could do with his own power? Perhaps Emile hadn't even come here at all. Perhaps the Reapers had lied about that at Apollion's behest, just to get them here, to this place, this moment—

Bryce angled her sword higher, ready to fight until the end. Hunt gazed at her for a moment, an avenging angel in her own right—and then slammed his hand onto the brass plaque of the Dead Gate.

Bryce dared only a glance behind her as Hunt bellowed again. He was standing, but his hand . . .

White, blinding firstlight—or was it secondlight?—flowed from the Dead Gate up his arm. Up his shoulder. And on the other side of the archway, the stone began to go dark. As if he were draining it.

The two hounds of the Shepherd merged back together, anticipating the next strike. Hunt's voice was a thunderclap as he said behind her, "Light it up, Bryce."

The words bloomed in Bryce's heart at the same moment Hunt shot a bolt of his power—the Dead Gate's power—into her. It burned and roared and blinded, a writhing ball of energy that Bryce broke to her will and funneled into the Starsword.

Forks of lightning cracked from Hunt, from her, from the sword.

The Shepherd turned tail and fled.

Bryce ran after it.

Wings flapped behind her, and then she was in Hunt's arms. He carried her high above the beast's back, then plunged down, lightning streaming around them, a meteorite crashing—

They slammed into the creature, and Bryce drove the sword into the Shepherd's nape. Into the skull beneath. Lightning and firstlight blasted through it, and the hound exploded into smoking smithereens.

Bryce and Hunt hit the ground panting and steaming, soaked with the Shepherd's blood. But Hunt was up again in a moment, running, a hand on Bryce's back as he hauled her with him. "The river," he panted, lightning skittering across his teeth, his cheeks. His wings drooped like he was wholly exhausted. Like flying was beyond him.

Bryce didn't waste breath to answer as they raced through the mist toward the Istros.

"Two more Vanir bodies this morning, Your Excellency," Tharion said by way of greeting, bowing at the waist as he stood in his queen's private study.

It was more biodome than study, really, full of plants and a deep, winding stream, studded with large pools. The River Queen swam among the lily pads, her black hair trailing like ink in the water behind her. Her day of meetings might require her to be inside the building, but she took all of them here, sitting in her element.

She turned toward Tharion, hair plastered down her ample, heavy breasts, her brown skin gleaming with water. "Tell me where." Her voice was lovely, but subdued. Cold.

"One left hanging upside down in an olive grove north of the city—drained and shot the same way as the selkie—the other crucified on the tree next to him. Also shot, with a slit throat. They'd clearly been tortured. Two human scents were present. Seems like this happened yesterday."

He'd gotten the report this morning over breakfast. Hadn't bothered to go to the sites or ask Holstrom to come with him, not when the Aux had been the ones to get the call, and would be the ones to handle the bodies.

"And you still believe the rebel Pippa Spetsos is behind these killings."

"The style is in line with what her Lightfall squad does to its victims. I think she's on Emile Renast's trail, and is torturing anyone who helped him on his way."

"Is the boy here, then?"

"Considering the proximity of the latest site, I have good reason to believe he has arrived." An otter looped and twirled past the windows, a message clenched in his fangs, neon-yellow vest glaringly bright in the cobalt blue.

"And Sofie Renast?" The River Queen toyed with a pink-and-gold lily that brushed against her soft stomach, running her elegant fingers over its petals. "Any sightings of her?"

"Not a ripple." No need to mention Bryce and Athalar going to the Bone Quarter for answers. There was nothing to tell yet. He could only hope the two of them would emerge alive.

"The Hind is here, in Lunathion. Do you believe she's also tracking Emile?"

"She's only arrived today." He'd gotten reports already that her wolves prowled the city, along with the Harpy. At least the Hawk, his spies said, had remained behind in Pangera, left to guard Ephraim's roost, apparently. "Her whereabouts have been public for the last few days—she doesn't have a human scent, and also wasn't in the city to commit these murders. All signs point to Pippa Spetsos."

The river-spirit plucked the lily and tucked it behind her ear. It glowed as if lit by a kernel of firstlight. "Find that boy, Tharion."

He bowed his head. "What about Ophion Command? If they find out we have Emile . . ."

"Make sure they don't find out." Her eyes darkened, and storms threatened. Lightning lashed the surface high above. "We are loyal to the House of Many Waters first and foremost."

"Why the boy?" he finally dared ask. "Why do you want him so badly?"

"You question me?" Only the Ocean Queen, Lady of Waters, Daughter of Ogenas, had that right. Or the Asteri. Tharion bowed.

Lightning illuminated the surface again, and Tharion's brows lowered. That wasn't his queen's power. And since the forecast hadn't called for storms . . .

Tharion bowed again. "I apologize for the impertinence. Your will is mine," he said, the familiar words falling from his lips. "I'll update you when I've apprehended the boy."

He made to leave, risking doing so without dismissal, and had nearly made it to the archway before the River Queen said, "Did you enjoy your punishment last night?"

He closed his eyes for a moment before he turned to face her.

She'd lowered herself into the stream again, no more than a dark, beautiful head among the lily pads. Like one of her sobeks, waiting to make a meal of the unworthy dead.

Tharion said, "It was a wise and fitting punishment for my ignorance and transgression."

Her lips curled upward, revealing slightly pointed white teeth. "It is diverting to see you tug at the leash, Tharion."

He swallowed his retort, his rage, his grief, and inclined his head.

More lightning. He had to go. Knew better than to reveal his impatience, though. "I have only your daughter's best interests in my heart."

Again, that ancient, cruel smile that informed him she'd seen too many males—some far smarter than he—come and go. "I suppose we shall see." With that, she dipped beneath the water, vanishing under the lily pads and among the reeds.

Hunt could barely stand.

The firstlight had flayed him, leaving a smoking ruin inside his body, his mind. But it had worked. He'd taken the power and converted it into his own. Whatever the fuck that meant. Apollion had known—or guessed enough to be right. And Bryce . . . the sword . . .

She'd been a conduit to his power. Fucking Hel.

They staggered through the mists, the obelisks. Screeching and hissing rose around them. Reapers. Would anyplace in Midgard be safe now, even after death? He sure as fuck didn't want his soul in the Bone Quarter.

The bone gates appeared overhead, carved from the ribs of some ancient leviathan, and beyond them, the steps to the river. Hunt's knees nearly buckled as he spied a familiar wave skimmer and the mer male atop it, beckoning frantically as he pivoted the wave skimmer toward Lunathion proper.

"I thought that was you, with all the lightning," Tharion panted as they rushed toward him and leapt down the steps. He slipped off the wave skimmer to make room for them, shifting as he went. The mer looked like Hel: haunted and tired and bleak.

Bryce climbed on first, and Hunt joined her, clasping her from behind. She gunned the engine and sped off into the mist, Tharion shooting under the surface beside them. Hunt nearly collapsed against her back, but Bryce veered to the left, so sharply he had to clutch her hips to keep from falling into the water. "Fuck!" she shouted as scaly, muscled backs broke the surface.

Sobeks.

Only the nutritious souls went to the Under-King. The ones given over to the beasts were snacks. Junk food. A broad snout full of thick, daggerlike fangs shot from the water.

Blood sprayed before the creature could rip into Hunt's leg. Bryce zigged to the right, and Hunt twisted to see Tharion on their tail, a deadly plume of water aimed above him. Pressurized, like a water cannon. So intense and brutal that it had carved a hole right through a sobek's head.

Another beast lunged for them, and again, Tharion struck, water breaking flesh as surely as it could eat away at stone.

A third, and Tharion attacked with brutal efficiency. The other beasts halted, tails lashing the water.

"Hang on!" Bryce shouted toward Tharion, who gripped the side of the wave skimmer as she hurtled them toward the Black Dock. The mist fell away behind them, and a wall of sunshine blinded Hunt.

They didn't stop, though. Not when they hit the dock. Not when Tharion leapt from the water and shifted, grabbing a spare Blue Court aquatic uniform from the seat-hatch in the wave skimmer. The three of them hurried down the streets to Bryce's apartment.

In the safety of her home, Bryce knelt on the floor, wet and bloody and panting. The slice along her spine was long but mercifully shallow, already clotting. It had missed the Horn tattoo by millimeters. Hunt had enough sanity remaining to avoid the white couch as Tharion said, "What happened? Any sign of Emile or Sofie?"

"No—we were stupid to even look for them in the Bone Quarter," Hunt said, sitting at the dining table, trying to reel his mind back in. Bryce filled the mer in on the rest.

When she finished, Tharion dropped onto one of the counter stools, face white. "I know I should be disappointed that Emile and Sofie weren't hiding in the Bone Quarter, but . . . that's what awaits us in the end?"

Hunt opened his mouth, but Bryce asked, "Where's Ruhn? He and Ithan should be back."

Hunt narrowed his eyes. "Call them."

Bryce did, but neither answered. Hunt fished out his phone, grateful he'd gotten the water-repellent spell Quinlan had needled him into purchasing. News alerts and messages filled the screen.

Hunt said a shade hoarsely, "Ephraim just got here. With the Hind."

Tharion nodded grimly. "She brought her pack of dreadwolves with her."

Bryce checked the clock on her phone again. "I need to find Ruhn."

33

Ruhn said nothing as the Hind produced a deck of cards from the pocket of her imperial uniform.

Ithan played the role of confused jock, alternating ignorance with bored distraction as he watched the game above the bar. The Hind shuffled the deck, cards cracking like breaking bones.

On the table's fourth side, the Harpy lounged in her seat and marked his every move. Her wings—a matte black, like they'd been built for stealth—spilled onto the floor. She wore the familiar battle-suit of the 45th—Sandriel's former prized legion. The Harpy, along with the Hammer, had been one of its notoriously cruel leaders.

"I don't believe we've met," the Hind said, flexing and breaking the cards again. Her hands were deft, unfaltering. Unscarred. She wore a gold ring crowned with a square, clean-cut ruby. A subtle hint of wealth.

Ruhn forced himself to smirk. "I'm flattered I was so high on your priority list today."

"You're my half sister's fiancé, are you not?" A lifeless smile. The opposite of Hypaxia's warmth and wisdom. The Hind was only about twenty years older than her sister—forty-seven years old—far closer in age than most Vanir siblings. But they shared nothing in common, it seemed. "It would be rude not to introduce myself upon arrival. I already visited your father's villa. He informed me that you were here."

Cormac must have arrived right before the Hind, to feed the lie to the Autumn King. Thank the gods.

Ruhn snorted. "Nice to meet you. I'm busy."

The Harpy's skin was as pale as the belly of a fish, set off by her jet-black hair and eyes. She said, "You're as impertinent as you appear, princeling."

Ruhn flicked his lip ring with his tongue. "I'd hate to disappoint."

The Harpy's features contorted in anger. But the Hind said mildly, "We'll play poker, I think. Isn't that what you play on Tuesday nights?"

Ruhn repressed his shiver of fear. The standing game wasn't a secret, but . . . how much did she know about him?

Ithan remained the portrait of boredom, gods bless him.

So Ruhn said to the Hind, "All right, you're keeping tabs on me for your sister's sake." Was it mere coincidence she'd sought him out now? What had Mordoc told her about Ithan's whereabouts this morning? Ruhn asked the Harpy, "But why the Hel are *you* here?"

The Harpy's thin lips stretched into a grotesque smile. She reached a pale hand toward Ithan's muscled shoulder as she said, "I wanted to survey the goods."

Without looking at her, the wolf snatched her fingers, squeezing hard enough to show that he could break bone if he wished. Slowly, he turned, eyes brimming with hate. "You can look, but don't touch."

"You break it, you buy it," the Harpy crooned, wriggling her fingers. She liked this—the edge of pain.

Ithan bared his teeth in a feral grin and released her hand. The pup had balls, Ruhn would give him that. Ithan looked at the TV again as he said, "Pass."

The Harpy bristled, and Ruhn said, "He's a little young for you."

"And what about you?" A killer's sharp smile.

Ruhn leaned back in his chair, swigging from his whiskey. "I'm engaged. I don't fuck around."

The Hind dealt the cards with a swift, sure grace. "Except with fauns, of course."

Ruhn kept his face unmoved. How did she know about the female at the party? He met her golden eyes. A perfect match for the Hammer in beauty and temperament. She hadn't been at the Summit this spring, thank the gods. The Harpy had been there, though, and Ruhn had done his damn best to stay away from her.

The Hind scooped up her cards without breaking his stare. "I wonder if my sister shall learn of that."

"Is this some sort of shakedown?" Ruhn fanned out his cards. A decent hand—not great, but he'd won with worse.

The Hind's attention bobbed to her cards, then back to his face. This female had most likely killed Sofie Renast. A silver torque glinted at the base of her throat. Like she'd killed and broken so many rebels that the collar of her uniform couldn't fit all the darts. Did the necklace grow with each new death she wrought? Would his own be marked on that collar?

The Hind said, "Your father suggested I meet you. I agreed." Ruhn suspected that his father hadn't just told her his location to provide an alibi, but also to warn him to keep the fuck out of trouble.

Ithan picked up his cards, scanned them, and swore. The Harpy said nothing as she examined her own hand.

The Hind held Ruhn's gaze as the game began. She was the spitting image of Luna, with her upswept chignon, the regal angle of her neck and jaw. As coldly serene as the moon. All she needed was a pack of hunting hounds at her side—

And she had them, in her dreadwolves.

How had someone so young risen in the ranks so swiftly, gained such notoriety and power? No wonder she left a trail of blood behind her.

"Careful now," the Harpy said with that oily smile. "The Hammer doesn't share."

The Hind's lips curved upward. "No, he doesn't."

"As Ithan said," Ruhn drawled, "pass."

The Harpy glowered, but the Hind's smile remained in place. "Where is your famed sword, Prince?"

With Bryce. In the Bone Quarter. "Left it at home this morning," Ruhn answered.

"I heard you spent the night at your sister's apartment."

Ruhn shrugged. Was this interrogation merely to fuck with him? Or did the Hind know something? "I didn't realize you had the authority to grill Aux leaders in this city."

"The authority of the Asteri extends over all. Including Starborn Princes."

Ruhn caught the bartender's eye, signaling for another whiskey. "So this is just to prove you've got bigger balls?" He draped an arm over the back of his chair, cards in one hand. "You want to head up the Aux while you're in town, fine. I could use a vacation."

The Harpy's teeth flashed. "Someone should rip that tongue from your mouth. The Asteri would flay you for such disrespect."

Ithan drew another card and said mildly, "You've got some nerve, coming to our city and trying to start shit."

The Hind replied with equal calm, "So do you, lusting after the female your brother loved."

Ruhn blinked.

Ithan's eyes turned dangerously dark. "You're full of shit."

"Am I?" the Hind said, drawing a card herself. "Of course, as my visit here will likely entail meeting the princess, I looked into her history. Found quite a chain of messages between you two."

Ruhn thanked the bartender as the male brought over a whiskey and then quickly retreated. Ruhn said into Ithan's mind, *She's trying to rile you. Ignore her.*

Ithan didn't answer. He only said to the Hind, voice sharpening, "Bryce is my friend."

The Hind drew another card. "Years of pining in secret, years of guilt and shame for feeling what he does, for hating his brother whenever he talks about Miss Quinlan, for wishing that *he* had been the one who'd met her first—"

"Shut up," Ithan growled, rattling the glasses on the table, pure feral wolf.

The Hind went on, unfazed, "Loving her, lusting for her from the sidelines. Waiting for the day when she would realize that *he* was the one she was meant to be with. Playing his little heart out on the sunball field, hoping she'd notice him at last. But then big brother dies."

Ithan paled.

The Hind's expression filled with cool contempt. "And he hates himself even more. Not only for losing his brother, for not being there, but because of the one, traitorous thought he had after learning the news. That the path to Bryce Quinlan was now cleared. Did I get that part right?"

"*Shut your fucking mouth*," Ithan growled, and the Harpy laughed.

Calm down, Ruhn warned the male.

But the Hind said, "Call."

Mind reeling, Ruhn laid out the decent hand he'd gotten. The Harpy put hers down. Good. He'd beaten her. The Hind gracefully spread hers across the table.

A winning hand. Beating Ruhn by a fraction.

Ithan didn't bother to show his cards. He'd already shown them, Ruhn realized.

The Hind smiled again at Ithan. "You Valbarans are too easy to break."

"Fuck you."

The Hind rose, gathering her cards. "Well, this has been delightfully dull."

The Harpy stood with her. Black talons glinted at the angel's fingertips. "Let's hope they fuck better than they play poker."

Ruhn crooned, "I'm sure there are Reapers who'll stoop to fuck you."

The Hind snickered, earning a glare from the Harpy that the deer shifter ignored. The Harpy hissed at Ruhn, "I do not take being insulted lightly, princeling."

"Get the Hel out of my bar," Ruhn snarled softly.

She opened her mouth, but the Hind said, "We'll see you soon, I'm sure." The Harpy understood that as a command to leave and stormed out the door onto the sunny street. Where life, somehow, continued onward.

The Hind paused on the threshold before she left, though. Peered over her shoulder at Ruhn, her silver necklace glinting in the sunlight trickling in. Her eyes lit with unholy fire.

"Tell Prince Cormac I send my love," the Hind said.

Bryce was one breath away from calling the Autumn King when the door to the apartment opened. And apparently, she looked a Hel of a lot worse than her brother or Ithan, because they immediately demanded to know what had happened to her.

Hunt, nursing a beer at the kitchen counter, said, "Emile and Sofie aren't in the Bone Quarter. But we found out some major shit. You'd better sit down."

Yet Bryce went up to her brother, scanning him from the piercings along his ear to his tattooed arms and ass-kicking boots. Not one sleek black hair out of place, though his skin was ashen. Ithan, standing at his side, didn't give her the chance to turn to him before approaching the fridge and grabbing a beer of his own.

"You're all right?" Bryce asked Ruhn, who was frowning at the dirt and blood on her—the wound on her back had thankfully closed, but was still tender.

Tharion said from where he sat on the couch, feet propped on the coffee table, "Everyone is fine, Legs. Now let's sit down like a good little rebel family and tell each other what the Hel happened."

Bryce swallowed. "All right. Yeah—sure." She scanned Ruhn again, and his eyes softened. "You scared the shit out of me."

"We couldn't answer our phones."

She didn't let herself reconsider before throwing her arms around her brother and squeezing tight. A heartbeat later, he gently hugged her back, and she could have sworn he shuddered in relief.

Hunt's phone buzzed, and Bryce pulled away from Ruhn. "Celestina wants me at the Comitium for Ephraim's arrival," Hunt said. "She wants her triarii assembled."

"Oh, Ephraim's already here." Ithan dropped onto the couch. "We learned the hard way."

"You saw him?" Bryce asked.

"His cronies," Ithan said, not looking at her. "Played poker with them and everything."

Bryce whirled on Ruhn. Her brother nodded gravely. "The Hind and the Harpy showed up to the bar where we were lying low. I can't tell if it was because Mordoc sniffed around the alley where Cormac made the intel drop or what. But it was . . . not great."

"Do they know?" Hunt asked quietly, storms in his eyes. "About you? About us?"

"No idea," Ruhn said, toying with his lip ring. "I think we'd be dead if they did, though."

Hunt blew out a sigh. "Yeah, you would be. They would have taken you in for questioning already."

"The Hind is a fucking monster," Ithan said, turning on the TV. "Her and the Harpy, both."

"I could have told you that," Hunt said, finishing his beer and striding to where Bryce stood before the glass dining table. She didn't stop him as he slid a hand over her jaw, cupping her cheek, and kissed her. Just a swift brush of their mouths, but it was a claiming and a promise.

"Rain check?" he murmured onto her lips. Right. The dinner and the hotel—

She frowned pitifully. "Rain check."

He chuckled, but grew deadly serious. "Be careful. I'll be back as soon as I can. Don't go looking for that kid without me." He kissed her forehead before leaving the apartment.

Bryce offered up silent prayers to Cthona and Urd to protect him.

"Glad you two finally sorted it out," Tharion said from the couch.

Bryce flipped him off. But Ruhn sniffed her carefully. "You . . . smell different."

"She smells like the Istros," Ithan said from the couch.

"No, it's . . ." Ruhn's brows twitched toward each other, and he scratched at the buzzed side of his head. "I can't explain it."

"Stop sniffing me, Ruhn." Bryce hopped onto the couch on Tharion's other side. "It's gross. Story time?"

How do I look?" Celestina whispered to Hunt as they stood in front of the desk in her private study. Isaiah flanked her other side, Naomi to his left, Baxian to Hunt's right. Baxian had barely done more than nod to Hunt when he'd entered.

Hunt had taken the flight over here to soothe his nerves, his residual rage and awe at what he and Bryce had done. What they'd learned. By the time he'd alighted on the landing veranda, his face had become impassive once more. The mask of the Umbra Mortis.

It cracked a little, however, upon seeing Pollux a step away from Naomi. Grinning with feral, anticipatory delight.

This was a reunion from Hel. The Hind and the Hammer, back together once more. Never mind the Harpy and the Helhound—things had always revolved around Pollux and Lidia, their twin shriveled souls, and no one else. Thank the gods the Hawk had stayed behind in Pangera.

Hunt murmured to Celestina, "You look like a female about to enter an arranged mating." He was amazed his words had come out so casually, considering how his morning had gone.

The Archangel, clad in dawn-soft pink, gold at her wrists and ears, threw him a sad, *What can you do?* kind of smile.

Hunt, despite himself, added, "But you do look beautiful."

Her smile gentled, light brown eyes with them. "Thank you. And thank you for coming in on your day off." She squeezed his hand, her fingers surprisingly clammy. She was truly nervous.

Down the hall, the elevator doors pinged. Celestina's fingers tightened on Hunt's before letting go. He could have sworn hers were shaking.

So Hunt said, "It's no problem at all. I'll be right here all night. You need to bail, just give me a signal—tug on your earring, maybe—and I'll make up some excuse."

Celestina smiled up at him, squaring her shoulders. "You're a good male, Hunt."

He wasn't so sure of that. Wasn't so sure he hadn't offered only to make her like him so that when shit hit the fan, if Baxian or the Hind or anyone suggested he and Quinlan were up to anything shady, she'd give him the benefit of the doubt. But he thanked her all the same.

The meeting between Ephraim and Celestina was as stiff and awkward as Hunt had expected.

Ephraim was handsome, as so many of the Archangels were: black hair cut close to his head in a warrior-like fashion, light brown skin that radiated health and vitality, and dark eyes that noted every person in the room, like a soldier assessing a battlefield.

But his smile was genuine as he looked upon Celestina, who strode toward him with outstretched hands.

"My friend," she said, peering up into his face. As if seeing it for the first time.

Ephraim smiled, white teeth straight and perfect. "My mate."

She ducked her head right at the moment he went in to kiss her cheek, and Hunt reined in his cringe as Ephraim's lips met the side of her head. Celestina jolted back, realizing the miscommunication, that people were witnessing this, and—

Isaiah, gods bless him, stepped forward, a fist on his heart. "Your Grace. I welcome you and your triarii." Ephraim had only brought Sandriel's triarii with him, Hunt realized. Had left his original members back in Pangera with the Hawk.

Ephraim recovered from the awkward kiss and tucked his blindingly white wings close to his toned, powerful body. "I thank you for your welcome, Commander Tiberian. And hope that your triarii will welcome mine as you so warmly did."

Hunt at last glanced at the Hind, standing a few feet behind Ephraim, and then at Pollux, staring at her with wolfish intensity from across the room. The Hind's golden eyes simmered, focused wholly on her lover. As if she were waiting for the go-ahead to jump his bones.

"Yuck," Naomi muttered, and Hunt suppressed his smile.

Celestina seemed to be searching for something to say, so Hunt spared her and said, "We shall treat your triarii as our brothers and sisters." The Harpy sneered at the last word. Hunt's lightning sparked in answer. "For however long they remain here." *For however long I let you live, you fucking psychopath.*

Celestina recovered enough to say, "Their alliance shall be only one of the many successes for our mating."

Ephraim voiced his agreement, even as he raked his stare over his mate once more. Approval shone there, but Celestina . . . Her throat bobbed.

She'd . . . been with a male, hadn't she? Come to think of it, Hunt didn't even know if she preferred males. Had the Asteri considered that? Would they care what her preferences were, what her experience was, before throwing her into bed with Ephraim?

Baxian's eyes remained on the Harpy and the Hind, cold and watchful. He didn't seem particularly pleased to see them.

"I have some refreshments prepared," Celestina said, gesturing to the tables against the wall of windows. "Come, let us drink to this happy occasion."

Bryce had just finished telling Ruhn and Ithan what had gone down in the Bone Quarter—both of them looking as sick as Tharion had to hear about the real fate of the dead—when someone knocked on the door.

"So Connor," Ithan was saying, rubbing his face. "He's . . . They fed his soul into the Gate to become firstlight? Secondlight? Whatever."

Bryce wrung her hands. "It seems like they'd wait until we're all dust, and even our descendants have forgotten him, but considering how much we pissed off the Under-King, I feel like there's a chance he might . . . move Connor up the list."

"I need to know," Ithan said. "I need to fucking *know*."

Bryce's throat ached. "I do, too. We'll try to find out."

Tharion asked, "But what can be done to help him—any of them?"

Silence fell. The knock on the door came again, and Bryce sighed. "We'll figure that out, too."

Ruhn toyed with one of the hoops through his left ear. "Is there someone we should . . . tell?"

Bryce unlocked the door. "The Asteri undoubtedly know about it and don't care. They'll say it's our civic duty to give back whatever power we can."

Ithan shook his head, looking toward the window.

Ruhn said, "We have to think carefully about this. Was the Prince of the Pit pushing you and Athalar to go there by sending those Reapers? Or by having his Reapers hint that Emile and Sofie might be hiding there? Why? To—activate your combined powers with that Gate trick? He couldn't have known that would happen. We have to think about how the Asteri would retaliate if this *is* something they want kept under wraps. And what they'd do if we do indeed find and harbor Emile and Sofie."

"We'll game it out," Bryce said, and finally opened the door.

A hand locked around her throat, crushing the air from her. "You little cunt," Sabine Fendyr hissed.

Ruhn should have considered who might need to knock on the front door. Instead, he'd been so focused on the truth Bryce had revealed about their lives—and afterlives—that he'd let her open it without checking.

Sabine hurled Bryce across the room, hard enough that she

slammed into the side of the sectional, scooting the behemoth couch back by an inch.

Ruhn was up instantly, gun aimed at the Alpha. Behind him, Tharion helped Bryce to her feet. Sabine's attention remained fixed on Bryce as she said, "What game are you playing, *Princess*?" That title was clearly what had kept Sabine from ripping out Bryce's throat.

Bryce's brows lowered, but Ithan stepped to Ruhn's side, violence gleaming in his eyes. "What the Hel are you talking about?"

Sabine bristled, but she didn't remove her focus from Bryce as she continued, "You just can't stay out of wolf business, can you?"

Bryce said coolly, "Wolf business?"

Sabine pointed a clawed finger toward Ithan. "He was exiled. And yet *you* decided to harbor him. No doubt part of some plan of yours to rob me of my birthright."

"So the big bad wolf came all the way here to yell at me about it?"

"The big bad wolf," Sabine seethed, "came all the way here to remind you that no matter what my father might have said, *you* are no wolf." She sneered at Ithan. "And neither is he. So stay the fuck out of wolf affairs."

Ithan let out a low growl, but pain seemed to ripple beneath it.

Ruhn snarled, "You want to talk, Sabine, then sit the fuck down like an adult." At his side, he was vaguely aware of Bryce thumbing in a message on her phone.

Ithan squared his shoulders. "Bryce isn't harboring me. Perry dropped me here."

"Perry's a moon-eyed fool," Sabine spat.

Bryce angled her head, though. "What about this arrangement, exactly, bothers you, Sabine?" The way her voice had iced over . . . Fuck, she sounded exactly like their father.

Ithan said, "Bryce has nothing to do with you and me, Sabine. Leave her out of it."

Sabine pivoted toward him, bristling. "You're a disgrace and a traitor, Holstrom. A spineless waste, if this is the company you choose to keep. Your brother would be ashamed."

Ithan snapped, "My brother would tell me good fucking riddance to you."

Sabine snarled, the sound pure command. "You might be exiled, but you still obey *me*."

Ithan shuddered, but refused to back down.

Tharion stepped forward. "You want to throw down with Holstrom, Sabine, go ahead. I'll stand as witness."

Ithan would lose. And Sabine would gut him so thoroughly there would be no hope of recovery. He'd wind up with his brother, his soul served up to the Under-King and the Dead Gate on a silver platter.

Ruhn braced himself—and realized he had no idea what to do.

Celestina should have laid out some hard alcohol rather than rosé. Hunt wasn't nearly drunk enough to deal with having to keep smiling in a room full of his enemies. To deal with watching two people who had no choice but to make an arranged mating work somehow. They wouldn't officially be mated until the party next month, but their life together was already beginning.

Beside him, at the doors to the private veranda off Celestina's study, Isaiah knocked back his pale pink wine and muttered, "What a clusterfuck."

"I feel bad for her," Naomi said on Isaiah's other side.

Hunt grunted his agreement, watching Celestina and Ephraim attempt to make small talk across the room. Beyond them, the Harpy seemed content to sneer at Hunt the whole night. Baxian lurked by the door to the hall. Pollux and Lidia talked near the Harpy with bent heads.

Naomi followed the direction of his gaze. "There's a terrifying match."

Hunt chuckled. "Yeah." His phone buzzed, and he fished it out of his pocket to see that a text had arrived from *Bryce Sucks My Dick Like a Champ.*

Hunt choked, scrambling to switch screens as Isaiah peered over his shoulder and laughed. "I assume you didn't put that name in there."

"No," Hunt hissed. He'd punish her thoroughly for that one.

After he finally got to fuck her. He hadn't forgotten that he was supposed to be doing exactly that right now. That he'd made dinner and hotel reservations that had been canceled for this awkward-ass shit. Hunt explained to Isaiah, "It's this stupid running joke we have."

"A joke, hmmm?" Isaiah's eyes danced with delight, and he clapped Hunt on the shoulder. "I'm happy for you."

Hunt smiled to himself, opening up her message, trying not to look at the name she'd put in and think about how accurate it was. "Thanks." But his smile faded as he read the message.

Sabine here.

Hunt's heartbeat kicked up a notch. Isaiah read the message and murmured, "Go."

"What about this?" Hunt jerked his chin at Celestina and Ephraim across the room.

"Go," Isaiah urged. "You need backup?"

He shouldn't, but Bryce's message had been so vague, and—shit. "You can't come with me. It'll be too obvious." He turned to Naomi, but she'd drifted off toward the bar cart again. If he grabbed her, it'd draw everyone's attention. He scanned the space.

Baxian looked right at him, reading the tension on his face, his body. Fucker. Now someone *would* know he'd left—

Isaiah sensed it, noted it. "I'll deal with that," his friend murmured, and sauntered off toward the black-winged angel. He said something to Baxian that had them both pivoting away from Hunt.

Seizing his chance, Hunt backed up a step, then another, fading into the shadows of the veranda beyond the study. He kept moving, stealthy, until his heels were at the edge of the landing. But as he stepped off, free-falling into the night, he caught Celestina looking at him.

Disappointment and displeasure darkened her eyes.

35

Bryce cursed herself for opening the door. For letting the wolf in. For letting it get to this so quickly: Ithan and Sabine, about to splatter this apartment with blood. Ithan's blood.

Bryce's mouth dried out. Think. *Think*.

Ruhn swiftly glanced at her, but didn't suggest any bright ideas mind-to-mind.

Sabine snarled at Ithan, "Your brother knew his place. Was content to be Danika's Second. You're not nearly as smart as he was."

Ithan didn't back down as Sabine advanced. "I might not be as smart as Connor," he said, "but at least I wasn't dumb enough to sleep with Mordoc."

Sabine halted. "Shut your mouth, boy."

Ithan laughed, cold and lifeless. Bryce had never heard him make such a sound. "We never learned during that last visit: Was it an arranged pairing between you two, or some drunk decision?"

Mordoc—the Hind's captain?

"I will rip out your throat," Sabine growled, stepping closer. But Bryce saw it—the glimmer of surprise. Doubt. He'd thrown Sabine off her game a little with that volley.

Again, Ithan didn't lower his eyes. "He's here in this city. Are you going to see him? Take him to the Black Dock to bid farewell to his daughter?"

Bryce's stomach dropped, but she kept her face neutral. Danika had never said. Had always claimed it was a . . .

A male not worth knowing or remembering.

Bryce had assumed it was some lesser wolf, some male too submissive to keep Sabine's interest, and Sabine had refused to let Danika see him because of it. Even when Danika had known the truth of Bryce's parentage, she'd never told Bryce about her own lineage. The thought burned like acid.

Sabine spat, "I know what you're trying to do, Holstrom, and it won't work."

Ithan flexed his broad chest. Bryce had seen that same intense expression while facing off against opponents on the sunball field. Ithan had usually been the one to walk away from the encounter. And he'd *always* walked away if a teammate joined in the fight.

So Bryce stepped up. Said to Sabine, "Was Danika a rebel?"

Sabine whipped her head to her. "*What?*"

Bryce kept her shoulders back, head high. She outranked Sabine in position and power now, she reminded herself. "Did Danika have contact with the Ophion rebels?"

Sabine backed away. Just one step. "Why would you ever ask that?"

Ithan ignored the question and countered, "Was it because of Mordoc? She was so disgusted by him that she helped the rebels to spite him?"

Bryce shoved from the other side, "Maybe she did it out of disgust for you, too."

Sabine backed away one more step. Predator turning into prey. She snarled, "You're both delusional."

"Is that so?" Bryce asked, and then took a stab in the dark. "I'm not the one who ran all the way here to make sure Ithan and I weren't plotting some kind of wolf-coup against you."

Sabine bristled. Bryce pushed, getting no small delight out of it, "That's the fear, right? That I'm going to use my fancy princess title to get Holstrom to replace you somehow? I mean, you've got no heir beyond Amelie right now. And Ithan's as dominant as she is. But I don't think the Den likes Amelie—or you, for that matter—nearly as much as they love him."

Ithan blinked at her in surprise. But Bryce smiled at Sabine, who'd gone stone-faced as she snarled, "*Stay out of wolf business.*"

Bryce taunted, "I wonder how hard it would be to convince the Prime and the Den that Ithan is the bright future of the Valbaran wolves—"

"Bryce," Ithan warned. Had he truly never considered such a thing?

Sabine's hand drifted to something at her back, and Ruhn aimed his gun. "Nah," Bryce's brother said, smiling wickedly. "I don't think so."

A familiar ripple of charged air filled the room a moment before Hunt said, "Neither do I," and appeared in the doorway so silently Bryce knew he'd crept up. Relief nearly buckled her knees as Hunt stepped into the apartment, gun pointed at the back of Sabine's head. "You're going to leave, and never fucking bother us again."

Sabine seethed, "Allow me to give you a bit of advice. You tangle with Mordoc, and you'll get what's coming to you. Ask him about Danika and see what he does to get answers out of you."

Ithan's teeth flashed. "Get out, Sabine."

"You don't give me orders."

The wolves faced off: one young and brokenhearted, the other in her prime—and heartless. Could someone like Ithan, if he wanted it, ever win in a battle for dominance?

But then another figure stepped into the apartment behind Hunt.

Baxian. The angel shifter had a gun drawn, aimed at Sabine's legs to disable her if she tried to run.

Only a glimmer of surprise on Hunt's face told Bryce this wasn't a planned appearance.

Sabine turned slowly. Recognition flared in her eyes. And something like fear.

Baxian's teeth gleamed in a feral grin. "Hello, Sabine."

Sabine simmered with rage, but hissed, "You're all carrion," and stormed from the apartment.

"You all right?" Hunt asked Bryce as he looked her over. The redness around her throat was fading before his eyes.

Bryce scowled. "I could have done without being hurled into the side of the couch."

Baxian, still by the door, huffed a laugh.

Hunt turned toward him, lightning at the ready. "You got nothing better to do with your time than follow me around?"

"It seemed like you had an emergency," Baxian retorted. "I figured you might need backup. Especially considering where you were this morning." A slash of a smile. "I worried something had followed you back across the Istros."

Hunt clenched his jaw hard enough to hurt. "What about Isaiah?"

"You mean his pathetic distraction attempt?" Baxian snorted.

Before Hunt could reply, Ithan asked the Helhound, "You know Sabine?"

Baxian's face darkened. "In passing." From the way Sabine had acted, there was definitely more to it than that.

But Bryce suddenly asked Ithan, "Mordoc is . . . was . . . He's Danika's *father*?"

Ithan gazed at his feet. "Yeah."

"As in, the male who sired her. Like, gave her his genetic material."

Ithan's eyes blazed. "Yeah."

"And no one thought to fucking tell me?"

"I only knew because he visited the Den once, a year before we met you. She got her bloodhound gift from him. It was her secret to keep, but now that she's gone—"

"Why wouldn't she tell me?" Bryce rubbed at her chest. Hunt took her hand. Brushed his thumb over her knuckles.

"Would you want that asshole for a father?" Hunt asked.

"I have an asshole father already," Bryce said, and Ruhn grunted his agreement. “I’d have understood.” Hunt squeezed her hand in gentle reassurance.

“I don’t know why she didn’t say anything to you.” Ithan dropped onto the couch and ran his hands through his hair. “Danika would have become my Alpha one day, and Sabine ruler of us all, so if they wanted it kept quiet, I had no choice.” Until Sabine had exiled him, freeing Ithan from those restrictions.

“Would you have taken Sabine down just now?” Tharion asked.

“I might have tried,” Ithan admitted.

Hunt whistled. But it was Baxian who said, “You wouldn’t have won tonight.”

Ithan growled, “Did I ask for your opinion, dog?”

Hunt glanced between them. Interesting, that Ithan saw him as a dog, not an angel. His animal form took precedence for another shifter, apparently.

Baxian growled right back. “I said you wouldn’t have won *tonight*. But another day, give yourself a few more years, pup, and maybe.”

“And you’re an expert in such things?”

Ithan was still itching for a fight. Perhaps Baxian was about to give him one, sensing his need for it. Baxian’s wings tucked in. Definitely primed for a fight.

Bryce massaged her temples. “Go to the gym or the roof if you’re going to brawl. Please. I can’t afford to lose any more furniture.” She scowled at Ithan at that.

Hunt snickered. “We’ll get through the mourning process together, Quinlan. Have a proper send-off for the coffee table. Holstrom should give the eulogy, since he broke it.”

His phone buzzed, and he checked it to find Isaiah’s message. *All ok?*

He wrote back, *Yeah. You?*

She’s upset you left. Didn’t say anything, but I can tell. Baxian bailed, too.

Fuck. He replied, *Tell her it was an emergency and that Baxian needed to help me.*

He trailed you?

Just busting my balls, Hunt lied.

All right. Be careful.

Ithan said to Ruhn, "I'm accepting your offer."

Hunt's brows twitched toward each other. Bryce asked, "What offer?"

Ruhn sized her up before saying, "To come live with me and the guys. Because of your thin-ass walls."

Tharion said with mock outrage, "I had dibs on the pup as *my* friend."

"Sorry for sexiling you, Ithan," Bryce muttered. Hunt laughed, but Ithan didn't. He didn't look at Bryce at all. Weird.

Ruhn said to Ithan, "All right. You fighting that asshole first, or can we go?" He nodded to Baxian.

Hunt kept perfectly still. Ready to either intervene or referee.

Ithan surveyed the angel with that athletic precision and focus. Baxian only smiled at him in invitation. How many times had Hunt seen that expression on the Helhound's face before he ripped into someone?

But Ithan wisely shook his head. "Another time."

Three minutes later, Ithan was stepping into the hallway with Ruhn and Tharion, who had to go report to his queen once more.

"Ithan," Bryce said before he could leave. From the kitchen, Hunt watched her take a step into the hall, then halt, as if catching herself. "We made a good team."

From his angle, Hunt couldn't see Ithan's face, but he heard the quiet "Yeah," right before the elevator doors dinged. Then, "We did." For all the world, Hunt could have sworn the wolf sounded sad.

A moment later, Bryce walked back into the apartment and aimed right for Hunt, looking like she'd drop into his arms with exhaustion. She drew up short upon seeing Baxian. "Enjoying the view?"

Baxian stopped his surveying. "Nice place. Why'd Sabine come here?"

Bryce examined her nails. "She was pissed that I've been harboring Ithan after she kicked his ass to the curb."

"You know about her and Mordoc, though." It wasn't exactly a question.

"*You* know?" Hunt asked.

Baxian shrugged one shoulder. "I've spent years with the Hind and those who serve her. I picked up a few interesting details."

"What happened when Mordoc visited Danika?" Bryce asked.

"It didn't go well. He came back to Sandriel's castle . . ." Baxian said to Hunt, "Remember the time he ate that human couple?"

Bryce choked. "He *what*?"

Hunt said roughly, "Yeah."

"That was when he'd returned from the visit to the Den," Baxian explained. "He was in such a rage that he went out and killed a human couple he found on the street. Started eating the female while the male was still alive and begging for mercy."

"Burning fucking Solas," Bryce breathed, her hand finding Hunt's.

"Sabine was right to warn you away from him," Baxian said, aiming for the door.

Hunt grunted. "I never thought he'd be in this city."

"Let's hope he's gone soon, then," Baxian said, not looking back.

Bryce said, hand sliding from Hunt's, "Why did *you* come here, Baxian?"

The angel-shifter halted. "Athalar seemed like he needed help. We're partners, after all." His grin was savage, mocking. "And watching Celestina and Ephraim pretend to be into each other was too torturous, even for me."

Bryce was having none of it, though. "You were also at the Black Dock this morning."

"Are you asking if I'm spying on you?"

"Either that or you desperately want in on the cool kids' club."

"A good spy would tell you no, and say you were being paranoid."

"But you're . . . not a good spy?"

"I'm not a spy at all, and you're being paranoid."

Bryce rolled her eyes, and Hunt smiled to himself as she walked to the door, making to shut it behind Baxian. As she closed the door, he heard her say to the Helhound, "You're going to fit right in around here."

"Why'd you say that to him?" Hunt asked as he slumped onto the bed beside her later that night.

Bryce rested her head on Hunt's shoulder. "Say what?"

"That thing to Baxian about fitting in."

"Jealous?"

"I just . . ." His chest heaved as he sighed. "He's a bad male."

"I know. Don't think too much about my nonsense, Hunt."

"No, it's not that. It's . . . He's a bad male. I know he is. But I was no better than him."

She touched his cheek. "You're a good person, Hunt." She'd assured him of that so many times now.

"I told Celestina I'd have her back with Ephraim and then bailed. Good people don't do that."

"You bailed to come rescue your mate from the big bad wolf."

He flicked her nose, shifting onto his side, wings a wall of gray behind him. "I can't believe Mordoc is Danika's father."

"I can't believe our souls get turned into firstlight food," she countered. "Or that the Hind brought her dreadwolves here. Or that the Under-King is a fucking psychopath."

Hunt's laugh rumbled through her. "Rough day."

"What do you think happened in the Bone Quarter—with your lightning and the firstlight and everything?"

"What were you even thinking, jumping in front of my lightning?"

"It worked, didn't it?"

He glared. "You know that scar on Baxian's neck? I did that to him. With my lightning. With a blow a fraction of what I unleashed on the Starsword."

"Yeah, yeah, you're the tough, smart male who knows best and I'm an impulsive female whose feelings get her in trouble—"

"For fuck's sake, Quinlan."

She propped her head on a hand. "So you had no idea you could do that? Take the energy from the Dead Gate and transform it into lightning and all that?"

"No. It never occurred to me to channel anything into my lightning until the Prince of the Pit suggested it the other night. But . . . it made sense: you took the power out of the Heart Gate this spring, and Sofie Renast, as a thunderbird, could do something similar, so . . . even if the push came from the Prince of the Pit, trying it out seemed like a good alternative to being eaten."

"You went . . ." She wiggled her fingers in the air. "All lightning-berserker."

He kissed her brow, running a hand down her hip. "I get a little hysterical when your safety is involved."

She kissed the tip of his nose. "Such an alphahole." But she flopped back on the bed, tucking her arms under her head. "You think there actually *is* a resting place for our souls?" She sighed at the ceiling. "Like, if we died and didn't go to those places . . . what would happen?"

"Ghosts?"

She scowled. "You're not helping."

He chuckled, tucking his hands behind his own head. She crossed her ankle over his shin, and they lay there in silence, staring at the ceiling.

He said after a while, "You traded your resting place in the Bone Quarter for Danika's."

"Given what happens to everyone over there, I feel kind of relieved about that now."

"Yeah." He took one of her hands in his and laid their interlaced fingers atop his heart. "But wherever you're headed when this life is over, Quinlan, that's where I want to be, too."

36

The bridge was blissfully quiet compared to the absolute insanity of Ruhn's day.

He'd brought Holstrom back to his place, where Flynn and Dec had been gobbling down five pizzas between the two of them. The former had arched a brow at Ruhn's announcement that the fourth bedroom—a disgusting heap of crap thanks to years of throwing their messes in there before parties—was now Ithan's. He'd have the couch tonight, and tomorrow they'd clean out all the shit. Declan had only shrugged and tossed Ithan a beer, then pulled his laptop over, presumably to continue combing through the gallery footage.

Flynn had eyed the wolf, but shrugged as well. The message was clear enough: Yeah, Holstrom was a wolf, but so long as he didn't mouth off about Fae, they'd get along just fine. And a wolf was always better than an angel.

Guys were simple like that. Easy.

Not like the female burning across from him on the bridge.

"Hey, Day." He wished he had someplace to sit. For one fucking moment. He was technically sleeping, he supposed, but . . .

Well, damn. A deep-cushioned armchair appeared a foot away. He slumped into it and sighed. Perfect.

Her snort rippled toward him, and another chair appeared. A red velvet fainting couch.

"Fancy," he said as Day draped herself over it. She looked so much like Lehabah that his chest ached.

"Seeing me like this causes you distress."

"No," he said, puzzled as to how she'd read his emotions when night and stars covered his features. "No, it's . . . I, ah, lost a friend a few months ago. She loved to sit on a couch like that one. She was a fire sprite, so your whole fire thing . . . struck a little close to home."

She angled her head, flame shifting with her. "How did she die?"

He checked himself before he could reveal too much. "It's a long story. But she died saving my—someone I love."

"Then her death was noble."

"I should have been there." Ruhn leaned back against the cushions and gazed toward the endless black above them. "She didn't need to make that sacrifice."

"You would have traded your life for a fire sprite's?" There was no condescension in the question—merely bald curiosity.

"Yeah. I would have." He lowered his stare back to her. "Anyway, we made the intel drop-off. Nearly got caught, but we did it."

She straightened slightly. "By whom?"

"Mordoc. The Hind. The Harpy."

She stilled. Her fire guttered to that violet blue. "They are *lethal.* If you're caught, you will be lucky to just be killed."

Ruhn crossed an ankle over a knee. "Believe me, I know that."

"Mordoc is a monster."

"So's the Hind. And the Harpy."

"They're all . . . Where you are now?"

He hesitated, then said, "In Lunathion. Might as well tell you—you could have turned on the news and figured out where they are."

She shook her head, flame flowing. "You say too much."

"And you too little. Any other intel about the shipment on the Spine?"

"No. I thought you called me here to tell me something."

"No. I . . . I guess my mind reached for yours."

She watched him. And even though he couldn't see her face, and she couldn't see his, he'd never felt so naked. She said quietly, "Something's riled you."

How could she tell? "My day was . . . difficult."

She sighed. Tendrils of fire rippled around her. "Mine too."

"Yeah?"

"Yeah."

The word was teasing, a reminder of their earlier conversation. She did have a sense of humor, then.

Day said, "I work with people who are . . . Well, they make Mordoc seem like one of those sweet little otters in your city. There are days when it wears on me more than others. Today was one of them."

"Do you at least have friends to lean on?" he asked.

"No. I've never had a true friend in my life."

He winced. "That's . . . really sad."

She snorted. "It is, isn't it?"

"I don't think I'd have made it this far without my friends. Or my sister."

"For those of us with neither friends nor family, we find ways to make do."

"No family, eh? A true lone wolf." He added, "My father's a piece of shit, so . . . a lot of the time I wish I were like you."

"I have a family. A very influential one." She propped her head on a burning fist. "They're pieces of shit, too."

"Yeah? Your dad ever burn you for speaking out of turn?"

"No. But he did flog me for sneezing during prayers."

She wasn't an Asteri, then. Asteri had no family. No children. No parents. They just *were*.

He blinked. "All right. We're even."

She laughed quietly, a low, soft sound that ran delicate fingers over his skin. "A truly tragic thing to have in common."

"It really is." He smiled, even if she couldn't see it.

She said, "Since you are in a position of power, I'm assuming your father must be as well."

"Why can't I be self-made?"

"Call it intuition."

He shrugged. "All right. What about it?"

"Does he know of your rebel sympathies?"

"I think my work has gone beyond sympathies now, but . . . no. He'd kill me if he knew."

"Yet you risk your life."

"What's the question, Day?"

Her mouth quirked to the side. Or what he could see of it did. "You could use your power and rank to undermine people like your father, you know. Be a secret agent for the rebellion in that sense, rather than doing this message-carrying."

She didn't know who he was, right? Ruhn shifted in his chair. "Honestly? I'm shit at those deception games. My father is the master of them. This is far more my speed."

"And yet your father is allowed to stay in power?"

"Yeah. Aren't all of these assholes allowed to stay in power? Who's going to stop them?"

"Us. People like us. One day."

Ruhn snorted. "That's some idealistic shit right there. You know that if this rebellion is triumphant, we'll likely have a war for dominance between all the Houses, don't you?"

"Not if we play the game well." Her tone was completely serious.

"Why tell me any of this? I thought you were all . . . no-personal-stuff."

"Let's chalk it up to a difficult day."

"All right," he repeated. He leaned back in his chair once more, letting himself fall quiet. To his surprise, Day did the same. They sat in silence for long minutes before she said, "You're the first person I've spoken to normally in . . . a very long time."

"How long?"

"So long that I think I've forgotten what it feels like to be myself. I think I've lost my true self entirely. To destroy monsters, we become monsters. Isn't that what they say?"

"Next time, I'll bring us some psychic beers and a TV. We'll get you normal again."

She laughed, the sound like clear bells. Something male and primal in him sat up at the sound. "I've only ever had wine."

He started. "That's not possible."

"Beer wasn't deemed appropriate for a female of my position. I did have a sip once I was old enough to . . . not answer to my family, but I found it wasn't to my liking anyway."

He shook his head in mock horror. "Come visit me in Lunathion sometime, Day. I'll show you a good time."

"Given who is present in your city, I think I'll decline."

He frowned. Right.

She seemed to remember, too. And why they were here. "Is it confirmed where the rebels are making the strike on the Spine shipment?"

"Not sure. I'm the go-between, remember?"

"You told them what I said about the Asteri's new mech-suit prototype?"

"Yeah."

"Don't forget that it's the most valuable thing on that train. Leave the rest."

"Why not blow up the entire Spine and break their supply lines?"

Her fire sizzled. "We've tried multiple times. With each attempt, we've been thwarted. Either by betrayal or things simply going wrong. An attack like that requires a lot of people, and a lot of secrecy and precision. Do *you* know how to make explosives?"

"No. But there's always magic to do that."

"Remember that the rebellion is mostly humans, and their Vanir allies like to remain hidden. We are dependent on human resourcefulness and abilities. Simply compiling enough explosives to enact a serious hit on the Spine takes a great deal of effort. Especially considering the great losses Ophion has taken to its numbers lately. They're on the ropes." She added, oozing disgust, "This isn't a video game."

Ruhn growled. "I'm aware of that."

Her flame banked a fraction. "You're right. I spoke out of turn."

"You can just say 'I'm sorry.' No need for the fancy talk."

Another soft laugh. "Bad habit."

He saluted her. "Well, until next time, Day."

He half hoped she'd counter with something to keep them talking, keep him here.

But Day and her couch faded into embers drifting on a phantom wind. "Goodbye, Night."

Ithan Holstrom had never been inside a full-fledged Fae's house. There'd only been two Fae males on his CCU sunball team, and both were from cities across the territory, so he'd never had the chance to go to their homes and meet their families.

But Prince Ruhn's house was cool. It reminded him of the apartment Connor and Bronson and Thorne once had—a few blocks from here, actually: crappy old furniture, stained walls with posters of sports teams taped on them, an overly large TV, and a fully stocked bar.

He hadn't minded crashing on the couch last night. Would have slept on the porch, if it meant being far away from where Bryce and Hunt slept together.

The clock beneath the TV read seven in the morning when Ithan rose and showered. He helped himself to Tristan Flynn's array of fancy shampoos and body products, all marked *FLYNN'S. DO NOT TOUCH, RUHN. I MEAN IT THIS TIME.*

Ruhn had written beneath the scribbling on one of the bottles: *NO ONE LIKES YOUR WEIRD SHAMPOO ANYWAY.*

Flynn had scrawled, right along the bottom edge of the bottle, *THEN WHY IS IT NEARLY EMPTY? AND WHY IS YOUR HAIR SO SHINY? ASSHOLE!!!*

Ithan had snickered, even as his heart squeezed. He'd had that kind of dynamic once with his brother.

His brother, who was either already turned into secondlight—or on his way there.

The thought had any rising interest in breakfast melting into nausea. By the time Ithan had dressed and gone downstairs—the three Fae males who lived in the house were still asleep—he'd raised his phone to his ear.

Hey, this is Tharion, if you can't get me, send an otter.

All right, then.

An hour later, after a quick check of the program scanning the gallery footage for Danika, Ithan had headed for the Istros, grabbing an iced coffee on his way. He suppressed a smile as he handed over a silver mark to a whiskery otter whose name tag on his yellow vest said *Fitzroy*. Ithan parked his ass on a bench beside the Istros and stared across the river.

He'd wanted to fight Sabine last night. Had actually contemplated how her blood would taste when he ripped out her throat with his teeth, but . . . the Helhound's words lingered.

Connor had been an Alpha who'd accepted the role of Second because he'd believed in Danika's potential. Ithan had fallen in with Amelie's pack because he'd had nowhere else to go.

But last night, just for a moment, when Bryce had stepped up and the two of them had Sabine backing away . . . he'd remembered what it'd been like. To not only be a wolf in a pack, but a player on a team, working in unison, as if they were one mind, one soul.

Never mind that he'd once thought of himself and Bryce that way.

The fucking Hind could go to Hel. He had no idea how she'd pieced that together, but he'd kill her if she ever mentioned it to anyone again. Especially Bryce.

It was no one's business but his, and it was ancient history now anyway. He'd had two years without Bryce to sort his shit out, and being near her again had been . . . hard, but he'd never told anyone about his feelings before Connor died, and he sure as Hel wasn't going to start now.

The Hind had been right, though: he'd walked into Connor's dorm that day early in his brother's freshman year at CCU, intending to meet the awesome, gorgeous, hilarious hallmate Con talked about endlessly. And on his way down the dingy, carpeted hall, he'd run into . . . well, an awesome, gorgeous, hilarious hallmate.

He'd been struck stupid. She was the hottest person he'd ever seen, no joke. Her smile had warmed some gods-forsaken place in Ithan's chest that had been icy and dark since his parents had died, and those whiskey eyes had seemed to . . . *see* him.

Him, not the sunball player, not the star athlete or anything like that. Just him. Ithan.

They spoke for ten minutes in the hall without exchanging names. He'd just been Connor's little brother, and she hadn't given her name and he'd forgotten to ask for it, but by the time Connor poked his head into the hall, Ithan had decided he was going to marry her. He'd attend CCU, play sunball for them and not Korinth U, who'd already been wooing him, and he'd find this girl and marry her. He suspected they might even be mates, if he was right about that gut tug toward her. And that would be that.

Then Connor had said, "Looks like you met Ithan already, Bryce," and Ithan had wanted to dissolve into that disgusting dorm carpet.

He knew it was fucking stupid. He'd spoken to Bryce for ten minutes before finding out she was the girl his brother was obsessed with, but . . . it had messed with him. So he'd thrown himself into the role of irreverent friend, pretended to be into Nathalie so he had something to complain to Bryce about. He'd suffered on the sidelines watching Connor tiptoe around Bryce for years.

He'd never told Bryce that the reason why Connor had finally asked her out that night was because Ithan had told him to shit or get off the pot.

Not in those terms, and he'd said it without raising his brother's suspicions, as he'd always done when talking about Bryce, but he'd had it. Had just *had it* with his brother hesitating while Bryce dated a string of losers.

If Connor didn't step up to the line, then Ithan had decided he'd finally come forward. Take a gamble and see if that spark between them might lead somewhere.

But Bryce had said yes to Connor. And then Connor had died.

And while Connor was being murdered, she'd been fucking someone else in the White Raven bathroom.

Ithan had no idea how there wasn't some black hole where he'd been standing the moment he'd found out about that night. That was how hard he'd imploded, like the star he'd been gave the fuck up and bailed.

Ithan leaned back against the bench, sighing. These last few days, he'd felt like he was poking his head out of that black hole. Now this bullshit about Connor and the Pack's souls being fed into the Dead Gate threatened to pull him back in.

He knew Bryce was pissed about it. Upset. But she had Athalar now.

And no part of Ithan resented them for it. No, that history was behind him, but . . . he didn't know what to do with himself when he spoke to her. The girl he'd been so convinced would be his wife and mate and mother to his kids.

How many times had he allowed himself to picture that future: him and Bryce opening presents with their children on Winter Solstice eve, traveling the world together while he played sunball, laughing and growing old in this city, their friends around them.

He was glad to not be living in her apartment anymore. He'd had nowhere else to go after Sabine and Amelie had kicked him out, and he sure as fuck wasn't planning to stage any kind of coup with her, as Sabine seemed to fear, but . . . he was grateful Ruhn had offered him a place to stay instead.

"A little early, isn't it?" Tharion called from the river, and Ithan stood from the bench to find the mer treading water, powerful fin swirling beneath him.

Ithan didn't bother with pleasantries. "Can you get me to the Bone Quarter?"

Tharion blinked. "No. Unless you want to be eaten."

"Just get me to the shore."

"I can't. Not if I don't want to be eaten, either. The river beasts will attack."

Ithan crossed his arms. "I have to find my brother. See if he's okay."

He hated the pity that softened Tharion's face. "I don't see what you can do either way. If he's fine or if he's . . . not."

Ithan's throat dried out. "I need to know. Swim me past the Sleeping City and I'll see if I can glimpse him."

"Again, river beasts, so no." Tharion slicked back his hair. "But . . . I need to find that kid, if he's not in the Sleeping City. Maybe we can kill two birds with one stone."

Ithan angled his head. "Any idea where to look instead?"

"No. So I desperately need a hint in the right direction."

Ithan frowned. "What do you have in mind?"

"You're not going to like it. Neither is Bryce."

"Why does she need to be involved?" Ithan couldn't stop his voice from sharpening.

"Because I know Legs, and I know she'll want to come."

"Not if we don't tell her."

"Oh, I'm going to tell her. I like my balls where they are." Tharion grinned and jerked his chin to the city behind Ithan. "Go get some money. Gold marks, not credit."

"Tell me where we're going." Somewhere shady, no doubt.

Tharion's eyes darkened. "To the mystics."

37

Keep holding, hold, hold!" Madame Kyrah chanted, and Bryce's left leg shook with the effort of keeping her right leg aloft and in place.

Beside her, Juniper sweated along, face set with focused determination. June held perfect form—no hunched shoulders, no curved spine. Every line of her friend's body radiated strength and grace.

"And down into first position," the instructor ordered over the thumping music. Totally not the style that ballet was usually danced to, but that was why Bryce loved this class: it combined the formal, precise movements of ballet with dance club hits. And somehow, in doing so, it helped her understand both the movements and the sound better. Merge them better. Let her *enjoy* it, rather than dance along to music she'd once loved and daydreamed about getting to perform onstage.

Wrong body type had no place here, in this bright studio on an artsy block of the Old Square.

"Take a five-minute breather," said Madame Kyrah, a dark-haired swan shifter, striding to the chair by the wall of mirrors to swig from her water bottle.

Bryce wobbled over to her pile of crap by the opposite wall, ducking under the barre to pick up her phone. No messages. A blissfully quiet morning. Exactly what she'd needed.

Which was why she'd come here. Beyond *wanting* to come here twice a week, she needed to be here today—to work out every swirling thought. She hadn't told Juniper what she'd learned.

What could she say? *Hey, just FYI, the Bone Quarter is a lie, and I'm pretty sure there's no such thing as a true afterlife, because we all get turned into energy and herded through the Dead Gate, though some small bit of us gets shoved down the gullet of the Under-King, so . . . good fucking luck!*

But Juniper was frowning at her own phone as she drank a few sips from her water bottle.

"What's up?" Bryce asked between pants. Her legs shook simply standing still.

Juniper tossed her phone onto her duffel bag. "Korinne Lescau got tapped to be principal."

Bryce's mouth dropped open.

"*I know,*" Juniper said, reading the unspoken outrage on Bryce's face. Korinne had entered the company two years ago. Had only been a soloist for this season. And the CCB had claimed it wasn't promoting anyone this year.

"This is definitely a *fuck you,*" Bryce seethed.

June's throat bobbed, and Bryce's fingers curled, as if she could rip the face off of every director and board member of the CCB for putting that pain there. "They're too afraid to fire me, because the shows where I'm a soloist always bring in a crowd, but they'll do what they can to punish me," June said.

"All because you told a bunch of rich jerks that they were being elitist monsters."

"I might bring in money for the shows, but those rich jerks donate millions." The faun drained her water. "I'm going to stick it out until they *have* to promote me."

Bryce tapped her foot on the pale wood floor. "I'm sorry, June."

Her friend squared her shoulders with a quiet dignity that cracked Bryce's heart. "I do this because I love it," she said as Kyrah summoned the class back into their lines. "They're not worth my anger. I have to keep remembering that." She tucked a stray curl back into her bun. "Any word about that kid?"

Bryce shook her head. "Nope." She'd leave it at that.

Kyrah started the music, and they got back into position.

Bryce sweated and grunted through the rest of the class, but Juniper had become razor-focused. Every movement precise and flawless, her gaze fixed on the mirror, as if she battled herself. That expression didn't alter, even when Kyrah asked June to demonstrate a perfect series of thirty-two fouettés—spins on one foot—for the class. Juniper whipped around like the wind itself propelled her, her grounding hoof not straying one inch from its starting point.

Perfect form. A perfect dancer. Yet it wasn't enough.

Juniper left class almost as soon as it had finished, not lingering to chat like she usually did. Bryce let her go, and waited until most of the class had filtered out before approaching Kyrah by the mirror, where the instructor was panting softly. "Did you see the news about Korinne?"

Kyrah tugged on a loose pink sweatshirt against the chill of the dance studio. Even though she hadn't danced on CCB's stage in years, the instructor remained in peak form. "You seem surprised. I'm not."

"You can't say anything? You were one of CCB's prized dancers." And now one of their best instructors when she wasn't teaching her outside classes.

Kyrah frowned. "I'm as much at the mercy of the company's leadership as Juniper. She might be the most talented dancer I've ever seen, and the hardest-working, but she's going up against a well-entrenched power structure. The people in charge don't appreciate being called out for what they truly are."

"But—"

"I get why you want to help her." Kyrah shouldered her duffel and aimed for the double doors of the studio. "I want to help her, too. But Juniper made her choice this spring. She has to face the consequences."

Bryce stared after her for a minute, the doors to the studio banging shut. As she stood alone in the sunny space, the silence pressed on her. She looked to the spot where Juniper had been demonstrating those fouettés.

Bryce pulled out her phone and did a quick search. A moment later, she was dialing. "I'd like to speak to Director Gorgyn, please."

Bryce tapped her feet again as the CCB receptionist spoke. She clenched her fingers into fists before she answered, "Tell him that Her Royal Highness Princess Bryce Danaan is calling."

Push-ups bored Hunt to tears. If it hadn't been for the earbuds playing the last few chapters of the book he was listening to, he might have fallen asleep during his workout on the training roof of the Comitium.

The morning sun baked his back, his arms, his brow, sweat dripping onto the concrete floors. He had a vague awareness of people watching, but kept going. Three hundred sixty-one, three hundred sixty-two . . .

A shadow fell across him, blocking out the sun. He found the Harpy smirking down at him, her dark hair fluttering in the wind. And those black wings . . . Well, that's why there was no more sun.

"What," he asked on an exhale, keeping up his momentum.

"The pretty one wants to see you." Her sharp voice was edged with cruel amusement.

"Her name is Celestina," Hunt grunted, getting to three hundred seventy before hopping to his feet. The Harpy's gaze slid down his bare torso, and he crossed his arms. "You're her messenger now?"

"I'm Ephraim's messenger, and since he just finished fucking her, I was the closest one to retrieve you."

Hunt held in his cringe. "Fine." He caught Isaiah's attention from across the ring and motioned that he was leaving. His friend, in the middle of his own exercises, waved a farewell.

He didn't bother waving to Baxian, despite his help last night. And Pollux hadn't come up to the ring for their private hour of training—he was presumably still in bed with the Hind. Naomi had waited for him for thirty minutes before bailing and going to inspect her own troops.

Hunt stepped toward the glass doors into the building, wiping the sweat from his brow, but the Harpy followed him. He sneered over a shoulder. "Bye."

She gave him a slashing grin. "I'm to escort you back."

Hunt stiffened. This couldn't be good. His body going distant, he kept walking, aiming for the elevators. If he sent a warning message to Bryce right now, would she have enough time to flee the city? Unless they'd already come for her—

The Harpy trailed him like a wraith. "Your little disappearing act last night is going to bite you in the ass," she crooned, stepping into the elevator with him.

Right. That.

He tried not to look too relieved as the acid in his veins eased. That had to be why Celestina was summoning him. A chewing-out for bad behavior, he could deal with.

If only the Harpy knew what he'd really been up to lately.

So Hunt leaned against the far wall of the elevator, contemplating how he'd best like to kill her. A lightning strike to the head would be swift, but not as satisfying as plunging his sword into her gut and twisting as he drove upward.

The Harpy tucked in her black wings. She'd been built wiry and long, her face narrow and eyes a bit too large for her features. She went on, "You always did think more with your cock than your head."

"One of my most winning attributes." He wouldn't let her bait him. She'd done it before, when they'd both served Sandriel, and he'd always paid for it. Sandriel had never once punished the female for the brawls that had left his skin shredded. He'd always been the one to take the flaying afterward for "disturbing the peace."

The Harpy stepped onto the Governor's floor like a dark wind. "You'll get what's coming to you, Athalar."

"Likewise." He trailed her to the double doors of Celestina's public office. She halted outside, knocking once. Celestina murmured her welcome, and Hunt stepped into the room, shutting the door on the Harpy's pinched face.

The Archangel, robed in sky blue today, was immaculate—glowing. If she'd been kept up all night with Ephraim, she didn't reveal it. Or any emotion, really, as Hunt stopped before her desk and said, "You asked for me?" He took a casual stance, legs apart, hands behind his back, wings high but loose.

Celestina straightened a golden pen on her desk. "Was there an emergency last night?"

Yes. No. "A private matter."

"And you saw fit to prioritize that over assisting me?"

Fuck. "You seemed to have the situation under control."

Her lips thinned. "I had hoped that when you promised to have my back, it would be for the entire night. Not for an hour."

"I'm sorry," he said, and meant it. "If it had been for anything else—"

"I'm assuming it had to do with Miss Quinlan."

"Yeah."

"And are you aware that you, as one of my triarii, chose to assist a Princess of the Fae instead of your Governor?"

"It wasn't for anything political."

"That was not how my . . . mate perceived it. He asked why two of my triarii had ditched our private celebration. If they thought so little of me, of him, that they could leave without permission to help a Fae royal."

Hunt ran his hands through his hair. "I'm sorry, Celestina. I really am."

"I'm sure you are." Her voice was distant. "This shall not happen again."

Or what? he almost asked. But he said, "It won't."

"I want you staying in the barracks for the next two weeks."

"*What?*" Hunt supposed he could always quit, but what the fuck would he do with himself then?

Celestina's gaze was steely. "After that time, you may return to Miss Quinlan. But I think you need a reminder of your . . .

priorities. And I'd like you to fully commit to helping Baxian adjust." She shuffled some papers on her desk. "You're dismissed."

Two weeks here. Without Quinlan. Without getting to touch her, fuck her, lie next to her—

"Celestina—"

"Goodbye."

Despite his outrage, his frustration, he looked at her. Really looked.

She was alone. Alone, and like a ray of sunshine in a sea of darkness. He should have had her back last night. But if it was between her and Bryce, he'd always, *always* pick his mate. No matter what it cost him.

Which was apparently two weeks without Bryce.

But he asked, "How'd it go with Ephraim?" *You don't look too happy for a female who recently bedded her mate.*

Her head snapped up. Again, that distance in her eyes that told him he'd been shut out before she even said, "That's a private matter, to use your words."

Fine. "I'll be around today if you need me." He aimed for the door, but added, "Why send the Harpy to get me?"

Her caramel eyes shuttered. "Ephraim thought she might be the most effective."

"Ephraim, huh?"

"He is my mate."

"But not your master."

Power glowed along her wings, her tightly curling hair. "Careful, Hunt."

"Noted." Hunt strode into the hall, wondering if he'd done something to piss off Urd.

Two weeks here. With all the shit happening with Bryce and the rebels and Cormac . . . Fuck.

As if the mere thought of the word *rebels* had summoned her, he found the Hind leaning against the far wall. There was no sign of the Harpy. The Hind's beautiful face was serene, though her golden eyes seemed lit with Helfire. "Hello, Hunt."

"Here to interrogate me?" Hunt aimed for the elevator that

would take him back to the training ring. He kept his pace casual, arrogant. Utterly unfazed.

Even if Danaan had been freaked out by her, Hunt had seen and dealt with Lidia Cervos enough to know which buttons to push. Which to avoid. And that if he got her away from Mordoc, from Pollux, from her entire dreadwolf retinue, he'd leave her in smoking ruin. Fancy that—she was alone right now.

The Hind knew it, too. That was what made her dangerous. She might appear unarmed, vulnerable, but she carried herself like someone who might whisper a word and have death fly to defend her. Who might snap her fingers and unleash Hel upon him.

He'd been in Sandriel's possession when the Hind had signed on—recruited by the Archangel herself to serve as her spymaster. Lidia had been so young: barely into her twenties. She'd just made the Drop, and had no apparent deep well of magic, other than her swiftness as a deer shifter and her love of cruelty. Her appointment to such a high position had been a blaring alarm to stay the fuck away from her—she was a Vanir who'd cross any line, if she pleased Sandriel so greatly. Pollux had courted her almost immediately.

"What the fuck do you want?" Hunt asked, stabbing the elevator button. He blocked any thought of Ophion, of Emile, of their activities from his mind. He was nothing but the Umbra Mortis, loyal to the empire.

"You're friends with Ruhn Danaan, are you not?"

Burning fucking Solas. Hunt kept his face neutral. "I wouldn't say he's a friend, but yeah. We hang out."

"And Ithan Holstrom?"

Hunt shrugged. Calm—stay calm. "He's a decent guy."

"And what of Tharion Ketos?"

Hunt made himself blow out a loud sigh. It served to loosen the growing tightness in his chest. "Isn't it a little early for interrogating?"

Fuck, had she gone after Bryce already? Was one of her goons—Mordoc, even—at the apartment while she cornered Hunt here, at the elevator?

The Hind smiled without showing her teeth. "I woke up refreshed this morning."

"I didn't realize fucking Pollux is so boring that you could sleep through it."

She snickered, to his surprise. "Sandriel might have done so much more with you, if she'd only had the vision for it."

"Too bad she liked gambling more than torturing me." He could only thank the gods that Sandriel had gotten so buried in her debts that she'd had to sell him to Micah to pay them off.

"Too bad she's dead." Those golden eyes gleamed. Yeah, the Hind knew who was responsible for that death.

The elevator opened, and Hunt stepped in, the Hind following him. "So why the questions about my friends?" How much time would he have to warn them? Or would all of them fleeing the city confirm that they were guilty?

"I thought they were merely people you hung out with."

"Semantics."

Her small, bland smile raked down Hunt's temper. "An unusual group, even in a city as progressive as Lunathion. An angel, a wolf, a Fae Prince, a mer, and a half-human whore." Hunt growled at the last word, rage shaking him from his dread. "It sounds like the start to a bad joke."

"You want to ask me something, Lidia, then fucking say it. Don't waste my time." The elevator opened into the hall of the training floor, bringing the scent of sweat.

"I'm merely observing an anomaly. Wondering what might be so . . . compelling that so many people of power, from different species and Houses, are *hanging out* at Bryce Quinlan's apartment."

"She's got one Hel of a video-gaming system."

The Hind chuckled, the sound laced with menace. "I'll find out, you know. I always do."

"I look forward to it," Hunt said, stalking toward the doors. A dark figure loomed ahead of them—Baxian. His eyes were on the Hind. Stony, and yet seeking.

She stopped short. The *Hind* stopped short.

Baxian said, "Lidia."

The Hind replied flatly, "Baxian."

"I was looking for you." He inclined his head to Hunt in dismissal. He'd take over from here.

"Is it to explain why you vanished into the night with Hunt Athalar?" she asked, folding her hands behind her back in a perfect imperial stance. A good little soldier.

Hunt passed Baxian. "Not a word," Hunt said so softly it was barely more than a breath. Baxian nodded subtly.

Hunt had barely pushed open the doors to the training area when he heard Baxian say carefully to the Hind, as if remembering who she was, "I don't answer to you."

Her voice was smooth as silk. "Not to me, or Ephraim, but you still answer to the Asteri." Her true masters. "Whose will is mine."

Hunt's stomach churned. She was right.

And he'd do well to remember it before it was too late.

38

This is a dumb fucking idea."

"You really love to say that, Legs."

Bryce peered at the two-story iron doors in the back alley of the Old Square, the surface embossed with stars and planets and all matter of heavenly objects. "There's a reason no one comes to the mystics anymore." Hel, she'd suggested it while working on Danika's case this spring, but Hunt had convinced her not to come.

The mystics are some dark, fucked-up shit, he'd said.

Bryce glowered at Tharion and Ithan, standing behind her in the alley. "I mean it. What's behind those doors is not for the faint of heart. Jesiba knows this guy, but even she doesn't mess with him."

Ithan countered, "I can't think of another alternative. The Oracle only sees the future, not present. I need to know what's going on with Connor."

Tharion drawled, "If you can't stomach it, Legs, then sit out here on the curb."

She sighed through her nose, trying again. "Only lowlifes use the mystics these days."

They'd had this conversation twice already on the walk over. She was likely going to lose this round as well, but it was worth a shot. If Hunt had been with her, he'd have gotten his point across in that alphahole way of his. But he hadn't answered his phone.

He'd probably give her Hel for coming here without him.

Bryce sighed to the baking-hot sky. "All right. Let's get this over with."

"That's the spirit, Legs." Tharion clapped her on the back. Ithan frowned at the doors.

Bryce reached for the door chime, a crescent moon dangling from a delicate iron chain. She yanked it once, twice. An off-kilter ringing echoed.

"This is a really bad idea," she muttered again.

"Yeah, yeah," Ithan said, tipping his head back to study the building. The tattoo of Amelie's pack was glaringly dark in the sun. She wondered if he wanted to tear the flesh off and start anew.

Bryce set the question aside as one of the planets carved in the door—the five-ringed behemoth that was Thurr—swung away, revealing a pale gray eye. "Appointment?"

Tharion held up his BCIU badge. "The Blue Court requires your assistance."

"Does it, now?" A croaking laugh as that eye—eerily sharp despite the wrinkles around it—fixed on the mer. It narrowed in amusement or pleasure. "One of the river folk. What a treat, what a treat."

The planet slammed shut, and Tharion stepped onto the slate front step as the doors cracked open a sliver. Cold air rippled out, along with the tang of salt and the smothering dampness of mold.

Ithan trailed Bryce, swearing under his breath at the scent. She twisted, throwing him a reproachful glare. He winced, falling into step beside her with that sunball player's grace as they entered the cavernous space beyond.

A gray-robed old male stood before them. Not human, but his scent declared nothing other than some sort of Vanir humanoid. His heavy white beard fell to the thin band of rope that served as a belt, his wispy hair long and unbound. Four rings of silver and gold glinted on one of his withered, spotted hands, with small stars blazing in the center of each, trapped in the nearly invisible glass domes.

No—not stars.

Bryce's stomach turned over at the minuscule hand that pressed against the other side of the glass. There was no mistaking the desperation in that touch.

Fire sprites. Enslaved, all of them. Bought and sold.

Bryce struggled to keep from ripping that hand clean off the arm that bore it. She could feel Ithan watching her, feel him trying to puzzle out why she'd gone so still and stiff, but she couldn't tear her gaze from the sprites—

"It is not every day that one of the mer crosses my doorstep," the old male said, his smile revealing too-white teeth, still intact despite his age. Unless they'd come from someone else. "Let alone in the company of a wolf and a Fae."

Bryce gripped her purse, mastering her temper, and lifted her chin. "We need to consult your . . ." She peered past his bony shoulder to the dim space beyond. "Services." *And then I'll take all four of those rings and smash them open.*

"I shall be honored." The male bowed at the waist to Tharion, but didn't bother to extend the courtesy to Bryce and Ithan. "This way."

Bryce kept a hand within casual distance of the knife in her purse as they entered the dimness. She wished she had the reassuring weight and strength of Danika's sword, but the blade would have stood out too much.

The space consisted of two levels, bookshelves crammed with tomes and scrolls rising to the dark-veiled ceiling, an iron ramp winding up the walls in a lazy spiral. A great golden orb dangled in the center of the room, lit from within.

And beneath them, in tubs built into the slate floor . . .

To her left, Ithan sucked in a breath.

Three mystics slept, submerged in greenish, cloudy water, breathing masks strapped to their faces. Their white shifts floated around them, doing little to hide the skeletal bodies beneath. One male, one female, one both. That was how it always was, how it had always been. Perfect balance.

Bryce's stomach turned over again. She knew the sensation wouldn't stop until she left.

"May I interest you in a hot tea before we begin the formalities?" the old male asked Tharion, gesturing to a thick oak table to the right of the ramp's base.

"We're pressed for time," Ithan lied, stepping up to Tharion's side. Fine. Let them deal with the old creep.

Ithan set a pile of gold marks on the table with a clink. "If that doesn't cover the cost, give me the bill for the remainder." That drew Bryce's attention. Ithan spoke with such . . . authority. She'd heard him talk to his teammates as their captain, had seen him in command plenty, but the Ithan she'd known these past few days had been subdued.

"Of course, of course." The male's filmy eyes swept around the room. "I can have my beauties up and running within a few minutes." He hobbled toward the walkway and braced a hand on the iron rail as he began the ascent.

Bryce glanced back to the three mystics in their tubs, their thin bodies, their pale, soggy skin. Built into the floor beside them was a panel covered in a language she had never seen.

"Pay them no heed, miss," the old male called, still winding his way toward a platform about halfway up the room, filled with dials and wheels. "When they're not in use, they drift. Where they go and what they see is a mystery, even to me."

It wasn't that the mystics could see all worlds—no, the gift wasn't the unnerving thing. It was what they gave up for it.

Life. True life.

Bryce heard Tharion's swallow. She refrained from snapping that she'd warned him. Ten fucking times.

"The families are compensated handsomely," the old male said, as if reciting from a script designed to calm skittish patrons. He reached the controls and began flipping switches. Gears groaned and a few more lights flickered on in the tanks, further illuminating the mystics' bodies. "If that is of any concern to you."

Another switch flipped, and Bryce staggered back a step as a full holographic replica of their solar system exploded into view, orbiting the dangling sun in the center of the space. Tharion blew out what she could only assume was an impressed breath. Ithan scanned above them, like he could find his brother in that map.

Bryce didn't wait for them before trailing the old male up the walkway as the seven planets aligned themselves perfectly, stars glittering in the far reaches of the room. She couldn't keep the sharpness from her voice as she asked, "Do their families ever see them?"

She really had no right to demand these answers. She'd been complicit in coming here, in using their services.

"It would be upsetting for both parties," the male said distantly, still working his switches.

"What's your name?" Bryce advanced up the ramp.

Tharion murmured, "Legs." She ignored the warning. Ithan kept quiet.

Yet the old male replied, utterly unfazed, "Some people call me the Astronomer."

She couldn't keep the bite from her voice. "What do other people call you?" The Astronomer didn't answer. Up and up, Bryce ascended into the heavens, Tharion and Ithan trailing her. Like the assholes were second-guessing this.

One of the mystics twitched, water splashing.

"A normal reaction," the Astronomer said, not even looking up from his dials as they approached. "Everyone is always so concerned for their well-being. They made the choice, you know. I didn't force them into this." He sighed. "To give up life in the waking world to glimpse wonders of the universe that no Vanir or mortal shall ever see . . ." Stroking his beard, he added, "This trio is a good one. I've had them for a while now with no issues. The last group . . . One drifted too far. Too far, and for too long. They dragged the others with them. Such a waste."

Bryce tried to block out the excuses. Everyone knew the truth: the mystics came from all races, and were usually poor. So poor that when they were born with the gift, their families sold them to people like the Astronomer, who exploited their talent until they died, alone in those tubs. Or wandered so deep into the cosmos they couldn't find their way back to their minds.

Bryce clenched her hands into fists. Micah had allowed it to happen. Her piece-of-shit father turned a blind eye, too. As Autumn King, he had the ability to put an end to this practice or, at the least, advocate to stop it, but he didn't.

Bryce set aside her outrage and waved a hand to the drifting planets. "This space map—"

"It is called an orrery."

"This *orrery*." Bryce approached the male's side. "It's tech—not magic?"

"Can it not be both?"

Bryce's fingers curled into fists. But she said, a murky memory rippling from her childhood, "The Autumn King has one in his private study."

The Astronomer clicked his tongue. "Yes, and a fine one at that. Made by craftsmen in Avallen long ago. I haven't had the privilege to see it, but I hear it is as precise as mine, if not more so."

"What's the point of it?" she asked.

"Only one who does not feel the need to peer into the cosmos would ask such a thing. The orrery helps us answer the most fundamental questions: Who are we? Where do we come from?"

When Bryce didn't say anything more, Tharion cleared his throat. "We'll be quick with our own questions, then."

"Each one will be billed, of course."

"Of course," Ithan said through his teeth, stopping at Bryce's side. He peered through the planets to the mystics floating beneath. "Does my brother, Connor Holstrom, remain in the Bone Quarter, or has his soul passed through the Dead Gate?"

The Astronomer whispered, "Luna above." He fiddled with one of the faintly glowing rings atop his hand. "This question requires a . . . riskier method of contact than usual. One that borders on the illegal. It will cost you."

Bryce said, "How much?" Scam-artist bullshit.

"Another hundred gold marks."

Bryce started, but Ithan said, "Done."

She turned to warn him not to spend one more coin of the considerable inheritance his parents had left him, but the Astronomer hobbled toward a metal cabinet beneath the dials and opened its small doors. He pulled out a bundle wrapped in canvas.

Bryce stiffened at the moldy, rotten earth scent that crept from the bundle as he unfolded the fabric to reveal a handful of rust-colored salt.

"What the fuck is that?" Ithan asked.

"Bloodsalt," Bryce breathed. Tharion looked to her in question, but she didn't bother to explain more.

Blood for life, blood for death—it was summoning salt infused with the blood from a laboring mother's sex and blood from a dying male's throat. The two great transitions of a soul in and out of this world. But to use it here . . . "You can't mean to add that to their water," Bryce said to the Astronomer.

The old male hobbled back down the ramp. "Their tanks already contain white salts. The bloodsalt will merely pinpoint their search."

Tharion muttered to Bryce, "You might be right about this place."

"*Now* you agree with me?" she whisper-yelled as the Astronomer sprinkled the red salt into the three tanks.

The water clouded, and then turned rust colored. Like the mystics were now submerged in blood.

Ithan murmured, "This isn't right."

"Then let's take our money and go," she urged.

But the Astronomer returned and Tharion asked, "Is it safe for the mystics to contact the resting dead?"

The Astronomer typed on the pad mounted on a gold-plated lectern fashioned after an exploding star, then hit a black button on a panel nearby. "Oh yes. They do love to talk. Have nothing else to do with their time." He shot Bryce a sharp glare, gray eyes gleaming like cold knives. "As for your money . . . there is a no-refunds policy. Says so right there on the wall. You might as well stay to hear your answer."

Before Bryce could respond, the floor below slid away, leaving the mystics in their tubs. And creating a considerable gap between the base of the ramp and the entryway.

The tubs rested atop narrow columns, rising from a sublevel lined with more books and another walkway descending down, down—to a black pit in the center of the floor. And filling the sublevel, layer after layer of darkness revealed itself, each one blacker than the last.

Seven of them. One for each level of Hel.

"From the highest stars to the Pit itself." The Astronomer sighed, and typed again into the pad. "Their search may take a while, even with the bloodsalt."

Bryce sized up the gap between the base of the ramp and the entryway. Could she jump it? Ithan definitely could—Tharion, too.

She found Tharion watching her with crossed arms. "Just enjoy the show, Legs."

She scowled. "I think you've lost the right to call me that after this."

Ithan said quietly, face pained, "Bryce. I know this sucks. This is . . . This is not okay." His voice turned hoarse. "But if it's the only way to learn what's going on with Connor . . ."

She opened her mouth to snap that Connor would have condemned this place and told Ithan to find some other way, but . . . she could see him. Connor. Shining right there in Ithan's face, in his eyes—the same hue—and in those broad shoulders.

Her throat ached.

What line wouldn't she cross to help Connor and the Pack of Devils? They would have done the same for her. Connor might have condemned this place, but if their positions were reversed . . .

Tharion jerked his chin to the exit far below. "Go ahead, Princess. We'll see you later."

"Fuck you," Bryce snapped. She braced her feet apart. "Let's get this over with." From the corner of her eye, she saw Ithan's shoulders sag. In relief or shame, she didn't know.

The old male cut in, as if he hadn't heard a word of their hissed argument. "Most astronomers and mystics have been put out of business these days, you know. Thanks to fancy tech. And self-righteous busybodies like you," he spat toward Bryce. She snarled at him, the sound more primal Fae than she liked, but he waved that hateful, ring-encrusted hand toward the mystics in their pools. "*They* were the original interweb. Any answer you wish to know, they can find it, without having to wade through the slog of nonsense out there."

The female mystic twitched, dark hair floating around her in the suspension pool, black tendrils among the red salt. Dried salt water crusted the slate rim of the tub, as if she'd thrashed earlier and soaked the stones. Salt for buoyancy—and to protect them from the demons and beings they spied on or conversed with. But would those protections fade with the bloodsalt in the water?

The mystic who was both male and female jolted, their long limbs flailing.

"Oh," the Astronomer observed, scanning the pad. "They're going far this time. Very far." He nodded to Bryce. "That was high-quality bloodsalt, you know."

"For a hundred marks, it had better be," Ithan said, but his attention remained on the mystics below, his breathing shallow.

Another push of a button, and the holographic planets began to shift, becoming smaller as they drifted away. The sun rose into the ceiling, vanishing, and distant stars came into view. Different planets.

"The mystics made the first star-maps," the Astronomer said. "They charted more extensively than anyone had before. In the Eternal City, I heard they have a thousand mystics in the palace catacombs, mapping farther and farther into the cosmos. Speaking with creatures we shall never know."

Hunt had been in those catacombs—their dungeons, specifically. Had he ever heard a whisper of this?

Something beeped on the screen and Bryce motioned toward it. "What's that?"

"The male is reaching Hel's orbit." The Astronomer clicked his tongue. "He's much faster today. Impressive."

"Connor's soul wound up in *Hel*?" Horror laced Ithan's every word.

Bryce's throat closed up. It—it wasn't possible. How would that have even happened? Had she done something with the Gate this spring that had transported his soul over there?

Silence fell, the temperature dropping with it. She demanded, "Why is it getting colder?"

"Sometimes their powers manifest the environment they're encountering." Before anyone replied, the Astronomer twisted a brass dial. "What do you see, what do you hear?"

The male twitched again, red water splashing over the edge of the tub and dribbling into the pit beneath. Tharion peered over the iron rail. "His lips are turning blue."

"The water is warm." The Astronomer tutted. "Look." He pointed to the screen. A graph of rising and falling lines, like sound waves, appeared. "I'll admit the new tech has some advantages. The old way of transcribing was much harder. I had to reference every single brain wave to find the correlation to the right letter or word. Now the machine just does it for me."

I don't care about brain waves, Bryce thought. *Tell me what's happening with Connor.*

But the Astronomer rambled on, almost absentmindedly, "When you speak, your brain sends a message to your tongue to form the words. This machine reads that message, that signal, and interprets it. Without you needing to say a word."

"So it's a mind reader," Tharion said, face pale in the lights. Bryce drifted closer to Ithan—the wolf radiated dread.

"Of a sort," the Astronomer said. "Right now, it is more of an eavesdropper, listening to the conversation the mystic is having with whoever is on the other end of the line."

Tharion asked, hands behind his back as he peered at the machines, "How does it know what the other person is saying?"

"The mystic is trained to repeat back the words so that we may transcribe them." The screen began to flash a series of letters—words.

"*Too dark*," the Astronomer read. "*It is too dark to see. Only hear.*"

"Can you pinpoint where in Hel your mystic is?" Ithan indicated the holographic levels far below.

"Not precisely, but judging by the cold, I'd say deep. Perhaps the Chasm itself."

Bryce and Ithan swapped glances. His eyes were as wide as her own.

The Astronomer kept reading. "*Hello?*" Silence. Nothing but endless silence. "This is very common," the Astronomer assured them, gesturing them to move closer. Despite herself, despite her objections, Bryce leaned in to read the feed.

The mystic said, *I am searching for the soul of a wolf called Connor Holstrom.*

Someone, something answered.

No wolves have roamed these lands for eons. No wolf by that name dwells here, living or dead. But what are you?

Ithan shuddered, swaying a step. With relief, Bryce realized—because that was the dizzying, rushing sensation in her body, too.

"Strange," the Astronomer said. "Why were we drawn to Hel if your friend isn't there?"

Bryce didn't want to know. Tried and failed to open her mouth to say they should go.

I am a mystic, the male said.

From where?

A faraway place.

Why are you here?

To ask questions. Will you oblige me?

If I can, mystic, then I shall.

What is your name?

A pause. Then, *Thanatos.*

Bryce sucked in a sharp breath.

"The Prince of the Ravine." Tharion fell back a step.

Do you know if Connor Holstrom remains in the Bone Quarter of Midgard?

A long, long pause, the sound waves flatlining. Then—

Who sent you here?

A wolf, a mer, and a half-Fae, half-human female.

How the mystics had known of their presence, Bryce had no idea.

Didn't want to know what sort of perception they possessed while in those isolation tanks.

Thanatos asked, *What are their names?*

I do not know. Will you answer my questions?

Another long pause. "We need to stop this." Ithan nodded toward the male's tub. Ice was beginning to inch over the water.

They are listening, are they?

Yes.

Again, silence.

And then the demon prince said, *Let me see them. Let them see me.*

The mystic's eyes flew open in the tank below.

39

A shuddering inhale was the only sign of discomfort Bryce would allow herself as she stared at the hologram displayed in the center of the orrery. The male now contained inside its dark border.

Thanatos's tightly curled black hair was cropped close to his head, displaying the handsome, unsmiling face above the powerful body bedecked in dark, ornate armor. He gazed right at Bryce. As if he could indeed see through the mystic's eyes.

The Astronomer fell back a step, murmuring a prayer to Luna.

The feed kept going, in time to Thanatos's moving mouth. Hunger filled the demon's expression.

I can smell the starlight on you.

The Prince of the Ravine knew her. Somehow.

The Astronomer took another step back, then another, until he was pressed against the wall behind him, shaking in terror.

Thanatos's dark eyes pierced to her soul. *You're the one my brothers speak about.*

Ithan and Tharion glanced between her and the demon, hands within easy reach of their weapons—little as they could do.

"I came to ask about a friend's soul. I don't know why I'm talking to you," Bryce said, and added a bit quietly, "Your Highness."

I am a Prince of Death. Souls bow to me.

This male had none of Aidas's slickness or what Hunt had told her of Apollion's smug arrogance. Nothing that indicated mercy or humor.

Ithan blurted, teeth clattering with the cold, "Can you tell if Connor Holstrom's soul somehow got lost in Hel?"

Thanatos frowned at his knee-high boots, like he could see all the way down to the Pit levels below.

The wolf is your brother, I take it, he said to Ithan.

"Yes." Ithan's throat bobbed.

His soul is not in Hel. He is . . . His attention snapped again to Bryce. Ripped away skin and bone to the being beneath. *You slew one of my creations. My beloved pet, kept for so long on your side of the Crossing.*

Bryce managed to ask, breath clouding in front of her, "You mean the Reapers? Or the Shepherd?" A shepherd of souls—for a prince who peddled them. "The Under-King said you abandoned it after the First Wars."

Abandoned, or intentionally planted?

Great. Fantastic.

"I had no interest in being its lunch," Bryce said.

Thanatos's eyes flared. *You cost me a key link to Midgard. The Shepherd reported faithfully to me on all it heard in the Bone Quarter. The souls of the dead talk freely of their world.*

"Boo-hoo."

You mock a Prince of Hel?

"I just want answers." And to get the fuck out of here.

Thanatos studied her again—as if he had all the time in the universe. Then he said, *I will give them to you only out of respect for a warrior capable of slaying one of my creations. Shall I meet you on the battlefield, however, I will take vengeance for the Shepherd's death.*

Bryce's mouth dried out. "It's a date."

Connor Holstrom remains in the Bone Quarter. My Shepherd observed him on its rounds the night before you slew it. Unless . . . Ah, I see now. His eyes went distant. *An order was dispatched from the dark. He shall be left alone with the others until the usual amount of time has passed.*

"Who gave the order?" Ithan demanded.

It is not clear.

Bryce demanded, "Is there a way to help souls like Connor?" Whether he was ushered through the Dead Gate tomorrow or in five hundred years, it was a horrible fate.

Only the Asteri would know.

Tharion—the asshole—cut in, "Can you determine the location of a human boy named Emile Renast in Lunathion?"

Bryce stiffened. If Apollion was actually seeking Emile . . . had they just dragged another Prince of Hel into the hunt?

"That is not how this works," the Astronomer hissed from where he still cowered by the wall.

I do not know this name or person.

Thank the gods. And thank the gods the prince's words held no hint of awareness about what Emile was, or what Apollion might want from him.

Tharion drawled, "Know anyone who might?"

No. Those are matters of your world.

Bryce tried and failed to calm her racing heartbeat. At least Connor remained in the Bone Quarter, and they'd gotten a cease-fire.

"Kid's a thunderbird," Tharion said. "Ring any bells?"

"Tharion," Ithan warned, apparently on the same page as Bryce.

I thought the Asteri destroyed that threat long ago.

Bryce cleared her throat. "Maybe," she hedged. "Why were they a threat?"

I grow tired of these questions. I shall feast.

The room plunged into blackness.

The Astronomer whispered, "Luna guard me, your bow bright against the darkness, your arrows like silver fire shooting into Hel—"

Bryce lifted a hand wreathed in starlight, casting the room in silver. In the space where Thanatos's hologram had been, only a black pit remained.

The male mystic jerked violently, submerging and arching

upward. Red liquid splashed. The other two lay still as death. The machine began blaring and beeping, and the Astronomer halted his praying to rush to the controls. "He has snared him," the male gasped, hands shaking.

Bryce flared her light brighter as the feed began running again.

It has been a long while since a mortal fly buzzed all the way down to Hel. I will taste this one's soul, as I once sipped from them like fine wine.

Frost spread over the floor. The male mystic arched again, thin arms flailing, chest rising and falling at a rapid pace.

"Cut him loose!" Bryce barked.

Please, the mystic begged.

How sad and lonely and desperate you are. You taste of rainwater.

Please, please.

A little more. Just a taste.

The Astronomer began typing. Alarms wailed.

"What's happening?" Tharion shouted. Down below, the ice crept over the other two mystics in their tubs.

The prince continued, *You have gone too deep. I think I shall keep you.*

The male thrashed, sending waves of red water cascading into the void below.

"Turn off the machines," Ithan ordered.

"I cannot—not without the proper extraction. His mind might shatter."

Bryce protested, "He's fucked if you don't."

The Prince of the Ravine said, *I do not care for my brothers' agenda. I do not heed their rules and restraints and illusions of civilization. I shall taste all of you like this—you and your masters—once the door between our worlds is again open. Starting with you, Starborn.*

Ice exploded across the walls, crusting over the submerged mystics. The machines groaned, planets flickering, and then—

Every firstlight and piece of tech went out. Even Bryce's starlight vanished. Bryce swore. "What—"

The Astronomer panted in the darkness. Buttons clacked hollowly. "Their respirators—"

Bryce yanked out her phone and fumbled for its light. It was dead. Another curse from Tharion, and she knew his was, too. Every muscle and tendon in her body went taut.

Shimmering, golden light glowed from the Astronomer's upraised hand. The fire sprites trapped in his rings simmered steadily.

Apparently, it was all Ithan needed to see by as he launched himself over the rail and aimed for the male's iced-over tub. He landed gracefully, balancing his feet on either side. A pound of his fist had the ice cracking.

The male was convulsing, no doubt drowning without a functioning respirator. Ithan hauled him up, ripping the mask from his face. A long feeding tube followed. The male gagged and spasmed, but Ithan propped him over the rim, lest he slide back under.

Leaping with that athletic grace, Ithan reached the tub in the middle, freeing the mystic within. Then on to the female in the third.

The Astronomer was shrieking, but it seemed Ithan barely heard the words. The three mystics shook, soft cries trembling from their blue mouths. Bryce shook with them, and Tharion put a hand on her back.

Something groaned below, and the lights sputtered back on. Metal whined. The floor began to rise, pulling toward the tubs again. The sun fixture descended from the ceiling as the Astronomer hobbled down the walkway, cursing.

"You had no right to pull them out, *no right*—"

"They would have drowned!" Bryce launched into motion, storming after the male. Tharion stalked a step behind her.

The female stirred as the slate floor locked into place around the tubs. On reed-thin arms, she raised up her chest, blinking blearily at Ithan, then the room.

"Back," the mystic wheezed, her voice broken and raspy. Unused for years. Her dark eyes filled with pleading. "*Send me back.*"

"The Prince of the Ravine was about to rip apart your friend's soul," Ithan said, kneeling before her.

"*Send me back!*" she screamed, the words barely more than a hoarse screech. "*Back!*"

Not to Hel, Bryce knew—not to the Prince of the Ravine. But into the watery, weightless existence. Ithan got to his feet, inching away.

"Get out," the Astronomer seethed, hurrying toward his mystics. "All of you."

Bryce reached the bottom of the ramp, the Astronomer's still-glowing rings blazing bright. Fury boiled in her chest. "You would have sacrificed them—"

"*BACK!*" the female screamed again. The other two mystics stirred to consciousness, moaning. Bryce reached Ithan's side and looped her arm through his, pulling him toward the doors. The wolf gaped at the mystics, the mess they'd made.

The Astronomer knelt by the female, reaching for the tubes that Ithan had ripped free. "They cannot exist in this world anymore. *Do not want* to exist in this world." He glared at her, cold fire in his pale gray eyes.

Bryce opened her mouth, but Tharion shook his head, already heading to the exit. "Sorry for the trouble," he said over a broad shoulder.

"*Send me back*," the female whimpered to the Astronomer.

Bryce tried to hustle Ithan along, but the wolf gazed at the female, at the old male. His muscles tensed, like he might very well throw the Astronomer off the girl and haul her away.

"Soon," the old male promised, stroking the young woman's wet hair. "You'll be drifting again soon, my lamb." Each of his rings glimmered, projecting rays around the mystic's head like a corona.

Bryce stopped tugging on Ithan's arm. Stopped moving as she saw the pleading little hands pushing against the glass orbs on the Astronomer's fingers.

Do something. Be something.

But what could she do? What authority did she have to free

the sprites? What power could she wield beyond blinding him and snatching the rings off his fingers? She'd make it a block before the Aux or 33rd were called in, and then she'd have a fucking mess on her hands. And if Hunt was the one called to apprehend her . . . She knew he'd back her in an instant, but he also answered to the law. She couldn't make him choose. Not to mention that they couldn't afford the scrutiny right now. In so many ways.

So Bryce turned, hating herself, towing Ithan along. He didn't fight her this time. The Astronomer was still murmuring to his charges when Ithan shut the heavy doors behind them.

The street seemed unchanged in the light summer rain that had started. Tharion's face was haunted. "You were right," he admitted. "It was a bad idea."

Bryce opened and closed her fingers into fists. "You're a fucking asshole, you know that?"

Tharion threw her a mocking grin. "You're in the gray with us, Legs. Don't get boring now that you've got a fancy crown."

A low growl slipped from her throat. "I always wondered why the River Queen made you her Captain of Intelligence. Now I know."

"What does that mean?" Tharion advanced a step, towering over her.

Like Hel would she back down. "It means that you pretend to be Mr. Charming, but you're just a ruthless backstabber who will do anything to achieve his ends."

His face hardened. Became someone she didn't know. Became the sort of mer that people wisely stayed away from. "Try having your family at the mercy of the River Queen and then come cry to me about morals." His voice had dropped dangerously low.

"My family is at the mercy of *all* Vanir," she snapped. Starlight flared around her, and people down the alley paused. Turned their way. She didn't care. But she kept her voice whisper-soft as she hissed, "We're done working with you. Go find someone else to drag into your shit."

She turned to Ithan for backup, but the wolf had gone pale as he gazed toward a brick wall across the alley. Bryce followed his stare and went still. She'd seen the male before them on the news and in photos, but never in the flesh. She immediately wished she still had the distance of a digital screen between them. Her starlight guttered and went out.

Mordoc smiled, a slash of white in the shadows. "Causing trouble so early in the day?"

Nothing of Danika showed in Mordoc's craggy face. Not one shade or curve or angle.

Only—there. The way the wolf captain pushed off the wall and approached. She'd seen Danika make that movement with the same power and grace.

Ithan and Tharion fell into place beside her. Allies again, if only for this.

"What do you want, Mordy?" Tharion drawled, again that irreverent, charming mer.

But the wolf only sneered at Bryce. "Curious, for a little princess to visit a place like this."

Bryce admired her nails, grateful her hands weren't shaking. "I needed some questions answered. I'm getting married, after all. I want to know if there are any blemishes on my future husband's pristine reputation."

A harsh laugh with too many teeth. "I was warned you had a mouth on you."

Bryce blew him a kiss. "Happy not to disappoint my fans."

Ithan cut in, snarling softly, "We're going."

"The disgraced pup," Mordoc said, his chuckle like gravel. "Sabine said she'd thrown you out. Looks like you landed right with the trash, eh? Or is that from lurking in so many alleys lately? Care to explain that?"

Bryce sighed as Ithan bristled and said, "I don't know what you're talking about."

Before Mordoc could reply, Tharion said with that winning smile, "Unless you have some sort of imperial directive to interrogate us, we're done here."

The wolf grinned back at him. "I ran a mer male like you to shore once. Drove him into a cove with a net and learned what happens to mer when they're kept a few feet above the water for a day. What they'll do to reach one drop so they don't lose their fins forever. What they'll give up."

A muscle ticked in Tharion's jaw.

Bryce said, "Awesome story, dude."

She looped arms with Tharion, then Ithan, and hauled them down the alley with her. She might be pissed as fuck at the former, but she'd take the mer any day over Mordoc. They'd always be allies against people like him.

Danika's father . . . She started shaking when they turned the block's corner, leaving Mordoc in the shadows of the alley. She could only pray the Astronomer was as discreet as rumor claimed. Even in the face of one of the empire's worst interrogators.

They walked in silence back into the bustling heart of the Old Square, most of the tourists too busy snapping photos of the various decorations in honor of Celestina and Ephraim to notice them. A block away from the Heart Gate, Bryce halted, turning to Tharion. He looked at her with a frank, cool assessment. Here was the male who'd ruthlessly ripped apart his sister's murderer. The male who . . .

Who had jumped right into Fury's helicopter to come help during the attack last spring.

"Aw, Legs," Tharion said, reading her softening features. He reached out a hand to toy with the ends of her hair. "You're too nice to me."

She quirked her mouth to the side. Ithan remained a few steps away, and made himself busy scrolling through his phone. She said to Tharion, "I'm still mad at you."

Tharion grinned crookedly. "But you also still love me?"

She huffed a laugh. "We didn't get answers about Emile." Only more questions. "Are you going back there?"

"No." Tharion shuddered. She believed him.

"Let me know if you come up with any ideas about where the kid might be hiding."

He tugged on her hair. "I thought we weren't working together anymore."

"You're on probation. You can thank your abs for that."

He took her face in his hands, squeezing her cheeks as he pressed a chaste kiss to her brow. "I'll send you some photos later. Don't show Athalar."

Bryce shoved him. "Send me an otter and we'll be even." She might not approve or agree with Tharion's methods, might not entirely trust him, but they had far more dangerous enemies at their backs. Sticking together was the only choice.

"Done." Tharion flicked her nose with a long finger. He nodded at Ithan. "Holstrom." Then he sauntered down the street, presumably back to the Istros to check in with his queen.

Alone with Ithan on the sun-baked sidewalk, Bryce asked the wolf, "Where are you going now? Back to Ruhn's?"

Ithan's face was shadowed. Bleak. "I guess. You going to search for Emile?"

She pulled a postcard from her purse. Ithan's eyes brightened with recognition at her old tradition. "I'm actually sending this off to my mom." She studied her once-friend as he again turned solemn. "You all right?"

He shrugged. "I got my answers, didn't I?"

"Yeah, but . . ." She rubbed at her forehead, skin sticky with the remnants of sweat from her dance class hours ago. Years ago, it seemed.

"I mean, it all sounds fine, doesn't it? Connor's in the Bone Quarter, and with a don't-touch order, so . . ."

But she could tell, from the way he paced a step, that this

didn't sit well. She squeezed his shoulder. "We'll find something. Some way to help him." And everyone else trapped in the eternal slaughterhouse.

It might have been the worst lie she'd ever told, because as Ithan left, he looked like he actually believed her.

"Two weeks isn't that long," Isaiah consoled Hunt from across the glass table in the 33rd's private cafeteria in the Comitium. They sat at the table reserved exclusively for the triarii, next to the wall-to-ceiling windows overlooking the city.

Normally, Hunt didn't bother with the cafeteria, but Isaiah had invited him for an early lunch, and he'd needed to talk. He'd barely sat down when he burst out with his recap of his conversation with Celestina.

Hunt bit into his turkey-and-Brie sandwich. "I know it's not long," he said around the food, "but . . ." He swallowed, turning pleading eyes to his friend. "Bryce and I decided not to wait until Winter Solstice."

Isaiah burst out laughing, the sound rich and velvety. A few soldiers turned their way, then quickly resumed eating their meals. It might have bothered Hunt any other day, but today . . . "I'm glad you find my blue balls amusing," he hissed at his friend.

Isaiah laughed again, handsome as Hel in his suit. Given how many meetings he attended with Celestina—and now Ephraim—it was a miracle from Urd that his friend had found the time today to grab lunch with him. "I never thought I'd see the day when the Umbra Mortis came crying to me about a relatively light punishment because it interferes with his sex life."

Hunt drained his water. Isaiah had a point there. Of all the punishments he'd ever been given, this was the mildest.

Isaiah sobered, voice quieting. "So what happened last night? Everything okay?"

"It's fine now. Sabine came to the apartment looking for Ithan Holstrom. Bryce got spooked. I arrived in time to convince Sabine not to start shit."

"Ah," Isaiah said. Then asked, "And Baxian?"

"He took it upon himself as my so-called partner to provide backup. However unwanted."

Isaiah snorted. "Points for trying?"

Hunt chuckled. "Sure."

Isaiah dug into his own food, and for a moment, Hunt's chest strained with the effort of keeping every truth inside. Isaiah had been with him throughout the Fallen's rebellion. He'd have valuable insight into this shit with Ophion. Even if his advice was to stay the fuck out of it.

"What's wrong?" Isaiah asked.

Hunt shook his head. His friend was too good at reading him. "Nothing." He scrambled for another truth. "It's weird to think that two weeks without Bryce is a punishment. If I so much as blinked at Sandriel the wrong way, she pulled out my feathers one by one."

Isaiah shivered. "I remember." His friend had been the one to bandage his ravaged wings again and again, after all.

"You like working for her? Celestina, I mean?"

Isaiah didn't hesitate. "Yes. A great deal."

Hunt blew out a long breath. He couldn't tell Isaiah. Or Naomi. Because if they knew, even if they agreed to keep the shit with the rebels secret and stay out of it . . . they'd be killed, too. As it was, they might be tortured a little, but it'd become clear they knew nothing. And they might stand a chance.

"You know you can talk to me about anything, right?" Isaiah asked. Kindness shone in his dark eyes. "Even stuff with Celestina. I know it's weird with the rankings between us, but . . . I'm the middle man between the 33rd and her. Whatever you need, I'm here."

He'd never really deserved a friend like Isaiah. "It's not weird with the rankings between us," he said. "You're the leader of the 33rd. I'm happy to work for you."

Isaiah studied him. "I'm not the one who wields lightning. Or the one with a fancy nickname."

Hunt waved off the weight of what his friend said. "Trust me, I'd rather you be in charge."

Isaiah nodded, but before he could reply, silence rippled through the cafeteria. Hunt looked up on instinct, past all the wings and armor. "Great," he muttered. Baxian, tray in hand, walked toward them. Ignored the soldiers who gave him a wide berth or fell silent entirely as he passed by.

"Play nice," Isaiah murmured back, and made a show of beckoning the male over. Not for Baxian's sake, but for that of all the people witnessing this. The soldiers who needed to be presented with a unified leadership.

Hunt finished off his sandwich just as the shape-shifting angel slid into a chair beside Isaiah. Hunt met his stare. "How'd it go with the Hind?" He knew the male could read between his words. *Did you talk, you fucker?*

"Fine. I know how to handle Lidia." *No, I didn't, you asshole.*

Hunt found Isaiah watching them with raised brows. "What happened with Lidia?"

The Helhound answered smoothly, "She wanted to grill me about why I left last night. I didn't feel like explaining to her that I'm Athalar's understudy, and where he goes, I go."

Isaiah's eyes darkened. "You weren't so antagonistic toward her under Sandriel's rule."

Baxian dug into his platter of lamb kofta and herbed rice. "You've been in Lunathion for a while, Tiberian. Things changed after you left."

Isaiah asked, "Like what?"

Baxian gazed toward the glistening city roasting in the midday heat. "Things."

"I think that means we should mind our own fucking business," Hunt said.

Isaiah snickered. "He's taking a page out of your book, Hunt."

Hunt grinned. "You're confusing me with Naomi. I at least will tell you straight up to mind your own business. She'll only imply it."

"With a death glare."

"And maybe a gun set on the table for emphasis."

They laughed, but Hunt sobered as he noted Baxian observing their volley, something like envy on his face. Isaiah noted it, too, because he said to the Helhound, "You can laugh, you know. We do that kind of stuff here."

Baxian's mouth pressed into a thin line. "You've had more than ten years here. Forgive me if it takes a while to forget the rules of Sandriel's territory."

"As long as you don't forget that you're in Lunathion now." The threat of violence rumbled in Isaiah's every word, belying the impeccable suit he wore. "That scar Athalar put on your neck will be nothing compared to what I do to you if you hurt anyone in this city."

Baxian's eyes glittered. "Just because you weren't interesting enough to merit being part of Sandriel's triarii, don't take it out on me with bullshit threats."

Isaiah's teeth gleamed. "I had no interest in getting that close to a monster."

Hunt tried not to gape. He'd seen Isaiah lay down the law countless times. His friend wouldn't have gotten to where he was without the ability to draw a line and hold it. But it was rare these days to see that vicious warrior shine through. Soldiers were turning their way.

So Hunt cut in, "Sandriel would be thrilled to know that she's still pitting us against each other all these years later."

Isaiah blinked, as if surprised he'd tried to intervene. Baxian watched him cautiously.

Hunt took another deep breath. "Fuck, that sounded preachy." Baxian let out a snort, and the tension dissolved.

Isaiah threw Hunt a grateful smile, then rose. "I need to head out. I have a meeting with the Aux Heads."

Hunt winked. "Give Ruhn my love."

Isaiah laughed. "Will do."

With that, his friend strode off toward the trash receptacles. Angels lifted their heads as he passed; a few waved at him. The white-winged angel waved back, pausing at various tables to swap pleasantries. Isaiah's smile was wide—genuine.

Baxian said quietly, "Your friend was born for this."

Hunt grunted his agreement.

"No interest in leading again?" Baxian asked.

"Too much paperwork."

Baxian smirked. "Sure."

"What's that supposed to mean?"

"You led once, and it went poorly. I don't blame you for not stepping up again."

Hunt clenched his jaw but said nothing else as he finished off his meal. Baxian was right on his heels as they strode to empty their plates and dump their trays. Hunt didn't dare turn to tell the Helhound to back the fuck off. Not with so many eyes on them. He could hear soldiers whispering as they passed.

Hunt didn't bother to engage as Isaiah had. He couldn't bear to look at the other soldiers. The people who'd be summoned to fight against Ophion.

People he'd kill if they threatened Bryce. Fuck, if he replicated what he'd done at the Bone Quarter, he could fry them all in a second. No wonder the Asteri had considered the thunderbirds a threat—that kind of power was nothing short of lethal.

If Ophion got their hands on Emile . . . Yeah, that was a weapon to kill for.

Hunt reached the elevator bay beyond the doors. The five angels clustered there quickly aimed for the stairs.

"Tough crowd, huh?" Baxian said behind him as Hunt stepped into the elevator. To his displeasure, the Helhound got in with him. The space was wide enough to accommodate many beings with wings, but Hunt kept his tucked in tight.

"You get used to it," Hunt said, pushing the button for the triarii's barracks. He might as well assess his room to see what weapons he had left. What clothes he needed to send for. Knowing Bryce, she'd send him a pair of her underwear along with them.

"I thought you were Mr. Popular," Baxian said, watching the rising numbers above them.

"What the fuck would make you think that?" Hunt didn't wait for a reply as the elevator doors opened and he stepped into the quiet hall.

"You seem friendly with everyone outside this place."

Hunt arched a brow, pausing outside his old room. "What does that mean?"

Baxian leaned against his own door, across from Hunt's. "I mean, I hear you party with Prince Ruhn and his friends, you have a girlfriend, you seem to be on good terms with the wolves . . . But not the angels?"

"Isaiah and I are on good terms." And Naomi.

"I mean the others. The grunts. No friends there?"

"Why the Hel do you care?"

Baxian casually pulled in his wings. "I want to know what's in it for me. What kind of life I can look forward to."

"It's what you make of it," Hunt said, opening his door. Stale, dusty air greeted him. A far cry from the scent of coffee that filled Bryce's apartment.

He peered over a shoulder to find Baxian surveying his room. The emptiness of it. A peek into Baxian's room across the hall revealed an identically empty space.

Hunt said, "That's what my life was like, you know."

"Like what?"

"Vacant."

"Then what happened?"

"Bryce happened."

Baxian smiled slightly. Sadly. Was it—was it possible the Helhound was *lonely*?

"I'm sorry you have to stay apart from her for so long." Baxian sounded like he meant it.

Hunt's eyes narrowed. "Did Celestina punish you?"

"No. She said it was your bad influence, so it was your punishment to take."

Hunt chuckled. "Fair enough." He stepped into his room and made quick work of assessing his weapons and clothes.

When he reemerged into the hallway, Baxian was sitting at the pine desk in his room, going over what appeared to be reports. Every instinct screamed at Hunt to walk out and not say anything, to Hel with this male who'd been more of an enemy than a friend over the years, but . . .

Hunt braced a hand on the doorjamb. "What do they have you working on?"

"Progress reports for the new recruits. Seeing if there are any promising angels to pull up through the ranks."

"Are there?"

"No."

"Angels like us don't come around that often, I guess."

"Apparently not." Baxian went back to his paperwork.

The quiet of the hall, the room, settled on Hunt. Pushed on him. He could hear Bryce saying, *Come on. Try. It won't kill you.* She bossed him around even in his imagination. So Hunt said, "We've still got twenty minutes left of lunch. Want to play some *SUL Sunball*?"

Baxian turned. "What's that?"

"You really don't know anything about modern life, huh?" Baxian gave him a flat look. "SUL," Hunt explained. "Sunball United League. It's their video game. You can play from the point of view of any player, on any team. It's fun."

"I've never played a video game."

"Oh, I know." Hunt grinned.

Baxian surveyed him, and Hunt waited for the rejection, but Baxian said, "Sure. Why not?"

Hunt headed for the common room. "You might regret that in a few."

Indeed, ten minutes later, Baxian was cursing, fingers stumbling over the controller clenched in his hands. Hunt nimbly dodged Baxian's avatar.

"Pathetic," Hunt said. "Even worse than I thought."

Baxian growled, "This is so stupid."

"And yet you keep playing," Hunt countered.

Baxian laughed. "Yeah. I guess I do."

Hunt scored. "It's not even satisfying playing against a novice."

"Give me a day and I'll wipe the floor with you, Athalar." Baxian's thumbs flicked the controls. His avatar ran right into a goalpost and rebounded, sprawling onto the grass.

Hunt snickered. "Maybe two days."

Baxian glanced at him sidelong. "Maybe." They kept playing,

and when the clock above the door read twelve, Baxian asked, "Time to work?"

Hunt listened to the quiet dorm around them. "I won't tell if you don't."

"Didn't I prove this morning that I'm the soul of discretion?"

"I'm still waiting for your motive, you know."

"I'm not here to make an enemy of you."

"I don't get why."

Baxian ran into the goalpost again, his avatar ricocheting onto the field. "Life's too short to hold grudges."

"That's not a good enough reason."

"It's the only one you'll get." Baxian managed to gain control of the ball for all of ten seconds before Hunt took it from him. He cursed. "Solas. You can't go easy on me?"

Hunt let the subject drop. The gods knew he'd had plenty he hadn't wanted to talk about when he first arrived here. And the gods knew he'd done plenty of terrible shit on Sandriel's orders, too. Maybe he should take his own advice from earlier. Maybe it was time to stop letting Sandriel's specter haunt them.

So Hunt smiled roughly. "Where would the fun be in that?"

"This sucks," Bryce muttered into the phone that night, splayed out on her bed. "You really aren't allowed to leave?"

"Only for official 33rd work," Hunt said. "I forgot how crappy the barracks are."

"Your sad little room with its lack of posters."

His laugh rumbled in her ear. "I'm going to be extra good so she'll let me go early."

"I won't have anyone to watch *Beach House Hookup* with. You sure I can't come over there?"

"Not with Pollux and the Hind here. No fucking way."

Bryce toyed with the hem of her T-shirt. "Even if we stayed in your room?"

"Oh?" His voice dropped low, getting the gist of what she was suggesting. "To do what?"

She smiled to herself. She needed this, after the insanity of today. She hadn't even dared tell Hunt what had happened with the mystics, not over the phone, where anyone could listen in. But the next time she saw him face-to-face, she'd tell him about everything.

Including the otter Tharion had sent to her two hours ago, as promised, with a note that said, *Forgive me yet, Legs? Shall we kiss and make up?* She'd laughed—but sent a note back with the screamingly cute otter: *Start with kissing my ass and we'll see how it goes.* Another otter had arrived before ten with a note that said, *With pleasure.*

Now Bryce said to Hunt, mood significantly lifted despite the news, "Things."

His wings rustled in the background. "What kind of things?"

Her toes curled. "Kissing. And . . . more."

"Hmm. Explain what *more* means."

She bit her lip. "Licking."

His laugh was like dark velvet. "Where would you like me to lick you, Quinlan?"

They were doing this, then. Her blood heated. Syrinx must have scented what was up, and took it upon himself to leap off the bed and head into the living room.

Bryce swallowed. "My breasts."

"Mmm. They are delicious."

She slickened between her thighs, and rubbed her legs together, nestling further into the pillows. "You like to taste them?"

"I like to taste all of you." She could barely get a breath down. "I like to taste you, and touch you, and when I can leave these barracks again, I'm going to fly in a straight line to wherever you are so I can thoroughly fuck you."

She whispered, "Are you touching yourself?"

A hiss. "Yes."

She whimpered, rubbing her thighs together again.

"Are you?"

Her hand drifted beneath the waistband of her shorts. "Now I am."

He groaned. "Are you wet?"

"Soaking."

"Gods," he begged. "Tell me what you're doing."

She flushed. She'd never done anything like this, but if she and Hunt couldn't be together . . . she'd take what she could get.

She slid her finger into her sex, moaning softly. "I'm . . . I have a finger inside myself."

"Fuck."

"I wish it was yours."

"Fuck."

Was he close, then? "I'm adding another," she said as she did, and her hips bucked off the bed. "It still doesn't feel as good as you."

His breathing turned sharp. "Open up that nightstand, sweetheart."

Frantic, she grabbed a toy from the drawer. She shimmied off her shorts and her drenched underwear and positioned the vibrator at her entrance. "You're bigger," she said, the phone discarded beside her.

Another primal sound of pure need. "Yeah?"

She pushed the vibrator in, her back arching. "Oh gods," she panted.

"When we fuck for the first time, Quinlan, do you want it hard or do you want a long, smooth ride?"

"Hard," she managed to say.

"You want to be on top?"

Release gathered through her body like a wave about to break. "I want my turn on top, and then I want you behind me, fucking me like an animal."

"*Fuck!*" he shouted, and she heard flesh slapping against flesh in the background.

"I want you to ride me so hard I'm screaming," she went on, driving the vibrator in and out. Gods, she was going to explode—

"Anything you want. Anything you want, Bryce, I'll give it to you—"

That did it. Not the words, but her name on his tongue.

Bryce moaned, deep in her throat, her pants coming quick and wild, her core clenching around the vibrator as she pumped it in and out, working through her climax.

Hunt groaned again, cursing, and then he fell silent. Only their breathing filled the phone. Bryce lay limp against the bed.

"I want you so badly," he ground out.

She smiled. "Good."

"Good?"

"Yeah. Because I'm going to fuck your brains out when you come home to me."

He laughed softly, full of sensual promise. "Likewise, Quinlan."

Tharion sat atop the smooth rock half-submerged by a bend in the middle of the Istros and waited for his queen to respond to his report. But the River Queen, lounging on a bed of river weeds like a pool float, kept her eyes closed against the morning sun, as if she hadn't heard a single word of what he'd been explaining about the Bone Quarter and the Under-King.

A minute passed, then another. Tharion asked at last, "Is it true?"

Her dark hair floated beyond her raft of weeds, writhing over the surface like sea snakes. "Does it disturb you, to have your soul sent back into the light from whence it came?"

He didn't need to be Captain of Intelligence to know she was avoiding his question. Tharion said, "It disturbs me that we're told we rest in peace and contentment, yet we're basically cattle, waiting for the slaughter."

"And yet you have no problem with your body being sent back to feed the earth and its creatures. Why is the soul any different?"

Tharion crossed his arms. "Did you know?"

She cracked open a warning eye. But she propped her head on a fist. "Perhaps there is something beyond the secondlight. Someplace our souls go even after that."

For a glimmer, he could see the world she seemed to want: a world without the Asteri, where the River Queen ruled the waters, and the current system of soul-recycling remained, because hey, it kept the lights on. Literally.

Only those in power would change. Perhaps that was all she wanted Emile for: a weapon to ensure her survival and triumph in any upcoming conflict between Ophion and the Asteri.

But Tharion said, "The search for Emile Renast continues. I thought I had an easier way to find him, but it was a dead end." Tracking Pippa's string of bodies would have to remain his only path toward the kid.

"Report when you have anything." She didn't look back at him as the river weeds fell apart beneath her and she gently sank into the blue water.

Then she was gone, dissolving into the Istros itself and floating away as glowing blue plankton—like a trail of stars soared through the river.

Was a rebellion worth fighting, if it only put other power-hungry leaders in charge? For the innocents, yes, but . . . Tharion couldn't help but wonder if there was a better way to fight this war. Better people to lead it.

41

A week later, Ruhn stood beside Cormac and smiled as Bryce sweated in the Aux facility's private training ring.

"You're not concentrating," Cormac scolded.

"My head literally *aches*."

"Focus on that piece of paper and simply step there."

"You say that like it's easy."

"It is."

Ruhn wished this were the first time he'd heard this conversation. Witnessed this song-and-dance number between Bryce and Cormac as the prince tried to teach her to teleport. But in the week since all that major shit had gone down, this had been the main highlight. Their enemies had been unnervingly quiet.

When Cormac wasn't attending various Fae functions, Ruhn knew his cousin had been hunting for Emile. Ruhn had even gone with him twice, Bryce in tow, to wander the various parks of Moonwood, hoping the boy was camping out. All to no avail. Not a whisper of the kid anywhere.

Tharion had reported yesterday that he couldn't find the boy, either. From Tharion's unusually haggard face, Ruhn had wondered if the mer's queen was breathing down his neck about it. But no more bodies had been found. Either the kid was here, in hiding, or someone else had gotten him.

Bryce inhaled deeply, then shut her eyes on the exhale. "All right. Let's try this again."

Her brow bunched, and she grunted. Nothing.

Cormac snorted. "Stop straining. Let's return to summoning shadows."

Bryce held up a hand. "Can I have a hall pass, please?"

Ruhn laughed. She'd had little luck with the shadows, either. Starlight, yes. Lots and lots of starlight. But summoning darkness . . . she couldn't manage so much as a bit of shade.

If Apollion wanted an epic opponent, Ruhn was inclined to tell the Prince of the Pit that it might take a while.

"I think my magic's broken," Bryce said, bending over her knees and sighing.

Cormac frowned. "Try again." They'd had no word from anyone, even Agent Daybright, about what had happened with the shipment of ammo and the new mech-suit prototype. The news hadn't covered it, and none of Cormac's agents had heard anything.

That quiet had Cormac worried. Had Ruhn on edge, too.

Ithan had settled easily into Ruhn's house, weirdly enough. He stayed up late playing video games with Dec and Flynn, as if they'd been friends their entire lives. What the wolf did with his time while they were all at the Aux, Ruhn had no idea.

Ruhn hadn't asked him about what the Hind had said at the bar regarding Bryce, and Ithan sure as Hel hadn't mentioned it. If the wolf had a thing for his sister, it wasn't Ruhn's business. Ithan was a good housemate: cleaned up after himself, cleaned up after Flynn, and was excellent at beer pong.

Bryce sucked in a sharp breath. "I can *feel* it—like, this giant cloud of power right *there*." She ran a finger over the eight-pointed star scarred between her breasts. Starlight pulsed at her fingertip. Like an answering heartbeat. "But I can't access it."

Cormac gave her a smile Ruhn assumed he meant to be encouraging. "Try one more time, then we'll take a break."

Bryce began to grumble, but was interrupted by Ruhn's phone ringing.

"Hey, Dec."

"Hey. Bryce with you?"

"Yeah. Right here." Bryce jumped to her feet at the mention of her name. "What's up?"

Bryce leaned in to hear as Declan said, "My program finally finished analyzing all the footage of Danika at the gallery. Jesiba was right. It found something."

Bryce didn't know whether it was a good thing or not that Declan had finally concluded his search. Sitting around her new coffee table—a sad imitation of the original, but one Ithan had paid for—an hour later, she watched Declan pull up the feed.

She hadn't dared call Hunt. Not when one wrong move with Celestina could keep him away even longer.

Declan said to her, Ruhn, and Cormac, "It took so long because once it compiled all the footage I had to go through all the shots with Danika." He smirked at Bryce. "Did you *ever* work?"

Bryce scowled. "Only on Tuesdays."

Declan snorted, and Bryce braced herself for the sight of Danika, of Lehabah, of the old gallery library as he clicked play. Her heart twanged at the familiar corn-silk blond hair with its vibrant dyed streaks, braided down Danika's back. At the black leather jacket with the words *Through love, all is possible* stamped on it. Had the flash drive already been sewn into it?

"This is from two months before she died," Declan said quietly.

There was Bryce, in a tight green dress and four-inch heels, talking with Lehabah about *Fangs and Bangs*.

Danika was lounging at the desk, boots propped up, hands tucked behind her head, smirking at Bryce's regular argument that porn with a plot did not equal award-winning television. Lehabah was countering that sex didn't cheapen a show, and her voice—

Ruhn's hand slid across Bryce's back, squeezing her shoulder.

On the screen, Bryce motioned to Lehabah to follow her upstairs, and the two of them left. She had no memory of this day, this moment. She'd probably gone to grab something and hadn't wanted to leave Lehabah alone with Danika, who was prone to riling the sprite into the hottest of blue flames.

A second passed, then two, then three—

Danika moved. Swift and focused, like she'd been using the time lounging at the table to pinpoint where she needed to go. She headed straight to a lower shelf and pulled off a book. Glancing at the stairs, she flipped it open and began snapping photos with her phone of the inside. Page after page after page.

Then it was back on the shelf. Danika returned to her chair and lounged, pretending to be half-asleep when Bryce and Lehabah returned, still arguing about the stupid show.

Bryce leaned in toward the screen. "What book was that?"

"I clarified the image." Declan pulled up a frame of the book right before Danika's black-sparkle-painted nails grabbed it: *Wolves Through Time: Lineage of the Shifters.*

"You can see her finger going to some text here," Declan went on, clicking to another frame. Danika had opened the book, skimming over the text with a finger. Tapping something right near the top of the page.

As if it were exactly what she'd been looking for.

Bryce, Declan, and Ruhn studied the still frame of the book in Danika's hands. Cormac had departed upon getting a call that he would not—or could not—explain. The book was leather-bound and old, but the title indicated that it had been written after the arrival of the Vanir.

"It's not a published book," Declan said. "Or at least it predates our current publishing system. But as far as I can tell, no other libraries on Midgard have it. I think it must be a manuscript of some sort, perhaps a vanity project that got bound."

"Any chance there's a copy at the Fae Archives?" Ruhn asked her.

"Maybe," Bryce said, "but Jesiba might still have this one at the storage unit." She pulled out her phone and dialed quickly.

Jesiba answered on the second ring. "Yes, Quinlan?"

"You had a book at the old gallery. *Wolves Through Time*. What is it?"

A pause. Ruhn and Dec picked up every word with their Fae hearing.

"So you did look into the footage. Curious, wasn't it?"

"Just . . . please tell me. What is it?"

"A history of wolf genealogy."

"Why did you have it?"

"I like knowing the history of my enemies."

"Danika wasn't your enemy."

"Who said I was talking about Danika?"

"Sabine, then."

A soft laugh. "You are so very young."

"I need that book."

"I don't take demands, even from Starborn Princesses. I've given you enough." Jesiba hung up.

"That was helpful," Declan groused.

But twenty minutes later, Marrin buzzed to say that a messenger had dropped off a package from Miss Roga.

"I'm disturbed and impressed," Ruhn murmured as Bryce opened the nondescript package and pulled the leather tome free. "We owe Jesiba a drink."

"Danika snapped photos of the beginning pages," Declan said, now reviewing the footage on his phone. "Maybe only the first three, actually. But I think the page she tapped was the third."

Bryce opened the book, the hair on her arms rising. "It's a family tree. Going back . . . Does this go all the way back to when the Northern Rift opened?" Fifteen thousand years ago.

Ruhn peered over her shoulder as Bryce skimmed. "Gunthar Fendyr is the latest—and last—name here."

Bryce swallowed. "He was the Prime's father." She flipped to the third page, the one Danika had been most interested in.

"Niklaus Fendyr and Faris Hvellen. The first of the Fendyr line." She chewed on her lip. "I've never heard of them."

Declan tapped away on the computer. "Nothing comes up."

"Try their kids," Bryce suggested, giving him the names.

"Nothing."

They went through generation after generation until Dec said, "There. Katra Fendyr. From here . . . Yeah, there's an actual historical record and mentions of Katra from there on out. Starting five thousand years ago." He ran a finger up the tree, along the generations, counting silently. "But nothing on any of these Fendyrs before her."

Ruhn asked, "Why would Danika feel the need to be secretive about this, though?"

Bryce examined the first two names on the list, the ones Danika had tapped like she'd discovered something, and countered, "Why were their names lost to history?"

"Would Ithan know?" Declan asked.

"No idea." Bryce chewed on a hangnail. "I need to talk to the Prime."

Ruhn protested. "Need I remind you that Sabine tried to kill you last week?"

Bryce grimaced. "Then I'll need you two to make sure she's not at home."

Bryce didn't dare inform Hunt over the phone what she was doing, why she was doing it. She'd risked enough by calling Jesiba. But not having Hunt at her side as she slipped past the guards at the Den's gate felt like a phantom limb. Like she might find him in the shadows beside her at any moment, assessing a threat.

Declan was currently arguing with the Den guards about some imagined slight. And at the Aux headquarters . . . Well, if they were lucky, Sabine had already arrived to meet with Ruhn about an "urgent matter."

Bryce found the Prime without much trouble, sitting in the shade of a towering oak in the park that occupied the central space of the Den. A gaggle of pups played at his feet. No other wolves in the area.

She darted from the shadows of the building's columns to the wooden chair, a few curious pups perking up at the sight of her. Her chest squeezed at their fuzzy little ears and waggly tails, but she kept her gaze on the ancient male.

"Prime," she said, kneeling on his far side, hidden from the view of the guards still arguing with Dec at the gates. "A moment of your time, please."

He cracked open age-clouded eyes. "Bryce Quinlan." He tapped his bony chest. "A wolf."

Ruhn had told her what the Prime had said during the attack. She'd tried not to think of how much it meant to her. "Your bloodline—the Fendyr lineage. Can you think of why Danika might have been interested in it?"

He hesitated, then motioned to the pups and they scattered. She figured she had about five minutes until one of them blabbed to an adult that a red-haired Fae female was here.

The Prime's chair groaned as he faced her. "Danika enjoyed history."

"Is it forbidden to know the names of your first ancestors?"

"No. But they are largely forgotten."

"Do Faris Hvellen and Niklaus Fendyr ring any bells? Did Danika ever ask about them?"

He fell silent, seeming to scan his memory. "Once. She claimed she had a paper for school. I never learned what became of it."

Bryce blew out a breath. There hadn't been any papers about wolf genealogy in the secret coffee table stash. "All right. Thank you." This had been a waste of her time. She got to her feet, scanning the park, the gates beyond. She could make a run for it now.

The Prime halted her with a dry, leathery hand on her own. Squeezed. "You did not ask why we have forgotten their names."

Bryce started. "You know?"

A shallow nod. "It is one scrap of lore most of my people were careful to ensure never made it into the history books. But word of mouth kept it alive."

Brush crackled. Shit. She had to go.

The Prime said, "We did unspeakable things during the First

Wars. We yielded our true nature. Lost sight of it, then lost it forever. Became what we are now. We say we are free wolves, yet we have the collar of the Asteri around our necks. Their leashes are long, and we let them tame us. Now we do not know how to get back to what we were, what we might have been. That was what my grandfather told me. What I told Sabine, though she did not care to listen. What I told Danika, who . . ." His hand shook. "I think she might have led us back, you know. To what we were before we arrived here and became the Asteri's creatures inside and out."

Bryce's stomach churned. "Is that what Danika wanted?" It wouldn't have surprised her.

"I don't know. Danika trusted no one." He squeezed her hand again. "Except you."

A snarl rattled the earth, and Bryce found a massive female wolf approaching, fangs exposed. But Bryce said to the Prime, "You should talk to Sabine about Ithan."

He blinked. "What about Ithan?"

Did he not know? Bryce backed away a step, not letting the advancing female out of her sight. "She kicked him out, and nearly killed him. He's living with my brother now."

Those fogged eyes cleared for a moment. Sharp—and angry.

The female lunged, and Bryce ran, sprinting through the park to the gates. Past the guards still arguing with Declan, who winked at them and then burst into a run beside her, into the bustle of Moonwood. More questions dragged along behind her with each block they sprinted.

She had every intention of collapsing on her couch and processing things for a long while, but when they got back, Cormac was waiting outside her apartment.

Bloody and dirty, and—"What happened to you?" Declan said, as Bryce let them into the apartment, flinging the door open wide.

Cormac helped himself to a bag of ice from the freezer, pressing it to his cheek as he sat at the kitchen table. "Mordoc nearly snared me at an intel pickup. Six other dreadwolves were with him."

"Did Mordoc scent you?" Bryce asked, scanning the battered prince. If he had, if Cormac was tracked back here . . .

"No—I kept downwind, even for his nose. And if any of his soldiers did, they're not a problem anymore." Was the blood on his hands not his own, then? Bryce tried not to sniff it.

"What'd the intel say?" Declan asked, going to the window to scan the street beyond, presumably for anyone who might have followed Cormac.

"The hit on the Spine was successful," Cormac said, face hard beneath the blood and bruises. "The Asteri's new mech-suit prototype was attained, along with an invaluable amount of ammunition."

"Good," Declan said.

Cormac sighed. "They're shipping the prototype here."

Bryce started. "To Lunathion?"

"To the Coronal Islands." Close enough—two hours away by boat. "To a base on Ydra."

"Shit," Dec said. "They're going to start something here, aren't they?"

"Yes, likely with Pippa and her Lightfall squadron at the head."

"Don't they know she's nuts?" Bryce asked.

"She's successful with her ops. That's all that matters."

"What about Emile?" Bryce pushed. "Was she successful with him?"

"No. He's still out there. The agent said the hunt for him continues."

"So what do we do?" Dec asked Cormac. "Go to Ydra and convince them *not* to let Pippa have access to all those weapons?"

"Yes." Cormac nodded to Bryce. "Send an otter to Captain Ketos. And I believe we're also going to need Hunt Athalar's expertise."

42

Bryce was just walking down the shining hallway to Celestina's office when her phone rang.

Juniper. Bryce sent her to audiomail. A message came through instead. *Call back now.*

Dread burning like acid through her, Bryce dialed, praying nothing had happened with Fury—

Juniper answered on the first ring. "How *dare* you?"

Bryce halted. "What?"

"How *dare* you call Gorgyn?"

"I . . ." Bryce swallowed. "What happened?"

"I'm principal, that's what happened!"

"And that's a bad thing?" She was due to meet with Celestina in one minute. She couldn't be late.

"It's a bad thing because *everyone* knows that *Princess Bryce Danaan* put in a call and threatened to pull the Autumn King's donations if CCB didn't *recognize my talent*!"

"So what?" Bryce hissed. "Isn't this the only bit of good that being a princess entails?"

"No! It's the *opposite*!" Juniper was absolutely screaming with rage. Bryce started shaking. "I have worked my entire life for this, Bryce! My *entire life*! And you step in and take that accomplishment away from me! Make yourself—not me, not my talent—into the reason I got this promotion, the reason I made history! *You*, not me. Not me sticking it out, fighting through it, but my Fae Princess friend, who couldn't leave well enough alone!"

The clock chimed in the hallway. Bryce had to go. Had to talk to the Archangel.

"Look, I'm about to go into a meeting," she said as evenly as she could, though she thought she might puke. "But I'll call you back right after, I promise. I'm so sorry if—"

"Don't bother," June snapped.

"Juniper—"

The faun hung up.

Bryce focused on her breathing. She needed one of Kyrah's dance classes. Immediately. Needed to sweat and breathe and majorly unload and analyze the tornado wreaking havoc inside her. But this meeting . . . She squared her shoulders, putting away the fight, the fact that she'd fucked everything up, had been so arrogant and stupid and—

She knocked on the door to Celestina's office. "Enter," came the sweet female voice.

Bryce smiled at the Governor as if she hadn't destroyed a friendship moments ago. "Your Grace," Bryce said, inclining her head.

"Your Highness," Celestina answered, and Bryce reined in a wince. It was how she'd gotten this meeting, too. She'd asked the Archangel to meet not as Bryce Quinlan, but as a Princess of the Fae. It was an invitation even an Archangel had to agree to.

She wondered how it'd come back to haunt her.

"Just for this meeting," Bryce said, sitting down. "I've come to make a formal request."

"For the return of Hunt Athalar, I take it." A tired, sad sort of light gleamed in the Governor's eyes.

"A temporary return," Bryce said, and leaned back in her chair. "I know he bailed on you at your party. If I'd been aware he was doing that, I would never have asked him to assist me that night. So—totally feel free to punish him. You have my blessing."

It was a lie, but Celestina's lips twitched upward. "How long do you want him for?"

"A night." To go to the Coronal Islands and back before Pippa Spetsos and her cabal could get there. To convince whoever Command sent *not* to give Spetsos free rein to unleash those weapons on Valbara. "We figured we'd take the arrow train instead of driving the eight hours each way. I promised my mother I'd bring him home with me. If he doesn't come, there will be Hel to pay." Another lie.

But the Governor smiled fully at that. "Your mother is . . . a fearsome creature?"

"Oh yeah. And if Hunt's not there, every bad thing she thinks about him will be confirmed."

"She doesn't like him?"

"She doesn't like *any* male. No one is good enough for me, according to her. You have no idea how hard dating was when I was younger."

"Try being an Archangel in a small community," Celestina said, and smiled genuinely.

Bryce grinned. "Everyone was intimidated?"

"Some ran screaming."

Bryce laughed, and marveled that she did so. Hated that she had to lie to this warm, kind female.

Celestina hooked a curl behind her ear. "So a great deal is riding on Athalar's visit."

"Yeah. It's not like I need her permission to be with him, but it . . . It'd be nice to have her approval."

"I'm sure it would." Celestina's smile turned sad.

Bryce knew it wasn't her place, but she asked, "How are you and Ephraim getting along?"

A shadow flickered across Celestina's face, confirmation that she wasn't contented. "He's a thorough lover."

"But?"

She said deliberately, warning sharpening her voice, "But he has been my friend for many years. I find that I am now getting to know him in a whole new way."

Celestina deserved so much more than that. Bryce sighed. "I know you're, like . . . an Archangel, but if you ever need some girl talk . . . I'm here."

The last Governor she'd spoken to had tried to kill her. And she'd put a bullet in his head. This was a nice change.

Celestina smiled again, that warmth—and relief—returning to her features. "I'd like that very much, Your Highness."

"Bryce in this instance."

"Bryce." Her eyes twinkled. "Take Athalar home. And keep him there."

Bryce's brows rose. "Permanently?"

"Not at your parents' house. I mean take him with you to your family, and then he may live with you once more. He's been moping around so much that he's bringing down morale. I'll send him your way tomorrow morning. Let him stew one more night before I tell him at dawn."

Bryce beamed. "Thank you. I mean it, thank you *so* much."

But the Governor waved a hand. "You're doing me a favor, trust me."

Bryce made a call on her way to her next stop.

Fury answered right before it went to audiomail. "You fucked up, Bryce."

Bryce cringed. "I know. I'm really sorry."

"I get why you did it. I really do. But she is *devastated*."

Bryce stepped off the elevator and swallowed the lump in her throat. "Please tell her I'm so sorry. I'm so freaking sorry. I was trying to help, and I didn't think."

"I know," Fury said. "But I'm not getting in the middle of this."

"You're her girlfriend."

"Exactly. And you're her friend. And mine. I'm not playing the messenger. Give her some time, then try to talk it out."

Bryce sagged against a worn wall. "Okay. How long?"

"A few weeks."

"That's ages!"

"Devastated. Remember?"

Bryce rubbed at her chest, the unlit scar there. "Fuck."

"Start thinking of big ways to apologize," Fury said. Then added, "You ever figure that thing out with Danika or the kid?"

"Not yet. Want to help?" It was as much as she'd risk saying on the phone.

"No. I'm not getting in the middle of that shit, either."

"Why?"

"I have a lot of good things going on right now," Fury said. "June is one of them. I'm not jeopardizing any of it. Or her safety."

"But—"

"Big apology. Don't forget." Fury hung up.

Bryce swallowed her nausea, her self-disgust and hatred. She walked down the quiet hall to a familiar door, then knocked. She was rewarded by the sight of Hunt opening the door, shirtless and wearing his backward sunball hat. Gleaming with sweat. He must have just returned from the gym.

He jolted. "What are you—"

She cut him off with a kiss, throwing her arms around his neck.

He laughed, but his hands encircled her waist, lifting her high enough that she wrapped her legs around his middle. He slowed the kiss, his tongue driving deep, exploring her mouth. "Hi," he said against her lips, and kissed her again.

"I wanted to tell you the news," she said, kissing his jaw, his neck. He'd already hardened against her. She went molten.

"Yeah?" His hands roamed over her ass, kneading and stroking.

"Tomorrow morning," she said, kissing his mouth again and again. "You're outta here."

He dropped her. Not entirely, but swiftly enough that her feet hit the ground with a thud. "What?"

She ran her hands down his sweat-slick, muscled chest, then toyed with the band of his pants. Ran a finger up the length of him jutting out with impressive demand. "We're going on a little vacation. So do a good job of seeming like you're still brooding tonight."

"What?" he repeated.

She kissed his pec, running her mouth over the taut brown nipple. He groaned softly, his hand sliding into her hair. "Pack a swimsuit," she murmured.

A male voice chuckled behind them, and Bryce went rigid, whirling to find Pollux, arm slung around a beautiful female's shoulders, walking by. "Is he paying you by the hour?" the Hammer asked.

The female—the *Hind*—snickered, but said nothing as they approached. Solas, she was . . . beautiful and terrible. She'd tortured countless people. Killed them—probably including Sofie Renast. If Cormac saw her, if he got this close, would he take the risk and try to end her?

The Hind's amber eyes gleamed as they met Bryce's, as if she knew every thought in her head. The deer shifter smiled in invitation.

But the Hind and the Hammer continued on, for all the world looking like a normal couple from behind. Bryce couldn't help herself as she said to Pollux's back, "You really need to come up with some new material, Pollux."

He glared over a shoulder, white wings tucking in tight. But Bryce smiled sweetly and he, mercifully, kept walking, his wretched lover with him.

Bryce found Hunt smiling beside her, and it lightened any guilt about Juniper, any frustration with Fury, any fear and dread at being so close to the Hind, even as she yearned to tell him everything. Hunt tugged her hand, making to pull her into his room, but she planted her feet. "Tomorrow morning," she said hoarsely, her very bones aching with need. "Meet me at home."

She'd tell him everything then. All the insane shit that had gone on since they'd last seen each other.

Hunt nodded, hearing what she didn't say. He tugged her again, and she went to him, tilting back her head to receive his kiss. His hand slipped down the front of her leggings. He growled against her mouth as his fingers found the slickness waiting for him.

She whimpered as he rubbed over her clit in a luxurious, taunting circle. "I'll see you at dawn, Quinlan."

With a nip at her bottom lip, Hunt stepped back into his room. And as he shut the door, he licked his fingers clean.

* * *

Ithan blinked at the phone ringing in his hand.

Prime.

Every Valbaran wolf had the Prime's number in their phones. But Ithan had never once called it, and the Prime of Wolves had never once called him. It couldn't be good.

He halted midway down the alley, neon signs casting pools of color on the cobblestones beneath his boots. Sucking in a breath, he answered, "Hello?"

"Ithan Holstrom."

He bowed his head, even though the Prime couldn't see him. "Yes, Prime."

The withered old voice was heavy with age. "I was informed today that you are no longer residing at the Den."

"On Sabine's order, yes."

"Why?"

Ithan swallowed. He didn't dare say why. Sabine would deny it anyway. Sabine was the male's daughter.

"Tell me why." A hint of the Alpha the Prime had been during his younger years came through in his voice. This male had made the Fendyr family a force to be reckoned with in Valbara.

"Perhaps ask your daughter."

"I want to hear it from you, pup."

Ithan's throat worked. "It was punishment for disobeying her orders during the attack this spring and helping the humans in Asphodel Meadows. And punishment for praising Bryce Quinlan's actions during the attack in a magazine article."

"I see." Apparently, that was all the Prime needed. "What do you plan to do now?"

Ithan straightened. "I'm, ah, living with Prince Ruhn Danaan and his friends. Helping them out in the Fae division of the Aux." Helping with a rebellion.

"Is that where you wish to be?"

"Is there an alternative?"

A drawn-out, too-tense pause. "I would make you Alpha of your own pack. You have it in you—I've sensed it. For too long, you have suppressed it so others might lead."

The ground beneath Ithan seemed to rock. "I . . . What about Sabine?" Ithan's head swirled.

"I shall deal with my daughter, if this is what you choose."

Ithan had no fucking idea who'd even be in his pack. He'd locked himself out so thoroughly from old friends and family after Connor's death that he'd only bothered to associate with Amelie's pack. Perry was the closest thing he had to a friend at the Den, and she'd never leave her sister's side. Ithan swallowed hard. "I'm honored, but . . . I need to think about this."

"You have been through a great deal, boy. Take the time you need to decide, but know the offer stands. I would not lose another wolf of worth—especially to the Fae." Before Ithan could say goodbye, the old wolf hung up. Stunned and reeling, Ithan leaned against one of the brick buildings in the alley. Alpha.

But . . . an Alpha in Sabine's shadow, once the Prime was gone. Sabine would be *his* Prime. Amelie would reign as her Prime Apparent. And then Prime, when Sabine herself was gone.

He had little interest in serving either of them. But . . . was it a betrayal of the wolves, of his brother's legacy, to leave the Valbaran packs to Sabine's cruelty?

He brushed his hair back from his face. It was longer than it'd ever been while playing sunball. He couldn't tell if he liked it or not.

Fuck, he couldn't tell if he liked *himself* or not.

Straightening, Ithan pushed off the wall and finished his walk, arriving at his destination. The towering doors to the Astronomer's building of horrors were shut. Ithan pulled the crescent moon door chime once.

No answer.

He pulled it a second time, then pressed an ear to one of the metal doors, listening for any hint of life. Not even a footstep, though he could make out the hum of the machines beyond. He knocked twice, and then pressed his shoulder into the door. It opened with a groan, nothing but darkness beyond. Ithan slipped in, silently shutting the heavy door behind him. "Hello?"

Nothing. He aimed for the faint, pale glow of the three tanks in the center of the cavernous space. He'd never seen anything so strange and unsettling—the three beings who'd been sold into this life. Existence. This sure as fuck wasn't a life.

Not that he'd know. He hadn't had one in two years.

Their visit last week had lingered like an unhealed wound.

He might have walked out of here condemning everything he'd seen, but he'd still given the Astronomer his money. Kept this place running.

He knew it bugged Bryce, but she'd been swept back into the shit with Danika, and as a princess, her hands were tied as far as a public scene. Especially when she walked such a dangerous line these days—any additional bit of scrutiny might be her downfall.

But no one gave a fuck about him. No matter what the Prime had said.

"Hello?" he called again, the word echoing into the dimness.

"He's not here," rasped a hoarse female voice.

Ithan whirled, reaching for his gun as he scanned the darkness. His wolf-sight pierced through it, allowing him to make out the speaker's location. His hand dropped from his hip at the sight of her.

Long chestnut-brown hair draped over her too-thin, pale limbs, her body clad in that white shift that all three mystics wore. Her dark eyes were still—like she was only half-there. A face that might have been pretty, if it weren't so gaunt. So haunted.

Ithan swallowed, slowly approaching where she huddled against the wall, bony knees clutched to her chest. "I wanted to see your . . . boss."

He couldn't say *owner*, even though that's what the old creep was. In the gloom, he could make out a worktable beyond the mystic sitting on the floor, with a small box atop it. Light filtered out from the box, and he had a good idea of what was kept inside it. Who were kept inside, trapped in those four rings, which were apparently valuable enough that the old male had left them behind, rather than risk them in the city at large.

The mystic's rasping voice sounded as if she hadn't spoken in ages. "He put the other two back in, but didn't have the part he needed to fix my machine. He's at the Meat Market, meeting with the Viper Queen."

Ithan sniffed, trying to get a read on her. All he could get from this distance was salt. Like it had brined the scent right out of her. "You know when he'll be back?"

She only stared at him, like she was still hooked up to the machine beyond them. "You were the one who freed me." Solas, she sat with such . . . Vanir stillness. He'd never realized how much *he* moved until he stood before her. And he'd considered himself capable of a wolf's utter stillness.

"Yeah, sorry." But the word stuck—*freed*. She'd been pleading to go back. He'd assumed she'd meant into the between-place where the mystics roamed, but . . . What if she'd meant this world—back to her life before? The family who had sold her into this?

Not his problem, not his issue to solve. But he still asked, "Are you okay?" She didn't look okay. She sat the way he had in his dorm bathroom the night he'd learned that Connor was dead.

The mystic only said, "He will be back soon."

"Then I'll wait for him."

"He will not be pleased."

Ithan offered her a reassuring smile. "I can pay, don't worry."

"You've caused him a great deal of inconvenience. He'll kick you out."

Ithan took a step closer. "Can you help me, then?"

"I can't do anything unless I'm in the tank. And I don't know how to use the machines to ask the others."

"All right."

She angled her head. "What do you want to know?"

He swallowed hard. "Was it true, what the demon prince said, about my brother being safe for now?"

She frowned, her full mouth unnaturally pale. "I could only sense the other's terror," she said, nodding toward the tanks. "Not what was said."

Ithan rubbed the back of his neck. "All right. Thanks. That's all I needed." He had to know for sure that Connor was safe. There had to be some way to help him.

She said, "You could find a necromancer. They would know the truth."

"Necromancers are few and far between, and highly regulated," Ithan said. "But thanks again. And, uh . . . good luck."

He turned back toward the doors. The mystic shifted slightly, and the movement sent a whisper of her scent toward him. Snow and embers and—

Ithan went rigid. Whirled to her. "You're a wolf. What are you doing here?"

She didn't answer.

"Your pack allowed this to happen?" Rage boiled his blood. Claws appeared at his fingertips.

"My parents had no pack," she said hoarsely. "They roamed the tundra of Nena with me and my ten siblings. My gifts became apparent when I was three. By four, I was in there." She pointed to the tank, and Ithan recoiled in horror.

A wolf family had *sold* their pup, and she'd gone into that tank—

"How long?" he asked, unable to stop his trembling anger. "How long have you been in here?"

She shook her head. "I . . . I don't know."

"When were you born? What year?"

"I don't know. I don't even remember how long it's been since I made the Drop. He had some official come here to mark it, but . . . I don't remember."

Ithan rubbed at his chest. "Solas." She appeared as young as him, but among the Vanir, that meant nothing. She could be hundreds of years old. Gods, how had she even made the Drop here? "What's your name? Your family name?"

"My parents never named me, and I never learned their names beyond Mother and Father." Her voice sharpened—a hint of temper shining through. "You should leave."

"You can't be in here."

"There's a contract that suggests otherwise."

"You are a *wolf*," he snarled. "You're kept in a fucking *cage* here." He'd go right to the Prime. Make him order the Astronomer to free this unnamed female.

"My siblings and parents are able to eat and live comfortably because I am here. That will cease when I am gone. They will again starve."

"Too fucking bad," Ithan said, but he could see it—the determination in her expression that told him he wasn't going to pry her out of here. And he could understand it, that need to give over all of herself so that her family could survive. So he amended, "My name is Ithan Holstrom. You ever want to get out of here, send word." He had no idea how, but . . . maybe he'd check in on her every few months. Come up with excuses to ask her questions.

Caution flooded her eyes, but she nodded.

It occurred to him then that she was likely sitting on the cold floor because her thin legs had atrophied from being in the tank for so long. That old piece of shit had left her here like this.

Ithan scanned the space for anything resembling a blanket and found nothing. He only had his T-shirt, and as he reached for the hem, she said, "Don't. He'll know you were here."

"Good."

She shook her head. "He's possessive. If he even thinks I've had contact with someone other than him, he'll send me down to Hel with an unimportant question." She trembled slightly. He'd done it before.

"Why?"

"Demons like to play," she whispered.

Ithan's throat closed up. "You sure you don't want to leave? I can carry you right now, and we'll figure out the other shit. The Prime will protect you."

"You know the Prime?" Her voice filled with whispered awe. "I only heard my parents speak of him, when I was young."

So they hadn't been entirely shut off from the world, then. "He'll help you. I'll help you."

Her face again became aloof. "You must go."

"Fine."

"Fine," she echoed back, with a hint of that temper again. A bit of dominance that had the wolf in him perking up.

He met her stare. Not just a bit of dominance . . . that was a glimmer of an *Alpha*'s dominance. His knees buckled slightly, his wolf instinct weighing whether to challenge or bow.

An Alpha. Here, in a tank. She would likely have been her family's heir, then. Had they known what she was, even at age four? He suppressed a growl. Had her parents sent her here *because* she'd be a threat to their rule over the family?

But Ithan shoved the questions aside. Backed toward the doors again. "You should have a name."

"Well, I don't," she shot back.

Definitely Alpha, with that tone, that glimmer of unbending backbone.

Someone the wolf in him would have liked to tangle with.

And to leave her here . . . It didn't sit right. With him, with the wolf in his heart, broken and lonely as it might have been. He had to do something. Anything. But since she clearly wasn't going to leave this place . . . Maybe there was someone else he could help.

Ithan eyed the small box on the worktable, and didn't question himself as he snatched it up. She tried and failed to rise, her weakened legs betraying her. "He will *kill* you for taking them—"

Ithan strode to the doors, the box of fire sprites trapped inside their rings in hand. "If he's got a problem with it, he can take it up with the Prime." And explain why he was holding a wolf captive in here.

Her throat bobbed, but she said nothing more.

So Ithan stalked outside, onto the jarringly normal street beyond, and shut the heavy door behind him. But despite the distance he quickly put between himself and the mystics, his thoughts circled back to her, again and again.

The wolf with no name, trapped in the dark.

"I'm requesting an aquatic team of twenty-five for tomorrow," Tharion said to his queen, hands clenched behind his back, tail fanning idly in the river current. The River Queen sat in her humanoid form among a bed of rocky coral beside her throne, weaving sea nettle, her dark blue gown drifting around her.

"No," she said simply.

Tharion blinked. "We have solid intel that this shipment is coming from Pangera, *and* that Pippa Spetsos is likely already there. You want me to capture her, to interrogate her about Emile's whereabouts, I'm going to need backup."

"And have so many witnesses mark the Blue Court's involvement?"

What is *our involvement?* Tharion didn't dare ask. *What's your stake in this beyond wanting the kid's power?*

His queen went on, "You will go, and go alone. I take it your current cadre of . . . people will be with you."

"Yes."

"That should be enough to question her, given your companions' powers."

"Even five mer agents—"

"Just you, Tharion."

He couldn't stop himself as he said, "Some people might think you were trying to kill me off, you know."

Slowly, so slowly, the River Queen turned from her weaving. He could have sworn a tremor went through the riverbed. But her voice was dangerously smooth as she said, "Then defend my honor against such slander and return alive."

He clenched his jaw, but bowed his head. "Shall I say goodbye to your daughter, then? In case it is my last chance to do so?"

Her lips curled upward. "I think you've caused her enough distress already."

The words struck true. She might be a monster in so many ways, but she was right about him in that regard. So Tharion swam into the clear blue, letting the current pound the anger from his head.

If there was a chance of attaining Emile's power, the River Queen would snatch it up.

Tharion hoped he had it in himself to stop her.

The chairs had turned into velvet couches on the dream bridge.

Ruhn slid into his, surveying the endless dark surrounding him.

He peered past the fainting couch to Day's "side." If he were to follow her that way, would he wind up in her mind? See the things she saw? Look through her eyes and know who she was, where she was? Would he be able to read every thought in her head?

He could speak into someone's mind, but to actually *enter* it, to read thoughts as his cousins in Avallen could . . . Was this how they did it? It seemed like such a gross violation. But if she invited him, if she wanted him in there, could he manage it?

Flame rippled before him, and there she was, sprawled on the couch.

"Hey," he said, sitting back in his couch.

"Any information to report?" she said by way of greeting.

"So we're doing the formal thing tonight."

She sat up straighter. "This bridge is a path for information. It's our first and greatest duty. If you're coming here for someone to flirt with, I suggest you look elsewhere."

He snorted. "You think I'm flirting with you?"

"Would you say *hey* in that manner to a male agent?"

"Probably, yeah." But he conceded, "Not with the same tone, though."

"Exactly."

"Well, you caught me. I'm ready for my punishment."

She laughed, a full, throaty sound that he'd never heard before. "I don't think you could handle the sort of punishment I dole out."

His balls tightened; he couldn't help it. "We talking . . . restraints? Flogging?"

He could have sworn he got a flash of teeth biting into a lower lip. "Neither. I don't care for any of that in bed. But what do *you* prefer?"

"It's always the lady's choice with me. I'm game for anything."

She angled her head, a waterfall of flame spilling down the side of the couch, as if she draped long, lovely hair over it. "So you're not a . . . dominant male."

"Oh, I'm dominant," he said, grinning. "I'm just not into pressuring my partners into doing anything they don't like."

She studied him at that. "You say *dominant* with such pride. Are you a wolf, then? Some sort of shifter?"

"Look who's trying to figure me out now."

"Are you?"

"No. Are *you* a wolf?"

"Do I seem like one to you?"

"No. You seem like . . ." Someone crafted of air and dreams and cold vengeance. "I'm guessing you're in Sky and Breath."

She went still. Had he struck true? "Why do you say that?"

"You remind me of the wind." He tried to explain. "Powerful and able to cool or freeze with half a thought, shaping the world itself though no one can see you. Only your impact on things." He added, "It seems lonely, now that I'm saying it."

"It is," she said, and he was stunned that she'd admitted it. "But thank you for the kind words."

"Were they kind?"

"They were accurate. You see me. It's more than I can say about anyone else."

For a moment, they stared at each other. He was rewarded by a shifting of her flame, revealing large eyes that swept upward at the edges—crafted of fire, but he could still make out their shape. The clarity in them before her flame veiled her once more. He cleared his throat. "I guess I should tell you that the rebels were successful with their hit on the Spine. They're bringing over the Asteri's mech prototype to the Coronal Islands tomorrow night."

She straightened. "Why?"

"I don't know. I was told by—my informant. A rebel contingent will be there to receive the shipment. Where it goes from there, I don't know." Cormac wanted Athalar to examine the Asteri's prototype—see how it differed from the humans' that the angel had faced so often in battle.

Because Athalar was the only one among them who'd faced off against a mech-suit. Who'd apparently spent time in Pangera taking them apart and putting them back together again. Cormac, as he'd been fighting alongside the human rebels, had never battled one—and he wanted an outside opinion on whether replicating the Asteri's model would be beneficial.

And because Athalar was going, Bryce was going. And because Bryce was going, Ruhn was going. And Tharion would join them, as the River Queen had ordered him to.

Flynn, Dec, and Ithan would remain—too many people going would raise suspicions. But they'd been pissed to learn of it. *You're benching poor Holstrom,* Flynn had complained. Dec had added, *Do you know what that does to a male's ego?* Ithan had only grunted his agreement, but hadn't argued, a distant expression on his face. Like the wolf's mind was elsewhere.

"Who's going to be there?"

He angled his head. "We got word that Pippa Spetsos and her Lightfall squadron will also be present. We have some questions for her about . . . a missing person."

She straightened. "Is Spetsos being given command of the Valbaran front?"

"I don't know. But we're hoping we can convince whoever is there from Command otherwise. We suspect that she and Lightfall have left a trail of bodies all around the countryside."

Day was quiet for a moment, then asked, "Do you know the name of the ship that's carrying the prototype?"

"No."

"What island?"

"Why are you grilling me on this?"

"I want to make sure it's not a trap."

He grinned. "Because you'd miss me if I died?"

"Because of the information they'd squeeze from you before you did."

"Cold, Day. Real cold."

She laughed softly. "It's the only way to survive."

It was. "We're going to Ydra. That's all I know."

She nodded, like the name meant something to her. "If they catch you, running is your best option. Don't fight."

"I'm not programmed that way."

"Then reprogram yourself."

He crossed his arms. "I don't think I—"

Day hissed, bending over. She twitched, almost convulsing.

"Day?"

She sucked in a breath, then was gone.

"Day!" His voice echoed across the void.

He didn't think. Launching over the fainting couch, he sprinted down her end of the bridge, into the dark and night, flinging himself after her—

Ruhn slammed into a wall of black adamant. Time slowed, bringing with it flashes of sensation. No images, all . . . *touch.*

Bones grinding in her left wrist from where it was being squeezed tight enough to hurt; it was the pain that had awoken her, pulled her away from the bridge—

Willing herself to yield, give over, become his, to find some way to savor this. Teeth scraping at her nipple, clamping down—

Ruhn collided with the ground, the sensations vanishing. He surged to his feet, pressing a palm against the black wall.

Nothing. No echo to tell him what was happening.

Well, he *knew* what was happening. He'd gotten the sense of very rough sex, and though he had the distinct feeling that it was consensual, it wasn't . . . meaningful. Whoever slept at her side had woken her with it.

The impenetrable black loomed before him. The wall of her mind.

He had no idea why he waited. Why he stayed. Had no idea how much time passed until a flame once more emerged from that wall.

Her fire had banked enough that he could make out long legs walking toward him. Halting upon finding him kneeling. Then she dropped to her knees as well, flame again swallowing her whole.

"Are you all right?" he asked.

"Yes." The word was a hiss of embers being extinguished.

"What was that?"

"You've never had sex before?"

He straightened at the slicing question. "Are you all right?" he asked again.

"I said I was."

"You weren't—"

"No. He asked, albeit a bit suddenly, and I said yes."

Ruhn's insides twisted at the utter iciness. "You don't seem to have enjoyed it."

"Is it your business whether I find release or not?"

"Did you?"

"Excuse me?"

"Did you orgasm?"

"That's absolutely none of your business."

"You're right."

Again, silence fell, but they remained kneeling there, face-to-face. She said after a tense moment, "I hate him. No one knows it, but I do. He disgusts me."

"Then why sleep with him?"

"Because I . . ." A long sigh. "It's complicated."

"Indulge me."

"Do you only sleep with people you like?"

"Yes."

"You've never fucked someone you hate?"

He considered, even as the sound of her saying the word *fucked* did something to his cock. "All right. Maybe once. But it was an ex." A Fae female he'd dated decades ago, who he hadn't cared to remember until now.

"Then you can think of this like that."

"So he's—"

"I don't want to talk about him."

Ruhn blew out a breath. "I wanted to make sure you're okay. You scared the shit out of me."

"Why?"

"One moment you were here, the next you were gone. It seemed like you were in pain."

"Don't be a fool and get attached enough to worry."

"I'd be a monster not to care whether another person is hurt."

"There's no place for that in this war. The sooner you realize it, the less pain you'll feel."

"So we're back to the ice-queen routine."

She drew up. "Routine?"

"Where's the wild and crazy female I was talking about bondage with earlier?"

She laughed. He liked the sound—it was low and throaty and predatory. Fuck, he liked that sound a lot. "You are such a typical Valbaran male."

"I told you: Come visit me in Lunathion. I'll show you a good time, Day."

"So eager to meet me."

"I like the sound of your voice. I want to know the face behind it."

"That's not going to happen. But thank you." She added after a moment, "I like the sound of your voice, too."

"Yeah?"

"*Yeah.*" She chuckled. "You're trouble."

"Is it cliché if I say that *Trouble* is my middle name?"

"Oh yes. Very."

"What would *your* middle name be?" he teased.

Her flames pulled back, revealing those eyes of pure fire. "Retribution."

He grinned wickedly. "Badass."

She laughed again, and his cock hardened at the sound. "Goodbye, Night."

"Where are you going?"

"To sleep. Properly."

"Isn't your body resting?"

"Yes, but my mind is not."

He didn't know why, but he gestured to her fainting couch. "Then sit back. Relax."

"You want me to stay?"

"Honestly? Yeah. I do."

"Why?"

"Because I feel calm around you. There's so much shit going down, and I . . . I like being here. With you."

"I don't think most females would be flattered to be called 'calming' by a handsome male."

"Who says I'm handsome?"

"You talk like someone who's well aware of his good looks."

"Like an arrogant asshole, then."

"Your words, not mine."

Day rose to her feet, striding to the fainting couch. Her flames rippled as she lay upon it, and Ruhn jumped onto his own couch.

"All I need is a TV and a beer and I'm set," he said.

She snickered, curling on her side. "As I said: typical Valbaran male."

Ruhn closed his eyes, bathing in the timbre of her voice. "You gotta work on those compliments, Day."

Another chuckle, sleepier this time. "I'll add it to my to-do list, Night."

43

Hunt breathed in the cool air off the turquoise sea, admiring the pristine water, so clear that he could see the corals and rocks and the fish darting among them.

Down in the quay, hidden in a massive cavern, the cargo ship was still being unloaded. The sea cave, tucked into an isolated, arid part of Ydra, one of the more remote Coronal Islands, ran at least a mile inland. It had been selected because the water flowing within it ran so deep—deep enough for massive cargo ships to slide into its stone-hewn dock and unload their contraband.

Hunt stood in the shadows just within the mouth of the cave, focusing on the bright, open water ahead and not the reek of the oil on the ancient mech-suits currently helping to unload the ship into the fleet of awaiting vehicles: laundry trucks, food trucks, moving trucks . . . anything that might reasonably inch along one of the island's steeply curving roads or board one of the auto-ferries shuttling vehicles between the hundred or so islands of this archipelago without raising too much suspicion.

Cormac had teleported everyone to Ydra an hour ago. Hunt had nearly puked during the five-minute-long trip with several stops—when they'd finally arrived, he'd sat his ass on the damp concrete, head between his knees. Cormac had gone back, again and again, until all of them were here.

And then the poor fuck had to go head-to-head with whoever was in charge from Command, to convince them Pippa Spetsos shouldn't be anywhere near this shit.

Cormac had been unsteady on his feet, pale from the teleporting, but had left them with the promise to return soon. Bryce, Tharion, and Ruhn all sat on the ground—apparently not trusting their legs yet, either. Hunt hadn't failed to notice that Ruhn kept reaching over his shoulder—as if to seek the reassuring presence of the Starsword. But the prince had left the blade back in Lunathion, not wanting to risk losing it here if all Hel broke loose. It seemed the male was missing his security blanket as their stomachs and minds settled.

"I shouldn't have eaten breakfast," Tharion was saying, a hand on his abs. He wore only tight black aquatic leggings, equipped along the thighs with holsters for knives. No shoes or shirt. If he needed to shift into his mer form, he'd said upon arriving at Bryce's place this morning, he didn't want to lose much.

Tharion's timing had been unfortunate—he'd arrived at the apartment right after Hunt. Bryce was already propped up on the counter, gripping Hunt's shoulders while he lazily licked up her neck. Tharion's knock on the door was . . . unwelcome.

That would all have to wait. But his mate had gotten him out of the barracks—he'd repay her generously tonight.

Bryce now patted Tharion's bare shoulder. "I'm weirdly satisfied that a mer can get airsick, considering how many of us suffer from seasickness."

"*He's* still green, too," Tharion said, pointing to Hunt, who grinned weakly.

But Tharion went back to idly observing the cave around them. Perhaps *too* idly. Hunt knew Tharion's main objective: get Pippa to talk about Emile. Whether that interrogation would be friendly was up to the mer captain.

Ruhn murmured, "Incoming."

They all turned toward the cargo ship to see Cormac striding over to them. Still pale and drained—Hunt had no idea how he'd get them all out of here when this was over.

But Hunt tensed at the fury simmering off Cormac. "What's up?" Hunt said, eyeing the cave interior beyond Cormac. Tharion's attention drifted that way as well, his long body easing into a crouch, ready to spring into action.

Cormac shook his head and said, "Pippa's already got her claws in them. They're all eating out of her hand. The weapons are hers, and she's now in charge of the Valbaran front."

Tharion frowned, but scanned the space behind the Avallen Prince. "Anything about Emile or Sofie?"

"No. She didn't say a word about them, and I couldn't risk asking. I don't want her to know we're on the hunt as well." Cormac paced. "A confrontation about Emile in front of the others would likely lead to bloodshed. We can only play along."

"Any chance of isolating her?" Tharion pressed.

Cormac shook his head. "No. Believe me, she'll be on her guard as much as we are. You want to drag her off for questioning, you're going to have a battle on your hands."

Tharion swore, and Bryce patted his knee in what Hunt could only guess was an attempt at consolation.

Cormac faced Hunt. "Athalar, you're up." He jerked his head to the massive ship. "They're unloading the new prototype right now."

In silence, they followed the prince, Hunt keeping close to Bryce. The rebels—all in black, many with hats or masks on—stared at them as they passed. None of them smiled. One man grumbled, "Vanir pricks."

Tharion blew him a kiss.

Ruhn growled.

"Play nice," Bryce hissed at her brother, pinching his side through his black T-shirt. Ruhn batted her away with a tattooed hand.

"Real mature," Hunt muttered as they halted at the foot of the loading platform. Ruhn subtly flipped him off. Bryce pinched Hunt's side, too.

But Tharion let out a low whistle as four rusty mech-suits emerged from the ship's hold, each carrying the corner of a massive box.

It looked like a metal sarcophagus, carved with the insignia of the Asteri: seven stars around *SPQM*. The humans piloting the old-model mech-suits didn't so much as glance to the side as they carried the box down the ramp, the ground thudding beneath the machines' massive feet.

"Those suits are for battle, not manual labor," Tharion murmured.

"Twelve-gunners. They're the strongest of the human models." Hunt inclined his head to the twin double guns at the shoulder, the guns on each of the forearms. "Six visible guns, six hidden ones—and one of those is a cannon."

Bryce grimaced. "How many of these suits do the humans have?"

"A few hundred," Cormac answered. "The Asteri have bombed enough of our factories that these suits are all old, though. The imperial prototype that they're carrying could give us new technology, if we can study it."

Bryce murmured, "And no one is worried about giving this stuff over to trigger-happy Pippa?"

"No," Cormac replied gravely. "Not one of them."

"But they're cool with us examining the suit?" Bryce asked.

"I told them Athalar would have some insight into how they're constructed."

Hunt clicked his tongue. "No pressure, huh?" He suppressed the memory of Sandriel's face, her cruel amusement as she watched what he'd done to the suits on her orders.

The suits and their pilots reached the concrete quay, and someone barked an order that dispersed the various rebels working the docks until only a unit of twelve rebels—all humans—lingered behind Hunt and the others.

Hunt liked that about as much as the fact that they were here at all, on a fucking rebel base. Officially aiding Ophion. He kept his breathing slow and steady.

The unit of rebels marched past them, climbing into the vessel, and the mech-pilots stomped off, leaving the sarcophagus behind. A heartbeat later, a human female, brown-haired and freckled, emerged from the shadows beside the boat.

From the way Cormac tensed, Hunt knew who it was. He noted that she wore the uniform of the Lightfall squadron. All the rebels who'd gone by had borne armbands with the sinking sun emblem.

Hunt put his hand in easy reach of the gun at his thigh, lightning writhing in his veins. Bryce angled her body, already eyeing up the best shot. Tharion drifted a few feet to the left, positioning Pippa between himself and the water. As if he'd tackle her into it.

But Pippa moved casually to the other side of the sarcophagus as she said to Cormac, "The code to that box is seven-three-four-two-five."

Her voice was smooth and fancy—like she was some rich Pangeran kid playing at being a rebel. She said to Hunt, "We're waiting with bated breath for your analysis, Umbra Mortis." It was practically an order.

Hunt stared at her from under lowered brows. He knew he was recognizable. But the way she said his name definitely carried a threat. Pippa shifted her attention to Cormac. "I wondered when you'd try to turn them against me."

Hunt and Bryce drew close, guns at their fingertips now. Ruhn kept a step back, guarding their rear. And Tharion . . .

The mer had silently shifted positions again, putting himself within a few easy bounds of tackling Pippa.

"I haven't said anything to them about you yet," Cormac said with impressive iciness.

"Oh? Then why were you in such a rush to get here? I can only assume it was for one of two reasons: to convince them to put *you* in charge of the Valbaran front, presumably by slandering me, or to try to capture me so I can tell you everything I know about Emile Renast."

"Who says both can't be true?" Cormac countered.

Pippa grunted. "You needn't have bothered with capturing me. I would have worked with you to find him. But you wanted the glory for yourself."

"We're talking about a child's life," Cormac snarled. "You only want him as a weapon."

"And you don't?" Pippa sneered at them all. "It must make it easier for you if you pretend you're better than I am."

Tharion said, deadly soft, "We're not the ones torturing people to death for intel on the kid."

She frowned. "Is that what you think I've been up to? Those gruesome murders?"

"We found human scents *and* a piece of one of your soldiers on the kid's trail," Tharion growled, a hand drifting to his knives.

Her lips curved into a cold smile. "You arrogant, narrow-minded Vanir. Always thinking the worst of us humans." She shook her head in mock sympathy. "You're too coiled up in your own snake's nest to see the truth. Or to see who among you has a forked tongue."

True to form, Bryce stuck out her tongue at the soldier. Pippa only sneered.

"Enough, Pippa." Cormac punched the code into the small box at the foot of the sarcophagus. Bryce's eyes had narrowed, though. She held Pippa's gaze—and a chill went down Hunt's spine at the pure dominance in Bryce's face.

Pippa drawled, "It is of no concern now. anyway. The boy has been deemed a waste of resources. Especially now that we have . . . better weapons to wield."

As if in answer, the lid popped open with a hiss, and Hunt threw an arm in front of Bryce as it slid aside. Smoke from dry ice billowed out, and Cormac cleared it away with a brush of his hand.

Pippa said, "Well, Umbra Mortis? I await your insights."

"I'd mind how you speak to him, Pippa," Cormac warned her, voice sharp with authority.

Pippa faced Bryce, though. "And you're Cormac's bride, yes?" No kindness, no warmth filled her tone.

Bryce flashed the female a smile. "You can have the job if you want it so badly."

Pippa bristled, but Cormac gestured Hunt forward as the last of the smoke cleared.

Hunt surveyed the suit in the box and swore. "The Asteri designed this?" he asked. Pippa nodded, lips pursed tight. "For Vanir to pilot?" he pushed.

Another nod. Pippa said, "I don't see how it can possess more power than ours, though. It's smaller than our models." The quicksilver-bright suit would stand about seven feet high.

"You know what you're looking at?" Ruhn asked Hunt, scratching his head.

"It's like a robot," Bryce said, peering into the box.

"It's not," Hunt said. He rocked back on his heels, mind racing. "I heard rumors about this kind of thing being made, but I always thought it was a long shot."

"What is it?" Pippa demanded.

"Impatient, are we?" Hunt mocked. But he tapped a finger on the suit. "This metal has the same makeup as gorsian stones." He nodded to Bryce. "Like what they did with the synth—they were seeking ways to weaponize the gorsian stones."

"We already have them in our bullets," Pippa said smugly.

He ground out, "I know you do." He had a scar on his stomach from one.

Perhaps that threat alone was what had kept Tharion from making his move. The mer had a clear shot toward Pippa. But could he run faster than she could draw her gun? Hunt and Bryce could help him, but . . . Hunt really didn't want to outright attack an Ophion leader. Let Tharion and the River Queen deal with that shit.

Pippa shifted a few inches out of Tharion's range once more.

Hunt went on, "This metal . . . The Asteri have been researching a way to make the gorsian ore absorb magic, not suppress it."

Ruhn said, "Seems like ordinary titanium to me."

"Look closer," Hunt said. "There are slight purple veins in it. That's the gorsian stone. I'd know it anywhere."

"So what can it do?" Bryce asked.

"If I'm right," Hunt said hoarsely, "it can draw the firstlight from the ground. From all the pipes of it crisscrossing the land. These suits would draw up the firstlight and turn it into weapons. Brimstone missiles, made right there on the spot. The suit would never run out of ammo, never run out of battery life. Simply find the underground power lines, and it'd be charged up and ready to kill. That's why they're smaller—because they don't need all the extra tech and room for the arsenal that the human suits require. A Vanir warrior could climb inside and essentially wear it like an exoskeleton—like armor."

Silence.

Pippa said, voice full of awe, "Do you know what this would mean for the cause?"

Bryce said dryly, "It means a Hel of a lot more people would die."

"Not if it's in our hands," Pippa said. That light in her eyes—Hunt had seen it before, in the face of Philip Briggs.

Pippa went on, more to herself than to any of them, "We'd at last have a source of magic to unleash on them. Make them understand how we suffer." She let out a delighted laugh.

Cormac stiffened. So did Tharion.

But Hunt said, "This is a prototype. There might be some kinks to work out."

"We have excellent engineers," Pippa said firmly.

Hunt pushed, "This is a death machine."

"And what is a gun?" Pippa snapped. "Or a sword?" She sneered at the lightning zapping at his fingertips. "What is your magic, angel, but an instrument of death?" Her eyes blazed again. "This suit is simply a variation on a theme."

Ruhn said to Hunt, "So what's your take on it? Can Ophion use it?"

"No one should fucking use it," Hunt growled. "On either side." He said to Cormac, "And if you're smart, you'll tell Command to track down the scientists behind this and destroy them and their plans. The bloodshed on both sides will become monstrous if you're all using these things."

"It's already monstrous," Cormac said quietly. "I just want it ended."

But Pippa said, "The Vanir deserve everything that's coming to them."

Bryce grinned. "So do you, terrorizing that poor boy and then deciding he's not worth it."

"Emile?" Pippa laughed. "He's not the helpless baby you think he is. He found allies to protect him. By all means, go retrieve him.

I doubt he'll help the Vanir win this war—not now that we have this technology in our hands. Thunderbirds are nothing compared to this." She ran a hand over the rim of the box.

Tharion cut in, "Where's the kid?"

Pippa smirked. "Somewhere even you, mer, would fear to tread. I'm content to leave him there, and so is Command. The boy is no longer our priority."

Bryce seethed, "You're deluded if you think this suit is anything but a disaster for everyone."

Pippa crossed her arms. "I don't see how you have any right to judge. While you're busy getting your nails painted, Princess, good people are fighting and dying in this war."

Bryce wiggled her nails at the rebel. "If I'm going to associate with losers like you, I might as well look good doing it."

Hunt shook his head, cutting off Pippa before she could retort. "We're talking machines that can make *brimstone missiles* within seconds and unleash them at short range." His lightning now sizzled at his hands.

"Yes," Pippa said, eyes still lit with predatory bloodlust. "No Vanir will stand a chance." She lifted her attention to the ship above them, and Hunt followed her focus in time to see the crew appearing at the rails. Backs to them.

Five mer, two shifter-types. None in an Ophion uniform. Rebel sympathizers, then, who'd likely volunteered their boat and services to the cause. They raised their hands.

"What the fuck are you doing?" Hunt growled, just as Pippa lifted her arm in a signal to the human Lightfall squadron standing atop the ship. Herding the Vanir crew to the rails.

Guns cracked.

Blood sprayed, and Hunt flung out a wing, shading Bryce from the mist of red.

The Vanir crumpled, and Ruhn and Cormac began shouting, but Hunt watched, frozen, as the Lightfall squadron on deck approached the fallen crew, pumping their heads full of bullets.

"First round is always a gorsian bullet," Pippa said mildly in the terrible silence that followed as the Lightfall soldiers drew long knives and began severing heads from necks. "To get the Vanir down. The rest are lead. The beheading makes it permanent."

"Are you fucking *insane*?" Hunt burst out, just as Tharion spat, "You're a murdering psycho."

But Cormac snarled at Pippa, getting in her face, blocking Tharion's direct path. "I was told the crew would be unharmed. They helped us out of their belief in the cause."

She said flatly, "They're Vanir."

"And that's an excuse for this?" Ruhn shouted. Blood gleamed on his neck, his cheek, from where it had sprayed down. "They're Vanir who are *helping you*."

Pippa only shrugged again. "This is war. We can't risk them telling the Asteri where we are. The order to put the crew down came from Command. I am their instrument."

"You and Command are going to lead these people to ruin." Shadows gathered at Ruhn's shoulders. "And like Hel am I going to help you do it."

Pippa only snickered. "Such lofty morals." A phone buzzed in her pocket, and she checked the screen before saying, "I'm due to report to Command. Care to join me, Cormac?" She smiled slightly. "I'm sure they'd *love* to hear your concerns."

Cormac only glared, and Pippa let out a sharp whistle—an order. With that, she sauntered down the quay toward the side cavern, where the rest of the rebels had gone. A moment later, the human Lightfall squadron walked off the ship, guns at their sides. Ruhn snarled softly, but they followed Pippa without so much as glancing toward them.

The humans were bold as Hel to stride past them, putting their backs to Vanir after what they'd done.

When Pippa and Lightfall had vanished, Tharion said, "She knows where Emile is."

"If you can trust her," Bryce countered.

"She knows," Cormac said. He gestured to Tharion. "You want to interrogate her, go ahead. But with her and Lightfall now in charge of the Valbaran front, your queen will have a mess on her hands if you move against them. I'd think twice if I were you, mer."

Bryce hummed her agreement, mouth twisting to the side. "I'd stay the Hel away from her."

Hunt tucked in his wings. Assessed his mate.

She slid her gaze to him. Innocently. Too innocently.

She knew something.

She dropped the *Who, me?* expression and glared at him. As if to say, *Don't you fucking rat me out, Athalar.*

He was stunned enough that he inclined his head. He'd get the truth out of her later.

Tharion was asking, "All this ammo they unloaded . . . Ophion is bringing it into this region. To do what—stage some big battle?"

"No one would tell me," Cormac said. "If they let Pippa have free rein, she'll commit atrocities that will make that leopard massacre seem merciful."

"You think she'd start shit in Lunathion?" Ruhn asked.

"I don't see why you'd bring in guns and missiles for a tea party," Tharion said, rubbing his jaw. Then he added, "They already had this base set up. How long has it been here on Ydra?"

"Not sure," Cormac said.

"Well, with Pippa at the helm, it seems like they're ready to strike," Ruhn said.

Hunt said, "I can't let them do that. Even if I wasn't in the 33rd, I can't let them attack innocent people. They want to go head-to-head on some muddy battlefield, fine, but I'm not going to let them hurt anyone in my city."

"Me neither," Ruhn said. "I'll lead the Aux against you—against Ophion. Tell Command that if they make one move, they can say goodbye to their contact with Daybright."

Tharion didn't say anything. Hunt didn't blame him. The mer would have to follow the River Queen's orders. But his face was grim.

Cormac said, "You warn anyone in Lunathion, they'll ask how you know."

Hunt observed the bodies slumped against the boat railing. "That's a risk I'm willing to take. And one of us is a master of spinning bullshit." He pointed to Bryce.

Bryce scowled. Yeah, she knew he didn't just mean spinning lies for the authorities about their involvement with the rebels. *As soon as we're out of here*, he silently conveyed, *I want to know everything* you *know.*

She glowered, even if she couldn't read his thoughts. But that glower turned into icy determination as the others noticed the look. She lifted her chin. "We can't let the Asteri get this suit. Or Ophion—especially the Lightfall squadron."

Hunt nodded. At least on this, they were on the same page. "They're going to be so fucking pissed."

"I guess that means it's business as usual," Bryce said, winking despite her pale face. She said to him, "Light it up, Hunt."

Cormac whirled. "What are you—"

Hunt didn't give the prince time to finish before he laid a hand on the suit and blasted it apart with his lightning.

Hunt didn't stop at destroying the suit. His lightning slammed the parked trucks, too. Every single one of them. Bryce couldn't help but marvel at the sight of him—like a god of lightning. Like Thurr himself.

He looked *exactly* like that statuette that had sat on her desk a couple weeks ago—

Ruhn bellowed at her to get down, and Bryce hit the ground, covering her head with her arms as truck after truck exploded across the cavern. The walls shook, stones falling, and then there were wings blocking her, protecting her.

"There are brimstone missiles on those trucks!" Cormac roared.

Bryce raised her head as Hunt pointed to the untouched truck marked *Pie Life*. "Only on that one." He must have somehow figured it out during the few minutes they'd been here. Hunt grinned wickedly at Tharion. "Let's see what you got, Ketos."

Tharion grinned back, pure predator. The male behind the charming mask.

A wall of water slammed into the pie truck, sending it toppling over the quay. Tharion's power sucked it swiftly and deeply below, and then created a small eddy, forming an open tunnel to the truck—

Hunt's lightning speared through it. The water slammed shut in its wake, covering the lightning's path as the truck exploded beneath the surface.

Water sprayed through the cave, and Bryce ducked again.

People were shouting now, rushing from far inside the cave, guns pointed toward where the trucks burned, a wall of flame licking toward the cave's distant ceiling.

"Time to go," Hunt said to Cormac, who was gaping at them. He hadn't gone for his sword, which was a good sign, but—

The prince whirled to the rebels, shouting across the chaos, "It was an accident!"

There was no use in covering their asses, Bryce thought as Hunt grabbed her to him, wings spreading in anticipation of a mad dash through the cave and out into the open air. Like he wouldn't wait for Cormac to teleport them.

"We're leaving," Hunt ordered Ruhn, who fell into a defensive position behind him. Hunt said to Tharion, "You want Pippa, it's now or never."

Tharion scanned the chaos beyond the trucks, the rebels advancing with their guns. No sign of Pippa. "I'm not running a foot closer to that shit," Tharion murmured.

Cormac had raised his hands as he approached his Ophion allies. The prince shouted to them, "The suit came to life, and launched its power—"

A gunshot cracked. Cormac went down.

Ruhn swore, and Hunt held Bryce tight to his side as Cormac struggled on the ground, a hand to his shoulder. No exit wound.

"Fuck," Cormac cursed as Pippa Spetsos emerged from the shadows. She likely wanted the Avallen Prince alive for questioning.

And if Hunt flew into the air . . . he'd be an easy target. Especially while still inside the confines of the cave, no matter how massive. Tharion went for a knife at his side. Water wreathed his long fingers.

"Don't be dumb," Hunt warned Tharion. He whirled on Cormac. "Teleport us out."

"Can't," Cormac panted. "Gorsian bullet."

"Fuck," Bryce breathed, and Hunt prepared to take their chances in the sky, bullets be damned. He was a fast flier. He'd get her out. Then return to help the others. He just had to get her to safety—

Pippa snarled from across the cavern, "You are all *dead*, Vanir filth." Hunt's back muscles tensed, wings readying for a mighty leap upward, then a sharp bank to the left.

But at that moment, Bryce began glowing. A light that radiated from her star, then outward through her body. "Run on my mark," she said quietly, sliding her hand into Hunt's.

"Bryce," Ruhn started.

Stars glinted in Bryce's hair. "Close your eyes, boys."

Hunt did, not waiting to see if the others followed. Even with his eyes shut, he could see light sparking, blinding. Humans screamed. Bryce shouted, "Go!"

Hunt opened his eyes to the fading brightness, clenched her still-glowing hand, and ran toward the wide cave entrance and open sea.

"Grab that boat!" Tharion said, pointing toward a skiff moored a few yards inside the cave—presumably how so many rebels had arrived secretly.

Hunt swept Bryce into his arms and jumped into the air, flapping for it, reaching the boat and untying it before the others could arrive, then gunning the engine. It was ready to go by the time they leapt in, and he made sure Bryce was securely seated before speeding off.

"This boat won't make it back to the coast," Tharion said, taking over the steering. "We'll need to stop at a fuel dock."

Cormac gazed toward the billowing smoke rippling from the broad cave mouth. Like some giant was exhaling a mouthful of mirthroot. "They'll hunt us down and kill us."

"I'd like to see them try," Bryce spat, wind whipping her hair.

"Psychotic *assholes*." She seethed at the prince, "You want to fight alongside those people? They're no better than Philip fucking Briggs!"

Cormac shot back, "Why do you think I was doing all I could to find Emile? I don't want him in their hands! But this is a war. If you can't handle the game, then stay the fuck out of it."

"Their methods mean that even if they do win," Bryce shouted, "there will be nothing left of them that's human at all!"

"This was a bad day," Cormac said. "This whole encounter—"

"*A bad day?*" Bryce yelled, pointing to the smoldering cave. "All those people just got murdered! Is that how you treat your allies? Is that what you'll do to us when we have no more value to you? We'll be pawns for you to murder and then you'll manipulate some other decent people into helping you? You're Vanir, for fuck's sake—don't you realize they'll do this to *you* as well?"

Cormac only stared at her.

Bryce hissed at Cormac, "You can fuck off. You and Pippa and the rebels. Let the Hind tear you to shreds. I want nothing to do with this. We're done." She said to Tharion, "And I'm done with helping you and your queen, too. I'm done with all of this."

Hunt tried not to sag with relief. Maybe they could now wipe their hands clean of any damning association.

Tharion said nothing to her, to any of them, his face grave.

Bryce turned on Ruhn. "I'm not going to tell you what to do with your life, but I'd think twice about associating with Agent Daybright. She'll stab you right in the back, if the way these people treat their allies is any indication."

"Yeah," Ruhn said, but he didn't sound convinced.

For a moment, it seemed like she might fight him on it, but she kept quiet. Thinking it through, no doubt. Along with whatever other secrets she'd been keeping.

Hunt turned to monitor the island's shoreline. No boats came after them, and nothing lay ahead except open water. But—

He went still at the sight of the sleek black dog running along one of the dry, white cliffs of the island. Its coat was a strange, matte black.

He knew that dog. That particular shade of black. Like the wings it bore in its other form. The hound ran along the cliffs, barking.

"Fuck," Hunt said softly.

He lifted an arm to signal to the dog that he'd seen it. Seen him. The dog pointed with a massive paw westward, the direction they were headed. He barked once. As if in warning.

"Is that—" Ruhn asked, seeing the dog as well.

"Baxian." Hunt scanned the western horizon. "Head northward, Tharion."

"If Baxian's on those cliffs . . ." Bryce looped an arm through Hunt's and pressed tight.

Hunt could think of only one enemy Baxian might be summoned to work alongside. "The Hind can't be far away."

44

You have to teleport us out," Bryce ordered Cormac, who pressed a hand to his bloody shoulder. "Let me get that gorsian bullet out of you and—"

"You can't. They're designed to split apart into shrapnel on impact to make sure that the magic is suppressed for as long as possible. I'll need surgery to get every last shard out of me."

"How did the Hind find us?" Bryce demanded, breathing hard.

Cormac pointed to the smoke. "Someone must have tipped her off that there was something going down here today. And Athalar just let her know our precise location."

Hunt bristled, lightning flaring around his head like a bright twin of the halo. Bryce grabbed his shoulder in warning, but said to Cormac, "I'll try, then. Teleporting."

"You'll wind up in the sea," Cormac hissed.

"I'll try," she repeated, and clenched Hunt's hand harder. Only a little guilt stabbed her that it was his and not Ruhn's that she grabbed, but if it came down to it . . . she'd get Hunt out first.

Tharion cut in, "I could protect us in the water, but we'd need to jump in first."

Bryce shut out his voice as the others began arguing, and then—

"*Fuck,*" Hunt snarled, and she knew even before she opened her eyes that the Hind had appeared on the horizon. Guns cracked from a distance at a steady beat, but Bryce kept her eyes closed, willing herself to concentrate. Hunt said, "They want to keep me from flying."

Ruhn asked, "Do they know who we are?"

"No," Cormac said, "but the Hind always has snipers do this. You get airborne," he said to Hunt as Bryce gritted her teeth, *ordering* her power to move them away, "and you'll be vulnerable."

"Can we make it to the next island before they reach us?" Ruhn asked Tharion.

Tharion rifled through the compartment beside the steering wheel. "No. They're on a faster boat. They'll be on us when we hit open water." He pulled out a pair of binoculars. "A good two miles from shore."

"Shit," Ruhn said. "Keep going. We'll run until there's no other option."

Bryce tried to calm her frantic breathing. Hunt squeezed her hand in encouragement, lightning zapping into her fingers, but Cormac said to her quietly, "You can't do it."

"I can." But she opened her eyes, blinking at the brightness. This was such a beautiful place to die, with the turquoise sea and white islands behind them.

"Pollux and the Harpy are with the Hind," Tharion announced, lowering the binoculars.

"Get down," Hunt warned, ducking low. They all went with him, the water from the floor of the boat soaking into the knees of Bryce's leggings. "If we can see them, they can see us."

"You say that as if there's a chance of us somehow getting away unseen," Bryce muttered. She said to Tharion, "You can swim. Get the Hel out of here."

"No way." The wind tossed the mer's red hair as they bounded over the swells, the boat steered on a current of his power. "We're in this until the bitter end, Legs." But then the mer stiffened and roared, "*Into the water!*"

Bryce didn't second-guess him. She flung herself over the boat's side, Hunt splashing in with her, wings spraying water wide. The others followed. Tharion used his water magic to propel them a safe distance away, a wave of power that had Bryce sputtering as she emerged, salt stinging her eyes.

Right as something massive and glowing shot beneath her legs.

The torpedo struck the boat.

The tremor in the water rippled through her, and Tharion propelled them farther out as the boat exploded into smithereens, a plume of spray shooting sky-high.

Then it subsided, a field of debris and lashing waves left in its wake.

Exposed and adrift in the water, Bryce scanned for anywhere to go. Hunt was doing the same.

But Ruhn said, "Oh gods."

She looked to where her brother was treading water. Beheld the three massive black shapes aiming for them.

Omega-boats.

Ruhn had never once in his life felt as useless as he did treading water, flotsam drifting past, Ydra distant behind them and the next island not even a smudge on the horizon.

Even if Athalar could manage to get airborne with waterlogged wings, snipers were waiting to down him—and Bryce. Cormac couldn't teleport, and Tharion might be able to move them a little with his water, but against three Omega-boats . . .

He met Hunt's stare over the bobbing swells, the angel's soaking face grim with determination. Hunt asked, "Shadows?"

"Sun's too bright." And the waves shifted them too much.

Two of the Omega-boats peeled off for Ydra, presumably to prevent any Ophion boats from escaping. But that still left one massive submersible against them. And the Hind, the Harpy, and the Hammer on that approaching speedboat.

Once their faces became clear, it'd be over. Sandriel's old triarii would know who they were, and they'd be dead fucking meat. The Helhound, apparently, had tried to help them, but the rest of those assholes . . .

"Get out of here," Bryce scolded Tharion again.

Tharion shook his head, water spraying. "If Athalar can down their boats—"

"I can't," Hunt cut in, and Ruhn raised his brows. Hunt explained, "Even if it wouldn't give away my identity, you're in the water with me. If I unleash my lightning . . ."

Ruhn finished, "We're deep-fried."

Hunt said to Bryce, "You can't blind them, either. They'll know it's you."

"That's a risk I'm willing to take," she countered, treading water. "Lightning, they'd know it's you. But a bright burst of light . . . there are more ways to excuse it. I can blind them, and when they're down, we seize their boat."

Hunt nodded grimly, but Ruhn countered, "That doesn't handle the Omega-boat. It doesn't have windows."

"We'll take our chances," Hunt said.

"Right." Bryce focused on the approaching death squad. "How close do we let them get?"

Hunt eyed their enemies. "Close enough that we can leap on board when they're blinded."

Ruhn muttered, "So really damn close."

Bryce blew out a breath. "All right. All right." Light began flickering from her chest, building, casting the water around her into palest blue. "Just tell me when," she said to Hunt.

"Someone's coming," Tharion said, pointing with a clawed hand to the fleet. A wave skimmer broke away from the speedboat. A familiar golden head appeared atop it, bouncing across the waves.

"The Hind," Cormac said, blanching.

"At least she's alone."

"There goes our plan," Bryce hissed.

"No," Hunt said, though lightning began to glow in his gaze. Burning Solas. "We hold to it. She's coming to talk."

"How do you know that?"

Hunt growled, "The others are holding back."

Ruhn asked, hating that he didn't know, "Why would the Hind do that?"

"To torment us," Cormac guessed. "She toys with enemies before slaughtering them."

Athalar said to Bryce, the general incarnate, "Blind her when I give the signal." He ordered Tharion, "Use one of those knives as soon as she's down." The mer drew a blade. Bryce's light fluttered in the water, reaching down in the depths.

The Omega slowed behind the Hind, but continued to creep closer.

"Say nothing," Cormac warned them as the wave skimmer slowed, engine quieting.

And then the Hind was there, in her impeccable imperial uniform, black boots shining with water. Not one hair on her golden head lay out of place, and her face was the portrait of cruel calm as she said, "What a surprise."

None of them said a word.

The Hind slung one of her lean legs over the wave skimmer so she sat sidesaddle, and braced her elbows on her knees. Put her delicate chin in her hands. "This is the fun part of my job, you know. Finding the rats who nibble away at the safety of our empire."

Such a dead, hateful face. Like she was a statue, flawless and carved, brought to life.

The Hind nodded to Bryce, though. Her red lips curved upward. "Is that little light for me?"

"Come closer and find out," Bryce said, earning a warning look from Hunt. What was he waiting for?

But the Hind surveyed Tharion. "Your presence is . . . troublesome."

The water around him thrashed, roiled by his magic, but the mer kept silent. For some reason, he hadn't yet shifted. Was it some attempt to remain unrecognized for what he was? Or maybe a predator's instinct to hide one of his biggest assets until he could strike?

But the Hind sized up Tharion again. "I'm glad to see the River Queen's Captain of Intelligence is indeed smart enough to know that if he used his power to do something stupid like overturn this wave skimmer, my companions would unleash Hel upon all of you."

Tharion's teeth flashed. But he didn't attack.

Then the Hind met Ruhn's stare, and all that he was diluted to pure, lethal rage.

He'd kill her, and do it gladly. If he could get on that wave skimmer before Tharion, he'd rip out her throat with his teeth.

"Two Fae Princes," the Hind purred. "Crown Princes, no less. The future of the royal bloodlines." She clicked her tongue. "Not to mention that one of them is a Starborn heir. What a scandal this shall be for the Fae. What shame this will bring."

"What do you want?" Hunt challenged, lightning skittering over his shoulders. Bryce twisted toward him with alarm, and Ruhn tensed.

Athalar's power glowed along the tops of his wings, twining in his hair. Each breath seemed to summon more of it, keeping it well above the waves' reach. Readying for the strike.

"I already have what I want," the Hind said coolly. "Proof of your treachery."

Bryce's light shimmered and built, rippling into the depths below. And Hunt . . . If he unleashed his power, he'd electrocute all of them.

Ruhn said to his sister, mind-to-mind, *Get on that wave skimmer and run.*

Fuck that. Bryce slammed her mind shut to him.

The Hind reached into her pocket, and the lightning above Athalar flared, a whip readying to strike whatever gun the deer shifter possessed. Still he didn't give the signal.

But the Hind pulled out a small white stone. Held it up.

She smiled slightly at Cormac. "I showed one of these to Sofie Renast before she died, you know. Made this same demonstration."

Died. The word seemed to clang across the water. The Hind had truly killed her, then.

Cormac spat, "I'm going to rip you to pieces."

The Hind laughed softly. "From where I'm sitting, I don't see much chance of that." She extended her arm over the water. Her slim, manicured fingers splayed, and the stone plunged. It left barely a ripple on the waves as it fluttered down, down, down, shimmering white in Bryce's light, and then vanishing into the deep.

"Long way to the bottom," the Hind observed dryly. "I wonder if you'll drown before you reach it." The Omega-boat surged closer.

"Choose wisely," the Hind crooned. "Come with me," she said to Hunt, to Bryce, "or see what the seafloor has to offer you."

"Get fucked," Hunt seethed.

"Oh, I plan to, once this is done," she said, smiling wickedly.

Hunt's lightning flickered again. Glowed in his eyes. Shit—Athalar was walking a fine line of control.

Bryce murmured Hunt's name in warning. Hunt ignored her, but Tharion cursed softly.

What is it? Ruhn asked the male, who didn't look his way as Tharion replied, *Something big. Gunning for us.*

Not the Omega-boat?

No. It's . . . What the fuck is it?

"Hurry now," the Hind drawled. "Not much time."

Lightning wrapped around Hunt's head. Ruhn's heart stalled a beat as it lingered—like a crown, making of Hunt an anointed, primal god. Willing to slaughter any in his path to save the female he loved. He'd fry every single one of them if it meant getting Bryce out alive.

Some intrinsic part of Ruhn trembled at it. Whispered that he should get far, far away and pray for mercy.

But Bryce didn't balk from the knee-wobbling power surging around Athalar. Like she saw all of him and welcomed it into her heart.

Hunt, eyes nothing but pure lightning, nodded at Bryce. As if to say, *Blind the bitch.*

Bryce sucked in a breath, and began to glow.

Something solid and metal hit Bryce's legs, her feet, and before she could fully release her light, she was hurled up with it. When the water washed away, she lay on the hull of an Omega-boat.

No—it wasn't imperial. The insignia on it was of two entwined fishes.

Hunt lay beside her, wings dripping wet—lightning still crackling around him. His eyes . . .

Holy fuck, his eyes. Pure lightning filled them. No whites, no irises. Nothing but lightning.

It snapped around him, vines wreathing his arms, his brow. Bryce had the vague sense of the others behind them, but she kept her focus on Hunt.

"Hunt," she gasped out. "Calm down."

Hunt snarled toward the Hind. Lightning flowed like tongues of flame from his mouth. But the Hind had fallen back, revving her wave skimmer and retreating toward her line of boats. Like she knew what kind of death Hunt was about to unleash on her.

"*Hunt,*" Bryce said, but something metal clanked against the broad snout of the ship, and then a female voice was bellowing, "*Down the hatch! Now!*"

Bryce didn't question their good luck. Didn't care that the Hind had seen them, knew them, and they'd let the spy-breaker live. She hurtled to her feet, slipping on the metal, but Hunt was there, a hand under her elbow. His lightning danced up her arm, tickling, but not hurting. His eyes still blazed with power as they assessed the unknown female ahead, who—to her credit—didn't run screaming.

Bryce glanced behind to find Ruhn helping Cormac along, Tharion at their backs, a wave of water now towering between him and the Hind. Hiding them from the view of the approaching speedboat, with Pollux and the Harpy on it.

It didn't matter now. The Hind knew.

A dark-haired female waved to them from a hatch midway along the massive length of the ship—as large as an Omega-boat. Her brown skin gleamed with ocean spray, her narrow face set with grim calm as she gestured for them to hurry.

Yet Hunt's lightning still didn't ease. Bryce knew it wouldn't, until they were sure what the fuck was happening.

"Hurry," the female said as Bryce reached the hatch. "We

have less than a minute to get out of here." Bryce gripped the rungs of a ladder and propelled herself downward, Hunt right behind her. The female swore, presumably at the sight of Hunt's current state.

Bryce kept going down. Lightning slithered along the ladder, but didn't bite. Like Hunt was holding himself in check.

One after another, they entered, and the female had barely shut the hatch when the ship shuddered and swayed. Bryce clenched the ladder as the craft submerged.

"We're diving!" the female shouted. "Hold on!"

Bryce's stomach lurched with the ship, but she kept descending. People milled about below, shouting. They halted as Hunt's lightning surged over the floor. A vanguard of what was to come.

"If they're Ophion, we're fucked," Ruhn muttered from above Hunt.

"Only if they know about what we did," Tharion breathed from the end of their party.

Bryce rallied her light with each step downward. Between facing the two enemies now at their throats, she'd take Ophion, but . . . Could she and Hunt take down this ship, if they needed to? Could they do it without drowning themselves and their friends?

She dropped into a clean, bright white chamber—an air lock. Rows of underwater gear lined it, along with several people in blue uniforms by the door. Mer. The female who had escorted them joined the others waiting for them.

A brown-haired, ample-hipped female stepped forward, scanning Bryce.

Her eyes widened as Hunt dropped to the wet floor, lightning flowing around him. She had the good sense to hold up her hands. The people behind her did, too. "We mean you no harm," she said with firm calm.

Hunt didn't back down from whatever primal wrath he rode. Bryce's breathing hitched.

Ruhn and Cormac dropped on Bryce's other side, and the female scanned them, too, face strained as she noted the injured Avallen Prince, who sagged against Ruhn. But she smiled as Tharion entered on Hunt's right. Like she'd found someone of reason in this giant clusterfuck that had just tumbled down the hatch.

"You called for us?" she asked Tharion, glancing nervously toward Hunt.

Bryce murmured to Hunt, "Chill the fuck out."

Hunt stared at each of the strangers, as if sizing up a kill. Lightning sizzled through his hair.

"Hunt," Bryce muttered, but didn't dare reach for his hand.

"I . . ." Tharion drew his wide eyes from Hunt and blinked at the female. "What?"

"Our Oracle sensed we'd be needed somewhere in this vicinity, so we came. Then we got your message," she said tightly, an eye still fixed on Hunt. "The light."

Ruhn and Tharion turned to Bryce, Cormac nearly a dead weight of exhaustion in her brother's arms. Tharion smiled roughly. "You're a good luck charm, Legs."

It was the stupidest stroke of luck she'd ever had. Bryce said, "I, uh . . . I sent the light."

Hunt's lightning crackled, a second skin over his body, his soaked clothes. He didn't show any signs of calming down. She had no idea *how* to calm him down.

This was how he was that day with Sandriel, Ruhn said into her mind. *When he ripped off her head.* He added tightly, *You were in danger then, too.*

And what's that supposed to mean?

Why don't you tell me?

You seem like you know what the fuck is happening with him.

Ruhn glared at her as Hunt continued to glow and menace. *It means that he's going ballistic in the way that only mates can when the other is threatened. It's what happened then, and what's happening now. You're true mates—the way Fae are mates, in your bodies and souls. That's what was different about your scent the other day. Your scents have merged. As they do between Fae mates.*

She glared right back at her brother. *So what?*

So find some way to calm him down. Athalar's your fucking problem now.

Bryce sent a mental image of her middle finger back in answer.

The mer female squared her shoulders, unaware of Ruhn and Bryce's conversation, and said to Tharion, "We're not out of this yet. There's an Omega on our tail." She spoke like Hunt wasn't a living thunderstorm standing two feet away.

Bryce's heart strained. True mates. Not only in name, but . . . in the way that Fae could be mates with each other.

Ruhn said, *Athalar was dangerous before. But as a mated male, he's utterly lethal.*

Bryce countered, *He was always lethal.*

Not like this. There's no mercy in him. He's gone lethal in a Fae way.

In that predatory, kill-all-enemies way. *He's an angel.*

Doesn't seem to matter.

One look at Hunt's hard face, and she knew Ruhn was right. Some small part of her thrilled at it—that he'd descended this far into some primal instinct to try to save her.

Alphaholes can have their uses, she said to her brother with a bravado she didn't feel, and returned to the conversation at hand.

Tharion was saying to the female, "Captain Tharion Ketos of the Blue Court, at your service."

The female saluted as the people with her opened an airtight door to reveal a shining glass hallway. Blue stretched around it, a passageway through the ocean. A few fish shot past—or the ship shot past the fish. Faster than Bryce had realized. "Commander Sendes," the female said.

"What mer court do you come from?" Bryce asked. Hunt walked at her side, silent and blazing with power.

Commander Sendes glanced over a shoulder, face still a little pale at the sight of Hunt. "This one." Sendes gestured to the glass walkway around them, the behemoth of a ship that Bryce could now make out through it.

They hadn't entered along the flat back of the ship as Bryce had thought, but rather at the tip of it. As if the ship had pierced the surface like a lance. And now, with a view of the rest of the ship expanding beyond—below—the glass passage, what she could see of it appeared to be shaped like some sort of squid as it shot into the gloom below. A squid as large as the Comitium, and made of glass and matte metal for stealth.

Sendes lifted her chin. "Welcome to the *Depth Charger.* One of the six city-ships of the Ocean Queen's court Beneath."

45

All right, so you'll be charged with breaking and entering, and probably theft. Tell me again how you think you've still got grounds to go after this old creep?" Declan's boyfriend, Marc, leaned against the couch cushions, muscled arms crossed as he grilled Ithan.

Ithan blew out a breath. "When you put it like that, I can see what you mean about it being a tough case to win."

Flynn and Declan, beside them, attempted to murder each other in a video game, both cursing under their breath. "It's admirable," Marc admitted. The leopard shifter frowned toward the small black box Ithan had taken from the Astronomer's lair. "But you just waded knee-deep into shit."

"It's not right that she's trapped in there. What choice did she even have as a kid?"

"No arguments from me against that," Marc said. "But there's a legal contract involved, so she's technically owned by the Astronomer. She's not a slave, but she might as well be, legally. And theft of slaves is a big fucking crime."

"I know," Ithan said. "But it feels wrong to leave her there."

"So you took the fire sprites instead?" Marc arched a brow. "You wanna take a guess at how much they cost?" He nodded at the box in the center of the table. "What were you even thinking?"

"I wasn't thinking," Ithan muttered, swigging from his beer. "I was pissed."

Declan cut in, not tearing his attention from the screen and his shooting, "There were no cameras, though, right?"

"None that I saw."

"So it all comes down to whether the girl in the tank tells on you," Declan said, thumbs flying against the controller. Flynn swore at whatever Dec did to his avatar.

"You could return them," Marc suggested. "Say you were drunk, apologize, and send them back."

Ithan opened his mouth, but the box on the table rattled.

Rattled. Like the beings inside had heard. Even Declan and Flynn paused their game.

"Um," Declan said, wincing.

"Hello?" Flynn said, eyeing the box.

It rattled again. They all flinched.

"Well, someone has an opinion," Marc said, chuckling softly, and leaned forward.

"Careful," Dec warned. Marc threw him a wry look and opened the black box.

Light, golden and red, erupted, washing over the walls and ceiling. Ithan shielded his eyes, but the light was immediately sucked back in, revealing four rings nestled in black velvet, the tiny glass bubbles atop them glowing.

The glow inside faded and faded, until . . .

Declan and Marc glanced at each other in horror.

"Solas," Flynn swore, tossing aside his controller. "That old fuck should be crucified for this."

"All right," Marc murmured to Ithan. "I get why you took them."

Ithan grunted in answer, and peered at the four female figures inside the rings. He'd never met Lehabah face-to-face, as Bryce had never let him into the library beneath the gallery, but he'd seen Bryce's photos.

Three of the sprites were just like her—flames shaped into female bodies. Two were slim, one as sinfully curvy as Lehabah had been. The fourth globe was pure fire.

That fourth ring rattled. Ithan recoiled. That was clearly the one who'd shaken the box.

"So do we let them out?" Flynn asked, studying the box and the sprites trapped inside.

"Fuck yeah, we do," Declan said, shooting to his feet.

Ithan stared at the sprites, especially the fourth, radiant one who seemed so . . . angry. He didn't blame her. He murmured to his roommates, "You sure you're cool with freeing a bunch of pissed-off fire sprites in your house?"

But Flynn waved him off. "We've got sprinklers and smoke alarms."

"I'm not reassured," Marc said.

"Got it," Declan called, trotting from the kitchen with a hammer.

Marc rubbed his temples and leaned back against the cushions. "This cannot end well."

"Ye of little faith," Flynn said, catching the hammer as Declan tossed it to him.

Ithan winced. "Just . . . be careful."

"I don't think that word's in either of their vocabularies," Marc quipped, earning an elbow in the ribs from Declan as the male settled onto the couch beside him.

Flynn tugged the box toward him and said to the sprites, "Cover your heads." The three visible ones crouched down. The fourth one remained a ball of flame, but shrank slightly.

"Careful," Ithan warned again. Flynn, with a snap of the wrist, cracked the top of the first ring. It splintered, and he tapped it again. It broke into three pieces on the third rap of the hammer, but the sprite remained crouched.

Flynn moved onto the next, then the next.

By the time he'd cracked open the third ring, the sprites were poking their fiery heads out like chicks emerging from eggs. Flynn moved the hammer above the fourth one. And as it came down, Ithan could have sworn one of the sprites shouted, in a voice almost too hoarse to hear, "*Don't!*"

Too late.

All it took was one crack, and the flame within shoved outward, rupturing the glass.

They all leapt over the couch with a shout, and *fuck*, it was hot and bright and wind was roaring and something was screeching—

Then something heavy thudded on the coffee table. Ithan and the others peeked over the couch.

"What the fuck?" Flynn breathed, smoke curling from where the shoulders of his shirt had been singed.

The three sprites cowered in their shattered orbs. All shrinking from the naked, human-sized female smoldering on the coffee table beside them.

The female pushed up onto her arms, hair like darkest iron falling in curling waves around her delicately featured face. Her tan body simmered, the wood table beneath her charring everywhere her nude, luscious form touched. She lifted her head, and her eyes—fucking Hel.

They blazed crimson. More boiling blood than flame.

Her back heaved with each long, sawing breath, ripples of what seemed like red-and-gold scales flowing beneath her skin.

"He is going to kill you," she said in a voice rasping with disuse. But her eyes weren't on Ithan. They were on Flynn, his hammer raised again, as if it would do anything against the sort of fire she bore. "He is going to find you and kill you."

But Flynn, stupid, arrogant asshole that he was, got to his feet and grinned cheerfully down at the curvy female on the coffee table. "Good thing a dragon now owes me a debt."

Athalar was a time bomb—one that Ruhn had no idea how to defuse. He supposed that honor went to his sister, who kept a step away from the angel, one eye on him and the other on the unfolding race for the seafloor.

His sister was *mated*. It was rare enough among the Fae, but finding a mate who was an angel . . . His mind reeled.

Ruhn shook off the thought, approaching Commander Sendes and saying, "I don't hear any engine noise."

"You won't," Sendes said, opening an air lock door at the end of the long glass tunnel. "These are stealth ships, fueled by the Ocean Queen's power."

Tharion whistled, then asked, "So you think we can outrun an Omega in something this big?"

"No. But we're not outrunning it." She pointed through a wall of thick glass to the dimness below. "We're going into the Ravel Canyon."

"If you can fit," Ruhn challenged, hoisting Cormac up a little higher as the male groaned, "then so can the Omega-boats."

Sendes gave him a secret, knowing smile. "Watch."

Ruhn nodded to the prince hanging off his shoulder. "My cousin needs a medwitch."

"One is already coming to meet us," Sendes said, opening another air lock. The tunnel beyond was massive, with halls branching out in three directions like the arteries of a mighty beast. The hall directly ahead . . . "Well, that's a sight," Ruhn murmured.

A cavernous biodome bloomed at the end of the hall, brimming with lush tropical trees, streams winding through the fern-covered floor, and orchids blooming in curling mists. Butterflies flitted around, and hummingbirds sipped from the orchids and neon-colored flowers. He could have sworn he spied a small, furred beast running beneath a drooping fern.

"We have desalinators on this ship," Sendes explained, pointing to the biodome, "but should they ever fail, this is a wholly separate ecosystem that generates its own fresh water."

"How?" Tharion asked, but Sendes had halted at the intersection of the three halls. "The River Queen has a similar one, but nothing that can do this."

"I doubt your bleeding friend would appreciate the lengthy explanation right now," Sendes said, turning down the hallway to their right. People—mer, from their scents—walked past them, a few gaping, a few throwing confused looks their way, some waving to Sendes, who waved back.

Their surroundings had the air of a corporate building—or a city block. People going about their days, dressed in business or casual clothes, some exercising, some sipping from coffee cups or smoothies.

Bryce's head swiveled this way and that, taking it all in. Athalar just kept crackling with lightning.

"No one's concerned about who's on our tail?" Ruhn asked Sendes.

She halted before another massive window, again pointing. "Why should they be?"

Ruhn braced his feet as the ship plowed right for a dark, craggy wall rising from the seafloor. But as easy as a bird shifting directions, it pulled up alongside the wall and drifted down—then halted, hovering.

Ruhn shook his head. "They'll find us like this."

"Look down the body of the ship."

Pressing against the glass, Cormac a ballast on his other side, Ruhn obeyed. Where a mammoth ship had been, now . . . there was only black rock. Nothing else.

"This ship can become invisible?"

"Not invisible. Camouflaged." Sendes smiled with pride. "The Ocean Queen imbued her vessels with many gifts from the seas. This one has a squid's ability to blend into its surroundings."

"But the lights inside—" Tharion started.

"The glass is one-way. It blocks the light and any glimpse within once the camouflaging is activated."

"What about radar?" Ruhn asked. "You might be invisible to the naked eye, but surely the imperial ships would pick you up."

Another one of those proud smiles. "Again, the Ocean Queen's power fuels our ship, not the firstlight that the Omega radar is programmed to pick up. We register no signs of life, either—not even as a whale or a shark might on a radar. We are completely undetectable. To a passing Omega-boat, we are only a cluster of rock."

"What if they run into you?" Tharion asked.

"We can simply drift up or down, to avoid it." She pointed again. "Here they come."

Ruhn's heart leapt into his throat. Athalar's lightning snaked along his body once more. Bryce muttered something to him that apparently did nothing to calm the angel down.

But Ruhn was too busy monitoring the enemy's approach. Like a wolf stepping from the shadows of a kelp forest, the Omega-boat stalked for the canyon. Its firstlights blared into the dark, broadcasting its location.

People continued walking past, a few glancing to the enemy closing in, but not paying it much mind.

What the actual fuck.

The imperial ship plunged right after them. A wolf on the hunt, indeed.

"Watch," Sendes said.

Ruhn held his breath, as if it'd somehow keep them from detection, as the Omega-boat crept closer. A slow, strategic sweep.

He could make out the paint along its sides—the imperial insignia flaking off—the slices and dents from previous battles. Along its hull was written, *SPQM Faustus*.

"The *Faustus*," Tharion breathed, dread in his voice.

"You know the ship?" Sendes asked him.

"Heard of it," Tharion said, monitoring the warship inching past. Utterly unaware of them. "That vessel alone has downed sixteen rebel ships."

"At least they sent someone impressive after us this time," Sendes said.

Tharion ran a hand through his damp hair, claws retracting. "They're drifting right by us. This is incredible."

Cormac grunted, stirring in Ruhn's arms, "Does Ophion know about this?"

Sendes stiffened. "We are not aligned with Ophion." Thank fuck. Bryce sagged, and Hunt's lightning dimmed slightly.

"What about the Asteri? Are they aware of this technology?" Ruhn asked, gesturing to the boat around them, now vanishing into the deep, the Omega-boat blindly passing overhead.

Sendes continued walking, and they followed her. "No. And given the circumstances under which we found you, I trust you will not pass on the information. Just as we shall keep your presence confidential."

You fuck us, we'll fuck you. "Got it," Ruhn said, offering a smile that Sendes didn't return. The ship began drifting farther into the canyon's depths.

"Here she is," Sendes announced as a medwitch came running, a team of three with a stretcher close behind her.

"Cthona spare me," Cormac muttered, managing to lift his head. "I don't need all that."

"Yes, you do," Tharion and Ruhn said together.

If the medwitch and her team recognized any of them, they didn't let on. The next few minutes were a flurry of getting Cormac onto the stretcher and bustled to the medical center, with a promise that he'd be out of surgery within an hour and they could see him soon after that.

Through it all, Bryce kept back with Athalar. Lightning still skimmed over his wings, sparked at his fingertips.

Calm down, Ruhn said into Athalar's mind.

Thunderstorms boomed in answer.

All right, then.

The city-ship began sailing along the floor of the canyon, the seabed unusually flat and broad between the towering cliffs. They passed a half-crumbling pillar, and—

"Are those carvings?" Ruhn asked as Sendes led them back down the hall.

"Yes," she said a shade softly. "From long, long ago."

Tharion said, "What was down here?" He scanned the passing walls of the canyon floor—all of them carved with strange symbols.

"This was a highway. Not as you will find above the surface, but a grand avenue the mer once used to swim between great cities."

"I never heard of anything out here."

"It's from long ago," she said again, a bit tightly. Like it was a secret.

Bryce said from the back, "I used to work in an antiquities gallery, and my boss once brought in a statue from a sunken city. I always thought she was fudging the dates, but she said it was almost fifteen thousand years old. That it came from the original Beneath." As old as the Asteri—or at least their arrival in Midgard.

Sendes's expression remained neutral. "Only the Ocean Queen can verify that."

Ruhn peered through the glass again. "So the mer once had a city down here?"

"We once had many things," Sendes said.

Tharion shook his head at Ruhn, a silent warning to lay off the subject. Ruhn nodded back. "Where are we going, exactly?" Ruhn asked instead.

"I assume you want to rest for a moment. I'm bringing you to private quarters in our barracks."

"And from there?" Ruhn dared ask.

"We need to wait until the Omegas have cleared the area, but once that has happened, we'll return you wherever you wish."

"The mouth of the Istros," Tharion said. "My people can meet us there."

"Very well. We shall likely arrive at dawn, given our need for secrecy."

"Get me a radio and I'll put out a coded signal."

She nodded, and Ruhn admired the mers' innate trust in one another. Would she have so easily let *him* use a radio to contact anyone beyond this ship? He doubted it.

But Bryce halted at the hallway intersection. Glanced at Hunt before saying to Sendes, "You mind if me and my glowing friend here go into the biodome for a while?"

Sendes warily considered Hunt. "I'll close it to the public temporarily. As long as he does no harm in there."

Hunt bared his teeth, but Bryce smiled tightly. "I'll make sure he doesn't."

Sendes's gaze drifted down to the scar on her chest. "When you are done, ask for Barracks Six, and someone will point you that way."

"Thanks," Bryce said, then pivoted to Ruhn and Tharion. "Stay out of trouble."

"You too," Ruhn said, arching a brow.

Then Bryce was walking toward the lush biodome, Hunt trailing, lightning in his wake.

Sendes pulled a radio from her pocket. “Clear the biodome and seal off its doors.”

Ruhn started. “What?”

Sendes continued onward, boots clicking on the tiled floors. “I think she and the angel should have a little privacy, don’t you?”

46

There was only his power, and Bryce. The rest of the world had become an array of threats to her.

Hunt had the vague notion of being brought onto an enormous mer ship. Of talking with its commander, and noticing the people and the Omega-boat and Cormac being wheeled off.

His mind had drifted, riding some storm without end, his magic screaming to be unleashed. He'd ascended into this plane of existence, of primal savagery, the moment the Hind had appeared. He knew he had to take her out, if it meant getting Bryce to safety. Had decided that it didn't matter if Danaan or Cormac or Tharion got cooked in the process.

He couldn't turn away from that precipice.

Even as Bryce walked down a quiet, warm hallway toward a lush forest—pines and ferns and flowers; birds and butterflies of every color; little streams and waterfalls—he couldn't settle.

He needed his magic out, needed to scream his wrath and then hold her and know she was fine, they were fine—

He followed Bryce into the greenery, across a trickling stream. It was dim in here, mist curling along the floor. Like they'd walked into some ancient garden at the dawn of the world.

She halted in a small clearing, the floor covered with moss and small, white flowers shaped like stars. She turned to him, her eyes glowing. His cock stirred at the glittering intent in them.

Her lips curved upward, knowing and taunting. Without saying a word, she lifted her soaked T-shirt over her head. Another second and her purple lace bra was gone too.

The world, the garden, vanished at the sight of her full breasts, dusk-rose nipples already peaked. His mouth watered.

She unfastened her pants. Her shoes. And then she was shimmying out of her purple underwear.

She stood totally naked before him. Hunt's heart pounded so wildly he thought it'd burst from his chest.

She was so beautiful. Every lush line, every gleaming inch of skin, her beckoning sex—

"Your turn," she said huskily.

His magic howling, begging, Hunt had the vague sense of his fingers removing his clothes and shoes. He didn't care that he was already fully at attention. Only cared that her eyes dipped to his cock and a pleased sort of smile graced her mouth.

Naked, they faced each other in that garden beneath the sea.

He wanted to please his mate. His beautiful, strong mate. Hunt must have said it aloud, because Bryce said gently, "Yes, Hunt. I'm your mate." The star on her chest fluttered like an ember sputtering to life. "And you are mine."

The words rang through him. His magic burned his veins like acid, and he grunted against it.

Her eyes softened, like she could sense his pain. She said hoarsely, "I want you to fuck me. Will you do that?"

Lightning sparked over his wings. "Yes."

Bryce ran a hand up her torso, circling the glowing star between her full breasts. His cock throbbed. She took one step toward him, bare feet cushioned by the moss.

Hunt backed away a step.

She lifted a brow. "No?"

"Yes," he managed to say again. His head cleared a fraction. "This garden . . ."

"Closed to the public," she purred, the star's light shining through her fingers. She took another step, and Hunt didn't retreat this time.

He couldn't get a breath down. "I . . ." He swallowed. "My power—"

She paused a foot from him. The scent of her arousal wrapped invisible fingers around his cock and stroked hard. He shuddered. "Whatever you need to throw at me, Hunt, I can take it."

He let out a low groan. "I don't want to hurt you."

"You won't." She smiled softly—lovingly. "I trust you."

Her fingers brushed over his bare chest, and he shivered again. She closed the distance between them, mouth grazing over his pec—his heart. Hunt's lightning flared, casting the garden in silver. Bryce lifted her head.

"Kiss me," she breathed.

Hunt's eyes were pure lightning. His *body* was pure lightning as Bryce opened her mouth to him and his tongue swept in, tasting of rain and ether.

His power flowed over her, around her, a million sensual caresses, and she arched into it, gave herself over to it. He palmed her breast, power zapping at her nipple, and she gasped. He drove his tongue deeper, like he'd lap up the sound.

She knew Hunt needed a way to work off his magic, a way to reassure him that she was safe and his. *My beautiful, strong mate,* he'd growled as he looked at her naked body.

His other hand kneaded her ass, pulling her against him, pinning his cock between their bodies. He groaned at the touch of her stomach against him, and she writhed—just enough to drive him wild.

Lightning danced down her skin, along her hair, and she basked in it. Took it into herself, let herself become it, become *him*, and let him become her, until they were two souls twining together at the bottom of the sea.

Bryce had the vague sense of falling through air, through time and space, and then she found herself laid gently, reverently, on the mossy ground. Like even in his need, his fury, he wanted her safe and well. Feeling only pleasure.

She wrapped her arms around his neck, arching into him as she nipped at his lip, sucked on his tongue. More. She needed more. He clamped his teeth on the side of her throat, sucking hard, and she arched again, right as he settled between her legs.

The brush of his velvety cock against her bare sex had her shaking. Not with fear, but at his closeness, that nothing now lay between them and would never lie between them again.

He slickened himself with her wetness, his wings twitching. Lightning spiderwebbed on the moss around them, then up the trees overhead.

"Hunt," Bryce gasped. They could explore and play later. Right now, when death had been hovering so close, right now she needed him with her, in her. Needed his strength and power and gentleness, needed that smile and humor and love—

Bryce wrapped a hand around the base of his cock, pumping him once, angling him toward where she was absolutely drenched for him.

Hunt stilled, though. Gritted his teeth as she pumped the magnificent length of him again. His eyes met hers.

Only lightning filled them. An avenging god.

The star on her chest flared, merging with his lightning. He laid a hand atop it. Claiming the star, the light. Claiming her.

Bryce positioned him at her entrance, panting at the brush of the blunt head of his cock. But she released him. Let him decide whether this was what he wanted. This final bridge between their souls.

The lightning cleared from his eyes—as if he willed it. As if he wanted her to see the male beneath.

Pure Hunt. No one and nothing else.

It was a question, somehow. As if he were showing her every scar and wound, every dark corner. Asking if this—if he—was what she really wanted. Bryce only smiled softly. "I love you," she whispered. Shuddering, Hunt kissed her and slid home.

Nothing had ever felt so right.

Hunt worked himself into her, filling her deliciously, perfectly. With each gentle thrust, each inch gained into her, her light flared brighter. His lightning cracked, over and around them.

His back flexed beneath her fingers, his wings tucking in tight. His chest heaved in great bellows, pushing against her breasts, the star between them.

Another inch, another shudder of pleasure. And then he slid out. And out. And out.

His tongue flicked against hers as he slammed back, right to the hilt. Light spilled from her like an overflowing cup, rippling across the forest floor.

Bryce clawed at his back, his neck, and Hunt's teeth found her breast, clamping down. She went wild, hips driving up to meet him, power clashing with power.

Hunt set a steady, punishing pace, and she laid her hands on his ass just to feel the muscles clenching with each thrust, to *feel* him pushing into her—

He claimed her mouth again, and Bryce wrapped her legs around his waist. She moaned as he sank in, and his thrusts turned harder, faster. Lightning and starlight ricocheted between them.

She needed him wilder. Needed him to release that edge of fear and rage and become her Hunt again. She tightened her legs around him, and flipped them. The world spun, and then she was staring down at him, his cock buried so deep—

Lightning flowed over his teeth as he panted, all those abs flexing. Gods, he was beautiful. And hers. Utterly hers.

Bryce lifted her hips, rising off his cock—and then plunged back down. She arched as he kissed the star on her chest. She rose again, a steady, taunting slide, and then impaled herself.

He snarled against her skin. "Merciless, Quinlan."

Close. So close. She rose once more, luxuriating in each inch of his cock, nearly pulling herself from his tip. And as she drove down, she clenched her delicate inner muscles around him.

Hunt roared, and she was again on her back as he slammed into her. His power flowed over her, filled her, and she was him, and he was her, and then his cock hit that perfect spot deep in her, and the world was only light—

Release blasted through her, and Bryce might have been laughing, or sobbing, or shouting his name. Hunt rode her through it all, nursing every last drop of pleasure, and then he was moving again, punishing thrusts that sent them sliding across the mossy floor. His wings were a wall of gray above them, his wings were—glowing.

They filled with iridescent light. *He* filled with light.

Bryce reached a hand toward his blazing wings. Her own fingers, her hand, her arm—they radiated the same light. As if they had become filled with power, as if her light had leaked into him, and his into her—

"Look at you," he breathed. "Bryce."

"Look at *us*," she whispered, and lifted up to kiss him. He met her halfway, tongues tangling. His thrusts turned wilder. He was close.

"I want to go with you," he said against her mouth. Sounding . . . almost normal again.

"Then make it happen," she said, hand sliding for his balls. His fingers caressed her clit. Began stroking.

Bryce kneaded his balls, and a shudder went through him. Another. On the third stroke, she squeezed hard, right as lightning streamed from his fingers and—

She was falling. Had the distant sense of screaming her pleasure to the surface miles above, of an orgasm rocking through her, reducing her mind to rubble. She was vaguely conscious of Hunt pumping into her, spilling into her, over and over—

Falling through time and space and light and shadow—

Up was down and down was up, and they were the only beings in existence, here in this garden, locked away from time—

Something cold and hard pushed into her back, but she didn't care, not as she clenched Hunt to her, gasping down air, sanity. He was shaking, wings twitching, whispering, "Bryce, Bryce, Bryce," in her ear.

Sweat coated their bodies, and she dragged her fingers down his spine. He was hers, and she was his, and—

"*Bryce*," Hunt said, and Bryce opened her eyes.

Harsh, blinding light greeted them. White walls, diving equipment, and—a ladder. No hint of a garden.

Hunt was instantly up, whirling to assess their surroundings, cock still jutting out and gleaming. Bryce needed a moment to get her knees operational, bracing against the cold floor.

She knew this room.

Hunt's eyes remained wild, but—no lightning danced around them. No trace of that primal fury. Just a glowing, iridescent handprint on his chest, a remnant of starlight. It faded with each breath.

He asked between pants, "How the *fuck* did we wind up in the air lock?"

"Okay," Flynn said, clapping his hands together. "So to make sure I have this right . . ." He pointed to the slender fire sprite floating in the air to his left. "You're Ridi."

"Rithi!" she squeaked.

"Rithi," Flynn amended with a smile. He pointed to the full-bodied sprite before him. "You're Malana." She beamed. He pointed to the sprite to the right of her. "And you're Sasa. And you're triplets."

"Yes," Malana said, long hair floating in the air around her. "Descendants of Persina Falath, Lady of Cinders."

"Right," Ithan said, as if that meant anything to him. He knew nothing about sprites and their hierarchies. Only that they'd been banished from Sky and Breath ages ago for a failed rebellion. They'd been deemed Lowers ever since.

"And *you*," Flynn drawled, pivoting to the naked female on the other end of the sectional, a blanket draped around her shoulders, "are . . ."

"I haven't given you my name," came the answer, her red eyes now faded to a charred black. She'd stopped burning—at least enough to avoid singeing the couch.

"Exactly," Flynn said, as if the Fae lord weren't taunting a dragon. A fucking *dragon*. A Lower, yes, but . . . fuck. They weren't true shifters, switching between humanoid and animal bodies at will. They were more like the mer, if anything. There was a biological or magical difference to explain it—Ithan vaguely remembered learning about it in school, though he'd promptly forgotten the details.

It didn't matter now, he supposed. The dragon could navigate two forms. He'd be a fool to underestimate her in this one.

The dragon stared Flynn down. He gave her a charming smile back. Her chin lifted. "Ariadne."

Flynn arched a brow. "A dragon named Ariadne?"

"I suppose you have a better name for me?" she shot back.

"Skull-Crusher, Winged Doom, Light-Eater." Flynn ticked them off on his fingers.

She snorted, and the hint of amusement had Ithan realizing that the dragon was . . . beautiful. Utterly lethal and defiant, but—well, damn. From the gleam in Flynn's eyes, Ithan could tell the Fae lord was thinking the same.

Ariadne said, "Such names are for the old ones who dwell in their mountain caves and sleep the long slumber of true immortals."

"But you're not one of them?" Ithan asked.

"My kin are more . . . modern." Her gaze sharpened on Flynn. "Hence Ariadne."

Flynn winked. She scowled.

"How did all of you"—Declan cut in, motioning to Ariadne, her body similar to that of a Fae female's—"fit into that tiny ring?"

"We were bespelled by the Astronomer," Sasa whispered. "He's an ancient sorcerer—don't let him deceive you with that feeble act. He bought us all, and shoved us into those rings to light the way when he descends into Hel. Though Ariadne got put into the ring by . . ." She trailed off when the dragon cut her a scathing, warning look.

A chill went down Ithan's spine. He asked them, "Is there anything to be done to free the others he still controls? The mystics?"

"No," Ariadne answered. She peered down at her tan wrist. The brand there. *SPQM.* A slave's mark. The sprites also bore it. "He owns them, as he owns us. The mystic you spoke to, the wolf . . ." Her black eyes shifted toward red again. "He favors her. He will never let her go. Not until she grows old in that tank and dies."

Centuries from now, possibly. Ithan's gut twisted.

"Please don't make us go back," Rithi whispered, clinging to Malana.

"Hush," Malana warned.

Marc studied them. "Look, ladies. You're in a tough spot. You're not only slaves, but stolen slaves." A warning look at Ithan, who shrugged. He had no regrets. "Yet there are laws about your treatment. It's archaic and nonsensical that anyone can be owned, but if you can prove severe maltreatment, it might allow for you to be . . . purchased by someone else."

"Not freed?" Sasa whispered.

"Only your new owner could do that," Marc said sadly.

"So buy them and be done with it." Ariadne crossed her arms.

"What about you, sweetheart?" Flynn purred at the dragon, like the Fae male literally couldn't help himself.

Her eyes burned crimson. "I'm beyond your pay grade, lordling."

"Try me."

But the dragon turned back to staring at the TV, still paused on the video game. Ithan swallowed and asked her, "It's bad, then—what he does to the mystics?"

"He tortures them," Ariadne said flatly, and Rithi whimpered her agreement. "The wolf female is . . . defiant. She did not lie about his punishments. I've sat on his hand for years and witnessed him send her into the darkest corners of Hel. He lets the demons and their princes taunt her. Terrify her. He thinks he'll break her one day. I'm not so sure."

Ithan's stomach turned.

Ariadne went on, "She spoke true today about the necromancer, too." Flynn, Marc, and Declan turned toward Ithan, brows high. "You want answers about your dead brother, then you should find one."

Ithan nodded. The dragon belonged to the House of Flame and Shadow, even if the slave tattoo removed her from its protections. She'd have knowledge of a necromancer's ability.

Declan announced, "Well, since we're now harboring stolen slaves, we might as well make you ladies comfortable. Feel free to claim Ruhn's room—second bedroom at the top of the stairs."

The three sprites zoomed for the staircase, as if they were no more than three excited children. Ithan couldn't help his smile. He'd done some good today, at least. Even if it would land him in a heap of trouble.

Ariadne slowly got to her feet. They rose with her.

Flynn, standing closest, said to the dragon, "You could run, you know. Shift into your other form and take off. We won't tell anyone where you went."

Her red eyes again dimmed to black. "Don't you know what this does?" She lifted her arm to reveal the tattoo there. She laughed bitterly. "I can't shift unless he allows it. And even if I manage it, anywhere I go, anywhere on Midgard, he can track me in that form."

"You teleported," Cormac said to Bryce an hour later as she and Hunt stood beside his cot in the city-ship's hospital. The prince was pale, but alive. Every shard of the gorsian bullet had been removed. Another hour and he'd be back to normal.

Hunt didn't particularly care. They'd only come to Cormac for answers.

Hunt was still recovering from the sex that had blasted him apart mind and body and soul, the sex that Bryce had known would bring him back from the brink, that had made his magic sing.

Had made their magics merge.

He didn't know how to describe it—the feeling of her magic wending through him. Like he existed all at once and not at all, like he could craft whatever he wished from thin air and nothing would be denied to him. Did she live with this, day after day? That pure sense of . . . possibility? It had faded since they'd teleported, but he could still feel it there, in his chest, where her handprint had glowed. A slumbering little kernel of creation.

"*How?*" Bryce asked. She'd had no shame, not even a blush, striding in here—the two of them wearing navy-blue aquatic body armor they'd taken from the air lock to cover themselves. Ruhn had looked thoroughly uncomfortable, but Tharion had laughed at Hunt's disheveled hair and whatever stupid happiness was on his face, and said, "Good work bringing our boy back, Legs."

Bryce had gone right to Cormac and explained what had happened in the most Quinlan-like way Hunt could imagine: "Right at the end of banging Hunt's brains out, *right* when we came together, we wound up in the air lock."

Cormac studied her, then Hunt. "Your powers merged, I take it."

"Yeah," Bryce said. "We both went all glowy. Not in the way that he was glowing during his . . ." She frowned. "Rage-daze." She waved a hand. "This was like . . . we glowed with my starlight. Then we teleported."

"Hmm," Cormac said. "I wonder if you need Athalar's power for teleporting."

"I can't tell if that's an insult or not," Bryce said.

Hunt lifted his brows. "In what way?"

"If my powers only work if my big, tough male helps me out—"

"It can't be romantic?" Hunt demanded.

Bryce huffed. "I'm an independent female."

"All right," Hunt said, laughing softly. "Let's just say that I'm like some magic token in a video game and when you . . . use me, you level up."

"That is the dorkiest thing you've ever said," Bryce accused, and Hunt sketched a bow.

"So Hunt's magic is the key to Bryce's?" Ruhn asked Cormac.

"I don't know if it's Hunt specifically, or simply energy," Cormac said. "Your power came from the Gates—it's something we don't understand. It's playing by unknown rules."

"Great," Bryce muttered, sinking into the chair beside Ruhn's near the window. Black, eternal water spread beyond.

Hunt rubbed his jaw, frowning. "The Prince of the Pit told me about this."

Bryce's brow scrunched. "Sex teleporting?"

Hunt snorted. "No. He told me that you and I hadn't . . . explored what our powers could do. Together."

Ruhn said, "You think this is what he had in mind?"

"I don't know," Hunt admitted, marking the gleam of worry on Bryce's face. They still had a lot to talk about.

"Is it wise," Tharion drawled, "to do as he says?"

"I think we should wait to see if our theory is correct," Bryce said. "See if it really was our powers . . . merging." She asked Hunt, "How do you feel?"

"Fine," he said. "I think I kept a kernel of your power in me for a while, but it's gone quiet."

She smiled slightly. "We definitely need to do more research."

"You just want to bang Athalar again," Tharion countered.

Bryce inclined her head. "I thought that was a given."

Hunt stalked toward her, fully intending to drag her to some quiet room to test out the theory. But the door to the room slid open, and Commander Sendes appeared. Her face was grim.

Hunt braced himself. The Asteri had found them. The Omegas were about to attack—

But her gaze fell on Cormac. She said quietly, "The medwitch told me that in your delirium, you were talking about someone named Sofie Renast. That name is known to us here—we've heard of her work for years now. But I thought you should know that we were summoned to rescue an agent from the North Sea weeks ago. It wasn't until we reached her that we realized it was Sofie."

The room went utterly silent. Cormac's swallow was audible as Sendes went on, "We were too late. Sofie had drowned by the time our divers picked her up."

47

The morgue was cold and quiet and empty, save for the female corpse lying on the chrome table, covered by a black cloth.

Bryce stood by the doorway as Cormac knelt beside the body, preserved by a medwitch until the ship could hand Sofie over to the Ophion rebels for claiming. The prince was silent.

He'd been this way since Sendes had come to his room.

And though Bryce's body still buzzed with all she and Hunt had done, seeing that slender female body on the table, the prince kneeling, head bowed . . . Her eyes stung. Hunt's fingers found hers and squeezed.

"I knew," Cormac said roughly. His first words in minutes. "I think I always knew, but . . ."

Ruhn stepped to his cousin's side. Put a hand on his shoulder. "I'm sorry."

Cormac leaned his brow against the rim of the examination table. His voice shook. "She was good, and brave, and kind. I never deserved her, not for one minute."

Bryce's throat ached. She let go of Hunt's hand to approach Cormac, touching his other shoulder. Where would Sofie's soul go? Did it linger near her body until they could give her a proper Sailing? If she went to one of the resting places, they'd be dooming her to a terrible fate.

But Bryce didn't say any of that. Not as Cormac slid his fingers beneath the black cloth and pulled out a blue-tinged, stiff hand. He clasped it in his own, kissing the dead fingers. His shoulders began to shake as his tears flowed.

"We met during a recon report to Command," Cormac said, voice breaking. "And I knew it was foolish, and reckless, but I had to speak to her after the meeting was over. To learn everything I could about her." He kissed Sofie's hand again, closing his eyes. "I should have gone back for her that night."

Tharion, who'd been poring over the coroner's files on Sofie at the desk by the far wall, said gently, "I'm sorry if I gave you false hope."

"It kept her alive in my heart a little longer," Cormac said, swallowing back his tears. He pressed her stiff hand against his brow. "My Sofie."

Ruhn squeezed his shoulder.

Tharion asked carefully, "Do you know what this means, Cormac?" He rattled off a series of numbers and letters.

Cormac lifted his head. "No."

Tharion held up a photo. "They were carved on her upper biceps. The coroner thinks she did it while she drowned, with some sort of pin or knife she might have had hidden on her."

Cormac shot to his feet, and Bryce stepped into Hunt's awaiting arms as the Fae Prince folded back the sheet. Nothing on the right arm he'd held, but the left—

The assortment of numbers and letters had been carved roughly an inch below her shoulder, left unhealed. Cut deep.

"Did she know someone was racing to save her?" Hunt asked.

Cormac shook his head. "I have no idea."

"How did the mer know to pick her up?"

"She could have signaled them with her light," Cormac mused. "Or maybe they saw Emile's, like they did with Bryce's. It lit up the whole sea taking down those Omegas. It must have signaled them somehow."

Bryce made a note to ask Commander Sendes. She said to Hunt, "Do those numbers and letters mean anything to you?"

"No." He stroked his thumb over Bryce's hand, as if reassuring himself that she stood there, and wasn't the one on that table.

Cormac covered Sofie with the sheet again. "Everything Sofie did, it was for a reason. You remind me of her in some ways."

Ruhn said, "I'll put Declan on the hunt as soon as we're home."

"What about the Ophion rebels and Pippa?" Bryce asked. "And the Hind?"

Hunt said, "We're everyone's enemy now."

Cormac nodded. "We can only meet the challenge. But knowing for sure that Sofie is gone . . . I must redouble my efforts to find Emile."

"Pippa seemed to know where he was lying low," Tharion said. "No idea if that's the safe place that Danika mentioned, though."

Cormac's eyes flashed. "I'm not letting him fall into your queen's hands. Or Ophion's control."

"You ready to be a single dad?" Bryce drawled. "You're just going to take the kid in and what . . . bring him to Avallen? That'll be a *really* great place for him."

Cormac stiffened. "I hadn't planned that far. Are you suggesting I leave that child alone in the world?"

Bryce shrugged, studying her nails. Felt Hunt looking at her closely. "So do we warn our families?" Gods, if the Hind had already headed to her mom's house—

"The Hind won't go after them," Cormac consoled her. Then amended, "Not yet. She'll want you in her clutches first, so she can breathe in your suffering while you know she's hunting them down."

"So we go home and pretend nothing happened?" Ruhn asked. "What's to stop the Hind from arresting us when we get back?"

"Do you think we could get away with convincing the Asteri that we were at the rebel base to *stop* Pippa and Ophion?" Bryce asked.

Hunt shrugged. "I blasted the shit out of that base, so the evidence is in our favor. Especially if Pippa is now hunting us."

"The Hind won't buy that," Cormac challenged.

But Bryce said, smiling faintly, "Master of spinning bullshit, remember?"

He didn't smile back. Just looked at Sofie, dead and gone before him.

So Bryce touched the prince's hand. "We'll make them all pay."

The star on her chest glowed in promise.

The *Depth Charger* glided between the darkest canyons of the seafloor. In the glass-domed command center, Tharion hung back by the arching doorway into the bustling hall beyond and marveled at the array of tech and magic, the uniformed mer operating all of it.

Sendes lingered at his side, approval on her face as she monitored the team keeping the ship operational.

"How long have you guys had these ships?" Tharion asked, his first words in the minutes since Sendes had invited him down here, where only high-ranking mer officials were allowed. He supposed that being the River Queen's Captain of Intelligence granted him access, but . . . he'd had no idea any of this existed. His title was a joke.

"Around two decades," Sendes said, straightening the lapel of her uniform. "They took twice that to conceptualize and build, though."

"They must have cost a fortune."

"The ocean deeps are full of priceless resources. Our queen exploited them cleverly to fund this project."

"Why?"

She faced him fully. She had a wonderfully curvy body, he'd noticed. With the sort of ass he'd like to sink his teeth into. But . . . the River Queen's cold face rippled through his mind, and Tharion turned to the windows behind the commander.

Beyond the wall of glass, a bioluminescent cloud—some sort of jellyfish—bobbed by. Suitably unsexy.

Sendes asked, "Why does your queen involve herself with the rebels?"

"She's not involving herself with them. I think she merely

wants something that *they* want." Or used to want, if Pippa was to be believed—though after they'd blown the suit to pieces, maybe Ophion would be back on the hunt for the kid. "I don't think her motivations for wanting it are necessarily to help people, though." He winced as he said it. Too bold, too reckless—

Sendes huffed a laugh. "Your opinion is safe here, don't worry. The Ocean Queen is aware that her sister in the Blue River is . . . moody."

Tharion blew out a breath. "Yeah." He took in the control room again. "So all this . . . the ships, the rescuing of rebels . . . Is it because the Ocean Queen wants to overthrow the Asteri?"

"I'm not close enough to her to know whether that's her true motive, but these ships have indeed aided the rebels. So I'd say yes."

"And she intends to make herself ruler?" Tharion asked carefully.

Sendes blinked. "Why would she ever do that?"

"Why not? That's what the River Queen would do."

Sendes stilled, completely earnest as she said, "The Ocean Queen would not set herself up as a replacement for the Asteri. She remembers a time before the Asteri. When leaders were fairly elected. That is what she wishes to achieve once more."

The dark ocean passed beyond the glass. Tharion couldn't suppress his bitter laugh. "And you believe her?"

Sendes gave him a pitying look. "I'm sorry that the River Queen has abused your trust so much that you don't."

"I'm sorry that you're naïve enough to believe everything your queen says," he countered.

Sendes gave him that pitying look again, and Tharion tensed. He changed the subject, though. "What are the odds that either you guys or Cormac will release Sofie's body to me?"

Her brows lifted. "Why do you want it?"

"My queen wants it. I don't get to ask questions."

Sendes frowned. "What use could she have with a thunderbird's corpse?"

He doubted Cormac would appreciate Sofie being referred to as a *corpse,* but he said, "Again, no idea."

Sendes fell silent. "Does . . . does your queen have any necromancers in her employ?"

Tharion started. "What? No." The only one he knew was hundreds of miles away, and she sure as shit wasn't going to help out the River Queen. "Why?"

"It's the only reason I can think of to go to such lengths to retrieve a thunderbird's body. To reanimate it."

Cold horror sluiced through him. "A weapon without a conscience or soul."

Sendes nodded gravely. "But what does she need it for?"

He opened his mouth, but shut it. Speculating on his queen's motives in front of a stranger, even a friendly one, would be foolish. So he shrugged. "Guess we'll find out."

Sendes saw right through him, though. "We have no claim on the body, but Prince Cormac, as her lover and a member of Ophion, does. You'll have to take it up with him."

Tharion knew precisely how that would end. With a giant, burning *NO*. So, short of becoming a body snatcher—not high on his list of life goals—he wasn't delivering the goods. "Time to begin the spin cycle," Tharion murmured, more to himself than to Sendes. He'd have to either lie about ever finding Sofie's body or lie about why he couldn't steal it. Fuck.

"You could be more, you know," Sendes said, seeming to read the dread on his face. "At a place like this. We don't need to lie and scheme here."

"I'm content where I am," Tharion said quickly. His queen would never let him leave anyway.

But Sendes inclined her head knowingly—sadly. "You ever need anything, Captain Ketos, we're here for you."

The kindness stunned him enough that he had no reply.

Sendes was called over by one of the deck officers, and Tharion observed the mer at the controls. Serious, but . . . smiling. No tension, no walking on eggshells.

He glanced at the clock. He should go back to the sleeping quarters Sendes had arranged for them. Check in with the others.

Yet once he did, he'd sleep. And when he woke, he'd return to Lunathion.

To the Blue Court.

It was getting harder to ignore the part of him that didn't want to go home at all.

Ruhn slept miles beneath the surface, a fitful sort of slumber from which he rose frequently to ensure his companions were all piled into the small room with him on the cots and bunk beds. Cormac had opted to remain in the morgue with Sofie, wanting to mourn in private, to say all the prayers to Cthona and Luna that his lover was owed.

Tharion dozed on the bottom bunk across from Ruhn's, sprawled across the top of the sheets. He'd wandered off after dinner to explore the ship, and returned hours later, quiet. He hadn't said anything about what he'd seen other than *It's mer-only*.

So Ruhn had sat with the lovebirds, Bryce nestled between Hunt's legs as they ate dinner on the floor of the room, the sea drifting by their window. They'd reach the mouth of the Istros at dawn, and Tharion's people would be waiting there to transport them upriver to Lunathion.

What would happen then . . . Ruhn could only pray it'd work out in their favor. That Bryce could play their cards well enough to avoid their doom.

Night?

Day's voice floated into his mind, faint and—worried.

He let his mind relax, let himself find that bridge, the two couches. She already sat on hers, burning away. "Hey."

"Are you all right?"

"Worried about me, huh?"

She didn't laugh. "I heard about an attack on the rebel base on Ydra. That people were killed, and the shipment of ammo and the suit destroyed. I . . . thought you might have been among the ones lost."

He surveyed her.

"Where are you now?" she asked.

He let her change the subject. "Somewhere safe." He couldn't say more. "I watched Pippa Spetsos and the Ophion rebels kill innocent Vanir in cold blood today. You want to tell me what the fuck that's about?"

She stiffened. "Why did she kill them?"

"Does it matter?"

She considered. "No. Not if the victims were innocent. Pippa did it herself?"

"A group of soldiers under her command did."

Her flame guttered to hottest blue. "She's a fanatic. Dedicated to the rebel cause, yes—but to her own cause most of all."

"She was a friend of Agent Cypress, apparently."

"She was no friend to Sofie. Or anyone." Her voice had gone cold. Like she was angry enough that she forgot to use Sofie's code name.

"Sofie's dead, by the way."

Day started. "You're sure of this?"

"Yes. She drowned."

"She . . ." Day's legs curled beneath her. "She was a brave agent. Far better and braver than Ophion deserved." Genuine sorrow laced Day's words.

"You liked her."

"She went into the Kavalla death camp to save her brother. Did everything the Ophion commanders asked her just so she could get scraps of information about him. If Pippa serves only herself, then Sofie was her opposite: all the work she did was for others. But yes. I did like her. I admired her courage. Her loyalty. She was a kindred spirit in many ways."

Ruhn slumped against the back of his couch. "So, what—you hate Pippa and Ophion, too? If everyone hates her and the group, why the fuck do you bother working with them?"

"Do you see anyone else leading the cause? Has anyone else stepped up to the line?"

No. No one else would dare.

Day said, "They're the only ones in recent memory to have ever mustered such a force. Only Shahar and General Hunt Athalar ever did anything close, and they were decimated in one battle."

And Athalar had suffered for centuries afterward.

Day went on, "To be free of the Asteri, there are things that we all must do that will leave a mark on our souls. It's the cost, so that our children and their children won't ever need to pay it. So they'll know a world of freedom and plenty."

The words of a dreamer. A glimpse beneath that hard-ass facade.

So Ruhn said, the first time he'd said it aloud, "I'm not going to have children."

"Why?"

"I can't."

She angled her head. "You're infertile?"

He shrugged. "Maybe. I don't know. The Oracle told me when I was a kid that I was to be the last of my bloodline. So either I die before I can sire a child, or . . . I'm shooting blanks."

"Does it bother you?"

"I'd prefer not to be dead before my time, so if her words just mean that I'm not going to be a father . . . I don't know. It doesn't change a lick of who I am, but I still try not to think about it. No one in my life knows, either. And considering the father I have . . . maybe it's good that I won't be one. I wouldn't know the first thing about how to be a decent dad."

"That doesn't seem true."

He snorted. "Well, anyway, that was my stupid way of saying that while I might not be having kids, I . . . I get what you're saying. I have people in my life who will, and for their kids, their families . . . I'll do whatever I have to."

But she was having none of his deflecting. "You are kind, and caring. And seem to love those around you. I can't think of anything else needed to be a father."

"How about growing the Hel up and not partying so much?"

She laughed. "All right. Maybe that."

He smiled slightly. Faint, distant stars glowed in the darkness around them.

She said, "You seem unsettled."

"I saw a bunch of fucked-up shit today. I was having a hard time sleeping before you knocked."

"Knocked?"

"Whatever you want to call it. Summoned me."

"Shall I tell you a story to help you sleep?" Her voice was wry.

"Yeah." He'd call her bluff.

But she only said, "All right."

He blinked. "Really?"

"Why not?" She motioned for him to lie down. So Ruhn did, closing his eyes.

Then, to his shock, she came and sat beside him. Brushed a burning hand through his hair. Warm and gentle—tentative.

She began, "Once upon a time, before Luna hunted the heavens and Solas warmed Cthona's body, before Ogenas blanketed Midgard with water and Urd twined our fates together, there lived a young witch in a cottage deep in the woods. She was beautiful, and kind, and beloved by her mother. Her mother had done her best to raise her, with her only companions being the denizens of the forest itself: birds and beasts and the babbling brooks . . ."

Her voice, lovely and fair and steady, flowed through him like music. Her hand brushed through his hair again and he reined in his purr.

"She grew older, strong and proud. But a wandering prince passed by her clearing one day when her mother was gone, beheld her beauty, and wanted her desperately to be his bride."

"I thought this was supposed to be a comforting story," Ruhn muttered.

She laughed softly, tugging on a strand of his hair. "Listen."

Ruhn figured to Hel with it and shifted, laying his head on her lap. The fire did not burn him, and the thigh beneath was firm with muscle, yet supple. And that scent . . .

Day went on, "She had no interest in princes, or in ruling a kingdom, or in any of the jewels he offered. What she wanted was a true heart to love her, to run wild with her through the forest. But the prince would not be denied. He chased her through the wood, his hounds following."

Ruhn's body relaxed, limb by limb. He breathed in her scent, her voice, her warmth.

"As she ran, she pleaded with the forest she loved so dearly to help her. So it did. First, it transformed her into a deer, so she might be as swift as the wind. But his hounds outraced her, closing in swiftly. Then the forest turned her into a fish, and she fled down one of the mountain streams. But he built a weir at its base to trap her. So she became a bird, a hawk, and soared for the skies. But the prince was a skilled archer, and he fired one of his iron-tipped arrows."

Ruhn drifted, quiet and calm. When was the last time anyone had told him a story to lull him to sleep?

"It struck her breast, and where her blood fell, olive trees sprouted. As her body hit the earth, the forest transformed her one last time . . ."

Ruhn woke, still on the mind-bridge. Day lay on the couch across from him, asleep as well, her body still veiled with flame.

He stood, crossing the distance to her.

A princess of fire, sleeping, waiting for a knight to awaken her. He knew that story. It tugged at the back of his mind. A sleeping warrior-princess surrounded by a ring of fire, damned to lie there until a warrior brave enough to face the flames could cross them.

Day turned over, and through the flame, he glimpsed a hint of long hair draped over the arm of the couch—

He backed away a step. But somehow she heard, and shot upright. Flame erupted around her as Ruhn retreated to his own couch. "What were you doing?"

Ruhn shook his head. "I . . . I wanted to know how the story ended. I fell asleep as the witch was pierced with an arrow."

Day jumped up from her couch, walking around it—putting it between them. Like he'd crossed some major line.

But she said, "The forest turned the witch into a monster before she hit the earth. A beast of claws and fangs and bloodlust. She ripped the prince and hounds who pursued her into shreds."

"And that's it?" Ruhn demanded.

"That's it," Day said, and walked into the darkness, leaving only embers drifting behind.

PART III

THE PIT

48

Ruhn paced in front of Bryce's TV, his phone at his ear. The tattoos on his forearms shifted as he clenched the phone tight. But his voice was calm, heavy, as he said, "All right, thanks for looking, Dec."

Bryce watched Ruhn's face as her brother hung up, and knew exactly what he was going to say. "No luck?"

Ruhn slumped back against her couch cushions. "No. What we saw on Sofie's arm doesn't come up anywhere."

Bryce nestled into Hunt on the other end of the couch while the angel talked to Isaiah on the phone. Upon arriving back in Lunathion courtesy of a few Blue Court wave skimmers, Tharion had gone Beneath to see his queen. It was unlikely that the River Queen would know what the numbers and letters carved onto Sofie's biceps meant, but it was worth a shot.

Cormac had found thirty messages from his father waiting for him, asking after his whereabouts, so he'd gone off to the Autumn King's villa to convince the male—and therefore his father—that he'd been accompanying Bryce to Nidaros.

Bryce supposed she should clue her parents in about the official cover story, but she couldn't quite bring herself to do it. She needed to settle—calm her racing mind—a bit first.

Frankly, it was a miracle the Hind and her dreadwolves hadn't been waiting at the apartment. That the news wasn't broadcasting all of their faces with a *REBEL TRAITORS* banner slapped beneath it. But a skim of the news while Ruhn had talked to Dec showed nothing.

So she'd spent the last few minutes trying hard to teleport from the couch to the kitchen.

Nothing. How had she done it during sex? She wasn't due for her lesson with Ruhn and Cormac until tomorrow, but she wanted to show up with *some* idea.

Bryce concentrated on the kitchen stools. *I am here. I want to go there.* Her magic didn't so much as budge. *Two points in space. I'm folding a piece of paper, joining them. My power is the pencil that punctures through the paper, linking them—*

Hunt said, "Yeah. Ember grilled me, but we're good. We had a nice time." He winked at Bryce, even though the casual gesture didn't quite light his eyes. "All right. I'll see you at the meeting later." Hunt hung up the phone and sighed. "Unless they've got a dagger digging into his back, it seems like Isaiah has no clue about what went down at Ydra. Or that the Hind saw any of us."

"What game is she playing?" Ruhn said, toying with his lip ring. "You really think Isaiah wasn't playing it cool to lure you to the Comitium later?"

"If they wanted to arrest us, they'd have been waiting for us," Hunt said. "The Hind is keeping this to herself."

"But why?" Bryce asked, frowning deeply. "To mess with our minds?"

"Honestly?" Hunt said. "That's a distinct possibility. But if you ask me, I think she knows we're . . . up to something. I think she wants to see what we do next."

Bryce considered. "We've been so focused on Emile and Ophion and the demons that we've forgotten one key thing: Sofie died knowing vital intel. The Hind knew that—was afraid enough of it that she killed her to make sure the intel died with Sofie. And if it didn't take much for Tharion to piece together that Sofie and Danika knew each other and come to us, I bet the Hind has figured that out, too. She has hackers who could have found the same emails between them."

Hunt's wing brushed her shoulder, curving around her. "But how does it even tie to Danika? Sofie didn't get the intel until two years after Danika died."

"No idea," Bryce said, leaning her head against Hunt's shoulder. A casual, steadying sort of intimacy.

The sex on the ship had been life-altering. Soul-altering. Just . . . altering. She couldn't wait to have him again.

But she cleared the thought from her head as Ruhn asked, "Any chance this somehow ties into Danika researching that Fendyr lineage?" Her brother rubbed his temples. "Though I don't see how anything about that would be war-changing intel worth killing to hide."

"Me neither," Bryce said, sighing. She'd slept last night curled beside Hunt in their bunk, limbs and wings and breath mingling, but she was still exhausted. From the shadows under Hunt's eyes, she knew the same weariness weighed on him.

A knock sounded on her door, and Ruhn rose to get it. Hunt's hand tangled in her hair, and he tugged on the strands, getting Bryce to look up at him. He kissed her nose, her chin, her mouth.

"I might be tired," he said, as if he'd sensed her thoughts, "but I'm ready for round two when you are."

Her blood heated. "Good," she murmured back. "I'd hate for you to be unable to keep up in your old age."

They were interrupted by Ruhn standing over them. "Sorry to break up the lovefest, but the Helhound's outside."

Baxian gave them no time to prepare as he burst in after Ruhn, black wings splaying slightly. "How the fuck did you call that ship?"

"What are you doing here?" Hunt asked quietly.

Baxian blinked. "Making sure you're all still in one piece."

"Why?" Ruhn asked.

"Because I want in." Baxian helped himself to a stool at the counter.

Bryce coughed, but said innocently, "On what?"

The Helhound threw her a dry look. "On whatever it was that had you all going to meet with Ophion, then blasting their shit to Hel."

Bryce said smoothly, "We thought to cut off Ophion before they could ruin Valbara's peace."

Baxian snorted. "Yeah, sure. Without backup, without alerting anyone."

"There are rebel sympathizers in the 33rd," Hunt said firmly. "We couldn't risk tipping them off."

"I know," Baxian replied with equal cool. "I'm one of them."

Bryce stared at the shifter and said as calmly as she could, "You realize we could go right to Celestina with this. You'd be crucified before nightfall."

"I want you to tell me what's going on," Baxian countered.

"I already told you. And you just royally fucked yourself over," Bryce said.

"If they start asking questions about how you know I'm a sympathizer, you think anyone's going to buy your bullshit about going there to save Valbara from the big bad human rebels? Especially when you lied to Celestina about going to your parents' house?" Baxian laughed. Hunt had gone so still that Bryce knew he was a breath away from killing the male, even though no lightning zapped around him. "The Asteri will let the Hind start on you right away, and we'll see how long those lies hold up under her ministrations."

"Why isn't the Hind here yet?" Bryce asked. She'd confirm nothing.

"Not her style," Baxian said. "She wants to give you enough rope to hang yourself."

"And Ydra wasn't enough?" Ruhn blurted.

Bryce glared at him. Her brother ignored it, his lethal attention on Baxian.

"If I were to guess, I'd say that she thinks you'll lead her toward whatever it is she wants."

Ruhn growled, "What do *you* want?"

Baxian leaned back against the counter. "I told you: I want in."

"No," Hunt said.

"Did I not warn your asses yesterday?" Baxian said. "Did I not back you up when Sabine came raging in here? Have I said anything to anyone about it since then?"

"The Hind plays games that span years," Hunt countered with soft menace. "Who knows what you're planning with her? But we're not rebels anyway, so there's nothing for you to join."

Baxian laughed—without joy, without any sort of amusement—and hopped off the stool. Aimed right for the front door. "When you fools want actual answers, come find me." The door slammed behind him.

In the silence that fell in his wake, Bryce closed her eyes.

"So . . . we play casual," Ruhn said. "Figure out how to outsmart the Hind."

Hunt grunted, not sounding convinced. That made two of them.

A buzz sounded, and Bryce opened her eyes to see Ruhn scanning his phone. "Flynn needs me back at the house. Call me if you hear anything."

"Be careful," Hunt warned him, but her brother just patted the hilt of the Starsword before striding out. As if the blade would do anything against the Hind.

Alone in their apartment, truly alone at last, Bryce waggled her brows at Hunt. "Want to take our minds off everything with a little tumble in the sheets?"

Hunt chuckled, leaning to brush a kiss on her mouth. He paused millimeters from her lips, close enough that she could feel his smile as he said, "How about you tell me what the fuck you know about Emile?"

Bryce pulled back. "Nothing."

His eyes blazed. "Oh? Spetsos practically blabbed it, didn't she? With her talk about snakes." Lightning shimmered along his wings. "Are you fucking insane? Sending that kid to the Viper Queen?"

49

How'd it go?"

Ruhn stood before Flynn and Dec, his friends sitting on the sectional with too-innocent smiles. Ithan sat on Dec's other side—and his wary face tipped Ruhn off.

"I'm wondering if I should ask you three the same thing," Ruhn said, arching a brow.

"Well, you're alive, and not captured," Dec said, tucking his hands behind his head and leaning back against the couch. "I'm assuming it went . . . well?"

"Let's leave it at that," Ruhn said. He'd fill them in later. When he was a little less exhausted and a little less worried about those innocent expressions.

"Good, great, fantastic," Flynn said, leaping to his feet. "So, you know how you're always saying that it's pretty sexist that we don't have any female roommates . . ."

"I've never said tha—"

Flynn gestured to the foyer behind him. "Well, here you go."

Ruhn blinked as three fire sprites zoomed in, landing on Flynn's broad shoulders. A full-bodied one cuddled up against his neck, smiling.

"Meet the triplets," Flynn said. "Rithi, Sasa, and Malana."

The taller of the slender ones—Sasa—batted her eyelashes at Ruhn. "Prince."

"Our insurance rates will go sky-high," Ruhn said to Declan, appealing to the slightly-less-insane of his roommates.

"When the fuck did you become a grown-up?" Flynn barked.

Ithan jerked his chin toward the doorway again. "Wait to have your meltdown until after you meet the fourth new roommate."

A short, curvy female walked in, her wavy black hair nearly down to her waist. Most of her tan skin was hidden by the plaid blanket wrapped around her naked body. But her eyes—burning Solas. They were bloodred. Glowing like embers.

"Ariadne, meet Ruhn," Flynn crooned. "Ruhn, meet Ariadne."

She held Ruhn's stare, and he stilled as he caught a glimmer of something molten course beneath the skin of her forearm, making her flesh look like . . . scales.

Ruhn whirled on Dec and Flynn. "I was gone for a day! Sunrise to sunrise! And I come back to *a dragon*? Where did she come from?"

Dec and Flynn, the three sprites with them, pointed to Ithan.

The wolf winced.

Ruhn glanced back at the dragon, at the hand clutching the blanket around her. The slight hint of the brand on her wrist. He studied the sprites.

"Please tell me they're at least here legally," Ruhn said quietly.

"Nope," Flynn said cheerfully.

Hunt had two options: start shouting or start laughing. He hadn't decided which one he wanted to do as they walked down a narrow hallway of the most lethal warehouse in the Meat Market, aiming for the door at the far end. The blank-faced Fae guards at the door didn't so much as blink. If they knew who Bryce was to them, they gave no sign.

"How'd you figure it out?" Bryce's brows bunched. She hadn't denied it on the flight over here. That she'd somehow gotten Emile to the Viper Queen. And Hunt had been too fucking pissed to ask any questions.

So fucking pissed that it had driven away any lingering lust from last night.

Hunt said under his breath, "I told you. You're not as slick as you think. The way you got so tense with Pippa talking about snakes was a dead giveaway." He shook his head. "It wasn't Pippa killing those people to track Emile, was it?"

Bryce winced. "No. It was the Viper Queen's henchmen. Well, henchwoman. She sent one of her human lackeys—some merc—to hunt him down. Hence the female human scent."

"And you were fine with this? Not simply killing those people, but framing Pippa?" Granted, Pippa was awful, but . . . Something crumpled in his chest.

Was this any different from his time with Shahar? Falling for a beautiful, powerful female—only to have her hide her innermost thoughts—

"No," Bryce said, paling. She halted ten feet from the guards. Touched Hunt's arm. "I wasn't fine with that part at all." Her throat bobbed. "I told her to find him by any means necessary. I didn't realize it'd entail . . . that."

"That was a stupid fucking thing to do," Hunt snarled, and immediately hated himself for the bruised look that came into her eyes. But he continued toward the door, pulling out of her grip.

The guards wordlessly let them enter the lushly appointed apartment. Definitely a far cry from her ramshackle office levels below. A foyer of carved wood flowed ahead, the crimson rug leading toward a large sitting room with a massive, floor-to-ceiling interior window overlooking the Viper Queen's notorious fighting pit.

Bryce murmured coldly as they aimed for the sitting room, "I'm not letting this poor kid fall into anyone's hands. Even Cormac's."

"So that night we came here with Juniper and Fury—was Emile here already?"

"The Viper Queen was supposed to have apprehended him by that point. But then Tharion told us about the dead selkie, and it was clear she hadn't yet found him. So I came here to see what the Hel had happened, and to inform her that leaving a trail of bodies . . . that was *not* what I had intended. When I walked past the guards after we separated to search, I might have muttered a few questions for them to convey to their queen. And they might have had one of their undercover guards come up to me at the butcher where I bought the meat for Syrinx and tell me that the kid was still at large, and they'd last seen him near the Black Dock. Which made me doubt everything I'd assumed about him coming here, and I knew that I just . . . I needed to go to the Bone Quarter to make sure he *wasn't* there. While the Viper Queen kept searching. But apparently either she or her henchwoman ignored my demand to stop the killing, and added a few more to the list before they grabbed Emile."

"So coming here that night was a big waste of time?"

She shook her head. "No. I also needed everyone to think I was looking for Emile, and that we'd cleared this space, so if the Viper Queen did manage to get him, no one would come here again. And I needed you and Fury with me so that the Viper Queen would remember who would come fuck her up if she hurt the kid in the process."

That queen now stood before them, a slim female in a neon-green silk jumpsuit beside a large, plush couch. Her glossy black bob reflected the golden flames from the fireplace to her right. And seated on the couch before her, small and thin and wide-eyed, was a boy.

"Come to collect your package or make more threats about Athalar cooking me alive?" the Viper Queen asked, puffing on a cigarette between her purple-painted lips.

"Nice sneakers" was all Bryce said, gesturing to the snake shifter's white-and-gold high-tops. But Bryce offered Emile a gentle smile. "Hey, Emile. I'm Bryce."

The boy said nothing. Rather, he looked up at the Viper Queen, who drawled, "Red's the one who got you here. Ignore the angel. He's all bark, no bite."

"Oh, he likes to bite," Bryce murmured, but Hunt was in no mood to laugh. Or even smile. He said to the Viper Queen, power sparking in his veins, "Don't think for one moment that I'll ever forget how you screwed me over that night with Micah. Vik's suffering and Justinian's death are on you."

The queen had the audacity to look down at herself, as if searching for guilt.

But before Hunt could contemplate roasting her, Emile squeaked, "Hi."

He was just a kid, alone and afraid. The thought doused any lightning in Hunt's veins.

Bryce nodded at the Viper Queen. "I'd like a moment with Emile, please." It was a command. From a princess to another ruler.

The Viper Queen's slitted pupils widened—with amusement or predatory intent, Hunt didn't know. But she said, "Emile, holler if you need anything." She sauntered down an ornate, wood-paneled hallway and vanished through a door.

Bryce plopped onto the couch beside Emile and said, "So what's up?" The boy—and Hunt—blinked at her.

Emile said quietly, "My sister's dead, isn't she?"

Bryce's face softened, and Hunt said, "Yeah. She is. We're so sorry."

Emile gazed at his pale, bony hands. "The Vipe said you were looking, but . . . I knew." Hunt scanned the boy for any hint of that thunderbird gift. Any hint of a magic able to harvest and transform power to his will.

Bryce put a hand on Emile's shoulder. "Your sister was a badass. A brave, brilliant badass."

Emile offered a wobbly smile. Gods, the boy was scrawny. Way too thin for his lanky frame. If this was how thin he remained after a few weeks outside the death camp's barbed-wire fences . . . This boy had seen and endured things that no child—no person—should face.

Shame flooded Hunt, and he sat down beside Bryce.

No wonder she'd worked alone to arrange this—none of the rest of them had really stopped to think about the kid himself. Just his power, and what it might mean if the wrong person got hold of it.

Hunt tried to catch her eye, to show her that he understood, and he didn't hold any of this against her, but she kept her focus on the boy.

Bryce said quietly, "I lost a sister, too. Two years ago. It was hard, and you never stop feeling the loss, but . . . you learn to live with it. I'm not going to tell you time heals all wounds, because for some people it doesn't." Hunt's heart strained at the pain in her voice, even now. "But I get it. What you're feeling."

Emile said nothing. Hunt suppressed the urge to gather both of them in his arms and hug them tightly.

"And look," Bryce went on, "no matter what the Viper Queen says to you, don't take her threats too seriously. She's a psycho, but she's not a kid killer."

"Real reassuring," Hunt muttered.

Bryce scowled at him. "It's true."

But Hunt knew why the Viper Queen wouldn't have harmed the kid. He turned to the fighting pit beyond the window. It was dim and quiet now, too early in the day for the fights that drew hundreds—and made millions—for the snake shifter.

Alarm flared. Hunt blurted, "You didn't sign any contracts with her, right?"

"Why would she want me to sign anything?" Emile said, toeing the carpet.

Hunt said quietly, "Thunderbirds are insanely rare. A lot of people would want that power." He extended a hand toward Emile, and lightning wreathed his fingers, wending between them. "I'm not a thunderbird," Hunt said, "but I've got a similar gift. Made me, ah . . . valuable." He tapped the branded-out slave's mark on his wrist. "Not in any way that counts, deep down, but it made certain people willing to do a lot of bad things to attain me." The Viper Queen would kill—had killed—to own that power.

Emile's eyes widened at the lightning. Like he was seeing Hunt for the first time. "Sofie said something like that about her power once. That it didn't change who she was inside."

Hunt melted a bit at the trust in the kid's face. "It didn't. And your power doesn't, either."

Emile glanced between them. Then down the hall. "What power?"

Hunt slowly, slowly turned to Bryce. Her face revealed nothing. "Your . . . thunderbird power? The power that downed those Omega-boats?"

The kid's face shuttered. "That was Sofie."

Bryce lifted her chin in challenge. "Emile doesn't have any powers, Hunt."

Hunt looked like she'd dumped a bucket of ice water on him.

"What do you mean?" he asked, voice low. He didn't wait for her to reply before he pushed, "How do *you* know, Bryce?"

"I didn't know for sure," Bryce said. The small, scared boy now cringed away from the angel. She continued, "But I figured it was a good possibility. The only thing Vanir care about is power. The only way to get them to care about a human boy was to spin a story about him having powers like Sofie's. The only way to make sure he got to safety was to craft a lie about him being valuable. I had a feeling Sofie knew that all too well." She added with a soft smile to the boy, "Emile was—*is* valuable. To Sofie. To his family. As all loved ones are."

Hunt blinked. Blinked again. Anger—and fear—warred in his eyes. He whispered, "Does the Viper Queen know this?"

Bryce didn't hide her disdain. "She never asked." Bryce had been sure to word the bargain between them very carefully, so Emile could walk out of here whenever he wished.

Hunt's lightning writhed across his brow. "Any protection she's offering this kid will vanish the moment she knows." His gaze shifted to Emile, who watched the lightning not in fear, but with sorrow. The lightning immediately vanished. Hunt rubbed his face. Then said to Bryce, "You did all of this on a guess?"

"Sofie was part-human. Like me." Cormac himself had said they were alike. She explained as gently as she could, "You've never spent a moment of your life as a human, Hunt. You always had value to Vanir. You just said so yourself."

His wings rustled. "And what was the Vipe's asking price?"

"She'd retrieve Emile, hold him here—in comfort and safety—until I came to pick him up. And in return, I'd owe her a favor."

"That was reckless," he said through his teeth.

"It's not like I have piles of gold lying around." This wasn't the time or place for this fight. "You can have your alphahole fit later," she seethed.

"Fine," Hunt shot back. He leaned forward to address the boy, that thunderous expression easing. "Sorry, Emile. I'm glad you're safe, however insanely Bryce acted to make that happen. You game to answer a few questions?"

Emile nodded shallowly. Bryce braced herself.

Hunt gave Bryce another dirty look before he said, "How did you keep the Viper Queen from knowing you don't have any power?"

Emile shrugged. "When she talked about fights and stuff, I didn't answer. I think she thought I was scared."

"Good call," Bryce said. But Hunt cut in, "Were you originally heading to this city to find some sort of meeting place that you and your sister had agreed on beforehand?"

Emile nodded again. "We were supposed to meet here, actually."

Hunt murmured, "A place *where the weary souls find relief* . . ."

Bryce explained, "The Meat Market is drug central. I figured if Danika had suggested it as a hiding spot, then she might have thought the Viper Queen would be . . . amenable to helping them out. Turns out Danika was right."

Emile added, "The Vipe's agent picked me up before I could make it to the city proper. She said it wasn't safe anywhere but with them."

"It wasn't," Bryce said, smiling gently, "but now you're safe with us."

Well, at least they could agree on that. Hunt asked, "Did your sister ever mention anything secret about the Asteri? Anything super valuable to the rebels?"

Emile considered, brow scrunching. "No."

Bryce blew out a heavy breath. It had been a long shot anyway.

Emile wrung his fingers. "But . . . I do recognize that name. Danika. She was the wolf, right?"

Bryce went still. "You knew Danika?"

Emile shook his head. "No, but Sofie told me about her the night we separated. The blond wolf, who died a couple years ago. With the purple and pink streaks in her hair."

50

Bryce struggled to breathe. "How did Danika and Sofie know each other?"

"Danika found Sofie using her Vanir powers," Emile said. "She could smell Sofie's gift, or something. She needed Sofie to do something for her—Danika couldn't do it because she was too recognizable. But Sofie . . ." Emile toed the carpet. "She wasn't . . ."

Bryce cut in, "Sofie was a human. Or passed as one. She'd be ignored by most. What did Danika need her to do?"

Emile shook his head. "I don't know. I wasn't able to talk to Sofie for very long when we were in Kavalla."

Hunt's wide eyes shone with surprise, his anger at her seemingly forgotten for the moment. She pulled a slip of paper from her pocket. "These letters and numbers were found on your sister's body. Any idea what they mean?"

Emile bounced his knee. "No."

Damn it. Bryce twisted her mouth to the side.

Head bowed, Emile whispered, "I'm sorry I don't know anything else."

Hunt cleared his throat. Reached in front of Bryce to clasp the boy's shoulder. "You did good, kid. Really good. We owe you."

Emile offered Hunt a wobbly smile.

Yet Bryce's mind spun. Danika had needed Sofie to find something *big.* And though it had taken her years after Danika had died, Sofie had finally found it. And it had indeed been big enough that the Hind had killed her, rather than risking Sofie spreading it . . .

Hunt said, drawing her from her thoughts, "Bryce."

Her mate nodded pointedly to the window a few feet away.

"Give us a minute," she said to Emile with a smile, and walked over to the window, Hunt trailing her.

Hunt whisper-hissed, "What do we do with him now? We can't leave him here. It's only a matter of time until the Viper Queen figures out that he doesn't have powers. And we can't bring him with us. Pippa might very well come sniffing now that we destroyed that suit and they really do need a thunderbird's power—"

"Pippa Spetsos is a bad woman," Emile said from the couch, paling. Hunt had the good sense to look embarrassed that his little fit had been overheard. "Sofie warned me about her. After I got on the boat, she wanted to question me . . . I ran the moment no one was looking. But she and her Lightfall unit tracked me—all the way to the marshes. I hid in the reeds and was able to shake them there."

"Smart." Bryce pulled out her phone. "And we know all about Pippa, don't worry. She won't get anywhere near you." She glared at Hunt. "You really think I didn't plan this out?"

Hunt crossed his arms, brows high, but Bryce was already dialing. "Hey, Fury. Yeah, we're here. Bring the car around."

"You brought Axtar into this?"

"She's one of the few people I trust to escort him to his new home."

Fear flooded Emile's eyes. Bryce walked back to the couch and ruffled his hair. "You'll be safe there. I promise." She gave Hunt a warning look over her shoulder. She wasn't going to reveal more until they'd left. But she said to Emile, "Go use the bathroom. You're in for a long ride."

Hunt was still sorting through his racing feelings when they walked out of the Meat Market, Emile hidden beneath the shadows of a hooded sweatshirt. As promised, the Viper Queen had let them leave, no questions asked.

She'd only smiled at Bryce. Hunt suspected, with a sinking feeling, that she already knew Emile had no powers. That she'd taken in the kid because, despite his potential, there was one thing that might be more valuable to her one day: Bryce owing her a favor.

Hel yeah, he was going to have his little alphahole fit.

But he tucked away the thoughts when he found Fury Axtar leaning against a sleek black sedan, her arms crossed. Emile stumbled a step. Hunt didn't blame the kid.

Bryce threw her arms around her friend, saying, "Thank you *so* much."

Fury pulled back and turned to survey Emile as if she were looking at a particularly nasty bug. "Not much meat on him."

Bryce nudged her with an elbow. "So get him some snacks on the road."

"Snacks?" Fury said, but opened one of the rear doors.

"You know," Bryce drawled, "garbage food that provides zero nutrition for our bodies, but *lots* of nutrition for our souls."

How could she be so . . . glib about what she'd done? Any number of people would likely kill her for it. If not Cormac, then the River Queen or Ophion or the Hind—

Fury shook her head, chuckling, but beckoned to the boy. "In you go."

Emile balked.

Fury flashed a feral smile, "You're too short for the front. Airbag safety regulations."

"You just don't want him messing with the radio," Bryce muttered. Fury didn't deny it, and Emile didn't say anything as he climbed into the back seat. He had no bag, no belongings.

Hunt remembered that feeling. After his mother had died, he'd had no traces or reminders or comforts of the child he'd been, the mother who had sung him to sleep.

Nausea churned in his gut. Hunt said to the kid, "Don't let Fury boss you around."

Emile lifted wide, pleading eyes to Hunt. Gods, how had everyone forgotten that he was only a kid? Everyone except Bryce.

Shahar would never have done something like this, risked so much for someone who could do her absolutely no good. But Bryce . . . Hunt couldn't stop himself from stepping closer to her. From brushing his wing against her in a silent apology.

Bryce stepped beyond his reach. Fair enough. He'd been an asshole. She asked Fury, "You've got the address?"

"Yes. We'll be there in eight hours. Seven, if we don't bother with snacks."

"He's a kid. He needs snacks," Hunt cut in.

But Fury ignored him and stalked around the car, sliding into the driver's seat. Two handguns were buckled to her thighs. He had a feeling more were in the glove compartment and trunk. And then there was whatever Vanir power she possessed that made Fury Axtar, well . . . Fury Axtar. "You're lucky I love you, Quinlan. And that Juniper didn't want this kid here for another minute."

Hunt caught the way Bryce's throat bobbed, but she lifted a hand in farewell. Then she approached the still-open back door, where she said to Emile, "Your name isn't Emile Renast anymore, okay?"

Panic sparked in the kid's face. Bryce touched his cheek, as if she couldn't help it. The last of Hunt's anger dissolved entirely.

Bryce was saying, "All the documents will be waiting for you. Birth certificate, adoption papers . . ."

"Adoption?" Emile croaked.

Bryce grinned winningly at the kid. "You're part of the Quinlan-Silago clan now. We're a crazy bunch, but we love each other. Tell Randall to make you chocolate croissants on Sundays."

Hunt had no words. She hadn't only found a place for this lost kid. She'd found him a new family. *Her* family. His throat tightened to the point of pain, his eyes stinging. But Bryce kissed Emile's cheek, shut the door, and thumped the car roof. Fury sped off down the cobblestone street, hooked a sharp left, and was gone.

Slowly, Bryce turned back to him.

"You're sending him to your parents," he said quietly.

Her eyes iced over. "Did I miss the memo where I needed your approval to do so?"

"For Urd's sake, that's not why I was mad."

"I don't care if you're mad," she said, flickering with light. "Just because we're fucking doesn't mean I answer to you."

"Pretty sure it's a little bit more than fucking."

She bristled, and his anger bristled with it. But he remembered where they were—right in front of the Viper Queen's headquarters. Where anyone might see. Or try to start shit.

"I have to go to work," Bryce said, practically biting out each word.

"Fine. So do I."

"Fine." She didn't wait for him before striding off.

Hunt rubbed his eyes and shot skyward. He knew Bryce was well aware that he trailed her from above as she wove through the tangle of streets that made up the Meat Market, banking northward toward the CBD only when she'd crossed Crone Street into the safety of the Old Square.

But she didn't look up. Not once.

"I only have ten minutes before I need to go to the archives," Bryce said to her brother as he ushered her into his house an hour later. "I'm already behind as Hel at work."

Steaming at Hunt, she'd used the long walk to process all that had happened with Emile and the Viper Queen. To pray that Fury didn't scare the living daylights out of the kid before he reached her parents' house in Nidaros. And contemplate whether she'd maybe overreacted a smidgen to Hunt's anger at her not telling him.

Bryce had been just turning down the block to the archives when Ruhn called with his vague request to come over immediately. She'd thumbed in a quick message to her boss about a doctor's appointment running late, and raced right over here.

She dumped her purse beside the front door. "Please start explaining why this was so urgent that you needed me to— Oh."

She'd assumed it had something to do with Ithan, or that maybe Declan had found something. Which was why she'd sprinted from FiRo, in her stupid heels, in the stupid heat, and was now a sweaty mess.

She hadn't expected a beautiful female clad in nothing but a blanket, standing against the foyer wall like some trapped animal. Her crimson eyes narrowed with warning.

Bryce offered a smile to the female against the wall. "Uh, hey. Everything . . . all right?" She hissed to Ruhn over her shoulder, "*Where are her clothes?*"

"*She wouldn't wear them,*" Ruhn hissed back. "Believe me, Dec tried." He pointed to an untouched pile of male clothes by the stairs.

But the female was scanning Bryce from her heels to her head. "You came to see the mystics. You blazed with starlight."

Bryce peered back. It wasn't the female mystic, but . . . she turned to see Ithan, looking guilty, on the couch. With three fire sprites floating around his head.

Her blood turned to acid. A plump sprite sprawled on his knee, beaming at Bryce. The memory of Lehabah burned bright and searing.

"So, Ithan *might* have gotten pissed when he went back to the Astronomer and found out that the female mystic is a wolf," Ruhn was saying, "and he *might* have done something rash and taken something he shouldn't have, and then these morons freed them from the rings . . ."

Bryce whirled to the female against the wall. "You were in one of the rings?"

The red eyes flared again. "Yes."

Bryce asked Ithan, "Why did you go back there?"

"I wanted to be sure about Connor," he said. She didn't miss the tone of accusation—that she hadn't been as concerned as he was. Neither did Ruhn, who tensed at her side.

Bryce swallowed hard. "Is he . . . okay?"

Ithan dragged a hand through his hair. "I don't know. I need to find out."

Bryce nodded gravely, then managed to face the three sprites in the living room. Managed to lift her chin and ask, voice shaking only slightly, "Do you know a sprite named Lehabah?"

"No," said Malana, the full-bodied sprite so similar to Lele that Bryce could barely stand to face her. "What clan is she?"

Bryce inhaled a shuddering breath. The males had hushed. "Lehabah claimed she was a descendant of Queen Ranthia Drahl, Queen of Embers."

One of the slender sprites—Rithi, maybe?—puffed with red flame. "An heir of Ranthia?"

A chill went down Bryce's arms. "She said so."

"Fire sprites do not lie about their lineage," said the third sprite, Sasa. "How do you know her?"

"I knew her," Bryce said. "She died three months ago. She gave her life to save mine."

The three sprites floated toward Bryce. "The Drahl line has long been scattered to the winds," Sasa said sadly. "We don't know how many remain. To lose even one . . ." She bowed her head, flame dimming to a soft yellow.

The dragon in the hall said to Bryce, "You were a friend to this sprite."

Bryce twisted to the female. "Yes." Damn her tight throat. To the three sprites, she said, "I freed Lehabah before she died. It was her . . ." She could barely get the words out. "It was her first and final act of freedom to choose to save me. She was the bravest person I've ever met."

Malana drifted to Bryce, pressing a warm, burning hand to her cheek. "In her honor, we shall call you an ally of our people."

Bryce didn't miss the slave tattoo on Malana's wrist. The other two sprites bore the same marking. She slowly turned to Ithan. "I'm glad you stole them from that creep."

"It didn't feel right to leave them."

Something in her chest melted, and she suppressed the urge to hug her old friend, to cry at the glimmer of the male she'd once known. Bryce asked Ruhn instead, "Can't we find some way out of this, Mr. Fancy Prince?"

"Marc's on it," Declan said, holding up his phone. "He thinks you two might be able to use your royal sway to either commandeer them on behalf of the royal household or get the Astronomer to accept payment for them rather than press charges."

"Payment?" Bryce blurted.

"Relax," Flynn said, smirking. "We got the money, Princess."

"Yeah, I've seen your daddy's fancy house," Bryce quipped, earning a scowl from Flynn and an *oooooh* from the sprites.

Bryce suppressed her smile and lifted a brow at Ruhn. She'd fucked up one friendship thanks to pulling princess rank, but this . . . For Lehabah, she'd do it. "You in, Chosen One?"

Ruhn's mouth quirked to the side. "Hel yeah, Starborn."

Bryce waved him off and turned fully to the dragon in the hallway. "I'm guessing you cost . . . a lot."

"More than even a prince and princess can afford," the dragon said with a note of bitterness. "I was a gift to the Astronomer from an Archangel."

"Must have been some reading the Astronomer did for them," Flynn muttered.

The dragon hedged, "It was."

Her eyes cooled to jet-black cinders. To leave her at the Astronomer's mercy, to go back into that tiny little ring to sit on his filthy old fingers . . .

"Look," Bryce said, "if Marc's right about the commandeering slaves thing for royal services, then Ruhn and I can make up some shit to explain why we need you."

"Why help me?" the dragon asked.

Bryce tapped her wrist. "My mate was a slave. I can't turn a blind eye to it anymore. No one should." And since she'd already helped out one lost soul today, why not add a few more?

"Who is your mate?" the dragon said.

"Wait," Flynn objected. "You guys are mates? Like, mates-mates?"

"Mates-mates," Ruhn said.

"Does the Autumn King know?" Declan asked.

Bryce could have sworn Ruhn glanced at Ithan, who was busy with something on his phone, before she said, "Let's say it was officially confirmed last night."

Flynn whistled.

Bryce rolled her eyes, but faced the dragon again. "His name is Hunt Athalar."

Recognition kindled in the dragon's eyes. "Orion Athalar?"

"One and the same," Bryce said. "You know him?"

Her mouth pressed into a thin line. "Only by reputation."

"Ah." Bryce asked, a shade awkwardly, "What's your name?"

"Ariadne."

"Ari for short," Flynn chimed in.

"Never Ari," the dragon snapped.

Bryce's mouth twitched. "Well, Ariadne, expect these idiots to piss you off on an hourly basis. But try not to burn the place down." She winked at the dragon. "Feel free to toast Flynn when he's a smart-ass, though."

Flynn flipped her off, but Bryce turned toward the door—only to find three sprites in her face. "You should speak to our queen about Lehabah's bravery," Sasa said. "Irithys is not a descendant of Ranthia, but she would like to hear your tale."

"I'm pretty busy," Bryce said quickly. "Gotta go to work."

But Malana said to her sister, "She'd need to *find* Irithys first." She explained to Bryce, "Last we heard, before we went into the rings all those years ago, she had been sold to one of the Asteri. But perhaps they'd let you speak to her."

"Why would I need to speak to her?" Bryce asked as she kept heading for the door, aware of Ariadne's keen gaze.

"Because princesses need allies," Rithi said, and Bryce halted.

Bryce sighed. "I'm going to need a really big drink after work," she said, and walked out the door, her phone already at her ear.

"What?" Jesiba said by way of answering.

"The Astronomer. You know him?" Bryce had zero idea what

the old male was, but . . . he seemed like he'd be in the House of Flame and Shadow.

There was silence from the sorceress before she said, "Why?"

"Looking for some strings to pull."

Jesiba laughed quietly. "You're the one who stole his rings?"

Maybe they had some sorcerer message-board support group. "Let's say a friend did."

"And now you want—what? My money to pay for them?"

"I want you to convince him to accept the money my friends will pay for them."

"One of those rings is priceless."

"Yeah, the dragon. Ariadne."

"Is that what she calls herself?" A low laugh. "Fascinating."

"You know her?"

"Of her."

Bryce crossed a busy intersection, keeping her head down as a passing tourist gawked too long in her direction. At least no dreadwolves prowled the streets. "So? Can you help or not?"

Jesiba grunted. "I'll make a call. No promises."

"What are you going to say?"

"That he owes me a favor." Dark promise glittered in the words. "And now you do, too."

"Get in line," Bryce said, and hung up.

By the time Bryce reached her little office in the archives, relieved she hadn't needed to pull her princess rank again, she was ready to bask in the AC and kick back in her chair. Ready to maybe send a message to Hunt to feel out whether he was still pissed. But all plans vanished at the sight of the envelope on her desk.

It contained an analysis of dragon fire, dating back five thousand years. It was in a language Bryce didn't know, but a translation had been included. Jesiba had scribbled *Good luck* at the top.

Well, now she knew why the Astronomer kept Ariadne in a ring. Not for light—but for protection.

Among its many uses, the ancient scholar had written, *dragon fire is one of the few substances proven to harm the Princes of Hel. It can burn even the Prince of the Pit's dark hide.*

Yeah, Ariadne was valuable. And if Apollion was readying his armies . . . Bryce had no intention of letting the dragon return to the Astronomer's clutches.

51

Hunt knew he'd been a fool to think this would end once they found Emile. Once the kid was safe. Bryce clearly had no intention of dropping this. Not with Danika somehow involved.

But he tucked all that aside. He had other shit to take care of right now.

He had to meet with Celestina first. Make an appearance, maintain the facade that all was well. Ensure that the Hind hadn't told the Archangel anything. His meeting with Isaiah wasn't for an hour—plenty of time.

Plenty of time to also stew over Bryce, and how well she'd played all of them. How she'd helped Emile, but she'd hidden her plans from him. Plans that had cost lives. And yeah, Bryce could take care of herself, but . . . He'd thought they were a team.

Again: he knew he'd been a fool.

Hunt soothed his wild blood, and only when he was certain his lightning wasn't about to erupt did he knock on the Governor's door.

Celestina smiled in greeting—a good sign. No hint of Ephraim or the others. Good as well. Her smile widened as Hunt stepped closer. "Congratulations," she said warmly.

Hunt angled his head. "On what?"

She gestured to him. "I take it from your scent that you and Bryce are mated."

He hadn't realized the sex would be broadcast like that. Apparently, the bond between them *had* gone to that biological level. "I, ah. Yeah. Since the overnight at her parents' house."

Even if they'd just been at each other's throats. And not in the good way.

"So visiting her parents went well, then."

"I thought her mom would cut off my balls at one point, but get Ember talking about sunball, and she'll become your best friend." It was true, though he'd learned it months ago. Even if some part of him recoiled at having to answer Celestina's question with a blatant lie.

Celestina laughed merrily. There was no wariness or displeasure in it—no indication that she might know the truth. "Good. I'm happy for you. For both of you."

"Thank you," Hunt said. He added, to cover his bases, "Ruhn and Prince Cormac joined us, though. It made things . . . slightly awkward."

"Because Cormac is technically Bryce's fiancé?" Celestina asked wryly.

Hunt snorted. "That, too, but mostly because Ember isn't . . . a fan of the Fae. She asked Ruhn to come, since she hadn't seen him in years, but it was still tense at times."

"I've heard of her history with the Autumn King. I'm sorry that it still haunts her."

"So am I," Hunt said. "Anything happen here while I was gone?"

"Only if you count overseeing party preparations for the equinox."

Hunt chuckled. "That fun, huh?"

"Riveting," Celestina said, then seemed to remember herself because she added, "Of course, it's for a joyous occasion, so it's not entirely a chore."

"Of course."

The sun through the windows behind her turned her white

wings radiant. "Baxian might have something more interesting to report. He was barely here yesterday."

It took all of Hunt's training to keep his own face neutral as he said, "I've got a meeting with Isaiah, but my next stop after that is to check in with him."

Everything between them was a lie. And one word from the Hind . . . Hunt suppressed the surge of his power as it crackled through him.

Baxian might have claimed he was a rebel sympathizer, might have helped them enough to garner some trust, but . . . he'd be a fool to trust him entirely.

"What's wrong?" Celestina asked, brow furrowing with worry.

Hunt shook his head. "Nothing." He clasped his hands behind his back and asked casually, "Anything for me to do today?"

Hunt emerged from the Archangel's office five minutes later with a stack of preliminary reports on demon activity at the Northern Rift. She wanted his expertise in examining the types of demons caught, as well as an analysis on whether the breeds and frequency meant Hel was planning something.

The answer was a definite yes, but he'd find some way to draw out the task to buy himself more time. To decide how much to tell her about Hel.

Apollion had spoken true, about him and Bryce and their powers. And if the Prince of the Pit had been honest about that, what else had he been honest about? Some shit with Hel was stirring. Hunt's gut twisted.

But he still had one more thing to do before descending into all of that. He hunted down the Hind in ten minutes, finding her in the barracks bathroom, applying red lipliner, of all things. He'd never thought she might actually have to put on her makeup. Somehow, he pictured her permanently coiffed and painted.

"Hunter," she crooned without breaking her stare from the mirror. They were alone.

"Don't call me that."

"You never did like Sandriel's nickname for you."

"I had no interest in being part of her club."

The Hind kept drawing her lipliner with a steady hand. "To what do I owe this pleasure?"

Hunt leaned against the bathroom door, blocking any exit. She slid a kohl-lined eye in his direction.

"What are you going to do about what happened yesterday?" he asked.

She opened a tube of lipstick and began filling in the precise outline she'd drawn. "If you're referring to when I fucked Pollux in the showers, I'm afraid I'm not going to apologize to Naomi Boreas for leaving the stall door open. I did invite her to join, you know."

"That's not what I'm talking about."

She started on her top lip. "Then enlighten me."

Hunt stared at her. She'd seen him. Spoken to him, to all of them, while they'd been in the water. He'd gone ballistic, ready to slaughter her. Had needed his mate's touch and body to calm down afterward.

Hunt growled, "Is this some sort of cat-and-mouse game?"

She set the golden lipstick tube on the counter and pivoted. Beautiful and cold as a statue of Luna. "You're the hunter. You tell me."

This female had killed Sofie Renast. Drowned her. And had tortured so many others that the silver torque around her neck practically screamed the names of the dead.

When Hunt said nothing, the Hind inspected herself in the mirror, tucking a stray tendril of hair into her elegant chignon. She then stalked toward him—to the door. He stepped away silently. The Hind said as she exited, "Perhaps you'll stop prattling on about nonsense once you see what the Harpy did by the Angels' Gate. It's rather extraordinary."

Ten minutes later, Hunt learned what she meant.

The crystal Gate in the heart of the CBD was muted in the midmorning light, but no one was looking at it anyway. The gathered crowd was snapping pictures and murmuring about the two figures lying facedown on the ground beneath it.

It had been a long while since Hunt had seen anyone blood-eagled.

The corpses wore black stealth clothes—or shreds of them. Rebels. That was the Ophion crest on their red armbands, and the sinking sun of the Lightfall squadron above it.

Across the Gate's square, someone vomited, then sprinted away, crying softly.

The Harpy had started down their backs. Taken her knives and sawed through the ribs, cleaving each bone from the spine. And then she'd reached through the incisions and yanked their lungs through them.

Leaving a pair of bloody wings draped over their backs.

Hunt knew the victims would have still been alive. Screaming.

Ephraim had brought this into his city. *This* was what the Hind, the Asteri would unleash upon him and Bryce. It wouldn't be crucifixion. It'd be something far more creative.

Had the Harpy left the blood eagles as a message for Ophion, or for all of Valbara?

Celestina had allowed this to happen here. Allowed the Harpy to do this and then display the bodies. Hadn't even mentioned it in their meeting. Because she agreed with these methods, or because she had no choice?

Hunt swallowed against the dryness in his mouth. But others had noticed him now. *The Umbra Mortis,* they murmured. Like he'd helped the Harpy create this atrocity.

Hunt swallowed his answer. *We might be triarii, but I will* never *be like that monster.*

They wouldn't have believed him.

It had been a weird fucking day, but Ruhn heaved a sigh of relief when Athalar called. *All clear,* the angel had said, and it had eased Ruhn's exhaustion and dread, if only by a fraction. He hadn't told Athalar about the sprites and the dragon. He'd let Bryce tell her mate those details. He wondered if she'd even told him yet about the mystics.

Ruhn toyed with his lip ring as he returned to the living room, where Flynn was flirting with the sprites while Dec asked them questions about their lives in the rings. The dragon sat on the stairs, and Ruhn ignored her, even if it went against every primal instinct to do so. Ithan lifted his brows as Ruhn entered.

"We're good," Ruhn told the males, who all muttered prayers of thanks to the gods. He faced the dragon, bracing himself, but was interrupted by the sound of the doorbell.

Brows lowering, hand drifting to the gun tucked into his back waistband, Ruhn strode to the front door. A lovely, familiar female scent hit him a moment before he registered who stood there, broom in hand.

Queen Hypaxia Enador smiled faintly. "Hello, Prince. I'd hoped to find you here."

52

Tharion finished his report to the River Queen, his fin holding him steady in the current of the river depths. She lounged among a bed of river oysters, long fingers trailing over the ridges and bumps.

"So my sister has a fleet of ships that elude the Asteri's Omega-boats." The waters around them swirled, and Tharion fought to keep in place, tail swishing hard.

"Only six."

"Six, each one the size of the Comitium." Her eyes flashed in the dim depths.

"Does it make a difference?" He'd had no choice but to tell her everything—it was the only way to explain why he'd returned without Pippa Spetsos in tow. Or at least answers regarding Emile Renast's whereabouts.

"Do sisters not share everything?" She dragged a finger along the jagged edge of an oyster and it opened, revealing the pearl within. "They mock me, with these ships. They suggest I am not trustworthy."

"No one said anything like that." He clenched his jaw. "I don't think they've told anyone else."

"Yet this Commander Sendes saw fit to inform *you*."

"Only of the vague details, and only because we stumbled onto her ship."

"They rescued you. They could have let you drown and kept their secrets, yet they saved you." His blood chilled. She would have let them drown. "I want you to find out everything you can about these ships."

"I don't think that will be easy," Tharion cautioned.

"Who is to say my sister won't use them against me?"

She rules the oceans. I doubt she wants one stupid river. But Tharion said, "That didn't seem to be on anyone's mind."

"Perhaps not now, but I wouldn't put it past her."

He refrained from telling her she was being paranoid. Instead, he tried his best weapon: diverting her attention. "Shall I continue hunting for Emile Renast?"

The River Queen eyed him. "Why wouldn't you?"

He tried to hide his relief that she'd pivoted with him, even though he knew she'd return to the subject of the Ocean Queen's ships soon enough. "Even with the ammo and mech-suit prototype destroyed, Pippa Spetsos just became a lot more powerful—her position in Ophion has changed. Capturing her, interrogating her . . . We do that, and we risk having Ophion deem us enemies."

"I do not care what Ophion deems us. But very well." She motioned to the surface. "Go Above. Find another way to collect the boy."

"As you will it," he said, bowing in the current.

She flicked a hand in dismissal. "I shall make your excuses to my daughter."

"Give her my love."

She didn't answer, and Tharion made a beeline to the surface and open world above.

He'd finished tugging on the clothes he'd left in a nook of the quay near Moonwood's River Gate when wings rustled on the walkway above him. He peered over the stone rim to find Athalar standing with crossed arms.

"We need to talk," said the Umbra Mortis.

Ruhn stared at the witch-queen. At his bride.

Hypaxia Enador was as beautiful as he remembered: luxurious, dark hair falling in soft curls down to her slim waist; brown skin that glowed as if moonlight ran beneath it; large, dark eyes that noticed too much. Her mouth, full and inviting, parted in a lovely smile as she stepped into the foyer.

The witch touched a knot in the wood on her broom. It was a stunning piece of art: every inch of its handle carved with intricate designs of clouds and flowers and stars, each twig in the base carved as well and bound together with golden thread.

But with the touch on that knot, the broom vanished.

No, it shrank. Into a golden brooch of Cthona, the earth goddess ripe with child. Hypaxia pinned the brooch onto the shoulder of her gauzy blue robes and said, "A convenient bit of witch-magic. I found that carrying a broom around the city is . . . cumbersome. And attracts the notice of many. Especially a broom such as mine."

"That is . . . really fucking cool," Ruhn admitted.

She began to answer, but her eyes slid to the dragon sitting at the foot of the stairs, and she stopped. She blinked once before turning to Ruhn. "A friend?"

"Yeah," Ruhn lied, and then Flynn and Declan and Ithan were there, sprites in tow, gawking at the queen.

Ithan cleared his throat, likely at the stunning beauty of the witch.

Ruhn hadn't been much better when he'd first seen her. Yet she'd hardly given him the time of day at the Summit. Even if she'd helped out majorly during the shit that had gone down in this city. Had been willing to fly here to help save its citizens—and Bryce.

Ruhn straightened, remembering himself. That he was a prince, and owed her the respect due to her rank. He bowed deeply. "Welcome, Your Majesty."

Flynn smirked, and Ruhn threw him a warning glare as he rose. "Allow me to introduce my . . . companions. Tristan Flynn, Lord Hawthorne." Flynn sketched an irreverent bow—a mockery of the one Ruhn had made. "Declan Emmet, super-genius." Dec grinned, bowing with more gravitas. They'd both been at the Summit when Ruhn had formally met Hypaxia—as a queen, and not the medwitch he'd believed her to be—but had never officially been presented to her. "Ithan Holstrom . . . wolf," Ruhn continued. Ithan gave him a look as if to say, *Really, asshole?* But Ruhn moved on to the sprites, the dragon. "And, uh, our guests."

Hypaxia gave the dragon another wary glance. Flynn stepped forward, slinging an arm around Hypaxia's shoulders. "Welcome. Let's talk about all those times Ruhn tried to talk to you at the Summit and you ignored him."

Declan chuckled, taking up a position at Hypaxia's other side. She furrowed her brow, as if the two males spoke another language entirely.

The queen seemed to note the details of his house as she was escorted to the sectional. His disgusting, beer-soaked house. Solas, a half-smoked mirthroot blunt sat in the ashtray on the coffee table a mere foot from Hypaxia.

Ruhn said to Ithan, *Get that fucking mirthroot out of here.*

Ithan lunged for it.

Not right now! When she's not looking.

Ithan caught himself with that sunball player's grace and relaxed against the cushions as Hypaxia sat, nestled between Flynn and Declan. If Ithan had to pick one word to describe the queen's expression, it would have been baffled. Utterly baffled.

Ruhn rubbed his neck, approaching the couch. "So, ah. Good to see you."

Hypaxia smiled in that wise, knowing way. Fucking Hel, she was lovely. But her voice darkened as she said, "I'd like to have a word with you. Alone."

Ithan rose, subtly swiping the mirthroot from the table. "Room's yours. We'll be upstairs."

Flynn opened his mouth, presumably to say something mortifying, but Ithan grabbed him by the shoulder and hauled him up, shoving the mirthroot into the lord's hands. The sprites fell into line behind them as Declan joined the fray, and then they were all gone, Ariadne stalking up the stairs after them. Ruhn had no doubt they'd try to eavesdrop.

He took a seat on the stained, reeking couch, reining in his cringe as Hypaxia adjusted the folds of her blue robes. "So . . . how are you?"

Hypaxia angled her head. She didn't wear her crown of cloudberries, but every line of her radiated grace and calm and care. She was about fifty years younger than he was, yet he felt like a whelp in front of her. Had she known her fiancé lived in a place like this, had a lifestyle like this?

"I wanted to ask you for a favor." Ruhn stilled. She went on, "I've come to Lunathion for the mating celebration in a few weeks. I'll be staying at the witches' embassy, but . . ." She twisted her hands, the first sign of doubt he'd ever seen from her. "I was wondering if you might spare me an escort."

"Why? I mean, sure, yes, but . . . everything okay?"

She didn't answer.

Ruhn asked, "What about your coven?" They should protect their queen at any cost.

Her long lashes bobbed. "They were my mother's coven. It was one of her last wishes that I inherit them, rather than select my own."

"So you don't like them?"

"I don't trust them."

Ruhn considered. "You want me to give you an escort to protect you from your own coven?"

Her mouth tightened. "You think I'm mad."

"I thought witches lived and died for their loyalty."

"The loyalty of these witches began and ended with my mother. She raised me in isolation—from the world, but also from them. My tutors were . . . unconventional."

It was the most they'd ever spoken to each other. Ruhn asked, "In what way?"

"They were dead."

A chill went down his spine. "Right. Necromancer stuff, huh?"

"Enadors can raise the dead, yes. My mother summoned three ancient, wise spirits to teach me. One for battle and physical training, one for mathematics and sciences, and the other for history, reading, and languages. She oversaw my magical training herself—especially the healing."

"And this freaked her coven out?"

"It estranged us. My only companions while growing up were the dead. When my mother passed, I found myself surrounded by strangers. And they found themselves with a queen whose unorthodox education unnerved them. Whose gifts of necromancy unnerved them further."

"But you're the last Enador. Who would they replace you with?"

"My sister."

Ruhn blinked. "The *Hind*?"

"Lidia has no witch gifts, so she would be a figurehead. She'd wear the crown, but my mother's general, Morganthia, would rule."

"That's insane."

"Lidia was born first. She is the spitting image of my mother." Hypaxia's father must have passed along the genes for her darker coloring, then. "Even while I was growing up, I sometimes heard whispers from my mother's coven wondering if . . . perhaps Lidia should not have been given away."

"Why?"

"Because they're more comfortable with a half-shifter than a half-necromancer. They fear the influence of the House of Flame and Shadow, though I have sworn no vows to any but Earth and Blood. But Lidia is Earth and Blood, through and through. Exactly as they are. They loved my mother, I have no doubt, but they have different plans for the future than she did. That became apparent by the end."

"What sort of plans?"

"A closer bond with the Asteri. Even at the cost of our relative autonomy."

"Ah." That was a potential minefield. Especially considering the shit that he was doing for Ophion. Or had been doing for them—he had no idea where they stood now, after Ydra.

Hypaxia went on, "Your kindness is why I've come here. I know you to be a male of bravery and dedication. While I'm in this city for the Governors' celebration, especially with Lidia in town, I fear my mother's coven might make a move. They presented a unified front with me at the Summit, but the last few months have been strained."

"And since we're technically engaged, it won't be seen as a declaration of your distrust if I send one of my people to look after you. It'll be deemed some protective male bullshit."

Her lips twitched. "Yes. Something like that."

"All right. No problem."

She swallowed, bowing her head. "Thank you."

He dared to touch her hand, her skin velvety smooth. "We'll take care of this. Don't worry."

She patted his hand in a *Thanks, friend* sort of way.

Ruhn cleared his throat, glancing at the ceiling—the distinctive, worrisome *thumping* coming from it. "Since you were raised by ghosts, I'm hoping you won't mind having a bit of an unorthodox guard."

Her brows rose.

Ruhn smiled. "How do you feel about sunball players?"

No one bothered them, but plenty of people stared as Tharion and Hunt meandered through the ornate water garden along the river in Moonwood, a hundred rainbows glimmering in the mists around them. Tharion loved this part of the city—though the Old Square's grit still called to him.

"So what's up?" Tharion said as Athalar paused beneath a towering elm, its leaves shimmering in the spray from a massive fountain of Ogenas lounging in an oyster shell.

The angel pulled his phone from a hidden pocket in his battlesuit. "I had a meeting with the Governor." His fingers flew over the phone, presumably summoning whatever the information was. He handed it to Tharion. "She had me go over some of the latest demon reports from Nena. I wanted to pass them along to the Blue Court."

Tharion took the phone and scrolled through the photos. "Anything interesting?"

"That one. The tail—just out of the shot here." Hunt pointed to the picture, face stony. "It's a deathstalker."

Even the burbling fountain beyond them seemed to quiet at the name.

"What's that?"

"Lethal assassins bred by the Prince of the Pit. He keeps them as pets." Athalar's wings rustled. Had a shadow passed over the sun? "I've only dealt with them once. I've got a scar down my back from it."

If the encounter had left Athalar scarred . . . Cthona spare them all. "One was in Nena?"

"Three days ago."

"Shit. Where did it go?"

"No idea. Report says there's been no breach of Nena's borders. Tell your people to be alert. Warn your queen, too."

"I will." Tharion glanced sidelong at the angel. Noticed that they weren't near cameras or other people. "Any further updates?" Tharion asked carefully.

"Maybe," Hunt said.

"I thought so," Tharion said. The warning about the demons seemed true—but also a convenient cover.

"I know where Emile is," Athalar said quietly.

Tharion nearly stumbled a step. "Where?"

"Can't say. But he's safe." Athalar remained grave despite the beauty of Moonwood around them. "Call off your search. Spin some bullshit to your queen. But you're done hunting for that kid."

Tharion surveyed the angel, the mist beading on the gray wings. "And you think it's wise to tell me that *you* know where he is?"

Hunt bared his teeth in a feral smile. "You going to torture it out of me, Ketos?"

"The thought had crossed my mind."

Lightning licked across Hunt's forehead as he motioned to the fountains, the water all around. "Not the best place for a lightning fight."

Tharion began to pace. "The River Queen won't give up. She wants that kid."

"It's a dead end. And a gigantic waste of your time." Tharion arched a brow. Hunt said, voice low, "Emile Renast has no powers. His sister staged things to make it seem that way, hoping that arrogant Vanir like us would find the kid important enough to look after."

Something glimmered in Athalar's face that Tharion couldn't place. Pain. Sorrow. Shame?

"And I'm supposed to take your word for it," Tharion said.

"Yeah, you are."

Tharion knew that tone. The merciless voice of the Umbra Mortis.

"I can think of only one person who'd make you this intense," Tharion drawled, unable to resist. "Legs knows where the kid is, too, huh?" He laughed to himself. "Did she arrange this? I should have seen that coming." He chuckled again, shaking his head. "What's to stop me from going to ask *her* some questions?"

"Hard to ask Bryce any questions when you don't have a head attached to your body," Hunt said, violence glittering in his eyes.

Tharion held up his hands. "Threat received." But his mind spun with all he'd learned. "Let's say I do trust you. Emile really has no powers?"

"Not even a drop. He might be descended from a thunderbird, but Sofie was the only one with the gifts."

"Fuck." The River Queen would be livid, even if she'd been the one who'd ordered him to spend weeks on a wild goose chase. Hel, she'd be pissed that he hadn't figured out the truth sooner. "And the intel?"

"Kid knows nothing." Hunt seemed to consider, then added, "He confirmed that Danika and Sofie had contact. But nothing else."

Tharion dragged his hands through his still-wet hair. "Fuck," he said again, pacing a step.

Athalar tucked in his wings. "How badly is she going to punish you for this?"

Tharion swallowed. "I'm going to have to spin it carefully."

"Even though none of it is your fault?"

"She'll deem it a failure. Rational thinking is second to her need to feel like she's won."

"I really am sorry." The angel tilted his head to the side. "Any chance she'll fire you and let that be that?"

Tharion let out a humorless laugh. "I wish. But . . ." He paused, an idea sparking. He glanced up and down the sun-baked concrete quay. "Who says she has to know today?"

A corner of Athalar's mouth kicked up. "As far as I know, you and I met up to swap status reports."

Tharion began walking toward the city proper, the hustle and bustle that set his blood thrumming. Athalar fell into step beside him. "It could take days to learn that Emile isn't worth our time. Weeks."

The angel winked. "Months, if you do it right."

Tharion grinned, a thrill shooting through his bones as they entered Moonwood's tree-lined streets. It was a dangerous game, but . . . he'd play it. Milk every second of freedom he could from this. Stay Above as often as he liked, so long as he checked in Below every now and then. "Got any ideas where I can crash?"

53

Ithan didn't think of himself as an eavesdropper. But sometimes he couldn't help it if his keen wolf's hearing picked up stuff being said, even a floor below.

This time, it had been some big, *big* stuff.

Ithan used all his training, all those years of practice and games, to keep from pacing as Ruhn went on and on about the witch-queen needing an escort in the city. Yes, fine, he'd do it, he'd guard her back, but—

"You may speak, Ithan Holstrom," the stunningly beautiful witch said, cutting off Ruhn, who blinked at them. Ithan hadn't realized he'd broadcast his impatience so clearly.

Flynn and Declan had remained upstairs with the sprites and Ariadne, booing when Ruhn had asked only Ithan to come downstairs.

Ithan cleared his throat. "You can talk to the dead, right? You're . . . a necromancer? I'm sorry—I couldn't help but overhear." He offered Ruhn an apologetic look, too. But at Hypaxia's cautious nod, he pressed on, "If I agree to guard you, would you . . ." Ithan shook his head. "Would you try to make contact with my brother, Connor?"

For a long moment, Hypaxia only stared at him. Her dark eyes beheld everything. Too much. "I can feel the disturbance in your heart, Ithan. You don't wish to speak to him merely from longing and loss."

"No. I mean, yeah, I miss him like crazy, but . . ." He paused. Could they tell her everything Bryce had learned?

Ruhn spared him the effort of deciding and said, "Do you know what happens to the dead after they've been in the Bone Quarter for a while?"

Her face paled. "You learned of the secondlight."

"Yeah," Ruhn said, lip ring glinting. "Ithan is pretty worried about what happened to his brother and the Pack of Devils, especially after they helped my sister. If you've got any ability to learn what's happened to Connor Holstrom, or to warn him, even if it's to no avail . . . we'd appreciate it. But Ithan will gladly escort you either way you choose."

Ithan tried not to appear too grateful. He'd spent years thinking Ruhn was a dick, mostly thanks to Bryce and Danika constantly dissing him, but . . . this guy had let him into his house, trusted him with his secrets, and now seemed intent on helping him. He wondered if the Fae knew how lucky they were.

Hypaxia nodded sagely. "There is a ritual I could perform . . . It'd need to be on the Autumnal Equinox, though."

"When the veil between realms is thinnest," Ruhn said.

"Yes." Hypaxia smiled sadly at Ithan. "I'm sorry for your loss. And that you've learned the truth."

"How do *you* know the truth?" Ithan asked.

"The dead have little reason to lie."

Ice skittered down Ithan's spine. "I see." The chandelier rattled above.

Ruhn rubbed at his face, the tattoos on his arm shifting with the movement. He lowered his hand and looked at the witch-queen. His fiancée. Lucky male.

"You cool with a dragon joining you?" the prince asked Hypaxia.

"*That* dragon?" Hypaxia peered at the ceiling.

"A lawyer friend of mine says I need a royal, official reason to commandeer someone else's slave. A very important, powerful slave. Protecting my fiancée is about as important as it gets."

Hypaxia's lips curled, though doubt kindled in her dark eyes. That made two of them. She asked Ithan, "How do you feel about it?"

Ithan gave her a half smile, flattered that she'd even asked. "If you can contact my brother on the equinox, then it doesn't really matter what I feel."

"Of course it does," she said, and sounded like she meant it.

A few weeks until the equinox. And then he could see Connor again. Even if it was just one last time.

Even if it was only to deliver a warning that might do him no good.

Bryce might have avoided going home for as long as possible. Might have stayed at the archives right until closing and been one of the last people exiting the building as night fell. She'd made it down the sweeping marble steps, breathing in the dry, warm night air, when she saw him.

Hunt leaned against a car across the narrow street, wings folded elegantly. People hurrying home from work gave him a wide berth. Some outright crossed the street to avoid him.

He'd worn his hat. That fucking sunball hat she couldn't resist.

"Quinlan." He pushed off the car and approached her where she'd halted at the foot of the stairs.

She lifted her chin. "Athalar."

He huffed a soft laugh. "So that's how it's gonna go, huh?"

"What do you want?" They'd had little fights over the months, but nothing this important.

He waved a hand to the building looming behind her. "I need to use the archives to look something up. I didn't want to disturb you during working hours."

She jabbed a thumb at the building, now beautifully illuminated against the starry night. "You waited too long. The building is closed."

"I didn't realize you'd hide inside until closing. Avoiding something, Quinlan?" He smiled savagely as she bristled. "But you're good at sweet-talking people into doing your bidding. Getting us in will be a walk in the park, won't it?"

She didn't bother to look pleasant, though she pivoted and began marching back up the steps, heels clacking on the stone. "What do you need?"

He gestured to the cameras mounted on the massive pillars of the entrance. "I'll explain inside."

"So you think Hel's planning something?" Bryce asked two hours later when she found Hunt where she'd left him, the massive expanse of the archives quiet around them. There had been no need to sweet-talk her way in after all. She'd discovered another perk to working here: getting to use this place after hours. Alone. Not even a librarian to monitor them. They'd gotten past the security guards with barely a word. And her boss wouldn't show up until night was fully overhead—not for at least another hour.

Hunt had said he needed to peruse some newly translated Fae texts on ancient demons, so she'd gotten him set up at a table in the atrium and then gone back to her office on the other side of the floor.

"The demons in the reports Celestina gave me are bad news," Hunt said. He was working at the desk, sunball hat bright in the moonlight streaming through the glass ceiling. "Some of the worst of the Pit. All rare. All lethal. The last time I saw so many clustered together was during the attack this spring."

"Hmm." Bryce slid into the chair across from him.

Was he going to ignore what happened earlier? That wouldn't do. Not at all.

She casually extended her foot beneath the table. Drifted it up Hunt's muscled leg. "And now they need the big, tough angel to dispatch them back to Hel."

He slammed his legs together, trapping her foot. His eyes lifted to hers. Lightning sparked there. "If Aidas or the Prince of the Pit is planning something, this is probably the first hint."

"Aside from them literally saying that Hel's armies are waiting for me?"

Hunt squeezed her foot harder, those powerful thigh muscles shifting. "Aside from that. But I can't tell Celestina about that shit without raising questions about Hel's interest in *you*, so I need to find a way to warn her with the intel she gave me."

Bryce studied her mate and considered the way he'd spoken of the Archangel. "You like Celestina, huh?"

"Tentatively." His shoulders were tight, though. He explained, "I might like her, but . . . the Harpy blood-eagled two Ophion rebels today. Celestina allowed that shit to go down here."

Bryce had seen the news coverage of it already. It had been enough to turn her stomach. She said, "So you'll play faithful triarii, get her info on the demons, and then . . ."

"I don't know." He released her foot. She traced her toes over his knee. "Stop it. I can't think if you're doing that."

"Good."

"Quinlan." His voice dropped low. She bit her lip.

But Hunt said softly, "Any word from Fury?"

"Yeah. Package was delivered, safe and sound." She could only pray her mom wasn't showing Emile her weird babies-in-plants sculptures.

"Tharion's off the hunt," Hunt said.

She stiffened. "You told him?"

"Not the details. Only that the search isn't worth his time, and he won't find what he's seeking."

"And you trust him?"

His voice went quieter. "I do." He returned to the documents he'd been poring over.

Bryce grazed her toes over his other knee, but he clapped a hand on top of her foot, halting its progress. "If Hel's amassing armies, then these demons must be the vanguard, coming to test the defenses around Nena."

"But they'd need to find a way to open the Northern Rift entirely."

"Yeah." He eyed Bryce. "Maybe Aidas has been buttering you up for that."

Bryce's blood chilled. "Cthona spare me."

He frowned. "Don't think for one moment that Aidas and the Prince of the Pit have forgotten the Horn in your back. That Thanatos didn't have it in mind when you spoke to him."

She rubbed at her temple. "Maybe I should cut it out of my skin and burn it."

He grimaced. "That's a real turn-on, Quinlan."

"Were you getting turned on?" She wiggled her toes beneath his hand. "I couldn't tell."

He gave her a half smile—finally, a crack in that pissed-off exterior. "I was waiting to see how high your foot was going to get."

Her core heated. "Then why'd you stop me?"

"I thought you'd like a little challenge."

She bit her lip again. "There was an interesting book in those stacks over there." She inclined her head to the darkness behind them. "Maybe we should check it out."

His eyes simmered. "Might be useful."

"Definitely useful." She rose from the desk and strode into the dimness, deep enough into the stacks that none of the cameras in the atrium where they'd been sitting could pick them up.

Hands wrapped around her waist from behind, and Hunt pressed against her. "You drive me fucking crazy, you know that?"

"And you're a domineering alphahole, you know that?"

"I'm not domineering." He nibbled at her ear.

"But you'll admit you're an alphahole?"

His fingers dug into her hips, tugging her back against him. The hardness there. "You want to fuck it out, then?"

"Are you still mad at me?"

He sighed, his breath hot against her neck. "Bryce, I needed to process everything."

She didn't turn around. "And?"

He kissed under her ear. "And I'm sorry. For how I acted earlier."

She didn't know why her eyes stung. "I wanted to tell you, I really did."

His hands began to rove up her torso, loving and gentle. She arched against him, exposing her neck. "I understand why you didn't." He dragged his tongue up her throat. "I was . . . I was upset that you didn't trust me. I thought we were a team. It rattled me."

She made to turn around at that, but his hands tightened, holding her in place. So she said, "We are a team. But I wasn't sure if you'd agree with me. That an ordinary human boy was worth the risk."

He let her twist in his arms this time. And—shit. His eyes were wounded.

His voice hoarsened. "Of course I would have thought a human was worth the risk. I was too wrapped up in other shit to see the whole picture."

"I'm sorry I didn't give you enough credit." She cupped his face. "Hunt, I'm really sorry."

Maybe she'd fucked up by not telling him, not trusting him. She regretted that the Viper Queen had killed those people, but she'd be damned if she felt bad about how things had ended up . . .

Hunt turned his head, kissing her palm. "I still don't understand how you pieced it all together. Not just Sofie lying about Emile's powers, but how you knew the Viper Queen would be able to find him."

"She's got an arsenal of spies and trackers—I figured she was one of the few people in this city who could do it. Especially if she was motivated enough by the idea that Emile had powers that could be useful to her. And *especially* when his trail was picked up in the marshes."

He shook his head. "Why?"

"She's a queen of snakes—and reptiles. I know she can communicate with them on some freaky psychic level. And guess what the marshes are full of?"

Hunt swallowed hard. "Sobeks?"

Bryce nodded.

He hooked a strand of her hair behind her ear. Kissed its pointy tip. Forgiveness that she hadn't realized she needed filled the gesture.

Hunt asked softly, "What about the others? Are you going to tell them?"

She slowly shook her head. "No. You and Fury and Juniper are the only ones who will ever know." Not even Ruhn.

"And your parents."

"I meant the other people in this city, currently doing shady shit."

He kissed her temple. "I can't believe your mom didn't freak out and drag you home."

"Oh, she wanted to. I think Randall had to stage an intervention."

"Don't take this the wrong way, but . . . why Nidaros?"

"It's the safest and best place I can think of. He'll be protected there. Hidden. The local sun-priest owes Randall a favor and is having all the relevant documents forged. My parents . . . They weren't able to have a kid of their own. I mean, other than me. So even though my mom was freaked as fuck about the whole rebel thing, she's already gone crazy decorating a room for Emile."

"Emile-who-is-not-Emile anymore." His smile lit something iridescent in her chest.

"Yeah," she said, unable to stop her answering smile. "Cooper Silago. My half brother."

He studied her, though. "How'd you manage to communicate about it?" There was no way she or her parents would have ever risked discussing this over email or phone.

She smiled slightly. "Postcards."

Hunt choked on a laugh. "That was all a lie?"

"No. I mean, my mom sent me the postcard after our fight, but when I wrote back, I used a code that Randall taught me in case of . . . emergencies."

"The joys of a warrior for a parent."

She chuckled. "Yeah. So we've been swapping postcards about this for the past two weeks. To anyone else, it would have seemed like we were talking about sports and the weather and my mom's weird baby sculptures. But that's why Emile stayed at the Viper Queen's for so long. Sending postcards back and forth isn't the fastest method of communication."

"But it's one of the more brilliant ones." Hunt kissed her brow, wings curling around them. "I love you. You're crazy and shady as all Hel, but I love you. I love that you did this for that kid."

Her smile widened. "Glad to impress, Athalar."

His hands began drifting down her sides, thumbs stroking over her ribs. "I've been aching for you all day. Aching to show you how sorry I am—and how much I fucking love you."

"All is forgiven." She grabbed one of his hands, dragging it down her front, along her thigh—and up under her dress. "I've been wet for hours," she whispered as his fingers brushed her soaked underwear.

He growled, teeth grazing her shoulder. "All this, just for me?"

"Always for you." Bryce turned again and rubbed her ass against him, feeling the hard, proud length of his cock jutting against her.

Hunt hissed, and his fingers slipped beneath her underwear, circling her clit. "You want me to fuck you right here, Quinlan?"

Her toes curled in her heels. She curved back against him, and his other hand went up to her breast, sliding beneath her neckline to cup the aching flesh beneath. "Yes. Right now."

He nipped at her ear, drawing a gasp as his fingers slid down to her entrance, dipping in. "Say please," he breathed.

She arched, moaning softly, and he hushed her. "Please," she gasped.

She trembled with anticipation at the click of his belt buckle, the zip of his pants. Shivered as he set her hands upon the nearest shelf and gently bent her over. Then slid her dress up her thighs. Exposed her ass to the cool air.

"Gods-damn," Hunt breathed, running his hands over her rear. Bryce writhed.

He hooked his fingers in her underwear, sliding the lace down her thighs, letting them fall between her ankles. She stepped out of them, spreading her legs wide in invitation. But Hunt dropped to his knees behind her, and before Bryce could inhale, his tongue was at her sex, lapping and dipping inside.

She moaned again, and he gripped her thighs, holding her in place as he feasted on her. His wings brushed her ass, her hips as he leaned forward, tasting and suckling, and—

"I'm going to come if you keep doing that," she rasped.

"Good," he growled against her, and as he slid two fingers into her, she did exactly that.

She bit her lip to keep from crying out, and he licked her, drawing out each ripple of her climax. She panted, dizzy with pleasure, clinging to the shelf as he rose behind her once more.

"Now be *very* quiet," he whispered in her ear, and pushed inside her.

From behind, at this angle, the fit was luxuriously tight and deep. As he had last night, Hunt eased his way into her with care, and she gritted her teeth to keep from groaning at each inch he claimed for himself. He stilled when he was fully seated, her ass pressed entirely against his front, and ran a possessive hand down her spine.

The fullness of him, the size, simply smelling him and knowing it was Hunt inside her—release threatened again. Bigger and mightier than before. Her star began to glow, silvering the shelves, the books, the darkness of the stacks.

"You like that?" He withdrew nearly to the tip before pushing back in. She buried her face against the hard shelf to stay quiet. "You like how my cock feels in you?"

She could only get out a garbled *yesIdopleasemore.* Hunt laughed, dark and rich, and thrust in—a little harder this time. "I love you undone like this," he said, moving again. Setting the pace. "Utterly at my mercy."

Yesyesyes, she hissed, and he laughed again. His balls slapped against her ass.

"You know how much I thought about doing this all those months ago?" he said, bending to press a kiss to her neck.

"Likewise," she managed to say. "I wanted you to fuck me on my desk at the gallery."

His thrusts turned a little uneven. "Oh yeah?"

She moved her hips back against him, angling him in deeper. He groaned now. She whispered, "I knew you'd feel like this. So fucking perfect."

His fingers dug into her hips. "All yours, sweetheart. Every piece of me." He thrust harder. Faster.

"Gods, I love you," she breathed, and that was his undoing.

Hunt yanked her from the shelf, pulling her to the ground with him, positioning her on all fours. His knees spread her own even wider, and Bryce bit her hand to hold in her scream of pleasure as he rammed into her, over and over and over. "I fucking love you," he said, and Bryce cracked.

Light exploded from her as she came, driving back onto his cock, so deep he touched her innermost wall. Hunt shouted, and his cock pulsed in her, following her into that blinding pleasure like he couldn't stop, like he'd keep spilling into her forever.

But then he stilled, and they remained there, panting, Hunt buried in her.

"No teleporting this time, huh?" he said, bending to kiss her neck.

She leaned her forehead against her hands. "Must need your power to join mine or something," she mumbled. "Good thing you didn't do that, though—probably would have burned the building down. But I don't care right now." She wiggled her ass against him, and he hissed. "Let's go home and have more makeup sex."

Night.

Ruhn opened his eyes, finding himself on the couch on the bridge, with Daybright seated across from him.

"Hey," he said. He'd passed out on the sectional while Declan and Ithan argued about sunball crap. Flynn had been busy fucking a nymph upstairs.

Ariadne and the sprites had claimed Declan's bedroom, as the male had planned to spend the night at Marc's, and gone to sleep soon after a painfully awkward evening meal. The dragon had picked at her dinner like she'd never seen food before. The sprites had drunk an entire bottle of wine between them and spent the meal burping up embers.

How any of them were sleeping with Flynn's escapades down the hall was beyond Ruhn.

Day drummed a flaming hand on the rolled arm of the fainting couch. "I have information for you to pass along."

Ruhn straightened. "Good or bad?"

"That's for you to decide."

She watched him intently. He wasn't sure if he'd see her after that colossal bit of weirdness last night. But she said nothing of it as she declared, "I have it on good authority that Pippa Spetsos is planning something big in retaliation for losing so much ammunition and the imperial mech-suit prototype. Ophion is fully behind her. They believe the unit that sabotaged the shipment has gone rogue, and appointed Spetsos to send a clear message to both those rebels and the empire."

Ruhn kept his face carefully blank. "What's she up to? Where?"

"I'm not sure. But given that her last known location was Ydra, I thought you should pass it along to your cohorts in Crescent City, lest she attack there."

"Do the Asteri know about her plans?"

"No. Only I do."

"How'd you learn about them?"

"That's none of your concern."

Ruhn studied her. "So we're back to the distance. No more bedtime stories?"

Again, she drummed her fingers. "Let's chalk that up to a moment of insanity."

"I didn't see anything."

"But you wanted to."

"I don't need to. I don't give a shit what you look like. I like talking to you."

"Why?"

"Because I feel like I can be real with you, here."

"Real."

"Yeah. Honest. I've told you shit no one else knows."

"I don't see why."

He rose from his couch and crossed to hers. He leaned against the arm of the sofa, peering down at her blazing face. "See, I think you like me, too."

She shot to her feet, and he backed away a step. She came closer, though. Near enough for her chest to brush his. Flame and darkness twined, stars turning into embers between them. "This is not some game, where you can flirt and seduce your way through it," she hissed. "This is war, and one that will claim many more lives before it is through."

A growl worked its way up his throat. "Don't patronize me. I know the cost."

"You know *nothing* of cost, or of sacrifice."

"Don't I? I might not have been playing rebel all my life, but believe me, shit has never been easy." Her words had found their mark, though.

"So your father doesn't like you. You're not the only one. So your father beat you, and burned you. So did mine."

Ruhn snarled, getting in her face. "What the fuck is your point?"

She snarled right back. "My point is that if you are not careful, if you are not smart, you will find yourself giving up pieces of your soul before it's too late. You will wind up *dead*."

"And?"

She stilled. "How can you ask that so cavalierly?"

He shrugged. "I'm nobody," he said. It was the truth. Everything he was, the worth by which the world defined him . . . it had all been *given* to him. By pure luck of being born into the "right" family. If he'd done anything of value, it had been through the Aux. But as a prince . . . he'd been running his entire life from that title. Knew it to be utterly hollow.

And Bryce had kept her power a secret so he might hold on to that scrap of specialness.

Ruhn turned away from Day, disgusted with himself.

Bryce loved him far more than she hated their father. Had given up privilege and power for him. What had he ever done for anyone on that scale? He'd die for his friends, this city—yeah. But . . . who the fuck was he, deep down?

Not a king. His father wasn't a fucking king, either. Not in the way that mattered.

"Message received," he said to Day.

"Night—"

Ruhn opened his eyes.

The living room was dark, the TV off, Ithan presumably long gone to sleep.

Ruhn turned over on the couch, tucking his arms behind his head and staring at the ceiling, watching beams of headlights drift across it from passing cars.

Who the fuck was he?

Prince of Nothing.

54

Sitting in her office at the archives, phone at her ear, Bryce drained the last sips of her third coffee of the day, and debated whether a fourth cup would have her crawling on the ceiling by lunchtime.

"So, um—Cooper's good?" she asked her mother, setting her coffee cup atop the paper that held the sequence of numbers and letters from Sofie's arm. Randall had now deemed it safe enough to discuss the boy on the phone. Bryce supposed it'd be weird not to, since her parents had just publicly adopted the kid.

"He's an exceptionally bright boy," Ember said, and Bryce could hear the smile in her voice. "*He* appreciates my art."

Bryce sighed at the ceiling. "The surest test of intelligence out there."

"Do you know he hasn't been to school in more than three years?" Ember's voice sharpened. "*Three years*."

"That's awful. Has he . . . ah . . . talked about his . . . previous home?"

Her mom caught her meaning. "No. He won't talk about it, and I'm not going to push. Milly Garkunos said to let him bring it up on his own time."

"Milly Garkunos suddenly became a child psychiatrist?"

"Milly Garkunos is a good neighbor, Bryce Adelaide Quinlan."

"Yeah, and a busybody. Don't tell her anything." Especially about this.

"I wouldn't," Ember hissed.

Bryce nodded, even though her mom couldn't see through the phone. "Let the kid quietly adjust."

"Am I his caretaker, or are you, Bryce?"

"Put Randall on the phone. He's the voice of reason."

"Randall is beside himself with happiness at having another child in the house, and is currently on a walk through the woods with Cooper, showing him the lay of the land."

Bryce smiled at that. "I loved doing that with him."

Ember's voice softened. "He loved doing that with you, too."

Bryce sighed again. "Thanks again, Mom. I know this was a shock—"

"I'm glad you included us, Bryce. And gave us this gift." Bryce's throat ached. "Please be careful," Ember whispered. "I know you think I'm overbearing and annoying, but it's only because I want the best for you. I want you to be safe, and happy."

"I know, Mom."

"Let's plan on a girls' weekend this winter. Someplace nice and cold. Skiing?"

"Neither of us skis."

"We can learn. Or sit by the fire and drink spiked hot chocolate."

Here was the mom she adored, the one she'd worshipped as a kid. "It's a plan."

A ripple of fire, of pure power, shuddered through the building. Silence flowed in its wake, the usual background noise halting. "I gotta get back to work," Bryce said quickly.

"Okay, love you."

"Love you," Bryce said, and had barely hung up when the Autumn King walked in.

"Trash gets dumped in the back," she said without looking up.

"I see your irreverence has not been altered by your new immortality."

Bryce lifted her head. This wasn't how she wanted to start her day. She'd already spent her walk to work with Ruhn, needing him to explain to her twice about the plan to have Queen Hypaxia escorted by Ithan and the dragon in exchange for the witch-queen contacting Connor's spirit on the equinox. She'd been slightly nauseated at that, but had grunted her approval before she left him on the street, telling him to give Hypaxia her number in case she needed anything. A few minutes later, Ruhn had forwarded the queen's contact information.

Her father sniffed her. "Would you like to explain to me *why* you have mated with Athalar, when you are betrothed to a Fae Prince?"

"Because he's my mate?"

"I didn't know half-breeds could have such things."

She bared her teeth. "Real classy."

Fire filled his eyes. "Did you not consider that I arranged for your union with Cormac out of your best interests? The interests of your offspring?"

"You mean *your* best interests. As if I'd ever let you within a hundred miles of any child of mine."

"Cormac is powerful, his household strong. I want you in Avallen because it is a *safehold*. Even the Asteri cannot pierce its mists without permission, so old is the magic that guards it."

Bryce stilled. "You're full of shit."

"Am I? Did you not kill an Archangel this spring? Are you not now at the mercy of the Asteri? Are demons not once more creeping through the Northern Rift—in greater numbers than ever before?"

"Like you give a single fuck about my safety."

Flame rippled around him, then vanished. "I am your father, whether you like it or not."

"You didn't seem to care about that until I surpassed you in power."

"Things change. I found watching Micah harm you to be . . . unsavory."

"Must have really bothered you, since you've seemed to have no issue with harming others yourself."

"Explain."

"Oh, come on. Don't give me that blank fucking look. The last Starborn Prince. You killed him because he was special and not you, and everyone knows it."

Her father threw back his head and laughed. "Is that what you think? That I killed my rival for spite?"

She said nothing.

"Is that what prompted you to hide your gift all these years? Concern that I'd do the same to you?"

"No." It was partly true. Her mother had been the one who'd thought that.

The Autumn King shook his head slowly and sat in the chair opposite her desk. "Ember fed you too many lies born of her irrational fears."

"And what about the scar on her face? Was that a lie, too? Or an irrational fear?"

"I have already told you that I regret that more than you know. And that I loved Ember deeply."

"I don't think you know what that word means."

Smoke curled from his shoulders. "At least I understand what it means to use my household name."

"What?"

"Princess Bryce Danaan. That was the name you gave the Governor, as well as the director of the Crescent City Ballet, isn't it? And what your lawyer—Marc, is it?—called you in his letter to the Astronomer, justifying the fact that you and your brother had commandeered four of his slaves."

"So?"

Her father smiled faintly. "You purchased influence with my name. The royal name. You bought it, and there are no returns, I'm afraid."

Her blood went cold.

"The legal paperwork for your official name change is already filed."

"You fucking change my name and I will *kill* you." Starlight flared at her chest.

"Threatening your king is punishable by death."

"You will never be my king."

"Oh, I am. You declared fealty by using my name, your title. It is done." Rage surged through her, rendering her mute. He went on, enjoying every second of it, "I wonder how your mother shall react."

Bryce shot out of her chair, slamming her hands on the desk. Light shimmered at her fingertips.

Her father didn't so much as flinch. He looked at her hands, then her face, and said blandly, "You are now officially a Princess of the Fae. I expect you to act as such."

Her fingers curled on the desk, her long nails gouging the wood. "You have *no right*."

"I have every right. And you had the right not to use your royal privileges, but you chose otherwise."

"I didn't *know*." He couldn't get away with this. She'd call Marc immediately. See if he and his team could find some way out of it.

"Ignorance is no excuse," her father said, cold amusement frosting his face. "You are now Bryce Adelaide Danaan."

Bile burned her throat. She'd never heard anything more hateful. She was Bryce Adelaide Quinlan. She'd never stop being a Quinlan. Her mother's daughter.

Her father continued, "You will maintain appearances with Cormac for as long as I command you to." He rose, glancing again at her hands—the lines she'd gouged in the desk thanks to that new Vanir strength. His eyes narrowed. "What is that number there?"

She flipped over the piece of paper on which she'd written the sequence of numbers and letters on Sofie's body. But despite her rage and disgust, she managed to ask, "You know it?"

He scanned her face. "I will admit to turning a blind eye to the recklessness of your brother, but I would think you, Princess, would be more careful. The Asteri won't come to kill me first. Or even Athalar. They'll go right to Nidaros."

Her stomach twisted. "I don't know what you're talking about." What did the sequence from Sofie's arm have to do with this? Had he known Sofie? She didn't dare ask. Her father stalked for her office door, graceful as a leopard.

But he paused on the threshold, attention going to the star on her chest. "I know what it is you're searching for. I've been seeking it for a long, long time."

"Oh?" she sneered. "And what is that?"

The Autumn King stepped into the dimness of the stacks. "The truth."

Juniper didn't attend dance class that evening, and Madame Kyrah didn't so much as look at Bryce.

Though everyone else did. There were glares and whispers.

So inappropriate.

What an entitled brat.

Can you imagine *ever doing that to a friend?*

Bryce left class during the five-minute break and didn't return.

She found a bench in a quiet part of the Oracle's Park and slumped onto the wooden slats, tugging her hat low over her face.

She was a fucking princess. Yes, she'd been one before today, but . . .

A folder full of documents had been delivered right before she'd gone to class. In it had been a new scooter registration, proof of name change, and a credit card. A sleek, black credit card with *HRH Bryce Danaan* stamped on the front. A long, golden leash stretched from it to her father. And his bank account. She'd shoved everything into a drawer in her desk and locked it.

How could she tell her mother? How could she tell Randall?

She'd been so fucking *stupid*. She wished Danika were with her. Wished June didn't hate her guts, that Fury wasn't hundreds of miles to the north. With her parents, who already had enough to deal with, without her telling them about this spectacular fuckup.

And yeah, she knew if she called Hunt, he'd find her in two seconds, but . . . She wanted to talk to another female. Someone who might understand.

She dialed before she could second-guess herself.

Thirty minutes later, Bryce waited at a pizza counter, nursing a beer, watching people begin to queue at the alley food stalls as night fell, the baking temperature with it.

The witch-queen entered so casually that Bryce might not have noticed if it hadn't been for Ithan's presence. He sat at one of the small tables in the alley, clad in an old sunball T-shirt and track pants, looking for all the world like a guy out to meet a friend. Except for the outline of the handgun tucked into the back of his waistband. The knife she knew was in his boot.

No sign of the dragon, though. Unless Ariadne was somewhere out of sight.

Bryce said to Hypaxia, "Nice jeans."

The witch peered down at herself, the light green blouse, charcoal biker jacket, and tight black jeans, the sensible flats and pretty gold bracelet. A matching gold brooch of Cthona adorned the lapel of her jacket. "Thank you. Ithan suggested I blend in."

"He's not wrong," Bryce said, glancing at the wolf sizing up every person on the street. She said to Hypaxia, "Order what you want and we'll pay the tab when we leave."

The witch strode the ten feet to the display in the tiny shop, then quietly ordered. If the male behind the counter recognized her, he didn't let on.

Hypaxia took a position at the counter overlooking the alley. Ithan lifted his brows high. She nodded. All was fine.

Bryce said to her, "He's pretty intense about the guard duty."

"Very professional," Hypaxia said approvingly.

Bryce offered a friendly smile. "Thanks for coming. I know my call was super random. I just . . . I had a crazy day. And thought you might have some advice."

Hypaxia smiled at last. "I'm pleased you did. I've wished to see you since our encounter this spring." When the queen had been playing medwitch. And . . .

It all came rushing back.

Hypaxia had freed Hunt from the halo. Had removed it. Had given him the ability to slay Sandriel and come aid Bryce—

"Thank you for what you did," Bryce said, throat tight. "For helping Hunt."

Hypaxia's smile only widened. "From your scent, it seems as if you and he have made things . . . permanent. Congratulations."

Bryce casually rocked back on her heels. "Thank you."

"And how's your thigh?"

"No more pain. Also thanks to you."

"I'm glad to hear it."

Bryce sipped from her beer as the server brought over the queen's pizza. She murmured to him, and the male brought the second slice out to Ithan, who grinned over at Hypaxia and held up the slice in a long-distance cheers. Still no sign of the dragon. Maybe that was a good thing.

When Hypaxia had taken a bite, Bryce said, "So, I, uh . . ."

"Ah. The reason you asked me here?"

Bryce sighed. "Yeah. My father—the Autumn King—visited today. Said that because I used his name for a few things, it meant I had accepted my royal title. I tried to refuse, but he'd already done the paperwork. I'm now officially a princess." She almost choked on the last word.

"Judging from your expression, this is not good news."

"No. I know you're pretty much a stranger, and that you were born into your title and never had the choice to be normal, but . . . I feel like I'm drowning here."

A gentle, warm hand landed atop hers. "I am sorry he did that to you."

Bryce studied a stain on the counter, unsure if she could look at the witch without crying.

Hypaxia said, "Why do you think I came here this spring? I wanted to be normal. If only for a few months. I know what you're feeling."

Bryce shook her head. "Most people wouldn't get it. They'd think, *Oh, poor you, you have to be a princess*. But I've spent my entire life avoiding this male and his court. I *hate* him. And I just walked right into his clutches like a fucking idiot." She heaved a shuddering breath. "I think Hunt's answer to all of this would be to go flambé my father until he reversed this bullshit, but . . . I wanted to see if you had any alternate ideas."

The queen took another bite of her pizza, contemplating. "While I might enjoy the sight of Hunt Athalar flambéing the Autumn King . . ." Bryce's mouth quirked up at that. "I think you're right that a more diplomatic method is required."

"So you think there's a way out of this?" Marc had agreed to help, but hadn't sounded hopeful.

"I think there are ways to manage this. Manage your father."

Bryce nodded. "Ruhn mentioned you had some . . . drama with your coven."

A soft laugh. "I suppose that's a good way to put it."

"He also mentioned that you had some unusual tutors growing up." Ghosts, he'd told her on the phone this morning.

"Yes. My dearest friends."

"No wonder you wanted to bust out and escape, if you had only the dead for company."

Hypaxia chuckled. "They were wonderful companions, but yes. They encouraged me to come here, actually."

"Are they with you on this trip?"

"No. They cannot leave the confines of the keep where I was raised. My mother's summoning spell bound them there. It is . . . Perhaps it's the reason I returned to my homelands again."

"Not to be queen?"

"That too," Hypaxia said quickly. "But . . . they are my family."

"Along with the Hind," Bryce said carefully.

"I do not count her as kin."

Bryce was grateful for the shift in their conversation, even if for a few minutes. She needed time to sort through her raging feelings. "You look nothing alike."

"That is not why I don't consider her a sister."

"No, I know that."

"Our mother was as golden-haired and tan-skinned as she. My father, however—I take after his coloring."

"And who was the Hind's father?"

"A rich and powerful stag shifter in Pangera. My mother never told me the details of how they came to breed. Why she agreed to it. But the Hind inherited her father's powers, not the witch gifts, and thus she was sent at age three to live with him."

"That's horrible." When Bryce had been three . . . her mother had fought nearly to the death to keep her from the Autumn King's clutches. Her mother had done all that, only for Bryce to wind up right here. Shame and dread filled her. She knew it was only a matter of time until her mom found out, but she couldn't tell her—not yet.

"It was part of their deal," Hypaxia explained. "Whatever gift Lidia inherited, that was where she would live. She spent the first three years with my mother, but when the shifter gifts manifested, his kin came to claim her. My mother never saw her again."

"Was your mom bothered by what she became?"

"I was not privy to those thoughts," Hypaxia said tightly enough that Bryce knew to drop it. "But it has never sat well with me."

"Are you going to see her while she's here?"

"Yes. I've never met her before. I was born several years after she was sent away."

Bryce drank again. "I'd suggest not getting your hopes up."

"I'm not. But we digress from your troubles." The queen sighed. "I don't know Fae royal laws, so I'm afraid I can't tell you definitively, but . . . at this point, I think the only ones who might be able to stop your father are the Asteri."

"I was afraid of that." Bryce rubbed her temples. "Just wait until Hunt hears."

"He won't be pleased?"

"Why the Hel would he be pleased?"

"Because you are mated. And now your father has made you a princess. Which makes him . . ."

"Oh gods," Bryce said, choking. "Hunt is a fucking *prince*." She laughed bitterly. "He's going to go ballistic. He'll hate it even more than I do." She laughed again, a bit hysterically. "Sorry. I'm, like, literally imagining his face when I tell him tonight. I need to record it or something."

"I can't tell if this is a good or bad thing."

"Both. The Autumn King expects me to keep up my engagement with Prince Cormac."

"Even though your scent makes it clear you're with another?"

"Apparently." She didn't want to think about that. She finished the beer, then gathered up her plate and Hypaxia's to toss in the trash. She quickly paid their tab, and as she pocketed the receipt, she asked the queen, "Wanna walk a little? It's not as hot as it was."

"I'd like that very much."

They kept silent, unnoticed by those around them as they entered the alley. Ithan fell into step a polite distance behind. The dragon, if she was there, was nowhere to be seen.

"So your brother told you of the situation with my mother's coven, then."

"Yeah. That sucks. I'm sorry."

They reached the river a block away and turned down the quay. Dry, warm wind rustled the palms lining it. Hypaxia studied the stars. "I had such visions for what the future would be like. Of witches returning to power. Of being with the person who I . . ." She cleared her throat.

"You're seeing someone?" Bryce asked, brows lifting.

The queen's face shuttered. "No." Hypaxia blew out a long breath. "The relationship wasn't possible anymore. I might have continued it, but it was not . . . They didn't want to."

Bryce blinked. If Hypaxia was in love with someone else . . . Fuck. "Poor Ruhn," she said.

Hypaxia smiled sadly. "I think your brother wants to marry me as little as I want to marry him."

"Ruhn's hot, though. So are you. Maybe the attraction will kick in." Bryce owed her brother at least an attempt to try to play up his good attributes.

A laugh. "It takes far more than that."

"Yeah, but he's a good guy. Like, a *really* good guy. And I can't believe I'm even saying this, but . . . while I'm sure the person you love is great, you really couldn't do better than Ruhn."

"I'll remember those words." Hypaxia toyed with one of her long curls. “The engagement to your brother was an attempt to prevent my mother’s coven from gaining too much power.”

Bryce said, “But you said you *want* the witches to return to power. Or is it that you want your people to regain their power—but you want your mother’s coven to . . . be excluded from that?” Hypaxia nodded gravely. Bryce’s brows knit. “Aren’t the witches already powerful?”

“Not as we once were. For generations now, mighty bloodlines have run dry, magic withering. Like they are . . . siphoned into nothing. My mother’s coven has no interest in discovering why. They only want us to become even more subservient to the Asteri.”

This female had freed Hunt in pure defiance of the Asteri. Was Hypaxia a rebel? Did she dare ask her? How much had Ithan and Ruhn told her yesterday?

Dark mists curled on the other side of the river. She asked quietly, “Did your mom summon your tutors from the Bone Quarter? Or another eternal resting place?”

“Such things did not exist when my tutors walked the earth.”

Bryce gaped. “Your tutors predate the Asteri’s arrival?”

Hypaxia narrowed her eyes in warning for Bryce to keep her voice down. “Yes. They were already long dead when the Northern Rift opened.”

“They remember a time before the Asteri—when Parthos still stood?” Bryce ventured.

“Yes. One of my tutors, Palania, taught mathematics and science at its academy. She was born in the city surrounding it, and died there, too. So did generations of her family.”

“The Asteri don’t like people talking about these things. That humans accomplished so much before their arrival.”

“They are classic conquerors.” Hypaxia gazed toward the Bone Quarter. “They have conquered even death in this world. Spirits that once rested peacefully are now herded into these . . . zones.”

Bryce started. “You know about that?”

“The dead speak to me of their horrors. When my mother died, I had to do some things that . . . Let’s say my mother’s coven was not happy that I found a way for my mother to avoid going to an eternal resting place. Even if doing so sacrificed my ability to speak with her forever." Shadows darkened her eyes. "But I could not send her to a zone like the Bone Quarter. Not when I knew what would become of her."

"Why not tell everyone? Why not tell the whole world?"

"Who would believe me? Do you know what the Asteri would do to me? To my people? They would slaughter every single witch to punish me. My mother knew it as well—and also chose not to say anything. If you are wise, you will not, either. I shall help Ithan Holstrom and his kin as best I can on the equinox, but there are limits."

Bryce halted by the rail overlooking the night-dark river. "Where did the dead go before the Asteri arrived? Did your tutors ever tell you that?"

Her mouth softened into a smile. "No. But they told me it was . . . good. Peaceful."

"Do you think the souls that are harvested here ever wind up there?"

"I don't know."

Bryce blew out a breath. "Well, this is the most depressing girl talk I've ever had."

"It's the first girl talk I've ever had."

"Normal girls dish about normal shit."

"You and I are not normal girls."

No, they weren't. They were . . . a queen and a princess. Meeting as equals. Talking about things that could get them killed.

"It can be very lonely, to wear a crown," Hypaxia said quietly, as if reading her thoughts. "But I'm glad to have you to speak with, Bryce."

"Me too." And she might not be anywhere near done fighting her father's bullshit, but . . . it was a comfort to know that she had the witch-queen on her side, at least. And other allies.

Ithan stood guard twenty feet behind. His stare met hers, bright in the dimness. She opened her mouth to call him over, to ask how much he'd heard.

But at that moment, a massive, scaled gray beast leapt over the quay railing.

And before Bryce could shout, it barreled into Ithan and closed its jaws around his throat.

55

Bryce didn't have time to scream. Didn't have time to do anything but fall back on her ass, scrambling away from Ithan, his blood spraying, gurgling as his throat—

The beast—the *demon*—ripped out Ithan's throat.

Tipped back its broad, flat head and swallowed the chunk of flesh between black, curved fangs.

"Get up," Hypaxia ordered from where she stood above Bryce, a knife in her hand. Where it'd come from, Bryce had no idea.

Ithan—

She couldn't do this again. Couldn't endure it.

The demon stepped away from Ithan's twitching, dying body. Would he survive that kind of a blow? If the demon had poison on its fangs like the kristallos—

This thing might have been some relative. Its matte gray scales flowed over a muscular, low-slung body; a tail as long as Bryce whipped back and forth, its spiked end carving grooves in the stone. People along the quay, the streets beyond, started fleeing.

Her body couldn't move. Shock—she knew this was shock, and yet—

Help would come soon. Someone, either in the Aux or the 33rd, would arrive. Hunt—

"*Get up*," Hypaxia said, gripping Bryce under a shoulder to haul her to her feet. Slowly, the witch-queen dragged Bryce back—

A snarl reverberated through the stones behind them.

Bryce twisted to find a second demon, twin to the one that had ripped out Ithan's throat, approaching at their rear. The two of them were closing in on the prey now trapped between them.

Fear, cold and sharp, sliced through her. Shattered the shock rooting her into uselessness. Clarified her fogged, bloody vision.

"Back-to-back," Hypaxia ordered, voice low and calm. One knife—that's all they had. Why the fuck didn't she carry a gun?

But Ithan had a gun. On his lifeless body, Bryce could make out the gun he hadn't had a chance to draw. How many rounds did it hold? If the demon was fast enough to sneak up on him, though, she didn't stand a chance. Not unless . . .

"What kind of magic do you have?" Bryce murmured, pressing her back to Hypaxia as she eyed the second demon. She'd kill these fuckers. Rip them apart piece by piece for this.

"Does it matter?" Hypaxia asked, angling her knife at the first demon.

"Is it energy? Like lightning?"

"Healing and wind—and the necromancy, which I can't even begin to explain."

"Can you pinpoint it? Shoot it into me?"

"What?"

"I need a charge. Like a battery," Bryce said, the scar on her chest glowing faintly.

The demon before her bayed to the night sky. Her ears rang.

"To do what?"

"Just—do it now, or we are going to be royally fucked."

The first demon howled. Like so many beings from the Pit, their eyes were milky—blind. As if they'd been in the dark so long they'd ceased to need them. So blinding wasn't an option. But a bullet . . . "You think a knife is going to work on them?" Bryce demanded.

"I . . ." Hypaxia guided them toward the quay railing. Three feet remained until there was nowhere to go but the water. Bryce shuddered, remembering the sobeks that had attacked them that day fleeing the Bone Quarter.

"Use your healing power and hit my fucking chest," Bryce snarled. "Trust me." They had no other choice. If Hunt's power had charged her up, maybe . . .

The creature nearest the witch-queen lunged, snapping. The two females slammed into the railing.

"Now!" Bryce shouted, and Hypaxia whirled, shoving a shining palm to Bryce's chest. Warmth flowed into her, soft and gentle, and—

Stars erupted in Bryce's mind. Supernovas.

Ithan.

It was as easy as taking a step.

One breath, Bryce stood against the quay. The next, she was beside Ithan's body, behind the creatures, who pivoted toward her, sensing that her scent had shifted away.

Hypaxia tapped the golden brooch on the lapel of her jacket. With a *woomph* of air, her broom appeared before her, and the queen leapt onto it, shooting skyward—

Bryce grabbed the gun from Ithan's waistband, clicked off the safety, and fired at the closest demon. Brain matter splattered as the bullet plowed between its sightless eyes.

The second demon charged at her, Hypaxia forgotten as she hovered on her broom in the air above. Bryce fired, and the beast dodged the blow—as if it could feel the air itself parting for the bullet. It was onto her, aware of what weapon she bore—

The demon leapt for her, and Bryce rallied her power.

Stepped from her place beside Ithan's body to the open walkway behind the charging creature.

It hit the ground and spun, claws gouging deep. Bryce fired again, and the demon used those preternatural senses to veer left at the last millisecond, taking the bullet in the shoulder. The shot did nothing to slow it.

The demon jumped for her again, and Bryce moved. Slower this time—Hypaxia's power was already funneling out of her.

"Thirty feet behind you!" Hypaxia ordered from above,

pointing, and Bryce gritted her teeth, mapping out how to get there. The dance she had to lead the creature into.

It leapt, claws out, and Bryce teleported back ten feet. It leapt again and she moved, body shaking against the strain. Another ten feet back. She could make the last jump. Had to make the last jump as the demon sprang—

Roaring, Bryce flung all of herself, all that remained of the spark of Hypaxia's power, into her desire to step, to move—

She appeared ten feet back, and the creature, sensing her pattern, jumped.

It didn't look up. Didn't see the witch-queen plunging to the earth, dagger aloft.

Bryce hit the ground as Hypaxia jumped from her broom and landed atop the beast, slamming her blade into its skull. Witch and demon went down, the former astride it like a horse from Hel. But the demon didn't so much as twitch.

Scraped palms and knees already healing, Bryce panted, shaking. She'd done it. She'd—

Ithan. Oh gods, Ithan.

On wobbling legs, she scrambled to her feet and rushed for him. His throat was healing—slowly. He stared unseeingly at the night sky.

"Move back," Hypaxia said, breathing heavily, broom discarded beside her. "Let me see him."

"He needs a medwitch!"

"I am a medwitch," Hypaxia said, and knelt.

Wings filled the skies, sirens blaring from the streets. Then Isaiah was there, hands on Bryce's shoulders. "Are you all right? Is that Holstrom? Where's Athalar?" The rapid-fire questions pelted her.

"I'm here," Hunt said from the darkness, landing with enough force that the ground shook. Lightning skittered over the concrete. He assessed Bryce, then Ithan, the wolf's body glowing under Hypaxia's hands. Then he registered the two demons and went pale. "Those . . ." He scanned Bryce again.

"You know what they are?" Isaiah asked.

Hunt rushed to Bryce and tucked her into him. She leaned into his warmth, his strength. He said quietly, "Deathstalkers. Personal pets of the Prince of the Pit. They were seen in Nena four days ago. They somehow crossed the border."

Bryce's stomach hollowed out.

Isaiah held up a hand to keep the other advancing angels and Aux at bay. "You think these two came here all the way from Nena? And why attack Bryce?"

Bryce wrapped her arms around Hunt's waist, not caring that she was clinging. If she let go, her knees might very well give out. Hunt lied smoothly, "Isn't it obvious? Hel's got a score to settle with her after this spring. They sent their best assassins to kill her."

Isaiah seemed to buy that theory, because he said to Bryce, "How did you even bring them down?"

"Ithan had a gun. I got a lucky shot on the first. Queen Hypaxia took care of the second."

It was mostly true.

"There," Hypaxia announced, stepping back from Ithan's healed, limp body. "He'll wake when he's ready." She gathered her broom and, with a touch—or some of her witch-power—it shrank back into the golden brooch of Cthona. She pinned it onto her gray jacket as she pivoted to Isaiah. "Can your soldiers transport him to the witches' embassy? I'd like to tend to him personally until he's conscious."

Bryce couldn't argue with that. But . . . there was no one to call for Ithan. No family, no friends, no pack. No one except—

She dialed Ruhn.

Deathstalkers. He should have sent out a warning the moment he'd IDed the tail of one in that photo from Nena. Should have had every soldier in this city on alert.

But Bryce . . . by some miracle, she didn't have a scratch on her.

It wasn't possible. Hunt knew how fast the deathstalkers were. Even Fae couldn't outrun them. They'd been bred that way by Apollion himself.

Hunt waited to speak until he and Bryce stood in the golden hall of the witches' embassy. Ithan had already been handed over from the two angels who'd flown him here to Ruhn and Declan, who'd gently carried the wolf into a small room to recover. "So, let's hear the real story."

Bryce turned to him, eyes bright with fear—and excitement. "I did it. Teleported." She explained what Hypaxia had done—what she had done.

"That was one Hel of a risk." He wasn't sure whether to kiss her or shake her for it.

"My options were limited," Bryce said, crossing her arms. Through the open doorway, Ruhn and Dec set Ithan on the cot, Hypaxia instructing them to position his body in a certain way. "Where the Hel was the dragon?"

"Fucking coward told Holstrom she'd climb up to the rooftops to provide a second set of eyes, and then bailed," Flynn said, face dark as he stepped into the hall.

"Do you blame her?" Bryce said.

"Yeah." Flynn glowered. "We did her a favor, and she fucked us over. She could have torched those demons." Before Bryce could counter, the lord stalked away with a disgusted shake of his head.

Bryce waited until the hall was empty again before asking Hunt, "You think these were the appetizers the Prince of the Pit threatened to send to test us?"

"Yes. They answer only to him."

"But they were about to kill me. He didn't seem to want us dead. And it seems reckless to do it just to test me." She gestured between them. "His epic opponents, remember?"

Ruhn stepped into the hall and murmured, "Unless you weren't the one they were supposed to kill." He jerked his chin toward Hypaxia, lowering his voice. He assessed the quiet halls of the embassy—no witches in sight—before saying, "Maybe her coven summoned them, somehow."

Bryce frowned. "Why?"

Ruhn paced a step. "You'd be the perfect cover story. She was walking beside someone Hel has a score to settle with—someone who'd pissed Hel off this spring. Deathstalkers imply the Prince of the Pit's involvement. If she'd died, all eyes would be on Hel. Everyone would think they'd targeted you, and she'd be the unfortunate additional loss."

"What about Ithan, though?"

Hunt picked up Ruhn's thread. "Also collateral. After this spring, I doubt Sabine would be stupid enough to summon a demon. That leaves our enemies or Hypaxia's. But given what Apollion threatened . . . I'd say odds are it was him. Maybe he was willing to take the risk that you'd die during his little test—maybe he supposed that if you died, you wouldn't be worthy of battling him anyway."

Bryce rubbed her face. "So where does that leave us?"

Hunt interlaced their fingers. "It leaves us with the realization that this city needs to be on high alert and you need to be armed at all times."

She glared. "That's not helpful."

Ruhn, wisely, kept his mouth shut.

"You didn't have any weapons tonight," Hunt snarled. "You two had *one knife* between you. You were lucky Ithan carried that gun. And you were even luckier in your guess that Hypaxia could charge up your ability to teleport."

Ruhn grunted his agreement.

"So that's how you did it," Declan said, walking back into the hall. The warrior shut the door behind him, giving Hypaxia and Ithan privacy.

Bryce sketched a bow. "It'll be my special solo act during the school talent show."

Declan snorted, but Ruhn was assessing her. "You really teleported?"

Bryce explained everything again, and Hunt couldn't keep himself from tugging her closer. When she finished, Ruhn echoed Hunt's words. "We got lucky tonight. *You* got lucky tonight."

Bryce winked at Hunt. "And I plan to get lucky again."

"Gross," Ruhn said as Declan snickered.

Hunt flicked Bryce's nose and said to Ruhn, "Let's set up watches around the apartment and this embassy—assign your most trusted soldiers. I'll get Isaiah and Naomi on it, too."

"The 33rd and the Aux teaming up to guard little old me?" Bryce crooned. "I'm flattered."

"This is not the time to debate alphahole politics," Hunt ground out. "Those were fucking deathstalkers."

"And I dealt with them."

"I wouldn't be so dismissive," he growled. "The Prince of the Pit will send hordes of them through the Northern Rift if he ever gets it fully open, rather than shoving one or two through at a time for fun. They hunt down whoever they're ordered to stalk. They're assassins. You get marked by them for execution, and you are *dead*."

She blew on her fingers, as if chasing off dust. "All in a day's work for me, then."

"Quinlan—"

Ruhn started laughing.

"What?" Hunt demanded.

Ruhn said, "You know who I was talking to before I got your call? My father." Bryce went still, and Hunt knew it was bad. Ruhn grinned at him. "*Your* father in-law."

"Excuse me?"

Ruhn didn't stop grinning. "He told me the wonderful news." He winked at Bryce. "You must be so happy."

Bryce groaned and turned to Hunt. "It's not official—"

"Oh, it's official," Ruhn said, leaning against the wall beside the door.

"What the fuck are you two talking about?" Hunt growled.

Ruhn smirked at Hunt. "She's been bandying about the royal name, apparently. Which means she's accepted her position as princess. And as you're her mate, that makes you son-in-law to the Autumn King. And my brother."

Hunt gaped at him. Ruhn was completely serious.

Bryce blurted, "Did you ask him about Cormac? The Autumn King insists the engagement is still on."

Ruhn's amusement faded. "I don't see how it could be."

"I'm sorry," Hunt cut in, "but what the fuck?" His wings splayed. "You're now officially a *princess*?"

Bryce winced. "Surprise?"

56

Ithan groaned, his body giving a collective throb of pain.

His throat—jaws and fangs and claws, the queen and *Bryce*—

He lunged up, hand at his neck—

"You're safe. It's over." The calm female voice came from his right, and Ithan twisted, finding himself on a narrow bed in a gilded room he'd never seen.

Queen Hypaxia sat in a chair beside him, a book in her lap, wearing her blue robes once again. No sign of the casual, modern female he'd been trailing earlier. His voice was like gravel as he asked, "You all right?"

"Very well. As is Miss Quinlan. You're at my embassy, in case you were wondering."

Ithan sagged back against the bed. He'd been ambushed, like a fucking novice. He'd always prided himself on his reflexes and instincts, but he'd had his ass handed to him. The queen opened her mouth, but he demanded, "What about the dragon?"

Hypaxia's mouth tightened. "Ariadne was nowhere to be found. It appears she has taken her chances with the law and fled."

Ithan growled. "She bailed?" The dragon had claimed she couldn't. That there was nowhere in Midgard she could go without the Astronomer finding her.

Gods. One guarding assignment and he'd fumbled it. Badly.

He deserved to have his throat ripped out. Deserved to be lying here, like a weak fucking child, for his ineptitude.

Hypaxia nodded gravely. "The city cameras picked it up: Ariadne left the moment I entered the pizza shop. But nothing more—even the cameras can't find her."

"She's likely halfway across the planet by now," Ithan grumbled. The Fae males were going to be so pissed.

"You liberated her from the ring. From serving a terrible master. Are you surprised that she is not willing to wait for someone to purchase her again?"

"I thought she'd be grateful, at least."

Hypaxia frowned with disapproval. But she said, "She is a dragon. A creature of earth and sky, fire and wind. She should never have been contained or enslaved. I hope she stays free for the rest of her immortal life."

The tone brooked no room for argument, and—well, Ithan agreed with the queen anyway. He sighed, gently rubbing at his tender throat. "So what the fuck attacked us? A demon?"

"Yes, an extremely deadly one." She explained what had happened.

Ithan eased into a sitting position once more. "I'm sorry I fucked this one up so badly. I . . . I don't like making mistakes like this." Losing grated on his very soul. The queen and Bryce were safe, but he was a fucking *loser.*

"You have nothing to apologize for," the queen said firmly. "Considering the gravity of the situation, I'm assuming your friends know more about the motives behind this attack than they have told me."

Well, she was definitely right on that one. Ithan blew out a breath that set his throat aching. It'd be another few hours until it was totally healed.

He had no idea how long it'd take until he forgave himself for fucking up tonight.

"So you can really contact Connor on the Autumnal Equinox?" he asked quietly, hating that he needed to change the subject. Not that this new one was much better.

"Yes." She angled her head, curls spilling over her shoulder. "You worry for him."

"Wouldn't you? I don't care if we've been told that he's, like, off-limits. I want to make sure he's okay. I heard what you said to Bryce—about ensuring your mom didn't go to one of the sleeping realms. I want you to do that for him." He swallowed, then amended, "If you're cool with that, Your Majesty."

Her eyes twinkled with amusement. "I shall do my best."

Ithan sighed again, staring at the tall windows on the other side of the room, the drapes shut for the night. "I know you're already doing a lot for me, but . . . the Astronomer has a wolf enslaved to him as one of his mystics. Is there anything you could do for her?"

"What do you mean?" He took it as a good sign that she didn't say no.

He said, "I can't just leave her there."

"Why is it your burden to free her?"

"Wolves don't belong in cages. That's what the mystics' tanks are. Watery cages."

"And what if she wants to be in there?"

"How could she?" Before the queen could answer, he plowed on, "I know it's random. There are so many other people suffering out there. But it doesn't sit right with me."

He'd screwed up enough in the past two years—he wouldn't drop the ball on this. An Alpha wolf in captivity—the idea was abhorrent. He'd do whatever he could to help her.

She seemed to read whatever lay on his face. "You're a good male, Ithan Holstrom."

"You met me yesterday." And after tonight, he sure as fuck didn't deserve that claim.

"But I can tell." She touched his hand gently. "I do not think there is much I can do to help the mystic, unfortunately, beyond what your other royal friends might be able to accomplish."

Ithan knew she was right. He'd find another way, then. Somehow. "Well, this is fucked."

"It sure is," said a male voice from the doorway, and Ithan

blinked, surprised to find Flynn and Declan standing there, Tharion a step behind them.

"Hey," Ithan said, bracing for the ridicule, the ribbing, the questioning about how the Hel he'd mangled protection duty.

But Declan bowed his head to the queen before sauntering over to Ithan. "How you feeling, pup?"

"Fine," Ithan said, then admitted, "A little sore."

"Getting your throat ripped out does that to a male," Flynn said. He winked at Hypaxia. "But she fixed you up pretty good, didn't she?"

Hypaxia smiled up at him. Tharion, lingering by the door, chuckled.

Ithan said quietly, "Yeah, she did."

Declan clapped his hands together. "Okay, well, we just wanted to make sure you were all right."

Hypaxia added, "They've been in and out all night."

"You'll give them away as big old softies, Pax," Tharion said to the queen, who shook her head at the name. As if Tharion often used it to annoy her.

Declan asked the queen, "When can he come home?"

Home. The word rang through Ithan. He'd been their roommate for only a week and a half. When had he last had a true home? The Den hadn't been one since his parents had died.

But . . . that was genuine concern on Declan's face. On Flynn's. Ithan swallowed hard.

"Tomorrow morning," Hypaxia said, and rose from her chair. "I'll do my final check then, and if you're cleared, you'll be on your way, Ithan."

"I'm supposed to guard you," Ithan countered, his voice thick.

But she patted his shoulder before walking to the door. Tharion fell into step beside her, like he planned to converse in private. The witch-queen said to Ithan as she and the mer left, "Take tomorrow off."

Ithan opened his mouth to object, but she'd already left, the mer with her.

Flynn slung himself into the seat the queen had vacated. "Don't tell Ruhn, but I'd love to have that female do a check on *me*."

Ithan scowled, but refrained from explaining what he'd overheard. The queen loved another and seemed pretty cut up about it. But what good was love, in the face of duty?

He'd keep Hypaxia's romance quiet. She'd agreed to her union with Ruhn, and he could do nothing but admire that she'd chosen to do so even when her heart lay with someone else.

Fuck, he knew how that felt. He blocked out Bryce's face from his mind.

Declan was saying to Flynn, "Do yourself a favor and don't hit on her. Or tease her."

"She's Ruhn's fiancée," Flynn said, propping his boots on the edge of Ithan's bed and tucking his hands behind his head. "That entitles me to some ribbing."

Ithan laughed, eyes stinging. No one ever joked in Amelie's pack. He might coax a smile from Perry every once in a while, but mostly they were all serious. Humorless. They never laughed at themselves.

But these guys had come to check on him. Not to rip into him for failing. They didn't even seem to view it as a failure.

Flynn asked a shade seriously, "You're really feeling all right, though?"

Ithan mastered himself. "Yeah."

"Good," Declan said.

Ithan's throat tightened. He hadn't realized how much he missed it—people having his back. Caring if he lived or died. The Pack of Devils had been that for him, yes, but his sunball team, too. He hadn't spoken to any of them since Connor's death.

Flynn's eyes softened slightly, as if seeing something on Ithan's face, and Ithan straightened, clearing his throat. But Flynn said, "We got you, wolf."

"Why?" The question slipped out before Ithan could wonder whether he should ask. But there were probably dozens of Fae who'd spent years trying to squeeze into the trio that was Ruhn, Flynn, and Declan. Why they'd brought Ithan into their little circle was beyond him.

Flynn and Dec swapped glances. The latter shrugged. "Why not?"

"I'm a wolf. You're Fae."

"So old-fashioned." Flynn winked. "I had you pegged as more progressive than that."

"I don't want your pity," Ithan said.

Declan drew back. "Who the fuck said anything about pity?"

Flynn put up his hands. "We're only friends with you because we want good sunball tickets."

Ithan looked between the males. Then burst out laughing.

"All right." He rubbed at his sore throat again. "That's a good enough reason for me."

Ruhn monitored his sister as they waited for Athalar to finish briefing some senior members of the 33rd on what had gone down with the deathstalker.

It felt like last spring all over again. Granted, Micah had been the one summoning those kristallos demons, but . . . this couldn't be good. The Horn was tattooed on Bryce's back now—what wouldn't Hel do to attain it?

"The answer," Bryce said to Ruhn, "is that I'm not going to allow any sort of security detail."

Ruhn blinked. And said silently, *I wasn't thinking that.*

She glared at him sidelong. *I could* feel *you brooding about the attack. It's the logical conclusion from an overly aggressive Fae male.*

Overly aggressive?

Protective?

Bryce. This is some serious-ass shit.

I know.

And you're a princess now. An official one.

She crossed her arms, watching Hunt talk with his friends. *I know.*

How do you feel about it?

How do you *feel about it?*

Why the fuck would it make any difference what I feel? He scowled at her.

Because now you have to share the crown.

I'm glad I can share it with you. Selfishly, pathetically glad, Bryce. But . . . isn't this what you wanted to avoid?

It is. Her mental voice hardened into sharp steel.

Are you going to do something about it?

Maybe.

Tread carefully. There are so many laws and rules and shit that you don't know about. I can fill you in, but . . . this is a whole new level of the game. You have to be on alert.

She faced him, offering a broad grin that didn't meet her eyes before taking a few steps toward Athalar. "If dear old dad wants a princess," she said, looking more like their father than he'd ever witnessed, "then he'll get one."

"Dreadwolves prowling the Old Square," Hypaxia hissed under her breath to Tharion as she peered out the window of her private suite on the second floor of the elegant embassy.

Despite the plush furniture, the room definitely belonged to a witch: a small crystal altar to Cthona adorned the eastern wall, covered in various tools of worship; a large obsidian scrying mirror hung above it; and the fireplace built into the southern wall had various iron arms, presumably to hold cauldrons during spells. A royal suite, yes, but a workroom as well.

"I hate the sight of them," the queen went on, the streetlights casting her beautiful face in golden hues. "Those uniforms. The silver darts on their collars." He wondered how many people ever saw her so unguarded. "Rebel-hunters. That's what they are."

Indeed, where they walked, revelers fell silent. Tourists stopped snapping photos.

"Tell me how you really feel, Pax," Tharion said, crossing his arms.

The queen whirled toward him. "I wish you'd stop using that nickname. Ever since the Summit—"

"Ever since then, you've missed me using it?" He gave her his most charming smile.

She rolled her eyes, but he caught the slight curl of her lips.

He asked, "Have you kept up the tally? How many times has Prince Ruhn gawked at you since you arrived?"

She flushed. "He doesn't gawk."

"I think our final tally at the Summit was . . . thirty? Forty?"

She whacked him on the chest.

"I missed you," he said, grinning.

She grinned back. "What does your fiancée have to say about that?" She was one of the few people who knew. During their initial meeting at the Summit—an accidental encounter late one night when she'd sought some solitude at one of the mer's subterranean pools and found him seeking the same—they'd spoken of their various . . . obligations. A friendship had immediately sprung up.

Tharion countered, "What does *your* fiancé have to say about it?"

The witch laughed softly, the sound like silver bells. "You're the one who's been associating with him. You tell me."

He chuckled, but his amusement fell away, his voice becoming serious. "He's concerned enough about you that he told some of us about your coven. Why didn't you tell me?" He'd grab any one of them who harmed her and drown them. Slowly.

She searched his face. He let her. "What could you have done?"

Well, that stung. Especially because she was right. He let out a long sigh. He wished he could tell her—about the fact that he'd bought himself a small stretch of freedom. That he would only go back to the Blue Court to keep up appearances, that he'd pretend Emile Renast was still on the loose for as long as he could, but . . . Would he go back after that? *Could* he go back?

Maybe he'd get in touch with the Ocean Queen's people and beg for asylum. Maybe they'd shelter his family, too.

He'd opened his mouth to speak when a ripple went through the street below. People stopped. Some pressed against buildings.

"What the fuck are they doing here?" Tharion growled.

Mordoc and the Hammer stalked down the street, wolf and angel sneering at all in their path. They seemed to savor the quiet and dread that trailed in their wake.

Hypaxia's brows raised. "Not friends of yours?"

He put a hand on his heart. "You wound me, Pax."

The queen's mouth thinned as Pollux and Mordoc crossed the intersection. "It's an ill omen, to see them here."

"Maybe they want to make sure all is well, considering what attacked tonight."

Mighty Ogenas, creatures straight from the Pit. He'd been enjoying a drink with a pride of lioness shifters at a wine bar when he'd gotten the call. He'd come here, claiming an investigative visit from the Blue Court, but . . . "You sure you're all right?" he asked, glad to pivot from the two monsters on the street.

"I'm fine," Hypaxia said, turning weary, sad eyes toward him. "Miss Quinlan proved herself a valuable ally in a fight." He liked the idea of the two of them becoming friendly. They'd be a formidable pair against any opponent.

"What'd your coven say about the attack?" Tharion asked, glancing to the shut double doors across the room. Pollux and Mordoc vanished down the street. As if they'd all been frozen, people suddenly began moving again. None went in the direction the Hammer and the dreadwolf had gone.

"My coven feigned outrage, of course. It's not worth recounting."

Fair enough. "You should get some sleep. You must be exhausted from healing Holstrom."

"Not at all." Her gaze again lifted to his face. "But you . . . you should go. Another few minutes and suspicions will be raised."

"Oh?" He couldn't resist teasing. "Like what?"

She flushed again. "Like we're doing things we shouldn't."

"Sounds naughty."

She playfully shoved him toward the door. He let her, walking backward as he said, "I'll see you soon, okay? You have my number."

Her eyes shone like stars. "Thank you for checking on me."

"Anything for you, Pax." Tharion shut the door behind him and found himself face-to-face with three witches. All members of her coven, if his memory of the Summit served him. All cold-faced and unamused. "Ladies," he said, inclining his head.

None of them answered, and as they converged on the queen's suite with a knock on her door, he suppressed the instinct to return to her side.

But it wasn't his place, and he still had one more task tonight. First, though, he needed a dip in the Istros to make sure his fins stayed intact.

Thirty minutes later, still wet, Tharion walked up to the peeling front door of the near-collapsing house off Archer Street, music blasting from the windows despite the late hour. Tharion knocked, loudly enough to be heard over the bass.

A moment later, the door opened. Tharion smiled crookedly at Ruhn, and waved to Tristan Flynn and Declan Emmet standing in the foyer behind him. "Got space for one more roommate?"

57

Hunt waited until he and Bryce had entered the apartment, the door firmly shut behind them, before he said, “I’m a *prince* now?”

Bryce slumped onto the couch. “Welcome to the club.”

“Your father really did this?”

She nodded glumly. “My mom is going to freak.”

Hunt stalked to the couch. “What about you, Bryce? Your mom can deal with it. I can deal with this, believe it or not. But . . . are you okay?”

She only stroked Syrinx’s coat.

He scented salt and water, then, and sat on the new coffee table, lifting her chin between his thumb and forefinger to find tears running down her cheeks. Ones he had no doubt she’d been holding back for hours.

He’d turn the Autumn King into smoldering carrion for putting those tears, the fear and panic and sorrow, in her eyes.

“I spent my whole life avoiding this. And I just feel . . .” She wiped angrily at her face. “I feel so fucking *stupid* for having walked into his net.”

“You shouldn’t. He bent the rules to his will. He’s a snake.”

“He’s a snake and now technically, legally, my king.” She choked on a sob. “I will never have a normal life again. I’ll never be free of him, and—”

Hunt gathered her into his arms, moving to the couch and pulling her into his lap. "We'll fight him on this. You want a normal life, a life with me—we'll make it happen. You're not alone. We'll fight him together."

She buried her face against his chest, tears splashing onto the black armor of his battle-suit. He stroked her silken hair, letting the smooth strands slide through his fingers.

"I could handle the Starborn shit. I could handle the magic," she said, voice muffled against his chest. "But this . . . I can't fucking handle this." She lifted her head, dread and panic flooding her expression. "He *owns* me. I'm chattel to him. If he wanted me to marry Cormac tonight, he could sign the marriage documents without even my presence. If I wanted a divorce, he'd be the one to grant it, not that he would. I'm a commodity—either I belong to him, or I belong to Cormac. He can do whatever he wants, and no amount of bravado from me can stop it."

Lightening skittered down his wings. "I'll fucking kill him."

"And what will that do, beyond get you executed?"

He leaned his brow against hers. "We'll think of a way out of this."

"Hypaxia said only the Asteri could override him. Considering our status with them, I doubt they'll help."

Hunt blew out a long breath. Tightened his arms around his mate. He'd slaughter anyone who tried to take her from him. King, prince, Fae, or Asteri. He'd fucking *kill*—

"Hunt."

He blinked.

"Your eyes went all . . . rage-dazey." She sniffled.

"Sorry." The last thing she needed right now was to have to handle his fury, too. He kissed her cheek, her temple, her neck.

She rested her brow on his shoulder, shuddering. Syrinx whimpered from where he had cuddled up on her other side.

For long minutes, Hunt and Bryce sat there. Hunt savored every place his body touched hers, the warmth and scent of her. Racked his mind for anything he might do, any path out of this.

Her fingers curled against the nape of his neck. He loosened his grip, pulling back to scan her face.

Starlight and fire sparked there. "Tell me that look means you came up with some brilliant yet painless way out of this," he said.

She kissed him softly. "You're not going to like it."

Ruhn wasn't at all shocked when he found himself standing before that mental couch.

After the night he'd had, nothing could shock him.

On the bridge, Day surveyed Ruhn without saying a word. Somehow, he could have sworn she sensed his turmoil.

But Ruhn said, "Anything for me?" He hadn't forgotten their last conversation. She'd told him he was a worthless, do-nothing loser who'd never known sacrifice or pain.

"You're angry with me."

"I don't care about you enough to be angry with you," he said coldly.

"Liar."

The word was an arrow shot between them. The night around him rippled. His temper hadn't improved when he discovered that Ariadne had straight up bailed. Fled the moment no one was looking and gone the gods knew where. He didn't blame the dragon. He was just . . . pissed he hadn't anticipated it.

He asked Day, "What the fuck do you want me to say?"

"I owe you an apology for last time. I'd had a rough day. My temper got the better of me."

"You spoke the truth. Why bother apologizing for it?"

"It's not the truth. I . . ." She seemed to struggle for words. "Do you know when I last spoke honestly with someone? When I last spoke to someone as I do to you, as close to my real self as I've ever come?"

"I'm guessing it's been a while."

She crossed her arms, wrapping them around herself. "Yes."

"Can I ask you a question?"

She angled her head. "What?"

He rubbed his neck, his shoulder. "What do you think makes a good leader?" The question was ridiculous—an essay for a second-grader. But after all that had gone down . . .

She didn't balk. "Someone who listens. Who thinks before acting. Who tries to understand different viewpoints. Who does what is right, even if the path is long and hard. Who will give a voice to the voiceless."

His father was none of those things. Except for thinking before acting. That male had schemes that had been in play for decades. Centuries.

"Why do you ask?"

Ruhn shrugged. "All this rebel stuff has me thinking about it. Who we'd replace the Asteri with. Who we'd *want* to replace them with."

She studied him, her gaze a brand on his skin. "What do *you* think makes a good leader?"

He didn't know. Only that he wasn't entirely sure he fit the bill of what she'd described, either. Where would that leave his people? "I'm trying to figure that out." If he became king one day, what sort of ruler would he be? He'd try to do right, but . . .

Silence fell, companionable and comfortable.

But then Day blew out a breath, blue flame rippling from her mouth. "I'm not used to this sort of thing."

He lowered himself onto his couch. "What sort of thing?"

"Friendship."

"You consider me a friend?"

"In a world full of enemies, you're my only friend."

"Well, maybe I should give you friendship lessons, because you fucking blow at it."

She laughed, and the sound wasn't entirely joyous. "All right. I deserved that."

He gave her a half smile, even if she couldn't see it. "Lesson one: don't shit on your friends when you have a bad day."

"Right."

"Lesson two: Your true friends won't mind when you do, so long as you own up to it and apologize. Usually in the form of buying them a beer."

Another laugh, softer this time. "I'll buy you a beer, then."

"Yeah? When you come to visit me?"

"Yeah," she said, the word echoing. "When I come visit you."

He rose and crossed to her couch, peering down at her. "Which will be when, Day?"

She tipped her head back, as if staring up at him. "On the Autumnal Equinox."

Ruhn stilled. "You . . . What?"

She brought her burning hand to her head—her ear. Like she was tucking a strand of hair behind it. She stood, walking around the couch. Putting it between them as she said, "I must attend the ball for the Archangels. I could . . . meet you somewhere."

"I'm going to that ball," he said, unsure why his voice went hoarse. For her to be invited there, she had to be important, precisely as they'd suspected. "The equinox fete is always a masked ball. We can meet there."

She backed up a step as he rounded the couch. "In front of so many?"

"Why not? We'll both be in masks. And we're both invited to the party, so why would it be suspicious for two people to talk there?"

He could have sworn he heard her heart pounding. She asked, "How will I know you?"

"The party's in the conservatory on the rooftop garden of the Comitium. There's a fountain on the western side of it—right off the stairs from the conservatory. Meet me there at midnight."

"But how can I be sure not to mistake someone else for you?"

"If I think it's you, I'll say 'Day?' And if you answer 'Night,' we'll know."

"We shouldn't."

Ruhn took a step toward her, his breathing uneven. "Is it so bad if I know who you are?"

"It jeopardizes everything. For all I know, you could be baiting me for the Asteri—"

"Look at me and tell me you think that's true."

She did. Ruhn came close enough that the heat of her flame warmed his body.

And, deciding to Hel with it, he reached for her hand. The flame warmed his night-skin, but did not burn. The hand beneath the fire was slender. Delicate.

Her fingers contracted against his own, but he held firm. "I'll be waiting for you."

"And if I'm not what you expect?"

"What do you think I'm expecting?"

Again, her fingers twitched, like she'd yank away. "I don't know."

He tugged on her arm, pulling her a little closer. When was the last time he'd had to work for a female's attention like this? Fuck, he *was* working for it, wasn't he? He wanted to see her face. Know who was bold and brave enough to risk her life again and again to defy the Asteri.

Ruhn stared down at the veil of flame between him and Day. "I want to smell your scent. See you. Even for a moment."

"That ball will be swarming with our enemies."

"Then we won't stay long. But . . . just meet me, all right?"

She was silent, as if she were trying to pierce the blanket of stars he wore. "Why?"

His voice dropped. "You know why."

She hesitated. Then she said softly, "Yes."

Her flames seemed to reach for his stars and shadows. "Midnight."

She faded into embers on the wind. "Midnight," she promised.

58

Two weeks later, Hunt scowled at his reflection in the mirror. He tugged at the white bow tie of his tux, already feeling strangled by the stupid thing.

He'd wanted to wear his battle-suit to the party, but Bryce had staged an intervention last week and demanded he wear something "halfway normal." *Then you can go back to being the predator-in-the-night we all love so much*, she'd said.

Hunt growled, giving himself a final once-over before calling across the apartment, "I'm as good as I'm going to get, so let's leave. The van's downstairs."

He sure as fuck couldn't cram his wings into the usual black sedan the Autumn King would have sent for Bryce. But at least the asshole had sent a van instead. Cormac was her official escort to the party, and was no doubt waiting in the vehicle. It had likely been Cormac who'd convinced the Autumn King to switch to a van so Bryce's "plus-one" could join them.

Bryce had bristled at every new order that had come from the Autumn King: the jewelry she was expected to wear, the clothes, the height of her heels, the length of her nails, the type of car they'd take, who would exit the car first, how *she* would exit the car—apparently, her ankles and knees were to be forever glued together in public—and lastly, most outrageously, what and how she was allowed to eat.

Nothing. That was the short answer. A Fae Princess did not eat in public, was the long answer. Maybe a sip of soup or one solitary, small bite to be polite. And one glass of wine. No hard liquor.

Bryce had read the list of commandments one night after they'd fucked in the shower, and had been so wound up that Hunt had gone down on her to take the edge off. He'd taken his time tasting her, savoring each lick of her delicious, enticing sex.

Even fucking her at night and before work, he couldn't get enough. Would find himself in the middle of the day aching for her. They'd already fucked twice in her office, right on her desk, her dress bunched at her waist, his pants barely unbuckled as he pounded into her.

They hadn't been caught, thank the gods. Not just by her coworkers, but by anyone who'd report it to Cormac, to the Autumn King. She'd already had one battle with her father over Hunt still living here with her. But after tonight . . .

He scooped up the golden mask from where he'd left it on the dresser—so fucking ridiculous and dramatic—and stepped into the great room, toes wriggling in his patent leather shoes. When was the last time he'd worn anything but his boots or sneakers? Never. He'd literally never worn shoes like this. When he was young, it had been lace-up sandals or boots—and then it had been boots for centuries.

What would his mother make of this male in the mirror? He strained to recall her smile, to imagine how her eyes might have sparkled. He wished she were here. Not only to see him, but to know that all she'd struggled to provide had paid off. To know that he could take care of her now.

Bryce let out a whistle from the other side of the great room, and Hunt looked up, tucking away the old ache in his chest.

All the breath left his chest. "Holy shit."

She was . . .

"Holy shit," he said again, and she laughed. He swallowed. "You're so fucking beautiful."

She blushed, and his head began roaring, cock aching. He wanted to lick that blush, wanted to kiss every inch of her smile.

"I couldn't bring myself to wear the tiara," Bryce said, lifting a wrist and twirling the crown around it with typical irreverence.

"You don't need it."

She really didn't. The sparkling black dress hugged every luscious curve before loosening around the knee, spilling into a train of solid night. The plunging neckline stopped below her breasts, framing the star between them, drawing the eye to the remarkable scar.

Black gloves flowed up to her elbows, and her satin-clad fingers toyed with one of the diamond chandelier earrings sparkling against the column of her neck. She'd left her hair down, a diamond comb pinning back one side, the silken mass of hair draping over her opposite shoulder. In her other hand she clutched the stem of a silver mask.

Full, bloodred lips smiled at him beneath eyes framed with a swoop of kohl. Simple makeup—and utterly devastating.

"Solas, Quinlan."

"You clean up pretty good yourself."

Hunt straightened the lapels of his tux. "Yeah?"

"Want to stay home and fuck instead?"

Hunt laughed. "Very regal of you. Any other night, my answer would be yes." He offered his arm. "Your Highness."

Bryce smirked and took it, pressing close to him. Hunt breathed in her scent, the jasmine of her perfume. She set her tiara on her head at a jaunty angle, the little peak of solid diamond glittering as if lit by starlight. Hunt straightened it for her, and led her out the door.

Toward the world waiting for them.

Ruhn bowed before the seated Archangels. Hypaxia, at his side, bowed as well.

He was a lying piece of shit, he'd thought ruefully as he'd donned a black-on-black tux an hour ago. He'd agreed to be Hypaxia's date to this thing—as her fiancé, and as Crown Prince he didn't really have a choice but to be here—but he hadn't been able to stop thinking about Day. About whether she'd show up in a mere few hours.

He'd already scoped out the fountain through the western doors. It lay in shadow beyond the massive glass conservatory, about fifteen feet from the stairs leading out of the building and into the starry night.

He hadn't spoken to Day since they'd made their arrangement. He'd tried to talk to her, but she hadn't answered. Would she be here tonight, as promised? Was she already in the packed conservatory?

He'd removed his carved black mask to make his formal greeting to the Archangels, and as he turned from Celestina and Ephraim, Ruhn scanned the crowd once more.

Beautiful gowns, beautiful ladies—they were masked, but he knew most of them. Of course, Day could be someone he knew. He had no idea what to look for. *Where* to even look for her in the vast, candlelit space, bedecked in garlands and wreaths of autumnal leaves brought from the colder climes up north. Winged skulls and scythes were interspersed with a rainbow of fall gourds on every table. Day could be anywhere.

Security had been insane getting in here. It was the 33rd's show, and they ran it like the paranoid psychos they were. Soldiers stood stationed outside the doors and hovered in the skies. Baxian and Naomi had checked IDs and invites at the doors. They'd remain there all night, even while other members of the triarii reveled. None of Ephraim's people had been tapped to stand guard. Either from a lack of trust or as a privilege, Ruhn didn't know.

There had been no sign of Pippa Spetsos or her Lightfall squadron, or any other Ophion unit recently, but dreadwolves still prowled the streets. And this ballroom.

Ruhn slipped on his mask and said to Hypaxia, "Can I get you anything?"

She was resplendent in a royal-blue ball gown, her cloudberry crown gleaming amid her dark, upswept hair. Heads turned to remark on her beauty, visible even with the white-winged mask she'd donned. "I'm fine, thank you." She smiled pleasantly.

Ithan, in a traditional tux behind her, stepped up, his silver wolf mask glittering in the little firstlights strung throughout the lush conservatory. "The River Queen's daughter wishes to meet you," he murmured, gesturing to where Tharion stood stone-faced beside a stunning, curly-haired young female. The former looked a bit stiff for once, but the female, clad in gauzy turquoise, brimmed with energy. Excitement.

That had been a minor bomb the other night. Tharion had settled quite comfortably into life with Ruhn and his friends . . . until he'd gotten the otter's note from the River Queen instructing him to come to this ball with her daughter.

Apparently, the leash only stretches so far, Tharion had said when Ruhn had asked, and that had been that.

Hypaxia smiled at Ithan. "Of course. I'd love to meet her." Ithan offered his arm, and Hypaxia said to Ruhn, "I suppose we'll dance later?"

"Yeah," Ruhn said, then bowed quickly. "I mean, yes. I'd be honored." Hypaxia gave him a strange, assessing glance, but left with Ithan.

He needed a drink. A big fucking drink.

He was halfway to one of the six open bars throughout the space, each one of them packed, when his sister and Cormac walked in.

Bryce looked like a princess, and it had nothing to do with the crown, an heirloom of the Danaan house that their father had ordered her to wear tonight. People stared at her—many unkindly.

Or maybe their attention was on Athalar. The angel entered a few steps behind the royal couple. Apparently, he'd been given the night off by Celestina. But how the male could stand walking behind them, seeing Bryce's hand on another male's arm . . .

Athalar's face revealed nothing, though. He was the Umbra Mortis once more.

A flash of red across the space drew Ruhn's gaze. His father made his way toward Bryce and Cormac. The Avallen Prince seemed inclined to meet him halfway, but Bryce tugged on his arm and steered them right to the Archangels instead.

A few Fae gasped at the snub—Flynn's parents among them. Flynn, the traitor, had claimed he had a headache to avoid coming tonight. From his parents' pinched faces upon seeing Ruhn arrive without Flynn in tow, he knew his friend hadn't told them. Too bad for all the eligible young ladies they'd no doubt lined up to woo their son tonight.

Ignoring the dismayed Fae, Bryce strode right up to the dais where the Archangels sat, bypassing the line of well-wishers. No one dared call her out for it. Athalar followed her and Cormac, and Ruhn noted his father's stormy face and moved closer, too.

Bryce and Cormac bowed before the Archangels, Celestina's brows high as she turned between Hunt and Cormac. Bryce said, "My congratulations to you both."

"Thank you," Ephraim answered, bored and eyeing the bar.

Cormac added, "Avallen extends its wishes and hopes for your happiness."

It had been a relief to discover that Mordoc wouldn't be attending the party tonight—wouldn't be able to put faces to the scents he'd probably detected in the alley all those days ago. But the Hind was here. Ruhn had already warned his cousin to stay away from the female, no matter how his blood might howl for vengeance.

"And we extend our wishes to you, too," Celestina said.

"Thank you," Bryce said, smiling widely. "Prince Hunt and I plan to be quite happy."

A gasp rippled through the room.

Bryce half turned toward Hunt and extended a hand. The angel walked to her, eyes dancing with wicked amusement. Cormac seemed caught between surprise and fury.

The room seemed to be spinning. Bryce wouldn't dare. She wouldn't fucking dare pull a stunt like this. Ruhn swallowed a laugh of pure shock.

"Prince?" Celestina asked.

Bryce looped her arm through Hunt's, pressing close. "Hunt and I are mates." A charming, brilliant smile. "That makes him my prince. Prince Cormac was good enough to escort me tonight, as we've become close friends this month." She turned to the crowd. Immediately pinpointed the Autumn King, glaring white-faced at her. "I thought you told her, Father."

Holy shit.

She'd played along with the rules so far to reach this point. A public declaration that she was with Hunt. That Hunt was a prince—a Prince of the Fae.

And their father, who hated public scenes . . . he could either risk calling his own daughter a liar—thus embarrassing himself—or play along.

The Autumn King said into the stunned crowd, "My apologies, Your Graces. My daughter's union must have slipped my mind." His eyes threatened Helfire as he glowered at Bryce. "I hope her excitement in announcing her union with Hunt Athalar is not interpreted as an attempt to upstage your joy tonight."

"Oh, no," Celestina said, covering her mouth with a hand to hide a smile. "I congratulate and bless you and Hunt Athalar, Bryce Quinlan." It didn't get more official than that.

Ephraim grunted and motioned to the nearest server for a drink. Taking that as her cue, Bryce bowed to them again, and pivoted Hunt toward the crowd. Cormac had the wits to follow, but left them near a pillar after a word to Bryce. He stalked for the Autumn King.

So Ruhn went up to them, and Bryce snorted. "Nice crown."

He jerked his chin at her. "That's all you have to say?"

She shrugged. "What?"

But she frowned over his shoulder. Right. There were a lot of people with Vanir hearing listening. He'd yell at her later.

Though . . . he didn't really need to yell at all. She'd found her way out of this clusterfuck. Her own brilliant, daring way. "I'm really glad you're my sister," Ruhn said.

Bryce smiled so broadly it showed all her teeth.

Ruhn shook off his shock and said to Athalar, "Sweet tux." He added, just to be a dick, "Your Highness."

Athalar pulled at his collar. "No wonder you got all those piercings, if this is how you're expected to dress at these things."

"First rule of being a prince," Ruhn said, grinning. "Rebel where you can." Considering what they were all doing these days, it was the understatement of the year.

Hunt growled, but Ephraim and Celestina stood from their thrones at the rear of the conservatory, a massive screen dropping from a panel in the glass ceiling. A projector began to hum.

"Friends." Celestina's clear voice rang out over the crowd. Anyone still speaking shut the fuck up. "We thank you for coming to celebrate our union this lovely evening."

Ephraim's deep voice boomed, "It is with much joy that Celestina and I announce our mating." He smiled faintly at his gorgeous mate. "And with much joy that we remotely welcome our guests of honor."

The lights dimmed, leaving only soft candlelight that made the decorative skulls all the more menacing. Then the screen flickered on, revealing seven thrones. A sight more harrowing than any skull or scythe.

Six of the thrones were full. The seventh had been left vacant, as always—thanks to the Prince of the Pit.

A chill skittered up Ruhn's arms as the Asteri coldly surveyed the party.

59

Bryce couldn't get a breath down.

The Asteri stared at them all like they could see through the screen. See them gathered here.

They must be able to, Bryce realized. Her hand slipped into Hunt's, and he squeezed tight, a gray wing tucking around her. Gods, he was gorgeous tonight.

She'd figured this party was the only setting where her father wouldn't dare challenge her. Where any union with Hunt could be verified and recognized by Archangels. She'd worn and done everything he'd ordered . . . all so she could get here tonight. Had raced up to the dais upon arriving so that she could announce Hunt as her mate before her father could introduce her as Cormac's bride.

Relief and excitement—and a bit of smugness—had coursed through her. Her father would bring down the hammer later. But tonight . . . she'd celebrate her victory. She knew Hunt had as little interest in being a prince as she did in being a princess. But he'd done it. For her. For them.

She'd been about to drag Hunt into a closet or a cloakroom to fuck his brains out when the screen descended. And now, staring at the six immortal figures, at Rigelus's boyish face . . .

Thankfully, other people in the room were shaking, too. Her heart pounded like a drum.

Celestina and Ephraim bowed, and everyone followed suit. Bryce's legs wobbled on her heels as she did so. Hunt squeezed her hand again, but she kept her focus on the ground, hating the primal fear, the terror of knowing that these beings judged them, and with one word they might slay everyone, might slay her family—

"Our congratulations to you, Celestina and Ephraim," Rigelus crooned in that voice that didn't belong to the teenage body his twisted soul inhabited. "We extend our wishes for a happy mating, and a fertile one."

Celestina and Ephraim lowered their heads in thanks. "We are grateful for your wisdom and kindness in pairing us," Celestina said. Bryce tried and failed to detect the undercurrent of her tone. Was it sincere? Was the slight tightness from a lie, or from being before the Asteri?

Octartis, the Southern Star—the Asteri to Rigelus's right—spoke, her voice like ancient, cracking ice. "I understand other congratulations are in order, too."

A chill shot along Bryce's spine as Rigelus said, "Princess Bryce Danaan and Prince Hunt Athalar." It was an order. A command.

The crowd fell back. Giving the Asteri a clear shot at them.

Oh gods. Bryce's blood rushed from her face. How did they already know? Had the cameras on their end been running the whole time, letting the Asteri watch and listen unseen?

But then the Autumn King was there, bowing at her side. "I present my daughter to you, Holy Ones," he intoned.

She wondered if he hated bowing to them. It satisfied the fuck out of her to see him do it, but there was no time to dwell on that now. Bryce bowed, too, as she murmured, "Hail the Asteri."

Cormac appeared on her father's other side, bowing low. As Crown Prince of Avallen, he had no other choice.

He'd been furious at her stunt. Not that she'd ended their engagement, but that she hadn't warned him ahead of time. *Any other surprises tonight, Princess?* he'd snapped at her before striding off to speak to her father. *You broke our deal. I won't forget that.*

She hadn't responded, but . . . Did the Asteri know one of their fiercest rebels stood before them, playing prince? Did they know how she'd helped him, worked with him? She supposed if they did, they'd all be dead.

"And I present her mate and consort, Prince Hunt Athalar," the Autumn King was saying sharply, his disapproval palpable. He might very well kill her for this. If Cormac didn't do it first.

But, according to Fae law, she was now Hunt's property. Recognized in the past few minutes by both Archangels and the Asteri. If it made Hunt uncomfortable, if he resented his new title or the beings before him, he showed no sign as he bowed, his wing brushing over her back. "Hail the Asteri."

"Rise," the Asteri said, and so Bryce, Hunt, and her father did. There were so many eyes upon them. In this room, in that chamber in the Eternal City. Rigelus's, especially, bore into her. He smiled slightly. Like he knew everything she'd done these weeks. Every rebel activity, every mutinous thought.

Bryce hated herself for lowering her gaze. Even as she knew Hunt stared Rigelus down.

But the Bright Hand of the Asteri said, "So many happy unions tonight. It is our wish that you all partake in the revelry. Go, and celebrate Death's Day in peace."

Everyone bowed again, and the screen went dark. More than a few people whimpered, as if they'd been holding in the sound.

No one spoke for several seconds as the lights brightened. Then the band began once more slightly off-tempo, like the musicians needed a minute to get their shit together. Even the Archangels were a little pale as they took their seats.

Bryce faced her father. The Autumn King said in a voice so low no one else could hear, "You little bitch."

Bryce smiled broadly. "It's 'You little bitch, *Your Highness.*'" She stalked into the crowd. She didn't miss Hunt smirking at the king, throwing him a wink that clearly said: *Make a move and I'll fry you, asswipe.*

But she had to suck down a few long breaths as she halted at the edge of the dance floor, trying to regain her composure.

"You all right?" Hunt asked, gripping her shoulder.

"Yes, Your Highness," she muttered.

He chuckled, and leaned to whisper in her ear, "I thought you only called me that in bed, Quinlan." She did. *You are my fucking prince,* she'd panted last night as he drove his cock up into her.

Bryce leaned against him, shaking off the last of the Asteri's ice. "I can't believe we did it."

Hunt let out a low laugh. "There's going to be Hel to pay." From her father. But tonight, he could do nothing. Here, in front of all these people, he could do nothing at all.

So Bryce said, "Dance with me?"

He raised a brow. "Really?"

"You do know how to dance, right?"

"Of course I do. But . . . It's been a long while since I've danced with anyone."

Since Shahar, probably. She interlaced their fingers. "Dance with me."

The initial steps were stilted, hesitant. His arm slid around her waist, his other hand clutching hers as he led her into the sweet ballad coming from the band. With so many watching, it took a verse or two to get their rhythm.

Hunt murmured, "Just look at me, and fuck all the rest of them."

His eyes shone with desire and joy, and that spark that was pure Hunt. The star on her chest gleamed, on full display. Someone gasped, but Bryce kept her attention on Hunt. He smiled again.

It was all that mattered, that smile. They fell into easy movement, and when Hunt spun her, she smiled back.

She whipped into his arms, and Hunt didn't falter a step, sweeping her around the floor. She had the vague sense of Ruhn and Hypaxia dancing, Celestina and Ephraim, too, of Baxian and Naomi—Isaiah now with them—on guard by the doors, but she couldn't look away from Hunt.

He pressed a kiss to her mouth. The entire universe melted away with it. It was only them, would only be them, dancing together, souls twining. "Everything that ever happened to me, it was all so I could meet you, Quinlan. Be here with you. I'm yours. Forever."

Her throat tightened, and the star on her chest flared, lighting up the entire conservatory like a small moon. Bryce kissed him back, not caring who saw, only that he was here.

"Everything I am is yours," she said against his lips.

Hypaxia seemed distracted as Ruhn danced with her, trying his best to avoid watching Hunt and Bryce make moon-eyes at each other. To avoid hearing the comments that trailed in their wake.

The Umbra Mortis—now a Fae Prince. What a disgrace. The slurs and nastiness flowed past Ruhn from Fae mouths, bold enough to run free behind the safety of their masks. Not that the masks would hide their scents. Ruhn marked each one of them.

Athalar was his brother now, by law. And Ruhn didn't put up with people talking shit about his family. The family he liked, anyway.

Cormac had already left, slipping into a shadow and teleporting out. A small mercy—Cormac had been so distracted by Bryce's little surprise that he hadn't bothered to confront the Hind. But Ruhn didn't blame his cousin for bailing. After the stunt Bryce had pulled, Cormac would have been swarmed by Fae families eager to present their daughters. Flynn's parents—a sharp-eyed Sathia in tow—were clearly scouring the ballroom for any hint of the Avallen Prince.

Ruhn suppressed his smile at the thought of their fruitless hunt and focused on his partner. Hypaxia seemed to be scanning the crowd.

His heart skipped a beat. He asked quietly, "You looking for someone?"

She cleared her throat. "My sister. The Hind."

His chest loosened. "Over by the foot of the dais. Next to Pollux."

Hypaxia glanced over on their next turn. The Hind and the Hammer stood together, both in matte black masks, the angel in a white imperial uniform edged in gold. The Hind's golden, sparkling dress clung to her hips before falling to the floor. Her blond hair had been swept up, and for once, no silver torque adorned her neck. Only slender gold earrings brushed her shoulders.

"They make a beautiful pair," Hypaxia murmured. "As monstrous inside as they are lovely outside, though."

Ruhn grunted. "Yeah."

Hypaxia chewed on her lip. "I was waiting until tonight to approach her."

He studied her face. "You want me to go with you?" He could offer nothing less.

"Do you think she'll . . . react badly?"

"She's too smart to cause a scene. And I don't think the Hind is the sort to do that anyway. She's cut from the same cloth as my father. The worst thing that happens is that she ignores you."

Hypaxia stiffened in his arms. "I suppose you're right. I'd rather get this meeting over with. It will spoil the rest of my night to stew over it."

"Why meet with her at all?"

"Because she is my sister. And I've never spoken to her. Or seen her in the flesh."

"I felt that way when I learned about Bryce's existence."

She nodded distractedly, her eyes darting around the room again. "You're sure you don't mind coming with me?"

Ruhn checked the massive clock at the rear of the conservatory. Eleven fifty. He had time. A few minutes. He needed something to distract himself with anyway. "I wouldn't have offered if I didn't mean it."

They slipped from the dance floor, the crowd parting for the beautiful queen as she aimed for her sister. The Hind marked her approach without smiling. Pollux, however, grinned at Hypaxia, then at Ruhn.

Hypaxia, to her credit, squared her shoulders as she halted. "Lidia."

The Hind's mouth curled upward. "Hypaxia." Her voice was low, smooth. It was a blatant show of disrespect, not to use the queen's title. Not to even bow.

Hypaxia said, "I wished to formally greet you." She added, "Sister."

"Now, *that* is a name no one has ever called me," Lidia said.

Pollux sneered. Ruhn bared his teeth in warning and received a mocking smile in return.

Hypaxia tried once more. "It is a name that I hope we can both hear more often."

Not one ounce of kindness or warmth graced the Hind's beautiful face, even with the mask. "Perhaps," Lidia said, and went back to staring at the crowd. Bored and disinterested. A dismissal and an insult.

Ruhn glanced at the clock. He should go. Make his way slowly to the garden doors, then slip outside. But he couldn't leave Hypaxia to face her sister alone.

"Are you enjoying Lunathion?" Hypaxia tried.

"No," the Hind drawled. "I find this city tediously plebian."

The Hammer snickered, and Hypaxia said to him with wondrous authority, "Go lurk somewhere else."

Pollux's eyes flashed. "You can't give me orders."

But the Hind turned her cool, amused gaze on the Hammer. "A minute, Pollux."

The Hammer glared at Hypaxia, but the witch-queen remained unbowed before a male who'd slaughtered his way through the world for centuries.

Ruhn saw his opening and said to Hypaxia, "I'll give you two a moment as well."

Before the queen could object, he backed into the crowd. He was a piece of shit for abandoning her, but . . .

He walked, unnoticed and unbothered, to the western doors. Slipped out of them and down the five steps to the gravel ground. He strode to the fountain bubbling away in the shadows beyond the reach of the conservatory's lights and leaned against it, his heart pounding.

Two minutes now. Would Day be here?

He monitored the doors, forcing himself to breathe in and out slowly.

Maybe this was a bad idea. He'd been talking to the Hind and the Hammer, for fuck's sake. This place *was* swarming with enemies, all of whom would slaughter him and Day if they were found out. Why had he risked her like this?

"Looking for someone?" a female voice crooned.

Ruhn whirled, his stomach bottoming out as he beheld the masked figure before him.

The Harpy stood in the shadows beyond the fountain. As if she'd been waiting.

60

Ruhn scanned the face in the darkness. It couldn't be her.

The fucking *Harpy*? He took in her dark hair, the lean body, the taunting mouth—

"What are you doing out here?" the Harpy asked, stalking closer, her dark wings blacker than the night.

Ruhn forced himself to take a breath. "Day?" he asked quietly.

The Harpy blinked. "What's that supposed to mean?"

The breath nearly whooshed from him. Thank the fucking gods it wasn't her, but if the Harpy was here, and Agent Daybright was about to appear . . . The Harpy and the Hind had shown up at the bar that day, but he'd seen nothing of the former since. And yeah, meeting by the fountain with another person wouldn't scream *rebel liaison*, but if the Harpy had any suspicions about him, or whoever Daybright was, if she saw them meeting together . . .

He had to get out of here. Walk back into the conservatory and not endanger Day.

What an idiot he was.

"Enjoy the party," Ruhn said to the Harpy.

"No stolen kisses for me in the garden?" she mocked as he stormed up the steps.

He'd explain to Day later. The clock read two minutes past

twelve—she hadn't come. Or maybe she'd seen who was in the garden and decided to hang back.

Seen who also observed from the shadows at the top of the stairs.

The Hind's golden eyes gleamed in the dimness through her mask. She'd followed him. *Fuck.* Had she suspected that he was slipping away to meet with someone? She hadn't said a word, as far as he knew, about the shit that had gone down at Ydra—was it so she could ultimately follow them to a bigger prize?

To the greatest prize a spy-catcher could find. Agent Daybright.

Ruhn stared down the Hind as he passed her. She watched him with serene indifference.

He tugged at his collar as he entered the noise and heat of the party. He'd come that close to being caught by the Hind and the Harpy—to getting Day caught by them.

Ruhn didn't say goodbye to anyone before bailing.

Hunt licked his way up Bryce's neck, a hand sliding over her mouth to muffle her moan as he tugged her down the dim hallway. "You want someone to find us?" His voice was guttural.

"We're official now. I don't care." But she fumbled with the handle of the cloakroom door. Standing behind her, mouth at her throat, Hunt suppressed a groan of his own as her ass pushed into his aching cock. Another few seconds, and they'd be in the cloakroom. And within a few seconds of that, he planned to be balls-deep in her.

He knew Baxian and Naomi had been well aware they weren't going down this hall to use the bathroom, but the angels guarding the door had only smirked at them.

"It's locked," she mumbled, and Hunt huffed a laugh against her warm skin.

"Good thing you've got a big, tough alphahole with you, Quinlan," he said, pulling away from her. Gods, if anyone walked down this hallway, they'd get a glimpse at his pants and know what was about to go down. He'd lasted all of three dances before needing to slip away with her. They'd return to the party soon. Once they got in a good, solid fuck.

He'd be damned if he'd ever call himself Prince Hunt, but . . . it had been worth it. The wild plan she'd spun for him more than two weeks ago, when she'd honored him by asking if he'd do this.

Hunt dragged his teeth down the column of her neck, then tugged her a step back. Bryce, panting softly, face flushed with desire that set his cock pounding, grinned fiendishly at him.

"Watch and learn, sweetheart," Hunt said, and rammed his shoulder into the door.

The lock splintered, and Hunt didn't hesitate before tugging her in with him. Her arms slid around his neck, all of her lining up with him, and he hefted her leg to wrap around his waist, bracing to hoist her up—

A squeak of surprise halted him.

Hunt whirled, mind trying to match up with what his senses were blaring.

But there it was. There they were.

Celestina's dress had been tugged down, baring one full, round breast. Gleaming as if someone had been licking it.

But it wasn't Ephraim who stood before the Archangel, positioned between the female and Hunt. It wasn't Ephraim whose own clothes were askew, hair mussed, lips swollen.

It was Hypaxia.

Hunt had no idea what to say.

Bryce cleared her throat and stepped in front of Hunt, blocking his raging erection from view. "I guess the locked door means *already occupied*, huh?"

Hypaxia and Celestina just stared at them, their hair half falling out of their elegant arrangements.

Hunt slowly, quietly shut the door behind them. Lifted his hands. Because that was a faint glow of power beginning to shimmer around Celestina. An Archangel's wrath, priming to strike down any enemy.

Hunt couldn't stop his own lightning from answering, its zap searing through him. If Celestina was going to throw down, he'd match her.

Bryce said breathlessly to Hypaxia, as she sensed the brewing storm in the cloakroom, "I've, uh, never been in this kind of situation before."

Hypaxia glanced to the Governor, whose eyes had turned white, flaring with power, and said to Bryce, an attempt at casualness, "Me neither."

The only way in and out was the door at Hunt's back. Unless Celestina blasted apart the entire top of the building. Hunt put a hand on Bryce's shoulder.

But his mate said brightly, "In case we need to clarify, we aren't going to say anything."

Hypaxia nodded sagely. "We thank you." She peered up at the Archangel—at her lover. "Celestina."

The Governor didn't take her gaze from Hunt. If he so much as breathed wrong, she'd kill him. In two fucking seconds. Hunt grinned, though. She could *try* to kill him. "My lips are sealed."

Her wings glowed, so bright the entire cloakroom was illuminated. "You endanger the person I love," Celestina said, her voice echoing with power. "For infringing on what he considers his, Ephraim will end her. Or the Asteri will kill her to make a statement."

Bryce kept her hands up. "The Asteri are probably going to kill me, too, at some point." Hunt whipped his head to her. She wouldn't— "I like you," she said instead, and Hunt tried not to sag with relief that she hadn't explained their rebel activities. "I think you're good for this city. Ephraim and his loser cabal, not so much, but once he's gone home, I think you're going to make Lunathion even more . . .. awesome." Hunt threw her an incredulous look. She shrugged. Bryce's eyes met Celestina's. Her star flared.

Power to power. Female to female. Governor to . . . *Princess* wasn't the right word for the expression that came across Bryce's face, the shift of her posture.

Another word formed on his tongue, but Hunt didn't let it

take root, didn't let himself think of all the deadly implications that the other word would entail.

Bryce said, with that more-than-princess bearing, "I have no plans to fuck you over. Either of you." She faced Hypaxia, who was giving Bryce that more-than-princess look, too. "We're allies. Not only politically, but . . . as females who have had to make some shitty, hard choices. As females who live in a world where most powerful males see us only as breeding tools." Hypaxia nodded again, but Celestina continued to stare at Bryce. A predator surveying the best place to strike.

Hunt rallied his power again. Bryce continued, "I'm no one's prize mare. I took a gamble with this idiot"—she jerked a thumb toward Hunt, who gaped at her—"and luckily, it paid off. And I just want to say that"—she swallowed—"if you two want to make a gamble with each other, say fuck it to the arrangements with Ephraim and Ruhn, then I'm with you. We'd have to go against the Asteri, but . . . look what I did tonight. Whatever I can do, whatever clout I have, it's yours. But let's start by walking out of this closet in one piece."

Silence fell.

And slowly, like a setting sun, the Archangel's power dimmed until only her silhouette glowed with it. Hypaxia laid a hand on her lover's shoulder, proof that they were safe.

Celestina said, setting her fine clothing to rights, "We weren't without choices in this. When the Autumn King came asking for Hypaxia's hand for his son, I was the one who encouraged her to accept. But who I love, who I am mated to . . . those are decisions that I am not entitled to make, as an Archangel."

Hunt grunted. "I know how that feels." At Celestina's arched brow, he pointed to his branded-out wrist. "Slave, remember?"

"Perhaps there's a thin line between Governor and slave," Hypaxia mused.

Celestina admitted, "I thought that Hypaxia might wed the prince, perhaps in a political sense, and when enough time had passed, we could . . . resume our relationship. But then the Asteri gave the order about Ephraim, and I found myself with little choice but to say yes."

Bryce asked quietly, "Did Ephraim . . ."

"I agreed to it," the Governor said firmly. "Though I can't say I found it enjoyable." Hypaxia kissed her cheek.

That was why Celestina had seemed so unsettled before her first night with Ephraim, so haunted afterward—because her heart lay elsewhere.

Bryce said to the females, "For however long you want and need to keep this secret, we won't breathe a hint to anyone. You have my word."

And it occurred to Hunt, as both females nodded, that Bryce had somehow earned their trust—had become someone who people trusted unfailingly.

A more-than-princess, indeed.

Hunt smiled at his mate and said, "Well, we should probably leave. Before someone comes in and finds us all in here and thinks I'm having the night of my life." Hypaxia and Bryce laughed, but Celestina's answering smile was subdued.

Bryce seemed to note that, and looped her arm through the witch-queen's, steering her toward the door and murmuring, "Let's discuss how much this evening will piss off the Autumn King and how wonderful that will be," as they left, leaving Hunt and Celestina alone.

His Archangel observed him. Hunt didn't dare move.

"So you're truly a prince now," Celestina said.

Hunt blinked. "Uh, yeah. I guess."

The Governor walked past him, toward where her lover had gone into the hall. "There's a fine line between prince and slave, too, you know."

Hunt's chest tightened. "I know."

"Then why accept the burden?" she asked, pausing.

Bryce seemed thick as thieves with the witch-queen as they walked arm-in-arm. "She's worth it."

But Celestina said, face solemn, "Love is a trap, Hunt." She shook her head, more at herself than at him. "One I can't figure out how to free myself from."

"You *want* to be free of it?"

The Archangel stepped into the hall, wings still glowing with a remnant of power. "Every single day."

Tharion tried not to glance at his watch—technically his grandfather's waterproof watch, given to him upon high school graduation—as the night wore on. Bryce's betrothal coup had provided five minutes of glorious amusement before he'd been sucked into boredom and impatience.

He knew it was an honor to be here, to escort the River Queen's daughter, who was sparkling with delight and joy. But it was hard to feel that privilege when he'd been ordered to attend the ball at her side.

Tharion had waited at the docks by the River Gate at sundown, dressed to the nines. The River Queen's daughter had emerged from the mists in a pale oak boat pulled by a bevy of snow-white swans. Tharion hadn't failed to notice the sobeks lurking fifty feet beyond them. Sentinels for this journey of their queen's most precious daughter.

"Is it not magical?" his companion was saying for the fifth time that night, sighing at the lights and dancing couples.

Tharion drained the rest of his champagne. *She is allowed to have one glass of wine*, her mother had said in her letter via otter. *And she is to be home by one.*

Tharion finally glanced at his watch. Twelve twenty. Another fifteen minutes and he could start ushering her toward the door. He handed his flute to a passing server, but found his companion's expression had turned dangerously pouty.

He offered her a charming, bland smile, but she said, "You do not seem to be enjoying yourself."

"I am," he assured her, taking her hand and pressing a kiss to her knuckles.

"Your friends do not come to speak with us."

Well, considering that he'd seen Bryce and Hunt slip off somewhere, that was no surprise. Ithan was chatting with Naomi Boreas and the Helhound at the doors, and the others . . . Ruhn and Cormac had bailed. No sign of Hypaxia.

Though the witch-queen had already come to speak with them. He'd had a hard time meeting her gaze throughout the awkward conversation, while she could see how stupid he'd been in tying himself to this female. But Hypaxia had been kind to the River Queen's daughter, who herself had been all smiles. Tharion hadn't dared call her Pax.

"My friends have a lot of glad-handing to do," he hedged.

"Oh." She fell silent, lurking on the edge of the dance floor as couples swept past. Maybe it was all the champagne, but he really looked at her: the dark eyes full of longing and quiet happiness, the eager energy buzzing from her, the sense that she was some creature crafted into mortal form only for this night, and would dissolve into river silt as soon as the clock struck one.

Was he any better than her mother? He'd been stringing this girl along for ten years now. Had held her back tonight because *he* didn't feel like enjoying himself.

She must have felt the weight of his stare, because she twisted to him. Tharion offered her another bland smile, then turned to one of the bodyguards lurking in the shadows behind them. "Hey, Tritus, can you take over for this dance?"

The guard glanced between them, but Tharion smiled down at the River Queen's daughter, whose brows were raised. "Go dance," he told her. "I'll be right back." He didn't let her object before handing her off to the guard, who was actually blushing as he extended his arm.

And Tharion didn't look back as he strode off into the crowd, wondering how much shit he'd be in for this. But . . . even if he was flayed for it, he wasn't going to string her along any further.

He paused on the outskirts of the crowd, finally turning to see the guard and the River Queen's daughter dancing, both of them smiling. Happy.

Good. She deserved that. Mother or not, temper or not, she deserved someone to make her happy.

Tharion made his way over to the nearest open bar, and was about to order a whiskey when he noticed a curvy female—a leopard shifter from the scent of her—lounging against the counter beside him.

He'd always noticed a good ass, and this female . . . Hel yes.

"Come here often?" he asked her with a wink. The leopard turned her head toward him, light brown skin radiant in the soft lights. Her eyes were thick-lashed, utterly gorgeous above high cheekbones and full lips, all of it framed by golden-brown hair that fell around her heart-shaped face in soft waves. She had the ease and grace of a movie star. Probably was one, if she was important enough to be here. That full mouth curled in a smile. "Is that your attempt at a pickup line?"

He knew that sultry tone. So Tharion ordered his whiskey and said to the stranger, "You want it to be?"

61

"Are you all right?" Ithan asked Hypaxia as the clock neared three thirty in the morning. She'd complained of some stomach cramps and had left the party for about twenty minutes, returning pale-faced.

The witch-queen now tucked a dark curl behind her ear, then adjusted the fall of her jet-black robes, having pulled them over her gown moments before. Even standing in the small clearing of an olive grove nestled in the hills beyond the city, the sounds of revelry reached them: booming bass, cheering, strobing lights. A far cry from the whispering leaves and dry ground around him, the stars glinting beyond the silvery canopy.

Another world away from that glittering party where so many powers had come together tonight. Where Bryce had somehow outmaneuvered the Autumn King and had declared Hunt her prince. He hadn't known what to think in that moment.

He'd done his best to stay the fuck away from Sabine and Amelie tonight. Thankfully, they had been present only long enough to see the Asteri speak, then left. He hated himself for being so relieved about it. The Prime hadn't attended—he usually avoided such functions.

"So this is it?" Ithan asked Hypaxia, gesturing with a hand to the seven candles she'd arranged on the ground. "Light the candles and wait?"

Hypaxia drew out a long dagger. "Not quite," she said, and Ithan kept a step back as she used the knife to draw lines between the candles.

Ithan angled his head. "A six-pointed star," he said. Like the one Bryce had made between the Gates this spring, with the seventh candle at its center.

"It's a symbol of balance," she explained, moving away a foot, but keeping the dagger at her side. Her crown of cloudberries seemed to glow with an inner light. "Two intersecting triangles. Male and female, dark and light, above and below . . . and the power that lies in the place where they meet." Her face became grave. "It is in that place of balance where I'll focus my power." She motioned to the circle. "No matter what you see or hear, stay on this side of the candles."

A chill went up Ithan's spine, even as his heart lightened. If he could just talk to Connor . . . He'd thought over and over about what he'd say, but he couldn't remember any of it.

Hypaxia read whatever lay in his gaze, her face again solemn.

But a bargain was a bargain. Hypaxia lifted both arms, holding the dagger aloft, and began chanting.

Day appeared far down the bridge and stayed there, like she didn't want to come near him.

Ruhn sat on his couch, forearms on his knees. He'd been reeling from what had gone down in the garden for hours now. Was surprised he'd even fallen asleep in his physical body.

He rushed to her. "I'm sorry I endangered you."

Day said nothing. Just stood there, burning.

He tried again. "I . . . It was a really dumb idea. I'm sorry if you showed and I wasn't there. I got to the garden and the Harpy and the Hind had trailed me, and I think they might have suspected me, or I don't know, but I'm . . . I'm so sorry, Day."

"I was there," she said quietly.

"What?"

"I saw you," she said, and stalked forward. "Saw the threat, too. And stayed away."

"Where? In the garden?"

She came closer. "I saw you," she said again. Like she was still processing it.

"You came." He shook his head. "I thought you might not have, and we didn't talk since we made that plan, and I was worried—"

"Ruhn." His name on her lips rocked through him.

He shuddered. "You know who I am."

"Yes."

"Say my name again."

She came closer. "Ruhn." Her flames parted enough for him to get a glimpse of a smile.

"Are you still in the city? Can I meet you somewhere?" It was the middle of the night—but it was the equinox. People would be partying until dawn. But they'd be masked—he and Day could fit right in.

"No." Her voice flattened. "I'm gone."

"Liar. Tell me where you are."

"Did you learn nothing tonight? Did you not see how close we came to disaster? The Asteri's servants are everywhere. One mistake, even for a moment, and we are *dead*."

His throat worked. "When the Harpy came out of the shadows, I thought she was you. I . . . I panicked for a moment."

A quiet laugh. "That would have been awful for you? To have me be someone you hate so much?"

"It would take some adjustment."

"So you do have a notion of what you expect me to be like."

"I don't. I just . . . don't want you to be *her*."

Another laugh. "And you're a Fae Prince."

"Does it gross you out?"

"Should it?"

"It grosses me out."

"Why?"

"Because I've done nothing to deserve that title."

She studied him. "The Autumn King is your father. The one who hurt you."

"The one and only."

"He's a disgrace of a king."

"You should talk to my sister. I think she'd like you."

"Bryce Quinlan."

He tensed at her knowing Bryce's name so readily, but if she'd been at the party tonight, she'd know without a doubt. "Yeah. She hates my father even more than I do."

But Day's flame dimmed. "You're engaged to Queen Hypaxia."

He almost laughed it off, but her voice was so grave. "It's complicated."

"You danced with her like it wasn't."

"You saw me?"

"Everyone saw you."

That sharpness in her voice . . . was it jealousy? He said carefully, "I'm not the two-timing sort. Hypaxia and I are betrothed in name only. I don't even know if we'll marry. She has as little attachment to me as I do to her. We like and admire each other, but . . . that's about it."

"Why should I care?"

He studied her, then took a step closer, until only a handsbreadth separated them. "I wanted to see you tonight. I spent the entire time watching the clock."

Her breathing hitched. "Why?"

"So I could do this." Ruhn lifted her chin and kissed her. The mouth beneath the fire was soft, and warm, and opened for him.

Flaming fingers twined through his hair, tugging him close, and Ruhn slid his arms around a slim, curving body, hands feeling her ample backside. Fuck yes.

His tongue brushed over hers, and she shuddered in his arms. But she met him stroke for stroke, as if she couldn't hold back, as if she wanted to know every inch of him, his every taste and nuance.

Her hand slid along his jaw, fingers exploring the shape of his face. He willed his night to pull back to show his eyes, his nose, his mouth. Thankfully, it obeyed him. Beyond the veil of flame covering her features, he could feel her watching him. Seeing his bared face.

Her fingers traced the bridge of his nose. The bow of his lips. Then she kissed him again, with sheer abandon, and Ruhn gave himself entirely to it.

"You remind me that I'm alive," she said, voice thick. "You remind me that goodness can exist in the world."

His throat ached. "Day—"

But she hissed, stiffening against his grip. She glanced back toward her end of the bridge.

No. That male who'd once dragged her from sleep to have sex with her—

Day whipped her head back to Ruhn and the flame rippled, revealing pleading eyes of solid fire. "I'm sorry," she whispered, and vanished.

Hunt was still drunk when he and Bryce returned to the apartment at three in the morning. She carried her heels in one hand, the train of her dress in the other. They'd left the party soon after Ruhn had bailed, and headed to a dive bar in the heart of the Old Square, where they'd proceeded to play pool and drink whiskey in their ridiculous finery.

They didn't talk about what they'd discovered in the cloakroom. What more was there to say?

"I'm plastered," Bryce announced to the dim apartment, slumping onto the couch.

Hunt chuckled. "Very princess-ish."

She removed her earrings, chucking the diamonds onto the coffee table as if they were cheap costume jewelry. The comb in her hair followed, gems glinting in the soft firstlights.

She stretched out her legs, bare feet wiggling on the coffee table. "Let's never do that again."

"The whiskey or outsmarting your father or the party?" Hunt

tugged his white bow tie free of its knot as he approached the couch and peered down at her.

She huffed a laugh. "The party. Outsmarting my father and the whiskey will *always* be a repeat activity."

Hunt sat on the coffee table, adjusting his wings around it. "It could have been a lot worse."

"Yeah. Though I can't think of anything much worse than gaining multiple enemies for the price of one." That the Asteri's appearance had only been a footnote said plenty about their night. "Though Celestina isn't our enemy, I guess."

Hunt picked up one of her feet and began rubbing the insole. She sighed, sinking back into the cushions. Hunt's cock stirred at the pure pleasure she radiated.

"Can I tell you something?" Hunt said, massaging the arch of her foot. "Something that might be deemed alphahole-ish?"

"As long as you keep rubbing my foot like that, you can say whatever the Hel you want."

Hunt laughed. "Deal." He picked up her other foot, starting on that one. "I liked being at the party tonight. Despite all the fancy clothes and the Asteri and the stuff with Hypaxia and Celestina. Despite all the prince bullshit. I liked being seen. With you."

Her mouth quirked to the side. "You liked staking your territory?"

"Yeah." He let her see the predator in him. "I've never had that with anyone."

She frowned. "Shahar never showed you off?"

"No. I was her general. At public functions, we didn't appear together. She never wanted that. It would have positioned me as an equal, or at least someone she deemed . . . important."

"I thought your movement was all about equality," Bryce said, frown deepening.

"It was. But we still had to play by the old rules." Rules that continued to govern and dictate people's lives. Celestina's and Hypaxia's lives.

"So she never came out and said, *Hey, world! He's my boyfriend!*"

Hunt laughed, and marveled that he did so. He'd never thought he'd be able to laugh about anything related to Shahar. "No. It's why I was so . . . honored when you asked me to do this."

Bryce studied him. "Do you want to go outside so we can get caught fooling around in public by the press? That'll make us *really* official."

"Maybe another time." Hunt lifted her foot to his mouth, pressing a kiss to the instep. "So, we're, like . . . married."

"Are we?" She held out a hand before her, studying her splayed fingers. "I don't see a ring, Athalar."

He nipped at her toes, earning a squeal from her. "You want a ring, I'll get you one." Another kiss. "You want iron, steel, or titanium?" Wedding bands in Lunathion were simple, their value derived from the strength of the metal used to forge them.

"Titanium all the way, baby," she crowed, and Hunt bit her toes again.

She squirmed, but he held her firm. "These little toes make me think some dirty things, Quinlan," he said against her foot.

"Please tell me you don't have a foot fetish."

"No. But everything where you're involved is a fetish for me."

"Oh?" She leaned back farther into the cushions, her dress slipping up her legs. "So I make you want to get a little kinky?"

"Uh-huh." He kissed her ankle. "Just a little."

She arched into the touch. "Want to have drunk, sloppy sex, Prince Hunt?"

He rumbled a laugh against her calf. Only from her lips would he tolerate that title. "Fuck yeah."

She pulled her leg from his touch and stood with that dancer's grace. "Unzip me."

"Romantic."

She gave him her back, and Hunt, still seated, reached up to tug at the zipper hidden down the length of her spine. The tattoo of the Horn appeared, along with inches of golden skin, until the first tendrils of lace from her thong were revealed. The zipper ended before he could get a view of what he wanted.

But Bryce peeled the dress from her front, letting it drop. She hadn't worn a bra, but the black thong . . .

Hunt ran his hands over the firm cheeks of her ass, bending to bite at a delicate strap of her underwear. She let out a soft, breathy sound that had him kissing the base of her spine. Her long hair brushed his brow, silken and as lovely as a caress.

Bryce turned in his grip, and—what luck—he found himself right where he wanted to be. From where it sat high on her hips, her thong plunged into a dramatic vee, a veritable arrow pointing to paradise.

He kissed her navel. Flicked her nipples with his thumbs as he licked up toward them. Her fingers slid into his hair, her head tipping back as he closed his mouth around a taut bud. He rolled her nipple over his tongue, savoring the weight and taste of it, his hands drifting around her waist, tangling in the straps of her thong. Tugging it down her hips. Her thighs. He moved to her other breast, sucking it into his mouth. Bryce groaned, and his cock pushed against the front of his dress pants.

He liked having her at his mercy. Liked this image, of her wholly naked and resplendent before him, his to touch and pleasure and worship. Hunt smiled against her breast. He liked it a lot.

He rose, scooping her into his arms and carrying her to the bedroom, his bow tie dangling around his neck.

He laid her on the mattress, cock pulsing at the sight of her heavy-lidded with desire, sprawled there naked and his for the taking. He pulled the tie free. "Want to get a little kinky with me, Quinlan?"

She glanced to the iron posts of the headboard, and her red lips parted in a feline grin. "Oh yes."

Hunt made quick work of binding her hands to the bedposts. Light enough not to hurt, but tight enough that getting any ideas about touching him while he feasted on her was out of the question.

Bryce lay stretched out before him, and Hunt could hardly get a breath down as he unbuttoned his shirt. Then his pants. He shed his shoes, his socks—all the trappings of civility, until he stood before her naked, and Bryce bit her lip. Then he propped up her knees and spread them wide.

"Fuck," he said, taking in her gleaming sex, already drenched for him. Its heady scent hit him, and he shuddered, cock now a steady ache.

"Since I can't touch myself," she said huskily, "maybe you'll do the honors."

"Fuck," he said again, unable to think of anything else. She was so beautiful—every single part of her.

"Are you articulating what you'd like to do to me, or has your brain short-circuited?"

He snapped his gaze to her own. "I wanted to draw this out. Really torment you."

Her legs spread a little wider, a taunting invitation. "Oh?"

"I'll save that for another day," he growled, and crawled on top of her. The tip of his cock nudged at her wet, hot entrance, and a shiver of anticipatory pleasure went down his spine. But he ran a hand down the length of her torso, fingers tracing the silken swells of her breasts, the plane of her stomach. She writhed, tugging on the restraints.

"So defiant." He dipped to kiss her neck. He pushed in a little, his mind blacking out at the perfect tightness. But he withdrew—and eased back in a little more. Even when every instinct screamed to plunge into her, unless she asked for it, he'd be careful. He wanted her to feel only ecstasy.

"Stop teasing," she said, and Hunt raked his teeth down her left breast, sucking in her nipple as he sank a bit further into her sheer perfection. "*More*," she snarled, hips rising as if she'd impale herself on him.

Hunt laughed. "Who am I to deny a princess?"

Her eyes flashed with desire hot enough to sear his soul. "I'm issuing a royal decree for you to fuck me, Hunt. Hard."

His balls tightened at the words, and he gave her what she wanted. They both groaned as he sank all the way home in a thrust that had him seeing stars. She felt like bliss, like eternity—

Hunt withdrew and thrust again, and there were indeed stars around them—no, it was her, she was glowing like a star—

Her hips undulated, meeting his, driving him deeper.

Fuck yes. She was his, and he was hers, and now the whole fucking world knew it—

He sent out a fizzle of his lightning, snapping the restraints on her wrists. Her hands instantly came around his back, fingers grappling hard enough to draw sweet slices of pain. Hunt's wings twitched, and she wrapped her legs around his middle. He sank even deeper, and holy *fuck*, the squeeze of her—

She flexed those inner muscles. His eyes nearly rolled back in his head.

"Solas, Quinlan—"

"*Hard*," she breathed in his ear. "Fuck me like the prince you are."

Hunt lost it. He pulled back enough to grip her ass in both hands, tilting her pelvis upward—and plunged in. She moaned, and everything he was transformed into something primal and animalistic. *His*. His mate to touch and fuck and fill—

Hunt let himself go, pounding into her again and again and again.

Bryce's moans were sweet music, a temptation and a challenge. She glowed, and Hunt looked at his cock, sliding in and out of her, shining with her wetness—

He was glowing, too. Not with her starlight, but . . . fuck, his lightning was crackling down his arms, his hands, skittering over her hips, up to her breasts.

"Don't stop," she gasped as his lightning flared. "Don't stop."

Hunt didn't. He yielded to the storm, riding it, riding her, and there was only Bryce, her soul and her body and the flawless fit of them—

"Hunt," she pleaded, and he knew from her breathy tone that she was close.

He didn't let up. Didn't give her one ounce of mercy. The slap and slide of their bodies meeting filled the room, but the sounds were distant, the world was distant as his power and essence flowed into her. Bryce cried out, and Hunt turned frenzied, pounding once, twice—

On the third, mightiest thrust, he ruptured, his power with him.

Lightning filled the room, filled her as surely as his seed, and he kissed her through it, tongues meeting, ether flooding his senses. He could never get enough of this—this connection, this sex, this power flowing between them. He needed it more than he needed food, water—needed this sharing of magic, this twining of souls; he'd never stop craving it—

Then he was falling, amid black wind and lightning and stars. He came through all of it, roaring his pleasure to the skies.

Because those *were* skies above them. And city lights. Booming bass from a nearby party.

Hunt stilled, gaping down at Bryce. At the surface beneath her—the apartment building's roof.

Bryce grinned sheepishly. "Oops."

62

Hypaxia's chants rose in volume and complexity, the full moon with them. It silvered the orchard.

Ithan shivered against the cold. He knew that it wasn't due to the night around them, or the autumn unfolding. No, the air had been pleasantly warm a moment ago. Whatever Hypaxia's magic was doing, it was bringing the frigid temperatures with it.

"I can feel . . . a presence," the witch-queen whispered, arms lifted toward the moon, beautiful face solemn. "Someone is coming."

Ithan's mouth dried out. What would he even say to Connor? *I love you* would likely be the first. *I miss you every minute of every damn day* would be the second. Then the warning. Or should it be the warning first? He shook out his trembling fingers at his sides.

"Get ready to say your piece. Your brother's spirit is . . . strong. I'm not sure how long I can hold the star."

Something weirdly like pride rose in him at that. But Ithan stepped closer, breathing evenly. Exactly as he had before important games, during game-winning shots. Focus. He could do this. He'd deal with the repercussions later.

The star she'd drawn glowed a faint blue, illuminating the trees around them.

"One more moment . . ." Hypaxia hissed, panting, a faint sheen on her temples. Like this was draining the power out of her.

Light ruptured from the star, blinding and white, a great wind shaking the trees around them, sending olives scattering in a pitter-patter. Ithan squeezed his eyes shut against it, letting his claws slide free.

When the wind stopped, he blinked, adjusting his vision. His brother's name died in his throat.

A creature, tall and thin and robed, lurked in the center of the six-pointed star. Hypaxia let out a soft gasp. Ithan's stomach clenched. He'd never seen the male, but he'd seen drawings.

The Under-King.

"You were not summoned," Hypaxia said, mastering her surprise. She lifted her chin, every inch the queen. "Return to the misty isle over which you rule."

The Under-King laughed at the witch. Her body shimmered with pale blue light. Like she was rallying her power. But the Under-King slowly turned his head to Ithan. Let out another dry, husky laugh.

"Young fools. You play with powers beyond your ken." His voice was horrible. Full of dusty bones and the pleading screams of the dead.

Yet Hypaxia didn't back down an inch. "Be gone, and let us see the one whom I have summoned."

Ithan's hand drifted toward his gun. It wouldn't do anything. His wolf form would protect him better with its speed, but even losing that split second to shifting might make him vulnerable, and cost Hypaxia her life.

The Under-King extended a bony hand. Light rippled where it met the edge of the star. "Do not fear, wolf pup. I cannot harm you. Here, at least." He grinned, exposing too-large brown teeth.

Ithan bristled and he found his voice at last as he growled, "I want to speak to my brother."

Beside him, Hypaxia was murmuring under her breath, the light around her building.

"Your brother is well cared for." Dark fire danced in the Under-King's milky eyes. "But whether that remains so now depends entirely on you."

"What the Hel does that mean?" Ithan demanded. But the

witch-queen had tensed. Wind stirred her curly hair, as if she were readying her defenses.

The Under-King lifted a bony hand, and an eerie, greenish light wreathed his fingers. Ithan could have sworn ancient, strange symbols swirled in that light. "Let's play a little game first." He inclined his head to Hypaxia, whose face had gone stony—anticipatory. "The House of Flame and Shadow has long been curious about your . . . abilities, Your Majesty."

Bryce knew she was dreaming. Knew she was physically in her bed. Knew she was currently tucked up against Hunt's side. But she also knew that the being in front of her was real—even if the setting was not.

She stood on a vast, dusty plain before an azure, cloudless sky. Distant dry mountains studded the horizon, but she was surrounded only by rock and sand and emptiness.

"Princess." The voice was like Hel embodied: dark and icy and smooth.

"Prince." Her voice shook.

Apollion, Prince of the Pit, had chosen to appear in a golden-haired, golden-skinned body. Handsome in the way that ancient statues were handsome, in the way that Pollux was handsome.

His black eyes, however, gave him away. No whites anywhere. Only unending darkness.

The Star-Eater himself.

She asked, trying to master her shaking, "Where are we?"

"Parthos. Or what remains of it."

The barren land seemed to stretch on forever. "In the real world, or in, like, dreamworld?"

He angled his head, more animal than humanoid. "Dreamworld. Or what you consider to be dreams."

She wasn't going to touch that one. "All right, then. Um . . . nice to meet you."

Apollion's mouth curved upward. "You do not cower before me."

"Aidas kind of ruined your scary-monster vibe."

A soulless laugh. "My brother has the tendency to be a thorn in my side."

"Maybe he should join this conversation."

"Aidas would be angry with me for speaking with you. That's why I picked this moment, when he is conveniently occupied."

"With what?"

"Raising Hel's armies. Readying them."

Her breath hitched. "To invade Midgard?"

"It's been long in the making."

"I'm going to make a request on behalf of my planet and say please stay in your own world."

Another twitch of his mouth. "You do not trust us. Good. Theia did. It was her downfall."

"The Starborn Queen?"

"Yes. Aidas's great love."

Bryce started. "His *what*?"

Apollion waved a broad hand to the ruined world around them. "Why do you think I slew Pelias? Why do you think I went on to devour Sirius? All for him. My foolish, lovesick brother. In such a rage over Theia's death at Pelias's hands. His folly lost us that phase of the war."

Bryce had to blink. "I'm sorry, but please back up. You summoned me into this dream to tell me about how Aidas, Prince of the Chasm, was the lover of Theia, the first Starborn Queen, even though they were enemies?"

"They were not enemies. We were her allies. She and some of her Fae forces allied with us—against the Asteri."

Her mouth dried out. "Why didn't he tell me this? Why are *you* telling me this?"

"Why are you not yet master of your powers? I was very clear: I told your mate you must both explore your potential."

"Did you send those Reapers to jump me and Ruhn?"

"What Reapers?" She could have sworn his confusion was sincere.

"The ones who told me the same exact thing, to master my powers."

"I did no such thing."

"That's what the Under-King said. I'm guessing one of you is lying."

"This is not a useful debate. And I do not appreciate being called a liar." Pure threat laced the words.

But Bryce steeled herself. "You're right—it's not a useful debate. So answer my question: Why the Hel are you telling me any of this stuff about Aidas and Theia?" If he spoke true, and Hel hadn't been their enemy back then . . . Whatever side Theia had ruled, she'd been . . . against the Asteri. And Pelias had killed her—fighting *for* the Asteri.

Her mind spun. No wonder nobody knew about Theia. The Asteri had likely erased her from history. But a Fae Queen had loved a demon prince. And he had loved her enough to . . .

"I am telling you this because you are racing blind toward your doom. I am telling you this because tonight the veil between our worlds is thinnest and I might finally speak to you."

"You spoke to Hunt before."

"Orion was bred to be receptive to our kind. Why do you think he is so adept at hunting us? But that is of no matter. This night, I might appear to *you*—as more than a vision." He reached out a hand, and Bryce flinched as it touched her. Truly *touched* her, ice so cold it ached. "Hel is nearly ready to finish this war."

She took a step back. "I know what you're going to ask, and my answer is *no*."

"Use the Horn. The power Athalar gives you can activate it." His eyes danced with storms. "Open the doors to Hel."

"Absolutely fucking not."

Apollion chuckled, low and lethal. "What a disappointment." The plain that had been Parthos began to fade into nothing. "Come find me in Hel when you learn the truth."

Ithan pivoted slowly, eyeing the shadows where the Under-King had stood—and vanished.

"Don't move from this spot," Hypaxia warned him, voice low.

"I can feel his power all around us. He's turned this clearing into a labyrinth of wards."

Ithan sniffed, as if it'd give him some sense of what the Hel she was talking about. But nothing appeared to have changed. No creatures jumped out at them. Still, he said, "I'll follow your lead."

Hypaxia scanned the sky. "He warded above us, too. To keep us grounded." She crinkled her nose. "Right. On foot it is."

Ithan swallowed. "I, ah . . . got your back?"

She chuckled. "Just keep up, please."

He gave her a determined smile. "You got it."

Ithan braced himself as Hypaxia took a step forward, hand extended. Her fingers recoiled at whatever ward she encountered, right as a low snarl sounded from the trees beyond.

The hair on his neck rose. His wolf senses told him it wasn't an animal's snarl. But it sounded . . . hungry.

Another one rippled from nearby. Then another. All around them.

"What is that?" Ithan breathed, even his Vanir eyes failing to pierce the darkness.

Hypaxia's hands glowed white-hot with magic. She didn't take her gaze off the trees ahead of them. "The hunting hounds of the House of Flame and Shadow," she said grimly before slamming her hand against the ward in front of them.

63

He was a micromanaging fucking nightmare," Bryce ranted the next day as she stood with Hunt, Ruhn, and Declan in the Aux training center during her lunch break. Tharion lay sprawled on a bench against the wall, napping. Cormac, standing across the space, frowned.

Her brother was pale. "You really think Theia and a bunch of Fae sided with Hel during the war?"

Bryce suppressed a shiver of cold at the memory. "Who knows what's true?"

Across the vast, empty room, Hunt rubbed his jaw. She hadn't even mentioned what Apollion had said—that little tidbit about Hunt being *bred*. She'd tackle that later. Hunt mused, "What's the benefit in convincing us of a lie? Or the truth, either, I suppose. All that matters is that Hel is definitely on the move."

Declan said, "Can we pause for a moment and remark on the fact that both of you have *spoken* to the Prince of the Pit? Is no one else about to puke at the thought?"

Ruhn held up a hand, and Tharion lazily lifted one from the bench, but Bryce high-fived Hunt. "Special kids club," she said to the angel, who winked at her. She leapt back a step, rallying her power. "Again." They'd been in here for twenty minutes already, practicing.

Hunt's lightning flared at his fingertips, and Bryce set her feet apart. "Ready?" he asked.

Tharion roused himself enough to turn over, propping his head on a fist. Bryce scowled at him, but the mer only waggled his brows in encouragement.

She faced Hunt again, right as the angel hurled his lightning at her like a spear. It zinged against her chest, a direct hit, and then she was glowing, power singing, soaring—

Two feet in front of the windows.

She'd no sooner thought the command than she appeared across the space. Exactly two feet from the windows. *Back to a foot before Hunt.*

She appeared before him, so suddenly that he staggered back.

Ruhn. She moved again, slower this time. But her brother yelped.

Declan braced himself, like he thought he'd be next, so Bryce thought, *A foot behind Hunt.*

She pinched her mate's butt so fast he didn't have time to whirl before she'd moved again. This time in front of Declan, who cursed when she poked him in the ribs, then teleported once more.

Cormac called from where he'd been standing in the far corner, "You're slowing." She was. Damn it, she was. Bryce rallied her power, Hunt's energy. She appeared in front of Tharion's bench, but the mer was waiting.

Fast as a striking shark, Tharion grabbed her face and planted a smacking kiss on her lips.

Hunt's laugh boomed across the space, and Bryce joined him, batting the mer away.

"Too slow, Legs," Tharion drawled, leaning back against the bench and crossing an ankle over a knee. He draped an arm along the back of the plastic bench. "And too predictable."

"Again," Cormac ordered. "Focus."

Bryce tried, but her bones weighed her down. Tried again to no avail. "I'm out."

"Concentrate, and you could hold on longer. You use too much at once, and don't reserve the energy for later."

Bryce put her hands on her hips as she panted. "Your teleporting works differently than mine. How can you know that?"

"Mine comes from a source of magic, too. Energy, just a different form. Each jump takes more out of me. It's a muscle that you need to build up."

She scowled, wiping her brow as she walked back over to Hunt.

"It does seem like he's right," Declan said to Bryce. "Your teleporting works when your power gets charged up by energy—considering what I heard about how quickly you ran out of steam with Hypaxia, Hunt's is the best form of it."

"Damn right it is," Hunt growled, earning a smack on the arm from Bryce.

"Do you think the power will . . . stay in me if I don't use it?" she asked Dec.

"I don't think so," Dec said. "Your power came from the Gate—with a shit-ton of firstlight mixed in. So your magic—beyond the light, I mean—needs to be powered up. It relies on firstlight, or any other form of energy it can get. You're literally a Gate: you can take in power and offer it. But it seems the similarity ends there. The Gates can store power indefinitely, while yours clearly peters out after a while." He faced Hunt. "And your power, Athalar, as pure energy, is able to draw from her, like she did from the Gate. Bryce, when you draw from a source, it's the same way the Gates zap power from people using them to communicate."

Bryce blinked. "So I'm like some magical leech?"

Declan laughed. "I think only of certain kinds of magic. Forms of pure energy. Throw in the Horn, which relies on a blast of power to activate it . . ."

"And you're a liability," Ruhn said darkly. Tharion grunted his agreement.

Declan rubbed his chin. "You told Ruhn after the attack that Hypaxia aimed for your scar to supercharge your powers, right? I wonder what would happen if you were struck on the Horn."

"Let's not find out," Bryce said quickly.

"Agreed," Cormac said from across the room. He pointed to the obstacle course he'd laid out in the center of the space. "Back to work. Follow the track."

Bryce pivoted toward the Avallen Prince, and said as casually as she could, "I'm shocked you're even here."

Cormac said icily, "Because you decided to end our engagement without consulting me?"

Hunt muttered to her, "Anything to avoid your exercises, huh?"

She glared at her mate, especially as Ruhn chuckled, but said to Cormac, "I had no other choice."

Shadows rippled around Cormac. "You could have let me know while you were plotting."

"There was no plotting. Athalar and I decided, and then just waited."

The Avallen Prince snarled low. Hunt let out a warning growl of his own. Tharion said nothing, though she knew the mer was monitoring every breath and word. But Cormac didn't take his eyes from her. "Do you have any idea what the phone call with my father was like?"

"I'm assuming it was similar to the Autumn King telling me I'm a little bitch?"

Cormac shook his head. "Let's be clear: I'm only here today because I'm well aware that if I'm not, then your brother will cease contacting Agent Daybright."

"I'm flattered you know me so well," Ruhn drawled, his arms crossed. He'd moved into a position on Cormac's other side—without her even noticing. Placing himself between the Avallen Prince and Bryce. Oh please.

Cormac glowered at him, but then focused upon Bryce again. "I'm willing to move beyond this, on the condition that you don't surprise me again. We have too many enemies as it is."

"One," she said, "don't give me conditions. But two . . ." She made a show of examining her bare arms. "Nothing up my sleeves. No other secrets to hide, I swear."

Except for that itsy-bitsy thing about Emile. Hunt gave her a dry look, as if to say, *Liar,* but she ignored him.

Cormac, however, did not. Catching that look, the Avallen Prince said, "There's something else."

"Nope."

But even Ruhn now lifted his brows at her. Hunt said casually, "Don't be paranoid."

"You have something planned," Cormac pressed. "For fuck's sake, tell me."

"I don't have anything planned," Bryce said, "other than figuring out this teleporting crap."

One moment, Cormac was glancing between her and Hunt. The next, he'd vanished.

Only to reappear at Bryce's back with a knife to her throat.

Bryce stiffened. "Come on, Cormac. There's no need for this." Lightning shone in Hunt's eyes. Ruhn had drawn his gun. Tharion remained sprawled across the bench, but—that was a knife now gleaming in his hand. His focus was fixed on the Avallen Prince.

"*Tell me,*" Cormac snarled, and cool metal bit into her throat.

Trying not to breathe too deeply, Bryce laid a finger on the blade. "I made the Drop. I'll survive."

Cormac hissed at her ear. "Tell me what the fuck you have planned, or you'll lose your head. Good luck growing that back."

"You draw blood and you lose your head, too," Hunt growled with lethal menace.

She could blind Cormac, she supposed. But would his shadows muffle the impact? She doubted he'd truly kill her, but if he tried . . . Hunt would definitely attack. Ruhn would, too.

And she'd have an even bigger mess on her hands.

So Bryce said, "Fine. It's about Emile."

Hunt started. So did Tharion as the mer said, "Bryce."

Cormac didn't remove the knife. "*What* about Emile?"

"I found him. At the Viper Queen's warehouse." She sighed loudly. "I learned he was there, that all the reptiles and gross things in the marshes had told her where he was and she'd gone to retrieve him. She was the one who killed the people who helped him, and intended to control him. But when I went to the warehouse two days ago, he was already gone."

Cormac whirled her to face him with rough hands. "Gone where?"

"Somewhere safe. Apparently, the Vipe found it in herself to put him into the care of people who will look after him."

"*Who?*" His face was white with rage. Tharion's eyes had widened.

"I don't know. She wouldn't tell me."

"Then I'll make her tell *me*."

Ruhn laughed. "No one makes the Viper Queen do anything."

Into her mind, her brother said, *Cormac might not know you well enough to tell when you're lying, but I do.*

It's not a lie. Emile is safe.

He's just not where you're claiming.

Oh, he was with the Viper Queen. And now he's somewhere else.

Cormac shook his head. "Why would the Viper Queen have any interest in that boy?"

"Because she likes to collect powerful beings to fight in her pits," Hunt snarled. "Now put the fucking knife away."

To her relief, the prince lowered the knife from her neck with an easy flip of the blade. "But why would she let go of someone so powerful, if she likes to use them in fights?"

Bryce said, "Because Emile has no powers."

Are you shitting me? Ruhn asked.

Nope. Kid's totally human.

Cormac's eyes narrowed. "Sofie said—"

"She lied," Bryce said.

Cormac's shoulders slumped. "I need to find him. I shouldn't have put off questioning Spetsos—"

"Emile is safe, and cared for," Bryce interrupted, "and that's all you need to know."

"I owe it to Sofie—"

"You owe it to Sofie to keep Emile out of this rebellion. Your life is hardly what I'd call a stable environment. Let him stay hidden."

Cormac said to Tharion, "What are *you* going to tell your queen?"

Tharion offered him a razor-sharp smile. "Absolutely nothing." A threat of violence simmered beneath the words. If Cormac breathed anything to the mer, to the River Queen, the Avallen Prince would find himself in a watery grave.

Cormac sighed. And to her shock, he said, "I apologize for the knife." To Hunt, he said, "And I apologize for threatening your mate."

Ruhn asked, "Don't I get an apology?" Cormac bristled, but Ruhn grinned.

Bryce caught Hunt watching her, his expression proud. Like she'd done something worthy. Had it been her smooth weaving of lies and truth?

"Apology accepted," Bryce said, forcing herself to sound chipper. Steering away from the topic of Emile. "Now back to training."

Cormac shrugged, pointing to the spots he'd taped off: X's on the floor, atop chairs, atop piled mats, beneath a table.

Bryce groaned, but marked them, cataloged the path she'd take.

"Well, that was exciting," Tharion announced, groaning as he got to his feet. "Right. I'm out."

Hunt arched a brow. "Where to?"

"I'm still technically employed by the River Queen. Regardless of what happened with Emile, there are other matters to attend to."

Bryce waved at him. But Ruhn said, "Dinner tonight?"

Tharion winked. "You got it." Then he sauntered through the metal doors and was gone.

"All right, Athalar," Bryce muttered when the mer had shut the doors. "Time to level up."

Hunt laughed, but his lightning flared again. "Let's do this, Your Highness."

There was something in the way he said *Your Highness* that made her realize that the expression on his face a moment before hadn't been pride in her manipulation—it had been pride in the way she'd defused things without violence. Like he thought she might actually deserve the title she now bore.

Bryce tucked the thought aside. By the time the bolt of lightning slammed into her chest, she was already running.

Despite the exhaustion weighing on his very bones, despite the urgency that had sent him and Hypaxia racing here, Ithan couldn't help gaping from the doorway as the party girl he'd loved moved through the Aux training space like the wind, vanishing and appearing at will. At his side, Hypaxia monitored the remarkable feats, studying Bryce intently.

Bryce finished the obstacle course and halted at Hunt's side, bending over her knees to catch her breath.

Hypaxia cleared her throat, stepping into the gymnasium. Even the queen looked . . . ruffled after the endless, terrifying night they'd had.

They'd passed Tharion on his way out. The mer had been speaking in low tones to someone on the phone, and had raised his brows with concern at the sight of the dirt and sweat on them. But whoever had been on the phone must have been important enough that he couldn't hang up, and Tharion had only continued on after Hypaxia had given him a gesture that seemed to assure him that she was fine. The mer had stopped and peered back over a shoulder at Ithan, as if needing to confirm the queen's claim, but Ithan had nothing to offer him. What the Hel could he say? They weren't fine. Not at all. So they'd left Tharion in the hall, the mer staring after them for a long moment.

"What's up?" Ruhn asked Ithan, waving his greeting to Hypaxia. Then the prince did a double take. "What the Hel happened to you two? I thought you were summoning Connor."

The others in the training space halted.

"We did indeed try to summon Connor Holstrom last night," Hypaxia said gravely.

Bryce paled as she hurried over. "What happened? Is Connor all right? Are you guys all right?"

Ithan's throat worked. "Ah . . ."

Hypaxia replied for him, “We did not encounter Connor. The Under-King answered.”

“What happened?” Bryce asked again, voice rising.

Ithan met her stare. Pure predatory wolf gleamed there. “He detained us for his amusement. Sicced Flame and Shadow’s nightmare dogs on us and warded us into an olive grove with them. It took Hypaxia until now to figure out an exit through the wards that wouldn’t get us ripped to shreds. We’re fine, though.” Ruhn whirled with alarm to his fiancée, and the witch-queen nodded solemnly, shadows in her eyes. Ithan scrubbed at his face before he added, “He wants to see you at Urd’s Temple.”

Hunt’s lightning sparked at his fingertips. “Fuck no.”

Ithan swallowed hard. “You don’t have a choice.” He turned, pleading and exhausted, to Bryce. “Connor is safe for right now, but if you don’t show within an hour, the Under-King will throw him and the rest of the Pack of Devils through the Gate immediately. He’ll make secondlight of them all.”

64

Tharion strolled through the Meat Market, casually browsing the stalls. Or at least, he tried to appear casual. While surveying an array of luck stones, he kept an ear open. In the midday bustle, the general assortment of lowlifes had come here for lunch, shopping, or fucking, and at this point, they'd likely have downed at least a few drinks. Which meant loose tongues.

I hear the bitch is already pregnant, one satyr grunted to another as they sat around a barrel converted into a table, smoked kebabs half-eaten in front of them. *Ephraim's been fucking her good.*

Tharion pushed aside his disgust at the crude words. He hated that word—*bitch*. How many times had it been thrown at his sister whenever she'd ventured Above? She'd always laughed it off, and Tharion had laughed it off with her, but now . . . He shook off the pang of guilt and moved to the next stall, full of various types of mushrooms from the damp forests to the northeast.

He checked his phone—the quick message exchange between him and Pax.

What happened? Are you all right? he'd written nearly an hour ago, after running into her and Holstrom in the hall of the Aux training center. She'd been dirty and tired-looking, and he hadn't been able to so much as ask if she was okay, because he'd been on the phone with the River Queen. Who had wanted updates on Emile.

Which was why he had come here. To maintain the fiction that he was hunting for the kid. He figured he'd do some listening to the idle chatter while pretending, though. Pick up gossip from the city creeps.

His phone buzzed, and Tharion scanned the message on the screen before loosing a long breath. Hypaxia had written, *I'm fine. Just some Flame and Shadow posturing.*

He didn't like that one bit. But what the Hel could he do about any of it?

"Lion's head is in season," said the gnome perched on a stool behind the baskets of fungi, drawing Tharion from his thoughts. "Morels finished their run, but I've got one last basket left."

"Only browsing," Tharion said, flashing a smile at the rosy-cheeked, red-capped male.

"Let me know if you have any questions," the gnome said, and Tharion again tuned in to the tables behind him.

Fight last night was brutal. There was nothing left of that lion after—

I drank so much I can't remember who the Hel I was fucking—

—that dragon finished with them. Only embers—

I need more coffee. They should give us the day off after *a holiday, you know?*

Tharion stilled. Slowly turned, pinpointing the speaker who'd snagged his attention.

Dragon.

Well, *that* was interesting. And . . . fortunate.

He'd been lounging on that bench while Legs trained, needing the company of others as a distraction from the shuddering earthquake of nerves after last night. He'd fucked the leopard shifter in the garden shadows. Had enjoyed every second of it, and from her two orgasms, she had, too.

He might have walked away from the River Queen's daughter last night, but he hadn't told her that. As far as the River Queen and her daughter knew, and judging by the former's tone on the phone earlier when she'd called to ask about the hunt for Emile, they were still engaged. But if either of them found out . . .

If they found out, wouldn't it be convenient to have a dragon to offer as an apology present? Wouldn't a dragon be perfect in lieu of Emile?

"This place isn't nearly as fun when you're sober," Flynn observed from behind him thirty minutes later as he approached in civilian clothes, precisely as Tharion had requested. The attire did little to hide the gun tucked down the back of his shorts.

Tharion hadn't dared say much on the phone when he'd asked the Fae lord to meet him here. And while Flynn might act like an unworried frat boy, Tharion knew he was too smart to risk asking questions on an open phone line.

Tharion rose from a table in the midst of the food stalls, where he'd been sipping coffee and filing old emails, and began a casual walk through the market. Low enough that no one—not even the fennec-fox shifter working a row over—would be able to hear, he said, "I found something you might be interested in."

Flynn feigned typing into his phone. "Yeah?"

Tharion muttered out of the corner of his mouth, "Remember how your new best friend with the . . . fiery temperament went missing?"

"You found Ari?" Flynn's voice had become dangerously solemn. A voice that few ever heard, Tharion knew. Unless they were about to die.

Tharion pointed toward the wooden walkway built above the market. Leading toward an ordinary door that he knew opened into a long hallway. Two blank-faced Fae guards armed with semiautomatic rifles stood before it. "I've got a wild guess about where she might be."

Now he had to figure out how to get the dragon Beneath.

Tharion eyed the bare-bones wooden hallway as he and Flynn strode down the worn planks, aiming for a round door at its far end. It looked like the entry to a vault, solid iron that didn't reflect the dim firstlights.

They'd been halted at the first door by the Viper Queen's guards. Flynn had snarled at them, but the males had ignored him, their drug-hazed eyes unblinking as they radioed their leader. That Tharion knew of this door at all told her guards he was important enough to warrant a call.

And here they were. About to go into the Viper Queen's nest.

The massive vault door swung open when they were about ten feet away, revealing ornate red carpets—definitely Traskian—over marble floors, three tall windows with heavy black velvet drapes held back with chains of gold, and low-slung couches designed for lounging.

The Viper Queen was sitting on one of them in a white jumpsuit, feet bare, toenails painted a purple so dark it was almost black. The same color as her lipstick. Her gold-tipped nails, however, glinted in the soft lights as she lifted a cigarette to her mouth and puffed away.

But beside her, sprawled on the couch . . .

He'd been right. The Viper Queen did like to collect valuable fighters.

"Ari," Flynn said tightly, halting just beyond the door. Mirthroot hung heavy in the air, along with a secondary, cloying scent that Tharion could only assume was another drug.

The dragon, clad in black leggings and a tight black tank top, didn't take her eyes off the massive TV mounted above the dark fireplace across the room. But she replied, "Tristan."

"Good to see you," Flynn said, voice taking on that dangerously low quality that so few lived to tell about. "Glad you're in one piece."

The Viper Queen chuckled, and Tharion braced himself. "The lion she fought last night can't say the same. Even confined to her humanoid form, she is . . . formidable."

Tharion grinned sharply at the ruler of the Meat Market. "Did you capture her?" He needed to know how she'd done it. If only so he could do it himself.

The Viper Queen's snake eyes flared to a nearly neon green. "I'm not in the business of snatching slaves. Unlike some people I know." She smirked at Ariadne. The dragon continued to stare at the TV with fixed intent. "She sought me out and asked for asylum, since she realized there was nowhere on Midgard she might flee from her captor. We reached a bargain that suited us both."

So the dragon had come of her own free will. Maybe he could convince her to go Beneath. It'd be a Hel of a lot easier.

Even if once he got her down there, she'd never get out again.

"You'd rather be here," Flynn asked the dragon, "fighting in her pit, than with us?"

"You threw me on guard duty," Ari spat, at last snapping her attention from the TV to Flynn. Tharion didn't envy the male as she fixed her burning gaze on him. "Is that any better than fighting in the pit?"

"Uh, yeah. A fuck-ton better."

"You sound like someone who's grown accustomed to his life being dull as dust," Ari said, turning back to the TV.

"You've been trapped inside a *ring* for the gods know how long," Flynn exploded. "What the Hel do you know about anything?"

Molten scales flowed under her skin, then vanished. Her face remained placid. Tharion wished he had some popcorn. But he caught the Viper Queen's narrowed eyes on him.

She said coolly, "I remember you: dead sister. Rogue shifter."

Tharion suppressed the flicker of ire at the casual reference to Lesia and threw the snake shifter his most charming smile. "That's me."

"And the River Queen's Captain of Intelligence."

"The one and only." He winked. "Care to have a word?"

"Who am I to deny the wishes of the River Queen's daughter's beloved?" Tharion tensed, and her purple lips curled, the razor-sharp bob swaying as she rose. "Don't roast the Faeling," she said to Ariadne, then curled a finger at Tharion. "This way."

She led him through a narrow hall lined with doors. He could see ahead that the corridor opened into another chamber. All he could make out of it was more carpets and couches as they approached. "Well, mer?"

Tharion huffed a laugh. "A few questions."

"Sure." She tapped ash from her cigarette into a glass ashtray atop the coffee table.

He opened his mouth, but they'd reached the room at the other end of the hall. It was a near-twin to the other, only its windows overlooked the fighting pit.

But sitting on one of the couches, with a pile of white powder that seemed a Hel of a lot like lightseeker on a small brass scale on the table before her . . .

"Let me guess," Tharion drawled at the Harpy, who lifted her head from where a Fae male weighed out the drugs, "it's not yours; it's for a friend."

The Harpy's dark eyes narrowed with warning as she eased to her feet. "Here to narc on me, fish?"

Tharion smiled slowly. "Just paying a friendly visit."

She turned her menacing stare to the Viper Queen, who slid her hands into her pockets and leaned against the far wall. "Did you sell me out?"

"This pretty hunk of meat waltzed in. Wanted a word. He knows the rules."

Tharion did. This was the Viper Queen's space. Her word was law. He had as little authority over her as he did the Asteri. And if he pulled anything, she had as much authority as the Asteri to end him. Likely by throwing him into that fighting pit and seeing how many of her fighters it took to kill him.

Tharion gestured to the doorway in a mockery of a bow. "I won't trouble you."

The Harpy glanced at the male who now scooped her lightseeker into a black velvet bag lined with plastic.

"VIP service, huh?" Tharion said to the Viper Queen, whose lips curved again.

"Only the best for my most valued clients," she said, still leaning against the wall.

The Harpy snatched the bag from the Fae male, her black wings rustling. "Keep your mouth shut, mer. Or you'll wind up in pieces like your sister."

He let out a low growl. “Keep talking, hag, and I’ll show you what I did to the male who killed her.”

The Harpy chuckled, tucking her drugs into the pocket of her jacket, and walked out, wings a black cloud behind her.

“Buying or selling?” the Viper Queen asked him quietly as the Fae male packed up his drugs and scale and bustled out.

Tharion turned to her, willing the rage riding his temper to ease off. “You know that psychopath made blood eagles out of two rebels, don’t you?”

“Why do you think I invited her to be a client? Someone who does that kind of shit needs to take the edge off. Or keep it on, I suppose.”

Tharion shook off his disgust. “She talk to you about what those rebels were doing in this city?”

“Are you asking me to play spy, Captain?”

“I’m asking you whether you’ve heard anything about Ophion, or a commander named Pippa Spetsos.” He needed to know if and when Pippa and her Lightfall unit would make a move, even without that mech-suit prototype. If he could save innocent lives in this city, he would.

“Of course I have. Everyone’s heard of Ophion.”

Tharion ground his teeth. “You know what they’re up to?”

She took a long drag from her cigarette. “Information isn’t free.”

“How much?”

“The dragon’s good for business.” Her snake eyes didn’t move from his. “Fight last night brought in a lot of money. I worked out a deal with her: she’ll get a portion of profits from her wins, and it can go toward buying her freedom.”

“You don’t own her.” No matter that *he* wanted to hand her over to his queen like . . .

Fuck, like a slave.

“No, I don’t. That’s why I’ll need you to spin whatever bullshit your friends and their lawyer gave to the Astronomer. Something about royal commandeering?” The Viper Queen admired her immaculate nails. “Tell everyone her fighting here is a matter of imperial security.”

"No one will believe that." And fuck, he needed that dragon. He needed her as an exit strategy out of this Emile situation. And any fallout for leaving the queen's daughter.

"People believe anything when presented correctly."

Tharion sighed at the mirrored ceiling. The dragon had at least agreed to be here, to fight toward her freedom, but . . .

The Viper Queen said, as if somehow reading or guessing his thoughts, "Even in that humanoid form, she can turn you into ashes if you try to bring her to the Blue Court." Tharion glowered, but said nothing. She went on, "You and your little gaggle of friends have been awfully active lately. I might have let Quinlan talk me into a bargain for the kid, but I have no plans to let this dragon slip out of my hands." A sharp smile. "You fools should have kept a tighter leash on her."

Tharion gave her a sharp smile of his own. "It's not my call whether she can stay here or not."

"Get your royal friends and their legal team to spin their bullshit and we'll be good, mer."

Fuck. He was really going to walk out of here empty-handed, wasn't he. His mind raced as he tried to think up some other prize to bring back to his queen, something to save his hide . . .

He'd figure it out later. When he wasn't in front of a notoriously lethal Vanir.

He sighed and said, "If the dragon agrees, then whatever. We'll spin our bullshit."

"She already has." Another sly smile.

"So tell me what Spetsos is up to." If he could appear competent in his job as Captain of Intelligence, maybe the information about a rebel threat would keep his queen's wrath at bay.

The Viper Queen pulled out her phone, checking the digital clock. "Call your friends and find out."

"What?"

But the Viper Queen had already turned back to the hall, to the dragon and Flynn at its other end.

Tharion dialed Hypaxia. Hunt. Then Bryce. Ithan. Ruhn. No one answered.

He didn't dare put it into a message, but . . . He dialed Hunt again. "Pick the fuck up," he murmured. "Pick the fuck up."

For a moment, he flashed back to another day, when he'd tried and tried to call his sister only to get her audiomail, so he'd called his parents, asking if they'd spoken to her, if they knew where she was—

Tharion reached Flynn, who was sitting on the couch, engaging in a silent staring contest with Ariadne. He couldn't keep the edge from his voice as he said, "Call Ruhn. See if he'll pick up for you."

"What's wrong?" Flynn was instantly on his feet.

"Not sure," Tharion said, heading for the door. He swallowed down those awful memories and his rising dread. "Any idea where they were today?"

The Viper Queen said behind them, sinking onto the couch again, "Good luck."

Tharion and Flynn paused at the doorway. The Fae lord pointed to the dragon. "We're not done here."

Ariadne only watched the TV again, ignoring him.

Flynn snarled. "I'm coming back for you."

Tharion tucked away the knowledge of what he'd done, what he'd bargained for this measly tip-off about Ophion and Spetsos. He'd tell Flynn later.

Ariadne's stare turned to Flynn as the vault door swung open again. Black turned to red. "Spare your high-handedness for someone who wants it, lordling."

Tharion stepped into the hall, phone again at his ear. Bryce didn't answer.

But Flynn looked back at the dragon lounging in the Viper Queen's nest. "We'll see about that, sweetheart," the Fae lord growled, and followed Tharion out.

Bryce had been to Urd's Temple in Moonwood all of one time since moving to Crescent City years ago. She and Juniper had drunkenly taken a cab over here one night during college to make an offering to the goddess of fate to make sure their destinies were epic.

Literally, that was what she'd said.

Benevolent and Farseeing Urd, please make our destinies as epic as possible.

Well, she'd gotten it, Bryce thought as she strode up the steps of the gray marble temple. So had June, though . . . Sorrow and guilt and longing swarmed her at the thought of her friend.

The quiet street was empty of cars. Like the Under-King had cleared everything out.

Or maybe that was due to the other menacing presence they'd dodged near the intersection of Central and Laurel on their walk over here from the training center: Pollux and Mordoc. Two monsters abroad in the city, a unit of the Hind's dreadwolves trailing behind them.

Searching for something. Or someone.

Hunt made sure no one was on the street behind the temple as Bryce, Ruhn, and Hypaxia entered. The Under-King had been very specific—only those four people were permitted to come. Ithan and Cormac hadn't been happy to stay behind.

Beyond the temple's courtyard—not a priestess in sight—the open doors to the inner sanctum beckoned, shadows and smoke within.

Bryce checked that the rifle across her back was in place, the handgun ready at her hip. Ruhn, on her left, carried the Starsword. She'd argued that it was impolite to arrive at a meeting bearing a weapon designed to kill Reapers, but the others overruled her. Ruhn would stay within arm's reach at all times, in case she needed to draw the blade. Lightning crackled around Hunt as they stepped into the gloom.

Not trusting how long it could last—or whether she could even contain it within herself—she hadn't asked him to transfer a charge to her. If it was needed, he could power her up in seconds.

A pyre smoked atop a black stone altar in the center of the temple. A stone throne on a dais loomed at the rear of the space. No statues ever adorned Urd's Temple—no depiction of the goddess had ever been made. Fate took too many forms to capture in one figure.

But someone *was* sitting on the throne.

"Punctual," the Under-King intoned, his bony fingers clicking on the stone arm of the throne. "I appreciate that."

"You desecrate that throne," Ruhn warned. "Get your rotting carcass off it."

The Under-King rose, black robes drifting on a phantom wind. "I thought the Fae bowed to Luna, but perhaps you remember the old beliefs? From a time when Urd was not a goddess but a force, winding between worlds? When she was a vat of life, a mother to all, a secret language of the universe? The Fae worshipped her then."

Bryce feigned yawning, earning an alarmed look from Ruhn, who'd blanched at the sight of the Under-King descending from the dais. Hunt, at least, didn't seem surprised. He'd grown accustomed to her antics, she supposed.

Hypaxia monitored every movement from the Under-King, wind stirring her hair. She had a score to settle after last night, it seemed.

"So," Hunt drawled, "here to finish our business?"

The Under-King drifted to the black altar, his horrific face contorting with pleasure as he breathed in the smoldering bones atop it. "I wished to inform you that the Reapers you so hatefully accused me of sending after you were in fact not Apollion's at all. I've discovered that they hailed from the Eternal City."

Bryce stiffened. "Reapers can cross oceans?"

"Reapers once crossed worlds. I don't see how some water might deter them."

"Why come here to attack us?" Hunt demanded.

"I don't know."

"And why tell us this at all?" Bryce went on.

"Because I do not appreciate my territory being infringed upon."

"Bullshit," Ruhn said. Hypaxia trailed a few steps behind him. "You told them the horrible truth about what happens after death, and yet you're willing to let them live now because you're pissed that someone stepped on your toes?"

His eyes—his dead, milky eyes—fixed on Bryce. "You are officially a princess now, I hear. I suspect you will learn a great deal of equally unpleasant truths."

"You're hedging," Ruhn growled.

But Bryce asked, "Did Jesiba speak to you?"

"Who?"

"Jesiba Roga. Antiquities dealer. She has—had—a few Death Marks. She must know you. She knows everyone."

The Under-King's eyes glowed. "I do not know her by that name, but yes. I know of her." His gaze drifted behind her, to Hypaxia at last. "You did well last night. Few could have worked their way through that labyrinth of spells. The House of Flame and Shadow will welcome you."

The breeze around Hypaxia rose to a chill wind, but she didn't deign to speak. Bryce made a note to herself to never get on the queen's bad side.

Hunt cut in, "You summoned us here to give us this convenient update about those Reapers, and now you want to play nice? I don't buy it."

The Under-King only smiled, revealing those too-large brown teeth.

Bryce said, "What does this sequence mean?" She rattled off what had been on Sofie's arm.

The Under-King blinked. "I don't know." He smiled again, wider. "But perhaps you should ask them." He pointed behind her to the doorway. The world beyond.

Where Pippa Spetsos was marching into the courtyard of the temple, flanked by Lightfall soldiers.

Hunt's lightning flared. "You tipped off Ophion," he snarled, even as he began calculating the fastest route out of the temple.

Ruhn, already at the inner sanctum doors, slammed them shut and barred them. Locking them in with the Under-King.

Pippa's voice came through the doors. *"Come play, Vanir scum. We'll show you what happens when you turn on us."*

Hypaxia's face paled. "You were . . . working with the rebels?"

"Emphasis on *were*," Bryce muttered. Not that it made a difference right now.

The Under-King's figure began to fade away. An illusion. A projection. Hunt didn't bother to wonder how he had done it, had made the details seem so real. "War means death. Death means souls—and more secondlight. Who am I to turn away from a feeding trough? Commander Spetsos's first act upon arriving in Crescent City was to kneel before me. When she mentioned the enemies in their ranks, I took it upon myself to inform her of our . . . altercation. We made a deal that is in both of our best interests."

The rebels would claim the kill, sparing the Under-King any political fallout, but the creep would be satisfied that he'd played a role in slaughtering them, and receive whatever souls would wind up in his realm. A whole lot of them, if Pippa was on the move.

Bryce bristled, starlight shimmering from her. "And were you lying when you claimed you didn't send the Reapers after me and Ruhn those weeks ago?"

"I spoke true then and I speak true now. I had no involvement in that. Why should I lie to you, when I have already revealed so much?"

"Keep playing these games, and you'll make enemies of all of us," Ruhn warned the king.

The Under-King faded into shadows. "Death is the only victor in war." Then he was gone.

A bullet boomed against the metal door. Then another. Pippa was still shouting her vitriol.

"Any ideas?" Hunt asked. If the rebels had gorsian bullets, this would get messy very quickly. And bring a huge crowd to witness the disaster.

Bryce grabbed Hunt's hand. Pushed it on her chest. "Level me up, Athalar."

Ruhn jerked his chin toward Hypaxia. "Take her with you."

The witch-queen glared at the Fae Prince in reproach, but Bryce shook her head, keeping her hand over Hunt's. Her fingers tightened, the only sign of her nerves as she said, "I've never brought anyone along. I need all my focus right now."

Good. At least she was being smart about this. Hunt held his mate's gaze, letting her see his approval, his encouragement. He wouldn't waste time asking what she planned. Bryce was brilliant enough to have something figured out. So Hunt let his lightning flow, setting it zinging through his hand and into her chest.

Her star began glowing beneath his fingers, as if in greedy anticipation. Another barrage of bullets clanged against the door.

His lightning flowed into her like a river, and he could have sworn he heard a beautiful sort of music between their souls as Bryce said, "We need reinforcements."

Ruhn contained his panic as his sister, charged up with a spike of Athalar's lightning, vanished into nothing.

An impact rocked the metal doors into the inner sanctum. Why hadn't the Aux been summoned yet? He reached for his phone. If he called in help, there would be questions about why they'd even been here in the first place. He'd already tried Cormac, but the male had sent him to audiomail, and then messaged that he was talking to the King of Avallen. There was no way the prince would interrupt that call.

They were trapped.

He pivoted to Hypaxia, who was scanning the sanctum, searching for any hidden doors. "There has to be another exit," she said, running her hands over the walls. "No temple ever has just one way in and out."

"This one might," Hunt grumbled.

Bryce reappeared, and Ruhn marked every detail of his panting sister. "Easy peasy," Bryce declared, but her face was sweaty, her eyes dim with exhaustion. What the Hel had she gone off to do?

Another bang on the doors, and the metal dented.

"What the fuck was that?" Ruhn drew the Starsword.

"We need to get out of here now," Bryce said, going to Hunt's side. "We have time, but not much."

"Then teleport us out."

She shook her head. "I don't know if I can do it—"

"You can," Athalar said, absolutely certain. "You just teleported in and out. You've got this. Steady your breathing, block out the noise, and focus."

Her throat bobbed. But she reached for Athalar's hand.

Hunt took a step away. "Hypaxia first. Then Ruhn."

"I might not have enough strength—"

"You do. Go."

Wariness and apprehension flooded his sister's face. But Bryce kissed Athalar's cheek, then grabbed the witch by the arm. "Hold on. I've never taken anyone with me like this and it might be . . ." Her words cut off as they disappeared.

Thank the gods. Thank the gods Bryce had made it out again, with Hypaxia in tow.

Hunt held his breath.

Ruhn said, "You should go next. You're her mate."

"You're her brother. And heir to the Fae throne."

"So is she."

Hunt blinked at the prince, but then Bryce was back, panting. "Oh gods, that fucking sucked." She retched, and reached a hand for Ruhn. "Come on."

"Rest," her brother ordered, but the doors dented further inward. Another few blows and they'd be open. And if Bryce's plan didn't get them a little more time . . .

Bryce grabbed Ruhn's arm and before her brother could object, they vanished. Alone, Hunt monitored the door, rallied his lightning. He could charge her up again, but she was clearly exhausted. Would it do any good?

The doors shuddered, and light cracked in as they peeled apart a few inches.

Hunt ducked behind the altar, away from the spray of bullets that followed, blindly aiming for whoever was within. "*There!*" Pippa shouted, and guns trained on him.

Where the fuck was Bryce—

The doors blew open, throwing three Lightfall soldiers to the ground.

Pollux stood between the doors, white wings luminescent with power, laughing to himself as he brought a clenched fist down upon the head of a female rebel sprawled before him. Bone and blood sprayed. Beyond him, in the courtyard, rebels fired at Mordoc and the dreadwolves. And out in the street, standing beneath a palm tree, away from the fray, Hunt could see the Hind, surveying the brawl.

Bryce appeared and slid behind the altar. Her skin had gone ashen, her breaths uneven. Sharp. She lifted a shaking hand toward him. "I . . ." She collapsed to her knees. She didn't need to say the rest. She was tapped out. Yet she'd come back to him. To fight her way out with him.

"Another charge?" he asked, lightning twining down his arms as he lifted her to her feet.

"I don't think my body can take it." She leaned against him. "I feel like overcooked meat."

Hunt peered around the altar. "How'd you manage to buy us time?"

"The Gates," Bryce panted. "I had to teleport to a few of them before I found one that was pretty empty and unwatched. I used the dial pad to broadcast a report that Ophion was sacking Urd's Temple—right in the middle of one of those stupid daily announcements. I figured a unit would be sent here. Probably the biggest and baddest they had, which happened to also be the closest."

He remembered now—they'd avoided Pollux and Mordoc, along with the Hind's dreadwolves, on the walk over here. "Your voice will be recognized—"

"I recorded the message, then played it through the Gate using a voice-warping app," she said with a grim smile. "And I made sure to move fast enough that the cameras couldn't pick it up as more than a blur, don't worry."

He could only gape at her, his clever, brilliant Bryce. Gods, he loved her.

Crouching behind the altar again as the fighting pressed into the temple, Hunt breathed, "We have to find some way to get through those doors unseen."

"If you can give me a minute . . ." She brushed a shaking hand to her chest. The scar there.

But Hunt knew. Only time would allow her to gain back her strength, and it would sure as fuck take longer than they had to spare.

Hunt banked his lightning, fearful Pollux would spy it. The Hammer drew closer, Mordoc a menacing shadow behind him. Where they walked, rebels died. Hunt couldn't get a visual on Pippa.

Bryce panted, and Hunt scented her blood before he looked. Her nose was bleeding. "What the fuck?" he exploded, covering her with his body as a stray spray of bullets shot over the top of the altar.

"My brain might be soup," she hissed, though fear shone in her eyes.

If he could unleash his lightning, he might be able to fry their way out. No matter that everyone would know who'd been there, especially if Mordoc picked up on the scents afterward, but . . . he'd take that chance. For Bryce, he'd risk it.

They could, of course, say that they had been fighting Ophion, but there was a chance that the Hind would decide this was the moment to reveal what she knew.

"Hold on to me," Hunt warned, reaching for Bryce as something crept out of the shadows behind Urd's throne.

A black dog. Massive, with fangs as long as Hunt's hand.

The Helhound motioned to the throne with a clawed paw. Then he vanished behind it.

There was no time to think. Hunt scooped up Bryce and ran, ducking low through the shadows between the altar and the dais, praying no one saw them in the chaos and smoke—

He whipped behind the throne to find the space empty. No sign of Baxian.

A growl came behind him, and Hunt whirled to the back of the throne. It wasn't solid stone at all, but an open doorway, leading into a narrow stairwell.

Hunt didn't question their luck as he sprinted through the stone doorway. Baxian, now in angelic form, shoved it shut behind him. Sealing them entirely in darkness.

Baxian lit the tight steps downward with his phone. Hunt held on to Bryce. From the way she clung to him, he wasn't entirely certain she could walk.

"I heard Pollux give the order to come here over the radio," Baxian said, hurrying ahead, wings rustling. Hunt let the male lead, glancing behind them to ensure the door didn't open. But the seal was perfect. Not so much as a crack of light shone. "Given how pissed Pippa was after Ydra, I figured it was you lot involved. I researched the history of this temple. Found rumors about the door hidden in the throne. It's what took me some time—finding the tunnel entrance in. Some priestess must have used it recently, though. Her scent was all over the alley and fake wall that leads in here."

Hunt and Bryce said nothing. That was twice now that Baxian had interfered to save them from the Hind and Pollux. And now Pippa.

"Is Spetsos dead?" Baxian asked, as they reached the bottom of the stairs and entered a long tunnel.

"Don't know," Hunt grunted. "She probably escaped and left her people to die."

"Lidia will be pissed she didn't catch her, but Pollux seemed to be enjoying himself," Baxian said, shaking his head. They walked until they hit a crossroads flanked by skulls and bones placed in tiny alcoves. Catacombs. "I don't think they had any clue you were there," Baxian went on, "though how they got tipped off—"

Bryce moved, so fast Hunt didn't have time to stop her from dropping out of his arms.

To stop her from unslinging her rifle and pointing it at Baxian. "Stop right there."

Bryce wiped the blood dripping from her nose on her shoulder as she aimed the rifle at the Helhound, paused in the catacombs' crossroads.

Her head pounded relentlessly, her mouth felt as dry as the

Psamathe Desert, and her stomach was a churning eddy of bile. She was never teleporting again. Never, ever, *ever.*

"Why the fuck do you keep popping up?" Bryce seethed, not taking her attention off the Helhound. Hunt didn't so much as move at her side. "Hunt says you're not spying for the Hind or the Asteri, but I don't fucking believe it. Not for one second." She clicked off the safety. "So tell me the gods-damned truth before I put this bullet through your head."

Baxian walked to one of the curved walls full of skulls. Didn't seem to care that he was a foot away from the barrel of her gun. He ran a finger down the brown skull of what seemed to be some fanged Vanir, and said, "Through love, all is possible."

The rifle nearly tumbled from her fingers. "What?"

Baxian peeled back the collar of his battle-suit, revealing brown, muscled flesh. And a tattoo scrawled over the angel's heart in familiar handwriting.

Through love, all is possible.

She knew that handwriting. "Why," she asked carefully, voice shaking, "do you have Danika's handwriting tattooed on you?"

Baxian's dark eyes became pained. Empty. "Because Danika was my mate."

65

Bryce aimed the rifle at Baxian again. "You are a fucking *liar.*"

Baxian left his collar open, Danika's handwriting inked there for all to see. "I loved her. More than anything."

Hunt said harshly, words echoing in the dry catacombs around them, "This isn't fucking funny, asshole."

Baxian turned pleading eyes to him. Bryce wanted to claw the male's face off. "She was my mate. Ask Sabine. Ask her why she ran the night she burst into your apartment. She's always hated and feared me—because I saw how she treated her daughter and wouldn't put up with it. Because I've promised to turn her into carrion one day for what Danika endured. That's why Sabine left the party last night so fast. To avoid me."

Bryce didn't lower the gun. "You're full of shit."

Baxian splayed his arms, wings rustling. "Why the fuck would I lie about this?"

"To win our trust," Hunt said.

Bryce couldn't get a breath down. It had nothing to do with the teleporting. "I would have known. If Danika had a mate, I would have *known*—"

"Oh? You think she would have told you that her mate was someone in Sandriel's triarii? The Helhound? You think she'd have run home to dish about it?"

"Fuck you," Bryce spat, focusing the scope right between his eyes. "And fuck your lies."

Baxian walked up to the gun. To the barrel. Pushed it down and against his heart, right up against the tattoo in Danika's handwriting. "I met her two years before she died," he said quietly.

"She and Thorne—"

Baxian let out a laugh so bitter it cracked her soul. "Thorne was delusional to think she'd ever be with him."

"She fucked around," Bryce seethed. "You were no one to her."

"I had two years with her," Baxian said. "She didn't fuck anyone else during that time."

Bryce stilled, doing the mental tally. Right before her death, hadn't she teased Danika about . . .

"Two years," she whispered. "She hadn't gone on a date in two years." Hunt gaped at her now. "But she . . ." She racked her memory. Danika had hooked up constantly throughout college, but a few months into their senior year and the year after . . . She'd partied, but stopped the casual sex. Bryce choked out, "It's not possible."

Baxian's face was bleak, even in the dimness of the catacombs. "Believe me, I didn't want it, either. But we saw each other and knew."

Hunt murmured, "That's why your behavior changed. You met Danika right after I left."

"It changed *everything* for me," Baxian said.

"How did you even meet each other?" Bryce demanded.

"There was a gathering of wolves—Pangeran and Valbaran. The Prime sent Danika as his emissary."

Bryce remembered that. How pissed Sabine had been that Danika had been tapped to go, and not her. Two weeks later, Danika had come back, and she'd seemed subdued for a few days. She'd said it was exhaustion but . . .

"You're not a wolf. Why were you even there?" Danika couldn't have been with Baxian, couldn't have had a *mate* and not told her about it, not smelled like it—

She was a bloodhound. With that preternatural sense of smell, she'd know better than anyone how to hide a scent—how to detect if any trace of it had remained on her.

"I wasn't at the gathering. She sought me out while she was there."

"Why?"

"Because she was researching shifter ancestry. Mine is . . . unique."

"You shift into a dog," Bryce raged. "What's unique about that?" Even Hunt gave her a disapproving frown. She didn't care. She was sick of these surprises about Danika, about all the things she'd never known—

"She wanted to know about my shifter ancestry. Really old shifter ancestry that manifested in me after years of lying dormant. She was examining the most ancient bloodlines in our world and saw a name on an early ancestor's family tree that could be traced all the way to the last living descendant: me."

"What the Hel could you even tell her if it was that ancient?" Hunt asked.

"Ultimately, nothing. But once we knew we were mates, once we'd sealed it . . . She started to open up about what she was looking into."

"Was it about the synth?" Bryce asked.

"No." Baxian clenched his jaw. "I think the synth was a cover for something else. Her death was because of the research she was doing."

Through love, all is possible. One last clue from Danika. To look where she'd stamped the phrase—right on this male.

So Bryce said, "Why did she care about any of this?"

"She wanted to know where we came from. The shifters, the Fae. All of us. She wanted to know what we'd once been. If it might inform our future." Baxian's throat worked. "She was also . . . She told me she wanted to find an alternative to Sabine."

"*She* was the alternative to Sabine," Bryce snapped.

"She had a feeling she might not live long enough for that," Baxian said hoarsely. "Danika didn't want to leave the wolves' future in Sabine's hands. She was seeking a way to protect them by uncovering a possible alternative in the bloodline to challenge Sabine."

It was so . . . so *Danika.*

"But after we met," Baxian went on, "she started hunting for a way into a world where we could be together—since there was no way Sabine or Sandriel, or even the Asteri, would have allowed it."

Bryce clicked the safety back on the gun and lowered it to the ground.

Baxian said with quiet ferocity, "I was so fucking glad when you killed Micah. I knew . . . I had this *feeling* that prick was involved in her death."

Glad someone finally put a bullet through Micah's head, Baxian had said when they'd first met. Bryce surveyed the male who'd loved her friend—the male she'd never known about. "Why wouldn't she have told me?"

"She wanted to. We didn't dare talk on the phone or write to each other. We had a standing agreement to meet at a hotel in Forvos—I could never get away from Sandriel for long—on a given day every two months. She worried that the Asteri would use me against her to keep her in line, if they found out about us."

"Did she tell you she loved you?" Bryce pushed.

"Yes," Baxian replied without a moment of hesitation.

Danika had once claimed she'd only said those words to Bryce. To *her,* not to this . . . stranger. This male who'd freely and willingly served Sandriel. Hunt had been given no choice in that matter. "She didn't care that you're a monster?"

Baxian flinched. "After I met Danika, I tried my best to counteract all I did for Sandriel, though sometimes all I could do was . . . lessen Sandriel's evil." Yet his eyes softened. "She loved you, Bryce. You were the most important person in the world to her. You were—"

"Shut up. Just . . . shut the fuck up," Bryce whispered. "I don't want to hear it."

"Don't you?" he challenged. "Don't you want to know all of it? Isn't that why you've been digging around? You want to know—*need* to know what Danika knew. What she was up to, what she kept secret."

Her face hardened into stone. She said flatly, "Fine. Let's start with this one, if you knew her so well. How did Danika meet Sofie

Renast? You ever hear that name in all your secret little conversations? What did Danika want from her?"

Baxian bristled. "Danika learned about Sofie's existence while investigating thunderbird lineage as part of her research into shifters and our origins. She traced the bloodlines—and then confirmed it by tracking her down and scenting her. Being Danika, she didn't let Sofie walk away without answering some questions."

Bryce stilled. "What kind of questions?" Hunt put a hand on her shoulder.

Baxian shook his head. "I don't know. And I don't know how they pivoted to working together on the Ophion stuff. But I think Danika had some theories about thunderbirds beyond the lineage thing. About their power in particular."

Bryce frowned. "Do you know why Sofie Renast might have felt the need to carve a series of numbers and letters on herself while she drowned a few weeks ago?"

"Solas," Baxian murmured. And then he recited the sequence from Sofie's body, down to the last numeral. "Was that it?"

"What the fuck are you playing at, Baxian?" Hunt growled, but Bryce snapped at the same time, "What *is* it?"

Baxian's eyes flashed. "It's a system of numbering rooms used in only one place on Midgard. The Asteri Archives."

Hunt swore. "And how in Urd's name do you know that?"

"Because I gave it to Danika."

Bryce was surprised enough that words failed her.

"Sandriel was the Asteri's pet." Baxian turned to Hunt. "You know that, Athalar. She made me serve as escort on one of her visits to their palace. When they brought her down to the archives for a meeting, I saw them go through that door. When Sandriel emerged, she was pale. It was odd enough that I memorized the series of numbers and letters and passed it to Danika later as something to look into. Danika became . . . obsessed with it. She wouldn't tell me why, or what she thought might be in there, but she had theories. Ones that she said would alter this very world. But she couldn't go in herself. She was too recognizable. She knew the Asteri were already watching her."

"So after she met Sofie, Danika gave her the information, and had Sofie sneak in to investigate," Bryce murmured. "Since Sofie's record wouldn't have shown anything suspicious about her."

Baxian nodded. "From what I gleaned from the Hind's reports, it took Sofie three years of work to get in. Three years of spying and going undercover as one of the archivists. I'm assuming she finally found a way to sneak into that room—and ran to Kavalla soon after. By that time, Danika was . . . gone. She died without ever learning what was in the room."

"But Sofie did," Bryce said quietly.

"Whatever she learned was in that room," Hunt agreed. "That must have been the intel Sofie planned to use as leverage against Ophion—and against the Asteri."

"Something war-changing," Bryce said. "Something big."

"Why wouldn't this room identifier come up on search engines?" Hunt asked Baxian.

The Helhound tucked in his wings. "The Asteri don't have any of their palace blueprints on the interweb. Even their library cataloging system is secret. Anything digitized is highly encrypted."

"And if we had someone who could hack into anything?" Bryce asked.

Baxian again smiled bitterly. "Then I guess you'd have a chance at finding out what was in that room."

"This is a totally nonsensical way of numbering rooms," Declan muttered, typing away on the sectional couch in Ruhn's house. Bryce had run there with Hunt after leaving Baxian in the alley the tunnel had led to, a few blocks from Urd's Temple. She was still reeling.

She'd turned on her phone to find several missed calls from Tharion. The Viper Queen had given him a heads-up about Ophion—only a few minutes too late. Flynn had nearly thrown a fit when Ruhn had explained what had happened.

At least no word had emerged about their connection to the rebel attack on Urd's Temple, as the news was calling it. Pollux, Mordoc, and the Hind were hailed as heroes for stopping Pippa's forces from desecrating the sacred space. The only failure: Pippa had escaped.

Bryce would deal with that later. Would deal with a lot of other shit later.

Declan scratched his head. "You realize that what we're doing right now amounts to treason."

"We owe you big-time," Hunt said, sitting on the arm of the sofa.

"Pay me in booze," Declan said. "It'll be a comfort while I worry about when the dreadwolves will show up at my door."

"Here," Ruhn said, handing the male a glass of whiskey. "This'll start you off." Her brother dropped onto the cushions beside her. Across the couch, Hypaxia sat next to Ithan, quiet and watchful.

Bryce had let Hunt explain what they'd learned from Baxian. And let Ruhn explain the whole truth to the witch-queen and the sprites, who had draped themselves around Flynn's shoulders where he sat on Declan's other side.

But it was to Ithan that Bryce's attention kept returning. And as Declan focused, Bryce said quietly to the wolf, "Did you know about Danika and Baxian?" His face had revealed nothing.

"Of course not," Ithan said. "I thought she and Thorne . . ." He shook his head. "I have no idea what to make of it. I never once scented anything on her."

"Me neither. Maybe she was able to hide it with her bloodhound gift somehow." She cleared her throat. "It wouldn't have mattered to me."

"Really? It would have mattered to me," Ithan countered. "To everyone. Not only is Baxian not a wolf, he's . . ."

"An asshole," Hunt supplied without looking up from his phone.

"Yeah," Ithan said. "I mean, I get that he just saved your hides, but . . . still."

"Does it matter now?" Flynn asked. "I mean, no offense, but Danika's gone."

Bryce gave him a flat look. "Really? I had no idea."

Flynn flipped her off, and the sprites *oooh*ed at his shoulder.

Bryce rolled her eyes. Exactly what Flynn needed: his own flock of cheerleaders trailing him at all hours. She said to Flynn, "Hey, remember that time you set a dragon free and were dumb enough to think she'd follow your orders?"

"Hey, remember that time you wanted to marry me and wrote *Lady Bryce Flynn* in all your notebooks?"

Hunt choked.

Bryce countered with, "Hey, remember when you pestered me for years to hook up with you, but I have something called standards—"

"This is highly unusual behavior for royals," Hypaxia observed.

"You have no idea," Ruhn muttered, earning a smile from the queen.

Noting the way her brother's face lit up, then dimmed . . . Did he know? About Hypaxia and Celestina? She had no idea what else might dampen his expression.

"Where's Tharion?" Hunt asked, surveying the house. "Shouldn't he be here?"

"He's upstairs," Ruhn said. They could fill Tharion in later, she supposed. And Cormac, once he'd finished with whatever his father wanted.

Declan suddenly cursed, frowning. Then he said, "There's good news and bad news."

"Bad news first," Bryce said.

"There's no way in Hel I can ever hack into this archival system. It's ironclad. I've never seen anything like it. It's gorgeous, actually."

"All right, tone down the fanboying," Ruhn grumbled. "What's the good news?"

"Their camera system in the Eternal Palace is *not* ironclad."

"So what the fuck does that get us?" Hunt asked.

"At the very least, I can confirm whether Sofie Renast ever gained access to that room."

"And where that room might be," Bryce murmured. Ithan and Hypaxia both nodded. "All right. Do it."

"Settle in," Declan warned. "We're in for a long night."

Ithan was dispatched to get Tharion after an hour, and Bryce was rewarded with the sight of a sleep-tousled mer entering the living room wearing nothing but his jeans.

Tharion plopped onto the couch beside Hypaxia, slinging his arm around the queen's shoulders and saying, "Hi, Pax."

Hypaxia waved off the mer. "Sleeping all afternoon?"

"Life of a playboy," Tharion said. Apparently, they'd become fast friends during the Summit. Bryce might have wondered if there was more between them, had she not found the witch with the Archangel the night before. She wondered if Tharion knew.

Wondered if it rankled her brother that the witch and the mer had stayed in touch since the Summit, and he'd had only silence from her. Ruhn didn't so much as frown.

Around midnight, Declan said, "Well, holy shit. There she is."

Hunt nearly trampled Ruhn as they hurried over. Bryce, of course, made it to Declan's side first, and swore. Hunt shoved Ruhn out of the way with an elbow and claimed the seat next to his mate. Ithan, Tharion, Hypaxia, and Flynn—sprites in tow—pressed in around them.

"She looks so young," Hunt murmured.

"She was," Ruhn said. Dec had pulled up the photo from Sofie's old university ID and had the program search for any faces that resembled hers in the footage.

Bryce had tried to call Cormac, but the prince hadn't answered his phone.

So they kept silent as Declan played the footage of the wood-and-marble subterranean library. From the camera mounted on the ceiling, they could see Sofie Renast, clad in some sort of white uniform that could only belong to one of the archivists, stalk by the ancient shelves.

"Door Seven-Eta-Dot-Three-Alpha-Omega," Declan said, pointing to a wooden door beyond the shelf. "You can make out the writing faintly beside it."

They could. Sofie slipped inside the room, using some sort of ID card to bypass the modern lock, then shut the carved door behind her.

"Fifteen minutes pass," Declan said, zooming ahead. "And then she's out again." Sofie walked from the room the same way she had entered it: calmly.

"She doesn't have anything on her," Hunt observed.

"I can't make out anything under her clothes, either," Ruhn agreed.

"Neither did the computer," Declan said. "She carried nothing in, nothing out. But her face is white as death." Just as Baxian claimed Sandriel's had been.

"When is this dated?" Bryce asked. Hunt squeezed her knee, like he needed to touch her, remind himself she was here and safe with him.

"Two months ago," Declan said. "Right before she went into Kavalla."

"It took *three years* of working undercover to get access to this room?" Ruhn said.

"Do you know how intense the security is?" Hunt asked. "I can't believe she made it in at all."

"I know it's fucking intense, Athalar," Ruhn said tightly.

Bryce said, "Well, we're going to have to beat her time."

They all faced her. Bryce's attention remained fixed on the screen, though. On the young woman walking out of the ancient library.

Hunt's stomach twisted. He had a feeling he knew what she was going to say even before Bryce declared, "We need to get to the Eternal City—and into those archives."

"Bryce," Hunt started, dread rushing through him. He might have made peace with their involvement with Cormac and Ophion, but this . . . this was on a whole new level. Perilously close to what he'd done leading the Fallen.

"I want to know what Sofie knew," Bryce said through her teeth. "What Danika was willing to risk so much to discover."

After the truth Baxian had dropped, she needed the full story more than ever. It didn't only have to do with wanting to use the intel as leverage against the Asteri. Danika had thought this information could change the world. Save it, somehow. How could she walk away from it now?

"You're talking about breaking into the most secure place on Midgard," Tharion interjected carefully. "Breaking into an enemy's stronghold."

"If Sofie Renast did it, I can, too."

Ruhn coughed. "You realize none of us know our way around the palace, Bryce. We'll be operating blind."

Hunt tensed beside her, and Bryce knew that particular sort of tautness on his face. Knew he was shutting out his vivid memories of the throne room, the dungeons. Blood and screaming and pain—that's all he recalled, he'd told her.

She leaned into his side. Offered what love she could through the touch.

"We won't be operating blind," Bryce said to Ruhn, lifting her chin. "I know someone who's intimately familiar with its layout."

Ithan sat on the couch long after Bryce and Athalar had gone home, and Ruhn, Dec, and Flynn had left for their Aux duties. The sprites had opted to follow Flynn, leaving Ithan and Tharion alone in the house.

"You ready for the shitshow we're about to enter?" the mer asked him, forearms on his knees as he leaned forward to play the video game on the big screen.

"I don't really have a choice but to be ready, right?" Ithan, playing on the split screen beside him, jammed his thumbs onto the controller buttons.

"You're probably used to high-stakes situations. You went to finals a couple times."

"Twice. And three times in high school."

"Yeah, I know. I mean, I watched you." Tharion flicked the switch on the controller, seemingly content to focus on the game. Like he wasn't a male who'd walked in and out of the Viper Queen's lair today. "You seem remarkably calm about everything that's been going down."

"Flynn said it doesn't make a difference if Danika was Baxian's mate, since she's, you know, dead." His chest ached. "I guess he's right."

"I meant about the rebels and the Under-King, but that's good to know."

Ithan shrugged. "After this spring, what the fuck is normal anyway?"

"True." They played for a few more minutes.

"What's the deal with you and the River Queen's daughter?" Ithan asked finally.

Tharion didn't take his eyes off the screen. "I've been betrothed to her for years. End of story."

"You love her?"

"Nope."

"Why get engaged to her, then?"

"Because I was horny and stupid and wanted to fuck her so badly that I swore myself to her, thinking I could undo it in the morning. Turns out, I couldn't."

"Rough, dude."

"Yep." Tharion paused the game. "You seeing anyone?"

Ithan had no idea why, but the wolf in the Astronomer's tank emerged before him. But he said carefully, "Ruhn didn't tell you about, uh, my past?"

"You mean about you having a thing for Bryce? No."

"Then how the fuck do you know?"

"She's Bryce. *Everyone* has got a thing for her."

"I used to like her."

"Uh-huh."

Ithan exposed his teeth. "I don't feel that way about her anymore."

"Good, because Athalar would probably kill you, then barbecue your corpse."

"He could try."

"He'd try, and he'd win, and I doubt slow-roasted wolf would taste that good, even doused in sauce."

"Whatever."

Tharion chuckled. "Don't do anything tragically romantic to prove yourself to her, okay? I've seen that shit go down before and it never works. Definitely not if you're dead."

"Not on my agenda, but thanks."

Tharion's expression turned serious. "I mean it. And . . . look, I bet Bryce will kick my balls into my throat for this, but if you have any unresolved business with anyone, I'd get it done before we go to the Eternal City. Just in case."

In case they didn't come back. Which seemed likely.

Ithan sighed. Set down his controller. Got up from the couch. Tharion arched a brow.

Ithan said, "There's something I have to do."

66

You have to be ten kinds of stupid," Fury hissed at Bryce from where they sat at the dive bar's counter, nursing their drinks. Fury had initially refused to meet up when Bryce had called her last night, but Bryce had pestered her enough throughout the following morning that she'd agreed to meet here.

Bryce had barely been able to sleep, though Hunt had done a good job exhausting her. Her mind couldn't stop turning over the things she'd learned. Danika had a *mate*. Sabine had known about it. Danika's mate still loved her.

And Danika had never told Bryce about any of it.

"I know it's insane," Bryce murmured, swirling her whiskey and ginger beer. "But any help you can give me . . ."

"You need a *shit*-ton of help, but not with this. You're out of your mind." Fury leaned closer, getting in Bryce's face. "Do you know what they'll do to you if you're caught? What they might do to your family, to Juniper, to punish you? Did you see what the Harpy did to those rebels? Do you know what Mordoc likes to do to *his* victims? I make sure to stay well out of his path. These people are soulless. The Asteri will gladly let them go to work on you and everyone you love."

"I know," Bryce said carefully. "So help me make sure I don't get caught."

"You're assuming I just have blueprints of the crystal palace lying around."

"I know you've been there. You have a better memory than anyone I know. You mean to tell me you didn't take mental notes while you were there? That you didn't notice the exits, the guards, the security systems?"

"Yeah, but you're talking about the archives. I can only give you a vague layout. I've only ever walked the halls—never gone into the rooms."

"So don't you want to know what's *in* those rooms? What Danika suspected might be inside that one room in particular?"

Fury swigged from her vodka on the rocks. "Don't try to convert me to your bullshit cause. I've done work for both sides and neither is worth the time of day. They're certainly not worth your life."

"We're not working for either side."

"Then what side are you working for?"

"Truth," Bryce said simply. "We want the truth."

Fury studied her, and Bryce withstood the searing assessment. "You've definitely lost your mind, then. I'm going to take June out of this city for a while. Lie low."

"Good." Bryce wished she could warn her parents without raising suspicions. She tapped her foot on the bronze footrest beneath the bar.

"Can you take Syrinx with you?" She wouldn't leave without knowing he'd be cared for.

"Yeah." Fury sighed and signaled the bartender for another vodka. "I'll get you what intel I can."

Tharion found his fiancée sitting on the edge of the quay off the Bone Quarter, her delicate feet dipping into the turquoise water, sending waves splashing in the sunlight. Her black hair was unbound, cascading down her slim back in a luxurious fall.

Once, that beauty had staggered him, snagged him. Now it merely . . . weighed.

"Thank you for meeting me." He'd sent the otter an hour ago. She twisted, looking back at him, a pretty smile lighting her face.

Tharion swallowed hard. She'd been so . . . starry-eyed at the party the other night. So elated to be there, dancing and laughing.

A decade. A decade wasted for him—and for her.

He'd advised Holstrom to settle any unfinished business. He needed to do the same.

"I, ah . . ." Tharion paced a step, keenly aware of the sobeks lurking in the river, appraising them with slitted eyes. The mer guards positioned near the dock, spears within throwing range, ready to impale him. "I wanted to talk to you."

Her look turned wary. He could have sworn the sobeks drifted closer. Tourists spotted them and began snapping photos along the quay. Saw the River Queen's daughter and began snapping photos of the beauty, too.

This was an awfully public place for this kind of meeting, but he knew if he did this at the Blue Court, if her mother got word of it before he could leave, she'd keep him Beneath, as trapped as any of the mortals who'd once been dragged below by the mer.

"You wish to call off our betrothal," she said. Thunderclouds threatened in her eyes.

Instinct had him fumbling for soothing lies to comfort her. But . . . if he was going to die, either at the Asteri's or her mother's hand, he wanted to do it knowing he'd been honest. "Yes."

"You think I did not know? All this time? A male who wanted to marry me would have acted by now." Her nose crinkled in anger. "How many years did I spend trying to coax some affection, some intimacy from you? Something to heal this?"

He refrained from saying that she'd also been vindictive and childish and sullen.

The water at her feet thrashed. "Yet it was always *I'm busy working on a case.* Then it was the next case, and the next. Then your wave skimmer would break, then your mother would need you, then your friends would require you." Power stirred around her. "You believe it is not obvious to all of the Blue Court that you don't *want* to come back home?"

His breathing stalled. He'd vastly underestimated her. He dared ask, "Why didn't you call it off, if you knew all that, then?"

"Because I harbored a shred of hope you might change. Like a fool, I prayed to Ogenas every day that you might come to me of your own free will. But that hope has withered now." She stood, somehow towering over him even though she was more than a foot shorter. Her words were a chill wind skittering over the water. "You want to stay here, amid this filth and noise?"

"I . . ." He scrambled for the words. "I do."

But she slowly shook her head. "My mother warned me of this. Of you. You do not have a true heart. You never did."

Good. At least she finally knew the truth. But he said as gently as he could, "I have to leave the city for a while, but let's talk about this more when I'm back. I feel like there's a lot of air to clear here."

"No more talking." She retreated a step to the edge of the quay, bristling with power. Waves crashed against the stones, spraying her feet. "Come Beneath with me."

"I can't." He wouldn't.

Her teeth flashed, more shark than humanoid. "Then we'll see what my mother has to say about this," she hissed, and leapt into the river.

Tharion debated jumping in after her, but—why? His palms slickened with sweat. He had thirty minutes, he supposed. Thirty minutes until he was hauled Beneath by his fin, and he'd never, ever leave again.

Tharion dragged his hands through his hair, panting. He peered westward toward the low-lying buildings beyond the CBD. Celestina would never interfere, and Bryce and Ruhn didn't have the authority. And there was no chance in Hel that Commander Sendes and the *Depth Charger* would get here in thirty minutes.

Only one person in Crescent City might stand up to the River Queen and survive. One person even the River Queen might balk at crossing. One person who valued powerful fighters and would hide them from their enemies. And one person he could reach in thirty minutes.

Tharion didn't think twice before he began running.

"Thanks again for getting me in here," Ithan said to Hypaxia, who sat in the waiting room of the Prime's study at the Den. It was weird to have needed to ask a veritable stranger to get him safely into his own home, but . . . this was the only way.

The witch-queen offered him a soft smile. "It's what friends do, isn't it?"

He bowed his head. "I'm honored to be called your friend." He'd been proud to walk through the gates moments before at the side of this strong, kind female. No matter that the wolves on duty had sneered as he'd passed.

A reedy voice grunted his name, and Ithan rose from the leather chair, offering Hypaxia a smile. "I'll be quick."

She waved him off, and Ithan braced himself as he entered the old wolf's formal study. Wood-paneled walls crammed with bookshelves gleamed in the midday light. The Prime sat at his desk, hunched over what seemed to be a stack of paperwork. Sabine stood above him. Monitoring every shaking stroke of his hand.

Ithan stiffened. Sabine's teeth gleamed.

Yet the old wolf lifted his head. "It is good to see you, boy."

"Thank you for meeting with me." Sabine knew that Danika had been sworn to a mate. That Baxian was in this city. Ithan shoved the thought away. "I know you're busy, so—"

"Out with it," Sabine snarled.

Ithan let her see the wolf in him, the dominance he didn't shove down like he always had. But the Prime said, "Go ahead, Ithan."

Ithan squared his shoulders, tucking his hands behind his back. The same pose he'd taken when getting instructions from Coach. To Hel with it, then.

"One of the Astronomer's mystics is a wolf. An *Alpha* wolf." The words were met with silence, but Sabine's eyes narrowed. "She's from Nena—sold so young she doesn't know her name, or her age. I'm not even sure if she knows she's an Alpha. But she's a wolf, and she's no better than a slave in that tank. I . . . We can't leave her there."

"What business is it of ours?" Sabine demanded.

"She's a wolf," Ithan repeated. "That should be all we need to help her."

"There are plenty of wolves. And plenty of Alphas. They are not all our responsibility." Sabine exposed her teeth again. "Is this part of some scheme you and that half-breed whore are concocting?"

She sneered as she said it, but . . . Sabine had come to Bryce's apartment that night to warn her to stay out of wolf business. Out of some fear, however unfounded, that Bryce would somehow back Ithan—as if Sabine herself could be at risk of being overthrown.

Ithan tucked that aside. Tossing out wild accusations wouldn't help his cause right now. So he said carefully, "I just want to help the mystic."

"Is this what you've dedicated your time to now, Holstrom? Charity cases?"

Ithan swallowed his retort. "Danika would have done something."

"Danika was an idealistic fool," Sabine spat. "Don't waste our time with this."

Ithan looked to the Prime, but the old wolf said nothing. Did nothing. Ithan turned to the door again and strode out.

Hypaxia rose to her feet as he appeared. "Done so soon?"

"Yeah, I guess." He'd told someone about the mystic. He supposed . . . Well, now he supposed he could go to Pangera with few regrets.

Sabine strutted out of the study. She growled low in her throat at Ithan, but faltered upon seeing Hypaxia. Hypaxia held the wolf's stare with steely calm. Sabine only snorted and stalked away, slamming the hall door behind her.

"Let's go," Ithan said to Hypaxia.

But the door to the study opened again, and the Prime stood there, a hand on the jamb to support himself. "The mystic," the

Prime said, panting slightly, as if the walk from his desk to the door had winded him. "What did she look like?"

"Brown hair. Medium brown, I think. Pale skin." A common enough description.

"And her scent? Was it like snow and embers?"

Ithan stilled. The ground seemed to sway. "How do you know that?"

The old wolf bowed his silvery head. "Because Sabine is not the only Fendyr heir."

Ithan rocked back on his heels at that. Was that why Sabine had come to the apartment that night to warn off Bryce? Not to keep Ithan from becoming the Prime Apparent, but to scare Bryce away before she could discover there was a true alternative to Sabine. A legitimate one.

Because Bryce would stop at nothing to find that other heir.

And Sabine would kill them to prevent it.

67

Tharion burst into the Viper Queen's nest. He had only minutes until all Hel broke loose.

Ariadne was sprawled on her belly on the carpet, a book splayed open before her, bare feet bobbing above her ample backside. The sort of ample backside that on any other day, he'd truly appreciate. The dragon didn't remove her focus from her book as she said, "She's in the back."

Tharion ran for the rear room. The Viper Queen lounged on a couch before the window overlooking the fighting pit where the current match was unfolding, reading something on her electronic tablet. "Mer," she said by way of greeting.

"I want to be one of your prize fighters."

She slowly turned her head toward him. "I don't take freelancers."

"Then buy me."

"You're not a slave, mer."

"I'll sell myself to you."

The words sounded as insane as they felt. But he had no other options. His alternative was another form of slavery. At least here, he'd be away from that stifling court.

The Viper Queen set down her tablet. "A civitas selling himself into slavery. Such a thing is not done."

"You're law unto yourself. You can do it."

"Your queen will flood my district for spite."

"She isn't dumb enough to fuck with you."

"I take it that's why you're rushing into my care."

Tharion checked his phone. Ten minutes left at most. "It's either be trapped in a palace down there or trapped up here. I choose here, where I won't be required to breed some royal offspring."

"You are becoming a *slave*. To be free of the River Queen." Even the Vipe looked like she was wondering if he'd gone mad.

"Is there another way? Because I'm out of ideas."

The Viper Queen angled her head, bob shifting with the movement. "A good businessperson would tell you no, and accept this absurd offer." Her purple lips parted in a smile. "But . . ." Her gaze swept across the room, to the Fae males standing guard by an unmarked door. He had no idea what lay beyond. Possibly her bedchamber. Why it needed to be guarded when she wasn't inside was beyond him. "They defected from the Autumn King. Swore allegiance to me. They've proved loyal."

"So I'll do it. I hereby defect. Give me some way to immerse myself in water once a day and I'm set."

She chuckled. "You think you're the first mer fighter I've had? There is a tub a few levels down, with water piped in right from the Istros. It's yours. But defecting . . . That is not as easy as simply saying the words." She stood, rolling back the sleeve of her black jumpsuit to expose her wrist. A tattoo of a snake twining around a crescent moon lay there. She lifted her wrist to her mouth and bit, and blood—darker than usual—welled where her teeth had been. "Drink."

The floor began rumbling, and Tharion knew it wasn't from the fight. Knew something ancient and primordial was coming for him, to drag him back to the watery depths.

He grabbed her wrist and brought it to his mouth.

If he defected from the River Queen, then he could defect from the Viper Queen one day, couldn't he?

He didn't ask. Didn't doubt it as he laid his lips on her wrist, and her blood filled his mouth.

Burned his mouth. His throat.

Tharion staggered back, choking, grabbing at his neck. Her blood, her venom dissolved his throat, his chest, his heart—

Cold, piercing and eternal, erupted through him. Tharion crashed to his knees.

The rumbling halted. Then retreated. Like whatever it had been hunting for had vanished.

Tharion panted, bracing for the icy death that awaited him.

But nothing happened. Only that vague sense of cold. Of . . . calm. He slowly lifted his eyes to the Viper Queen.

She smiled down at him. "Seems like that did the trick." He struggled to his feet, swaying. He rubbed at the hollow, strange place in his chest. "Your first fight is tonight," she said, still smiling. "I suggest you rest."

"I need to help my friends finish something first."

Her brows rose. "Ah. This business with Ophion."

"Of a sort. I need to be able to help them."

"You should have bargained for that freedom before swearing yourself to me."

"Allow me this and I'll come back and fight for you until I'm chum."

She laughed softly. "Fine, Tharion Ketos. Help your friends. But when you are done . . ." Her eyes glowed green, and his body turned distant. Her will was his, her desires his own. He'd crawl through coals to fulfill her orders. "You return to me."

"I return to you." He spoke in a voice that was and wasn't his own. Some small part of him screamed.

The Viper Queen flicked a hand toward the archway. "Go."

Not entirely of his own volition, he stalked back down the hallway. Each step away from her had that distance lessening, his thoughts again becoming his own, even as . . .

Ariadne peered up from her book as he stalked past. "Are you mad?"

Tharion retorted, "I could ask the same of you." Her face tightened, but she returned to her book.

With each step toward his friends, he could have sworn a long, invisible chain stretched. Like an endless leash, tethering him—no matter where he went, no matter how far—back to this place.

Never to return to the life he'd traded away.

Ithan sat on a park bench in Moonwood, a few blocks from the Den, still reeling from the world-shattering revelation the Prime had dropped on him.

The wolf mystic was a Fendyr. An *Alpha* Fendyr.

Ithan hadn't been able to get any more than that out of the Prime before the male's gaze had gone murky, and he'd needed to sit down again. Hypaxia had worked some healing magic to ease whatever pains ailed him, and he'd been asleep at his desk a moment later.

Ithan breathed in the fall day. "I think I've put her in grave danger."

Hypaxia straightened. "In what way?"

"I think Sabine knows. Or has already guessed." Another Alpha in the heritage bloodline could destroy the wolves. But how the fuck had she wound up in that tank? And in Nena? "Sabine will kill her. Even if Sabine thinks she *might* be a Fendyr Alpha, if there have been rumors about it before now . . . Sabine will destroy any threat to her power."

"So the mystic isn't some sister or long-lost daughter?"

"I don't think so. Sabine had an elder brother, but she defeated him in open combat decades before I was born. Took his title as Prime Apparent and became Alpha. I thought he died, but . . . maybe he was exiled. I have no idea."

Hypaxia's face turned grave. "So what can be done?"

He swallowed. "I don't like going back on my promises."

"But you wish to leave my side to look into this."

"Yes. And"—he shook his head—"I can't go to Pangera with the others. If there's a Fendyr heir who isn't Sabine . . ." It might mean that the future Danika had hoped for could come to pass. If he could find some way to keep the mystic alive. And get her free of the Astronomer's tank.

"I need to stay here," he said finally. "To guard her." He didn't care if he had to camp on the street outside of the Astronomer's place. Wolves didn't abandon each other. Granted, friends didn't abandon each other, either, but he knew Bryce and the others would get it.

"I need to find the truth," Ithan said. Not just for his people. But for his own future.

"I'll tell the others," Hypaxia offered. "Though I'll miss you as my guard."

"I'm sure Flynn and his backup singers will be happy to protect you." Hypaxia laughed softly. But Ithan said, "Don't tell them—don't tell Bryce, I mean. About the other Fendyr heir. She'd be distracted by it, at a time when she needs to focus elsewhere."

And this task . . . this task was *his*.

He hadn't been there to help Danika that night she'd died. But he was here now. Urd had left him alive—perhaps for this. He'd fulfill what Danika had left unfinished. He'd protect this Fendyr heir—no matter what.

"Just tell the others that I need to stay here for wolf stuff."

"Why not tell them yourself?"

He got to his feet. He might already be too late. "There's no time to waste," he said to the queen, and bowed to her. "Thanks for everything."

Hypaxia's mouth curled upward in a sad smile. "Be careful, Ithan."

"You too."

He broke into a jog, pulling out his phone as he did. He sent the message to Bryce before he could second-guess it. *I've got something important to do. Hypaxia will fill you in. But I wanted to say thanks. For not hating my guts. And having my back. You always had my back.*

She replied immediately. *Always will.* She added a few hearts that had his own cracking.

Pocketing his phone, breathing in that old ache, Ithan shifted.

For the first time in weeks, he shifted, and it didn't hurt one bit. Didn't leave him feeling the ache of exile, of being packless. No, his wolf form . . . it had focus. A purpose.

Ithan darted through the streets, running as fast as he could toward the Astronomer's place to begin his long watch.

Ruhn hadn't seen Day since the night of the ball. Since he'd kissed her. Since that other male had dragged her away, and pain had filled her voice.

But now she sat on the couch before him. Quiet and wary.

"Hey," Ruhn said.

"I can't see you anymore," she said in answer.

Ruhn drew up short. "Why?"

"What happened between us on the equinox is never to happen again." She rose. "It was dangerous, and reckless, and utter madness. Pippa Spetsos was in your city. Attacked your temple with her Lightfall unit. Lunathion is soon to become a battlefield."

He crossed his arms. Drew his focus inward, to the instinctual veil of night and stars. He'd never figured out where it had come from, why his mind had automatically hidden him, but—there. A neat little knot in his mind.

A tug on it, and it fell away, dropping all the night and stars. Letting her see all of him. "What happened to you? Are you hurt?"

"I'm fine." Her voice was tight. "I can't jeopardize all I've sacrificed for."

"And kissing me is a threat to that?"

"It distracts me from my purpose! It throws me from my vigilance! *It will catch up to me.*" She paced a few feet. "I wish I were normal. That I had met you under any other circumstances, that I had met you long ago, before I got tangled in this." Her chest heaved, flames flickering. She lifted her head, no doubt meeting his stare through the barrier of flames. "I told you that you remind me that I am alive. I meant that. Every word. But it's because of that feeling that I'll likely wind up dead, and you with me."

"I don't understand the threat," he said. "Surely a kiss that's good enough to distract you isn't a bad thing." He winked, desperate for her to smile.

"The male who . . . interrupts us. He will slaughter you if he finds out. He'll make me watch."

"You fear him." Something primal stirred in Ruhn.

"Yes. His wrath is terrible. I've seen what he does to enemies. I wouldn't wish it upon anyone."

"Can't you leave him?"

She laughed, harsh and hollow. "No. My fate is bound to his."

"Your fate is bound to mine." The words echoed into the darkness.

Ruhn reached for her hand. Took the flames within his own. They parted enough for him to see her slim, fiery fingers as he stroked his thumb over them. "My mind found yours in the darkness. Across an ocean. No fancy crystal required. You think that's nothing?"

He glimpsed enough of her eyes to see that they were closed. Her head bowed. "I can't."

But she didn't stop him when he stepped closer. When his other hand slid around her waist. "I'm going to find you," he said against her burning hair. "I'll find you one day, I promise." She shuddered, but melted into him. Like she'd yielded any attempt at restraint. "You remind me that I'm alive, too," he whispered.

Her arms came around him. She was slender—on the taller side, but with a delicate frame. And insane curves. Lush hips, full breasts that pushed against his chest with tantalizing softness. That sweet, tempting ass.

She murmured against his pec, "I never told you the ending of the story from the other night."

"With the witch-turned-monster?"

"It didn't end badly." He didn't dare breathe. "As the witch fell to the earth, the prince's arrow through her heart, the forest transformed her into a monster of claws and fangs. She ripped the prince and his hounds to shreds." Her fingers began trailing up his spine. "She remained a monster for a hundred years, roaming the forest, killing all who drew near. A hundred years, so long that she forgot she had once been a witch, had once possessed a home and a forest she loved."

Her breath was warm against his chest. "But one day, a warrior arrived in the forest. He'd heard of the monster so vicious none could kill it and live. She set out to slaughter him, but when the warrior beheld her, he was not afraid. He stared at her, and she at him, and he wept because he didn't see a thing of nightmares, but a creature of beauty. He saw her, and he was not afraid of her, and he loved her." She released a shuddering breath. "His love transformed her back into a witch, melting away all that she'd become. They dwelled in peace in the forest for the rest of their immortal lives."

"I like that ending much better," he said, and she huffed a soft laugh.

He dipped his head, kissing her neck, breathing in the subtle scent of her. His cock instantly hardened. Fuck yes. This scent, this female—

A sense of rightness settled into his bones like a stone dropped in a pond. Her hand began stroking up his spine again. His balls tightened with each trailing caress.

Then her mouth was on his pec, flaming lips grazing over the swirling tattoo there. The pierced nipple on his left pec. Her tongue flicked at the hoop, and his brain went haywire as he realized he was naked, or had somehow willed his clothes gone, because that was his bare skin she was touching, kissing.

And she . . . He ran his hands over her waist again. Smooth, velvety soft skin greeted him.

"You want to do this?" he ground out.

She kissed his other nipple. "Yes."

"I'm not even sure we can have sex like this."

"I don't see why not." Her fingers skated down to the top of his ass, taunting.

Ruhn's cock throbbed. "Only one way to find out," he managed to say.

Day huffed another breathy laugh and lifted her head. Ruhn just took her face between his hands and kissed her. She opened for him, and their tongues met, and she was as sweet as summer wine, and he needed to be in her, needed to touch and savor all of her.

Ruhn hoisted her up, and she wrapped her legs around his middle, his cock dangerously close to where it wanted to be. But he carried her to the fainting couch, gently laying her down before climbing atop her. "Let me see your face," he breathed, sliding a hand between her legs.

"Never," she said, and Ruhn didn't care, not as his fingers slicked through her soaked sex. Utterly ready for him.

He spread her knees and knelt between them. Dragged his tongue up her center—

He bucked, like his cock had a mind of its own, like it *needed* to be in her, or it was going to fucking erupt right there—

Ruhn fisted himself, pumping slowly as he licked her again.

Day moaned, her chest heaving, and he was rewarded with the sight of her breasts. Then her arms. Then her stomach and legs, and finally—

She was still crafted of fire, but he could clearly see the body now. Only her head remained in those flames, which shrank until they were no more than a mask over her features.

Long hair cascaded down her torso, and he ran a hand through it. "You're beautiful," he said.

"You haven't seen my face."

"I don't need to," he said. He laid a hand on her heart. "What you do, every minute of every single day . . . I've never met anyone like you."

"I've never met a male like you, either."

"Yeah?"

"*Yeah,*" she said, and he punished her for the sass in her voice by licking her again, drawing another gasp. "Ruhn."

Fuck, he loved his name on her lips. He slipped a finger into her, finding her mind-meltingly tight. She was going to drive him wild.

She tugged on his shoulders, hauling him up. "Please," she said, and he hissed as her fingers wrapped around his cock and guided him to her entrance.

He halted there, poised on the brink. "Tell me what you like," he said, kissing her neck. "Tell me how you want it."

"I like it true," she said, hands running down his face. "I want it real."

So Ruhn slid home, crying out at the sheer perfection of her. She groaned, arching, and Ruhn stilled. "Did I hurt you?"

"No," she whispered, hands framing his face as he hovered above her. "No. Not at all."

The pressure of her around his cock was too much, too gloriously intense—"I can go slow." He couldn't. He really fucking couldn't, but for her, he'd try.

She laughed softly. "Please don't."

He withdrew nearly to the tip and pushed back in with a smooth, steady thrust. He nearly leapt out of his skin at the rippling pleasure.

Her hands dug into his shoulders, and Day said, "You feel better than I even dreamed."

Ruhn smiled into her neck. "You dreamed about this?"

He thrust again, sinking to the hilt, and she gasped. "Yes," she said, as if his cock had wrung the word from her. "Every night. Every time I had to . . ." She trailed off. But Ruhn claimed her mouth, kissing her as deeply as he fucked her. He didn't need her to say the rest, the part that would smash something in his chest.

Ruhn angled her hips so he could drive deeper still, and she reached up above her to clutch at the rolled arm of the chaise. "Ruhn," she moaned again, a warning that she was close—and echoed it with a flex of her delicate inner muscles.

The squeeze had him grabbing her hands in his and slamming home. Her hips undulated in perfect rhythm with his, and nothing had ever felt so good, so real as their souls twining here—

"Come for me," he breathed against her mouth, as he reached between them to rub the bud of her clit in a taunting circle.

Day cried out, and those inner muscles fluttered and clenched around his cock, milking him—

Release barreled through him, and Ruhn didn't hold back as he pounded into her, wringing the pleasure from both of them.

They kept moving, one orgasm rolling into the next, and he had no fucking idea how it was even possible, but he was still hard, still going, and he needed more and more and more of her—

He erupted again, hauling her with him.

Their breaths echoed against each other like crashing waves, and she was shaking as she held him. He lowered himself so his head rested upon her chest. Her heartbeat thundered into his ear, and even the melody of that was beautiful.

Her fingers tangled in his hair. "I . . ."

"I know," Ruhn said. It had never been like that with anyone. Sex had been good, yeah, but this . . . He was fairly certain his soul lay in splinters around them. He kissed the skin above her breast. "I should have asked you if you had anything to report first."

"Why?"

"Because my mind's too fried to remember anything after this point."

Another one of those soft laughs. "All is quiet. No word on Pippa Spetsos after she eluded capture at Urd's Temple."

"Good. Though I guess we could use a distraction to keep attention elsewhere."

"From what?"

Ruhn toyed with the strands of her long hair, trying to make out the texture, the color. All was pure flame. "I'm coming your way."

She stilled. "What do you mean?"

"We need to get into the Asteri Archives."

"Why?"

"The vital intel Sofie Renast possessed is likely in one of the rooms there."

She pushed up onto her elbows. "What?"

He pulled out of her and said, "Any intel on the layout of the crystal palace or the archives, since you're so familiar with them . . . we'd appreciate it."

"You're going to break into the crystal palace. Into the archives."

"Yes."

"Ruhn." She grabbed his face in her hands. "Ruhn, do *not* go there. They will kill you. All of you."

"Hence the need for attention to be elsewhere while we break in."

Her fingers dug into his cheeks, and her heart pounded so wildly he could hear it. "It's got to be a trap."

"No one knows except people I trust. And now you."

She shot to her feet, again wholly veiled in flame. "If you're caught, I cannot help you. I won't be able to risk saving you. Or your sister. You're on your own."

His temper began simmering. "So you won't tell me anything useful about the layout."

"Ruhn, I—"

Again, that awful hiss of surprise and pain. That glance behind her.

To him. The male.

Ruhn grabbed her hand, like she could stay with him. But she began panting, wild and frantic. Terrified. "Ruhn, they know. *I*—" Her voice cut out for a moment. "The dungeons—"

She vanished.

Like she'd been snatched away.

68

We leave for the crystal palace tomorrow," Ruhn snarled at Hunt in the great room of Bryce's apartment. "At dawn."

"Let me get this straight," the angel said with maddening calm. "You've been meeting mind-to-mind with Agent Daybright—and dating her?"

Bryce sat at the dining table as she nursed a cup of coffee—which she needed desperately, since Ruhn had burst in at four in the morning. "Banging her, apparently."

Ruhn growled at his sister. "Does it matter?"

"It does," Hunt said, "because you're suggesting that we break into the crystal palace not only to get into the archives, but to save your lady love. That adds a shit-ton of risk."

"I'll get her myself," Ruhn shot back. "I just need to get in with you two first."

"Absolutely not," Bryce countered. "I get that you want to play rescuing hero, but what you're talking about is suicide."

"Would you hesitate to go in after Athalar?" He pointed to the angel. "Or you to go after Bryce?"

"You've known her for a month," Bryce protested.

"You knew Athalar for barely more than that before you offered to sell yourself into slavery for him." Ruhn snapped before they could speak, "I don't need to justify my feelings or my plans to you. I came here to tell you that I'm going with you. Once we're inside the palace, we'll go our separate ways."

"See, that's the part that bugs me," Bryce said, draining her coffee. "This whole 'separate ways' thing. We all go in, we all go out."

Ruhn blinked, but Bryce said to the angel, "Honestly, you should stay here."

"*Excuse me?*" Hunt demanded.

Ruhn kept silent as Bryce said, "The more of us go in, the better the chance of getting noticed. Ruhn and I can manage."

"One, no. Two, fuck no. Three . . ." Hunt grinned wickedly. "Who's going to level you up, sweetheart?" She scowled, but Hunt plowed on, "I'm going with you."

She crossed her arms. "It'd be safer with two people."

"It'd be safer not to go at all, but here we are, going," Hunt said. Ruhn wasn't entirely sure what to do with himself as the angel crossed the room and knelt before Bryce, grabbing her hands. "I want a future with you. *That's* why I'm going. I'm going to fight for that future." His sister's eyes softened. Hunt kissed her hands. "And to do so, we can't play by other people's rules."

Bryce nodded, and faced Ruhn. "We're done playing by Ophion's rules, or the Asteri's rules, or anyone else's. We'll fight our own way."

Ruhn smirked. "Team Fuck-You." Bryce grinned.

Hunt said, "All right, Team Fuck-You." He stood and patted a hand-drawn map of the crystal palace on the dining table. "Fury dropped this off earlier, and now we're all wide awake, so time to get studying. We need to create a distraction to make the Asteri look elsewhere, and we need to know where we're going once we're in there."

Ruhn tried not to marvel at the commander mode Athalar had slipped into. "It has to be something big," he said, "if it'll buy us enough time to get into the archives and find Day."

"She's probably in the dungeons," Hunt said. He added, as if reading Ruhn's worry, "She's alive, I'm sure of it. The Hind will be dispatched to work on her—they're not going to kill her right away. Not when she's got so much valuable information."

Ruhn's stomach churned. He couldn't get the sound of Day's panicked voice out of his mind. His very blood roared to go to her, find her.

Bryce said a shade gently, "We'll get her out, Ruhn."

"That doesn't give us much time to plan something big, though," Hunt said, sliding into the seat beside Bryce.

Ruhn scratched his jaw. They didn't have time to wait weeks. Even hours might be lethal. Minutes. "Day said that Pippa is lying low—but she has to have something planned. Ophion has taken enough hits to its numbers and bases lately that they'll likely let her do whatever she wants, either as some final-stand effort or to rally old and new recruits. Maybe we can prompt Pippa to do whatever she's planning a little earlier."

Bryce drummed her fingers on the table. "Call Cormac."

Bryce was fully awake when Cormac arrived thirty minutes later, Tharion in tow. She'd called him, too. He'd started them on this bullshit—he could damn well help finish it.

Yet Tharion . . . something was off about his scent. His eyes. He said nothing when Bryce asked, so she dropped it. But he seemed different. She couldn't place it, but he was different.

Cormac said when Ruhn had filled them in, "I have it on good authority as of last night that Pippa is planning a raid in a few weeks on the Pangeran lab where the Asteri's engineers and scientists work—where they made that new mech prototype. She wants their plans for it, and the scientists themselves."

"To build the new mech-suits?" Tharion asked.

Cormac nodded.

"And you were going to tell us this when?" Ruhn challenged.

Cormac's eyes blazed. "I heard at midnight. I figured it could wait until morning. Besides, you lot haven't bothered to loop me in on anything since the ball, have you?" He directed this last bit at Bryce.

She smiled sweetly. "I thought you were licking your wounds."

Cormac seethed, "I've been dealing with my father, finding a way to convince him to let me remain here after the *humiliation* of my engagement being called off."

Tharion let out a whistle at that. Bryce asked, "And did you?"

"I wouldn't be here if I hadn't," Cormac hurled back. "He thinks I'm currently trying to woo you from Athalar."

Hunt snorted at this, earning a glare from Cormac. Bryce cut in before it could escalate to blows, "So how do we convince Pippa to make her move now? We're not exactly on good terms with her."

Tharion said, "What if she's not the one initiating the raid?"

Bryce angled her head. "You mean . . . *us*?"

"I mean me and Cormac and whoever else we can trust. *We* carry out the raid, and Pippa and her cronies come running before we can steal the plans and suits they want."

"And where does that get us?" Hunt asked.

"It gets us in a lab with Pippa and Ophion—and if we time it right, a pack of dreadwolves will arrive right after they do."

"Solas," Bryce said, scrubbing at her face. "How are you going to get out of that?"

Cormac smiled at Tharion, as if sensing the direction of his thoughts. "That's the big distraction. We blow it all to Hel."

Ruhn blew out a breath. "That'll certainly get the Asteri's attention."

"The lab's twenty miles north of the Eternal City," Cormac said. "It might even draw them out to inspect the site. Especially if Pippa Spetsos has been captured."

"You're cool with handing over a fellow rebel?" Hunt asked the prince.

"I don't see any other options."

"Keep the casualties to a minimum," Hunt said to Cormac, to Tharion. "We don't need their blood on our hands."

Bryce massaged her chest. They were really doing this. She got to her feet, and they all looked at her as she said, "I'll be right back," and padded into her bedroom.

She shut the door and strode to a photo on her dresser, staring at it for several long minutes. The door opened behind her, and Hunt was there. "You all right?"

Bryce kept staring at the photo. "We were really happy that night," she said, and Hunt approached to study the photo of her, Danika, Juniper, and Fury, all grinning in the White Raven nightclub, drunk and high and gorgeous. "I thought we were really happy, at least. But when that photo was taken, Fury was still . . . doing what she does, Juniper was quietly in love with her, and Danika . . . Danika had a *mate*, had all these secrets. And I was stupid and drunk and convinced we'd party until we were dust. And now I'm here."

Her throat ached. "I feel like I have no idea who I am. I know that's so fucking cliché, but . . . I *thought* I knew who I was then. And now . . ." She lifted her hands, letting them fill with starlight. "What's the end goal in this? Somehow, someway, overthrowing the *Asteri*? What then? Rebuilding a government, an entire world? What if it triggers another war?"

Hunt tugged her into his arms and rested his chin atop her head. "Don't worry about that shit. We focus on the now, then deal with everything else afterward."

"I thought a general always planned ahead."

"I do. I am. But the first step in making those plans is finding out what the fuck Sofie knew. If it's nothing, then we reassess. But . . . I know how it feels to wake up one day and wonder how you got so far from that carefree person you were. I mean, yeah, my life in the slums with my mom wasn't easy, but after she died . . . It was like I'd had some illusion ripped away from me. It's how I wound up with Shahar. I was reeling and angry, and . . . it took me a long, long while to sort myself out. I'm still sorting it out."

She leaned her brow against his chest. "Can I admit that I'm scared shitless?"

"Can I admit that I am, too?"

She laughed, squeezing him tight around the middle, breathing in his scent. "I'd be slightly less scared if you were staying here, and I could go in knowing you're safe."

"Likewise."

She pinched his ass. "Then I guess we're stuck with each other, venturing into the lion's den."

"More like a sobek nest."

"Great. Really reassuring."

He chuckled, the sound rumbling into her bones, warming them. "Ruhn talked to Declan. He's going to hack into the security cameras at the palace—turn away the cameras while we're in there. We need to give him our route through the building so he can turn them without being noticed by anyone monitoring the system. Flynn will run support for him."

"What if we wind up needing to take a different hall?"

"He'll have backup plans, but . . . we'll really need to try to stick to ours."

Nausea roiled her gut, but she said, "Okay."

Hunt kissed her cheek. "Take your time, Quinlan. I'll be with the others." Then he was gone.

Bryce stared at the photo again. She pulled out her phone from her bathrobe and dialed. Unsurprisingly, Juniper's phone went to audiomail. It was five thirty in the morning, but—she knew Juniper would have picked up before.

"Hey, this is Juniper Andromeda. Leave a message!"

Bryce's throat closed up at her friend's lovely, cheerful voice. She took a breath as the audiomail beeped. "Hey, June. It's me. Look, I know I fucked up, and . . . I'm so sorry. I wanted to help, but I didn't think it through, and everything you said to me was absolutely right. I know you might not even listen to this, but I wanted you to know that I love you. I miss you so much. You've been a rock for me for so long, and I should have been that for you, but I wasn't. I just . . . I love you. I always have, and always will. Bye."

She rubbed at her aching throat as she finished. Then removed the photo from the frame, folded it, and slipped it inside her phone case.

69

Ruhn found Cormac sitting alone in an Old Square dive bar, face stony as he watched the late-night news show, a glossy-haired celebrity laughing her way through some interview—a shameless promo for her recent movie.

"What are you doing here?" the Avallen Prince asked him as Ruhn slid onto the stool beside him.

"Flynn was notified of your location. Thought I'd see why you were up so late. Considering our appointment tomorrow."

Cormac studied him sidelong, then drained his beer. "I wanted some quiet."

"And you came to a dive in the Old Square for that?" Ruhn indicated the blasting music, the wasted patrons around them. The sylph puking green liquid into the trash can by the pool table in the back.

His cousin said nothing.

Ruhn sighed. "What's wrong?"

"Does it matter to you?" Cormac signaled for another beer.

"It matters to me when we're relying on you tomorrow." When Day and Bryce were relying on the prince to be alert and ready.

"This isn't my first big . . . appointment." Ruhn glanced at the male—the immaculate blond hair, the unfailingly arrogant angle of his chin.

Cormac caught him looking and said, "I don't know how your father never managed to do it."

"Do what?" Ruhn leaned his forearms on the oak bar.

"Break you. The kindness in you."

"He tried," Ruhn choked out.

"My father did, too. And won." Cormac snorted, taking his fresh beer from the bartender. "I wouldn't have bothered to check on you."

"Yet you expended a lot of time and risk on finding . . . her."

The prince shrugged. "Perhaps, but deep down, I am what I've always been. The male who would have gladly killed you and your friends."

Ruhn tugged on his lip ring. "You're telling me this right before we head off?"

"I suppose I'm telling you this to . . . to apologize."

Ruhn tried not to gape. "Cormac—"

His cousin blankly watched the TV. "I was jealous of you. Then and now. For your friends. For the fact that you have them. That you don't let your father . . . corrupt what is best in you. But had I been forced to marry your sister . . ." His mouth twisted to the side. "I think, with time, she might have undone the damage my father did to my soul."

"Bryce has that effect on people."

"She will be a good princess. As you are a good prince."

"I'm starting to get disturbed by all this niceness."

Cormac drank again. "I'm always pensive the night before an appointment."

For a glimmer, Ruhn could see the male his cousin might have become—might yet become. Serious, yes, but fair. Someone who understood the cost of a life. A good king.

"When all this shit is done," Ruhn said hoarsely, tucking even thoughts of Day aside as he settled himself more comfortably on the stool, "I want us to start over."

"Us?"

"You and me. Prince to prince. Future king to future king. Screw the past, and screw that shit with the Starsword. Screw our fathers.

We don't let them decide who we get to be." Ruhn extended his hand. "We'll carve our own paths."

Cormac smiled almost sadly. Then took Ruhn's hand, clasping firmly. "It'd be an honor."

The barracks were dim. No one lounged in the common area, from what Hunt could tell down the hall as he entered his room.

Good. No one but the cameras to see him come and go.

He'd left Quinlan sleeping, and hadn't told anyone where he was going.

His room was cold and soulless as he shut the door behind him. Just as he'd been when he'd first met Quinlan. He'd displayed no traces of his life, put no art on the walls, done absolutely nothing to declare that this space was his. Perhaps because he'd known it truly wasn't.

Hunt strode to his desk, setting his empty duffel on it. He made quick work of loading up the extra knives and guns he'd kept in here, not wanting to be noticed checking out a stock of weapons from the armory. Thank the gods Micah had never bothered with enforcing the sign-out rules. Hunt had enough here to . . . well, to sneak into the crystal palace, he supposed.

He zipped the duffel, his gaze catching on the helmet on his desk. The skull painted on its front stared at him, unholy Hel in its black pits for eyes. The face of the Umbra Mortis.

Hunt picked up the helmet and set it on his head, the world shading into hues of red and black through the visor. He didn't let himself second-guess it as he stalked out of his room and into the night.

Celestina was standing at the elevator bay.

Hunt drew up short. Did she know? Had someone tipped her off? The duffel of weapons burned against his hip. He reached to pull off the helmet.

"Leave it," she said, and though her words were firm, her expression was contemplative. "I've always wondered what it looked like."

Hunt lowered his hand. "Everything all right?"

"I'm not the one sneaking in at five in the morning."

Hunt shrugged. "I couldn't sleep." The Archangel remained in front of the elevator bay, blocking his access. Hunt asked, "How are things with Ephraim?"

Her wings snapped shut. A clear warning. Whether it was to keep his mouth shut about Hypaxia or something else, he didn't know. Celestina only said, "He departs tomorrow. I shall visit his keep next month if there is not . . . a change in my situation by then."

If she hadn't gotten pregnant.

"Your silence speaks volumes about your dismay, Athalar." Power crackled in her voice. "I go to the mating bed willingly."

Hunt nodded, even as disgust and rage curled through him. The Asteri had ordered this, done this. They'd make Celestina keep going to Ephraim until she was pregnant with the child they wanted her to bear. Another little Archangel for them to mold into a monster. Would Celestina fight to keep her child free from their influence? Or would Ephraim hand the kid over to the Asteri and the secretive training centers they had for young Archangels? Hunt didn't want to know.

Celestina asked, "Why couldn't you sleep?"

He blew out a breath through his nose. "Is it pathetic to say it's because of the prince stuff?"

She offered him a pitying wince. "I thought that might come up."

Hunt tapped the side of his helmet. "I . . . weirdly missed it. And I wanted to clear out the last of my stuff from the room before it became a public spectacle." It was partially true.

She smiled softly. "I haven't had the chance to ask, but will you be leaving us?"

"I honestly have no idea. Bryce and I are giving the Autumn King a few days to cool down before asking him to define my royal duties. The thought of having to act fancy and take meetings with a bunch of assholes makes me want to puke."

Another quiet laugh. "But?"

"But I love Bryce. If doing that shit is what will allow us to be together, then I'll grin and bear it."

"Does she want to do such things?"

"Hel no. But . . . we don't really get much say. The Autumn King forced her hand. And now we're pretty much stuck with things as they are."

"Are you? The Umbra Mortis and the Starborn Princess don't seem the types to accept things as they are. You proved that with your surprise at the party."

Was there an edge to her voice? A gleam of suspicion?

They'd trusted Hypaxia not to say a word of their activities to her lover, had believed the witch when she said Celestina didn't know, but . . . the gods knew he talked when Bryce fucked the Hel out of him. Mistakes happened. Especially with a gorgeous set of tits involved.

But he made himself shrug again. "We're trying to get a better picture of the battle ahead before deciding where to start fighting the royal nonsense."

Her mouth quirked to one side. "Well, I hope that if you need an ally, you'll come to me."

Was that code for something? He scanned her face but could pick up nothing beyond reserved concern. He had to get out of here. So Hunt bowed his head. "Thank you."

"A prince doesn't need to bow to a Governor, you know." She walked over to the landing veranda doors, opening them for him. All right. He'd fly home.

Hunt stalked into the night, that bag of weapons a millstone hanging off his shoulder. He spread his wings. "Old habits."

"Indeed," she said, and a shiver went down his spine.

He didn't look back as he launched skyward.

Hunt slowly sailed over the city. Dawn remained a whisper on the horizon, and only a few delivery trucks rumbled along to bakeries and coffee shops. He had the skies to himself.

Hunt tugged off his helmet, tucking it into the crook of his elbow, and breathed in the open, clean breeze off the Istros. In a few hours, they'd leave for Pangera—Tharion had already reached out to Commander Sendes and arranged for transport across the ocean.

By tomorrow morning, they'd reach the Eternal City.

Tomorrow morning, he'd again wear this helmet. And pray that he and his mate walked away alive.

70

Tharion had commanded plenty of raids for the River Queen. He'd gone in solo, led teams small and large, and usually emerged unscathed. But riding shotgun beside Prince Cormac in the open-air jeep as they approached the security checkpoint down the cypress-lined road, he had the distinct feeling that he might not get so lucky today.

The imperial uniform they each wore lay heavy and smothering in the sun, but at least the hot day would disguise any glimmer of nervous sweat on them.

No one had seemed to notice the change he felt with every breath: the invisible tether, now stretched tight, linking whatever remained of his heart—that cold, dead thing—to the Viper Queen in Valbara. A constant reminder of his promise. His new life.

He tried not to think of it.

He'd been grateful for the wonders of the *Depth Charger*'s swift submersible-pod as it hurtled their group across the ocean. Sendes had told him when he contacted her that the city-ship was too slow to make it in time, but one of its makos—sleek little transport pods—could do it. So they'd boarded the pod at the coast, then spent their time either planning or sleeping, keeping themselves mostly separate from the mer who steered the ship.

Cormac waved with impressive casualness to the four guards—ordinary wolves, all of them—at the gate. Tharion kept his right hand within swift reach of the gun strapped to the side of his seat.

"Hail the Asteri." Cormac spoke with such offhanded ease that Tharion knew he'd said it a thousand times. Perhaps in similar settings.

"Hail the Asteri," the female guard who stepped forward said. She sniffed, marking what her eyes confirmed: a Fae male and a mer male, both in officer's uniforms. She saluted, and Tharion nodded for her to stand down.

Cormac handed over their forged papers. "We're to meet with Doctor Zelis. Have they radioed that he's ready?"

The guard scanned the clipboard in her hands. The three others with her didn't take their attention off the car, so Tharion gave them a glare he usually reserved for field agents who'd royally fucked up. The wolves, however, didn't back down.

"There's no appointment on here with Zelis," the guard said.

Tharion drawled, "It wouldn't be in writing."

She studied him, and Tharion smirked. "Rigelus's orders," he added.

The female's throat bobbed. To question the actions of an Asteri, or to risk letting two officers in who weren't on the security roster . . .

Cormac pulled out his phone. "Shall I call him?" He showed her a contact page that merely read: *Bright Hand*.

The wolf paled a little. But she saluted again, waving them through.

"Thank you," Cormac said, gunning the engine and driving through the gates before they'd finished lifting.

Tharion didn't dare speak to Cormac. Not with the wolves so nearby. They just stared ahead at the dirt road winding through the forest. At the sprawling concrete compound that appeared around the next bend, where guards were already waving them through the barbed-wire fencing.

He had to keep an eye on the clock today. The spray of the water from the mako's passage had extended the amount of time he could stay Above, but a familiar itching had started an hour ago. Another fucking headache to deal with: five more hours until he had to truly submerge. The coast was a two-hour drive from here. So . . . they'd better get this shit done within three. Two, to be safe.

Tharion nodded to the wolves in front of the lab and took in the enormous, low building. It hadn't been built for beauty, but for function and storage.

Smokestacks billowed behind the lab, which seemed to be at least half a mile long and perhaps twice as wide. "Look at this place," Tharion murmured as Cormac pulled up to the steel front doors. They opened as if by invisible hands—another guard must have pressed the security button to allow them in. Tharion whispered, "You think Pippa's going to come?" How the Hel would she get in?

Cormac cut the engine and threw open his door, stepping crisply into the morning sun. "She's already here."

Tharion blinked, but followed Cormac's military-precise motions as he climbed from the car. Cormac turned toward the open doors to the lab. "They're in the trees."

Declan had spent the previous day covertly planting information on rebel networks: the anti-Ophion rebels who'd destroyed the base on Ydra were making a move on this lab before Pippa and her agents could do so. She must have had Lightfall hauling ass to get here in time.

Tharion suppressed the urge to peer into the trees. "What about the dreadwolves?"

"This place reeks of humans, can't you smell it?"

"No."

Cormac stalked toward the open doors, black boots shining. "They're using human labor. Carted in and out every dawn and dusk. Pippa would have timed their arrival with it, so their scents are hidden from the dreadwolves below."

Solas. "So why wait for us to arrive, then?"

Cormac growled, "Because Pippa has a score to settle."

Bryce had no idea why anyone would want to live in the Eternal City. Not simply because it lay in the shadow of the crystal palace of the Asteri, but because it was . . . old. Dusty. Worn. No skyscrapers, no neon lights, no music blasting from passing cars. It seemed to have been trapped in time, stuck in another century, its masters unwilling to bring it forward.

As she, Hunt, and Ruhn lurked in the shadows of an olive grove a mile to the west of the palace, she steadied her nerves by imagining the Asteri as a bunch of cranky old people, shouting for everyone to keep the noise down, complaining that the lights were too bright and the youngsters too whippersnappery.

It definitely helped. Just a little.

Bryce glanced at Hunt, who kept his attention on the olive grove, the skies. He'd worn his black battle-suit, along with the Umbra Mortis helmet, to her shock. A warrior going back into battle.

Was this the right move? This risk, this danger they were plunging into? Maybe they'd have been better off staying in Lunathion, keeping their heads down.

Maybe she was a coward for thinking that.

She flicked her attention to Ruhn, her brother's face tight as he monitored the olive grove as well. He'd worn his Aux battle-suit, too, his black hair tied back in a braid that flowed down his spine, along the length of the Starsword strapped there. He clutched the comm-crystal in a fist, occasionally opening his fingers to study it. As if it might offer some hint about Day's welfare. He'd said he hadn't used it since that first contact with her, but he'd grabbed it before they left in case it could help locate her, if she had its twin on her.

Ruhn shifted from foot to foot, black boots crunching on the rocky, dry earth. "Cormac should be here by now."

She knew every second since Agent Daybright had gone dark pressed on her brother. Bryce didn't want to think about what was probably happening to the agent Ruhn seemed to care so much for. If they were lucky, she'd be alive. If they were luckier, there would be enough of her to salvage. Any attempts Ruhn had made to contact her—even going so far as to use the crystal—had been futile.

"Give him a minute," Bryce said. "It's a long jump." Too far for her to make—or attempt. Especially with others in tow. She needed all her strength for what was to come.

"You're a teleporting expert now?" Ruhn asked, brows high. The ring in his bottom lip glinted in the hot morning light. "Dec's on standby. I don't want to throw off his calculations. Even by a minute."

Bryce opened her mouth, but Cormac appeared in the small clearing ahead. They'd studied a satellite map of the grove yesterday and Cormac had committed the location to memory, plotting out the jumps he'd need to make to get here from the lab. And the jumps he'd need to make from this grove into the palace itself.

Cormac announced, "We're in. Tharion's in the waiting room. I slipped off to the bathroom. All plans are a go. Ready, Athalar?" Hunt, then Bryce, then Ruhn. That had been the order they'd settled on, after an hour of arguing.

Hunt drew his gun, keeping it at his thigh. That helmeted head turned to Bryce, and she could feel his gaze even through the visor. "See you on the other side, Quinlan," Hunt said, taking Cormac's gloved hand.

Prince to prince. She marveled at it.

Then they were gone, and Bryce struggled to get down a breath.

"I feel like I can't breathe, either," Ruhn said, noticing. "Knowing that Day's in there." He added, "And knowing that you're about to go in there, too."

Bryce gave him a wobbly smile. And then decided to Hel with it and threw her arms around her brother, squeezing him hard. "Team Fuck-You, remember? We'll kick ass."

He chuckled, holding her tightly. "Team Fuck-You forever."

She pulled away, scanning her brother's violet-blue eyes. "We'll get her out. I promise."

Ruhn's golden skin paled. "Thanks for helping me, Bryce."

She nudged him with an elbow. "We Starborn have each other's backs, you know?"

But her brother's face turned grave. "When we get home, I think we need to talk."

"About what?" She didn't like that serious expression. And didn't like that Cormac was taking so long.

Ruhn's mouth tightened. "All right, since we might very well die in a few minutes—"

"That is *so* morbid!"

"I wanted to wait until shit had calmed down, but . . . You outrank the Autumn King in power."

"And?"

"I think it's time his reign comes to an end, don't you?" He was completely serious.

"You want me to back you in a coup? A Fae coup?"

"I want to back *you* in a Fae coup. I want you as Autumn Queen."

Bryce recoiled. "I don't want to be a queen."

"Let's ditch the whole reluctant royal thing, okay? You saw what the Fae did during the attack this spring. How they shut out innocents and left them to die, with our father's blessing. You mean to tell me that's the best our people can do? You mean to tell me that's what we're supposed to accept as normal Fae behavior? I don't buy that for a second."

"*You* should be king."

"No." Something else shone in his eyes, some secret she didn't know, but she could sense. "You have more power than I do. The Fae will respect that."

"Maybe the Fae should rot."

"Tell that to Dec. And Flynn. And my mother. Look at them and tell me that the Fae aren't worth saving."

"Three. Out of the entire population."

Ruhn's face turned pleading, but then Cormac appeared, panting and covered in sweat. "Athalar's waiting."

"Think about it," Ruhn murmured as she approached Cormac. "All clear?"

"No issues. The intel was right: they don't even have wards around the place," Cormac reported. "Arrogant worms." He extended a hand to Bryce. "Hurry."

Bryce grabbed the prince's hand. And with a last look at her brother, she vanished into wind and darkness, stomach whipping around and around. Cormac said over the roaring of the space between places, "He asked you to be queen, didn't he?"

Bryce blinked up at him—though it was difficult with the force of the storm around them. "How did you know?"

"I might have caught the end of your conversation." Bryce clung harder as the wind pressed. Cormac said, "He's right."

"Spare me."

"And you were right, too. When we first met, and you said the Oracle's prophecy was vague. I understand that now. She didn't mean our union in marriage would bring prosperity to our people. She meant our union as allies. Allies in this rebellion."

The world took form at the edges of the darkness.

"But after today . . ." Cormac's words grew heavy. Weary. "I think the choice about whether to lead our people forward will be up to you."

Hunt couldn't shake the tremor from his hands. Being here, in this palace . . .

It smelled the same. Even in the hallway directly outside the archives, where he hid in an alcove, the stale odor of this place dragged claws down his temper, set his knees wobbling.

Screaming, pain blinding as they sawed off his wings slowly—

Shahar was dead, her broken body still dust-covered from Sandriel dragging it through the streets on her way in here—

Pollux laughing as he pissed on Shahar's corpse in the middle of the throne room—

His wings, his wings, his wings—

Hunt swallowed, shutting out the memories, focusing his mind on the hall. No one was around.

Bryce and Cormac appeared, and she'd hardly thanked him before he vanished, off to grab Ruhn before teleporting back to the lab. Sweat gleamed on the prince's face, his skin sallow. He had to be exhausted.

"All right?" Hunt murmured, brushing back her hair with a gloved hand. She nodded, eyes full of worry—and something else. But Hunt flicked her chin and went back to monitoring.

They stood in tense silence, and then Ruhn was there, Cormac with him. Cormac's skin was ashen now. He disappeared immediately, back to the lab.

"Tell Declan we're a go," Hunt said.

Ruhn's shadows cloaked them from sight as he thumbed in a message on a secure phone that Declan had retrofitted against tracking. In five minutes, Tharion would contact them on it to tell them whether or not to move.

Bryce's fingers slid into Hunt's, clutching tight. He squeezed back.

He had no idea how five minutes passed. He was barely breathing, monitoring the hall ahead. Bryce held his gloved hand through all of it, her jaw tense.

Then Ruhn lifted his head. "Tharion said Cormac just blew up the jeep."

Hunt nudged her with a wing. "Your turn, Quinlan."

Ruhn said, "Remember: Every minute in there risks detection. Make them count."

"Thanks for the pep talk," she said, but smiled grimly up at Hunt. "Light it up, Athalar."

Hunt pressed a hand to her heart, his lightning a subtle flare that was sucked into the scar. As the last of it faded, Bryce teleported into the archives.

To find whatever truth might lie within them.

71

Bryce's breathing turned so jagged that she could barely think as she tumbled alone through the darkness.

They were in the Asteri's palace. In their sacred, forbidden archives.

And she was . . . in a stairwell?

Bryce took steadying inhales as she surveyed the spiral staircase, crafted entirely of white quartz. Firstlight glimmered, golden and soft, lighting the carved steps downward. At her back was a door—the other side of the one they'd watched Sofie walk through on the surveillance footage.

The one labeled with the number Sofie had etched into her biceps.

Bryce began to creep down the stairs, her black utility boots nearly silent against the quartz steps. She saw no one. Heard no one.

Her heart raced, and she could have sworn the veins of firstlight in the quartz throbbed with each beat. As if in answer.

Bryce halted after a turn in the stairs and assessed the long hallway ahead. When it revealed no guards, she stepped into it.

There were no doors. Only this hall, perhaps seventy feet long and fifteen feet wide. Likely fourteen feet, to be a multiple of seven. The holy number.

Bryce scanned the hall. The only thing in it was a set of crystal pipes shooting upward into the ceiling, with plaques beneath them, and small black screens beside the plaques.

Seven pipes.

The crystal floor glowed at her feet as she approached the nearest plaque.

Hesperus. The Evening Star.

Brows rising, Bryce strode to the next pipe and plaque. *Polaris*. The North Star.

Plaque after plaque, pipe after pipe, Bryce read the individual names of each Asteri.

Eosphoros. Octartis. Austrus.

She nearly tripped at the penultimate. *Sirius*. The Asteri the Prince of the Pit had devoured.

She knew what the last plaque would say before she reached it. *Rigelus*. The Bright Hand.

What the Hel was this place?

This was what Danika had felt was important enough for Sofie Renast to risk her life for? What the Asteri had wanted to contain so badly they'd hunted Sofie down to preserve the secret?

The crystal at her feet flared, and Bryce had nowhere to go, nowhere to hide, as firstlight, pure and iridescent, ruptured.

She squeezed her eyes shut, dropping into a crouch.

But nothing happened. At least, not to her.

The firstlight faded enough that Bryce cracked open her eyes to see it shooting up six of the pipes.

The little black screens beside each plaque flared to life, filled with readings. Only Sirius's pipe remained unlit. Out of commission.

She went rigid as she read the Bright Hand's screen: *Rigelus Power Level: 65%.*

She whirled to the next plaque. The screen beside it said, *Austrus Power Level: 76%.*

"Holy gods," Bryce whispered.

The Asteri fed on firstlight. The Asteri . . . *needed* firstlight. She looked at her feet, where light flowed in veins through the crystal before funneling into the pipes. The quartz.

A conduit of power. Exactly like the Gates in Crescent City.

They'd built their entire palace out of it. To fuel and harness the firstlight that poured in.

She'd studied Fury's rough map of the palace layout. This area was seven levels below the throne room, where the Asteri sat on crystal thrones. Did those thrones fill them with power? In plain sight, they fueled up like batteries, sucking in this firstlight.

Nausea constricted her throat. All the Drops people made, the secondlight the dead handed over . . . All the power of the people of Midgard, the power the people *gave* them . . . it was gobbled up by the Asteri and used against its citizens. To control them.

Even the Vanir rebels who were killed fighting had their souls fed to the very beasts they were trying to overthrow.

They were all just food for the Asteri. A never-ending supply of power.

Bryce began shaking. The veins of light wending beneath her feet, glowing and vibrant . . . She traced them down as far as she could see through the clear stone, into a brilliantly shining mass. A core of firstlight. Powering the entire palace and the monsters that ruled it.

This was what Sofie had learned. What Danika had suspected.

Did the Asteri even possess holy stars in their chests, or was it firstlight, stolen from the people? Firstlight that they *mandated* be given over in the Drop to fuel cities and technology . . . and the overlords who ruled this world. Secondlight that was ripped from the dead, squeezing every last drop of power from the people.

Cut off the firstlight, destroy this funnel of power, get people to stop handing over their power through the Drop in those centers that funneled off their energy, stop the dead from becoming secondlight . . .

And they could destroy the Asteri.

72

Athalar paced in a tight circle. "She should be back."

"She's got two minutes," Ruhn growled, clenching the comm-crystal so hard in his fist it was a wonder the edges weren't permanently etched into his fingers.

Hunt said, "Something happened. She should be here by now."

Ruhn eyed the watch on his wrist. They had to make it down to the dungeons. And if they didn't start immediately . . . He peered at the crystal in his hand.

Day, he said, throwing her name out into the void. But no answer came. Like every other attempt to reach her recently.

"I'm going to get a head start," he murmured, pocketing the crystal. "I'll cloak myself in my shadows. If I'm not back in ten minutes, leave without me."

"We all go together," Hunt shot back, but Ruhn shook his head. "We'll come find you."

Ruhn didn't reply before he slipped down the hall, blending into the darkness, and aimed for the passageways that would take him across the palace compound. To the dungeons and the agent trapped within them.

* * *

Bryce raced back to the top of the stairs, bile burning her throat.

She'd been here too long. Could only spare a minute or two more.

She reached the door and the landing, rallying what remained of Hunt's charge to teleport back to him and Ruhn, but the door handle seemed to gleam. What else lay down here? What else might she uncover? If this was her only opportunity . . .

Bryce didn't let herself doubt as she slipped into the main archives hallway. It was dim and dusty. Utterly silent.

Shelves crammed with books loomed around her, and Bryce scanned their titles. Nothing of interest, nothing of use—

She sprinted through the library, reading titles and names of sections as fast as she could, praying that Declan had kept up and was moving the cameras away from her. She scanned the vague section titles above the stacks. *Tax Records, Agriculture, Water Processing* . . .

The doors along this stretch had been named similarly to each other—not in code, but along a theme.

Dawn. Midnight. Midday. She had no idea what any of the names meant, or what lay behind the door. But one in the center snared her eye: *Dusk.*

She slipped inside.

Bryce was late. Hunt stayed put only because his secure phone had flashed with a message from Declan. *She's okay. She went into a room called Dusk. I'll keep you posted.*

Of course Quinlan was doing *extra* research. Of course she couldn't listen to the rules and be back when she was supposed to—

Then again, *Dusk* could have something to do with Dusk's Truth. No wonder Bryce had entered.

Hunt paced again. He should have gone with her. Made her teleport him in, even if it would have drained her at a time when they'd need all her gifts.

Ruhn had already been gone for three minutes. A lot could happen in that time.

"Come on, Bryce," Hunt murmured, and prayed to Cthona to keep his mate safe.

Cloaked in shadows, Ruhn raced down the halls, encountering no one. Not one guard.

It was too quiet.

The hall opened into a wide fork: To the left lay the dungeons. To the right, the stairs up to the palace proper. He went left without hesitation. Down the stairs that turned from cloudy quartz to dark stone, like the life had been sucked from the rock. His skin chilled.

These dungeons . . . Athalar had made it out, but most never did.

Ruhn's stomach churned, and he slowed his pace, readying himself for the gauntlet ahead. Checkpoints of guards—easy enough to avoid with his shadows—locked doors, and then two halls of cells and torture chambers. Day had to be somewhere in there.

Screams began leaking out. Male, thankfully. But they were wrenching. Pleading. Sobbing. He wished he could plug his ears. If Day was making a similar sound, in such agony . . .

Ruhn kept going—until Mordoc stepped into his path with a feral grin. He sniffed once, that bloodhound gift no doubt feeding him a host of information before he said, "You're a long way from cavorting with spies in the alleys of Lunathion, Prince."

Tharion raced behind Cormac, a shield of water around them as the prince hurled ball after ball of fire into the chaotic, smoky lab. Chunks of rupturing machines flew toward them, smoldering—and Tharion intercepted them as best he could.

The doctor had led them right into the lab without a second thought. Cormac had put a bullet through the male's head a moment later, then ended the lives of the screaming scientists and engineers around him.

"Are you fucking insane?" Tharion screamed as they ran. "You said we'd limit the casualties!"

Cormac ignored him. The bastard had gone rogue.

Tharion snarled, half debating whether to overpower the prince. "Is this any better than what Pippa Spetsos does?"

Tharion got his answer a second later. Gunfire crackled behind them, and rebels stormed in. Right on time.

Imperial Vanir reinforcements roared as they rushed in—and were drowned out by the barrage of guns. An ambush.

Would it be enough to draw the Asteri's attention away? Cormac had incinerated the jeep with his fire magic moments before they'd shot the doctor—surely that would warrant a message to the Asteri. And this shitshow unfolding . . .

Cormac skidded to a stop, Tharion with him. Both of them fell silent.

A familiar female, clad in black and armed with a rifle, stepped into their path.

Pippa pointed the gun at Cormac. "I've been looking forward to this." Her rifle cracked, and Cormac teleported, but too slowly. His powers were drained.

Blood sprayed a moment before Cormac vanished—then appeared behind Pippa.

The bullet had passed through his shoulder, and Tharion launched into movement as Pippa twisted toward the prince.

Tharion was stopped by shaking ground, though. A glowing, electrified sword plunged into the floor in front of him.

A mech-suit sword.

Cormac shouted to Tharion, "*Get out of here!*" The prince faced off against Pippa as the woman fired again.

Tharion knew that tone. Knew that look. And it was then that he understood.

Cormac hadn't just gone rogue. He'd never intended to get out of here alive.

The door marked *Dusk* had been left unlocked. Bryce supposed she had Declan to thank for the dead electronic keypad.

Braziers of firstlight glowed in the corners of the room, dimly illuminating the space. A round table occupied the middle. Seven seats around it.

Her blood chilled.

A small metal machine sat in the center of the table. A projection device. But Bryce's attention snagged on the stone walls, covered in paper.

Star-maps—of constellations and solar systems, marked up with scribbled notations and pinned with red dots. Her mouth dried out as she approached the one nearest. A solar system she didn't recognize, with five planets orbiting a massive sun.

One planet in the habitable zone had been pinned and labeled.

Rentharr. Conq. A.E. 14000.

A.E. She didn't know that dating system. But she could guess what *Conq.* meant.

Conquered . . . by the Asteri? She'd never heard of a planet called Rentharr. Scribbled beside it was a brief note: *A bellicose, aquatic people. Primordial land life. Little supply. Terminated A.E. 14007.*

"Oh gods," Bryce breathed, and went to the next star-map.

Iphraxia. Conq. A.E. 680. Lost A.E. 720.

She read the note beside it and her blood iced over. *Denizens learned of our methods too quickly. We lost many to their unified front. Evacuated.*

Somewhere out in the cosmos, a planet had managed to kick out the Asteri.

Map to map, Bryce read the notes. Names of places that weren't known in Midgard. Worlds that the Asteri had conquered, with notations about their use of firstlight and how they either lost or controlled those worlds. Fed on them until there was nothing left.

Fed on their power . . . like she had with the Gate. Was she no better than them?

The rear wall of the chamber held a map of this world.

Midgard, the map read. *Conq. A.E. 17003.*

Whatever *A.E.* was, if they'd been on *this* planet for fifteen thousand years, then they'd existed in the cosmos for far, far longer than that.

If they could feed off firstlight, generate it somehow on each planet . . . could they live forever? Truly immortal and undying? Six ruled this world, but there'd originally been a seventh. How many existed beyond them?

Pages of notes on Midgard had been pinned to the wall, along with drawings of creatures.

Ideal world located. Indigenous life not sustainable, but conditions prime for colonization. Have contacted others to share bounties.

Bryce's brow furrowed. What the Hel did that mean?

She peered at a drawing of a mer beside a sketch of a wolf shifter. *The aquatic shifters can hold a hybrid form far more easily than those on land.*

She read the next page, with a drawing of a Fae female. *They did not see the old enemy who offered a hand through space and time. Like a fish to bait, they came, and they opened the gates to us willingly. They walked through them—to Midgard—at our invitation, leaving behind the world they knew.*

Bryce backed away from the wall, crashing into the table.

The Asteri had lured them all into this world from other planets. Somehow, using the Northern and Southern Rifts, or whatever way they traveled between worlds, they'd . . . drawn them into this place. To farm them. Feed off them. Forever.

Everything was a lie. She'd known a lot of accepted history was bullshit, but this . . .

She twisted to the projector device in the center of the table and stretched an arm to hit the button. A three-dimensional, round map of the cosmos erupted. Stars and planets and nebulas. Many marked with digital notes, as the papers on the walls had been.

It was a digital orrery. Like the metal one she'd glimpsed as a kid in the Autumn King's study. Like the one in the Astronomer's chamber.

Was this what Danika had learned in her studies on bloodlines? That they'd all come from elsewhere—but had been lured and trapped here? And then fed on by these immortal leeches?

The map of the universe rotated above her. So many worlds. Bryce reached out to touch one. The digital note immediately appeared beside it.

Urganis. Children were ideal nutrition. Adults incompatible.

She swallowed against the dryness in her throat. That was it. All that remained of a distant world. A note about whether its people made for good eating and what the Asteri had done to its young.

Was there a home planet? Some original world the Asteri had come from, bled so dry that they'd needed to go hunting in the wilds of space?

She began flicking through planets, one after another after another, clawing past the stars and cosmic clouds of dust.

Her heart stopped at one.

Hel.

The ground seemed to slide away from beneath her.

Hel. Lost A.E. 17001.

She had to sink into one of the chairs as she read the note. *A dark, cold world with mighty creatures of night. They saw through our lures. Once warring factions, the royal armies of Hel united and marched against us. We were overwhelmed and abandoned their world, but they gave chase. Learned from our captured lieutenants how to slip between the cracks in realms.*

Bryce was dimly aware of her shaking body, her shallow breaths.

They found us on Midgard in 17002. Tried to convince our lured prey of what we were, and some fell to their charms. We lost a third of our meals to them. War lasted until nearly the end of 17003. They were defeated and sent back to Hel. Far too dangerous to allow them access to this world again, though they might try. They developed attachments to the Midgard colonists.

"Theia," Bryce whispered hoarsely. Aidas had loved the Fae queen, and . . .

Hel had come to help, exactly as Apollion had said. Hel had kicked the Asteri from their own world, but . . . Tears stung her eyes. The demon princes had felt a moral obligation to chase after the Asteri so they might never prey upon another world. To spare others.

Bryce began sifting through planets again. So many worlds. So many people, their children with them.

It had to be here—the Asteri's home world. She'd find it and tell the Princes of Hel about it, and once they were done beating these assholes into dust here on Midgard, they'd go to that home world and they'd blow it the fuck up—

She was sobbing through her teeth.

This empire, this world . . . it was just one massive buffet for the six beings ruling it.

Hel had tried to save them. For fifteen thousand years, Hel had never stopped trying to find a way back here. To free them from the Asteri.

"Where the *fuck* did you come from?" she seethed.

Worlds ripped past her fingertips, along with the Asteri's dispassionate notes. Most planets were not as lucky as Hel had been.

They rose up. We left them in cinders.

Firstlight tasted off. Terminated world.

Denizens launched bombs at us that left planet and inhabitants too full of radiation to be viable food. Left to rot in their waste.

Firstlight too weak. Terminated world but kept several citizens who produced good firstlight to sustain us on travels. Children proved hearty, but did not take to our travel method.

These psychotic, soulless *monsters*—

"You will not find our home world there," a cold voice said through the intercom on the table. "Even we have forgotten where its ruins lie."

Bryce panted, only rage coursing through her as she said to Rigelus, "*I am going to fucking kill you.*"

73

Rigelus laughed. "I was under the impression that you were only here to access the information for which Sofie Renast and Danika Fendyr died. You're going to kill me as well?"

Bryce squeezed shaking hands into fists. "Why? Why do any of this?"

"Why do you drink water and eat food? We are higher beings. We are *gods*. You cannot blame us if our source of nutrition is inconvenient for you. We keep you healthy, and happy, and allow you to roam free on this planet. We have even let the humans live all this time, just to give you Vanir someone to rule over. In exchange, all we ask is a little of your power."

"You're parasites."

"What are all creatures, feeding off their resources? You should see what the inhabitants of some worlds did to their planets—the rubbish, the pollution, the poisoned seas. Was it not fitting that we returned the favor?"

"You don't get to pretend that this is some savior story."

Rigelus chuckled, and the sound knocked her from her fury enough to remember Hunt and Ruhn, and, oh gods, if Rigelus knew she was here, he'd find them—

"Isn't that what you're doing?"

"What the fuck is that supposed to mean?"

"You left such a noble audiomail to your friend Juniper. Of course, once I heard it, I knew there was only one place you could be going. Here. To me. Precisely as I had hoped—and planned."

She shut away her questions, instead demanding, "Why do you want me here?"

"To reopen the Rifts."

Her blood froze. "I can't."

"Can't you?" The cold voice slithered through the intercom. "You are Starborn, and have the Horn bound to your body and power. Your ancestors wielded the Horn and another Fae object that allowed them to enter this world. Stolen, of course, from their original masters—our people. Our people, who built fearsome warriors in that world to be their army. All of them prototypes for the angels in this one. And all of them traitors to their creators, joining the Fae to overthrow my brothers and sisters a thousand years before we arrived on Midgard. They slew my siblings."

Her head spun. "I don't understand."

"Midgard is a base. We opened the doors to other worlds to lure their citizens here—so many powerful beings, all so eager to conquer new planets. Not realizing we were *their* conquerors. But we also opened the doors so we might conquer those other worlds as well. The Fae—Queen Theia and her two foolish daughters—realized that, though too late. Her people were already here, but she and the princesses discovered where my siblings had hidden the access points in their world."

Rage rippled through his every word. "Your Starborn ancestors shut the gates to stop us from invading their realm once more and reminding them who their true masters are. And in the process, they shut the gates to all other worlds, including those to Hel, their stalwart allies. And so we have been trapped here. Cut off from the cosmos. All that is left of our people, though our mystics beneath this palace have long sought to find any other survivors, any planets where they might be hiding."

Bryce shook. The Astronomer had been right about the host of mystics here. "Why are you telling me this?"

"Why do you think we allowed you to live this spring? You are the key to opening the doors between worlds again. You will undo the actions of one ignorant princess fifteen thousand years ago."

"Not a chance."

"Are your mate and brother not here with you?"

"No."

Rigelus laughed. "You're so like Danika—a born liar."

"I'll take that as a compliment." She lifted her chin. "You knew she was onto you."

"Of course. Her quest for the truth began with her bloodhound gift. Not a gift of the body's strength, but of *magic*, such as the shifters should not have. She could scent other shifters with strange powers."

Like Sofie. And Baxian. Danika had found him through researching his bloodline, but had she scented it, too?

"It prompted her to investigate her own bloodline's history, all the way back to the shifters' arrival in this world, to learn where her gifts came from. And she eventually began to suspect the truth."

Bryce's throat worked. "Look, I already did the whole villain monologuing thing with Micah this spring, so cut to the chase."

Rigelus chuckled again. "We shall get to that in a moment." He went on, "Danika realized that the shifters are Fae."

Bryce blinked. "What?"

"Not your kind of Fae, of course—your breed dwelled in a lovely, verdant land, rich with magic. If it's of any interest to you, your Starborn bloodline specifically hailed from a small isle a few miles from the mainland. And while the mainland had all manner of climes, the isle existed in beautiful, near-permanent twilight. But only a select few in the entirety of your world could shift from their humanoid forms to animal ones. The Midgard shifters were Fae from a different planet. All the Fae in that world shared their form with an animal. The mer descended from them, too. Perhaps they once shared a world with your breed of Fae, but they had been alone on their planet for long enough to develop their own gifts."

"They don't have pointed ears."

"Oh, we bred that out of them. It was gone within a few generations."

An isle of near-permanent twilight, the home world of *her* breed of Fae . . . A land of Dusk.

"Dusk's Truth," Bryce breathed. It wasn't just the name of this room that Danika had been talking about with Sofie.

Rigelus didn't answer, and she didn't know what to make of it. But Bryce asked, "Why lie to everyone?"

"Two breeds of Fae? Both rich in magic? They were ideal food. We couldn't allow them to unify against us."

"So you turned them against each other. Made them two species at odds."

"Yes. The shifters easily and swiftly forgot what they had once been. They gladly gave themselves to us and did our bidding. Led our armies. And still do."

The Prime had said something similar. The wolves had lost what they had once been. Danika had known that. Danika had *known* the shifters had once been Fae. Were still Fae—but a different kind.

"And Project Thurr? Why was Danika so interested in that?"

"Thurr was the last time someone got as far as Danika did in learning about us. It didn't end well for them. I suppose she wanted to learn from their mistakes before acting."

"She was going to tell everyone what you were."

"Perhaps, but she knew she had to do it slowly. She started with Ophion. But her research into the bloodlines and the origins of the shifters, her belief that they'd once been a different type of Fae, from a different Fae world, was important enough that they put her in touch with one of their most talented agents: Sofie Renast. From what I gather, Danika was *very* intrigued by Sofie and her powers. But Sofie, you see, had a theory, too. About energy. What her thunderbird gifts sensed while using firstlight. And even better for Danika: Sofie was an unknown. Danika would be noticed poking about, but Sofie, as a passing human working in the archives, was easily missed. So Danika sent her to learn more, to go undercover, as you call it."

She'd made an enormous mistake coming here.

"We were eventually notified by one of our mystics here, who learned it from prying into the mind of one of Ophion's Command. So we did a little tugging. Pointed Micah toward synth. Toward Danika."

"No." The word was a whisper.

"You think Micah acted alone? He was a brash, arrogant male. All it took was some nudging, and he killed her for us. Had no idea it was on our behalf, but it played out as we planned: he was eventually caught and killed for disturbing our peace. I thank you for that."

Bryce shot from her chair. They'd killed Danika—to keep all of this secret. She would rip them to shreds.

"You can try to run," Rigelus said. "If that will make you feel better."

Bryce didn't give him a chance to say more before she teleported back to the alcove, Hunt's power fading like a dimming flame inside her.

No sign of Ruhn. But Hunt—

He was on his knees, Umbra Mortis helmet discarded on the stone floor beside him. Hands behind his head, bound with gorsian manacles.

His eyes turned wild, pleading, but there was nothing Bryce could do as freezing stone clamped around her wrists as well, and she found herself face-to-face with a grinning Harpy.

74

Tharion ran—or tried to. The mech-suit blocked his exit with a giant gun.

The pilot inside grinned. "Time to fry, fish."

"Clever," Tharion ground out, and leapt back as the cannon-gun fired. Only a smoking pile of rubble remained of the concrete where he'd stood.

"*Go!*" Cormac yelled again, and Pippa's rifle thundered.

Tharion twisted to see the prince collapse to his knees, a gaping hole in his chest.

He had to get him out. Couldn't leave him like this, where recovery would likely be thwarted by a beheading. But if he stayed, if he wasn't killed outright . . .

He had four hours to reach water. The rebels would use that against him. And he might have sold his life away to the Viper Queen, but to live without his fins . . . He wasn't ready to lose that piece of his soul.

Cormac's eyes rippled with fire as he met Tharion's stare. *Run*, that gaze said.

Tharion ran.

The mech-suit behind him fired again, and he rolled between its massive legs. Shooting to his feet, he sped for the hole the mech-suit had made in the wall. Daylight poured in through the billowing smoke.

That tether in his chest—the Viper Queen's leash—seemed to whisper, *Get to water, you stupid bastard, then return to me.*

Tharion dared a glance back as he leapt through the opening. The mech-suit was advancing on Cormac. Pippa marched beside it now, smiling in triumph.

Beyond them, row after row of half-made mech hybrids slumbered. Waiting for activation and slaughter. It didn't matter which side they fought for.

Cormac managed to lift a bloody hand to point behind Pippa. She drew up short and whirled to face the five glowing beings at the far end of the space.

The Asteri. Oh gods. They'd come.

Cormac gave no warning as he erupted into a ball of fire.

Pippa was consumed by it first. Then the mech-pilot, who burned alive in his suit.

But the ball kept growing, spreading, roaring, and Tharion began running again, not waiting to see if it could somehow, against all odds, take out the Asteri.

He ran into the open air, following the tug of that leash back to the water, to Valbara, dodging the wolf guards now racing to the building. Sirens blared. White light rippled into the sky—the Asteri's rage.

Tharion cleared the trees. Kept running for the coast. Maybe he'd get lucky and find a vehicle before then—even if he had to steal it. Or put a gun to the driver's head.

He was half a mile away when the entire building exploded, taking Cormac, the suits, and the rebels with it.

Slumped on the cell floor, Ruhn's body ached from the beating he'd taken. Mordoc had surrounded him with dreadwolves—no shadows would have been able to hide Ruhn from the bloodhound anyway. He'd have been sniffed out immediately.

Had Day betrayed him? Pretended to be captured so he'd come here? He'd been so blind, so fucking *blind*, and now—

The door to the cell far beneath the Asteri's palace opened. Ruhn, chained to the wall with gorsian shackles, looked up in horror as Bryce and Athalar entered, similarly shackled. His sister's face was wholly white.

Athalar bared his teeth at the Harpy as she shoved him in. Since Mordoc still lurked by the cell archway, grinning at them both, Ruhn had no doubt that the Hind was somewhere close by—that she'd be the one who got to work on them.

Neither Athalar nor Bryce fought their captors as they, too, were chained to the wall. Bryce was shaking. With fear or rage, Ruhn didn't know.

He met Mordoc's stare, letting the dreadwolf see just who the fuck he was tangling with. "How did you know I'd be here?"

The dreadwolf captain pushed off from the archway, violence in every movement. "Because Rigelus planned it that way. I still can't believe you walked right into his hands, you stupid fuck."

"We came here to assist the Asteri," Ruhn tried. "You've got the wrong idea."

From the corner of his eye, he could sense Bryce trying to catch his attention.

But Mordoc's face twisted with cruel delight. "Oh? Was that the excuse you were going to use in that alley? Or with the mystics? You forget who you're speaking to. I never forget a scent." He sneered at Bryce and Hunt. "I tracked you all around Lunathion—Rigelus was all too happy to hear about your activities."

"I thought you reported to the Hind," Athalar said.

The silver darts along Mordoc's collar glinted as he stepped closer. "Rigelus has a special interest in you lot. He asked me to sniff around." He made a show of smelling Hunt. "Maybe it's because your scent is wrong, angel."

Athalar growled, "What the fuck does that mean?"

Mordoc angled his head with mocking assessment. "Not like any other angel I've scented."

The Harpy rolled her eyes and said to the captain, "Enough. Leave us."

Mordoc's lip curled. "We're to wait here."

"*Leave us,*" the Harpy snapped. "I want a head start before she ruins my fun. Surely you know a thing or two about that, if you're sneaking around her to report to Rigelus." Mordoc bristled, but stalked off with a low snarl.

Ruhn's mind raced. They should never have come here. Mordoc *had* remembered his scent—and tracked them these past weeks. Had fed every location to Rigelus. Fuck.

The Harpy grinned. "It's been a while since I've played with you, Athalar."

Hunt spat at her feet. "Come and get it."

Ruhn knew he was trying to keep her from going for Bryce. Buying them whatever time he could to find a way out of this shitstorm. Ruhn met Bryce's panicked look.

She couldn't teleport, thanks to the gorsian shackles. Could Cormac get back here? He was their only shot at getting out of these chains—their only shot at survival. Had Dec seen the capture? Even if he had, there were no reinforcements to send.

The Harpy drew a short, lethal knife. The kind so precise that it could carve skin from the most delicate places. She flipped it in her hand, keeping back from Athalar's reach, even with the chains. Her focus slid to Ruhn. Hate lit her eyes.

"Not so cocky now, are you, princeling?" she asked. She pointed her knife toward his crotch. "You know how long it takes for a male to grow back his balls?"

Pure dread shot through him.

Bryce hissed, "Keep your fucking hands off him."

The Harpy laughed. "Does it bother you, Princess, to see your males so roughly handled?" She approached Ruhn, and he could do nothing as she ran the side of the blade down his cheek. "So pretty," she murmured, her eyes like blackest Hel. "It will be a shame to ruin such beauty."

Hunt growled, "Come play with someone interesting."

"Still the noble bastard," the Harpy said, running the knife down the other side of Ruhn's face. If she came close enough, he could try to rip out her throat with his teeth, but she was too wary. Kept far enough back. "Trying to distract me from harming others. Don't you remember how I cut up your soldiers piece by piece despite your pleading?"

Bryce lunged against her chains, and Ruhn's heart cracked as she screamed, "*Get the fuck away from him!*"

"Listening to you squeal while I carve him will be a delight," the Harpy said, and slid the knife to the base of Ruhn's throat.

It was going to hurt. It would hurt, but because of his Vanir blood, he wouldn't die—not yet. He'd keep healing while she sliced him apart.

"*GET OFF HIM!*" Bryce bellowed. A guttural roar thundered in the words. As Fae as he'd ever heard his sister.

The tip of the knife pierced Ruhn's throat, its sting blooming. He dove deep, into the place where he'd always run to avoid his father's ministrations.

They'd walked in here so foolishly, had been so blind—

The Harpy sucked in a breath, muscles tensing to shove in the knife.

Something golden and swift as the wind barreled into her side and sent the Harpy sprawling.

Bryce shouted, but all the noise, all the thoughts in Ruhn's head eddied away as a familiar, lovely scent hit him. As he beheld the female who leapt to her feet, now a wall between him and the Harpy.

The Hind.

75

You fucking *cunt*," the Harpy cursed, rising to draw a long, wicked sword.

Ruhn couldn't move from the floor as the Hind unsheathed her own slim blade. As her beckoning scent floated to him. A scent that was somehow entwined with his own. It was very faint, like a shadow, so vague that he doubted anyone else would realize the underlying scent belonged to him.

And her scent had been familiar from the start because Hypaxia was her half-sister, he realized. Family ties didn't lie. He'd been wrong about her being in House of Sky and Breath—the Hind could claim total allegiance to Earth and Blood.

"I knew it. I always *knew* it," the Harpy seethed, wings rustling. "Traitorous bitch."

It couldn't be.

It . . . it couldn't be.

Bryce and Hunt were frozen with shock.

Ruhn whispered, "Day?"

Lidia Cervos looked over a shoulder. And she said with quiet calm in a voice he knew like his own heartbeat, a voice he had never once heard her use as the Hind, "Night."

"The Asteri will carve you up and feed you to your dreadwolves," the Harpy crooned, sword angling. "And I'm going to help them do it."

The golden-haired female—Lidia, *Day*—only said to the Harpy, "Not if I kill you first."

The Harpy lunged. The Hind was waiting.

Sword met sword, and Ruhn could only watch as the shifter deflected and parried the angel's strike. Her blade shone like quicksilver, and as the Harpy brought down another arm-breaking blow, a dagger appeared in Lidia's other hand.

The Hind crossed dagger and sword and met the blow, using the Harpy's movement to kick at her exposed stomach. The angel went down in a pile of wings and black hair, but she was instantly up, circling. "The Asteri will let Pollux have at you, I think." A bitter, cruel laugh.

Pollux—the male who'd . . . A blaring white noise blasted through Ruhn's head.

"Pollux will get what's coming to him, too," the Hind said, blocking the attack and spinning on her knees so that she was behind the Harpy. The Harpy twirled, meeting the blow, but backed a step closer to Ruhn.

Their blades again met, the Harpy pressing. The Hind's arms strained, the sleek muscles in her thighs visible through her skin-tight white pants as she pushed up, up, to her feet. She kept her black boots planted—the Harpy's stance was nowhere near as solid.

Lidia's golden eyes slid to Ruhn's. She nodded shallowly. A command.

Ruhn crouched, readying.

"Lying filth," the Harpy raged, losing another inch. Just a little further . . . "When did they turn you?"

Ruhn's heart raced.

The two females clashed and withdrew with horrifying skill, then clashed again. "Liar I might be," Lidia growled, smiling savagely, "but at least I'm no fool."

The Harpy blinked as the Hind shoved her another inch.

Right to the edge of Ruhn's reach.

Ruhn grabbed the Harpy's ankle and *yanked*. The angel shouted, tumbling down again, wings splaying.

The Hind struck.

Swift as a cobra, Lidia plunged her sword into the top of the Harpy's spine, right through her neck. The tip of her blade hit the floor before the Harpy's body collided with it.

The Harpy tried to scream, but the Hind had angled the blow to pierce her vocal cords. The next blow, with her parrying dagger, plunged through the Harpy's ear and into the skull beneath. Another move, and her head rolled away.

And then silence. The Harpy's wings twitched.

Ruhn slowly lifted his gaze to the Hind.

Lidia stood over him, splattered with blood. Every line of the body he'd seen and felt was taut. On alert.

Hunt breathed, "You're a double agent?"

But Lidia launched into motion, grabbing Ruhn's chains, unlocking them with a key from her imperial uniform. "We don't have much time. You have to get out of here."

She'd sworn she wouldn't come for him if he got into trouble. But here she was.

"Was this a trap?" Bryce demanded.

"Not in the way you're thinking," Lidia said. As the Hind, she'd kept her voice low and soft. Day's voice—*this* person's voice—sounded higher. She came close enough while she freed Ruhn's feet that he could scent her again. "I tried to warn you that I believed Rigelus *wanted* you to come here, that he knew you would, but . . . I was interrupted." By Pollux. "When I was finally able to reach out to you again, it was clear that only those of us in Sandriel's triarii knew about Rigelus's plan, and that Mordoc had been feeding him information regarding your whereabouts. To warn you off would have been to give myself away."

Hunt glowered as Ruhn stared at the Hind. "And we couldn't have that," the angel said.

Mordoc—how had the bloodhound not noticed the subtle shift in Lidia's scent? In Ruhn's? Or had he, and been biding his time to spring the trap shut?

Lidia shot Hunt a glare, not backing down as she started on Bryce's chains. "There is a great deal that you do not understand."

She was so beautiful. And utterly soulless.

You remind me that I'm alive, she'd told him.

"You killed Sofie," Bryce hissed.

"No." Lidia shook her head. "I called for the city-ship to save her. They arrived too late."

"What?" Athalar blurted.

Ruhn blinked as the Hind pulled a white stone from her pocket. "These are calling stones—beacons. The Ocean Queen enchanted them. They'll summon whatever city-ship is closest when dropped into the water. Her mystics sense when the ships might be needed in a certain area, and the stones are used as a precise method of location."

She'd done it that day in Ydra, too. She'd summoned the ship that saved them.

"Sofie drowned because of you," Ruhn growled, his voice like gravel. "People died at your hands—"

"There is so much to tell you, Ruhn," she said softly, and his name on her tongue . . .

But Ruhn looked away from her. He could have sworn the Hind flinched.

He didn't care. Not as Hunt asked Bryce, "Did you find out the truth?"

Bryce paled. "I did. I—"

Steps sounded down the hall. Far away, but approaching. The Hind went still. "Pollux."

Her hearing had to be better than his. Or she knew the cadence of the bastard's steps so well she could tell from a distance.

"We have to make it appear real," she said to Bryce, to Ruhn, voice pleading, utterly desperate. "The information lines *can't* be broken." Her voice cracked. "Do you understand?"

Bryce did, apparently. She smirked. "I shouldn't enjoy this so much."

Before Ruhn could react, his sister punched the shifter in the face. Sent her sprawling. He shouted, and those footsteps down the hall turned into a run.

Bryce leapt upon the Hind, fists flying, and the Harpy's blood on the floor smeared all over them both. Hunt struggled against his chains, and Ruhn got to his feet, lunging toward the females—

Pollux appeared in the doorway.

He beheld the dead Harpy, beheld Bryce bloodied with the Hind beneath her, being pummeled, beheld Ruhn advancing, and drew his sword.

Ruhn could have sworn the Hind whispered something in Bryce's ear before Pollux grabbed Bryce by the neck and hauled her off the other female.

"Hello, Princess," the monster crooned.

Hunt had no words in his head as the male he hated above all others grabbed his mate by the neck. Held her off the floor so that the tips of her sneakers dragged on the bloodied stone.

"Look what you did to my friend," Pollux said in that dead, soulless voice. "And to my lover."

"I'll do the same to you," Bryce managed to say, feet kicking blindly.

"*Put her the fuck down,*" Hunt snarled.

Pollux sneered at him, and did no such thing.

The Hind had managed to pull her sword from the Harpy's body and point it at Ruhn. "Back against the wall or she dies." Her voice was flat and low—as Hunt had always heard it. Not at all like the softer, higher register of a moment before.

Agent Daybright hadn't needed saving after all. And the Hind . . . the female that Hunt had seen so mercilessly stride through the world . . .

She was a rebel. Had saved their asses that day in the waters off Ydra by summoning the city-ship with the calling stone. It hadn't been Bryce's light at all. *We got your message,* they'd said.

Ruhn looked like he'd been punched in the gut. In the soul.

But Pollux finally lowered Bryce to the ground, an arm wrapping around her middle as he grinned at Hunt. He sniffed Bryce's hair. Hunt's vision went black with rage as Pollux said, "This is going to be so satisfying."

Bryce was shaking. She knew—whatever the truth was about the Asteri, about all of this, she knew. They had to get her out, so that information wouldn't die here.

So she wouldn't die here.

The next few minutes were a blur. Guards flowed in. Hunt found himself being hauled to his feet, Bryce chained beside him, Ruhn on her other side, the Hind stalking next to Pollux as they walked from the dungeons to an elevator bay.

"Their Graces await you," the Hind said with such unfeeling ice that even Hunt bought it, and wondered if he'd imagined the female helping them. Imagined that she'd risked everything to save Ruhn from the Harpy.

From the way Ruhn was glaring at the Hind, Hunt could only guess what the prince was thinking.

They entered the elevator, the Hind and Pollux facing them. The Hammer smirked at Hunt.

If they could kill Pollux . . . But cameras monitored this elevator. The halls. The Hind would be revealed.

Bryce was still shaking beside him. He hooked his fingers through hers, sticky with blood—as much movement as his chains would allow.

He tried not to glance down when he felt her own chains. The manacles were loose. Unlocked. Only Bryce's fingertips held them in place—the Hind hadn't secured them. Bryce met Hunt's stare. Pained and full of love.

The Hind had known it, too. That Bryce, with the intel she carried, had to get out.

Was the Hind planning something? Had she whispered a plan in Bryce's ear?

Bryce said nothing. Just held his hand—for the last time, he realized as the elevator shot up through the crystal palace.

He was holding his mate's hand for the last time.

Ruhn stared at the female he'd thought he knew. At her impassive, beautiful face. Her empty golden eyes.

It was a mask. He'd seen the real face moments ago. Had joined his body and soul with hers days ago. He knew what fire burned there.

Night.

Her voice was a distant, soft plea in his mind. Like Lidia was trying to find a way to link their thoughts again, like the crystal in his pocket had yet again forged a path. *Night.*

Ruhn ignored the begging voice. The way it broke as she said, *Ruhn.*

He fortified the walls of his mind. Brick by brick.

Ruhn. Lidia banged on the walls of his mind.

So he encased it with iron. With black steel.

Pollux smiled at him. Slid a hand around the Hind's blood-splattered throat and kissed under her ear. "Do you like the way my lover looks, princeling?"

Something lethal snapped free at that hand on her neck. The way it squeezed, and the slight glimmer of pain in Lidia's eyes—

He'd hurt her. Pollux had hurt her, again and again, and she'd voluntarily submitted so she could keep feeding the rebels intel. She'd endured a monster like Pollux for this.

"Maybe we'll put on a show for you before the end," Pollux said, and licked up the column of Lidia's neck, lapping up the blood splattered there.

Ruhn bared his teeth in a silent snarl. He'd kill him. Slowly and thoroughly, punishing him for every touch, every hand he'd put on Lidia in pain and torment.

He had no idea where that landed him. Why he wanted and needed that steel-clad wall between him and Lidia, even as his blood howled to murder Pollux. How he could abhor her and need her, be drawn to her, in the same breath.

Pollux laughed against her skin, then pulled away. Lidia smiled coolly. Like it all meant nothing, like she felt nothing at all.

But that voice against the walls of his mind shouted, *Ruhn!*

She banged against the black steel and stone, over and over. Her voice broke again, *Ruhn!*

Ruhn locked her out.

She'd taken countless lives—but she'd worked to save them, too.

Did it change anything? He'd known Day was someone high up—he'd have been a fool to think anyone with that level of clearance with the Asteri would come without complications. But for it to be her . . . What the Hel did it even say about him, that he was capable of feeling what he did for someone like *her*?

His ally was his enemy. His enemy was his lover. He focused on the gore splattered on her.

Lidia had so much blood on her hands that there would never be any washing it away.

Bryce knew no one was coming to save them. Knew it was likely her fault. She could barely stand to feel Hunt's fingers against hers as they walked down the long crystal hallway. Couldn't stand the stickiness of the Harpy's blood as it dried on her skin.

She'd never seen a hall so long. A wall of windows stretched along one side, overlooking the palace grounds and ancient city beyond. On the other side, busts of the Asteri in their various forms frowned down upon them from atop pedestals.

Their masters. Their overlords. The parasites who had lured them all into this world. Who had fed off them for fifteen thousand years.

Rigelus wouldn't have told her so much if he planned to ever let her go again.

She wished she'd called her mom and Randall. Wished she could hear their voices one more time. Wished she'd made things right with Juniper. Wished she'd lain low and been normal and lived out a long, happy life with Hunt.

It wouldn't have been normal, though. It would have been contented ignorance. And any children they had . . . their power would one day have also been siphoned off to fuel these cities and the monsters who ruled them.

The cycle had to stop somewhere. Other worlds had managed to overthrow them. *Hel* had managed to kick them out.

But Bryce knew she and Hunt and Ruhn wouldn't be the ones to stop the cycle. That task would be left to others.

Cormac would continue to fight. Maybe Tharion and Hypaxia and Ithan would pick up the cause. Perhaps Fury, too.

Gods, did Jesiba know? She'd kept Parthos's remaining books—knowing the Asteri would want to wipe out the narrative that contradicted their own sanctioned history. So Jesiba *had* to know what kind of beings ruled here, didn't she?

The Hind led their group down the hall, Pollux at their backs. At the far, far end of the passage, Bryce could make out a small arch.

A quartz Gate.

Bryce's blood chilled. Did Rigelus plan to have her open it as some sort of test before cracking wide the Rifts?

She'd do it. Rigelus had Hunt and Ruhn in his claws. She knew her mate and brother would tell her that their lives weren't worth it, but . . . weren't they?

The Hind turned a third of the way down the hall, toward a pair of colossal open doors.

Seven thrones towered on a dais at the far end of the cavernous, crystal space. All but one lay empty. And the center throne, the occupied one . . . it glowed, full of firstlight. Funneling it right into the being who sat atop it.

Something feral opened an eye in Bryce's soul. And snarled.

"I suppose you're pleased to have added yet another angel to your kill list with the death of the Harpy," the Bright Hand of the Asteri drawled to Bryce, stare sweeping over the blood caked on her. "I do hope you're ready to pay for it."

76

Hunt stared at his severed wings, mounted on the wall high above the Asteri's thrones.

Shahar's pristine white wings were displayed above his, still glowing after all these centuries, right in the center of the array. Isaiah's were to the left of Hunt's. So many wings. So many Fallen. All preserved here.

He'd known the Asteri had kept them. But seeing them . . .

It was proof of his failure. Proof that he should never have come here, that they should have told Ophion and Tharion and Cormac to fuck off—

"I did you a favor, killing the Harpy," Bryce said to Rigelus, who watched her with lifeless eyes. At least the five others weren't here. "She was a drag."

Hunt blinked at his blood-splattered mate. Her eyes smoldered like coals, defiant and raging. She'd seen his wings, too.

Rigelus propped his slender chin on a fist, leaning a bony elbow against his throne. He appeared as a Fae boy of seventeen or so, dark-haired and gangly. A weak facade to veil the ancient monster beneath. "Shall we banter some more, Miss Quinlan, or can I get to the part where I order you to confess the names of your allies?"

Bryce smirked, and Hunt had never loved her more. On her

other side, Ruhn glanced between the Asteri and his sister, as if trying to formulate a plan.

Hunt caught a familiar scent, and he twisted to see Baxian and Mordoc enter behind them. They walked to where the Hind and the Hammer stood by the pillars. Blocking the way out.

Rigelus had known of their mission here before they'd even reached Pangera's shores—before they'd even set out. Mordoc had tracked their scents with that bloodhound's gift all around the city, marking each location and reporting directly to the Bright Hand.

And Hunt had left his phone in Lunathion, for fear of it being tracked here. Baxian wouldn't have been able to warn him, if he'd even been willing to risk doing so.

Hunt's eyes met Baxian's. The male revealed nothing. Not one bit of recognition.

Had everything he'd told them been a trap? A long con to get them here?

Bryce said to Rigelus, drawing Hunt's attention away, "There is no one else. But let's talk about how you're intergalactic parasites who trick us into making the Drop so you can feed off our firstlight. And then feed off our souls' secondlight when we die."

Hunt went still. He could have sworn someone behind him—Baxian or the Hind, perhaps—started.

Rigelus snorted. "Is this your way of telling your companions what you know?"

Bryce didn't avert her gaze. "Hel yeah, it is. Along with the fact that if we destroy that core of firstlight beneath this palace—"

"Silence," Rigelus hissed, and the room shuddered with power.

But Hunt's mind reeled. The Asteri, the firstlight . . . Bryce caught his stare, her eyes brimming with rage and purpose. There was more, she seemed to say. So much more to be used against the Asteri.

Rigelus pointed at Ruhn. "I'm sure you could enlighten me as to who has been helping you. I know of Prince Cormac—I'd hoped his rebel activities might be of use someday. When we learned of his treachery, the others wanted to kill him and be done with it, but I thought it might be . . . valuable to see where and to whom he led us. A Prince of the Fae would no doubt wind up around other powerful Vanir, perhaps even try to recruit some of them, and thus root out the corruption among our most loyal subjects. So why kill one traitor, when we could eventually kill many? Alas, he's dead now. That's where my other siblings are—drawn out to the lab, as you no doubt expected. But they reported that another male was with the prince, and fled."

Bryce made a low sound in her throat.

Rigelus turned to her. "Oh yes. Cormac incinerated himself and the lab. A great setback, considering how useful he was, but one we shall overcome, of course. Especially with Pippa Spetsos among the dead."

At least Tharion had escaped unidentified.

"Perhaps we shall call in your father to assist with the questioning," Rigelus went on to Ruhn, bored and cool. "He was so skilled at wielding his fire to get things out of you when you were a boy."

Ruhn stiffened.

Hunt took in Bryce's blood-flecked features. He'd only once seen this level of rage on her face. Not toward Rigelus, but the male who'd sired her. It was the same rage he'd beheld that day she'd killed Micah.

"Isn't that what so many of the tattoos are for?" Rigelus continued. "To hide the scars he left on you? I'm afraid we'll have to ruin some of the ink this time around."

Fucking Hel. Bryce's lips had gone white from pressing them together so hard. Her eyes were bright with unshed tears.

Ruhn looked at his sister and said softly, "You brought so much joy into my life, Bryce."

It was perhaps the only goodbye they'd be able to make.

Hunt reached for Bryce's fingers, but she stepped forward. Lifted her chin in that defiant, fuck-you way he loved so much. "You want me to open a portal for you? Fine. But only if you let them go and agree to leave them unharmed. Forever."

Hunt's blood iced over. "That was why you lured us here?" he found himself demanding of the Asteri, even as he roared with outrage at Bryce's offer.

Rigelus said, "I couldn't very well snatch you off the streets. Not such notorious, public figures. Not without the right charges to bring you in." A smirk at Bryce. "Your friend Aidas will be terribly disappointed to learn you couldn't tell the difference between the real Prince of the Chasm and myself. He's terribly vain in that way."

Hunt started, but Bryce seethed, "You pretended to be Aidas that night."

"Who else could break through the wards on your apartment? You didn't even suspect anything when he encouraged you toward rebellious activities. Though I suppose credit for that goes to me—I played his rage about Theia and Pelias quite well, don't you think?"

Fuck. He'd anticipated their every move.

Rigelus went on, "And you didn't even look that hard into the Reapers I sent from this city to nudge you. The Bone Quarter was a testing ground for your true power, you see—since you seemed to have little awareness or interest in it all summer. You were to hone your powers, all so we might put them to good use. You played along beautifully."

Hunt's fingers curled into fists. He should have seen it—should have pushed Bryce away from this mess, should have taken her at the first hint of trouble and gone to a place where no one could ever find them.

But this was Midgard. No matter where they went, no matter how far from Lunathion or the Eternal City, the Asteri would always find them.

Rigelus sighed dramatically at their stunned silence. "This all seems very familiar, doesn't it? A Starborn queen who allied with a Prince of Hel. Who trusted him deeply, and ultimately paid the price."

Hunt mastered himself enough to nod toward the seventh, always empty throne. "Hel got one on you in the end, though, I think."

Rigelus's body glowed with ire, but his voice remained silky smooth. "I look forward to facing Apollion again. Mordoc suspected that the Star-Eater had been trying to get your attention these past weeks—to prod you along in his own way."

So one Prince of Hel had been a fake, the other true. Apollion really had sent the deathstalkers, presumably to test Bryce's powers—just as Rigelus also wanted—and Hunt's own. And wanted it so badly that he was willing to risk her death should she not be up to the task.

But she'd teleported that night. Used that ability to defeat the deathstalkers. Had started to grasp the gift and progressed in leaps and bounds since then. Literally.

Apollion must have known she'd need those skills. Perhaps for this very moment.

The gorsian chains on Bryce's wrists were unlocked. If she could throw them off, she could get out. If the Hind could somehow get his own chains off, he'd block the Asteri and Bryce could keep running.

Hunt said, one last try, "You're full of shit, and Mordoc should get his nose checked. We're not rebels. Celestina can vouch for us."

Rigelus laughed, and Hunt bristled. "Celestina? You mean the Archangel who reported to me that you'd lied about going to visit Miss Quinlan's family a few weeks ago, and then reported to me immediately when she saw you leave the barracks heavily armed?" The words landed like a phantom punch to Hunt's gut.

Love is a trap, Celestina had told him. Was this her way of protecting what she loved? Proving her trustworthiness to the Asteri by selling Hunt and his friends out so that they might react kindly if they learned about Hypaxia? Had she any idea the witch she loved was involved?

Rigelus seemed to read those questions on Hunt's face, because he said, "She might have once been a friend of Shahar, Orion, but with so much personally on the line for her, she is no friend to you. At least, not when it comes to protecting those she cherishes most."

"Why are you doing this?" Ruhn asked hoarsely.

Rigelus frowned with distaste. "It is a matter of survival." A glance at Bryce. "Though her first task for us shall be one of . . . a personal matter, I think."

"You're going to attack Hel," Hunt breathed. Was that what Apollion was anticipating? Why he'd kept telling them, again and again, that Hel's armies were readying?

Not to attack this world, but to defend Hel itself. To ally with any who'd stand against the Asteri.

"No," Rigelus said. "Even Hel is not at the top of our list of those from whom we shall exact vengeance." Again, that smile at Bryce. "The star on your chest—do you know what it is?"

"Let's assume I know nothing," Bryce said grimly.

Rigelus inclined his head. "It's a beacon to the world from which the Fae originally came. It sometimes glows when nearest the Fae who have undiluted bloodlines from that world. Prince Cormac, for example."

"It glowed for Hunt," Bryce shot back.

"It also glows for those who you choose as your loyal companions. Knights."

"So what?" Bryce demanded.

"So that star will lead us back to that world. Through you. They overthrew our brethren who once ruled there—we have not forgotten. Our initial attempt at revenge was foiled by your ancestor who also bore that star on her chest. The Fae have still not atoned for the deaths of our brothers and sisters. Their home world was rich in magic. I crave more of it."

Bryce shook, but Hunt's heart cracked as she squared her shoulders. "My bargain holds. You let Hunt and Ruhn go freely and unharmed—forever—and I'll help you."

"Bryce," Ruhn pleaded, but Hunt knew there was no arguing with her.

"Fine," Rigelus said, and smiled, triumph on every line of his lanky body. "You may say goodbye, as a sign of my gratitude for your assistance."

Bryce turned to Hunt, and the terror and pain and grief on her gore-splattered face threatened to bring him to his knees. He slipped his chained hands around her head, pulling her close. Whispered in her ear. Her fingers bunched in his shirt, as if in silent confirmation.

So Hunt pulled back. Stared into his mate's beautiful face for the last time.

He laughed softly, a sound of wonder at odds with the crystal throne room and the monsters in it. "I love you. I wish I'd said it more. But I love you, Quinlan, and . . ." His throat closed up, his eyes stinging. His lips brushed her brow. "Our love is stronger than time, greater than any distance. Our love spans across stars and worlds. I will find you again. I promise."

He kissed her, and she shuddered, silently crying as her mouth moved against his own. He savored the warmth and taste of her, etching it into his soul.

Then he stepped back, and Bryce faced Ruhn.

She couldn't do this.

Her heart was shattering; her bones were screaming that this was *wrong, wrong, wrong.*

She couldn't leave them. Couldn't go through with what Hunt had whispered to her.

She clung to her brother, unable to stop her sobbing. Even as a small weight dropped into her pocket.

But Ruhn whispered in her ear, "I lied to the Autumn King about what the Oracle told me as a boy." She stilled. Ruhn went on, swift and urgent, "The Oracle told me that the royal line would end with me. That I am the last of the line, Bryce." She tried to pull back to gape at him, but he held her firm. "But maybe she didn't see that *you* would come along. That you would walk this path. You have to live. I can see it on your face—you don't want to do any of this. But you *have* to live, Bryce. You have to be queen."

She'd guessed what the Autumn King had done to Ruhn, how he'd tortured him as a boy, though she'd never confirmed it. And that debt . . . she'd make her sire repay it, someday.

"I don't accept that," Bryce breathed to Ruhn. "I *don't.*"

"I do. I always have. Whether I die right now or whether I'm just infertile, I don't know." He chuckled. "Why do you think I partied so hard?"

She couldn't laugh. Not about this. "I don't buy that bullshit for one second."

"It doesn't matter now."

Then Ruhn said into her mind, *Grab the Starsword when you go.*

Ruhn—

It's yours. Take it. You'll need it. You got the chains unhooked?

Yes. She'd used the key the Hind had slipped her to unlock Hunt's and Ruhn's manacles while she held them.

Good. I told Athalar the signal. You're ready?

No.

Ruhn pressed his brow against hers. *We need armies, Bryce. We need you to go to Hel through that Gate, and bring Hel's armies back with you to fight these bastards. But if Apollion's cost is too high . . . don't come back to this world.*

Her brother pulled away. And Ruhn said, shining with pride, "Long live the queen."

Bryce didn't give the others a chance to puzzle it out.

She flicked her wrists, chains falling to the floor as she grabbed the Starsword from Ruhn and whirled toward Rigelus.

She plunged into her power in a blink. And before the Bright Hand could shout, she blasted him with starlight.

Hunt threw his chains to the ground the moment Ruhn said the word *queen*. And as his mate launched her blinding power at Rigelus, Hunt hurled his at the male, too.

Lightning struck the marble pillar just above the crystal throne.

It was a gamble: directing his initial blast of power at Rigelus, to keep him down, rather than charging up Bryce and risking an attack from Rigelus before it was done.

Behind them, shouting rose, and Hunt twisted to see Bryce running toward the doors, Starsword in hand.

Pollux lunged for her, but Baxian was there. He tackled the male to the crystal floor. Behind him, Mordoc was bleeding from a gash in his throat. The Hind was on the floor, unconscious. Had Baxian's treachery been a surprise to her? Hunt supposed he didn't care. Not as Baxian got Pollux down, and Bryce raced through the doors, out into the endless hallway. She turned left, red hair streaming behind her, and then she was gone.

Hunt whirled back toward Rigelus, but too late.

Power, hot and aching, blasted him into a nearby pillar. Glowing like a god, Rigelus leapt off the dais, the crystal floor splintering beneath him, and barreled after Bryce, death raging in his eyes.

Bryce's heart cracked piece by piece with each step she ran from that throne room.

As she sped down the long hall, the busts of the Asteri damned her with their hateful faces.

A tidal wave of power rose behind her, and she dared a look over her shoulder to find Rigelus on her tail. He blazed white with magic, fury radiating from him.

Come on, Hunt. Come on, come on . . .

Rigelus sent out a blast of power, and Bryce zoomed left. The Asteri's power smashed through a window, glass spraying. Bryce slipped on the shards, but kept running toward the arch at the end of the hall. The Gate she'd open to take her to Hel.

She'd take her chances with Aidas and Thanatos and Apollion. Get their armies and bring them back to Midgard.

Rigelus shot another spear of power, and Bryce ducked, sliding low just as it shattered a marble bust of Austrus. Fragments sliced her face, her neck, her arms, but then she was up and running again, clenching the Starsword so hard her hand ached.

The slide had cost her.

Rigelus was ten feet behind. Five. His hand stretched for her trailing hair.

Lightning speared down the hall, shattering windows and statues in its wake.

Bryce welcomed it into her heart, her back. Welcomed it into the tattoo there as Hunt's power singed her very blood—and left it sparking.

Lightning ruptured from her scar like a bullet passing through. Right into the archway of the Gate.

She didn't dare see if Hunt still stood after his flawless shot. Not as the air of the Gate's arch turned black. Murky.

Rigelus's fingers snared in her hair.

Bryce gave herself to the wind and darkness, and teleported for the Gate.

Only to land ten feet ahead of Rigelus, as if her powers had hit a wall. Bryce could sense them now—a series of wards, like those Hypaxia had said the Under-King had used to entrap her and Ithan.

But Rigelus shouted in rage and surprise, as if shocked she'd even managed to get that far, and slung his power again.

Ten feet at a time, then. Bryce teleported, and another statue lost its head.

Again, and again, and again, Rigelus shot his power at her and Bryce leapt through space, ward to ward, zigging and zagging, glass and countless statues to the Asteri's egos shattering, the Gate nearing—

Bryce leapt *back*—right behind Rigelus.

He whirled, and she blasted a wall of light into his face. He howled, and she teleported once more—

Bryce landed ten feet from the Gate's gaping maw and kept running.

Rigelus roared as Bryce jumped into the awaiting darkness.

It caught her, sticky like a web. Time slowed to a glacial drip.

Rigelus was still roaring, lunging.

Bryce thrust her power out, willed the Gate to take her and her alone, and she was falling, falling, falling while standing still, suspended in the archway, sucked backward so that her hair trailed outward, toward Rigelus's straining fingers—

"*NO!*" he bellowed.

It was the last sound Bryce heard as the darkness within the Gate swallowed her whole.

She fell, slowly and without end—and sideways. Not a plunge down, but a yank *across*. The pressure in her ears threatened to pulp her brain, and she was screaming into wind and stars and emptiness, screaming to Hunt and Ruhn, left behind in that crystal palace. Screaming—

77

Hunt could barely get a breath down around the stone gag. A gorsian stone, to match the ones clamped around his wrists and neck. The same kind contained Ruhn and Baxian as the two males were led toward the doors of the throne room by Rigelus and his underlings.

Not one flicker of lightning remained in Hunt's body.

The Hind strode beside Rigelus, speaking softly as they walked past where Hunt was on his knees outside the doors. She didn't so much as look at Ruhn. The prince only stared ahead.

Baxian was escorted over, bloodied and bruised from the fight with Pollux. Mordoc was recovering from his slit throat, hate simmering from him as he lay bleeding on the floor. Hunt gave the bloodhound a savage smile as a ribbon of Rigelus's power hauled Hunt to his feet.

"A short stop before the dungeons, I think," Rigelus announced, turning left—toward the shattered ruin along the hall. Toward the now-empty Gate.

Hunt was powerless to do anything but follow, Ruhn and Baxian with him. He'd been at the end of the hall when Bryce had made her spectacular run, teleporting as fast as the wind toward the black hole that had opened within the small Gate. No trace of the blackness or Bryce remained now.

Hunt could only pray that Bryce had reached Hel. That she'd

locate Aidas and he'd protect her as they rallied Hel's armies and brought them back through the Rift into Midgard. To save them.

Hunt doubted he'd be around to see it. Doubted Ruhn or Baxian would, either.

Rigelus halted before the Gate. "Get the angel on his knees."

Bryce's scent still lingered in the air of the empty space framed by the Gate. Hunt focused on that scent and that scent alone as Pollux shoved him to the floor before the Gate.

If this was it, he could die knowing Bryce had gotten away. She'd gone from one Hel to a literal one, but . . . she'd gotten away. Their last chance at salvation.

"Go ahead, Hammer," Rigelus said, smiling at Hunt, cold death in his ageless eyes.

Hunt could feel Ruhn and Baxian watching in muted horror. Hunt bowed over his knees, waiting for the blow to his neck.

Bryce, Bryce, Bryce—

Pollux's hands clamped onto either side of his face. Holding it upright, like he'd snap Hunt's neck with his bare hands.

Pollux laughed softly.

Hunt knew why a moment later as Rigelus approached, a hand lifted and near-blinding with white light. "I don't think I need one of the crones this time," the Bright Hand said.

No. *No.* Anything but this.

Hunt thrashed, but Pollux held him firm, smile unfaltering.

Rigelus laid his glowing hand on Hunt's brow and pain erupted through his skull, his muscles, his blood. As if the very marrow of his bones were being burned into mist.

The Asteri's power slithered and spiderwebbed across Hunt's brow, piercing into him with every spike of the halo's thorns that Rigelus tattooed there.

Hunt screamed then. It echoed off the stones, off the Gate.

Beside him, Baxian started inhaling sharp, jagged breaths. Like the Helhound knew he was next.

The pain across Hunt's brow became blinding, his vision splintering.

The halo kept spreading over his skull, worse than any gorsian shackle. His power writhed in its iron grip, no longer his to fully command. Just as his own life, his freedom, his future with Bryce . . . Gone.

Hunt screamed again, and as darkness swept in to claim him, he wondered if that soul-scream, not the halo, was what Rigelus wanted. If the Asteri believed the sound of his suffering might carry through the Gate and into Hel itself, where Bryce could hear him.

Then Hunt knew nothing at all.

78

Hel had grass. And mist.

Those were Bryce's first two thoughts as she landed—or appeared. One moment she was falling sideways, and then her right shoulder collided with a wall of green that turned out to be the ground.

She panted, mind spinning so violently she could only lie amid the drifting, chill fog. Her fingers dug into the verdant grass. Blood coated her hands. Crusted beneath her nails.

She had to get up. Had to start moving before one of Hel's creatures sniffed her out and ripped her to shreds. If those deathstalkers found her, they'd kill her in an instant.

The Starsword—

There. A foot beyond her head.

Bryce trembled as she eased onto her knees, bending to hold them tight.

Hunt . . . She could have sworn she heard his screams echoing in the mist as she fell.

She had to get up. Find a way to Aidas.

Yet she couldn't move. To get up would be to walk away from her world, from Hunt and Ruhn, and whatever the Asteri were doing to them—

Get up, she told herself, gritting her teeth.

The mists parted ahead, peeling back to reveal a gentle turquoise river perhaps fifty feet from where she knelt, flowing right past the . . . lawn.

She was on someone's clipped, immaculate lawn. And across the river, emerging from the mist . . .

A city. Ancient and beautiful—like something on a Pangeran postcard. Indistinct shapes meandered through the mist on the other side of the river—the demons of Hel.

Get up.

Bryce swallowed hard, as if she could drink down her shaking, and slid out a leg to rise. The Harpy's blood still soaked her leggings, the fabric sticky against her skin.

Something icy and sharp pressed against her throat.

A cool male voice spoke above her, behind her, in a language she did not recognize. But the curt words and tone were clear enough: *Don't fucking move.*

Bryce lifted her hands and reached for her power. Only splintered shards remained.

The male voice demanded something in that strange language, and Bryce stayed on her knees. He hissed, and then a strong hand clamped on her shoulder, hauling her up and twisting her to face him.

She glimpsed black boots. Dark, scalelike armor over a tall, muscled body.

Wings. Great, black wings. A demon's wings.

But the male face that stared through the mists, grave and lethal . . . it was beautiful, despite the fact that his hazel eyes held no mercy. He spoke again, in a soft voice that promised pain.

Bryce couldn't stop her chest from heaving wildly. "Aidas. I need to see Aidas. Can you take me to him?" Her voice broke.

The winged male swept his gaze over her—assessing and wary. Noted that the blood covering her was not her own. His attention drifted to the Starsword lying in the grass between them. His eyes widened slightly.

Bryce lunged a step toward him, making to grab the front of

his intricate armor. He easily sidestepped the move, face impassive as she asked, "Can you take me to Prince Aidas?" She couldn't stop her tears then. The male's brows knitted.

"Please," Bryce begged. "Please."

The male's face didn't soften as he picked up the sheathed Starsword, then gestured for her to step closer.

Bryce obeyed, shaking, wondering if she should be fighting, screaming.

With scarred hands, the demon pulled a scrap of black cloth from a hidden pocket in his armor. Held it up to his face, feigning putting it on. A blindfold.

Bryce breathed in, trying to calm herself as she nodded. The male's hands were gentle but thorough as he fitted it tightly over her eyes.

Then hands were at her knees and back, and the ground was gone—they were flying.

Only the flap of his leathery wings and the sighing mist filled her ears. So different from the rippling hush of Hunt's feathers in the wind.

Bryce tried to use the time in the air to stop shaking, but she couldn't. Couldn't even form a solid thought.

They glided downward, her stomach tipping with the movement, and then they landed, the thump of the demon's boots hitting the ground echoing through her. He set her down, taking her by the hand. A door creaked open. Warm air greeted her, then the door shut. He said something she didn't understand, and then she was toppling forward—

He caught her, and sighed. She could have sworn he sounded . . . exasperated. He gave no warning as he hauled her over a shoulder and tromped down a set of stairs before entering somewhere . . . nice-smelling. Roses? Bread?

They ate bread in Hel? Had flowers? *A dark, cold world,* the Asteri had said in their notes on the planet.

Floorboards groaned beneath his boots, and then Bryce found herself again on solid ground, carpets cushioning her feet. He led her by the hand and pushed her downward. Bryce tensed, fighting it, but he did it again, and she sat. In a comfy chair.

He spoke in that silken voice, and she shook her head. "I don't understand you," she said rawly. "I don't know Hel's languages. But . . . Aidas? Prince Aidas?"

He didn't reply.

"Please," she repeated. "I need to find Prince Aidas. My world, Midgard—it's in grave danger, and my mate . . ." Her voice broke, and she doubled over in the darkness. *I will find you again*, Hunt had promised.

But he wouldn't. He couldn't. He had no way to get here. And she had no way to get home.

Unless Aidas or Apollion knew how to use the Horn. Had magic that could charge it.

She'd left Hunt and Ruhn. Had run and left them, and . . . Bryce sobbed. "Oh gods," she wept. She tore off the blindfold, baring her teeth. *"Aidas!"* she shouted at the cold-faced male. "Get fucking *AIDAS*."

He didn't so much as blink. Didn't reveal one hint of emotion, that he cared.

But—this room. This . . . house?

Dark oak wood floors and furniture. Rich, velvet fabrics. A crackling fire. Books on the shelves lining one wall. A cart of liquor in crystal decanters beside the black marble fireplace. And through the archway beyond the winged male, a foyer and a dining room.

Its style could have fit in with her father's study. With Jesiba's gallery.

The male watched cautiously. She swallowed down her tears, straightening her shoulders. Cleared her throat. "Where am I? What level of Hel?"

"Hel?" he said at last.

"Hel, yes, Hel!" She gestured to the house. The complete opposite of what she'd expected. "What level? Pit? Chasm?"

He shook his head, brow furrowing. The front door in the foyer opened, and multiple people rushed in, males and females, all speaking that strange language.

Bryce beheld the first one and shot to her feet.

The petite, dark-haired female with angular eyes like Fury's drew up short. Her red-painted mouth dropped open, no doubt at the blood all over Bryce's face and body.

This female was . . . Fae. Clad in beautiful, yet thoroughly old-fashioned clothes. Like the stuff they wore on Avallen.

Another winged male, broader than the other, swaggered in, a pretty female with brown-gold hair at his side. Also Fae. Also wearing clothes that seemed out of some sort of fantasy film.

Bryce blurted, "I've been trying to ask him, but he doesn't understand. Is this Hel? I need to see Prince Aidas."

The dark-haired one turned to the others and said something that had them all angling their heads at Bryce. The swaggering male sniffed, trying to read the scent of the blood on her.

Bryce swallowed hard. She knew only one other language, and that one . . .

Her heart thundered. Bryce said in the ancient language of the Fae, of the Starborn, "Is this world Hel? I need to see Prince Aidas."

The petite, dark-haired female staggered back, a hand to her mouth. The others gaped. As if the small female's shock was a rare occurrence. The female eyed the Starsword then. Looked to the first winged male—Bryce's captor. Nodded to the dark-hilted knife at his side.

The male drew it, and Bryce flinched.

Flinched, but—"What the fuck?" The knife could have been the twin of the Starsword: black hilted and bladed.

It *was* its twin. The Starsword began to hum within its sheath, glittering white light leaking from where leather met the dark hilt. The dagger—

The male dropped the dagger to the plush carpet. All of them retreated as it flared with dark light, as if in answer. Alpha and Omega.

"Gwydion," the dark-haired female whispered, indicating the Starsword.

The broader male sucked in a breath. Then said something in

that language she couldn't comprehend. The brunette at his side snapped something back that sounded like a reprimand.

"Is this Hel?" Bryce asked again in the old tongue of the Fae.

The dark-haired female observed Bryce from head to toe: the clothes so thoroughly at odds with their own attire, the blood and cuts. Then she replied in the old tongue, "No one has spoken that language in this world for fifteen thousand years."

Bryce rubbed at her face. Had she traveled in time, somehow? Or did Hel occupy a different time and—

"Please," she said. "I need to find Prince Aidas."

"I do not know who that is."

"Apollion, then. Surely you know the Prince of the Pit."

"I do not know of such people. This world is not Hel."

Bryce slowly shook her head. "I . . . Then where am I?" She surveyed the silent others, the winged males and the other Fae female, who stared coolly. "*What world is this?*"

The front door opened again. First, a lovely female with the same brown-gold hair as the one already standing before Bryce entered. She wore a loose white shirt over brown pants, both splattered with paint. Her hands were tattooed to the elbows in intricate swirls. But her blue-gray eyes were wary—soft and curious, but wary.

The winged, dark-haired male who stepped in behind her . . .

Bryce gasped. "Ruhn?"

The male blinked. His eyes were the same shade of violet blue as Ruhn's. His short hair the same gleaming black. This male's skin was browner, but the face, the posture . . . It was her brother's. His ears were pointed, too, though he also possessed those leathery wings like the two other males.

The female beside him asked the petite female a question in their language.

But the male continued to stare at Bryce. At the blood on her, at the Starsword and the knife, the blades still gleaming with their opposite lights.

He lifted his gaze to her, stars in his eyes. Actual stars.

Bryce pleaded with the petite female, "My world . . . Midgard . . .

It's in grave danger. My mate, he . . ." She couldn't get the words out. "I didn't mean to come here. I meant to go to Hel. To get aid from the princes. But I don't know what this world is. Or how to find Hel. I need your help."

It was all there was left to do: throw herself at their mercy and pray they were decent people. That even if she'd come from another world, they'd recognize her as Fae and be compassionate.

The petite female seemed to repeat Bryce's words to the others. The female with the tattooed hands asked Bryce a question in their language. The petite one translated: "She wants to know what your name is."

Bryce glanced from the tattooed female to the beautiful male at her side. They both possessed an air of quiet, gentle authority. The others all seemed to wait for their cues. So Bryce addressed the two of them as she lifted her chin. "My name is Bryce Quinlan."

The male stepped forward, tucking in his wings. He smiled slightly and said in the Old Language, in a voice like glorious night, "Hello, Bryce Quinlan. My name is Rhysand."

EPILOGUE

Ithan Holstrom crouched, a hulking wolf among the rain-lashed shadows outside the Astronomer's building, monitoring the few people in the alley braving the storm.

No word had come from Pangera. Just a mention of an explosion at a lab outside the city, and that was it. He didn't expect to hear anything from Bryce and the others at least until the next day.

But he couldn't help the urge to pace, even as he guarded the doors across the alley. He'd seen no glimpse of the Astronomer. No patrons had entered. Had Mordoc dragged the wretch off for an interrogation about why Ithan and his friends had visited him? And left the mystics here—unguarded and alone?

He'd fucked up guard duty with Hypaxia. He wouldn't make that mistake again. Not with the mystic caged beyond those doors.

Another Fendyr heir to the Prime. An Alpha to challenge Sabine.

Something moved in the shadows far down the alley, beyond the neon glow of the signs above the tattoo parlors and bars. Swift and hulking and— He sniffed the air. Even with the rain, he knew that scent. Knew the golden eyes that glowed in the rainy darkness.

Ithan's growl rumbled over the slick cobblestones, his wet fur bristling.

Amelie Ravenscroft, his former Alpha, only snarled back, sending whatever patrons were on the streets scattering into the buildings, and melted into the dimness.

Ithan waited until her scent had faded before letting out a breath. He'd been right to come here, then. If he hadn't been here . . . He glanced to the doors again.

He couldn't stay here indefinitely. He'd need others to keep watch while he rested.

His phone rang from where he'd left it on the stoop of an alley doorway, and Ithan shifted into his humanoid body before answering. "Flynn. I was about to call you." To beg for a massive favor. If Sabine came here, or Amelie returned, packs in tow . . .

The Fae lord didn't reply immediately. Ithan could have sworn he heard the male swallow.

He stilled. "What is it?" Flynn's breathing turned harsh. Jagged. "Flynn."

"Shit went down." The Fae lord seemed to be struggling for words. And to hold back tears.

"Is . . ." He couldn't face this. Not again. Not—

"Ruhn and Athalar have been taken prisoner by the Asteri. Dec saw it on the palace feeds. Tharion called from the *Depth Charger* pod to say Cormac's dead."

Ithan began shaking his head, even as he contemplated the risk of discussing this on the phone. Breathing was somehow impossible as he whispered, "Bryce?"

A long, long pause.

Ithan slid to the soaking ground.

"She disappeared. You . . . you gotta come hear it from Dec."

"Is she alive?" Ithan's snarl tore through the rain, bouncing off the bricks.

"The last we saw her in this world . . . she was."

"What do you mean, *in this world*?" But he had a terrible feeling that he already knew.

"You have to see it for yourself," Flynn croaked.

"I can't," Ithan bit out. "I've got something to do."

"We need you," Flynn said, and his voice was full of an authority that people outside the Aux rarely heard. "We're friends now, wolf. Get your furry ass over here."

Ithan peered toward the towering doors. Felt himself being pulled apart by Urd herself.

"I'll be there in fifteen," Ithan said, and hung up. Slid his phone into his pocket. Stalked across the street.

A blow from his fist dented the metal doors. The second one broke the locks. The third sent them crumpling inward.

No sign of the Astronomer. Too bad. He was in the mood for blood tonight.

But Ithan stormed to the nearest tub. The wolf mystic floated in the murky, salt-laden water, hair spread around her, eyes closed. Breathing mask and tubes back in place.

"Wake up." His words were a low growl. "We're going."

The mystic didn't respond, lost to wherever her mind took her.

"I know you can hear me. I need to go somewhere, and I'm not leaving you behind. People are lurking out there who want you dead. So you can either get the fuck up right now or I can do it for you."

Again, no response. His fingers flexed, claws sliding free, but he kept his hand at his side. It was only a matter of time until someone came to investigate why the doors had been ripped open, but to tear her from that dream state . . . she'd been so tormented the last time.

"Please," he said softly, head bowing. "My friends need me. My . . . my pack needs me."

That's what they'd become.

He'd lost his brother, his brother's pack—the pack that would have one day been his—but this one . . .

He wouldn't lose it. Would fight until the bitter end to protect it.

"Please," Ithan whispered, voice breaking. Her hand twitched, the water rippling. Ithan's breath caught in his throat.

Her brow furrowed. The feeds on her tank began blaring and beeping, flashing red. The hair on Ithan's arms rose.

And then, lids fluttering, like the Alpha fought for every inch toward awakening, the lost Fendyr heir opened her eyes.

ACKNOWLEDGMENTS

To Robin Rue: How can I even convey my gratitude for all that you do as both an agent and a friend? (Dedicating this book to you is a feeble attempt at doing so!) Thank you from the bottom of my heart for your wisdom and encouragement, and for being there at the drop of a hat. And thank you, as always, for being a kindred spirit in all things fine food and wine!

To Noa Wheeler: I thank the universe every single day that our paths crossed. From your brilliant feedback to your unparalleled attention to detail, you are the most incredible editor I've ever worked with. (And the only person out there who truly understands my *NYT* crossword and Spelling Bee obsessions.) Here's to many more books together!

To Erica Barmash: Working with you again is such a pleasure! Thank you for all the years spent championing my books and being such a great friend!

To Beth Miller, an all-around gem of a human being, and a fellow marine biology fangirl: Thank you for all your hard work and for being a constant ray of sunshine! (And for the amazing marine wildlife photos!)

To the global Bloomsbury team: Nigel Newton, Kathleen Farrar, Adrienne Vaughn, Ian Hudson, Rebecca McNally, Valentina

Rice, Nicola Hill, Amanda Shipp, Marie Coolman, Lauren Ollerhead, Angela Craft, Lucy Mackay-Sim, Emilie Chambeyron, Donna Mark, David Mann, Michal Kuzmierkiewicz, Emma Ewbank, John Candell, Donna Gauthier, Laura Phillips, Melissa Kavonic, Oona Patrick, Nick Sweeney, Claire Henry, Nicholas Church, Fabia Ma, Daniel O'Connor, Brigid Nelson, Sarah McLean, Sarah Knight, Liz Bray, Genevieve Nelsson, Adam Kirkman, Jennifer Gonzalez, Laura Pennock, Elizabeth Tzetzo, Valerie Esposito, Meenakshi Singh, and Chris Venkatesh. I can't imagine working with a better group of people. Thank you for all your dedication and tremendous work! And tons of gratitude and love to Grace McNamee for jumping on board so quickly to help with this book! An especially big thank-you to Kaitlin Severini, copyeditor extraordinaire, and to Christine Ma, eagle-eyed proofer!

Cecilia de la Campa: You are one of the hardest-working and loveliest people I know. Thank you for all that you do! To the entire Writers House team: You guys are incredible, and I'm honored to work with you.

Thank you to the fierce and lovely Jill Gillett (and Noah Morse!), for making so many of my dreams come true and being an absolute delight to work with! To Maura Wogan and Victoria Cook: I'm so grateful to have you in my corner.

To Ron Moore and Maril Davis: working with you two rock stars has been the highlight of my *life*. And thank you so much to Ben McGinnis and Nick Hornung—you guys are amazing!

To my sister Jenn Kelly: What would I do without you? You bring such joy and light into my life. I love you.

I could write another thousand pages about the marvelous and talented women who keep me going, and who I am honored to call friends: Steph Brown, Katie Webber, Lynette Noni, and Jillian Stein. I adore you all!

Thank you, as always, to my family and in-laws for the unwavering love.

To Annie, faithful friend and writing companion: I love you forever, babypup.

To Josh and Taran: Thank you for always making me smile and laugh. I love you both more than there are stars in the sky.

And thank *you*, dear reader, for reading and supporting my books. None of this would be possible without you.

DISCOVER MORE OF THE WORLD OF SARAH J. MAAS!

CRESCENT CITY

THRONE OF GLASS

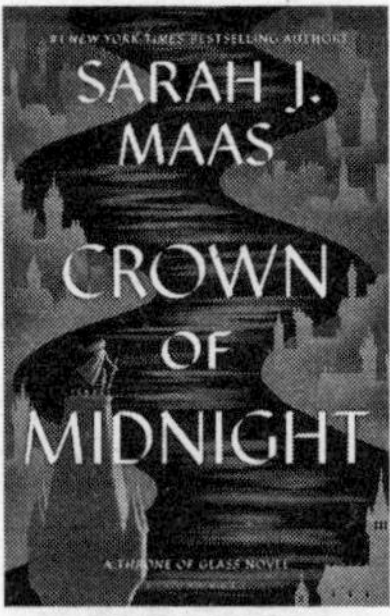

A COURT OF THORNS AND ROSES

CRESCENT CITY

HOUSE of FLAME and SHADOW

Books by Sarah J. Maas

The Throne of Glass series

The Assassin's Blade
Throne of Glass
Crown of Midnight
Heir of Fire
Queen of Shadows
Empire of Storms
Tower of Dawn
Kingdom of Ash
•
The Throne of Glass Coloring Book

The Court of Thorns and Roses series

A Court of Thorns and Roses
A Court of Mist and Fury
A Court of Wings and Ruin
A Court of Frost and Starlight
A Court of Silver Flames
•
A Court of Thorns and Roses Coloring Book

The Crescent City series

House of Earth and Blood
House of Sky and Breath
House of Flame and Shadow

CRESCENT CITY

HOUSE of FLAME and SHADOW

SARAH J. MAAS

BLOOMSBURY PUBLISHING
NEW YORK • LONDON • OXFORD • NEW DELHI • SYDNEY

BLOOMSBURY PUBLISHING
Bloomsbury Publishing Inc.
1385 Broadway, New York, NY 10018, USA
29 Earlsfort Terrace, Dublin 2, Ireland

BLOOMSBURY, BLOOMSBURY PUBLISHING, and the Diana logo are trademarks of Bloomsbury Publishing Plc

First published in the United States 2024

Map by Virginia Allyn
Endpapers and interior art by Carlos Quevedo

ISBN: HB: 978-1-63557-410-4; eBook: 978-1-68119-309-0
Special editions: 978-1-63973-286-9; 978-1-63973-294-4; 978-1-63973-296-8; 978-1-63973-297-5; 978-1-63973-295-1; 978-1-63973-298-2; 978-1-63973-293-7; 978-1-63973-382-8; 978-1-63973-368-2

Library of Congress Cataloging-in-Publication Data is available

2 4 6 8 10 9 7 5 3

Typeset by Westchester Publishing Services
Printed and bound in Great Britain by CPI (UK) Ltd, Croydon CR0 4YY

For Sloane,
who lights up entire universes with her smile

LUNATHION
CRESCENT CITY
THE ANGELS' GATE
CENTRAL BUSINESS DISTRICT
THE MEAT MARKET
THE MERCHANTS' GATE
WESTERN ROAD
ISTROS RIVER

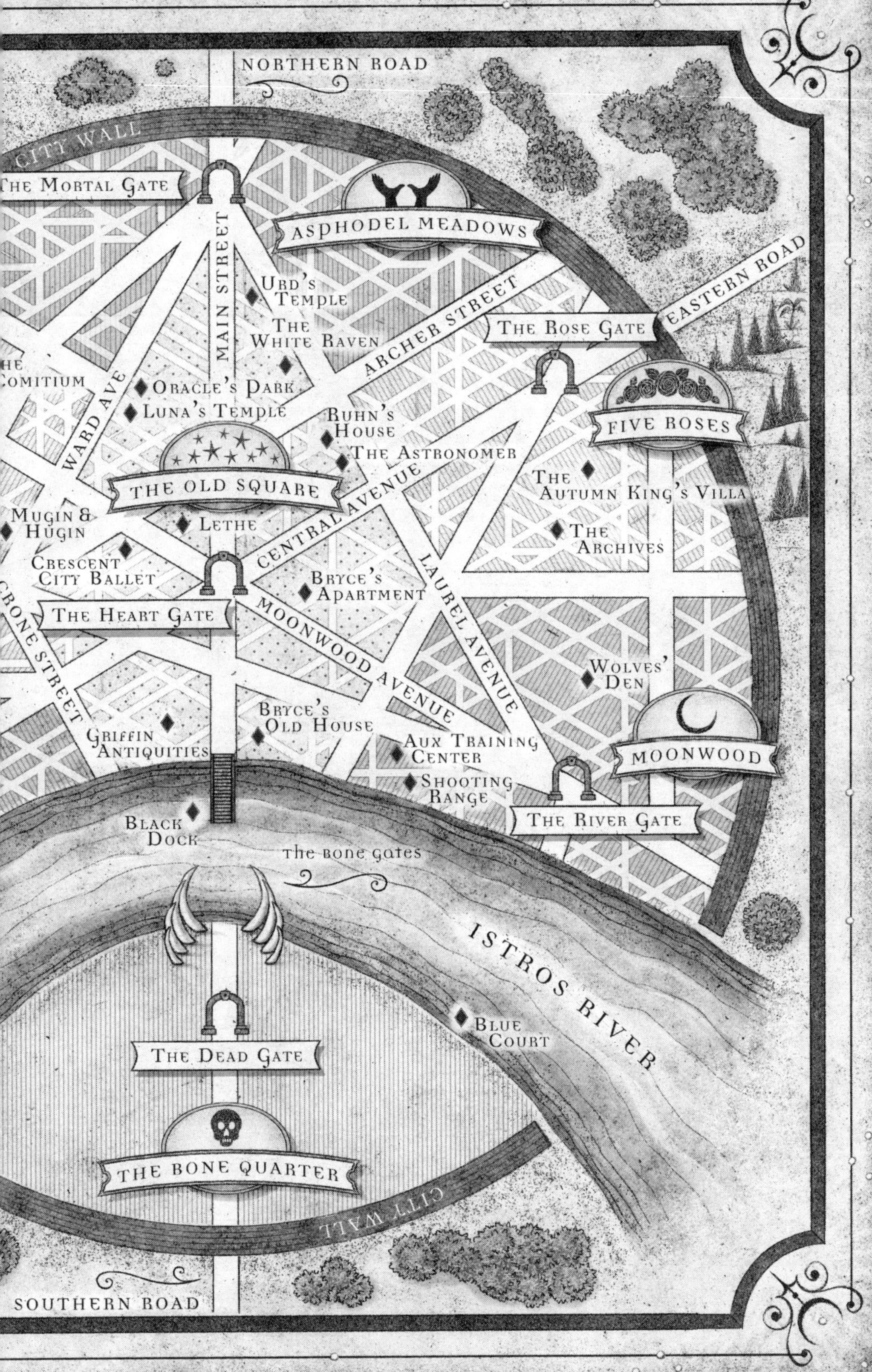

Northern Road
City Wall
The Mortal Gate
Asphodel Meadows
Main Street
Urd's Temple
The White Raven
Archer Street
Eastern Road
The Rose Gate
The Comitium
Ward Ave
Oracle's Park
Luna's Temple
Five Roses
Ruhn's House
The Astronomer
The Old Square
Central Avenue
The Autumn King's Villa
Mugin & Hugin
Lethe
The Archives
Crescent City Ballet
Bryce's Apartment
Laurel Avenue
The Heart Gate
Moonwood Avenue
Crone Street
Wolves' Den
Bryce's Old House
Griffin Antiquities
Aux Training Center
Moonwood
Shooting Range
The River Gate
Black Dock
The Bone Gates
Istros River
Blue Court
The Dead Gate
The Bone Quarter
City Wall
Southern Road

THE FOUR HOUSES OF MIDGARD

As decreed in 33 V.E. by the Imperial Senate in the Eternal City

HOUSE OF EARTH AND BLOOD

Shifters, humans, witches, ordinary animals, and many others to whom Cthona calls, as well as some chosen by Luna

HOUSE OF SKY AND BREATH

Malakim (angels), Fae, elementals, sprites,* and those who are blessed by Solas, along with some favored by Luna

HOUSE OF MANY WATERS

River-spirits, mer, water beasts, nymphs, kelpies, nøkks, and others watched over by Ogenas

HOUSE OF FLAME AND SHADOW

Daemonaki, Reapers, wraiths, vampyrs, draki, dragons, necromancers, and many wicked and unnamed things that even Urd herself cannot see

**Sprites were kicked out of their House as a result of their participation in the Fall, and are now considered Lowers, though many of them refuse to accept this.*

PROLOGUE

The Hind knelt before her undying masters and contemplated how it would feel to tear out their throats.

Around her own throat, a silver torque lay cool and heavy. It never warmed against her skin. As if the taken lives it symbolized wanted her to endure death's icy grip as well.

A silver dart on a dreadwolf uniform: the trophy for a rebel wiped off the face of Midgard. Lidia had acquired so many that her imperial grays couldn't hold them all. So many that they'd been melted down into that torque.

Did anyone in this chamber see the necklace for what it truly was?

A collar. With a golden leash leading right to the monsters before her.

And did those monsters ever suspect that their faithful pet sat at their feet and pondered the taste and texture of their blood on her tongue? On her teeth?

But here she would kneel, until given leave to rise. As this world would kneel until the six enthroned Asteri drained it dry and left its carcass to rot in the emptiness of space.

The staff of the Eternal Palace had cleaned the blood from the shining crystal floor beneath her knees. No coppery tang lingered in the sterile air, no errant drops marred the columns flanking the chamber. As if the events of two days ago had never occurred.

But Lidia Cervos could not let herself dwell on those events. Not while surrounded by her enemies. Not with Pollux kneeling beside her, one of his shining wings resting atop her calf. From another, it might have been a gesture of comfort, of solidarity.

From Pollux, from the Hammer, it meant nothing but possession.

Lidia willed her eyes dead and cold. Willed her heart to be the same, and focused on the two Fae Kings pleading their cases.

"My late son acted of his own accord," declared Morven, King of the Avallen Fae, his bone-white face grave. The tall, dark-haired male wore all black, but no heavy air of mourning lay upon him. "Had I known of Cormac's treason, I would have handed him over myself."

Lidia flicked her gaze to the panel of parasites seated on their crystal thrones.

Rigelus, veiled as usual in the body of a Fae teenage boy, propped his delicate chin on a fist. "I find it difficult to believe that you had no knowledge of your son's activities, considering how tightly you held his reins."

Shadows whispered over Morven's broad shoulders, trailing off his scaled armor. "He was a defiant boy. I thought I'd beaten it out of him long ago."

"You thought wrong," sneered Hesperus, the Evening Star, who'd taken on the shape of a blond nymph. Her long, slim fingers tapped the glimmering arm of her throne. "We can only assume that his treachery stemmed from some decay within your royal house. One that must now be scourged."

For the first time in the decades the Hind had known him, King Morven held his tongue. He'd had no choice but to answer the Asteri's summons yesterday, but he clearly did not appreciate the reminder that his autonomy was a mere illusion, even on the misty isle of Avallen.

Some small part of her relished it—seeing the male who'd strutted through Summits and meetings and balls now weighing his every word. Knowing it might be his last.

Morven growled, "I had no knowledge of my son's activities or of his craven heart. I swear it upon Luna's golden bow." His voice rang clear as he added with impressive fury, "I condemn all that Cormac was and stood for. He shall not be honored with a grave nor a burial. There will be no ship to sail his body into the Summerlands. I will ensure that his name is wiped from all records of my house."

For a heartbeat, Lidia allowed herself a shred of pity for the Ophion agent she'd known. For the Fae Prince of Avallen who'd given everything to destroy the beings before her.

As she had given everything. Would still give everything.

Polaris, the North Star—wearing the body of a white-winged, dark-skinned female angel—drawled, "There will be no ship to sail Cormac's body to the Summerlands because the boy immolated himself. And tried to take us with him." Polaris let out a soft, hateful laugh that raked talons down Lidia's skin. "As if a paltry flame might do such a thing."

Morven said nothing. He'd offered what he could, short of getting on his knees to plead. It might very well come to that, but for now, the Fae King of Avallen held his head high.

Legend claimed that even the Asteri could not pierce the mists that shrouded Avallen, but Lidia had never heard of it being tested. Perhaps that was also why Morven had come—to keep the Asteri from having a reason to explore whether the legend was true.

If they were somehow repelled by whatever ancient power lay around Avallen, that would be a secret worth abasing oneself to keep.

Rigelus crossed an ankle over his knee. Lidia had seen the Bright Hand order entire families executed with the same casual air. "And you, Einar? What have you to say for your son?"

"Traitorous shit," spat Pollux from where he knelt beside Lidia. His wing still rested on her leg like he owned it. Owned her.

The Autumn King ignored the Hammer. Ignored everyone except Rigelus as he flatly replied, "Ruhn has been wild since birth. I did what I could to contain him. I have little doubt that he was lured into this business through his sister's machinations."

Lidia kept her fingers loose, even as they ached to curl into fists. Steadied her heart into a sluggish, ordinary beat that no Vanir ears would detect as unusual.

"So you would seek to spare one child by damning the other?" Rigelus asked, lips curling into a mild smile. "What sort of father are you, Einar?"

"Neither Bryce Quinlan nor Ruhn Danaan has the right to call themselves my children any longer."

Rigelus angled his head, his short, dark hair shimmering in the glow of the crystal room. "I thought she had claimed the name Bryce Danaan. Have you revoked her royal status?"

A muscle ticked in the Autumn King's cheek. "I have yet to decide a fitting punishment for her."

Pollux's wings rustled, but the angel kept his head down as he snarled to the Autumn King, "When I get my hands on your cunt of a daughter, you'll be glad to have disavowed her. What she did to the Harpy, I shall do to her tenfold."

"You'd have to find her first," the Autumn King said coolly. Lidia supposed Einar Danaan was one of the few Fae on Midgard who could openly taunt an angel as powerful as the Malleus. The Fae King's amber eyes, so like his daughter's, lifted to the Asteri. "Have your mystics discovered her whereabouts yet?"

"Do you not wish to know where your son is?" asked Octartis, the Southern Star, with a coy smile.

"I know where Ruhn is," the Autumn King countered, unmoved. "He deserves to be there." He half turned toward where Lidia knelt, and surveyed her coldly. "I hope you wring every last answer from him."

Lidia held his stare, her face like stone, like ice—like death.

The Autumn King's gaze flicked over the silver torque at her throat, a faint, approving curve gracing his mouth. But he asked Rigelus, with an authority that she could only admire, "Where is Bryce?"

Rigelus sighed, bored and annoyed—a lethal combination. "She has chosen to vacate Midgard."

"A mistake we shall soon rectify," Polaris added.

Rigelus shot the lesser Asteri a warning look.

The Autumn King said, his voice a shade faint, "Bryce is no longer in this world?"

Morven glanced warily at the other Fae King. As far as anyone knew, there was only one place that could be accessed from Midgard—there was an entire wall circling the Northern Rift in Nena to prevent its denizens from crossing into this world. If Bryce was no longer on Midgard, she had to be in Hel.

It had never occurred to Lidia that the wall around the Rift would also keep Midgardians from getting *out*.

Well, most Midgardians.

Rigelus said tightly, "That knowledge is not to be shared with anyone." The edge sharpening his words implied the rest: *under pain of death.*

Lidia had been present when the other Asteri had demanded to know how it had happened: how Bryce Quinlan had opened a gate to another world in their own palace and slipped through the Bright Hand's fingers. Their disbelief and rage had been a small comfort in the wake of all that had happened, all that was still churning through Lidia.

A silvery bell rang from behind the Asteri's thrones in a polite reminder that another meeting had been scheduled shortly.

"This discussion is not yet finished," Rigelus warned the two Fae Kings. He pointed with a skinny finger to the double doors open to the hall beyond. "Speak of what you have heard today, and you will find that there is no place on this planet where you will be safe from our wrath."

The Fae Kings bowed and left without another word.

The weight of the Asteri's gazes landed upon Lidia, singeing her very soul. She withstood it, as she had withstood all the other horrors in her life.

"Rise, Lidia," Rigelus said with something that bordered on affection. Then, to Pollux, "Rise, my Hammer." Lidia shoved down the bile that burned like acid and got to her feet, Pollux with her. His white wing brushed against her cheek, the softness of his feathers at odds with the rot of his soul.

The bell tinkled again, but Rigelus lifted a hand to the attendant waiting in the shadows of the nearby pillars. The next meeting could wait another moment.

"How go the interrogations?" Rigelus slouched on his throne as if he had asked about the weather.

"We are in the opening movements," Lidia said, her mouth somehow distant from her body. "Athalar and Danaan will require time to break."

"And the Helhound?" asked Hesperus, the nymph's dark eyes gleaming with malice.

"I am still assessing him." Lidia kept her chin high and tucked her hands behind her back. "But trust that I shall get what we need from all of them, Your Graces."

"As you always do," Rigelus said, gaze dipping to her silver collar. "We give you leave to do your finest work, Hind."

Lidia bowed at the waist with imperial precision. Pollux did the same, wings folding elegantly. The portrait of a perfect soldier—the one he'd been bred to become.

It wasn't until they'd entered the long corridor beyond the throne room that the Hammer spoke. "Do you think that little bitch really went to Hel?" Pollux jerked his head behind them, toward the dull, silent crystal Gate at the opposite end of the hall.

The busts lining the walkway—all the Asteri in their various forms throughout the centuries—had been replaced. The windows that had been shattered by Athalar's lightning had been repaired.

As in the throne room, not one hint of what had occurred remained here. And beyond the crystal walls of this palace, no whisper had surfaced in the news.

The only proof: the two Asterian Guards now flanking either side of the Gate. Their white-and-gold regalia shone in the streaming sunlight, the tips of the spears gripped in their gloved hands like fallen stars. With their golden helmets' visors down, she could make out nothing of the faces beneath. It didn't matter, she supposed. There was no individuality, no life in them. The elite, highborn angels had been bred for obedience and service. Just as they'd been bred to bear those glowing white wings. As the angel beside her had.

Lidia maintained her unhurried pace toward the elevators. "I won't waste time trying to find out. But Bryce Quinlan will no doubt return one day, regardless of where she wound up."

Beyond the windows, the seven hills of the Eternal City rippled under the sunlight, most of them crusted with buildings crowned by terra-cotta roofs. A barren mountain—more of a hill, really—lay among several nearly identical peaks just north of the city border, the metallic gleam atop it like a beacon.

Was it an intentional taunt to Athalar that the mountain, Mount Hermon—where he and the Archangel Shahar had staged the doomed first and final battle of their rebellion—today housed scores of the Asteri's new hybrid mech-suits? Down in the dungeons, Athalar would have no way of seeing them, but knowing Rigelus, the positioning of the new machines was definitely symbolic.

Lidia had read the report yesterday morning about what the Asteri had cooked up these last few weeks, despite Ophion's attempts to stop it. Despite *her* attempts to stop it. But the written details had been nothing compared to the suits' appearance at sunset. The city had been abuzz as the military transports had crested the hill and deposited them, one by one, with news crews rushing out to report on the cutting-edge tech.

Her stomach had churned to see the suits—and did so again now as she gazed at their steel husks glinting in the sun.

Further proof of Ophion's failure. They'd destroyed the mech-suit on Ydra, obliterated the lab days ago—yet it had all been too late. In secret, Rigelus had crafted this metal army and stationed it atop Mount Hermon's barren peak. An improvement on the hybrids, these did not even require pilots to operate them, though they still had the capacity to hold a single Vanir soldier, if need be. As if the hybrids had been a well-calculated distraction for Ophion while Rigelus had secretly perfected *these*. Magic and tech now blended with lethal efficiency, with minimal cost to military life. But those suits spelled death for any remaining rebels, and damned the rest of the rebellion.

She should have caught Rigelus's sleight of hand—but she hadn't. And now that horror would be unleashed on the world.

The elevator opened, and Lidia and Pollux entered in silence. Lidia hit the button for the lowest sublevel—well, second lowest. The elevators did not descend to the catacombs, which could only be accessed by a winding crystal staircase. There, one thousand mystics slumbered.

Each of whom were now focused on a single task: *Find Bryce Quinlan.*

It begged the question: If everyone knew that the Northern Rift and other Gates only opened to Hel, why did the Asteri bother to expend such resources in hunting for her? Bryce had landed in Hel—surely there was no need to order the mystics to find her.

Unless Bryce Quinlan had wound up somewhere *other* than Hel. A different world, perhaps. And if that was the case . . .

How long would it take? How many worlds existed beyond Midgard? And what were the odds of Bryce surviving on any of them—or ever getting back to Midgard?

The elevators opened into the dank dimness of the dungeons. Pollux prowled down the stone walkway, wings tightly furled. Like he didn't want one speck of dirt from this place marring their pristine white feathers. "Is that why you're keeping them alive? As bait for that bitch?"

"Yes." Lidia followed the screams past the guttering firstlight sconces along the wall. "Quinlan and Athalar are mates. She will return to this world because of that bond. And when she does, she will go straight to him."

"And the brother?"

"Ruhn and Bryce are Starborn," Lidia said, heaving open the iron door to the large interrogation chamber beyond. Metal grated against stone, its shriek eerily similar to the sounds of torment all around them. "She will want to free him—as her brother and her ally."

She stalked down the exposed steps into the heart of the chamber, where three males hung from gorsian shackles in the center of the room. Blood pooled beneath them, dribbling into the grate below their bare feet.

She shut down every part of her that felt, that breathed.

Athalar and Baxian dangled unconscious from the ceiling, their torsos patchworks of scars and burns. And their backs . . .

A constant drip sounded in the otherwise silent chamber, like a leaking faucet. The blood still oozed from the stumps where their wings had been. The gorsian shackles had slowed their healing to near-human levels—keeping them from dying entirely, but ensuring that they suffered through every moment of pain.

Lidia couldn't look at the third figure hanging between them. Couldn't get a breath down near him.

Leather whispered over stone, and Lidia dove deep within herself as Pollux's whip cracked. It snapped against Athalar's raw, bloody back, and the Umbra Mortis jolted, swaying on his chains.

"Wake up," the Hammer sneered. "It's a beautiful day."

Athalar's swollen eyes cracked open. Hate blazed in their dark depths.

The halo inked anew upon his brow seemed darker than the shadows of the dungeon. His battered mouth parted in a feral smile, revealing bloodstained teeth. "Morning, sunshine."

A soft, broken rasp of a laugh sounded to Athalar's right. And though she knew it was folly, Lidia looked.

Ruhn Danaan, Crown Prince of the Valbaran Fae, was staring at her.

His lip was swollen from where Pollux had torn out his piercing. His eyebrow was crusted with blood from where that hoop had been ripped out, too. Across his tattooed torso, along the arms above his head, blood and dirt and bruises mingled.

The prince's striking blue eyes were sharp with loathing.

For her.

Pollux slashed his whip into Athalar's back again, not bothering with questions. No, this was the warm-up. Interrogation would come later.

Baxian still hung unconscious. Pollux had beaten him into a bloody pulp last night after severing his and Athalar's wings with a blunt-toothed saw. The Helhound didn't so much as stir.

Night, Lidia tried, casting her voice into the moldy air between herself and the Fae Prince. They'd never spoken mind-to-mind outside of their dreaming, but she'd been trying since he'd arrived here. Again and again, she'd cast her mind toward his. Only silence answered.

Just as it had from the moment Ruhn had learned who she was. What she was.

She knew he could communicate, even with the gorsian stones halting his magic and slowing his healing. Knew he'd done so with his sister before Bryce had escaped.

Night.

Ruhn's lip pulled back in a silent snarl, blood snaking down his chin.

Pollux's phone rang, a shrill, strange sound in this ancient shrine to pain. His ministrations halted, a terrible silence in their wake. "Mordoc," the Hammer said, whip still in one hand. He pivoted from Athalar's swinging, brutalized body. "Report."

Lidia didn't bother to protest the fact that her captain was reporting to the Hammer. Pollux had taken the Harpy's death personally—he'd commandeered Mordoc and the dreadwolves to find any hint of where Bryce Quinlan might have gone.

That he still believed Bryce was responsible for the Harpy's death was only because Athalar and Ruhn hadn't revealed that it was Lidia who'd murdered the Harpy. They knew who she was, and only the fact that she was vital to the rebellion kept them from spilling her secrets.

For a moment, with Pollux turned away, Lidia let her mask drop. Let Ruhn see her true face. The one that had kissed his soul and shared her own with him, their very beings melding.

Ruhn, she pleaded into his mind. *Ruhn.*

But the Fae Prince did not answer. The hate in his eyes did not lessen. So Lidia donned her Hind's mask once again.

And as Pollux pocketed his phone and angled his whip anew, the Hind ordered the Hammer in the low, lifeless voice that had been her shield for so long now, "Get the barbed wire instead."

PART I

THE DROP

Bryce Quinlan sat in a chamber so far beneath the mountain above that daylight must have been a myth to the creatures who dwelled there.

For a place that apparently *wasn't* Hel, her surroundings sure appeared like it: black stone, subterranean palace, even-more-subterranean interrogation cell . . . The darkness seemed inherent to the three people standing across from her: a petite female in gray silk, and two winged males clad in black scalelike armor, one of them—the beautiful, powerful male in the center of the trio—literally rippling with shadows and stars.

Rhysand, he'd called himself. The one who looked so much like Ruhn.

It couldn't be coincidence. Bryce had leapt through the Gate intending to reach Hel, to finally take up Aidas's and Apollion's repeated offers to send their armies to Midgard and stop this cycle of galactic conquest. But she'd wound up here instead.

Bryce glanced to the warrior beside Ruhn's almost-twin. The male who'd found her. Who'd carried the black dagger that had reacted to the Starsword.

His hazel eyes held nothing but cold, predatory alertness.

"Someone has to start talking," the short female said—the one who'd seemed so shocked to hear Bryce speak in the Old

Language, to see the sword. Flickering braziers of something that resembled firstlight gilded the silken strands of her chin-length bob, casting the shadow of her slender jaw in stark relief. Her eyes, a remarkable shade of silver, slid over Bryce but remained unimpressed. "You said your name is Bryce Quinlan. That you come from another world—Midgard."

Rhysand murmured to the winged male beside him. Translating, perhaps.

The female went on, "If you are to be believed, how is it that you came here? *Why* did you come here?"

Bryce surveyed the otherwise empty cell. No table glittering with torture instruments, no breaks in the solid stone beyond the door and the grate in the center of the floor, a few feet away. A grate from which she could have sworn a hissing sound emanated.

"What world is this?" Bryce rasped, the words gravelly. After Ruhn's body double had introduced himself in that lovely, cozy foyer, he'd grabbed her hand. The strength of his grip, the brush of his calluses against her skin had been the only solid things as wind and darkness had roared around them, the world dropping away—and then there was only solid rock and dim lighting. She'd been brought to a palace carved beneath a mountain, and then down the narrow stairs to this dungeon. Where he'd pointed to the lone chair in the center of the room in silent command.

So she'd sat, waiting for the handcuffs or shackles or whatever restraints they used in this world, but none had come.

The short female countered, "Why do you speak the Old Language?"

Bryce jerked her chin at the female. "Why do you?"

The female's red-painted lips curved upward. It wasn't a reassuring sight. "Why are you covered in blood that is not your own?"

Score: one for the female.

Bryce knew her blood-soaked clothes, now stiff and dark, and her blood-crusted hands did her no favors. It was the Harpy's blood, and a bit of Lidia's. All coating Bryce as a part of a careful game to keep her alive, to keep their secrets safe, while Hunt and Ruhn had—

Her breath began sawing in and out. She'd left them. Her mate and her brother. She'd left them in Rigelus's hands.

The walls and ceiling pushed in, squeezing the air from her lungs.

Rhysand lifted a broad hand wreathed in stars. "We won't harm you." Bryce found the rest of the sentence lurking within the dense shadows around him: *if you don't try to harm us.*

She closed her eyes, fighting past the jagged breathing, the crushing weight of the stone above and around her.

Less than an hour ago, she'd been sprinting away from Rigelus's power, dodging exploding marble busts and shattering windows, and Hunt's lightning had speared through her chest, into the Gate, opening a portal. She'd leapt toward Hel—

And now . . . now she was here. Her hands shook. She balled them into fists and squeezed.

Bryce took a slow, shuddering breath. Another. Then opened her eyes and asked again, her voice solid and clear, "What world is this?"

Her three interrogators said nothing.

So Bryce fixed her eyes on the female, the smallest but by no means the least deadly of the group. "You said the Old Language hasn't been spoken here in fifteen thousand years. Why?"

That they were Fae and knew the language at all suggested some link between here and Midgard, a link that was slowly dawning on her with terrible clarity.

"How did you come to be in possession of the lost sword Gwydion?" was the female's cool reply.

"What . . . You mean the Starsword?" Another link between their worlds.

All of them just stared at her again. An impenetrable wall of people accustomed to getting answers in whatever way necessary.

Bryce had no weapons, nothing beyond the magic in her veins, the Archesian amulet around her neck, and the Horn tattooed into her back. But to wield it, she needed power, needed to be fueled up like some stupid fucking battery—

So talking was her best weapon. Good thing she'd spent years as a master of spinning bullshit, according to Hunt.

"It's a family heirloom," Bryce said. "It's been in my world since it was brought there by my ancestors . . . fifteen thousand years ago." She let the last few words land with a pointed glance at the female. Let her do the math, as Bryce had.

But the beautiful male—Rhysand—said in a voice like midnight, "How did you find this world?"

This was not a male to be fucked with. None of these people were, but this one . . . Authority rippled off him. As if he was the entire axis of this place. A king of some sort, then.

"I didn't." Bryce met his star-flecked stare. Some primal part of her quailed at the raw power within his gaze. "I told you: I meant to go to Hel. I landed here instead."

"How?"

The things far below the grate hissed louder, as if sensing his wrath. Demanding blood.

Bryce swallowed. If they learned about the Horn, her power, the Gates . . . what was to stop them from using her as Rigelus had wanted to? Or from viewing her as a threat to be removed?

Master of spinning bullshit. She could do this.

"There are Gates within my world that open into other worlds. For fifteen thousand years, they've mostly opened into Hel. Well, the Northern Rift opens directly into Hel, but . . ." Let them think her rambling. An idiot. The party girl most of Midgard had labeled her, that Micah had believed her to be, until she was vacuuming up his fucking ashes. "This Gate sent me here with a one-way ticket."

Did they have tickets in this world? Transportation?

She clarified into their silence, "A companion of mine gambled that he could send me to Hel using his power. But I think . . ." She sorted through all that Rigelus had told her in those last moments. That the star on her chest somehow acted as a beacon to the original world of the Starborn people.

Grasping at straws, she nodded to the warrior's dagger. "There's a prophecy in my world about my sword and a missing knife. That when they're reunited, so will the Fae of Midgard be."

Master of spinning bullshit, indeed.

"So maybe I'm here for that. Maybe the sword sensed that dagger and . . . brought me to it."

Silence. Then the silent, hazel-eyed warrior laughed quietly.

How had he understood without Rhysand translating? Unless he could simply read her body language, her tone, her scent—

The warrior spoke with a low voice that skittered down her spine. Rhysand glanced at him with raised brows, then translated for Bryce with equal menace, "You're lying."

Bryce blinked, the portrait of innocence and outrage. "About what?"

"You tell us." Darkness gathered in the shadow of Rhysand's wings. Not a good sign.

She was in another world, with strangers who were clearly powerful and wouldn't hesitate to kill her. Every word from her lips was vital to her safety and survival.

"I just watched my mate and my brother get captured by a group of intergalactic parasites," she snarled. "I have no interest in doing anything except finding a way to help them."

Rhysand looked to the warrior, who nodded, not taking his gaze off Bryce for so much as a blink.

"Well," Rhysand said to Bryce, crossing his muscled arms. "*That's* true, at least."

Yet the petite female remained unmoved. In fact, her features had tightened at Bryce's outburst. "Explain."

They were Fae. There was nothing to suggest that they were better than the pieces of shit Bryce had known for most of her life. And somehow, despite appearing to be stuck a few centuries behind her own world, they seemed even more powerful than the Midgardian Fae, which could only lead to *more* arrogance and entitlement.

She needed to get to Hel. Or at the very least back to Midgard. And if she said too much . . .

The female noted her hesitation and said, "Just look in her mind already, Rhys."

Bryce went rigid. Oh gods. He could pry into her head, see anything he wanted—

Rhysand glanced at the female. She held his stare with a ferocity that belied her small stature. If Rhysand was in charge, his underlings certainly weren't expected to be silent cronies.

Bryce eyed the lone door. No way to reach it in time, even on the off chance they'd left it unlocked. Running wouldn't save her. Would the Archesian amulet provide any protection? It hadn't prevented Ruhn's mind-speaking, but—

I do not pry where I am not willingly invited.

Bryce lurched back in the chair, nearly knocking it over at the smooth male voice in her mind. Rhysand's voice.

But she answered, thanking Luna for keeping her own voice cool and collected, *Code of mind-speaking ethics?*

She felt him pause—as if almost amused. *You've encountered this method of communication before.*

Yes. It was all she'd say about Ruhn.

May I look in your memories? To see for myself?

No. You may not.

Rhysand blinked slowly. Then he said aloud, "Then we'll have to rely on your words."

The petite female gaped at him. *"But—"*

Rhysand snapped his fingers and three chairs appeared behind them. He sank gracefully onto one, crossing an ankle over a knee. The epitome of Fae beauty and arrogance. He glanced up at his companions. "Azriel." He motioned lazily to the male. Then to the female. "Amren."

Then he motioned to Bryce and said neutrally, "Bryce . . . Quinlan."

Bryce nodded slowly.

Rhysand examined his trimmed, clean nails. "So your sword . . . it's been in your world for fifteen thousand years?"

"Brought by my ancestor." She debated the next bit, then added,

"Queen Theia. Or Prince Pelias, depending on what propaganda's being spun."

Amren stiffened slightly. Rhysand slid his eyes to her, clocking the movement.

Bryce dared to push, "You . . . know of them?"

Amren surveyed Bryce from her blood-splattered neon-pink shoes to her high ponytail. The blood smeared on Bryce's face, now stiff and sticky. "No one has spoken those names here in a very, very long time."

In fifteen thousand years, Bryce was willing to bet.

"But you have heard of them?" Bryce's heart thundered.

"They once . . . dwelled here," Amren said carefully.

It was the last scrap of confirmation Bryce needed about what this planet was. Something settled deep in her, a loose thread at last pulling taut. "So this is it, then. This is where we—the Midgard Fae—originated. My ancestors left this world and went to Midgard . . . and we forgot where we came from."

Silence again. Azriel spoke in their own language, and Rhysand translated. Perhaps Rhysand had been translating for Azriel mind-to-mind these last few minutes.

"He says we have no such stories about our people migrating to another world."

Yet Amren let out a small, choked sound.

Rhysand turned slowly, a bit incredulous. "Do we?" he asked smoothly.

Amren picked at an invisible speck on her silk blouse. "It's murky. I went in before . . ." She shook her head. "But when I came out, there were rumors. That a great number of people had vanished, as if they had never been. Some said to another world, others said they'd moved on to distant lands, still others said they'd been chosen by the Cauldron and spirited away somewhere."

"They must have gone to Midgard," Bryce said. "Led by Theia and Pelias—"

Amren held up a hand. "We can hear your myths later, girl.

What I want to know"—her eyes sharpened, and it was all Bryce could do to weather the scrutiny—"is why *you* came here, when you meant to go elsewhere."

"I'd like to know that, too," Bryce said, perhaps a bit more boldly than could be deemed wise. "Believe me, I'd like nothing more than to get out of your hair immediately."

"To go to . . . Hel," Rhysand said neutrally. "To find this Prince Aidas."

These people weren't her friends or allies. This might be the home world of the Fae, but who the fuck knew what they wanted or aspired to? Rhysand and Azriel *looked* pretty, but Urd knew the Fae of Midgard had used their beauty for millennia to get what they wanted.

Rhysand didn't need to read her mind—no, he seemed to read all that on her own face. He uncrossed his legs, bracing both feet on the stone floor. "Allow me to lay out the situation for you, Bryce Quinlan."

She made herself meet his star-flecked stare. She'd taken on the Asteri and Archangels and Fae Kings and walked away. She'd take him on, too.

The corner of Rhysand's mouth curled upward. "We will not torture it from you, nor will I pry it from your mind. If you choose not to talk, it is indeed your choice. Precisely as it will be *my* choice to keep you down here until you decide otherwise."

Bryce couldn't stop herself from coolly surveying the room, her attention lingering on the grate and the hissing that drifted up from it. "I'll be sure to recommend it to my friends as a vacation spot."

Stars winked out in Rhysand's eyes. "Can we expect any others to arrive here from your world?"

She gave the truest answer she could. "No. As far as I know, they've been looking for this place for fifteen thousand years, but I'm the only one who's ever made it back."

"Who is *they*?"

"The Asteri. I told you—intergalactic parasites."

"What does that mean?"

"They are . . ." Bryce paused. Who was to say these people

wouldn't hand her right over to Rigelus? Bow to him? Theia had come from this world and fought the Asteri, but Pelias had bought what they were selling and gleefully knelt at their immortal feet.

Her pause said enough. Amren snorted. "Don't waste your breath, Rhysand."

Rhysand angled his head, a predator studying prey. Bryce withstood it, chin high. Her mother would have been proud of her.

He snapped his fingers again, and the blood, the dirt on her, disappeared. A stickiness still coated her skin, but it was clean. She blinked down at herself, then up at him.

A cruel half smile graced his mouth. "To incentivize you."

Amren and Azriel remained stone-faced. Waiting.

She'd be stupid to believe Rhysand's *incentive* meant anything good about him. But she could play this game.

So Bryce said, "The Asteri are ancient. Like tens of thousands of years old." She winced at the memory of that room beneath their palace, the records of conquests going back millennia, complete with their own unique dating system.

Her captors didn't reply, didn't so much as blink. Fine—insane old age wasn't totally nuts to them.

"They arrived in my world fifteen thousand years ago. No one knows from where."

"What do you mean by *arrived*?" Rhysand asked.

"Honestly? I have no idea how they first got to Midgard. The history they spun was that they were . . . liberators. Enlighteners. According to them, they found Midgard little more than a backwater planet occupied by non-magical humans and animals. The Asteri chose it as the place to begin creating a perfect empire, and creatures and races from other worlds soon flocked to it through a giant rip between worlds called the Northern Rift. Which now only opens to Hel, but it used to open to . . . anywhere."

Amren pushed, "A rip. How does that happen?"

"Beats me," Bryce said. "No one's ever figured out how it's even possible—why it's at that spot in Midgard, and not others."

Rhysand asked, "What happened after these beings arrived in your world?"

Bryce sucked her teeth before saying, "In the *official* version of this story, another world, Hel, tried to invade Midgard. To destroy the fledgling empire—and everyone living in it. But the Asteri unified all these new people under one banner and pushed Hel back to its own realm. In the process, the Northern Rift was fixed with its destination permanently on Hel. After that, it remained mostly closed. A massive wall was erected around it to keep any Hel-born stragglers from getting through the cracks, and the Asteri built a glorious empire meant to last for eternity. Or so we're all ordered to believe."

The faces in front of her remained impassive. Rhysand asked quietly, "And what is the unofficial story?"

Bryce swallowed, the room in the archives flashing through her memory. "The Asteri are ancient, immortal beings who feed on the power of others—they harvest the magic of a people, a world, and then eat it. We call it firstlight. It fuels our entire world, but mostly them. We're required to hand it over upon reaching immortality—well, as close to immortality as we can get. We seize our full, mature power through a ritual called the Drop, and in the process, some of our power is siphoned off and given over to the firstlight stores for the Asteri. It's like a tax on our magic."

She wasn't even going to touch upon what happened after death. How the power that lingered in their souls was eventually harvested as well, forced by the Under-King into the Dead Gate and turned into secondlight to fuel the Asteri even more. Whatever reached them after the Under-King ate his fill.

Amren angled her head, sleek bob shifting with the movement. "A tax on your magic, taken by ancient beings for their own nourishment and power." Azriel's gaze shifted to her, Rhysand presumably still translating mind-to-mind. But Amren murmured to herself, as if the words triggered something, "A tithe."

Rhysand's brows rose. But he waved a broad, elegant hand at Bryce to continue. "What else?"

She swallowed again. "Midgard is only the latest in a long line of worlds invaded by the Asteri. They have an entire archive of different planets they've either conquered or tried to conquer. I saw it right before I came here. And, as far as I know, there were only three planets that were able to kick them out—to fight back and defeat them. Hel, a planet called Iphraxia, and . . . a world occupied by the Fae. The original, Starborn Fae." She nodded to the dagger at Azriel's side, which had flared with dark light in the presence of the Starsword. "You know my sword by a different name, but you recognize what it is."

Only Amren nodded.

"I think it's because it came from this world," Bryce said. "It seems connected to that dagger somehow. It was forged here, became part of your history, then vanished . . . right? You haven't seen it in fifteen thousand years, or spoken this language in nearly as long—which lines up perfectly with the timeline of the Starborn Fae arriving in Midgard."

The Starborn—Theia, their queen, and Pelias, the traitor-prince who'd usurped her. Theia had brought two daughters with her into Midgard: Helena, who'd been forced to wed Pelias, and another, whose name had been lost to history. Much of the truth about Theia had been lost as well, either through time or the Asteri's propaganda. Aidas, Prince of the Chasm, had loved her—that much Bryce knew. Theia had fought alongside Hel against the Asteri to free Midgard. Had been killed by Pelias in the end, her name nearly wiped from all memory. Bryce bore Theia's light—Aidas had confirmed it. But beyond that, even the Asteri Archives had provided no information about the long-dead queen.

"So you believe," Amren said slowly, silver eyes flickering, "that *our* world is this third planet that resisted these . . . Asteri."

It was Bryce's turn to nod. She motioned to the cell, the realm above it. "From what I learned, long before the Asteri came to my world, they were *here*. They conquered and meddled with and ruled this world. But eventually the Fae managed to overthrow them—to defeat them." She loosed a tight breath, scanning each of their faces. "How?" The question was hoarse, desperate. "How did you do it?"

But Rhysand glanced warily to Amren. She had to be some sort of court historian or scholar if he kept consulting her about the past. He said to her, "Our history doesn't include an event like that."

Bryce cut in, "Well, the Asteri remember your world. They're still holding a grudge. Rigelus, their leader, told me it's his personal mission to find this place and punish you all for kicking them to the curb. You're basically public enemy number one."

"It is in our history, Rhysand," Amren said gravely. "But the Asteri were not known by that name. Here, they were called the Daglan."

Bryce could have sworn Rhysand's golden face paled slightly. Azriel shifted in his chair, wings rustling. Rhysand said firmly, "The Daglan were all killed."

Amren shuddered. The gesture seemed to spark more alarm in Rhysand's expression. "Apparently not," she said.

Bryce pushed Amren, "Do you have any record about how they were defeated?" A kernel of hope glowed in her chest.

"Nothing beyond old songs of bloody battles and tremendous losses."

"But the story . . . it rings true to you?" Bryce asked. "Immortal, vicious overseers once ruled this world, and you guys banded together and overthrew them?"

Their silence was confirmation enough.

Yet Rhysand shook his head, as if still not quite believing it. "And you think . . ." He met Bryce's stare, his eyes once again full of that predatory focus. Gods, he was terrifying. "You believe the Daglan—these *Asteri*—want to come back here for revenge. After at least fifteen thousand years." Doubt dripped from every word.

"That's, like, five minutes for Rigelus," Bryce countered. "He's got infinite time—and resources."

"What kind of resources?" Cold, sharp words—a leader assessing the threat to his people.

How to begin describing guns or brimstone missiles or mech-suits or Omega-boats or even the Asteri's power? How to convey the ruthless, swift horror of a bullet? And maybe it was reckless, but . . . She extended her hand to Rhysand. "I'll show you."

Amren and Azriel cut him sharp looks. Like this might be a trap.

"Hold on," Rhysand said, and vanished into nothing.

Bryce started. "You—you can teleport?"

"We call it winnowing," Amren drawled. Bryce could have sworn Azriel was smirking. But Amren asked, "Can you do it?"

"No," Bryce lied. If Azriel sensed her lie, he didn't call her out this time. "There are only two Fae who can."

It was Amren's turn to start. "Two—on your entire planet?"

"I'm guessing you have more?"

Azriel, without Rhysand to translate, watched in silence. Bryce could have sworn shadows wreathed him, like Ruhn's, yet . . . wilder. The way Cormac's had been.

Amren's chin dipped. "Only the most powerful, but yes. Many can."

As if on cue, Rhysand appeared again, a small silver orb in one hand.

"The Veritas orb?" Amren said, and Azriel lifted an eyebrow.

But Rhysand ignored them and extended his other hand, in which lay a small silver bean.

Bryce took it, peering at the orb he laid on the floor. "What are these?"

Rhysand nodded to the orb. "Hold it, think of what you want to show us, and the memories shall be captured within for us to view."

Easy enough. Like a camera for her mind. She gingerly approached the orb and picked it up. The metal was smooth and cold. Lighter than it should have been. Hollow inside.

"Here goes," she said, and closed her eyes. Pictured the weapons, the wars, the battlefields she'd seen on television, the mech-suits, the guns she'd learned to fire, the lessons with Randall, the power Rigelus had blasted down the hall after her—

She shut it off at that point. Before she leapt into the Gate, before she left Hunt and Ruhn behind. She didn't want to relive that. To show what she could do. To reveal the Horn or her ability to teleport.

Bryce opened her eyes. The ball remained quiet and dim. She put it back on the floor and rolled it toward Rhysand.

He floated it on a phantom wind to his hand, then touched its top. And all that had been in her mind played out.

It was worse, seeing it as a sort of memory-montage: the violence, the brutality of how easily the Asteri and their minions killed, how indiscriminately.

But whatever she felt was nothing compared to the surprise and dread on her captors' faces.

"Guns," Bryce said, pointing to the rifle Randall fired in her displayed memory, landing a perfect bulls-eye shot in a target half a mile off. "Brimstone missiles." She pointed to the blooming golden light of destruction as the buildings of Lunathion ruptured around her. "Omega-boats." The *SPQM Faustus* hunted through the dark depths of the seas. "Asteri." Rigelus's white-hot power blasted apart stone and glass and the world itself.

Rhysand mastered himself, a cool mask sliding into place. "You live in such a world."

It wasn't entirely a question. But Bryce nodded. "Yes."

"And they want to bring all of that . . . here."

"Yes."

Rhysand stared ahead. Thinking it through. Azriel just kept his eyes on the space where the orb had displayed the utter destruction of her world. Dreading—and yet calculating. She'd seen that look before on Hunt's face. A warrior's mind at work.

Amren turned to Rhys, meeting his stare. Bryce knew that look, too. A silent conversation passing between them. As Bryce and Ruhn had often spoken.

Her heart wrenched to see it, to remember. It steadied her, though. Sharpened her focus.

The Asteri had been here—under a different name, but they'd been here. The ancestors of these Fae had defeated them. And Urd had sent her here—here, not Hel. Here, where she'd instantly encountered a dagger that made the Starsword sing. Like it had been the lodestone that had drawn her to this world, to that riverbank. Could it really be the knife from the prophecy?

She'd believed that destroying the Asteri would be as simple as obliterating that firstlight core, yet Urd had sent her here. To the original world of the Midgardian Fae. She had no choice but to trust Urd's judgment. And pray that Ruhn, that Hunt, that everyone she loved in Midgard could hold on until she found a way to get home.

And if she couldn't . . .

Bryce examined the silver bean that lay smooth and gleaming in her hand. Amren said without looking at her, "You swallow it, and it will translate our mother tongue for you. Allow you to speak it, too."

"Fancy," Bryce murmured.

She had to find a way home. If that meant navigating this world first . . . language skills would be useful, considering the extent of bullshit still to be spun. And, sure, she didn't trust these people for one moment, but considering all the questions they kept lobbing her way, she highly doubted they were going to poison her. Or go to such lengths to do so, when a slit throat would be way easier.

Not a comforting thought, but Bryce nonetheless popped the silver bean into her mouth, worked up enough saliva, and swallowed. Its metal was cool against her tongue, her throat, and she could have sworn she felt its slickness sliding into her stomach.

Lightning cleaved her brain. She was being ripped in two. Her body couldn't hold all the searing light—

Then blackness slammed in. Quiet and restful and eternal.

No—that was the room around her. She was on the floor, curled over her knees, and . . . glowing. Brightly enough to illuminate Rhysand's and Amren's shocked faces.

Azriel was already poised over her, that deadly dagger drawn and gleaming with a strange black light.

He noted the darkness leaking from the blade and blinked. It was the most shock Bryce had seen him display.

"Put it away, you fool," Amren said. "It sings for her, and by bringing it close—"

The blade vanished from Azriel's hand, whisked away by a shadow. Silence, taut and rippling, spread through the room.

Bryce stood slowly—as Randall and her mom had taught her to move in front of Vanir and other predators.

And as she rose, she found it in her brain: the knowledge of a language that she had not known before. It sat on her tongue, ready to be spoken, as instinctual as her own. It shimmered along her skin, stinging down her spine, her shoulder blades—wait.

Oh no. No, no, no.

Bryce didn't dare reach for the tattoo of the Horn, to call attention to the letters that formed the words *Through love, all is possible.* She could feel them reacting to whatever had been in that spell that set her glowing and could only pray it wasn't visible.

Her prayers were in vain.

Amren turned to Rhysand and said in that new, strange language—*their* language: "The glowing letters inked on her back . . . they're the same as those in the *Book of Breathings.*"

They must have seen the words through her T-shirt when she'd been on the floor. With every breath, the tingling lessened, like the glow was fading. But the damage was already done.

They once again assessed her. Three apex killers, contemplating a threat.

Then Azriel said in a soft, lethal voice, "Explain or you die."

2

Tharion's blood dripped into the porcelain sink of the hushed, humid bathroom, the roar of the crowd a distant rumble through the cracked green tiles. He breathed in through his nose. Out through his mouth. Pain rippled along his aching ribs.

Stay upright.

His hands clenched the chipped edges of the sink. He inhaled again, focusing on the words, willing his knees not to buckle. *Keep standing, damn you.* He'd taken a beating tonight.

The minotaur he'd faced in the Viper Queen's ring had been twice his weight and at least four feet taller than him. He had a hole in his shoulder leaking blood down the sink drain thanks to the horns he hadn't been fast enough to avoid. And several broken ribs thanks to blows from fists the size of his head.

Tharion loosed another breath, wincing, and reached for the small medkit on the lip of the sink. His fingers shook, fumbling with the vial of potion that would blunt the edge of the pain and accelerate the healing his Vanir body was already doing.

He chucked the cork into the trash can beside the sink, atop the wads of bloodied cotton bandages and wipes he'd used to clean his face. It had somehow been more important than addressing the pain—the hole in his shoulder—that he should be able to see his face, the male beneath.

The reflection wasn't kind. Purple smudges beneath his eyes matched the bruises along his jaw, the cuts on his lip, his swollen nose. All things that would fade and heal swiftly enough, but the hollowness in his eyes . . . It was his face, and yet a stranger's.

Tharion didn't meet his own gaze in the mirror as he tipped back the vial and chugged it. Silky, tasteless liquid coated his mouth, his throat. He'd once done shots with the same abandon. In the span of a few weeks, everything had gone to shit. His whole fucking life had gone to shit.

He'd given up everything he was and had been and ever would be.

He'd chosen this, being chained to the Viper Queen. He'd been desperate, but the burden of his decision weighed on him. He hadn't been allowed to leave the warren of warehouses in the two days since arriving—hadn't really wanted to, anyway. Even the need to return to the water was taken care of for him: a special tub had been prepared below this level with water pumped in directly from the Istros.

So he hadn't been in the river, or felt the wind and the sun, or heard the chatter and rhythmic beats of normal life in days. Hadn't so much as found an exterior window.

The door groaned open, and a familiar female scent announced the identity of the new arrival. As if at this hour, in this bathroom, it could be anyone else.

The Viper Queen had a crew of fighters. But the two of them . . . she treated them like prized racehorses. They fought during the prime-time slots. This bathroom was for their private use, along with the suite upstairs.

The Viper Queen owned them. And she wanted everyone to know it.

"I warmed them up for you," Tharion rasped over a shoulder at Ariadne. The dark-haired dragon, clad in a black bodysuit that accentuated her luscious curves, turned toward him.

Tharion and Ariadne were required to look sexy and stylish,

even as the Viper Queen bade them to bloody themselves for the crowd's amusement.

Ariadne halted at a sink a few feet away, surveying the angles of her face in the mirror as she washed her hands.

"Still as pretty as ever," Tharion managed to tease.

That earned him a sidelong assessment. "You look like shit."

"Nice to see you, too," he drawled, the healing potion tingling through him.

Her nostrils flared delicately. It wasn't wise to taunt a dragon. But he'd been on a hot streak of making stupid decisions lately, so why stop now?

"You have a hole in your shoulder," she said without taking her gaze from his.

Tharion peered at the ghastly wound, even as his skin knitted closed, the sensation like spiders crawling over the area. "Builds character."

Ariadne snorted, returning to her reflection. "You know, you throw around your attraction to females quite a bit. I'm starting to think it's a shield."

He stiffened. "Against what?"

"Don't know, don't really care."

"Ouch."

Ariadne continued examining herself in the mirror. Was she hunting for herself—the person she'd been before coming here—as well? Or maybe the person she'd been before the Astronomer had trapped her inside a ring and worn her on his finger for decades?

Tharion had done what the Viper Queen had asked regarding Ari: he'd woven a web of lies to his Aux contacts about the dragon being commandeered for security purposes. So the Viper Queen didn't technically own Ari as a slave—Ari remained a slave owned by someone else. She just . . . lived here now.

"Your adoring public awaits," Tharion said, grabbing another cotton wipe and holding it under the running water before beginning to clean the blood from his bare chest. He could have jumped in one of the showers to his left, but it would have stung like Hel on his still-mending wounds. He twisted, straining for the particularly nasty slice along his left shoulder blade. It remained out of reach, even for his long fingers.

"Here," Ariadne said, taking the wipe from his hand.

"Thanks, Ar—Ariadne." He'd almost called her Ari, but it didn't seem wise to antagonize her when she'd offered to help him.

Tharion braced his hands on the sink. Ariadne dabbed along the wound, wiping up blood, and he clenched the porcelain hard enough for it to groan beneath his fingers. He gritted his teeth against the stinging, and into the silence, the dragon said, "You can call me Ari."

"I thought you hated that nickname."

"Everyone seems inclined to use it, so it might as well be my choice for you to do so."

"Was that your thinking when you abandoned my friends right before a deathstalker attacked them?" He couldn't keep the bite from his voice, antagonizing her be damned. "Everyone expected the worst of you, so why not just be the worst?"

She snorted. "Your friends . . . you mean the witch and the redhead?"

"Yes. Real honorable of you to ditch them."

"They seemed capable of looking after themselves."

"They are. But you bailed all the same."

"If you're so invested in their safety, perhaps you should have been there." Ari tossed the wipe in the trash and grabbed another one. "Who taught you to fight, anyway?"

He let the argument drop—it'd get them nowhere. He couldn't even have said why he'd felt inclined to bring it up now, of all times. "Here I was, thinking you didn't care to know anything about me."

"Call it curiosity. You don't seem . . . serious enough to be the River Queen's Captain of Intelligence."

"Such a flatterer."

But embers sparked in her eyes, so Tharion shrugged. "I learned how to fight the usual way: I enrolled in the Blue Court Military

Academy after school, and have spent the years since honing those skills. Nothing cool. You?"

"Survival."

He opened his mouth to respond, but the dragon turned on a booted heel. "Ari—" he called before she could reach the door. "We didn't, you know."

She turned, eyebrows rising. "Didn't what?"

"Expect the worst of you."

Her face twisted—rage and sorrow and a drop of shame. Or maybe he was imagining that last bit. She didn't answer before stalking out.

The dripping of his blood again filled the bathroom.

Tharion waited until the potion patched most of the holes in his skin, and didn't bother tugging the upper half of the black bodysuit on before following the dragon back to the heat and smells and light of the fighting ring.

Ari was just getting started. With impressive calm, she squared off against three male lion shifters, the enormous cats circling her with deadly precision. She turned with them, not letting the lions get behind her, her skin beginning to glow with molten scales, her black eyes flickering red.

Across the pit, the one-way window that peered over the ring reflected the glaring spotlights. But Tharion knew who stood on the other side of it, amid the plush finery of her private quarters. Who watched the dragon fight, assessing the intensity of the crowd's roar.

"Traitor," someone hissed to his left.

Tharion found two young mer males glaring at him from the risers above. Both clutched beers and had the glazed look of guys who'd already downed a few.

Tharion gave them a bland nod and faced the ring again.

"Fucking loser," the other male spat.

Tharion kept his eyes on Ari. Steam rippled from the dragon's mouth. One of the lions lunged, swiping with fingers that ended in curved claws, but she ducked away. The concrete floor singed where her feet had been. Preliminary blast marks.

"Some fucking captain," the first male taunted.

Tharion ground his teeth. This wasn't the first time in the past few days that one of his people had recognized him and told him precisely how they felt. Everyone knew Tharion had defected from the Blue Court. Everyone knew he'd defected and come *here* to serve the Meat Market's depraved ruler. The River Queen and her daughter had made sure of it.

Captain Whatever, Ithan Holstrom had once called him. It seemed he truly embodied it now.

You gave that up, he reminded himself. He could never again so much as set foot in the Istros. The moment he did, his former queen would kill him. Or order her sobeks to rip him to shreds. Something twisted in his gut.

He was aware that his parents lived only because he'd gotten messages from them expressing their outrage and disappointment. *We already lost one child,* his mother had written. *Now we lose another. Defecting, Tharion? What in Ogenas's depths were you thinking?*

He didn't write back. Didn't apologize for being so reckless and selfish that he hadn't thought of their safety before committing this act of insanity. He'd not only sworn himself to the Viper Queen, he'd bound himself to her, too. After all the shit that had gone down in Pangera . . . no place else was safe for him, anyway. Only here, where the Viper Queen was allowed to rule.

He watched Ari pace in the ring. *You gave that up,* he told himself again firmly. *For this.*

"You're a disgrace," the other mer male went on.

Something liquid and foamy splashed on Tharion's head, his bare shoulders. The fucker had thrown his beer.

Tharion snarled up at them, and the males had the good sense to back up a step, like they might have finally remembered what Tharion was capable of when provoked. But before he could beat the living shit out of them, one of the Viper Queen's personal guards—one of those glassy-eyed Fae defectors—said, "Fishboy. Boss wants you. Now."

Tharion stiffened, but he had no choice. The tugging sensation in his gut would only worsen the longer he resisted. Best to get this over with now.

So he left the assholes behind. Left Ari with the lions, who'd be deep-fried in about twenty minutes, or whenever the dragon had put on enough of a show to please the audience and did what she could have accomplished without so much as stepping into the ring.

He had no doubt there'd be some vendor waiting in the wings to scoop up the cooked carcasses and sell them in a food stall nearby. It wasn't called the Meat Market for nothing.

The walk upstairs, to the room behind that one-way window, was long and quiet. He willed his mind to be that way, too. To stop caring.

It was easier said than done, when everything kept circling: the failed attack on the lab, Cormac's death . . . They'd all been so fucking dumb, thinking they could take on the Asteri. And now here he was.

Honestly, he'd been headed this way for a while before that. Starting with the debacle with the River Queen's daughter. Then Lesia's death a year ago. This last month had been a culmination of that shit. Of what a pathetic, weak failure he'd always been beneath the surface.

Tharion knocked once on the wooden door, then entered.

The Viper Queen stood at the window overlooking the pit, where Ari had switched to taunting the lions. They were now frantic to escape. Everywhere the cats lunged to flee the ring, a wall of flame blocked their exit.

"She's a natural performer," the Viper Queen observed without turning. The ruler of the Meat Market wore a white silk romper cut to her slim figure, feet bare. A cigarette dangled from her manicured hand. "You could learn from her."

Tharion leaned against the wooden doorframe. "Is that an order or a suggestion?"

The Viper Queen pivoted, shiny dark hair swaying with her. Her lips were painted their usual dark purple, offsetting the snake shifter's pale skin. "Do you know the lengths I went to in procuring that minotaur for you tonight?"

Tharion kept his mouth shut. How many times had he stood like this in front of the River Queen, silent while she ripped into him? He'd lost count long ago.

The Viper Queen's teeth flashed, delicate fangs stark against the purple of her lips. "Five minutes, Tharion?" Her voice dropped to a deadly purr. "A great deal of effort on my part, and all I get out of it, all my crowd gets, is a five-minute fight?"

Tharion gestured to his shoulder. "I'd think goring me and then hurling me across the ring was spectacle enough."

"I'd have liked to see that several more times. Not witness you flying into a rage and snapping the bull's neck."

She crooked a finger. That tugging in his gut increased. As if they possessed a mind of their own, his feet and legs moved. They carried him to the window, to her side.

He hated it—not the summoning, but the fact that he'd stopped any attempt at defying it.

"To make up for you blowing your load," the Viper Queen drawled, "I told Ari to drag out her fight." She inclined her head to the ring. Ari's face had gone empty and cold as she made the lions scream under her flames.

Tharion's gut churned. No wonder Ari hadn't stayed long to talk to him. But she'd helped him anyway. He had no idea how to unpack that.

"Try a little harder next time," the Viper Queen hissed in his ear, lips brushing his skin. She sniffed. "The mer punks really drenched you."

Tharion stepped away. "Is there a reason you called me up here?" He wanted a shower, and the relief that only sleep could offer him.

Her lips curled upward. She tugged back the pristine sleeve of her romper, exposing her moon-pale wrist. "Considering how little heart you put into your performance, I thought you might need a pick-me-up."

Tharion clenched his teeth. He wasn't a slave—though he'd

been stupid and desperate enough to offer himself as such to her. But instead she'd offered him something nearly as bad: the venom only she could produce.

And now, after that initial taste of it . . . His mouth filled with saliva. The scent of her skin, the blood and venom beneath it—he was helpless before her, a hungry fucking animal.

"Maybe if I offered you some before your fights," she mused, forearm extended to him like a personal feast, "you would find a bit more . . . stamina."

With every scrap of will left in him, Tharion lifted his eyes to hers. Let her see how much he hated this, hated her, hated himself.

She smiled. She knew. Had known when he'd defected to her, to this life. He'd told himself that this was a place of refuge, but it was getting harder to hide from what it really was.

A long-overdue punishment.

The Viper Queen slid one of her gold-painted nails down her wrist. Opened a vein churning with that milky, opalescent venom that made him see the gods themselves.

"Go ahead," she urged, and Tharion wanted to scream, to weep, to run, as he grabbed her arm to his mouth and sucked in a mouthful of the venom.

It was beautiful. It was horrific. And it punched through him. Stars flickered in the air. Time slowed to a syrupy, languid scroll. Exhaustion and pain faded to nothing.

He'd heard the whispers long before he'd come here: her venom was the best high an immortal could ever attain. Having tasted it, he didn't disagree. Didn't blame those Fae defectors who served as her bodyguards in exchange for hits of this.

He'd once pitied them, scorned them.

Now he was one of them.

The Viper Queen's hand trailed up his chest to his neck, tracing over the spot where his gills usually appeared. She scraped her painted nails over it—a mark of pure ownership. Not only of his body, but of who he was, who he'd once been.

Her fingers tightened on his throat. An invitation, this time.

The Viper Queen's lips brushed against his ear again as she whispered, "Let's see what kind of stamina you have now, Tharion."

"We can't just leave Tharion in here."

"Trust me, Holstrom, Captain Whatever can look after himself."

Ithan frowned deeply at Tristan Flynn from across the rickety table. Declan Emmet and his boyfriend, Marc, were chatting up a vendor at one of the Meat Market's many stalls. The owl-headed Vanir was the third person they'd spoken to tonight, hoping to get news of their imprisoned friends—the twelfth lowlife they'd contacted in the past two days.

And Ithan was getting sick enough of their fruitless talking that he taunted Flynn, "Is this what Fae do? Leave their friends to suffer?"

"Fuck you, wolf," Flynn said, but didn't take his eyes off where Declan and Marc worked their charm. Even the usually unflappable Flynn now had bags beneath his eyes. He'd rarely smiled in the past few days. Seemed to be sleeping as little as Ithan was.

Yet despite all that, Ithan went for the throat. "So Ruhn's life means more—"

"Ruhn is in a fucking *dungeon* being tortured by the Asteri," Flynn snarled. "Tharion is here because he defected. He made that choice."

"Technically, Ruhn also made a choice to go to the Eternal City—"

Flynn dragged his hands through his brown hair. "If you're going to complain, then get the fuck out of here."

"I'm not complaining. I'm just saying that we've got a friend in a bad situation literally *right there* and we're not even trying to help him." Ithan pointed to the second level of the cavernous warehouse, the nondescript door that led into the Viper Queen's private quarters.

"Again, Ketos defected. Not much we can do."

"He was desperate—"

"We're all fucking desperate," Flynn murmured, eyeing a passing draki male carrying a sack of what smelled like elk meat. He sighed. "Seriously, Holstrom—go back to the house. Get some rest." Again, Ithan noted the Fae lord's exhausted face. "And," Flynn added, "take that one with you." Flynn nodded to the female sitting ramrod straight at a nearby table, alert and tense. The three fire sprites lay draped around her shoulders, dozing.

Right. The other source of Ithan's frustration these days: playing babysitter for Sigrid Fendyr.

It would have been smarter to leave her back at the Fae males' house—his house now, he supposed—but she'd refused. Had insisted on accompanying them.

Sigrid insisted on seeing and knowing *everything*. If he'd thought she'd crawl out of her mystic's tank and cower, he'd thought wrong. She'd been a pain in his ass for two days now, wanting the complete history of the Fendyrs, their enemies, Ithan's enemies . . . anything and everything that had happened while she'd been the Astronomer's captive.

She hadn't offered up much of her own past—not even a crumb about her father, whose history she hadn't known until Ithan had filled her in, how the male had long ago been Prime Apparent until his sister, Sabine, had challenged him and won. Ithan had thought she'd killed him, but she'd apparently sent Sigrid's father off into exile instead, where Sigrid had been born. Anything other than that was a complete mystery. Part of Ithan didn't want to know what circumstances had been so dire as to make a Fendyr sell his heir—sell an *Alpha*—to the Astronomer.

That heir was only sitting quietly right now because she'd taken two steps into the Meat Market and sneered, *Who'd want to shop at a disgusting place like this?* Promptly making Declan and Marc's work infinitely harder by earning the ire of any vendor within earshot.

The whisper network here put them all within earshot.

So Flynn had ordered her to sit alone. Well, alone apart from her fiery little cabal. Wherever Sigrid went, the sprites went with her.

Ithan had no idea if that bond was from the years in the

tank, or from a shared trauma, or just because they were females living in a very male house, but the four of them together were a headache.

"It's too dangerous for her to be out in the open," Flynn went on. "Anyone can report a sighting."

"No one knows who she is. To them, she's a random wolf."

"Yeah, and all it takes is one mention to Amelie or Sabine that a female wolf is in your company, and they'll know. I'm shocked they haven't run right over here already."

"Sabine's ruthless, but she's not dumb. She wouldn't start shit on the Viper Queen's turf."

"No, she'll wait until we cross into the CBD and then ambush us." The angels had long ignored anything that went on at street level in their district, too preoccupied with the comings and goings in their lofty towers.

Ithan glared at the male. Normally, he got along fine with Flynn. Liked him, even. But since Ruhn and Hunt and Bryce had disappeared . . .

Disappeared wasn't the right word, at least for Ruhn and Hunt. They'd been taken prisoner, but Bryce . . . no one knew what had happened to her. Hence their presence here, seeking any intel they could get their hands on after Declan's computer searches had been fruitless.

Any information on Bryce, on Ruhn, on Athalar . . . they were desperate for it. For a direction. A spark to light the way. Something that was better than sitting on their asses, not knowing.

Ithan glanced at the chair beneath him. *He* was currently sitting on his ass. Not knowing anything.

Before he could let self-loathing sink its teeth into him, he rose and stalked over to where Sigrid sat monitoring the patrons of the Meat Market. She lifted brown eyes full of irritation and disdain to him. "This is a bad place."

No shit, he refrained from saying. "It has it uses," he hedged.

He'd gone straight to the Fae males' house when he'd hauled Sigrid out of the Astronomer's tank. They'd stayed there while Flynn and Declan pretended that all was normal in their world. While they continued working for the Aux, Prince Ruhn's absence dismissed as a much-needed vacation.

Ithan had been waiting for soldiers to show up. Or assassins, sent by the Asteri or Sabine or the Astronomer.

Yet there had been no questions. No interrogations. No arrests. The Autumn King hadn't even grilled Flynn and Dec, though he no doubt knew something had happened to his son. And that where Ruhn went, his two best friends went with him.

The public had no idea what had happened in the Eternal City. Granted, Ithan and the Fae warriors didn't know much either, but they knew that their friends had gone into the Asteri stronghold and hadn't come out again. The Asteri, the other powers at play . . . they knew that Ithan and the others had also been involved, even if they hadn't been present. And yet they hadn't made a move to punish them.

It wasn't a comforting thought.

Sigrid angled her head with lupine curiosity. "Do you come here often?"

With anyone else, he might have made a joke about pickup lines, but Sigrid didn't know or care about humor. He couldn't blame her, after what she'd been through. So Ithan said, "When my work for the Aux or my pack demands it. But rarely, thank the gods."

Her mouth tightened. "The Astronomer frequented this place." That day Ithan had gone back to the Astronomer's place to free her, he remembered, the ancient male had been over here buying some part for her tank.

"Any idea who he patronizes?" It was more of a casual question than anything.

Sigrid peered around. If she'd been in wolf form, he had no doubt her ears would have been flicking, picking up every sound. She replied without taking her focus off the teeming market, "A satyr, I heard him say once. Who sells salts and other things."

Ithan glanced to the balcony level—to the shut green door where the satyr lived. He knew who she was talking about, thanks to all those past visits on behalf of the Aux. The lowlife peddled in all kinds of contraband.

Sigrid marked his shift in attention, tracing his line of sight. "That's his place?"

Ithan gave a slow nod.

Sigrid shot to her feet, eyes gleaming with predatory intent.

"Where are you going?" Ithan demanded, stepping into her path.

The sprites jolted from their nap, clinging to Sigrid's long brown hair to keep from being thrown off her shoulders.

"Are we done?" Malana asked, yawning.

"We're terribly bored," Sasa agreed, stretching her plump body along Sigrid's neck. Rithi, the third sister, hummed in agreement.

Ignoring the sprites, Sigrid's teeth flashed as she faced Ithan. "I want to see why this satyr thinks it appropriate to supply people like the Astrono—"

"We're not here to cause trouble," Ithan said, and didn't move an inch from her path. But she stomped around him, pure Fendyr. A force of nature—one he'd just begun to see unleashed.

Despite that noble bloodline, Ithan grabbed her arm. "Do *not* go up there," he snarled softly, fingers digging into her bony arm.

She looked down at his hand, then up at his face. Her nose crinkled with anger. "Or what?"

The steel of an Alpha rang in her voice. Ithan's very bones cried out to submit, to bow away, to step aside.

But he fought it, pushed against it—met it with his own dominance. The Fendyrs might have been Alphas for generations, but the Holstroms weren't pushovers. They were Alphas, too—leaders and warriors in their own right.

Like Hel would he let this female push him around, Fendyr or no.

Flynn's chair scraped the ground, but Ithan didn't take his eyes from Sigrid as the Fae male stalked over and hissed, "What the fuck is wrong with you two? Go snarl at each other somewhere it won't be noticed by everyone in the gods-damned Meat Market."

Ithan bared his teeth at Sigrid. She bared hers right back.

He said to Flynn, still not breaking Sigrid's stare, "She wants to go confront the salt dealer about his association with the Astronomer. The satyr who got in all that trouble last year."

Flynn sighed at the wooden ceiling. "Now's not the time to go on a self-righteous warpath, sweetheart."

Sigrid looked away from Ithan at last, though the wolf part of him knew she wasn't conceding in their battle of wills. No, it was because she'd found another opponent to face. "Don't speak to me like I'm some common female," Sigrid raged at Flynn, who held up his hands. She whipped her head back to Ithan, "It's within my rights—"

"You have no rights," a male voice said. Marc. The leopard shifter had stalked up behind them with preternatural grace. Though he was in jeans and a long-sleeved T-shirt, the male still had an air of sleek professionalism. "Since you technically don't even exist. You're a ghost, for all intents and purposes."

Sigrid slowly turned, lip curling. "Did I ask for your opinion, *cat*?"

Normally, Ithan would have been glad to engage in some intershifter rivalry. But Marc was a good male—her disdain was utterly misplaced. Declan sauntered up beside his boyfriend and slung an arm around his broad shoulders. "I think it's past someone's bedtime."

Sigrid growled. But the sprites drifted from her shoulders to float in front of her face as Sasa said carefully, "Siggy, we *are* here to . . . do other things. Perhaps we could come back another time."

Ithan almost laughed at the nickname. Someone as intense as the female before him had no business being called *Siggy*.

"The next time they let us out of the house," Sigrid said, bristling. "In days or weeks."

"I'll remind you," Declan drawled, "that you're currently Sabine's primary enemy."

"Let her come find me," Sigrid said without an ounce of fear. "I've a score to settle."

"Luna spare me," Flynn muttered. Ithan could have sworn he caught the sprites nodding their agreement as they resettled themselves on Sigrid's shoulders. The Fae lord turned to Declan and Marc. "Anything?"

The couple shook their heads. "No. It really does seem like the Asteri put a lock on the information. Nothing's getting in or out." Silence fell, heavy and tense.

It was Sigrid who said, "So what now?"

Only two days out of the tank and she was already assuming the mantle of leader, whether she knew it or not. A true Alpha, expecting to be answered . . . and obeyed.

"We keep trying to find out what's going on," Declan said with a one-shouldered shrug.

Flynn blew out an exasperated breath and plopped onto his chair again. "We're no closer than we were two days ago: Ruhn and Athalar are being held as traitors. That's all we know." That was all Marc's inside source at the Eternal City had been able to glean. Nothing else.

Declan sank into a seat and rubbed his eyes with his thumb and index finger. "Honestly? We're lucky we aren't in those dungeons, too."

"We have to break them out," Flynn said, crossing his muscled arms. Rithi, on his left shoulder, made an identical gesture.

"Urd knows what shape they're in," Declan said bleakly. "We'd need medwitches on hand, probably."

"You've got healing magic," Flynn countered.

"Yeah," Dec said, shaking his head, "but the kind of injuries they'd have . . . I'd need to be working alongside a team of trained professionals."

The thought of what those injuries might be to require such a team of medwitches made them all fall silent again. A heavy, miserable sort of quiet.

"And," Declan challenged, head lifting, "where would we even go once we rescued them? There's no one on Midgard who could hide or harbor us."

"What about that mer ship?" Flynn mused. "The one that picked them up at Ydra. It outran the Omega-boats. Seems pretty damned good at hiding from the Asteri, too."

"Flynn," Marc warned with a glance at the teeming market. All those listening ears.

Ithan kept his voice low. "Tharion could get us onto that ship."

He expected Flynn to roll his eyes at the mention of helping Ketos, but the male glanced to the second level. "He can't set foot beyond this market."

None of them had seen or heard from the mer male since he'd left for Pangera. But they'd learned of his whereabouts thanks to a neon-green piece of paper taped to a lamppost, advertising an upcoming match in the Viper Queen's fighting pit with Tharion as the main event. It was clear enough what had happened: the male had defected from the Blue Court and run straight here.

Ithan countered, "Then we ask Tharion how to get a message to them."

Declan shook his head. "And what then? We all live under the ocean forever?"

Ithan shifted on his feet. The wolf in him would go insane. No ability to run freely, to respond to the moon calling his name—

"*She* lived in a tank for the gods know how long," Flynn said, gaze darting to Sigrid. "I think we can manage a cushy, city-sized submarine."

Sigrid flinched—a crack in her usually cocky exterior.

"Careful," Ithan warned Flynn.

The sprites murmured their comfort to Sigrid, their flames now a deep raspberry. But Sigrid silently rose from her seat and walked toward a nearby vendor selling opals. The sweatshirt and pants Ithan had given her hung off her lean frame, swishing with each step.

"You need to remind her to shower," Dec said a shade quietly, eyes shining with concern.

She hadn't known what shampoo was. Or soap. Or conditioner. Hadn't even known what a shower was, and had refused to step into the stream until Ithan had done so himself, fully clothed, to demonstrate that it was safe. That it wasn't some version of a tank.

She'd never slept in a proper bed before, either. Or at least not one that she remembered.

"Okay," Declan said, drawing attention back to the matter at hand. "We're clearly not learning anything by asking around, but let's think about it . . . Ruhn has to be alive. The Asteri wouldn't kill him right away—he's too big of a political presence."

"Yeah, so let's go rescue him," Flynn pushed. "Him and Athalar."

"What about Bryce?" Declan asked so softly it was barely a whisper.

"She's gone," Flynn said tightly. "Went wherever."

Ithan didn't like that tone—not one bit. "What, you think Bryce bailed?" he demanded. "You think she'd willingly leave Ruhn and Hunt to the Asteri? Come on."

Flynn leaned back in his chair. "You got a better guess about where she might be?"

Ithan restrained the urge to punch the Fae lord in the throat. Flynn was angry and hurting and scared, Ithan reminded himself. "Bryce doesn't give up on the people she loves. If she went somewhere, it's gotta be important."

"Doesn't matter where she went," Flynn said. "All I know is we have to get Ruhn out before it's too late."

Ithan glanced at the second level again, that sunball captain part of his mind calculating, thinking it through . . .

Dec gripped Flynn's shoulder, squeezing tight. "Look, the mer ship isn't a bad idea, but we need to think long-term. Need to consider our families, too."

"My parents and sister can go to Hel for all I care," Flynn said.

"Well, I want my family to be safe," Declan snapped. "*If* we're going to rescue Ruhn and Athalar, we need to make sure no one else gets caught in the cross fire."

Dec looked to Ithan, and Ithan shrugged. He had no one left to warn. Would anyone even miss him if he were gone? His duty was to protect the wolf at the stall across the way. Out of some stupid hope that she might . . . He had no idea. Challenge and defeat Sabine? Correct the dangerous path Sabine was leading the wolves down? Fill the void that Danika had left?

Sigrid was a loose cannon. An Alpha, yes, but she had no training.

Her impulses were all over the place, too unpredictable. With time, she might learn the necessary skills, but time wasn't their ally these days.

So Ithan said, "You want to save Ruhn and Athalar? That mer ship is the only way we can cross the ocean unnoticed. Maybe the mer on it will have some idea how to break them out. They might even help us if we're lucky." He pointed to the second level. "Tharion's our way in."

"Seems convenient," Flynn said at last, "given that you were insisting we needed to spring him loose from here."

"Two birds, one stone."

"Tharion can't leave," Marc mused, "but nothing's stopping him from talking to us. Maybe he can provide contact information."

"Only one way to find out," Ithan said.

Flynn sighed, which Ithan took as acceptance. "Someone's gotta tell her to go home." He jabbed a thumb over his shoulder toward Sigrid.

"And be her escort," Dec added.

"Not it," Flynn and Ithan said at the same moment.

Declan whipped his head to Marc and said, "Not it," before the leopard could grasp what was going on.

Marc rubbed his temples. "Remind me how it is that the three of you are considered some of the most feared warriors in this city?"

Dec just kissed his cheek.

Marc sighed. "If I have to bring *Siggy* home, then Holstrom has to be the one to tell her."

Ithan opened his mouth, but . . . fine. With a mocking smile to the males, he walked over to retrieve the Alpha. And spare the opal dealer from her endless questions.

How do you know *it bestows luck or love or joy? What do the colors have to do with anything? What proof do you have that these work?*

He couldn't tell if it was curiosity, pent up from years in that tank, or sheer Alphaness, needing to question everyone and everything. Needing order in the world.

Ithan put a hand on Sigrid's elbow to alert her of his presence, but again she flinched. Ithan backed away a step, hands up as the opal dealer watched warily. "Sorry."

She didn't like being touched. She'd only let him touch her to wash her hair that first night, when she'd had no idea how to do it.

Ithan motioned her to walk back toward the males, and she fell into step beside him, a healthy distance away. Most wolves needed touch—craved it. Had the instinct been robbed from her by those years in the tank?

It made it hard to be annoyed with her when he thought about it like that.

"How do you get used to it?" Sigrid asked over the hiss of cooking meat and bartering shoppers. Behind her, the sprites were still hovering by the array of opals, exclaiming over the stones. How the three sprites had adapted so quickly to this strange, open world was beyond him. They'd been trapped by the Astronomer, too, locked in his rings.

Ithan asked, "Used to what?"

Sigrid peered at her hands, her thin body beneath the sweats. Passing shoppers noted her—him—and gave them a wide berth. "Feeling like you're stranded in a rotting corpse."

He blinked. "I, ah . . ." He couldn't imagine himself in her shoes, suddenly a body of flesh and blood and bone after the weightless years in the isolation tank. "You just need time."

Her eyes lowered. It didn't seem to be the answer she was looking for.

"Sigrid," he said again. "You're . . . you're doing great."

"Why do you keep calling me that?" she asked.

"That's the name Sasa chose for you," Ithan said, offering a friendly smile.

"Why do I need a name? I've lived this long without one."

"An Alpha should have one. A *person* should have one. The Astronomer let you take the Drop—you'll be alive for centuries."

When pressed, she'd revealed that she'd somehow made the Drop in the isolation tank. She couldn't tell him when or how, but he'd been relieved to hear she had that protection.

"I don't want to talk about the Drop." Her voice was flat, dead.

"Neither do I." He would have liked some answers about what she'd experienced, but not now. Not when they'd reached the three waiting males. The sprites, finally emerging from the depths of the opal stall, raced over, three plumes of flame streaming across the bone-dry warehouse.

"So, do we go knock?" Flynn asked, pointing to the metal, vault-like door at the top of the stairs. The entrance to the Viper Queen's private lair.

Marc caught Ithan's eye. Had he explained to Sigrid that Marc would escort her home?

Ithan cringed. No, he hadn't.

Marc glared. *Coward,* the leopard's look seemed to say. But he tensed, going still. "Stay quiet."

The others obeyed, the two Fae males reaching for the guns at their sides. The Meat Market bustled on unawares, selling and trading and feeding, and yet . . .

Marc's tawny eyes scanned the warehouse, the skylights. He sniffed.

Ithan did the same. As shifters, their senses were sharper than those of the Fae.

From the doorway behind them, the blend of smells from the open night leaked in, the reek of the sewers beyond . . .

And the scent of converging wolves.

I don't know what language the tattoo is in," Bryce insisted. "My friend got it inked on me when I was blackout—"

"Do not *lie*," Rhysand warned with soft menace. He'd kill her. Whatever the language was, it was apparently so bad that it might as well say *Stick knife here*.

Amren stalked around Bryce, peering at the tattoo no doubt still glowing from beneath the material of her white shirt. "I can feel something in the letters . . ." Bryce tensed. "Get Nesta."

Azriel murmured, "Cassian won't be happy."

"Cassian will deal. Nesta will be able to sense this better than I can." Bryce turned, placing Amren and Azriel back in her line of sight right as the former insisted, "Get her, Rhysand."

Bryce's knees bent into a defensive crouch. How much would this hurt? Would she stand any chance of—

Rhysand vanished again.

Before Bryce had finished rising to her feet, he returned, a familiar female with golden-brown hair in tow. As she had earlier in the foyer, the female wore dark leathers akin to those on Azriel and Rhysand, and stood with an unruffled, cool sort of calm. A warrior.

Her blue-gray eyes slid over Bryce.

Bryce slowly, almost numbly sank back into her chair. Whatever was in those eyes—

The female said quietly to the others, voice flat, almost bored, "I told you earlier: There's something Made on her. Beyond that sword she carried."

"Made?" Bryce, caution be damned, asked the newcomer—Nesta, she could only assume—at the same time Amren pointed to Bryce's back and asked, "Is it that tattoo?"

Nesta just said, "Yes."

All of them stared at Bryce once more, expressions unreadable. Which one would strike first? Four against one—she wasn't getting out of here alive.

Amren said quietly to Rhysand, "What do you want to do with her, Rhys?"

Bryce clenched her jaw. Even if she stood zero chance of winning, like Hel would she take her death lying down. She'd fight in whatever way she could—

Nesta jerked her chin at Bryce, haughty and aloof. "You can fight us, but you'll lose."

Fuck that. Bryce held the female's stare, finding a will of pure steel gleaming in it. "You try to touch that tattoo and you'll find out why the Asteri want me dead so badly."

She regretted the retort instantly. Azriel's hand drifted toward the dagger at his side. But Nesta stepped closer, unimpressed and unintimidated.

"What is it?" Nesta asked Bryce, motioning to her back. "How is a bit of writing on your skin . . . Made?"

"I can't answer the question until you tell me what the fuck *Made* means."

"Don't tell her anything," Amren warned Nesta. She pointed to the doorway. "You did your job and told us what we needed. We'll see you later."

Nesta's brows rose at the dismissal. But she looked at Bryce and smiled sharply. "It's in your best interests to cooperate with them, you know."

"So they've told me," Bryce said, fingers curling into fists at the sides of her chair. She tucked them under her thighs to keep from doing anything stupid.

Nesta's eyes gleamed with amusement, marking the movement.

"Our . . . visitor needs rest," Rhysand said, and gracefully stalked to the door. Order given, Amren and Azriel strode after him, Nesta following only after staring at Bryce for another heartbeat. A taunting, daring look.

Yet as Azriel reached the threshold, Bryce blurted to the winged warrior, "The sword—where is it?"

Azriel paused, glancing over a shoulder. "Somewhere safe."

Bryce held Azriel's gaze, meeting his ice with her own—with that expression she knew Ruhn always thought looked so much like their father's. The face she'd let the world see so very rarely. "The sword is mine. I want it back."

Azriel's mouth kicked up at the corners. "Then give us a good reason to return it to you."

Time dripped by. Trays of simple food appeared at fairly regular intervals: bread, beef stew—or what she assumed was beef stew—hard cheese. Foods similar to ones back home.

Even the herbs were familiar—had the Fae of this world introduced them to Midgard? Or were plants like thyme and rosemary somehow universal? Strewn across space?

Or maybe the Asteri had brought those herbs from their own home world and planted them on all their conquered planets.

She knew it was a stupid thing to contemplate. That she had way bigger things to consider than an intergalactic garden. But she quickly lost interest in eating, and thinking about everything else was . . . too much.

No one else came to see her. Bryce entertained herself by tossing peas from her stew into the grate in the center of the floor, counting the long seconds until she heard a faint *plink,* and then the hiss and roar of whatever lurked down there.

She didn't want to know. Her imagination conjured plenty of options, all with sharp teeth and ravenous appetites.

She tried the door only once. It wasn't locked, but a wall of black night filled the doorway, obscuring the hall beyond from sight. Blocking anyone from going in or out. She'd flared her starlight, but even it had muted in the face of that darkness.

Maybe it was some kind of fucked-up test. To see if she could get through their strongest powers and wards. To feel her out as an opponent. Maybe to see what the Horn—whatever was *Made* about it—could do. But she didn't need to throw her starlight against that darkness to know it wasn't budging. Its might thundered in her very bones.

Bryce scoured her memory for any alternative escape tactic, reviewing everything Randall had taught her, but none of it was applicable to getting through that impenetrable power.

So Bryce sat. And ate. And threw peas at the monsters below.

Even if she got out of here, she couldn't get off-planet. Not without someone to power her up, activating the Horn in the process. And from Apollion's hints, Hunt's power was far more compatible with hers than most. Granted, Hypaxia had powered her up against the deathstalker, but there was no guarantee the witch-queen's magic would have been enough to open a gate.

And did she *need* a gate to get home? Micah had used the Horn in her back to open all seven Gates in Crescent City, blocks away. When she'd landed here, there had been no gate-like structure nearby. Just a grassy front lawn, the river, and the house she could barely make out through the dense mists.

Only the dagger—and Azriel wielding it—had been there. Like *that* was where she'd needed to be.

"When knife and sword are reunited, so shall our people be," Bryce murmured into the quiet.

To what end, though? The Fae were horrible. The ones here weren't much different from the ones she knew, as far as she could tell. And the Fae on Midgard had proved their moral rot again this spring, locking vulnerable people out of their villas during the demon attack. Proved it with their laws and rules keeping females oppressed, little more than chattel. Bryce had twisted their rules against them at the Autumn Equinox to marry Hunt, but according to those same rules, she now technically *belonged* to him. She was a princess, for Urd's sake, and yet she was still the property of the untitled male she'd married.

Maybe the Fae weren't worth uniting.

But it still left her with the problem of getting off this planet—one of the few worlds to have ever succeeded in ousting the Asteri. Daglan. Whatever they were called.

Bryce leaned against a wall of the cell, knees to her chest, and tried to sort through it all, laying out the pieces before her.

Hours stretched on. Nothing came to her.

Bryce rubbed at her face. She'd stumbled into the home world of the Fae. The world from which the Starborn Fae—Theia and Pelias and Helena—had come. From which the Starsword had come, and where its knife had been waiting. If Urd had some intention in sending her here . . . she sure as fuck had no idea what it was.

Or how she'd get out of this mess.

"We shouldn't have brought her with us," Flynn murmured as they hurried through the stalls of the Meat Market, aiming for an alternate exit on the quieter side of the warehouse. "I fucking *told* you, Holstrom—"

"I ordered him to bring me," Sigrid cut in, keeping pace beside Ithan, the sprites dimmed to a pale yellow as they hunched on her shoulders. Something in Ithan twinged at that—an Alpha, defending him. Taking the responsibility, even if it implied that he *could* be ordered. The Alphas he'd lived under for the past few years had used their power and dominance for themselves. Danika had used her position to support those under her, in her own brash way, but Danika was gone. He'd thought he'd never encounter another like her, but maybe—

"Sabine would have found us anyway," Ithan said, "whether we were here or at the house. It was only a matter of time."

They entered a long service corridor with a dented metal door at its other end, a half-assed *EXIT* painted on it in white lettering.

Definitely not up to code. Though he doubted a city health and safety inspector had ever set foot in this warren of misery.

"Do we split up?" Dec asked. "Try to shake them that way?"

"No," Marc said, claws glinting at his fingertips. "Their sense of smell's too good. They'll be able to tell which of us she's with."

As if in answer, howls rent the warehouse proper. Ithan's entire body locked up. He knew the tenor of those howls. *Prey on the run.* He gritted his teeth to keep from answering, to clamp his responding howl inside his body.

Beside him, Sigrid was a live wire. Like the howls had triggered a response in her, too.

"So we make a run for it," Flynn said. "Where do we rendezvous if we get separated?"

The question hung in the air. Where the fuck was safe in this city, on this planet? Considering their connections to imprisoned traitors, the list of options was short as fuck. Where would Bryce have gone? She would have found someone bigger and badder . . . or smarter, at least. She would have gone to the gallery, maybe, to its protective wards, but Jesiba Roga's sanctum was gone. Griffin Antiquities had never been repaired or reopened. Which left—

"We make it to the Comitium," Ithan said. "Isaiah Tiberian will shelter us."

Dec lifted a brow. "You know Tiberian?"

"No, but Athalar's his friend. And I've heard he's a good male."

"For an angel," Flynn muttered.

Sigrid demanded, "We're going to the angels?" Disdain and distrust spiked each word.

The howls in the warehouse closed in: *We stalk the darkness together.*

"I don't see another option," Dec admitted. "It's a gamble, though. Tiberian might go right to Celestina."

"The Governor's cool," Flynn said.

"I don't trust any Archangel," Marc said. "They're bred and raised into unchecked power. They go to those secretive academies, ripped away from any family. It's not conducive to raising well-balanced people. *Good* people."

At the exit, they paused, listening carefully to the sounds beyond. They couldn't smell anything through the metal door, but the howls behind them drew closer. Whoever was in the warehouse would reach this hall in a matter of moments.

Another howl—this one familiar. "Amelie," Ithan breathed. If they turned back, they'd face a fight with the second-most powerful wolf pack in Lunathion. Yet to go through that door into the unforgiving city, no certain allies to shelter them—

Sigrid did them all a favor and shoved the door open.

And there, standing in the alley beyond, stood Sabine Fendyr.

Sabine let out a joyless laugh. Her eyes met Ithan's, filled with nothing but hate, and then she faced Sigrid, Ithan's dismissal clear. He was nothing and no one to her. Not even a wolf to acknowledge.

Ithan bared his teeth. Flynn, Dec, and Marc clicked off the safeties on their guns.

But Sabine just said to Sigrid through a mouth full of fangs, "You look exactly like him."

4

Pain and dark and quiet. That was the entirety of Hunt Athalar's world.

No, that wasn't true.

Those things were the entirety of the world beyond his tortured body, his sawed-off wings, the aching hunger writhing in his stomach and thirst burning his throat, the slave brand stamped on his wrist. The halo inked anew upon his brow by Rigelus himself, its oppressive power somehow heavier and oilier than the first. All that he had achieved, regained . . . wiped away. His very existence belonged to the Asteri once more.

But inside him, beyond that sea of pain and despair, Bryce was the entirety of his world.

His mate. His wife. His princess.

Prince Hunt Athalar Danaan. He would have hated the last name were it not for the fact that it was a marker of her ownership over his soul, his heart.

There was Bryce, and nothing else. Not even Pollux's barbed-wire whips could rip her face from his mind. Not even that blunt-toothed saw had severed it from him, even as it had hewn through his wings.

Bryce, who had gotten away. Gone to Hel to seek aid. He'd stay here, let Pollux rip him to shreds, cut through his wings again and again, if it meant that the Asteri's attention stayed away from her. If it bought her time to rally the force needed to take on these fuckers.

He'd die before he told them where she was. His only consolation was that Ruhn would do the same.

Baxian, bloody and swaying on the other side of Ruhn, didn't know where Bryce had gone, but he knew plenty about what Bryce had been up to lately. Yet the Helhound hadn't given Pollux an inch. Hunt would have expected nothing less of a male Urd had chosen to be Danika Fendyr's mate.

It was quiet now—the only sound the clank of their chains. Blood and piss and shit coated the floor beneath them, the smell almost as unbearable as the pain.

Pollux was creative, Hunt would give him that. Where others might have gone for stabbing in the gut and twisting, the Hammer had learned the exact points on the feet to whip and burn to cause maximum agony while keeping his victims conscious.

Or maybe it was the Hind who'd learned those tricks. She stood behind her lover and watched with dead eyes as the Hammer slowly—so slowly—took them apart.

That was the other secret he and Danaan would keep. The Hind—what and who she was.

Oblivion beckoned, a sweet release Hunt had come to crave as much as Bryce's body entwined with his. He pretended, sometimes, that when he fell into the blackness, he was falling into her arms, into her sweet, tight heat.

Bryce. Bryce. Bryce.

Her name was a prayer, an order.

He had little hope of leaving this place alive. His only job was to make sure he held out long enough for Bryce to do what she had to do. After his series of colossal fuckups over the centuries . . . it was the least he could offer up.

He should have seen it coming—part of him *had* seen it coming a few weeks ago, when he'd tried to convince Bryce not to go down this road. He should have fought harder. Should have told her this outcome was inevitable, especially if he was involved.

He'd *known* not to trust Celestina with her whole *new Governor, new rules* bullshit. He'd let her win him over, and the Archangel had fucking betrayed them. All that talk about being a friend of Shahar's—he'd eaten it up. Let the memory of his long-dead lover cloud his instincts, as Celestina had surely gambled it would.

What was this but another Fallen rebellion? On a smaller scale, yes, but the stakes had been so much higher this time. Then, he'd lost an army, lost his lover—had known she was dying as time had stretched and slowed around him. Had known she was dead when time had resumed its normal speed once more, and the whole world had changed.

Yet the ties that now bound him to others—not only Bryce, but to the two males in this dungeon with him—had become unbearable. Their pain was his pain. Perhaps worse than what he endured before.

Shahar had been given the easy end. To die at Sandriel's hand, to die on the battlefield, swift and final . . . It had been easier.

A few feet away, Baxian groaned softly.

Hunt's arms had gone numb, shoulders popping out of their sockets from trying to support the weight of their bodies. He mustered his energy, his focus, enough to say to Baxian, "How . . . how you doing?"

Baxian let out a wet cough. "Great."

Next to Hunt, Ruhn grunted. It might have been a laugh. Their only options were screaming and sobbing, or laughing at this giant fucking disaster.

Indeed, Ruhn said, "Wanna . . . hear a . . . joke?" The prince didn't wait for a reply before he continued, "Two angels . . . and a Fae Prince . . . walk into . . . a dungeon . . ."

Ruhn didn't finish, and didn't need to. A broken, rasping laugh came out of Hunt. Then Baxian. Then Ruhn.

Though every heave shrieked through his arms, his back, his broken body, Hunt couldn't stop laughing. The sound bordered on hysteria. Soon tears were leaking down his cheeks, and he knew from the scent that the others were laughing and crying as well, like it was the funniest fucking thing in the world.

The door to the chamber banged open, echoing off the stones like a thunderclap.

"Shut the fuck up," Pollux barked, stalking down the stairs, wings blazing in the dimness.

Hunt laughed louder. Footsteps trailed behind the Hammer—a dark-haired, brown-skinned male followed him in: the Hawk. The final member of Sandriel's triarii. "What the Hel is wrong with them?" he sneered at Pollux.

"They're stupid shits, that's what," Pollux said, strutting to the rack of torture devices and grabbing an iron poker. He thrust it into the embers of the fire, the light gilding his white wings into a mockery of a heavenly aura.

The Hawk prowled closer, peering at the three of them with a close scrutiny that echoed his namesake. Like Baxian, the Hawk hailed from two peoples: angels, who had granted him his white wings, and hawk shifters, who'd granted him his ability to transform into a bird of prey.

Those were about all the similarities between the two males. For starters, Baxian had a soul. The Hawk . . .

The Hawk's gaze lingered on Hunt. Nothing of life, of joy, lay in those eyes.

"Athalar."

Hunt nodded to the male in greeting. "Asshole."

Ruhn snickered. The Hawk pivoted to the rack, where he pulled out a long, curving knife. The kind that was designed to yank out organs on the withdraw. Hunt remembered that one—from last time.

Ruhn laughed again, as if almost drunk. "Creative."

"We'll see how you laugh in a moment, princeling," the Hawk said, earning a grin from Pollux as the Hammer waited for the poker to heat. "I heard your cousin Cormac pleaded for mercy before the end."

"Fuck you," Ruhn snarled.

The hawk shifter weighed the knife in his hands. "His father has disowned him. Or whatever's left of his body." A wink at Ruhn. "Your father has done the same."

Hunt didn't miss the shock that rippled over Ruhn's face. At his father's betrayal? Or at his cousin's demise? Did such things even matter down here?

Baxian rasped to the Hawk, "You're a fucking liar. Always were . . . always will be."

The Hawk smiled up at Baxian. "How about we start with your tongue today, traitor?"

To Baxian's credit, he stuck out his tongue toward the Hawk in invitation.

Hunt smirked. Yeah—they were all in this together. To the bitter end.

The Hawk cut his stare toward Hunt. "You'll be next, Athalar."

"Come and get it," Hunt gasped. Ruhn extended his tongue as well.

The Hawk simmered with rage at their defiance, white wings glowing with unearthly power. But slowly, a smile lit his face—horrific in its calculation, its gradual delight as Pollux turned, the poker white-hot and rippling with heat.

"Who's first?" the Hammer crooned. The angel stood poised, silhouetted against the blazing fire behind him.

Hunt opened his mouth, his last bit of bravado before the shitshow began, but in the shadows behind Pollux, beyond the fireplace, something dark moved. Something darker than shadow.

Not Ruhn's shadows. The prince didn't seem to be able to access those when constrained by the gorsian shackles. Only the prince's mind-speaking abilities remained.

This shadow was different—darker, older. Watching them.

Watching Hunt.

Hallucinations: Bad, because it meant he had some infection that even his immortal body couldn't fight off. Good, because it meant he might quietly slip away into death's embrace. Bad, because it meant the Asteri might turn their attention fully to Bryce. Good, because the pain would be gone. Bad, because he still held out some stupid, fool's hope deep in his heart of seeing her again. Good, because Bryce wouldn't come looking for him if he was dead.

Across the room, the thing in the shadows moved. Just slightly. Like it had crooked a finger at him.

Death. That was the thing in the shadows.

And now it beckoned.

Night.

Borne on a raft of oblivion, Ruhn drifted across a sea of pain.

The last thing he remembered was the sound and sight of his small intestine splattering on the ground, pain as sharp as—well, as sharp as the curved knife the Hawk had plunged into his gut.

He wondered when the shifter would disembowel them with his talons in his hawk form, as he was fond of doing. Ruhn could imagine it easily: the Hawk perching on his torso and clawing out his organs, pecking at them with that razor-sharp beak. He'd heal, and then the Hawk would begin again. Over and over—

Ruhn had been a fool to think nothing that happened down here could be worse than the years of torture at his father's hands. The burns, the gorsian shackles his father had put him in to keep him from fighting back, keep him from healing—then, at least, he'd developed his own ways of surviving, of recovering. But now there was only pain, then oblivion, then pain again.

Had he died? Or been a whisper away from death, as Vanir could be if the blow wasn't truly fatal? His Fae body would regenerate the organs, even slowed by the gorsian shackles.

Night.

The female voice echoed across the starlit sea. Like a lighthouse shining in the distance.

Night.

Here, there was no escape from her voice. If he roused himself, the pain would wash over the raft and he'd drown in it. So he had no choice but to listen, to drift toward that beacon.

Gods, what did he do to you?

Anger and grief filled the question as it came from all around him, from inside him.

Ruhn managed to say, *Nothing you haven't done a thousand times yourself.*

Then she stood there with him, on his raft. Lidia. Fire streamed off her body, but he could see her perfect face. The most beautiful female he'd ever seen. A flawless mask over a rotted heart.

His enemy. His lover. The soul he'd thought was—

She knelt and extended a hand toward him. *I'm so sorry.*

Ruhn shifted beyond her reach. As much movement as he could manage, even here. Something like agony flashed in her eyes, but she didn't try to touch him again.

He must have been killed today. Or come close to it, if she was here. If he had no defenses left and she'd broken through that mental wall for the first time since he'd learned who she was.

What had they done to Cormac to render him irrevocably dead?

He couldn't stop the memory from flooding him, of sitting beside Cormac in that bar before they went to the Eternal City, of that one moment he thought he'd glimpsed the person his cousin might have been. The friend Cormac might have become, if he hadn't been systematically stripped of kindness by King Morven.

It shouldn't have been a shock to Ruhn, that the two kings had disowned their sons. Though one king had fire in his veins and the other shadows, Einar and Morven were more alike than anyone realized.

Ruhn had always held some scrap of hope that his father saw the Asteri for what they truly were, and that if it ever came down to it, his father would make the right choice. That the orrery in his study, the years spent looking for patterns in light and space . . . that it had meant something larger. That it wasn't simply the idle studying of a bored royal who needed to feel more important in the grand scheme of things than he actually was.

That hope was dead. His father was a spineless fucking coward.

Ruhn, Lidia said, and he hated the sound of his name on her lips. He hated *her.* He turned on his side, putting his back to her.

I understand why you're angry, why you must hate me, she began hoarsely. *Ruhn, the . . . the things I've done . . . I need you to understand why I did them. Why I'll keep doing them.*

Save your sob story for someone who gives a shit.

Ruhn, please.

The raft groaned, and he knew she was reaching for him again. But he couldn't bear that touch, the pleading in her voice, the emotion that no one else in the world but him had ever heard from the Hind.

So Ruhn said, *Fuck your excuses.* And rolled off that mental raft to let the sea of pain drown him.

5

Ithan's heart stalled as Sabine smiled savagely, advancing toward the warehouse's side door. The alley behind her was empty—no witnesses. Exactly what Ithan and all those who served under Sabine had been trained to ensure.

Sigrid backed up a step, right into Declan. The sprites clung to her neck, yellow flames trembling.

"I knew my brother let me find him and your sister too easily," Sabine snarled, eyes fixed wholly on Sigrid, as if the two Fae warriors with guns pointed at her head were nothing. "I *knew* he lied about how many pups he had."

Sigrid halted her retreat. Ithan didn't dare take his eyes off Sabine to read her face.

"All that effort—for *you*?" Sabine surveyed her curving claws. "I promise to make this quick, at least. It's more than I can say for your sister. Poor pup."

"Leave her alone," Ithan snarled, balancing on the balls of his feet, readying to leap for Sabine. To make this final, disastrous stand.

Sabine laughed humorlessly, acknowledging his existence at last. "Some guard, Holstrom."

"You have two fucking seconds, Sabine, to get lost," Declan said.

Sabine's smile crinkled her nose—sheer lupine fury. "You'll need more than bullets to down me, Faeling." Ithan had told Flynn that Sabine wasn't dumb enough to start shit on the Viper Queen's turf, but at the sight of the Prime Apparent's hateful expression, he wondered if her rage and fear had overridden any scrap of common sense.

He unsheathed his claws. "How about these?" He snarled again. "You're dead fucking meat when we tell the authorities about this."

Sabine's smile became icy cold. "Who will you tell? Celestina won't care. And the Autumn King wants a clean slate for the Valbaran Fae. He'll have nothing to do with this."

A low, thunderous growl rattled from behind Ithan.

The hair on his arms rose. It was a growl of pure challenge. One he'd heard from Danika. From Connor. The challenge of a wolf who wouldn't back down.

Sabine glanced to Sigrid in surprise.

"I went into the tank for my sister," Sigrid rasped, agony and rage contorting her face. "To keep her fed. To keep her safe. And you killed her." Her voice rose, full of command that had the wolf in him sitting up, readying to strike at her signal. "I'll rip out your throat, you soulless thief. I'm going to piss on your rotting *corpse*—"

Sabine leapt.

Declan fired his gun at the same time Flynn unleashed a second, blasting shot.

Sigrid dropped to her knees, claws scratching at her face as she shielded her ears against the noise. Flynn advanced, gun at the ready, firing again at the downed wolf leaking blood onto the grimy alley pavement.

Dec's shot had been for Sabine's knee—to incapacitate her. But Flynn had blasted Sabine's face clean off.

"Hurry," Flynn said, grabbing Sigrid's arm. The trembling sprites leapt onto his shoulders. "We have to get to the river—we'll grab one of the boats."

Yet Ithan could only stare at Sabine's body, the blood and gore splattered around the alley. She would no doubt heal from this wound, but not soon enough to stop them from leaving.

Every muscle in his body locked up. As if screaming, *Help her!*

Protect and save your Alpha! Even if something in his gut whispered, *Rip her to pieces.*

The others began running for the alley, but Ithan didn't move.

"Stop," he said. They didn't hear him. "*Stop!*" His shout echoed over stone and corpse and blood—and they halted within steps of the alley exit.

"What?" Marc said, his cat's eyes gleaming in the dimness.

"The other wolves . . . they went quiet." The howls that had been closing in behind them had stopped entirely.

"Glad someone finally noticed," drawled a female voice from the end of the alley.

The Viper Queen lounged against a filthy wall, cigarette smoldering between her fingers, her white jumpsuit glowing like the moon in the flickering firstlight from the lampposts. Her eyes dropped to Sabine's body. Her purple-painted lips curved upward as her gaze lifted to Ithan's.

"Bad dog," she purred.

"This is a most unorthodox request, Lidia."

Lidia kept her chin high, hands tucked behind her back as she walked with clipped precision along the crystal hallway. The perfect imperial soldier. "Yes, but I believe Irithys might be . . . motivating for Athalar."

Rigelus kept pace beside her, graceful despite his long, gangly legs. The teenage Fae body masked the immortal monster beneath.

As they began to descend a winding staircase, lit only by firstlights guttering in tiny alcoves, Rigelus sniffed, "She is mostly cooperative, but she might balk at the order."

Now a step behind him, Lidia fixed her gaze on his scrawny neck. It would be so easy, were he any other being, to wrap her hands around it and twist. She could almost feel the echo of his crunching bones reverberating against her palms.

"Irithys will do what she's told," Lidia said as they descended into the gloom.

Rigelus said nothing more as they wound around and around,

into the earth beneath the Eternal Palace. Even deeper than the dungeons where Ruhn and the others were kept. Most believed this place little more than myth.

Rigelus at last halted before a metal door. Lead—six inches thick.

Lidia had been here only once over her time with the Asteri. Accompanied by Rigelus then as well, along with her father.

A private tour of the palace, given by the Bright Hand himself to one of his most loyal subjects—and one of his wealthiest. And Lidia, young and still brimming with hate and disdain for the world, had been all too willing to join them.

She became that person again as Rigelus laid a hand on the door. The lead glowed, and then the door swung open.

The oppressive heat and humidity of this place hadn't changed since that first visit. As Lidia stepped inside after Rigelus, it once again pushed with damp fingers on her face, her neck.

The hall stretched ahead, the one thousand sunken tubs in the stone floor shining with pale light that illuminated the bodies floating within. Masks and tubes and machines hummed and hissed; salt crusted the stones between the tanks, some sections piled thick with it. And before the machines, already bowing at the waist to Rigelus . . .

A withered humanoid form, veiled and dressed in gray robes, the material gauzy enough to reveal the bony body beneath, stood at the massive desk at the entrance of the room. The Mistress of the Mystics. If she had a name, Lidia had never heard it uttered.

Above her veiled head, a hologram of images spun, stars and planets whizzing by. Every constellation and galaxy the mystics now searched for Bryce Quinlan. How many corners of the universe remained?

That wasn't Lidia's concern—not today. Not as Rigelus said, "I have need of Irithys."

The mistress lifted her head, but her body remained stooped with age, so thin the knobs of her spine jutted from beneath her gauzy robe. "The queen has been sullen, Your Brilliance. I fear she will not be amenable to your requests."

Rigelus only gestured to the hall, bored. "We shall try, nonetheless."

The mistress bowed again and hobbled past the sunken tubs and machinery, the trail of her robes white with salt.

Rigelus strode past the mystics without so much as a downward glance. They were mere cogs in a machine to help facilitate his needs. But Lidia couldn't help assessing the watery faces as she passed. All slumbering, whether they wanted to or not.

Where had they come from, the dreamers locked down here? What Hel had they or their families endured to make it worth it? And what skills did they possess to warrant this alleged honor of honors, to serve the Asteri themselves?

Rigelus neared the dimly glowing center of the hall. There, in a crystal bubble the size of a cantaloupe, a female made of pure flame slumbered.

Her long hair lay draped around her in golden waves and curls of fire, her lean, graceful limbs nude. The Sprite Queen was perhaps no bigger than Lidia's hand, yet even in repose, she had a presence. Like she was the small sun around which this place orbited.

It was close to the truth, Lidia supposed.

The mistress hobbled to the warded and bespelled orb and rapped on it with her knobbly knuckles. "Get up. Your master's here to see you."

Irithys opened eyes like glowing coals. Even crafted of flame, she seemed to simmer with hate. Especially as her gaze landed on Rigelus.

The Bright Hand inclined his head mockingly. "Your Majesty."

Slowly, with dancer-like grace, Irithys sat up. Her eyes slid from Rigelus to her mistress to Lidia. Nothing but calculation and resentment shone on her face—an uncommonly plain face, considering the usual beauty of her kind.

Rigelus gestured to Lidia, the golden rings on his long fingers sparkling in Irithys's light. "My Hind has a request of you."

My Hind. Lidia ignored the possession in the words. The way they raked down her very soul.

She stepped closer to the bubble, hands once again clasped behind her back. "I have three prisoners in the dungeon who will find your sort of fire particularly motivating. I require you to come to the dungeons, to help me convince them to talk."

The Mistress of the Mystics whipped her head to Lidia. "You can't mean for her to *leave* here—"

Not sparing the crone a look, Lidia said, "Surely, as mistress of this place, you can find it in yourself to protect your wards for a few hours."

Beneath the thin veil, she could have sworn the mistress's eyes sparked with hostility. "Irithys is here *because* of the need for her specific kind of protection. Because of her light, a beacon against the darkness of Hel—"

Lidia only leveled a bored look at Rigelus.

He smirked, always amused by the cruelty of others, and said to the mistress, "Should Hel come knocking, send word and I will assist you personally." A huge honor—and an indication of how badly he needed Athalar broken. Ruhn and Baxian, she wasn't entirely sure about, but Athalar . . .

The mistress bowed her head. Leaving Irithys now staring at Lidia.

Lidia lifted her chin. "Will you be amenable to assisting me?"

Irithys glanced down at herself, as if she could see the small band of tattoos around her throat. A halo of sorts—inked on the Sprite Queen by an imperial hag to keep her power in check.

The queen's gesture was a silent question.

Rigelus said, "The ink remains. You can wield enough of your powers to prove useful."

Lidia kept quiet. Let Irithys study her.

She'd been kept down here more than a century. Had not seen daylight or left that crystal bubble in all that time. There was a good chance that behind the glimmering eyes, the queen had gone mad.

But Lidia didn't need her sanity. She could do the thinking for the two of them.

Irithys's chin dipped slightly.

Rigelus turned to Lidia. "You have a week with her."

Lidia held the sprite's blazing stare, let her see the cold fire within her own soul. "Breaking Athalar won't take that long."

Bryce left what she assumed was dinner—roast chicken, more bread, and some herbed potatoes—uneaten on the tray. No one had come by in the hours that had passed, so she assumed they'd either check in with her tomorrow, or perhaps wait until she was banging on that wall of night and howling for someone to come talk to her.

Neither of which seemed like an appealing option.

That left two choices, really. See if she could break through the magical barrier, then make her way out of this mountain and into a strange new world with no idea where she was going, or . . .

She glanced down. Or she could see what lay at the bottom of the grate, if there was some opening beyond the beasts that might take her out of this place . . . and into a strange new world with no idea where she was going.

Hours, and that was the best she could come up with.

"Pathetic," she muttered, zipping the Archesian amulet along its chain. "Fucking pathetic."

What was happening to Hunt? To Ruhn? Were they even—

She wouldn't let herself think about it.

Her captors had taken her phone before bringing her here, so she had no idea what time it was. Or at least what time it was on Midgard. She didn't even want to wade into the tangle of how time might pass faster or slower on this world. And how long had actually passed since that run down the hallway in the Eternal Palace—

Bryce stood from her crouched position against the wall. Stalked to the grate in the center of the room. A chorus of hissing rose from it as she approached.

"Yeah, yeah, I hear you," she murmured, kneeling and prying the grate out of the floor, her fingers straining painfully with the effort. But inch by inch, it pulled away, scraping too loudly against the stone floor.

She waited a moment, listening for the sounds of her approaching captors. When no one came to investigate the noise, Bryce peered into the yawning dark pit she'd opened.

She lowered her head a little toward the hole. The hissing stopped.

Bryce willed starlight to her hand and held it up. Nothing but emptiness waited below. Bryce fisted her palm, balling the starlight into an orb, and dropped it down—

A writhing sea of black, scaled bodies silvered by her light appeared.

Bryce scrambled back.

Sobeks—or their dark twins. Tharion had faced them when they'd escaped the Bone Quarter, concentrating his water magic into lethal spears that pierced their thick hides, but . . ."Fuck," she breathed.

She glanced over a shoulder to the door. To the shield that echoed there with a sense of Rhysand. Power the likes of which she'd never encountered—at least, other than from the Asteri.

If he had as much power as an Asteri . . . It was all a hunch, really, but if he could be manipulated into helping her, somehow coming back to Midgard with her and kicking ass—

She might very well replace six conquerors for another. And something had to change, the cycle had to stop *now,* but not if it began anew with another overlord. And if Rhysand did indeed have that much power, she doubted these interrogations would continue so peaceably for much longer. Especially now that they knew she had something of importance tattooed on her back. Whatever *Made* meant, it held considerable weight with them. She had little doubt their patience would soon wear thin.

And whether it'd manifest in Rhysand going against his oh-so-polite insistence on her consent to be mentally probed or in Azriel carving her up with that black knife . . . she didn't want to be around to find out.

Bryce peered at the hole, the beasts below.

That kernel of magic that had altered the language in her

brain and set the Horn glowing had left something in her chest. Just enough fuel.

She'd have a nanosecond to teleport—winnow, as they called it here—down to the beasts. To that sliver of rock she'd noted jutting above them, little wider than her foot. Then she'd have to see if there was any way out. Some tunnel through which they moved beneath this place.

Unless it was only a pit, a veritable cage where they sat in darkness and waited for meat—dead or alive—to be thrown to them.

It would be a true leap of faith.

Her hands shook, but she balled them into fists. She'd outrun an Asteri. Granted, that was with Hunt's lightning, but . . .

Every minute here counted. Every minute left Hunt and Ruhn in Rigelus's hands. If they were even still alive.

"Hunt. Ruhn. Mom. Dad. Fury. June. Syrinx." She whispered their names, fighting the tightness in her throat.

She had to get out of here. Before these people decided the risk she posed was too great, and dealt with her the smart way. Or before they decided they liked the sound of Midgard, of Rigelus, and knew she'd be a wonderful peace offering—

"Get the fuck up," she grunted. "Get the fuck up and do something."

Hunt would tell her she was out of her mind. Ruhn would tell her to try to spin some more bullshit, try to win her captors over. But Danika . . .

Danika would have jumped.

Danika *had* jumped—down into the depths of the Drop with Bryce. Knowing there'd be no return trip for her.

Danika, whose death Rigelus had engineered, manipulating Micah into killing her.

A white haze blurred Bryce's vision. Primal wrath pumped through her, the sort only the Fae could descend into. It sharpened her vision. Tautened her muscles. The star on her chest flared with soft light.

"Fuck this," she growled.

And teleported into the pit.

Tharion supposed he was still high, still hallucinating, when Ithan Holstrom, Declan Emmet, Tristan Flynn, Marc Rosarin, and an unfamiliar female wolf—carrying three *very* familiar sprites—walked into the suite. They were escorted by the Viper Queen and six of her drugged-out Fae bodyguards.

Lying on the couch in front of the TV, so chill it was as if his very bones had melted into the cushions, Tharion could barely lift his head as the group filed in. He gave them a lazy, blissed-out smile. "Hi, friends."

Declan blew out a breath. "Burning fucking Solas, Tharion."

Tharion's face heated. He had a good idea how he looked. But he couldn't convince his body to move. His head was too heavy, limbs too limp. He closed his eyes, sinking back into that sweet heaviness.

"What the fuck is happening here?" Flynn growled. "Did you do that to him?"

Tharion only realized that Ari had entered the living space when she hissed at Flynn, "*Me?* You think I go around drugging helpless people?"

"You go around abandoning them," Flynn countered. "Or was that reserved for Bryce and Hypaxia?"

"Go back to your partying, pretty boy," Ari spat.

"I'll leave you all to catch up," the Viper Queen crooned, and stalked out, shutting the door behind her with a soft click.

Tharion managed to open his eyes. "Why are you guys here?" Ogenas, his mouth felt so far away.

Declan paced a few steps. "Bryce, Athalar, and Ruhn didn't make it out of the Eternal Palace."

Was it the news or the venom that made his entire world spin? "Dead?" The word was like ash on his tongue.

"No," Declan said. "As far as we know. Bryce disappeared, and Ruhn and Hunt are now being held in the Asteri's dungeons."

Tharion just stared at the Fae warrior—Declan's form blurring at the edges—and let the news sink in.

"Dude, your pupils are huge," Flynn said. No wonder his vision was so foggy. "What are you on?"

"You don't want to know."

"Her venom," Ari snapped. "That's what he's on."

"You look terrible," Declan said, stepping closer to peer down at Tharion. "Your shoulder—"

"Minotaur," Tharion grunted. "It's healing. And I don't want to talk about it. Where did Bryce go?"

"We don't know," Declan said.

"Fuck." Tharion said the word on a long exhale. It echoed in every bone and blood vessel. Before he could ask more, he noticed Ari sizing up the group, her gaze landing on the female wolf beside Holstrom. "I know you."

The female wolf's chin lifted. "Likewise, dragon."

Tharion must have made a confused face, because Holstrom said, "This is Sigrid . . . Fendyr."

Yeah, he was hallucinating. There was only *one* Fendyr other than the Prime: Sabine. And he was pretty sure she didn't have any secret daughters.

"We'll get to the particulars later," Declan said, and slumped into the nearest chair. His boyfriend stood beside him, a hand on his shoulder. "We have to sort through this clusterfuck."

Flynn swore. "What is there to sort through? We killed Sabine."

Tharion jolted—or tried to. His body wouldn't move.

"*You* killed Sabine," Declan said. "I shot her in the leg."

"She's not dead-dead," Flynn said.

"She doesn't have a *face,*" Dec countered. "That's pretty—"

"What happened to the other wolves?" Holstrom asked none of them in particular.

Oh, wait—he was asking Tharion and Ari. Ari gave Holstrom a blank look. "What wolves?"

"We were being chased by the Black Rose Pack," Ithan explained, "and then . . . we weren't. Where did the Viper Queen take them?"

"Start looking in the river," Tharion mumbled.

"She wouldn't have killed them," Marc said. "It'd be a headache, even for her. Her goons must have knocked them out and moved them elsewhere."

"What about Sabine?" Holstrom asked.

Gods, Tharion's head was throbbing. This had to be some weird dream.

"The Viper Queen will twist this to her own advantage somehow," Marc said. "She'll either present herself as Sabine's rescuer or hand us over."

Tharion lifted his brows at Marc.

Marc caught the look and explained, "I've had a few clients get into trouble with the Viper Queen over the years. I learned a thing or two about her tactics."

Tharion nodded, as if this was perfectly fucking normal, and closed his eyes again.

"Pathetic," Ari hissed—probably at him. But then she asked the others, "So you're all the Viper Queen's captives?"

"Not sure," Declan said. "She caught us in the act of, uh . . . downing Sabine. When she told us to follow, it seemed like an order."

"But she said nothing else?" Ari asked. Tharion cracked an eye, fighting to stay present.

"Just that we can crash here tonight," Flynn said, plopping on the couch beside Tharion and grabbing the remote. He flipped to some sports highlights.

"We should make a run for Tiberian or for the river," Declan said.

"You're not getting out if the Viper Queen doesn't want you to," Tharion rasped.

"So we're trapped?" Sigrid's voice hitched with something like panic.

"No," Holstrom said. "But we need to think through our steps carefully. It's a question of strategy."

"Lead on, oh great sunball captain," Flynn intoned with mock solemnity.

Ithan rolled his eyes, and the gesture was so normal, so friendly, that something in Tharion's chest tightened. He'd thrown all this away, any shot at a normal life. And now his friends were here . . . seeing him like this.

Tharion closed his eyes once more, this time because he couldn't stand the sight of his friends. Couldn't stand the worry and pity in Holstrom's eyes as the wolf took in his sorry state.

Captain Whatever. More like Captain Worthless.

The beasts were much larger, much fouler-smelling up close. Bryce's magic sputtered as they turned her way. She teetered on the rock ledge before steadying herself.

One leap upward, and they'd devour her. Her star illuminated only the closest ones, all hissing mouths, writhing bodies, slashing tails—

She rallied her power, but . . . nothing. Just glittering stardust in her veins. Only enough to keep that star glowing on her chest. No teleporting, then. Could these creatures see enough to be blinded? They dwelled in the darkness. Could they have evolved past the need for sight?

The thoughts raced and crashed through her. The grate was thirty feet up—no way to go back now. And the floor of the pit was covered with these things, all smelling her, assessing her.

But not . . . advancing. Like something about her gave them pause.

Made. Maybe it also meant something to these creatures.

Bryce tugged the neckline of her T-shirt down, revealing the star in all its glory. The beasts shrank back, hissing, tossing massive, scaled heads. Their teeth glinted in the starlight.

A tunnel stretched on either side of the pit. She could only make out the cavernous mouths, but it seemed like this pit sat in the middle of a passage. To where, though? This was the stupidest thing she'd ever done. In a life full of stupid ideas and mistakes, that was saying something, but . . .

Bryce turned toward one of the tunnels, trying to better see what lay beyond. The star in her chest dimmed. Like her magic was rapidly fading. She whirled toward the other tunnel, trying to see what she could before the magic vanished—

The star flared brightly again.

"Huh," she murmured. Bryce turned back the other way. The star faded. To the opposite side: it brightened.

Rigelus had said the star reacted to people—those loyal to her, her chosen knights or whatever. He'd also said that Theia herself had borne this star on her chest. And in this world, this home planet of Theia and the Starborn . . .

Bryce had no choice but to trust that star.

"That way, then," she said, her voice echoing in the chamber. But she still had to get over the gulf of those beasts between her and the next rocky outcropping in the tunnel wall.

She'd never before wished for wings, but fuck if they wouldn't have been handy right then. If Hunt had been here with her—

Her throat closed up. The beasts hissed, tails lashing. As if they could sense her shift in attention.

Bryce focused on her breathing, as she'd learned to do in the wake of losing Danika, as she'd learned to do in the face of all those Vanir and Fae who'd sneered at her. The star kept glowing, pointing the way. The creatures settled, as if her emotions were theirs.

She willed herself to calm. To feel no fear. The creatures settled further. Some laid their heads down.

She glanced at the star in her chest. Still glowing brightly. *They are your champions, too,* it seemed to say. The star hadn't been wrong about Hunt. Or Cormac.

So Bryce stuck one foot over the ledge. The beasts didn't move. She let her foot drop a little lower, dangling bait—

Nothing.

Her heartbeat ratcheted up, and a massive head rose, pivoting her way—

Through love, all is possible. She called up the memory of Danika's love and let it course through her, steady her as she lowered herself onto the ground.

Into the beasts' nest.

They lay before her like obedient dogs. She didn't question it. Didn't think of anything but the star on her chest and the tunnel it pointed toward and the desire to see the faces of those she loved once more.

Bryce took a step, her neon-pink sneaker outrageously bright amid the dark scales so terrifyingly close. Then another step. The creatures watched, but they didn't move a single talon.

Ruhn had called her a queen before she left. And for the first time in her life, as she walked through that sea of death . . . she might have lifted her chin a bit higher. Might have felt a mantle settle on her shoulders, a train of starlight in her wake.

Might have felt something like a crown settle upon her head. Guiding her into the dark.

Tharion finally worked up enough concentration and energy to get to his feet and amble toward his room. Holstrom cornered him a second later.

"What the Hel happened?" the wolf asked, halting Tharion on the threshold.

"The River Queen was gunning for me." Gods, his voice sounded dead, even to his ears. "It was either death or imprisonment at her hands or . . . this."

"You should have come to me."

"For what?" Tharion's laugh was as dead as his voice. "You're a defector, too. We're packless wolves." Tharion nodded to the wolf now sitting on the couch beside Flynn. "Speaking of which . . . Sigrid *Fendyr*?"

"Long story. She's Sabine's niece." Ithan's mouth tightened. "She was the female mystic in the Astronomer's place. I pulled her out two days ago."

Tharion's head spun. "So what are you doing here?"

"Before Sabine showed up to kill Sigrid, we were just getting to the part where I convinced everyone to come free you from this shithole so we could get onto the *Depth Charger* and save Ruhn and Athalar."

"That's . . . a lot of words." Tharion's heart was swimming with them.

Or maybe that was the venom. His stomach was churning, and he really needed a toilet or a bed or a single moment of peace.

"You can't stay here," Ithan said, but his voice seemed distant as Tharion walked to his bed and collapsed face-first onto the mattress. "We're gonna find a way to get you out."

"Too late, wolf," Tharion said, words muffled against the pillows. They slurred further as sleep grabbed him with sharp talons and tugged him down. "There's no saving me."

Ithan found Sigrid pacing before the window overlooking the now-dim fighting pit. It was late enough that even its lights had been shut off.

"You should sleep—the couch is yours."

Dec, Flynn, and Marc had all claimed spots on the floor—though from their breathing patterns, Ithan knew they were awake. After the night they'd had, how could any of them sleep?

Sigrid wrapped her arms around her thin body. "We're trapped here."

"No," Ithan insisted. "I won't let that happen."

"I can't be trapped again." Her voice broke. "I *can't*."

"You're getting out of here," Ithan said. "No matter what."

"Then why not go for the door right now?" she demanded, waving a hand toward the exterior door to the suite.

"Because there are six drugged-up Fae assassins on the other side, waiting to kill us if we do."

Her face blanched and she rubbed at her chest. "*Trapping us.* I need to get out."

"You will."

She closed her eyes, breathing shallowly, losing herself in panic.

Ithan glanced across the room. The three sprites—now curled up beside Flynn and dozing as violet balls of flame—hadn't seemed too panicked. Quiet, but . . . focused. Like they were accustomed to facing fear. It made his guts twist to think about it.

"Sabine will come for me again," Sigrid said. "Won't she?"

"She'll try, but we'll be long out of the city by the time she recovers."

Her eyes narrowed. "Why didn't we leave immediately? When you took me out of the tank?"

Ithan stiffened. "Because I didn't know where else to go."

"A house with those *buffoons* was the best—"

"Those buffoons are my friends, and some of the best fighters I know," Ithan warned, temper flaring. "Those buffoons risked their lives for you tonight—*saved* you tonight."

Her teeth bared. "If Sabine will recover, then let me get to her body and rip it to—"

"Believe me, the thought crossed my mind. But . . ."

He didn't finish the thought.

"But what?"

He shook his head, not letting himself go there, even mentally. "It's late," he said. "You should sleep."

"I won't be able to."

"Then try," he said, perhaps a bit more sharply than necessary.

Sigrid glared at him, then glanced toward the door to Tharion's bedroom. "Was *that* the mer you wanted to get to help us?"

"Yes."

She snorted. "I don't think he'll be much help to anyone. Not even himself."

"You should sleep," he said again. He'd had enough of this.

"Is this a thing you do frequently?" she asked suddenly. "Liberate people enslaved to others?"

"Only recently," he said wearily.

He didn't wait for her to reply before he walked to Tharion's room, threw himself on the ground beside the heavily sleeping male, and closed his eyes.

6

About twenty feet into the tunnel, the beasts tapered off. They remained still, watchful, until Bryce had passed the last of them. Until she found bars blocking the way, save for a small door on the left side of the barrier. The door swung open at the touch of her hand. She had to stoop to get through, but it had clearly been designed to keep the beasts from getting out.

She made sure to shut the door behind her.

The metal groaned, and then hissing, like a swarm of angry wasps, filled the tunnel.

The beasts were writhing again, snapping jaws and heaving bodies scraping against each other, as if shutting the door had knocked them from their stupor. Bryce stumbled back in time to see one particularly massive beast lunge for the bars.

The iron shook with the impact—but held.

Bryce panted, surveying the sinuous death once again in motion. But the beasts were far too large to squeeze through the bars.

She let out a shaky breath and surveyed the tunnel ahead. The star flared brighter, as if urging her onward.

"All right," she said, patting her chest. "All right."

* * *

Bryce walked for hours. Or what she assumed was hours, judging by how sore her legs became, how her feet ached, even with the cushioning of her sneakers.

The tunnel could lead nowhere. It could last for a hundred miles.

She should have grabbed some supplies—stuffed some of the food from her tray into her pockets and bra. Filled up on water.

She saw no deviations, no alternate tunnels or crossroads. Just one long, endless stretch into the dark.

Her mouth dried out, and though she knew she shouldn't, Bryce stopped. Sitting down against the age-worn wall, she swallowed the dryness in her mouth. She had no choice but to keep going.

She closed her eyes for a heartbeat. Only one—

Bryce's eyes flew open.

She'd fallen asleep. Somehow, she'd *fallen asleep*, so fucking exhausted from the last gods knew how many hours that she hadn't even realized it, and—

The star on her chest was still glowing beneath her T-shirt. She remained in the tunnel.

But it was no longer empty.

Nesta stood over her, a sword strapped down her back. The female's blue-gray eyes seemed to gleam with power in the starlight.

Bryce didn't dare move.

Nesta tossed her a leather-wrapped canteen. "Do yourself a favor and drink before you pass out again."

Bryce sipped from the canteen of what seemed to be—thankfully—water, and watched the other female over the rim of the bottle. Nesta sat against the opposite wall of the tunnel, monitoring Bryce with a feline curiosity.

They'd been silent in the minutes since Bryce had awoken. Nesta had barely moved, other than to take a seat.

At last, Bryce capped the canteen and tossed it back to Nesta.

The female caught it with ease. "How'd you learn that I left the cell?" No need to reveal that she could teleport.

Nesta gave her a bored look—as if Bryce should have already known the answer. "We have people who can talk to shadows. They told us you went through the grate."

Interesting—and creepy. But Bryce asked, "So you're here to drag me back to the cell?"

Nesta shoved the canteen into her pack and rose, the movement sure and graceful. The sword strapped down her back . . . it wasn't the Starsword, though Bryce could have sworn there was something similar about the blade. A kind of presence, a tug toward it.

The female inclined her head to the tunnel behind them—the way back. "I was sent to escort you."

"Semantics." Bryce got to her feet. Her versus this female . . . decent odds, but the sword presented a problem. As did whatever sort of presence thrummed from Nesta, apparently able to detect the Horn in Bryce's back. Battling an opponent whose skills and powers were unknown, if not wholly alien, was probably unwise. "Look. I'm not here to start trouble—"

"Then don't. Walk back with me."

Bryce eyed the tunnel behind them. "How'd you even get past the beasts?"

A slight smile. "It pays to know people with wings."

Bryce grunted, despite the ache in her chest. "So someone flew you to the gate—"

"And will fly us out." A corner of her mouth kicked up. "Or haul you, if you decide to do this the hard way."

Bryce scanned the path behind Nesta. Only deep shadows lingered. No sign of anyone with wings waiting to snatch her. "You might be bluffing."

She could have sworn silver fire danced in Nesta's eyes. "Do you want to find out?"

Bryce held her stare. Clearly, they didn't want her dead, if they'd sent someone to retrieve her, not hunt her down. But if she returned to that cell, how long would they keep her there? Even hours could make a difference for Hunt and Ruhn—

"I'm always up for a day of discovery," Bryce said.

Then she erupted with light.

Nesta cursed, but Bryce didn't wait to see if the light had blinded her before bolting down the passage. Without any weapons, a running head start was her best chance of making it.

A force like a stone wall hit her from behind. The world tilted, her breath rushing from her as she collided with the stone ground, bones barking in pain. Shadows had wrapped around her, pinning her, and she thrashed, kicking and swatting at them.

She flared her light, a blast of incandescence that sent the shadows splintering in every direction.

She might not have enough magic left in her veins to teleport, but she could buy herself some time with this, at least. She scrambled to her feet, the shadows leaping upon her again, a pack of wolves set on devouring her.

She let them swarm her for just a moment before her magic exploded outward, a bomb of light in every direction. It sent those shadows flying into the ceiling, the walls. Where shadow met stone, debris tumbled from the ceiling. The mountain shook.

Bryce ran. Deeper into the tunnel, into the dark, her star flaring as she raced away from the crumbling rock all around—

The world shook and roared again, sending her sprawling amid a cloud of dust.

And then there was silence, interrupted only by the skittering rocks from the wall of stones now blocking the way back. But a cave-in wouldn't stop Vanir or Fae for long. Bryce lunged upward—

Metal bit into her throat. Icy, deathly cold.

"Do not," Nesta said quietly, panting, "move."

Bryce glared up at the female but didn't shove the blade from her throat. Her very bones roared at her not to touch the sword more than necessary. "Neat trick with the shadows."

Nesta just stared imperiously at her. "Get up."

"Put down your sword and I will."

Their gazes clashed, but the sword moved a fraction. Bryce got to her feet, wiping dust and debris from her clothes. "What now?"

Her knees buckled with exhaustion. Her magic was spent, her veins utterly devoid of starlight.

Nesta glanced to the cave-in. Whatever shadow magic she possessed seemed to have little ability to move it. The warrior nodded to the tunnel ahead. "I suppose you're getting your way."

"I didn't mean to cause that—"

"It doesn't matter. There's only one way out now. If there's a way out at all."

Bryce sighed, frowning at the star on her chest, still gleaming into the dark through her T-shirt. Illuminating all the dirt now smeared on the white cotton. "I didn't intend to drag anyone else into this with me."

"Then you should have stayed in the Hewn City."

Bryce tucked away that kernel of knowledge—the place she'd been kept was called the Hewn City. "Look, this star . . ." She tapped her chest. "It's pointing me this way. I have no idea why, but I have to follow it."

Nesta gestured with her blade to the dark path ahead. Bryce could have sworn the sword sang through the air. "So lead on."

"You won't stop me?"

Nesta sheathed the sword down her back with enviable grace. "We're trapped down here. We might as well see what lies ahead."

It was a better reaction than Bryce could have hoped for. Especially from the Fae.

With a shrug, Bryce walked into the dark, one eye on the female at her side. And prayed Urd knew where she was leading them.

7

Lidia carried the crystal bubble containing the Queen of the Fire Sprites through the dim halls, Irithys's flame splashing gold upon the marble floors and walls.

She said nothing to the sprite—not with all the cameras mounted throughout the Asteri's palace. Irithys didn't seem to care. She rested on the bottom of the orb with her legs folded serenely. After several long minutes, though, the sprite said, "The dungeons aren't this way."

"And you're so familiar with the layout of this place?"

"I have a keen memory," the queen said flatly, her long hair floating above her head in a twirl of yellow flame. "I need only see something once to remember it. I recall the entire walk down here to the mystics in perfect detail."

A helpful gift. But Lidia said, "We're not going to the dungeons."

From the corner of her eye, she noted Irithys peering at her. "But you told Rigelus—"

"It has been a long while since you left your bubble . . . and used your powers." Whatever embers were left with the halo's constraints. "I think it wise that we warm you up a bit before the main event."

"What do you mean?" the queen demanded, flame shifting to a wary orange, but Lidia said nothing as she unlocked an unmarked iron door on a quiet lower level. Lidia offered up silent thanks to Luna that her hands didn't shake as she reached for the handle, the gold-and-ruby ring on her finger shimmering in Irithys's light.

Between one breath and the next, Lidia buried that part of her that begged to distant gods, the part that doubted. She became still and flat, expression as undisturbed as the surface of a forgotten forest pool.

The door creaked open to reveal a table, a chair in front of it, and on the other side of the table, chained with gorsian shackles, an imperial hag.

The hag lifted baleful, yellow-tinged eyes to Lidia as the Hind shut the door behind her. Those eyes lowered to the bubble, the Sprite Queen glowing orange inside it.

Lidia slid into the chair across from the prisoner, setting the sprite's crystal on the table between them as if it were no more than a handbag. "Thank you for meeting me, Hilde."

"I had no choice in the matter," the hag rasped, her thinning white hair glimmering like strands of wispy moonlight. A wretched, twisted creature, but one of hidden beauty. "Ever since your *dogs* arrested me on trumped-up charges—"

"You were found in possession of a comm-crystal known to be used by Ophion rebels."

"I never saw that crystal in all my life," Hilde snapped, shards of brown teeth glinting. "Someone framed me."

"Yes, yes," Lidia said, waving a hand. Irithys watched every movement, still that alert shade of orange. "You can plead your case before Rigelus."

The imperial hag had the good sense to look nervous. "Then why are you here?"

Lidia smirked at Irithys. "To warm you up."

The Sprite Queen caught her meaning, and simmered into a deep, threatening red.

But the hag let out a hacking laugh. She still wore her imperial uniform, the crest of the Republic frayed over her sagging breasts. "I've got nothing to tell you, *Lidia*."

Lidia crossed one leg over the other. "We'll see."

Hilde hissed, "You think yourself so mighty, so untouchable."

"Is this the part where you tell me you'll have your revenge?"

"I knew your mother, girl," the hag snapped.

Lidia had enough training and self-control to keep her face blank, tone utterly bored. "My mother was a witch-queen. Plenty of people knew her."

"Ah, but I *knew* her—flew in her unit in our fighting days."

Lidia angled her head. "Before or after you sold your soul to Flame and Shadow?"

"I swore allegiance to Flame and Shadow *because* of your mother. Because she was weak and spineless and had no taste for punishment."

"I suppose my mother and I differ on that front, then."

Hilde swept her rheumy gaze over Lidia. "Better than that disgrace of a sister who now calls herself queen."

"Hypaxia is half Flame and Shadow—she should have your allegiance on both fronts."

Lidia knew Irithys monitored each word. If she could remember things after seeing them only once, did it also apply to what she heard?

"Your mother was a fool to give you away," Hilde grumbled.

Lidia arched a brow. "Is that a compliment?"

"Take it as you will." The hag flashed her rotting teeth in a nightmare of a smile. "You're a born killer—like any true witch. That girl on the throne is as softhearted as your mother. She'll bring down the entire Valbaran witch-dynasty."

"Alas, my father was a smart negotiator," Lidia said, making a good show of admiring the ruby ring on her finger, the stone as red as Irithys's flame. "But enough about me." She gestured to the hag, then to the sprite. "Irithys, Queen of the Sprites. Hilde, Grand Hag of the Imperial Coven."

"I know who you are," Irithys said, her voice quiet with leashed rage. She now floated in the center of the orb, her body bloodred. "You put this collar on me."

Hilde again smiled, wide enough to reveal her blackened gums. A lesser person would have cowered at that smile. "I had the honor of doing it to the little bitch who bore the crown before you, too."

Hilde didn't mean Irithys's mother, who had never been queen at all. No, when the last Sprite Queen had died, the line had passed to a different branch of the family, with Irithys first to inherit.

A damned inheritance—she'd gained the title and a prison sentence in the same breath. Irithys had barely had her crown for a day before Rigelus had her brought into the dungeons.

Lidia said blandly, "Yes, Hilde. We all know how skilled you are. Athalar himself can thank you for his first halo. But let's talk about why you chose to betray us."

"I did no such thing." Even with the gorsian shackles, a crackling sort of energy leaked from the hag.

Lidia sighed at the ceiling. "I do have appointments today, Hilde. Shall we speed this up?"

She gave no warning before tapping the top of Irithys's crystal. It melted away to nothing, leaving only air between the hag and the Sprite Queen.

Irithys didn't move. Didn't try to run or erupt. She just stood there like a living, burning ruby. As if being free of the crystal after all these years—

Lidia shut down the thought, her voice as dead as her eyes as she said, "Let's see how motivational you can be, Your Majesty."

Hilde glared daggers, but didn't cower or tremble.

Yet Irithys turned to Lidia, hair swirling above her. "No."

Lidia arched a brow. "No?"

Across the table, Hilde was still bristling—but listening carefully.

Irithys said boldly, unafraid, "No."

"It wasn't a request." Lidia nodded to the hag. "Burn her hand."

Hilde snatched her gnarled hands off the table. As if that could save her.

Irithys's chin lifted. "I may be your captive, but I do not have to obey you."

"Hilde is a traitor to the Republic—"

"These are *lies*," Hilde interrupted.

"Your pity is wasted on her," Lidia went on.

"It is not pity," Irithys said, ruby flame darkening to a color like rich wine. "It is honor. There is none in attacking a person who cannot fight back, enemy or no."

Lidia's upper lip curled back from her teeth. "Burn. Her."

Irithys glowed a violet blue, like hottest flame. "*No.*"

Hilde let out a caw of laughter.

Lidia said with a calm that usually made enemies start begging, "I will ask you one more time—"

"And I will tell you a thousand more times: no. On my honor, no."

"You have no honor down here. It means nothing in this place."

"Honor is all I have," Irithys said, the heat of her indigo flames strong enough to warm Lidia's chilled hands. "Honor, and my name. I will not sully or yield them. No matter what my enemy has done. Or what you threaten me with, Hind."

Lidia held the sprite's blazing stare and found only unbreaking, unrelenting will there.

So Lidia inclined her head mockingly at the queen. And with a wave of her hand, she activated the magic Rigelus had gifted her for the week. Like a ball of ice melting in reverse, the crystal orb formed around Irithys again.

"Then I have no need of you," Lidia said, and picked up the crystal, stalking for the door.

Irithys said nothing, but her flame burned a bright, royal blue.

Lidia had just opened the metal door again when Hilde called from the table, "And what of me?"

Lidia threw the imperial hag a cool look. "I suggest you beg Rigelus for mercy." She didn't let the hag reply before slamming the door behind her.

Mercy. Lidia had held none in her heart two days ago, when she'd walked past Hilde in the upper corridors and slipped her own comm-crystal into the hag's pocket. With Ruhn in the dungeons, no one was accessing the other end of the line, anyway. The crystal was, for all intents and purposes, dead. But in Hilde's possession, when Mordoc had sniffed it out on Lidia's suspicion . . . the crystal once again became invaluable.

She could think of no one, other than the Asteri themselves, that Irithys might hate more than the hag who had inked the tattoo on her burning throat. No one that Irithys might enjoy hurting more than Hilde.

And yet the Sprite Queen had refused.

The mistress was nowhere to be found when Lidia returned to the heat and humidity of the mystics' hall, nor when Lidia set Irithys back on her stand in the center of it.

"What of the other prisoners?" Irithys demanded as Lidia stepped back.

Lidia paused, sliding her hands into her pockets. "Why should I waste my time trying to convince you to assist me with them?"

Indeed, time was running thin. She had places to be, and quickly.

"You went to an awful lot of trouble to get me out today. For nothing."

Lidia shrugged, then began prowling for the exit. "I know when I'm losing a battle." She tossed over a shoulder, "Enjoy your name and honor. I hope they're good company in that crystal ball."

Bryce and Nesta walked in fraught, heavy silence for ages.

Bryce's feet had begun aching again, the soreness continuing all the way up her legs. Normally, she would have resorted to talking to distract herself from the discomfort, but Bryce knew better than to ask prying questions about this world, about Nesta's people.

It would be too suspicious. If she sought to tell them as little as possible about herself and Midgard, then they probably wished to do the same regarding their home.

Without warning, Nesta stopped, holding up a fist.

Bryce halted beside her, glancing sidelong to find Nesta's blue-gray eyes making a slow sweep over the tunnel ahead. Icy calm had settled on her face.

Bryce murmured, "What is it?"

Nesta's eyes again flicked over the terrain.

As Bryce stepped forward, her star illuminated what had given the warrior pause: the tunnel widened into a large chamber, its ceiling so high even Bryce's starlight didn't reach it. And in the center of it . . . the path dropped away on either side, leaving only a sliver of a rocky bridge over what seemed to be an endless chasm.

Bryce knew it wasn't endless only because far, far below, water roared. A large subterranean river, if the sound was this loud even up here. Bits of spray floated from the darkness, the damp air laced with a thick, metallic scent—iron. There must have been deposits of it down here.

Nesta said with equal quiet, "That bridge is the perfect place for an ambush."

"From *who*?" Bryce hissed.

"I haven't lived long enough to know every horror in this world, but I can tell you that dark places tend to breed dark things. Especially ones as old and forgotten as this."

"Great. So how do we get across without attracting said dark things?"

"I don't know—this tunnel is foreign to me."

Bryce turned to her in surprise. "You've never been down this way?"

Nesta cut her a look. "No. No one has."

Bryce snorted, surveying the chasm and bridge ahead. No movement, no sound other than the rushing water far below. "Who'd you piss off to get sent to retrieve me, anyway?"

She could have sworn Nesta's lips curved into a smile. "On a good day, too many people to count. But today . . . I volunteered."

Bryce arched a brow. "Why?"

That silvery flame flashed in Nesta's eyes. A shiver slithered along Bryce's spine. Fae and yet . . . not.

"Call it intuition," Nesta said, and stepped onto the bridge.

They'd made it halfway across the narrow bridge—Bryce doing everything she could not to think about the lack of railings, the seemingly endless drop to that thundering river—when they heard it. A new noise, barely audible above the rapids' roar.

Talons skittering over stone.

From above *and* below.

"Hurry." Nesta drew that plain-yet-remarkable sword. At the touch of her hand, silver flames skittered down the blade and—

The breath whooshed out of Bryce. The sword pulsed, as if all the air around it had vanished. It was like the Starsword, somehow. A sword, but more. Just as Nesta was Fae but more.

"What is your sword—"

"Hurry," Nesta repeated, stalking across the rest of the bridge.

Bryce mastered herself enough to obey, moving as fast as she dared given the plunge gaping on either side.

Leathery wings fluttered. Those talons scraped along the stone mere feet ahead—

Bryce damned caution to Hel and jogged toward the tunnel mouth beyond, where Nesta was waving at her to hurry the fuck up, sword gleaming faintly in her other hand.

Then Bryce's star illuminated the rock framing the tunnel's mouth.

She ran.

A teeming mass of *things* crusted the entrance, smaller than the beasts beneath the dungeon, but almost worse. Cruder, more leathery. Like some sort of primordial bat-lizard hybrid. Black tongues tasted the air between flesh-shredding, clear teeth. Like the kristallos, bred and raised for eons in darkness—

A few of the creatures leapt, swooping into the void below, off on the hunt—

The tunnel, the bridge, rumbled.

Bryce staggered, the drop looming sickeningly closer, and a white wave of panic blinded every sense—

Training and Fae grace caught her, and Bryce could have wept with relief that she hadn't tumbled into that void. Especially as something massive and slimy lurched from below, the size of two city buses.

An enormous worm, gleaming with water and mud.

A mouth full of rows of teeth opened wide and *snapped*—

Bryce fell back on her ass as the worm caught three of the flying lizards between those teeth. Swallowed them all in one bite.

Her starlight flared, casting the whole cavern in light and shadow.

The creatures on the walls screeched—either at the worm or the light—flapping off their perches and right into the creature's opening jaws. Another snapping bite, river water and metallic-reeking mud spraying with the movement, and more vanished down the worm's throat.

Bryce could only stare.

One twist of its behemoth body and it'd be upon her. One bite and she'd be swallowed. Her starlight could do nothing against it. It had no eyes. It likely operated on smell, and there she was, a trembling treat offered up on that bridge—

A strong, slim hand grabbed Bryce under the shoulder and dragged her back.

Sensations pelted her: rock scraping beneath her as she was dragged, light and shadows and shrieking flying things, her back stinging as debris sliced her skin, the wet slap of the worm's massive body as it surged from the depths again, snatching at the beasts—

She couldn't stop shaking as Nesta dropped her a safe distance into the tunnel. The worm took a few more bites at the air, the cavern shuddering with each of its powerful thrusts upward. The iron smell grew stronger—blood. It misted the air alongside the river water.

Every snap of the worm's jaws boomed through the rock, through Bryce's bones.

She could only watch in mute horror as more creatures disappeared between those teeth. As the tang of more blood filled the air. Until the worm at last began sinking down, down, down. Back toward the river and wherever its lair lay below.

Nesta's breathing was as harsh as Bryce's, and when Bryce finally peered at the warrior, she found Nesta's gaze already on her. Displeasure and something like disappointment filled Nesta's pretty face as she said, "You froze out there."

Hot anger washed away Bryce's lingering shudders, the stinging from her scraped skin, and she shoved to her feet. "What the fuck was that thing?"

Nesta glanced to the shadows behind Bryce, as if someone stood there. But she said, "A Middengard Wyrm."

"Middengard?" Bryce started at the word. "Like—*Midgard*? Did they come from my world originally?"

Horrific as the creature was, to have another being from her world here was . . . oddly comforting. And maybe finding a scrap of comfort in that fact proved how fucking desperate she was.

"I don't know," Nesta said.

"Are they common around here?" If they were, no wonder the Fae had bailed on this world.

"No," Nesta said, a muscle ticking in her jaw. "As far as I know, they're rare. But I've seen my sister's paintings of the one she defeated. I thought her renderings exaggerated, but it was as monstrous as she depicted it." She shook her head, shock honing into something cold and sharp once more. "I didn't know more than one existed." Her eyes swept over Bryce in a warrior's wary assessment. "What manner of power is it that you possess? What sort of light is this?"

Bryce slowly shook her head. "Light. Just . . . light." Strange, terrible light from another world, she'd once been told.

From this world.

Nesta's eyes glimmered. "What court did your ancestors hail from?"

"I don't know. The Fae ancestor whose powers I bear, Theia—she was Starborn. Like me."

"That term means nothing here." Nesta pulled Bryce to her

feet with ease. "But Amren told me what you said of Theia, the queen who went to your world from ours."

Bryce brushed the dust and rock off her back, her ass. Her ego. "My ancestor, yes."

"Theia was High Queen of these lands. Before she left," Nesta said.

"She was?" A powerful ruler here as well as in Midgard. Her ancestor had been *High* Queen. Bryce carried not only Theia's starlight—she carried her royal ties to this world. Which could land her in some major hot water with these people, if they felt threatened by Bryce's lineage—if they believed she might have some sort of claim to their throne.

Nesta's eyes drifted to the star on Bryce's chest, then to the shadows behind her. But she let the subject drop, turning toward the tunnel ahead. "If we encounter something that wants to eat us again," the warrior said, "don't stare at it like a startled deer. Either run, or fight."

Randall would like this female. The thought pained her. But she snapped back, "I've been doing that my entire life. I don't need a lesson from you about it."

"Then don't make me risk my neck dragging you out of danger next time," Nesta said coolly.

"I didn't ask you to save me," Bryce growled.

But Nesta began walking into the tunnel once more—not waiting for Bryce or her star to light the way. "You've gotten us into enough of a mess as it is," the warrior said without looking back. "Keep close."

8

The shadows were watching him again.

Baxian and Ruhn had passed out, and Hunt had thought he'd lost consciousness, too, but . . . here he was. Watching a shadow watch him back. It stood beside the rack of devices Pollux and the Hawk had used on him.

Lidia hadn't appeared today. He didn't know whether that was a good sign. Didn't dare ask Ruhn for his take on it. Hunt supposed that, out of all of them, he himself should be the one to know whether it was a good sign. He'd lived through this shit for years.

But he should have known a lot of other things, too.

Hunt had lost feeling in his hands, his shoulders. The itching from his slowly regenerating wings continued, though. Like streams of ants tickling down his spine. No writhing could help it.

He should have known not to tangle with Archangels, with the Asteri. He should have warned Bryce more strongly—should have tried harder to get her to back down from this insane path.

Isaiah had tried to convince him all those centuries ago. Hunt hadn't listened . . . and he'd lived with the consequences. He should have learned.

His blood cooled as it ran along his body. Dripped to the floor.

But he hadn't learned a fucking thing, apparently. One didn't take on the Asteri and their hierarchies and win. *He should have known.*

The shadow smiled at him.

So Hunt smiled back. And then the shadow spoke.

"You would do well in Hel."

Too drugged with agony, Hunt didn't even quiver at the familiar male voice. One he'd already heard in another dream, another life.

"Apollion," he grunted. Not Death at all, then.

He tried not to let disappointment sink in his gut.

"What a sorry state you're in," the Prince of the Pit purred. He remained hidden in the shifting shadows. The demon prince inhaled, as if tasting the air. "What delicious pain you feel."

"I'd be happy to share."

A terrifyingly soft laugh. "Your good humor, it seems, remains intact. Even with the halo inked anew upon your brow."

Hunt smiled savagely. "I had the honor of having it done by Rigelus's hand this time."

"Interesting that he would do it himself, rather than employ an imperial hag. Do you detect a difference?"

Hunt's chin dipped. "This one . . . stings. The hag's halo felt like cold iron. This burns like acid." He'd just finished voicing the last word when a thought slammed into him. "Bryce. Is she . . . is she with you?" If they'd hurt her, if Apollion gave one suggestion that—

"No." The shadow seemed to blink. "Why?"

Horror leached through Hunt, colder than ice. "Bryce didn't make it to Hel?" Where was she, then? Had she made it anywhere, or was she tumbling through time and space, forever trapped—

He must have made some pitiful noise because Apollion said, "One moment before the hysterics, Athalar," and vanished.

Hunt couldn't breathe. Maybe it was the weight of his body crushing his lungs, but . . . Bryce hadn't made it. She hadn't fucking made it to Hel, and he was stuck here, and—

Apollion appeared again, a second shadow at his side. Taller and thinner, with eyes like blue opals.

"Where is Bryce?" hissed the Prince of the Chasm.

"She went to find you." Hunt's voice broke. Beside him, Ruhn groaned, stirring. "She went to fucking find *you*, Aidas." The Princes of Hel looked at each other, some wordless conversation passing between them. Hunt pushed, "You two told her to find you. Fed us all that bullshit about armies and wanting to help and getting her ready—"

"Is it possible," Aidas said to his brother, ignoring Hunt entirely, "after everything . . . ?"

"Don't fall into romanticism," Apollion cautioned.

"The star might have guided her," Aidas countered.

"Please," Hunt cut in, not caring if he was begging. *"Tell me where she is."* Baxian grunted, rising to consciousness.

Aidas said quietly, "I have a suspicion, but I can't tell you, Athalar, lest Rigelus wring it from you. Though he has likely already arrived at the same conclusion."

"Fuck you," Hunt spat.

But Apollion said to his brother, "We must leave."

"Then what was the point of all this watching me from the shadows?" Hunt demanded.

"To ensure that we can continue to rely on you when the time comes."

"To do what?" Hunt ground out.

"What you were born to do—to accomplish the task for which your father brought you into existence," Apollion said before fading into nothing, leaving Aidas standing alone before the prisoners.

Shock reared up in Hunt, dampened by the weight of an old, unbidden hurt. "I have no father."

Aidas's expression was sad as he stepped out of the shadows. "You spent too long asking the wrong questions."

"What the fuck does *that* mean?"

Aidas shook his head. "The black crown once again circling your brow is not a new torment from the Asteri. It has existed for millennia."

"Tell me the fucking truth for *once*—"

"Stay alive, Athalar." The Prince of the Chasm followed his brother, vanishing into darkness and embers.

* * *

Tharion woke with a pounding headache that echoed through every inch of his body.

From the smell in his room, Holstrom had slept there, likely on the floor, but the space was empty. Squinting against his headache, Tharion padded into the main living space to find Holstrom on the couch, Flynn beside him, and Declan and Marc nursing coffees at the small table by the window overlooking the fighting pit. Ariadne sat in a chair, reading a book, her demeanor completely at odds with the female who'd roasted those lions last night.

No sign of the Fendyr heir. Or the sprites. Maybe he'd hallucinated that part.

"Morning," he grumbled, shutting one eye against the brightness of the room.

None of them answered.

Fine. He'd deal with them in a moment. After coffee. He padded to the wet bar across the room, the glare of the muted television sending a spike of pain through his left eye, and turned on the coffee machine by muscle memory. Tharion shoved a cup under the nozzle and hit a button that vaguely resembled the main one.

"You really do look like shit," Flynn drawled as Tharion inhaled the aroma of the coffee. "Ari, of course, looks gorgeous as always."

The dragon kept her attention on her book, ignoring the Fae lord. She didn't move a muscle, as if she wanted them to forget she was there. Like such a thing was even possible.

But Flynn focused on Tharion again. "Why didn't you come to us for help?"

Tharion sipped his coffee, wincing at the heat that burned his mouth. "It's too early for this conversation."

"Bullshit," Holstrom said. "We would have helped you. Why come here?"

Tharion couldn't keep the snap from his voice. "Because the River Queen would have wiped you guys off the map. I didn't want that on my conscience."

"And this is better?" Ithan demanded.

Flynn added, "Now you're stuck here, taking whatever she

dishes out, not to mention the shit she's offering you on the side. How could you be so fucking dumb?"

Tharion cut him a look. "You're one to talk about doing dumb shit, Flynn."

Flynn's eyes flickered—a rare glimmer of the powerful Fae lord lurking beneath the casual facade. "Even I would never sell my soul to the Viper Queen, Ketos."

Holstrom added, "There's gotta be some way to get you out of this. You defected from the Blue Court. Who's to say you can't defect from—"

"Look," Tharion said, grinding his teeth, "I know you've got some savior complex, Holstrom—"

"Fuck you. You're my friend. You don't get to ignore the danger you're drowning in."

Tharion couldn't decide whether to glare at the wolf or hug him. He drank from his boiling-hot coffee again. Welcomed its sear down his throat.

Ithan said hoarsely, "We're all that's left. It's only us now."

Declan said quietly from the table, "It's all fucked up. Ruhn, Athalar, Bryce . . ." Marc laid a comforting hand on his shoulder.

"I know," Tharion said. "And Cormac's dead."

"What?" Flynn spat his coffee back into his mug.

Tharion filled them in on what had gone down in the lab, and fuck—he really could have used some of that venom right now. By the time he'd finished explaining his arrangement with the Viper Queen, they were all silent again.

Until Flynn said, "Okay. Next steps: We need to get to the *Depth Charger*, and then to Pangera. To the Eternal City." He nodded to Tharion. "Before we got ambushed by Sabine, we had just decided to seek you out—to bail you out of this shit, and to see if you could get us in with the mer on the ship."

"There's no way in Hel the Vipe lets him go," Ari said, breaking her silence.

The males blinked at her, as if they'd indeed forgotten that a dragon sat in their midst. Marc's mouth tightened as he realized how much she'd heard.

But Flynn asked her, brow arching, "And you're an authority on the Vipe now?"

"I'm an authority on assholes," Ari countered smoothly, giving Flynn a look as if to indicate that he was included on that list. "And by asking her to free him, you'll make her cling tighter."

"She's right," Tharion said. "I can try to think of a way to contact Commander Sendes—"

"No," Ithan said. "We *all* go."

"I'm touched," Tharion said, setting his coffee down on the counter behind him. "Really. But it's not as easy as saying *I defect* and walking out."

Ithan bristled, but Sigrid appeared in the bathroom doorway, steam rippling out. She must have showered. "What would it take?"

Tharion eyed the female. Definitely an Alpha, with that solid stance, those bright eyes. The lack of fear in them. "The Vipe's all about business."

"You're rich," Ari said to Flynn.

"It's not about money for her," Marc said. "She's got more than she knows what to do with. It'd take a trade."

Tharion frowned toward the hallway—the door that led to the Viper Queen's private chambers. "Who's with her right now?"

"Some female," Ari answered, rising to her feet and padding toward the hall. She reached the door to her room and said over a shoulder, "Pretty blond in an imperial uniform." The dragon didn't say anything else as she shut her bedroom door. Then locked it.

"We need to get out of here," Declan said, voice low. "Immediately."

"What's wrong?" Flynn asked. Declan was already reaching for his handgun, Marc easing to his feet beside him with feline grace.

Tharion peered down the hall in time to see the door swing open. The Viper Queen, clad in a blue silk tracksuit and white high-top sneakers, sauntered toward them, hooped gold earrings swaying beneath her black bob. "Just a moment," she said to whoever was in the room behind her. "Your kind of poison's downstairs. Takes a minute to get."

Tharion stiffened as the snake shifter entered the room, surveying his friends.

"You missed a spot of Sabine's blood on your hands," she drawled to Flynn.

They all glared at her. But it was the Fendyr heir who shot to her feet and snapped, "You're no better than the Astronomer, keeping these people here, drugging and—"

The Viper Queen cut her off. "Lower the hackles, little Fendyr." She surveyed Sigrid from her wet hair to her baggy sweats. "Staying here's free, but a wardrobe upgrade will cost you."

"Let them go," Sigrid commanded, voice like thunder. "The dragon and the mer—let them go."

Tharion didn't let the Alpha's ferocity get his hopes up. Not as the Viper Queen laughed. "Why would I do that? They bring in good business." She cut Tharion a mocking smirk as she stalked for the door, headed to get whatever drugs her client down the hall wanted. "When they're not blowing their load after a few minutes."

Tharion bristled, crossing his arms. But as soon as the Viper Queen had shut the door, vanishing outside, clipped footsteps sounded from down the hall.

Dec and Flynn drew their guns. Holstrom had his claws out. Tharion unsheathed his own, his entire body tensing.

"Put those away," said a cool female voice. Terror stole any last traces of Tharion's brain fog.

"Oh fuck," Flynn breathed.

"You open that door," the Hind said mildly, "and Prince Ruhn dies."

9

Bryce and Nesta pushed through the tunnel for hours, tense silence filling the space between them again. Worse than before.

It was typical, Bryce realized, of her interactions with the Fae she knew from her own world. She didn't know why it somehow . . . disappointed her to realize it.

They paused once, Nesta wordlessly tossing her a water canteen along with a roll of dark bread.

"You brought provisions," Bryce said around a mouthful of the faintly sweet, moist roll. "Seems weird, considering you intended to bring me right back to the cell."

Nesta only swigged from her canteen. "I had a feeling I might be running around after you for a while."

"Long enough to need to stop to eat?" Their gazes met, Nesta's silvered in Bryce's starlight.

"We don't know these caves. I prepared for anything."

"Not the Wyrm, apparently."

"You're alive, aren't you?"

Bryce couldn't help her snort. "Fair enough."

There was no more talk after that.

It was possible they could walk right into a dead end and have wasted miles and hours down here. But the tunnel seemed . . . intentional. And Bryce wasn't about to pose a question about the potential fruitlessness of their trek if it would make Nesta try to drag her back to the cave-in to wait to be dug out.

She was getting her way—for better or worse.

Bryce was deep enough in her thoughts that she didn't notice the fork in the tunnel until she'd nearly passed the tunnel that veered to the right. She drew up short, the halt of Nesta's footsteps behind her telling her the warrior had done the same.

Bryce tugged the neck of her T-shirt down to reveal more of her starlight, illuminating the two options gaping before them.

To the left, the tunnel continued, old, rough rock walls curving into the gloom.

To the right . . . Around the natural archway, an array of stars and planets had been carved, crowned at its apex by a large setting or rising sun. Bryce's star glowed brighter as she faced it, guiding her there.

She could dimly make out more scenes of violence and bloodshed covering the walls inside the tunnel.

"I'm going to take a guess and say let's go right." Bryce sighed, covering her star again with her shirt.

"Very well," Nesta said, and strode for the archway.

Bryce lunged before Nesta could clear it, grabbing the warrior by the back of her collar. With a twirl and a flash, Nesta was on her, sword at Bryce's throat. Its metal was impossibly cold.

Bryce held up her hands, trying not to breathe too loudly, to bring her skin into any more contact with that horrific blade than necessary. "No—look." She nodded as minutely as she could to the carvings in the tunnel just beyond the archway.

Nesta didn't remove the blade, which seemed to throb against Bryce's skin, like the sword was alive and aware. But Nesta's gaze shifted to where Bryce had indicated.

"What is it?"

"Those carvings," Bryce breathed. "Back home, my job is to look at ancient art, to study it and sell it, and . . . never mind, that's not really relevant. I just mean I've seen a *lot* of ancient Fae artwork, and that stuff on the walls—it's spelling out a warning. So if you want to get impaled by a bunch of rusty spears, keep walking."

Nesta blinked, head angling, more feline than Fae. But the sword lowered.

Bryce tried not to gasp in relief as that icy metal left her skin, her soul. She never wanted to endure anything like it again.

Nesta either didn't know or didn't care about the sword's impact on Bryce as she surveyed the carvings. The one closest to them.

A female, clearly Fae nobility from the ornate robes and fancy jewelry, stared out from the wall. As if she were addressing an audience, welcoming the newcomers to the tunnel. She was young and beautiful, yet stood with a presence that seemed regal. Long hair flowed around her like a silent river, framing her delicate, heart-shaped face.

Bryce shook off the last of her dread and translated the inscription. "Her name was Silene."

Nesta peered at the writing beneath the image. "That's all it says?"

Bryce shrugged. "Old-school Fae. Lots of fancy titles and lineage. You know how they liked to preen."

Nesta's lips quirked upward. Bryce motioned at the embossed panels that continued onward.

"The warning is in the story she's telling here," Bryce said.

A field of corpses had been carved into the wall, a battlefield stretching ahead. Crucifixes loomed over the battlefield, bodies hanging from them. Great, dark beasts of scales and talons—the ones from the pit beneath her cell, she realized with a shudder—feasted on screaming victims. Blood eagles were splayed out on stone altars.

"Mother above," Nesta murmured.

"Those holes along the corpses there—the ones that look like wounds . . . I'd bet anything there are mechanisms in them to send weapons at passersby," Bryce said. "As some fucked-up 'artistic' way of making the viewer experience the pain and terror of these Fae victims."

Bryce could have sworn something like surprise and embarrassment—that perhaps the warrior herself hadn't spotted the threat—crossed Nesta's face.

"How do you propose we get through, then?" A weighted question. A test.

Like Hel would Bryce *freeze* again. She held out a hand. "Pass me something heavy. I'll see if I can trigger the mechanism to fire."

Nesta sighed, as if annoyed again. Bryce turned to her, about to snap something about having a better idea, when Nesta lifted an arm. Silver flame wreathed her fingers. Bryce backed away a step.

It was fire but not fire. It was like ice turned into flame. It echoed in Nesta's eyes as she laid her hand on the stone wall. Silver fire rippled over the carvings.

Mechanisms clicked—and misfired. Rusty metal bolts shot from the walls. Or tried to. They barely cleared the wall before they melted into dust.

Nesta's power shivered down the walls, disappearing into the dark. Faint clicking and hissing faded away into the gloom; the sound of the traps turned to ashes.

Nesta met Bryce's stare. The fire wreathing her hand winked out, but the silver flame still flickered in her eyes. "You have my gratitude" was all Nesta said before striding ahead.

Later, Bryce and Nesta again dined on hard cheese and more of that dark bread, their resting place a small alcove in the tunnel wall. Bryce's starlight still provided the only glow, muted through her T-shirt. It was cold enough that she looked with envy at Nesta's dark cape, wrapped tightly around the warrior.

She distracted herself by peering at the carvings etched into the walls: Fae kneeling before impossibly tall, robed humanoids, glowing bits of starlight in their upraised hands. Magic. An offering to the crowned creatures before them. One of the beings was reaching a hand toward the nearest Fae, her fingers stretching toward that offered light.

Bryce's stomach twisted as she noted that behind the supplicating Fae, chained humans lay prostrate on the earth, their crudely carved faces a sharp contrast to the otherworldly, pristine beauty of the Fae. Another bit of fucked-up artistry: Humans were little more than rock and dirt compared to the Fae and their godlike masters. Not even worth the effort of carving them. Present only for the Fae to lord their power over them, to crush the humans beneath their heels.

From far away, Rigelus's voice sounded in Bryce's memory. The Asteri had once given the humans to the Vanir to have someone to rule over, to keep them from thinking about how they were hardly better off, all of them slaves to the Asteri. It continued on Midgard today, this false sense of superiority and ownership. And it seemed it existed in this world as well.

Nesta finished her cheese, gnawing it right down to the rind, and said without looking at Bryce, "Your star always glows like that?"

"No," Bryce said, swallowing down the bread. "But down here, it seems to."

"Why?"

"That's what I wanted to find out: What it's leading me toward in this tunnel. *Why* it's leading me there."

"Why you stumbled into our world." Rhysand or the others must have filled Nesta in on everything before siccing her on Bryce.

Bryce motioned to the tunnel and its ancient carvings. "What is this place, anyway?"

"I told you earlier: We don't know. Until you crept past the beasts, even Rhys didn't know this tunnel existed. He certainly didn't know there were carvings down here."

"And Rhysand is . . . your king?"

Nesta snorted. "He'd like to be. But no. He's the High Lord of the Night Court."

Bryce arched a brow. "So he serves a king?"

"We have no kings in these lands. Only seven courts, each ruled by a High Lord. Sometimes a High Lady beside them."

A rock skittered in the distance. Bryce twisted toward it, but—nothing. Only darkness.

She found Nesta watching her carefully. Nesta asked, "Why not let me get impaled earlier? You could have let me walk right into a trap and run."

"I have no reason to want you dead."

"Yet you ran from the cell."

"I know how interrogations tend to end."

"No one was going to torture you."

"Not yet, you mean."

Nesta didn't reply. At the sound of another scuff in the darkness, Bryce whipped her head to it and found Nesta watching her once more.

"What is that?" Bryce asked quietly.

Nesta's eyes gleamed like a cat's in the dimness. "Just the shadows."

10

Tharion knew this wouldn't end well. Not with Flynn and Dec pointing guns at the Hind, Marc's claws gleaming and poised to shred flesh. Not with Holstrom crouched, teeth bared, angled in front of Sigrid. The Fendyr heir glanced between them all with predatory assessment, understanding a threat at hand but not what it was.

Well, fuck. That left him as the voice of reason.

So Tharion did what he did best: dragged up the smile of the person he'd once been and sauntered over to Tristan Flynn.

He laid a claw-tipped finger on the barrel of the Fae lord's gun, pushing it down. "Take a breath," Tharion crooned. "We're all on neutral territory. Even Lidia wouldn't be so stupid as to harm you here." He winked at the Hind, though his insides trembled. "Would you?"

The Hind's face held no emotion, but her chin dipped.

Sigrid stepped forward. "Who are you?"

The Hind's golden eyes swept over the female wolf. Her nostrils flared delicately. "I think," she murmured quietly, "the better question is who are *you*?"

"None of your business," Ithan cut in.

The Hind gave him a look that said she had her suspicions but it wasn't her priority—yet. She said to the Fendyr heir, "A moment of privacy, if you will."

Holstrom growled. "Whatever you have to say, you can say it in front of her."

Declan said quietly, "Holstrom, maybe she can . . . go join the dragon for a minute."

Ithan turned outraged eyes on Declan but then seemed to relent. If this was about Ruhn, if the only way for the Hind to talk was to get Sigrid out of earshot . . .

Tharion chimed in, "Ari locked her door, so I'm pretty sure that means *alone time*." He nodded to the door beside Ari's. "But go ahead and take my room."

Sigrid scoffed. "I'm not some pup to be ordered about—"

"Please," Declan said with a helpless gesture. Marc again laid a gentle hand on his shoulder.

There was a moment, then, when Ithan and Sigrid looked at each other—when Tharion could have sworn some sort of battle of wills passed between them.

Sigrid bristled, then spat, "Fine," and stalked off toward Tharion's bedroom.

The sprites zoomed after her, but the Hind halted them. "You three—wait."

Sasa, Malana, and Rithi turned, wide eyes on the Hind. But she didn't speak again until Sigrid had slammed the door to Tharion's room. Perhaps a bit petulantly.

Tharion didn't miss Ithan's sigh.

The Hind glanced at her watch, likely calculating how much time remained until the Viper Queen returned, then said to Flynn and Dec, "I went looking for you two, but no one was at your . . . house." Her tone dripped with enough disdain that it was clear what she thought of their house off Archer Street. "But I knew that Ketos had defected and come to the Meat Market for refuge—so I guessed you might be hiding here as well."

"Guessed?" Declan demanded. "Or someone sold us out?"

"Don't flatter yourself," the Hind said, crossing her arms. "You're extremely predictable."

"Well, you're fucking wrong," Flynn said, still not holstering his gun. "We're not here to hide."

Declan coughed, as if to say, *This is what you choose to lie about?* Marc hid a smile.

"I don't care why you're here," the Hind said. "We don't have much time. Ruhn's life depends on you listening to me."

"What the fuck have you done to Ruhn?" Flynn cut in.

Tharion could have sworn something like pain flashed across the Hind's face. "Ruhn lives. As do Athalar and Argos."

"Bryce?" Ithan asked hoarsely.

"I don't know. She . . ." The Hind shook her head.

But Declan asked, "Baxian got involved? The Helhound?"

Before she could finish, Flynn demanded, "Why are you *here*?" His voice broke. "To arrest us? To rub our failure in our faces?"

The Hind pivoted to the Fae lord, and—yes, that was pain shining in her eyes. "I'm here to help you rescue Ruhn."

Even Tharion blinked.

"This is a trap," Declan said.

"It's no trap." The Hind surveyed them bleakly. "Athalar, Baxian, and Ruhn are being held in the dungeons beneath the Asteri's palace. The Hammer and the Hawk torture them daily. They . . ." A muscle ticked in her slim jaw. "Your friends haven't talked. But I'm not sure how much longer the Asteri will be entertained by their suffering."

"I'm sorry," Declan spat, "but aren't *you* their lead interrogator?"

The Hind turned her unnaturally perfect face toward the Fae warrior. "The world knows me as such, yes. I don't have time to tell you everything. But I require your help, Declan Emmet. I'm one of a few people on Midgard who can get into those dungeons unchallenged. And I'm the only one who can get them out. But I need *you* to help hack the cameras in the palace. I know you've done so once before."

"Yeah," Dec muttered. "But even with the cameras hacked, our plans haven't exactly turned out great lately. Ask Cormac how well our last big adventure went."

The words pelted Tharion like stones. The memory of the Fae

Prince immolating himself slammed into him. A flash, and Cormac was dead—

"It only failed because Rigelus knew they were coming," the Hind said, not unkindly. "Celestina sold them out."

Shock rippled through the room. But Marc murmured to Declan, "I told you: Archangels are creeps."

Flynn threw up his hands. "Am I the only one who feels like they're on a bad acid trip?"

Tharion scrubbed at his face. "I'm still on one, I think." Flynn snorted, but Tharion mastered himself, clearing his throat before saying to the Hind, "Allow me to clarify a few things: You are the Asteri's most skilled interrogator and spy-breaker. You and your dreadwolves tormented us nonstop not so long ago, in this very city. You are, not to put too fine a point on it, pretty much the soul of evil. Yet you're asking us to help you free our friends. And you expect us not to be suspicious?"

She surveyed them all for a long moment, and Tharion had the good sense to sit down before she said evenly, "I'm Agent Daybright."

"Bullshit," Flynn spat, angling his gun at her again.

Daybright, who was high up in the Asteri's innermost circles. Daybright, who knew of their plans before the Asteri ever acted. Daybright, the most vital link in the rebels' information chain . . .

"She smells like Ruhn," Ithan murmured. They all blinked at him. The wolf sniffed again. "Just barely. Smell her—it's there."

To Tharion's shock, a bit of color stained the Hind's cheeks. "He and I . . ."

"Don't for one fucking second believe this," Flynn snapped. "She probably rolled around in his blood in the dungeons."

Her teeth flashed in a snarl, the first hint of a crack in that cool exterior. "I would never hurt him. Everything I've done recently, everything I'm doing now, has been to keep Ruhn alive. Do you know how hard it is to keep Pollux at bay? To convince him to go slow? Do you have *any idea what that's like*?" She screamed the last part at Flynn, who backed away a step. The Hind heaved a breath, shaking. "I need to get him out. If you don't help me, then his death is on you. And I will *destroy you*, Tristan Flynn."

Flynn slowly shook his head, confusion and disbelief stark on his face.

The Hind turned to Tharion, and he withstood her blazing look. "I made sure the *Depth Charger* was there to pick you up after Agent Silverbow sacrificed himself, trying to bring the Asteri down with him; I filled Commander Sendes in about Ruhn and Athalar and Baxian being captured, and Bryce going missing. I'm the one who's kept Rigelus off your scent, kept the Asteri from killing anyone who has ever meant anything to Ruhn, Bryce, or Athalar."

"Or you're the one," Tharion said, "who got the information out of the real Agent Daybright and are here to entrap us, too."

"Believe what you want," the Hind said, and true exhaustion slumped her shoulders. For a heartbeat, Tharion pitied her. "But in three days, I am going to free them. And I will fail if I don't have your help."

"Even if we believe you," Declan said, "we have families who the Asteri would kill without a thought. People we love."

"Then use this time to get them into hiding. But the more people who know, the more likely we will be discovered."

"You can't be fucking serious," Flynn said to Declan. "You're trusting this monster?"

Declan met the Hind's eyes, and Tharion knew he was weighing whatever he found there. "It makes sense, Flynn. Everything Ruhn told us about Daybright . . . it adds up."

"Does Ruhn know what you are?" Flynn spat.

Lidia ignored him, and instead looked to Tharion. "I need you, too, Ketos."

Tharion shrugged with a nonchalance he didn't feel. "Unfortunately, I can't leave the building."

"Find a way out. I need you to be my ally and advocate on the *Depth Charger* after we have completed the rescue."

Holstrom said, "The Viper Queen's apparently your drug dealer—why don't you ask her to let Tharion go?"

Lidia held his stare with a dominance that belied her deer-shifter heritage. "Why don't you, Ithan Holstrom?"

There was something in her voice that Tharion didn't quite understand—a challenge, perhaps. A gauntlet thrown.

"Does Ruhn know?" Flynn demanded again.

"Yes," the Hind said. "He, Athalar, and Bryce know. Baxian doesn't."

Flynn's throat bobbed. "You lied to Ruhn."

"We lied to each other," she said, some sort of emotion flickering in her golden eyes. "Our identities weren't supposed to be revealed. We both . . . went too far."

"Why bother to save them?" Declan asked. "Ruhn and Hunt have no value to Ophion, other than being good fighters. And Argos isn't connected with Ophion at all."

"Hunt Athalar is valuable to Bryce Quinlan, and to activating her power. Baxian Argos is a powerful warrior and skilled spy. He is therefore valuable to all of us."

"And Ruhn?" Ithan asked, brows high.

"Ruhn is valuable to me," the Hind said without an ounce of doubt. "At sunrise in two days' time, a skiff will be waiting for you at Ionia's harbor, at the very end of the north dock. Get on it, and the captain will take you a few miles offshore. Throw this into the water and wait." She chucked a small white stone to Tharion.

He'd seen one like it before—that day in the sea off Ydra. She'd thrown one into the water then, and the *Depth Charger* had appeared.

She must have noted his shock, because she said, "I summoned the ship that day after what happened at Ydra. Drop that stone into the ocean, and the *Depth Charger* will come again and carry you to Pangera."

Silence filled the room.

Lidia looked to the sprites crouching at Flynn's neck and said, "I have questions for you three."

"Us?" Sasa squawked, ducking behind Flynn's left ear. Her flame illuminated it, casting his skin a glowing red.

Lidia said, "About your queen."

"Irithys?" Malana said, flaring a deep violet. "Where—"

"I know where she is," Lidia said calmly, though Tharion noted with surprise that her hands were shaking. "But I want to know what *you* know about her. Her temperament."

"Where have the Asteri been keeping her?" Sasa demanded, turning white-hot with anger.

Lidia tipped her chin upward. "Answer my questions, and I'll tell you."

"We only know of her through rumor," Rithi said, poking her head out from behind Flynn's right ear. "She is noble, and brave—"

"Is she trustworthy?" Lidia asked.

Rithi ducked behind Flynn's ear again, but Sasa snapped, "She is our queen. She is honor itself."

Lidia looked coolly at the sprite. "I know plenty of rulers who don't embody that virtue one bit." Tharion could only stare at the Hind—Agent Daybright. Their . . . ally. "What else?"

"That is all we know," Malana said, "all we have heard. Now tell us: Where *is* she?"

Lidia's mouth curved upward. "Would you rush to free her?"

"Don't patronize them," Flynn snapped with rare gravitas. The sprites huddled closer to him.

To Tharion's shock, Lidia inclined her head. "Apologies. Your courage and loyalty are commendable. I wish I had a thousand like you at my disposal."

"To Hel with your compliments," Sasa snarled, her flame blazing bright. "You promised—"

"The Asteri have her in their palace."

"Beyond that!" Sasa cried, flaring white-hot again.

"You should have bargained better if you wanted to know more."

Tharion tensed. This female might be an ally, but fuck, she was slippery.

In the furious silence, the Hind walked to the door. She halted before opening it, and didn't turn around as she said to them all, "I know you don't trust me. I don't blame you. That you don't tells me I've done my job very well. But . . ."

She looked over a shoulder, and Tharion saw her throat bob.

"Ruhn and Athalar are in danger. As we speak, Rigelus is debating which one of them will die. It all boils down to how it might impact Quinlan. But once he decides, there will be nothing I can do to stop it. So I am . . ." Her voice caught. "I am begging you. Before it's too late. Help me pull this off. Find a way out of this situation with the Viper Queen"—a nod to Tharion, then a nod to Declan—"be ready at a moment's notice from me to hack into the cameras at the Eternal Palace"—and finally a look toward the rest of them—"and for Luna's sake, be on that dock in two days' time."

With that, she left. For a long moment, none of them could speak.

"Well, Flynn," Declan finally rasped, "looks like you got your wish."

11

Rushing water roared through the cavern, its spray coating Bryce's face with drops so cold they were kisses of ice.

The strange carvings had continued all the way here, showing great Fae battles and lovemaking and childbirth. Showing a masked queen, a crown upon her head, bearing instruments in her hand and standing before an adoring crowd. Behind her, a great mountaintop palace rose toward the sky, winged horses soaring among the clouds. No doubt some religious iconography of her divine right to rule. Beyond the mountaintop palace, a lush archipelago spread into the distance, rendered with remarkable detail and skill.

Scenes of a blessed land, a thriving civilization. One relief had been so similar to the frieze of the Fae male forging the sword at the Crescent City Ballet that Bryce had nearly gasped. The last carving before the river had been one of transition: a Fae King and Queen seated on thrones, a mountain—different from the one with the palace atop it—behind them with three stars rising above it. A different kingdom, then. *Some ancient High Lord and Lady,* Nesta had suggested before approaching the river.

She hadn't commented on the lower half of the carving, which depicted a Helscape beneath their thrones, some kind of underworld. Humanoid figures writhed in pain amid what looked like icicles and snapping, scaly beasts—either past enemies conquered or an indication of what failure to bow to the rulers would bring upon the defiant.

The suffering stretched throughout, lingering even underneath that archipelago and its mountaintop palace. Even here, in paradise, death and evil remained. A common motif in Midgardian art, too, usually with the caption: *Et in Avallen ego.*

Even in Avallen, there am I.

A whispered promise from Death. Another version of *memento mori.* A reminder that death was always, always waiting. Even in the blessed Fae isle of Avallen.

Maybe all the ancient art that glorified the idea of *memento mori* had been brought to Midgard by these people.

Maybe she was thinking too much about shit that really didn't matter at the moment. Especially with an impassable river before her.

Bryce and Nesta peered down at the cascade rushing past, the night-dark waters flowing deeper into the caverns. The scent of iron was stronger here, likely because they now stood closer to the river than they had before. It didn't matter. All that mattered was the fact that the tunnel continued on the other side, and the gap was large enough that jumping wasn't an option.

"Now would be a good time for your friends with wings to find us," Bryce muttered. Her star shone ahead, faint but still pointing the way to the path across the river.

Nesta glanced over a shoulder. "You winnowed out of the cell." So the shadows *had* told Nesta and the others everything. "You can't do so again?"

"I, ah . . . It drained me." She hated to reveal any sort of weakness, but didn't see a way around it. "I'm still recovering."

"Surely your magic should have replenished by now. You were able to use some against me before the cave-in. And the star on your chest still glows. Some magic must remain in you."

"I was always able to get it to glow," Bryce confessed, "long before I ever had true power." For a heartbeat, Bryce debated telling Nesta how she'd attained her depth of power, how she could get even *more* if someone fueled her up. Just to let the warrior know she wasn't some loser who froze in the face of an enemy, giant Wyrm or no.

But that would reveal more about her abilities than was wise.

"You can't, uh . . . winnow?" Bryce asked Nesta.

"I've never tried," Nesta admitted. "My powers are unusual amongst the High Fae."

"High Fae? As opposed to . . . normal Fae?"

Nesta shrugged. "They use the *High* part to make themselves sound more important than they are."

Bryce's mouth twitched upward. "Sounds like the Fae in my world." She angled her head. "But you're High Fae. You . . . talk about them like you're not."

"I'm new to the Fae realms," Nesta said, her focus again on the river. "I was born human and turned High Fae against my will." She sighed. "It's a long story. But I've only lived in the faerie lands for a handful of years now. Much of this is still strange to me."

"I know the feeling," Bryce said. "My mother is human, my father Fae. I've lived between two worlds my entire life."

Nesta nodded shallowly. "None of that helps us get across the river."

Bryce surveyed her companion. If Nesta was originally human and had been turned Fae—however the fuck *that* was possible—maybe her sympathies still lay with humankind. Maybe she'd understand how it was to be powerless and frightened in a world designed to oppress and kill her—

Or maybe she'd been sent to win Bryce's sympathy and trust, working for a so-called High Lord. Everything she'd said in these tunnels could have been a lie. And she was powerful enough that she'd been called in to look at the Horn on Bryce's back—she was no defenseless lamb.

"Up for a swim?" Bryce asked the warrior, kneeling to dip a hand into the river. She hissed at its ice-cold bite.

Great. Just . . . great.

She frowned at the dark, rushing water, illuminated by the light from her star. Smooth white pebbles glimmered brightly far beneath the surface. *Really* brightly.

Bryce glanced at her star. It was glowing more strongly now. She stood, wiping her wet, chilled hand on the thigh of her leggings. The star dimmed.

"What is it?" Nesta took a step closer, a hand rising toward the sword at her back.

Bryce knelt again, plunging her hand back into the frigid river. Her star glowed brighter as she angled its light over the water. She twisted on her knees, toward the gloom downriver. The starlight flared in answer. It faded to a dull light when she pivoted back toward the tunnel ahead.

"You've gotta be kidding me," Bryce muttered, rising to her feet again.

"What?" Nesta asked, scanning the river, the darkness around them.

Bryce didn't reply. The star had led her this far. If it wanted her in the river . . .

Bryce glanced over a shoulder to Nesta. "See you at the bottom." And with a wink, Bryce jumped into the roaring water.

The cold knocked the breath from Bryce.

The thrashing river was illuminated by her star, the water a clear, striking blue in the small bubble of her light. It glazed the high cavern ceiling, and it was all Bryce could do to keep her head above the rapids, from being smashed against the boulders spiking up throughout the twisting length of the river.

Behind her, Nesta had jumped in—as Bryce had rounded a bend a moment ago, she'd heard Nesta's snapped *"Reckless idiot!"* before the roar of the river swallowed all sounds once more.

The star had to be leading her somewhere. To something.

Bryce was hurled around another bend in the caverns, and as she struggled to keep her head clear of the water, her star seemed to extend a beam into the darkness.

The ray of silvery light landed upon a small pool bulging out of the opposite side of the river. A break in the rapids. Right in front of a small bank . . . and another looming tunnel entrance beyond.

Bryce began swimming for the pool, her body screaming with the effort of pushing perpendicular to the current, racing to reach that sliver of calm water before she was swept past. Stroke after stroke, kick after kick, she aimed for that narrow shore.

She turned to warn Nesta to make for the shore, too, but found that the female was a few feet behind her, swimming like mad for the bank. So Bryce continued swimming, arms straining as the river pulled her forward mercilessly. If she and Nesta didn't reach the little pool soon, they'd miss it entirely—

The tug of the water relented. Bryce's strokes became easier, her pace faster.

And then she was in the pool, the water still and light compared to the raging beast behind her. She clawed at the rocky shore, hauling herself onto it.

Rocks scraped against each other beside her, and then Nesta's heavy, wet breathing sounded. "What . . ." Nesta panted. "The . . ." Another breath. *"Fuck."*

Bryce inhaled all that beautiful, wonderful air, even as intense cold began to shake through her very bones. "The star said to go this way," she managed to say.

"Some warning would have been good," Nesta growled.

Bryce rose onto her elbows, gasping down breath after breath. "Why? You would have tried to talk me out of it."

"Because," Nesta bit out, wiping the water from her eyes as she got to her knees, "we could have come down here without having to get wet. I'm not to let you out of my sight—not even for a moment, so I had no choice but to go after you. But since you jumped in so damned fast . . . Now we're freezing."

"How could we have reached here without getting wet?" Bryce asked, shuddering with cold, teeth already clacking against each other.

Nesta rolled her eyes and said to the shadows, "You might as well come out now."

Bryce whirled on her knees, reaching for a weapon that wasn't there as Azriel landed from above them.

His wings were spread so wide they nearly touched either side of the cavern, and the black dagger hung at his hip, its dark hilt gleaming faintly in the light of her star. And peeking above a broad shoulder, its matching dark hilt like shadow given form, was the Starsword.

"What the fuck do you mean Bryce isn't in Hel?" Ruhn managed to say around what was left of his tongue, every breath like shards of glass slicing down his throat.

Hunt gave no answer, and Ruhn supposed he hadn't really expected one, anyway.

Baxian grunted, "Where?" It was about all the angel could get out, Ruhn realized.

"Dunno," Hunt said, voice gravelly from screaming.

The Hawk had yanked the lever that sent them all plunging, laughing when they'd yelped as their injuries collided with cold stone. As reeking puddles of their own blood and waste splashed onto them. But at least they were on the floor.

Still chained at the wrists and ankles, Ruhn had only been able to lie there, shuddering, tears leaking from his eyes at the relief in his shoulders, his arms, his lungs.

The Hawk had slid a tray of food toward them before he left—but kept it far enough away that they'd have to crawl through their piss and shit to get to it before the rats converged.

Baxian was currently trying to reach the tray, legs pushing against the stones, the half-grown stumps of his wings stained red. He stretched a filthy hand toward the broth and water, and groaned deeply. Blood leaked from a wound in his ribs.

Ruhn wasn't sure he could eat, though his body screamed for food. He took breath after sawing breath.

The Oracle had told him that the royal bloodline ended with him. Had she seen that he'd wind up here—and never walk out alive? Cold worse than the dungeons' damp chill crept through him.

He had come to peace with the possibility of this fate for himself a long time ago. Granted, not this particular demise, but an untimely end in some vague sense. But now that Bryce was a true royal, the prophecy shed light on her fate, too. If she hadn't made it to Hel . . . perhaps she hadn't made it anywhere. Thus ending the royal bloodline with both of their deaths.

He couldn't share his suspicions with Athalar. Couldn't offer up that bit of despair that would break the Umbra Mortis worse than any of Pollux's tools. It would be Ruhn's secret to keep. His own wretched truth, left to fester in his heart.

The smell of stale bread filled his nostrils, rising above the stench as the tray slid in front of him. Splashing through a puddle of—Ruhn didn't want to know what the liquid was. Though his nose offered up a few unpleasant suggestions.

"Gotta eat," Hunt said, hands shaking as he brought a cup of broth to his mouth.

"Don't want us dead, then," Baxian said, slowly lifting a piece of bread.

"Not yet." Athalar sipped slowly. Like he didn't trust his body not to chuck it all up. "Eat, Danaan."

It was a command, and Ruhn found himself reaching his weak, trembling fingers toward the broth. It took all his focus, all his strength, to raise it to his lips. He could barely taste it. Right—his tongue was still regrowing. He sipped again.

"I don't know where Bryce is," Hunt said, voice raw. He picked up a piece of bread with his good hand. The burned fingers on his other hand were twisted at different angles. Some were missing nails.

Fuck, how had their lives come to this?

Athalar took the last bite of bread and lay back—right in the reeking piles and puddles. He closed his eyes. The halo gleamed darkly on the angel's brow. Ruhn knew Athalar's relaxed posture belied his thoughts. Knew the angel was probably frantic with worry and dread.

Guilt was likely eating Athalar alive. Guilt that wasn't his to bear—they'd all made choices that had landed them here. But the words were too heavy, too painful for Ruhn to voice.

Baxian finished and lay down as well, instantly asleep. The Hammer and the Hawk had come down especially hard on the Helhound.

It was personal with them—Baxian had been one of their own. A brother-in-arms, a partner in cruelty. Now they'd take him apart piece by piece.

Ruhn lifted his cup again—a silicone one that couldn't be broken to use as a weapon—and peered into the water within. Watched it ripple with his breath.

"We need to get out of here," Ruhn said, and nothing had ever sounded more stupid. Of course they needed to get out of here. For so many fucking reasons.

But Athalar cracked open an eye. Met his stare. Pain and rage and determination shone there, unbroken despite the halo and slave brand on his wrist. "Then talk to your . . . person." *Girlfriend,* the angel didn't say.

Ruhn ground his teeth, and his ravaged mouth gave a burst of pain. He'd rather die here than beg the Hind for help. "Another way."

"I was in these dungeons . . . for seven years," Hunt said. "No way out. Especially not with Pollux so invested in ripping us apart."

Ruhn glanced again at the halo. He knew the angel didn't only mean a way out of the dungeons. The Asteri owned them now.

Baxian stirred from his slumber to wearily rasp, "I never appreciated it, Athalar. What you went through."

"I'm surprised I didn't get a badge of honor when I left here." The light words were at odds with the utter emptiness of Hunt's stare. Ruhn couldn't stand to see it there, in the eyes of the Umbra Mortis.

Baxian chuckled brokenly, playing along. "Maybe Pollux will give you one this time."

If Ruhn got free, Pollux would be the first asshole he ended. He didn't dwell on why. Didn't dwell on the rage that coursed through him whenever he saw the white-winged angel.

He'd been so stupid. Naïve and reckless and *stupid* to let himself get in so deep with Day—with Lidia—and forget the Oracle's warning. Delude himself into thinking that it probably meant he wouldn't have kids. He'd been so fucking pathetic and lonely that he'd needed to think the best, even though it was clear he'd always had a one-way ticket to disaster.

The only thing left to do was put an end to it.

So Ruhn said, "You were alone then, Athalar."

Hunt met Ruhn's stare, as if to say, *Oh yeah?* Ruhn just nodded. Friends, brothers, whatever—he had Athalar's back.

Something glimmered in Athalar's eyes. Gratitude, maybe. Or hope. Much better than what had been there moments ago. It sharpened Ruhn's focus. Cleared the pain-fogged bits of his brain. This might be a one-way ticket for him, but it didn't have to be for Hunt. And Bryce . . .

Ruhn looked away before Hunt could read the fear that filled his eyes, his heart.

Thankfully, Baxian added, "And you weren't . . . the Umbra Mortis back then, either. You've changed, Athalar."

Hunt let out a grating laugh, full of challenge and defiance. Thank the gods for that. "What are you thinking, Danaan?"

12

You've been here this whole time?" Bryce eyed the shadow-wreathed warrior as they left the river behind, walking through the lower tunnel passage. They followed the light of Bryce's star, once again pointing ahead, faintly illuminating the carvings all around them. Her teeth chattered with cold, but moving helped warm her frozen body—just a fraction.

Azriel, striding a few feet behind Bryce as Nesta led the way through the tunnel, said, "Yes."

Nesta snorted. "That's about all you'll get out of him."

Bryce peered over a shoulder at the male, trying to calm her shivers. "Those were your shadows against my light earlier?"

"Yes," Azriel said again.

Nesta chuckled. "And he's probably been put out about it ever since."

"Seeing you go into that freezing river helped," Azriel said mildly, and Bryce could have sworn she caught a hint of a smile gracing his beautiful face.

But she asked, "Why keep hidden at all?"

"To observe," Nesta answered for him, stride unfaltering. "To see what you'd do. Where you'd lead me. As soon as we realized there was a tunnel, we got supplies together and followed you." Hence her pack of food.

They passed by more carvings—all disarmed well ahead of their approach by Nesta's silver flame. These were more peaceful: They showed small children playing. Time passing with trees blooming, then barren, then blooming again. Pretty, perfect scenes at odds with the conversation at hand.

Bryce gestured to the passageway and the carvings. "Your guess remains as good as mine. I'm just following the light."

"Right into the river," Nesta grumbled. Azriel snickered behind her.

Bryce glanced at him again, at the wings and armor. At his ears—she realized now that they weren't arched, but round like a human's. There had been carvings earlier of warriors that looked like him—armies of them. "Do you have Vanir in this world?"

His eyes narrowed. "What's that?"

Bryce slowed her pace, allowing herself to fall into step beside him. Though perhaps he allowed it as well. "In Midgard—my world—it's a term for all magical, non-human beings. Fae, angels, shifters, mer, sprites . . ." Azriel's brows rose with each word. "Basically, they're the top of the food chain."

"In this world," Nesta said from ahead, rubbing her wet, cold arms to get some semblance of warmth into them, "we have the humans and the Fae. But amongst the Fae, there are High Fae, like . . . me. Amren. And what some call lesser faeries: any other magical creatures. And then there are people like Azriel, who is just . . . Illyrian."

"So Rhysand is Illyrian, too?" Bryce pried. "He's got the wings."

"Half," Nesta corrected. "Half High Fae, half Illyrian." Azriel cleared his throat as if to warn her to stop talking so much, and Nesta added sharply, "And with the combined arrogance of both."

Azriel *really* cleared his throat then, and Bryce couldn't help her smile, despite her clacking teeth.

Her gaze flicked to the Starsword strapped to Azriel's back, then to his side, to the knife hanging there. Her ears hollowed out for a moment, a dull thump sounding once, and her hand spasmed, seemingly tugged toward those blades.

Azriel's wings twitched at the same moment, and he rolled his shoulders, like he was shaking off some phantom touch. A peek at Nesta revealed her studying the male, as if such a display was unusual.

Bryce put aside her questions, rubbing her frozen hands together for warmth. *Eyes on the prize,* she reminded herself as they continued on. *Master of spinning bullshit.*

Carrying both the dagger and the Starsword was clearly bothering Azriel.

As they pushed into the gloom, clothes slowly drying, bodies slowly thawing, Bryce counted his wings twitching or shoulders rolling no less than six times.

Not to mention the occasional hollow thump in her own ears if she drew too near to him.

They crossed a stream, wide enough to be a river, but shallow and rocky all the way across. Her blazing star, thankfully, pointed to the tunnel on the other side. No swimming necessary this time. As they crossed, the star illuminated slimy white creatures slithering out of their path. Bryce reined in the urge to cringe down at them. Or at the iron-rich water scent that stuffed itself up her nose. She said, if only to distract herself from the gross fauna of the stream, "Did the Fae make these tunnels?"

A few steps ahead, Nesta said nothing. But Azriel, trailing behind, mused after a moment, "I don't think so. From the consistent size of them, I'd guess that a Middengard Wyrm originally made these passages. Maybe it even used these waterways to get around."

"Does it matter?" Nesta said without looking back.

"Possibly," Azriel murmured. "We should be on alert. It might still use them to access the tunnel system."

Alarm flared through Bryce. "What makes you say that?"

Azriel nodded to a pile of white things that she'd mistaken for more of the writhing, newt-like creatures. "Bones. Of those things from the bridge chamber, probably."

Bryce stumbled on a slippery rock, going down into the frigid water, palms and knees smarting—

A strong hand was instantly at her back, but too late to avoid the stinging cuts that now peppered her hands and legs. "Careful," Azriel warned, setting her on a sturdier rock.

Bryce's stomach hollowed out with her ears this time, and the dagger was right there, the sword so close—

Azriel let out a grunt, going rigid. Like he could feel it, too, the weapons' demand to be together or apart or whatever it was, the strange power of them in proximity to each other—

"Watch your footing" was all the male said before stepping back. Far enough away that the sword and the dagger halted their strange tugging at Bryce. Her stomach eased, her hearing with it.

Reaching the bank, she shook off the stinging in her palms, the scent of her blood stronger than that of the river, and wiped the blood from her torn knees. She'd liked these leggings, damn it. Mud came away with the blood, and she clicked her tongue as she wiped her hand along the rock wall, trying to smear it away.

She realized too late that she'd smudged the blood and dirt over a carving of two serene, lute-playing Fae females. With an apologetic look to them and their long-dead carver, Bryce continued on. And on. And on.

"Your hands aren't healing," Azriel said from behind Bryce the next day. Or whenever it was now, considering that they'd all slept for a few hours with nothing in the darkness to indicate the passing of time. Bryce had dozed lightly, fitfully, aware of every drip of moisture and scrape of rock in the tunnel, the breathing from the warriors beside her.

She knew they'd been monitoring *her* every breath.

After a quick meal, they'd been on their way. And apparently, Azriel hadn't missed the scent of her hands still leaking blood.

Nesta halted ahead, as if concerned by Azriel's words, and when the female backtracked, hand outstretched, Bryce showed her scraped-up palms.

"Something in the water?" Nesta murmured to Azriel.

"Her knees healed," Azriel murmured back.

Bryce didn't want to know how he knew that. She peered at her raw, scraped hands, the smeared blood and lingering mud on them. "Maybe my magic's weird down here. It'd explain why the star is doing its . . . GPS thing."

Her tongue stumbled over the *GPS* pronunciation in their language, but if they had no idea what the Hel she was talking about, they didn't let on.

Instead, Azriel asked, "How fast do you usually heal?" He reached for her hand, her starlight washing over the golden skin of his own hands . . . and the scars there. Covering every inch.

She'd seen them during their first encounter on that misty riverbank, but had forgotten until now. She'd never seen such extensive burn scars.

The sword and dagger, so close now, began their thrumming and tugging. Her hearing hollowed out, her gut with it.

Azriel's wings twitched once again.

But Bryce said of her bleeding hands, blocking out the blades' call, "I'm half-human, so I'm used to slower healing, but since making the Drop, I've been healing at relatively normal Vanir speeds."

Nesta must have been filled in on the Drop as well, because she didn't question what it was. She only said, "Maybe it has something to do with your magic needing so long to replenish, too."

"Again," Azriel reminded them, "her knees have healed."

Bryce glanced at the thick scarring over his fingers. What—who—had done such a brutal thing to him? And though she knew it was dumb to open up, to show any vulnerability, she said quietly, "The male who fathered me . . . he used to burn my brother to punish him. The scars never healed for him, either." Ruhn had just tattooed over them. A fact she'd only learned right before she'd come here, and knowing about the pain he'd suffered—

Azriel dropped her hand. But he said nothing as he stepped back, far enough away that the sword and dagger stopped chattering to Bryce. If they continued plaguing him, he made no sign. He only motioned them to keep moving before prowling off into the gloom, taking the lead this time. Bryce watched him for a moment before following, heart heavy in her chest for some reason she couldn't place.

Nesta continued down the tunnel, this time staying a little closer to Bryce. The female said a shade quietly, "I'm sorry about your brother's suffering."

The words steadied Bryce, focused her. "I'll make sure my sire pays for it one day."

"Good" was all Nesta said. "Good."

"Tell me about the Daglan." Bryce's voice echoed too loudly in the otherwise silent cave from where she sat against the tunnel wall, a carving of three dancing Fae females above her. The scent of her blood filled the cave, the wounds on her hands still open and bleeding. Not enough to be alarming, but a small, steady ooze every now and then.

Azriel and Nesta, sitting beside each other with the ease of familiarity, both frowned. Nesta said, "I don't know anything about them." She considered, then added, "I slew one of their contemporaries, though. About seven months ago."

Bryce's brows rose. "So not an Asteri—Daglan, I mean?"

Azriel shifted. Nesta glanced sidelong at him, marking the movement, but said to Bryce, "I don't think so. The creature—Lanthys—was a breed unto himself. He was . . . horrible."

Bryce angled her head. "How did you kill him?"

Nesta said nothing.

Bryce's gaze lifted to the sword hilt peeking above the warrior's shoulder. "With that?"

Nesta just said, "Its name is Ataraxia."

"That's an Old Language word." Nesta nodded. Bryce murmured, "Inner Peace—that's your sword's name?"

"Lanthys laughed when he heard it, too."

"I'm not laughing," Bryce said, meeting the female's stare.

She found nothing but open curiosity on Nesta's face. Nesta said, "The scar your light comes from . . . it's shaped like an eight-pointed star. Why?"

Bryce peered at where the light was muffled by her T-shirt. "It's the symbol of the Starborn, I think."

"And the magic marked you in this way?"

"Yes. When I . . . revealed who I was, what I am, to the world, I drew the star out of my chest. It left that scar in its wake." She glanced to Azriel. "Like a burn."

His face was an unreadable mask. But Nesta asked, "So you have a star *within* you? An actual star?"

Bryce shrugged with one shoulder. "Yeah? I mean, not literally. It's not like a giant ball of gas spinning in space. But it's starlight."

Nesta didn't seem particularly impressed. "And you said these Asteri of yours . . . they also have stars within them?"

Bryce winced. "Yes."

"So what's the difference between you and them?" Nesta asked.

"Aside from the fact that I'm not an intergalactic colonialist creep?"

She could have sworn Nesta's mouth kicked up at a corner. That Azriel chuckled, the sound soft as shadow. "Right," Nesta said.

"I, uh . . . I don't know." Bryce considered. "I never really thought about it. But . . ." Those final moments running from Rigelus flashed in her memory, the bursts of his power rupturing marble and glass, searing past her cheek—

"My light is just that," Bryce said. "Light. The Asteri claim their powers are from holy stars inside themselves, but they can physically manipulate things with that light. Kill and destroy. Is starlight that can shatter rock actually light? Everything they've told us is basically a lie, so it's possible they don't have stars inside them at all—that it's merely bright magic that *looks* like a star, and they called it a holy star to wow everyone."

Azriel said, wings rustling, "Does it matter what their power is called, then?"

"No," Nesta admitted. "I was only curious."

Bryce chewed on her lip. What *was* the Asteri's power? Or hers? Hers was light, but perhaps theirs was actually the brute force of a star—a sun. So hot and strong it could destroy all in its path. It wasn't a comforting thought, so Bryce asked Nesta, in need of a new subject, "What kind of sword is that, anyway?" Its simple, ordinary hilt jutted above Nesta's shoulder.

"One that can kill the unkillable," Nesta answered.

"So is the Starsword," Bryce said quietly, then nodded to Azriel's side. "Can your dagger kill the unkillable, too?"

"It's called Truth-Teller," he said in that soft voice, like shadows given sound. "And no, it cannot."

Bryce arched a brow. "So does it . . . tell the truth?"

A hint of a smile, more chilling than the frigid air around them. "It gets people to do so."

Bryce might have shuddered had she not caught Nesta rolling her eyes. It gave her enough courage to dare ask the winged warrior, "Where did the dagger come from?"

Azriel's hazel eyes held nothing but cool wariness. "Why do you want to know?"

"Because the Starsword"—she motioned to the blade he had down his back—"sings to it. I know you're feeling it, too." *Let it be out in the open.* "It's driving you nuts, right?" Bryce pushed. "And it gets worse when I'm near."

Azriel's face again revealed nothing.

"It is," Nesta answered for him. "I've never seen him so fidgety."

Azriel glowered at his friend. But he admitted, "They seem to want to be near each other."

Bryce nodded. "When I landed on that lawn, they instantly reacted when they were close together."

"Like calls to like," Nesta mused. "Plenty of magical things react to one another."

"This was unique. It felt like . . . like an answer. My sword blazed with light. That dagger shone with darkness. Both of them are crafted of the same black metal. Iridium, right?" She jerked her chin to Azriel, to the dagger at his side. "Ore from a fallen meteorite?"

Azriel's silence was confirmation enough.

"I told you guys back in that dungeon," Bryce went on. "There's literally a prophecy in my world about my sword and a dagger reuniting our people. *When knife and sword are reunited, so shall our people be.*"

Nesta frowned deeply. "And you truly think this is that particular dagger?"

"It checks too many boxes not to be." Bryce lifted a still-bloody hand, and she didn't miss the way they both tensed. But she furled her fingers and said, "I can feel them. It gets stronger the closer I get to them."

"Then don't get too close," Nesta warned, and Bryce lowered her hand.

Bryce surveyed the carved walls, pivoting. "These reliefs tell a narrative, too, you know."

Nesta peered up at the images: the three dancing Fae in the foreground, the stars overhead, the scattered islands. The mountain island with the castle atop its highest peak. And again, always the reminder of that suffering underworld beneath it. *Memento mori. Et in Avallen ego.* "What sort of narrative?"

Bryce shrugged. "If I had a few weeks, I could walk the whole length and analyze it."

"But you don't know our history," Nesta said. "It'd have no context for you."

"I don't need context. Art has a universal language."

"Like the one tattooed on your back?" Nesta said.

All right. Their turn to ask questions. "Your friend—Amren. She said it was the same as the language in some book?"

Azriel asked, stone-faced, "What do you call it in your world—that language?"

Bryce shook her head. "I don't know. I told the truth earlier. My friend and I got . . . We had a lot to drink one night." And smoked a fuck-ton of mirthroot, but they didn't need to know that, or need an explanation about the drugs of Midgard. "I barely remember it. She said it meant *Through love, all is possible.*"

Nesta clicked her tongue, but not with disdain. Something like understanding.

Bryce went on, "She claimed she picked the alphabet out of a book in the tattoo shop, but . . . I don't think that was the case." She needed to steer this away from the Horn. Quickly. Especially since Nesta had been the one they'd called to inspect her tattoo.

Azriel asked, "How did your friend know the language?"

"I still don't know. I've been trying to figure out what she knew for months now."

"Why not just ask her?" Nesta countered.

"Because she's dead." The words came out flatter than Bryce had intended. But something cracked in her to say them, even if she'd lived with that reality every day for more than two years now. "The Asteri had her assassinated, then had it framed as a demonic murder. She was getting close to discovering some major truth about the Asteri and our world, so they had her killed."

"What truth?" This from Azriel.

"I've been trying to uncover that, too," Bryce said.

"Was the language of your tattoo part of it?" Azriel pressed.

"I don't know—I only got as far as learning that she'd uncovered what the Asteri truly are, what they do to the worlds they conquer. If I ever get home . . ." Her heart became unbearably heavy. "If I ever get home, maybe I'll learn the rest."

Silence fell. Then Nesta nodded to the three dancing Fae figures above Bryce. "So what does that mean, then? If you don't need the context."

Bryce examined the relief. Took in the dancing, the stars, the idyllic islands in the background. And she said softly, "It means that there was once joy in this world."

Silence. Then Nesta said, "That's it?"

Bryce kept her eyes on the dancers, the stars, the lush lands. Ignored the darkness beneath. Focused on the good—always the good. "Isn't that all that matters?"

13

It took five hours for the Viper Queen to deign to meet Ithan.

Five hours, plus the fact that Ithan had opened the door to the hallway where two Fae assassins stood posted and threatened to start ripping apart the warehouse.

Then and only then was he escorted here, to her office.

He'd left Flynn, Dec, Marc, and Tharion quietly debating not only how the fuck they'd get out of the Meat Market, but also whether to trust the Hind. The sprites, shocked by her mention of their lost queen, had retreated into Tharion's bedroom with Sigrid. The dragon hadn't yet emerged from her own.

But Ithan had had enough of debating, of asking questions. He'd never been good with that shit. Maybe it was the athlete in him, but he just wanted to *do* something.

It didn't matter if they could trust the Hind or not. If she could get them to Pangera, closer to their friends . . . he'd take that. But he had to get one friend out first.

Ithan sat in an ancient green chair in a truly derelict office, watching the Viper Queen type key by key into a computer that could have doubled as a cement block.

A statue of Luna sat atop that computer, arrow pointed at the Viper Queen's face. A few more deliberate *click-clacks* of her long nails on the keyboard, and then her green eyes slid to Ithan.

"So what was all the yelping about?"

Ithan crossed his arms. On the desk itself sat a statuette of Cthona, carved from black stone. In one arm the goddess cradled an infant to her bare breast. In the other, she extended an orb—Midgard—out into the room. Cthona, birther of worlds. He touched it idly, gathering his courage.

"I want to discuss what you're going to do about Sabine," he said.

The Viper Queen leaned back in her seat, sleek bob swaying. "As far as I know, when Amelie Ravenscroft woke up from having her throat cut by my guards, she tracked down the Prime Apparent, dragged her carcass home, and has been feeding Sabine a steady diet of firstlight to regenerate her. She's already back on her feet."

Ithan's blood curdled. "So Sabine recovered quickly."

The Viper Queen cocked her head. "Were you hoping otherwise?"

He didn't answer. Instead, he asked, "And you're going to hand Sigrid and me over to her?"

The Viper Queen opened a drawer, pulled out a silver tin of cigarettes, and lifted one to her mouth. "Depends on how nicely you ask me not to, Holstrom." The cigarette rose and fell with the words. She lifted a lighter and ignited the tip, taking a long drag.

"What'll it take?"

Smoke rippled from her mouth as the Viper Queen sized him up. Her tongue darted over her purple lower lip. Tasting—scenting. The way snakes smelled.

"Let's introduce ourselves first. We've never met, have we?"

"Hi. Nice to meet you."

"So testy. I thought you'd be a big old softy."

He flashed his teeth. "I don't know why you'd assume that."

She took another long drag of her cigarette. "Did you not go against Sabine's orders and lead a small group of wolves into Asphodel Meadows to save humans? To save the most vulnerable of the House of Earth and Blood?"

He growled. "I was doing a nice thing. There wasn't much more to it than that."

The Viper Queen exhaled a plume of smoke, more dragon than the one upstairs. "That remains to be seen."

Ithan challenged, "You sent your people to help that day, too."

"I was doing a nice thing," the Viper Queen echoed mildly. "There wasn't much more to it than that."

"Maybe you'll feel inclined to do the nice thing today, too."

"Buying or selling, Holstrom?"

Ithan leashed the wolf inside howling at him to start shredding things. "Look, I don't play games."

"Pity." She examined her manicured nails. "Sabine doesn't, either. All you wolves are so *boring*."

Ithan opened his mouth, then shut it. Considered what she'd said, what she'd done. "You don't like Sabine."

Her lips curved slowly. "Does anyone?"

He clenched his hands into fists. "If you don't like her, why let her go?"

"I'd ask the same of you, pup. You had her down—why not finish the kill?" Ithan couldn't help the way his body tensed. "Of course," the Viper Queen went on, "the Fendyr heir—Sigrid, is it?—should be the one to do it. Don't you wolves call it . . . challenging?"

"Only in open combat, when witnessed by pack-members of the Den. If Sigrid had killed Sabine last night, it would have been an assassination."

"Semantics."

A chill skittered down his spine. "You want Sabine truly dead." She said nothing. "Is this your cost, then? You want me to kill—"

"Oh, no. I wouldn't *dare* tangle in politics like that."

"Just drugs and misery, right?"

Again, that slow smile. "What would your dear brother say if he knew you were here with the likes of me?"

Ithan wouldn't give her the satisfaction of a reaction. "Tell me what it'll take to get all of us out of here."

"A fight." She extinguished her cigarette. "Just one fight. From you. A private event," the Viper Queen purred. "Only for me."

"Why?" Ithan demanded.

"I place a high value on amusement. Especially my own." She smiled again. "One fight for safe passage—and Ketos's freedom. You win, and it's all yours. Nothing more required beyond that."

Fuck, he should have brought Marc with him—he'd have thought this through, would have spotted any pitfalls a mile off.

But Ithan knew if he walked out, if he went to get someone else, the option would be off the table. It came down to him, and him alone.

"I fight, and you'll let us all go. Immediately."

Her chin dipped. "I'll even provide a car to take you wherever you want to go."

One fight. He'd fought plenty in his life. "I'm not taking your venom," Ithan said.

"Who said I was offering?" Her lips curled.

"You'll let Tharion free of that, too," Ithan added. "No more enthralling bullshit."

"I'm offended, Holstrom. It's a sacred bond amongst my kind."

"Nothing is sacred to you."

The Viper Queen lifted a finger and turned the statuette of Luna toward him, the arrow now pointing his way. "Oh?"

"The trappings mean nothing if you don't follow it up with actions."

Another little smile. "So self-righteous."

Ithan held her stare, letting her see the wolf within, whatever bones of it remained.

There had to be a catch. But time was running out—and he didn't see an alternative to getting out of this mess.

"Fine," Ithan said. "One fight."

"It's a deal," the Viper Queen crooned. She rose and stalked to the door, body moving with sinuous grace. "The fight's at ten tomorrow night. Your friends can come watch, if they want." She opened the door, an order to leave. Ithan obeyed, and she pulled out yet another cigarette tin—this one gold—and flicked it open. He was passing over the threshold when she said, "I'll give you a worthy opponent, don't worry."

The Viper Queen smirked. And then added before she slammed the door shut in his face, "Make your brother proud."

Lidia Cervos brushed out her hair, seated at her vanity in her ornate room in the Asteri's palace. A monstrosity of gold silk, ivory velvet, and polished oak overlooking the seven hills of the city. The perfect room for the pampered, loyal pet of the Asteri.

No one had thought twice or even questioned her when she'd gone to Lunathion earlier to deliver a message to Celestina and make a pit stop at the Meat Market to pick up some "party favors." Even Mordoc hadn't cared.

But her allies believed she was their enemies' faithful pet, too.

So here she was. Alone. Praying that Declan Emmet and his friends would meet her. Praying that she'd correctly judged the Sprite Queen, many levels below.

The door to the bathroom opened, steam rippling out, and Pollux emerged, wholly naked and gleaming from the shower.

"You're not dressed?" he asked, frowning at her dove-gray silk dressing robe. The frown deepened as his eyes drifted over her hair, still down and unstyled. "We're leaving in fifteen minutes."

Here it was—the beginning of an intricate dance.

"My cycle is starting," she said, putting a hand to her lower abdomen. "Make excuses for me."

Pollux slicked back his blond hair and stalked over to her, his heavy cock swinging with each step. His white wings dripped a trail of water over the cream carpet. "Rigelus personally asked us to be there. Take a tonic."

"I did," she said, letting a bit of her temper show. It wasn't a lie. She *had* taken a potion—one of her emergency contraceptives, lest her usual plan fail. It had jump-started her cycle two weeks ahead of schedule.

Right on cue, Pollux sniffed, scenting her blood. "You're early."

He knew, because he didn't like to fuck her when she was bleeding. She'd come to cherish her cycle. Pollux usually tormented someone else that week.

She met his stare, if only because his cock was in her face and she had little interest in looking at it for another second of her existence. The tonic did its job in that moment, and nausea churned in her gut—along with a slice of pain.

She didn't have to fake her wince. "Tell Rigelus I apologize."

Pollux observed her without an ounce of mercy. To the contrary—his cock thickened. A cat enjoying the suffering of its dinner.

But she ignored it, going back to the mirror. A broad, powerful hand stroked down her hair, brushing it aside. Then lips found her neck, his tongue flicking beneath her ear. "I hope you'll feel better soon."

Lidia made herself lift a hand to his hair. Run her fingers through the damp strands and let out a low sound. It might have been pain or lust. To the Malleus, it was all the same. He pulled back, a hand pumping his cock as he headed into the dressing room, wings glowing white behind him.

She was in their bed—a great mass of down pillows and silken sheets—when Pollux left fifteen minutes later, wearing a tux with devastating effect. Such a beautiful exterior, this monster.

"Lidia," the Hammer purred, possession in his rich voice, and then he was gone.

She lay in bed, fighting past the twisting in her gut, the nausea that wasn't solely from her cycle. Only after ten minutes had gone by did she rise from the mattress.

She hurried into the bathroom, still humid from Pollux's shower—usually so hot she wondered if he was trying to scald the evil from himself—and pulled out the bag of feminine hygiene products that she knew he'd never open. As if touching a tampon might make his cock shrivel up and drop off.

Inside the bag lay a burner phone. A different one arrived in a box of tampons every month. She ran the shower again, blocking out any identifying noises that could be picked up from the palace's cameras on the walls outside or by anyone on the other end of the line. Then she dialed.

An operator answered. "Fincher Tiles and Flooring."

She shifted her voice into a lilting, sweet croon. "I'm looking for custom ash-wood floors, seven-by-seven pieces?"

"One moment, please."

Another ring. Then another female said, "This is Custom Ash-Wood Floors, Seven by Seven."

Lidia let out a small breath. She had only called once before, long ago. They'd sent her burner phone after burner phone, in case of an emergency. Each month she'd destroyed them, unused.

Well, this was an emergency.

"This is Daybright," she said in her normal voice.

The female on the line sucked in a breath. "Solas."

Lidia continued quickly, "I need all agents mobilized and ready to move in three days."

The female on the line cleared her throat. "I . . . Agent Daybright, I don't think there's anyone to mobilize."

Lidia blinked slowly. "Explain."

"We've taken too many hits, lost too many people. And after the death of Agent Silverbow, a good number abandoned the cause."

"How many are left?"

"A couple hundred, perhaps."

Lidia closed her eyes. "And none can be spared right now to—"

"Command's put an end to all missions. They're going into hiding."

"Patch me through to Command, then."

"I . . . I'm not authorized to do that."

Lidia opened her eyes. "Tell Command I'll speak to them and only them. This information is something that might buy them a shot at survival."

The dispatcher paused, considering. "If it's not—"

"It is. Tell them it's about something they've wanted to do for a very long time."

Another pause. Thinking through all she knew, probably. "One moment."

It was the work of a few minutes to get the human male on the phone. For Lidia to use the passcodes to identify herself and verify her identity, as well as his. To explain the plan she'd slowly been forming. For Ophion to survive another day, yes . . . but even more so, for their unwitting help in making sure Ruhn survived.

Two days. Lidia left him with a time, a start location, and an order to be ready. There'd be no missing the signal. She could only hope Ophion would show up as the commander had promised.

Lidia ended the call, and crushed the phone in her fist until only shards of plastic and glass remained. Then she opened the bathroom window, pretending to air out the steam as the tiny pieces blew into the starry night.

Bryce faced another river, this one waist-deep and frigid. But at least the star kept pointing ahead this time, no swimming required. They splashed through the water in silence, Bryce's still-bleeding hands stinging at the river's kiss, and she shivered as they emerged on the other side.

"So that eight-pointed star," Nesta said into the quiet as they began walking again, shoes squishing, "it's a symbol of the Starborn people in your world. It means nothing else?"

"Why all the questions about it?" Bryce asked through chattering teeth. Azriel walked a few steps behind, silent as death, but she knew he was listening to every word.

Nesta went silent, and Bryce thought she might not answer, but then she said, "I had a tattoo on my back—recently. A magical one, now gone. But it was of an eight-pointed star."

"And?"

"And the magic, the power of the bargain that caused the tattoo to appear . . . it chose the design. The star meant nothing to me. I thought maybe it was related to my training, but its shape was identical to the scar on your chest."

"So we're obviously destined to be best friends," Bryce teased. Nesta didn't smile or laugh. Bryce asked, "Is that . . . is that why you volunteered to come to get me?"

"I've been in the Fae realms long enough to know that there are forces that sometimes guide us, push us along. I've learned to let them. And to listen." Nesta smirked. "It's why I didn't kill you for following your starlight into the river. You were doing the same thing."

Bryce's chest tightened. The female had a story to tell, and one Bryce would, in any other circumstance, like to hear. But before she could even consider asking, something massive and white appeared ahead. A skeleton of enormous bones.

"The Wyrm?" Bryce asked, even as she realized it wasn't. This thing was different, with a body like a sobek's. Each tooth was as large as Bryce's hand.

"No," Azriel said from behind them, the rushing river muffling his soft words. "And I don't think the Wyrm ate it, if its skeleton is intact like this."

"Do you know what it is?" Bryce asked.

"No," Azriel said again. "And part of me is glad not to."

"You think there are more down here?" Nesta asked Azriel, scanning the dark.

"I hope not," Azriel answered. Bryce shuddered and took the opportunity to continue onward, leading the way, leaving those ancient, terrifying bones far behind.

The river was still a thunderous roar when the carvings changed. Normally, they were full of life and action and movement. But this one was simple, clearly meant to be the sole focus. Something of great importance to whoever had carved it.

An archway had been etched, stars glimmering around it. And in that archway stood a male figure, the image created with impressive depth. His hand was upraised in greeting.

And Bryce might have looked closer, had the Middengard Wyrm not exploded from the river behind them.

14

The Middengard Wyrm had arrived at last. Precisely according to Bryce's plan.

She'd been dripping blood for it all this way, leaving a trail, constantly scraping off her scabs to reopen her wounds—ones she'd intentionally inflicted on herself by "falling" into the stream. If the Wyrm relied on scent to hunt, then she'd left a veritable neon sign leading right to them. She hadn't known when or how it would attack, but she'd been waiting.

And she was ready.

Bryce fell back as not only shadows, but blue light flared from Azriel—right alongside the ripple of silver flame from Nesta. Back-to-back, they faced the massive creature with razor-sharp focus. Ataraxia gleamed in Nesta's hand. Truth-Teller pulsed with darkness in Azriel's.

Now or never. Her legs tensed, readying to sprint.

Nesta's eyes slid to Bryce's for a heartbeat. As if understanding at last: Bryce's "unhealing" hand. The blood she'd wiped on the walls. Her musing about the linked river system in these caves, sussing out what they knew regarding the terrain and the Wyrm. To unleash this thing—on *them*.

"I'm sorry," Bryce said to her. And ran.

She meant them no harm—she hadn't lied about that. They could undoubtedly face the Wyrm and live. Nesta had said her sister had done exactly that.

But Bryce needed to learn whatever Urd had sent her to discover. If it was intel that could help or harm her world . . . she didn't want these people knowing. Using it against her. Offering it up to the Asteri. Or wielding it against Midgard for their own gain. Whatever lay ahead was for her alone.

Bryce raced down the tunnel, her path lit by flashes of silver flame and blue magic. Nesta's and Azriel's powers, flaring like lightning against the nightmare of the Wyrm.

The faces of the tunnel carvings watched Bryce's flight with cold, damning eyes. Her breath sawed in her throat. She had no idea how far she had to run, but if she could get a little farther—

A shout bounced off the rocks behind her. Not one of pursuit, but of pain. Azriel. She glanced over a shoulder just as his blue light went out.

Then a female shout resounded through the cavern, and Nesta's silver flame vanished, too, leaving Bryce's starlight to illuminate the way. Leaving only darkness and silence behind her.

She had to keep going. They were seasoned warriors. They were fine.

But that silence, interrupted by Bryce's breathing, her rushing steps . . .

She was the master of spinning bullshit. She'd kept them distracted, kept them from thinking her a manipulative little shit, but . . .

Bryce slowed to a stop. The darkness behind her loomed.

She found herself face-to-face with a scene depicting a great battlefield before the high walls of a city, Fae and winged horrors and snarling beasts all at war, entrenched in pain and suffering. One of the Fae stood in the foreground, spearing a fellow Fae warrior in the mouth.

Fae against Fae. It shouldn't have bothered her. Shouldn't have grabbed her as it did: the warrior-female's merciless expression as she embedded her spear in the agonized face of the female soldier before her. It shouldn't have unsettled something in Bryce to see it.

She'd long ago understood that this kind of thing wasn't beyond the Fae. She took comfort in knowing she wasn't like them, would never be that way.

Yet what she'd just done . . .

She wasn't a monster. Was she?

Maybe she'd regret it. She knew Hunt would have yelled at her for setting a trap only to go help the people she'd ensnared.

But Bryce began running again, hurtling through the cave. Back toward Nesta and Azriel.

And prayed there was something left for her to save.

Bryce realized now, as she retraced her steps, that what she'd earlier thought to be the roaring of the river was in fact the thunderous movement of the Wyrm's massive body. Azriel and Nesta must have made the same mistake.

In the dark, her starlight silvered the walls, casting the world into stark relief.

Her starlight hadn't felt so . . . empty before. While it had been guiding them, it had been comforting, had brought some color and spark to this realm of eternal night. Now, bobbing with every sprinting step, it seemed harsh. Devoid of color.

Like even the light was disgusted by her.

Nesta and Azriel weren't in the tunnel by the carving of the archway. From the shaking of the ground and the snapping of jaws ahead, they'd driven the Wyrm back to the river.

Bryce checked herself in time to slow to a walk before reaching the bank, reminding herself of Randall's training.

Observe, assess, decide.

So she crept up the last few feet toward the rushing water, a hand over her star to dim it, and—

They weren't there. No sign of the Wyrm or its meal. Her stomach dropped. They'd seemed supremely badass and capable. Surely that Wyrm couldn't have . . .

It had.

Nesta lay sprawled on a large rock in the river not ten feet away. No sign of the Wyrm or Azriel. Perhaps it had eaten him already. And would soon return for the other part of its meal.

Oh gods, she'd done this, she'd fucked up beyond forgiveness—

Bryce raced to Nesta's prone form, splashing through the icy water, slipping over stones, the river foaming around her waist in a strong current as she reached to turn the female over—

Nesta's eyes were open. And blazing with fury.

A hand wrapped around Bryce's throat. A blade poked into her back. And Azriel's voice was whisper-soft as he snarled, "Give me one reason not to bury this knife in your spine."

Bryce bared her teeth. "Because I came back to help?"

Nesta snorted, getting to her feet. Utterly unharmed.

"The Wyrm?" Bryce managed to ask, trying not to think about the knife angled to slide into her body. Or about the tug and thrum of the Starsword and the dagger, so near to her now.

"It's hunting us," Nesta seethed, eyeing the river, the tunnel.

"Then fucking *run*," Bryce panted. "The tunnel's open—"

"We're not leaving that thing alive in the world," Azriel said with quiet venom. Nesta unsheathed Ataraxia, the blade glowing faintly. Her demeanor was calm, as if this was all in a day's work.

Solas burn her. Randall would kill her for being so stupid. "You lured me here."

Nesta nodded to Azriel, who withdrew his blade but kept a hand on Bryce's shoulder, either to prevent her from moving or to hold her steady in the river's current. "You saved me from the traps in the walls. It only made sense that you'd have a guilty conscience to go with that soft heart."

Scratch that: her *mother* would kill her for being so stupid.

"I—" Bryce began, but Nesta said, "Save it."

The sharp tone was enough to make Bryce peer into the river's darkness, the tunnel on either side. Even the call of the Starsword and Truth-Teller became secondary as she asked, "How did it disappear?"

"Deep pits in the riverbed," Azriel murmured. "It got one whiff of Nesta's power and dove into one. But from the shaking of the stone . . . it's staying close. Watching us."

"Then why the fuck are we standing in the river?"

Nesta smirked at her. "Bait."

Make your brother proud.

The Viper Queen might as well have shot Ithan in the fucking gut. Like she knew precisely how ashamed Connor would have been of how far he'd fallen.

"What's she going to do about Sabine?" Tharion asked Ithan as he entered the suite once more. Right—he'd told them that was what he wanted to learn from her.

"Nothing," Ithan said.

Sigrid sat on the couch beside Declan, watching his fingers fly over his phone.

"Where's Marc?" Ithan asked.

"Pulled the lawyer privileges card," Flynn answered for Dec. "Fed the guards some crap about legal stuff. He got a message from the Viper Queen a minute after you left, saying he was free to go."

So that was what the Viper Queen had been typing on her computer.

"Go where?"

"To his firm," Dec said, still focusing on his phone. "He's going to look into whether there's a legal way to get us all out of this shitshow."

"I might have a solution for that," Ithan said. They all looked at him.

Tharion asked quietly, "What did she offer you, pup?"

"Nothing I can't handle."

Tharion stood from the table by the fighting ring window. "Did you—"

"One fight—from me. Tomorrow night."

Sigrid's eyes widened. "What sort of fight?"

Ithan pointed to the window behind Tharion. "One of her fancy ones. Down there."

"Did she say *who*?" He'd never seen Ketos's face so serious. "You should have made her specify. She's going to screw you over—screw us all over somehow." Tharion's voice sharpened. "What the Hel were you thinking?"

"I was thinking," Ithan shot back, "that *you* made a stupid choice, and I was trying to get you out of it. Get us all out of this mess."

Tharion blinked at him, eyes dark. Cold. "I didn't ask you to get me out of it. You think I can just walk out of here? I *can't*."

"The Viper Queen said you could—"

"And what then?" The mer got to his feet. "I'll be right back at the mercy of the River Queen. The Viper Queen knows that—she knows I don't have any choice but to stay here, with her." Tharion shook his head in disgust. "You dumb fucking idiot." With that, the mer stalked out of the room.

Silence reigned for a moment. Then Declan said, "You should have talked to us first."

"Yeah, well, I didn't," Ithan snapped. Then sighed. "The Hind gave us two days. Marc's a genius and all that, but legal shit takes time. We don't have that."

"The mer is right," Sigrid said darkly. "You shouldn't trust someone like her. Anyone who traffics in lives has no honor."

"I know," Ithan said. And for a moment, he could see it in Sigrid's eyes—the rigid, yet fair Alpha she might be. With the emotional scars to understand the importance and value of each life.

Maybe he should have encouraged her to kill Sabine last night. Ithan sighed again.

Flynn walked to the wet bar. "Better drink up, Holstrom."

"I never drink before a game," Ithan said. "Even the day before."

"Trust me," Flynn said, pressing a glass of whiskey into Ithan's hand, "with the Vipe hand-selecting your opponent, you'll want something to take the edge off."

"You left your blood all over the place to lead it along," Nesta said. "It's after you—not us. So *you're* going to draw it back here."

Bryce glanced between Nesta and Azriel. They were completely serious.

Bryce pointed to the boulder Nesta had been lying upon moments ago. "So, what, I'm supposed to sit on this rock and wait for the Wyrm to show up and eat me?"

"That last bit is up to you," Nesta said, turning toward the other end of the river. "But from what I just saw, you're a fast runner. You'll get away in time. Probably."

Asshole.

Azriel murmured, "Quiet," and Bryce, without much of an alternative, obeyed.

It didn't matter how brightly her starlight shone. The Wyrm was blind. And it was only a matter of time until it came sniffing again—

It was a matter of seconds, actually.

One moment, there was only the rushing river. The next, a wall of water exploded in front of Azriel, the behemoth body of the Wyrm dwarfing even the warrior's powerful form.

Bryce had never seen such a horrible creature, even during the attack on Crescent City this spring. Rays of blue light flared from Azriel, spearing for the creature—

They pierced its dark, wet skin and vanished.

It was all Bryce saw before she leapt off the rock, splashing through the water, aiming for the tunnel archway.

Nesta shot past her, Ataraxia in hand, silver fire wreathing the other. But the Wyrm vanished—as fast as it had appeared, it went back into the sinkhole.

"Where is it?" Nesta shouted to Azriel, who pivoted, scanning the river, the tunnel—

Behind them, closer to Bryce, the Wyrm erupted from the water again from another sinkhole. Silver fire blasted past her. The Wyrm screeched as the raw power slammed into its side, setting the caverns shaking, debris and rock splashing into the river.

Then the fire vanished, sucked into its skin. The Wyrm again plunged beneath the water, into the sinkhole.

Azriel and Nesta returned to their back-to-back position, and Bryce gathered her wits enough to say, "What happened?"

"It . . . it ate my power," Nesta murmured.

"That's not possible," Azriel said, eyes fixed on the river.

"It *did*," Nesta snapped. "I felt it."

"Shit," Azriel said.

"We need to run," Bryce said.

"No," Nesta said, silver fire in her eyes again. "That thing doesn't get out of this fight alive."

As if in answer and challenge, the Wyrm leapt from the water, a massive, powerful surge, jaws opening wide toward Nesta and Azriel and Bryce—

A flap of Azriel's wings and the three of them were airborne, faster than even the Wyrm could attack. It narrowly missed Azriel's booted feet as it dove again, vanishing once more.

"We need it restrained," Nesta said to Azriel. "So I can get close with Ataraxia."

"If your power didn't kill it, there's no saying Ataraxia will, either," Azriel panted, landing them on the bank. "It breaks through my tethers like they're spiderwebs."

"Then we get something else to do the fighting for us," Nesta said, and Azriel whirled to her, as if in alarm.

But Bryce said, "Fine." And reached a hand out to Azriel. "Give me the Starsword." She'd led them into this mess—she could try to get them out of it. The Starsword had killed Reapers. Maybe it would kill this thing, too.

"Don't you dare," Azriel began—but not to Bryce. Dread paled his golden skin. "Nesta—"

Something metallic gleamed like sunshine in Nesta's hand. A mask.

"Nesta," Azriel warned, panic sharpening his voice, but too late. She closed her eyes and shoved it onto her face. A strange, cold breeze swept through the tunnel.

Bryce had endured that wind before, in the Bone Quarter. A wind of death, of decay, of quiet. The hair on her arms rose. And her blood chilled to ice as Nesta opened her eyes to reveal only silver flame shining there.

Whatever that mask was, whatever power it had . . . death lay within it.

"Take it off," Azriel snarled, but Nesta extended a hand into the darkness of the tunnel.

Mortal, an ancient, bone-dry voice whispered in Bryce's head. *You are mortal, and you shall die. Memento mori. Memento mori, memento—*

Bone clicked in the darkness. The earth shook.

Azriel grabbed Bryce, tugging her back against him as he retreated toward the wall, as if it'd offer any shelter from whatever approached. The Starsword and Truth-Teller hummed and pulled at Bryce's spine, and her hands itched, like she could feel the weapons in her palms—

She didn't see what it was that Nesta drew from the dark before the Wyrm found them.

As it had before, it leapt from the river, thrashing into the narrow tunnel, blocking the way back. Azriel's shield glowed blue around them. Jaws open wide to reveal rows of flesh-shredding teeth, the Wyrm shot right for them.

But something massive and white slammed into the Wyrm instead. A creature of pure bone, larger than the Wyrm.

The skeleton they'd encountered down the tunnel. Reanimated.

Its jaws snapped for the Wyrm, long arms ending in claws finding purchase on either side of the Wyrm's unholy mouth.

The Wyrm shrieked, but the creature held firm, biting down on the Wyrm's head and shaking, shaking, *shaking*—

Azriel dragged Bryce back, sword and dagger calling to her to draw them, use them. But he kept pulling her away, deeper into the tunnel as the undead thing and the Wyrm grappled with each other. The ceiling shook, debris shattering on the floor. Azriel arched a wing, shielding them both from its slicing rain.

But there was nothing in that world to shield them from the being standing a few feet away.

Hair drifting on a phantom breeze, Nesta glowed with silver fire. Still wearing her mask. A finger pointed toward the fight. Commanding that creature of bone and death to attack the Wyrm. Again. Again.

"What is she—" Bryce began, but Azriel clamped a hand over her mouth, hauling her farther down the tunnel.

So Bryce could only watch in awe and utter terror as Nesta's fingers closed into a fist.

The beast's jaws encircled the Wyrm's entire front end and smashed it down into the earth, pinning it. The ground rocked with the impact, and even Azriel stumbled, his hand flying from Bryce's mouth.

The Wyrm thrashed, but the undead creature held it firm. Held it down as Nesta drew Ataraxia once more and approached.

"We need to help her," Bryce panted to Azriel.

"I promise you, she's fine," Azriel countered, urging them further into the tunnel. Out of the impact zone, Bryce realized.

The Wyrm must have sensed the sword's approach, because it bucked against the bones and claws pinning it to the rock.

It managed to nudge the undead creature back, but only for a heartbeat.

Nesta raised her free hand again, and the undead creature slammed the Wyrm back into the ground. The Wyrm thrashed, desperate now.

With a dancer's grace, Nesta scaled the undead beast's tail, running along the knobs of its spine like rocks in a stream. Getting to higher ground, to a better angle.

The Wyrm shrieked, but Nesta had reached the undead beast's white skull. And then she was jumping, sword arcing above her, then down, down—

Straight into the head of the Wyrm.

A shudder of silver fire rushed down the Wyrm. That cold, dry wind shivered through the caves again, death in its wake.

The Wyrm slumped to the ground.

The silence was worse than the sound.

Azriel was instantly gone, wings tucking in tight as he rushed toward Nesta and the undead beast that still held the Wyrm in its grip.

"Take it off," Azriel ordered her.

The female turned her head toward him with a smooth motion that Bryce had only seen from possessed dolls in horror movies.

"Take it off," Azriel snarled.

Still staring at him, Nesta yanked Ataraxia from the Wyrm's body and slid down its side, landing with that preternatural ease on the rock.

Every muscle in Bryce's body went taught, that voice whispering over and over to her, *Mortal. You shall die. You shall die. You shall die.*

She hated how she shook at Nesta's stalking approach. How both the human and Vanir parts of her trembled at this thing, whatever it was, contained within the mask.

Azriel didn't yield a single step. Nesta came to a stop before him. Nothing human or Fae looked out through the eyeholes of the mask.

"Take it off," he said, voice pure ice. "Let the creature rest again."

A blink, and the undead creature collapsed once more into a pile of bones.

"Cassian's waiting for you, Nesta," Azriel said—tone gentling. "Take off the Mask." Nesta stayed silent, Ataraxia ready in her hand. One swipe, and Azriel would be dead. "He's waiting for you at the House of Wind," Azriel went on. "At home."

Another blink from Nesta. The silver fire banked a little.

Like whoever Cassian was, and whatever the House of Wind was . . . they might be the only things capable of fighting the siren song of the Mask.

"Gwyn and Emerie are waiting," Azriel pushed. "And Feyre and Elain." The silver flame flared at that. Then Azriel said, "Nyx is waiting, too."

The silver flame went out entirely.

The Mask fell from Nesta's face, clattering on the stone.

Nesta swayed, but Azriel was there, catching her, bringing her to his chest, scarred hands stroking her hair. "Thank the Mother," he breathed. "Thank the Mother."

Bryce began to turn away, sensing that she was witnessing something deeply personal.

But Nesta pulled back from Azriel. Steadied her feet before facing Bryce, Ataraxia still in one hand. She flicked the fingers of her other hand and the Mask instantly vanished, off to wherever she'd summoned it from.

Bryce had so many words in her head that none of them came out.

Nesta just sheathed Ataraxia down her spine again and said to Bryce, "Keep walking."

15

It took Bryce hours to stop shaking. To chase that cold, deadly wind from her skin. To stop hearing the whispering of her death, the death of all things.

She'd never encountered anything like that mask. Nesta had seemed at its mercy, brought back to herself only by Azriel's list of whoever those people were—clearly people Nesta cared about.

Through love, all is possible. Even getting free of death-masks.

Nesta didn't speak, staying close beside Azriel. Or maybe he was the one staying close to her. The male didn't seem to want her farther away than he could grab.

Eventually, Bryce could stand it no longer. "I'm sorry," she said.

At their silence, she twisted to look back at them. They wore twin expressions of ice.

"I'm . . . I'm really fucking sorry," Bryce said, heart thundering.

"You're proving," Nesta said tightly, "to be more trouble than you're worth."

"Then why not just kill me?" Bryce snapped.

"Because whatever you think you'll find at the end of these tunnels," Azriel said with lethal quiet, "whatever warrants the effort of trying to kill us . . . that has to be something worth seeing."

"You could leave me here and go ahead yourselves." She probably shouldn't have suggested that. Too late now.

"That star on your chest suggests otherwise," Nesta said, and left Azriel's side at last to head into the dark. "We've put this much effort into seeing what you'll do. Might as well see it through."

"Effort?" But even as she spoke, Bryce understood. "You knew I'd go through the grate."

"Rhysand guessed, yes—and you made him smug as hell when you winnowed. Granted, he was surprised that you could winnow at all, but . . . the bastard sent us after you." Nesta spoke without turning around, striding with that unfaltering confidence into the gloom. "He had us make sure there was only one path forward. Make sure *you* believed there was only one path forward, too. So you'd show your hand—show us what you truly wanted here."

"You caused the cave-in."

Nesta shrugged. "Azriel caused it. But yes."

"Why—why do any of this? Why do you *care*?"

Nesta was quiet for a beat. Azriel didn't say a word, a wall of silent menace at her back. Then Nesta said, "Because I've seen that star on your chest before."

"Yeah, you said that," Bryce said. "Your tattoo—"

"Not my tattoo."

"Then where?" Bryce breathed. If she could get answers—

But Nesta strode ahead again into the darkness. "No place good."

After another fitful rest, Azriel and Nesta were both still clearly pissed at Bryce. Rightly so, but wasn't she allowed to be pissed, too? They'd manipulated her every step of the way, watching her like some animal in a zoo, making her think she'd caused that cave-in when they'd engineered it themselves . . .

She shot Azriel a sidelong glare as they walked through the tunnel. He gave her a cool look in return.

Behind him, the carvings continued, showing Fae frolicking over hills and thriving in ancient-looking walled cities. A scene of growth and change. But Azriel's eyes slid ahead—and he nodded at where Nesta had stopped.

"We have a problem," Nesta murmured as they stepped up to her side.

A chasm stretched before them, Bryce's starlight glowing in a single ray straight across it. Bryce swallowed.

Yeah, they really fucking did.

Ruhn managed to keep his food down, and that was about all he could say for himself as he lay on the filthy, reeking floor and slept.

Maybe it was because he hadn't managed to truly sleep in days. Maybe it was because Athalar had asked him to do it, and he knew, deep down, that he needed to grow the fuck up. But here he was. On a familiar-looking mental bridge. Staring at a burning female figure.

Ruhn? Lidia's voice caught. *What happened?*

"I need to pass along intel." Each word was cold and clipped.

The flame around Lidia banked until it was nothing but her flowing golden hair, and it killed him. She was so fucking beautiful. It wouldn't have mattered to him, *hadn't* mattered to him during those weeks they'd gotten to know each other, but . . .

She kept ten feet away. He hadn't bothered with his stars and night. He didn't care.

"Bryce . . . was trying to go to Hel to ask for help. She didn't make it there."

Lidia's face was impassive. "How can you possibly know this?"

"The Prince of the Pit paid Hunt a visit. He confirmed that Bryce isn't with him—or his brothers."

To her credit, Lidia didn't balk at the mention of Apollion—she didn't even question why Hunt was in contact with him. "Where did she go?"

"We don't know. The plan was for her to head there to raise their armies and bring them back, but if she's not there, we're shit out of luck."

"Was there . . . was there a chance that Hel might have actually allied with you?" Disbelief laced every word.

"Yeah. There still is."

"Why tell me any of this?"

He clenched his jaw. "We weren't sure if you or Command had any suspicions about where Bryce went, or if you were hoping she'd carry out some sort of miracle when she got back here. But we figured you should know that doesn't seem like an option."

Lidia swore. She looked at her hands, as if she could see whatever plans Ophion might have had crumbling away. "We weren't counting on any assistance from your sister or Hel, but I'll pass along the warning nonetheless." Her eyes churned with worry. "Is she . . ."

Trust Day to get right to the heart of the matter.

"I don't know." His flat tone conveyed everything.

She angled her head, and he knew her well enough to know she was considering all he'd told her. The Oracle's warning.

But Lidia said, "She's not dead." Nothing but pure confidence filled her words.

"Oh yeah?" He couldn't keep his snide tone in check. "What makes you so sure?"

She took his nastiness in stride. "Rigelus has his mystics hunting for her. He wants her found."

"He doesn't know what I know."

"No—he knows *more* than you. He wouldn't waste the effort if he believed Bryce was dead. Or in Hel. He knows she's somewhere else."

Ruhn ignored the kernel of hope in his chest. "So what does it mean, then?"

"It means he thinks Bryce's location might make some difference." She crossed her arms. "It means wherever he suspects she might be . . . it has him worried."

"I don't see how it *could* make any difference."

"Then you underestimate your sister."

"Fuck you," he snapped.

"Rigelus isn't underestimating Bryce for one moment," she went on, tone sharpening. "One thousand mystics, Ruhn—all looking for her. Do you know how many tasks he usually has them doing? But they are all focused on finding her. That tells me he's very, very scared."

Ruhn swallowed hard. "What would happen if his mystics found her location?"

Lidia shook her head, flames twining through the strands. "I don't know. But he must have some plan in mind."

Ruhn asked, "Why can't they find her? I thought his mystics could find anything."

"The universe is vast. Even a thousand mystics need some time to comb every galaxy and star system."

"How much time?"

Her eyes simmered. "Not as much as Bryce likely needs—if she is indeed trying to do the impossible."

"Which is what?"

"Find help."

It was about as much as Ruhn could take. He turned back toward his end of the bridge. "Ruhn."

He halted, shuddering at the way she spoke his name, the memory of how it had felt to hear it the first time, after the equinox ball, when she'd learned who he was.

But that was the problem, wasn't it? She knew who he was . . . and he knew who *she* was. Knew that while she might be Agent Daybright, she'd been the Hind for decades before she'd decided to turn rebel. Had committed plenty of despicable acts for Sandriel and the Asteri long before she'd killed the Harpy to save his life. Did changing sides erase the stain?

She said quietly, "I'm doing what I can to help you."

Ruhn looked over a shoulder. She'd wrapped her arms around her middle. "I don't give a fuck what you're doing. I'm only here because other people's lives might depend on it."

Hurt flashed in her eyes, and it was kindling to his temper. How dare she look that way, look like *she* was hurt, when it was *his* fucking heart—

"You're dead to me," Ruhn hissed, and vanished.

16

Too narrow for me to fly," Azriel said, assessing the seemingly endless chasm between them and the rest of the tunnel. No bridge this time. Only a narrow, endless drop. Far too slim for Azriel to spread his wings. Far too wide for any of them to jump.

"Is this another manipulation?" Bryce asked Nesta coolly.

Nesta snorted. "The rock doesn't lie. He can't even spread his wings halfway."

To get this far and turn back with no answers, nothing to help her get home . . . The star still blazed ahead. Pointing to the tunnel across the chasm.

"No one's got any rope?" Bryce asked pathetically. She was met with incredulous silence. Bryce nodded to Azriel. "Those shadows of yours could take form—they caused that cave-in. Can't you, like, make a bridge or something? Or your blue light . . . you seemed to think it could have restrained the Wyrm. Make a rope with that."

His brows rose. "Neither of those things is remotely possible. The shadows are made of magic, just very condensed. These"—he motioned to the blue stones in his armor—"concentrate my power and allow me to craft it into things that resemble weapons. But they're still only magic—power."

Bryce's mouth twisted to the side. "So it's like a laser?" With the language now imprinted on her brain, her tongue stumbled over *laser* like it was truly the foreign word it was for them. She spoke it like she did in Midgard, but with the accent of this world layered over it, warping the word slightly.

"I don't know what that is," Azriel said, at the same time Nesta declared, "This still doesn't solve the issue of getting over there."

But Bryce frowned deeply at Azriel. "Do you ever use that power to, uh, charge people up?"

"Charge?"

"Fuel. Um. Give your power to someone else to help *their* power."

"Are you implying that I could do such a thing to you?"

"I'm pretty sure the concept of a battery won't have much meaning here, but yeah. My magic can be amplified by someone else's power." The other untranslatable word—*battery*—lay heavy on her tongue.

But Nesta looked her over. "For what purpose?"

"So I can teleport." Another word that didn't translate. "Winnow." She pointed to the other side of the divide. "I could winnow us over there."

Azriel said, "Give me a reason to believe you won't winnow out of here and leave us."

"I can't. You'll have to trust me."

"After what you just pulled?"

"Remember that I'll be trusting you not to blast a hole through my heart." She tapped the star. "Aim right there."

"I told you already: we don't want to kill you."

"Then aim carefully."

Azriel and Nesta exchanged a glance.

Bryce added, "Look, I'd offer you something in return if I could. But you literally took everything of value from me." She pointed to the sword at Azriel's back.

Nesta angled her head. Then reached into her pocket. "What about this?"

Her phone.

Her *phone*. With Nesta's movement, the lock screen came on, blaring bright in the gloom, with Hunt's face right there. His beautiful, wonderful face, so full of joy—

Azriel and Nesta were blinking at the bright light, the photo, and then the phone was gone, stashed in Nesta's pocket again.

"There's a portrait hidden inside its encasing," Nesta added. "Of you and three females."

The photo of Bryce, Danika, June, and Fury. She'd forgotten she'd put it in there before heading to Pangera. But there, in Nesta's pocket, shielded by those fancy-ass waterproofing spells she'd purchased, was her only link back to Midgard. To the people who mattered. And if she was stuck in this fucking world . . . that might very well be all she had left of her own.

"Were you waiting to dangle that in front of me?" Bryce asked.

A shrug from Nesta. "I guessed you might find it valuable."

"Who's to say I'm not playing you? Making you think it means something to me so I can leave you down here anyway?"

"Same reason you came running back to see if we were alive," Azriel said coolly.

Fine. She'd exposed herself with that one. So she said to Azriel, "Hit the star."

"How much power?"

Gods, this was potentially a really bad idea. Experimenting with power she didn't know or understand—

"A little. Just make sure you don't deep-fry me."

After the shit with the Wyrm, he'd probably like nothing more than to do exactly that. But Azriel's lips tugged upward. "I'll try my best."

Bryce braced herself, sucking in a deep breath—

Azriel struck before she could exhale. Searing, sharp power, a bolt of blue right into her star. Bryce bent over, coughing, breathing around the burn, the alien strangeness of the power.

"Are you all right?" Nesta asked with something like concern.

Was it his power? Or something about this world? Even Hunt's hadn't felt like this—so undiluted, like one-hundred-proof liquor.

Bryce closed her eyes and counted to ten, breathing hard. Letting it ease into her blood. Her bones. It tingled along her limbs.

Slowly, she straightened, opening her eyes. From the way the others' faces were illuminated, she knew her gaze had turned incandescent.

They tensed, reaching for their weapons, bracing for her to flee or attack. But Bryce extended her hands—now glowing white—to them.

Nesta took one first. Then Azriel's hand, battered and deeply scarred, slid around hers. Light leaked from where their skin met. She could have sworn his shadows hovered, watching like curious snakes.

Bryce pictured the tunnel mouth. She wanted to go there—

A blink, and it was done.

The raw power in her faded with the jump. Enough that the incandescence vanished and her skin returned to its normal state. Until only her star remained glowing once more.

But she found Azriel and Nesta observing her with different expressions than before. Wariness, yet something like respect, too.

"Let's go," Azriel said, and released her hand. Because the sword and dagger weren't merely tugging now. They were singing, and all she had to do was reach out for them—

But before she could give in to temptation, Azriel stalked into the dark.

Staying a few feet behind him still wasn't enough to block out the blades' song. But Bryce tried to ignore it, well aware of Nesta's watchful gaze. Tried to pretend that everything was totally fine.

Even if she knew that it wasn't. Not even close. And she had a feeling that whatever waited at the end of these tunnels would be way worse.

"The Cauldron," Nesta said hours later, pointing to yet another carving on the wall. It indeed showed a giant cauldron, perched atop what seemed to be a barren mountain peak with three stars above it.

Azriel halted, angling his head. "That's Ramiel." At Bryce's questioning look, he explained, "A mountain sacred to the Illyrians."

Bryce nodded to the carving. "What's the big deal about a cauldron?"

"*The* Cauldron," Azriel amended. Bryce shook her head, not understanding. "You don't have stories of it in your world? The Fae didn't bring that tradition with them?"

Bryce surveyed the giant cauldron. "No. We have five gods, but no cauldron. What does it do?"

"All life came and comes from it," Azriel said with something like reverence. "The Mother poured it into this world, and from it, life blossomed."

Nesta said quietly, "But it is also real—not a myth." Her swallow was audible. "I was turned High Fae when an enemy shoved me into it. It's raw power, but also . . . sentient."

"Like that mask you put on earlier."

Azriel folded his wings tightly, clearly wary of discussing such a powerful instrument with a potential enemy. But Nesta asked, "You detected a sentience in the Mask?"

Bryce nodded. "It didn't, like, talk to me or anything. I could just . . . sense it."

"What did it feel like?" Nesta asked quietly.

"Like death," Bryce breathed. "Like death incarnate."

Nesta's eyes grew distant, grave. "That's what the Mask can do. Give its wearer power over Death itself."

Bryce's blood chilled. "And this is a . . . normal type of weapon here?"

"No," Azriel said from ahead, shoulders tense. "It is not."

Nesta explained, "The Mask is one of three objects of catastrophic power, Made by the Cauldron itself. The Dread Trove, we call it."

"And the Mask is . . . yours?"

"I was also Made by the Cauldron," Nesta said, "which allows me to wield it." She spoke with no pride or boasting. Merely cold resignation and responsibility.

"Made," Bryce mused. "You said that my tattoo was Made."

"It is a mystery to us," Nesta said. "You'd need to have had the ink Made by the Cauldron, in this world, for it to be so."

The Horn had come from here. Had been brought by Theia

and Pelias into Midgard. Perhaps it, too, had been forged by the Cauldron.

Bryce tucked away the knowledge, the questions it raised. "We don't have anything like the Cauldron on Midgard. Solas is our sun god, Cthona his mate and the earth goddess. Luna is his sister, the moon; Ogenas, Cthona's jealous sister in the seas. And Urd guides all—she's the weaver of fate, of destiny." Bryce added after a moment, "I think she's the reason I'm here."

"Urd," Nesta murmured. "The Fae say the Cauldron holds our fates. Maybe it became this Urd."

"I don't know," Bryce said. "I always wondered what happened to the gods of the original worlds, when their people crossed into Midgard. Did they follow them? Did I bring Urd or Luna or any of them with me?" She gestured to the caves. "Are they here, or am I alone, stranded in your world with no gods to call my own?"

They began walking again, the questions hanging there unanswered.

Bryce asked, because some small part of her had to know after what she'd seen of the Mask, "When you die, where do your souls go?" Did they even believe in the concept of a soul? Maybe she should have led with that.

But Azriel said softly, "They return to the Mother, where they rest in joy within her heart until she finds another purpose for us. Another life or world to live in." He glanced sidelong at her. "What about your world?"

Bryce's gut twisted. "It's . . . complicated."

With nothing else to do as they walked, she explained it: the Bone Quarter and other Quiet Realms, the Under-King and the Sailings. The black boats tipping or making it to shore. The Death Marks that could purchase passage. And then she explained the secondlight, the meat grinder of souls that churned their lingering energy into more food for the Asteri.

Her companions were silent when she finished. Not with contemplation, but with horror.

"So that is what awaits you?" Nesta asked at last. "To become . . . food?"

"Not me," Bryce said quietly. "I, ah . . . I don't know what's coming for me."

"Why?" Azriel asked.

"That friend I mentioned—the one who learned the truth about the Asteri? When she died, I worried that she might not be given the honor of making it to shore during her Sailing. I . . . couldn't let her bear that final disrespect. I didn't know then about the secondlight. So I bargained with the Under-King: my soul, my place in the Bone Quarter in exchange for hers." Again, that horrified quiet. "So when I die, I won't rest there. I don't know where I'll go."

"It has to be a relief," Nesta said, "to at least know you won't go to the Bone Quarter. To be harvested." She shuddered.

"Yeah," Bryce agreed. "But what's the alternative?"

"Do you still have a soul?" Nesta asked.

"Honestly? I don't know," Bryce admitted. "It feels like I do. But what will live on when I die?" She blew out a breath. "And if I were to die in this world . . . what would happen to my soul? Would it find its way back to Midgard, or linger here?" The words sounded even more depressing out loud.

Something glaringly bright blinded her—her phone. Hunt's face smiled up at her.

"Here," Nesta said. Bryce wordlessly took the phone, blinking back her tears at the sight of Hunt. "You kept your word and winnowed us. So take it."

Bryce knew it was for more than that, but she nodded her thanks all the same.

She flashed the screen at Nesta and Azriel. "That's Hunt," she said hoarsely. "My mate."

Azriel peered at the picture. "He has wings."

Bryce nodded, throat unbearably tight. "He's an angel—a malakh." But talking about him made the burning in her eyes worse, so she slid the phone into her pocket.

As they walked on, Nesta said, "When we stop again . . . can you show me how that contraption works?"

"The phone?" The word couldn't be translated into their language, and it sounded outright silly in their accent.

But Nesta nodded, her eyes fixed on the tunnel ahead. "Trying to figure out what it does has been driving us all crazy."

Tharion cornered the dragon in the pit's bathroom. He could barely stand on his left leg thanks to a gash he'd taken in his thigh from the claws of the jaguar shifter he'd faced as the lunchtime entertainment. No prime time for him tonight, though—not with Ithan in the pit.

"Do not fucking kill Holstrom," he warned Ariadne.

She tilted her head back, eyes flashing as they met his. "Oh? Who said I'm facing him?"

Tharion and the others had spent most of the last twenty-four hours debating who the Viper Queen would select to face Ithan. And now, with less than an hour left until the fight and no opponent announced . . . "Who else would the Vipe unleash on him? You're the only one here who's stronger. The only one worth a fight."

"So flattering."

"Don't kill him," Tharion snarled.

She batted her eyelashes. "Or what?"

Tharion clenched his teeth. "He's a good male, and a valuable one to a lot of people, and if you kill him, you'll be playing into the Vipe's hands. Make the fight fast, and make it as painless as you can."

Ari let out a cool laugh that belied the blazing heat in her eyes. "You don't give me orders."

"No, I don't," Tharion said. "But I'm giving you advice. You kill Ithan, you hurt him beyond repair, and you will have more enemies than you know what to do with. Starting with Tristan Flynn—who might seem like an irreverent idiot, but is fully capable of ripping you apart with his bare hands—and ending with me."

Ariadne let out a snort and tried to stride around him. Tharion gripped her by the arm, the claws at the tips of his fingers digging into her soft flesh. "I mean it."

"And what about me?" she sneered.

"What about you?"

"Are you warning Ithan Holstrom not to harm me?"

He blinked. "You're a *dragon*."

Another one of those humorless laughs. "I have a job to do. I swore oaths, too."

"Always looking out for number one."

She tried to pry her arm free, but he dug his fingers in further. She hissed, "I'm not a part of your little cabal, and I don't want to be. I don't give a shit about you, or whatever you're trying to pull against the Asteri. It's clearly going to get you all killed."

"Then what *do* you want, Ari? A life of *this*?"

Her skin heated, searing his palm, and he had no choice but to release her. She stalked toward the hall door that led to the eerily quiet pit. As the Viper Queen had promised, only she would watch.

Ariadne opened the door, but tossed over a shoulder, "Do you like your wolf cooked with barbecue sauce or gravy?"

"So a phone," Nesta said, overpronouncing the word as they crossed yet another small stream, hopping from stone to stone, "can take these *photographs* that capture a moment in time, but not the people in it?"

"Phones have cameras," Bryce answered, "and the camera is the thing that . . . yeah. It's like an instant drawing of the moment." Gods, so many words and terms from her own language to explain. She forged ahead. "But with all the details rendered perfectly. And don't ask me more than that, because I seriously have no idea how it actually works."

Nesta chuckled as she landed gracefully on the opposite bank. Azriel strode ahead into the dark, the carvings around him lit by Bryce's star: more war, more death, more suffering . . . this time on a larger scale, entire cities burning, people screaming in pain, devastation and grief on a whole new level. No paradise to counter the suffering. Just death.

Nesta paused on the stream bank to wait for Bryce to finish crossing. "And it also holds music. Like a Symphonia?"

"I don't know what that is, but yes, it holds music. I've got a few thousand songs on here."

"Thousand?" Nesta whirled as Bryce jumped from the last stone onto the bank, pebbles skittering from beneath her sneakers. "In that tiny thing? You recorded it all?"

"No—there's a whole industry of people whose job it is to record it, and again, I don't know how it works." Finding her footing, Bryce followed Azriel, now a hulking shadow silhouetted against the larger dark.

Nesta fell into step beside her. "And it's a way of talking mind-to-mind with other people."

"Sort of. It can connect to other people's phones, and your voices are linked in real time . . ."

"And let me guess: you don't know exactly how it works."

Bryce snorted. "Pathetic, but true. We take our tech and don't ask what the Hel makes it operate. I couldn't even tell you how the flashlight in the phone works." To demonstrate, she hit the button and the cave illuminated, the battle scenes and suffering on the walls around them even more stark. Azriel hissed from up ahead, whirling their way with his eyes shielded, and Bryce quickly turned it off.

Nesta smirked. "I'm surprised it can't cook you food and change your clothes, too."

"Give it a few years, and maybe it will."

"But you have magic to do these things?"

Bryce shrugged. "Yeah. Magic and tech kind of overlap in my world. But for those of us without much in the way of the former, tech really helps fill the gap."

"And that weaponry you showed us," Azriel said quietly, pausing his steps to let them catch up. "Those . . . guns."

"That's tech," Bryce said, "not magic. But some Vanir have found ways to combine magic and machine to deadly effect."

Their silence was heavy.

"We're here," Azriel said, motioning to the darkness ahead. The reason, it turned out, that he had halted.

A massive metal wall now blocked their way, thirty feet high and thirty feet wide at least, with a colossal eight-pointed star in its center.

The carvings continued straight up to it: battle and suffering, two females running on either side of the passage, as if running for this very wall . . . Indeed, around the star, an archway had been etched. Like this was the destination all along.

Bryce glanced back at Nesta. "Is this where you saw my star?"

Nesta slowly shook her head, eyeing the wall, the embossed star, the cave that surrounded them. "I don't know where this place is. What it is."

"Only one way to find out," Bryce said with a bravado she didn't feel, and approached the wall. Azriel, a live wire beside her, approached as well, a hand already on Truth-Teller.

The lowest spike of the star extended down, right in front of Bryce. So she laid a hand on the metal and pushed. It didn't budge.

Nesta stalked to Bryce's side, tapping a hand on the metal. A dull thud reverberated against the cave walls. "Did you really think it'd move?"

Bryce grimaced. "It was worth a shot."

Nesta opened her mouth to say something—to make fun of Bryce, probably—but was silenced by groaning metal. She staggered back a step. Azriel threw an arm in front of her, blue light wreathing his scarred hand.

Leaving Bryce alone before the door.

But she couldn't have moved if she'd wanted. Couldn't take her eyes away from the shifting wall.

The spikes of the star began to expand and contract, as if it were breathing. Metal clicked behind it, like gears shifting. Locks opening.

And in the lowest spike of the star, a triangle of a door slid open.

17

Only dry, ancient darkness waited beyond the star door. No sound or hint of life. Just more darkness. Older, somehow, than the tunnel behind them. Heavier. More watchful.

Like it was alive. And hungry.

Bryce stepped into it anyway.

"What is this place?" Bryce breathed, daring another step into the tunnel that lay on the door's other side. Azriel and Nesta quickly fell into step behind her.

A shriek of metal sliced through the air, and Bryce whirled—

Too late. Even Azriel, now mid-stride, hadn't been fast enough to stop the door from sliding shut. Its thud echoed through her feet, up her legs. Dust swirled.

They'd been sealed in.

Bryce's star flared . . . and went out.

A chill rippled up her arms, some primal instinct screaming at her to *run* without knowing why—

Light flared at Azriel's hand—faelight, he'd told her earlier. Two orbs of it drifted ahead, illuminating a short passageway. At its other end lay a vast, circular chamber, its floor carved with symbols and drawings akin to those on the walls of the tunnel.

Nesta whispered, voice breathy with fear, "*This* is the place I last saw the star on your chest." She drew Ataraxia, and the blade gleamed in the dimness. "We call it the Prison."

It was like game day, Ithan told himself. The same restlessness coursing through his body, the same razor-sharp focus settling into place.

Except there would be no ref. No rules. No one to call a time-out.

He stood at the edge of the empty ring in the center of the fighting pit, surrounded by his friends and Sigrid. The sprites, unable to stomach the violence, had opted to stay away.

There was no sign of the dragon.

He hadn't dared research how bad third-degree burns were. If he'd be in any shape to go help free Athalar and Ruhn. And the Helhound, apparently—what was that about?

Focus. Survive the fight, win, and they could be out of here tonight. He was good at winning. Or he had been, once upon a time.

"She'll try to distract you," Flynn said from beside him, staring at the empty ring. "But get around her flames, and I think you can take her."

"I thought you had the hots for the dragon," Declan muttered. "No pun intended."

"Not when she's about to toast my friend."

Ithan tried and failed to smile.

"Ari won't go easy on you," Tharion finally chimed in. He'd returned to the suite an hour ago, but he'd gone into his bedroom and shut the door. At least he'd come down for the fight.

"So he's supposed to—what, Ketos?" Flynn asked. "Stand there and be burned to a crisp?"

"I bet the Viper Queen would find that *highly* amusing," Declan said grimly.

Ithan, despite himself, finally smiled at that.

Tharion's face remained grave, though, as he said to Ithan,

"Odds are, Ari's going to hurt you. Badly. But she's arrogant—use it against her."

Ithan felt Sigrid's gaze on him, but he nodded at the mer. "Promise to wield that water magic of yours to douse the flames and I'll be fine."

Tharion was in no mood to joke, though. "Holstrom, I . . . Look, I said some shit earlier that I—" He shook his head. "If you can get me out of here, I'll make it count. It means a lot that you'd even try. That you care."

"We're a pack," Ithan said to Tharion, Flynn, and Dec. "It's what we do for each other." None of them contradicted it. His heart strained.

Tharion's eyes glimmered with emotion. "Thanks."

The double doors on the other side of the space creaked open to reveal the Viper Queen in a metallic gold jumpsuit and matching high-tops.

"She'll probably have Ari jump down from the rafters in a ball of flame," Tharion murmured as the snake shifter moved across the chamber with sinuous, unhurried grace. Ithan looked up, but the shadowed top of the ring remained empty as far as his wolf-sharp eyes could see.

The Viper Queen halted a few feet away and frowned at Ithan. "That's what you chose to wear?" He examined his T-shirt and jeans. The same ones he'd been wearing since arriving in this Hel-hole. But she nodded to Tharion. "You should have spruced him up a bit."

Tharion said nothing, his face like stone.

The Viper Queen turned, jumpsuit glimmering like molten gold, and strutted toward the nearest riser. She plunked herself down and waved an elegant hand to Ithan. "Begin."

Ithan glanced to the empty ring. "Where's the dragon?"

The Viper Queen pulled out her phone and typed into it, the screen casting her already pale face in an unearthly pallor. "Ariadne? Oh, she's no longer in my employ."

"*What?*" Tharion and Flynn blurted at the same time.

The Viper Queen didn't look up from her phone, thumbs flying.

The light bounced off her long nails, also painted a metallic gold. “An offer too good to refuse came in an hour ago.”

“She’s not your slave,” Tharion snapped, face more livid than Ithan had ever seen. “You don’t fucking own her.”

“No,” the Viper Queen agreed, typing away, “but the arrangement was . . . advantageous to us both. She agreed.” She at last lifted her head. Nothing remotely kind lay within her green eyes as she surveyed Tharion. “If you ask me, I think she said yes in order to avoid having to toast Holstrom to a crisp. I wonder who might have made her feel bad about that?”

They all turned to the mer, who gaped at the Viper Queen.

“Of course,” the Vipe went on, typing again on her phone, “I didn’t inform her new employer that the dragon’s a softhearted worm. But given her new surroundings, I think she’ll harden up quickly.” The *swish* of a message being sent punctuated her words.

Tharion looked like he was going to be sick. Ithan didn’t blame him.

But Ithan willed himself to focus, his breathing to steady. She wanted him off-balance. Wanted him reeling. He squared his shoulders. “So who am I fighting, then?”

The Viper Queen slid her phone into her pocket and smiled, revealing those too-white teeth.

“The Fendyr heir, of course.”

“We should get Rhys.”

“We’d have to hike up through the mountain, climb down past the wards, then hope we’re not too far to reach him mind-to-mind.”

Bryce listened to Azriel and Nesta quietly argue, content to let them debate while she took in the chamber.

“This place is lethal,” Azriel insisted gravely. “The wards in there are sticky as tar.”

“Yes,” Nesta admitted, “but we’ve come all this way, so let’s see why we’ve been dragged here.”

“Why *she*’s been dragged here—by that star.” They both turned toward her at last, expressions taut.

Bryce composed her own face into the portrait of innocence as she asked, "What *is* the Prison?"

Nesta's lips pursed for a heartbeat before she said, "A misty island off the coast of our lands." She glanced at Azriel and mused, "Do you think we somehow walked beneath the ocean?"

Azriel slowly shook his head, his dark hair shining in the faelights bobbing overhead. "There's no way we walked that far. The door must have been a portal of some sort, moving us from the mainland out here."

Nesta's brows lifted. "How is that possible?"

"There are caves and doors throughout the land," Azriel said, "that open into distant places. Maybe that was one of them." His gaze flicked to Bryce, noting how closely she was listening to all that, and said, "Let's go in."

He took Bryce's hand in his broad, callused one, pulling her toward the chamber beyond.

His face was a mask of cold determination in the light of the golden orbs floating over them, his hazel eyes darting around to monitor the gloom.

This close to him, hand in hand, she could feel the sword and dagger again thrumming and pulsing. They throbbed against her eardrums—

The hilt of the Starsword shifted in her direction—she could have reached out and touched it with her other hand. One movement, and its hilt would be in her grip.

Azriel shot her a warning look.

Bryce kept her face bland, bored. Had his glance been to warn her to be careful for her own safety, or for her not to make one wrong move?

Maybe both.

Too soon, too quickly, they neared the entrance to the large, round chamber at the end of the short passage. The faelight danced over carvings etched and embossed onto the stone floor, as ornate and detailed as those in the tunnels leading here. The entire floor of the chamber was covered with them.

But between her and that room hung a sense of foreboding, of heaviness, of *keep the fuck out.*

Even the sword and dagger seemed to go quiet. Her star remained extinguished. Like their task was done. They'd arrived at the place they'd been compelled to bring her.

Bryce sucked in a breath. "I'm going in. Keep a step back," she warned Azriel.

"And miss the fun?" Azriel muttered. Nesta chuckled behind them.

"I mean it," Bryce said, trying to tug her hand from his. "You stay here."

His fingers tightened on hers, not letting go. "What do you sense?"

"Wards," Bryce replied, again scanning the arena-sized cavern ahead. And there, right in the center of the space . . .

Another eight-pointed star.

It must have been the one Nesta had seen before. As if in answer, the star on Bryce's chest flared, then dimmed.

Nesta stepped up beside them, pointing. "The Harp sat atop that star."

"Harp?" Bryce asked, not missing the glare that Azriel directed at Nesta. But Nesta's eyes remained on the star as she said, more to herself than to them, "It was held there by those wards."

Azriel scanned the chamber, still not letting go of Bryce's hand as he said to Nesta, "We don't know what else might be kept at bay in here."

"I didn't sense anything except the Harp last time," Nesta replied, but she still assessed the chamber with a warrior's focus.

"We also didn't sense that there was a second entrance into this place," Azriel countered. "We can assume nothing right now."

Bryce fingered the Archesian amulet around her neck. It had protected her at the gallery . . . had allowed her to walk through Jesiba's grade A wards . . .

There had to be an answer here, somewhere. About something. Anything.

Bryce's fingers tightened around the amulet. Then she looked over Azriel's shoulder, and her eyes widened. "Watch out!"

He dropped her hand instantly, whirling to the unseen, unsensed opponent.

The nonexistent opponent.

Bryce moved with Fae swiftness, and by the time Azriel realized there was nothing there, she'd already crossed the ward line.

Cold fury tightened his features, but Nesta was smirking with something like approval.

"You're on your own now," Azriel said, blue stones glimmering at his hands with a cold fury that matched his expression.

Bryce's brows lifted, walking backward a few steps. "You really can't get through?"

He crouched to trace a scarred hand along the stone floor, anger fading in the face of his curiosity. "No." He peered up at Bryce, mouth twisting to the side. "I don't know whether to be impressed or worried." He rose and jerked his chin at Nesta. "You going in?"

Nesta crossed her arms and remained at his side. "Let's see what happens first."

Bryce scowled. "Thanks."

Nesta didn't smile. She only urged, "Be quick. Look around, but don't linger."

Bryce tried, "I'd feel better if I had my sword."

Azriel said nothing, face impassive. Fine. Sighing, Bryce surveyed the carvings on the floor. Whorls and faces and—

The hair on her arms rose.

"These are Midgard's constellations." Bryce pointed to a cluster. "That's the Great Ladle. And that . . . that's Orion. The hunter."

Hunt. Her Hunt.

Her companions, the tunnels, the world faded away as she traced the stars, plotting their path. The Archesian amulet warmed against her skin, as if working to clear the wards around her.

"The Archer," she breathed. "The Scorpion and the Fish . . . This is a map of *my* cosmos." Her boot knocked against a raised half-orb, a screaming face carved into it. "Siph." The outermost planet. She went to the next, a similar mound with a grave male face. "Orestes."

"Orestes?" Azriel asked sharply, drawing her attention back to where he and Nesta still stood at the tunnel archway. "The warrior?"

She blinked. "Yes."

"Interesting," Nesta said, head angling. "Perhaps the name came from the same source."

Bryce indicated the next mound, the face of a bearded old man. "Oden." The next, closer to the center of the room, was a young, laughing male. "Lakos." Another mound rose on the other side of the star, massive and helmeted. "Thurr," she said. Then she pointed to a mound with a female head. "Farya." And beyond Farya, a large, raised mound with snaking tendrils. "Sol," she whispered, indicating the sun-shaped thing.

She scanned the room again and turned to the eight-pointed star. Directly between Lakos and Thurr. "Midgard." The name seemed to echo in the chamber. "Someone went to an awful lot of trouble to make this floor. Someone who'd been to my world and then came back here." Bryce glanced over a shoulder to Nesta, the warrior's face unreadable. "You said there was a harp on the eight-pointed star?" A shallow nod. "What kind of harp? Was it special in any way?"

"It can move its player between physical places," Nesta said, a shade too quickly.

"What else?" Bryce asked, and her chest glowed again.

Azriel lifted a hand toward Nesta, as if he'd cover her mouth to shut her up, but she said, "The Harp is Made. It can stop time itself."

"It stops *time*?" Bryce's knees wobbled.

She could think of only one group of people in her own world who'd be able to create stuff like that. Who, if they had indeed Made such objects, had a really good reason for wanting to get back into this world. To claim them.

"Was there ever," Bryce ventured, a sudden hunch taking form in her mind, "a Made object called the Horn?"

"I don't know," Nesta said. "Why?"

Bryce gazed at the eight-pointed star, the very heart of this chamber, of this map of the cosmos. "Someone put your Harp there for a reason."

"To keep it hidden," Azriel said.

"No," Bryce said quietly, facing the star fully, her free hand drifting to touch the matching scar on her chest.

It had led her all the way here. To this exact spot, where the Harp had been.

"It was left for someone like me."

"What do you mean?" Nesta demanded, voice bouncing off the rock.

But Bryce went on, the words tumbling out of her faster than she could sort them, "I think . . . I think all those carvings in the tunnels might be to remind us of what happened." She pointed to where they stood, the passage behind them. "The carvings tell a story. And they're an invitation to come *here*."

"Why?" Azriel asked with that lethal softness.

Bryce stared at the eight-pointed star for a moment before she said, "To find the truth."

"Bryce," Nesta cautioned, as if reading her thoughts.

Bryce didn't so much as look back as she stepped onto the star.

18

Hunt coughed, seeing stars with every heave as he sprayed blood.

"Fuck, Athalar," Baxian grunted from where he hung on the other side of Danaan, though he wasn't much better.

They'd had all of a few hours on the floor before Pollux had returned and hauled them back up. Hunt hadn't been able to stop screaming as his shoulders dislocated again.

But Pollux had been called away somewhere, and apparently there was no one else in the palace suitably fucked up to torture them, so they'd been left here.

Bryce. Her name came and went with his wet, rasping breaths. He'd wanted so many things with her. A normal, happy life. Children.

Gods, how many times had he thought about her beautiful face as it would look when she held their little winged children? They'd have their mother's hair and temper, and his gray wings, and occasionally, he'd catch a glimpse of his own mother's smile on their cherubic faces.

The last time he'd been in these dungeons, he'd had no visions of the future to cling to. Shahar had been dead, most of the Fallen with her, and all his dreams with them. But maybe this was worse. To have come *so* close to those dreams, to be able to see them so vividly, to know Bryce was out there . . . and he was not.

Hunt shoved aside the thoughts, the pain that ached worse than his shoulders, his breaking body, and grunted, "Danaan. You're up."

The Hammer's early departure today had left an opening. Everything else, what Apollion and Aidas had implied, that shit about his father and the black crown—the halo—on him . . . it was all secondary.

All his failures on Mount Hermon, the Fallen who'd died, losing Shahar, being enslaved . . . Secondary.

All the repeated failures these past few months, leading them toward disaster, toward this . . . Secondary.

If this was their one shot, he'd put it all behind him. He had been alone the last time. Seven years down here, alone. Only the screams of his fellow tortured Fallen in other chambers to keep him company, to remind him hourly of his failures. Then the two years in Ramuel's dungeons. Nine years alone.

He wouldn't let the two friends beside him endure it.

"Do it now, Danaan," Hunt urged Ruhn.

"Give me . . . a moment," Ruhn panted.

Fuck, the prince had to be in bad shape to have even asked that. Proud bastard.

"Take a few," Hunt said, gentle but firm, even as guilt twisted his gut. To his credit, Ruhn took only a minute, then the creaking of his chains began again.

"Keep it quiet," Baxian warned as Ruhn swayed his body back and forth, swinging his weight. Aiming for the rack of weapons and devices just beyond the reach of his feet.

"Too . . . far," Ruhn said, legs straining toward the rack. Trying to grab the iron poker that, if the prince's abs held out, he could curl upward and position with his feet, nestling it inside the chain links—and twist it until they hopefully snapped free.

It was a long shot—but any shot was worth a try.

"Here," Hunt said, and lifted himself up on his screaming shoulders, feet out. Blocking out the agony, breathing through it, Hunt kicked as Ruhn collided with him. The prince muffled a cry of pain, but arced farther this time, closer to the rack.

"You got this," Baxian murmured.

Ruhn swung back, and Hunt kicked him again, eyes watering at what the movement did to every part of his body.

The rack was still too far. Another few inches and Ruhn's feet could grab the handle of the iron poker, but those inches were insurmountable.

"Stop," Hunt ordered, breathing hard. "We need a new plan."

"I can reach it," Ruhn growled.

"You can't. Not a chance."

Ruhn's swinging came to a gradual halt. And in silence, they hung there, chains clanking. Then Ruhn said, "How strong is your bite, Athalar?"

Hunt stilled. "What the fuck do you mean?"

"If I . . . swing into you . . . ," Ruhn said, gasping. "Can you bite off my hand?"

Shock fired through Hunt like a bullet. From the other side of Ruhn, Baxian protested, *"What?"*

"I'd have more range," Ruhn said, voice eerily calm.

"I'm not biting off your fucking hand," Hunt managed to say.

"It's the only way I'll reach it. It'll grow back."

"This is insane," Baxian said.

Ruhn nodded to Hunt. "We need you to be the Umbra Mortis. He's a badass—he wouldn't hesitate."

"A badass," Hunt said, "not a cannibal."

"Desperate times," Ruhn said, meeting Hunt's stare.

Determination and focus filled the prince's face. Not one trace of doubt or fear.

Pollux probably wouldn't return until morning. It might work.

And the guilt already weighing on Hunt, on his shredded soul . . . What difference would this make, in the end? One more burden for his heart to bear. It was the least he could offer, after all he'd done. After he'd led them into this unmitigated disaster.

Hunt's chin dipped.

"Athalar," Baxian cut in roughly. *"Athalar."*

Hunt dragged his eyes to the Helhound, expecting disgust and dismay. But he found only intense focus as Baxian said, "I'll do it."

Hunt shook his head. Though Baxian could probably reach if Ruhn stretched toward him—

"I'll do it," Baxian insisted. "I've got sharper teeth." It was a lie. Perhaps his teeth were sharper in his Helhound form, but—

"I don't care who fucking does it," Ruhn snarled. "Just do it before I change my mind."

Hunt scanned Baxian's face again. Found only calm—and sorrow. Baxian said softly, "Let me shoulder this burden. You can get the next one."

The Helhound had been Hunt's enemy at Sandriel's fortress for so many years. Where had that male gone? Had he ever existed, or had it been a mask all along? Why had Baxian even fallen in with Sandriel in the first place?

Maybe it didn't matter now. Hunt nodded to Baxian in acceptance and thanks. "You were a worthy mate to Danika," he said.

Pain and love flooded Baxian's eyes. Perhaps the words had touched on a wound, a doubt that had long plagued him.

Hunt's heart strained. He knew the feeling.

But Baxian jerked his chin at Ruhn, holding the prince's stare with the unflinching determination he'd been known for as one of Sandriel's triarii.

Here was the male Hunt had tangled with back then—to devastating results. Including that snaking scar down Baxian's neck, courtesy of Hunt's lightning.

"Get ready," Baxian said quietly to Ruhn. "You can't scream."

With the excuse of her cycle, Lidia found a shred of privacy to think through her plan, to fret over whether it would work, to pace her room and debate whether she'd put her trust in the right people.

Trust was a foreign concept to her—even before she'd turned into Agent Daybright. Her father had certainly never instilled such a thing in her. And after her mother had sent her away at age three, right into the arms of that monstrous man . . . Trust didn't exist in her world.

But right now, she had no choice but to rely on it.

Lidia had just changed her tampon and washed her hands when Pollux strutted into the bathroom.

"Good news," he announced, flashing a dazzling smile. He seemed lighter on his feet than he had since Quinlan had escaped.

She leaned against the bathroom door, inspecting her immaculate uniform. "Oh?"

"I'm surprised you didn't hear it from Rigelus first." Pollux stripped off his bloodied shirt.

Ruhn's blood clung to him, its scent screaming through the room. Ruhn's *blood—*

Muscles rippling under his golden skin, Pollux stalked to the shower, where untold gallons of blood had washed away from his body. A wild sort of excitement seemed to pulse from him as he cranked on the water.

"Rigelus and the others were able to fix the Harpy."

At first, nothing happened as Bryce stood atop the eight-pointed star.

"Well—" Nesta began.

Light flared from the star at Bryce's feet, from her chest, merging and blending, and then a hologram of a dark-haired young female—High Fae—appeared. As if she were addressing an audience.

Bryce knew that heart-shaped face. The long hair.

"Silene," Bryce murmured.

"From the carving?" Nesta asked, and as Bryce glanced to her, the warrior stepped through the wards as if they were nothing. Like she could have done so all along. Azriel didn't try to stop her, but remained standing inside the tunnel mouth. "At the beginning of the tunnels," Nesta said, "there was that carving of a young female . . . you said her name was Silene."

"The carving's an exact likeness," Bryce said, nodding. "But who is she?"

Azriel said softly, voice tinged with pain, "She looks like Rhysand's sister."

Nesta peered back at him with something like curiosity and sympathy. Bryce might have asked what the connection meant, but the hologram spoke.

"My story begins before I was born." The female's voice was heavy—weary. Tired and sad. "During a time I know of only from my mother's stories, my father's memories." She lifted a finger to the space between her brows. "Both of them showed me once, mind-to-mind. So I shall show you."

"Careful," Azriel warned, but too late. Silene's face faded, and mist swirled where she'd stood. It glowed, casting light upon Nesta's shocked face as she came to a stop beside Bryce.

Bryce swapped a look with the female. "First sign of trouble," Nesta said under her breath, "and we run."

Bryce nodded. She could agree to that much. Then Silene's voice spoke from the fog. And any promise of running faded from Bryce's mind.

We were slaves to the Daglan. For five thousand years, our people—the High Fae—knelt before them. They were cruel, powerful, cunning. Any attempt at rebellion was quashed before forces could be rallied. Generations of my ancestors tried. All failed.

The fog cleared at last.

And in its wake spread a field of corpses under a gray sky, the twin to the one carved miles behind in the tunnels: crucifixes, beasts, blood eagles—

The Daglan ruled over the High Fae. And we, in turn, ruled the humans, along with the lands the Daglan allowed us to govern. Yet it was an illusion of power. We knew who our true masters were. We were forced to make the Tithe to them once a year. To offer up kernels of our power in tribute. To fuel their own power—and to limit our own.

Bryce's breath caught in her throat as an image of a Fae female kneeling at the foot of a throne appeared, a seed of light in her upheld hands. Smooth, delicate fingers closed around the Fae female's droplet of power. It flickered, illumining pale skin.

The hand that had claimed the power lifted, and Bryce stilled as the memory zoomed out to reveal the hand's bearer: a black-haired, white-skinned Asteri.

There was no mistaking the cold, otherworldly eyes. She lounged in golden robes, a crown of stars upon her head. Her red lips pulled back in a cold smile as her hand closed tightly around the seed of power.

It faded into nothing, absorbed into the Asteri's body.

The Daglan became arrogant as the millennia passed, sure of their unending dominion over our world. But their overconfidence eventually blinded them to the enemies amassing at their backs, a force like none that had been gathered before.

Bryce's breath remained caught in her throat, Nesta still as death at her side, as the scene shifted to show a golden-haired High Fae female standing a step behind the Asteri's throne. Her chin was lifted, her face as cold as her mistress's.

My mother served at that monster's side for a century, a slave to her every sick whim.

Bryce knew who it was before Silene spoke again. Knew whose truth she'd been led here, across the stars, to learn at last.

Theia.

Lidia froze at Pollux's words as he stepped into the steaming spray of the shower. "What do you mean they've fixed the Harpy?"

The Hammer said over the noise of the water, tipping back his head to soak his golden hair, "They've been working on her as a pet project of sorts—Rigelus just told me. Apparently, it's looking good."

"*What* is looking good?" Lidia asked, using all her training to keep her heartbeat calm.

"That she'll wake up. Rigelus needs one more thing." Pollux opened the shower door and reached out a hand for her. An order more than an invitation.

With fingers that felt far away, Lidia unbuttoned her uniform. "What about my cycle?" she asked, as coyly as she could stomach.

"Water will wash the blood away," Pollux said, and she hated the weight of his eyes on her as she stripped. Stepping in, she winced at the burning heat of the water. Pollux only tugged her to his naked body, his erection already pressing into her.

"When will the Harpy wake up?" Lidia asked as Pollux's mouth found her throat and he bit deeply enough for her to wince again.

If the Harpy returned and spoke of what she'd seen, of who had really killed her . . .

None of Lidia's plans, however well laid, would matter.

Pollux's hand slid to her ass, cupping and squeezing. He nipped her ear, wholly unaware of the dread creeping through her as he said against her wet skin, "Soon." Another squeeze, harder this time. "Another day or two and we'll have her back."

The Viper Queen's announcement might as well have been a brimstone missile dropped into the room.

Tharion looked between Ithan, Sigrid, and the snake shifter. The Fendyr heir was staring at the female, face pale with shock.

The Viper Queen drawled to her, "What was it you said to me? That I was no better than the Astronomer?" She waved a manicured hand toward the ring, gold nails glinting. "Well, here's a shot to free yourself. I believe that's more than he ever offered you."

"I'm not fighting Sigrid," Ithan snarled, bristling.

"Then you and your friends will stay here," the Viper Queen said, leaning back on her hands. "And whatever urgent rescue mission you want to stage for your other friends will fail."

This bitch knew everything.

"Let me fight Holstrom," Tharion snapped.

"No," the Viper Queen said with sweet venom. "Holstrom and the girl go into the ring, or the deal's off."

"You fucking—" Flynn started.

"I'll do it," Sigrid said, fingers curling into fists at her sides.

They all turned to the Fendyr heir. Ithan's face twisted, a portrait of anguish.

Tharion noted that pain, and wished he'd never been born. His choices had led them here. His fuckups.

"Good," the Viper Queen said to Sigrid, who bared her teeth at the snake. But the ruler of the Meat Market gave the wolf a serpent's smile. "Looks like it might be your last night on Midgard. Maybe you should have gotten that wardrobe upgrade after all."

* * *

Bryce stared at the hard-faced, beautiful female who could have rivaled the Hind for sheer badassery and beauty. Theia.

Silene's next words only confirmed how alike the ancient Fae Queen and the Hind were:

But my mother, Theia, used the time she served the Daglan to learn all she could about their instruments of conquest. The Dread Trove, we called it in secret. The Mask, the Harp, the Crown, and the Horn.

From the corner of her vision, Bryce spied Nesta glancing her way at the last word.

The Horn had been sister to the Mask, and the Harp Nesta had mentioned. It had come from *here,* and worse, was part of some deadly arsenal of the Asteri—

And Theia.

The carving in the tunnel of the crowned, masked queen—Theia—flashed in Bryce's memory. She'd been holding two instruments: a horn and a harp.

The Daglan, Silene went on, *always quarreled over who should control the Trove, so more often than not, the Trove went unused. It was their downfall.*

Was this it, then? Why she'd been sent to this world? To learn about this Trove—that it might possibly be the thing to destroy the Asteri? But Bryce could only watch as the vision showed Theia's hands snatching the objects from black pedestals. Spiriting them away from the subterranean mountain holds where they were kept, using cave archways to move swiftly across the lands.

Caves like this one. Capable of moving people great distances in a matter of hours. Or an instant.

Snow drifted across the image, and then Theia was standing atop a mountain, a black monolith rising behind her.

"Ramiel," Azriel whispered from behind them, from beyond the wards.

Theia embraced a handsome, broad-shouldered man amid the swirling snow.

My mother and father, Fionn, had kept their love a secret through the years, knowing the Daglan would find it amusing to tear them apart if they learned of the affair. But they were able to meet in secret—and to plan their uprising.

"Fionn . . . ," Azriel murmured, awe lacing his voice, "was your ancestor."

Nesta turned from the vision, frowning toward Azriel. "You might as well come in," she muttered, and pointed. Silver flame rippled in a straight line, spearing for Azriel. He didn't flinch away, only tucking in his wings tightly as streams of smoke filtered up from the floor.

A path through the wards. The spells shimmered against the flames, as if trying to close in on the road she'd made, but Nesta's power held them at bay.

Azriel inclined his head to Nesta as he stepped through that slender passage lined with silver flames, not one ounce of fear on his beautiful face. Only when Azriel had passed through did Nesta release her power, the wards slamming back into place in a shimmering rush, like a wave washing over the shore.

Bryce pointed to the hologram—to the golden-haired Fae male. "Who is he?" she asked quietly. There had never been any mention of Fionn in the histories of Midgard, the lore.

"The first and last High King of these lands," Azriel breathed.

Before Bryce could contemplate this further, Silene went on, *But my mother and father knew they needed the most valuable of all the Daglan's weapons.*

Bryce tensed. This *had* to be the thing that had given them the edge—

The snows around Ramiel parted, revealing a massive bowl of iron at the foot of the monolith. Even through the vision, its presence leaked into the world, a heavy, ominous thing.

"The Cauldron," Nesta said, dread lacing her voice.

Not a useful weapon, then. Bryce braced herself as Silene continued.

The Cauldron was of our world, our heritage. But upon arriving here, the Daglan captured it and used their powers to warp it. To turn it from what it had been into something deadlier. No longer just a tool of creation, but of destruction. And the horrors it produced . . . those, too, my parents would turn to their advantage.

Another shift of memory, and Fionn pulled a long blade from the Cauldron, dripping water. A black blade, whose dark metal absorbed any trace of light around it. Bryce's knees weakened.

The Starsword.

Two other figures stood there, veiled in the thick snow, but Bryce hardly got a chance to wonder about them before Silene's narration began anew.

They fought the Daglan and won, she went on. *Using the Daglan's own weapons, they destroyed them. Yet my parents did not think to learn the Daglan's other secrets—they were too weary, too eager to leave the past behind.*

"Wait," Bryce cut in. "How did they use those weapons?" Nesta and Azriel cast wary looks her way. "How the fuck did they use them? And what other secrets—"

But Silene kept speaking, history unspooling from her lips.

My father became High King, and my mother his queen, yet this island on which you stand, this place . . . my mother claimed it for herself. The very island where she had once served as a slave became her domain, her sanctuary. The Daglan female who'd ruled it before her had chosen it for its natural defensive location, the mists that kept it veiled from the others. So, too, did my mother. But more than that, she told me many times that she and her heirs were the only ones worthy of tending this island.

Nesta murmured to Azriel, "The Prison was once a royal territory?"

Bryce didn't care—and Azriel didn't reply. Silene had glossed over how Theia and Fionn had used the Trove and Cauldron against the Asteri, and why the Hel had she come to this planet if not to learn about that?

Yet once again, Silene's memory plowed forward.

And with the Daglan gone, as the centuries passed, as the Tithe was no longer demanded of us or the land, our powers strengthened. The land *strengthened. It returned to what it had been before the Daglan's arrival millennia before. We returned to what we'd been before that time, too, creatures whose very magic was tied to this land. Thus the land's powers became my mother's. Dusk, twilight—that's what the island was in its long-buried heart, what her power bloomed into, the lands rising with it. It was, as she said, as if the island had a soul that now blossomed under her care, nurtured by the court she built here.*

Islands, like those they'd seen in the carvings, rose up from the sea, lush and fertile.

Bryce couldn't take her gaze off the wondrous sight, even as Silene continued. *After centuries with an empty womb, my mother bore both my sister and me within a span of five years. My father was fading by then—he was centuries older than my mother. But Fionn did not consider my mother a worthy successor. The crown should go to the eldest child, he said—to my sister, Helena. It was time, he thought, for a new generation to lead.*

It did not sit well with my mother, or with many of those in her court—especially her general, Pelias. He agreed with my mother that Helena was too young to inherit our father's throne. But my mother was still in her prime. Still ripe with power, and it was clear that she'd been blessed by the gods themselves, since she had been gifted children at long last.

So it was just as it had been before: those behind the throne worked to upend it.

The image shifted to some sort of marsh—a bog. Fionn rode a horse between the islands of grass, bow at the ready as he ducked beneath trees in bloom.

My parents often went hunting in the vast slice of land the Daglan had kept for their private game park, where they had crafted terrible monsters to serve as worthy prey. It was there that he met his death.

A dark-haired, pale creature that could have been the relative of the nøkk in Jesiba's gallery dragged a bound and gagged Fionn into the inky depths of the bog, the once-proud king screaming as he went under.

Horror rooted Bryce to the spot.

Theia and Pelias stood at the water's edge, faces impassive.

Petals began falling from the trees. Leaves with them. Birds took flight. As if sudden winter gripped the bog. As if the land had died with its king.

Then the Starsword was thrust from the center of the pool,

sparkling in the gray light. A heartbeat later, a scaled hand lifted a dagger—Truth-Teller. Debris or a gift from the creature, Bryce could only guess as they sparkled in the grayish light, dripping water. It didn't matter—in the face of such treachery and brutality, who fucking cared?

My father had never shown himself to be giving—long had he kept Gwydion and never once offered it to my mother. The dagger that had belonged to his dear friend, slain during the war, hung at his side, unused. But not for long.

Theia extended her hands toward the water, the offered blades. And on phantom wings, sword and dagger soared for her. Summoned to her hands.

Starlight flared from Theia as she snatched the sword and knife out of the air, the blades glowing with their own starlight.

My mother returned that day with only Pelias and my father's blades. As she had helped Make them, they answered to the call in her blood. To her very power.

Bryce knew that call. Had been hearing it since she arrived in this world. A chill rippled down her spine.

And then she took the Trove for herself.

Theia sat, enthroned, the Harp and Horn beside her, the Mask in her lap, and the Crown atop her head.

Unchecked, limitless power sat upon that throne. Bryce could barely get a breath down.

The Theia who Aidas had spoken so highly of . . . she was a murdering *tyrant*?

As if in answer, Silene said, *Our people bowed—what other option did they have in the face of such power? And for a short span, she ruled. I cannot say whether the years were kind to my people—but there was no war. At least there was that.*

"Yeah," Bryce seethed, more to Silene than the others, "at least you guys had that."

My sister and I grew older. My mother educated us herself, always reminding us that though the Daglan had been vanquished, evil lived on. Evil lurked beneath our very feet, always waiting to devour us. I believe she told us this in order to keep us honest and true, certainly more than she had ever been. Yet as we aged and grew into our power, it became clear that only one throne could be inherited. I loved Helena more than anything. Should she have wanted the throne, it was hers. But she had as little interest in it as I did.

It was not enough for my mother. Possessing all she had ever wanted was not enough.

"Classic stage mom," Bryce muttered.

My mother remembered the talk of the Daglan—their mention of other worlds. Places they had conquered. And with two daughters and one throne . . . only entire worlds would do for us. For her legacy.

Bryce shook her head again. She knew where this was going.

Remembering the teachings of her former mistress, my mother knew she might wield the Horn and Harp to open a door. To bring the Fae to new heights, new wealth and prestige.

Bryce rolled her eyes. Same corrupt, delusional Fae rulers, different millennium.

Yet when she announced her vision to her court, many of them refused. They had just overthrown their conquerors—now they would turn conqueror, too? They demanded that she shut the door and leave this madness behind her.

But she would not be deterred. There were enough Fae throughout her lands, along with some of the fire-wielders from the south, who supported the idea, merchants who salivated at the thought of untapped riches in other worlds. And so she gathered a force.

It was Pelias who told her where to cast her intention. Using old, notated star maps from their former masters, he'd selected a world for them.

Bryce's gut churned. The Asteri must have kept archives and records on this world, too. Exactly like the room Bryce had found in the palace, full of notes on conquered planets. *Dusk,* they'd labeled the room—as if out of all the worlds mentioned within, *this* world remained their focus. This place.

Pelias told her it was a world the Daglan had long coveted but had not had the chance to conquer. An empty world, but one of plenty.

She had no way of knowing that he had spent our era of peace learning ancient summoning magic and searching the cosmos for whatever remained of the Daglan on other worlds. What he wanted from them, I can only guess—perhaps he knew that to wrest the Trove from Theia and seize power for himself, he needed someone more powerful than he was.

"You idiot," Bryce spat at the image of Pelias and Theia hovering over a table full of star charts. "Both of you: fucking idiots."

And after all that searching, someone finally answered. A Daglan who had been using his army of mystics to scour galaxies for our world. The Daglan promised him every reward, if only he could nudge my mother toward this moment, to use the Dread Trove to open a portal to the world he indicated.

A step beside her, Nesta clicked her tongue in disgust.

My mother did not question Pelias, her conspirator and ally, when he told her to will the Horn and Harp to open a doorway to this world. She did not question how and why he knew that this island, our misty home, was the best place to do it. She simply gathered our people, all those willing to conquer and colonize—and opened the doorway.

In a chamber—*this* chamber, if the eight-pointed star on the floor was any indication, though the celestial carvings had not yet been added—beside red-haired Fae who looked alarmingly like Bryce's father, Helena and Silene appeared, grown and beautiful, and yet still young—gangly. Teenagers.

In the center of the chamber, a gate opened into a land of green and sunshine. And standing there among the greenery, waiting for them . . .

"Oh fuck." Bryce's mouth dried out. "Rigelus."

The teenage Fae boy, appearing no older than Helena and Silene, smiled at Theia. Raised a hand in greeting.

My mother did not recognize the enemy when they wore a friendly face, beckoning her and the others through the portal. Had she any hesitations upon finding that the empty world she'd been promised was indeed populated, they were calmed when the strangers claimed to be Fae as well, long separated from our world by the Daglan, whom they too claimed to have overthrown. And they had waited all this time to reunite our people.

With a few words from the Daglan, my mother's doubts melted away, and our exodus into Midgard began.

Long lines of Fae passed through the chamber, through the portal, and into Midgard.

Nausea twisted through Bryce. "She opened the front door to the Asteri. Brought the Trove right to them."

"Fool," Nesta growled at the image. "Power-hungry fool."

But if Theia had opened the door to this realm, if she had the Horn and Harp, why hadn't the Asteri immediately pounced on both? They'd wanted this world, wanted the Trove, and Theia had practically hand-delivered both to them. The Asteri were too smart, too wicked, to have forgotten either fact. So there must have been some plan in place—

By the grace of the Mother, she was paranoid enough about any new allies or companions that she hid the Horn and Harp. She created a pocket of nothingness, she told me, and stashed them there. Only she could access that pocket of nothingness—only she could retrieve the Horn and Harp from its depths. But she remained unaware that Pelias had already told the Daglan of their presence. She had no idea that she was allowed to live, if only for a time, so they might figure out where she'd concealed them. So Pelias, under their command, might squeeze their location out of her.

Just as she had no idea that the gate she had left open into our home world . . . the Daglan had been waiting a long, long time for that, too. But they were patient. Content to let more and more of Theia's forces come into the new world—thus leaving her own undefended. Content to wait to gain her trust, so she might hand over the Horn and Harp.

It was a trap, to be played out over months or years. To get the instruments of power from Theia, to march back into our home world and claim it again . . . It was a long, elegant trap, to be sprung at the perfect moment.

And, distracted by the beauty of our new world, we did not consider that it all might be too *easy. Too simple.*

Midgard was a land of plenty. Of green and light and beauty. Much like our own lands—with one enormous exception. The memory spanned to a view from a cliff of a distant plain full of creatures. Some winged, some not. *We were not the only beings to come to this world hoping to claim it. We would learn too late that the other peoples had been lured by the Daglan under similarly friendly guises. And that they, too, had come armed and ready to fight for these lands. But before conflict could erupt between us all, we found that Midgard was already occupied.*

Theia and Pelias, with Helena and Silene trailing, warriors ten deep behind them, stood atop the cliff, surveying the verdant land and the enormous walled city on the horizon.

Bryce's breath caught. She'd spent years working in the company of the lost books of Parthos, knowing that a great human civilization had once flourished within its walls, but here, before her, was proof of the grandeur, the human skill that had existed on Midgard. And had been entirely wiped away.

She braced herself, knowing what came next, hating it.

We found cities in Midgard carved by human hands. This world had been mostly populated by humans, and only a handful of unusual creatures that had kept mostly to themselves. It was a blank slate, as far as worlds went. Little native magic to fight the Daglan's power.

"Fuck you," Bryce breathed. Nesta grunted her agreement. "Blank slate, my ass." Bryce balled her hands into fists, a familiar, long-simmering rage building under her skin.

Yet the humans were not pleased at our arrival. A legion of armored humans lined the exterior of a walled city, built of pale stone. Bryce didn't want to watch—but couldn't tear her eyes away from the sight.

My mother had dealt with human uprisings before. She knew what to do.

Humans lay slaughtered, the sand beneath them bloody. Bryce trembled, jaw clenched so tightly it hurt. So many dead—both soldiers and civilians. Adults and . . . Gods, she couldn't stand the sight of the smallest bodies.

Azriel swore, low and dirty. Nesta was breathing jaggedly.

Yet Silene spoke on, voice unwavering, as if the memory of the merciless bloodshed didn't faze her one bit.

City to city, we moved. Taking the land as we wished. Taking human slaves to build for us.

But some humans resisted, their city-states uniting as we Fae had once united against our masters.

Bryce didn't let her heart lift at the bronze-armored legions in lines and phalanxes ranged against the glimmering armor of the Fae. She knew how this particular tale ended.

Knew it would be wiped from official history.

But had Aidas known what Theia—what Helena and Silene and the Fae—had done? He must have—he'd loved Theia, after all. And yet he still had the fucking *nerve* to talk about her as if she wasn't a murdering piece of shit. To talk about Bryce having her light as if it was something good.

That star in her chest . . . it was the light of a butcher. Her ancestor.

Was this what she had been sent here to learn? That she wasn't some brave savior's scion, but a descendent of a morally corrupt bloodline?

It didn't matter if that was what the star had wanted her to learn or not—she knew it now, and there'd never be any unlearning it.

There would never be any atoning for what her ancestors had done.

The thoughts sliced her heart like shards of glass, and Bryce might have walked out right then and there, might have told Silene's memory to fuck off with her history lesson—but if this unbearable history could offer some hint about how to save Midgard's future . . .

Bryce kept listening.

20

Standing at the edge of the ring, Ithan found he couldn't move.

He was doing this. This ultimate disgrace, this betrayal of all that he was as a person, as a wolf—

Across the ring, Sigrid was so small. So thin and frail and *new* to this world. This reality. Had he freed her from the tank for this? Only to wind up here?

"Begin," the Viper Queen intoned.

Flynn, Dec, and Tharion stood at the sidelines, barely containing their rage.

Tharion had been right. He'd been so fucking stupid to tangle with the Viper Queen like this, to think it'd be as easy as bloodying himself, maybe getting a few burns—

And now Ariadne had been traded away because of it, too. He barely knew the dragon, yet that was also his burden to carry.

"I said *begin*," the Viper Queen snapped.

Ithan met Sigrid's light brown gaze.

Alpha. Fendyr. Prime. That's what he was taking on. All that he'd bowed to, stood for—

Ithan didn't let himself think. Didn't broadcast his moves. He launched himself at her before he could back away from this precipice.

He swung a punch for Sigrid's face and she lunged aside with surprising speed. An Alpha's speed.

Ithan struck again, and she ducked once more, all instinct.

Sigrid leapt—a swipe of claw-tipped hands.

Shock blasted through Ithan at the sight of those claws, so readily drawn. He stood rooted to the floor—a second too long.

She slashed across his ribs, sharp pain blasting like acid through him—

He bounced away to the sound of Flynn cursing. Ithan pushed a hand to his side. Warm blood leaked over his fingers.

Something sharpened in him. Steadied him. They were doing this: wolf to wolf. Alpha to . . . whatever he was. A wolf without a pack.

Ithan lunged again, reaching low—

His fist collided with Sigrid's soft belly, but she didn't go down. She twisted, elbow slamming directly into his nose. It wasn't an elegant maneuver, but it was a smart one. Bone crunched, blood spurted, and then claws were raking at his face—

He staggered back again. She'd gone for his fucking *eyes*. Ithan tackled her, throwing her to the floor.

"Holstrom!" Tharion shouted, and he couldn't tell if it was a warning or a reprimand, but there was no time to think about it as Sigrid's claws punched through his shoulder. Ithan reared back, roaring, wrenching her claws free.

She brought her legs up and *kicked*. Ithan grabbed her ankles, but too slow. Her feet connected with his gut, and then he was soaring back, back—

He hit the other side of the ring with a thud that echoed through his very bones.

Mired in shame, Tharion watched the bloodbath unfold before him.

He deserved to be here, in this place, with the Viper Queen. He didn't deserve to be freed, to be fought for.

Ariadne. Her name clanged through him. Sold—or traded,

whatever the fuck that meant. Because of him. Because of what he'd said to her, apparently.

Everything he touched turned to shit.

"This isn't going to end well," Flynn murmured. "Even if Ithan wins . . ." Whatever state Sigrid would be in, they wouldn't be able to leave tonight.

Yet even through his shame, Tharion had to admit that she was fighting better than he'd expected. Sloppy and untrained, yes, but she was giving as good as she got. Holding her own.

She and Ithan rolled on the floor, claws out, blood spraying—

Ithan took a hit to the jaw, lacerating his skin. Sigrid seemed inclined to rip him to shreds.

"Solas," Flynn muttered, rubbing his jaw in sympathy.

Tharion dug his nails into his palms, drawing blood.

He couldn't watch this. Couldn't let this happen. Not for his sake—not even for his freedom.

Sigrid slashed again, and Ithan rolled to the side, narrowly missing her wrath. But Sigrid was on him in an instant, and Holstrom's roar of pain as her claws connected with his thigh had Flynn lunging for the ring.

Tharion grabbed the Fae lord, fingers grappling into hard muscle. "Easy," he murmured. "He's fine."

Total fucking lie. Neither Ithan nor Sigrid were fine. Not even close.

Flynn struggled, thrashing out of Tharion's grip and whirling on the Viper Queen. "This ends *now*."

"It ends," the ruler of the Meat Market drawled from the stands, "when I give the order."

Tharion stilled. "It ends at a knockout."

"It ends with one of them on their way to the Bone Quarter," the Viper Queen said, taking out her phone and snapping a photo of the bloodied wolves squaring off in the ring.

A fight to the death. Tharion choked out, "Holstrom won't—"

"We'll see," the Viper Queen said, and a grunt from Ithan had Tharion spinning back to the fight. From the rage flickering in

Ithan's eyes as he dodged another onslaught of blows from Sigrid, the wolf had heard everything.

"Please," Tharion said to the Vipe. "Let me swap in for the Fendyr heir—"

"Enough, fish," the Viper Queen said, pocketing her phone in her gold jumpsuit.

Tharion might have begged, had Ithan not panted from the ring, "It's done, Tharion." Holstrom was already back on his feet, circling Sigrid, leaking blood everywhere. He'd barely touched her.

He wouldn't touch her, Tharion knew. To harm this female who'd faced such misery . . . Holstrom would never do it.

Tharion couldn't get a breath down, his anger a violent sea churning through his body, drowning him. He'd fucking kill the Viper Queen for putting his friends through this. Even if he only needed to look in the mirror to find the person at fault for this mess.

Sigrid slashed her claws again, and Ithan ducked low with athletic grace.

Sigrid launched an offensive then, powerful and steady in a way that told Tharion it was pure instinct. Swipe, punch, duck—

She wasn't just an heir to the Fendyr line. She *was* the Fendyr line, at its most potent.

It was clearly all Ithan could do to keep ahead of each blow. Blood coated his mouth, his teeth. His brown eyes shone bright and furious. Not at the wolf attacking him, but at the female who'd led them to this.

"Fuck, fuck, fuck," Flynn chanted, pulling at his hair.

Ithan's back hit the ropes, and there was nowhere to go, absolutely nowhere at all, as Sigrid slammed her fist toward his face.

Tharion's stomach flipped. This was all for *him*, and he was the biggest fucking loser on the planet—

Ithan had been waiting, though. He ducked—and punched his claws into the Fendyr heir's gut.

Sigrid screamed, staggering back, collapsing to her knees.

Ithan halted, panting hard. His face was empty as he walked

toward the female clutching her bleeding stomach. It had been a hard blow—but not a fatal one. Claws glinted at his fingertips.

Tharion couldn't breathe as Ithan raised his hand to make the final blow.

Silene's voice remained as steady, unmoved, as it had been throughout. A bored immortal, blandly reciting a history of others' suffering.

We were still waging our war on the humans when the door between worlds opened again. More Fae appeared—from another world this time.

Tall, beautiful beings entered. Even Bryce's rage and despair stalled.

Fae from another world—but they looked so similar to the ones from this place. How was it possible? Another ancient conquest of the Asteri? Another place they'd colonized and tampered with, and eventually lost?

They were Fae like us, but not. The ears, the grace, the strength were identical, but they were shape-shifters, all of them. Each capable of turning into an animal. And each, even in their humanoid body, equipped with elongated canine teeth.

It was a puzzle—enough of one that my mother paused her warmongering. There were two types of Fae. From two seemingly unconnected and distant worlds. These new Fae bore elemental magic, strong enough to make Pelias wary of them. They were more aggressive than the Fae we knew—wilder. And they answered directly to Rigelus.

It seemed, in fact, like they'd known Rigelus a long while.

My mother soon began to suspect that our host was not as benevolent as he claimed. But by the time she learned just how wrong she had been about him, it was too late.

"No shit," Nesta growled, disgust coating her voice, and Bryce could only manage a nod.

My mother would trust only us. Pelias, she might have once included, but he had taken to the pleasures of this new world too eagerly, championed by Rigelus himself.

A glimpse through a curtain of Pelias dumping a human woman's body into a river beside a white-stoned villa. Bruised and naked and dead.

Bryce nearly fell to her knees as the brutalized woman's corpse drifted and sank beneath the clear river, Pelias already long gone.

"They've got some nerve," Nesta grated out. "They were murdering children in those human cities."

"It's still going on today," Bryce said hoarsely. "Humans tossed in dumpsters after the Vanir have tormented and killed them. It goes on every single day in Midgard, and it started with *that* fucker." She pointed a shaking finger at the memory. "With him, and Theia, and all those monsters."

She might have truly erupted then, but Silene continued her story.

My mother eventually trusted only Helena and myself to seek the truth. She knew we could be of great use to her, because we bore the shadows as well as starlight.

Helena and Silene crept through the dimness of a mighty crystal palace. Down a winding crystal staircase. "That's the Asteri's palace," Bryce whispered to Azriel and Nesta. "In the Eternal City."

We spent a month hidden in the enemy's stronghold, no more than shadows ourselves. By the time we returned to our mother, we'd learned the truth: Rigelus and his companions were not Fae at all, but parasites who conquered world after world, feeding off the magic and lives of their citizens. The Daglan, now under their true name: the Asteri.

It was then that my mother told us, showed us, what had happened so long ago. All that she had done since. But she did not waste time apologizing for the past. If we had indeed walked into an enemy's trap, she said, then we must defeat them.

Bryce placed a hand over the star-shaped scar on her chest, fingers curling into the fabric of her shirt. Could she carve it out of herself, the connection to these two-faced hypocrites, and walk away from it forever?

My mother had kept the star map that the Daglan had long ago annotated. And a world on it had caught her attention—a world, like ours, that had overthrown the Daglan.

In an elaborate bedroom, standing before a desk with her two daughters, Theia waved a hand. As if she'd pulled them from that pocket of nothingness, the Harp and Horn appeared on the desk, glimmering alongside the Starsword and the knife.

Theia nodded once, slowly, as if making a decision, and then played the Horn and Harp. A portal between worlds swirled. It solidified, an archway to nowhere. A handsome, golden-haired male stood before it, with eyes like blue opals.

Bryce inhaled sharply.

Prince Aidas only asked my mother one thing when she opened the gate to his world: "Have you come to ask for Hel's help, then?"

Hunt cringed as Baxian vomited blood and flesh and bone. All of it splattered on the floor below them, and the smell—

Ruhn was gasping, shaking, but the prince hadn't asked the Helhound to stop.

"A little more," Baxian said, panting hard. Hunt's own stomach churned at the blood sliding down the male's chin. "Two more bites and it'll be off."

Ruhn whimpered but nodded grimly. They swung into each other, legs locking tight, and Baxian gave no warning before he bit down again. There was no time to waste.

Hunt shut out the sounds. The smells. Bryce and his future and those beautiful kids—that was the image he held in his mind instead. Escape—survival—was the goal. Bryce was the goal.

Even if he had no idea how he'd face her again after failing to protect them from this fate. After agreeing to let his friends do this. He had no idea how he'd look her in the eye.

Ruhn let out a muffled shout, and Baxian retched again, mouth still around Ruhn's wrist. Balking.

They'd come too fucking far to stop now. So Hunt said, voice hardening into that cold, flat tone of the Umbra Mortis, just as Ruhn had said they needed, "Again, Baxian."

"Please," Ruhn moaned, and it wasn't a request to stop, but to hurry. To get it over with.

"Again," the Umbra Mortis ordered Baxian.

Baxian, who'd shouldered this unspeakable task for Hunt so he didn't have to endure it—

The Helhound heaved forward, teeth clamping down, and *crunched.*

Ruhn screamed, swinging away wildly.

Hunt didn't know where to look first. At Baxian, spewing blood and flesh onto the stones beneath him. At the hand and part of a wrist still attached to the chain, or at Ruhn surging for the rack, sobbing through his teeth at all the weight now on one arm, feet straining—

Hunt acted, lifting his feet and *pushing*. Ruhn's toes nudged the top of the iron.

"More," Hunt barked. He'd become the Umbra Mortis, become that fucking monster again if it gave his friends a shot at survival—

Ruhn swung toward Hunt, blood everywhere, and Hunt steeled himself, then gave him another kick. The prince's toes connected with the iron poker. Held. And as he swung back—the poker came with him.

Ruhn came to a halt, dangling from that one arm. How the fuck would Ruhn curl upward with *one* arm, not two? Hunt began swinging for him. If he could use his legs and help Ruhn twist—

"What acrobatics," drawled a familiar male voice from the doorway. "And what determination."

Cold horror cracked through Hunt as Rigelus approached, flanked by Pollux and the Hawk.

Ithan panted as he stood over Sigrid, claws raised. The Fendyr heir's face was white with pain, her hand still clutching her bloodied side.

"Kill her, Holstrom," the Viper Queen purred from the sidelines, rising to her feet in a ripple of gold. "And it's done."

The Viper Queen had wanted him to be presented with this choice—this true *amusement*: deciding between saving his friends, saving Athalar and Ruhn and possibly Bryce . . . and Sigrid. The future of the Fendyr line. An alternative to Sabine.

On the ground, Sigrid lifted her head to look at him. Blood dribbled from her nose.

He'd done that to her. He'd never felt so dirty, so worthless as when he'd punched his claws through her stomach.

But Sigrid said with a mouth full of bloody teeth, "I never thanked you."

The entire world stilled. The Viper Queen faded into nothing. "For what?" Ithan panted.

"For getting me out." Her eyes were so trusting, so sad—

Make your brother proud.

If Connor were here . . .

Ithan lowered his claws. Slowly, he turned to the Viper Queen, whose face was tight with displeasure. "Fuck you, and fuck this bargain. If you don't let—"

Sigrid struck.

A cheap, cruel lunge for his throat, designed to rip it out. Ithan barely blocked the blow, her claws sinking into his forearm with a blinding flash of pain.

"Fendyr through and through," the Viper Queen said approvingly. It wasn't a compliment. Ithan wrenched his arm away, flesh tearing with it, and he could hardly breathe around the pain—

Sigrid slashed for his throat again. Then again. She hurled him against the ropes with strength only a Fendyr Alpha could wield. And as he rebounded, shooting right for her, he saw it. The death in her eyes.

She'd kill him. He might have pulled her from the tank, but she was, first and last, an Alpha.

And Alphas did not lose. Not to lesser wolves.

Make your brother proud.

They were the only words in his head as Ithan hurtled through the air. As he met Sigrid's eyes. The primal, intrinsic dominance there that took no prisoners. Had no mercy. Could never have mercy.

Make your brother proud.

Ithan aimed his clawed fist for her shoulder, a blow that would send her to her knees.

But Sigrid was fast—too fast. And did not yet understand how swiftly she could move.

Neither did Ithan.

One moment, his claws were heading for her shoulder. The next, she'd managed to bob to the right, planning to sidestep the blow—

Ithan saw it in slow motion. As if watching someone else—another wolf, caught in this ring.

One moment, Sigrid was dodging him, so swift he didn't have time to pull the punch. The next, she was still, eyes wide with shock and pain.

His claws hadn't gone through her shoulder.

They'd punched straight through her throat.

21

Aidas was a Prince of Hel, Silene went on.

Bryce's breath caught in her throat.

Using rare summoning salts that facilitated communication between worlds, his spies in Midgard had kept him well informed since the Asteri had failed to conquer his planet. Aidas had been assigned to hunt for the Asteri ever since. So their evil might never triumph again. On his world, or any other.

Hel was somehow the force for *good* in all this. How had Aidas been able to see past Theia's atrocities? And more than that, to love her? It made no sense. Unless Aidas was just like Theia, a murdering hypocrite—

Long hours did my mother and Aidas speak through the portal, neither daring to cross into the other's world. For many days afterward, in secret, they planned.

It soon became clear that we needed more troops. Any Fae that were loyal to us . . . and humans. The very enemies my mother had slaughtered and enslaved, she now needed. Their final stronghold lay at Parthos, where all the scholars and thinkers of their day had holed up in the great library. And so it was to Parthos we next went, winnowing under cover of darkness.

"Unbelievable," Nesta seethed.

The white-stoned city rose like a dream from a vast, black-soiled river delta.

Parthos was more beautiful than any city currently on Midgard, adorned with elegant spires and columns, massive obelisks in the market squares, sparkling fountains and complex networks of aqueducts, and humans milling about in relative peace and ease, not fear.

At the edge of the city, overlooking the marshes to the north, sat a massive, columned building—no, a complex of several buildings.

The library of Parthos.

It hadn't only been a place to hold books, Bryce knew. The compound had housed several academies for various fields of study—the arts, sciences, mathematics, philosophy—as well as the vast collection of books, a treasure trove of thousands of years' worth of learning.

Bryce's heart ached to see it—what had once been. What had been lost.

Crowded into an amphitheater in the center of the complex stood a mix of humans and Fae arguing—pointing and shouting.

The meetings did not go well, Silene said. *But my mother stood firm. Explained what she had learned. What the humans had long known, though they had been ignorant of the details.*

The arguing parties slowly sat on the stone benches, quietly listening to Theia.

And when she had finished, the humans revealed their own discovery—one that showed us our doom.

As a lone human woman stood from the crowd, Bryce reminded herself to keep breathing, to steady herself—

The Asteri had infected the water we consumed with a parasite. They'd poisoned the lakes and streams and oceans. The parasites burrowed their way into our bodies, warping our magic.

Holy gods.

The Asteri created a coming-of-age ritual for all magical creatures who had entered Midgard, and their descendants. A blast of magic would be released and then contained—and then fed to the Asteri. It was a greater, more concentrated dose than the seeds of power they'd sucked off us for years in the Tithe. They spun it into a near-religious experience, explained it away as a method to harness energy for fuel, and had been feeding off it ever since.

"The Drop," Bryce whispered, dismay rocking through her. She knew Nesta and Azriel were staring at her, but she couldn't look away from the memory.

Should anyone with power opt out of the ritual, the parasites would suck immortals dry until they withered away to nothing—like humans. It would be dismissed as old age. Lies were planted about the dangers of performing the ritual in any place other than one of the Asteri's harvesting sites, where the power could be contained and filtered to them, and to their cities and their technology.

Bryce was going to be sick.

The Asteri's hold on the people of her world wasn't merely based in military and magical might. These parasites ensured that they fucking *owned* each person, their very power. Their tyranny had wormed itself into the blood of every being on Midgard.

The humans had learned this—the Asteri had been careless in spilling knowledge around them, because without magic, the humans were unaffected. And they'd watched in smug silence while we, their gleeful oppressors, had unwittingly become oppressed. With one sip of water from this world, we belonged to the Asteri. There was no undoing it.

The despair nearly broke us then and there.

At last, Bryce could truly relate. She'd gone somewhere far away from her body. Listened as if from a distance as the last acts of this damned history played out.

But we convinced the humans to trust us. And my mother began reaching out to some of those Fae who had followed us into Midgard—those she hoped she could trust.

In the end, my mother had ten thousand Fae willing to march, most hailing from our dusk-bound lands. And when my mother fully opened the doorway to Hel, Aidas and his brothers brought fifty thousand soldiers with them.

I do not have the words for the war's brutality. For the lives lost, the torment and fear. But my mother did not break.

The Asteri mounted their counteroffensive swiftly, and wisely put Pelias in charge of their forces. Pelias knew my mother and her tactics well.

And though Hel's armies fought valiantly, our people with them, it was not enough.

I was never privy to the story of how my mother and Prince Aidas became lovers. I know only that even in the midst of war, I had never seen my mother so at peace. She told me once, when I marveled at our luck that the portal had opened to Aidas that day, that it was because they were mates—their souls had found each other across galaxies, linking them that fateful day, as if the mating bond between them was indeed some physical thing. That was how deeply they loved each other. And when this war was over, she promised me, we would go to Hel with Aidas. Not to rule, but to live. When this was over, she promised, she would spend the rest of her existence atoning.

She did not get to fulfill that promise.

"Too bad," Nesta said pitilessly.

But Bryce had moved beyond words. Beyond anything other than pure despair and dread.

Word came from the enemy right before they attacked in the dead of night: Surrender, and we would be spared. Fight, and we would be slaughtered.

Our camp had been erected high in the mountains, where we thought the winter snows would protect us from advancing enemies. Instead, we were cold and hungry, with barely any time to ready our forces. Aidas had returned to Hel to recruit more soldiers, so we were spending a rare night with our mother alone.

Hel did not have the chance to come to our aid. My mother did not even bother to try to open a portal to their world. Our forces on Midgard were already depleted—the new recruits wouldn't be amassed for days. We begged her to open the portal anyway, to at least get the princes' help, but my mother believed it would do little good. That what was coming that night was inevitable.

"Fool," Nesta said again, and Bryce nodded numbly.

But my mother didn't ask us to fight.

A bloodied Theia pressed the Horn into Helena's hands, and urged Silene to take the Harp and the dagger. She kept the Starsword for herself.

The place where we had first entered this world was nearby. We'd been camping here in part so that my mother could eventually open a portal again and recruit more Fae to fight. She still did not understand much about voyaging between worlds—she wasn't sure, if she opened a portal in another spot, if it would open to a different place in our world. So she'd gambled on our entry point in Midgard opening precisely into our court once more. From there, she'd planned to take the tunnels that leapt across the lands and build Fae armies. Even knowing they'd opposed her before, knowing they'd probably refuse her or kill her, she had no other options.

But there was no time for that now.

"Play the Horn and Harp," our mother ordered, pulling them out of that pocket of nothingness, "and get out of this world." It would be swift, a momentary opening, too fast for Rigelus to pounce on. We'd open it and be gone before he would even catch wind of what we'd done—and then we would seal the door between worlds forever.

Theia pressed a kiss to each of their brows.

She warned that Pelias was coming. For both of us. Rigelus had made him Prince of the Fae, and Pelias would use us to legitimize his reign. He meant to father children on us.

Even with all they had done, the crimes they'd committed against humans, Bryce's chest still tightened in panic for the sisters.

Pulling her daughters close, Theia flared with starlight. And in the small space between their bodies, Bryce could just make out Theia plucking a low string on the Harp. In answer, a star—akin to the one Bryce could pull from her own chest—emerged from Theia's body. It split into three shimmering balls of light, one drifting into Silene's chest and another to Helena's before the final one, as if it were the mother from which the other two stars had been born, returned to Theia's body.

For a moment, all three of them glowed. Even Truth-Teller,

in Silene's hand, seemed to ripple, a dark countermelody to how Gwydion flashed in Theia's hand, its light a heartbeat.

She gave us what protection her magic could offer, transferring it from her body into our own using the Harp. Another secret she had learned from her long-ago masters: that the Harp could not only move its bearer through the world, but move things from one place to another—even move magic from her soul to ours.

Gwydion in hand, Theia left the tent. With Fae grace and surety, she leapt onto the back of a magnificent winged horse and was airborne in seconds, soaring into the battle-filled night.

Bryce drew in a sharp breath. Silene hadn't shown the creatures in the earlier memories, or in the initial crossing into Midgard, but there they were. The pegasuses in the tunnels' carvings hadn't been religious iconography, then. And they'd lived long enough in Midgard to grace early art, like the frieze at the Crescent City Ballet. They must have all died out, becoming nothing more than myth and a line of sparkly toys.

Another beautiful thing that Theia and her daughters had destroyed.

Helena's eyes filled with panic as she turned to Silene in the memory.

To escape, it was worth the risk of going back to our home world, even if the Fae there might kill us for our connections to the Asteri, our foolishness in trusting them.

Helena grabbed Silene's hand and hauled her toward the far edge of the camp. Toward the snow-crusted peak ahead—a natural archway of stone. A gateway.

But no matter how fast we ran, it was not fast enough.

Far below, Fae were rushing up the mountain. Not the advancing enemy, but members of their court racing for them, realizing what Helena and Silene were doing. Still glowing with their mother's magic, both princesses stood atop the slope like silver beacons in the night. The Fae masses sprinted for them, bearing small children in their arms, bundled against the cold.

Bryce couldn't endure it, this last atrocity. But she made herself watch. For the memory of those children.

We would not stop. Not even for our people.

Hatred coursed through Bryce at Silene's words, the rage so violent it threatened to consume her as surely as any flame.

Helena lifted the Horn to her lips as Silene plucked a string on the Harp. A shuddering, shining light rippled in the archway, and then a stone room appeared beyond it, dim and empty.

That was when the wolves found us. The shape-shifting Fae, closing in from the other side of the mountain, barreled through the snow. *The Asteri had sent their fiercest warriors to capture us.*

In the back of her mind, Bryce marveled at it: that the wolves, the shifters . . . they had once been *Fae*. So similar to Bryce's sort of Fae, yet so different—

I lifted the Harp again, Silene said, voice finally hitching with emotion, *but my sister did not sound the Horn. And when I turned . . .*

Silene paused, finding Helena standing yards away. Facing the enemy advancing from the snow, the skies. Their frantic, desperate people surging up the side of the mountain, pleas for their children on their lips.

Helena eyed the fleeing people, the wolves closing in. She leaned over to Silene, plucked the shortest string, and shoved her sister, still holding the Harp, backward.

She used the Harp to send me the last of the distance to the archway.

Silene landed in the snow, hundreds of feet now between her and her sister. Wolves advanced on Helena below.

Helena didn't look back as she charged down the mountain, away from the pass. Buying me time. But I took one moment to look. At her, at the wolves giving chase. And at our mother—farther down the mountain, now locked in combat with Pelias, her winged horse dead beside her.

Power blasted from Pelias, power such as I had never seen from him.

The power struck her mother—struck true.

Even their fleeing people halted, looking behind them at the figure lying prone in the gore. At Pelias, stooping to pick up the Starsword.

With an easy, almost graceful flip of his hand, he plunged the sword through Theia's head.

There was a choice for me, then. To stay and avenge my mother, fight alongside my sister . . . or to survive. To shut the door behind me.

Silene jumped through the portal toward the chamber beyond, plucking the Harp as she went.

And as I tumbled between worlds . . . the Horn sounded.

Silene fell and fell and fell, down and sideways. The Horn's keening was cut off abruptly, and then she lay awkwardly on a stone floor, surrounded by darkness.

She was home.

Sobbing, Silene scrambled to her feet, snow spraying from her clothes. Not one shred of pity stirred in Bryce's heart at Silene's tears.

Not as screaming echoed through the walls. Through the stone. Silene's people had reached the pass, and now banged on the rock, begging to be let through.

Silene covered her ears, sinking again to the floor. She clutched the Harp to her chest.

Mother above, open up! a male roared. *We have children here! Take the children!*

Bryce shook her head in mute horror as the screams and pleading faded. Then stopped entirely. As if sucked into the very stones of this place. Right along with the melting snow around Silene.

"You fucking coward," Bryce breathed at last. Her voice broke on the last word. *This* was her heritage.

Heavy quiet fell in the chamber, interrupted only by Silene's broken rasping as she knelt, cradling the Harp.

At that moment, Silene said, *I had only one thought in my mind. That this knowledge would die with me. This world would continue as if the Fae who had gone into Midgard had never been. They would become a story whispered around campfires about people who had vanished. It was the only thing I could think to do to protect this world. To atone.*

Too little, too late. And of course, Silene would have benefitted from hiding her past—if she didn't tell anyone who she was or what she and her family had done, she couldn't be punished for it. How convenient. How *noble.*

Silene studied the spot where she knelt on the eight-pointed star in the center of the room. The only adornment.

She slowly set the Harp atop the star. Snow still melting in her hair, she got to her feet and wiped her tears, then rallied her magic, the sheer concentrated power of her light. It sliced through the stone like a knife through warm butter—a laser.

Light that wasn't just light—light, as the Asteri could wield their power.

Silene carved planets and stars and gods. A map of the cosmos. Of the world she had abandoned. When she finished, she lay beside the Harp, curled around the dagger sheathed at her waist.

Silene traced her fingers over the stone, like she could somehow reach across the stars to her sister. A seed of starlight began to form at her fingertip—

The vision went dark. Then Silene's face appeared again—older, worn. Her clear blue eyes looked out with a steady gaze. *My strength wanes,* she said. *I hope that my life has been spent wisely. Atoning for my mother's crimes and foolishness and love—and trying to make it right. I carved these tunnels, the path here, so some record might exist of what we were, what we did. But first I had to erase all of it from recent memory.*

Her face faded away, and more images began. A faster montage.

Silene, walking away from the Harp and through the empty, beautiful halls of a palace carved into the mountain—*this* mountain.

Our home had been left empty since we'd vanished. As if the other Fae thought it cursed. So I made it truly cursed. Damned it all.

She wandered through rooms that must once have been familiar to her, pausing as if lost in memory. Then she waved a hand, and entire hallways were walled off with natural rock. Another wave, and ornate throne rooms were swallowed by the mountain, until only the lowermost passages, the dungeons and this chamber far beneath, remained.

Despite my efforts to hide what this place had once been, a terrible, ancient power hung in the air. It was as my mother had warned us when we were children: evil always lingered, just below us, waiting to snatch us into its jaws.

So I went to find another monster to conceal it.

Beneath another mountain, far to the south, I found a being of blood and rage and nightmares. Once a pet of the Asteri, it had long been in hiding, feeding off the unwitting. With the dagger and my power, I laid a trap for it. And when it came sniffing, I dragged it back here. Locked it in one of the cells. Warded the door.

One after another, I hunted monsters—the remaining pets of the Daglan—until many of the lowest rooms were filled with them. Until my once-beautiful home became a prison. Until even the land was so disgusted by the evil I'd gathered here that the islands shriveled and the earth became barren. The winged horses who hadn't gone with my mother to Midgard, who had once flown in the skies, playing in the surf . . . they were nearly gone. Not a single living soul remained, except for the monstrosities in the mountain.

No pity or compassion stirred in Bryce. She didn't buy Silene's "for the common good" bullshit. It had all been to cover her own ass, to make sure the Fae in this world never learned how close she and her mother and sister had come to damning them. How Silene and Helena *had* damned the Fae of Midgard, locking them out along with their children. Another few seconds of keeping the portal open and she could have saved dozens of lives. But she hadn't.

So boo-fucking-hoo and to Hel with her atonement.

I left, wandering the lands for a time, seeing how they had moved on without Theia's rule. They'd splintered into several territories, and though they were not at war, they were no longer the unified kingdom I had known.

I will spare you the details of how I came to wed a High Lord's son. Of the years before and after he became the High Lord of Night, and I his lady. He wanted me to be High Lady, as the other lords' mates were, but I refused. I had seen what power had done to my mother, and I wanted none of it.

Yet when my first son was born, when the babe screamed and the sound was full of night, I brought him to the Prison and keyed the wards into his blood. No one knew that the infant who sometimes glowed with starlight had inherited it from me. That it was the light of the evening star. The dusk star.

And this island that had become barren and empty . . . this, too, was his. I told him, when he was old enough, what I had left here for him. So that someone might be able to access this record, to know the risks of using the Trove and the threat of the Asteri, always waiting to return here. I made sure he knew that the buried weapon he'd need against the Asteri was down here. I only asked that he not tell his father, my mate. To my knowledge, he never has. And one day, he has promised to tell his son, and his son after him. A secret shame, a secret history, a secret weapon—all hidden within our bloodline. Our burden to carry forward, carved and recounted here so that if the original history becomes warped or parts of it lost to time . . . here it is, etched in stone.

Nesta murmured to Azriel, "Does Rhys . . . does he know?"

"No," Azriel replied without an ounce of doubt. "Somewhere along the line . . . all this was forgotten, and never passed on."

Bryce couldn't bring herself to care. She knew the truth now, and all that mattered was getting home to Midgard to share it with others. With Hunt.

But to the rest of the world, Silene said, *I ensured that my mother and her lands became a whisper. Then a legend. People wondered if Theia had ever existed. The old generation died off. I clung to life, even after my mate had passed. As an elder, I spun lies for my people and called them truth.*

"No one knows what became of Theia and General Pelias," I told countless generations. "They betrayed King Fionn, and Gwydion was forever lost, his dagger with it." I lied with every breath.

"Theia and Fionn had two daughters. Unimportant and unimpressive." That was the hardest, perhaps. Not that my own name was gone. But that I had to erase Helena's, too.

Bryce glowered. Erasing her sister's name was worse than butchering human families?

My son had sons, and I lived long enough to see my grandsons have sons of their own. And then I returned here. To the place that had once been full of light and music, and now housed only terrors.

To leave this account for one whose blood will summon it, child of my child, heir of my heir. To you—I leave my story, your story. To you, in this very stone, I leave the inheritance and the burden that my own mother passed to me.

The image blurred, and there she was again. That old, weary face.

I hope the Mother will forgive me, Silene said, and the hologram dissolved.

"Well, I fucking don't," Bryce spat, and flipped off the place where Silene had stood.

22

Hunt could only watch in despair as the Bright Hand of the Asteri swept into the chamber, followed by Pollux and the Hawk. The Hawk noted the hand still dangling from the chains and laughed.

"Just like a rat," the Hawk taunted, "gnawing off a limb when caught in a trap."

"Get fucked," Baxian spat, Ruhn's blood coating his face, his neck, his chest.

"Language," Rigelus chided, but didn't interfere as Pollux snatched the iron poker from where Ruhn still clutched it between his feet. Ruhn, to his credit, tried to hold on to it, legs curling upward to tuck it close. But weakened and bleeding . . . there was nothing he could do. Pollux ripped it away, beating Ruhn's back once with it—prompting a pained grunt from the prince—then used the poker to prod Ruhn's severed hand from the shackle above.

It landed on the filthy ground with a sickening thump.

Smiling, the Hawk picked it up like it was a shiny new toy.

Observing the three of them, Rigelus said mildly, "If I'd known you were so bored down here, I would have sent Pollux back sooner. Here I was, thinking you'd had enough of pain."

Pollux stalked to the lever, wings glowingly white. With a smirk, the Hammer pulled it and sent all three of them dropping heavily to the ground.

The agony that blasted through Hunt drowned out Ruhn's scream as the prince landed on his severed wrist.

Hunt gave himself one breath, one moment on that filthy floor to sink down into the icy black of the Umbra Mortis. To fight past the pain, the guilt, to focus. To lift his head.

Rigelus stared down at them impassively. "I'm hoping that I will soon have further insight into where Miss Quinlan might have gone," he crooned. "But perhaps you might feel inclined now to talk?"

Ruhn spat, "Fuck off."

Behind Rigelus's back, the Hawk folded the fingers of Ruhn's severed hand until only the middle one remained upright.

Hunt snarled softly. The snarl of the Umbra Mortis.

Yet Rigelus stepped closer to Hunt, immaculate white jacket almost obscenely clean in this place. The golden rings on his fingers glimmered. "It brings me no joy to see you with the halo and slave brand again, Athalar."

"Halo," Hunt asked as solidly as he could, "or black crown?"

Rigelus blinked—the only sign of his surprise—but the term clearly landed with the Bright Hand.

"Been talking to shadows, have you?" Rigelus hissed.

"Umbra Mortis and all that," Hunt said. "Makes sense for the Shadow of Death."

Baxian chuckled.

Rigelus narrowed his eyes at the Helhound, then turned back to Hunt. "What lengths would the Umbra Mortis go to in order to keep these two pathetic specimens alive, I wonder?"

"What the fuck do you want?" Hunt growled. Pollux flashed him a warning look.

"A small task," Rigelus said. "A favor. Unrelated to Miss Quinlan entirely."

"Don't fucking listen to him," Baxian muttered, then cried out as a whip cracked, courtesy of the Hawk.

"I'd be willing to offer a . . . reprieve," Rigelus said to Hunt, ignoring the Helhound entirely. "If you do something for me."

That was what this had been about, then. His mystics would find Bryce—he didn't need the three of them for that. But the torture, the punishment . . . Hunt willed his foggy head to clear, to listen to every word. To cling to that Umbra Mortis he'd once been, what he'd been so happy to leave behind.

"Your lightning is a gift, Athalar," Rigelus continued. "A rare one. Use it once, on my behalf, and perhaps we can find you three more comfortable . . . arrangements."

Ruhn spat, "To do *what*?"

"A side project of mine."

Hunt snapped, "I'm not agreeing to shit."

Rigelus smiled sadly. "I assumed that would be the case. Though I'm still disappointed to hear it." He pulled a sliver of pale rock from his pocket—a crystal. Uncut and about the length of his palm. "It'll be harder to extract it from you without your consent, but not impossible."

Hunt's stomach flipped. "Extract what?"

Rigelus stalked closer, crystal in hand. The Asteri halted steps from Hunt, fingers unfurling so he could examine the hunk of quartz in his palm. "A fine natural conduit," the Bright Hand said thoughtfully. "And an excellent receptacle for power." Then he lifted his gaze up to Hunt. "I'll give you a choice: offer me a sliver of your lightning, and you and your friends will be spared the worst of your suffering."

"No." The word rose from deep in Hunt's gut.

Rigelus's expression remained mild. "Then choose which one of your friends shall die."

"Go to Hel." The Umbra Mortis slipped away, too far to reach.

Rigelus sighed, bored and weary. "Choose, Athalar: Shall it be the Helhound or the Fae Prince?"

He couldn't. Wouldn't.

Pollux was grinning like a fiend, a long knife already in his hand. Whichever of Hunt's friends was chosen, the Hammer would draw out their deaths excruciatingly.

"Well?" Rigelus asked.

He'd do it—the Bright Hand would do this, make him choose between his friends, or just kill both of them.

And Hunt had never hated himself more, but he reached inward, toward his lightning, suppressed and suffocated by the gorsian shackles, but still there, under the surface.

It was all Rigelus needed. He pressed the quartz against Hunt's forearm, and the stone cut into his skin. Searing, acid-sharp lightning surged out of Hunt, ripped from his soul, twisted through the confines of the gorsian shackles, extracted inch by inch into the crystal. Hunt screamed, and he had a moment of brutal clarity: this was what his enemies felt when he flayed them alive, what Sandriel had felt when he'd destroyed her, and oh *gods*, it burned—

And then it stopped.

Like a switch being flipped, only darkness filled him. His lightning sank back into him, but in Rigelus's hands, the crystal now glowed, full of the lightning he'd wrenched from Hunt's body. Like a firstlight battery—like the scrap of power extracted during the Drop.

"I think this will do for now," Rigelus crooned, sliding the stone back into his pocket. It illuminated the dark material of his pants, and Hunt's throat constricted, bile rising.

The Bright Hand turned away, and said to the Hammer and the Hawk without looking back, "I think two out of three will still be a good incentive for Miss Quinlan to return, don't you? Executioner's choice."

"You bastard," Hunt breathed. "I did what you asked."

Rigelus strode for the stairs that led out of the chamber. "Had you agreed to give me your lightning from the start, both of your companions would have been spared. But since you made me go to all that effort . . . I think you need to learn the consequences of your defiance, however short-lived it was."

Baxian seethed, "He'll never stop defying you—and neither will we, asshole."

It meant more than it should have that the Helhound spoke up for him. And also made it worse.

Last time he'd been here, he'd been alone. He'd had only the screams of soldiers to endure. His guilt had devoured him, but it was different than this. Than having to be here with two brothers and bear their suffering along with his own.

Being alone would have been better. So much better.

Rigelus knew it, too. It was why he'd waited this long to come down here, giving Hunt time to comprehend the bind he was in.

The Bright Hand ascended the steps with feline grace. "We shall see what Athalar is willing to give up when it really comes down to it. Where even the Umbra Mortis draws the line."

Lidia's time had run out. If she was to act, it had to be now. There was no margin for error. She needed the prisoners ready—in whatever way she could manage.

But she'd gotten no farther than two steps into the dungeon when the breath whooshed from her body at the sight of the stump where Ruhn's hand should have been.

The prince hung, unconscious, from his chains. Athalar and Baxian were out, too. All three were caked in blood.

Pollux and the Hawk were panting, smiling like fiends. "You missed the fun, Lidia," the Hawk said, and held up—

Held up—

That broad, tattooed hand—Ruhn's hand—had touched her. On that mental plane, soul to soul, those hands had caressed her, gentle and loving.

"Well done," she managed, though she screamed inside. Clawed at the walls of her being and shrieked with fury. "Which one of you claimed the prize?"

"Baxian, actually," the Hammer said, chuckling. "Chewed it off like the dog he is in an attempt to get free."

Lidia made herself turn. Look at the Helhound like she was impressed. Some small part of her was. But the pain Ruhn had endured . . .

She put a hand to her stomach, and her wince wasn't entirely feigned.

"Lidia?" the Hawk asked, white wings rustling.

"Her cycle," Pollux answered for her, disdain coating his voice.

"I'm fine," she snapped, to make the show complete. The Hawk and Pollux swapped looks, as if to say, *Females*. She pulled a velvet case from an interior pocket of her uniform jacket. When she flicked it open, firstlight glowed from the two syringes strapped within.

"What's that?" The Hawk stalked a step closer, peering at the needles.

Lidia made herself smirk at him, then at Pollux. "It seems a shame to me that Athalar and the Helhound's wings are no longer able to be . . . targeted. I thought we'd bring them back into play."

A shot of a medwitch healing potion, laced with firstlight, would regrow their wings within a day or two, even under the repressive power of the gorsian shackles. If she'd known about Ruhn's hand, she would have brought three, but now there would be no way to casually explain the need for it, not without drawing too much attention.

And she needed Athalar and Baxian able to fly.

Pollux smiled. "Clever, Lidia." He jerked his chin toward the unconscious angels. "Do it."

She didn't need the Hammer's permission, but she didn't protest. "Wait until they're fully regrown," she warned Pollux and the Hawk. "Let them savor the hope of having their wings again before you find some interesting way to remove them anew."

Athalar and Baxian were too deeply unconscious to even feel the prick of the needle at the center of their spines. Firstlight glowed along their backs, stretching like shining roots toward the stumps of their wings. The wounds in between healed over slowly, but she'd bade the medwitch who'd crafted the potion to weave a spell in it to target the wings specifically. If she'd healed them both completely, it would have been too suspicious.

Slowly, before her eyes, the stumps on their backs began to rebuild, flesh and sinew and bone creeping together, multiplying.

Lidia turned from the gruesome sight. She could only pray they'd be healed in time.

"I'll take it from here," she said to Pollux and the Hawk, striding to the rack.

"I thought you were here to heal them." The Hawk glanced between her and the angels.

"Only the wings," Lidia said. "Why not play with other parts while they mend?"

The Hammer smiled. "Can I watch?"

"No."

Ruhn stirred, groaning softly, and it was all she could do to keep from pulling one of the long blades from the rack and plunging it through Pollux's gut.

"You know how I like to watch," Pollux purred, and the Hawk chuckled. What an utter waste of life. He'd stood by while the Hammer committed his bloody atrocities. Had delighted in watching during those years with Sandriel, too.

The Malleus's eyes gleamed with naked lust. "Why don't you put on a show for us?"

"Get out," she said, unamused. Pollux might pretend he had control, but he knew who the Asteri favored. Her orders were not to be ignored. "I don't need distractions."

The Hawk snickered, but obeyed, stalking out. A true minion, through and through.

The Hammer, however, walked over to her. With a lover's gentleness, he put a hand on the side of her neck. And then squeezed tight enough to bruise as he said against her mouth, "I'll fuck that disrespect out of you, Lidia. Bloody cunt or not."

Then he was striding up the steps, wings glowing with his wrath. He slammed the door behind him.

Lidia waited, listening. When she was convinced they were both gone, she pulled the lever that sent the prisoners crashing to the floor and rushed to where Ruhn lay sprawled.

"Get up." She kept her voice hard, cold. But the prince opened his beautiful blue eyes.

She scanned his face. *Ruhn.* No one answered. As if pain had carved him up and hollowed him out. *Ruhn, listen to me.*

You're dead to me, he'd said. It seemed he'd killed the connection between them, too. But Lidia still cast her thoughts toward his mind.

Ruhn, I don't have much time. I managed to make contact with people who can help get you out of here, but the Harpy is somehow about to be resurrected, and once she is, the truth will come out. If my plan's to go off without a hitch, if you are to survive, you need to listen—

Ruhn only closed his eyes and didn't open them again.

Silence, heavy and unbearable, filled the chamber beneath the Prison. Bryce stared at the eight-pointed star, revulsion coursing through her in an oily slide.

"They were horrible," she rasped. "Self-serving, reckless monsters."

"Silene and Helena did shut the portal," Nesta countered carefully.

Bryce's gaze snapped to the female. "Only after they opened it again—to *escape.* It was open because they wanted to run. And they left all those people behind. They could have held it open a little longer, could have saved them. But Silene chose herself. She's a fucking *disgrace.*"

"Surely their fate at Pelias's hands," Azriel said, "would explain some of their motivation in acting quickly."

Bryce pointed to the place where Silene had stood. "That fucking *bitch* locked out children to save herself and then tried to justify it."

It was no different than what the Valbaran Fae had done this spring in Crescent City—locking the innocents out of their villas while they cowered inside, protected by their wards.

"What did you . . . ," Nesta began, a shade gently. "What was it that you expected to find here?"

"I don't know." Bryce let out a bitter laugh. "I thought maybe . . . maybe they'd have some answer about how to kill the Asteri. But she glossed over *that* part. I thought that in the thousands of years since then, maybe the Fae of Midgard had evolved into the reprehensible shitheads they are. Not that they were reprehensible all along."

She scrubbed at her face, eyes stinging. "I thought having Theia's light was . . . good. Like she was somehow better than Pelias. But she wasn't." And Aidas had *loved* her? "I thought it'd somehow give me an edge in this shitshow. But it fucking doesn't. It just means I'm the heir to a legacy of selfish, scheming assholes."

And worse, that parasite in Midgard's waters . . . what could even be done against that? Bryce sucked in a shuddering breath.

A gentle hand rested on her shoulder. Nesta.

"We need to tell Rhys," Azriel said hoarsely. Like he was still reeling from all he'd heard. "Immediately."

Bryce's gaze snapped to his face. The concern and determination there. Everything he'd seen . . . it was a threat to this world, to the people in it.

Azriel asked her with terrifying calm, "What happened to the Horn?"

Bryce held his stare, seething, beyond trying to spin any bullshit.

But Nesta said, "She *is* the Horn, Azriel. It's inked into her flesh." She lowered her hand from Bryce's shoulder and peered at her. "Isn't that right? It's the only thing that would have made your tattoo react that way earlier."

Azriel's hazel eyes flickered with predatory intent. He'd carve it out of her fucking back.

If she ran for the exit tunnel . . . They'd said something about a climb out of here, then a hike down a mountain.

But this court was an island. She wouldn't be able to get away from them.

Azriel began circling her with an unhurried, calculating precision. Bryce turned with him, keeping him in sight, but doing so exposed her back to Nesta, who she suspected might be the apex predator in the room.

"That's how you got to this world," Nesta went on, backing up a step—no doubt to provide space to draw Ataraxia. "Why you, and no one else, can come. Why you said no one would be able to follow you here. Because only you have the Horn. Only you can move between worlds."

"You got me," Bryce said, throwing up her hands in mock surrender and taking a step out of Nesta's range. "I'm a big, bad, world-jumping monster. Like my ancestors."

"You're a liability," Nesta said flatly, eyes taking on that silvery sheen—that otherworldly fire.

"I told you guys a hundred times already: I didn't even want to come here—"

"It doesn't matter," Nesta said. "You *did* come here, to the place where the Daglan are still apparently dead set on returning."

"The Asteri would need the Horn to open a portal. They might find me, but they can't get in."

"But you want to go home," Nesta said, "and for that you'll have to open a door to Midgard. What if Rigelus is right there? Waiting to come through?"

Bryce turned to keep facing Azriel, but—

Only shadows surrounded her.

Nesta had distracted her, enough that her focus had slipped and Azriel had vanished. They'd worked in silent, perfect tandem.

Not to attack, she realized, as a shadow darker than the ones around it raced for the tunnel across the chamber. But to go get reinforcements.

"No!" Bryce threw out a hand, and light ruptured from her fingers. It slammed into Azriel's shadows, fracturing the darkness and revealing the warrior beneath. But not enough to stop his sprint—

She needed more power.

The eight-pointed star at her feet glimmered. As if her magic had nudged something within it. Like embers flaring in stirred ashes. What if her star hadn't been guiding her to the knowledge, but to something . . . different? Something tangible.

Like calls to like.

To you, in this very stone, Silene had said, *I leave the inheritance and the burden that my own mother passed to me.*

This place, this Prison and the court it had once been, was

Bryce's inheritance. Hers to command, as Silene had commanded it.

And that memory, of Silene lying next to the Harp in the center of this room, reaching for one of the carvings with a kernel of light forming at her finger . . .

In this very stone . . .

Silene had warped her former palace and home into this Prison. She must have imbued some magic in the rock to do it. Must have given over some part of her power to not only change the terrain, but to house the monsters in their cells.

Theia had shown her how to do it. In those last moments with her daughters, Theia had used the Harp to transfer magic from herself into Silene and Helena, to protect them. It had appeared as a star. Had Silene replicated that here?

Was it possible that the Harp, in that moment that Silene reached for it, power at the ready, had been able to transfer her magic to this place?

. . . I leave the inheritance and the burden that my own mother passed to me.

And precisely as Theia had gifted her own power to Silene . . . perhaps Silene had in turn left that same power here, to be claimed by a future scion.

One by one, rapid as shooting stars, the thoughts raced through Bryce. More on instinct than anything else, she dropped to her knees and slammed her hand atop the eight-pointed star. Bryce reached with her mind, through layers of rock and earth—and there it was. Slumbering beneath her.

Not firstlight, not as she knew it on Midgard—but raw Fae power from a time before the Drop. The power ascended toward her through the stone, like a glimmering arrow fired into the dark—

Azriel flapped his wings and was instantly airborne, swooping for the tunnel exit.

Like a small sun emerging from the stone itself, a ball of light burst from the floor. A star, twin to the one in Bryce's chest. Her starlight at last awoke again, as if reaching with shining fingers for that star hovering inches away.

With trembling hands, Bryce guided the star to the one gleaming on her chest. Into her body.

White light erupted everywhere.

Power, uncut and ancient, scorched through her veins. The hair on her head rose. Debris floated upward. She was everywhere and nowhere. She was the evening star and the last rays of color before the dark.

Azriel had nearly reached the tunnel. Another flap of his wings and he'd be swallowed by its dark mouth.

But at a mere thought from Bryce, stalactites and stalagmites formed, closing in on him. The room became a wolf, its jaws snapping for the winged warrior—

The rock had moved for her, as it had for Silene.

"Stop him," she said in a voice that was more like her father's than anything she'd ever heard come out of her mouth.

Azriel swept for the tunnel archway—and slammed into a wall of stone. The exit had sealed.

Slowly, he turned, wings rustling. Blood trickled out of his nose from his face-first collision with the rock now in his path. He spread his wings, bracing for a fight.

The mountain shook, the chamber with it. Debris fell from the ceiling. Walls began shifting, rock groaning against rock. As if the place this had once been was fighting to emerge from the stone.

But Nesta raced at Bryce, Ataraxia drawn, silver flame wreathing the blade.

Bryce lifted a hand, and spike after spike of rock ruptured from the ground, blocking Nesta's advance. The chamber shuddered again—

"*Stop,*" Azriel roared, something like panic in his voice. "The cells—"

From far away, she could sense it: the *things* lurking within the mountain, her mountain. Twisted, wretched creatures. Some had been here since Silene had trapped them. Had been contemplating their escape and revenge all this time. She'd let them out if she restored the mountain to its former glory.

And in that moment, the mountain—the island—spoke to her.

Alone. It was so alone—it had been waiting all this time. Cold and adrift in this thrashing gray sea. If she could reach out, if she could open her heart to it . . . it might sing again. Awaken. There was a beating, vibrant heart locked away, far beneath them. If she freed it, the land would rise from its slumber, and such wonders would spring again from its earth—

The mountain shook again. Nesta and Azriel had halted ten feet away, Ataraxia a blazing light, Truth-Teller enveloped by shadows. The Starsword remained sheathed at Azriel's back—but she could have sworn it twitched. As if urging Azriel to draw it.

Nesta warned Bryce, her eyes on the shaking earth, "If you open those cells—"

"I don't want to fight you," Bryce said, voice oddly hollow, like the surge of magic she'd taken from Silene's store had emptied out her soul. "I'm not your enemy."

"Then let us bring you back to our High Lord," Nesta snapped. Ataraxia flashed in answer.

"To do what? Lock me up? Cut the Horn out of my skin?"

"If that's what's necessary," Nesta said coldly, knees bending, readying to strike. "If that's what it takes to keep our world safe."

Bryce bared her teeth in a feral grin. More spikes of rock shot up from the ground, angling toward Nesta and Azriel. "Then come and take it."

With a flap of his wings, Azriel burst toward her, fast as a striking panther—

Bryce stomped her foot. Those spikes of stone stretched higher, blocking his way. Blue light flared from him, smashing through the stones.

Bryce stomped her foot again, summoning more lethal spears of rock—but there were none left. Only a vast, gaping void.

Bryce had only a second to realize there literally *was* a void below her feet, before the ground beneath them collapsed entirely.

23

If the prisoners had done something as drastic as biting off Ruhn's hand, they had to be dangerously close to breaking. Which left Lidia with too little time, and too few options.

The one before her now seemed the wisest and swiftest. She could only trust that Declan Emmet had gotten the coded message she'd sent through her secure labyrinth of channels and was turning the cameras away at this very moment.

The Mistress of the Mystics had scuttled off as soon as Lidia had stalked through the doors to the dank hall—surely to grouse to Rigelus about Lidia's unexpected arrival. She'd ordered Lidia to wait at the front desk.

Lidia had lingered long enough to ensure the mistress had indeed left, then promptly ignored her order.

"Irithys," Lidia said to the sprite lying on the bottom of the crystal ball. Curled on her side, the queen remained asleep. Or pretended to be. "I need your help."

The Sprite Queen cracked open an eye. "To torture more people?"

"To torture *me*."

Irithys opened both eyes this time. Slowly sat up. "What?"

Lidia brought her face close to the crystal and said quietly, "There is an angel in the dungeon. Hunt Athalar."

Irithys sucked in a breath—she knew him. How could she not, as one of the Fallen in her own way? Though Irithys hadn't fought in the failed rebellion, she'd been born into the consequences: heir to a damned people, a queen enslaved upon the moment of her crowning. She'd know every key player in the saga—know every decision that had led to the punishment that rippled across generations of sprites.

"He has begun the fight anew. And this spring, a sprite befriended him; she died to save his mate. Her name was Lehabah. She claimed to be a descendent of Queen Ranthia Drahl." Just as Lidia had seen the footage of Athalar slaying Sandriel, so, too, had she witnessed the final stand of the fire sprite who had saved Bryce Quinlan. Rigelus had considered it imperative that Lidia know everything about the threat to the Asteri's power.

Irithys's eyes widened at the mention of their long-dead queen's line. The bloodline believed gone. The queen whose decision to rebel alongside Athalar and his Archangel had led to this enslaved fate for all sprites, for Irithys herself. But she said evenly, "So?"

Lidia said, "I need you to help me free Hunt Athalar and two of his companions."

Irithys stood, flame a mistrusting yellow. "Is this another *warm-up*?"

Lidia didn't have time for lies, for games. "The warm-up with Hilde was a test. Not to see what you could do, but who you are."

The queen's head angled. The yellow hue remained.

Lidia said, "To see if you were as honorable as I had hoped. As trustworthy."

"For what?" The sprite spat the words, sparks of pure red flying from her.

"To help me with a diversion—one that might save more lives than the three in the dungeon."

Irithys sniffed. "You are Rigelus's pet." She waved with a burning hand to the mystics slumbering in their tanks. "No better than them, obeying him in all things. They would lie if he commanded them to. Would drown themselves, if he so much as breathed the word."

"I can explain later. Right now I only have"—she choked on the word—"trust to offer."

"What of the cameras?" Irithys glanced to the ever-watchful eyes mounted throughout the space.

"I have people in my employ who have ensured that they are looking elsewhere right now," Lidia said, praying that it was true.

And with an appeal to Luna, she tapped the crystal ball, dissolving it. She still had the access Rigelus had granted in her blood to open the ball—she could still make this happen.

She'd intended to use the Sprite Queen to attempt to melt the gorsian shackles off Ruhn, Baxian, and Athalar, but things had changed. She needed Irithys for something far bigger.

Irithys stood in the open air, arms crossed, now a familiar, wary orange shade. "And this?" She gestured to the ink on her neck.

Lidia said quietly, as calmly as she could, "I made a bargain with Hilde for her freedom. She need only do one favor for me when the time comes, and she'll walk free."

Irithys angled her head again. "And the part about me torturing you . . . ?"

"Will come after that. To make it believable."

"Make *what* believable?"

Lidia checked her watch. Not much time. "I need to know if you're in or out."

To her credit, the Sprite Queen didn't waste time. Lidia held her stare, and let the queen see all that lay beneath it. Surprise lit Irithys's face . . . but she nodded slowly, turning a determined hue of ruby.

"Get the hag," the queen said.

It was a matter of a few minutes to get Hilde brought down. The guards didn't question the Hind, and her luck had held—the mistress was still off complaining to Rigelus.

Hilde glared at Lidia as she stood before the sprite, the queen free of her crystal and burning a bright bloodred. "And I walk free as soon as I do this favor for you?"

"No one shall stop you."

Hilde weighed Lidia's expression. "What is it, then?"

Lidia nodded toward Irithys. "Undo what you did years ago. Remove the tattoo from her neck."

Hilde showed no shock, not even a glimmer. Instead, she again glanced between Lidia and the sprite, who remained silent and watchful. "Won't your master punish you for that?"

Lidia said, "All I do is in service of Rigelus's will, even if he cannot always see it." A pretty lie.

But Hilde nodded slowly, her wispy silver hair gleaming with the red of Irithys's flame. "I shall seek shelter in my House until you have officially cleared my name, then."

Lidia produced a key to the hag's gorsian shackles. Irithys simmered beside her, now a tense violet, as the lock clicked.

The hag's shackles fell free.

Before they could hit the floor, Hilde whirled toward Lidia, mouth opening in a scream of fury—

Lidia drew her gun faster than the eye could follow and pressed it against the side of the hag's head. "I don't think so."

"You're a traitorous pile of filth. Rigelus will reward me handsomely when I tell him about this."

Lidia pushed the barrel of the gun into the hag's temple. "Free the queen now, or this bullet goes into your brain. And the shackles go back on."

The injury would be permanent with gorsian shackles slowing the healing. Death would find her almost instantaneously.

Hilde spat, a wad of greenish-brown phlegm splattering at Lidia's feet. "Who's to say you won't kill me afterward?"

"I swear on Luna's golden bow that I shall not kill you."

There were few stronger vows, short of the blood oath of the Fae. It seemed to do the trick for the hag, who bared her rotted teeth but said, "Fine."

A wave of a gnarled hand and some chanted, guttural words, and the ink melted down Irithys's fiery neck. Like black rain, it sluiced down her flaming blue body, dripping to the stones below.

And in its wake, as it cleared, the sprite began to blaze a blinding white.

Lidia lowered the gun from the hag's head. "As promised."

Hilde sneered, "What now? I leave, knowing you have some scheme afoot?"

Lidia slid her gaze to Irithys. "Your move, sprite."

Irithys smiled, and crooked a small, white-hot finger.

Hilde burst into flames. The hag didn't even have time to scream before she was ash on the floor. Amid the acrid smoke curling through the room, Irithys glowed like a newborn star.

"And now, Hind?" the Sprite Queen asked, bright as Solas himself.

Lidia held out her forearm. "Now you make it look like an accident."

"What?"

"Burn me." She nodded to Hilde's ashes. "Not like that, but . . . enough. So it looks convincing when I tell the others you overpowered me and Hilde when I fetched you for more help torturing the prisoners, and then you got away."

Irithys's white flame again turned yellow. "Got away to do *what*, though?"

"Create a diversion."

"It will hurt."

Lidia held the sprite's stare. "Good. In order to be real, it needs to hurt."

She laid out her plan for the queen as quickly as she could, telling her how to navigate the path of disabled cameras to get out of the palace, where to hide, and when and where to strike. And if somehow, against all odds, she succeeded . . . she laid out what would be required of Irithys after that. As insane and unlikely as it was.

All of it relied on the queen. When Lidia had finished, Irithys was shaking her head—not with refusal, but with shock.

"Can I trust you?" Lidia asked the sprite.

Irithys began to glow white again—white-hot. "You don't have any other choice now, do you?"

Lidia extended her arm once more. "Make it hurt, Your Majesty."

Darkness and debris and dust. Coughs and groans.

From the sounds behind her, Bryce knew Nesta and Azriel were alive. What state they were in . . . Well, she didn't particularly care at the moment.

The power she'd siphoned from this place, from Silene herself, thrummed through her body, familiar and yet foreign. It was part of her now—not like a temporary charge from Hunt, but rather something that had *stuck* to her own power, bound itself there.

Like called to like. As if her star had known this magic existed and drawn her toward it, as if they were sister powers—

And they were. Bryce bore Theia's light through Helena's line. And this light . . . it was Theia's light through Silene. Two sisters, united at last. But Silene's light, now mixed with Bryce's . . .

It was light, but it wasn't quite the same as the power she'd possessed before. She couldn't figure it out, didn't have the time to explore its nuances, as she got to her feet and beheld the faint shimmer filling the chamber they'd fallen into. The one that had been hidden a level below the star.

A sarcophagus made of clear quartz lay in the center of the space. And inside it, preserved in eternal youth and beauty, lay a dark-haired female.

Bryce's mind sped through possibilities. This place had once been an Asteri palace before Theia had claimed it. And in the tunnel carvings, made by Silene to depict her mother's teachings . . .

Evil always waited below them.

What if Silene had never realized what, exactly, Theia had meant? That it wasn't just a metaphor?

That here, literally right under them, slumbering in that forgotten coffin . . .

Here lay the evil beneath.

24

Bryce's breath came fast and shallow as she surveyed the crystal coffin in the center of the otherwise empty chamber.

There were no doors into the room. As far as she could discern, the only entrance was through the ceiling that had just collapsed beneath them.

In the crystal sarcophagus, the female lay preserved with unnerving detail.

No, not preserved. Her slim chest rose and fell. Sleeping.

The hair on the back of Bryce's neck rose.

One of the inmates she'd been warned not to release from the Prison. Some ancient, strange being held down here, in a cell beneath their feet, so dangerous she'd been encased in crystal—

That crystal coffin revealed the features of the sleeping female: humanoid, pale-skinned, and slender. Her silky golden gown accentuated every delicate curve of her body.

Bryce had never seen skin that pale. It glowed like a full moon. Her dark hair . . . it was *too* dark, somehow. It didn't reflect the light at all. It shouldn't have existed in nature.

And—was she wearing lipstick? No one had lips that vibrantly red. *Blow Job Red,* Danika had once quipped about a similar shade Bryce had worn.

"What have you done?" Azriel rasped, and Bryce twisted to

find him on his feet, wings tucked in, Nesta leaning against him as if wounded, Ataraxia dangling from her grip. The male now held the Starsword at the ready, Truth-Teller gripped in his other hand.

He must have had some sort of Starborn blood in him, then—a distant ancestor, maybe. Or maybe his possession of the knife somehow allowed him to also bear the Starsword.

As if in answer to Azriel's question, the female in the coffin opened her eyes. They were a crushing blue—and they *glowed*.

Bryce tried to scramble away, but she remained frozen in place as the female's gaze slid toward hers. As those red lips curved upward in a small smile that held no joy. As the female lifted a long, slender hand to the lid of the crystal sarcophagus and said, "Release me, slave."

Even muffled by the crystal, the voice was cold, merciless.

"Have you lost your senses?" Nesta seethed at Bryce, hobbling a step closer.

"I didn't mean to open a cell—" Bryce started.

"This isn't one of the cells," Azriel snarled. "We didn't even know this chamber existed."

The female in the coffin ignored their arguing. "How long have I slumbered?" Again, she pushed against the crystal of her sarcophagus.

Or had it been a cage?

Azriel growled at Bryce, "Did you know she was down here?"

Bryce didn't take her eyes off the coffin and the monster within it. "No."

The female in the coffin banged on the lid, its dull thump echoing off the dark stone walls. "Slave, do as you are told."

"Get fucked," Bryce snapped toward the coffin.

"You dare defy me?" Through the quartz, Bryce could only watch as the encased female's nostrils flared. Sniffing. "Ah. You are a mongrel. Both slave and the slave of our slaves. No wonder your manners are coarse."

Nesta rasped, hefting Ataraxia higher, "What *are* you?"

The female's long nails scraped along the lid of the coffin. She didn't look at them as she tested the lid for weaknesses. "I am your god. I am your master. Do you not know me?"

"We don't have any fucking master," Bryce snarled.

The female's nails gouged deep lines into the crystal, but the lid held. She searched beyond Bryce, her gaze falling upon Azriel. Her lips curled. "A foot soldier. Excellent. Kill this insolent female and free me." She pointed to Bryce.

Azriel didn't move. The caged female hissed, "Kneel, soldier. Make the Tithe so I may regain my strength and leave this cage."

Bryce knew then. Knew what evil had been kept in this coffin all this time.

Beside Azriel, Nesta steadied her stance. Like she'd figured it out, too. The motion drew the creature's gaze—and her eyes flared in pure rage. She glanced between Nesta and Bryce, and her white teeth flashed as she asked the latter, "Was it Theia who stole the Horn for you? Who put it in your flesh?" Her gaze slid back to Nesta. "And you—you are linked to the other parts of the Trove. Did she give them to you?"

"I don't know what you're talking about," Nesta said flatly.

The creature snickered, and drawled to Nesta, "I can smell them on you, girl. Do you not think a blacksmith knows their own creation?"

Bryce's mouth dried out.

The female in the sarcophagus was an Asteri.

Tharion had no words as they walked down the halls of the Meat Market to the car supposedly waiting for them in a side alley. None of them did.

Ithan hadn't spoken since he'd torn out Sigrid's throat.

It had been an accident. Tharion had seen Ithan aiming that blow for Sigrid's shoulder, but the female had dodged so quickly—and chosen the wrong fucking direction, by stupid chance—that the blow had become fatal.

Silence had fallen as Ithan stared at the fist and claws he'd punched clean through Sigrid's throat. His hand was the only thing keeping her body upright as her eyes went vacant—

"Remove your fist," the Viper Queen had commanded.

Ithan's face had gone dead, and the wolf snatched his claws and hand out of Sigrid's throat.

It was the final indignity. The removal of his hand and claws severed what remained of her thin neck.

And as he yanked his bloody fist back, as her body collapsed to the ring floor . . . Sigrid's head rolled away.

Ithan had just stared at what he'd done. And Tharion hadn't been able to find the words to say that they'd all *seen* what Holstrom had intended, all knew he hadn't meant to kill her.

The Viper Queen's assassins stood at the alley door, holding it open. As promised, a black sedan had been parked there.

Tharion took one step—only one—out into the night before the sweet, beckoning scent of the Istros hit him. Every muscle and instinct in his body came alive, begging him to go to the water, to submerge himself in its wildness and magic, to shed legs in favor of fins, to let the river ripple through his gills, into his very blood—

Tharion shut down the demand, the longing. Kept moving toward the sedan, one foot after another.

Still silent, they filed into the car, Flynn taking the wheel, Dec sliding into the passenger seat. Tharion sat in the back beside the male who'd taken on this unholy burden for him.

"You, ah . . . ," Flynn began as he started the car and peered over his shoulder to reverse out of the alley. "You all right, Holstrom?"

Ithan said nothing.

Declan announced quietly, looking down at his phone, "Marc's handling our family stuff. Making sure everyone's safe."

Small fucking consolation.

Three bright lights slammed into the windshield, and they all jumped. But—the sprites. They'd forgotten the sprites.

Flynn rolled down his window and Rithi, Sasa, and Malana sped in. Sasa breathed, *"Go, go, go,"* and Flynn didn't waste time questioning as they reversed out of the alley at full speed. In a smooth shift, he pulled onto a main street and switched into drive—and then they were zooming off through the labyrinth of streets Tharion had thought he'd never see again.

"What's happening?" Declan asked the sprites, who had nestled into the drink holders up front.

"We burned it," Sasa said, a deep orange.

"Burned *what*?" Flynn demanded.

Tharion could only gape as Malana pointed through the rear window, to where flames were now licking the night sky above the Meat Market.

"She'll kill you." Tharion's voice was hoarse. Like he'd been screaming. Maybe he had been. He didn't know.

"She'll have to find us to do that," said Rithi grimly, then turned to Ithan. "She engineered that perfectly. She used you."

"I played right into her hands." Ithan's voice was soft, broken.

No one spoke. No one seemed inclined to. So Tharion figured he might as well ask, "How so?"

Ithan shook his head and looked out the window, face blank, still blood-splattered. He said nothing more.

They drove on through the city, somehow unchanged despite what had just occurred. Drove all the way to the Rose Gate and the Eastern Road beyond it. To the coast, and the ship that would be waiting for them.

And all the consequences that would follow.

Bryce backed away as Azriel advanced a step toward the crystal coffin, Truth-Teller now glowing with black light in his left hand.

Bryce had seen the gold-clad creature who now slumbered in the coffin before, she realized: when Silene had related her mother's story. This female before them . . . she was the Asteri who'd ruled here. Theia's mistress.

The Asteri's blue eyes lowered to the dagger. "You dare draw a weapon before me? Against those who crafted you, soldier, from night and pain?"

"You are no creator of mine," Azriel said coldly. The Starsword gleamed in his other hand. If they bothered him, if they called to him, he didn't let on. Neither hand so much as twitched.

The Asteri's eyes flared with recognition at the long blade. "Did Fionn send you, then? To slay me in my sleep? Or was it that traitor Enalius? I see that you bear his dagger—as his emissary? Or his assassin?"

The words must have meant something to Azriel. The warrior let out a small noise of shock.

"Fionn indeed sent us to finish you off," Nesta lied with impressive menace. "But it looks like now we'll have the pleasure of killing you awake."

The Asteri smiled again. "You'll have to open this sarcophagus to get me."

Bryce smiled back at her, all teeth. "Fionn sent them. But Theia sent *me*."

Blue fire simmered in the creature's eyes. "That traitorous bitch will be dealt with after I handle you."

Azriel started to move along the coffin. Assessing the best way to attack the Asteri, no doubt. "Unfortunately for you," Bryce taunted, "Theia's been dead for fifteen thousand years. So have the rest of your buddies. Your people are little more than a half-forgotten myth in this world."

For a heartbeat, it was the creature's turn to blink. As if a memory had cleared, she said, more to herself than them, "Theia was so charming that day. Told me I looked tired, and to replenish myself in the crystal here, above the well. But she sealed me within instead. To let me starve to death over the eons." Teeth, white as snow, flashed. "And in my dreams, she danced upon the stones above me. Danced upon my grave while I starved beneath her feet."

"Give me the Starsword," Bryce murmured to Azriel. The blade had killed Reapers. Maybe it could kill an Asteri. Maybe that was what she'd come here to learn.

"No," Azriel snarled. "You brought this terror upon us."

"I had no idea she was here—"

"Release me, slaves," the Asteri cut in. "I grow impatient."

Why hadn't Theia warned her daughters that this thing was down here? Why be so irresponsible, so reckless—

Et in Avallen ego. Even here, on this island that had been a paradise during Theia's reign, this evil had existed. And Theia *had* warned her children about it—that evil was always lurking beneath them, waiting to grab them. Literally.

The taint of the Asteri who had ruled here, Silene had claimed, had lingered about this place—a terrible, ancient power. Enough so that it had needed to be concealed by the Prison's wickedness. Silene just hadn't figured out that it remained because an Asteri was still present.

And here, against all odds, was a living link to the past, to answers Bryce needed. If Urd had guided her this far . . .

Bryce said calmly, "I have questions for you. If you don't answer them, I'm happy to leave you down here until the end of eternity."

"Oh, this planet will be long dead before eternity has ended. Its star will expand, and expand, and eventually devour everything in its path. Including this world."

"Thanks for the astronomy lesson."

A slow smile. "I shall answer your questions . . . if you release me from this tomb."

Bryce held her stare.

"Don't you fucking dare," Azriel murmured.

But time pressed down on her. With every minute, Hunt suffered. She was sure of it.

The very stones and wards of this place answered to her will . . .

Azriel lunged for Bryce, but she'd already pointed to the crystal coffin. *"Get up, then."*

A click, loud as thunder, and the lid unlocked.

25

Opening the coffin had been as easy as commanding the stones of the mountain to move.

"What have you done?" Nesta said, silver fire flaring in her eyes, down Ataraxia's blade.

The Asteri laid a hand on the unlocked coffin lid and began to push.

Like Hel would she face this thing unarmed. Bryce extended a hand toward Azriel, casting her will with it.

The Starsword flew from his hand and into hers.

Azriel started, shadows flashing at his shoulders, readying to strike, but Bryce said, "Theia showed me that trick in Silene's little memory montage." It was the feeling she'd been sensing, of the blade calling to her. Being willing to leap into her hand.

Azriel bared his teeth, but drew another sword that had been sheathed in a concealed panel at his back and hefted Truth-Teller in his other hand as Nesta lifted Ataraxia—

Bryce twisted to the coffin in time to see the Asteri slowly climb out, like a hatching spider.

Bryce's chest provided the only light, making the monster's pale skin even whiter, deepening the red of her lips to a near-purple hue. Her long black hair draped down her slim form, pooling on the stone beneath her like liquid night.

But she remained on the floor, hunched over herself. Like she didn't have the strength to stand.

"You go left," Azriel murmured to Nesta, power blazing around them.

"No," Bryce said, not looking back as she approached the Asteri on the floor and sat down, setting the Starsword on the cold stone beside her.

To her shock, Azriel and Nesta didn't attack. But they remained only a step away, weapons at the ready.

"Your companions think you mad for releasing me," the Asteri said, picking at an invisible speck on her golden silk gown as she settled herself into a proper seated position.

"They don't realize that you haven't fed in thousands of years, and I can kick your ass."

"We realized it," Nesta muttered.

"Let's start with the basics, leech," Bryce said to the Asteri. "Where did—"

"You may call me Vesperus." The creature's eyes glowed with irritation.

"Are you related to Hesperus?" Bryce arched a brow at the name, so similar to one of Midgard's Asteri. "The Evening Star?"

"*I* am the Evening Star," Vesperus seethed.

Bryce rolled her eyes. "Fine, we'll call you the Evening Star, too. Happy?"

"Is it not fitting?" A wave of long fingers capped in sharp nails. "I drank from the land's magic, and the land's magic drank from me."

"Where did you come from, before you arrived here?"

Vesperus folded her hands in her lap. "A planet that was once green, as this one is."

"And that wasn't good enough?"

"We grew too populous. Wars broke out between the various beings on our world. Some of us saw the changes in the land beginning—rivers run dry, clouds so thick the sun could not pierce them—and left. Our brightest minds found ways to bend the fabric of worlds. To travel between them. Wayfarers, we called them. World-walkers."

"So you trashed your planet, then went to feed off others?"

"We had to find sustenance."

Bryce's fingers curled against the rock floor, but her voice remained steady. "If you knew how to open portals between worlds, why did you need to rely on the Dread Trove?"

"Once we left our home world, our powers began to dim. Too late, we realized that we had been dependent on our land's inherent magic. The magic in other worlds was not potent enough. Yet we could not find the way back home. Those of us who ventured here found ways to amplify that power, thanks to the gifts of the land. We pooled our power, and imbued those gifts into the Cauldron so that it would work our will. We Made the Trove from it. And then bound the very essence of the Cauldron to the soul of this world."

Solas. "So destroy the Cauldron . . ."

"And you destroy this world. One cannot exist without the other."

Behind them, Nesta sucked in a sharp breath. But Bryce said, "You gave this world a kill switch."

"We gave many worlds . . . kill switches. To protect our interests." She said it with such calm, such surety.

"Do you know Rigelus?"

"You speak his name very casually for a worm."

"We're closely acquainted."

A slight pursing of the lips. "I knew him in passing. I'm assuming you wish to slay him—and have come to ask me how to do it."

Bryce said nothing.

Vesperus leveled a cold look at her. "I will not help you in that regard. I will not betray the secrets of my people."

"Was this sort of compassion the reason Theia didn't kill you?"

Vesperus glowered. "Theia knew that for my kind, this sort of punishment would be far worse than death. To be confined, yet live. To neither breathe, nor eat, nor drink—but to be left in half slumber, starving." That gleam in her eyes—it wasn't solely rage. It was madness. "It would have been a mercy to kill me. Theia did not understand the word. I raised her from childhood not to. She would come down here every now and then and stare at me—I slept, but I could sense her there. Gloating over me. Convinced of her triumph."

A chill skittered down Bryce's spine. "She kept you down here as a trophy."

Vesperus's chin dipped in a nod. "I believe she drew pleasure from my suffering."

"I don't blame her," Bryce snapped, even as a sick feeling filled her stomach. Theia might have helped Midgard in the end, but she was no better than the monster who'd raised her.

"I have questions for you, too, mongrel."

"By all means," Bryce said, waving her hand.

"If we lost the war to Theia, if my people are now a mere myth, how is it that you know Rigelus intimately? Do the Asteri still dwell here?"

"No," Bryce said. "I came from another world. One where the Asteri remain in control."

"How long have the Asteri ruled?"

"Fifteen thousand years."

"Rigelus must be very pleased with himself."

"Oh, he is."

But the Asteri looked from Bryce to Azriel and Nesta behind her, brows lifting. "Is life so unbearable under our rule that you must always defy us?"

Yes. No. For Bryce, life had been fine. Shitty in spots, but fine. But for so many others . . .

"Does it matter," Vesperus pushed on, addressing Bryce once more, "that we take a little of your power? What would you even do with it?"

"It matters that we're lied to," Bryce said. "That our power is not yours for the taking. That your supremacy is unchecked and unearned."

"There is a natural order to the universe, girl. The strong rule the weak, and the weak benefit from it. Everything in nature preys and is preyed upon. You Fae somehow consider this an affront only when it is applied to you."

"I'm not going to debate the ethics of conquest with you. Rigelus and the others have no right to my world, but they've poisoned the water in Midgard—it's full of some sort of parasite that leaches our magic and requires us to offer it up to the Asteri. How do I undo it?"

Vesperus's eyes glowed with delight. "We'd hoped for something of this nature, rather than the Tithe, which required the *consent*"—she spat the word as if it tasted foul—"of our subjects, but we never figured out how . . . The water supply, you say?" A soft laugh. "Rigelus always was clever."

"How the *fuck* do I undo it?"

"You seem to think me inclined to help you, when I would receive nothing in return."

"I know what you want, and you're not getting it."

"And if I were to say that I have no wish to rule, only to live?"

"You'd still be a leech, who'd need to feed on these people. You don't deserve to go free."

"They have a place in this land for creatures like me. The unwanted. It is called the Middle. I have dreamt of it, seen it in my long slumber."

"That's not my decision to make."

"Use the Crown that Made scum over there possesses." Vesperus nodded to Nesta. "You could forge a path to enact your vision by clearing the minds of those before you."

She had no idea what Vesperus meant, but Bryce countered coolly, "You guys had a long fucking time to figure out every way to justify your actions, huh?"

"We are superior beings. We do not need to justify anything."

"You'd fit right in on Midgard."

"If Rigelus has held on to his power for so long, then your world is firmly in his grasp. He will not abandon it. He will have learned from the mistakes my companions and I made on this world and on others."

Bryce's hand curled into a fist. The force of holding her power at bay sang through her.

Vesperus's gaze darted to Bryce's glowing fist. "Is it time for us to battle, then?"

Power thrummed from the Asteri, a steady beat against Bryce's skin.

Even depriving Vesperus of her magic sustenance for this long hadn't killed her. What would taking out that massive core of firstlight under the Asteri's palace in the Eternal City do, other than remove their source of nutrition? It wouldn't be enough.

So Bryce let some of her power shimmer to the surface. She could have sworn her starlight was . . . heavier. Different, somehow, with the addition of what she'd claimed from Silene.

"I know you can die," Bryce said, and felt the power glowing in her eyes. "The Fae killed you losers once, and on my world, Apollion ate one of you."

"Ate?" Vesperus's amusement banked.

Bryce smiled slowly. "They call him the Star-Eater. He ate Sirius. I have him on standby, waiting to come eat you, too."

"You lie."

"I wish I could show you the empty throne Rigelus still keeps for Sirius. It's sort of sweet."

"What manner of creature is this Apollion?"

"We call them demons, but you probably know them by some other name. Your kind tried to invade their world, Hel. It didn't go well for you."

"Then Hel and this Apollion shall pay for such sacrilege," Vesperus hissed.

"Somehow, I don't think you'll be the one to make him."

Vesperus's fingers tapped her gold-clad knee. Her eyes guttered to midnight blue, promising death. She braced her hands on the ground and began to push upward—to stand.

"Don't move," Bryce warned, hand closing around the Starsword's hilt. Azriel and Nesta pointed their blades at the Asteri.

But Vesperus completed the motion. Stood to her full height. Bryce had no choice but to shoot to her feet as well. Vesperus swayed, but remained upright.

The Asteri advanced a tentative, testing step. Bryce held her ground.

Vesperus took another step, steadier now, and smiled past Bryce. At Azriel, at Truth-Teller. "You don't know how to use it, do you?"

Azriel pointed the dagger toward the advancing Asteri. "Pretty sure this end's the one that'll go through your gut."

Vesperus chuckled, her dark hair swaying with each inching step closer. "Typical of your kind. You want to play with our weapons, but have no concept of their true abilities. Your mind couldn't hold all the possibilities at once."

Azriel snarled softly, wings flaring, "Try me."

Vesperus took one more step, now barely a foot from Bryce. "I can smell it—how much of what we created here went unused. Ignorant fools."

Bryce let her magic flow. A thought, and her hair drifted around her head, borne aloft once more by the currents of her power, still amplified by what she'd seized from this mountain. She angled the Starsword before her, light rippling along the blade.

Vesperus backed up a half step, hissing at the gleaming weapon. "We hid pockets of our power throughout the lands, in case the vermin should cause . . . problems. It seems our wisdom did not fail us."

"There are no such places," Azriel countered coldly.

"Are there not?" Vesperus grinned broadly, showing all of her too-white teeth. "Have *you* looked beneath every sacred mountain? At their very roots? The magic draws all sorts of creatures. I can sense them even now, slithering about, gnawing on the magic. *My* magic. They're as much vermin as the rest of you."

Bryce carefully didn't glance at Nesta, who was creeping around the crystal coffin. Nesta had claimed earlier that the Middengard Wyrm had eaten her power—was that the sort of creature Vesperus meant?

And perhaps more importantly: Was Nesta still weakened? Or had her power returned?

Bryce clutched the Starsword tighter. Its power thudded into her palms like a heartbeat. "But why store your power *here*? It's an island—not exactly an easy pit stop."

"There are certain places, girl, that are better suited to hold power than others. Places where the veil between worlds is thin, and magic naturally abounds. Our light thrives in such environments, sustained by the regenerative magic of the land." She gestured around them. "This island is a thin place—the mists around it declare it so."

Bryce continued, buying Nesta more time to get closer to Vesperus, "We don't have anything like that on Midgard."

But didn't they? The Bone Quarter, surrounded by impenetrable mists, held all that secondlight.

"Every world has at least one thin place," Vesperus drawled. "And there are always certain people more suited to exploit it—to claim its powers, to travel through them to other worlds."

The Northern Rift was wreathed in mist, too, Bryce realized. A tear between worlds—a thin place. And the riverbank where she'd landed in this world . . . it had been misty there, as well.

"Theia had the gift," Vesperus said, "but did not understand how to claim the light. I made sure never to reveal how during her training—how she might light up entire worlds, if she wished, if she seized the power to amplify her own. But you, Light-Stealer . . . She must have passed the gift down to you. And it seems you have learned what she did not."

Vesperus peered at her bare feet, the rock beneath. "Theia never learned how to access the power I cached beneath my palace. She had no choice but to leave it there, buried in the veins of this mountain. Her loss—and my gain."

Oh gods. There was a fucking firstlight core here, far beneath their feet—

Vesperus smiled. "You really should have killed me when you had the chance."

Light shot up the Asteri's legs, into her body. A blinding flash, and then—

Vesperus's red mouth opened in joy and triumph, but no sound came out. Only black blood.

Bryce blinked at the crunch. The wet spray. The glint of silver that appeared between Vesperus's shining breasts.

The firstlight flowing up the Asteri's body shivered—and vanished.

Nesta had plunged Ataraxia right through Vesperus's chest.

26

Ithan didn't deserve to exist. To breathe.

And yet here he was, sitting in the back of a car as they approached the docks at Ionia. Here he was, praying the Hind hadn't sold them out and that the ship would be waiting to bring them to Pangera.

Kin-slayer. Murderer. The thoughts echoed through his very bones.

Ithan had killed the one person who might have led the Valbaran wolves to a different future, an alternative to Sabine.

It didn't matter that it had been accidental. He'd ripped out her throat. And decapitated her in the process of removing his fist.

To save his friends, he'd done this unspeakable, unforgivable thing. He was no better than the Hind.

Ithan caught a glimpse of his reflection in the car window, and hastily turned away.

Ataraxia had slain the Middengard Wyrm—but there was no indication the blade could also kill an Asteri. That anything, in any world, could do that except for Apollion.

"*Get out of range*—" Bryce warned Nesta, but the warrior snarled at Bryce, "She was keeping you talking until she got an opportunity to kill you with that cache of light, you fool."

Black blood dribbled from Vesperus's lips. "You are indeed a fool, girl."

The power slipped from Bryce's grip as Vesperus placed a hand at Ataraxia's tip and shoved. The sword punched back through her chest. The movement was hard enough that Nesta stumbled, shock whitening her face.

Slowly, Vesperus turned. Smiled at Nesta. Then down at the gaping hole between her breasts, already healing. All that firstlight was grade A healing magic. Taken in such a big dose—

"Ataraxia didn't work," Nesta breathed, shock still stark on her face. "The Trove—"

"Do *not* summon the Trove," Azriel ordered. "Don't bring it near her."

Nesta shook her head. "But—"

"Not even for our lives," Azriel snarled.

"Oh, I'll get the Trove soon enough," Vesperus said, and peered at the hole above her coffin, the ruined chamber beyond.

For a heartbeat, Bryce wasn't in the tomb, but back in Griffin Antiquities. A heartbeat, and she was in the library below the gallery, Micah held at bay, Lehabah begging her to go—

She'd found a way then. She'd killed a fucking Archangel.

There were two blades practically screaming for her to use them. Bryce again reached out a hand, her will, toward Azriel. And as surely as the Starsword had done, Truth-Teller flew from his grip. He tried to grab it, but even his swift lunge wasn't fast enough to stop it. To stop Bryce as the knife soared for her fingers.

The dagger's hilt landed in her palm, cool and heavy.

Her body began to hum. Like having one blade in each hand—the Starsword and Truth-Teller—electrified her.

Bryce stepped toward Vesperus. Vesperus swayed back slightly. Just as Bryce had suspected.

Behind her, Nesta and Azriel unleashed twin bolts of magic, one silver, one blue—arcing toward Vesperus from two directions. Splitting Vesperus's attention for a heartbeat—

The heartbeat Bryce had used to kill Micah.

The heartbeat that she used now to spring at the Asteri, sword in one hand, dagger in the other.

Bone collided with metal, and Vesperus screeched in rage as Bryce plunged Truth-Teller and the Starsword into her chest.

Bryce threw her power into the Starsword, light ripping through the black blade, willing it to tear this fucking monster apart—

She willed it into Truth-Teller, and shadows flowed—

And where the two blades met, where Bryce's light merged at their nexus, power met power.

Her ears hollowed out. Magic like lightning surged through her, from her. The chamber rippled, a muffled *boom* echoing through Bryce.

Her blood roared, a beast howling at the moon. She was vaguely aware of a glow, of radiating light that flowed through the Starsword, the dagger—

Vesperus thrashed, falling beyond Bryce's grip, sinking to her knees.

The Asteri hunched over, hands grappling on the hilts of the blades. She hissed as her skin touched the black metal. "I shall *kill* you for this."

But the words were slow . . . dragged out.

No, that was *time* slowing, rippling, as it had with Micah, as if the blades were killing the Asteri, a great world power—

A whip of blue magic shot through the world, a ribbon of cobalt piercing the starlight and darkness. She could see every loop and coil as it wrapped around Vesperus's neck.

Time resumed—sped up to its normal rate. "Stop!" Bryce shouted, but too late.

Vesperus lifted a hand to her neck as Azriel's blue light dissolved into her skin. She let out a strangled laugh as blood leaked from her mouth. "Still so ignorant. Your power is and will always be mine."

Blue magic appeared at her fingertips, absorbed from the Illyrian's attack. She wrapped it around one hand like a glove and grasped the Starsword's handle.

As if it provided the barrier she needed, allowing her to touch the blade, Vesperus yanked the Starsword free and let it clatter to the stones, coated with gore.

It . . . it hadn't worked. The sword and dagger united hadn't killed her.

Hand glowing blue, Vesperus studied the dagger still in her chest and then smiled at Bryce as she wrapped her fingers, still wreathed in lightning, around the hilt. "I'm going to carve you up with this, girl."

Nesta rotated Ataraxia in her hand and swung upward. Azriel shouted at her, "Throw your power in the blade!"

"No!" Bryce screamed. The Starsword and Truth-Teller had clearly been weakening the Asteri. If she could figure out how to amplify their power, she'd know how to kill them all—

Vesperus had just yanked Truth-Teller from her chest in a smooth slide when Ataraxia severed flesh and bone, dark blood—or whatever ichor flowed in an Asteri's veins—spraying.

Vesperus's dark head tumbled to the stones.

Silver fire wreathed Ataraxia as Nesta plunged the blade into the Asteri's fallen head. Again. And again. Ichor and light leaked from the broken body, and between one stab and the next, Nesta's arm slowed, slowed, slowed—

That was time slowing again. Bryce could see every spark of silver flame coiling about the blade, see it reflected in Nesta's eyes.

The sword descended into Vesperus's head one last time. Inch by inch, shattering bone and spraying gore—

Time snapped back into movement, but Vesperus did not.

Vesperus, the only Asteri left on this world, lay dead.

There was a small boat waiting for them. That much had gone right.

Tharion couldn't stand to look at Ithan. At any of his friends, even the sprites, who'd done so much for him.

The captain was waving to them, a silent order to hurry up while they still had the cover of darkness. Dawn was beginning to turn the sky gray.

They ditched the car at the end of the dock and walked quickly toward the small boat. Once they were on the *Depth Charger*, they'd be untraceable, even if the Viper Queen tracked the car here.

Tharion slid a hand into his pocket and fingered the white stone that would summon the ship. Dec, Flynn, and the sprites jumped into the boat, Dec quietly talking to the captain, but Holstrom had paused at the edge of the dock.

Silently, Tharion came up beside him.

The water was clear, even twenty feet above the bottom. Where he might have once jumped in, luxuriated in the crisp ocean water . . .

He didn't dare send a ripple through the waters of the world announcing his presence. Coward.

Flynn called to them, "Get on, assholes!"

Tharion glanced to Ithan, but the wolf was staring at the eastern horizon. The rising sun.

"Ready?" Tharion asked.

"I have to go back," Holstrom rasped.

"What?" Tharion faced him fully. "What do you mean?"

The wolf slowly turned to look at him, his eyes bleak. Tharion felt the weight of his guilt at what he'd done to this male, in having Holstrom fight for him.

"To Crescent City," Ithan said, face like stone. "I have to go back."

"Why?"

"Holstrom! Ketos!" Dec hollered as the boat's engine churned.

Ithan just said quietly, "To make it right."

A shudder of muscle and a ripple of light, and the human form became a massive wolf.

"Ithan—" Tharion started.

The wolf turned and sprinted down the dock, back toward the arid countryside, golden in the rising light.

Flynn bellowed, "Holstrom, what the *fuck*!"

But the wolf had already reached the shore. Then the main building of the marina. Then the alley beside it . . . and then he vanished.

Silence fell, interrupted only by the grumble and splash of the engine. Tharion turned back toward the boat, toward the two friends onboard, the sprites gleaming like three small stars between them.

"What the fuck happened?" Flynn demanded.

Tharion shook his head, at a loss for words, and stepped onto the boat.

His fault—all of it. He lifted his face to the sky as the boat peeled toward the open ocean, and wondered if he'd ever see Valbara again.

If he even deserved to.

27

Bryce couldn't move for a moment. Vesperus was dead.

Nesta slashed her hand and the creature's body burned with that strange silver fire.

As the Asteri was reduced to ashes, Bryce grabbed the sword and dagger from the ground, both blades dripping with Vesperus's blood.

She whirled on Nesta, on Azriel. "You shouldn't have killed her. If we could have gotten her under control, the amount of information that we could have pried from her—"

"Do you have any idea what you almost did here?" Nesta raged, covered in Vesperus's dark ichor. She still gripped Ataraxia in one hand, as if not yet decided whether she was done killing. "What you unleashed?"

"Trust me, I know better than you guys what the Asteri can do."

"Then you have even less of an excuse for your actions," Nesta snapped. Her sword rose.

Azriel extended a scarred hand to Bryce, panting hard. "Open the passage out of here. You're coming back with us. Right now."

To that cell under a different mountain. Where she had no doubt she'd be subjected to the interrogation Vesperus should have received.

Bryce snorted. "Like Hel I am." Debris began floating around her. "You killed the one person here who might have given me the answer I needed."

"You're looking for ways to kill the Daglan. Well, *I* just killed that monster," Nesta said. "Isn't that answer enough?"

"No," Bryce said. "You've only left me with more questions."

She let her power flow outward from the star in her chest. From the Horn in her back.

"Don't you *dare*," Azriel warned with lethal softness.

But Bryce shoved out a slice of her power. Sharp and targeted, as Silene had used to carve the stones. As Azriel had focused his own power on her star earlier.

Light cut through stone and sizzled, a line literally drawn at Azriel's feet.

Whatever had changed in her power with the addition of Silene's magic . . . Fuck yeah. This would be useful.

"I won't tell them about you," Bryce said coolly, even as part of her marveled at the laser she'd created out of pure magic. The other part of her cringed from it—from the power that was eerily similar to what Rigelus had used against her before she jumped through the Gate in the Eternal Palace. "I swear it on my mate's life. Even if Rigelus . . ." She shook her head. "I won't breathe a word to them about this place."

Azriel dared to put one foot over the line she'd blasted into the floor. "They'll pry it from you. People like me, like them . . . we always get the information we need." His gaze darkened with the promise of unending pain.

"I won't let it come to that," Bryce said, and sent her power searing through her star again—right into the crystal sarcophagus.

Crystal like the Gate that had opened the way to this world.

The sarcophagus glowed . . . and then darkened into a pit.

"Please," Azriel said, his gaze now on her hands. On the Starsword—and on Truth-Teller. Something like panic filled his hazel eyes.

Shaking her head, Bryce backed toward the hole she'd made in the world. In the universe. She could only pray it would lead her to Midgard.

She met Nesta's stare. Raging silver fire flickered there.

"You're as much of a monster as they are," Nesta accused.

Bryce knew. She'd always known. "Love will do that to you."

Silver flames roared for her in a tidal wave, but Bryce was already leaping, sheathing the blades as she moved. Cold like nothing she'd known tore past her head, her spine—

And then the light from Nesta's silver flame winked out as the gate shut above Bryce, nothing but darkness surrounding her as she plunged deeper and deeper into the pit.

Toward home.

PART II
THE SEARCH

28

Hours after Pollux and the Hawk had left with Rigelus, Hunt was no closer to knowing who they would select to die. His bet was on Baxian, but there was a good chance Pollux would realize that killing Ruhn would devastate Bryce. If Bryce ever got back home to learn of it.

He'd been surprised and disturbed to stir from unconsciousness to find a familiar, growing weight at his back. A glance to Baxian had shown him the source: their wings were somehow regrowing at rapid speed, despite the gorsian shackles. Someone had to have given them something to orchestrate the healing—though it couldn't mean anything good.

He wondered if their captors had realized that the relentless itching would be a torment as awful as the whips and brands. Gritting his teeth against it, Hunt writhed, arching his spine, as if it'd help ease the merciless sensation. He'd give anything, anything, for one scratch—

"Orion." Aidas's voice sounded in his head, in the chamber. A cat with eyes like blue opals crouched on the floor, amid the blood and waste. The same form Rigelus had used to deceive Hunt months ago.

"Aidas . . . or Rigelus?" Hunt groaned.

Aidas was smart enough to get it—Hunt needed proof. The

demon prince said, "Miss Quinlan first met me on a park bench outside of the Oracle's Temple when she was thirteen. I asked her what blinds an Oracle."

The real thing, then. Not some trick of the Asteri.

"Bryce," Hunt moaned.

"I'm looking for her," Aidas said. Hunt could have sworn the cat looked sad.

"What does Rigelus want from my lightning?"

Aidas's tail swished. "So that's why he's working so hard to break you."

"He threatened to kill one of them if I didn't give some to him." A nod to Ruhn and Baxian.

Aidas bristled. "You mustn't do so, Athalar."

"Too late. He harvested it into a crystal like firstlight. And the fucker's going to kill one of them anyway."

Aidas's blue eyes filled with worry, but the prince said nothing.

So Hunt said again, "What does he want from my lightning?"

"If I were to guess . . . The same thing Sofie Renast's lightning was hunted for: to resurrect the dead."

Hunt's head swam. "My lightning can't do that. We didn't even know Sofie's lightning could do that."

Aidas blinked. "Well, apparently, Rigelus thinks both sources of lightning can."

"How did you find that out? *We* didn't discover that, and we were trying to dig up information about Sofie for weeks." Hunt fought the fog in his head. No, he knew this wasn't possible.

"I don't just sit around waiting for you to contact me," Aidas said. "My spies hear whispers around Midgard . . . and when some concern me, I go to investigate."

"So the River Queen was on the hunt for Sofie to . . . engage in some necromancy? Why not go to the Bone Quarter?"

"I don't know what the River Queen wanted."

Hunt scoured his memory for what had happened to Sofie's corpse after they'd found it in the morgue aboard the *Depth Charger*. What had Cormac done with it? Was it still on the ship? And if so, did the Ocean Queen know what she had in her possession?

The questions swarmed, but one rose to the forefront. "Why didn't Rigelus just hunt down Sofie's body? Why bother going after me?"

"You presented yourself to him rather conveniently, Athalar. Not to mention that you're alive, and much easier to command than a corpse."

"There are some Archangels who might disagree with you."

Aidas's mouth twitched upward, but he said, "It will likely take time for Rigelus to figure out a way to wield the lightning he extracted from you. Though I admit I am . . . disturbed to learn of his new experimentation. It does not bode well for any of us, if Rigelus is tangling with the dead."

"Why now?" Hunt asked. "I've been enslaved to them for centuries, for Urd's sake."

"Perhaps they've at last learned what your father bred you to be."

Even the miserable itching in his back was forgotten at those words. "What the *fuck* does that mean?"

But Aidas only shook his head. "A tale for another time, Athalar."

"A tale for *now*, Aidas. These cryptic mentions of my father, the *black crown*, secrets about my powers—"

"Mean nothing, if you do not get out of these dungeons."

"Then stop fucking popping out of the shadows and find a key."

"I cannot. My body isn't real here."

"It was real enough in Quinlan's apartment."

"That was a portal, a summoning. This is like . . . a phone call."

"Then send one of your buddies through the Northern Rift to help us—"

"The distance from Nena is too great. They wouldn't arrive in time to make a difference. You will get answers, Athalar, I promise. If you survive. But if the Asteri can use your lightning to raise the dead, in ways swifter and less limited than traditional necromancy, then the armies they might create—"

"You're not making me feel any better about giving some over." Another bit of guilt to burden his soul. He didn't know how he wasn't already broken beneath the sheer weight of it.

"Try not to give him more, then." But Aidas threw him a

pitying look. "I am sorry that one of your companions will die tomorrow."

"Fuck," Hunt said hoarsely. "Any idea who they've picked?"

Aidas angled his head, more feline than princely. Like he could hear things Hunt couldn't. "The one whose death will mean the most to both you and Bryce." Hunt closed his eyes. "The Fae Prince."

This was all Hunt's fault. He'd learned nothing since the Fallen. And he'd been fine with taking on the punishment himself, but for others to do it, for Ruhn to—

"I'm sorry," the Prince of the Chasm said again, and sounded like he meant it.

But Hunt said hoarsely, "If you find her . . . if you see her again . . . tell her . . ."

Not to come back. Not to dare enter this world of pain and suffering and misery. That he was so damn sorry for not stopping all of this.

"I know," Aidas said, not needing Hunt to finish before he vanished into darkness.

29

Bryce had dropped down between worlds. And yet when she landed, she collided sideways with a wall.

Apparently, magical interstellar travel didn't care about physics.

Her head throbbed; her mouth was painfully dry. The rough fibers of a carpet scraped her cheek, muffling the sounds of an enclosed space. It was dry, vaguely musty. Familiar-smelling.

"Isn't this interesting," drawled a male voice in her own language. It was the most wonderful sound she'd ever heard.

Though she'd have wished, perhaps, for the words to have come from someone other than the Autumn King.

He loomed over her, his hands wreathed in flame. Above him, a golden orrery clicked and whirred. She'd landed in her father's private study.

The Autumn King's lips curled in that familiar cruel smile. "And where have *you* been, Bryce Quinlan?"

Bryce opened her mouth, power rallying—

And sputtering out.

"For an old bastard, you move fast," she groaned, straining against the gorsian shackles on her wrists. No chains attached to them, at least—just the cuffs of the shackles. But it was enough. Bryce couldn't so much as summon a flicker of starlight.

Her father knew it. He strolled to his giant wooden desk like he had all the time in the world.

In those initial seconds when she'd landed here, in the worst fucking place in the whole fucking world, he'd not only disabled her power with those shackles—he'd also disarmed her. The Starsword and Truth-Teller now lay behind him on his desk. Along with her phone.

Bryce lifted her chin, though she remained sitting on the ground. "Are Ruhn and Hunt alive?"

Something like distaste flashed in the Autumn King's eyes. As if such mortal bonds should be the least of her concerns. "You show your hand, Bryce Quinlan."

"I thought my name was *Bryce Danaan* now," she seethed.

"To the detriment of the line, yes," the Autumn King said, his eyes sparking. "Where have you been?"

"There was a sample sale at the mall," Bryce said flatly. *"Are Ruhn and Hunt still alive?"*

The Autumn King's head angled, gaze sweeping over her filthy T-shirt, her torn leggings. "I was informed that you were no longer on this planet. Where did you go?"

Bryce declined to answer.

Her father smiled slightly. "I can connect the dots. You arrive from off-world, bearing a knife that matches the Starsword. The dagger from the prophecy, no?" His eyes gleamed with greed. "Not seen since the First Wars. If I were to guess, you managed to reach a place I have long desired to go." He glanced up at the orrery.

"You might want to reconsider before packing your bags," Bryce said. "They don't take kindly to assholes."

"Your journey hasn't impacted that smart mouth of yours, I see."

She smiled with saccharine sweetness. "You're still an absolute bastard, *I see*."

The Autumn King pursed his lips. "I'd be careful if I were you." He pushed off his desk and stalked toward her. "No one knows you're here."

"Taking your daughter hostage: excellent parenting."

"You are my guest here until I see fit to release you."

"Which will be when?" She batted her eyelashes with exaggerated innocence.

"When I have the reassurances I seek."

Bryce made a show of tapping her chin in contemplation. "How about this: You let me go, and I don't fucking kill you for delaying me?"

A soft, taunting laugh. How had her mother ever loved this cold-blooded reptile?

"I've already sealed off the wards around this villa, and sent away my servants and sentries."

"You mean to tell me we're going to do all our own cooking?"

The intensity on his face didn't falter. "No one shall even know that you are back in this world until I see fit."

"And then you'll tell the Asteri?" Her heart skipped a beat. She couldn't let that happen.

Her father smiled again. "That depends entirely on you."

Ithan ran himself into the ground all the way back to the eastern gate of Crescent City, hundreds of miles from the dock in Ionia where he'd left Tharion and the others.

Make your brother proud.

He hadn't been able to get on that boat. Ketos might be able to walk away from the consequences of his actions, but Ithan couldn't.

Gilded by the setting sun, Crescent City bustled on as usual, unaware of what he'd done. How everything had changed.

He took the coward's path through the city, cutting through FiRo rather than going right to the Istros through Moonwood. If he saw another wolf right now . . .

He didn't want to know what he'd do. What he'd say.

He was no one in the hustle of rush hour, but he kept to the alleys and side streets. He didn't spare a glance for the Heart Gate as he sprinted past it, nor did he let himself look eastward toward Bryce and Danika's old apartment when he passed that, too.

He only looked ahead, toward the approaching river. Toward the Black Dock at the end of the street.

Despite the chaotic throngs of evening commuters in the rest of the city, the Black Dock was silent and empty, wreathed in mist. Down the quay, a few mourners wept on benches, but no one stood on the dock itself.

Ithan couldn't bring himself to look deeper into the mists, toward the Bone Quarter. He prayed Connor wasn't looking his way from across the river.

Ithan shifted into his humanoid form before walking a block westward along the quay. Ithan knew where the entrance was—everyone did.

No one ever went there, of course. No one dared.

The great black door sat in the middle of a matching black marble building—a facade. The building had been styled after an elaborate mausoleum. The door was the focus, the main reason for its existence: to lead one not into the building, but below it.

No one stood guard at the door. Ithan supposed nobody was needed. Anyone who wanted to rob this place would deserve all that they'd face inside.

Crude, ancient markings covered the black door. Like scratches carved by inhuman fingernails. At its center, an etching of a horned, humanoid skull engulfed in flames stared out at him.

Ithan knocked on its hateful face once. Twice. The metal thudded dully.

The door yawned open, silent as a grave. Only darkness waited beyond, and a long, straight staircase into the gloom.

It might as well have been Hel on Midgard.

Ithan felt nothing, was nothing, as he strode in. As the door shut behind him, sealing him in solid, unending night.

Locking him inside the House of Flame and Shadow.

30

If the Autumn King was indeed cooking their meals, then Bryce had to admit that he wasn't a bad chef. Roast chicken, green beans, and some thickly sliced bread waited on the marble table in the vast dining room.

Apparently, she'd arrived around three in the afternoon on a Friday. That was all she'd been able to get out of him while he'd led her from his office to a bedroom on the second floor. Not what the date was, or even the month. Or year.

Nausea coursed through her. Hunt had been kept in the Asteri dungeons for *years* the last time . . . Was he still there? Was he even alive? Was Ruhn? Her family?

There was nothing in her bedroom, an elegant—if bland—blend of marble and overstuffed furniture in varying shades of gray and white, to aid in answering these questions. Her father wanted her cut off from the world, and so it was: No TV. No phone—not even a landline. A glamour shimmered on the floor-to-ceiling windows overlooking an interior lavender garden, blocking prying eyes from seeing in. A peek toward the sky showed an iridescent bubble over the whole place—wards. Like the ones the Fae had established to lock down their territory during the attack this spring.

But it was the screams of pleading Fae parents as Silene locked them out of their home world, leaving their children to the Asteri's cruelty, that echoed through Bryce's head.

And now, sitting across the massive dining table from her father hours later, having showered and changed into a pair of jeans, a T-shirt, and a skintight navy blue athletic jacket that he'd given her—she really fucking hoped they weren't left over from a booty call—Bryce asked, "So is this the plan? Lock me up here until I get so bored that I tell you everything? Or is it to deprive me of information so that I'll tell you anything in exchange for a snippet of news about Hunt?"

Her father sliced into his chicken with a precision that told her exactly how he dealt with his enemies. But he sighed through his nose. "Your hosts in the other world must have had a high tolerance for irreverent nonsense, if you're still alive."

"Most people call it charm."

He sipped from his wine. "How long were you there?"

"Tell me about Ruhn and Hunt."

He sipped again. "That wasn't even a good attempt to surprise me into answering."

"You know, only a real piece of shit would withhold that information."

He set down his wine. "Here is how this shall work. For every question of mine that you answer, *you* shall receive an answer to one of your questions. If I sense that you are lying, you shall not get a reply from me."

"You know, I just played this game with someone even more horrible than you—shocking, I know—and it didn't end well for her. So I suggest we skip the Q and A and you tell me what I want to know."

He only stared. He'd sit here all fucking night.

Bryce tapped her foot on the marble floor, weighing it out. "Fine."

"Did you truly go to the home world of the Fae?"

"Yes."

A muscle ticked in his jaw. "Athalar and Ruhn are still alive."

Bryce tried not to sag with relief. "How long—"

He held up a finger. "My turn."

Fucker.

"What was their world like?"

"I don't know—I only saw a holding cell and some tunnels and caverns. But . . . it seemed free. Of the Asteri, at least." And then, because she knew it would upset him, she said, "The Fae there are stronger than we are. The Asteri take a chunk of our power through the Drop—it feeds them, sustains them. In that other world, the Fae retain their full, pure power."

She could have sworn his face had paled, even under the flattering golden glow of the twin iron chandeliers dangling above. It made her more smug than she'd expected.

"How long was I gone?" she asked.

"Five days."

The timelines between their worlds were similar, then. "And—"

"What did you learn while you were there?"

How to reply? To give him the truth . . . "I'm still processing."

"That's not an acceptable answer."

"I learned," she snapped, "that most of the Fae, no matter what world they're on, are a bunch of selfish assholes."

His eyebrows lifted. "Oh?"

She crossed her arms. "Let's just say that I know a female who could wipe your sorry ass from existence and not break a sweat."

And yet Nesta hadn't done that to Bryce. She'd thought it luck, but was it possible the female had pulled her punches? Nesta hadn't been anything like Silene or Theia.

It didn't matter now, but the thought lingered.

"That still doesn't answer my question. You must have gone to that world for a reason—what did you learn?"

"One, I wound up there by accident. Two, *technically*, I did answer your question, so be more specific next time."

Something dark and lethal passed over her father's face. "How—"

Bryce held up a finger, mocking him. "What happened after I left?"

Her father's whiskey-colored eyes simmered with flame at the sight of that finger, the command and insistence of the right to speak it conveyed. The sight must have been especially galling from a female.

But he seemed to tamp down his anger and said with a smugness of his own, like he was savoring the bad news as much as she had while giving hers, "The Asteri threw Athalar and your brother into their dungeons, and managed to contain the knowledge of what occurred at their palace. They only informed those of us who needed to know." He drained his wine. "Did you bring these Fae back into Midgard with you?"

"Did you *see* them arrive here with me?" No need to tell him that she didn't part on good terms. Azriel might very well have killed her if she'd stayed a moment longer.

Bryce braced her forearms on the table, gorsian shackles thudding against the cool marble. "So you've known Ruhn is in the Asteri's dungeons for five days and have done nothing to help him?"

"Ruhn deserves all that is coming his way. He chose his fate."

Her fingers curled into fists, nails digging into her flesh. "He's your son, for fuck's sake."

"I can have others."

"Not if I kill you first." A familiar white haze crept over her vision.

Her father smiled, as if noting the primal fury of the Fae—but purely human rage. "You're so like your mother." He smirked. "No questions about *her* fate?"

"I know you wouldn't be able to keep from telling me if something had happened to her. You'd take too much pleasure in it. Why have the Asteri kept Hunt and Ruhn alive?"

"I believe it is my turn."

"*I* believe it's *my* turn. *No questions about* her *fate?* counts as a question, asshole."

Her father's eyes flickered, as if amused despite himself—and impressed. "Very well."

"Why have they kept Ruhn and Hunt alive?"

"To use them against you, I assume, though I cannot say for sure." He poured himself more wine, the fading sunlight streaming through the windows making the liquid glow like fresh blood. "Tell me about the knife—it is the one from our prophecies, the sibling to the Starsword?"

"The one and only. They call it Truth-Teller." He opened his mouth again, but she tapped her fingers on the table. Better get the lay of the land, assess where any allies might be—if they survived. "What's the status of Ophion?"

"No attacks since the one on the lab. Their numbers are nearly depleted. Ophion is, for all intents and purposes, dead."

Bryce reined in her wince.

The Autumn King drank from his wine again. At this rate, he'd get through the whole bottle before the sun had fully set. "How did you attain Truth-Teller?"

"I stole it." She smiled slightly at his frown of distaste. "What of my other friends—are they all alive?"

"If you counted that traitor Cormac amongst your friends, then no. But the rest of them, as far as I have heard, are alive and well." Bryce reeled. Cormac was— "Did you steal the dagger to fulfill the prophecy?"

She shrugged with what nonchalance she could muster and set down her fork. "I'm tired of this game."

Cormac was dead. Had he died that day at the lab, or had it been afterward—perhaps in the Asteri's dungeons, under their questioning? Or had they simply sent the male home to his shitty father and let the King of Avallen rip him to shreds for dishonoring his household?

The Autumn King smiled like he'd won. "Then you are dismissed. I shall see you tomorrow."

She pushed past her twisting grief to say, "Fuck you."

He merely inclined his head and resumed eating in silence.

Ithan strode down the steps of the House of Flame and Shadow in darkness so pure that even his wolf eyes couldn't pierce it.

He'd never heard anything about what waited at the bottom of the stairs. But he figured he was out of options.

He lost track of how long he walked downward, the air tight and dry. Like a tomb.

The scuff of his sneakers against the steps echoed off the black walls. His eyes strained with the effort of trying to see, to no avail. If the steps ended in a plunge, he'd have no idea. No warning.

It was true, in the end, that he had no warning. But not for a drop. Metal clanked, and his skull with it, as Ithan slammed into a wall. He rebounded, swearing—

Light, golden and soft, cracked through the stairwell.

It wasn't a wall. It was a door, and beyond it, silhouetted by the light, was a slim female figure. Even before he could make out her face, he knew the voice. Arch, cultured, bored.

"Well, that's one way of knocking," drawled Jesiba Roga.

31

Jesiba Roga led Ithan through a subterranean hall of black stone, lit only by crackling fires in hearths shaped like roaring, fanged mouths. In front of those fireplaces lounged draki of varying hues, vampyrs drinking goblets of blood, and daemonaki in business suits typing away on laptops.

A weirdly . . . normal place. Like a private club.

He supposed it *was* a private club, of sorts. The headquarters of any House were open to all its members, at any time. Some chose to dwell within them, mostly the workers who ran the House's daily operations. But some just came to hang out, to meet, to rest.

Ithan, to his embarrassment, had never been to Lunathion's House of Earth and Blood headquarters. Hadn't been to its main headquarters, either, up in Hilene. Bryce had as a kid, he remembered, but he couldn't recall the details.

Ithan followed Jesiba down the long hall, past people who barely looked his way, and then through a set of double doors of black wood carved with the horned skull sigil of the House.

He didn't know what he'd expected. A council chamber, some fancy office . . .

Not the sleek, onyx bar, lit with deep blue lighting, like the heart of a flame. A jazz quartet played on a small stage beneath an archway in the rear of the space, the many high tables—all adorned with glass votives of that blue light—oriented toward the music. But Roga headed right for the obsidian glass bar, the gilded stools before it.

A golden-scaled draki female in a gauzy black dress worked the bar, and nodded toward Roga. The sorceress nodded back shallowly as she took a seat and patted the stool beside her, ordering Ithan, "Sit."

Ithan threw the sorceress a glare at the blatant reference to his canine nature, but he obeyed.

A moment later, the bartender slid two dark glasses toward them, both rippling with smoke. Jesiba knocked hers back in one go, smoke curling from her mouth as she said, "I thought the porters had smoked too much mirthroot when they told me that Ithan Holstrom was walking down the entry steps."

Ithan peered into his dark glass, at the amber liquid that looked and smelled like whiskey, though he'd never seen whiskey with smoke rising from it.

"It's called a smokeshow," Roga drawled. "Whiskey, grated ginger, and a little draki magic to make it look fancy."

Ithan took her word for it and swallowed the whole thing in one mouthful. It burned all the way down—burned through the nothingness in him.

"Well," Roga said, "based on how eagerly you drank that and the fact that you're here at all, I can assume things are . . . not going well for you."

"I need a necromancer."

"And I need a new assistant, but you'd be surprised how few competent ones are out there."

Ithan didn't hide his glower. "I'm serious."

Roga signaled the bartender for another round. "As am I. Ever since Quinlan left me to go work at the Fae Archives, I've been up to my neck in paperwork."

Ithan was pretty sure that wasn't how it had gone down with Bryce and Jesiba, but he said, "Look, I didn't come here to talk to you—"

"Yes, but you're lucky as Hel that the porters called me to deal with you, and not someone else. One of the vamps might have taken a taste by now."

She nodded to the nearest high table behind them, where two gorgeous blonds in skintight black dresses perched, no drinks before them. They were surveying the people in the room, as if looking over a menu.

Ithan cleared his throat. "I need a necromancer," he said again. "Immediately."

Jesiba sighed, and nodded her thanks to the bartender as she slid over another smokeshow. "Your brother's been dead for too long."

"Not for my brother," Ithan said. "For someone else."

Jesiba drank slowly this time. Smoke fluttered from her lips as she swallowed. "Whatever it is, pup, I'd suggest making peace with it."

"There's *no making peace with it*," Ithan snarled. He could have sworn the glasses rattled, that the jazz quartet faltered, that the two vamps turned his way. A glance from Jesiba, and the room resumed its rhythms.

"Who did you kill?" Jesiba asked, voice so low it was barely audible.

Ithan's throat constricted. He couldn't breathe—

"Holstrom." Her eyes glowed like the flames in the sconces behind the bar.

There was no fixing this, no undoing it. He was a traitor and a murderer and—

"Who do you need to raise?" Roga's question was cold as ice.

Ithan made himself meet her gaze, made himself face what he'd done.

"A lost Fendyr heir."

"I'm assuming the food last night was reheated leftovers, if that shitty little yogurt you left outside my door this morning counts as breakfast," Bryce said to the Autumn King as she plopped into a red leather armchair and watched his orrery tick away.

Her father, sitting across the oversized desk, ignored her.

"How long are you going to keep me here?"

"Are we playing the question game again? I thought you'd tired of it last night." He didn't look up from what he was writing, his sheet of red hair slipping over a broad shoulder.

She clenched her teeth. "Just trying to calculate how much borrowed time I have left."

His golden pen—a fountain pen, for fuck's sake—slashed across the paper. "I shall procure more groceries, if my breakfast provisions are inadequate."

Bryce crossed her legs, the leather chair creaking as she leaned back. "Look at you: cooking your own meals and grocery shopping. Why, you could almost pass as a functional adult and not some pampered brat."

The fabric of his gray T-shirt pulled over his chest as his shoulders tensed.

Bryce pointed to the orrery. "The Astronomer said you had some Avallen craftsmen make that for you. Fancy." The Autumn King's eyes narrowed at the mention of the Astronomer, but he didn't look up from his paper. Bryce plowed on, "He said the orrery is to contemplate fundamental questions about ourselves, like who we are and where we came from. I have a hard time believing you're in here all day, thinking about anything that profound."

His pen stalled on the paper. "The Fae bloodlines have been weakening for generations now. It is my life's work to investigate why. This orrery was built in pursuit of answering that question."

She blew on her nails. "Especially after little old me became a certified Starborn Princess, huh?"

His fingers tightened on his pen, hard enough that she was surprised the gold plating didn't dent. "The question of our failing bloodlines plagued me long before you were born."

"Why? Who cares?"

He lifted his head at last, his eyes cold and dead. "I care if our people are weakening. If we become lesser than the angels, the shifters, the witches."

"So it's about your ego, then."

"It's about our survival. The Fae stand in a favorable position with the Asteri. If our power wanes, they will lose interest in maintaining that. Others will creep in to take what we have, predators around a carcass. And the Asteri won't lift a finger to stop them."

"And this is why you and Morven schemed to throw me and Cormac together?"

"*King* Morven has noticed the fading as well. But he has the luxury of hiding behind Avallen's mists."

Bryce drummed her fingers on the smooth rolled arm of her chair. "Is it true that the Asteri can't pierce the mists around Avallen?"

"Morven is almost certain they can't. Though I don't know if Rigelus has ever tried to breach the barriers." He glanced toward the tall windows to his left, toward the dome of the glamour shimmering above the olive trees and lavender beds. As much of a barrier as he could ever hope to hide behind.

Bryce weighed her options, and ultimately dared to go for it as she asked, "Does the term *thin place* mean anything to you?"

He angled his head, and damn if it didn't freak her the fuck out to see how similar the motion was to her own habits. "No. What is it?"

"Just something I heard once."

"You lie. You learned of it in the home world of the Fae."

Maybe she shouldn't have asked. Maybe it was too dangerous to have revealed this to him. Not for her, but for the world she'd left. Bryce halted her fingers' drumming, laying her hand flat on the cool, smooth leather arm. "I only heard the phrase, not the definition."

He surveyed her, sensing that lie as well, but something like admiration brightened his eyes. "Defiant to a fault."

Still seated, she sketched a half bow.

The Autumn King went on, idly twirling the pen between his fingers, "I always knew your mother was hiding something about you. She went to such lengths to conceal you from me."

"Maybe because you're a sociopath?"

His fingers tightened around the pen once more. "Ember loved me, once upon a time. Only something enormous would have severed that love."

Bryce propped her chin on a fist, all innocent curiosity. "Like when you hit her? Something enormous like that?"

Fire licked along his shoulders, in his long hair. But his voice remained flat. "Let us not retread old ground. I have told you my feelings on the matter."

"Yeah, you're *so* sorry about it. Sorry enough that now you've done exactly what she was so scared of all along: locked me up in your villa."

He motioned to the windows. "Has it occurred to you that here, hidden from the world and any spying eyes, you are safe? That should anyone on Midgard have learned of your return, word would soon have reached the Eternal Palace and you would be dead?"

Bryce put a hand on her chest. "I totally love how you're building yourself up as my savior—really, A for effort on that front—but let's cut the bullshit. I'm locked up here because you want something from me. What is it?"

He didn't answer, and instead twisted to adjust one of the settings on some sort of prism-like device. Whatever he'd done sent the sunlight piercing through the orrery's assortment of planets.

A prism—the total opposite of what she'd done with her powers when she'd fought Nesta and Azriel. Where she'd condensed light, the prism fractured it.

She glanced at her hands, so pale against the bloodred of the leather chair. She'd been riding on adrenaline and despair and bravado. How had she managed to make her light into a laser in those last moments in the Fae world? It had been intuitive in the moment, but now . . . Maybe it was better not to know. Not to think about how her light seemed to be edging closer to the properties of an Asteri's destructive power.

"Ruhn told me that you hole up in here all day looking for patterns," Bryce said, nodding to the orrery, the prism device, the assortment of golden tools on the desk. "What sort of patterns?" She and Ruhn had enjoyed a good laugh over that—the thought of the mighty Autumn King as little more than a conspiracy theorist.

What does he think he's going to find? Ruhn had asked, snickering. *That the universe is playing a giant game of tic-tac-toe?*

Bryce's heart twanged with the memory.

The Autumn King jotted down another note, pen scraping too loudly in the heavy quiet. "Why should I trust a loud-mouthed child with no discretion to keep my secrets?"

"It's a secret, huh? So this is some controversial shit?"

Disdain warped his handsome face. "I once asked your brother to provide me with a seed of his starlight."

"Gross. Don't call it that."

His nostrils flared. "What little *seed* he was able to produce allowed me to use this in a way I found . . . beneficial." He patted the gold-plated device that held the prism.

"I didn't realize making rainbows on the wall was so important to you."

He ignored her. "This device refracts the light, pulling it apart so I might study every facet of it." He pointed to a sister device positioned directly across from it. "That device gathers it back into one beam again. I am attempting to add *more* to the light in the process of re-forming it. If the light might be pulled apart and strengthened in its most basic form, there's a chance that it will coalesce into a more powerful version of itself."

She refrained from mentioning the blue stones Azriel had wielded—how they'd condensed and directed his power. Instead, she drawled, "And this is a good use of your time because . . . ?"

His silence was biting.

"Let me do the math." She began ticking items off on her fingers. "The Asteri are made of light. They feed on firstlight. You are studying light, its properties, beyond what science can already tell us . . ."

A muscle ticked in his jaw.

"Am I getting warm?" Bryce asked. "But if you have such questions about the Asteri, why not ask them yourself?" She hummed in contemplation. "Maybe you want to use this against them?"

He arched a brow. "Your imagination does run rampant."

"Oh, totally. But you took zero interest in me as a kid. And now suddenly, once I revealed my magic light, you want me to be part of your fucked-up little family."

"My only interest in you lies in the bloodline you stand to pass on."

"Too bad Hunt complicates that."

"More than you know."

She paused, but didn't fall for the trap of asking about it. She continued to lead him down the path of her rambling, resuming her counting on her fingers.

"So your daughter has light powers, you're interested in *patterns* in light . . . you want the information hidden from the Asteri . . ." She chuckled, lowering her hand at last. "Oh, don't even try to deny it," she said when he opened his mouth. "If you wanted to help them, you'd have turned me over to them already."

The Autumn King smiled. It was a thing of nightmarish beauty. "You truly are my child. More so than Ruhn ever was."

"That's not a compliment." But she went on, content to needle him with her guesses. "You want to know if I can kill them, don't you? The Asteri. If the Starborn light is different from their light, and *how* it is different. That's where the orrery comes in: contemplating where we come from . . . what sort of light we have, how it can be weaponized."

His nostrils flared again. "And did you learn such things on your journey?"

Bryce tapped her gorsian-shackled wrist. "Remove these and I can show you what I learned."

He smirked, and picked up the prism device again. "I'll wait."

She hadn't thought for a second that would work—but it seemed he knew it, too. That this was a game, a dance between them.

Bryce nodded to where he'd left the Starsword and Truth-Teller on the desk the day before. According to Ruhn, the Autumn King had rarely dared to touch the sword. It seemed like that was true, if he hadn't moved the blades since her crash landing. "Let's talk about how we can add another notch to my Magical Starborn Princess belt: I united the sword and knife. Prophecy fulfilled."

"You don't know anything about that prophecy," the Autumn King said, and returned to his work.

She asked sweetly, "So my interpretation is wrong? *When knife and sword are reunited, so shall our people be.* Well, I went to our old world. Met some people. Reminded them we exist. Came back here. Thus, two people reunited."

He shook his head in pure disgust. "You know as little about those blades as you do your own true nature."

She made a show of yawning. "Well, I do know that only the Chosen One can handle the blades. Wait—does that mean you can't? Since last I checked . . . only Ruhn and I got the Chosen One membership cards."

"Ruhn doesn't possess the raw power to handle such a thing correctly."

"But I do?" she asked innocently. "Is *that* why I'm here? We're going to cooperate in some kind of training montage so I can take down the Asteri for you?"

"Who says I want to get rid of the Asteri?"

"You've been really careful not to mention one way or another how you feel about them. One moment, you're protecting me from them, the next you're trying to keep the Fae in their good graces. Which is it?"

"Can it not be both?"

"Sure. But if you get rid of the Asteri, it'd give you even more power than whatever scheme you had planned that involved my marrying Cormac."

He adjusted a dial on his device, the light shifting a millimeter to the right. "Does it matter who is in power, so long as the Fae survive?"

"Um, yeah. One option is a parasitic blight upon this world. Let's not go with that choice."

He set the device down again. "Explain this . . . parasite. You mentioned something about the Asteri taking some of our power through the Drop."

Bryce debated it. He held her stare, seeing that debate rage in her.

Who would he tell, though? At this point, the more people who knew, even the assholes, the better it was. That way the secret couldn't die with her.

And after all the shit she'd learned and been through . . . maybe it'd help to lay out all the pieces at once.

So Bryce told him. Everything she'd learned about the Asteri, their history, their feeding patterns, the firstlight and secondlight. Gods, it was worse saying it aloud.

She finished, slumping back in the armchair. "So we're basically a giant buffet for the Asteri."

He'd been still and watchful while she'd related the information, but now he said quietly, "Perhaps the Asteri have been taking too much, for too long, from our people. That is why the bloodlines have weakened, generation after generation." He spoke more to himself than to her, but his eyes snapped to Bryce's as he said, "So all the water on Midgard is contaminated."

"I don't think a filter's gonna help you, if that's what you're planning."

He cut her a glare. "Yet the Fae in the other world do not have this affliction?"

"No. The Asteri hadn't developed this nasty little method of theft when they occupied their world." She rubbed her temples. "Maybe that sword and dagger can cleanse the parasite, though." She hummed again, as if thinking it over. "Maybe you should let me impale you with them and we can see what happens."

"You will never understand how they work," he said flatly.

"So you do?" She let her skepticism show in her voice. "How?"

"You're not the only one with access to ancient texts. Jesiba Roga's collection is but a fraction of mine—and a fraction of what lies in Avallen. I have studied the lore long enough to draw some conclusions."

"Good for you. You're a genius."

Fire crackled at his fingertips—the same flame he'd used to burn Ruhn as a kid. She shut down the thought as he warned, "I wouldn't be so impertinent if I were you. Your survival depends entirely upon my goodwill."

Oily, churning nausea coursed through her gut. Whatever game or dance they'd been engaging in . . . he could have this round. "Gods, you're the worst."

He picked up a nearby notebook and cracked open its green cover. It was full of scribbling. His research records and thoughts. A stack of paper lay underneath it, also covered with his writing. Leafing through the notebook, his voice was bland as he said, "I tire of you. Take your leave."

32

Hunt knew what was coming when the Hawk left the door to the dungeons open. Knew it would be bad when they were all dumped to the filthy ground again, Ruhn moaning at what it did to his arm.

All this, to break Hunt to Rigelus's will. A slow sapping of Hunt's resolve, to suffer and see these males suffer beside him, to wear him down to this point, so he'd beg them to stop, would offer up anything to make it cease, to save them—

"Get the fuck up," the Hawk ordered from the doorway as Mordoc and several of his dreadwolves stalked into the chamber. They didn't wait for Hunt to obey the Hawk's command before they reached for him, the silver darts in their imperial uniforms glinting.

Hunt bared his teeth. A few of them stepped back at the expression on his face. At the presence of the Umbra Mortis, still unbroken.

Even Mordoc, with all those silver darts crusting his collar, paused, considering.

Hunt's legs shook, his body roared in pain, but he stood. His barely formed wings twitched, trying to spread in angelic wrath. This might all be his fault, but he'd go down swinging.

"Rigelus requests an audience," the Hawk drawled, tapping an invisible watch on his slender wrist. "Best not to keep His Holiness waiting."

Hunt had no idea how Ruhn or Baxian managed to stand beside him. But groaning, hissing, they did. A sidelong glance to Baxian showed him the Helhound's wings—fully formed, but still as weak as Hunt's own—were tucked in protectively.

Hunt had little hope either of them would keep their wings today. But losing them again would be better than losing Ruhn. Would Bryce ever forgive him if he let Ruhn die? Would he ever forgive himself?

He already knew the answer.

Mordoc aimed a gun at Hunt's head, and the other dreadwolves followed suit with Baxian and Ruhn as their chains were unanchored from the wall.

Hunt caught Ruhn's agonized, exhausted stare. How the fuck would they even make it up the small flight of stairs to where the Hawk stood?

Nice knowing you, Athalar.

The prince's voice was muffled. Like even the energy to talk mind-to-mind was too much. Or maybe that was all the gorsian stone on them.

But somehow . . . Ruhn seemed to know his fate. He didn't appear inclined to fight it.

"One foot at a time, friends," Baxian murmured as they reached the bottom of the stairs. Hunt hated the hand he had to brace on the cold stone wall to help him get up the steps. Hated his jagged breathing, the screaming in his body, the effort required to lift each foot.

But he did as Baxian said. One foot at a time.

And then the Hawk was in front of them, still sneering. Mordoc and the dreadwolves kept their guns trained as the motherfucker bowed mockingly. "This way, friends."

Mordoc snickered, the fucker.

Hunt staggered into the hall, head spinning. The cup of thin broth and dry bread had been a pathetic excuse for a meal. Quinlan would have had some smart remark about it. He could almost hear her saying to the Hawk, *Where's my pizza, bird-boy?*

Hunt laughed to himself, earning a quizzical look over the shoulder from the Hawk.

Ruhn stumbled, nearly eating stone. The dreadwolves swept in, hauling him up before he could collapse. The prince's feet scraped and pushed feebly at the floor, trying to stand, but his body failed him.

Hunt could do nothing but watch as two dreadwolves dragged Ruhn along like a fucking duffel bag.

Maybe it would be a mercy for Ruhn to die. The thought was abhorrent, but—

"Please let us take the elevator," Baxian muttered from behind him, and Hunt chuckled again. He might have been on the verge of hysteria.

"Shut the fuck up," Mordoc snarled, and Baxian grunted, no doubt from a blow the dreadwolf had landed on his battered body.

Thank the gods, they were indeed herded down the hall toward the elevator bay. As if on cue, the gold-plated doors parted to reveal the Hind in her pristine uniform.

"Good morning, boys," she purred, face cold as death as she held the door open with a slender hand. Her other arm was in a sling, heavily bandaged.

"Lidia," the Hawk drawled, and nodded to her injured arm. "How are the burns healing up?"

Limping into the elevator beside Lidia, Hunt eyed the Hind's sling. Had she finished playing rebel and gone back to her true self? Maybe she'd been using fire to persuade a prisoner to talk and gotten a little too enthusiastic. Ruhn's face remained wholly blank. He was back on his feet again, slowly approaching the elevator.

"Fine." Lidia leaned against the button panel, fire in her golden eyes. She sniffed at Baxian, then said to the Hawk, "You couldn't wash them first?"

"Rigelus said immediately," the Hawk said, shoving Ruhn in.

The prince hit the glass wall at the rear of the elevator and slumped to the floor with a groan. The Hawk reached to push in Baxian, but the Helhound bared his teeth, and even the Hawk didn't try anything as the Helhound took up a place beside Hunt, limping only slightly.

How much had changed since those years with Sandriel. And how little.

"Room for two," Lidia snapped at her dreadwolves, and a pair of stone-faced soldiers slipped in. Each had at least a dozen silver darts along the collars of their gray uniforms. Lidia ordered Mordoc, "Be waiting outside the bay upstairs."

Mordoc nodded, golden eyes bright with anticipated bloodshed, and snarled something to the dreadwolf unit that had them marching swiftly for the stairs. With feral delight dancing over his face, Mordoc trailed them out.

Lidia waited until the dreadwolves and their captain had left the landing before removing her hand from the door. The elevator sealed shut, and the car began to slide upward.

They emerged from the underground levels, rising into the crystal palace above.

Blinding light pierced Hunt's eyes—daylight. His eyes, accustomed to the dark, couldn't focus—he couldn't make out anything of the world around him. He lifted a wing to block out the light, body barking in pain with the movement. Ruhn and Baxian hissed, recoiling from the light as well.

The Hawk snickered. "Just a taste of what Rigelus will do to you." The two dreadwolves chuckled with him.

Hunt squinted as he lowered his wing and met the shithead's eyes. "Fuck you." Like Hel would these assholes make him beg and grovel—either for his own life or Ruhn's.

Lidia said mildly, "I couldn't have said it better myself, Athalar." Hunt looked, but not fast enough.

The Hawk certainly didn't look fast enough.

And Hunt knew he'd treasure this moment forever: the moment when Lidia Cervos pulled out her gun and fired it right between the Hawk's eyes.

33

All Ruhn knew was blinding light, and the blast of gunshots.

Three bodies hit the floor. The Hawk, followed by two dreadwolves. And before them, lowering her gun to her side . . . Lidia.

"What the *fuck*!" Baxian shouted.

He didn't know—Ruhn had never told him. Even in his rage and loathing, he'd never dared risk sharing the knowledge of Daybright's identity with another person who could betray her.

Using her good hand, Lidia hit a button on the elevator. "We have one minute and thirty-five seconds to get to the car." She yanked a ring of keys from her pocket and knelt in front of Athalar. Fumbling a bit with her bandaged hand, she freed first his ankles, then his wrists from the gorsian shackles. Then Baxian's.

Ruhn blinked and she was in front of him, eyes bright and clear. "Hang on," she whispered. Her slender fingers brushed his skin, and gorsian stone fell away. His magic swelled, a tide of starlight rising within him.

It stopped at the end of his arm. He was missing his fucking *hand*—

He swayed. Lidia caught him, hauling him upright with ease. But he didn't miss the grunt of pain from whatever it did to her arm, now free of its sling.

Her scent hit him, wrapping around him, holding him awake as surely as she wrapped her arm around his middle to help keep him standing.

"How long, Lidia?" Baxian asked. "How long since you've turned?" His face was slack with shock.

"There'll be time enough to trade rebel background stories," she said shortly, watching the changing floor numbers. "When the doors open, go left, then take the first door, then down two flights, take the door after that, then jump into the car. It's large enough to fit all of you—and the wings." She glanced over a shoulder, gaze sweeping over Hunt, then Baxian. "Are they healed enough to fly? Did the firstlight injection work?"

She was the one to thank for the angels' healing—in anticipation of this escape?

"Weak, but functional," Baxian panted. "But you're insane if you believe we can get out—"

"Shut up," she snapped, her good arm tightening around Ruhn's side before she angled him toward the door. "We only have one minute now."

The elevator dinged, and Ruhn knew he should be bracing himself as Hunt and Baxian were, but he couldn't move his body, his agonized, weak body, even when the doors opened—

Lidia moved him instead. She charged into the hall, half dragging him, and cut left, Athalar and Baxian behind her.

Sparks flickered in Ruhn's vision, blackness creeping in at the edges. It was all he could do to keep his feet under him, keep them moving, as Lidia raced them down the corridor to that door she'd indicated, then the stairs—

Ruhn stumbled on the first step, and she was there, heaving him over her slender back, lifting him. Fucking *carrying* him, despite that injured arm. He might have been mortified had each movement not set every nerve in his arm screaming.

Down, then through the glass door into the above-ground parking garage. An imperial open-air jeep with an unmanned gunner mounted in the back waited at the curb.

"Baxian: gunner," Lidia ordered as she dumped Ruhn into the front passenger seat, pain threatening to tear his fragile consciousness from him.

The Helhound needed no further explanation before crawling up to the machine gun. Athalar threw himself across the back row, wings barely able to squeeze in with him. And then Lidia slung herself into the driver's seat. A stomp of her feet on the pedals as she slammed the stick shift into place, and the car rocketed off.

The many-tiered garage was crammed full of military vehicles. Someone was going to see them, someone was going to come—

On a downward turn, Ruhn collided with the side paneling, and the impact reverberated painfully through his body as Lidia let the car drift, drift—then punched it forward, flying down a ramp. Hunt let out a broken laugh, apparently impressed. Athalar cut it short, though.

Ruhn saw why a second later. The guard station. Six guards had been stationed around it: two angels, four wolves. They'd heard the racing car.

They hardly had time to notice Baxian at the gunner. They didn't even manage to raise their rifles or summon a spark of magic before the Helhound unleashed a hundred rounds of bullets. With the angle of the down-ramp, they stood right in his line of fire.

Blood sprayed in a mist as Lidia sailed through them—the car bumping over their bodies with sickening thuds. She shattered the barrier.

They burst into the sunlight, but there was no relief. They were now in the middle of the city, with enemies all around. Ruhn couldn't get a breath down.

A voice crackled over the radio—Declan Emmet's voice. "Daybright, you read?"

Hot tears began to streak down Ruhn's face.

Lidia shot the car down the long, wide stone bridge between the palace and the towering iron gates at its far end. Another guard station threatened ahead.

"Copy, Emmet," Lidia said into the radio, wincing as she had to take the wheel with her bandaged arm. Whatever had happened to her had to be brutal if she was still in pain. Something in his chest twisted to think of it. "We're approaching the bridge gates."

"Camera feeds are wonky. We lost track of you in the elevator bay. All there?" Dec said.

"All here," Lidia said, glancing at Ruhn.

"Thank fuck," Dec said, and Ruhn choked on a sob. Then Dec said, "Camera's showing twelve guards at the gate. Do not stop, Daybright. Go. I repeat, go, go, *go*."

They sped toward the guard station, headed directly for the array of soldiers with guns aimed at them. They looked uncertain at the sight of the Hind driving the car. Everyone knew that to piss her off was to die.

"Lidia," Baxian warned. There were too many to shoot at once, no matter how uncertain they were.

Lidia punched the jeep into the highest gear.

The nearest soldier—an angel—catapulted himself into the sky, aiming his rifle down at them. Athalar's lightning sparked, a feeble attempt to halt the death about to come down.

But it was Baxian, unleashing the machine gun again, who downed the soldier. The angel's wings flared as he plummeted, blood showering them in a ruby rain.

Lidia charged through the fray, ducking low as bullets flew. They careened through the barricade, wood exploding, the crystal palace of the Asteri looming behind them, a grim reminder of what they fled.

Then they were past the gates, splinters of wood still falling into the jeep as they cut hard down the nearest avenue. Tearing out of a nondescript alley, a white van fell in line with them, the sliding door open to reveal—

"Where *the fuck* is your hand?" Tristan Flynn shouted to Ruhn over the gunfire, a rifle at his shoulder. He fired behind them, again and again, and Baxian pivoted the gunner to the rear, unloading bullets onto the pursuing enemy.

Ruhn was well and truly crying then.

The van veered, and Flynn shouted, "Shit!" as it narrowly dodged a pedestrian—a draki female who shrieked, falling back against the wall of a building.

The radio crackled again, and a stranger's voice filled it. "Daybright, we're a go at Meridan."

Another voice: "We're a go at Alcene."

Another: "Ready at Ravilis."

On and on. Eleven locations total.

Then a soft female voice said, "This is Irithys. Set to ignite at the Eternal City."

"What the fuck is happening, Lidia?" Hunt breathed. They raced through the narrow city streets, the van with Flynn falling into line behind them. Hunt grunted, "Those are all places on the Spine."

Athalar was right: Every single city mentioned was a major depot along the vital railway that funneled imperial weapons to the front.

Lidia didn't take her eyes off the road as she picked up the radio. "This is Daybright. Blast it to Hel, Irithys."

Ruhn knew that name. He remembered the three sprites telling Bryce just a few weeks ago that their queen, Irithys, would want to hear of Lehabah's bravery. The lost Queen of the Fire Sprites.

"Consider it done," Irithys said.

And as they took another sharp turn onto a broad street, Ruhn's body bleating with pain as he again collided with the car door, an explosion bloomed on the other end of the city. An explosion so big that only someone made of fire might have caused it—

In the distance, another eruption sounded.

Ruhn could see it in his mind's eye: The line of exploding orange and red that raced up the continent. One depot after another after another, all exploding into nothing. The Hind had broken the Spine of Pangera with one fatal blow, ignited by the fire from the lost Sprite Queen.

Ruhn couldn't help but admire the symbolism of it, for the only race of Vanir who'd universally stood with Athalar during the Fallen rebellion to have lit this match. He caught a glimpse of Athalar's face—the awe and grief and pride shining there.

The entire land seemed to be rumbling with the impact from

the explosions. Lidia said, "We needed a distraction. Ophion and Irithys obliged."

Indeed, not one pedestrian or driver looked at the jeep or the van racing for the city walls. All eyes had turned to the north, to the train station.

Angels in imperial uniforms flew for it, blotting out the sun. Sirens wailed.

Even if word had gone out about their escape, the Eternal City—and all of Pangera—had bigger things to deal with.

"And Ophion needed a shot at survival," Lidia added. "So long as the Spine remained intact, they couldn't gain any ground."

She'd once told Ruhn that Ophion had been trying and failing to blow up the Spine for years now. Yet she'd done it. Somehow, she'd done it . . . for all of them.

They turned onto an even larger avenue, this one leading right out of the city, and Flynn's van pulled up beside them again. "We'll cover the highway. Get to the port!" he shouted. Lidia saluted the male, and Flynn winked at Ruhn before the van peeled away and the Fae lord slid the door shut.

But ahead of them, at the gate through the city walls, a light began flashing. An alarm blaring atop another guard station.

From the massive stone archway, a metal grate began to descend, preparing to seal the city. Trapping those responsible for the station attack inside—or trapping *them.*

The guards, all wolves in imperial uniforms, whirled toward them, and Ruhn winced as Baxian unleashed his bullets before they could draw their weapons. People shrieked along the sidewalks, fleeing into buildings and ducking behind parked cars.

"We're not going to make it," Baxian called as Lidia zoomed toward the guard station.

"Lidia," Athalar warned.

"Get down!" Lidia barked, and Ruhn shut his eyes, sinking low as the grate lowered at an alarming rate. Metal screamed and exploded right above them, the car rocking, shuddering—

Yet Lidia kept driving. She raced onto the open road beyond the city as the grate slammed shut behind them.

"Cutting it a little close, don't you think?" Hunt shouted to Lidia, and Ruhn opened his eyes to find that the gunner had been ripped clean off. Baxian was clinging for dear life to the back of the jeep, a manic grin on his face.

They had made it, and the closure of the city gate had sealed in any land-bound cars or patrols. Precisely as Lidia had planned, no doubt.

"That was the easy part," Lidia called over the wind, and the jeep sailed out into the countryside, into the olive groves and rolling hills beyond.

Ruhn stirred from where he'd collapsed against the side paneling. His wrist bled—the wound had reopened.

Declan said over the radio, "Let me talk to him."

For a heartbeat, Ruhn met Lidia's bright, golden eyes. Then she extended the radio to him. It was all Ruhn could do to clutch the radio in his good hand. *Good* being relative. His fingernails were gone.

"Hey, Dec," he groaned.

Declan laughed thickly—like he might have been holding back tears. "It's so fucking good to hear your voice."

Ruhn squeezed his eyes shut, throat working. "I love you. You know that?"

"Tell me again when I see you in an hour. You've got a Hel of a drive ahead. Put Daybright back on."

Ruhn silently handed the radio to Lidia, careful not to touch her. Not to look at her.

"This is Daybright," Lidia said, and Ruhn glanced behind them. A pillar of smoke rose from the part of the city where the glass domes of the train depot used to gleam.

"You want good news or bad news first?" Dec asked over the radio.

"Good."

"Most of the imperial security forces are at the train station, and the city is under lockdown. Irithys made it out—she vanished into the countryside. Off to wherever."

"I gave her instructions on where to go—what to do," Lidia said quietly. But then asked, "What's the bad news?"

"Mordoc and two dozen dreadwolves also made it out of the southwestern gate before it shut. I think they've figured out you're headed for the coast."

"Fuck," Athalar spat from the back seat.

"Flynn?" Lidia asked.

"Flynn's behind them. Mordoc and company are crossing onto your road. They'll be on your tail within ten minutes at your current speed. So go faster."

"I'm already driving at top speed."

"Then you'll have to find a way to ditch them."

Cold washed through Ruhn that had nothing to do with his injuries or bleeding arm. He dared himself to look at Lidia—really look at her.

She merely stared at the road ahead. The wind ripped strands of her golden hair free from the chignon high on her head. Calculation swirled in her eyes.

Baxian said over the wind, "They'll have every guard between here and the coast watching the road."

And they'd just lost their machine gun. Lidia reached for the holster at her thigh and handed her sidearm back to Athalar.

"That's all we have?" Athalar demanded, checking the bullets. Ruhn didn't need to look to know there weren't enough in the gun to get them through this.

"If I'd packed more, someone would have been suspicious," Lidia said coolly.

Declan's voice crackled over the radio. "What's the plan, Daybright?"

Ruhn watched her beautiful, perfect face. Watched as determination set her features. "Have the ship at the planned coordinates," she told Declan. "Ready the hatch for an aerial landing."

34

The Autumn King stayed holed up in his study for the rest of the day, so Bryce took the opportunity to go poking about. First in the kitchen, which was utilitarian enough that it was clearly built for a team of chefs. The walk-in fridge was, thankfully, stocked with freshly cooked food. She helped herself to some poached trout and herbed rice for lunch, along with a glass of the fanciest champagne she could find—swiped from a cold case in the massive wine cellar—and tried all the door handles to the outside once before settling for a walk through the villa halls.

She wandered past white columns and soaring atriums, expanses of floor-to-ceiling windows, and artfully concealed panels for tech. She'd opened a few of the latter as she walked, hoping for something to connect her to the outside world, but so far they had revealed only controls for the radiant flooring, the automatic blinds, and the air conditioner.

Bryce swigged directly from the bottle as she meandered through the basement. A gym, steam room, massage room, and a sauna occupied one wing. The other wing held an indoor lap pool, a screening room, and what seemed to be the Autumn King's security office. All the computers and cameras were dark and locked. No amount of trying to turn them on worked.

He'd thought of everything.

Cursing him to darkest Hel, she wandered through the ground level: a formal living room, the dining room, his study—doors shut in a quiet message to keep the fuck out—the kitchen again, a den, and a game room complete with a pool table and shuffleboard table.

None of the TVs worked. A check revealed that their power cords were missing. No interweb routers to be found, either.

She tried not to picture her mom here, young and innocent and trusting.

On the next level up, doors had been left open to reveal various guest rooms, all as beautiful and bland as her own. One wing was locked—surely her father's private suite.

Yet the double doors at the end of the other wing had been left unlocked. She opened them to a familiar scent that had her heart clenching.

Ruhn.

Posters of rock bands still hung on the walls. The massive four-poster bed with its black silk sheets was really the only sign of princely wealth. The rest screamed rebellious youth: ticket stubs taped by the mirror, a record of all the concerts he'd ever been to. A closet full of black shirts and jeans and boots, mixed with a jumble of discarded knives and swords.

It was a time capsule, frozen right before Ruhn returned from Avallen after enduring his Ordeal and emerging victorious with the Starsword. Had he even come back here, or had he immediately found a new place to live, knowing the sword gave him some degree of leverage over his father?

Or maybe it hadn't gone down like that at all. Maybe the Autumn King had kicked him out, jealous and bitter over the Starsword. Or maybe Ruhn had just up and left one day.

She'd never asked Ruhn about it. About so many things.

She opened the drawers of the desk by the window to discover a lighter, various drug paraphernalia, chewed-up cheap pens, and . . .

Her chest tightened as she pulled out the tub of silver nitrate balm. Grade A medwitch stuff—to treat burns. Her fingers clenched around the plastic, so hard it groaned. She set the tub carefully back into the drawer and sank onto Ruhn's bed. The gorsian shackles at her wrists shone faintly in the dim light.

Ruhn had gotten out of this festering place, and she was glad of it. She offered up a silent prayer to Cthona that she'd get to tell her brother that.

For right now, though, she was alone in this. And it was only a matter of time until the Autumn King's patience wore thin.

It was nothing short of miraculous, what the Hind had done. Declan, Flynn, and Ophion had helped, but Hunt knew that the female driving the car had orchestrated it all.

She'd somehow found Irithys, Queen of the Fire Sprites . . . and convinced her to be the spark to ignite this enormous, unheard-of attack. For the Fallen, for the sprites who had become Lowers for standing with them—the smallest among the Vanir, the outcasts—this blow had been for them. Struck by the person who would hold the most meaning to those looking for a sign.

Irithys was not only free in the world. She was on the attack.

Hunt shook his head in wonder and glanced to Ruhn, slumped against the passenger-side door.

The strike had been for the rebellion, Hunt knew, but the escape—the escape had been entirely for Ruhn.

"What do you mean, *aerial landing*?" Baxian demanded, panting heavily.

Lidia veered the car off the paved road, down a dirt lane that wended between the dry hills, and toward the mountains near the shore. The car bumped and shook on the dusty ground, and each of Hunt's injuries screamed. Ruhn moaned.

Lidia didn't answer, and pushed the car to its limit, winding up and around the hills, through the patchy shade of the olive trees flanking the road, the wind in their faces hot and dry.

Without warning, Lidia slammed on the brakes, the car skidding on the loose gravel. Hunt crashed into the back of the driver's seat, grimacing at the impact.

"Shit," Lidia hissed amid the swirling dust. "*Shit.*"

The dust cleared enough that Hunt could finally see what had triggered her sudden stop. A few feet ahead, the road had ended. A thick grove of olive trees blocked the way, too dense to even try to drive through.

"Lidia," Baxian demanded, and she twisted in her seat, looking at them.

"I'd hoped this road would take us closer to the water," she said, out of breath for the first time since Hunt had known her. She peered over a shoulder at Hunt, then at Baxian. "You'll have to get into the skies from here."

"What?" Ruhn demanded, trying to push himself up from where he'd been thrown against the passenger door.

But Lidia leapt out of the car without opening her own door. Her eyes were wild as she asked Hunt and Baxian, flinging open the back door, "Do you think you can fly?"

Hunt managed to crawl out of the back seat and stand, head spinning with pain and exhaustion. With a hand braced on the side of the car, he spread his newly formed wings.

Pain lanced down his back, sharp and deep. Gritting his teeth, Hunt made them move. Made them flap—once, twice. Their beats stirred the dirt and dust into clouds that gathered at their feet. "Yeah," he said roughly, fighting through the agony. "I think so."

On the other side of the jeep, Baxian was doing the same, black wings coated in dust. The Helhound nodded in agreement.

Lidia rushed over to the passenger door, dirt crunching beneath her boots, and heaved it open. Ruhn nearly fell into the dirt at her feet, but she caught him with her good arm. Hauled him over to Hunt, earning a glare from the Fae Prince as he fought to regain his footing. Lidia didn't so much as look down at Ruhn as she ordered Hunt and Baxian, "Carry him between you. The *Depth Charger* is waiting."

Hunt blinked, stepping up to help Ruhn stand. Pain again tore through him at the effort.

"What about you?" Baxian demanded, limping to Ruhn's other side. His dark wings dragged in the dirt.

Lidia lifted her chin. The sunlight danced over the silver of her torque as she did so. "I'm the bigger prize. Mordoc will go after me. It'll buy you time."

"I can carry you," Baxian insisted, even as he slid an arm under Ruhn's shoulders. Hunt could have sighed with relief at having the burden lessened.

Ruhn said nothing. Didn't even move as Baxian and Hunt kept him upright.

Lidia shook her head at the Helhound. "You're both at death's door. Take Ruhn and go." Her expression held no room for argument. *"Now,"* she snarled, and apparently the discussion was over, because she shifted.

Hunt had never seen Lidia in her deer form. She was lovely—her coat a gold so pale it was nearly white. Her golden eyes were framed by thick, dark lashes. A slice of darker gold slashed up between her eyes like a lick of flame.

Lidia looked at Ruhn, though. Only at him.

Half-dangling between Hunt and Baxian, Ruhn stared at her. Still said nothing.

The world seemed to hold its breath as the elegant doe walked up to Ruhn and gently, lovingly, nuzzled his neck.

Ruhn didn't so much as move. Not a blink as Lidia pulled away, those golden eyes lingering on his face—just a moment longer.

Then she bounded off into the trees, a streak of sunlight that was there and gone.

Like she'd never been.

Ruhn scanned the forest where Lidia had vanished, his hand rising to his neck. The skin there was warm, as if her touch still lingered.

"Right," Athalar grunted, stooping to reach for Ruhn's legs. "On three." Baxian tightened his grip under Ruhn's shoulders.

Wings stirred, and Ruhn stirred with them. "Lidia," he croaked.

But Athalar and Baxian jumped into the skies, both males groaning in agony, the world tilting—and then they were airborne, Athalar holding Ruhn's legs, Baxian at his shoulders.

Ruhn hung like a sack of potatoes. His stomach flipped at the dizzying drop to the arid ground far below. The mountain rising before them. The glittering blue sea stretching beyond.

Behind them, shooting among the olive trees like a bolt of lightning, raced that beautiful, near-white doe. A hind.

To reach the sea, she'd have to ascend through the hilly groves, and then right up the rocky mountain itself.

Was there a way down on the other side? She'd only mentioned an aerial landing when she'd spoken to Dec. Not a sea rescue. Or a land rescue.

Lidia wasn't coming.

The realization clanged through Ruhn like a death knell.

"Oh fuck," Athalar spat, and Ruhn followed the direction of the angel's gaze behind them.

A pack of two dozen dreadwolves streamed like ants through the forest. All headed straight for that deer.

A wolf larger than the others led the pack—Mordoc. Closing in fast on Lidia as the hills slowed her.

"Stop," Ruhn rasped. "We have to go back."

"No," Athalar said coldly, his grip tightening on Ruhn's legs.

Which was faster—a deer or a wolf?

If they caught up to her, it'd be over. Lidia had known that, and gone anyway.

"Put me down," Ruhn snarled, but the malakim held him firm, so hard his bones ached.

The wolves narrowed the distance, as if the hills were nothing to them. But Athalar and Baxian had caught an air current and were soaring swiftly enough now that Lidia rapidly shrank in the distance—

"PUT ME DOWN!" Ruhn roared, or tried to. His voice, hoarse from screaming, could barely rise above a whisper.

"Aerial legion from the east," Baxian announced to Hunt.

Ruhn looked up, following Athalar's line of sight. Sure enough, like a cloud of locusts, soldiers surged for them.

"Fuckers," Athalar hissed, wings beating faster. Baxian kept pace as they swooped toward the sea.

Farther from Lidia, who now neared the top of the towering

mountain. That was the last Ruhn saw of her as they soared over the arid peak.

Open ocean spread before them. Ruhn twisted, trying to keep an eye on Lidia.

His stomach dropped.

As if Ogenas herself had sliced it in half, the mountain's seaward side had been shaved off. There was nothing waiting for Lidia but a straight, lethal plunge to the water hundreds of feet below.

35

Hunt blocked out Ruhn's screams and cursing. He knew he'd have been in the same state if it had been Bryce out there, being run aground by two dozen dreadwolves. He'd made those sounds once, long ago—when Shahar and Sandriel had plummeted toward the earth, Shahar's blood streaming—

The glare of the sun on the sea made his head throb. Or maybe that was his injuries and exhaustion. Each flap of his wings sent agony rocking through him, threatening to steal his breath. He took it into his heart, though. Embraced the pain. He deserved every pulse of it.

But there, emerging from the water like a breaching whale . . .

A shining metal hatch cleared the surface. Then a person burst through it, waving frantically. And Hunt could only wonder if he was hallucinating as he realized it was Tharion signaling to them, urging them on from the narrow exterior deck atop the *Depth Charger.*

Hunt and Baxian dove, and Ketos leapt onto the nose of the mighty ship, shouting something that the wind devoured.

Toward the coast, angels were gaining speed, closing in. The cool spray of waves stung every inch of Hunt, salt burning in his open wounds. He half fell the last ten feet onto the soaked metal of the ship.

Tharion raced forward, face stark with urgency. "I said land *in* the hatch!" the mer yelled.

Hunt ground his teeth, but Ruhn had shot to his feet, swaying, dangerously close to falling into the water. "Lidia," he gasped to Tharion, pointing to the cliffs. He swayed again, and Tharion caught him. Ruhn gripped the mer's muscled forearm with his good hand. Tharion's eyes dropped to the prince's missing hand. The mer paled.

But Ruhn groaned, "You have to help her."

"This ship can't get any closer to shore," Tharion said placatingly.

"Not this ship," Ruhn snarled with impressive menace. *"You."*

Hunt eyed the mountain—the cliff looming like a giant at the distant shore. "Ruhn, even if Lidia can make it to the edge . . . that's a deadly drop." She'd be splattered on the surface of the water.

"Please," Ruhn said, voice breaking as he scanned Tharion's face.

Tharion looked to Hunt. Then Baxian. Apparently realized they were in no shape to fly another foot.

Tharion sighed but declared, "Always happy to provide the heroics." The mer passed the prince over to Baxian, and stripped out of his clothes. Utterly unconcerned by his nudity, the mer leapt into the cobalt swells and, a heartbeat later, his massive tail splashed the surface. He didn't look back before he disappeared under the water, a flash of orange against the blue.

Baxian began murmuring a prayer to Ogenas. It was all Hunt could do to join him.

Maybe this was his fault, too. If he'd stopped Bryce, stopped the others, from going up against the Asteri . . . none of them would be in this position. None of this would have happened.

But Ruhn stayed silent throughout. Eyes fixed on the shore, face pale as death. As if he could see all the way to the shifter on the cliffs, racing for her life.

Every breath burned Lidia's lungs.

Each galloping step was uphill, nothing but dry, treacherous stones and snaking roots underneath. So many roots, all intent on tripping her delicate hooves.

This hadn't been part of the plan. She'd been a fool to take that road, not knowing where it would end, that it would strand her in the arid foothills with a mountain to climb.

But Ruhn and the angels had made it. Would be on the ship by now.

Irithys had made it out, to go do what needed doing. At least her trust in the queen hadn't been misplaced. At least that much had gone right.

Snarls filled the scrub behind her, and Lidia recognized them all.

Her dreadwolves. Her soldiers. The deepest snarl, unnervingly close behind, was Mordoc.

Lidia pushed herself faster, harder. Found a switchback trail—a deer path, ironically enough—up the mountain. A legion of angels loomed like thunderclouds in the sky.

She had to get to the water. If she could make it to the sea, she might stand a chance at swimming to the ship.

Brush snapped to her left, and Lidia leapt toward a boulder just as Mordoc crashed through the scrub and trees, jaws snapping.

He missed her by inches.

Mordoc rebounded against the rock below and leapt upward again. He'd clear the boulder and be on her soon. Right on his tail were Vespasian and Gedred, his favored torturers and hunters—*her* favored torturers and hunters. Foam streamed from their maws as they scaled the rocks.

Lidia leapt again, higher onto the boulder, then atop it. The wolves couldn't jump as far, but she didn't wait to see them try as she dashed across the rock's broad top, then upward again.

Branches and thorns ripped at her fur, her legs.

The scent of her own blood filled her nose, coppery and thick. Her hooves slipped against the loose stones, the sound like bones clacking. There had to be some path around the side of the mountain, some way to round it and get down its other side to the water below—

There. Up another quarter mile. A ledge that curved around the mountain. She plunged ahead, and the snarls behind her closed in again. She had to get to the ledge. Had to reach the water.

She couldn't cry in this body, but she nearly did as she at last reached the curve around the mountain. As the ledge jutted out before her.

Like a long finger, it stretched high above the sea and rock five hundred feet below. The rest of the mountain was a sheer cliff face.

There was no other way down. No way back.

From the way her hooves dug into the stone, she could tell the rock was some sort of soft material that would crumble in her hands if she tried to climb down the cliff in her humanoid form. That is, if Mordoc and the others didn't shoot her off it first.

Mordoc's vicious snarl sounded behind her, and Lidia looked back, then, right as he shifted. The wolves behind him did the same.

So Lidia shifted into her humanoid form as well. Panting hard, reorienting her senses to this body, she backed a step toward the edge.

Vespasian, at Mordoc's left, drew a rifle. Pointed it at her.

"This seems familiar," Mordoc panted, a wild light in his eyes. "What was it that you told that thunderbird bitch?"

Lidia backed away another step, as Gedred, too, drew and aimed her rifle.

Mordoc spat on the dry ground, then wiped his mouth with the back of his hand. "Are you faster than a bullet? That's what you asked Sofie Renast that night." Her captain laughed, too-large teeth flashing. "Let's see, *Lidia*. Let's see how fast you are now, you traitorous cunt."

Lidia's gaze darted between Vespasian and Gedred. She found no mercy on their faces. Only hate and rage. They were dreadwolves who had let a hind lead them. And she had betrayed them.

Now they'd make her pay.

The shots wouldn't be to kill her. They'd lame her, as she had done with Sofie Renast, so they could drag her back to the Asteri to be ripped to shreds. Either by them or Pollux.

The shouts of the aerial legion drew closer from above. Was Pollux with them? Leading the swarm of angels to grab her?

Death lay behind her, at the end of the ledge. Swift, forgiving death.

The sort she'd be denied by the Asteri. If she could make it to the end of the cliff . . . it would be fast.

She'd fall, and her head would splatter on the rocks, and she'd likely feel very little. Perhaps a swift burst of pain, then nothing.

Even if she would never see what she had worked for, hoped for.

Lidia shoved that thought behind her. As she had always done.

Gedred knelt, rifle braced against a shoulder. Ready to fire.

So Lidia reached up to the silver torque around her neck. A flick of her fingers and it snapped free. "Since we're repeating the past, I suppose I'll tell you what Sofie told me that night." She flung the torque, that hateful collar, into the dirt and smiled at Mordoc, at the dreadwolves. *"Go to Hel."*

Then she broke into a run. Faster than she'd ever sprinted in this human form, hurtling toward the cliff edge. Two bullets landed at her heels, and she veered to the side, easily dodging the third.

She'd taught these dreadwolves everything they knew. She used it against them now.

"Shoot that bitch!" Mordoc screamed at his snipers.

Lidia's life diluted into each step. Each pump of her arms. Bullets sprayed rock and shrapnel at her feet. Only a few more steps.

"END HER!" Mordoc roared.

But the cliff edge was there—and then she was over it.

Lidia sobbed as she leapt, as the open air embraced her. As the rocks and surf spread below.

For a heartbeat, she thought the water might be rising to meet her.

But that was her. Falling.

A gunshot cracked like a thunderhead breaking. Pain ruptured through her chest, bone shattering, red washing over her vision.

Lidia let out a choked, bloody laugh as she died.

36

Jesiba Roga moved Ithan from the bar pretty damn quickly after he'd said precisely who he wanted to raise from the dead. He found himself transported to an office—her office, apparently—crammed full of crates and boxes of what had to be relics for her business.

She shoved him into a chair in front of a massive black desk, took a seat on the other side in a tufted white velvet armchair, and ordered him to tell her everything.

Ithan did. He needed her help, and he knew he wouldn't get it without honesty.

When he finished, Roga leaned back in her seat, the dim golden light from her desk lamp gilding her short platinum hair.

"Well, this wasn't how I expected my evening to go," the sorceress said, rubbing her groomed brows. On the built-in bookshelf behind her sat three glass terrariums filled with various small creatures. People she had turned into animals? For their sake, he hoped not.

But maybe she could turn him into a worm and step on him. That'd be a mercy.

Jesiba's eyes gleamed, as if sensing his thoughts. But she said quietly, "So you want a necromancer to raise this Sigrid Fendyr."

"It hasn't been very long," Ithan said. "Her body is probably still fresh enough that—"

"I don't need a wolf to tell me the rules of necromancy."

"Please," Ithan rasped. "Look, I just . . . I fucked up."

"Did you?" A cold, curious question.

He swallowed against the dryness in his throat as he nodded. "I was supposed to rescue her—and she was supposed to make the Fendyrs better, to save everyone."

Roga crossed her arms. "From what?"

"From Sabine. From how fucking *awful* the wolves have become—"

"As far as I remember, the wolves were the ones who raced to Asphodel Meadows this spring."

"Sabine refused to let us go."

"Yet you defied her and went anyway. The others followed you."

"I'm not here to debate wolf politics."

"But this *is* politics. You raise Sigrid, and . . . what then? Have you thought that through?"

Ithan growled, "I need to fix it."

"And you think a necromancer will solve that problem."

He bared his teeth. "I know what you're thinking—"

"You don't even know what *you're* thinking, Ithan Holstrom."

"Don't talk to me like—"

She lifted a finger. "I will remind you that you are in *my* House, and asking for a gargantuan favor. You came here uninvited, which itself is a violation of our rules. So unless you want me to hand you over to the vamps to be sucked dry and left to rot on the dock, I suggest you check that tone, pup."

Ithan glared, but shut his mouth.

Roga smiled slightly. "Good dog."

Ithan reined in his growl. She smiled wider at that.

But after a moment she said, "Where's Quinlan?"

"I don't know."

Roga nodded to herself. "I do nothing for free, you know."

He met her stare, letting her see that he'd give her whatever she wanted. Her lips pursed with distaste at his desperation. He didn't care.

"Most necromancers," she continued, "are arrogant pricks who will fuck you over."

"Great," he muttered.

"But I know one who might be trustworthy."

"Name your price. And theirs."

"I told you already: I need a competent assistant. As far as memory serves, you were a history major at CCU." At his questioning look, she said, "Quinlan used to prattle on and *on* about how proud of you she was." His chest ached unbearably. Roga rolled her eyes, either at her words or at whatever was on his face, then gestured to the crates and boxes around her. "As you can see, I have goods that need sorting and shipping."

Ithan slowly blinked. "You mean . . . work for you, and you'll get me in touch with this necromancer?"

A dip of her chin.

"But I need it done *now*," he said, "while her body's still fresh—"

"I shall arrange to have the body transported from wherever the Viper Queen has thrown it, and keep it . . . on ice, as it were. Safe and sound. Until the necromancer becomes available."

"Which is how long?"

Her lips curved. "What's the rush?"

He couldn't answer. He didn't believe *The weight of my own guilt is killing me and I can't stand it another moment* would make any difference to her.

"Let's start with a couple days, Holstrom. A couple honest days of work . . . and we'll assess whether you do a good enough job to merit the aid you seek."

"I could walk right out of here and ask the nearest necromancer—"

"You could, but the vamps might take a bite before you can. Or you might ask the wrong necromancer and wind up . . . unsatisfied."

Jesiba opened her laptop. She typed in her password, then said without looking up from the screen, "That big crate marked *Lasivus* needs unpacking and cataloging. There's an extra laptop on the credenza over there. Password *JellyJubilee*. Both words capitalized, no spaces. Don't give me that look, Holstrom. Quinlan set it."

Ithan blinked again. But slowly got to his feet. Walked to the crate.

He summoned his claws, using them in lieu of a crowbar, and pried the lid off the crate. It landed on the carpeted floor with a dull thud and a spray of dust.

"You break it, Holstrom," the sorceress drawled from her desk as she typed away, "you buy it."

Wasn't that the truth.

Bryce didn't see the Autumn King for the rest of the day. She foraged dinner from the kitchen so she didn't need to endure another meal and game of twenty questions with him.

She was carrying her plate up to her bedroom when her captor appeared at the top of the stairs. "I was looking for you."

Bryce lifted the plate and the ham-and-butter sandwich atop it. "And I'm looking to eat. Bye."

The Autumn King remained directly in her path as she crested the stone steps. "I want to talk to you."

She peered up at him, hating that he stood taller than her. But she managed to give him a look down her nose—one that had worked wonders on irritating Hunt when they'd first met. And despite herself and all that had happened between them, she asked, "Why haven't you cleared out Ruhn's old room?"

He angled his head. Clearly, he hadn't been expecting a question like that. "Is there a reason I should have done so?"

"Seems awfully sentimental of you."

"I have ten other bedrooms in this house. Should I ever need his, I will have it cleared."

"That's not an answer."

"Is there a specific answer you're looking for?"

She opened her mouth to bite out a reply, but shut it. She surveyed him coolly.

He said a shade quietly, "Go ahead and ask."

"Do you ever wonder?" she blurted. "What might have happened if you hadn't sent your goons to hunt us down, or hadn't tossed me to the curb when I was thirteen?"

His eyes flickered. "Every single day."

"Then why?" Her voice cracked a bit. "You hit her, and then felt bad about it—you still feel bad about it. Yet you hunted us down, nearly killed her in the process. And when I showed up years later, you were nice to me for, like, two days before you kicked me out."

"I don't answer to you."

She shook her head, disgust chasing away any trace of appetite. "I don't get it—get *you*."

"What is there to get? I am a king. Kings do not need to explain themselves."

"Fathers do."

"I thought you wanted nothing to do with me."

"And that hasn't changed. But why not be a nice fucking person?"

He stared at her for a long, unbearable moment with that look she knew she so often had on her own face. The expression she'd inherited from him, cold and merciless.

He said, "Here I was, thinking you had a *real* father in Randall Silago and didn't have any need of me whatsoever."

She nearly dropped her plate. "Are you—are you *jealous* of Randall?"

His face was like stone, but his voice hoarsened as he said, "He got your mother in the end. And got to raise you."

"That sounds awfully close to regret."

"I have already told you: I live with that regret every day." He surveyed her, the plate of food in her hands. "But perhaps we might eventually move past it." He added after a moment, "Bryce."

She didn't know what to feel, to think, as he spoke her name.

Without her last name attached, without any sort of sneer. But she cleared her throat and replied, "You help me find a way to get Hunt and Ruhn out of the Asteri dungeons, and then we can talk about you becoming a better dad." She said the last words as she stepped around him, heading for her bedroom. Even if she no longer wanted to eat, she needed to put some distance between them, needed to think—

Her father called after her, "Who said Athalar and Ruhn are still in the dungeons? They haven't been since this morning."

Bryce halted and turned slowly.

"Where are they?" Her voice had gone dead—quiet. The way she knew his voice went when his temper flared.

But her father only crossed his arms, smug as a cat. "That's the big question, isn't it? They escaped. Vanished into the sea, if rumor is to be believed."

Bryce let the words sink in. "You . . . you let me think they were in the dungeons. When you knew all along they were free."

"They *were* in the dungeons when you arrived. Their status has now changed."

"Did you know it was about to change?" White, blinding fury filled her head, her eyes. Even as part of her wondered if he, too, had needed some distance between them after their conversation, and revealing this truth . . . it was his best way to shove her away again.

"I answered your questions, as you stipulated. You asked where the Asteri took them after your encounter. I told you the truth. You didn't ask for an update today, so—"

One heartbeat, the plate and sandwich were in her hands. The next, they were hurling through the air toward his head. "You *asshole*."

Her father blasted away both plate and food with a wall of fire. Cinders of crisped bread and meat fell to the floor among shards of broken ceramic.

"Such tantrums," he said, surveying the mess on the carpet, "from someone who just learned her brother and mate are free."

"How about this," Bryce seethed, hating the gorsian shackles around her wrists more than ever. "You let me go right now, and I'll toss your ass straight through a portal and into the original Fae world. Go pack your bags."

He chuckled. "You'll bring me to that Fae world whether I let you go or not."

"Oh yeah?"

"I hear your mother and Randall have adopted a son. It'd be a shame if something happened to the boy."

She rolled her eyes. "Don't come crying to me when Mom and Randall kick your ass. They did it once—I'm sure they'll be happy to remind you what they're capable of."

"Oh, it wouldn't be me darkening their doorstep." He smirked, wholly confident. "A whisper to Rigelus, let's say, of your parents harboring a rebel boy . . ."

Bryce rolled her eyes again. "Did you take some sort of class in school? Intro to Bad Guys? Get fucking serious. You're not going to conquer any world."

"If you should open a door between worlds at my behest, Rigelus may be grateful enough to me that he grants me a good chunk of it."

Bryce eyed the shards of broken plate. Sharp enough to slit his throat.

He gave her a condescending smile, like he knew what she was contemplating.

Her father wasn't for or against the Asteri. He was just an opportunist. If removing them got him more power, he'd fight them. If bowing to the Asteri proved more lucrative, he'd prostrate himself before their crystal thrones. For all his talk of helping the Fae, he believed in nothing except advancing himself.

She said tightly, "You're already a king here."

"Of a continent. What is that to an entire planet?"

"You know, you might not be the Starborn Chosen One, but I think out of all of us, you've got the most in common with Theia. She thought the same damn thing. But she learned too late that Rigelus doesn't share."

"With the knife you brought back in play, he might find himself willing to bargain."

Bryce gave him a flat look. "What makes you think the blades will do anything to him?"

"Those blades, united, would end him."

"Trust me: I tried it on an Asteri and it didn't do anything." At least, not before Nesta had interfered.

If he was shocked by her confession, he didn't let on. "Did you *order* them to work?"

"Hard to order them, shithead, when I don't know what they can even do."

"Open a portal to nowhere," the Autumn King said, the flame guttering in his eyes.

"What do you mean?" Bryce demanded.

"The Starsword is Made, as you called it." He waved an idle hand, sparks at his fingertips. "The knife can Unmake things. Made and Unmade. Matter and antimatter. With the right influx of power—a command from the one destined to wield them—they can be merged. And they can create a place where no life, no light exists. A place that is nothing. Nowhere."

Her knees wobbled. "That's not . . . that's not possible."

"It is. I read about it in the Avallen Archives centuries ago."

"Then how do I do it? Just say 'merge into nowhere' and that's that?"

"I don't know," he admitted. "My research has not revealed the steps to merge the blades. Only what they could do."

Bryce stared at the male before her for a long moment. Glanced down the steps to the lower level—toward his study. "I want to see this research myself."

"It is on Avallen, and females are not allowed beyond the lobby of the archives."

"Yeah, our periods would probably get all over the books."

His lip curled. "Perhaps it is lucky you weaseled out of your engagement to Cormac. Your coarseness wouldn't have been well tolerated in Avallen."

"Oh, they'd warm up to me once they saw me swinging around the Starsword and remembered who and what I am."

"That would be an affront all on its own. A female has never possessed the blade."

"What?" She barked a laugh that echoed off the stone walls. "In fifteen thousand years, you mean to tell me only males have claimed it?"

"As females are not allowed in the Cave of Princes, they had no opportunity to attempt to claim it, even if they had the starlight in their veins."

Bryce gaped at him. "Are you fucking kidding me? They banned females from the Cave of Princes to keep us from getting our hands on the sword?"

His silence was answer enough.

She snapped, "I'm pretty sure there are rules, even in this shitty empire, against treating females like that."

"Avallen has long been left mostly to govern itself, its ways hidden from the modern world behind its mists."

"But there's information, somewhere on Avallen, about what these blades can do."

"Yes, but you must be invited in order to cross the mists. And considering where you stand with Morven . . ."

She was never getting in. Certainly not without the assistance of the male before her.

Her head swam, and for a heartbeat, everything that she had done and still had to do weighed so heavily she could barely breathe.

"I need to go lie down," she rasped.

The Autumn King didn't stop her as she again turned toward her bedroom. Like he knew he'd won.

She strode in silence down the hall, steps muffled by the stone.

But not to her room. Instead, she walked all the way to Ruhn's room, where she collapsed onto the bed. She didn't move for a long while.

37

Ruhn's life had become beeping machines and flickering monitors and an uncomfortable vinyl chair that served as both seat and bed.

He technically had a bed, but it was too far from this room. A few times, Flynn and Dec had come to sedate him and drag him there for a restorative treatment, as his hand was still recovering.

His fingers had formed again, but they were pale and weak. The medwitches had a small store of firstlight potions—a rarity on a ship where firstlight was banned and they relied on some sort of jacked-up bioluminescence to light everything—but Ruhn had refused them. Had demanded that they give every last drop to Lidia. His hand would heal the old-fashioned way. Whether he and Baxian would ever recover from the ordeal that had led to his hand being chewed off was another story.

But one he'd deal with later.

"Get some sleep," Flynn said from the doorway, a cup of what smelled like coffee in hand. His friend nodded to the bed and wires and machines before Ruhn. "I can take watch."

"I'm fine," Ruhn rasped. He'd barely spoken since yesterday. Didn't want to talk to anyone. Not even Flynn and Dec, though they'd come for him. Had saved him.

All because of this female before him.

While they'd been rebuilding what was left of her body, she'd flatlined twice. Even with the firstlight potion having healed the wounds to her heart. Both times, Ruhn had been sleeping in his own bed, halfway across the damned ship.

So he'd stopped leaving this room.

That there was anything left of Lidia at all was thanks to Tharion, whose cushioning plume of water had shielded her from the full impact of landing on the rocks—but the mer had still been far enough away that it hadn't stopped her plunge entirely.

It didn't matter though, because a hole as big as a fist had already been shot through her heart.

The hole was gone, healed now thanks to that rare, precious firstlight potion. And she had a functioning heart again, if the monitor marking every beat was any indication. Lungs: repaired. Ribs: rebuilt. Cracked skull: patched together. Brains stuffed back in.

Ruhn couldn't stop seeing it. How Lidia had looked when Tharion had hauled her onto the *Depth Charger.* Her limp body. So . . . small. He'd never realized how much smaller she was than him.

Or what the world might be like without her living in it.

Because Lidia had been dead. When Tharion had carried her back from the coast, she'd been completely dead. Even her Vanir healing abilities had been overtaxed.

Something had broken in Ruhn at the sight of it. Something even Pollux and the Hawk and the Asteri's dungeons hadn't managed to reach.

So the ship's medwitches had emptied their stores of firstlight potions on Lidia. Then Athalar had used his lightning to jumpstart her heart, because even liquid miracles weren't enough to get it beating again. Had used it three times now, because the crash cart had taken too long to fire up when she'd flatlined.

When Ruhn asked how he knew to try such a thing, the angel had muttered something about thanking Rigelus for the idea, and left it at that. Ruhn had been too relieved at the sound of Lidia's thumping heart to ask more.

"Ruhn, buddy—you gotta sleep." Flynn finally stepped into the room, dropping into the chair beside his. "If she gets up, I'll call you. If she even *moves*, I will call you."

Ruhn just stared at the too-pale female on the bed.

"Ruhn."

"The last thing I said to her," Ruhn whispered, "was that she was dead to me."

Flynn blew out a breath. "I'm sure she knew you didn't mean it."

"I did mean it."

His friend swallowed. "I didn't realize things between you guys had become so . . . intense."

"She did all this to save me anyway," he said, ignoring Flynn's unspoken request to fill him in.

The guilt of it would eat him alive. She'd done horrible things as the Hind, both before and after becoming Daybright, things he couldn't forget, yet . . . his head was spinning with it. The rage and guilt and that other thing.

Flynn squeezed his shoulder. "Go sleep, Ruhn. I've got your girl."

She wasn't his girl. She wasn't anything to him.

Yet he still ignored Flynn. Didn't move from the chair, though he closed his eyes. Focused on his breathing until sleep loomed.

"Stubborn asshole," Flynn muttered, but threw a blanket over Ruhn anyway.

Day, Ruhn said into the void between them, as he had nearly every hour now. *Day—can you hear me?*

No answer.

Lidia.

He'd never addressed her by her name before. Even in here.

He tried again, sending it out into the void like a plea. *Lidia.*

But the darkness only howled in answer.

"So," Hunt said to Tharion as they sat in the empty mess hall of the *Depth Charger*, "the Viper Queen, huh?"

Tharion picked at his poached fish and fine strands of seaweed salad. "Let's not get into it, Athalar." They'd missed lunch, but had been able to scrounge up plates of leftovers from the cooks.

"Fair enough." Hunt flexed his wings, now fully back to their usual strength, thanks to that firstlight Lidia had manipulated her way into giving him. "Thanks for coming to pick us up."

Tharion lifted his stare—bleak, empty.

Hunt knew the feeling. Was trying not to feel that way every second of every minute. Was drowning under it, now that he and his friends were here, safe, without the physical torture to distract him.

"Holstrom said we're a pack," Tharion said. "I don't necessarily appreciate the canine comparison, but I like the sentiment. As soon as Lidia told us you guys were days away from being executed . . . we had to do what was necessary." Sort of. It hadn't been as easy as that, of course, but once he'd been out of the Meat Market, he'd been all in.

Hunt had gotten the rundown yesterday of all that had happened. Or at least some of it. Considering that Lidia remained unconscious, he still had no idea what she'd done on her end to organize everything.

It was all so unlikely, so impossible.

He'd awoken last night, drenched in sweat, convinced he was back in those dungeons. It had taken him switching the lights on to accept the reality of his surroundings. Those initial seconds in the pitch black, when he couldn't tell where he was, were unbearable.

He wished Bryce were with him. Not just to sleep beside him, and to remind him that he'd made it out, but . . . he needed his best friend.

Bryce was gone, though. And that fact, too, woke him from slumber. Dreams of her tumbling through space, alone and lost forever.

Tharion seemed to sense the shift in his thoughts, because he asked quietly, "How you holding up, Athalar?"

"Wings are back to normal," Hunt said, folding them tightly behind him. "Emotionally . . . ?" He shrugged. He'd sat in the shower for an hour last night, the water near-scalding as it rinsed away the filth and blood of the dungeon. As he had in those days before Bryce, he'd let the water scourge the dirt and the darkness from him. But there was one marking that couldn't be washed away.

Tharion's eyes now drifted to Hunt's brow. "They're monsters to do that to you again." Hot anger sharpened the mer's face.

"They're monsters with or without putting the halo back on me." Hunt lifted his wrist, exposing the brand. The *C* that had been stamped there, negating it, was gone. "You think a slave can still be a prince?"

"I'm sure those Fae assholes have some regulations forbidding it," Tharion said with a wry smile, "but if there's anyone who could get around them, it's Bryce."

Hunt blocked out the pain in his chest. He couldn't bear to imagine the look of sorrow and rage that would creep over her face when she saw the halo, the brand. If she ever came back.

That last thought was more unbearable than any other.

Hunt forced himself past it and asked Tharion, "How are you doing?"

"About the same as you, but hanging in there." Tharion picked at his food again. Shadows seemed to swim in his brown eyes. "Taking it hour by hour."

"No word from Holstrom?"

Tharion shook his head, dark red hair shifting with the motion. The mer set down his fork at last. "What now?"

"Honestly?" Hunt braced his forearms on the metal table. "I don't know. Yesterday, my main goal was not dying. Today? All I can think about is where Bryce is, how to find her." And how he'd live with himself in the meantime.

"You really think she's in some other world?"

The blazing lights of the mess hall bounced off the metallic surface of the table in a bright blur. "If she's not in Hel, then yes—I hope she's in another world, and safely so."

"We'll figure out some way to get her back here."

Hunt didn't bother telling the mer it was likely impossible. Bryce was the one person on Midgard who could open a portal capable of bringing her home.

He just said, "Bryce would want me to get the word out—about what she learned regarding the Asteri. So I figure I'll start with the Ocean Queen. She's not allied with Ophion, but she seems to . . . help them." He gestured to the ship around them.

"Ah," Ketos said wryly. "And I thought you found me in my bunk to do lunch."

"I did. I wanted to see how you were," Hunt said, then admitted, "but I also wanted to see if you had any sort of in."

"With the Ocean Queen?" Tharion laughed, cold and hollow. "Might as well ask if I've got an in with Ogenas herself."

"She's gone to all this trouble to help the enemies of the Asteri," Hunt said, drumming his fingers on the table. "I want to know why."

Tharion studied his face with a scrutiny that reminded Hunt why Ketos had been made the River Queen's Captain of Intelligence. Hunt let the mer see the pure determination that flowed through him.

"All right," Tharion said gravely. "I'll see what I can do. Though . . ." He winced.

"What?"

"Considering what happened with her sister and niece . . . it might not go well."

"You're on this ship, and no one has tried to kill you or send you back to the River Queen—that must mean something."

"I think it has more to do with Lidia's importance than mine, much as that kills me to say." Tharion sighed through his nose. "And believe me, from the moment I got onto this ship, I've taken no shortage of shit about defecting from the River Queen. I'm pretty much a pariah."

"Well . . . maybe there's a way to use it to your advantage to lure the Ocean Queen here for a meeting."

Tharion crossed his muscular arms. "I'd rather not."

"Think about it," Hunt said. "Whatever you can stomach doing . . . I'd appreciate it."

Tharion dragged his long fingers through his red hair. "Yeah. Yeah, I know." Tharion shifted on the metal bench to pull a phone from his skintight wetsuit. He began typing. "I'll see if Sendes is free to talk." He got to his feet with fluid grace. "I'll let you know if I get anywhere."

Not an ember of the mer's usual spark lit his eyes.

"Thanks," Hunt said. "Keep me posted." Tharion nodded and strode off, still typing away.

Hunt finished his own plate of fish, then the rest of Tharion's, before he left the mess hall. The ship halls were quiet. Using the walk to stretch and test the strength of his healed wings, he strode in silence along the glass-lined corridors, nothing but dark ocean beyond. All that crushing water held back by the Ocean Queen's magic. Hunt could only marvel.

He hadn't gone back to the biodome a few levels up. Couldn't bear to see where he and Bryce had officially become mates.

He found Baxian in the gym they'd been assigned—one of dozens on this ship, and the closest to their living quarters—doing chest presses.

"You need a spotter for that much weight," Hunt warned, pausing near the bench where the angel shifter grunted under the bar, dark wings splayed beneath him. "You should have asked."

"You weren't in your room," Baxian said as he lowered the bar to his bare, muscled chest. Sweat dribbled down the groove between his pecs, his brown skin gleaming. Shreds of the tattoo across his heart—*Through love, all is possible*, inked in Danika's handwriting—remained. How he'd ever get it replaced . . . Hunt's own heart strained.

Baxian went on, "And when I asked the sprites if they'd seen you, they said you were off *doing lunch*."

Hunt had stopped by the small interior room where Malana, Sasa, and Rithi had holed up since arriving, to ask if they wanted to join him and Tharion. They were at a low, constant level of panic being down here, under the water. But they hadn't wanted to come to lunch. Didn't want to see the ship, or any indication that an endless ocean was all around them. So they stayed in their windowless room, binge-watching some inane reality TV show about realtors selling beach villas in the Coronal Islands, and pretended they weren't surrounded by a giant death trap for their kind.

It had pained him to see them gathered around the TV earlier. Lehabah would have loved them. Lehabah should have been there, with them. With all of them.

Baxian kept his eyes on the weights he'd been lifting. "I needed to get in here for a bit."

"Why?"

"Bad thoughts" was all Baxian said.

"Ah." Likely ones that included the taste of Ruhn's blood in his mouth. Hunt silently stepped behind the bench, within reach of the bar as Baxian lifted it again, arms shaking. He easily had six hundred pounds on it. "What number is this?"

"Eighty," Baxian grunted, arms straining, wings splayed beneath him. Hunt took it upon himself to guide the bar back to its posts. "I want to get to a hundred."

"Baby steps, buddy."

Baxian panted up at the ceiling, then his eyes slid toward Hunt, watching him upside down. "What's up?"

"Just checking in on a friend."

"I'm fine," Baxian said, curling upward and bracing his hands on his thighs. His wings drooped to the black plastic tiles.

Hunt knew it was a lie, but he nodded anyway. If Baxian wanted to talk, he'd talk.

He'd told Baxian everything while they'd lain in the medwitch's room yesterday, in between stitches and potions and pain. Told him about Bryce, and the Hind, and all the shit they'd learned.

Baxian had taken it well, though he clearly remained in shock about the Hind's involvement. Hunt didn't blame him. He still had trouble believing it himself. But Baxian had been working with Lidia for even longer than Hunt—it'd probably take longer to adjust his image of her.

Baxian nodded to Hunt's face. "Any luck getting that shit removed?"

Hunt didn't dare look at the wall of mirrors behind the Helhound. Hadn't been able to stand the sight of his face with that halo once again marring his brow. He could have sworn its ink seared him every now and then. It had never done that before—but this halo, inked by Rigelus, felt different. Worse. Alive, somehow.

"No," Hunt said. "Hypaxia Enador got rid of it the last time. So unless there's a witch-queen hiding on this ship, I've gotta learn to live with it for the time being."

"Rigelus is a fucking asshole. Always was." Baxian wiped the sweat from his brow with the back of his hand.

Hunt angled his head. "What changed with you, really? Is this new Baxian Argos just the result of learning Danika was your mate?"

It was a potential minefield, to bring up his dead mate. To lose a mate was to lose half of your soul; to live without them was torture.

"I don't want to talk about the past," Baxian said, wings snapping in tight to his body, and Hunt let it drop.

"Then let's talk about next steps," Hunt said, folding his own wings with a lingering whisper of tightness. Another day and he'd be totally back to normal.

"What's there to talk about? Big picture: the Asteri have to go."

Hunt snorted. "Glad we're on the same page." He could only pray that Tharion was able to get Sendes to contact the Ocean Queen—and that she might be on the same page as them, too.

He surveyed the male he thought he'd known for so many years. "Is it too much to hope that some of Sandriel's old triarii might also be secret anti-imperialists?"

"Don't push your luck. Two's already huge. Three, if we include you."

Thankfully, he'd never been in her actual triarii—just had to put up with their shit while surviving the years he'd been shackled to Sandriel. Hunt ignored the familiar shiver of dread at the memory of those years and asked, "But you and Lidia never had any idea that you both were—"

"No. None. I thought she was no better than Pollux." Baxian wiped more sweat from his brow, his breath steadying. "You think Lidia will make it?"

Hunt rubbed his jaw. "I hope so. We need her."

"For what?"

Hunt gave his old enemy—now friend, he supposed—a slash of a smile. "To make these fuckers pay for what they've done."

Tharion told himself to snap out of it. To focus on the fact that, against all odds, they'd succeeded in rescuing their friends from the Asteri dungeons—had even gone a step beyond and saved Lidia Cervos from certain death.

It didn't matter, though. Holstrom had stayed behind. Holstrom, whose life Tharion had wrecked.

And not only Holstrom's life, but the future of the wolves, too. That Fendyr heir was dead because of him. Technically because of Holstrom, but . . . none of it would have happened if it weren't for Tharion's own choices.

He hadn't let anyone catch wind of the past day he'd spent since getting on this ship puking up his guts. Partially from the withdrawal to the Viper Queen's venom, but also from sheer disgust at all he'd done, what he'd become.

Ariadne had been sold off, the gods knew where. To whom. And fine, she hadn't been technically *sold*, because the Viper Queen hadn't owned her, but . . . she'd left to avoid having to kill Holstrom. Or so the Viper Queen had let her believe, getting the advantageous trade while planning all along to put Sigrid in the ring against Ithan.

If there was a level below rock bottom, Tharion had found it.

He forced himself to stop grinding his teeth and concentrate on Sendes. She stood in the center of the bridge, taking a report from one of her soldiers.

None of the other technicians or officers on the bridge spoke to him. None even looked his way.

At least no one here called him a traitor. But they all knew he'd defected from the River Queen. And given how little she was liked on this ship, he knew it had more to do with the fact that he'd defected from the *mer*. From them.

He wanted to shout to this whole bridge that if he could, he'd defect from himself.

Sendes turned at last when she'd dismissed her soldier. "Sorry about that."

Tharion waved her off. Considering how much they owed Sendes and this ship, she never needed to apologize to him for anything. "I feel like this is all I say these days, but I wanted to ask for a favor."

She smiled faintly. "Go ahead."

He braced himself. "If I wanted to get in touch with the Ocean Queen, arrange a meeting between her, me, and Hunt Athalar . . . could you facilitate it?"

Sendes's throat bobbed. Not a good sign.

"If it'll put you in a weird position," Tharion amended, "don't worry about it. But I told Athalar I'd ask you, and—"

"You'll get your wish," she said ruefully. "The Ocean Queen is coming here tomorrow."

Tharion swallowed his surprise. "Okay," he said carefully. "You sound . . . worried?"

Sendes tugged at the neck of her collar. "She wants to see you. All of you."

His brows rose. "Then problem solved."

"I got the sense from her call that she isn't . . . entirely pleased you're here." Sendes grimaced. "Something to do with the Viper Queen *and* the River Queen threatening war for harboring you?"

Well, shit.

38

Ithan lunged for the book that had somehow skittered for the office doorway, landing atop it with a thud that echoed through his bones.

To his dismay, the book squirmed under him, trying to wriggle for the door and the world beyond.

"Keep it down over there," Jesiba growled above her typing.

Ithan grunted, pressing all his considerable weight onto the errant book—

"Enough," Jesiba snapped, and the book stilled at the command in her voice.

Yet Ithan didn't move until he was certain the book had fully obeyed its mistress. Uncurling to peer down at the blue leather-bound book, he tensed, then reached a hand for it.

But the book just lay there. Dormant. Like any other book—

It snapped for his fingers, and Ithan lunged again.

"Lehabah was much more effective—and ate far less. Where does all that food go, wolf?"

Ithan couldn't answer as he again wrestled the book into submission, wrapping the tome in his arms. Clutching it to his chest, he eased to his feet, then stomped toward the shelf where it was *supposed* to have stayed while he unpacked yet another crate—

"I said *enough*," Jesiba snapped again, and the book froze in

Ithan's arms. He shoved it back on the shelf before it could get away. Then gave it another shove as a *fuck you.*

The book shoved back, as if it'd leap off the shelf and go at him for round three, but a golden ripple of light shimmered down its spine—a barrier falling back into place. Wards to seal the magical books in. The book thudded against it—and could go no further.

Jesiba said from the desk, "I thought I'd outsmarted it with the previous ward, but let's see it try to get through that one."

As if in answer, the book again rattled on the shelf. Ithan flipped it off, then faced the sorceress.

He'd been working nonstop for the past day, unpacking crates, inspecting the goods, cataloging the contents, rewrapping the artifacts inside, attaching new shipping labels . . . Busywork, but it kept him occupied.

Kept him from thinking about the blood on his hands. The body he could only hope was indeed on ice somewhere in this subterranean warren.

He didn't leave Roga's office. She had food delivered from the House's private kitchens—and if he needed to rest, she ordered him to curl up on the carpet like the dog he was.

He did, ignoring the insult, and slept deeply enough that she'd had to prod him with a foot to wake him.

He might have objected had she not been the bearer of good news: Hunt Athalar, Ruhn Danaan, and Baxian Argos had escaped from the Asteri's dungeons during a rescue operation that had incinerated the entirety of the Spine.

The Hind had done it. Tharion and Flynn and Dec had done it. Somehow, they'd pulled it off. Relief had tightened his throat to the point of pain, even as shame for not helping them twisted his gut.

Since then, Ithan and Jesiba had spoken little. Roga had mostly been on calls with clients or off at House meetings she didn't tell him about, but now . . . Ithan peered at the shelf, at the magic book again shuddering against the wards holding it in place.

"During the Summit," Ithan said, ignoring the belligerent volume, "Micah said your books were from the Library of Parthos."

Amelie had gossiped about it afterward. "That they're all that's left of it."

"Mmm," Jesiba murmured, continuing to clack away at her keyboard.

Ithan threw himself into the chair before her desk. "I thought Parthos was a myth."

"The books say otherwise, don't they?"

"What's the truth, then?"

"Not one that's easy to swallow for Vanir." But she stopped typing. Her eyes lifted above the computer screen to find his.

"Amelie Ravenscroft claimed that Micah said the library held two thousand years of human knowledge *before* the Asteri."

"And?" Her face revealed nothing.

He pointed to the pissed-off book. "So the humans had magic?"

She sighed through her nose. "No. The magic books here . . . they were *supposed* to be guardians of the library itself. At least, that's what I enchanted them to do, centuries ago. To attack those who tried to steal the books, to defend them." One such book, Ithan recalled Bryce telling him, had helped save her when she fought Micah. "But the volumes took on lives and desires of their own. They became . . . aware." She glared at the misbehaving book. "And by the time I tried to unweave the spells of life on them, their existence had become too permanent to undo. So I needed monitors such as Lehabah to guard the guardians. To make sure they didn't escape and become more of a nuisance."

"Why not sell them?"

She gave him a withering look. "Because *my* spells are written in there. I'm not letting that knowledge loose in the world." Roga had been a witch before she'd defected to the House of Flame and Shadow and called herself a sorceress instead. He could only imagine what she'd seen in her long, long life.

"So what do they say? The Parthos books?"

The clacking keys resumed. "Nothing. And everything."

Ithan snorted. "Cryptic, as usual."

Her typing stopped again. "They'd bore most people. Some are books on complex mathematics, entire volumes on imaginary numbers. Some are philosophical treatises. Some are plays—tragedies, comedies—and some are poetry."

"All from human life before the Asteri?"

"A great civilization lived on Midgard long before the Asteri conquered it." He could have sworn she sounded sad. "One that prized knowledge in all its forms. So much so that a hundred thousand humans marched at Parthos to save these books from the Asteri and Vanir who came to burn them." She shook her head, face distant. "A world where people loved and valued books and learning so much that they were willing to die for them. Can you imagine what such a civilization was like? A hundred thousand men and women marched to defend a *library*—it sounds like a bad joke these days." Her eyes blazed. "But they fought, and they died. All to buy the library priestesses enough time to smuggle the books out on ships. The Vanir armies intercepted most of them, and the priestesses were burned, their precious books used as kindling. But one ship . . ." Her lips curved upward. "The *Griffin*. It slipped through the Vanir nets. Sailed across the Haldren and found safe harbor in Valbara."

Ithan slowly shook his head. "How do you know all this, when no one else does?"

"The mer know some of it," she hedged. "The mer aided the *Griffin* across the sea, at the behest of the Ocean Queen."

"Why?"

"That's the mer's story to tell."

"But why do *you* know this? How do you have this collection?"

"I'll refrain from making the comparison to a dog with a bone." Jesiba closed her laptop with a soft click. Interlaced her fingers and set them upon the computer. "Quinlan knew when to keep her mouth shut, you know. She never asked why I have these books, why I have the Archesian amulets that the Parthos priestesses wore."

Ithan's mouth dried out. He whispered, "What—who are you?"

Jesiba burst out laughing, and several of the books on the shelf shuddered. Ithan was barely breathing as Jesiba snapped her fingers.

Her short hair flowed out—down into long, curling tresses that softened her face. Her makeup washed away, revealing features that somehow seemed younger . . . more innocent.

It was Jesiba, yet it wasn't. It was Jesiba, as if she'd been trapped in the bloom of youth. Of innocence. But her voice was as jaded as he'd always heard it as she said, "Lest you think me lying . . . This is the state I will always revert to—can revert to, at a mere wish."

"So you're . . . able to do magical makeovers?"

She didn't smile. "No. I was cursed by a demon. By a prince who intercepted my ship and the books on it."

Ithan's heart thundered.

"We had almost reached the Haldren Sea when Apollion found the *Griffin*." Her voice was flat. "He'd heard about the doomed stand at Parthos, and the ships, and the priestesses burned with their books. He was curious about what might be so valuable to the humans that we were willing to die for it. He didn't understand when I told him it was no power beyond knowledge—no weapon beyond learning." Her smile turned bitter. "He refused to believe me. And cursed me for my impudence in denying him the truth."

Ithan swallowed hard. "What kind of a curse?"

She gestured to her longer hair, her softer face. "To live, unchanging, until I showed him the true power of the books," she said simply. "He still believes they're a weapon, and that I'll one day grow tired enough of living that I'll hand them over and reveal all their supposed secret weapons."

"But . . . I thought you were a witch."

She shrugged. "I was, for a time. How do you categorize a human woman who stops aging? Who always reverts to the same age, the same physical condition as she was when she was cursed? I'd cherished my years with my fellow priestesses at Parthos. When the witch-dynasties rose, I thought I might find similar companionship with them. A home."

"You . . . you were a *priestess* at Parthos?"

She nodded. "Priestess, witch . . . and now sorceress."

"But if you were human, where'd your magic come from?" She'd said Apollion granted her long life, not power.

Her gray eyes darkened like the stormy sea she'd sailed across long ago. "When Apollion found my ship, he was ripe with power. He'd just consumed Sirius. I don't think he intended it, but when his magic . . . touched me, something transferred over."

From the way she said *touched*, Ithan knew exactly how she viewed what he'd done to her.

"It took me a while to realize I had powers beyond the stasis of eternal youth," she said blandly. "And fortunately, I've had fifteen thousand years to master them. To let them become part of me, take on a life of their own, as the books did."

Horror sluiced through him. "Do you want to . . . start aging again?"

It was a dangerously personal question, but to his surprise, she answered. "Not yet," Jesiba said a shade quietly. "Not until it's time."

"For what?" he dared ask.

She looked over a shoulder at the small library, at the feisty book that had at last simmered down, as if sulking. "For a world to emerge where these books will be truly safe at last."

39

Bryce found the Autumn King in his study, his red hair aglow in the morning light. Contemplating the Starsword and Truth-Teller on his desk.

What she'd said the other night must have struck a nerve, then. Good.

"So close," she purred as she shut the door and approached the desk, "but so far. So unworthy."

Flames danced in his eyes. "What is it you want, girl?"

She swept around the desk to stand beside his chair, peering at the weapons from his angle. He frowned, as if her mere proximity was distasteful. "Did my mom ever tell you what happened that night she was trying to get me to safety? When your goons caught up to her and Randall?"

"I'd consider your words carefully," he snarled.

Bryce smiled. "Randall hadn't picked up a gun in years. Not since he'd gotten home from the front and vowed he'd never use one again. He was on the verge of swearing his vows to Solas when he got the request from the High Priest to go help a single mom and her three year-old daughter get away from you. And that night your loser guards caught up with us . . . that was the first time Randall picked up a gun again. He put a bullet right through your chief security officer's head. Randall hated every single fucking second of it. But he did it. Because in that moment, even after only three days on the run, he knew that he was already in love with my mom. And that there was nothing he wouldn't do for her."

The Autumn King's nose crinkled with annoyance. "Is there a point to this story?"

"My point," she said, leaning closer to her father, "is that I didn't just learn about love from my mom. I learned about it from my dad, too. My *true* dad. My weak human dad who you're so jealous of that you can't stand it. He taught me to fight like Hel for the people I love."

"I grow bored of this." The Autumn King made to pull away, but Bryce grabbed his arm.

"Way ahead of you there. I grew bored of you the instant you opened your mouth."

Stone clicked.

The Autumn King reeled back, but too late. The gorsian shackle had already clamped on his wrist.

"You little bitch," he hissed, and Bryce let the shackle from her other wrist tumble to the ground. "You have no idea who you're fucking with—"

"I do. A useless, pathetic loser."

He lunged to his feet, but she'd already snatched up both Truth-Teller and the Starsword. He halted as she unsheathed the blades and pointed both at him.

Bryce said smoothly, the knife and sword steady in her hands, "Here's the bargain: you don't put up a fight, and I don't impale you with these and experiment on how to open a portal to nowhere in your gut."

Flame burned and then died out in his eyes as the shackle held him firm.

She smiled, inclining her head. "Thanks for that intel about the blades, by the way. I thought you might know something of use. It's really too bad that you sent all the servants away, isn't it? No one to hear you scream."

His face whitened with rage. "You arrived here intentionally."

"Guilty as charged," she said, shaking her hair over a shoulder with a toss of her head. "I knew you'd been doing all this research for centuries. You're the one person who's obsessed with the Starsword and its secrets, sad Chosen One reject that you are. So I came here for answers. To learn what, exactly, a weapon like this could do. How to get rid of our little intergalactic friends." She grinned. "And you assumed I landed here because . . . ?"

He glowered.

"Oh right," she said. "Because I'm your stupid, bumbling daughter. I landed here by accident—is that it?" She laughed, unable to help herself. "You probably even convinced yourself it was Luna sending you some sort of gift. That you were given the gods' favor and this was destined by Urd."

His silence was confirmation enough.

She made an exaggerated pout. "Tough luck. And *really* tough luck about the shackle. Though I guess it's fitting that I used the key Ruhn kept in his room. He told me about it once, you know. That's what he had to use when you'd bind him with these and burn him. You put these delightful things on him so he couldn't fight back. And it happened often enough that he invested in a disarming key that he left in his desk so he could free himself when you sent him back to his room to suffer."

Again, the Autumn King said nothing. The bastard wouldn't deny it.

Bryce flashed her teeth, searing white rage creeping over her vision. But her voice was cold as ice as she said, "To be honest, I'd really like to kill you right now. For my mom, but also for Ruhn. And for me, too, I guess." She nodded to the doorway. "But we do have a bargain, don't we? And I've got a hot date today."

Pure death loomed in his eyes. "The Asteri will kill you."

"Maybe. But you're not going to help them by telling them about this." She extended the Starsword toward his face. He didn't dare move as she bopped him on the nose with its tip. "It's a real shame that you unplugged all your electronics and shut off your interweb. There'll be no way to call for help from the basement closet."

He choked on his outrage. "The—"

"Oh, don't worry," she drawled. "I put a bucket and some water in there for you. Probably enough to last until one of your meathead guards wonders what's going on in here and comes to check." She pretended to think. "They might have a bitch of a time getting through your wards, though."

"As will you."

"Unfortunately for you, no, I won't. You didn't ward against teleporting. Such a rare gift here—you didn't even think to spell against it, did you? Lucky me."

"I would consider your next moves *very* carefully if—"

"Yeah, yeah." She pointed with the sword to the door. "Let's go. Your subterranean abode awaits."

He didn't try anything as she escorted him down, clearly wary of the power of the weapons she held.

Ever since Vesperus had writhed under the two blades, there had been a thought niggling at the back of Bryce's mind. Remembering all Ruhn had told her about the Autumn King's obsession with the Starsword, she'd gambled that he might know about the dagger, too.

It had been the hardest decision she'd ever made: to come here, to play this game, rather than to will the portal to take her right to Hunt. But Hunt, as she had feared, had still been in the dungeons, and to appear there would have been too risky. And this knowledge was too important.

But now she knew a little more. The Starsword and Truth-Teller could open a portal to nowhere, whatever that was. Now she just needed to learn how to make them do it.

Good thing he'd also told her where on Midgard to find more information about the blades.

The Autumn King balked as Bryce pointed with the sword to the open closet in the basement. Like so much of the house, it was fireproof. The heavy steel door would likely take him a while to break out of, if he even managed to free himself from the gorsian shackle.

The Autumn King growled as he backed into the closet, "I will kill you and your bitch mother for this."

She motioned him further inside. "I'll pencil you in for tomorrow."

With that, she slammed the door shut in his face and locked it. He barreled into it a second later, the door shuddering, but it held.

Whistling to herself, propping the Starsword on a shoulder, Bryce strode out of the basement.

There was so much more to do. Places to be. People to see.

And more to learn.

Five minutes later, Bryce pulled her phone out of the desk drawer in the Autumn King's study. It was dead, and a quick search of his office showed no hint of charging cords to get it working again. She slipped it into the band of her leggings, then picked up the Starsword and Truth-Teller from where she'd placed them on the desk.

The Autumn King's prism device sat where he'd left it. An idle beam of sunlight shone through the windows, catching in the prism and refracting a rainbow onto one of the golden planets of the orrery—on Midgard. Light pulled apart. Light stripped bare.

In the chaos of those final moments with Vesperus and these days with the Autumn King, she hadn't yet had a chance to explore the magic she'd taken from Silene's store.

She'd claimed the magic, she supposed, as Silene had surely left it there for future heirs to take. But why hadn't they? Why hadn't her son, who'd heard the truth directly from her mouth? Bryce knew she might never know the answer now. But she could try to learn something about the power she now held within her.

With a sharp inhale, Bryce rallied her magic. On the exhale, she sent a stream of her starlight into the prism, her power faster than ever before.

Starlight hit the prism, passed through it, and—

"Huh."

It wasn't a rainbow that emerged from the other side. Not even close.

It took her a moment to process what she was seeing: a gradient beam of starlight. Where the rainbow would have been full of color, this one began in shimmering white light and descended into shadow.

An anti-rainbow, as it were. Light falling into darkness, droplets of starlight raining from the highest beam into the shadowy band at the bottom, devoured by the darkness below.

Like the fading light of day—of dusk.

What did it mean? She was pretty sure her light had been pure before, but now, with Silene's power mixed in . . . there was darkness there, too. Hidden beneath.

Et in Avallen ego.

Did it make a difference to her power? To her? To now have that layer of darkness?

Bryce buried the questions. She could think about it later. Right now . . .

She took the notebook on the desk and slid it into the inside pocket of her athletic jacket.

Then she nudged the prism on the desk a few inches to the side, angling it toward the device across the room. The one the Autumn King said might be able to recapture the light, possibly with more power added to it. But what if light blasted from either prism, meeting in the middle? What would happen in the collision of all that magic?

All that smashing light, those little bits of magic bashing into each other, would produce energy. And fuel her up like a battery.

She hoped.

"Only one way to find out," she muttered to herself.

With a prayer to Cthona, she sent twin beams of light arcing around the prisms, shooting straight into them.

Twin bursts of that light flared from either prism, gunning for each other. Bands of light falling into darkness, her power stripped to its most elemental, basic form. They shot for each other, and where they met, light and darkness and darkness and light slamming into each other—

Bryce stepped into the explosion in the heart of it.

Stepped into her power.

It lit her up from the inside, lit up her very blood. Her hair drifted above her head, pens and papers and other office detritus flowing upward with it.

Such light and darkness—the power lay in the meeting of the

two of them. She understood it now, how the darkness shaped the light.

But all that colliding power . . . it was the boost she needed.

With a parting middle finger to the floor at her feet and the Autumn King sulking beneath it, she teleported out of the villa to the place she wanted to be the most.

Home. Wherever that was in Midgard.

Because her home was no longer just a physical place, but a person, too.

Silene had claimed as much when she spoke of Theia and Aidas—their souls had found each other across worlds, because they were mates. They were each other's homes.

And for Bryce, home was—and always would be—Hunt.

Exhaustion weighed so heavily on Ruhn that despite his aching neck, he couldn't be bothered to shift into a more comfortable position in the chair. Machines beeped endlessly, like metal crickets marking the passing of the night.

He had a vague sense of Declan replacing Flynn. Then Dec left and it was Flynn again.

He didn't know what woke him. Whether it was some hitch in the machine or some shift in the cadence of her breathing, but . . . a stillness went through him. He cracked his eyes open, sore and gritty, and looked to the bed.

Lidia still lay unconscious. Ghastly pale.

Lidia.

No answer. Ruhn leaned over his knees and rubbed his face. Maybe he could crash on the tiled floor. It'd be better than contorting himself in the chair.

"Morning," Flynn said. "Want some coffee?"

Ruhn grunted his assent. Flynn clapped him on the back and slipped out, the door hissing open and shut.

Gods, his whole body hurt. His hand . . . He examined the thin, strangely pale fingers, the lack of tattoos or scars. Still weak.

Like it was still rebuilding the strength stored in his immortal blood on the day of his Drop.

He flexed his fingers, wincing, then slowly sat up and rolled his neck. He was on his third rotation when he looked at the bed and noticed Lidia staring at him.

He went wholly still.

Her golden eyes were hazy with pain and exhaustion, but they were open, and she was . . . she was . . .

Ruhn blinked, making sure he wasn't dreaming.

Lidia rasped, "Am I dead or alive?"

His chest caved in. "Alive," he whispered, hands beginning to shake.

Lidia's lips curled faintly, like it took all her effort to do so. The weight of it hit him—of what she was and who she was and what she had done.

The Hind lay before him—the fucking *Hind*. How could he feel such relief about someone he hated so much? How could he hate someone whose life mattered more to him than his own?

Her glazed eyes shifted from his. Glanced around the windowless room, taking in the machines and her IV. Her nostrils flared, scenting the room beneath the antiseptics and various potions. Something sharpened in her stare. Something like recognition.

Then Lidia asked very quietly, "Where are we?"

The question surprised him. She'd planned this escape. Had her injury affected her mind? Gods, he hadn't even thought about the potential damage from going without oxygen for so long. Ruhn said softly, "On the *Depth Charger*—"

She moved.

Tubing and monitors came flying off her, ripped from her arm so fast blood sprayed. Machines blared, and Ruhn couldn't act quickly enough to stop her as she leapt out of the bed, feet slipping on the floor as she hurtled to the door.

The glass hissed open, revealing Flynn with two cups of coffee in hand. He dodged to the side with a "What the fuck!"

Lidia barreled out, hardly able to stand, and it was all Ruhn could do to race after her.

The few medwitches in the hall at this hour let out surprised cries at the deer shifter stumbling past in her pale blue medical gown, careening into the walls with the grace of a newborn colt. Her legs had been rebuilt—she'd never used these ones before.

"What the *Hel*," Flynn said, a step behind Ruhn, smelling of the coffee that had spilled on him when he'd dived out of Lidia's way.

Lidia hit the stairwell, and just before the door shut behind her, Ruhn saw her trip, falling to her knees on the steps, then surge up again.

"Lidia," he panted, each step singeing his lungs. *Fuck* his still-healing body—

He slammed into the stairwell door, but she was already half-way up, long legs pale and thin against the gray tiles.

She charged up and up, around and around, either unaware or uncaring that Ruhn ran close behind. She threw open an unmarked door, then bolted down the hall. People in civilian clothes pressed back against the walls at the sight of her—then him. The walls here were covered with bright art and flyers.

Sharp inhales came from Lidia. She was sobbing, craning her neck to see through the windows of the rooms she passed. Ruhn read the words on each wooden door: *Year Three. Year Seven. Year Five.*

She skidded to a halt, gripping a doorjamb. Ruhn reached her side as she shoved her face up to the glass.

Year Nine.

A group of teenagers—most of them mer, with striped skin and various coloring—sat in rows of desks in the classroom. Lidia pressed a hand against the door. Tears rolled down her cheeks.

And then a boy, golden-haired and blue-eyed, looked away from his teacher and toward the window. The kid wasn't mer.

The ground slid out from under Ruhn. The boy had Lidia's face. Her coloring.

Another boy to his left, also not mer, had dark hair and golden eyes. Lidia's eyes.

Behind them, Flynn grunted with surprise. "You've got brothers on this ship?"

"They're not my brothers," Lidia whispered. Her fingers curled on the glass. "They're my sons."

Hunt leaned against the wall of the massive tactical room on the *Depth Charger,* arms crossed. Tharion and Baxian flanked him, the former feigning nonchalance, the latter the portrait of menace.

Only a conference table occupied the room, and though they'd been told to take a seat upon walking in five minutes ago, they all remained standing.

Hunt ran through all the things he needed to say. The Ocean Queen had told Sendes that she wanted Tharion presented to her, but Hunt knew he wouldn't get a better opportunity to ask her his questions. Assuming Tharion wasn't turned into a bloody pulp before Hunt could start talking. That would throw a wrench in his plans.

If Tharion was nervous, the mer didn't show it. He just removed invisible flecks of lint from his aquatic suit and glanced at the digital clock on the far wall every now and then. But Hunt had noted his dead-eyed stare. A male prepared to face his end. Who might think he deserved it.

Power shuddered through the ship, like an undersea earthquake. As menacing and deadly as a tsunami. Ancient and cold as the bottom of an oceanic trench.

"She's here," Tharion murmured.

Baxian's dark wings tucked in tighter, and he glanced sidelong at Hunt. "You ever meet the Ocean Queen?"

"Nope," Hunt said, folding in his own wings. He wished he had a weapon—any weapon. Even with his lightning and brute strength, there was something comforting in the weight of a gun or sword at his side. Though neither would be helpful against the being who'd arrived on the ship. "Never even seen her. You?"

Baxian ran a hand over his tightly curled black hair. "No. Ketos?"

"No," was the mer's only reply, his eyes again fixed on the clock.

It was no surprise that even Tharion hadn't met the Ocean Queen. She was more of an enigma than the River Queen, rumored to have been born of Ogenas herself. The daughter of a goddess, who could likely bring the force of this entire ocean crashing down upon this ship and—

The door clicked open. Sendes appeared on the threshold and announced, "Her Depthless Majesty, the Ocean Queen." The commander stepped aside, bowing at the waist as a tiny female entered behind her.

Hunt blinked. Even Tharion seemed to be restraining his shock, his breath shallow.

Her luscious body measured barely more than four feet. Her skin was as pale as the belly of a fish; her angular eyes as dark as a shark's. Her heart-shaped face was neither pretty nor plain, and the rosebud-shaped lips were the reddish pink of a snapper. She walked with a strange sort of lightness—like she was unused to being on solid ground—and the gown of kelp and sea fans she wore trailed behind her, the shells and coral in the train tinkling as she moved.

Pushing off the wall, the three of them followed Sendes's lead and bowed.

Hunt watched the Ocean Queen as he did so, though, and noted the slow sweep of her eyes over them. She only moved her eyes—nothing else. An apex predator assessing her prey.

When she'd decided they had suitably worshipped her, she stalked to the head of the table. Each step left behind a wet footprint on the tiles, though she appeared entirely dry. Barnacles adorned some strands of her hair like beads.

"Sit," she ordered, voice deep and rolling and utterly chilling.

Wings rustled and chairs groaned as they obeyed. Hunt could only wonder if he'd pissed off Urd today as he realized *he* had claimed the chair nearest to the head of the table—to the monarch standing there. Baxian sat on his other side, and Tharion, the worm, had wriggled his way to the seat farthest away—within leaping distance of the door.

Adjusting his wings around the chair back, Hunt caught Baxian's eye. The Helhound gave him a look that pretty much said: *Well, I'm shitting my pants.*

Hunt glanced pointedly at his own chair, as if to say, *You're not the one sitting closest to her.*

The queen surveyed them with ageless, pitiless eyes.

Hunt couldn't help his swallow. He'd never felt so small, so insignificant. Even in front of the Asteri, he'd remembered that he was a warrior, and a damned good one, and might at least make a last stand against them. But before this female . . . He saw it in her eyes, sensed it in his blood: one thought from her, and she'd wipe him from existence with a tidal wave of power.

Sendes cleared her throat and said, voice shaking, "May I present Hunt Athalar, Baxian Argos, and Tharion Ketos."

"Our guests from Valbara," the Ocean Queen acknowledged. Squalls howled in her words, even as her tone remained mild. Hunt's entire body tensed.

As fast as a storm sweeping in over the sea, she seemed to grow—no, she *was* growing, taller and taller, until she towered over Sendes, nearly Hunt's own height.

Her power surged, filling the room, dragging their meager souls down into its airless heart like a maelstrom. The Ocean Queen slid her attention to Tharion and said with knee-trembling menace, "You have brought a heap of trouble to my doorstep."

* * *

Ruhn tried and failed to process what he'd heard. Lidia had . . . children?

A female voice behind them said, "Miss Cervos."

Lidia didn't turn. Just stared at the boys in the classroom.

But Ruhn looked, and found a full-bodied, dark-skinned mer female with a kind face standing there. She said to Ruhn, "I'm Director Kagani, the head of this school."

Lidia's fingers contracted on the glass of the door's window. "Can I meet them?" The question was very, very quiet. Broken.

Kagani sighed softly. "I think it would be disruptive, and too public, for them to be pulled out of class right now."

Lidia finally turned at that, teeth flashing. "I want to meet my children."

Ruhn's mind spun at her expression. Rage and pain and a mother's unbreaking ferocity.

"I know you do," Kagani said with unflappable calm. "But it would be best if we talk in my office after school. It's right down the hall."

The Hind didn't so much as move.

"Consider what is best for *them*, Lidia," Kagani encouraged. "I understand, I truly do—I'm a mother, myself. If I had . . ." Her throat worked. "I would want the same if I had made your choices. But I'm also an educator, and an advocate for these children. Please put the twins first today. Just as you have every day for the past fifteen years."

Lidia scanned the female's face with an openness Ruhn had never seen from her. She looked over a shoulder, back into the classroom. The blond boy now stood at his desk, staring at her with wide eyes. The dark-haired one watched carefully, but remained seated.

So much of Lidia was written all over their features. When they were away from her, it was unlikely that anyone would draw a connection, but it was impossible to miss the relation when seeing them in close proximity.

"All right," Lidia whispered, lowering her hand from the window. "All right."

Kagani let out a small sigh of relief. "Why don't you go get cleaned up. School isn't out for another five hours, so take your time. Have some food. Maybe get cleared by your medwitch." A nod to the half-healed holes in Lidia's arm where she'd torn out her IV.

"All right," Lidia said a third time, and stepped away. As if Ruhn and Flynn didn't exist.

Director Kagani added gently, "I'll contact Brann and Actaeon's adoptive parents to see if they can come in, too."

Lidia nodded silently, and kept walking.

Ruhn glanced to Flynn, whose brows were high. Ruhn raised his own brows in silent agreement.

A sudden movement snared his attention and Ruhn whirled toward Lidia, blindly reaching for her.

But he wasn't swift enough to catch her as she fainted, crumpling to the floor.

Tharion had never met anyone as petrifying and alluring as the Ocean Queen. Never wanted to cry and laugh and scream at the same time . . . though he was leaning toward the latter as the queen bestowed the full force of her displeasure upon him.

"Tharion Ketos." She spoke his name like it left a foul taste in her mouth. "How is it that you have not one, but *two* queens demanding your head?"

He winced and put forth his brightest charm—his first and best line of defense. "I tend to have that effect on females?"

The monarch didn't smile, but he could have sworn Sendes, stationed in the doorway, was trying not to.

The Ocean Queen folded her hands in front of her curved, soft belly. "I have received reports that the Viper Queen of Lunathion has put a bounty on your head for three million gold marks." Athalar, the bastard, let out a low whistle. "*Five* million if you're alive, so she can punish you herself."

Tharion choked on a breath. "For what?" He added hastily, "Your Majesty."

"I don't know the particulars, nor do I care to," the Ocean Queen said, pearlescent teeth flashing behind her vivid red lips. "But I believe it has something to do with your presence bringing certain individuals who then caused untold damage to her property. She holds *you* responsible."

He was so, so fucked.

"But that is not the end of my problems," the queen went on. He could have sworn those glistening teeth sharpened. "My so-called sister in the Istros is demanding your return as well. She is threatening war upon me—*me*—if you are not handed over. Presumably to be executed."

He could scarcely get a breath down. "Please," he whispered, "my parents—"

"Oh, I wouldn't worry about your family if I were you," the Ocean Queen seethed. Her teeth were now hooked and razor-like. Pure shark. "The River Queen and Viper Queen only want *you*. I would like one good reason why I shouldn't hand you over—let them squabble over your carcass."

He scrambled for some way to disarm the moment, to win her, but came up empty. His unnaturally deep pool of luck had finally and officially run dry—

"You hand him over," a female voice drawled from the open doorway, "and you'll have a third queen pissed at you."

Tharion's stomach bottomed out.

Bryce Quinlan swept through the doorway and winked at the Ocean Queen. "Tharion serves me."

41

Hunt had left his body. Maybe he'd died. That was *Bryce* in the doorway, smirking at the Ocean Queen.

She was Bryce and yet she was . . . not.

She wore her usual casual attire—skintight jeans and a soft white T-shirt topped with a navy athletic jacket. Hel, she even sported those neon-pink sneakers. But there was something different in her posture, in the way the light seemed to shimmer from her.

She was older, somehow. Not in any line or wrinkle, but in her eyes. Like she'd been through some major shit, good and bad. Hunt recognized it, because he knew it lay etched in his own face, too.

The Ocean Queen eyed Bryce unflinchingly. "And who, pray tell, are *you*?"

Bryce didn't miss a beat. "I'm Bryce Danaan, Queen of the Valbaran Fae."

Hunt let out a strangled sound—a sob.

Bryce looked at him then, scanning his face, the tears he couldn't stop. Her gaze flicked to the halo, then down to his wrist—but her expression yielded nothing. She just walked up to where he sat, and it *was* her, her fucking scent, and that was her soft skin brushing his hand as she peered down into his face.

"Hey," he said, voice rough, eyes stinging.

Bryce squeezed his hand, tears filling her eyes as well. "Hey." She blinked her tears away, twisting back to the Ocean Queen, who monitored every move. Every breath.

The Ocean Queen said to Bryce, shark's teeth flashing, "I recognize no queen bearing that title."

"I do," Hunt said, folding his wings behind him as he stood, coming to Bryce's side. Her fingers grazed his own, and a chill of pleasure soared through him. "She's my mate." He sketched a bow to the Ocean Queen. "Prince Hunt Athalar Danaan, at your service. I can testify that Tharion Ketos serves my queen and mate. Any other claims to him are false."

Bryce shot him a wry glance that seemed to say, *You're a big fucking liar, but I love you.*

The Ocean Queen still surveyed Bryce with a face as cold as the northern reaches of the Haldren Sea. "That remains to be seen." She pointed to Tharion, her fingernail made of pure nacre. "Tharion Ketos, you are confined to this ship until I decide otherwise."

Tharion bowed his head, but remained still and silent.

The Ocean Queen lowered her finger and shot a sharp glance at Bryce. It was instinct for Hunt's knees to bend, to prepare to leap between them, to shield his mate. But there was no amount of lightning, no gun, no weapon that could save Bryce, should the Ocean Queen bring the full wrath of the sea down upon them. This deep, they'd have no chance of reaching the surface in time. That is, if their bodies didn't explode first from the pressure.

But the near-divine being declared, a shade haughtily, "Queen or no queen, you are all now guests on my ship—and will leave only when I bid you to."

Hunt refrained from saying that her checkout policy wasn't very guest friendly. Especially as the Ocean Queen asked Bryce, dark eyes narrowing, "Does your father the Autumn King still draw breath?"

Bryce smiled slowly. "For the time being."

The Ocean Queen weighed the words—then answered Bryce's

smile with her own, revealing all those hooked shark's teeth. "I don't recall inviting you onto this ship."

Bryce checked her nails—it was such a thoroughly Bryce movement that Hunt's chest tightened. "Well, *someone* sent me an e-vite."

Hunt lowered his head to keep the grin from his face. He'd forgotten how fun it was—to see Bryce in her element. Leading these shitheads along by the nose. It lightened some of that weight in his chest, some of that primal terror—just a fraction.

The Ocean Queen said flatly, "I do not know of any such thing."

Amusement glimmered in Bryce's whiskey-colored eyes, but her tone was dead serious as she explained, "I teleported here. I needed to find my mate."

"You and your mate are dismissed," the Ocean Queen said, waving that nacre-tipped hand. A hermit crab skittered through her dark locks and then vanished again. "I have important matters to discuss with Captain Ketos."

Tharion looked up, grimacing. Maybe his death sentence hadn't been delayed after all.

But again, Bryce didn't miss a beat. "Yeah, see, *my* matters are a bit more pressing."

"I find that highly unlikely."

Two queens facing off. And there was no doubt in Hunt's mind that Bryce *was* a queen now. The poise, the strength radiating from her . . . She didn't need a crown to rule this room.

Bryce sucked in a breath, the only sign of nerves. And said to the ruler of the seas, "You're wrong."

It was only through sheer will that Bryce didn't throw her arms around Hunt immediately and kiss him silly. Only through sheer will that she didn't start raging and crying at the halo inked anew on his brow, the brand stamped on his wrist.

She'd kill the Asteri for this.

She'd already planned to, of course, but after what they'd done to Hunt while she'd been gone . . . she'd make sure they died slowly.

That is, once she figured out how to kill them.

And as soon as she held Hunt, she wasn't letting go. Ever. But they had so much shit to do right now that giving in wasn't an option, holding him and loving him weren't options.

She didn't dare ask where Ruhn was, not with the Ocean Queen present. Baxian was with Hunt, so maybe her brother was nearby, too. The Autumn King had said they were all rescued. Ruhn had to be here. Somewhere.

But she couldn't wait for her brother. He'd have to be filled in later.

"I journeyed to the original world of the Fae," she began, "through a Gate in the Eternal Palace. I possess Luna's Horn, which helped clear the pathway between worlds."

Stunned, breathless silence filled the room. Hunt practically thrummed with lightning and curiosity, but Bryce kept her eyes on the Ocean Queen as the female said neutrally, "I'm assuming you learned something."

Bryce gave a shallow nod. "I knew already that the Asteri are intergalactic parasites. But I learned that the Asteri infected Midgard's waters upon invading this world."

"Infected," the Ocean Queen mused.

Bryce nodded again. "The Asteri put an actual parasite in the water—or something like a parasite. I don't really know what it is, specifically. Whatever it is, it makes everyone on Midgard *have* to offer up firstlight via the Drop. Or else we'll lose our powers—we'll wither and die."

"Fuck," Hunt breathed. Bryce still didn't look at him, though. At Tharion or Baxian or Sendes, who were all gaping in absolute dread.

Only the Ocean Queen didn't appear surprised.

Bryce said, narrowing her eyes in realization, "You—you knew this."

The Ocean Queen shook her head. "No. I always wondered, though, why my people still needed to make the Drop, even down here. But now that you have revealed this terrible truth, what shall *you* do?"

"I guess I'll take on the Asteri," Bryce said. "Banish them from this world."

"How?" The Ocean Queen shifted, the coral beading on her gown tinkling.

Bryce hedged, not quite willing to lay out *everything* for this stranger. "I don't suppose an eviction notice would do the trick?"

The three males around them didn't bat an eye, but Sendes shifted on her feet.

The Ocean Queen said plainly, "This is folly. You'd need entire armies to fight the Asteri."

"Care to supply one?" Bryce countered.

"My people are skilled in the water, not on land. But Ophion has forces, what little remain. I believe Lidia Cervos mustered them the other day to devastating effect. Though I have not yet learned how many survived the mission."

Bryce said to the queen, "So you *do* work with Ophion?"

"We assist each other when we can—I harbor their agents if they make it here. But Ophion is as prejudiced against us as a Vanir against a mortal. They find accepting our help to be . . . unsavory."

"Plenty of Vanir have helped Ophion over the years," Baxian cut in with soft strength.

Bryce's heart tightened as Danika's face flashed through her mind. If Danika could not be here, it was only fitting that her mate stood here instead.

"And Ophion resents all of them," Commander Sendes said from where she still stood beside the doorway. "We'd need a solid bridge between us to get talks going about unifying armies."

Hunt turned to Bryce and asked quietly, "What about Briggs?"

Her blood chilled. "No fucking way. He'll turn around and kill us." The former rebel leader's gaunt, hollow face flashed in her mind, along with those deep blue eyes that had seemed to bore right through her.

"She is correct," the Ocean Queen said, folding her hands over her stomach once more in a portrait of regal poise. "Another route is required."

Bryce said as casually as she could, "Hel will aid us."

The Ocean Queen scoffed. "You trust those demons?"

"I do." At the ruler's raised brows, Bryce said, jaw clenching, "Hel's known all this stuff for millennia. And tried their best to make it right. To help liberate us. That's what they were trying to do during the First Wars."

Again, her friends were stunned into silence.

But the Ocean Queen let out a small, disbelieving snort. "You learned that in this other world as well?"

"Yes." Bryce kept her tone even, refusing to be baited.

"You trust Hel enough to fully open the Northern Rift to allow their armies through?"

"If it's our only shot at defeating the Asteri."

"You'd trade one evil for another."

Bryce couldn't stop the starlight that began pulsing under her skin, condensing and sharpening into that *thing* that could cleave through stone. "I'd hardly call the Princes of Hel evil, when they've refused to let the Asteri win all these years. When they've gone out of their way to try to help us, even though it'll cost them. Hel owes us nothing, yet they're so convinced of the importance of ridding the universe of the Asteri that they've been at this for thousands of years. I'd say that's a pretty solid commitment."

The Ocean Queen seemed to grow an inch, then another. She jerked her chin toward Hunt. "Your mate hunted demons for centuries—has seen their brutality and bloodlust up close. What does he have to say about their supposed altruism?"

Hunt squared his shoulders, utterly unshakable. Bryce's throat tightened to see it—to know even before he spoke that he had her back. "It's tough for me to accept, especially when they wrecked Lunathion this spring, but if Bryce trusts them, I trust them. Besides, we're out of options."

Bryce spared him from dwelling further on the topic by saying, "There is another thing."

All of them turned to her. Hunt, at least, had the good sense to look nervous.

Bryce kept her gaze on the Ocean Queen as she said, "We need to head to Avallen."

"Why?" the Ocean Queen demanded. A tsunami roared in her tone.

"There's some research I need to do in its archives that might help our cause." It was at least *partially* the truth. "About the First Wars and Hel's involvement."

Okay, the last part was a lie. But she wasn't about to explain what she really needed on the mist-shrouded isle.

The Ocean Queen drawled, "I don't recall becoming a ferry service. Do you assume my city-ship is at your disposal?"

"Do you want to win this war or not?"

Shock rippled through the room at her words. Hunt tensed, readying for a physical confrontation.

But Bryce blazed with starlight as she said, "Look, I know nothing is free. But for fuck's sake, let's talk plainly. Name your price. You've gone out of your way to try to help people for years, working toward bringing down the Asteri. So why are you making things more difficult when we finally have a chance at beating them?"

"This is becoming tedious," the Ocean Queen said. "I did not come here to be ordered about by an impostor queen."

"Call me what you want," Bryce said, "but the longer we don't act, the easier it will be for Rigelus and the rest of the Asteri to move against us."

"Everything seems urgent to the young."

"Yeah, I get that, but—"

"I was not done speaking."

Bryce hid her wince as the Ocean Queen surveyed her. "You *are* young. And idealistic. And inexperienced."

"Don't forget ill qualified and always inappropriately dressed."

The female cut her a warning glare. Bryce held up her hands in mock surrender.

The Ocean Queen loosed a long breath. "I do not know you, Bryce Danaan, and so far have seen little to recommend you as a reliable ally. My people have managed to evade the Asteri's influence for millennia now—to remain safe down here, fighting against them as best we can. And yet you have informed me that even here, we are not untouched. Even here, in my domain, the Asteri's parasite infects us all."

"I'm sorry to have been the bearer of bad news," Bryce said, "but would you rather I had kept it from you?"

"Honestly? I don't know." The Ocean Queen studied her hand—a banded sea krait twined around her wrist like a living black-and-white bracelet. Poisonous as Hel. The ruler said quietly, "Have you thought about an evacuation?"

Bryce started. "To where? There's nowhere on Midgard, except maybe this ship, that isn't under their control." Avallen was apparently shielded by its mists, yes, but King Morven still bowed to the Asteri.

The queen lifted her head. "To the home world of the Fae."

Hunt shifted, wings rustling. "You mean leave this planet completely?"

The Ocean Queen didn't take her eyes from Bryce's as she said, "Yes. Use the Horn, allow as many through as you can, and then seal the way forever."

Horror twisted through her. "And what—abandon the rest here? To be slaves and feeding troughs for the Asteri?" She'd be no better than Silene.

The Ocean Queen asked, "Isn't it better for some to be free, than for all to be dead?"

Hunt let out a low laugh, stepping closer to Bryce's side as he said to the Ocean Queen, "You can't mean that. Who the fuck would even get chosen to come? Your people? Our families? In what universe is that fair?"

Seated at the conference table, Baxian nodded his agreement, but Tharion kept still as stone. Maybe he didn't want to attract the queen's attention or ire once more. Spineless asshole. But Bryce squashed her distaste. She needed all the allies she could get.

"I do not say it is fair," the Ocean Queen said, stroking the sea krait on her wrist. "But it might be what is necessary."

Bryce swallowed the dryness in her mouth. "I came back here to help everyone, not to abandon them to the mercy of the Asteri."

"Perhaps Urd sent you to that other world to establish a safe harbor. Have you considered that?"

Bryce exploded, "What was all this for, then? The stealth, the ships, the Ophion contacts? What the fuck was it for if you just want to run away from the Asteri in the end?"

Eyes blacker than the Melinoë Trench pinned her to the spot. "Do not dare question my dedication, girl. I have fought and sacrificed for this world when no one else would. Once, my kingdom was vaster than you can imagine—but the Asteri came, and entire islands withered into the sea in despair, taking the very heart of this world with it. The very heart of the mer, too. If there is anyone who understands how futile it is to stand against the Asteri, it is I."

Bryce's breath caught in her throat. "Wait—you were here *before* the Asteri? The mer were here? I thought only humans lived on Midgard then."

The Ocean Queen's face became distant with memory. "They had the land—we had the seas. Our people met only occasionally, the root of the humans' legends about the mer." A wistful smile, then her eyes again focused on Bryce, sharp and calculating. "But yes, we have always been here. Midgard has always had magic, as all nature has inherent magic. The Asteri just did not deign to recognize it."

Bryce filed away the information. "Fine—you win the award for longest-suffering people on Midgard. That doesn't entitle you to jump to the front of the Evacuate Midgard line." Hunt touched her shoulder lightly, a gentle warning. But Bryce ignored him and laid her hands flat on the table, leaning over it to breathe in the Ocean Queen's face. "I *refuse* to open a gate like that. I won't help you condemn the majority of Midgard's people while a select few dance off into the sunset."

The sea krait on the Ocean Queen's wrist hissed at Bryce. Even as its mistress's face remained as cold as the ice floes of the north. "You will come around to the idea when your friends and loved ones start dying around you."

"Don't you dare condescend to her," Hunt growled at the queen.

Sendes cleared her throat, trying to bail them out of this

clusterfuck, but all Bryce could hear was a roaring in her ears, all she could see was a blinding white creeping over her vision—

"You're a coward," Bryce spat at the Ocean Queen. "You hide behind your power, but you're a *coward*."

The ship shuddered, as if the very sea tensed with rage.

But the Ocean Queen said, "Against my better instincts, I will deposit you and yours in Avallen, as requested. Consider that my last gift."

Bryce ground her teeth so hard her jaw hurt.

"But when you fail in whatever uprising you think you can muster," the Ocean Queen said by way of dismissal, striding for the door, leaving a trail of water in her wake, "when you realize that I am right and fleeing is the best option, I ask only this in exchange for my services: take as many of my people as you can."

42

Bryce couldn't help but be impressed that Hunt, Tharion, and Baxian held their shit together until they got back to a cabin barely big enough to fit all of them, let alone so many egos. She certainly had a Hel of a time with it.

But as soon as the door shut, absolute chaos erupted.

"What the *fuck*—" Hunt exploded.

"Are you all right—" she started.

"The *home world of the Fae*?" Tharion demanded at the same time Baxian chuckled, "That was epic."

Tharion sank onto one of the bunks, his normally tan skin pale. "Only you would tangle with the Ocean Queen, Legs."

Baxian said to the mer, "Confined to the ship, huh?"

Tharion winced. "I'm fucked."

Bryce turned to Hunt, who was leaning against the door he'd shut. She arched her brows at her mate, at his too-calm expression. She knew that look. He was no doubt debating how soon he could kick everyone out and fuck her senseless.

Her toes curled in her sneakers, and she gave him a wink. Hunt rolled his eyes, a corner of his mouth kicking up despite himself.

She hadn't failed to see that glimmer of darkness in his gaze, though. Whatever had happened to him while she'd been gone, it had left a mark on the inside, too.

But they'd talk about it later. Bryce asked, "Where's Ruhn?"

"With Lidia," Hunt said quietly.

"Lidia?"

Baxian nodded, sitting beside Tharion, his black wings gleaming like raven feathers. "Yeah. She got us all out. She's, uh . . . a bit worse for wear. Ruhn's been watching over her."

Bryce's chest tightened. "Will she—"

Before Bryce could finish, the door blasted open. Hunt's lightning was an instant crackling wall in front of her.

But Bryce let out a low sound of joy when she saw Ruhn panting in the doorway, her brother's eyes wide with shock.

Then they were hugging and laughing, and such joy poured from her that her starlight glowed brightly, casting stark shadows in the cramped room. "Bryce," he said, grinning, and the pride in his voice had her throat closing up. She grabbed his hand, unable to come up with the words, but then she saw his arms.

His tattoos were in ribbons. Like his skin had been split open so deep—

Her starlight winked out. "Ruhn," she breathed.

"All in one piece," Ruhn said, and glanced to Baxian. "Again."

"I don't want to know what that look means," Bryce said as Baxian winced apologetically.

"You really don't," Hunt said, sliding an arm around her shoulders and guiding her to the bunk opposite where Baxian and Tharion rested. He sat close enough that his thigh pressed into hers, and went so far as to drape a wing over her. Like he'd never let her out of his sight again.

She breathed in his scent, his warmth, over and over again. The most wonderful things in the universe.

Ruhn blinked at Bryce, as if not convinced she was really there. "I'm not hallucinating, right?" he asked.

"No." Bryce patted the bed beside her.

But Ruhn lingered by the door, his face grim. "It kills me to say this, but I can't stay long."

"What happened?" Baxian asked.

"Lidia woke up," Ruhn said. "And, ah . . . she had some surprises to share."

"So," Hunt said to Ruhn in the stunned quiet five minutes later. "Your girlfriend has . . . kids."

Bryce's mind reeled from all her brother had said.

Ruhn only lifted baleful eyes to Hunt. All right: no teasing. She let out a low whistle. "How the Hel did Lidia hide it? When did she even *have* these kids?"

Baxian said ominously, "I think the better question is whether they're Pollux's."

"They didn't have wings," Ruhn said tensely. "But that doesn't mean anything."

"She's all right, though?" Bryce asked. She owed the female everything. *Everything.* If there was anything she could do to help her—

"She's sleeping again," Ruhn said. "I think the run upstairs drained her."

"Adrenaline fueled it, probably," Tharion mused.

Ruhn's eyes went hazy, worried, so Bryce supposed Hunt did him a favor when he changed the subject. He turned to her. "Okay, let's hear it. How the *fuck* did you get onto this ship? How did you find us?"

To distract Ruhn, she could play along. "I told you: I teleported." She met Hunt's eyes, registering the love and pain there, and said quietly, "You're my home, Hunt. Our love spans across stars and worlds, remember?" She smiled slightly. "I'll always find you."

His throat worked, no doubt recalling that he'd said those same words to her before she'd jumped through the Gate in the Eternal Palace. But he dropped her stare like he couldn't bear it, and asked, "*Where* did you teleport from?"

Fine, then. She'd give him some space to sort out his shit. "From dear old Dad's house. Where he thought he was keeping me hostage."

"He *thought*?" Ruhn demanded.

Bryce shrugged.

Hunt threw her a bone this time. "Can you explain what you said to the Ocean Queen in there? About the parasites in the water and the Asteri?"

"What else is there to say? They infected the waters of Midgard with it. It's in all of us. It forces us to make the Drop, otherwise it sucks away our power."

"Excuse me?" Ruhn blurted.

Bryce sighed. And explained it again.

All of it, this time—from the start. Arriving in the other world, being held in the dungeon. Escaping and traveling the tunnels with Azriel and Nesta. Then what she'd learned in that secret chamber: of the world of the Fae, of the Daglan, of Theia and Fionn and Pelias, of Silene and Helena, of Hel's assistance. Of claiming Silene's power, and how her own starlight now felt different. Then the encounter with Vesperus and stealing Truth-Teller from Azriel.

It took an hour to explain it all, though she omitted any mention of the Mask or the Trove. The fewer people who knew about them, the better. When she got to the part about how she'd been able to zero in on Hunt and jump right to him, his eyes gleamed, so full of love that her chest ached.

Ruhn had been silent through all of it, though his phone buzzed frequently while she spoke. She had a feeling that he was getting updates from someone about Lidia's current state.

Hunt leaned forward, bracing his forearms on his thighs. He exhaled a long breath. "Okay. That is . . . a lot. Just give me a moment."

Bryce absently rubbed at her chest, the eight-pointed star scar there. She said quietly, "Tell me what happened here. Please."

Bryce needed a minute when they finished.

Ten minutes, actually.

She left the room with a quiet "I'm so sorry" and then she was in the hall, stomach churning, breath stalling—

"Bryce," Hunt said from a few steps behind, boots thudding on the tiled floor.

She couldn't turn to face him. She'd left them, and they had suffered so much—

"Quinlan," he growled. His hand wrapped around her elbow, halting her. The hall was empty, its window overlooking the crushing black sea beyond the glass.

"Bryce," he said again, and gently turned her. She couldn't stop her face from crumpling.

Hunt was there in an instant, wrapping her in his arms, wings folding around them, surrounding her with that familiar, beckoning scent of rain on cedar.

"Shhh," he whispered, and she realized she'd begun crying, the full force of all that had happened to him, to her, crashing down.

Bryce slid her arms around his waist, clinging tight. "I was so worried—"

"I'm fine."

She scanned his face, his silver-lined eyes. "Those dungeons weren't . . . fine, Hunt."

"I survived."

But shadows darkened his face with the words. He bowed his head, leaning his brow against hers. That hateful halo pressed against her skin. "Barely," he admitted. She tightened her arms around him, shaking. "The thought of you kept me going."

He might as well have punched her in the heart. "You kept me going, too."

"Yeah?" The love in his voice threatened to shatter her heart. "I knew these smoldering good looks would come in handy one day."

She laughed brokenly. Lifted a hand to his face and traced its strong, beautiful lines.

"I'm sorry," he breathed, and the pain in the words nearly knocked her to the ground.

"For *what*?"

He shut his eyes, throat bobbing. "For getting us into this mess."

She pulled back. "*You? You* got us into this mess?"

He opened his eyes again, his gaze bleak as the sea beyond the wall of windows at their backs. "I should have warned you, should have made us all think before we jumped into this nightmare—"

She gaped. "You did warn me. You warned us all." She cupped his cheek in a hand. "But the only ones to blame for any of this are the Asteri, Hunt."

"I should have tried harder. None of us would be in this situation—"

"I'm going to stop you right there," she said hotly, laying her palm on his chest. "Do I regret the pain and suffering that you all went through? Solas, yes. I can barely think about it. But do I regret that we took a stand, that we *are* taking a stand? No. Never. And you couldn't have stopped me from starting that fight." She frowned. "I thought we were on the same page about doing what needs to be done."

His expression shuttered. "We were—are."

"You don't sound too sure of that."

"You didn't have to see your friends carved apart."

The second the words were out, she knew from his wide eyes that he regretted them. But it didn't stop them from hurting, from pelting her heart like stones. From sending her anger boiling up within her.

But she stared at the black ocean pressing against the glass, all that death held a few inches away. She said quietly, "I had to live with the terror of possibly never getting home, never seeing you again, wondering if you were even alive, every second I was gone." She glanced at him sidelong in time to see something cold pass over his face. She hadn't seen that coldness in a long, long time.

The face of the Umbra Mortis.

His voice was chilled, too, as he said, "Good thing we both made it, then."

It wasn't a resolution. Not even close. But this wasn't the conversation she wanted to have with him. Not right now. So she said blandly, turning from the wall of windows, "Yeah. Good thing."

"So we're really headed to Avallen?" Hunt asked carefully,

letting it drop as well, that Umbra Mortis face vanishing. "You ready to deal with King Morven?"

Bryce nodded, crossing her arms. "We won't accomplish anything against the Asteri if I can't learn what that portal to nowhere is and how it could possibly kill them. The Autumn King suggested that the Avallen Archives have a trove of information about the blades. And as for Morven . . . I just spent a few days with one asshole Fae King. Morven won't be any worse."

Hunt shifted on his feet, wings tucking in tight. "I'm down with the plan and all, but . . . you really think there's anything in the Avallen Archives that hasn't already been discovered?"

"If there's any place on Midgard that might have clues, it's there. The heart of all things Starborn. And that's where the Autumn King said he read about the portal to nowhere in the first place."

"I'll take whatever edge we can get, but again: King Morven isn't exactly friendly."

Bryce glanced down at her chest, the star-shaped scar barely peeking above the dip of her T-shirt. "He'll welcome us."

"Why are you so sure?"

She reached a hand into the interior pocket of her black athletic jacket. With a flourish, she pulled out her father's notebook. "Because I've got the Autumn King's dirty little secrets."

43

Lidia Cervos stared at her sons. Their mer foster parents were seated on either side of them, watching her with predatory focus. Davit and Renki. She'd never learned their names until now. But judging by the way they sat poised to strike, her boys had been well cared for. Loved.

Director Kagani sat across her desk from them, hands interlaced before her. The silence was palpable. Lidia had no idea how to break it.

Had no idea who she was, sitting here in one of the *Depth Charger*'s dark blue tactical bodysuits. A far comfier uniform than her old one, designed for an aquatic lifestyle. No sign of her silver torque or imperial medals or any of the trappings of that fake life she'd created.

She'd woken again a few hours after collapsing, in a different hospital bed, free of tubes and ports. She hoped the medwitch who'd helped her out of bed assumed her shaking legs were from lingering weakness.

Even if the feeling continued now, as she sat before her sons.

Brann, golden-haired and blue-eyed, wearing a forest-green T-shirt and jeans with holes in the knees, held her stare. Didn't balk from it as Actaeon, dark-haired and golden-eyed, did. But it was to Actaeon, in his black T-shirt and matching jeans, that she spoke, gentling her voice as much as she could. "There is . . . a great deal to tell you. Both of you."

Actaeon glanced to the foster father on his left. Davit. The brown-skinned male in a dark blue officer's uniform nodded encouragingly. Lidia's chest tightened. This had been her choice. One she'd had no option but to accept, yet . . .

She looked to Brann, whose eyes glowed with inner fire. Fearless—reckless. A natural leader. She'd seen that look on his face before, even as a baby.

Brann said, "So, what—we're supposed to live with you now?"

Actaeon whipped his head to his parents in alarm. Lidia suppressed the sting at that expression, but answered, "No." It was all she could manage to say.

Renki, pale-skinned and dark-haired, assured Actaeon, "This doesn't change anything. You guys are staying with us. And besides that, your mom has to take care of some stuff." He was clad in the navy-blue coveralls of a ship medic—he must have run right over from work.

Brann's brows lifted, as if he'd ask what kind of stuff, but Actaeon said quietly, "She's not our mom."

The words landed in her gut like a physical blow.

Davit said a shade sharply, "Yes, she is, Ace."

An oily sort of jealousy wended its way through her at the nickname. Her dark-haired son lifted his head, and—

Pure power glimmered in his eyes. She'd seen that look on his face before, too—long, long ago. The thoughtful, quiet stone to Brann's wildfire.

Lidia couldn't help her smile, despite the hurtful words. She said to Actaeon, to Brann, "You're exactly as you were as infants."

Brann smiled back at her. Actaeon didn't.

Director Kagani interrupted, "We're not going to put labels on anything or anyone right now. Lidia does indeed have . . . work that will keep her from settling down yet, and even once she does, we will all have another discussion about what is best for you two. And your fathers."

Lidia met Renki's gaze. The dominance and protectiveness in it. She still saw the glimmer of pleading beneath it. *Please don't take my sons away from me.*

It was the same sentiment she'd once conveyed to the Ocean Queen. A plea that had fallen on deaf ears.

They were her boys, her babies for whom she had changed the course of her life, but they had been raised by these males. Actaeon and Brann *were* their sons. Not by blood, but through love and care. They had protected them, raised them well.

She could have asked for nothing more—that the boys possessed such an attachment to their parents went beyond any hope she'd harbored.

So Lidia said, even as something in her soul crumbled, "I have no intention of taking you away from your parents." Her heart thundered, and she knew they could all hear it. But she raised her chin anyway. "I don't know when my work will be over, if ever. But if it is, if I am allowed to return here . . . I would like to see you again." She looked to the twins' parents. "All of you."

Renki nodded, gratitude in his eyes. Davit put a hand on Actaeon's shoulder.

Brann said, "You mean the work you do . . . as the Hind?"

Lidia glanced to Director Kagani in alarm. She had made them promise not to tell the boys who and what she was—

"We have TV down here," Brann said, reading her surprise and dismay. "We recognized you today. Had no idea you were our birth mom until now, but we know what you do. Who you work for."

"I work for the Ocean Queen," Lidia said. "For Ophion."

"You serve the Asteri," Actaeon cut in coldly. "You kill rebels for them."

"Ace," Davit warned again.

But Actaeon didn't back down. He looked to his twin and demanded, "You're cool with this? With her? You know what she does to people?"

Fire sparked in Brann's gaze once more. "Yeah, asshole, I do."

"Language," Renki warned.

Actaeon ignored him and pressed Brann, "Her boyfriend's the *Hammer*."

"Pollux is not my boyfriend," Lidia cut in, back stiffening.

"Your fuck buddy, then," Actaeon snapped.

"Actaeon," Renki snarled.

Director Kagani said quellingly, "That is enough, Actaeon." The director sighed, facing Lidia. "And perhaps that is enough for all of us for one day."

Actaeon let out a humorless laugh. "I'm just getting started." He pointed to his brother. "You want to play loyal dog, go ahead. You'll fit right in with her dreadwolves."

"You're a dick, you know that?" Brann seethed.

"Boys," Davit said. "That is *enough*." The male winced at Lidia. "I'm really sorry about this. We raised them to behave better."

Lidia nodded, throat closing up. But she said to Actaeon, "I understand. I really do."

She stood, the weight of their stares threatening to send her to her knees. But she said to Davit and Renki, "Thank you for taking care of them. For loving them."

Her eyes stung, and something massive began to implode in her chest, so Lidia said nothing else before walking out of the director's office, shutting the door behind her. She nodded her farewell to the administrative assistant sitting beyond the door, then she was out in the hall, gasping down air, fighting that implosion—

"Lidia," said a male voice behind her, and she turned to find Renki walking after her.

The male's face was pained. "I'm so sorry about how that went down. Davit and I have discussed this possibility for years, and we never planned it to be like that." He ran a hand through his dark hair. "I don't want you to think we, like . . . tried to turn the boys against you."

She shook her head. "The thought never crossed my mind."

Renki shifted on his feet, black work boots squeaking softly on the tiled floor. "We didn't know who you were, either. Until today.

We knew their mom was deep undercover for Ophion, but we didn't know *how* undercover."

"Only Director Kagani and the Ocean Queen knew."

"I'd love to hear the full story, if you're allowed to tell it. Davit would, too."

She swallowed hard. "Perhaps another day."

"Yeah—definitely get some rest." He grimaced, surveying her. "I'm, ah, a medic here. I was on the team that brought you in, actually. I'm glad to see you're back on your feet."

She nodded, unsure what to say.

Renki went on, "Davit captains one of the submersible-pods that runs recon, so he's occasionally away for days or weeks at a time—sometimes it's just me and the boys." He added, "Well, me, and both sets of our parents, who help out a lot. They adore the boys."

Grandparents. Something the boys wouldn't have had otherwise.

"Do you have siblings?" she asked the male.

Renki nodded. "I have two brothers, and Davit has a sister. So there are lots of cousins running around. The boys grew up in a veritable pack of them."

She smiled slightly. "Was it hard for them to live here without being mer?"

"At times," Renki said. "When they were toddlers, they didn't get why they couldn't just jump into the water with the other kids. There were lots of tantrums. Especially from Brann." A soft, loving laugh. "But Actaeon's a bit of a genius. He devised helmets and fins for them to use so they can keep up with the others. Even in the depths."

Pride bloomed in her chest. "Is that why you call him Ace?"

Renki grinned. "Yeah. He's been taking things apart and putting them back together into something smarter and cooler since he was a baby."

"I remember that," she said softly. "He'd always pull apart every toy I gave him . . ." She cut herself off.

But Renki's smile remained. "Still does. It's the one downside to living on this ship. Director Kagani gets the best teachers she can, but we're limited in what kind of higher ed we can offer him."

"And Brann?"

Renki let out a laugh. "Brann is . . . Well, he's a what-you-see-is-what-you-get kind of guy. A natural athlete—fearless. Quick to anger, and quick to laugh. He does okay in school, but right now, he's more interested in hanging out with his buddies. He's the stereotypical jock. We're both content to let him be who he is."

"They're like the sun and moon, then," she said quietly.

Renki's smile softened. "Yeah. Exactly." He reached into his pocket and pulled out a business card. "This has my contact information, in case you need anything. If you want to chat with me, or Davit, or have any questions . . ."

Lidia took his card, nodding her gratitude, unable to find words.

Renki said, "Ace might have said some . . . not-nice stuff in there, but don't for one moment think that he hasn't been wondering about you all this time. The two of them have some foggy memories of you, I think. Director Kagani says they were too young at the time, but I swear they do. They told me once that you had hair like Brann's and eyes like Ace's. Since they never learned who you were until today, I'm going to finally believe them."

"You're very kind for saying that."

Renki held her stare, sorrow and something else in his gaze. "I'll work on Ace for you. But for now, give him time."

She bowed her head. "Thank you."

She didn't trust herself to say more before she turned away, walking down the hall.

Lidia had nearly reached the stairwell, nearly tamped down the tears threatening to rise within her, when hurrying feet scuffed behind her. She slowed her pace, and stopped before the stairwell door, not opening it.

Only when the messenger extended a folded piece of kelp to her did Lidia turn.

The messenger, a young mer male who regarded her with a

mix of curiosity and wariness, announced, "From Her Depthless Majesty," before stepping aside to wait for a response.

Lidia unfolded the broad, flat kelp leaf. She read what was within, then nodded to the messenger. "I'll go right to her."

She didn't let herself look back at the hall, toward her sons behind the office door halfway down it, before walking into the stairwell. But as the door slammed behind her, it echoed through her entire being.

Five minutes later and ten floors down, Lidia found herself before the ruler of the seas. The Ocean Queen stood at a wall of windows overlooking the eternal dark of the deep ocean, her black hair floating around her as if she were indeed underwater.

It had been fifteen years since Lidia had last seen her. Last spoken to her.

As she had then, the Ocean Queen stood no taller than Lidia's chest, but Lidia steeled her spine against the power that filled the room.

She'd spent decades enduring the Asteri's presence. This female's power, however mighty . . . she'd weather it, too. Maybe that was why the Ocean Queen had bothered with her in the first place, all those years ago: Lidia had been able to face her and not tremble.

"I heard you have been reunited with your young," the Ocean Queen said without turning.

Lidia inclined her head anyway. "I thank Ogenas for such a gift."

"I do not recall granting you leave to abandon your post."

Lidia lifted her chin, keeping her breathing steady as the Ocean Queen slowly, slowly pivoted. Her eyes were black as the ocean outside.

The Ocean Queen went on, "I do not recall granting you leave to bring all these fugitives onto one of my city-ships."

Lidia remained silent, well aware that she had not been given leave to speak, either.

The Ocean Queen's eyes flickered. She was pleased by this small show of obedience, at least. "Our work relies upon our secrecy—it relies upon the Asteri considering us too vague a threat to bother investigating. We evade the Omega-boats, we offer sanctuary to the occasional Ophion agent. Nothing more. No attacks, no direct conflict. But you have now given the Asteri cause to start wondering what, exactly, swims in the deep. What *I* am doing down here."

When Lidia didn't reply, the Ocean Queen waved a hand. Permission to speak.

"I had no choice," Lidia said, keeping her eyes on the tiled floor. "We could not risk losing such valuable assets to our cause. But I can assure you that before I left, Rigelus and the others still did not consider you and your people a priority."

"Perhaps not," the Ocean Queen said, growing a few inches taller, ripping away nearly all the air in the room. "But now their most wanted enemies are on this ship. It will be only a matter of days before his mystics find us."

"Then it should be a relief that they shall depart for Avallen tomorrow."

The insolent words were out before Lidia could rein them in. She'd overheard the news from a passing group of officers—who'd all given her a wide berth when they noticed who was walking down the hall toward them. But the Ocean Queen only smiled. A shark's smile.

"And *you*," the ruler said with menacing softness, "shall depart tomorrow, too."

Every word eddied out of Lidia's head. Despite her years of training, of self-restraint, all she could say was, "My sons—"

"You have seen them." The ruler's sharp teeth flashed. "Consider yourself Ogenas-blessed indeed for that. Now you will resume your duties."

The unbearable, soul-shredding departure had nearly broken Lidia fifteen years ago. And now . . .

"You loathe me," the Ocean Queen said, as if delighted.

Lidia shoved every bit of despair, every bit of defiance, down deep. Her feelings didn't matter. Only Actaeon and Brann mattered.

So her tone was bland, empty, when she spoke. As hollow and soulless as it had been all these years with the Asteri, with Pollux. "Tell me what I must do."

Ruhn paced his room, grinding his teeth until they ached. Bryce had gone to the home world of their people. And their father had held her hostage. Granted, she'd engineered it, but . . .

The true weight of it had only sunk in later, once they'd parted.

Maybe he should hit the gym. Work out some of this aggression roaring through his system, overriding any joy from seeing Bryce. To out-sweat the need to find his father and wipe him from the face of Midgard for what he'd tried to do to Bryce. For the fact that Ruhn hadn't been there to stop it, to shield her from him.

He untied his boots, then slung off his long-sleeved shirt, aiming for the small locker at the opposite end of his room, where he'd been provided with clothes and sneakers. A ten-mile run on the treadmill followed by a fuck-ton of weights would help. Maybe he'd get lucky and someone would be in the gym to spot him.

Ruhn yanked out a white T-shirt, carrying it with him as he flung open the door, intending to pull it on as he walked to the gym—

He ran smack into Lidia.

Her scent hit him, addling his senses, and he took a step back, out of it. "Hey," he said, then blurted, "You're up."

She lifted her chin, eyes a bit glassy. "Yes."

Ruhn twisted his shirt in his hands. She was wearing one of the ship's aquatic bodysuits that left nothing to the imagination. He might not have explored her body—on this plane, anyway—but their souls had definitely fucked, and he had no idea where the Hel that put them.

"I, um, was about to go to the gym," he said, and held up the shirt. His palms turned sweaty. "How are you feeling?"

"Stronger." It wasn't an answer, not really. She nodded to a door directly across the hall from his. "I've been moved to that room."

Ruhn stepped further into the corridor, shutting his door behind him. As he did, her smell wrapped around him, dizzying and heady and so fucking enticing that his mouth watered—and then he beheld the ice in her eyes.

He stepped back, brows lifting. "These are appropriate digs for Agent Daybright?"

Lidia looked at him without any humor, any sense that they'd shared their souls. Two passing officers skirted around them. He caught a few of their whispers as they headed for the elevator bay at the end of the hall. *There she is. Holy shit, it's her.*

Lidia ignored them.

The elevator opened down the hall, and Ruhn couldn't help but think of the last time he and Lidia had been in one. When she'd put a bullet through the Hawk's head and killed those dreadwolves. Then, her eyes had been open and pleading. None of that remained.

He couldn't stop himself from asking, "Did you see your sons yet?"

"Yes." She fit a key in her lock.

"How . . . ah . . . how'd it go?"

She didn't face him. "I am a stranger to them." Not one shred of emotion laced the words.

"How are the foster parents?"

The lock clicked. "A nice mer couple."

What happened? Who was the father? How did you wind up here? He wanted to know so many things. How had she ever kept this hidden? Her family—

Fuck, her family. These boys were male heirs to the Enador line. Hypaxia was their aunt.

But Lidia said distantly, turning to face him at last, "Everything I did was for them, you know."

His chest ached. "For your kids?"

She studied her hands, the imposing ruby ring on one of her

fingers. "I haven't seen them since they were eighteen months old. Not even a picture."

But she'd known them on sight today. Had known what grade they'd be in, remembered where the school was on this ship, and run directly there.

He lingered at his doorway. For a heartbeat, he allowed himself to look at her face. The impossible perfection of it, the light of her golden eyes, the glint of her hair. The most beautiful female he'd ever seen, and yet it didn't even fucking matter. None of that had ever mattered when it came to her.

He asked, "What happened?"

"What difference does it make?" she asked, wary and sharp. "I thought you didn't wish to hear my *sob story*, as you put it."

Well, he'd earned that. "Look," he said tightly, "you can't expect me to learn who you are, what you are, and be immediately cool with it, okay? I'm still processing all this shit."

"What is there to process? I am who I am, and I've done what I've done. The fact that I have children doesn't erase that."

All right. She was pissed off. "It's almost like you want me to resent you."

"I wanted you to *listen*," she snapped, "but you wouldn't. Yet now that I fit some sort of acceptably sad female backstory, you're willing to hear me out."

"That's bullshit." Fuck, she and Bryce would get along well. The fact that both of them were on this ship . . . Part of him wanted to run and hide.

Lidia went on, "Would you have listened if I had no backstory other than realizing what was right and wanting to fight for it? Of doing whatever it took to make sure that good prevailed against tyranny? Or does my being a mother somehow make my choices more palatable to you?"

"Most dudes run when they find out the female they're into has kids."

Her eyes flickered with cold fire. "That's male strength for you."

"You seemed to like my strength plenty, sweetheart."

She snorted, turning back toward her door. Dismissing him.

His temper coiled. "So what's the *sob story*, Lidia?"

Slowly, she looked back, her face a mask of utter contempt, and said before she shut the door in his face, "You don't deserve to hear it."

44

Ithan was carefully setting down a figurine of Cthona giving birth on all fours—the planet Midgard crowning between her legs—when Jesiba's phone rang. The shrill sound shattered the silence, but Ithan's sunball reflexes kept him from dropping the fragile marble.

"What."

Even Ithan's wolf-keen hearing couldn't make out the person on the other end.

"Fine."

She hung up, gaze instantly shooting to Ithan. He gently nestled the figurine into a crate, packing peanuts rustling. "What is it?" he asked carefully.

"Come with me." She got to her feet and strode across the room with surprising speed considering her dark blue four-inch heels. She hadn't bothered to change her hair back to its usual short length, and the sight of her swaying golden locks was . . . odd. So was the face free of its usual makeup. She might very well have been a few years older than Ithan for all she appeared.

She halted at the doorway and pointed to the wall adjacent to the bookshelf. "Bring that with you. It's loaded."

Ithan glanced over at the weapon mounted there. He'd heard what Bryce had done to Micah with it.

But Ithan didn't hesitate as he crossed the room and grabbed the Godslayer Rifle off the wall.

Jesiba led Ithan through a dark-stoned warren, lit by simmering golden fires. The hallways were strangely quiet, and it occurred to him that he had no idea what time it was. Judging by the quiet, he guessed it was the middle of the night. But in the House of Flame and Shadow, where so many nocturnal predators dwelled, that might not have been accurate.

It didn't matter, really.

The sounds of a gathered crowd rumbled down the stones long before he reached the round chamber.

Pillars had been formed from stalactites and stalagmites that had merged together—he scoured his brain and came up short on what *those* were called—and unlike the cut, polished glory of the other halls, the walls were raw stone. The domed ceiling was rough-hewn, and it echoed the murmuring and chattering of the crowd, too thick to identify individual words.

People quieted as Jesiba strutted through the natural archway into the room, Ithan a step behind her, that notorious gun in his hands. It was lighter than he'd thought it would be, yet he'd never held anything more electric.

The crowd parted to allow Jesiba through. She looked straight ahead as she strode into the center of the room, her dark blue skirt trailing behind her, heels beating a rolling, take-no-shit beat. If anyone was shocked by her new hairdo and lack of makeup, no one dared say anything. Or keep their stare on her for too long.

But Ithan glanced ahead to what—who—stood in the center of the chamber, and his heart stumbled.

The Astronomer lifted a knobbly finger and pointed at Ithan.

"You're dead, thief," the old man snarled.

Tharion knew he'd dodged a bullet. Knew Bryce's arrival had spared him from the Ocean Queen sending him right back to Lunathion.

A bounty on his head. Fuck.

But to be confined to this ship . . . was it any better than being held by the River Queen or the Viper Queen? Confined as a *guest*, the Ocean Queen had claimed. But he knew what she'd meant.

"Avallen has always given me the creeps," Flynn was saying as they all squeezed around a table in their deck's mess hall, discussing the next day's arrival on the misty isle. At this hour of the evening, every table was crammed with people for dinner, their conversations and laughter so loud it made it nearly impossible for Tharion to hear his companions. "But Morven's terrible. I've known him since I was a kid, and he's a fucking snake. Him, and the Murder Twins."

"Murder Twins?" Athalar asked with a mix of alarm and amusement from where he sat beside Bryce, an arm looped around her waist, his fingers idly toying with the ends of her hair. Tharion knew that even if they hadn't been short on space around the table, the mates would have kept close together.

"A nickname we gave my distant cousins," Ruhn said around a mouthful of bread. "After they joined Cormac in trying to kill us multiple times in the Cave of Princes." The prince's eyes flickered with regret as he spoke Cormac's name.

Tharion blocked out the image that flashed—of Cormac's final moments, of running while the Fae male immolated himself. His grip clenched around his fork, so tight his knuckles turned white.

But Ruhn went on, "They can read minds . . . whether you want them to or not." He pointed with his half-eaten chunk of bread to Bryce. "They're not going to ask for permission like that Night Court dude."

Bryce grimaced. "Can anyone defend against their skills?"

"Yeah," Ruhn said, "but you have to be vigilant at all times, even when you can't see them near you. And they obey Morven unconditionally."

Bryce examined her nails. "I love me some good old-fashioned goons."

Tharion smiled, grip loosening on his fork.

But Ruhn shook his head. "They're not your usual goons, and Morven's not your usual sort of asshole. During my Ordeal—"

"I know," Bryce said, scooping up some rice, grown in one of the ship's many hydroponic gardens. "Big, bad uncle. You pissed him off, he sent you into the Cave of Princes to punish you, you showed him up . . ."

"He's Cormac's father," Declan said carefully. "Don't forget that he's just lost a son and heir."

Tharion stared down at his platter of rice and fish, though his appetite had vanished like seafoam on the sand.

"He was quick to disown him," Lidia Cervos said from the far end of the table.

Tharion had nearly keeled over in shock when she'd sat down with them. But . . . where else would she sit in the packed hall?

He didn't fail to note that Ruhn sat at the opposite end of the table.

Lidia added, "But I will echo the warning: King Morven only agrees to things that are advantageous to him. If you're going to convince him not to immediately sell you out to the Asteri, you need to spin it the right way."

"I'd planned to go right to the archives," Bryce said. "No royal visit required."

"The mists," Ruhn said, "tell him everything. He'll know we've arrived. It'll infuriate him if you don't . . . pay tribute."

"So we play nice," Athalar said, draining his glass of water. The other diners kept glancing toward their table—with awe, with dread, with curiosity. All of them pretended not to notice.

"And," Ruhn added, wincing, "females aren't permitted in the archives."

Tharion rolled his eyes. "Please," he muttered.

"Yeah, yeah," Bryce said, waving a dismissive hand. "The Autumn King made *sure* I was aware of their No Girls Allowed rules. But too bad for Morven: I'm going in."

Hunt nudged her with a gray wing. "I'm assuming you have some plan up your sleeve that you're going to spring on us at the worst possible moment."

"I think you mean the coolest possible moment," Bryce said, and Tharion, despite himself, smiled again.

"Note how she didn't answer that," Hunt said darkly to Baxian, who chuckled and said, "Danika was the same."

An undercurrent of longing and sorrow flowed beneath the Helhound's light tone. A male who'd lost his mate. It was, rumor claimed, worse than losing one's soul. Tharion couldn't decide whether he pitied the male for the loss, or envied him for being lucky enough to have found his mate in the first place. He wondered what Baxian would have preferred: to have never known Danika, or this, to have had their centuries together cut so brutally short.

Bryce reached across the table and squeezed the Helhound's hand, love and pain on her face. Tharion turned his gaze from the matching expression Baxian gave her as he squeezed her hand back. A private, intimate moment of grieving.

After a moment of silence for the two of them to mourn the wolf they'd both loved, Flynn said, "Avallen is an old and fucked-up place. We need to be fast so we can get the Hel out of there."

Bryce let go of Baxian's hand and said primly, "Research takes time." The perfect imitation of a schoolmarm. But she dropped the act as she added quickly, "Plus I want to visit the Cave of Princes."

Tharion had heard only legends regarding the famed caves—none of them good.

Ruhn gaped. "And you think you can do this without even saying hello to Morven? Females aren't allowed in there, either."

Bryce crossed her arms, leaning into Athalar's side. "Okay, maybe we'll drop in for tea."

Her brother was having none of it. "The Cave of Princes . . . why? What's that got to do with the portal-to-nowhere stuff?"

Bryce shrugged, going back to her food. "It's where the Starsword has always been held. I think there might be some information there."

"Again . . . not actually answering," Hunt said under his breath to Baxian. Tharion stifled his grin of amusement. Especially as Bryce glared at her mate. Athalar just pressed a kiss to her brow, a casual bit of love that had Baxian glancing away.

Tharion wished he had something to offer the Helhound, some sort of comfort. But the gods knew he wasn't the one to dispense any sort of advice regarding love. Loss, maybe—he'd learned to live with the hole in his chest after Lesia had been murdered—but he doubted Baxian wanted to hear someone try to liken losing a sister to losing one's mate.

"We shouldn't stay on Avallen a moment longer than necessary," Flynn insisted, drawing Tharion's attention once more. "I'm telling you, every time I've been on the island, it's made my magic . . . unhappy." In emphasis, a delicate vine wrapped around his hand, between his fingers. "It literally shrivels up and dies when I'm there." The vine did just that, withering into dust that sprinkled over his half-eaten plate of fish and rice. Flynn took a bite anyway.

"I always forget you actually have magic," Bryce said. "But I'll refrain from making the obvious dig about failing to perform on Avallen."

"Thanks," Flynn muttered, shoveling another forkful of food into his mouth.

"We should split up when we arrive," Declan declared, pushing around his own meal. "Some of us can hit up the archives, and the others can go to the Cave of Princes. We'll all look for any extra intel about the Starsword and its connection to the dagger."

With a glance to the massive window at the rear of the mess hall, overlooking the crushing black ocean beyond, Tharion said, "And I'll be here, praying to Ogenas that you find something useful about how to destroy the Asteri with those blades."

Ogenas—Keeper of Mysteries. If there was a god to beg for knowledge, it'd be her.

"Archives," Ruhn, Flynn, and Declan said, raising their hands.

Bryce glowered at them. "Shitheads. I was counting on some guidance from you, since you've actually been in the Cave of Princes before." She turned to Athalar and Baxian and sighed. "Looks like we get to do some spelunking."

"Just so you know," Ruhn said, "during our Ordeal, it took the three of us a while to get to Pelias's tomb and the Starsword. But that was also because we were being chased and hunted by ghouls and

Cormac and the Murder Twins. So there might be a more direct route—though there are mists that try to confuse you every step of the way."

"Great," Bryce said, but Tharion didn't miss how her eyes had seemed to brighten, as if her brother's words had sparked something.

"And," Ruhn added, "there are carvings throughout the caves—including in the burial chamber. It could take you a while to find anything. Make sure you bring a few days' worth of supplies with you."

"Noted," Athalar said grimly.

"Fantastic," Baxian grumbled beside him.

Tharion's heart strained, his own words from a moment ago sinking in. He *would* be here, on this ship. While they left. Tomorrow they'd part ways. These people Urd had brought into his life, who he didn't deserve . . .

"I'm going with you," Lidia said. "To Avallen." She'd been so silent that Tharion had forgotten she sat at the other end of the table.

Ruhn didn't so much as look at her as she spoke. Tharion noted that the Hind was deliberately not looking at him, either. Only at Bryce.

"Why?" Bryce asked. "You, ah . . . Your kids are on this ship."

Lidia's spine stiffened. "The Ocean Queen has made it very clear that if I do not resume my duties as Agent Daybright, the protection she has given them will . . . cease." They all looked at her in surprise, but Lidia continued, "The Asteri have created a new, worse type of mech-suit—worse than the hybrids from a few weeks ago. This one no longer requires a pilot to operate it, only techs in a distant room. Rigelus has ordered the suits stationed atop Mount Hermon." A glance toward Hunt, whose face was stony at the news. "The Ocean Queen wants me to learn how to stop them, but I fear there's little that I can glean beyond what the news networks have all been reporting. The suits are already built, and ready to be unleashed. We can do nothing."

"Avallen's the opposite direction from the Eternal City," Hunt growled. "We'd be taking you way too far north."

Lidia shook her head. "It is useless to expend my time looking for a way to stop the mech-suits—a solution that in all odds probably doesn't exist. I convinced the Ocean Queen that I'm of better use to her if I accompany you to Avallen and learn whatever you uncover there."

"So," Bryce said, "you've offered to—what, spy on us for the Ocean Queen? And are telling us about it?"

A shallow nod. "You've made her nervous, Bryce Quinlan, and that is not a good thing. But because I have . . . connections to your group, she's seen the advantage in sending me." A glance toward Ruhn at last. The Fae Prince continued to ignore her.

"Do you really think nothing can be done about those new suits?" Bryce asked. "They sound dangerous."

Lidia's face remained solemn. "Destroying them would require assembling a force to march on the Eternal City. A force we do not have. So I will be going with you, for the time being. Until we figure out how we're all going to end this."

Stunned silence filled the room. Tharion's breathing hitched at the thought of what Lidia was implying.

"Well, great," Flynn muttered, earning a sharp look from Lidia. "Are you on Team Archives or Team Caves?"

"That remains to be seen," Lidia said coolly. "As it remains to be seen whether you can convince Morven to even allow you to enter either place. *Especially* if females are not allowed."

"We'll convince him," Bryce said, flashing that disarming smile. Tharion didn't fail to catch the suspicious look Hunt slid her way.

Tharion would worry about it later. His friends were leaving. And he'd remain on this ship, under the control of the Ocean Queen. It didn't matter if Bryce claimed him as her subject—there was no standing up to the ruler of the seas.

It wouldn't have surprised him to glance down and find his chest caving in.

But his friends continued talking, and Tharion tried to savor it—the easy camaraderie, the tones and rhythms of their voices.

Too soon, he'd likely never see them again.

"This ship is just one big version of the Astronomer's ring," Sasa said quietly from where she floated above the glass conference table. "Malana's been sick about it since we got on board." Indeed, there was no sign of the third sprite.

"Is she okay?" Bryce asked.

"She'll be okay when we leave," Rithi said, admiring her reflection in the glass surface of the table. But the sprite suddenly peered up at Bryce's face. "When we're in open air again."

"That's what we came to talk about," Lidia said, glancing between the sisters from where she sat on the other side of the table. "Your next move."

Bryce had been surprised and a little unnerved when Lidia had pulled her aside after dinner and explained her plan. Bryce had an intimate connection to the sprite community, and Lidia needed the triplets sent on an essential task. It would be best if that request came from someone they trusted, the Hind insisted.

The sprites now swapped looks. "We had planned to follow you to Avallen," Sasa said, chin lifting. "Unless you would rather not have three sprites—"

"It would be an honor and a joy to have three sprites with me," Bryce said, hoping her earnest tone proved how much she meant it. How her heart had been aching since Lidia had grabbed her earlier, and the memory of Lehabah's beautiful face had glowed brightly in her mind. "And honestly, where we're going, you guys would be super useful." In the darkness of the Cave of Princes, even with Bryce's starlight, three extra flames would have been *very* helpful. "But . . ." She considered her next words carefully.

Lidia spared her the effort. "Irithys is free."

The sprites gasped, both going vibrant orange. "Free?" Rithi breathed.

"Escaped," Lidia amended. "I helped her get out of the Asteri palace, in exchange for her assistance with rescuing our friends from the dungeons."

"Where is she now?" Sasa demanded, flame warming—paling to a lighter hue.

"That is why we came to talk to you," Bryce said. "We don't know where she is."

"You . . . lost our queen?" Sasa said softly.

"When we parted ways," Lidia added quickly, as Rithi and Sasa were now turning white-hot with anger, "I suggested that Irithys go find a stronghold of your people. She seemed . . . hesitant to do so. I think she might be worried about how she'll be received."

The sprites bristled with anger.

"So," Bryce cut in quickly, "we were wondering if you guys would go find her. Make sure she's, ah . . . safe. And offer her your companionship."

"Our queen doesn't want to see her people?" Rithi's voice was dangerously low, her flame still a simmering white.

"Irithys," Lidia said calmly, "has spent the majority of her existence locked within a crystal ball. As you, perhaps, can understand better than anyone else on Midgard . . . to suddenly be free of captivity, to be alone in the world, is no easy thing. So I"—a glance at Bryce—"*we* are asking you to find her. To offer her companionship and guidance, yes, but also . . ."

"To help us," Bryce finished. "We need you three to advocate for Midgard—help her understand what we're fighting for. And maybe convince her to help against the Asteri again. When the time's right."

The sprites studied them for a long moment.

Sasa said, "You would trust Lowers and slaves with this?"

"We would trust no one else for so important a task," Lidia said.

There weren't many Vanir on Midgard who would say it—and believe it. Bryce felt herself slide dangerously toward liking the Hind.

But Rithi asked, "You can't believe that some fire sprites would make a difference against the Asteri. Our ancestors didn't during the battle with the Fallen . . . and that was against malakim."

"Lehabah made a difference against Micah," Bryce said, throat unbearably tight. "One fire sprite took on an Archangel and handed his ass to him. Her presence bought me the time to kill him. To kill an Archangel."

The sprites' eyes widened. "You *killed* Micah?" Rithi breathed.

Lidia didn't seem surprised—as the Hind, she'd probably heard about the whole thing right after it happened. "With Lehabah's help," Bryce said. "*Because* of Lehabah's help." She swallowed down the ache in her throat. "So yes—I believe that the fire sprites can and will make a difference against the Asteri."

The sisters looked at each other, as if they could mind-speak like Ruhn.

Then Sasa met Bryce's stare. And said without an ounce of fear, "We will find Irithys." The sprites burned to a deep, true blue. "And fight with her against the Asteri when the time comes."

"That went well," Bryce said minutes later as she and Lidia walked down the hall, back toward their sleeping quarters. "I'm glad you had me talk to them."

The Hind said nothing, gaze fixed on the passage ahead.

"You all right?" Bryce dared ask. The Hind had sat with them at dinner, but had been mostly quiet. And definitely hadn't even looked once at Ruhn. Nor had her brother acknowledged Lidia's presence.

"Fine," Lidia said, and Bryce knew it for the lie it was.

They said nothing more for the rest of the way, stopping only when they reached the sleeping quarters. Hunt was waiting for Bryce in their room. But Bryce paused and said before Lidia could walk into her own cabin, "Thank you."

Lidia halted, turning her way. "For what?"

"Saving my mate. My brother. My best friend's mate. You know, three of the most important people in my life." She offered a tentative smile.

Lidia inclined her head, regal and graceful. "It was the least I could do." She turned back to open her door.

"Hey," Bryce said. Lidia paused again. Bryce jerked her chin at Lidia, and the cabin beyond the Hind—where she'd be staying alone. "I know we don't, uh, know each other or anything, but if you need someone to talk to . . . Someone who's *not* Ruhn . . ." She shrugged. "I'm a door away."

Gods, that sounded stupid.

But Lidia's mouth quirked upward, something like surprise in her eyes. "Thank you," she said, and walked into her room, quietly shutting the door behind her.

All day, Hunt had been practically counting down the minutes until he could get Bryce alone in their room, then get her naked. But now that he was lying in the too-narrow bunk with her, lights out and the only sound their breathing . . . he didn't know where to start.

That fucked-up conversation between them earlier didn't help. He'd told her his truth, and she didn't want to hear it. Couldn't accept it.

But it *was* his fault—out of all of them, he should have known better than to lead them down this road again. He didn't get how she couldn't see that.

"Can I be honest about something?" she said into the darkness. She didn't wait for his answer before she said, "Aside from dangling the Autumn King's notes in front of Morven, I don't have a solid game plan for dealing with him. Or a solid backup plan should he not go for the notebooks."

Hunt put aside thoughts of their earlier fight and said, "Oh, I know. You didn't have nearly as much insufferable swagger about this as you usually do when you have a genius secret plan."

She whacked his shoulder. "I mean it. Aside from the Autumn King's notes, my only other bargaining chip with him is my breeding potential. And since you and I are married . . ."

"Are you asking for a divorce?"

She chuckled. "No. I'm saying that I've got no worth to these shitheads. Since my uterus is . . . spoken for."

"Mmm. Sexy." He nipped at her ear. "I missed you." They could get into the nitty-gritty of their argument later. Tomorrow. Never.

He trailed a hand down her hip, her thigh. His cock stirred at the softness of her, the sweet smell of lilac and nutmeg.

"As much as I want to bang your brains out, Athalar," she said, and Hunt laughed into her hair, "can we just . . . hold each other tonight?"

"Always," he said, heart aching. He tucked her in tighter, so fucking grateful for her scent in his nose, the lushness of her body against his. He didn't deserve it. "I love you."

She pressed even closer, arm wrapping around his waist. "I love you, too," she whispered back. "Team Caves, all the way."

He huffed a laugh. "Let's get T-shirts."

"Don't tempt me. If Avallen wasn't a backwater island with no interweb, I would have already ordered them to arrive at Morven's castle."

He grinned, that weight in his chest lifting for a precious moment. "There's really no interweb?"

"Nope. The mists block all. Legend has it that even the Asteri can't pierce them." She made a silly little eerie *woooooo* noise and wriggled her fingers. Then she paused, as if considering, before adding, "Vesperus mentioned things called *thin places*—wreathed in mist. The Prison in the Fae world was one. And it seems too coincidental that the ancient Starborn Fae *also* established a stronghold in a place wreathed by mist that keeps out enemies."

Hunt's brows rose. "How can the mists possibly keep a wall up against the Asteri?"

"The better question is why would the Asteri leave Avallen alone for so long if it *is* capable of keeping them out."

Hunt pressed a kiss to the top of her head. "I suspect you'll find out the answers in the most dramatic way possible."

She snuggled closer to him, and he held her tighter. "You know me well, Athalar."

Ithan didn't dare point the Godslayer Rifle at the Astronomer. But he remained poised to do so as Jesiba said, "What is this about?"

The crowd—draki, vamps, daemonaki, and many others he couldn't name—was silent as death. They had all come to witness this retribution. Ithan's mouth dried out.

The Astronomer's slate-gray eyes blazed with hatred. "The wolf stole something of mine."

Jesiba shrugged. "The matter of the sprites and the dragon has been settled between us."

"Do not toy with me, Jesiba," the Astronomer snapped. "We both know he took more than those firelings."

Ithan stepped up. His hands grew sweaty against the sleek wood and metal of the rifle. "A tank is no place for a wolf." *Or anyone,* he thought. "And besides, she wasn't yours to begin with. She had no slave mark."

"Her father sold her to me. It was an unofficial passing of ownership."

"She was a child, and you had no right—"

Ithan had killed her. *He* had no right to speak of her like he wasn't as bad as this man before him—

"You are a *thief,* wolf, and I demand payment! I demand her returned to me!"

Words were suddenly impossible. Ithan couldn't speak.

But a lovely, lilting female voice said from behind the crowd, "The Fendyr heir shall never again be yours, Astronomer."

The crowd hissed, and parted to reveal Queen Hypaxia Enador walking into the chamber, robes floating behind her on a phantom wind.

From the corner of his eye, Ithan caught Jesiba's smirk. "Hypaxia," the sorceress said. "Just the necromancer I was looking for."

45

That Jesiba was able to clear the crowd without so much as a word was testament to her grip on this place, this House.

Ithan found himself torn between looking at Hypaxia and the Astronomer—and avoiding both of their gazes.

The Astronomer waited until the crowd had left before saying to the witch-queen, "If you know where the wolf is and withhold that information, then the law says you are—"

"No law applies here," Hypaxia cut in, "as the Fendyr heir was not a legal slave. Just as you said." Gods, Ithan wished he had one fraction of her steadiness, that serene intelligence. Hypaxia went on, "So there was nothing for Ithan Holstrom to steal. He merely allowed a free civitas to make a choice about whether to remain in that wretched tank . . . or to leave."

And then he'd killed her.

Jesiba was giving him a warning look, as if to say, *Do not fucking breathe a word about that.* Ithan returned her a look, as if to say, *Do you think I'm that dumb?*

She glanced pointedly at his *CCU SUNBALL* T-shirt.

He rolled his eyes and turned to the witch-queen facing off against the Astronomer.

"That wolf cost me untold sums of gold. The loss of one mystic—"

"I'll pay it," Ithan said hoarsely. His parents had made some wise investments before their deaths. He had more money than he knew what to do with.

"I require ten million gold marks."

Ithan burst out coughing. He was well off, but—

"Paid," Jesiba said coolly.

Ithan whirled to her, but the sorceress was smiling blandly at the Astronomer. "Add it to my monthly tab."

The Astronomer glared at her, then at Ithan, and finally at Hypaxia, who looked at him with icy disdain. But he only spat on the ground and stalked out, long stringy hair flowing behind him.

In the silence, Jesiba faced Hypaxia and said, "I called you days ago and told you to come *immediately*. Is your broom not working?"

Ithan whirled on Jesiba. "*This* is the necromancer you had in mind?"

Honestly, he didn't know why he hadn't thought of it himself. He'd just worked with her, for fuck's sake, when they'd tried to conjure Connor at the Autumn Equinox. Maybe because it *hadn't* worked and the Under-King had arrived instead, he'd written her off, but—

"Hypaxia's father was the finest necromancer I've ever known," Jesiba said, crossing her arms. "She has his gift. If there's anyone to trust with your task, Holstrom, it's her."

Hypaxia's brows lifted in faint surprise—as if the praise was unusual. But she said to Jesiba, "We should talk in your office."

"Why?"

Hypaxia seemed to debate whether to answer, but finally said, "You want to know what delayed me these days? What I feared this fall has come to pass. Morganthia Dragas and her coven have staged a coup in the name of what they consider the preservation of witchkind's old ways. I am Queen of the Valbaran Witches no longer." She touched her breast, where her usual golden pin of Cthona was broken in two. "To escape their executioners, I have sworn fealty to the House of Flame and Shadow."

* * *

Lidia had let Renki decide on the place for this early-morning meeting. Somewhere neutral, somewhere private, somewhere "chill," as the mer male had described it.

Lidia wished she had some *chill* herself as she sat on the couch in the quiet student rec area—Director Kagani had closed it to everyone else for an hour—and looked at her sons. They sat on the opposite couch, which was stained and sagging, befitting a student lounge.

Davit had been called away for work late last night, so only Renki had come. The male now sat at the beverage counter on the opposite end of the room. Giving them space. An illusion of privacy.

She wished he'd sat with them.

There was a good chance Morven wouldn't let them leave Avallen alive. She'd needed to see her boys before she left, just one more time, but that didn't mean this was comfortable.

Ace leaned back against the cushions, arms crossed, staring at the TV blasting sunball highlights above the foosball table. But Brann surveyed her frankly, gaze bright with his keen intellect and fighting nature. A warrior indeed. He said without preamble, "Why did you want to meet us so early?"

Lidia subtly wiped her sweaty palms on the legs of her tactical bodysuit. She knew both boys marked the motion. "I thought I might make myself available to you, in case you had any questions about me. My past."

She'd faced down horrors without flinching, and yet this—this had her heart thundering.

Brann's mouth twisted to the side as he thought about it. Without taking his eyes off the TV, Actaeon said, "It's because she's leaving."

Too smart for his own good. Lidia looked at him, though Ace wouldn't acknowledge her, and said, "Yes. Today."

Brann glanced between them. "Where?"

Ace answered before she could. "She's not going to tell you. Don't bother asking. She doesn't know what the word *honesty* means."

Lidia clenched her jaw. "I wish I could tell you. But our mission relies on secrecy."

Ace slid his eyes to her then. "And us kids will go blabbing your location to everyone, right?"

Gods help her. "I wish I could tell you," she repeated.

Brann asked, voice thick, "Are you coming back?"

Lidia said frankly, "I hope so."

Actaeon returned to the TV. "You've managed to slither out of every scrape so far. I don't see why this would be any different."

The words hit like a blow to some soft, unguarded part of her.

Brann gave his twin a warning glare. "Come on, Ace." Clearly, they'd had some sort of conversation beforehand. About how they'd behave.

And clearly, Ace hated her.

Fine. She could live with that. He was safe, and loved. For that, she could endure his resentment.

"We're at war," Lidia told them. "And it's about to get uglier. I cannot tell you where I am going, but I can tell you I may not come back. Every time I venture out, especially now that my enemies know the truth about me, there is a good chance I will not return."

Ace snapped, "Are we supposed to feel bad and cry for our mommy?"

It took all her will not to break down. Mustering that coolness she'd perfected over the years, she said, "You claimed I didn't know what honesty was a moment ago. Well, I'm giving it to you. If you interpret this as manipulation, I cannot help that. But I wanted to see you—both of you—before I left today. To say goodbye."

Brann again glanced between them. Then said, "I guess my biggest question is why. Why you left us here."

"I didn't have a choice," she said plainly, keenly aware of Renki across the room. "It was either leave you here, safe and with people who would love you, or risk bringing you into a world that would have offered the opposite. I . . . I've thought about you every single day since."

This was veering into territory she wanted to avoid. She hadn't planned on approaching it during this visit. Maybe ever. And she knew that if she stayed for one more moment, she'd likely say more than was wise, things she wasn't ready to say aloud—things the boys might not be ready to hear.

Instead, with slightly trembling fingers, she pulled her ruby ring from her finger and laid it on the table between them. "I want you to have this." She fought past the tightness in her throat. "It's an heirloom of my father's household. He's not anyone worth remembering, but that ruby . . ." She couldn't bear to see what expression might be on their faces. "It's very valuable. You can sell it to pay for university, housing . . . when you're old enough, I mean. If you ever leave this ship. Not that you should." She was rambling. She swallowed, and at last looked at them. Ace's face was blank, but Brann was staring with wide eyes at the obscenely huge ruby. "Or if you want to keep it," she said quietly, "that's fine, too."

She wished she had something else to leave them, some other piece of her that wasn't connected to the monster who'd sired her, but this was all she possessed.

Task complete, Lidia stood, and Renki glanced her way. She nodded to him.

She faced her sons—fierce and strong and capable, no thanks to her. "I know it won't matter to you," she said, staring at Ace as he again pointedly watched the TV, "but I'm so very proud of how you turned out. Of the males you are, and are still becoming. I look at you both and know that . . . that I made the right choice." She smiled softly at Brann.

Brann's eyes gleamed. "Thanks for that. For giving us our parents." He motioned to Renki. Lidia bowed her head. "Good luck out there," Brann said. "Wherever you're going."

She put a hand on her heart.

Brann jabbed Ace with an elbow. Ace slid his golden eyes back to her and said, "Bye."

Lidia kept her hand on her heart, tapping it once, and turned away.

She left, not knowing where she was going, only that she had to keep moving or else she'd find some place to crumple up and die.

She walked through the gleaming halls of the ship. Walked and walked and walked, and did not let herself look back.

Ithan only waited until the door to Jesiba's office shut before he whirled on Hypaxia.

"What happened?" Ithan demanded.

Jesiba had warned him before setting off through the halls to *keep quiet*, and he'd obeyed, even while they'd stopped in the dark dining hall for the former witch-queen to get some food. Apparently, she hadn't eaten in days—that alone had banked his rising impatience. But now, safely behind the locked doors to Jesiba's office, they'd get answers.

"It's as I said," Hypaxia replied, voice a bit flat as she laid the tray of food on the table. "My mother's former general, Morganthia, had her forces surround my fortress. They gave me their terms: yield the cloudberry crown or die. I offered the crown, but they somehow heard *die*."

"Can they do that?" Ithan demanded. "Just . . . kick you out?"

"Yes," Jesiba said, claiming her leather desk chair. "The witch-dynasties were founded in fairness, in the right to remove an unfit ruler. It was meant to protect the people, but Morganthia has used it to her advantage."

Hypaxia sank into one of the chairs before Jesiba's desk and rubbed her eyes with her thumb and forefinger. It was the most normal-looking gesture Ithan had ever seen the queen make. "Morganthia's first act as queen was to order my execution. Her second was to undo my mother's animation spell for my tutors." She added at Ithan's raised brows, "They are—were—ghosts."

How it was possible, he had no idea, but he still said, "I'm sorry."

She nodded her thanks, voice weighted with grief. "The spell was bound to the crown. And once that crown was hers . . ." She looked up at Jesiba, her face full of pleading.

"You mourn for three people long dead," Jesiba said coolly, and Ithan hated her for it. "Mourn for your people instead, now beholden to an unhinged queen and her coven."

Hypaxia straightened. "You sound as if you think I should have fought her."

"You should have," Jesiba shot back, dark fire flashing in her eyes. A seed of Apollion's power—transformed into something new. "Did you even try to hold on to your crown before conceding?"

"I would have died."

"And retained your honor. Your mother would have been proud."

"A bloodless coup was a better alternative to fighting, to bringing in innocents to die in my name—"

"Once she gets her reign underway, Morganthia will spill far more blood than what might have been shed for you." Jesiba closed her eyes and shook her head with pure disgust.

"I did not come here for your judgment, Jesiba," Hypaxia hissed, wilder than Ithan had ever witnessed her.

"As I am second in command of this House, you now answer to me."

Ithan reined in the shock that reared through him. Jesiba was *second* in command of the House of Flame and Shadow?

And she thought *Hypaxia* was the best necromancer for Ithan? When she had all those others at her disposal?

"And," Jesiba went on to Hypaxia, heedless of Ithan's surprise, "as someone who spent centuries with the witches, I have insights worthy of your attention."

Hypaxia snapped, "You abandoned our people."

"So did you."

Fraught, miserable silence filled the room. Hypaxia took one bite—just one—of her ham-and-cheese sandwich.

Hypaxia didn't know, Ithan realized, what Jesiba was, deep down. She still thought her a witch defector. "Look," he said, "I know you guys have some baggage to sort out, but . . . I do have a pressing matter."

The former witch-queen turned to him, and her eyes softened. She took another bite of her sandwich, and said after she'd swallowed, "Jesiba apprised me of the situation when she called. I must admit, I was surprised by my sister's involvement. But I am sorry for what happened."

He bowed his head, shame washing through him.

Hypaxia went on, finishing off the sandwich in a few more bites, "But necromancy is no easy thing, Ithan."

"I remember," he said.

Her lips thinned. Yeah, she remembered every minute of their little encounter with the Under-King, too. But Hypaxia said, eyes bright with determination, "I will try to help you."

The breath nearly went out of him.

Hypaxia added, "I'll begin tomorrow. Today I have obligations. Oaths to swear."

Oaths to the Under-King, who'd been impressed enough by her skill at the Autumn Equinox that he'd told her he'd welcome her here. Even Morganthia Dragas would hesitate before tangling with the Under-King.

"I don't have much time," Ithan said.

"These oaths cannot wait," Jesiba said. She pointed to the door of her office, an order to Hypaxia. "They must be sworn at the Black Dock before sunup, girl. You had your last meal. Now go."

Hypaxia didn't hesitate. She left, robes flowing behind her, and shut the door.

"Fool," Jesiba said, slumping in her chair. "Innocent, idealistic fool."

Ithan stayed still, wondering if she'd forgotten he was there.

But Jesiba raised her eyes to him. "She's always been that way. Worse than Quinlan. Letting her heart lead her around like a dog on a leash. I blame her mother for keeping her locked away. No wonder Celestina swept her off her feet when—"

Ithan started. "Wait. Hypaxia and Celestina?" Jesiba nodded. Ithan angled his head to one side. "The Hind said that Celestina was the reason the Asteri knew Bryce was headed for the Eternal City. Hypaxia wouldn't—"

"It's over now," Jesiba said shortly. "I have it on good authority that Hypaxia was . . . not pleased when she found out that Celestina had sold out your friends. But even that betrayal didn't open Hypaxia's eyes enough to see Morganthia's move coming."

"She saw it," Ithan said. "She came here this spring, asking Ruhn for protection from Morganthia. I guarded her—"

"Protection," Jesiba snapped. "*Guarding.* Not *acting.* She knew Morganthia was a threat and chose to wait for her to attack rather than strike her own blow against her. Rather than find allies, she played medwitch in the city, made love to that Archangel. Rather than gather power, she ran to a Fae Prince and a wolf to shield her." She shook her head again. "Hecuba meant to protect her all these years by keeping her isolated from the corrupt covens. She hobbled her in the process." Jesiba crossed her arms and stared at nothing, fury and disdain tightening her face.

Ithan dared ask, "Why did you defect from the witches?"

"I didn't like the direction they were headed."

"Was this when Hecuba was queen?"

"Long before that. The witches have been in decline for generations. A magical and moral rot." She leaned her head against the back of her chair. "Naïve girl," Jesiba murmured to herself.

"What sort of oaths does Hypaxia need to swear at the Black Dock before sunrise?"

"Old ones."

"That's not—"

"The mysteries of the House of Flame and Shadow are not for you to know."

"Will Hypaxia . . . change?"

"No. Her oaths are nothing like those the Reapers swear. The establishment of allegiance is a legal process, but one that must be honored as the Under-King has decreed."

The Under-King . . . whom Jesiba served as second in command. "I didn't know you were so important here."

"I'm flattered. And before you ask, no, Quinlan isn't aware. People in this House don't talk. But the City Heads know."

"And the Astronomer . . . he knows." She nodded. "What's your deal with him? You said you have a monthly bill." He blew out a breath. "Fuck, I can't pay you all that money—"

"It's a tax write-off for the House," Jesiba said, waving a hand.

"And I'm growing tired of all these questions from you. You're asking things you have no right to know."

"Then stop telling me so much."

She smirked. "You're not as boring as you seem."

"I'm flattered," he echoed.

Jesiba laughed quietly. And then said, "A few centuries after Apollion changed me, he heard whispers that I had . . . powers. Being a lazy wretch, he sent his brother Aidas to investigate. And presumably to kill me if I was indeed a threat."

She spoke the names of the demon princes like they were people she knew well.

"But Aidas found that I posed no threat, and discovered that I still had the library and remained defiant to his brother's demands to reveal its so-called power. In the strange way of things, Aidas and I became friends, of a sort. We still are. I suppose it's because we're so used to each other now. It's been . . . a long time."

"So what did he report to Apollion?"

"That I was to be respected, but left alone."

"And did Apollion listen?"

A half shrug. "He sends Aidas to check in every once in a while."

"What does this have to do with the Astronomer?"

"I've paid the Astronomer for years now to look for a way to undo Apollion's grip on my soul."

Disgust roiled through him. "So you pay him and he does your bidding?"

"I pay him," she said blandly, "but he also stands to benefit from any discovery."

"Why?"

"He wants to find the answer so he might use it to become young himself. He is human—or used to be, before so much foul magic tainted his soul. He fears death more than anything. He stands to gain a great deal should he succeed in his search. I suppose we're two miserable creatures feeding off each other." She cut Ithan a look. "He might seem frail, but he's slippery. He'll be seeking other ways to fuck you over."

He nodded to where he'd replaced the Godslayer Rifle on the wall. "Would you have given me the order to kill him today?"

"No," Jesiba said. "The rifle was just a threat. I still need him."

"I think scientists call it a symbiotic relationship."

"Well, it's one I've been building toward long before he came into existence."

"So you've been using this creep and his hold on innocents—"

"You didn't seem to have any qualms about using him when you went for information about your brother."

The Astronomer must have told her about that visit. Ithan pressed on. "Can you . . . elaborate?" At her flat look, he added, "Please? Why did you even use the Astronomer in the first place?"

"I thought it was the cats who had a problem with curiosity."

"Blame it on the part of me that chose to be a history major in college."

Her lips curled upward, but she sighed at the ceiling and said, "In my own research over the millennia, I learned that dragon fire is one of the few things that can make a Prince of Hel balk."

"You meant to use it against *Apollion*?" Ithan couldn't help but gape at her sheer audacity.

She studied her manicured nails. "I thought it might be a good . . . negotiating tool."

Ithan let out an impressed laugh. "Wow. So what happened?"

"Rumor spread in the city that the Astronomer had possession of a dragon. I sought him out and offered to buy Ariadne on the spot." She crossed her arms again. "The bastard wouldn't sell her, not for anything in the world. But I realized that day that I might have another opportunity on my hands: I could use his mystics to hunt in Hel for answers on how to free me, and have the mystics guarded by Ariadne while they did so."

"But you said you wanted to wait to . . . not be young until the books were safe."

"Yes. But when that time comes, I want the solution in hand."

"Why?"

"So I don't talk myself out of it." He felt, more than saw, the weight of all those years bowing her shoulders. "You're not like most wolves I've known."

"Is that an insult or a compliment?" He honestly couldn't tell.

She uncrossed her arms and drummed her fingers on the desk. "There's a lot you don't know, Ithan Holstrom, about the truth. Too much for me to delve into here and now." Her fingers halted, and her gaze simmered with ancient pain and anger. "But it was the wolf packs who reached Parthos first. Who started the slaughter and burnings. It was the wolf packs, led by Asteri-bred bloodhounds, who hunted down my sisters. I've never forgotten that."

Ithan's stomach churned at the shameful history of his people, but he asked, "Bred?"

A wry smile. "The gift already existed amongst the wolves, but the Asteri encouraged it. Bred it into certain lines. They still do."

"Like Danika."

Jesiba's fingers resumed their drumming. "The Fendyrs have been a . . . carefully cultivated line for the Asteri."

"How so?"

She fixed her blazing eyes on him. This female had lived through all of Midgard's Asteri history. He could hardly wrap his mind around it. "Didn't you ever wonder why the Fendyrs are so dominant? Generation after generation?"

"Genetics."

"Yes, genetics bred by the Asteri. Sabine and Mordoc were ordered to breed."

"But Sabine took the title from her brother—"

"At whose urging? She's an angry, small-minded female. Her brother was smarter, but clearly no male of worth, if he sold his daughter to the Astronomer. He was likely deemed unfit by the Asteri, who coaxed Sabine into challenging him. And when Sabine's dominance won out, they made sure Mordoc was sent to produce a line of more . . . *competent* Fendyrs."

"Well, Micah fucked that up for them."

"And who do you think pulled Micah's strings?"

Ithan was glad he was sitting. "You think the Asteri had Micah kill Danika? After all that trouble to breed her into existence?"

Never mind that Connor and the Pack of Devils had been destroyed as a result of that scheming—

"I think Danika was reckless and willful, and the Asteri knew they could never control her as they could Sabine. I think they realized that with Danika, they'd produced a wolf so powerful she rivaled the ones I faced in the First Wars. *True* wolves. And she was not on their side. She had to be eliminated."

Ithan sagged in his seat, but then a thought struck him. "The Under-King told Hypaxia and me that Connor . . . that the Under-King had been given a command not to touch my brother. Why?"

Jesiba's face was unreadable. "I don't know. In all likelihood, it's because he was an asset in life, and remains so in death."

"To who?"

"The Asteri. They know what Connor means to Quinlan, to you—that makes his soul very, very valuable."

Ithan reeled. "I'm nobody."

Jesiba gave him a disdainful look, but her phone rang before she could answer him. She picked up after one trill.

She listened silently until she said in a clipped tone, "Fine." The sorceress hung up and fixed Ithan with a stare. "You're wanted downstairs at the morgue."

"You guys have a private morgue here?"

She rolled her eyes. "Hypaxia finished her vows in record time—she's waiting down there for you. With Sigrid's corpse."

46

This is as far as the ship can take you," Commander Sendes said as Bryce and Hunt steadied themselves on the wave-tossed top of the *Depth Charger*. A gray sea crashed around them, the damp, howling wind blasting right through Bryce's feeble jacket to bite at her bones.

It wasn't exactly how Bryce had pictured the entrance to the fabled Fae homeland.

Hunt's wings, nearly the same hue as the water, stretched wide, as if testing the air currents. On his other side, Baxian peered out over the water, his black wings braced against the wind.

Not that they had far to fly.

The wall of mist rose from the sea itself, stretching all the way into the clouds. Perhaps it continued above them. It was impossible to see.

As she'd suspected, the mists were nearly identical to those around the Bone Quarter. Impenetrable, ominous . . . Were these truly thin places between worlds? And what the Hel was it about *these* mists that the Asteri couldn't cross?

"You can't cruise under the mist?" Hunt asked Sendes, nodding toward the swirling mass ahead.

Sendes shook her head, the bitter wind ripping strands of her dark hair free from its tight braid. "No. There's no mist under the water, but there is a barrier—invisible, yet solid as stone."

"So they're wards?" Bryce asked, shivering again. The fire sprites, who had been perched on her shoulders when she climbed into the freezing air, had left moments ago, three flames zooming out across the waves toward the distant landmass of Pangera. She'd offered up a prayer to Solas as they quickly vanished over the horizon.

"Not wards in the way we know them," Sendes explained, barely flinching at the frigid wave that slammed into the side of the ship, showering her. Bryce, a few steps away, hissed at the spray, leaping back a step. "They seem . . . naturally occurring, rather than spell-made. Even the Ocean Queen's never given the order to attempt to breach the mists here. It's like Midgard itself made these."

Bryce slid her chilled, wet hands into the pockets of her jacket. It did little to warm them. "Told you the mists are worth looking at."

Last night in bed, she'd wanted to talk to him about their quarrel. But she'd been exhausted, and so grateful to just be lying next to him, that she hadn't said anything.

Hunt peered up at the towering barrier of mist, feathers rippling in the wind. "So how'd the Fae get access in the first place?"

"Those sleazeballs can wriggle their way into anything. The ancient ones were no different," Bryce said.

Sendes grunted in agreement, but her phone pinged, and the commander stepped away to read whatever message had come in.

Baxian stepped up to Hunt's other side, grimacing as another wave roared, showering them all this time. *Fuck* it was cold. "So what's the plan?" the Helhound asked them. He jerked his chin to Hunt. "You and I fly recon along the wall, looking for a way in?"

Hunt nodded grimly and said, "Maybe we'll find a doorbell somewhere."

"Your brother's late," Baxian said to Bryce. "We shouldn't stay here any longer than necessary. There are probably Omega-boats nearby."

"The ship knows how to avoid them," Bryce countered, dodging behind Hunt to avoid another shower of icy water.

"Yeah, but we don't want them tipped off that we're heading into Avallen," Baxian said. He spread his wings, flapping them once, spraying droplets off his black feathers. "I'll head west along the wall," the Helhound said to Hunt. "Meet back here in ten?"

Before Baxian could leap into the skies, the hatch behind them groaned, and Ruhn appeared through it, Flynn and Dec behind him. All three armed, as Bryce, Hunt, and Baxian were, with weapons from the *Depth Charger*'s arsenal. Handguns and knives, mostly—but better than nothing.

"Sorry, sorry," Ruhn said upon seeing Hunt's frown. "Flynn and Dec discovered the waffle station in the mess hall and went crazy."

Flynn patted his stomach. "You mer know how to do breakfast," he said to Sendes, who slid her phone into her pocket and sauntered over.

Bryce might have laughed if Tharion hadn't emerged from the hatch behind them, tight-faced and pale. He met Bryce's stare as he came to her side—bleak and exhausted.

Bryce reached out and cupped the mer's strong jaw. "Hang in there," she murmured.

"Thanks, Legs." Tharion stepped back to the rail's edge, his face becoming unreadable.

She wished she had more to say, more comfort to offer him. After all he'd done to help them these past several months, this was the best she could do? Leave him behind?

Movement in the hatch caught her eye again, and Lidia's golden head emerged. Though Ruhn and his friends continued to debate whether waffles went better with syrup or whipped cream—of all the fucking things to talk about right now—she could have sworn her brother tensed.

Lidia didn't look at Ruhn, though. Didn't say anything, only stared up at the swirling mist. If she was surprised at its ominous presence, her face revealed nothing. She offered no explanation, no apology for her own tardiness.

The Hind glanced back at the open hatch. No doubt thinking about her sons far below.

Baxian was watching her—like she puzzled him. Bryce didn't blame him. The Helhound had worked closely with her as the Hind, and yet here she stood, so different underneath the same exterior he'd always known. Even if he, too, had hidden his true allegiances behind his own mask.

She couldn't begin to imagine how Lidia might feel, though. Bryce walked up to her and said quietly, "I'm sorry you can't stay with them."

Lidia's golden eyes snapped to her face. For a moment, Bryce steadied herself for a biting response. But then Lidia's shoulders slumped slightly, and she said, "Thank you." Her gaze softened, like she remembered Bryce's offer to talk last night, and she said again, quieter this time, "Thank you."

Bryce nodded, and turned to find Ruhn watching them closely. His face instantly became as unreadable as stone. Whatever was between him and Lidia, she wouldn't poke it with a ten-foot pole. A hundred-foot pole.

Bryce instead said to her brother, to Flynn and Dec, "We were about to run some recon, but it occurs to me that you three have actually been here before." She gestured to the mists. "How do we get in?"

A particularly large wave rocked the *Depth Charger*, and Hunt was instantly there, a hand at Bryce's back to steady her.

"Alphahole," she muttered up at him, but let him see the light dancing in her eyes.

Ruhn and his two friends were frowning at each other, though. Her brother said, "Normally, you need an invite from Morven. But I learned during my Ordeal that having the Starsword grants you . . . entry privileges."

Bryce's brows lifted, but she winced as another blast of cold, wet wind slammed into her. She stepped closer into Hunt's warmth, her mate curling a gray wing around her to block the gusts. "How?"

Ruhn jerked his chin to where the sword was sheathed down her back. "Draw it and you'll see." Bryce and Hunt swapped wary glances, and Ruhn sighed. "What, you think this is some sort of prank?"

Bryce said, "I don't know! You're being awfully cryptic!"

Baxian chuckled from Hunt's other side, enjoying the show. Gods, he and Danika had been made for each other.

Despite the pang of loss at the thought, Bryce glared at the Helhound, then drew the sword in one smooth movement. The black blade didn't so much as gleam in the gray light. The dagger at her side seemed to weigh heavier, as if being dragged toward the blade—

"Well, look at that," Tharion drawled, peering up at the wall of mist.

"Doorbell indeed," Hunt murmured.

A triangle of a door—like the one in Silene's caves—had slid open.

The hair on Bryce's arms rose as a white boat, the opposite of those at the Black Dock, sailed out. The arching prow had been carved like a stag's head, twin lanterns hanging from the branches of its mighty horns.

And then the stag itself spoke, eyes glowing, its mouth moving as a deep male voice came from inside it—no doubt broadcast from a king miles away.

"Welcome, Bryce Danaan. I've been expecting you."

Tharion watched his friends climb into the white boat, the angels furling their wings tightly. The boat held steady on the bobbing waves, guided by whatever magic had sent it here in the first place. Flynn kept a wary eye on Lidia as she leapt in after Ruhn, but hesitated before jumping himself. He turned back to Tharion and offered a hand. "See you around, mer."

Tharion studied the male's broad, callused hand, its golden skin flecked with sea spray. Behind Tharion, Sendes had already waved to his friends and was now heading for the hatch.

If he was to make his move, it had to be now. Because if he stayed on this ship another day . . . it wouldn't end well for him.

Which left him with one choice, really.

Sendes paused at the open hatch and beckoned Tharion below. Places to be and all that.

Flynn frowned at the hand he still held extended, at Tharion, standing there—

Tharion moved.

Bracing his hands on the rail, he vaulted over the side, landing in the white boat with a thud that had the others cursing at him.

"Ketos," Athalar demanded, a steadying hand on the side of the boat as it rocked, "what the fuck?"

But Flynn landed behind Tharion a second later, saying, *"Go, go, go,"* to the boat or whatever magic controlled it.

Tharion's blood raced in his veins as the boat began to pull away from the *Depth Charger*, and then Sendes was at the rail, her eyes wide with shock.

"She'll *kill* you," Sendes cried. "Tharion—"

Tharion flashed the commander a grin. "She'll have to breach the mists first."

He barely got the last word out before the prow of the boat entered the famed mists.

Yet he could have sworn a shudder went through the ocean behind them, as if a great leviathan of power was already surging, rising for him—

They crossed into the dense mists. The sense of pure power vanished. Nothing remained except the gray water around the boat and the drifting mists, too thick to see more than a few feet beyond the glow of the stag's eyes.

Tharion faced forward at last and found his friends staring at him in varying degrees of alarm. Lidia Cervos was slowly shaking her head—like she understood the gravity of what he'd done better than any of them.

"Well," he said as casually as he could, sitting down and crossing his legs, "not to invite myself to the party, but I'm coming with you guys as well."

47

You have no idea how many people I had to convince not to eat her carcass on her way down here," Jesiba drawled as Ithan stared blankly at the shape of the body beneath the white sheet in the morgue.

At the sagging place between neck and head.

Hypaxia, working on something at the counter, called over, "This might take a while."

Ithan peered around the sterile, tiled morgue and managed to say, "Why *do* you guys have a morgue down here?"

Jesiba sat on a medical-looking stool, back straight. "Where else are we supposed to raise dead bodies?"

"I don't know why I asked."

"You did a number on her, you know."

Ithan glared at the sorceress. Jesiba winked at him.

But Hypaxia turned to them, and Ithan got his first good look at her face since coming down here. Exhaustion etched deep lines into it, and her eyes were bleak. Hopeless.

What had swearing her allegiance to this House cost her? Jesiba had claimed the ritual had been unusually fast—was that why she looked so drained? Part of him didn't want to know.

He opened his mouth to tell her she didn't have to do this for him, that she should rest, but . . . he didn't have time. The longer they waited, the less chance they had to be successful at raising the decapitated—

Decapitated—

Nausea churned in his gut.

"Take a seat, Ithan," Hypaxia said gently. Greenish light wreathed her fingers as she approached the table holding a bundle in her hands.

"Is that a sewing kit?" He was going to puke everywhere.

Jesiba snorted. "You'd better hope her head's back on when Hypaxia wakes her."

The former witch-queen pulled a glowing syringe of firstlight from a cabinet and laid it on a tray atop a wheeled cart. "As soon as she wakes, an injection of firstlight will heal the damage. But the head needs to be attached first so that the tendons can regrow and latch on."

"Okay," Ithan said, taking a deep breath against his rising nausea. "Okay." Fuck, he was a monster for having made this necessary.

"Here we go," Hypaxia said.

Jesiba caught Ithan's eye. "Sure you want to resurrect a Fendyr?"

He didn't answer. Couldn't face the answer. So he said nothing.

Hypaxia began chanting.

Hunt had been in Morven Donnall's throne room for all of ten seconds and he already hated it.

After the shining white boat had guided them through the mists, he'd expected some sort of summer paradise to lie beyond. Not a cloudy sky above a land of dense green hills and a gray-stoned castle perched on a cliff above a winding—also gray—river. In the distance, thatched-roof cottages marked farmsteads, and a small city of two- and three-story buildings crusted the hill, up to the castle itself.

No skyscrapers. No highways. No cars. The lamps he could make out were flame, not firstlight.

The boat sailed down the river toward the cliff, entering the castle through a yawning cave at its base. Everyone had stayed silent throughout the journey, assuming the stag on the prow had ears that worked as well as its mouth, and could broadcast every word to the male waiting in the castle for them.

A male now seated before them, on a throne seemingly crafted from a single set of antlers. The beast who'd grown them had to have been colossal, the likes of which didn't exist elsewhere on Midgard. Did stags that big roam around here? The thought was . . . not comforting.

But neither were the shadows that curled like snakes around the king, wild and twining. A coiled crown of them sat atop Morven's dark head, blacker than the Pit.

Bryce and Ruhn stood at the head of their little group, and Hunt swapped a look with Baxian, whose frown told Hunt he was deeply unimpressed by this place.

"Could use a reno, if you ask me," Tharion muttered from Hunt's other side, and Hunt's mouth twitched upward.

The mer had some nerve, cracking jokes when he'd just acted directly against the Ocean Queen's orders. Yeah, Hunt was glad to have Ketos with them, but fuck—what had the mer been thinking, jumping into the boat?

Hunt knew what he'd been thinking, actually. And didn't blame the mer for his choice, but they had enough enemies out there as it was. If this somehow provoked the Ocean Queen to work against them . . .

From the glares the others kept throwing Ketos's way, they weren't happy about this development, either. But right now, they had another ruler to deal with.

"You bring traitors and enemies of the empire to my home," the Fae King intoned. The shadows around him halted their twining—predators readying to attack.

But Bryce pointed to herself, then to Ruhn, the portrait of innocent confusion, and said, "Are you talking to me or him?"

Baxian ducked his head, as if trying not to smile. Hunt felt inclined to do the same, but he didn't dare take his focus off the stone-faced ruler or the shadows at his command.

"This male"—a disdainful look at Ruhn—"has been disowned by his father. You are the only royal standing before me."

"Oof," Bryce said to Ruhn. "So harsh." Ruhn's eyes glittered, but he said nothing. She gestured to the dim, small castle around them. "You know, I'm surprised by all this doom and gloom. Cormac said it'd be nicer."

Morven's dark eyes flashed. The shadow-crown atop his head seemed to darken further. "That name is no longer recognized or acknowledged here."

"Yeah?" Ruhn said, crossing his arms. "Well, it is with us. Cormac gave his life to make this world a better place."

"He was a liar and a traitor—not just to the empire, but to his birthright."

"And we can't have that," Bryce crooned. "All that precious breeding stock—gone."

"I will remind you that royal you might be, but you are still female. And Fae females speak only when spoken to."

Bryce smiled slowly.

"Now you've done it," Hunt grumbled, and decided it was a good time to step up to his mate's side. He said to the king, "Telling her to shut up doesn't end well for anyone. Trust me."

"I will not be addressed by a slave," Morven seethed, nodding toward Hunt's wrist, the mark barely visible past his black sleeve. Then he nodded to Hunt's haloed brow. "Least of all a Fallen angel, disgraced by the world."

"Oh boy," Bryce said, sighing at the ceiling. She whirled to their group. "Okay, let's do a head count. If you're disowned, disgraced, or both, raise your hand."

Tharion, Baxian, Lidia, Hunt, and Ruhn raised their hands. Bryce surveyed Flynn and Dec, both still in their usual black jeans and T-shirts, and sighed again. She gestured expansively, giving them the floor.

Flynn smirked, sauntering to Bryce's side. "Far as I know, I'm still my father's heir. Good to see you again, Morven."

Hunt could have sworn Morven's shadows hissed. "It would be in your best interests, Tristan Flynn, to speak to me with the utmost respect."

"Oh?" Flynn crossed his arms, brimming with entitled arrogance.

Morven motioned to someone behind them, the delicate silver embroidery along the wrists and collar of his immaculately cut black jacket gleaming in the firelight, and Hunt whirled as two hulking guards prowled from the shadows. He hadn't sensed them, hadn't heard them—

From Tharion's and Baxian's shocked faces, he knew they were equally surprised.

But Ruhn, Flynn, and Declan glowered. Like they recognized the approaching males, both towering and armed to the teeth. They were clearly twins.

The Murder Twins Ruhn had mentioned, capable of prying into minds as they saw fit.

But that wasn't Hunt's top concern—not yet.

Because between them, in black leggings and a white sweater, light brown hair down around her face . . . Hunt had no idea who the Fae female was. She was fuming, though, outright seething at the guards, the king, and—

"What the fuck?" Flynn exploded.

"Sathia?" Declan said, gaping.

"It seems," Morven drawled as the Murder Twins dragged the Fae female forward, their grips white-knuckled on her arms, hard enough to bruise, "that your sister has landed in a heap of trouble, Tristan Flynn."

48

Bryce didn't know who to focus on: Sathia Flynn bristling with fury in Morven's throne room, or Tristan's shocked face as he processed the scene before them. Bryce opted for the latter, especially as Flynn snapped at the King of Avallen, "What do you mean, *trouble*?"

Morven drawled, "Many of the Valbaran Fae sense . . . unrest on the horizon, and have been seeking shelter within my lands." Those serpentine shadows writhed around his neck, over his shoulders, with unnerving menace. The king's shadows, the Murder Twins' . . . they felt different from Ruhn's: wilder, meaner. Ruhn's shadows were gentle, stealthy night; theirs were the dark of lightless caves.

"If you pitched this place as a luxury vacation, you're about to get a bunch of one-star reviews," Bryce muttered, earning a chuckle from Tharion. She didn't smile at the mer, though. He'd added another nearly all-powerful ruler to their list of enemies—she didn't want to talk to him right now. From the way Tharion's chuckle quickly died off, he knew she wasn't happy.

So Bryce watched as Flynn, dead serious perhaps for the first time in his life, said to the Stag King, voice dripping with disdain, "Let me guess, my parents came running right over." He glanced around the throne room. "Where's my oh-so-brave father? And everyone else, for that matter?"

Morven's face might as well have been carved from stone. "A select few have been allowed in. Most have been sent back to Lunathion. But for those who remain here, there is a price to be paid, of course."

Flynn slowly turned toward his sister. "What did you promise him?" Pure rage and a hint of fear laced his question. But Flynn didn't go for the female or the twins holding her.

Bryce sized them up, and found both males already smiling at her. And then, deep in her mind, twin dark shadows snarled, readying to strike—

She incinerated them with a mental wall of starlight.

The twins hissed, one of them blinking as if that light had physically blinded him. Bryce bared her teeth, and kept that shining wall in her mind. A second later, there was a polite tap against it and Ruhn said, *Keep this up. No matter what.*

Tell Hunt and the others to put up a wall as well, Bryce replied, glaring daggers at the twins.

Already did, Ruhn replied. *You should see the lightning around Athalar's mind. He burned their probes into crisps.*

Yuck. Don't say probes.

Ruhn snorted, and his presence faded from her mind just as Morven continued, "Sathia has promised me nothing. In fact, she has refused to pay my asking price. A generous one, at that: her choice between the males who stand beside her. And as a female has no worth here beyond the offspring she might bear Avallen, I don't see a reason why your sister should remain in this haven another moment."

Morven's words sank in. "I'm sorry," Bryce said, glancing between Sathia's outraged, pretty face and the Stag King and his feral shadows, "but to clarify: Are you saying you're requiring any females who seek refuge here to *marry*?"

"It would be unsafe for so many unwed females to be running about without a male relative or husband," Morven said, picking at an invisible fleck of dirt on his night-black pants.

"Yeah," Bryce said, "the gods know what would happen if all us females were unsupervised. Absolute anarchy. Cities would crumble."

But Flynn said to Morven, "So bring their brothers and husbands over."

Bryce glared at him, but Morven declared, "I have no need for more males in this land."

Bryce ground her teeth hard enough to hurt. This was the male who'd agreed with her father that Bryce and Cormac should marry, injecting more power and dignity into the Fae royal line.

Flynn said, "And my parents?"

Morven sniffed. "I have allowed Lord and Lady Hawthorne to remain here, as our ties date back to the First Wars. They are currently residing at my private hunting lodge up north."

"So send Sathia to my dad," Flynn snapped.

"He won't," Sathia said at last. Though her Fae voice was soft and cultured, Bryce didn't miss the backbone of steel running through it. "It's either marry here, or go back to Lunathion."

"So go back," Flynn ordered his sister.

Sathia slowly shook her head. "It's not safe."

"You've got your cushy villa," Ruhn said with unusual harshness. "You'll be fine."

Sathia shook her head again, gaze fixing on her brother. "It's not safe because of *you*."

"What?" Flynn blurted.

"Word has spread," Morven said from his antler-and-shadow throne, "of your assistance in that one's"—a nod toward Ruhn—"escape. Along with the escape of two other enemies of the empire." A flick of his cold eyes to Baxian and Hunt, who glared back with impressive menace. "The entire Hawthorne family is now wanted by the Asteri for questioning."

"They want to kill us to punish you," Sathia burst out, pointing a damning finger at Flynn. "We had to leave in the middle of the night, when we got an alert that the 33rd was coming to bring us in. These clothes are the only ones I have with me."

"What a sacrifice for you," Flynn sneered. But Bryce caught the guilt darkening his eyes. Declan had already pulled out his phone, no doubt to check on his family and Marc—

"There's no reception here, thanks to the mists," Sathia said to Declan.

The male's face paled, and he muttered, "I forgot."

But Sathia added quietly, "I put in a call to your parents before we left. They said they'd get in touch with your boyfriend, too."

Flynn gaped at her, but Declan bowed his head in thanks.

"What?" Sathia glared at her brother. "You think I'm that much of a monster?"

Flynn gave her another sneer that said, *Yes*, and Bryce stepped in to spare everyone from their bickering. "Okay," she said to Morven, "so you're insisting that Flynn's sister marry one of . . . these creeps?" Bryce gestured to the Murder Twins holding Sathia, making sure that mental wall of starlight was still intact. She wasn't letting their minds anywhere near hers.

"Seamus and Duncan are lords of the Fae," Morven snapped at Bryce. "You will address them with a female's proper tone of deference."

For fuck's sake. "You didn't answer my question," Bryce said. Sathia's expression had become downright panicked. "You're really forcing her into marriage or deporting her to be killed by the Asteri?"

Morven twirled a shadow around one of his long, broad fingers. "Her father has agreed it is in her best interest to wed. And has agreed that should she refuse, she shall be sent back to Lunathion." He clenched his fist, crushing the shadow within. "For too long, she has refused any males he has presented to her for marriage. Her father's patience has come to an end, and he has begged me to oversee this matter."

"Dad of the year," Baxian growled.

Bryce grunted her agreement.

Sathia said with impressive coldness, "It is within my rights to refuse any suitor presented to me."

Morven gave her a look dripping with distaste. "It is, girl. Just as it is within your father's rights to disown you for failing in your duty to continue the family bloodline."

Bryce grumbled, "So what's the point of giving females refusal rights at all if you punish them for it?"

"This isn't our problem," Flynn grumbled, and even Ruhn whirled to him in shock. "We didn't come here to deal with this."

"So you're not here to beg asylum as well?" Morven asked, propping his chin on a fist.

"No," Hunt growled, stepping forward, wings flaring. "We're not." He glanced to Bryce, motioning her forward again.

Swapping a look with Ruhn that said they'd deal with the issue of Sathia later, Bryce set aside her concern and lifted her chin as she stepped to Hunt's side. "I'm here to access the Avallen Archives and the Cave of Princes."

"Access denied," Morven said.

"You mistake me," Bryce said in that voice that brooked no argument. "I wasn't asking your permission." The star on her chest began to glow, illuminating her T-shirt and athletic jacket. "As a Starborn Princess, no part of Avallen is denied to me."

"I shall decide who is worthy of accessing my realm," Morven snarled.

"The starlight says otherwise," Bryce said. She drew the Starsword—and the dagger. "And so do these."

As if their sheaths had kept their power contained, the naked metal now throbbed against her palm, up her arms, tugging toward each other so violently it took all her strength to keep them apart.

Morven paled. Even his shadows receded. "What is that in your left hand?" Even the Murder Twins and Sathia had their eyes trained on her, as if they couldn't look away.

"Some major prophecy fulfillment," Bryce said, hoping to Hel she was hiding the tremble in her arms from keeping the black blades steady, from ignoring that instinct murmuring to her to bring them together, not keep them apart.

"Where did you get that knife?" Morven hissed.

"So you know what it is, then?" Bryce said.

"Yes," he seethed. "I can feel its power."

"Well, that makes it easier," Bryce said. She sheathed both weapons. Mercifully, the pulling eased with the action. "Less explaining for me." She nodded to Morven, and he glowered. "I'll be in and out of here before you know it."

His shadows returned, darkening the air behind his antler-throne until it seemed Morven sat before a void. "Females are forbidden in both the Avallen Archives and the Cave of Princes."

"I don't really care," Bryce said.

"You spit on our sacred traditions."

"Get over it."

Morven's nostrils flared. "I'll remind you, girl, that one word from me and the Asteri will have you in their grasp."

"You'd have to open the mists to them first," Bryce countered. "And it seems like you've worked *really* hard not to do that—or give them a reason to come here at all."

"You can be removed by guards."

Bryce gestured to Hunt, then Baxian, then the others. "My own guards might make that difficult."

"This is *my* kingdom—"

"I'm not challenging that. I just want to look through your archives. A few days, then we'll all be out of your hair." She pulled the Autumn King's notebook from her jacket. "I'll even sweeten the deal: Here's my sire's private journal. Well, his most current one. All his recent scheming, written down. It's pretty stupid, if you ask me. *Dear Diary, today I made a list of all my enemies and how I plan to kill them. It's so hard being king—I wish I had a friend!*"

She grinned as Morven's eyes narrowed on the leather-bound notebook, and she flashed him the first page, where her father's distinctive handwriting was visible. He'd know it well, as the two old losers communicated mostly through written letters, since Avallen had no computers. "You let us stay here and it's yours when we leave."

Morven's fingers drummed on the arm of his throne. Fish on a line.

But he said, shadows lightening at last, "Your presence here threatens to bring the Asteri's wrath upon me."

Bryce considered, blinking. "Well, it seems you've got no problem harboring fugitives, if you're letting in Flynn's parents."

He glared, pure darkness in his eyes.

Bryce went on, "I mean, you could probably make up for Cormac's *dishonor* by selling us out to the Asteri . . . but if you hand us over, you'd have to turn in Flynn's parents and the other nobles, too. And I doubt it'd win you any points with your own people if you betrayed some fancy-ass nobles." She crossed her arms. "You're in a real pickle, huh?"

Morven tapped his booted foot on the ground.

"It's super hard," Bryce commiserated, "to try to play both sides, isn't it?"

"I am not playing either side," Morven said. "I am loyal to the Asteri."

"Then open the mists—invite them here. Let's have them over for brunch."

Morven's silence was damning.

Bryce smiled. "I thought so." She nodded to Sathia. "One more thing: she doesn't marry anyone, and she comes with us."

Sathia gaped at Bryce. But Bryce threw the Fae female a warning look. Bryce had only seen Sathia Flynn from a distance at parties. Usually, the female's hair was dyed varying shades of shining dark brown or blond. Now her locks were an ordinary light brown—her natural color, perhaps. It was like seeing a glimpse of the real female beneath.

"I cannot allow that," Morven said. "She is an unwed female."

"Her brother is here," Bryce said, nodding to Flynn. "Irresponsible party boy that he is, at least he has the parts that matter to you."

Flynn glared, but Dec elbowed him hard enough that he stepped up and said, "I'll, uh, take responsibility for Sathia."

Sathia bristled like an angry cat, but kept her mouth shut.

"No," Morven said, a shadow wrapping itself around his wrist like a bracelet. An idle, bored bit of magic. "You are an unsuitable chaperone, as you have demonstrated time and again."

Hunt gave Bryce a look, and she knew what he was thinking. It was the same thing Ruhn said into her mind a heartbeat later:

As much as it kills me to say this . . . we might have to let this go. Sathia is Flynn's sister and all, but it's not our battle to fight.

Bryce subtly shook her head. *You really want to leave her to Morven's mercy?*

Trust me, Bryce, Sathia can handle herself.

But Bryce glanced back at Lidia, who'd been watching all this with a cold, clear focus. Staying completely silent in that way of hers that made others forget her presence. Even Morven, it seemed, hadn't noticed who stood in his throne room—because he now let out a low grunt of surprise at the sight of her.

Yet the Hind met Bryce's gaze. *What would you do?* Bryce tried to convey.

Lidia seemed to grasp the general direction of her thoughts, because she said quietly, "I never had anyone to fight for me."

Well, that did it.

Bryce opened her mouth, rallying power to her star, but Tharion spoke from behind them.

"I'll marry Sathia."

It took Hypaxia seven hours, seven minutes, and seven seconds to raise Sigrid.

Ithan barely moved from his stool the entire time Hypaxia stood over the corpse and chanted. Jesiba left, came back with her laptop, and worked for some of the time. She even offered Ithan some food, which he refused.

He had no appetite. If this didn't work . . .

Hypaxia's now-hoarse chanting stopped suddenly. "I—"

Ithan hadn't been able to watch as she'd sewed Sigrid's head back on. Only when she'd covered the body again had he returned his gaze to the spectacle.

Hypaxia staggered back from the examination table. From the shape under the sheet. Ithan was instantly up, catching her smoothly.

"What have you done?" Jesiba demanded, laptop shutting with a click.

Ithan set Hypaxia on her feet, and the former witch-queen

looked between them, helpless and—terrified. Out of the corner of his eye, something white shifted.

Ithan turned as the body on the table sat up. As the sheet rippled away, revealing Sigrid's grayish face, her eyes closed. The thick, unforgiving stitches in an uneven line along her neck. She still wore her clothes, stiff with old blood.

Stitches popping, Sigrid slowly turned her head.

But her chest . . . it didn't rise and fall. She wasn't breathing.

The lost Fendyr heir opened her eyes. They burned an acid green.

"Reaper," Jesiba breathed.

49

I'm telling you, Ketos, she is the *worst*," Flynn growled at Tharion in the shadows of the pillars flanking one side of the throne room. Normal shadows, thankfully. Not the awful ones the Fae King commanded. "This is a terrible idea. It will ruin your life."

"My life is already ruined," Tharion said, voice as hollow as he felt. "If we live through this, we can get a divorce."

"The Fae don't divorce." Flynn gripped his arm hard. "It's literally marriage until death."

"Well, I'm not Fae—"

"She is. If you divorce her, she won't have any chance of ever marrying again. She'll be sullied goods. After the first marriage, the only ways out are death or widowhood. A widow can remarry, but a divorcée . . . it's not even a thing. She'd be persona non grata."

On the opposite side of the room, Declan and Ruhn were talking to Sathia in hushed tones. Likely having the same conversation.

Morven glowered away on his throne, shadows like a hissing nest of asps around him, the monstrous twins now flanking him on either side. Tharion had detected the oily shadows creeping toward his mind the moment the twins had arrived. He'd instinctively thrown up a roaring river of water, creating a mental moat around himself. He had no idea what he was doing, but it had worked. The shadows had drowned.

It only made this decision easier. To have anyone forced to endure the Murder Twins' presence, to *marry* someone who could pry into minds—

Tharion now said to Flynn, "Your sister would be a pariah amongst the Fae only. Normal people won't have a problem with divorce."

Flynn didn't back down one inch, his teeth flashing. "She is the daughter of *Lord Hawthorne*. She's always going to want to marry within the Fae."

"She accepted my offer." With the quietest and blandest *yes* he'd ever heard, but still. A clear acceptance.

Flynn snapped, "Because she's desperate and scared—you think that's a good state of mind to make an informed decision?"

Tharion held the male's stare. "I don't see anyone else stepping forward to help her."

Flynn growled. "Look, she's spoiled and petty and mean as a snake, but she's my little sister."

"So find some alternative that doesn't involve her death to get her out of this."

Flynn glared, and Tharion glared right back.

Across the way, Sathia shoved past Dec and Ruhn and stormed toward them. She was short—but stood with a presence that commanded the room. Her dark eyes were pure fire as they met Tharion's. "Are we doing this?"

Gone was that quiet, bland tone.

Bryce, Athalar, and Baxian were watching from the rear of the room, the Hind a few steps to the side.

None of them had expected the day to go this way. Starting with Tharion bailing on the Ocean Queen, and culminating in this shitshow. But if it had been Lesia in Sathia's stead . . . he would have wanted someone to step up to help her, faithless soldier or no.

So Tharion said to Sathia, "Yeah. Let's do it."

Morven wasted no time in summoning a Priestess of Cthona. Like the bastard was trying to call Tharion's bluff.

Not five minutes later, Tharion found himself with a wife.

"You," Sigrid growled at Ithan, her rasping voice barely more than a whisper.

Ithan could hardly process what he was hearing—seeing.

"What happened?" Jesiba shouted at Hypaxia, who was still clinging to Ithan—who, in turn, was backing them toward the door.

But it was Sigrid who answered, more stitches popping as her neck moved, revealing a brutal scar now etched there. "We came to a doorway. *She* wanted to go one way . . ." A smile twisted her face. "I went the other."

Hypaxia shook her head, frantic. "She wouldn't come, she slipped through my fingers—"

"I had no interest in letting such a prize go," intoned a cold voice.

Even Jesiba got to her feet as the Under-King appeared in the morgue doorway.

As he had on the night of the Autumnal Equinox, he wore dark, fraying robes that floated on a phantom breeze.

"You had no right," Hypaxia challenged, pushing past Ithan as his every sense went into overdrive at the Under-King's unearthly presence, his ageless might. "No right to turn her—"

"Am I not lord of the dead?" He remained in the doorway, hovering as if standing on air. "She had no Sailing. Her soul was there for the claiming. You offered her one option, witch. I gave her another."

He beckoned to Sigrid, who moved off the table as if she were alive. As if she had never been dead. Were it not for the acid-green eyes, the scars, Ithan might have believed it.

A Fendyr was a *Reaper.* A half-life, a walking corpse—

It was sacrilege. A disgrace.

And it was all his fault.

"Which is the more attractive choice?" the Under-King mused

as Sigrid took his hand. "To have been raised by you, Hypaxia, to be under your command and thrall . . . or to be free?"

"To be your servant," Hypaxia corrected with impressive steel.

"Better mine than yours," the Under-King countered. He then inclined his head to Ithan. "Young Holstrom. You have my gratitude. Her soul might have drifted forever. She's in capable hands now."

"What—what are you going to do?" Ithan dared ask.

The Under-King peered down at Sigrid and smiled, revealing too-large, brown teeth. "Come, my pet. You have much to learn."

But Sigrid turned to Ithan, and he'd never known such self-loathing as he did when she said in that rasping Reaper's voice, "You killed me."

"I'm sorry." The words didn't even cover it. Would never cover it.

"I won't forget this."

Neither would he. As long as he lived. He held her stare, hating those acid-green eyes, the deadness in them—

"We will speak soon," the Under-King said to Jesiba, more warning than invitation. Before Jesiba could reply, the Under-King and Sigrid vanished on a dark wind.

Only when its scraps of shadow had faded from the morgue did Jesiba say, "What a disaster."

Hypaxia was staring at her hands, as if trying to walk herself through her mistake.

Ithan couldn't stop the shaking that overtook him from head to toe, right down to his very bones. "Fix this."

Hypaxia didn't look up.

Ithan growled, his heart racing swiftly, "*Fix* this."

Jesiba clicked her tongue. "What's done is done, pup."

"I don't accept that." Ithan bared his teeth at her, then pointed at Hypaxia. "Undo what you just did."

Slowly, Hypaxia lifted her eyes to his. Bleak, pleading, tired. "Ithan—"

"FIX IT!" Ithan roared, the witch's necromantic instruments rattling in the wake of the sound. He didn't care. Nothing fucking mattered but this. *"FIX HER!"* He whirled on Jesiba. "Did you know this would happen?" His voice broke.

Jesiba gave him a flat look. "No. And if you take that tone with me again—"

"There might be a way," Hypaxia said quietly.

Even Jesiba blinked, turning with Ithan to survey the former witch-queen. "Once the dead have crossed that threshold into Reaperdom—"

Hypaxia's gaze met Ithan's and held, the pain bleeding away to pure determination. "Necromancy can lead her to that threshold; it can haul her back again, too."

"How?" Jesiba asked. Ithan could barely breathe.

"We need a thunderbird."

Jesiba threw up her hands. "There are none left."

"Sofie Renast was a thunderbird," Ithan said, more to himself than to the others. "We thought her brother might be one, too, but—"

"Sofie Renast is dead," Jesiba said.

Hypaxia only asked, "Where's her body?" The question rang like a death knell through the morgue.

Jesiba got it before Ithan did. "After that debacle," she said, pointing to the examination table where Sigrid had laid moments before, the sheet now discarded on the floor beside it, "you really want to try raising the dead again?"

"Sofie's been dead for too long to raise," Ithan said, nausea churning in his gut. And, he didn't add, he couldn't help but agree with Roga about Hypaxia's track record.

"If she hasn't been given a Sailing, then it should work—though the decayed state of her body will be . . . gruesome." Hypaxia paced the room. "She should still have enough lightning lingering in her veins to bridge the gap between life and death. The thunderbirds were once able to aid necromancers, to use their lightning to hold the souls of the dead. They could even imbue their power into ordinary objects, like weapons, and give them magical properties—"

"And you think it can somehow undo Sigrid becoming a Reaper?" Ithan said.

"I think the lightning might be able to pull her soul back toward life," Hypaxia said. "And give her the chance to make the choice again. A few days as a Reaper might change her mind."

Silence fell. Ithan looked to Jesiba, but the sorceress was silent, as if weighing Hypaxia's every word.

Ithan swallowed hard. "Will it work?"

Jesiba didn't take her eyes from Hypaxia as she said quietly, "It might."

"But where's her body?" Ithan pushed. "The last I heard from my friends, the Ocean Queen had it on her ship. She could have sent it out the air lock for all we know—"

"Give me thirty minutes," Jesiba said, and didn't wait for a reply before stalking out of the room.

There was nothing to do but wait. Ithan didn't feel like doing anything except sitting at the desk and looking at his hands.

His inept, bloodstained hands.

He'd tried to save Sigrid from the Astronomer, and had only succeeded in killing her. And then turning her corpse into a Reaper. Every choice he'd made had led them from bad to worse to catastrophic.

Jesiba breezed through the metal doors of the morgue exactly thirty minutes later. "Well, it took more bribes than I'd have liked, but I have good news and bad news," she declared.

"Good first," Ithan said, looking up from his hands at last. Hypaxia had sat in the other desk chair the entire time, silent and thoughtful.

"I know where Sofie's body is," Jesiba said.

"And the bad news?" Hypaxia asked quietly.

Jesiba glanced between them, gray eyes blazing. "It's on Avallen. With the Stag King."

50

Ruhn had no idea how Bryce managed to not kill Morven. He honestly had no idea how he didn't, either.

But they wasted no time getting to work. Though Bryce was apparently on Team Caves, she insisted on checking out the archives first.

The Avallen Archives were as imposing and massive as Ruhn remembered from his last and only visit to Avallen. Granted, he'd never been allowed inside, but from its looming gray exterior, the building rivaled the *Depth Charger* in sheer size. A city of learning, locked behind the lead doors.

Only for the royal bloodlines—the royal males—to access.

"We really have to *work*?" Flynn groused, rubbing his head. "Can't we relax for a bit? This place gives me the creeps—I need to decompress."

Athalar gave Flynn a look. "It gives all of us the creeps."

"No," Flynn said gravely, shaking his head. "I told you—my magic *hates* this place."

"What do you mean?" Bryce asked, peering at him over a shoulder.

Flynn shrugged. "The earth feels . . . rotted. Like there's nothing for my magic to grab on to, or identify with. It's weird. It bothered me the first time we were here, too."

"He whined about it the entire time," Declan agreed, earning an elbow in the ribs from Flynn.

But Flynn jerked his chin at Sathia, standing by herself a few feet away. "You sense it, too, right?"

His sister twisted her rosebud mouth to the side, then admitted, "My magic is also uneasy on Avallen. My brother's claims are not totally without merit."

"Well," Bryce said, "buck up, Flynn. I think a big, tough Fae male like you can power through. We'll *decompress* tonight. Tomorrow we split into Team Archives and Team Caves and work as fast as we can."

She lifted a hand to one of the lead doors, but didn't touch it yet. "Trust me, though, I don't want to stay on this miserable island for a moment more than necessary."

"Agreed," Athalar muttered, stepping up beside Bryce. "Let's find what we need and get the fuck out."

"What are we looking for, exactly?" Sathia asked. "Everything you told me about the other Fae world and all you've learned . . . I'm sorry, but I need a bit more direction to go on when we get in there."

Since we're all known enemies of the Asteri, what's another person who knows our shit? Bryce had asked when Flynn had demanded that Sathia stay behind.

And Sathia had refused to be left alone, even with the safety of her married status now granting her the right to move freely. *I'm not going to be locked up in some room to rot,* she'd said, and stomped after Bryce, who had begun explaining everything she'd learned about Theia and her daughters and the Fae history in and outside of Midgard. She hadn't spoken a word to Tharion since they'd exchanged their vows—and the mer had seemed just fine about that, too.

It was all fucking nuts. But Ruhn had heard what Lidia had said to Bryce—about never having had anyone to fight for her. It hadn't sat well.

Ruhn dared a look over at where Lidia stood, peering up at the towering entrance to the archives. He hadn't failed to note

Morven's shock upon realizing she stood in his throne room. And as they'd departed, the Stag King had seemed poised to speak to Lidia, but the Hind had breezed past him before he could.

Her golden eyes slid to Ruhn's, and he could have sworn pure fire pulsed through him—

He quickly looked away.

Sathia asked Bryce, "What if you don't find the answers you seek?"

"Then we're fucked," Bryce said plainly, and finally laid her palm flat against the doors to the archives. A shudder seemed to go through the metal.

On a groan, the doors swung inward, revealing nothing but sunlight-dappled gloom beyond. Ruhn swapped glances with Dec, whose brows were high at the display of submission from the building. But Bryce breezed through, Athalar and Baxian on her heels.

"So you really intend to go into the Cave of Princes?" Sathia asked Bryce as they entered the dim space.

"I know my female presence will probably cause the caves to collapse from sheer outrage," Bryce said, voice echoing off the massive dome above them, "but yes."

Ruhn snickered and peered up at the dome. It was a mosaic of onyx stones, interrupted by bits of opal and diamond—stars. A crescent moon of pure nacre occupied the apex of it, gleaming in the dimness. Eerily similar to the Ocean Queen's sharp nails.

Sathia trailed Bryce and asked softly, "And—that's really it? The knife?"

"Shocking, I know," Bryce said. "Party girl bearing the prophesied—"

"No," Sathia said. "I wasn't thinking that."

Bryce paused, turning, and Ruhn knew Athalar was monitoring every word, every move from Sathia as Flynn's sister clarified, "I was thinking about what it means. Not just in regard to the Asteri and your conflict with them. But what it means for the Fae."

"Whole lot of nothing," Flynn snorted.

"We were told our people would be united with the return of that knife," Sathia countered sharply. Her tone gentled as she asked Bryce, "Is that part of . . . whatever plan you have? To unite the Fae?"

Bryce surveyed the rows and rows of shelves and said coldly, "The Fae don't deserve to be united."

Even Ruhn froze. He'd never thought about what Bryce might do as leader, but . . .

"Come on, Quinlan," Athalar said, slinging his arm around her shoulders and decisively changing the subject, "let's get to exploring."

"Yeah, yeah," Bryce muttered. "I suppose it's too much to hope for a digital catalog here, so . . . I guess we'll have to do it the old-fashioned way." She pointed ahead, to the entire wall taken up by a card catalog. "Look for any mention of the sword and knife, anything about the mists guarding this place, Pelias and Helena . . . Maybe even stuff about the earliest days of Avallen, either during the First Wars or right after."

"That is . . . a lot to look for," Flynn said.

"Bet you're wishing you'd learned to read," Sathia trilled, striding for the catalog.

"I can read!" Flynn sulked. Then mumbled, "It's just boring."

Ruhn snorted, and the sound was echoed nearby—Lidia.

Again, that look between them. Ruhn said a shade awkwardly to her, "We should get cracking."

A catalog that massive could take days to comb through. Especially since there was no librarian or scholar in sight. Come to think of it, the entire place had an air of neglect. Emptiness. The castle did, too, as well as the small city and surrounding lands.

It had all seemed so mysterious, so strange when he'd come here decades ago: the famed misty isle of Avallen. Now he could only think of Cormac, growing up in the gloom and quiet. All that fire, dampened by this place.

And yet he'd loved his people—wanted to do right by them. By everyone on Midgard, too.

There had to be something good here, if Cormac had come out of it. Ruhn just couldn't for the life of him figure out what.

The Fae don't deserve to be united.

Bryce's words hung in the air, as if they still echoed off the dome above. And Ruhn didn't know why, but as the words settled into the darkness . . . they made him sad.

After a few tense minutes, Declan declared, "Well, *this* is interesting."

He stood at the nearest table, what looked like a stack of maps unrolled before him. A large one—of Midgard—was spread across the top.

Ruhn strode for his friend, grateful for the break. "What is?" The others followed suit, gathering around the table.

Dec pointed at Avallen on the map, the paper yellow with age despite the preserving spells upon it. "I thought looking at old maps might give us some hints about the mists—you know, see how old cartographers represented them and stuff. And then I found this."

Athalar rubbed his neck and said, "At the risk of being ridiculed . . . what am I looking at?"

"There are islands here," Declan said. "Dozens."

It clicked. "There shouldn't be any islands around Avallen," Ruhn said.

Bryce leaned closer, running her fingers across the archipelago. "When's this map from?"

"The First Wars," Dec said, and pulled another map from the bottom of the pile. "This is Midgard now. No islands in this area except the one we're on."

"So . . . ," Baxian said.

"So," Dec said, annoyed, "isn't it weird that there *were* islands fifteen thousand years ago, and now they're gone?"

Tharion cleared his throat. "I mean, sea levels do rise—"

Dec gave them all a withering look, and pulled out a third map. "This map's from a hundred years after the First Wars." Ruhn scanned it. No islands at all.

Across the table, Lidia was silently assessing the different maps. She lifted her eyes to Ruhn's, and he couldn't stop his heartbeat from jacking up, his blood from thrumming at her nearness—

"All those islands," Bryce murmured, "disappeared within a hundred years."

"Right after the Asteri arrived," Athalar added, and Ruhn looked away from Lidia long enough to consider what was before them.

He said, "Well, despite its mists, Avallen clearly has had no problem revealing its shape and coastline to the Asteri for the empire's official maps. Why hide the islands?"

"There are no islands," Sathia said quietly. "The ones on that first map . . ." She pointed along the northwestern coast. "We sailed in from that direction. We didn't see a single island. The mists could have obscured some of them, but we should have seen at least a few."

"I've never seen or heard any mention of additional islands here," Flynn agreed.

Silence fell, and they all glanced between the three maps as if they'd reveal some big secret.

Dec finally shook his head. Something happened here a long time ago—something big. But what?"

"And," Lidia murmured, the cadence of her voice sending shivers of pleasure down Ruhn's spine, "is this knowledge at all useful to us?"

Bryce tapped a hand on the oldest map, and Ruhn could practically see the wheels turning in her head.

"Silene said something in her memories about the island that had once been her court." Bryce's face took on a faraway look, as if she were trying to remember the exact words. "She said that the land . . . shriveled. That when she started to house those monsters to hide the Harp's presence, the island of the Prison became barren. And the Ocean Queen said islands literally withered into the sea in despair when the Asteri arrived."

"So?" Flynn asked.

Bryce's gaze sharpened again. "It seems weird that two Fae strongholds, both islands, were once archipelagos, and then *both* lost all but the central island in the wake of the arrival of . . . unpleasant forces."

Ruhn raised his eyebrows. "I can't believe you actually told us what you were thinking, for once."

Bryce flipped him off as Athalar snickered. She nodded decisively. "Team Archives: keep looking into this."

The others dispersed again to resume their researching, but Bryce grabbed Ruhn by the elbow before he could move. "What?" he asked, glancing down at her grip.

Bryce's look was resolute. "We don't have the luxury of time."

"I know," Ruhn said. "We'll search as quickly as we can."

"A few days," Bryce said, letting go of his arm. She glanced toward the sealed front doors of the archives, the island beyond. "I don't think we have more than that before Morven decides it's in his best interest to tell the Asteri we're here, risks to his people be damned. Or before the Asteri's mystics pinpoint our location."

"Maybe the mists can keep out mystic eyes as well," Ruhn suggested.

"Maybe, but I'd rather we not find out the hard way. A few days, Ruhn—then we're out of here."

"The caves could take longer than that to navigate," Ruhn warned. "You sure there's anything in there worth finding? As far as I could tell, it was some decorative crap on the walls and a lot of misty tunnels. We'd get through the archives way faster if we all tackled the catalog together."

"I have to look at the caves," Bryce said quietly. "Just in case."

It hit him then, like a bucket of ice water. Bryce wasn't entirely sure she *could* find anything to help her unite the blades. To kill the Asteri.

So Ruhn squeezed her shoulder. "We'll figure it out, Bryce."

She offered him a grim smile. It was all Ruhn could do to offer one back.

They found nothing else regarding the missing islands, the mists, or the sword and the knife in the hours they spent combing through the catalog. They'd barely made a dent in the collection by the time Bryce called it quits for dinner, her hands so achingly dry from all the dust that they burned.

In silence, the group walked to the castle dining room. What a long, fucking day. Each of their trudging steps seemed to echo the sentiment.

The dining room was empty, though a small buffet of food had been laid out for them.

"Guess we're early," Tharion said as the group surveyed the firelit room, its faded tapestries depicting long-ago Fae hunts. Their quarry lay at the center of one: a chained, collared white horse.

Bryce jolted. It wasn't a horse. It was a *winged* horse.

So they'd survived here, then—at least for a few generations. Before they'd either died out or the Fae had hunted them to extinction.

"We're not early," Sathia said beside Tharion, her face tight. "The formal dinner started fifteen minutes ago. If I were to guess, it's been moved to another location for everyone else."

"No one wants to eat with us?" Hunt asked.

Bryce said, "They probably consider it beneath them to mingle with our ilk." Hunt, Baxian, and Tharion turned to her with incredulous expressions. Bryce shrugged. "Welcome to my life." Hunt was frowning deeply, and Bryce added to him, unable to help herself, "You don't need to feel guilty about that one, you know."

He glared at her, and the others made themselves scarce.

"What does that mean?" Hunt asked quietly.

It wasn't the time or place, but Bryce said, "I can't get a read on you. Like, if you even want to be here or not."

"Of course I do," Hunt growled, eyes flashing.

She didn't back down. "One moment you're all in, the next you're all broody and guilty—"

"Don't I have the right to feel that way?" he hissed. The others had already reached the table.

"You do," she said, keeping her voice low, though she knew the others could hear them. One of the downfalls of hanging with Vanir. "But each of us made choices that led us to all this. The weight of that's not only on you, and it isn't—"

"I don't want to talk about this." He started walking toward the center of the room.

"Hunt," she started. He kept walking, wings tucking in tight.

Across the room, she met Baxian's stare from where he was pulling out a chair at the table. *Give him time,* the Helhound's look seemed to say. *Be gentle with him.*

Bryce sighed, nodding. She could do that.

They served themselves, and sat at random spots along the massive table, large enough to seat forty: Ruhn, Flynn, Sathia, and Dec in one cluster; Tharion, Baxian, Hunt, and Bryce in another. Lidia claimed a chair beside Bryce, definitely *not* looking to where Ruhn watched them from down the table.

"So this is Avallen," Lidia said, breaking the awkward silence.

"I know," Bryce muttered. "I'm trying to scrape my jaw off the floor."

"It reminds me of my father's house," Lidia said quietly, digging into her potatoes and mutton. Hearty, simple food. Definitely not the fine feast Morven and his court were indulging in elsewhere.

"They must both have a subscription to *Medieval Living*," Bryce said, and Lidia's mouth curved toward a smile.

It was so weird to see the *Hind* smile. Like a person.

The males must have been thinking the same thing, because Baxian asked, "How long, Lidia? How long since you turned spy?"

Lidia gracefully carved her meat. "How long since *you* started believing in the cause?"

"Since I met my mate, Danika Fendyr. Four years ago."

Bryce's chest ached at the pride in his voice—and the pain. Her fingers itched with the urge to reach across the table to take his hand, just as she had last night.

But Lidia blinked slowly. And said softly, "I'm sorry, Baxian."

Baxian nodded in acknowledgment. Then said to Lidia and Hunt, "I kind of can't get over being here with the two of you. Considering where we were not that long ago. Who we were."

"I bet," Bryce murmured.

Hunt tested the edge of a knife with his thumb, then cut into his own meat. "Urd works in mysterious ways, I guess."

Lidia's eyes glimmered. Hunt lifted his glass of water to her. "Thanks for saving our asses."

"It was nothing," she replied, slicing into the mutton again.

Baxian put down his fork. "You put everything on the line. We owe you."

Bryce glanced down the table and noticed Ruhn watching them. She gave him a pointed glance, as if to say, *Chime in, asshole,* but Ruhn ignored her.

Lidia's mouth kicked into a half smile. "Find a way to kill the Asteri, and we're even."

The rest of dinner was mostly quiet, and Bryce found herself growing weary enough that by the time she'd finished her plate, she just wanted to lie down somewhere. Thankfully, *one* person in the castle deigned to engage with them: an older Fae woman who gruffly said she'd show them to their rooms.

Even if they weren't welcome, at least they were given decent accommodations, all along the same hall. Bryce didn't really mark who bunked with whom, focusing solely on being shown to her own room, but she didn't fail to notice the awkward beat when Tharion and Sathia were shown through a door together halfway down the hall.

Bryce sighed once she and Hunt entered their own chamber. She wished she'd had the energy to talk to Ruhn, to really delve into what it had been like for him here, what he was feeling, but . . .

"I need to lie down," Bryce said, and slumped face-first onto the bed.

"Today was weird," Hunt said, helping to remove her sheathed sword and dagger. He placed them with expert care at the side of the bed, then gently turned her over. "You all right?"

Bryce peered up into his face—the halo on his brow. "I really hope we find something here to make it worthwhile."

Hunt sat beside her, removing his own weapons and setting them on a side table. "You're suddenly worried we won't?"

Bryce got to her feet, unable to sit still despite her exhaustion. She paced in front of the crackling fire. "I don't know. It's not like I was expecting a giant neon sign in the archives that said *Answers Here!* But if the Asteri are going after Flynn's family . . ." She hadn't let herself think about it earlier. There was nothing she could do from here, without phone or interweb service. "Then they're going after mine."

"Randall and Ember can look after themselves." But Hunt rose, walking to her and taking her hands. "They'll be okay." His hands were warm around hers, solid. She closed her eyes at the touch, savoring its love and comfort. "We'll get there, Quinlan. You traveled between worlds, for fuck's sake. This is nothing by comparison."

"Don't tempt Urd."

"I'm not. I'm just telling you the truth. Don't lose faith now."

Bryce sighed, examining his tattooed brow again. "We need to find some way to get this off you."

"Not a big priority."

"It is. I need you at your full power." The words came out wrong, and she amended, "I need you to be free of them."

"I will be. We all will be."

Staring into his dark eyes, she believed him. "I'm sorry about earlier. If I pushed you too hard."

"I'm fine." His voice didn't sound fine.

"I wasn't trying to tell you how to feel," she said. "I just want you to know that none of us, especially me, hold you responsible for all this shit. We're a team."

He lowered his stare, and she hated the weight pressing on his head, drooping his wings. "I don't know if I can do this again, Bryce."

Her heart strained. "Do what?"

"Make choices that cost people their lives." His eyes lifted to hers again, bleak. "It was easier for Shahar, you know. She didn't care about other people's lives, not really. And she died so fast, she didn't have to endure the weight of the guilt that might have come later. Sometimes I envy her for it. I did envy her for it, back then. For escaping it all by dying."

"That's the old Umbra Mortis talking," Bryce said, fumbling for humor amid the cold wash of pain and worry at his words, his dead tone.

"Maybe we need the Umbra Mortis right now."

She didn't like that. Not one bit. "I need Hunt, not some helmeted assassin. I need my mate." She kissed his cheek. "I need *you*."

The darkness in his eyes lightened, and it eased her heart, relief washing through her.

She kissed his cheek again. "I know we should go wash up for bed and use the chamber pot or whatever excuse they have for a toilet in this museum, but . . ."

"But?" He lifted his brows.

Bryce rose onto her toes, brushing her mouth against his. And the taste of him . . . Gods, yes. "But I need to feel you first."

His hands tightened around her waist. "Thank fuck."

There was more to be discussed, of course. But right now . . .

He lowered his face to hers, and Bryce met him, the kiss thorough and open, and just . . . bliss. Home and eternity and all she'd fought for. All she'd keep fighting for.

From the way he returned the kiss, she knew he realized it, too. Hoped he let it burn through any lingering scraps of remorse.

"I love you," he said against her mouth, and deepened the kiss. She stifled a sob of relief, arms winding around his neck. Hunt's hands slid around to her ass and he hefted her up, smoothly walking them over to the enormous, curtained bed.

Clothes were peeled away. Mouths met, and explored, and tasted. Fingers caressed and stroked. Then Hunt was over her, and Bryce let her joy, her magic shine through her.

"Look at you," Hunt breathed, hips flexing beneath her hands, cock teasing her entrance. "Look at you."

Bryce smiled as she let more of that power shine through her: Starborn light so silvery bright it cast shadows upon the bed. "Like it?"

Hunt's thrust, driving himself in to the hilt, was his response. "You're so fucking beautiful," he whispered. Lightning gathered around his wings, his brow. Like his power couldn't help but answer hers, even with the halo's damper on it.

Bryce moaned as he withdrew, nearly pulling out of her, then plunged back in.

Hunt angled her hips to drive himself deeper. And as his cock brushed her innermost wall, as lightning flickered above her, in her . . .

Mate. Husband. Prince. *Hunt.*

"Yes," Hunt said, and she must have voiced her thoughts aloud, because his thrusts turned deeper, harder. "I fucking love you, Bryce."

Her magic rose at his words, a surging wave. Or maybe that was her climax, rising along with it. She couldn't get enough of him, couldn't get close enough to him, needed to be *in* him, his very blood—

"Solas, Bryce," Hunt growled, pumping into her in a long, luxurious stroke. "I can't—" She didn't want him to. She gripped his ass, nails digging in deep in silent urging. "Bryce," he warned, but he didn't stop moving in her. Lightning crackled and snaked around them, an avalanche racing toward her.

"Don't stop," she pleaded.

Their magics collided—their souls. She scattered across the stars, across galaxies, lightning skittering in her wake.

She had the dim sense of Hunt being thrown with her, of his shout of ecstasy and surprise. Knew that their bodies remained joined in some distant world, but here, in this place between places, all they were melted into one, crossed over and transferred and becoming something *more.*

Stars and planets and rainbow clouds of nebulas swirled around them, darkness cut with lightning brighter than the sun. Sun and moon held together in perfect balance, suspended in the same sky. And beneath them, far below, she could see Avallen, thrumming with their magic, so much magic, as if Avallen were the very source of it, as if *they* were the very source of all magic and light and love—

Then it ebbed away. Receded into muted color and warm air and heavy breathing. The weight of Hunt's body atop hers, his cock pulsing inside her, his wings splayed open above them.

"Holy shit," Hunt said, lifting himself enough to look at her. "Holy . . . *shit.*"

It had been more then fucking, or sex, or lovemaking. Hunt stared down at her, starlight shimmering in his hair. Just as she knew lightning licked through her own.

"It felt like my power went into you," Hunt said, eyes tracking the lightning as it slithered down her body. "It's . . . yours."

"As mine is yours," she said, touching a fleck of starlight glittering between the sable locks of his hair.

"I feel weird," he admitted, but didn't move. "I feel . . ."

She sensed it, then. Understood it at last. What it had always been, what she'd learned to call it in that other world.

"Made," Bryce whispered with a shade of fear. "That's what it feels like. Whatever power can flow between us . . . my Made power from the Horn can, too."

Hunt looked down at himself, at where their bodies remained joined. She had a pang of guilt, then, for not telling him all she knew yet about the other Made objects in the universe—about the Mask, the Trove. "I guess it flows both ways: my power into you, and yours into me."

Hunt smiled and surveyed the room around them. "At least we seem to be past ending up somewhere new every time we fuck."

Bryce snorted. "That's a relief. I don't think Morven would have appreciated our naked asses landing in his room."

"Definitely not," Hunt agreed, kissing her brow. He brushed back a strand of her hair. "But what difference does it make? That we're connected this way?"

Bryce lifted her head to kiss him. "Another thing for us to figure out."

"Team Caves all the way," he said against her mouth.

She laughed, their breath mingling, twining together like their souls. "I told you I should have ordered T-shirts."

51

Tharion stood in the old-timey stone bedroom, complete with a curtained bed and tapestries on the wall, and had no idea what to say to his wife.

Apparently, Sathia Flynn had no idea what to say to him, either, because she took a seat in a carved wooden chair before the crackling hearth and stared at the fire.

They'd barely exchanged more than a word all day. But now, having to share a room—

"You can take the bed," he said, the words too loud, too big in the chamber.

"Thank you," she said, arms wrapping around herself. The firelight danced on her light brown hair, setting golden strands within it shining.

"I don't, uh—I don't expect anything."

That earned him a wry look over her shoulder. "Good. Neither do I."

"Good," he echoed, and winced, walking to the window. The starless night was a black wall beyond, interrupted only by a few glimmering fires at farmstead cottages. "Does it ever get . . . not gloomy here?"

"This is my first visit, so I can't say." Her tone was a bit sharp, as if unused to speaking normally to people, but she added, "I hope so."

Tharion walked to the wooden chair opposite hers and sank onto it. The damn thing was hard as Hel. He shifted, trying to find a more comfortable angle, but gave up after a second and said, "Let's start from the beginning. I'm Tharion Ketos. Former Captain of Intelligence for the River Queen—"

"I know who you are," she said quietly, her soft tone belied by the steely calm in her eyes.

He arched a brow. "Oh? Good or bad?"

She shook her head. "I'm Sathia Flynn, daughter of Lord Hawthorne."

"And?"

She cocked her head to the side, strands of her long hair slipping over a shoulder. "What else is there?"

He feigned contemplation. "Favorite color?"

"Blue."

"Favorite food?"

"Raspberry tarts."

He let out a laugh. "Really?"

She frowned. "What's wrong with that?"

"Nothing," he said, then added, "Mine's cheese puffs."

She let out a hint of a laugh. But it faded as she said, "Why?"

He ticked the reasons off on his fingers. "They're crispy, they're cheesy—"

"No. I mean—why did you do this?" She gestured between them.

Tharion debated how to spin his story, but . . . "This arrangement of ours might as well be an honest one." He sighed. "I'm a wanted male. The Viper Queen has a bounty of five million gold marks on my head."

She choked. "What?"

"Surprise," he said. Then added, "Sorry. I feel like . . . maybe I should have mentioned that before."

"You think?" But she mastered herself, a practiced, calm

demeanor stealing over her pale features before she said for a third time, "Why?"

"I . . . may have been indirectly responsible for burning down the Meat Market, and now she wants to kill me. That was after I defected from the River Queen, who, uh, also wants to kill me. And then the Ocean Queen harbored me and forbade me from leaving her ship, but I disobeyed her order and bailed, and now here I am and . . . I'm really not doing a good job of making myself seem appealing, am I?"

"My father is going to keel over dead," Sathia said. Something like wicked amusement glinted in her eyes.

He could work with a sense of humor.

"As glad as I am to hear that," Tharion said, earning another few millimeters of smile, "it's a long way of saying . . . I've fucked up a lot." Sigrid's dead body flashed before his eyes, and he shoved it away. "Too much," he amended.

"So this is some attempt at redemption?" Any amusement faded from her face.

"It's an attempt to be able to look at myself in the mirror again," he said plainly. "To know I did something good, at some point, for someone else."

"All right," she said, then looked back at the fire.

"You seem, uh . . . relatively cool with this whole marriage thing."

"I've grown up knowing my fate would lead me to the marriage altar." The words were flat.

"But you thought that would be marriage to a Fae—"

"I don't particularly want to talk about the things that have been expected of me my entire life," she said with the imperiousness of a queen. "Or the doors that are now closed to me. I am alive, and I didn't have to marry Goon One or Goon Two, so—yes, I'm *cool* with that."

"The mind-prying thing didn't woo you, huh?"

"They're brutes and bullies, even without their mind gifts. I abhor them."

"Good to know you have standards." Tharion extended his hand to her. "It's nice to meet you, Sathia."

She gingerly took the offered hand, her fingers delicate against his. But her handshake was firm—unflinching. "It's nice to meet you, too . . . husband."

Dawn broke over Avallen, though Lidia had never seen such a gloomy sunrise. Granted, given her fitful sleep last night, she wasn't exactly in the mood to appreciate any sunrise, clear or cloudy. But as she stood on one of the small castle balconies overlooking the hilly countryside, her arms braced against the lichen-crusted stone rail, she couldn't help but wonder if Avallen ever saw sunshine.

The city—more of a town, really—had been built atop a craggy hill, and offered views from every street of the surrounding green countryside, the land a patchwork of small farms and quaint homesteads. A land lost in time, and not in a good way.

Even Ravilis, Sandriel's former stronghold, had been more modern than this. There wasn't so much as a trace of firstlight anywhere. The Fae here used candles.

And had apparently been given an order, considering the unusually quiet streets, to shun the visitors at every turn. But she could have sworn that countless Fae were watching her from the shuttered windows of the ancient-looking town houses flanking the streets winding up to the castle. She'd always known Morven ruled with an iron fist, but this submission was beyond what she'd expected.

She'd barely been able to sleep last night. Hadn't been able to stop seeing her sons' faces as she'd left that room, or how they'd blended with the memory of their faces as babies, how they'd been sleeping so peacefully, so beautifully, in their cribs that last night, when she'd looked at them one final time and left. Walked off the *Depth Charger* and into the submersible pod.

It had felt like dying, both then and now. Felt like Luna had shot her with a poisoned arrow and she was bleeding out, an invisible wound leaking into the world, and there was nothing that could ever be done to heal it.

Lidia scrubbed her hands over her face, finding her cheeks chilled. Maybe it would have been better to have not seen them again. To have never returned to the ship, and not reopened that wound.

There was no torture that Pollux or Rigelus could have devised for her that hurt worse than this. The chill wind whipped past, moaning through the narrow streets of the ancient, mist-wreathed city.

Below her, in the courtyard, Bryce and Athalar, Baxian, Tharion, and the mer's new bride were preparing to leave. Ruhn and his two friends stood with them, speaking in low voices. No doubt running over all they knew regarding the Cave of Princes once more.

She didn't really know why she'd come out here—they hadn't bothered to tell her they'd be leaving, or invite her to the send-off. Baxian at last looked up, either sensing or spotting Lidia, and lifted a hand in farewell. Lidia returned the gesture.

The rest of the group turned, too, Bryce waving a bit more enthusiastically than the others.

Flynn and Dec just nodded to her. Ruhn merely glanced up before averting his eyes. With a final embrace for his sister, the Fae Prince stalked back into the castle and disappeared from view, his two friends with him. Bryce and her crew aimed for the castle gates. For the countryside beyond, still half asleep under the grayish light.

Shadows whispered over the stones of the balcony, and Lidia didn't turn to acknowledge Morven as he stepped up beside her. "So sentimental of you, to see them off."

Lidia kept her gaze on the departing group, headed for a cluster of taller hills rising against the horizon. "Is there something you want?"

A hiss at her impudence. "You're a filthy traitor."

Lidia slid her stare to the Fae King at last. Beheld his pale, hateful face. "And you're a spineless coward who disavowed his own child at the first sign of trouble."

"Had you any honor, any understanding of royal duty, you would understand why I did so." Shadows twined over the shoulders of his fine black jacket, the silver embroidery. The Stag King, they called him. It was an insult to deer shifters. The Fae male had no affinity for the beasts, despite his throne, crafted from the bones of some noble, butchered beast. "You would know there are more important things than even one's own children."

There was nothing more important. Nothing. She was here today, on this island, back in the field once more, because there would never be anything more important than the two boys she'd left on the *Depth Charger.*

"I enjoyed watching you grovel, you know," Lidia said. And she had—despite everything, she'd loved every second of Morven kneeling before the Asteri. Just as she loved seeing him bristle with fury as she threw his humiliation in his face.

"I have no doubt a blackheart like you did," Morven sneered. "But I wonder: Should a better offer come along, will you betray these friends as easily as you did your masters?"

Lidia's fingers curled at her sides, but she kept her face impassive. "Are you sulking because you did not see me for what I truly am, Morven, or because I witnessed you in your moment of shame? In the moment you traded loyalty to your son for your own life?"

He seethed, shadows poised to strike. "You know nothing of loyalty."

Lidia let out a low laugh, and glanced toward the five figures heading out into the greenery of the countryside. Toward the red-haired female in the center of the group. "I've never had a leader to stir the sentiment."

Morven noted the direction of her gaze and scowled. "You're a fool to follow her."

Lidia gave him a sidelong look, pushing off the stone wall of the balcony. "You're a fool not to," she said quietly, striding for the archway into the castle proper. "It will be your doom. And Avallen's."

Morven snarled, "Is that a threat?"

Lidia kept walking, leaving her enemy and the miserable dawn behind. "Just some professional advice."

"So all that talk, all those myths and hand-wringing about the Cave of Princes," Hunt said to Bryce, sweating lightly from their hours-long trek across the rolling fields to this craggy cluster of hills, the castle now a lone spike on the horizon behind them, "and *this* is it?"

Bryce looked around. "Underwhelming, isn't it?"

The entrance to the cave was little more than a sliver between two boulders. Ancient, weatherworn runes were etched into the stones, but that was all that set this place apart from any other crack in the rock face.

That, and the tongue of mist slithering out from the gloom.

"Morven needs a decorator," Tharion said, peering into the darkness beyond. "I think he could really move beyond his ancestors' shadows-and-misery theme."

"This is how he likes it," Sathia said. "The way Avallen was when it was first built—right after the First Wars ended. His father kept it that way, and his father before him, going all the way back to Pelias himself."

Hunt swapped a look with Bryce. That was precisely why they'd come. If there was a place any bit of truth might be preserved, it was here. He didn't relish the thought of going into a cave; some intrinsic part of him bucked at the idea of being so far from the wind, so far belowground, trapped once again. But he forced himself past the bolt of fear and dread and said to Sathia, "Do *you* have any idea how the mists keep the Asteri out of Avallen?" She hadn't volunteered the information yesterday, but maybe it was because they hadn't thought to ask.

"No," Sathia said. "The rumor is that the magic of the mists is so old, it predates even the Asteri's arrival."

"Well," Tharion said, gesturing dramatically, "ladies first, Legs."

"Such chivalry," Bryce retorted.

"You're the one with a built-in flashlight," Hunt reminded her.

She rolled her eyes and said to a wary Sathia, "Word of advice: don't let them push you around."

"I won't," Sathia said. For some reason, Hunt believed her.

Bryce was looking at Flynn's sister as if she was thinking the same thing. "It's good to have another female around here." She nodded to Baxian, Tharion, and Hunt. "The Alphahole Club was getting too crowded for my liking."

Bryce halted at the line between light and shadow. The mist trickling along the cave floor reached for her pink sneakers with white, curving claws. Her starlight didn't pierce the darkness beyond a few feet ahead. It only illuminated a thicker cloud of mist. Masking any threats waiting beyond.

She couldn't bring herself to cross that line.

"This place feels wrong," Baxian murmured, coming up beside Bryce.

"Here's hoping we see daylight again," Tharion said with equal quiet from a step behind them.

"We will," Hunt said, adjusting the heavy pack strapped between his wings. "Nothing to worry about except some ghouls. And wraiths. And 'scary shit,' Ruhn claimed."

"Oh, just that," Bryce said, throwing him a wry glance. She added to Sathia, pointing to the spires barely poking over the green horizon, "It's not too late to head back to the castle."

"I'm not going to sit around with those mind-reading bastards lurking about," Sathia hissed.

They all turned toward her.

"Did something . . . happen?" Hunt asked carefully. Tharion was watching her closely.

"I'm not going to be left alone in that castle," Sathia insisted, wrapping her arms around herself, fingers digging into her white sweater, and Bryce knew she didn't want to discuss it further.

"Fair enough," Hunt said, reading Sathia's tone, too. "But Ruhn warned me that most of what's in here is old, and wicked, and likes to drink blood. And eat souls. I'm not sure of the order, though."

"Sounds like your run-of-the-mill Fae nobility, then," Bryce said, hefting her heavy pack higher. She winked at Sathia. "You'll be right at home."

The Fae female gave her a watery smile, but to her credit, didn't run screaming from the cave and its grasping, misty fingers. If Sathia did indeed prefer to face what lurked in this cave over the Murder Twins, maybe Bryce owed it to her and females everywhere to kick some ass when they got back.

If they got back.

"Right," Hunt said. "According to Declan, Pelias's tomb and the Starsword's resting place lie right in the center of the cave network." They'd swiped food and water from the surprised-looking kitchen staff, preparing for a few days' journey. "But there are lots of things that will try to eat us along the way."

Bryce ignored the twisting in her stomach. She'd gone to another world, she'd faced an Asteri—she could deal with a few ghouls and wraiths. She had three badasses with her. Plus Sathia. She could do this.

Bryce faced the others and held out her hand at waist level. "Go Team Caves on three?"

They all looked at her, but didn't cover her hand with theirs. Not even Hunt, the bastard. After the way they'd fucked last night, the least he could do was indulge her with some team spirit. But he gave her a look, as if to say, *Gravitas, Quinlan.*

Fuck that. She lifted her hand in the air and shouted, "Gooooo Team Caves!"

The words echoed off the boulders, down the passage, and into the misty darkness beyond. Where they suddenly cut off, as if the caves themselves had devoured them.

"That's not creepy at all," Hunt murmured.

"Totally normal," Baxian agreed.

"Don't worry," Bryce crooned. "I'll protect you from the scary cave." And with that, she strode into the dark.

Morven cornered Ruhn outside the dining hall just before he and his friends left for the archives again after breakfast.

"A word," Morven said, hooking a finger toward him. The mass of shadows from the day before was gone, but the crown of them remained floating atop his head.

"Here I was," Ruhn drawled, nodding at Flynn and Dec to keep going down the hall, "thinking I didn't exist to you."

Morven leveled a cold look at him—it made Ruhn's father seem downright cheerful. But Ruhn noticed that the king waited to speak until Lidia had walked past, out the door, not sparing a glance for either of them.

"What are your sister's intentions in coming here?"

"Bryce told you," Ruhn said tightly. "She wants information."

"On what?"

"The sword and knife, for one thing. The rest is classified." *Asshole,* he didn't need to add.

Morven's eyes darkened to blackest night. "And does she plan to claim Avallen for herself?"

Ruhn burst out laughing. "What? No. If she did, I wouldn't tell you, but trust me: this place . . ." He surveyed the dark, crypt-like hall. "This isn't her style. Just ask my father."

"That is another thing: Your sister must have done something to him. How else would she come to possess his journal?"

"If she has, it didn't involve trying to claim his crown. She's said nothing about it." Ruhn glared at the king. "And again: If she was planning some sort of Fae coup, why the Hel would I tell you about it?"

"Because you are *true* Fae, not some half-breed—"

"I'd mind how you speak about my sister."

Morven's shadows gathered at his fingers, his shoulders. Wild, angry shadows that Ruhn's own balked to meet. They seemed corrupted somehow, like those Seamus and Duncan wielded mentally. "You are Starborn. You have an obligation to our people."

"To do what?"

"To ensure they survive."

"Bryce is Starborn, too."

Ruhn, Dec, and Flynn had given his sister and the others all the pointers they could regarding what they'd face in the dark labyrinth of the Cave of Princes, but their own journey through the misty cave network had been so chaotic that they had little to offer when it came to a direct route to Pelias's tomb. Bryce hadn't seemed too concerned, despite her comment last night about time running out. But maybe she was putting on a brave face.

"Yes," Morven sneered, "and what has your sister done with her Starborn heritage except show contempt for the Fae?"

"You don't know a damn thing about her."

"I know she spat on her Fae lineage when she announced her union with that *angel*." His shadows quivered with rage.

"All right," Ruhn said, turning to go. "I'm officially done. Bye."

Morven grabbed him by the arm. Shadows slithered up from his hand onto Ruhn's forearm, squeezing tight. "After dealing with your sister yesterday, I prayed all night to Luna for guidance." His eyes gleamed with a fanatic's fervor. "She allowed me to see that you, despite your . . . transgressions . . . are our people's only hope of regaining some credibility in future generations."

Ruhn sent his own shadows racing down his arm, biting at Morven's and snapping free of their grip with satisfying ease. "Luna doesn't strike me as the type who'd stoop to talking to assholes like you."

Despite his shredded shadows, Morven's fingers dug into his arm. "There are females here who—"

"Nope." Ruhn shrugged off his uncle's hand. Kept a wall of shadows at his back as he walked away. *"Bye."*

"Selfish fool," Morven hissed. Ruhn could have sworn the king's shadows hissed, too.

But Ruhn lifted his arm above his head and flipped him off without looking back. He found Dec and Flynn waiting by a courtyard fountain outside, a safe distance from Lidia.

"What was that all about?" Flynn asked, falling into step beside Ruhn.

"Not worth explaining," Ruhn replied, keeping his eyes on the archives dome a few streets away.

Declan asked Lidia, "Any chance Morven will run to the Asteri?"

"Not yet," she said quietly. "Bryce's claims yesterday were true—she handled him well." She added, turning toward Ruhn, "You could learn a thing or two from your sister."

"What's that supposed to mean?" Ruhn demanded.

Flynn and Dec pretended to be busy looking into a closed butcher shop as they passed by.

"You're a prince," Lidia said coolly. "Start acting like one."

52

You're a prince. Start acting like one.

Fuck, Lidia knew precisely what to say to piss him off. To keep him thinking about her in the hours that passed, during all the fruitless searching for anything about the missing islands, the Starsword, the dagger, or the mists.

She'd gone on a walk for half an hour and then come back, smelling of the sea, and still hadn't said anything to him.

"You could, uh, talk to her," Flynn said from beside Ruhn, shutting yet another useless drawer full of catalog cards. "I can literally feel you brooding."

"I'm not brooding."

"You're brooding," Declan said from Ruhn's other side.

"*You're* brooding," Ruhn said, nodding to Dec's taut face.

"I have good reason to. I can't get in touch with my family or Marc—"

Ruhn softened. "I'm sure they're fine. You warned them to lie low before all that shit at the Meat Market, and Sathia said she reached out to them. Marc will make sure they stay safe."

"It doesn't make it any easier, knowing I can't even check in with them thanks to this medieval playland."

Ruhn and Flynn grunted their agreement.

"This place sucks," Dec said, and slammed the drawer he'd

been combing through closed. "And so does this library's cataloging system." Dec peered down the long, long row and called, "Anything?"

Ruhn tried but failed not to look at Lidia. She'd taken the far end of the catalog, definitely on purpose, and had yet to say a word to them in the hours they'd been here together. "No," she said, and continued her work.

Fine.

Just fine.

"Well," Hunt whispered, voice echoing off the slick black stone before being swallowed by the dense mists, "this is terrifying."

The reek of mold and rot was already giving him a headache, unsettling every instinct that told him to get out of the misty enclosed space and into the skies, into the safety of the wind and clouds—

"Once you've seen a Middengard Wyrm feeding," Bryce muttered in the soupy darkness, waving away the mist in front of her face to no avail, "nothing's as bad."

"I don't want to know what that is," Baxian said.

Hunt appreciated that Baxian hadn't needed to be asked before flanking Bryce's exposed side. Tharion and Sathia walked close behind, saying little as the pathway descended. Ruhn had said the carvings on the walls started a little ways in, but they hadn't found a hint of them yet. Just rock—and mist, so thick they could only see a few feet ahead.

Bryce said, "Think an earthworm with a mouth full of double rows of teeth. The size of two city buses."

"I *said* I didn't want to know what that was," Baxian grumbled.

"It's not even that bad, compared to some of the other shit I saw," Bryce went on. And then admitted, if only because they had followed her into the deadly dark and deserved to know the whole truth, "They have a thing called the Mask—a tool that can literally raise the dead. No necromancers needed. No fresh bodies, either."

They all stared at her. "Really?" Tharion asked.

Bryce nodded gravely. "I saw the Mask used to animate a skeleton that had been dead for ages. And give it enough strength that it could take on the Wyrm."

Hunt blew out a whistle. "That's some mighty powerful death-magic."

He refrained from complaining that she hadn't mentioned it until now, because he certainly wasn't mentioning how Rigelus had taken his lightning to do something similar, and Baxian, thankfully, didn't say anything, either. They'd heard nothing about what had come of it, but it couldn't be good.

Another thing he'd have to atone for.

He'd heard what Bryce was trying to tell him last night, about all of them bearing a piece of the blame for their collective actions. But it didn't stop him from harboring the guilt. He didn't want to talk about it anymore. Didn't want to feel it anymore.

"Yeah," Bryce said, continuing into the dark, "the powers in that Fae world are . . . off the charts."

"And yet the Asteri want to tangle with them again," Baxian said.

"Rigelus knows how to hold a grudge," Bryce said. She halted abruptly.

Hunt's every instinct went on alert. "What?" he asked, scanning the misty darkness ahead. But Bryce's gaze was on the wall to her left, where a carving had been etched into the stone with startling precision.

"An eight-pointed star," Baxian said.

Bryce's hand drifted to her chest, fingers silhouetted against the brightness shining there.

Hunt surveyed the star, then the images that began a few feet beyond it, plunging onward into the mists, as if this place marked the beginning of a formal walkway. Bryce merely began walking again, head swiveling from side to side as she took in the ornate, artistic carvings along the black rock. It was all Hunt could do to keep up with her, not letting the mists veil her from sight.

Fae in elaborate armor had been carved into the walls, many holding what seemed to be ropes of stars. Ropes that had been looped around the necks of flying horses, the beasts screaming in fury as they were hauled toward the ground. Some sank into what looked like the sea, drowning.

"A hunt," Bryce said quietly. "So the early Fae did kill all of Theia's pegasuses, then."

"Why?" Sathia asked.

"They weren't fans of the Starlight Fancy dolls," Hunt answered.

But Bryce didn't smile. "These carvings are like the ones in Silene's caves. Different art, but the storytelling style is similar."

"It'd make sense," Tharion said, running his fingers over a thrashing, drowning horse, "considering that the art's from the same time period."

"Yeah," Bryce muttered, and pressed on, her starlight now flaring a beam through the mists. Pointing straight ahead. There was no privacy to corner her and ask what the Hel she was *really* thinking—certainly not as something shifted in the shadows to Hunt's left.

He reached over a shoulder for his sword, lightning at the ready. Or as ready as it could be with the gods-damned halo suppressing it—

"Ghouls," Baxian said, drawing his sword in an easy motion. The shadows writhed, hissing like a nest of snakes.

"They're not coming any closer," Sathia whispered, her fear thick as the fog around them.

Hunt wrapped his lightning around his fist, the sparks making the damp walls glisten like the surface of a pond. But light flared from Bryce, and the ghouls shrank back further.

"Benefits of being the Super Powerful and Special Magic Starborn Princess," Bryce drawled, sashaying past the nooks and alcoves in the stone where the ghouls teemed. "Ruhn said they ran from his starlight during his Ordeal. Looks like they're not fans of mine, either."

Sathia inched past the nearest cluster of ghouls, keeping a step behind Bryce.

A scabbed, jet-colored hand skittered from a deep pocket of shadows, its nails long and cracked, digging into the stone—

Before Hunt's lightning could strike, Bryce's starlight flared again. The hand fell back, a low hiss skimming over the rocks. "Super Powerful and Special Magic Starborn Princess, indeed," Hunt said, impressed.

But Bryce turned toward the lines the ghoul had gouged into the rock, running a hand over them. She rubbed the bits of dust and debris between her forefinger and thumb, sniffed it once, then slid her gaze to Hunt. "Flynn's right: I don't like it here." She licked—fucking *licked*—the dark substance on her fingers and grimaced. "Nope. Not at all."

Sathia, still a few steps behind Bryce, shivered. "Can you feel it, then? How . . . dead it all seems? Like there's something festering here."

Hunt had no idea what the Hel either female was talking about, and from Tharion's and Baxian's baffled expressions, they didn't, either.

Bryce only moved on into the dark and mists. They had no choice but to keep pace with her, to stay in that protective bubble of starlight.

"There's water ahead," Baxian said, his advanced hearing picking it up before Hunt could detect it. "A river—a big one, from the sound of it."

Bryce slid Hunt a look. "Good thing we've got two hunky dudes with wings."

And there it was again—that gleam in her eyes. There and gone, but . . . he could almost hear her brain working. Connecting some dots he couldn't see.

"Stay close," Bryce murmured, leading them deeper into the cave. "I've spent a disgusting amount of time underground lately, and I can tell you there's nothing good coming our way."

Flynn and Dec left to grab everyone lunch, and Ruhn resigned himself to working in silence with Lidia, only the rustle of paper and slamming of fruitless drawers for sound.

He found nothing. Neither did she, he concluded from her occasional sighs of frustration. So different from the contented, near-purring sighs she'd made in his arms that time their souls had merged, as he'd moved in her—

Cousin.

Ruhn slowly, slowly turned toward the towering open doorway. No one stood there. Only the gray day lay beyond.

On your left.

Seamus leaned against a nearby stack, arms crossed. A dagger was buckled over his broad chest, just as it had been all those decades ago. As it had been then, the male's dark hair was cut close to his head—to avoid an enemy getting a grip on it, Ruhn knew. And if Seamus was there, then that meant—

On your right, Duncan said into his mind, and Ruhn glanced the other way to find Seamus's brother leaning in a mirror position on the opposite stack. In lieu of a dagger, Duncan carried a slender sword strapped down his spine.

Ruhn kept both of them in his line of sight. *What do you want?*

Instinct had already kept his mind veiled in stars and shadows, but he did a quick mental scan to ensure his walls were intact.

Duncan sneered. *Our uncle sent us to make sure the female was behaving herself.*

Ruhn glanced at Lidia, still searching the catalog. *Fuck,* her mind was unguarded—

It was second nature, really, to leap for her mind. As if he could somehow shield her from them.

But on the other end of that mental bridge, a wall of fire smoldered. It wasn't just fire—it was a conflagration that swirled sky-high, as if generating its own winds and weather. Magma seemed to churn beneath it, visible through cracks in the whirling storm of flame.

Well, he didn't need to worry about her, then.

You spoil our fun, cousin, Seamus said.

She'd be fun to rummage through, Duncan added.

Ruhn eyed the males. *Get lost.*

Her presence defiles this place, Seamus said, attention sliding to

Lidia and fixing on her shoulder blades with an intensity Ruhn didn't like one fucking bit.

So does yours, Ruhn shot back.

Seamus's dark eyes shifted toward Ruhn once more. *We can smell you on her, you know.* Seamus's teeth flashed. *Tell me: Was it like fucking a Reaper?*

A low growl slipped out of Ruhn, and Lidia turned at the sound. She showed no surprise. As if she'd been aware of their presence this whole time, and had been waiting for some sort of signal to interfere.

She looked coolly between his cousins. "Seamus. Duncan. I'll thank you to stay out of my mind."

Seamus bristled, pure Fae menace. "Did we talk to you, bitch?"

Ruhn clenched his jaw so hard it hurt, but Lidia lifted those golden eyes to the twin princes and said, "Shall I demonstrate how I *make* males like you talk to me?"

Duncan snarled. "You're lucky our uncle gave the word to stand down. Or else we'd have already told the Asteri you're here, Hind."

"Good dogs," Lidia said. "I'll be sure to advise Morven to give you both a treat."

Ruhn's lips twitched upward. But—she'd told him to act like the prince he was. So he schooled his face into icy neutrality. A mask as hard as Lidia's. "Tell Morven we'll send word if we require his assistance," he said to his cousins.

The dismissal found its mark better than any taunt. Duncan pushed off the bookshelf, hand curling at his side—shadows wrapping around his knuckles. Darker, wilder than Ruhn's. As if they'd been captured from a storm-tossed night.

"You're an embarrassment to our people," Duncan said. "A disgrace."

Seamus stalked over to his twin, his identical face displaying matching disdain. "Don't waste your breath on him."

Seamus said into Ruhn's mind, *You'll get what's coming to you.*

Ruhn kept his face impassive—*princely,* some might say. "Good to see you both."

Again, his failure to snap back at them only riled them further, and both of his cousins growled before turning as one and striding from the archives.

Only when they'd vanished through the massive doors did Ruhn say quietly to Lidia, "You all right?"

"Yes," she said, her golden eyes meeting his. Ruhn's breath caught in his throat. "They're no different from any other brute I've encountered." Like Pollux. She turned back to the catalog. "They'd get along with Sandriel's triarii."

"I'll remind you that a good chunk of that triarii has since proved to be on our side," Ruhn said. But he could think of nothing else to say, and silence once more fell—inside his head and in the archives—so he began to search again.

After several long minutes, it became unbearable. The silence. The tension. And simply to say something, to break that misery, he blurted, "Why fire?"

She slowly turned toward him. "What?"

"You always appeared as a ball of fire to me. Why?"

She angled her head, eyes gleaming faintly. "Stars and night were already taken." She smirked, and something eased in his chest at this bit of normalcy. Of what it had been like when they were just Day and Night. Despite himself, he found himself smiling back.

But she studied him. "How . . ."

He met her wide, searching stare. "How what?"

"How did you wind up like this?" she asked, voice soft. "Your father is . . ."

"A psychotic dickbag."

She laughed. "Yes. How did you escape his influence?"

"My friends," he said, nodding toward the door they'd exited through. "Flynn and Dec kept me sane. Gave me perspective. Well, maybe not Flynn, but Dec did. Still does."

"Ah."

He allowed himself the luxury of taking in her face, her expression. Noted the kernel of worry there and asked, "How did it go with your sons before we left yesterday?" He'd heard she'd gone to say goodbye, but nothing about the encounter. And given how haunted her face had looked when they'd left the *Depth Charger* . . .

"Great." The word was terse enough that he thought she wouldn't go on, but then she amended, "Terrible." A muscle ticked in her jaw. "I think Brann would want to get to know me, but Ace—Actaeon . . . He loathes me."

"It'll take time."

She changed the subject. "Do you think your sister will actually find something of use against the Asteri?"

Given how many people over the centuries had probably looked for such a thing, Ruhn didn't resent her question. "Knowing Bryce, she's up to something. She always has a few cards up her sleeve. But . . ." He blew out a breath. "Now that she's in the fucking Cave of Princes, part of me doesn't want to know what those cards might entail."

"Your sister is a force of nature." Nothing but admiration shone through the words.

Pride glimmered in his chest at the praise, but Ruhn merely said, "She is." He let that be that.

But the silence that followed was different. Lighter. And he could have sworn he caught Lidia glancing toward him as often as he looked toward her.

Ithan strode down the halls of the House of Flame and Shadow, Hypaxia at his side, his stomach full and contented after a surprisingly good breakfast in its dim dining hall. They'd been early enough that most people hadn't yet arrived.

He'd eaten an insane amount, even for him, but given that they were leaving for Avallen tomorrow, he'd wanted to fuel up as much as possible. He'd demanded that they go *now,* but Jesiba apparently had to arrange transportation and permission for them to enter the island, and since they weren't telling anyone the truth about why they were going, she also had to weave a web of lies to whoever her contact on the Fae island was.

But soon he could right this awful wrong. They'd find Sofie's body, get her lightning, and then fix this. It was a slim shard of hope, but one he clung to. One that kept him from crumbling into absolute ruin.

One he could only thank the female beside him for—the female who hadn't thought twice before helping him so many times. It was for her sake that he made himself keep his tone light as he patted his rock-hard stomach and said, "Did you know they had such good food here?"

Hypaxia smirked. "Why do you think I defected so easily?"

"In it for the food, huh?"

Hypaxia grinned, and he knew the expression was rare for the solemn queen. "I'm *always* in it for the—"

A shudder rumbled through the black halls, clouds of dust drifting from the ceiling. Ithan kept his footing, wrapping a hand around Hypaxia's elbow to steady her.

"What the Hel was that?" Ithan murmured, scanning the dark stone above them.

Another *boom*, and Ithan began running, Hypaxia hurrying behind him, aiming for Jesiba's office. He was through the double doors a moment later, revealing Jesiba at her desk, her face taut, eyes wide—

"What the Hel is going on?" Ithan demanded, rushing over to where she had a feed up on her computer, showing exploding bombs.

Another impact hit, and Ithan motioned Hypaxia to get under the desk. But the former witch-queen did no such thing, instead asking, "Is that feed right above us?"

"No," Jesiba said, her voice so hoarse she almost sounded like a Reaper. "Omega-boats pulled into the Istros." On the feed, buildings crumbled. "Their deck launchers just fired brimstone missiles into Asphodel Meadows."

53

Ithan and Hypaxia raced across the city, the blocks either full of panicking residents and tourists or deathly, eerie quiet. People sat on the sidewalks in stunned shock. Ithan steeled himself for what he'd find in the northeastern quarter, but it wasn't enough to prepare him for the bloodied humans, ghostlike with all the dust and ash on them, streaming out of it. Children screamed in their arms. As he crossed into Asphodel Meadows, the cracked streets were filled with bodies, lying still and silent.

Further into the smoldering ruin, cars had been melted. Piles of rubble remained where buildings had stood. Bodies lay charred. Some of those bodies were unbearably small.

He drifted someplace far, far away from himself. Didn't hear the screams or the sirens or the still-collapsing buildings. At his side, Hypaxia said nothing, her grave face streaked with silent tears.

Closer to the origin of the blasts, there was nothing. No bodies, no cars, no buildings.

There was nothing left in the heart of Asphodel Meadows beyond a giant crater, still smoldering.

The brimstone missiles had been so hot, so deadly, that they'd melted everything away. Anyone who'd taken a direct hit would have died instantly. Perhaps it had been a small mercy to be taken out that fast. To be wiped away before understanding the nightmare that was unfolding. To not be scared.

Ithan's wolf instinct had him focusing. Had him snapping to attention as Hypaxia pulled a vial of firstlight healing potion from her bag and ran to the nearest humans beyond the blast radius—two young parents and a small child, covered head to toe in gray dust, huddling in the doorway of a partially collapsed building.

Hypaxia might have defected from being queen, but she was, first and foremost, a healer. And with his Aux and pack training, Ithan could make a difference, too. Even though he was a wolf without a pack, a disgraced exile and murderer. He could still help. *Would* still help, no matter what the world called him. No matter what unforgivable things he'd done.

So Ithan sprinted for the nearest human, a teenage girl in her school uniform. The fuckers had chosen to strike in the morning, when most people would be out in the streets on their way to work, kids on their way to school, all of them defenseless in the open air—

A snarl slipped out of him, and the girl, bleeding from her forehead, half-pinned under a chunk of cement, cringed away. She scrambled to push the cement block off her lower legs, and it was him—*his* presence that was terrifying her—

He shoved the wolf, the rage down. "Hey," he said, kneeling beside her, reaching for the chunk of cement. "I'm here to help."

The girl stopped her frantic shoving against the block, and lifted her bloodied eyes to him as he easily hauled it off her shins. Her left leg had been shredded down to the bone.

"Hypaxia!" he called to the witch, who was already rising to her feet.

But the girl grabbed Ithan's hand, her face ghastly white as she asked him, "Why?"

Ithan shook his head, unable to find the words. Hypaxia threw herself to her knees before the girl, fishing another firstlight vial from her satchel. One of a scant few, Ithan saw with a jolt. They'd need so many more.

But even if all the medwitches of Crescent City showed up . . . would it be enough?

Would it ever be enough to heal what had been done here?

"You getting anything?" Hunt asked Tharion as they stood on the bank of a deep, wide river rushing through the cave system. Bryce, standing a few feet away, let the males talk as she studied the river, the mists blocking its origin and terminus; the carved walls continuing on the other side of the river; the musty, wet scent of this place.

Nothing so far that would tell her anything new about the blades, mist, or how to kick some Asteri ass, but she filed away everything she saw.

"No," the mer said. Bryce was half listening to him. "My magic just senses that it's . . . cold. And flows all through these caves."

"I guess that's good," Baxian said, tucking in his wings. He winked at Bryce, drawing her attention. "No Wyrms swimming about."

Bryce glowered. "You wouldn't be joking if you'd seen one." She didn't give the Helhound time to reply before she said to him and Hunt, "Wings up to carry us?"

Her mind was racing too much for conversation as they awkwardly crossed the river, Hunt flying Sathia and Bryce together, Baxian carrying Tharion. Bryce extended her bubble of starlight so they could all remain within it, which was about as much extra activity as she could be bothered with while she took in the carvings.

They didn't tell the story that Silene's carvings had narrated—there was no mention of a slumbering evil beneath their feet. Just a river of starlight, into which the long-ago Fae had apparently dragged those pegasuses and drowned them.

Yeah, the Fae here had been no better than the ones in Nesta's world.

They walked for hours and hours—miles and miles. There were occasional stops, alternating who took watch, but sleep was difficult.

The ghouls lurked in crevices and alcoves all around, scraps of malevolent shadow. They hissed with hunger for warm blood—and in abject fear of her starlight. Only someone with the Starborn gift—or someone under their protection—could survive here.

The Starsword pressed on her back; the dagger dug into her hip. They burdened each step, locked in some strange battle to be near each other that intensified as she got farther into the cave.

Bryce ignored them, and instead tracked the carvings on the walls. On the ceilings. Brutal images carved with care and precision: Merciless, unending battles and bloodshed. Cities in ruins. Lands crumbling away. All falling into that river of starlight, as if the Starborn power had swept it away in a tide of destruction.

"I have a question." Sathia's voice echoed through the tunnel. "It might be considered impertinent."

Bryce snorted. "Didn't you know? That's the motto of Team Caves."

Sathia increased her pace until she was at Bryce's side. "Well, you don't seem to want anything to do with the Fae."

"Bingo," Bryce said.

"Yet you're here, bearing our two most sacred artifacts—"

"Three, if you count the Horn in my back."

Sathia's stunned silence seemed to bounce through the cave. "The . . . the *Horn*? How?"

"Fancy magic tattoo," Bryce said, waving a hand. "But go on."

Sathia's throat worked. "You bear *three* of our most sacred artifacts. Yet you plan to . . . do what with the Fae?"

"Nothing," Bryce said. "You're right: I want nothing to do with them." The carvings around them only strengthened that resolve. Especially the ones of the pegasus slaughter. She glanced sidelong at the female. "No offense."

But Sathia said, "Why?"

This really wasn't a conversation Bryce felt like having, and she gave the female a look that said as much. But Sathia held her stare, frank and unafraid.

So Bryce sighed. "The Fae are . . . not my favorite people. They never have been, but after this spring even more so. I *really* don't want to associate with a group of cowards who locked out innocents the day demons poured into our city, and who seem intent on doing that again on a larger scale here on Avallen."

"Some of us had no choice but to be locked in our villas," Sathia said tightly. "My parents forbade me from—"

"I never let something being forbidden stop me from doing it," Bryce said.

Sathia glared, but went on. "If you . . . if we . . . survive all this, what then?"

"What do you mean, *what then*?"

"What do you do with the sword and knife? With the Horn? Let's say your wildest hopes about the Asteri come true, and we find the knowledge here or in the archives to help defeat them. Once they're gone, do you keep these objects, when you want nothing to do with our people?"

"Are you saying I shouldn't keep them?"

"I'm asking you what *you* plan to do—with them, and yourself."

"I'm changing the motto of Team Caves," Bryce announced. "It's now *Mind Your Own Business*."

"I mean it," Sathia said, not taking Bryce's shit for one second. "You'll walk away from it all?"

"I don't see much of a reason to hang around," Bryce said coldly. "I don't see why you'd want to, either. You're chattel to them. To the Autumn King, to Morven, to your dad. Your only value comes from your breeding potential. They don't give a fuck if you're smart or brave or kind. They only want you for your uterus, and Luna spare you if you have any troubles with it."

"I know that," Sathia answered with equal ice. "I've known that since I was a child."

"And you're cool with it?" Bryce countered, unable to stop the sharpness in her voice. "You're cool with being used and treated like that? Like you're lesser than them? You're cool with having no rights, no say in your future? You're cool with a life where you either belong to your male relatives or your husband?"

"No, but it is the life I was born into."

"Well, you're Mrs. Ketos now," Bryce said, nodding back at Tharion, who was watching them carefully. "So brace yourself for all that entails."

"What does *that* mean?" Tharion demanded.

But Sathia ignored her taunts and said, "What are you going to do to the Fae?"

"Do?" Bryce asked, halting.

Sathia didn't back down. "With all that power you have. With who you are, what you bear."

Hunt let out a low whistle of warning.

But Bryce seethed at Sathia, "I just want the Fae to leave me the fuck alone. And I'll leave them the fuck alone."

Sathia pointed at the Starsword on Bryce's back. "But the prophecy—when those blades are reunited, so shall our people be. That has to mean you, uniting all the Fae peoples—"

"I already did that," Bryce cut in. "I connected the Fae of Midgard to the ones in our home world. Prophecy fulfilled. Or were you hoping for something else?"

Sathia's gaze simmered. An unbroken female, despite the life she'd led. "I was hoping for a Fae Queen. Someone who might change things for the better."

"Well, you got me instead," Bryce said, and continued into the dark, fingers curling at her sides. Maybe she'd use her laser power to wipe these carvings from the walls. As easily as Rigelus had shattered the statues in the Eternal Palace. Maybe she'd send out a blast of her light so vicious it would obliterate all the hissing ghouls around them. "The Fae dug their own graves. They can lie in them."

Sathia let it drop.

Hunt fell into step beside Bryce, putting a hand on her shoulder as if to offer his support, but she could have sworn that even her mate was disappointed in her.

Whatever. If they wanted to preserve a long, fucked-up line of Fae tyrants, that was on them.

Flynn and Dec abandoned Ruhn the moment they called it quits at the archives, leaving him and Lidia to share a painfully quiet meal in the castle's empty dining room.

There was so much he wanted to ask her, to talk to her about, to know. He couldn't find the words. So he ate, fork unbearably loud against his plate, each bite like crunching glass. And when they finished, they walked back to their rooms in silence, each step echoing in the hallway, loud as a thunderclap.

But before they parted ways, as Ruhn was about to enter his room, he blurted, "You think my sister's okay?"

"You're the one who's been in the Cave of Princes," Lidia said, but turned toward him. "You tell me."

He shook his head. "Honestly, I don't know. Bryce has got a lot of shit going on right now. Those caves are confusing on a good day. If you're not focused, they can be deadly."

Lidia crossed her arms. "Well, I have faith that between her, Athalar, and Baxian, your sister will be fine."

"Tharion will be insulted."

"I don't know Ketos well enough as a warrior to judge him."

"Ithan Holstrom calls him Captain Whatever, but I think it's selling him a bit short. Tharion's a badass when he feels like it."

She smiled, and damn if it didn't do funny things to Ruhn's chest. She said again, "Your sister will be fine."

He nodded, blowing out a breath. "Do you and Hypaxia have any contact?"

"No. Not since the ball."

His mouth moved before he could think through his next question. "That night . . . were you ever going to meet me in the garden?"

Surprise flickered in her eyes, then vanished. Her mouth pursed, like she was debating her answer. "The Harpy got there before I did," she said finally.

He stepped toward her, the hall suddenly too small. "But were you going to show up like we'd planned?"

"Does it matter?"

He dared another step. He hadn't realized how her hips swelled so invitingly before dipping to her waist.

His hands curled, and he hated himself for the punch of lust that went through him, nearly knocking the breath from his lungs. He wanted her. Wanted her naked and under him and moaning his name, wanted her to tell him *everything*, and wanted . . . wanted his friend back. The friend he could speak honestly to, who knew things about him that no one else knew.

He took one more step, and he could see her trembling. With fear or restraint, he had no idea.

"Lidia," he murmured, in front of her at last, and she closed her eyes, the pulse in her throat fluttering.

Her scent shifted—like flowers unfurling under the morning sun. That scent was pure arousal. His cock tightened painfully.

He didn't care that they were in the middle of a hallway with his awful cousins running amok. He slid a hand onto her waist, nearly groaning at the steep curve, the way it fit his hand perfectly.

She kept her eyes closed, her pulse still flickering. So he took his other hand and tilted her head to the side. Leaned down and brushed his mouth over that fluttering spot.

Her breathing hitched, and his eyes nearly rolled back in his head. She tasted . . . fuck. He needed more. His teeth grazed the soft skin of her throat, and his tongue skimmed along the space just under her ear. His cock throbbed in answer.

Her body loosened, pliant in his hands, and her head tipped a little further to the side. An invitation. He licked up the column of her throat, hand drifting from her waist down to her ass—

She stiffened. Pulled away.

Like she'd caught herself. Remembered who she was. Who he was.

He stood there like a fucking moron, panting slightly, cock fully hard and straining against his pants, and she just . . . stared at him. Wide-eyed.

"I . . ." He had no idea what to say. What to do.

His head swam. This female had so much blood on her hands, yet—

"Good night," he rasped, and turned to his own room before he could make a greater fool of himself.

She didn't stop him.

54

Bryce lay on the hard, cold ground and tried to pretend she was back in her bed, that a rock wasn't poking into her hip bone, that her arm was the *most* comfortable pillow—

From Sathia's tossing and turning nearby, she knew the female was having the same amount of success getting settled for the night.

Hunt had fallen asleep right away, his deep breathing now a gentle rhythm that she tried to focus on, to lure her to sleep. She supposed his warrior days had made him used to rougher conditions, but . . . no. She didn't want to think about all the things Hunt had endured so that sleeping on this unforgiving surface was easy for him. Especially when the misplaced guilt from so many of those things was now clearly eating him alive.

It had been easier in the Fae world, as exhaustion had been riding her so hard that she'd had no choice *but* to pass out. But here, even well protected by Baxian on watch, sleep remained elusive.

Bryce flipped onto her back, her starlight shifting with her, broadcasting every one of her movements like a lighthouse beacon. Fuck, how she'd sleep with *that* blazing in her eyes—

She stared miserably up at the ceiling, carved here to resemble the branches of a forest. Beautiful, remarkable work that had never been documented, never been revealed to the world at large. Only to the few Fae royal males who'd sought the Starsword.

That blade was currently lying to her left, a thrumming, pulsing presence made worse by Truth-Teller on her right, which pulsed in a counter-beat. Like the blades were talking.

Just fucking great. It was a regular old sleepover here. Bryce ignored the chattering blades as best she could, focusing instead on the caves, the carvings.

Females had never been allowed in here. Now *two* Fae females had entered. She hoped all the long-dead princes buried in the caves were thrashing in their sarcophagi.

Such fear of females—such hatred. Why? Because of Theia? Pelias had been the one to found the Starborn line here on Midgard. Had all the bans and restrictions stemmed from his fear of someone like her rising again?

Bryce supposed scholars and activists had spent centuries researching and debating it, so the likelihood of finding an answer herself, even knowing the truth about Theia, was slim to none. It didn't make it any easier to swallow, though.

So she curled on her side, gazing at the carved river of stars that her starlight illuminated. The river of her lineage, meant to last through the millennia. Her bloodline, in its literal, starry form. Her bloodline, running straight through these caves. An inheritance of cruelty and pain.

She wished Danika were with her. If there was one person who might have understood the complexity of such a fucked-up inheritance, of having the future of a people weighing on her, it would have been Danika.

Danika, who'd wanted more for this world, for Bryce.

Light it up.

But maybe the Fae and their bloodline didn't deserve Bryce's light. Maybe they deserved to fall forever into darkness.

Flynn and Dec, the bastards, didn't show up to breakfast. Leaving Ruhn and Lidia to dine alone again.

Ruhn had lain awake most of the night, hard and aching—then fretting about what Bryce and the others were facing in the Cave of Princes. Maybe he should have gone with them. Maybe staying here had been cowardly, even if they did need information from the archives. Flynn and Dec could have found it.

The dining room doors opened as they were finishing their meal, and Ruhn braced himself for his asshole cousins. But a tall Fae male walked in, glancing about before quietly shutting the door behind him. As if he didn't want to be seen.

"Lidia Cervos." The male's voice shook.

Ruhn reached a hand toward the knife in his boot as the male approached the table. Lidia watched him, expression unreadable. Ruhn tried and failed to control his thundering heart. He opened his mouth. To order the stranger to announce himself, to demand he leave—

"I came to thank you," the male said, and reached for his pocket. Ruhn drew his knife, but the male only pulled out a piece of paper. A small portrait of a female and three young children. All Fae.

But Lidia didn't look. Like she couldn't bear to.

The male said, "Ten years ago, you saved my life."

Ruhn didn't know what to do with his body. Lidia just stared at the floor.

The male went on, "My unit was up in the base at Kelun. It was the middle of the night when you burst in, and I thought we were all dead. But you told us that the Hammer was coming—that we had to run. All seven of us are alive today, with our families, because of you."

Lidia nodded, but it seemed like a *thank you, please stop* motion. Not from any humility or embarrassment—it was pain on her lowered face. Like she couldn't endure listening.

He extended the portrait of his family again.

"I thought you might like to see what your choice that night achieved."

Still, Lidia didn't look up. Ruhn couldn't move. Couldn't get a breath down.

The male went on, "There are a few of us from my unit still

here, in secret. Prince Cormac convinced us all to join the cause. But we never told him, or anyone, who saved us. We didn't want to jeopardize whatever you were doing. But when we heard through the rumor mill that you—the Hind, I mean—had defied the Asteri, some of us contacted each other again."

The male at last noticed Lidia's discomfort and said, "Perhaps it is too soon for you to acknowledge all you have done, the lives you saved, but . . . I wanted to tell you that we are grateful. We owe you a debt."

"There is no debt," Lidia said, finally meeting the male's eyes. "You should go."

Ruhn blinked at the dismissal, but Lidia clarified to the stranger, "I assume you have kept your activities and associations secret from Morven. Don't risk his wrath now."

The male nodded, understanding. "Thank you," he said again, and was gone.

In the silence that followed, Ruhn asked, "You let them see who you really were?"

"It was either risk my identity being revealed to the world, or let them die," Lidia said quietly as they headed for the door. "I couldn't have lived with myself if I'd chosen the latter."

Ruhn arched a brow. "Not to sound totally callous, but why? There were only seven of them. It wouldn't have made a difference in the rebellion."

"Maybe not for Ophion as a whole, but it would have made a difference for their families." She didn't look at him. "Partners, children, parents—all hoping for their safe return."

"There had to be more to it than that," he pushed. "There was way more than that on the line for you."

She opened the door, and didn't speak again until they'd stepped into the hallway. "I guess I hoped that . . . that if my sons were ever in a similar situation, someone would do the same for them."

His heart twisted at the words, her truth. "Your path was difficult, Lidia—Hel, I don't think I could have endured any of it. But what you did was incredible. Don't lose sight of that."

"I could have saved more," she said softly, eyes on the floor as they strode down the empty hall. "I should have saved more."

Lidia had no idea what to make of the encounter with the former rebel this morning.

Maybe Urd had sent him to her, to remind her that her choices and sacrifices had, in fact, made some difference in the world. Even if they had gutted her.

The Ocean Queen hadn't given her a choice in leaving the ship, both all those years ago and now. But here, on this cheerless Fae island . . . here, at least, were some people who'd benefitted from that impossible position.

Flynn and Declan hadn't yet arrived in the archives, and as the silence became unbearable while she and Ruhn started their search, the only scents the musty catalog cards and Ruhn's inviting, reassuring smell, Lidia found herself calling down the line of the card catalog, "I'm going to go hunt for some coffee. Want to join me?"

Ruhn looked over, and gods, he was handsome. She'd never really let herself think about the sheer beauty of him. Even with his tattoos in ribbons, proof of what Pollux had done—

His blue eyes flickered, as if noting the direction of her thoughts. "Sure, let's go."

Even the way he spoke, the timbre of his voice . . . she could luxuriate in that all day. And when he'd touched her last night, licked her—

Did he have any idea how close she'd come to begging him to strip her naked, to lick her from head to toe and spend a long while between her legs?

"What's that look about?" Ruhn asked, voice low, thick. She noted every shifting muscle in his shoulders, his arms, his powerful thighs as he walked toward her. The way the sunlight gleamed on his long dark hair, turning it into a silken cascade of night. That buzzed side of his head seemed to be begging for her fingers to slide over the velvet-soft hair while she nipped at his pointed ear—

She began walking as he reached her, because the alternative was to wrap herself around him. "Brain fog. I need a cup of coffee."

She'd slept poorly again last night. At first, it had been thanks to the memory of what they'd done in the hallway, but then her thoughts had shifted to Brann and Actaeon, to that last conversation with them, and she'd wished that she could find herself on that mental bridge, her friend Night sitting in his armchair beside her.

Not just to have someone to talk to, but to have *him* to talk to. About . . . everything.

Ruhn fell into step beside her. "Who would have thought the Hind had a caffeine addiction?"

His half smile did something funny to her knees. But he said nothing more as they explored the back hallway of the archives, opening and closing doors. A closet crammed with half-rotted brooms and mops, another closest adorned with trays of various quartz crystals—no doubt some sort of scholarly recording device needed for this technology-free island—and a few empty cells with chipped desks that must have once been private studies.

"Morven really needs to invest in a new break room," Ruhn said as they finally beheld the kitchen. "This can't be good for employee morale."

Lidia took in the dark, dusty space, the wooden counter against the wall littered with mouse droppings, the cobwebs spun under the row of cabinetry. "This is like some bad medieval cliché," she said, approaching the filth-crusted cauldron in the darkened hearth. "Is this . . . gruel?"

Ruhn stepped up beside her, and his scent had her going molten between her legs. "I don't know why everyone thought Avallen would be some fairy-tale paradise. I've been telling Bryce for years that it's horrible here."

Lidia turned from the days-old goop in the cauldron and began opening cabinets. A mouse had made a home in a box of stale crackers, but at least there was a sealed jar of tea bags. "I should have known there would be no coffee." She peered around for a kettle and found Ruhn standing with one by the ancient sink, pumping water into it.

"Your sister," Lidia said, "was right to wonder what was going on with this place. Do you think Morven's hiding anything?"

"You're the super spy-breaker," Ruhn said, going to the hearth and tossing a few logs into the ashes. "You tell me."

The muscles in his forearm shifted as he grabbed some kindling and flint and lit the fire with a sort of efficiency that shouldn't have made her mouth water. He glanced over a shoulder, those blazingly blue eyes curious, and she realized he'd asked her a question, and she'd just been . . . staring at him. At his arms.

She cleared her throat and went about hunting for two mugs. "Morven never gave the Asteri or me cause to look into this place. He always appeared when summoned, and offered his services without question. He was, as far as Rigelus was concerned, a perfect minion."

"So there was never any discussion about these mists and Morven getting to hide behind them whenever he wanted?" The fire sparked to life, and Ruhn rose, stepping back to monitor it.

"No," Lidia said. "I think Rigelus believes the mists to be some . . . charming quirk of Midgard and the Fae. Something that added a bit of personality to this world. And since Morven and his forefathers played nice, they were left alone."

Ruhn slid his hands into the pockets of his black jeans. "I guess I'm surprised that after the truth about Cormac came out, the Asteri still didn't come poking around Avallen to see what might have caused the prince to turn rebel."

"Morven slithered right to the Eternal City," Lidia said, clenching her jaw. "And disavowed his son immediately."

"Right, with my dad in tow."

She scanned his face, the pain and anger that he didn't hide. "Yesterday, when I said you should act more like a prince . . ."

"Don't worry about it."

"I know the kind of monsters you're going up against." She dipped her eyes to his forearms, where the childhood burn scars were now mostly gone, but a few shiny pink streaks remained, untouched even by Pollux's ministrations.

"I can look after myself," he said tightly, fitting the kettle onto the hook over the fire and swinging it above the flame.

"I know you can," she tried, failing miserably at explaining. "I'm just . . . I see how good you are, Ruhn. You wear your emotions on your face because you *feel* in a way that Morven and the Autumn King do not. I don't want them to use that against you. To figure out how to hurt you."

He slowly faced her, those beautiful blue eyes wary, yet tender. "I think that's a compliment?"

She huffed a laugh, and plopped two tea bags into the least dusty mugs she'd found. "It's a compliment, Ruhn." She met his gaze, and offered him a small smile. "Take it and move on."

They found nothing new that day. Flynn and Dec seemed content to let them do the work, because they didn't show up. Or perhaps they'd gone off on some important errand and couldn't let them know, with no way to text or call.

"Listen to this," Lidia said, and Ruhn stopped his endless browsing to walk over to where she'd opened an ancient scroll. He'd noticed the way she'd been looking at him earlier—the pure desire in her eyes, her scent. It had distracted him so much that he'd barely been able to light the fire in that sorry excuse for a kitchen.

But Ruhn reined in the urge to scent her, to bury his face in her neck and lick that soft skin. Lidia pointed at the unfurled scroll before her. "The catalog listed this scroll's title as *The Roots of Earthen Magic*."

"And?"

Her mouth quirked to the side. "I think it's strange that both Flynn and Sathia can't stand Avallen."

"What does that have to do with defeating the Asteri?"

"I figured it might be worthwhile to pull out some of the

earliest writings about earth magic—what role it played in the First Wars, or soon after. This scroll was the oldest I could find."

Flynn had picked a Hel of a time to not show up. "And . . . ?"

"This doesn't offer more than what we already know about the usual sort of earth magic the Fae possess, but it *does* mention that those with earth magic were sent ahead to scout lands, to sense where to build. Not only the best geographical locations, but magical ones, too. They could sense the ley lines—the channels of energy running throughout the land, throughout Midgard. They told the Asteri to build their cities where several of the lines met, at natural crossroads of power, and picked those places for the Fae to settle, too. But they selected Avallen *just* for the Fae. To be their personal, eternal stronghold."

Ruhn considered. "Okay, so if Flynn and Sathia say this place is dead and rotting . . ."

"It doesn't line up with the claims recorded here about Avallen."

"But why would the ancient Fae lie about there being ley lines here?"

"I don't think they lied," Lidia said, and pointed to the maps on the other table, where Dec had discarded them. "I think the Avallen they first visited, with all those ley lines and magic . . . I think it existed. But then something changed."

"We knew that already, though," Ruhn said carefully. "That something changed."

"Yes," Lidia said, "but the mists haven't. Could that be intentional? They left the mists intact, but the rest was altered—entire islands gone, the earth itself festering."

"But that would only have hurt the Fae—and we all know they're self-serving bastards. They'd never willingly part with any sort of power."

"Maybe they weren't willing," Lidia mused. "Whatever happened, the mists kept it hidden from the Asteri."

"What do you think they wanted to hide? Why rot their own land?"

Lidia gestured to the catalog behind them. "Maybe the answer's in there somewhere."

Ruhn nodded. Even as he wondered if they'd be ready for whatever that answer might be.

Bryce stood with Baxian on the bank of a second river, surveying the path on its distant side, her star glowing dimly toward it. The river passageway was narrow enough that she would have to teleport them across. She kept her starlight blazing bright, the ghouls a whispering malice around them.

There had been nothing helpful in the carvings so far. Fae slaying dragons, Fae dancing in circles, Fae basking in their own glory. Nothing of use. All surface-level shit. Bryce ground her teeth.

"Danika was the same, you know," Baxian said quietly so the others wouldn't hear. "With the wolves. She hated what so many of them were, and wanted to understand how they had become that way."

Bryce turned toward him, her starlight flaring a bit brighter as it illuminated the downward sweep of the river. It dimmed as she faced the Helhound fully. "The wolves are by and large *way* better than the Fae."

"Maybe." Baxian glanced to her. "But what of your brother? Or Flynn and Declan?" A nod to where Sathia, Tharion, and Hunt sat together. "What of her? Do you think they're all a lost cause?"

"No," Bryce admitted. Baxian waited. She let out a long breath. "And the Fae I met in the other world weren't so bad, either. I might have even been friends with them if circumstances had been different."

"So the Fae aren't inherently bad."

"Of course not," Bryce hissed. "But most of the ones in this world—"

"You know every Fae on Midgard?"

"I can judge them by their collective actions," Bryce snapped. "How they locked people out during the attack—"

"Yeah, that was fucked up. But until Holstrom defied orders, the wolves weren't helping, either."

"What's your point?"

"That the right leader makes all the difference."

Bryce recoiled at the words: *the right leader.* Baxian went on, "The Valbaran Fae might not be the most charitable people in our world, but think about who's led them for the last five hundred years. And long before that. Same with the wolves. The Prime isn't bad, but he's only one decent guy in a string of brutal leaders. Danika was working to change that, and she was killed for it."

"Rigelus told me they killed her to keep the information about their true nature contained," Bryce said.

Baxian cut her a look. "And you believe everything Rigelus says? Besides, why can't it be both? They wanted to keep their secrets to themselves, yes, but also to destroy the kernel of hope Danika offered. Not only to the wolves, but all of Midgard. That things could be different. Better."

Bryce massaged her aching chest, the starlight unusually dim. "They definitely would have killed her for that, too."

Baxian's face tightened with pain. "Then make her death count for something, Bryce."

He might as well have punched her in the face. "And what," she demanded, "try to redeem the *Fae*? Get them some self-help books and make them sit in circles to talk about their feelings?"

His face was like stone. "If you think that would be effective, sure."

Bryce glowered. But she loosed a long breath. "If we survive this shit with the Asteri, I'll think about it."

"They might go hand in hand," he said.

"If you start spewing some bullshit about rallying a Fae army to take on the Asteri—"

"No. This isn't some epic movie." He cocked his head. "But if you think you could manage—"

Bryce, despite herself, laughed. "Sure. I'll add it to my to-do list."

Baxian smiled slightly. "I just wanted you to know that Danika was thinking about a lot of the same things."

"I wish she'd talked to me about it." Bryce sighed. "About a lot of stuff."

"She wanted to," he said gently. "And I think putting that Horn in your back was her way of perhaps . . . manipulating you onto a similar path."

"Typical Danika."

"She saw it in you—what you could mean for the Fae." His voice grew unbearably sad. "She was good about seeing that kind of thing in people."

Bryce touched his arm. "I'm glad she had you to talk to. I really am."

He gave her a sorrowful smile. "I'm glad she had you, too. I couldn't be there with her, couldn't leave Sandriel, and I'm so fucking grateful that she had someone there who loved her unconditionally."

Bryce's throat closed up. She might have offered some platitude about them reuniting in the afterlife, but . . . the afterlife was a sham. And Danika's soul was already gone.

"Guys," Hunt said from where he and the others had risen to their feet. "We need to keep going."

"Why?" Bryce asked, walking over. Her starlight dimmed, as if telling her she was headed in the wrong direction. *I know,* she told it silently.

"We shouldn't linger, even with the Magical Starborn Princess watching over us," Tharion said, winking. "I think it's getting too tempting for the ghouls." He jerked his head toward the writhing mass of shadows barely visible within the mists. Their hissing had risen to such a level that it reverberated against her bones.

"All right," Bryce said, resisting the urge to plug her ears against the unholy din. "Let's go."

"That's the first wise decision you've made," drawled a deep male voice from the tunnel behind them.

And there was nowhere to run, nothing to do but stand and face the threat, as Morven stalked out of the mists. And behind him, flame simmering in his eyes, strode the Autumn King.

55

Hunt let his lightning gather at his fingers, let it wind through his hair as the two Fae Kings approached, one wreathed in flame, the other in shadow. The hissing of the ghouls, their stench, had veiled the kings' approach. Unless Morven had *willed* the ghouls to make such a racket, so they could creep up this close without even Baxian's hearing picking it up.

Hunt's lightning was a spark of what he'd command without the halo, but it was enough to fry these fuckers—

The Autumn King only stared at Bryce, pure hatred twisting his face. "Did you think that closet could hold me?"

Hunt's lightning sizzled around him, twining up his forearm. He was dimly aware of Tharion forming a plume of water straight from the river they'd been about to cross and aiming it at the kings. Of Baxian, sword out and snarling—

Seeming supremely unconcerned, Bryce said to her father, "I imprisoned Micah in a bathroom, so a closet seemed good enough for you. I have to admit that I'd hoped you'd stay in there a bit longer, though."

Morven's shadows thrashed around him like hounds straining at the leash. "You will return to my castle with us to face the consequences for treating your sovereign so outrageously."

Bryce laughed. "We're not going anywhere with you."

Morven smiled, and his shadows stilled. "I think you will."

Dark, scabby hands dragged Flynn and Declan out of the shadows. The males struggled, but the ghouls held them in check. Only the creatures' hands were visible—the rest of their bodies remained hidden in the shadows, as if unable to stand being so close to Bryce's starlight.

Sathia let out a low noise of shock. But Hunt demanded, "Where the fuck is Ruhn?"

"Occupied with wooing that traitorous bitch," Morven said. "He didn't even notice my nephews stealing these idiots away."

Two voices said into Hunt's mind, *We'll kill you and then breed your mate until she's—*

Starlight flared, silencing the voices but revealing the Murder Twins lurking behind the two kings. Steps away from Dec and Flynn, like the brothers commanded the ghouls to hold the males.

Bryce blazed, bright white against the blue and gold of the Autumn King's flames, the impenetrable dark of Morven's shadows. "What the fuck do you want?"

Flynn and Declan let out high, keening sounds. Though the ghouls' hands hadn't shifted, blood was trickling from her friends' noses. Dripping onto the ground.

Seamus and Duncan smiled. Whatever those fucks were doing to Dec's and Flynn's minds—

"You treacherous little brat," Morven spat at Bryce, shadows now at the ready once more. "Trying to win me over with your sire's research. He would never have let you get your dirty hands on it if you hadn't incapacitated him somehow. I went to investigate immediately."

Hunt could only gape as Bryce feigned a yawn. "My mistake. I assumed you'd want a leg up on this asshole here." She pointed with her thumb at the Autumn King. "But I didn't bargain on you being too dumb to interpret what was in his notes without his help."

Hunt had to stifle a chuckle, despite the danger they were in. Morven's affronted look was a little too forced—Bryce had clearly hit home. The Autumn King shot him a nasty glare.

"Let them go," Bryce said, "and then we'll talk like adults."

"They will be released when you have returned to my castle," Morven said.

"Then kill them now, because I'm not going back with you."

Flynn and Dec turned outraged eyes on her, but the ghouls held them firm. Morven said nothing. Even his shadows didn't move. The Murder Twins just eyed Bryce, readying for a fight.

Bring it, fuckers, Hunt wanted to say. From the way the twins glared at him, he wondered if they'd picked up his thoughts.

Yet Bryce smiled mockingly at Morven. "But I know you won't kill them. They're too valuable as breeding assets. Which is what all this comes down to, right? Breeding."

The Autumn King said coldly, even as red-hot flame simmered at his fingertips, "The Fae must retain our power and birthright. The royal bloodlines have been fading, turning watery and weak in your generation."

"Cormac proved that with his spinelessness," Morven bit out. "We must do everything we can to strengthen them."

"Cormac was more of a warrior than you'll ever be," Tharion snapped, that plume of water narrowing to needle-like sharpness. It'd punch a hole through the face of whoever got in front of it.

"Too bad I'm married now," Bryce mused. "And you guys don't do divorce."

Morven sneered. "Exceptions can be made for the sake of breeding."

Hunt's rage roared through him.

"All this breeding talk is *awfully* familiar," Bryce said, yawning again. "And come to think of it, this whole Fae King versus Fae Queen thing seems like history repeating itself, too." She scrunched up her features, pretending to think. "But you know . . ." She patted Truth-Teller's hilt. "Some things might be different these days." Hunt could have sworn the Starsword hummed faintly, as if in answer.

"You disgrace our people and history by bearing those blades," Morven accused.

"Don't forget that I also bear this," Bryce said, and held up a hand. Light—pure, concentrated light—fizzed there.

"Oh, you believe mere light can best true darkness?" Morven seethed, shadows rising behind him in a black wave. They were deep, suffocating—lifeless.

Hunt gathered his lightning again, a chain twining around his wrist and forearm. One whip of it, and he'd fry the ghouls holding Dec and Flynn, freeing up two more allies in this fight—

But the Autumn King beheld that concentrated seed of light at Bryce's finger. His flames banked. Any amusement or rage leached from his expression as he murmured to Morven, "Run."

"Now *that's* the first wise decision *you've* made," Bryce mocked.

A beam of slicing, burning light shot from her hand toward the ceiling.

Then solid rock rained down upon them all.

Ruhn had just decided that he really should go see where his friends had disappeared to all day, and was about to do so after leaving the archives that night when he found himself walking back toward the bedrooms with Lidia.

"I know it's an unusual situation," she said when they reached his door, "but I liked working with you today."

He halted, throat working before he managed to say, "Must be nice, to finally get to . . . be yourself. Out in the open."

"It's complicated," she said quietly.

She shifted on her feet, like she wanted to say more but didn't know how, so Ruhn decided to do her a favor and asked, "Wanna come in for a minute?" At her arched brow, he added, "Just to talk."

Her lips curved, but she nodded. He opened his door, stepping aside to let her in. They found seats in the threadbare armchairs before the crackling fire, and for a moment, Lidia stared at the flames as if they were speaking to her.

Ruhn was about to offer her a drink when she said, "Everything in my life is complicated. All the relationships, real and faked . . . sometimes I can't even tell them apart." Her voice was soft—sad. And utterly exhausted.

Ruhn cleared his throat. "When you and I . . ." *Fucked.* "Slept together, you knew who I was. Beyond the code name, I mean."

Her eyes found his, dancing with flame. "Yes."

"Did it complicate things for you?"

She held his stare, her eyes as gold as the flames before them, and his heart thundered. "No. I was shocked, but it didn't complicate anything."

"Shocked?"

She gestured to him. "You're . . . you."

"And that's . . . bad?"

She huffed a laugh, and it was so much like Day that he couldn't get a breath down.

"You're the defiant, partying prince. You have all those piercings and tattoos. I didn't have you down for being a rebel."

"Trust me, it wasn't on my five-year plan, either."

She laughed again, and the breathy sound went right to his cock, wrapping tight. Her voice had always done that. "Why risk it?"

"At first?" He shrugged, fighting past the rising lust pounding through his body. "Cormac blackmailed me. Said he'd tell my father about my mind-speaking abilities. But then I realized it was . . . it was the right thing to do."

"Agent Silverbow will be sorely missed. He already is."

"You knew Cormac, then?"

"No, but I knew of the things he accomplished for Ophion, and the people caught up in the war. He was a good male." She glanced to the shut door. "His father did not deserve a son like him."

Ruhn nodded.

She looked at him intently. "Your father, too—he does not deserve a son like you."

The words shouldn't have meant anything, especially coming from the Hind, but Ruhn's throat tightened at the raw honesty in her voice.

"Can I ask," he ventured, "about your deal with the Ocean Queen?"

Lidia's jaw tightened. "I was young, and afraid, when I made my bargain with her. But even now, I'd make the same choices. For my sons."

"What happened?" He met her eyes. "I know it's not my business, but . . ."

"Pollux isn't their father." He nearly sighed with relief. "It . . ." She struggled for words. "I come from a long line of powerful stag shifters. We have rituals. Secret ones, old ones. We don't necessarily worship the same gods that you do. I think our gods predate this world, but I've never confirmed it."

"Let me guess: You participated in some kind of secret sex rite and got pregnant?"

Her eyes widened, then she laughed—a full, throaty sound this time. "Essentially, yes. A fertility rite, deep in the Aldosian Forest. I was selected from the females of my family. A male from another family was chosen. Neither of our identities were known to each other, or to each other's families. It was quick, and not particularly interesting, and if there was fertility magic, I couldn't tell you what the Hel it was."

"Were you already with Pollux then?"

"Ruhn . . ." She looked at her hands. "My father took me from my mother when I was three. I remember being taken, and not understanding, and only learning later, when I was old enough, that my father was a power-hungry monster. He's not worth the breath it takes to speak of him, and I blamed my mother for letting him take me away. I became his little protégé, I think out of some hope that it would wound her when she heard I had turned out exactly like him."

She took a shaky breath. "I trained, and I schemed, and I wound up in Sandriel's triarii, a high honor for my family. I'd been serving Sandriel for ten years when my father chose me for this ritual. I had become adept at . . . getting people to talk. Pollux and I were dancing around each other, but I had not yet decided to let him into my bed. So I went to the ritual."

Ruhn couldn't move, couldn't have spoken even if he wanted to.

"A few weeks later, I knew I was pregnant. A baby from a sacred ritual would have been celebrated. I should have rushed right to my father to announce the good news, but I hesitated. For the first time in my life, I hesitated. And I didn't know *why* I couldn't tell him. Why, when I thought of the baby inside of me, when I thought of handing that child over to him, I couldn't."

She hooked a stray lock of hair behind her ear, the restless motion at odds with her usual poised demeanor. Ruhn refrained from putting a hand on her shoulder.

"I knew that within a matter of days, Pollux or the others—Athalar was still with us then—would scent the pregnancy. So I staged my own kidnapping and disappearance. I made it look like Ophion had grabbed me. I didn't even know where I was running to. But I couldn't stop thinking of the babies—I knew it was twins, by that point—and how I would do anything to keep them out of my father's hands. Out of Sandriel's hands. I knew, deep down, what sort of monsters I served. I had always known. And I didn't want to be like them. Not just for the babies' sake, but my own. So I ran."

"And that's when the Ocean Queen found you?" His voice was hoarse.

"I found her. When I finally paused to breathe, I remembered what some rebels had claimed while I . . . interrogated them. That the ocean itself would come to help them. It seemed strange enough that I took a chance. I walked into a known rebel base and surrendered. I begged to be taken to the ocean."

He couldn't imagine what she'd felt in that moment—knowing her children's lives hung in the balance.

"Their highest commanders understood, and got me onto the *Depth Charger.* The Ocean Queen welcomed me, but with a caveat. I could stay on her ship, bear the babies, and remain for a time. But in exchange for her protection, and the continued protection of my children . . . I had to go back. I would spin a lie about being interrogated and held prisoner for more than two years, and I would go back. Work my way up in the Asteri's esteem, gain their trust. I would feed any intel to Ophion—and by extension, the Ocean Queen."

"And you could not see your sons."

"No. I would not see my sons again. At least, not until the Ocean Queen allowed me to."

"That's terrible."

"It kept them safe."

"And kept you in her service."

"Yes. I tried to save the rebels who crossed my path, though."

"Was it your idea or hers to save them?" He didn't realize how vital her answer was until he asked the question.

"I told you, my eyes had been opened. And while I had to play the part of interrogator and loyal servant, I did everything I could to mitigate the damage. There were agents who were about to talk, to spill vital secrets. Those, I had to kill. 'Accidents' during torture. But I gave them swift, merciful deaths. The ones who held out, or who stood a chance . . . I tried to get them out. Sometimes it didn't work."

"Like Sofie Renast."

"Like Sofie Renast," she said quietly. "I did not intend for her to drown. The mistake in timing . . . I carry that."

He took her hand—slowly, making sure she'd allow the touch. "What happened when you returned?"

"Pollux confessed his feelings. Said he'd been frantic to find me for the two years I'd been gone. That he'd slaughtered countless rebels trying to find me. The old Lidia would have slept with him. And I knew it would make my cover complete. The rest is history."

She lifted her gaze to his. "I'm not wholly innocent, you see," she said. "Had it not been for my sons, I might very well have become the person the world believes me to be, forever ignoring that small voice whispering that it was wrong."

"It must have been so . . . lonely," he said.

Surprise lit her eyes at his understanding. It shamed him. "Then you came along," she said. "This nearly inept, reckless agent."

He snickered.

She smiled. "And you saw me. For the first time, you saw *me*.

I could talk to you as I hadn't spoken to anyone. You reminded me that I was—I am—alive. I hadn't felt that way in a very long time."

He scanned her face. Saw past that remarkable beauty and into the burning soul inside.

"Don't look at me like that," she whispered.

"Like what?" he murmured.

But she shook her head and got to her feet, walking to the door.

Ruhn caught up to her before she could reach for the knob. "Lidia."

She paused, but didn't look at him.

He laid a hand on her cheek. Gently turned her face back to his. Her skin was so soft, so warm. "Lidia," he said roughly. "Finding out who you are . . . it fucked with my head. To know you're the Hind, but also Lidia—also Day. *My* Day. But now . . ." He swallowed.

"Now?" Her gaze dipped to his mouth.

His cock tightened at that gaze. He said, voice near guttural, "Now I don't fucking care who you are, so long as you're mine." Her eyes shot to his, again full of surprise. "Because I'm yours, Day. I'm fucking yours."

Her face crumpled. And he couldn't stand the sight of her crying, the relief and joy. So he leaned forward, bringing his mouth to hers.

The kiss didn't start sweetly. It was openmouthed—teeth clacking, tongues clashing. Her hands wrapped around his neck, and he hauled her to him, pulling her flush against his chest.

Yes, yes, yes.

His hand coasted over her ass and he squeezed, drawing a moan from deep in her throat. She pulled her mouth from his, though. "Ruhn."

He stilled. "What?" If she wanted to stop, he'd stop. Whatever she wanted, he'd give her.

She ran her fingers over his pecs. He shuddered as she asked, "Are you sure?"

"Yes," he breathed, nipping at her bottom lip. He guided her toward the bed, then onto it. She traced her finger over where his lip ring had been ripped out. Then his brow ring.

"I couldn't stand it," she whispered, putting her mouth to his brow. "I couldn't . . ." She began shaking. He tightened his arms around her.

"I'm here," he said. "We made it."

She trembled harder, as if all that she had experienced and done were now breaking free in aftershocks.

"I'm here," he said again, and leaned down to kiss the side of her neck. "I'm here." He kissed below her ear. Her hands came up, caressing a line down his back. She stopped shaking. "I'm here," he said, kissing the base of her throat. Tugging down the zipper on the front of her tactical bodysuit.

She wasn't wearing a bra. Her breasts, lush, high palmfuls tipped in rosy pink, spilled out into his hands. He swore, and couldn't stop himself from dipping his head to suck one into his mouth.

She inhaled sharply, and the sound was kindling to his cock. He grazed his teeth over her nipple, tugging lightly.

Her hands wandered around his waist, aiming toward his front, and—yeah, not happening. He wanted to explore first. Not removing his mouth from that delicious breast, he grabbed her wrists in one hand and pinned them above her head, settling more firmly between her legs.

She flinched.

It was barely more than a flicker, but he felt it. The slight tightening in her body. He halted, raised his head. Looked down at her. At the hands he'd pinned—

That *fucker.*

Ruhn let go immediately.

He'd kill him. He'd rip Pollux limb from limb, feather by feather for putting that flinch there, for hurting her—

Her eyes softened. She laid her palms on either side of his face and whispered, "Just an old memory."

One that shouldn't be there. One that Pollux had put there.

"Ruhn."

He took her wrists in his hands and gently pressed a kiss to each one. Then laid them on her chest, hands over her heart, kissing her as he did so.

"Ruhn," she said again, but he sprawled out beside her. Looped an arm over her middle.

"Stay here with me tonight," he said quietly. A tendril of his shadows curled around the flames of the sconces, dimming them. "No sex. Just . . . stay with me."

He could feel her eyes on him in the dark. But then she moved—zippers hissing as she shrugged out of her clothes. He tugged off his pants, nestling under the blankets.

Then her warm, soft, lush body curled into his.

And yeah, he wanted to be inside of her so badly he had to grind his teeth, but her scent soothed him. Steadied him. He slid a hand over her bare waist, tucking her in close, her breasts flush against his chest. His hand drifted lower, to her ass, and all it would have taken was a shift in angle and he would have been between her legs.

But this wasn't about sex. And as their breathing evened out, as they stared at each other in the near-dark, he'd never felt more seen.

Eventually, her eyes closed. Her breathing deepened.

But Ruhn lay awake, holding her tight, and did not let go until dawn.

"Is that a *laser*?" Tharion shouted as rock crumbled from where the light had sliced into it, the cave-in now cutting off access to the two Fae Kings, Flynn and Dec, and the Murder Twins. And a bunch of ghouls. But Bryce ordered, "The river!"

"What?" Hunt barked. Bryce was already running for the dark, rushing water.

"Jump in," Bryce called, starlight bobbing with each step.

"Teleport us across!" Hunt countered. Flynn and Declan had been stranded on the other side of that cave-in, and they needed to figure out how to get them away from the kings and the twins—

"Jump in *now*," Bryce ordered, and didn't wait before she ran for the ledge. Hunt grabbed for her, to stop her from this pure insanity—

She leapt. Right into the river. He could have sworn the starlight glowed brighter as she did, as if agreeing with her decision.

Then the light in her chest went out.

And in the sudden dark, with only Hunt's lightning flickering around them, the ghouls began to hiss, drawing nearer, as if coming through the rock itself.

"River," Tharion said, grabbing Sathia and racing for it. He dove, and she shrieked as he dragged her with him. The roar of the river swallowed the sound—and them—in half a second.

There was no choice left, really. Hunt met Baxian's stare and saw his own annoyance mirrored there. They could have taken the kings. Bryce surely knew that. And yet . . .

If Bryce had chosen to cause a cave-in, to block the kings but not kill them, to opt for going downriver instead of teleporting across . . . she hadn't told him why, likely due to their fight. She hadn't told him, which meant his mate probably no longer trusted him, and he had no idea how to start fixing that—

"Athalar," Baxian growled. "Snap out of it!"

Hunt blinked. He'd been frozen in place, reeling. Baxian's eyes were wide. Hunt shook off his shame. It pissed him off to no end, but Bryce did nothing without reason.

Hunt didn't wait to see if Baxian followed before he tucked his wings in tight and leapt.

56

Hunt shuddered with cold, teeth chattering, as he hauled himself onto a dark bank illuminated dimly by Bryce's star.

After a rushing, disorienting downhill journey, the river had calmed and emptied into the pool around them, a small bank providing the lone path of escape. Tharion was already near Bryce, a shivering Sathia between them, and Baxian was just crawling onto the shore a few feet from Hunt, dark wings dragging on the rock beside him.

Hunt exploded at his mate, "What the *fuck*?"

"Later, Athalar," Bryce murmured, turning from the pool and facing a natural archway of stone, with a tunnel beyond. Her star blazed bright—brighter than it had upriver.

"No, *now*," he warned, scrambling to his feet, water sloshing from his boots, his waterlogged wings impossibly heavy. "You say we're all in this together, making decisions *together*, and then you go and pull that shit?"

She whirled, teeth bared. "Well, *someone* has to lead."

His temper flared. "What the fuck does that mean?"

"It means that I'm not letting my fear and guilt swallow me whole." The others stayed silent, several feet away. "It means that I'm putting all that shit aside and focusing on what needs to be done!"

"And I'm not?" He splayed his arms, motioning to the caves around them. Lightning flickered over his hands. "I'm here, aren't I?"

"Do you even *want* to be?" Her voice echoed off the rocks. "Because it seems like your fear of the consequences outweighs your desire to defeat the Asteri."

"It *does*," he snarled, unable to stop the words from coming out. "It will be hard to enjoy freedom if we're *dead*."

"I'd rather die trying to bring them down than spend the rest of my life knowing the truth and doing nothing."

He could barely hear above the roaring in his head. "Everyone we love will die, too. You're willing to risk that? Your mom and dad? Cooper? Syrinx? Fury and June? You're willing to let them be tortured and killed?"

She stiffened, shaking with anger.

Hunt took a deep breath, collecting himself, and shook the water out of his wings. "Look, I'm sorry." He took another deep breath. "I know this isn't the time to pick a fight. This whole thing might be a colossal fucking mistake, might get everyone we know killed, but . . . I'll go along with it. I have your back. I promise."

She blinked. Then blinked again. "That's not good enough for me," she said quietly. "That isn't good enough for me—that you'll just go along with it."

"Well, get used to the feeling," he said.

"Get over yourself, *Umbra Mortis*." With that, she stormed into the misty gloom, star illuminating the way.

"Yeesh," Tharion said lightly to Sathia and Baxian, but Hunt didn't smile as they continued after Bryce, trailing water everywhere.

"How the fuck did you know to get out here, anyway?" Baxian asked Bryce, likely trying to lighten the tension now filling the caves as surely as the mist smothering them.

"Because I've been here before," Bryce said, her voice still a little rough around the edges.

Even Hunt's anger eased enough for him to wonder if she'd hit her head in the river. Especially as they approached a solid wall of rock.

Bryce pushed a hand against the wall. A wedge of an archway opened beneath her palm. Her starlight flared, lighting up the wall and the carving that surrounded the triangular doorway.

An eight-pointed star. Twin to the scar on her chest.

"These caves," Bryce said, pointedly not looking at him, "are nearly identical to the ones I walked through in the original world of the Fae." She took a step into the star's doorway. "The river there flowed throughout them—provided shortcuts. The Wyrm used them to sneak up on us. But my star glowed brighter whenever it wanted me to go a certain way, like it does here. It guided me into one of the rivers in the Fae world. I listened to it, jumped in, and it led me down to a passage that took me exactly where I needed to be to learn Silene's truth. Just now, my star was glowing brighter when I faced downriver. I figured this river might lead down to another passage. Maybe one that's got another bit of truth. Anything to help against the Asteri."

"That was an insane leap of logic," Tharion said. "And what about Flynn and Dec? The Autumn King and Morven and the Murder Twins still have them, those fucking *ghouls* still have them—"

"That confrontation will come." Bryce walked calmly into the waiting darkness and swirling mist, adjusting Truth-Teller at her side. "But not yet."

They had no choice but to follow her. "What does it all mean?" Baxian asked Hunt, almost plaintively.

Hunt cast aside his lingering anger and kept his focus pinned on his mate. "I think we're about to find out."

Flynn and Dec still weren't at breakfast the next morning. And Ruhn's quick jog through the castle and its grounds revealed no sign of them. Or of the Murder Twins. Just some Fae nobles and servants, unsure what to make of him, whether to sneer or bow. He ignored them, and was hurrying back to his room when Lidia emerged from it.

She took one look at his face and asked, "What's wrong?"

He didn't wonder how she'd guessed it—she'd had to be

excellent at reading people her whole adult life. Her survival had depended on it.

Ruhn checked that his various blades were in place. "Flynn and Dec . . . I don't think they're here. And neither are my creep cousins. Or Morven."

Her eyes sharpened with caution. "It might be unconnected."

"It's not. My friends don't bail on me." And he'd been so fucking distracted by her, by wanting her, that he hadn't let himself think about it.

She put a hand on his arm. "Where do you think they went?"

Ruhn sucked in a breath. "Morven and the twins have to be involved. They must have taken Flynn and Dec to the Cave of Princes."

"To make a move against Bryce?"

Ruhn's stomach churned. "Maybe. But I think Morven took them as bait—for me. He expects me to follow."

"If it's a trap, then we shouldn't rush in—"

"My friends rushed to save me from the Asteri dungeons," he said, holding her beautiful gaze. "You found them, and they ran to help. I can't leave them in Morven's hands."

"I wasn't suggesting we leave them," she said, striding to her own room. She left the door open so he could see her as she grabbed two guns off her night table and holstered them at her thighs. "I'm saying let's think through a strategy before we go rescue them."

Something burned in Ruhn's chest, and he didn't dare name it.

But he felt it all the same as they armed themselves and went to save his friends.

Hunt didn't let his guard down, not for one second. Even with every word of his fight with Quinlan hanging in the air like the residue of fireworks. Lightning flickered in one fist; his sword was clenched in another. He didn't put either aside as they entered a chamber at the other end of the tunnel.

He scanned its intricately carved walls of black stone, the exquisite landscapes depicted there, as they stepped in—

Stone grated against itself, and before Hunt could whirl, faster even than his lightning, the triangular door shut behind them. Tharion, a step ahead, let out a low whistle.

Baxian just swapped a look with Hunt that told him the Helhound suspected the same thing he did: only Bryce could get that door to open. It wasn't a calming thought. Not as Hunt surveyed what lay ahead.

The lone object in the chamber was a sarcophagus carved from white marble, the hue striking against the deep black of the stone walls. A statue of an armored Fae male lay atop the sarcophagus, hands clasped around a missing object.

Bryce nodded to it. "That must be where the Starsword lies when not in use." Her voice was flat, as if drained from their argument.

Sathia staggered a step closer. "Prince Pelias's tomb," she breathed.

"Ruhn told me his creepster descendants line the walls of the main passages in here," Bryce said, pointing to the only other way out: another archway of stone across the chamber, barely visible through the mists. She adjusted the Starsword across her back, and a hand fidgeted with Truth-Teller at her side—like the blades were bothering her.

Hunt surveyed the domed space, examining the stories told on the walls: an archipelago nestled above a sea of starlight, an idyllic, serene land—all that the world believed Avallen to be. "I don't see anything about the Starsword or Truth-Teller, let alone how to unify them," Hunt admitted. "Or the mists. The islands are here, but nothing else." Maybe this was a dead end for information.

"There could be something out in the main passage," Tharion offered.

But Bryce approached the sarcophagus. Peered down at the perfectly carved, handsome face of the first Starborn Prince.

"Hello, you rapist fuck," she said, her voice cold with fury.

Hunt barely breathed. He wondered if Urd were watching, if the heaviness in the room wasn't the mists, but rather the goddess's presence, having guided them here.

"You thought you won," Bryce whispered to the sarcophagus. "But she got one over on you in the end. She got the last laugh."

"Bryce?" Hunt ventured.

She looked up from Pelias's carved rendering, and there was nothing of her human heart in those eyes. Only icy, Fae hatred for the long-dead male before her.

Offering a rope of neutral ground, Hunt said, "Can you, uh, fill us in?"

Yet it was Tharion who gestured to the empty death chamber. "Maybe Pelias built another chamber around here that's actually got something about the sword and dagger and that portal to nowhere—"

"No," Bryce said quietly. "We're exactly where we need to be." She pointed to the floor, the carving of rivers of stars winding throughout. "And this place wasn't built by Pelias. He had nothing to do with these tunnels, the carvings." She laid a hand on the floor. Her starlight flowed through the carvings in the stone, the walls, the ceiling—

What had looked like etched seas or rivers of stars now filled in with starlight, became . . . alive. Moving, cascading, coursing. A secret illustration, only for those with the gifts and vision to see it.

The rippling river of starlight flowed right to the sarcophagus in the center of the chamber. Swirled around it like an eddy.

Bryce threw herself against the coffin, legs straining as she pushed—

And the sarcophagus slid away. Revealing a small, secret staircase beneath.

Bryce panted for a moment, and then smiled grimly. "This place was built by Helena."

57

The sword and knife pulsed more strongly with each step downward into the secret stairwell. Like they wanted to be here—*needed* to be here. Just when Bryce thought she honestly might chuck them off her for a moment of relief, her feet touched the bottom.

Amid the mists, trickling water sounded from a narrow stream in the center of the chamber. Some offshoot of the river a level up, filtered through the black rock. And beside the stream, a black ewer and bowl rested upon an etching of an eight-pointed star.

"What the fuck is this?" Hunt murmured, sticking close to her. As if, despite their fight, he still wanted to protect her. But maybe it was that need to protect her that was leading to the guilt, the fear devouring him whole.

She'd meant every word she'd said to him—it wasn't good enough for him to go along with things. She needed Hunt, all of him, fighting at her side. She didn't know how to convey that. How to make him understand and embrace that.

Her teeth chattered with the cold, but even that seemed secondary as Bryce surveyed the stream and pitcher and bowl. The eight-pointed star. Two of its points had been hollowed out into slits—one small, one larger.

There was nothing else in the room.

"You don't know what this is?" she asked Hunt. She could play Situation Normal with him—at least for now.

"I'm getting really fucking sick of surprises," Tharion burst out, arriving at the bottom of the stairs with Sathia in tow.

Bryce held up a finger, and let her light condense there.

"And then there's *that*," Tharion said, but Bryce held Hunt's stare as she pointed it at the ground and sliced a small line. An inch, and that was it.

"Helena used the same gifts to carve this place as her sister, Silene, used in their home world. But there's one big difference. One reason why she chose this place for the caves."

She knelt, and rubbed her fingers through the debris she'd left on either side of the cut. Brought it up to Hunt's face. "Do you recognize it?"

Hunt studied the black, glittering dust on her fingers and paled. "That's black salt."

Bryce nodded slowly. Baxian blew out a breath that sounded suspiciously like *Oh fuck*.

"These caves are made entirely of black salt," Bryce said. She'd seen it as soon as the ghoul had gouged lines in the wall. Knew its smell, its rotting, oily feel. A taste of it had confirmed her suspicions.

Hunt frowned. "You think Helena was trying to summon her sister from their home world?"

"No," Bryce said, shaking her head. "She sent Silene back to be safe—she was an asshole, but she would never have done anything to jeopardize that."

"So what is this place, then?" Tharion asked.

It was Sathia who got it first. "It's to summon demons. To commune with Hel."

Stunned silence rocked the room.

"They were her only remaining allies," Bryce explained.

Helena might have done some unforgivable things, but Bryce could admit the female had been a fighter. Until the very end, if this chamber was any indication.

Hunt asked, wings twitching, "But why make an entire underground warren of caves? And why dedicate it to her rapist husband?"

Bryce shrugged. "As a reason to keep coming here. She built him a tomb that would last, where his sword might lie forever until a worthy successor came along."

"You can't possibly know that," Hunt said carefully. Like he was afraid of getting into another fight.

It did something to her heart, that caution, but Bryce said, "The caves are nearly identical to the ones in her home world—caves she grew up navigating. And Avallen, like her childhood home, is wreathed in mist. It's a thin place as well. Judging by all the mists in here, maybe Avallen, these caves, are an even *stronger* thin place than the one in the Fae world. The Prison—the court it had been before that . . . Vesperus said that she chose it originally because it was a thin place, good for traveling between worlds. Theia knew this, too. She must have told Helena."

Tharion cleared his throat. "So Helena made all these caves just to have a private line to Hel?"

"Pretty much," Bryce said. "Avallen had everything she needed. But for her to have built the caves this way suggests resources. Helena couldn't have done it in secret. She had to have had approval from Pelias. And what better way to hide this, to protect it through the ages, than to wrap it up in a temple to the patriarchy?" Bryce pointed to the sarcophagus room above them. To the bones she'd have liked to scatter into a septic tank. "She knew the Fae males would never tear this place down or disturb it—for fuck's sake, Morven refuses to update Avallen in *any way* because he wants it to stay the same as it was when Pelias was alive. Helena knew these males well. She knew if she hid this under here, it'd be preserved, and remain undisturbed."

"Okay, assuming for a moment that we believe all that," Tharion said, "how do you know this was some secret chamber she used to commune with Hel, of all places? What do the pitcher and bowl mean?"

"She'd get thirsty with all the salt down here?" Baxian quipped, and Hunt grunted.

But Sathia walked up to the stream. "That water filters straight through the black salt, and this chamber is thick with it." She met Bryce's stare, brows knotting. "Can you summon a demon if you drink water laced with black salt?"

"I've never heard of anything like that, even during my demon-hunting years," Hunt said.

"If Helena was summoning demons here, someone would have noticed," Baxian said. "The temperature would have dropped enough that anyone else in the caves would have felt it, even a level above."

"Maybe she wasn't summoning them *here*," Bryce said, walking to the pitcher and bowl, to the eight-pointed star they sat upon. The slits in two of the points had been deeply carved—too deep for her to see how far into the rock they went. But Bryce tapped the side of her head. "But in here."

"What?" Hunt asked.

Bryce knelt and dipped the ewer into the dark, icy water. The vessel and bowl, too, had been carved from black salt. "The Starborn could mind-speak. Still can." She nodded up toward the river a level above, with the Murder Twins lurking somewhere on its other side. "Maybe the salt helped her mind-speak with Hel. Maybe someone in Hel can tell us how to kill the Asteri. Apollion himself ate Sirius . . . Maybe he's had the answer all along."

Hunt blurted, "Don't you dare—"

Bryce lifted the jug to her lips, but lightning smashed the vessel apart before she could drink.

She whirled, temper searing through her.

Hunt was glowing with lightning, furious as he advanced on her. "Do *not* drink from that—"

"This is *not* the time to go Alphahole!"

"—without me," he finished.

Bryce could only gape at her mate as he grabbed the drinking bowl and held it out to her.

Ready to follow her into Hel.

* * *

Together, then. As their powers, their souls, were linked, so they'd drink the salt-laced water together.

"This . . . might be a very bad idea," Tharion said as Bryce and Hunt sat facing each other, knee to knee and hand to hand.

Hunt was inclined to agree. But he said, "Apollion appeared to both me and to Bryce in dream states. Maybe he was using the same communication method he'd used with Helena."

"So, what," Baxian said as Sathia gathered the water in the drinking bowl. "You're going to drink and hope you pass out and . . . talk to Hel? Ask them for answers about the sword and knife that they might have somehow forgotten to tell you until now?"

"Helena left this here," Bryce said, holding Hunt's stare. No doubt or fear—only steely focus gleamed in his mate's eyes. "Just as Silene left everything in the caves of her home world. For someone to find. Someone who could bear the Starsword, and whose starlight would lead them down here. Someone who might also have learned the truth . . . and known where to look." Bryce turned her gaze to the ceiling, the stairs upward. "I think Helena left this to help us."

"Helena and Silene weren't . . . good people," Baxian warned.

"No, but they hated the Asteri," Bryce said. "They wanted to get rid of them as much as we do." And it was hope that brimmed in her eyes then, so bright it nearly stole Hunt's breath away. For a moment, not even a full heartbeat, he nearly believed they might succeed. "If this buys us a shot, whatever it might be, we have to try. I want answers. I want the truth."

Bryce lifted the bowl to her lips and drank.

Bryce was falling backward, and yet not moving. Her body remained kneeling, yet her soul fell, icing over, into the dark, into nothing and nowhere. A presence around her, beside her, flickered with lightning. Hunt.

He was with her. Soul-falling alongside her.

It was a leap. All of it was a leap, but she had to believe that Urd had led her here. That Helena had been as smart as her sister, and would have fought the male who abused her until the very end. That Helena had played the game not only for her lifetime, but for future generations.

Hoping that maybe one day, millennia from her death, another female might come along with starlight—Theia's starlight—in her veins. Passed down not from Pelias, but from Helena herself. Theia's starlight.

Passed down to her. Bryce Adelaide Quinlan.

And maybe she wasn't who Helena or Silene would have chosen, certainly not with their anti-human bullshit, but that wasn't her problem.

The falling sensation stopped. There was only blackness, frigid and dry. Her starlight flickered, a pale, feeble light in the impenetrable dark. A hand found hers, and she didn't need to look to know Hunt stood beside her in . . . whatever this place was. This dreamworld.

Two blue lights glowed in the distance, closing in on them. Hunt's fingers tightened on hers in warning. His lightning flickered. But the lights drew nearer. And nearer. And when they crossed into the light of her star . . .

Aidas was smiling faintly—joy and hope brightening his remarkable eyes. "It seems you got a little lost on your way to find me, Bryce Quinlan. But welcome to Hel."

58

It took two days of working without rest to help the people of the Meadows. But Ithan didn't mind, barely thought about the need to go to Avallen to find Sofie's body or the exhaustion as he dug through the rubble, or carried out the dead or dying, or held down the wounded long enough for Hypaxia or another medwitch to save them. And still there were more. So many more humans, hurt or dead.

There was no sign of the Governor, but the 33rd showed up, at least. The Aux—Fae and a scant number of wolves—arrived soon after. Ithan kept clear of the latter, both to avoid conflict and to avoid being spotted by any Asteri sympathizers who might have come to gloat over the ruins.

But he kept his head down. Kept working. Doing what little he could to help or clear or at least respectfully move the fallen.

There were no Sailings, not for the humans. There'd never been Sailings for them. So their bodies were laid out in rows upon rows inside the lobby of the nearest intact office building.

Barely a dozen wolves had shown up. Only the equivalent of two packs had come to help. It was a disgrace.

Something in this world had to change. And as Ithan piled up the dead, as he laid child after child in that building lobby, he realized that change had to start with him.

Make your brother proud.

He had to get to Avallen. Had to get Sigrid back. Only with her, with an alternate Fendyr heir to lead the wolves . . . Only then could changes begin.

A new future. For all of them.

For the first five minutes, Tharion didn't stop monitoring Bryce's and Hunt's breathing.

Baxian and Tharion had caught them as they'd suddenly toppled backward, unconscious, and laid them gently on the black salt ground. They didn't move. Only the rise and fall of their chests showed any signs of life. Whatever was happening, it indeed took place in their minds.

Tharion, Sathia, and Baxian sat a few cautious feet away from their friends. "How long do we give them?" Sathia asked. "Until we try to wake them, I mean."

Tharion swapped a look with Baxian. "Fifteen minutes?"

"Give them thirty," Baxian said. Then added, "We'll keep monitoring them, though."

Silence fell, interrupted only by their breathing and the sound of the stream trickling through the cavern. Beside Tharion, Sathia was turning the black salt drinking bowl over in her slender hands, again and again. Lost in thought.

"You ever done anything like this?" Baxian asked, noting her unease.

"No," she said. "I'm not the adventurous sort."

"Have you gone through your Ordeal?" Baxian asked.

She nodded shallowly. Not a good experience, then.

Part of Tharion wanted to ask about it, but he said, "What happened with you and your brother to put such a divide between you?"

Her eyes slashed to his. "What happened between you and the River Queen to put such a high bounty on your head?"

He gave her an indolent smile. "You don't know?"

"I've pieced bits of it together. You upset her prissy daughter, and had to run. But what did you do to upset her in the first place?"

Tharion drummed his fingers on the cold stone floor. "I wanted to call off our engagement. She didn't."

Sathia straightened. "You were *engaged*? To the River Queen's daughter?"

"For ten years."

She set the bowl on the ground. "And she didn't realize that after ten years, you didn't want to marry her?"

Tharion glanced to where Bryce and Hunt lay, deathly still. "I don't really feel like talking about this."

Yet Sathia pushed, "So you called it off, but she . . . tried to keep it?"

"And keep me. Beneath. Forever."

The dismay on her face set him laughing. Laughter was the sole alternative to crying. "Yeah."

"But you could have swum away."

"You can't just *swim away* from the River Queen. She denies her daughter nothing. She'd have locked me in my humanoid form, to ensure I couldn't swim out."

Again, that dismay on her face. "She'd do that to one of her own kind? Destroy your fins to confine you?"

"She isn't mer," he said. "She's an elemental. And yes, she does it to punish mer all the time."

"That's barbaric."

"So is treating Fae females like broodmares and forcing them to marry."

Sathia only angled her head. "You ran away from marriage to the River Queen's daughter . . . only to wind up married to a stranger."

He knew Baxian was listening closely, though the Helhound kept his focus on Bryce and Athalar. "It seemed like a better option."

"It doesn't make sense."

He sighed. And maybe because they were on some cursed island in the middle of the Haldren, maybe because they were hundreds of feet underground with only Cthona to witness it, he said, "My little sister. Lesia. She, ah, died last year."

Sathia seemed taken aback at the turn the conversation had taken. "I'm sorry, Tharion," she said gently. She sounded sincere.

Baxian murmured, "I didn't know that. My condolences, Ketos."

Tharion couldn't stop the memory of Lesia from flashing bright in his mind. Red-haired and beautiful and alive. His chest ached, threatening to cave in on itself.

But it was better than the other memory of her—of the photographs her murderer had snapped of her body. What he'd done to her when Tharion hadn't been there to protect her.

Tharion went on, "I know you and Flynn have a . . . tense relationship. But you're still his little sister. You were in trouble. And I knew that if Lesia had been in the same spot, I'd have wanted a decent male to help her out."

Sathia's eyes softened. "Well, thank you. If we make it through all this"—she waved a hand to the caves, the world beyond—"I'll see if there's a way to liberate you from this . . . situation."

"Trust me, it's in my best interest to stay married to you until the River Queen's daughter moves on to some other poor bastard. If I'm single . . ."

"She'll come after you."

Tharion nodded. "It's cowardly and pathetic, I know. And I mean, her mother will probably come after me and kill me anyway. But at least I won't have to spend my life as a royal concubine."

"All right." Sathia squared her shoulders. "Marriage it is, then." She gave him a small smile. "For now." Then she glanced to Bryce and Hunt. "You think they're really in Hel?"

"Part of me hopes yes, the other part hopes no," Tharion answered.

"They're in Hel," Baxian said quietly.

Sathia twisted toward him. "How do you know?"

Baxian pointed to their slumbering friends. "Look."

Bryce and Hunt lay peacefully on the black salt ground, hands entwined, their bodies covered in a thin layer of frost.

The black boat that Aidas led Bryce and Hunt into was a cross between the one that had brought them into Avallen and the ones that carried bodies to the Bone Quarter. But in lieu of a stag's head, it was a stag's skull at the prow, greenish flame dancing in its eyes as it sailed through the cave. The eerie green light illuminated black rock carved into pillars and buildings, walkways and temples.

Ancient. And empty.

Bryce had never seen a place so void of life. So . . . still. Even the Bone Quarter had a sense of being lived in, albeit by the dead. But here, nothing stirred.

The river was wide, yet placid. The lap of water against the hull seemed to echo too loudly over the stones, over the ceiling so far above that it faded into the gloom.

"It's like a city of the dead," Hunt murmured, draping a wing around Bryce.

Aidas turned from where he stood at the prow, holding in his hands a long pole that he'd used to guide them. "That's because it is." He gestured with a pale hand to the buildings and temples and avenues. "This is where our beloved dead come to rest, with all the comforts of life around them."

"But we're not . . . here-here," Bryce said. "Right? We're just dreaming?"

"In a sense," Aidas said. "Your physical body remains in your world." He glanced over a shoulder. "In Helena's cave."

"You knew about it this whole time," Hunt accused.

Aidas's eyes gleamed. "Would you have believed me?"

This close to Hunt, Bryce felt every muscle in his body tense. Her mate said, "The truth might have been a good start toward that."

Before Aidas could answer, the boat approached a small quay leading to what appeared to be a temple. A figure emerged from between the pillars of the temple and descended its front steps. Golden-haired, golden-skinned.

Hunt's lightning sparked, illuminating the whole city and river.

Apollion lifted a hand. Pure, sizzling lightning danced around it, arcing out to meet Hunt's.

"Welcome, son," said the Prince of the Pit.

59

Every word eddied from Hunt's head. Apollion, Prince of the Pit, had called him—

Bryce leapt out of the boat and onto the shore, chest blazing with starlight. "What the Hel did you just say?"

No matter what tension or argument might lie between them, she'd go down swinging for him. Hunt jumped after her, wings steadying him as his boots hit the loose black stones. Apollion had called him *son*—

The Prince of the Pit swept down the stairs, his every step seeming to echo through the vast cavern. Another male in dark armor followed him, his tightly curled hair almost hidden by his war helmet.

"Thanatos," Bryce said, drawing up short, pebbles skittering under her neon-pink sneakers.

Hunt had enough sense left in him to get to his mate's side, but Aidas was already there, lifting a hand. "We are here to talk. There will be no violence."

From within the ornate helm, Thanatos's eyes blazed with murderous rage.

"Do as he says," Apollion ordered the Prince of the Ravine, halting at the base of the temple steps.

Hunt's lightning twined up his forearms, ready to strike as

he growled at the Prince of the Pit, "What the fuck did you mean by—"

He didn't finish his words as Aidas reached to touch Bryce's shoulder. Acting on instinct, Hunt lunged, intending to shove the Prince of the Chasm away from his mate.

He went right through the demon prince.

Hunt stumbled and lifted his hands. His fingers shimmered faintly with a pale, bluish light. Bryce had the same aura around her.

They were ghosts here.

Apollion let out a low chuckle as Hunt backed toward Bryce's side once more. "You will find that you cannot harm us, nor we you, in such a state." His deep voice pealed like thunder off the walls.

Son. It wasn't possible—

"Helena planned it that way," Aidas said. His gaze remained fixed on Bryce while he explained, "During my time with Theia, Helena was a quiet girl, but she always listened."

"You spoke too much," Thanatos snapped.

Aidas ignored him. "Helena learned black salt would allow her to commune with us while protecting her mind and her soul."

Just like the barrier of it that Bryce had sprinkled in her apartment, that day she'd summoned Aidas. When Hunt had still thought her a frivolous party girl, playing with fire.

"Fine," Hunt cut in. "Great, we're protected." He eyed the Prince of the Pit. His very bones shook, but he forced himself past his fear, his dread. "What the fuck did you mean by calling me son?"

Thanatos scoffed. "You are no son of his." He yanked off his war helmet, cradling it under an arm. "If anything, you are mine."

Hunt's knees buckled. "*What?*"

"Let us sit and be civilized about this," Aidas said to Bryce, but she was peering into the shadows of the temple looming at the top of the steps.

"I think we're good here," she hedged. Hunt cleared his reeling thoughts enough to follow her line of vision.

He saw them, then. The dogs. Their milky eyes glowed from the gloom between the pillars.

"They will not harm you," Aidas said, nodding toward the hounds that looked an awful lot like the Shepherd that Bryce and Hunt had fought in the Bone Quarter. "They are Thanatos's companions."

Hunt reached for his lightning, little that it could do in this insubstantial form. It zapped against his fingers, normally a familiar, comforting presence, but . . .

No one had ever known who had sired him. Where this lightning had come from.

"My concern exactly," Bryce said, not taking her attention off the hounds. She nodded to Thanatos. "He eats *souls*—"

"The Temple of Chaos is a sacred place," Apollion said sharply. "We shall never defile it with violence." The words rumbled like thunder again.

Hunt sized up Apollion, then Thanatos. What the fucking *fuck*—

But Thanatos sniffed toward Bryce, almost as canine as the hounds in the shadows, and said, "Your starlight smells . . . fresher."

The hunger lacing the male's words stilled Hunt's chaotic mind—honing him into a weapon primed for violence. He didn't give a shit if he never got answers about his parentage. If that asshole made one move against Bryce, ghostly forms or no—

Bryce said nonchalantly, "New deodorant."

"No," Thanatos said, missing the joke entirely, "I can smell it on your spirit. I am the Prince of Souls—such things are known to me. Your power has been touched by something new."

Bryce rolled her eyes, but for a heartbeat, Hunt wondered if Thanatos was right: Bryce had explained how the prism in the Autumn King's office had revealed her light to now be laced with darkness, as if it had become the fading light of day, of twilight—

"We don't have much time," Aidas said irritably. "The dreaming draft will only last so long. Please—come into the temple." He inclined his head in a half bow. "On my honor, no harm shall come to you."

Hunt opened his mouth to say the Prince of the Chasm's honor meant shit, but Bryce's whiskey eyes assessed Aidas in a long, unhurried sweep. And then she said, "All right."

Pushing aside every raging thought and question for the moment, Hunt kept one eye on the exit behind them as they traded the pebbled shore for the smooth temple steps. As they walked up those steps and entered a space that was a near-mirror to temples back home—indeed, its layout was identical to the last temple Hunt had stood in: Urd's Temple.

He shut down the memory of Pippa Spetsos's ambush, the desperate scramble for their lives. How they'd hidden behind the altar, barely escaping. In lieu of the black stone altar in the center of the temple, a bottomless pit was the main focal point. Five chairs of carved black wood encircled it.

Hunt and Bryce claimed the chairs closest to the stairs behind them—closest to the river and the boat still idling at the shore. Aidas took the one on Bryce's other side, sitting with a smooth, feline grace. The braziers bounced their bluish light off his blond hair.

Apollion's eyes glimmered like coals as he said to Hunt, "I am disappointed to see that you have not yet freed yourself from the black crown, Orion Athalar."

"Someone explain what the fuck that is," Hunt snapped. Of all the things he'd ever imagined for his life, sitting in a circle with three Princes of Hel hadn't been anywhere on the list.

"The black crowns were collars in Hel," Thanatos answered darkly. His powerful body seemed primed to leap across that pit to attack. Hunt monitored his every breath. "Spells, crafted by the Asteri to enslave us. They were a binding, one the Asteri adapted in their next war—upon Midgard."

Hunt turned to Aidas. "You seemed surprised to see one on me that first time we met. Why?"

But before Aidas could begin, Apollion answered, "Because the Princes of Hel cannot be contained by the black crowns. The Asteri learned that—it was their downfall. As you were made by Hel's princes, it should not be able to hold you."

Made by them? By these fuckers?

Hunt had no idea what to say, what to do as everything in his life swirled and diluted, his heartbeat ratcheting up to a thunderous beat. "I—I don't . . ."

"Start talking," Bryce snapped at Apollion, scooting her chair an inch or two closer to Hunt's. Not from fear, Hunt knew—but from solidarity. It settled something in him, soothed a jagged edge. "Hunt's mother was an angel."

His mother's loving, tired face flashed before Hunt's eyes, twisting his heart.

"She was," Apollion said, and the way he smiled . . .

White rage blinded every one of Hunt's senses. "Did you *dare*—"

"She was not ill used," Aidas said, holding up an elegant hand. "We might command nightmares, but we are not monsters."

"Explain," Bryce ordered the demon princes, starlight rippling from her. Thanatos sniffed the air once more, savoring it, and earned a glare from Aidas. "From the beginning."

Despite the heated words they'd exchanged earlier, Hunt had never loved her more—had never been so grateful that Urd had chosen such a loyal, fierce badass for his mate. He could trust her to get the answers they needed.

"How much do you know?" Aidas asked her. "Not just about Athalar, but about the whole history of Midgard."

"Rigelus has a little conquest room," Bryce said, the softness fading from her face as she crossed her arms. "He's got a whole section about invading your planet. And I know Hel once had warring factions, but you sorted out your shit and marched as one to kick the Asteri out of Hel. A year later, you hunted them down across the stars and found them on Midgard. You fought them again, and it didn't go well that time. You got jettisoned from Midgard and have been trying to creep back through the Northern Rift ever since."

"Is that all?" Apollion drawled.

Bryce said warily to Aidas, "I know you loved Theia. That you fought for her."

The Prince of the Chasm studied his long, slender hands. "I did. I continue to do so, long after her death."

Hunt had a feeling that the darkness in the pit before them was breathing.

"Even though she was hardly any better than the Asteri?" Bryce challenged.

Aidas lifted his head. "There is no denying how Theia spent most of her existence. But there was goodness in her, Bryce Quinlan. And love. She came to regret her actions, both in her home world and on Midgard. She tried to make things right."

"Too little, too late," Bryce said.

"I know," Aidas admitted. "Believe me, I know. But there is much that I regret, too." He swallowed, the strong column of his throat working.

"What happened?" Bryce pressed. Hunt almost didn't want to know.

Aidas sighed, the sound weighted with the passing of countless millennia. "The Asteri ordered Pelias to use the Horn to close the Northern Rift, to defend themselves against attack. He did, sealing out all the other worlds in the process, but the Horn broke before he could close it entirely on Hel. The tiniest of wedges was left in the Rift for my kind to sneak through. Helena used black salt to contact me, hoping to launch another offensive against the Asteri, but we couldn't find a way. Unless the Rift was fully opened, we could not strike. And our numbers were so depleted that we would not have stood a chance."

Thanatos picked up the narrative, resting his helmet on a knee. "The vampyrs and Reapers had defected to the Asteri. They betrayed us, the cowards." From the shadows behind him, his hounds snarled, as if in agreement. "They'd been our captains and lieutenants, for the most part. Our armies were in shambles without them. We needed time to rebuild."

"I believe Helena realized," Aidas went on, "that the war would not be won in her lifetime. Nor by any of her sons. They had too much of their father in them. And they, too, greatly enjoyed the benefits of being in the Asteri's favor."

Bryce uncrossed her arms, leaning forward. "I'm sorry, but I still don't understand why Helena built the Cave of Princes. Just to talk to you guys like long-distance pen pals?"

Aidas's full mouth kicked up at a corner. "In a way, yes. Helena needed our counsel. But by that point, she'd also figured out what Theia had done in her last moments alive."

60

The Cave of Princes was as foul and disorienting as Ruhn remembered. But at least he had a kernel of starlight to keep the ghouls at bay in the misty dark. Even if it took most of his concentration to summon it and keep it glimmering.

He and Lidia had entered hours ago, and he'd immediately smelled Flynn's and Dec's scents hanging in the air. Along with Morven's and the Murder Twins'. But it was the sixth scent that had sent Ruhn running down the passages, Lidia easily keeping pace with him. A scent that haunted his nightmares, waking and asleep.

Somehow, the Autumn King was here. And his father wasn't lying in wait for Ruhn, but heading deeper into the caves, after Bryce. Ruhn pushed ahead, even when his legs demanded a break.

Morven's and his father's scents—with the others in tow—cut through nearly hidden tunnels and steeply descending passageways, as if the Stag King knew every secret, direct route. He probably did, as King of Avallen. Or maybe the ghouls showed him the way.

Eventually, Ruhn's body screamed for water, and he paused. Lidia didn't complain—didn't do anything but follow him, always alert to any threat. Yet as they once again rushed down the passage, Lidia said quietly, "I apologize for last night."

Despite every instinct roaring at him to hurry, Ruhn halted. "What do you mean?"

Her throat worked, her face almost luminous in his starlight. "When I . . . flinched."

He blinked. "Why the Hel would you apologize for that?" Pollux should be the one to apologize. Hel, Ruhn would *make* the fucker apologize to Lidia—on his knees—before putting a bullet in his head.

Color stained her cheeks, a rosy glow against the misty darkness behind them. "I like to think myself immune to . . . lingering memories."

Ruhn shook his head, about to object, when she went on. "Everything I did with Pollux, I did willingly. Even if I found his brand of entertainment hard to stomach at times."

"I get it," Ruhn said a shade hoarsely. "I really do. I'm not judging, Lidia. We don't have to do anything you don't want to do. Ever."

"I want to, though." Lidia glanced at his mouth.

"Want to what?" he asked, voice dropping an octave.

"Know what your body feels like. Your mouth. In reality. Not in some dreamworld."

His cock hardened, and he shifted on his feet. He didn't mask the arousal in his tone, his scent, when he said, "Anytime you want, Lidia."

Except, of course, right now. But after he sorted through whatever shitshow was about to go down in these caves—

The pulse in her throat seemed to flutter in answer. "I want you all the time."

Gods damn. Ruhn leaned in. Ran his mouth, his tongue, up her neck. Lidia let out a breathy little sound that had his balls drawing tight.

Ruhn said against her soft skin, "When we get out of these caves, you'll show me exactly where you want me, and how you want me."

She squirmed a little, and he knew that if he slid his hand between her legs, he'd find her wet. "Ruhn," she murmured.

He kissed her neck again, watching through heavily lidded eyes as her nipples pebbled, poking against the thin material of her shirt. He'd explore *those* a lot. Maybe do a little exploring right now—

A rasping, ancient *hiss* sounded from the rocks nearby.

And this was so not the place. Ruhn peeled away from Lidia, meeting her eyes. They were glazed with lust.

But she cleared her throat. "We have to keep going."

"Yeah," he said.

"Maybe you should, ah, take a moment," she said, smirking at the bulge in his pants.

He threw her a wry look. "You don't think the ghouls will appreciate it?"

Lidia snickered. Then grabbed his hand, tugging him back into a steady, paced run. "I want to be the only one who gets to appreciate it from now on."

He couldn't stop the purely male smugness that flooded him. "I can live with that."

"I know what Theia did," Bryce said, shaking her head. "She tried to send her daughters back to their home world, but only Silene made it."

Aidas arched a brow. "I'm assuming you have gleaned something of the truth, if you know of Silene by name. Did you learn what happened to her?"

"She left a . . . a magical video that explained everything." Bryce pulled Truth-Teller from the sheath at her side. Here, at least, the blades didn't pull at each other. "Silene had this with her when she returned to her home world. And now I've brought it back to Midgard."

Aidas started at the sight of the dagger. "Did Silene account for what happened during that last encounter with her mother?"

Bryce rolled her eyes. "Just tell me, Aidas."

Thanatos and Apollion shifted in their seats, annoyed at her irreverence, but Aidas's mouth curved toward a smile. "It took me—and Helena—years to understand what Theia actually did with her magic."

"She shielded her daughters," Bryce said, recalling how Theia's star had split in three, with an orb going to each of her children. "She used the Harp to carry her magic over to them as a protection spell of sorts."

Aidas nodded. "Theia used the Harp to divide her magic—*all* her magic—between the three of them. A third to Silene. A third to Helena. And the remainder stayed with Theia." His eyes dimmed with an old sorrow. "But she did not keep enough to protect herself. Why do you think Theia fell to Pelias that day? With only a third of her power, she did not stand a chance against him."

"And the sword and knife?" Bryce asked.

"Theia endeavored to keep the Asteri from being able to wield her power to use the sword and knife. Both weapons were keyed to her power, thanks to Theia's assistance in their Making," Aidas explained calmly. "It is why the Starsword calls to the descendants of Helena—of Theia. But only to those with enough of Theia's starlight to trigger its power. Your ancestors called these Fae Starborn. The Asteri have no power over the blades; they lack Theia's connection to the weapons. Since the Starsword and the knife were both Made by Theia at the same moment, their bond has always linked them. They have long sought to be reunited, as they were in their moment of their Making."

"Like calls to like," Bryce murmured. "That's why the Starsword and Truth-Teller keep wanting to be close to each other. Why they keep freaking out."

Aidas nodded. "I believe that when you opened the Gate, despite your desire to come to Hel, the Starsword's desire to reach the knife—and vice versa—was so strong that the portal was redirected to the world where they were Made. With the door closed between worlds, they had been unable to reunite. But once you opened it, the blades' pull toward each other was stronger than your untrained will."

With the Starsword in hand, she'd gone right to Truth-Teller, landing on that lawn mere feet away from Azriel and the dagger.

Bryce winced down at the blades. "I'm trying not to be creeped out that these things are, like . . . sentient." But she'd felt it, hadn't she? That pull, that call between them. She'd sworn they were *talking* last night, for fuck's sake. Like two friends who'd been apart, now rushing to catch up on every detail of their lives.

Over fifteen thousand years of separation.

Aidas went on, "But it wasn't just the blades that you reunited in the home world of the Fae, was it?"

Bryce's hands glowed faintly with that ghostly aura. "No," she admitted. "I think . . . I think I claimed some of Theia's magic. Silene left it waiting there." She'd thought it was another star, not a piece of a larger one.

Aidas did not seem surprised, but the other two princes wore such similar expressions of confusion that she almost smiled. Bryce glanced to Hunt, who nodded shallowly. *Go ahead,* he seemed to say.

So Bryce explained how she had claimed the power from the Prison, what she'd seen and learned from Silene's memory, her confrontation with Vesperus.

Bryce finished, "I thought Silene had left *her* power, yet she still had magic afterward. It must have been Theia's power that she left in the stones. It absorbed into mine—like it *was* mine. And when my light shone through the Autumn King's prism, it had transformed. Become . . . fuller. Now tinged with dark."

Aidas mused, "I'd say you had a third of Theia's power already, the part that originally was given to Helena—that came down to you through Helena's bloodline, and you took another third from where Silene stashed it. But if you can find the last third, the part that Theia originally kept for herself . . . I wonder how your light might appear then. What it might do."

"You knew Theia," Bryce said. "You tell me."

"I believe you've already begun to see some glimpses of it," Aidas said, "once you attained what Silene had hidden."

Bryce considered. "The laser power?"

Aidas laughed. "Theia called it starfire. But yes."

Bryce frowned. "Is it—is it the same as the Asteri's?" She hadn't realized how much the question had been weighing on her. Eating at her.

"No," Apollion cut in, scowling. "They are similar in their ability to destroy, but the Asteri's power is a blunt, wicked tool of destruction."

Aidas added, eyes shining with sympathy, "Starfire's ability to destroy is but one facet of a wonderous gift. The greatest difference, of course, lies in how the bearer chooses to use it."

Bryce offered him a small smile as that weight lifted.

Hunt cut in, "So just to clarify: There's still a third well of Theia's power out there—or was?"

"Helena knew that her own portion of her mother's magic would be passed down to future generations," Aidas said. "But when Theia died, all that remained of Theia's power lay in the Starsword. Theia put it into the blade after she parted from her daughters."

Bryce shook her head. "Let me get this straight. Theia divided her power into three parts: one to each of her daughters, and she transferred the last part to the Starsword. So the final piece of her magic is . . . in this blade? It's been waiting all this time?"

"No," Aidas said. "Helena removed it."

Bryce groaned. "Really? It can't be easy?"

Aidas snorted. "Helena did not deem it wise to leave what remained of Theia's star in the sword, even in secret."

"But how would the Asteri have been able to wield Theia's power to use the sword and knife," Bryce protested, "if she was dead?"

"They could have resurrected her," Hunt said quietly.

Aidas nodded gravely. "Theia didn't want them to be able to access the full strength of the star in her bloodline, even through her corpse. So she split it in three, putting only enough into the Starsword for her to face Pelias—long enough to buy her daughters time to run. She gave her magic to her daughters, thinking they would both escape to their home world and be beyond the reach of the Asteri forever."

"Why not send the Starsword with them, too?"

"Because then the knife and sword would have been together," Thanatos said.

"But what sort of threat do they pose?" Bryce said, practically shouting with impatience. "The Autumn King said they can open a portal to nowhere—is that it?"

"Yes," Aidas confirmed. "And together, they can unleash ultimate destruction. Theia separated them to keep the Asteri from ever having that ability. She did not know of a way they could be united by someone not of her bloodline, but the Asteri have been known to be . . . creative."

"How did Helena transfer the power out of the sword? She didn't have the Harp," Bryce said.

"No," Aidas agreed. "But Helena knew that Midgard possessed its own magic. A raw, weaker sort of magic than that in her home world, but one that could be potent in high concentrations. She learned that it flowed across the world in great highways, natural conduits for magic."

"Ley lines," Bryce breathed.

Aidas nodded. "These lines are capable of moving magic, but also carrying communications across great distances." Like those between the Gates of Crescent City, the way she'd spoken to Danika the day she'd made the Drop. "There are ley lines across the whole of the universe. And the planets—like Midgard, like Hel, like the home world of the Fae—atop those lines are joined by time and space and the Void itself. It thins the veils separating us. The Asteri have long chosen worlds that are on the ley lines for that exact purpose. It made it easier to move between them, to colonize those planets. There are certain places on each of these worlds where the most ley lines overlap, and thus the barrier between worlds is at its weakest."

Everything slotted together. *"Thin places,"* Bryce said with sudden certainty.

"Precisely," Apollion answered for Aidas with an approving nod. "The Northern Rift, the Southern Rift—both lie atop a tremendous knot of ley lines. And while those under Avallen are not as strong, the island is unique as a thin place thanks to the presence of black salt—which ties it to Hel."

"And the mists?" Hunt asked. "What's the deal with them?"

"The mists are a result of the ley lines' power," Aidas said. "They're an indication of a thin place. Hoping to find a ley line strong enough to help her transfer and hide Theia's power, Helena sent a fleet of Fae with earth magic to scour every misty place they could find on Midgard. When they told her of a place wreathed in mists so thick they could not pierce them, Helena went to investigate. The mists parted for her—as if they had been waiting. She found the small network of caves on Avallen . . . and the black salt beneath the surface."

Aidas smiled darkly. "She returned to the Eternal City and convinced Pelias that only such a place would be a worthy burial location for him. He was vain and arrogant enough to believe her. So they established the Fae kingdom on Avallen, and she carved his royal tomb into the rock. She spun lies about wanting future generations to worship him, to have to be born with the *right* blood to have the privilege of attaining his sword, which would be buried with him."

Aidas gestured toward the Starsword, sheathed down Bryce's back. "Helena knew Pelias would never part with his trophy, not until he died. And when he did, she at last drew upon the raw power of Avallen's ley lines to take the star her mother had imbued in the Starsword and hide it."

"So why the prophecy about the sword and knife?" Hunt asked. "If Theia was so scared of them being reunited, why all this crap about trying to get them back together?"

Aidas crossed his legs. "Helena planted that prophecy, seeded it in Fae lore. She knew that despite her mother's fears, the sword and knife *are* needed to destroy the Asteri. She knew that if a scion came along who could claim all three pieces of magic, they'd need the sword and knife to make that power *count*. Theia's power, when whole, is the only thing that can unite and activate the true power of those blades and stop the Asteri's tyranny."

Bryce's mouth dried out. A real path to ending the Asteri, at last.

"So where is it?" Bryce asked. "Where's the last part of Theia's power?"

"I don't know," Aidas said sadly. "Helena told no one, not even me."

Bryce let out a long, frustrated breath, but Hunt kept pushing the princes. "So to unite the sword and knife, Bryce needs to find the starlight Helena took from the Starsword—the last third of Theia's power—which is stashed somewhere on Avallen?"

"Yes," Aidas said simply.

"But how do I make them open that portal to nowhere—and what the Hel does that mean, anyway?" Bryce griped.

Thanatos said roughly, "We've been wondering that for eons."

Aidas dragged a hand through his golden hair. "*Ultimate destruction* was the best any of us could guess."

"Fantastic," Bryce grumbled.

Yet Hunt asked, "If Avallen is one of the stronger thin places, why did the Asteri even allow the Fae to live here?"

"The black salt, in such high quantity, keeps them away. They never realized that its presence drew us as much as it repelled them," Apollion said with satisfaction. "It has the same properties that made us immune to the thrall of their black crowns."

Bryce tensed at that, glancing at Hunt, but her mate asked, setting aside his own questions for now, "Did Helena know the Asteri were repelled from this place?"

Aidas nodded. "Once she figured it out, it confirmed her decision to hide Theia's power here."

Bryce angled her head. "But why did the mists open for Helena to get through in the first place?"

"The black salt only repels the Asteri; the mists repel everyone else. But certain people, with certain gifts, can access the power of thin places—on any world. World-walkers." Aidas gestured gracefully to Bryce. "You are one of them. So were Helena and Theia. Their natural abilities lent themselves to moving through the mists."

Bryce brushed invisible dirt off her shoulders,

"Add it to Bryce's list of Magical Starborn Princess crap," Hunt said, chuckling. But then he frowned deeply. "If the sword and knife could open a portal to nowhere all along, why didn't Theia use them herself in the First Wars?"

"Because she was scared," Aidas said, his voice suddenly tense. "For everyone."

"Right," Bryce said. "Ultimate destruction."

"Yes," Aidas said. Thanatos gave a disdainful snort, but Apollion looked at Aidas with something like compassion. "Theia," Aidas explained, "had theorized about what uniting the blades would do, but never put it into practice. She was afraid that if she opened a portal to nowhere, all of Midgard might get drawn in. She might succeed in trapping the Asteri in another world only to damn this world to follow them right in. So she opted for caution. And by the time she should have damned caution to the wind . . . it was too late for her. For us. It was safer, wiser, for her to separate the blades, and her power."

"But Helena felt differently," Bryce said.

"Helena believed the risk worthwhile," Aidas said. "She suffered greatly in the years following the First Wars—and saw the suffering of others, too. I came to agree with her. She wouldn't tell me where she moved Theia's power, but I know she left it accessible for the future scion who might emerge, bearing Helena's own third of Theia's light. The person who could somehow, against all odds, unite the pieces of Theia's power—and then the two blades."

"What blinds an Oracle?" Bryce whispered.

"Theia's star," Aidas said softly. "I told you: The Oracle did not see that day . . . but I did. I saw you, so young and bright and brave, and the starlight Helena had told me to wait for. That third of Theia's power, passed down through Helena's line."

Hunt demanded, "But what is Bryce supposed to *do*? Find that last piece of Theia's power, use it on the blades, and open this portal to nowhere while praying we don't all get locked in with the Asteri, too?"

"That's about the sum of it," Aidas said, his eyes fixed on Bryce.

"But there was one thing Theia and Helena did not anticipate: that you would bear the Horn, reborn, in your body. Another way to open doors between worlds."

"And what's she supposed to do with that?" Hunt snarled.

Aidas smiled slightly. "Fully open the Northern Rift, of course."

61

So," Bryce said slowly, as if letting the words sink in, "why not use the Horn to open the portal to nowhere?"

"Because no one knows what that is—*where* it is. The sword and knife are pinpointed to its location, somehow. They are the only way to get to that nowhere-place."

Hunt's head spun. Hel, his head had been spinning nonstop for the past ten minutes. But Bryce was having none of it. "What if I never got the knife back? What if I never came to Avallen? What if I never got the chance, or refused to come here, or whatever?"

Apollion and Thanatos shifted in their seats, either bored or on edge, but Aidas continued speaking. "I do not know how Helena hoped you would be able to retrieve the knife from her home world. As for Avallen . . . Helena wanted me to nudge you along. But you harbored such hatred for the Fae—you would never have trusted me if I had pushed you to travel to their stronghold."

"That's true," Bryce muttered.

"My brothers and I had doubts about Helena's plans. We continued to rest our hopes on reopening the Northern Rift so that we could continue the fight against the Asteri. If someone like you, a world-walker, did come along and Avallen was somehow not accessible for you to claim Theia's power, we still needed a way to . . . fuel you up, as it were." He faced Hunt at last.

Hunt could barely breathe. Here—after all this waiting . . . here were the answers.

"You are the son of my two brothers only in the vaguest sense," Aidas said.

Something in Hunt's chest eased—even as his stomach roiled.

"Thanatos refused to help at first," Apollion added, glaring at his brother.

"I did not approve of the plan," Thanatos snapped, gripping his helmet tight. "I still do not."

"My brother," Aidas said, nodding to Thanatos, "has long excelled at crafting things."

"Funny," Bryce said, "I didn't take you for a quilter."

Hunt gave her an incredulous look, but Aidas smiled before he said to Hunt, "During the First Wars, as you call them, Thanatos helped Apollion breed new types of demons to fight on our side. The kristallos, designed to hunt for the Horn—so we might find a way into Midgard unobstructed. The Shepherd. The deathstalkers." A nod to Hunt, like he knew of the scar down Hunt's back from one of them. "They were but a few of my brothers' creations."

Bryce shook her head. "But the kristallos venom can negate magic. If you knew how to do that, why did you not use it against the Asteri in the war?"

"We tried," Aidas said. "It did not have the same effect on their powers."

"I'm sorry," Hunt interrupted, "but are you implying that I was made by *you two assholes*? As some sort of pet?" He pointed to Thanatos, then to Apollion.

"Not a pet," Apollion said darkly. "A weapon." He nodded to Bryce. "For her, whenever she might come along."

"But you didn't know the timelines would overlap," Bryce said a bit breathlessly.

"No. There were previous experiments," Apollion said. "We hoped they would spread and multiply throughout Midgard, but the Asteri caught wind of our plan and removed them."

"The thunderbirds," Bryce said, gaping. "You guys made them, too?"

"We did," Aidas said matter-of-factly, "and sent them through the cracks in the Northern Rift. But they were hunted to near-extinction generations ago. Blessing an angel with their power, a perfect soldier . . . it was a gift of poisoned honey. The Asteri believed they had somehow, through their selective breeding of the malakim, finally achieved a flawless soldier to serve them. That it was their own brilliance that brought someone like Hunt Athalar into the world."

"But you rebelled," Apollion said to Hunt with no small hint of pride. "You were too valuable to kill, but they wanted you broken. Your servitude was that attempt."

Hunt could barely feel his body.

"Can we please rewind for a moment?" Bryce cut in. "You guys made the thunderbirds to complement my power—in case I never got the sword and knife, and if I ever needed a boost to open the Rift. But when they were hunted down, you . . . made Hunt, and then I was born . . ."

"Athalar was already enslaved by then," Aidas said, "but we kept a close watch."

Apollion nodded to Hunt. "Why do you think you're so adept at hunting demons? It's in your blood—part of *me* is in your blood."

Nausea clawed its way up Hunt's throat. The thought of owing anything at all to the Prince of the Pit . . .

"Just as he gave over some of his essence for the kristallos," Thanatos said, "so he gave something to me for you. His Helfire."

"Helfire?" Bryce demanded.

"The lightning," Thanatos said, waving an irritated hand. "Capable of killing almost anything. Even an Asteri."

"That's how you killed Sirius?" Bryce asked. "With your . . . Helfire?"

"Yes," Apollion said, then added to Hunt, "Your name was a nod to that, whispered in your mother's ear as you were born. Orion . . . master of Sirius."

"Clever," Hunt snapped, then demanded, "Wait—my lightning can kill the Asteri?" Hope bloomed, bright and beautiful in his chest.

"No," Apollion said. "It is . . . diluted from my own. It could harm them, but not kill them. I believe your mother's angelic blood tempered my power."

That hope withered. And something darker took its place as he asked, "How did my mother play into this?" He could handle some genetic meddling, but—

"There was a scientist at the Asteri Archives," Aidas said. "An angel who was delving into the origins of the thunderbirds, how strange their power was. He named the project after a near-forgotten god of storms."

"Project Thurr," Bryce said. "Was Danika investigating it, too? I found mentions of it, after she died."

"I don't know," Aidas said, "but the angel was researching thunderbirds at the behest of the Asteri, who worried they might return. It led him to us instead. When we told him the truth, he offered to help in whatever way he could. Thanatos was finishing up his work then. And with a male volunteer, only a female to breed with was needed."

Hunt couldn't breathe. Bryce laid a hand on his knee.

"Your father knew your mother briefly," Aidas said. "And he knew having a partner would help lift her from her poverty. He had every intention of staying. Of leaving behind his life and raising you in secret."

Hunt could barely ask, "What happened?"

"The mystics told Rigelus of your father's connection to us. They didn't discover everything—nothing about you or your mother. Only that he had been speaking to us. Rigelus had him brought in, tortured, and executed."

Hunt's heart stalled.

"He didn't break," Apollion said with something like kindness. "He never mentioned your mother, or her pregnancy. The Asteri never knew you were tied to him in any way."

"What . . . what was his name?"

"Hyrieus," Aidas answered. "He was a good male, Hunt Athalar. As you are."

Bryce squeezed his knee, her hand so warm—or was he unnaturally cold? "Okay, so Hunt was made to be a backup battery for me—"

"Can I do the same for Ruhn, then?" Hunt interrupted.

"No," Thanatos said. "The prince's light, his affinity for these thin places, isn't strong enough. Not like hers."

Hunt gripped Bryce's hand atop his knee. "Is it in my DNA that Bryce and I are mates? Was that engineered, too?"

"No," Aidas said quickly, "that was never intended. I think that was left to higher powers. Whatever they may be."

Hunt turned to Bryce and found nothing but love in her eyes. He couldn't stand it.

Horror cracked through him, as chilled as hoarfrost. He'd been created by these males to give and to suffer, and where the fuck did that leave him? Who the fuck did that make him?

"Okay," Bryce said, "Helfire and starfire: a potent combination. But Helena left all this shit to help end this conflict. It sounds like *you guys* just want me to open a gods-damned door for you to come in and save the day instead."

"Is it so bad," Thanatos purred, "to have us do your dirty work?"

Bryce glowered at him. "This is my world. I want to fight for it."

"Then fight alongside us," Thanatos challenged.

Tense silence stretched between them. Hunt had no idea how to even begin processing this insanity. But that cold in his veins . . . that felt good. Numbing.

"I could have used a bit more time to prepare," Bryce muttered.

Aidas only shook his head. "You weren't ready before. And what if you had told the wrong person? You know what the Asteri do to those who challenge their divinity. I could not risk it. Risk you. I had to wait for you to find the answers for yourself. But haven't I told you from the start to find me? That I will help you? That is what Apollion was attempting to do, too, in his misguided way: to ready you both for all this—to battle the Asteri."

"But how," Hunt asked, fighting past that numbing, blissful

chill in his chest, "did you kick the Asteri out of Hel the first time?"

"They had trouble feeding off our magic," Thanatos said, voice thick with disgust. "And found that our powers rivaled their own. They fled before we could kill them."

Bryce swallowed audibly as she surveyed Apollion. "And you really *ate* Sirius? Like, ingested her?"

But it was Aidas who answered, pride flaring on his face. Apollion slew her with his Helfire when she attacked him—he pulled her burning heart from her chest and ate it."

Hunt shuddered. But Bryce said, "How is that even possible?"

"I am darkness itself," Apollion said softly. "True darkness. The kind that exists in the bowels of a black hole."

Hunt's bones quaked. The male wasn't boasting.

"So why can't you just . . . eat the rest of them?" Bryce asked.

"It requires proximity," Aidas said. "And the Asteri are well aware of my brother's talents. They will avoid him at all costs."

The princes flickered, like they were on a screen that had glitched.

"We're running low on time," Thanatos said. "The black salt is wearing off."

Bryce focused on Apollion. "You guys have been telling me nonstop about having your armies ready to go." She gestured to the temple, the dead city beyond. "This place looks pretty empty."

Apollion's eyes grew ever darker. "We have allowed you to see only a fraction of Hel. Our lands and armies are elsewhere. They are ready."

"So if I open the Northern Rift with the Horn . . . ," Bryce said. Hunt cleared his throat in warning. "All seven of you and your armies will come through?"

"The three of us," Aidas amended. "Our four other brothers are currently engaged in other conflicts, helping other worlds."

"I didn't realize you guys were, like, intergalactic saviors," Bryce said.

Aidas's mouth quirked upward. She could have sworn Apollion's did, too.

"But yes," Aidas went on, "opening the Northern Rift is the only way for our armies to fully and quickly enter Midgard."

"After what happened this spring," Hunt said to his mate, "you trust them not to fucking *eat* everyone?"

"Those were our pets," Aidas insisted, "not our armies. And they have been severely punished for it. They will stay in line this time, and follow our orders on the battlefield."

Bryce glanced to Hunt, but he couldn't read the expression on her face. The princes flickered once more, the temple shimmering and paling. A tug pulled at Hunt's gut, yanking him back toward the body he'd left in Avallen.

"I'll think about it," Bryce answered.

"This is no game, girl," Thanatos snapped.

Bryce leveled a cool look at the Prince of the Ravine. "I'm sick and tired of people using *girl* as an insult."

Thanatos opened his mouth to respond, but abruptly vanished—his connection had been severed.

Apollion said to Hunt, "Do not squander the gifts that have been given to you—by me, by my brother." His gaze drifted to the halo on Hunt's brow. "No true son of Hel can be caged."

Then he was gone, too.

Son of Hel. Hunt's very soul iced over at the thought.

Only Aidas remained, seeming to cling to the connection as he spoke to Bryce, his blue eyes intense on her face. "If you find that final piece of Theia's power . . . if the cost of uniting the sword and knife is too much, Bryce Quinlan, then don't do it. Choose life." He glanced to Hunt. "Choose each other. I have lived with the alternative for millennia—the loss never gets easier to bear."

Bryce reached a ghostly hand toward Aidas, but the Prince of the Chasm was gone.

And all of Hel with him.

62

Bryce opened her eyes to fire. Blazing, white-hot fire.

Hunt's lightning instantly surrounded her, but it was too late.

The Autumn King and Morven stood in the chamber, somehow having caught up with them. Shadows wreathed the latter, but her father raged with flame.

And in the center of the room, surrounded by fire that even Tharion's water could not extinguish, stood her friends.

Bryce gave herself one breath to take in the sight: Tharion, Baxian, Sathia, Flynn, and Declan, all huddled close and ringed by fire. There was no sign of the ghouls in the shadows, but the Murder Twins stood just outside the perimeter, smirking like the assholes they were.

The Autumn King didn't bother to encircle her and Hunt with fire, knowing that even Hunt's lightning couldn't stop him if he chose to burn their prisoners to ashes. It was protection enough.

"Get up," Morven ordered Bryce, shadows like whips in the Stag King's hands. "We've been waiting long enough for you to snap out of that stupor."

Hunt hissed, and Bryce glanced over to find angry, blistered weals along her mate's forearm. They'd been *burning* Hunt to try to wake him up—

Bryce lifted her eyes to the shadow-crowned King of Avallen. To her sire, standing cold-faced beside him despite the fire at his fingertips. "What did you do with that black salt?" the Autumn King asked quietly. "Who did you see?"

Bryce drew the Starsword and Truth-Teller.

"Relinquish those weapons," Morven snapped. "You've sullied them long enough."

The fire closed in tighter around their friends. Baxian swore as a lick of it singed his black feathers.

"Sorry," Bryce said to the kings, not lowering her weapons, "but the blades don't work for rejected losers."

The Autumn King sneered, "Their taste is questionable. We shall remedy that at last."

"Right," Bryce said thoughtfully. "I forgot that you killed the last Starborn Prince because you couldn't deal with how jealous you were of him."

The Autumn King, as he had the last time she'd accused him of this, only chuckled. Morven glanced at him, as if in sudden doubt.

But the Autumn King said, "Jealous? Of that sniveling whelp? He was unworthy of that sword, but no more unworthy than *you*."

Bryce flashed him a winning smile. "I'll take that as a compliment."

The Autumn King went on, "I killed the boy because he wanted to put an end to the bloodline. To all that the Fae are." The male jerked his chin at Bryce. "Like you, no doubt."

She shrugged. "Not gonna deny it."

"Oh, I know your heart, Bryce *Quinlan*," the Autumn King seethed. "I know what you'd do, if left to your own devices."

"Binge an obscene amount of TV?"

His flame rose higher, herding her friends closer together. Dangerously little space remained between their bodies and the fire. "You are a threat to the Fae. Raised by your mother to abhor us, you are not fit to bear the royal name."

Bryce let out a harsh, bitter laugh. "You think my mom turned me against you? I turned against you the moment you sent your goons after us to kill her and Randall. And every moment since then, you pathetic loser. You want someone to blame for me thinking the Fae are worthless pieces of shit? Look in the mirror."

"Ignore her hysterical prattling," Morven warned the Autumn King.

The Autumn King bared his teeth at her. "You've let a little bit of inherited power and a title go to your head."

Morven's shadows rose behind him, ready to obliterate all in their path. "You'll wish for death when the Asteri get their hands on you."

Bryce tightened her grip on the blades. They hummed, pulling toward each other. Like they were begging her for that final reunification. She ignored them, and instead asked the Fae Kings, "Finally going to hand us over?"

"The worms you associate with, yes," the Autumn King said without an ounce of pity. "But you . . ."

"Right, breeding," Bryce said, and didn't miss Hunt's incredulous look at her tone. Her arms strained with the effort of keeping the blades apart. "I'm assuming Sathia, Flynn, and Dec will be kept for breeding, too, but any non-Fae are out of luck. Sorry, guys."

"This is not a joke," Morven spat.

"No, it's not," Bryce said, and met his stare. "And I'm done laughing at you fools."

Morven didn't flinch. "That little light show might have surprised us last time, but one spark from you, and your friends burn. Or shall we demonstrate an alternate method?" Morven gestured with a shadow-wreathed hand to the Murder Twins.

Bryce checked that her mental wall of starlight was intact, but like the bullies they were, the twins struck the person they assumed was weakest.

One heartbeat, Sathia was wide-eyed and monitoring the showdown. The next, she'd snatched a knife from Tharion's side.

And held it against her own throat.

"Stop it," Tharion snarled toward the twins, who were snickering.

Sathia's hand shook, and she pressed the dagger into her neck a little harder, drawing a trickle of blood.

"You make one move toward her, fish, and that knife slides home," Morven said.

"Leave her alone," Bryce said, and stepped forward—just one foot. The sword and dagger in her hands now seemed to tug forward, too—toward the center of the room. She tightened her grip on them.

Fire blazed brighter around her friends. One of Baxian's feathers caught fire, and Dec only just managed to pat it out before it could spread. "Drop the blades, and they'll release her mind," the Autumn King countered.

Bryce glanced to the sword and knife, fighting that tug from both weapons toward the center of the room.

Sathia stood on the other side of that burning ring, pure, helpless terror on her face, blood streaming down her neck. One thought from Seamus or Duncan, one motion, and that knife would slide into her throat.

Bryce tossed the blades to the ground.

Their dark metal clanked against the stone with brutal finality as they skittered to a stop nearly atop the eight-pointed star. Out of reach.

Neither king advanced, though, as if afraid to pick them up—or even walk over to them.

The Murder Twins pouted at their spoiled fun, but Sathia lowered the knife. Her fingers still clenched it at her side, though—clearly at the twins' direction. None of the others dared to pry it from her fingers.

But Bryce only stared at the Autumn King as she snarled, "You were giving me all that bullshit about how much you loved my mom and regretted having hit her—yet this is what you're doing to your own daughter? And to the daughter of one of your Fae buddies?"

"You stopped being my daughter the moment you locked me in my own home."

"Ouch," Bryce said. "That hit me right in the heart." She tapped on her chest for emphasis, and the star glowed in answer.

"She is stalling for time," the Autumn King said to Morven. "She did precisely this with Micah—"

"Oh yeah," Bryce said, advancing a step, "when I kicked his ass. Did he tell you?" she asked Morven. "It's supposed to be a big secret." She stage-whispered, taking another step closer, "I cut that fucker into pieces for what he did to Danika."

The Murder Twins seemed to start in surprise.

Bryce smiled at them, at Morven, at the Autumn King, and said, "But what I did to Micah is *nothing* compared to what I'll do to you."

She extended her hands. Starsword and Truth-Teller flew to them, as they had in the Fae world. Like calling to like.

But she hadn't been stalling for time for herself. She'd been stalling for Hunt.

As the sword and dagger flew to her, Hunt's lightning, gathering in a wave behind her, launched for the Murder Twins.

They had a choice, then: let go of their hold on Sathia to intercept the two whips of lightning that lashed for them, or allow Hunt's lightning to obliterate them.

The twins opted to live. A shield of shadows slammed against the reaching spears of lightning. It was all Bryce needed to see before she burst into motion.

The Autumn King shouted in warning, but Bryce was already running for them. For him.

She didn't hold back as she erupted with starlight.

The entire cave shook as lightning and shadow collided. Hunt gritted his teeth.

Tharion had managed to get the knife away from Sathia before she dropped it and impaled her own foot, and now the female crouched in the circle of fire, head gripped in her hands.

The blast of starlight that shot from Bryce as she ran for their enemies threatened to bring down the cavern. Her hair rose above her head, her fingertips shining white-hot with starfire.

Hunt gaped at her power, the beauty and condensed might of it.

But one of the Murder Twins laughed, a spiteful sound that promised his mate would suffer. Six ghouls burst from the shadows, little more than shadows themselves in their dark, tattered robes and reaching, scabbed hands.

What unholy things had the twins done, to become masters of these wretched beings?

Hunt glimpsed jaws stocked with three-inch, curving teeth opening wide, aiming for a distracted Bryce—

With a roar of fury, he sent half a dozen spears of lightning crackling for the ghouls and a seventh—a lucky one—for the twins' shadows.

Where lightning met ancient malice, the ghouls exploded into sizzling dust. But his lightning fractured against the twins' wall of darkness. It kept them from joining the fight with Bryce, though it didn't destroy their shield.

"Help her," Baxian hissed over the crackling flame, but Hunt shook his head, throwing more of his lightning at the twins, who were now pushing back with a slowly advancing wall of shadow. Hunt dared a glance at Sathia, who watched with wide eyes as Bryce launched herself at the two Fae Kings.

Bryce flew like a shooting star through the dim cavern.

"She doesn't need my help," Hunt whispered.

Fire met starlight met shadows, and Bryce loosed herself on the world.

It ended today. Here. Now.

This had nothing to do with the Asteri, or Midgard. The Fae had festered under leaders like these males, but her people could be so much more.

Bryce carried the weight of that with each punch of starfire toward the Autumn King that had him dancing away, with each smothering spate of shadows Morven sent to herd her back toward the stream.

She hadn't gone to that other world only because of the sword and knife, or to find some magic bullet to stop the rot in her own world. She knew that now.

Urd had sent her there to see, even in the small fraction of their world that she'd witnessed, that Fae existed who were kind and brave. She might have had to betray Nesta and Azriel, trick them . . . but she knew that at their cores, they were good people.

The Fae of Midgard were capable of more.

Ruhn proved it. Flynn and Dec proved it. Even Sathia proved it, in the short time Bryce had known her.

Bryce launched a line of pure starfire at Morven, gouging deep in the black-salt floor. He dodged, rolling out of reach with a warrior's skill.

It stopped today.

The pettiness and chauvinism and arrogance that had been the hallmarks of the Fae of Midgard for generations. Pelias's legacy.

It all fucking stopped *today*.

The starlight flared around Bryce, the darkness of Silene's—Theia's—dusk power giving it shape, transforming it into that starfire. If she could find that final third piece and make the star whole—

She was already whole. What she had—who she was . . . it was enough. She'd always been enough to take on these bastards, power or no power. Starborn crap or no.

She was enough.

The Murder Twins were returning Hunt's ambush now. From his angle, Bryce knew Hunt couldn't see what they were up to behind their wall of shadows, pushing his way, blasting apart his lightning.

But from over here . . . Bryce could see how they used that wall against Hunt. Used it to shield themselves from view as they turned her way.

Even Hunt's lightning wasn't fast enough as the Murder Twins sprang for her with swords drawn. Right as their shadowy talons scraped down the wall of her mind.

It stopped today.

Bryce exploded—into the twins's minds, their bodies. Flooding them with starfire. A part of her recoiled in horror as their huge forms crumpled to the ground, steaming holes where their eyes had been. Where their brains had been. She'd melted their minds.

Morven screamed in fury—and something like fear.

She'd done that. With only two-thirds of Theia's star, she'd managed to—

"Bryce!" Hunt shouted, but he was too late—Morven had sent a whip of shadow, hidden beneath a plume of the Autumn King's flame, for her. It wrapped around her legs and *yanked.* Bryce slammed into stone, starlight blinking out.

The impact cracked through her skull, setting the world spinning. Or maybe that was the shadows, dragging her closer to the wall of flame.

Bryce slashed down at the leash of shadows with a hand wreathed in starfire.

It tore the darkness into ribbons. Bryce was up in a heartbeat, but not fast enough to dodge the punch of flame the Autumn King sent toward her gut—

Bryce teleported, swift and instinctive as a breath. Right to the Autumn King.

It ended now.

The Autumn King staggered in shock as she grabbed his burning fist in one hand. As she held firm, her nails digging in hard. His fire singed into her skin, blinding her with pain, but she dug her nails in deeper and sent her starfire blasting into him.

Her father roared in agony, falling to his knees. Morven, so stunned he'd been frozen in place, swore brutally.

Bryce stared at what she had done to the Autumn King's fist. What had once been his hand.

Only melted flesh and bone remained.

The Autumn King retched at the pain, bowing over his knees, hand cradled to his chest.

"Do you think those gifts make you special?" Morven raged, shaking free of his stupor. A swarming nest of shadows teemed around him. "My son could do the same—and he was trash in the end. Just like you."

Morven's shadows launched for her like a flock of ravens.

Bryce blasted out a wall of starlight, destroying those shadow birds, but more came, from everywhere and nowhere, from below—

The Autumn King got to his feet, face gray with agony, cradling his charred remnant of a hand. "I'm going to teach you a new definition of pain," he spat.

And there was no amount of training that could have prepared Bryce, no time to teleport to avoid the two swift attacks from the Fae Kings, matched in power.

She dodged the bone-searing blast of fire from her father, only to have Morven's shadows grab her again. Hands of pure darkness hurled her onto the stone so hard the breath went out of her. The Starsword and Truth-Teller flew from her fingers.

A female cried out, and for a moment, Bryce thought it might have been Cthona, maybe Luna herself.

But it was Sathia.

It was Sathia, on her feet again, and yet it wasn't. It was every Fae female who'd come before them.

Bryce exploded her light outward, shredding Morven's shadows apart. They cleared to reveal the Autumn King standing above her, a sword of flame in his undamaged hand.

"I should have done this a long time ago," her father snarled, and plunged his burning sword toward her exposed heart.

The Autumn King only made it halfway before light burst from his chest.

Hunt's lightning had—

No.

It wasn't Hunt's lightning that shone through the Autumn King's rib cage.

It was the Starsword. And it was Ruhn wielding it, standing behind him.

Ruhn, who had driven the sword right through their father's cold heart.

Ruhn knew in his bones why he'd walked through these caves. He was a Starborn Prince, and he'd come to right an ancient wrong.

With the Starsword in his hand, piercing his father's heart . . . Ruhn knew he was exactly where he was meant to be.

The Autumn King let out a shocked grunt, blood dribbling from his mouth.

"I know *every* definition of pain thanks to you," Ruhn spat, and yanked out the sword.

His father collapsed face-first onto the stone floor.

Even Morven's shadows halted as the Autumn King struggled to raise himself onto his hands. Lidia, guarding Ruhn's back against the Stag King, said nothing.

No pity stirred in Ruhn's heart as his father gurgled blood. As it dribbled onto the stones. The Autumn King lifted his head to meet Ruhn's stare.

Betrayal and hatred burned in his face.

Ruhn said into his mind, into all their minds, *I lied about what the Oracle said to me.*

His father's eyes flared with shock at Ruhn's voice in his head, the secret his son had kept all these years. Ruhn didn't care what Morven made of it, didn't even bother to look at the Stag King. Bryce and Athalar could handle the shadows, if Morven was dumb enough to attack.

So Ruhn stared into his father's hateful face and said, *The Oracle didn't tell me that I would be a fair and just king. She told me that the royal bloodline would end with me.*

He had the sense that his friends were watching with wide eyes. But he only had words for the pathetic male before him.

I thought it meant your *bloodline.*

Ruhn lifted the bloodied Starsword. Flame simmered along his father's body, limning his powerful form. But Ruhn was no longer a cowering boy, inking himself with tattoos to hide the scarring.

I was wrong. I think the Oracle meant all of them, Ruhn went on, mind-to-mind. *The* male *lines. The Starborn Princes included—all you fucks who have corrupted and stolen and never once apologized for it. The entire system. This bullshit of crowns and inheritance.*

His father's sneering voice filled his mind. *You're a spoiled, ungrateful brat who never deserved to carry my crown—*

I don't want it, Ruhn snapped, and shut down the bridge between their minds that allowed his father to speak. He'd had enough of listening to this male.

Blood trickled from his father's lips as his Vanir body sought to heal him—to rally his strength to attack.

The line will end with me, you fucking prick, Ruhn said into his father's mind, *because I yield my crown, my title, to the queen.*

True fear turned his father's face ashen. And out of the corner of his eye, Ruhn saw Bryce's star begin to glow.

A serene peace bloomed in him. *I always assumed the Oracle's prophecy meant that I would die.* He let his kernel of starlight flicker down the blade, an answer to Bryce's beckoning blaze. One last time.

But I am going to live, he said to his father. *And I am going to live well—without you.*

Even Morven's shadows weren't fast enough as Ruhn whipped the Starsword through the air again. And sliced clean through his father's neck.

Bryce had no words as Ruhn severed the Autumn King's head. As her brother skewered the skull on the Starsword before it even hit the stone.

She got to her feet. Came up beside Ruhn where he stood rigid, still holding the bloodied sword, their father's head impaled on it.

The fire around their friends remained, an impenetrable prison. As if the Autumn King had imbued the flames with energy he'd cast outside himself, to linger even past his death. A final punishment. Lidia rushed over, as if she could somehow find a way to undo the flames—

"Let them go," Bryce said to Morven in a voice she didn't entirely recognize. "Before we skewer you as well."

Morven bared his teeth. But despite the blazing hate in his eyes, he lowered himself to his knees and lifted his hands in submission. "I yield."

The fire vanished. Morven blinked, as if surprised, but said nothing.

Their friends were instantly on their feet, Hunt putting a hand on Sathia's back to steady her. Then they all came to stand, as one, behind Bryce and Ruhn. And she saw it, for a glimmering heartbeat. Not a world divided into Houses . . . but a world united.

Bryce walked a few steps to pick up Truth-Teller from where it lay near the Autumn King's decapitated corpse. She didn't look at the body, at the blood still pooling outward, as she said to Ruhn, "Helena created the prophecy to explain what these weapons could do, the power needed to take on the Asteri. But I think, in her own way, the prophecy was also her hope for *me*. What I might do, beyond wielding the power."

Confusion swirled in Ruhn's bright blue eyes.

"Sword," Bryce said, nodding to the Starsword in his hand. She lifted Truth-Teller in her own. "Knife." And then she pointed to their friends, to the Fae and angel and mer and shifter behind them. "People."

"It wasn't only about the Fae," Ruhn said quietly.

"It doesn't have to be," Bryce amended. "It can mean what we want it to." She smiled slightly. "*Our* people," she said to Ruhn, to the others. "The people of Midgard. United against the Asteri."

It had taken all this time, a journey through the stars and under the earth . . . but here they were.

Morven spat on the ground. "If you plan to fight the Asteri, you will fail. It doesn't matter if you unify every House. You will be wiped from the face of Midgard."

Bryce surveyed the king on his knees. "I appreciate your confidence."

Morven's shadows began to seethe along his shoulders again. Rippling down his arms. "I yield now, girl, but the Fae shall never accept a half-breed by-blow as queen, even a Starborn one."

Ruhn lunged for him, Starsword angling, but Bryce blocked him with an arm. For a long moment, she stared down into Morven's face. Really, truly looked at it. At the male beneath the crown of shadows.

She found only hate.

"If we win," Bryce said quietly, "this new world will be a fair one. No more hierarchies and bullshit." The very things Hunt had fought for. That he and the Fallen had suffered for. "But right now," Bryce said, "I'm Queen of the Valbaran Fae." She nodded to the Autumn King's body cooling on the ground, then smirked at Morven. "And of Avallen."

Morven hissed, "You'll be Queen of Avallen over my dead . . ." He trailed off at the smile on her face. And paled.

"As I was saying," Bryce drawled, "for the moment, I'm queen. I'm judge, jury . . ."

Bryce looked to Sathia, still shaken and wide-eyed from the twins' attack—yet unafraid. Unbroken, despite what the males in her life, what this male, had tried to do to her.

So Bryce peered down at Morven and finished sweetly, "And I'm your motherfucking executioner."

The King of Avallen was still blazing with hate when Bryce slid Truth-Teller into his heart.

It was a matter of a few strokes of Truth-Teller through Morven's neck for Bryce to behead him. And as she rose to her feet, it was a Fae Queen who stood before Ruhn, wreathed in starlight, unflinching before her enemies. From the love shining on Athalar's face as he beheld Bryce, Ruhn knew the angel saw it as well.

But it was Sathia who approached Bryce. Who knelt at her feet, bowing her head, and declared, "Hail Bryce, Queen of the Midgardian Fae."

"Oof," Bryce said, wincing. "Let's start with Avallen and Valbara and see where we wind up."

But Flynn and Declan knelt, too. And Ruhn turned to his sister and knelt as well, offering up the Starsword with both hands.

"To right an old wrong," Ruhn said, "and on behalf of all the Starborn Princes before me. This is yours."

No words had ever sounded so right. Nor had anything felt so right as when Bryce took the Starsword from him, a formal claiming, and weighed it in her hands.

Ruhn watched his sister glance between the Starsword and Truth-Teller, one blade blazing with starlight, the other with darkness. "What now?" she asked quietly.

"Other than taking a moment to process the deaths of those two assholes over there?" Ruhn said. He nodded toward Morven and his father.

Bryce offered a watery smile. "We learned some things, at least."

"Yeah?" The others were all crowding around them now, listening.

"Turns out," Athalar said with what Ruhn could have sworn was forced casualness, "Theia did some weird shit with her star magic, divvying it up between herself and her daughters. Long story short, Bryce has two of those pieces, but Helena used Avallen's nexus of ley lines and natural magic to hide the third piece somewhere on Avallen. If Bryce can get that piece, the sword and knife will be able to open a portal to nowhere, and we can trap the Asteri inside it."

Bryce gave Hunt a look as if to say there was a *lot* more to it than that, but she said, "So . . . new mission: find the power Helena hid. Aidas claimed that Helena used Midgard's ley lines to hide it in these caves after Pelias died." She sighed, scanning all their faces. "Any thoughts on where it might be?"

Ruhn blinked at her. "Yeah," he said hoarsely. "I do have a thought."

"Really?" Athalar said, frowning.

"Don't look so shocked," Ruhn grumbled.

Lidia came up to his side, adding, "After Pelias died, you say?"

"Yeah. It's complicated—"

"I think it's part of the land," Lidia interrupted. "In the very bones of Avallen."

Bryce and Athalar raised their eyebrows, but Ruhn glanced to Lidia and nodded. "It explains a lot."

Bryce cut in, "Like . . . ?"

"Like why Avallen was once part of an archipelago, but now it's only one island," Ruhn said. "You said Helena drew upon Avallen's ley lines to contain her mother's star—to hide it here, right? I think doing so drained *all* the land's magic from its ley lines, and repurposed it to encage Theia's power. It made the land wither. Just as you said Silene's own lands withered around the Prison while it held her own share of power."

Bryce mused, "Silene had the Horn, but Helena had to use the ley lines instead. Yet both had a disastrous effect on the land itself." She peered down at the blades again.

"How do you propose getting the magic out?" Lidia challenged. "We have no idea how to access it."

No one answered. And, fuck, Morven and the Autumn King were lying there, dead and dismembered, and—

"Anyone got any bright ideas?" Tharion asked into the fraught silence.

Ruhn stifled his laugh, but Bryce slowly turned toward the mer, as if in surprise.

"Bright," she murmured. Then looked at Athalar, scanning his face. "Light it up," she whispered. As if it was the answer to everything.

Bright.

Light.

Light it up.

The world seemed to pause, as if Urd herself had slowed time as each thought pelted Bryce.

She glanced at the walls. At the river of starlight that Helena had depicted at the bottom of every carving.

Mere hours ago, she'd thought it was the bloodline of the Starborn in artistic form.

But Silene had depicted the evil running beneath the Prison in her carvings, unwittingly warning about Vesperus . . . Perhaps Helena, too, had left a clue.

A final challenge.

Bryce peered down at the eight-pointed star in the center of the room. The two strange slits in the points. One small, one larger.

She looked at the weapons in her hands: a small dagger, and a large sword. They'd fit right into the slits in the floor, like keys in a lock.

Keys to unlock the power stored beneath. The last bit of power she needed to open the portal to nowhere.

That power had originally belonged to the worst sort of Fae, but it didn't have to. It could belong to anyone. It could be Bryce's for the taking.

To light up this world.

"Bryce?" Hunt asked, a hand on her back.

Bryce rallied herself, breathing deep. Bits of debris and rock from her battle with the Fae Kings began drifting upward.

She walked through it, right to that eight-pointed star on the ground, identical to the one on her chest. The debris and rock swirled, a maelstrom with her at its center.

Bryce inhaled deeply, bracing herself as she whispered, "I'm ready."

"For *what*?" Hunt demanded, but Bryce ignored him.

On an exhale, she plunged the weapons into the slits in the eight-pointed star. The small one for the knife. The larger one for the sword.

And like a key turning in a lock, they released what lay beneath.

63

Light blasted up through the blades into her hands, her arms, her heart. Bryce could hear it through her feet, through the stone. The song of the land beneath her. Quiet and old and forgotten, but there.

She heard how Avallen had yielded its joy, its bright green lands and skies and flowers, so it might hold the power as it was bid, waiting all this time for someone to unleash it. To free it.

"Bryce!" Hunt shouted, and she met her mate's eyes.

None of what the Princes of Hel had said about him scared her. They hadn't made Hunt's soul. That was all hers, just as her own soul was his.

Helena had bound the soul of this land in magical chains. No more. No more would Bryce allow the Fae to lay claim over anything.

"You're free," Bryce whispered to Avallen, to the land and the pure, inherent magic beneath it. "Be free."

And it was.

Light burst from the star, and the caves shook again. They rolled and rattled and trembled—

The walls were buckling, and she had the sense that Hunt lunged for her, but fell to his knees as the ground moved upward. Stone crumbled away around them, burying Pelias's sarcophagus, the corpses of the two newly dead kings, and all their other hateful ancestors below. It churned them into dust. Sunlight broke through, the very earth parting as Bryce and the others were thrust upward.

Sunlight—not gray skies.

They emerged in the hills less than a mile from the castle and royal city. As if the caves had been backtracking all this way.

And from the rocky ground beneath them, spreading from the star at Bryce's feet, grass and flowers bloomed. The river from the caverns burst forth, dancing down the newly formed hill.

Sathia and Flynn laughed, and both siblings knelt, putting their fingers in the grass. The earth magic in their veins surged forth as an oak burst from Flynn's hands, shooting high over them, and from Sathia's hands tumbled runners of strawberry and brambles of blackberry, tangles of raspberries and thickets of blueberries—

"Holy gods," Tharion said, and pointed out to the sea.

It was no longer gray and thrashing, but a vibrant, clear turquoise. And rising from the water, just as they had seen on the map Declan had found, were islands, large and small. Lush and green with life.

Forests erupted on the island they stood on, soon joined by mountains and rivers.

So much life, so much magic, freed at last of Vanir control. A place not only for the Fae, but for everyone. All of them.

Bryce could feel it—the joy of the land at being seen, at being freed. She looked at Ruhn, and her brother's face was bright with awe. As if their father didn't lie beneath the earth, lost forever to the dark, his bones to be eaten by worms.

It was only awe, and freedom, lighting Ruhn's face.

No more pain. No more fear.

Bryce didn't know when she started crying, only that the next moment Ruhn was there, his arms around her, and they were both sobbing.

Their friends gave them space, understanding that it wasn't pure joy that coursed through them—that their joy was tempered by grief for the years of pain, and hope for the years ahead.

The world might very well end soon, Bryce knew, and they

might all die with it, but right now the paradise blooming around them, this awakened land, was proof of what life had been like before the Asteri, before the Fae and the Vanir.

Proof of what might be afterward.

Ruhn pulled back, cupping her face in his hands. Tears ran down his face. She couldn't stop crying—crying and laughing—with all that flowed from her heart.

Her brother only pressed a kiss to her brow and said, "Long live the queen."

64

The land had awoken, and the Fae of Avallen were terrified.

Hunt tried not to be smug at the sight of the destroyed castle. The occupants and the town had been spared, but vines and trees had burst through Morven's castle and turned it into rubble.

"A last *fuck you* from the land," Bryce murmured to Hunt as the two of them arrived at a hill overlooking the ruins. At their far end, a group of Fae stood in apprehensive silence around the demolished building.

Beside him, Bryce thrummed with power—from Helena and her cursed bloodline, but also from whatever lingering soul-wound had healed the moment Ruhn had cut off their father's head.

Hunt slid an arm around his mate's waist, taking in the Fae who were gawking at the ruins, the island of Avallen—and the new islands surrounding it.

Bryce peered up at him. "Are you . . . okay?"

He was silent for a long moment, looking out at the landscape. "No."

She pressed closer into his side.

His throat worked for a moment. "I'm some weird demonic test-tube baby."

"Maybe that's where you came from, Hunt," she said, offering him a gentle smile, "but it's not who you are—who you became."

He glanced at her. "Earlier, you seemed to not like the person I became."

She sighed. "Hunt, I get it—all the shit you're feeling. I really do. But I can't do this without you. *All* of you."

His heart ached as he looked at her fully. "I know. I'm trying. It's just . . ." He struggled for the words. "My worst nightmare would be to see you in the Asteri's hands. To see you dead."

"And avoiding that fate is worth letting them rule forever?" There was no sharpness to her question—just curiosity.

"Part of me says yes. A very, very loud part of me," he admitted. "But another part of me says that we need to do whatever it takes to end this. So future generations, future mates . . . they don't have to make the same choices, suffer the same fates, as we have."

He *would* try to put his fear behind him. For her, for Midgard.

"I know," she said gently. "If you need to talk, if you need someone to listen . . . I'm here."

He scanned her face, pure love aching in his heart. Some of that lingering darkness and pain remained, yes, but he'd fight through it. And he knew she'd give him the space he needed to do so. "Thanks, Quinlan."

She rose up on her toes to kiss his cheek. A sweet, soft brush of her lips that warmed the final numbed shards of his soul.

Then she surveyed the ruins once more, taking his hand as they began walking down toward their friends gathered at the foot of the hill. "I got the last piece of Theia's power, but what now? How do we take on the Asteri? How do we get close enough to them to use the knife and sword and toss them through that portal?"

He kissed her temple. "Give it a rest for today. For now, enjoy being leveled up."

She snorted. "That doesn't sound like a strategy from the Umbra Mortis."

"I can't tell if that's an insult or not." He nudged her with a wing. "We've got some other urgent stuff to sort out first, Bryce."

"Yeah, I know," she said as they came to a stop among their friends. She addressed all of them. "Since this place can hold out against the Asteri, we need to get as many people here as possible. Without tipping off imperial forces."

"The *Depth Charger* could help," Flynn suggested. Tharion grimaced but didn't object.

Lidia asked, "But how would they pierce the mists?"

Bryce lifted a hand, and in the distance, the mists parted—then sealed. "Didn't you hear? I'm a fancy world-walker who can do this shit innately. Plus . . ." She gave a crooked grin. "I'm now Queen of Avallen. Wielding the mists is a perk of the job."

"Of course," Hunt said, rolling his eyes and earning a jab to the ribs.

But Ruhn warned, "The Fae won't be happy to share."

Bryce motioned to the ruins, the damage she'd unleashed, however unknowingly. "They don't have any choice."

Ruhn snorted. "Long live the queen, indeed."

Declan gave a shout from up on the hill, and they all turned toward him.

"Whatever you did with those mists, Bryce," Declan shouted, "I got service!" He lifted his phone in triumph, and then lowered his head to read whatever messages he had.

"Small victories," Bryce said. Lidia and Tharion laughed.

The Hind's amusement faded, though, as she turned to Tharion, as if drawn by the mer's own chuckle. "You could hide here, you know. The Ocean Queen can't pass through these mists unless Bryce allows it."

"Hide," Tharion said, as if the word tasted foul.

"The alternative is begging her not to kill you," Lidia said, "and then doing everything she says for the rest of your life."

"No different from the River Queen," Tharion said. Sathia was watching him carefully—curiously. The mer shrugged, and asked Lidia baldly, "How do you live with it? Being at her mercy?"

Lidia's mouth tightened, and they all pretended they weren't listening to her every word as she said at last, "I had no other choice." She looked to Ruhn, eyes bright. "But I'm not going to anymore."

Ruhn started, whirling to her. "What?"

Lidia said to him, to all of them, "If we survive the Asteri, I'm not going back."

Hunt had seen enough of the Ocean Queen to know how well that would go down.

Bryce said cautiously, "But your sons . . ."

"If we survive, my enemies will be dead," Lidia said, chin lifting with queenly grace. "And surely she will have no need of my services anymore." She nodded to Tharion. "I'm not going back, and neither should you. The age of unchecked rulers is over." She motioned to the ruins. "This is the first step."

A chill went down Hunt's spine at the surety of her words. Bryce opened her mouth like she might say something.

But Baxian pivoted toward Declan, as if he'd sensed something off. A second later, Declan's head snapped up.

A foreboding quiet settled over Hunt. Over all of them.

No one spoke as Declan approached. As the male's throat bobbed. And when he looked at Ruhn, at Bryce, tears shone in his eyes.

"The Asteri made their move."

Bryce grabbed Hunt's arm, as if it would keep her from falling.

"Tell me," Lidia said, pushing through them to get to Declan.

Declan glanced at the Hind, then back to Bryce. "The Asteri organized a hit, led by Pollux and Mordoc, on every Ophion base. They wiped them off the map."

"Fuck," Hunt breathed.

But Declan was shaking his head. "They wiped out everyone in their camps, too."

Hunt's knees shook.

And when Declan looked to Bryce, Hunt knew immediately that it would be bad. Wished he could undo it, whatever it was—

"And they dispatched their Asterian Guard to Asphodel Meadows. They . . . they said it was a hotbed of rebel activity."

Bryce began shaking her head, backing away.

Declan's voice broke as he said, "They unleashed ten brimstone missiles on the Meadows. On everyone living there."

PART III

THE ASCENT

65

Ithan stood on the deck of a fishing boat that had seen better decades, Hypaxia at his side. Apparently, Jesiba Roga didn't think the two of them needed to travel in style.

But at least the shark-shifter crew hadn't asked questions. And had kept their own counsel as they cut the engine and the boat bobbed in the gray swells of the Haldren, right in front of the impenetrable, sky-high wall of mist.

Ithan nodded to the broken brooch on Hypaxia's cloak. "Any chance your broom still works? We could fly over them."

"No," Hypaxia said. "And besides, only Morven can let us through."

Ithan reached a hand toward the mists, twining it through his fingers. "So how do we contact him? Knock on the barrier? Send up a flare?"

His tone was more cheerful than he felt. Somewhere beyond these mists lay Sofie's body. Apparently, Morven had told Jesiba they could have it—his late son had shipped it to his home, and the Fae King hadn't yet bothered to have it tossed into the garbage. A stroke of luck sent from Urd herself. Jesiba had promised that Morven wouldn't touch it—that he'd be glad to dump the body into their hands.

That is, if they could get through the barrier. Hypaxia lifted a light brown hand to the mists, as if testing them. "They feel . . ."

As if in answer, the curtain of the mists shuddered and parted.

Sunlight flooded through. Gray seas turned turquoise. The wind warmed to a balmy, gentle breeze. A paradise lay beyond.

Even the gruff shark shifters gasped in shock. But Ithan glanced at Hypaxia, who was wide-eyed as well. "What's wrong?"

Hypaxia slowly shook her head. "This is not the Avallen I have visited before."

"What do you mean?" Every instinct went on alert, his wolf at the ready.

Hypaxia motioned to the captain to start sailing through the parted mists, toward the lush, beckoning land. Prettier than even the Coronal Islands. The former witch-queen breathed, "Something tremendous has occurred here."

Ithan sighed. "Please tell me it was a *good* tremendous change?"

Her silence wasn't reassuring.

Hunt found Bryce sitting atop the ruins of what had once been a tower, tangles of blooming vines and roses all around her. A beautiful, surreal place for a Fae Queen to rest.

The land seemed to know her, small blooming flowers nestling around her body, some of them even curling in the long strands of her hair.

Yet her face when Hunt sat beside her was hollow. Devastated.

Dried tears had left salty tracks down her cheeks. And her whiskey-colored eyes, usually so full of life and fire, were vacant. Vacant in a way he hadn't seen since that time he'd found her at Lethe, drinking away her grief at Danika's death, the wound reopened when she realized her father had withheld vital information that would have helped with the investigation.

Hunt sat at her side on an uneven bit of tumbled stone and slid a wing around her. From up here, he could see the scattering of islands amid the vibrant teal of the ocean. Avallen had awoken into a paradise, and part of him ached to leap into the skies and explore every inch of it, but . . .

"All that new power from Theia," Bryce said hoarsely, "and it didn't amount to shit. I didn't find it in time to help anyone—save anyone."

Hunt kissed her temple and promised, "We'll make it count, Bryce."

"I'm sorry," she said quietly. "For being a dick to you about what you're going through."

"Bryce . . . ," he began, scrambling for the words.

"I apologize for everything I said to you about getting over it," she went on. "But . . ." Her lips pressed into a thin line, as if keeping in a sob that wanted to work itself free.

"What just happened," he said roughly, "isn't your fault. It's no one's fault but the Asteri's. You've always been right about that."

She said dully, as if she hadn't heard a word he'd said, "Fury and June are getting into a helicopter with my parents, Emile—Cooper, I mean—and Syrinx," A glance down at where she'd discarded her phone in the blossoms beside her. "The Asteri didn't find them before the attack, but I want them all here, kept safe."

"Good," Hunt said. They'd all spent the past hour making frantic phone calls to family and friends. Hunt had debated for a long while about whether to risk calling Isaiah and Naomi, but had opted not to in the end, lest it raise any trouble if their phones were tapped. Which was part of why he'd sought Bryce out now, even though he knew she'd come up here to be alone.

The others were finding lodgings for the night, now that Morven's castle lay in ruins. From Ruhn's grim face, it seemed the Fae weren't being welcoming. *Tough fucking luck,* Hunt wanted to say. They were about to get a whole influx of people.

"We could stay here," Bryce murmured, and Hunt knew that the words were ones she'd only speak in front of him. "We could get all our friends and family, anyone who can make it across the Haldren—and just . . . stay here, protected. Forever. It's basically what the Ocean Queen asked for. And would make me little better than my ancestors—to hide like that. But at least people would be safe. Some people on Midgard, at least." While the majority remained at the mercy of the Asteri.

Hunt leaned forward to peer at her face. "Is that what you want to do?"

"No," Bryce said, and her eyes lifted to the island-dotted horizon. To the wall of mist beyond it. "I mean, anyone who can make it here, any refugees, they'll be allowed in. I willed the mists to make it so."

He would normally have ribbed her about how very Super Powerful and Special Magic Starborn Fae Queen that was, but he kept his mouth shut. Let her keep talking.

"But us . . ." The bleak look on her face had him folding his wing more tightly around her. "We can't hide here forever."

"No," he agreed. "We can't." He let her see how much he meant it. That he'd fight until the very end.

She leaned her head against his shoulder. "I can't even think about what they did. To Ophion and the camps . . . to the Meadows . . ." Her voice broke.

He couldn't process it, either. The innocents killed. The children.

"We have an obligation," Bryce said, and lifted her head. "To those people. To Midgard. And to other worlds, too. We have an obligation to end this."

It was Bryce's beloved face looking at him, but it was also the face of a queen. His lightning stirred in answer. And it didn't matter to him if those fucks Apollion and Thanatos had made him, made his power. If his lightning could help her, save her, save Midgard from the Asteri . . . that was all that mattered.

Bryce said, "*I* have an obligation to end this."

Her gaze swept over the peaceful archipelago, and for a moment, Hunt could see it: a life here, with their kids and their friends. A life they could build for themselves in this untouched place.

It shimmered there, so close he could nearly touch it.

Bryce said, as if thinking the same thing, "I think Urd needed me to come here."

"To know it could be a refuge?"

She shook her head. "I wondered why the mists kept out the Asteri, how we could use those mists against them. I thought we'd come here and find answers, maybe some secret weapon—like some major Asteri-repelling device."

She slid her exhausted gaze to him at last.

"But it's the sheer quantity of black salt that keeps the Asteri out, not the mists, and we can't replicate that. I think Urd wanted me to see that a society could thrive here. That I could be safe here, along with everyone I love."

Her mouth trembled, but she pressed it into a thin line.

"I think Urd wanted me to see and learn all that," she went on, "and have to decide whether to stay, or leave this safety behind and fight. Urd wanted to tempt me."

"Maybe it was a gift," Hunt offered. "Not a test or challenge, Bryce, but a gift." At her raised eyebrows, he explained, "For Urd to let the people you love be safe here—while you go kick some Asteri ass."

Her smile was unspeakably sad. "To know they'll be protected here . . . even if we fail."

He didn't try to reassure her that they'd succeed. Instead, he promised gently, "We'll do it together. You and me—we'll end it together." He brushed a strand of her hair behind a delicately pointed ear. "I'm with you. All of me. You and I, we'll finish this."

Her chin lifted, and he could have sworn a crown of stars glimmered around her head. "I want to wipe them off the face of the planet," she said, and though her voice was soft, nothing but pure, predatory rage filled it.

"I'll get the mop and bucket," he said, and flashed her a smile.

She looked at him, all regal fury and poise—and laughed. The first moment of normalcy between them, joyous and beautiful. Another thing for him to fight for. Until the very end.

Tendrils of night-blooming purple flowers unfurled around her in answer, despite the daylight. Had it always been leading toward this? In the night garden, before they were attacked by the kristallos all those months ago, he could have sworn the flowers had opened for her. Were they sensing this power, the dusk-born heritage in her veins?

"This is remarkable," he said, nodding to the island that seemed to respond to her every emotion.

"I think it's what the Prison—the island in the Fae's home world—once was. When Theia ruled it, I mean. Before Silene fucked it all up. Maybe they're linked in some way through being thin places and spilled over to each other a bit. Maybe back in that other world . . . maybe I woke up the land around the Prison, too."

Hunt's brows rose. "Only one way to find out, I guess."

She huffed. "I don't think they'll ever let me set foot back in that world."

"Do you think there's any chance we could recruit them to fight for us?"

"No. I mean, I don't know what they'd say, but . . . I wouldn't ask that of them. Of anyone."

"I take back what I said earlier, about giving the planning a rest: we need to start thinking through our strategy." He hated putting the burden on her, but they had to make a move. She was right—they couldn't hide here. "The Asteri clearly want us to retaliate for what they did. Rigelus probably expects us to try to rally an army and attack them, but it'll never work. We'll always be outgunned and outnumbered." He took her hand. "I . . . Bryce, I lost one army already."

"I know," she said.

But he pushed, "We're also talking about taking on *six* Asteri. If it was us versus Rigelus, maybe . . . but all six? Do we separate them? Pick them off one by one?"

"No. It'd give the others time to rally. We strike them all at once—together."

He considered. "It's time to let Hel in, isn't it?"

The sweet breeze ruffled her hair as she nodded.

"So where does that leave us?" he asked.

The star on her chest glowed. "We're going to Nena. To open the Northern Rift."

"Fuck. Okay. Ignoring the enormity of that, and assuming it all goes right, what happens next? Do we walk into the palace and start fighting?"

Her gaze had again lifted to the islands and glimmering sea. That regal expression spread over her face, and he knew he was getting a glimpse of the leader she'd become. If they got through this.

"What is the one thing Rigelus has constantly told us?" Bryce asked.

"That we suck?"

She chuckled. "He went out of his way to offer you freedom," she said, nodding to where the brand was back on his wrist, "as a way to entice me to keep my mouth shut about killing Micah. And keep you quiet about killing Sandriel."

He angled his head. "You want to go public about it?"

"I think Rigelus and the Asteri are nervous about the world finding out what we did. That their precious Archangels could be killed. By two apparent randos, no less."

It was Hunt's turn to chuckle. "We're not exactly randos."

"Yeah, but I'm still going to show Midgard that even Archangels can be killed."

"Okay, that's . . . that's awesome," Hunt said, his blood pumping at the thought. Rigelus would lose his fucking mind. "But what will it accomplish?"

"They'll be so busy dealing with the media they won't think about us for a little while," Bryce said, smiling cruelly. Just a hint of the father who now lay dead beneath the earth here. "It will be more of a distraction than any army from Hel."

"I think it's a good idea," Hunt said, mulling it over. "I really do. But how are you going to prove it? Everyone would have to take your word for it, and the Asteri would deny it immediately."

"That's why I need to talk to Jesiba."

"Oh?"

She got to her feet and offered him a hand to rise. "Because she has the video footage of what I did to Micah."

* * *

What lay before Ithan was truly a paradise on Midgard. Crystal clear water, lush vegetation, streams and waterfalls pouring into the sea, powdery sand, birds singing . . .

He remained on alert, however, as the boat pulled up to a cove, close enough to the shore that he and Hypaxia jumped out and waded the few feet onto the beach.

"Which way?" he asked the former queen, scanning the dense foliage bordering the beach, the rising hills. "Jesiba said the castle was a few miles inland, but I didn't see anything while we were sailing in—"

Wings flapped above, and Ithan shifted on instinct, his powerful wolf's body nudging Hypaxia behind him as he snarled up at the sky.

Two scents hit him a heartbeat later.

And Ithan's head emptied out entirely as Hunt Athalar landed in the sand, Bryce in his arms.

66

Back in his humanoid form, Ithan sat across from Bryce and Hunt in the grass, unable to get words out. Hypaxia, seated beside him, gave him space to think.

Beyond Bryce sat Ruhn, Flynn, Dec, and Tharion—and Lidia and Baxian. Along with a female who was apparently Tharion's wife and Flynn's sister.

Some crazy shit had happened. Ithan knew that. But they didn't offer any explanations, instead waiting for him to get into why he'd come here. What had happened.

His throat became unbearably tight.

"I . . ." They were all staring at him. Waiting. "I need Sofie Renast's body."

"Well," Hunt said, whistling, "that wasn't what I expected to hear."

Ithan lifted pleading eyes to the Umbra Mortis. "Jesiba said King Morven has the body—"

"Had the body," Ruhn amended, crossing his arms. His tattoos looked like they'd been put through a paper shredder. Ithan had noticed that immediately upon seeing his friends, upon hugging them all so tightly they'd complained about his grip. Ruhn went on, "The body is now technically Bryce's."

Ithan shook his head, not understanding.

Hunt drawled, "Morven is dead, and Bryce is Queen of Avallen."

Ithan just blinked at Bryce, who was watching him. Carefully. Like she knew something had—

"The Meadows," he blurted. Had they heard about it here? Had they—

"We know," Flynn said.

"Fucking bastards," Tharion murmured.

Bryce only asked Ithan, "How bad?"

Ithan couldn't talk about the small bodies, so many of them—

"As one might expect," Hypaxia answered grimly, "and then some." Heavy silence fell.

"Whatever took you away from helping the city," Lidia said, eyes on her sister, "must be important indeed. Why do you need Sofie's body?"

Again, they all looked at him. And he couldn't contain his misery as he said, "Because I fucked up."

It all came out. How he'd found an alternate heir to the Fendyr line, freed her from the Astronomer . . . and then killed her.

None of it was news to Tharion, Flynn, or Dec. But judging from the way Bryce and Ruhn were glowering at the trio . . . Apparently, they had forgotten to mention this information in the chaos of the last few days.

How they'd forgotten to mention the thing that had literally shredded apart Ithan's life was beyond him, but he didn't dwell on it. He plowed on to the part of his story that was news for all of them: How he and Hypaxia had attempted to raise Sigrid. And now the Fendyr heir was a Reaper.

When he reached the end of his account, they were all staring at him wide-eyed. No one more so than Bryce, who hadn't said anything when he'd spoken of an alternative to Sabine, someone Danika might have liked.

Ithan finished, "So if Sofie's body is intact—"

"It's not," Bryce said quietly.

Something crumpled in Ithan's chest as he met her whiskey-colored eyes.

"Morven's castle collapsed," Bryce said sadly. "Sofie's body is underneath tons of rubble, even if it *is* intact."

Ithan put his face in his hands and breathed hard.

Flynn put a consoling arm around his shoulders, squeezing. "Maybe there's another way—"

"We needed a thunderbird," Ithan said through his hands. There was no fixing this. No undoing it. He'd brought this upon an innocent wolf, upon his people—

"Look," Bryce said, and the gentleness in her tone almost killed him. She blew out a long breath. "An alternate Fendyr heir would have been amazing. But . . ."

Ithan lowered his hands from his face. "But *what*?"

Hunt's eyes flashed at Ithan's snarl. But Bryce didn't back down as she said, "We have bigger problems right now. And time isn't our ally."

"I killed her," Ithan said, voice cracking. "I fucking *killed* her—"

But Athalar said to Hypaxia, "Rigelus collected some of my lightning—for a similar purpose, I think." Bryce started, as if this was news to her. "Are you sure it wouldn't help with Sigrid?"

"It might be worth a try," Hypaxia admitted, "but I don't have any of the supplies I'd need to contain your sort of power."

Ruhn's head lifted. "Like a bunch of crystals?"

They all turned to the prince, but he was looking at Lidia. The Hind explained, "We found a cache of them in the archives."

Ruhn added, "Rigelus used one to grab Athalar's power in the dungeons. Would it work for you, too?"

Hypaxia nodded slowly and said to Hunt, "I wouldn't require much."

Bryce glanced around at the others. Ruhn took her meaning and motioned to his friends. "Come on. Let's grab those crystals from the archives. Hopefully it's still standing."

Flynn, Dec, Lidia, Baxian, and Tharion—his wife in tow—headed down the hill with Ruhn. Only Tharion glanced back, just once, his eyes full of pity. Like the mer understood what it was to have fucked up so royally. To regret.

But Bryce grabbed Ithan's hand, bringing his attention back to her. "What's done is done, Ithan."

"Jesiba said the same thing," he said glumly.

"And she's right," Bryce said. At her side, Athalar nodded. But Bryce motioned with a hand to Hypaxia. "The whole fucking world's changing so rapidly—we're all changing, faster than we can process. For Cthona's sake, Hypaxia isn't even queen anymore. Have either of you really reflected on that?" A punch of guilt went through Ithan. He'd been so focused on himself that he hadn't thought to check in with the witch. But Hypaxia's face remained grave, determined. And Bryce went on to Ithan, "So look: you killed Sigrid, and she's a Reaper, and I think it's . . . really admirable that you're trying to raise her—"

"Don't patronize me," he snarled, and again Athalar threw him that warning glare.

"I'm not," Bryce said. She was the Queen of Avallen, and Ithan could see it in her eyes: the leader glimmering there. "Part of why I love you is because you'll stop at nothing to do the right thing."

"Trying to do the right thing led me to the debacle with Sigrid," he said, shaking his head in disgust.

"Maybe," Bryce said, and glanced at Hypaxia. "But the two of you . . . I need your help. I have to believe that Urd sent you here for this."

"For what?" Hypaxia said, head angling.

Bryce and Hunt swapped glances. The angel motioned to his mate, as if to say, *Your story to tell.*

"I, uh," Bryce said, pulling at some blades of grass, "have a lot to update you guys about."

"You weren't kidding about the big update," Ithan said when Bryce had finished.

"Where do we factor into this, though?" Hypaxia asked. "If

you're thinking to raise an army to aid Hel, I have no sway with the witches, and Ithan wouldn't be able to muster the wolves—"

"No armies from Midgard," Bryce said. "We don't have the time for that, anyway."

Hypaxia pulled on a tightly coiled curl. "What, then?"

Bryce's eyes seemed to glow. "I need you to make an antidote for the Asteri's parasite."

Hypaxia blinked slowly. That bit of Bryce's story had been the hardest to swallow. That they were all infected by something in the water, their magic cut off at the knees.

Bryce pushed on, "You figured out an antidote for the synth, Hypaxia. I need you to do it again. Help us level up before we take on the Asteri. Get us free of their restraints."

"You place an awful lot of faith in my abilities. I'll need to study the parasite before I can even start mapping out the properties of an antidote—"

"We don't have time for the full-blown scientific method," Bryce said.

"I'd hesitate to give you anything that hadn't been fully tested," Hypaxia countered.

"We don't have that luxury," Athalar said firmly. "Anything you can rig up, even if it's temporary, even if it just holds the parasite at bay for a bit . . ."

"I don't know if that's possible," Hypaxia said, but Ithan could see the ideas gleaming in her eyes. "And I'd need a lab. Considering the state of Avallen after your . . . claiming of it, I don't think there's anything here I could use."

"And no power, anyway," Bryce said. "So you'll have to head back to the Lunathion House of Flame and Shadow—it seems like you guys will be hidden and protected there. Especially if Jesiba's around."

Ithan hadn't told Bryce about who—what—Jesiba really was. That was Jesiba's secret to tell.

Her words settled. Ithan said, "What do you mean *you guys*? I don't know shit about science. I can't help Hypaxia with this."

"You know how to fight," Athalar said. "And defend. Hypaxia will need someone to guard her while she works."

Ithan turned to Bryce, who was watching him with a grim expression. "But Sigrid—"

"We need that antidote, Ithan," Bryce said gently, but firmly. "More than anything. Hunt will give you the lightning for Sigrid, but we need that antidote first." She added to Hypaxia, "As fast as you can make it."

Hypaxia and Bryce stared at each other for a long moment. "Very well," Hypaxia said, inclining her head.

Ithan closed his eyes. To abandon his quest, to leave Sigrid as a Reaper . . .

But his friends needed him. They were asking for his help. To deny them, even if it was to save Sigrid . . . He'd already screwed up Sigrid's life. He wouldn't do the same to his friends.

So Ithan opened his eyes and said, "When do we head back to Crescent City?"

Bryce's face remained grim as she said, "Right now."

"Now?" Hypaxia said, the first bit of shock she'd shown.

"That boat's still waiting for you," Athalar said, pointing to the ocean in the distance. "We'll go get the crystals from the others, and I'll fire up the stones. Once I bring them back here, get on that boat and sail for Lunathion."

"And if—when—I come up with an antidote to the parasite?" Hypaxia asked Bryce and Hunt. "How do I contact you?"

"Call us," Bryce said. "If you can't reach us, get the antidote to the Eternal City. There's a fleet of mech-suits on Mount Hermon—hide near there, and we'll find you."

"When, though?"

Bryce's face hardened. "You'll know when it's too late to help us."

Ithan started, "Bryce—"

But Bryce nodded toward the glimmering sea. "As fast as you can," she repeated to the former witch-queen. "I'm begging you."

With that, she walked to Athalar, and he leapt into the skies, flying them in the direction the others had headed.

There was no chance to talk to Tharion or Flynn or Dec. No

chance to even say goodbye. From the way Hypaxia was watching the angel and Bryce vanish toward the distant ruins, he suspected she was thinking the same thing about Lidia.

Twenty minutes later, Bryce and Athalar were back, half a dozen quartz crystals sizzling in the angel's hands. Bottled lightning.

Hypaxia pocketed them, promising to use them well. Bryce kissed her cheek, then Ithan's.

Once, he would have done anything for that kiss. But now it left him hollow, reeling.

Athalar only clapped Ithan on the shoulder before launching skyward with Bryce again, soon no more than a speck against the blue.

When they were alone, Hypaxia motioned to the path they'd taken up from the beach. "We must rise to meet this challenge, Ithan," she said, her voice sure. She patted the lightning-filled crystals now glowing through the pockets of her dark blue robes.

With that, she started off for the boat and the task before them.

Ithan lingered for a moment longer. He'd failed in this quest, too. He'd had a second shot at fixing Sigrid, and he'd failed. It was important to help their friends—and all of Midgard—but the decision weighed on him.

He'd always thought of himself as a good guy, but maybe he wasn't. Maybe he'd been deluding himself.

He didn't know where that left him.

Ithan followed Hypaxia, turning his back on Avallen and the sliver of hope it had offered. To have the lightning in hand, but to have to postpone any effort to help Sigrid . . .

He had no choice but to keep putting one foot in front of the other.

Maybe at some point, he'd stop leaving a trail of absolute destruction in his wake.

67

Hunt found Baxian arranging fresh bundles of hay in the castle stables. They remained intact, located just far enough away from the castle to have been spared during its collapse. "You got the lightning to the wolf and the witch?" Baxian asked by way of greeting.

"They're on their way back to Lunathion with it. But the priority is to try to find a cure for the parasite."

"Good," Baxian grunted. "I hope they have more success than I've had with finding us housing for tonight."

"That bad, huh?" Hunt said, leaning against the doorway.

"No one wants to loan us a room or even a bed, so short of kicking people out of their homes . . ." The Helhound gestured grandly to the stables. "Welcome to Hotel Horseshit."

Hunt chuckled, surveying the woodwork. "Honestly, I've slept in way worse. These horses have a nicer home than the one I grew up in."

Sad, but true.

"Same," Baxian said, and it surprised Hunt enough that he lifted a brow. Baxian said, "I, ah . . . grew up in one of the poorer parts of Ravilis. Being half-shifter—half-*Helhound* shifter—and half-angel . . . it didn't make my parents popular with either the

House of Earth and Blood or the House of Sky and Breath. Made it hard for them to keep their jobs."

"Which one of your parents was the angel?"

"My dad," Baxian said. "He served as a captain in Sandriel's 45th. He had it easier than my mom, who was shunned by everyone she ever knew for 'sullying' herself with an angel. But they both paid the price for being together."

From the way his tone darkened, Hunt knew it had to have been bad. "I'm sorry," he said.

"I was eight. I still don't know how the mob started, but . . ." Baxian's throat worked, yet he finished one pallet of hay and moved on to start another. "It ended with my mom torn to shreds by her fellow Helhounds, and my father seized by the very angels he commanded and given the Living Death."

Hunt blew out a breath. "Fuck."

"They were in such a frenzy, they, ah . . ." Baxian shook his head. "They kept cutting off his wings every time they tried to heal. He lost so much blood in the end that he didn't make it."

"I'm sorry," Hunt said again. "I never knew."

"No one did. Not even Sandriel." Baxian laid a blanket over the next pallet. "From then on, I was on my own. Neither side of the family would take a *half-breed,* as they made sure to call me, so I learned how to fend for myself in the slums. How to keep hidden, how to listen for valuable information—how to sell that information to interested parties. I became good enough at it that I made a name for myself. The Snake, they called me, because I fucked over so many people. And Sandriel eventually heard about me and recruited me for her triarii—to be her spy-master and tracker. The Snake became the Helhound, but . . . I kept a few touches."

The memory of Baxian's reptilian armor flashed through Hunt's mind.

"I hated it, hated Sandriel, hated Lidia, who I always thought could see through me, but . . . what else was I going to do with myself?" Baxian finished with all the pallets and faced Hunt. "Serving in Sandriel's triarii was better than living in the slums, always looking over my shoulder for whoever wanted to knife me. But the shit she had us do . . ." He tapped his neck, the scar Hunt had given him. "I deserved this."

"We all did fucked-up shit for Sandriel," Hunt said roughly.

"Yeah, but you didn't have a choice. I did."

"You chose to turn away from it, to mitigate the damage when you could."

"Thanks to Danika," Baxian said.

"What better excuse than love?" Hunt asked.

Baxian smiled sadly. "I told her everything, you know. Danika, I mean. And she understood—she didn't judge. She told me she had a half-human, half-Fae friend who had faced similar troubles. I think her love for Bryce allowed her to see past all my shit and still love me."

Hunt smiled. "You should tell Bryce that."

Baxian eyed him. "You guys . . . ah, you guys okay? Things seemed kind of rough for a while, down in the caves."

"Yeah," Hunt said, letting out a long breath. "Yeah, we are. We talked."

"And the Hel stuff . . ." Bryce had filled everyone in about what the Princes of Hel had claimed about Hunt's origins. "You doing okay with that?"

Hunt considered. "It seems secondary to everything else that's going on, you know? Poor me, with my daddy issues. Daddies? I don't even know."

Baxian huffed a laugh. "Does it matter? Your exact genetic makeup?"

Hunt considered again. "No. That's just stuff in my blood, my magic. It's not who I am." He shrugged. "That's what Bryce says, anyway. I'm working on believing it."

Baxian nodded to the halo on Hunt's brow. "So how come you haven't taken it off yet? They claimed you've had the power all along."

Hunt glanced toward the raftered ceiling. "I will," he hedged.

Baxian gave Hunt a look that said he saw right through him. That right now, Hunt needed a breather. Just some time to process everything. He wanted to be free of the halo, but to go full Prince of Hel or whatever . . . he wasn't ready for that. Not yet.

But Baxian said, "Bryce is right, though. Who you are isn't about what's biologically in your system. It's about who raised you. Who you are now."

Hunt's mother's face flashed before his eyes, and he fixed the memory of her close to his heart. "Have you and Bryce been exchanging notes on how to give me a pep talk?"

Baxian laughed, then glanced around. "Where is she, anyway? Off making more gardens?"

Hunt laughed quietly. "Probably. But I came here to find you—we're having a council of war in a minute, but I wanted to ask you something first."

Baxian crossed his powerful arms, giving Hunt his full attention. "What?"

"Some shit's going down soon. I need someone to run things if I'm not around."

"And where would you be?"

"You'll hear about everything from Bryce," Hunt said, holding his stare. "But I need a second in command right now."

Baxian raised his brows. For a moment, Hunt was in a war tent again, giving orders to his soldiers before battle. He shook off the chill of the memory and folded his wings.

Baxian smirked, though. "Who said you're in charge?"

Hunt rolled his eyes. "My wife, that's who." But he pressed, "So . . . will you? I need someone who can fight. On the ground and in the air."

"Oh, you're only asking because I have wings?" Baxian ruffled his black feathers for emphasis.

"I'm asking," Hunt said, noting the spark of amusement on the Helhound's face, "because I trust you, asshole. For some weird reason."

"Asteri dungeon bonding at its finest." The tone was light, though the shadows of all they'd been through darkened Baxian's eyes. "But I'm honored. Yeah—you can trust me. Tell me what needs to get done and I'll do it."

"Thanks," Hunt said, and motioned to the exit. "You might regret that in a few minutes . . . but thanks."

"Let me get this straight," Ruhn said. They had all gathered around a campfire in the middle of an open plain—about the only privacy they could find from spying ears. Just for the Hel of it, Flynn had grown a small grove of oak trees around them. His earth-based magic seemed to be exploding here now, as if the reborn land were calling to him to fill it, adorn it.

But Ruhn fixed his stare on his sister as he said, "We're going to *Nena*. To open the *Northern Rift*."

Bryce, seated on a large stone with Hunt beside her, said, "*I* am going to Nena. With Hunt. And my parents—I need Randall's particular brand of expertise. Baxian will stay here with Cooper until they get back. *You* are going to take those two buzzards"—she nodded to Flynn and Declan, who glared at her—"and go back to Lunathion."

Ruhn blinked slowly. "To . . . die? Because that's what will happen if we're caught."

"To find Isaiah and Naomi. See if they can come join us. Their phones and emails are no doubt tapped—we don't have any other way to contact them."

"You want us to go convince two members of Celestina's triarii to go rogue?" Dec said.

Hunt said, "They won't need much convincing, but yes. We need them."

Ruhn shook his head. "If you're thinking of rallying some sort of angelic host to take on the Asteri, forget it. No angel is going to follow any of us—even Athalar—into battle."

Bryce held her ground. This was her plan, and there'd be no shaking her or Athalar from it, Ruhn knew. He opened his mouth to keep arguing anyway, but Dec cut him off.

"What about him?" Dec asked, pointing to Baxian. "He's got a better in with the angels."

Bryce shook her head. "Baxian will stay here to help coordinate the arriving refugees, and lead in our stead." Bryce gestured to herself and Hunt.

"We could do that," Flynn said.

"No," Bryce said coolly. "You can't. The Fae are more scared of him, so he'll be the most effective."

"Says who?" Flynn demanded. "We're plenty scary."

"Says the fact that he, at least, was able to get us the stables to sleep in," Hunt growled. Baxian waggled his eyebrows at the Fae lord. "The rest of you struck out completely."

Flynn and Dec scowled. But Ruhn's breath caught as Bryce looked to Lidia. "I'm not going to presume to give you orders. I know you have an obligation to the Ocean Queen. Do what you must."

"I go with Ruhn," Lidia said quietly, and something in his chest sparked at that.

Bryce just nodded, and he didn't miss the gratitude in his sister's eyes.

"And me?" Tharion asked at last, brows high.

"I need you to go back to the River Queen," Bryce said softly. "And convince her to shelter as many people Beneath as possible."

Tharion paled. "Legs, I'd love to do that, but she'll kill me."

"Then find some way to convince her not to," Athalar said, nothing but pure general as he fixed his stare on the mer. "Use those Captain Whatever skills and figure out something she wants more than killing you."

Tharion glanced to Sathia, who was watching attentively. "She, uh . . . won't be pleased by my new marital status."

"Then find something," Hunt said again, "to please her."

Tharion's jaw clenched, but Ruhn could see him thinking through his options.

"The Blue Court was the only faction in Crescent City that sheltered people during the attack this spring," Bryce said. "You guys went out of your way to help innocents get to safety. Appeal to that side of the River Queen. Tell her a storm is coming, and that after what went down in Asphodel Meadows, we need her to take in as many people as the Blue Court can accommodate. If there's anyone who's got the charm to sway her, it's you, Tharion."

"Ah, Legs," Tharion said, rubbing his face. "How can I resist when you ask like that?"

Sathia, to Ruhn's surprise, laid a hand on the mer's knee and promised Bryce, "We'll both go."

"Then she'll definitely kill Tharion," Flynn said.

Sathia glared at her brother. "I know a thing or two about dealing with arrogant rulers." Her chin lifted. "I'm not afraid of the River Queen." Tharion looked like he might warn her against that, but kept his mouth shut.

"Good," Bryce said to Sathia. "And thank you."

"So that's it, then," Ruhn said. "Come dawn, we're scattering to the winds?"

"Come dawn," Bryce said, and her chest flared with starlight that lit up the entire countryside, "we're retaliating."

Ruhn was still mulling it over—what Bryce wanted to do. Opening the Northern Rift to *Hel*. She had to be insane . . . yet he trusted her. And Athalar. They surely had some other sneaky-ass shit up their sleeves, but they'd reveal it when the time was right.

Ruhn tossed and turned on his crunchy, spiky pallet of hay, unable to sleep. Perhaps that was because Lidia lay across from him, staring up at the raftered ceiling.

Her eyes slid over to his, and Ruhn said into her mind, *Can't sleep?*

I'm thinking about all the Ophion agents I encountered over the years. I never knew them in person, but the people who helped me organize the strike on the Spine, and worked with me for years before that . . . they're all gone now.

It wasn't your fault.

Asphodel Meadows was aimed at your sister. But butchering Ophion, the people in the camps . . . that was to punish me. Ophion aided me in your escape, and Rigelus wanted revenge.

Ruhn's heart ached. *We'll make the Asteri pay for it.*

She turned on her side, looking at him full in the face. Gods, she was beautiful.

How are you feeling? Her question was gentle. *After . . . what happened with your father.*

I don't know, Ruhn said. *It felt right in the moment, felt good, even. But now . . .* He shook his head. *I keep thinking about my mother, of all people. And what she'll say. She might be the only person who'll mourn him.*

She loved him?

She was attached to him, even if he treated her as little more than a broodmare. But he kept her in comfort all these years, as a reward for birthing him a son. She was always grateful for that.

Lidia reached a hand across the narrow space between them and found his own—his fingers still strangely pale and uncalloused. But her skin was so soft and warm, the bones beneath so strong. *You'll find a way to live with what you did to your father. I did.*

Ruhn lifted a brow. *You . . . ?*

I killed him, yes. The words were frank, yet weary.

Why?

Because he was a monster—to me, and to so many others. I made it look like a rebel attack. Told Ophion to get their mech-suits and be waiting for him when his car drove through a mountain pass on its way to a meeting with me. They left a flattened vehicle and a corpse in their wake. Then burned the whole thing.

Ruhn blinked. *Beheading my father seems like it was much . . . faster.*

It certainly was. Her eyes held nothing but cold anger. *I told the Ophion agents in the mech-suits to take their time squashing him in his car. They did.*

Cthona, Lidia.

But I, too, wondered, about my mother after that, she said quietly. *About Hecuba. Wondered what the Queen of the Valbaran Witches made of her ex-lover's death. If she thought of me. If she had any interest, any at all, in reaching out to me after he died. But I never heard from her. Not once.*

I'm sorry, he offered, and squeezed her hand. After a beat he asked, *So you're really not going back to the Ocean Queen?*

No. Not as her spy. I meant every word earlier. I serve no one.

Is it weird to say I'm proud of you? Because I am.

She huffed a laugh and interlaced their fingers, her thumb stroking over the back of his hand. *I see you, Ruhn,* she said gently. *All of you.*

The words were a gift. His chest tightened. He couldn't stop himself from leaning across the space and quietly, so no one around them might hear, pressing his mouth to hers.

The kiss was gentle, near silent. He pulled away after a heartbeat, but her free hand slid to his cheek. Her eyes glowed golden, even in the moonlit dimness of the stables. *When we're not sleeping in a stable surrounded by people,* she said, mind-voice low—a purr that curled around his cock and gripped tight—*I want to touch you.*

His cock hardened at that, aching. He shut his eyes, fighting it, but her lips brushed his, silently teasing.

I want to ride you, she whispered into his mind, and slipped her hand from his to palm him through his pants. Ruhn bit down on his lower lip to keep from groaning. Her fingers slid down the length of him. *I want this inside of me.* She dug the heel of her palm along him, and he stifled a moan. *I want* you *inside of me.*

Fuck yeah was all he could manage to say, to think.

Her laughter echoed in his mind, and her lips slid from his to find the spot beneath his ear. Her teeth grazed over his too-hot skin, and he writhed against the hand she still had on him, the crackling hay so gods-damned loud—

"Please don't fuck right next to us," Flynn muttered from a few feet away.

"Ugh," Bryce called from across the stables. "Really?"

Ruhn squeezed his eyes shut, fighting his arousal.

But Lidia laughed quietly. "Sorry."

"Pervs," Declan muttered, hay crinkling as he turned over.

Ruhn looked back to Lidia and saw her smiling, delight and mischief brightening her face.

And damn if it wasn't the most beautiful thing he'd ever seen.

68

You're hovering."

"Sorry, sorry." Ithan paced the morgue that Hypaxia had swiftly converted into a lab. "I just don't know what to *do* with myself while you're working on all that science stuff."

Hunched over the desk, Hypaxia was setting up the things she'd need to begin her experiments.

She said idly, without lifting her head, "I could use a sample of the parasite."

He halted. "How?" He answered his own question. "Oh. A glass of water." He glanced to the sink. "You think there are tons of them swimming around?"

"I doubt it's that obvious, considering how many scientists and medwitches have studied our water over the years. But it must be in there somewhere, if we're all infected."

Ithan sighed and walked over to the sink, grabbing a mug that said *Korinth University College of Mortuary Science.* He filled it with water and plunked it down beside Hypaxia. "There. The Istros's finest."

"That mug could be contaminated," Hypaxia said, using a ruler to sketch out a grid on a piece of paper. "We need a sterile container first. And samples from several different water sources."

"Did I mention that I hate science?"

"Well, I love it," Hypaxia said, still without looking up. "There are sterile cups in the cabinet along the back wall. Get multiple samples from this tap, from the Istros itself, and one from a bottle of store-bought water. We'll need a wider sample base, but that'll do for the initial phases." Ithan gathered a bunch of the sterile containers and headed for the door.

He was a glorified water boy. He'd never hear the end of it from his sunball buddies. That is, if he ever talked to them again.

But Ithan said nothing before slipping out, and Hypaxia didn't call after him.

Ithan bottled and labeled the various samples, gave Hypaxia a few vials of his blood as a base for an infected person, and then she sent him back out for *more* water samples from different sources. The dining hall, a nearby restaurant, and—best of all—the sewers.

He was on his way back through the dark door of the House of Flame and Shadow when the hair on the back of his neck rose. He knew that eerie, unsettled feeling. He whirled—

It wasn't Sigrid. A different female Reaper, veiled head to toe in black, glided smoothly over the quay. People outright fled—the street behind her was wholly empty.

But she continued toward the door, where Ithan stood frozen. He had no option, really, but to hold the door open for her.

The Reaper drifted by, black veils billowing. Acid-green eyes gleamed beneath the dark fabric over her face, and her rasping voice turned his bowels watery as she said, "Thank you," and continued into the stairwell.

Ithan waited five whole minutes before following. She had no scent at all. Not even the reek of a corpse. As if she'd ceased to exist in any earthly way. It drove his wolf nuts.

But—

Ithan sniffed the air of the stairwell again as he descended toward the lowest levels of the House and the morgue-lab. As he slipped into the lab and shut the door behind him, he asked, "What happens to the parasite when we die?"

Hypaxia finally looked up from her papers and vials and forms. "What?"

"I just saw a Reaper," he said. "They're dead. Well, they died. So do they still have the parasite? They don't eat or drink, so they couldn't be reinfected, right? But does the parasite disappear when we die? Does it die, too?"

Hypaxia blinked slowly. "That's an interesting question. And if the parasite does indeed die when the host does, then Reapers might provide a way to locate the parasite simply by the lack of it in their own bodies."

"Why do I feel like you're going to ask me to—"

"I need you to get me a Reaper."

Dawn broke, purple and golden, over the islands of Avallen. But Bryce only had eyes for the helicopter making its descent onto the grassy, blooming field before the ruins of Morven's castle. She smiled grimly.

The roar was deafening to her Fae ears, but she had insisted on being here. On seeing this: Fury waving from the pilot's seat, June waving frantically from beside her.

Bryce waved back, her throat tight to the point of pain, and then the side door to the helicopter slid open, and a yip cut through the air.

There was no stopping Syrinx as he bounded off the helicopter and raced for her through the high grasses. She dropped to her knees to hug him, kiss him, let him lick all over her face as he wiggled his little lion's tail and yowled with joy.

Boots crunched in the grass, and Randall was walking toward her, a pack on his back and a rifle slung over his shoulder. His eyes were bright as he beheld her, and he clapped the tall boy at his side—Emile, now Cooper—on the shoulder.

And Bryce couldn't stop her laugh of pure joy as her mother leapt out of the helicopter behind them, took one look at Bryce kneeling in the meadow, and said, "Bryce Adelaide Quinlan, what's all this talk about you jumping around between worlds?"

69

Ithan knew he'd have no luck convincing a Reaper on his own. At least without risking getting his soul sucked out and eaten. But fortunately, there were plenty of Reapers who would answer Jesiba Roga's summons. Unfortunately, one arrived at the morgue within an hour of Jesiba's request to the Under-King.

Ithan kept reminding himself of every exit, of his strength, of where the knife in his boot was, of how quickly he could summon claws or shift—

The male Reaper was relatively fresh, judging by the way he'd strutted—only a hint of a glide—into the morgue. This one seemed inclined to play rock star, with his torn black jeans dangling precariously off his prominent hip bones and an array of tattoos scattered over his unnervingly pale torso. No shirt to be seen. He'd bothered with ass-kicking black boots, left partially untied at the tops, and he'd strapped twin black leather bracelets at his wrists.

Gods, Bryce would have had a field day with this guy—his long golden hair was *very* carefully mussed. That is, until she beheld the acid-green eyes, and the throat that revealed precisely where his death blow had been. The wound had sealed over, but the scars remained.

"Thank you for coming," Hypaxia said, standing beside the

examination table with queenly grace. "This will only take a few moments."

The Reaper glanced between her and Ithan, but sauntered over to the table, hopping on with a thud that set the metal shuddering. "Heard you defected, witchy-witch." His voice was a hoarse, wicked rasp. It might have been dismissed as a result of the death wound to his throat, but it was typical of a Reaper. Exactly how Sigrid's voice had sounded—

"Welcome to the House," the Reaper continued, bluish lips quirking up in a sneer. He nodded to Ithan. "What's a wolf pup doing here?"

Ithan mastered his primal fear of the creature before them and crossed his arms. "What's it to you?"

"You're Holstrom, right?" That sneer didn't fade. If this shithead said anything about Connor—

"I was in the Aux," the Reaper said, tapping one of his tattoos. "Lion-shifter pack."

Oh shit. Ithan had heard of this guy. A low-level lion who'd shown up with his pack a few months ago on a routine Aux inspection of a vampyr nest in the Meat Market. The wounds on his neck corresponded with what the vamps had done to the guy. But to have chosen to become a Reaper, in the same House as the ones who'd killed him . . .

From the gleam in the Reaper's eyes, Ithan couldn't help but wonder if he had turned Reaper not to elude true death, but to one day exact vengeance.

Hypaxia approached the Reaper and said, "May I touch your head?"

The Reaper kept his eyes on the former queen. "Touch me all you want, sweetheart."

For fuck's sake. Ithan suppressed a growl, but Hypaxia remained unruffled as she placed her brown hands on his shining golden hair.

Ithan refrained from reaching for the knife in his boot as the Reaper inhaled deeply. Getting a whiff of her scent? Or preparing to eat her spirit? "Your soul smells like rain clouds and mountain berries." The creep licked his lips. "Anyone ever tell you that?"

How Hypaxia kept her hands on his head, Ithan had no idea. He was half inclined to rip the shithead's arms out of their sockets and use them to beat the guy senseless.

The Reaper inhaled again. "A little bit of witch, a little bit of necromancer, huh?"

"She needs to concentrate," Ithan said through his teeth.

The Reaper slid those acid-green eyes over to him. He asked Hypaxia, "Am I distracting you, honey?"

She didn't answer. The expression on her face was distant as she focused on what lay within the Reaper's mind.

The Reaper inhaled deeply again, his eyes rolling back in his head. "Gods, your scent's like fucking *wine*—"

"We're done, thank you," Hypaxia said politely, stepping back and making notes on the papers stacked on her desk. "Please give my regards to your master."

The Reaper stared at her for a long moment, practically feral. Ithan barely breathed, ready to pounce, even though this lowlife was unkillable—

"I'll see you around," the Reaper said, more of a promise than a parting, and hopped off the table. He strutted again for the doors, this time with a bit of that Reaper's floating gait, as if trying to show off for the witch.

Only when he left did Ithan let out a long breath. "What a fucking creep."

Hypaxia leaned against the examination table. "Your guess was right, though. He didn't have the parasite." She crossed her arms. "I didn't sense anything like one, anyway. I didn't sense anything living inside him at all."

"So what now?"

"I compare what I detected in him to what I discovered in your blood. See what stands out. See if I can isolate where in *you* the parasite lies."

Good. At least he'd contributed that much.

"How could you stand it?" Ithan asked, unable to contain his curiosity. "Being that close to him?"

"I've had to endure plenty of uncomfortable situations and difficult people in my life," Hypaxia said, pushing off the table and walking to the computer. She clicked the monitor on. "A lonely, scared Reaper, new to the afterlife, doesn't bother me."

"Lonely? Scared?" Ithan choked on a laugh.

But Hypaxia glanced over a shoulder, her face unreadable. "You couldn't see it? What lay beneath the bravado? His clothes and attitude show how desperately he's trying to cling to his mortal life. He's frightened out of his mind."

"You pity him."

"Yes." She turned back to her computer. "I pity him, and all Reapers."

Sigrid included, no doubt. Guilt tightened his chest, but Ithan said, "Most half-lifes seem to enjoy terrorizing the rest of us."

"They might, but their existence is what their name implies: It is half a life. Not true living. It seems sad to me."

Ithan considered. "You're . . . you're a really good person." She chuckled. "I mean it," he insisted. "The witches are worse off without you."

She glanced over a shoulder again, and this time her eyes were full of sorrow. "Thank you." She nodded to the door. "I need to focus for a while. Without your, ah . . . hovering."

He saluted her. "Message received. I'll be down the hall if you need me."

"Queen of all this, huh?"

Bryce didn't stop sorting through the trunks of supplies Fury had brought on the helicopter, even though her friend's question came with a shit-eating grin.

"Did you get the goggles?" Bryce asked, pushing past a layer of winter hats. All the snow gear was there, just as she'd requested. On short notice, Fury had pieced together a remarkable array of jackets, pants, hats, gloves, underlayers—everything they'd need to survive the subzero temperatures of Nena.

Bryce intended to leave Avallen as soon as her parents had a rest from the helicopter journey—as soon as they were able to get Cooper settled with Baxian, and process all she'd told them upon their arrival.

Her parents sat in the grass on the other side of the field, talking quietly, Syrinx lounging in Randall's lap. So Bryce gave them space, using the time to check the gear Fury had brought—not that she didn't trust Fury to have thought of every detail.

But she should check, anyway. Just to make sure that they had all the gear they might need. So many things could go wrong, and she was taking her human parents with her, she was really going to do this—

A slender brown hand touched Bryce's wrist. "B—you okay?"

Bryce looked up at last, finding Juniper standing beside her, a deep frown on her beautiful face. A few feet away, Fury stood with crossed arms, brows high.

Bryce sighed, turning from the three massive trunks that would be loaded onto the helicopter looming behind them.

Her friends were safe here. It should have eased something in her chest—a gift from Urd, Hunt had claimed—but seeing them here . . .

There was a fourth trunk, resting in the grass close to the helicopter. Fury had only been able to gather so much before the quick takeoff from Valbara, but still . . . there were a considerable number of weapons here.

Handguns. Rifles. Knives.

A joke, really, considering that they were going up against six intergalactic, nearly all-powerful beings. Most of the weapons would be for the others—to buy them any shot at surviving.

Everything else would come down to her.

Fury and Juniper were watching. Waiting. Like they could see all of that on her face. Just as Juniper, that bleak winter, had sensed from Bryce's tone alone that despair had pushed her to the brink.

Juniper—whose last audiomail to Bryce had been so angry, after Bryce had done such an unforgivable thing by calling the director of the Crescent City Ballet. Only love and relief showed on her face now.

Juniper silently opened her arms, and Bryce rushed into them.

Her throat closed up, eyes stinging, at her friend's warmth, her scent. Fury's scent and arms wrapped around them a moment later, and Bryce shut her eyes, savoring it.

"I'm so sorry you both got dragged into this," Bryce said hoarsely. "June, I'm sorry for all of it. I'm so fucking sorry."

Juniper's arms tightened around her. "We've got bigger problems to face—you and I are good."

Bryce pulled back, glancing between her two friends. She'd updated them, and her parents—Cooper in tow—about as much as she could.

Fury frowned. "I should be coming with you guys. I'm of more use in the field."

Bryce would have given anything to have someone as talented as Fury watching her back. But this wasn't about Bryce's own safety, her own comfort.

"You're precisely where you should be," Bryce insisted. "When people hear that Fury Axtar's guarding Avallen, they'll think twice before fucking with this place."

Fury rolled her eyes. "Babysitting."

Bryce shook her head. "It's not. I need you guys here—helping any of the people who can make it. Helping Baxian."

"Yeah, yeah," Fury said, jerking her chin toward the rest of their friends, standing on the other side of the helicopter. "I'll admit, I'm looking forward to grilling Baxian about him and Danika."

They stared toward the handsome male, who must have sensed their attention and turned from where he'd been talking to Tharion and Ruhn. Baxian winced.

Juniper laughed. "We won't bite!" she called to the Helhound.

"Liar," Fury muttered, earning another laugh from Juniper.

Baxian wisely went back to his conversation. Though Bryce didn't fail to notice how Tharion poked the angel shifter in the side, grinning.

"I can't believe she never told us about him," Juniper said quietly, sadly.

"Danika didn't tell us a lot of stuff," Bryce said with equal softness.

"Neither did you," Fury teased, nudging Bryce with an elbow. "And again: Queen of Avallen?"

Bryce rolled her eyes. "If you want the job, it's yours."

"Oh, not for all the gold in the world," Fury said, dark eyes dancing with amusement. "This is your shitshow to run."

Juniper scowled at her girlfriend. "What Fury means is that we have your back."

Bryce kissed June's velvet-soft cheek. "Thanks." She looked between her friends again. "If we don't make it back . . ."

"Don't think like that, B," Juniper insisted, but Fury said nothing.

Fury had dealt in the shadows of the empire for years. She was well aware of the odds.

Bryce went on, "If I don't make it back, you'll be safe here. The mists will allow any true refugee through—but I'd still keep an eye out for any Asteri agents. There are plenty of natural resources to sustain everyone, and yeah, there's no firstlight to fuel your tech, but—"

Juniper laid a hand on Bryce's wrist again. "We got this, B. You go do . . . what you need to do."

"Save the world," Fury said, chuckling.

Bryce grimaced. "Yeah. Basically."

"We got this," Juniper repeated, hand tightening on Bryce's wrist. "And so do you, Bryce."

Bryce took out her phone. Popped it free of the case, revealing the photograph she'd tucked in there of them. Of how it had been when there were four. "Keep this for me," she said, handing it to Fury. "I don't want to lose it."

Fury studied the photo—how happy they'd all been, how

seemingly young. She folded Bryce's fingers around the photo. "Take it." Fury's eyes shone bright. "So we'll all be with you."

Bryce's throat tightened again, but she slid the photo into the back pocket of her jeans. And allowed herself to look at June and Fury one last time, to memorize every line of their faces.

Friends worth fighting for. Worth dying for.

Ember Quinlan was waiting on the hill where Bryce and her friends had risen from beneath the Cave of Princes.

Ember peered at the grassy ground, face tight. No trace of the caves remained. "So his body is just . . . under there."

Bryce nodded. She knew who her mother meant. "Ruhn decapitated him and, um, impaled his head before the ground swallowed him. There's no chance of him coming back."

Ember didn't smile as she stared at the earth, the Autumn King's corpse far beneath it.

"I spent so long running from him, fearing him. To imagine a world where he doesn't exist . . ." Her mom lifted her eyes to Bryce's face, and at the pain and relief in them, Bryce threw her arms around her and held tight.

"I'm so proud of you," Ember whispered. "Not for . . . dealing with him, but for all of it. I'm so, so proud, Bryce."

Bryce couldn't stop the stinging in her eyes. "I could only do it because I was raised by a badass mom."

Ember chuckled, pulling back to clasp Bryce's face in both hands. "You look different."

"Good different or bad different?"

"Good. Like a functioning adult."

Bryce smiled. "Thanks, Mom."

Ember wrapped her arms around Bryce and squeezed. "But it doesn't matter if you're Queen of the Fae or the Universe or whatever crap . . ." Bryce laughed at that, but Ember said, "You'll always be my sweet baby."

Bryce hugged her mother tightly, all thoughts of the hateful male lying dead far below them fading away.

In the distance, the helicopter started roaring again, this time piloted by Randall, thanks to his compulsory years in the peregrini army. All humans were forced to serve. The skills he'd learned during those years remained useful, especially now, but Bryce knew the experience weighed on his soul.

Bryce looked up at last from her mother's embrace and saw Hunt motioning for them to get on board—obnoxiously tapping his wrist, as if to say, *Time is of the essence, Quinlan!*

Bryce scowled, knowing that with his angel-sharp eyes he could see it from this distance, but she held her mom for another moment. Breathed in her mom's smell, so familiar and calming. Like home.

Ember hugged her back, content to be there—to hold her daughter for one moment longer.

This was what really mattered in the end.

70

Ithan was thoroughly sick of playing bodyguard, even from a floor below. While Hypaxia had been comparing what she'd observed in the Reaper to the water samples and Ithan's own blood, he'd been packing up artifacts in Jesiba's office. And glancing at the door every other minute as if Hypaxia would burst in and declare that she'd developed an antidote to the parasite. She never did.

When he entered the morgue, he found Hypaxia at the desk, head in her hands. Vials of all sizes and shapes littered the metal surface beside her.

Ithan dared to lay a hand on her shoulder. "Don't give up. You're exhausted—you've been working for hours. You'll find a cure."

"I already found it."

It took him a moment to process what she'd said. "You . . . Really?"

Her head bobbed, and she nudged a vial of clear liquid with a fingertip. "It went faster than I had even dared to hope. I was able to use the synth antidote as a template. Synth and the parasite have magic-altering properties in common—I'll spare you the details. With the changes I made, though, I think this will isolate the parasite and kill it the same way the synth antidote worked." She pointed at more small vials on a low table behind her. "I made as much as I could. But . . ."

"But?" He could barely breathe.

She sighed. "But it's far from perfect. I had to use Athalar's lightning to bind it together. I had to use all of it, I'm afraid."

She motioned to her desk, where six quartz crystals now lay. Dormant. Empty.

His heart twisted. "It's okay." Sigrid would remain a Reaper for the time being, but he wouldn't give up on trying to help her.

"Athalar's lightning holds it together, but not permanently," Hypaxia went on. "The antidote is highly unstable—a little jostling, and it might go completely stale. If I had more time, I might find a way to stabilize it, but for right now . . ."

He squeezed her shoulder. "Just tell me."

Her mouth twisted to the side before she said, "The antidote's not a permanent fix. Its effect will wear off—and since the water of Midgard is still contaminated with the parasite, we will be reinfected as soon as it does."

"How long will a dose work?"

"I don't know. A few weeks? Months? Longer than a few days, I think, but I'll need to keep refining it. Find some way to make it permanent."

"But it'll work for now?"

"In theory. So long as Athalar's lightning binds it together. But I haven't gathered the nerve to test it on myself. To see if it works and is safe, but also . . . to find out who I might be without this thing feeding on me." She raised her head and met his stare, her face bleak and exhausted. "If we remove this parasite, what will it accomplish? What will *you* do with the extra power?"

"I'll help my friends, for whatever good it'll do."

"And the wolves?"

"What about them?"

"If you get more power, it could put you beyond Sabine's abilities. Make you strong enough that you could challenge her." She looked at him seriously. "You might be able to end Sabine's tyranny, Ithan."

"I . . ." He couldn't find the right words. "I didn't really think about what we'd do next."

She wasn't impressed. "You need to. All of us do."

He stiffened. "I'm not a planner. I'm a sunball player, for fuck's sake—"

"You *were* a sunball player," she said. "And I suspect you haven't thought about the implications of having the most power among the wolves because you're avoiding thinking about what you really want."

He glared at her. "And what is that?"

"You want Sabine gone. No one but you is going to come along and do it."

He felt sick. "I don't want to lead anyone."

She gave him a look, as if seeing through him. But she said, with a disappointment that cut right to his heart, "All this arguing's of no use. We don't even know if the antidote works." She eyed the vial.

She would do it, he knew. She'd try it, risk herself—

Ithan didn't broadcast his moves before he snatched up the vial. Before he lifted it to his mouth and swallowed.

Hypaxia whirled toward him, eyes wide with apprehension—

Then there was only black.

There was his body . . . and more than his body.

His wolf, and him, and power, like he could leap between entire continents in one bound—

Ithan's eyes flew open. Had the world always been so sharp, so clear? Had the morgue smelled so strongly of antiseptic? Was there a body rotting away in one of the boxes? When had *that* arrived? Or had it been lying there all along?

And that smell, of lavender and eucalyptus . . .

Hypaxia was kneeling over him, breathing hard. "Ithan—"

A blink, and a flash, and he shifted. She staggered back at the wolf that appeared, faster than he'd ever changed before.

Another blink and flash, and he was back in his humanoid body.

As easy as breathing. Fast as the wind. Something was different, something was . . .

His blood howled toward an unseen moon. His fingers curled on the floor as he sat up, claws scraping.

"Ithan?" The witch's voice was a whisper.

"It worked." The words echoed through the room, the world. "It's gone—I can tell."

Somehow, a barrier had been removed. One that had ordered him to stand down, to obey . . . It was nothing but ashes now. Only dominance remained. Untethered.

But filling the void of that barrier with a rising, raging force—

Ithan held out his hand and willed the *thing* under his skin to come forward. Ice and snow appeared in his palm. They did not melt against his skin.

He could fucking summon *snow*. The magic sang in him, an old and strange melody.

Wolves didn't have magic like this. Never had, as far as he'd heard. Shifting and strength, yes, but this elemental power . . . it shouldn't exist in a wolf, yet there it was. Rising in him, filling the place where he'd never realized the parasite had existed.

Ithan said roughly, "We need to get this to our friends."

Hypaxia smiled grimly. "What are you going to do?"

Ithan eyed the door to the hall. "I think it's time for me to start making some plans."

"Only my daughter would drag us up to Nena," Ember groused, shivering against the cold that stole even Hunt's breath away. "You couldn't have done this in, oh, I don't know, the Coronal Islands?"

"The Northern Rift, Mom," Bryce said through chattering teeth, "is in the *north*."

"There's a southern one," Ember muttered.

"It's even colder down there," Bryce said, and looked to Hunt and Randall for help.

Hunt chuckled despite the frigid temperatures and howling wind that had hit them from the moment they'd stepped out of the helicopter.

They could fly no further. The massive black wall stretched for miles in either direction before curving northward, with wards protecting the airspace above it. Hunt knew from maps that the area the wall encircled was forty-nine miles in diameter—seven times seven, the holiest of numbers—and that at its center, somewhere in the barren, snow-blasted terrain, lay the Northern Rift, shrouded in mist. Barriers upon barriers protected Midgard from the Rift, and Hel beyond it.

"We better get going," Randall said, nodding to the lead doors in the wall before them.

"There aren't any sentries," Hunt observed, falling into step beside the male, grateful for the snow gear Axtar had somehow procured for all of them. "There should be at least fifteen here."

"Maybe they bailed because it was too fucking cold," Bryce said, shivering miserably.

"An angelic guard never *bails,*" Randall said, tugging the faux-fur-lined hood of his parka further over his face. "If they're not here . . . it's not a good sign."

Hunt nodded to the rifle in Randall's gloved hands. "That work in these temperatures?"

"It'd better," Ember grumbled.

But Hunt caught Bryce's look, and summoned his lightning to the ready. He knew her starfire was already warming beneath her gloves. With Theia's power now united within her . . . he couldn't decide if he was eager to see what that starfire could do, or dreading it.

"Is it a trap?" Ember said as they approached the towering, sealed gates and abandoned guard post.

Hunt peered into the frosted window of the booth, then yanked open the door. The ice was crusted so thickly he had to use a considerable amount of strength to pry it free. A swift examination of the interior revealed rime coating the controls, the chairs, the water station. "No one's been here for a while."

"I don't like this," Ember said. "It's too easy."

Hunt glanced to Bryce, her eyes teary with cold, the tip of her nose bright red. In these temperatures, they wouldn't last ten more minutes before frostbite set in. He and his mate would recover, but Ember and Randall, with their human blood . . .

"Let's get this booth warmed up," Bryce said. She stepped inside and began brushing frost off the switches. "Maybe the heater still works."

Ember gave her daughter a look that said she was well aware Bryce and Hunt had avoided addressing her concerns, but stepped inside as well.

They got the heater working—just one of them. The others were too frosted over to sputter to life. But it was enough to warm the small space and offer her parents a sliver of shelter as Bryce and Hunt again explored the frigid terrain, studying the wall and its gate.

"You think it's a trap?" Bryce said through the scarf she'd tugged up over her mouth and nose. She'd found some pairs of snow goggles in the booth, and the world was sharp through the stark clarity of the lenses. Was this how it had looked through Hunt's Umbra Mortis helmet?

Hunt said, wearing polarized goggles of his own, "I've never known the guard station at the Northern Rift to be empty, so . . . something's up, for sure."

"Maybe Apollion did us a favor and sent a few deathstalkers to clear it out." As she spoke the demon prince's name, the wind seemed to quiet. "Well, that's not spooky at all."

"This far north," Hunt said, turning in place to survey the terrain, "maybe all those bullshit warnings about not speaking his name on this side of the Rift are true."

Bryce didn't dare test it out again. But she walked to the lead gates in the wall and laid a gloved hand on them. "I heard the wall and the gates both had white salt built into them." For protection against Hel.

"Hasn't stopped the demons from slipping through," Hunt noted, face unreadable with the goggles and his own scarf over his mouth. "I hunted down enough of them to know how fallible the wall is. And the guards, I suppose."

"I hate to imagine what's been getting past *without* guards here." Hunt said nothing, which wasn't remotely comforting. "So how do we get through?" Bryce asked.

"There's a button inside the booth," Hunt said. "Nothing fancy."

Bryce nudged him. "Easy-peasy, for once." A blast of icy wind slammed into her back, as if throwing her toward the wall. Even with the layers of winter gear, she could have sworn the cold bit her very bones.

"We should go before we lose the light." Hunt nodded at the sun already sinking toward the horizon. "Daylight's only a few hours up here."

"Bryce?" her dad called from the booth. "You guys need to see this."

They found Ember and Randall in front of a flickering monitor.

"The security footage." Ember pointed with a shaking gloved finger. Bryce knew the trembling wasn't from cold. Her mom hit a key on the computer and the footage began rolling.

"Is that . . . ," Bryce breathed.

"We need to get to the Rift," Hunt growled. *"Now."*

71

You set foot in that Den without an invitation from the Prime or Sabine and you're dead, pup."

"I know," Ithan said, packing yet another crate for Jesiba. The task was stupidly mundane given all the shit that was going down. But when he'd burst into the office moments ago to tell her the good news, Jesiba had refused to speak to him until he *earned his keep* for a few minutes. So here he was, packing and talking at the same time. "But if Hypaxia and I are heading off to the Eternal City, we might . . . die." He choked on the word. "I want them to know the truth."

"And what truth is that?"

Ithan straightened from where he'd been bent over the crate. "The truth of what I did to Sigrid. That Sigrid exists, I guess, even if she is a Reaper. That—"

"So it's about you easing your guilty conscience."

Ithan cut her a look. "I want them to know what happened. That yeah, Sigrid is a Reaper, and I totally failed at trying to undo that, but . . . they do technically have an alternative to Sabine—even if it's a half-life. It'd be radical and unheard of to accept a Reaper as Prime, but stranger things have happened, right?"

Jesiba began typing away on her computer. "Why do you care?"

"Because the wolves have to change. They need to know they

can choose someone other than Sabine." He looked down at his palm, willing ice to form there. It cracked over his skin in a thin film before melting away. "They need to know there's an antidote that might grant them powers beyond hers. That they don't need to be subservient to her."

"The wolves will need proof regarding that bit," Jesiba said, "or you won't walk out of there alive."

"Isn't this enough?" He formed a shard of ice on his fingertip, as much as he could reliably control. He supposed he'd need to seek out the Fae or some sort of ice sprite to teach him how to command this new ability.

Hypaxia had taken the antidote minutes after him. She'd blacked out, as he had, but awoken thrumming with power. He could have sworn a light, playful breeze now played about her hair constantly—and that a steady sort of power seemed to emanate from her, even when she wasn't using it.

He'd offered Jesiba a vial upon telling her the news, but the sorceress had said, *It won't help me, pup.* And then ordered him to begin this miserable work while he explained the rest.

Jesiba now said, "Knowing the wolves, they'll think Quinlan asked me to do something to you that made you . . . unnatural."

"They know Bryce is a good person."

"Do they? As far as I recall, they've been anything but kind to her since Danika and the Pack died. You included."

Ithan's cheeks warmed. "It was a rough time. For all of us."

"Danika Fendyr would have skewered all of you to the front gates of the Den for how you treated Quinlan."

"Danika would have . . ." Ithan trailed off as a thought struck him. "Danika questioned the wolf power structure, you know. Even she thought it was weird that the Fendyrs went unchecked for so long."

"Did she?"

Ithan turned toward the sorceress's desk. "Bryce and I found some research papers Danika had hidden. She wanted to know why the Fendyrs were so dominant—I don't think she approved of it, either." He nodded to himself. "She would have encouraged the others to take the antidote. To kick Sabine to the curb."

Jesiba's brows rose. "If you say so. You knew Danika far better than I ever did."

"I know she hated her mother—and thought the hierarchies were grossly unfair." Ithan paced a few steps. "I have to get those papers. I'll bring them to the Den to show everyone that it's not just *me* questioning this, but that even one of the Fendyrs disagreed with their unchecked dominance. It might help sway them toward accepting an alternative to Sabine. Sigrid's a Fendyr, but she's not in the direct line. That might help them accept her as an alternative."

"They'll say you forged them." Jesiba typed away at her keyboard.

"That's a risk I have to take," Ithan said, striding to the door. "The days of Sabine keeping the wolves down, of making us stand by while innocents suffer . . . that has to end. We need a change. A big one. And maybe, if Urd's got our backs, what's most important within Sigrid still remains intact, unchanged by becoming a Reaper. If that's the case, I'll take Sigrid over Sabine any day."

Maybe it wasn't a matter of undoing what had been done, but rather of playing the bad hand that had been dealt to him. Of adapting.

"Open-minded as that is, Holstrom," Jesiba said, shutting her laptop, "do you really think it's a wise decision to not only go to the Den utterly defenseless, but to start preaching that they accept a *Reaper* as their Prime Apparent? Let's not forget that some of the wolves might still like Sabine and her style of leadership. Many probably do, in fact."

"Yeah, but it's time to give them the chance to choose otherwise. To break free of her control."

"You forget," Jesiba said darkly, "that from the very start, they've been the Asteri's chief enforcers. They've never shown any inclination to *break free* of anyone's control."

"It's a risk I have to take," he insisted. "And I can't sit around."

"Quinlan told you to protect Hypaxia."

"This won't take long. Keep an eye on her for me—please."

He walked to the door, and Jesiba spoke as he wrapped his

fingers around the knob. Her voice was heavy, resigned. "Be careful, pup."

Ithan snuck over to Bryce's apartment using the House of Flame and Shadow's unnervingly accurate map of the sewers. He didn't want to think about who else made regular use of those tunnels.

Even with the access that Danika had long ago granted him, he entered the building through the roof door. There was no doubt the building was being watched, and he kept to the shadows as much as he could. If the guard downstairs saw him on the cameras, no one came to investigate.

Danika's papers remained where he and Bryce had left them: in the junk mail drawer. He leafed through them just to make sure they did indeed say all he'd remembered.

They did. It could be a convenient bit of backup for his claims. *See? Even Danika wanted all this to change. And, yes, Sigrid is a Fendyr—but she's also* different*—she could be a step in the right direction.*

He'd find some way to say it more eloquently, but Danika's name still carried weight.

Ithan gently folded the pile of papers and slid them into the back pocket of his jeans. Outside, the city remained quiet—hushed. Grieving.

And inside this building . . .

Gods, it was weird to see this apartment, so empty and stale without its occupants.

Ithan glanced to the white sectional, like he'd find Athalar and Bryce sitting there, Syrinx curled up with them.

How far away that existence seemed now. He doubted it'd ever return. Wondered if his friends would ever return. If Bryce was—

He didn't let himself finish the thought.

He had no choice but to keep going. However it played out. And Jesiba was right. To walk into the Den was likely suicide, but . . . He glanced down the hall. To Bryce's bedroom door.

Maybe he didn't need to go in unarmed.

72

It took too long—way too fucking long—for the gates to yawn open, ice and snow cracking off and falling to the ground. Bryce wedged through them first, starfire blazing under her gloves.

"I don't understand," Ember was saying as she squeezed through behind Bryce, Randall hot on her tail. Hunt came last. "What is the *Harpy* doing out here?"

"She's not the Harpy anymore," Bryce said. "She's like . . . some weird necromantically raised thing made by the Asteri thanks to whatever they managed to do with some of Hunt's lightning. I don't know, but we don't want to meet whatever she is now."

Bryce caught the worry and guilt on Hunt's face. They didn't have the time, though, for her to assure him that this wasn't his fault. He'd had no choice but to give Rigelus his lightning. It had been used for some fucked-up shit, but that wasn't on him.

Ember protested, "But the Harpy *ate* the guards—"

"Which is why we're going to the Rift," Bryce said, nodding to Hunt, whose eyes shone with steely determination. "Right fucking now."

Hunt didn't wait before lifting her mother in his arms and spreading his wings. Bryce grabbed Randall and said, "Surprise: I can teleport. Don't barf."

Thankfully, Randall didn't vomit as she teleported them the

twenty-four and a half miles to the center of the walled ring. But he did when they arrived.

They beat Hunt and her mother there, leaving Bryce with nothing to do but watch her dad puke his guts up in the snow as the dizziness of teleporting hit him again and again.

"That is . . . ," Randall said, and retched again. "Useful, but horrible."

"I think that sums me up in a nutshell," Bryce said.

Randall laughed, vomited again, then wiped his mouth and stood. "You're not horrible, Bryce. Not by a long shot."

"I guess. But this is," she said, and gestured up at the structure before them. At the swirling mists.

A massive arch of clear quartz rose forty feet into the air, its uppermost part nearly hidden by the drifting mist. They could see straight through the archway, though, and nothing lay within it except what could only be described as a ripple in the world. Between worlds. And more mist on its other side.

"The Asteri must have built the archway around the Rift to try to contain it," Bryce said. "Or try to control it, I guess."

"I'll say this once, and that's it," Randall said. Behind him, closing in, Hunt and Ember approached from above. "But is opening the Rift . . . the best idea?"

Bryce blew out a long, hot breath that faded into the mists wafting past. "No. But it's the only idea I have."

There wasn't one black ribbon of mourning in the Den. No keening dirges offered up to Cthona, beseeching the goddess to guide the newly dead. In fact, somewhere in the compound, a stereo was blasting a thumping dance beat.

Trust Sabine to proceed as if nothing had changed. As if an atrocity hadn't occurred in a neighboring district.

At this time of year, it was tradition for many of the Den families to scatter into the countryside to enjoy the changing of the leaves and the crisp autumn mountains, so only a skeleton crew of packs remained. Ithan knew which ones would be there—just as he knew that only Perry Ravenscroft, the Black Rose's Omega and Amelie's little sister, would be on guard duty at the gates.

A bronze rendering of the Embrace—the sun sinking or rising out of two mountains—was displayed in the window of the guard station. And it was because he knew Perry so well that he understood that this small decoration was her way of telling the city that there were some in the Den who mourned, who were praying to Cthona to comfort the dead.

Perry's large emerald eyes widened at the sight of Ithan as he prowled up to the guard booth. To her, it must have seemed like he'd materialized out of thin air. In fact, his stealth was courtesy of his new speed and preternatural quiet—furthered by the fact that he'd traveled through the sewers, needing to remain out of sight until the last possible minute.

Perry lunged for the radio on the desk, long brown hair flashing in the afternoon sunlight, but Ithan held up a hand. She paused.

"I need to talk," he said through the glass.

Those green eyes scanned his face, then drifted to a spot over his shoulder, to the sword he carried. Perry stared at him—then opened the door to the booth. Her cinnamon-and-strawberry scent hit him a heartbeat later.

This close, he could count the smattering of freckles across the bridge of her nose. The pale skin beneath them seemed to blanch further as she processed what he'd said.

"Sabine's in a meeting—"

"Not Sabine. I need to talk to everyone else." Ithan pushed, "You were the only one who checked in to see if I was alive after . . . everything." She'd texted him occasionally—not much, but with Amelie as her Alpha and sister, he knew she didn't dare risk more communication than that. "Please, Perry. Just let me into the courtyard."

"Tell me what you want to talk to us about, and I'll consider it." Even as Omega, the lowest of the Black Rose Pack, she didn't back down.

It was for that courage alone that Ithan told her his secret first. "A new future for the wolves."

Ithan knew it was due to how loved and trusted Perry was within the Den that so many wolves arrived in the courtyard quickly, as soon as her message went out about a last-minute announcement.

He kept to the shadows of the pillars under the building's north wing, watching the people he'd counted as friends, almost family, congregate in the grassy space. The red and gold trees of the small park behind them swayed in the crisp autumn breeze, the wind luckily keeping his scent hidden from the wolves.

When enough of a crowd had assembled—a hundred wolves, or so—Perry stepped out onto the few steps in front of the building doors and said, "So, uh . . . almost everyone's here."

People smiled at her, bemused yet indulgent. It'd always been that way for Perry, the resident artist of the Den, who at age four had painted her room every color of the rainbow despite her parents' order to pick one hue.

Perry glanced toward him, eyes bright with fear. For him or for herself, he had no idea.

"Go ahead," she said quietly, and stepped off the stairs and into the grass.

Make your brother proud.

Though those words had come from the Viper Queen, Ithan held them close to his heart as he stepped out of the shadows.

Snarls and growls and shouts of surprise rose. Ithan held up his hands. "I'm not here to start trouble."

"Then get the fuck out!" someone—Gideon, Amelie's third—shouted from the back. Amelie herself was striding through the crowd, fury twisting her face—

"Everything we are is a lie," Ithan said before Amelie could reach him and start swinging.

Some people quieted. Ithan plunged on, because Amelie's canines were lengthening, and he knew she'd be making the full shift soon.

"Danika Fendyr questioned this, too. She died before she could find the truth."

The words had their desired effect. The crowd went silent. But Amelie still charged forward, shoving people out of the way now, Gideon a menacing, hulking mass close behind—

Ithan looked at Perry, standing at the front of the crowd, her green eyes trained on him. It was to her that he said, "The Asteri planted a parasite in our brains that repressed our inherent magic, reducing it to its most basic components: shifting and strength. Yet even those abilities have been cut off at the knees. All so we can remain their faithful enforcers, as we've been since the Northern Rift opened."

Amelie was ten feet away, muscles tensing to jump onto the stairs, to pin him and shred him—

"Look," Ithan said, and held out a hand. Ice swirled in his palm.

A gasp went through the crowd. Even Amelie stumbled in shock.

Ithan said, letting the ice crust his fingers, "Magic—*elemental* magic. It was lying there, dormant in my veins all this time." He found Perry's eyes again, noted the shock and something like yearning in them. "A friend of mine, a medwitch, made an antidote for me. I took it and discovered what I really am. *Who* I really am. What sleeps in the bloodline of all wolves, repressed by the Asteri for fifteen thousand years."

"It's a witch-trick," Amelie spat, making to shove past her little sister. "Move," she ordered Perry. Not as her sister, but as her Alpha.

But Perry, despite her slim frame, held firm. And said to Amelie, her voice carrying, "I want to hear what he has to say."

Ithan spoke as quickly as he could, giving the wolves an overview of the parasite and what it did to their magic. And then, because they were still looking doubtful, he explained what really happened in the Bone Quarter: Secondlight. The meat grinder of souls.

When he was done, Ithan found Perry's face again. She'd gone ghostly white.

"Queen Hypaxia Enador can verify all I've told you," Ithan said.

"She's not queen anymore!" a wolf called. "She's been kicked out—like you, Holstrom."

Ithan bared his teeth. "She's brilliant. She figured out how to fix this *thing* in our brains, to give us this magic back. So don't you take that fucking tone about her."

And at the snarl in his voice, the order, the wolves in the crowd straightened. Not with anger or fear, but . . .

"What did you do?" Perry said, staggering forward a step. "Ithan, you're—"

"There is another Fendyr," Ithan said, plowing ahead, bracing himself.

The crowd stirred. Perry gaped at him. "What do you mean?" she asked. He couldn't stand the confusion and hope in her voice, her bright eyes.

"Her name is Sigrid," Ithan said, throat tightening painfully. "She . . . she's the daughter of Sabine's late brother. And she—"

"That is enough," Amelie spat, shoving forward at last. "This insane rambling stops *now*."

Ithan growled, low and deep, and even Amelie halted, one foot on the step.

He held her gaze, let her see everything in it.

"Why is this traitor still alive?" Sabine's voice slithered over the courtyard.

Ithan pivoted, carefully keeping Amelie in his sights as he surveyed the approaching Prime Apparent.

A step behind her, emerging from the shadows, strode Sigrid and the Astronomer.

73

Reaper," Perry breathed, falling back. Not to run, but to protect a young wolf a few steps behind her, who shook in pure terror at the acid-green eyes of the Reaper in their midst.

Judging by Sigrid's fairly normal gait, she was still in the middle of her transition. But there was an oddness to her movements already. The beginnings of that unnaturally smooth glide that only Reapers could effect.

And she'd left on her wrecked, bloodied clothes. As proof, he realized—because his blood was also on them. And the wolves would know that with one sniff.

Struggling for the right words as he pointed at Sigrid, Ithan said, "It's—she's no threat to you all."

"That is a *Reaper*!" someone shouted at him from the back.

The Astronomer was grinning at Ithan. How had the old bastard managed to get her away from the Under-King? He'd somehow orchestrated this, right down to bringing his former mystic to Sabine. All for vengeance on Ithan.

"Whatever story Holstrom is spinning for you," Sabine said loudly, "don't listen to a word of it." The crowd was recoiling, desperate to get away from the Reaper at Sabine's side. "Ithan Holstrom is a liar," Sabine declared, "and a traitor to all we stand for."

"That's not true," Ithan growled.

"Isn't it?" Sabine pointed to where Sigrid stood beside her, gazing out at the crowd with an impassive face. "Look at what you did to my dear niece."

The word hit the crowd like a rogue wave. He practically felt them piecing it together—that the Reaper before them was the same Fendyr heir he'd been telling them about moments ago.

Niece, people whispered. *Is it possible that—*

The Astronomer folded his withered hands before him, the portrait of serene old age. "It is true," he announced. "Twenty years ago, Lars Fendyr sought me out and sold his eldest pup into my service." He motioned to Sigrid. "She was my faithful companion, as dear to me as my own daughter." His dark eyes slid to Ithan, sharp with hate. "Until that boy kidnapped her and turned her into *that.*"

The crowd shifted away, all their focus now on Ithan, their eyes distrusting, damning—

"My brother's daughter," Sabine said, raising her voice to be heard over the murmuring, shifting crowd. "Killed in cold blood by that male." She pointed to Ithan. "Just as he and his Fae friends tried to kill me."

"That's—" Ithan started, noting how pale Perry had become.

"It's the truth," Sabine sneered. "I have the video footage of it, courtesy of the Viper Queen. I'd be happy to show everyone how brutally you executed a defenseless young wolf."

Horror stole any words from Ithan's throat.

It had always been a long game for the Viper Queen. Not only to amuse herself, but to use the knowledge of what he'd done to her advantage. Her relationship with Sabine was strained—so why not sweeten it with a little peace offering?

Marc had even told Ithan that the Viper Queen dealt not in money, but in favors and intel. He'd walked right into that trap.

"He then tried to have a necromancer raise her from the dead," Sabine went on, gesturing to the Reaper. "So she might be his puppet for usurping me."

"That is *not*—"

The Astronomer added, "And when I heard what had befallen

her . . ." The Astronomer gave Sigrid a pitying look. "I petitioned the Under-King for her release so that I could immediately bring her to the Den, to you good people."

This couldn't be happening.

Sabine grinned. It sure as fuck was happening. "This morning, Sigrid informed me that when she was faced with this unspeakable enslavement," Sabine said, "she wanted to protect her people, so she chose the existence of a Reaper instead. And she has made her way here at last, to be my heir."

There was a shocked silence.

He'd been a stupid fucking fool to think that Sigrid would be like Danika, that she might have chosen to be a Reaper and still want joy and peace and what was best for the wolves—instead of the pure hate that now gleamed in her eyes as she glowered at Ithan.

But Amelie was blinking at Sabine. *She* was Sabine's heir. To name another, and a Reaper, at that . . .

Perry glanced between her sister and Sabine, then at the Reaper. "Why don't you let your new heir speak for herself, Sabine?"

Sabine snarled at Perry, and Perry backed away a step.

Ithan's hackles rose at the fear, the submission.

"Everyone knows the Holstroms have long desired to replace the Fendyrs," Sabine went on.

"Bullshit," Ithan spat.

"Our traditions continue because they are *strong*," Sabine said to the crowd. The Astronomer stepped closer to Sigrid's side, eyeing the wolves. "To listen to this boy spew the propaganda of a renegade witch—"

"Go to the Bone Quarter," Ithan cut in. "Plead with the Under-King to grant you an audience with my brother. Connor will tell you—"

"Only the scum of the House of Flame and Shadow can do such things," Sabine sneered.

"Your *heir*," Perry said with quiet authority, "is in that House, Sabine."

Sabine gave Perry a simpering smile that made Ithan see red. "Sigrid has defected to Earth and Blood." The crowd murmured again. "And," Sabine continued, "she will dwell here from now on. As your future Prime Apparent."

The Astronomer nodded, his long beard grazing the belt around his draped robes. "After convincing the Under-King to release her into my care, it pains me to again part with my daughter-of-the-heart, but for your benefit, I shall. Sigrid is henceforth a part of your Den—a true wolf."

"I don't recall approving the request," said an old, withered voice. The crowd hushed as the Prime hobbled through the doors. Even the Astronomer lowered his head in deference.

Sabine must have coached Sigrid, because the wolf dropped to her knees before the Prime and bowed her head. "Grandfather," she rasped.

People gasped at the sound of her voice. The hoarse whisper of a Reaper.

The Prime peered down at Sigrid's sallow face. Her acid-green eyes. The wounds on her throat, her neck.

He said nothing as his milky eyes slid to Ithan. Sorrow and pain filled them.

Ithan swallowed hard, but held his ground. "I'm sorry. I . . . I didn't mean for it to turn out like this." The attention of the crowd pushed on his skin like a weight. "I was trying to make things right."

"At the expense of the wolves' future," Sabine snapped.

Ithan reached over his shoulder and drew the weapon he'd brought from Bryce's bedroom.

The Fendyr sword whined as it came free of its sheath. Sabine's eyes flared with fury and longing—

But Ithan knelt before the ancient Prime and bowed his head, lifting the blade in offering.

"I have no intention of usurping the Fendyrs," Ithan said, keeping his gaze on the ground. "I only want what's best for our people. I thought Sigrid might be . . . different, but I was wrong. I was so wrong, and I am so sorry."

Sabine seethed, "Father, don't listen to this trash—"

"Silence," the Prime ordered, in a voice Ithan had not heard in years. He dared to look up at the old male. "I heard what you said," the Prime told Ithan. "Over the cameras." His milky eyes seemed to clear for a heartbeat, revealing a glimpse of the powerful, righteous wolf he'd been. "Danika did indeed guess at what you have told everyone. She suspected it, and asked me about it, and though I had long thought the same, I shied away from the truth. It was . . . easier to continue than to face a painful reality. To keep stability, rather than risk an uncertain future."

The Prime took the sword Ithan offered, his withered hand shaking with the effort of holding the heavy blade. "I allowed our people to be forced to serve in the Aux," he continued, looking now to Perry, "even when their artist's souls abhor it." Perry's eyes shone with pain. "What Ithan has said to you is true. It has always been true, going back to the First Wars and the unspeakable atrocities our people committed on behalf of the Asteri. My daughter"—a glance at Sabine, who was snarling softly—"did not care to listen when I mentioned that the wolves might be more—better—than we have been. But my granddaughter did."

The old wolf let out a heavy sigh. "Danika might have led us back to what we were before we allowed ourselves to be collared by the Asteri. I have long believed that she was killed for this goal—by the powers who wish the status quo to remain in place." The Prime looked down at the wolf kneeling at his feet. "But it must be broken." He extended the sword to Ithan. "Ithan Holstrom is my heir."

Stunned silence rippled through the crowd, the world. Ithan couldn't get a breath down.

"And no one else," the Prime finished.

Sabine had gone white as death. "Father—"

The Prime leveled a cold look at his daughter. "For too long I've left you unchecked."

"I've kept our people, this city safe—"

"You are hereby stripped of your title, your rank, and your authority."

Sabine just stared. At her side, Sigrid's blazing green eyes darted between the two wolves.

The Astronomer was now glancing at the distant eastern gates, as if starting to wonder if he'd backed the wrong horse.

"Take it," the Prime said to Ithan. He extended the sword again.

Ithan shook his head. "I didn't come here to—"

"I offered to make you Alpha once, Ithan Holstrom. I now offer to make you Prime. Don't walk away from it."

Ithan didn't reach for the sword. "I—"

He didn't get the chance to finish his refusal.

One moment, he was staring at the sword. The next, Sabine had snatched it from her father's hands.

She plunged it through the Prime's ancient face.

The crowd exploded into screams and shouts. From the corner of his eye, Ithan saw Amelie dragging a struggling Perry away, out of range.

The Prime crumpled to the ground before Ithan, eyes unseeing, coated with blood. If a medwitch got here soon enough, maybe—

Sigrid moved.

Ithan couldn't contain his cry of dismay as she leapt onto her grandfather's body and pressed her mouth to his withered lips. She inhaled deeply.

Light flared up through the Prime's mouth, illumining his hollowed cheeks, and then Sigrid was breathing it in, drinking it.

His soul, his firstlight—

She cocked her head back and swallowed that light, his essence. Her skin gleamed as the light passed down the column of her throat, inch by inch.

There was no coming back for the Prime.

Sabine cut off his head anyway. The Astronomer, slack-jawed and sprayed with blood, had stumbled back a step, gaping at Sigrid as she leveled her green stare on him, ravenous—

Ithan had only a heartbeat to pivot, to leap off the stairs before Sabine swung the bloodied sword at him. He couldn't take his eyes off the Prime, though. Off Sigrid, the Reaper he'd created who had eaten the old wolf's soul, as hungry as a vampyr—

"Ithan!" Perry shouted, and he snapped to attention as Sabine launched for him again, sword arcing.

He leapt back, narrowly missing being gutted.

"This sword," Sabine panted, brandishing it, "is mine. The title is *mine*."

Ithan shifted, so fast even Sabine blinked.

Make your brother proud.

Sabine swung the sword as Ithan charged, a powerful blow that would cleave even his wolf's skull in two.

Ithan leapt straight at the blade. His jaws closed around it.

Sabine's eyes flared with shock as Ithan bit down, tasting metal.

And shattered the Fendyr sword between his teeth.

74

Most of the crowd had fled as soon as Sigrid had started feeding on the Prime's soul. But Perry and Amelie, Gideon with them, remained near the trees, watching Sabine and Ithan.

Sabine stared down at the seven shards the Fendyr sword had broken into, then lifted her furious gaze to Ithan.

Ithan shifted back into his humanoid body with a near-instant flash. "It's just a piece of steel," he said, panting, the metallic tang of the blade lingering in his mouth. "All those years you obsessed over it, resented Danika for having it . . . It's just a piece of metal."

Sabine's claws glinted. Her lips curled back from her fangs as she snarled.

But behind her, Sigrid was closing in on the Astronomer, who had fallen to the ground and was now crawling backward, hands up. The male pleaded, "Did I not treat you well, deliver you from the Under-King's grasp—"

The Astronomer didn't get the chance to plead his case. Sigrid, either from spite or lost to her hunger, left the old man no time to scream as she leapt upon him and fitted her mouth against his.

Even Sabine paused to watch as Sigrid plunged her clawed hand into his chest, ripping out his still-beating heart in the same moment that she inhaled deeply, and that glimmering light—the secondlight—of his soul rose up through his body, into their fused mouths—

Not Ithan's problem. Not right now. He whipped his head back to Sabine, and let out a long, deep snarl of his own.

Sabine's nose crinkled. "You are no Alpha, pup," she growled, and lunged.

Ithan charged. A straight sprint into death's awaiting claws.

Sabine leapt for him, and Ithan ducked low, sliding, grabbing the longest of the sword's shards and lifting it high—

Blood rained down, and Sabine screamed as she hit the grass with a thud. Ithan sprang to his feet and whirled. Sabine crouched on the ground, a hand pressed to her gut. As if it'd keep the organs now spilling on the grass from tumbling out.

He had a dim awareness of Sigrid, behind him, swallowing down the Astronomer's dying soul and dropping his limp corpse to the stones of the stairs.

But Ithan slowly approached Sabine, and there was no one else in the world, no task but this. Sabine lifted raging, pain-filled eyes to him.

"Everything I have done," Sabine panted up at him, "has been for the wolves."

"It's been for yourself," Ithan spat, stopping before her.

She sneered, revealing blood-coated teeth. "You will lead them to ruin."

"We'll see" was all Ithan said before shifting once more into his wolf's body with that preternatural speed.

Sabine looked his wolf in the eyes—and beheld her death there. She opened her mouth to speak, but Ithan didn't give her the chance. Enough of her vitriol had poisoned the world.

A leap, a crunch of his impossibly strong jaws, and it was done.

With that extra strength he'd gained, he'd broken through the steel of the sword. Breaking through flesh and bone was nothing by comparison.

But once her blood hit his tongue, red washed over his vision, blazing, burning. He was rage and snarls and fangs. He was blood and entrails and primal fury—

"Ithan."

Perry's quavering voice shook him from the daze. From what he'd done to Sabine's body. Her blood coated his mouth, her flesh was stuck between his teeth—

"They're watching," Perry breathed, stepping up to him.

Still in his wolf form, Ithan started to turn toward the witnesses of his savagery, but Perry said, "Don't look," and dropped to her knees before him. Tilted back her head and exposed her neck. "I yield." She added a heartbeat later, "I yield to the Prime."

The words struck a chord in him, one of despair and suffocation. But he couldn't stop it—the instinct to reach forward and lightly clamp his teeth around Perry's slender throat. To take that cinnamon-and-strawberry taste into his mouth.

To accept her submission to him. Her recognition.

Footsteps thudded nearby. Then Amelie stood there, shock paling her face—

But she, too, dropped to her knees. Exposed her neck.

It was either submit to him, or die. As a potential rival, he'd have had no choice but to kill her. A glance behind him revealed the corpse of the Astronomer sprawled across the stairs, leaking blood that trickled down the steps. But Sigrid had vanished. As if she knew he would be coming for her.

Something relaxed in him as he gently closed his jaws around Amelie's throat, too, accepting her surrender. A bitterer, staler taste than Perry's sweetness. But he accepted it all the same.

"Hail Ithan," Amelie said, loud enough for all to hear, "Prime of the Valbaran Wolves."

In answer, a chorus of howls went up from around the Den. Then the city. Then the wilderness beyond the city walls. As if all of Midgard hailed him.

When it ceased, Ithan tipped his wolf's head to the sky and loosed a howl of his own. Triumph and pain and mourning.

Make your brother proud.

And as his howl finished echoing, he could have sworn he heard a male wolf's cry float up from the Bone Quarter itself.

75

Ruhn didn't recognize his city.

Imperial battleships filled the Istros. Dreadwolves prowled the streets. The 33rd had been joined by the Asterian Guard.

And the Meadows still smoldered in the north, lines of smoke rising to the jarringly blue sky.

But it was the quiet that unnerved him the most as he and Lidia crept through the sewers, making their way toward the Comitium. Flynn and Dec had peeled off a few blocks back to go scope out the Aux headquarters for any whisper of where Isaiah and Naomi might be. If they could intercept Isaiah and Naomi at the Comitium, they'd save themselves hours of searching.

Then came the hard part: finding a secure place to meet with them, long enough to explain everything. But for right now, his focus was on finding the two members of Celestina's triarii. And trying not to get caught in the process.

"This should open up into a tunnel that will lead right under the Comitium," Ruhn told Lidia, keeping his voice low. The sewers appeared empty, but in Crescent City there was always someone watching. Listening.

"Once we're in the building," she said, "I can get us to their barracks."

"You're sure you know where the cameras—"

She gave him a look. "It was my job when Ephraim visited to know where they were. Both as the Hind and as Agent Daybright. I could navigate this place blindfolded."

Ruhn blew out a breath. "All right. But when we get to the barracks—"

"Then those shadows of yours come into play, and we hide until Isaiah and Naomi appear. Unless they're already there and we can get them alone."

"Right. Got it." He rolled his neck.

She eyed him. "You seem . . . nervous."

He snorted. "It's my first mission with my girlfriend. I want to impress her."

Her lips quirked up, and Ruhn led the way down another tunnel. "Am I your girlfriend, then?" she asked.

"Is that . . . okay with you?"

She gave him a true smile. It made her seem younger, lighter—the person she might have been if Urd hadn't taken her down her particular fucked-up life path. It knocked the breath from him. "*Yeah*, Ruhn. It's okay with me."

He smiled back, remembering how she'd chastised him when they'd first met for saying "Yeah," for being so casual.

Ahead, Ruhn saw that they were approaching a dented metal door marked *Do Not Enter*. "Now, that's practically an invitation," he said, earning a laugh from Lidia as he kicked in the door.

The sight of the imperial battleships in the Istros robbed Tharion of any joy at the river's familiar, beckoning scent. So did the presence of the Omega-boats docked with them. And right by the Black Dock . . . the *SPQM Faustus*. The very Omega-boat they'd barely outrun that day on Ydra.

He hadn't dared venture into the northernmost part of the city to see the damage to Asphodel Meadows. They weren't here for that, and he knew he'd see nothing that would make him feel any better. The city was eerily quiet. As if in mourning.

Face and hair hidden under a sunball cap, Tharion glowered at the armada for long enough as he stood on the quay that Sathia warned, "You'll draw attention to us with all that glaring."

"I should slip into the water and blast holes in all their hulls," Tharion snarled.

"Focus," she said. "You do that, and we won't accomplish what we came here to do." She frowned at the ships. "Which is clearly still necessary."

"They're holding the city hostage."

"All the more reason to plead with the River Queen to take people in."

Tharion found only cool determination on Sathia's heart-shaped face. "You're right," he said. He let out a low whistle, and waited.

An otter in a bright yellow vest leapt onto the quay, dripping everywhere. It rose onto its hind legs in front of Tharion, whiskers twitching, spraying droplets of water.

Sathia grinned.

"Stop it," Tharion muttered. "It only encourages them to be cuter."

She bit her lip, and though it was thoroughly distracting, Tharion got his act together enough to say to the otter, "Tell the River Queen that Tharion Ketos wants a meeting."

The whiskers twitched again.

Sathia added, "Please."

Tharion avoided the urge to roll his eyes, but also added, "Please." He fished out a gold coin. "And make it speedy, friend."

The otter took the coin in his little black fingers and turned it over, eyes brightening at the outrageous sum. With a flick of his long tail, he leapt back into the clear turquoise water with barely a ripple and was gone.

Tharion watched him gracefully swim out into the depths, then vanish over the drop into the dark, to the Blue Court Beneath. Only tiny, glimmering lights showed any signs of life there.

"What now?" Sathia asked, again eyeing the warships docked in the river. If just one of the soldiers on them recognized Tharion . . .

He tugged his sunball hat over his hair. "Now we lurk in the shadows and wait."

"This doesn't seem safe," Ember said for the fifth time as Bryce stood before the Northern Rift's archway. Hunt waited ten paces behind her, freezing his feathers off. "This seems like the opposite of safe. You're opening *the Northern Rift to Hel*. And we're supposed to believe these demons—the princes, for Urd's sake—are *good*?"

"I'm not sure they're good," Bryce said. "But they're on our side. Just trust me, Mom."

"Trust her, Ember," Randall said, but from the tightness in his voice, Hunt knew the man wasn't too happy, either.

"When you're ready, Athalar," Bryce called to him.

"I thought you didn't need me to fuel you up anymore," Hunt said. "Especially with all that extra power you've got now."

"I don't want to try it on my own for this," Bryce said. "Seems like a high-stakes situation to test out my new abilities."

"I bet you could do it," Hunt called over the wind, "but all right. On three." Bryce stilled, squaring her shoulders.

Hunt rallied his lightning. Prayed to every god, even if they'd mostly fucked him over until this point. The power of his lightning was familiar, yet suddenly foreign. *Helfire*, Apollion had called it.

Answers—at long last, answers about why he was what he was, about why he and no one else had the lightning. Even the thunderbirds, made by Hel, had been hunted to extinction by the Asteri. With Sofie's death, they were truly gone.

Though the Harpy's resurrection—another thing that was his fucking fault—suggested that the Asteri now had other methods of raising the dead.

Only if they could get their hands on more of his lightning. He'd sooner die.

"One . . . ," Hunt breathed, and lifted a hand wreathed in lightning.

Lord of Lightning, the Oracle had called him.

"Two . . ."

Had the Oracle seen what he was, where his power came from, that day?

You remind me of that which was lost long ago. The thunderbirds, hunted to extinction.

Was that the wind ruffling her parka, or was Bryce shaking as she waited for the blow? Hunt didn't give himself a moment to reconsider. To halt.

"Three."

He launched a spear of lightning at his mate.

76

As it had that day at the Asteri's palace, when she had leapt from her own world to another, Hunt's lightning lanced through Bryce's back, through the Horn, into the star on her chest—and out into the Gate.

Ember shouted in fear, and even Randall stumbled back a step, but Hunt let his lightning flow into Bryce, kept a steady stream of it surging between them.

"Open," Bryce said, her voice carrying on the wind. A sliver of darkness began to spread in the middle of the Gate.

Hunt funneled more lightning into her, and the sliver widened, inch by inch.

The Northern Rift had been fixed on Hel—until now. Until his power had passed through not only the Horn on Bryce, but the star on her chest, too—that link to a different world. Reorienting the Gate, as it had that day in the Eternal Palace, to open elsewhere. That was their theory, at least. No one had ever tried to manipulate the Northern Rift to open somewhere other than Hel, but—

"That's enough, Hunt," Ember warned.

Hunt ignored her and sent another spike of power into his mate. Bryce's hair floated up, snow and ice drifting with it, but she maintained an eerie calm until the void filled the entirety of the massive Gate.

Hunt cut off his lightning, running to where Bryce stood before the wall of darkness.

Darkness—flecked by starlight.

A female with golden-brown hair sat in an armchair before a fireplace on the other side of it. All that darkness was the starry night beyond her windows.

And her face was a portrait of pure shock as Bryce lifted a hand in greeting and said, "Hello, Nesta."

The River Queen sat in a chair before a computer panel in the control room connected to the west air lock, a makeshift throne in the sterile, utilitarian space. The tech who operated the computer had vacated the chamber in a near-sprint at the queen's snapped command.

Tharion was well aware that the air lock could be easily hosed down to remove any and all traces of blood. A body flushed out through it would go straight to the sobeks circling outside like Reapers.

If Sathia noted those details, if she understood that she and Tharion had been brought here purely for the convenience of getting rid of his corpse, she didn't let on.

His wife simply curtsied, a graceful swoop downward, at odds with her casual leggings and white sweater, the cashmere now streaked with dirt and torn along the bottom hem. "Your Majesty," Sathia said, her voice cultured yet unthreatening. "It is an honor to meet you."

The River Queen's dark eyes swept over Sathia. "Am I supposed to open my arms to the female who usurped my daughter?"

Sathia didn't so much as flinch. "If my union with Tharion has brought you grief or offense, then I offer my wholehearted apologies."

A beat, too long to be comforting. Tharion lifted his gaze to the River Queen and found her watching him. Her gaze was cold, cruel. Unimpressed.

"I take it," the River Queen said, "you want something very badly from me, if you have come back to risk my wrath."

Tharion bowed his head. "Yes, Your Majesty."

"And yet you have brought your *wife*—for what? To soften me? Or as a shield to hide behind?"

"Considering she's barely up to my chest," Tharion said dryly, "I don't think she'd make much of a shield."

Sathia glared at him, but the River Queen frowned. "Always making jokes. Always playing the fool." She waved a hand adorned in rings of shell and coral toward Sathia. "I suppose I should wish you congratulations on your nuptials, but I instead wish you luck. With a male like that for a husband, you'll need it in droves."

"I thank you," Sathia said with such sincerity that Tharion nearly bought it, too. "May your good wishes fly straight to Urd's ears."

Okay, maybe he'd underestimated his wife. She seemed more comfortable in this setting than he was.

Indeed, the River Queen seemed intrigued enough by Sathia's grace under fire that she said, "Well, Tharion. Let's hear what was so important that you dared enter my realm again."

He clasped his hands behind his back, exposing his chest like he knew the River Queen preferred. He didn't see her jagged sea-glass knife anywhere, but she always had it on her. "I am here on behalf of Bryce Quinlan, Queen of the Fae of Valbara and Avallen, to request asylum in the Blue Court for the people of Crescent City."

Another long pause.

"Queen, is it?" the River Queen said. "Of Valbaran and Avallen Fae?" Her eyes slid to Sathia—the Fae representative, he supposed.

Sathia's chin dipped. "Bryce Quinlan now rules both territories. I serve her, as does Tharion."

Eyes as black and depthless as a shark's slid to Tharion. The same eyes as her sister, the Ocean Queen, he realized. "Am I supposed to be pleased to hear you have yet again defected?"

"I did what my morals demanded," Tharion said.

"Morals," the River Queen mused. "What morals do you have other than ensuring your own survival at any cost? Was it your *morals* that guided you when you took my daughter's maidenhead, swearing to love her until you died, and then toyed with her affections for the next decade?"

Fuck. But Sathia answered for him with that unflinching calm, "These are the mistakes of youth—ones Tharion has reflected upon and learned from."

The River Queen fixed her attention on Sathia again. "Has he? Or was that the poisoned honey he poured into your ear to woo you?"

"He brought me before you," Sathia countered. "Proof that he is willing to own up to his actions."

It took a special sort of person to talk like that to the River Queen. To not back down one inch, not tremble at her power, her ageless face.

The River Queen's eyes narrowed, clearly thinking along the same lines. "And this *Queen Bryce* thought Tharion the best emissary to beg me for such an enormous favor?"

Sathia's chin didn't lower. "She remembered how Tharion and your people so bravely and selflessly carried innocents down here to safety during the attack this spring."

Damn, she was good.

The River Queen waved a hand toward the window overlooking the depths and the monsters prowling beyond. "And does she have a good reason why I shouldn't kill Tharion where he stands and send his body out to the river beasts?"

Sathia didn't even glance toward the circling sobeks. "Because he is now in Queen Bryce's employ. You strike him down, and you shall have the Fae to deal with."

A flash of little pointed teeth. "They'll have to get Beneath first."

Sathia didn't miss a beat. "I believe it would not be in your best interest to become a city under siege."

Holy gods, his wife had balls. Tharion wisely wiped any sort of reaction from his face, but Ogenas damn him, if they survived this meeting, he wanted Sathia to teach him everything she knew.

The River Queen scoffed, but angled her head before changing the subject. "How does the girl suddenly wield such power?"

"That is her own story to tell," Sathia said, folding her hands behind her back, "but she has powerful allies. In this world and in others."

"Others?"

Tharion dared say, turning his voice into a mirror of his wife's poised calm, "Bryce counts the Princes of Hel as allies."

"Then she is an enemy to Midgard. And an imbecile as well, if she is seeking to hide the people of this city from the demons she'd ally with."

"She doesn't seek to hide people from Hel," Tharion said, "but from the Asteri's wrath."

The River Queen blinked slowly. "You ask me to take a stand against the Republic itself."

"What happened in Asphodel Meadows was a disgrace," Tharion said, voice dangerously low. "If you don't stand against the Republic for something of this nature, then you're complicit in their slaughter."

Sathia cut him a warning glance, but the River Queen studied him. Like she hadn't really seen him until this point.

She opened her mouth, and hope surged in Tharion's chest—

But then the interior door to the room hissed open, and the River Queen's daughter was charging in, rage and sorrow crumpling her beautiful face as she screamed, *"How could you?"*

"Is that a Prince of Hel?" Ember whispered from a few steps behind Bryce, her teeth clacking with cold.

"Does she *look* like a prince?" Randall hissed back, snow crunching as he hopped from one foot to another to keep warm.

"Bryce said Aidas appeared to her as a cat, so who's to say—"

"Guys," Bryce murmured as Nesta slowly, slowly rose from her chair by the fireplace. A dagger had somehow appeared in the female's hand, as if it had been concealed under the cushion.

It had worked. They'd managed to make the Northern Rift open to a place other than Hel.

"What are you doing?" Nesta said, and it occurred to Bryce in that moment that none of the others could understand her. Which left Bryce as translator.

So Bryce muttered to Hunt, wide-eyed but poised to leap into action, "Give me a minute," and faced Nesta.

"I'm not going to harm you, or your world," Bryce said in Nesta's own language.

"Then why is there a giant portal in my living room?" Nesta's blue-gray eyes were gleaming with predatory violence. Some of that silver flame was starting to build at her fingertips. Would it withstand Bryce's starfire? Especially with the force of that leveled-up power in her body behind it?

But she hadn't come here for that. "I needed to talk to you."

"How did you know I'd be alone?"

"I didn't. Urd threw me a bone."

The dagger and the silver flame didn't vanish. "Shut that portal."

"Not until I say what I need to say."

The silver flame now flickered in Nesta's eyes. "Then say it, and be gone." Her gaze lowered to Bryce's side. "And leave the dagger you stole."

Bryce ignored that and swallowed hard.

Ember hissed to Randall, *"I don't think it's going well."* Randall hushed her.

But Nesta's eyes slid to Hunt—to the feathered wings, the lightning dancing at his hand, the halo on his brow. "Is that your mate?"

Bryce nodded, and motioned Hunt to step forward. "Hunt Athalar." She'd never fucking use *Danaan* again. For either of them.

Hunt approached and inclined his head. Bryce could have sworn lightning lashed across his eyes, as if the power he'd summoned, enough to open the Northern Rift, was riding him hard.

But Nesta only observed him imperiously, then turned to Bryce. "What do you want?"

Bryce squared her shoulders. "I need you to give me the Mask."

77

Is that a request or a threat?" Nesta asked quietly, and even with a portal between them, the ground seemed to shudder at the female's power.

"It's a plea. A desperate fucking plea," Bryce said, and exposed her palms to the female in supplication. "I need it to give me an edge against the Asteri. To destroy them."

"No." Nesta's eyes held no mercy. "Now shut the portal and be gone." She glanced over a shoulder, where the stars seemed to be winking out in the far distance. "Before the High Lord gets here and rips you to shreds."

"What is that?" Hunt murmured, marking the darkness sweeping in.

"Rhysand," Bryce murmured back, then said to Nesta, "Please. I don't need the Mask forever. Just . . . until it's done. Then I'll return it."

Nesta laughed, pure ice. "You expect me to trust a female who tried to deceive and outsmart us at every turn?"

"I *did* outsmart you," Bryce said coolly, and Nesta's eyes sparked at the challenge. "But that's neither here nor there. Look, I get it—the Mask is insanely powerful and dangerous. I wouldn't trust someone who asked me to use the Horn, either. But my world needs this."

Nesta said nothing.

The darkness crept closer. Fury leaked from it, along with a primal rage. Bryce took a step forward, and Nesta's dagger angled upward.

"Please," Bryce said again. "I promise I'll return the Mask—and Truth-Teller. After I've done what I need to do here."

"You must think me a fool if you believe I'd hand over one of the deadliest weapons in my world. Especially when the monsters in *your* world have wanted to get their hands on it and the rest of the Dread Trove for millennia. Not to mention that few people can use the Mask and live. You put it on, and you might very well die."

"That's a risk I'm willing to take," Bryce said calmly.

"And I'm supposed to trust that you, after all you did here, are going to return the Mask out of the goodness of your heart?"

Bryce nodded. "Yes."

Nesta laughed joylessly, glancing at the approaching darkness. "All I have to do is wait until he gets here, you know. Then you'll wish you'd shut that portal."

"I know," Bryce said, and her throat tightened. "But I'm begging you. The Asteri just exterminated an entire human community in my city. Families." Her eyes burned with tears, and the frigid wind threatened to freeze them. "They killed *children.* To punish me. To punish my mate"—Bryce gestured to Hunt—"for escaping their clutches. This has to end—it has to stop *somewhere.*"

The cold anger in Nesta's eyes flickered.

Bryce couldn't stop the tears that slid down her cheeks, turning instantly to ice. "I know you don't trust me. You have no reason to. But I promise I'll return the Mask. I brought collateral—to prove that my intentions are good. That I *will* give it back."

And with that, Bryce ushered her parents forward. Ember and Randall gave her wary glances, but edged closer to the portal.

It tore Bryce's heart out to do it, but she said firmly to Nesta, "These are my parents. Ember Quinlan and Randall Silago. I'm giving them to you—to stay in your world, until I destroy the Asteri and return the Mask to you."

Nesta's eyes flared with shock, but she mastered it instantly, squaring her shoulders. "And if you die in the process?"

"Then my parents will be safer stuck in your world than in mine."

"But the Mask will be in yours. In the hands of the Asteri."

"I don't have anything greater to offer you than this," Bryce said, voice cracking.

"It's not about offering me anything."

Bryce bit back her sob, and her parents turned to her, confused and trusting, angry on her behalf without knowing why.

"Bryce," Hunt said, eyeing that approaching storm. "We should shut the connection." Only Hunt knew the horrible thing she was doing. How it had killed her to leave Cooper behind, because it would have been too suspicious to insist he come on so dangerous a mission. But Baxian, Fury, and June would look after him—and Syrinx.

"Bryce?" her mom asked. "What's going on?"

Bryce couldn't stop her tears as she looked at her mom, at her dad. Possibly for the last time. "Nothing," she said, and faced Nesta again.

"If you won't give me the Mask," she said to the female, "then take them anyway."

Nesta blinked.

"Take my parents," Bryce said, voice breaking. "They have no idea why they're here or who you are or what your world is. They think I'm talking to someone in Hel. But take them, and keep them safe. I ask only that."

Nesta studied Bryce, then Bryce's mother and father. She set her dagger down on the side table near her chair. "You'd leave them in my world . . . and possibly never see them again."

"Yes," Bryce said. "I need Hunt to help me against the Asteri. But my parents are human. They'll be easy targets for the Asteri—they're already being hunted by them. They're good people." She fought back another sob. "They're the best people."

"Bryce," Randall said, enough warning in his voice that she knew he'd spied the encroaching darkness and could tell that something was not right with this plan.

But Bryce couldn't look at her parents. Only at Nesta.

The silver fire in the female's gray-blue eyes banked. Then vanished.

Nesta extended her hand toward Bryce. Something golden glittered in it.

The Mask.

"For whatever good it can do you," Nesta said quietly, "it's yours to borrow." A glance at her parents told Bryce enough: she'd take the collateral.

Bryce's throat bobbed. Hunt murmured, "What the fuck *is* that thing?" As if he could sense the ancient, depthless power leaking from the Mask in Nesta's hand.

But Bryce said, "Thank you," and reached toward Nesta. She could have sworn the very world—all worlds—shuddered as Nesta's hand crossed into Midgard and passed the Mask to Bryce.

Then it was in Bryce's gloved fingers, and it was unholy and empty and cruel—but the star in her chest seemed to purr in its presence.

Bryce tucked it into her jacket, zipping it up inside. It thrummed against her body, its ancient beat echoing in her bones. Her starlight seemed to flicker in answer. Like whatever piece of Theia remained in it knew the Mask, and was glad to see it once more.

"Thank you," Bryce said again. The darkness was now blotting out the city below Nesta's window.

"Good luck," Nesta whispered.

Bryce inclined her head in thanks. And with a subtle nod to Hunt . . .

His power struck her parents. Not lightning, but a storm wind at their backs. Shoving them through the portal, through the Northern Rift, and into Nesta's world.

"Bryce!" her mother shouted, stumbling—but Bryce didn't wait. Didn't say anything as she willed the Horn to sever the connection, to collapse the bridge between their worlds. The last image she had was of the darkness, of Rhysand's power, slamming into the windows of Nesta's room, her mother's outraged face, Randall reaching for his rifle—

Snow and mist returned. The Rift was shut. And her parents were on the other side of it.

Bryce's knees wobbled. Hunt put a hand to her elbow. "We have to get out of here."

She had the Mask. And the Horn. And Theia's star. And the blades. It would have to be enough to take on living gods.

"Bryce, we have to go," Hunt said, stronger now. "Can you teleport us back to the wall?"

It should have been a relief, to know her parents were in that other world, with people who she had learned were decent and kind, but her mom would never forgive her. Randall would never forgive her. Not just for throwing them into that world, but for leaving Cooper behind.

"What the *fuck*," Hunt hissed, and Bryce whirled as he hauled her behind him.

Right as the Harpy, clad in white to camouflage her against the snow, dove from the mists. Even her black wings had been painted white to blend in.

Amid the swirling mists, she was as awful as Bryce remembered, yet her face . . . There was nothing alive there, nothing remotely aware. She was a husk. A host. With one mission: *kill*.

78

Any hope of succeeding died in Tharion as the River Queen's daughter threw herself into her mother's lap and sobbed. "You married *her*?"

They were the only words he could discern among the weeping.

Sathia just stared at the girl. Like she was completely out of politesse to spin to their advantage. The River Queen stroked her daughter's dark hair, murmuring gentle reassurances, but her eyes blazed with pure hate for Tharion.

Tharion began, "I . . ." He couldn't find the right words.

The River Queen's daughter lifted her head at his voice, her face streaked with tears. The river outside trembled, shaking the Blue Court. "You sold yourself to some Fae harlot?" She sniffed at Sathia. "With *dirt* in her veins? Not even a drop of water to call to you?"

Sathia took the insults, stone-faced, granting him a window into the way she'd been treated in her life. It didn't sit well.

It was enough to goad him into responding, "Her magic is that of growing things, of life and beauty. Not of drowning and stifling."

The River Queen's daughter stood slowly. "You *dare* speak to me in such a way?"

And at her petulant fury, at her mother's rage . . . he'd had it. He'd fucking *had* it.

Tharion pointed to the window. Not at the sobeks, but at the surface too far above to see. "There are *imperial battleships* in this river! Asphodel Meadows is a smoldering *ruin*, with the bodies of children strewn in the streets!"

He'd never yelled like this. At anyone, least of all his former queen and princess.

But he couldn't stop it, the pure rage and desperation that ruptured from him. "And all you care about is who one stupid fucking male is married to? There are babies in that rubble! And you cry only for *yourself*!"

Sathia was gaping, warning etched on her face, but Tharion spoke directly to the River Queen. "Bryce sent me to beg you to help, but I'm asking you personally, too. Not as mer, not as someone in the Blue Court, but as a living being who loves this city. There is nowhere else on Valbara that might weather the storm. This place, Beneath . . . it can withstand at least the initial brunt. Give the children of Crescent City a safe harbor. A chance. If you won't let all the people come, then at least take the children."

"No," the River Queen's daughter sniveled. "You used and discarded me. You don't have the right to ask such favors of us, of the Blue Court."

"I'm *sorry*," Tharion burst out. "I am sorry that I misled you, and slept with you, and realized too late that I had gone too far. I'm sorry I strung you along for years—I didn't know how to talk to you, or be an adult, and I'm sorry. It wasn't right of me, and it was immature, and I hate that I did that to you, to anyone."

She glowered at him, sniffling.

Tharion said, "And I married Sathia to bail her out of a shitty situation. King Morven of Avallen was forcing her into marriage with a Fae brute, and the only options were face the Asteri's wrath and die, or wed. I offered her a way out. Marriage to me. I owed it to my sister to help a female in trouble. Our marriage isn't a comment on how I feel about you *or* her."

"And the fact that she is a Fae beauty held no sway over you?" sneered the River Queen's daughter.

"No," Tharion said honestly. "I . . ." He looked toward his wife, who was indeed pretty. Beautiful. But that hadn't entered into his decision to offer his aid. "She was a person in trouble, who needed help."

The River Queen's daughter seethed.

Tharion said, voice breaking, "But if you take in the people of this city, if you shelter them against whatever storm the Asteri might bring . . . when this is over, if I am alive . . ." He held her stare. "I will divorce my wife and marry you."

Sathia whirled to him, but he couldn't face her, couldn't bear to see her reaction to how he'd abandon her, too—

The River Queen's daughter sniffed, a child calming from a tantrum. "I accept. I shall marry you once you're rid of her."

"You shall not." The River Queen's voice shook the room, the river. "My daughter does not accept this offer. Nor do I."

Tharion's chest crumpled. "Please," he begged. "If you could just—"

"I am not done speaking," she said, and held up a hand. Tharion obeyed. "I no longer wish my daughter to be tied to the likes of you, in truth or in promise. As far as marriage between you is concerned, it shall never happen."

"Mother—"

"You are your wife's problem now," the River Queen said to Tharion.

Tharion shut his eyes against the stinging in them, hating this, hating that he'd lost this opportunity, this safe haven for the people of Crescent City, due to his own bullshit.

"But your willingness to sacrifice your freedom to live Above is no small thing," the River Queen went on. She tilted her head to the side, and one of the shells in her hair sprouted legs and skittered under the tresses. A hermit crab. "You never asked me why I sent you to look for Sofie Renast's body, and to find her brother."

Tharion opened his eyes and found her staring curiously at him. Not with kindness, but with something like respect. "It . . . it wasn't my place to question," he said.

"You are frightened of me, as all wise beings are," she said a shade smugly. "But I have fears, too. Of this world, at the mercy of the Asteri."

Tharion tried not to gape.

"Our people are ancient," the River Queen said. "My sisters and I remember a world before the Asteri arrived and caused the land's magic to wither. Entire islands vanished into the sea, our civilizations with them. And though we were limited in our power to stop them . . . we have tried, each in our own way."

Her daughter was staring at her like she didn't know her.

But the River Queen went on, "We remember the power the thunderbirds wielded. How the Asteri hunted them down. Because they *feared* them. And when I learned one had been killed, her thunderbird brother on the loose . . . I knew those were assets the Asteri would seek to recover at any cost. I might not have known why, but I had no intention of letting them attain either Sofie or her brother."

Tharion blinked. "You . . . you wanted them in order to stop the Asteri?"

A shallow nod. "It might not have made a difference in the greater sense, but keeping them safe was my attempt, however small, at thwarting the Asteri's plans."

Tharion had no idea what to do other than bow his head and admit, "Emile wasn't a thunderbird. Only a human. He's in hiding now."

"And yet you kept this from me." The river shuddered at her displeasure.

"I thought it would be best for the boy to disappear from the world completely."

The ruler scanned his face again for a long, long moment.

"I see the male that you are," the River Queen said, and it was more gentle than he'd ever heard her. "I see the male that you shall become." She nodded to Sathia. "Who sees a female in trouble and does not think of the consequences to his own life before helping." A nod, grave and contemplative. "I wish I had seen more of that male here. I wish you had been that male for my daughter. But if you are that male now, and you are that male for the sake of this city . . ."

She waved a hand, and the sobeks swam away on a silent command.

"Then the Blue Court shall help. Any who we can bring down here before the warships catch wind of it . . . any person, from any House: I shall harbor them."

The Harpy was a horror. Hunt could *feel* her lack of presence. The emptiness leaking from her.

The Asteri had raised her from the dead, but left her soul by the wayside.

They'd bypassed the necromancers, who used one's soul for resurrection, and instead created a perfect soldier to station here: one who did not feel cold, who did not need to eat, and who had no scruples whatsoever.

And it had all come from his lightning. His Helfire. He knew, deep down, that it wasn't his fault, but . . . he'd given Rigelus that lightning.

And it had created this nightmare.

Rigelus had to have guessed they'd come to the Northern Rift, and planted the Harpy to lie in wait.

Hunt rallied his lightning, making the mists glow eerily around him, but Bryce said, "What did they do to you?"

The Harpy didn't answer. She didn't show any sign that she'd heard or cared. As if she'd lost her voice. Her very identity.

"Fry the bitch," Bryce muttered to Hunt, and he didn't wait before sending a plume of lightning for the Harpy.

She dodged it, those white-painted wings as fast as they had ever been—

No, they hadn't been painted white. They'd *turned* white. As if whatever the Asteri had done to her with Hunt's lightning had bleached the color out of them.

Hunt threw another bolt of lightning, then another, and he might have lit up the whole fucking sky if not for that gods-damned halo—

"Athalar!" A familiar male voice rang from the mists above

them. Hunt didn't dare take his focus off the Harpy as the voice clicked.

Isaiah.

"What the *Hel*—" an equally familiar female voice said. Naomi.

But it was the third voice, coming from behind him as its owner landed in the snow, that made Hunt's blood go cold. "What new evil is this?"

The Governor of Valbara had arrived.

Bryce didn't know which was worse: Celestina or the Harpy. The female who'd stabbed them in the back, or the one who'd literally tried to slit Ruhn's throat.

She and Hunt couldn't take on two enemies at once—not in subfreezing temperatures, totally drained from opening the Rift, with the mists obscuring almost everything.

The Harpy swooped, and Hunt launched his lightning, so fast only the swiftest of angels could evade the strike. The Harpy did, and plunged earthward, mist streaming off her white wings, straight for Bryce. Bryce rolled out of the way and the Harpy hit the ground, snow exploding around her, but she was instantly up, lunging for Bryce again.

Isaiah blasted the Harpy with a wall of wind, knocking her back. But Celestina stood three yards away, and Hunt was already whirling to face her—

Bryce unzipped her thick jacket, the cold wind instantly biting into her skin. She grabbed the Mask.

And gave no warning at all as she fitted the icy gold to her face.

Wearing the Mask was like being underwater, or at a very high altitude. Her head was full of its power, her blood thrumming, pulsing in time with the presence in her head, her bones. The world seemed to dilute into its basics: alive or dead. She was alive, but with the Mask, she might escape even death itself and live forever.

The star in her chest hummed, welcoming that power like an old friend.

Bryce shoved aside her revulsion. Hunt was readying his lightning for Celestina, the mists glowing with each crackle, and the Harpy had broken through Isaiah's power and was diving for Bryce again—

"Stop," Bryce said to the Harpy. It was her voice, but not.

The Harpy halted.

Everyone halted.

"Bryce," Hunt breathed, but he was far away. He was alive, and her business was with the dead.

"Kneel."

The Harpy fell to her knees in the snow.

Celestina started, "What evil weapon have you—"

"I shall deal with you later," Bryce said in that voice that resonated through her and created ripples in the mist.

Even the Archangel fell silent as Bryce approached the Harpy. Peered down into her narrow, hateful face. Truly soulless.

A body with no pilot.

Cold horror lurched through Bryce, despite the Mask's unholy embrace. Maybe it was a mercy, she thought as she stared into the vacant, raging face of the Harpy. Maybe it was a mercy to do this.

There was no soul to grab onto, to command. Only the body. But the Mask seemed to understand what was needed. "Your work is done," Bryce said, her voice reverberating through the frozen landscape. "Be at rest."

It was sickening—and yet it was a relief as the Harpy's eyes closed and she collapsed to the ground. As her skin began to wither, her body reclaiming the form it had known in death.

The cheekbones sank, decaying over the Harpy's face. Bryce knew that beneath the angel's white gear, her body would be doing the same.

When the Harpy lay desiccated in the snow, Bryce finally peeled the Mask off—only to find Naomi, Isaiah, and Celestina staring at her, awash in shock and dread.

79

Nah," Ruhn said into the phone as he and Lidia once again wended through the sewers, "they weren't at the triarii's private barracks. We waited for hours, but they're deserted. No one came or went. From the look of Isaiah's and Naomi's rooms, no one's been there for days."

Lidia trudged ahead, neck bent forward as she checked a burner phone she'd brought with her from the *Depth Charger*—years ago, it seemed.

"So what do we do?" Flynn asked. "Keep waiting? Dec was able to hack into the Aux's computers while I scouted around the area, but he found nothing about their movements, either. It doesn't seem like the Aux even knows they're gone." With the Asteri out to punish anyone caught associating with them, it had been safest to observe the Aux from a distance, rather than directly talk to anyone. Not to mention the risk of being sold out to the Asteri by any enterprising sorts.

Ruhn considered. "If Isaiah and Naomi are missing, Celestina probably wants to keep their absence unnoticed."

In the background, Declan said, "You think she killed them?"

"It's possible," Ruhn said as Flynn switched him to speakerphone. "We're going to circle back there tomorrow. See if we can pick up anything else. You two be on the lookout for any sign of them. Check the squares where they do the crucifixions."

"Fuck," Flynn said.

"I'll try to access the security footage from the Comitium," Dec volunteered. "Maybe there's something there that can point us in the right direction."

Ruhn sighed. "Be careful. Let's rendezvous at sunset—the northeastern corner of the intersection just past the shooting range."

"Copy," Flynn and Dec said, and hung up.

Ruhn and Lidia walked another block or so in the reeking quiet before he said, "You lulled me to sleep with a story once. About a witch who turned into a monster."

"What of it?" She glanced sidelong at him.

"Is it a real story, or did you make it up?"

"It was a story my mother told me," she said softly. "The only story I remember her telling me as a child before she . . . let me go."

He'd been about to ask if the similarities between the evil prince and Pollux, the kind knight and himself, had been meant prophetically, but at the sadness in her voice . . . "I'm really sorry you went through that, Lidia. I can't imagine doing that to a child. The thought of letting my own kid go into the arms of a stranger—"

"I did it, though," she said, staring ahead at nothing. "What my mother did to me, I did exactly the same thing to my sons."

His heart ached at the pain and guilt in her voice. "You entrusted your sons to a loving family—"

"I didn't know that. I had no idea who they were going to be living with."

"But the alternative was taking them with you."

"Maybe I should have. Maybe I should have run into the wilds and hidden forever with them."

"What kind of life would that have been? You gave them a real life, and a happy one, on the *Depth Charger*."

"A true mother would have—"

"You *are* a true mother," he said, and grabbed her hand, turning her to face him. "Lidia, you made an impossible choice—you decided to protect your children, even if it meant you wouldn't see them grow up. Fuck, if that doesn't make you a true mother, then I don't know what does."

Pain rippled across her face, and he wrapped his arms around her as she leaned against his chest. "They were the one thing that kept me going," she said. "Through every horror, it was just knowing that they were there, and safe, and that my choices were keeping them that way."

He slid a hand down her back, luxuriating in the feel of her, offering up whatever comfort he could. They stood there for long minutes, just holding each other.

"I told you before," she said against his chest, "that you remind me that I'm alive."

He kissed the top of her head in answer, her golden hair silky against his mouth.

"For a long time, I wasn't," she said. "I did my work as the Hind, as Daybright—all to keep my sons safe and do what I thought was right. But I felt nothing. I was essentially a wraith most days, occupying a shell of a body. But then I met you, and it was like I was back in my body again. Like I was . . . awake." She pulled back, scanning his face. "I don't think I'd ever been truly awake," she said, "until I met you."

He smiled down at her, his heart too full for words. So he kissed her, gently, lovingly.

She slid her hand into his as they continued onward. But Ruhn paused her again, long enough to tip her head back and kiss her once more. "I know we have some shit to sort out still," he said against her mouth, "but . . . girlfriend, lover, whatever you want to be, I'm all in."

Her lips curved against his in a smile. "I thank Urd every single day that Cormac asked you to be my contact."

He pulled away, grinning. "I still owe you a beer."

"If we get through this, Ruhn," she said, "I'll buy *you* a beer."

Ruhn grinned again, and slid an arm around her waist as they walked on into the gloom. They strode in warm, companionable quiet for several blocks before Lidia's phone buzzed, and she pulled it from her pocket to glance at the screen. "It's from the *Depth Charger*," she said, and paused to open the message.

He watched her eyes dart over the screen—then halt. Her hands shook.

"Pollux," Lidia breathed, and Ruhn stilled. Her eyes lifted to his, and pure panic filled them as she whispered, "He's taken my sons."

Hunt didn't let himself dwell on it—the unholy majesty that was Bryce wearing the Mask. On what she'd been able to do to the Harpy.

He faced Celestina, Isaiah and Naomi behind her, all clad in heavy winter gear. Isaiah's and the Governor's white wings were nearly invisible against the snow. All their faces, however, were taut with shock. "What are you doing here?" Hunt said.

"What is that?" Naomi breathed, ignoring his question, eyes on the golden object in Bryce's hands.

"Death," Isaiah answered, face ashen. "That mask . . . it's death."

Hunt demanded again, "What are you doing here?"

Isaiah's eyes shot to Hunt's. "We've been tracking that *thing*." He gestured to the pile of clothes that had been the resurrected Harpy moments before. "Celestina's old contacts up here reported that the guard station at the wall had been attacked by some new terror, so we all raced up here, fearing it was something from Hel—"

"Why not send a legion?" Hunt asked, eyeing the two angels who'd once been his closest companions. "Why come yourselves?"

"Because the Asteri ordered us to stand down," Naomi said. "But someone still had to stop this carnage."

Hunt met Celestina's eyes, the Archangel's flawless face a mask of stone. "Going off-leash, huh?"

Temper sparked in her gaze. "I regret what I did to you and yours, Hunt Athalar, but it was necessary to—"

"Spare me," Hunt snapped. "You fucking betrayed us to the Asteri—"

"Hunt," Isaiah said, holding up a hand, "look, there's a lot of bad blood here—"

"Bad blood?" Hunt exploded. "I fucking went to the *dungeons* because of her!" He pointed at the Governor. Bryce moved closer to him, a comforting presence at his side. He gestured to his forehead, barely visible with his gear. "I have this *halo* on my fucking head again because of her!"

Celestina just stood there, shivering. "As I said, I regret what I did. It has cost me more than you know." She seemed to blink back tears. "Hypaxia has . . . ended things between us."

"What, your girlfriend didn't like that you're a two-faced snake?" Hunt said.

"Hunt," Bryce murmured, but he didn't fucking care.

"You were supposed to be *good*," Hunt said, voice breaking. "You were supposed to be the good Archangel. And you're even worse than Micah." He spat, and it turned to ice before it could hit the snow. "At least he made it clear when he was fucking someone over."

His lightning thrashed in his veins, looking for a way out.

"Hunt," Naomi said, "what the Governor did was fucked up, but—"

"She went against Asteri orders to be here," Isaiah finished. "Let's get out of the cold and talk—"

"I'm done fucking talking," Hunt said, and his power stirred. "I am *done* with Archangels and your fucking *bullshit*."

His lightning hissed along the snow. And as his vision flashed, he knew lightning forked across his eyes.

Celestina held up her gloved hands. "I want no quarrel with you, Athalar."

"Too bad," Hunt said, and lightning skittered over his tongue. "I want one with you."

He didn't give any further warning before he hurled his power at the Archangel. He gave everything, yet it wasn't enough. His power choked at its limits, restrained by the halo.

A leash to hold demons in check.

It hadn't worked on the princes. He'd be damned if he allowed it to keep working on him.

Hunt let his power build and build and build. The snow around him melted away.

Apollion had given his essence, his Helfire, to Hunt. And if that made him a son of Hel, so be it.

Hunt closed his eyes, and saw it there—the black band of the halo, imprinted across his very soul. Its scrolling vine of thorns. The spell to contain him.

Everyone knew the enslavement spell couldn't be undone. Hunt had never even tried. But he was done playing by the Asteri's rules. By anyone's rules.

Hunt reached a mental hand toward the black thorns of the halo. Wreathed his fingers in lightning, in Helfire, in the power that was his and only his.

And sliced through it.

The thorns of the halo shivered and bled. Black ink dripped down, dissolving into nothing, gobbled up by the power that was now surging in him, rising up—

Hunt opened his eyes to see Isaiah gaping at him in fear and awe. The halo still marred his friend's brow.

No more.

Knowing where it was, how to destroy it, made it easier. Hunt reached out a tendril of his power for Isaiah, and before his friend could recoil, he sliced a line through the halo on his brow.

Isaiah hissed, staggering back. A roaring, raging wind rose from his feet as his halo, too, crumbled away from his brow.

Celestina was looking between them, terror stark on her face. "That's not—that's not—"

"I suggest you run," Hunt said, his voice as frozen as the wind that bit at their faces.

But Celestina straightened. Held her ground. And with bravery he didn't expect, she said, "Why are *you* here?"

As if he'd be distracted by the question, as if it'd keep her fate at bay—

Bryce answered for him. "To open the Northern Rift to Hel."

Naomi whirled on Bryce and said, "What?"

Isaiah, too stunned at his halo's removal to pay much attention to the conversation, was staring at his hands—as if he could see the unleashed power they now commanded.

Celestina shook her head. "You've lost your minds." She planted her feet, and white, shining power glowed around her. "You want to fight me, Athalar, go ahead. But you're not opening the Rift."

"Oh, I think we are," Hunt said, and launched his lightning at her.

The world ruptured as it collided with a wall of her power, and Hunt poured more lightning in, snow melting away, the very stone beneath them buckling and warping as his lightning struck and struck and struck—

"Athalar!" Naomi shouted. "What the fuck—"

Celestina blasted out her power, a wall of glowing wind.

Hunt snapped his lightning through it. He was done with the Archangels. With their hierarchies. Done with—

Isaiah stepped into the fray, hands up.

"Stop," he said, and power glowed in his friend's eyes. "Athalar, stop."

"She deserves to die—every fucking Archangel deserves to die for what they do to us," Hunt said through his teeth. But it registered, suddenly, that Bryce was no longer by his side.

She was running back toward the Rift, her star blazing. So bright—with the two other pieces of Theia's star now united with what Bryce had been born with, her star blazed as bright as the sun. The sun *was* a star, for fuck's sake—

"No!" Celestina shouted, and her power flared.

Hunt slammed his lightning into the Archangel so hard it shattered her power, sending her flying back into the snow with a satisfying thud.

Celestina's wings splayed wide, flinging snow in all directions, blood leaking from her nose and mouth. "Don't!" she cried to Bryce. "I've dedicated *years* of my life to preventing the Rift from opening," she panted. "Find another way. Don't do this."

Bryce halted, snow spraying with the swiftness of her stop.

That magnificent star blazed from her chest, casting a brilliant glimmer over the snow. Breathing hard, Bryce said to the Archangel, "The Princes of Hel have offered their help, and Midgard needs it, whether you know it or not. Hunt and I have already killed two Archangels. Don't make us kill you, too."

Hunt glanced to Bryce in question. As if there was an alternative to killing Celestina—

"You . . . ," Celestina said. "You killed Micah and Sandriel," she whispered.

"They were stronger than you," Hunt said, "so I don't think much of your chances."

Hunt's lightning flared around him, poised to strike, to flay her from the inside out, as he had done with Sandriel.

But Celestina's brown eyes widened at his lightning, released from its bonds and spreading through the world. She'd never seen the full extent of what he could do—she'd never had the chance during those weeks they'd worked together. "How is it . . . how is it that you have the power of Archangels but are not one yourself?" she asked.

"Because I'm the Umbra Mortis," Hunt said, voice unyielding as the ice around them. And he'd never felt more like it as he stared at Celestina, and knew that with one strike to her heart, she'd be smoldering, bloody ruins.

Celestina's gaze lowered, and she dropped to her knees. Like she knew it, too.

A plume of pure, uncut lightning rose above Hunt's shoulder, an asp ready to strike true. He looked to Bryce, waiting for the nod to incinerate her.

But Bryce was staring at him sadly. Softly, lovingly, she said, "You're not, Hunt."

He didn't understand the words. He blinked at her.

Bryce stepped forward, snow crunching under her feet. "You're not the Umbra Mortis," she said. "You never were, deep down. And you never will be."

Hunt pointed a lightning-wreathed finger at Celestina. "She and all her kind should be blasted off the face of Midgard."

"Maybe," Bryce said gently, taking another step. Her starlight faded into nothing. "But not by you."

Disgust roiled through him. He'd never once hated Bryce, but in that moment, as she doubted him, he did.

"She doesn't deserve to die, Hunt."

"Yes, she fucking does," Hunt spat. "I remember each and every one of them—all the angels who marched against us on Mount Hermon, all the Senate, the Asteri, and the Archangels at my sentencing. I remember *all* of them, and she's no better than they were. She's no better than Sandriel. Than Micah."

"Maybe," Bryce said again, her voice still gentle, soothing. He hated that, too. "No one is forgiving her. But she doesn't deserve to die. And I don't want her blood on your hands."

"Where was this mercy when it came to the Autumn King? You didn't stop Ruhn then."

"The Autumn King had done nothing in his long, miserable life except inflict pain. He didn't merit my notice, let alone my mercy. She does."

"Why?" He looked to his mate, his rage slipping a notch. *"Why?"*

"Because she made a mistake," Naomi said, stepping forward, expression pained. "And has been trying to make it right ever since. Isaiah and I didn't come up here with her because she ordered us to. We wanted to help her."

Hunt pointed to the Rift mere feet from Bryce. "She's going to stop you from opening it."

"I will not," Celestina promised, keeping her head bowed. "I yield."

"Let her go, Hunt," Bryce said.

"Morven yielded, and you killed him," Hunt snapped at her.

"I know," Bryce said. "And I'll live with that. I wouldn't wish the same burden on you. Hunt . . . We have enough enemies. Let her go."

"I swear upon Solas himself," Celestina said, the highest oath an angel could invoke, "that I will help you, if it is within my power."

"I'm not going to take the word of an Archangel."

"Well, we're going to need this Archangel," Bryce said, and Hunt's rage slipped further as he looked to her again.

"What?"

Bryce glanced at the Harpy's body, half-melted from Hunt's lightning clashing with Celestina's power. The rock around it had been warped—his lightning had altered the stone itself. Bryce closed the distance between her and Hunt, reaching out to take his hand.

His lightning crawled over her skin, but he didn't let it hurt. He could never hurt her.

"You said you're with me—all of you," Bryce murmured, staring at him and only him. "Put the past behind you. Focus on what's ahead. We have a world to save, and I need my mate at my side to do it. No one else—not a son of Hel, not the Umbra Mortis, not even Hunt fucking Athalar. I need my *mate*. Just Hunt."

He saw it all in her eyes—that no matter what had happened, who he'd been and what he'd done . . . it really didn't matter to her. Being made in Hel didn't matter to her. But she'd captured who he was, deep down, in those photos last spring. The person she'd brought into the world. The person she loved.

Just Hunt.

So he let go. Let go of the lightning, of the death singing in his veins. Let go of Apollion's and Thanatos's smirking faces. Let go of his rage at the Archangel before him, and the Archangels who'd existed before her.

Just Hunt. He liked that.

His lightning faded, fizzling away entirely. And he said to Bryce, as if she were the only person on Midgard, in any galaxy, "I love you, Just Bryce."

She snickered, and kissed him lightly on the cheek. "Now, if you don't plan on killing Celestina anymore . . ." Bryce pulled the Mask from her jacket again. "We're going to raise an army."

"What army?" Isaiah whispered.

"We're going to raise the Fallen," Bryce said, tossing the Mask in the air and catching it like it was a fucking sunball.

Hunt's knees buckled. "You said we were going to use the Mask to fight the Asteri."

"And we are," Bryce said, pitching the Mask up and catching it once more. "It's your fault you didn't ask for specifics on *how* we'd use it against them."

No, he'd assumed she'd put it on and it would give her some edge to kill them.

Hunt shook his head. "You're out of your mind."

Bryce halted her tossing at that, voice gentling. "We need a distraction for the Asteri. Hel won't be enough. But an army of the dead, an army of the Fallen, will work nicely. An army that won't have to die again. And Isaiah and Naomi are going to lead them."

"That's why you sent Ruhn and Lidia to get them," Hunt said quietly, fighting through his shock.

Isaiah gave him a questioning look, but Bryce replied, "Yes. I thought if we could get them, and get the Mask from Nesta . . . it might work."

"But how can you raise them?" Hunt demanded. Nesta had used the bones of a beast, Bryce had told him. "Their bodies are gone—"

"The Asteri kept their wings," Bryce said, disgust lacing every word. "They kept *your* wings, like trophies. But because they didn't have Sailings, I think part of their souls might still be attached."

Hunt rubbed at his frozen face. "And what—you're just going to have a bunch of wings flying around?"

She cut him a sharp look. "No. Well, yes—but only to get them to where we need their souls."

"You said the Mask can reanimate dead bodies—not give souls new ones."

"That's what I saw Nesta do," Bryce said. "But Theia's star . . ."

Cupping her hands before her chest, she drew out the blazing, beautiful star. It illuminated the mists, set the snow at their feet sparkling.

"Wow," Naomi breathed.

What Bryce had taken from her chest that day during the

attack last spring was a fraction of the star she now held between her palms.

"This," Bryce said, face glowing in the starlight, "seems to recognize the Mask, somehow. When I put the Mask on, I could feel the pull between the two powers. Maybe it's something about Theia's star. I think it can command the Mask to do . . . different things."

"This isn't the time to experiment," Hunt warned.

"I know," Bryce conceded. "But I think all it would take is a bit of the deceased, and I could Make them anew. Not give them true life, but their souls would be returned—given new forms. Unlike . . . unlike what the Asteri did to the Harpy."

"That mask can truly raise the dead, then," Naomi said hoarsely.

Bryce nodded. "The Fallen wouldn't be given new, breathing bodies, but yes—they'd be able to help us."

"What sort of bodies, then?" Isaiah asked, glancing nervously at Hunt.

"Ones the Asteri already made for us," Bryce said a shade quietly. "Perfect blends of magic and tech."

"The new mech-suits," Hunt realized. "The ones the Asteri stationed on Mount Hermon."

Bryce nodded gravely. "I think Rigelus stationed those suits up there to taunt you guys, but it's about to blow up in his stupid fucking face. Lidia said the suits don't need pilots to operate, so we don't have to worry about any physical interference. Dec can hack into their computer system and block imperial access while the souls of the Fallen fuse with the mech-suits and pilot them under Naomi and Isaiah's command."

But to do what she was suggesting . . .

"We can't," Hunt rasped, wings slumping. "*I can't* ask them to die for us again. Even if they're already dead. The Fallen have given too much."

Bryce walked over to him. Took his hand. "We need those suits piloted by the Fallen, or they'll be used against *us* by the Asteri. We need the Asteri and their forces entirely occupied."

But Hunt's heart twisted. "Bryce."

"It will be their choice whether to return, to pilot those suits. I'll give them that choice, when I raise them. And I'll be with you for every moment of it." She nodded to Isaiah and Naomi. "They'll command the Fallen. You don't need to shoulder that burden anymore. I'll need you with me—in the Asteri's palace."

He closed his eyes, breathing in her scent. Celestina could have struck, he supposed, but she remained kneeling.

And just as he had that day when Hunt had given Sandriel her due, Isaiah suddenly knelt before him. Naomi joined him on her knees.

"I'm not an Archangel," Hunt blurted. "And I haven't agreed to lead you two. So get up."

It was Celestina who said, "Perhaps the age of Archangels is over."

"You sound happy about it."

"I would be, if it were to come to pass," Celestina said, and got to her feet. "I told you once: Shahar was my friend. I might not have had the courage to fight alongside her then . . ." Her chin lifted. "But I do now."

He was having none of it. "And what are *you* going to do during all this?"

Bryce answered before Celestina could reply. "She's going to Ephraim's fortress." At Hunt's surprised look, echoed by Celestina, Bryce explained, "He's the closest Archangel to the Eternal City. We need him occupied. If Ephraim joins the fight, it will complicate everything."

Celestina nodded gravely. "I will make sure he does not come within a hundred miles of the capital."

"How?" Hunt demanded. "Tie him up?"

"I will do whatever is necessary to end this," Celestina said, chin high.

Hunt pointed to the Rift. "We're going to open the Rift to *Hel*. You didn't seem too keen on that a moment ago."

Celestina glanced between Hunt and Bryce. "It goes against everything I've worked for, but . . . it does seem that all you two have done has been in the best interest of the innocents of

Midgard. I don't believe that you would open the Rift if it would jeopardize the most vulnerable."

"Yeah?" Hunt snapped. "And where the fuck were *you* when Asphodel Meadows was blasted into nothing?"

That brought a measure of ice to Bryce's stare. True grief filled Celestina's eyes.

"It was the final straw, Hunt," Isaiah said. "Why we—she—disobeyed the Asteri. They gave no warning. The ships pulled into the Istros, and they said it was for our protection. I didn't even know the ships could send aerial missiles that far."

Naomi's lashes were pearled with tears that quickly turned to ice as she added, "It was the most cowardly, unforgivable . . . We don't stand for that. None of us. Not Celestina, and certainly not the 33rd."

Hunt looked back to Bryce, and found only pain and cold resolve staring back at him. She was right. They had enough enemies. Ones who had to pay.

And he might not have trusted one word out of an Archangel's mouth, but if Isaiah and Naomi believed Celestina, that meant something. Isaiah, who had suffered under Archangels as much as Hunt had, was here, helping Celestina, knowing she had betrayed his friend. Isaiah wasn't some spineless asshole—he was good and smart and brave.

And Isaiah was here.

So Hunt said, "All right. Let's ring Hel's doorbell."

Hunt had enough lightning left to blast Bryce again. It passed through her and into the Gate—into the heart of the Northern Rift.

Her will, blazing with that undiluted starlight, changed its location once more.

Celestina, Isaiah, and Naomi held back a step, all glowing with power, readying for the worst.

Impenetrable darkness spread within the archway, broken only by two glowing blue eyes.

Prince Aidas stood there, impeccably dressed in his jet-black clothes, not one golden hair on his head out of place. He surveyed the icy terrain, the sun now setting after a brief window of daylight.

Bryce swung her arm out in a grand, sweeping gesture as the Prince of the Chasm stepped through the Northern Rift. "Welcome back to Midgard," she said. "Hope you have a pleasant stay."

80

So," Jesiba said, drumming her fingers on her desk, "the pup goes to pitch a deworming medicine to a bunch of wolves and comes home Prime."

Ithan ignored the jab. "I need you to get me in with the Under-King," he said. He'd showered in the barracks at the Den and changed into nondescript Aux clothes, then swiftly checked on Perry and the others before running back to the House of Flame and Shadow. He was Prime, yes, and all that entailed, but—

"Why?"

"I need to see my brother. And considering that it was a fucking disaster the last two times I tangled with the dead . . . I'm not going to make mistakes this time. I need the Under-King's help." Ithan paced her office.

"Again: Why?"

He looked straight at her. "Because Connor is trying to reach me." He'd heard that howl from the Bone Quarter and known whose it was. Who was calling to him.

While Ithan had changed, Hypaxia had handed out the antidote at the Den, to those who'd take it. Perry had been first in line, apparently. And it hadn't been an Omega standing before Ithan when he'd checked on her as he left the Den.

Ithan hadn't stayed long enough to find out what Perry was—what powers she and the others had gained, long buried in the wolves' bloodline. He'd given the order that this new knowledge was to be contained to the Den, and the wolves had agreed.

Obeyed him.

"You were right," Ithan said to Jesiba, "about needing a plan. I have no idea what I'm doing."

"You could take some lessons from Quinlan about thinking two steps ahead."

Ithan glared at her. "Any updates from Avallen?"

"She called two hours ago. Wanting a favor, as always. And an update on your progress." The sorceress smirked. "And when I told her what Hypaxia had accomplished, of course, she requested that you bring that antidote to her."

"When—where?"

Jesiba smirked again. "The Eternal City. Tomorrow. I think Quinlan's had enough of being pushed around. She said to bring some wolves, if you have any to back you up."

Ithan stared. To not only *be* Prime, but to *act* as Prime . . . "Is there going to be a battle?"

"I don't know." Jesiba fixed him with a grave look. "But if I were you, I'd get the pups and vulnerable wolves to safe hiding places. Not the Den, not in Lunathion. Get them evacuated deep into the wild. Go to ground. And then take the best fighters you have to the Eternal City."

"There aren't many at the Den—most are away."

"Then take whoever's around. It will be better than nothing."

Ithan paced a step, then another. "Maybe I should have left Sigrid in that tank. It'd be better than being a Reaper." There was no one to blame for her predicament but himself. Ithan rubbed his forehead. "Look, I need to see my brother. One last time."

"That's impossible."

Ithan's teeth flashed. "I know you can ask the Under-King." He didn't wait for her reply before he asked, "Do you know—about the secondlight? That our souls are food for the Under-King and the Asteri?"

"Yes."

Ithan shook his head. "And it doesn't bother you?"

"Of course it bothers me. It's bothered me for fifteen thousand years. But it is just one branch of the many-headed beast of the Asteri rule."

Ithan scrubbed at his face. "Can you help me or not?" He'd need all the help he could get. He wasn't a leader. Judging by the mess he'd brought upon Sigrid, he wasn't fit to make decisions for anyone. He'd tried to save her and failed—utterly and completely failed. That had been only one life. With all the Valbaran wolves now his responsibility . . .

He pushed back against the crushing panic and dread.

Jesiba was silent for a moment. Then she said quietly, "Let me see what I can do, pup." Her mouth twisted to the side. "Bring Hypaxia with you."

Bryce had just entered the guard booth when her phone rang. She'd needed one second—one fucking moment by herself—to process the enormity of what she'd done.

She'd thrown her parents into the Fae world.

Bryce had always found a sense of comfort in knowing that no matter what she did, or where she was, Ember Quinlan and Randall Silago were in Nidaros—that Ember and Randall *existed* and would always be there to fight for her. Fight *with* her, if she was being honest about her mom. Knowing that was a comfort, too.

And now they were . . . gone. Alive, yes, but on the other side of the universe.

They could have stayed on Avallen, safe with everyone else, with Cooper . . . but she'd needed them. Needed them to bargain with Nesta, but she also needed to know that her parents were forever beyond the Asteri's reach.

It was selfish, she knew. Cowardly. But she didn't regret it.

Though she really wanted *one second* to process it all. Hence the guard booth.

Until the phone rang.

She'd been out of range beyond the wall, so she had no idea if it was Urd's timing or if her brother had been trying to reach her nonstop. She answered on the first ring.

"Ruhn?"

"I need you back here."

"What's wrong?"

Panic edged his every word. "Pollux intercepted the *Depth Charger* as it dropped people off at the edge of Avallen's mists. He slaughtered a bunch of mer, and . . . I don't know how, but he knew about Lidia's sons. He took them. He's holding them at the palace."

Bryce nearly dropped her phone. Outside, Hunt was a shadow against the darkness and snow, their companions more shadows around him.

"I guess the Asteri figured out how to lure us to them," Bryce said quietly.

"The *Depth Charger* sent us a transport pod—we're about to get on it with Flynn and Dec and head to the Eternal City," Ruhn said hoarsely. "But if those kids are in the dungeons—"

Her stomach flipped. "Okay," she breathed. "Yes, of course. Okay. We'll get on the helicopter immediately."

Ruhn let out a shaking breath. "Did you . . . do what you needed to up there?"

"Yes," Bryce said, and stepped out into the howling wind and brutal cold. Hunt and Aidas were huddled together, planning. Isaiah and Naomi stood a few feet away, chiming in, but keeping their distance, as if not quite comfortable with the idea that they were in the presence of a Prince of Hel. Celestina had flown off to Ephraim's fortress in Ravilis moments ago, her white wings blindingly bright with the light off the snow. She'd keep him occupied, she'd promised again before leaving—with a final nod to Hunt that he hadn't returned.

Beyond Hunt and the others, stretching into the distance, marched the armies of Hel. They covered all twenty-four and a half miles from the wall to the still-open Rift.

Unholy terrors—especially those pets that had been unleashed in Crescent City this spring. Bryce had never been more glad to have the Archesian amulet around her neck—though she wondered if it could hold off *this* many demons, should they choose to have a little snack.

From Hunt's tense shoulders, she knew the horde was as unnerving for him as it was for her. Leathery-winged, horned humanoids that seemed to be grunt soldiers. Bone-white reptilian beasts that crawled on all fours—hounds of war. Skeletal beings with too-large jaws, stacked with needlelike teeth that gleamed with greenish slime. There were more—so many more: things that slithered, things that flew, things that surveyed Midgard with milky, sightless eyes and bayed at the anticipated bloodlust.

Hunt offered no commentary on the endless lines of nightmares. He'd spent a lifetime hunting down the very creatures now fighting for them—how many of Hel's marching forces knew that, too? How many of them had crossed into Crescent City just a few months ago and gleefully unleashed pain and death?

But this time, true to the princes' word, the beasts stayed in line. As for the soldiers, Bryce didn't look too closely at the faces beneath their armor. At the spiky wings poking above the lines, the taloned hands gripping spears. But they did not speak, did not snarl. Their breath curled from beneath the visors of their helmets with each step through the frigid air. Each step deeper into Midgard.

All of Hel, ready to strike.

She had to trust that it would prove to be the right choice.

"Tell Lidia we're coming," Bryce said to Ruhn, still on the line. The thundering of their feet and hooves and claws shook the snowy earth. "And tell her we're not coming alone."

81

This seems familiar," Ithan muttered to Hypaxia as they stood on the Black Dock, each clutching a Death Mark in their hands. "You, me, the Under-King . . ."

"Our best friend," Hypaxia said wryly, the mists from the Bone Quarter an impenetrable wall across the river. She gestured to the water. "Shall we?"

Ithan nodded, and they flicked their Death Marks into the river. They landed with a soft plunk, and ripples spread outward in only one direction—south. Toward the Bone Quarter. They vanished into the mist.

In the ensuing silence, Ithan dared say, "Jesiba said you and the Governor were, ah . . . together. How long?"

She threw him a pained wince. "A while. But not anymore."

"Even while she was with Ephraim?"

"Her arrangement with Ephraim is a political contract. What she and I have . . . had . . ." She shook her head, the moonlight silvering her dark curls. "I'm sure Jesiba said I was naïve."

"Maybe," he hedged.

Hypaxia looked at where her Death Mark had disappeared under the surface. "Everyone told me, you know. That Archangels aren't to be trusted. That they've got those secret training camps that indoctrinate them, that they're puppets for the Asteri. But she spent all that time in Nena, and I thought it had removed her from their influence." She chewed on her lip, then added, "Apparently it gave her incentive to do whatever it took to get her off that frozen bit of land."

"We . . . we all make bad decisions." He blew out a breath. "Gods, that sounded dumb."

Hypaxia laughed quietly. "It's appreciated nonetheless." She sobered. "But when I learned what she'd done . . . Well. I miss my mother most days, but especially lately. Especially after everything with Celestina." She indicated the mists across the way. "So I understand why you seek out your brother."

"I'm sorry about your mother," he offered.

"Most people tell me I should be over her passing. But . . ." Her shoulders bowed. "I don't know if there will ever come a day when I don't feel like there's a hole in my heart where she used to be."

"Yeah," he said quietly, his own chest aching. "I know the feeling." He cleared his throat. "So you couldn't, uh, raise your mom with your necromancy?"

"No," Hypaxia said gravely. "She took steps to ensure that her soul did not fall into the clutches of the Under-King. And even if I could, she would resent me for using it for something so . . . selfish."

"She's your mom, though."

"She was also my queen." Hypaxia's chin lifted. "And she would be ashamed to learn that I have defected from the witches and yielded my crown. So, no. I don't want to see her. I couldn't face her, even if I had the chance."

"Aren't you still a witch, though? I mean, yeah—you're now in Flame and Shadow, but you didn't stop being a witch." Jesiba may have rejected the title, but that had been her choice.

"I'm still a witch," Hypaxia said, hands curling at her sides. "That can never be taken away from me."

Ithan surveyed the black planks beneath his feet. He had to arrange the Sailing for the Prime. For Sabine, too, he supposed.

Did he, though? The Prime's soul was gone. There was nothing to offer up to the Bone Quarter beyond an empty body. And if the people of Lunathion saw the Prime's boat tip, not understanding why . . . he couldn't allow it.

He'd gladly give Sabine the indignity of letting everyone see her boat tip. He'd also be glad to let her soul live on in the Bone Quarter until it was time to be turned into mystery meat for the Asteri, but he'd have to decide whether she deserved a Sailing in the first place.

Gods, he wished Bryce was with him. She'd have an idea. *Just cut her up real small and shove her down the garbage disposal.*

Ithan snorted and offered up a prayer to Luna's bright face above him that his friend was indeed safe—and on the move.

A black boat glided out of the mists ahead, aiming straight for Ithan and Hypaxia, waiting on the dock. Exactly as Jesiba had promised it would.

Ithan swallowed hard. "Cab's here."

Ithan knew he was Prime of the Valbaran Wolves, but he certainly didn't feel like it. The whole thing was a joke. He was just . . . a dude. Granted, one with more power than he'd realized, but now there were people depending on him. He had to make decisions.

At least as sunball captain, he'd had coaches telling him what to do. Now he was coach and captain rolled into one.

And, given how much he'd fucked up lately, how every choice to help Sigrid had only led her toward an absolutely disastrous fate . . . Gods, he really didn't feel like Prime at all.

But he tried to at least look like it—back straight, shoulders squared—as he and Hypaxia stood before the Under-King in a gray-stoned temple to Urd.

The Under-King lounged on a throne beneath a behemoth statue of a figure holding a black metal bowl between her upraised hands. Symbols were carved all over the bowl, continuing down her fingers, her arms, her body. Ithan could only assume it was meant to represent Urd. No other temples ever depicted the goddess, no one even dared—most people claimed that fate was impossible to portray in any one form. But it seemed that the dead, unlike the living, had a vision of her. And those symbols running from the bowl onto her skin . . . they were like tattoos.

They looked oddly familiar. Ithan didn't have time to ponder it as he and Hypaxia inclined their heads to the Under-King.

"Thank you for the audience," Ithan said, trying to keep his breathing normal. Praying that none of those hounds the Under-King had sent after them on the Autumnal Equinox were lurking around in the misty shadows.

At least there weren't any Reapers. No sign of Sigrid, wherever she'd gone. One more clusterfuck for him to deal with—but another day. If he managed to live another day, of course.

The Under-King's bony, withered fingers clicked on the stone arms of his throne. "Prime," he said to Ithan, "I'm honored to be your first political visit. Though I believe protocol dictates that a meeting with the Governor should have been your priority." A knowing glance at Hypaxia. "Unless present company makes such things . . . uncomfortable."

Hypaxia's eyes flickered, but she said nothing.

They'd come here for a reason, so Ithan ignored the Under-King's mocking and said, "Look, uh . . . Your Majesty." The Under-King gave him a smile that was all browned, aged teeth. Ithan tried not to shudder. "Jesiba Roga said you agreed that we could make a request. I'd like to speak to my brother, Connor Holstrom."

The Under-King turned to Hypaxia. "Did I not give you duties to attend to?"

"Handing out blood bags to vampyrs isn't a good use of my time," Hypaxia said with impressive authority.

"Shall I reassign you to waiting on the Reapers?" A cruel smile. "They'd enjoy a taste or two of you, girl."

"I only want five minutes with my brother," Ithan interrupted.

"To do what?" The Under-King leaned forward.

"I need to tell him a few things."

"The goodbye you never got to say," the Under-King taunted.

"Yes," Ithan said sharply.

The Under-King angled his head. "And you promise not to warn him of what awaits?"

"Does it matter if I do? He's trapped here already," Ithan said, gesturing to the temple, the barren land beyond.

"I have no interest in civil unrest—even amongst the dead," the Under-King said. "And too much unrest would bring unwanted attention and questions." From the Asteri, no doubt.

Ithan crossed his arms. "That didn't seem to be your position when you sold my friends out to Pippa Spetsos."

"Pippa Spetsos stood to assist in expanding my kingdom significantly," the creature said. "It was an investment for my Reapers—to keep them contented and fed."

Ithan blocked out the flash of the Prime's broken body, the way Sigrid had sucked out his soul.

Hypaxia said calmly, "Why did the Reapers first defect from Apollion and join you?"

The Under-King flinched. "Do not speak his name here."

"My apologies," Hypaxia murmured. She didn't sound at all sorry.

But the Under-King settled himself. "In Hel, the Reapers fed on and ruled the vampyrs, and when the vampyrs defected to this world, the Reapers followed their food source. And found the other beings on Midgard to be a veritable feast. So they have left the vampyrs to themselves, feeding as they please on the rest of the populace."

Ithan couldn't stop his shudder this time. He couldn't imagine what Hel was like, if Reapers and vampyrs had just been walking about—

"But you are not from Hel," Hypaxia said.

"No." The Under-King's milky eyes settled on Ithan. "I was birthed by the Void, but my people . . ." He smiled cruelly at Ithan. "They were not unknown to your own ancestors, wolf. I crept through when they charged so blindly into Midgard. This place is much better suited to my needs than the caves and barrows I was confined to."

Ithan reeled. "You came from the shifters' world?"

"You were not known as shifters then, boy."

"Then what—"

"And she," the Under-King went on, gesturing to that unusual depiction of Urd towering above him, "was not a goddess, but a force that governed worlds. A cauldron of life, brimming with the language of creation. Urd, they call her here—a bastardized version of her true name. Wyrd, we called her in that old world."

"That is all well and good," Hypaxia said, "but my friend's request—"

"Go speak to your brother, boy," the Under-King drawled, almost melancholy. As if all the talk of his old world had exhausted him. "You have seven minutes."

Ithan's mouth dried out. "But where—"

The Under-King pointed to the exit behind them. "There."

Ithan turned. And there was Connor, as vibrant as he'd ever been in life, standing in the temple doorway.

82

Ithan didn't know whether to laugh or cry as he sat beside his brother on the front steps of the temple. Hypaxia remained inside, speaking quietly with the Under-King.

Connor appeared exactly as he had the day Ithan had last seen him, cheering in the stands at his sunball game . . . except for the bluish light around his body. The mark of a ghost.

Ithan had found out the hard way what that meant—he'd tried to hug his brother, but his arms went right through him.

Seven minutes. Less than that now.

"There's so much I wanted to say to you," Ithan began.

Connor opened his mouth, but no sound came out.

Ithan blinked. "You can't . . . you can't talk?"

Connor shook his head.

"Ever? Or just—now?"

Connor mouthed *ever.*

"But Danika talked to Bryce—"

Connor tapped his chest. As if to say, *In here.*

Ithan rubbed at his face. "The Under-King fucking *knew* you couldn't talk, and—"

Blue glowed in his vision as Connor laid a hand on his shoulder. It didn't have any weight. But the look his brother gave him, pitying and worried—

"I'm sorry I wasn't there," Ithan said, voice breaking.

Connor slowly shook his head.

"I should have been there."

Connor laid a finger on his lips. *Don't say another word.*

Ithan swallowed down the tightness in his throat. "I miss you every single day. I wish you were with me. I . . . Fuck, I'm knee-deep in shit, and I could really use my brother right now."

Connor angled his head. *Tell me.*

Ithan did. As succinctly as he could, aware of each second counting down. About Sigrid and Sabine and the Prime. About what he was now. About the parasite and its antidote.

Ithan glanced at his phone when he finished. Only two minutes left. Connor was smiling faintly.

"What?" Ithan said.

His brother laid a hand on his heart and bowed his head, a mark of respect to the Prime.

Ithan glowered. "It's not funny."

Connor lifted his head, shaking it. There was nothing but pride in his eyes.

Ithan's throat closed up. "I don't know what to do now. How to be Prime. How to fix this shit with Sigrid—if it can even *be* fixed. We're all out of Athalar's lightning now, anyway. Maybe I'm an asshole for not making Sigrid a priority. But I need to help Bryce and the others first. I'm so fucking far out of my league. And . . . there's more I can't tell you. I wish I could, but—"

Connor glanced behind them, to the temple and the Under-King inside it.

When he was assured that they were truly alone, he extended a hand toward Ithan. A sparkling seed of light filled it. Connor lifted it to his mouth and mimicked eating it.

"You know?" Ithan whispered. "About the secondlight?"

Connor nodded once.

Ithan snorted. "Trust the Pack of Devils to figure it out."

But Connor reached into a pocket and laid something on the ground between them.

A bullet.

It was crafted of the same reeking metal as a Death Mark. As if it had been created from all those coins tossed into the river. Whatever properties its metal held must have allowed it to be touched and moved by the dead.

"I don't understand," Ithan said. "What is it?"

Connor began gesturing, too fast for Ithan to follow.

But robes rustled on stone, and Ithan grabbed the black bullet before the Under-King appeared from between the temple pillars and declared, "Your time has come to an end."

Connor looked to Ithan's hand, then up at him, eyes pleading with him to catch his meaning.

"Just one more minute," Ithan begged. "Please."

"You have already been granted more than most mortals ever receive. Be grateful."

"Be grateful," Ithan breathed as Hypaxia stepped beside the Under-King. "For what? For my brother being *here*?" His shout echoed off the gray pillars, the gravel, the empty mists.

Connor signaled to shut up. Ithan ignored him.

"I refuse to accept this," Ithan seethed, claws glinting at his fingertips. "That *this* is the best it gets—"

"Remember your vow, pup," the Under-King warned.

Ithan bristled. "What are you but some freak alien from another world who capitalized on this one?"

Connor was staring at him now—eyes wide, urging him to be quiet, to stand down.

But that thing that had awoken in Ithan the moment the parasite had vanished wouldn't go away. It stared down this creature, this *thing* from his people's home world, and it knew the Under-King for what he truly was.

Enemy, his blood sang, and it spoke of caves beneath hills, of plundered graves and musty darkness. *Enemy.*

Ithan's snarl cleaved the mists, bounced off the temple. Frost curled at his fingertips. Even Connor backed away in surprise.

"What is that?" the Under-King said, backing away a step as well, toward the temple interior. Ithan peered down at his hands. The ice crusting them.

Enemy.

The silent dead, the suffering—Ithan would stand for it no more.

"Get out of my realm," the Under-King said, and Ithan scented his fear. His surprise and dread. Like he knew Ithan for that ancient enemy as well.

The Under-King backed away another step, nearly inside the temple now, and slipped on pure ice. Righting himself, robes fluttering, he lifted a bony hand, and Ithan knew in his gut it would be to summon the hunting hounds.

Ithan didn't give him the chance.

Ice crusted the Under-King's withered hand. Then his arm. Then his shoulder—

"Stop this *now*!" the Under-King bellowed.

But the ice kept crawling over him. Ithan let it. Let this male see what a ruthless fucking murderer he was, let him see that he wouldn't tolerate this shit for his brother, for his parents, for *anyone* he loved.

No more Sailings. He'd never go to another.

He'd single-handedly destroyed the Fendyr line. Why not destroy Death, too?

The Under-King opened his mouth to shout, but Ithan's ice covered his face, his body. An encasing cold so complete, Ithan could feel it in his heart. Hear its frigid wind, capable of killing in seconds.

Ithan yielded to it. Poured it into the being now trapped on the stairs before him like a statue.

He knew Connor was watching in horror. And he didn't dare take his focus off the Under-King long enough to read Hypaxia's face.

Ithan became so cold he forgot what warmth was. Forgot fire and sun and—

Connor got in front of him. Snarling.

Ithan's focus slipped. But instead of the disgust and dismay he thought would be on Connor's face, there was only sorrow and worry.

"Well, that's one way to shut the old windbag up," Jesiba Roga said, stalking from the shadows of the temple interior.

Ithan whirled. But Jesiba said to Hypaxia, who was tense and thrumming with power by the nearest pillar, "Do it."

The former witch-queen didn't strike with her shimmering power. She merely lifted an unlit brazier from beside the temple entrance. With a face like stone, Hypaxia swung the dark metal.

And the Under-King exploded into sparkling shards of ice.

83

There was a ringing silence as Ithan took in the pile of ice that had once been the Under-King . . . and felt nothing.

The Under-King was dead. Gone.

Ithan had killed him.

"Looks like we'll need a new Head of House," Jesiba said calmly to Hypaxia, who was staring down at the Under-King, clearly appalled at what she'd done.

What they'd done.

"When I swung at him," Hypaxia said quietly to Ithan, ignoring Jesiba, "I put a bit of my power behind the blow."

Hypaxia held out a bloodied hand to Ithan, and he realized that he, too, was bleeding all over, from the explosion of razor-like ice shrapnel. Rivers of red ran down his hands, his face. Hypaxia didn't look much better.

He slid his bloodied hand into hers. Her hand glowed, and they were both healed. The cuts on her face vanished—along with his, judging by the tingle that washed over his skin. Faster than he'd ever seen any other medwitch work.

"Play later," Jesiba said. "We have work to do."

"What work?" Ithan asked.

"You kill it, you become it," Jesiba said to Hypaxia. "You are now, for all intents and purposes, Head of the House of Flame and Shadow. And this place."

Her face paled. "That's not possible. I don't want that burden."

"Too bad. You killed him."

Hypaxia advanced on Jesiba, her face twisted in anguish and fury. "You knew this would happen," she accused. "You made me escort Ithan not to help him, but—"

"I suspected things might shake out in your favor," Jesiba said mildly. "But even though you've inherited this place by right, you must make some decisions quickly. Before Rigelus becomes aware."

"Like what?" Ithan demanded, looking to Connor, who still stood nearby at the top of the stairs, watching them all with awe on his ghostly face.

"Like what to do with the souls here," Jesiba said, nodding to Connor.

"We let them go," Ithan said. "We don't even need the Quiet Realms at all, do we?"

"No," Jesiba said. "Death worked just fine without them before the Asteri came."

But Connor was shaking his head.

"No?" Ithan asked.

His brother nodded to Ithan's clenched fist, clutching the black bullet. Connor opened his mouth, but still, no sound emerged.

"Oh, please," Jesiba said, and turned to Hypaxia. "Order him to speak already."

Hypaxia's brows rose. "Speak."

Connor blew out a breath, distinctly audible. Hypaxia was truly the mistress of this place. Ithan marveled at it.

And it was his brother's voice, the voice he'd known his whole life, that insisted, "Don't send us off into the ether."

"Connor . . . ," Ithan started.

Connor held Hypaxia's stare. "Don't miss this opportunity." He began walking down the stairs—nearly running—and it was all they could do to follow him. With that strong, sure grace, his brother stalked down the empty avenue flanked with strangely carved obelisks. All the way to the Dead Gate, its crystal muted in the dimness.

Only when they stood before it did Connor speak again. "That bullet," Connor said, nodding to where Ithan held it, "was made by us—the dead. For Bryce." A soft, pained smile crossed his face at her name. "To use with the Godslayer Rifle."

"What's so special about it?" Jesiba demanded.

"Nothing yet. But it was crafted to hold us. Our secondlight." As if in answer, the Gate began to glow. "We had planned to make contact with Jesiba—to ask her, through her role in Flame in Shadow, to get in touch with one of you." Connor shrugged with one shoulder. "But when you appeared earlier, Ithan, with the Under-King distracted . . . Well, it was a little earlier than we'd planned, but everyone was ready. I think Urd made it so." After all Ithan had heard and experienced, he didn't doubt his brother's claim. "So they began the exodus through this Gate. They were finishing when I was summoned to you."

A conduit, like the one Bryce had drawn from in the spring.

"All of our secondlight, from every soul here," Connor said quietly. "It's yours to put in that bullet. Use it well."

Ithan's throat constricted. "But if you . . . if you turn into secondlight—"

"I'm already gone, Ithan," Connor said gently. "And I can think of no better way to end my existence than by striking a blow for all our ancestors who've been trapped and consumed by the Asteri." He nodded to the bullet, the glowing Gate illuminating his face. "Look at the engraving."

Memento Mori. The letters gleamed in the Gate's pale light.

Jesiba let out a quiet laugh. "Got the idea from me, did you?"

Connor's mouth quirked up at a corner. Ithan nearly broke down at that half smile. Gods, he'd missed it. Missed his big brother.

But the Dead Gate glowed brighter—as if the time had come. As if it couldn't hold all those souls, the secondlight they'd become, much longer.

Connor said to Ithan, "You do make me proud, you know. Every day before now, and every day after. Nothing you do will ever change that."

Something ruptured in Ithan's chest. "Connor—"

"Tell Bryce," Connor said, eyes shining as he stepped toward the glowing Gate, a wall of light now shimmering in the empty arch, "to make the shot count."

Connor stepped into the archway and faded into that wall of light.

He was gone. And this time it was just as unbearable, as unfathomable to have had his brother here, to see him and speak to him and lose him again—

The light began shrinking and contracting, pulsating, and Ithan could have sworn he heard the hissing of Reapers rushing toward them in the distance. The light shivered and imploded, condensing into a tiny seed of pure light.

It floated in the Gate's archway, thrumming with such power that the hair on Ithan's arms rose.

"Put it in the bullet," Jesiba ordered Ithan, who unscrewed its cap and gingerly approached the seed.

All the souls of the people here . . . the dreams of the dead, their love for the living . . .

Ithan gently slid the bullet around the seed of light and replaced the cap. He lifted the bullet between his thumb and forefinger, its point digging into his skin.

As the light floated up through the bullet, *Memento Mori* was briefly illuminated, letter by letter.

Then it faded, the dark metal stark in the gray light.

"What now?" Ithan rasped, barely able to speak.

Connor had been here, and now he was gone. Forever.

"I have Reapers to sort out," Hypaxia murmured, staring off into the distant mists, to where the hissing was growing louder.

Ithan mastered the hole in his heart enough to ask, "What about Sigrid?"

Hypaxia said carefully, "What would you like me to do with her?"

"Just, ah . . ." Fuck, he had no idea. "Tell her I want to talk to her." He clarified, "I need to talk to her. But only once I'm back from the Eternal City." If he ever came back.

Hypaxia nodded solemnly. "If I encounter her, I will convey the message."

"The Reapers won't take the power shift well," Jesiba warned Hypaxia.

"Then I appoint you my second in command and order you to help me," Hypaxia said flatly.

"Happy to oblige," Jesiba said, examining her red-painted nails.

"You can't kill them," Hypaxia warned the sorceress.

Jesiba gave the witch a wry smile, and nodded to Ithan, who pulled himself from his grief long enough to meet her steely gaze. "Get your ass to Pangera, Prime. And get that bullet to Bryce Quinlan."

Tharion didn't speak, barely breathed, until he and Sathia were back in the open air. It had taken a few hours to coordinate with his former colleagues about how they'd conduct the exodus from the city, how they'd get the message around without alerting anyone to the plan. Word was bound to leak at some point about the Blue Court harboring refugees, but hopefully by then they'd have a good number of people Beneath. And then the Blue Court would go into lockdown, praying that the River Queen's power could hold out against the brimstone torpedoes of the Omega-boats docked in the river. It was risky . . . but it was a plan.

Only when they'd ducked for cover in a shadowy alley did Tharion say to Sathia, "We did it. We fucking did it—"

She smiled, and it was beautiful. *She* was beautiful.

But a voice crooned from the shadows of the alley, "Isn't this an interesting turn of events?"

It was all Tharion could do to draw the knife at his side and step in front of Sathia as the Viper Queen emerged into the light, her drugged-out, hulking Fae assassins flanking her.

"I don't have any quarrel with you," Tharion said to the Viper Queen, who was clad in one of her usual jumpsuits—ocean blue this time, with high-top sneakers in an amethyst suede with maroon laces.

"You burned my house down," the Viper Queen said, her snake's eyes glowing green. Like a Reaper's eyes. The Fae assassins behind her shifted, as if they were an extension of her wrath.

"Colin?" Sathia blurted, and Tharion found her gaping at one of the Fae males. "*Colin?* I thought you . . ."

The Viper Queen glanced between the towering Fae male and Sathia and said to the latter, "Who the fuck are you?"

"Sathia Flynn, daughter of Padraig, Lord Hawthorne." Sathia's chin rose, pure disdain in every word. "I know who you are, so don't bother to introduce yourself, but I want to know why my friend is in your employ."

It was a different face from the one of courtly grace she'd poured on for the River Queen. This one was imperious and icy and a little bit terrifying.

The Viper Queen snorted.

Sathia bared her teeth. "Colin. Get away from this trash and come home."

The towering Fae male stared blankly ahead. As he had this whole time. Like he didn't hear her.

"Colin," Sathia said, voice sharpening with something like panic.

"McCarthy won't respond unless I give him the order," the Viper Queen drawled, walking to the male and running her manicured hands over his broad chest. Her metallic gold nails glinted against the black leather of his jacket. "But let me guess: Childhood friend? Handsome, poor Fae guard, spoiled little rich girl . . ." Her purple-painted lips curved in a smile, and she patted the male's cheek, purring to him, "Is that why you came crawling to me? Would her daddy not let you court her?"

Tharion's heart stalled at the pain that washed over Sathia's face as she breathed, more to herself than to anyone, "Father said you had found a new position in Korinth."

"Padraig Flynn has always been an excellent liar," the Viper Queen said. "And a better client. He introduced me to McCarthy, of course." She gestured to the blank-faced assassin.

Sathia paled. "Come home, Colin." Her voice broke. "Please."

Tharion had no idea how anyone, the drugged-out male included, could resist the pleading in that voice. Her face.

"It's too late for that," the Viper Queen said, and nodded to Tharion. "But you and I have unfinished business, mer."

"Leave him alone," Sathia snapped, teeth flashing as she stepped closer to Tharion. "Don't you *dare* touch him."

Tharion's fingers slid toward hers, squeezing once in warning to be quiet.

"And what authority do you have, girl, to order me away from him?"

"I'm his wife," Sathia spat.

The Viper Queen burst out laughing. And Tharion could have sworn that something like pain shown in McCarthy's bright blue eyes—just a glimmer.

"You leave him alone," Sathia said again, and vines curled at her fingers. "Him *and* Colin."

"That's not an option I'm interested in, girl," the Viper Queen said, and inclined her head to one side. The assassins, Colin included, aimed their guns. Did he imagine it, or was McCarthy's weapon trembling slightly?

Tharion sheathed his knife and held up his hands, again stepping in front of Sathia. "Your business is with me."

He'd accomplished what he needed to with the River Queen. And if Sathia became a widow . . . she could remarry, by Fae law. Maybe even find some way to save that poor bastard McCarthy and marry him. So Tharion said, "Let her walk out of here before you put a bullet in my head."

"Oh, I'm not going to kill you that quickly," the Viper Queen said. "Not a chance, Ketos."

She advanced a step, her assassins flowing with her.

"You take one more step toward my friend," said a familiar female voice, "and you die."

Tharion's knees wobbled as he glanced over a shoulder—and found Hypaxia Enador striding in from the quay, Ithan Holstrom bristling with menace at her side.

84

I don't take orders from former witch-queens," the Viper Queen said. Her guards didn't back down an inch. But Colin McCarthy's gun was definitely trembling, like he was fighting the order with everything he had.

"What about from the Head of the House of Flame and Shadow?" Hypaxia countered. Tharion's knees gave out abruptly at the greenish light that flared in her eyes.

Sathia caught him around the waist, grunting as she held him up.

Tharion whispered, "Pax?"

But his friend—this female who had been his friend from the moment they'd met each other at the Summit, who always seemed to see the real male beneath his veneer of charm—only glowered at the Viper Queen. "You touch him, or his friend, and you bring down the wrath of Flame and Shadow upon you."

Holstrom stepped up to her side, brimming with power—with *magic*, cold and foreign—and added, "And the wrath of all Valbaran Wolves."

There was only one person who could claim that.

The male before him was Prime. There was no doubt about it. But that strange power rippling from him . . . what the Hel was *that*?

The Viper Queen stared long and hard at Ithan, then at Hypaxia.

"Power shift," she murmured, pulling a cigarette from her jumpsuit pocket and putting it in her mouth. "Interesting." The cigarette bobbed with the word, and she lit it, taking a long drag. She fixed her snake's eyes on Tharion. "Your bounty still stands."

"Drop the bounty," Ithan ordered, pure Alpha echoing in his voice.

"I won't forgive or forget what Ketos did to me and mine. But he'll walk out of here today—I'll allow that much."

Hypaxia gave her a look dripping with disdain. "*You* will walk out of here today. *We* will allow that much."

The Viper Queen took another long drag of her cigarette and blew the air toward Hypaxia. "Give a witch a scrap of true power and it goes right to her pretty little head."

"Fuck you," Ithan snarled.

But the Viper Queen stepped back into the alley, whistling sharply to her assassins before striding away. They turned as one and marched after her.

Colin McCarthy didn't so much as look back.

"What the *fuck*?" Tharion exploded at Ithan, at Hypaxia. The Prime of the Valbaran Wolves and the Head of the House of Flame and Shadow. "What happened?"

"What happened to *you*?" Ithan countered. "Where are the others? Is Bryce here?"

"Bryce? No—she's in Nena. She . . ." Now wasn't the time for a catch-up.

But Ithan said, "Nena?" He dragged his hands through his hair. "Fuck."

"Why?" Tharion asked.

Hypaxia said gravely, "We need to get to Bryce. Immediately."

"Okay," Tharion said. "I'll see if I can reach her or Athalar."

Hypaxia and Ithan began walking, and Tharion followed, Sathia a few feet behind. When the door to the House of Flame and Shadow loomed before them, Hypaxia lifted a hand and it swung open silently. Hers to command.

Ithan walked right in. But Tharion at last mastered his shock enough to ask Hypaxia, "How did you wind up—"

"It's a long story," she said, tucking a dark curl behind her ear. "But get inside first. It's the only safe place in this city."

Tharion glanced back at Sathia, who was pale-faced at the open door before them. "Give me a minute," he said, and Hypaxia nodded and walked into the gloom.

"Hypaxia is a friend," Tharion explained softly to Sathia. "No harm will come to you in there."

Sathia lifted her gaze, bleak and despairing, to his face. Like she'd seen a ghost.

And maybe she had. "It was my Ordeal." Her lips were so, so white. "I only realized it afterward," she murmured. "After Colin . . . left. Losing him was my Ordeal."

Tharion laid a gentle hand on her back, surprised by the strange tightness in his gut, and eased her toward the doorway. "I'm sorry," he said, and led his wife into the gloom.

It was all he could offer her.

"The reception in Nena is shit—there's some weird interference happening right now," Tharion announced. They stood in Jesiba Roga's office, of all places. "But from the few words I managed to make out, they're heading for the Eternal City immediately."

"Good," Holstrom said, pacing in front of Roga's desk. "That's what Jesiba told me earlier. But where do we rendezvous?"

"That's the tough part," Tharion admitted, sliding into one of the chairs. Sathia sat quietly in the other one, lost in thought. "The reception cut off before we could get to that. I tried calling him back, and Quinlan, and her parents, but . . . nothing."

"Maybe they got the Rift open," Hypaxia mused. "Magic pouring into Midgard from Hel could be disrupting the connection. Demons cause power outages sometimes with their presence. Imagine what a lot of them all at once might do."

"It's possible, but doesn't change the issue at hand," Holstrom said. The wolf had changed—somehow, in the span of a day, he'd gone from lost to focused. From lone wolf to Prime. Tharion had gotten a vague story out of him about facing Sabine, and Hypaxia taking on the Under-King to become Head of the House of Flame and Shadow, but even beyond that, they seemed like they'd leveled up. Majorly.

Especially Ithan. Even the most powerful of wolves only had shifting abilities and super strength—not actual *magic*. And yet Holstrom, suddenly, had the ability to wield ice. Like the power had been locked in his bloodline all this time. But Tharion put aside the thought as Holstrom added, "We need to figure out how to link up with them."

"I'm sure if the Rift is open, we'll see them coming a mile off," Tharion said.

"We need to find Hunt and Bryce *before* they enter into any kind of confrontation with the Asteri," Ithan insisted. He picked up a vial of clear liquid from the desk. "Hypaxia found a cure for the Asteri's parasite. We need to distribute it to everyone we can."

Tharion blinked in shock. Sathia stopped her brooding to listen.

Then Ithan pulled out a long, dark bullet from his pocket. "And we need to get this to Bryce as soon as possible."

"What is that?" Tharion asked as a strange, ancient sort of power thrummed from the black bullet.

Ithan's face was grim. "A gift from the dead."

85

Well, friends," Bryce said to Hunt, to Declan and Flynn, to Ruhn and Lidia. They had all gathered in a nondescript white van—one of a fleet Ophion had kept stashed throughout Pangera should an agent on the run ever need an escape vehicle—on the edge of the Eternal City. And though Lidia was frantic with urgency to rescue her sons, this step was necessary. "Ready to change the world?"

Jesiba had just sent over the footage of Micah's demise.

"Let's burn this fucker down," Flynn said, and Dec nodded, typing away on his laptop.

"We're recording in thirty seconds," Dec warned Bryce, and she looked to where Hunt sat next to her, so quiet, so thoughtful. Terrified, she realized.

He glanced up, bleak fear in his eyes as he said hoarsely, "The last time I took a stand like this, with the Fallen . . . it cost me everything." He swallowed hard, but he kept his gaze on her. She could have sworn lightning sparked along his wings. "But this time I have Bryce Adelaide Quinlan at my side."

She took his hand in hers, squeezing tightly. "I've got you, sweetheart," she whispered to him, and his eyes flickered in recognition. He'd said the same thing to her once—that day she'd had the kristallos venom removed from her leg.

He squeezed her hand back. "Let's light it up."

Declan signaled, and the red light on his laptop camera turned on.

Bryce stared into the camera's lens and said, "I am Bryce Quinlan. Heir to the Starborn Fae, Queen of the Fae in Avallen and Valbara, but most importantly . . . the half-human daughter of Ember Quinlan and Randall Silago."

Hunt barely seemed to be breathing as Bryce said, "This is my mate and husband, Hunt Athalar. And we're here to show you . . ."

It hit her, right then—a wave of nerves.

Hunt sensed it and picked up her thread without missing a beat. "We're here to show you that the Republic is not as all-powerful as you've been led to believe." He lifted his chin. "Centuries ago, I led a legion—the Fallen—against the Archangels, against the Asteri. You know how it ended. That day on Mount Hermon, only one other group of Vanir came to our aid: the sprites. We all suffered for it, and those of us who survived are still punished to this day." His throat worked, and Bryce had never loved him more as he continued, "But today we're here to tell you that it's worth it. Fighting back. That it's possible to defy them and live. That their hierarchies, their rules . . . it's all bullshit. And it's time to put a stop to it."

Bryce might have smiled had she not finally found the right words. "What happened in Asphodel Meadows was an atrocity. What happened to those innocent families . . ." She bared her teeth. "It must never be allowed to happen again. *We*, the people of Midgard, can never allow it to happen again."

She looked the camera dead in its dark eye, looked at the world beyond. "The Asteri lie to you, all of you, every second of every single day. For the past fifteen thousand years, they've lied to us, enslaved us, and we haven't even known the half of it. They use a parasite in the water to control and harvest our magic under the guise of the Drop. Because they need that magic—they need *us*, our power. Without the power from the people of Midgard, the Asteri are nothing."

She squared her shoulders. Hunt's pride was a warmth that practically seeped into her side, but he let her keep talking, let her take the lead as she said, "The Asteri don't want you to know this. They have schemed and murdered to keep their secrets." Danika's face, the faces of the Pack of Devils, flashed before her eyes. It was for them that she spoke, for Lehabah, for all those in the Meadows. "We've been told we're too weak, and they're too powerful, for us to fight back. But that's just another lie."

Bryce continued, "So we're here to show you that it can be done. I fought back, and I killed an Archangel who the Asteri used like a puppet to murder Danika Fendyr and the Pack of Devils. I fought back, and I won—I have the footage to prove it."

And with a flick of a switch from Declan, the video played.

Bryce peered around the small, bare-bones room in the safe house near the northernmost section of wall around the Eternal City. "Lidia's certain this is secure?"

Hunt, wings tucked in tight in the cramped space, nodded to the sliver of a bed. "Yeah. And I'm pretty sure all the five-star hotels would report our asses to the Asteri anyway."

"That's not what I meant," Bryce grumbled, plopping onto the creaky, lumpy bed. More of a cot, really. "I mean, all of Ophion's . . . dead." She choked on the word. "Who's to say this place hasn't been compromised? Lidia's not exactly in a calm state of mind. She might not be thinking clearly."

"Dec and Flynn are on guard," Hunt said, sitting down beside her with a groan. "I think we're good to rest tonight."

Bryce scrubbed at her face. "I'm not sure I can sleep, knowing that video's going out soon." And soon after that, Hel would begin its journey to the Eternal City. She could only pray the armies' presence would remain unnoticed until the right moment. She'd taken steps to ensure that.

Hunt waggled his eyebrows at her. "Want to do something other than sleeping?"

Despite all that weighed on her, despite what awaited them the next day, Bryce smirked. "Oh?" She half reclined, leaning back on her elbows. The bed let out a wailing *creaaak*.

"Oof," Bryce said, wincing. "If anyone has any doubt that we're about to fuck each other's brains out, this bed will clue them right in."

Hunt's mouth kicked up at a corner, but his eyes had darkened, going right to her mouth. "I'm down for some noisy sex." He braced a hand on one side of her, bringing his lips within grazing distance of her own. "Might be our last night on—"

She put a hand over his mouth. "Don't." Her throat closed up. "Don't say that."

He pulled back, his own gaze unbearably tender. "We're going to survive, Quinlan. All of us. I promise."

She leaned forward, brushing her mouth against his. "I don't want to think about tomorrow right now."

It was his turn to say, "Oh?"

She traced her tongue over the seam of his lips, and he opened for her. She swept her tongue in, tasting the essence that was Hunt, her mate and husband—"I want to think about you," she said, pulling back, grazing a hand over his pecs, his rock-hard stomach. "About you on top of me."

He shuddered, head bowing. She kissed the place where his halo had been, where he'd freed himself from its grasp.

Her hand trailed lower, to his black jeans and the hardness already pushing against them. "I want to think about this," she said, palming him, "inside of me."

"Fuck," he breathed, and pivoted them, laying her out flat beneath him. "I love you."

She lifted her hand to cup his face, drawing his gaze to her own. "I love you more than anything in this world—or any other."

He closed his eyes, pressing a kiss to her temple. "I thought you said no goodbyes."

"It's not a goodbye." She ran her hands down the groove of his spine, his wings like velvet against her fingertips. "It's the truth."

His mouth found her neck, and his teeth grazed over her pulse. "You're my best friend, you know that?" He pulled away, staring down at her, and she couldn't stop her star from flaring with light. "I mean, you're my mate and wife—fuck, that still sounds weird—but you're my best friend, too. I never thought I'd have one of those."

She ran her fingers over his strong jaw, his cheeks. "After Danika, I didn't think . . ." Her eyes prickled, and she reached up to kiss him again. "You're my best friend, too, Hunt. You saved me—literally, I guess, but also . . ." She tapped her heart, the glowing star. Another reference to this past spring, to all that had grown between them, the words spoken during what she'd thought had been her final phone call. "In here."

He scanned her eyes, and there was so much love in her that she couldn't stand it, so much love that it washed over any fear and dread of what tonight and tomorrow would bring. For the moment, it was just them—Bryce and Hunt. For the moment, it was only their souls, their bodies, and nothing else mattered.

Just Hunt. And Just Bryce.

So she kissed him again, and there was no more talking after that.

Hunt met her tongue stroke for stroke, and the weight of his body on hers was joy and comfort and home. Home—he *was* home. Her ability to teleport to him had only proved that. Home wasn't a place or a thing, but *him*. Wherever Hunt was . . . that was where home was. She'd find him across galaxies, if need be.

He tugged off her long-sleeved shirt, gently, lovingly. Bryce practically ripped his black shirt off his shoulders.

Hunt chuckled, rising up to unbuckle his belt, then unzipping his pants. "So impatient."

She rubbed her thighs together, desperate for any friction. Especially as his impressive length sprang free, and—

"Commando?" Bryce said, choking.

Hunt smirked. "All the underwear they gave me on the *Depth Charger* was too small for this." He palmed himself, pumping, and she groaned at the sight of the small bead of moisture at the tip of his cock. "Now let's see what underwear *you're* wearing, Quinlan," he said, eyes dark with lust, and tugged down her leggings. She lifted her hips off the bed, coils screeching, and Hunt laughed at the sound.

But his laugh died in his throat as he beheld the cherry-red thong. "*This* is what they gave you on the *Depth Charger*?"

"Not the *Depth Charger*." She grinned as he peeled off her leggings, exposing the tiny red lace thong. "I grabbed these from Morven's castle—the guest rooms had whole unopened packs of them."

Hunt's booming laugh set her star glowing, and the breath whooshed out of her as he gripped her knees in either hand and spread her legs wide. "If that asshole wasn't dead, I'd send him a thank-you note."

Hunt pressed his mouth to the front of her underwear and huffed a hot breath.

"Damn, Quinlan," he said against her, and she buried a hand in his silken hair. He slipped a finger around the front of her underwear, toying with her entrance. "Gods-damn."

She clawed at her underwear, beyond words.

Hunt obliged her by removing the thong with cruel, brutal slowness. She growled, but he dangled the underwear on one finger before setting it aside. "I wouldn't want to damage this precious thing."

"I'm going to damage *you* if you don't get in me right now," she managed to say, opening her legs wider.

She nearly climaxed at the raw need, the ravenous hunger on Hunt's face. Especially as he slowly, slowly lifted his gaze to hers, filled with pure lightning.

"Hunt," she begged, and he lunged for her.

He gripped her hips, lifting her off the mattress, angling her precisely how he wanted as he slid into her in a long, smooth glide.

Bryce moaned at the size of him, filling every part of her, and she dug her fingers into the hard muscles of his ass, pinning him there for a moment. Luxuriating in the stretch of herself around him, the weight of his body against hers.

"How?" he panted against her hair. "How the fuck can it feel this good every time?"

Her fingers clenched harder, urging him to move. He withdrew almost to the tip, and plunged back in, hard enough that another moan slipped out of her.

"You like that?" He angled her hips again, his to play with. "You like my cock this deep in you?"

She couldn't manage anything more than a nod. He rewarded her with another long stroke that had her seeing stars.

Those were . . . those were *actual* stars dancing around them, filling the room.

"Quinlan," he breathed, eyes wide at the stars floating by. But she needed more friction, more pleasure. She palmed her breast, squeezing, rolling her hard nipple between her fingers.

"Fuck," he exploded, and thrust into her again, so deep and strong that it pushed them up the bed. Another stroke, and then his lightning was sparking over his shoulders, across his wings, a band of it over his brow like a crown—

She lifted a glowing hand, and his lightning twined over her fingers, zapping her delicately.

He withdrew, and her moan of protest turned into one of pure pleasure as he flipped her onto her front and plunged into her again, the fit of his cock so tight in her that she could barely stand it.

Starlight poured out of her, and his lightning skittered over her spine, ecstasy in its wake.

"Hunt," she cried, release hovering just over the horizon.

His fingers dug into her hips. "Come for me, Bryce."

Release crashed into her, out of her, her starlight flaring, and the room was blindingly bright. Hunt pounded into her in sure, steady strokes, and his lightning was between her thighs, his lightning was in her very blood, and all that she was and he was blended into such light, such power—

His hoarse shout was the only warning before he spilled into her, and it sent her climaxing again, knowing how deeply he was seated in her, marking her.

His fingers slid to her clit, stroking her through the throes, amplifying it. She reared up against him, pressing back into his chest as his fingers circled and swirled, and nothing had ever felt so perfect as wave after wave of pleasure washed over and out of her.

And then the world stilled, the light fading, and they were kneeling on the bed, Bryce leaning fully back against Hunt, one of his hands resting between her legs, the other looped around her middle. He pressed kiss after kiss to the space between her neck and shoulder. "Bryce," he murmured against her skin, his chest heaving into her spine. "Bryce."

She slid a hand over his, holding him between her legs, as if she could freeze this moment, stop the next sunrise from coming.

He shuddered, kissing her again. "I can . . . Fuck, I can *feel* you. Like, in me."

She twisted enough to peer up at his stunned, devastated face.

"It's like that part of you that's . . . Made, or whatever you called it," he breathed. "It's in me. Like this piece of you is nestled there."

"Good," she said, kissing his jaw. Inside her, his lightning lingered, fueling her up like a small sun. "No matter what happens tomorrow," she said, breathing hard, "I'll have this piece of you with me. Strengthening me." She could almost summon it, that lightning. It flowed under her skin, so full of possibility that she had no idea how she'd sleep.

Hunt tugged her back against him, holding her tight as he brought them both down onto the creaky bed. "Sleep, Quinlan," he whispered into her hair. "I'm with you no matter what."

86

Ithan left Tharion recovering from the dose of the antidote the mer had taken. His reaction had been strong enough that the pipes in the House of Flame and Shadow had burst from the surge in his water magic. Hypaxia had her hands full, keeping her House in order.

So Ithan had come to the Den. Which was now . . . his.

Well, it would never be his, since it belonged to all the wolves who called it home, but it was his responsibility.

He found Perry in the guard booth again, doodling in a notebook. He rapped on the glass, drawing her attention, and at her wide eyes, he gave her a half smile.

"Hard at work or hardly working?" he teased.

But she jumped to her feet, flinging open the door. "Sorry, I was just—"

"Per, it's me," he said, alarmed.

She straightened, standing at attention, as Sabine had liked. For fuck's sake. He'd deal with that later. For now . . . He sniffed, trying to read the subtle change in her scent. It remained that strawberries-and-cinnamon blend he'd known his whole life, but with the antidote . . . He couldn't put a finger on it. It had been so strong, right in those moments after she'd taken the antidote, yet now it had dimmed.

There wasn't time to ponder it, to wonder why an Omega once again stood before him. Ithan peered through the open gates of the Den. "Where is everyone?"

Perry shifted on her feet. "They, uh . . . they left."

Ithan slowly blinked. "What do you mean they left?" Had the River Queen started her evacuation already? He'd come here to inform everyone that it might be best to lie low in the Blue Court for a few weeks, but maybe she had already gotten a message to them.

"What happened shook them," Perry said. "They're loyal to you, Ithan, but they're worried. They all headed out of town. Said they wanted to wait until after the new year to see how things, um . . . turned out." In a few *months*.

Ithan weighed the fear in her eyes. Not for him, but . . . "And where's your sister?" he asked quietly. The wolf in him began bristling, snarling for the opponent he knew was coming.

"Amelie led them out," Perry said, throat bobbing. "I think she wanted to make sure everyone got to where they're going." But her eyes dropped to the pavement.

"Sure," Ithan said. Perry shifted on her feet. "Why didn't you go?"

"Someone had to stay to tell you," she mumbled, a blush creeping over her cheeks.

"I have a hard time believing your sister made you stay."

"She wanted me to go, but . . . I couldn't abandon the Den. They moved the Prime into the lobby—I think some wanted to stay for the Sailing, but the spooked ones wanted to leave. It didn't feel right to abandon his body there. Alone." Tears gleamed in her emerald eyes, genuine grief for the old wolf.

Any aggression rising in Ithan stalled out at the pain, the loyalty in her face. He squeezed her shoulder. "Thanks for staying, Per."

She followed him into the Den, hitting an interior button to shut the gates behind them. Ithan paused in the grassy meadow, watching the trees of the park bend in the cool breeze. The blood had been cleaned away from the building's entrance. The bodies of Sabine and the Astronomer—

"I dumped them in the sewer," Perry said with quiet rage,

reading Ithan's glance toward where the corpses had been. "They don't deserve a Sailing. Especially Sabine."

Surprise sparked in him at the normally peaceful wolf's act of defiance, but he nodded. "Rotting in the shit of the city seems like a good place for Sabine to wind up," he said, and Perry huffed a laugh. It wasn't real amusement. They were both far beyond that.

"Where did you go?" Perry asked, tentatively enough that he knew she was still feeling him out. As a friend, and as her Alpha and Prime. Learning how much she could push.

"It's a long story," he said. "But I came back here to get everyone to safety." He explained about the River Queen and the Blue Court.

"But now," he finished, "I have to head to the Eternal City."

Perry studied him, clearly understanding more than he'd said. "So we're going up against the Asteri?"

"*We* aren't doing anything," he said. "I'm going up against them."

"But you're Prime," she insisted. "You speak for all Valbaran wolves. Your choices are our choices. If you stand against the Asteri, *we* stand against the Asteri."

"Then disavow me," he said. "But I'm going."

"That's not what I'm saying," she said. "I don't disagree with you—things have to change, and change for the better. But the wolves are scattered at the moment. At vacation homes, on trips . . . too far to reach the Blue Court before you go off to the Eternal City."

"So?"

"So get the word out to them before you go. Give them a few hours to find shelter, either by getting to the Blue Court, or by finding somewhere in the wilds to lie low. The second the Asteri see you, the Prime, standing against them in any capacity, they'll go after the wolves to punish you. And after what happened at the Meadows . . ." Her eyes flooded with pain. "I don't think there's any atrocity they wouldn't commit."

Ithan opened his mouth to object. He had to get that bullet and antidote to Bryce *now*. It might even be too late already.

But he couldn't live with one more wolf death on his conscience.

And if a single pup were harmed because he hadn't given them time to hide . . .

"Three hours," Ithan agreed. "You know how to send encrypted messages?"

Perry nodded.

"Then start getting the word out." He looked to the building lobby beyond the pillars and the stairs up to it. "And I'll start digging a grave."

"A grave?" Perry protested. "But the Sailing—"

"There are no more Sailings," Ithan said quietly. "The Under-King is dead."

He was met with stunned silence. Then Perry said, "But—the Bone Quarter."

"Is a lie. All of it." Ithan gestured to the phone already in her hand. "Get the word out, then we'll talk. I'll tell you everything I know."

Perry held his stare, her own full of worry and shock and determination. Then she began typing into her phone. "I'm glad, Ithan," she said quietly, "that you're Prime."

That makes one of us, he almost said, but just nodded his thanks.

Tharion shoved the last gun into a rucksack and turned to where Hypaxia was nesting vials of the antidote into a satchel. "How many do you have?" he asked.

Water whispered in his ears, his heart, his veins. A steady flow of magic, as if a raging river coursed through him. Half a thought and it'd be unleashed.

"Two dozen, give or take a few," she said quietly. "Not enough."

"You're going to need entire factories dedicated to getting it out there," Tharion said.

She handed him the bag. "Here. Don't jostle it too much on the trip. Athalar's lightning holds them together—a little agitation can destabilize the doses to the point where they won't work."

He angled his head. "You're not coming?" He planned to make his way to the Asteri's palace itself—the most likely place for a confrontation between Bryce and the Asteri. Gods, the very notion of it was insane. Suicidal. But for his friends, for Midgard, he'd go, antidote in tow.

Hypaxia's eyes gleamed with that greenish light. "No—I'm staying here."

Tharion weighed the heaviness in that one word and took a seat on the edge of Roga's desk. The sorceress was off handling some squabble between vampyrs and city medwitches over the vampyrs' raid of a blood bank, apparently. "Why?"

"Someone has to deal with all the broken pipes in this House," Hypaxia teased.

Tharion blushed slightly. His eruption after ingesting the antidote would take a long while to live down. But there had been so much *power*—all of a sudden, he'd been overflowing with water, and it was music and rage and destruction and life. But he said, "Come on, Pax. Tell me why."

Her gaze lowered to her hands. "Because if all goes poorly over there, someone needs to remain here. To help Lunathion."

"If it goes poorly over there, everyone is fucked anyway," he said. "You being here, I'm sorry to say, won't make much of a difference."

"I want to keep making the antidote," she added. "We need a better way to stabilize it. I want to start on it *now*."

He looked at his friend—really looked at her. "You okay?"

Her eyes, so changed since taking Flame and Shadow's throne for herself, dipped to the floor. "No."

"Pax—"

"But I have no choice," she said, and squared her shoulders. She nodded to the doors. "You should get your wife and go."

"Is that a note of disapproval I detect?"

Hypaxia smiled gently. "No. Well, I disapprove of much of what led you to marry her, but not . . . the marriage itself."

"Yeah, yeah, get in line to lecture me."

"I think Sathia might be good for you, Tharion."

"Oh?"

Her smile turned secretive. "Yes."

Tharion gave her a smile of his own. "Knock 'em dead, Pax."

"Hopefully not literally," Hypaxia said with a wink.

Grinning despite himself, Tharion exited Roga's office. He'd left Sathia in a small guest room to wash up and rest, though they both knew that no amount of rest would prepare her for the insanity they were about to face.

He'd offered to send her down to the Blue Court, but she'd refused. And dropping her off in Avallen would have taken them too far out of their way. So she'd be coming with him.

Tharion knocked on the door to the guest room and didn't wait for her to reply before he opened it.

The room was empty. There was only a note on the bed, laced with her lingering scent. Tharion read it once. Then a second time, before it really set in.

I can't leave Colin in her hands. I hope you understand.

Good luck. And thank you for all you've done for me.

Sathia had left him. That's what the *thank you* at the end was. It was fitting—he'd done worse to the River Queen's daughter, and yet . . .

Tharion carefully laid the note back on the bed. He didn't blame her. It was her choice to go save her ex-boyfriend from being a drugged-out assassin—and a noble choice, at that. No, he didn't blame her at all.

It was better she didn't come with him to the Eternal City, in any case. She'd be safer that way.

Still, Tharion looked at the note on the bed for a long, long moment.

And though he knew he was heading off to challenge the Asteri, likely to die in the attempt . . . as Tharion left the House of Flame and Shadow, then Lunathion itself, he couldn't stop thinking about her.

The video Hunt and Bryce had recorded was due to go out at any moment. Ruhn was so fucking proud of his sister. She knew how to make the most of a bad hand.

That moment came soon after midnight, with a stroke of a key from Declan.

And now, sitting on the floor of the windowless bedroom in the safe house Lidia had procured for them, Ruhn peered over at where she sat beside him and said, "Just a few hours until dawn, then we'll make our move."

Lidia stared at nothing, knee bobbing nervously. She'd spoken little since they'd gotten the news of her sons' abduction. And though Ruhn had been aching to touch her in the quiet moments, he'd kept his hands to himself. She had other things on her mind.

"I never should have gone back onto the *Depth Charger*," Lidia said at last.

"If Pollux was able to learn about your kids," Ruhn objected, "he would have found out whether you were on the ship or off it."

"You should have let me die in the Haldren Sea," she said. "Then he'd have had no reason to go after them."

"Hey." Ruhn grabbed her hand, squeezing tight. She dragged her gaze over to him. "None of this is your fault."

She shook her head, and Ruhn gently touched her face. "You are allowed to feel whatever you need to right now. But come dawn, when we walk out of here, you'll have to bury it and become the Hind again. One last time. Without the Hind, we're not going to get into that palace."

She scanned his gaze, and leaned forward, her brow pressing against his.

Ruhn breathed in her scent, taking it deep into his body—but he found it already marking him. It had been there, hidden in him, since that first time.

"Can I . . ." She swallowed hard. "Can we . . ."

"Tell me what you want," he said, kissing her cheek.

She pulled back, and slid a hand against his jaw. "You. I want you."

"You sure?" She had so much burdening her. With her sons in the Asteri's hands, he didn't blame her if—

"I need to not think for a while," she said, then added, "and . . .

I need to touch you." She traced her fingers over his lips. "Your real body."

He closed his eyes against her touch. "Tell me what you want, Lidia."

Her lips grazed his, and he shuddered. "I want you—all of you. In me."

A grin spread across Ruhn's face. "Happy to oblige."

He followed her lead, letting her set the pace. Each kiss, he answered with his own. Let her show him where she wanted him to touch, to lick, to savor.

Thankfully, the parts where she wanted him to *really* focus were the ones Ruhn had been especially interested in. The taste of her sweetness on his tongue had him nearly coming in his pants—and that was before her breathy moans filled his ears like the most beautiful music he'd ever heard.

"Ruhn," she said, but didn't give him the order to halt, so he kept working her in long strokes of his tongue, wishing to the gods he still had his lip piercing, knowing he could have driven her to distraction with it—but there would be time later.

She arched off the bed, and her orgasm sent him writhing, desperate for any sensation against his cock.

She put him out of his misery a moment later, her eyes nearly pure flame as she unzipped him, and her slender hand wrapped around him—

He bucked against her first stroke, and was about to start begging when she pushed him back onto the bed. When she climbed over him, straddling him, and that hand around his cock guided him to her entrance.

Ruhn slid his hands into Lidia's golden hair, the silken strands spilling through his fingers, and held her gaze as she sank down onto him.

He gritted his teeth at the warmth and tightness of her, panting through the rush of pleasure, the sense of perfection, the flawless fit—

She settled against him, seated fully, and her chest rose and fell so rapidly that Ruhn grabbed her hands, pressing kisses to her fingertips. Her eyes fluttered shut, and then her hips moved—and there was nothing more to say, to do, as she rode him.

He lifted his hips, and her moans heightened. He wished he could devour the sound. He made do by rising up, kissing her thoroughly, her legs wrapping around his middle. It plunged him impossibly deeper, and he lost it. Went positively feral at being so far inside her, at the smell and taste of her—

Lidia met him stroke for stroke, met his savagery with her own, teeth grazing his neck, his chest. Every thrust had him rubbing an inner wall, and fuck, he was going to *die* from this pleasure—

Then her head tipped back, and her delicate muscles tightened around him as she came, sending him spiraling after her. He pounded into her through it, that feral part of him relishing spilling into her, and she was *his* and he was hers, and there was a word for it, but it eluded him.

She stilled, and Ruhn took her weight as she leaned against him, their bodies now a tangle of arms and legs, his cock still buried to the hilt. Her every breath pushed against him, and he stroked his fingers down the column of her spine, over and over.

She was here. He was here.

For as long as Urd would allow them to be.

Lidia lay in Ruhn's arms as the hours passed, sleep eluding her.

It had been everything she'd wanted, needed, this joining with him. She'd never felt so safe, so cherished. And yet her sons remained in the Asteri's hands. In Pollux's hands.

The hours dripped by. Lidia shut down the part of her that cataloged every possible torment that might be inflicted on Brann and Actaeon. The torments that she herself had inflicted on so many others.

Maybe this was her punishment for that. Her punishment for so many things.

Ruhn stirred, and Lidia nestled closer to him, breathing in his scent, savoring the strength of his body around hers.

And tried not to think about tomorrow.

87

Hiding out in the unmarked van parked in a dusty alley of the Eternal City the next morning, Ruhn peered over at where Lidia sat stone-faced against the metal siding, and slid closer.

She'd barely slept, and Ruhn didn't blame her. A glimpse at her haggard face this morning as they'd crept out of the safe house and back into the van had kept him close to her, offering what comfort he could. Now he laid a hand on her knee and said, "Another hour or so. Then we'll head into the palace."

Another hour until Declan could confirm that the Asteri were well and truly distracted by the video they'd unleashed into the world. From Dec's initial reports this morning, it was a giant clusterfuck. The footage had been blasted on every news channel and social media site. Dec had also confirmed that he'd hacked into the imperial network and learned that this morning, the Asteri and their advisors would all be meeting to discuss the fallout. The news about the parasite had really resonated. All media outlets were abuzz with chatter about it. And the footage of Bryce killing Micah, her claims about how Danika and the pack had died . . .

It didn't matter that the imperial network had pulled the footage almost immediately. It was already out there, circulating on private servers, being downloaded onto phones. Being watched and analyzed over and over again. Imperial trolls tried to insist it was fake, planting comments that it was a manipulated video, but Dec made sure that footage of Bryce running through the streets of Lunathion this spring, saving the whole city, made it out, too.

And there were people out there who remembered that, who had seen her running to save them. They vouched for her, confirming not only that she had saved the city from Hel, but also from the brimstone missiles the Asteri had launched.

The Asteri had a lot on their hands that morning. Exactly as planned. And once their emergency meeting had begun, it would be time to make a move.

"A single misstep and my sons . . . ," Lidia began, swallowing hard.

"Set the fear aside," Ruhn said, offering her the honesty she'd so often given him. "Focus on the task, not the what-ifs."

"He's right," Bryce added from where she and Athalar sat nearby, leaning against each other. Flynn and Dec sat in the front, the former monitoring the streets, the latter with a laptop on his knees, hacking his way into the imperial military controls for the mech-suits. Another few hours, and they'd be in. "Leave the baggage behind today."

Lidia straightened. "My sons are not *baggage*—"

"No," Bryce amended, "they're not. But you know that palace better than anyone. Any distractions are going to cost us."

"I know Pollux better than anyone," Lidia said, staring ahead at nothing. "And that's why it's unbearable to sit here."

"Rest up while you can, Lidia," Athalar advised. "All Hel is going to break loose pretty damn soon."

"Literally," Bryce said with unnerving cheer.

Ithan buried the Prime in the heart of the meadow, so his soul might feel the romping joy of pups for generations to come.

If any of them survived this.

Tharion had called him, asking where the fuck he was, and Ithan told the mer to head to the Eternal City without him. To try to find Bryce and Athalar and get the antidote to them or any of their friends before they went full-tilt at the Asteri. If the antidote had leveled him up, then he couldn't even imagine what it would do to Bryce and Athalar.

Ithan shouldered his backpack and the Godslayer Rifle that Roga had loaned, and left the main building of the Den. Perry was again standing guard at the booth outside the gates.

"Did you get any rest?" Ithan asked, poking his head in. From the bruises under her eyes, he knew the answer before she nodded. "I told you to get some sleep."

"I wanted to be here," she said, "in case anyone came looking for help or had questions."

His chest tightened at her thoughtfulness—her kindness. "And did anyone?"

"No," she said, rubbing her eyes.

"You should get down to the Blue Court."

Her gaze found his. "You're leaving?"

"Yeah," he said. He hadn't slept much either, but he'd forced his body to rest. He knew he had to be at full strength for what was to come.

Perry's phone buzzed, and she glanced at the screen. Her brows knitted.

"What is it?"

She opened up her phone and read aloud, "'Bryce Quinlan and Hunt Athalar killed the Archangels Micah and Sandriel this spring.' There's . . . there's video footage of Bryce . . ."

Ithan's heart began racing. He was too late. Bryce was already making her move.

"I need to go," he said. "I have to help her however I can."

Perry rose from her seat in the booth. "Good luck, Ithan. I . . . I really hope I see you again."

He wrapped his arms around her in a tight hug, her cinnamon-and-strawberry scent washing over him. Just as it always had—like she hadn't taken the antidote. He set aside his curiosity about it again. "I hope I see you again, too," he said against her hair, and pulled back.

Her eyes shone with tears. "Please be careful."

He adjusted the straps on his backpack. "Get to the Blue Court, Perry."

"I'm in the imperial network," Declan announced a couple hours later.

Hunt finished arming himself with the few weapons he'd taken from what Fury Axtar had managed to bring in that helicopter: two handguns and a long knife. It wasn't much, but Axtar had chosen the weapons well. They were all solid, reliable pieces.

"Those mech-suits are no fucking joke." Dec shuddered. "But I'm ready to go when you guys are."

Hunt checked the gun holstered at his thigh. The clip was loaded. Reloads sat in his back pocket. He could have used the comfort of his Umbra Mortis suit with its twin swords nestled in the sheaths down its back. But two handguns, a knife in his boot, and his lightning would have to do. *He* would have to do.

Just Hunt. He could live with that.

He ran an eye over Bryce. The hilt of the Starsword rose above her ponytail, and Truth-Teller had been strapped on one thigh. She had a handgun on the other, only one clip for a reload.

Hel had brought its armies, but they fought with power and fangs and teeth and brute strength.

"Right," Bryce said, "we all clear on the plan?"

"Which one?" Ruhn muttered. "You have, like, seven."

"Better to over-prepare," Bryce trilled. "Plan's simple: keep the Asteri distracted by unleashing Hel and the Fallen . . . while Athalar and I sneak into the palace and destroy that firstlight core."

"Don't forget," Hunt cut in wryly, "rescue Lidia's sons, destroy Pollux, get close enough to the Asteri to eliminate them from the planet . . ." He ticked off the items on his fingers.

"Yeah, yeah," Bryce said, waving a hand. She winked at Lidia, flashing a grin that Hunt knew was designed to put the Hind at ease. "You ready to beat the shit out of these assholes?"

Lidia's chin lifted. She had a knife at her side and a handgun. That was it.

It was laughable that they were heading into the fucking Asteri's palace armed so lightly, but it didn't bear dwelling upon. They didn't have a choice.

"The moment we leave this truck, we have two minutes until the street cameras alert the Asteri's techs that we're in the city if they identify us," Lidia said.

"Which is why it's my job," Declan said from his station in the back of the van, "to keep those cameras away from you guys."

"And my job," Flynn said from the driver's seat, "to keep us moving around the city to avoid detection."

"As soon as I message you," Ruhn said, "be ready for a pickup."

"We did this once before, remember?" Flynn said to Ruhn. "Meeting up with Lidia once she'd sprung you and Athalar was a trial run for the big show."

"I don't care what you have to do," Lidia said to Flynn, to Dec, "or who you have to leave behind. But you get my sons out of this city and to the coast." She met their stare and added, "Please."

Dec nodded. "We've got you covered, Lidia." The name seemed to trip Dec up, but he got over it and said, "We'll protect your kids. Just do what you have to do, and we'll be where you need us."

She nodded back, eyes glittering. "Thank you."

Hunt glanced to Bryce, who was watching all this silently. Not a good sign.

Lidia noted Bryce's look and said, "You remember the way to their throne room?"

"Yes," Bryce said, and faced Hunt. "The wings were all still there a couple weeks ago—let's hope Rigelus hasn't redecorated."

"He won't have touched them," Lidia answered. "He abhors change."

The words hung in the air. Hunt swallowed against the dryness in his throat. They were doing this. He was doing this.

Hadn't he learned his fucking lesson *twice* now? With the Fallen, then with recent events? To go back for a third helping . . .

"I remember," Bryce said quietly—just to him, even with the

others listening. "Every movement of Micah's sword when he cut off your wings. How there was nothing we could do to stop him—stop *them.* I remember how they sold you back to Sandriel, and that time, too, there was nothing we could do to stop them. I remember every fucking moment of it, Hunt." Her eyes glimmered with pure rage and focus. "But today we finally fucking *stop them.*"

Hunt held his mate's stare, and let her courage be his courage, let her strength be his guiding light.

"I promised myself that day Micah cut off your wings," Bryce said, still just for him, "that they'd pay for it. For what they've done." Starlight flickered around her head in a shadow of that crown of stars.

No one spoke. Bryce got to her feet, heading for the back doors of the van. The world, the Asteri, the end waited beyond.

She looked back at all of them. Her eyes met Hunt's.

And Bryce said before she stepped into the light, "Through love, all is possible."

88

It was too easy to get into the Asteri's palace. Lidia knew every entrance, but even with her unrivaled knowledge, it was too easy for them to get in through the service doors that led to the extensive garbage-processing dock.

Too easy to slip down one of the reeking chutes and land in a trash room a level below.

But only when the four of them were in the tiny, malodorous closet on the sublevel did they pause. Look at each other.

"Good luck," Ruhn said to his sister, perhaps for the last time.

But Bryce smiled gently, softly, and though she had been all fierce determination in the van a few minutes ago, it was love in her face now as she said to him, "You brought so much joy into my life, too, Ruhn."

He remembered, then, saying those words to her before she'd vanished through the Gate. *You brought so much joy into my life, Bryce.* It felt like a lifetime ago.

She said nothing more, and Ruhn had no words in him as Bryce, Athalar in tow, cracked open the door and slipped out.

Ruhn waited a moment in silence with Lidia, the reek of the trash threatening to send his meager breakfast of bread and olive oil back up. He met Lidia's stare in the dimness, though.

And while she might need to be the Hind today, might need to become that stone-cold female again, he leaned in to brush his mouth to hers. Only once, and then he whispered, at last naming that feeling he hadn't dared acknowledge until now, "If I don't get the chance to tell you later . . . I love you."

Lidia blinked, golden eyes glimmering. "Ruhn."

But he didn't wait for a response or a refusal or a denial. He eased open the door an inch and peered into the hallway.

"Clear," he murmured, drawing his handgun. With any luck, Dec was doing his job.

Praying that the Asteri, distracted with trying to tamp down the effects of Bryce and Hunt's message, wouldn't even consider that Hel was about to be unleashed in their own home, Ruhn stepped into the hall, Lidia right behind them.

And then, wreathed in his shadows as they stole through the heart of the empire, they began the hunt to find her sons.

They had a few close calls, and Hunt wished again for his Umbra Mortis suit, if only for the helmet's heightened hearing to detect any passing politicians or workers.

The politicians could get fucked for all Hunt cared. But the workers . . . Gods willing, when the time came, the workers would be able to escape. That when Declan hacked into the Asteri alert system, their phones would buzz with the evacuation order to get the fuck out of the palace, and they would heed the warning.

Hunt's heart was thundering through every inch of him as he and Bryce hid in the shadows of a massive statue of Polaris, the female's hands upraised in victory.

Beyond the statue rose a familiar set of doors. The whole hallway was precisely as it had been the last time Hunt had seen it, before his lightning and Rigelus's power had blasted it to smithereens: busts of the Asteri lining one wall, the windows overlooking the seven hills of the Eternal City on the other. And somewhere out there, inching along the main road of the Sacra Via . . . Dec and Flynn would be waiting.

But not for them. Hunt knew he and Bryce might never come back from this fight.

If they succeeded in destroying the firstlight core and cutting off the Asteri's renewable source of power, then they'd have to get close enough to those bastards for Bryce to use the sword and knife. To unite them using that star, and risk whatever might happen with a portal to nowhere.

Theia had been afraid of it. Aidas had warned them to *choose life*, for fuck's sake, if the portal was too dangerous. It didn't bode well. But what other options did they have?

There were too many ifs, too many unknowns. It was an even flimsier plan than the last time they'd snuck into this palace. And while they'd all agreed on the plan together, if it failed, if Bryce or any of them died . . .

No. He wouldn't go down that road again. He had made mistakes in the past, bad calls, but fighting against tyranny, against brutality, would never be the wrong choice.

Hunt glanced to his mate, her attention fixed on the hallway. On the Gate at its far end. Sensing his attention, she mouthed, *Go*, and motioned him along. And Hunt went, as he'd go anywhere, so long as it was with her.

For the first time in his life, it seemed that Urd was listening as he and Bryce slipped past the doors into the empty throne room. He gazed at the towering wall of the Fallen's wings behind the seven crystal thrones.

And there, at its center, pinned like a new trophy, was his Umbra Mortis helmet and suit.

Bryce held the Mask in her hands, its gold surface shimmering among the crystal of the sterile throne room. The wings of the Fallen hung on the wall, a fluttering array of colors and shapes and sizes. So many lives, given toward this moment.

Hunt buckled the last bit of his suit into place, fitting the Umbra Mortis helmet over his head. Bryce hadn't questioned him when he took it off the wall. She knew why he wanted it.

Just as she knew that his wings, pinned right above Rigelus's throne, could not remain.

He'd wear that suit and helmet one more time. It wouldn't be the Umbra Mortis wearing that suit, but Hunt. Her Hunt.

And together they would end this.

She wished Ithan had made it in time with Hypaxia's antidote. But they couldn't delay this—not by a single minute.

Bryce ran her thumbs over the Mask's smooth brow. It looked like a death mask for some long-dead king. Had it been crafted around the mold of some Asteri's face? Fashioned after the hateful visage of a Daglan in that other world?

"Bryce," Hunt warned, his voice low and warped through the helmet.

She beheld the Shadow of Death standing there. He drew his twin swords from the back of his suit, flipping them in his hands. "Do it now."

All she'd ever done in her life, every step . . . it had led here.

Here, to this chamber, with the wings of the noble Fallen around her. With Hunt, one of the few remaining warriors.

But no longer.

Bryce lifted the Mask to her face, and closed her eyes as she slid it on. The metal adhered to her skin. It sucked at her face, her soul—

The world diluted again. Alive, not-alive. Breathing, not-breathing. Dead . . . undead.

The star inside her flared brightly, as if to say, *Hello, old friend.* Yes, the ancient magic knew the Mask. It understood its deepest secrets.

Bryce turned to the wings. And in the shadow-vision of the Mask, where the wings were pinned, most held a twinkling light. The kernel of a soul. The last scraps of their existences, shining like a wall of stars.

She'd been right: They had never been given Sailings. It had been the final insult to the dead warriors, the shame of being denied a blessed afterlife. It would prove to be the Asteri's downfall. These souls, left to wander for centuries, were now hers to claim.

A thought, and her will was their will. The Mask called, and the souls of the Fallen answered, drifting from the wall like a swarm of fireflies.

Rustling filled the air. The wings began to beat slowly at first, like butterflies testing out their new bodies. The flapping of wings filled the throne room, the world. A storm wind from Hunt had the pins ripping free. All but two sets—one a familiar gray, one shiningly white—loosed into the world.

And then the throne room was full of wings—white and gray and black, soaring, their sparks of soul shining brightly within them, visible only to Bryce as she looked through the Mask.

Hunt and Bryce stood in the center of the storm, her hair whipped about by their wind, skin grazed by their downy feathers.

A spark of Hunt's lightning struck the two pairs of wings still pinned to the wall. His own wings, and Isaiah's. They caught fire, burning until they were nothing but ashes floating on the breeze of a thousand wings, freed at last from this place.

Another storm wind from Hunt and the doors to the hall opened. The windows lining the hall exploded.

And the wings of the Fallen soared for the open blue sky beyond.

The throne room emptied of them, like water down a drain, leaving a lone figure in the doorway. Staring at them.

Rigelus.

Feathers floated in the air around him.

"What," the Bright Hand seethed, glowing with power, "do you think you're doing?"

He stepped in, and his eyes went right to Bryce's face. Maybe it was the Mask, maybe she had been pushed beyond her limits, but she felt no fear, absolutely none, as she looked at the Bright Hand of the Asteri and said, "Righting a wrong."

But Rigelus narrowed his eyes at the Mask. "You bear a weapon you have no business wielding."

In the streets beyond, people were shouting at the sight of the host of wings flying overhead.

Dead and undead—Rigelus's nature confused the Mask. Alive and not-alive. Breathing and not-breathing. It couldn't get a grip on the Bright Hand, and it seemed to be recoiling, pulling away from Bryce—

She focused. *You obey me.*

The Mask halted. And remained in her thrall.

Rigelus eyed Hunt in his battle-suit and helmet. But he said to Bryce, "You traveled a long way from home, Bryce Quinlan." He advanced one step. That he hadn't attacked yet was proof of his wariness.

Hunt's lightning slithered over the floor.

But Bryce pointed behind Rigelus. To one of the hills beyond the city walls, where the wings had landed in the dry grass. They coated the hilltop, wings flapping idly, a flock of butterflies come down to rest.

And Bryce commanded them, *Rise, as you once were.*

Ice colder than that in Nena flowed through her, toward the now-distant wings. She could sense Hunt's pain, but Bryce didn't take her eyes from Rigelus.

"You have no idea what powers you toy with, girl," Rigelus said. "The Mask will curse your very soul—"

"Let's spare ourselves the idle threats this time," Bryce said, and pointed out the window again. This time to the army that had crept up to stand among the wings bearing those souls. "I think you have bigger issues to deal with."

She smiled then—a predator's smile, a queen's smile—as the armies of Hel crested the hill.

"Right on time," Bryce said.

Rigelus said nothing as more and more of those dark figures appeared atop the hill. Spilling out from the portal she'd opened for them just over its other side, hidden from view.

At the sight of the teeming hordes cresting the hills, seemingly from nowhere, at the sight of the three princes marching at their front . . .

People began screaming in the streets. Another signal—for Declan. To get the evacuation order out under the guise of an Imperial Emergency Alert. Every phone in this city would buzz with the command to escape beyond the city walls—to the coast, if they could.

Rigelus stared toward the armies of Hel now assembled on his doorstep.

"Surprise," Hunt said.

Rigelus slowly, slowly turned back toward Bryce and Hunt. And smiled.

"Did you think I didn't know the moment you opened the Northern Rift?" Bryce braced herself, rallied her power as Rigelus lifted a glowingly bright hand and said, "I have been waiting for your arrival. And have prepared accordingly."

A horn sounded, a clear note echoing across the city.

And in answer, the Asterian Guard exploded into the streets of the Eternal City.

89

I knew as soon as you reached the Rift—my Harpy told me, and I watched you through her eyes before you ended her." Rigelus advanced another step into the throne room, power brewing in his hand, dancing along the golden rings on each long finger.

Bryce and Hunt tensed, eyeing the distance to the exit. A smaller door lay behind the thrones, but to reach it they'd have to put their backs to Rigelus.

In the city, light sparked and boomed—brimstone missiles. Made and fired by the Asterian Guard on the rooftops, spearing toward the demons of Hel's armies. Arcing, golden, the missiles slammed into the dark ranks atop Mount Hermon. Earth and rock shattered, light blooming upward.

"And like the rodents you are," Rigelus said, "I knew you'd leave an escape route for yourselves and your allies. Right to Hel. I knew you'd leave the Rift open."

Hunt grabbed Bryce's hand, preparing to get them out.

"So I sent three legions of my Asterian Guard to the Rift last night. I think they and their brimstone missiles will find Hel quite unguarded, with all its armies here."

"We have to warn Aidas," Hunt said, squeezing her hand. Bryce looked at Rigelus once more—at his smirk of triumph at outwitting them—

And with a shove of her power, she teleported herself and Hunt out of the palace.

Right to the chaos of the hills beyond the city.

Ruhn and Lidia raced along the palace corridors, veiled in his shadows.

They'd found no sign of her sons. Nothing in the dungeons, the sight of which had given Ruhn such a jolt of pure terror he had nearly dropped their concealing shadows. And nothing in any of the holding cells. They'd made their way through the palace as quickly as they could while staying undetected. Dec had disabled many of the cameras, and Ruhn's shadows took care of the rest. But after twenty minutes of fruitless searching, Ruhn grabbed Lidia's arm before they could race down yet another hallway.

"We need to stop and reconsider where they might be," Ruhn said, breathing hard.

"They're here—he's got them *here*," Lidia snarled, struggling against his grip.

Ruhn held firm, though. "We can't keep running around blindly. Think: Where would Pollux take them?"

She panted, eyes wide with panic, but took a breath. Another.

And that cold, Hind's mask slid over her face. "I know how to find them," she said. And Ruhn didn't question her as she took off again, this time heading back down the stairs, down, down, down until—

The heat and humidity hit him first. Then the smell of salt.

The one thousand mystics of the Asteri slumbered in their sunken tubs, in regimented lines between the pillars of the seemingly endless hall.

"Traitor," a withered, veiled female hissed from a desk in front of the doors, rising to her feet.

Lidia pulled out her handgun and sent a bullet through the female's skull without hesitation. The blast rocked like thunder through the hall, but the mystics didn't stir.

Ruhn stared at Lidia, at the place where the old female had been standing, at the blood now sprayed on the stones—

But Lidia was already heading for the nearest tank, for the controls beside it. She began typing. Then moved to the next mystic, then the next, and the next.

"We don't have long until someone comes down here to investigate that gunshot," Ruhn warned. But Lidia kept moving from tank to tank, and he peered at the first monitor to see the question she'd written. *Where are Lidia Cervos's sons?*

She stopped typing at the seventh mystic, and stalked along the rows of tubs.

Ruhn moved to the doorway to keep watch, hiding himself in shadows as he monitored the hall, the stairs at their far end. They'd be lucky if it took even a minute for inquiring ears to get down here—

Lidia gasped. Ruhn whirled toward her, but she was already running.

"Pollux has got them under the palace," she said as she reached the door and raced out, Ruhn running alongside her.

"Under?" Ruhn asked, trailing her down the stairs.

"In the hall with the firstlight core that your sister discovered—under the archives."

"Lidia," Ruhn said, grabbing her arm. "It has to be a trap. To have them at the core—"

She pointed the gun at his head. "I'm going. If it's a trap, then it's a trap. But I'm going."

Ruhn held up his hands. "I know, and I'm going with you, but we have to think through the—"

She was already sprinting again, the gun back at her side. The castle had filled with sound now, a cacophony of shouting, scared people trying to get out as fast as possible. It masked the sound of their creeping about, but . . . Lidia was frantic—desperate. Which made for a dangerous ally, Hind or no. She'd get herself killed, and her sons, too.

He couldn't let her jeopardize herself like that. If anyone was going to put themselves in that lethal danger . . .

It'd be him.

Ruhn vaulted down the stairs behind Lidia. And when he caught up to her, he clicked the safety off his gun.

Lidia heard that click and halted. Turned to him—slow, disbelieving. She didn't glance at the gun. She already knew it was there. Her eyes were on his. Unreadable, cold. The eyes of the Hind.

Ruhn rasped, "I can't let you get yourself killed."

"I will never forgive you for this," she said, voice like ice itself. *"Never."*

"I know," Ruhn said. And fired.

One shot, right to her thigh.

She shouted in pain as she crumpled, the bullet passing through the wound and ricocheting off the stairs behind her, the thunder of the gun and her scream spinning into a chorus that shredded his soul. A chorus that, thankfully, was muffled by the chaos unfolding levels above.

She pressed her palm to the open wound, which he'd inflicted far from any dangerous artery, and her eyes blazed with pure, flaming rage. "I will *kill* you—"

She reached for the gun at her other thigh, as if she really would blast his face off.

Ruhn bolted down the stairs before she could take aim. Holstering his own gun, he raced onward, leaving her to bleed behind him.

The waterways of the Eternal City were old, and strange, and unfriendly.

Tharion hated them. Especially with the amplified power in his veins, freed from its bonds. His body and soul recognized the very essence of his surroundings. They did not like what they encountered.

There was no mer court in the river wending like a snake through the city. There was barely any life at all beyond bottom-feeders and skittering things that clung to the shadows.

Above, the world was chaos. Armies and missiles and wings.

Here, the sounds were muffled. The water whispered to him where to go, where to bring the bag of sealed antidotes. Flowed with him, guided his powerful tail, right to the grate in the river-bank. His gills flared as he hauled away the metal. As he swam into the dark, lightless tunnel and switched on the aquatic headlamp he'd had the good sense to bring.

And with the water guiding him, Tharion swam like Hel for the Asteri's palace.

Bombs ruptured, and it was so much worse than the past spring. Brimstone missiles rose from the city, from the Asterian Guard hidden within it, from the mech-suits stirring to life atop Mount Hermon—

So much destruction. Hyperconcentrated angelic wrath.

Atop one of the hills beyond the city, Bryce was gasping for breath, a bit dizzy, as she yanked the Mask from her face. Hunt ran for where the Prince of the Chasm stood overlooking the dark beasts swarming toward the city walls and said, "Phase Two starts now."

Bryce mastered herself enough to stagger up to Aidas and Hunt. The armies of Hel, both terrestrial and airborne, all hungry and raging, were no fucking joke.

She knew it had been the only way. To stand a chance, unleashing Hel had been the only way. Even so, its army was petrifying, allies or not. She had to trust that Aidas and the other princes had them on tight leashes.

"They're almost close enough," Aidas said, clad in black armor akin to Thanatos's. Bryce could only assume that his brothers were either among the fray or overseeing their own divisions of the teeming black mass.

There was nothing to do for a moment but watch the Asterian Guard decide they had the beasts on the run and begin advancing beyond the city walls.

Wings fluttered nearby, and Isaiah and Naomi touched down beside Hunt.

"Ready?" Isaiah asked, clad in the black battle-suit of the 33rd.

"Soon," Aidas said. The angels still maintained a healthy distance from him, but had at least lost their disbelieving, wary expressions in his presence.

The Asterian Guard swept out into the hills and valleys below, their mech-suits marching among them, and where they struck, demons died.

"Do you think," Aidas mused, "that they have any idea what's about to happen to them?"

"No," Hunt said, smiling darkly. "And neither does Rigelus."

Bryce slid the Mask back on, and its ungodly, leeching presence ate into her soul. But the star inside her seemed to hold the Mask at bay.

"That'll teach him to think he can outsmart us," Naomi said.

The Asterian Guard, white plumes of horsehair on their helmets shining bright in the daylight, advanced through the field of demons. The feet of the scores of mech-suits among them shook the earth.

"I think the three legions he sent to Nena," Naomi said, "will be in for quite a surprise when they find that half of Hel's army is still there and waiting for them."

Isaiah said, with no small amount of satisfaction, "They should be getting word to the Asteri right about"—he checked his phone—"now."

"Perfect," Aidas purred. "Then we're ready."

"Messaging Declan," Naomi said, typing into her phone. The Fae warrior was waiting in the van, the hacked imperial military network laid bare at his fingertips.

The Asteri's mech-suits halted mid-stride. The Asterian Guard paused, glancing at the fancy new machines that had malfunctioned all at once. The glowing eyes of the mech-suits faded and died out.

"Magic and machines," Isaiah said. "Never a good combination."

"It's a go," Naomi said, reading a message on her phone. "Do your thing, Quinlan."

They all looked to Bryce.

Alive and not-alive. Dead and undead. Bryce reached out a hand toward the stilled metal army below. Cold, awful power went through her. But her will was their will. Her will was everything.

Rise, Bryce said, blasting the thought out. *Fight. Obey Isaiah Tiberian and Naomi Boreas. Hel is your ally—you fight beside them.*

Only she could see the twinkling souls of the Fallen, drifting toward those suits from the nearby hilltop, alighting on them one by one by one.

The eyes of the suits blazed again. Bryce saw the nearest mech-suit lift its metal arm in front of its face. Watch its fingers wriggle with something like wonder.

Then it turned to the closest Asterian Guard and bashed the soldier's head in.

"Holy gods," Naomi breathed as the mech-suits, one after another, began to march away from the Asterian Guard.

The souls of the Fallen had waited for the moment the Asterian Guard and their mech-suits had begun to march toward the city below.

And the remaining souls of the Fallen that didn't have a mech-suit to slip into . . . Well, there were plenty of dead demons and Asterian Guards with bodies intact enough for occupying. Twitching, as if adjusting to the new limbs, those corpses lurched to their feet. Came to stand beside their Fallen brethren in their mech-suit hosts.

"You're up," Hunt said to Isaiah and Naomi. "Time to get into the city."

The angels bowed their heads. And with a great thrust of their wings, they launched skyward. Isaiah's voice boomed out. *"Fallen, you are now Risen! To the gates!"*

Isaiah looked back at Hunt, his eyes brimming with pride and determination. The warrior touched his heart and flew off. Hunt lifted his arm in salute and farewell, as if beyond words.

It was indeed a sight beyond words—beyond any description. An army of the undead, of machines and demons, marched for the city walls.

"Incoming," Hunt said. "Seems like that footage kept them distracted until now."

"Right on time," Aidas confirmed, as the glowing figures approached the battlefield spread before the northern gates of the Eternal City, come to exterminate this threat themselves.

The Asteri.

And walking toward them, the armies parting before him, was the Prince of the Ravine, with the Prince of the Pit trailing close behind.

90

Hunt refrained from heaving a sigh of relief, even if his helmet would have masked the sound.

Bryce had freed the souls of the Fallen from the throne room and placed them into those mech-suit bodies, but the hardest and most dangerous part of their plan started now. Hunt fought to keep his breathing steady, his focus on the unfolding battle and chaos. His helmet blared with alerts and assessments.

Aidas unsheathed a shining silver blade that seemed to glow with bluish light. "My turn," the demon prince said, the dry breeze whipping his pale blond hair. He asked Bryce, "A ride?"

Hunt had only a moment to glimpse the worry, the fear in her eyes as she grabbed Aidas's hand, then Hunt's, and teleported them. With the power of Theia's star, it barely took a moment. Barely seemed to drain her. But what arose around them as they reappeared on the battlefield was a scene straight from a nightmare.

Kristallos demons, deathstalkers, hounds like the Shepherd, and worse . . . the pets of Thanatos, all racing past the Asteri and into the city itself. Hunt's helmet turned them all into distant figures, the world awash in red and black.

But the Asteri had bigger fish to fry: The three princes now before them. Especially Apollion, standing between his brothers.

There was no sign of Rigelus. He'd sent the other five Asteri to do his dirty work.

"You shall pay for marching on our city," Polaris snapped at them.

Hunt unfurled his power, lightning bright even from behind the visor of his helmet. Beside him, Bryce had already peeled off the Mask. And beyond them, around them, the Fallen—*his* Fallen, now in bodies of metal and nightmares, all still bound by the command to follow Isaiah and Naomi—engaged the Asterian Guard. Swarmed them.

Miniature brimstone missiles launched from the mech-suits' shoulder guns, fired at the Asterian Guard. Floating feathers and cinders were all that remained.

It had been Hunt's idea to play on Rigelus's arrogance. He thought them reckless and stupid—thought they'd be dumb enough to believe that they could somehow smuggle an army down from Nena and launch a surprise attack on the Eternal City. That they'd be dumb enough to leave Hel open and vulnerable.

So they'd let the Asteri split their Asterian Guard in two, sending half to Nena to conquer Hel . . . only to be slaughtered by a host of demons awaiting them there, under the command of one of Apollion's captains.

And this half of the guard, the most elite and trained of all angels . . .

They wouldn't stand a chance, either.

Three Princes of Hel faced off against five Asteri in the dry scrub beyond the city walls, war exploding all around them.

It was Polaris who looked to Bryce. "You shall die for this impertinence," she sneered, and launched a blinding blast of raw power for her. Apollion stepped forward, a hand raised. Pure, devouring darkness destroyed Polaris's light.

And satisfaction like Hunt had never known coursed through him at the way the Asteri halted. Stepped back.

Apollion inclined his golden head to the Asteri. "It has been an age."

"Do not let him get any closer," Polaris hissed to the others, and as one, the Asteri attacked.

The ground ruptured, and light met dark met light—

Hunt whirled to Bryce, a shield of pure lightning crackling between them and the fighting. His voice was partially muffled by his helmet. "We need to get out of here—"

"No," Bryce said, eyes on the Asteri.

"That's not the plan," Hunt growled, reaching for her elbow, intending to fly them away from the battlefield if she wouldn't teleport them. They needed to destroy the firstlight core, or else all this would be pointless. With it still functional, the Asteri could run back to the palace, regenerate their powers, their bodies. "Bryce," Hunt warned.

But Bryce drew the Starsword and Truth-Teller, starlight and darkness flowing down the black blades. She didn't unite them, though. At least there was still time to stick to the plan—

Polaris burst through the fray, eyes burning with white light fixed on Bryce. "You should have run when you had the chance," the North Star snarled.

The air seemed to pulse with the power from those blades, from Bryce. Like they knew the time to unite had come at last.

No running, then. Only adapting.

So Hunt rallied his own power, rising to meet his mate.

Polaris launched herself toward them, and Hunt struck: a blast of pure lightning at her feet, warping the very stone there, opening a pit for her to trip into—

Bryce teleported. Slowly enough that Hunt knew she was already tiring, despite the extra power from the star, but then she was there, in front of Polaris as the Asteri hit the ground, and only Hunt's lightning shield kept the blast of power from frying Bryce as she lifted the sword and the dagger above her head.

Polaris's eyes widened as Bryce plunged the blades into her chest. And as those blades thrust through skin and bone, the star in Bryce's own chest flared out to meet them.

It collided with the blades, and both sword and knife blazed bright, as if white-hot. The light extended up through Bryce's hands, her arms, her body, turning her incandescent—

Into a star. A sun.

Polaris screamed, her mouth opening unnaturally wide.

The slowing of the world when a great power died was familiar to Hunt from Micah's death, from Shahar's, from Sandriel's, but this was so much worse.

With the helmet, Hunt could truly see everything: the particles of dust drifting by, the droplets of Polaris's blood rising upward like a red rain as Bryce shoved her blades deeper and deeper—

The demon princes were turning toward them, their Asteri opponents with them.

Gone were the princes' humanoid skins. Creatures of darkness and decay stood there, mouths full of sharp teeth, leathery wings splayed. A great black mass lay within Apollion's yawning open mouth as he surged for Octartis—

The Asteri male flung up a wall of light.

The brimstone missiles from the shoulders and forearms of the mech-suit hybrids sparked again, ember by ember by ember, and Hunt could see with perfect clarity as the spiraling missiles launched into the world, toward the panicking Asterian Guard.

A deathstalker raced past, one galloping step lasting an age, a lifetime, an eon as it seemed to balance on one foot mid-stride.

And Bryce was still there, falling with Polaris, those two black blades meeting in the Asteri's chest, Theia's star uniting them in power and purpose—

Debris skittered toward Bryce, toward Polaris. Like whatever was happening at that intersection of the blades was drawing the world in, in, in.

To the portal to nowhere.

A primal chill sang down Hunt's spine. Theia had been right; Aidas was right. That portal to nowhere, opening somehow inside Polaris, was dangerous not just to the Asteri, but to anyone in its reach.

He had to stop it. He had to shut it fast, or else he knew, instinctively, that all of them would perish—

Time dripped by as Polaris contorted in pain. Bryce's hair was sucked toward the Asteri, toward the blades and wherever they were opening to—

Too slow. Whatever Theia's star was summoning, the portal was opening too slowly, and every second that it yawned wider threatened to swallow Bryce, too.

He'd been made by Hel to help her. To end this. *Helfire and starfire: a potent combination*, Bryce had said in Hel.

It was pure instinct. Pure desperation, too. Hunt unleashed his lightning, directed it toward the nexus where those blades met. It flowed like a sizzling ribbon through the world, past the death-stalkers, past the Princes of Hel, past the mech-suits—

Hunt watched it collide with the sword and dagger right where they crossed, where Theia's star still glowed between them, binding them in unholy union. And where his Helfire met starfire, where lightning met blades, it bloomed with blinding light.

Polaris's face twisted with agony. And still the world kept slowing, slowing—

Tendrils of Hunt's Helfire twined down the blade, into Polaris herself. Lightning danced over Bryce's teeth, over her shocked eyes.

He expected an outward explosion, expected to see every last bit of Asteri bone and brain rupture, shard by shard.

But instead, Polaris imploded. Her chest caved in, sucked into the blades as if by a powerful vacuum. Followed by her abdomen and shoulders, and Polaris was screaming and screaming—

Until he saw it, just a flash, so fast that in real time he'd never have witnessed it: the tiny, inky dot the two blades had made, right where they met.

The *thing* Polaris had been sucked into. A black dot.

It was there and then gone as Bryce stumbled forward, and the blades separated, and time resumed, so fast Hunt lost his breath. He touched a button on the side of his helmet, raising his visor, offering him lungfuls of fresh air.

One of the Asteri roared, and the world itself shook, the city walls with it.

But Bryce was staring down at the place where Polaris had been. At the blades in her hands, still wreathed in his Helfire and her starlight.

A portal to nowhere. To a black hole.

No wonder it had started to suck in Bryce as well. And the rest of the world. No wonder Theia had hesitated, if that was what she'd suspected would happen at the joining of the blades.

Hunt's body was vibrating with power as Bryce lifted her face to his. Pure, savage delight lit her eyes. She'd seen it, too—she knew she'd sent Polaris straight into the nothingness of a black hole.

And—there. A kernel of worry sparked. Like it was setting in how dangerous it would be to open another one, let alone five more. What they'd risk each time.

Still, they stared at each other, just for a moment. They'd killed a gods-damned Asteri.

Hunt's power buzzed through him again, in his very bones—

No. That wasn't his power buzzing through him. It was his phone. The interior speakers on his helmet patched Ruhn through.

"Danaan."

"You need to get to the hall with the firstlight core," Ruhn said. "We've . . . We need help." The line went dead.

"Bryce—" Hunt began, but when he turned to her, he found that pure light had again filled her eyes.

He'd seen that face only once before—the day she'd killed Micah. When she'd looked at the cameras and shown the world what lurked under the freckles and smile: the apex predator beneath. Wrath's bruised heart.

Whatever it took to end this . . . she'd do it. His blood pumped through him, sparking at that look, at what she had done—

"Go," shouted the thing Aidas had become, identifiable only by those blazing blue eyes as he faced Octartis beside Apollion.

The princes looked like the worst of horrors, but Hunt knew their true nature now. They had come to help. And for a single heartbeat, pride at being a son of Hel threaded through him.

Hunt looked back to Bryce, shutting the helmet's visor over his eyes again. "We have to get to the hall with the firstlight core," he said, but she was already reaching for him. Grabbing his hand, primal fury blazing on her face, the Starsword and Truth-Teller again sheathed.

A blink, and they were gone.

She was draining fast. They landed in a hallway three levels up, if the number on the nearby stairwell entrance was any indication.

Blood leaked from her nose, and Hunt might have fretted had he not heard the snarls surrounding them. Had his helmet not blared with alerts.

They'd teleported into a corridor full of deathstalkers.

Thanatos had sent his pets into the palace to distract and occupy any Asteri who might have stayed away from the battlefield, but his grip on them must have been weak, or he simply did not care.

Taking on just one had left a scar down Hunt's back. Granted, he'd been bound by the halo, but even at full power, taking on this many would be no mean feat. Beside him, Bryce panted. She needed a breather. After her fight with Polaris, after managing to avoid the black hole she'd opened, after the teleporting . . . his mate needed rest.

Hunt eyed the snarling pack. The thought of wasting his power to kill an ally's beast rankled him.

But in the end, he didn't have to decide—a wall of water crashed through the corridor.

And roared straight for him and Bryce.

91

There was no way out. No window, no exit, no place to breathe as water flooded the hall up to the ceiling.

Hunt grabbed Bryce, his lightning rendered useless in the water, and swam toward where he guessed the stairs might be in the tumbling dark. His helmet filled with water, warping his vision—

A light shone. He hadn't thought Bryce had that kind of power left—but no. It wasn't Bryce. Tharion was swimming toward them through the hall. Ketos had never commanded enough power to control this much water, and with such force, yet here he was, clearly the master of this flood.

An air bubble formed around Hunt and Bryce. He yanked off his helmet, splashing water down his front. "What the fuck," Hunt spat, choking on the water.

But Bryce got it before Hunt did, and yelled at Tharion through the air bubble now saving their asses, "Don't drown them all! We need them on the battlefield!"

"I had a bag of antidotes," Tharion shouted, his powerful, tiger-striped tail thrashing, "but the force of the water snapped the strap. It's down here somewhere, just wait for me to—"

"No time!" Bryce shouted back. "Find it, then find us!"

Bryce was right: to delay getting to that room, cutting off the Asteri's power at the knees . . . it wasn't a risk worth taking, even for the antidote.

The water roared past, into the stairwell. "Go!" Tharion called as the water vanished from the hall, the mer and the demons swept upward in its current. "I'll be right behind you!"

Hunt and Bryce landed hard on the stones, soaking wet and sputtering, but they didn't wait.

"Hurry," Bryce said, grabbing his arm to haul him to his feet. "The firstlight core's below us."

It was all Hunt could do to shake the water from his eyes, grab his helmet, and race after her.

Ruhn had fucked up. In so many ways, he'd fucked up.

He could think of nothing else as he stood before Pollux, hands raised, before the door down to the hall with the firstlight core running underneath it.

There was no sign of Actaeon or Brann.

"Where's Lidia?" Pollux sneered, pointing a gun at Ruhn's face, his white wings glowing with power.

Ruhn had left her bleeding and wounded on the stairs, utterly vulnerable, hating him—

"Where are the boys?" he growled.

"Someplace else," Pollux said, and Ruhn's stomach churned at what that might imply. "Rigelus guessed you'd seek out his mystics, so he instructed them to feed the lie to you. Which you swallowed so fucking easily, because you're a gullible fool." The Hammer stepped forward and jerked his chin at Ruhn. "Move. I know Lidia's around here somewhere."

Ruhn had little choice but to obey. To let the Hammer lead him away from the firstlight core, out of the archives, then back down that hall to where Lidia would be lying bleeding on the stairs.

Pollux's breathing hitched as the scent of her blood filled the hall. "Lidia," he called in a singsong. Her scent became overpowering as they turned the corner to where Ruhn had left her—

There was no trace of her.

Tharion helped Lidia limp along, a band of living water wrapped around the hole in her thigh. Chasing down the satchel and antidotes, he'd found both bag and Hind on the stairs, right before they'd heard the Hammer snarling.

Only two vials had made it. The rest had burst, thanks to either the impact or the volatility of Athalar's lightning. But Lidia had been shot—by Ruhn, she'd told him. Tharion didn't know whether to admire or curse Danaan for it. The idiot had done it to keep her from harm, so he'd face Pollux alone.

Tharion hadn't needed to ask what she and Ruhn were doing down here in the first place. Why they'd risked everything to be here, why they'd separated from Bryce and Hunt.

Pollux had gloated about Lidia's sons to Ruhn, how the mystics had been ordered to lie about where they were, leading her into a trap. But that meant her sons remained captive elsewhere in this palace—and Pollux knew how to find them.

"Lidia . . . ," the Hammer crooned. "Lidia . . ." He practically sang her name.

Lidia gritted her teeth. With a surge upward, she launched for the hall, for the Hammer, but Tharion grabbed her, hauling her back down beside him.

"We need to regroup," he hissed.

"I need to get to my *sons*," she hissed back, and tried to move again. They spoke so quietly that their words were barely more than whispers of breath.

Tharion held her still. "You're in no shape—"

She tried once more, and Tharion decided to Hel with it. He willed the water band around her thigh to push in tighter, to send a tendril into the hole in her skin for emphasis.

She clapped a hand over her mouth, swallowing a scream.

Tharion pulled back the tendril, hating himself for the pain he'd caused, but he held his magic in place to keep any hint of her blood from showing where she'd gone. Her eyes widened, surprise replacing pain as the water eased up at his command. A simple, normal bit of magic, but he knew his eyes blazed with power—with the raging rapids of the Istros itself.

He said, low and swift, "Hypaxia managed to develop an antidote for the parasite. It temporarily returns the magic the Drop took from us—more than that, actually."

Tharion could have sworn something like pride gleamed in her eyes. "I knew she'd figure it out," Lidia murmured.

"Here." He used a plume of water to free the case of antidotes from his pack. He lifted one of the precious two remaining vials. "Take it. You'll black out for a sec, but . . ."

But to face the monster in that hallway, she would need to be fully healed. Need that wound gone. Lidia didn't hesitate as she grabbed the vial, uncorked it, and drank.

She swayed, and gold flashed in her eyes. He caught her as she blacked out, counting the breaths: one, two—

Her gunshot wound healed instantly. Lidia's eyes flew open, blazing gold. She looked down at her hands, flexing her fingers. "I knew she'd figure it out," Lidia repeated, more to herself than to him.

Tharion gently set her down and motioned for her to keep quiet as steps sounded once more, far closer than before.

"We do this slow and smart," Tharion warned, and helped her to her feet. She rose without a grimace or wince, all traces of pain now gone. But she nodded.

On silent feet, with Tharion's magic sending little particles of mist to evaporate the trail of their scent, they descended the steps.

"Lidia . . . ," Pollux crooned again.

A glance between them, and they halted at the bottom of the stairwell. Tharion peered around the corner to the long hall beyond, where Pollux held Danaan at gunpoint in front of him.

"Lidia . . . ," Pollux sang again. "I found your *companion*, so you can't be far away . . ."

Tharion withdrew. Lidia shook with rage and power. Tharion could feel it shuddering around him, rising up like a behemoth from the deep.

What had that antidote woken in her? What had been taken during the Drop? And what had lain dormant, all this time? His water seemed to quail at it—like it knew something he didn't.

"You're here," Pollux said. "I can sense your soul nearby. It is entwined with mine, you know."

Lidia's teeth flashed, her power growing around them like a physical presence. Tharion sliced his hand in front of them, indicating that she should stand down. Until he had a clear shot at the Hammer, they couldn't give away their position—

"Very well," Pollux said. A whistle through his teeth, and a door down the hall groaned open. Footsteps sounded, approaching them, approaching Pollux.

Tharion dared risk another glance around the corner. Two angels in imperial armor had stepped out. And between them . . .

Two teenage boys, both bound and gagged.

Lidia didn't need to look. She inhaled, scenting whatever was coming—

Her eyes flared as she recognized her sons' scents. Pure, murderous rage filled her gaze, and Tharion was suddenly very, very glad she was on their side.

So he knew better than to stop Lidia as she emerged from their hiding spot, rounded the corner, and said, power ringing through her voice, "Let them go."

Bryce had enough strength to make it to a hall a level above the archives. From there, she and Hunt snuck down on foot, trailing water, as quickly and quietly as they could. She might have pushed herself to teleport them down to the hallway with the firstlight core, but she needed to conserve her strength. Only one Asteri was currently down—

She'd killed Polaris.

The realization kept rippling through her. How it had felt,

how Polaris's blood had felt, showering her, the primal, raging satisfaction in seeing the other Asteri's outrage as Bryce impaled their sister with the sword and dagger, ignited by Hunt's Helfire.

And then Polaris had been sucked into nothing.

Into *nowhere.* The blades, fueled by her starlight and sped along by Hunt's Helfire, had opened a portal to a place that wasn't a place.

One Asteri had been banished from Midgard. But would she be lucky enough to get near the others? Now that they knew what she could do, what she bore, they'd avoid her, as they'd avoided Apollion.

The thoughts shot through Bryce's mind, dread sinking in her stomach, as they ran through the palace.

There was no point in staying hidden. Everyone knew they were here. A nod to Hunt, and her mate blasted open the doors into the archives.

Glass shattered, spraying everywhere, and a shield of Hunt's lightning kept the shards from shredding them as they raced through it, Bryce leading them toward the door to the hallway where the power of Midgard was held—

The glow of the room spilled up the stairs, leading the way down.

There was no sign of Lidia's sons. Indeed, the hall was exactly as it had been before. A crystal floor. The seven pipes, each with an Asteri's name on an engraved plaque beneath, and next to the plaques, small screens showing their power levels.

Sirius and Polaris were now dark. But the others were nearly full.

One of them, the seventh, was at full power. And standing before it was its bearer, smiling faintly at them.

Rigelus.

92

Rigelus unleashed a wall of white-hot power, and Bryce had enough sense to blast up a wall of her own, matching the lightning Hunt hurled between them and the Asteri.

The entire palace above them shook at the impact.

And as it cleared, Bryce drew the Starsword and Truth-Teller. "It didn't end well for Polaris," she told the Bright Hand, sending starfire rippling down the blades. "It won't end well for you."

"Polaris was weak," Rigelus said. "And a fool to let you draw close with those blades." Without warning, he launched his power at them again.

Bryce grabbed Hunt this time and teleported to the other side of the room.

Rigelus's power hit the stairs behind them, and they buckled. A true blow from the Bright Hand might collapse the entire palace, but that strike still would have seared their skin down to the bone.

"We have to get to that core under the crystal," Bryce said, and Rigelus attacked again.

"Kill him first," Hunt grunted, nodding toward the blades in her hands.

"He won't let us get near enough." She gathered her strength to teleport them to the core, and Hunt erupted with his lightning as they reappeared, firing right for Rigelus—

It hit a barrier of light and scattered.

"Your lightning," Bryce said quickly. "It warped stone earlier when you shot it at Polaris. Do you think it can warp crystal?" They stood about thirty feet above the glowing core below. To even get through that block of crystal, they'd need precious, uninterrupted minutes. She'd thought her starfire could eventually chisel away at it, but they didn't have the luxury of time.

"I need a good shot at the floor—a few, probably," Hunt said, as Rigelus attacked once more. Again, Bryce teleported. "Can you buy me time?"

Her mouth had dried out, and blood was dribbling from her nose again, but she nodded.

"What is it you're whispering?" Rigelus said calmly from where he stood in front of the pipes, but Bryce teleported them again.

They appeared right in front of Rigelus, and from his shocked face, he hadn't expected that. No, he'd thought her power tapped out.

The distraction cost him.

Hunt's Helfire slammed into the crystal floor. Bryce didn't wait to see what happened, how Rigelus reacted, before teleporting them back to the center of the room, and Hunt's Helfire boomed as it collided with the stone, which had indeed warped, and was now splintering under the monstrous heat.

Crystal peeled away, melting.

And beneath it, a tunnel to the core of firstlight began to form.

The Eternal City was a chaos of brimstone missiles, mech-suits, demons, the Asterian Guard, and every imaginable nightmare. Light and darkness warred across every inch of the city.

But Ithan sprinted through the streets, heading toward the crystal palace. Toward the white light flashing from it like some massive strobe.

It had to be Bryce. But the palace was massive, as big as the Comitium, and to find her in it . . .

No one had answered his phone calls. With the battle, he didn't think they would, but he'd kept trying, all the way here on the boat he'd quickly hired, then running from the coast without rest, without food or water.

A brimstone missile sailed overhead, sparking with golden light. It hit a building nearby, and the world ruptured.

Even Ithan, with his speed and grace, was thrown. His bones cracked against the building, the Godslayer Rifle swinging from his shoulder. And something else had cracked behind him, not bone but—

Ithan slid to the ground among the screaming people, reaching for his pack. Frantically, he pulled out the container with the vials of antidote for Bryce and Hunt.

Liquid leaked from them. Only shards of the vials remained.

Tharion had more, but Luna knew where the mer was in this mess. The rifle, at least, was unharmed—scraped up along the barrel, but nothing that would affect its usefulness.

He struggled to his feet, but a strong hand gripped him. Helped him up.

Ithan whirled, teeth out, only to find a human woman standing there, her eyes blazing with determination. And behind her, helping the wounded or running for the battle, were more humans. Some in their work clothes, some unarmed, but all heading for the conflict. For this first and possibly last shot against the Asteri.

And he knew. Bryce's message hadn't only been a distraction for the Asteri. It had been a rallying cry. For the people who had suffered most at the Asteri's hands.

So Ithan began hurtling for the palace again. Past all those humans, valiantly helping and fighting—despite the odds, despite the cost. The antidotes for his friends were gone. But he still had the rifle and its bullet.

Make your brother proud.

Lidia didn't bother with bullets. She holstered her gun and drew her sword.

She knew the odds against Pollux. But she'd been studying him for years now. Had learned his moves, his arrogance, his tricks.

She hadn't let him learn hers.

So Lidia glanced sidelong at Ruhn and said, "Get out of here. This is between him and me."

She wanted nothing to do with Ruhn. He'd shot her—he'd *shot* her, in some male fit of dominance, and it had kept her from her sons. She'd never forgive him—

"No fucking way." Ruhn eyed the two guards flanking her sons. As if he could take them, as if Pollux's gun wasn't pointed right at the back of his skull.

It'd be a bullet for Ruhn, but Pollux wouldn't blast her apart with a gun, or with his power. Not right away. He'd want to bloody her up right. Hurt her slow and hard and make her beg for mercy.

The palace shuddered.

"Lidia," Pollux said with hideous satisfaction. "You look well for someone who's been knee-deep in trash lately."

"Fuck you," Ruhn spat.

Behind Pollux, still several feet down the hallway, her sons stood tall, even as they trembled. The sight short-circuited something in her brain.

But Pollux sneered at Ruhn. "Was it for you that she left, then? Betrayed all she knew? For a Fae princeling?"

"Don't give him that much credit," Lidia snarled. She'd say anything to keep Pollux's attention on her—away from the boys. Ruhn could go to Hel for all she cared. But Lidia gestured between herself and Pollux. "This reckoning was years in the making."

"Oh, I know," Pollux said, and motioned to the two angels behind him. "See, the Ocean Queen's fleet isn't all that secure. Catch a mer spy, threaten to fillet them, and they'll tell you anything. Including where the *Depth Charger* is headed. And the two *very* interesting children aboard it—their true heritage at last revealed and the talk of the ship."

Lidia considered every scenario in which she could take on Pollux and get her sons out of here. Few of them ended with her walking out of here alive, too.

"They put up an admirable fight, you know," Pollux said. "But they couldn't keep their mouths *shut*, could they?" He glared at Actaeon. A bruise bloomed on his temple. "You learned quick enough how effective a gag is."

A flame lit deep inside her, crackling and blazing.

"After all the trouble these two brats gave me," Pollux said, white wings glimmering with brute power, "I'm really going to enjoy killing them in front of you."

93

Ruhn kept perfectly still as Brann and Actaeon, bound in gorsian shackles, were shoved to their knees before Pollux by those two imperial guards.

The Hammer smiled at Lidia, who'd gone utterly still and pale. "I knew instantly that they weren't mine, of course. No sons of my blood could be captured so easily. Pathetic," he sneered at a seething Brann, who was sporting a bloody nose. The kid would take on the Hammer with his bare hands.

Actaeon, however, watched Pollux carefully, though the boy was equally battered. His golden eyes missing nothing. Assessing all. Trying to find an opening.

Lidia rasped, "Please."

Pollux laughed. "Too late for niceties now, Lidia."

Ruhn's mind raced, sifting through every angle and advantage they might have. The math was damning.

Even if Pollux lowered the gun pointed at Ruhn's head, he still stood close enough to kill the boys with one strike. There was no way either Lidia or Ruhn could reach the boys in time, physically or magically. A bullet would be slower than the striking Hammer.

And even with Tharion at Lidia's side . . . No, there was no chance.

"Go get Rigelus," Pollux said to the two guards, not taking his gaze off Lidia, off Ruhn. "He'll enjoy watching this, I think."

Without question, without so much as a blink at the atrocities they were leaving behind, the guards departed down the hall. Turned into the stairwell and out of sight.

Tharion struck.

A blast of water, so concentrated it could have shattered stone, speared for Pollux. Ruhn darted to the left as Pollux fired his gun. But not for him, he realized as the bullet raced, faster than it should have, borne on a wave of angelic power—

Pollux dove aside, the plume of water missing his wing. But his bullet and power struck true.

Tharion grunted, going down before Ruhn could see where the mer had been hit. Somewhere in the chest—

As water dripped off the walls and ceiling around them, Lidia said, "Let them go, Pollux. Your quarrel is with me."

He snickered. "And what better way to destroy you? I suppose I can make one allowance: you can choose which boy dies first."

Brann snarled through his gag at Pollux, but Actaeon looked at his mother, eyes sharp, as if telling her to kill this asshole.

"They're children," Lidia said, voice cracking. Ruhn couldn't stand it—the pure desperation in her face. The agony.

"They're *your* children," Pollux said, power flickering at his hand. "Ordinarily, I'd like to make this last a while, but sacrifices must be made in battle." As if in answer, the very building around them shuddered. "I hear there are deathstalkers loose in here. Perhaps I'll feed the brats to them."

"Don't," Lidia said, falling to her knees. "Tell me what you want, what I must do, and I'll do it—anything—"

Ruhn's heart cleaved in two. For the boys; for her, debasing herself for this prick.

He rallied his shadows. But if Tharion hadn't been able to hit his mark . . .

Pollux smiled at Lidia. "I always liked you on your knees, you know."

"Whatever you want," Lidia pleaded. "Please, Pollux. I am *begging* you—"

She'd do it. Give Pollux whatever he wanted.

Her boys stiffened. Seeing that, too. Perhaps finally understanding what—who—their mother was. What had guided her all these years, and would continue to guide her in her final moments.

Ruhn just saw Lidia. Lidia, who had given so much, too much. Who would do this without a thought.

So Ruhn stepped forward. "I'll trade you. Me, for them."

Any other opponent would have dismissed it. But Pollux looked him over with a cruel, hungry sort of curiosity.

Ruhn snarled, saying the words he hadn't dared voice until now, "She's my mate, you fucker."

Lidia inhaled a sharp breath.

Ruhn taunted the Hammer, "You want me to tell you how she said we measured up?" Crass, crude words—but ones he knew would strike the Hammer's fragile ego.

The blow landed. "I'll kill the lot of you," Pollux seethed, his beautiful face ugly with rage.

"Nah," Ruhn said. "You touch her or the boys, and your attention will be split. Giving me the opening I need to blast you to Hel."

He should have taken that shot when Tharion attacked. He'd wasted the mer's blow—and now Tharion was lying on the ground, alarmingly still, blood leaking from a hole in his chest.

"Ruhn," Lidia warned.

"But," Ruhn went on smoothly, "you hand over the boys unharmed, you let them and Lidia and Tharion go, and I'll walk right up to you. With no guns, no magic. You can pull me apart piece by piece. Take all the time you want."

"Ruhn," Lidia's voice broke.

He didn't look at her. Didn't have the strength to see whatever was in her eyes. He knew she hated him for putting that bullet in her thigh—but it had been to save her. To keep them from this terrible fate that they'd all arrived at anyway.

So he said to her, mind-to-mind, *I love you. I fell in love with you in the depths of my soul, and it's my soul that will find yours again in the next life.*

He shut off the connection between them before she could reply.

Then Ruhn faced the white-winged angel, lifting his hands. "All yours, Hammer."

94

Unarmed, Ruhn kept his gaze on the Malleus. "What's it gonna be, Pollux?"

Lidia's sons were watching him closely. Lidia said nothing. But the Hammer looked toward her. "I don't see why I can't have everything I want," the angel said. Then grinned at Ruhn. "Wait your turn, princeling."

It happened so fast.

Pollux pivoted to the boys. Fixed his stare on Brann. Pure, brute power flared around the angel.

Lidia screamed as Pollux unleashed a lethal spear of his power toward Brann.

Ruhn couldn't turn away. Didn't want to watch, and yet he knew he had to witness this crime, this unforgivable atrocity—

But Lidia ran, swift as the wind. Swifter than a bullet.

Ruhn didn't understand what he saw next: How Lidia reached Brann in time. How she threw herself over her son, knocking him to the ground as she burst into white-hot flames.

They erupted from her like a brimstone missile, blasting Pollux off his feet. Not some freak accident or bomb, but fire magic, pouring out of Lidia. Searing from her.

"Brann," she was panting down at her son, the boy untouched by the flame, scanning his stunned face, tugging the gag from his mouth. "*Brannon.*" She stifled a sob around the boy's full name, but then Actaeon was there, hauling his brother away as best he could with the bonds still restraining them.

"What are you?" Ace breathed.

Still panting, blazing with fire, Lidia said, "An old bloodline," and got to her feet.

It was Daybright, as Ruhn had seen her in his mind. She'd presented herself—her *true* self—to him all this time.

"Get them out of here," Lidia said to Ruhn, hair floating up in a golden halo, embers swirling around her head. "Get the mer to a healer." It was a miracle that Tharion wasn't already dead, given the hole blasted through him.

Pollux got to his feet. "You cunt," he spat. "What the fuck is this?"

"Shifters, as they used to be," Lidia said, fire rippling from her mouth. "As Danika Fendyr told me we were. Now free of the Asteri's parasite."

Ruhn gaped at her. She was free of the parasite? She must have gotten that antidote, somehow—from Tharion?

Lidia was glorious, wreathed in flame and blazing with fury.

Pollux's power surged again. "I'll kill you all the same, bitch."

"You can try," Lidia said, smiling.

Pollux ran at her, striking with his magic. The hallway shook, debris raining down—

A wall of blue fire leapt between them. Pollux collided with it, then stuck. A fly in a burning web.

Lidia stalked toward the angel as Pollux struggled against the flames.

"You signed your death warrant when you touched my sons," she said. And exhaled a breath.

Flame rippled from her mouth into Pollux's flesh. The angel screamed—or tried to.

Freed of any secrets, of any need to keep them, Lidia seemed to unleash all that she was. Ruhn could only watch as fire poured down Pollux's throat. Into his body. Roasting him from the inside out until he was nothing but smoldering cinders, a pillar of brimstone standing mid-strike, mouth still open.

She'd incinerated him.

Lidia held out a finger. And poked the towering pillar that had once been Pollux.

It sent Pollux's ash-statue crumbling to the ground.

Her sons got to their feet, shock stark on their battered faces. The knife in Ruhn's boot helped him make quick work of prying open their gorsian shackles, but it was Actaeon who whispered to Lidia, "Mom?"

She looked over a shoulder to her son. Her lips curved upward—at what he'd called her, Ruhn guessed.

The palace shook again—whatever was going on outside, it had to be bad.

"Get the mer to Declan to be healed. Even after taking the antidote, I don't think Ketos's own body can save him," Lidia ordered. "And that's the last vial of the antidote in his bag. My sister figured it out. Don't jostle it, though—it's volatile."

"Lidia," Ruhn said, but her eyes blazed with true fire.

"I need to help the others." She launched into a run for the stairs. "Get my sons to safety, and we're even. Save them, and I forgive you for shooting me."

She glanced back at her boys, and then vanished up into the palace. Into the battle-torn world beyond.

Lidia had known, even as a child, that she was pure power, and she'd kept that power buried in her veins.

Not witch-power. She knew her flames were . . . different. Her father didn't have them, either.

She'd kept them secret, even from the Asteri. Especially from the Asteri. No other shifters had them, to her knowledge, and she knew what revealing them would mean: becoming an experiment to be pulled apart by the Asteri.

Then she had run into Danika Fendyr, who had somehow learned things about Lidia's paternal bloodline, and wanted to know if Lidia had any strange gifts. Fae-like, elemental gifts.

She'd debated killing Danika then and there to keep the gift secret. And what else did Danika know—could she know about her sons?

The shifters were Fae from another world, Danika had explained. Blessed with a Fae form and a humanoid one, gifted with elemental powers.

It confirmed what Lidia had long guessed. Why she had named Brannon after the oldest legends from her family's bloodline: of a Fae King from another world, fire in his veins, who had created stags with the power of flame to be his sacred guards.

Lidia hadn't mentioned any of that as Danika had filled her in on how they'd become shifters, and the Asteri's experimentation with them on Midgard, which had eventually erased their pointed ears. She'd been glad when Danika had died, all her questions with her.

No longer.

After ingesting the antidote that her brilliant, brave sister had made, the fire had surged so close to the surface that she couldn't deny it. Didn't want to deny it.

Flame rippled from Lidia as she raced out of the palace, through the city, and onto the battlefield beyond. Untethered, unconquerable.

The dreadwolves scented her first, no doubt thanks to Mordoc's keen bloodhound senses. Spotted her standing before the gates to the city. They knew her, even with the fire, and they raced for her in humanoid form, teeth bared. Mordoc led the pack, the hate practically radiating off him. Behind him, as always, ran Gedred and Vespasian, sniper rifles aimed.

It was time for Lidia to clean house.

"You—" Mordoc barked.

Lidia didn't give him the chance to finish. No longer would this male, Danika Fendyr's sire, spew his vitriol into the world. He was done inflicting pain upon Midgard.

Lidia turned Mordoc and the two snipers into ashes with a thought. Until all that remained of them was the molten silver from the darts in their collars, pooled on the ground. Another thought, and the pack of dreadwolves, now skidding to a halt in panic, met the same fate.

Angels in the Asterian Guard shot from the skies, power blasting.

Lidia obliterated them, too.

Demons paused, their long-dead Fallen allies with them, mech-suits going utterly still.

The Asterian Guard's war-machines shifted directions and rumbled toward her, each mammoth tank armed with brimstone missiles. The angels manning them aimed their rifles at her and unleashed a barrage of bullets.

Her fire a song in her blood, Lidia walked across the battlefield. Bullets melted before they could reach her.

It was so much more natural than it had ever been. In the Cave of Princes, it had taken nearly all her concentration to douse the flames of the Autumn King around her companions. Only Morven had seemed to be surprised—the others hadn't questioned how the flames had disappeared. There had been too much chaos for anyone to piece it together.

Now her fire flowed and flowed. Her truth was freed.

The war-machines halted. Angled their guns and bombers toward her. They'd wipe her from Midgard.

But she'd keep going until the end. She didn't look behind her at the palace, where she could only pray that Ruhn—her mate—was getting her sons to safety.

For the first time in her miserable existence, she let the world see her for what she was. Let herself see all that she was.

The missile launchers turned white-hot. Lidia rallied her flames. Even if she intercepted the missiles in midair, the shrapnel alone could kill her allies—

There was one way to stop it. To get there first. Before the missiles launched. And take them all out, herself included.

She began running.

She wished she'd been able to say goodbye to her sons. To Ruhn. To tell him her answer to what he'd said.

I love you.

She cast the thought behind her, toward the Fae Prince she knew would keep her sons safe.

The war-machines followed her movements with their launchers. They'd try to blast her into Hel before she could reach them.

Emphasis on *try*.

It had been a short life, as far as Vanir were concerned, and a bad one, but there had been moments of joy. Moments that she now gathered and held close to her heart: cradling her newborn sons, smelling their baby-sweet scents. Talking with Ruhn for hours, when she knew him only as Night. Lying in his arms.

So few happy memories, but she wouldn't have traded them for anything.

Would have done it all again, just for those memories.

Lidia dove deep, all the way into the simmering dregs of her power.

The war-machines loomed, black and blazing with power. Ready for her. Launch barrels stared her down, brimstone missiles glowing golden in their throats.

Lidia unleashed her own fire, ready for her final incineration.

But before her flame could touch those war-machines, before the brimstone missiles could fire, the launch barrels melted. Iron dripped away, sizzling on the dry earth.

And those brimstone missiles, caught in the melting machinery . . .

The explosions shook the very world as the missiles ruptured, turning the war-machines into death traps for the soldiers within. They melted into nothing. The heat of it singed Lidia's face, and amid the burning and billowing smoke—

Three tiny white lights burned bright.

Fire sprites. Simmering with power.

Through the fire and smoke and drifting embers, Lidia recognized them. Sasa. Rithi. Malana. Blazing, raging with fire. They must have crept up unseen from behind enemy lines. Too small to be noticed, to ever be counted by arrogant Vanir.

Another war-machine rumbled forward, rolling over the ruins of the front line.

A stupid mistake. The metal treads melted, too, pinning the machine in place. Trapping the soldiers and pilots within it.

They tried to fire their missiles at Lidia, at the three sprites now coming to her side, but they never got the chance. One moment, the war-machine was there, missile launchers primed with their payload. The next, the metal of the machine flared white, and then melted.

Where the machine had been, a fourth sprite glowed, a hot, intense blue.

Irithys.

She lifted a small hand in greeting.

Lidia raised one back.

"We found her," Sasa said to Lidia, breathless with adrenaline or hope or fear or all of them at once. "We told her what you and Bryce said."

Malana added as Irithys zoomed for them, leaving a trail of blue embers in her wake, "But it did not take much convincing to get her here."

"How did you know to come today?" Lidia asked as Irithys joined them, a blue star in the midst of the three shimmering lights of the others.

Irithys grinned, the first true smile Lidia had seen from the Sprite Queen. "We didn't. They reached me yesterday, and we talked long into the night." A fond smile at the three sprites, who turned raspberry pink with pleasure. "We were still awake when Bryce Quinlan and Hunt Athalar's video went out. We raced down from Ravilis, hoping to help in any way we could."

"We arrived in the nick of time, it seems," Sasa said, nodding to the smoldering ruins.

"We wouldn't have wanted to miss all the fun," Rithi added with a wicked smile.

Irithys's smile was more subdued as she studied Lidia. The queen's flame set Lidia's own sparking in answer. Dancing over her fingertips, her hair, in joyful recognition. "I sensed the fire in you the moment we met," the queen said. "I didn't think yours would manifest so brilliantly, though."

Lidia sketched a bow, but refrained from telling the queen about the antidote just yet, how it would make Irithys's flame even more lethal. Later—if they survived. But right now . . . Lidia smirked at the queen, at their gathering enemies. "Let's burn it all down."

Because ahead of them, dozens strong, an entire line of war-machines headed their way. Missile launchers groaned into position. All aiming for where they stood.

"With pleasure," Irithys said, and even from a few feet away, Lidia's skin seared with the heat of the queen's flame. "We shall build a new world atop their ashes."

Rithi, Sasa, and Malana turned blue, matching their queen's fire with their own. The four fire sprites unleashed their power on the war-machines and the Vanir powering them. Lidia's white-hot flames joined theirs, twining and dancing around it, as if every moment of recognition until now had built toward this, as if her flames had known theirs for millennia.

And as one flame, one unified people, as Bryce Quinlan had promised, their fire struck the enemy line.

Machines ruptured. Lidia staggered back, back, back with the force of it, still unfamiliar with the fire in her veins, after it had been so long suppressed.

But the sprites kept their fire concentrated on the machines and their pilots. And as Lidia hit the ground, as the missiles exploded upon contact with the flames, she cast the last of her power upward. To shield the allied forces fighting behind them and the fire sprites now ahead of her from the shrapnel, which melted until it became raining, molten metal.

It hissed where it hit the earth.

Irithys blazed like a blue star, shooting from machine to machine, leaving burning death in her wake. The three other sprites followed suit. Where they shimmered, imperial forces died.

And as the enemy melted at their fingertips . . . for a moment, just one, Lidia allowed herself to kindle a spark of hope.

* * *

"I'm okay," Tharion panted, blood leaking from his mouth. "I'm okay."

"I call bullshit," Ruhn said, kneeling beside the mer, fumbling through his pack for the vial Lidia had mentioned. The mer would be dead already without the antidote in his veins. But if Ruhn didn't do something to help Tharion now, he'd surely be dead in a few minutes.

"Get him into a sitting position," Actaeon was saying to his brother. "Get his head above his chest so the blood doesn't go out too fast."

"We have to help her," Brann said. "She's out on the battlefield—"

"You guys aren't going anywhere," Ruhn said to the boys. He found the clear vial and knocked it back. "Help me get Ketos up. We've got two seconds before those shithead guards come back, maybe with Rigelus in tow—"

They didn't have two seconds.

From the stairwell at the far end of the hall, the two angels who'd held the boys captive emerged. No sign of Rigelus, thank the gods, but right then, whatever was in that potion hit Ruhn's stomach, his body, and the world tilted, surging, blacking out—

A moment, long enough so that when his vision returned, it was to see the two angels reaching for their guns.

Ruhn exploded.

Starlight, two beams of it straight to their eyes, blinded them. Just as Bryce had done to the Murder Twins. Twin whips of his shadows wrapped around their necks and squeezed.

"What the fuck," Brann said, but Ruhn barely heard him. There was only power, surging as it never had before. His mind was starkly clear as he willed the shadows to begin slicing through angelic flesh.

Blood spurted. Bone cracked. Two heads rolled to the ground.

"Holy shit," Brann breathed. Actaeon was gaping at Ruhn.

"The mer," the kid said, whirling back to where Tharion had passed out again.

"Fuck," Ruhn spat, and put a hand to Tharion's chest to staunch the bleeding—

Warm, bright magic answered. *Healing* magic, rising to the surface as if it had been dormant in his blood.

He had no idea how to use it, how to do anything other than will it with a simple *Save him*.

In answer, light poured from his hands, and he could *feel* Tharion's flesh and bone knitting back together beneath his fingers, mending, healing . . .

It had been a clean shot through the chest and out the back. And this new healing magic seemed to know what to do, how to close both entry and exit wounds. It couldn't replace the blood, but if Ketos was no longer leaking . . . he might survive.

A shudder rocked the palace, and time slowed.

For a heartbeat, Ruhn thought it might be his own power, but no. He'd felt this before. Just a short time ago, when the world had rippled with what he knew, deep in his bones, was the impact of an Asteri dying. Like an Archangel's death, but worse.

Another Asteri must be going down.

He willed that lovely, bright power to keep healing Ketos, though. To use the stretch of time to buy more of it for the mer, to heal, heal, heal—

It was eternity, and yet it was nothing. Time resumed, so fast that the boys lost their grip on Tharion, but the wound had healed over. Ruhn grunted as he hoisted the unconscious mer over a shoulder and said to the boys, "We gotta get out of here."

Half of him wanted to dump the twins somewhere safe and race to wherever Lidia was, but his mate had asked him to protect the two most precious people in her world.

He wouldn't break a gesture of trust so great. Not for anything.

They tore through the palace, its halls eerily empty. People must have gotten the evacuation order and fled. The guards had even left their stations at the doors and the front gates.

Ruhn and the boys made it into the city streets, and Ruhn reached for his phone to dial Flynn, praying the male had the van nearby. Only then did he get a look at the battlefield beyond the city. The cloud of darkness above the glowing lights.

That darkness was pure Pit. Fires blazed on the other side of the field—that had to be Lidia.

"Ruhn!" He knew that voice.

He turned, Tharion a limp weight on his shoulder, and found Ithan Holstrom sprinting toward them, a rifle over his shoulder.

He knew that rifle, too. The Godslayer Rifle.

Ithan's face was splattered with dirt and blood, like he'd fought his way up here. "Is Ketos alive?" At Ruhn's nod, Ithan asked, "Where's Bryce?"

As if in answer, light flared from the palace above and behind them.

Ruhn's blood turned to ice. "We told her and Athalar to meet us. But it was a trap . . . fuck."

"I need to get to Bryce," Ithan said urgently.

Ruhn pointed to the palace, and couldn't find the words, any words, to say that the wolf might already be too late.

Ace and Brann looked up at him, at the palace, at the battlefield.

His charges. His to protect through the storm.

"Run," Ruhn told Ithan, and motioned to the twins. "Keep close, and follow my lead."

95

Bryce's breath sawed through her lungs, but she gave herself over to it. To the wind and movement and propulsion of herself and Hunt through the small space as Rigelus launched strike after strike.

She was not the scared female she'd been a week ago, running from him down the hall. She knew Theia's star gave her enough of an edge to keep one step ahead of Rigelus as she teleported again and again and again.

They just had to deactivate the core, and then she'd take the sword and knife and go after the Asteri. One by one.

Hunt's lightning slammed continuously into the floor. But she and Hunt kept moving, so fast that one boom hadn't finished sounding before another began. The sound was monstrous, all-consuming, and the room rained stone and crystal.

But in the center of the room, the tunnel of warped, melted crystal was almost complete.

Minutes had passed, maybe years. It was a dance, keeping one step ahead of Rigelus, and she knew that it would come to its crashing finale soon enough.

Another blow, and the glow of the firstlight core blazed, casting Rigelus's furious face in stark relief.

Bryce teleported them away, but it was slower—too slow—

Rigelus snapped his power at them.

A wall like burning acid sent them careening into the stairwell, and Bryce knew only Hunt's lightning kept it from being fatal. She rallied her power to teleport, but it sputtered out.

"Perhaps you should not have expended so much of your strength against Polaris." Rigelus smirked, and lifted his gleaming hand—

It was a choice of death or survival.

Bryce teleported herself and Hunt—but not to the center of the room. They crashed to the floor a level above, clear of the core.

"One more strike!" Hunt was shouting. "Bryce, one more fucking strike and we're through—"

Bryce's knees buckled, and her head swam. Her power had dissolved into stardust in her veins.

Hunt caught her as she swayed. "Bryce." Her nose stung; she could taste the blood in her mouth, metallic and sharp. "Fuck," Hunt hissed, and grabbed her face in his hands. "Bryce—look at me."

It took effort. Too much effort.

"I'm sorry," she panted, and the words were barely a rasp. "I'm sorry." All that power she'd attained . . . what good had it done? And what good would having the Starsword and the knife be if she had no starlight left to unite them?

"One more, Bryce," Hunt said, breathing hard. Blood leaked from his own nostrils. The cost of all that power, without cease. "Just one more blow, I can feel it . . ."

"Okay," she said. "Okay."

They had to get back down there before Rigelus could find some way to repair the damage they'd done. "Okay," she said again, but her power wouldn't rally. She looked to Hunt. "A boost?"

From the concern in his eyes, she knew he didn't have much left, either. But his lightning sparked, a crown about his head, making a primal god of him.

Rather than strike her with his Helfire, he hauled her to him and kissed her.

Lightning flowed from him into her, a living river of song and power. She pulled back, panting hard, and it hadn't been much, but it was there, it was enough—

"Stop," called an exhausted male voice from down the hall.

And though she'd leapt between worlds and ended Archangels and Asteri, nothing had prepared her to see Ithan Holstrom racing down the palace hallway with the Godslayer Rifle slung over his shoulder.

Hunt had no energy left to dwell on the fact that Holstrom seemed . . . leveled up. Older, more powerful somehow, even though he'd just seen the wolf. He didn't fucking care about any of it as the wolf reached them and said to Bryce, "I was sent to give you this." He handed her the rifle.

With shaking hands, Bryce took it. "Jesiba gave it to you?"

"No. I mean, yes, but . . ." Ithan's eyes were wide. "There's a bullet in there, full of the secondlight of the dead of Crescent City. Connor gave it to me. For you."

"Connor?" Bryce swayed again, and Hunt caught her.

"There's no time to explain," Ithan said, "but the dead sent me to give you that rifle, and that bullet." Ithan's eyes shone bright. "Connor said to make it count, Bryce."

Bryce looked down at the rifle in her hands, weighing it. Hunt asked, "What use is one bullet of secondlight against an Asteri?"

"Not against an Asteri," Bryce said. "That bullet is a secondlight bomb."

Ithan nodded, apparently getting what she meant more than Hunt did.

"I don't have enough strength to teleport both of us back to the core," Bryce said, and took Hunt's hand. She pressed something cold into it.

Her words struck, and Hunt spat, "Fuck that." His temper flared. "Fuck that, Bryce, let's go blast that monster to Hel—"

"Get out of the palace," Bryce warned, and teleported. Alone.

Taking the Godslayer Rifle with her, and leaving the Mask in Hunt's hand.

She had one shot.

Last time, Lehabah had bought her the two seconds it cost to line up that shot.

This time, there was no fire sprite to save her. No synth to fuel her. Only training that Randall had hammered into her over the years. She sent a silent prayer of thanks to him.

One shot, straight down into the tunnel that Hunt had made, to blast apart the last of the crystal around the core and release all that firstlight.

She knew what lining up the shot would cost her. Knew that in the second it took to aim, Rigelus would launch his power at her, and there would be no wall of Hunt's lightning to keep it at bay.

Bryce savored the whipping, wild wind around her as she teleported—one last time, propelling herself through the world.

She lifted the rifle to her shoulder, clicking off the safety, and then she was there in the core room, debris and crystal everywhere, her rifle already aimed at the hole in the center.

But Rigelus was not alone. The three other remaining Asteri now stood with him, the four of them a solid wall between Bryce and the firstlight core. At least another one was dead, if the slowing of the world a few minutes ago was any indication. But four remained.

Bryce's finger stalled on the trigger. To waste the bullet on them—

"Don't you want to know what you risk, before you act so recklessly?" Rigelus said smugly. He didn't wait for her to answer. "You destroy the firstlight core, and you destroy Midgard itself."

96

Bryce didn't lower the Godslayer Rifle. She kept it aimed at the Asteri's feet. At the hole just behind them. To get close enough, she'd have to teleport right to them, and fire straight into the hole.

"That core is tied to Midgard's very soul," Rigelus said. "You destroy it, and this entire planet will wink out of existence."

Bryce's blood chilled. She might have called bullshit had it not been for Vesperus's claims about the Cauldron.

"You made the core a kill switch for this world," Bryce breathed.

The Asteri to Rigelus's left—Eosphoros, the Morning Star—sneered, "To prevent rodents like *you* from getting any ideas about destroying us."

"Our fate," Rigelus said to Bryce, folding his hands in front of him almost beatifically, "is tied to that of this planet. You kill our source of nourishment, and you doom every living soul on Midgard as well."

"And if I call your bluff?" Bryce demanded, buying whatever time she could to sort out all she'd heard and witnessed and endured—

"Then a darkness like none you have ever known shall devour this planet, and you will all cease to exist," said the Asteri to Rigelus's right—Hesperus, the Evening Star.

"So you'd rather die," Bryce said, "than see any of us freed from you?"

"If we are denied our food, then we shall die; there is no purpose to your existence, if not to sustain us. You are chattel."

"You're fucking delusional." Bryce kept the rifle aimed at their feet. "How about I kill all of you, and leave the core here? How about that?"

"You'd have to get close enough with those blades to do so, girl," Eosphoros sneered, death in her eyes as she glanced to the Starsword at Bryce's back, to Truth-Teller sheathed at her side. "We shall not make Polaris's mistake."

They were right—Bryce knew that if she set down the gun, if she drew the blades . . . Well, they'd kill her so fast she probably wouldn't be able to draw the weapons in time.

"Think very carefully, Bryce Quinlan," Rigelus said, stepping forward with his hands raised. "One bullet from you into the core, and this world and all its innocents will be sucked into a void with no end."

The same Void that Apollion had claimed allowed him to devour the Asteri? Polaris's body had been sucked into nothing—

"You seemed so outraged in your little video," Rigelus purred, "at the deaths of those innocents in Asphodel Meadows. But what are a few hundred children compared to the millions you damn by firing that bullet?"

A void with no end . . .

"Kill her, brother," hissed the fourth Asteri, Austrus, glowing with power. "Kill her, and let us return to battle the princes before they find us down here—"

"What will it be, Bryce Quinlan?" Rigelus asked, extending a hand. "You have my word that if you do not fire that bullet, you and yours shall go free. And remain so."

The other Asteri whirled on him, outraged.

"I can teach you things you've never even dreamed of," Rigelus promised. "The language inked on your back—it is *our* language. From our home world. I can teach you how to wield it. *Any* world might be open to you, Bryce Quinlan. Name the world, and it shall be yours."

"I only want this world to be free of you," Bryce said through her teeth. "Forever."

One of the Asteri began, "How dare you speak to—" but Rigelus interrupted, attention only on Bryce, "That, too, might be possible. A Midgard of your imagining." He smiled, so earnestly she almost believed him. "Yours will be a life of comfort. I shall set you up as a *true* queen—not only of the Fae, but of all Valbara. No more Governors. No more angelic hierarchies, if that is what you and Athalar wish. If you desire the dead to be freed, then we shall find a way around death, too. They were always simply dessert to us."

"Dessert," Bryce said, hands shaking with anger. She gripped the rifle tighter.

"The secondlight shall be the dead's to keep," Rigelus went on.

But Bryce said, a familiar white haze of pure rage creeping over her vision, "They're not *dessert*. They're people. People the inhabitants of this planet knew and loved."

"A poor choice of words," Rigelus acknowledged, "and I apologize. But what you wish, you shall have. And if you desire to—"

"Enough of this catering to vermin," Eosphoros snapped. "She dies."

"I don't think so," Bryce said, and teleported directly to the Asteri. Right to the hole in the floor that Hunt had made. "I think it's your turn for that."

She fired the Godslayer Rifle into the firstlight core.

The Asteri screamed, and time dripped by as the bullet fired from the rifle, slow enough that Bryce could see the writing on its side: *Memento Mori*.

Powered by the souls of the dead, of Connor and the Pack of Devils and so many more . . . the dead sacrificing for the sake of the living. The dead, yielding eternity so Midgard might be free.

The bullet spiraled downward, into the light, toward that final crystal barrier.

Rigelus lunged for her, his hands incandescent with uncut power. Once he touched her, she'd be dead—

And maybe this was what Danika had planned all along, in putting the Horn in her, wanting her to claim that other piece of Theia's star from Avallen. Maybe this was what Urd had planned for her, had whispered she might do ever since she had accessed her power, or what Hel had imagined she and Hunt might one day do.

She wished she'd had a bit more time with Hunt. With her parents and friends. A bit more time to savor the sun, and the sky, and the sea. To listen to music, all the music she could ever hear. To dance—just one more step or spin—

Rigelus was still reaching for her arm with his bright hands; the bullet was still spiraling. And as that bullet of secondlight smashed through that final layer of crystal, as it tunneled down and down—

Bryce wished she'd had more time.

But she didn't. And if this was the time that she had been given . . . she'd make it count.

I believe it all happened for a reason. I believe it wasn't for nothing.

From far away, the words she'd spoken at the Gate the previous spring echoed.

All that had happened had been for this. Not for her, but for Midgard. For the safety and future of all worlds.

And as the bullet erupted in the firstlight core, as Rigelus's hand wrapped around her wrist and pure acid burned her skin and bones where he touched her—

Like the battery she was, she grabbed his power. Sucked it into herself.

Light met light and yet—Rigelus's starlight wasn't light at all.

It was power, yes. But it was *firstlight.* It was the power of Midgard. Of the people.

It flowed into her, so much power that it nearly knocked the breath out of her lungs. Time slowed further, and still she seized more of Rigelus's power.

His power indicator on the wall plummeted.

Rigelus reeled back, releasing her, either in pain or rage or fear, she didn't know—

His light was not his own. His light had been stolen from the people of Midgard. He was a living gate, storing that power, and just as she'd taken it from the Gates this spring, just as it had fueled her Ascent, fueled her own power to new levels . . . now it became hers.

Without the firstlight, without the people of Midgard and every other planet they'd bled dry . . . without the power of the people, these Asteri fuckers were *nothing*.

And with that knowledge, that undeniable truth, Bryce sent all that power through the Horn in her back.

Right as the core ruptured.

Midgard's kill switch flipped on. Mere feet away, the world began to cave in, sucking itself inward, obliterating everything—

Bryce willed it, and the Horn obeyed.

A portal opened—right in front of the core and the dark dot that was emerging from it, vacuuming in all life. Bryce sent the core, that lifeless, growing dot, through her portal.

The Asteri screamed again, and didn't stop. Like they knew she'd conjured her own kill switch.

A thought, and Bryce widened her portal enough that it sucked in the Asteri, their screams vanishing as they went. Rigelus and his bright hands were now a dim glow, still reaching for Midgard, clinging to it as he was pulled in.

Bryce had a heartbeat to take in what—where—she'd opened a portal to: a black, airless place, dotted with small, distant stars. A heartbeat, and then she was yanked in, too.

Straight to deep space.

97

The Asteri's crystal palace was collapsing.

Near the city walls, a crack and boom hollowed out Ruhn's ears, rocking through him. He looked back over a shoulder to see the palace's towers begin to sway and topple.

"Bryce," he gasped out.

Tharion, now awake and walking gingerly, halted, the twins—who'd been helping him along—pausing with him.

The entire world halted as a shudder went through it. As light ruptured from below the palace. A great force, like a whirlpool sucking them in, in, in, began pulling at their edges.

"Run," Tharion breathed, sensing it, too.

Nodding, Ruhn grabbed both boys by the hand. They raced the last few blocks to the city gates, Tharion struggling to keep up.

Even as Ruhn felt that tug toward the collapsing palace, and knew there would be no escaping.

Bryce had left him.

She had left him, and teleported down to those monsters alone. Hunt hadn't made it far, Holstrom on his heels, before that *boom* had rocked the palace, and the skies had opened up above somehow, and the palace was collapsing down, down, down—

It was a choice between letting Holstrom die or keep trying to make it to Bryce.

And because he knew his mate would never forgive him if he abandoned Ithan, Hunt grabbed the wolf and launched into the air, dodging falling blocks of crystal and stone and metal.

He had no idea where they landed, only that it was on the rim of a giant crater that had not been there before. It reminded him of the news footage he'd seen of what remained of Asphodel Meadows—he could only wonder if Bryce had done so intentionally.

But as Hunt shook the blood and dust from his eyes, he saw what lay at the crater's heart: a gaping void. Stars beyond it.

The force of the void yanked him inward, tugged him toward it—

"*Go,*" he ordered Holstrom. "Get as many people as you can out of the way."

Because on the other side of the portal that Bryce had somehow opened into the stars, there was a wall of impenetrable darkness. Hunt could just make out the glowing figures being sucked toward it.

Bryce had opened a black hole in the middle of Midgard.

Had she done it with the blades? Or had the joining of the Starsword and Truth-Teller merely given her the idea of how she might capture all the Asteri at once, rather than picking them off individually?

It didn't matter.

Nothing mattered, because there was a fucking black hole on the other side of that portal, and the force of it was so strong that *this* side of the portal was being sucked toward it, too—

But that didn't matter, either.

Because there, among those glowing lights of the Asteri . . . that was Bryce's starlight.

And she was headed to that black hole as well.

Bryce knew she should be dead. There was no air here, no warmth.

Maybe it was the Horn in her flesh, the Made essence of her, that kept her alive—just enough.

It had been a gamble. But she'd seen what the Starsword and Truth-Teller had done to Polaris. They had created a void that had sucked the Asteri in—the only sort of prison that might destroy a being of light. The only force in the universe that *ate* light, so strong no light could ever escape it. A portal to nowhere.

To a black hole.

Wasn't that the unholy power that Apollion possessed? The power of the Void. The antithesis of light.

The only thing that could kill a planet in one bite. Destroy the Asteri, and Midgard with them.

The Asteri knew it as well—they'd always known it, and employed it for their kill switch, to be activated upon destruction of the firstlight core.

So she'd met their black hole with one of her own. A bigger one. A black hole—a void—to *eat* other black holes.

Because Bryce couldn't let that happen to Midgard. She'd opened her portal to her black hole only wide enough for those who were right next to the core to be sucked in with it.

And now she was here, careening through space with the Asteri.

Light poured from the glowing beings around her, their screams silenced from lack of air. Behind her, the only light snuck in through a sliver she'd left behind . . . a sliver she still needed to close. One small window to Midgard. She couldn't bring herself to do it. Not yet.

She let herself look at that sliver of light, of blue sky. The last trace of home.

I believe it all happened for a reason. I believe it wasn't for nothing.

Ahead of the Asteri was the glowing mass that was the firstlight core, the black, growing hole in the heart of it . . .

The light stretched and bent as it was pulled into the yawning maw of the larger black hole. And then was gone.

Not one trace of it remained. No more kill switch, no more firstlight. Midgard was free of them.

That sliver of light thinned further. It was now too far for her to reach. She had no way of getting back to the portal. No way of propelling herself there. There was just this, the slow drift toward the event horizon of the black hole. The inevitable, crushing end.

Ahead of her, the first two Asteri, Hesperus and Eosphoros, were nearing that line of no return. They were clawing at nothing, trying to find any sort of purchase in the emptiness of space to haul them away from the yawning mouth of the black hole—

But their glowing fingers found nothing at all as they slid over that line and vanished.

Time slowed for a heartbeat—only one, time dragging, dragging—and then resumed. Their deaths had been fast. A swift swallow.

I believe it all happened for a reason. I believe it wasn't for nothing.

Rigelus and Austrus were next, but the two were clinging to each other.

No, she saw all at once: it was Austrus who was clinging, frantic as a drowning person, and Rigelus was trying to pry himself free, blasting his fellow Asteri with remnants of power that Austrus absorbed—

Perhaps if she hadn't drained Rigelus to the dregs, he might have succeeded. The Bright Hand seemed to realize it, too. Decided on a different route to free himself, because he got his feet up between them and *kicked*.

Austrus went tumbling back—straight for the event horizon. His screams made no sound.

Time slowed and shuddered as the black hole devoured him, too.

And then there was only Rigelus, still glowing—but weakly. That kick he'd given Austrus had propelled him toward Bryce. There was nothing she could do to escape him, no way to paddle out of his range—

Rigelus's expression revealed undiluted hate as he collided with her. As they spun out through space, with no meaning to *up* or *down*, and whatever protection the Horn gave her seemed to buckle in the Asteri's presence.

The Horn would bow to its maker, its master.

She needed air. She needed *air*—

Bryce shoved at him, freeing a bit of space between their bodies. Not severing contact, but enough that the Horn's protection snapped back into place, and she could breathe.

Rigelus was speaking, shouting in her face, but no words reached her. There was no sound in space. But loathing twisted his face, and she knew he beheld the same in hers as she sucked in a breath. Her last, she knew. She'd make it count, too.

Bryce grabbed his scrawny torso and wrapped her arms, then her legs around it.

Rigelus had a one-way ticket for that black hole—she'd make sure of it.

Even if she went with him.

98

His Umbra Mortis helmet discarded in the rubble beside him, Hunt stared at the giant, dark *thing* that had appeared in the center of the city and was slowly devouring everything around it.

Bryce was in that hole. A dark wind whipped at Hunt's hair, and he knew without looking who had arrived at his side.

"I told her to choose to live," Aidas murmured sadly, gazing toward the starry black expanse.

"She wouldn't be Bryce if she had chosen herself," Hunt said hoarsely. He wouldn't love her this much if she wasn't the sort of person who would have jumped in. "We have to help her," he growled, wings braced against the tug of the black hole trying to pull all of Midgard in with it.

"There's nothing that can be done," Aidas said, his voice full of sorrow.

"I have to try." Hunt's knees bent, his wings spread, preparing himself for that leap into space. To Bryce. And that eternal wall of black beyond where his mate glowed.

"You go in there, and you will die," Aidas said. "There is no air to propel you, nothing for your wings to grasp onto to carry you forward to her. You will drift, and she will still wind up with Rigelus in the Void, and you will follow her in, helpless, a few minutes later."

"But she left the portal open," Hunt said. "To Midgard."

Aidas turned those weary eyes to him. "I believe it shall shut when she and the Horn in her back are obliterated."

"She left it open to *come home*," Hunt snarled. He studied the Mask in his hands. She'd left it with him . . . why? He'd have no ability to get it back to the Fae in their home world. Hel, he couldn't even wield the damn thing. He wasn't Made; he couldn't command it.

"She is likely already dead from lack of oxygen," Aidas said softly. "I'm sorry."

"I don't accept that for one minute," Hunt raged. "I *refuse* to accept that—"

"Then go die with her," Aidas said, not unkindly. "If that's your wish, then do so now. She and Rigelus already approach the Void's edge."

Hunt studied the Mask again.

Bryce did nothing without a reason. She had left him with the Mask, knowing she was headed to her death. She'd left it with her mate . . . her mate, who had a little bit of her Made essence in him thanks to their lovemaking last night.

Which might make him capable of wielding it. For just long enough.

She had given everything for Midgard. For him.

That day last spring, when all hope had been lost, she had made the Drop alone. To save him, and to save the city—and she had done it from pure love. She had done it without expecting to come back.

Just as she must have jumped through this portal suspecting she'd never return.

Demons were spilling into the streets, and the Asterian Guard was still fighting, unaware that their remaining masters were headed toward obliteration. The mech-suits of the Fallen and their enemies clashed.

Bryce had gone into death itself for him that day in the spring.

Hunt could do no less for her.

"Athalar," Aidas said as he gazed at the hole in the world. "It is done. Come—we must finish this. Even with the Asteri gone, there are other battles to fight before the day is won."

The words might have sunk in then—*the Asteri gone*—but the ground shook behind him.

Hunt turned. A mech-suit stood there, towering over him. No pilot—this was one of the Fallen. The glowing green eyes shifted between him and the hole in the universe, the small bit of light drifting, drifting toward that infinite darkness.

The mech-suit held out a hand, and Hunt knew.

He knew which of the Fallen controlled this suit, whose soul had come to offer a hand. To help him do the impossible.

"Shahar," he said, tears falling.

The mech-suit, the Archangel's soul within it, inclined its head. Aidas took a step back, as if surprised.

In the streets, the other suits halted. Fell to their knees, bowing. Hunt could feel them—the souls of the Fallen. Swarming around him, around the suit.

But Shahar simply knelt before Hunt and opened the pilot's door.

His wings might not work in space, but the propulsion from the suit's weapons would.

Hunt didn't hesitate. He climbed in, wings furled tight in the small interior, and yanked the metal door shut.

"Thank you," he said to the Archangel, to the Fallen he now felt pressing around him.

He'd once been forced to take mech-suits apart on the battlefield to help Shahar's sister destroy humans. Now this one would help him save a life. The life that mattered to him more than any other.

Hunt didn't look at Aidas, at the collapsed palace sending debris skittering toward the portal, the black hole so enormous its pull threatened to drag them all in. Hunt just stared directly at the void as he began running, suit thundering around him, straight for that portal.

And leapt in after his mate.

It was too far.

Not for the suit, whose blasts of power sent Hunt careening

toward Bryce and Rigelus, but for the oxygen systems. They screamed at him on the screens, flashing red. Air became thin; his lungs ached—

Hunt did the only thing he could think to do. He slid the Mask onto his face.

To escape death, he'd don its trappings. The Umbra Mortis in truth.

The Mask ripped apart his soul.

Life and death—that was all that space, the universe, really was. But that chasm yawning wide, so close to Bryce and Rigelus . . . that was death incarnate.

They were struggling. He could see that now. Light flaring between them, rippling into nothing, both trying to get away from the other, to blast away—

There was only one brimstone missile left in the suit. Hunt took aim toward his mate and Rigelus. They were moving too swiftly, too closely. To shoot one would be to shoot the other.

He could have sworn a light, ghostly hand guided his to the release button.

"She'll get thrown in, too," Hunt whispered to Shahar.

That ghostly hand pressed—lightly, as if it was all she could manage—on his hand. On the button.

As if to say, *Fire.*

And the gods had never done him any favors, Urd had certainly never helped him, yet . . .

Maybe they had.

Maybe that day he'd first met Bryce, the gods had sent him there. Not to be some instrument of Hel, but because Urd knew that there would be a female who would be kind and selfless and brave, who would give everything for her city, for her planet. And that she would need someone to give everything back to *her.*

Bryce had given him a life, and a beautiful one. He didn't need all the photo evidence that had streamed in front of his face when he'd been in the Comitium's holding cell to realize it. She had brought joy, and laughter, and love, had pried him free of that cold, dark existence and pulled him into the light. Her light.

He wouldn't let it be extinguished.

So Hunt pushed the missile-launch button. One push, and it blasted from the shoulder panel on the mech-suit.

And as it left the suit, spiraling through space, golden with all that angelic wrath . . .

He felt Shahar leave with it.

Could have sworn he saw great, shining wings wrap around that missile as it spiraled through space, straight for Bryce and Rigelus.

The Fallen's cause, ended at last with this final blow.

Bryce and Rigelus halted their struggle at the glowing missile's approach.

And Hunt knew it was Shahar, it was every one of the Fallen, it was all who'd stood against the Asteri, who guided that missile for a direct hit into Rigelus's face.

It didn't explode. It launched him away from Bryce, the Bright Hand now tumbling for the event horizon, the missile with him—

And Bryce was free. Drifting.

But still too close to the edge.

Using the suit's precious cache of firepower for momentum, Hunt propelled himself forward, racing through space for his mate, his wife, his love—

The missile and Rigelus crossed the event horizon.

Time slowed.

It stretched and rippled as a flare of light plumed, either Rigelus or the erupting missile, Shahar and the Fallen's cause vanishing with it into darkness.

And then Bryce was before him, her hair floating like she was underwater. Face crusted—frozen. Unconscious.

The Mask said a different word, but he ignored it.

Ignored it and reached and reached, time still so fucking slow—

The metal hands of the suit wrapped around her waist just as time resumed. He deployed the remaining small artillery and blasted toward home. Toward the portal, now beginning to slide shut.

It could only mean one thing. The Mask had been trying to tell him, but he refused to believe it. He wouldn't believe it for one second.

But the portal was closing, getting smaller and smaller, and—

A glowing, black figure filled it. Then another.

Aidas and Apollion.

Their power grabbed the edges of the portal and held it a little wider. Held it open a moment longer.

And with what little strength he had left, Hunt threw a desperate, raging, blazing-hot rope of lightning toward Apollion. The only being on Midgard who could handle his power.

Apollion caught it, in that humanoid form once more, and pulled.

Aidas flared with black light, pushing back against the sealing portal, against Urd's wishes. Hunt was close enough to see the princes' strained faces, Apollion's teeth flashing as he dragged Hunt by his lightning, inch by inch, closer and closer. Aidas was sweating, panting as he fought to keep the portal open—

And then Ruhn was there. Starlight flaring. Pushing back against the impossible. Lidia was beside him, crackling with fire.

Tharion. Holstrom. Flynn and Dec. A fire sprite, her small body bright with flame. Isaiah and Naomi.

So many hands, so many powers, from almost every House.

The friends they'd made were what mattered in the end. Not the enemies.

Through love, all is possible.

It was love that was holding the portal open. That held it open until the very end, until Hunt and Bryce were through, crashing into the dirt of Midgard, the blue sky filling his sight and all that beautiful air filling his lungs—

The portal shut, sealing the black hole and all of space behind it.

The Asteri were gone.

Hunt was out of the mech-suit in a heartbeat, shattering the metal panel, swinging down to where Bryce lay on the ground. She wasn't moving. Wasn't breathing.

And he finally let the Mask say the word he'd been ignoring since he'd grabbed her in the depths of space.

Dead.

99

It was too long," Declan was saying as Hunt worked on Bryce's heart, his lightning slamming into her, over and over. "She was without oxygen for too long, even for Vanir. There's nothing my healing magic can do if she's already—"

Hunt blasted his lightning into her chest again.

Bryce arced off the ground, but her heart didn't start beating.

Their friends were gathered around them, shadows to his grief, this unfathomable pain.

Get up, he willed the Mask, willed her. *Get the fuck up.*

But it did not respond. Like one final *fuck you*, the Mask tumbled off his face. As if her Made essence had faded from him with her death.

"Bryce," he ordered, voice cracking. This wasn't happening, this couldn't be happening to him, not when they'd been so close—

"Blessed Luna, so bright in the sky," Flynn whispered, "spare your daughter—"

"No prayers," Hunt growled. "No *fucking* prayers."

She couldn't be dead. She had fought so hard and done so much . . .

Hunt crashed his lightning into her heart again.

It had worked before. That day of the demon attack in the spring—he'd brought her back to life.

But her heart did not answer this time.

Rigelus had used his gods-damned lightning to resurrect the Harpy—why the fuck didn't it work now? What had Rigelus known about Hunt's own power that Hunt didn't?

"Do something," Hunt snarled up at Apollion and Aidas. "You've got a black hole in your fucking mouth—you've got all the power in the galaxy," he spat at the Prince of the Pit. *"Save her."*

"I cannot," Apollion said, and Hunt had never hated anything more than he hated the grief in the prince's eyes. The tears on Aidas's face. "We do not have such gifts."

"Then find Thanatos," Ruhn ordered. "He goes around calling himself the *Prince of Souls* or whatever bullshit. Find him and—"

"He cannot save her, either," Aidas said softly. "None of us can."

Hunt looked down at his mate, so still and cold and lifeless.

The scream that came out of him shook the very world.

There was nothing but that scream, and the emptiness where she had been, where the life they were supposed to have had together should have been. And when his breath ran out, he was just . . . done. There was nothing left, and what the fuck was the point of it all if—

A gentle hand touched his shoulder. "I might be able to try something," said a female voice.

Hunt looked up to find Hypaxia Enador somehow standing beside him, the Bone Crown of the House of Flame and Shadow atop her shining black curls.

His sister was gone. Ruhn looked at Bryce's face and knew she was dead. Beyond dead.

He had no sound in his mind. Lidia stood beside him, her hand in his, her sons behind them. The boys had been the ones who'd convinced him to come back—had refused to go another step until they helped in some way.

But none of it had made a difference. Even Athalar's lightning hadn't revived Bryce.

And then Hypaxia had stepped forward, wearing that crown of bones. Somehow, she was now the Head of the House of Flame and Shadow. Offering to help.

"She'll never forgive me if you raise her into some shadow of herself," Hunt said, voice strained with tears, with his screams.

"I'm not proposing to raise her," Hypaxia assured him.

Hunt dragged his hands through his hair. "She doesn't have a soul—I mean, she does, but she sold it to the Under-King, so if that's what you need, then you're shit out of luck—"

"The Under-King is gone," Hypaxia said. Ruhn's knees wobbled. "Any bargains he made with the living or the dead are now null and void. Bryce's soul is hers to do with as she wills."

"Please—help her," Ruhn blurted, desperate. "Help her if you can."

Hypaxia met his eyes, then looked to Lidia beside him, their hands linked. She smiled.

Athalar whispered, "Anything. Whatever you need, I'll give anything."

The witch looked down at Bryce, and said to Athalar, "Not a sacrifice. A trade."

She beckoned behind her, summoning Jesiba Roga to her side.

Hunt stared at the sorceress, but Roga was only gazing at Bryce.

"Oh, Quinlan," Roga said, and there were tears gathering on her lashes.

"Priestess," Apollion hissed, and Roga lifted eyes brimming with disdain and disgust to the Prince of the Pit.

"Still wondering if I'm going to do anything with those books?" Roga snapped at Apollion. She pointed to Bryce, dead on the ground. "Don't you think if they had some power, I'd be using it *right now* to save that girl?"

Apollion glowered at her. "You're a born liar, priestess—"

"We don't have much time," Hypaxia interrupted, and even the Prince of the Pit halted at the command in her voice. "We need to act before too much damage is done to her body."

"Please," Ruhn rasped, "just explain. I know you said we didn't need to, but if we can offer something—"

"It is for me to offer," Jesiba said, and looked down again at Bryce. Tears covered the sorceress's cheeks. *Priestess,* Apollion had called her.

"To offer what?" Lidia asked.

"My life," Roga said. "My long, wicked life." She raised her eyes to Apollion again.

"That is not possible," Apollion said.

"You cursed me," Jesiba said, and as puzzled as Hunt was, he couldn't bring himself to interrupt. "You cursed me to immortality. Now I'm making it a gift: the gift of a Vanir's long life. I give it freely to Bryce Quinlan, if she wants it."

Apollion snapped, "That curse is for the *living.*"

"Then it is a good thing I have a way with the dead," Hypaxia declared.

Perhaps for the first time in his existence, Apollion looked surprised. Aidas asked, "Is . . . is such a thing possible?"

Hunt said, "I offer my life, then."

"What would be the point?" Jesiba said, laughing harshly. "Save her, only to be dead yourself?"

"You . . . you'll die?" Ruhn blurted.

Jesiba smiled softly. "After fifteen thousand years, I've had my fill of Midgard."

"We must do it now," Hypaxia said. "I can feel her thinning."

Hunt didn't like that word one bit, so he said to Jesiba, "Thank you. I never knew that Quinlan . . . that she meant anything to you."

Jesiba's brows rose, and a bit of the prickly sorceress he knew returned. "Of course she does. Do you know how hard it is to find a competent assistant?"

Hunt was beyond laughter, though. "Thank you," he said again. "I . . . I hope you find peace."

Jesiba's face bloomed in a smile, and it was perhaps the first true one he'd ever seen from her. "I've already found it, Athalar. Thanks to you both." With a nod to him and Bryce, she walked up to Hypaxia and offered her hand. "Lead the House of Flame and Shadow back to the light," she said to the witch, who bowed her head.

None of them dared speak as Hypaxia began to chant.

This place was the opposite of where she'd gone during the Drop. Rather than an endless chasm, it was just . . . light. Soft, golden light. Gentle and easy on the gaze.

It was warm and restful, and she had nowhere else she really wanted to be except . . .

Except . . .

Bryce looked behind her. More light glowed in that direction.

"Looking for the exit?" said a dry female voice. "It's that way."

Bryce turned, and Jesiba was there.

The golden light rippled and faded, and they stood upon a green hill in a lush, gentle land. The land she'd glimpsed that day after the attack in the spring—when she had believed Connor and the Pack of Devils had been safe and protected in the Bone Quarter.

It was real.

"Quinlan."

She turned to Jesiba. "Are we dead?"

"Yes."

"Did the others—"

"Alive, though the Asteri are not." A wry nod. "Thanks to you."

Bryce smiled, and felt it beam through her. "Good. Good." She breathed in a lungful of the sweet, fresh air, noted the tang of salt, a hint of sea nearby—

"Quinlan," Jesiba said again. "You have to go back."

Bryce angled her head. "What do you mean?"

"To life," Jesiba said, irritable as always. "Why else do you think I'm here? I traded my life for yours."

Bryce blinked. "What? Why?"

"Holstrom can fill you in on the particulars of my existence. But let's just say . . ." Jesiba walked up to her and took her hand.

"That Archesian amulet isn't merely for protection against my books or against demons. It's a link to Midgard itself."

Bryce glanced down at her chest, the slender gold chain and delicate knot of circles dangling from it. "I don't understand."

"The amulets first belonged to the librarian-priestesses of Parthos. Each was imbued with Midgard's innate magic—the very oldest. The sort every world has, for those who know where to look."

"So?"

"So I think Midgard knows what you did, in whatever way a planet can be sentient. How you freed Avallen, not because you wanted to claim the land for yourself, but because you believed it was right."

At Bryce's surprised expression, Jesiba said, "Come, Quinlan. I know how ridiculously soft-hearted you can be." The words were dry, but her face was soft.

"What does that have to do with"—Bryce gestured around them—"all this?"

"As thanks for what you did for Midgard . . . we are being allowed this trade, as it were."

Bryce blinked, still not getting it. "A trade?"

Jesiba plowed ahead, ignoring her question. "The Parthos books are yours now. Protect them, cherish them. Share them with the world."

Bryce stammered, "*How* can you possibly, and *why* would you possibly—"

"A hundred thousand humans marched at Parthos to save the books—to save their centuries of knowledge from the Asteri. They all knew they wouldn't walk away. I had to run, that day. To protect the books, I ran from my friends and my family, who fought to buy me time." Her eyes gleamed. "You went into that portal today knowing you wouldn't walk away, either. I can offer now what I couldn't then, all those years ago. My family and friends are long gone, but I know they'd want to offer this to you, too. As our own thanks for freeing our world."

Bryce reeled. Jesiba had been at Parthos *when it fell*?

"The books are yours," Jesiba said again. "And so is the gallery's collection. The paperwork's done."

"But how did you know I'd wind up—"

"You've got one of the worst self-sacrificing streaks I've ever encountered," Jesiba said. "I had a feeling an intervention might be needed here today." She peered up at the blue sky, and smiled to herself. "Go home, Bryce. This will all be here when you're ready."

"My soul—"

"Free. The Under-King is dead. Again, Holstrom will fill you in."

Bryce's eyes stung. "I don't . . . I don't understand. I was happy to give my life—well, not *happy*, but willing—"

"I know," Jesiba said, and squeezed her hand. "That's why I'm here." She gestured behind Bryce, where a crystal doorway, reminiscent of Crescent City's Gates, now glowed. "The angel is waiting for you, Quinlan."

The angel. *Hunt.*

The thing she'd left behind. The thing that she'd been looking for, the reason she'd hesitated . . .

"This will all be here when you're ready," Jesiba repeated, then motioned to the green hills beyond. "We'll all be here when you're ready."

Far out, on a distant hill, stood seven figures.

Bryce knew them by shape, knew them by their heights and the glow around them. She picked out Connor standing tall at the back. And standing at their front, a hand upraised . . .

Bryce began crying, and it was pure joy and love that burst from her as she lifted a hand in greeting toward Danika.

Danika, here—with everyone. Safe and loved.

She heard the words on the wind, carried from her friend's soul to hers.

Light it up, Bryce.

And Bryce was laughing, laughing and sobbing as she yelled back across the lush plain and hills, *"Light it up, Danika!"*

Wolfish laughter flowed to her. And then there was a spark of light by Danika's shoulder, and Bryce knew that fire . . .

She blew a kiss to Lehabah. Through her tears, she turned back to Jesiba. "How? The secondlight—"

"It took their power. But what is eternal, what is made of love . . . that can never be destroyed."

Bryce stared at her in wonder.

Jesiba laughed. "And that's about as sentimental as I'll ever get, even here." She gave Bryce a nudge toward the crystal archway. "Live your life, Quinlan. And live it well."

Bryce nodded, and hugged Jesiba, conveying all that was in her heart.

Jesiba hugged her back—first awkwardly, then wholeheartedly. And as Bryce hugged her, she looked one more time toward the hill where Danika and Lehabah and Connor and the Pack of Devils had waved.

But they were already gone. Off to enjoy the wonders and peace of this place. It filled her heart with joy to know it.

So Bryce turned from Jesiba. From what awaited them, all of them, and walked back toward the archway.

Toward life.

Toward Hunt.

100

Bryce opened her eyes.

There were . . . a lot of people standing over her. Most of them were crying.

"This," she groaned, "is like some fucked-up version of attending your own Sailing."

Everyone was gaping at her. And Hunt—he was real, he was right there, and the shock on his face was so genuine that Bryce just laughed.

The Asteri were gone. And with them, their firstlight, secondlight, their prison of an afterlife, and those she'd loved and lost . . . they were safe, too.

All of Danika's work, fulfilled.

Bryce looked from Hunt to Ithan, also hovering over her, and gave the wolf a long, assessing look. "Who died and made you Prime?"

Ithan gaped at her, but Hypaxia—crowned with bones, for fuck's sake—smirked and said, "Sabine."

And Bryce laughed again.

"What the fuck, Quinlan?" Hunt muttered, and she looked back at her mate, whose face was so wan, his eyes so full of wonder—

She had the sense of others being there. Of Ruhn and Lidia and Flynn and Dec and Tharion and the Princes of Hel, but they all faded away before Hunt.

Bryce lifted a hand to his cheek, wiping away a tear with her thumb. "Look at my big, tough Alphahole," she said quietly, but tears thickened her voice, too.

"How can you joke at a time like this?" Hunt said, and Bryce surged forward and kissed him.

It was light and love and *life*.

She had a dim awareness of a stirring in the air around them and Ruhn saying, "Does someone, uh, want to put Jesiba's ashes in a . . . cup or something?"

But Bryce just kissed Hunt, and his arms slid around her, holding her tight to him.

Like he'd never let go.

Hunt allowed Bryce out of his sight only for a few minutes. So he could do this last, final task.

Wings of every color and the husks of the mech-suits still lay where they'd collapsed hours earlier, instantly crashing to the ground the moment the Fallen souls had vacated them.

He didn't have any particular suit in mind, but he walked among the field of them—stepping over the bodies of fallen demons and Asterian angels alike, feathers scattered everywhere, and finally halted before a hulking suit, its eyes now darkened.

"Thanks," he said quietly to the Fallen, even if their souls were now gone. Off to the place Bryce claimed they'd all go, in the end. "For having my back this one last time."

The battlefield beyond the city walls was eerily silent save for the calls of carrion-feeders, but the city behind him was a symphony of sirens and wails and screams. Of news helicopters circling, trying to find some way to convey what had happened.

Naomi had gone off to meet them, to attempt to establish some semblance of order.

"We did it," Hunt said, throat thick. "At last, we did it. The hierarchies are still here, I guess, but I promise you . . ." He swallowed hard, surveying all the cold, empty metal littering the field around him. "It's going to change from here on out."

Wings flapped overhead, and then Isaiah was there, wounds already healed beneath the blood crusted on his dark skin. His brow remained wonderfully clear of the halo.

Isaiah surveyed the mech-suits, the empty eyes, and bowed his head in silent thanks.

"Wherever they've gone," Isaiah said after a moment, "I hope it's the paradise they deserve."

"It is," Hunt said, and knew it in his heart to be true. He eyed the angel. "What's up?"

Isaiah smiled slightly. "I heard you came out here and thought you might want company. You know, someone to brood with."

Hunt chuckled. "Thanks. I always appreciate a partner-in-brooding."

Isaiah's smile broadened. But his eyes gleamed as he said, "So, after all this time, all this suffering . . . we finally saw the Fallen's cause fulfilled."

"I was just telling them that," Hunt said, gesturing to the empty husks of metal.

Isaiah clapped Hunt on the shoulder. "Thank you—for fighting for us until the end. Your mom would be proud, I think. Really damn proud, Hunt."

Hunt didn't have words, so he nodded, swallowing against the tightness in his throat. "Where do we go from here, though? I don't know shit about building governments. Do you?"

"No," Isaiah said. "But I think we're about to get a crash course."

"That's not reassuring." Hunt turned back toward the city. It was a shock to his system, as great as a zap of his lightning, to see the familiar skyline without the spires of the crystal palace.

The Asteri were *gone*.

He needed to get back to Bryce. To hold her, smell her, kiss her. No other reason than that. Than the fact that he'd come so, so close to losing her.

"Hunt," Isaiah said. The white-winged angel's eyes were solemn. "You could rule the angels, you know."

Hunt blinked slowly.

Isaiah went on, "We'll dismantle the Archangels and their schools and the hierarchies, and it'll take years, but in the meantime, we'll need a leader. Someone to guide us, rally us. Give us courage to turn from the old ways and toward something new. Something fair." He folded his wings. "That should be you."

Twice now, angels had bowed to him. Twice now, they'd given him that acknowledgment and permission. And yeah, with the Helfire in his veins, he could lead. Could blast any holdout Archangel or faction into submission.

But . . .

His phone buzzed, and he pulled it from his pocket to glance down.

Bryce Gives Me Magical Orgasms, Literally had messaged him.

Where are you?? I'm having separation anxiety! Get back here!!!

Another buzz, and she added, *After you do whatever you need to, I mean. Like, I'm supportive of you taking space for yourself and doing what has to be done.*

Another buzz.

But also get back here right now.

Hunt choked on his laugh. He had everything he needed. Everything he'd ever want.

Don't get your panties in a twist, Quinlan, he answered. *I'll be back soon.*

Then he added, *Actually, do me a favor and take your panties off altogether.*

He didn't wait for her response as he slid his phone into his back pocket and grinned at Isaiah.

His friend's eyebrows were high, no doubt surprised that he'd answered texts instead of replying to such a serious suggestion.

But Hunt had his answer. He'd had it for some time now.

He clapped Isaiah on the shoulder and said, "The angels already have a leader to steer them through this, Isaiah."

"Celestina—"

"Not Celestina." He squeezed his friend's shoulder once, then stepped back, wings flapping, readying to carry him to his wife, his mate, his best friend. To the future that awaited them. "You."

"Me?" Isaiah said, choking. "Athalar—"

Hunt lifted a few feet off the ground, hovering a beat as the autumn breeze ruffled his wings, his hair, singing of the newness of the world to come. "Lead the angels, Isaiah. I'm here if you need me."

"Hunt."

But Hunt shot into the skies, headed for Bryce and whatever tomorrow might bring.

Bryce's soul was hers. It had always been hers, she supposed, but it had been . . . on loan.

Now that it was fully hers again, there was a whole new world to explore without the Asteri lurking about. A whole new afterlife, when she and Hunt were ready.

But not for a long, long time. Not while they still had so much to sort out.

There was one task she had to do immediately, though. How Isaiah managed to commandeer a helicopter to fly to Nena so quickly, Bryce had no idea. But maybe it had something to do with Celestina's pull, even from Ephraim's keep. Or maybe it was more about Celestina wanting to impress Hypaxia, who was now apparently the Head of the House of Flame and Shadow. And who didn't seem opposed to the idea of speaking to Celestina again, if the looks they'd been sneaking each other's way were any indication.

The Ocean Queen and her fleet had brought the witch over here—Hypaxia had intercepted the monarch on her way to beat the shit out of the Asteri for kidnapping Lidia's two sons. The Ocean Queen might be a piece of work, but she stood by her own. And when two children had been kidnapped from her care, she'd shown up prepared to wash the entire city away in their defense.

She and her commanders remained in the Eternal City, the threat of the tsunami she held leashed around the perimeter keeping any Asteri loyalists at bay. At least the ruler seemed too busy with the new world to deal with her petty bullshit with Tharion. For now.

It *was* a new world. In almost every sense.

Declan was already working with a team on the math of how long Midgard could run on what remained of the firstlight before it went dark, without new firstlight being fed into the power grid. Before they had to pull out the candles and watch their mobile phones slowly die. Not that they'd have any service once the grids failed.

They'd all be back to Avallen-style living. Too bad Morven wasn't around to enjoy it.

But they'd have to figure it out soon. Whether they wanted to restore the firstlight power system or try to find an alternate method. Whether they'd require people to hand over their power, or perhaps tax the uber-powerful. Require Archangels, who had power in spades, to donate some of their power to the grid. The powerful, serving the weak.

Or some shit like that. Honestly, Bryce planned to leave it to smarter minds than hers to sort out. Though she had little hope that she wouldn't have to step in to kick some ass before all was said and done. For right now . . . There was a capital city in chaos. A world turned upside down. Yet she set her sights northward.

Bryce found Nesta in the same room the female had been in before. With Ember and Randall and a handsome, vaguely familiar winged male beside them, who smelled like Nesta's mate. Sitting around a table and talking over tea and chocolate cake.

Chocolate cake, for fuck's sake.

Nesta was instantly on her feet, a long dagger in her hand. The male beside her also reached for a concealed weapon, swift as a thought.

But Bryce only gazed at her parents. Happy and at home with the Fae.

Her mom stared back at her like she'd seen a ghost. The teacup she was holding began rattling against its saucer.

Hunt spared Ember from guessing at what had passed by saying, "The Asteri are gone. Midgard is free."

A tear fell from Ember's eye. Bryce didn't think twice before stepping into that world and wrapping her arms around her mother. Holding her tight.

Ember clasped Bryce's face in her hands. "I am so proud to be your mother."

Bryce beamed, her own eyes stinging with tears, and Randall leaned in to press a kiss to her head. "You did good, kid."

Bryce threw her arms around her dad and hugged him, too. Hugged the human warrior who had served in the Asteri's armies, shredded apart his soul for them, until her mom had put him back together.

Nesta and her mate tensed, and Bryce knew Hunt had stepped into their world.

He peered around the room. Glanced at the city sparkling far below, a ribbon of river winding through it. They had to be high up on a mountain for this kind of view.

Nesta's mate said, "You have one minute before Rhys gets here and explodes."

"Oh, Rhys will be fine, Cassian," Ember said—in the Fae's language.

At Bryce's shocked face, Randall said in the same language, "It got too hard to mime everything. They gave us that bean-thing they offered you."

But Bryce shook her head. "Rhysand will be *fine*? The guy who brings darkness incarnate—"

"He and Randall bonded about being overprotective dads," Ember said. "So now Rhys knows *exactly* the sort of shit you like to pull, which apparently you pulled here, too . . ."

Bryce glanced to Nesta, who was watching warily. So Bryce reached into her jacket and pulled out the Mask. "Here. As promised."

Everyone fell silent.

And then Bryce drew Truth-Teller, and Cassian looked like he'd jump between her and Nesta. Hunt set his feet into a fighting stance in response, but Bryce just said, "Alphaholes," and laid the dagger on the table between their tea set and treats.

"You brought them back." Nesta's voice was quiet.

"Did you think I wouldn't?"

"I don't know what I thought," Nesta said, but smiled slightly.

"Poor Nesta's been in the doghouse since you took their weapons and dumped us here," Ember explained. "I tried telling Rhysand and Azriel how there's no stopping you when you've got your mind set on something, and I think Feyre—Rhysand's mate—believed me, but . . ." Ember glanced at Nesta and winced. "I apologize *again* for my daughter's behavior."

"I made the choice to give her the Mask," Nesta reminded Ember. To Bryce, she added wryly, "Your mother somehow doesn't believe that I did so willingly."

Bryce rolled her eyes at her mother. "Great. Thanks for that." She gestured to the portal shimmering behind them. "Shall we?"

Ember smiled softly. "They're truly gone, then."

"Gone, and never to be heard from again," Bryce said, her heart lifting with the words.

Ember's eyes gleamed with tears, but she turned, taking Nesta's hands and clenching them tightly in her own. "Despite the fact that my daughter lied and schemed and basically betrayed us . . . ," she started.

"Tell us how you really feel, Mom," Bryce muttered, earning an amused sidelong glance from Nesta.

But Ember continued, looking only at Nesta, "I am glad of one thing: that I was able to meet you."

Nesta's lips pressed into a thin line, and she glanced down at their joined hands.

Bryce cut in, if only to spare Nesta from her mom's increasingly weepy-looking expression, "Next time I take on intergalactic evil, I'll try to accommodate your bonding schedule."

Ember finally looked over at Bryce, glaring. "You and I are going to have *words* when we get home, Bryce Adelaide Quinlan. Leaving Cooper behind like that—"

"I know," Bryce said. She had a *lot* to answer for on that front. And apologizing to do.

"Your mother loves you," Nesta said quietly, reading the exasperation on Bryce's face. "Don't for one second take that for granted."

Bryce could only incline her head to Nesta. "I'm lucky," she admitted. "I've always been lucky to have her as a mom."

Ember really looked like she might cry now, especially as she turned back to Nesta and said, "This time with you was a gift, Nesta. It truly was."

With that, she pulled Nesta to her in a tight embrace, and Bryce could have sworn something like pain and longing crossed Nesta's expression. Like she hadn't experienced a mom-hug for a long, long time.

So Bryce gave the female some privacy to enjoy every second of that motherly embrace and turned to where Randall and Cassian stood behind them. The males had clasped arms warmly. "Thanks, friend," Randall was saying to the warrior. "For everything."

Cassian grinned, and, well, Bryce could see why Nesta might be into a male who looked like that. "Maybe we'll meet again one day, under less . . . strange circumstances."

"I hope so," Randall said, and as he passed by where Ember and Nesta were still hugging, he clapped the latter on the shoulder with fatherly affection.

Bryce's heart swelled to the point of pain as Randall approached Hunt and hugged him, too. Hunt returned the embrace, thumping her father on the back before they separated to pass through the portal together.

Ember at last pulled away from Nesta. But she gently put a hand to the female's cheek and whispered, "You'll find your way," before walking toward the portal.

Bryce could have sworn there were tears in Nesta's eyes as her mother stepped back into Midgard.

But those tears were gone when Nesta met Bryce's stare. And Cassian, like any good mate, sensed when he wasn't wanted, and walked over to the fireplace to pretend to read some sort of old-looking manuscript. Bryce knew that, *also* like any good mate, if she made one wrong move, he'd rip her to shreds. Which was precisely why Hunt had come back into the room, and was watching Nesta carefully.

"Alphaholes," Nesta echoed, eyes gleaming with amusement.

Bryce chuckled and drew the Starsword. Again, Cassian tensed, but Bryce just offered the blade to Nesta. The female took it, blinking.

"You said you had an eight-pointed star tattooed on you," Bryce explained. "And you found the chamber with the eight-pointed star in the Prison, too."

Nesta lifted her head. "So?"

"So I want you to take the Starsword." Bryce held the blade between them. "Gwydion—whatever you call it here. The age of the Starborn is over on Midgard. It ends with me."

"I don't understand."

But Bryce began backing toward the portal, taking Hunt's hand, and smiled again at the female, at her mate, at their world, as the Northern Rift began to close. "I think that eight-pointed star was tattooed on you for a reason. Take that sword and go figure out why."

101

The *Depth Charger* had anchored offshore, since the nearest port to the Eternal City was too shallow to accommodate the city-ship. Standing beside Ruhn, Lidia stared at her sons as they waited on the concrete pier while the transport pod surfaced, water sloshing off its glass dome top.

Revealing Renki and Davit, both waving wildly at the two boys standing beside Lidia.

At her sons, who were smiling at their dads, Brann enthusiastically waving back, Ace giving a smaller—but no less earnest—wave as well.

Ruhn placed a gentle hand on Lidia's back, and she leaned into the reassuring, loving touch. Her mate. Yes, she knew it without a doubt.

The glass top of the pod opened, and then Renki and Davit leapt gracefully onto the pier, Brann and Ace running for them—

It was pure love and joy, the embraces shared between the boys and their fathers. Renki had tears of relief running down his face, and Davit was holding both boys to him as if he'd never let them go again.

But Davit did let go. He crossed to Lidia in two strides and wrapped his arms around her, too. "Thank you," the male said, voice choked with tears. "Thank you." Renki was there the moment Davit pulled back, hugging her as tightly.

Lidia found herself smiling, even as her heart was again aching, and leaned away to survey her sons.

They were both considering her, Brann frowning deeply, Ace more unreadable. It was the former who said, "So this is goodbye?"

Lidia glanced to Renki and Davit, who both nodded. They'd spoken on the phone yesterday to coordinate this reunion—and what lay ahead. "Until things settle down a bit up here," Lidia said. "Above the surface, I mean."

Because even in the day since the Asteri had been vanquished, shit was already hitting the fan. The drainage of the firstlight grid was going to be a huge problem. But the Ocean Queen had fueled all her city-ships and their various pods without firstlight. With her own power. Maybe the ruler had some insight into how they might adapt their tech to move beyond consuming firstlight.

The Ocean Queen, of course, hadn't been happy when Lidia had sent a messenger to the *Depth Charger.* Lidia had kept her note short and efficient:

I trust that my services are no longer required and henceforth resign from your employ.

With gratitude for your compassion,

Lidia Cervos

The Ocean Queen had dispatched her reply—again on a briny piece of kelp—an hour later.

I have bigger issues to consider than your loyalty, Lidia Cervos. I accept your resignation, but do not fool yourself into thinking that this is the last we shall cross paths. For now, you may live your life Above.

It was the best Lidia could hope for.

Now, Lidia glanced between her sons and added, "But I'd like to see you both again. If that's okay with you."

Brann nodded, and she had no words in her head as he walked up to her and threw his arms around her.

Her son's scent, his warmth and nearness, threatened to bring her to her knees. But she managed to stay standing, knowing

Ruhn was beside her, would always be there, supporting her, as Brann pulled back, grinning.

"You're a badass," Brann said, and added, "Mom."

Even as her heart glowed with joy at the word, Lidia dared glance over his shoulder to find that Renki and Davit were grinning as broadly as Brann. Happy for her—for all of them. Her boys had a beautiful family, and perhaps, if everyone was all right with it, it was one she could find a place in. Find joy in.

Brann leaned in, pressing a kiss to Lidia's cheek that she knew she'd cherish for the rest of her existence. Then he walked over to Ruhn, and Lidia could only blink as Brann threw his arms around Ruhn, too, hugging him tight. "Thanks," Brann said. "For what you were gonna do. To save us—and our mom."

Ruhn clapped Brann on the back, and Lidia's chest filled with so much brightness she could barely contain it all. "No worries," Ruhn said. "All in a day's work for us Aux grunts."

Brann grinned, then walked back to his parents, hugging Renki again.

Lidia glanced to Ace, who was watching her warily. Knowing he wouldn't rush into her arms as Brann had, Lidia walked up to him. Slowly. Giving him time to decide what he wanted to do.

Ace held his ground, but his eyes weren't cold as he said, "Thanks for coming for us." His mouth quirked to the side. "Take care of yourself."

"I've got Ruhn watching my back," Lidia said, glancing to Ruhn. "I'll be fine."

"He *shot* you," Ace said, frowning at Ruhn.

"I shouldn't have told you that," Ruhn muttered.

Lidia smirked, but faced Ace again. "He'll pay for it, don't worry."

Ace didn't look so sure, staring Ruhn down for a moment. But when he began walking toward his dads, he stumbled, as if . . .

Lidia glared at Ruhn, who whistled innocently at the sky. Fine—let him keep his mind-speaking secrets.

Ruhn slid a hand around her waist as the boys and their parents boarded the pod. Davit slid into the pilot's seat, flicking on switches, and Brann claimed the seat beside him. Renki and Ace took the back seats, and as the pod whirred to life, they all looked at her.

Lidia offered them a small, hopeful smile. Her fingers found Ruhn's, and she gripped his hand tightly. Ruhn didn't let go.

Her sons were alive, and free, and in her life again, and it was more than she'd ever hoped for.

So the future, whatever it held . . . she'd cherish every moment of it.

Bryce was thoroughly sick of Nena's endless chill when she opened the Northern Rift again. Not to the home world of the Fae, but to Hel.

Only blackness awaited the army marching through. The beasts and flying things and the princes, who went one by one, Thanatos giving her a look that said she might have destroyed the Asteri but he was still mad about his dog, until only Apollion and Aidas stood before her in the ice and snow.

They did not seem to require coats or hats or gloves. They didn't even shiver.

Apollion said to Hunt, "Hel has no hold on you, and you have no obligation to us."

"Uh, thank you?" Hunt said. "Likewise."

Apollion threw him a half smile, then glanced to Bryce. "You did better than expected."

Bryce snapped her fingers, the sound muffled by her gloves. "*That* is what I want on my new business cards. *Bryce Quinlan: Better than Expected.*"

Apollion just smirked and walked toward the dark.

"Hey," Bryce called after the Prince of the Pit.

Apollion paused, raising a brow at her.

Bryce threw him a grin and said, "Thanks for not giving up on Midgard."

She could have sworn a kernel of compassion warmed Apollion's face before he glanced to Aidas and said, "I shall be happy to lay the matter to rest. And to see my brother at peace."

With that, he strode through the Rift.

Bryce's teeth were chattering now, but she faced Aidas. "Will we see you again?"

Aidas smiled wickedly. "Do you wish to?"

"No," Bryce said, and meant it. "Grateful as we are . . . I think we have different definitions for the word *pet*."

Aidas smiled fully this time. "Then I shall give you my gratitude, Bryce Quinlan. And bid you farewell."

"I'll be forever grateful," Bryce said to the Prince of the Chasm, "for your kindness that day at the Oracle."

His smile turned gentler. "Theia would be proud of you."

"And of you," Bryce said, the only gift she could offer to a Prince of Hel. She refrained from saying that Theia's pride meant shit to her, though. "I think you might get to hear it from her lips one day."

Aidas angled his head. Bryce had told all of them about what Jesiba had claimed. What she'd seen in that land of glowing light. "You think a Prince of Hel shall be allowed in?"

Bryce walked up to him and kissed his cheek. Icy skin met her lips. "I think a good male, regardless of where he is from, will always be allowed in."

Aidas's eyes glowed bright blue—with gratitude or longing or love, she didn't know. But the prince only nodded to her, then to Hunt, and walked through the Northern Rift into the dark.

Apollion was waiting just inside, and he took up a place beside his brother. Bryce's hand slid into Hunt's, and she lifted her other hand in farewell.

To her surprise, both princes returned the gesture.

With a ripple of thought and power, she closed the Rift. Locked it securely, leaving no cracks to slip through. Though the Asteri were gone, all their crystal Gates throughout Midgard remained intact. But for now, at least *this* particular Gate was shut completely. At long last.

"Looks like your demon-hunting days might be over," she said to Hunt.

Her mate grinned down at her, and kissed her gently, and even the frigid winds of Nena seemed to warm around them. "Guess I should file for unemployment."

Tharion Ketos stood on the outskirts of the Meat Market, looking for his wife.

Thanks to the water sprites in her employ, the Viper Queen had apparently been able to put out the blazing main building before the fire had spread, leaving the bulk of the Meat Market's interconnected warehouses intact.

Indeed, it seemed as if it was business as usual—albeit already adjusted to a new world. From the back of a truck, shady-looking grunts unloaded cannisters glowing with firstlight. Already stocking up on a product that would soon be in high demand.

Tharion didn't really know why he'd come here, when Sendes had informed him that the Ocean Queen had forgiven his disobedience. In fact, she'd made him a perfectly good offer to be a commander in her forces and work aboard the *Depth Charger*, but he'd found himself saying he had something to do first.

And then made his way back here.

The world was in upheaval. The Asteri were gone, but there was an Imperial Senate to contend with, and Archangels, and the various House Heads, and . . . maybe he should have stayed on that ship.

He didn't know why he had expected peace and comfort. Why he'd thought everyone would be happy and just . . . chill. But there were plenty of greedy fucks out there in the world, who were happy to use the shake-up to grab for power.

And he knew that the fuck who ruled the Meat Market was probably one of them. He'd have to contend with her at some point, probably someday soon.

But right now he needed to find his wife. Just to make sure she was okay. Then he could be on his way. Go to the *Depth Charger*. Or do something else, he didn't know. He figured Ogenas would guide him at some point. Maybe help him figure out his mess of a life.

Tharion slipped on the hood of his sweatshirt, checking that the gun concealed at his side was secure and ready, and walked into the warren of the Meat Market. To whatever Urd had in store for him.

He only made it one block before a female voice said from the shadows, "You have to be ten kinds of dumb to go back in there."

He halted, peering into the alley from which the voice had spoken. Two crimson eyes smoldered in the darkness.

Tharion inclined his head. "Hello, Ariadne."

102

Bryce stood in the foyer of the Autumn King's villa, surveying the field of flashing cameras, the haughty Fae nobility, and the confused-looking guards glancing between her and the crowd.

For the occasion, she'd chosen a pink dress that she knew drove Hunt to distraction. It had been either that or leggings and a T-shirt, and given that she wanted to avoid anything taking away from what she was actually doing, she'd opted for formal.

Of course, settling on the pink dress had been an ordeal in itself. There was now a giant heap of clothing in her bedroom for her to put away when she got home, which was incentive enough to draw this out for as long as possible.

But she took one look at Sathia and Flynn's sneering parents, the Lord and Lady Hawthorne having recently returned from Avallen, and decided to Hel with waiting. To Hel with all the other Fae nobility who had gathered at her invitation this morning.

She'd set foot in the city late last night, had gone right to the ruins of Asphodel Meadows, and called for this meeting the next day.

She would have done it last night, but Hunt had told her to take the time to sort out what she wanted to say. To let Marc get the paperwork ready.

The leopard shifter and Declan now stood beside the desk that had been hauled into the foyer, Ruhn and Flynn with them.

She glanced to Hunt, and he nodded subtly. It was time.

So Bryce stepped up to the desk and said to the cameras, to the Fae aristocrats, "I'll make this short and sweet, for all the busy nobles here who have to get back to champagne lunches and spa treatments."

Silence, and a frantic clicking of cameras. The videographers pressed in closer, angling their mics to pick up her every breath. One of the camera guys—a draki male—was smirking.

But Bryce kept her gaze on the cameras, on the world listening. "This is my first and only decree as the Fae Queen of Valbara and Avallen: the royal houses are ended."

She ignored the gasps and protests, and tapped the paperwork on the desk. "I've had the documents drawn up. Allow me to be perfectly clear: I am not abdicating either throne. I am no longer queen, but with this document, *no one* shall ever wear the crown again. The Fae monarchy is abolished. Forever."

From the corner of her eye, she could see Hunt grinning broadly. She wished her mom was here, but they'd decided that Ember Quinlan's presence might cause too much speculation that her human mother had pushed her to do this.

"I am donating all the Autumn King's residences in this city," Bryce said, gesturing to the elegant space around them, "to house those displaced by the attack on Asphodel Meadows. This villa in particular will be used to house children orphaned by the massacre."

One of the Fae nobles choked.

"As for the royal properties elsewhere—in Valbara and on Avallen—they will be sold to anyone who can stomach their tacky-ass decor, and the profits will go toward rebuilding Asphodel Meadows."

Bryce picked up the golden fountain pen she'd swiped from the Autumn King's study after chucking all his prisms into the trash. She planned to dismantle the orrery and sell it for scrap metal. She knew enough about how light traveled and formed—how it could break apart and come back together. She never wanted to learn another thing about light again, even her own.

"The Asteri are gone," Bryce said to the listening world, "and the Fae kingdoms with them. In their place, we will build a government built on equality and fairness. This document grants me the right to represent the Fae in the building of such a government. And nothing more."

"Traitor," hissed a Fae noble who Bryce could have sworn had sneered at her once in a restaurant, years ago.

Bryce hummed to herself, flipping the Autumn King's beloved pen between her fingers. "You guys shouldn't have granted your royals such absolute power in your quest to keep everyone else down in the dirt." She leaned over the documents. "Maybe then you could have stopped me from doing this."

The golden pen touched paper, ink blooming on the parchment.

"But you're in the mud with the rest of us now," Bryce said to the Fae as she signed her name. "Better get used to the smell."

Thus, with the stroke of the Autumn King's golden pen, the royal bloodlines of the Fae were wiped from existence.

Ruhn flicked on the lights in the apartment—for however long the place would even have power. "Bryce is going to throw a fit, but I swear it was the only one available furnished on short notice," he said to Lidia as they stepped inside the home literally a floor below Bryce's.

Lidia smiled, though, surveying the apartment that was the mirror image of Bryce's layout save for the furniture. She approached the white, gleaming kitchen. "It's lovely—really. I'll get the money wired to your account."

"Nah," Ruhn said. "Consider it a thank-you present. For bailing me out of the dungeons."

Lidia turned from the kitchen, brows high. "I think we're even by now. After . . . everything." After that shit with Pollux, which he knew would haunt his dreams for a long fucking time.

But there would be joy to light the dark memories. When he'd gone with her to return the boys to their parents, Ruhn had been content to watch the happy reunion, especially as Lidia was hugged with equal welcome and love by the boys' parents. As the boys had, in their own ways, made it clear that Lidia would be welcome in their lives.

Brann, he had no doubt, would be the easier one. But Ace . . .

Ruhn smiled to himself at the memory of how Ace had looked over at Ruhn before leaving, his dark eyes knowing. Sharp. As if to say, *Take care of my mom.*

Ruhn had answered into the kid's mind, *She can take care of herself, but I will.*

Ace's eyes had widened in shock, and he'd stumbled a step, but—with an assessing, impressed glance at Ruhn—had continued to the transport pod.

Ruhn and Lidia had spent *one* night in his shithole house, aching to fuck each other within an inch of their lives but all too conscious of his friends a thin wall away, before he'd called up a realtor and asked about finding an apartment. Immediately. With a few specific requests.

"The bedroom over there's got two beds in it," he said, pointing across the great room. "For your boys."

Her eyes were lined with silver as she faced the guest bedroom.

That had been Ruhn's main demand to the realtor: find an apartment with a guest room that had two beds. "They can visit whenever they—and you—want."

Her smile was so soft and hopeful that his heart ached. But she walked to the couch in front of the TV and sat down, as if testing it out. Testing out this house, this life.

"I think their dads will want to keep them close for a while after what happened," Lidia said, "but yes . . . I would love for them to be here sometimes."

Ruhn sank beside her on the couch. "They're going to raise Hel when they're older."

"I'm fine with that, so long as it's not literally." Lidia sighed. "I've had enough of demons for a while, however friendly."

Ruhn chuckled. "Me too."

For a few minutes, they sat in companionable silence, the apartment—*their* apartment—settling in around them.

"I can't believe we're alive," Lidia said at last.

"I can't believe the Asteri are gone."

The past few days had been such a whirlwind that he hadn't really processed all that had happened. Or the current state of the world.

Lidia said carefully, "Your sister and Athalar's intentions are good, but it's going to take a lot more than one meeting with a bunch of world leaders to sort out an entirely new system of government. Or dismantle slavery."

"I know. Bryce knows."

"Are you . . . What do you plan to do?"

It was a loaded question, but Ruhn answered, "I'll help her. I'll head up the Aux with Holstrom, I guess. Since the Fae throne's gone as of this morning." It had been a wonder to behold—Bryce standing in front of the crowd of cameras and nobles, ending the monarchies with a stroke of a pen. Their father's favorite pen, no less.

Ruhn had never been so proud to be Bryce's brother.

He smiled slightly. "The Oracle was right in a lot of ways, I guess." Lidia lifted a brow. "It wasn't just that the crown would go to Bryce, but that she'd end it. The Danaan royal line is finished."

Lidia clicked her tongue. "You're not dead or childless, after all."

"Not yet," Ruhn said, laughing again. All that time spent dreading the prophecy, worrying over his fate . . .

Lidia looked at him, in that way that no one else on Midgard did—like she saw *him*. "Are you prepared to not be a prince anymore, though? To be . . . normal?"

"I think so," he said, nudging her knee with his own. "Are you?"

"I have no idea. I don't even know what normal is," Lidia admitted.

Ruhn took her hand, linking their fingers. "How about we figure it out together, then?"

"How to be normal?"

"How to live a normal life. The normal, adult apartment's a good start. For both of us." No more veritable frat house living.

But wariness flooded her eyes. "My life is complicated."

"Whoever said normal isn't complicated?" he countered. "All I know is that whatever tomorrow or next year or the next millennium has in store for this world, I want to face it at your side."

Her expression softened. She leaned closer, brushing a strand of his hair back with her free hand.

They weren't the Hind and a Crown Prince of the Fae. Weren't Day and Night. Right then, there, they were simply Lidia and Ruhn. He wouldn't have it any other way.

But Ruhn got to his feet and walked to the kitchen, opening the fridge. The other request he'd made of the realtor: stock the fridge with one thing and one thing only.

Maybe the veritable frat house wasn't entirely gone. He walked back to the couch and handed Lidia a beer.

"As promised, Day," he said, twisting off the cap on his bottle. "One beer."

She looked at the bottle, pure delight shining on her face. She twisted the cap off her own beverage, but got to her feet and clinked her bottle against his before drinking. "To a normal life, Ruhn."

Ruhn leaned in to kiss her, and Lidia met him halfway. And the love and joy in him glowed brighter than starlight as he said against her mouth, "To a normal life, Lidia."

It would take the wolves of the Den a few days to come back from where they'd been lying low. But they *were* coming back.

Ithan didn't know if it was Amelie's order or if Perry had asked them, but everyone was returning. Perhaps just to see how shitty he'd be at leading them as Prime.

Or to assess the dynamic without the Fendyrs.

Or to get their stuff before the firstlight power grid failed and chaos reigned.

Ithan stood in the command center of the Aux headquarters,

Flynn and Dec across from him, the former eyeing Perry with an interest Ithan didn't entirely appreciate.

Perry was blushing, and Ithan didn't appreciate that, either.

But Ruhn and Lidia walked in before Ithan could say anything stupid, and the former Fae Prince said, "So, first things first: I think it sucks that we save the world and still have to be back at work two days later."

Perry laughed, and . . . okay, maybe Ithan liked the sound.

But Lidia said, grave and yet serene, "I'm expecting a report tonight regarding the status of the firstlight power grid and how we might stop it from failing. Lunathion's engineers have been meeting with the Ocean Queen to learn how she powers her ships without it and will present those findings to us. But in the meantime, we need to start assessing allies inside the city and out of it. Celestina's still dealing with Ephraim, trying to garner his support, but the other Archangels are going to start jockeying for power. If we don't want to fall back into the old ways, we need a solid plan."

"Shouldn't Athalar be here for this?" Flynn said.

"He's on his way," Ruhn said. "With Bryce. But they told us to start without them."

Dec and Flynn made kissing noises at each other, and Ithan laughed, Perry joining him.

Maybe it wouldn't be so bad. Not the being Prime part, that part he didn't particularly like, but this new future. It'd probably be batshit crazy for a while, and they'd have no shortage of enemies, but . . .

They'd also have each other. A pack. Of all Houses.

Which was why they were here. No more splintered Aux, divided among Houses and species. They'd lead by example. Starting today.

So Ithan said to Lidia and Ruhn, to Flynn and Dec and Perry, "Whatever these assholes want to throw at us, we'll throw right back at them."

"Spoken like a true sunball captain," Dec teased.

Ithan said, "Yeah." He let the word settle, and for a moment he felt it—that urge to set foot on the field, to grip that ball in his hands.

A glimmer, and it was gone, but . . . after years of nothing, he felt it. Wanted it. So Ithan grinned and added, "I am."

"That was Hypaxia on the phone," Bryce said in the sunny, open atrium of the elegant town house that would soon be the new Griffin Antiquities.

Hunt, unpacking a statue of Thurr from a crate, asked over a winged shoulder, "What'd she say?"

"That if she can find a way to stabilize the antidote, we could have it rolling out to everyone by the Spring Equinox. That is, if we still have power by then. She wants more of your lightning, by the way. She's already out of this batch of antidotes."

Bryce and Hunt had both gotten doses. The surge of magic that had resulted had been intense enough that apparently a whole new island had risen in Avallen—as if the island was now bound to her very soul. As if she and Midgard were, as Jesiba had claimed, bound together, Archesian amulet or no.

And thanks to Hunt, there had been a day straight of thunderstorms. Of course, he was fined by the city for illegal and improper weather manipulation, but *He blew his magical load* didn't really seem to hold sway when Bryce tried to explain it to the authorities.

The new power in their veins, as if returned from what the Asteri had taken, required some getting used to. And new training. Bryce could teleport in one jump between the city and her parents' house now. Which was . . . good and bad.

Good, because she could see Cooper whenever she wanted, and steal him away to the city for a hint of *real* fun. Bad, because her parents now expected her and Hunt for weekly dinners. Bryce had negotiated it down to monthly, but she knew Ember would be making a full-court press for at *least* once every two weeks.

But all of it depended on what they did next—if the firstlight power grid could hold. If it'd collapse. If they'd all have to start over again, squatting over fires in the darkness. But she—they—would proceed as usual. Let the geniuses and scientists find a way to save them this time.

"Well," Hunt said, "if Hypaxia needs someone to go beat the shit out of the Redners, I'm game. They're creeps." The former witch-queen had reluctantly partnered with Redner Industries, hoping to mass-produce the antidote.

"Scary Asshole, Part Two?"

"Happily." He turned from the crate to where Bryce was shelving books on the towering built-in unit behind her desk.

The books. The Parthos collection. No longer in darkness and hiding, but here, in the daylight, for anyone to come see. She couldn't bear to keep them locked away.

Thankfully, she'd found three new employees to help her manage the unwieldy collection. Sasa, Rithi, and Malana currently perched on a takeout container, watching an episode of *Veiled Love* on Hunt's phone where he'd propped it up against his water bottle.

They'd never replace Lehabah, but it filled something in her heart to see them. To hear Syrinx, snoring beneath her new desk, in the little nest of blankets he'd made down there. Like something had finally slid into place. Like she was exactly where she was meant to be.

"So," Hunt said, going back to unloading all the crates Hypaxia had sent over from the House of Flame and Shadow. Apparently, Jesiba had been anticipating this transfer of ownership—she'd made Ithan pack most of the artifacts up.

Bryce thought Jesiba would appreciate the Godslayer Rifle now mounted behind Bryce's desk. As much a warning to anyone who might try to steal the books as in honor of the priestess who'd guarded them for so long. That is, if the fire sprites didn't roast any would-be thief.

She didn't know where Irithys had gone, and she still wished to talk to the queen, to tell her about Lehabah, but from what Sasa had said, it sounded as if the Sprite Queen was now traveling the world, intent on freeing every last one of her people. Especially those who might be held by owners averse to the new worldwide ban on slavery.

"So . . . what?" Bryce asked Hunt, sliding a tome onto the shelf.

"So . . . are you gonna talk about the whole no-more-Fae-monarchy thing?"

"What's there to talk about?" Bryce said. "I sent out my decree. It's over. No longer my problem."

"Others might not see it that way."

"That's why, Athalar . . . ," she began, shelving another book that tried to wriggle out of her hands. She smacked it back over and shoved it onto the shelf. "That's why we're going to establish a Fae democracy. A senate, and all that crap. So the Fae can go complain to *them* about their problems."

"A senate and all that crap, huh?" Hunt said. "Sounds real official."

She turned toward him. "And what about you? How come you get to walk away from the 33rd and the angel stuff, but somehow I can't bail on the Fae drama?"

"I didn't make magic islands come flying out of the ocean and resurrect a whole territory."

"Well, Avallen's different," she sniffed.

"You just don't want to lose your new vacation home," he teased, crossing the room toward her. She let him crowd her against the bookshelf, loving his size and strength and the wall of power that was pure Hunt.

"Maybe I don't," she said, not backing down an inch. "But until the Fae can show me that they'll share Avallen with everyone, it's mine." She'd debated sending the Parthos books there, to the Avallen Archives, but she wanted them close. Wanted them accessible to everyone, not locked away on a remote island. "Or, at least, it's my responsibility," she amended.

"Yeah, well, Baxian's dying to get off the island and back into civilization, so maybe look into hiring a caretaker." Fury and June had already returned to Crescent City. There was only so much medieval living her friends could take, apparently. But Baxian had stuck it out.

She winced. The angel had been keeping the Fae in line since she and Hunt had left Avallen in his hands, taking good care of any and all refugees who made it there. Danika would have been proud. Bryce had made sure to tell the Helhound that—and about seeing his mate in the afterworld. He'd been silent enough during that call that she knew he was crying, but all he had said to Bryce was "Thank you."

"Okay, okay," Bryce said to Hunt. "Set up a democracy, find a new babysitter for Avallen, play Scary Asshole with you . . . Anything else for me to do? In addition to starting my new business?" She gestured to the soon-to-be-open gallery.

"How about hiring a sexy assistant?"

She didn't miss the heat in his eyes. The spark.

She bit her lip. "Sexy assistant, huh? You cool with going from the Umbra Mortis to fetching my coffee?"

"If it comes with the perk of kinky office sex, I'm cool with anything," Hunt growled, nipping at her ear.

"Oh, the position *definitely* comes with kinky office sex," she purred.

She felt the hardness of him push into her hip before he said, low and wicked, "Sprites—go find somewhere else to be for a while."

They grumbled, but zoomed out to the stairs, all blushing a bright pink. Syrinx dashed after them, yelping.

Bryce didn't care where they went. Not as Hunt pressed his cock against her center, and she writhed. "Get on the desk," he said, voice like gravel.

Her blood thrummed through her. "We're already late for our meeting with Ruhn and the others at the Aux."

"They can deal." His voice was pure, unrelenting sex. Her knees wobbled.

But Bryce had only taken one step toward the desk when her phone rang. Baxian.

"Call back later," Hunt said, coming to stand behind her. Sliding his hands up her thighs, bunching her skirt as he went. Yes—*fuck* yes.

Hunt's phone rang. Baxian again.

"Maybe we should . . . answer," Bryce said, though she almost didn't, considering that Hunt had a fistful of her skirt in one hand and her bare ass palmed in his other—

Hunt groaned and reached for his phone, answering with a snapped *"What."*

With her Fae ears, Bryce could hear perfectly clearly as Baxian asked, "Where's your mate?"

It was the low note of panic and urgency that had Hunt putting him on speakerphone and saying, "We're both here."

Baxian let out a shuddering breath, and Bryce's arousal vanished, cold dread filling her gut. If something had happened already, an attack on Avallen—

"I . . ." Baxian choked on the word. "There are about two dozen of them."

Bryce swapped a confused glance with Hunt and asked, "Them?"

Baxian let out a laugh that verged on hysteria. "I swear, it's like they sprang out of the earth, like they were hibernating or hiding there, I don't fucking know—"

"Baxian," Bryce said, heart thundering. *"What is it?"*

"Flying horses. Horses with *wings.*"

Bryce blinked slowly. "Horses . . . with wings."

"Yes," Baxian said, his voice rising. "They're flying around and trampling everything and eating all the crops and I think you might need to come here because they seem to be the sort of thing that might belong to a Super Magical Fancy Starborn Princess . . ."

Bryce looked at Hunt, pure wonder flooding her.

"There are flying horses in Avallen," Hunt said, eyes as wide as her own, pure joy sparking there.

"In Silene's account," Bryce breathed, "she talked about her mother having flying horses. How some came here . . . and there were depictions of them in the Cave of Princes and Morven's castle. I thought they'd all been killed, but maybe . . ." Bryce shook her head. "Is it possible?" Had Helena somehow secretly kept them alive, suspended, waiting until it was safe again?

She didn't care. Not right now. "There are flying horses in Avallen," Bryce repeated to Hunt. "There are *pegasuses* in Avallen."

"Please come help me," Baxian said miserably.

"We'll be there by dawn," Bryce said, and hung up for Hunt. She met her mate's blazingly bright eyes. No more shadows, no more halo, no more pain. Never again. "Rain check on the desk sex?"

"For Jelly Jubilee in the flesh?" Hunt grinned. "Anything."

Bryce threw her arms around his neck, kissing him thoroughly, then dashed for the door.

There was an angel in her office, and a pegasus herd on Avallen. And the Asteri were gone and the dead were free . . . and though she knew there was work to do to heal Midgard, the world was out there. *Life* was out there.

So Bryce and Hunt ran out to live it.

Together.

ACKNOWLEDGMENTS

Even after so many books, I still wake up every day thankful for the incredible people that I have the honor of knowing and working with, and, with that in mind, my love and deepest gratitude go out to:

The magnificent global team at Bloomsbury: Noa Wheeler (whose editorial genius is unparalleled!), Nigel Newton, Kathleen Farrar, Adrienne Vaughan, Ian Hudson, Rebecca McNally, Valentina Rice, Erica Barmash, Angela Craft, Nicola Hill, Amanda Shipp, Marie Coolman, Lauren Ollerhead, Rebecca McGlynn, Grace McNamee, Eleanor Willis, Katie Ager, Ben McCluskey, Holly Minter, Sam Payne, Donna Mark, David Mann, John Candell, Donna Gauthier, Laura Phillips, Jaclyn Sassa, Britt Hopkins, Claire Henry, Michael Young, Nicholas Church, Brigid Nelson, Sarah McLean, Sarah Knight, Joe Roche, Fabia Ma, Sally Wilks, Inês Figueira, Jack Birch, Fliss Stevens, Claire Barker, Cristina Cappelluto, Genevieve Nelsson, Adam Kirkman, Jennifer Gonzalez, Laura Pennock, Elizabeth Tzetzo, Valerie Esposito, and Meenakshi Singh.

To Kaitlin Severini for copyediting, and Andrea Modica and Hannah Bowe for proofreading. To Elizabeth Evans, for her stellar audio adaptations, and to Carlos Quevedo, for his stunning cover art.

To the badass and brilliant team at Writers House: Robin Rue (marvelous agent and wonderful friend), Beth Miller, Cecilia de la Campa, Maja Nikolic, Kate Boggs, Maria Aughavin, Albert Araneo, Sydnee Harlan, Alessandra Birch, Sofia Bolido, Angelamarie Malkoun, Melissa Vasquez, Rosie Acacia, Lisa Castiglione, and Angela Kafka.

To the amazing team at Frankfurt Kurnit Klein & Selz: Maura Wogan, Victoria Cook, Kimberly Maynard, Louise Decoppet, Mark Merriman, Michael Ling, Michael Williams, Gregory Boyd, Edward Rosenthal, Molly Rothschild, Amanda Barkin, and Nicole Bergstrom. To Jill Gillett for her wisdom and guidance.

To my sister, Jenn, who inspires me every day, and to my dear friends who always make me smile: Julie, Megan, Katie, Steph, and Lynette. To Laura and Louisse, whose emails never fail to brighten my day.

To Ana, who takes such amazing care of my babies, allowing me to write these books.

To Josh, Taran, Sloane, and Annie: you are the greatest gifts in my life, and I love you more than words can say.

And to the readers who make all of this even possible: thank you for *everything*.